国外优秀数学著作
原 版 系 列

梅林变换手册

Handbook of Mellin Transforms

［俄罗斯］Yu. A. 布里奇科夫 (Yu. A. Brychkov)
［白俄］O. I. 马里切夫 (O. I. Marichev)
［俄罗斯］N. V. 萨维申科 (N. V. Savischenko)

著

（英文）

HITP
哈爾濱工業大學出版社
HARBIN INSTITUTE OF TECHNOLOGY PRESS

黑版贸登字 08-2021-062 号

图书在版编目(CIP)数据

梅林变换手册=Handbook of Mellin Transforms:
英文/(俄罗斯)Yu. A. 布里奇科夫(Yu. A. Brychkov),
(白俄)O. I. 马里切夫(O. I. Marichev),(俄罗斯)N. V.
萨维申科(N. V. Savischenko)著. —哈尔滨:哈尔滨
工业大学出版社,2024.3
ISBN 978-7-5767-1286-5

Ⅰ.①梅… Ⅱ.①Y… ②O… ③N… Ⅲ.①梅林变换-
手册-英文 Ⅳ.①O177.6-62

中国国家版本馆 CIP 数据核字(2024)第 050310 号

MEILIN BIANHUAN SHOUCE

策划编辑 刘培杰 杜莹雪
责任编辑 宋 淼 李兰静
封面设计 孙茵艾
出版发行 哈尔滨工业大学出版社
社 址 哈尔滨市南岗区复华四道街 10 号 邮编 150006
传 真 0451-86414749
网 址 http://hitpress.hit.edu.cn
印 刷 哈尔滨博奇印刷有限公司
开 本 787 mm×1 092 mm 1/16 印张 39 字数 652 千字
版 次 2024 年 3 月第 1 版 2024 年 3 月第 1 次印刷
书 号 ISBN 978-7-5767-1286-5
定 价 128.00 元

(如因印装质量问题影响阅读,我社负责调换)

Contents

Preface

The Mellin transformation was introduced by a Finnish mathematician Robert Hjalmar Mellin in his paper "Über die fundamentale Wichtigkeit des Satzes von Cauchy für die Theorien der Gamma– und der hypergeometrischen Funktionen. Acta Soc. Fennicae, 1896, 21, 1–115." At present, it is widely used in various problems of pure and applied mathematics, in particular, in the theory of differential and integral equations, and the theory of Dirichlet series. It found extensive applications in mathematical physics, number theory, mathematical statistics, theory of asymptotic expansions, and especially, in the theory of special functions and integral transformations. Using the Mellin transformation, many classical integral transforms can be represented as compositions of direct and inverse Laplace transforms.

This handbook contains tables of the direct Mellin transforms of the form

$$F(s) = \mathfrak{M}[f(x); s] = \int_0^\infty x^{s-1} f(x)\, dx, \qquad s = \sigma + i\tau.$$

Since the majority of integrals can be reduced to the form of the corresponding Mellin transforms with a specific choice of parameters, this book can also be considered as a handbook of definite and indefinite integrals. By changes of variables, the Mellin transform can be turned into the Fourier and Laplace transforms.

The inverse Mellin transform has the form

$$f(x) = \mathfrak{M}^{-1}[F(s); x] = \frac{1}{2\pi i} \int_{\sigma - i\infty}^{\sigma + i\infty} x^{-s} F(s)\, ds, \qquad \alpha < \sigma < \beta;$$

see Appendix I.

The main text is introduced by a fairly detailed list of contents, from which the required formulas can easily be found. The tables are arranged in two columns. The left-hand column of each page shows function $f(x)$ and the right-hand column gives the corresponding Mellin transform $F(s)$. For the sake of compactness, abbreviated notation is used. For example, the formula 3.14.9.1 (the formula 1 of the Subsection 3.14.9)

No.	$f(x)$	$F(s)$
1	$\left\{ \begin{matrix} S(ax) \\ C(ax) \end{matrix} \right\} K_\nu(bx)$	$\dfrac{2^{s+\delta-1}\, a^{\delta+1/2}}{3^\delta \sqrt{\pi}\, b^{s+\delta+1/2}} \Gamma\left(\dfrac{2s - 2\nu + 2\delta + 1}{4} \right) \Gamma\left(\dfrac{2s + 2\nu + 2\delta + 1}{4} \right)$ $\times\, {}_3F_2\left(\begin{matrix} \frac{2\delta+1}{4},\ \frac{2s-2\nu+2\delta+1}{4},\ \frac{2s+2\nu+2\delta+1}{4} \\ \frac{2\delta+1}{2},\ \frac{2\delta+5}{4}; \ -\frac{a^2}{b^2} \end{matrix} \right)$ $[a,\ \mathrm{Re}\, b > 0;\ \mathrm{Re}\, s > |\mathrm{Re}\, \nu| - (2 \pm 1)/2]$

where $\delta = \left\{ \begin{matrix} 1 \\ 0 \end{matrix} \right\}$, is a contraction of the two formulas

1	$S\left(ax\right)K_{\nu}\left(bx\right)$	$\dfrac{2^{s}\,a^{3/2}}{3\sqrt{\pi}\,b^{s+3/2}}\,\Gamma\left(\dfrac{2s-2\nu+3}{2}\right)\Gamma\left(\dfrac{2s+2\nu+3}{2}\right)$
		$\times\ {}_{3}F_{2}\left(\begin{array}{c}\frac{3}{4},\ \frac{2s-2\nu+3}{2},\ \frac{2s+2\nu+3}{2}\\ \frac{3}{2},\ \frac{7}{4};\ -\frac{a^{2}}{b^{2}}\end{array}\right)$
		$\left[a,\ \operatorname{Re}b>0;\ \operatorname{Re}s>\left|\operatorname{Re}\nu\right|-3/2\right]$

(in which only the upper sign and the upper expression in the curly brackets are taken) and

2	$C\left(ax\right)K_{\nu}\left(bx\right)$	$\dfrac{2^{s-1}\,a^{1/2}}{\sqrt{\pi}\,b^{s+1/2}}\,\Gamma\left(\dfrac{2s-2\nu+1}{2}\right)\Gamma\left(\dfrac{2s+2\nu+1}{2}\right)$
		$\times\ {}_{3}F_{2}\left(\begin{array}{c}\frac{1}{4},\ \frac{2s-2\nu+1}{2},\ \frac{2s+2\nu+1}{2}\\ \frac{1}{2},\ \frac{5}{4};\ -\frac{a^{2}}{b^{2}}\end{array}\right)$
		$\left[a,\ \operatorname{Re}b>0;\ \operatorname{Re}s>\left|\operatorname{Re}\nu\right|-1/2\right]$

(in which only the lower sign and the lower expression in the curly brackets are taken).

The formula $a,\ b<\operatorname{Re}s<c,\ d$ is an abbreviated form of the inequality

$$\max\left(a,\ b\right)<\operatorname{Re}s<\min\left(c,\ d\right).$$

In all chapters, unless other restrictions are indicated, $k,\ l,\ m,\ n,\ p,\ q=0,\ 1,\ 2,\ldots$

Some integrals are considered in the sense of the principal value.

Various functional relations that will be useful for evaluation of Mellin transforms are given at the beginning of every section. More formulas can be found at `http://functions.wolfram.com`.

In the preparation of this handbook, use was made, above all, of the books of H. Bateman, A. Erdélyi, W. Magnus, F. Oberhettinger, and F. G. Tricomi [1], Yu. A. Brychkov [3], O. I. Marichev [14], I. S. Gradshteyn and I. M. Ryzhik [13], V. A. Ditkin and A. P. Prudnikov [10], F. Oberhettinger [15], and A. P. Prudnikov, Yu. A. Brychkov, and O. I. Marichev [18–23]. An appreciable part of the formulas were obtained by the authors.

Appendix I contains some properties of Mellin transforms and examples of their application.

Appendix II is devoted to conditions of convergences of integrals.

The bibliographic sources and notations are given at the end of the book.

This handbook is intended for researchers, engineers, post-graduate students, university students, and generally for anyone who uses mathematical methods.

Chapter 1
General Formulas

1.1. Transforms Containing Arbitrary Functions

1.1.1. Basic formulas

Notation: $F_1(s) = \mathfrak{M}[f_1(x); s]$, $F_2(s) = \mathfrak{M}[f_2(x); s]$.

No.	$f(x)$	$F(s)$
1	$\dfrac{1}{2\pi i} \displaystyle\int_{c-i\infty}^{c+i\infty} F(s)\, x^{-s}\, ds$	$F(s)$
2	$\displaystyle\int_0^\infty f_1\left(\dfrac{x}{t}\right) f_2(t)\, \dfrac{dt}{t}$	$F_1(s)\, F_2(s)$

1.1.2. $f(ax^r)$ and the power function

Condition: $\operatorname{Im}\beta = 0$, $\beta \neq 0$.

1	$f(ax)$	$a^{-s} F(s)$
2	$x^\alpha f(x)$	$F(s+\alpha)$
3	$f(x^\beta)$	$\dfrac{1}{|\beta|} F\left(\dfrac{s}{\beta}\right)$
4	$f(ax^\beta)$	$\dfrac{1}{|\beta|} a^{-s/\beta} F\left(\dfrac{s}{\beta}\right)$
5	$x^\alpha f(x^\beta)$	$\dfrac{1}{|\beta|} F\left(\dfrac{s+\alpha}{\beta}\right)$
6	$x^\alpha f(ax^\beta)$	$\dfrac{1}{|\beta|} a^{-(s+\alpha)/\beta} F\left(\dfrac{s+\alpha}{\beta}\right)$

1.1.3. $f(ax^r)$ and elementary functions

Condition: $\operatorname{Im} \beta = 0$, $\beta \neq 0$.

1	$\ln x \, f(x)$	$F'(s)$
2	$\ln^m x \, f(x)$	$F^{(m)}(s)$
3	$x^\alpha \ln^m x \, f(x)$	$F^{(m)}(s+\alpha)$
4	$\ln^m x \, f(x^\beta)$	$\dfrac{\operatorname{sgn}\beta}{\beta^{m+1}} F^{(m)}\left(\dfrac{s}{\beta}\right)$
5	$\ln x \, f(ax)$	$a^{-s}\left[F'(s) - \ln a\, F(s)\right]$
6	$\ln^m x \, f(ax)$	$(-1)^m a^{-s} \displaystyle\sum_{k=0}^{m} (-1)^k \binom{m}{k} \ln^{m-k} a\, F^{(k)}(s)$
7	$\ln^m x \, f(ax^\beta)$	$\dfrac{(-1)^m \operatorname{sgn}\beta}{\beta^{m+1}} a^{-s/\beta} \displaystyle\sum_{k=0}^{m} (-1)^k \binom{m}{k} \ln^{m-k} a\, F^{(k)}\left(\dfrac{s}{\beta}\right)$
8	$x^\alpha \ln^m x \, f(x^\beta)$	$\dfrac{\operatorname{sgn}\beta}{\beta^{m+1}} F^{(m)}\left(\dfrac{s+\alpha}{\beta}\right)$
9	$x^\alpha \ln x \, f(ax^\beta)$	$\dfrac{\operatorname{sgn}\beta}{\beta^2} a^{-(s+\alpha)/\beta} \left[-\ln a\, F\left(\dfrac{s+\alpha}{\beta}\right) + F'\left(\dfrac{s+\alpha}{\beta}\right)\right]$
10	$x^\alpha \ln^m x \, f(ax^\beta)$	$\dfrac{(-1)^m \operatorname{sgn}\beta}{\beta^{m+1}} a^{-(s+\alpha)/\beta} \displaystyle\sum_{k=0}^{m} (-1)^k \binom{m}{k} \ln^{m-k} a\, F^{(k)}\left(\dfrac{s+\alpha}{\beta}\right)$
11	$x^\alpha e^{bx} f(ax^\beta)$	$\dfrac{\operatorname{sgn}\beta}{\beta} a^{-(s+\alpha)/\beta} \displaystyle\sum_{n=0}^{\infty} \dfrac{(a^{-1/\beta}b)^n}{n!} F\left(\dfrac{s+n+\alpha}{\beta}\right)$

1.1.4. Derivatives of $f(x)$

1	$f'(x)$	$(1-s)F(s-1)$ $\qquad \left[x^{s-1}f(x)\big|_{x=0} = x^{s-1}f(x)\big|_{x=\infty} = 0\right]$
2	$f^{(n)}(x)$	$(-1)^n \Gamma\begin{bmatrix} s \\ s-n \end{bmatrix} F(s-n) = \Gamma\begin{bmatrix} n+1-s \\ 1-s \end{bmatrix} F(s-n)$ $\left[\begin{array}{l} x^{s-k}f^{(n-k)}(x)\big|_{x=0} = x^{s-k}f^{(n-k)}(x)\big|_{x=\infty} = 0, \\ k = 1, 2, \ldots, n \end{array}\right]$

No.	$f(x)$	$F(s)$
3	$\left(x\dfrac{d}{dx}\right)^n f(x)$	$(-s)^n F(s)$
		$\left[\begin{array}{l} x^s\left(x\dfrac{d}{dx}\right)^k f(x)\bigg|_{x=0} = x^s\left(x\dfrac{d}{dx}\right)^k f(x)\bigg|_{x=\infty} = 0, \\ k=0,1,\ldots,n-1 \end{array}\right]$
4	$\left(\dfrac{d}{dx}x\right)^n f(x)$	$(1-s)^n F(s)$
		$\left[\begin{array}{l} x^s\left(\dfrac{d}{dx}x\right)^k f(x)\bigg|_{x=0} = x^s\left(\dfrac{d}{dx}x\right)^k f(x)\bigg|_{x=\infty} = 0, \\ k=0,1,\ldots,n-1 \end{array}\right]$
5	$\left(x^{1-\alpha}\dfrac{d}{dx}\right)^n f(x)$	$(-\alpha)^n \Gamma\left[\begin{array}{c} \frac{s}{\alpha} \\ \frac{s-n\alpha}{\alpha} \end{array}\right] F(s-n\alpha)$
6		$= \alpha^n \Gamma\left[\begin{array}{c} \frac{(n+1)\alpha-s}{\alpha} \\ \frac{\alpha-s}{\alpha} \end{array}\right] F(s-n\alpha) \qquad\qquad [\alpha\neq 0]$
		$\left[\begin{array}{l} x^{s-k\alpha}\left(x^{1-\alpha}\dfrac{d}{dx}\right)^{n-k} f(x)\bigg|_{x=0} \\ \qquad = x^{s-k\alpha}\left(x^{1-\alpha}\dfrac{d}{dx}\right)^{n-k} f(x)\bigg|_{x=\infty} = 0, \\ k=1,2,\ldots,n \end{array}\right]$
7	$\left(\dfrac{d}{dx}x^{1-\beta}\right)^n f(x)$	$\beta^n \Gamma\left[\begin{array}{c} \frac{1-s+n\beta}{\beta} \\ \frac{1-s}{\beta} \end{array}\right] F(s-n\beta) \qquad\qquad [\beta\neq 0]$
		$\left[\begin{array}{l} x^{s-k\beta}\left(\dfrac{d}{dx}x^{1-\beta}\right)^{n-k} f(x)\bigg|_{x=0} \\ \qquad = x^{s-k\beta}\left(\dfrac{d}{dx}x^{1-\beta}\right)^{n-k} f(x)\bigg|_{x=\infty} = 0, \\ k=1,2,\ldots,n \end{array}\right]$
8	$\left(x^{1-\alpha}\dfrac{d}{dx}x^{1-\beta}\right)^n f(x)$	$(\alpha+\beta-1)^n \Gamma\left[\begin{array}{c} \frac{n(\alpha+\beta-1)+\alpha-s}{\alpha+\beta-1} \\ \frac{\alpha-s}{\alpha+\beta-1} \end{array}\right] F(s-n\alpha-n\beta+n)$
		$[\alpha+\beta-1\neq 0]$
9		$= \displaystyle\prod_{k=0}^{n-1}[\alpha-s+k(\alpha+\beta-1)]\, F(s-n\alpha-n\beta+n)$
		$\left[\begin{array}{l} x^{s-k(\alpha+\beta-1)}\left(x^{1-\alpha}\dfrac{d}{dx}x^{1-\beta}\right)^{n-k} f(x)\bigg|_{x=0} \\ \qquad = x^{s-k(\alpha+\beta-1)}\left(x^{1-\alpha}\dfrac{d}{dx}x^{1-\beta}\right)^{n-k} f(x)\bigg|_{x=\infty} = 0, \\ k=1,2,\ldots,n \end{array}\right]$

No.	$f(x)$	$F(s)$
10	$\left(x^{1-\alpha}\dfrac{d}{dx}x^{\alpha}\right)^{n}f(x)$	$(\alpha-s)^{n}F(s)$
		$\left[\begin{array}{l} x^{s}\left(x^{1-\alpha}\dfrac{d}{dx}x^{\alpha}\right)^{n-k}f(x)\bigg|_{x=0} \\ \qquad = x^{s}\left(x^{1-\alpha}\dfrac{d}{dx}x^{\alpha}\right)^{n-k}f(x)\bigg|_{x=\infty}=0, \\ k=1,2,\ldots,n \end{array}\right]$
11	$\dfrac{\partial}{\partial a}f(x,a)$	$\dfrac{\partial}{\partial a}F(s,a)$

1.1.5. Integrals containing $f(x)$

Notation: $F_{1}(s)=\mathfrak{M}\left[f_{1}(x);s\right]$, $F_{2}(s)=\mathfrak{M}\left[f_{2}(x);s\right]$.

No.		
1	$\displaystyle\int_{0}^{\infty}f_{1}(xt)\,f_{2}(t)\,dt$	$F_{1}(s)\,F_{2}(1-s)$
2	$\displaystyle\int_{0}^{\infty}t^{\alpha}f_{1}(xt)\,f_{2}(t)\,dt$	$F_{1}(s)\,F_{2}(1-s+\alpha)$
3	$\displaystyle x^{\alpha}\int_{0}^{\infty}f_{1}(xt)\,f_{2}(t)\,dt$	$F_{1}(s+\alpha)\,F_{2}(1-s-\alpha)$
4	$\displaystyle x^{\alpha}\int_{0}^{\infty}t^{\beta}f_{1}(xt)\,f_{2}(t)\,dt$	$F_{1}(s+\alpha)\,F_{2}(1-s-\alpha+\beta)$
5	$\displaystyle\int_{0}^{\infty}f_{1}\left(\frac{x}{t}\right)f_{2}(t)\,dt$	$F_{1}(s)\,F_{2}(s+1)$
6	$\displaystyle\int_{0}^{\infty}t^{\alpha}f_{1}\left(\frac{x}{t}\right)f_{2}(t)\,dt$	$F_{1}(s)\,F_{2}(s+\alpha+1)$
7	$\displaystyle x^{\alpha}\int_{0}^{\infty}f_{1}\left(\frac{x}{t}\right)f_{2}(t)\,dt$	$F_{1}(s+\alpha)\,F_{2}(s+\alpha+1)$
8	$\displaystyle x^{\alpha}\int_{0}^{\infty}t^{\beta}f_{1}\left(\frac{x}{t}\right)f_{2}(t)\,dt$	$F_{1}(s+\alpha)\,F_{2}(s+\alpha+\beta+1)$
9	$\displaystyle\int_{0}^{\infty}f_{1}\left(\frac{t}{x}\right)f_{2}(t)\,dt$	$F_{1}(-s)\,F_{2}(s+1)$
10	$\displaystyle\int_{0}^{\infty}f_{1}\left(x^{\alpha}t^{\beta}\right)f_{2}(t^{\gamma})\,dt$	$\dfrac{1}{|\alpha|}F_{1}\left(\dfrac{s}{\alpha}\right)\dfrac{1}{|\gamma|}F_{2}\left(\dfrac{\alpha-\beta s}{\alpha\gamma}\right)$ $[\alpha,\beta,\gamma\neq 0]$

No.	$f(x)$	$F(s)$
11	$\displaystyle\int_0^x f(t)\,dt$	$-\dfrac{1}{s}F(s+1)$ $\qquad\qquad\qquad$ [$\operatorname{Re}s < 0$]
12	$\displaystyle\int_0^x \cdots \int_0^x f(t)\,(dt)^n$ $= \displaystyle\int_0^x \frac{(x-t)^{n-1}}{(n-1)!}f(t)\,dt$	$\dfrac{(-1)^n}{(s)_n}F(s+n)$ $\qquad\qquad\qquad$ [$\operatorname{Re}s < 1-n$]
13	$\displaystyle\int_0^x \frac{(x-t)^{\alpha-1}}{\Gamma(\alpha)}f(t)\,dt$ $\equiv \left(I_{0+}^\alpha f\right)(x)$	$\Gamma\!\begin{bmatrix}1-s-\alpha\\1-s\end{bmatrix}F(s+\alpha)$ $\quad$ [$\operatorname{Re}\alpha > 0;\ \operatorname{Re}(s+\alpha)<1$]
14	$\displaystyle\int_x^\infty f(t)\,dt$	$\dfrac{1}{s}F(s+1)$ $\qquad\qquad\qquad$ [$\operatorname{Re}s > 0$]
15	$\displaystyle\int_x^\infty \cdots \int_x^\infty f(t)\,(dt)^n$ $= \displaystyle\int_x^\infty \frac{(t-x)^{n-1}}{(n-1)!}f(t)\,dt$	$\dfrac{1}{(s)_n}F(s+n)$ $\qquad\qquad\qquad$ [$\operatorname{Re}s > 0$]
16	$\displaystyle\int_x^\infty \frac{(t-x)^{\alpha-1}}{\Gamma(\alpha)}f(t)\,dt$ $\equiv \left(I_-^\alpha f\right)(x)$	$\Gamma\!\begin{bmatrix}s\\s+\alpha\end{bmatrix}F(s+\alpha)$ $\qquad$ [$\operatorname{Re}\alpha,\ \operatorname{Re}s > 0$]
17	$x^\gamma\left(I_{0+}^\alpha x^\beta f\right)(x)$	$\Gamma\!\begin{bmatrix}1-s-\alpha-\gamma\\1-s-\gamma\end{bmatrix}F(s+\alpha+\beta+\gamma)$ $\qquad\qquad\qquad$ [$\operatorname{Re}\alpha > 0;\ \operatorname{Re}(s+\alpha+\gamma)<1$]
18	$x^\gamma\left(I_-^\alpha x^\beta f\right)(x)$	$\Gamma\!\begin{bmatrix}s+\gamma\\s+\alpha+\gamma\end{bmatrix}F(s+\alpha+\beta+\gamma)$ $\qquad\qquad\qquad$ [$\operatorname{Re}\alpha,\ \operatorname{Re}(s+\gamma)>0$]
19	$\displaystyle\int_0^\infty e^{-xt}f(t)\,dt$	$\Gamma(s)\,F(1-s)$ $\qquad\qquad\qquad$ [$\operatorname{Re}s > 0$]
20	$x^\alpha\displaystyle\int_0^\infty t^\beta e^{-xt}f(t)\,dt$	$\Gamma(s+\alpha)\,F(1-s-\alpha+\beta)$ $\quad$ [$\operatorname{Re}(s+\alpha) > 0$]
21	$\displaystyle\int_0^\infty e^{-t/x}f(t)\,dt$	$\Gamma(-s)\,F(s+1)$ $\qquad\qquad\qquad$ [$\operatorname{Re}s < 0$]
22	$x^\alpha\displaystyle\int_0^\infty t^\beta e^{-t/x}f(t)\,dt$	$\Gamma(-s-\alpha)\,F(s+\alpha+\beta+1)$ $\quad$ [$\operatorname{Re}(s+\alpha) < 0$]
23	$\displaystyle\int_0^\infty e^{-x/t}f(t)\,dt$	$\Gamma(s)\,F(s+1)$ $\qquad\qquad\qquad$ [$\operatorname{Re}s > 0$]

No.	$f(x)$	$F(s)$
24	$x^\alpha \displaystyle\int_0^\infty t^\beta e^{-x/t} f(t)\, dt$	$\Gamma(s+\alpha)\, F(s+\alpha+\beta+1) \qquad\qquad\qquad [\operatorname{Re}(s+\alpha)>0]$
25	$\displaystyle\int_0^\infty \cos(xt) f(t)\, dt$	$\cos\dfrac{s\pi}{2}\,\Gamma(s)\,\mathfrak{M}[f(x);1-s] \qquad\qquad\qquad [\operatorname{Re} s>0]$
26	$\displaystyle\int_0^\infty \sin(xt) f(t)\, dt$	$\sin\dfrac{s\pi}{2}\,\Gamma(s)\,\mathfrak{M}[f(x);1-s] \qquad\qquad\qquad [\operatorname{Re} s>0]$
27	$\displaystyle\int_0^\infty \sqrt{xt}\, J_\nu(xt) f(t)\, dt$	$2^{s-1/2}\,\Gamma\begin{bmatrix}\frac{2s+2\nu+1}{4}\\ \frac{3-2s+2\nu}{4}\end{bmatrix}\mathfrak{M}[f(x);1-s]$
28	$\displaystyle\int_0^\infty \sqrt{xt}\, K_\nu(xt) f(t)\, dt$	$2^{s-3/2}\,\Gamma\left(\dfrac{2s+2\nu+1}{4}\right)\Gamma\left(\dfrac{2s-2\nu+1}{4}\right)\mathfrak{M}[f(x);1-s]$
29	$\displaystyle\int_0^\infty \sqrt{xt}\, Y_\nu(xt) f(t)\, dt$	$\dfrac{2^{s-1/2}}{\pi}\sin\dfrac{(2\nu-2s-3)\pi}{4}\,\Gamma\left(\dfrac{2s-2\nu+1}{4}\right)$ $\times\,\Gamma\left(\dfrac{2s+2\nu+1}{4}\right)\mathfrak{M}[f(x);1-s]$
30	$\displaystyle\int_0^\infty \sqrt{xt}\, \mathbf{H}_\nu(xt) f(t)\, dt$	$2^{s-1/2}\tan\dfrac{(2s+2\nu+1)\pi}{4}\,\Gamma\begin{bmatrix}\frac{2s+2\nu+1}{4}\\ \frac{3-2s+2\nu}{4}\end{bmatrix}\mathfrak{M}[f(x);1-s]$

Chapter 2
Elementary Functions

2.1. Algebraic Functions

More formulas can be obtained from the corresponding sections due to the relations

$$\frac{1}{\sqrt{z+1}+1} = \frac{1}{2}\,{_2}F_1\left(\begin{matrix}\frac{1}{2},\,1\\2;\,-z\end{matrix}\right), \qquad \frac{1}{\sqrt{\sqrt{z+1}+1}} = \frac{1}{\sqrt{2}}\,{_2}F_1\left(\begin{matrix}\frac{1}{4},\,\frac{3}{4}\\\frac{3}{2};\,-z\end{matrix}\right),$$

$$\frac{1}{\sqrt{1-\sqrt{z}}} + \frac{1}{\sqrt{1+\sqrt{z}}} = 2\,{_2}F_1\left(\begin{matrix}\frac{1}{4},\,\frac{3}{4}\\\frac{1}{2};\,z\end{matrix}\right), \qquad \frac{1}{(1-\sqrt{z})^{3/2}} + \frac{1}{(1+\sqrt{z})^{3/2}} = 2\,{_2}F_1\left(\begin{matrix}\frac{3}{4},\,\frac{5}{4}\\\frac{1}{2};\,z\end{matrix}\right),$$

$$(z+1)^a = {_1}F_0\left(\begin{matrix}-a\\-z\end{matrix}\right) = {_2}F_1\left(\begin{matrix}-a,\,b\\b;\,-z\end{matrix}\right), \qquad (z+1)^a = \frac{1}{\Gamma(-a)}\,G^{11}_{11}\left(z\,\middle|\,\begin{matrix}a+1\\0\end{matrix}\right),$$

$$\frac{1}{1-z} = \pi\,G^{11}_{22}\left(z\,\middle|\,\begin{matrix}0,\,1/2\\0,\,1/2\end{matrix}\right), \qquad (1-x)^{\alpha-1}_+ = \Gamma(\alpha)\,G^{10}_{11}\left(x\,\middle|\,\begin{matrix}\alpha\\0\end{matrix}\right), \qquad (x-1)^{\alpha-1}_+ = \Gamma(\alpha)\,G^{01}_{11}\left(x\,\middle|\,\begin{matrix}\alpha\\0\end{matrix}\right).$$

2.1.1. $(a^r - x^r)^{\alpha}_+$ and $(x^r - a^r)^{\alpha}_+$

No.	$f(x)$	$F(s)$	
1	$\theta(a-x)$	$\dfrac{a^s}{s}$	$[a,\ \mathrm{Re}\,s > 0]$
2	$\theta(x-a)$	$-\dfrac{a^s}{s}$	$[a > 0;\ \mathrm{Re}\,s < 0]$
3	$\theta(x-a) - \theta(x-b)$	$\dfrac{b^s - a^s}{s}$	$[0 < a < b;\ \mathrm{Re}\,s > 0]$
4	$\theta(a-x)\,x^\alpha$	$\dfrac{a^{s+\alpha}}{s+\alpha}$	$[a,\ \mathrm{Re}\,(s+\alpha) > 0]$
5	$\theta(x-a)\,x^\alpha$	$-\dfrac{a^{s+\alpha}}{s+\alpha}$	$[a > 0;\ \mathrm{Re}\,(s+\alpha) < 0]$

No.	$f(x)$	$F(s)$
6	$(a-x)_+^{\alpha-1}$	$a^{s+\alpha-1} \operatorname{B}(\alpha, s)$ $\qquad\qquad\qquad [a,\ \operatorname{Re}\alpha,\ \operatorname{Re}s > 0]$
7	$(x-a)_+^{\alpha-1}$	$a^{s+\alpha-1} \operatorname{B}(\alpha, 1-\alpha-s)$ $\qquad\qquad [a,\ \operatorname{Re}\alpha > 0;\ \operatorname{Re}(\alpha+s) < 1]$
8	$(a^r-x^r)_+^{\alpha-1}$	$\dfrac{a^{s+(\alpha-1)r}}{r} \operatorname{B}\left(\dfrac{s}{r}, \alpha\right)$ $\qquad\quad [a,\ r,\ \operatorname{Re}\alpha,\ \operatorname{Re}s > 0]$
9	$(x^r-a^r)_+^{\alpha-1}$	$\dfrac{a^{s+(\alpha-1)r}}{r} \operatorname{B}\left(\alpha, 1-\alpha-\dfrac{s}{r}\right)$ $\qquad\qquad\qquad\qquad\qquad [a,\ r,\ \operatorname{Re}\alpha > 0;\ \operatorname{Re}s < r(1-\operatorname{Re}\alpha)]$
10	$x^\alpha (a-x)_+^{\beta-1}$	$a^{s+\alpha+\beta-1} \operatorname{B}(s+\alpha, \beta)$ $\qquad\qquad [a,\ \operatorname{Re}\beta,\ \operatorname{Re}(s+\alpha) > 0]$
11	$x^\alpha (x-a)_+^{\beta-1}$	$a^{s+\alpha+\beta-1} \operatorname{B}(1-s-\alpha-\beta, \beta)$ $\qquad [a,\ \operatorname{Re}\beta,\ \operatorname{Re}(s+\alpha+\beta) < 1]$

2.1.2. $(ax+b)^\rho$ and $|x-a|^\rho$

No.	$f(x)$	$F(s)$
1	$\dfrac{1}{a-x}$	$\pi a^{s-1} \cot(s\pi)$ $\qquad\qquad [a > 0;\ 0 < \operatorname{Re}s < 1]$
2	$\dfrac{a}{a-x} - \displaystyle\sum_{k=0}^{n} \left(\dfrac{x}{a}\right)^k$	$\pi a^s \cot(s\pi)$ $\qquad\qquad [a > 0;\ -n-1 < \operatorname{Re}s < -n]$
3	$\dfrac{1}{(ax+b)^\rho}$	$\dfrac{b^{s-\rho}}{a^s} \operatorname{B}(s, \rho-s)$ $\qquad [0 < \operatorname{Re}s < \operatorname{Re}\rho;\ |\arg a|,\ |\arg b| < \pi]$
4	$\dfrac{1}{(a-x)^n}$	$-\dfrac{\pi(-a)^{s-n}}{(n-1)!\sin(s\pi)} \displaystyle\prod_{k=1}^{n-1}(s-k)$ $\qquad\qquad\qquad\qquad [0 < \operatorname{Re}s < n;\ n = 1, 2, \ldots;\ |\arg(-a)| < \pi]$
5	$\dfrac{1}{(x+a)^\rho} - \dfrac{1}{x^\rho}$	$a^{s-\rho} \operatorname{B}(s, \rho-s)$ $\qquad [-1 < \operatorname{Re}s < 0,\ \operatorname{Re}\rho;\ |\arg a| < \pi]$
6	$\dfrac{a^\rho}{(x+a)^\rho} + \dfrac{\rho x}{a} - 1$	$a^s \operatorname{B}(s, \rho-s)$ $\qquad [-2 < \operatorname{Re}s < -1,\ \operatorname{Re}\rho;\ |\arg a| < \pi]$
7	$\dfrac{a^\rho}{(x+a)^\rho}$ $\quad - \displaystyle\sum_{k=0}^{n} \binom{-\rho}{k} \left(\dfrac{x}{a}\right)^k$	$a^s \operatorname{B}(s, \rho-s)$ $\qquad [-n-1 < \operatorname{Re}s < -n,\ \operatorname{Re}\rho;\ |\arg a| < \pi]$

No.	$f(x)$	$F(s)$
8	$\dfrac{1}{\lvert x-a\rvert^{\rho}}$	$a^{s-\rho}\sec\dfrac{\rho\pi}{2}\cos\dfrac{(2s-\rho)\pi}{2}\,\mathrm{B}(s,\rho-s)$
9		$=\dfrac{\pi a^{s-\rho}}{\Gamma(\rho)}\sec\dfrac{\rho\pi}{2}\,\Gamma\!\left[\begin{array}{c}s,\ \rho-s\\ \frac{2s-\rho+1}{2},\ \frac{1-2s+\rho}{2}\end{array}\right]$ $[a>0;\ 0<\operatorname{Re}s<\operatorname{Re}\rho<1]$
10	$\dfrac{\operatorname{sgn}(a-x)}{\lvert x-a\rvert^{\rho}}$	$\pi\,a^{s-\rho}\csc\dfrac{\rho\pi}{2}\,\Gamma\!\left[\begin{array}{c}s,\ \rho-s\\ \rho,\ \frac{2s-\rho+2}{2},\ \frac{\rho-2s}{2}\end{array}\right]$ $[a>0;\ 0<\operatorname{Re}s<\operatorname{Re}\rho<1]$

2.1.3. $(ax+b)^{\rho}(cx+d)^{\sigma}$

1	$\dfrac{1}{(ax+b)(cx+d)}$	$\dfrac{\pi(ac)^{1-s}}{(bc-ad)\sin(s\pi)}\left[(ad)^{s-1}-(bc)^{s-1}\right]$ $[0<\operatorname{Re}s<2;\ \lvert\arg(b/a)\rvert,\ \lvert\arg(d/c)\rvert<\pi]$
2	$\dfrac{1}{(x+a)(b-x)}$	$\dfrac{\pi}{a+b}\left[\dfrac{a^{s-1}}{\sin(s\pi)}+b^{s-1}\cot(s\pi)\right]$ $[b>0;\ 0<\operatorname{Re}s<2;\ \lvert\arg a\rvert<\pi]$
3	$\dfrac{1}{(x-a)(x-b)}$	$\pi\cot(s\pi)\dfrac{a^{s-1}-b^{s-1}}{b-a}$ $[a>b>0;\ 0<\operatorname{Re}s<2]$
4	$\dfrac{1}{(x+a)^{\rho}(x-b)}$	$a^{-\rho}(-b)^{s-1}\,\mathrm{B}(s,\rho-s+1)\,{}_2F_1\!\left(\begin{array}{c}\rho,\ s;\ \frac{a+b}{a}\\ \rho+1\end{array}\right)$ $[a\neq0;\ 0<\operatorname{Re}s<\operatorname{Re}\rho+1;\ \lvert\arg a\rvert<\pi,\ \lvert\arg(-b)\rvert<\pi]$
5	$\dfrac{1}{(x+a)^{\rho}(x-b)}$	$-\dfrac{\pi b^{s-1}}{(a+b)^{\rho}}\cot[(s-\rho)\pi]-\dfrac{a^{s-\rho}}{a+b}\,\mathrm{B}(s,\rho-s)\,{}_2F_1\!\left(\begin{array}{c}1,\ 1-\rho;\ \frac{a}{a+b}\\ s-\rho+1\end{array}\right)$ $[a\neq0;\ b>0;\ 0<\operatorname{Re}s<\operatorname{Re}\rho+1]$
6	$\dfrac{1}{(ax+b)^{\rho}(cx+d)^{\sigma}}$	$\dfrac{d^{s-\sigma}}{b^{\rho}c^{s}}\,\mathrm{B}(s,\rho+\sigma-s)\,{}_2F_1\!\left(\begin{array}{c}\rho,\ s;\ \frac{bc-ad}{bc}\\ \rho+\sigma\end{array}\right)$ $[0<\operatorname{Re}s<\operatorname{Re}(\rho+\sigma);\ \lvert\arg(b/a)\rvert,\ \lvert\arg(d/c)\rvert<\pi]$

2.1.4. $(a-x)_{+}^{\rho}(bx+c)^{\sigma}$ **and** $(x-a)_{+}^{\rho}(bx+c)^{\sigma}$

1	$\dfrac{\theta(a-x)}{x+a}$	$\dfrac{a^{s-1}}{2}\left[\psi\!\left(\dfrac{s+1}{2}\right)-\psi\!\left(\dfrac{s}{2}\right)\right]$ $[a,\ \operatorname{Re}s>0]$
2	$\dfrac{\theta(a-x)}{(bx+c)^{\rho}}$	$\dfrac{a^{s}}{sc^{\rho}}\,{}_2F_1\!\left(\begin{array}{c}\rho,\ s;\ -\frac{ab}{c}\\ s+1\end{array}\right)$ $\left[\begin{array}{c}a,\ \operatorname{Re}s>0;\\ \lvert\arg(bx+c)\rvert<\pi\ \text{for}\ 0\le x\le a\end{array}\right]$

No.	$f(x)$	$F(s)$
3	$\dfrac{\theta(x-a)}{(bx+c)^\rho}$	$\dfrac{a^{s-\rho}b^{-\rho}}{\rho-s}\,{}_2F_1\!\left(\begin{matrix}\rho,\ \rho-s;\ -\frac{c}{ab}\\ 1-s+\rho\end{matrix}\right)$ $[a>0;\ b\neq 0;\ \operatorname{Re}s<\operatorname{Re}\rho;\ |\arg(bx+c)|<\pi\ \text{for}\ x\geq a]$
4	$(a-x)_+^\rho\,(bx+c)^\rho$	$\left(\dfrac{ac}{b}\right)^{(s+\rho)/2}(ab+c)^\rho\,\Gamma(\rho+1)\,\Gamma(s)\,\mathrm{P}_\rho^{-s-\rho}\!\left(\dfrac{c-ab}{c+ab}\right)$ $[a,\ \operatorname{Re}s>0;\ \operatorname{Re}\rho>-1;\ |\arg(bx+c)|<\pi\ \text{for}\ 0\leq x\leq a]$
5	$(a-x)_+^\rho\,(bx+c)^\sigma$	$a^{s+\rho}c^\sigma\,\mathrm{B}(\rho+1,s)\,{}_2F_1\!\left(\begin{matrix}-\sigma,\ s;\ -\frac{ab}{c}\\ s+\rho+1\end{matrix}\right)$ $[a,\ \operatorname{Re}s>0;\ \operatorname{Re}\rho>-1;\ |\arg(bx+c)|<\pi\ \text{for}\ 0\leq x\leq a]$
6	$(x-a)_+^\rho\,(bx+c)^\rho$	$\left(\dfrac{ac}{b}\right)^{(s+\rho)/2}(ab+c)^\rho\,\Gamma(\rho+1)\,\Gamma(-s-2\rho)\,\mathrm{P}_\rho^{s+\rho}\!\left(\dfrac{ab-c}{ab+c}\right)$ $\left[\begin{matrix}a>0;\ \operatorname{Re}\rho>-1;\ \operatorname{Re}s<-2\operatorname{Re}\rho;\\ |\arg(bx+c)|<\pi\ \text{for}\ x\geq a\end{matrix}\right]$
7	$(x-a)_+^\rho\,(bx+c)^\sigma$	$a^{s+\rho+\sigma}\,b^\sigma\,\mathrm{B}(\rho+1,-s-\rho-\sigma)\,{}_2F_1\!\left(\begin{matrix}-\sigma,\ -s-\rho-\sigma\\ 1-s-\sigma;\ -\frac{c}{ab}\end{matrix}\right)$ $\left[\begin{matrix}a>0;\ \operatorname{Re}\rho>-1;\ \operatorname{Re}s<-\operatorname{Re}(\rho+\sigma)\\ |\arg(bx+c)|<\pi\ \text{for}\ x\geq a\end{matrix}\right]$
8	$\dfrac{(a-x)_+^\rho}{(bx+c)^{\rho+1/2}}$	$\dfrac{a^{s+\rho}}{c^{\rho+1/2}}\,\mathrm{B}(s,\rho+1)\,{}_2F_1\!\left(\begin{matrix}\frac{2\rho+1}{2},\ s;\ -\frac{ab}{c}\\ s+\rho+1\end{matrix}\right)$ $[a,\ \operatorname{Re}s>0;\ \operatorname{Re}\rho>-1;\ |\arg(bx+c)|<\pi\ \text{for}\ 0\leq x\leq a]$
9	$\dfrac{(a-x)_+^\rho}{(bx+c)^{\rho+3/2}}$	$\dfrac{a^{s+\rho}}{c^{\rho+3/2}}\,\mathrm{B}(s,\rho+1)\,{}_2F_1\!\left(\begin{matrix}\frac{2\rho+3}{2},\ s;\ -\frac{ab}{c}\\ s+\rho+1\end{matrix}\right)$ $[a,\ \operatorname{Re}s>0;\ \operatorname{Re}\rho>-1;\ |\arg(bx+c)|<\pi\ \text{for}\ 0\leq x\leq a]$
10	$\dfrac{(x-a)_+^\rho}{(bx+c)^{\rho+1/2}}$	$\dfrac{a^{s-1/2}}{b^{\rho+1/2}}\,\mathrm{B}\!\left(\dfrac{1-2s}{2},\rho+1\right)\,{}_2F_1\!\left(\begin{matrix}\frac{2\rho+1}{2},\ \frac{1-2s}{2}\\ \frac{3-2s+2\rho}{2};\ -\frac{c}{ab}\end{matrix}\right)$ $\left[\begin{matrix}a>0;\ \operatorname{Re}\rho>-1;\ \operatorname{Re}s<1/2;\\ |\arg(bx+c)|<\pi\ \text{for}\ x\geq a\end{matrix}\right]$
11	$\dfrac{(x-a)_+^\rho}{(bx+c)^{\rho+3/2}}$	$\dfrac{a^{s-3/2}}{b^{\rho+3/2}}\,\mathrm{B}\!\left(\dfrac{3-2s}{2},\rho+1\right)\,{}_2F_1\!\left(\begin{matrix}\frac{2\rho+3}{2},\ \frac{3-2s}{2}\\ \frac{5-2s+2\rho}{2};\ -\frac{c}{ab}\end{matrix}\right)$ $\left[\begin{matrix}a>0;\ \operatorname{Re}\rho>-1;\ \operatorname{Re}s<3/2\\ |\arg(bx+c)|<\pi\ \text{for}\ x\geq a\end{matrix}\right]$

2.1.5. $(ax^\mu + b)^\rho (cx^\nu + d)^\sigma$

1	$\dfrac{1}{(ax^\mu + 1)^\rho (bx^\mu + 1)^r}$	$\dfrac{a^{-s/\mu}}{\mu} \, \mathrm{B}\left(\dfrac{s}{\mu}, \rho + r - \dfrac{s}{\mu}\right) {}_2F_1\left(\genfrac{}{}{0pt}{}{r, \frac{s}{\mu}; \frac{a-b}{a}}{\rho + r}\right)$
		$[\mu > 0; \; 0 < \mathrm{Re}\, s < \mu \, \mathrm{Re}\,(\rho + r)\,; \; |\arg a|, \; |\arg b| < \pi]$
2	$\dfrac{1}{(x + a)(x^2 + b^2)}$	$\dfrac{\pi}{2(a^2 + b^2)}\left[\dfrac{ab^{s-2}}{\sin(s\pi/2)} - \dfrac{b^{s-1}}{\cos(s\pi/2)} + \dfrac{2a^{s-1}}{\sin(s\pi)}\right]$
		$[\mathrm{Re}\, b > 0; \; 0 < \mathrm{Re}\, s < 3; \; |\arg a| < \pi]$
3	$\dfrac{1}{(x^2 + a^2)(b^2 - x^2)}$	$\dfrac{\pi}{2(a^2 + b^2)}\left(a^{s-2}\csc\dfrac{s\pi}{2} + b^{s-2}\cot\dfrac{s\pi}{2}\right)$
		$[a^2 + b^2 \neq 0; \; 0 < \mathrm{Re}\, s < 4]$
4	$\dfrac{1}{(x^2 + a)(x^2 + b)}$	$\dfrac{\pi}{2(a - b)}\csc\dfrac{s\pi}{2}\left(b^{s/2-1} - a^{s/2-1}\right)$
		$[0 < \mathrm{Re}\, s < 4; \; |\arg a| < \pi; \; |\arg b| < \pi]$
5	$\dfrac{1}{(x^{1/n} + a^{1/n})^\rho}$	$na^{s-\rho/n}\,\mathrm{B}\,(ns, \rho - ns)$ $\qquad$ $[a > 0; \; 0 < n\,\mathrm{Re}\, s < \mathrm{Re}\,\rho]$
6	$\dfrac{(x/a)^\alpha - (x/a)^\beta}{x - a}$	$\pi\, a^{s-1}\dfrac{\sin[(\alpha - \beta)\pi]}{\sin[(s + \alpha)\pi]\sin[(s + \beta)\pi]}$
		$[a > 0; \; -\mathrm{Re}\,\alpha, \; -\mathrm{Re}\,\beta < \mathrm{Re}\, s < 1 - \mathrm{Re}\,\alpha, \; 1 - \mathrm{Re}\,\beta]$
7	$\dfrac{x^\mu - 1}{x^\nu - 1}$	$\dfrac{\pi}{\nu}\sin\dfrac{\mu\pi}{\nu}\csc\dfrac{s\pi}{\nu}\csc\dfrac{(s + \mu)\pi}{\nu}$ $\qquad$ $[0 < \mathrm{Re}\, s < \nu - \mu]$
8	$\dfrac{x^\mu - 1}{x^{\mu n} - 1}$	$\dfrac{\pi}{\mu n}\sin\dfrac{\pi}{n}\csc\dfrac{s\pi}{\mu n}\csc\dfrac{(s + \mu)\pi}{\mu n}$ $\qquad$ $[0 < \mathrm{Re}\, s < (n - 1)\mu; \; n \geq 2]$
9	$\dfrac{x - 1}{x^n - 1}$	$\dfrac{\pi}{n}\sin\dfrac{\pi}{n}\csc\dfrac{s\pi}{n}\csc\dfrac{(s + 1)\pi}{n}$ $\qquad$ $[0 < \mathrm{Re}\, s < n - 1; \; n \geq 2]$
10	$\dfrac{x^\mu - a^\mu}{x - a}$	$\pi a^{s+\mu-1}\sin(\mu\pi)\csc(s\pi)\csc[(s + \mu)\pi]$
		$[a > 0; \; 0 < \mathrm{Re}\, s < 1; \; 0 < \mathrm{Re}\,(s + \mu) < 1]$
11	$\dfrac{x^\mu - x^{-\mu}}{x^\nu - x^{-\nu}}$	$\dfrac{\pi\sin(\mu\pi/\nu)}{\nu[\cos(\mu\pi/\nu) + \cos(s\pi/\nu)]}$
		$[-\mathrm{Re}\,(\mu + \nu), \; \mathrm{Re}\,(\mu - \nu) < \mathrm{Re}\, s < \mathrm{Re}\,(\mu + \nu), \; \mathrm{Re}\,(\nu - \mu)]$

2.1.6.　$(a-x)_+^{\alpha-1}\left(x^n+b^n\right)^r$ **and** $(x-a)_+^{\alpha-1}\left(x^n+b^n\right)^r$

1	$(a-x)_+^{\alpha-1}\left(x^n+b^n\right)^r$	$a^{s+\alpha-1}b^{nr}\,\mathrm{B}\left(s,\alpha\right)\,_{n+1}F_n\left(\begin{array}{c}-r,\frac{s}{n},\frac{s+1}{n},\ldots,\frac{s+n-1}{n};-\left(\frac{a}{b}\right)^n\\[4pt]\frac{s+\alpha}{n},\frac{s+\alpha+1}{n},\ldots,\frac{s+\alpha+n-1}{n}\end{array}\right)$
		$\left[a,\ \mathrm{Re}\,\alpha>0;\ b\neq 0;\ \mathrm{Re}\,s>0;\ n=1,2,\ldots\right]$
2	$(x-a)_+^{\alpha-1}\left(x^n+b^n\right)^r$	$a^{s+nr+\alpha-1}\,\mathrm{B}\left(1-s-nr-\alpha,\alpha\right)$
		$\times\,_{n+1}F_n\left(\begin{array}{c}-r,-\frac{s+nr+\alpha-1}{n},-\frac{s+nr+\alpha-2}{n},\ldots,-\frac{s+nr+\alpha-n}{n}\\[4pt]-\frac{s+nr-1}{n},-\frac{s+nr-2}{n},\ldots,-\frac{s+nr-n}{n};-\left(\frac{b}{a}\right)^n\end{array}\right)$
		$\left[a,\ \mathrm{Re}\,\alpha>0;\ b\neq 0;\ \mathrm{Re}\,s<1-nr-\alpha;\ n=1,2,\ldots\right]$

2.1.7.　$\left(ax^2+bx+c\right)^\rho(dx+e)$

1	$\dfrac{1}{ax^2+bx+c}$	$-\dfrac{\pi}{\sqrt{b^2-4ac}}\left[\csc\left(s\pi\right)\left(\dfrac{\sqrt{b^2-4ac}+b}{2a}\right)^{s-1}\right.$
		$\left.+\cot\left(s\pi\right)\left(\dfrac{\sqrt{b^2-4ac}-b}{2a}\right)^{s-1}\right]$
		$\left[\begin{array}{l}a,b,c\text{ are real};\ a>0;\ b^2-4ac>0;\\-\sqrt{b^2-4ac}-b<0<\sqrt{b^2-4ac}-b;\ 0<\mathrm{Re}\,s<2\end{array}\right]$
2		$=\dfrac{\pi\cot\left(s\pi\right)}{\sqrt{b^2-4ac}}\left[\left(\dfrac{-\sqrt{b^2-4ac}-b}{2a}\right)^{s-1}-\left(\dfrac{\sqrt{b^2-4ac}-b}{2a}\right)^{s-1}\right]$
		$\left[\begin{array}{l}a,b,c\text{ are real};\ a>0;\ b^2-4ac>0;\\\sqrt{b^2-4ac}+b<0;\ 0<\mathrm{Re}\,s<2\end{array}\right]$
3		$=\dfrac{\pi\csc\left(s\pi\right)}{\sqrt{b^2-4ac}}\left[\left(\dfrac{b-\sqrt{b^2-4ac}}{2a}\right)^{s-1}-\left(\dfrac{\sqrt{b^2-4ac}+b}{2a}\right)^{s-1}\right]$
		$\left[\begin{array}{l}(|\mathrm{Im}\,a|+|\mathrm{Im}\,b|+|\mathrm{Im}\,c|\neq 0)\text{ or }\left(a,b,c\text{ are real};\ a>0;\right.\\\left.b^2-4ac>0;\ \sqrt{b^2-4ac}-b<0;\ 0<\mathrm{Re}\,s<2\right)\end{array}\right]$
4	$\dfrac{1}{ax^2+bx+a}$	$\dfrac{2\pi\cot\left(s\pi\right)}{\sqrt{b^2-4a^2}}\sinh\left[(s-1)\ln\dfrac{-\sqrt{b^2-4a^2}-b}{2a}\right]$
		$\left[\begin{array}{l}a,b\text{ are real};\ a>0;\ b^2-4a^2>0;\\\sqrt{b^2-4a^2}+b<0;\end{array}\right]$
5		$=\dfrac{2\pi\csc\left(s\pi\right)}{\sqrt{b^2-4a^2}}\sinh\left[(s-1)\ln\dfrac{b-\sqrt{b^2-4a^2}}{2a}\right]$
		$\left[|\mathrm{Im}\,a|+|\mathrm{Im}\,b|\neq 0;\ 0<\mathrm{Re}\,s<2\right]$
6	$\dfrac{1}{x^2+2x\cos\left(\beta\pi\right)+1}$	$-\dfrac{\pi}{\sin\left(\beta\pi\right)}\,\Gamma\left[\begin{array}{c}s,\,1-s\\\beta s-\beta,\,1-\beta s+\beta\end{array}\right]$　　$\left[|\beta|<1;\ 0<\mathrm{Re}\,s<2\right]$

No.	$f(x)$	$F(s)$
7	$\dfrac{x+a}{(x+b)(x+c)}$	$\dfrac{\pi}{\sin(s\pi)}\left[\dfrac{b-a}{b-c}b^{s-1}+\dfrac{c-a}{c-b}c^{s-1}\right]\quad\begin{bmatrix}0<\operatorname{Re}s<1;\\|\arg b|,\ |\arg c|<\pi\end{bmatrix}$
8	$\dfrac{x+a}{(x+a)^2+b^2}$	$\dfrac{\pi}{\sin(s\pi)}\left(a^2+b^2\right)^{s/2-1/2}\cos\left[(1-s)\arctan\dfrac{b}{a}\right]$ $[ab\neq 0;\ 0<\operatorname{Re}s<1]$
9	$\dfrac{1}{(ax^2+2bx+c)^\rho}$	$a^{-s/2}c^{s/2-\rho}\,\mathrm{B}\,(s,2\rho-s)\ {}_2F_1\left(\begin{matrix}\frac{s}{2},\ \frac{2\rho-s}{2}\\\frac{2\rho+1}{2};\ 1-\frac{b^2}{ac}\end{matrix}\right)$ $[a>0;\ b^2<ac;\ 0<\operatorname{Re}s<2\operatorname{Re}\rho]$

2.1.8. Algebraic functions of $\sqrt{ax+b}$

No.	$f(x)$	$F(s)$
1	$\dfrac{1}{\left(\sqrt{x+a}\pm\sqrt{a}\right)^\rho}$	$\pm\rho\,(4a)^{s-\rho/2}\,\Gamma\left[\begin{matrix}\frac{2s-(1\mp1)\rho}{2},\ \rho-2s\\\frac{2-2s+(1\pm1)\rho}{2}\end{matrix}\right]$ $[(1\mp1)\operatorname{Re}\rho/2<\operatorname{Re}s<\operatorname{Re}\rho/2;\ |\arg a|<\pi]$
2	$\dfrac{1}{\left(\sqrt{x+a}\pm\sqrt{x}\right)^\rho}$	$\pm\rho\,2^{-2s}a^{s-\rho/2}\,\Gamma\left[\begin{matrix}2s,\ \frac{\pm\rho-2s}{2}\\\frac{2s\pm\rho+2}{2}\end{matrix}\right]$ $[0<\operatorname{Re}s<\pm\operatorname{Re}\rho/2;\ |\arg a|<\pi]$
3	$\dfrac{1}{\sqrt{x+a}\left(\sqrt{x+a}\pm\sqrt{a}\right)^\rho}$	$2^{2s-\rho}a^{s-(\rho+1)/2}\,\mathrm{B}\left(\dfrac{2s-(1\mp1)\rho}{2},\ 1-2s+\rho\right)$ $[(1\mp1)\operatorname{Re}\rho/2<\operatorname{Re}s<(\operatorname{Re}\rho+1)/2;\ |\arg a|<\pi]$
4	$\dfrac{1}{\sqrt{x+a}\left(\sqrt{x+a}\pm\sqrt{x}\right)^\rho}$	$2^{1-2s}a^{s+(\rho-1)/2}\,\mathrm{B}\left(2s,\ \dfrac{1-2s\mp\rho}{2}\right)$ $[0<\operatorname{Re}s<(1\mp\operatorname{Re}\rho)/2;\ |\arg a|<\pi]$
5	$\dfrac{1}{\left(\sqrt{x}+\sqrt{a}\right)^\rho}+\dfrac{1}{|\sqrt{x}-\sqrt{a}|^\rho}$	$2\sqrt{\pi}\,a^{s-\rho/2}\,\Gamma\left[\begin{matrix}\frac{1-\rho}{2},\ \frac{\rho-2s}{2},\ s\\\frac{\rho}{2},\ \frac{2s-\rho+1}{2},\ \frac{1-2s}{2}\end{matrix}\right]$ $[a>0;\ 0<\operatorname{Re}s<\operatorname{Re}\rho/2<1/2]$
6	$\dfrac{1}{\left(x+a+\sqrt{a(2x+a)}\right)^\rho}$	$\rho 2^{s-\rho+1}a^{s-\rho}\,\Gamma\left[\begin{matrix}2\rho-2s,\ s\\1-s+2\rho\end{matrix}\right]\quad[0<\operatorname{Re}s<\operatorname{Re}\rho;\ |\arg a|<\pi]$

No.	$f(x)$	$F(s)$
7	$\dfrac{(2x+a)^{-1/2}}{\left[x+a+\sqrt{a(2x+a)}\right]^{\rho}}$	$2^{s-\rho}\,a^{s-\rho-1/2}\,\mathrm{B}\left(1-2s+2\rho,\,s\right)$ $\qquad\qquad\qquad [0<\operatorname{Re}s<\operatorname{Re}\rho+1/2;\ \lvert\arg a\rvert<\pi]$
8	$\dfrac{(x+a)^{-1/2}}{\left[x+a+b+2\sqrt{b\,(x+a)}\,\right]^{\rho}}$	$2^{2s-2\rho}a^{s-\rho-1}\sqrt{b}\;\mathrm{B}\left(1-2s+2\rho,\,s\right){}_2F_1\!\left(\genfrac{}{}{0pt}{}{\frac{2\rho+1}{2},\,1-s+\rho}{1-s+2\rho;\,\frac{a-b}{a}}\right)$ $\qquad [0<\operatorname{Re}s<\operatorname{Re}\rho+1/2;\ \lvert\arg a\rvert,\ \lvert\arg b\rvert,\ \lvert\arg(b/a)\rvert<\pi]$

2.1.9.   Algebraic functions of $\sqrt{ax^2+bx+c}$

No.	$f(x)$	$F(s)$
1	$\dfrac{1}{\sqrt{x^2+2x\cos\beta+1}}$	$\dfrac{\pi}{\sin(s\pi)}\,P_{s-1}(\cos\beta)\qquad\qquad [\lvert\beta\rvert<\pi;\ 0<\operatorname{Re}s<1]$
2	$\dfrac{1}{\left(\sqrt{x^2+a^2}\pm a\right)^{\rho}}$	$\pm 2^{s-\rho-1}\rho a^{s-\rho}\,\Gamma\!\left[\genfrac{}{}{0pt}{}{\frac{s-(1\mp 1)\rho}{2},\,\rho-s}{\frac{2-s+(1\pm 1)\rho}{2}}\right]$ $\qquad\qquad\qquad [\operatorname{Re}a>0;\ (1\mp 1)\rho<\operatorname{Re}s<\operatorname{Re}\rho]$
3	$\dfrac{1}{\left(\sqrt{x^2+a^2}\pm x\right)^{\rho}}$	$\pm\dfrac{\rho a^{s-\rho}}{2^{s+1}}\,\Gamma\!\left[\genfrac{}{}{0pt}{}{s,\,\frac{\pm\rho-s}{2}}{\frac{s\pm\rho+2}{2}}\right]\qquad [\operatorname{Re}a>0;\ 0<\operatorname{Re}s<\pm\operatorname{Re}\rho]$
4	$\dfrac{1}{\sqrt{x^2+1}\left(\sqrt{x^2+1}+a\right)^{\rho}}$	$\dfrac{a^{-\rho}}{2}\,\mathrm{B}\!\left(\dfrac{1-s}{2},\dfrac{s}{2}\right){}_2F_1\!\left(\genfrac{}{}{0pt}{}{\frac{\rho}{2},\,\frac{\rho+1}{2}}{\frac{s+1}{2};\,\frac{1}{a^2}}\right)$ $\qquad + a^{s-\rho-1}\,\mathrm{B}\left(s-1,\,1-s+\rho\right){}_2F_1\!\left(\genfrac{}{}{0pt}{}{\frac{1-s+\rho}{2},\,\frac{2-s+\rho}{2}}{\frac{3-s}{2};\,\frac{1}{a^2}}\right)$ $\qquad\qquad\qquad [\operatorname{Re}a>-1;\ 0<\operatorname{Re}s<\operatorname{Re}\rho+1]$
5	$\dfrac{\left(x^2+1\right)^{-1/2}}{\left(\cos\beta\pm i\sin\beta\sqrt{x^2+1}\right)^{\rho}}$	$\left(\dfrac{\sin\beta}{2}\right)^{(1-s)/2}\Gamma\!\left[\genfrac{}{}{0pt}{}{\frac{s}{2},\,1-s+\rho}{\rho}\right]$ $\quad\times\left[\dfrac{1}{\sqrt{\pi}}\,Q^{(s-1)/2}_{\rho-(s+1)/2}(\cos\beta)\mp\dfrac{i\sqrt{\pi}}{2}\,P^{(s-1)/2}_{\rho-(s+1)/2}(\cos\beta)\right]$ $\qquad\qquad\qquad [0<\operatorname{Re}s<\operatorname{Re}\rho+1]$
6	$\dfrac{\left(x^2+1\right)^{-1/2}}{\left(\sqrt{(a^2-1)(x^2+1)}+a\right)^{\rho}}$	$\dfrac{\left(a^2-1\right)^{-\rho/2}}{2}\,\mathrm{B}\!\left(\dfrac{s}{2},\dfrac{1-s+\rho}{2}\right){}_2F_1\!\left(\genfrac{}{}{0pt}{}{\frac{\rho}{2},\,\frac{1-s+\rho}{2}}{\frac{1}{2};\,\frac{a^2}{a^2-1}}\right)$ $\quad-\dfrac{\left(a^2-1\right)^{-(\rho+1)/2}}{2a\,(1-s+\rho)}\,\mathrm{B}\!\left(\dfrac{s}{2},\dfrac{2-s+\rho}{2}\right)\Bigg[{}_2F_1\!\left(\genfrac{}{}{0pt}{}{\frac{\rho+1}{2},\,\frac{2-s+\rho}{2}}{-\frac{1}{2};\,\frac{a^2}{a^2-1}}\right)$ $\quad-\left(1+a^2(2-s+2\rho)\right){}_2F_1\!\left(\genfrac{}{}{0pt}{}{\frac{\rho+1}{2},\,\frac{2-s+\rho}{2}}{\frac{1}{2};\,\frac{a^2}{a^2-1}}\right)\Bigg]$ $\qquad\qquad [\operatorname{Re}a>1;\ \operatorname{Re}\rho>0;\ \operatorname{Re}s<\operatorname{Re}\rho+1]$

No.	$f(x)$	$F(s)$
7	$\dfrac{1}{\sqrt{x^2+a^2}\left(\sqrt{x^2+a^2}+a\right)^{\rho}}$	$(2a)^{s-\rho-1}\,\mathrm{B}\left(\dfrac{s}{2},\,1-s+\rho\right)\qquad[\operatorname{Re}a>0;\,0<\operatorname{Re}s<\operatorname{Re}\rho+1]$
8	$\dfrac{1}{\sqrt{x^2+a^2}\left(\sqrt{x^2+a^2}+b\right)^{\rho}}$	$(2a)^{s-\rho-1}\,\mathrm{B}\left(\dfrac{s}{2},\,1-s+\rho\right)\,{}_2F_1\left(\begin{matrix}1-s+\rho,\,\rho\\ \frac{2-s+2\rho}{2};\,\frac{a-b}{2a}\end{matrix}\right)$ $\left[\begin{matrix}\operatorname{Re}a>0;\,0<\operatorname{Re}s<\operatorname{Re}\rho+1;\\ |\arg(b/a+1)|<\pi\end{matrix}\right]$
9	$\dfrac{1}{\sqrt{x^2+a^2}\left(\sqrt{x^2+a^2}-a\right)^{\rho}}$	$(2a)^{s-\rho-1}\,\mathrm{B}\left(\dfrac{s}{2}-\rho,\,1-s+\rho\right)$ $[\operatorname{Re}a>0;\,2\operatorname{Re}\rho<\operatorname{Re}s<\operatorname{Re}\rho+1]$
10	$\dfrac{1}{\sqrt{x^2+a^2}\left(\sqrt{x^2+a^2}\pm x\right)^{\rho}}$	$2^{-s}a^{s-\rho-1}\,\mathrm{B}\left(s,\,\dfrac{1-s\pm\rho}{2}\right)$ $[\operatorname{Re}a>0;\,0<\operatorname{Re}s<1\pm\operatorname{Re}\rho]$
11	$\dfrac{1}{\sqrt{x^2+a^2}\left(\sqrt{x^2+a^2}+bx\right)^{\rho}}$	$2^{-s}a^{s-\rho-1}\,\mathrm{B}\left(s,\,\dfrac{1-s+\rho}{2}\right)\,{}_2F_1\left(\begin{matrix}\rho,\,s;\,\frac{1-b}{2}\\ \frac{s+\rho+1}{2}\end{matrix}\right)$ $[\operatorname{Re}a>0;\,0<\operatorname{Re}s<\operatorname{Re}\rho+1;\,|\arg(b+1)|<\pi]$
12	$\dfrac{1}{\left(x+a+\sqrt{(x+a)^2-a^2}\right)^{\rho}}$	$2^{1-s}\rho a^{s-\rho}\,\Gamma\left[\begin{matrix}2s,\,\rho-s\\ s+\rho+1\end{matrix}\right]\qquad[0<\operatorname{Re}s<\operatorname{Re}\rho;\,|\arg a|<\pi]$
13	$\dfrac{1}{\left(x+a+\sqrt{(x+a)^2-b^2}\right)^{\rho}}$	$2^{-\rho}a^{s-\rho}\,\mathrm{B}(s,\,\rho-s)\,{}_2F_1\left(\begin{matrix}\frac{\rho-s}{2},\,\frac{\rho-s+1}{2}\\ \rho+1;\,\frac{b^2}{a^2}\end{matrix}\right)$ $[|b|\le|a|;\,0<\operatorname{Re}s<\operatorname{Re}\rho;\,|\arg a|<\pi]$
14		$=\dfrac{\rho\left(a^2-b^2\right)^{s/2}}{(ib)^{\rho}}\,\Gamma(s)\,\Gamma(\rho-s)\,\mathrm{P}_s^{-\rho}\left(\dfrac{a}{\sqrt{a^2-b^2}}\right)$ $[0<b<a;\,0<\operatorname{Re}s<\operatorname{Re}\rho]$
15	$\dfrac{1}{\left(x+a+\sqrt{(x+a)^2-b^2x^2}\right)^{\rho}}$	$2^{-\rho}a^{s-\rho}\,\mathrm{B}(s,\,\rho-s)\,{}_2F_1\left(\begin{matrix}\frac{s}{2},\,\frac{s+1}{2}\\ \rho+1;\,b^2\end{matrix}\right)$ $[|b|\le1;\,0<\operatorname{Re}s<\operatorname{Re}\rho;\,|\arg a|<\pi]$
16	$\dfrac{(x+2a)^{-1/2}}{\left(x+a+\sqrt{x^2+2ax}\right)^{\rho}}$	$\dfrac{a^{s-\rho-1/2}}{2^{s-1/2}}\,\mathrm{B}\left(2s,\,\dfrac{1-2s+2\rho}{2}\right)$ $[0<\operatorname{Re}s<\operatorname{Re}\rho+1/2;\,|\arg a|<\pi]$
17	$\dfrac{\left(x^2+2ax\right)^{-1/2}}{\left(x+a+\sqrt{x^2+2ax}\right)^{\rho}}$	$\dfrac{2^{s-1}a^{s-\rho-1}}{\sqrt{\pi}}\,\Gamma\left[\begin{matrix}s,\,1-s+\rho,\,\frac{2s-1}{2}\\ s+\rho\end{matrix}\right]$ $[1/2<\operatorname{Re}s<\operatorname{Re}\rho+1;\,|\arg a|<\pi]$

No.	$f(x)$	$F(s)$
18	$\dfrac{\left[(x+a)^2-b^2\right]^{-1/2}}{\left[x+a+\sqrt{(x+a)^2-b^2}\right]^\rho}$	$2^{-\rho}a^{s-\rho-1}\,\mathrm{B}\left(s,1-s+\rho\right)\,{}_2F_1\left(\begin{matrix}\frac{1-s+\rho}{2},\ \frac{2-s+\rho}{2}\\ \rho+1;\ \frac{b^2}{a^2}\end{matrix}\right)$
		$\left[\lvert b\rvert<\lvert a\rvert;\ 0<\mathrm{Re}\,s<\mathrm{Re}\,\rho+1;\ \lvert\arg a\rvert<\pi\right]$
19	$\dfrac{\left[(x+a)^2-b^2x^2\right]^{-1/2}}{\left[x+a+\sqrt{(x+a)^2-b^2x^2}\right]^\rho}$	$2^{-\rho}a^{s-\rho-1}\,\mathrm{B}(s,\rho-s+1)\,{}_2F_1\left(\begin{matrix}\frac{s}{2},\ \frac{s+1}{2}\\ \rho+1;\ b^2\end{matrix}\right)$
		$\left[\lvert b\rvert<1;\ 0<\mathrm{Re}\,s<\mathrm{Re}\,\rho+1;\ \lvert\arg a\rvert<\pi\right]$
20	$\dfrac{1}{\left(\sqrt{x^2+a^2}+\sqrt{b^2x^2+a^2}\right)^\rho}$	$2^{-\rho-1}a^{s-\rho}\,\mathrm{B}\left(\dfrac{s}{2},\dfrac{\rho-s}{2}\right)\,{}_2F_1\left(\begin{matrix}\frac{\rho+1}{2},\ \frac{s}{2}\\ \rho+1;\ 1-b^2\end{matrix}\right)$
		$\left[\mathrm{Re}\,a,\ \mathrm{Re}\,b>0;\ 0<\mathrm{Re}\,s<\mathrm{Re}\,\rho\right]$
21	$\dfrac{1}{\left(\sqrt{x^2+a^2}+\sqrt{x^2+b^2}\right)^\rho}$	$2^{-\rho-1}a^{s-\rho}\,\mathrm{B}\left(\dfrac{s}{2},\dfrac{\rho-s}{2}\right)\,{}_2F_1\left(\begin{matrix}\frac{\rho-s}{2},\ \frac{\rho+1}{2}\\ \rho+1;\ \frac{a^2-b^2}{a^2}\end{matrix}\right)$
		$\left[\mathrm{Re}\,a,\ \mathrm{Re}\,b>0;\ 0<\mathrm{Re}\,s<\mathrm{Re}\,\rho\right]$
22	$\dfrac{(x+a)^{-1/2}}{\left(x+bx+a+2\sqrt{bx(x+a)}\right)^\rho}$	$\dfrac{a^{s-\rho-1/2}\sqrt{b}}{2^{2s-1}}\,\mathrm{B}\left(2s,\dfrac{1-2s+2\rho}{2}\right)\,{}_2F_1\left(\begin{matrix}\frac{2\rho+1}{2},\ \frac{2s+1}{2}\\ \frac{2s+2\rho+1}{2};\ 1-b\end{matrix}\right)$
		$\left[0<\mathrm{Re}\,s<\mathrm{Re}\,\rho+1/2;\ \lvert\arg a\rvert,\ \lvert\arg b\rvert<\pi\right]$
23	$\dfrac{(x^2+a^2)^{-1/2}(x^2+b^2)^{-1/2}}{\left(\sqrt{x^2+a^2}+\sqrt{x^2+b^2}\right)^\rho}$	$\dfrac{a^{s-\rho-2}}{2^{\rho+1}}\,\mathrm{B}\left(\dfrac{s}{2},\dfrac{2-s+\rho}{2}\right)\,{}_2F_1\left(\begin{matrix}\frac{\rho+1}{2},\ \frac{2-s+\rho}{2}\\ \rho+1;\ \frac{a^2-b^2}{a^2}\end{matrix}\right)$
		$\left[\mathrm{Re}\,a,\ \mathrm{Re}\,b>0;\ 0<\mathrm{Re}\,s<\mathrm{Re}\,\rho+2\right]$
24	$\dfrac{(x^2+a^2)^{-1/2}(b^2x^2+a^2)^{-1/2}}{\left(\sqrt{x^2+a^2}+\sqrt{b^2x^2+a^2}\right)^\rho}$	$\dfrac{a^{s-\rho-2}}{2^{\rho+1}}\,\mathrm{B}\left(\dfrac{s}{2},\dfrac{2-s+\rho}{2}\right)\,{}_2F_1\left(\begin{matrix}\frac{\rho+1}{2},\ \frac{s}{2}\\ \rho+1;\ 1-b^2\end{matrix}\right)$
		$\left[\mathrm{Re}\,a,\ \mathrm{Re}\,b>0;\ 0<\mathrm{Re}\,s<\mathrm{Re}\,\rho+2\right]$

2.1.10. Various algebraic functions

No.	$f(x)$	$F(s)$
1	$(a-x)_+^{-\alpha}$ $+\dfrac{\sin\left[(c-\alpha)\pi\right]}{\sin(c\pi)}(x-a)_+^{-\alpha}$	$\dfrac{\pi a^{s-\alpha}}{\sin(c\pi)\,\Gamma(\alpha)}\,\Gamma\left[\begin{matrix}s,\ \alpha-s\\ s-c+1,\ c-s\end{matrix}\right]$ $\left[a>0;\ 0<\mathrm{Re}\,s<\mathrm{Re}\,\alpha<1\right]$
2	$\dfrac{\sin\left[(c-\alpha)\pi\right]}{\sin(c\pi)}(a-x)_+^{-\alpha}$ $+(x-a)_+^{-\alpha}$	$\dfrac{\pi a^{s-\alpha}}{\sin(c\pi)\,\Gamma(\alpha)}\,\Gamma\left[\begin{matrix}s,\ \alpha-s\\ s+c-\alpha,\ 1-s-c+\alpha\end{matrix}\right]$ $\left[a>0;\ 0<\mathrm{Re}\,s<\mathrm{Re}\,\alpha<1\right]$

No.	$f(x)$	$F(s)$
3	$\theta(a-x)\left(\sqrt{a-x}+\sqrt{a}\right)^{-1/2}$ $+\theta(x-a)x^{-1/2}\left(\sqrt{x}+\sqrt{x-a}\right)^{1/2}$	$\dfrac{\sqrt{\pi}\,a^{s-1/4}}{2^{3/2}}\,\Gamma\left[\begin{array}{c}\frac{1-4s}{4},\,s\\ \frac{4s+1}{4},\,\frac{3-2s}{2}\end{array}\right]\quad[a>0;\,0<\operatorname{Re}s<1/4]$
4	$\theta(a-x)\left(\sqrt{a-x}+\sqrt{a}\right)^{1/2}$ $+\sqrt{a}\,\theta(x-a)\left(\sqrt{x}+\sqrt{x-a}\right)^{-1/2}$	$\dfrac{\sqrt{\pi}\,a^{s+1/4}}{2^{3/2}}\,\Gamma\left[\begin{array}{c}\frac{1-4s}{4},\,s\\ \frac{4s+5}{4},\,\frac{1-2s}{2}\end{array}\right]\quad[a>0;\,0<\operatorname{Re}s<1/4]$
5	$(a-x)_+^{-1/2}\sqrt{\sqrt{a-x}+\sqrt{a}}$ $+(x-a)_+^{-1/2}\sqrt{\sqrt{x}+\sqrt{x-a}}$	$\sqrt{2\pi}\,a^{s-1/4}\,\Gamma\left[\begin{array}{c}\frac{1-4s}{4},\,s\\ \frac{4s+1}{4},\,\frac{1-2s}{2}\end{array}\right]\quad[a>0;\,0<\operatorname{Re}s<1/4]$
6	$(a-x)_+^{-1/2}\sqrt{\sqrt{a}-\sqrt{a-x}}$ $-(x-a)_+^{-1/2}\sqrt{\sqrt{x}+\sqrt{x-a}}$	$-\sqrt{2\pi}\,a^{s-1/4}\,\Gamma\left[\begin{array}{c}\frac{1-4s}{4},\,\frac{2s+1}{2}\\ \frac{4s+1}{4},\,1-s\end{array}\right]$ $[a>0;\,-1/2<\operatorname{Re}s<1/4]$
7	$(a-x)_+^{-1/2}\sqrt{\sqrt{a-x}+\sqrt{a}}$ $-(x-a)_+^{-1/2}\sqrt{\sqrt{x}-\sqrt{x-a}}$	$\sqrt{2\pi}\,a^{s-1/4}\,\Gamma\left[\begin{array}{c}\frac{3-4s}{4},\,s\\ \frac{4s+3}{4},\,\frac{1-2s}{2}\end{array}\right]$ $[a>0;\,0<\operatorname{Re}s<3/4]$
8	$(a-x)_+^{-1/2}\left[\left(\sqrt{a}+\sqrt{a-x}\right)^{\rho}\right.$ $\left.+\left(\sqrt{a}-\sqrt{a-x}\right)^{\rho}\right]$	$2\sqrt{\pi}\,a^{s+(\rho-1)/2}\,\Gamma\left[\begin{array}{c}s,\,s+\rho\\ \frac{2s+\rho}{2},\,\frac{2s+\rho+1}{2}\end{array}\right]$ $[a,\,\operatorname{Re}s>0,\,-\operatorname{Re}\rho]$
9	$(x-a)_+^{-1/2}\left[\left(\sqrt{x}+\sqrt{x-a}\right)^{\rho}\right.$ $\left.+\left(\sqrt{x}-\sqrt{x-a}\right)^{\rho}\right]$	$2\sqrt{\pi}\,a^{s+(\rho-1)/2}\,\Gamma\left[\begin{array}{c}\frac{1-2s-\rho}{2},\,\frac{1-2s+\rho}{2}\\ 1-s,\,\frac{1-2s}{2}\end{array}\right]$ $[a>0;\,\operatorname{Re}s<(1-|\operatorname{Re}\rho|)/2]$
10	$(x^2-a^2)_+^{-1/2}\left[\left(x+\sqrt{x^2-a^2}\right)^{\rho}\right.$ $\left.+\left(x-\sqrt{x^2-a^2}\right)^{\rho}\right]$	$2^{-s}a^{s+\rho-1}\,\mathrm{B}\left(\dfrac{1-s-\rho}{2},\,\dfrac{1-s+\rho}{2}\right)$ $[\operatorname{Re}s<|\operatorname{Re}\rho|+1]$
11	$(a^2-x^2)_+^{-1/2}\left[\left(a+\sqrt{a^2-x^2}\right)^{\rho}\right.$ $\left.+\left(a-\sqrt{a^2-x^2}\right)^{\rho}\right]$	$(2a)^{s+\rho-1}\,\mathrm{B}\left(\dfrac{s}{2},\,\dfrac{s+2\rho}{2}\right)$ $[\operatorname{Re}s>0,\,-2\operatorname{Re}\rho]$

No.	$f(x)$	$F(s)$
12	$\dfrac{\left(\sqrt{a}+\sqrt{a-x}\right)^{\rho}-\left(\sqrt{a}-\sqrt{a-x}\right)^{\rho}}{\sqrt{a-x}}$	$2^{2s+\rho}\dfrac{\sin(\rho\pi)}{\pi}a^{s+(\rho-1)/2}\Gamma(1-2s-\rho)\Gamma(s)$ $\times\,\Gamma(s+\rho)\quad\begin{bmatrix}0,\,-\operatorname{Re}\rho<\operatorname{Re}s<(1-\operatorname{Re}\rho)/2;\\ -\pi<\arg a\le\pi\end{bmatrix}$
13	$\dfrac{\left(\sqrt{x}+\sqrt{x-a}\right)^{\rho}-\left(\sqrt{x}-\sqrt{x-a}\right)^{\rho}}{\sqrt{x-a}}$	$2^{1-2s}\dfrac{\sin(\rho\pi)}{\pi}a^{s+(\rho-1)/2}\Gamma(2s)\Gamma\left(\dfrac{1-2s-\rho}{2}\right)$ $\times\,\Gamma\left(\dfrac{1-2s+\rho}{2}\right)\quad\begin{bmatrix}0<\operatorname{Re}s<(1-|\operatorname{Re}\rho|)/2;\\ -\pi<\arg a\le\pi\end{bmatrix}$
14	$\dfrac{\left(x+\sqrt{x^2-a^2}\right)^{\rho}-\left(x-\sqrt{x^2-a^2}\right)^{\rho}}{\sqrt{x^2-a^2}}$	$2^{-s}\dfrac{\sin(\rho\pi)}{\pi}a^{s+\rho-1}\Gamma\left(\dfrac{1-s-\rho}{2}\right)\Gamma\left(\dfrac{1-s+\rho}{2}\right)$ $\times\,\Gamma(s)\quad\begin{bmatrix}0<\operatorname{Re}s<1-|\operatorname{Re}\rho|;\\ -\pi/2<\arg a\le\pi/2\end{bmatrix}$
15	$\theta(a-x)\left[\left(\sqrt{a}+\sqrt{a-x}\right)^{\rho}\right.$ $\left.-\left(\sqrt{a}-\sqrt{a-x}\right)^{\rho}\right]$	$2^{2s+\rho}\rho\,a^{s+\rho/2}\Gamma\begin{bmatrix}s,\,s+\rho\\ 2s+\rho+1\end{bmatrix}$ $[a>0;\ \operatorname{Re}s>0,\,-\operatorname{Re}\rho]$
16	$\theta(a-x)\left[\left(\sqrt{a+x}+\sqrt{a-x}\right)^{\rho}\right.$ $\left.-\left(\sqrt{a+x}-\sqrt{a-x}\right)^{\rho}\right]$	$2^{s+\rho-2}\rho\,a^{s+\rho/2}\Gamma\begin{bmatrix}\frac{s}{2},\,\frac{s+\rho}{2}\\ \frac{2s+\rho+2}{2}\end{bmatrix}$ $[a>0;\ \operatorname{Re}s>0,\,-\operatorname{Re}\rho]$
17	$\theta(a-x)\left[\left(\sqrt{\sqrt{a}+\sqrt{x}}-\sqrt{\sqrt{a}-\sqrt{x}}\right)^{\rho}\right.$ $\left.-a^{-\rho/4}\left(\sqrt{\sqrt{a}+\sqrt{x}}+\sqrt{\sqrt{a}-\sqrt{x}}\right)^{\rho}\right]$	$-2^{2s+\rho-1}\rho\,a^{s+\rho/4}\Gamma\begin{bmatrix}s,\,\frac{2s+\rho}{2}\\ \frac{4s+\rho+2}{2}\end{bmatrix}$ $[a>0;\ \operatorname{Re}s>0,\,-\operatorname{Re}\rho/2]$
18	$\dfrac{\theta(a-x)}{\sqrt{a-x}}\left[\left(\sqrt{\sqrt{a}+\sqrt{x}}-\sqrt{\sqrt{a}-\sqrt{x}}\right)^{\rho}\right.$ $\left.+\left(\sqrt{\sqrt{a}+\sqrt{x}}+\sqrt{\sqrt{a}-\sqrt{x}}\right)^{\rho}\right]$	$2^{2s+\rho}a^{s+(\rho-2)/4}\,\mathrm{B}\left(s,\,\dfrac{2s+\rho}{2}\right)$ $[a>0;\ \operatorname{Re}s>0,\,-\operatorname{Re}\rho/2]$
19	$\dfrac{\theta(a-x)}{\sqrt{a-x}}\left[\left(\sqrt{a}-\sqrt{a-x}\right)^{\rho}\right.$ $\left.+\left(\sqrt{a}+\sqrt{a+x}\right)^{\rho}\right]$	$2^{2s+\rho}a^{s+(\rho-1)/2}\,\mathrm{B}(s,\,s+\rho)$ $[a>0;\ \operatorname{Re}s>0,\,-\operatorname{Re}\rho]$
20	$\dfrac{\theta(a-x)}{\sqrt{a^2-x^2}}\left[\left(\sqrt{a+x}-\sqrt{a-x}\right)^{\rho}\right.$ $\left.+\left(\sqrt{a+x}+\sqrt{a-x}\right)^{\rho}\right]$	$2^{s+\rho-1}a^{s+(\rho-2)/2}\,\mathrm{B}\left(\dfrac{s}{2},\,\dfrac{s+\rho}{2}\right)$ $[a>0;\ \operatorname{Re}s>0,\,-\operatorname{Re}\rho]$
21	$\theta(a-x)\left[\left(a-\sqrt{a^2-x^2}\right)^{\rho}\right.$ $\left.-\left(a+\sqrt{a^2-x^2}\right)^{\rho}\right]$	$-2^{s+\rho-1}\rho\,a^{s+\rho}\Gamma\begin{bmatrix}\frac{s}{2},\,\frac{s+2\rho}{2}\\ s+\rho+1\end{bmatrix}$ $[a>0;\ \operatorname{Re}s>0,\,-2\operatorname{Re}\rho]$

No.	$f(x)$	$F(s)$
22	$\dfrac{\theta(a-x)}{\sqrt{a^2-x^2}}\left[\left(a-\sqrt{a^2-x^2}\right)^\rho \right.$ $\left.+\left(a+\sqrt{a^2-x^2}\right)^\rho\right]$	$(2a)^{s+\rho-1}\;\mathrm{B}\left(\dfrac{s}{2},\dfrac{s+2\rho}{2}\right)$ $[a>0;\ \mathrm{Re}\,s>0,\,-2\,\mathrm{Re}\,\rho]$
23	$\theta(x-a)\left[\left(\sqrt{x}-\sqrt{x-a}\right)^\rho\right.$ $\left.-\left(\sqrt{x}+\sqrt{x-a}\right)^\rho\right]$	$-2^{-2s}\rho\,a^{s+\rho/2}\,\Gamma\left[\begin{array}{c}\frac{-2s-\rho}{2},\,\frac{-2s+\rho}{2}\\ 1-2s\end{array}\right]$ $[a>0;\ \mathrm{Re}\,s<-\lvert\mathrm{Re}\,\rho\rvert/2]$
24	$\theta(x-a)\left[\left(\sqrt{x+a}-\sqrt{x-a}\right)^\rho\right.$ $\left.-\left(\sqrt{x+a}+\sqrt{x-a}\right)^\rho\right]$	$-2^{-s+\rho/2-2}\rho\,a^{s+\rho/2}\,\Gamma\left[\begin{array}{c}\frac{-2s-\rho}{4},\,\frac{-2s+\rho}{4}\\ 1-s\end{array}\right]$ $[a>0;\ \mathrm{Re}\,s<-\lvert\mathrm{Re}\,\rho\rvert/2]$
25	$\theta(x-a)\left[\left(\sqrt{\sqrt{x}+\sqrt{a}}+\sqrt{\sqrt{x}-\sqrt{a}}\right)^\rho\right.$ $\left.-\left(\sqrt{\sqrt{x}+\sqrt{a}}-\sqrt{\sqrt{x}-\sqrt{a}}\right)^\rho\right]$	$2^{-2s+\rho/2-1}\rho\,a^{s+\rho/4}\,\Gamma\left[\begin{array}{c}\frac{-4s-\rho}{4},\,\frac{-4s+\rho}{4}\\ 1-2s\end{array}\right]$ $[a>0;\ \mathrm{Re}\,s<-\lvert\mathrm{Re}\,\rho\rvert/4]$
26	$\dfrac{\theta(x-a)}{\sqrt{x-a}}\left[\left(\sqrt{\sqrt{x}+\sqrt{a}}-\sqrt{\sqrt{x}-\sqrt{a}}\right)^\rho\right.$ $\left.+\left(\sqrt{\sqrt{x}+\sqrt{a}}+\sqrt{\sqrt{x}-\sqrt{a}}\right)^\rho\right]$	$2^{-2s+\rho/2+1}a^{s+(\rho-2)/4}\,\mathrm{B}\left(\dfrac{2-4s-\rho}{4},\dfrac{2-4s+\rho}{4}\right)$ $[a>0;\ \mathrm{Re}\,s<(2-\lvert\mathrm{Re}\,\rho\rvert)/4]$
27	$\dfrac{\theta(x-a)}{\sqrt{x-a}}\left[\left(\sqrt{x}-\sqrt{x-a}\right)^\rho\right.$ $\left.+\left(\sqrt{x}+\sqrt{x-a}\right)^\rho\right]$	$2^{1-2s}a^{s+(\rho-1)/2}\,\mathrm{B}\left(\dfrac{1-2s-\rho}{2},\dfrac{1-2s+\rho}{2}\right)$ $[a>0;\ \mathrm{Re}\,s<(1-\lvert\mathrm{Re}\,\rho\rvert)/2]$
28	$\dfrac{\theta(x-a)}{\sqrt{x^2-a^2}}\left[\left(\sqrt{x+a}-\sqrt{x-a}\right)^\rho\right.$ $\left.+\left(\sqrt{x+a}+\sqrt{x-a}\right)^\rho\right]$	$2^{-s+\rho/2}a^{s+(\rho-2)/2}\,\mathrm{B}\left(\dfrac{2-2s-\rho}{4},\dfrac{2-2s+\rho}{4}\right)$ $[a>0;\ \mathrm{Re}\,s<(2-\lvert\mathrm{Re}\,\rho\rvert)/2]$
29	$\theta(x-a)\left[\left(x-\sqrt{x^2-a^2}\right)^\rho\right.$ $\left.-\left(x+\sqrt{x^2-a^2}\right)^\rho\right]$	$-2^{-s-1}\rho\,a^{s+\rho}\,\Gamma\left[\begin{array}{c}\frac{-s-\rho}{2},\,\frac{-s+\rho}{2}\\ 1-s\end{array}\right]$ $[a>0;\ \mathrm{Re}\,s<-\lvert\mathrm{Re}\,\rho\rvert]$
30	$\dfrac{\theta(x-a)}{\sqrt{x^2-a^2}}\left[\left(x-\sqrt{x^2-a^2}\right)^\rho\right.$ $\left.+\left(x+\sqrt{x^2-a^2}\right)^\rho\right]$	$2^{-s}a^{s+\rho-1}\,\mathrm{B}\left(\dfrac{1-s-\rho}{2},\dfrac{1-s+\rho}{2}\right)$ $[a>0;\ \mathrm{Re}\,s<1-\lvert\mathrm{Re}\,\rho\rvert]$
31	$\left[a^2x^2+(bx-x-1)^2\right.$ $\left.-2ax(bx+x+1)\right]^{-1/2}$	$\pi\csc(s\pi)\,F_4(1,s;1,1;a,b)\qquad[0<\mathrm{Re}\,s<1]$

2.2.   The Exponential Function

More formulas can be obtained from the corresponding sections due to the relations

$$a^z = e^{z \ln a}, \quad e^z = {}_0F_0(z) = {}_1F_1(a; a; z), \quad e^{-z} = G_{01}^{10}\left(z \left|\begin{matrix} \cdot \\ 0 \end{matrix}\right.\right).$$

2.2.1. $e^{-ax^r - bx^p}$

No.	$f(x)$	$F(s)$
1	e^{-ax}	$\dfrac{\Gamma(s)}{a^s}$ $\qquad$ $[\operatorname{Re} a,\ \operatorname{Re} s > 0 \text{ or } (\operatorname{Re} a = 0;\ 0 < \operatorname{Re} s < 1)]$
2	$e^{-ax} - \displaystyle\sum_{k=0}^{n-1} \dfrac{(-ax)^k}{k!}$	$\dfrac{\Gamma(s)}{a^s}$ $\qquad$ $[\operatorname{Re} a \geq 0;\ -n < \operatorname{Re} s < 1 - n;\ n = 1, 2, \ldots]$
3	e^{iax}	$\dfrac{2^{s-1}\sqrt{\pi}}{a^s}\left(\Gamma\!\left[\begin{matrix} \frac{s}{2} \\ \frac{1-s}{2} \end{matrix}\right] + i\,\Gamma\!\left[\begin{matrix} \frac{s+1}{2} \\ \frac{2-s}{2} \end{matrix}\right]\right)$ $\qquad$ $[a > 0;\ 0 < \operatorname{Re} s < 1]$
4	$e^{-(a+ib)x}$	$\dfrac{\Gamma(s)}{(a^2 + b^2)^{s/2}}\exp\!\left(-is \arctan \dfrac{b}{a}\right)$ $[a,\ \operatorname{Re} s > 0 \text{ or } (a > 0;\ 0 < \operatorname{Re} s < 1)]$
5	$\left\{\begin{matrix} \theta(a-x) \\ \theta(x-a) \end{matrix}\right\} e^{-bx}$	$b^{-s}\left\{\begin{matrix} \gamma(s, ab) \\ \Gamma(s, ab) \end{matrix}\right\}$ $\qquad$ $\left[a > 0;\ \left\{\begin{matrix} \operatorname{Re} s > 0 \\ \operatorname{Re} b > 0 \end{matrix}\right\}\right]$
6	$e^{-ax^2 - bx}$	$\dfrac{\Gamma(s)}{(2a)^{s/2}}\, e^{b^2/(8a)} D_{-s}\!\left(\dfrac{b}{\sqrt{2a}}\right)$ $\left[\begin{matrix}(\operatorname{Re} a, \operatorname{Re} s > 0) \text{ or } (\operatorname{Re} b, \operatorname{Re} s > 0;\ \operatorname{Re} a = 0) \text{ or} \\ (0 < \operatorname{Re} s < 2;\ \operatorname{Re} a = \operatorname{Re} b = 0;\ \operatorname{Im} a \neq 0)\end{matrix}\right]$
7	$e^{ax - bx^n}$	$\dfrac{b^{-s/n}}{n}\displaystyle\sum_{k=0}^{n-1}\dfrac{a^k b^{-k/n}}{k!}\,\Gamma\!\left(\dfrac{s+k}{n}\right){}_2F_n\!\left(\begin{matrix}1, \frac{s+k}{n};\ \frac{a^n}{bn^n} \\ \Delta(n, k+1)\end{matrix}\right)$ $[\operatorname{Re} b > 0;\ n \geq 2]$
8	$e^{-ax - b/x}$	$2\left(\dfrac{b}{a}\right)^{s/2} K_s\!\left(2\sqrt{ab}\right)$ $\qquad$ $[\operatorname{Re} a,\ \operatorname{Re} b > 0]$
9	$e^{-ax - b/x^2}$	$\dfrac{b^{s/2}}{2}\,\Gamma\!\left(-\dfrac{s}{2}\right){}_0F_2\!\left(\begin{matrix}-\frac{a^2 b}{4} \\ \frac{1}{2}, \frac{s+2}{2}\end{matrix}\right) - \dfrac{ab^{(s+1)/2}}{2}\,\Gamma\!\left(-\dfrac{s+1}{2}\right){}_0F_2\!\left(\begin{matrix}-\frac{a^2 b}{4} \\ \frac{3}{2}, \frac{s+3}{2}\end{matrix}\right)$ $+ a^{-s}\,\Gamma(s)\,{}_0F_2\!\left(\begin{matrix}-\frac{a^2 b}{4} \\ \frac{1-s}{2}, \frac{2-s}{2}\end{matrix}\right)$ $\qquad$ $[\operatorname{Re} a,\ \operatorname{Re} b > 0]$
10	$e^{ia(x+b/x)/2}$	$i\pi b^{s/2}\, e^{-is\pi/2} H_{-s}^{(1)}\!\left(a\sqrt{b}\right)$ $\qquad$ $[\operatorname{Im} a > 0;\ \operatorname{Im}(ab) > 0]$

No.	$f(x)$	$F(s)$
11	$\left\{\begin{matrix}\theta(a-x)\\\theta(x-a)\end{matrix}\right\}e^{-b/x^\mu}$	$\dfrac{b^{s/\mu}}{\mu}\left\{\begin{matrix}\Gamma(-s/\mu,\,b/a^\mu)\\\gamma(-s/\mu,\,b/a^\mu)\end{matrix}\right\}$ $\qquad [a,\,\operatorname{Re}b,\,\operatorname{Re}\mu>0;\ \operatorname{Re}s<0]$
12	e^{-ax^μ}	$\dfrac{a^{-s/\mu}}{\mu}\Gamma\left(\dfrac{s}{\mu}\right)$ $\qquad [\mu,\,\operatorname{Re}a,\,\operatorname{Re}s>0]$
13	$1-e^{-ax^{\pm\mu}}$	$-\dfrac{a^{\mp s/\mu}}{\mu}\Gamma\left(\pm\dfrac{s}{\mu}\right)$ $\qquad\left[\begin{matrix}\mu,\,\operatorname{Re}a>0;\\-(1\pm1)\,\mu/2<\operatorname{Re}s<(1\mp1)\,\mu/2\end{matrix}\right]$

2.2.2. $e^{bx^m(a-x)^n}$ and algebraic functions

No.	$f(x)$	$F(s)$
1	$\left\{\begin{matrix}\theta(a-x)\\\theta(x-a)\end{matrix}\right\}x^\alpha e^{-bx}$	$b^{-s-\alpha}\left\{\begin{matrix}\gamma(s+\alpha,\,ab)\\\Gamma(s+\alpha,\,ab)\end{matrix}\right\}$ $\qquad [a,\,\operatorname{Re}b,\,\operatorname{Re}(s+\alpha)>0]$
2	$(a-x)_+^{\alpha-1}e^{bx}$	$a^{s+\alpha-1}\,\mathrm{B}(s,\alpha)\,{}_1F_1\left(\begin{matrix}s;\ ab\\s+\alpha\end{matrix}\right)$ $\qquad [\operatorname{Re}\alpha,\,\operatorname{Re}s>0]$
3	$(x-a)_+^{\alpha-1}e^{-bx}$	$a^{s+\alpha-1}e^{-ab}\,\Gamma(\alpha)\,\Psi(\alpha,\,s+\alpha;\,ab)$ $\qquad [\operatorname{Re}b,\,\operatorname{Re}s>0]$
4	$(a^2-x^2)_+^{\alpha-1}e^{-bx}$	$\dfrac{a^{s+2\alpha-2}}{2}\mathrm{B}\left(\alpha,\dfrac{s}{2}\right){}_1F_2\left(\begin{matrix}\frac{s}{2};\ \frac{a^2b^2}{4}\\\frac{1}{2},\,\frac{s}{2}+\alpha\end{matrix}\right)$ $-\dfrac{a^{s+2\alpha-1}b}{2}\mathrm{B}\left(\alpha,\dfrac{s+1}{2}\right){}_1F_2\left(\begin{matrix}\frac{s+1}{2};\ \frac{a^2b^2}{4}\\\frac{3}{2},\,\frac{s+1}{2}+\alpha\end{matrix}\right)$ $[a,\,\operatorname{Re}s,\,\operatorname{Re}\alpha>0]$
5	$(x^2-a^2)_+^{\alpha-1}e^{-bx}$	$\dfrac{a^{s+2\alpha-2}}{2}\mathrm{B}\left(\alpha,1-\alpha-\dfrac{s}{2}\right){}_1F_2\left(\begin{matrix}\frac{s}{2};\ \frac{a^2b^2}{4}\\\frac{1}{2},\,\alpha+\frac{s}{2}\end{matrix}\right)$ $-\dfrac{a^{s+2\alpha-1}b}{2}\mathrm{B}\left(\alpha,\dfrac{1-s}{2}-\alpha\right){}_1F_2\left(\begin{matrix}\frac{s+1}{2};\ \frac{a^2b^2}{4}\\\frac{3}{2},\,\alpha+\frac{s+1}{2}\end{matrix}\right)$ $+b^{-s-2\alpha+2}\,\Gamma(s+2\alpha-2)\,{}_1F_2\left(\begin{matrix}1-\alpha;\ \frac{a^2b^2}{4}\\\frac{3-s-2\alpha}{2},\,\frac{4-s-2\alpha}{2}\end{matrix}\right)$
6		$=\dfrac{\Gamma(\alpha)}{\sqrt{\pi}}\left(\dfrac{2a}{b}\right)^{\alpha-1/2}K_{\alpha-1/2}(ab)$ $\qquad [a,\,\operatorname{Re}b,\,\operatorname{Re}\alpha>0]$
7	$\dfrac{e^{-bx}}{(x+a)^\rho}$	$a^{s-\rho}\,\Gamma(s)\,\Psi(s,\,s-\rho+1;\,ab)$
8		$=\dfrac{a^{(s-\rho-1)/2}}{b^{(s-\rho+1)/2}}\,e^{ab/2}\,\Gamma(s)\,W_{(1-\rho-s)/2,\,(s-\rho)/2}(ab)$ $[\operatorname{Re}b,\,\operatorname{Re}s>0;\ |\arg a|<\pi]$

No.	$f(x)$	$F(s)$
9	$\dfrac{e^{-bx}}{x+a}$	$a^{s-1}e^{ab}\Gamma(s)\Gamma(1-s,\,ab)$ $\left[\begin{array}{l}(\operatorname{Re}b,\ \operatorname{Re}s>0)\ \text{or}\\ (\operatorname{Re}b=0;\ 0<\operatorname{Re}s<1);\ |\arg a|<\pi\end{array}\right]$
10	$\dfrac{e^{-bx}}{x-a}$	$\dfrac{\pi e^{-ab}\csc(s\pi)}{b^{s-1}\Gamma(1-s)}E_s(-ab)+i\pi e^{-ab}a^{s-1}\qquad[a,\ \operatorname{Re}b,\ \operatorname{Re}s>0;\ s\neq 1]$
11	$\dfrac{e^{-bx}}{(x^2+a^2)^{\rho}}$	$\dfrac{\Gamma(s-2\rho)}{b^{s-2\rho}}\,{}_1F_2\left(\begin{array}{c}\rho;\ \frac{2\rho-s+1}{2}\\[2pt]\frac{2\rho-s+2}{2};\ -\frac{a^2b^2}{4}\end{array}\right)$ $+\dfrac{a^{s-2\rho}}{2}\,\mathrm{B}\left(\dfrac{s}{2},\dfrac{2\rho-s}{2}\right){}_1F_2\left(\begin{array}{c}\frac{s}{2};\ -\frac{a^2b^2}{4}\\[2pt]\frac{1}{2},\ \frac{s-2\rho+2}{2}\end{array}\right)$ $-\dfrac{a^{s-2\rho+1}b}{2}\,\mathrm{B}\left(\dfrac{s+1}{2},\dfrac{2\rho-s-1}{2}\right){}_1F_2\left(\begin{array}{c}\frac{s+1}{2};\ -\frac{a^2b^2}{4}\\[2pt]\frac{3}{2},\ \frac{s-2\rho+3}{2}\end{array}\right)$ $\left[\begin{array}{l}\operatorname{Re}a,\ \operatorname{Re}b,\ \operatorname{Re}s>0\ \text{or}\\ (\operatorname{Re}b=0;\ \operatorname{Re}(s-2\rho)<1)\end{array}\right]$
12	$\dfrac{e^{-bx}}{(x^2+a^2)^n}$	$\dfrac{(-1)^n\Gamma(s-1)}{2(n-1)!}\,D_t^{n-1}\Big[t^{(s-2)/2}\big(e^{ib\sqrt{t}+i\pi s/2}\Gamma\big(2-s,\,ib\sqrt{t}\big)$ $+e^{-ib\sqrt{t}-i\pi s/2}\Gamma\big(2-s,\,-ib\sqrt{t}\big)\big)\Big]\Big|_{t=a^2}$ $[\operatorname{Re}a,\ \operatorname{Re}b,\ \operatorname{Re}s>0;\ n=1,2,\dots]$
13	$\dfrac{e^{-bx}}{x^2-a^2}$	$\dfrac{\Gamma(s-2)}{b^{s-2}}\,{}_1F_2\left(\begin{array}{c}1;\ \frac{a^2b^2}{4}\\[2pt]\frac{3-s}{2},\ \frac{4-s}{2}\end{array}\right)-\dfrac{\pi a^{s-2}}{2\sin(s\pi)}\left[e^{ab}+e^{-ab}\cos(s\pi)\right]$ $[a,\ \operatorname{Re}b,\ \operatorname{Re}s>0]$
14	$(a-x)_+^{\alpha-1}(b-x)^{-\alpha}e^{cx}$	$a^{s+\alpha-1}b^{-\alpha}\,\mathrm{B}(s,\alpha)\,\Phi_1\left(s,\alpha;s+\alpha;\dfrac{a}{b},ac\right)$ $[0<a<|b|;\ \operatorname{Re}s,\ \operatorname{Re}\alpha>0]$
15	$\left(\sqrt{x+a}+\sqrt{a}\right)^{\rho}e^{-bx}$	$\dfrac{\rho\sqrt{a}}{b^{s+(\rho-1)/2}}\,\Gamma\left(\dfrac{2s+\rho-1}{2}\right){}_2F_2\left(\begin{array}{c}\frac{1+\rho}{2},\ \frac{1-\rho}{2};\ ab\\[2pt]\frac{3}{2},\ \frac{3-2s-\rho}{2}\end{array}\right)$ $+b^{-s-\rho/2}\Gamma\left(\dfrac{2s+\rho}{2}\right){}_2F_2\left(\begin{array}{c}\frac{\rho}{2},\ -\frac{\rho}{2};\ ab\\[2pt]\frac{1}{2},\ \frac{2-2s-\rho}{2}\end{array}\right)$ $-2^{2s+\rho}\rho a^{s+\rho/2}\Gamma\left[\begin{array}{c}s,\ -2s-\rho\\ 1-s-\rho\end{array}\right]{}_2F_2\left(\begin{array}{c}s,\ s+\rho;\ ab\\[2pt]\frac{2s+\rho+1}{2},\ \frac{2s+\rho+2}{2}\end{array}\right)$ $[\operatorname{Re}b,\ \operatorname{Re}s>0;\ |\arg a|<\pi]$

No.	$f(x)$	$F(s)$
16	$\left(\sqrt{x+a}-\sqrt{a}\right)^{\rho} e^{-bx}$	$-\dfrac{\rho\sqrt{a}}{b^{s+(\rho-1)/2}}\,\Gamma\left(\dfrac{2s+\rho-1}{2}\right)\,{}_2F_2\left(\begin{matrix}\frac{1+\rho}{2},\ \frac{1-\rho}{2};\ ab\\ \frac{3}{2},\ \frac{3-2s-\rho}{2}\end{matrix}\right)$
		$+\,b^{-s-\rho/2}\,\Gamma\left(\dfrac{2s+\rho}{2}\right)\,{}_2F_2\left(\begin{matrix}\frac{\rho}{2},\ -\frac{\rho}{2};\ ab\\ \frac{1}{2},\ \frac{2-2s-\rho}{2}\end{matrix}\right)$
		$+\,2^{2s+\rho}\rho a^{s+\rho/2}\,\Gamma\left[\begin{matrix}s+\rho,\ -2s-\rho\\ 1-s\end{matrix}\right]\,{}_2F_2\left(\begin{matrix}s,\ s+\rho;\ ab\\ \frac{2s+\rho+1}{2},\ \frac{2s+\rho+2}{2}\end{matrix}\right)$
		$[\operatorname{Re}b,\ \operatorname{Re}(s+\rho)>0;\ |\arg a|<\pi]$
17	$\dfrac{\left(\sqrt{x+a}-\sqrt{a}\right)^{\rho}}{\sqrt{x+a}}\,e^{-bx}$	$b^{(1-\rho)/2-s}\,\Gamma\left(\dfrac{2s+\rho-1}{2}\right)\,{}_2F_2\left(\begin{matrix}\frac{1+\rho}{2},\ \frac{1-\rho}{2};\ ab\\ \frac{1}{2},\ \frac{3-2s-\rho}{2}\end{matrix}\right)$
		$-\,\dfrac{\rho\sqrt{a}}{b^{s+\rho/2-1}}\,\Gamma\left(\dfrac{2s+\rho-2}{2}\right)\,{}_2F_2\left(\begin{matrix}\frac{2+\rho}{2},\ \frac{2-\rho}{2};\ ab\\ \frac{3}{2},\ \frac{4-2s-\rho}{2}\end{matrix}\right)$
		$+\,2^{2s+\rho}\,a^{s+(\rho-1)/2}\,\mathrm{B}\left(1-2s-\rho,\ s+\rho\right)\,{}_2F_2\left(\begin{matrix}s,\ s+\rho;\ ab\\ \frac{2s+\rho}{2},\ \frac{2s+\rho+1}{2}\end{matrix}\right)$
		$[\operatorname{Re}b,\ \operatorname{Re}(s+\rho)>0;\ |\arg a|<\pi]$
18	$\left(\sqrt{x+a}\pm\sqrt{x}\right)^{\rho} e^{-bx}$	$\mp\dfrac{\rho a^{s+\rho/2}}{2^{2s}}\,\Gamma\left[\begin{matrix}2s,\ \frac{-2s\mp\rho}{2}\\ \frac{2s\mp\rho+2}{2}\end{matrix}\right]\,{}_2F_2\left(\begin{matrix}s,\ \frac{2s+1}{2};\ ab\\ \frac{2s-\rho+2}{2},\ \frac{2s+\rho+2}{2}\end{matrix}\right)$
		$+\,\dfrac{2^{\pm\rho}a^{(\rho\mp\rho)/2}}{b^{s\pm\rho/2}}\,\Gamma\left(s\pm\dfrac{\rho}{2}\right)\,{}_2F_2\left(\begin{matrix}\mp\frac{\rho}{2},\ \frac{1\mp\rho}{2};\ ab\\ 1\mp\rho,\ \frac{2-2s\mp\rho}{2}\end{matrix}\right)$
		$[\operatorname{Re}b,\ \operatorname{Re}s>0;\ |\arg a|<\pi]$
19	$\dfrac{\left(\sqrt{x+a}+\sqrt{x}\right)^{\rho}}{\sqrt{x+a}}\,e^{-bx}$	$-\dfrac{\pi a^{s+(\rho-1)/2}}{2^{2s-1}}\,\csc\dfrac{(2s+\rho-1)\pi}{2}\,\Gamma\left[\begin{matrix}2s\\ \frac{2s-\rho+1}{2},\ \frac{2s+\rho+1}{2}\end{matrix}\right]$
		$\times\,{}_2F_2\left(\begin{matrix}s,\ \frac{2s+1}{2};\ ab\\ \frac{2s-\rho+1}{2},\ \frac{2s+\rho+1}{2}\end{matrix}\right)-\dfrac{2^{\rho}\pi}{b^{s+(\rho-1)/2}}\,\sec\dfrac{(2s+\rho)\pi}{2}$
		$\times\left[\Gamma\left(\dfrac{3-2s-\rho}{2}\right)\right]^{-1}\,{}_2F_2\left(\begin{matrix}\frac{1-\rho}{2},\ \frac{2-\rho}{2};\ ab\\ 1-\rho,\ \frac{3-2s-\rho}{2}\end{matrix}\right)$
		$[\operatorname{Re}b,\ \operatorname{Re}s>0;\ |\arg a|<\pi]$
20	$\dfrac{\left(\sqrt{x+a}-\sqrt{x}\right)^{\rho}}{\sqrt{x+a}}\,e^{-bx}$	$-\dfrac{\pi a^{s+(\rho-1)/2}}{2^{2s-1}}\,\csc\dfrac{(2s-\rho-1)\pi}{2}\,\Gamma\left[\begin{matrix}2s\\ \frac{2s-\rho+1}{2},\ \frac{2s+\rho+1}{2}\end{matrix}\right]$
		$\times\,{}_2F_2\left(\begin{matrix}s,\ \frac{2s+1}{2};\ ab\\ \frac{2s-\rho+1}{2},\ \frac{2s+\rho+1}{2}\end{matrix}\right)-\dfrac{2^{-\rho}\pi a^{\rho}}{b^{s-(\rho+1)/2}}\,\sec\dfrac{(2s-\rho)\pi}{2}$
		$\times\left[\Gamma\left(\dfrac{3-2s+\rho}{2}\right)\right]^{-1}\,{}_2F_2\left(\begin{matrix}\frac{1+\rho}{2},\ \frac{2+\rho}{2};\ ab\\ 1+\rho,\ \frac{3-2s+\rho}{2}\end{matrix}\right)$
		$[\operatorname{Re}b,\ \operatorname{Re}s>0;\ |\arg a|<\pi]$

No.	$f(x)$	$F(s)$
21	$\left(\sqrt{x^2+a^2}+a\right)^{\rho} e^{-bx}$	$-2^{s+\rho-1}\rho a^{s+\rho}\,\Gamma\!\left[\begin{array}{c}\frac{s}{2},\,-s-\rho\\ \frac{2-s-2\rho}{2}\end{array}\right]{}_2F_3\!\left(\begin{array}{c}\frac{s}{2},\,\frac{s+2\rho}{2};\,-\frac{a^2b^2}{4}\\ \frac{1}{2},\,\frac{s+\rho+1}{2},\,\frac{s+\rho+2}{2}\end{array}\right)$
		$+\,2^{s+\rho}\rho a^{s+\rho+1}b\,\Gamma\!\left[\begin{array}{c}\frac{s+1}{2},\,-s-\rho-1\\ \frac{1-s-2\rho}{2}\end{array}\right]{}_2F_3\!\left(\begin{array}{c}\frac{s+1}{2},\,\frac{s+2\rho+1}{2};\,-\frac{a^2b^2}{4}\\ \frac{3}{2},\,\frac{s+\rho+2}{2},\,\frac{s+\rho+3}{2}\end{array}\right)$
		$+\,\dfrac{\rho a\,\Gamma(s+\rho-1)}{b^{s+\rho-1}}\,{}_2F_3\!\left(\begin{array}{c}\frac{1+\rho}{2},\,\frac{1-\rho}{2};\,-\frac{a^2b^2}{4}\\ \frac{3}{2},\,\frac{2-s-\rho}{2},\,\frac{3-s-\rho}{2}\end{array}\right)$
		$+\,\dfrac{\Gamma(s+\rho)}{b^{s+\rho}}\,{}_2F_3\!\left(\begin{array}{c}\frac{\rho}{2},\,-\frac{\rho}{2};\,-\frac{a^2b^2}{4}\\ \frac{1}{2},\,\frac{1-s-\rho}{2},\,\frac{2-s-\rho}{2}\end{array}\right)\qquad[\operatorname{Re}a,\ \operatorname{Re}b,\ \operatorname{Re}s>0]$
22	$\left(\sqrt{x^2+a^2}-a\right)^{\rho} e^{-bx}$	$2^{s+\rho-1}\rho a^{s+\rho}\,\Gamma\!\left[\begin{array}{c}\frac{s+2\rho}{2},\,-s-\rho\\ \frac{2-s}{2}\end{array}\right]{}_2F_3\!\left(\begin{array}{c}\frac{s}{2},\,\frac{s+2\rho}{2};\,-\frac{a^2b^2}{4}\\ \frac{1}{2},\,\frac{s+\rho+1}{2},\,\frac{s+\rho+2}{2}\end{array}\right)$
		$-\,2^{s+\rho}\rho a^{s+\rho+1}b\,\Gamma\!\left[\begin{array}{c}\frac{s+2\rho+1}{2},\,-s-\rho-1\\ \frac{1-s}{2}\end{array}\right]{}_2F_3\!\left(\begin{array}{c}\frac{s+1}{2},\,\frac{s+2\rho+1}{2};\,-\frac{a^2b^2}{4}\\ \frac{3}{2},\,\frac{s+\rho+2}{2},\,\frac{s+\rho+3}{2}\end{array}\right)$
		$-\,\dfrac{\rho a}{b^{s+\rho-1}}\,\Gamma(s+\rho-1)\,{}_2F_3\!\left(\begin{array}{c}\frac{1+\rho}{2},\,\frac{1-\rho}{2};\,-\frac{a^2b^2}{4}\\ \frac{3}{2},\,\frac{2-s-\rho}{2},\,\frac{3-s-\rho}{2}\end{array}\right)$
		$+\,\dfrac{\Gamma(s+\rho)}{b^{s+\rho}}\,{}_2F_3\!\left(\begin{array}{c}\frac{\rho}{2},\,-\frac{\rho}{2};\,-\frac{a^2b^2}{4}\\ \frac{1}{2},\,\frac{1-s-\rho}{2},\,\frac{2-s-\rho}{2}\end{array}\right)$
		$\qquad\qquad\qquad\qquad\qquad\qquad[\operatorname{Re}a,\ \operatorname{Re}b,\ \operatorname{Re}(s+2\rho)>0]$
23	$\dfrac{\left(\sqrt{x^2+a^2}+a\right)^{\rho}}{\sqrt{x^2+a^2}}\,e^{-bx}$	$(2a)^{s+\rho-1}\,\Gamma\!\left[\begin{array}{c}\frac{s}{2},\,1-s-\rho\\ \frac{2-s-2\rho}{2}\end{array}\right]{}_2F_3\!\left(\begin{array}{c}\frac{s}{2},\,\frac{s+2\rho}{2};\,-\frac{a^2b^2}{4}\\ \frac{1}{2},\,\frac{s+\rho}{2},\,\frac{s+\rho+1}{2}\end{array}\right)$
		$-\,(2a)^{s+\rho}b\,\Gamma\!\left[\begin{array}{c}\frac{s+1}{2},\,-s-\rho\\ \frac{1-s-2\rho}{2}\end{array}\right]{}_2F_3\!\left(\begin{array}{c}\frac{s+1}{2},\,\frac{s+2\rho+1}{2};\,-\frac{a^2b^2}{4}\\ \frac{3}{2},\,\frac{s+\rho+1}{2},\,\frac{s+\rho+2}{2}\end{array}\right)$
		$+\,\dfrac{\Gamma(\rho+s-1)}{b^{s+\rho-1}}\,{}_2F_3\!\left(\begin{array}{c}\frac{1+\rho}{2},\,\frac{1-\rho}{2};\,-\frac{a^2b^2}{4}\\ \frac{1}{2},\,\frac{2-s-\rho}{2},\,\frac{3-s-\rho}{2}\end{array}\right)$
		$+\,\dfrac{\rho a}{b^{s+\rho-2}}\,\Gamma(s+\rho-2)\,{}_2F_3\!\left(\begin{array}{c}\frac{2+\rho}{2},\,\frac{2-\rho}{2};\,-\frac{a^2b^2}{4}\\ \frac{3}{2},\,\frac{3-s-\rho}{2},\,\frac{4-s-\rho}{2}\end{array}\right)$
		$\qquad\qquad\qquad\qquad\qquad\qquad[\operatorname{Re}a,\ \operatorname{Re}b,\ \operatorname{Re}s>0]$
24	$\dfrac{\left(\sqrt{x^2+a^2}-a\right)^{\rho}}{\sqrt{x^2+a^2}}\,e^{-bx}$	$(2a)^{s+\rho-1}\,\mathrm{B}\!\left(\frac{s+2\rho}{2},\,1-s-\rho\right){}_2F_3\!\left(\begin{array}{c}\frac{s}{2},\,\frac{s+2\rho}{2};\,-\frac{a^2b^2}{4}\\ \frac{1}{2},\,\frac{s+\rho}{2},\,\frac{s+\rho+1}{2}\end{array}\right)$
		$-\,(2a)^{s+\rho}b\,\mathrm{B}\!\left(\frac{s+2\rho+1}{2},\,-s-\rho\right){}_2F_3\!\left(\begin{array}{c}\frac{s+1}{2},\,\frac{s+2\rho+1}{2};\,-\frac{a^2b^2}{4}\\ \frac{3}{2},\,\frac{s+\rho+1}{2},\,\frac{s+\rho+2}{2}\end{array}\right)$
		$+\,\dfrac{\Gamma(s+\rho-1)}{b^{s+\rho-1}}\,{}_2F_3\!\left(\begin{array}{c}\frac{1+\rho}{2},\,\frac{1-\rho}{2};\,-\frac{a^2b^2}{4}\\ \frac{1}{2},\,\frac{2-s-\rho}{2},\,\frac{3-s-\rho}{2}\end{array}\right)$
		$-\,\dfrac{\rho a}{b^{s+\rho-2}}\,\Gamma(s+\rho-2)\,{}_2F_3\!\left(\begin{array}{c}\frac{2+\rho}{2},\,\frac{2-\rho}{2};\,-\frac{a^2b^2}{4}\\ \frac{3}{2},\,\frac{3-s-\rho}{2},\,\frac{4-s-\rho}{2}\end{array}\right)$
		$\qquad\qquad\qquad\qquad\qquad\qquad[\operatorname{Re}a,\ \operatorname{Re}b,\ \operatorname{Re}(s+2\rho)>0]$

No.	$f(x)$	$F(s)$
25	$\left(\sqrt{x^2+a^2}+x\right)^\rho e^{-bx}$	$-\dfrac{\rho\,a^{s+\rho}}{2^{s+1}}\,\Gamma\left[\begin{matrix}s,\ -\frac{s+\rho}{2}\\ \frac{s-\rho+2}{2}\end{matrix}\right]\,{}_2F_3\left(\begin{matrix}\frac{s}{2},\ \frac{s+1}{2};\ -\frac{a^2b^2}{4}\\ \frac{1}{2},\ \frac{s+\rho+2}{2},\ \frac{s-\rho+2}{2}\end{matrix}\right)$
		$\quad+\dfrac{\rho\,a^{s+\rho+1}\,b}{2^{s+2}}\,\Gamma\left[\begin{matrix}s+1,\ -\frac{s+\rho+1}{2}\\ \frac{s-\rho+3}{2}\end{matrix}\right]\,{}_2F_3\left(\begin{matrix}\frac{s+1}{2},\ \frac{s+2}{2};\ -\frac{a^2b^2}{4}\\ \frac{3}{2},\ \frac{s+\rho+3}{2},\ \frac{s-\rho+3}{2}\end{matrix}\right)$
		$\quad\quad+\dfrac{2^\rho\Gamma(s+\rho)}{b^{s+\rho}}\,{}_2F_3\left(\begin{matrix}-\frac{\rho}{2},\ \frac{1-\rho}{2};\ -\frac{a^2b^2}{4}\\ 1-\rho,\ \frac{1-s-\rho}{2},\ \frac{2-s-\rho}{2}\end{matrix}\right)$
		$[\operatorname{Re}a,\ \operatorname{Re}b,\ \operatorname{Re}s>0]$
26	$\left(\sqrt{x^2+a^2}-x\right)^\rho e^{-bx}$	$\dfrac{\rho\,a^{s+\rho}}{2^{s+1}}\,\Gamma\left[\begin{matrix}s,\ \frac{\rho-s}{2}\\ \frac{s+\rho+2}{2}\end{matrix}\right]\,{}_2F_3\left(\begin{matrix}\frac{s}{2},\ \frac{s+1}{2};\ -\frac{a^2b^2}{4}\\ \frac{1}{2},\ \frac{s-\rho+2}{2},\ \frac{s+\rho+2}{2}\end{matrix}\right)$
		$\quad-\dfrac{\rho a^{s+\rho+1}\,b}{2^{s+2}}\,\Gamma\left[\begin{matrix}s+1,\ \frac{\rho-s-1}{2}\\ \frac{s+\rho+3}{2}\end{matrix}\right]\,{}_2F_3\left(\begin{matrix}\frac{s+1}{2},\ \frac{s+2}{2};\ -\frac{a^2b^2}{4}\\ \frac{3}{2},\ \frac{s-\rho+3}{2},\ \frac{s+\rho+3}{2}\end{matrix}\right)$
		$\quad\quad+\dfrac{a^{2\rho}\Gamma(s-\rho)}{2^\rho b^{s-\rho}}\,{}_2F_3\left(\begin{matrix}\frac{\rho}{2},\ \frac{\rho+1}{2};\ -\frac{a^2b^2}{4}\\ \rho+1,\ \frac{1-s+\rho}{2},\ \frac{2-s+\rho}{2}\end{matrix}\right)$
		$[\operatorname{Re}a,\ \operatorname{Re}b,\ \operatorname{Re}s>0]$
27	$\dfrac{\left(\sqrt{x^2+a^2}+x\right)^\rho}{\sqrt{x^2+a^2}}\,e^{-bx}$	$\dfrac{a^{s+\rho-1}}{2^s}\,\Gamma\left[\begin{matrix}s,\ \frac{1-s-\rho}{2}\\ \frac{s-\rho+1}{2}\end{matrix}\right]\,{}_2F_3\left(\begin{matrix}\frac{s}{2},\ \frac{s+1}{2};\ -\frac{a^2b^2}{4}\\ \frac{1}{2},\ \frac{s+\rho+1}{2},\ \frac{s-\rho+1}{2}\end{matrix}\right)$
		$\quad-\dfrac{a^{s+\rho}b}{2^{s+1}}\,\Gamma\left[\begin{matrix}s+1,\ -\frac{s+\rho}{2}\\ \frac{s-\rho+2}{2}\end{matrix}\right]\,{}_2F_3\left(\begin{matrix}\frac{s+1}{2},\ \frac{s+2}{2};\ -\frac{a^2b^2}{4}\\ \frac{3}{2},\ \frac{s+\rho+2}{2},\ \frac{s-\rho+2}{2}\end{matrix}\right)$
		$\quad\quad+\dfrac{2^\rho\Gamma(s+\rho-1)}{b^{s+\rho-1}}\,{}_2F_3\left(\begin{matrix}\frac{1-\rho}{2},\ \frac{2-\rho}{2};\ -\frac{a^2b^2}{4}\\ 1-\rho,\ \frac{2-s-\rho}{2},\ \frac{3-s-\rho}{2}\end{matrix}\right)$
		$[\operatorname{Re}a,\ \operatorname{Re}b,\ \operatorname{Re}s>0]$
28	$\dfrac{\left(\sqrt{x^2+a^2}-x\right)^\rho}{\sqrt{x^2+a^2}}\,e^{-bx}$	$\dfrac{a^{s+\rho-1}}{2^s}\,\mathrm{B}\left(s,\ \frac{1-s+\rho}{2}\right)\,{}_2F_3\left(\begin{matrix}\frac{s}{2},\ \frac{s+1}{2};\ -\frac{a^2b^2}{4}\\ \frac{1}{2},\ \frac{s-\rho+1}{2},\ \frac{s+\rho+1}{2}\end{matrix}\right)$
		$\quad-\dfrac{a^{s+\rho}b}{2^{s+1}}\,\mathrm{B}\left(s+1,\ \frac{\rho-s}{2}\right)\,{}_2F_3\left(\begin{matrix}\frac{s+1}{2},\ \frac{s+2}{2};\ -\frac{a^2b^2}{4}\\ \frac{3}{2},\ \frac{s-\rho+2}{2},\ \frac{s+\rho+2}{2}\end{matrix}\right)$
		$\quad\quad+\dfrac{2^{-\rho}a^{2\rho}}{b^{s-\rho-1}}\,\Gamma(s-\rho-1)\,{}_2F_3\left(\begin{matrix}\frac{\rho+1}{2},\ \frac{\rho+2}{2};\ -\frac{a^2b^2}{4}\\ \rho+1,\ \frac{2-s+\rho}{2},\ \frac{3-s+\rho}{2}\end{matrix}\right)$
		$[\operatorname{Re}a,\ \operatorname{Re}b,\ \operatorname{Re}s>0]$
29	$(a-x)_+^{\alpha-1}\,e^{bx^2}$	$a^{s+\alpha-1}\,\mathrm{B}(s,\alpha)\,{}_2F_2\left(\begin{matrix}\frac{s}{2},\ \frac{s+1}{2};\ a^2b\\ \frac{s+\alpha}{2},\ \frac{s+\alpha+1}{2}\end{matrix}\right)\qquad[a,\ \operatorname{Re}\alpha,\ \operatorname{Re}s>0]$
30	$(a-x)_+^{\alpha-1}\,e^{bx^n}$	$a^{s+\alpha-1}\,\mathrm{B}(\alpha,s)\,{}_nF_n\left(\begin{matrix}\Delta(n,s);\ a^nb\\ \Delta(n,s+\alpha)\end{matrix}\right)$
		$[a,\ \operatorname{Re}\alpha,\ \operatorname{Re}s>0;\ n=1,2,\ldots]$

No.	$f(x)$	$F(s)$
31	$(a-x)_+^{\alpha-1}\, e^{bx(a-x)}$	$a^{s+\alpha-1}\, \mathrm{B}(s,\alpha)\, {}_2F_2\left(\begin{matrix} s,\ \alpha;\ \frac{a^2b}{4} \\ \frac{s+\alpha}{2},\ \frac{s+\alpha+1}{2} \end{matrix}\right)$ $\qquad$ $[a,\ \mathrm{Re}\,\alpha,\ \mathrm{Re}\,s > 0]$
32	$(a-x)_+^{\alpha-1}\, e^{bx^2(a-x)^2}$	$a^{s+\alpha-1}\, \mathrm{B}(s,\alpha)\, {}_4F_4\left(\begin{matrix} \frac{s}{2},\ \frac{s+1}{2},\ \frac{\alpha}{2},\ \frac{\alpha+1}{2};\ \frac{a^4b}{16} \\ \frac{s+\alpha}{4},\ \frac{s+\alpha+1}{4},\ \frac{s+\alpha+2}{4},\ \frac{s+\alpha+3}{4} \end{matrix}\right)$ $\quad$ $[a,\ \mathrm{Re}\,s > 0]$
33	$(a-x)_+^{\alpha-1}\, e^{b(a-x)^n}$	$a^{s+\alpha-1}\, \mathrm{B}(\alpha,s)\, {}_nF_n\left(\begin{matrix} \Delta(n,\alpha);\ a^nb \\ \Delta(n,s+\alpha) \end{matrix}\right)$ $\qquad$ $[a,\ \mathrm{Re}\,\alpha,\ \mathrm{Re}\,s > 0;\ n = 1,2,\dots]$

2.2.3. $e^{\varphi(x)}$ and algebraic functions

No.	$f(x)$	$F(s)$
1	$(x-a)_+^{\alpha-1}\, e^{b/x}$	$a^{s+\alpha-1}\, \mathrm{B}(1-s-\alpha,\alpha)\, {}_1F_1\left(\begin{matrix} 1-s-\alpha \\ 1-s;\ \frac{b}{a} \end{matrix}\right)$ $\quad$ $[a>0;\ \mathrm{Re}\,(s+\alpha) < 0]$
2	$\dfrac{e^{-b/x}}{(x+a)^\rho}$	$a^{s-\rho}\, \Gamma(\rho-s)\, \Psi\left(\rho-s;\ \frac{b}{a};\ 1-s\right)$ $\qquad$ $[\mathrm{Re}\,b > 0;\ \mathrm{Re}\,\rho > \mathrm{Re}\,s > 0;\ |\arg a| < \pi]$
3	$\dfrac{e^{-b/x}}{x+a}$	$a^{s-1}\, e^{b/a}\, \Gamma(1-s)\, \Gamma\left(s,\ \frac{b}{a}\right)$ $\qquad$ $[\mathrm{Re}\,b > 0;\ \mathrm{Re}\,s < 1;\ |\arg a| < \pi]$
4	$(x-a)_+^{\alpha-1}\, e^{b/x^2}$	$a^{s+\alpha-1}\, \mathrm{B}(1-s-\alpha,\alpha)\, {}_2F_2\left(\begin{matrix} \frac{1-s-\alpha}{2},\ \frac{2-s-\alpha}{2} \\ \frac{1-s}{2},\ \frac{2-s}{2};\ \frac{b}{a^2} \end{matrix}\right)$ $\qquad$ $[a>0;\ \mathrm{Re}\,(s+\alpha) < 0]$
5	$(1-x)_+^{\alpha}\, e^{-a/(1-x)}$	$e^{-a}\, \Gamma(s)\, \Psi(s;a;-\alpha)$ $\qquad$ $[\mathrm{Re}\,a,\ \mathrm{Re}\,s > 0]$
6	$(1-x)_+^{-1/2}\, e^{-a/(1-x)}$	$2^s e^{-a/2}\, \Gamma(s)\, D_{-2s}\left(\sqrt{2a}\right)$ $\qquad$ $[\mathrm{Re}\,a,\ \mathrm{Re}\,s > 0]$
7	$\left(1-x^2\right)_+^{-1/2}\, e^{-a/(1-x)}$	$e^{-a/2}\, \Gamma(s)\, D_{-s}^2\left(\sqrt{a}\right)$ $\qquad$ $[\mathrm{Re}\,a,\ \mathrm{Re}\,s > 0]$
8	$(x-1)_+^{\alpha}\, e^{-a/(x-1)}$	$\Gamma(-s-\alpha)\, \Psi(-s-\alpha;-\alpha;a)$ $\qquad$ $[\mathrm{Re}\,a > 0;\ \mathrm{Re}\,s < -\,\mathrm{Re}\,\alpha]$
9	$(x-1)_+^{-1/2}\, e^{-a/(x-1)}$	$\dfrac{e^{a/2}}{2^{s-1/2}}\, \Gamma\left(\frac{1}{2}-s\right)\, D_{2s-1}\left(\sqrt{2a}\right)$ $\qquad$ $[\mathrm{Re}\,a > 0;\ \mathrm{Re}\,s < 1/2]$
10	$\left(x^2-1\right)_+^{-1/2}\, e^{-a/(x-1)}$	$e^{a/2}\, \Gamma(1-s)\, D_{s-1}^2\left(\sqrt{a}\right)$ $\qquad$ $[\mathrm{Re}\,a > 0,\ \mathrm{Re}\,s < 1]$

No.	$f(x)$	$F(s)$
11	$\dfrac{e^{b/(x+a)}}{(x+a)^{\rho}}$	$a^{s-\rho}\,\mathrm{B}\left(s,\rho-s\right){}_1F_1\!\left(\begin{matrix}\rho-s\\ \rho;\ \frac{b}{a}\end{matrix}\right)$ $\qquad[0<\operatorname{Re}s<\operatorname{Re}\rho;\ |\arg a|<\pi]$
12	$\dfrac{e^{bx/(x+a)}}{(x+a)^{\rho}}$	$a^{s-\rho}\,\mathrm{B}\left(s,\rho-s\right){}_1F_1\!\left(\begin{matrix}s\\ \rho;\ b\end{matrix}\right)$ $\qquad[0<\operatorname{Re}s<\operatorname{Re}\rho;\ |\arg a|<\pi]$
13	$(a-x)_+^{\alpha-1}\,(b-x)^{-\alpha}$ $\times e^{c/(b-x)}$	$a^{s+\alpha-1}b^{-\alpha}e^{c/(b-a)}\,\mathrm{B}\left(\alpha,s\right)\Phi_1\!\left(\alpha,s;s+\alpha;\dfrac{a}{b},\dfrac{ac}{b(a-b)}\right)$ $\qquad[0<a<b;\ \operatorname{Re}s,\ \operatorname{Re}\alpha>0]$
14	$\left(x^2+1\right)^{\alpha}e^{-a/(x^2+1)}$	$\dfrac{e^{-a}}{2}\,\mathrm{B}\left(\dfrac{s}{2},-\dfrac{s}{2}-\alpha\right){}_1F_1\!\left(\begin{matrix}\frac{s}{2};\ a\\ -\alpha\end{matrix}\right)$ $\qquad[0<\operatorname{Re}s<-2\operatorname{Re}\alpha]$
15	$\left(1-x^2\right)_+^{-1/2}e^{-ax/(1-x)}$	$e^{a/2}\,\Gamma\left(s\right)D_{-s}^2\left(\sqrt{a}\right)$ $\qquad[\operatorname{Re}a,\ \operatorname{Re}s>0]$
16	$\left(1-x^2\right)_+^{-1/2}$ $\times e^{-a(1+x)/(1-x)}$	$\Gamma\left(s\right)D_{-s}^2\left(\sqrt{2a}\right)$ $\qquad[\operatorname{Re}a,\ \operatorname{Re}s>0]$
17	$\left(x^2-1\right)_+^{-1/2}$ $\times e^{-a(x+1)/(x-1)}$	$\Gamma\left(1-s\right)D_{s-1}^2\left(\sqrt{2a}\right)$ $\qquad[\operatorname{Re}s<1]$
18	$\left(1-x^2\right)_+^{-1/2}e^{a(x-x^{-1})}$	$\dfrac{\sqrt{\pi^3 a}}{2\sqrt{2}}\left[J_{s/2}(a)\,Y_{(s-1)/2}(a)-J_{(s-1)/2}(a)\,Y_{s/2}(a)\right]$ $\qquad[\operatorname{Re}a>0]$
19	$\left(x^2-1\right)_+^{-1/2}e^{a(x^{-1}-x)}$	$\dfrac{\sqrt{\pi^3 a}}{2\sqrt{2}}\left[J_{(1-s)/2}(a)\,Y_{-s/2}(a)-J_{-s/2}(a)\,Y_{(1-s)/2}(a)\right]$ $\qquad[\operatorname{Re}a>0]$
20	$\left(1-x^2\right)_+^{-1/2}$ $\times e^{-(ax+b)/(1-x^2)}$	$e^{-b/2}\,\Gamma\left(s\right)D_{-s}\!\left(\sqrt{b+\sqrt{b^2-a^2}}\right)D_{-s}\!\left(\sqrt{b-\sqrt{b^2-a^2}}\right)$ $\qquad[\operatorname{Re}(a+b),\ \operatorname{Re}s>0]$
21	$\left(x^2-1\right)_+^{-1/2}$ $\times e^{-(ax+b)/(x^2-1)}$	$e^{b/2}\,\Gamma\left(1-s\right)D_{s-1}\!\left(\sqrt{b+\sqrt{b^2-a^2}}\right)D_{s-1}\!\left(\sqrt{b-\sqrt{b^2-a^2}}\right)$ $\qquad[\operatorname{Re}(a+b)>0;\ \operatorname{Re}s<1]$
22	$\left(1+x^2\right)^{\alpha}$ $\times e^{-a(1-x^2)/(1+x^2)}$	$\dfrac{1}{2}(2a)^{\alpha/2}\,\mathrm{B}\left(\dfrac{s}{2},-\dfrac{s+2\alpha}{2}\right)M_{-(s+\alpha)/2,-(\alpha+1)/2}(2a)$ $\qquad[\operatorname{Re}a>0;\ 0<\operatorname{Re}s<-2\operatorname{Re}\alpha]$

No.	$f(x)$	$F(s)$
23	$\left(1-x^2\right)_+^{\alpha} e^{-ax^2/(1-x^2)}$	$\dfrac{a^{\alpha/2}}{2}\, e^{a/2}\, \Gamma\left(\dfrac{s}{2}\right) W_{-(s+\alpha)/2,\,-(\alpha+1)/2}\left(a\right)$ $\qquad$ $[\mathrm{Re}\,a,\ \mathrm{Re}\,s>0]$
24	$\left(1-x^2\right)_+^{-1/2}$ $\times e^{-(ax+b)^2/(1-x^2)}$	$e^{(a^2-b^2)/2}\, \Gamma\left(s\right) D_{-s}\left(\sqrt{2}\,a\right) D_{-s}\left(\sqrt{2}\,b\right)$ $\qquad$ $[\mathrm{Re}\,(a+b),\ \mathrm{Re}\,s>0]$
25	$\left(1-x^2\right)_+^{-1/2}$ $\times e^{-(bx^2+ax+b)/(1-x^2)}$	$\Gamma\left(s\right) D_{-s}\left(\sqrt{2b+\sqrt{4b^2-a^2}}\right) D_{-s}\left(\sqrt{2b-\sqrt{4b^2-a^2}}\right)$ $\qquad$ $[\mathrm{Re}\,(a+2b),\ \mathrm{Re}\,s>0]$
26	$\left(1-x^2\right)_+^{-1/2}$ $\times e^{-(bx^2+ax)/(1-x^2)}$	$e^{b/2}\Gamma\left(s\right) D_{-s}\left(\sqrt{b+\sqrt{b^2-a^2}}\right) D_{-s}\left(\sqrt{b-\sqrt{b^2-a^2}}\right)$ $\qquad$ $[\mathrm{Re}\,(a+b),\ \mathrm{Re}\,s>0]$
27	$\left(x^2-1\right)_+^{-1/2}$ $\times e^{-(bx^2+ax+b)/(x^2-1)}$	$\Gamma\left(1-s\right) D_{s-1}\left(\sqrt{2b+\sqrt{4b^2-a^2}}\right) D_{s-1}\left(\sqrt{2b-\sqrt{4b^2-a^2}}\right)$ $\qquad$ $[\mathrm{Re}\,(a+2b)>0;\ \mathrm{Re}\,s<1]$
28	$e^{-b\sqrt{x+a}}$	$\dfrac{b}{\sqrt{\pi}}\left(\dfrac{2\sqrt{a}}{b}\right)^{s+1/2} \Gamma\left(s\right) K_{s+1/2}\left(\sqrt{a}\,b\right)$ $\qquad$ $[\mathrm{Re}\,a,\ \mathrm{Re}\,b,\ \mathrm{Re}\,s>0]$
29	$\dfrac{e^{-b\sqrt{x+a}}}{\sqrt{x+a}}$	$\dfrac{2}{\sqrt{\pi}}\left(\dfrac{2\sqrt{a}}{b}\right)^{s-1/2} \Gamma\left(s\right) K_{s-1/2}\left(\sqrt{a}\,b\right)$ $\qquad$ $[a,\ \mathrm{Re}\,b,\ \mathrm{Re}\,s>0]$
30	$\dfrac{e^{ia\sqrt{x^2+1}}}{\sqrt{x^2+1}}$	$\dfrac{i\sqrt{\pi}}{2}\left(\dfrac{a}{2}\right)^{(1-s)/2} \Gamma\left(\dfrac{s}{2}\right) H^{(1)}_{(1-s)/2}\left(a\right)$ $\qquad$ $[\mathrm{Im}\,a,\ \mathrm{Re}\,s>0]$
31	$\theta\left(x-a\right) e^{-b\sqrt{x^2-a^2}}$	$\dfrac{a^{(s+1)/2}}{b^{(s-1)/2}}\, S_{(s-3)/2,\,(s+1)/2}\left(ab\right)$ $\qquad$ $[a,\ \mathrm{Re}\,b>0]$
32	$\left(a^2-x^2\right)_+^{-1/2} e^{-b\sqrt{a^2-x^2}}$	$\dfrac{\sqrt{\pi}}{2}\left(\dfrac{2a}{b}\right)^{(s-1)/2} \Gamma\left(\dfrac{s}{2}\right)\left[I_{(s-1)/2}\left(ab\right) - \mathbf{L}_{(s-1)/2}\left(ab\right)\right]$ $\qquad$ $[a,\ \mathrm{Re}\,b,\ \mathrm{Re}\,s>0]$
33	$\left(x^2-a^2\right)_+^{-1/2} e^{-b\sqrt{x^2-a^2}}$	$\dfrac{\sqrt{\pi}}{2}\left(\dfrac{2a}{b}\right)^{(s-1)/2} \Gamma\left(\dfrac{s}{2}\right)\left[\mathbf{H}_{(s-1)/2}\left(ab\right) - Y_{(s-1)/2}\left(ab\right)\right]$ $\qquad$ $[a,\ \mathrm{Re}\,b>0]$

2.2.4. $\left(e^{ax} \pm c\right)^{\rho} e^{-bx}$

1	$\dfrac{1}{e^{ax} + 1}$	$\dfrac{1 - 2^{1-s}}{a^s} \Gamma(s)\, \zeta(s)$	$[\operatorname{Re} a,\ \operatorname{Re} s > 0]$
2	$\dfrac{1}{e^{ax} - 1}$	$\dfrac{\Gamma(s)}{a^s} \zeta(s)$	$[\operatorname{Re} a > 0;\ \operatorname{Re} s > 1]$
3	$\dfrac{1}{e^{ax} - c}$	$\dfrac{\Gamma(s)}{a^s c} \operatorname{Li}_s(c)$	$[\operatorname{Re} s > 1;\ \lvert \arg(1 - c) \rvert < \pi]$
4	$\dfrac{e^{-bx}}{e^{ax} + 1}$	$\dfrac{\Gamma(s)}{(2a)^s} \left[\zeta\left(s, \dfrac{a+b}{2a}\right) - \zeta\left(s, \dfrac{2a+b}{2a}\right) \right]$ $[\operatorname{Re} a,\ \operatorname{Re}(a+b),\ \operatorname{Re} s > 0]$	
5	$\dfrac{e^{-bx}}{e^{ax} - 1}$	$\dfrac{\Gamma(s)}{a^s} \zeta\left(s, \dfrac{a+b}{a}\right)$	$[\operatorname{Re} a,\ \operatorname{Re}(a+b) > 0;\ \operatorname{Re} s > 1]$
6	$\left(\dfrac{1}{e^x - 1} - \dfrac{1}{x} + \dfrac{1}{2}\right) e^{-ax}$	$\Gamma(s) \left[\zeta(s, a) - \dfrac{a^{-s}}{2} + \dfrac{a^{1-s}}{1-s} \right]$	$[\operatorname{Re} a > 0;\ \operatorname{Re} s > -1]$
7	$\left(\dfrac{1}{e^x - 1} - \dfrac{1}{x}\right) e^{-ax}$	$\Gamma(s) \left[\zeta(s, a) - a^{-s} + \dfrac{a^{1-s}}{1-s} \right]$	$[\operatorname{Re} a,\ \operatorname{Re} s > 0]$
8	$\dfrac{e^{-bx}}{e^{ax} - c}$	$\dfrac{\Gamma(s)}{a^s} \Phi\left(c, s, \dfrac{a+b}{a}\right)$ $\left[\begin{array}{l}(\operatorname{Re} a,\ \operatorname{Re}(a+b) > 0;\ \operatorname{Re} s > 0;\ \lvert \arg(1 - c) \rvert < \pi)\ \text{or} \\ (\lvert c \rvert \le 1;\ c \ne 1;\ \operatorname{Re} s > 0)\ \text{or}\ (c = 1;\ \operatorname{Re} s > 1)\end{array}\right]$	
9	$\dfrac{1}{\left(e^{ax} - 1\right)^2}$	$\dfrac{\Gamma(s)}{a^s} \left[\zeta(s - 1) - \zeta(s) \right]$	$[\operatorname{Re} a > 0;\ \operatorname{Re} s > 2]$
10	$\dfrac{e^{-bx}}{\left(e^{ax} - 1\right)^2}$	$\dfrac{\Gamma(s)}{a^{s+1}} \left[a\, \zeta\left(s - 1, \dfrac{a+b}{a}\right) - (a+b)\, \zeta\left(s, \dfrac{a+b}{a}\right) \right]$ $[\operatorname{Re} a,\ \operatorname{Re}(a+b) > 0;\ \operatorname{Re} s > 2]$	
11	$\dfrac{e^{-bx}}{\left(e^{ax} - c\right)^2}$	$\dfrac{\Gamma(s)}{a^{s+1} c} \left[a\Phi\left(c, s - 1, \dfrac{a+b}{a}\right) - (a+b)\,\Phi\left(c, s, \dfrac{a+b}{a}\right) \right]$ $\left[\begin{array}{l}(\operatorname{Re} a,\ \operatorname{Re}(a+b) > 0;\ \operatorname{Re} s > 0;\ \lvert \arg(1 - c) \rvert < \pi)\ \text{or} \\ (\lvert c \rvert \le 1;\ c \ne 1;\ \operatorname{Re} s > 0)\ \text{or}\ (c = 1;\ \operatorname{Re} s > 1)\end{array}\right]$	
12	$\left(e^{bx} + c\right)^n e^{-ax}$	$c^n\, \Gamma(s) \displaystyle\sum_{k=0}^{n} \binom{n}{k} \dfrac{(a - bk)^{-s}}{c^k}$	$[\operatorname{Re} s > 0;\ \operatorname{Re} a > n \operatorname{Re} b]$

2.3.   Hyperbolic Functions

More formulas can be obtained from the corresponding sections due to the relations

$$\sinh z = -\sinh(-z) = \frac{e^z - e^{-z}}{2} = -i\sin(iz), \quad \cosh z = \cosh(-z) = \frac{e^z + e^{-z}}{2} = \cos(iz),$$

$$\sinh z = z\, {}_0F_1\left(\frac{3}{2}; \frac{z^2}{4}\right), \quad \cosh z = {}_0F_1\left(\frac{1}{2}; \frac{z^2}{4}\right),$$

$$\sinh z = \frac{\sqrt{\pi}\, z}{2}\, G_{02}^{10}\left(-\frac{z^2}{4}\ \Big|\ \genfrac{}{}{0pt}{}{\cdot}{0,\,-1/2}\right), \quad \cosh z = \sqrt{\pi}\, G_{02}^{10}\left(-\frac{z^2}{4}\ \Big|\ \genfrac{}{}{0pt}{}{\cdot}{0,\,1/2}\right).$$

2.3.1.   Rational functions of $\sinh x$ and $\cosh x$

No.	$f(x)$	$F(s)$	
1	$\sinh(ax)$	$i(-ia)^{-s}\sin\dfrac{s\pi}{2}\,\Gamma(s)$	$[\operatorname{Re} a = 0;\ \|\operatorname{Re} s\| < 1]$
2	$\cosh(ax)$	$(ia)^{-s}\cos\dfrac{s\pi}{2}\,\Gamma(s)$	$[\operatorname{Re} a = 0;\ 0 < \operatorname{Re} s < 1]$
3	$\sinh(ax) - ax$	$i(-ia)^{-s}\sin\dfrac{s\pi}{2}\,\Gamma(s)$	$[\operatorname{Re} a = 0;\ -3 < \operatorname{Re} s < -1]$
4	$\cosh(ax) - 1$	$(ia)^{-s}\cos\dfrac{s\pi}{2}\,\Gamma(s)$	$[\operatorname{Re} a = 0;\ -2 < \operatorname{Re} s < 0]$
5	$\cosh(ax) - \dfrac{a^2 x^2}{2} - 1$	$(ia)^{-s}\cos\dfrac{s\pi}{2}\,\Gamma(s)$	$[\operatorname{Re} a = 0;\ -4 < \operatorname{Re} s < -2]$
6	$\sinh(ax)$ $\displaystyle -\sum_{k=0}^{n}\frac{(ax)^{2k+1}}{(2k+1)!}$	$i(-ia)^{-s}\sin\dfrac{s\pi}{2}\,\Gamma(s)$	$[\operatorname{Re} a = 0;\ -2n - 3 < \operatorname{Re} s < -2n - 1]$
7	$\cosh(ax) - \displaystyle\sum_{k=0}^{n}\frac{(ax)^{2k}}{(2k)!}$	$(ia)^{-s}\cos\dfrac{s\pi}{2}\,\Gamma(s)$	$[\operatorname{Re} a = 0;\ -2(n+1) < \operatorname{Re} s < -2n]$
8	$\operatorname{sech}(ax)$	$\dfrac{2^{1-2s}}{a^s}\,\Gamma(s)\left[\zeta\left(s, \dfrac{1}{4}\right) - \zeta\left(s, \dfrac{3}{4}\right)\right]$	$[\operatorname{Re} a,\ \operatorname{Re} s > 0]$
9	$\operatorname{csch}(ax)$	$\dfrac{2^s - 1}{2^{s-1} a^s}\,\Gamma(s)\zeta(s)$	$[\operatorname{Re} a > 0;\ \operatorname{Re} s > 1]$
10	$\operatorname{csch}(ax) - \dfrac{1}{ax}$	$2\left(1 - 2^{-s}\right) a^{-s}\,\Gamma(s)\,\zeta(s)$	$[\operatorname{Re} a > 0;\ \|\operatorname{Re} s\| < 1]$
11	$\operatorname{sech}^2(ax)$	$\dfrac{4}{(2a)^s}\left(1 - 2^{2-s}\right)\Gamma(s)\,\zeta(s - 1)$	$[\operatorname{Re} a,\ \operatorname{Re} s > 0]$

No.	$f(x)$	$F(s)$
12	$\operatorname{csch}^2(ax)$	$\dfrac{2^{2-s}}{a^s}\,\Gamma(s)\,\zeta(s-1)$ $\qquad$ [$\operatorname{Re} a,\ \operatorname{Re} s > 2$]
13	$\dfrac{\sinh(ax)}{\sinh(bx)}$	$\dfrac{\Gamma(s)}{(2b)^s}\left[\zeta\left(s,\dfrac{b-a}{2b}\right)-\zeta\left(s,\dfrac{b+a}{2b}\right)\right]$ $\quad$ [$\operatorname{Re} b > |\operatorname{Re} a|;\ \operatorname{Re} s > 0$]
14	$\dfrac{\cosh(ax)}{\sinh(bx)}$	$\dfrac{\Gamma(s)}{(2b)^s}\left[\zeta\left(s,\dfrac{b-a}{2b}\right)+\zeta\left(s,\dfrac{b+a}{2b}\right)\right]$ $\quad$ [$\operatorname{Re} b > |\operatorname{Re} a|;\ \operatorname{Re} s > 1$]
15	$\dfrac{\sinh(ax)}{\cosh(bx)}$	$\dfrac{\Gamma(s)}{(4b)^s}\left[\zeta\left(s,\dfrac{b-a}{4b}\right)-\zeta\left(s,\dfrac{b+a}{4b}\right)+\zeta\left(s,\dfrac{3b+a}{4b}\right)\right.$ $\left.-\zeta\left(s,\dfrac{3b-a}{4b}\right)\right]$ $\quad$ [$\operatorname{Re} b > |\operatorname{Re} a|;\ \operatorname{Re} s > -1$]
16	$\dfrac{\cosh(ax)}{\cosh(bx)}$	$\dfrac{\Gamma(s)}{(4b)^s}\left[\zeta\left(s,\dfrac{b-a}{4b}\right)+\zeta\left(s,\dfrac{b+a}{4b}\right)-\zeta\left(s,\dfrac{3b+a}{4b}\right)\right.$ $\left.-\zeta\left(s,\dfrac{3b-a}{4b}\right)\right]$ $\quad$ [$\operatorname{Re} b > |\operatorname{Re} a|;\ \operatorname{Re} s > 0$]
17	$\dfrac{\sinh(ax)}{\cosh(bx)}$	$\dfrac{\Gamma(s)}{(2b)^s}\left[\Phi\left(-1,s,\dfrac{b-a}{2b}\right)-\Phi\left(-1,s,\dfrac{b+a}{2b}\right)\right]$ $\quad$ [$\operatorname{Re} b > |\operatorname{Re} a|;\ \operatorname{Re} s > 1$]
18	$\dfrac{\sinh(ax)}{\cosh^2(ax)}$	$\dfrac{2^{3-2s}\Gamma(s)}{a^s}\left[\zeta\left(s-1,\dfrac{1}{4}\right)-\zeta\left(s-1,\dfrac{3}{4}\right)\right]$ $\quad$ [$\operatorname{Re} a > 0;\ \operatorname{Re} s > 1$]
19	$\dfrac{\cosh(ax)}{\sinh^2(ax)}$	$\dfrac{2}{a^s}\left(1-2^{1-s}\right)\Gamma(s)\,\zeta(s-1)$ $\qquad$ [$\operatorname{Re} a > 0;\ \operatorname{Re} s > 2$]
20	$\dfrac{1}{\cosh x+\cos\theta}$	$2^{s-1}\pi^s\csc\theta\,\csc\dfrac{s\pi}{2}\left[\zeta\left(1-s,\dfrac{\pi-\theta}{2\pi}\right)-\zeta\left(1-s,\dfrac{\pi+\theta}{2\pi}\right)\right]$ $\quad$ [$|\theta|<\pi;\ \operatorname{Re} s > 0$]
21	$\dfrac{\sinh(x/2)}{\cosh x+\cos\theta}$	$2^{2s-3}\pi^s\csc\dfrac{\theta}{2}\sec\dfrac{s\pi}{2}\left[\zeta\left(1-s,\dfrac{\pi-\theta}{4\pi}\right)-\zeta\left(1-s,\dfrac{\pi+\theta}{4\pi}\right)\right.$ $\left.+\zeta\left(1-s,\dfrac{3\pi+\theta}{4\pi}\right)-\zeta\left(1-s,\dfrac{3\pi-\theta}{4\pi}\right)\right]$ $\quad$ [$|\theta|<\pi;\ \operatorname{Re} s > 0$]
22	$\dfrac{\cosh(x/2)}{\cosh x+\cos\theta}$	$2^{2s-3}\pi^s\sec\dfrac{\theta}{2}\csc\dfrac{s\pi}{2}\left[\zeta\left(1-s,\dfrac{\pi-\theta}{4\pi}\right)+\zeta\left(1-s,\dfrac{\pi+\theta}{4\pi}\right)\right.$ $\left.-\zeta\left(1-s,\dfrac{3\pi+\theta}{4\pi}\right)-\zeta\left(1-s,\dfrac{3\pi+\theta}{4\pi}\right)\right]$ $\quad$ [$|\theta|<\pi;\ \operatorname{Re} s > 0$]

No.	$f(x)$	$F(s)$
23	$\dfrac{\sinh(ax)\sinh(bx)}{\cosh(2ax)+\cosh(2bx)}$	$\dfrac{2^{-1-2s}\Gamma(s)}{(a^2-b^2)^{s/2}}\left[\left(\dfrac{a+b}{a-b}\right)^{s/2}-\left(\dfrac{a+b}{a-b}\right)^{-s/2}\right]$ $\times\left[\zeta\left(s,\dfrac{1}{4}\right)-\zeta\left(s,\dfrac{3}{4}\right)\right]$ $\quad$ [Re a, Re $b>0$; Re $s>-2$]
24	$\tanh(ax)$	$\dfrac{2^{1-s}-1}{2^{s-1}a^s}\Gamma(s)\zeta(s)$ $\quad$ [Re $a>0$; $-1<$ Re $s<0$]
25	$\tanh(ax)-1$	$\dfrac{2^{1-s}-1}{2^{s-1}a^s}\Gamma(s)\zeta(s)$ $\quad$ [a, Re $s>0$]
26	$\coth(ax)-1$	$\dfrac{\Gamma(s)}{2^{s-1}a^s}\zeta(s)$ $\quad$ [$a>0$; Re $s>1$]

2.3.2. Hyperbolic and algebraic functions

Notation: $\delta=\left\{\begin{matrix}1\\0\end{matrix}\right\}$.

1	$(a-x)_+^{\alpha-1}\left\{\begin{matrix}\sinh(bx)\\\cosh(bx)\end{matrix}\right\}$	$\dfrac{a^{s+\alpha-1}}{2}\mathrm{B}(\alpha,s)\left[{}_1F_1\left(\begin{matrix}s;\ ab\\s+\alpha\end{matrix}\right)\mp{}_1F_1\left(\begin{matrix}s;\ -ab\\s+\alpha\end{matrix}\right)\right]$ $\quad$ [a, Re $\alpha>0$; Re $s>-(1\pm1)/2$]
2	$(a^2-x^2)_+^{\alpha-1}$ $\times\left\{\begin{matrix}\sinh(bx)\\\cosh(bx)\end{matrix}\right\}$	$\dfrac{a^{s+2\alpha+\delta-2}b^\delta}{2}\mathrm{B}\left(\alpha,\dfrac{s+\delta}{2}\right){}_1F_2\left(\begin{matrix}\frac{s+\delta}{2};\ \frac{a^2b^2}{4}\\\frac{2\delta+1}{2},\ \frac{s+2\alpha+\delta}{2}\end{matrix}\right)$ $\quad$ [a, Re $\alpha>0$; Re $s>-\delta$]
3	$\dfrac{1}{(x+a)^\rho}\sinh\dfrac{b}{x+a}$	$a^{s-\rho-1}b\,\mathrm{B}(s,\rho-s+1)\,{}_2F_3\left(\begin{matrix}\frac{\rho-s+1}{2},\ \frac{\rho-s+2}{2}\\\frac{3}{2},\ \frac{\rho+1}{2},\ \frac{\rho+2}{2};\ \frac{b^2}{4a^2}\end{matrix}\right)$ $\quad$ [$0<$ Re $s<$ Re $\rho+1$; $|\arg a|<\pi$]
4	$\dfrac{1}{(x+a)^\rho}\cosh\dfrac{b}{x+a}$	$a^{s-\rho}\mathrm{B}(s,\rho-s)\,{}_2F_3\left(\begin{matrix}\frac{\rho-s}{2},\ \frac{\rho-s+1}{2}\\\frac{1}{2},\ \frac{\rho}{2},\ \frac{\rho+1}{2};\ \frac{b^2}{4a^2}\end{matrix}\right)$ $\quad$ [$0<$ Re $s<$ Re ρ; $|\arg a|<\pi$]
5	$\dfrac{1}{(x+a)^\rho}\sinh\dfrac{bx}{x+a}$	$a^{s-\rho}b\,\mathrm{B}(s+1,\rho-s)\,{}_2F_3\left(\begin{matrix}\frac{s+1}{2},\ \frac{s+2}{2};\ \frac{b^2}{4}\\\frac{3}{2},\ \frac{\rho+1}{2},\ \frac{\rho+2}{2}\end{matrix}\right)$ $\quad$ [$-1<$ Re $s<$ Re ρ; $|\arg a|<\pi$]
6	$\dfrac{1}{(x+a)^\rho}\cosh\dfrac{bx}{x+a}$	$a^{s-\rho}\mathrm{B}(s,\rho-s)\,{}_2F_3\left(\begin{matrix}\frac{s}{2},\ \frac{s+1}{2};\ \frac{b^2}{4}\\\frac{1}{2},\ \frac{\rho}{2},\ \frac{\rho+1}{2}\end{matrix}\right)$ $\quad$ [$0<$ Re $s<$ Re ρ; $|\arg a|<\pi$]

No.	$f(x)$	$F(s)$
7	$\dfrac{1}{(x^2+a^2)^\rho}\sinh\dfrac{bx}{x^2+a^2}$	$\dfrac{a^{s-2\rho-1}b}{2}\,\mathrm{B}\left(\dfrac{s+1}{2},\dfrac{1-s+2\rho}{2}\right)\,{}_2F_3\left(\begin{smallmatrix}\frac{s+1}{2},\ \frac{1-s+2\rho}{2};\ -\frac{b^2}{16a^2}\\ \frac{3}{2},\ \frac{\rho+1}{2},\ \frac{\rho+2}{2}\end{smallmatrix}\right)$ $[\mathrm{Re}\,a>0;\ -1<\mathrm{Re}\,s<2\,\mathrm{Re}\,\rho+1]$
8	$\dfrac{1}{(x^2+a^2)^\rho}\cosh\dfrac{bx}{x^2+a^2}$	$\dfrac{a^{s-2\rho}}{2}\,\mathrm{B}\left(\dfrac{s}{2},\dfrac{2\rho-s}{2}\right)\,{}_2F_3\left(\begin{smallmatrix}\frac{s}{2},\ \frac{2\rho-s}{2};\ \frac{b^2}{16a^2}\\ \frac{1}{2},\ \frac{\rho}{2},\ \frac{\rho+1}{2}\end{smallmatrix}\right)$ $[\mathrm{Re}\,a>0;\ 0<\mathrm{Re}\,s<2\,\mathrm{Re}\,\rho]$
9	$(a-x)_+^{(\delta-1)/2}(bx+1)^\alpha$ $\times\left\{\begin{matrix}\sinh\left(c\sqrt{a-x}\right)\\\cosh\left(c\sqrt{a-x}\right)\end{matrix}\right\}$	$\dfrac{\sqrt{\pi}\,a^{s+\delta-1/2}c^\delta}{\delta+1}\,\Gamma\left[\begin{matrix}s\\\frac{2s+2\delta+1}{2}\end{matrix}\right]$ $\times\,\Xi_2\left(-\alpha,\,s;\,\dfrac{2s+2\delta+1}{2};\,-ab,\dfrac{ac^2}{4}\right)$ $[a,\ \mathrm{Re}\,s>0;\ |\arg(ab+1)|<\pi]$
10	$(x-a)_+^{(\delta-1)/2}(1-x+a)_+^\alpha$ $\times\left\{\begin{matrix}\sinh\left(b\sqrt{x-a}\right)\\\cosh\left(b\sqrt{x-a}\right)\end{matrix}\right\}$	$\dfrac{\sqrt{\pi}\,(a+1)^{s-1}b^\delta}{\delta+1}\,\Gamma\left[\begin{matrix}\alpha+1\\\frac{2\alpha+2\delta+3}{2}\end{matrix}\right]$ $\times\,\Xi_2\left(1-s,\,\alpha+1;\,\dfrac{2\alpha+2\delta+3}{2};\,\dfrac{1}{a+1},\dfrac{b^2}{4}\right)$ $[a,\ \mathrm{Re}\,s>0]$
11	$(a-x)_+^{\alpha-1}$ $\times\left\{\begin{matrix}\sinh\left(b\sqrt{x(a-x)}\right)\\\cosh\left(b\sqrt{x(a-x)}\right)\end{matrix}\right\}$	$a^{s+\alpha+\delta-1}b^\delta\,\mathrm{B}\left(\dfrac{2\alpha+\delta}{2},\dfrac{2s+\delta}{2}\right)\,{}_2F_3\left(\begin{smallmatrix}\frac{2\alpha+\delta}{2},\ \frac{2s+\delta}{2};\ \frac{a^2b^2}{16}\\ \frac{2\delta+1}{2},\ \frac{s+\alpha+\delta}{2},\ \frac{s+\alpha+\delta+1}{2}\end{smallmatrix}\right)$ $[a>0;\ \mathrm{Re}\,\alpha,\ \mathrm{Re}\,s>-\delta/2]$

2.3.3. Hyperbolic functions and e^{ax}

No.	$f(x)$	$F(s)$
1	$e^{-ax}\sinh(ax)$	$-\dfrac{a^{-s}}{2^{s+1}}\,\Gamma(s)$ $\qquad[-1<\mathrm{Re}\,s<0;\ |\arg a|\le\pi/2]$
2	$e^{-ax}\left\{\begin{matrix}\sinh(bx)\\\cosh(bx)\end{matrix}\right\}$	$\dfrac{\Gamma(s)}{2}\left[(a-b)^{-s}\mp(a+b)^{-s}\right]$ $\left[\begin{matrix}(\mathrm{Re}\,a>|\mathrm{Re}\,b|;\ \mathrm{Re}\,s>-(1\pm1)/2)\ \text{or}\\(\mathrm{Re}\,a+|\mathrm{Re}\,b|=0;\ \mathrm{Re}\,s<1)\end{matrix}\right]$
3	$e^{-ax}\left\{\begin{matrix}\sinh(bx)\\\cosh(bx)\end{matrix}\right\}^n$	$\dfrac{\Gamma(s)}{2^n}\sum_{k=0}^{n}(\mp1)^{n-k}\binom{n}{k}\left[a+(n-2k)b\right]^{-s}$ $[\mathrm{Re}\,a>n\,|\mathrm{Re}\,b|;\ \mathrm{Re}\,s>-(1\pm1)/2]$

No.	$f(x)$	$F(s)$
4	$e^{-ax}\sinh^{2n}(bx)$	$\dfrac{(-1)^n\Gamma(s)}{2^{2n}a^s}\dbinom{2n}{n}+\dfrac{\Gamma(s)}{2^{2n}}\displaystyle\sum_{k=0}^{n-1}(-1)^k\dbinom{2n}{k}$
		$\times\left[(a-(2n-2k)b)^{-s}+(a+(2n-2k)b)^{-s}\right]$
		$[\operatorname{Re}(a-2nb)>0;\ \operatorname{Re}s>-2n]$
5	$e^{-ax}\sinh^{2n+1}(bx)$	$\dfrac{\Gamma(s)}{2^{2n+1}}\displaystyle\sum_{k=0}^{n}(-1)^k\dbinom{2n+1}{k}\left[(a-(2n-2k+1)b)^{-s}\right.$
		$\left.-(a+(2n-2k+1)b)^{-s}\right]$
		$[\operatorname{Re}(a-(2n+1)b)>0;\ \operatorname{Re}s>-2n-1]$
6	$e^{-ax}\cosh^{n}(bx)$	$\dfrac{(1+(-1)^n)\Gamma(s)}{2^{n+1}a^s}\dbinom{n}{n/2}+\dfrac{\Gamma(s)}{2^n}\displaystyle\sum_{k=0}^{[(n-1)/2]}\dbinom{n}{k}$
		$\times\left[(a-(n-2k)b)^{-s}+(a+(n-2k)b)^{-s}\right]$
		$[\operatorname{Re}(a-nb),\ \operatorname{Re}s>0]$
7	$\dfrac{e^{-ax}}{\sinh(bx)}$	$\dfrac{2^{1-s}}{b^s}\Gamma(s)\zeta\left(s,\dfrac{a+b}{2b}\right)\qquad[\operatorname{Re}a>-|\operatorname{Re}b|;\ \operatorname{Re}s>1]$
8	$\dfrac{e^{-ax}}{\cosh(bx)}$	$\dfrac{2^{1-2s}}{b^s}\Gamma(s)\left[\zeta\left(s,\dfrac{b+a}{4b}\right)-\zeta\left(s,\dfrac{3b+a}{4b}\right)\right]$
		$[\operatorname{Re}a>-|\operatorname{Re}b|;\ \operatorname{Re}s>0]$
9	$\dfrac{e^{-ax}}{\cosh(ax)}$	$\dfrac{2^{1-s}}{a^s}\left(1-2^{1-s}\right)\Gamma(s)\zeta(s)\qquad[\operatorname{Re}a,\ \operatorname{Re}s>0;\ s\neq1]$
10	$e^{-ax}\tanh(bx)$	$\dfrac{\Gamma(s)}{2^{2s-1}b^s}\left[\zeta\left(s,\dfrac{a}{4b}\right)-\zeta\left(s,\dfrac{a+2b}{4b}\right)\right]-\dfrac{\Gamma(s)}{a^s}$
		$[\operatorname{Re}a>0;\ \operatorname{Re}s>-1]$
11	$e^{-ax}\coth(bx)$	$\dfrac{2^{1-s}}{b^s}\Gamma(s)\zeta\left(s,\dfrac{a}{2b}\right)-\dfrac{\Gamma(s)}{a^s}\qquad[b,\ \operatorname{Re}a>0;\ \operatorname{Re}s>1]$
12	$\dfrac{1}{e^{ax}+1}\left\{\begin{array}{l}\sinh(bx)\\\cosh(bx)\end{array}\right\}$	$\dfrac{\Gamma(s)}{2(2a)^s}\left[\zeta\left(s,\dfrac{a-b}{2a}\right)\mp\zeta\left(s,\dfrac{a+b}{2a}\right)-\zeta\left(s,\dfrac{2a-b}{2a}\right)\right.$
		$\left.\pm\zeta\left(s,\dfrac{2a+b}{2a}\right)\right]\qquad[\operatorname{Re}a>|\operatorname{Re}b|;\ \operatorname{Re}s>-(1\pm1)/2]$
13	$\dfrac{1}{e^{ax}-1}\left\{\begin{array}{l}\sinh(bx)\\\cosh(bx)\end{array}\right\}$	$\dfrac{\Gamma(s)}{2a^s}\left[\zeta\left(s,\dfrac{a-b}{a}\right)\mp\zeta\left(s,\dfrac{a+b}{a}\right)\right]$
		$[\operatorname{Re}a>|\operatorname{Re}b|;\ \operatorname{Re}s>(1\mp1)/2]$

No.	$f(x)$	$F(s)$
14	$\dfrac{e^{-ax}}{\cosh(ax)+\cos\theta}$	$\left(\dfrac{2\pi}{a}\right)^{s}\csc\theta\csc(s\pi)\left[\cos\dfrac{2\theta+s\pi}{2}\,\zeta\left(1-s,\dfrac{\pi+\theta}{2\pi}\right)\right.$ $\left.-\cos\dfrac{2\theta-s\pi}{2}\,\zeta\left(1-s,\dfrac{\pi-\theta}{2\pi}\right)\right]\qquad[|\theta|<\pi;\ \operatorname{Re}a,\ \operatorname{Re}s>0]$
15	$\dfrac{e^{-ax}}{\cosh(ax)-\cos\theta}$	$\dfrac{i\Gamma(s)}{a^{s}\sin\theta}\left[e^{i\theta}\operatorname{Li}_{s}\left(e^{-i\theta}\right)-e^{-i\theta}\operatorname{Li}_{s}\left(e^{i\theta}\right)\right]$ $[|\theta|\neq 2\pi n;\ \operatorname{Re}a,\ \operatorname{Re}s>0]$
16	$\theta(a-x)\,e^{bx}\sinh(a-x)$	$e^{-a}a^{s+1}\,\Gamma\!\begin{bmatrix}s\\s+2\end{bmatrix}\Phi_{2}(s,1;s+2;ab+a,2a)\qquad[a,\ \operatorname{Re}s>0]$
17	$(a-x)_{+}^{-1/2}\,e^{cx}$ $\times\begin{Bmatrix}\sinh\left(b\sqrt{a-x}\right)\\\cosh\left(b\sqrt{a-x}\right)\end{Bmatrix}$	$\dfrac{\sqrt{\pi}}{2^{\delta}}\,a^{s+\delta-1/2}b^{\delta}\,\Gamma\!\begin{bmatrix}s\\\frac{2s+2\delta+1}{2}\end{bmatrix}\Phi_{3}\left(s;\dfrac{2s+2\delta+1}{2};ac,\dfrac{ab^{2}}{4}\right)$ $[a,\ \operatorname{Re}s>0]$

2.3.4. Hyperbolic functions and $e^{\varphi(x)}$

Notation: $\delta=\begin{Bmatrix}1\\0\end{Bmatrix}$.

No.	$f(x)$	$F(s)$
1	$e^{-ax^{2}}\begin{Bmatrix}\sinh(bx)\\\cosh(bx)\end{Bmatrix}$	$\dfrac{e^{b^{2}/(8a)}}{2^{s/2+1}a^{s/2}}\,\Gamma(s)\left[D_{-s}\left(-\dfrac{b}{\sqrt{2a}}\right)\mp D_{-s}\left(\dfrac{b}{\sqrt{2a}}\right)\right]$ $[\operatorname{Re}a>0;\ \operatorname{Re}s>-(1\pm1)/2]$
2	$e^{-ax^{2}-bx}\begin{Bmatrix}\sinh(cx)\\\cosh(cx)\end{Bmatrix}$	$\dfrac{e^{(b^{2}+c^{2})/(8a)}}{2^{s/2+1}a^{s/2}}\,\Gamma(s)\left[e^{-bc/(4a)}D_{-s}\left(\dfrac{b-c}{\sqrt{2a}}\right)\mp e^{bc/(4a)}\right.$ $\left.\times D_{-s}\left(\dfrac{b+c}{\sqrt{2a}}\right)\right]\qquad[\operatorname{Re}a>0;\ \operatorname{Re}s>-(1\pm1)/2]$
3	$e^{-ax-b/x}\begin{Bmatrix}\sinh(cx)\\\cosh(cx)\end{Bmatrix}$	$\left(\dfrac{b}{a-c}\right)^{s/2}K_{s}\left(2\sqrt{ab-bc}\right)\mp\left(\dfrac{b}{a+c}\right)^{s/2}K_{s}\left(2\sqrt{ab+bc}\right)$ $[\operatorname{Re}a>|\operatorname{Re}c|;\ \operatorname{Re}b>0]$
4	$(a^{2}-x^{2})_{+}^{-1/2}\,e^{-b/(a^{2}-x^{2})}$ $\times\begin{Bmatrix}\sinh\left[cx/(a^{2}-x^{2})\right]\\\cosh\left[cx/(a^{2}-x^{2})\right]\end{Bmatrix}$	$\dfrac{2^{(2s-3)/4+\delta}a^{s-1}}{\sqrt{c}}\,e^{-b/(2a^{2})}\left(b+\sqrt{b^{2}-a^{2}c^{2}}\right)^{1/4}\Gamma\left(\dfrac{s+\delta}{2}\right)$ $\times D_{-s}\left(\dfrac{\sqrt{b+\sqrt{b^{2}-a^{2}c^{2}}}}{a}\right)M_{(1-2s)/4,\pm1/4}\left(\dfrac{b-\sqrt{b^{2}-a^{2}c^{2}}}{2a^{2}}\right)$ $[a>0;\ b>ac>0;\ \operatorname{Re}s>-\delta]$

No.	$f(x)$	$F(s)$
5	$\left(x^2 - a^2\right)_+^{-1/2} e^{-b/(x^2 - a^2)}$ $\times \left\{ \begin{array}{l} \sinh\left[cx/(x^2 - a^2)\right] \\ \cosh\left[cx/(x^2 - a^2)\right] \end{array} \right\}$	$\dfrac{a^{s-1}}{2^{(2s+1)/4 - \delta}\sqrt{c}}\, e^{b/(2a^2)} \left(b + \sqrt{b^2 - a^2 c^2}\right)^{1/4} \Gamma\left(\dfrac{1 - s + \delta}{2}\right)$ $\times D_{s-1}\left(\dfrac{\sqrt{b + \sqrt{b^2 - a^2 c^2}}}{a}\right) M_{(2s-1)/4,\,\pm 1/4}\left(\dfrac{b - \sqrt{b^2 - a^2 c^2}}{2a^2}\right)$ $[a > 0;\ b > ac > 0;\ \operatorname{Re} s < \delta + 1]$
6	$\left(a^2 - x^2\right)_+^{-1/2}$ $\times e^{-b(a^2 + x^2)/(a^2 - x^2)}$ $\times \left\{ \begin{array}{l} \sinh\left[cx/(a^2 - x^2)\right] \\ \cosh\left[cx/(a^2 - x^2)\right] \end{array} \right\}$	$\dfrac{2^{(2s-3)/4 + \delta} a^{s - 3/4}}{\sqrt{c}} \left(2ab + \sqrt{4a^2 b^2 - c^2}\right)^{1/4}$ $\times \Gamma\left(\dfrac{s + \delta}{2}\right) D_{-s}\left(\dfrac{\sqrt{2ab + \sqrt{4a^2 b^2 - c^2}}}{\sqrt{a}}\right)$ $\times M_{(1-2s)/4,\,\pm 1/4}\left(\dfrac{2ab - \sqrt{4a^2 b^2 - c^2}}{2a}\right)$ $[a > 0;\ 2ab > c > 0;\ \operatorname{Re} s > -\delta]$
7	$\left(x^2 - a^2\right)_+^{-1/2}$ $\times e^{-b(x^2 + a^2)/(x^2 - a^2)}$ $\times \left\{ \begin{array}{l} \sinh\left[cx/(x^2 - a^2)\right] \\ \cosh\left[cx/(x^2 - a^2)\right] \end{array} \right\}$	$\dfrac{a^{s - 3/4}}{2^{(2s+1)/4 - \delta}\sqrt{c}} \left(2ab + \sqrt{4a^2 b^2 - c^2}\right)^{1/4}$ $\times \Gamma\left(\dfrac{1 - s + \delta}{2}\right) D_{s-1}\left(\dfrac{\sqrt{2ab + \sqrt{4a^2 b^2 - c^2}}}{\sqrt{a}}\right)$ $\times M_{(2s-1)/4,\,\pm 1/4}\left(\dfrac{2ab - \sqrt{4a^2 b^2 - c^2}}{2a}\right)$ $[a > 0;\ 2ab > c > 0;\ \operatorname{Re} s < \delta + 1]$
8	$\dfrac{1}{\sqrt{x^2 + a^2}}\, e^{-b/(x^2 + a^2)}$ $\times \left\{ \begin{array}{l} \sinh\left[cx/(x^2 + a^2)\right] \\ \cosh\left[cx/(x^2 + a^2)\right] \end{array} \right\}$	$\dfrac{2^{\delta - 1/2} a^{s - 1/2}}{\sqrt{c}}\, e^{-b/(2a^2)}\, \mathrm{B}\left(\dfrac{1 - s + \delta}{2}, \dfrac{s + \delta}{2}\right)$ $\times M_{(2s-1)/4,\,\pm 1/4}\left(\dfrac{\sqrt{b^2 + a^2 c^2} - b}{2a^2}\right)$ $\times M_{(1-2s)/4,\,\pm 1/4}\left(\dfrac{\sqrt{b^2 + a^2 c^2} + b}{2a^2}\right)$ $[\operatorname{Re} a,\, b,\, c > 0;\ -\delta < \operatorname{Re} s < \delta + 1]$
9	$\dfrac{1}{\sqrt{x^2 + a^2}}\, e^{-b(a^2 - x^2)/(a^2 + x^2)}$ $\times \left\{ \begin{array}{l} \sinh\left[cx/(x^2 + a^2)\right] \\ \cosh\left[cx/(x^2 + a^2)\right] \end{array} \right\}$	$\dfrac{2^{\delta - 1/2} a^{s - 1/2}}{\sqrt{c}}\, \mathrm{B}\left(\dfrac{1 - s + \delta}{2}, \dfrac{s + \delta}{2}\right)$ $\times M_{(2s-1)/4,\,\pm 1/4}\left(\dfrac{\sqrt{4a^2 b^2 + c^2} - 2ab}{2a}\right)$ $\times M_{(1-2s)/4,\,\pm 1/4}\left(\dfrac{\sqrt{4a^2 b^2 + c^2} + 2ab}{2a}\right)$ $[\operatorname{Re} a,\, b,\, c > 0;\ -\delta < \operatorname{Re} s < \delta + 1]$

2.4. Trigonometric Functions

More formulas can be obtained from the corresponding sections due to the relations

$$\sin z = -\sin(-z) = \cos\left(\frac{\pi}{2} - z\right) = -\cos\left(z + \frac{\pi}{2}\right) = \frac{e^{iz} - e^{-iz}}{2i} = -i\sinh(iz),$$

$$\cos z = \cos(-z) = \sin\left(\frac{\pi}{2} - z\right) = \sin\left(z + \frac{\pi}{2}\right) = \frac{e^{iz} + e^{-iz}}{2} = \cosh(iz),$$

$$\begin{Bmatrix} \sin z \\ \cos z \end{Bmatrix} = \sqrt{\frac{\pi z}{2}}\, J_{\pm 1/2}(z), \quad \sin z = z\,_0F_1\left(\frac{3}{2}; -\frac{z^2}{4}\right), \quad \cos z = \,_0F_1\left(\frac{1}{2}; -\frac{z^2}{4}\right),$$

$$\sin z = \frac{\sqrt{\pi}\, z}{\sqrt{z^2}}\, G_{02}^{10}\left(\frac{z^2}{4}\,\Big|\, \begin{matrix} \cdot \\ 1/2,\, 0 \end{matrix}\right), \quad \cos z = \sqrt{\pi}\, G_{02}^{10}\left(\frac{z^2}{4}\,\Big|\, \begin{matrix} \cdot \\ 0,\, 1/2 \end{matrix}\right).$$

2.4.1. $\sin(ax + b)$ and $\cos(ax + b)$

Notation: $\delta = \begin{Bmatrix} 1 \\ 0 \end{Bmatrix}$.

No.	$f(x)$	$F(s)$	
1	$\begin{Bmatrix} \sin(ax) \\ \cos(ax) \end{Bmatrix}$	$a^{-s}\begin{Bmatrix} \sin(s\pi/2) \\ \cos(s\pi/2) \end{Bmatrix}\Gamma(s)$	$[a > 0;\ -\delta < \operatorname{Re} s < 1]$
2	$\begin{Bmatrix} \sin(ax) \\ \cos(ax) \end{Bmatrix}$	$a^{-s}\begin{Bmatrix} \sin(s\pi/2) \\ \cos(s\pi/2) \end{Bmatrix}\Gamma(s)$	$[a > 0;\ -\delta < \operatorname{Re} s < 1]$
3	$\sin(ax) - ax$	$a^{-s}\sin\dfrac{s\pi}{2}\Gamma(s)$	$[a > 0;\ -3 < \operatorname{Re} s < -1]$
4	$\cos(ax) - 1$	$a^{-s}\cos\dfrac{s\pi}{2}\Gamma(s)$	$[a > 0;\ -2 < \operatorname{Re} s < 0]$
5	$\cos(ax) + \dfrac{a^2 x^2}{2} - 1$	$a^{-s}\cos\dfrac{s\pi}{2}\Gamma(s)$	$[a > 0;\ -4 < \operatorname{Re} s < -2]$
6	$\sin(ax)$ $- \displaystyle\sum_{k=0}^{n} \frac{(-1)^k (ax)^{2k+1}}{(2k+1)!}$	$a^{-s}\sin\dfrac{s\pi}{2}\Gamma(s)$	$[a > 0;\ -2n - 3 < \operatorname{Re} s < -2n - 1]$
7	$\cos(ax)$ $- \displaystyle\sum_{k=0}^{n} \frac{(-1)^k (ax)^{2k}}{(2k)!}$	$a^{-s}\cos\dfrac{s\pi}{2}\Gamma(s)$	$[a > 0;\ -2(n+1) < \operatorname{Re} s < -2n]$
8	$\theta(a - x)\begin{Bmatrix} \sin(bx) \\ \cos(bx) \end{Bmatrix}$	$\dfrac{i^{(1\pm 1)/2}}{2} b^{-s}\left[e^{-is\pi/2}\gamma(s, iab) \mp e^{is\pi/2}\gamma(s, -iab)\right]$ $[a > 0;\ \operatorname{Re} s > -(1 \pm 1)/2;\ |\arg b| < \pi]$	

No.	$f(x)$	$F(s)$
9	$\left\{\begin{array}{l}\sin(ax+b)\\\cos(ax+b)\end{array}\right\}$	$\dfrac{\Gamma(s)}{a^s}\left\{\begin{array}{l}\sin(s\pi/2+b)\\\cos(s\pi/2+b)\end{array}\right\}$ $\qquad [a>0;\ 0<\operatorname{Re}s<1]$
10	$\left\{\begin{array}{l}\sin(ax+\theta\pi)\\\cos(ax+\theta\pi)\end{array}\right\}$	$\dfrac{\sqrt{\pi}}{2}\left(\dfrac{2}{a}\right)^s\Gamma\left[\begin{array}{c}\frac{s}{2},\ \frac{s+1}{2}\\\frac{s+2\theta-\delta+1}{2},\ \frac{-s-2\theta+\delta+1}{2}\end{array}\right]$ $\qquad [a>0;\ 0<\operatorname{Re}s<1]$
11	$b\sin(ax)+c\cos(ax)$	$b\sqrt{\dfrac{b^2+c^2}{b^2}}\dfrac{\Gamma(s)}{a^s}\sin\left(\dfrac{s\pi}{2}+\arctan\dfrac{c}{b}\right)$ $\qquad [a>0;\ 0<\operatorname{Re}s<1]$

2.4.2.   Trigonometric and algebraic functions

Notation: $\delta=\left\{\begin{array}{l}1\\0\end{array}\right\}$.

No.	$f(x)$	$F(s)$
1	$(a-x)_+^{\alpha-1}\left\{\begin{array}{l}\sin(bx)\\\cos(bx)\end{array}\right\}$	$\dfrac{i^{(1\pm1)/2}}{2}a^{s+\alpha-1}\mathrm{B}(\alpha,s)\left[{}_1F_1\left(\begin{array}{c}s;\ -iab\\s+\alpha\end{array}\right)\mp{}_1F_1\left(\begin{array}{c}s;\ iab\\s+\alpha\end{array}\right)\right]$
		$[a,\ \operatorname{Re}\alpha>0,\ \operatorname{Re}s>-(1\pm1)/2]$
2	$(a^2-x^2)_+^{\alpha-1}\left\{\begin{array}{l}\sin(bx)\\\cos(bx)\end{array}\right\}$	$\dfrac{a^{s+2\alpha+\delta-2}b^\delta}{2}\mathrm{B}\left(\alpha,\dfrac{s+\delta}{2}\right){}_1F_2\left(\begin{array}{c}\frac{s+\delta}{2};\ -\frac{a^2b^2}{4}\\\frac{2\delta+1}{2},\ \frac{s+2\alpha+\delta}{2}\end{array}\right)$
		$[a,\ \operatorname{Re}\alpha>0;\ \operatorname{Re}s>-\delta]$
3	$\dfrac{\sin(bx)}{(x+a)^\rho}$	$a^{s-\rho+1}b\,\mathrm{B}(s+1,\rho-s-1)\,{}_2F_3\left(\begin{array}{c}\frac{s+1}{2},\ \frac{s+2}{2};\ -\frac{a^2b^2}{4}\\\frac{3}{2},\ \frac{s-\rho+2}{2},\ \frac{s-\rho+3}{2}\end{array}\right)$
		$+\,b^{\rho-s}\sin\dfrac{(s-\rho)\pi}{2}\Gamma(s-\rho)\,{}_2F_3\left(\begin{array}{c}\frac{\rho}{2},\ \frac{\rho+1}{2};\ -\frac{a^2b^2}{4}\\\frac{1}{2},\ \frac{1-s+\rho}{2},\ \frac{2-s+\rho}{2}\end{array}\right)$
		$+\,\dfrac{\rho a}{b^{s-\rho-1}}\Gamma(s-\rho-1)\cos\dfrac{(\rho-s)\pi}{2}\,{}_2F_3\left(\begin{array}{c}\frac{\rho+1}{2},\ \frac{\rho+2}{2};\ -\frac{a^2b^2}{4}\\\frac{3}{2},\ \frac{2-s+\rho}{2},\ \frac{3-s+\rho}{2}\end{array}\right)$
		$[b>0;\ -1<\operatorname{Re}s<\operatorname{Re}\rho+1;\ |\arg a|<\pi]$
4	$\dfrac{\cos(bx)}{(x+a)^\rho}$	$a^{s-\rho}\mathrm{B}(s,\rho-s)\,{}_2F_3\left(\begin{array}{c}\frac{s}{2},\ \frac{s+1}{2};\ -\frac{a^2b^2}{4}\\\frac{1}{2},\ \frac{s-\rho+1}{2},\ \frac{s-\rho+2}{2}\end{array}\right)$
		$+\,b^{\rho-s}\Gamma(s-\rho)\cos\dfrac{(s-\rho)\pi}{2}\,{}_2F_3\left(\begin{array}{c}\frac{\rho}{2},\ \frac{\rho+1}{2};\ -\frac{a^2b^2}{4}\\\frac{1}{2},\ \frac{1-s+\rho}{2},\ \frac{2-s+\rho}{2}\end{array}\right)$
		$+\,\dfrac{\rho a}{b^{s-\rho-1}}\Gamma(s-\rho-1)\sin\dfrac{(\rho-s)\pi}{2}\,{}_2F_3\left(\begin{array}{c}\frac{\rho+1}{2},\ \frac{\rho+2}{2};\ -\frac{a^2b^2}{4}\\\frac{3}{2},\ \frac{2-s+\rho}{2},\ \frac{3-s+\rho}{2}\end{array}\right)$
		$[b>0;\ 0<\operatorname{Re}s<\operatorname{Re}\rho+1;\ |\arg a|<\pi]$
5	$\dfrac{1}{x+a}\left\{\begin{array}{l}\sin(bx)\\\cos(bx)\end{array}\right\}$	$\dfrac{i^{(1\pm1)/2}}{2}a^{s-1}\Gamma(s)\left[e^{iab}\Gamma(1-s,iab)\mp e^{-iab}\Gamma(1-s,-iab)\right]$
		$[b>0;\ -(1\pm1)/2<\operatorname{Re}s<2;\ |\arg a|<\pi]$

No.	$f(x)$	$F(s)$
6	$\dfrac{1}{x-a}\begin{Bmatrix}\sin(bx)\\\cos(bx)\end{Bmatrix}$	$-\dfrac{a}{b^{s-2}}\Gamma(s-2)\begin{Bmatrix}\sin(s\pi/2)\\\cos(s\pi/2)\end{Bmatrix}{}_1F_2\left(\begin{matrix}1;\ -\frac{a^2b^2}{4}\\\frac{3-s}{2},\ \frac{4-s}{2}\end{matrix}\right)$

$$\mp\,\frac{\Gamma(s-1)}{b^{s-1}}\begin{Bmatrix}\cos(s\pi/2)\\\sin(s\pi/2)\end{Bmatrix}{}_1F_2\left(\begin{matrix}1;\ -\frac{a^2b^2}{4}\\\frac{2-s}{2},\ \frac{3-s}{2}\end{matrix}\right)$$

$$-\,\pi a^{s-1}\cot(s\pi)\begin{Bmatrix}\sin(ab)\\\cos(ab)\end{Bmatrix}$$

$$[a,\,b>0;\ -\delta<\operatorname{Re}s<2]$$

| 7 | $\dfrac{1}{(x^2+a^2)^\rho}\begin{Bmatrix}\sin(bx)\\\cos(bx)\end{Bmatrix}$ | $\dfrac{a^{s-2\rho+\delta}b^\delta}{2}\,\mathrm{B}\left(\dfrac{s+\delta}{2},\dfrac{2\rho-s-\delta}{2}\right){}_1F_2\left(\begin{matrix}\frac{s+\delta}{2};\ \frac{a^2b^2}{4}\\\frac{2\delta+1}{2},\ \frac{s-2\rho+\delta+2}{2}\end{matrix}\right)$ |

$$+\,b^{2\rho-s}\begin{Bmatrix}\sin[(s-2\rho)\pi/2]\\\cos[(s-2\rho)\pi/2]\end{Bmatrix}\Gamma(s-2\rho)\,{}_1F_2\left(\begin{matrix}\rho;\ \frac{a^2b^2}{4}\\\frac{2\rho-s+1}{2},\ \frac{2\rho-s+2}{2}\end{matrix}\right)$$

$$[b,\ \operatorname{Re}a>0;\ -\delta<\operatorname{Re}s<2\operatorname{Re}\rho+1]$$

| 8 | $\dfrac{1}{x^2+a^2}\begin{Bmatrix}\sin(bx)\\\cos(bx)\end{Bmatrix}$ | $\dfrac{\pi a^{s-2}}{2}\begin{Bmatrix}\sinh(ab)\sec(s\pi/2)\\\cosh(ab)\csc(s\pi/2)\end{Bmatrix}$ |

$$-\,\frac{\Gamma(s-2)}{b^{s-2}}\begin{Bmatrix}\sin(s\pi/2)\\\cos(s\pi/2)\end{Bmatrix}{}_1F_2\left(\begin{matrix}1;\ \frac{a^2b^2}{4}\\\frac{3-s}{2},\ \frac{4-s}{2}\end{matrix}\right)$$

$$[b,\ \operatorname{Re}a>0;\ -(1\pm1)/2<\operatorname{Re}s<3]$$

| 9 | $\dfrac{1}{x^2-a^2}\begin{Bmatrix}\sin(bx)\\\cos(bx)\end{Bmatrix}$ | $\pm\dfrac{\pi a^{s-2}}{2}\begin{Bmatrix}\sin(ab)\tan(s\pi/2)\\\cos(ab)\cot(s\pi/2)\end{Bmatrix}$ |

$$-\,\frac{\Gamma(s-2)}{b^{s-2}}\begin{Bmatrix}\sin(s\pi/2)\\\cos(s\pi/2)\end{Bmatrix}{}_1F_2\left(\begin{matrix}1;\ -\frac{a^2b^2}{4}\\\frac{3-s}{2},\ \frac{4-s}{2}\end{matrix}\right)$$

$$[a,\,b>0;\ -(1\pm1)/2<\operatorname{Re}s<3]$$

| 10 | $\dfrac{1}{x^4+a^4}\sin(bx)$ | $b^{4-s}\sin\dfrac{s\pi}{2}\,\Gamma(s-4)\,{}_1F_4\left(\begin{matrix}1;\ -\frac{a^4b^4}{256}\\\frac{5-s}{4},\ \frac{6-s}{4},\ \frac{7-s}{4},\ \frac{8-s}{4}\end{matrix}\right)+\dfrac{\pi a^{s-4}}{2}\sec\dfrac{s\pi}{2}$ |

$$\times\left(\cos\frac{s\pi}{4}\sinh\frac{ab}{\sqrt2}\cos\frac{ab}{\sqrt2}-\sin\frac{s\pi}{4}\cosh\frac{ab}{\sqrt2}\sin\frac{ab}{\sqrt2}\right)$$

$$[b>0;\ -1<\operatorname{Re}s<5;\ |\arg a|<\pi/4]$$

| 11 | $\dfrac{1}{x^4+a^4}\cos(bx)$ | $b^{4-s}\cos\dfrac{s\pi}{2}\,\Gamma(s-4)\,{}_1F_4\left(\begin{matrix}1;\ -\frac{a^4b^4}{256}\\\frac{5-s}{4},\ \frac{6-s}{4},\ \frac{7-s}{4},\ \frac{8-s}{4}\end{matrix}\right)$ |

$$+\,\frac{\pi a^{s-4}}{4}\left(\csc\frac{s\pi}{4}\cosh\frac{ab}{\sqrt2}\cos\frac{ab}{\sqrt2}-\sec\frac{s\pi}{4}\sinh\frac{ab}{\sqrt2}\sin\frac{ab}{\sqrt2}\right)$$

$$[b>0;\ 0<\operatorname{Re}s<5;\ |\arg a|<\pi/4]$$

No.	$f(x)$	$F(s)$

12 $\left(\sqrt{x^2+a^2}+a\right)^{\nu}\sin(bx)$

$$-2^{s+\nu}\nu\pi a^{s+\nu+1}b\csc\left[(s+\nu)\pi\right]$$

$$\times\Gamma\left[\begin{matrix}\frac{s+1}{2}\\ \frac{1-s-2\nu}{2},\ s+\nu+2\end{matrix}\right]\,{}_2F_3\left(\begin{matrix}\frac{s+1}{2},\ \frac{s+2\nu+1}{2};\ \frac{a^2b^2}{4}\\ \frac{3}{2},\ \frac{s+\nu+2}{2},\ \frac{s+\nu+3}{2}\end{matrix}\right)$$

$$+\frac{\nu\pi ab^{-s-\nu+1}}{2\,\Gamma(2-s-\nu)}\csc\frac{(s+\nu)\pi}{2}\,{}_2F_3\left(\begin{matrix}\frac{1-\nu}{2},\ \frac{1+\nu}{2};\ \frac{a^2b^2}{4}\\ \frac{3}{2},\ \frac{2-s-\nu}{2},\ \frac{3-s-\nu}{2}\end{matrix}\right)$$

$$+\frac{\pi b^{-s-\nu}}{2\,\Gamma(1-s-\nu)}\sec\frac{(s+\nu)\pi}{2}\,{}_2F_3\left(\begin{matrix}-\frac{\nu}{2},\ \frac{\nu}{2};\ \frac{a^2b^2}{4}\\ \frac{1}{2},\ \frac{1-s-\nu}{2},\ \frac{2-s-\nu}{2}\end{matrix}\right)$$

$$[b,\ \operatorname{Re}a>0;\ -1<\operatorname{Re}s<1-\operatorname{Re}\nu]$$

13 $\left(\sqrt{x^2+a^2}+a\right)^{\nu}\cos(bx)$

$$2^{s+\nu-1}\nu\pi a^{s+\nu}\csc\left[(s+\nu)\pi\right]$$

$$\times\Gamma\left[\begin{matrix}\frac{s}{2}\\ \frac{2-s-2\nu}{2},\ s+\nu+1\end{matrix}\right]\,{}_2F_3\left(\begin{matrix}\frac{s}{2},\ \frac{s+2\nu}{2};\ \frac{a^2b^2}{4}\\ \frac{1}{2},\ \frac{s+\nu+1}{2},\ \frac{s+\nu+2}{2}\end{matrix}\right)$$

$$+\frac{\pi b^{-s-\nu}}{2\,\Gamma(1-s-\nu)}\csc\frac{(s+\nu)\pi}{2}\,{}_2F_3\left(\begin{matrix}-\frac{\nu}{2},\ \frac{\nu}{2};\ \frac{a^2b^2}{4}\\ \frac{1}{2},\ \frac{1-s-\nu}{2},\ \frac{2-s-\nu}{2}\end{matrix}\right)$$

$$-\frac{\nu\pi ab^{-s-\nu+1}}{2\,\Gamma(2-s-\nu)}\sec\frac{(s+\nu)\pi}{2}\,{}_2F_3\left(\begin{matrix}\frac{1-\nu}{2},\ \frac{1+\nu}{2};\ \frac{a^2b^2}{4}\\ \frac{3}{2},\ \frac{2-s-\nu}{2},\ \frac{3-s-\nu}{2}\end{matrix}\right)$$

$$[b,\ \operatorname{Re}a>0;\ 0<\operatorname{Re}s<1-\operatorname{Re}\nu]$$

14 $\left(\sqrt{x^2+a^2}+x\right)^{\nu}\sin(bx)$

$$2^{-s-2}\nu\pi a^{s+\nu+1}b\sec\frac{(s+\nu)\pi}{2}$$

$$\times\Gamma\left[\begin{matrix}s+1\\ \frac{s-\nu+3}{2},\ \frac{s+\nu+3}{2}\end{matrix}\right]\,{}_2F_3\left(\begin{matrix}\frac{s+1}{2},\ \frac{s+2}{2};\ \frac{a^2b^2}{4}\\ \frac{3}{2},\ \frac{s-\nu+3}{2},\ \frac{s+\nu+3}{2}\end{matrix}\right)$$

$$+\frac{2^{\nu-1}\pi b^{-s-\nu}}{\Gamma(1-s-\nu)}\sec\frac{(s+\nu)\pi}{2}\,{}_2F_3\left(\begin{matrix}\frac{1-\nu}{2},\ -\frac{\nu}{2};\ \frac{a^2b^2}{4}\\ 1-\nu,\ \frac{1-s-\nu}{2},\ \frac{2-s-\nu}{2}\end{matrix}\right)$$

$$[b,\ \operatorname{Re}a>0;\ -1<\operatorname{Re}s<1-\operatorname{Re}\nu]$$

15 $\left(\sqrt{x^2+a^2}+x\right)^{\nu}\cos(bx)$

$$2^{-s-1}\nu\pi a^{s+\nu}\csc\frac{(s+\nu)\pi}{2}$$

$$\times\Gamma\left[\begin{matrix}s\\ \frac{s-\nu+2}{2},\ \frac{s+\nu+2}{2}\end{matrix}\right]\,{}_2F_3\left(\begin{matrix}\frac{s}{2},\ \frac{s+1}{2};\ \frac{a^2b^2}{4}\\ \frac{1}{2},\ \frac{s-\nu+2}{2},\ \frac{s+\nu+2}{2}\end{matrix}\right)$$

$$+\frac{2^{\nu-1}\pi b^{-s-\nu}}{\Gamma(1-s-\nu)}\csc\frac{(s+\nu)\pi}{2}\,{}_2F_3\left(\begin{matrix}\frac{1-\nu}{2},\ -\frac{\nu}{2};\ \frac{a^2b^2}{4}\\ 1-\nu,\ \frac{1-s-\nu}{2},\ \frac{2-s-\nu}{2}\end{matrix}\right)$$

$$[b,\ \operatorname{Re}a>0;\ 0<\operatorname{Re}s<1-\operatorname{Re}\nu]$$

No.	$f(x)$	$F(s)$
16	$\dfrac{\left(\sqrt{x^2+a^2}+a\right)^{\nu}}{\sqrt{x^2+a^2}}\sin(bx)$	$-2^{s+\nu}\pi a^{s+\nu}b\,\csc\left[(s+\nu)\,\pi\right]$

$$\times\,\Gamma\left[\begin{matrix}\frac{s+1}{2}\\[2pt]\frac{1-s-2\nu}{2},\;s+\nu+1\end{matrix}\right]\,{}_2F_3\left(\begin{matrix}\frac{s+1}{2},\;\frac{s+2\nu+1}{2};\;\frac{a^2b^2}{4}\\[2pt]\frac{3}{2},\;\frac{s+\nu+1}{2},\;\frac{s+\nu+2}{2}\end{matrix}\right)$$

$$+\,\frac{\pi b^{-s-\nu+1}}{2\,\Gamma(2-s-\nu)}\,\csc\frac{(s+\nu)\,\pi}{2}\,{}_2F_3\left(\begin{matrix}\frac{1-\nu}{2},\;\frac{1+\nu}{2};\;\frac{a^2b^2}{4}\\[2pt]\frac{1}{2},\;\frac{2-s-\nu}{2},\;\frac{3-s-\nu}{2}\end{matrix}\right)$$

$$-\,\frac{\nu\pi ab^{-s-\nu+2}}{2\,\Gamma(3-s-\nu)}\,\sec\frac{(s+\nu)\,\pi}{2}\,{}_2F_3\left(\begin{matrix}\frac{2-\nu}{2},\;\frac{2+\nu}{2};\;\frac{a^2b^2}{4}\\[2pt]\frac{3}{2},\;\frac{3-s-\nu}{2},\;\frac{4-s-\nu}{2}\end{matrix}\right)$$

$$[b,\ \mathrm{Re}\,a>0;\ -1<\mathrm{Re}\,s<2-\mathrm{Re}\,\nu]$$

No.	$f(x)$	$F(s)$
17	$\dfrac{\left(\sqrt{x^2+a^2}+a\right)^{\nu}}{\sqrt{x^2+a^2}}\cos(bx)$	$-2^{s+\nu-1}\pi a^{s+\nu-1}\,\csc\left[(s+\nu-1)\,\pi\right]$

$$\times\,\Gamma\left[\begin{matrix}\frac{s}{2}\\[2pt]\frac{2-s-2\nu}{2},\;s+\nu\end{matrix}\right]\,{}_2F_3\left(\begin{matrix}\frac{s}{2},\;\frac{s+2\nu}{2};\;\frac{a^2b^2}{4}\\[2pt]\frac{1}{2},\;\frac{s+\nu}{2},\;\frac{s+\nu+1}{2}\end{matrix}\right)$$

$$-\,\frac{\nu\pi ab^{-s-\nu+2}}{2\,\Gamma(3-s-\nu)}\,\csc\frac{(s+\nu)\,\pi}{2}\,{}_2F_3\left(\begin{matrix}\frac{2-\nu}{2},\;\frac{2+\nu}{2};\;\frac{a^2b^2}{4}\\[2pt]\frac{3}{2},\;\frac{3-s-\nu}{2},\;\frac{4-s-\nu}{2}\end{matrix}\right)$$

$$-\,\frac{\pi b^{-s-\nu+1}}{2\,\Gamma(2-s-\nu)}\,\sec\frac{(s+\nu)\,\pi}{2}\,{}_2F_3\left(\begin{matrix}\frac{1-\nu}{2},\;\frac{1+\nu}{2};\;\frac{a^2b^2}{4}\\[2pt]\frac{1}{2},\;\frac{2-s-\nu}{2},\;\frac{3-s-\nu}{2}\end{matrix}\right)$$

$$[b,\ \mathrm{Re}\,a>0;\ 0<\mathrm{Re}\,s<2-\mathrm{Re}\,\nu]$$

No.	$f(x)$	$F(s)$
18	$\dfrac{\left(\sqrt{x^2+a^2}+x\right)^{\nu}}{\sqrt{x^2+a^2}}\sin(bx)$	$-2^{-s-1}\pi a^{s+\nu}b\,\csc\frac{(s+\nu)\,\pi}{2}$

$$\times\,\Gamma\left[\begin{matrix}s+1\\[2pt]\frac{s-\nu+2}{2},\;\frac{s+\nu+2}{2}\end{matrix}\right]\,{}_2F_3\left(\begin{matrix}\frac{s+1}{2},\;\frac{s+2}{2};\;\frac{a^2b^2}{4}\\[2pt]\frac{3}{2},\;\frac{s-\nu+2}{2},\;\frac{s+\nu+2}{2}\end{matrix}\right)$$

$$+\,\frac{2^{\nu-1}\pi b^{-s-\nu+1}}{\Gamma(2-s-\nu)}\,\csc\frac{(s+\nu)\,\pi}{2}\,{}_2F_3\left(\begin{matrix}\frac{1-\nu}{2},\;\frac{2-\nu}{2};\;\frac{a^2b^2}{4}\\[2pt]1-\nu,\;\frac{2-s-\nu}{2},\;\frac{3-s-\nu}{2}\end{matrix}\right)$$

$$[b,\ \mathrm{Re}\,a>0;\ -1<\mathrm{Re}\,s<2-\mathrm{Re}\,\nu]$$

No.	$f(x)$	$F(s)$
19	$\dfrac{\left(\sqrt{x^2+a^2}+x\right)^{\nu}}{\sqrt{x^2+a^2}}\cos(bx)$	$-2^{-s}\pi a^{s+\nu-1}\,\csc\frac{(s+\nu-1)\,\pi}{2}$

$$\times\,\Gamma\left[\begin{matrix}s\\[2pt]\frac{s-\nu+1}{2},\;\frac{s+\nu+1}{2}\end{matrix}\right]\,{}_2F_3\left(\begin{matrix}\frac{s}{2},\;\frac{s+1}{2};\;\frac{a^2b^2}{4}\\[2pt]\frac{1}{2},\;\frac{s-\nu+1}{2},\;\frac{s+\nu+1}{2}\end{matrix}\right)$$

$$-\,\frac{2^{\nu-1}\pi b^{-s-\nu+1}}{\Gamma(2-s-\nu)}\,\sec\frac{(s+\nu)\,\pi}{2}\,{}_2F_3\left(\begin{matrix}\frac{1-\nu}{2},\;\frac{2-\nu}{2};\;\frac{a^2b^2}{4}\\[2pt]1-\nu,\;\frac{2-s-\nu}{2},\;\frac{3-s-\nu}{2}\end{matrix}\right)$$

$$[b,\ \mathrm{Re}\,a>0;\ 0<\mathrm{Re}\,s<2-\mathrm{Re}\,\nu]$$

No.	$f(x)$	$F(s)$
20	$\left(x^2 - a^2\right)_+^{-1/2}$ $\times \left[\left(x + \sqrt{x^2 - a^2}\right)^\nu \right.$ $+ \left(x - \sqrt{x^2 - a^2}\right)^\nu\right]$ $\times \sin(bx)$	$\dfrac{a^{s+\nu}b}{2^{s+1}} \Gamma\left[\begin{matrix} -\frac{s+\nu}{2}, \frac{\nu-s}{2} \\ -s \end{matrix}\right] {}_2F_3\left(\begin{matrix} \frac{s+1}{2}, \frac{s+2}{2}; -\frac{a^2b^2}{4} \\ \frac{3}{2}, \frac{s-\nu+2}{2}, \frac{s+\nu+2}{2} \end{matrix}\right)$ $+ \dfrac{2^{\nu-1}\pi b^{-s-\nu+1}}{\Gamma(2-s-\nu)}$ $\times \csc\dfrac{(s+\nu)\pi}{2} {}_2F_3\left(\begin{matrix} \frac{1-\nu}{2}, \frac{2-\nu}{2}; -\frac{a^2b^2}{4} \\ 1-\nu, \frac{2-s-\nu}{2}, \frac{3-s-\nu}{2} \end{matrix}\right)$ $+ \dfrac{2^{-\nu-1}\pi a^{2\nu}b^{-s+\nu+1}}{\Gamma(2-s+\nu)} \csc\dfrac{(s-\nu)\pi}{2}$ $\times {}_2F_3\left(\begin{matrix} \frac{\nu+1}{2}, \frac{\nu+2}{2}; -\frac{a^2b^2}{4} \\ 1+\nu, \frac{2-s+\nu}{2}, \frac{3-s+\nu}{2} \end{matrix}\right)$ $[a, b > 0;\ \mathrm{Re}\,s < 2 - |\mathrm{Re}\,\nu|]$
21	$\left(x^2 - a^2\right)_+^{-1/2}$ $\times \left[\left(x + \sqrt{x^2 - a^2}\right)^\nu \right.$ $+ \left(x - \sqrt{x^2 - a^2}\right)^\nu\right]$ $\times \cos(bx)$	$\dfrac{a^{s+\nu-1}}{2^s} \Gamma\left[\begin{matrix} \frac{1-s-\nu}{2}, \frac{1-s+\nu}{2} \\ 1-s \end{matrix}\right] {}_2F_3\left(\begin{matrix} \frac{s}{2}, \frac{s+1}{2}; -\frac{a^2b^2}{4} \\ \frac{1}{2}, \frac{s-\nu+1}{2}, \frac{s+\nu+1}{2} \end{matrix}\right)$ $- \dfrac{2^{\nu-1}\pi b^{-s-\nu+1}}{\Gamma(2-s-\nu)}$ $\times \sec\dfrac{(s+\nu)\pi}{2} {}_2F_3\left(\begin{matrix} \frac{1-\nu}{2}, \frac{2-\nu}{2}; -\frac{a^2b^2}{4} \\ 1-\nu, \frac{2-s-\nu}{2}, \frac{3-s-\nu}{2} \end{matrix}\right)$ $- \dfrac{2^{-\nu-1}\pi a^{2\nu}b^{-s+\nu+1}}{\Gamma(2-s+\nu)} \sec\dfrac{(s-\nu)\pi}{2} {}_2F_3\left(\begin{matrix} \frac{\nu+1}{2}, \frac{\nu+2}{2}; -\frac{a^2b^2}{4} \\ 1+\nu, \frac{2-s+\nu}{2}, \frac{3-s+\nu}{2} \end{matrix}\right)$ $[a, b > 0;\ \mathrm{Re}\,s < 2 - |\mathrm{Re}\,\nu|]$
22	$\dfrac{1}{(x+a)^\rho} \begin{Bmatrix} \sin[b/(x+a)] \\ \cos[b/(x+a)] \end{Bmatrix}$	$a^{s-\rho-\delta}b^\delta\, \mathrm{B}(s, \rho-s+\delta)\, {}_2F_3\left(\begin{matrix} \frac{\rho-s+\delta}{2}, \frac{\rho-s+\delta+1}{2}; -\frac{b^2}{4a^2} \\ \frac{2\delta+1}{2}, \frac{\rho+\delta}{2}, \frac{\rho+\delta+1}{2} \end{matrix}\right)$ $[0 < \mathrm{Re}\,s < \mathrm{Re}\,\rho + \delta;\ |\arg a| < \pi]$
23	$\dfrac{1}{(x+a)^\rho}$ $\times \begin{Bmatrix} \sin[bx/(x+a)] \\ \cos[bx/(x+a)] \end{Bmatrix}$	$a^{s-\rho}b^\delta\, \mathrm{B}(s+\delta, \rho-s)\, {}_2F_3\left(\begin{matrix} \frac{s+\delta}{2}, \frac{s+\delta+1}{2}; -\frac{b^2}{4} \\ \frac{2\delta+1}{2}, \frac{\rho+\delta}{2}, \frac{\rho+\delta+1}{2} \end{matrix}\right)$ $[-\delta < \mathrm{Re}\,s < \mathrm{Re}\,\rho;\ |\arg a| < \pi]$
24	$\left(1 - x^2\right)_+^{-1/2}$ $\times \begin{Bmatrix} \sin(ax - a/x) \\ \cos(ax - a/x) \end{Bmatrix}$	$\mp\sqrt{\dfrac{\pi a}{2}} \begin{Bmatrix} I_{s/2}(a)\, K_{(s-1)/2}(a) \\ I_{(s-1)/2}(a)\, K_{s/2}(a) \end{Bmatrix}$ $[a > 0;\ \mathrm{Re}\,s > -1]$
25	$\left(x^2 - 1\right)_+^{-1/2}$ $\times \begin{Bmatrix} \sin(ax - a/x) \\ \cos(ax - a/x) \end{Bmatrix}$	$\sqrt{\dfrac{\pi a}{2}} \begin{Bmatrix} I_{(1-s)/2}(a)\, K_{s/2}(a) \\ I_{-s/2}(a)\, K_{(s-1)/2}(a) \end{Bmatrix}$ $[a > 0;\ \mathrm{Re}\,s < 2]$

No.	$f(x)$	$F(s)$
26	$(a-x)_+^{(\delta-1)/2}(bx+1)^{\alpha}$ $\times\left\{\begin{array}{c}\sin\left(c\sqrt{a-x}\right)\\\cos\left(c\sqrt{a-x}\right)\end{array}\right\}$	$\dfrac{\sqrt{\pi}\,a^{s+\delta-1/2}c^{\delta}}{\delta+1}\,\Gamma\left[\begin{array}{c}s\\\frac{2s+2\delta+1}{2}\end{array}\right]$ $\times\,\Xi_2\left(-\alpha,\,s;\,\dfrac{2s+2\delta+1}{2};\,-ab,\,-\dfrac{ac^2}{4}\right)$ $[a,\ \mathrm{Re}\,s>0;\ |\arg(ab+1)|<\pi]$
27	$(x-a)_+^{(\delta-1)/2}(1-x+a)_+^{\alpha}$ $\times\left\{\begin{array}{c}\sin\left(b\sqrt{x-a}\right)\\\cos\left(b\sqrt{x-a}\right)\end{array}\right\}$	$\dfrac{\sqrt{\pi}\,(a+1)^{s-1}b^{\delta}}{\delta+1}\,\Gamma\left[\begin{array}{c}\alpha+1\\\frac{2\alpha+2\delta+3}{2}\end{array}\right]$ $\times\,\Xi_2\left(1-s,\,\alpha+1;\,\dfrac{2\alpha+2\delta+3}{2};\,\dfrac{1}{a+1},\,-\dfrac{b^2}{4}\right)$ $[a,\ \mathrm{Re}\,s>0]$
28	$(a-x)_+^{\alpha-1}$ $\times\left\{\begin{array}{c}\sin\left(b\sqrt{x(a-x)}\right)\\\cos\left(b\sqrt{x(a-x)}\right)\end{array}\right\}$	$a^{s+\alpha+\delta-1}b^{\delta}\,\mathrm{B}\left(\dfrac{2\alpha+\delta}{2},\dfrac{2s+\delta}{2}\right){}_2F_3\left(\begin{array}{c}\frac{2\alpha+\delta}{2},\frac{2s+\delta}{2};-\frac{a^2b^2}{16}\\\frac{2\delta+1}{2},\frac{s+\alpha+\delta}{2},\frac{s+\alpha+\delta+1}{2}\end{array}\right)$ $[a>0;\ \mathrm{Re}\,s>-\delta/2]$
29	$\left\{\begin{array}{c}\sin\left(b\sqrt{x^2+a^2}\right)\\\cos\left(b\sqrt{x^2+a^2}\right)\end{array}\right\}$	$\pm\dfrac{2^{(s-3)/2}\sqrt{\pi}\,a^{(s+1)/2}}{b^{(s-1)/2}}\,\Gamma\left(\dfrac{s}{2}\right)\left[\left\{\begin{array}{c}\cos\left(s\pi/2\right)\\\sin\left(s\pi/2\right)\end{array}\right\}J_{(s+1)/2}\left(ab\right)\right.$ $\mp\left\{\begin{array}{c}\sin\left(s\pi/2\right)\\\cos\left(s\pi/2\right)\end{array}\right\}Y_{(s+1)/2}\left(ab\right)\Bigg]\quad[\mathrm{Re}\,a,\,b>0;\,0<\mathrm{Re}\,s<1]$
30	$\dfrac{1}{\sqrt{x^2+a^2}}$ $\times\left\{\begin{array}{c}\sin\left(b\sqrt{x^2+a^2}\right)\\\cos\left(b\sqrt{x^2+a^2}\right)\end{array}\right\}$	$\pm2^{(s-3)/2}\sqrt{\pi}\left(\dfrac{a}{b}\right)^{(s-1)/2}\Gamma\left(\dfrac{s}{2}\right)\left\{\begin{array}{c}J_{(1-s)/2}\left(ab\right)\\Y_{(1-s)/2}\left(ab\right)\end{array}\right\}$ $[\mathrm{Re}\,a,\,b>0;\,0<\mathrm{Re}\,s<2]$
31	$\theta(a-x)$ $\times\left\{\begin{array}{c}\sin\left(b\sqrt{a^2-x^2}\right)\\\cos\left(b\sqrt{a^2-x^2}\right)\end{array}\right\}$	$\pm\dfrac{a^{(s+1)/2}}{b^{(s-1)/2}}\left\{\begin{array}{c}2^{(s-3)/2}\sqrt{\pi}\,J_{(s+1)/2}\left(ab\right)\\s_{(s-3)/2,\,(s+1)/2}\left(ab\right)\end{array}\right\}$ $[a,\ \mathrm{Re}\,s>0]$
32	$(a^2-x^2)_+^{-1/2}$ $\times\sin\left(b\sqrt{a^2-x^2}\right)$	$\dfrac{\sqrt{\pi}}{2}\left(\dfrac{2a}{b}\right)^{(s-1)/2}\Gamma\left(\dfrac{s}{2}\right)\mathbf{H}_{(s-1)/2}\left(ab\right)\qquad[a,\ \mathrm{Re}\,s>0]$
33	$(a^2-x^2)_+^{-1/2}$ $\times\cos\left(b\sqrt{a^2-x^2}\right)$	$2^{(s-3)/2}\sqrt{\pi}\left(\dfrac{a}{b}\right)^{(s-1)/2}\Gamma\left(\dfrac{s}{2}\right)J_{(s-1)/2}\left(ab\right)\qquad[a,\ \mathrm{Re}\,s>0]$

No.	$f(x)$	$F(s)$
34	$\theta(x-a)\sin\left(b\sqrt{x^2-a^2}\right)$	$\dfrac{2^{(s-1)/2}a^{(s+1)/2}}{\sqrt{\pi}\,b^{(s-1)/2}}\sin\dfrac{s\pi}{2}\Gamma\left(\dfrac{s}{2}\right)K_{(s+1)/2}(ab)\quad [a,\,b>0;\ \mathrm{Re}\,s<1]$
35	$\theta(x-a)\cos\left(b\sqrt{x^2-a^2}\right)$	$\dfrac{2^{(s-3)/2}\sqrt{\pi}\,a^{(s+1)/2}}{b^{(s-1)/2}}\Gamma\left(\dfrac{s}{2}\right)\Big[I_{-(s+1)/2}(ab)$ $-\,\mathbf{L}_{(s+1)/2}(ab)-\dfrac{(ab)^{(s-1)/2}}{2^{(s-3)/2}\sqrt{\pi}\,s\,\Gamma\left(\frac{s}{2}\right)}\Big]\quad [a,\,b>0;\ \mathrm{Re}\,s<1]$
36	$\left(x^2-a^2\right)_+^{-1/2}$ $\times\sin\left(b\sqrt{x^2-a^2}\right)$	$\dfrac{\sqrt{\pi}}{2}\left(\dfrac{2a}{b}\right)^{(s-1)/2}\Gamma\left(\dfrac{s}{2}\right)\left[I_{(1-s)/2}(ab)-\mathbf{L}_{(s-1)/2}(ab)\right]$ $[a,\,b>0;\ \mathrm{Re}\,s<2]$
37	$\left(x^2-a^2\right)_+^{-1/2}$ $\times\cos\left(b\sqrt{x^2-a^2}\right)$	$\dfrac{1}{\sqrt{\pi}}\left(\dfrac{2a}{b}\right)^{(s-1)/2}\sin\dfrac{s\pi}{2}\Gamma\left(\dfrac{s}{2}\right)K_{(s-1)/2}(ab)$ $[a>0;\ \mathrm{Re}\,s<2]$
38	$\dfrac{1}{(x^2+a^2)^\rho}\,\cos\dfrac{bx}{x^2+a^2}$	$\dfrac{a^{s-2\rho}}{2}\,\mathrm{B}\left(\dfrac{s}{2},\,\rho-\dfrac{s}{2}\right){}_2F_3\left(\begin{matrix}\frac{s}{2},\,\rho-\frac{s}{2};\,-\frac{b^2}{16a^2}\\[2pt]\frac{1}{2},\,\frac{\rho}{2},\,\frac{\rho+1}{2}\end{matrix}\right)$ $[\mathrm{Re}\,a>0;\ 0<\mathrm{Re}\,s<2\,\mathrm{Re}\,\rho]$
39	$\dfrac{1}{(x^2+a^2)^\rho}\,\sin\dfrac{bx}{x^2+a^2}$	$\dfrac{a^{s-2\rho-1}b}{2}\,\mathrm{B}\left(\dfrac{s+1}{2},\,\dfrac{1-s+2\rho}{2}\right){}_2F_3\left(\begin{matrix}\frac{s+1}{2},\,\frac{1-s+2\rho}{2};\,-\frac{b^2}{16a^2}\\[2pt]\frac{3}{2},\,\frac{\rho+1}{2},\,\frac{\rho+2}{2}\end{matrix}\right)$ $[\mathrm{Re}\,a>0;\ -1<\mathrm{Re}\,s<2\,\mathrm{Re}\,\rho+1]$

2.4.3. Trigonometric and the exponential functions

Notation: $\delta=\left\{\begin{matrix}1\\0\end{matrix}\right\}$.

No.	$f(x)$	$F(s)$	
1	$e^{-ax}\left\{\begin{matrix}\sin(ax)\\\cos(ax)\end{matrix}\right\}$	$2^{-s/2}a^{-s}\left\{\begin{matrix}\sin(s\pi/4)\\\cos(s\pi/4)\end{matrix}\right\}\Gamma(s)$	$\left[\begin{matrix}(\mathrm{Re}\,s>-\delta;\ \lvert\arg a\rvert<\pi/4)\ \text{or}\\(-\delta<\mathrm{Re}\,s<1;\ \lvert\arg a\rvert=\pi/4)\end{matrix}\right]$
2	$e^{-ax/\sqrt{3}}\left\{\begin{matrix}\sin(ax)\\\cos(ax)\end{matrix}\right\}$	$2^{-s}3^{s/2}a^{-s}\left\{\begin{matrix}\sin(s\pi/3)\\\cos(s\pi/3)\end{matrix}\right\}\Gamma(s)$ $\left[\begin{matrix}(\mathrm{Re}\,s>-\delta;\ \lvert\arg a\rvert<\pi/6)\ \text{or}\\(-\delta<\mathrm{Re}\,s<1;\ \lvert\arg a\rvert=\pi/6)\end{matrix}\right]$	
3	$e^{-ax}\left\{\begin{matrix}\sin(bx)\\\cos(bx)\end{matrix}\right\}$	$\dfrac{\Gamma(s)}{(a^2+b^2)^{s/2}}\left\{\begin{matrix}\sin[s\arctan(b/a)]\\\cos[s\arctan(b/a)]\end{matrix}\right\}$ $\left[\begin{matrix}(\mathrm{Re}\,a>\lvert\mathrm{Im}\,b\rvert;\ \mathrm{Re}\,s>-(1\pm1)/2)\ \text{or}\\(\mathrm{Re}\,a+\lvert\mathrm{Im}\,b\rvert=0;\ \mathrm{Re}\,s<1)\end{matrix}\right]$	

No.	$f(x)$	$F(s)$
4	$e^{-\sqrt{3}\,ax}\begin{Bmatrix}\sin(ax)\\\cos(ax)\end{Bmatrix}$	$(2a)^{-s}\begin{Bmatrix}\sin(s\pi/6)\\\cos(s\pi/6)\end{Bmatrix}\Gamma(s)\quad\begin{bmatrix}(\operatorname{Re}s>-\delta;\ \lvert\arg a\rvert<\pi/3)\text{ or}\\(-\delta<\operatorname{Re}s<1;\ \lvert\arg a\rvert=\pi/3)\end{bmatrix}$
5	$e^{-(\sqrt{2}+1)ax}\begin{Bmatrix}\sin(ax)\\\cos(ax)\end{Bmatrix}$	$2^{-s}\left(1+\dfrac{1}{\sqrt{2}}\right)^{-s/2}a^{-s}\begin{Bmatrix}\sin(s\pi/8)\\\cos(s\pi/8)\end{Bmatrix}\Gamma(s)$ $\begin{bmatrix}(\operatorname{Re}s>-\delta;\ \lvert\arg a\rvert<3\pi/8)\text{ or}\\(-\delta<\operatorname{Re}s<1;\ \lvert\arg a\rvert=3\pi/8)\end{bmatrix}$
6	$e^{-\sqrt{1+2/\sqrt{5}}\,ax}\begin{Bmatrix}\sin(ax)\\\cos(ax)\end{Bmatrix}$	$\left(2+\dfrac{2}{\sqrt{5}}\right)^{-s/2}a^{-s}\begin{Bmatrix}\sin(s\pi/5)\\\cos(s\pi/5)\end{Bmatrix}\Gamma(s)$ $\begin{bmatrix}(\operatorname{Re}s>-\delta;\ \lvert\arg a\rvert<3\pi/10)\text{ or}\\(-\delta<\operatorname{Re}s<1;\ \lvert\arg a\rvert=3\pi/10)\end{bmatrix}$
7	$e^{-ax\cos\theta}\begin{Bmatrix}\sin(ax\sin\theta)\\\cos(ax\sin\theta)\end{Bmatrix}$	$\dfrac{\Gamma(s)}{a^s}\begin{Bmatrix}\sin(s\theta)\\\cos(s\theta)\end{Bmatrix}\qquad[a>0;\ \lvert\theta\rvert<\pi/2;\ \operatorname{Re}s>-(1\pm1)/2]$
8	$e^{-x\cos(\theta\pi)}$ $\times\begin{Bmatrix}\sin[x\sin(\theta\pi)]\\\cos[x\sin(\theta\pi)]\end{Bmatrix}$	$\pi\,\Gamma\begin{bmatrix}s\\\frac{1-\delta}{2}+\theta s,\ \frac{1+\delta}{2}-\theta s\end{bmatrix}\qquad[\lvert\theta\rvert<1/2;\ \operatorname{Re}s>-\delta]$
9	$\theta(a-x)\,e^{-bx}\begin{Bmatrix}\sin(cx)\\\cos(cx)\end{Bmatrix}$	$\dfrac{i^{(1\pm1)/2}}{2}\left[(b+ic)^{-s}\gamma(s,ab+iac)\mp(b-ic)^{-s}\gamma(s,ab-iac)\right]$ $[a>0;\ \operatorname{Re}s>-(1\pm1)/2]$
10	$\theta(x-a)\,e^{-bx}\begin{Bmatrix}\sin(cx)\\\cos(cx)\end{Bmatrix}$	$\dfrac{i^{(1\pm1)/2}}{2}\left[(b+ic)^{-s}\Gamma(s,ab+iac)\mp(b-ic)^{-s}\Gamma(s,ab-iac)\right]$ $[a,\ \operatorname{Re}b>0]$
11	$e^{-ax^2}\begin{Bmatrix}\sin(bx)\\\cos(bx)\end{Bmatrix}$	$\dfrac{b^\delta}{2a^{(s+\delta)/2}}\Gamma\left(\dfrac{s+\delta}{2}\right){}_1F_1\left(\dfrac{s+\delta}{2}{\atop\dfrac{2\delta+1}{2}};-\dfrac{b^2}{4a}\right)\quad[\operatorname{Re}a>0;\ \operatorname{Re}s>-\delta]$
12	$e^{-ax^2-bx}\begin{Bmatrix}\sin(cx)\\\cos(cx)\end{Bmatrix}$	$\dfrac{i^{(1\pm1)/2}\Gamma(s)}{2\,(2a)^{s/2}}e^{(b^2-c^2)/(8a)}\left[e^{ibc/(4a)}D_{-s}\left(\dfrac{b+ic}{\sqrt{2a}}\right)\right.$ $\left.\mp\,e^{-ibc/(4a)}D_{-s}\left(\dfrac{b-ic}{\sqrt{2a}}\right)\right]\quad[\operatorname{Re}a>0;\ \operatorname{Re}s>-(1\pm1)/2]$
13	$e^{-c/x}\begin{Bmatrix}\sin(bx)\\\cos(bx)\end{Bmatrix}$	$i^{(1\pm1)/2}\left(\dfrac{c}{b}\right)^{s/2}\left[e^{-is\pi/4}K_s\left(2e^{i\pi/4}\sqrt{bc}\right)\right.$ $\left.\mp\,e^{is\pi/4}K_s\left(2e^{-i\pi/4}\sqrt{bc}\right)\right]\quad[b,\ \operatorname{Re}c>0;\ \operatorname{Re}s<1]$
14	$e^{-ax-c/x}\begin{Bmatrix}\sin(bx)\\\cos(bx)\end{Bmatrix}$	$i^{(1\pm1)/2}c^{s/2}\left[(a+ib)^{-s/2}K_s\left(2\sqrt{ac+ibc}\right)\right.$ $\left.\mp\,(a-ib)^{-s/2}K_s\left(2\sqrt{ac-ibc}\right)\right]\quad[\operatorname{Re}a>\lvert\operatorname{Im}b\rvert;\ \operatorname{Re}c>0]$

No.	$f(x)$	$F(s)$
15	$e^{-a/x^2} \left\{ \begin{matrix} \sin(bx) \\ \cos(bx) \end{matrix} \right\}$	$\dfrac{\Gamma(s)}{b^s} \left\{ \begin{matrix} \sin(s\pi/2) \\ \cos(s\pi/2) \end{matrix} \right\} {}_0F_2 \left(\begin{matrix} -; & \frac{ab^2}{4} \\ \frac{1-s}{2}, & \frac{2-s}{2} \end{matrix} \right)$ $+ \dfrac{a^{(s+\delta)/2}b^\delta}{2} \Gamma\left(-\dfrac{s+\delta}{2} \right) {}_0F_2 \left(\begin{matrix} -; & \frac{ab^2}{4} \\ \frac{2\delta+1}{2}, & \frac{s+\delta+2}{2} \end{matrix} \right)$ $[b,\ \operatorname{Re} a > 0;\ \operatorname{Re} s < 1]$
16	$e^{-a\sqrt{x}} \left\{ \begin{matrix} \sin(bx) \\ \cos(bx) \end{matrix} \right\}$	$i^{(1\pm1)/2} \dfrac{\Gamma(2s)}{(2b)^s} \left[e^{-i(a^2+4bs\pi)/(8b)} D_{-2s}\left(\dfrac{ae^{-\pi i/4}}{\sqrt{2b}} \right) \right.$ $\left. \mp e^{i(a^2+4bs\pi)/(8b)} D_{-2s}\left(\dfrac{ae^{\pi i/4}}{\sqrt{2b}} \right) \right]$ $[b,\ \operatorname{Re} a > 0;\ \operatorname{Re} s > -(1\pm1)/2]$
17	$\dfrac{1}{e^{ax}-1} \left\{ \begin{matrix} \sin(bx) \\ \cos(bx) \end{matrix} \right\}$	$\dfrac{i^{(1\pm1)/2}}{2a^s} \Gamma(s) \left[\zeta\left(s, \dfrac{a+ib}{a} \right) \mp \zeta\left(s, \dfrac{a-ib}{a} \right) \right]$ $[\operatorname{Re} a > |\operatorname{Im} b|;\ \operatorname{Re} s > (1\mp1)/2]$
18	$\dfrac{1}{e^{ax}+1} \left\{ \begin{matrix} \sin(bx) \\ \cos(bx) \end{matrix} \right\}$	$\dfrac{i^{(1\pm1)/2}}{2^{s+1}a^s} \Gamma(s) \left[\zeta\left(s, \dfrac{a+ib}{2a} \right) \mp \zeta\left(s, \dfrac{a-ib}{2a} \right) \right.$ $\left. - \zeta\left(s, \dfrac{2a+ib}{2a} \right) \pm \zeta\left(s, \dfrac{2a-ib}{2a} \right) \right]$ $[\operatorname{Re} a > |\operatorname{Im} b|;\ \operatorname{Re} s > -(1\pm1)/2]$
19	$(a-x)_+^{(\delta-1)/2} e^{cx}$ $\times \left\{ \begin{matrix} \sin\left(b\sqrt{a-x}\right) \\ \cos\left(b\sqrt{a-x}\right) \end{matrix} \right\}$	$\dfrac{\sqrt{\pi}}{2^\delta} a^{s+\delta-1/2} b^\delta \Gamma\left[\begin{matrix} s \\ \frac{2s+2\delta+1}{2} \end{matrix} \right] \Phi_3\left(s;\ \dfrac{2s+2\delta+1}{2};\ ac, -\dfrac{ab^2}{4} \right)$ $[a,\ \operatorname{Re} s > 0]$
20	$e^{-ax} \left\{ \begin{matrix} \sin(bx^2+ax) \\ \cos(bx^2+ax) \end{matrix} \right\}$	$\dfrac{\Gamma(s)}{(2b)^{s/2}} e^{a^2/(4b)} \left\{ \begin{matrix} \sin(s\pi/4) \\ \cos(s\pi/4) \end{matrix} \right\} D_{-s}\left(\dfrac{a}{\sqrt{b}} \right)$ $[b > 0;\ \operatorname{Re} s > -(1\pm1)/2;\ |\arg a| < \pi/4]$
21	$(a^2-x^2)_+^{-1/2} e^{-b/(a^2-x^2)}$ $\times \left\{ \begin{matrix} \sin\left[cx/(a^2-x^2)\right] \\ \cos\left[cx/(a^2-x^2)\right] \end{matrix} \right\}$	$\dfrac{2^{(2s-3)/4+\delta} a^{s-1}}{\sqrt{c}} e^{-b/(2a^2)} \left(\sqrt{b^2+a^2c^2}+b \right)^{1/4} \Gamma\left(\dfrac{s+\delta}{2} \right)$ $\times D_{-s}\left(\dfrac{\sqrt{\sqrt{b^2+a^2c^2}+b}}{a} \right) M_{(2s-1)/4,\pm1/4}\left(\dfrac{\sqrt{b^2+a^2c^2}-b}{2a^2} \right)$ $[a,\ b,\ c > 0;\ \operatorname{Re} s > -\delta]$

No.	$f(x)$	$F(s)$
22	$\left(x^2 - a^2\right)_+^{-1/2}$ $\times e^{-b/(x^2-a^2)}$ $\times \left\{ \begin{array}{l} \sin\left[cx/\left(x^2-a^2\right)\right] \\ \cos\left[cx/\left(x^2-a^2\right)\right] \end{array} \right\}$	$\dfrac{a^{s-1}}{2^{(2s+1)/4-\delta}\sqrt{c}} e^{b/(2a^2)} \left(\sqrt{b^2+a^2c^2}+b\right)^{1/4}$ $\times \Gamma\left(\dfrac{1-s+\delta}{2}\right) D_{s-1}\left(\dfrac{\sqrt{\sqrt{b^2+a^2c^2}+b}}{a}\right)$ $\times M_{(1-2s)/4,\,\pm 1/4}\left(\dfrac{\sqrt{b^2+a^2c^2}-b}{2a^2}\right)$ $[a,\,b,\,c>0;\ \operatorname{Re}s<\delta+1]$
23	$\left(a^2 - x^2\right)_+^{-1/2}$ $\times e^{-b(a^2+x^2)/(a^2-x^2)}$ $\times \left\{ \begin{array}{l} \sin\left[cx/\left(a^2-x^2\right)\right] \\ \cos\left[cx/\left(a^2-x^2\right)\right] \end{array} \right\}$	$\dfrac{2^{(2s-3)/4+\delta}a^{s-3/4}}{\sqrt{c}} \left(\sqrt{4a^2b^2+c^2}+2ab\right)^{1/4}$ $\times \Gamma\left(\dfrac{s+\delta}{2}\right) D_{-s}\left(\dfrac{\sqrt{\sqrt{4a^2b^2+c^2}+2ab}}{\sqrt{a}}\right)$ $\times M_{(2s-1)/4,\,\pm 1/4}\left(\dfrac{\sqrt{4a^2b^2+c^2}-2ab}{2a}\right)$ $[a,\,b,\,c>0;\ \operatorname{Re}s>-\delta]$
24	$\left(x^2 - a^2\right)_+^{-1/2}$ $\times e^{-b(x^2+a^2)/(x^2-a^2)}$ $\times \left\{ \begin{array}{l} \sin\left[cx/\left(x^2-a^2\right)\right] \\ \cos\left[cx/\left(x^2-a^2\right)\right] \end{array} \right\}$	$\dfrac{a^{s-3/4}}{2^{(2s+1)/4-\delta}\sqrt{c}} \left(\sqrt{4a^2b^2+c^2}+2ab\right)^{1/4}$ $\times \Gamma\left(\dfrac{1-s+\delta}{2}\right) D_{s-1}\left(\dfrac{\sqrt{\sqrt{4a^2b^2+c^2}+2ab}}{\sqrt{a}}\right)$ $\times M_{(1-2s)/4,\,\pm 1/4}\left(\dfrac{\sqrt{4a^2b^2+c^2}-2ab}{2a}\right)$ $[a,\,b,\,c>0;\ \operatorname{Re}s<\delta+1]$
25	$\dfrac{1}{\sqrt{x^2+a^2}} e^{-b/(x^2+a^2)}$ $\times \left\{ \begin{array}{l} \sin\left[cx/\left(x^2+a^2\right)\right] \\ \cos\left[cx/\left(x^2+a^2\right)\right] \end{array} \right\}$	$\dfrac{2^{\delta-1/2}a^{s-1/2}}{\sqrt{c}} e^{-b/(2a^2)} \operatorname{B}\left(\dfrac{1-s+\delta}{2},\dfrac{s+\delta}{2}\right)$ $\times M_{(1-2s)/4,\,\pm 1/4}\left(\dfrac{b-\sqrt{b^2-a^2c^2}}{2a^2}\right)$ $\times M_{(1-2s)/4,\,\pm 1/4}\left(\dfrac{b+\sqrt{b^2-a^2c^2}}{2a^2}\right)$ $[\operatorname{Re}a,\,b,\,c>0;\ -\delta<\operatorname{Re}s<\delta+1]$
26	$\dfrac{1}{\sqrt{x^2+a^2}}$ $\times e^{-b(a^2-x^2)/(a^2+x^2)}$ $\times \left\{ \begin{array}{l} \sin\left[cx/\left(x^2+a^2\right)\right] \\ \cos\left[cx/\left(x^2+a^2\right)\right] \end{array} \right\}$	$\dfrac{2^{\delta-1/2}a^{s-1/2}}{\sqrt{c}} \operatorname{B}\left(\dfrac{1-s+\delta}{2},\dfrac{s+\delta}{2}\right)$ $\times M_{(1-2s)/4,\,\pm 1/4}\left(\dfrac{2ab-\sqrt{4a^2b^2-c^2}}{2a}\right)$ $\times M_{(1-2s)/4,\,\pm 1/4}\left(\dfrac{2ab+\sqrt{4a^2b^2-c^2}}{2a}\right)$ $[\operatorname{Re}a,\,b,\,c>0;\ -\delta<\operatorname{Re}s<\delta+1]$

2.4.4. Trigonometric and hyperbolic functions

Notation: $\delta = \begin{Bmatrix} 1 \\ 0 \end{Bmatrix}$.

1	$(a-x)_+^{\alpha-1}$ $\times \begin{Bmatrix} \sinh(bx)\sin(bx) \\ \cosh(bx)\cos(bx) \end{Bmatrix}$	$a^{s+\alpha+2\delta-1}b^{2\delta}\,\mathrm{B}\,(\alpha,\,s+2\delta)$ $\times\,{}_4F_7\left(\begin{matrix} \Delta(4,\,s+2\delta);\,\pm\frac{a^4b^4}{64} \\ \frac{2\delta+1}{4},\,\frac{2\delta+3}{4},\,\frac{2\delta+1}{2},\,\Delta(4,\,s+\alpha+2\delta) \end{matrix}\right)$ $[a,\,\mathrm{Re}\,\alpha>0;\,\mathrm{Re}\,s>-2\delta]$
2	$(a-x)_+^{\alpha-1}$ $\times \begin{Bmatrix} \cosh(bx)\sin(bx) \\ \sinh(bx)\cos(bx) \end{Bmatrix}$	$a^{s+\alpha}b\,\mathrm{B}\,(\alpha,\,s+1)\,{}_4F_7\left(\begin{matrix} \Delta(4,\,s+1);\,-\frac{a^4b^4}{64} \\ \frac{1}{2},\,\frac{3}{4},\,\frac{5}{4},\,\Delta(4,\,s+\alpha+1) \end{matrix}\right)$ $\pm\,\dfrac{a^{s+\alpha+2}b^3}{3}\,\mathrm{B}\,(\alpha,\,s+3)\,{}_4F_7\left(\begin{matrix} \Delta(4,\,s+3);\,-\frac{a^4b^4}{64} \\ \frac{1}{4},\,\frac{1}{2},\,\frac{3}{4},\,\Delta(4,\,s+\alpha+3) \end{matrix}\right)$ $[a,\,\mathrm{Re}\,\alpha>0;\,\mathrm{Re}\,s>-1]$
3	$(a^2-x^2)_+^{\alpha-1}$ $\times \begin{Bmatrix} \sinh(bx)\sin(bx) \\ \cosh(bx)\cos(bx) \end{Bmatrix}$	$\dfrac{a^{s+2\alpha+2\delta-2}b^{2\delta}}{2}\,\mathrm{B}\left(\alpha,\,\frac{s+2\delta}{2}\right)$ $\times\,{}_2F_5\left(\begin{matrix} \frac{s+2\delta}{4},\,\frac{s+2\delta+2}{4};\,-\frac{a^4b^4}{64} \\ \frac{2\delta+1}{4},\,\frac{2\delta+3}{4},\,\frac{2\delta+1}{2},\,\frac{s+2\alpha+2\delta}{4},\,\frac{s+2\alpha+2\delta+2}{4} \end{matrix}\right)$ $[a,\,\mathrm{Re}\,\alpha>0;\,\mathrm{Re}\,s>-2\delta]$
4	$(a^2-x^2)_+^{\alpha-1}$ $\times \begin{Bmatrix} \cosh(bx)\sin(bx) \\ \sinh(bx)\cos(bx) \end{Bmatrix}$	$\dfrac{a^{s+2\alpha-1}b}{2}\,\mathrm{B}\left(\alpha,\,\frac{s+1}{2}\right)\,{}_2F_5\left(\begin{matrix} \frac{s+1}{4},\,\frac{s+3}{4};\,-\frac{a^4b^4}{64} \\ \frac{1}{2},\,\frac{3}{4},\,\frac{5}{4},\,\frac{s+2\alpha+1}{4},\,\frac{s+2\alpha+3}{4} \end{matrix}\right)$ $\pm\,\dfrac{a^{s+2\alpha+1}b^3}{6}\,\mathrm{B}\left(\alpha,\,\frac{s+3}{2}\right)\,{}_2F_5\left(\begin{matrix} \frac{s+3}{4},\,\frac{s+5}{4};\,-\frac{a^4b^4}{64} \\ \frac{5}{4},\,\frac{3}{2},\,\frac{7}{4},\,\frac{s+2\alpha+3}{4},\,\frac{s+2\alpha+5}{4} \end{matrix}\right)$ $[a,\,\mathrm{Re}\,\alpha>0;\,\mathrm{Re}\,s>-1]$
5	$e^{-ax}\begin{Bmatrix} \sinh(bx)\sin(bx) \\ \cosh(bx)\cos(bx) \end{Bmatrix}$	$a^{-s-2\delta}b^{2\delta}\,\Gamma(s+2\delta)\,{}_4F_3\left(\begin{matrix} \Delta(4,\,s+2\delta);\,-\frac{4b^4}{a^4} \\ \frac{2\delta+1}{4},\,\frac{2\delta+3}{4},\,\frac{2\delta+1}{2} \end{matrix}\right)$ $[\mathrm{Re}\,a>|\mathrm{Re}\,b|+|\mathrm{Im}\,b|;\,\mathrm{Re}\,s>-2\delta]$
6	$e^{-ax}\begin{Bmatrix} \cosh(bx)\sin(bx) \\ \sinh(bx)\cos(bx) \end{Bmatrix}$	$a^{-s-1}b\,\Gamma(s+1)\,{}_4F_3\left(\begin{matrix} \Delta(4,\,s+1) \\ \frac{1}{2},\,\frac{3}{4},\,\frac{5}{4};\,-\frac{4b^4}{a^4} \end{matrix}\right)$ $\pm\,\dfrac{a^{-s-3}b^3}{3}\,\Gamma(s+3)\,{}_4F_3\left(\begin{matrix} \Delta(4,\,s+3) \\ \frac{5}{4},\,\frac{3}{2},\,\frac{7}{4};\,-\frac{4b^4}{a^4} \end{matrix}\right)$ $[\mathrm{Re}\,a>|\mathrm{Re}\,b|+|\mathrm{Im}\,b|;\,\mathrm{Re}\,s>-1]$
7	$e^{-ax^2}\begin{Bmatrix} \sinh(bx)\sin(bx) \\ \cosh(bx)\cos(bx) \end{Bmatrix}$	$\dfrac{a^{-(s+2\delta)/2}b^{2\delta}}{2}\,\Gamma\left(\frac{s+2\delta}{2}\right)\,{}_2F_3\left(\begin{matrix} \frac{s+2\delta}{4},\,\frac{s+2\delta+2}{4};\,-\frac{b^4}{16a^2} \\ \frac{2\delta+1}{4},\,\frac{2\delta+3}{4},\,\frac{2\delta+1}{2} \end{matrix}\right)$ $[\mathrm{Re}\,a>0;\,\mathrm{Re}\,s>-2\delta]$

No.	$f(x)$	$F(s)$
8	$e^{-ax^2}\left\{\begin{array}{l}\cosh{(bx)}\sin{(bx)}\\ \sinh{(bx)}\cos{(bx)}\end{array}\right\}$	$\dfrac{a^{-(s+1)/2}b}{2}\Gamma\left(\dfrac{s+1}{2}\right){}_2F_3\left(\begin{array}{c}\frac{s+1}{4},\frac{s+3}{4}\\ \frac{1}{2},\frac{3}{4},\frac{5}{4};-\frac{b^4}{16a^2}\end{array}\right)$ $\pm\dfrac{a^{-(s+3)/2}b^3}{6}\Gamma\left(\dfrac{s+3}{2}\right){}_2F_3\left(\begin{array}{c}\frac{s+3}{4},\frac{s+5}{4}\\ \frac{5}{4},\frac{3}{2},\frac{7}{4};-\frac{b^4}{16a^2}\end{array}\right)$ $[\operatorname{Re}a>0;\ \operatorname{Re}s>-1]$

2.4.5. Products of trigonometric functions

Notation: $\lambda_n=\dfrac{1+(-1)^n}{2}$, $\mu_n=\dfrac{(-1)^m+(-1)^n}{2}$.

No.	$f(x)$	$F(s)$	
1	$\sin^2(ax)$	$-\dfrac{a^{-s}}{2^{s+1}}\cos\dfrac{s\pi}{2}\Gamma(s)$	$[a>0;\ -2<\operatorname{Re}s<0]$
2	$\sin^2(ax)-\dfrac{1}{2}$	$-\dfrac{a^{-s}}{2^{s+1}}\cos\dfrac{s\pi}{2}\Gamma(s)$	$[a>0;\ 0<\operatorname{Re}s<1]$
3	$\cos^2(ax)-\dfrac{1}{2}$	$\dfrac{a^{-s}}{2^{s+1}}\cos\dfrac{s\pi}{2}\Gamma(s)$	$[a>0;\ 0<\operatorname{Re}s<1]$
4	$\cos^2(ax)-1$	$\dfrac{a^{-s}}{2^{s+1}}\cos\dfrac{s\pi}{2}\Gamma(s)$	$[a>0;\ -2<\operatorname{Re}s<0]$
5	$\sin^2(ax)-a^2x^2$	$-\dfrac{a^{-s}}{2^{s+1}}\cos\dfrac{s\pi}{2}\Gamma(s)$	$[a>0;\ -4<\operatorname{Re}s<-2]$
6	$\cos^2(ax)+a^2x^2-1$	$\dfrac{a^{-s}}{2^{s+1}}\cos\dfrac{s\pi}{2}\Gamma(s)$	$[a>0;\ -4<\operatorname{Re}s<-2]$
7	$\sin^3(ax)$	$\dfrac{3^{s+1}-1}{4}(3a)^{-s}\sin\dfrac{s\pi}{2}\Gamma(s)$	$[a>0;\ -2<\operatorname{Re}s<0]$
8	$\cos^3(ax)$	$\dfrac{3^{s+1}+1}{4}(3a)^{-s}\cos\dfrac{s\pi}{2}\Gamma(s)$	$[a>0;\ 0<\operatorname{Re}s<1]$
9	$\cos^3(ax)+\dfrac{3}{2}a^2x^2-1$	$\dfrac{3^{s+1}+1}{4}(3a)^{-s}\cos\dfrac{s\pi}{2}\Gamma(s)$	$[a>0;\ -4<\operatorname{Re}s<-2]$
10	$\sin^n(ax)$	$2^{s-n}\sqrt{\pi}\,|a|^{-s}\operatorname{sgn}^n a\,\Gamma\left[\begin{array}{c}\frac{s+2\lambda}{2}\\ \frac{2\lambda-s+1}{2}\end{array}\right]$ $\times\displaystyle\sum_{j=0}^{[(n-1)/2]}(-1)^{[n/2]+j}\dfrac{n!\,(n-2j)^{-s}}{j!\,(n-j)!}$ $\left[\begin{array}{l}\lambda=(1-(-1)^n)/4;\ s\neq-2(\lambda+k);\\ \operatorname{Im}a=0,\ a\neq0;\ -n<\operatorname{Re}s<2\lambda;\ n\geq1\end{array}\right]$	

No.	$f(x)$	$F(s)$
11	$\sin^{2n}(ax)$	$\dfrac{\sqrt{\pi}}{2^{2n}a^s}\Gamma\left[\begin{array}{c}\frac{s}{2}\\\frac{1-s}{2}\end{array}\right]\sum\limits_{k=0}^{n-1}(-1)^{n+k}\dfrac{(2n)!}{k!\,(2n-k)!}(n-k)^{-s}$ $[a>0;\ -2<\operatorname{Re}s<0;\ n\geq 1]$
12	$\sin^{2n+1}(ax)$	$\dfrac{\sqrt{\pi}}{2^{2n-s+1}a^s}\Gamma\left[\begin{array}{c}\frac{s+1}{2}\\\frac{2-s}{2}\end{array}\right]\sum\limits_{k=0}^{n}(-1)^{n+k}\dfrac{(2n+1)!}{k!\,(2n-k+1)!}$ $\times(2n-2k+1)^{-s}\qquad[a>0;\ |\operatorname{Re}s|<1]$
13	$\cos^{2n+1}(ax)$	$2^{s-2n-1}\sqrt{\pi}\,(2n+1)!\,a^{-s}\Gamma\left[\begin{array}{c}\frac{s}{2}\\\frac{1-s}{2}\end{array}\right]$ $\times\sum\limits_{k=0}^{n}\dfrac{(2n-2k+1)^{-s}}{k!\,(2n-k+1)!}\qquad[a>0;\ 0<\operatorname{Re}s<1]$
14	$\cos^n(ax)-1$	$2^{1-n}a^{-s}\cos\dfrac{s\pi}{2}\,\Gamma(s)\sum\limits_{k=0}^{\frac{n}{2}-1}\binom{n}{k}(n-2k)^{-s}$ $[a>0;\ -2<\operatorname{Re}s<0]$
15	$\cos^{2n}(ax)-1$	$2^{-2n}(2n)!\sqrt{\pi}\,a^{-s}\Gamma\left[\begin{array}{c}\frac{s}{2}\\\frac{1-s}{2}\end{array}\right]\sum\limits_{k=0}^{n-1}\dfrac{(n-k)^{-s}}{k!\,(2n-k)!}$ $[a>0;\ -2<\operatorname{Re}s<0;\ n\geq 1]$
16	$\sin^n(ax)-\dfrac{(-1)^n+1}{2^{n+1}}\binom{n}{n/2}$	$\sqrt{\pi}\,\Gamma\left[\begin{array}{c}\frac{2s+(-1)^{n+1}+1}{4}\\\frac{-2s+(-1)^{n+1}+3}{4}\end{array}\right]$ $\times\sum\limits_{k=0}^{[(n-1)/2]}(-1)^{[n/2]-k}\binom{n}{k}\dfrac{2^{s-n}}{[a(n-2k)]^s}$ $[a>0;\ ((-1)^n-1)/2<\operatorname{Re}s<1]$
17	$\cos^n(ax)-\dfrac{(-1)^n+1}{2^{n+1}}\binom{n}{n/2}$	$2^{1-n}a^{-s}\cos\dfrac{s\pi}{2}\,\Gamma(s)\sum\limits_{k=0}^{[(n-1)/2]}\binom{n}{k}(n-2k)^{-s}$ $[a>0;\ 0<\operatorname{Re}s<1]$
18	$\sin^m(ax)$ $-2^{1-m}\sum\limits_{j=0}^{n}\dfrac{(-1)^j(ax)^{m+2j}}{(m+2j)!}$ $\times\sum\limits_{k=0}^{[(m-1)/2]}\binom{m}{k}\dfrac{(-1)^k}{(m-2k)^{-m-2j}}$	$\sqrt{\pi}\,\Gamma\left[\begin{array}{c}-\frac{s+m+2n}{2},\ \frac{s+m+2n+2}{2}\\\frac{1-s}{2},\ \frac{2-s}{2}\end{array}\right]$ $\times\sum\limits_{k=0}^{[(m-1)/2]}(-1)^{n+k+1}\binom{m}{k}\dfrac{2^{s-m}}{[a(m-2k)]^s}$ $[a>0;\ -m-2n-2<\operatorname{Re}s<-m-2n]$

No.	$f(x)$	$F(s)$
19	$\cos^m(ax)$ $-2^{1-m}\sum\limits_{j=1}^{n}\dfrac{(-1)^j(ax)^{2j}}{(2j)!}$ $\times\sum\limits_{k=0}^{[(m-1)/2]}\binom{m}{k}(m-2k)^{2j}-1$	$2^{1-m}a^{-s}\cos\dfrac{s\pi}{2}\,\Gamma(s)\sum\limits_{k=0}^{[(m-1)/2]}\binom{m}{k}(m-2k)^{-s}$ $[a>0;\ -2n-2<\operatorname{Re}s<-2n]$
20	$\left\{\begin{array}{c}\sin(ax)\sin(bx)\\ \cos(ax)\cos(bx)\end{array}\right\}$	$\dfrac{1}{2}\cos\dfrac{s\pi}{2}\,\Gamma(s)\left[|a-b|^{-s}\mp(a+b)^{-s}\right]$ $[a,b>0;\ a\neq b;\ -(1\pm1)<\operatorname{Re}s<1]$
21	$\sin(ax)\cos(bx)$	$\dfrac{1}{2}\sin\dfrac{s\pi}{2}\,\Gamma(s)\left[(a+b)^{-s}+|a-b|^{-s}\operatorname{sgn}(a-b)\right]$ $[a,b>0;\ a\neq b;\ |\operatorname{Re}s|<1]$
22	$\sin^m(ax)\left[\sin^n(bx)\right.$ $\left.-2^{-n}\lambda_n\binom{n}{n/2}\right]$	$(-2)^{-m-n+1}\dfrac{(s-1)^{\lambda_{m+1}\lambda_{n+1}}}{s^{\lambda_m\lambda_n}}\sin\dfrac{(s-\mu_n)\pi}{2}\,\Gamma(s+\mu_n)$ $\times\left\{\sum\limits_{k=0}^{[(m-1)/2]}(-1)^{[m/2]-k}\binom{m}{k}\sum\limits_{j=0}^{[(n-1)/2]}(-1)^{[n/2]-j}\binom{n}{j}\right.$ $\times\left[[a(m-2k)+b(n-2j)]^{-s}\right.$ $\left.\left.+\dfrac{(-1)^{m+(n-m)\theta(a(m-2k)-b(n-2j))}}{|a(m-2k)-b(n-2j)|^s}\right]\right\}+\dfrac{(-1)^{n-1}}{2^{m+n-1}}\binom{m}{m/2}$ $\times\dfrac{\lambda_m}{b^s}\,\Gamma(s)\sin\dfrac{(s-\lambda_n)\pi}{2}\sum\limits_{k=0}^{[(n-1)/2]}\binom{n}{k}\dfrac{(-1)^{[n/2]-k}}{(n-2k)^s}$ $[a,b,m,n>0;\ -m-n\lambda_{n+1}<\operatorname{Re}s<1]$
23	$\sin^m(ax)\left[\cos^n(bx)\right.$ $\left.-2^{-n}\lambda_n\binom{n}{n/2}\right]$	$2^{-m-n+1}\binom{m}{m/2}\dfrac{\lambda_m}{b^s}\cos\dfrac{s\pi}{2}\,\Gamma(s)\sum\limits_{k=0}^{[(n-1)/2]}\binom{n}{k}(n-2k)^{-s}$ $-(-1)^m2^{-m-n+1}\sin\dfrac{(s-\lambda_m)\pi}{2}$ $\times\Gamma(s)\sum\limits_{k=0}^{[(m-1)/2]}(-1)^{[m/2]-k}\binom{m}{k}$ $\times\sum\limits_{j=0}^{[(n-1)/2]}\binom{n}{j}\left\{[a(m-2k)+b(n-2j)]^{-s}\right.$ $\left.+\dfrac{(-1)^{m\theta(b(n-2j)-a(m-2k))}}{|a(m-2k)-b(n-2j)|^s}\right\}$ $[a,b,m,n>0;\ -m<\operatorname{Re}s<1]$

No.	$f(x)$	$F(s)$
24	$\cos^n(bx)\left[\sin^m(ax)\right.$ $\left. - 2^{-m}\lambda_m\begin{pmatrix} m \\ m/2 \end{pmatrix}\right]$	
25	$\cos^m(ax)\left[\cos^n(bx)\right.$ $\left. - 2^{-n}\lambda_n\begin{pmatrix} n \\ n/2 \end{pmatrix}\right]$	
26	$\sin^m(ax)\sin^{2n}(bx)$	

24

$$(-1)^{m-1}2^{-m-n+1}\begin{pmatrix} n \\ n/2 \end{pmatrix}\frac{\lambda_n}{a^s}\sin\frac{(s-\lambda_m)\pi}{2}$$

$$\times\Gamma(s)\sum_{k=0}^{[(m-1)/2]}\begin{pmatrix} m \\ k \end{pmatrix}\frac{(-1)^{[m/2]-k}}{(m-2k)^s}$$

$$-(-1)^m 2^{-m-n+1}\sin\frac{(s-\lambda_m)\pi}{2}$$

$$\times\Gamma(s)\sum_{k=0}^{[(m-1)/2]}(-1)^{[m/2]-k}\begin{pmatrix} m \\ k \end{pmatrix}\sum_{j=0}^{[(n-1)/2]}\begin{pmatrix} n \\ j \end{pmatrix}$$

$$\times\left\{[b(n-2j)+a(m-2k)]^{-s}+\frac{(-1)^{m\theta(b(n-2j)-a(m-2k))}}{|b(n-2j)-a(m-2k)|^s}\right\}$$

$$[a,b,m,n>0;\ -m\lambda_{m+1}<\operatorname{Re}s<1]$$

25

$$2^{-m-n+1}\begin{pmatrix} m \\ m/2 \end{pmatrix}\frac{\lambda_m}{b^s}\cos\frac{s\pi}{2}\Gamma(s)\sum_{k=0}^{[(n-1)/2]}\begin{pmatrix} n \\ k \end{pmatrix}(n-2k)^{-s}$$

$$+2^{-m-n+1}\cos\frac{s\pi}{2}\Gamma(s)\sum_{j=0}^{[(m-1)/2]}\begin{pmatrix} m \\ j \end{pmatrix}$$

$$\times\sum_{k=0}^{[(n-1)/2]}\begin{pmatrix} n \\ k \end{pmatrix}\left\{[b(n-2j)+a(m-2k)]^{-s}\right.$$

$$\left. + |b(n-2j)-a(m-2k)|^{-s}\right\}$$

$$[a,b,m,n>0;\ 0<\operatorname{Re}s<1]$$

26

$$(-1)^{n+[(m+1)/2]}2^{-m-2n+1}s^{-\lambda_m}\sin\frac{(\lambda_m-s)\pi}{2}$$

$$\times\Gamma(\lambda_m+s)\sum_{k=0}^{[(m-1)/2]}(-1)^k\begin{pmatrix} m \\ k \end{pmatrix}\sum_{j=0}^{n-1}(-1)^j\begin{pmatrix} 2n \\ j \end{pmatrix}$$

$$\times\left\{[a(m-2k)+2b(n-j)]^{-s}\right.$$

$$\left. +\frac{(-1)^{m+(2n-m)\theta(a(m-2k)-2b(n-j))}}{|a(m-2k)-2b(n-j)|^s}\right\}$$

$$+2^{-m-2n-s+1}\begin{pmatrix} m \\ m/2 \end{pmatrix}\frac{\lambda_m}{b^s}\cos\frac{s\pi}{2}\Gamma(s)$$

$$\times\sum_{k=0}^{n-1}\begin{pmatrix} 2n \\ k \end{pmatrix}\frac{(-1)^{k+n}}{(n-k)^s}+(-1)^{[m/2]}2^{-m-2n+1}a^{-s}$$

$$\times\begin{pmatrix} 2n \\ n \end{pmatrix}\sin\frac{(\lambda_m+s)\pi}{2}\Gamma(s)\sum_{k=0}^{[(m-1)/2]}\begin{pmatrix} m \\ k \end{pmatrix}\frac{(-1)^k}{(m-2k)^s}$$

$$[a,b,m,n>0;\ -m-2n<\operatorname{Re}s<\lambda_{m+1}]$$

No.	$f(x)$	$F(s)$
27	$\sin^m(ax)\cos^n(bx)$	$(-1)^{m+1}2^{-m-n+1}\dbinom{n}{n/2}\dfrac{\lambda_n}{a^s}\sin\dfrac{(s-\lambda_m)\pi}{2}$ $\times\Gamma(s)\displaystyle\sum_{k=0}^{[(m-1)/2]}\binom{m}{k}\dfrac{(-1)^{k+[m/2]}}{(m-2k)^s}$ $+2^{-m-n+1}\dbinom{m}{m/2}\dfrac{\lambda_m}{b^s}\cos\dfrac{s\pi}{2}\Gamma(s)\displaystyle\sum_{k=0}^{[(n-1)/2]}\binom{n}{k}\dfrac{1}{(n-2k)^s}$ $-(-1)^m2^{-m-n+1}\sin\dfrac{(s-\lambda_m)\pi}{2}\Gamma(s)\displaystyle\sum_{k=0}^{[(m-1)/2]}(-1)^{[m/2]-k}\binom{m}{k}$ $\times\displaystyle\sum_{j=0}^{[(n-1)/2]}\binom{n}{j}\Big\{[b(n-2j)+a(m-2k)]^{-s}$ $+\dfrac{(-1)^{m\theta(b(n-2j)-a(m-2k))}}{\lvert a(m-2k)-b(n-2j)\rvert^s}\Big\}$ $[a,b,m,n>0;\ -m<\operatorname{Re}s<1-\delta_{(-1)^n+(-1)^m-2,0}]$
28	$\cos^m(ax)\cos^{2n-1}(bx)$	$2^{-m-2n+2}\dbinom{m}{m/2}\dfrac{\lambda_m}{b^s}\cos\dfrac{s\pi}{2}\Gamma(s)\displaystyle\sum_{k=0}^{n-1}\binom{2n-1}{k}\dfrac{1}{(2n-2k-1)^s}$ $+2^{-m-2n+2}\cos\dfrac{s\pi}{2}\Gamma(s)\displaystyle\sum_{k=0}^{n-1}\binom{2n-1}{k}$ $\times\displaystyle\sum_{j=0}^{[(m-1)/2]}\binom{m}{j}\Big\{[a(m-2j)+b(2n-2k-1)]^{-s}$ $+\lvert a(m-2j)-b(2n-2k-1)\rvert^{-s}\Big\}$ $[a,b,m,n>0;\ 0<\operatorname{Re}s<1]$
29	$\left\{\begin{array}{c}\sin(ax^2)\\\cos(ax^2)\end{array}\right\}\sin(bx)$	$\dfrac{a^{-(s+1)/2}b}{2}\Gamma\!\left(\dfrac{s+1}{2}\right)\left\{\begin{array}{c}\cos[(1-s)\pi/4]\\\sin[(1-s)\pi/4]\end{array}\right\}$ $\times\,{}_2F_3\!\left(\begin{array}{c}\frac{s+1}{2},\,\frac{s+3}{2};\,-\frac{b^4}{64a^2}\\[2pt]\frac{1}{2},\,\frac{3}{4},\,\frac{5}{4}\end{array}\right)\mp\dfrac{a^{-(s+3)/2}b^3}{12}\Gamma\!\left(\dfrac{s+3}{2}\right)$ $\times\left\{\begin{array}{c}\cos[(s+1)\pi/4]\\\sin[(s+1)\pi/4]\end{array}\right\}{}_2F_3\!\left(\begin{array}{c}\frac{s+3}{4},\,\frac{s+5}{4};\,-\frac{b^4}{64a^2}\\[2pt]\frac{5}{4},\,\frac{3}{2},\,\frac{7}{4}\end{array}\right)$ $[a,b>0;\ -1-(1\pm1)<\operatorname{Re}s<2]$
30	$\left\{\begin{array}{c}\sin(ax^2)\\\cos(ax^2)\end{array}\right\}\cos(bx)$	$\dfrac{a^{-s/2}}{2}\Gamma\!\left(\dfrac{s}{2}\right)\left\{\begin{array}{c}\sin(s\pi/4)\\\cos(s\pi/4)\end{array}\right\}{}_2F_3\!\left(\begin{array}{c}\frac{s}{4},\,\frac{s+2}{4};\,-\frac{b^4}{64a^2}\\[2pt]\frac{1}{4},\,\frac{1}{2},\,\frac{3}{4}\end{array}\right)$ $\mp\dfrac{a^{-s/2-1}b^2}{4}\Gamma\!\left(\dfrac{s+2}{2}\right)\left\{\begin{array}{c}\cos(s\pi/4)\\\sin(s\pi/4)\end{array}\right\}{}_2F_3\!\left(\begin{array}{c}\frac{s+2}{4},\,\frac{s+4}{4};\,-\frac{b^4}{64a^2}\\[2pt]\frac{3}{4},\,\frac{5}{4},\,\frac{3}{2}\end{array}\right)$ $[a,b>0;\ -(1\pm1)<\operatorname{Re}s<2]$

No.	$f(x)$	$F(s)$
31	$\left\{ \begin{array}{l} \sin(ax)\sin(b/x) \\ \cos(ax)\cos(b/x) \end{array} \right\}$	$\pm\dfrac{\pi}{4}\left(\dfrac{b}{a}\right)^{s/2}\csc\dfrac{s\pi}{2}\Big[J_s\left(2\sqrt{ab}\right) - J_{-s}\left(2\sqrt{ab}\right)$ $\pm\dfrac{2\sin(s\pi)}{\pi}K_s\left(2\sqrt{ab}\right)\Big] \qquad [a,\,b>0;\ |\operatorname{Re} s| < (3\pm1)/2]$
32	$\left\{ \begin{array}{l} \sin(ax)\cos(b/x) \\ \cos(ax)\sin(b/x) \end{array} \right\}$	$\dfrac{\pi}{4}\left(\dfrac{b}{a}\right)^{s/2}\sec\dfrac{s\pi}{2}\Big[J_s\left(2\sqrt{ab}\right) + J_{-s}\left(2\sqrt{ab}\right)$ $\pm\dfrac{2\sin(s\pi)}{\pi}K_s\left(2\sqrt{ab}\right)\Big] \qquad [a,\,b>0;\ |\operatorname{Re} s| < 1]$
33	$\sin(ax)\sin(bx)\sin(cx)$	$\dfrac{\Gamma(s)}{4}\sin\dfrac{s\pi}{2}\Big[\dfrac{1}{(a+b-c)^s} - \dfrac{1}{(a+b+c)^s} +$ $+\dfrac{\operatorname{sgn}(a-b+c)}{|a-b+c|^s} - \dfrac{\operatorname{sgn}(a-b-c)}{|a-b-c|^s}\Big]$ $\begin{bmatrix} a>0;\ \operatorname{Im} b = \operatorname{Im} c = 0;\ b > |c|; \\ a - b \neq |c|;\ -3 < \operatorname{Re} s < 1 \end{bmatrix}$
34	$\sin(ax)\sin(bx)\cos(cx)$	$\dfrac{\Gamma(s)}{4}\cos\dfrac{s\pi}{2}\Big[-\dfrac{1}{(a+b-c)^s} - \dfrac{1}{(a+b+c)^s} +$ $+\dfrac{1}{|a-b+c|^s} + \dfrac{1}{|a-b-c|^s}\Big]$ $\begin{bmatrix} a>0;\ \operatorname{Im} b = \operatorname{Im} c = 0;\ b > |c|; \\ a - b \neq |c|;\ -2 < \operatorname{Re} s < 1 \end{bmatrix}$
35	$\sin(ax)\cos(bx)\cos(cx)$	$\dfrac{\Gamma(s)}{4}\sin\dfrac{s\pi}{2}\Big[\dfrac{1}{(a+b-c)^s} + \dfrac{1}{(a+b+c)^s} +$ $+\dfrac{\operatorname{sgn}(a-b+c)}{|a-b+c|^s} + \dfrac{\operatorname{sgn}(a-b-c)}{|a-b-c|^s}\Big]$ $\begin{bmatrix} a>0;\ \operatorname{Im} b = \operatorname{Im} c = 0;\ b > |c|; \\ a - b \neq |c|;\ -1 < \operatorname{Re} s < 1 \end{bmatrix}$
36	$\cos(ax)\cos(bx)\cos(cx)$	$\dfrac{\Gamma(s)}{4}\cos\dfrac{s\pi}{2}\Big[\dfrac{1}{(a+b-c)^s} + \dfrac{1}{(a+b+c)^s} +$ $+\dfrac{1}{|a-b+c|^s} + \dfrac{1}{|a-b-c|^s}\Big]$ $\begin{bmatrix} a>0;\ \operatorname{Im} b = \operatorname{Im} c = 0;\ b > |c|; \\ a - b \neq |c|;\ 0 < \operatorname{Re} s < 1 \end{bmatrix}$
37	$e^{-ax}\left\{ \begin{array}{l} \sin^n(bx) \\ \cos^n(bx) \end{array} \right\}$	$\left\{ \begin{array}{l} (-i)^n \\ 1 \end{array} \right\}\dfrac{\Gamma(s)}{2^n}\displaystyle\sum_{k=0}^{n}(\mp1)^{n-k}\binom{n}{k}[a+ib(n-2k)]^{-s}$ $[\operatorname{Re} a > n\,|\operatorname{Im} b|;\ \operatorname{Re} s > -(1\pm1)n/2]$

No.	$f(x)$	$F(s)$
38	$e^{-ax}\sin^{2n}(bx)$	$\dfrac{\Gamma(s)}{2^{2n}a^s}\dbinom{2n}{n}+\dfrac{(-1)^n\,\Gamma(s)}{2^{2n}}\displaystyle\sum_{k=0}^{n-1}(-1)^k\dbinom{2n}{k}$ $\times\left[(a-i(2n-2k)b)^{-s}+(a+i(2n-2k)b)^{-s}\right]$ $[\operatorname{Re}(a-2inb)>0;\ \operatorname{Re}s>-2n]$
39	$e^{-ax}\sin^{2n+1}(bx)$	$-\dfrac{(-1)^n\,i\,\Gamma(s)}{2^{2n+1}}\displaystyle\sum_{k=0}^{n}(-1)^k\dbinom{2n+1}{k}$ $\times\left[(a-i(2n-2k+1)b)^{-s}-(a+i(2n-2k+1)b)^{-s}\right]$ $[\operatorname{Re}(a-i(2n+1)b)>0;\ \operatorname{Re}s>-2n-1]$
40	$e^{-ax}\cos^n(bx)$	$\dfrac{[1+(-1)^n]\,\Gamma(s)}{2^{n+1}a^s}\dbinom{n}{n/2}+\dfrac{\Gamma(s)}{2^n}\displaystyle\sum_{k=0}^{[(n-1)/2]}\dbinom{n}{k}$ $\times\left[(a-i(n-2k)b)^{-s}+(a+i(n-2k)b)^{-s}\right]$ $[\operatorname{Re}(a-inb)>0;\ \operatorname{Re}s>0]$

2.4.6. $\operatorname{sinc}^n(bx)$ and elementary functions

No.	$f(x)$	$F(s)$
1	$\operatorname{sinc}(ax)$	$\dfrac{2^{s-2}\sqrt{\pi}}{a^s}\Gamma\left[\begin{array}{c}\frac{s}{2}\\\frac{3-s}{2}\end{array}\right]$ $\qquad[a>0;\ 0<\operatorname{Re}s<2]$
2	$e^{-ax}\operatorname{sinc}(ax)$	$\dfrac{2^{3s/2-4}}{\sqrt{\pi}\,a^s}\Gamma\left[\begin{array}{c}\frac{s}{4},\ \frac{s+1}{4},\ \frac{s+2}{4}\\\frac{5-s}{4}\end{array}\right]$ $\left[\begin{array}{l}(|\arg a|<\pi/4;\ \operatorname{Re}s>0)\ \text{or}\\(|\arg a|=\pi/4;\ 0<\operatorname{Re}s<2)\end{array}\right]$
3	$e^{-ax}\operatorname{sinc}(bx)$	$\dfrac{\Gamma(s-1)}{b(a^2+b^2)^{(s-1)/2}}\sin\left[(s-1)\arctan\dfrac{b}{a}\right]$ $\left[\begin{array}{l}(\operatorname{Re}a>|\operatorname{Im}b|;\ \operatorname{Re}s>0)\ \text{or}\\(\operatorname{Re}a=|\operatorname{Im}b|;\ 0<\operatorname{Re}s<2)\end{array}\right]$
4	$e^{-ax^2}\operatorname{sinc}(bx)$	$\dfrac{a^{-s/2}}{2}\Gamma\left(\dfrac{s}{2}\right){}_1F_1\left(\begin{array}{c}\frac{s}{2}\\\frac{3}{2}\end{array};-\dfrac{b^2}{4a}\right)$ $\qquad[\operatorname{Re}a,\ \operatorname{Re}s>0]$
5	$e^{-ax^2-bx}\operatorname{sinc}(cx)$	$\dfrac{i\,\Gamma(s-1)}{2c(2a)^{(s-1)/2}}e^{(b^2-c^2)/(8a)}\left[e^{ibc/(4a)}D_{1-s}\left(\dfrac{b+ic}{\sqrt{2a}}\right)\right.$ $\left.\mp\,e^{-ibc/(4a)}D_{1-s}\left(\dfrac{b-ic}{\sqrt{2a}}\right)\right]\quad[\operatorname{Re}a,\ \operatorname{Re}s>0]$

No.	$f(x)$	$F(s)$
6	$\sin(ax)\operatorname{sinc}(ax)$	$-(2a)^{-s}\sin\dfrac{s\pi}{2}\,\Gamma(s-1)$ $\qquad\qquad [a>0;\ |\operatorname{Re}s|<1]$
7	$\cos(ax)\operatorname{sinc}(ax)$	$-(2a)^{-s}\cos\dfrac{s\pi}{2}\,\Gamma(s-1)$ $\qquad\qquad [a>0;\ 0<\operatorname{Re}s<2]$
8	$\operatorname{sinc}^2(ax)$	$2^{1-s}a^{-s}\cos\dfrac{s\pi}{2}\,\Gamma(s-2)$ $\qquad\qquad [a>0;\ 0<\operatorname{Re}s<2]$
9	$\operatorname{sinc}^3(ax)$	$\dfrac{a^{-s}}{4}\left(3-3^{3-s}\right)\cos\dfrac{s\pi}{2}\,\Gamma(s-3)$ $\qquad [a>0;\ 0<\operatorname{Re}s<4]$
10	$\operatorname{sinc}^{2n}(ax)$	$\dfrac{\sqrt{\pi}}{2^{2n}a^s}\Gamma\left[\begin{array}{c}\frac{s-2n}{2}\\\frac{1-s+2n}{2}\end{array}\right]\displaystyle\sum_{k=0}^{n-1}(-1)^{n+k}\dfrac{(2n)!}{k!\,(2n-k)!}(n-k)^{2n-s}$ $\qquad\qquad\qquad [a>0;\ 0<\operatorname{Re}s<2n]$
11	$\operatorname{sinc}^{2n+1}(ax)$	$\dfrac{\sqrt{\pi}}{2^{4n-s+2}a^s}\Gamma\left[\begin{array}{c}\frac{s-2n}{2}\\\frac{3-s+2n}{2}\end{array}\right]\displaystyle\sum_{k=0}^{n}(-1)^{n+k}\dfrac{(2n+1)!}{k!\,(2n-k+1)!}$ $\times(2n-2k+1)^{2n-s+1}\qquad [a>0;\ 0<\operatorname{Re}s<2n+2]$
12	$\operatorname{sinc}^n(ax)$ $-\dfrac{(-1)^n+1}{2^{n+1}}\dfrac{\binom{n}{n/2}}{(ax)^n}$	$\dfrac{\sqrt{\pi}}{a^s}\Gamma\left[\begin{array}{c}\frac{2s-2n+(-1)^{n+1}+1}{4}\\\frac{-2s+2n+(-1)^{n+1}+3}{4}\end{array}\right]$ $\times\displaystyle\sum_{k=0}^{[(n-1)/2]}(-1)^{[n/2]-k}\binom{n}{k}2^{s-2n}(n-2k)^{n-s}$ $[a>0;\ (2n+(-1)^n-1)/2<\operatorname{Re}s<n+1]$
13	$e^{-ax}\operatorname{sinc}^n(bx)$	$(-i)^n\dfrac{\Gamma(s-n)}{(2b)^n}\displaystyle\sum_{k=0}^{n}(-1)^{n-k}\binom{n}{k}[a+ib(n-2k)]^{n-s}$ $\qquad\qquad\qquad [\operatorname{Re}a>n\,|\operatorname{Im}b|;\ \operatorname{Re}s>0]$
14	$\operatorname{sinc}\left(b\sqrt{x^2+a^2}\right)$	$\dfrac{2^{(s-3)/2}\sqrt{\pi}\,a^{(s-1)/2}}{b^{(s+1)/2}}\Gamma\left(\dfrac{s}{2}\right)J_{(1-s)/2}(ab)\quad [\operatorname{Re}a>0;\ 0<\operatorname{Re}s<2]$
15	$\theta(a-x)$ $\times\operatorname{sinc}\left(b\sqrt{a^2-x^2}\right)$	$\dfrac{2^{(s-3)/2}\sqrt{\pi}\,a^{(s-1)/2}}{b^{(s+1)/2}}\Gamma\left(\dfrac{s}{2}\right)\mathbf{H}_{(s-1)/2}(ab)\qquad\qquad [a,\ \operatorname{Re}s>0]$
16	$\theta(x-a)$ $\times\operatorname{sinc}\left(b\sqrt{x^2-a^2}\right)$	$\dfrac{2^{(s-3)/2}\sqrt{\pi}\,a^{(s-1)/2}}{b^{(s+1)/2}}\Gamma\left(\dfrac{s}{2}\right)\left[I_{(1-s)/2}(ab)-\mathbf{L}_{(s-1)/2}(ab)\right]$ $\qquad\qquad\qquad [a,b>0;\ \operatorname{Re}s<2]$

2.5. The Logarithmic Function

More formulas can be obtained from the corresponding sections due to the relations

$$\ln{(z+1)} = z\,{}_2F_1\left(1, 1; 2; -z\right), \quad \ln\left(\sqrt{z+1} + \sqrt{z}\right) = \sqrt{z}\,{}_2F_1\left(\frac{1}{2}, \frac{1}{2}; \frac{3}{2}; -z\right),$$

$$\ln\frac{1+\sqrt{z}}{1-\sqrt{z}} = 2\sqrt{z}\,{}_2F_1\left(\frac{1}{2}, 1; \frac{3}{2}; z\right), \quad \frac{\ln\left(\sqrt{z+1}+\sqrt{z}\right)}{\sqrt{z+1}} = \sqrt{z}\,{}_2F_1\left(1, 1; \frac{3}{2}; -z\right),$$

$$\ln^2\left(\sqrt{z+1}+\sqrt{z}\right) = z\,{}_3F_2\left(1, 1, 1; \frac{3}{2}, 2; -z\right),$$

$$\ln{(z+1)} = G^{12}_{22}\left(z\left|\begin{matrix}1, 1\\1, 0\end{matrix}\right.\right), \quad \ln\left(\sqrt{z+1}\pm\sqrt{z}\right) = \pm\frac{1}{2\sqrt{\pi}}\,G^{12}_{22}\left(z\left|\begin{matrix}1, 1\\1/2, 0\end{matrix}\right.\right),$$

$$\frac{\ln\left(\sqrt{z+1}+\sqrt{z}\right)}{\sqrt{z+1}} = \frac{\sqrt{\pi}}{2}\,G^{22}_{33}\left(z\left|\begin{matrix}1/2, 1/2,\\1/2, 1/2, 0\end{matrix}\right.\right),$$

$$\ln^2\left(\sqrt{z+1}+\sqrt{z}\right) = \frac{\sqrt{\pi}}{2}\,G^{13}_{33}\left(z\left|\begin{matrix}1, 1, 1\\1, 0, 1/2\end{matrix}\right.\right).$$

2.5.1. $\ln{(bx)}$ and algebraic functions

No.	$f(x)$	$F(s)$
1	$\left\{\begin{matrix}\theta(a-x)\\\theta(x-a)\end{matrix}\right\}\ln\dfrac{x}{a}$	$\mp\dfrac{a^s}{s^2}$ $\qquad\qquad\qquad\qquad [a>0;\ \pm\operatorname{Re}s>0]$
2	$\left\{\begin{matrix}\theta(a-x)\\\theta(x-a)\end{matrix}\right\}\ln{(bx)}$	$\mp\dfrac{a^s[1-s\ln{(ab)}]}{s^2}$ $\qquad [a>0;\ \pm\operatorname{Re}s>0;\ \lvert\arg b\rvert<\pi]$
3	$(a-x)^{\alpha-1}_{+}\ln{(bx)}$	$a^{s+\alpha-1}\,\mathrm{B}(s, \alpha)\left[\psi(s)-\psi(s+\alpha)+\ln{(ab)}\right]$ $\qquad\qquad [a,\ \operatorname{Re}\alpha,\ \operatorname{Re}s>0;\ \lvert\arg b\rvert<\pi]$
4	$(x-a)^{\alpha-1}_{+}\ln{(bx)}$	$a^{s+\alpha-1}\,\mathrm{B}(1-s-\alpha, \alpha)\left[\psi(1-s)-\psi(1-s-\alpha)+\ln{(ab)}\right]$ $\qquad\qquad [a,\ \operatorname{Re}\alpha>0;\ \operatorname{Re}(s+\alpha)<1;\ \lvert\arg b\rvert<\pi]$
5	$(a^2-x^2)^{\alpha-1}_{+}\ln{(bx)}$	$\dfrac{a^{s+2\alpha-2}}{2}\,\mathrm{B}\left(\alpha, \dfrac{s}{2}\right)\left[\dfrac{1}{2}\psi\left(\dfrac{s}{2}\right)-\dfrac{1}{2}\psi\left(\dfrac{s}{2}+\alpha\right)+\ln{(ab)}\right]$ $\qquad\qquad [a,\ \operatorname{Re}\alpha,\ \operatorname{Re}s>0;\ \lvert\arg b\rvert<\pi]$
6	$(x^2-a^2)^{\alpha-1}_{+}\ln{(bx)}$	$\dfrac{a^{s+2\alpha-2}}{2}\,\mathrm{B}\left(\alpha, \dfrac{2-s-2\alpha}{2}\right)\left[\dfrac{1}{2}\psi\left(\dfrac{2-s}{2}\right)-\dfrac{1}{2}\psi\left(\dfrac{2-s-2\alpha}{2}\right)\right.$ $\left.+\ln{(ab)}\right]\qquad [a,\ \operatorname{Re}\alpha>0;\ \operatorname{Re}(s+2\alpha)<2;\ \lvert\arg b\rvert<\pi]$
7	$\theta(a-x)\dfrac{\ln x}{x+a}$	$\dfrac{a^{s-1}}{4}\left\{2\ln a\left[\psi\left(\dfrac{s+1}{2}\right)-\psi\left(\dfrac{s}{2}\right)\right]+\psi'\left(\dfrac{s+1}{2}\right)-\psi'\left(\dfrac{s}{2}\right)\right\}$ $\qquad\qquad\qquad\qquad\qquad\qquad [a,\ \operatorname{Re}s>0]$

No.	$f(x)$	$F(s)$
8	$\dfrac{\ln x}{x+a}$	$\pi a^{s-1}\csc(s\pi)\left[\ln a - \pi\cot(s\pi)\right]$ $\qquad$ $[0 < \operatorname{Re} s < 1;\ |\arg a| < \pi]$
9	$\dfrac{\ln x}{a-x}$	$\pi a^{s-1}\left[\ln a\cot(s\pi) - \dfrac{\pi}{\sin^2(s\pi)}\right]$ $\qquad$ $[a > 0;\ 0 < \operatorname{Re} s < 1]$
10	$\dfrac{\ln x}{(x+a)(x-1)}$	$\dfrac{\pi\csc^2(s\pi)}{a+1}\left\{\pi - a^{s-1}\left[\sin(s\pi)\ln a - \pi\cos(s\pi)\right]\right\}$ $[0 < \operatorname{Re} s < 2;\ s \neq 1;\ |\arg a| < \pi]$
11	$\dfrac{\ln x}{(x+a)^2}$	$\dfrac{\pi(1-s)a^{s-2}}{\sin(s\pi)}\left[\ln a - \pi\cot(s\pi) + \dfrac{1}{s-1}\right]$ $[0 < \operatorname{Re} s < 2;\ s \neq 1;\ |\arg a| < \pi]$
12	$\dfrac{\ln x}{(x+a)(x+b)}$	$\dfrac{\pi\csc(s\pi)}{a-b}\left[b^{s-1}\ln b - a^{s-1}\ln a - \pi\left(b^{s-1} - a^{s-1}\right)\cot(s\pi)\right]$ $[0 < \operatorname{Re} s < 2;\ s \neq 1;\ |\arg a|,\ |\arg b| < \pi]$
13	$\dfrac{\ln(x/b)}{(x+a)(x+b)}$	$\dfrac{\pi}{(b-a)\sin(s\pi)}\left[a^{s-1}\ln\dfrac{a}{b} + \pi\left(b^{s-1} - a^{s-1}\right)\cot(s\pi)\right]$ $[0 < \operatorname{Re} s < 2;\ |\arg a|,\ |\arg b| < \pi]$
14	$\dfrac{\ln x}{(x+a)(x+b)(x+c)}$	$\pi\csc(s\pi)\left[\dfrac{a^{s-1}\left(\pi\cot(s\pi) - \ln a\right)}{(a-b)(c-a)} + \dfrac{b^{s-1}\left(\pi\cot(s\pi) - \ln b\right)}{(a-b)(b-c)}\right.$ $\left. + \dfrac{c^{s-1}\left(\pi\cot(s\pi) - \ln c\right)}{(a-c)(c-b)}\right]$ $[0 < \operatorname{Re} s < 3;\ s \neq 1;\ |\arg a|,\ |\arg b|,\ |\arg c| < \pi]$

2.5.2. $\ln(bx+c)$ **and algebraic functions**

No.	$f(x)$	$F(s)$
1	$\theta(a-x)\ln(x+a)$	$\dfrac{a^s}{s}\left\{\ln(2a) - \dfrac{1}{2}\left[\psi\left(\dfrac{s+2}{2}\right) - \psi\left(\dfrac{s+1}{2}\right)\right]\right\}$ $\qquad$ $[a,\ \operatorname{Re} s > 0]$
2	$\theta(a-x)\ln(bx+c)$	$\dfrac{a^s}{s}\left[\ln\left(\dfrac{ab}{c}+1\right) + \ln c - \dfrac{ab}{c}\,\Phi\left(-\dfrac{ab}{c}, 1, s+1\right)\right]$ $\left[\begin{array}{l} a,\ \operatorname{Re} c,\ \operatorname{Re} s > 0;\ \operatorname{Re}(c/b) \geq 0\ \text{or} \\ \operatorname{Re}(c/b) \leq -1;\ \operatorname{Im}(c/b) \neq 0 \end{array}\right]$
3	$\left.\begin{array}{l}\ln(ax+1)\\ \ln|ax-1|\end{array}\right\}$	$\dfrac{\pi a^{-s}}{s}\left\{\begin{array}{l}\csc(s\pi)\\ \cot(s\pi)\end{array}\right\}$ $\qquad$ $[-1 < \operatorname{Re} s < 0;\ |\arg a| < \pi]$
4	$\dfrac{\ln(x+a)}{(x+a)^{\rho}}$	$a^{s-\rho}\operatorname{B}(s, \rho-s)\left[\psi(\rho) - \psi(\rho-s) + \ln a\right]$ $[0 < \operatorname{Re} s < \operatorname{Re}\rho;\ |\arg a| < \pi]$

No.	$f(x)$	$F(s)$
5	$(a-x)_+^{\alpha-1}\ln(bx+c)$	$\dfrac{a^{s+\alpha}b}{c}\,\mathrm{B}(s+1,\alpha)\,{}_3F_2\left(\begin{matrix}1,\,1,\,s+1;\,-\frac{ab}{c}\\2,\,s+\alpha+1\end{matrix}\right)+a^{s+\alpha-1}\ln c\,\mathrm{B}(s,\alpha)$
		$[a,\ \operatorname{Re}\alpha,\ \operatorname{Re}s>0;\ |\arg(bx+c)|<\pi \text{ at } 0<x<a]$
6	$(x-a)_+^{\alpha-1}\ln(bx+c)$	$\dfrac{a^{s+\alpha-2}c}{b}\,\mathrm{B}(\alpha,2-s-\alpha)\,{}_3F_2\left(\begin{matrix}1,\,1,\,2-s-\alpha\\2,\,2-s;\,-\frac{c}{ab}\end{matrix}\right)+a^{s+\alpha-1}$
		$\times\,\mathrm{B}(\alpha,1-s-\alpha)\left[\psi(1-s)-\psi(1-s-\alpha)+\log\dfrac{ab}{c}+\log c\right]$
		$[a,\ \operatorname{Re}\alpha>0;\ \operatorname{Re}(s+\alpha)<1;\ |\arg(bx+c)|<\pi \text{ at } x>a]$
7	$(a^2-x^2)_+^{\alpha-1}\ln(bx+c)$	$\dfrac{a^{s+2\alpha+1}b^3}{6c^3}\,\mathrm{B}\left(\alpha,\dfrac{s+3}{2}\right)\,{}_3F_2\left(\begin{matrix}1,\,\frac{3}{2},\,\frac{s+3}{2};\,\frac{a^2b^2}{c^2}\\\frac{5}{2},\,\frac{s+2\alpha+3}{2}\end{matrix}\right)$
		$-\dfrac{a^{s+2\alpha}b^2}{4c^2}\,\mathrm{B}\left(\alpha,\dfrac{s+2}{2}\right)\,{}_3F_2\left(\begin{matrix}1,\,1,\,\frac{s+2}{2};\,\frac{a^2b^2}{c^2}\\2,\,\frac{s+2\alpha+2}{2}\end{matrix}\right)$
		$+\dfrac{a^{s+2\alpha-1}b}{2c}\,\mathrm{B}\left(\alpha,\dfrac{s+1}{2}\right)+\dfrac{a^{s+2\alpha-2}\ln c}{2}\,\mathrm{B}\left(\alpha,\dfrac{s}{2}\right)$
		$[a,\ \operatorname{Re}\alpha,\ \operatorname{Re}s>0;\ |\arg(bx+c)|<\pi \text{ at } 0<x<a]$
8	$(x^2-a^2)_+^{\alpha-1}\ln(bx+c)$	$\dfrac{a^{s+2\alpha-5}c^3}{6b^3}\,\mathrm{B}\left(\alpha,\dfrac{5-s-2\alpha}{2}\right)\,{}_3F_2\left(\begin{matrix}1,\,\frac{3}{2},\,\frac{5-s-2\alpha}{2}\\\frac{5}{2},\,\frac{5-s}{2};\,\frac{c^2}{a^2b^2}\end{matrix}\right)$
		$-\dfrac{a^{s+2\alpha-4}c^2}{4b^2}\,\mathrm{B}\left(\alpha,\dfrac{4-s-2\alpha}{2}\right)\,{}_3F_2\left(\begin{matrix}1,\,1,\,\frac{4-s-2\alpha}{2}\\2,\,\frac{4-s}{2};\,\frac{c^2}{a^2b^2}\end{matrix}\right)$
		$+\dfrac{a^{s+2\alpha-3}c}{2b}\,\mathrm{B}\left(\alpha,\dfrac{3-s-2\alpha}{2}\right)$
		$+\dfrac{a^{s+2\alpha-2}}{2}\,\mathrm{B}\left(\alpha,\dfrac{2-s-2\alpha}{2}\right)\left[\dfrac{1}{2}\,\psi\left(\dfrac{2-s}{2}\right)\right.$
		$\left.-\dfrac{1}{2}\,\psi\left(\dfrac{2-s-2\alpha}{2}\right)+\log\dfrac{ab}{c}+\log c\right]$
		$[a,\ \operatorname{Re}\alpha>0;\ \operatorname{Re}(s+2\alpha)<2;\ |\arg(bx+c)|<\pi \text{ at } x>a]$
9	$(a-x)_+^{\alpha-1}$	$a^{s+\alpha}b\,\mathrm{B}(s,\alpha+1)\,{}_3F_2\left(\begin{matrix}1,\,1,\,s+1\\2,\,s+\alpha+1;\,-ab\end{matrix}\right)$
	$\times\ln[b(a-x)+1]$	$[a,\ \operatorname{Re}s>0;\ \operatorname{Re}\alpha>-1]$
10	$\theta(a-x)(bx+1)^\alpha$	$\dfrac{a^{s+1}c}{s(s+1)}\,F_3(-\alpha,1,s,1;s+2;-ab,-ac)$
	$\times\ln[c(a-x)+1]$	$[a,\ \operatorname{Re}s>0;\ |\arg b|,\ |\arg(1+ac)|<\pi]$

2.5.3. $\ln \dfrac{ax+b}{cx+d}$, $\ln\left|\dfrac{ax+b}{cx+d}\right|$ **and algebraic functions**

1	$\ln \dfrac{ax+b}{ax+c}$	$\dfrac{\pi a^{-s}}{s}\left(b^s-c^s\right)\csc\left(s\pi\right)$
		$[0<\operatorname{Re}s<1;\ |\arg a|,\ |\arg b|,\ |\arg c|<\pi]$

2	$\ln\left|\dfrac{ax+b}{ax-c}\right|$	$\dfrac{\pi a^{-s}}{s}\csc\left(s\pi\right)\left[b^s-c^s\cos\left(s\pi\right)\right]$ $\qquad[a,\,b,\,c>0;\ 0<\operatorname{Re}s<1]$

3	$\ln\left|\dfrac{x+a}{x-a}\right|$	$\dfrac{\pi a^s}{s}\tan\dfrac{s\pi}{2}$ $\qquad\qquad[a>0;\ |\operatorname{Re}s|<1;\ s\neq0]$

4	$\theta\left(a-x\right)\ln\left[\dfrac{c(a-x)}{b-x}+1\right]$	$\dfrac{a^{s+1}c}{s\left(s+1\right)b}\,F_1\left(1,\,s,\,1;\,s+2;\,\dfrac{a}{b},\,-\dfrac{ac}{b}\right)$
		$[0<a<b;\ \operatorname{Re}s>0;\ |\arg c|<\pi]$

5	$\dfrac{1}{(x+a)^{\rho}}\ln\left(\dfrac{b}{x+a}+1\right)$	$a^{s-\rho-1}b\,\mathrm{B}\left(s,\,1-s+\rho\right)\,{}_3F_2\!\left(\begin{matrix}1,\,1,\,1-s+\rho\\2,\,\rho+1;\,-\dfrac{b}{a}\end{matrix}\right)$
		$[0<\operatorname{Re}s<\operatorname{Re}\rho+1;\ |\arg a|,\ |\arg b|<\pi]$

6	$\dfrac{1}{(x+a)^{\rho}}\ln\dfrac{x+a+b}{x+a-b}$	$a^{s-\rho-1}b\,\mathrm{B}\left(s,\,1-s+\rho\right)\,{}_4F_3\!\left(\begin{matrix}\dfrac{1}{2},\,1,\,\dfrac{1-s+\rho}{2},\,\dfrac{2-s+\rho}{2}\\\dfrac{3}{2},\,\dfrac{\rho+1}{2},\,\dfrac{\rho+2}{2};\,\dfrac{b^2}{a^2}\end{matrix}\right)$
		$[0<\operatorname{Re}s<\operatorname{Re}\rho+1;\ |\arg a|,\ |\arg b|<\pi]$

7	$\dfrac{1}{(x+a)^{\rho}}\ln\dfrac{(1+b)\,x+a}{(1-b)\,x+a}$	$2a^{s-\rho}b\,\mathrm{B}\left(s+1,\,\rho-s\right)\,{}_4F_3\!\left(\begin{matrix}\dfrac{1}{2},\,1,\,\dfrac{s+1}{2},\,\dfrac{s+2}{2}\\\dfrac{3}{2},\,\dfrac{\rho+1}{2},\,\dfrac{\rho+2}{2};\,b^2\end{matrix}\right)$
		$[-1<\operatorname{Re}s<\operatorname{Re}\rho;\ |\arg a|,\ |\arg b|<\pi]$

8	$(a-x)_+^{\alpha-1}\ln\dfrac{1+bx}{1-bx}$	$a^{s+\alpha}b\,\mathrm{B}\left(s+1,\,\alpha\right)\,{}_4F_3\!\left(\begin{matrix}\dfrac{1}{2},\,\dfrac{1}{2},\,\dfrac{s+1}{2},\,\dfrac{s+2}{2};\,a^2b^2\\\dfrac{3}{2},\,\dfrac{s+\alpha+1}{2},\,\dfrac{s+\alpha+2}{2}\end{matrix}\right)$
		$[a,\,\operatorname{Re}\alpha>0;\ \operatorname{Re}s>-1]$

9	$(a-x)_+^{\alpha-1}\ln\dfrac{1+b\,(a-x)}{1-b\,(a-x)}$	$a^{s+\alpha}b\,\mathrm{B}\left(s,\,\alpha+1\right)\,{}_4F_3\!\left(\begin{matrix}\dfrac{1}{2},\,\dfrac{1}{2},\,\dfrac{\alpha+1}{2},\,\dfrac{\alpha+2}{2};\,a^2b^2\\\dfrac{3}{2},\,\dfrac{s+\alpha+1}{2},\,\dfrac{s+\alpha+2}{2}\end{matrix}\right)$
		$[a,\,\operatorname{Re}s>0;\ \operatorname{Re}\alpha>-1]$

10	$\left(a^2-x^2\right)_+^{\alpha-1}\ln\dfrac{1+bx}{1-bx}$	$\dfrac{a^{s+2\alpha-1}b}{2}\,\mathrm{B}\left(\dfrac{s+1}{2},\,\alpha\right)\,{}_3F_2\!\left(\begin{matrix}\dfrac{1}{2},\,\dfrac{1}{2},\,\dfrac{s+1}{2};\,a^2b^2\\\dfrac{3}{2},\,\dfrac{s+2\alpha+1}{2}\end{matrix}\right)$
		$[a,\,\operatorname{Re}\alpha>0;\ \operatorname{Re}s>-1]$

2.5.4. $\ln(ax^2 + bx + c)$ and algebraic functions

1	$\ln\left(x^2 + 1\right)$	$\dfrac{\pi}{s}\,\csc\dfrac{s\pi}{2}$	$[-2 < \operatorname{Re} s < 0]$
2	$\ln\left[(x-1)^2\right]$	$\dfrac{2\pi}{s}\,\cot\left(s\pi\right)$	$[-1 < \operatorname{Re} s < 0]$
3	$\ln\left(x^2 + 2ax + 1\right)$	$\dfrac{2\pi\cos\left(s\arccos a\right)}{s\sin\left(s\pi\right)}$	$[-1 < a \le 1;\ -1 < \operatorname{Re} s < 0]$

4	$\dfrac{\ln\left(x^2 + a^2\right)}{x + a}$	$\pi a^{s-1}\left\{\dfrac{2}{s}\csc\dfrac{s\pi}{2} - \dfrac{2}{s+1}\sec\dfrac{s\pi}{2} + \left[\ln\left(4a^4\right) - 4\pi\cot\left(s\pi\right)\right]\csc\left(s\pi\right)\right.$
		$\left. + \sec\dfrac{s\pi}{2}\,\Phi\left(-1, 1, \dfrac{s+3}{2}\right) - \csc\dfrac{s\pi}{2}\,\Phi\left(-1, 1, \dfrac{s+2}{2}\right)\right\}$
		$[0 < \operatorname{Re} s < 1;\ \operatorname{Re} a > 0]$

5	$(a - x)_+^{\alpha - 1}\ln\left(bx^2 + 1\right)$	$a^{s+\alpha+1}b\,\mathrm{B}\left(s+2, \alpha\right)\,{}_4F_3\left(\begin{matrix}1, 1, \frac{s+2}{2}, \frac{s+3}{2};\ -a^2 b\\ 2, \frac{s+\alpha+2}{2}, \frac{s+\alpha+3}{2}\end{matrix}\right)$
		$[a,\ \operatorname{Re}\alpha > 0;\ \operatorname{Re} s > -2;\ |\arg b| < \pi]$
6	$(a - x)_+^{\alpha - 1}$ $\times \ln\left[b(a-x)^2 + 1\right]$	$a^{s+\alpha+1}b\,\mathrm{B}\left(s, \alpha+2\right)\,{}_4F_3\left(\begin{matrix}1, 1, \frac{\alpha+2}{2}, \frac{\alpha+3}{2};\ -a^2 b\\ 2, \frac{s+\alpha+2}{2}, \frac{s+\alpha+3}{2}\end{matrix}\right)$
		$[a,\ \operatorname{Re} s > 0;\ \operatorname{Re}\alpha > -2;\ |\arg b| < \pi]$
7	$(a - x)_+^{\alpha - 1}$ $\times \ln\left(bx\left(a - x\right) + 1\right)$	$a^{s+\alpha+1}b\,\mathrm{B}\left(s+1, \alpha+1\right)\,{}_4F_3\left(\begin{matrix}1, 1, s+1, \alpha+1;\ -\frac{a^2 b}{4}\\ 2, \frac{s+\alpha+2}{2}, \frac{s+\alpha+3}{2}\end{matrix}\right)$
		$[a > 0;\ \operatorname{Re} s,\ \operatorname{Re}\alpha > -1;\ |\arg\left(4 + a^2 b\right)| < \pi]$

2.5.5. $\ln\dfrac{ax^2 + bx + c}{dx^2 + ex + f}$ and algebraic functions

1	$\ln\dfrac{x^2 + 2x\cos\theta + 1}{x^2}$	$-2\pi\,\Gamma\left[\begin{matrix}s, -s\\ \frac{\pi+2\theta s}{2\pi}, \frac{\pi-2\theta s}{2\pi}\end{matrix}\right]$ $\qquad [|\theta| < \pi;\ 0 < \operatorname{Re} s < 1]$
2	$\ln\dfrac{(x+a)^2 + c^2}{(x+b)^2 + c^2}$	$\dfrac{2\pi}{s\sin\left(s\pi\right)}\left[\left(a^2 + c^2\right)^{s/2}\cos\left(s\arctan\dfrac{c}{a}\right)\right.$
		$\left. - \left(b^2 + c^2\right)^{s/2}\cos\left(s\arctan\dfrac{c}{b}\right)\right]$ $\quad [a, b, c > 0;\ 0 < \operatorname{Re} s < 1]$
3	$\ln\dfrac{x^2 + 2abx + a^2}{(x+a)^2}$	$\dfrac{2\pi a^s}{s}\csc\left(s\pi\right)\left[\cos\left(s\arccos b\right) - 1\right]$
		$[a > 0;\ -1 < b \le 1;\ |\operatorname{Re} s| < 1]$

No.	$f(x)$	$F(s)$
4	$(a-x)_+^{\alpha-1}$ $\times\ln\dfrac{1+bx(a-x)}{1-bx(a-x)}$	$2a^{s+\alpha+1}b\,\mathrm{B}(s+1,\alpha+1)\ _6F_5\left(\begin{matrix}\frac{1}{2},\,1,\,\Delta(2,\alpha+1),\,\Delta(2,s+1)\\[2pt] \frac{3}{2},\,\Delta(4,s+\alpha+2);\,\frac{a^4b^2}{16}\end{matrix}\right)$ $[a>0;\ \mathrm{Re}\,s,\ \mathrm{Re}\,\alpha>-1]$
5	$\dfrac{1}{(x+a)^\rho}\ln\left[\dfrac{b}{(x+a)^2}+1\right]$	$a^{s-\rho-2}b\,\mathrm{B}(s,\rho-s+2)\ _4F_3\left(\begin{matrix}1,\,1,\,\frac{\rho-s+2}{2},\,\frac{\rho-s+3}{2}\\[2pt] 2,\,\frac{\rho+2}{2},\,\frac{\rho+3}{2};\,-\frac{b}{a^2}\end{matrix}\right)$ $[0<\mathrm{Re}\,s<\mathrm{Re}\,\rho+2;\ |\arg a|,\,|\arg b|<\pi]$
6	$\dfrac{1}{(x+a)^\rho}\ln\left[\dfrac{bx^2}{(x+a)^2}+1\right]$	$a^{s-\rho}b\,\mathrm{B}(s+2,\rho-s)\ _4F_3\left(\begin{matrix}1,\,1,\,\frac{s+2}{2},\,\frac{s+3}{2}\\[2pt] 2,\,\frac{\rho+2}{2},\,\frac{\rho+3}{2};\,-b\end{matrix}\right)$ $[-2<\mathrm{Re}\,s<\mathrm{Re}\,\rho;\ |\arg a|,\,|\arg b|<\pi]$

2.5.6. $\ln(\varphi(x))$ and algebraic functions

No.	$f(x)$	$F(s)$	
1	$\ln\dfrac{\sqrt{x+a}\pm\sqrt{a}}{\sqrt{x}}$	$\pm\dfrac{a^s}{2\sqrt{\pi}\,s}\,\Gamma(s)\,\Gamma\left(\dfrac{1}{2}-s\right)$	$[0<\mathrm{Re}\,s<1/2;\ |\arg a|<\pi]$
2	$\ln\dfrac{\sqrt{x+a}\pm\sqrt{x}}{\sqrt{a}}$	$\mp\dfrac{a^s}{2\sqrt{\pi}\,s}\,\Gamma(-s)\,\Gamma\left(s+\dfrac{1}{2}\right)$	$[-1/2<\mathrm{Re}\,s<0;\ |\arg a|<\pi]$
3	$\theta(a-x)\ln\dfrac{\sqrt{a-x}+\sqrt{a}}{2\sqrt{a}}$	$\dfrac{\sqrt{\pi}a^s}{2s}\,\Gamma\left[\begin{matrix}s\\ \frac{2s+1}{2}\end{matrix}\right]-\dfrac{a^s}{s^2}\left(s\ln 2+\dfrac{1}{2}\right)$	$[a,\ \mathrm{Re}\,s>0]$
4	$\dfrac{1}{\sqrt{x+a}}\ln\dfrac{\sqrt{x+a}\pm\sqrt{x}}{\sqrt{a}}$	$\pm\dfrac{\pi^{3/2}a^{s-1/2}}{2}\,\sec(s\pi)\,\Gamma\left[\begin{matrix}\frac{1-2s}{2}\\ 1-s\end{matrix}\right]$	$[|\mathrm{Re}\,s|<1/2;\ |\arg a|<\pi]$
5	$\dfrac{1}{\sqrt{x+a}}\ln\dfrac{\sqrt{x+a}\pm\sqrt{a}}{\sqrt{x}}$	$\pm\dfrac{\pi^{3/2}a^{s-1/2}}{2}\,\csc(s\pi)\,\Gamma\left[\begin{matrix}s\\ \frac{2s+1}{2}\end{matrix}\right]$	$[0<\mathrm{Re}\,s<1;\ |\arg a|<\pi]$
6	$\dfrac{\ln(\sqrt{x+a}\pm\sqrt{a})}{\sqrt{x+a}}$	$2^{2s-1}a^{s-1/2}\,\mathrm{B}(s,1-2s)\left[\psi(1-s)-\psi\left(\dfrac{1-2s}{2}\right)+\ln a\right.$ $\left.-\left\{\begin{matrix}0\\ 2\pi\cot(s\pi)\end{matrix}\right\}\right]$	$[0<\mathrm{Re}\,s<1/2;\ |\arg a|<\pi]$
7	$\dfrac{\ln(\sqrt{x+a}\pm\sqrt{x})}{\sqrt{x+a}}$	$2^{-2s}a^{s-1/2}\,\mathrm{B}\left(2s,\dfrac{1-2s}{2}\right)[\ln a\pm\pi\tan(s\pi)]$ $\left[\begin{matrix}(0<\mathrm{Re}\,s<1/2;\ |\arg a|<\pi;\ a\neq1)\ \text{or}\\ (|\mathrm{Re}\,s|<1/2\ \text{for}\ a=1)\end{matrix}\right]$	
8	$\dfrac{1}{(x+a)^\rho}\ln\dfrac{\sqrt{x+a}+b}{\sqrt{x+a}-b}$	$2a^{s-\rho-1/2}b\,\mathrm{B}\left(s,\rho-s+\tfrac{1}{2}\right)\ _3F_2\left(\begin{matrix}\frac{1}{2},\,1,\,\rho-s+\frac{1}{2}\\ \frac{3}{2},\,\rho+\frac{1}{2};\,\frac{b^2}{a}\end{matrix}\right)$ $\left[0<\mathrm{Re}\,s<\mathrm{Re}\,\rho+1/2;\ |\arg(1-b^2/a)|<\pi\right]$	

No.	$f(x)$	$F(s)$
9	$\left(\sqrt{x+a}\pm\sqrt{x}\right)^{\rho}$ $\times\ln\left(\sqrt{x+a}\pm\sqrt{x}\right)$	$\mp\dfrac{2^{-2s}\rho a^{s+\rho/2}}{2s\mp\rho}\,\mathrm{B}\left(2s,\dfrac{\mp\rho-2s}{2}\right)$ $\times\left[\ln a\mp\psi\left(\dfrac{\mp\rho-2s}{2}\right)\pm\psi\left(\dfrac{2s\mp\rho+2}{2}\right)+\dfrac{2}{\rho}\right]$ $\left[\begin{array}{l}0<\operatorname{Re}s<\mp\operatorname{Re}\rho/2;\\ (\operatorname{Re}s>-1/2\text{ for }a=1);\ \left|\arg a\right|<\pi\end{array}\right]$
10	$\dfrac{\left(\sqrt{x+a}\pm\sqrt{x}\right)^{\rho}}{\sqrt{x+a}}$ $\times\ln\left(\sqrt{x+a}\pm\sqrt{x}\right)$	$2^{-2s}a^{s+(\rho-1)/2}\,\mathrm{B}\left(2s,\dfrac{1\mp\rho-2s}{2}\right)$ $\times\left[\ln a\mp\psi\left(\dfrac{1\mp\rho-2s}{2}\right)\pm\psi\left(\dfrac{1\mp\rho+2s}{2}\right)\right]$ $\left[\begin{array}{l}0<\operatorname{Re}s<1\mp\operatorname{Re}\rho/2;\\ (\operatorname{Re}s>-1\text{ for }a=1);\ \left|\arg a\right|<\pi\end{array}\right]$
11	$\theta(x-a)\ln\dfrac{\sqrt{x-a}+\sqrt{x}}{\sqrt{a}}$	$-\dfrac{\sqrt{\pi}a^{s}}{2s}\,\Gamma\left[\begin{array}{c}-s\\ \frac{1}{2}-s\end{array}\right]$ $\qquad [a>0;\ \operatorname{Re}s<0]$
12	$\theta(a-x)\ln\dfrac{\sqrt{a-x}+\sqrt{a}}{\sqrt{x}}$	$\dfrac{\sqrt{\pi}a^{s}}{2s}\,\Gamma\left[\begin{array}{c}s\\ s+\frac{1}{2}\end{array}\right]$ $\qquad [a,\ \operatorname{Re}s>0]$
13	$\theta(x-a)\ln\dfrac{\sqrt{x-a}+\sqrt{x}}{\sqrt{x}}$	$-\dfrac{a^{s}}{2s^{2}}-\dfrac{\sqrt{\pi}\,a^{s}}{2s}\,\Gamma\left[\begin{array}{c}-s\\ \frac{1}{2}-s\end{array}\right]$ $\qquad [a>0;\ \operatorname{Re}s<0]$
14	$\theta(a-x)\ln\dfrac{\sqrt{a}+\sqrt{a-x}}{\sqrt{a}-\sqrt{a-x}}$	$\dfrac{\sqrt{\pi}a^{s}}{s}\,\Gamma\left[\begin{array}{c}s\\ s+\frac{1}{2}\end{array}\right]$ $\qquad [a,\ \operatorname{Re}s>0]$
15	$\theta(x-a)\ln\dfrac{\sqrt{x}+\sqrt{x-a}}{\sqrt{x}-\sqrt{x-a}}$	$-\dfrac{\sqrt{\pi}a^{s}}{s}\,\Gamma\left[\begin{array}{c}-s\\ \frac{1}{2}-s\end{array}\right]$ $\qquad [a>0;\ \operatorname{Re}s<0]$
16	$(a-x)_{+}^{\alpha-1}\ln\dfrac{1+b\sqrt{a-x}}{1-b\sqrt{a-x}}$	$a^{s+\alpha-1/2}b\,\mathrm{B}\left(s,\dfrac{2\alpha+1}{2}\right)\,_3F_2\left(\begin{array}{c}\frac{1}{2},\,\frac{1}{2},\,\frac{2\alpha+1}{2};\,ab^{2}\\ \frac{3}{2},\,\frac{2s+2\alpha+1}{2}\end{array}\right)$ $\left[a,\ \operatorname{Re}s>0;\ \operatorname{Re}\alpha>-1/2;\ \left|\arg\left(1-ab^{2}\right)\right|<\pi\right]$
17	$\theta(a-x)(bx+1)^{\nu}$ $\times\ln\dfrac{\sqrt{a}+\sqrt{a-x}}{\sqrt{x}}$	$\dfrac{\sqrt{\pi}\,a^{s}}{2s}\,\Gamma\left[\begin{array}{c}s\\ \frac{2s+1}{2}\end{array}\right]\,_3F_2\left(\begin{array}{c}-\nu,\,s,\,s;\,-ab\\ \frac{2s+1}{2},\,s+1\end{array}\right)$ $\left[a,\ \operatorname{Re}s>0;\ \left|\arg\left(1+ab\right)\right|<\pi\right]$
18	$\theta(a-x)(bx+1)^{\alpha}\ln\big(c\sqrt{a-x}$ $+\sqrt{c^{2}(a-x)+1}\big)$	$\dfrac{\sqrt{\pi}\,a^{s+1/2}c}{2}\,\Gamma\left[\begin{array}{c}s\\ \frac{2s+3}{2}\end{array}\right]F_3\left(-\alpha,\,\dfrac{1}{2},\,s,\,\dfrac{1}{2};\,\dfrac{2s+3}{2};\,-ab,\,-ac^{2}\right)$ $\left[a,\ \operatorname{Re}s>0;\ \left|\arg b\right|,\ \left|\arg\left(1+ac^{2}\right)\right|<\pi\right].$

No.	$f(x)$	$F(s)$
19	$\theta(a-x)(bx+1)^{\alpha}$ $\times \ln\dfrac{c+\sqrt{a-x}}{c-\sqrt{a-x}}$	$\dfrac{\sqrt{\pi}\,a^{s+1/2}}{c}\,\Gamma\!\left[\begin{matrix}s\\\frac{2s+3}{2}\end{matrix}\right]F_3\!\left(-\alpha,\frac{1}{2},s,1;\frac{2s+3}{2};-ab,\frac{a}{c^2}\right)$ $\qquad\qquad\left[a,\ \mathrm{Re}\,s>0;\ |\arg b|,\ |\arg(1-a/c^2)|<\pi\right]$
20	$\theta(a-x)\ln\dfrac{\sqrt{b-x}+c\sqrt{a-x}}{\sqrt{b-x}-c\sqrt{a-x}}$	$a^{s+1/2}\sqrt{\dfrac{\pi}{b}}\,c\,\Gamma\!\left[\begin{matrix}s\\\frac{2s+3}{2}\end{matrix}\right]F_1\!\left(\frac{1}{2},s,1;\frac{2s+3}{2};\frac{a}{b},\frac{ac^2}{b}\right)$ $\qquad\qquad\left[a,\ \mathrm{Re}\,s>0;\ |\arg(1-a/b)|,\ |\arg(1-ac^2/b)|<\pi\right]$
21	$\theta(a-x)\ln\!\left(c\sqrt{\dfrac{a-x}{b-x}}\right.$ $\left.+\sqrt{\dfrac{c^2(a-x)}{b-x}+1}\right)$	$\dfrac{1}{2}\,a^{s+1/2}\sqrt{\dfrac{\pi}{b}}\,c\,\Gamma\!\left[\begin{matrix}s\\\frac{2s+3}{2}\end{matrix}\right]F_1\!\left(\frac{1}{2},s,\frac{1}{2};\frac{2s+3}{2};\frac{a}{b},-\frac{ac^2}{b}\right)$ $\qquad\qquad\left[a,\ \mathrm{Re}\,s>0;\ |\arg(1-a/b)|,\ |\arg(1+ac^2/b)|<\pi\right]$
22	$\theta(a-x)\ln\!\left(a+\sqrt{a^2-x^2}\right)$	$\dfrac{a^s}{s}\left[\dfrac{\sqrt{\pi}}{2}\Gamma\!\left[\begin{matrix}\frac{s}{2}\\\frac{s+1}{2}\end{matrix}\right]-\dfrac{1}{s}+\ln a\right]$ $\qquad\qquad[a,\ \mathrm{Re}\,s>0]$
23	$\ln\dfrac{\sqrt{a^2+x^2}+a}{2a}$	$\dfrac{a^s}{2\sqrt{\pi}\,s}\,\Gamma\!\left(\dfrac{1-s}{2}\right)\Gamma\!\left(\dfrac{s}{2}\right)$ $\qquad[\mathrm{Re}\,a>0;\ -2<\mathrm{Re}\,s<0]$
24	$\ln\dfrac{\sqrt{x^2+a^2}+x}{a}$	$-\dfrac{a^s}{2s}\,\mathrm{B}\!\left(\dfrac{s+1}{2},-\dfrac{s}{2}\right)$ $\qquad[\mathrm{Re}\,a>0;\ -1<\mathrm{Re}\,s<0]$
25	$\theta(x-a)\ln\dfrac{\sqrt{x}+\sqrt{x-a}}{\sqrt{x}-\sqrt{x-a}}$	$\sqrt{\pi}\,a^s\,\Gamma\!\left[\begin{matrix}-s,\,-s\\\frac{1}{2}-s,\,1-s\end{matrix}\right]$ $\qquad[a>0;\ \mathrm{Re}\,s<0]$
26	$\theta(a-x)\ln\dfrac{\sqrt{a^2-x^2}+a}{x}$	$\dfrac{\sqrt{\pi}\,a^s}{2s}\,\Gamma\!\left[\begin{matrix}\frac{s}{2}\\\frac{s+1}{2}\end{matrix}\right]$ $\qquad[a,\ \mathrm{Re}\,s>0]$
27	$\theta(x-a)\ln\dfrac{\sqrt{x^2-a^2}+x}{a}$	$-\dfrac{\sqrt{\pi}\,a^s}{2s}\,\Gamma\!\left[\begin{matrix}-\frac{s}{2}\\\frac{1-s}{2}\end{matrix}\right]$ $\qquad[a>0;\ \mathrm{Re}\,s<0]$
28	$\ln\dfrac{\sqrt{x^2+a^2}+x}{2x}$	$-\dfrac{a^s}{2\sqrt{\pi}\,s}\,\Gamma\!\left(-\dfrac{s}{2}\right)\Gamma\!\left(\dfrac{s+1}{2}\right)$ $\qquad[\mathrm{Re}\,a>0;\ 0<\mathrm{Re}\,s<2]$
29	$\dfrac{\ln\!\left(\sqrt{x^2+a^2}\pm x\right)}{\sqrt{x^2+a^2}}$	$2^{-s}a^{s-1}\mathrm{B}\!\left(s,\dfrac{1-s}{2}\right)\left(\ln a\pm\dfrac{\pi}{2}\tan\dfrac{s\pi}{2}\right)$ $\qquad\qquad[\mathrm{Re}\,a>0;\ 0<\mathrm{Re}\,s<1]$
30	$\left(\sqrt{x^2+a^2}+x\right)^{\alpha}$ $\times \ln\!\left(\sqrt{x^2+a^2}+x\right)$	$\dfrac{2^{-s}a^{s+\alpha}}{s-\alpha}\,\mathrm{B}\!\left(s,-\dfrac{s+\alpha}{2}\right)\left[\dfrac{\alpha}{2}\,\psi\!\left(-\dfrac{s+\alpha}{2}\right)\right.$ $\left.-\dfrac{\alpha}{2}\,\psi\!\left(\dfrac{s-\alpha+2}{2}\right)-\alpha\ln a-1\right]$ $\qquad\left[\begin{matrix}\mathrm{Re}\,a>0;\ 0<\mathrm{Re}\,s<-\mathrm{Re}\,\alpha\\(\mathrm{Re}\,s>-1\ \text{for}\ a=1)\end{matrix}\right]$

No.	$f(x)$	$F(s)$
31	$(a-x)_+^{\alpha-1}\ln\dfrac{b+\sqrt{x(a-x)}}{b-\sqrt{x(a-x)}}$	$\dfrac{2a^{s+\alpha}}{b}\,\mathrm{B}\left(\dfrac{2\alpha+1}{2},\dfrac{2s+1}{2}\right)\,{}_4F_3\left(\begin{matrix}\frac{1}{2},\,1,\,\frac{2\alpha+1}{2},\,\frac{2s+1}{2};\,\frac{a^2}{4b^2}\\ \frac{3}{2},\,\frac{s+\alpha+1}{2},\,\frac{s+\alpha+2}{2}\end{matrix}\right)$ $[a>0;\ \mathrm{Re}\,s,\ \mathrm{Re}\,\alpha>-1;\ |\arg(1-a^2/(4b^2))|<\pi]$
32	$(a-x)_+^{\alpha-1}\ln\Big[bx(a-x)$ $\qquad+\sqrt{b^2x^2(a-x)^2+1}\,\Big]$	$a^{s+\alpha+1}b\,\mathrm{B}(s+1,\alpha+1)$ $\times{}_6F_5\left(\begin{matrix}\frac{1}{2},\,\frac{1}{2},\,\Delta(2,\alpha+1),\,\Delta(2,s+1)\\ \frac{3}{2},\,\Delta(4,s+\alpha+2);\,-\frac{a^4b^2}{16}\end{matrix}\right)$ $[a>0;\ \mathrm{Re}\,s,\ \mathrm{Re}\,\alpha>-1;\ |\arg(1+a^4b^2/16)|<\pi]$
33	$(a-x)_+^{\alpha-1}\ln\big(b\sqrt{a-x}$ $\qquad+\sqrt{b^2(a-x)+1}\,\big)$	$a^{\alpha+s-1/2}b\,\mathrm{B}\left(s,\dfrac{2\alpha+1}{2}\right)\,{}_3F_2\left(\begin{matrix}\frac{1}{2},\,\frac{1}{2},\,\frac{2\alpha+1}{2};\,-ab^2\\ \frac{3}{2},\,\frac{2s+2\alpha+1}{2}\end{matrix}\right)$ $[a,\ \mathrm{Re}\,s>0;\ \mathrm{Re}\,\alpha>-1/2;\ |\arg(1+ab^2)|<\pi]$
34	$(a-x)_+^{\alpha-1}$ $\qquad\times\ln\left(bx+\sqrt{b^2x^2+1}\right)$	$a^{\alpha+s}b\,\mathrm{B}(s+1,\alpha)\,{}_4F_3\left(\begin{matrix}\frac{1}{2},\,\frac{1}{2},\,\frac{s+1}{2},\,\frac{s+2}{2};\,-a^2b^2\\ \frac{3}{2},\,\frac{s+\alpha+1}{2},\,\frac{s+\alpha+2}{2}\end{matrix}\right)$ $[a,\ \mathrm{Re}\,\alpha>0;\ \mathrm{Re}\,s>-1;\ |\arg(1+a^2b^2)|<\pi]$
35	$(a-x)_+^{\alpha-1}\ln\big[b(a-x)$ $\qquad+\sqrt{b^2(a-x)^2+1}\,\big]$	$a^{\alpha+s}b\,\mathrm{B}(s,\alpha+1)\,{}_4F_3\left(\begin{matrix}\frac{1}{2},\,\frac{1}{2},\,\frac{\alpha+1}{2},\,\frac{\alpha+2}{2};\,-a^2b^2\\ \frac{3}{2},\,\frac{s+\alpha+1}{2},\,\frac{s+\alpha+2}{2}\end{matrix}\right)$ $[a,\ \mathrm{Re}\,s>0;\ \mathrm{Re}\,\alpha>-1;\ |\arg(1+a^2b^2)|<\pi]$
36	$(a^2-x^2)_+^{\alpha-1}$ $\qquad\times\ln\left(bx+\sqrt{b^2x^2+1}\right)$	$\dfrac{a^{2\alpha+s-1}b}{2}\,\mathrm{B}\left(\dfrac{s+1}{2},\alpha\right)\,{}_3F_2\left(\begin{matrix}\frac{1}{2},\,\frac{1}{2},\,\frac{s+1}{2};\,-a^2b^2\\ \frac{3}{2},\,\frac{s+2\alpha+1}{2}\end{matrix}\right)$ $[a,\ \mathrm{Re}\,\alpha>0;\ \mathrm{Re}\,s>-1;\ |\arg(1+a^2b^2)|<\pi]$
37	$\theta(x-a)$ $\qquad\times\ln\dfrac{cx+\sqrt{x^2+c^2x^2-b^2}}{\sqrt{x^2-b^2}}$	$-\dfrac{a^sc}{s}\,F_2\left(\dfrac{1}{2},\dfrac{1}{2},-\dfrac{s}{2};\dfrac{3}{2},\dfrac{2-s}{2};-c^2,\dfrac{b^2}{a^2}\right)$ $\left[\begin{matrix}a>0;\ \mathrm{Re}\,s<0;\\ |\arg(1-b^2/a^2)|,\ |\arg(1+c^2)|<\pi\end{matrix}\right]$
38	$\theta(a-x)\ln\dfrac{a+\sqrt{a^2-x^2}}{a-\sqrt{a^2-x^2}}$	$\dfrac{\sqrt{\pi}\,a^s}{s}\,\Gamma\left[\begin{matrix}\frac{s}{2}\\ \frac{s+1}{2}\end{matrix}\right]$ $[a,\ \mathrm{Re}\,s>0]$
39	$\theta(x-a)\ln\dfrac{x+\sqrt{x^2-a^2}}{x-\sqrt{x^2-a^2}}$	$-\dfrac{\sqrt{\pi}}{s}\,a^s\,\Gamma\left[\begin{matrix}-\frac{s}{2}\\ \frac{1-s}{2}\end{matrix}\right]$ $[a>0;\ \mathrm{Re}\,s<0]$
40	$\dfrac{1}{\sqrt{a+x}}\ln\dfrac{x-(b-c)^2x+a}{x-(b+c)^2x+a}$	$\dfrac{4bc}{a^{1/2-s}}\,\mathrm{B}\left(s+1,\dfrac{1}{2}-s\right)F_4\left(1,s+1;\dfrac{3}{2},\dfrac{3}{2};b^2,c^2\right)$ $[-1<\mathrm{Re}\,s<1/2;\ |\arg a|,\ |\arg b|,\ |\arg c|<\pi]$

2.5.7. $\ln(\varphi(x))$ and the exponential function

1	$e^{-ax}\ln x$	$a^{-s}\,\Gamma(s)\,[\psi(s)-\ln a]$ $\qquad$ [Re a, Re $s>0$]
2	$\theta(a-x)\,e^{bx}\ln(1+c(a-x))$	$\dfrac{a^{s+1}c}{s(s+1)}\,\Xi_1(1,\,s,\,1;\,s+2;\,-ac,\,ab)$ $\qquad$ [a, Re $s>0$; $|\arg(ac+1)|<\pi$]
3	$\theta(a-x)\,e^{bx}\ln\dfrac{\sqrt{a}+\sqrt{a-x}}{\sqrt{x}}$	$\dfrac{a^s\sqrt{\pi}}{2s}\,\Gamma\!\left[\begin{matrix}s\\\frac{2s+1}{2}\end{matrix}\right]\,{}_2F_2\!\left(\begin{matrix}s,\,s;\,ab\\\frac{2s+1}{2},\,s+1\end{matrix}\right)$ $\qquad$ [a, Re $s>0$]
4	$\theta(a-x)\,e^{bx^2}\ln\dfrac{\sqrt{a}+\sqrt{a-x}}{\sqrt{x}}$	$\dfrac{\sqrt{\pi}\,a^s}{2s}\,\Gamma\!\left[\begin{matrix}s\\\frac{2s+1}{2}\end{matrix}\right]\,{}_3F_3\!\left(\begin{matrix}\frac{s}{2},\,\frac{s}{2},\,\frac{s+1}{2};\,a^2b\\\frac{2s+1}{4},\,\frac{2s+3}{4},\,\frac{s+2}{2}\end{matrix}\right)$ $\qquad$ [a, Re $s>0$]
5	$\theta(a-x)\,e^{bx}\ln\dfrac{1+c\sqrt{a-x}}{1-c\sqrt{a-x}}$	$\sqrt{\pi}\,a^{s+1/2}c\,\Gamma\!\left[\begin{matrix}s\\\frac{2s+3}{2}\end{matrix}\right]\,\Xi_1\!\left(\dfrac{1}{2},\,s,\,1;\,s+\dfrac{3}{2};\,ac^2,\,ab\right)$ $\qquad$ [a, Re $s>0$; $|ac^2|<1$]
6	$\dfrac{\ln x}{e^x+1}$	$\Gamma(s)\left\{\left[2^{1-s}\ln 2+\left(1-2^{1-s}\right)\psi(s)\right]\zeta(s)\right.$ $\left.+\left(1-2^{1-s}\right)\zeta'(s)\right\}$ $\qquad$ [Re $s>0$]
7	$\ln\left(1+e^{-ax}\right)$	$\dfrac{1-2^{-s}}{a^s}\,\Gamma(s)\,\zeta(s+1)$ $\qquad$ [Re a, Re $s>0$]
8	$\ln\left(1-e^{-ax}\right)$	$-\dfrac{\Gamma(s)}{a^s}\,\zeta(s+1)$ $\qquad$ [Re a, Re $s>0$]

2.5.8. The logarithmic and hyperbolic or trigonometric functions

Notation: $\delta=\left\{\begin{matrix}1\\0\end{matrix}\right\}$.

1	$\ln\tanh(ax)$	$\dfrac{2^{-s}-2}{(2a)^s}\,\Gamma(s)\,\zeta(s+1)$ $\qquad$ [a, Re $s>0$]
2	$\theta(1-x)\left\{\begin{matrix}\sin(ax)\\\cos(ax)\end{matrix}\right\}\ln^n x$	$\dfrac{(-1)^n n!a^\delta}{(s+\delta)^{n+1}}\,{}_{n+1}F_{n+2}\!\left(\begin{matrix}\frac{s+\delta}{2},\,\frac{s+\delta}{2},\,\ldots,\,\frac{s+\delta}{2};\,-\frac{a^2}{4}\\\delta+\frac{1}{2},\,\frac{s+\delta+2}{2},\,\frac{s+\delta+2}{2},\,\ldots,\,\frac{s+\delta+2}{2}\end{matrix}\right)$ $\qquad$ [$a>0$; Re $s>-\delta$]
3	$\left\{\begin{matrix}\sin(ax)\\\cos(ax)\end{matrix}\right\}\ln x$	$\dfrac{\Gamma(s)}{a^s}\left\{\begin{matrix}\sin(s\pi/2)\\\cos(s\pi/2)\end{matrix}\right\}\left[\psi(s)-\ln a\pm\dfrac{\pi}{2}\tan^{\mp1}\dfrac{s\pi}{2}\right]$ $\qquad$ [$a>0$; $-(1\pm1)/2<$ Re $s<1$]

No.	$f(x)$	$F(s)$
4	$e^{-ax}\sin(bx)\ln x$	$\dfrac{\Gamma(s)}{(a^2+b^2)^{s/2}}\sin\left(s\arctan\dfrac{b}{a}\right)\left[\psi(s)-\dfrac{1}{2}\ln(a^2+b^2)\right.$ $\left.+\arctan\dfrac{b}{a}\cot\left(s\arctan\dfrac{b}{a}\right)\right]$ $\qquad[\operatorname{Re}a>|\operatorname{Im}b|;\ \operatorname{Re}s>-1]$
5	$e^{-ax}\cos(bx)\ln x$	$\dfrac{\Gamma(s)}{(a^2+b^2)^{s/2}}\cos\left(s\arctan\dfrac{b}{a}\right)\left[\psi(s)-\dfrac{1}{2}\ln(a^2+b^2)\right.$ $\left.-\arctan\dfrac{b}{a}\tan\left(s\arctan\dfrac{b}{a}\right)\right]$ $\qquad[\operatorname{Re}a>|\operatorname{Im}b|;\ \operatorname{Re}s>0]$
6	$\theta(a-x)\begin{Bmatrix}\sinh(bx)\\\cosh(bx)\end{Bmatrix}$ $\times\ln\dfrac{\sqrt{a}+\sqrt{a-x}}{\sqrt{x}}$	$\dfrac{\sqrt{\pi}\,a^{s+\delta}b^{\delta}}{2(s+\delta)}\Gamma\left[\begin{matrix}s+\delta\\\frac{2s+2\delta+1}{2}\end{matrix}\right]\,{}_3F_4\left(\begin{matrix}\frac{s+\delta}{2},\ \frac{s+\delta}{2},\ \frac{s+\delta+1}{2};\ \frac{a^2b^2}{4}\\\frac{2\delta+1}{2},\ \frac{2s+2\delta+1}{4},\ \frac{2s+2\delta+3}{4},\ \frac{s+\delta+2}{2}\end{matrix}\right)$ $\qquad[a>0;\ \operatorname{Re}s>-\delta]$
7	$\theta(a-x)\begin{Bmatrix}\sin(bx)\\\cos(bx)\end{Bmatrix}$ $\times\ln\dfrac{\sqrt{a}+\sqrt{a-x}}{\sqrt{x}}$	$\dfrac{\sqrt{\pi}\,a^{s+\delta}b^{\delta}}{2(s+\delta)}\Gamma\left[\begin{matrix}s+\delta\\\frac{2s+2\delta+1}{2}\end{matrix}\right]\,{}_3F_4\left(\begin{matrix}\frac{s+\delta}{2},\ \frac{s+\delta}{2},\ \frac{s+\delta+1}{2};\ -\frac{a^2b^2}{4}\\\frac{2\delta+1}{2},\ \frac{2s+2\delta+1}{4},\ \frac{2s+2\delta+3}{4},\ \frac{s+\delta+2}{2}\end{matrix}\right)$ $\qquad[a>0;\ \operatorname{Re}s>-\delta]$
8	$\theta(a-x)\begin{Bmatrix}\sin(bx)\\\cos(bx)\end{Bmatrix}$ $\times\ln\dfrac{a+\sqrt{a^2-x^2}}{x}$	$\dfrac{\sqrt{\pi}\,a^{s+\delta}b^{\delta}}{2(s+\delta)}\Gamma\left[\begin{matrix}\frac{s+\delta}{2}\\\frac{s+\delta+1}{2}\end{matrix}\right]\,{}_2F_3\left(\begin{matrix}\frac{s+\delta}{2},\ \frac{s+\delta}{2};\ -\frac{a^2b^2}{4}\\\frac{2\delta+1}{2},\ \frac{s+\delta+1}{2},\ \frac{s+\delta+2}{2}\end{matrix}\right)$ $\qquad[a>0;\ \operatorname{Re}s>-\delta]$
9	$\theta(a-x)$ $\times\begin{Bmatrix}\sinh(bx)\sin(bx)\\\cosh(bx)\cos(bx)\end{Bmatrix}$ $\times\ln\dfrac{\sqrt{a}+\sqrt{a-x}}{\sqrt{x}}$	$\dfrac{\sqrt{\pi}\,a^{s+2\delta}b^{2\delta}}{2(s+2\delta)}\Gamma\left[\begin{matrix}s+2\delta\\\frac{2s+4\delta+1}{2}\end{matrix}\right]$ $\times\,{}_5F_8\left(\begin{matrix}\frac{s+2\delta}{4},\ \Delta(4,\ s+2\delta);\ -\frac{a^4b^4}{64}\\\frac{2\delta+1}{4},\ \frac{2\delta+3}{4},\ \frac{2\delta+1}{2},\ \Delta\left(4,\ \frac{2s+4\delta+1}{2}\right),\ \frac{s+2\delta+4}{4}\end{matrix}\right)$ $\qquad[a>0;\ \operatorname{Re}s>-2\delta-1]$
10	$\theta(a-x)$ $\times\begin{Bmatrix}\sinh(bx)\sin(bx)\\\cosh(bx)\cos(bx)\end{Bmatrix}$ $\times\ln\dfrac{a^2+\sqrt{a^4-x^4}}{x^2}$	$\dfrac{\sqrt{\pi}\,a^{s+2\delta}b^{2\delta}}{2(s+2\delta)}\Gamma\left[\begin{matrix}\frac{s+2\delta}{4}\\\frac{s+2\delta+2}{4}\end{matrix}\right]$ $\times\,{}_2F_5\left(\begin{matrix}\frac{s+2\delta}{4},\ \frac{s+2\delta}{4};\ -\frac{a^4b^4}{64}\\\frac{2\delta+1}{4},\ \frac{2\delta+3}{4},\ \frac{2\delta+1}{2},\ \frac{s+2\delta+2}{4},\ \frac{s+2\delta+4}{4}\end{matrix}\right)$ $\qquad[a>0;\ \operatorname{Re}s>-2\delta]$

No.	$f(x)$	$F(s)$
11	$\theta(a-x)$ $\times \left\{ \begin{array}{l} \sinh(bx)\cos(bx) \\ \cosh(bx)\sin(bx) \end{array} \right\}$ $\times \ln \dfrac{\sqrt{a}+\sqrt{a-x}}{\sqrt{x}}$	$\dfrac{\sqrt{\pi}\,a^{s+1}b}{2(s+1)}\Gamma\left[\begin{array}{c} s+1 \\ \frac{2s+3}{2} \end{array}\right] {}_5F_8\left(\begin{array}{c} \frac{s+1}{4},\ \frac{s+1}{4},\ \frac{s+2}{4},\ \frac{s+3}{4},\ \frac{s+4}{4};\ -\frac{a^4b^4}{64} \\ \frac{1}{2},\ \frac{3}{4},\ \frac{5}{4},\ \frac{2s+3}{8},\ \frac{2s+5}{8},\ \frac{2s+7}{8},\ \frac{2s+9}{8},\ \frac{s+5}{4} \end{array}\right)$ $\mp \dfrac{\sqrt{\pi}\,a^{s+3}b^3}{6(s+3)}\Gamma\left[\begin{array}{c} s+3 \\ \frac{2s+7}{2} \end{array}\right]$ $\times {}_5F_8\left(\begin{array}{c} \frac{s+3}{4},\ \frac{s+3}{4},\ \frac{s+4}{4},\ \frac{s+5}{4},\ \frac{s+6}{4};\ -\frac{a^4b^4}{64} \\ \frac{5}{4},\ \frac{3}{2},\ \frac{7}{4},\ \frac{2s+7}{8},\ \frac{2s+9}{8},\ \frac{2s+11}{8},\ \frac{2s+13}{8},\ \frac{s+7}{4} \end{array}\right)$ $[a>0;\ \mathrm{Re}\,s>-1]$
12	$e^{-x}\sin(a\ln x)$	$-i\,\Gamma(s+ia)\sinh\ln\dfrac{\Gamma(s+ia)}{|\Gamma(s+ia)|}$ $\qquad [\mathrm{Re}\,s>|\mathrm{Im}\,a|]$
13	$e^{-x}\cos(a\ln x)$	$\Gamma(s+ia)\cosh\ln\dfrac{\Gamma(s+ia)}{|\Gamma(s+ia)|}$ $\qquad [\mathrm{Re}\,s>|\mathrm{Im}\,a|]$
14	$\theta(1-x)\left\{ \begin{array}{l} \sin(a\ln x) \\ \cos(a\ln x) \end{array} \right\}$	$\mp \dfrac{1}{s^2+a^2}\left\{ \begin{array}{l} a \\ s \end{array} \right\}$ $\qquad [\mathrm{Re}\,s>0]$
15	$\theta(a-x)\sin\left(b\ln\dfrac{x}{a}\right)$	$-\dfrac{a^s b}{s^2+b^2}$ $\qquad [a>0;\ \mathrm{Re}\,s>|\mathrm{Im}\,b|]$
16	$\theta(x-a)\sin\left(b\ln\dfrac{x}{a}\right)$	$\dfrac{a^s b}{s^2+b^2}$ $\qquad [a>0;\ \mathrm{Re}\,s<-|\mathrm{Im}\,b|]$

2.5.9. Products of logarithms

No.	$f(x)$	$F(s)$
1	$\ln x\ln(x^2+1)$	$-\dfrac{\pi}{2s^2}\csc\dfrac{s\pi}{2}\left(\pi s\cot\dfrac{s\pi}{2}+2\right)$ $\qquad [-2<\mathrm{Re}\,s<0]$
2	$\ln^2 x\ln(x^2+1)$	$\dfrac{\pi}{8s^3}\csc^3\dfrac{s\pi}{2}\left[3\pi^2s^2+\left(\pi^2s^2-8\right)\cos(s\pi)+4\pi s\sin(s\pi)+8\right]$ $\qquad [-2<\mathrm{Re}\,s<0]$
3	$\theta(a-x)\ln^2(a-x)$	$\dfrac{a^s}{s}\left\{ [\psi(s+1)-\ln a+\mathbf{C}]^2-\psi'(s+1)+\dfrac{\pi^2}{6} \right\}$ $\qquad [a,\ \mathrm{Re}\,s>0;\ \mathrm{Re}\,s>-2 \text{ for } a=1]$
4	$\theta(x-a)\ln^2(x-a)$	$-\dfrac{a^s}{s}\left\{ [\psi(-s)-\ln a+\mathbf{C}]^2+\psi'(-s)+\dfrac{\pi^2}{6} \right\}$ $\quad [a>0;\ \mathrm{Re}\,s<0]$
5	$\theta(a-x)\ln^n(a-x)$	$a^s\dfrac{\partial^n}{\partial\beta^n}\left[a^\beta\,\mathrm{B}(\beta+1,s)\right]\Big|_{\beta=0}$ $\qquad [a,\ \mathrm{Re}\,s>0;\ \mathrm{Re}\,s>-n \text{ for } a=1]$

No.	$f(x)$	$F(s)$
6	$(a-x)_+^{\alpha-1}\ln^n(a-x)$	$a^{s-1}\dfrac{\partial^n}{\partial\alpha^n}\left[a^\alpha\,\mathrm{B}\,(\alpha,\,s)\right]$ $\qquad [a,\ \mathrm{Re}\,\alpha,\ \mathrm{Re}\,s>0;\ \mathrm{Re}\,s>-n\ \text{for}\ a=1]$
7	$(x-a)_+^{\alpha-1}\ln^n(x-a)$	$a^{s-1}\dfrac{\partial^n}{\partial\alpha^n}\left[a^\alpha\,\mathrm{B}\,(\alpha,\,1-s-\alpha)\right]\quad [a,\ \mathrm{Re}\,\alpha>0;\ \mathrm{Re}\,s<1-\mathrm{Re}\,\alpha]$
8	$\dfrac{\theta\,(a-x)}{(bx+c)^\rho}\ln^n(a-x)$	$\dfrac{a^s}{c^\rho}\dfrac{\partial^n}{\partial\beta^n}\left[a^\beta\,\mathrm{B}\,(\beta+1,\,s)\ {}_2F_1\!\left(\begin{matrix}\rho,\,s;\,-\frac{ab}{c}\\ s+\beta+1\end{matrix}\right)\right]\Bigg|_{\beta=0}$ $\qquad [a,\ \mathrm{Re}\,s>0;\ |\arg(bx+c)|<\pi\ \text{for}\ 0\le x\le a]$
9	$\dfrac{\theta\,(x-a)}{(bx+c)^\rho}\ln^n(x-a)$	$\dfrac{a^{s-\rho}}{b^\rho}\dfrac{\partial^n}{\partial\beta^n}\left[a^\beta\,\mathrm{B}\,(\beta+1,\,\rho-s-\beta)\ {}_2F_1\!\left(\begin{matrix}\rho,\,\rho-s-\beta\\ 1-s+\rho;\,-\frac{c}{ab}\end{matrix}\right)\right]\Bigg|_{\beta=0}$ $\qquad [a>0;\ \mathrm{Re}\,s<\mathrm{Re}\,\rho;\ |\arg(bx+c)|<\pi\ \text{for}\ a\le x<\infty]$
10	$(a-x)_+^{\alpha-1}\ln^n(bx+c)$	$a^{s+\alpha-1}\,\mathrm{B}\,(\alpha,\,s)\,\dfrac{\partial^n}{\partial\beta^n}\left[c^\beta\,{}_2F_1\!\left(\begin{matrix}-\beta,\,s;\,-\frac{ab}{c}\\ s+\alpha\end{matrix}\right)\right]\Bigg|_{\beta=0}$ $\qquad [a,\ \mathrm{Re}\,\alpha,\ \mathrm{Re}\,s>0;\ |\arg(bx+c)|<\pi\ \text{for}\ 0\le x\le a]$
11	$\dfrac{\theta\,(x-a)}{(bx+c)^\rho}\ln^n(bx+c)$	$(-1)^n\dfrac{\partial^n}{\partial\rho^n}\left[\dfrac{a^{s-\rho}b^{-\rho}}{\rho-s}\ {}_2F_1\!\left(\begin{matrix}\rho,\,\rho-s;\,-\frac{c}{ab}\\ 1-s+\rho\end{matrix}\right)\right]$ $\qquad [a>0;\ \mathrm{Re}\,s<\mathrm{Re}\,\rho;\ |\arg(bx+c)|<\pi\ \text{for}\ a\le x<\infty]$
12	$\dfrac{1}{(bx+c)^\rho}\ln^n(bx+c)$	$(-1)^n\left(\dfrac{c}{b}\right)^s\dfrac{\partial^n}{\partial\rho^n}\left[c^{-\rho}\,\mathrm{B}\,(\rho-s,\,s)\right]$ $\qquad\left[\begin{matrix}a>0;\ 0<\mathrm{Re}\,s<\mathrm{Re}\,\rho;\\ |\arg(bx+c)|<\pi\ \text{for}\ 0\le x<\infty\end{matrix}\right]$
13	$\dfrac{\theta\,(a-x)\ln^\alpha(a/x)}{b^2x^2-2abx\cos\theta+a^2}$	$\dfrac{ia^{s-2}\Gamma\,(\alpha+1)}{2b\sin\theta}\left[\Phi\,(be^{-i\theta},\,\alpha+1,\,s-1)-\Phi\,(be^{i\theta},\,\alpha+1,\,s-1)\right]$ $\qquad [a,\,b,\ \mathrm{Re}\,\alpha>0;\ 0<\mathrm{Re}\,s<2;\ |\theta|<\pi]$
14	$\theta\,(a-x)\ln\dfrac{\sqrt{a-x}+\sqrt{a}}{\sqrt{x}}$ $\times\ln(bx+1)$	$\dfrac{\sqrt{\pi}\,a^{s+1}b\,\Gamma\,(s+1)}{2s\,(s+1)\,\Gamma\left(\frac{2s+3}{2}\right)}\left[(s+1)\,{}_3F_2\!\left(\begin{matrix}1,\,1,\,s+1\\ 2,\,\frac{2s+3}{2};\,-ab\end{matrix}\right)\right.$ $\left.-\,{}_3F_2\!\left(\begin{matrix}1,\,s+1,\,s+1\\ \frac{2s+3}{2},\,s+2;\,-ab\end{matrix}\right)\right]\qquad [a>0;\ \mathrm{Re}\,s>-1;\ |\arg b|<\pi]$
15	$\theta\,(a-x)\ln\dfrac{\sqrt{a-x}+\sqrt{a}}{\sqrt{x}}$ $\times\ln\dfrac{1+bx}{1-bx}$	$\dfrac{\sqrt{\pi}\,a^{s+1}b\,\Gamma\,(s+1)}{s\,(s+1)\,\Gamma\left(\frac{2s+3}{2}\right)}\left[(s+1)\,{}_4F_3\!\left(\begin{matrix}\frac{1}{2},\,1,\,\frac{s+1}{2},\,\frac{s+2}{2};\,a^2b^2\\ \frac{3}{2},\,\frac{2s+3}{4},\,\frac{2s+5}{4}\end{matrix}\right)\right.$ $\left.-\,{}_4F_3\!\left(\begin{matrix}1,\,\frac{s+1}{2},\,\frac{s+1}{2},\,\frac{s+2}{2};\,a^2b^2\\ \frac{2s+3}{4},\,\frac{2s+5}{4},\,\frac{s+3}{2}\end{matrix}\right)\right]$ $\qquad [a>0;\ \mathrm{Re}\,s>-1;\ |\arg(1-a^2b^2)|<\pi]$

No.	$f(x)$	$F(s)$
16	$\theta(a-x)\ln\dfrac{\sqrt{a-x}+\sqrt{a}}{\sqrt{x}}$ $\times\ln\left(bx+\sqrt{b^2x^2+1}\right)$	$\dfrac{\sqrt{\pi}\,a^{s+1}b\,\Gamma(s+1)}{2(s+1)\Gamma\left(\frac{2s+3}{2}\right)}\,{}_5F_4\left(\begin{array}{c}\frac{1}{2},\,\frac{1}{2},\,\frac{s+1}{2},\,\frac{s+1}{2},\,\frac{s+2}{2};\,-a^2b^2\\ 1,\,\frac{2s+3}{4},\,\frac{2s+5}{4},\,\frac{s+3}{2}\end{array}\right)$ $\left[a>0;\ \mathrm{Re}\,s>-1;\ \left|\arg\left(1+a^2b^2\right)\right|<\pi\right]$
17	$\dfrac{\theta(a-x)}{\sqrt{b^2x^2+1}}\ln\dfrac{\sqrt{a-x}+\sqrt{a}}{\sqrt{x}}$ $\times\ln\left(bx+\sqrt{b^2x^2+1}\right)$	$\dfrac{\sqrt{\pi}\,a^{s+1}b\,\Gamma(s+1)}{2(s+1)\Gamma\left(\frac{2s+3}{2}\right)}\,{}_5F_4\left(\begin{array}{c}1,\,1,\,\frac{s+1}{2},\,\frac{s+1}{2},\,\frac{s+2}{2};\,-a^2b^2\\ \frac{3}{2},\,\frac{2s+3}{4},\,\frac{2s+5}{4},\,\frac{s+3}{2}\end{array}\right)$ $\left[a>0;\ \mathrm{Re}\,s>-1;\ \left|\arg\left(1+a^2b^2\right)\right|<\pi\right]$
18	$\theta(a-x)\ln\dfrac{\sqrt{a-x}+\sqrt{a}}{\sqrt{x}}$ $\times\ln\left(bx^2+1\right)$	$\dfrac{\sqrt{\pi}\,a^{s+2}b\,\Gamma(s+2)}{2s(s+2)\Gamma\left(\frac{2s+5}{2}\right)}\left[(s+2)\,{}_4F_3\left(\begin{array}{c}1,\,1,\,\frac{s+2}{2},\,\frac{s+3}{2};\,-a^2b\\ 2,\,\frac{2s+5}{4},\,\frac{2s+7}{4}\end{array}\right)\right.$ $\left.-2\,{}_4F_3\left(\begin{array}{c}1,\,\frac{s+2}{2},\,\frac{s+2}{2},\,\frac{s+3}{2};\,-a^2b\\ \frac{2s+5}{4},\,\frac{2s+7}{4},\,\frac{s+4}{2}\end{array}\right)\right]$ $\left[a>0;\ \mathrm{Re}\,s>-2;\ \left|\arg\left(1-a^2b^2\right)\right|<\pi\right]$
19	$(a-x)_+^{\alpha-1}\ln^2\left[bx(a-x)\right.$ $\left.+\sqrt{b^2x^2(a-x)^2+1}\right]$	$a^{s+\alpha+3}b^2\,\mathrm{B}(s+2,\,\alpha+2)$ $\times\,{}_7F_6\left(\begin{array}{c}1,\,1,\,1,\,\Delta(2,\,\alpha+2),\,\Delta(2,\,s+2)\\ \frac{3}{2},\,2,\,\Delta(4,\,s+\alpha+4);\,-\frac{a^4b^2}{16}\end{array}\right)$ $\left[\mathrm{Re}\,\alpha,\ \mathrm{Re}\,s>-2;\ \left|\arg\left(16+a^4b^2\right)\right|<\pi\right]$
20	$(a-x)_+^{\alpha-1}\ln^2\left[b(a-x)\right.$ $\left.+\sqrt{b^2(a-x)^2+1}\right]$	$a^{s+\alpha+1}b^2\,\mathrm{B}(s,\,\alpha+2)\,{}_4F_3\left(\begin{array}{c}1,\,1,\,\frac{\alpha+2}{2},\,\frac{\alpha+3}{2};\,-a^2b^2\\ \frac{3}{2},\,\frac{s+\alpha+2}{2},\,\frac{s+\alpha+3}{2}\end{array}\right)$ $\left[a,\ \mathrm{Re}\,s>0;\ \mathrm{Re}\,\alpha>-2;\ \left|\arg\left(1+a^2b^2\right)\right|<\pi\right]$
21	$(a-x)_+^{\alpha-1}\ln^2\left[b\sqrt{a-x}\right.$ $\left.+\sqrt{b^2(a-x)+1}\right]$	$a^{s+\alpha}b^2\,\mathrm{B}(s,\,\alpha+1)\,{}_4F_3\left(\begin{array}{c}1,\,1,\,1,\,\alpha+1;\,-ab^2\\ \frac{3}{2},\,2,\,s+\alpha+1\end{array}\right)$ $\left[a,\ \mathrm{Re}\,s>0;\ \mathrm{Re}\,\alpha>-1;\ \left|\arg\left(1+ab^2\right)\right|<\pi\right]$
22	$(a-x)_+^{\alpha-1}\ln^2\left[b\sqrt{x(a-x)}\right.$ $\left.+\sqrt{1+b^2x(a-x)}\right]$	$a^{s+\alpha+1}b^2\,\mathrm{B}(s+1,\,\alpha+1)\,{}_5F_4\left(\begin{array}{c}1,\,1,\,1,\,\alpha+1,\,s+1;\,-\frac{a^2b^2}{4}\\ \frac{3}{2},\,2,\,\frac{s+\alpha+2}{2},\,\frac{s+\alpha+3}{2}\end{array}\right)$ $\left[a>0;\ \mathrm{Re}\,\alpha,\ \mathrm{Re}\,s>-1;\ \left|\arg\left(4+a^2b^2\right)\right|<\pi\right]$
23	$(a-x)_+^{\alpha-1}$ $\times\ln^2\left(bx+\sqrt{b^2x^2+1}\right)$	$a^{s+\alpha+1}b^2\,\mathrm{B}(s+2,\,\alpha)\,{}_4F_3\left(\begin{array}{c}1,\,1,\,\frac{s+2}{2},\,\frac{s+3}{2};\,-a^2b^2\\ \frac{3}{2},\,\frac{s+\alpha+2}{2},\,\frac{s+\alpha+3}{2}\end{array}\right)$ $\left[a,\ \mathrm{Re}\,\alpha>0;\ \mathrm{Re}\,s>-2;\ \left|\arg\left(1+a^2b^2\right)\right|<\pi\right]$
24	$(a^2-x^2)_+^{\alpha-1}$ $\times\ln^2\left(bx+\sqrt{b^2x^2+1}\right)$	$\dfrac{a^{s+2\alpha}b^2}{2}\,\mathrm{B}\left(\dfrac{s+2}{2},\,\alpha\right)\,{}_4F_3\left(\begin{array}{c}1,\,1,\,1,\,\frac{s+2}{2};\,-a^2b^2\\ \frac{3}{2},\,2,\,\frac{s+2\alpha+2}{2}\end{array}\right)$ $\left[a,\ \mathrm{Re}\,\alpha>0;\ \mathrm{Re}\,s>-2;\ \left|\arg\left(1+a^2b^2\right)\right|<\pi\right]$

No.	$f(x)$	$F(s)$

25 $\quad \theta(a-x) \ln \dfrac{a+\sqrt{a^2-x^2}}{x}$

$\qquad\qquad \times \ln \dfrac{b+x}{b-x}$

$$\frac{2\sqrt{\pi}\,a^{s+1}}{bs^2(s+1)}\Gamma\left[\begin{array}{c}\frac{s+1}{2}\\\frac{s}{2}\end{array}\right]\left[(s+1)\,{}_3F_2\left(\begin{array}{c}\frac{1}{2},\,1,\,\frac{s+1}{2}\\\frac{3}{2},\,\frac{s+2}{2};\,\frac{a^2}{b^2}\end{array}\right)\right.$$

$$\left.-\,{}_3F_2\left(\begin{array}{c}1,\,\frac{s+1}{2},\,\frac{s+1}{2}\\\frac{s+2}{2},\,\frac{s+3}{2};\,\frac{a^2}{b^2}\end{array}\right)\right]\quad\left[\begin{array}{c}a>0;\ \operatorname{Re}s>-1;\\|\arg(1-a^2/b^2)|<\pi\end{array}\right]$$

26 $\quad \theta(a-x)\ln\dfrac{a+\sqrt{a^2-x^2}}{x}$

$\qquad\qquad \times \ln\left(bx+\sqrt{b^2x^2+1}\right)$

$$\frac{\sqrt{\pi}\,a^{s+1}b}{s^2(s+1)}\Gamma\left[\begin{array}{c}\frac{s+1}{2}\\\frac{s}{2}\end{array}\right]\left[(s+1)\,{}_3F_2\left(\begin{array}{c}\frac{1}{2},\,\frac{1}{2},\,\frac{s+1}{2}\\\frac{3}{2},\,\frac{s+2}{2};\,-a^2b^2\end{array}\right)\right.$$

$$\left.-\,{}_3F_2\left(\begin{array}{c}\frac{1}{2},\,\frac{s+1}{2},\,\frac{s+1}{2}\\\frac{s+2}{2},\,\frac{s+3}{2};\,-a^2b^2\end{array}\right)\right]\quad\left[\begin{array}{c}a>0;\ \operatorname{Re}s>-1;\\|\arg(1+a^2b^2)|<\pi\end{array}\right]$$

27 $\quad \dfrac{\theta(a-x)}{\sqrt{b^2x^2+1}}\ln\dfrac{a+\sqrt{a^2-x^2}}{x}$

$\qquad\qquad \times\ln\left(bx+\sqrt{b^2x^2+1}\right)$

$$\frac{\sqrt{\pi}\,a^{s+1}b}{2(s+1)}\Gamma\left[\begin{array}{c}\frac{s+1}{2}\\\frac{s+2}{2}\end{array}\right]{}_4F_3\left(\begin{array}{c}1,\,1,\,\frac{s+1}{2},\,\frac{s+1}{2}\\\frac{3}{2},\,\frac{s+2}{2},\,\frac{s+3}{2};\,-a^2b^2\end{array}\right)$$

$$[a>0;\ \operatorname{Re}s>-1;\ |\arg(1+a^2b^2)|<\pi]$$

28 $\quad \theta(a-x)\ln\dfrac{a+\sqrt{a^2-x^2}}{a-\sqrt{a^2-x^2}}$

$\qquad\qquad \times\ln\left(bx+\sqrt{b^2x^2+1}\right)$

$$\frac{4\sqrt{\pi}\,a^{s+1}b}{s^2(s+1)^2}\Gamma\left[\begin{array}{c}\frac{s+3}{2}\\\frac{s}{2}\end{array}\right]\left[(s+1)\,{}_3F_2\left(\begin{array}{c}\frac{1}{2},\,\frac{1}{2},\,\frac{s+1}{2}\\\frac{3}{2},\,\frac{s+2}{2};\,-a^2b^2\end{array}\right)\right.$$

$$\left.-\,{}_3F_2\left(\begin{array}{c}\frac{1}{2},\,\frac{s+1}{2},\,\frac{s+1}{2}\\\frac{s+2}{2},\,\frac{s+3}{2};\,-a^2b^2\end{array}\right)\right]\quad\left[\begin{array}{c}a>0;\ \operatorname{Re}s>-1;\\|\arg(1+a^2b^2)|<\pi\end{array}\right]$$

29 $\quad \theta(1-x)\,e^{ax}\ln^n x$

$$\frac{(-1)^n\,n!}{s^{n+1}}\,{}_{n+1}F_{n+1}\left(\begin{array}{c}s,\,s,\ldots,\,s;\,a\\s+1,\,s+1,\ldots,\,s+1\end{array}\right)\qquad[\operatorname{Re}s>0]$$

30 $\quad e^{-ax^\alpha}\ln^n x$

$$\frac{1}{\alpha}\left(\frac{\partial}{\partial s}\right)^n\left[a^{-s/\alpha}\Gamma\left(\frac{s}{\alpha}\right)\right]\qquad[\alpha,\ \operatorname{Re}a,\ \operatorname{Re}s>0]$$

31 $\quad e^{-ax}\ln^2 x$

$$\frac{\Gamma(s)}{a^s}\left\{[\psi(s)-\ln a]^2+\psi'(s)\right\}\qquad[\operatorname{Re}a,\ \operatorname{Re}s>0]$$

32 $\quad e^{-ax}\ln^3 x$

$$\frac{\Gamma(s)}{a^s}\left\{[\psi(s)-\ln a]^3+3[\psi(s)-\ln a]\psi'(s)+\psi''(s)\right\}$$

$$[\operatorname{Re}a,\ \operatorname{Re}s>0]$$

33 $\quad \dfrac{e^{-ax}}{(bx+c)^\rho}\ln^n(bx+c)$

$$(-1)^n\left(\frac{c}{b}\right)^s\Gamma(s)\frac{\partial^n}{\partial\rho^n}\left[c^{-\rho}\Psi\left(s,\,s-\rho+1;\,\frac{ac}{b}\right)\right]$$

$$\left[\begin{array}{c}(\operatorname{Re}a,\ \operatorname{Re}s>0)\ \text{or}\ (\operatorname{Re}s>-n\ \text{for}\ c=1);\\|\arg(bx+c)|<\pi\ \text{for}\ x\geq 0\end{array}\right]$$

34 $\quad e^{-ax^2-bx}\ln^n x$

$$\frac{\partial^n}{\partial s^n}\left[(4a)^{-s/2}\Gamma(s)\Psi\left(\frac{s}{2},\,\frac{1}{2};\,\frac{b^2}{4a}\right)\right]$$

$$\left[\begin{array}{c}\operatorname{Re}a,\ \operatorname{Re}s>0\ \text{or}\ (\operatorname{Re}a=0;\ \operatorname{Re}b,\ \operatorname{Re}s>0)\\\text{or}\ (\operatorname{Re}a=\operatorname{Re}b=0;\ \operatorname{Im}a\neq 0;\ 0<\operatorname{Re}s<2)\end{array}\right]$$

No.	$f(x)$	$F(s)$
35	$e^{-ax-b/x}\ln^n x$	$2\dfrac{\partial^n}{\partial s^n}\left[\left(\dfrac{b}{a}\right)^{s/2}K_s\left(2\sqrt{ab}\right)\right]$ $\qquad$ [Re a, Re $b>0$]
36	$\theta(1-x)\left\{\begin{array}{c}\sinh(ax)\\\cosh(ax)\end{array}\right\}\ln^n x$	$\dfrac{(-1)^n\,n!a^\delta}{(s+\delta)^{n+1}}\,{}_{n+1}F_{n+2}\left(\begin{array}{c}\frac{s+\delta}{2},\frac{s+\delta}{2},\dots,\frac{s+\delta}{2};\frac{a^2}{4}\\\frac{2\delta+1}{2},\frac{s+\delta+2}{2},\frac{s+\delta+2}{2},\dots,\frac{s+\delta+2}{2}\end{array}\right)$ $\qquad$ [$a>0$; Re $s>-\delta$]
37	$\left\{\begin{array}{c}\sin(ax)\\\cos(ax)\end{array}\right\}\ln^2 x$	$\dfrac{\Gamma(s)}{a^s}\left\{\begin{array}{c}\sin(s\pi/2)\\\cos(s\pi/2)\end{array}\right\}\left[\left(\psi(s)-\ln a\pm\dfrac{\pi}{2}\tan^{\mp 1}\dfrac{s\pi}{2}\right)^2\right.$ $\left.+\psi'(s)-\dfrac{\pi^2}{4}\left\{\begin{array}{c}\csc(s\pi/2)\\\sec(s\pi/2)\end{array}\right\}^2\right]$ $\qquad$ [$a>0$; $-(1\pm 1)/2<$ Re $s<1$]
38	$\left\{\begin{array}{c}\sin(ax)\\\cos(ax)\end{array}\right\}\ln^n x$	$\dfrac{\partial^n}{\partial s^n}\left[\dfrac{\Gamma(s)}{a^s}\left\{\begin{array}{c}\sin(s\pi/2)\\\cos(s\pi/2)\end{array}\right\}\right]$ $\qquad$ [$a>0$; $-(1\pm 1)/2<$ Re $s<1$]
39	$\theta(a-x)\ln\dfrac{\sqrt{a}+\sqrt{a-x}}{\sqrt{x}}$ $\times\ln^2\left(bx+\sqrt{b^2x^2+1}\right)$	$\dfrac{\sqrt{\pi}\,a^{s+2}b^2}{2s(s+2)}\Gamma\left[\begin{array}{c}s+2\\\frac{2s+5}{2}\end{array}\right]\left[(s+2)\,{}_5F_4\left(\begin{array}{c}1,1,1,\frac{s+2}{2},\frac{s+3}{2};-a^2b^2\\\frac{3}{2},2,\frac{2s+5}{4},\frac{2s+7}{4}\end{array}\right)\right.$ $\left.-2\,{}_5F_4\left(\begin{array}{c}1,1,\frac{s+2}{2},\frac{s+2}{2},\frac{s+3}{2};-a^2b^2\\\frac{3}{2},\frac{2s+5}{4},\frac{2s+7}{4},\frac{s+4}{2}\end{array}\right)\right]$ $\qquad$ [$a>0$; Re $s>-2$]
40	$\theta(a-x)\ln\dfrac{a+\sqrt{a^2-x^2}}{x}$ $\times\ln^2\left(bx+\sqrt{b^2x^2+1}\right)$	$\dfrac{\sqrt{\pi}\,a^{s+2}b^2}{2(s+2)}\Gamma\left[\begin{array}{c}\frac{s+2}{2}\\\frac{s+3}{2}\end{array}\right]\,{}_5F_4\left(\begin{array}{c}1,1,1,\frac{s+2}{2},\frac{s+2}{2}\\\frac{3}{2},2,\frac{s+3}{2},\frac{s+4}{2};-a^2b^2\end{array}\right)$ $\qquad$ [$a>0$; Re $s>-2$]
41	$\dfrac{\theta(1-x)\ln^n x}{\ln^2 x+a^2}$	$\dfrac{1}{a}\dfrac{\partial^n}{\partial s^n}\left[\sin(as)\,\mathrm{ci}(as)-\cos(as)\,\mathrm{si}(as)\right]$ $\qquad$ [a, Re $s>0$]
42	$\dfrac{\theta(1-x)\ln x}{\ln^2 x+a^2}$	$\sin(as)\,\mathrm{si}(as)+\cos(as)\,\mathrm{ci}(as)$ $\qquad$ [a, Re $s>0$]
43	$\dfrac{\theta(1-x)}{(\ln x-a)^n}$	$\dfrac{1}{(n-1)!}\left[s^{n-1}e^{as}\,\mathrm{Ei}(-as)-\sum_{k=1}^{n-1}(n-k-1)!\dfrac{s^{k-1}}{(-a)^{n-k}}\right]$ $\qquad$ [a, Re $s>0$]
44	$\dfrac{\theta(1-x)}{\ln x\left[\ln^2(-\ln x)+\pi^2\right]}$	$\nu(s)-e^s$ $\qquad$ [Re $s>0$]
45	$\dfrac{\theta(1-x)\ln(-\ln x)}{\sqrt{-\ln x}\left[\ln^2(-\ln x)+\pi^2\right]}$	$\pi\left[\nu\left(s,-\dfrac{1}{2}\right)-e^s\right]$ $\qquad$ [Re $s>0$]

2.6.   Inverse Trigonometric Functions

More formulas can be obtained from the corresponding sections due to the relations

$$\arcsin z = z\,{}_2F_1\left(\frac{1}{2},\frac{1}{2};\frac{3}{2};z^2\right), \quad \arccos z = \frac{\pi}{2} - z\,{}_2F_1\left(\frac{1}{2},\frac{1}{2};\frac{3}{2};z^2\right),$$

$$\frac{\arcsin z}{\sqrt{1-z^2}} = z\,{}_2F_1\left(1,1;\frac{3}{2};z^2\right), \quad \frac{\arccos z}{\sqrt{1-z^2}} = \frac{\pi}{2\sqrt{1-z^2}} - z\,{}_2F_1\left(1,1;\frac{3}{2};z^2\right),$$

$$\arcsin^2 z = z^2\,{}_3F_2\left(1,1,1;\frac{3}{2},2;z^2\right), \quad \arctan z = z\,{}_2F_1\left(1,\frac{1}{2};\frac{3}{2};-z^2\right),$$

$$\operatorname{arccot} z = \frac{\pi z}{2}\sqrt{\frac{1}{z^2}}\sqrt{\frac{1}{z^2+1}}\sqrt{z^2+1} - z\,{}_2F_1\left(\frac{1}{2},1;\frac{3}{2};-z^2\right),$$

$$\operatorname{arccsc} z = \frac{1}{z}\,{}_2F_1\left(\frac{1}{2},\frac{1}{2};\frac{3}{2};\frac{1}{z^2}\right), \quad \operatorname{arcsec} z = \frac{\pi}{2} - \frac{1}{z}\,{}_2F_1\left(\frac{1}{2},\frac{1}{2};\frac{3}{2};\frac{1}{z^2}\right),$$

$$\arcsin z = -\frac{1}{2\sqrt{\pi}\,z}G_{22}^{12}\left(-z^2\left|\begin{array}{c}3/2,3/2\\1,1/2\end{array}\right.\right), \quad \arcsin^2 z = -\frac{\sqrt{\pi}}{2}G_{33}^{13}\left(-z^2\left|\begin{array}{c}1,1,1\\1,0,1/2\end{array}\right.\right),$$

$$\operatorname{arccsc} z = \frac{\sqrt{-z^2}}{2\sqrt{\pi}\,z}G_{22}^{21}\left(-z^2\left|\begin{array}{c}1/2,1\\0,0\end{array}\right.\right), \quad \operatorname{arcsec} z = \frac{\pi}{2} - \frac{1}{2\sqrt{\pi}\,z}G_{22}^{12}\left(-\frac{1}{z^2}\left|\begin{array}{c}1/2,1/2\\0,-1/2\end{array}\right.\right),$$

$$\arctan z = \frac{1}{2z}G_{22}^{12}\left(z^2\left|\begin{array}{c}1,3/2\\1,1/2\end{array}\right.\right).$$

2.6.1. $\arcsin(\varphi(x))$, $\arccos(\varphi(x))$, and algebraic functions

No.	$f(x)$	$F(s)$	
1	$\arcsin(ax)$	$\dfrac{i(ia)^{-s}}{2\sqrt{\pi}\,s}\Gamma\left(\dfrac{s+1}{2}\right)\Gamma\left(-\dfrac{s}{2}\right)$	$[-1 < \operatorname{Re} s < 0]$
2	$\arccos(ax) - \dfrac{\pi}{2}$	$\dfrac{(-a)^{-(s+1)/2}a^{(1-s)/2}}{2\sqrt{\pi}\,s}\Gamma\left(\dfrac{s+1}{2}\right)\Gamma\left(-\dfrac{s}{2}\right)$	$[-1 < \operatorname{Re} s < 0]$
3	$\arcsin(ax) - ax$	$-\dfrac{i(ia)^{-s}}{\sqrt{\pi}\,s^2}\Gamma\left(\dfrac{2-s}{2}\right)\Gamma\left(\dfrac{s+1}{2}\right)$	$[\operatorname{Re}(ia) > 0; -3 < \operatorname{Re} s < -1]$
4	$\arccos(ax) + ax - \dfrac{\pi}{2}$	$-\dfrac{i(ia)^{-s}}{2\sqrt{\pi}\,s}\Gamma\left(\dfrac{s+1}{2}\right)\Gamma\left(-\dfrac{s}{2}\right)$	$[\operatorname{Im} a < 0; -3 < \operatorname{Re} s < -1]$
5	$\arcsin(ax)$ $-\displaystyle\sum_{k=0}^{n}\dfrac{(1/2)_k\,(ax)^{2k+1}}{(2k+1)\,k!}$	$-\dfrac{i\sqrt{\pi}\,(ia)^{-s}}{s^2}\sec\dfrac{s\pi}{2}\Gamma\left[\begin{array}{c}\frac{2-s}{2}\\\frac{1-s}{2}\end{array}\right]$ $[\operatorname{Re}(ia) > 0; -3-2n < \operatorname{Re} s < -1-2n]$	
6	$\arccos(ax) - \dfrac{\pi}{2}$ $+\displaystyle\sum_{k=0}^{n}\dfrac{(1/2)_k\,(ax)^{2k+1}}{(2k+1)\,k!}$	$\dfrac{i\sqrt{\pi}\,(ia)^{-s}}{2s}\sec\dfrac{s\pi}{2}\Gamma\left[\begin{array}{c}-\frac{s}{2}\\\frac{1-s}{2}\end{array}\right]$ $[\operatorname{Im} a < 0; -2n-3 < \operatorname{Re} s < -2n-1]$	

No.	$f(x)$	$F(s)$
7	$\dfrac{1}{\sqrt{1-a^2x^2}}\arcsin(ax)$	$-\dfrac{i\pi^{3/2}(ia)^{-s}}{4}\sec\dfrac{s\pi}{2}\,\Gamma\!\left[\begin{matrix}\frac{1-s}{2}\\[2pt]\frac{2-s}{2}\end{matrix}\right]$ $\qquad$ $[\operatorname{Re}(ia)>0;\ \lvert\operatorname{Re}s\rvert<1]$
8	$\theta(a-x)\left\{\begin{matrix}\arcsin(x/a)\\ \arccos(x/a)\end{matrix}\right\}$	$\dfrac{(\pi\pm\pi)a^s}{4s}\mp\dfrac{\sqrt{\pi}\,a^s}{s^2}\,\Gamma\!\left[\begin{matrix}\frac{s+1}{2}\\[2pt]\frac{s}{2}\end{matrix}\right]$ $\qquad$ $[a>0;\ \operatorname{Re}s>-(1\pm1)/2]$
9	$(a-x)_+^{\alpha-1}\arcsin(bx)$	$a^{s+\alpha}b\,\mathrm{B}(s+1,\alpha)\ {}_4F_3\!\left(\begin{matrix}\frac{1}{2},\frac{1}{2},\frac{s+1}{2},\frac{s+2}{2};\,a^2b^2\\[2pt]\frac{3}{2},\frac{s+\alpha+1}{2},\frac{s+\alpha+2}{2}\end{matrix}\right)$ $\qquad\qquad\qquad\qquad\qquad\qquad [a,\ \operatorname{Re}\alpha>0;\ \operatorname{Re}s>-1]$
10	$(a^2-x^2)_+^{\alpha-1}\arcsin(bx)$	$\dfrac{a^{s+2\alpha-1}b}{2}\,\mathrm{B}\!\left(\dfrac{s+1}{2},\alpha\right){}_3F_2\!\left(\begin{matrix}\frac{1}{2},\frac{1}{2},\frac{s+1}{2};\,ab^2\\[2pt]\frac{3}{2},\frac{s+2\alpha+1}{2}\end{matrix}\right)$ $\qquad\qquad\qquad\qquad\qquad\qquad [a,\ \operatorname{Re}\alpha>0;\ \operatorname{Re}s>-1]$
11	$\dfrac{\theta(a-x)}{(x^2+b^2)^\rho}\arccos\dfrac{x}{a}$	$\dfrac{\pi a^s}{2^{s+1}b^{2\rho}}\,\Gamma\!\left[\begin{matrix}s\\[2pt]\frac{s+2}{2},\frac{s+2}{2}\end{matrix}\right]{}_3F_2\!\left(\begin{matrix}\rho,\frac{s}{2},\frac{s+1}{2}\\[2pt]\frac{s+2}{2},\frac{s+2}{2};\,-\frac{a^2}{b^2}\end{matrix}\right)$ $\qquad\qquad\qquad\qquad\qquad\qquad [a,\ \operatorname{Re}b,\ \operatorname{Re}s>0]$
12	$(a-x)_+^{\alpha-1}\arcsin(b(a-x))$	$a^{s+\alpha}b\,\mathrm{B}(s,\alpha+1)\ {}_4F_3\!\left(\begin{matrix}\frac{1}{2},\frac{1}{2},\frac{\alpha+1}{2},\frac{\alpha+2}{2};\,a^2b^2\\[2pt]\frac{3}{2},\frac{s+\alpha+1}{2},\frac{s+\alpha+2}{2}\end{matrix}\right)$ $\qquad\qquad\qquad\qquad\qquad\qquad [a,\ \operatorname{Re}s>0;\ \operatorname{Re}\alpha>-1]$
13	$(a-x)_+^{\alpha-1}\arcsin(bx(a-x))$	$a^{s+\alpha+1}b\,\mathrm{B}(s+1,\alpha+1)$ $\times{}_6F_5\!\left(\begin{matrix}\frac{1}{2},\frac{1}{2},\Delta(2,s+1),\Delta(2,\alpha+1)\\[2pt]\frac{3}{2},\Delta(4,s+\alpha+2);\,\frac{a^4b^2}{16}\end{matrix}\right)$ $\qquad\qquad\qquad\qquad\qquad\qquad [\operatorname{Re}s,\ \operatorname{Re}\alpha>-1]$
14	$(a-x)_+^{\alpha-1}\arcsin(b\sqrt{a-x})$	$a^{s+\alpha-1/2}b\,\mathrm{B}\!\left(s,\dfrac{2\alpha+1}{2}\right){}_3F_2\!\left(\begin{matrix}\frac{1}{2},\frac{1}{2},\frac{2\alpha+1}{2};\,ab^2\\[2pt]\frac{3}{2},\frac{2s+2\alpha+1}{2}\end{matrix}\right)$ $\qquad\qquad\qquad\qquad\qquad\qquad [a,\ \operatorname{Re}s>0;\ \operatorname{Re}\alpha>-1/2]$
15	$\theta(a-x)(bx+1)^\alpha$ $\times\arcsin(c\sqrt{a-x})$	$\dfrac{\sqrt{\pi}\,a^{s+1/2}c}{2}\,\Gamma\!\left[\begin{matrix}s\\[2pt]\frac{2s+3}{2}\end{matrix}\right]F_3\!\left(-\alpha,\dfrac{1}{2},s,\dfrac{1}{2};s+\dfrac{3}{2};-ab,ac^2\right)$ $\qquad\qquad\quad [a,\ \operatorname{Re}s>0;\ a\lvert b\rvert,a\lvert c^2\rvert<1;\ \lvert\arg(ab+1)\rvert<\pi]$
16	$\theta(a-x)\dfrac{(bx+1)^\alpha}{\sqrt{1-c^2(a-x)}}$ $\times\arcsin(c\sqrt{a-x})$	$\dfrac{\sqrt{\pi}\,a^{s+1/2}c}{2}\,\Gamma\!\left[\begin{matrix}s\\[2pt]\frac{2s+3}{2}\end{matrix}\right]F_3\!\left(-\alpha,1,s,1;s+\dfrac{3}{2};-ab,ac^2\right)$ $\qquad\qquad\quad\left[\begin{matrix}a,\ \operatorname{Re}s>0;\ a\lvert b\rvert,a\lvert c^2\rvert<1;\\ \lvert\arg(ab+1)\rvert,\ \lvert\arg(ac^2+1)\rvert<\pi\end{matrix}\right]$

No.	$f(x)$	$F(s)$
17	$(a-x)_+^{\alpha-1}$ $\times \arcsin\left(b\sqrt{x(a-x)}\right)$	$a^{s+\alpha}b\,\mathrm{B}\left(\dfrac{2s+1}{2},\dfrac{2\alpha+1}{2}\right) {}_4F_3\left(\begin{matrix}\frac{1}{2},\frac{1}{2},\frac{2s+1}{2},\frac{2\alpha+1}{2};\frac{a^2b^2}{4}\\\frac{3}{2},\frac{s+\alpha+1}{2},\frac{s+\alpha+2}{2}\end{matrix}\right)$ $[a,\ \mathrm{Re}\,s,\ \mathrm{Re}\,\alpha > -1/2]$
18	$\dfrac{1}{(x+a)^\rho}\arcsin\dfrac{b}{x+a}$	$a^{s-\rho-1}b\,\mathrm{B}\left(s,1-s+\rho\right){}_4F_3\left(\begin{matrix}\frac{1}{2},\frac{1}{2},\frac{1-s+\rho}{2},\frac{2-s+\rho}{2}\\\frac{3}{2},\frac{\rho+1}{2},\frac{\rho+2}{2};\frac{b^2}{a^2}\end{matrix}\right)$ $[0 < \mathrm{Re}\,s < \mathrm{Re}\,\rho+1;\ |\arg a| < \pi]$
19	$\dfrac{1}{\sqrt{(x+a)^2-b^2}\,(x+a)^\rho}$ $\times \arcsin\dfrac{b}{x+a}$	$a^{s-\rho-2}b\,\mathrm{B}\left(s,2-s+\rho\right){}_4F_3\left(\begin{matrix}1,1,\frac{2-s+\rho}{2},\frac{3-s+\rho}{2}\\\frac{3}{2},\frac{\rho+2}{2},\frac{\rho+3}{2};\frac{b^2}{a^2}\end{matrix}\right)$ $[0 < \mathrm{Re}\,s < \mathrm{Re}\,\rho+2;\ |\arg a| < \pi]$
20	$\dfrac{1}{(x+a)^\rho}\arcsin\dfrac{bx}{x+a}$	$a^{s-\rho}b\,\mathrm{B}\left(s+1,\rho-s\right){}_4F_3\left(\begin{matrix}\frac{1}{2},\frac{1}{2},\frac{s+1}{2},\frac{s+2}{2}\\\frac{3}{2},\frac{\rho+1}{2},\frac{\rho+2}{2};b^2\end{matrix}\right)$ $[-1 < \mathrm{Re}\,s < \mathrm{Re}\,\rho;\ |\arg a| < \pi]$
21	$\dfrac{(x+a)^{-\rho}}{\sqrt{1-\frac{b^2x^2}{(x+a)^2}}}\arcsin\dfrac{bx}{x+a}$	$a^{s-\rho}b\,\mathrm{B}\left(s+1,\rho-s\right){}_4F_3\left(\begin{matrix}1,1,\frac{s+1}{2},\frac{s+2}{2}\\\frac{3}{2},\frac{\rho+1}{2},\frac{\rho+2}{2};b^2\end{matrix}\right)$ $[-1 < \mathrm{Re}\,s < \mathrm{Re}\,\rho;\ |\arg a| < \pi]$
22	$\dfrac{1}{(x^2+a^2)^\rho}\arcsin\dfrac{bx}{x^2+a^2}$	$\dfrac{a^{s-2\rho-1}b}{2}\,\mathrm{B}\left(\dfrac{s+1}{2},\dfrac{1-s+2\rho}{2}\right){}_4F_3\left(\begin{matrix}\frac{1}{2},\frac{1}{2},\frac{s+1}{2},\frac{1-s+2\rho}{2}\\\frac{3}{2},\frac{\rho+1}{2},\frac{\rho+2}{2};\frac{b^2}{4a^2}\end{matrix}\right)$ $[\mathrm{Re}\,a > 0;\ -1 < \mathrm{Re}\,s < 2\,\mathrm{Re}\,\rho+1]$
23	$\dfrac{(x^2+a^2)^{-\rho}}{\sqrt{1-\frac{b^2x^2}{(x^2+a^2)^2}}}$ $\times \arcsin\dfrac{bx}{x^2+a^2}$	$\dfrac{a^{s-2\rho-1}b}{2}\,\mathrm{B}\left(\dfrac{s+1}{2},\dfrac{1-s+2\rho}{2}\right){}_4F_3\left(\begin{matrix}1,1,\frac{s+1}{2},\frac{1-s+2\rho}{2}\\\frac{3}{2},\frac{\rho+1}{2},\frac{\rho+2}{2};\frac{b^2}{4a^2}\end{matrix}\right)$ $[\mathrm{Re}\,a > 0;\ -1 < \mathrm{Re}\,s < 2\,\mathrm{Re}\,\rho+1]$
24	$\dfrac{(x+a)^{-\rho}}{\sqrt{a-b^2+x}}\arcsin\dfrac{b}{\sqrt{x+a}}$	$a^{s-\rho-1}b\,\mathrm{B}\left(s,1-s+\rho\right){}_3F_2\left(\begin{matrix}1,1,1-s+\rho\\\frac{3}{2},\rho+1;\frac{b^2}{a}\end{matrix}\right)$ $[|b^2| < a;\ 0 < \mathrm{Re}\,s < \mathrm{Re}\,\rho+1]$
25	$\theta(a-x)$ $\times \arcsin\left(c\sqrt{\dfrac{a-x}{b-x}}\right)$	$a^{s+1/2}\sqrt{\dfrac{\pi}{b}}\,c\,\dfrac{\Gamma(s)}{2\Gamma\left(s+\frac{3}{2}\right)}\,F_1\left(\dfrac{1}{2},s,\dfrac{1}{2};s+\dfrac{3}{2};\dfrac{a}{b},\dfrac{ac^2}{b}\right)$ $[a < |b|,\ |b/c^2|;\ a,\ \mathrm{Re}\,s > 0]$

No.	$f(x)$	$F(s)$
26	$\dfrac{\theta(a-x)}{\sqrt{c^2(x-a)+b-x}}$ $\times \arcsin\left(c\sqrt{\dfrac{a-x}{b-x}}\right)$	$\dfrac{\sqrt{\pi}a^{s+1/2}c}{2b}\dfrac{\Gamma(s)}{\Gamma\left(s+\frac{3}{2}\right)}F_1\left(1,s,1;s+\dfrac{3}{2};\dfrac{a}{b},\dfrac{ac^2}{b}\right)$ $[a<|b|,\ |b/c^2|;\ a,\ \mathrm{Re}\,s>0]$
27	$\theta(x-a)\arcsin\dfrac{cx}{\sqrt{x^2-b^2}}$	$-\dfrac{a^sc}{s}F_2\left(\dfrac{1}{2},\dfrac{1}{2},-\dfrac{s}{2};\dfrac{3}{2},1-\dfrac{s}{2};c^2,\dfrac{b^2}{a^2}\right)$ $[a>b>0;\ \mathrm{Re}\,s<0;\ |\arg c|<\pi]$
28	$\dfrac{\theta(x-a)}{\sqrt{x^2(1-c^2)-b^2}}$ $\times \arcsin\dfrac{cx}{\sqrt{x^2-b^2}}$	$\dfrac{a^{s-1}c}{1-s}F_2\left(1,1,\dfrac{1-s}{2};\dfrac{3}{2},\dfrac{3-s}{2};c^2,\dfrac{b^2}{a^2}\right)$ $[a>b>0;\ \mathrm{Re}\,s<0;\ |\arg c|<\pi]$
29	$\theta(x-a)\arccos\dfrac{a}{x}$	$\dfrac{\sqrt{\pi}\,a^s}{s^2}\Gamma\left[\begin{matrix}\frac{1-s}{2}\\-\frac{s}{2}\end{matrix}\right]$ $[a>0;\ \mathrm{Re}\,s<0]$
30	$\arccos\left(\sqrt{ax+1}-\sqrt{ax}\right)$	$\dfrac{a^{-s}}{\sqrt{\pi}\,s}\sin(s\pi)\Gamma(-2s)\Gamma\left(\dfrac{4s+1}{2}\right)$ $[-1/4<\mathrm{Re}\,s<0;\ |\arg a|<\pi]$
31	$\arccos\dfrac{\sqrt{ax}}{\sqrt{ax+1}+1}$	$\dfrac{a^{-s}}{\sqrt{\pi}\,s}\sin(s\pi)\Gamma\left(\dfrac{1}{2}-2s\right)\Gamma(2s)$ $[0<\mathrm{Re}\,s<1/4;\ |\arg a|<\pi]$
32	$\arccos\dfrac{\sqrt{ax+1}-1}{\sqrt{ax}}$	$\dfrac{a^{-s}}{\sqrt{\pi}\,s}\sin(s\pi)\Gamma\left(\dfrac{1}{2}-2s\right)\Gamma(2s)$ $[0<\mathrm{Re}\,s<1/4;\ |\arg a|<\pi]$
33	$\arccos\dfrac{1}{\sqrt{ax}+\sqrt{ax+1}}$	$\dfrac{a^{-s}}{\sqrt{\pi}\,s}\sin(s\pi)\Gamma(-2s)\Gamma\left(\dfrac{4s+1}{2}\right)$ $[-1/4<\mathrm{Re}\,s<0;\ |\arg a|<\pi]$

2.6.2. $\arcsin(\varphi(x))$, $\arccos(\varphi(x))$, and the exponential function

No.	$f(x)$	$F(s)$
1	$\theta(a-x)e^{bx}$ $\times \arcsin\left(c\sqrt{a-x}\right)$	$\sqrt{\pi}a^{s+1/2}c\dfrac{\Gamma(s)}{2\Gamma\left(s+\frac{3}{2}\right)}\Xi_1\left(\dfrac{1}{2},s,\dfrac{1}{2};s+\dfrac{3}{2};ac^2,ab\right)$ $[a,\ \mathrm{Re}\,s>0]$
2	$\dfrac{\theta(a-x)}{\sqrt{1-c^2(a-x)}}e^{bx}$ $\times \arcsin\left(c\sqrt{a-x}\right)$	$\sqrt{\pi}a^{s+1/2}c\dfrac{\Gamma(s)}{2\Gamma\left(s+\frac{3}{2}\right)}\Xi_1\left(1,s,1;s+\dfrac{3}{2};ac^2,ab\right)$ $[a,\ \mathrm{Re}\,s>0]$

No.	$f(x)$	$F(s)$
3	$\theta(a-x)\,e^{bx}\arccos\dfrac{x}{a}$	$\dfrac{(2a)^s}{s+1}\left[ab\,\Gamma\begin{bmatrix}\frac{s+2}{2},\ \frac{s+2}{2}\\ s+2\end{bmatrix}\,{}_2F_3\left(\begin{matrix}\frac{s+1}{2},\ \frac{s+2}{2};\ \frac{a^2b^2}{4}\\ \frac{3}{2},\ \frac{s+3}{2},\ \frac{s+3}{2}\end{matrix}\right)\right.$ $\left.+\dfrac{2}{s}\,\Gamma\begin{bmatrix}\frac{s+3}{2},\ \frac{s+3}{2}\\ s+2\end{bmatrix}\,{}_2F_3\left(\begin{matrix}\frac{s}{2},\ \frac{s+1}{2};\ \frac{a^2b^2}{4}\\ \frac{1}{2},\ \frac{s+2}{2},\ \frac{s+2}{2}\end{matrix}\right)\right]$ $[a,\ \mathrm{Re}\,s>0]$
4	$\theta(a-x)\,e^{bx^2}\arccos\dfrac{x}{a}$	$\dfrac{\sqrt{\pi}\,a^s}{2s}\,\Gamma\begin{bmatrix}\frac{s+1}{2}\\ \frac{s+2}{2}\end{bmatrix}\,{}_2F_2\left(\begin{matrix}\frac{s}{2},\ \frac{s+1}{2};\ a^2b\\ \frac{s+2}{2},\ \frac{s+2}{2}\end{matrix}\right)$ $[a,\ \mathrm{Re}\,s>0]$

2.6.3. $\arccos(bx)$ **and hyperbolic or trigonometric functions**

Notation: $\delta=\left\{\begin{matrix}1\\0\end{matrix}\right\}$.

No.	$f(x)$	$F(s)$
1	$\theta(a-x)\left\{\begin{matrix}\sinh(bx)\\ \sin(bx)\end{matrix}\right\}\arccos\dfrac{x}{a}$	$\dfrac{\sqrt{\pi}\,a^{s+1}b}{(s+1)^2}\,\Gamma\begin{bmatrix}\frac{s+2}{2}\\ \frac{s+1}{2}\end{bmatrix}\,{}_2F_3\left(\begin{matrix}\frac{s+1}{2},\ \frac{s+2}{2};\ \pm\frac{a^2b^2}{4}\\ \frac{3}{2},\ \frac{s+3}{2},\ \frac{s+3}{2}\end{matrix}\right)$ $[a>0;\ \mathrm{Re}\,s>-1]$
2	$\theta(a-x)\left\{\begin{matrix}\cosh(bx)\\ \cos(bx)\end{matrix}\right\}\arccos\dfrac{x}{a}$	$\dfrac{\sqrt{\pi}\,a^s}{s^2}\,\Gamma\begin{bmatrix}\frac{s+1}{2}\\ \frac{s}{2}\end{bmatrix}\,{}_2F_3\left(\begin{matrix}\frac{s}{2},\ \frac{s+1}{2};\ \pm\frac{a^2b^2}{4}\\ \frac{1}{2},\ \frac{s+2}{2},\ \frac{s+2}{2}\end{matrix}\right)$ $[a,\ \mathrm{Re}\,s>0]$
3	$\theta(a-x)\left\{\begin{matrix}\sinh(bx^2)\\ \cosh(bx^2)\end{matrix}\right\}\arccos\dfrac{x}{a}$	$\dfrac{\sqrt{\pi}\,a^{s+2\delta}b^{2\delta}}{(s+2\delta)^2}\,\Gamma\begin{bmatrix}\frac{s+2\delta+1}{2}\\ \frac{s+2\delta}{2}\end{bmatrix}$ $\times{}_3F_4\left(\begin{matrix}\frac{s+2\delta}{4},\ \frac{s+2\delta+1}{4},\ \frac{s+2\delta+3}{4};\ \frac{a^4b^2}{4}\\ \frac{2\delta+1}{2},\ \frac{s+2\delta+2}{4},\ \frac{s+2\delta+4}{4},\ \frac{s+2\delta+4}{4}\end{matrix}\right)$ $[a>0;\ \mathrm{Re}\,s>-2\delta]$
4	$\theta(a-x)\left\{\begin{matrix}\sin(bx)\sinh(bx)\\ \cos(bx)\cosh(bx)\end{matrix}\right\}$ $\times\arccos\dfrac{x}{a}$	$\dfrac{\sqrt{\pi}\,a^{s+2\delta}b^{2\delta}}{2(s+2\delta)}\,\Gamma\begin{bmatrix}\frac{s+2\delta+1}{2}\\ \frac{s+2\delta+2}{2}\end{bmatrix}$ $\times{}_3F_6\left(\begin{matrix}\frac{s+2\delta}{4},\ \frac{s+2\delta+1}{4},\ \frac{s+2\delta+3}{4};\ -\frac{a^4b^4}{64}\\ \frac{2\delta+1}{4},\ \frac{2\delta+3}{4},\ \frac{2\delta+1}{2},\ \frac{s+2\delta+2}{4},\ \frac{s+2\delta+4}{4},\ \frac{s+2\delta+4}{4}\end{matrix}\right)$ $[a>0;\ \mathrm{Re}\,s>-(2\delta+1)]$
5	$\theta(a-x)\left\{\begin{matrix}\cosh(bx)\sin(bx)\\ \sinh(bx)\cos(bx)\end{matrix}\right\}$ $\times\arccos\dfrac{x}{a}$	$\dfrac{\sqrt{\pi}\,a^{s+1}b}{2(s+1)}\,\Gamma\begin{bmatrix}\frac{s+2}{2}\\ \frac{s+3}{2}\end{bmatrix}\,{}_3F_6\left(\begin{matrix}\frac{s+1}{4},\ \frac{s+2}{4},\ \frac{s+4}{4};\ -\frac{a^4b^4}{64}\\ \frac{1}{2},\ \frac{3}{4},\ \frac{5}{4},\ \frac{s+3}{4},\ \frac{s+5}{4},\ \frac{s+5}{4}\end{matrix}\right)$ $\pm\dfrac{\sqrt{\pi}\,a^{s+3}b^3}{6(s+3)}\,\Gamma\begin{bmatrix}\frac{s+4}{2}\\ \frac{s+5}{2}\end{bmatrix}\,{}_3F_6\left(\begin{matrix}\frac{s+3}{4},\ \frac{s+4}{4},\ \frac{s+6}{4};\ -\frac{a^4b^4}{64}\\ \frac{5}{4},\ \frac{3}{2},\ \frac{7}{4},\ \frac{s+5}{4},\ \frac{s+7}{4},\ \frac{s+7}{4}\end{matrix}\right)$ $[a>0;\ \mathrm{Re}\,s>-1]$

No.	$f(x)$	$F(s)$
6	$\theta(a-x)\left\{\begin{matrix}\sinh(b\sqrt{x})\sin(b\sqrt{x})\\\cosh(b\sqrt{x})\cos(b\sqrt{x})\end{matrix}\right\}$ $\times \arccos\dfrac{x}{a}$	$\dfrac{\sqrt{\pi}\,a^{s+\delta}b^{2\delta}}{2(s+\delta)}\Gamma\!\left[\begin{matrix}\frac{s+\delta+1}{2}\\\frac{s+\delta+2}{2}\end{matrix}\right]$ $\times {}_2F_5\!\left(\begin{matrix}\frac{s+\delta}{2},\ \frac{s+\delta+1}{2};\ -\frac{a^2b^4}{64}\\\frac{2\delta+1}{4},\ \frac{2\delta+3}{4},\ \frac{2\delta+1}{2},\ \frac{s+\delta+2}{2},\ \frac{s+\delta+2}{2}\end{matrix}\right)$ $[a>0;\ \operatorname{Re}s>-\delta]$
7	$\theta(a-x)\left\{\begin{matrix}\cosh(b\sqrt{x})\sin(b\sqrt{x})\\\sinh(b\sqrt{x})\cos(b\sqrt{x})\end{matrix}\right\}$ $\times \arccos\dfrac{x}{a}$	$\dfrac{\sqrt{\pi}\,a^{s+1/2}b}{2s+1}\Gamma\!\left[\begin{matrix}\frac{2s+3}{4}\\\frac{2s+5}{4}\end{matrix}\right]{}_2F_5\!\left(\begin{matrix}\frac{2s+1}{4},\ \frac{2s+3}{4};\ -\frac{a^2b^4}{64}\\\frac{1}{2},\ \frac{3}{4},\ \frac{5}{4},\ \frac{2s+5}{4},\ \frac{2s+5}{4}\end{matrix}\right)$ $\pm\dfrac{\sqrt{\pi}\,a^{s+3/2}b^3}{3(2s+3)}\Gamma\!\left[\begin{matrix}\frac{2s+5}{4}\\\frac{2s+7}{4}\end{matrix}\right]{}_2F_5\!\left(\begin{matrix}\frac{2s+3}{4},\ \frac{2s+5}{4};\ -\frac{a^2b^4}{64}\\\frac{5}{4},\ \frac{3}{2},\ \frac{7}{4},\ \frac{2s+7}{4},\ \frac{2s+7}{4}\end{matrix}\right)$ $[a>0;\ \operatorname{Re}s>-1/2]$

2.6.4. Trigonometric functions of inverse trigonometric functions

No.	$f(x)$	$F(s)$	
1	$\theta(a-x)\sin\left(\nu\arccos\dfrac{x}{a}\right)$	$\dfrac{\nu\pi a^s}{2^{s+1}}\Gamma\!\left[\begin{matrix}s\\\frac{s-\nu+1}{2},\ \frac{s+\nu+1}{2}\end{matrix}\right]$	$[a,\ \operatorname{Re}s>0]$
2	$\dfrac{1}{\sqrt{a^2-x^2}}\sin\left(\nu\arccos\dfrac{x}{a}\right)$	$\dfrac{a^{s-1}}{2^{s+1}\pi}\sin(\nu\pi)\Gamma\!\left[s,\ \dfrac{1-s-\nu}{2},\ \dfrac{1-s+\nu}{2}\right]$ $[0<\operatorname{Re}s<1-|\operatorname{Re}\nu|;\ |\arg a|<\pi]$	
3	$\left(a^2-x^2\right)_+^{-1/2}\cos\left(\nu\arccos\dfrac{x}{a}\right)$	$\dfrac{\pi a^{s-1}}{2^s}\Gamma\!\left[\begin{matrix}s\\\frac{s+\nu+1}{2},\ \frac{s-\nu+1}{2}\end{matrix}\right]$	$[a,\ \operatorname{Re}s>0]$
4	$\left(x^2-a^2\right)_+^{-1/2}\cos\left(\nu\operatorname{arcsec}\dfrac{x}{a}\right)$	$\pi(2a)^{s-1}\Gamma\!\left[\begin{matrix}1-s\\\frac{2-s-\nu}{2},\ \frac{2-s+\nu}{2}\end{matrix}\right]$	$[a>0;\ \operatorname{Re}s<1]$
5	$\theta(a-x)\sin\left(\nu\arcsin\sqrt{1-\dfrac{x}{a}}\right)$	$\dfrac{\nu\sqrt{\pi}\,a^s}{2}\Gamma\!\left[\begin{matrix}s,\ \frac{2s+1}{2}\\\frac{2s+\nu+2}{2},\ \frac{2s-\nu+2}{2}\end{matrix}\right]$	$[a,\ \operatorname{Re}s>0]$
6	$\left(a^2-x^2\right)_+^{-1/2}\cos\left(\nu\arccos\dfrac{x^2-a^2}{a^2}\right)$	$\dfrac{\pi a^{s-1}}{2^s}\Gamma\!\left[\begin{matrix}s\\\frac{s+2\nu+1}{2},\ \frac{s-2\nu+1}{2}\end{matrix}\right]$	$[a,\ \operatorname{Re}s>0]$
7	$\left(x^2-a^2\right)_+^{-1/2}\cos\left(\nu\arccos\dfrac{a}{x}\right)$	$\pi(2a)^{s-1}\Gamma\!\left[\begin{matrix}1-s\\\frac{2-s-\nu}{2},\ \frac{2-s+\nu}{2}\end{matrix}\right]$	$[a>0;\ \operatorname{Re}s<1]$
8	$(1-x)_+^{-1/2}\left(1+\sqrt{1-x}\right)^\nu\cos\dfrac{\pi\nu}{2}$ $-\,x^{\nu/2}(x-1)_+^{-1/2}\sin\left(\nu\arcsin\dfrac{1}{\sqrt{x}}\right)$	$\sqrt{\pi}\,\Gamma\!\left[\begin{matrix}s,\ \frac{2-2s-\nu}{2}\\\frac{2s+\nu+1}{2},\ 1-s-\nu\end{matrix}\right]$	$[0<\operatorname{Re}s<1-\operatorname{Re}\nu/2]$

No.	$f(x)$	$F(s)$
9	$(1-x)_+^{-1/2}\left(1+\sqrt{1-x}\right)^\nu \sin\dfrac{\pi\nu}{2}$ $+\, x^{\nu/2}(x-1)_+^{-1/2}\cos\left(\nu\arcsin\dfrac{1}{\sqrt{x}}\right)$	$\sqrt{\pi}\,\Gamma\left[\begin{matrix} s,\ \frac{1-2s-\nu}{2} \\ \frac{2s+\nu}{2},\ 1-s-\nu \end{matrix}\right]$ $[0<\operatorname{Re}s<(1-\operatorname{Re}\nu)/2]$
10	$(1-x)_+^{-1/2}\sin\left(\nu\arcsin\sqrt{x}\right)$ $-\cos\dfrac{\nu\pi}{2}(x-1)_+^{-1/2}\left(\sqrt{x}+\sqrt{x-1}\right)^\nu$	$-\sqrt{\pi}\,\Gamma\left[\begin{matrix} \frac{2s+1}{2},\ \frac{1-2s-\nu}{2} \\ \frac{2s-\nu+1}{2},\ 1-s \end{matrix}\right]$ $[-1/2<\operatorname{Re}s<(1-\operatorname{Re}\nu)/2]$
11	$(1-x)_+^{-1/2}\cos\left(\nu\arcsin\sqrt{x}\right)$ $+\sin\dfrac{\nu\pi}{2}(x-1)_+^{-1/2}\left(\sqrt{x}+\sqrt{x-1}\right)^\nu$	$\sqrt{\pi}\,\Gamma\left[\begin{matrix} s,\ \frac{1-2s-\nu}{2} \\ \frac{2s-\nu+1}{2},\ \frac{1-2s}{2} \end{matrix}\right]$ $[0<\operatorname{Re}s<(1-\operatorname{Re}\nu)/2]$
12	$\theta(1-x)\sin\left(\nu\arcsin\sqrt{x}\right)$ $+\sin\dfrac{\pi\nu}{2}\theta(x-1)\left(\sqrt{x}+\sqrt{x-1}\right)^\nu$	$\dfrac{\nu\sqrt{\pi}}{2}\,\Gamma\left[\begin{matrix} \frac{2s+1}{2},\ -\frac{2s+\nu}{2} \\ \frac{2s-\nu+2}{2},\ 1-s \end{matrix}\right]$ $[-1/2<\operatorname{Re}s<-\operatorname{Re}\nu/2]$
13	$\theta(1-x)\left(1+\sqrt{1-x}\right)^\nu\sin\dfrac{\nu\pi}{2}$ $+\,\theta(x-1)x^{\nu/2}\sin\left(\nu\arcsin\dfrac{1}{\sqrt{x}}\right)$	$\dfrac{\nu\sqrt{\pi}}{2}\,\Gamma\left[\begin{matrix} s,\ \frac{1-2s-\nu}{2} \\ \frac{2s+\nu+2}{2},\ 1-s-\nu \end{matrix}\right]$ $[0<\operatorname{Re}s<(1-\operatorname{Re}\nu)/2]$
14	$\theta(1-x)\cos\left(\nu\arcsin\sqrt{x}\right)$ $+\cos\dfrac{\nu\pi}{2}\theta(x-1)\left(\sqrt{x}+\sqrt{x-1}\right)^\nu$	$-\dfrac{\nu\sqrt{\pi}}{2}\,\Gamma\left[\begin{matrix} s,\ -\frac{2s+\nu}{2} \\ \frac{2s-\nu+2}{2},\ \frac{1-2s}{2} \end{matrix}\right]$ $[0<\operatorname{Re}s<-\operatorname{Re}\nu/2]$
15	$\theta(1-x)\left(1+\sqrt{1-x}\right)^\nu\cos\dfrac{\nu\pi}{2}$ $+\,\theta(x-1)x^{\nu/2}\cos\left(\nu\arcsin\dfrac{1}{\sqrt{x}}\right)$	$-\dfrac{\nu\sqrt{\pi}}{2}\,\Gamma\left[\begin{matrix} s,\ -\frac{2s+\nu}{2} \\ \frac{2s+\nu+1}{2},\ 1-\nu-s \end{matrix}\right]$ $[0<\operatorname{Re}s<-\operatorname{Re}\nu/2]$
16	$(1-x)_+^{-1/2}\sin\left(\nu\arccos\sqrt{x}\right)$ $+\,(x-1)_+^{-1/2}\sinh\left(\nu\operatorname{arccosh}\sqrt{x}\right)$	$\dfrac{\sin(\nu\pi)}{2\pi^{3/2}}\,\Gamma\left[\begin{matrix} s,\ \dfrac{2s+1}{2},\ \dfrac{1-2s-\nu}{2},\ \dfrac{1-2s+\nu}{2}\end{matrix}\right]$ $[|\operatorname{Re}\nu|<1;\ 0<\operatorname{Re}s<(1-|\operatorname{Re}\nu|)/2]$
17	$(1-x)_+^{-1/2}\sinh\left(\nu\operatorname{arccosh}\dfrac{1}{\sqrt{x}}\right)$ $+\,(x-1)_+^{-1/2}\sin\left(\nu\arccos\dfrac{1}{\sqrt{x}}\right)$	$\dfrac{\sin(\nu\pi)}{2\pi^{3/2}}\,\Gamma\left[\begin{matrix}\dfrac{2s+\nu}{2},\ \dfrac{2s-\nu}{2},\ \dfrac{1-2s}{2},\ 1-s\end{matrix}\right]$ $[|\operatorname{Re}\nu|<1;\ |\operatorname{Re}\nu|/2<\operatorname{Re}s<1/2]$

2.6.5. $\arcsin(\varphi(x))$, $\arccos(\varphi(x))$, **and the logarithmic function**

1 $\theta(a-x)\ln(bx+1)\arccos\dfrac{x}{a}$

$$\frac{\sqrt{\pi}\,a^{s+1}b}{2(s+1)}\Gamma\left[\begin{array}{c}\frac{s+2}{2}\\\frac{s+3}{2}\end{array}\right]{}_6F_5\left(\begin{array}{c}\frac{1}{2},\frac{1}{2},1,1,\frac{s+1}{2},\frac{s+2}{2}\\\frac{1}{2},1,\frac{3}{2},\frac{s+3}{2},\frac{s+3}{2};\,a^2b^2\end{array}\right)$$

$$-\frac{\sqrt{\pi}\,a^{s+2}b^2}{4(s+2)}\Gamma\left[\begin{array}{c}\frac{s+3}{2}\\\frac{s+4}{2}\end{array}\right]{}_6F_5\left(\begin{array}{c}1,1,\frac{3}{2},\frac{3}{2},\frac{s+2}{2},\frac{s+3}{2}\\\frac{3}{2},\frac{3}{2},2,\frac{s+4}{2},\frac{s+4}{2};\,a^2b^2\end{array}\right)$$

$$[a>0;\ \mathrm{Re}\,s>-1;\ |\arg b|<\pi]$$

2 $\theta(a-x)\ln\dfrac{\sqrt{a}+\sqrt{a-x}}{\sqrt{x}}$

$\times\arcsin(bx)$

$$\frac{\sqrt{\pi}\,a^{s+1}b}{2(s+1)}\Gamma\left[\begin{array}{c}s+1\\\frac{2s+3}{2}\end{array}\right]{}_5F_4\left(\begin{array}{c}\frac{1}{2},\frac{1}{2},\frac{s+1}{2},\frac{s+1}{2},\frac{s+2}{2};\,a^2b^2\\\frac{3}{2},\frac{2s+3}{4},\frac{2s+5}{4},\frac{s+3}{2}\end{array}\right)$$

$$[a>0;\ \mathrm{Re}\,s>-1]$$

3 $\theta(a-x)\ln\dfrac{\sqrt{a}+\sqrt{a-x}}{\sqrt{x}}$

$\times\dfrac{\arcsin(bx)}{\sqrt{1-b^2x^2}}$

$$\frac{\sqrt{\pi}\,a^{s+1}b}{2(s+1)}\Gamma\left[\begin{array}{c}s+1\\\frac{2s+3}{2}\end{array}\right]{}_5F_4\left(\begin{array}{c}1,1,\frac{s+1}{2},\frac{s+1}{2},\frac{s+2}{2};\,a^2b^2\\\frac{3}{2},\frac{2s+3}{4},\frac{2s+5}{4},\frac{s+3}{2}\end{array}\right)$$

$$[a>0;\ \mathrm{Re}\,s>-1]$$

4 $\theta(a-x)\ln\dfrac{a+\sqrt{a^2-x^2}}{x}$

$\times\arcsin(bx)$

$$\frac{\sqrt{\pi}\,a^{s+1}b}{s^2(s+1)}\left[\begin{array}{c}\frac{s+1}{2}\\\frac{s}{2}\end{array}\right]\left[(s+1)\,{}_3F_2\left(\begin{array}{c}\frac{1}{2},\frac{1}{2},\frac{s+1}{2};\,a^2b^2\\\frac{3}{2},\frac{s+2}{2}\end{array}\right)\right.$$

$$\left.-{}_3F_2\left(\begin{array}{c}\frac{1}{2},\frac{s+1}{2},\frac{s+1}{2};\,a^2b^2\\\frac{s+2}{2},\frac{s+3}{2}\end{array}\right)\right]$$

$$[a>0;\ \mathrm{Re}\,s>-1;\ |\arg(1+a^2/b^2)|<\pi]$$

5 $\theta(a-x)\ln\dfrac{a+\sqrt{a^2-x^2}}{x}$

$\times\dfrac{\arcsin(bx)}{\sqrt{1-b^2x^2}}$

$$\frac{\sqrt{\pi}\,a^{s+1}b}{2(s+1)}\Gamma\left[\begin{array}{c}\frac{s+1}{2}\\\frac{s+2}{2}\end{array}\right]{}_4F_3\left(\begin{array}{c}1,1,\frac{s+1}{2},\frac{s+1}{2};\,a^2b^2\\\frac{3}{2},\frac{s+2}{2},\frac{s+3}{2}\end{array}\right)$$

$$[a>0;\ \mathrm{Re}\,s>-1;\ |\arg(1+a^2b^2)|<\pi]$$

6 $(a-x)_+^{-1/2}\arcsin\sqrt{\dfrac{a-x}{a}}$

$+(x-a)_+^{-1/2}$

$\times\ln\dfrac{\sqrt{x}+\sqrt{x-a}}{\sqrt{a}}$

$$\frac{a^{s-1/2}}{2\sqrt{\pi}}\Gamma\left[s,\frac{2s+1}{2},\frac{1-2s}{2},\frac{1-2s}{2}\right] \quad [a>0;\ 0<\mathrm{Re}\,s<1/2]$$

7 $(x-a)_+^{-1/2}\arcsin\sqrt{\dfrac{x-a}{x}}$

$+(a-x)_+^{-1/2}$

$\times\ln\dfrac{\sqrt{a}+\sqrt{a-x}}{\sqrt{x}}$

$$\frac{a^{s-1/2}}{2\sqrt{\pi}}\Gamma\left[s,s,1-s,\frac{1-2s}{2}\right] \quad [a>0;\ 0<\mathrm{Re}\,s<1/2]$$

No.	$f(x)$	$F(s)$
8	$\theta(a-x)\ln(bx^2+1)$ $\times \arccos\dfrac{x}{a}$	$\dfrac{\sqrt{\pi}\,a^{s+2}b}{s(s+2)^2}\Gamma\!\left[\begin{matrix}\frac{s+3}{2}\\\frac{s+2}{2}\end{matrix}\right]\!\left[(s+2)\,_3F_2\!\left(\begin{matrix}1,1,\frac{s+3}{2}\\2,\frac{s+4}{2};-a^2b\end{matrix}\right)\right.$ $\left.-2\,_3F_2\!\left(\begin{matrix}1,\frac{s+2}{2},\frac{s+3}{2}\\\frac{s+4}{2},\frac{s+4}{2};-a^2b\end{matrix}\right)\right]$ $[\operatorname{Re}s>-2;\ |\arg(1+a^2b)|<\pi]$
9	$\theta(a-x)\ln\dfrac{b+x}{b-x}\arccos\dfrac{x}{a}$	$\dfrac{\sqrt{\pi}\,a^{s+1}}{2b(s+1)}\Gamma\!\left[\begin{matrix}\frac{s}{2}\\\frac{s+3}{2}\end{matrix}\right]\!\left[(s+1)\,_3F_2\!\left(\begin{matrix}\frac{1}{2},1,\frac{s+2}{2};\frac{a^2}{b^2}\\\frac{3}{2},\frac{s+3}{2}\end{matrix}\right)\right.$ $\left.-\,_3F_2\!\left(\begin{matrix}1,\frac{s+1}{2},\frac{s+2}{2};\frac{a^2}{b^2}\\\frac{s+3}{2},\frac{s+3}{2}\end{matrix}\right)\right]$ $[a>0;\ \operatorname{Re}s>-1;\ |\arg(b^2-a^2)|<\pi]$
10	$\theta(a-x)\arccos\dfrac{x}{a}$ $\times\ln\left(bx+\sqrt{1+b^2x^2}\right)$	$\dfrac{\sqrt{\pi}\,a^{s+1}b}{4(s+1)}\Gamma\!\left[\begin{matrix}\frac{s}{2}\\\frac{s+3}{2}\end{matrix}\right]\!\left[(s+1)\,_3F_2\!\left(\begin{matrix}\frac{1}{2},\frac{1}{2},\frac{s+2}{2}\\\frac{3}{2},\frac{s+3}{2};-a^2b^2\end{matrix}\right)\right.$ $\left.-\,_3F_2\!\left(\begin{matrix}\frac{1}{2},\frac{s+1}{2},\frac{s+2}{2}\\\frac{s+3}{2},\frac{s+3}{2};-a^2b^2\end{matrix}\right)\right]$ $[a>0;\ \operatorname{Re}s>-1;\ |\arg(1+a^2b^2)|<\pi]$
11	$\theta(a-x)\arccos\dfrac{x}{a}$ $\times\ln^2\left(bx+\sqrt{1+b^2x^2}\right)$	$\dfrac{\sqrt{\pi}\,a^{s+2}b^2}{2s(s+2)}\Gamma\!\left[\begin{matrix}\frac{s+3}{2}\\\frac{s+4}{2}\end{matrix}\right]\!\left[(s+2)\,_4F_3\!\left(\begin{matrix}1,1,1,\frac{s+3}{2};-a^2b^2\\\frac{3}{2},2,\frac{s+4}{2}\end{matrix}\right)\right.$ $\left.-2\,_4F_3\!\left(\begin{matrix}1,1,\frac{s+2}{2},\frac{s+3}{2};-a^2b^2\\\frac{3}{2},\frac{s+4}{2},\frac{s+4}{2}\end{matrix}\right)\right]$ $[a>0;\ \operatorname{Re}s>-2;\ |\arg(1+a^2b^2)|<\pi]$
12	$\dfrac{\theta(a-x)}{\sqrt{1+b^2x^2}}\arccos\dfrac{x}{a}$ $\times\ln\left(bx+\sqrt{1+b^2x^2}\right)$	$\dfrac{\sqrt{\pi}\,a^{s+1}b}{2(s+1)}\Gamma\!\left[\begin{matrix}\frac{s+2}{2}\\\frac{s+3}{2}\end{matrix}\right]\,_4F_3\!\left(\begin{matrix}1,1,\frac{s+1}{2},\frac{s+2}{2};-a^2b^2\\\frac{3}{2},\frac{s+3}{2},\frac{s+3}{2}\end{matrix}\right)$ $[a>0;\ \operatorname{Re}s>-1;\ |\arg(1+a^2b^2)|<\pi]$

2.6.6. $\arctan(\varphi(x))$ **and** $\operatorname{arccot}(bx)$

No.	$f(x)$	$F(s)$	
1	$\left\{\begin{matrix}\arctan(ax)\\\operatorname{arccot}(ax)\end{matrix}\right\}$	$\mp\dfrac{\pi a^{-s}}{2s}\sec\dfrac{s\pi}{2}$	$[\operatorname{Re}a>0;\ 0<\mp\operatorname{Re}s<1]$
2	$\arctan(ax)-ax$	$-\dfrac{\pi a^{-s}}{2s}\sec\dfrac{s\pi}{2}$	$[\operatorname{Re}a>0;\ -3<\operatorname{Re}s<-1]$

No.	$f(x)$	$F(s)$
3	$\operatorname{arccot}(ax) + ax$ $- \dfrac{\pi}{2}\, ax\sqrt{\dfrac{1}{a^2x^2}}$	$\dfrac{\pi a^{-s}}{2s}\sec\dfrac{s\pi}{2}$ $\qquad [\operatorname{Re} a > 0;\ -3 < \operatorname{Re} s < -1]$
4	$\arctan(ax)$ $- \sum_{k=0}^{n}(-1)^k\dfrac{(ax)^{2k+1}}{2k+1}$	$-\dfrac{\pi a^{-s}}{2s}\sec\dfrac{s\pi}{2}$ $\qquad [\operatorname{Re} a > 0;\ -2n - 3 < \operatorname{Re} s < 2n - 1]$
5	$\operatorname{arccot}(ax) - \dfrac{\pi}{2}\, ax\sqrt{\dfrac{1}{a^2x^2}}$ $+ \sum_{k=0}^{n}(-1)^k\dfrac{(ax)^{2k+1}}{2k+1}$	$\dfrac{\pi a^{-s}}{2s}\sec\dfrac{s\pi}{2}$ $\qquad [\operatorname{Re} a > 0;\ -2n - 3 < \operatorname{Re} s < -2n - 1]$
6	$\theta(a - x)\left\{\begin{array}{l}\arctan(x/a)\\ \operatorname{arccot}(x/a)\end{array}\right\}$	$\dfrac{a^s}{4s}\left[\pi \pm \psi\left(\dfrac{s+1}{4}\right) \mp \psi\left(\dfrac{s+3}{4}\right)\right]$ $\qquad [a > 0;\ \operatorname{Re} s > -(1 \pm 1)/2]$
7	$(a - x)_+^{\alpha-1}\arctan(bx)$	$a^{s+\alpha}b\,\mathrm{B}(s+1, \alpha)\,{}_4F_3\!\left(\begin{matrix}\frac{1}{2},\, 1,\, \frac{s+1}{2},\, \frac{s+2}{2};\, -a^2b^2\\ \frac{3}{2},\, \frac{s+\alpha+1}{2},\, \frac{s+\alpha+2}{2}\end{matrix}\right)$ $\qquad [a,\ \operatorname{Re}\alpha > 0;\ \operatorname{Re} s > -1]$
8	$(a^2 - x^2)_+^{\alpha-1}\arctan(bx)$	$\dfrac{a^{s+2\alpha-1}b}{2}\,\mathrm{B}\!\left(\dfrac{s+1}{2}, \alpha\right){}_3F_2\!\left(\begin{matrix}\frac{1}{2},\, 1,\, \frac{s+1}{2};\, -a^2b^2\\ \frac{3}{2},\, \frac{s+2\alpha+1}{2}\end{matrix}\right)$ $\qquad [a,\ \operatorname{Re}\alpha > 0;\ \operatorname{Re} s > -1]$
9	$(a - x)_+^{\alpha-1}\arctan[b(a - x)]$	$a^{s+\alpha}b\,\mathrm{B}(s, \alpha+1)\,{}_4F_3\!\left(\begin{matrix}\frac{1}{2},\, 1,\, \frac{\alpha+1}{2},\, \frac{\alpha+2}{2};\, -a^2b^2\\ \frac{3}{2},\, \frac{s+\alpha+1}{2},\, \frac{s+\alpha+2}{2}\end{matrix}\right)$ $\qquad [a,\ \operatorname{Re} s > 0;\ \operatorname{Re}\alpha > -1]$
10	$(a - x)_+^{\alpha-1}$ $\times \arctan(b\sqrt{a - x})$	$a^{s+\alpha-1/2}b\,\mathrm{B}\!\left(s, \alpha+\dfrac{1}{2}\right){}_3F_2\!\left(\begin{matrix}\frac{1}{2},\, 1,\, \frac{2\alpha+1}{2};\, -ab^2\\ \frac{3}{2},\, \frac{2s+2\alpha+1}{2}\end{matrix}\right)$ $\qquad [a,\ \operatorname{Re} s > 0;\ \operatorname{Re}\alpha > -1/2]$
11	$\theta(a - x)(bx + 1)^\alpha$ $\times \arctan(c\sqrt{a - x})$	$\dfrac{\sqrt{\pi}a^{s+1/2}c}{2}\,\Gamma\!\left[\begin{matrix}s\\ \frac{2s+3}{2}\end{matrix}\right]F_3\!\left(-\alpha, \dfrac{1}{2}, s, 1;\, \dfrac{2s+3}{2};\, -ab, -ac^2\right)$ $\qquad [a,\ \operatorname{Re} s > 0;\ |\arg b| < \pi]$
12	$(a - x)_+^{\alpha-1}$ $\times \arctan\!\big(b\sqrt{x(a - x)}\big)$	$a^{s+\alpha}b\,\mathrm{B}\!\left(s+\dfrac{1}{2}, \alpha+\dfrac{1}{2}\right){}_4F_3\!\left(\begin{matrix}\frac{1}{2},\, 1,\, \frac{2s+1}{2},\, \frac{2\alpha+1}{2};\, -\frac{a^2b^2}{4}\\ \frac{3}{2},\, \frac{s+\alpha+1}{2},\, \frac{s+\alpha+2}{2}\end{matrix}\right)$ $\qquad [a > 0;\ \operatorname{Re} s,\ \operatorname{Re}\alpha > -1/2]$

No.	$f(x)$	$F(s)$
13	$\dfrac{1}{(x+a)^\rho} \arctan \dfrac{b}{x+a}$	$a^{s-\rho-1}b\,\mathrm{B}\left(s,1-s+\rho\right)\,{}_4F_3\left(\begin{matrix}\frac{1}{2},1,\frac{1-s+\rho}{2},\frac{2-s+\rho}{2}\\\frac{3}{2},\frac{\rho+1}{2},\frac{\rho+2}{2};-\frac{b^2}{a^2}\end{matrix}\right)$ $[0<\mathrm{Re}\,s<\mathrm{Re}\,\rho+1;\ |\arg a|<\pi]$
14	$\dfrac{1}{(x+a)^\rho} \arctan \dfrac{b}{\sqrt{x+a}}$	$a^{s-\rho-1/2}b\,\mathrm{B}\left(s,\frac{1}{2}-s+\rho\right)\,{}_3F_2\left(\begin{matrix}\frac{1}{2},1,\frac{1-2s+2\rho}{2}\\\frac{3}{2},\frac{2\rho+1}{2};-\frac{b^2}{a}\end{matrix}\right)$ $[0<\mathrm{Re}\,s<\mathrm{Re}\,\rho+1/2;\ |\arg a|<\pi]$
15	$\dfrac{1}{(x+a)^\rho} \arctan \dfrac{bx}{x+a}$	$a^{s-\rho}b\,\mathrm{B}\left(s+1,\rho-s\right)\,{}_4F_3\left(\begin{matrix}\frac{1}{2},1,\frac{s+1}{2},\frac{s+2}{2}\\\frac{3}{2},\frac{\rho+1}{2},\frac{\rho+2}{2};-b^2\end{matrix}\right)$ $[-1<\mathrm{Re}\,s<\mathrm{Re}\,\rho;\ |\arg a|<\pi]$
16	$\theta\left(x-a\right) \arctan \dfrac{bx}{\sqrt{x^2-c^2}}$	$-\dfrac{a^s b}{s}\,F_2\left(\frac{1}{2},1,-\frac{s}{2};\frac{3}{2},\frac{2-s}{2};-b^2,\frac{c^2}{a^2}\right)$ $[a>c>0;\ \mathrm{Re}\,s<0;\ |\arg b|<\pi]$
17	$\theta\left(a-x\right)$ $\times \arctan\left(c\sqrt{\dfrac{a-x}{b-x}}\right)$	$\dfrac{\sqrt{\pi}\,a^{s+1/2}c}{2\sqrt{b}}\Gamma\left[\begin{matrix}s\\\frac{2s+3}{2}\end{matrix}\right]F_1\left(\frac{1}{2},s,1;s+\frac{3}{2},\frac{a}{b},-\frac{ac^2}{b}\right)$ $[b>a>0;\ \mathrm{Re}\,s>0]$
18	$\dfrac{1}{\sqrt{a+x}} \arctan\left[2bcx\right.$ $\times \left.\dfrac{1}{x-i\left(b^2+c^2\right)x+a}\right]$	$2a^{s-1/2}bc\,\mathrm{B}\left(s+1,\frac{1}{2}-s\right)F_4\left(1,s+1;\frac{3}{2},\frac{3}{2};ib^2,ic^2\right)$ $[-1<\mathrm{Re}\,s<1/2;\ |\arg a|<\pi]$
19	$\theta\left(1-x\right)\arctan\dfrac{\ln\left(-\ln x\right)}{\pi}$	$\dfrac{\pi}{s}\left[e^s-\nu\left(s\right)-\dfrac{1}{2}\right]$ $[\mathrm{Re}\,s>0]$
20	$\theta\left(1-x\right)\arctan\dfrac{\pi}{\ln\left(-\ln x\right)}$	$\dfrac{\pi}{s}\left[\nu\left(s\right)-2\sinh s\right]$ $[\mathrm{Re}\,s>0]$

2.6.7. $\arctan\left(\varphi\left(x\right)\right)$ and the exponential function

No.	$f(x)$	$F(s)$
1	$e^{-ax}\arctan\left(bx\right)$	$\dfrac{\pi}{2a^s}\Gamma\left(s\right)-\dfrac{a^{1-s}}{b}\Gamma\left(s-1\right)\,{}_2F_3\left(\begin{matrix}\frac{1}{2},1;-\frac{a^2}{4b^2}\\\frac{3}{2},\frac{2-s}{2},\frac{3-s}{2}\end{matrix}\right)-\dfrac{\pi ab^{-s-1}}{2\left(s+1\right)}\csc\dfrac{s\pi}{2}$ $\times\,{}_1F_2\left(\begin{matrix}\frac{s+1}{2};-\frac{a^2}{4b^2}\\\frac{3}{2},\frac{s+3}{2}\end{matrix}\right)-\dfrac{\pi b^{-s}}{2s}\sec\dfrac{s\pi}{2}\,{}_1F_2\left(\begin{matrix}\frac{s}{2};-\frac{a^2}{4b^2}\\\frac{1}{2},\frac{s+2}{2}\end{matrix}\right)$ $[b,\ \mathrm{Re}\,a>0;\ \mathrm{Re}\,s>-1]$

No.	$f(x)$	$F(s)$
2	$e^{-ax^2}\arctan(bx)$	$\dfrac{\pi a^{-s/2}}{4}\Gamma\left(\dfrac{s}{2}\right)-\dfrac{\pi b^{-s}}{2s}\sec\dfrac{s\pi}{2}\,{}_1F_1\left(\genfrac{}{}{0pt}{}{\frac{s}{2};\ \frac{a}{b^2}}{\frac{s+2}{2}}\right)$ $-\dfrac{a^{(1-s)/2}}{2b}\Gamma\left(\dfrac{s-1}{2}\right){}_2F_2\left(\genfrac{}{}{0pt}{}{\frac12,\,1;\ \frac{a}{b^2}}{\frac32,\,\frac{3-s}{2}}\right)$ $[b,\ \operatorname{Re}a>0;\ \operatorname{Re}s>-1]$
3	$\theta(a-x)e^{bx}$ $\times\arctan(c\sqrt{a-x})$	$\dfrac{\sqrt{\pi}\,a^{s+1/2}c}{2}\Gamma\left[\genfrac{}{}{0pt}{}{s}{s+\frac32}\right]\Xi_1\left(\dfrac12,\,s,\,1;\,s+\dfrac32;\,-ac^2,\,ab\right)$ $[a,\ \operatorname{Re}s>0]$
4	$\arctan(ae^{-x})$	$\dfrac{a}{2^{s+1}}\Gamma(s)\,\Phi\left(-a^2,\,s+1,\,\dfrac12\right)$ $[a,\ \operatorname{Re}s>0]$

2.6.8. $\arctan(\varphi(x))$ **and trigonometric functions**

No.	$f(x)$	$F(s)$
1	$\sin(ax)\arctan(bx)$	$\dfrac{\pi}{2a^s}\sin\dfrac{s\pi}{2}\Gamma(s)+\dfrac{\pi ab^{-s-1}}{2(s+1)}\csc\dfrac{s\pi}{2}\,{}_1F_2\left(\genfrac{}{}{0pt}{}{\frac{s+1}{2};\ \frac{a^2}{4b^2}}{\frac32,\,\frac{s+3}{2}}\right)$ $+\dfrac{a^{1-s}}{b}\cos\dfrac{s\pi}{2}\Gamma(s-1)\,{}_2F_3\left(\genfrac{}{}{0pt}{}{\frac12,\,1;\ \frac{a^2}{4b^2}}{\frac32,\,\frac{3-s}{2},\,1-\frac{s}{2}}\right)$ $[a,b>0;\ |\operatorname{Re}s|<1]$
2	$\cos(ax)\arctan(bx)$	$\dfrac{\pi}{2a^s}\cos\dfrac{s\pi}{2}\Gamma(s)-\dfrac{\pi b^{-s}}{2s}\sec\dfrac{s\pi}{2}\,{}_1F_2\left(\genfrac{}{}{0pt}{}{\frac{s}{2};\ \frac{a^2}{4b^2}}{\frac12,\,\frac{s+2}{2}}\right)$ $-\dfrac{a^{1-s}}{b}\sin\dfrac{s\pi}{2}\Gamma(s-1)\,{}_2F_3\left(\genfrac{}{}{0pt}{}{\frac12,\,1;\ \frac{a^2}{4b^2}}{\frac32,\,\frac{2-s}{2},\,\frac{3-s}{2}}\right)$ $[a,b>0;\ 0<\operatorname{Re}s<1]$
3	$\sin(ax)\arctan\dfrac{b}{x}$	$-\dfrac{\pi ab^{s+1}}{2(s+1)}\csc\dfrac{s\pi}{2}\,{}_1F_2\left(\genfrac{}{}{0pt}{}{\frac{s+1}{2};\ \frac{a^2b^2}{4}}{\frac32,\,\frac{s+3}{2}}\right)$ $-\dfrac{b}{a^{s-1}}\cos\dfrac{s\pi}{2}\Gamma(s-1)\,{}_2F_3\left(\genfrac{}{}{0pt}{}{\frac12,\,1;\ \frac{a^2b^2}{4}}{\frac32,\,\frac{2-s}{2},\,\frac{3-s}{2}}\right)$ $[a,b>0;\ -1<\operatorname{Re}s<2]$
4	$\cos(ax)\arctan\dfrac{b}{x}$	$\dfrac{\pi b^s}{2s}\sec\dfrac{s\pi}{2}\,{}_1F_2\left(\genfrac{}{}{0pt}{}{\frac{s}{2};\ \frac{a^2b^2}{4}}{\frac12,\,\frac{s+2}{2}}\right)$ $+\dfrac{b}{a^{s-1}}\sin\dfrac{s\pi}{2}\Gamma(s-1)\,{}_2F_3\left(\genfrac{}{}{0pt}{}{\frac12,\,1;\ \frac{a^2b^2}{4}}{\frac32,\,\frac{2-s}{2},\,\frac{3-s}{2}}\right)$ $[a,b>0;\ 0<\operatorname{Re}s<2]$

No.	$f(x)$	$F(s)$
5	$\dfrac{1}{(x^2+a^2)^{\nu/2}}$ $\times \left\{ \begin{array}{l} \sin(\nu \arctan(x/a)) \\ \cos(\nu \arctan(x/a)) \end{array} \right\}$	$a^{s-\nu} \left\{ \begin{array}{l} \sin(s\pi/2) \\ \cos(s\pi/2) \end{array} \right\} B(s, \nu-s)$ $[\operatorname{Re} a > 0;\ -(1\pm 1)/2 < \operatorname{Re} s < \operatorname{Re}\nu]$
6	$\dfrac{1}{(x^2+a^2)^{\nu/2}}$ $\times \left\{ \begin{array}{l} \sin[\nu \operatorname{arccot}(x/a)] \\ \cos[\nu \operatorname{arccot}(x/a)] \end{array} \right\}$	$a^{s-\nu} \left\{ \begin{array}{l} \sin[(\nu-s)\pi/2] \\ \cos[(\nu-s)\pi/2] \end{array} \right\} B(s, \nu-s)$ $[\operatorname{Re} a > 0;\ 0 < \operatorname{Re} s < (1\pm 1)/2 + \operatorname{Re}\nu]$
7	$(1-x)_+^{-1/2} \left[\left(1+\sqrt{1-x}\right)^\nu - \left(1-\sqrt{1-x}\right)^\nu \right]$ $+ 2x^{\nu/2}(x-1)_+^{-1/2}$ $\times \sin\left(\nu \arctan\sqrt{x-1}\right)$	$\dfrac{\sin(\nu\pi)}{\pi^{3/2}} \Gamma\left[s,\ s+\nu,\ \dfrac{1-2s-\nu}{2},\ \dfrac{2-2s-\nu}{2} \right]$ $[|\operatorname{Re}\nu| < 1;\ 0, -\operatorname{Re}\nu < \operatorname{Re} s < (1-\operatorname{Re}\nu)/2]$
8	$(x-1)_+^{-1/2} \left[\left(\sqrt{x}+\sqrt{x-1}\right)^\nu - \left(\sqrt{x}-\sqrt{x-1}\right)^\nu \right]$ $+ 2(1-x)_+^{-1/2}$ $\times \sin\left(\nu \arctan\sqrt{\dfrac{1-x}{x}}\right)$	$\dfrac{\sin(\nu\pi)}{\pi^{3/2}} \Gamma\left[s,\ \dfrac{2s+1}{2},\ \dfrac{1-2s-\nu}{2},\ \dfrac{1-2s+\nu}{2} \right]$ $[|\operatorname{Re}\nu| < 1;\ 0 < \operatorname{Re} s < (1-|\operatorname{Re}\nu|)/2]$
9	$\dfrac{1}{(x^2+2ax\cos\varphi+a^2)^\rho}$ $\times \left\{ \begin{array}{l} \sin u \\ \cos u \end{array} \right\}$ $u = 2\rho\arctan\dfrac{a\sin\varphi}{x+a\cos\varphi}$	$a^{s-2\rho} \left\{ \begin{array}{l} \sin[(2\rho-s)\varphi] \\ \cos[(2\rho-s)\varphi] \end{array} \right\} B(s, 2\rho-s)$ $[a > 0;\ 0 \le \varphi < \pi;\ 0 < \operatorname{Re} s < 2\operatorname{Re}\rho]$

2.6.9. $\arctan(\varphi(x))$ **and the logarithmic function**

No.	$f(x)$	$F(s)$
1	$\theta(a-x)\ln\dfrac{\sqrt{a}+\sqrt{a-x}}{\sqrt{x}}$ $\times \arctan(bx)$	$\dfrac{\sqrt{\pi}\,a^{s+1}b}{2s(s+1)} \Gamma\left[\begin{array}{c} s+1 \\ \frac{2s+3}{2} \end{array} \right] \left[(s+1)\ {}_4F_3\left(\begin{array}{c} \frac{1}{2},\ 1,\ \frac{s+1}{2},\ \frac{s+2}{2} \\ \frac{3}{2},\ \frac{2s+3}{4},\ \frac{2s+5}{4} \end{array}; -a^2b^2 \right) \right.$ $\left. -\ {}_4F_3\left(\begin{array}{c} 1,\ \frac{s+1}{2},\ \frac{s+1}{2},\ \frac{s+2}{2} \\ \frac{2s+3}{4},\ \frac{2s+5}{4},\ \frac{s+3}{2} \end{array}; -a^2b^2 \right) \right]$ $[a > 0;\ \operatorname{Re} s > -1;\ |\arg(1+a^2b^2)| < \pi]$

No.	$f(x)$	$F(s)$
2	$\theta(a-x)\ln\dfrac{a+\sqrt{a^2-x^2}}{x}$ $\times \arctan(bx)$	$\dfrac{\sqrt{\pi}\,a^{s+1}b}{s(s+1)}\Gamma\!\left[\begin{matrix}\frac{s+1}{2}\\ \frac{s}{2}\end{matrix}\right]{}_4F_3\!\left(\begin{matrix}\frac{1}{2},\,1,\,\frac{s+1}{2},\,\frac{s+1}{2}\\ \frac{3}{2},\,\frac{s+2}{2},\,\frac{s+3}{2}\end{matrix};\,-a^2b^2\right)$ $\left[a>0;\ \mathrm{Re}\,s>-1;\ \left|\arg\left(1+a^2b^2\right)\right|<\pi\right]$
3	$\theta(a-x)\ln\dfrac{a+\sqrt{a^2-x^2}}{a-\sqrt{a^2-x^2}}$ $\times \arctan(bx)$	$\dfrac{2\sqrt{\pi}\,a^{s+1}b}{s^2(s+1)}\Gamma\!\left[\begin{matrix}\frac{s+1}{2}\\ \frac{s}{2}\end{matrix}\right]\left[(s+1)\,{}_3F_2\!\left(\begin{matrix}\frac{1}{2},\,1,\,\frac{s+1}{2}\\ \frac{3}{2},\,\frac{s+2}{2}\end{matrix};\,-a^2b^2\right)\right.$ $\left.-\,{}_3F_2\!\left(\begin{matrix}1,\,\frac{s+1}{2},\,\frac{s+1}{2}\\ \frac{s+2}{2},\,\frac{s+3}{2}\end{matrix};\,-a^2b^2\right)\right]$ $\left[a>0;\ \mathrm{Re}\,s>-1;\ \left|\arg\left(1+a^2b^2\right)\right|<\pi\right]$

2.6.10. $\operatorname{arccsc}(\varphi(x))$ **and algebraic functions**

No.	$f(x)$	$F(s)$	
1	$\operatorname{arccsc}(ax)$	$\dfrac{i(ia)^{-s}}{2\sqrt{\pi}\,s}\Gamma\!\left(\dfrac{s}{2}\right)\Gamma\!\left(\dfrac{1-s}{2}\right)$	$[\mathrm{Im}\,a<0;\ 0<\mathrm{Re}\,s<1]$
2	$\theta(x-a)\operatorname{arccsc}\dfrac{x}{a}$	$-\dfrac{\sqrt{\pi}\,a^s}{s^2}\Gamma\!\left[\begin{matrix}\frac{1-s}{2}\\ -\frac{s}{2}\end{matrix}\right]-\dfrac{\pi a^s}{2s}$	$[a>0;\ \mathrm{Re}\,s<0]$
3	$\dfrac{\operatorname{arccsc}(ax)}{\sqrt{a^2x^2-1}}$	$-\dfrac{\pi^{3/2}(ia)^{-s}}{4}\csc\dfrac{s\pi}{2}\Gamma\!\left[\begin{matrix}\frac{s}{2}\\ \frac{s+1}{2}\end{matrix}\right]$	$[\mathrm{Im}\,a<0;\ 0<\mathrm{Re}\,s<2]$
4	$\theta(a-x)\operatorname{arccsc}\dfrac{a}{x}$	$-\dfrac{\sqrt{\pi}\,a^s}{s^2}\Gamma\!\left[\begin{matrix}\frac{s+1}{2}\\ \frac{s}{2}\end{matrix}\right]+\dfrac{\pi a^s}{2s}$	$[a,\ \mathrm{Re}\,s>0]$
5	$\operatorname{arccsc}^2(ax)$	$-\dfrac{\pi^{3/2}(ia)^{-s}}{2s}\csc\dfrac{s\pi}{2}\Gamma\!\left[\begin{matrix}\frac{s}{2}\\ \frac{s+1}{2}\end{matrix}\right]$	$[\mathrm{Im}\,a<0;\ 0<\mathrm{Re}\,s<2]$

2.6.11. $\operatorname{arcsec}(bx)$ **and algebraic functions**

No.	$f(x)$	$F(s)$	
1	$\theta(x-a)\operatorname{arcsec}\dfrac{x}{a}$	$\dfrac{\sqrt{\pi}\,a^s}{s^2}\Gamma\!\left[\begin{matrix}\frac{1-s}{2}\\ -\frac{s}{2}\end{matrix}\right]$	$[a>0;\ \mathrm{Re}\,s<0]$
2	$\operatorname{arcsec}(ax)-\dfrac{\pi}{2}$	$\dfrac{i}{2\sqrt{\pi}\,s}\left(-\dfrac{1}{a^2}\right)^{s/2}\Gamma\!\left(\dfrac{1-s}{2}\right)\Gamma\!\left(\dfrac{s}{2}\right)$	$[\mathrm{Re}\,a>0;\ 0<\mathrm{Re}\,s<1]$
3	$\operatorname{arcsec}^2(ax)-\dfrac{\pi^2}{4}$	$-\dfrac{\pi^{3/2}(ia)^{-s}}{s}e^{is\pi/2}\csc(s\pi)\Gamma\!\left[\begin{matrix}\frac{s}{2}\\ \frac{s+1}{2}\end{matrix}\right]$	$[\mathrm{Im}\,a<0;\ 0<\mathrm{Re}\,s<1]$

2.6.12. Products of inverse trigonometric functions

1	$\theta\left(a-x\right)\arcsin^2\left(bx\right)$	$\dfrac{a^s\arcsin^2\left(ab\right)}{s}-\dfrac{2a^{s+2}b^2}{s\left(s+2\right)}\,{}_3F_2\!\left(\begin{matrix}1,\,1,\,\frac{s+2}{2}\\\frac{3}{2},\,\frac{s+4}{2};\,a^2b^2\end{matrix}\right)$
		$\left[a>0;\ \operatorname{Re}s>-2;\ \left|\arg\left(1-a^2b^2\right)\right|<\pi\right]$
2	$\arcsin^2\left(ax\right)$	$-\dfrac{\pi^{3/2}\left(ia\right)^{-s}}{2s}\csc\dfrac{s\pi}{2}\,\Gamma\!\left[\begin{matrix}-\frac{s}{2}\\\frac{1-s}{2}\end{matrix}\right]\qquad\left[\operatorname{Im}a<0;\ -2<\operatorname{Re}s<0\right]$
3	$\arccos^2\left(ax\right)-\dfrac{\pi^2}{4}$	$-\dfrac{\pi^{3/2}\left(ia\right)^{-s}}{2s}e^{is\pi/2}\csc\left(s\pi\right)\Gamma\!\left[\begin{matrix}-\frac{s}{2}\\\frac{1-s}{2}\end{matrix}\right]\qquad\left[\operatorname{Im}a<0;\ -1<\operatorname{Re}s<0\right]$
4	$\theta\left(a-x\right)\arcsin\left(bx\right)$	$\dfrac{\sqrt{\pi}\,a^{s+1}b}{4\left(s+1\right)}\,\Gamma\!\left[\begin{matrix}\frac{s}{2}\\\frac{s+3}{2}\end{matrix}\right]\left[\left(s+1\right){}_3F_2\!\left(\begin{matrix}\frac{1}{2},\,\frac{1}{2},\,\frac{s+2}{2}\\\frac{3}{2},\,\frac{s+3}{2};\,a^2b^2\end{matrix}\right)\right.$
	$\times\arccos\dfrac{x}{a}$	$\left.-\,{}_3F_2\!\left(\begin{matrix}\frac{1}{2},\,\frac{s+1}{2},\,\frac{s+2}{2}\\\frac{s+3}{2},\,\frac{s+3}{2};\,a^2b^2\end{matrix}\right)\right]$
		$\left[a>0;\ \operatorname{Re}s>-1;\ \left|\arg\left(1-a^2b^2\right)\right|<\pi\right]$
5	$\dfrac{\theta\left(a-x\right)}{\sqrt{1-b^2x^2}}\arcsin\left(bx\right)$	$\dfrac{\sqrt{\pi}\,a^{s+1}b}{2\left(s+1\right)}\,\Gamma\!\left[\begin{matrix}\frac{s+2}{2}\\\frac{s+3}{2}\end{matrix}\right]{}_4F_3\!\left(\begin{matrix}1,\,1,\,\frac{s+1}{2},\,\frac{s+2}{2}\\\frac{3}{2},\,\frac{s+3}{2},\,\frac{s+3}{2};\,a^2b^2\end{matrix}\right)$
	$\times\arccos\dfrac{x}{a}$	$\left[a>0;\ \operatorname{Re}s>-1;\ \left|\arg\left(1-a^2b^2\right)\right|<\pi\right]$
6	$\theta\left(a-x\right)\arctan\left(bx\right)$	$\dfrac{\sqrt{\pi}\,a^{s+1}b}{4\left(s+1\right)}\,\Gamma\!\left[\begin{matrix}\frac{s}{2}\\\frac{s+3}{2}\end{matrix}\right]\left[\left(s+1\right){}_3F_2\!\left(\begin{matrix}\frac{1}{2},\,1,\,\frac{s+2}{2}\\\frac{3}{2},\,\frac{s+3}{2};\,-a^2b^2\end{matrix}\right)\right.$
	$\times\arccos\dfrac{x}{a}$	$\left.-\,{}_3F_2\!\left(\begin{matrix}1,\,\frac{s+1}{2},\,\frac{s+2}{2}\\\frac{s+3}{2},\,\frac{s+3}{2};\,-a^2b^2\end{matrix}\right)\right]$
		$\left[a>0;\ \operatorname{Re}s>-1;\ \left|\arg\left(1+a^2b^2\right)\right|<\pi\right]$
7	$\left(a-x\right)_+^{\alpha-1}\arcsin^2\left(bx\right)$	$a^{s+\alpha+1}b^2\,\mathrm{B}\left(s+2,\,\alpha\right){}_5F_4\!\left(\begin{matrix}1,\,1,\,1,\,\frac{s+2}{2},\,\frac{s+3}{2};\,a^2b^2\\\frac{3}{2},\,2,\,\frac{s+\alpha+2}{2},\,\frac{s+\alpha+3}{2}\end{matrix}\right)$
		$\left[a,\ \operatorname{Re}\alpha>0;\ \operatorname{Re}s>-2;\ \left|\arg\left(1-a^2b^2\right)\right|<\pi\right]$
8	$\left(a^2-x^2\right)_+^{\alpha-1}\arcsin^2\left(bx\right)$	$\dfrac{a^{s+2\alpha}b^2}{2}\,\mathrm{B}\!\left(\dfrac{s+2}{2},\,\alpha\right){}_4F_3\!\left(\begin{matrix}1,\,1,\,1,\,\frac{s+2}{2};\,a^2b^2\\\frac{3}{2},\,2,\,\frac{s+2\alpha+2}{2}\end{matrix}\right)$
		$\left[a,\ \operatorname{Re}\alpha>0;\ \operatorname{Re}s>-2;\ \left|\arg\left(1-a^2b^2\right)\right|<\pi\right]$
9	$\theta\left(a-x\right)\ln\dfrac{\sqrt{a}+\sqrt{a-x}}{\sqrt{x}}$	$\dfrac{\sqrt{\pi}\,a^{s+2}b^2}{2s}\,\Gamma\!\left[\begin{matrix}s+2\\\frac{2s+5}{2}\end{matrix}\right]\left[{}_5F_4\!\left(\begin{matrix}1,\,1,\,1,\,\frac{s+2}{2},\,\frac{s+3}{2}\\\frac{3}{2},\,2,\,\frac{2s+5}{4},\,\frac{2s+7}{4};\,a^2b^2\end{matrix}\right)\right.$
	$\times\arcsin^2\left(bx\right)$	$\left.-\,\dfrac{2}{s+2}\,{}_5F_4\!\left(\begin{matrix}1,\,1,\,\frac{s+2}{2},\,\frac{s+2}{2},\,\frac{s+3}{2}\\\frac{3}{2},\,\frac{2s+5}{4},\,\frac{2s+7}{4},\,\frac{s+4}{2};\,a^2b^2\end{matrix}\right)\right]$
		$\left[a>0;\ \operatorname{Re}s>-2;\ \left|\arg\left(1-a^2b^2\right)\right|<\pi\right]$

No.	$f(x)$	$F(s)$
10	$\theta(a-x)\ln\dfrac{a+\sqrt{a^2-x^2}}{x}$ $\times \arcsin^2(bx)$	$\dfrac{\sqrt{\pi}\,a^{s+2}b^2}{2(s+2)}\,\Gamma\!\begin{bmatrix}\frac{s+2}{2}\\\frac{s+3}{2}\end{bmatrix}{}_5F_4\!\left(\begin{matrix}1,1,1,\frac{s+2}{2},\frac{s+2}{2};\,a^2b^2\\\frac{3}{2},2,\frac{s+3}{2},\frac{s+4}{2}\end{matrix}\right)$ $\left[a>0;\ \operatorname{Re}s>-2;\ \left|\arg\left(1-a^2b^2\right)\right|<\pi\right]$
11	$(a-x)_+^{\alpha-1}$ $\times \arcsin^2(b(a-x))$	$a^{s+\alpha+1}b^2\,\mathrm{B}(s,\alpha+2)\,{}_5F_4\!\left(\begin{matrix}1,1,1,\frac{\alpha+2}{2},\frac{\alpha+3}{2};\,a^2b^2\\\frac{3}{2},2,\frac{s+\alpha+2}{2},\frac{s+\alpha+3}{2}\end{matrix}\right)$ $\left[a,\ \operatorname{Re}s>0;\ \operatorname{Re}\alpha>-2;\ \left|\arg\left(1-a^2b^2\right)\right|<\pi\right]$
12	$(a-x)_+^{\alpha-1}$ $\times \arcsin^2(bx(a-x))$	$a^{s+\alpha+3}b^2\,\mathrm{B}(s+2,\alpha+2)$ $\times\,{}_7F_6\!\left(\begin{matrix}1,1,1,\Delta(2,\alpha+2),\Delta(2,s+2)\\\frac{3}{2},2,\Delta(4,s+\alpha+4);\,\frac{a^4b^2}{16}\end{matrix}\right)$ $\left[a>0;\ \operatorname{Re}s,\ \operatorname{Re}\alpha>-2;\ \left|\arg\left(16-a^4b^2\right)\right|<\pi\right]$
13	$(a-x)_+^{\alpha-1}$ $\times \arcsin^2(b\sqrt{a-x})$	$a^{s+\alpha}b^2\,\mathrm{B}(s,\alpha+1)\,{}_4F_3\!\left(\begin{matrix}1,1,1,\alpha+1;\,ab^2\\\frac{3}{2},2,s+\alpha+1\end{matrix}\right)$ $\left[a,\ \operatorname{Re}s>0;\ \operatorname{Re}\alpha>-1;\ \left|\arg\left(1-ab^2\right)\right|<\pi\right]$
14	$(a-x)_+^{\alpha-1}$ $\times \arcsin^2\!\left(b\sqrt{x(a-x)}\right)$	$a^{s+\alpha+1}b^2\,\mathrm{B}(s+1,\alpha+1)\,{}_5F_4\!\left(\begin{matrix}1,1,1,\alpha+1,s+1;\,\frac{a^2b^2}{4}\\\frac{3}{2},2,\frac{s+\alpha+2}{2},\frac{s+\alpha+3}{2}\end{matrix}\right)$ $\left[a>0;\ \operatorname{Re}s,\ \operatorname{Re}\alpha>-1;\ \left|\arg\left(4-a^2b^2\right)\right|<\pi\right]$
15	$(a-x)_+^{\alpha-1}$ $\times \arcsin^2(bx\sqrt{a-x})$	$a^{s+\alpha+2}b^2\,\mathrm{B}(s+2,\alpha+1)\,{}_6F_5\!\left(\begin{matrix}1,1,1,\alpha+1,\frac{s+2}{2},\frac{s+3}{2};\,\frac{4a^3b^2}{27}\\\frac{3}{2},2,\frac{s+\alpha+3}{3},\frac{s+\alpha+4}{3},\frac{s+\alpha+5}{3}\end{matrix}\right)$ $\left[a>0;\ \operatorname{Re}\alpha>-1;\ \operatorname{Re}s>-2;\ \left|\arg\left(27-4a^3b^2\right)\right|<\pi\right]$
16	$\dfrac{1}{(x+a)^\rho}\arcsin^2\dfrac{b}{x+a}$	$a^{s-\rho-2}b^2\,\mathrm{B}(s,2-s+\rho)\,{}_5F_4\!\left(\begin{matrix}1,1,1,\frac{2-s+\rho}{2},\frac{3-s+\rho}{2}\\\frac{3}{2},2,\frac{\rho+2}{2},\frac{\rho+3}{2};\,\frac{b^2}{a^2}\end{matrix}\right)$ $\left[0<\operatorname{Re}s<\operatorname{Re}\rho+2;\ \left|\arg a\right|<\pi\right]$
17	$\dfrac{1}{(x+a)^\rho}\arcsin^2\dfrac{bx}{x+a}$	$a^{s-\rho}b^2\,\mathrm{B}(s+2,\rho-s)\,{}_5F_4\!\left(\begin{matrix}1,1,1,\frac{s+2}{2},\frac{s+3}{2}\\\frac{3}{2},2,\frac{\rho+2}{2},\frac{\rho+3}{2};\,b^2\end{matrix}\right)$ $\left[-2<\operatorname{Re}s<\operatorname{Re}\rho;\ \left|\arg a\right|<\pi\right]$
18	$\theta(a-x)\arcsin^2(bx)$ $\times \arccos\dfrac{x}{a}$	$\dfrac{\sqrt{\pi}\,a^{s+2}b^2}{2s(s+2)}\,\Gamma\!\begin{bmatrix}\frac{s+3}{2}\\\frac{s+4}{2}\end{bmatrix}\!\left[(s+2)\,{}_4F_3\!\left(\begin{matrix}1,1,1,\frac{s+3}{2}\\\frac{3}{2},2,\frac{s+4}{2};\,a^2b^2\end{matrix}\right)\right.$ $\left.-2\,{}_4F_3\!\left(\begin{matrix}1,1,\frac{s+2}{2},\frac{s+3}{2}\\\frac{3}{2},\frac{s+4}{2},\frac{s+4}{2};\,a^2b^2\end{matrix}\right)\right]$ $\left[a>0;\ \operatorname{Re}s>-2;\ \left|\arg\left(1-a^2b^2\right)\right|<\pi\right]$

2.7. Inverse Hyperbolic Functions

More formulas can be obtained from the corresponding sections due to the relations

$$\operatorname{arcsinh} z = \ln\left(z + \sqrt{z^2 + 1}\right); \quad \operatorname{arccosh} z = \ln\left(z + \sqrt{z^2 - 1}\right), \quad -\pi/2 < \arg z \le \pi/2;$$

$$\operatorname{arcsinh} z = z\,{}_2F_1\left(\frac{1}{2}, \frac{1}{2}; \frac{3}{2}; -z^2\right), \quad \operatorname{arccosh} z = \frac{\sqrt{z-1}}{\sqrt{1-z}}\left[\frac{\pi}{2} - z\,{}_2F_1\left(\frac{1}{2}, \frac{1}{2}; \frac{3}{2}; z^2\right)\right],$$

$$\frac{\operatorname{arcsinh} z}{\sqrt{z^2+1}} = z\,{}_2F_1\left(1, 1; \frac{3}{2}; -z^2\right); \quad \operatorname{arcsinh}^2 z = z^2\,{}_3F_2\left(1, 1, 1; \frac{3}{2}, 2; -z^2\right),$$

$$\operatorname{arctanh} z = \frac{1}{2}\left[\ln\left(1+z\right) - \ln\left(1-z\right)\right], \quad \operatorname{arctanh} z = z\,{}_2F_1\left(1, \frac{1}{2}; \frac{3}{2}; z^2\right),$$

$$\operatorname{arccoth} z = \frac{1}{2}\left[\ln\frac{z+1}{z} - \ln\frac{z-1}{z}\right],$$

$$\operatorname{arccoth} z = -\frac{\pi z}{2}\sqrt{-\frac{1}{z^2}}\sqrt{\frac{1}{1-z^2}}\sqrt{1-z^2} + z\,{}_2F_1\left(\frac{1}{2}, 1; \frac{3}{2}; z^2\right),$$

$$\operatorname{arccsch} z = \frac{1}{z}\,{}_2F_1\left(\frac{1}{2}, \frac{1}{2}; \frac{3}{2}; -\frac{1}{z^2}\right), \quad \operatorname{arcsech} z = \frac{\sqrt{z^{-1}-1}}{\sqrt{1-z^{-1}}}\left[\frac{\pi}{2} - \frac{1}{z}\,{}_2F_1\left(\frac{1}{2}, \frac{1}{2}; \frac{3}{2}; \frac{1}{z^2}\right)\right],$$

$$\operatorname{arcsinh} z = \frac{1}{2\sqrt{\pi}\,z}\,G_{22}^{12}\left(z^2 \left| \begin{array}{c} 3/2, 3/2 \\ 1, 1/2 \end{array}\right.\right),$$

$$\operatorname{arccosh} z = \frac{\sqrt{z-1}}{\sqrt{1-z}}\left[\frac{\pi}{2} - \frac{z}{2\sqrt{\pi}}\,G_{22}^{12}\left(-z^2 \left| \begin{array}{c} 1/2, 1/2 \\ 0, -1/2 \end{array}\right.\right)\right],$$

$$\operatorname{arctanh} z = -\frac{1}{2z}\,G_{22}^{12}\left(-z^2 \left| \begin{array}{c} 1, 3/2 \\ 1, 1/2 \end{array}\right.\right), \quad \operatorname{arccoth} z = \frac{1}{2z}\,G_{22}^{12}\left(-\frac{1}{z^2} \left| \begin{array}{c} 0, 1/2 \\ 0, -1/2 \end{array}\right.\right).$$

2.7.1. $\operatorname{arcsinh}^n\left(\varphi\left(x\right)\right)$ and elementary functions

No.	$f\left(x\right)$	$F\left(s\right)$
1	$\operatorname{arcsinh}\left(ax\right)$	$\dfrac{a^{-s}}{2s^2}\,\mathrm{B}\left(\dfrac{s+1}{2}, \dfrac{2-s}{2}\right)$ $\qquad$ [$\operatorname{Re} a > 0;\ -1 < \operatorname{Re} s < 0$]
2	$\operatorname{arcsinh}\left(ax\right) - ax$	$\dfrac{a^{-s}}{2s^2}\,\mathrm{B}\left(\dfrac{s+1}{2}, \dfrac{2-s}{2}\right)$ $\qquad$ [$\operatorname{Re} a > 0;\ -3 < \operatorname{Re} s < -1$]
3	$\operatorname{arcsinh}\left(ax\right)$ $-\sum\limits_{k=0}^{n}(-1)^k\,\dfrac{(1/2)_k}{k!\,(2k+1)}\,(ax)^{2k+1}$	$\dfrac{a^{-s}}{2s^2}\,\mathrm{B}\left(\dfrac{s+1}{2}, \dfrac{2-s}{2}\right)$ $\qquad$ [$\operatorname{Re} a > 0;\ -2n-3 < \operatorname{Re} s < -2n-1$]
4	$\operatorname{arcsinh}\left(ax\right) - \ln\left(2ax\right)$ $+\dfrac{1}{2}\sum\limits_{k=1}^{n}(-1)^k\,\dfrac{(1/2)_k}{k!\,k}\,(ax)^{-2k}$	$\dfrac{a^{-s}}{2s^2}\,\mathrm{B}\left(\dfrac{s+1}{2}, \dfrac{2-s}{2}\right)$ $\qquad$ [$\operatorname{Re} a > 0;\ 2n < \operatorname{Re} s < 2n+2$]

No.	$f(x)$	$F(s)$
5	$\theta(a-x)\operatorname{arcsinh}(bx)$	$-\dfrac{a^{s+1}b}{s(s+1)}\,{}_2F_1\left(\begin{matrix}\frac{1}{2},\ \frac{s+1}{2}\\[2pt]\frac{s+3}{2};\ -a^2b^2\end{matrix}\right)+\operatorname{arcsinh}(ab)\dfrac{a^s}{s}$ $[a>0;\ \operatorname{Re}s>-1]$
6	$(a-x)_+^{\alpha-1}\operatorname{arcsinh}(bx)$	$a^{s+\alpha}b\,\mathrm{B}(\alpha,s+1)\,{}_4F_3\left(\begin{matrix}\frac{1}{2},\ \frac{1}{2},\ \frac{s+1}{2},\ \frac{s+2}{2};\ -a^2b^2\\[2pt]\frac{3}{2},\ \frac{s+\alpha+1}{2},\ \frac{s+\alpha+2}{2}\end{matrix}\right)$ $[a,\ \operatorname{Re}\alpha>0;\ \operatorname{Re}s>-1]$
7	$\dfrac{1}{\sqrt{a^2x^2+1}}\operatorname{arcsinh}(ax)$	$\dfrac{\pi^{3/2}a^{-s}}{4}\sec\dfrac{s\pi}{2}\,\Gamma\!\left[\begin{matrix}\frac{1-s}{2}\\[2pt]\frac{2-s}{2}\end{matrix}\right]\qquad[\operatorname{Re}a>0;\ -1<\operatorname{Re}s<1]$
8	$\theta(a-x)\arccos\dfrac{x}{a}\operatorname{arcsinh}(bx)$	$\dfrac{\sqrt{\pi}a^{s+1}b}{2(s+1)}\,\Gamma\!\left[\begin{matrix}\frac{s+2}{2}\\[2pt]\frac{s+3}{2}\end{matrix}\right]\,{}_4F_3\left(\begin{matrix}\frac{1}{2},\ \frac{1}{2},\ \frac{s+1}{2},\ \frac{s+2}{2}\\[2pt]\frac{3}{2},\ \frac{s+3}{2},\ \frac{s+3}{2};\ -a^2b^2\end{matrix}\right)$ $[a>0;\ \operatorname{Re}s>-1]$
9	$\dfrac{1}{\sqrt{a^2x^2+1}}\operatorname{arcsinh}\dfrac{1}{ax}$	$\dfrac{\pi^{3/2}a^{-s}}{4}\csc\dfrac{s\pi}{2}\,\Gamma\!\left[\begin{matrix}\frac{s}{2}\\[2pt]\frac{s+1}{2}\end{matrix}\right]\qquad[\operatorname{Re}a>0;\ 0<\operatorname{Re}s<2]$
10	$\operatorname{arcsinh}\sqrt{\dfrac{\sqrt{ax+1}-1}{2}}$	$-\dfrac{a^{-s}}{4s}\,\mathrm{B}\left(s+\dfrac{1}{2},-s\right)\quad[-1/2<\operatorname{Re}s<0;\ |\arg a|<\pi]$
11	$\operatorname{arcsinh}\sqrt{\dfrac{\sqrt{ax+1}-\sqrt{ax}}{2\sqrt{ax}}}$	$\dfrac{a^{-s}}{4s}\,\mathrm{B}\left(s,\dfrac{1}{2}-s\right)\qquad[0<\operatorname{Re}s<1/2;\ |\arg a|<\pi]$
12	$\operatorname{arcsinh}^2(ax)$	$-\dfrac{\pi^{3/2}a^{-s}}{s^2}\csc\dfrac{s\pi}{2}\,\Gamma\!\left[\begin{matrix}\frac{2-s}{2}\\[2pt]\frac{1-s}{2}\end{matrix}\right]\quad[\operatorname{Re}a>0;\ -2<\operatorname{Re}s<0]$
13	$(a-x)_+^{\alpha-1}\operatorname{arcsinh}^2(bx)$	$a^{s+\alpha+1}b^2\,\mathrm{B}(\alpha,s+2)\,{}_5F_4\left(\begin{matrix}1,\ 1,\ 1,\ \frac{s+2}{2},\ \frac{s+3}{2};\ -a^2b^2\\[2pt]\frac{3}{2},\ 2,\ \frac{s+\alpha+2}{2},\ \frac{s+\alpha+3}{2}\end{matrix}\right)$ $[a,\ \operatorname{Re}\alpha>0;\ \operatorname{Re}s>-2]$
14	$\theta(a-x)\arccos\dfrac{x}{a}\operatorname{arcsinh}^2(bx)$	$\dfrac{\sqrt{\pi}a^{s+2}b^2}{2(s+2)}\,\Gamma\!\left[\begin{matrix}\frac{s+3}{2}\\[2pt]\frac{s+4}{2}\end{matrix}\right]\,{}_5F_4\left(\begin{matrix}1,\ 1,\ 1,\ \frac{s+2}{2},\ \frac{s+3}{2}\\[2pt]\frac{3}{2},\ 2,\ \frac{s+4}{2},\ \frac{s+4}{2};\ -a^2b^2\end{matrix}\right)$ $[a>0;\ \operatorname{Re}s>-2]$
15	$\operatorname{arcsinh}^2\sqrt{\dfrac{\sqrt{ax+1}-1}{2}}$	$\dfrac{\pi^{3/2}a^{-s}}{8s}\csc(s\pi)\,\Gamma\!\left[\begin{matrix}-s\\[2pt]\frac{1-2s}{2}\end{matrix}\right]\ [-1<\operatorname{Re}s<0;\ |\arg a|<\pi]$
16	$\operatorname{arcsinh}^2\sqrt{\dfrac{\sqrt{ax+1}-\sqrt{ax}}{2\sqrt{ax}}}$	$\dfrac{\pi^{3/2}a^{-s}}{8s}\csc(s\pi)\,\Gamma\!\left[\begin{matrix}s\\[2pt]\frac{2s+1}{2}\end{matrix}\right]\quad[0<\operatorname{Re}s<1;\ |\arg a|<\pi]$

2.7.2. $\operatorname{arccosh}^n (\varphi (x))$ and elementary functions

1	$\operatorname{arccosh} (ax) + \dfrac{i\pi}{2}$	$\dfrac{(ia)^{-s}}{2s^2} \mathrm{B} \left(\dfrac{s+1}{2}, 1-s \right)$ $[\operatorname{Im} a < 0; \, -1 < \operatorname{Re} s < 0]$
2	$\operatorname{arccosh} (ax) - \dfrac{\pi}{2} \dfrac{\sqrt{ax-1}}{\sqrt{1-ax}}$ $+ \dfrac{\sqrt{ax-1}}{\sqrt{1-ax}} \displaystyle\sum_{k=0}^{n} \dfrac{(1/2)_k}{k! \, (2k+1)} (ax)^{2k+1}$	$\dfrac{i\sqrt{a-1}}{2\sqrt{\pi}\sqrt{1-a}\,s^2} (ia)^{-s} \mathrm{B} \left(\dfrac{s+1}{2}, 1-s \right)$ $[\operatorname{Im} a < 0; \, -2n-3 < \operatorname{Re} s < -2n-1]$
3	$\operatorname{arccosh} (ax) - \dfrac{1}{2} \ln \left(-4a^2 x^2 \right)$ $+ \dfrac{\pi\sqrt{-a^2}}{2a} + \dfrac{1}{2} \displaystyle\sum_{k=1}^{n} \dfrac{(1/2)_k}{k\,k!} (ax)^{-2k}$	$\dfrac{a^{-s} e^{is\pi/2}}{2s^2} \mathrm{B} \left(\dfrac{s+1}{2}, 1-s \right)$ $[\operatorname{Im} a > 0; \, 2n < \operatorname{Re} s < 2n+2]$
4	$\operatorname{arccosh} \left(\sqrt{ax} + \sqrt{ax+1} \right)$	$-\dfrac{a^{-s}}{s} \cos (s\pi) \mathrm{B} \left(-2s, 2s + \dfrac{1}{2} \right)$ $[-1/4 < \operatorname{Re} s < 0; \, |\arg a| < \pi]$
5	$\operatorname{arccosh} \dfrac{1}{\sqrt{ax+1} - \sqrt{ax}}$	$-\dfrac{a^{-s}}{s} \cos (s\pi) \mathrm{B} \left(-2s, 2s + \dfrac{1}{2} \right)$ $[-1/4 < \operatorname{Re} s < 0; \, |\arg a| < \pi]$
6	$\operatorname{arccosh} \dfrac{\sqrt{ax}}{\sqrt{ax+1} - 1}$	$\dfrac{a^{-s}}{s} \cos (s\pi) \mathrm{B} \left(2s, \dfrac{1}{2} - 2s \right)$ $[0 < \operatorname{Re} s < 1/4; \, |\arg a| < \pi]$
7	$\operatorname{arccosh} \dfrac{\sqrt{ax+1} + 1}{\sqrt{ax}}$	$\dfrac{a^{-s}}{s} \cos (s\pi) \mathrm{B} \left(2s, \dfrac{1}{2} - 2s \right)$ $[0 < \operatorname{Re} s < 1/4; \, |\arg a| < \pi]$
8	$\operatorname{arccosh}^2 (ax) + \dfrac{\pi^2}{4}$	$\dfrac{\pi^{3/2}}{s} (ia)^{-s} e^{is\pi/2} \csc (s\pi) \Gamma \left[\begin{matrix} -\frac{s}{2} \\ \frac{1-s}{2} \end{matrix} \right]$ $[\operatorname{Im} a < 0; \, -1 < \operatorname{Re} s < 0]$

2.7.3. $\operatorname{arctanh} (ax)$ and elementary functions

1	$\operatorname{arctanh} (ax)$	$\dfrac{i\pi}{2s} (ia)^{-s} \sec \dfrac{s\pi}{2}$ $[\operatorname{Im} a < 0; \, -1 < \operatorname{Re} s < 0]$
2	$\operatorname{arctanh} (ax) - ax$	$\dfrac{i\pi}{2s} (ia)^{-s} \sec \dfrac{s\pi}{2}$ $[\operatorname{Im} a < 0; \, -3 < \operatorname{Re} s < -1]$

No.	$f(x)$	$F(s)$
3	$\operatorname{arctanh}(ax) - \sum_{k=0}^{n} \dfrac{(ax)^{2k+1}}{2k+1}$	$\dfrac{i\pi}{2s}(ia)^{-s}\sec\dfrac{s\pi}{2}$ $[\operatorname{Im} a < 0;\ -2n-3 < \operatorname{Re} s < -2n-1]$
4	$\operatorname{arctanh}(ax) - \dfrac{\pi i}{2} - \sum_{k=0}^{n} \dfrac{(ax)^{-2k-1}}{2k+1}$	$\dfrac{i\pi}{2s}\left(\dfrac{i}{a}\right)^{s}\sec\dfrac{s\pi}{2}\quad [\operatorname{Im} a > 0;\ 2n+1 < \operatorname{Re} s < 2n+3]$
5	$(a-x)_{+}^{\alpha-1}\operatorname{arctanh}(bx)$	$a^{s+\alpha}b\,\mathrm{B}(\alpha,\,s+1)\ _4F_3\left(\begin{matrix}\frac{1}{2},\,1,\,\frac{s+1}{2},\,\frac{s+2}{2};\,a^2b^2\\[2pt]\frac{3}{2},\,\frac{s+\alpha+1}{2},\,\frac{s+\alpha+2}{2}\end{matrix}\right)$ $[a,\ \operatorname{Re}\alpha > 0;\ \operatorname{Re} s > -1]$
6	$\theta(a-x)\ln\dfrac{\sqrt{a-x}+\sqrt{a}}{\sqrt{x}}$ $\times\operatorname{arctanh}(bx)$	$\dfrac{\sqrt{\pi}\,a^{s+1}b}{2s(s+1)}\Gamma\!\left[\begin{matrix}s+1\\2s+3\\2\end{matrix}\right]\left[(s+1)\ _4F_3\left(\begin{matrix}\frac{1}{2},\,1,\,\frac{s+1}{2},\,\frac{s+2}{2}\\[2pt]\frac{3}{2},\,\frac{2s+3}{4},\,\frac{2s+5}{4};\,a^2b^2\end{matrix}\right)\right.$ $\left.-\ _4F_3\left(\begin{matrix}1,\,\frac{s+1}{2},\,\frac{s+1}{2},\,\frac{s+2}{2}\\[2pt]\frac{2s+3}{4},\,\frac{2s+5}{4},\,\frac{s+3}{2};\,a^2b^2\end{matrix}\right)\right]$ $[a > 0;\ \operatorname{Re} s > -1]$
7	$\theta(a-x)\arccos\dfrac{x}{a}\operatorname{arctanh}(bx)$	$\dfrac{\sqrt{\pi}\,a^{s+1}b}{2(s+1)}\Gamma\!\left[\begin{matrix}\frac{s+2}{2}\\\frac{s+3}{2}\end{matrix}\right]\ _4F_3\left(\begin{matrix}\frac{1}{2},\,1,\,\frac{s+1}{2},\,\frac{s+2}{2}\\[2pt]\frac{3}{2},\,\frac{s+3}{2},\,\frac{s+3}{2};\,a^2b^2\end{matrix}\right)$ $[a > 0;\ \operatorname{Re} s > -1]$

2.7.4. $\operatorname{arccoth}(ax)$ **and algebraic functions**

No.	$f(x)$	$F(s)$
1	$\operatorname{arccoth}(ax)$	$-\dfrac{i\pi}{2s}(-ia)^{-s}\sec\dfrac{s\pi}{2}\qquad [\operatorname{Im} a > 0;\ 0 < \operatorname{Re} s < 1]$
2	$\operatorname{arccoth}(ax) - \dfrac{\pi i}{2} - ax$	$\dfrac{i\pi}{2s}(ia)^{-s}\sec\dfrac{s\pi}{2}\qquad [\operatorname{Im} a < 0;\ -3 < \operatorname{Re} s < -1]$
3	$\operatorname{arccoth}(ax) - \dfrac{\pi i}{2} - \sum_{k=0}^{n}\dfrac{(ax)^{2k+1}}{2k+1}$	$\dfrac{i\pi}{2s}(ia)^{-s}\sec\dfrac{s\pi}{2}$ $[\operatorname{Im} a < 0;\ -2n-3 < \operatorname{Re} s < -2n-1]$
4	$\operatorname{arccoth}(ax) - \sum_{k=0}^{n}\dfrac{(ax)^{-2k-1}}{2k+1}$	$-\dfrac{i\pi}{2s}\left(-\dfrac{i}{a}\right)^{s}\sec\dfrac{s\pi}{2}$ $[\operatorname{Im} a < 0;\ 2n+1 < \operatorname{Re} s < 2n+3]$

2.7.5. $\operatorname{arcsech}^n (\varphi (x))$ **and elementary functions**

1	$\operatorname{arcsech} (ax) + \dfrac{i\pi}{2}$	$\dfrac{a^{-s}}{2s^2} e^{is\pi/2} \operatorname{B} \left(\dfrac{s+2}{2}, \dfrac{1-s}{2} \right)$ $[\operatorname{Im} a > 0;\ 0 < \operatorname{Re} s < 1]$
2	$\operatorname{arcsech} (ax) - \dfrac{1}{2} \ln \left(-\dfrac{4}{a^2 x^2} \right)$ $+ \dfrac{\pi a}{2} \sqrt{-\dfrac{1}{a^2 x^2}} + \dfrac{1}{2} \sum\limits_{k=1}^{n} \dfrac{(1/2)_k}{k!\,k} (ax)^{2k}$	$\dfrac{(ia)^{-s}}{s^2} \operatorname{B} \left(\dfrac{s+2}{2}, \dfrac{1-s}{2} \right)$ $[\operatorname{Im} a < 0;\ -2n - 2 < \operatorname{Re} s < -2n]$
3	$\operatorname{arcsech} \left(\sqrt{ax+1} - \sqrt{ax} \right)$	$-\dfrac{a^{-s}}{s} \cos (s\pi) \operatorname{B} \left(2s + \dfrac{1}{2}, -2s \right)$ $[-1/4 < \operatorname{Re} s < 0;\ |\arg a| < \pi]$
4	$\operatorname{arcsech} \dfrac{1}{\sqrt{ax} + \sqrt{ax+1}}$	$-\dfrac{a^{-s}}{s} \cos (s\pi) \operatorname{B} \left(2s + \dfrac{1}{2}, -2s \right)$ $[-1/4 < \operatorname{Re} s < 0;\ |\arg a| < \pi]$
5	$\operatorname{arcsech} \dfrac{\sqrt{ax}}{\sqrt{ax+1} + 1}$	$\dfrac{a^{-s}}{s} \cos (s\pi) \operatorname{B} \left(2s, \dfrac{1}{2} - 2s \right)$ $[0 < \operatorname{Re} s < 1/4;\ |\arg a| < \pi]$
6	$\operatorname{arcsech} \dfrac{\sqrt{ax+1} - 1}{\sqrt{ax}}$	$\dfrac{a^{-s}}{s} \cos (s\pi) \operatorname{B} \left(2s, \dfrac{1}{2} - 2s \right)$ $[0 < \operatorname{Re} s < 1/4;\ |\arg a| < \pi]$
7	$\operatorname{arcsech} \left(\sqrt{a^2 x^2 + 1} - ax \right)$	$-\dfrac{a^{-s}}{s} \cos \dfrac{s\pi}{2} \operatorname{B} \left(s + \dfrac{1}{2}, -s \right)$ $[\operatorname{Re} a > 0;\ -1/2 < \operatorname{Re} s < 0]$
8	$\operatorname{arcsech} \dfrac{1}{ax + \sqrt{a^2 x^2 + 1}}$	$-\dfrac{a^{-s}}{s} \cos \dfrac{s\pi}{2} \operatorname{B} \left(s + \dfrac{1}{2}, -s \right)$ $[\operatorname{Re} a > 0;\ -1/2 < \operatorname{Re} s < 0]$
9	$\operatorname{arcsech} \dfrac{\sqrt{a^2 x^2 + 1} - 1}{ax}$	$\dfrac{a^{-s}}{s} \cos \dfrac{s\pi}{2} \operatorname{B} \left(s, \dfrac{1}{2} - s \right)$ $\quad [\operatorname{Re} a > 0;\ 0 < \operatorname{Re} s < 1/2]$
10	$\operatorname{arcsech} \dfrac{ax}{\sqrt{a^2 x^2 + 1} + 1}$	$\dfrac{a^{-s}}{s} \cos \dfrac{s\pi}{2} \operatorname{B} \left(s, \dfrac{1}{2} - s \right)$ $\quad [\operatorname{Re} a > 0;\ 0 < \operatorname{Re} s < 1/2]$
11	$\operatorname{arcsech}^2 (ax) + \dfrac{\pi^2}{4}$	$\dfrac{\pi^{3/2} a^{-s}}{s} \csc (s\pi) \Gamma \left[\begin{matrix} \frac{s}{2} \\ \frac{s+1}{2} \end{matrix} \right]$ $\quad [0 < \operatorname{Re} s < 1;\ |\arg a| < \pi]$

2.7.6. $\operatorname{arccsch}^n(\varphi(x))$ and elementary functions

1	$\operatorname{arccsch}(ax)$	$\dfrac{a^{-s}}{2s^2}\operatorname{B}\left(\dfrac{s+2}{2},\dfrac{1-s}{2}\right)$ $[\operatorname{Re}a>0;\ 0<\operatorname{Re}s<1]$
2	$\operatorname{arccsch}(ax)$ $-\sum\limits_{k=0}^{n}(-1)^k\dfrac{(1/2)_k}{(2k+1)\,k!}(ax)^{-2k-1}$	$\dfrac{a^{-s}}{2s^2}\operatorname{B}\left(\dfrac{s+2}{2},\dfrac{1-s}{2}\right)$ $[2n+1<\operatorname{Re}s<2n+3;\ -\pi/2\le\arg a<\pi/2]$
3	$\operatorname{arccsch}(ax)$ $-\dfrac{1}{2ax}\left(\dfrac{1}{a^2x^2}\right)^{-1/2}\ln\dfrac{4}{a^2x^2}$	$\dfrac{a^{-s-1}}{2s^2}\left(\dfrac{1}{a^2}\right)^{1/2}\operatorname{B}\left(\dfrac{s+2}{2},\dfrac{1-s}{2}\right)$ $[-2<\operatorname{Re}s<0;\ -\pi/2\le\arg a<\pi/2]$
4	$\operatorname{arccsch}(ax)$ $-\dfrac{1}{2ax}\left(\dfrac{1}{a^2x^2}\right)^{-1/2}\left[\ln\dfrac{4}{a^2x^2}\right.$ $\left.-\sum\limits_{k=1}^{n}(-1)^k\dfrac{(1/2)_k}{k!\,k}(ax)^{2k}\right]$	$\dfrac{a^{-s-1}}{2s^2}\left(\dfrac{1}{a^2}\right)^{1/2}\operatorname{B}\left(\dfrac{s+2}{2},\dfrac{1-s}{2}\right)$ $[-2n-2<\operatorname{Re}s<-2n;\ -\pi/2\le\arg a<\pi/2]$
5	$\dfrac{1}{\sqrt{a^2x^2+1}}\operatorname{arccsch}(ax)$	$\dfrac{\pi^{3/2}\left(a^2\right)^{(1-s)/2}}{4a}\csc\dfrac{s\pi}{2}\,\Gamma\!\left[\begin{array}{c}\frac{s}{2}\\\frac{s+1}{2}\end{array}\right]$ $[\operatorname{Re}a\ne0;\ 0<\operatorname{Re}s<2]$
6	$\dfrac{1}{\sqrt{a^2x^2+1}}\operatorname{arccsch}\dfrac{1}{ax}$	$\dfrac{\pi^{3/2}a^{-s}}{4}\sec\dfrac{s\pi}{2}\,\Gamma\!\left[\begin{array}{c}\frac{1-s}{2}\\\frac{2-s}{2}\end{array}\right]$ $[\operatorname{Re}a>0;\ -1<\operatorname{Re}s<1]$
7	$\operatorname{arccsch}\sqrt{\dfrac{2}{\sqrt{ax+1}-1}}$	$-\dfrac{a^{-s}}{4s}\operatorname{B}\left(s+\dfrac{1}{2},-s\right)$ $[-1/2<\operatorname{Re}s<0;\ |\arg a|<\pi]$
8	$\operatorname{arccsch}\sqrt{\dfrac{2\sqrt{ax}}{\sqrt{ax+1}-\sqrt{ax}}}$	$\dfrac{a^{-s}}{4s}\operatorname{B}\left(s,\dfrac{1}{2}-s\right)$ $[0<\operatorname{Re}s<1/2;\ |\arg a|<\pi]$
9	$\operatorname{arccsch}^2(ax)$	$\dfrac{\pi^{3/2}a^{-s}}{2s}\csc\dfrac{s\pi}{2}\,\Gamma\!\left[\begin{array}{c}\frac{s}{2}\\\frac{s+1}{2}\end{array}\right]$ $[\operatorname{Re}a>0;\ 0<\operatorname{Re}s<2]$
10	$\operatorname{arccsch}^2\sqrt{\dfrac{2}{\sqrt{ax+1}-1}}$	$\dfrac{\pi^{3/2}a^{-s}}{8s}\csc(s\pi)\,\Gamma\!\left[\begin{array}{c}-s\\\frac{1-2s}{2}\end{array}\right]$ $[-1<\operatorname{Re}s<0;\ |\arg a|<\pi]$
11	$\operatorname{arccsch}^2\sqrt{\dfrac{2\sqrt{ax}}{\sqrt{ax+1}-\sqrt{ax}}}$	$\dfrac{\pi^{3/2}a^{-s}}{8s}\csc(s\pi)\,\Gamma\!\left[\begin{array}{c}s\\\frac{2s+1}{2}\end{array}\right]$ $[0<\operatorname{Re}s<1;\ |\arg a|<\pi]$

2.7.7. Hypebolic functions of inverse hyperbolic functions

1	$\sinh\left(\nu\operatorname{arcsinh}\dfrac{x}{a}\right)$	$\dfrac{\nu a^s}{4\sqrt{\pi}}\cos\dfrac{\nu\pi}{2}\Gamma\left[\begin{matrix}\frac{s+1}{2},\ -\frac{s+\nu}{2},\ \frac{\nu-s}{2}\\ \frac{2-s}{2}\end{matrix}\right]$ $[\operatorname{Re}a>0;\ -1<\operatorname{Re}s<-|\operatorname{Re}\nu|]$
2	$\sinh\left(\nu\operatorname{arccsch}\dfrac{x}{a}\right)$	$\dfrac{\nu a^s}{4\sqrt{\pi}}\cos\dfrac{\nu\pi}{2}\Gamma\left[\begin{matrix}\frac{1-s}{2},\ \frac{s-\nu}{2},\ \frac{s+\nu}{2}\\ \frac{s+2}{2}\end{matrix}\right]$ $[\operatorname{Re}a>0;\ |\operatorname{Re}\nu|<\operatorname{Re}s<1]$
3	$\dfrac{1}{\sqrt{x^2+a^2}}\sinh\left(\nu\operatorname{arcsinh}\dfrac{x}{a}\right)$	$\dfrac{a^{s-1}}{2\sqrt{\pi}}\sin\dfrac{\nu\pi}{2}\Gamma\left[\begin{matrix}\frac{s+1}{2},\ \frac{1-\nu-s}{2},\ \frac{\nu-s+1}{2}\\ \frac{2-s}{2}\end{matrix}\right]$ $[\operatorname{Re}a>0;\ -1<\operatorname{Re}s<1-|\operatorname{Re}\nu|]$
4	$\dfrac{1}{\sqrt{x^2+a^2}}\sinh\left(\nu\operatorname{arccsch}\dfrac{x}{a}\right)$	$\dfrac{a^{s-1}}{2\sqrt{\pi}}\sin\dfrac{\nu\pi}{2}\Gamma\left[\begin{matrix}\frac{2-s}{2},\ \frac{s-\nu}{2},\ \frac{s+\nu}{2}\\ \frac{s+1}{2}\end{matrix}\right]$ $[\operatorname{Re}a>0;\ |\operatorname{Re}\nu|<\operatorname{Re}s<2]$
5	$|a-x|^\nu\sinh\left(\nu\operatorname{arctanh}\dfrac{2\sqrt{ax}}{a+x}\right)$	$-\sqrt{\pi}\,a^{s+\nu}\Gamma\left[\begin{matrix}\frac{2\nu+1}{2}\\ -\nu\end{matrix}\right]\Gamma\left[\begin{matrix}\frac{2s+1}{2},\ \frac{1-2\nu-2s}{2}\\ 1-s,\ s+\nu+1\end{matrix}\right]$ $\left[\begin{matrix}a>0;\ \operatorname{Re}\nu>-1/2;\\ -1/2<\operatorname{Re}s<1/2-\operatorname{Re}\nu\end{matrix}\right]$
6	$|a-x|^\nu\sinh\left(\nu\operatorname{arccoth}\dfrac{a+x}{2\sqrt{ax}}\right)$	$-\sqrt{\pi}\,a^{s+\nu}\Gamma\left[\begin{matrix}\frac{2\nu+1}{2}\\ -\nu\end{matrix}\right]\Gamma\left[\begin{matrix}\frac{2s+1}{2},\ \frac{1-2\nu-2s}{2}\\ 1-s,\ s+\nu+1\end{matrix}\right]$ $\left[\begin{matrix}a>0;\ \operatorname{Re}\nu>-1/2;\\ -1/2<\operatorname{Re}s<1/2-\operatorname{Re}\nu\end{matrix}\right]$
7	$\theta(a-x)\sinh\left(\nu\operatorname{arcsech}\dfrac{x}{a}\right)$	$\dfrac{\nu\sqrt{\pi}\,a^s}{4}\Gamma\left[\begin{matrix}\frac{s-\nu}{2},\ \frac{s+\nu}{2}\\ \frac{s+1}{2},\ \frac{s+2}{2}\end{matrix}\right]$ $\qquad[a>0;\ \operatorname{Re}s>|\operatorname{Re}\nu|]$
8	$\theta(x-a)\sinh\left(\nu\operatorname{arccosh}\dfrac{x}{a}\right)$	$\dfrac{\nu\sqrt{\pi}\,a^s}{4}\Gamma\left[\begin{matrix}\frac{-s-\nu}{2},\ \frac{-s+\nu}{2}\\ \frac{1-s}{2},\ \frac{2-s}{2}\end{matrix}\right]$ $\qquad[a>0;\ \operatorname{Re}s<-|\operatorname{Re}\nu|]$
9	$\theta(a-x)\sinh\left(\nu\operatorname{arctanh}\sqrt{1-\dfrac{x}{a}}\right)$	$\dfrac{\nu\sqrt{\pi}\,a^s}{2}\Gamma\left[\begin{matrix}\frac{2s-\nu}{2},\ \frac{2s+\nu}{2}\\ \frac{2s+1}{2},\ s+1\end{matrix}\right]$ $\qquad[a>0;\ \operatorname{Re}s>|\operatorname{Re}\nu|/2]$
10	$\theta(x-a)\sinh\left(\nu\operatorname{arctanh}\sqrt{1-\dfrac{a}{x}}\right)$	$\dfrac{\nu\sqrt{\pi}\,a^s}{2}\Gamma\left[\begin{matrix}\frac{-2s-\nu}{2},\ \frac{-2s+\nu}{2}\\ \frac{1-2s}{2},\ 1-s\end{matrix}\right]$ $\qquad[a>0;\ \operatorname{Re}s<-|\operatorname{Re}\nu|/2]$
11	$\dfrac{1}{\sqrt{x^2+a^2}}\cosh\left(\nu\operatorname{arcsinh}\dfrac{x}{a}\right)$	$\dfrac{a^{s-1}}{2\sqrt{\pi}}\cos\dfrac{\nu\pi}{2}\Gamma\left[\begin{matrix}\frac{s}{2},\ \frac{1-s-\nu}{2},\ \frac{1-s+\nu}{2}\\ \frac{1-s}{2}\end{matrix}\right]$ $[\operatorname{Re}a>0;\ 0<\operatorname{Re}s<1-|\operatorname{Re}\nu|]$

No.	$f(x)$	$F(s)$
12	$\dfrac{1}{\sqrt{x^2+a^2}}\cosh\left(\nu\,\mathrm{arccsch}\,\dfrac{x}{a}\right)$	$\dfrac{a^{s-1}}{2\sqrt{\pi}}\cos\dfrac{\nu\pi}{2}\,\Gamma\!\left[\begin{array}{c}\frac{1-s}{2},\ \frac{s-\nu}{2},\ \frac{s+\nu}{2}\\ \frac{s}{2}\end{array}\right]$ $\quad[\mathrm{Re}\,a>0;\ |\mathrm{Re}\,\nu|<\mathrm{Re}\,s<1]$
13	$|a-x|^{\nu}\cosh\left(\nu\,\mathrm{arctanh}\left(\dfrac{2\sqrt{ax}}{x+a}\right)\right)$	$\sqrt{\pi}\,a^{s+\nu}\,\Gamma\!\left[\begin{array}{c}\frac{2\nu+1}{2},\ -s-\nu,\ s\\ -\nu,\ \frac{1-2s}{2},\ \frac{2s+2\nu+1}{2}\end{array}\right]$ $\quad[a>0;\ \mathrm{Re}\,\nu>-1/2;\ 0<\mathrm{Re}\,s<-\mathrm{Re}\,\nu]$
14	$|a-x|^{\nu}\cosh\left(\nu\,\mathrm{arccoth}\left(\dfrac{x+a}{2\sqrt{ax}}\right)\right)$	$\sqrt{\pi}\,a^{s+\nu}\,\Gamma\!\left[\begin{array}{c}\frac{2\nu+1}{2},\ -s-\nu,\ s\\ -\nu,\ \frac{1-2s}{2},\ \frac{2s+2\nu+1}{2}\end{array}\right]$ $\quad[a>0;\ \mathrm{Re}\,\nu>-1/2;\ 0<\mathrm{Re}\,s<-\mathrm{Re}\,\nu]$
15	$\dfrac{\theta(a-x)}{\sqrt{a^2-x^2}}\cosh\left(\nu\,\mathrm{arcsech}\,\dfrac{x}{a}\right)$	$\dfrac{\sqrt{\pi}\,a^{s-1}}{2}\,\Gamma\!\left[\begin{array}{c}\frac{s-\nu}{2},\ \frac{s+\nu}{2}\\ \frac{s}{2},\ \frac{s+1}{2}\end{array}\right]$ $\quad[a>0;\ \mathrm{Re}\,s>|\mathrm{Re}\,\nu|]$
16	$\dfrac{\theta(a-x)}{\sqrt{a-x}}\cosh\left(\nu\,\mathrm{arctanh}\sqrt{1-\dfrac{x}{a}}\right)$	$\sqrt{\pi}\,a^{s-1}\,\Gamma\!\left[\begin{array}{c}\frac{2s-\nu}{2},\ \frac{2s+\nu}{2}\\ s,\ \frac{2s+1}{2}\end{array}\right]$ $\quad[a>0;\ \mathrm{Re}\,s>|\mathrm{Re}\,\nu|/2]$
17	$\dfrac{\theta(x-a)}{\sqrt{x^2-a^2}}\cosh\left(\nu\,\mathrm{arccosh}\,\dfrac{x}{a}\right)$	$\dfrac{\sqrt{\pi}\,a^{s-1}}{2}\,\Gamma\!\left[\begin{array}{c}\frac{1-s-\nu}{2},\ \frac{1-s+\nu}{2}\\ \frac{1-s}{2},\ \frac{2-s}{2}\end{array}\right]$ $\quad[a>0;\ \mathrm{Re}\,s<1-|\mathrm{Re}\,\nu|]$
18	$\dfrac{\theta(x-a)}{\sqrt{x-a}}\cosh\left(\nu\,\mathrm{arctanh}\sqrt{\dfrac{x}{a}-1}\right)$	$\sqrt{\pi}\,a^{s-1/2}\,\Gamma\!\left[\begin{array}{c}\frac{1-2s-\nu}{2},\ \frac{1-2s+\nu}{2}\\ \frac{1-2s}{2},\ 1-s\end{array}\right]$ $\quad[a>0;\ \mathrm{Re}\,s<(1-|\mathrm{Re}\,\nu|)/2]$

Chapter 3
Special Functions

3.1. The Gamma $\Gamma(z)$, Psi $\psi(z)$, and Zeta $\zeta(z)$ Functions

More formulas can be obtained from the corresponding sections due to the relations

$$\Gamma(z) = \lim_{w \to \infty} \frac{w^z}{z} \,{}_1F_1(z; z+1; -w),$$

$$\Gamma(1-z)\,\Gamma(1+z) = \frac{z\pi}{\sin(z\pi)}, \quad \Gamma\left(z+\frac{1}{2}\right)\Gamma\left(\frac{1}{2}-z\right) = \frac{\pi}{\cos(z\pi)},$$

$$\psi(z) = (z-1)\,{}_3F_2(1, 1, 2-z; 2, 2; 1) - \mathbf{C}, \quad \psi(-z) = \frac{1}{z} + \pi\cot(z\pi) + \psi(z),$$

$$\psi^{(n)}(z) = (-1)^{n+1}\,n!\,z^{-n-1}\,{}_{n+2}F_{n+1}(1, z, z, \ldots, z; z+1, z+1, \ldots, z+1; 1),$$

$$\psi^{(n)}(z \pm m) = \psi^{(n)}(z) \pm (-1)^n\,n! \sum_{k=(1\mp1)/2}^{m-(1\pm1)/2} \frac{1}{(z \pm k)^{n+1}},$$

$$\zeta(s) = \mathrm{Li}_s(1), \quad \mathrm{Re}\,s > 1; \quad \zeta(s, a+n) = \zeta(s, a) - \sum_{k=0}^{n-1} \frac{1}{\left((a+k)^2\right)^{s/2}},$$

$$\zeta(s, a-n) = \zeta(s, a) + \sum_{k=0}^{n-1} \frac{1}{\left((a+k-n)^2\right)^{s/2}}.$$

3.1.1. $\Gamma(\varphi(x))$

No.	$f(x)$	$F(s)$	
1	$\dfrac{a^x}{\Gamma(x+b)}$	$a^{1-b}\,\mu(a, s-1, b-1)$	$[a,\ \mathrm{Re}\,b,\ \mathrm{Re}\,s > 0]$
2	$\ln\dfrac{\sqrt{x}\,\Gamma(x)}{\Gamma\left(x+\frac{1}{2}\right)}$	$\dfrac{\sec(s\pi/2)}{(2\pi)^s}\left(1 - 2^{-s-1}\right)\Gamma(s)\,\zeta(s+1)$	$[0 < \mathrm{Re}\,s < 1]$
3	$\dfrac{x^c a^x}{\Gamma(x+b+1)}$	$a^{-b}\,\Gamma(s+c)\,\mu(a, s+c-1, b)$	$[\mathrm{Re}\,(s+c) > 0]$

No.	$f(x)$	$F(s)$
4	$\dfrac{\theta(1-x)}{\Gamma(1-\ln x)}$	$\nu(e^{-s})$
5	$\dfrac{\theta(1-x)}{\Gamma(b-\ln x+1)}$	$e^{bs}\nu(e^{-s},b)$
6	$\dfrac{\theta(1-x)(-\ln x)^c}{\Gamma(b-\ln x+1)}$	$\Gamma(c+1)e^{bs}\mu(e^{-s},c,b)$

3.1.2. $\psi(ax+b)$

1	$\psi(x+1)+\mathbf{C}$	$-\dfrac{\pi}{\sin(s\pi)}\zeta(1-s)$	$[-1<\operatorname{Re}s<0]$
2	$\psi(x+a)-\psi(x+b)$	$\dfrac{\pi}{\sin(s\pi)}[\zeta(1-s,b)-\zeta(1-s,a)]$	$[a,b>0;\,0<\operatorname{Re}s<1]$
3	$\ln x-\psi(x+1)$	$\dfrac{\pi}{\sin(s\pi)}\zeta(1-s)$	$[0<\operatorname{Re}s<1]$
4	$\ln x-\psi\left(x+\dfrac{1}{2}\right)$	$\dfrac{2^{1-s}-1}{\sin(s\pi)}\zeta(s)$	$[0<\operatorname{Re}s<1]$
5	$\ln(x+1)-\psi(x+1)$	$\dfrac{\pi}{\sin(s\pi)}\left[\zeta(1-s)+\dfrac{1}{s}\right]$	$[0<\operatorname{Re}s<1]$

3.1.3. $\psi^{(n)}(ax+b)$

1	$\dfrac{1}{x}-\psi'(x+1)$	$\dfrac{\pi(s-1)}{\sin(s\pi)}\zeta(2-s)$	$[1<\operatorname{Re}s<2]$
2	$\dfrac{1}{x+1}-\psi'(x+1)$	$\dfrac{\pi(s-1)}{\sin(s\pi)}\left[\zeta(2-s)+\dfrac{1}{s-1}\right]$	$[0<\operatorname{Re}s<2]$
3	$\psi^{(n)}(x+1)$	$\dfrac{(-1)^{n-1}\pi}{\sin(s\pi)}(1-s)_n\,\zeta(1-s+n)$	$[0<\operatorname{Re}s<n]$

3.1.4. $\zeta(\nu,ax+b)$

1	$\zeta(\nu,ax+b)$	$a^{-s}\mathrm{B}(s,\nu-s)\zeta(\nu-s,b)$	$[\operatorname{Re}\nu,\ \operatorname{Re}b>0;\,0<\operatorname{Re}s<\operatorname{Re}\nu-1]$
2	$\zeta(\nu,x)-\dfrac{1}{x^\nu}$	$\mathrm{B}(s,\nu-s)\zeta(\nu-s)$	$[0<\operatorname{Re}s<\operatorname{Re}\nu-1]$

3.2. The Polylogarithm $\mathrm{Li}_n(z)$

More formulas can be obtained from the corresponding sections due to the relations

$$\mathrm{Li}_n(z) = z\,_{n+1}F_n\left(1, 1, \ldots, 1; 2, 2, \ldots, 2; z\right),$$

$$\mathrm{Li}_n(-z) = -\,G^{1,\,n+1}_{n+1,\,n+1}\left(z\,\middle|\,\begin{matrix} 1, 1, \ldots, 1 \\ 1, 0, \ldots, 0 \end{matrix}\right).$$

3.2.1. $\mathrm{Li}_n(bx)$ and algebraic functions

No.	$f(x)$	$F(s)$
1	$\theta(a-x)\,\mathrm{Li}_2\left(\dfrac{x}{a}\right)$	$\dfrac{a^s}{s^2}\left[\dfrac{\pi^2 s}{6} - \psi(s+1) - \mathbf{C}\right]$ $\qquad [a > 0;\ \mathrm{Re}\,s > -1]$
2	$\mathrm{Li}_n(-ax)$	$(-1)^n\,\dfrac{\pi\csc(s\pi)}{a^s s^n}$ $\qquad [-1 < \mathrm{Re}\,s < 0;\ |\arg a| < \pi]$
3	$\theta(a-x)\,\mathrm{Li}_n(-bx)$	$\dfrac{a^{s+1}b}{s(s+1)}\,_{n+1}F_n\left(\begin{matrix} 1, 1,\ \ldots,\ 1, s+1 \\ 2,\ \ldots,\ 2, s+2;\ -ab \end{matrix}\right)$ $-\dfrac{a^{s+1}b}{s}\,_{n+1}F_n\left(\begin{matrix} 1, 1,\ \ldots,\ 1 \\ 2,\ \ldots,\ 2;\ -ab \end{matrix}\right)$ $[a > 0;\ \mathrm{Re}\,s > -1;\ |\arg b| < \pi]$
4	$(a-x)_+^{\alpha-1}\,\mathrm{Li}_n(-bx)$	$-a^{s+\alpha}b\,\mathrm{B}(\alpha, s+1)\,_{n+2}F_{n+1}\left(\begin{matrix} 1, 1,\ \ldots,\ 1, s+1;\ -ab \\ 2,\ \ldots,\ 2, s+\alpha+1 \end{matrix}\right)$ $[a,\ \mathrm{Re}\,\alpha > 0;\ \mathrm{Re}\,s > -1;\ |\arg b| < \pi]$
5	$(x-a)_+^{\alpha-1}\,\mathrm{Li}_n(-bx)$	$-a^{s+\alpha}b\,\mathrm{B}(\alpha, -s-\alpha)\,_{n+2}F_{n+1}\left(\begin{matrix} 1, 1,\ \ldots,\ 1, s+1;\ -ab \\ 2,\ \ldots,\ 2, s+\alpha+1 \end{matrix}\right)$ $+(-1)^{n+1}\dfrac{\pi\csc[(s+\alpha)\pi]}{b^{s+\alpha-1}(s+\alpha-1)^n}$ $\times\,_{n+1}F_n\left(\begin{matrix} 1-\alpha, 1-s-\alpha, \ldots, 1-s-\alpha \\ 2-s-\alpha,\ \ldots,\ 2-s-\alpha;\ -ab \end{matrix}\right)$ $[a,\ \mathrm{Re}\,\alpha > 0;\ \mathrm{Re}\,(s+\alpha) < 1;\ |\arg b| < \pi]$
6	$\dfrac{1}{(x+a)^\rho}\,\mathrm{Li}_n(-bx)$	$-a^{s-\rho+1}b\,\mathrm{B}(s+1, \rho-s-1)$ $\times\,_{n+2}F_{n+1}\left(\begin{matrix} 1, 1,\ \ldots,\ 1, s+1;\ ab \\ 2,\ \ldots,\ 2, s-\rho+2 \end{matrix}\right) + \dfrac{\pi\,b^{\rho-s}}{(\rho-s)^n}$ $\times\csc[(s-\rho)\pi]\,_{n+1}F_n\left(\begin{matrix} \rho, \rho-s,\ \ldots,\ \rho-s;\ ab \\ \rho-s+1,\ \ldots,\ \rho-s+1 \end{matrix}\right)$ $[-1 < \mathrm{Re}\,s < \mathrm{Re}\,\rho;\ |\arg a|,\ |\arg b| < \pi]$

No.	$f(x)$	$F(s)$
7	$\dfrac{1}{x-a}\,\mathrm{Li}_n\left(-bx\right)$	$\pi a^s b \cot\left(s\pi\right)\,{}_{n+1}F_n\left(\begin{matrix}1,\,1,\,\ldots,1;\,-ab\\2,\,2,\,\ldots,2\end{matrix}\right)$
		$\qquad -\dfrac{\pi\,b^{1-s}}{\left(1-s\right)^n}\,\csc\left(s\pi\right)\,{}_{n+1}F_n\left(\begin{matrix}1,\,1-s,\,\ldots,\,1-s;\,-ab\\2-s,\,\ldots,\,2-s\end{matrix}\right)$
		$[a>0;\ \lvert\mathrm{Re}\,s\rvert<1;\ \lvert\arg b\rvert<\pi]$
8	$(a-x)_+^{\alpha-1}\,\mathrm{Li}_2\left(-bx^2\right)$	$-a^{s+\alpha+1}b\,\mathrm{B}\left(\alpha,\,s+2\right)\,{}_5F_4\left(\begin{matrix}1,\,1,\,1,\,\frac{s+2}{2},\,\frac{s+3}{2};\,-a^2b\\2,\,2,\,\frac{s+\alpha+2}{2},\,\frac{s+\alpha+3}{2}\end{matrix}\right)$
		$[a,\ \mathrm{Re}\,\alpha>0;\ \mathrm{Re}\,s>-2]$
9	$\dfrac{1}{(x+a)^\rho}\,\mathrm{Li}_2\left(\dfrac{b}{x+a}\right)$	$a^{s-\rho-1}b\,\mathrm{B}\left(s,\,1-s+\rho\right)\,{}_4F_3\left(\begin{matrix}1,1,1,\,1-s+\rho\\2,2,\,\rho+1;\,\frac{b}{a}\end{matrix}\right)$
		$[0<\mathrm{Re}\,s<\mathrm{Re}\,\rho+1;\ \lvert\arg a\rvert<\pi]$
10	$\dfrac{1}{(x+a)^\rho}\,\mathrm{Li}_2\left(\dfrac{bx}{x+a}\right)$	$a^{s-\rho}b\,\mathrm{B}\left(s+1,\,\rho-s\right)\,{}_4F_3\left(\begin{matrix}1,1,1,\,s+1\\2,2,\,\rho+1;\,b\end{matrix}\right)$
		$[-1<\mathrm{Re}\,s<\mathrm{Re}\,\rho;\ \lvert\arg a\rvert<\pi]$
11	$(a-x)_+^{\alpha-1}\,\mathrm{Li}_2\left(bx\left(a-x\right)\right)$	$a^{s+\alpha+1}\,b\,\mathrm{B}(s+1,\,\alpha+1)\,{}_5F_4\left(\begin{matrix}1,\,1,\,1,\,s+1,\,\alpha+1;\,\frac{a^2b}{4}\\2,\,2,\,\frac{s+\alpha+2}{2},\,\frac{s+\alpha+3}{2}\end{matrix}\right)$
		$[a>0;\ \mathrm{Re}\,s,\ \mathrm{Re}\,\alpha>-1;\ \lvert\arg\left(4-a^2b\right)\rvert<\pi]$

3.2.2. $\mathrm{Li}_n\left(bx\right)$ and the logarithmic or inverse trigonometric functions

No.	$f(x)$	$F(s)$
1	$\theta\left(a-x\right)\ln\dfrac{\sqrt{a}+\sqrt{a-x}}{\sqrt{x}}$ $\times\,\mathrm{Li}_2\left(bx\right)$	$\dfrac{\sqrt{\pi}\,a^{s+1}b}{2s\left(s+1\right)}\,\Gamma\left[\begin{matrix}s\\\frac{2s+3}{2}\end{matrix}\right]\left[{}_3F_2\left(\begin{matrix}1,\,s+1,\,s+1\\\frac{2s+3}{2},\,s+2;\,ab\end{matrix}\right)\right.$ $\left.-\left(s+1\right)\,{}_3F_2\left(\begin{matrix}1,\,1,\,s+1\\2,\,\frac{2s+3}{2};\,ab\end{matrix}\right)+s\left(s+1\right)\,{}_4F_3\left(\begin{matrix}1,\,1,\,1,\,s+1\\2,\,2,\,\frac{2s+3}{2};\,ab\end{matrix}\right)\right]$ $[a>0;\ \mathrm{Re}\,s>-2;\ \lvert\arg\left(1-ab\right)\rvert<\pi]$
2	$\theta\left(a-x\right)\arccos\sqrt{\dfrac{x}{a}}$ $\times\,\mathrm{Li}_2\left(bx\right)$	$\dfrac{\sqrt{\pi}\,a^{s+1}b}{2s^2\left(s+1\right)}\,\Gamma\left[\begin{matrix}\frac{2s+3}{2}\\s+2\end{matrix}\right]\left[{}_3F_2\left(\begin{matrix}1,\,s+1,\,\frac{2s+3}{2}\\s+2,\,s+2;\,ab\end{matrix}\right)\right.$ $\left.-\left(s+1\right)\,{}_3F_2\left(\begin{matrix}1,\,1,\,s+1\\2,\,\frac{2s+3}{2};\,ab\end{matrix}\right)+s\left(s+1\right)\,{}_4F_3\left(\begin{matrix}1,\,1,\,1,\,\frac{2s+3}{2}\\2,\,2,\,s+2;\,ab\end{matrix}\right)\right]$ $[a>0;\ \mathrm{Re}\,s>-1;\ \lvert\arg\left(1-ab\right)\rvert<\pi]$

3.3. The Exponential Integral Ei (z)

More formulas can be obtained from the corresponding sections due to the relations

$$\text{Ei}\,(z) = -e^z\,\Psi\,(1;\,1;\,-z) + \frac{1}{2}\left(\ln z - \ln\frac{1}{z}\right) - \ln\,(-z)\,,$$

$$\text{Ei}\,(z) = z\,{}_2F_2\,(1,\,1;\,2,\,2;\,z) + \frac{1}{2}\left(\ln z - \ln\frac{1}{z}\right) + \mathbf{C}\,,$$

$$\text{Ei}\,(-z) = -G_{12}^{20}\left(z\,\middle|\,{1 \atop 0,\,0}\right)\,, \quad \text{Ei}\,(-z) = -e^{-z}G_{12}^{21}\left(z\,\middle|\,{0 \atop 0,\,0}\right)\,.$$

3.3.1. Ei $(\varphi\,(x))$ and algebraic functions

No.	$f\,(x)$	$F\,(s)$
1	Ei $(-ax)$	$-\dfrac{a^{-s}}{s}\,\Gamma\,(s)$ $\qquad\qquad[a,\ \text{Re}\,s > 0]$
2	Ei $(-ax - b)$	$-\left(\dfrac{b}{a}\right)^s\,\Gamma\,(s)\,\Gamma\,(-s,\,b)$ $\qquad[a,\ \text{Re}\,s > 0;\ |\arg b| < \pi]$
3	$(a - x)_+^{\alpha-1}\,\text{Ei}\,(-bx)$	$-a^{s+\alpha}b\,\text{B}\,(s+1,\,\alpha)\,{}_3F_3\!\left({s+1,\,1,\,1;\,-ab \atop s+\alpha+1,\,2,\,2}\right)$ $+\,a^{s+\alpha-1}\,\text{B}\,(s,\,\alpha)\,[\psi\,(s) - \psi\,(s+\alpha) + \ln\,(ab) + \mathbf{C}]$ $[a,\ \text{Re}\,\alpha,\ \text{Re}\,s > 0;\ |\arg b| < \pi]$
4	$(x - a)_+^{\alpha-1}\,\text{Ei}\,(-bx)$	$-a^{s+\alpha}b\,\text{B}\,(\alpha,\,-s-\alpha)\,{}_3F_3\!\left({1,\,1,\,s+1;\,-ab \atop 2,\,2,\,s+\alpha+1}\right)$ $-\,b^{-s-\alpha+1}\dfrac{\Gamma\,(s+\alpha-1)}{s+\alpha-1}\,{}_2F_2\!\left({1-\alpha,\,1-s-\alpha;\,-ab \atop 2-s-\alpha,\,2-s-\alpha}\right)$ $+\,a^{s+\alpha-1}\,\text{B}\,(\alpha,\,1-s-\alpha)\,[\psi\,(1-s) - \psi\,(1-s-\alpha) + \ln\,(ab) + \mathbf{C}]$ $[a,\ \text{Re}\,b,\ \text{Re}\,\alpha > 0;\ \text{Re}\,(s+\alpha) < 1]$
5	$\dfrac{1}{(x+a)^\rho}\,\text{Ei}\,(-bx)$	$-a^{s-\rho+1}b\,\text{B}\,(s+1,\,\rho-s-1)\,{}_3F_3\!\left({1,\,1,\,s+1;\,ab \atop 2,\,2,\,s-\rho+2}\right)$ $+\,\dfrac{b^{\rho-s}\,\Gamma\,(s-\rho)}{\rho-s}\,{}_2F_2\!\left({\rho,\,\rho-s;\,ab \atop \rho-s+1,\,\rho-s+1}\right)$ $+\,a^{s-\rho}\,\text{B}\,(s,\,\rho-s)\,[\psi\,(s) - \psi(\rho-s) + \ln\,(ab) + \mathbf{C}]$ $[\text{Re}\,b > 0;\ 0 < \text{Re}\,s < \rho;\ |\arg a| < \pi]$
6	$\dfrac{1}{x+a}\,\text{Ei}\,(-bx)$	$-\dfrac{b^{1-s}\,\Gamma\,(s-1)}{s-1}\,{}_2F_2\!\left({1,\,1-s;\,ab \atop 2-s,\,2-s}\right)$ $-\,\pi a^{s-1}\,\csc\,(s\pi)\left[\pi\cot\,(s\pi) + \Gamma\,(0,\,-ab) + \ln\dfrac{1}{a} + \ln\,(-a)\right]$ $[\text{Re}\,b > 0;\ 0 < \text{Re}\,s < 1;\ |\arg a| < \pi]$

No.	$f(x)$	$F(s)$
7	$\dfrac{1}{x-a}\,\mathrm{Ei}\,(-bx)$	$\pi a^{s-1}\cot(s\pi)\left[2\pi\csc(2s\pi)-\mathrm{Ei}\,(-ab)\right]+\dfrac{b^{1-s}}{1-s}\,\Gamma\,(s-1)$

$$\times\,{}_2F_2\!\left(\begin{matrix}1,\,1-s;\,-ab\\2-s,\,2-s\end{matrix}\right)\qquad[a,\ \mathrm{Re}\,b>0;\ 0<\mathrm{Re}\,s<1]$$

No.	$f(x)$	$F(s)$
8	$\left(a^2-x^2\right)_+^{\alpha-1}\,\mathrm{Ei}\,(-bx)$	$\dfrac{a^{s+2\alpha}b^2}{8}\,\mathrm{B}\!\left(\alpha,\dfrac{s+2}{2}\right){}_3F_4\!\left(\begin{matrix}1,\,1,\,\frac{s+2}{2};\,\frac{a^2b^2}{4}\\\frac{3}{2},\,2,\,2,\,\frac{s+2\alpha+2}{2}\end{matrix}\right)$

$$-\,\dfrac{a^{s+2\alpha-1}b}{2}\,\mathrm{B}\!\left(\alpha,\dfrac{s+1}{2}\right){}_2F_3\!\left(\begin{matrix}\frac{1}{2},\,\frac{s+1}{2};\,\frac{a^2b^2}{4}\\\frac{3}{2},\,\frac{3}{2},\,\frac{s+2\alpha+1}{2}\end{matrix}\right)$$

$$+\,\dfrac{a^{s+2\alpha-2}}{2}\,\mathrm{B}\!\left(\alpha,\dfrac{s}{2}\right)\left[\dfrac{1}{2}\,\psi\!\left(\dfrac{s}{2}\right)-\dfrac{1}{2}\,\psi\!\left(\dfrac{s+2\alpha}{2}\right)\right.$$

$$\left.+\ln(ab)+\mathbf{C}\right]\qquad[a,\ \mathrm{Re}\,\alpha,\ \mathrm{Re}\,s>0;\ |\arg b|<\pi]$$

No.	$f(x)$	$F(s)$
9	$\left(x^2-a^2\right)_+^{\alpha-1}\,\mathrm{Ei}\,(-bx)$	$\dfrac{a^{s+2\alpha}b^2}{8}\,\mathrm{B}\!\left(\alpha,-\dfrac{s+2\alpha}{2}\right){}_3F_4\!\left(\begin{matrix}1,\,1,\,\frac{s+2}{2};\,\frac{a^2b^2}{4}\\\frac{3}{2},\,2,\,2,\,\frac{s+2\alpha+2}{2}\end{matrix}\right)$

$$-\,\dfrac{a^{s+2\alpha-1}b}{2}\,\mathrm{B}\!\left(\alpha,-\dfrac{s+2\alpha-1}{2}\right){}_2F_3\!\left(\begin{matrix}\frac{1}{2},\,\frac{s+1}{2};\,\frac{a^2b^2}{4}\\\frac{3}{2},\,\frac{3}{2},\,\frac{s+2\alpha+1}{2}\end{matrix}\right)$$

$$-\,\dfrac{\Gamma\,(s+2\alpha-2)}{s+2\alpha-2}\,b^{-s-2\alpha+2}\,{}_2F_3\!\left(\begin{matrix}1-\alpha,\,-\frac{s+2\alpha-2}{2};\,\frac{a^2b^2}{4}\\-\frac{s+2\alpha-3}{2},\,-\frac{s+2\alpha-4}{2},\,-\frac{s+2\alpha-4}{2}\end{matrix}\right)$$

$$+\,\dfrac{a^{s+2\alpha-2}}{2}\,\mathrm{B}\!\left(\alpha,-\dfrac{s+2\alpha-2}{2}\right)\left[-\dfrac{1}{2}\,\psi\!\left(-\dfrac{s+2\alpha-2}{2}\right)+\ln(ab)\right.$$

$$\left.+\dfrac{1}{2}\,\psi\!\left(-\dfrac{s-2}{2}\right)+\mathbf{C}\right]\qquad[a,\ \mathrm{Re}\,b,\ \mathrm{Re}\,\alpha>0;\ \mathrm{Re}\,(s+2\alpha)<2]$$

3.3.2. $\mathrm{Ei}\,(\varphi\,(x))$ and the exponential function

No.	$f(x)$	$F(s)$
1	$e^{\pm ax}\,\mathrm{Ei}\,(\mp ax)$	$-\dfrac{\pi}{a^s}\left\{\begin{matrix}\csc(s\pi)\\\cot(s\pi)\end{matrix}\right\}\Gamma\,(s)\qquad\qquad\qquad[a>0;\ 0<\mathrm{Re}\,s<1]$
2	$e^{-ax}\,\mathrm{Ei}\,(-bx)$	$-\dfrac{\Gamma\,(s)}{s\,(a+b)^s}\,{}_2F_1\!\left(\begin{matrix}1,\,s;\,\frac{a}{a+b}\\s+1\end{matrix}\right)\qquad[\mathrm{Re}\,(a+b),\ \mathrm{Re}\,s>0;\ |\arg b|<\pi]$
3	$e^{-ax}\,\mathrm{Ei}\,(bx)$	$-\dfrac{\pi}{a^s}\cot(s\pi)\,\Gamma\,(s)+\dfrac{\Gamma\,(s-1)}{b\,(a-b)^{s-1}}\,{}_2F_1\!\left(\begin{matrix}1,\,1;\,\frac{b-a}{b}\\2-s\end{matrix}\right)$

$$[\mathrm{Re}\,a>b>0;\ \mathrm{Re}\,s>0]$$

No.	$f(x)$	$F(s)$
4	$e^{-a/x}\,\mathrm{Ei}\,(-bx)$	$a^s\,\Gamma\,(-s)\left[\dfrac{ab}{s+1}\,{}_2F_3\!\left(\begin{matrix}1,\,1;\,ab\\2,\,2,\,s+2\end{matrix}\right)-\psi\,(-s)+\ln(ab)+\mathbf{C}\right]$

$$-\,\dfrac{b^{-s}}{s}\,\Gamma\,(s)\,{}_1F_2\!\left(\begin{matrix}-s;\,ab\\1-s,\,1-s\end{matrix}\right)\qquad[\mathrm{Re}\,a,\ \mathrm{Re}\,b>0]$$

No.	$f(x)$	$F(s)$
5	$e^{-a\sqrt{x}}\,\mathrm{Ei}\,(-bx)$	$\dfrac{2a}{(2s+1)\,b^{s+1/2}}\Gamma\left(\dfrac{2s+1}{2}\right)\,{}_2F_2\left(\begin{matrix}\frac{2s+1}{2},\ \frac{2s+1}{2}\\ \frac{3}{2},\ \frac{2s+3}{2};\ \frac{a^2}{4b}\end{matrix}\right)$

$$-\frac{\Gamma(s)}{sb^s}\,{}_2F_2\left(\begin{matrix}s,\ s;\ \frac{a^2}{4b}\\ \frac{1}{2},\ s+1\end{matrix}\right)$$

$$\left[\begin{matrix}\left(\mathrm{Re}\,b,\ \mathrm{Re}\,s>0\right)\ \text{or}\ \left(\mathrm{Re}\,b=0;\ \mathrm{Re}\,a,\ \mathrm{Re}\,s>0\right)\ \text{or}\\ \left(\mathrm{Re}\,b=\mathrm{Re}\,a=0;\ 0<\mathrm{Re}\,s<2\right);\ (\mathrm{Im}\,b=0\ \text{or}\\ \left(\mathrm{Im}\,b\neq0;\ \mathrm{Re}\,a>0\right)\ \text{or}\ \left(\mathrm{Im}\,b\neq0;\ \mathrm{Re}\,a=0;\ 2\,\mathrm{Re}\,s<1\right))\end{matrix}\right]$$

No.	$f(x)$	$F(s)$
6	$e^{ax}\,\mathrm{Ei}\,(-ax-b)$	$-\dfrac{\pi a^{-s}}{\sin(s\pi)}\Gamma(s,b)$ $\qquad$ $[0<\mathrm{Re}\,s<1]$
7	$e^{ax}\big[\mathrm{Ei}\,(-2ax)$ $\ -\mathrm{Ei}\,(-ax)\big]$	$\dfrac{a^{-s}}{2}\Gamma(s)\left[\psi\left(\dfrac{2-s}{2}\right)-\psi\left(\dfrac{1-s}{2}\right)\right]$ $\quad[0<\mathrm{Re}\,s<1;\ |\arg a|<\pi]$
8	$e^{bx}\,\mathrm{Ei}\,(-u_+)$ $\ +e^{-bx}\,\mathrm{Ei}\,(u_-)$ $u_\pm=b\big(\sqrt{x^2+a^2}\pm a\big)$	$-\sqrt{\pi}\,a^{(s+1)/2}\left(\dfrac{b}{2}\right)^{(1-s)/2}\cot\dfrac{s\pi}{2}\,\Gamma\left(\dfrac{s}{2}\right)K_{(s+1)/2}\,(ab)$ $[b,\ \mathrm{Re}\,a>0;\ 0<\mathrm{Re}\,s<1]$

3.3.3. Ei (bx) **and hyperbolic or trigonometric functions**

Notation: $\delta=\left\{\begin{matrix}1\\0\end{matrix}\right\}$.

No.	$f(x)$	$F(s)$
1	$\left\{\begin{matrix}\sin(ax)\\\cos(ax)\end{matrix}\right\}\mathrm{Ei}\,(-bx)$	$-\dfrac{a^\delta}{(s+\delta)\,b^{s+\delta}}\Gamma(s+\delta)\,{}_3F_2\left(\begin{matrix}\frac{s+\delta}{2},\ \frac{s+\delta}{2},\ \frac{s+\delta+1}{2}\\ \frac{2\delta+1}{2},\ \frac{s+\delta+2}{2};\ -\frac{a^2}{b^2}\end{matrix}\right)$ $[a,\ b>0;\ \mathrm{Re}\,s>-\delta]$
2	$\left\{\begin{matrix}\sin(a\sqrt{x})\\\cos(a\sqrt{x})\end{matrix}\right\}\mathrm{Ei}\,(-bx)$	$-\dfrac{2a^\delta}{(2s+\delta)\,b^{s+\delta/2}}\Gamma\left(\dfrac{2s+\delta}{2}\right)\,{}_2F_2\left(\begin{matrix}\frac{2s+\delta}{2},\ \frac{2s+\delta}{2};\ -\frac{a^2}{4b}\\ \frac{2\delta+1}{2},\ \frac{2s+\delta+2}{2}\end{matrix}\right)$ $[\mathrm{Re}\,a,\ \mathrm{Re}\,(a+b),\ \mathrm{Re}\,s>0]$
3	$e^{bx}\sin(ax)\,\mathrm{Ei}\,(-bx)$	$\dfrac{a^{1-s}}{b}\Gamma(s-1)\cos\dfrac{s\pi}{2}\,{}_3F_2\left(\begin{matrix}\frac{1}{2},\ 1,\ 1;\ -\frac{a^2}{b^2}\\ \frac{2-s}{2},\ \frac{3-s}{2}\end{matrix}\right)$

$$-\frac{a^{2-s}}{b^2}\Gamma(s-2)\sin\frac{s\pi}{2}\,{}_3F_2\left(\begin{matrix}1,\ 1,\ \frac{3}{2};\ -\frac{a^2}{b^2}\\ \frac{3-s}{2},\ \frac{4-s}{2}\end{matrix}\right)$$

$$+\frac{\pi\csc(s\pi)}{(a^2+b^2)^{s/2}}\Gamma(s)\sin\left(s\arctan\frac{a}{b}\right)$$

$$[a>0;\ -1<\mathrm{Re}\,s<2;\ |\arg b|<\pi]$$

No.	$f(x)$	$F(s)$
4	$e^{-bx}\sin(ax)\,\text{Ei}(bx)$	$\dfrac{\pi a^{1-s}}{2b\,\Gamma(2-s)}\csc\dfrac{s\pi}{2}\,{}_3F_2\!\left(\begin{matrix}\frac{1}{2},\,1,\,1;\,-\frac{a^2}{b^2}\\ \frac{2-s}{2},\,\frac{3-s}{2}\end{matrix}\right)$
		$\qquad -\dfrac{\pi a^{2-s}}{2b^2\,\Gamma(3-s)}\sec\dfrac{s\pi}{2}\,{}_3F_2\!\left(\begin{matrix}1,\,1,\,\frac{3}{2};\,-\frac{a^2}{b^2}\\ \frac{3-s}{2},\,\frac{4-s}{2}\end{matrix}\right)$
		$-\dfrac{\pi\cot(s\pi)}{(a^2+b^2)^{s/2}}\,\Gamma(s)\sin\!\left(s\arctan\dfrac{a}{b}\right)\qquad [a,\,b>0;\ -1<\text{Re}\,s<2]$
5	$e^{bx}\cos(ax)\,\text{Ei}(-bx)$	$-\dfrac{a^{1-s}}{b}\,\Gamma(s-1)\sin\dfrac{s\pi}{2}\,{}_3F_2\!\left(\begin{matrix}\frac{1}{2},\,1,\,1;\,-\frac{a^2}{b^2}\\ \frac{2-s}{2},\,\frac{3-s}{2}\end{matrix}\right)$
		$\qquad -\dfrac{a^{2-s}}{b^2}\,\Gamma(s-2)\cos\dfrac{s\pi}{2}\,{}_3F_2\!\left(\begin{matrix}1,\,1,\,\frac{3}{2};\,-\frac{a^2}{b^2}\\ \frac{3-s}{2},\,\frac{4-s}{2}\end{matrix}\right)$
		$\qquad\qquad -\dfrac{\pi\csc(s\pi)}{(a^2+b^2)^{s/2}}\,\Gamma(s)\cos\!\left(s\arctan\dfrac{a}{b}\right)$
		$[a>0;\ 0<\text{Re}\,s<2;\ |\arg b|<\pi]$
6	$e^{-bx}\cos(ax)\,\text{Ei}(bx)$	$-\dfrac{\pi a^{1-s}}{2b\,\Gamma(2-s)}\sec\dfrac{s\pi}{2}\,{}_3F_2\!\left(\begin{matrix}\frac{1}{2},\,1,\,1;\,-\frac{a^2}{b^2}\\ \frac{2-s}{2},\,\frac{3-s}{2}\end{matrix}\right)$
		$\qquad -\dfrac{\pi a^{2-s}}{2b^2\,\Gamma(3-s)}\csc\dfrac{s\pi}{2}\,{}_3F_2\!\left(\begin{matrix}1,\,1,\,\frac{3}{2};\,-\frac{a^2}{b^2}\\ \frac{3-s}{2},\,\frac{4-s}{2}\end{matrix}\right)$
		$-\dfrac{\pi\cot(s\pi)}{(a^2+b^2)^{s/2}}\,\Gamma(s)\cos\!\left(s\arctan\dfrac{a}{b}\right)\qquad [a,\,b>0;\ 0<\text{Re}\,s<2]$
7	$\left.\begin{matrix}\sin(ax)\sinh(ax)\\ \cos(ax)\cosh(ax)\end{matrix}\right\}$ $\times\text{Ei}(-bx)$	$-\dfrac{a^{2\delta}}{b^{s+2\delta}(s+2\delta)}\,\Gamma(s+2\delta)\,{}_5F_4\!\left(\begin{matrix}\frac{s+2\delta}{4},\,\Delta(4,\,s+2\delta);\,-\frac{4a^4}{b^4}\\ \frac{2\delta+1}{4},\,\frac{2\delta+3}{4},\,\frac{2\delta+1}{2},\,\frac{s+2\delta+4}{4}\end{matrix}\right)$
		$[a,\,b>0;\ \text{Re}\,s>-2\delta]$
8	$\left.\begin{matrix}\cos(ax)\sinh(ax)\\ \sin(ax)\cosh(ax)\end{matrix}\right\}$ $\times\text{Ei}(-bx)$	$\pm\dfrac{a^3b^{-s-3}}{3(s+3)}\,\Gamma(s+3)\,{}_5F_4\!\left(\begin{matrix}\frac{s+3}{4},\,\Delta(4,\,s+3)\\ \frac{5}{4},\,\frac{3}{2},\,\frac{7}{4},\,\frac{s+7}{4};\,-\frac{4a^4}{b^4}\end{matrix}\right)$
		$\qquad -\dfrac{ab^{-s-1}}{s+1}\,\Gamma(s+1)\,{}_5F_4\!\left(\begin{matrix}\frac{s+1}{4},\,\Delta(4,\,s+1)\\ \frac{1}{2},\,\frac{3}{4},\,\frac{5}{4},\,\frac{s+5}{4};\,-\frac{4a^4}{b^4}\end{matrix}\right)$
		$[a,\,b>0;\ \text{Re}\,s>-1]$

3.3.4. $e^{ax}\ln^n x\,\text{Ei}(bx)$

1	$\ln(ax)\,\text{Ei}(-bx)$	$\dfrac{b^{-s}}{s}\,\Gamma(s)\left[\ln\dfrac{b}{a}-\psi(s)+\dfrac{1}{s}\right]\qquad\qquad [\text{Re}\,a,\,\text{Re}\,b,\,\text{Re}\,s>0]$

No.	$f(x)$	$F(s)$
2	$\ln^n x \, \mathrm{Ei}\,(-ax)$	$-\dfrac{d^n}{ds^n}\left[\dfrac{\Gamma(s)}{a^s s}\right]$ $\qquad\qquad$ $[\mathrm{Re}\,a,\ \mathrm{Re}\,s>0]$
3	$e^{ax}\ln x\,\mathrm{Ei}\,(-ax)$	$\dfrac{\pi\Gamma(s)}{a^s\sin(s\pi)}\left[\pi\cot(s\pi)-\psi(s)+\ln a\right]$ $\quad$ $[0<\mathrm{Re}\,s<1;\ |\arg a|<\pi]$
4	$e^{-ax}\ln x\,\mathrm{Ei}\,(-bx)$	$\dfrac{\Gamma(s)}{(a+b)^s}\left[\left[\ln(a+b)-\psi(s)\right]\Phi\left(\dfrac{a}{a+b},1,s\right)+\Phi\left(\dfrac{a}{a+b},2,s\right)\right]$ $[\mathrm{Re}\,(a+b),\ \mathrm{Re}\,s>0;\ |\arg b|<\pi]$
5	$e^{-ax}\ln^n x\,\mathrm{Ei}\,(-bx)$	$-\dfrac{d^n}{ds^n}\left[\dfrac{\Gamma(s)}{(a+b)^s}\Phi\left(\dfrac{a}{a+b},1,s\right)\right]$ $[\mathrm{Re}\,(a+b),\ \mathrm{Re}\,s>0;\ |\arg b|<\pi]$
6	$e^{\pm ax}\ln^n x\,\mathrm{Ei}\,(\mp ax)$	$-\pi\dfrac{d^n}{ds^n}\left[\dfrac{\Gamma(s)}{a^s}\left\{\begin{matrix}\csc(s\pi)\\\cot(s\pi)\end{matrix}\right\}\right]$ $\left[0<\mathrm{Re}\,s<1;\ \left\{\begin{matrix}|\arg a|<\pi\\a>0\end{matrix}\right\}\right]$

3.3.5. Products of Ei (ax)

No.	$f(x)$	$F(s)$
1	$\mathrm{Ei}^2\,(-ax)$	$\dfrac{a^{-s}\Gamma(s)}{2^{s-1}s}\Phi\left(\dfrac{1}{2},1,s\right)$ $\qquad\qquad$ $[a,\ \mathrm{Re}\,s>0]$
2	$\mathrm{Ei}\,(-ax)\,\mathrm{Ei}\,(-bx)$	$\dfrac{\Gamma(s)}{a^s}\left[\dfrac{bs}{a(s+1)}\,{}_4F_3\left(\begin{matrix}1,1,s+1,s+1\\2,2,s+2;\,-\frac{b}{a}\end{matrix}\right)\right.$ $\left.+\dfrac{1}{s}\left(\dfrac{1}{s}-\psi(s)-\mathbf{C}+\ln\dfrac{a}{b}\right)\right]$ $\quad[a+b,\ \mathrm{Re}\,s>0]$
3	$e^{ax}\,\mathrm{Ei}^2\,(-ax)$	$\dfrac{\Gamma(s)}{2a^s}\left[\dfrac{4\pi^2\cos(s\pi)}{\sin^2(s\pi)}+\psi'\left(\dfrac{1-s}{2}\right)-\psi'\left(\dfrac{2-s}{2}\right)\right]$ $\quad[a,\ \mathrm{Re}\,s>0]$
4	$e^{-ax}\,\mathrm{Ei}\,(-bx)\,\mathrm{Ei}\,(bx)$	$\dfrac{\pi}{sb^s}\cot\dfrac{s\pi}{2}\,\Gamma(s)\,{}_3F_2\left(\begin{matrix}\frac{s}{2},\frac{s}{2},\frac{s+1}{2}\\\frac{1}{2},\frac{s+2}{2};\,\frac{a^2}{b^2}\end{matrix}\right)+\dfrac{\pi a}{(s+1)b^{s+1}}\tan\dfrac{s\pi}{2}\,\Gamma(s+1)$ $\times{}_2F_1\left(\begin{matrix}\frac{s+1}{2},\frac{s+1}{2},\frac{s+2}{2}\\\frac{3}{2},\frac{s+3}{2};\,\frac{a^2}{b^2}\end{matrix}\right)-\dfrac{a^{2-s}\Gamma(s-2)}{b^2}\,{}_4F_3\left(\begin{matrix}1,1,1,\frac{3}{2};\,\frac{a^2}{b^2}\\2,\frac{3-s}{2},\frac{4-s}{2}\end{matrix}\right)$ $[b,\ \mathrm{Re}\,a,\ \mathrm{Re}\,s>0]$
5	$\ln(ax)\,\mathrm{Ei}^2\,(-bx)$	$\dfrac{2^{1-s}b^{-s}}{s}\Gamma(s)\left\{\dfrac{2}{s}\left[\psi(s)-\dfrac{1}{s}-\ln 2\right]{}_2F_1\left(\begin{matrix}1,1;\,-1\\s+1\end{matrix}\right)\right.$ $\left.+\ln\dfrac{a}{b}\,\Phi\left(\dfrac{1}{2},1,s\right)-\Phi\left(\dfrac{1}{2},2,s\right)\right\}$ $[b,\ \mathrm{Re}\,a,\ \mathrm{Re}\,s>0]$

3.4.   The Sine $\operatorname{si}(z)$, $\operatorname{Si}(z)$, and Cosine $\operatorname{ci}(z)$ Integrals

More formulas can be obtained from the corresponding sections due to the relations

$$\operatorname{si}(z) = \operatorname{Si}(z) - \frac{\pi}{2}; \quad \operatorname{ci}(z) = \frac{1}{2}\left[\operatorname{Ei}(-iz) + \operatorname{Ei}(iz)\right], \quad [\operatorname{Re} z > 0];$$

$$\operatorname{si}(z) = -\frac{\pi}{2}\left(\frac{\sqrt{z^2}}{z} + 1\right) + \frac{i}{2}\left[\operatorname{Ei}(-iz) - \operatorname{Ei}(iz)\right], \quad [\operatorname{Re} z \neq 0];$$

$$\operatorname{Si}(z) = z\,_1F_2\left(\frac{1}{2}; \frac{3}{2}, \frac{3}{2}; -\frac{z^2}{4}\right),$$

$$\operatorname{ci}(z) = -\frac{z^2}{4}\,_2F_3\left(1, 1; 2, 2, \frac{3}{2}; -\frac{z^2}{4}\right) + \ln z + \mathbf{C},$$

$$\operatorname{ci}(z) = -\frac{\sqrt{\pi}}{2}\,G_{13}^{20}\left(\frac{z^2}{4} \,\middle|\, \begin{matrix} 1 \\ 0,\,0,\,1/2 \end{matrix}\right) - \frac{\ln z^2}{2} + \ln z,$$

$$\operatorname{Si}(z) = \frac{\sqrt{\pi}z^2}{2z}\left[\sqrt{\pi} - G_{13}^{20}\left(\frac{z^2}{4} \,\middle|\, \begin{matrix} 1 \\ 0,\,1/2,\,0 \end{matrix}\right)\right], \quad \operatorname{Si}(z) = \frac{\sqrt{\pi}z^2}{2z}\,G_{13}^{11}\left(\frac{z^2}{4} \,\middle|\, \begin{matrix} 1 \\ 1/2,\,0,\,0 \end{matrix}\right),$$

$$\operatorname{Si}(z) = \frac{\sqrt{\pi}\,z}{4}\,G_{13}^{11}\left(\frac{z^2}{4} \,\middle|\, \begin{matrix} 1/2 \\ 0,\,-1/2,\,-1/2 \end{matrix}\right).$$

3.4.1. $\operatorname{si}(ax)$, $\operatorname{Si}(ax)$, and $\operatorname{ci}(ax)$

No.	$f(x)$	$F(s)$	
1	$\operatorname{si}(ax)$	$-\dfrac{\Gamma(s)}{a^s s}\sin\dfrac{s\pi}{2}$	$[a > 0;\ 0 < \operatorname{Re} s < 2]$
2	$\operatorname{ci}(ax)$	$-\dfrac{\Gamma(s)}{a^s s}\cos\dfrac{s\pi}{2}$	$[a > 0;\ 0 < \operatorname{Re} s < 2]$
3	$\operatorname{Si}(ax)$	$-\dfrac{\Gamma(s)}{a^s s}\sin\dfrac{s\pi}{2}$	$[a > 0;\ -1 < \operatorname{Re} s < 0]$

3.4.2. $\operatorname{si}(bx)$, $\operatorname{ci}(bx)$, and algebraic functions

1	$(a-x)_+^{\alpha-1}\,\operatorname{si}(bx)$	$a^{s+\alpha}b\,\mathrm{B}(\alpha, s+1)\,_3F_4\left(\begin{matrix} \frac{1}{2}, \frac{s+1}{2}, \frac{s+2}{2}; -\frac{a^2b^2}{4} \\ \frac{3}{2}, \frac{3}{2}, \frac{s+\alpha+1}{2}, \frac{s+\alpha+2}{2} \end{matrix}\right) - \dfrac{\pi}{2}a^{s+\alpha-1}\mathrm{B}(\alpha, s)$
		$[a,\ b,\ \operatorname{Re}\alpha,\ \operatorname{Re} s > 0]$
2	$(a-x)_+^{\alpha-1}\,\operatorname{ci}(bx)$	$-\dfrac{a^{s+\alpha+1}b^2}{4}\,\mathrm{B}(\alpha, s+2)\,_4F_5\left(\begin{matrix} 1, 1, \frac{s+2}{2}, \frac{s+3}{2}; -\frac{a^2b^2}{4} \\ \frac{3}{2}, 2, 2, \frac{s+\alpha+2}{2}, \frac{s+\alpha+3}{2} \end{matrix}\right)$
		$+ a^{s+\alpha-1}\mathrm{B}(\alpha, s)\left[\psi(s) - \psi(s+\alpha) + \log(ab) + \mathbf{C}\right]$
		$[a,\ b,\ \operatorname{Re}\alpha,\ \operatorname{Re} s > 0]$

No.	$f(x)$	$F(s)$
3	$\left(a^2 - x^2\right)_+^{\alpha-1} \mathrm{si}\,(bx)$	$\dfrac{a^{s+2\alpha-1}b}{2}\,\mathrm{B}\left(\alpha, \dfrac{s+1}{2}\right)\,{}_2F_3\left(\begin{matrix}\frac{1}{2}, \frac{s+1}{2};\ -\frac{a^2b^2}{4}\\ \frac{3}{2}, \frac{3}{2}, \frac{s+2\alpha+1}{2}\end{matrix}\right) - \dfrac{\pi a^{s+2\alpha-2}}{4}\,\mathrm{B}\left(\alpha, \dfrac{s}{2}\right)$

$$[a,\, b,\ \mathrm{Re}\,\alpha,\ \mathrm{Re}\,s > 0]$$

4	$\left(a^2 - x^2\right)_+^{\alpha-1} \mathrm{ci}\,(bx)$	$-\dfrac{a^{s+2\alpha}b^2}{8}\,\mathrm{B}\left(\alpha, \dfrac{s+2}{2}\right)\,{}_3F_4\left(\begin{matrix}1, 1, \frac{s+2}{2};\ -\frac{a^2b^2}{4}\\ \frac{3}{2}, 2, 2, \frac{s+2\alpha+2}{2}\end{matrix}\right)$

$$+\dfrac{a^{s+2\alpha-2}}{2}\,\mathrm{B}\left(\alpha, \dfrac{s}{2}\right)\left[\dfrac{1}{2}\,\psi\left(\dfrac{s}{2}\right) - \dfrac{1}{2}\,\psi\left(\dfrac{s+2\alpha}{2}\right) + \ln(ab) + \mathbf{C}\right]$$

$$[a,\, b,\ \mathrm{Re}\,\alpha,\ \mathrm{Re}\,s > 0]$$

5	$\dfrac{1}{(x^2 + a^2)^\rho}\,\mathrm{si}\,(bx)$	$-\dfrac{a^{s-2\rho+3}b^3}{36}\,\mathrm{B}\left(\dfrac{s+3}{2}, \dfrac{2\rho-s-3}{2}\right)\,{}_3F_4\left(\begin{matrix}1, \frac{3}{2}, \frac{s+3}{2};\ \frac{a^2b^2}{4}\\ 2, \frac{5}{2}, \frac{5}{2}, \frac{s-2\rho+5}{2}\end{matrix}\right)$

$$+\dfrac{a^{s-2\rho+1}b}{2}\,\mathrm{B}\left(\dfrac{s+1}{2}, \dfrac{2\rho-s-1}{2}\right)$$

$$-\dfrac{\pi a^{s-2\rho}}{4}\,\mathrm{B}\left(\dfrac{s}{2}, \dfrac{2\rho-s}{2}\right) + \dfrac{b^{2\rho-s}}{2\rho-s}\,\Gamma\left(s - 2\rho\right)$$

$$\times \sin\dfrac{(s-2\rho)\,\pi}{2}\,{}_2F_3\left(\begin{matrix}\rho, \frac{2\rho-s}{2};\ \frac{a^2b^2}{4}\\ \frac{2\rho-s+1}{2}, \frac{2\rho-s+2}{2}, \frac{2\rho-s+2}{2}\end{matrix}\right)$$

$$[b,\ \mathrm{Re}\,a > 0;\ 0 < \mathrm{Re}\,s < 2\,\mathrm{Re}\,\rho + 2]$$

6	$\dfrac{1}{(x^2 + a^2)^\rho}\,\mathrm{ci}\,(bx)$	$-\dfrac{a^{s-2\rho+2}b^2}{8}\,\mathrm{B}\left(\dfrac{s+2}{2}, \dfrac{2\rho-s-2}{2}\right)\,{}_3F_4\left(\begin{matrix}1, 1, \frac{s+2}{2};\ \frac{a^2b^2}{4}\\ \frac{3}{2}, 2, 2, \frac{s-2\rho+4}{2}\end{matrix}\right)$

$$+\dfrac{a^{s-2\rho}}{2}\,\mathrm{B}\left(\dfrac{s}{2}, \dfrac{2\rho-s}{2}\right)\left[\dfrac{1}{2}\,\psi\left(\dfrac{s}{2}\right) - \dfrac{1}{2}\,\psi\left(\dfrac{2\rho-s}{2}\right) + \ln(ab) + \mathbf{C}\right]$$

$$+\dfrac{b^{2\rho-s}}{2\rho-s}\,\Gamma\left(s - 2\rho\right)\cos\dfrac{(s-2\rho)\,\pi}{2}\,{}_2F_3\left(\begin{matrix}\rho, \frac{2\rho-s}{2};\ \frac{a^2b^2}{4}\\ \frac{2\rho-s+1}{2}, \frac{2\rho-s+2}{2}, \frac{2\rho-s+2}{2}\end{matrix}\right)$$

$$[b,\ \mathrm{Re}\,a > 0;\ 0 < \mathrm{Re}\,s < 2\,\mathrm{Re}\,\rho + 2]$$

7	$\dfrac{1}{x^2 - a^2}\,\mathrm{si}\,(bx)$	$-\dfrac{\pi b^{2-s}}{2\,(2-s)\,\Gamma\,(3-s)}\,\sec\dfrac{s\pi}{2}\,{}_2F_3\left(\begin{matrix}1, \frac{2-s}{2};\ -\frac{a^2b^2}{4}\\ \frac{3-s}{2}, \frac{4-s}{2}, \frac{4-s}{2}\end{matrix}\right)$

$$+\dfrac{\pi a^{s-2}}{2}\,\tan\dfrac{s\pi}{2}\,\mathrm{Si}\,(ab) + \dfrac{\pi^2 a^{s-2}}{4}\,\cot\dfrac{s\pi}{2}$$

$$[a,\, b > 0;\ 0 < \mathrm{Re}\,s < 4]$$

8	$\dfrac{1}{x^2 - a^2}\,\mathrm{ci}\,(bx)$	$-\dfrac{\pi b^{2-s}}{2\,(2-s)\,\Gamma\,(3-s)}\,\csc\dfrac{s\pi}{2}\,{}_2F_3\left(\begin{matrix}1, \frac{2-s}{2};\ -\frac{a^2b^2}{4}\\ \frac{3-s}{2}, \frac{4-s}{2}, \frac{4-s}{2}\end{matrix}\right)$

$$-\dfrac{\pi a^{s-2}}{2}\,\cot\dfrac{s\pi}{2}\,\mathrm{ci}\,(ab) + \dfrac{\pi^2 a^{s-2}}{4}\,\csc^2\dfrac{s\pi}{2}$$

$$[a,\, b > 0;\ 0 < \mathrm{Re}\,s < 4]$$

No.	$f(x)$	$F(s)$
9	$\dfrac{1}{(x+a)^\rho}\,\mathrm{Si}\left(\dfrac{b}{x+a}\right)$	$a^{s-\rho-1}b\,\mathrm{B}\left(s,1-s+\rho\right){}_3F_4\left(\begin{matrix}\frac12,\ \frac{1-s+\rho}{2},\ \frac{2-s+\rho}{2};\ -\frac{b^2}{4a^2}\\ \frac32,\ \frac32,\ \frac{\rho+1}{2},\ \frac{\rho+2}{2}\end{matrix}\right)$ $[0<\mathrm{Re}\,s<\mathrm{Re}\,\rho+1;\ |\arg a|<\pi]$
10	$\dfrac{1}{(x+a)^\rho}\,\mathrm{Si}\left(\dfrac{bx}{x+a}\right)$	$a^{s-\rho}b\,\mathrm{B}\left(s+1,\rho-s\right){}_3F_4\left(\begin{matrix}\frac12,\ \frac{s+1}{2},\ \frac{s+2}{2};\ -\frac{b^2}{4}\\ \frac32,\ \frac32,\ \frac{\rho+1}{2},\ \frac{\rho+2}{2}\end{matrix}\right)$ $[-1<\mathrm{Re}\,s<\mathrm{Re}\,\rho;\ |\arg a|<\pi]$
11	$\dfrac{1}{(x^2+a^2)^\rho}$ $\times\mathrm{Si}\left(\dfrac{bx}{x^2+a^2}\right)$	$\dfrac{a^{s-2\rho-1}b}{2}\,\mathrm{B}\left(\dfrac{s+1}{2},\dfrac{1-s+2\rho}{2}\right){}_3F_4\left(\begin{matrix}\frac12,\ \frac{s+1}{2},\ \frac{1-s+2\rho}{2};\ -\frac{b^2}{16a^2}\\ \frac32,\ \frac32,\ \frac{\rho+1}{2},\ \frac{\rho+2}{2}\end{matrix}\right)$ $[\mathrm{Re}\,a>0;\ -1<\mathrm{Re}\,s<2\,\mathrm{Re}\,\rho+1]$

3.4.3. si (bx), ci (bx), and the exponential function

No.	$f(x)$	$F(s)$
1	$e^{-ax}\left\{\begin{matrix}\mathrm{si}\,(bx)\\ \mathrm{ci}\,(bx)\end{matrix}\right\}$	$\pm\dfrac{a\,\Gamma(s+1)}{b^{s+1}(s+1)}\left\{\begin{matrix}\cos(s\pi/2)\\ \sin(s\pi/2)\end{matrix}\right\}{}_3F_2\left(\begin{matrix}\frac{s+1}{2},\ \frac{s+1}{2},\ \frac{s+2}{2}\\ \frac32,\ \frac{s+3}{2};\ -\frac{a^2}{b^2}\end{matrix}\right)$ $-\dfrac{\Gamma(s)}{b^s s}\left\{\begin{matrix}\sin(s\pi/2)\\ \cos(s\pi/2)\end{matrix}\right\}{}_3F_2\left(\begin{matrix}\frac{s}{2},\ \frac{s}{2},\ \frac{s+1}{2}\\ \frac12,\ \frac{s+2}{2};\ -\frac{a^2}{b^2}\end{matrix}\right)$ $[b,\ \mathrm{Re}\,a,\ \mathrm{Re}\,s>0]$
2	$e^{-ax^2}\,\mathrm{si}\,(bx)$	$-\dfrac{b^3}{36a^{(s+3)/2}}\Gamma\left(\dfrac{s+3}{2}\right){}_3F_3\left(\begin{matrix}1,\ \frac32,\ \frac{s+3}{2}\\ 2,\ \frac52,\ \frac52;\ -\frac{b^2}{4a}\end{matrix}\right)$ $+\dfrac{b}{2a^{(s+1)/2}}\Gamma\left(\dfrac{s+1}{2}\right)-\dfrac{\pi}{4a^{s/2}}\Gamma\left(\dfrac{s}{2}\right)$ $[b,\ \mathrm{Re}\,a,\ \mathrm{Re}\,s>0]$
3	$e^{-ax^2}\,\mathrm{ci}\,(bx)$	$-\dfrac{b^2}{8a^{(s+2)/2}}\Gamma\left(\dfrac{s+2}{2}\right){}_3F_3\left(\begin{matrix}1,\ 1,\ \frac{s+2}{2}\\ \frac32,\ 2,\ 2;\ -\frac{b^2}{4a}\end{matrix}\right)$ $+\dfrac{\Gamma(s/2)}{4a^{s/2}}\left[\psi\left(\dfrac{s}{2}\right)+\ln\dfrac{b^2}{a}+2\mathbf{C}\right]$ $[b,\ \mathrm{Re}\,a,\ \mathrm{Re}\,s>0]$

3.4.4. si (bx), ci (bx), and trigonometric functions

No.	$f(x)$	$F(s)$
1	$\sin(ax)\,\mathrm{si}\,(bx)$	$\dfrac{b\,\Gamma(s+1)}{a^{s+1}}\cos\dfrac{s\pi}{2}\,{}_3F_2\left(\begin{matrix}\frac12,\ \frac{s+1}{2},\ \frac{s+2}{2}\\ \frac32,\ \frac32;\ \frac{b^2}{a^2}\end{matrix}\right)-\dfrac{\pi\Gamma(s)}{2a^s}\sin\dfrac{s\pi}{2}$ $[0<b<a;\ -1<\mathrm{Re}\,s<2]$
2	$\sin(ax)\,\mathrm{si}\,(bx)$	$-\dfrac{a\,\Gamma(s+1)}{b^{s+1}(s+1)}\cos\dfrac{s\pi}{2}\,{}_3F_2\left(\begin{matrix}\frac{s+1}{2},\ \frac{s+1}{2},\ \frac{s+2}{2}\\ \frac32,\ \frac{s+3}{2};\ \frac{a^2}{b^2}\end{matrix}\right)$ $[0<a<b;\ -1<\mathrm{Re}\,s<2]$

No.	$f(x)$	$F(s)$
3	$\sin(ax)\,\mathrm{ci}(bx)$	$\dfrac{b^2\Gamma(s+2)}{4a^{s+2}}\sin\dfrac{s\pi}{2}\,{}_4F_3\left(\begin{matrix}1,\,1,\,\frac{s+2}{2},\,\frac{s+3}{2}\\ \frac{3}{2},\,2,\,2;\,\frac{b^2}{a^2}\end{matrix}\right)$
		$+\dfrac{\Gamma(s)}{a^s}\sin\dfrac{s\pi}{2}\left[\mathbf{C}+\psi(s)+\dfrac{\pi}{2}\cot\dfrac{s\pi}{2}+\ln\dfrac{b}{a}\right]$
		$[0<b<a;\ -1<\operatorname{Re}s<2]$
4	$\sin(ax)\,\mathrm{ci}(bx)$	$\dfrac{a\Gamma(s+1)}{b^{s+1}(s+1)}\sin\dfrac{s\pi}{2}\,{}_3F_2\left(\begin{matrix}\frac{s+1}{2},\,\frac{s+1}{2},\,\frac{s+2}{2}\\ \frac{3}{2},\,\frac{s+3}{2};\,\frac{a^2}{b^2}\end{matrix}\right)$
		$[0<a<b;\ -1<\operatorname{Re}s<2]$
5	$\cos(ax)\,\mathrm{si}(bx)$	$-\dfrac{b\,\Gamma(s+1)}{a^{s+1}}\sin\dfrac{s\pi}{2}\,{}_3F_2\left(\begin{matrix}\frac{1}{2},\,\frac{s+1}{2},\,\frac{s+2}{2}\\ \frac{3}{2},\,\frac{3}{2};\,\frac{b^2}{a^2}\end{matrix}\right)-\dfrac{\pi\Gamma(s)}{2a^s}\cos\dfrac{s\pi}{2}$
		$[0<b<a;\ 0<\operatorname{Re}s<2]$
6	$\cos(ax)\,\mathrm{si}(bx)$	$-\dfrac{\Gamma(s)}{b^s s}\sin\dfrac{s\pi}{2}\,{}_3F_2\left(\begin{matrix}\frac{s}{2},\,\frac{s}{2},\,\frac{s+1}{2}\\ \frac{1}{2},\,\frac{s+2}{2};\,\frac{a^2}{b^2}\end{matrix}\right)$ $[0<a<b;\ 0<\operatorname{Re}s<2]$
7	$\cos(ax)\,\mathrm{ci}(bx)$	$\dfrac{b^2\Gamma(s+2)}{4a^{s+2}}\cos\dfrac{s\pi}{2}\,{}_4F_3\left(\begin{matrix}1,\,1,\,\frac{s+2}{2},\,\frac{s+3}{2}\\ \frac{3}{2},\,2,\,2;\,\frac{b^2}{a^2}\end{matrix}\right)$
		$+\dfrac{\Gamma(s)}{a^s}\cos\dfrac{s\pi}{2}\left[\mathbf{C}+\psi(s)-\dfrac{\pi}{2}\tan\dfrac{s\pi}{2}+\ln\dfrac{b}{a}\right]$
		$[0<b<a;\ 0<\operatorname{Re}s<2]$
8	$\cos(ax)\,\mathrm{ci}(bx)$	$-\dfrac{\Gamma(s)}{b^s s}\cos\dfrac{s\pi}{2}\,{}_3F_2\left(\begin{matrix}\frac{s}{2},\,\frac{s}{2},\,\frac{s+1}{2}\\ \frac{1}{2},\,\frac{s+2}{2};\,\frac{a^2}{b^2}\end{matrix}\right)$ $[0<a<b;\ 0<\operatorname{Re}s<2]$
9	$\sin(ax)\,\mathrm{ci}(ax)$ $-\cos(ax)\,\mathrm{si}(ax)$	$\dfrac{\pi}{2a^s}\Gamma(s)\sec\dfrac{s\pi}{2}$ $[a>0;\ 0<\operatorname{Re}s<1]$
10	$\cos(ax)\,\mathrm{ci}(ax)$ $+\sin(ax)\,\mathrm{si}(ax)$	$-\dfrac{\pi}{2a^s}\Gamma(s)\csc\dfrac{s\pi}{2}$ $[a>0;\ 0<\operatorname{Re}s<2]$
11	$\cos(ax)\,\mathrm{ci}(ax)$ $+\sin(ax)\,\mathrm{Si}(ax)$	$-\dfrac{\pi}{2a^s}\cos\dfrac{s\pi}{2}\cot\dfrac{s\pi}{2}\Gamma(s)$ $[a>0;\ 0<\operatorname{Re}s<1]$
12	$\sin(ax)\,\mathrm{ci}(ax)$ $-\cos(ax)\,\mathrm{Si}(ax)$	$\dfrac{\pi}{2a^s}\sin\dfrac{s\pi}{2}\tan\dfrac{s\pi}{2}\Gamma(s)$ $[a>0;\ -1<\operatorname{Re}s<1]$

No.	$f(x)$	$F(s)$
13	$\sin\left(b\sqrt{x^2+a^2}\right)$	$-\dfrac{\pi a^{(s+1)/2}}{2^{(s+3)/2}b^{(s-1)/2}}\csc\dfrac{s\pi}{2}\,\Gamma(s)\,\Gamma\left(\dfrac{1-s}{2}\right)J_{-(s+1)/2}(ab)$
	$\times\,\mathrm{si}\left(b\sqrt{x^2+a^2}\right)$	$-\dfrac{2^{(s-5)/2}\pi^{3/2}a^{(s+1)/2}}{b^{(s-1)/2}}\Gamma\left(\dfrac{s}{2}\right)\left[\sec\dfrac{s\pi}{2}\,J_{(s+1)/2}(ab)\right.$
	$+\cos\left(b\sqrt{x^2+a^2}\right)$	$\left.+\csc\dfrac{s\pi}{2}\,\mathbf{H}_{(s+1)/2}(ab)\right]+\dfrac{\pi a^s}{2s}\csc\dfrac{s\pi}{2}$
	$\times\,\mathrm{ci}\left(b\sqrt{x^2+a^2}\right)$	$[a,\,b>0;\;0<\operatorname{Re}s<2]$
14	$e^{-ax}\left[\sin(bx)\operatorname{ci}(bx)\right.$	$\dfrac{\pi\,\Gamma(s)}{2b^s}\sec\dfrac{s\pi}{2}\,{}_2F_1\left(\begin{smallmatrix}\frac{s}{2},\,\frac{s+1}{2}\\\frac{1}{2};\,-\frac{a^2}{b^2}\end{smallmatrix}\right)+\dfrac{\pi a\,\Gamma(s+1)}{2b^{s+1}}\csc\dfrac{s\pi}{2}$
	$\left.-\cos(bx)\operatorname{si}(bx)\right]$	$\times\,{}_2F_1\left(\begin{smallmatrix}\frac{s+1}{2},\,\frac{s+2}{2}\\\frac{3}{2};\,-\frac{a^2}{b^2}\end{smallmatrix}\right)+\dfrac{\Gamma(s-1)}{a^{s-1}b}\,{}_3F_2\left(\begin{smallmatrix}\frac{1}{2},\,1,\,1\\\frac{2-s}{2},\,\frac{3-s}{2};\,-\frac{a^2}{b^2}\end{smallmatrix}\right)$
		$[b,\,\operatorname{Re}a,\,\operatorname{Re}s>0]$
15	$e^{-ax}\left[\cos(bx)\operatorname{ci}(bx)\right.$	$\dfrac{\pi a\,\Gamma(s+1)}{2b^{s+1}}\sec\dfrac{s\pi}{2}\,{}_2F_1\left(\begin{smallmatrix}\frac{s+1}{2},\,\frac{s+2}{2}\\\frac{3}{2};\,-\frac{a^2}{b^2}\end{smallmatrix}\right)-\dfrac{\pi\,\Gamma(s)}{2b^s}\csc\dfrac{s\pi}{2}$
	$\left.+\sin(bx)\operatorname{si}(bx)\right]$	$\times\,{}_2F_1\left(\begin{smallmatrix}\frac{s}{2},\,\frac{s+1}{2}\\\frac{1}{2};\,-\frac{a^2}{b^2}\end{smallmatrix}\right)-\dfrac{\Gamma(s-2)}{a^{s-2}b^2}\,{}_3F_2\left(\begin{smallmatrix}\frac{3}{2},\,1,\,1\\\frac{3-s}{2},\,\frac{4-s}{2};\,-\frac{a^2}{b^2}\end{smallmatrix}\right)$
		$[b,\,\operatorname{Re}a,\,\operatorname{Re}s>0]$

3.4.5. $\mathrm{Si}(bx)$ and the logarithmic or inverse trigonometric functions

No.	$f(x)$	$F(s)$
1	$\theta(a-x)\ln\dfrac{\sqrt{a-x}+\sqrt{a}}{\sqrt{x}}$	$\dfrac{\sqrt{\pi}\,a^{s+1}b}{2s}\Gamma\!\left[\begin{smallmatrix}s+1\\\frac{2s+3}{2}\end{smallmatrix}\right]\left[{}_3F_4\left(\begin{smallmatrix}\frac{1}{2},\,\frac{s+1}{2},\,\frac{s+2}{2};\,-\frac{a^2b^2}{4}\\\frac{3}{2},\,\frac{3}{2},\,\frac{2s+3}{4},\,\frac{2s+5}{4}\end{smallmatrix}\right)\right.$
	$\times\,\mathrm{Si}(bx)$	$\left.-\dfrac{1}{s+1}\,{}_3F_4\left(\begin{smallmatrix}\frac{s+1}{2},\,\frac{s+1}{2},\,\frac{s+2}{2};\,-\frac{a^2b^2}{4}\\\frac{3}{2},\,\frac{2s+3}{4},\,\frac{2s+5}{4},\,\frac{s+3}{2}\end{smallmatrix}\right)\right]$
		$[a>0;\;\operatorname{Re}s>-1]$
2	$\theta(a-x)\ln\dfrac{a+\sqrt{a^2-x^2}}{x}$	$\dfrac{\sqrt{\pi}\,a^{s+1}b}{2s(s+1)}\Gamma\!\left[\begin{smallmatrix}\frac{s+1}{2}\\\frac{s+2}{2}\end{smallmatrix}\right]\left[(s+1)\,{}_2F_3\left(\begin{smallmatrix}\frac{1}{2},\,\frac{s+1}{2};\,-\frac{a^2b^2}{4}\\\frac{3}{2},\,\frac{3}{2},\,\frac{s+2}{2}\end{smallmatrix}\right)\right.$
	$\times\,\mathrm{Si}(bx)$	$\left.-\,{}_2F_3\left(\begin{smallmatrix}\frac{s+1}{2},\,\frac{s+1}{2};\,-\frac{a^2b^2}{4}\\\frac{3}{2},\,\frac{s+2}{2},\,\frac{s+3}{2}\end{smallmatrix}\right)\right]$ $[a>0;\;\operatorname{Re}s>-1]$
3	$\theta(a-x)\arccos\dfrac{x}{a}\,\mathrm{Si}(bx)$	$\dfrac{\sqrt{\pi}\,a^{s+1}b}{2(s+1)}\Gamma\!\left[\begin{smallmatrix}\frac{s+2}{2}\\\frac{s+3}{2}\end{smallmatrix}\right]{}_3F_4\left(\begin{smallmatrix}\frac{1}{2},\,\frac{s+1}{2},\,\frac{s+2}{2};\,-\frac{a^2b^2}{4}\\\frac{3}{2},\,\frac{3}{2},\,\frac{s+3}{2},\,\frac{s+3}{2}\end{smallmatrix}\right)$
		$[a>0;\;\operatorname{Re}s>-1]$

3.4.6.　Si (bx), si (bx), ci (bx), **and** Ei $(-ax^r)$

1	Ei $(-ax)$ Si (bx)	$-\dfrac{b\,\Gamma(s)}{a^{s+1}}\left[{}_3F_2\left(\begin{matrix}\frac{1}{2},\ \frac{s+1}{2},\ \frac{s+2}{2}\\ \frac{3}{2},\ \frac{3}{2};\ -\frac{b^2}{a^2}\end{matrix}\right)-\dfrac{1}{s+1}\,{}_3F_2\left(\begin{matrix}\frac{s+1}{2},\ \frac{s+1}{2},\ \frac{s+2}{2}\\ \frac{3}{2},\ \frac{s+3}{2};\ -\frac{b^2}{a^2}\end{matrix}\right)\right]$
		$[a,\ b>0;\ \operatorname{Re}s>-1]$
2	Ei $(-ax)$ si (bx)	$\dfrac{b^3\Gamma(s+3)}{18a^{s+3}(s+3)}\,{}_5F_4\left(\begin{matrix}1,\ \frac{3}{2},\ \frac{s+3}{2},\ \frac{s+3}{2},\ \frac{s+4}{2}\\ 2,\ \frac{5}{2},\ \frac{5}{2},\ \frac{s+5}{2};\ -\frac{b^2}{a^2}\end{matrix}\right)-\dfrac{b\,\Gamma(s+1)}{a^{s+1}(s+1)}+\dfrac{\pi\,\Gamma(s)}{2a^s s}$
		$[b,\ \operatorname{Re}a,\ \operatorname{Re}s>0]$
3	Ei $(-ax)$ ci (bx)	$\dfrac{b^2\Gamma(s+2)}{4\,a^{s+2}(s+2)}\,{}_5F_4\left(\begin{matrix}1,\ 1,\ \frac{s+2}{2},\ \frac{s+2}{2},\ \frac{s+3}{2}\\ 2,\ 2,\ \frac{3}{2},\ \frac{s+4}{2};\ -\frac{b^2}{a^2}\end{matrix}\right)$
		$\qquad\qquad-\dfrac{\Gamma(s)}{a^s s}\left[\psi(s)-\dfrac{1}{s}+\ln\dfrac{b}{a}+\mathbf{C}\right]\qquad[b,\ \operatorname{Re}a,\ \operatorname{Re}s>0]$
4	Ei $(-ax^2)$ si (bx)	$\dfrac{b^3}{18a^{(s+3)/2}(s+3)}\,\Gamma\left(\dfrac{s+3}{2}\right){}_4F_4\left(\begin{matrix}1,\ \frac{3}{2},\ \frac{s+3}{2},\ \frac{s+3}{2}\\ 2,\ \frac{5}{2},\ \frac{5}{2},\ \frac{s+5}{2};\ -\frac{b^2}{4a}\end{matrix}\right)$
		$\qquad-\dfrac{b}{a^{(s+1)/2}(s+1)}\,\Gamma\left(\dfrac{s+1}{2}\right)+\dfrac{\pi}{2a^{s/2}s}\,\Gamma\left(\dfrac{s}{2}\right)\qquad[a,\ \operatorname{Re}b,\ \operatorname{Re}s>0]$
5	Ei $(-ax^2)$ ci (bx)	$\dfrac{b^2}{4a^{s/2+1}(s+2)}\,\Gamma\left(\dfrac{s+2}{2}\right){}_4F_4\left(\begin{matrix}1,\ 1,\ \frac{s+2}{2},\ \frac{s+2}{2}\\ 2,\ 2,\ \frac{3}{2},\ \frac{s+4}{2};\ -\frac{b^2}{4a}\end{matrix}\right)$
		$\qquad-\dfrac{\Gamma(s/2)}{a^{s/2}s}\left[\dfrac{1}{2}\psi\left(\dfrac{s}{2}\right)-\dfrac{1}{s}+\ln\dfrac{b}{\sqrt{a}}+\mathbf{C}\right]\qquad[b,\ \operatorname{Re}a,\ \operatorname{Re}s>0]$

3.4.7.　si^2 (bx) + ci^2 (bx) **and trigonometric functions**

1	si^2 (ax) + ci^2 (ax)	$\dfrac{\pi\Gamma(s)}{a^s s}\csc\dfrac{s\pi}{2}\qquad\qquad\qquad[a>0;\ 0<\operatorname{Re}s<2]$
2	sin (ax) [si^2 (bx)	$-\dfrac{a^{2-s}\Gamma(s-2)}{b^2}\sin\dfrac{s\pi}{2}\,{}_4F_3\left(\begin{matrix}1,\ 1,\ 1,\ \frac{3}{2};\ \frac{a^2}{b^2}\\ 2,\ \frac{3-s}{2},\ \frac{4-s}{2}\end{matrix}\right)$
	+ ci^2 (bx)]	$\qquad\qquad+\dfrac{\pi a\,\Gamma(s+1)}{b^{s+1}(s+1)}\sec\dfrac{s\pi}{2}\,{}_3F_2\left(\begin{matrix}\frac{s+1}{2},\ \frac{s+1}{2},\ \frac{s+2}{2}\\ \frac{3}{2},\ \frac{s+3}{2};\ \frac{a^2}{b^2}\end{matrix}\right)$
		$[a,\ b>0;\ -1<\operatorname{Re}s<2]$
3	cos (ax) [si^2 (bx)	$-\dfrac{a^{2-s}\Gamma(s-2)}{b^2}\cos\dfrac{s\pi}{2}\,{}_4F_3\left(\begin{matrix}1,\ 1,\ 1,\ \frac{3}{2};\ \frac{a^2}{b^2}\\ 2,\ \frac{3-s}{2},\ \frac{4-s}{2}\end{matrix}\right)$
	+ ci^2 (bx)]	$\qquad\qquad+\dfrac{\pi\,\Gamma(s)}{b^s s}\csc\dfrac{s\pi}{2}\,{}_3F_2\left(\begin{matrix}\frac{s}{2},\ \frac{s+1}{2},\ \frac{s}{2}\\ \frac{1}{2},\ \frac{s+2}{2};\ \frac{a^2}{b^2}\end{matrix}\right)$
		$[a,\ b>0;\ 0<\operatorname{Re}s<2]$

3.4.8.   Products of $\operatorname{si}(bx)$ and $\operatorname{ci}(bx)$

1	$\operatorname{si}(ax)\operatorname{si}(bx)$	$-\dfrac{a^{-s-1}b}{s+1}\cos\dfrac{s\pi}{2}\,\Gamma(s+1)\,{}_4F_3\!\left(\begin{matrix}\frac{1}{2},\,\frac{s+1}{2},\,\frac{s+1}{2},\,\frac{s+2}{2}\\[2pt]\frac{3}{2},\,\frac{3}{2},\,\frac{s+3}{2};\,\frac{b^2}{a^2}\end{matrix}\right)$

$$+\frac{\pi}{2a^s s}\sin\frac{s\pi}{2}\,\Gamma(s)$$

$$[0<b<a;\,0<\operatorname{Re}s<2]$$

2	$\operatorname{si}(ax)\operatorname{ci}(bx)$	$-\dfrac{a^{-s-2}b^2}{4(s+2)}\sin\dfrac{s\pi}{2}\,\Gamma(s+2)\,{}_5F_4\!\left(\begin{matrix}1,1,\,\frac{s+2}{2},\,\frac{s+2}{2},\,\frac{s+3}{2}\\[2pt]\frac{3}{2},\,2,\,2,\,\frac{s+4}{2};\,\frac{b^2}{a^2}\end{matrix}\right)$

$$-\frac{\Gamma(s)}{a^s s}\sin\frac{s\pi}{2}\left[\psi(s)+\frac{\pi}{2}\cot\frac{s\pi}{2}-\frac{1}{s}+\ln\frac{b}{a}+\mathbf{C}\right]$$

$$[0<b<a;\,0<\operatorname{Re}s<2]$$

3	$\operatorname{si}(ax)\operatorname{ci}(bx)$	$\dfrac{a^3 b^{-s-3}}{18(s+3)}\sin\dfrac{s\pi}{2}\,\Gamma(s+3)\,{}_5F_4\!\left(\begin{matrix}1,\,\frac{3}{2},\,\frac{s+1}{2},\,\frac{s+1}{2},\,\frac{s+4}{2}\\[2pt]2,\,\frac{5}{2},\,\frac{5}{2},\,\frac{s+5}{2};\,\frac{a^2}{b^2}\end{matrix}\right)$

$$+\frac{a}{b^{s+1}(s+1)}\sin\frac{s\pi}{2}\,\Gamma(s+1)+\frac{\pi}{2b^s s}\cos\frac{s\pi}{2}\,\Gamma(s)$$

$$[0<a<b;\,0<\operatorname{Re}s<2]$$

4	$\operatorname{ci}(ax)\operatorname{ci}(bx)$	$-\dfrac{a^{-s-2}b^2}{4(s+2)}\cos\dfrac{s\pi}{2}\,\Gamma(s+2)\,{}_5F_4\!\left(\begin{matrix}1,\,1,\,\frac{s+2}{2},\,\frac{s+2}{2},\,\frac{s+3}{2}\\[2pt]\frac{3}{2},\,2,\,2,\,\frac{s+4}{2};\,\frac{b^2}{a^2}\end{matrix}\right)$

$$-\frac{\Gamma(s)}{a^s s}\cos\frac{s\pi}{2}\left[\psi(s)-\frac{\pi}{2}\tan\frac{s\pi}{2}-\frac{1}{s}+\ln\frac{b}{a}+\mathbf{C}\right]$$

$$[0<b<a;\,0<\operatorname{Re}s<2]$$

5	$\big[\sin(x)\operatorname{ci}(2x)$	$\dfrac{2^{-s-4}}{s}\Gamma(s)\left\{\pi^2 s\,[3-\cos(s\pi)]\sec\dfrac{s\pi}{2}+4\pi\,[1+\cos(s\pi)]\right.$
	$-\cos(x)\operatorname{Si}(2x)\big]^2$	

$$\times\csc\frac{s\pi}{2}+4s\cos\frac{s\pi}{2}\left[\psi'\!\left(\frac{s+1}{2}\right)-\psi'\!\left(\frac{s}{2}\right)\right]\Big\}$$

$$[-2<\operatorname{Re}s<0]$$

6	$\big[\sin(x)\operatorname{ci}(2x)$	$2^{-s-3}\Gamma(s)\left\{\dfrac{\pi^2}{2}\,[\cos(s\pi)+3]\csc\dfrac{s\pi}{2}\right.$
	$-\cos(x)\operatorname{Si}(2x)\big]$	
	$\times\big[\cos(x)\operatorname{ci}(2x)$	
	$+\sin(x)\operatorname{Si}(2x)\big]$	

$$+\sin\frac{s\pi}{2}\left[3\psi'\!\left(\frac{s+1}{2}\right)-4\psi'(s)-\psi'\!\left(\frac{s}{2}\right)\right]\Big\}$$

$$[-1<\operatorname{Re}s<1]$$

3.5. Hyperbolic Sine shi (z) and Cosine chi (z) Integrals

More formulas can be obtained from the corresponding sections due to the relations

$$\text{shi}(z) = -i\,\text{Si}(iz), \quad \text{shi}(z) = z\,{}_1F_2\left(\frac{1}{2}; \frac{3}{2}, \frac{3}{2}; \frac{z^2}{4}\right),$$

$$\text{chi}(z) = \text{ci}(iz) - \frac{\pi i}{2}, \quad \text{chi}(z) = \frac{z^2}{4}\,{}_2F_3\left(1, 1; 2, 2, \frac{3}{2}; \frac{z^2}{4}\right) + \ln z + \mathbf{C},$$

$$\text{chi}(z) = -\frac{\sqrt{\pi}}{2}\,G_{13}^{20}\left(-\frac{z^2}{4}\,\middle|\,\begin{matrix}1\\0,\,0,\,1/2\end{matrix}\right) + \frac{1}{2}\left[\ln z - \ln(-z)\right].$$

3.5.1. shi (bx), chi (bx), and algebraic functions

No.	$f(x)$	$F(s)$
1	$(a-x)_+^{\alpha-1}\,\text{shi}(bx)$	$a^{s+\alpha}b\,\text{B}(\alpha,\,s+1)\,{}_3F_4\left(\begin{matrix}\frac{1}{2},\,\frac{s+1}{2},\,\frac{s+2}{2};\,\frac{a^2b^2}{4}\\\frac{3}{2},\,\frac{3}{2},\,\frac{s+\alpha+1}{2},\,\frac{s+\alpha+2}{2}\end{matrix}\right)$ $[a,\,\text{Re}\,\alpha,\,\text{Re}\,s>0]$
2	$(a-x)_+^{\alpha-1}\,\text{chi}(bx)$	$\dfrac{a^{s+\alpha+1}b^2}{4}\,\text{B}(\alpha,\,s+2)\,{}_4F_5\left(\begin{matrix}1,\,1,\,\frac{s+2}{2},\,\frac{s+3}{2};\,\frac{a^2b^2}{4}\\\frac{3}{2},\,2,\,2,\,\frac{s+\alpha+2}{2},\,\frac{s+\alpha+3}{2}\end{matrix}\right)$ $+\,a^{s+\alpha-1}\,\text{B}(\alpha,\,s)\left[\psi(s) - \psi(s+\alpha) + \log(ab) + \mathbf{C}\right]$ $[a,\,\text{Re}\,\alpha,\,\text{Re}\,s>0]$
3	$(a^2-x^2)_+^{\alpha-1}\,\text{shi}(bx)$	$\dfrac{a^{s+2\alpha-1}b}{2}\,\text{B}\left(\alpha,\,\frac{s+1}{2}\right)\,{}_2F_3\left(\begin{matrix}\frac{1}{2},\,\frac{s+1}{2};\,\frac{a^2b^2}{4}\\\frac{3}{2},\,\frac{3}{2},\,\frac{s+2\alpha+1}{2}\end{matrix}\right)$ $[a,\,\text{Re}\,\alpha,\,\text{Re}\,s>0]$
4	$(a^2-x^2)_+^{\alpha-1}\,\text{chi}(bx)$	$\dfrac{a^{s+2\alpha}b^2}{8}\,\text{B}\left(\alpha,\,\frac{s+2}{2}\right)\,{}_3F_4\left(\begin{matrix}1,\,1,\,\frac{s+2}{2};\,\frac{a^2b^2}{4}\\\frac{3}{2},\,2,\,2,\,\frac{s+2\alpha+2}{2}\end{matrix}\right)$ $+\,\dfrac{a^{s+2\alpha-2}}{2}\,\text{B}\left(\alpha,\,\frac{s}{2}\right)\left[\frac{1}{2}\psi\left(\frac{s}{2}\right) - \frac{1}{2}\psi\left(\frac{s+2\alpha}{2}\right) + \ln(ab) + \mathbf{C}\right]$ $[a,\,\text{Re}\,\alpha,\,\text{Re}\,s>0]$
5	$\dfrac{1}{(x+a)^\rho}\,\text{shi}\left(\dfrac{b}{x+a}\right)$	$a^{s-\rho-1}b\,\text{B}(s,\,1-s+\rho)\,{}_3F_4\left(\begin{matrix}\frac{1}{2},\,\frac{1-s+\rho}{2},\,\frac{2-s+\rho}{2};\,\frac{b^2}{4a^2}\\\frac{3}{2},\,\frac{3}{2},\,\frac{\rho+1}{2},\,\frac{\rho+2}{2}\end{matrix}\right)$ $[0<\text{Re}\,s<\text{Re}\,\rho+1;\,|\arg a|<\pi]$
6	$\dfrac{1}{(x+a)^\rho}\,\text{shi}\left(\dfrac{bx}{x+a}\right)$	$a^{s-\rho}b\,\text{B}(s+1,\,\rho-s)\,{}_3F_4\left(\begin{matrix}\frac{1}{2},\,\frac{s+1}{2},\,\frac{s+2}{2};\,\frac{b^2}{4}\\\frac{3}{2},\,\frac{3}{2},\,\frac{\rho+1}{2},\,\frac{\rho+2}{2}\end{matrix}\right)$ $[-1<\text{Re}\,s<\text{Re}\,\rho;\,|\arg a|<\pi]$

No.	$f(x)$	$F(s)$
7	$\dfrac{1}{(x^2+a^2)^\rho}\,\mathrm{shi}\left(\dfrac{bx}{x^2+a^2}\right)$	$\dfrac{a^{s-2\rho-1}b}{2}\,\mathrm{B}\left(\dfrac{s+1}{2},\dfrac{1-s+2\rho}{2}\right)\,{}_3F_4\left(\begin{matrix}\frac{1}{2},\ \frac{s+1}{2},\ \frac{1-s+2\rho}{2};\ \frac{b^2}{16a^2}\\ \frac{3}{2},\ \frac{3}{2},\ \frac{\rho+1}{2},\ \frac{\rho+2}{2}\end{matrix}\right)$
		$[\operatorname{Re}a>0;\ -1<\operatorname{Re}s<2\operatorname{Re}\rho+1]$

3.5.2. shi (bx), chi (bx), and the exponential function

No.	$f(x)$	$F(s)$
1	$e^{-ax}\,\mathrm{shi}\,(bx)$	$\dfrac{b^3}{18\,a^{s+3}}\,\Gamma(s+3)\,{}_4F_3\left(\begin{matrix}1,\ \frac{3}{2},\ \frac{s+3}{2},\ \frac{s+4}{2}\\ 2,\ \frac{5}{2},\ \frac{5}{2};\ \frac{b^2}{a^2}\end{matrix}\right)+\dfrac{b}{a^{s+1}}\,\Gamma(s+1)$
		$[\operatorname{Re}a>|\operatorname{Re}b|;\ \operatorname{Re}s>0]$
2	$e^{-ax}\,\mathrm{chi}\,(bx)$	$\dfrac{b^2}{4a^{s+2}}\,\Gamma(s+2)\,{}_4F_3\left(\begin{matrix}1,\ 1,\ \frac{s+2}{2},\ \frac{s+3}{2}\\ \frac{3}{2},\ 2,\ 2;\ \frac{b^2}{a^2}\end{matrix}\right)+\dfrac{\Gamma(s)}{a^s}\left[\psi(s)+\ln\dfrac{b}{a}+\mathbf{C}\right]$
		$[\operatorname{Re}a>|\operatorname{Re}b|;\ \operatorname{Re}s>0]$
3	$e^{-ax^2}\,\mathrm{shi}\,(bx)$	$\dfrac{b^3}{36a^{(s+3)/2}}\,\Gamma\left(\dfrac{s+3}{2}\right)\,{}_3F_3\left(\begin{matrix}1,\ \frac{3}{2},\ \frac{s+3}{2}\\ 2,\ \frac{5}{2},\ \frac{5}{2};\ \frac{b^2}{4a}\end{matrix}\right)+\dfrac{b}{2a^{(s+1)/2}}\,\Gamma\left(\dfrac{s+1}{2}\right)$
		$[\operatorname{Re}a,\ \operatorname{Re}s>0;\ |\arg b|<\pi]$
4	$e^{-ax^2}\,\mathrm{chi}\,(bx)$	$\dfrac{b^2}{8a^{s/2+1}}\,\Gamma\left(\dfrac{s+2}{2}\right)\,{}_3F_3\left(\begin{matrix}1,\ 1,\ \frac{s+2}{2}\\ \frac{3}{2},\ 2,\ 2;\ \frac{b^2}{4a}\end{matrix}\right)$
		$+\dfrac{1}{2a^{s/2}}\,\Gamma\left(\dfrac{s}{2}\right)\left[\dfrac{1}{2}\,\psi\left(\dfrac{s}{2}\right)+\ln\dfrac{b}{\sqrt{a}}+\mathbf{C}\right]$
		$[\operatorname{Re}a,\ \operatorname{Re}s>0;\ |\arg b|<\pi]$

3.5.3. shi (bx) and the logarithmic or inverse trigonometric functions

No.	$f(x)$	$F(s)$
1	$\theta(a-x)\ln\dfrac{\sqrt{a-x}+\sqrt{a}}{\sqrt{x}}$ $\times\,\mathrm{shi}\,(bx)$	$\dfrac{\sqrt{\pi}\,a^{s+1}b}{2s}\,\Gamma\left[\begin{matrix}s+1\\ \frac{2s+3}{2}\end{matrix}\right]\left[{}_3F_4\left(\begin{matrix}\frac{1}{2},\ \frac{s+1}{2},\ \frac{s+2}{2};\ \frac{a^2b^2}{4}\\ \frac{3}{2},\ \frac{3}{2},\ \frac{2s+3}{4},\ \frac{2s+5}{4}\end{matrix}\right)\right.$ $\left.-\dfrac{1}{s+1}\,{}_3F_4\left(\begin{matrix}\frac{s+1}{2},\ \frac{s+1}{2},\ \frac{s+2}{2};\ \frac{a^2b^2}{4}\\ \frac{3}{2},\ \frac{2s+3}{4},\ \frac{2s+5}{4},\ \frac{s+3}{2}\end{matrix}\right)\right]$ $[a>0;\ \operatorname{Re}s>-1]$
2	$\theta(a-x)\arccos\dfrac{x}{a}\,\mathrm{shi}\,(bx)$	$\dfrac{\sqrt{\pi}\,a^{s+1}b}{2(s+1)}\,\Gamma\left[\begin{matrix}\frac{s+2}{2}\\ \frac{s+3}{2}\end{matrix}\right]\,{}_3F_4\left(\begin{matrix}\frac{1}{2},\ \frac{s+1}{2},\ \frac{s+2}{2};\ \frac{a^2b^2}{4}\\ \frac{3}{2},\ \frac{3}{2},\ \frac{s+3}{2},\ \frac{s+3}{2}\end{matrix}\right)\quad [a>0;\ \operatorname{Re}s>-1]$

3.6.   erf (z), erfc (z), **and** erfi (z)

More formulas can be obtained from the corresponding sections due to the relations

$$\left\{ \begin{matrix} \operatorname{erf}(z) \\ \operatorname{erfc}(z) \end{matrix} \right\} = \frac{1}{\sqrt{\pi}} \left\{ \begin{matrix} \gamma\left(1/2, z^2\right) \\ \Gamma\left(1/2, z^2\right) \end{matrix} \right\}, \quad \left\{ \begin{matrix} \operatorname{erf}(z) \\ \operatorname{erfi}(z) \end{matrix} \right\} = \frac{2z}{\sqrt{\pi}} \, {}_1F_1\left(\frac{1}{2}; \frac{3}{2}; \mp z^2\right),$$

$$\left\{ \begin{matrix} \operatorname{erf}(z) \\ \operatorname{erfi}(z) \end{matrix} \right\} = \frac{z}{\sqrt{\pm z^2}} \left[1 - \frac{e^{-z^2}}{\sqrt{\pi}} \, \Psi\left(\frac{1}{2}; \frac{1}{2}; \pm z^2\right) \right], \quad \operatorname{erf}(z) = -i\operatorname{erfi}(iz) = 1 - \operatorname{erfc}(z),$$

$$\operatorname{erfc}(z) = \frac{z}{\sqrt{z^2}} \left[\frac{e^{-z^2}}{\sqrt{\pi}} \, \Psi\left(\frac{1}{2}; \frac{1}{2}; z^2\right) - 1 \right] + 1, \quad \operatorname{erfc}(z) = 1 - \frac{2z}{\sqrt{\pi}} \, {}_1F_1\left(\frac{1}{2}; \frac{3}{2}; -z^2\right),$$

$$\operatorname{erf}(z) = \frac{\sqrt{2}\,z}{\sqrt{-iz^2}} \left[C\left(-iz^2\right) - iS\left(-iz^2\right) \right],$$

$$\operatorname{erf}(z) = \frac{z}{\sqrt{\pi z^2}} \, G_{12}^{11}\left(z^2 \, \middle| \, \begin{matrix} 1 \\ 1/2, 0 \end{matrix}\right), \quad \operatorname{erfc}\left(\sqrt{z}\right) = \frac{1}{\sqrt{\pi}} \, G_{12}^{20}\left(z \, \middle| \, \begin{matrix} 1 \\ 0, 1/2 \end{matrix}\right),$$

$$\operatorname{erfi}(z) = \frac{z}{\sqrt{-\pi z^2}} \, G_{12}^{11}\left(-z^2 \, \middle| \, \begin{matrix} 1 \\ 1/2, 0 \end{matrix}\right).$$

3.6.1.   erf $(ax + b)$, erfc $(ax + bx^{-1})$

No.	$f(x)$	$F(s)$
1	$\operatorname{erf}(ax+b) - \operatorname{erf}(cx+b)$	$\dfrac{e^{-b^2}\left(c^{-s} - a^{-s}\right)}{2^s\sqrt{\pi}} \Gamma(s) \Psi\left(\begin{matrix}\frac{s+1}{2} \\ \frac{1}{2};\, b^2\end{matrix}\right)$ $\qquad [\operatorname{Re} s > 0;\ |\arg a|,\ |\arg c| < \pi/4]$
2	$\operatorname{erf}(ax+b) - \operatorname{erf}(cx+d)$	$\dfrac{\Gamma(s)}{2^{(s-1)/2}\sqrt{\pi}} \left[c^{-s}e^{-d^2/2} D_{-s-1}\left(\sqrt{2}\,d\right) - a^{-s}e^{-b^2/2} D_{-s-1}\left(\sqrt{2}\,b\right) \right]$ $\qquad [\operatorname{Re} s > 0;\ |\arg a|,\ |\arg c| < \pi/4]$
3	$\operatorname{erfc}\left(ax \pm \dfrac{b}{x}\right)$	$\dfrac{2b}{\sqrt{\pi}\,s} \left(\dfrac{b}{a}\right)^{(s-1)/2} e^{\mp 2ab} \left[K_{(s+1)/2}(2ab) \mp K_{(s-1)/2}(2ab) \right]$ $\qquad [b > 0;\ |\arg a| < \pi/4]$

3.6.2.   erf (bx), erfc (bx), **and algebraic functions**

No.	$f(x)$	$F(s)$
1	$\left\{ \begin{matrix} \operatorname{erf}(ax) \\ \operatorname{erfc}(ax) \end{matrix} \right\}$	$\mp \dfrac{a^{-s}}{\sqrt{\pi}\,s} \Gamma\left(\dfrac{s+1}{2}\right) \qquad \left[\left\{ \begin{matrix} -1 < \operatorname{Re} s < 0 \\ \operatorname{Re} s > 0 \end{matrix} \right\};\ |\arg a| < \pi/4 \right]$
2	$(a-x)_+^{\alpha-1} \left\{ \begin{matrix} \operatorname{erf}(bx) \\ \operatorname{erfc}(bx) \end{matrix} \right\}$	$\pm \dfrac{2a^{s+\alpha}b}{\sqrt{\pi}} \mathrm{B}(s+1, \alpha)\, {}_3F_3\left(\begin{matrix}\frac{1}{2}, \frac{s+1}{2}, \frac{s+2}{2};\ -a^2b^2 \\ \frac{3}{2}, \frac{s+\alpha+2}{2}, \frac{s+\alpha+1}{2}\end{matrix}\right)$ $+ \dfrac{1 \mp 1}{2} a^{s+\alpha-1} \mathrm{B}(s, \alpha) \qquad [a,\ \operatorname{Re}\alpha > 0;\ \operatorname{Re} s > -(1 \pm 1)/2]$

No.	$f(x)$	$F(s)$
3	$(x-a)_+^{\alpha-1} \begin{Bmatrix} \operatorname{erf}(bx) \\ \operatorname{erfc}(bx) \end{Bmatrix}$	$\pm \dfrac{2a^{s+\alpha}b}{\sqrt{\pi}} \, \mathrm{B}\left(\alpha, -s-\alpha\right) \, {}_3F_3\left(\begin{matrix} \frac{1}{2}, \frac{s+1}{2}, \frac{s+2}{2}; -a^2b^2 \\ \frac{3}{2}, \frac{s+\alpha+2}{2}, \frac{s+\alpha+1}{2} \end{matrix}\right)$

$$\pm \frac{\Gamma\left(\frac{s+\alpha}{2}\right)}{\sqrt{\pi}\,b^{s+\alpha-1}\,(1-s-\alpha)} \, {}_3F_3\left(\begin{matrix} \frac{1-\alpha}{2}, \frac{2-\alpha}{2}, \frac{1-s-\alpha}{2}; -a^2b^2 \\ \frac{1}{2}, \frac{2-s-\alpha}{2}, \frac{3-s-\alpha}{2}; \end{matrix}\right)$$

$$\pm \frac{a\,(1-\alpha)\,\Gamma\left(\frac{s+\alpha-1}{2}\right)}{\sqrt{\pi}\,b^{s+\alpha-2}\,(2-s-\alpha)} \, {}_3F_3\left(\begin{matrix} \frac{2-\alpha}{2}, \frac{3-\alpha}{2}, \frac{2-s-\alpha}{2}; -a^2b^2 \\ \frac{3}{2}, \frac{3-s-\alpha}{2}, \frac{4-s-\alpha}{2} \end{matrix}\right)$$

$$+ \frac{1\mp 1}{2}\,a^{s+\alpha-1}\,\mathrm{B}\left(\alpha, 1-\alpha-s\right)$$

$$\left[\operatorname{Re}\alpha > 0, \begin{Bmatrix} a>0; \ \operatorname{Re}(s+\alpha) < 1 \\ \operatorname{Re}a > 0 \end{Bmatrix}; \ |\arg b| < \pi/4\right]$$

No.	$f(x)$	$F(s)$
4	$(a^2-x^2)_+^{\alpha-1} \begin{Bmatrix} \operatorname{erf}(bx) \\ \operatorname{erfc}(bx) \end{Bmatrix}$	$\pm \dfrac{a^{s+2\alpha-1}b}{\sqrt{\pi}} \, \mathrm{B}\left(\dfrac{s+1}{2}, \alpha\right) \, {}_2F_2\left(\begin{matrix} \frac{1}{2}, \frac{s+1}{2}; -a^2b^2 \\ \frac{3}{2}, \frac{s+2\alpha+1}{2} \end{matrix}\right)$

$$+ \frac{1\mp 1}{4}\,a^{s+2\alpha-2}\,\mathrm{B}\left(\frac{s}{2}, \alpha\right)$$

$$[a, \ \operatorname{Re}\alpha > 0; \ \operatorname{Re}s > -(1\pm 1)/2]$$

No.	$f(x)$	$F(s)$
5	$(x^2-a^2)_+^{\alpha-1} \begin{Bmatrix} \operatorname{erf}(bx) \\ \operatorname{erfc}(bx) \end{Bmatrix}$	$\pm \dfrac{a^{s+2\alpha-1}b}{\sqrt{\pi}} \, \mathrm{B}\left(\dfrac{1-s-2\alpha}{2}, \alpha\right) \, {}_2F_2\left(\begin{matrix} \frac{1}{2}, \frac{s+1}{2}; -a^2b^2 \\ \frac{3}{2}, \frac{s+2\alpha+1}{2} \end{matrix}\right)$

$$\pm \frac{b^{2-s-2\alpha}}{\sqrt{\pi}\,(2-s-2\alpha)} \, \Gamma\left(\frac{s+2\alpha-1}{2}\right)$$

$$\times \, {}_2F_2\left(\begin{matrix} 1-\alpha, \frac{2-s-2\alpha}{2}; -a^2b^2 \\ \frac{3-s-2\alpha}{2}, \frac{4-s-2\alpha}{2} \end{matrix}\right)$$

$$+ \frac{1\mp 1}{4}\,a^{s+2\alpha-2}\,\mathrm{B}\left(\frac{2-s-2\alpha}{2}, \alpha\right)$$

$$\left[\operatorname{Re}\alpha > 0, \begin{Bmatrix} a>0; \ \operatorname{Re}(s+2\alpha) < 2 \\ a>0 \end{Bmatrix}; \ |\arg b| < \pi/4\right]$$

No.	$f(x)$	$F(s)$
6	$\dfrac{1}{(x+a)^{\rho}} \begin{Bmatrix} \operatorname{erf}(bx) \\ \operatorname{erfc}(bx) \end{Bmatrix}$	$\pm \dfrac{2a^{s-\rho+1}b}{\sqrt{\pi}} \, \mathrm{B}\left(s+1, \rho-s-1\right) \, {}_3F_3\left(\begin{matrix} \frac{1}{2}, \frac{s+1}{2}, \frac{s+2}{2}; -a^2b^2 \\ \frac{3}{2}, \frac{s-\rho+2}{2}, \frac{s-\rho+3}{2} \end{matrix}\right)$

$$\pm \frac{1}{\sqrt{\pi}\,b^{s-\rho}\,(\rho-s)} \, \Gamma\left(\frac{s-\rho+1}{2}\right) \, {}_3F_3\left(\begin{matrix} \frac{\rho}{2}, \frac{\rho+1}{2}, \frac{\rho-s}{2}; -a^2b^2 \\ \frac{1}{2}, \frac{\rho-s+1}{2}, \frac{\rho-s+2}{2} \end{matrix}\right)$$

$$\mp \frac{\rho a}{\sqrt{\pi}\,b^{s-\rho-1}\,(\rho-s+1)} \, \Gamma\left(\frac{s-\rho}{2}\right)$$

$$\times \, {}_3F_3\left(\begin{matrix} \frac{\rho+1}{2}, \frac{\rho+2}{2}, \frac{\rho-s+1}{2}; -a^2b^2 \\ \frac{3}{2}, \frac{\rho-s+2}{2}, \frac{\rho-s+3}{2} \end{matrix}\right) + \frac{1\mp 1}{2}\,a^{s-\rho}\,\mathrm{B}\left(s, \rho-s\right)$$

$$\left[\begin{Bmatrix} -1 < \operatorname{Re}s < \operatorname{Re}\rho \\ \operatorname{Re}s > 0 \end{Bmatrix}; \ |\arg a|, 4|\arg b| < \pi\right]$$

No.	$f(x)$	$F(s)$
7	$\dfrac{1}{x-a}\left\{\begin{array}{l}\mathrm{erf}\,(bx)\\\mathrm{erfc}\,(bx)\end{array}\right\}$	$\mp\dfrac{\pi a^{s-1}}{b}\cot(s\pi)\,\mathrm{erf}\,(ab)\pm\dfrac{\Gamma\left(\frac{s}{2}\right)}{\sqrt{\pi}\,b^{s-1}\,(1-s)}\,{}_2F_2\!\left(\begin{array}{c}1,\ \frac{1-s}{2};\ -a^2b^2\\\frac{2-s}{2},\ \frac{3-s}{2}\end{array}\right)$
		$\pm\dfrac{a\Gamma\left(\frac{s-1}{2}\right)}{\sqrt{\pi}\,b^{s-2}\,(2-s)}\,{}_2F_2\!\left(\begin{array}{c}1,\ \frac{2-s}{2};\ -a^2b^2\\\frac{3-s}{2},\ \frac{4-s}{2}\end{array}\right)-\dfrac{\pi\mp\pi}{2}\,a^{s-1}\cot(s\pi)$
		$[a>0;\ |\mathrm{Re}\,s|<1;\ |\arg b|<\pi/4]$
8	$\dfrac{1}{(x^2+a^2)^\rho}\left\{\begin{array}{l}\mathrm{erf}\,(bx)\\\mathrm{erfc}\,(bx)\end{array}\right\}$	$\pm\dfrac{a^{s-2\rho+1}b}{\sqrt{\pi}}\,\mathrm{B}\!\left(\dfrac{s+1}{2},\dfrac{2\rho-s-1}{2}\right)\,{}_2F_2\!\left(\begin{array}{c}\frac{1}{2},\ \frac{s+1}{2};\ a^2b^2\\\frac{3}{2},\ \frac{s-2\rho+3}{2}\end{array}\right)$
		$\pm\dfrac{b^{2\rho-s}}{\sqrt{\pi}\,(2\rho-s)}\,\Gamma\!\left(\dfrac{s-2\rho+1}{2}\right)\,{}_2F_2\!\left(\begin{array}{c}\rho,\ \frac{2\rho-s}{2};\ a^2b^2\\\frac{2\rho-s+1}{2},\ \frac{2\rho-s+2}{2}\end{array}\right)$
		$+\dfrac{(1\mp1)}{4}\,a^{s-2\rho}\,\mathrm{B}\!\left(\dfrac{s}{2},\dfrac{2\rho-s}{2}\right)$
		$\left[\mathrm{Re}\,a>0;\ \left\{\begin{array}{c}-1<\mathrm{Re}\,s<2\,\mathrm{Re}\,\rho\\\mathrm{Re}\,s>0\end{array}\right\};\ |\arg b|<\pi/4\right]$
9	$\dfrac{1}{x^2-a^2}\left\{\begin{array}{l}\mathrm{erf}\,(bx)\\\mathrm{erfc}\,(bx)\end{array}\right\}$	$\pm\dfrac{\pi a^{s-2}}{2}\,\tan\dfrac{s\pi}{2}\,\mathrm{erf}\,(ab)\pm\dfrac{b^{2-s}}{\sqrt{\pi}\,(2-s)}\,\Gamma\!\left(\dfrac{s-1}{2}\right)$
		$\times\,{}_2F_2\!\left(\begin{array}{c}1,\ \frac{2-s}{2};\ -a^2b^2\\\frac{3-s}{2},\ \frac{4-s}{2}\end{array}\right)-\dfrac{(1\mp1)\,\pi a^{s-2}}{4}\,\cot\dfrac{s\pi}{2}$
		$\left[a>0;\ \left\{\begin{array}{c}-1<\mathrm{Re}\,s<2\\\mathrm{Re}\,s>0\end{array}\right\};\ |\arg b|<\pi/4\right]$
10	$(ax^2+b)^n\,\mathrm{erfc}\,(cx)$	$\dfrac{b^n}{\sqrt{\pi}\,c^s s}\,\Gamma\!\left(\dfrac{s+1}{2}\right)\,{}_3F_1\!\left(\begin{array}{c}-n,\ \frac{s}{2},\ \frac{s+1}{2}\\\frac{s+2}{2};\ -\frac{a}{bc^2}\end{array}\right)\quad[\mathrm{Re}\,s>0;\ |\arg c|<\pi/4]$

3.6.3.   erf (bx), erfc (bx), **and the exponential function**

No.	$f(x)$	$F(s)$
1	$e^{-ax}\left\{\begin{array}{l}\mathrm{erf}\,(bx)\\\mathrm{erfc}\,(bx)\end{array}\right\}$	$\mp\dfrac{1}{\sqrt{\pi}\,b^s s}\,\Gamma\!\left(\dfrac{s+1}{2}\right)\,{}_2F_2\!\left(\begin{array}{c}\frac{s}{2},\ \frac{s+1}{2}\\\frac{1}{2},\ \frac{s+2}{2};\ \frac{a^2}{4b^2}\end{array}\right)\pm\dfrac{a}{\sqrt{\pi}\,b^{s+1}\,(s+1)}$
		$\times\,\Gamma\!\left(\dfrac{s+2}{2}\right)\,{}_2F_2\!\left(\begin{array}{c}\frac{s+1}{2},\ \frac{s+2}{2}\\\frac{3}{2},\ \frac{s+3}{2};\ \frac{a^2}{4b^2}\end{array}\right)+\dfrac{1\pm1}{2a^s}\,\Gamma\,(s)$
		$\left[\left\{\begin{array}{c}\mathrm{Re}\,a>0,\ \mathrm{Re}\,s>-1\\\mathrm{Re}\,s>0\end{array}\right\};\ |\arg b|<\pi/4\right]$
2	$e^{-ax^2}\left\{\begin{array}{l}\mathrm{erf}\,(bx)\\\mathrm{erfc}\,(bx)\end{array}\right\}$	$\pm\dfrac{b}{\sqrt{\pi}\,a^{(s+1)/2}}\,\Gamma\!\left(\dfrac{s+1}{2}\right)\,{}_2F_1\!\left(\begin{array}{c}\frac{1}{2},\ \frac{s+1}{2}\\\frac{3}{2};\ -\frac{b^2}{a}\end{array}\right)+\dfrac{1\mp1}{4a^{s/2}}\,\Gamma\!\left(\dfrac{s}{2}\right)$
		$[\mathrm{Re}\,a>0;\ \mathrm{Re}\,s>-(1\pm1)/2;\ |\arg b|<\pi/4]$
3	$e^{a^2x^2}\,\mathrm{erfc}\,(ax)$	$\dfrac{a^{-s}}{2}\,\Gamma\!\left(\dfrac{s}{2}\right)\sec\dfrac{s\pi}{2}\qquad\qquad[0<\mathrm{Re}\,s<1;\ |\arg a|<\pi/4]$

No.	$f(x)$	$F(s)$
4	$e^{-a^2x^2}\,\mathrm{erfi}\,(ax)$	$\dfrac{\pi}{2a^s\Gamma\left(\frac{2-s}{2}\right)}\sec\dfrac{s\pi}{2}$ $\qquad[|\mathrm{Re}\,s|<1;\ |\arg a|<\pi/4]$
5	$e^{ax^2}\,\mathrm{erfc}\,(bx)$	$\dfrac{b^{-s}}{\sqrt{\pi}\,s}\Gamma\left(\dfrac{s+1}{2}\right)\,_2F_1\left(\begin{matrix}\frac{s}{2},\ \frac{s+1}{2}\\ \frac{s+2}{2};\ \frac{a}{b^2}\end{matrix}\right)$ $\qquad\left[\mathrm{Re}\left(b^2-a\right),\ \mathrm{Re}\,s>0\right]$
6	$e^{-a/x}\left\{\begin{matrix}\mathrm{erf}\,(bx)\\ \mathrm{erfc}\,(bx)\end{matrix}\right\}$	$\dfrac{1\mp1}{2}\,a^s\,\Gamma\left(-s\right)\pm\dfrac{2a^{s+1}b}{\sqrt{\pi}}\,\Gamma\left(-s-1\right)\,_1F_3\left(\begin{matrix}\frac{1}{2};\ -\frac{a^2b^2}{4}\\ \frac{3}{2},\ \frac{s+2}{2},\ \frac{s+3}{2}\end{matrix}\right)$ $\mp\dfrac{1}{\sqrt{\pi}\,b^s\,s}\,\Gamma\left(\dfrac{s+1}{2}\right)\,_1F_3\left(\begin{matrix}-\frac{s}{2};\ -\frac{a^2b^2}{4}\\ \frac{1}{2},\ \frac{1-s}{2},\ \frac{2-s}{2}\end{matrix}\right)$ $\pm\dfrac{a}{\sqrt{\pi}\,b^{s-1}\,(s-1)}\,\Gamma\left(\dfrac{s}{2}\right)\,_1F_3\left(\begin{matrix}\frac{1-s}{2};\ -\frac{a^2b^2}{4}\\ \frac{3}{2},\ \frac{2-s}{2},\ \frac{3-s}{2}\end{matrix}\right)$ $\left[\left\{\begin{matrix}\mathrm{Re}\,a>0;\ \mathrm{Re}\,s<0\\ \mathrm{Re}\,a>0\end{matrix}\right\};\ |\arg b|<\pi/4\right]$
7	$e^{-a/x^2}\left\{\begin{matrix}\mathrm{erf}\,(bx)\\ \mathrm{erfc}\,(bx)\end{matrix}\right\}$	$\dfrac{1\mp1}{4}\,a^{s/2}\,\Gamma\left(-\dfrac{s}{2}\right)\pm\dfrac{a^{(s+1)/2}b}{\sqrt{\pi}}\,\Gamma\left(-\dfrac{s+1}{2}\right)\,_1F_2\left(\begin{matrix}\frac{1}{2};\ ab^2\\ \frac{3}{2},\ \frac{s+3}{2}\end{matrix}\right)$ $\mp\dfrac{1}{\sqrt{\pi}\,b^s\,s}\,\Gamma\left(\dfrac{s+1}{2}\right)\,_1F_2\left(\begin{matrix}-\frac{s}{2};\ ab^2\\ \frac{1-s}{2},\ \frac{2-s}{2}\end{matrix}\right)$ $\left[\left\{\begin{matrix}\mathrm{Re}\,a>0;\ \mathrm{Re}\,s<0\\ \mathrm{Re}\,a>0\end{matrix}\right\};\ |\arg b|<\pi/4\right]$
8	$e^{-ax-b^2x^2}\,\mathrm{erfi}\,(bx)$	$\dfrac{\Gamma\left(s-1\right)}{\sqrt{\pi}\,a^{s-1}b}\,_2F_2\left(\begin{matrix}\frac{1}{2},\ 1;\ \frac{a^2}{4b^2}\\ \frac{2-s}{2},\ \frac{3-s}{2}\end{matrix}\right)+\dfrac{\Gamma\left(s/2\right)}{2b^s}\tan\dfrac{s\pi}{2}\,_1F_1\left(\begin{matrix}\frac{s}{2};\ \frac{a^2}{4b^2}\\ \frac{1}{2}\end{matrix}\right)$ $+\dfrac{a}{2b^{s+1}}\,\Gamma\left(\dfrac{s+1}{2}\right)\cot\dfrac{s\pi}{2}\,_1F_1\left(\begin{matrix}\frac{s+1}{2};\ \frac{a^2}{4b^2}\\ \frac{3}{2}\end{matrix}\right)$ $[\mathrm{Re}\,a>0;\ \mathrm{Re}\,s>-1;\ |\arg b|<\pi/4]$
9	$e^{-ax+b^2x^2}\,\mathrm{erfc}\,(bx)$	$\dfrac{\Gamma\left(s-1\right)}{\sqrt{\pi}\,a^{s-1}b}\,_2F_2\left(\begin{matrix}\frac{1}{2},\ 1;\ -\frac{a^2}{4b^2}\\ \frac{2-s}{2},\ \frac{3-s}{2}\end{matrix}\right)+\dfrac{\Gamma\left(\frac{s}{2}\right)}{2b^s}\sec\dfrac{s\pi}{2}\,_1F_1\left(\begin{matrix}\frac{s}{2};\ -\frac{a^2}{4b^2}\\ \frac{1}{2}\end{matrix}\right)$ $+\dfrac{a}{2b^{s+1}}\,\Gamma\left(\dfrac{s+1}{2}\right)\csc\dfrac{s\pi}{2}\,_1F_1\left(\begin{matrix}\frac{s+1}{2};\ -\frac{a^2}{4b^2}\\ \frac{3}{2}\end{matrix}\right)$ $[\mathrm{Re}\,a,\ \mathrm{Re}\,s>0;\ |\arg b|<\pi/4]$
10	$e^{-ax-bx^2}\,\mathrm{erf}\,(cx)$	$\dfrac{c}{\sqrt{\pi}\,b^{(s+1)/2}}\,\Gamma\left(\dfrac{s+1}{2}\right)\Psi_1\left(\dfrac{s+1}{2},\dfrac{1}{2};\dfrac{3}{2},\dfrac{1}{2};-\dfrac{c^2}{b};\dfrac{a^2}{4b}\right)$ $-\dfrac{ac}{\sqrt{\pi}\,b^{(s+2)/2}}\,\Gamma\left(\dfrac{s+2}{2}\right)\Psi_1\left(\dfrac{s+2}{2},\dfrac{1}{2};\dfrac{3}{2},\dfrac{3}{2};-\dfrac{c^2}{b};\dfrac{a^2}{4b}\right)$ $[\mathrm{Re}\,b,\ \mathrm{Re}\left(b+c^2\right)>0;\ \mathrm{Re}\,s>-1]$

No.	$f(x)$	$F(s)$
11	$e^{-b^2x^2-a/x^2}\,\mathrm{erfi}\,(bx)$	$-\dfrac{\pi a^{s/4}}{2b^{s/2}}\sec\dfrac{s\pi}{2}\left[\mathbf{L}_{s/2}\left(2b\sqrt{a}\right)-I_{-s/2}\left(2b\sqrt{a}\right)\right]$ $\qquad\qquad[\operatorname{Re}a>0;\ \operatorname{Re}s<1;\ s\neq-1,-3,\dots;\ |\arg b|<\pi/4]$
12	$e^{b^2x^2-a/x^2}\,\mathrm{erfc}\,(bx)$	$\dfrac{\pi a^{s/4}}{2b^{s/2}}\sec\dfrac{s\pi}{2}\left[\mathbf{H}_{s/2}\left(2b\sqrt{a}\right)-Y_{s/2}\left(2b\sqrt{a}\right)\right]$ $\qquad\qquad[\operatorname{Re}a>0;\ \operatorname{Re}s<1;\ s\neq-1,-3,\dots;\ |\arg b|<\pi/4]$
13	$e^{a^2x^2}\,\mathrm{erfc}\,(ax+b)$	$\dfrac{\Gamma(s)}{\sqrt{\pi}\,(2a)^s}\,\Gamma\left(\dfrac{1-s}{2},b^2\right)\qquad\qquad[0<\operatorname{Re}s<1;\ |\arg a|<\pi/4]$
14	$e^{-a^2x}\,\mathrm{erfi}\,(a\sqrt{x})$	$a^{-2s}\,\Gamma\left[\begin{matrix}\frac{1-2s}{2},\ \frac{2s+1}{2}\\ 1-s\end{matrix}\right]\qquad\qquad[0<|\operatorname{Re}s|<1/2;\ |\arg a|<\pi/4]$
15	$\theta\,(a-x)\,e^{bx}\,\mathrm{erf}\left(c\sqrt{a-x}\right)$	$a^{s+1/2}c\,\Gamma\left[\begin{matrix}s\\ \frac{2s+3}{2}\end{matrix}\right]\Phi_2\left(s,\dfrac{1}{2};\dfrac{2s+3}{2};ab,-ac^2\right)\qquad[a,\ \operatorname{Re}s>0]$

3.6.4.   erf (bx), erfc (bx), erfi (bx), and algebraic or the exponential functions

1	$(a-x)_+^{\alpha-1}\,e^{b^2x^2}$ $\times\left\{\begin{matrix}\mathrm{erf}\,(bx)\\ \mathrm{erfc}\,(bx)\end{matrix}\right\}$	$\pm\dfrac{2a^{s+\alpha}b}{\sqrt{\pi}}\,\mathrm{B}\,(s+1,\alpha)\ {}_3F_3\left(\begin{matrix}1,\ \frac{s+1}{2},\ \frac{s+2}{2};\ a^2b^2\\ \frac{3}{2},\ \frac{s+\alpha+1}{2},\ \frac{s+\alpha+2}{2}\end{matrix}\right)$ $\qquad+\dfrac{1\mp1}{2}a^{s+\alpha-1}\mathrm{B}\,(s,\alpha)\ {}_2F_2\left(\begin{matrix}\frac{s}{2},\ \frac{s+1}{2};\ a^2b^2\\ \frac{s+\alpha}{2},\ \frac{s+\alpha+1}{2}\end{matrix}\right)$ $\qquad\qquad[a,\ \operatorname{Re}\alpha>0;\ \operatorname{Re}s>-(1\pm1)/2]$
2	$\left(a^2-x^2\right)_+^{\alpha-1}\,e^{b^2x^2}$ $\times\left\{\begin{matrix}\mathrm{erf}\,(bx)\\ \mathrm{erfc}\,(bx)\end{matrix}\right\}$	$\pm\dfrac{a^{s+2\alpha-1}b}{\sqrt{\pi}}\,\mathrm{B}\left(\dfrac{s+1}{2},\alpha\right)\ {}_2F_2\left(\begin{matrix}1,\ \frac{s+1}{2};\ a^2b^2\\ \frac{3}{2},\ \frac{s+2\alpha+1}{2}\end{matrix}\right)$ $\qquad+\dfrac{1\mp1}{4}a^{s+2\alpha-2}\mathrm{B}\left(\dfrac{s}{2},\alpha\right)\ {}_1F_1\left(\begin{matrix}\frac{s}{2};\ a^2b^2\\ \frac{s+2\alpha}{2};\end{matrix}\right)$ $\qquad\qquad[a,\ \operatorname{Re}\alpha>0;\ \operatorname{Re}s>-(1\pm1)/2]$
3	$\left(x^2-a^2\right)_+^{\alpha-1}\,e^{\mp b^2x^2}$ $\times\left\{\begin{matrix}\mathrm{erfi}\,(bx)\\ \mathrm{erfc}\,(bx)\end{matrix}\right\}$	$\pm\dfrac{a^{s+2\alpha-1}b}{\sqrt{\pi}}\,\mathrm{B}\left(\dfrac{1-s-2\alpha}{2},\alpha\right)\ {}_2F_2\left(\begin{matrix}1,\ \frac{s+1}{2};\ \mp a^2b^2\\ \frac{3}{2},\ \frac{s+2\alpha+1}{2}\end{matrix}\right)$ $\qquad+\dfrac{1\mp1}{4}a^{s+2\alpha-2}\mathrm{B}\left(\dfrac{2-s-2\alpha}{2},\alpha\right)\ {}_1F_1\left(\begin{matrix}\frac{s}{2};\ a^2b^2\\ \frac{s+2\alpha}{2};\end{matrix}\right)$ $\qquad\pm\dfrac{b^{2-s-2\alpha}}{2}\left\{\begin{matrix}\tan\left[(s+2\alpha)\,\pi/2\right]\\ \sec\left[(s+2\alpha)\,\pi/2\right]\end{matrix}\right\}$ $\qquad\times\Gamma\left(\dfrac{s+2\alpha-2}{2}\right){}_1F_1\left(\begin{matrix}1-\alpha;\ \mp a^2b^2\\ \frac{4-s-2\alpha}{2}\end{matrix}\right)$ $\qquad\qquad[a,\ \operatorname{Re}\alpha>0;\ \operatorname{Re}(s+2\alpha)<3;\ |\arg b|<\pi/4]$

No.	$f(x)$	$F(s)$

4 — $\dfrac{e^{\mp b^2 x^2}}{(x+a)^\rho} \left\{ \begin{matrix} \operatorname{erfi}(bx) \\ \operatorname{erfc}(bx) \end{matrix} \right\}$

$$\pm \frac{2a^{s-\rho+1}b}{\sqrt{\pi}}\, \mathrm{B}(s+1,\rho-s-1)\; {}_3F_3\left(\begin{matrix} 1,\ \frac{s+1}{2},\ \frac{s+2}{2};\ \mp a^2 b^2 \\ \frac{3}{2},\ \frac{s-\rho+2}{2},\ \frac{s-\rho+3}{2} \end{matrix} \right)$$

$$\mp \frac{b^{\rho-s}}{2} \left\{ \begin{matrix} \tan\left[(\rho-s)\,\pi/2\right] \\ \sec\left[(\rho-s)\,\pi/2\right] \end{matrix} \right\} \Gamma\left(\frac{s-\rho}{2}\right)$$

$$\times\, {}_2F_2\left(\begin{matrix} \frac{\rho}{2},\ \frac{\rho+1}{2};\ \mp a^2 b^2 \\ \frac{1}{2},\ \frac{\rho-s+2}{2} \end{matrix} \right) \pm \frac{\rho a b^{\rho-s+1}}{2} \left\{ \begin{matrix} \cot\left[(s-\rho)\,\pi/2\right] \\ \csc\left[(s-\rho)\,\pi/2\right] \end{matrix} \right\}$$

$$\times\, \Gamma\left(\frac{s-\rho-1}{2}\right) {}_2F_2\left(\begin{matrix} \frac{\rho+1}{2},\ \frac{\rho+2}{2};\ \mp a^2 b^2 \\ \frac{3}{2},\ \frac{3-s+\rho}{2} \end{matrix} \right)$$

$$+ \frac{1\mp 1}{2}\, a^{s-\rho}\, \mathrm{B}(s,\rho-s)\; {}_2F_2\left(\begin{matrix} \frac{s}{2},\ \frac{s+1}{2};\ a^2 b^2 \\ \frac{s-\rho+1}{2},\ \frac{s-\rho+2}{2} \end{matrix} \right)$$

$$\left[-\left(1\pm 1\right)/2 < \operatorname{Re}s < \operatorname{Re}\rho+1;\ |\arg a|,\ 4|\arg b| < \pi\right]$$

5 — $\dfrac{e^{-b^2 x^2}}{x+a}\,\operatorname{erfi}(bx)$

$$\frac{a^{s-1}}{2}\, e^{-a^2 b^2} \left[i^{s-1} \cot \frac{s\pi}{2}\, \Gamma\left(\frac{s+1}{2}\right) \gamma\left(\frac{1-s}{2}, -a^2 b^2\right) \right.$$

$$\left. -\, i^s \tan\frac{s\pi}{2}\, \Gamma\left(\frac{s}{2}\right) \gamma\left(\frac{2-s}{2}, -a^2 b^2\right) - \frac{2\pi}{\sin(s\pi)}\, \operatorname{erfi}(ab) \right]$$

$$\left[-1 < \operatorname{Re}s < 2;\ |\arg a|,\ 4|\arg b| < \pi\right]$$

6 — $\dfrac{e^{-b^2 x^2}}{x-a}\,\operatorname{erfi}(bx)$

$$-\pi a^{s-1} e^{-a^2 b^2} \cot(s\pi)\, \operatorname{erfi}(ab)$$

$$-\frac{b^{1-s}}{2} \cot\frac{s\pi}{2}\, \Gamma\left(\frac{s-1}{2}\right) {}_1F_1\left(\begin{matrix} 1;\ -a^2 b^2 \\ \frac{3-s}{2} \end{matrix} \right)$$

$$+\frac{ab^{2-s}}{2} \tan\frac{s\pi}{2}\, \Gamma\left(\frac{s-2}{2}\right) {}_1F_1\left(\begin{matrix} 1;\ -a^2 b^2 \\ \frac{4-s}{2} \end{matrix} \right)$$

$$\left[a > 0;\ -1 < \operatorname{Re}s < 2;\ |\arg b| < \pi/4\right]$$

7 — $\dfrac{e^{\mp b^2 x^2}}{(x^2+a^2)^\rho} \left\{ \begin{matrix} \operatorname{erfi}(bx) \\ \operatorname{erfc}(bx) \end{matrix} \right\}$

$$\pm \frac{a^{s-2\rho+1}b}{\sqrt{\pi}}\, \mathrm{B}\left(\frac{s+1}{2}, \frac{2\rho-s-1}{2}\right) {}_2F_2\left(\begin{matrix} 1,\ \frac{s+1}{2};\ \pm a^2 b^2 \\ \frac{3}{2},\ \frac{s-2\rho+3}{2} \end{matrix} \right)$$

$$\mp \frac{b^{2\rho-s}}{2} \left\{ \begin{matrix} \tan\left[(2\rho-s)\,\pi/2\right] \\ \sec\left[(2\rho-s)\,\pi/2\right] \end{matrix} \right\} \Gamma\left(\frac{s-2\rho}{2}\right) {}_1F_1\left(\begin{matrix} \rho;\ \pm a^2 b^2 \\ \frac{2-s+2\rho}{2} \end{matrix} \right)$$

$$+ \frac{1\mp 1}{4}\, a^{s-2\rho}\, \mathrm{B}\left(\frac{s}{2}, \frac{2\rho-s}{2}\right) {}_1F_1\left(\begin{matrix} \frac{s}{2};\ -a^2 b^2 \\ \frac{s-2\rho+2}{2}; \end{matrix} \right)$$

$$\left[\operatorname{Re}a > 0;\ -\left(1\pm 1\right)/2 < \operatorname{Re}s < 2\operatorname{Re}\rho+1;\ |\arg b| < \pi/4\right]$$

8 — $\dfrac{e^{b^2 x^2}}{x^2+a^2}\,\operatorname{erfc}(bx)$

$$\frac{\pi a^{s-2}}{2}\, e^{-a^2 b^2} \sec\frac{s\pi}{2} \left[\cot\frac{s\pi}{2} - \operatorname{erfi}(ab) \right.$$

$$\left. +\frac{i^{s-2}}{\pi}\, \Gamma\left(\frac{s}{2}\right) \gamma\left(\frac{2-s}{2}, -a^2 b^2\right) \right]$$

$$\left[\operatorname{Re}a > 0;\ 0 < \operatorname{Re}s < 3;\ |\arg b| < \pi/4\right]$$

No.	$f(x)$	$F(s)$
9	$\dfrac{e^{-b^2x^2}}{x^2+a^2}\,\mathrm{erfi}\,(bx)$	$\dfrac{\pi a^{s-2}}{2}\,e^{a^2b^2}\sec\dfrac{s\pi}{2}\left[\mathrm{erf}\,(ab)-\dfrac{1}{\Gamma\left(\frac{2-s}{2}\right)}\,\gamma\left(\dfrac{2-s}{2},a^2b^2\right)\right]$
		$[\mathrm{Re}\,a>0;\,-1<\mathrm{Re}\,s<3;\,|\arg b|<\pi/4]$
10	$\dfrac{e^{b^2x^2}}{x^2-a^2}\,\mathrm{erfc}\,(bx)$	$\dfrac{\pi a^{s-2}}{2}\,e^{a^2b^2}\tan\dfrac{s\pi}{2}\,\mathrm{erfc}\,(ab)-\dfrac{\pi a^{s-2}}{\sin(s\pi)}\,e^{a^2b^2}$
		$\qquad\qquad -\dfrac{b^{2-s}}{2}\sec\dfrac{s\pi}{2}\,\Gamma\left(\dfrac{s-2}{2}\right)\,{}_1F_1\left({1;\,a^2b^2 \atop \frac{4-s}{2}}\right)$
		$[a>0;\,0<\mathrm{Re}\,s<3;\,|\arg b|<\pi/4]$
11	$\dfrac{e^{-b^2x^2}}{x^2-a^2}\,\mathrm{erfi}\,(bx)$	$\dfrac{\pi a^{s-2}}{2}\,e^{-a^2b^2}\tan\dfrac{s\pi}{2}\,\mathrm{erfi}\,(ab)$
		$\qquad\qquad +\dfrac{b^{2-s}}{2}\tan\dfrac{s\pi}{2}\,\Gamma\left(\dfrac{s-2}{2}\right)\,{}_1F_1\left({1;\,-a^2b^2 \atop \frac{4-s}{2}}\right)$
		$[a>0;\,-1<\mathrm{Re}\,s<3;\,|\arg b|<\pi/4]$

3.6.5. erf $(\varphi(x))$, erfc $(\varphi(x))$, and algebraic functions

No.	$f(x)$	$F(s)$
1	$(a-x)_+^{\alpha-1}$	$\dfrac{2}{\sqrt{\pi}}\,a^{s+\alpha}b\,\mathrm{B}\left(\dfrac{2\alpha+1}{2},\dfrac{2s+1}{2}\right){}_3F_3\left({\frac{1}{2},\,\frac{2\alpha+1}{2},\,\frac{2s+1}{2};\,-\frac{a^2b^2}{4} \atop \frac{3}{2},\,\frac{s+\alpha+1}{2},\,\frac{s+\alpha+2}{2}}\right)$
	$\times\,\mathrm{erf}\left(b\sqrt{x(a-x)}\right)$	$[a>0;\,\mathrm{Re}\,\alpha,\,\mathrm{Re}\,s>-1/2]$
2	$(a-x)_+^{\alpha-1}\,\mathrm{erf}\,(bx(a-x))$	$\dfrac{2}{\sqrt{\pi}}\,a^{s+\alpha+1}b\,\mathrm{B}\,(s+1,\alpha+1)\,{}_5F_5\left({\frac{1}{2},\,\Delta(2,s+1),\,\Delta(2,\alpha+1) \atop \frac{3}{2},\,\Delta(4,s+\alpha+2);\,-\frac{a^4b^2}{16}}\right)$
		$[a>0;\,\mathrm{Re}\,\alpha,\,\mathrm{Re}\,s>-1]$
3	$\theta(1-x)\,\mathrm{erfc}\left(\dfrac{ax+b}{\sqrt{1-x^2}}\right)$	$\sqrt{\dfrac{2}{\pi}}\,e^{(a^2-b^2)/2}\,\Gamma\,(s)\,D_{-s}\left(\sqrt{2}\,a\right)D_{-s-1}\left(\sqrt{2}\,b\right)$
		$[\mathrm{Re}\,s,\,\mathrm{Re}\,b>0]$
4	$\theta(x-a)\,\mathrm{erf}\left(\dfrac{bx}{\sqrt{x^2-c^2}}\right)$	$-\dfrac{2a^sb}{\sqrt{\pi}\,s}\,\Psi_1\left(\dfrac{1}{2},-\dfrac{s}{2};\dfrac{2-s}{2},\dfrac{3}{2};\dfrac{c^2}{a^2},-b^2\right)$
		$[a>0;\,\mathrm{Re}\,s<0;\,|c|<a]$
5	$\dfrac{1}{(x+a)^\rho}\,\mathrm{erf}\left(\dfrac{bx}{x+a}\right)$	$\dfrac{2a^{s-\rho}b}{\sqrt{\pi}}\,\mathrm{B}\,(s+1,\rho-s)\,{}_3F_3\left({\frac{1}{2},\,\frac{s+1}{2},\,\frac{s+2}{2} \atop \frac{3}{2},\,\frac{\rho+1}{2},\,\frac{\rho+2}{2};\,-b^2}\right)$
		$[-1<\mathrm{Re}\,s<\mathrm{Re}\,\rho;\,|\arg a|<\pi]$

No.	$f(x)$	$F(s)$
6	$\dfrac{1}{(x^2+a^2)^\rho}\,\mathrm{erf}\left(\dfrac{bx}{x^2+a^2}\right)$	$\dfrac{a^{s-2\rho-1}b}{\sqrt{\pi}}\,\mathrm{B}\left(\dfrac{s+1}{2},\dfrac{1-s+2\rho}{2}\right)\,{}_3F_3\left(\begin{array}{c}\frac{1}{2},\ \frac{s+1}{2},\ \frac{1-s+2\rho}{2}\\ \frac{3}{2},\ \frac{\rho+1}{2},\ \frac{\rho+2}{2};\ -\frac{b^2}{4a^2}\end{array}\right)$
		$[\,\mathrm{Re}\,a>0;\ -1<\mathrm{Re}\,s<2\,\mathrm{Re}\,\rho+1\,]$

3.6.6. $\mathrm{erf}\,(\varphi(x))$, $\mathrm{erfc}\,(\varphi(x))$, **and the exponential function**

No.	$f(x)$	$F(s)$
1	$(a-x)_+^{\alpha-1}\,e^{b^2x(a-x)}$ $\times\,\mathrm{erf}\left(b\sqrt{x(a-x)}\right)$	$\dfrac{2}{\sqrt{\pi}}\,a^{s+\alpha}b\,\mathrm{B}\left(s+\dfrac{1}{2},\alpha+\dfrac{1}{2}\right)\,{}_3F_3\left(\begin{array}{c}1,\ \frac{2s+1}{2},\ \frac{2\alpha+1}{2};\ \frac{a^2b^2}{4}\\ \frac{3}{2},\ \frac{s+\alpha+1}{2},\ \frac{s+\alpha+2}{2}\end{array}\right)$ $[\,a>0;\ \mathrm{Re}\,\alpha,\ \mathrm{Re}\,s>-1/2\,]$
2	$(a-x)_+^{\alpha-1}\,e^{b^2x^2(a-x)^2}$ $\times\,\mathrm{erf}\,(bx(a-x))$	$\dfrac{2}{\sqrt{\pi}}\,a^{s+\alpha+1}b\,\mathrm{B}\,(s+1,\alpha+1)\,{}_6F_5\left(\begin{array}{c}1,\ \Delta(2,s+1),\ \Delta(2,\alpha+1)\\ \frac{3}{2},\ \Delta(4,s+\alpha+2);\ \frac{a^4b^2}{16}\end{array}\right)$ $[\,a>0;\ \mathrm{Re}\,s,\ \mathrm{Re}\,\alpha>-1\,]$
3	$\dfrac{\theta(x-a)}{\sqrt{x^2-b^2}}\,e^{a^2x^2/(x^2-b^2)}$ $\times\,\mathrm{erf}\left(\dfrac{cx}{\sqrt{x^2-c^2}}\right)$	$\dfrac{2a^{s-1}c}{\sqrt{\pi}\,(1-s)}\,\Psi_1\left(1,\dfrac{1-s}{2};\dfrac{3-s}{2},\dfrac{3}{2};\dfrac{c^2}{a^2},-b^2\right)$ $[\,a>0;\ \mathrm{Re}\,s<0;\ |c|<a\,]$
4	$\dfrac{1}{(x+a)^\rho}\,e^{b^2x^2/(x+a)^2}$ $\times\,\mathrm{erf}\left(\dfrac{bx}{x+a}\right)$	$\dfrac{2a^{s-\rho}b}{\sqrt{\pi}}\,\mathrm{B}\,(s+1,\rho-s)\,{}_3F_3\left(\begin{array}{c}1,\ \frac{s+1}{2},\ \frac{s+2}{2}\\ \frac{3}{2},\ \frac{\rho+1}{2},\ \frac{\rho+2}{2};\ b^2\end{array}\right)$ $[\,-1<\mathrm{Re}\,s<\mathrm{Re}\,\rho;\ |\arg a|<\pi\,]$
5	$\dfrac{1}{(x^2+a^2)^\rho}\,e^{b^2x^2/(x^2+a^2)^2}$ $\times\,\mathrm{erf}\left(\dfrac{bx}{x^2+a^2}\right)$	$\dfrac{a^{s-2\rho-1}b}{2\sqrt{\pi}}\,\mathrm{B}\left(\dfrac{s+1}{2},\dfrac{1-s+2\rho}{2}\right)\,{}_3F_3\left(\begin{array}{c}1,\ \frac{s+1}{2},\ \frac{1-s+2\rho}{2}\\ \frac{3}{2},\ \frac{\rho+1}{2},\ \frac{\rho+2}{2};\ \frac{b^2}{4a^2}\end{array}\right)$ $[\,\mathrm{Re}\,a>0;\ -1<\mathrm{Re}\,s<2\,\mathrm{Re}\,\rho+1\,]$

3.6.7. $\mathrm{erf}\,(bx)$, $\mathrm{erfc}\,(bx)$, **and trigonometric functions**

Notation: $\delta=\left\{\begin{array}{c}1\\0\end{array}\right\}$.

No.	$f(x)$	$F(s)$
1	$\left\{\begin{array}{c}\sin(ax)\\\cos(ax)\end{array}\right\}\,\mathrm{erf}\,(bx)$	$-\dfrac{a^\delta b^{-s-\delta}}{\sqrt{\pi}\,(s+\delta)}\,\Gamma\left(\dfrac{s+\delta+1}{2}\right)\,{}_2F_2\left(\begin{array}{c}\frac{s+\delta}{2},\ \frac{s+\delta+1}{2};\ -\frac{a^2}{4b^2}\\ \frac{2\delta+1}{2},\ \frac{s+\delta+2}{2}\end{array}\right)$ $+\dfrac{\Gamma(s)}{a^s}\left\{\begin{array}{c}\sin(s\pi/2)\\\cos(s\pi/2)\end{array}\right\}$ $[\,a>0;\ -\delta-1<\mathrm{Re}\,s<1;\ |\arg b|<\pi/4\,]$

No.	$f(x)$	$F(s)$
2	$\left\{ \begin{array}{c} \sin\left(ax^2\right) \\ \cos\left(ax^2\right) \end{array} \right\}$ erf (bx)	$-\dfrac{a^\delta b^{-s-2\delta}}{\sqrt{\pi}\,(s+2\delta)}\,\Gamma\left(\dfrac{s+2\delta+1}{2}\right)\,{}_3F_2\left(\begin{array}{c} \frac{s+2\delta}{4},\ \frac{s+2\delta+1}{4},\ \frac{s+2\delta+3}{4} \\ \frac{2\delta+1}{2},\ \frac{s+2\delta+4}{4};\ -\frac{a^2}{b^4} \end{array}\right)$ $+\dfrac{a^{-s/2}}{2}\,\Gamma\left(\dfrac{s}{2}\right)\left\{ \begin{array}{c} \sin\left(s\pi/4\right) \\ \cos\left(s\pi/4\right) \end{array} \right\}$ $[a>0;\ -2\delta-1 < \operatorname{Re} s < 2;\ |\arg b| < \pi/4]$
3	$\left\{ \begin{array}{c} \sin\left(ax^2\right) \\ \cos\left(ax^2\right) \end{array} \right\}$ erfc (bx)	$\dfrac{a^\delta b^{-s-2\delta}}{\sqrt{\pi}\,(s+2\delta)}\,\Gamma\left(\dfrac{s+2\delta+1}{2}\right)\,{}_3F_2\left(\begin{array}{c} \frac{s+2\delta}{4},\ \frac{s+2\delta+1}{4},\ \frac{s+2\delta+3}{4} \\ \frac{2\delta+1}{2},\ \frac{s+2\delta+4}{4};\ -\frac{a^2}{b^4} \end{array}\right)$ $[\operatorname{Re} s > -2\delta;\ \operatorname{Re} b^2 > |\operatorname{Im} a|]$
4	$\sin\left(a\sqrt{x}\right)$ erfc (bx)	$\dfrac{2ab^{-s-1/2}}{\sqrt{\pi}\,(2s+1)}\,\Gamma\left(\dfrac{2s+3}{4}\right)\,{}_2F_4\left(\begin{array}{c} \frac{2s+1}{4},\ \frac{2s+3}{4};\ \frac{a^4}{256b^2} \\ \frac{1}{2},\ \frac{3}{4},\ \frac{5}{4},\ \frac{2s+5}{4} \end{array}\right)$ $-\dfrac{a^3 b^{-s-3/2}}{3\sqrt{\pi}\,(2s+3)}\,\Gamma\left(\dfrac{2s+5}{4}\right)\,{}_2F_4\left(\begin{array}{c} \frac{2s+3}{4},\ \frac{2s+5}{4};\ \frac{a^4}{256b^2} \\ \frac{5}{4},\ \frac{3}{2},\ \frac{7}{4},\ \frac{2s+7}{4} \end{array}\right)$ $[\operatorname{Re} s > -1/2;\ |\arg b| < \pi/4]$
5	$\cos\left(a\sqrt{x}\right)$ erfc (bx)	$\dfrac{b^{-s}}{\sqrt{\pi}\,s}\,\Gamma\left(\dfrac{s+1}{2}\right)\,{}_2F_4\left(\begin{array}{c} \frac{s}{2},\ \frac{s+1}{2};\ \frac{a^4}{256b^2} \\ \frac{1}{4},\ \frac{1}{2},\ \frac{3}{4},\ \frac{s+2}{2} \end{array}\right)$ $-\dfrac{a^2 b^{-s-1}}{2\sqrt{\pi}\,(s+1)}\,\Gamma\left(\dfrac{s+2}{2}\right)\,{}_2F_4\left(\begin{array}{c} \frac{s+1}{2},\ \frac{s+2}{2};\ \frac{a^4}{256b^2} \\ \frac{3}{4},\ \frac{5}{4},\ \frac{3}{2},\ \frac{s+3}{2} \end{array}\right)$ $[\operatorname{Re} s > 0;\ |\arg b| < \pi/4]$
6	$\left\{ \begin{array}{c} \sin^{2n}\left(ax\right) \\ \cos^{2n}\left(ax\right) \end{array} \right\}$ erfc (bx)	$\dfrac{2^{-2n}b^{-s}}{\sqrt{\pi}\,s}\,\Gamma\left(\dfrac{s+1}{2}\right)\left[2\sum_{k=0}^{n-1}(\mp 1)^{n-k}\binom{2n}{k}\right.$ $\left.\times\,{}_2F_2\left(\begin{array}{c} \frac{s}{2},\ \frac{s+1}{2};\ -(n-k)^2\,\frac{a^2}{b^2} \\ \frac{1}{2},\ \frac{s+2}{2} \end{array}\right) + \binom{2n}{n}\right]$ $[a>0;\ \operatorname{Re} s > -2n\delta;\ |\arg b| < \pi/4;\ n \geq 1]$
7	$\left\{ \begin{array}{c} \sin^{2n+1}\left(ax\right) \\ \cos^{2n+1}\left(ax\right) \end{array} \right\}$ erfc (bx)	$\dfrac{2^{-2n}a^\delta b^{-s-\delta}}{\sqrt{\pi}\,(s+\delta)}\,\Gamma\left(\dfrac{s+\delta+1}{2}\right)\sum_{k=0}^{n}(\mp 1)^{n-k}(2n-2k+1)^\delta$ $\times\binom{2n+1}{k}\,{}_2F_2\left(\begin{array}{c} \frac{s+\delta}{2},\ \frac{s+\delta+1}{2};\ -\left(n-k+\frac{1}{2}\right)^2\frac{a^2}{b^2} \\ \frac{2\delta+1}{2},\ \frac{s+\delta+2}{2} \end{array}\right)$ $[a>0;\ \operatorname{Re} s > -(2n+3)\,\delta;\ |\arg b| < \pi/4]$
8	$\left\{ \begin{array}{c} \sinh\left(ax\right)\sin\left(ax\right) \\ \cosh\left(ax\right)\cos\left(ax\right) \end{array} \right\}$ $\times$ erfc (bx)	$\dfrac{a^{2\delta}b^{-s-2\delta}}{\sqrt{\pi}\,(s+2\delta)}\,\Gamma\left(\dfrac{s+2\delta+1}{2}\right)$ $\times\,{}_3F_4\left(\begin{array}{c} \frac{s+2\delta}{4},\ \frac{s+2\delta+1}{4},\ \frac{s+2\delta+3}{4} \\ \frac{2\delta+1}{4},\ \frac{2\delta+3}{4},\ \frac{2\delta+1}{2},\ \frac{s+2\delta+4}{4};\ -\frac{a^4}{16b^4} \end{array}\right)$ $[a>0;\ \operatorname{Re} s > -2\delta;\ |\arg b| < \pi/4]$

No.	$f(x)$	$F(s)$
9	$\left\{ \begin{matrix} \sinh(ax)\cos(ax) \\ \cosh(ax)\sin(ax) \end{matrix} \right\}$ $\times \operatorname{erfc}(bx)$	$\dfrac{ab^{-s-1}}{\sqrt{\pi}\,(s+1)}\Gamma\left(\dfrac{s+2}{2}\right){}_3F_4\left(\begin{matrix} \frac{s+1}{4},\ \frac{s+2}{4},\ \frac{s+4}{4} \\ \frac{1}{2},\ \frac{3}{4},\ \frac{5}{4},\ \frac{s+5}{4};\ -\frac{a^4}{16b^4}\end{matrix}\right)$ $\mp \dfrac{a^3 b^{-s-1}}{3\sqrt{\pi}\,(s+3)}\Gamma\left(\dfrac{s+4}{2}\right){}_3F_4\left(\begin{matrix} \frac{s+3}{4},\ \frac{s+4}{4},\ \frac{s+6}{4} \\ \frac{5}{4},\ \frac{3}{2},\ \frac{7}{4},\ \frac{s+7}{4};\ -\frac{a^4}{16b^4}\end{matrix}\right)$ $[a>0;\ \operatorname{Re} s>-1;\ |\arg b|<\pi/4]$

3.6.8.　erfc (bx), erfi (bx), **and the exponential or trigonometric functions**

Notation: $\delta = \left\{\begin{matrix} 1 \\ 0 \end{matrix}\right\}$.

1	$e^{-b^2 x^2}\left\{\begin{matrix}\sin(ax)\\ \cos(ax)\end{matrix}\right\}$ $\times \operatorname{erfi}(bx)$	$\mp\dfrac{\Gamma(s-1)}{\sqrt{\pi}\,a^{s-1}b}\left\{\begin{matrix}\cos(s\pi/2)\\ \sin(s\pi/2)\end{matrix}\right\}{}_2F_2\left(\begin{matrix}\frac{1}{2},\ 1;\ -\frac{a^2}{4b^2}\\ \frac{2-s}{2},\ \frac{3-s}{2}\end{matrix}\right)$ $\mp\dfrac{a^\delta}{2b^{s+\delta}}\left\{\begin{matrix}\cot(s\pi/2)\\ \tan(s\pi/2)\end{matrix}\right\}\Gamma\left(\dfrac{s+\delta}{2}\right){}_1F_1\left(\begin{matrix}\frac{s+\delta}{2};\ -\frac{a^2}{4b^2}\\ \frac{2\delta+1}{2}\end{matrix}\right)$ $[a>0;\ -\delta-1<\operatorname{Re} s<2;\ |\arg b|<\pi/4]$
2	$e^{b^2 x^2}\left\{\begin{matrix}\sin(ax)\\ \cos(ax)\end{matrix}\right\}$ $\times \operatorname{erfc}(bx)$	$\mp\dfrac{\Gamma(s-1)}{\sqrt{\pi}\,a^{s-1}b}\left\{\begin{matrix}\cos(s\pi/2)\\ \sin(s\pi/2)\end{matrix}\right\}{}_2F_2\left(\begin{matrix}\frac{1}{2},\ 1;\ \frac{a^2}{4b^2}\\ \frac{2-s}{2},\ \frac{3-s}{2}\end{matrix}\right)$ $\mp\dfrac{a^\delta}{2b^{s+\delta}}\left\{\begin{matrix}\csc(s\pi/2)\\ \sec(s\pi/2)\end{matrix}\right\}\Gamma\left(\dfrac{s+\delta}{2}\right){}_1F_1\left(\begin{matrix}\frac{s+\delta}{2};\ \frac{a^2}{4b^2}\\ \frac{2\delta+1}{2}\end{matrix}\right)$ $[a>0;\ -\delta<\operatorname{Re} s<2;\ |\arg b|<\pi/4]$
3	$e^{-b^2 x^2}\left\{\begin{matrix}\sin(ax^2)\\ \cos(ax^2)\end{matrix}\right\}$ $\times \operatorname{erfi}(bx)$	$\dfrac{1}{2\sqrt{\pi}\,a^{(s-1)/2}b}\left\{\begin{matrix}\sin[(s-1)\pi/4]\\ \cos[(s-1)\pi/4]\end{matrix}\right\}\Gamma\left(\dfrac{s-1}{2}\right){}_3F_2\left(\begin{matrix}\frac{1}{4},\ \frac{3}{4},\ 1;\ -\frac{a^2}{b^4}\\ \frac{3-s}{4},\ \frac{5-s}{4}\end{matrix}\right)$ $-\dfrac{1}{4\sqrt{\pi}\,a^{(s-3)/2}b^3}\left\{\begin{matrix}\sin[(s+1)\pi/4]\\ \cos[(s+1)\pi/4]\end{matrix}\right\}$ $\times\Gamma\left(\dfrac{s-3}{2}\right){}_3F_2\left(\begin{matrix}\frac{3}{4},\ 1,\ \frac{5}{4};\ -\frac{a^2}{b^4}\\ \frac{5-s}{4},\ \frac{7-s}{4}\end{matrix}\right)$ $+\dfrac{a^\delta}{2b^{s+2\delta}}\tan\dfrac{s\pi}{2}\Gamma\left(\dfrac{s+2\delta}{2}\right){}_2F_1\left(\begin{matrix}\frac{s+2\delta}{4},\ \frac{s+2\delta+2}{4}\\ \frac{2\delta+1}{2};\ -\frac{a^2}{b^4}\end{matrix}\right)$ $[a>0;\ -2\delta-1<\operatorname{Re} s<3;\ |\arg b|<\pi/4]$
4	$e^{b^2 x^2}\sin(ax^2)\operatorname{erfc}(bx)$	$-\dfrac{a^{(1-s)/2}}{4\sqrt{\pi}\,b}\cos\dfrac{s\pi}{2}\csc\dfrac{(s+1)\pi}{4}\Gamma\left(\dfrac{s-1}{2}\right){}_3F_2\left(\begin{matrix}\frac{1}{4},\ \frac{3}{4},\ 1;\ -\frac{a^2}{b^4}\\ \frac{3-s}{4},\ \frac{5-s}{4}\end{matrix}\right)$ $+\dfrac{a^{(3-s)/2}}{8\sqrt{\pi}\,b^3}\cos\dfrac{s\pi}{2}\sec\dfrac{(s+1)\pi}{4}\Gamma\left(\dfrac{s-3}{2}\right){}_3F_2\left(\begin{matrix}1,\ \frac{3}{4},\ \frac{5}{4};\ -\frac{a^2}{b^4}\\ \frac{5-s}{4},\ \frac{7-s}{4}\end{matrix}\right)$ $-\dfrac{1}{2}\left(a^2+b^4\right)^{-s/4}\sec\dfrac{s\pi}{2}\sin\left(\dfrac{s}{2}\arctan\dfrac{a}{b^2}\right)\Gamma\left(\dfrac{s}{2}\right)$ $[a>0;\ -2<\operatorname{Re} s<3;\ |\arg b|<\pi/4]$

No.	$f(x)$	$F(s)$
5	$e^{b^2x^2}\cos\left(ax^2\right)\operatorname{erfc}(bx)$	$-\dfrac{a^{(1-s)/2}}{4\sqrt{\pi}\,b}\cos\dfrac{s\pi}{2}\csc\dfrac{(s-1)\pi}{4}\Gamma\left(\dfrac{s-1}{2}\right){}_3F_2\left(\begin{matrix}\frac{1}{4},\frac{3}{4},1;\,-\frac{a^2}{b^4}\\ \frac{3-s}{4},\frac{5-s}{4}\end{matrix}\right)$ $+\dfrac{a^{(3-s)/2}}{8\sqrt{\pi}\,b^3}\cos\dfrac{s\pi}{2}\csc\dfrac{(s+1)\pi}{4}\Gamma\left(\dfrac{s-3}{2}\right){}_3F_2\left(\begin{matrix}1,\frac{3}{4},\frac{5}{4};\,-\frac{a^2}{b^4}\\ \frac{5-s}{4},\frac{7-s}{4}\end{matrix}\right)$ $+\dfrac{1}{2}\left(a^2+b^4\right)^{-(s+2)/4}\sec\dfrac{s\pi}{2}\Gamma\left(\dfrac{s}{2}\right)$ $\times\left[a\sin\left(\dfrac{s+2}{2}\arctan\dfrac{a}{b^2}\right)+b^2\cos\left(\dfrac{s+2}{2}\arctan\dfrac{a}{b^2}\right)\right]$ $[a>0;\,0<\operatorname{Re}s<3;\,|\arg b|<\pi/4]$

3.6.9.   erf (bx), erfc (bx), **and the logarithmic function**

No.	$f(x)$	$F(s)$
1	$\ln x\,\operatorname{erf}(ax)$	$\dfrac{a^{-s}}{\sqrt{\pi}\,s}\Gamma\left(\dfrac{s+1}{2}\right)\left[\ln a+\dfrac{1}{s}-\dfrac{1}{2}\psi\left(\dfrac{s+1}{2}\right)\right]$ $[-1<\operatorname{Re}s<0;\,|\arg a|<\pi/4]$
2	$\ln\left(x^2+a^2\right)\left\{\begin{matrix}\operatorname{erf}(bx)\\\operatorname{erfc}(bx)\end{matrix}\right\}$	$\mp\dfrac{a^2b^{2-s}}{\sqrt{\pi}\,s}\Gamma\left(\dfrac{s-1}{2}\right){}_2F_2\left(\begin{matrix}1,1;\,a^2b^2\\2,\frac{3-s}{2}\end{matrix}\right)$ $\mp\dfrac{2a^2b^{2-s}}{\sqrt{\pi}\,s(s-2)}\Gamma\left(\dfrac{s-1}{2}\right){}_2F_2\left(\begin{matrix}1,\frac{2-s}{2};\,a^2b^2\\ \frac{3-s}{2},\frac{4-s}{2}\end{matrix}\right)$ $\pm\dfrac{b^{-s}}{\sqrt{\pi}\,s}\Gamma\left(\dfrac{s+1}{2}\right)\left[\dfrac{2}{s}-\psi\left(\dfrac{s+1}{2}\right)+2\ln b\right]$ $\pm\left[\dfrac{\pi a^s}{s}\operatorname{erfi}(ab)+\dfrac{\sqrt{\pi}\,i^{1-s}}{s\,b^s}\gamma\left(\dfrac{s+1}{2},-a^2b^2\right)\right]\sec\dfrac{s\pi}{2}$ $+\left\{\begin{matrix}0\\1\end{matrix}\right\}\dfrac{\pi a^s}{s}\csc\dfrac{s\pi}{2}$ $\left[\operatorname{Re}a>0;\left\{\begin{matrix}-1<\operatorname{Re}s<0\\ \operatorname{Re}s>0\end{matrix}\right\};\,|\arg b|<\pi/4\right]$
3	$\ln\left|x^2-a^2\right|\left\{\begin{matrix}\operatorname{erf}(bx)\\\operatorname{erfc}(bx)\end{matrix}\right\}$	$\pm\dfrac{a^2b^{2-s}}{\sqrt{\pi}\,s}\Gamma\left(\dfrac{s-1}{2}\right){}_2F_2\left(\begin{matrix}1,1;\,-a^2b^2\\2,\frac{3-s}{2}\end{matrix}\right)$ $\pm\dfrac{2a^2b^{2-s}}{\sqrt{\pi}\,s(s-2)}\Gamma\left(\dfrac{s-1}{2}\right){}_2F_2\left(\begin{matrix}1,\frac{2-s}{2};\,-a^2b^2\\ \frac{3-s}{2},\frac{4-s}{2}\end{matrix}\right)$ $\pm\dfrac{b^{-s}}{\sqrt{\pi}\,s}\Gamma\left(\dfrac{s+1}{2}\right)\left[\dfrac{2}{s}-\psi\left(\dfrac{s+1}{2}\right)+\pi\tan\dfrac{s\pi}{2}+2\ln b\right]$ $\mp\left[\dfrac{\pi a^s}{s}\operatorname{erf}(ab)+\dfrac{\sqrt{\pi}\,b^{-s}}{s}\Gamma\left(\dfrac{s+1}{2},a^2b^2\right)\right]\tan\dfrac{s\pi}{2}$ $+\left\{\begin{matrix}0\\1\end{matrix}\right\}\dfrac{\pi a^s}{s}\cot\dfrac{s\pi}{2}$ $\left[a>0;\left\{\begin{matrix}-1<\operatorname{Re}s<0\\ \operatorname{Re}s>0\end{matrix}\right\};\,|\arg b|<\pi/4\right]$

No.	$f(x)$	$F(s)$
4	$\theta(a-x)\ln\dfrac{\sqrt{a}+\sqrt{a-x}}{\sqrt{x}}$ $\times\,\mathrm{erf}\,(bx)$	$\dfrac{a^{s+1}b}{s}\,\Gamma\!\begin{bmatrix}s+1\\\frac{2s+3}{2}\end{bmatrix}\,{}_3F_3\!\left(\begin{matrix}\frac{1}{2},\ \frac{s+1}{2},\ \frac{s+2}{2};\ -a^2b^2\\\frac{3}{2},\ \frac{2s+3}{4},\ \frac{2s+5}{4}\end{matrix}\right)$ $-\dfrac{a^{s+1}b}{s(s+1)}\,\Gamma\!\begin{bmatrix}s+1\\\frac{2s+3}{2}\end{bmatrix}\,{}_3F_3\!\left(\begin{matrix}\frac{s+1}{2},\ \frac{s+1}{2},\ \frac{s+2}{2};\ -a^2b^2\\\frac{2s+3}{4},\ \frac{2s+5}{4},\ \frac{s+3}{2}\end{matrix}\right)$ $[a>0;\ \mathrm{Re}\,s>-1]$
5	$\theta(a-x)\ln\dfrac{\sqrt{a}+\sqrt{a-x}}{\sqrt{x}}$ $\times\,e^{b^2x^2}\,\mathrm{erf}\,(bx)$	$\dfrac{a^{s+1}b}{s+1}\,\Gamma\!\begin{bmatrix}s+1\\\frac{2s+3}{2}\end{bmatrix}\,{}_4F_4\!\left(\begin{matrix}1,\ \frac{s+1}{2},\ \frac{s+1}{2},\ \frac{s+2}{2};\ a^2b^2\\\frac{3}{2},\ \frac{2s+3}{4},\ \frac{2s+5}{4},\ \frac{s+3}{2}\end{matrix}\right)$ $[a>0;\ \mathrm{Re}\,s>-1]$
6	$\theta(a-x)\ln\dfrac{a+\sqrt{a^2-x^2}}{x}$ $\times\,\mathrm{erf}\,(bx)$	$\dfrac{2a^{s+1}b}{s(s+1)}\,\Gamma\!\begin{bmatrix}\frac{s+1}{2}\\\frac{s}{2}\end{bmatrix}\,{}_3F_3\!\left(\begin{matrix}\frac{1}{2},\ \frac{s+1}{2},\ \frac{s+1}{2};\ -a^2b^2\\\frac{3}{2},\ \frac{s+2}{2},\ \frac{s+3}{2}\end{matrix}\right)$ $[a>0;\ \mathrm{Re}\,s>-1]$
7	$\ln^n x\,\mathrm{erf}\,(ax)$	$-\dfrac{1}{\sqrt{\pi}}\,\dfrac{\partial^n}{\partial s^n}\!\left[\dfrac{a^{-s}}{s}\,\Gamma\!\left(\dfrac{s+1}{2}\right)\right]$ $\quad[-1<\mathrm{Re}\,s<0;\ |\arg a|<\pi/4]$
8	$\theta(a-x)\ln^n\dfrac{x}{a}\,\mathrm{erf}\,(bx)$	$\dfrac{2(-1)^n\,n!\,a^{s+1}b}{\sqrt{\pi}\,(s+1)^{n+1}}\,{}_{n+2}F_{n+2}\!\left(\begin{matrix}\frac{1}{2},\ \frac{s+1}{2},\ \ldots,\ \frac{s+1}{2}\\\frac{3}{2},\ \frac{s+3}{2},\ \ldots,\ \frac{s+3}{2};\ -a^2b^2\end{matrix}\right)$ $[a>0;\ \mathrm{Re}\,s>0]$
9	$\theta(a-x)\,e^{b^2x^2}\ln^n\dfrac{x}{a}$ $\times\,\mathrm{erf}\,(bx)$	$\dfrac{2(-1)^n\,n!\,a^{s+1}b}{\sqrt{\pi}\,(s+1)^{n+1}}\,{}_{n+2}F_{n+2}\!\left(\begin{matrix}1,\ \frac{s+1}{2},\ \ldots,\ \frac{s+1}{2}\\\frac{3}{2},\ \frac{s+3}{2},\ \ldots,\ \frac{s+3}{2};\ a^2b^2\end{matrix}\right)$ $[a>0;\ \mathrm{Re}\,s>-1]$

3.6.10. $\mathrm{erf}\,(ax)$ and inverse trigonometric functions

No.	$f(x)$	$F(s)$
1	$\theta(1-x)\left\{\begin{matrix}\arcsin x\\\arccos x\end{matrix}\right\}$ $\times\,\mathrm{erf}\,(ax)$	$\dfrac{(1\pm1)\sqrt{\pi}}{4s}\left[\sqrt{\pi}\,\mathrm{erf}\,(a)-a^{-s}\gamma\!\left(\dfrac{s+1}{2},\,a^2\right)\right]$ $\mp\dfrac{a}{2(s+1)}\,\Gamma\!\begin{bmatrix}\frac{s}{2}\\\frac{s+3}{2}\end{bmatrix}\!\left[(s+1)\,{}_2F_2\!\left(\begin{matrix}\frac{1}{2},\ \frac{s+2}{2};\ -a^2\\\frac{3}{2},\ \frac{s+3}{2}\end{matrix}\right)\right.$ $\left.-\,{}_2F_2\!\left(\begin{matrix}\frac{s+1}{2},\ \frac{s+2}{2};\ -a^2\\\frac{s+3}{2},\ \frac{s+3}{2}\end{matrix}\right)\right]\quad[\mathrm{Re}\,s>0]$
2	$\theta(a-x)\arccos\dfrac{x}{a}$ $\times\,\mathrm{erf}\,(bx)$	$\dfrac{a^{s+1}b}{2}\,\Gamma\!\begin{bmatrix}\frac{s}{2}\\\frac{s+3}{2}\end{bmatrix}\!\left[{}_2F_2\!\left(\begin{matrix}\frac{1}{2},\ \frac{s+2}{2}\\\frac{3}{2},\ \frac{s+3}{2};\ -a^2b^2\end{matrix}\right)\right.$ $\left.-\dfrac{1}{s+1}\,{}_2F_2\!\left(\begin{matrix}\frac{s+1}{2},\ \frac{s+2}{2}\\\frac{s+3}{2},\ \frac{s+3}{2};\ -a^2b^2\end{matrix}\right)\right]$ $[a>0;\ \mathrm{Re}\,s>-1]$

No.	$f(x)$	$F(s)$
3	$\theta(a-x)\,e^{b^2x^2}\arccos\dfrac{x}{a}$ $\times \operatorname{erf}(bx)$	$\dfrac{a^{s+1}b}{s+1}\Gamma\!\begin{bmatrix}\frac{s+2}{2}\\ \frac{s+3}{2}\end{bmatrix}{}_3F_3\!\left(\begin{matrix}1,\ \frac{s+1}{2},\ \frac{s+2}{2}\\ \frac{3}{2},\ \frac{s+3}{2},\ \frac{s+3}{2}\,;\,a^2b^2\end{matrix}\right)$ $\qquad[a>0;\ \operatorname{Re}s>-1]$
4	$\arctan x\,\operatorname{erf}(ax)$	$\dfrac{a^{1-s}}{\sqrt{\pi}\,s}\Gamma\!\left(\dfrac{s}{2}\right)\left[\dfrac{1}{s-1}\,{}_2F_2\!\left(\begin{matrix}1,\ \frac{1-s}{2}\,;\,a^2\\ \frac{2-s}{2},\ \frac{3-s}{2}\end{matrix}\right)+{}_2F_2\!\left(\begin{matrix}\frac{1}{2},\ 1\,;\,a^2\\ \frac{3}{2},\ \frac{2-s}{2}\end{matrix}\right)\right]$ $+\dfrac{\pi}{2s}\csc\dfrac{s\pi}{2}\operatorname{erfi}(a)+\dfrac{\sqrt{\pi}\,(-a^2)^{(1-s)/2}}{2as}\csc\dfrac{s\pi}{2}$ $\times\gamma\!\left(\dfrac{s+1}{2},-a^2\right)-\dfrac{\sqrt{\pi}\,a^{-s}}{2s}\Gamma\!\left(\dfrac{s+1}{2}\right)$ $[-2<\operatorname{Re}s<0;\ |\arg a|<\pi/4]$

3.6.11. erf (bx) and Ei $\left(-ax^2\right)$

No.	$f(x)$	$F(s)$
1	$\operatorname{Ei}\left(-ax^2\right)\operatorname{erf}(bx)$	$-\dfrac{2a^{-(s+1)/2}b}{\sqrt{\pi}\,(s+1)}\Gamma\!\left(\dfrac{s+1}{2}\right){}_3F_2\!\left(\begin{matrix}\frac{1}{2},\ \frac{s+1}{2},\ \frac{s+1}{2}\\ \frac{3}{2},\ \frac{s+3}{2}\,;\,-\frac{b^2}{a}\end{matrix}\right)$ $[\operatorname{Re}a>0;\ \operatorname{Re}s>-1;\ |\arg b|<\pi/4]$
2	$e^{b^2x^2}\operatorname{Ei}\left(-ax^2\right)\operatorname{erf}(bx)$	$-\dfrac{2a^{-(s+1)/2}b}{\sqrt{\pi}\,(s+1)}\Gamma\!\left(\dfrac{s+1}{2}\right){}_3F_2\!\left(\begin{matrix}1,\ \frac{s+1}{2},\ \frac{s+1}{2}\\ \frac{3}{2},\ \frac{s+3}{2}\,;\,\frac{b^2}{a}\end{matrix}\right)$ $[\operatorname{Re}\left(a-b^2\right)>0;\ \operatorname{Re}s>-1;\ |\arg b|<\pi/4]$

3.6.12. erf (bx), erfc (bx), and si (ax), ci (ax), Si (ax)

No.	$f(x)$	$F(s)$
1	$\operatorname{si}(ax)\operatorname{erf}(bx)$	$\dfrac{a^3b^{-s-3}}{18\sqrt{\pi}\,(s+3)}\Gamma\!\left(\dfrac{s+4}{2}\right){}_4F_4\!\left(\begin{matrix}1,\ \frac{3}{2},\ \frac{s+3}{2},\ \frac{s+4}{2}\\ 2,\ \frac{5}{2},\ \frac{5}{2},\ \frac{s+5}{2}\,;\,-\frac{a^2}{4b^2}\end{matrix}\right)$ $-\dfrac{ab^{-s-1}}{\sqrt{\pi}\,(s+1)}\Gamma\!\left(\dfrac{s+2}{2}\right)-\dfrac{a^{-s}}{s}\sin\dfrac{s\pi}{2}\Gamma(s)+\dfrac{\sqrt{\pi}}{2b^s s}\Gamma\!\left(\dfrac{s+1}{2}\right)$ $[a>0;\ -1<\operatorname{Re}s<2;\ |\arg b|<\pi/4]$
2	$\operatorname{ci}(ax)\operatorname{erf}(bx)$	$\dfrac{a^2b^{-s-2}}{4\sqrt{\pi}\,(s+2)}\Gamma\!\left(\dfrac{s+3}{2}\right){}_4F_4\!\left(\begin{matrix}1,\ 1,\ \frac{s+2}{2},\ \frac{s+3}{2}\\ \frac{3}{2},\ 2,\ 2,\ \frac{s+4}{2}\,;\,-\frac{a^2}{4b^2}\end{matrix}\right)$ $+\dfrac{b^{-s}}{\sqrt{\pi}\,s}\Gamma\!\left(\dfrac{s+1}{2}\right)\left[\dfrac{1}{s}-\dfrac{1}{2}\psi\!\left(\dfrac{s+1}{2}\right)+\ln\dfrac{b}{a}-\mathbf{C}\right]$ $-\dfrac{a^{-s}}{s}\Gamma(s)\cos\dfrac{s\pi}{2}$ $[a>0;\ -1<\operatorname{Re}s<2;\ |\arg b|<\pi/4]$

No.	$f(x)$	$F(s)$
3	$\operatorname{Si}(ax)\operatorname{erfc}(bx)$	$\dfrac{a\,\Gamma(s/2)}{2\sqrt{\pi}\,b^{s+1}}\left[{}_2F_2\!\left(\begin{matrix}\frac{1}{2},\ \frac{s+2}{2}\\[2pt]\frac{3}{2},\ \frac{3}{2};\ -\frac{a^2}{4b^2}\end{matrix}\right)-\dfrac{1}{s+1}\,{}_2F_2\!\left(\begin{matrix}\frac{s+1}{2},\ \frac{s+2}{2}\\[2pt]\frac{3}{2},\ \frac{s+3}{2};\ -\frac{a^2}{4b^2}\end{matrix}\right)\right]$ $[a>0;\ \operatorname{Re}s>-1;\ |\arg b|<\pi/4]$

3.6.13. Products of $\operatorname{erf}(ax)$, $\operatorname{erfc}(bx)$, $\operatorname{erfi}(cx)$

No.	$f(x)$	$F(s)$
1	$\left\{\begin{matrix}\operatorname{erf}(ax)\operatorname{erf}(bx)\\[2pt]\operatorname{erfc}(ax)\operatorname{erfc}(bx)\end{matrix}\right\}$	$-\dfrac{2b}{\pi a^{s+1}(s+1)}\Gamma\!\left(\dfrac{s+2}{2}\right)\,{}_3F_2\!\left(\begin{matrix}\frac{1}{2},\ \frac{s+1}{2},\ \frac{s+2}{2}\\[2pt]\frac{3}{2},\ \frac{s+3}{2};\ -\frac{b^2}{a^2}\end{matrix}\right)$ $\mp\dfrac{1}{\sqrt{\pi}\,s}\left\{\begin{matrix}b^{-s}\\[2pt]a^{-s}\end{matrix}\right\}\Gamma\!\left(\dfrac{s+1}{2}\right)$ $\left[\left\{\begin{matrix}-2<\operatorname{Re}s<0\\[2pt]\operatorname{Re}s>0\end{matrix}\right\};\ |\arg a|,\ |\arg b|<\pi/4\right]$
2	$\operatorname{erfi}(ax)\operatorname{erfc}(ax)$	$\dfrac{a^{-s}}{\sqrt{\pi}\,s}\tan\dfrac{s\pi}{4}\,\Gamma\!\left(\dfrac{s+1}{2}\right)$ $[-1<\operatorname{Re}s<2;\ |\arg a|<\pi/4]$
3	$\operatorname{erf}(ax)\operatorname{erfc}(bx)$	$\dfrac{2b}{\pi a^{s+1}(s+1)}\Gamma\!\left(\dfrac{s+2}{2}\right)\,{}_3F_2\!\left(\begin{matrix}\frac{1}{2},\ \frac{s+1}{2},\ \frac{s+2}{2}\\[2pt]\frac{3}{2},\ \frac{s+3}{2};\ -\frac{b^2}{a^2}\end{matrix}\right)$ $+\dfrac{1}{\sqrt{\pi}\,s}\left(b^{-s}-a^{-s}\right)\Gamma\!\left(\dfrac{s+1}{2}\right)$ $[\operatorname{Re}s>-1;\ |\arg a|,\ |\arg b|<\pi/4]$
4	$1-\operatorname{erf}^2(ax)$	$\dfrac{2}{\pi a^s}\Gamma\!\left(\dfrac{s}{2}\right)\,{}_2F_1\!\left(\begin{matrix}\frac{1}{2},\ \frac{s+2}{2}\\[2pt]\frac{3}{2};\ -1\end{matrix}\right)$ $[\operatorname{Re}s>0;\ |\arg a|<\pi/4]$
5	$\operatorname{erf}^2(ax)$	$\dfrac{2}{\pi(1+s)a^s}\Gamma\!\left(\dfrac{s+2}{2}\right)\,{}_3F_2\!\left(\begin{matrix}\frac{1}{2},\ \frac{s+1}{2},\ \frac{s+2}{2}\\[2pt]\frac{3}{2},\ \frac{s+3}{2};\ -1\end{matrix}\right)-\dfrac{a^{-s}}{\sqrt{\pi}\,s}\Gamma\!\left(\dfrac{s+1}{2}\right)$ $[-2<\operatorname{Re}s<0;\ |\arg a|<\pi/4]$
6	$(a-x)_+^{\alpha-1}$ $\times\operatorname{erf}\!\left(b\sqrt[4]{x(a-x)}\right)$ $\times\operatorname{erfi}\!\left(b\sqrt[4]{x(a-x)}\right)$	$\dfrac{4}{\pi}a^{s+\alpha}b^2\,\mathrm{B}\!\left(\dfrac{2\alpha+1}{2},\dfrac{2s+1}{2}\right)\,{}_4F_5\!\left(\begin{matrix}\frac{1}{2},\ 1,\ \frac{2\alpha+1}{2},\ \frac{2s+1}{2};\ \frac{a^2b^2}{16}\\[2pt]\frac{3}{4},\ \frac{3}{2},\ \frac{5}{4},\ \frac{s+\alpha+1}{2},\ \frac{s+\alpha+2}{2}\end{matrix}\right)$ $[a>0;\ \operatorname{Re}s,\ \operatorname{Re}\alpha>-1/2]$
7	$\operatorname{erfi}(ax)\operatorname{erf}(ax)\operatorname{erfc}(bx)$	$\dfrac{4a^2b^{-s-2}}{\pi^{3/2}(s+2)}\Gamma\!\left(\dfrac{s+3}{2}\right)\,{}_5F_4\!\left(\begin{matrix}\frac{1}{2},\ 1,\ \frac{s+2}{4},\ \frac{s+3}{4},\ \frac{s+4}{4}\\[2pt]\frac{3}{4},\ \frac{5}{4},\ \frac{3}{2},\ \frac{s+6}{4};\ \frac{a^4}{4b^4}\end{matrix}\right)$ $[\operatorname{Re}(b^2-a^2)>0;\ \operatorname{Re}s>-2;\ |\arg a|,\ |\arg b|<\pi/4]$

3.6.14. Products of erf (ax), erfc (bx), erfi (cx), and algebraic functions

1	$(a-x)_+^{\alpha-1}$ $\times \operatorname{erf}(bx)\operatorname{erfi}(bx)$	$\dfrac{4a^{s+\alpha+1}b^2}{\pi}\,\mathrm{B}\left(\alpha,\,s+2\right)\,{}_6F_7\!\left(\begin{matrix}\frac{1}{2},\,1,\,\Delta\left(4,\,s+2\right);\,\frac{a^4b^4}{4}\\[2pt]\frac{3}{4},\,\frac{5}{4},\,\frac{3}{2},\,\Delta\left(4,\,s+\alpha+2\right)\end{matrix}\right)$ $[a,\ \mathrm{Re}\,\alpha>0;\ \mathrm{Re}\,s>-2]$
2	$(a^2-x^2)_+^{\alpha-1}$ $\times \operatorname{erf}(bx)\operatorname{erfi}(bx)$	$\dfrac{2a^{s+2\alpha}b^2}{\pi}\,\mathrm{B}\left(\alpha,\,\dfrac{s+2}{2}\right)\,{}_4F_5\!\left(\begin{matrix}\frac{1}{2},\,1,\,\frac{s+2}{4},\,\frac{s+4}{4};\,\frac{a^4b^4}{4}\\[2pt]\frac{3}{4},\,\frac{5}{4},\,\frac{3}{2},\,\frac{s+2\alpha+2}{4},\,\frac{s+2\alpha+4}{4}\end{matrix}\right)$ $[a,\ \mathrm{Re}\,\alpha>0;\ \mathrm{Re}\,s>-2]$

3.6.15. Products of erf (ax), erfc (bx), erfi (cx), and the exponential function

1	$e^{-ax^2}\operatorname{erfi}(bx)\operatorname{erf}(bx)$	$\dfrac{2b^2}{\pi a^{s/2+1}}\,\Gamma\!\left(\dfrac{s+2}{2}\right)\,{}_4F_3\!\left(\begin{matrix}\frac{1}{2},\,1,\,\frac{s+2}{4},\,\frac{s+4}{4}\\[2pt]\frac{3}{2},\,\frac{3}{4},\,\frac{5}{4};\,\frac{b^4}{a^2}\end{matrix}\right)$ $[\mathrm{Re}\,a>\mathrm{Re}\,b^2;\ \mathrm{Re}\,s>-2;\ |\arg b|<\pi/4]$
2	$e^{-a^2x^2}\operatorname{erfi}(ax)\operatorname{erf}(bx)$	$-\dfrac{2a}{\pi b^{s+1}(s+1)}\,\Gamma\!\left(\dfrac{s+2}{2}\right)\,{}_3F_2\!\left(\begin{matrix}1,\,\frac{s+1}{2},\,\frac{s+2}{2}\\[2pt]\frac{3}{2},\,\frac{s+3}{2};\,-\frac{a^2}{b^2}\end{matrix}\right)$ $+\dfrac{a^{-s}}{2}\,\Gamma\!\left(\dfrac{s}{2}\right)\tan\dfrac{s\pi}{2}$ $[-2<\mathrm{Re}\,s<1;\ |\arg a|,\ |\arg b|<\pi/4]$
3	$e^{-(a^2+b^2)x^2}\operatorname{erfi}(ax)$ $\times \operatorname{erfi}(bx)$	$-\dfrac{b}{\sqrt{\pi}\,a^{s+1}}\,\cot\dfrac{s\pi}{2}\,\Gamma\!\left(\dfrac{s+1}{2}\right)\,{}_2F_1\!\left(\begin{matrix}1,\,\frac{s+1}{2}\\[2pt]\frac{3}{2};\,-\frac{b^2}{a^2}\end{matrix}\right)$ $-\dfrac{b^{1-s}}{2\sqrt{\pi}\,a}\,\cot\dfrac{s\pi}{2}\,\Gamma\!\left(\dfrac{s-1}{2}\right)\,{}_2F_1\!\left(\begin{matrix}\frac{1}{2},\,1\\[2pt]\frac{3-s}{2};\,-\frac{b^2}{a^2}\end{matrix}\right)$ $[|\mathrm{Re}\,s|<2;\ |\arg a|,\ |\arg b|<\pi/4]$
4	$e^{b^2x^2}\operatorname{erfc}(ax)\operatorname{erfc}(bx)$	$-\dfrac{2b}{\pi a^{s+1}(s+1)}\,\Gamma\!\left(\dfrac{s+2}{2}\right)\,{}_3F_2\!\left(\begin{matrix}1,\,\frac{s+1}{2},\,\frac{s+2}{2}\\[2pt]\frac{3}{2},\,\frac{s+3}{2};\,\frac{b^2}{a^2}\end{matrix}\right)$ $+\dfrac{a^{-s}}{s\sqrt{\pi}}\,\Gamma\!\left(\dfrac{s+1}{2}\right)\,{}_2F_1\!\left(\begin{matrix}\frac{s}{2},\,\frac{s+1}{2}\\[2pt]\frac{s+2}{2};\,\frac{b^2}{a^2}\end{matrix}\right)$ $[\mathrm{Re}\,s>0;\ |\arg a|,\ |\arg b|<\pi/4]$
5	$e^{a^2x^2}\operatorname{erf}(ax)\operatorname{erfc}(bx)$	$\dfrac{2a}{\pi b^{s+1}(s+1)}\,\Gamma\!\left(\dfrac{s+2}{2}\right)\,{}_3F_2\!\left(\begin{matrix}1,\,\frac{s+1}{2},\,\frac{s+2}{2}\\[2pt]\frac{3}{2},\,\frac{s+3}{2};\,\frac{a^2}{b^2}\end{matrix}\right)$ $[\mathrm{Re}\,(b^2-a^2)>0;\ \mathrm{Re}\,s>-1;\ |\arg b|<\pi/4]$

No.	$f(x)$	$F(s)$
6	$e^{b^2 x^2} \operatorname{erf}(ax) \operatorname{erfc}(bx)$	$\dfrac{2b}{\pi a^{s+1}(s+1)} \Gamma\left(\dfrac{s+2}{2}\right) {}_3F_2\left(\begin{matrix} 1, \frac{s+1}{2}, \frac{s+2}{2} \\ \frac{3}{2}, \frac{s+3}{2}; \frac{b^2}{a^2} \end{matrix}\right)$
		$\qquad - \dfrac{1}{\sqrt{\pi}\, a^s s} \Gamma\left(\dfrac{s+1}{2}\right) {}_2F_1\left(\begin{matrix} \frac{s}{2}, \frac{s+1}{2} \\ \frac{s+2}{2}; \frac{b^2}{a^2} \end{matrix}\right) + \dfrac{b^{-s}}{2} \Gamma\left(\dfrac{s}{2}\right) \sec \dfrac{s\pi}{2}$
		$[|\operatorname{Re} s| < 1;\ |\arg a|,\ |\arg b| < \pi/4]$
7	$e^{-ax^4} \operatorname{erf}(bx) \operatorname{erfi}(bx)$	$\dfrac{b^2}{\pi a^{(s+2)/4}} \Gamma\left(\dfrac{s+2}{4}\right) {}_3F_3\left(\begin{matrix} \frac{1}{2}, 1, \frac{s+2}{4}; \frac{b^4}{4a} \\ \frac{3}{4}, \frac{5}{4}, \frac{3}{2} \end{matrix}\right)$
		$[\operatorname{Re} a > 0;\ \operatorname{Re} s > -2;\ |\arg b| < \pi/4]$

3.6.16.　Products of $\operatorname{erf}(ax)$, $\operatorname{erfc}(bx)$, $\operatorname{erfi}(cx)$, and the logarithmic function

1	$\theta(a-x) \ln \dfrac{\sqrt{a-x}+\sqrt{a}}{x}$ $\times \operatorname{erf}(bx) \operatorname{erfi}(bx)$	$\dfrac{2a^{s+2}b^2}{\sqrt{\pi}(s+2)} \Gamma\left[\dfrac{s+2}{\frac{2s+5}{2}}\right] {}_7F_8\left(\begin{matrix} \frac{1}{2}, 1, \frac{s+2}{4}, \Delta\left(4, \frac{s+4}{2}\right); \frac{a^4 b^4}{4} \\ \frac{3}{4}, \frac{5}{4}, \frac{3}{2}, \frac{s+6}{4}, \Delta\left(4, \frac{s+2}{2}\right) \end{matrix}\right)$
		$[a > 0;\ \operatorname{Re} s > -2]$
2	$\theta(a-x) \ln \dfrac{\sqrt{a^2-x^2}+a}{x}$ $\times \operatorname{erf}(bx) \operatorname{erfi}(bx)$	$\dfrac{a^{s+2}b^2}{\sqrt{\pi}} \Gamma\left[\dfrac{\frac{s}{2}}{\frac{s+3}{2}}\right]\left[{}_4F_3\left(\begin{matrix} \frac{1}{2}, 1, \frac{s+2}{4}, \frac{s+4}{4}; \frac{a^2 b^4}{4} \\ \frac{3}{4}, \frac{5}{4}, \frac{3}{2}, \frac{s+3}{4}, \frac{s+5}{4} \end{matrix}\right)\right.$
		$\qquad\qquad \left. - \dfrac{2}{s+2} {}_4F_3\left(\begin{matrix} 1, \frac{s+2}{4}, \frac{s+2}{4}, \frac{s+4}{4}; \frac{a^2 b^4}{4} \\ \frac{3}{4}, \frac{5}{4}, \frac{s+3}{4}, \frac{s+5}{4}, \frac{s+6}{4} \end{matrix}\right)\right]$
		$[a > 0;\ \operatorname{Re} s > -2]$
3	$\theta(a-x) \ln^n \dfrac{x}{a}$ $\times \operatorname{erf}(bx) \operatorname{erfi}(bx)$	$\dfrac{4(-1)^n n!\, a^{s+2} b^2}{\pi (s+2)^{n+1}} {}_{n+3}F_{n+4}\left(\begin{matrix} \frac{1}{2}, 1, \frac{s+2}{4}, \dots, \frac{s+2}{4}; \frac{a^4 b^4}{4} \\ \frac{3}{4}, \frac{5}{4}, \frac{3}{2}, \frac{s+8}{4}, \dots, \frac{s+8}{4} \end{matrix}\right)$
		$[a > 0;\ \operatorname{Re} s > -2]$

3.6.17.　Products of $\operatorname{erf}(ax)$, $\operatorname{erfc}(bx)$, $\operatorname{erfi}(cx)$, and inverse trigonometric functions

1	$\theta(a-x) \arccos \dfrac{x}{a}$ $\times \operatorname{erf}(bx) \operatorname{erfi}(bx)$	$\dfrac{2a^{s+2}b^2}{\sqrt{\pi}\, s} \Gamma\left[\dfrac{\frac{s+3}{2}}{\frac{s+4}{2}}\right]\left[{}_4F_5\left(\begin{matrix} \frac{1}{2}, 1, \frac{s+3}{4}, \frac{s+5}{4}; \frac{a^4 b^4}{4} \\ \frac{3}{4}, \frac{5}{4}, \frac{3}{2}, \frac{s+4}{4}, \frac{s+6}{4} \end{matrix}\right)\right.$
		$\qquad\qquad \left. - \dfrac{2}{s+2} {}_4F_5\left(\begin{matrix} 1, \frac{s+2}{4}, \frac{s+3}{4}, \frac{s+5}{4}; \frac{a^4 b^4}{4} \\ \frac{3}{4}, \frac{5}{4}, \frac{s+4}{4}, \frac{s+6}{4}, \frac{s+6}{4} \end{matrix}\right)\right]$
		$[a > 0;\ \operatorname{Re} s > -2]$

3.7. The Fresnel Integrals $S(z)$ and $C(z)$

More formulas can be obtained from the corresponding sections due to the relations

$$\begin{Bmatrix} S(z) \\ C(z) \end{Bmatrix} = \frac{1 \pm i}{4} \left[\operatorname{erf}\left(\frac{(1+i)\sqrt{z}}{\sqrt{2}} \right) \mp \operatorname{erfi}\left(\frac{(1+i)\sqrt{z}}{\sqrt{2}} \right) \right],$$

$$\begin{Bmatrix} S(z) \\ C(z) \end{Bmatrix} = \begin{Bmatrix} i \\ 1 \end{Bmatrix} \sqrt{z} \left\{ \frac{1}{2\sqrt{2iz}}\left[1 - \frac{e^{-iz}}{\sqrt{\pi}}\Psi\left(\frac{1}{2}, \frac{1}{2}, iz \right) \right] \mp \frac{1}{2\sqrt{-2iz}}\left[1 - \frac{e^{iz}}{\sqrt{\pi}}\Psi\left(\frac{1}{2}, \frac{1}{2}, -iz \right) \right] \right\},$$

$$S(z) = \frac{1}{3}\sqrt{\frac{2z^3}{\pi}}\,{}_1F_2\left(\frac{3}{4}; \frac{3}{2}, \frac{7}{4}; -\frac{z^2}{4} \right), \qquad C(z) = \sqrt{\frac{2z}{\pi}}\,{}_1F_2\left(\frac{1}{4}; \frac{1}{2}, \frac{5}{4}; -\frac{z^2}{4} \right),$$

$$S(z) = \frac{\pi z^{3/8}}{\sqrt{2}\,(-\sqrt{z})^{3/4}}\,G_{13}^{10}\left(-\frac{z^2}{4} \,\middle|\, \begin{matrix} 1 \\ 3/4,\,1/4,\,0 \end{matrix} \right), \qquad C(z) = \frac{\pi z^{1/8}}{\sqrt{2}\,(-\sqrt{z})^{1/4}}\,G_{13}^{10}\left(-\frac{z^2}{4} \,\middle|\, \begin{matrix} 1 \\ 1/4,\,3/4,\,0 \end{matrix} \right),$$

$$S(\sqrt{z^2}) = \frac{1}{2} - \frac{1}{2}G_{13}^{20}\left(\frac{z^2}{4} \,\middle|\, \begin{matrix} 1 \\ 0,\,3/4,\,1/4 \end{matrix} \right), \qquad C(\sqrt{z^2}) = \frac{1}{2} - \frac{1}{2}G_{13}^{20}\left(\frac{z^2}{4} \,\middle|\, \begin{matrix} 1 \\ 0,\,1/4,\,3/4 \end{matrix} \right),$$

$$S^2(\sqrt{z^2}) + C^2(\sqrt{z^2}) = \frac{1}{\sqrt{2}}G_{24}^{12}\left(\frac{z^2}{4} \,\middle|\, \begin{matrix} 1/2,\,1 \\ 1/2,\,3/4,\,1/4,\,0 \end{matrix} \right).$$

3.7.1. $S(\varphi(x))$, $C(\varphi(x))$, and algebraic functions

Notation: $\delta = \begin{Bmatrix} 1 \\ 0 \end{Bmatrix}$.

No.	$f(x)$	$F(s)$
1	$\begin{Bmatrix} S(ax) \\ C(ax) \end{Bmatrix}$	$-\dfrac{a^{-s}}{\sqrt{2\pi}\,s}\Gamma\left(\dfrac{2s+1}{2} \right)\begin{Bmatrix} \sin\left[(2s+1)\pi/4\right] \\ \cos\left[(2s+1)\pi/4\right] \end{Bmatrix}$ $\qquad [a>0;\ -1 \mp 1/2 < \operatorname{Re}s < 0]$
2	$\dfrac{1}{2} - \begin{Bmatrix} S(ax) \\ C(ax) \end{Bmatrix}$	$\dfrac{a^{-s}}{\sqrt{2\pi}\,s}\Gamma\left(\dfrac{2s+1}{2} \right)\begin{Bmatrix} \sin\left[(2s+1)\pi/4\right] \\ \cos\left[(2s+1)\pi/4\right] \end{Bmatrix}$ $\quad [a>0;\ 0 < \operatorname{Re}s < 3/2]$
3	$(a-x)_+^{\alpha-1}\begin{Bmatrix} S(bx) \\ C(bx) \end{Bmatrix}$	$\sqrt{\dfrac{2}{\pi}}\,\dfrac{a^{s+\alpha+\delta-1/2}b^{\delta+1/2}}{2\delta+1}\,\mathrm{B}\left(s+\delta+\dfrac{1}{2},\alpha \right)$ $\times {}_3F_4\left(\begin{matrix} \frac{2\delta+1}{4},\ \frac{2s+3}{4},\ \frac{2s+4\delta+1}{4};\ -\frac{a^2b^2}{4} \\ \frac{2\delta+1}{2},\ \frac{2s+5}{4},\ \frac{2s+2\alpha+3}{4},\ \frac{2s+2\alpha+4\delta+1}{4} \end{matrix} \right)$ $[a,\,b,\,\operatorname{Re}\alpha>0;\ \operatorname{Re}s > -\delta-1/2]$
4	$(a^2-x^2)_+^{\alpha-1}\begin{Bmatrix} S(bx) \\ C(bx) \end{Bmatrix}$	$\dfrac{a^{s+2\alpha+\delta-3/2}b^{\delta+1/2}}{(2\delta+1)\sqrt{2\pi}}\,\mathrm{B}\left(\dfrac{2s+2\delta+1}{4},\alpha \right)$ $\times {}_2F_3\left(\begin{matrix} \frac{2s+2\delta+1}{4},\ \frac{2\delta+1}{4};\ -\frac{a^2b^2}{4} \\ \frac{2\delta+1}{2},\ \frac{2\delta+5}{4},\ \frac{2s+4\alpha+2\delta+1}{4} \end{matrix} \right)$ $[a,\,b,\,\operatorname{Re}\alpha>0;\ \operatorname{Re}s > -\delta-1/2]$

No.	$f(x)$	$F(s)$
5	$\dfrac{1}{(x^2+a^2)^\rho}\left\{\begin{array}{c}S(bx)\\C(bx)\end{array}\right\}$	$\dfrac{a^{s-2\rho+\delta+1/2}b^{\delta+1/2}}{(2\delta+1)\sqrt{2\pi}}\,\mathrm{B}\left(\dfrac{4\rho-2s-2\delta-1}{4},\dfrac{2s+2\delta+1}{4}\right)$ $\times\,{}_2F_3\left(\begin{array}{c}\frac{2\delta+1}{4},\frac{2s+2\delta+1}{4};\frac{a^2b^2}{4}\\\frac{2\delta+5}{4},\frac{2\delta+1}{2},\frac{2s-4\rho+2\delta+5}{4}\end{array}\right)$ $+\dfrac{b^{2\rho-s}}{\sqrt{2\pi}\,(2\rho-s)}\left\{\begin{array}{c}\sin\left[(2s-4\rho+1)\,\pi/4\right]\\\cos\left[(2s-4\rho+1)\,\pi/4\right]\end{array}\right\}$ $\times\,\Gamma\left(s-2\rho+\dfrac{1}{2}\right){}_2F_3\left(\begin{array}{c}\rho,\frac{2\rho-s}{2};\frac{a^2b^2}{4}\\\frac{2-s+2\rho}{2},\frac{1-2s+4\rho}{4},\frac{3-2s+4\rho}{4}\end{array}\right)$ $[b,\ \mathrm{Re}\,a>0;\ -\delta-1/2<\mathrm{Re}\,s<2\,\mathrm{Re}\,\rho]$
6	$\dfrac{1}{x^2-a^2}\left\{\begin{array}{c}S(bx)\\C(bx)\end{array}\right\}$	$\dfrac{b^{2-s}}{\sqrt{2\pi}\,(s-2)}\,\Gamma\left(\dfrac{2s-3}{2}\right)\left\{\begin{array}{c}\sin\left[(2s+1)\,\pi/4\right]\\\cos\left[(2s+1)\,\pi/4\right]\end{array}\right\}$ $\times\,{}_2F_3\left(\begin{array}{c}1,\frac{2-s}{2};-\frac{a^2b^2}{4}\\\frac{4-s}{2},\frac{5-2s}{4},\frac{7-2s}{4}\end{array}\right)\pm\sqrt{\dfrac{\pi}{2}}\,\dfrac{a^{s+\delta-3/2}b^{\delta+1/2}}{2\delta+1}$ $\times\left(\tan\dfrac{(2s+1)\,\pi}{4}\right)^{\pm1}{}_1F_2\left(\begin{array}{c}\frac{2\delta+1}{4};-\frac{a^2b^2}{4}\\\frac{2\delta+1}{2},\frac{2\delta+5}{4}\end{array}\right)$ $[a,\ b>0;\ -\delta-1/2<\mathrm{Re}\,s<2]$
7	$(a-x)_+^{\alpha-1}$ $\times\left\{\begin{array}{c}S(bx(a-x))\\C(bx(a-x))\end{array}\right\}$	$\sqrt{\dfrac{2}{\pi}}\,\dfrac{a^{s+\alpha+2\delta}b^{\delta+1/2}}{2\delta+1}\,\mathrm{B}\left(s+\delta+\dfrac{1}{2},\alpha+\delta+\dfrac{1}{2}\right)$ $\times\,{}_5F_6\left(\begin{array}{c}\Delta\left(2,\frac{2s+2\delta+1}{2}\right),\Delta\left(2,\frac{2\alpha+2\delta+1}{2}\right),\frac{2\delta+1}{4}\\\frac{2\delta+1}{2},\frac{2\delta+5}{4},\Delta(4,s+\alpha+2\delta+1);-\frac{a^2b^2}{64}\end{array}\right)$ $[a,\ b>0;\ \mathrm{Re}\,\alpha,\ \mathrm{Re}\,s>-\delta-1/2]$
8	$(a-x)_+^{\alpha-1}$ $\times\left\{\begin{array}{c}S\!\left(b\sqrt{x(a-x)}\right)\\C\!\left(b\sqrt{x(a-x)}\right)\end{array}\right\}$	$\sqrt{\dfrac{2}{\pi}}\,\dfrac{a^{s+\alpha+\delta-1/2}b^{\delta+1/2}}{2\delta+1}\,\mathrm{B}\left(\dfrac{4s+2\delta+1}{4},\dfrac{4\alpha+2\delta+1}{2}\right)$ $\times\,{}_5F_6\left(\begin{array}{c}\frac{4s+2\delta+1}{4},\frac{4\alpha+2\delta+1}{2},\frac{2\delta+1}{4};-\frac{a^2b^2}{16}\\\frac{2\delta+1}{2},\frac{2\delta+5}{4},\frac{2s+2\alpha+3}{4},\frac{2s+2\alpha+4\delta+1}{4}\end{array}\right)$ $[a,\ b>0;\ \mathrm{Re}\,\alpha,\ \mathrm{Re}\,s>-(2\delta+1)/4]$

3.7.2. $S(bx)$, $C(bx)$, and the exponential function

Notation: $\delta=\left\{\begin{array}{c}1\\0\end{array}\right\}$.

No.	$f(x)$	$F(s)$
1	$e^{-ax}\left\{\begin{array}{c}S(bx)\\C(bx)\end{array}\right\}$	$\sqrt{\dfrac{2}{\pi}}\,\dfrac{b^{\delta+1/2}}{(2\delta+1)\,a^{s+\delta+1/2}}\,\Gamma\left(\dfrac{2s+2\delta+1}{2}\right){}_3F_2\left(\begin{array}{c}\frac{2\delta+1}{4},\frac{2s+3}{4},\frac{2s+4\delta+1}{4}\\\frac{2\delta+1}{2},\frac{2\delta+5}{4};-\frac{b^2}{a^2}\end{array}\right)$ $[b,\ \mathrm{Re}\,a>0;\ \mathrm{Re}\,s>-\delta-1/2]$

No.	$f(x)$	$F(s)$
2	$e^{-ax^2}\begin{Bmatrix} S(bx) \\ C(bx) \end{Bmatrix}$	$\dfrac{b^{\delta+1/2}}{\sqrt{2\pi}\,(2\delta+1)\,a^{(2s+2\delta+1)/4}}\,\Gamma\left(\dfrac{2s+2\delta+1}{4}\right)$ $\times\,{}_2F_2\left(\begin{matrix} \frac{2\delta+1}{4},\ \frac{2s+2\delta+1}{4} \\ \frac{2\delta+1}{2},\ \frac{2\delta+5}{4};\ -\frac{b^2}{4a} \end{matrix}\right)$ $[b,\ \operatorname{Re}a>0;\ \operatorname{Re}s>-\delta-1/2]$

3.7.3. $\ S(\varphi(x))$, $C(\varphi(x))$, and trigonometric functions

Notation: $\delta = \begin{Bmatrix} 1 \\ 0 \end{Bmatrix}$.

No.	$f(x)$	$F(s)$
1	$\begin{Bmatrix} \sin(ax) \\ \cos(ax) \end{Bmatrix} S(bx)$	$\dfrac{1}{3}\sqrt{\dfrac{2}{\pi}}\,\dfrac{b^{3/2}}{a^{s+3/2}}\,\sin\dfrac{(\pm1-2s)\pi}{4}\,\Gamma\left(s+\dfrac{3}{2}\right)\,{}_3F_2\left(\begin{matrix} \frac{3}{4},\ \frac{2s+3}{4},\ \frac{2s+5}{4} \\ \frac{3}{2},\ \frac{7}{4},\ \frac{b^2}{a^2} \end{matrix}\right)$ $[a>b>0;\ -(3\pm2)/2<\operatorname{Re}s<1]$
2	$\begin{Bmatrix} \sin(ax) \\ \cos(ax) \end{Bmatrix} C(bx)$	$\sqrt{\dfrac{2}{\pi}}\,\dfrac{b^{1/2}}{a^{s+1/2}}\,\cos\dfrac{(\pm1-2s)\pi}{4}\,\Gamma\left(s+\dfrac{1}{2}\right)\,{}_3F_2\left(\begin{matrix} \frac{1}{4},\ \frac{2s+1}{4},\ \frac{2s+3}{4} \\ \frac{1}{2},\ \frac{5}{4};\ \frac{b^2}{a^2} \end{matrix}\right)$ $[a>b>0;\ -(2\pm1)/2<\operatorname{Re}s<1/2]$
3	$\begin{Bmatrix} \sin(ax) \\ \cos(ax) \end{Bmatrix} S(bx)$	$\dfrac{a^{-s}}{2}\cos\dfrac{(s-\delta)\pi}{2}\,\Gamma(s)-\dfrac{a^{\delta}b^{-s-\delta}}{\sqrt{2\pi}\,(s+\delta)}\cos\dfrac{(2s+2\delta-1)\pi}{4}$ $\times\,\Gamma\left(\dfrac{2s+2\delta+1}{2}\right)\,{}_3F_2\left(\begin{matrix} \frac{2s+\delta+1}{4},\ \frac{2s+3}{4},\ \frac{2s+5\delta}{4} \\ \frac{2\delta+1}{2},\ \frac{s+\delta+2}{2};\ \frac{a^2}{b^2} \end{matrix}\right)$ $[b>a>0;\ -(2\delta+3)/2<\operatorname{Re}s<1]$
4	$\begin{Bmatrix} \sin(ax) \\ \cos(ax) \end{Bmatrix} C(bx)$	$\dfrac{a^{-s}}{2}\cos\dfrac{(s-\delta)\pi}{2}\,\Gamma(s)+\dfrac{a^{\delta}b^{-s-\delta}}{\sqrt{2\pi}\,(s+\delta)}\sin\dfrac{(2s+2\delta-1)\pi}{4}$ $\times\,\Gamma\left(\dfrac{2s+2\delta+1}{2}\right)\,{}_3F_2\left(\begin{matrix} \frac{2s+\delta+1}{4},\ \frac{2s+3}{4},\ \frac{2s+5\delta}{4} \\ \frac{2\delta+1}{2},\ \frac{s+\delta+2}{2};\ \frac{a^2}{b^2} \end{matrix}\right)$ $[b>a>0;\ -(2\delta+1)/2<\operatorname{Re}s<1]$
5	$\begin{Bmatrix} \sin(ax) \\ \cos(ax) \end{Bmatrix} C(ax)$ $\mp\begin{Bmatrix} \cos(ax) \\ \sin(ax) \end{Bmatrix} S(ax)$	$\dfrac{\pi a^{-s}}{2\sqrt{2}\,\Gamma(1-s)}\,\csc\left(\dfrac{\pi}{4}\mp\dfrac{s\pi}{2}\right)$ $[a>0;\ -(2\pm1)/2<\operatorname{Re}s<(3\mp1)/4]$

No.	$f(x)$	$F(s)$
6	$\begin{Bmatrix} \sin(ax) \\ \cos(ax) \end{Bmatrix} \left[\dfrac{1}{2} - S(ax)\right]$ $\pm \begin{Bmatrix} \cos(ax) \\ \sin(ax) \end{Bmatrix} \left[\dfrac{1}{2} - C(ax)\right]$	$\dfrac{\Gamma(s)}{2\sqrt{2}\,a^s}\,\csc\left(\dfrac{\pi}{4} \pm \dfrac{s\pi}{2}\right) \qquad [a>0;\ 0 < \operatorname{Re} s < (2\pm 1)/2]$
7	$\cos u \left[\dfrac{1}{2} - C(u)\right]$ $+ \sin u \left[\dfrac{1}{2} - S(u)\right]$ $u = b\sqrt{x^2 + a^2}$	$\dfrac{a^{(s+1)/2}}{4\sqrt{2\pi}\,b^{(s-1)/2}}\,\Gamma\left[\begin{matrix} \frac{s}{2},\ \frac{3-2s}{4} \\ \frac{3}{4} \end{matrix}\right] S_{s/2-1,\,(s+1)/2}(ab)$ $[a,b>0;\ 0 < \operatorname{Re} s < 3/2]$
8	$\cos u \left[\dfrac{1}{2} - S(u)\right]$ $- \sin u \left[\dfrac{1}{2} - C(u)\right]$ $u = b\sqrt{x^2 + a^2}$	$\dfrac{a^{(s+1)/2}}{2\sqrt{2\pi}\,b^{(s-1)/2}}\,\Gamma\left[\begin{matrix} \frac{s}{2},\ \frac{1-2s}{4} \\ \frac{1}{4} \end{matrix}\right] S_{s/2,\,(s+1)/2}(ab)$ $[a,b>0;\ 0 < \operatorname{Re} s < 1/2]$
9	$\dfrac{\cos u}{u}\left[\dfrac{1}{2} - C(u)\right]$ $+ \dfrac{\sin u}{u}\left[\dfrac{1}{2} - S(u)\right]$ $u = b\sqrt{x^2 + a^2}$	$-\dfrac{2\sqrt{2\pi}}{3}\,a^{s-1/2}b^{-1/2}\csc\dfrac{(2s-1)\pi}{4}\,\Gamma\left[\begin{matrix} \frac{s}{2} \\ -\frac{3}{4},\ \frac{2s+3}{4} \end{matrix}\right]$ $\times\ {}_1F_2\left(\begin{matrix} 1;\ -\frac{a^2b^2}{4} \\ \frac{5}{4},\ \frac{2s+3}{4} \end{matrix}\right) + 2^{-(s+2)/2}\left(\dfrac{a}{b}\right)^{(s-1)/2} b^{-1}$ $\times\ \left[\csc\dfrac{(2s-1)\pi}{4}\Gamma(s-1)\Gamma\left(\dfrac{3-s}{2}\right) J_{(1-s)/2}(ab)\right.$ $\left. + \sqrt{\pi}\,2^{s-3/2}\sec\dfrac{s\pi}{2}\Gamma\left(\dfrac{s}{2}\right) J_{(s-1)/2}(ab)\right]$ $[a,b>0;\ 0 < \operatorname{Re} s < 5/2]$
10	$\dfrac{\cos u}{u}\left[\dfrac{1}{2} - S(u)\right]$ $- \dfrac{\sin u}{u}\left[\dfrac{1}{2} - C(u)\right]$ $u = b\sqrt{x^2 + a^2}$	$\dfrac{\sqrt{2\pi}}{12}\,a^{s+1/2}b^{1/2}\csc\dfrac{(2s+1)\pi}{4}\,\Gamma\left[\begin{matrix} \frac{s}{2} \\ \frac{3}{4},\ \frac{2s+5}{4} \end{matrix}\right]$ $\times\ {}_1F_2\left(\begin{matrix} 1;\ -\frac{a^2b^2}{4} \\ \frac{7}{4},\ \frac{2s+5}{4} \end{matrix}\right) + 2^{-(s+2)/2}\left(\dfrac{a}{b}\right)^{(s-1)/2} b^{-1}$ $\times\ \left[\csc\dfrac{(2s+1)\pi}{4}\Gamma(s-1)\Gamma\left(\dfrac{3-s}{2}\right) J_{(1-s)/2}(ab)\right.$ $\left. + \sqrt{\pi}\,2^{s-3/2}\sec\dfrac{s\pi}{2}\Gamma\left(\dfrac{s}{2}\right) J_{(s-1)/2}(ab)\right]$ $[a,b>0;\ 0 < \operatorname{Re} s < 3/2]$

3.7.4. $S(bx)$, $C(bx)$, and the logarithmic function

Notation: $\delta = \left\{ \begin{matrix} 1 \\ 0 \end{matrix} \right\}$.

1	$\theta(a-x)\ln\dfrac{\sqrt{a-x}+\sqrt{a}}{\sqrt{x}}$ $\times\left\{ \begin{matrix} S(bx) \\ C(bx) \end{matrix} \right\}$	$\dfrac{a^{s+\delta+1/2}b^{\delta+1/2}}{(2\delta+1)\sqrt{2}\,s}\Gamma\left[\begin{matrix} \frac{2s+2\delta+1}{2} \\ s+\delta+1 \end{matrix} \right]$ $\times\left[{}_3F_4\left(\begin{matrix} \frac{2\delta+1}{4},\ \frac{2s+2\delta+1}{4},\ \frac{2s+2\delta+3}{4};\ -\frac{a^2b^2}{4} \\ \frac{2\delta+1}{2},\ \frac{2s+5}{4},\ \frac{s+\delta+1}{2},\ \frac{s+\delta+2}{2} \end{matrix} \right) \right.$ $\left. -\dfrac{2\delta+1}{2s+2\delta+1}\,{}_3F_4\left(\begin{matrix} \frac{2s+2\delta+1}{4},\ \frac{2s+2\delta+1}{4},\ \frac{2s+2\delta+3}{4};\ -\frac{a^2b^2}{4} \\ \frac{2\delta+1}{2},\ \frac{s+\delta+1}{2},\ \frac{s+\delta+2}{2},\ \frac{2s+2\delta+5}{4} \end{matrix} \right) \right]$ $[a>0;\ \operatorname{Re}s>-(2\delta+1)/2]$
2	$\theta(a-x)\ln\dfrac{\sqrt{a^2-x^2}+a}{x}$ $\times\left\{ \begin{matrix} S(bx) \\ C(bx) \end{matrix} \right\}$	$\dfrac{a^{s+\delta+1/2}b^{\delta+1/2}}{(2\delta+1)\sqrt{2}\,s}\Gamma\left[\begin{matrix} \frac{2s+2\delta+1}{4} \\ \frac{2s+2\delta+3}{4} \end{matrix} \right]$ $\times\left[{}_2F_3\left(\begin{matrix} \frac{2\delta+1}{4},\ \frac{2s+2\delta+1}{4};\ -\frac{a^2b^2}{4} \\ \frac{2\delta+1}{2},\ \frac{2s+5}{4},\ \frac{2s+2\delta+3}{2} \end{matrix} \right) \right.$ $\left. -\dfrac{2\delta+1}{2s+2\delta+1}\,{}_3F_4\left(\begin{matrix} \frac{2s+2\delta+1}{4},\ \frac{2s+2\delta+1}{4};\ -\frac{a^2b^2}{4} \\ \frac{2\delta+1}{2},\ \frac{2s+2\delta+3}{4},\ \frac{2s+2\delta+5}{4} \end{matrix} \right) \right]$ $[a>0;\ \operatorname{Re}s>-(2\delta+1)/2]$

3.7.5. $S(bx)$, $C(bx)$, and $\operatorname{si}(ax)$, $\operatorname{ci}(ax)$

1	$\operatorname{si}(ax)\,S(bx)$	$\dfrac{(2b)^{3/2}}{3\sqrt{\pi}\,a^{s+3/2}(2s+3)}\sin\dfrac{(2s-1)\pi}{4}\Gamma\left(\dfrac{2s+3}{2} \right)$ $\times {}_4F_3\left(\begin{matrix} \frac{3}{4},\ \frac{2s+3}{4},\ \frac{2s+3}{4},\ \frac{2s+5}{4} \\ \frac{3}{2},\ \frac{7}{4},\ \frac{2s+7}{4};\ \frac{b^2}{a^2} \end{matrix} \right)$ $\left[\begin{matrix} (0<b<a;\ -3/2<\operatorname{Re}s<2)\ \text{or} \\ (b=a>0;\ -3/2<\operatorname{Re}s<1) \end{matrix} \right]$
2	$\operatorname{si}(ax)\,S(bx)$	$\dfrac{a^3}{18\sqrt{2\pi}\,b^{s+3}(s+3)}\cos\dfrac{(2s+1)\pi}{4}\Gamma\left(\dfrac{2s+7}{2} \right)$ $\times {}_5F_4\left(\begin{matrix} 1,\ \frac{3}{2},\ \frac{s+3}{2},\ \frac{2s+7}{4},\ \frac{2s+9}{4} \\ 2,\ \frac{5}{2},\ \frac{5}{2},\ \frac{s+5}{2};\ \frac{a^2}{b^2} \end{matrix} \right)+$ $+\dfrac{a}{\sqrt{2\pi}\,b^{s+1}(s+1)}\cos\dfrac{(2s+1)\pi}{4}\Gamma\left(\dfrac{2s+3}{2} \right)$ $+\dfrac{\Gamma\left(\frac{2s+1}{2} \right)}{\sqrt{2\pi}\,b^s s}\cos\dfrac{(1-2s)\pi}{4}+\dfrac{\Gamma(s)}{2a^s s}\cos\dfrac{(s-1)\pi}{2}$ $[b>a>0;\ -3/2<\operatorname{Re}s<2]$

No.	$f(x)$	$F(s)$
3	si $(ax)\,C(bx)$	$\dfrac{2\sqrt{2b}}{\sqrt{\pi}\,a^{s+1/2}(2s+1)}\cos\dfrac{(2s-1)\pi}{4}\,\Gamma\!\left(\dfrac{2s+1}{2}\right)$ $\times\,_4F_3\!\left(\begin{matrix}\frac{1}{4},\ \frac{2s+1}{4},\ \frac{2s+1}{4},\ \frac{2s+3}{4}\\[2pt]\frac{1}{2},\ \frac{5}{4},\ \frac{2s+5}{4};\ \frac{b^2}{a^2}\end{matrix}\right)$ $\left[\begin{matrix}(0<b<a;\ -1/2<\operatorname{Re}s<2)\ \text{or}\\(b=a>0;\ -1/2<\operatorname{Re}s<1)\end{matrix}\right]$
4	ci $(ax)\,S(bx)$	$-\dfrac{(2b)^{3/2}}{3\sqrt{\pi}\,a^{s+3/2}(2s+3)}\sin\dfrac{(2s+1)\pi}{4}\,\Gamma\!\left(\dfrac{2s+3}{2}\right)$ $\times\,_4F_3\!\left(\begin{matrix}\frac{3}{4},\ \frac{2s+3}{4},\ \frac{2s+3}{4},\ \frac{2s+5}{4}\\[2pt]\frac{3}{2},\ \frac{7}{4},\ \frac{2s+7}{4};\ \frac{b^2}{a^2}\end{matrix}\right)$ $\left[\begin{matrix}(0<b<a;\ -3/2<\operatorname{Re}s<2)\ \text{or}\\(b=a>0;\ -3/2<\operatorname{Re}s<1)\end{matrix}\right]$
5	ci $(ax)\,C(bx)$	$\dfrac{2\sqrt{2b}\,a^{-s-1/2}}{\sqrt{\pi}\,(2s+1)}\cos\dfrac{(2s+1)\pi}{4}\,\Gamma\!\left(\dfrac{2s+1}{2}\right)$ $\times\,_4F_3\!\left(\begin{matrix}\frac{1}{4},\ \frac{2s+1}{4},\ \frac{2s+1}{4},\ \frac{2s+3}{4}\\[2pt]\frac{1}{2},\ \frac{5}{4},\ \frac{2s+5}{4};\ \frac{b^2}{a^2}\end{matrix}\right)$ $\left[\begin{matrix}(0<b<a;\ -1/2<\operatorname{Re}s<2)\ \text{or}\\(b=a>0;\ -1/2<\operatorname{Re}s<1)\end{matrix}\right]$

3.7.6. $S(bx)$, $C(bx)$, **and** erf $(a\sqrt{x})$, erfc $(a\sqrt{x})$

Notation: $\delta=\left\{\begin{matrix}1\\0\end{matrix}\right\}$.

No.	$f(x)$	$F(s)$
1	erf $(a\sqrt{x})\left\{\begin{matrix}S(bx)\\C(bx)\end{matrix}\right\}$	$-\dfrac{2^{3/2}b^{\delta+1/2}}{\pi(2\delta+1)(2s+2\delta+1)a^{2s+2\delta+1}}\,\Gamma(s+\delta+1)$ $\times\,_4F_3\!\left(\begin{matrix}\frac{2\delta+1}{4},\ \frac{s+\delta+1}{2},\ \frac{s+\delta+2}{2},\ \frac{2s+2\delta+1}{4}\\[2pt]\frac{2\delta+1}{2},\ \frac{2\delta+5}{4},\ \frac{2s+2\delta+5}{4};\ -\frac{b^2}{a^4}\end{matrix}\right)$ $-\dfrac{1}{\sqrt{2\pi}\,b^s s}\,\Gamma\!\left(\dfrac{2s+1}{2}\right)\left\{\begin{matrix}\sin[(2s+1)\pi/4]\\\cos[(2s+1)\pi/4]\end{matrix}\right\}$ $[b>0;\ -1-\delta<\operatorname{Re}s<0;\ |\arg a|<\pi/4]$
2	erfc $(a\sqrt{x})\left\{\begin{matrix}S(bx)\\C(bx)\end{matrix}\right\}$	$\dfrac{2^{3/2}b^{\delta+1/2}}{\pi(2\delta+1)(2s+2\delta+1)a^{2s+2\delta+1}}\,\Gamma(s+\delta+1)$ $\times\,_4F_3\!\left(\begin{matrix}\frac{2\delta+1}{4},\ \frac{s+\delta+1}{2},\ \frac{s+\delta+2}{2},\ \frac{2s+2\delta+1}{4}\\[2pt]\frac{2\delta+1}{2},\ \frac{2\delta+5}{4},\ \frac{2s+2\delta+5}{4};\ -\frac{b^2}{a^4}\end{matrix}\right)$ $[b>0;\ \operatorname{Re}s>-(2\delta+1)/2;\ |\arg a|<\pi/4]$

3.7.7. Products of $S(bx)$ and $C(bx)$

1	$S(ax)S(bx)$	$\dfrac{b^{3/2}}{3\pi s a^{s+3/2}}\sin\dfrac{s\pi}{2}\,\Gamma(s+2)\,{}_3F_2\left(\begin{matrix}\frac{3}{4},\,\frac{s+2}{2},\,\frac{s+3}{2}\\\frac{3}{2},\,\frac{7}{4};\,\frac{b^2}{a^2}\end{matrix}\right)$
		$-\dfrac{a^{-s-3/2}b^{3/2}}{\pi s(2s+3)}\sin\dfrac{s\pi}{2}\,\Gamma(s+2)\,{}_3F_2\left(\begin{matrix}\frac{s+2}{2},\,\frac{s+3}{2},\,\frac{2s+3}{4}\\\frac{3}{2},\,\frac{2s+7}{4};\,\frac{b^2}{a^2}\end{matrix}\right)$
		$-\dfrac{\sqrt{\pi}\,b^{-s}}{2^{5/2}s\,\Gamma\left(\frac{1-2s}{2}\right)}\csc\dfrac{(2s+3)\pi}{4}$
		$[a,\,b>0;\,-3<\operatorname{Re}s<0]$
2	$S(ax)C(bx)$	$\dfrac{b^{1/2}}{\pi a^{s+1/2}}\cos\dfrac{s\pi}{2}\,\Gamma(s)\,{}_3F_2\left(\begin{matrix}\frac{1}{4},\,\frac{s+1}{2},\,\frac{s+2}{2}\\\frac{1}{2},\,\frac{5}{4};\,\frac{b^2}{a^2}\end{matrix}\right)$
		$+\dfrac{b^{1/2}}{\pi(2s+1)a^{s+1/2}}\cos\dfrac{s\pi}{2}\,\Gamma(s)\,{}_3F_2\left(\begin{matrix}\frac{s+1}{2},\,\frac{s+2}{2},\,\frac{2s+1}{4}\\\frac{1}{2},\,\frac{2s+5}{4};\,\frac{b^2}{a^2}\end{matrix}\right)$
		$-\dfrac{\sqrt{\pi}\,b^{-s}}{2^{5/2}s\,\Gamma\left(\frac{1-2s}{2}\right)}\csc\dfrac{(2s+1)\pi}{4}$
		$[a,\,b>0;\,-2<\operatorname{Re}s<0]$
3	$C(ax)C(bx)$	$\dfrac{b^{1/2}}{\pi a^{s+1/2}}\sin\dfrac{s\pi}{2}\,\Gamma(s)\,{}_3F_2\left(\begin{matrix}\frac{1}{4},\,\frac{s+1}{2},\,\frac{s+2}{2}\\\frac{1}{2},\,\frac{5}{4};\,\frac{b^2}{a^2}\end{matrix}\right)$
		$-\dfrac{b^{1/2}}{\pi(2s+1)a^{s+1/2}}\sin\dfrac{s\pi}{2}\,\Gamma(s)\,{}_3F_2\left(\begin{matrix}\frac{s+1}{2},\,\frac{s+2}{2},\,\frac{2s+1}{4}\\\frac{1}{2},\,\frac{2s+5}{4};\,\frac{b^2}{a^2}\end{matrix}\right)$
		$-\dfrac{\sqrt{\pi}\,b^{-s}}{2^{5/2}s\,\Gamma\left(\frac{1-2s}{2}\right)}\csc\dfrac{(2s+1)\pi}{4}$
		$[a,\,b>0;\,-1<\operatorname{Re}s<0]$
4	$C^2(ax)-S^2(ax)$	$\dfrac{2}{\pi a^s}\sin\dfrac{s\pi}{2}\,\Gamma(s)\,{}_2F_1\left(\begin{matrix}\frac{1}{2},\,s+1\\\frac{3}{2};\,-1\end{matrix}\right)\qquad[a>0;\,0<\operatorname{Re}s<1]$
5	$C^2(ax)+S^2(ax)$	$-\dfrac{\sqrt{\pi}}{2sa^s\,\Gamma\left(\frac{1-2s}{2}\right)}\sec\dfrac{s\pi}{2}\qquad[a>0;\,-1<\operatorname{Re}s<0]$
6	$\left[\dfrac{1}{2}-C(ax)\right]^2$ $+\left[\dfrac{1}{2}-S(ax)\right]^2$	$\dfrac{a^{-s}}{2\sqrt{\pi}\,s}\sec\dfrac{s\pi}{2}\,\Gamma\left(\dfrac{2s+1}{2}\right)\qquad[a>0;\,0<\operatorname{Re}s<1]$

3.8.   The Incomplete Gamma Function $\Gamma(\nu, z)$ and $\gamma(\nu, z)$

More formulas can be obtained from the corresponding sections due to the relations

$$\Gamma(-1, z) = \text{Ei}(-z) + \frac{e^{-z}}{z} + \frac{1}{2}\left[\ln\left(-\frac{1}{z}\right) - \ln(-z)\right] + \ln z,$$

$$\Gamma\left(-\frac{1}{2}, z\right) = \frac{2e^{-z}}{\sqrt{z}} - 2\sqrt{\pi}\,\text{erfc}\left(\sqrt{z}\right),$$

$$\Gamma(0, z) = -\text{Ei}(-z) + \frac{1}{2}\left[\ln(-z) - \ln\left(-\frac{1}{z}\right)\right] - \ln z, \quad \Gamma\left(\frac{1}{2}, z\right) = \sqrt{\pi}\,\text{erfc}\left(\sqrt{z}\right),$$

$$\Gamma(1, z) = e^{-z}, \quad \Gamma(n, z) = (n-1)!\,e^{-z}\sum_{k=0}^{n-1}\frac{z^k}{k!},$$

$$\Gamma(\nu, z) = \Gamma(\nu) - \frac{z^\nu e^{-z}}{\nu}\,{}_1F_1(1; \nu+1; z), \quad \gamma(\nu, z) = \Gamma(\nu) - e^{-z}\,\Psi(1-\nu; 1-\nu; z),$$

$$\Gamma(\nu, z) = e^{-z}\,\Psi(1-\nu; 1-\nu; z), \quad \gamma(\nu, z) = \frac{z^\nu}{\nu}\,{}_1F_1(\nu; \nu+1; -z),$$

$$\Gamma(\nu, z) = G_{12}^{20}\left(z\,\middle|\begin{matrix}1\\0,\,\nu\end{matrix}\right), \quad \gamma(\nu, z) = G_{12}^{11}\left(z\,\middle|\begin{matrix}1\\\nu,\,0\end{matrix}\right).$$

3.8.1. $\Gamma(\nu, ax)$, $\gamma(\nu, ax)$, and algebraic functions

No.	$f(x)$	$F(s)$
1	$\left\{\begin{matrix}\Gamma(\nu, ax)\\\gamma(\nu, ax)\end{matrix}\right\}$	$\pm\dfrac{a^{-s}}{s}\Gamma(s+\nu) \qquad\qquad [\text{Re}\,a, \pm\text{Re}\,s, \text{Re}(s+\nu) > 0]$
2	$(a-x)_+^{\alpha-1}\left\{\begin{matrix}\Gamma(\nu, bx)\\\gamma(\nu, bx)\end{matrix}\right\}$	$\mp\dfrac{a^{s+\alpha+\nu-1}b^\nu}{\nu}\,\text{B}(\alpha, s+\nu)\,{}_2F_2\left(\begin{matrix}\nu, s+\nu; -ab\\\nu+1, s+\alpha+\nu\end{matrix}\right)$ $+\dfrac{1\pm1}{2}a^{s+\alpha-1}\Gamma\begin{bmatrix}s, \alpha, \nu\\s+\alpha\end{bmatrix}$ $\left[a, \text{Re}\,\alpha, \text{Re}(s+\nu) > 0, \left\{\begin{matrix}\text{Re}\,s > 0\\\text{Re}\,\nu > 0\end{matrix}\right\}\right]$
3	$(x-a)_+^{\alpha-1}\left\{\begin{matrix}\Gamma(\nu, bx)\\\gamma(\nu, bx)\end{matrix}\right\}$	$\mp\dfrac{a^{s+\alpha+\nu-1}b^\nu}{\nu}\,\text{B}(\alpha, 1-s-\alpha-\nu)\,{}_2F_2\left(\begin{matrix}\nu, s+\nu; -ab\\\nu+1, s+\alpha+\nu\end{matrix}\right)$ $\mp\dfrac{b^{1-s-\alpha}}{1-s-\alpha}\Gamma(s+\alpha+\nu-1)$ $\times{}_2F_2\left(\begin{matrix}1-\alpha, 1-s-\alpha; -ab\\2-s-\alpha-\nu, 2-s-\alpha\end{matrix}\right)$ $+\left\{\begin{matrix}1\\0\end{matrix}\right\}a^{s+\alpha-1}\Gamma(\nu)\,\text{B}(\alpha, 1-s-\alpha)$ $\left[a, \text{Re}\,\alpha > 0; \left\{\begin{matrix}\text{Re}\,b > 0\\\text{Re}\,b, \text{Re}\,\nu > 0; \text{Re}(s+\alpha) < 1\end{matrix}\right\}\right]$

No.	$f(x)$	$F(s)$
4	$\dfrac{1}{(x+a)^\rho}\left\{\begin{matrix}\Gamma(\nu, bx)\\\gamma(\nu, bx)\end{matrix}\right\}$	$\mp\dfrac{a^{s+\nu-\rho}b^\nu}{\nu}\,\mathrm{B}(s+\nu, -s-\nu+\rho)$

$$\times\,_2F_2\left(\begin{matrix}\nu,\ s+\nu;\ ab\\\nu+1,\ s+\nu-\rho+1\end{matrix}\right)\pm\frac{b^{-s+\rho}}{s-\rho}\,\Gamma(s+\nu-\rho)$$

$$\times\,_2F_2\left(\begin{matrix}\rho,\ -s+\rho;\ ab\\1-s+\rho,\ 1-s-\nu+\rho\end{matrix}\right)$$

$$+\frac{1\pm1}{2}\,a^{s-\rho}\,\Gamma(\nu)\,\mathrm{B}(s,-s+\rho)$$

$$\left[\begin{matrix}\mathrm{Re}\,(s+\nu)>0;\ |\arg a|<\pi;\\\left\{\begin{matrix}\mathrm{Re}\,b,\ \mathrm{Re}\,s>0\\\mathrm{Re}\,b,\ \mathrm{Re}\,\nu>0;\ 0<\mathrm{Re}\,s<\mathrm{Re}\,\rho\end{matrix}\right\}\end{matrix}\right]$$

| 5 | $\dfrac{1}{x-a}\left\{\begin{matrix}\Gamma(\nu, bx)\\\gamma(\nu, bx)\end{matrix}\right\}$ | $\pm\pi\,a^{s-1}\cot\left[(s+\nu)\,\pi\right]\gamma(\nu, ab)\mp\dfrac{b^{1-s}}{1-s}\,\Gamma(s+\nu-1)$ |

$$\times\,_2F_2\left(\begin{matrix}1,\ 1-s;\ -ab\\2-s,\ 2-s-\nu\end{matrix}\right)-\frac{\pi\pm\pi}{2}\,a^{s-1}\cot(s\pi)\,\Gamma(\nu)$$

$$\left[a,\ \mathrm{Re}\,(s+\nu)>0;\ \left\{\begin{matrix}\mathrm{Re}\,b,\ \mathrm{Re}\,s>0\\\mathrm{Re}\,b,\ \mathrm{Re}\,\nu>0;\ \mathrm{Re}\,s<1\end{matrix}\right\}\right]$$

| 6 | $(a-x)_+^{\alpha-1}$ $\times\left\{\begin{matrix}\Gamma(\nu, bx(a-x))\\\gamma(\nu, bx(a-x))\end{matrix}\right\}$ | $\mp\dfrac{a^{s+\alpha+2\nu-1}b^\nu}{\nu}\,\mathrm{B}(s+\nu, \alpha+\nu)$ |

$$\times\,_3F_3\left(\begin{matrix}\nu,\ \alpha+\nu,\ s+\nu;\ -\frac{a^2b}{4}\\\nu+1,\ \frac{s+\alpha+2\nu}{2},\ \frac{s+\alpha+2\nu+1}{2}\end{matrix}\right)$$

$$+\frac{1\pm1}{2}\,a^{s+\alpha-1}\,\Gamma(\nu)\,\mathrm{B}(s,\alpha)$$

$$[a,\ \mathrm{Re}\,\nu,\ \mathrm{Re}\,(\alpha+\nu),\ \mathrm{Re}\,(s+\nu)>0]$$

| 7 | $\theta(x-a)\,\gamma\left(\nu, \dfrac{cx}{x-b}\right)$ | $-\dfrac{a^s c^\nu}{\nu s}\,\Psi_1\left(\nu, -s;\ 1-s,\ \nu+1;\ \dfrac{b}{a}, -c\right)$ |

$$[a>0;\ |b|<a;\ \mathrm{Re}\,(s+\nu)<-1]$$

3.8.2. $\Gamma(\nu, ax)$, $\gamma(\nu, ax)$, **and the exponential function**

No.	$f(x)$	$F(s)$
1	$e^{ax}\,\Gamma(\nu, ax)$	$\dfrac{\pi\csc\left[(s+\nu)\,\pi\right]}{a^s}\,\Gamma\left[\begin{matrix}s\\1-\nu\end{matrix}\right]\qquad[\mathrm{Re}\,a,\ \mathrm{Re}\,s>0;\ 0<\mathrm{Re}\,(s+\nu)<1]$
2	$e^{-ax}\left\{\begin{matrix}\Gamma(\nu, bx)\\\gamma(\nu, bx)\end{matrix}\right\}$	$\dfrac{1\pm1}{2a^s}\,\Gamma(\nu)\,\Gamma(s)\mp\dfrac{b^\nu}{\nu a^{s+\nu}}\,\Gamma(s+\nu)\,_2F_1\left(\begin{matrix}\nu,\ s+\nu\\\nu+1;\ -\frac{b}{a}\end{matrix}\right)$

$$\left[\mathrm{Re}\,a,\ \mathrm{Re}\,b,\ \mathrm{Re}\,(s+\nu),\ \left\{\begin{matrix}\mathrm{Re}\,s\\\mathrm{Re}\,\nu\end{matrix}\right\}>0\right]$$

No.	$f(x)$	$F(s)$
3	$(a-x)_+^{\alpha-1} e^{bx} \Gamma(\nu, bx)$	$a^{s+\alpha-1}\Gamma(\nu)\,\mathrm{B}(\alpha, s)\,{}_1F_1\!\begin{pmatrix} s;\ ab \\ s+\alpha \end{pmatrix}$

$$-\frac{a^{s+\alpha+\nu-1}b^\nu}{\nu}\,\mathrm{B}(\alpha, s+\nu)\,{}_2F_2\!\begin{pmatrix} 1,\ s+\nu;\ ab \\ \nu+1,\ s+\alpha+\nu \end{pmatrix}$$

$$[a,\ \mathrm{Re}\,\alpha > 0;\ \mathrm{Re}\,s > 0,\ -\mathrm{Re}\,\nu;\ |\arg b| < \pi]$$

| 4 | $(x-a)_+^{\alpha-1} e^{bx} \Gamma(\nu, bx)$ | $-\dfrac{a^{s+\alpha+\nu-1}b^\nu}{\nu}\,\mathrm{B}(\alpha, 1-s-\alpha-\nu)\,{}_2F_2\!\begin{pmatrix} 1,\ s+\nu;\ ab \\ \nu+1,\ s+\alpha+\nu \end{pmatrix}$ |

$$+a^{s+\alpha-1}\Gamma(\nu)\,\mathrm{B}(\alpha, 1-s-\alpha)\,{}_1F_1\!\begin{pmatrix} s;\ ab \\ s+\alpha \end{pmatrix}$$

$$-\frac{\pi b^{1-s-\alpha}}{\sin\left[(s+\alpha+\nu)\pi\right]}\,\Gamma\!\begin{bmatrix} s+\alpha-1 \\ 1-\nu \end{bmatrix}{}_1F_1\!\begin{pmatrix} 1-\alpha;\ ab \\ 2-s-\alpha \end{pmatrix}$$

$$[a,\ \mathrm{Re}\,\alpha > 0;\ \mathrm{Re}\,(s+\alpha+\nu) < 2;\ |\arg b| < \pi]$$

| 5 | $\dfrac{e^{bx}}{(x+a)^\rho}\,\Gamma(\nu, bx)$ | $a^{s-\rho}\Gamma(\nu)\,\mathrm{B}(s, \rho-s)\,{}_1F_1\!\begin{pmatrix} s;\ -ab \\ s-\rho+1 \end{pmatrix} - \dfrac{a^{s+\nu-\rho}b^\nu}{\nu}$ |

$$\times\,\mathrm{B}(s+\nu, \rho-\nu-s)\,{}_2F_2\!\begin{pmatrix} 1,\ s+\nu;\ -ab \\ \nu+1,\ s+\nu-\rho+1 \end{pmatrix}$$

$$+\frac{\pi b^{\rho-s}}{\sin\left[(s+\nu-\rho)\pi\right]}\,\Gamma\!\begin{bmatrix} s-\rho \\ 1-\nu \end{bmatrix}{}_1F_1\!\begin{pmatrix} \rho;\ -ab \\ \rho-s+1 \end{pmatrix}$$

$$[\mathrm{Re}\,s > 0;\ 0 < \mathrm{Re}\,(s+\nu) < \mathrm{Re}\,\rho+1;\ |\arg a|,\ |\arg b| < \pi]$$

| 6 | $\dfrac{e^{bx}}{x-a}\,\Gamma(\nu, bx)$ | $-\pi a^{s-1}e^{ab}\Gamma(\nu)\cot(s\pi) + \pi a^{s-1}e^{-ab}\cot\left[(s+\nu)\pi\right]\gamma(\nu, ba)$ |

$$-\frac{\pi a^{s-1}e^{ab}}{\sin\left[(s+\nu)\pi\right]}\,\Gamma\!\begin{bmatrix} s \\ 1-\nu \end{bmatrix}\gamma(1-s, ab)$$

$$[a,\ \mathrm{Re}\,s > 0;\ 0 < \mathrm{Re}\,(s+\nu) < 1;\ |\arg b| < \pi]$$

| 7 | $e^{-ax^2}\left\{\begin{matrix} \Gamma(\nu, bx) \\ \gamma(\nu, bx) \end{matrix}\right\}$ | $\dfrac{1\pm 1}{4a^{s/2}}\Gamma(\nu)\,\Gamma\!\left(\dfrac{s}{2}\right) \mp \dfrac{a^{-(s+\nu)/2}b^\nu}{2\nu}\,\Gamma\!\left(\dfrac{s+\nu}{2}\right){}_2F_2\!\begin{pmatrix} \frac{\nu}{2},\ \frac{s+\nu}{2} \\ \frac{1}{2},\ \frac{\nu+2}{2};\ \frac{b^2}{4a} \end{pmatrix}$ |

$$\pm\frac{a^{-(s+\nu+1)/2}b^{\nu+1}}{2(\nu+1)}\,\Gamma\!\left(\frac{s+\nu+1}{2}\right){}_2F_2\!\begin{pmatrix} \frac{\nu+1}{2},\ \frac{s+\nu+1}{2} \\ \frac{3}{2},\ \frac{\nu+3}{2};\ \frac{b^2}{4a} \end{pmatrix}$$

$$\left[\mathrm{Re}\,a,\ \mathrm{Re}\,b,\ \mathrm{Re}\,(s+\nu),\ \left\{\begin{matrix} \mathrm{Re}\,s \\ \mathrm{Re}\,\nu \end{matrix}\right\} > 0\right]$$

| 8 | $e^{-a/x}\left\{\begin{matrix} \Gamma(\nu, bx) \\ \gamma(\nu, bx) \end{matrix}\right\}$ | $\dfrac{1\pm 1}{2}a^s\,\Gamma(\nu)\,\Gamma(-s) \mp \dfrac{a^{s+\nu}b^\nu}{\nu}\,{}_1F_2\!\begin{pmatrix} \nu;\ ab \\ \nu+1,\ s+\nu+1 \end{pmatrix}$ |

$$\times\,\Gamma(-s-\nu) \pm \frac{\Gamma(s+\nu)}{b^s s}\,{}_1F_2\!\begin{pmatrix} -s;\ ab \\ 1-s,\ 1-s-\nu \end{pmatrix}$$

$$\left[\mathrm{Re}\,a,\ \left\{\begin{matrix} \mathrm{Re}\,b \\ \mathrm{Re}\,\nu,\ \mathrm{Re}\,b,\ \mathrm{Re}\,(-s) \end{matrix}\right\} > 0\right]$$

No.	$f(x)$	$F(s)$
9	$e^{ax-b/x}\,\Gamma(\nu, ax)$	$2^{2-s-2\nu}\left(\dfrac{b}{a}\right)^{s/2}\Gamma(1-s-\nu)\,S_{s+2\nu-1,\,-s}\left(2\sqrt{ab}\right)$ $[\operatorname{Re} b > 0;\ \operatorname{Re}(s+\nu) < 1;\ |\arg a| < \pi]$
10	$\theta(a-x)\,e^{bx}$ $\times\,\gamma(\nu, c(a-x))$	$a^{s+\nu}c^\nu\,\Gamma\begin{bmatrix} s, \nu \\ s+\nu+1 \end{bmatrix}\Phi_2(s,\nu;\,s+\nu+1;\,ab,-ac)$ $[a,\ \operatorname{Re} s > 0;\ \operatorname{Re}\nu > -1]$
11	$(a-x)_+^{-\nu}\,e^{b(a-x)}$ $\times\,\gamma(\nu, b(a-x))$	$\dfrac{a^s b^\nu}{\nu s}\,{}_2F_2\!\left(\begin{matrix} 1, 1;\ ab \\ \nu+1, s+1 \end{matrix}\right)\qquad [a,\ \operatorname{Re} s > 0;\ 0 < \operatorname{Re}\nu < 1]$
12	$(a-x)_+^{\alpha-1}\,e^{bx(a-x)}$ $\times\left\{\begin{matrix} \Gamma(\nu, bx(a-x)) \\ \gamma(\nu, bx(a-x)) \end{matrix}\right\}$	$\mp\dfrac{a^{s+\alpha+2\nu-1}b^\nu}{\nu}\,B(s+\nu, \alpha+\nu)\,{}_3F_3\!\left(\begin{matrix} 1, \alpha+\nu, s+\nu;\ \frac{a^2 b}{4} \\ \nu+1, \frac{s+\alpha+2\nu}{2}, \frac{s+\alpha+2\nu+1}{2} \end{matrix}\right)$ $+\dfrac{1\pm1}{2}\,a^{s+\alpha-1}\,\Gamma(\nu)\,B(s,\alpha)\,{}_2F_2\!\left(\begin{matrix} s, \alpha;\ \frac{a^2 b}{4} \\ \frac{s+\alpha}{2}, \frac{s+\alpha+1}{2} \end{matrix}\right)$ $[a,\ \operatorname{Re}\nu,\ \operatorname{Re}(s+\nu),\ \operatorname{Re}(\alpha+\nu) > 0]$
13	$\dfrac{e^{b/(x+a)}}{(x+a)^\rho}\,\gamma\!\left(\nu, \dfrac{b}{x+a}\right)$	$\dfrac{a^{s-\nu-\rho}b^\nu}{\nu}\,B(s, \nu+\rho-s)\,{}_2F_2\!\left(\begin{matrix} 1, \nu+\rho-s \\ \nu+1, \nu+\rho;\ \frac{b}{a} \end{matrix}\right)$ $[0 < \operatorname{Re} s < \operatorname{Re}(\nu+\rho);\ |\arg a| < \pi]$
14	$\dfrac{e^{bx/(x+a)}}{(x+a)^\rho}\,\gamma\!\left(\nu, \dfrac{bx}{x+a}\right)$	$\dfrac{a^{s-\rho}b^\nu}{\nu}\,B(s+\nu, \rho-s)\,{}_2F_2\!\left(\begin{matrix} 1, s+\nu;\ b \\ \nu+1, \nu+\rho \end{matrix}\right)$ $[-\operatorname{Re}\nu < \operatorname{Re} s < \operatorname{Re}\rho;\ |\arg a| < \pi]$
15	$\theta(x-a)(x-b)^{\nu-1}$ $\times\,e^{cx/(x-b)}\,\gamma\!\left(\nu, \dfrac{cx}{x-b}\right)$	$\dfrac{a^{s+\nu-1}c^\nu}{\nu(1-s-\nu)}\,\Psi_1\!\left(1, 1-s-\nu;\, 2-s-\nu, \nu+1;\, \dfrac{b}{a}, c\right)$ $[a > 0;\ |b| < a;\ \operatorname{Re}(s+\nu) < -1]$

3.8.3. $\Gamma(\nu, ax)$, $\gamma(\nu, ax)$, and trigonometric functions

Notation: $\delta = \left\{\begin{matrix} 1 \\ 0 \end{matrix}\right\}$.

No.	$f(x)$	$F(s)$
1	$\sin(ax)\left\{\begin{matrix} \Gamma(\nu, bx) \\ \gamma(\nu, bx) \end{matrix}\right\}$	$\pm\dfrac{a\,\Gamma(s+\nu+1)}{b^{s+1}(s+1)}\,{}_3F_2\!\left(\begin{matrix} \frac{s+1}{2}, \frac{s+\nu+1}{2}, \frac{s+\nu+2}{2} \\ \frac{3}{2}, \frac{s+3}{2};\ -\frac{a^2}{b^2} \end{matrix}\right) + \dfrac{1\mp1}{2a^s}\sin\dfrac{s\pi}{2}\,\Gamma(s)\,\Gamma(\nu)$ $\left[a,\ \operatorname{Re} b > 0;\ \left\{\begin{matrix} \operatorname{Re} s > -1;\ \operatorname{Re}(s+\nu) > -1 \\ \operatorname{Re}\nu > 0,\ -\operatorname{Re}\nu-1 < \operatorname{Re} s < 1 \end{matrix}\right\}\right]$

No.	$f(x)$	$F(s)$
2	$\cos(ax)\begin{Bmatrix}\Gamma(\nu,bx)\\\gamma(\nu,bx)\end{Bmatrix}$	$\pm\dfrac{\Gamma(s+\nu)}{b^s s}\,{}_3F_2\left(\begin{matrix}\frac{s}{2},\frac{s+\nu}{2},\frac{s+\nu+1}{2}\\\frac{1}{2},\frac{s+2}{2};\,-\frac{a^2}{b^2}\end{matrix}\right)+\dfrac{1\mp1}{2a^s}\cos\dfrac{s\pi}{2}\Gamma(s)\Gamma(\nu)$ $\left[a,\ \mathrm{Re}\,b>0;\left\{\begin{matrix}\mathrm{Re}\,s,\ \mathrm{Re}\,(s+\nu)>0\\\mathrm{Re}\,\nu>0;\ -\mathrm{Re}\,\nu<\mathrm{Re}\,s<1\end{matrix}\right\}\right]$
3	$\sin(a\sqrt{x})\begin{Bmatrix}\Gamma(\nu,bx)\\\gamma(\nu,bx)\end{Bmatrix}$	$\pm\dfrac{2a}{(2s+1)b^{s+1/2}}\Gamma\left(\dfrac{2s+2\nu+1}{2}\right){}_2F_2\left(\begin{matrix}\frac{2s+1}{2},\frac{2s+2\nu+1}{2}\\\frac{3}{2},\frac{2s+3}{2};\,-\frac{a^2}{4b}\end{matrix}\right)$ $+\dfrac{1\mp1}{a^{2s}}\sin(s\pi)\Gamma(\nu)\Gamma(2s)$ $\left[a,\ \mathrm{Re}\,b>0;\left\{\begin{matrix}\mathrm{Re}\,s,\ \mathrm{Re}\,(s+\nu)>-1/2\\\mathrm{Re}\,\nu>0;\ -\mathrm{Re}\,\nu-1/2<\mathrm{Re}\,s<1/2\end{matrix}\right\}\right]$
4	$\cos(a\sqrt{x})\begin{Bmatrix}\Gamma(\nu,bx)\\\gamma(\nu,bx)\end{Bmatrix}$	$\pm\dfrac{\Gamma(s+\nu)}{b^s s}\,{}_2F_2\left(\begin{matrix}s,\,s+\nu;\,-\frac{a^2}{4b}\\\frac{1}{2},\,s+1\end{matrix}\right)+\dfrac{1\mp1}{a^{2s}}\cos(s\pi)\Gamma(\nu)\Gamma(2s)$ $\left[a,\ \mathrm{Re}\,b>0;\left\{\begin{matrix}\mathrm{Re}\,s,\ \mathrm{Re}\,(s+\nu)>0\\\mathrm{Re}\,\nu>0;\ -\mathrm{Re}\,\nu<\mathrm{Re}\,s<1/2\end{matrix}\right\}\right]$
5	$e^{bx}\begin{Bmatrix}\sin(a\sqrt{x})\\\cos(a\sqrt{x})\end{Bmatrix}$ $\times\Gamma(\nu,bx)$	$\dfrac{\pi a^\delta}{b^{s+\delta/2}}\csc\dfrac{(2s+2\nu+\delta)\pi}{2}\Gamma\left[\begin{matrix}\frac{2s+\delta}{2}\\1-\nu\end{matrix}\right]{}_1F_1\left(\begin{matrix}\frac{2s+\delta}{2};\,\frac{a^2}{4b}\\\frac{2\delta+1}{2}\end{matrix}\right)$ $-\dfrac{2b^{\nu-1}}{a^{2s+2\nu-2}}\Gamma(2s+2\nu-2)\begin{Bmatrix}\sin[(s+\nu)\pi]\\\cos[(s+\nu)\pi]\end{Bmatrix}$ $\times{}_2F_2\left(\begin{matrix}1,\,1-\nu;\,\frac{a^2}{4b}\\\frac{3-2s-2\nu}{2},\,2-s-\nu\end{matrix}\right)$ $\left[\begin{matrix}a>0;\ \mathrm{Re}\,s>-\delta/2;\\-\delta/2<\mathrm{Re}\,(s+\nu)<3/2;\ |\arg b|<\pi\end{matrix}\right]$

3.8.4. $\Gamma(\nu,ax)$, $\gamma(\nu,ax)$, **and the logarithmic function**

No.	$f(x)$	$F(s)$
1	$\theta(a-x)\ln\dfrac{\sqrt{a}+\sqrt{a-x}}{\sqrt{x}}$ $\times\begin{Bmatrix}\Gamma(\nu,bx)\\\gamma(\nu,bx)\end{Bmatrix}$	$\mp\dfrac{\sqrt{\pi}\,a^{s+\nu}b^\nu}{2\nu(s+\nu)}\Gamma\left[\begin{matrix}s+\nu\\\frac{2s+2\nu+1}{2}\end{matrix}\right]{}_3F_3\left(\begin{matrix}\nu,\,s+\nu,\,s+\nu;\,-ab\\\nu+1,\,\frac{2s+2\nu+1}{2},\,s+\nu+1\end{matrix}\right)$ $+\dfrac{1\pm1}{4s}\sqrt{\pi}\,a^s\Gamma\left[\begin{matrix}s\\\frac{2s+1}{2}\end{matrix}\right]$ $[a,\ \mathrm{Re}\,\nu,\ \mathrm{Re}\,(s+\nu+1)>0]$
2	$\theta(a-x)\ln\dfrac{\sqrt{a}+\sqrt{a-x}}{\sqrt{x}}$ $\times e^{bx}\begin{Bmatrix}\Gamma(\nu,bx)\\\gamma(\nu,bx)\end{Bmatrix}$	$\mp\dfrac{\sqrt{\pi}\,a^{s+\nu}b^\nu}{2\nu(s+\nu)}\Gamma\left[\begin{matrix}s+\nu\\\frac{2s+2\nu+1}{2}\end{matrix}\right]{}_3F_3\left(\begin{matrix}1,\,s+\nu,\,s+\nu;\,ab\\\nu+1,\,\frac{2s+2\nu+1}{2},\,s+\nu+1\end{matrix}\right)$ $+\dfrac{1\pm1}{4s}\sqrt{\pi}\,a^s\Gamma\left[\begin{matrix}s\\\frac{2s+1}{2}\end{matrix}\right]{}_2F_2\left(\begin{matrix}s,\,s;\,ab\\\frac{2s+1}{2},\,s+1\end{matrix}\right)$ $[a,\ \mathrm{Re}\,\nu,\ \mathrm{Re}\,(s+\nu+1)>0]$

3.8.5. $\gamma(\nu, ax)$ and inverse trigonometric functions

1	$\theta(a-x)\arccos\dfrac{x}{a}$ $\times \gamma(\nu, bx)$	$\dfrac{(2a)^{s+\nu}b^\nu}{\nu(s+\nu)}\Gamma\left[\begin{matrix}\frac{s+\nu+1}{2},\ \frac{s+\nu+3}{2}\\ s+\nu+2\end{matrix}\right]{}_3F_4\left(\begin{matrix}\frac{\nu}{2},\ \frac{s+\nu}{2},\ \frac{s+\nu+1}{2};\ \frac{a^2b^2}{4}\\ \frac12,\ \frac{\nu+2}{2},\ \frac{s+\nu+2}{2},\ \frac{s+\nu+2}{2}\end{matrix}\right)$ $-\dfrac{2^{s+\nu}a^{s+\nu+1}b^{\nu+1}}{(\nu+1)(s+\nu+1)}\Gamma\left[\begin{matrix}\frac{s+\nu+2}{2},\ \frac{s+\nu+2}{2}\\ s+\nu+2\end{matrix}\right]$ $\times {}_3F_4\left(\begin{matrix}\frac{\nu+1}{2},\ \frac{s+\nu+1}{2},\ \frac{s+\nu+2}{2};\ \frac{a^2b^2}{4}\\ \frac32,\ \frac{\nu+3}{2},\ \frac{s+\nu+3}{2},\ \frac{s+\nu+3}{2}\end{matrix}\right)$ $[a,\ \mathrm{Re}(s+\nu+1)>0]$
2	$\theta(a-x)e^{bx}\arccos\dfrac{x}{a}$ $\times\gamma(\nu, bx)$	$\dfrac{2^{s+\nu}a^{s+\nu+1}b^{\nu+1}}{\nu(\nu+1)(s+\nu+1)}\Gamma\left[\begin{matrix}\frac{s+\nu+2}{2},\ \frac{s+\nu+2}{2}\\ s+\nu+2\end{matrix}\right]$ $\times {}_3F_4\left(\begin{matrix}1,\ \frac{s+\nu+1}{2},\ \frac{s+\nu+2}{2};\ \frac{a^2b^2}{4}\\ \frac{\nu+2}{2},\ \frac{\nu+3}{2},\ \frac{s+\nu+3}{2},\ \frac{s+\nu+3}{2}\end{matrix}\right)+\dfrac{2^{s+\nu+1}a^{s+\nu}b^\nu}{\nu(s+\nu)(s+\nu+1)}$ $\times\Gamma\left[\begin{matrix}\frac{s+\nu+3}{2},\ \frac{s+\nu+3}{2}\\ s+\nu+2\end{matrix}\right]{}_3F_4\left(\begin{matrix}1,\ \frac{s+\nu+1}{2},\ \frac{s+\nu}{2};\ \frac{a^2b^2}{4}\\ \frac{\nu+1}{2},\ \frac{\nu+2}{2},\ \frac{s+\nu+2}{2},\ \frac{s+\nu+2}{2}\end{matrix}\right)$ $[a,\ \mathrm{Re}(s+\nu+1)>0]$

3.8.6. $\Gamma(\nu, ax)$, $\gamma(\nu, ax)$, and $\mathrm{Ei}(bx)$

1	$\mathrm{Ei}(-ax)\left\{\begin{matrix}\Gamma(\nu, bx)\\ \gamma(\nu, bx)\end{matrix}\right\}$	$\pm\dfrac{b^\nu\Gamma(s+\nu)}{\nu(s+\nu)a^{s+\nu}}{}_3F_2\left(\begin{matrix}\nu,\ s+\nu,\ s+\nu;\ -\frac{b}{a}\\ \nu+1,\ s+\nu+1\end{matrix}\right)-\dfrac{1\pm1}{2a^s s}\Gamma(\nu)\Gamma(s)$ $\left[\mathrm{Re}\,a,\ \mathrm{Re}\,b,\ \mathrm{Re}(s+\nu)>0;\ \left\{\begin{matrix}\mathrm{Re}\,s\\ \mathrm{Re}\,\nu\end{matrix}\right\}>0\right]$

3.8.7. $\Gamma(\nu, ax)$, $\gamma(\nu, ax)$, and $\mathrm{erf}(bx^r)$, $\mathrm{erfc}(bx^r)$, $\mathrm{erfi}(bx^r)$

1	$\mathrm{erfc}(ax)\left\{\begin{matrix}\Gamma(\nu, bx)\\ \gamma(\nu, bx)\end{matrix}\right\}$	$\mp\dfrac{a^{-s-\nu}b^\nu}{\sqrt{\pi}\,\nu(s+\nu)}\Gamma\left(\dfrac{s+\nu+1}{2}\right){}_3F_3\left(\begin{matrix}\frac{\nu}{2},\ \frac{s+\nu}{2},\ \frac{s+\nu+1}{2}\\ \frac12,\ \frac{\nu+2}{2},\ \frac{s+\nu+2}{2};\ \frac{b^2}{4a^2}\end{matrix}\right)$ $\pm\dfrac{a^{-s-\nu-1}b^{\nu+1}}{\sqrt{\pi}\,(\nu+1)(s+\nu+1)}\Gamma\left(\dfrac{s+\nu+2}{2}\right)$ $\times {}_3F_3\left(\begin{matrix}\frac{\nu+1}{2},\ \frac{s+\nu+1}{2},\ \frac{s+\nu+2}{2}\\ \frac32,\ \frac{\nu+3}{2},\ \frac{s+\nu+3}{2};\ \frac{b^2}{4a^2}\end{matrix}\right)+\dfrac{1\pm1}{2}\dfrac{a^{-s}}{\sqrt{\pi}\,s}\Gamma(\nu)\Gamma\left(\dfrac{s+1}{2}\right)$ $[\mathrm{Re}\,b,\ \mathrm{Re}(a^2+b)>0;\ \mathrm{Re}\,s>-\mathrm{Re}\,\nu,\ 0]$
2	$\mathrm{erf}(a\sqrt{x})\left\{\begin{matrix}\Gamma(\nu, bx)\\ \gamma(\nu, bx)\end{matrix}\right\}$	$\pm\dfrac{b^\nu}{\sqrt{\pi}\,\nu(s+\nu)a^{2s+2\nu}}\Gamma\left(s+\nu+\dfrac12\right){}_3F_2\left(\begin{matrix}\nu,\ s+\nu,\ s+\nu+\frac12\\ \nu+1,\ s+\nu+1;\ -\frac{b}{a^2}\end{matrix}\right)$ $-\dfrac{1\pm1}{2\sqrt{\pi}\,a^{2s}s}\Gamma(\nu)\Gamma\left(\dfrac{2s+1}{2}\right)\pm\dfrac{\Gamma(s+\nu)}{b^s s}$ $\left[\mathrm{Re}\,b>0;\ \mathrm{Re}(s+\nu)>-1/2;\ \left\{\begin{matrix}\mathrm{Re}\,s\\ \mathrm{Re}\,\nu\end{matrix}\right\}>0;\ |\arg a|<\pi/4\right]$

No.	$f(x)$	$F(s)$
3	$\operatorname{erfc}\left(a\sqrt{x}\right)\begin{Bmatrix}\Gamma\left(\nu,bx\right)\\\gamma\left(\nu,bx\right)\end{Bmatrix}$	$\mp\dfrac{b^{\nu}}{\sqrt{\pi}\,\nu\,(s+\nu)\,a^{2s+2\nu}}\,\Gamma\left(s+\nu+\dfrac{1}{2}\right){}_3F_2\left(\begin{matrix}\nu,\,s+\nu,\,s+\nu+\frac{1}{2}\\\nu+1,\,s+\nu+1;\,-\frac{b}{a^2}\end{matrix}\right)$ $+\dfrac{1\pm1}{2\sqrt{\pi}\,a^{2s}s}\Gamma\left(\nu\right)\Gamma\left(\dfrac{2s+1}{2}\right)$ $\left[\operatorname{Re}b,\ \operatorname{Re}(s+\nu),\ \begin{Bmatrix}\operatorname{Re}s\\\operatorname{Re}\nu\end{Bmatrix}>0;\ |\arg a|<\pi/4\right]$
4	$e^{bx}\operatorname{erfc}\left(a\sqrt{x}\right)\gamma\left(\nu,bx\right)$	$\dfrac{b^{\nu}}{\sqrt{\pi}\,\nu\,a^{2s+2\nu}\,(s+\nu)}\,\Gamma\left(s+\nu+\dfrac{1}{2}\right){}_3F_2\left(\begin{matrix}1,\,s+\nu,\,s+\nu+\frac{1}{2}\\\nu+1,\,s+\nu+1;\,\frac{b}{a^2}\end{matrix}\right)$ $\left[\operatorname{Re}\left(a^2-b\right),\ \operatorname{Re}\nu,\ \operatorname{Re}(s+\nu)>0;\ |\arg b|<\pi/4\right]$
5	$e^{a^2x}\operatorname{erf}\left(a\sqrt{x}\right)\Gamma\left(\nu,bx\right)$	$\dfrac{4a}{\sqrt{\pi}\,b^{s+1/2}\,(2s+1)}\,\Gamma\left(s+\nu+\dfrac{1}{2}\right){}_3F_2\left(\begin{matrix}1,\,s+\frac{1}{2},\,s+\nu+\frac{1}{2}\\\frac{3}{2},\,s+\frac{3}{2};\,\frac{a^2}{b}\end{matrix}\right)$ $\left[\operatorname{Re}\left(b-a^2\right)>0;\ \operatorname{Re}s,\ \operatorname{Re}(s+\nu)>-1/2;|\arg a|<\pi/4\right]$
6	$\operatorname{erfi}\left(a\sqrt{x}\right)\operatorname{erf}\left(a\sqrt{x}\right)$ $\times\Gamma\left(\nu,bx\right)$	$\dfrac{4a^2}{\pi\,b^{s+1}\,(s+1)}\,\Gamma\left(s+\nu+1\right){}_5F_4\left(\begin{matrix}\frac{1}{2},\,1,\,\frac{s+1}{2},\,\frac{s+\nu+1}{2},\,\frac{s+\nu+2}{2}\\\frac{3}{4},\,\frac{5}{4},\,\frac{3}{2},\,\frac{s+3}{2};\,\frac{a^4}{b^2}\end{matrix}\right)$ $\left[a,\ \operatorname{Re}b>0;\ \operatorname{Re}s,\ \operatorname{Re}(s+\nu)>-1\right]$

3.8.8. Products of $\Gamma\left(\mu,ax\right)$ and $\gamma\left(\nu,ax\right)$

No.	$f(x)$	$F(s)$
1	$\Gamma\left(\nu,-ax\right)\Gamma\left(\nu,ax\right)$	$\dfrac{\pi\,(-a)^{-s/2}\,a^{-s/2}}{s}\,\csc\dfrac{(s+2\nu)\,\pi}{2}\,\Gamma\begin{bmatrix}s+\nu\\1-\nu\end{bmatrix}$ $\left[\operatorname{Re}a>0;\ 0,\ -2\operatorname{Re}\nu<\operatorname{Re}s<2-2\operatorname{Re}\nu\right]$
2	$\Gamma\left(\mu,ax\right)\begin{Bmatrix}\Gamma\left(\nu,bx\right)\\\gamma\left(\nu,bx\right)\end{Bmatrix}$	$\mp\dfrac{b^{\nu}\,\Gamma\left(s+\mu+\nu\right)}{\nu\,(s+\nu)\,a^{s+\nu}}\,{}_3F_2\left(\begin{matrix}\nu,\,s+\nu,\,s+\mu+\nu\\\nu+1,\,s+\nu+1;\,-\frac{b}{a}\end{matrix}\right)+\dfrac{1\pm1}{2a^s s}\,\Gamma\left(\nu\right)\Gamma\left(s+\mu\right)$ $\left[\begin{matrix}\operatorname{Re}(s+\mu),\ \operatorname{Re}(s+\nu),\ \operatorname{Re}(s+\nu+\mu)>0;\\\begin{Bmatrix}\operatorname{Re}(a+b)>0\\\operatorname{Re}b,\ \operatorname{Re}(a+b)>0\end{Bmatrix}\end{matrix}\right]$
3	$\gamma\left(\mu,ax\right)\gamma\left(\nu,bx\right)$	$-\dfrac{b^{\nu}\,\Gamma\left(s+\mu+\nu\right)}{\nu\,(s+\nu)\,a^{s+\nu}}\,{}_3F_2\left(\begin{matrix}\nu,\,s+\nu,\,s+\mu+\nu\\\nu+1,\,s+\nu+1;\,-\frac{b}{a}\end{matrix}\right)$ $-\dfrac{\Gamma\left(\mu\right)\Gamma\left(s+\nu\right)}{b^s s}\ \left[\begin{matrix}\operatorname{Re}a,\ \operatorname{Re}b,\ \operatorname{Re}\mu,\ \operatorname{Re}\nu,\\\operatorname{Re}(s+\mu+\nu)>0;\ \operatorname{Re}s<0\end{matrix}\right]$
4	$e^{-ax}\gamma\left(\mu,bx\right)\gamma\left(\nu,cx\right)$	$\dfrac{b^{\mu}c^{\nu}\,\Gamma\left(s+\mu+\nu\right)}{\mu\nu\,a^{s+\mu+\nu}}\,F_2\left(s+\mu+\nu,\mu,\nu;\mu+1,\nu+1;-\dfrac{b}{a},-\dfrac{c}{a}\right)$ $\left[\begin{matrix}\operatorname{Re}a,\ \operatorname{Re}(a+b),\ \operatorname{Re}(a+c),\\\operatorname{Re}(a+b+c),\ \operatorname{Re}(s+\mu+\nu)>0\end{matrix}\right]$

3.9. The Parabolic Cylinder Function $D_\nu(z)$

More formulas can be obtained from the corresponding sections due to the relations

$$D_{-1/2}(z) = \frac{\sqrt{\pi}}{2}\left[\sqrt[4]{z^2}\, I_{-1/4}\left(\frac{z^2}{4}\right) - \frac{z}{\sqrt[4]{z^2}}\, I_{1/4}\left(\frac{z^2}{4}\right)\right], \quad D_0(z) = e^{-z^2/4},$$

$$D_{1/2}(z) = \frac{\sqrt{\pi}}{4}\left[z\sqrt[4]{z^2}\, I_{-1/4}\left(\frac{z^2}{4}\right) + \left(z^2\right)^{3/4} I_{-3/4}\left(\frac{z^2}{4}\right)\right.$$

$$\left. - \left(z^2\right)^{3/4} I_{1/4}\left(\frac{z^2}{4}\right) - z\sqrt[4]{z^2}\, I_{3/4}\left(\frac{z^2}{4}\right)\right], \quad D_1(z) = ze^{-z^2/4},$$

$$D_{2n+\varepsilon}(z) = (-1)^n\, 2^n n!\, z^\varepsilon e^{-z^2/4} L_n^{(2\varepsilon-1)/2}\left(\frac{z^2}{2}\right), \quad [\varepsilon = 0 \text{ or } 1;\, n = 0, 1, 2, \ldots];$$

$$D_\nu(z) = 2^{\nu/2} e^{-z^2/4} \Psi\left(-\frac{\nu}{2}; \frac{1}{2}; \frac{z^2}{2}\right) = 2^{(\nu-1)/2} z e^{-z^2/4} \Psi\left(\frac{1-\nu}{2}; \frac{3}{2}; \frac{z^2}{2}\right),$$

$$D_\nu(z) = 2^{\nu/2} e^{-z^2/4}\left[\frac{1}{\Gamma((1-\nu)/2)}\, {}_1F_1\left(-\frac{\nu}{2}; \frac{1}{2}; \frac{z^2}{2}\right) - \frac{\sqrt{2\pi}\, z}{\Gamma(-\nu/2)}\, {}_1F_1\left(\frac{1-\nu}{2}; \frac{3}{2}; \frac{z^2}{2}\right)\right],$$

$$D_\nu(z) = 2^{-\nu/2} e^{-z^2/4} H_\nu\left(\frac{z}{\sqrt{2}}\right), \quad D_\nu(\sqrt{2}z) = 2^{\nu/2} e^{z^2/2}\, G_{12}^{20}\left(z\left|\begin{array}{c}(1-\nu)/2\\0, 1/2\end{array}\right.\right).$$

3.9.1. $D_\nu(bx)$ and elementary functions

Notation: $\delta = \left\{\begin{array}{c}1\\0\end{array}\right\}$.

No.	$f(x)$	$F(s)$
1	$D_\nu(ax)$	$\dfrac{2^{(\nu-s)/2}\sqrt{\pi}}{a^s}\,\Gamma\left[\begin{array}{c}s\\\frac{s-\nu+1}{2}\end{array}\right]\, {}_2F_1\left(\begin{array}{c}\frac{s}{2}, \frac{s+1}{2}\\\frac{s-\nu+1}{2};\, \frac{1}{2}\end{array}\right)$ $[\operatorname{Re} s > 0;\, |\arg a| < \pi/4]$
2	$e^{a^2x^2/4} D_\nu(ax)$	$\dfrac{a^{-s}}{2^{(s+\nu)/2+1}}\,\Gamma\left[\begin{array}{c}s, -\frac{s+\nu}{2}\\-\nu\end{array}\right]$ $\left[\begin{array}{c}0 < \operatorname{Re} s < -\operatorname{Re}\nu;\\|\arg a| < 3\pi/4\end{array}\right]$
3	$e^{-a^2x^2/4} D_\nu(ax)$	$\dfrac{2^{(\nu-s)/2}\sqrt{\pi}}{a^s}\,\Gamma\left[\begin{array}{c}s\\\frac{s-\nu+1}{2}\end{array}\right]$ $[\operatorname{Re} s > 0;\, |\arg a| < \pi/4]$
4	$e^{-a^2x^2/4} D_\nu(-ax)$	$\dfrac{2^{(\nu-s)/2}}{\sqrt{\pi}\, a^s}\cos\dfrac{(s+\nu)\pi}{2}\,\Gamma\left(\dfrac{1-s+\nu}{2}\right)\Gamma(s)$ $[0 < \operatorname{Re} s < \operatorname{Re}\nu + 1;\, |\arg a| < \pi/4]$
5	$e^{-ax^2} D_\nu(bx)$	$\dfrac{2^{(\nu-s)/2}\sqrt{\pi}}{b^s}\,\Gamma\left[\begin{array}{c}s\\\frac{s-\nu+1}{2}\end{array}\right]\, {}_2F_1\left(\begin{array}{c}\frac{s}{2}, \frac{s+1}{2}\\\frac{s-\nu+1}{2};\, \frac{b^2-4a}{2b^2}\end{array}\right)$ $\left[\begin{array}{l}(\operatorname{Re} s,\, \operatorname{Re}(4a+b^2) > 0)\text{ or}\\(\operatorname{Re}(4a+b^2) = 0;\, 0 < \operatorname{Re} s < -\operatorname{Re}\nu)\end{array}\right]$

No.	$f(x)$	$F(s)$

6 $\left(a^2 - x^2\right)_+^{\alpha-1} e^{\pm b^2 x^2/4}$ $\times D_\nu(bx)$

$$\frac{2^{\nu/2-1}\sqrt{\pi}\, a^{s+2\alpha-2}}{\Gamma\left(\frac{1-\nu}{2}\right)} B\left(\alpha, \frac{s}{2}\right) {}_2F_2\left(\begin{matrix} \frac{\mp 2\nu+1\mp 1}{4}, \frac{s}{2} \\ \frac{1}{2}, \frac{s+2\alpha}{2}; \frac{a^2b^2}{2} \end{matrix}\right)$$

$$- \frac{2^{(\nu-1)/2}\sqrt{\pi}\, a^{s+2\alpha-1}b}{\Gamma\left(-\frac{\nu}{2}\right)} B\left(\alpha, \frac{s+1}{2}\right) {}_2F_2\left(\begin{matrix} \frac{\mp 2\nu+3\mp 1}{4}, \frac{s+1}{2} \\ \frac{3}{2}, \frac{s+2\alpha+1}{2}; \frac{a^2b^2}{2} \end{matrix}\right)$$

$$[a,\ \operatorname{Re}\alpha,\ \operatorname{Re}s > 0]$$

7 $\dfrac{e^{\pm b^2 x^2/4}}{(x^2+a^2)^\rho} D_\nu(bx)$

$$\frac{2^{\nu/2-1}\sqrt{\pi}\, a^{s-2\rho}}{\Gamma\left(\frac{1-\nu}{2}\right)} B\left(\frac{s}{2}, \frac{2\rho-s}{2}\right) {}_2F_2\left(\begin{matrix} \frac{1\mp 1\mp 2\nu}{4}, \frac{s}{2} \\ \frac{1}{2}, \frac{s-2\rho+2}{2}; \mp\frac{a^2b^2}{2} \end{matrix}\right)$$

$$- \frac{2^{(\nu-1)/2}\sqrt{\pi}}{\Gamma\left(-\frac{\nu}{2}\right)} a^{s-2\rho+1} b\, B\left(\frac{s+1}{2}, \frac{2\rho-s-1}{2}\right)$$

$$\times {}_2F_2\left(\begin{matrix} \frac{3\mp 1\mp 2\nu}{4}, \frac{s+1}{2} \\ \frac{3}{2}, \frac{s-2\rho+3}{2}; \mp\frac{a^2b^2}{2} \end{matrix}\right) + \frac{2^{\rho-(s\pm\nu)/2}\sqrt{\pi}}{[2\sqrt{\pi}\,\Gamma(-\nu)]^{(1\pm 1)/2}}$$

$$\times \frac{b^{2\rho-s}\Gamma(s-2\rho)}{\Gamma^{\mp 1}\left(\frac{1\mp 1-2\nu\pm 4\rho\mp 2s}{4}\right)} {}_2F_2\left(\begin{matrix} \rho, \frac{4\rho-2s\mp 2\nu+1\mp 1}{4} \\ \frac{2\rho-s+2}{2}, \frac{2\rho-s+1}{2}; \mp\frac{a^2b^2}{2} \end{matrix}\right)$$

$$\left[\operatorname{Re}a>0; \left\{\begin{matrix} 0<\operatorname{Re}s<\operatorname{Re}(2\rho-\nu) \\ \operatorname{Re}s>0 \end{matrix}\right\}; |\arg b| < (2\pm 1)\pi/4\right]$$

8 $e^{-ax+b^2x^2/4} D_\nu(bx)$

$$-\frac{\pi}{2^{(s+\nu+2)/2}b^s} \csc\frac{(s+\nu)\pi}{2} \Gamma\left[\begin{matrix} s \\ -\nu, \frac{s+\nu+2}{2} \end{matrix}\right]$$

$$\times {}_2F_2\left(\begin{matrix} \frac{s}{2}, \frac{s+1}{2}; -\frac{a^2}{2b^2} \\ \frac{1}{2}, \frac{s+\nu+2}{2} \end{matrix}\right) + \frac{\pi a}{2^{(s+\nu+3)/2}b^{s+1}}$$

$$\times \sec\frac{(s+\nu)\pi}{2} \Gamma\left[\begin{matrix} s+1 \\ -\nu, \frac{s+\nu+3}{2} \end{matrix}\right] {}_2F_2\left(\begin{matrix} \frac{s+1}{2}, \frac{s+2}{2}; -\frac{a^2}{2b^2} \\ \frac{3}{2}, \frac{s+\nu+3}{2} \end{matrix}\right)$$

$$+ \frac{\pi b^\nu \csc[(s+\nu)\pi]}{a^{\nu+s}\Gamma(1-s-\nu)} {}_2F_2\left(\begin{matrix} -\frac{\nu}{2}, \frac{1-\nu}{2}; -\frac{a^2}{2b^2} \\ \frac{1-s-\nu}{2}, \frac{2-s-\nu}{2} \end{matrix}\right)$$

$$[\operatorname{Re}a,\ \operatorname{Re}s>0; |\arg b| < 3\pi/4]$$

9 $e^{-a/x+b^2x^2/4} D_\nu(bx)$

$$\frac{b^{-s}}{2^{(s+\nu+2)/2}} \Gamma\left[\begin{matrix} s, -\frac{s+\nu}{2} \\ -\nu \end{matrix}\right] {}_1F_3\left(\begin{matrix} -\frac{s+\nu}{2}; \frac{a^2b^2}{8} \\ \frac{1}{2}, \frac{1-s}{2}, \frac{2-s}{2} \end{matrix}\right)$$

$$- \frac{b^{-s}}{2^{(s+\nu+1)/2}} \Gamma\left[\begin{matrix} s-1, -\frac{s+\nu-1}{2} \\ -\nu \end{matrix}\right] {}_1F_3\left(\begin{matrix} -\frac{s+\nu-1}{2}; \frac{a^2b^2}{8} \\ \frac{3}{2}, \frac{2-s}{2}, \frac{3-s}{2} \end{matrix}\right)$$

$$- \sqrt{\pi}\, 2^{(\nu+1)/2} a^{s+1} b\, \Gamma\left[\begin{matrix} -s-1 \\ -\frac{\nu}{2} \end{matrix}\right] {}_1F_3\left(\begin{matrix} \frac{1-\nu}{2}; \frac{a^2b^2}{8} \\ \frac{3}{2}, \frac{s+2}{2}, \frac{s+3}{2} \end{matrix}\right)$$

$$+ \sqrt{\pi}\, 2^{\nu/2} a^s\, \Gamma\left[\begin{matrix} -s \\ \frac{1-\nu}{2} \end{matrix}\right] {}_1F_3\left(\begin{matrix} -\frac{\nu}{2}; \frac{a^2b^2}{8} \\ \frac{1}{2}, \frac{s+1}{2}, \frac{s+2}{2} \end{matrix}\right)$$

$$[\operatorname{Re}a>0;\ \operatorname{Re}(s+\nu)<0; |\arg b| < 3\pi/4]$$

No.	$f(x)$	$F(s)$
10	$e^{-a/x-b^2x^2/4}D_\nu(bx)$	$\dfrac{\sqrt{\pi}\,b^{-s}}{2^{(s-\nu)/2}}\Gamma\!\left[\begin{matrix}s\\\frac{s-\nu+1}{2}\end{matrix}\right]{}_1F_3\!\left(\begin{matrix}-\frac{s-\nu-1}{2};&-\frac{a^2b^2}{8}\\\frac{1}{2},\ \frac{1-s}{2},\ \frac{2-s}{2}\end{matrix}\right)$ $-\dfrac{\sqrt{\pi}\,ab^{1-s}}{2^{(s-\nu-1)/2}}\Gamma\!\left[\begin{matrix}s-1\\\frac{s-\nu}{2}\end{matrix}\right]{}_1F_3\!\left(\begin{matrix}-\frac{s-\nu-2}{2};&-\frac{a^2b^2}{8}\\\frac{3}{2},\ \frac{2-s}{2},\ \frac{3-s}{2}\end{matrix}\right)$ $-\sqrt{\pi}\,2^{(\nu+1)/2}a^{s+1}b\,\Gamma\!\left[\begin{matrix}-s-1\\-\frac{\nu}{2}\end{matrix}\right]{}_1F_3\!\left(\begin{matrix}\frac{\nu+2}{2};&-\frac{a^2b^2}{8}\\\frac{3}{2},\ \frac{s+2}{2},\ \frac{s+3}{2}\end{matrix}\right)$ $+\sqrt{\pi}\,2^{\nu/2}a^{s}\,\Gamma\!\left[\begin{matrix}-s\\\frac{1-\nu}{2}\end{matrix}\right]{}_1F_3\!\left(\begin{matrix}\frac{\nu+1}{2};&-\frac{a^2b^2}{8}\\\frac{1}{2},\ \frac{s+1}{2},\ \frac{s+2}{2}\end{matrix}\right)$ $[\operatorname{Re}a>0;\ \lvert\arg b\rvert<\pi/4]$
11	$e^{-a/x^2\pm b^2x^2/4}D_\nu(bx)$	$2^{\nu/2-1}\sqrt{\pi}\,a^{s/2}\Gamma\!\left[\begin{matrix}-\frac{s}{2}\\\frac{1-\nu}{2}\end{matrix}\right]{}_1F_2\!\left(\begin{matrix}\frac{\mp2\nu+1\mp1}{4}\\\frac{1}{2},\ \frac{s+2}{2};\ \mp\frac{ab^2}{2}\end{matrix}\right)$ $-2^{(\nu-1)/2}\sqrt{\pi}\,a^{(s+1)/2}b\,\Gamma\!\left[\begin{matrix}-\frac{s+1}{2}\\-\frac{\nu}{2}\end{matrix}\right]$ $\times{}_1F_2\!\left(\begin{matrix}\mp\frac{\nu}{2}+\frac{3\mp1}{4}\\\frac{3}{2},\ \frac{s+3}{2};\ \mp\frac{ab^2}{2}\end{matrix}\right)+\dfrac{2^{-(s\pm\nu)/2}\sqrt{\pi}\,b^{-s}}{[2\sqrt{\pi}\,\Gamma(-\nu)]^{(1\pm1)/2}}$ $\times\Gamma(s)\,\Gamma^{\pm1}\!\left(\frac{\mp2s-2\nu+1\mp1}{4}\right){}_1F_2\!\left(\begin{matrix}\frac{\mp2\nu-2s+1\mp1}{4}\\\frac{1-s}{2},\ \frac{2-s}{2};\ \mp\frac{ab^2}{2}\end{matrix}\right)$ $\left[\left\{\begin{matrix}\operatorname{Re}a>0;\ \operatorname{Re}(s+\nu)<0\\\operatorname{Re}a>0\end{matrix}\right\};\ \lvert\arg b\rvert<(2\pm1)\pi/4\right]$
12	$e^{\pm b^2x^2/4}\sin(ax)\,D_\nu(bx)$	$\dfrac{2^{(\nu-s-1)/2}a\sqrt{\pi}}{b^{s+1}}\left[2^{\nu+1}\sqrt{\pi}\,\Gamma(-\nu)\right]^{-(1\pm1)/2}\Gamma(s+1)$ $\times\Gamma^{\pm1}\!\left(\frac{-2\nu\mp2s\mp3+1}{4}\right){}_2F_2\!\left(\begin{matrix}\frac{s+1}{2},\ \frac{s+2}{2};\ \pm\frac{a^2}{2b^2}\\\frac{3}{2},\ \frac{2s\pm2\nu+5\pm1}{4}\end{matrix}\right)$ $+\dfrac{1\pm1}{2a^{s+\nu}}b^\nu\sin\frac{(s+\nu)\pi}{2}\,\Gamma(s+\nu)\,{}_2F_2\!\left(\begin{matrix}-\frac{\nu}{2},\ \frac{1-\nu}{2};\ \frac{a^2}{2b^2}\\\frac{1-s-\nu}{2},\ \frac{2-\nu-s}{2}\end{matrix}\right)$ $\left[a>0;\left\{\begin{matrix}-1<\operatorname{Re}s<1-\operatorname{Re}\nu\\\operatorname{Re}s>-1\end{matrix}\right\};\ \lvert\arg b\rvert<(2\pm1)\pi/4\right]$
13	$e^{\pm b^2x^2/4}\cos(ax)$ $\times D_\nu(bx)$	$\dfrac{2^{(\nu-s)/2}\sqrt{\pi}}{b^{s}}\left[2^{\nu+1}\sqrt{\pi}\,\Gamma(-\nu)\right]^{-(1\pm1)/2}\Gamma(s)$ $\times\Gamma^{\pm1}\!\left(\frac{-2\nu\mp2s\mp1+1}{4}\right){}_2F_2\!\left(\begin{matrix}\frac{s}{2},\ \frac{s+1}{2};\ \pm\frac{a^2}{2b^2}\\\frac{1}{2},\ \frac{2s\pm2\nu+3\pm1}{4}\end{matrix}\right)$ $+\dfrac{1\pm1}{2a^{s+\nu}}b^\nu\cos\frac{(s+\nu)\pi}{2}\,\Gamma(s+\nu)\,{}_2F_2\!\left(\begin{matrix}-\frac{\nu}{2},\ \frac{1-\nu}{2};\ \frac{a^2}{2b^2}\\\frac{1-s-\nu}{2},\ \frac{2-\nu-s}{2}\end{matrix}\right)$ $\left[a>0;\left\{\begin{matrix}0<\operatorname{Re}s<1-\operatorname{Re}\nu\\\operatorname{Re}s>0\end{matrix}\right\};\ \lvert\arg b\rvert<(2\pm1)\pi/4\right]$

No.	$f(x)$	$F(s)$

14 $e^{b^2 x^2/4}\sin\left(ax^2\right)D_\nu\left(bx\right)$

$$\frac{\pi a}{2^{(s+\nu+4)/2}b^{s+2}}\csc\frac{(s+\nu)\pi}{2}\,\Gamma\left[\begin{matrix}s+2\\-\nu,\ \frac{s+\nu+4}{2}\end{matrix}\right]$$

$$\times\,{}_4F_3\left(\begin{matrix}\frac{s+2}{4},\ \frac{s+3}{4},\ \frac{s+4}{4},\ \frac{s+5}{4}\\\frac{3}{2},\ \frac{s+\nu+4}{4},\ \frac{s+\nu+6}{4}\end{matrix};\ -\frac{4a^2}{b^4}\right)+\frac{(\nu-1)\nu\,b^{\nu-2}}{4a^{(s+\nu-2)/2}}\cos\frac{(s+\nu)\pi}{4}$$

$$\times\,\Gamma\left(\frac{s+\nu-2}{2}\right){}_4F_3\left(\begin{matrix}\frac{2-\nu}{4},\ \frac{3-\nu}{4},\ \frac{4-\nu}{4},\ \frac{5-\nu}{4}\\\frac{3}{2},\ -\frac{s+\nu-4}{4},\ -\frac{s+\nu-6}{4}\end{matrix};\ -\frac{4a^2}{b^4}\right)$$

$$+\frac{\pi a^{-(s+\nu)/2}b^\nu}{4\,\Gamma\left(-\frac{s+\nu-2}{2}\right)}\sec\frac{(s+\nu)\pi}{4}\,{}_4F_3\left(\begin{matrix}-\frac{\nu}{4},\ \frac{1-\nu}{4},\ \frac{2-\nu}{4},\ \frac{3-\nu}{4}\\\frac{1}{2},\ -\frac{s+\nu-2}{4},\ -\frac{s+\nu-4}{4}\end{matrix};\ -\frac{4a^2}{b^4}\right)$$

$$[a>0;\ -2<\operatorname{Re}s<2-\operatorname{Re}\nu;\ |\arg b|<3\pi/4]$$

15 $e^{b^2 x^2/4}\cos\left(ax^2\right)D_\nu\left(bx\right)$

$$-\frac{\pi}{2^{(s+\nu+2)/2}b^s}\csc\frac{(s+\nu)\pi}{2}\,\Gamma\left[\begin{matrix}s\\-\nu,\ \frac{s+\nu+2}{2}\end{matrix}\right]$$

$$\times\,{}_4F_3\left(\begin{matrix}\frac{s}{4},\ \frac{s+1}{4},\ \frac{s+2}{4},\ \frac{s+3}{4}\\\frac{1}{2},\ \frac{s+\nu+2}{4},\ \frac{s+\nu+4}{4}\end{matrix};\ -\frac{4a^2}{b^4}\right)+\frac{(\nu-1)\nu\pi b^{\nu-2}}{8a^{(s+\nu-2)/2}\,\Gamma\left(-\frac{s+\nu-4}{2}\right)}$$

$$\times\,\sec\frac{(s+\nu)\pi}{4}\,{}_4F_3\left(\begin{matrix}\frac{2-\nu}{4},\ \frac{3-\nu}{4},\ \frac{4-\nu}{4},\ \frac{5-\nu}{4}\\\frac{3}{2},\ -\frac{s+\nu-4}{4},\ -\frac{s+\nu-6}{4}\end{matrix};\ -\frac{4a^2}{b^4}\right)$$

$$+\frac{b^\nu}{2a^{(s+\nu)/2}}\cos\frac{(s+\nu)\pi}{4}\,\Gamma\left(\frac{s+\nu}{2}\right)$$

$$\times\,{}_4F_3\left(\begin{matrix}-\frac{\nu}{4},\ \frac{1-\nu}{4},\ \frac{2-\nu}{4},\ \frac{3-\nu}{4}\\\frac{1}{2},\ -\frac{s+\nu-2}{4},\ -\frac{s+\nu-4}{4}\end{matrix};\ -\frac{4a^2}{b^4}\right)$$

$$[a>0;\ 0<\operatorname{Re}s<2-\operatorname{Re}\nu;\ |\arg b|<3\pi/4]$$

16 $e^{-b^2 x^2/4}\left\{\begin{matrix}\sin\left(ax^2\right)\\\cos\left(ax^2\right)\end{matrix}\right\}$

$$\frac{\sqrt{\pi}\,a^\delta b^{-s-2\delta}}{2^{(s-\nu+2\delta)/2}}\,\Gamma\left[\begin{matrix}s+2\delta\\\frac{s-\nu+2\delta+1}{2}\end{matrix}\right]{}_4F_3\left(\begin{matrix}\frac{s+2\delta}{4},\ \frac{s+2\delta+1}{4},\ \frac{s+2\delta+2}{4},\ \frac{s+2\delta+3}{4}\\\frac{2\delta+1}{2},\ \frac{s-\nu+2\delta+1}{4},\ \frac{s-\nu+2\delta+3}{4}\end{matrix};\ -\frac{4a^2}{b^4}\right)$$

$\times\,D_\nu\left(bx\right)$

$$[a>0;\ \operatorname{Re}s>-2\delta;\ |\arg b|<\pi/4]$$

3.9.2. $D_\nu\left(bx\right)$ **and** $\operatorname{erf}\left(ax\right),\ \operatorname{erfc}\left(ax\right)$

1 $e^{\pm b^2 x^2/4}\operatorname{erf}\left(ax\right)D_\nu\left(bx\right)$

$$\frac{2^{(\nu-s+1)/2}a}{b^{s+1}\left[2^{\nu+1}\sqrt{\pi}\,\Gamma\left(-\nu\right)\right]^{(1\pm1)/2}}\,\Gamma\left(s+1\right)$$

$$\times\,\Gamma^{\pm1}\left(\frac{1\mp2s-2\nu\mp3}{4}\right){}_3F_2\left(\begin{matrix}\frac{1}{2},\ \frac{s+1}{2},\ \frac{s+2}{2};\ \pm\frac{2a^2}{b^2}\\\frac{3}{2},\ \frac{2s\pm2\nu+5\pm1}{4}\end{matrix}\right)$$

$$-\frac{(1\pm1)\,a^{-s-\nu}b^\nu}{2\sqrt{\pi}\,(s+\nu)}\,\Gamma\left(\frac{s+\nu+1}{2}\right){}_3F_2\left(\begin{matrix}-\frac{\nu}{2},\ \frac{1-\nu}{2},\ -\frac{s+\nu}{2}\\\frac{2-s-\nu}{2},\ \frac{1-s-\nu}{2};\ \frac{2a^2}{b^2}\end{matrix}\right)$$

$$\left[\operatorname{Re}a>0;\ \left\{\begin{matrix}-1<\operatorname{Re}s<-\operatorname{Re}\nu\\\operatorname{Re}s>-1\end{matrix}\right\};\ |\arg b|<(2\pm1)\pi/4\right]$$

No.	$f(x)$	$F(s)$
2	$e^{\pm b^2 x^2/4}\operatorname{erfc}(ax)$ $\times\, D_\nu(bx)$	$\dfrac{2^{\nu/2}a^{-s}}{s}\,\Gamma\!\left[\begin{array}{c}\frac{s+1}{2}\\[2pt]\frac{1-\nu}{2}\end{array}\right]{}_3F_2\!\left(\begin{array}{c}\frac{1\mp1\mp2\nu}{4},\,\frac{s}{2},\,\frac{s+1}{2}\\[2pt]\frac{1}{2},\,\frac{s+2}{2};\,\pm\frac{b^2}{2a^2}\end{array}\right)$ $-\dfrac{2^{(\nu+1)/2}a^{-s-1}b}{s+1}\,\Gamma\!\left[\begin{array}{c}\frac{s+2}{2}\\[2pt]-\frac{\nu}{2}\end{array}\right]{}_3F_2\!\left(\begin{array}{c}\frac{3\mp1\mp2\nu}{4},\,\frac{s+1}{2},\,\frac{s+2}{2}\\[2pt]\frac{3}{2},\,\frac{s+3}{2};\,\pm\frac{b^2}{2a^2}\end{array}\right)$ $[\operatorname{Re}s>0;\ |\arg a|<\pi/4;\ |\arg b|<(2\pm1)\pi/4]$
3	$e^{-b^2 x^2/4}\operatorname{erfc}(ax)$ $\times\,[D_\nu(-bx)-D_\nu(bx)]$	$-\dfrac{2^{(\nu+3)/2}b}{\pi\,a^{s+1}(s+1)}\sin\dfrac{\nu\pi}{2}\,\Gamma\!\left(\dfrac{\nu+2}{2}\right)\Gamma\!\left(\dfrac{s+2}{2}\right){}_3F_2\!\left(\begin{array}{c}\frac{\nu+2}{2},\,\frac{s+1}{2},\,\frac{s+2}{2}\\[2pt]\frac{3}{2},\,\frac{s+3}{2};\,-\frac{b^2}{2a^2}\end{array}\right)$ $[\operatorname{Re}s,\ \operatorname{Re}(2a^2+b^2)>0;\ |\arg a|<\pi/4]$

3.9.3.   Products of $D_\mu(bx^r)$

No.	$f(x)$	$F(s)$
1	$D_{-\nu-1}(ax)\,D_\nu(ax)$	$\dfrac{\pi}{2^{s+1/2}a^s}\,\Gamma\!\left[\begin{array}{c}s\\[2pt]\frac{s-2\nu+2}{4},\,\frac{s+2\nu+4}{4}\end{array}\right]$ $[\operatorname{Re}s>0;\ |\arg a|<\pi/4]$
2	$D_\nu\!\left(e^{\pi i/4}ax\right)D_\nu\!\left(\dfrac{ax}{e^{\pi i/4}}\right)$	$\dfrac{\sqrt{\pi}}{2^{s+1}a^s}\,\Gamma\!\left[\begin{array}{c}s,\,-\frac{s+2\nu}{4}\\[2pt]-\nu,\,\frac{s-2\nu+2}{4}\end{array}\right]$ $[\operatorname{Re}a>0;\ 0<\operatorname{Re}s<-2\operatorname{Re}\nu]$
3	$e^{(a^2+b^2)x^2/4}D_\mu(ax)$ $\times\,D_\nu(bx)$	$\dfrac{\sqrt{\pi}}{2^{(s+\mu-\nu)/2+1}a^s}\,\Gamma\!\left[\begin{array}{c}s,\,-\frac{s+\mu}{2}\\[2pt]-\mu,\,\frac{1-\nu}{2}\end{array}\right]{}_3F_2\!\left(\begin{array}{c}-\frac{\nu}{2},\,\frac{s}{2},\,\frac{s+1}{2}\\[2pt]\frac{1}{2},\,\frac{s+\mu+2}{2};\,-\frac{b^2}{a^2}\end{array}\right)$ $-\dfrac{\sqrt{\pi}\,b}{2^{(s+\mu-\nu)/2+1}a^{s+1}}\,\Gamma\!\left[\begin{array}{c}s+1,\,-\frac{s+\mu+1}{2}\\[2pt]-\mu,\,-\frac{\nu}{2}\end{array}\right]{}_3F_2\!\left(\begin{array}{c}\frac{1-\nu}{2},\,\frac{s+1}{2},\,\frac{s+2}{2}\\[2pt]\frac{3}{2},\,\frac{s+\mu+3}{2};\,-\frac{b^2}{a^2}\end{array}\right)$ $+\dfrac{a^\mu}{2^{(s+\mu+\nu)/2+1}b^{s+\mu}}\,\Gamma\!\left[\begin{array}{c}s+\mu,\,-\frac{s+\mu+\nu}{2}\\[2pt]-\nu\end{array}\right]{}_3F_2\!\left(\begin{array}{c}-\frac{\mu}{2},\,\frac{1-\mu}{2},\,-\frac{s+\mu+\nu}{2}\\[2pt]\frac{1-s-\mu}{2},\,\frac{2-s-\mu}{2};\,-\frac{b^2}{a^2}\end{array}\right)$ $[0<\operatorname{Re}s<-\operatorname{Re}(\mu+\nu);\ |\arg a|,\,|\arg b|<3\pi/4]$
4	$e^{(a^2-b^2)x^2/4}D_\mu(ax)$ $\times\,D_\nu(bx)$	$\dfrac{\pi}{2^{(s-\mu-\nu)/2}b^s}\,\Gamma\!\left[\begin{array}{c}s\\[2pt]\frac{1-\mu}{2},\,\frac{s-\nu+1}{2}\end{array}\right]{}_3F_2\!\left(\begin{array}{c}-\frac{\mu}{2},\,\frac{s}{2},\,\frac{s+1}{2}\\[2pt]\frac{1}{2},\,\frac{s-\nu+1}{2};\,\frac{a^2}{b^2}\end{array}\right)$ $-\dfrac{\pi a}{2^{(s-\mu-\nu)/2}b^{s+1}}\,\Gamma\!\left[\begin{array}{c}s+1\\[2pt]-\frac{\mu}{2},\,\frac{s-\nu+2}{2}\end{array}\right]{}_3F_2\!\left(\begin{array}{c}\frac{1-\mu}{2},\,\frac{s+1}{2},\,\frac{s+2}{2}\\[2pt]\frac{3}{2},\,\frac{s-\nu+2}{2};\,\frac{a^2}{b^2}\end{array}\right)$ $[\operatorname{Re}s>0;\ |\arg a|<3\pi/4,\,|\arg b|<\pi/4]$
5	$e^{-(a^2+b^2)x^2/4}D_\mu(ax)$ $\times\,D_\nu(bx)$	$\dfrac{\pi}{2^{(s-\mu-\nu)/2}a^s}\,\Gamma\!\left[\begin{array}{c}s\\[2pt]\frac{1-\nu}{2},\,\frac{s-\mu+1}{2}\end{array}\right]{}_3F_2\!\left(\begin{array}{c}\frac{\nu+1}{2},\,\frac{s}{2},\,\frac{s+1}{2}\\[2pt]\frac{1}{2},\,\frac{s-\mu+1}{2};\,-\frac{b^2}{a^2}\end{array}\right)$ $-\dfrac{\pi b}{2^{(s-\mu-\nu)/2}a^{s+1}}\,\Gamma\!\left[\begin{array}{c}s+1\\[2pt]-\frac{\nu}{2},\,\frac{s-\mu+2}{2}\end{array}\right]{}_3F_2\!\left(\begin{array}{c}\frac{\nu+2}{2},\,\frac{s+1}{2},\,\frac{s+2}{2}\\[2pt]\frac{3}{2},\,\frac{s-\mu+2}{2};\,-\frac{b^2}{a^2}\end{array}\right)$ $[\operatorname{Re}s>0;\ |\arg a|,\,|\arg b|<\pi/4]$

3.10. The Bessel Function $J_\nu(z)$

More formulas can be obtained from the corresponding sections due to the relations

$$J_{\pm 1/2}(z) = \sqrt{\frac{2}{\pi}} \frac{1}{\sqrt{z}} \left\{ \begin{matrix} \sin z \\ \cos z \end{matrix} \right\}, \quad J_{\pm 3/2}(z) = \sqrt{\frac{2}{\pi}} \frac{1}{z^{3/2}} \left[\pm \left\{ \begin{matrix} \sin z \\ \cos z \end{matrix} \right\} - z \left\{ \begin{matrix} \cos z \\ \sin z \end{matrix} \right\} \right];$$

$$J_\nu(z) = \frac{1}{\sin(\nu\pi)} \left[Y_{-\nu}(z) - Y_\nu(z) \cos(\nu\pi) \right], \quad [\nu \neq 0, \pm 1, \pm 2, \dots];$$

$$J_\nu(z) = \frac{1}{2} \left[H_\nu^{(1)}(z) + H_\nu^{(2)}(z) \right], \quad J_\nu(z) = \frac{z^\nu}{(iz)^\nu} I_\nu(iz),$$

$$J_\nu(z) = \frac{(z/2)^\nu}{\Gamma(\nu+1)} \, {}_0F_1\left(\nu+1; -\frac{z^2}{4}\right), \quad J_\nu(z) = z^\nu \left(z^2\right)^{-\nu/2} G_{02}^{10}\left(\frac{z^2}{4} \left|\begin{matrix} \cdot \\ \nu/2, -\nu/2 \end{matrix}\right.\right),$$

$$J_\nu(z) = \pi \left(\frac{z}{2}\right)^\nu G_{13}^{10}\left(-\frac{z^2}{4} \left|\begin{matrix} 1/2 \\ 0, -\nu, 1/2 \end{matrix}\right.\right),$$

$$J_\nu(z) = \pi z^\nu \left(-z^2\right)^{-\nu/2} G_{13}^{10}\left(-\frac{z^2}{4} \left|\begin{matrix} (\nu+1)/2 \\ \nu/2, -\nu/2, (\nu+1)/2 \end{matrix}\right.\right).$$

3.10.1. $J_\nu(bx)$ and algebraic functions

No.	$f(x)$	$F(s)$
1	$1 - J_0(ax)$	$-\dfrac{2^{s-1}}{a^s} \Gamma\left[\begin{matrix} \frac{s+2}{2} \\ \frac{2-s}{2} \end{matrix}\right] \qquad\qquad\qquad [a > 0;\ -2 < \operatorname{Re} s < 0]$
2	$J_\nu(ax)$	$\dfrac{2^{s-1}}{a^s} \Gamma\left[\begin{matrix} \frac{s+\nu}{2} \\ \frac{2-s+\nu}{2} \end{matrix}\right] \qquad\qquad\qquad [a > 0;\ -\operatorname{Re}\nu < \operatorname{Re} s < 3/2]$
3	$J_\nu(ax) - \dfrac{2^{-\nu}(ax)^\nu}{\Gamma(\nu+1)}$	$-\dfrac{2^{s-1}}{a^s} \Gamma\left[\begin{matrix} -\frac{s+\nu}{2}, \frac{s+\nu+2}{2} \\ \frac{2-s-\nu}{2}, \frac{2-s+\nu}{2} \end{matrix}\right] \; [a > 0;\ -\operatorname{Re}\nu - 2 < \operatorname{Re} s < 3/2, -\operatorname{Re}\nu]$
4	$J_\nu(ax) \pm J_{-\nu}(ax)$	$\pm \dfrac{1}{\pi} \left(\dfrac{2}{a}\right)^s \left\{\begin{matrix} \cos(\nu\pi/2)\sin(s\pi/2) \\ \sin(\nu\pi/2)\cos(s\pi/2) \end{matrix}\right\} \Gamma\left(\dfrac{s-\nu}{2}\right) \Gamma\left(\dfrac{s+\nu}{2}\right)$ $[a > 0;\ |\operatorname{Re}\nu| < \operatorname{Re} s < 3/2]$
5	$(a-x)_+^{\alpha-1} J_\nu(bx)$	$a^{s+\alpha+\nu-1} \left(\dfrac{b}{2}\right)^\nu \Gamma\left[\begin{matrix} \alpha, s+\nu \\ \nu+1, s+\alpha+\nu \end{matrix}\right]$ $\times \, {}_2F_3\left(\begin{matrix} \frac{s+\nu}{2}, \frac{s+\nu+1}{2}; -\frac{ab^2}{4} \\ \nu+1, \frac{s+\alpha+\nu}{2}, \frac{s+\alpha+\nu+1}{2} \end{matrix}\right)$ $[a,\ \operatorname{Re}\alpha,\ \operatorname{Re}(s+\nu) > 0]$
6	$(a^2-x^2)_+^{\alpha-1} J_\nu(bx)$	$\dfrac{a^{s+2\alpha+\nu-2} b^\nu}{2^{\nu+1}} \Gamma\left[\begin{matrix} \alpha, \frac{s+\nu}{2} \\ \nu+1, \frac{s+2\alpha+\nu}{2} \end{matrix}\right] {}_1F_2\left(\begin{matrix} \frac{s+\nu}{2}; -\frac{a^2 b^2}{4} \\ \nu+1, \frac{s+2\alpha+\nu}{2} \end{matrix}\right)$ $[a,\ \operatorname{Re}\alpha,\ \operatorname{Re}(s+\nu) > 0]$

No.	$f(x)$	$F(s)$
7	$\dfrac{1}{(x+a)^\rho} J_\nu(bx)$	$a^{s+\nu-\rho}\left(\dfrac{b}{2}\right)^\nu \Gamma\left[\begin{matrix} s+\nu,\ \rho-\nu-s \\ \nu+1,\ \rho \end{matrix}\right] {}_2F_3\left(\begin{matrix} \frac{s+\nu}{2},\ \frac{s+\nu+1}{2};\ -\frac{a^2b^2}{4} \\ \nu+1,\ \frac{s+\nu-\rho+1}{2},\ \frac{s+\nu-\rho+2}{2} \end{matrix}\right)$ $+\dfrac{2^{s-\rho-1}}{b^{s-\rho}}\Gamma\left[\begin{matrix} \frac{s-\rho+\nu}{2} \\ \frac{2-s+\nu+\rho}{2} \end{matrix}\right] {}_2F_3\left(\begin{matrix} \frac{\rho}{2},\ \frac{\rho+1}{2};\ -\frac{a^2b^2}{4} \\ \frac{1}{2},\ \frac{2-s-\nu+\rho}{2},\ \frac{2-s+\nu+\rho}{2} \end{matrix}\right)$ $-\dfrac{\rho\, a 2^{s-\rho-2}}{b^{s-\rho-1}}\Gamma\left[\begin{matrix} \frac{s+\nu-\rho-1}{2} \\ \frac{3-s+\nu+\rho}{2} \end{matrix}\right] {}_2F_3\left(\begin{matrix} \frac{\rho+1}{2},\ \frac{\rho+2}{2};\ -\frac{a^2b^2}{4} \\ \frac{3}{2},\ \frac{3-s-\nu+\rho}{2},\ \frac{3-s+\nu+\rho}{2} \end{matrix}\right)$ $[b>0;\ -\operatorname{Re}\nu<\operatorname{Re}s<\operatorname{Re}\rho+3/2;\ |\arg a|<\pi]$
8	$\dfrac{1}{x+a} J_\nu(bx)$	$2^{s-2}b^{-s+1}\Gamma\left[\begin{matrix} \frac{s+\nu-1}{2} \\ -\frac{s-\nu-3}{2} \end{matrix}\right] {}_1F_2\left(\begin{matrix} 1;\ -\frac{a^2b^2}{4} \\ -\frac{s-\nu-3}{2},\ -\frac{s+\nu-3}{2} \end{matrix}\right)$ $-2^{s-3}ab^{2-s}\Gamma\left[\begin{matrix} \frac{s+\nu-2}{2} \\ -\frac{s-\nu-4}{2} \end{matrix}\right] {}_1F_2\left(\begin{matrix} 1;\ -\frac{a^2b^2}{4} \\ -\frac{s-\nu-4}{2},\ -\frac{s+\nu-4}{2} \end{matrix}\right)$ $+\pi a^{s-1}\csc[(s+\nu)\pi]J_\nu(ab)$ $[b>0;\ -\operatorname{Re}\nu<\operatorname{Re}s<5/2;\ |\arg a|<\pi]$
9	$\dfrac{1}{x-a} J_\nu(bx)$	$\dfrac{2^{s-2}}{b^{s-1}}\Gamma\left[\begin{matrix} \frac{s+\nu-1}{2} \\ \frac{3-s+\nu}{2} \end{matrix}\right] {}_1F_2\left(\begin{matrix} 1;\ -\frac{a^2b^2}{4} \\ \frac{3-s-\nu}{2},\ \frac{3-s+\nu}{2} \end{matrix}\right)$ $+\dfrac{2^{s-3}a}{b^{s-2}}\Gamma\left[\begin{matrix} \frac{s+\nu-2}{2} \\ \frac{4-s+\nu}{2} \end{matrix}\right] {}_1F_2\left(\begin{matrix} 1;\ -\frac{a^2b^2}{4} \\ \frac{4-s-\nu}{2},\ \frac{4-s+\nu}{2} \end{matrix}\right)$ $-\pi a^{s-1}\cot[(s+\nu)\pi]J_\nu(ab)$ $[a,b>0;\ -\operatorname{Re}\nu<\operatorname{Re}s<5/2]$
10	$\dfrac{1}{(x^2+a^2)^\rho} J_\nu(bx)$	$\dfrac{a^{s+\nu-2\rho}b^\nu}{2^{\nu+1}}\Gamma\left[\begin{matrix} \frac{s+\nu}{2},\ \frac{2\rho-\nu-s}{2} \\ \nu+1,\ \rho \end{matrix}\right] {}_1F_2\left(\begin{matrix} \frac{s+\nu}{2};\ \frac{a^2b^2}{4} \\ \nu+1,\ \frac{s+\nu-2\rho+2}{2} \end{matrix}\right)$ $+\dfrac{2^{s-2\rho-1}}{b^{s-2\rho}}\Gamma\left[\begin{matrix} \frac{s+\nu-2\rho}{2} \\ \frac{2-s+\nu+2\rho}{2} \end{matrix}\right] {}_1F_2\left(\begin{matrix} \rho;\ \frac{a^2b^2}{4} \\ \frac{2-s-\nu+2\rho}{2},\ \frac{2-s+\nu+2\rho}{2} \end{matrix}\right)$ $[\operatorname{Re}a,b>0;\ -\operatorname{Re}\nu<\operatorname{Re}s<2\operatorname{Re}\rho+3/2]$
11	$\dfrac{1}{x^2+a^2} J_\nu(bx)$	$2^{s-3}b^{2-s}\Gamma\left[\begin{matrix} \frac{s+\nu-2}{2} \\ \frac{4-s+\nu}{2} \end{matrix}\right] {}_1F_2\left(\begin{matrix} 1;\ \frac{a^2b^2}{4} \\ \frac{4-s-\nu}{2},\ \frac{4-s+\nu}{2} \end{matrix}\right)$ $+\dfrac{\pi a^{s-2}}{2}\csc\dfrac{(s+\nu)\pi}{2}I_\nu(ab)$ $[\operatorname{Re}a,b>0;\ -\operatorname{Re}\nu<\operatorname{Re}s<7/2]$
12	$\dfrac{1}{x^2-a^2} J_\nu(bx)$	$\dfrac{2^{s-3}}{b^{s-2}}\Gamma\left[\begin{matrix} \frac{s+\nu-2}{2} \\ \frac{4-s+\nu}{2} \end{matrix}\right] {}_1F_2\left(\begin{matrix} 1;\ -\frac{a^2c^2}{4} \\ \frac{4-s-\nu}{2},\ \frac{4-s+\nu}{2} \end{matrix}\right) - \dfrac{\pi a^{s-2}}{2}\cot\dfrac{(s+\nu)\pi}{2}J_\nu(ab)$ $[a,b>0;\ -\operatorname{Re}\nu<\operatorname{Re}s<7/2]$

No.	$f(x)$	$F(s)$

13 $\dfrac{1}{(x^4+a^4)^\rho}\,J_\nu(bx)$

$$\frac{2^{s-4\rho-1}}{b^{s-4\rho}}\,\Gamma\left[\begin{array}{c}\frac{s+\nu-4\rho}{2}\\\frac{2-s+\nu+4\rho}{2}\end{array}\right]$$

$$\times\,_1F_4\left(\begin{array}{c}\rho;\ -\frac{a^4b^4}{256}\\\frac{4-s-\nu+4\rho}{4},\ -\frac{s+\nu-4\rho-1}{4},\ \frac{2-s+\nu+4\rho}{4},\ \frac{4-s+\nu+4\rho}{4}\end{array}\right)$$

$$-\frac{a^{s+\nu-4\rho+2}b^{\nu+2}}{2^{\nu+4}}\,\Gamma\left[\begin{array}{c}\frac{s+\nu+2}{4},\ \rho-\frac{s+\nu+2}{4}\\\nu+2,\ \rho\end{array}\right]$$

$$\times\,_1F_4\left(\begin{array}{c}\frac{s+\nu+2}{4};\ -\frac{a^4b^4}{256}\\\frac{3}{2},\ \frac{\nu+2}{2},\ \frac{\nu+3}{2},\ \frac{s+\nu-4\rho+3}{4}\end{array}\right)$$

$$+\frac{a^{s+\nu-4\rho}b^\nu}{2^{\nu+2}}\,\Gamma\left[\begin{array}{c}\frac{s+\nu}{4},\ \rho-\frac{s+\nu}{4}\\\nu+1,\ \rho\end{array}\right]\,_1F_4\left(\begin{array}{c}\frac{s+\nu}{4};\ -\frac{a^4b^4}{256}\\\frac{1}{2},\ \frac{\nu+1}{2},\ \frac{\nu+2}{2},\ \frac{s+\nu-4\rho+4}{4}\end{array}\right)$$

$$[b>0;\ -\operatorname{Re}\nu<\operatorname{Re}s<4\operatorname{Re}\rho+3/2;\ |\arg a|<\pi/4]$$

14 $\dfrac{1}{x^4-a^4}\,J_\nu(bx)$

$$\frac{2^{s-5}}{b^{s-4}}\,\Gamma\left[\begin{array}{c}\frac{s+\nu-4}{2}\\\frac{6-s+\nu}{2}\end{array}\right]\,_1F_4\left(\begin{array}{c}1;\ \frac{a^4b^4}{256}\\\frac{8-s-\nu}{4},\ \frac{8-s+\nu}{4},\ \frac{6-s-\nu}{4},\ \frac{6-s+\nu}{4}\end{array}\right)$$

$$-\frac{\pi a^{s+\nu-2}b^{\nu+2}}{2^{\nu+4}\Gamma(\nu+2)}\,\tan\frac{(s+\nu)\pi}{4}\,_0F_3\left(\begin{array}{c}\frac{a^4b^4}{256}\\\frac{3}{2},\ \frac{\nu+2}{2},\ \frac{\nu+3}{2}\end{array}\right)$$

$$-\frac{\pi a^{s+\nu-4}b^\nu}{2^{\nu+2}\Gamma(\nu+1)}\,\cot\frac{(s+\nu)\pi}{4}\,_0F_3\left(\begin{array}{c}\frac{a^4b^4}{256}\\\frac{1}{2},\ \frac{\nu+1}{2},\ \frac{\nu+2}{2}\end{array}\right)$$

$$[a,\,b>0;\ -\operatorname{Re}\nu<\operatorname{Re}s<11/2]$$

15 $\left(\sqrt{x^2+a^2}+a\right)^\rho J_\nu(bx)$

$$\frac{2^{s+\rho-1}}{b^{s+\rho}}\,\Gamma\left[\begin{array}{c}\frac{s+\rho+\nu}{2}\\\frac{2-s+\nu-\rho}{2}\end{array}\right]\,_2F_3\left(\begin{array}{c}-\frac{\rho}{2},\ \frac{\rho}{2};\ \frac{a^2b^2}{4}\\\frac{1}{2},\ \frac{2-s-\nu-\rho}{2},\ \frac{2-s+\nu-\rho}{2}\end{array}\right)$$

$$+\frac{2^{s+\rho-2}\rho a}{b^{s+\rho-1}}\,\Gamma\left[\begin{array}{c}\frac{s+\rho+\nu-1}{2}\\\frac{3-s+\nu-\rho}{2}\end{array}\right]\,_2F_3\left(\begin{array}{c}\frac{1-\rho}{2},\ \frac{1+\rho}{2};\ \frac{a^2b^2}{4}\\\frac{3}{2},\ \frac{3-s-\nu-\rho}{2},\ \frac{3-s+\nu-\rho}{2}\end{array}\right)$$

$$-2^{s+\rho-1}\rho a^{s+\rho+\nu}b^\nu\,\Gamma\left[\begin{array}{c}-s-\rho-\nu,\ \frac{s+\nu}{2}\\\nu+1,\ 1-\frac{s+2\rho+\nu}{2}\end{array}\right]$$

$$\times\,_2F_3\left(\begin{array}{c}\frac{s+\nu}{2},\ \frac{s+2\rho+\nu}{2};\ \frac{a^2b^2}{4}\\\nu+1,\ \frac{s+\rho+\nu+1}{2},\ \frac{s+\rho+\nu+2}{2}\end{array}\right)$$

$$[b,\ \operatorname{Re}a>0;\ -\operatorname{Re}\nu<\operatorname{Re}s<-\operatorname{Re}\rho+3/2]$$

16 $\dfrac{\left(\sqrt{x^2+a^2}+a\right)^\rho}{\sqrt{x^2+a^2}}\,J_\nu(bx)$

$$\frac{2^{s+\rho-2}}{b^{s+\rho-1}}\,\Gamma\left[\begin{array}{c}\frac{s+\nu+\rho-1}{2}\\\frac{3-s+\nu-\rho}{2}\end{array}\right]\,_2F_3\left(\begin{array}{c}\frac{1-\rho}{2},\ \frac{1+\rho}{2};\ \frac{a^2b^2}{4}\\\frac{1}{2},\ \frac{3-s-\nu-\rho}{2},\ \frac{3-s+\nu-\rho}{2}\end{array}\right)$$

$$+\frac{2^{s+\rho-3}\rho a}{b^{s+\rho-2}}\,\Gamma\left[\begin{array}{c}\frac{s+\nu+\rho-2}{2}\\\frac{4-s+\nu-\rho}{2}\end{array}\right]\,_2F_3\left(\begin{array}{c}\frac{2-\rho}{2},\ \frac{2+\rho}{2};\ \frac{a^2b^2}{4}\\\frac{3}{2},\ \frac{4-s-\nu-\rho}{2},\ \frac{4-s+\nu-\rho}{2}\end{array}\right)$$

$$+2^{s+\rho-1}a^{s+\rho+\nu-1}b^\nu\,\Gamma\left[\begin{array}{c}1-s-\nu-\rho,\ \frac{s+\nu}{2}\\\nu+1,\ 1-\frac{s+\nu+2\rho}{2}\end{array}\right]$$

$$\times\,_2F_3\left(\begin{array}{c}\frac{s+\nu}{2},\ \frac{s+2\rho+\nu}{2};\ \frac{a^2b^2}{4}\\\nu+1,\ \frac{s+\nu+\rho}{2},\ \frac{s+\nu+\rho+1}{2}\end{array}\right)$$

$$[b,\ \operatorname{Re}a>0;\ -\operatorname{Re}\nu<\operatorname{Re}s<5/2-\operatorname{Re}\rho]$$

No.	$f(x)$	$F(s)$
17	$\left(\sqrt{x^2+a^2}\pm x\right)^\rho J_\nu(bx)$	$\dfrac{2^{s\pm2\rho-1}a^{\rho\mp\rho}}{b^{s\pm\rho}}\Gamma\!\left[\begin{matrix}\frac{s+\nu\pm\rho}{2}\\\frac{2-s+\nu\mp\rho}{2}\end{matrix}\right]{}_2F_3\!\left(\begin{matrix}\mp\frac{\rho}{2},\frac{1\mp\rho}{2};\frac{a^2b^2}{4}\\1\mp\rho,\frac{2-s-\nu\mp\rho}{2},\frac{2-s+\nu\mp\rho}{2}\end{matrix}\right)$
		$\mp\dfrac{\rho a^{s+\rho+\nu}b^\nu}{2^{s+2\nu+1}}\Gamma\!\left[\begin{matrix}s+\nu,-\frac{s+\nu\pm\rho}{2}\\\nu+1,\frac{s+\nu\mp\rho+2}{2}\end{matrix}\right]{}_2F_3\!\left(\begin{matrix}\frac{s+\nu}{2},\frac{s+\nu+1}{2};\frac{a^2b^2}{4}\\\nu+1,\frac{s+\nu+\rho+2}{2},\frac{s+\nu-\rho+2}{2}\end{matrix}\right)$
		$[b,\ \operatorname{Re}a>0;\ -\operatorname{Re}\nu<\operatorname{Re}s<3/2\mp\operatorname{Re}\rho]$
18	$\dfrac{\left(\sqrt{x^2+a^2}\pm x\right)^\rho}{\sqrt{x^2+a^2}}J_\nu(bx)$	$\dfrac{2^{s\pm2\rho-2}a^{\rho\mp\rho}}{b^{s\pm\rho-1}}\Gamma\!\left[\begin{matrix}\frac{s+\nu\pm\rho-1}{2}\\\frac{3-s+\nu\mp\rho}{2}\end{matrix}\right]{}_2F_3\!\left(\begin{matrix}\frac{1\mp\rho}{2},\frac{2\mp\rho}{2};\frac{a^2b^2}{4}\\1\mp\rho,\frac{3-s-\nu\mp\rho}{2},\frac{3-s+\nu\mp\rho}{2}\end{matrix}\right)$
		$+\dfrac{a^{s+\rho+\nu-1}b^\nu}{2^{s+2\nu}}\Gamma\!\left[\begin{matrix}s+\nu,-\frac{s+\nu\pm\rho-1}{2}\\\nu+1,\frac{s+\nu\mp\rho+1}{2}\end{matrix}\right]$
		$\times{}_2F_3\!\left(\begin{matrix}\frac{s+\nu}{2},\frac{s+\nu+1}{2};\frac{a^2b^2}{4}\\\nu+1,\frac{s+\nu+\rho+1}{2},\frac{s+\nu-\rho+1}{2}\end{matrix}\right)$
		$[b,\ \operatorname{Re}a>0;\ -\operatorname{Re}\nu<\operatorname{Re}s<5/2\mp\operatorname{Re}\rho]$

3.10.2. $J_\nu(\varphi(x))$ and algebraic functions

No.	$f(x)$	$F(s)$
1	$\theta(1-x)\,J_\nu\!\left(\dfrac{a}{x}-ax\right)$	$I_{(\nu+s)/2}(a)\,K_{(\nu-s)/2}(a)$ $\qquad[a>0;\ \operatorname{Re}(s+\nu)<3/2]$
2	$\theta(x-1)\,J_\nu\!\left(ax-\dfrac{a}{x}\right)$	$I_{(\nu-s)/2}(a)\,K_{(\nu+s)/2}(a)$ $\qquad[a>0;\ \operatorname{Re}\nu>-1;\ \operatorname{Re}s<3/2]$
3	$J_\nu\!\left(a\left|x-\dfrac{1}{x}\right|\right)$	$I_{(\nu-s)/2}(a)\,K_{(\nu+s)/2}(a)+I_{(\nu+s)/2}(a)\,K_{(\nu-s)/2}(a)$ $\qquad[a>0;\ \operatorname{Re}\nu>-1;\ |\operatorname{Re}s|<3/2]$
4	$J_\nu\!\left(ax+\dfrac{a}{x}\right)$	$-\dfrac{\pi}{2}\left[J_{(\nu-s)/2}(a)\,Y_{(\nu+s)/2}(a)+J_{(\nu+s)/2}(a)\,Y_{(\nu-s)/2}(a)\right]$ $\qquad[a>0;\ |\operatorname{Re}s|<3/2]$
5	$(a-x)_+^{\alpha-1}$ $\times J_\nu(bx(a-x))$	$a^{s+\alpha+2\nu-1}\left(\dfrac{b}{2}\right)^\nu\Gamma\!\left[\begin{matrix}s+\nu,\ \alpha+\nu\\\nu+1,\ s+\alpha+2\nu\end{matrix}\right]$ $\times{}_4F_5\!\left(\begin{matrix}\Delta(2,\alpha+\nu),\ \Delta(2,s+\nu)\\\nu+1,\ \Delta(4,s+\alpha+2\nu);\ -\frac{a^4b^2}{64}\end{matrix}\right)$ $\qquad[a,\ \operatorname{Re}(\alpha+\nu),\ \operatorname{Re}(s+\nu)>0]$
6	$\left(a^2-x^2\right)_+^{\nu/2}$ $\times J_\nu\!\left(b\sqrt{a^2-x^2}\right)$	$\dfrac{2^{s/2-1}a^{s/2+\nu}}{b^{s/2}}\Gamma\!\left(\dfrac{s}{2}\right)J_{s/2+\nu}(ab)$ $\qquad[a,\ \operatorname{Re}s>0;\ \operatorname{Re}\nu>-1]$

No.	$f(x)$	$F(s)$
7	$\left(x^2 - a^2\right)_+^{\nu/2}$ $\times J_\nu\left(b\sqrt{x^2 - a^2}\right)$	$\dfrac{a^{s/2+\nu}}{\Gamma\left(\frac{2-s}{2}\right)}\left(\dfrac{2}{b}\right)^{s/2} K_{s/2+\nu}\left(ab\right)$ $[a,\, b > 0;\; \operatorname{Re}\nu > -1;\; \operatorname{Re}s < 3/2 - \operatorname{Re}\nu]$
8	$\left(x^2 + a^2\right)^{\rho}$ $\times J_\nu\left(b\sqrt{x^2 + a^2}\right)$	$\dfrac{2^{s+2\rho-1}\pi\, b^{-s-2\rho}}{\Gamma\left(\frac{2-s+\nu-2\rho}{2}\right)\Gamma\left(\frac{2-s-\nu-2\rho}{2}\right)} \csc\dfrac{(s+\nu+2\rho)\pi}{2}$ $\times {}_1F_2\left(\begin{matrix}\frac{2-s}{2};\ -\frac{a^2b^2}{4}\\ \frac{2-s+\nu-2\rho}{2},\ \frac{2-s-\nu-2\rho}{2}\end{matrix}\right)$ $-\dfrac{\pi a^{s+\nu+2\rho}b^\nu}{2^{\nu+1}}\csc\dfrac{(s+\nu+2\rho)\pi}{2}$ $\times\Gamma\left[\begin{matrix}\frac{s}{2}\\ \nu+1,\ -\frac{\nu+2\rho}{2},\ \frac{s+\nu+2\rho+2}{2}\end{matrix}\right]{}_1F_2\left(\begin{matrix}\frac{\nu+2\rho+2}{2};\ -\frac{a^2b^2}{4}\\ \nu+1,\ \frac{s+\nu+2\rho+2}{2}\end{matrix}\right)$ $[\operatorname{Re}a,\, b > 0;\; 0 < \operatorname{Re}s < -2\operatorname{Re}\rho + 1/2]$
9	$\left(x^2 + a^2\right)^{\nu/2}$ $\times J_\nu\left(b\sqrt{x^2 + a^2}\right)$	$\dfrac{2^{s/2-1}a^{s/2+\nu}}{b^{s/2}}\Gamma\left(\dfrac{s}{2}\right)\left[J_{s/2+\nu}\left(ab\right)\cos\dfrac{s\pi}{2} - Y_{s/2+\nu}\left(ab\right)\sin\dfrac{s\pi}{2}\right]$ $[\operatorname{Re}a,\, b > 0;\; 0 < \operatorname{Re}s < 3/2 - \operatorname{Re}\nu]$
10	$\left(x^2 + a^2\right)^{-\nu/2}$ $\times J_\nu\left(b\sqrt{x^2 + a^2}\right)$	$\dfrac{2^{s/2-1}a^{s/2-\nu}}{b^{s/2}}\Gamma\left(\dfrac{s}{2}\right)J_{\nu-s/2}\left(ab\right)$ $[\operatorname{Re}a,\, b > 0;\; 0 < \operatorname{Re}s < \operatorname{Re}\nu + 3/2]$
11	$\dfrac{1}{(x+a)^\rho}J_\nu\left(\dfrac{b}{x+a}\right)$	$\dfrac{a^{s-\nu-\rho}}{\Gamma(\nu+1)}\left(\dfrac{b}{2}\right)^\nu \mathrm{B}\left(s,\, \nu+\rho-s\right){}_2F_3\left(\begin{matrix}\frac{\nu+\rho-s}{2},\ \frac{\nu+\rho-s+1}{2};\ -\frac{b^2}{4a^2}\\ \nu+1,\ \frac{\nu+\rho}{2},\ \frac{\nu+\rho+1}{2}\end{matrix}\right)$ $[0 < \operatorname{Re}s < \operatorname{Re}(\nu+\rho);\; |\arg a| < \pi]$
12	$\dfrac{1}{(x+a)^\rho}J_\nu\left(\dfrac{bx}{x+a}\right)$	$a^{s-\rho}\left(\dfrac{b}{2}\right)^\nu\dfrac{\mathrm{B}\left(s+\nu,\, \rho-s\right)}{\Gamma(\nu+1)}{}_2F_3\left(\begin{matrix}\frac{s+\nu}{2},\ \frac{s+\nu+1}{2};\ -\frac{b^2}{4}\\ \nu+1,\ \frac{\nu+\rho}{2},\ \frac{\nu+\rho+1}{2}\end{matrix}\right)$ $[-\operatorname{Re}\nu < \operatorname{Re}s < \operatorname{Re}\rho;\; |\arg a| < \pi]$
13	$\dfrac{1}{(x^2+a^2)^\rho}$ $\times J_\nu\left(\dfrac{bx}{x^2+a^2}\right)$	$\dfrac{2^{-\nu-1}a^{s-\nu-2\rho}b^\nu}{\Gamma(\nu+1)}\mathrm{B}\left(\dfrac{s+\nu}{2},\ \dfrac{\nu+2\rho-s}{2}\right)$ $\times {}_2F_3\left(\begin{matrix}\frac{s+\nu}{2},\ \frac{\nu+2\rho-s}{2};\ -\frac{b^2}{16a^2}\\ \nu+1,\ \frac{\nu+\rho}{2},\ \frac{\nu+\rho+1}{2}\end{matrix}\right)$ $[\operatorname{Re}a,\, b > 0;\; -\operatorname{Re}\nu < \operatorname{Re}s < \operatorname{Re}(\nu+2\rho)]$

3.10.3. $J_\nu(\varphi(x))$ and the exponential function

1	$e^{-ax} J_\nu(bx)$	$\dfrac{b^\nu}{2^\nu a^{s+\nu}} \Gamma \begin{bmatrix} s+\nu \\ \nu+1 \end{bmatrix} {}_2F_1 \left(\begin{matrix} \frac{s+\nu}{2}, \frac{s+\nu+1}{2} \\ \nu+1; -\frac{b^2}{a^2} \end{matrix} \right)$

$$[\operatorname{Re}(s+\nu) > 0;\ \operatorname{Re} a > |\operatorname{Im} b|]$$

2	$e^{-ax^2} J_\nu(bx)$	$\dfrac{2^{-\nu-1} b^\nu}{a^{(s+\nu)/2}} \Gamma \begin{bmatrix} \frac{s+\nu}{2} \\ \nu+1 \end{bmatrix} {}_1F_1 \left(\begin{matrix} \frac{s+\nu}{2}; -\frac{b^2}{4a} \\ \nu+1 \end{matrix} \right)$

$$[\operatorname{Re} a > 0;\ \operatorname{Re}(s+\nu) > 0;\ |\arg b| < \pi]$$

3	$e^{-a\sqrt{x}} J_\nu(bx)$	$\dfrac{2^{s-1}}{b^s} \Gamma \begin{bmatrix} \frac{s+\nu}{2} \\ \frac{2-s+\nu}{2} \end{bmatrix} {}_2F_3 \left(\begin{matrix} \frac{s-\nu}{2}, \frac{s+\nu}{2} \\ \frac{1}{4}, \frac{1}{2}, \frac{3}{4}; -\frac{a^4}{64b^2} \end{matrix} \right)$

$$- \frac{2^{s-1/2}a}{b^{s+1/2}} \Gamma \begin{bmatrix} \frac{2s+2\nu+1}{4} \\ \frac{3-2s+2\nu}{4} \end{bmatrix} {}_2F_3 \left(\begin{matrix} \frac{2s-2\nu+1}{4}, \frac{2s+2\nu+1}{4} \\ \frac{1}{2}, \frac{3}{4}, \frac{5}{4}; -\frac{a^4}{64b^2} \end{matrix} \right)$$

$$+ \frac{2^{s-1}a^2}{b^{s+1}} \Gamma \begin{bmatrix} \frac{s+\nu+1}{2} \\ \frac{1-s+\nu}{2} \end{bmatrix} {}_2F_3 \left(\begin{matrix} \frac{s-\nu+1}{2}, \frac{s+\nu+1}{2} \\ \frac{3}{4}, \frac{5}{4}, \frac{3}{2}; -\frac{a^4}{64b^2} \end{matrix} \right)$$

$$- \frac{2^{s-1/2}a^3}{3b^{s+3/2}} \Gamma \begin{bmatrix} \frac{2s+2\nu+3}{4} \\ \frac{1-2s+2\nu}{4} \end{bmatrix} {}_2F_3 \left(\begin{matrix} \frac{2s-2\nu+3}{4}, \frac{2s+2\nu+3}{4} \\ \frac{5}{4}, \frac{3}{2}, \frac{7}{4}; -\frac{a^4}{64b^2} \end{matrix} \right)$$

$$[b,\ \operatorname{Re} a,\ \operatorname{Re}(s+\nu) > 0]$$

4	$e^{-a/x} J_\nu(bx)$	$\dfrac{2^{s-1}}{b^s} \Gamma \begin{bmatrix} \frac{s+\nu}{2} \\ \frac{2-s+\nu}{2} \end{bmatrix} {}_0F_3 \left(\begin{matrix} -\frac{a^2b^2}{16} \\ \frac{1}{2}, \frac{2-s-\nu}{2}, \frac{2-s+\nu}{2} \end{matrix} \right)$

$$- \frac{2^{s-2}a}{b^{s-1}} \Gamma \begin{bmatrix} \frac{s+\nu-1}{2} \\ \frac{3-s+\nu}{2} \end{bmatrix} {}_0F_3 \left(\begin{matrix} -\frac{a^2b^2}{16} \\ \frac{3}{2}, \frac{3-s-\nu}{2}, \frac{3-s+\nu}{2} \end{matrix} \right)$$

$$+ \frac{a^{s+\nu}b^\nu}{2^\nu} \Gamma \begin{bmatrix} -s-\nu \\ \nu+1 \end{bmatrix} {}_0F_3 \left(\begin{matrix} -\frac{a^2b^2}{16} \\ \nu+1, \frac{s+\nu+1}{2}, \frac{s+\nu+2}{2} \end{matrix} \right)$$

$$[b,\ \operatorname{Re} a > 0;\ \operatorname{Re} s < 3/2]$$

5	$e^{-a/x^2} J_\nu(bx)$	$\dfrac{2^{s-1}}{b^s} \Gamma \begin{bmatrix} \frac{s+\nu}{2} \\ \frac{2-s+\nu}{2} \end{bmatrix} {}_0F_2 \left(\begin{matrix} \frac{ab^2}{4} \\ \frac{2-s-\nu}{2}, \frac{2-s+\nu}{2} \end{matrix} \right)$

$$+ \frac{a^{(s+\nu)/2}b^\nu}{2^{\nu+1}} \Gamma \begin{bmatrix} -\frac{s+\nu}{2} \\ \nu+1 \end{bmatrix} {}_0F_2 \left(\begin{matrix} \frac{ab^2}{4} \\ \nu+1, \frac{s+\nu+2}{2} \end{matrix} \right)$$

$$[b,\ \operatorname{Re} a > 0;\ \operatorname{Re} s < 3/2]$$

6	$(a-x)_+^{\alpha-1} e^{\pm ibx} J_\nu(bx)$	$a^{s+\alpha+\nu-1} \left(\dfrac{b}{2} \right)^\nu \Gamma \begin{bmatrix} \alpha, s+\nu \\ \nu+1, s+\alpha+\nu \end{bmatrix} {}_2F_2 \left(\begin{matrix} \frac{2\nu+1}{2}, s+\nu; \pm 2iab \\ 2\nu+1, s+\alpha+\nu \end{matrix} \right)$

$$[a, b,\ \operatorname{Re}\alpha,\ \operatorname{Re}(s+\nu) > 0]$$

7	$(a-x)_+^{\nu/2} e^{bx}$ $\times J_\nu(c\sqrt{a-x})$	$a^{s+\nu} \left(\dfrac{c}{2} \right)^\nu \Gamma \begin{bmatrix} s \\ s+\nu+1 \end{bmatrix} \Phi_3 \left(s; s+\nu+1; ab, -\dfrac{ac^2}{4} \right)$

$$[a,\ \operatorname{Re} s > 0;\ \operatorname{Re}\nu > -1]$$

No.	$f(x)$	$F(s)$
8	$\left(a^2 - x^2\right)_+^{-1} e^{-b/(a^2-x^2)}$ $\times J_\nu\left(\dfrac{cx}{a^2-x^2}\right)$	$\dfrac{a^{s-1}}{c} e^{-b/(2a^2)} \Gamma\begin{bmatrix}\frac{s+\nu}{2}\\\nu+1\end{bmatrix} M_{(s-1)/2,\,\nu/2}\left(\dfrac{\sqrt{b^2+a^2c^2}-b}{2a^2}\right)$ $\times W_{(1-s)/2,\,\nu/2}\left(\dfrac{\sqrt{b^2+a^2c^2}+b}{2a^2}\right)$ $[a,\,b,\,c,\ \mathrm{Re}\,(s+\nu)>0]$
9	$\left(x^2-a^2\right)_+^{-1} e^{-b/(x^2-a^2)}$ $\times J_\nu\left(\dfrac{cx}{x^2-a^2}\right)$	$-\dfrac{a^{s-1}}{c} e^{b/(2a^2)} \Gamma\begin{bmatrix}\frac{2-s+\nu}{2}\\\nu+1\end{bmatrix} M_{(1-s)/2,\,\nu/2}\left(\dfrac{\sqrt{b^2+a^2c^2}-b}{2a^2}\right)$ $\times W_{(s-1)/2,\,\nu/2}\left(\dfrac{\sqrt{b^2+a^2c^2}+b}{2a^2}\right)$ $[a,\,b,\,c>0;\ \mathrm{Re}\,s<\mathrm{Re}\,\nu]$
10	$\dfrac{e^{\pm 2a^2 b/(x^2+a^2)}}{x^2+a^2}$ $\times J_\nu\left(\dfrac{2cx}{x^2+a^2}\right)$	$\dfrac{a^{s-1}}{2c} e^{\pm b} \Gamma\begin{bmatrix}\frac{2-s+\nu}{2},\ \frac{s+\nu}{2}\\\nu+1,\ \nu+1\end{bmatrix} M_{\mp(1-s)/2,\,\nu/2}\left(\dfrac{ab-\sqrt{a^2b^2-c^2}}{a}\right)$ $\times M_{\mp(1-s)/2,\,\nu/2}\left(\dfrac{ab+\sqrt{a^2b^2-c^2}}{a}\right)$ $[\mathrm{Re}\,a,\,b,\,c>0;\ -\mathrm{Re}\,\nu<\mathrm{Re}\,s<\mathrm{Re}\,\nu+2]$

3.10.4. $J_\nu(bx)$ and trigonometric functions

Notation: $\delta = \begin{Bmatrix}1\\0\end{Bmatrix}$.

1	$\begin{Bmatrix}\sin(ax)\\\cos(ax)\end{Bmatrix} J_\nu(ax)$	$\dfrac{(2a)^{-s}}{\sqrt\pi}\begin{Bmatrix}\sin[(s+\nu)\,\pi/2]\\\cos[(s+\nu)\,\pi/2]\end{Bmatrix}\Gamma\begin{bmatrix}\frac{1-2s}{2},\ s+\nu\\1-s+\nu\end{bmatrix}$ $[a>0;\ -\mathrm{Re}\,\nu-\delta<\mathrm{Re}\,s<1/2]$
2	$\begin{Bmatrix}\sin(ax+b)\\\cos(ax+b)\end{Bmatrix} J_\nu(ax)$	$\dfrac{(2a)^{-s}}{\sqrt\pi}\begin{Bmatrix}\sin[(s+\nu)\,\pi/2+b]\\\cos[(s+\nu)\,\pi/2+b]\end{Bmatrix}\Gamma\begin{bmatrix}\frac{1-2s}{2},\ s+\nu\\1-s+\nu\end{bmatrix}$ $[a>0;\ -\mathrm{Re}\,\nu<\mathrm{Re}\,s<1/2]$
3	$\begin{Bmatrix}\sin(ax)\\\cos(ax)\end{Bmatrix} J_\nu(bx)$	$\dfrac{2^{s+\delta-1}a^\delta}{b^{s+\delta}}\Gamma\begin{bmatrix}\frac{s+\nu+\delta}{2}\\\frac{2-s+\nu-\delta}{2}\end{bmatrix}{}_2F_1\left(\dfrac{\frac{s-\nu+\delta}{2},\ \frac{s+\nu+\delta}{2}}{\frac{2\delta+1}{2};\ \frac{a^2}{b^2}}\right)$ $[0<a<b;\ -\mathrm{Re}\,\nu-\delta<\mathrm{Re}\,s<3/2]$
4	$\begin{Bmatrix}\sin(ax)\\\cos(ax)\end{Bmatrix} J_\nu(bx)$	$\dfrac{b^\nu}{2^\nu a^{s+\nu}}\begin{Bmatrix}\sin[(s+\nu)\,\pi/2]\\\cos[(s+\nu)\,\pi/2]\end{Bmatrix}\Gamma\begin{bmatrix}s+\nu\\\nu+1\end{bmatrix}{}_2F_1\left(\dfrac{\frac{s+\nu}{2},\ \frac{s+\nu+1}{2}}{\nu+1;\ \frac{b^2}{a^2}}\right)$ $[0<b<a;\ -\mathrm{Re}\,\nu-\delta<\mathrm{Re}\,s<3/2]$

No.	$f(x)$	$F(s)$
5	$\begin{Bmatrix} \sin(ax^2) \\ \cos(ax^2) \end{Bmatrix} J_\nu(bx)$	$\dfrac{b^\nu}{2^{\nu+1}a^{(s+\nu)/2}} \begin{Bmatrix} \sin[(s+\nu)\pi/4] \\ \cos[(s+\nu)\pi/4] \end{Bmatrix} \Gamma\begin{bmatrix} \frac{s+\nu}{2} \\ \nu+1 \end{bmatrix}$

$$\times\, {}_2F_3\left(\begin{matrix} \frac{s+\nu}{4}, \ \frac{s+\nu+2}{4}; \ -\frac{b^4}{64a^2} \\ \frac{1}{2}, \ \frac{\nu+1}{2}, \ \frac{\nu+2}{2} \end{matrix}\right)$$

$$\mp\, \dfrac{b^{\nu+2}}{2^{\nu+3}a^{(s+\nu)/2+1}} \begin{Bmatrix} \cos[(s+\nu)\pi/4] \\ \sin[(s+\nu)\pi/4] \end{Bmatrix} \Gamma\begin{bmatrix} \frac{s+\nu+2}{2} \\ \nu+2 \end{bmatrix}$$

$$\times\, {}_2F_3\left(\begin{matrix} \frac{s+\nu+2}{4}, \ \frac{s+\nu+4}{4}; \ -\frac{b^4}{64a^2} \\ \frac{3}{2}, \ \frac{\nu+2}{2}, \ \frac{\nu+3}{2} \end{matrix}\right)$$

$$[a,\, b>0; \ -\operatorname{Re}\nu - 2\delta < \operatorname{Re}s < 5/2]$$

| 6 | $\sin(a\sqrt{x})\, J_\nu(bx)$ | $\dfrac{2^{s-1/2}a}{b^{s+1/2}} \Gamma\begin{bmatrix} \frac{2s+2\nu+1}{4} \\ \frac{3-2s+2\nu}{4} \end{bmatrix} {}_2F_3\left(\begin{matrix} \frac{2s-2\nu+1}{4}, \ \frac{2s+2\nu+1}{4} \\ \frac{1}{2}, \ \frac{3}{4}, \ \frac{5}{4}; \ -\frac{a^4}{64b^2} \end{matrix}\right)$ |

$$-\, \dfrac{2^{s-1/2}a^3}{3b^{s+3/2}} \Gamma\begin{bmatrix} \frac{2s+2\nu+3}{4} \\ \frac{1-2s+2\nu}{4} \end{bmatrix} {}_2F_3\left(\begin{matrix} \frac{2s-2\nu+3}{4}, \ \frac{2s+2\nu+3}{4} \\ \frac{5}{4}, \ \frac{3}{2}, \ \frac{7}{4}; \ -\frac{a^4}{64b^2} \end{matrix}\right)$$

$$[a,\, b>0; \ -\operatorname{Re}\nu - 1/2 < \operatorname{Re}s < 3/2]$$

| 7 | $\cos(a\sqrt{x})\, J_\nu(bx)$ | $\dfrac{2^{s-1}}{b^s} \Gamma\begin{bmatrix} \frac{s+\nu}{2} \\ \frac{2-s+\nu}{2} \end{bmatrix} {}_2F_3\left(\begin{matrix} \frac{s-\nu}{2}, \ \frac{s+\nu}{2} \\ \frac{1}{4}, \ \frac{1}{2}, \ \frac{3}{4}; \ -\frac{a^4}{64b^2} \end{matrix}\right)$ |

$$-\, \dfrac{2^{s-1}a^2}{b^{s+1}} \Gamma\begin{bmatrix} \frac{s+\nu+1}{2} \\ \frac{1-s+\nu}{2} \end{bmatrix} {}_2F_3\left(\begin{matrix} \frac{s-\nu+1}{2}, \ \frac{s+\nu+1}{2} \\ \frac{3}{4}, \ \frac{5}{4}, \ \frac{3}{2}; \ -\frac{a^4}{64b^2} \end{matrix}\right)$$

$$[a,\, b>0; \ -\operatorname{Re}\nu < \operatorname{Re}s < 3/2]$$

| 8 | $\sin\dfrac{a}{x}\, J_\nu(bx)$ | $\dfrac{2^{s-2}a}{b^{s-1}} \Gamma\begin{bmatrix} \frac{s+\nu-1}{2} \\ \frac{3-s+\nu}{2} \end{bmatrix} {}_0F_3\left(\begin{matrix} \frac{a^2b^2}{16} \\ \frac{3}{2}, \ \frac{3-s-\nu}{2}, \ \frac{3-s+\nu}{2} \end{matrix}\right)$ |

$$-\, a^{s+\nu}\left(\frac{b}{2}\right)^\nu \sin\frac{(s+\nu)\pi}{2} \Gamma\begin{bmatrix} -s-\nu \\ \nu+1 \end{bmatrix}$$

$$\times\, {}_0F_3\left(\begin{matrix} \frac{a^2b^2}{16} \\ \nu+1, \ \frac{s+\nu+1}{2}, \ \frac{s+\nu+2}{2} \end{matrix}\right)$$

$$[a,\, b>0; \ -\operatorname{Re}\nu - 1 < \operatorname{Re}s < 5/2]$$

| 9 | $\cos\dfrac{a}{x}\, J_\nu(bx)$ | $\dfrac{2^{s-1}}{b^s} \Gamma\begin{bmatrix} \frac{s+\nu}{2} \\ \frac{2-s+\nu}{2} \end{bmatrix} {}_0F_3\left(\begin{matrix} \frac{a^2b^2}{16} \\ \frac{1}{2}, \ \frac{2-s-\nu}{2}, \ \frac{2-s+\nu}{2} \end{matrix}\right)$ |

$$+\, a^{s+\nu}\left(\frac{b}{2}\right)^\nu \cos\frac{(s+\nu)\pi}{2} \Gamma\begin{bmatrix} -s-\nu \\ \nu+1 \end{bmatrix}$$

$$\times\, {}_0F_3\left(\begin{matrix} \frac{a^2b^2}{16} \\ \nu+1, \ \frac{s+\nu+1}{2}, \ \frac{s+\nu+2}{2} \end{matrix}\right)$$

$$[a,\, b>0; \ -\operatorname{Re}\nu - 1 < \operatorname{Re}s < 3/2]$$

No.	$f(x)$	$F(s)$
10	$\sin(ax) J_\nu(ax)$	$-\dfrac{2^{2-s}a^{-s}}{\pi^{3/2}} \sin\dfrac{(2\nu \mp 1)\pi}{4} \cos\dfrac{(2s \mp 1)\pi}{4}$
	$\pm \cos(ax) J_{-\nu}(ax)$	$\times \cos\dfrac{(s-\nu)\pi}{2} \sin\dfrac{(s+\nu)\pi}{2} \Gamma\left[\dfrac{1}{2}-s,\, s-\nu,\, s+\nu\right]$
		$[a>0;\ -\operatorname{Re}\nu-1,\ \operatorname{Re}\nu < \operatorname{Re}s < (2\mp1)/2]$
11	$\cos(ax) J_\nu(ax)$	$\pm\dfrac{2^{2-s}a^{-s}}{\pi^{3/2}} \sin\dfrac{(2\nu \pm 1)\pi}{4} \cos\dfrac{(2s \mp 1)\pi}{4}$
	$\pm \sin(ax) J_{-\nu}(ax)$	$\times \sin\dfrac{(s-\nu)\pi}{2} \cos\dfrac{(s+\nu)\pi}{2} \Gamma\left[\dfrac{1}{2}-s,\, s-\nu,\, s+\nu\right]$
		$[a>0;\ \operatorname{Re}\nu-1,\ -\operatorname{Re}\nu < \operatorname{Re}s < (2\mp1)/2]$
12	$e^{-ax}\begin{Bmatrix}\sin(bx)\\\cos(bx)\end{Bmatrix} J_\nu(bx)$	$\dfrac{(2b)^{\nu+\delta}}{\sqrt{\pi}\,a^{s+\nu+\delta}} \Gamma\left[\begin{matrix}\frac{2\nu+2\delta+1}{2},\ s+\nu+\delta\\2\nu+\delta+1\end{matrix}\right]$
		$\times {}_4F_3\left(\begin{matrix}\frac{2\nu+3}{4},\ \frac{2\nu+4\delta+1}{4},\ \frac{s+\nu+1}{2},\ \frac{s+\nu+2\delta}{2}\\\frac{2\delta+1}{2},\ \nu+1,\ \frac{2\nu+2\delta+1}{2};\ -\frac{4b^2}{a^2}\end{matrix}\right)$
		$[b,\ \operatorname{Re}a>0;\ \operatorname{Re}(s+\nu)>-\delta]$
13	$e^{-a\sqrt{x}}\begin{Bmatrix}\sin(a\sqrt{x})\\\cos(a\sqrt{x})\end{Bmatrix}$	$\dfrac{2^{s+1/2}a^3}{3b^{s+3/2}} \Gamma\left[\begin{matrix}\frac{2s+2\nu+3}{4}\\\frac{1-2s+2\nu}{4}\end{matrix}\right] {}_2F_3\left(\begin{matrix}\frac{2s+2\nu+3}{4},\ \frac{2s-2\nu+3}{4}\\\frac{3}{2},\ \frac{5}{4},\ \frac{7}{4};\ \frac{a^4}{16b^2}\end{matrix}\right)$
	$\times J_\nu(bx)$	$\pm\dfrac{2^{s-1/2}a}{b^{s+1/2}} \Gamma\left[\begin{matrix}\frac{2s+2\nu+1}{4}\\\frac{3-2s+2\nu}{4}\end{matrix}\right] {}_2F_3\left(\begin{matrix}\frac{2s+2\nu+1}{4},\ \frac{2s-2\nu+1}{4}\\\frac{1}{2},\ \frac{3}{4},\ \frac{5}{4};\ \frac{a^4}{16b^2}\end{matrix}\right)$
		$\mp\dfrac{2^{s+\delta-1}a^{2\delta}}{b^{s+\delta}} \Gamma\left[\begin{matrix}\frac{s+\nu+\delta}{2}\\\frac{2-s+\nu-\delta}{2}\end{matrix}\right] {}_2F_3\left(\begin{matrix}\frac{s+\nu+\delta}{2},\ \frac{s-\nu+\delta}{2}\\\frac{3}{4},\ \frac{2\delta+1}{2},\ \frac{4\delta+1}{4};\ \frac{a^4}{16b^2}\end{matrix}\right)$
		$[b>0;\ \operatorname{Re}(s+\nu)>-\delta/2;\ |\arg a|<\pi/4]$

3.10.5. $J_\nu(bx)$ and the logarithmic function

No.	$f(x)$	$F(s)$
1	$\theta(a-x)\ln\dfrac{\sqrt{a}+\sqrt{a-x}}{\sqrt{x}}$	$\dfrac{\sqrt{\pi}\,a^{s+\nu}}{2(s+\nu)}\left(\dfrac{b}{2}\right)^\nu \Gamma\left[\begin{matrix}s+\nu\\\nu+1,\ \frac{2s+2\nu+1}{2}\end{matrix}\right]$
	$\times J_\nu(bx)$	$\times {}_3F_4\left(\begin{matrix}\frac{s+\nu}{2},\ \frac{s+\nu}{2},\ \frac{s+\nu+1}{2};\ -\frac{a^2b^2}{4}\\\nu+1,\ \frac{2s+2\nu+1}{4},\ \frac{2s+2\nu+3}{4},\ \frac{s+\nu+2}{2}\end{matrix}\right)$
		$[a,\ \operatorname{Re}(s+\nu)>0]$
2	$\theta(a-x)\ln\dfrac{a+\sqrt{a^2-x^2}}{x}$	$\dfrac{\sqrt{\pi}\,a^{s+\nu}}{2(s+\nu)}\left(\dfrac{b}{2}\right)^\nu \Gamma\left[\begin{matrix}\frac{s+\nu+1}{2}\\\nu+1,\ \frac{s+\nu}{2}\end{matrix}\right] {}_2F_3\left(\begin{matrix}\frac{s+\nu}{2},\ \frac{s+\nu}{2};\ -\frac{a^2b^2}{4}\\\nu+1,\ \frac{s+\nu+1}{2},\ \frac{s+\nu+2}{2}\end{matrix}\right)$
	$\times J_\nu(bx)$	$[a,\ \operatorname{Re}(s+\nu)>0]$

3.10.6. $J_\nu(bx)$ and inverse trigonometric functions

Notation: $\delta = \left\{ \begin{matrix} 1 \\ 0 \end{matrix} \right\}$.

1	$\theta(a-x) \arccos \dfrac{x}{a} J_\nu(bx)$	$\dfrac{\sqrt{\pi}\, a^{s+\nu}}{(s+\nu)^2} \left(\dfrac{b}{2}\right)^\nu \Gamma\!\left[\begin{matrix} \frac{s+\nu+1}{2} \\ \nu+1,\ \frac{s+\nu}{2} \end{matrix}\right] {}_2F_3\!\left(\begin{matrix} \frac{s+\nu}{2},\ \frac{s+\nu+1}{2};\ -\frac{a^2b^2}{4} \\ \nu+1,\ \frac{s+\nu+2}{2},\ \frac{s+\nu+2}{2} \end{matrix}\right)$
		$[a,\ \mathrm{Re}\,(s+\nu) > 0]$
2	$\theta(a-x) \left\{ \begin{matrix} \sin(bx) \\ \cos(bx) \end{matrix} \right\}$ $\times \arccos \dfrac{x}{a} J_\nu(bx)$	$\dfrac{\sqrt{\pi}\, a^{s+\nu+\delta} b^{\nu+\delta}}{2^{\nu+1}(s+\nu+\delta)} \Gamma\!\left[\begin{matrix} \frac{s+\nu+\delta+1}{2} \\ \nu+1,\ \frac{s+\nu+\delta+2}{2} \end{matrix}\right]$ $\times {}_4F_5\!\left(\begin{matrix} \frac{2\nu+2\delta+1}{2},\ \frac{2\nu+2\delta+3}{2},\ \frac{s+\nu+\delta}{2},\ \frac{s+\nu+\delta+1}{2};\ -a^2b^2 \\ \frac{2\delta+1}{2},\ \frac{2\nu+\delta+1}{2},\ \frac{2\nu+\delta+2}{2},\ \frac{s+\nu+\delta+2}{2},\ \frac{s+\nu+\delta+2}{2} \end{matrix}\right)$
		$[a>0;\ \mathrm{Re}\,(s+\nu) > -\delta]$

3.10.7. $J_\nu(bx)$ and $\mathrm{Ei}\,(ax^r)$

1	$\mathrm{Ei}\,(-ax) J_\nu(bx)$	$-\dfrac{a^{-s-\nu}}{s+\nu} \left(\dfrac{b}{2}\right)^\nu \Gamma\!\left[\begin{matrix} s+\nu \\ \nu+1 \end{matrix}\right] {}_3F_2\!\left(\begin{matrix} \frac{s+\nu}{2},\ \frac{s+\nu}{2},\ \frac{s+\nu+1}{2} \\ \nu+1,\ \frac{s+\nu+2}{2};\ -\frac{b^2}{a^2} \end{matrix}\right)$
		$\left[\begin{matrix} (\mathrm{Re}\,a > \lvert\mathrm{Im}\,b\rvert;\ \mathrm{Im}\,a = 0;\ \mathrm{Re}\,(s+\nu) > 0)\ \text{or} \\ (\mathrm{Re}\,a + \lvert\mathrm{Im}\,b\rvert = 0;\ \mathrm{Im}\,a = 0;\ -\mathrm{Re}\,\nu < \mathrm{Re}\,s < 5/2)\ \text{or} \\ (\mathrm{Re}\,a \ge 0;\ \mathrm{Im}\,a \ne 0;\ \mathrm{Im}\,b = 0;\ -\mathrm{Re}\,\nu < \mathrm{Re}\,s < 3/2) \end{matrix}\right]$
2	$\mathrm{Ei}\,(-ax^2) J_\nu(bx)$	$-\dfrac{a^{-(s+\nu)/2}}{s+\nu} \left(\dfrac{b}{2}\right)^\nu \Gamma\!\left[\begin{matrix} \frac{s+\nu}{2} \\ \nu+1 \end{matrix}\right] {}_2F_2\!\left(\begin{matrix} \frac{s+\nu}{2},\ \frac{s+\nu}{2};\ -\frac{b^2}{4a} \\ \nu+1,\ \frac{s+\nu+2}{2} \end{matrix}\right)$
		$[\mathrm{Re}\,a,\ \mathrm{Re}\,(s+\nu) > 0]$
3	$e^{\pm ax}\,\mathrm{Ei}\,(\mp ax) J_\nu(bx)$	$-\dfrac{\pi}{a^{s+\nu}} \left(\dfrac{b}{2}\right)^\nu \left\{ \begin{matrix} \csc[(s+\nu)\pi] \\ \cot[(s+\nu)\pi] \end{matrix} \right\} \Gamma\!\left[\begin{matrix} s+\nu \\ \nu+1 \end{matrix}\right] {}_2F_1\!\left(\begin{matrix} \frac{s+\nu}{2},\ \frac{s+\nu+1}{2} \\ \nu+1;\ -\frac{b^2}{a^2} \end{matrix}\right)$
		$\mp \dfrac{2^{s-2}}{ab^{s-1}} \Gamma\!\left[\begin{matrix} \frac{s+\nu-1}{2} \\ \frac{3-s+\nu}{2} \end{matrix}\right] {}_3F_2\!\left(\begin{matrix} \frac{1}{2},\ 1,\ 1;\ -\frac{b^2}{a^2} \\ \frac{3-s-\nu}{2},\ \frac{3-s+\nu}{2} \end{matrix}\right)$
		$+ \dfrac{2^{s-3}}{a^2 b^{s-2}} \Gamma\!\left[\begin{matrix} \frac{s+\nu-2}{2} \\ \frac{4-s+\nu}{2} \end{matrix}\right] {}_3F_2\!\left(\begin{matrix} 1,\ 1,\ \frac{3}{2};\ -\frac{b^2}{a^2} \\ \frac{4-s-\nu}{2},\ \frac{4-s+\nu}{2} \end{matrix}\right)$
		$[b,\ \mathrm{Re}\,a > 0;\ -\mathrm{Re}\,\nu < \mathrm{Re}\,s < 5/2]$
4	$e^{\pm ax^2}\,\mathrm{Ei}\,(\mp ax^2) J_\nu(bx)$	$-\dfrac{\pi b^\nu}{2^{\nu+1} a^{(s+\nu)/2}} \left\{ \begin{matrix} \csc[(s+\nu)\pi/2] \\ \cot[(s+\nu)\pi/2] \end{matrix} \right\} \Gamma\!\left[\begin{matrix} \frac{s+\nu}{2} \\ \nu+1 \end{matrix}\right] {}_1F_1\!\left(\begin{matrix} \frac{s+\nu}{2};\ \pm\frac{b^2}{4a} \\ \nu+1 \end{matrix}\right)$
		$\mp \dfrac{2^{s-3}}{ab^{s-2}} \Gamma\!\left[\begin{matrix} \frac{s+\nu-2}{2} \\ \frac{4-s+\nu}{2} \end{matrix}\right] {}_2F_2\!\left(\begin{matrix} 1,\ 1;\ \pm\frac{b^2}{4a} \\ \frac{4-s-\nu}{2},\ \frac{4-s+\nu}{2} \end{matrix}\right)$
		$[b,\ \mathrm{Re}\,a > 0;\ -\mathrm{Re}\,\nu < \mathrm{Re}\,s < 5/2]$

3.10.8. $J_\nu(bx)$ **and** $\operatorname{si}(ax^r)$, $\operatorname{Si}(ax)$, **or** $\operatorname{ci}(ax^r)$

Notation: $\delta = \left\{ \begin{matrix} 1 \\ 0 \end{matrix} \right\}$.

1	$\left\{ \begin{matrix} \operatorname{si}(ax) \\ \operatorname{ci}(ax) \end{matrix} \right\} J_\nu(bx)$	$-\dfrac{a^{-s-\nu}}{s+\nu} \left(\dfrac{b}{2}\right)^\nu \left\{ \begin{matrix} \sin\left[(s+\nu)\pi/2\right] \\ \cos\left[(s+\nu)\pi/2\right] \end{matrix} \right\} \Gamma\left[\begin{matrix} s+\nu \\ \nu+1 \end{matrix} \right]$

$$\times {}_3F_2\left(\begin{matrix} \frac{s+\nu}{2},\ \frac{s+\nu}{2},\ \frac{s+\nu+1}{2} \\ \nu+1,\ \frac{s+\nu+2}{2};\ \frac{b^2}{a^2} \end{matrix} \right)$$

$$[0 < b < a;\ -\operatorname{Re}\nu < \operatorname{Re}s < 5/2]$$

2	$\operatorname{si}(ax) J_\nu(bx)$	$\dfrac{2^s a}{b^{s+1}} \Gamma\left[\begin{matrix} \frac{s+\nu+1}{2} \\ \frac{1-s+\nu}{2} \end{matrix} \right] {}_3F_2\left(\begin{matrix} \frac{1}{2},\ \frac{s-\nu+1}{2},\ \frac{s+\nu+1}{2} \\ \frac{3}{2},\ \frac{3}{2};\ \frac{a^2}{b^2} \end{matrix} \right) - \dfrac{\pi 2^{s-2}}{b^s} \Gamma\left[\begin{matrix} \frac{s+\nu}{2} \\ \frac{2-s+\nu}{2} \end{matrix} \right]$

$$[0 < a < b;\ -\operatorname{Re}\nu < \operatorname{Re}s < 5/2]$$

3	$\operatorname{ci}(ax) J_\nu(bx)$	$\dfrac{2^{s-2}}{b^s} \Gamma\left[\begin{matrix} \frac{s+\nu}{2} \\ \frac{2-s+\nu}{2} \end{matrix} \right] \left[\dfrac{a^2(s^2-\nu^2)}{2b^2}\ {}_4F_3\left(\begin{matrix} 1,\ 1,\ \frac{s-\nu+2}{2},\ \frac{s+\nu+2}{2} \\ \frac{3}{2},\ 2,\ 2;\ \frac{a^2}{b^2} \end{matrix} \right) \right.$

$$\left. +\psi\left(\frac{s+\nu}{2}\right) + \psi\left(\frac{2-s+\nu}{2}\right) + 2\ln\frac{2a}{b} + 2\mathbf{C} \right]$$

$$[0 < a < b;\ -\operatorname{Re}\nu < \operatorname{Re}s < 5/2]$$

4	$\left\{ \begin{matrix} \operatorname{si}(ax^2) \\ \operatorname{ci}(ax^2) \end{matrix} \right\} J_\nu(bx)$	$-\dfrac{(b/2)^\nu}{a^{(s+\nu)/2}(s+\nu)} \left\{ \begin{matrix} \sin\left[(s+\nu)\pi/4\right] \\ \cos\left[(s+\nu)\pi/4\right] \end{matrix} \right\} \Gamma\left[\begin{matrix} \frac{s+\nu}{2} \\ \nu+1 \end{matrix} \right]$

$$\times {}_3F_4\left(\begin{matrix} \frac{s+\nu}{4},\ \frac{s+\nu}{4},\ \frac{s+\nu+2}{4};\ -\frac{b^4}{64a^2} \\ \frac{1}{2},\ \frac{\nu+1}{2},\ \frac{\nu+2}{2},\ \frac{s+\nu+4}{4} \end{matrix} \right)$$

$$\pm \dfrac{(b/2)^{\nu+2}}{a^{(s+\nu)/2+1}(s+\nu+2)} \left\{ \begin{matrix} \cos\left[(s+\nu)\pi/4\right] \\ \sin\left[(s+\nu)\pi/4\right] \end{matrix} \right\} \Gamma\left[\begin{matrix} \frac{s+\nu+2}{2} \\ \nu+2 \end{matrix} \right]$$

$$\times {}_3F_4\left(\begin{matrix} \frac{s+\nu+2}{4},\ \frac{s+\nu+2}{4},\ \frac{s+\nu+4}{4};\ -\frac{b^4}{64a^2} \\ \frac{3}{2},\ \frac{\nu+2}{2},\ \frac{\nu+3}{2},\ \frac{s+\nu+6}{4} \end{matrix} \right)$$

$$[a,\ b > 0;\ -\operatorname{Re}\nu < \operatorname{Re}s < 5/2]$$

5	$\left[\left\{ \begin{matrix} \sin x \\ \cos x \end{matrix} \right\} \operatorname{ci}(2x) \right.$	$-\dfrac{2^{-s-1}}{\sqrt{\pi}} \left\{ \begin{matrix} \sin\left[(s+\nu)\pi/2\right] \\ \cos\left[(s+\nu)\pi/2\right] \end{matrix} \right\} \Gamma\left[\begin{matrix} s+\nu,\ \frac{1-2s}{2} \\ 1-s+\nu \end{matrix} \right]$
	$\mp \left\{ \begin{matrix} \cos x \\ \sin x \end{matrix} \right\} \operatorname{Si}(2x) \Big]$	$\times \left[\psi\left(\dfrac{1-s-\nu+\delta}{2}\right) \mp \psi\left(\dfrac{1-s+\nu}{2}\right) \right.$
	$\times J_\nu(x)$	$\left. \pm \psi\left(\dfrac{2-s+\nu}{2}\right) - \psi\left(\dfrac{s+\nu+\delta}{2}\right) \right]$

$$[-\delta/2 < \operatorname{Re}(s+\nu) < 3/2]$$

3.10.9. $J_\nu(bx)$ **and** $\operatorname{erf}(ax^r)$, $\operatorname{erfc}(ax^r)$, **or** $\operatorname{erfi}(ax^r)$

Notation: $\delta = \left\{ \begin{matrix} 1 \\ 0 \end{matrix} \right\}$.

1	$\left\{ \begin{matrix} \operatorname{erf}(ax) \\ \operatorname{erfc}(ax) \end{matrix} \right\} J_\nu(bx)$	$\mp \dfrac{a^{-s-\nu}}{\sqrt{\pi}\,(s+\nu)} \left(\dfrac{b}{2}\right)^\nu \Gamma\left[\begin{matrix} \frac{s+\nu+1}{2} \\ \nu+1 \end{matrix}\right] {}_2F_2\left(\begin{matrix} \frac{s+\nu}{2}, \frac{s+\nu+1}{2}; -\frac{b^2}{4a^2} \\ \nu+1, \frac{s+\nu+2}{2} \end{matrix}\right)$ $+ 2^{s-2}\dfrac{1\pm 1}{b^s}\Gamma\left[\begin{matrix} \frac{s+\nu}{2} \\ \frac{2-s+\nu}{2} \end{matrix}\right]$ $\left[\left\{\begin{matrix} b>0; -1-\operatorname{Re}\nu < \operatorname{Re}s < 3/2 \\ \operatorname{Re}(s+\nu)>0 \end{matrix}\right\}; |\arg a| < \pi/4\right]$
2	$\left\{ \begin{matrix} \operatorname{erf}(a\sqrt{x}) \\ \operatorname{erfc}(a\sqrt{x}) \end{matrix} \right\} J_\nu(bx)$	$\mp \dfrac{a^{-2(s+\nu)}}{\sqrt{\pi}\,(s+\nu)} \left(\dfrac{b}{2}\right)^\nu \Gamma\left[\begin{matrix} \frac{2s+2\nu+1}{2} \\ \nu+1 \end{matrix}\right] {}_3F_2\left(\begin{matrix} \frac{s+\nu}{2}, \frac{2s+2\nu+1}{4}, \frac{2s+2\nu+3}{4} \\ \nu+1, \frac{s+\nu+2}{2}; -\frac{b^2}{a^4} \end{matrix}\right)$ $+ 2^{s-2}\dfrac{1\pm 1}{b^s}\Gamma\left[\begin{matrix} \frac{s+\nu}{2} \\ \frac{2-s+\nu}{2} \end{matrix}\right]$ $\left[b>0; \left\{\begin{matrix} -\operatorname{Re}\nu-1/2 < \operatorname{Re}s < 3/2 \\ \operatorname{Re}(s+\nu)>0 \end{matrix}\right\}; |\arg a| < \pi/4\right]$
3	$\operatorname{erf}\left(\dfrac{a}{x}\right) J_\nu(bx)$	$\dfrac{a^{s+\nu}}{\sqrt{\pi}\,(s+\nu)} \left(\dfrac{b}{2}\right)^\nu \Gamma\left[\begin{matrix} \frac{1-s-\nu}{2} \\ \nu+1 \end{matrix}\right] {}_1F_3\left(\begin{matrix} \frac{s+\nu}{2}; \frac{a^2 b^2}{4} \\ \nu+1, \frac{s+\nu+1}{2}, \frac{s+\nu+2}{2} \end{matrix}\right)$ $+ \dfrac{a}{\sqrt{\pi}}\left(\dfrac{2}{b}\right)^{s-1}\Gamma\left[\begin{matrix} \frac{s+\nu-1}{2} \\ \frac{3-s+\nu}{2} \end{matrix}\right] {}_1F_3\left(\begin{matrix} \frac{1}{2}; \frac{a^2 b^2}{4} \\ \frac{3}{2}, \frac{3-s-\nu}{2}, \frac{3-s+\nu}{2} \end{matrix}\right)$ $[b>0; -\operatorname{Re}\nu < \operatorname{Re}s < 5/2; |\arg a| < \pi/4]$
4	$e^{\mp a^2 x^2}\left\{\begin{matrix} \operatorname{erfi}(ax) \\ \operatorname{erfc}(ax) \end{matrix}\right\}$ $\times J_\nu(bx)$	$\dfrac{b^\nu}{2^{\nu+1}a^{s+\nu}}\Gamma\left[\begin{matrix} \frac{s+\nu}{2} \\ \nu+1 \end{matrix}\right]\left\{\begin{matrix} \tan[(s+\nu)\pi/2] \\ \sec[(s+\nu)\pi/2] \end{matrix}\right\} {}_1F_1\left(\begin{matrix} \frac{s+\nu}{2}; \mp\frac{b^2}{4a^2} \\ \nu+1 \end{matrix}\right)$ $+ \dfrac{2^{s-2}b^{1-s}}{\sqrt{\pi}\,a}\Gamma\left[\begin{matrix} \frac{s+\nu-1}{2} \\ \frac{3-s+\nu}{2} \end{matrix}\right] {}_2F_2\left(\begin{matrix} \frac{1}{2}, 1; \mp\frac{b^2}{4a^2} \\ \frac{3-s-\nu}{2}, \frac{3-s+\nu}{2} \end{matrix}\right)$ $[b>0; -\operatorname{Re}\nu-(1\pm 1)/2 < \operatorname{Re}s < 5/2; |\arg a| < \pi/4]$
5	$e^{-a^2 x}\operatorname{erfi}(a\sqrt{x})J_\nu(bx)$	$\dfrac{2^{s+1/2}ab^{-s-1/2}}{\sqrt{\pi}}\Gamma\left[\begin{matrix} \frac{2s+2\nu+1}{4} \\ \frac{3-2s+2\nu}{4} \end{matrix}\right] {}_3F_2\left(\begin{matrix} 1, \frac{2s-2\nu+1}{4}, \frac{2s+2\nu+1}{4} \\ \frac{3}{4}, \frac{5}{4}; -\frac{a^4}{b^2} \end{matrix}\right)$ $- \dfrac{2^{s+5/2}a^3 b^{-s-3/2}}{3\sqrt{\pi}}\Gamma\left[\begin{matrix} \frac{2s+2\nu+3}{4} \\ \frac{1-2s+2\nu}{4} \end{matrix}\right] {}_3F_2\left(\begin{matrix} 1, \frac{2s-2\nu+3}{4}, \frac{2s+2\nu+3}{4} \\ \frac{5}{4}, \frac{7}{4}; -\frac{a^4}{b^2} \end{matrix}\right)$ $[b>0; -\operatorname{Re}\nu-1/2 < \operatorname{Re}s < 2; |\arg a| < \pi/4]$
6	$e^{a^2 x}\operatorname{erfc}(a\sqrt{x})J_\nu(bx)$	$\dfrac{2^{1-2s-3\nu}a^{-2s-2\nu}b^\nu}{\sqrt{\pi}}\Gamma\left[\begin{matrix} \frac{1-2s-2\nu}{2}, 2s+2\nu \\ \nu+1 \end{matrix}\right] {}_2F_1\left(\begin{matrix} \frac{s+\nu}{2}, \frac{s+\nu+1}{2} \\ \nu+1; -\frac{b^2}{a^4} \end{matrix}\right)$ $+ \dfrac{2^{s-3/2}b^{1/2-s}}{a\sqrt{\pi}}\Gamma\left[\begin{matrix} \frac{2s+2\nu-1}{4} \\ \frac{5-2s+2\nu}{4} \end{matrix}\right] {}_3F_2\left(\begin{matrix} \frac{1}{4}, \frac{3}{4}, 1; -\frac{b^2}{a^4} \\ \frac{5-2s-2\nu}{4}, \frac{5-2s+2\nu}{4} \end{matrix}\right)$ $- \dfrac{2^{s-7/2}b^{3/2-s}}{a^3\sqrt{\pi}}\Gamma\left[\begin{matrix} \frac{2s+2\nu-3}{4} \\ \frac{7-2s+2\nu}{4} \end{matrix}\right] {}_3F_2\left(\begin{matrix} \frac{3}{4}, 1, \frac{5}{4}; -\frac{b^2}{a^4} \\ \frac{7-2s-2\nu}{4}, \frac{7-2s+2\nu}{4} \end{matrix}\right)$ $[b>0; -\operatorname{Re}\nu < \operatorname{Re}s < 2; |\arg a| < \pi/4]$

No.	$f(x)$	$F(s)$
7	$\left\{ \begin{array}{c} \sin(bx) \\ \cos(bx) \end{array} \right\} \operatorname{erfc}(ax)$ $\times J_\nu(bx)$	$\dfrac{(2b)^{\nu+\delta}}{\pi a^{s+\nu+\delta}(s+\nu+\delta)} \Gamma\left[\begin{array}{c} \frac{2\nu+2\delta+1}{2}, \frac{s+\nu+\delta+1}{2} \\ 2\nu+\delta+1 \end{array} \right]$ $\times {}_4F_4\left(\begin{array}{c} \frac{2\nu+3}{4}, \frac{2\nu+4\delta+1}{4}, \frac{s+\nu+1}{2}, \frac{s+\nu+2\delta}{2}; -\frac{b^2}{a^2} \\ \frac{2\delta+1}{2}, \nu+1, \frac{2\nu+2\delta+1}{2}, \frac{s+\nu+\delta+2}{2} \end{array} \right)$ $[\operatorname{Re}(s+\nu) > -(1\pm1)/2; \, |\arg a| < \pi/4]$

3.10.10. $J_\nu(bx)$ and $S(ax^r)$, $C(ax^r)$

Notation: $\delta = \left\{ \begin{array}{c} 1 \\ 0 \end{array} \right\}$.

1	$\left\{ \begin{array}{c} S(ax) \\ C(ax) \end{array} \right\} J_\nu(bx)$	$-\dfrac{2^{-\nu-1/2}b^\nu}{\sqrt{\pi}\,a^{s+\nu}(s+\nu)} \Gamma\left[\begin{array}{c} \frac{2s+2\nu+1}{2} \\ \nu+1 \end{array} \right]$ $\times \left\{ \begin{array}{c} \cos[(2s+2\nu+1)\pi/4] \\ \sin[(2s+2\nu+1)\pi/4] \end{array} \right\}$ $\times {}_3F_2\left(\begin{array}{c} \frac{s+\nu}{2}, \frac{2s+2\nu+1}{4}, \frac{2s+2\nu+3}{4} \\ \nu+1, \frac{s+\nu+2}{2}; \frac{b^2}{a^2} \end{array} \right) + \dfrac{2^{s-2}}{b^s} \Gamma\left[\begin{array}{c} \frac{s+\nu}{2} \\ \frac{2-s+\nu}{2} \end{array} \right]$ $\left[-(2\pm1)/2 - \operatorname{Re}\nu < \operatorname{Re}s < \left\{ \begin{array}{c} 3/2 \text{ for } 0 < b < a \\ 1 \text{ for } 0 < b = a \end{array} \right\} \right]$
2	$\left\{ \begin{array}{c} S(ax) \\ C(ax) \end{array} \right\} J_\nu(bx)$	$\dfrac{2^{s+\delta}a^{\delta+1/2}}{3^\delta \sqrt{\pi}\, b^{s+\delta+1/2}} \Gamma\left[\begin{array}{c} \frac{2\nu+2s+2\delta+1}{4} \\ \frac{2\nu-2s-2\delta+3}{4} \end{array} \right]$ $\times {}_3F_2\left(\begin{array}{c} \frac{2\delta+1}{4}, \frac{2s+2\delta+2\nu+1}{4}, \frac{2s+2\delta-2\nu+1}{4} \\ \frac{2\delta+5}{4}, \frac{2\delta+1}{2}; \frac{a^2}{b^2} \end{array} \right)$ $[0 < a < b; \, -(2\pm1)/2 - \operatorname{Re}\nu < \operatorname{Re}s < 3/2]$
3	$\left\{ \begin{array}{c} S(ax^2) \\ C(ax^2) \end{array} \right\} J_\nu(bx)$	$-\dfrac{a^{-(s+\nu)/2}b^\nu}{2^{\nu+1/2}\sqrt{\pi}(s+\nu)} \Gamma\left[\begin{array}{c} \frac{s+\nu+1}{2} \\ \nu+1 \end{array} \right] \left\{ \begin{array}{c} \sin[(s+\nu+1)\pi/4] \\ \cos[(s+\nu+1)\pi/4] \end{array} \right\}$ $\times {}_3F_4\left(\begin{array}{c} \frac{s+\nu}{4}, \frac{s+\nu+1}{4}, \frac{s+\nu+3}{4}; -\frac{b^4}{64a^2} \\ \frac{1}{2}, \frac{\nu+1}{2}, \frac{\nu+2}{2}, \frac{s+\nu+4}{4} \end{array} \right)$ $\pm \dfrac{a^{-(s+\nu)/2-1}b^{\nu+2}}{2^{\nu+5/2}\sqrt{\pi}(s+\nu+2)} \Gamma\left[\begin{array}{c} \frac{s+\nu+3}{2} \\ \nu+2 \end{array} \right]$ $\times \left\{ \begin{array}{c} \cos[(s+\nu+1)\pi/4] \\ \sin[(s+\nu+1)\pi/4] \end{array} \right\}$ $\times {}_3F_4\left(\begin{array}{c} \frac{s+\nu+2}{4}, \frac{s+\nu+3}{4}, \frac{s+\nu+5}{4}; -\frac{b^4}{64a^2} \\ \frac{3}{2}, \frac{\nu+2}{2}, \frac{\nu+3}{2}, \frac{s+\nu+6}{4} \end{array} \right) + \dfrac{2^{s-2}}{b^s} \Gamma\left[\begin{array}{c} \frac{s+\nu}{2} \\ \frac{2-s+\nu}{2} \end{array} \right]$ $[a, b > 0; \, -2\mp1 - \operatorname{Re}\nu < \operatorname{Re}s < 3/2]$

3.10.11. $\quad J_\nu(bx)$ **and** $\Gamma(\mu, ax^r)$, $\gamma(\mu, ax^r)$

Notation: $\delta = \left\{ \begin{matrix} 1 \\ 0 \end{matrix} \right\}$.

1	$\left\{ \begin{matrix} \gamma(\mu, ax) \\ \Gamma(\mu, ax) \end{matrix} \right\} J_\nu(bx)$	$\mp \dfrac{a^{-s-\nu}}{s+\nu} \left(\dfrac{b}{2}\right)^\nu \Gamma\left[\begin{matrix} s+\mu+\nu \\ \nu+1 \end{matrix} \right] {}_3F_2\left(\begin{matrix} \frac{s+\nu}{2}, \frac{s+\mu+\nu}{2}, \frac{s+\mu+\nu+1}{2} \\ \nu+1, \frac{s+\nu+2}{2}; -\frac{b^2}{a^2} \end{matrix} \right)$
		$+ \dfrac{2^{s-1}\delta}{b^s} \Gamma\left[\begin{matrix} \mu, \frac{s+\nu}{2} \\ \frac{2-s+\nu}{2} \end{matrix} \right]$
		$\left[b, \operatorname{Re} a, \operatorname{Re}(s+\mu+\nu) > 0; \left\{ \begin{matrix} \operatorname{Re}\mu > 0; \ \operatorname{Re}s < 3/2 \\ \operatorname{Re}(s+\nu) > 0 \end{matrix} \right\} \right]$
2	$\left\{ \begin{matrix} \gamma(\mu, ax^2) \\ \Gamma(\mu, ax^2) \end{matrix} \right\} J_\nu(bx)$	$\mp \dfrac{a^{-(s+\nu)/2}}{s+\nu} \left(\dfrac{b}{2}\right)^\nu \Gamma\left[\begin{matrix} \frac{s+2\mu+\nu}{2} \\ \nu+1 \end{matrix} \right] {}_2F_2\left(\begin{matrix} \frac{s+\nu}{2}, \frac{s+2\mu+\nu}{2}; -\frac{b^2}{4a} \\ \nu+1, \frac{s+\nu+2}{2} \end{matrix} \right)$
		$+ \dfrac{2^{s-1}\delta}{b^s} \Gamma\left[\begin{matrix} \mu, \frac{s+\nu}{2} \\ \frac{2-s+\nu}{2} \end{matrix} \right]$
		$\left[b, \operatorname{Re} a, \operatorname{Re}(s+2\mu+\nu) > 0; \left\{ \begin{matrix} \operatorname{Re}\mu > 0; \ \operatorname{Re}s < 3/2 \\ \operatorname{Re}(s+\nu) > 0 \end{matrix} \right\} \right]$

3.10.12. $\quad J_\nu(bx)$ **and** $D_\nu(ax^r)$

Notation: $\delta = \left\{ \begin{matrix} 1 \\ 0 \end{matrix} \right\}$.

1	$e^{-a^2x^2/4} D_\mu(ax) \, J_\nu(bx)$	$\dfrac{2^{(s+\mu-\nu)/2-1} b^\nu}{a^{s+\nu}} \Gamma\left[\begin{matrix} \frac{s+\nu}{2}, \frac{s+\nu+1}{2} \\ \nu+1, \frac{s+\nu-\mu+1}{2} \end{matrix} \right] {}_2F_2\left(\begin{matrix} \frac{s+\nu}{2}, \frac{s+\nu+1}{2}; -\frac{b^2}{2a^2} \\ \nu+1, \frac{s+\nu-\mu+1}{2} \end{matrix} \right)$
		$[\operatorname{Re}(s+\nu) > 0; \ |\arg a| < \pi/4]$
2	$e^{a^2x^2/4} D_\mu(ax) \, J_\nu(bx)$	$\dfrac{b^\nu}{2^{(s+\mu+3\nu)/2+1} a^{s+\nu}} \Gamma\left[\begin{matrix} s+\nu, -\frac{s+\nu+\mu}{2} \\ \nu+1, -\mu \end{matrix} \right] {}_2F_2\left(\begin{matrix} \frac{s+\nu}{2}, \frac{s+\nu+1}{2}; \frac{b^2}{2a^2} \\ \nu+1, \frac{s+\nu+\mu+2}{2} \end{matrix} \right)$
		$+ \dfrac{2^{s+\mu-1} a^\mu}{b^{s+\mu}} \Gamma\left[\begin{matrix} \frac{s+\nu+\mu}{2} \\ -\frac{s-\nu+\mu-2}{2} \end{matrix} \right] {}_2F_2\left(\begin{matrix} \frac{1-\mu}{2}, -\frac{\mu}{2}; \frac{b^2}{2a^2} \\ -\frac{s+\nu+\mu-2}{2}, -\frac{s-\nu+\mu-2}{2} \end{matrix} \right)$
		$[b > 0; \ -\operatorname{Re}\nu < \operatorname{Re}s < 3/2 - \operatorname{Re}\mu; \ |\arg a| < 3\pi/4]$
3	$e^{-a^2/(4x^2)} D_\mu\left(\dfrac{a}{x}\right)$	$\dfrac{\sqrt{\pi}\, 2^{(2s+\mu-2)/2}}{b^s} \Gamma\left[\begin{matrix} \frac{s+\nu}{2} \\ \frac{1-\mu}{2}, \frac{2-s+\nu}{2} \end{matrix} \right] {}_1F_3\left(\begin{matrix} \frac{\mu+1}{2}; \frac{a^2b^2}{8} \\ \frac{1}{2}, \frac{2-s-\nu}{2}, \frac{2-s+\nu}{2} \end{matrix} \right)$
	$\times J_\nu(bx)$	$- \dfrac{\sqrt{\pi}\, 2^{(2s+\mu-3)/2} a}{b^{s-1}} \Gamma\left[\begin{matrix} \frac{s+\nu-1}{2} \\ -\frac{\mu}{2}, \frac{3-s+\nu}{2} \end{matrix} \right] {}_1F_3\left(\begin{matrix} \frac{\mu+2}{2}; \frac{a^2b^2}{8} \\ \frac{3}{2}, \frac{3-s-\nu}{2}, \frac{3-s+\nu}{2} \end{matrix} \right)$
		$+ \sqrt{\pi}\, 2^{(s+\mu-\nu)/2} a^{s+\nu} b^\nu \Gamma\left[\begin{matrix} -\nu \\ s+\nu+1, \frac{1-s-\mu-\nu}{2} \end{matrix} \right]$
		$\times \sin(\nu\pi) \csc\left[(s+\nu)\pi \right] {}_1F_3\left(\begin{matrix} \frac{s+\mu+\nu+1}{2}; \frac{a^2b^2}{8} \\ \nu+1, \frac{s+\nu+1}{2}, \frac{s+\nu+2}{2} \end{matrix} \right)$
		$[b > 0; \ \operatorname{Re}(\mu-\nu) < \operatorname{Re}s < 3/2; \ |\arg a| < \pi/4]$

No.	$f(x)$	$F(s)$
4	$D_{-\mu-1}\left(a\sqrt{x}\right)D_\mu\left(a\sqrt{x}\right)$ $\times J_\nu\left(bx\right)$	$\dfrac{2^{1/2-2s-3\nu}\,\pi b^\nu}{a^{2s+2\nu}}\,\Gamma\left[\begin{matrix}2s+2\nu\\ \nu+1,\ \frac{s+\mu+\nu+2}{2},\ \frac{s-\mu+\nu+1}{2}\end{matrix}\right]$ $\times {}_4F_3\left(\begin{matrix}\frac{s+\nu}{2},\ \frac{s+\nu+1}{2},\ \frac{2s+2\nu+1}{4},\ \frac{2s+2\nu+3}{4}\\ \nu+1,\ \frac{s+\mu+\nu+2}{2},\ \frac{s-\mu+\nu+1}{2};\ -\frac{4b^2}{a^4}\end{matrix}\right)$ $[b,\ \mathrm{Re}\,(s+\nu)>0;\ |\arg a|<\pi/4]$

3.10.13. Products of $J_\mu\left(ax\right)$

No.	$f(x)$	$F(s)$	
1	$J_\nu^2\left(ax\right)$	$\dfrac{a^{-s}}{2\sqrt{\pi}}\,\Gamma\left[\begin{matrix}\frac{1-s}{2},\ \frac{s+2\nu}{2}\\ \frac{2-s}{2},\ \frac{2-s+2\nu}{2}\end{matrix}\right]$	$[a>0;\ -2\,\mathrm{Re}\,\nu<\mathrm{Re}\,s<1]$
2	$J_{\nu-1}\left(ax\right)J_\nu\left(ax\right)$	$\dfrac{a^{-s}}{2\sqrt{\pi}}\,\Gamma\left[\begin{matrix}\frac{2-s}{2},\ \frac{s+2\nu-1}{2}\\ \frac{3-s}{2},\ \frac{1-s+2\nu}{2}\end{matrix}\right]$	$[a>0;\ 1-2\,\mathrm{Re}\,\nu<\mathrm{Re}\,s<2]$
3	$J_{-\nu}\left(ax\right)J_\nu\left(ax\right)$	$\dfrac{a^{-s}}{2\sqrt{\pi}}\,\Gamma\left[\begin{matrix}\frac{s}{2},\ \frac{1-s}{2}\\ \frac{2-s-2\nu}{2},\ \frac{2-s+2\nu}{2}\end{matrix}\right]$	$[a>0;\ 0<\mathrm{Re}\,s<1]$
4	$J_{-\nu-1}\left(ax\right)J_\nu\left(ax\right)$ $+\dfrac{2\sin\left(\pi\nu\right)}{\pi ax}$	$-\dfrac{a^{-s}}{2\sqrt{\pi}}\,\Gamma\left[\begin{matrix}\frac{1-s}{2},\ \frac{2-s}{2},\ \frac{s+1}{2}\\ \frac{3-s}{2},\ \frac{1-s-2\nu}{2},\ \frac{3-s+2\nu}{2}\end{matrix}\right]$	$[a>0;\ |\mathrm{Re}\,s|<1]$
5	$J_{-\nu-2}\left(ax\right)J_\nu\left(ax\right)$ $-\dfrac{4\left(\nu+1\right)\sin\left(\pi\nu\right)}{\pi a^2x^2}$	$\dfrac{a^{-s}}{2\sqrt{\pi}}\,\Gamma\left[\begin{matrix}\frac{1-s}{2},\ \frac{2-s}{2},\ \frac{s+2}{2}\\ \frac{4-s}{2},\ -\frac{s+2\nu}{2},\ \frac{4-s+2\nu}{2}\end{matrix}\right]$	$[a>0;\ -2<\mathrm{Re}\,s<1]$
6	$J_{-n-\nu-1}\left(ax\right)J_\nu\left(ax\right)$ $-\dfrac{2}{\sqrt{\pi}}\displaystyle\sum_{k=0}^{[n/2]}\dfrac{(-1)^{[(n+1)/2]+k}}{k!}$ $\times\dfrac{\left([n/2]-k+1\right)_{n-[n/2]}}{(ax)^{n-2k+1}}$ $\times\Gamma\left[\begin{matrix}k-n+\left[\frac{n}{2}\right]+\frac{1}{2}\\ k+\nu+1,\ k-n-\nu\end{matrix}\right]$	$\dfrac{(-1)^{n+1}a^{-s}}{2\sqrt{\pi}}\,\Gamma\left[\begin{matrix}\frac{1-s}{2},\ \frac{2-s}{2},\ \frac{s+n+1}{2}\\ \frac{3-s+n}{2},\ -\frac{s+n+2\nu-1}{2},\ \frac{3-s+n+2\nu}{2}\end{matrix}\right]$	$[a>0;\ -n-1<\mathrm{Re}\,s<1]$
7	$J_\mu\left(ax\right)J_\nu\left(ax\right)$	$\dfrac{2^{s-1}}{a^s}\,\Gamma\left[\begin{matrix}1-s,\ \frac{s+\mu+\nu}{2}\\ \frac{2-s+\mu-\nu}{2},\ \frac{2-s-\mu+\nu}{2},\ \frac{2-s+\mu+\nu}{2}\end{matrix}\right]$	$[a>0;\ -\,\mathrm{Re}\,(\mu+\nu)<\mathrm{Re}\,s<1]$

No.	$f(x)$	$F(s)$
8	$J_\mu(ax) J_\nu(ax)$ $-\dfrac{2^{-\mu-\nu}(ax)^{\mu+\nu}}{\Gamma(\mu+1)\Gamma(\nu+1)}$	$\dfrac{2^{s-1}}{a^s}\Gamma\left[\begin{matrix}1-s,\ \frac{s+\mu+\nu}{2}\\ \frac{2-s+\mu-\nu}{2},\ \frac{2-s-\mu+\nu}{2},\ \frac{2-s+\mu+\nu}{2}\end{matrix}\right]$ $[a>0;\ -\operatorname{Re}(\mu+\nu)-2<\operatorname{Re}s<-\operatorname{Re}(\mu+\nu),\ 1]$
9	$J_\nu(ax) J_\nu(bx)$	$\dfrac{2^{s-1}(ab)^\nu}{(a+b)^{s+2\nu}}\Gamma\left[\begin{matrix}\frac{s+2\nu}{2}\\ \nu+1,\ \frac{2-s}{2}\end{matrix}\right]{}_2F_1\left(\begin{matrix}\frac{2\nu+1}{2},\ \frac{s+2\nu}{2}\\ 2\nu+1;\ \frac{4ab}{(a+b)^2}\end{matrix}\right)$ $[a,b>0;\ a\neq b;\ -2\operatorname{Re}\nu<\operatorname{Re}s<2]$
10	$J_\mu(ax) J_\nu(bx)$	$\dfrac{2^{s-1}b^\nu}{a^{s+\nu}}\Gamma\left[\begin{matrix}\frac{s+\mu+\nu}{2}\\ \nu+1,\ \frac{2-s+\mu-\nu}{2}\end{matrix}\right]{}_2F_1\left(\begin{matrix}\frac{s+\mu+\nu}{2},\ \frac{s-\mu+\nu}{2}\\ \nu+1;\ \frac{b^2}{a^2}\end{matrix}\right)$ $[0<b<a;\ -(\mu+\nu)<\operatorname{Re}s<2]$
11	$J_\mu(a\sqrt{x}) J_\nu(bx)$	$\dfrac{2^{s-\mu/2-1}a^\mu}{b^{s+\mu/2}}\Gamma\left[\begin{matrix}\frac{2s+\mu+2\nu}{4}\\ \mu+1,\ \frac{4-2s-\mu+2\nu}{4}\end{matrix}\right]{}_2F_3\left(\begin{matrix}\frac{2s+\mu-2\nu}{4},\ \frac{2s+\mu+2\nu}{4}\\ \frac{1}{2},\ \frac{\mu+1}{2},\ \frac{\mu+2}{2};\ -\frac{a^4}{64b^2}\end{matrix}\right)$ $-\dfrac{2^{s-\mu/2-2}a^{\mu+2}}{b^{s+\mu/2+1}}\Gamma\left[\begin{matrix}\frac{2s+\mu+2\nu+2}{4}\\ \mu+2,\ \frac{2-2s-\mu+2\nu}{4}\end{matrix}\right]$ $\times{}_2F_3\left(\begin{matrix}\frac{2s+\mu-2\nu+2}{4},\ \frac{2s+\mu+2\nu+2}{4}\\ \frac{3}{2},\ \frac{\mu+2}{2},\ \frac{\mu+3}{2};\ -\frac{a^4}{64b^2}\end{matrix}\right)$ $[a,b>0;\ -\operatorname{Re}(\nu+\mu/2)<\operatorname{Re}s<7/4]$
12	$J_\mu\left(\dfrac{a}{x}\right) J_\nu(bx)$	$\dfrac{a^\mu b^{\mu-s}}{2^{2\mu-s+1}}\Gamma\left[\begin{matrix}\frac{s-\mu+\nu}{2}\\ \mu+1,\ \frac{2-s+\mu+\nu}{2}\end{matrix}\right]{}_0F_3\left(\begin{matrix}\frac{a^2b^2}{16}\\ \mu+1,\ \frac{2-s+\mu-\nu}{2},\ \frac{2-s+\mu+\nu}{2}\end{matrix}\right)$ $+\dfrac{a^{s+\nu}b^\nu}{2^{s+2\nu+1}}\Gamma\left[\begin{matrix}\frac{\mu-\nu-s}{2}\\ \nu+1,\ \frac{s+\mu+\nu+2}{2}\end{matrix}\right]$ $\times{}_0F_3\left(\begin{matrix}\frac{a^2b^2}{16}\\ \nu+1,\ \frac{s-\mu+\nu+2}{2},\ \frac{s+\mu+\nu+2}{2}\end{matrix}\right)$ $[a,b>0;\ -\operatorname{Re}\nu-3/2<\operatorname{Re}s<\operatorname{Re}\mu+3/2]$
13	$J_\nu^2(ax)\pm J_{-\nu}^2(ax)$	$\pm\dfrac{a^{-s}}{\pi^{3/2}}\left\{\begin{matrix}\cos(\nu\pi)\sin(s\pi/2)\\ \sin(\nu\pi)\cos(s\pi/2)\end{matrix}\right\}\Gamma\left[\begin{matrix}\frac{1-s}{2},\ \frac{s}{2}-\nu,\ \frac{s}{2}+\nu\\ \frac{2-s}{2}\end{matrix}\right]$ $[a>0;\ 2|\operatorname{Re}\nu|<\operatorname{Re}s<(3\mp1)/2],$
14	$J_\mu(ax) J_\nu(ax)$ $\pm J_{-\mu}(ax) J_{-\nu}(ax)$	$\pm\dfrac{1}{\pi}\left(\dfrac{2}{a}\right)^s\left\{\begin{matrix}\cos[(\mu+\nu)\pi/2]\sin(s\pi/2)\\ \sin[(\mu+\nu)\pi/2]\cos(s\pi/2)\end{matrix}\right\}$ $\times\Gamma\left[\begin{matrix}1-s,\ \frac{s-\mu-\nu}{2},\ \frac{s+\mu+\nu}{2}\\ \frac{2-s+\mu-\nu}{2},\ \frac{2-s-\mu+\nu}{2}\end{matrix}\right]$ $[a>0;\ |\operatorname{Re}(\mu+\nu)|<\operatorname{Re}s<(3\mp1)/2]$

3.10.14. $J_\mu(bx)\, J_\nu(cx)$ and the exponential or trigonometric functions

Notation: $\delta = \left\{ \begin{matrix} 1 \\ 0 \end{matrix} \right\}$.

1	$e^{-ax} J_\mu(bx)\, J_\nu(bx)$	$a^{-s-\mu-\nu} \left(\dfrac{b}{2} \right)^{\mu+\nu} \Gamma \left[\begin{matrix} s+\mu+\nu \\ \mu+1,\ \nu+1 \end{matrix} \right]$

$$\times\ {}_4F_3 \left(\begin{matrix} \frac{\mu+\nu+1}{2},\ \frac{\mu+\nu+2}{2},\ \frac{s+\mu+\nu}{2},\ \frac{s+\mu+\nu+1}{2} \\ \mu+1,\ \nu+1,\ \mu+\nu+1;\ -\frac{4b^2}{a^2} \end{matrix} \right)$$

$$[\operatorname{Re} a > 2|\operatorname{Im} b|];\ \ \operatorname{Re}(s+\mu+\nu) > 0$$

2	$e^{-ax} J_\mu(bx)\, J_\nu(cx)$	$\dfrac{b^\mu c^\nu}{2^{\mu+\nu} a^{s+\mu+\nu}} \Gamma \left[\begin{matrix} s+\mu+\nu \\ \mu+1,\ \nu+1 \end{matrix} \right]$

$$\times\ F_4 \left(\frac{s+\mu+\nu}{2},\ \frac{s+\mu+\nu+1}{2};\ \mu+1,\ \nu+1;\ -\frac{b^2}{a^2},\ -\frac{c^2}{a^2} \right)$$

$$[\operatorname{Re} a > |\operatorname{Im} b| + |\operatorname{Im} c|;\ \operatorname{Re}(s+\mu+\nu) > 0]$$

3	$e^{-ax^2} J_\mu(bx)\, J_\nu(bx)$	$\dfrac{b^{\mu+\nu}}{2^{\mu+\nu+1} a^{(s+\mu+\nu)/2}} \Gamma \left[\begin{matrix} \frac{s+\mu+\nu}{2} \\ \mu+1,\ \nu+1 \end{matrix} \right]$

$$\times\ {}_3F_3 \left(\begin{matrix} \frac{s+\mu+\nu}{2},\ \frac{\mu+\nu+1}{2},\ \frac{\mu+\nu+2}{2};\ -\frac{b^2}{a} \\ \mu+1,\ \nu+1,\ \mu+\nu+1 \end{matrix} \right)$$

$$[\operatorname{Re} a,\ \operatorname{Re}(s+\mu+\nu) > 0]$$

4	$e^{-ax^2} J_\mu(bx)\, J_\nu(cx)$	$\dfrac{b^\mu c^\nu}{2^{\mu+\nu+1} a^{(s+\mu+\nu)/2}} \Gamma \left[\begin{matrix} \frac{s+\mu+\nu}{2} \\ \mu+1,\ \nu+1 \end{matrix} \right]$

$$\times\ \Psi_2 \left(\frac{s+\mu+\nu}{2};\ \mu+1,\ \nu+1;\ -\frac{b^2}{4a},\ -\frac{c^2}{4a} \right)$$

$$[\operatorname{Re} a,\ \operatorname{Re}(s+\mu+\nu) > 0]$$

5	$\left\{ \begin{matrix} \sin(ax) \\ \cos(ax) \end{matrix} \right\}$ $\times\ J_\mu(bx)\, J_\nu(bx)$	$\dfrac{(b/2)^{\mu+\nu}}{a^{s+\mu+\nu}} \Gamma \left[\begin{matrix} s+\mu+\nu \\ \mu+1,\ \nu+1 \end{matrix} \right] \left\{ \begin{matrix} \sin[(s+\mu+\nu)\pi/2] \\ \cos[(s+\mu+\nu)\pi/2] \end{matrix} \right\}$

$$\times\ {}_4F_3 \left(\begin{matrix} \frac{\mu+\nu+1}{2},\ \frac{\mu+\nu+2}{2},\ \frac{s+\mu+\nu}{2},\ \frac{s+\mu+\nu+1}{2} \\ \mu+1,\ \nu+1,\ \mu+\nu+1;\ \frac{4b^2}{a^2} \end{matrix} \right)$$

$$\left[\begin{matrix} (0 < 2b < a;\ \operatorname{Re} s < 2;\ \operatorname{Re}(s+\mu+\nu) > -(1\pm 1)/2) \\ \text{or}\ (a = 2b > 0;\ \operatorname{Re} s < 1) \end{matrix} \right]$$

6	$\left\{ \begin{matrix} \sin(ax) \\ \cos(ax) \end{matrix} \right\}$ $\times\ J_\mu(bx)\, J_\nu(bx)$	$\dfrac{2^{s+\delta-1} a^\delta}{b^{s+\delta}} \Gamma \left[\begin{matrix} 1-s-\delta,\ \frac{s+\mu+\nu+\delta}{2} \\ \frac{2-s+\mu-\nu-\delta}{2},\ \frac{2-s-\mu+\nu-\delta}{2},\ \frac{2-s+\mu+\nu-\delta}{2} \end{matrix} \right]$

$$\times\ {}_4F_3 \left(\begin{matrix} \frac{s-\mu-\nu+\delta}{2},\ \frac{s+\mu-\nu+\delta}{2},\ \frac{s-\mu+\nu+\delta}{2},\ \frac{s+\mu+\nu+\delta}{2} \\ \frac{2\delta+1}{2},\ \frac{s+\delta}{2},\ \frac{s+\delta+1}{2};\ \frac{a^2}{4b^2} \end{matrix} \right)$$

$$-\ \frac{(\mu^2-\nu^2)\, a^{2-s}}{2\pi b^2} \sin \frac{(\mu-\nu)\pi}{2} \left\{ \begin{matrix} \sin(s\pi/2) \\ \cos(s\pi/2) \end{matrix} \right\}$$

$$\times\ \Gamma(s-2)\ {}_4F_3 \left(\begin{matrix} \frac{2-\mu-\nu}{2},\ \frac{2-\mu+\nu}{2},\ \frac{\mu-\nu+2}{2},\ \frac{\mu+\nu+2}{2} \\ \frac{3}{2},\ \frac{3-s}{2},\ \frac{4-s}{2};\ \frac{a^2}{4b^2} \end{matrix} \right) \mp$$

No.	$f(x)$	$F(s)$
		$$\mp \frac{a^{1-s}}{\pi b} \cos \frac{(\mu-\nu)\pi}{2} \left\{ \begin{matrix} \cos(s\pi/2) \\ \sin(s\pi/2) \end{matrix} \right\}$$ $$\times \Gamma(s-1)\ {}_4F_3\left(\begin{matrix} \frac{1-\mu-\nu}{2}, \frac{1-\mu+\nu}{2}, \frac{\mu-\nu+1}{2}, \frac{\mu+\nu+1}{2} \\ \frac{1}{2}, \frac{2-s}{2}, \frac{3-s}{2}; \frac{a^2}{4b^2} \end{matrix} \right)$$ $$[0 < a < 2b;\ \mathrm{Re}\,s < 2;\ \mathrm{Re}\,(s+\mu+\nu) > -\delta]$$

3.10.15. $J_\mu(bx)\,J_\nu(bx)$ and the logarithmic function

No.	$f(x)$	$F(s)$
1	$\theta(a-x)$ $\times \ln \dfrac{\sqrt{a-x}+\sqrt{a}}{\sqrt{x}}$ $\times J_\mu(bx)\,J_\nu(bx)$	$$\frac{\sqrt{\pi}\,a^{s+\mu+\nu}b^{\mu+\nu}}{2^{\mu+\nu+1}(s+\mu+\nu)}\Gamma\left[\begin{matrix} s+\mu+\nu \\ \mu+1,\ \nu+1,\ s+\mu+\nu+\frac{1}{2} \end{matrix}\right]$$ $$\times {}_5F_6\left(\begin{matrix} \frac{\mu+\nu+1}{2}, \frac{\mu+\nu+2}{2}, \frac{s+\mu+\nu}{2}, \frac{s+\mu+\nu}{2}, \frac{s+\mu+\nu+1}{2}; -a^2b^2 \\ \mu+1,\ \nu+1,\ \mu+\nu+1,\ \Delta\left(2, \frac{2s+2\mu+2\nu+1}{2}\right),\ \frac{s+\mu+\nu+2}{2} \end{matrix}\right)$$ $$[a>0;\ \mathrm{Re}\,(s+\mu+\nu)>0]$$
2	$\theta(a-x)$ $\times \ln \dfrac{\sqrt{a^2-x^2}+a}{x}$ $\times J_\mu(bx)\,J_\nu(bx)$	$$\frac{\sqrt{\pi}\,a^{s+\mu+\nu}b^{\mu+\nu}}{2^{\mu+\nu+1}(s+\mu+\nu)}\Gamma\left[\begin{matrix} \frac{s+\mu+\nu}{2} \\ \mu+1,\ \nu+1,\ \frac{s+\mu+\nu+1}{2} \end{matrix}\right]$$ $$\times {}_4F_5\left(\begin{matrix} \frac{\mu+\nu+1}{2}, \frac{\mu+\nu+2}{2}, \frac{s+\mu+\nu}{2}, \frac{s+\mu+\nu}{2}; -a^2b^2 \\ \mu+1,\ \nu+1,\ \mu+\nu+1,\ \frac{s+\mu+\nu+1}{2},\ \frac{s+\mu+\nu+2}{2} \end{matrix}\right)$$ $$[a>0;\ \mathrm{Re}\,(s+(\mu+\nu)/2)>0]$$

3.10.16. $J_\mu(bx)\,J_\nu(bx)$ and inverse trigonometric functions

No.	$f(x)$	$F(s)$
1	$\theta(a-x)\arccos\dfrac{x}{a}$ $\times J_\mu(bx)\,J_\nu(bx)$	$$\frac{2^{-\mu-\nu-1}\sqrt{\pi}\,a^{\mu+\nu+s}b^{\mu+\nu}}{\Gamma(\mu+1)\Gamma(\nu+1)(s+\mu+\nu)}\Gamma\left[\begin{matrix} \frac{s+\mu+\nu+1}{2} \\ \frac{s+\mu+\nu+2}{2} \end{matrix}\right]$$ $$\times {}_4F_5\left(\begin{matrix} \frac{\mu+\nu+1}{2}, \frac{\mu+\nu+2}{2}, \frac{s+\mu+\nu}{2}, \frac{s+\mu+\nu+1}{2}; -a^2b^2 \\ \mu+1,\ \nu+1,\ \mu+\nu+1,\ \frac{s+\mu+\nu+2}{2},\ \frac{s+\mu+\nu+2}{2} \end{matrix}\right)$$ $$[a,\ \mathrm{Re}\,(s+\mu+\nu)>0]$$

3.10.17. $J_\mu(bx)\,J_\nu(bx)$ and $\mathrm{Ei}(-ax^r)$

No.	$f(x)$	$F(s)$
1	$\mathrm{Ei}(-ax)\,J_\mu(bx)\,J_\nu(bx)$	$$-\frac{2^{-\mu-\nu}a^{-s-\mu-\nu}b^{\mu+\nu}}{s+\mu+\nu}\Gamma\left[\begin{matrix} s+\mu+\nu \\ \mu+1,\ \nu+1 \end{matrix}\right]$$ $$\times {}_5F_4\left(\begin{matrix} \frac{\mu+\nu+1}{2}, \frac{\mu+\nu+2}{2}, \frac{s+\mu+\nu}{2}, \frac{s+\mu+\nu}{2}, \frac{s+\mu+\nu+1}{2} \\ \mu+1,\ \nu+1,\ \mu+\nu+1,\ \frac{s+\mu+\nu+2}{2}; -\frac{4b^2}{a^2} \end{matrix}\right)$$ $$[\mathrm{Re}\,(s+\mu+\nu)>0;\ \mathrm{Re}\,s>|\mathrm{Im}\,b|]$$

No.	$f(x)$	$F(s)$
2	$\mathrm{Ei}\left(-ax^2\right)J_\mu(bx)J_\nu(bx)$	$-\dfrac{a^{-(s+\mu+\nu)/2}}{s+\mu+\nu}\left(\dfrac{b}{2}\right)^{\mu+\nu}\Gamma\left[\begin{array}{c}\frac{s+\mu+\nu}{2}\\ \mu+1,\ \nu+1\end{array}\right]$

$$\times\ {}_4F_4\left(\begin{array}{c}\frac{\mu+\nu+1}{2},\ \frac{\mu+\nu+2}{2},\ \frac{s+\mu+\nu}{2},\ \frac{s+\mu+\nu}{2};\ -\frac{b^2}{a}\\ \mu+1,\ \nu+1,\ \mu+\nu+1,\ \frac{s+\mu+\nu+2}{2}\end{array}\right)$$

$$\left[\mathrm{Re}\,a,\ \mathrm{Re}\,(s+\mu+\nu)>0\right]$$

3.10.18. $J_\mu(bx)\,J_\nu(bx)$ **and** $\mathrm{erfc}\,(ax),\ \mathrm{erf}\,(a/x),\ \Gamma(\lambda,\,ax)$

No.	$f(x)$	$F(s)$
1	$\mathrm{erfc}\,(ax)\,J_\mu(bx)\,J_\nu(bx)$	$\dfrac{a^{-s-\mu-\nu}}{\sqrt{\pi}\,(s+\mu+\nu)}\left(\dfrac{b}{2}\right)^{\mu+\nu}\Gamma\left[\begin{array}{c}\frac{s+\mu+\nu+1}{2}\\ \mu+1,\ \nu+1\end{array}\right]$

$$\times\ {}_4F_4\left(\begin{array}{c}\frac{\mu+\nu+1}{2},\ \frac{\mu+\nu+2}{2},\ \frac{s+\mu+\nu}{2},\ \frac{s+\mu+\nu+1}{2};\ -\frac{b^2}{a^2}\\ \mu+1,\ \nu+1,\ \mu+\nu+1,\ \frac{s+\mu+\nu+2}{2}\end{array}\right)$$

$$\left[\mathrm{Re}\,(s+\mu+\nu)>0;\ |\arg a|<\pi/4\right]$$

No.	$f(x)$	$F(s)$
2	$\mathrm{erf}\left(\dfrac{a}{x}\right)J_\mu(bx)\,J_\nu(bx)$	$\dfrac{2^{s-1}ab^{1-s}}{\sqrt{\pi}}\Gamma\left[\begin{array}{c}2-s,\ \frac{s+\mu+\nu-1}{2}\\ \frac{3-s+\mu-\nu}{2},\ \frac{3-s-\mu+\nu}{2},\ \frac{3-s+\mu+\nu}{2}\end{array}\right]$

$$\times\ {}_3F_5\left(\begin{array}{c}\frac{1}{2},\ \frac{2-s}{2},\ \frac{3-s}{2};\ a^2b^2\\ \frac{3}{2},\ \frac{3-s-\mu-\nu}{2},\ \frac{3-s+\mu-\nu}{2},\ \frac{3-s-\mu+\nu}{2},\ \frac{3-s+\mu+\nu}{2}\end{array}\right)$$

$$+\ 2^{s-1}a^{s+\mu+\nu}b^{\mu+\nu}\sec\frac{(s+\mu+\nu)\pi}{2}$$

$$\times\ \Gamma\left[\begin{array}{c}\frac{s+\mu+\nu}{2}\\ \mu+1,\ \nu+1,\ s+\mu+\nu+1\end{array}\right]$$

$$\times\ {}_3F_5\left(\begin{array}{c}\frac{\mu+\nu+1}{2},\ \frac{\mu+\nu+2}{2},\ \frac{s+\mu+\nu}{2};\ a^2b^2\\ \mu+1,\ \nu+1,\ \mu+\nu+1,\ \frac{s+\mu+\nu+1}{2},\ \frac{s+\mu+\nu+2}{2}\end{array}\right)$$

$$\left[b>0;\ -\mathrm{Re}\,(\mu+\nu)<\mathrm{Re}\,s<2;\ |\arg a|<\pi/4\right]$$

No.	$f(x)$	$F(s)$
3	$\Gamma(\lambda,\,ax)\,J_\mu(bx)\,J_\nu(bx)$	$\dfrac{a^{-(s+\mu+\nu)}\,(b/2)^{\mu+\nu}}{s+\mu+\nu}\Gamma\left[\begin{array}{c}s+\lambda+\mu+\nu\\ \mu+1,\ \nu+1\end{array}\right]$

$$\times\ {}_5F_4\left(\begin{array}{c}\frac{\mu+\nu+1}{2},\ \frac{\mu+\nu+2}{2},\ \frac{s+\mu+\nu}{2},\ \frac{s+\lambda+\mu+\nu}{2},\ \frac{s+\lambda+\mu+\nu+1}{2}\\ \mu+1,\ \nu+1,\ \mu+\nu+1,\ \frac{s+\mu+\nu+2}{2};\ -\frac{4b^2}{a^2}\end{array}\right)$$

$$\left[\begin{array}{c}\left(\mathrm{Re}\,a>0;\ \mathrm{Re}\,a>2|\mathrm{Im}\,b|,\ -\mathrm{Re}\,(\lambda+\mu+\nu),\right.\\ \left.-\mathrm{Re}\,(\mu+\nu)<\mathrm{Re}\,s\right)\ \mathrm{or}\\ \left(\mathrm{Re}\,a>0;\ \mathrm{Re}\,a+2|\mathrm{Im}\,b|=0;\ -\mathrm{Re}\,(\lambda+\mu+\nu),\right.\\ \left.-\mathrm{Re}\,(\mu+\nu)<\mathrm{Re}\,s<3-\mathrm{Re}\,\nu\right)\ \mathrm{or}\\ \left(\mathrm{Re}\,a=0;\ b>0;\ -\mathrm{Re}\,(\lambda+\mu+\nu),\right.\\ \left.-\mathrm{Re}\,(\mu+\nu)<\mathrm{Re}\,s<3-\mathrm{Re}\,\nu\right)\end{array}\right]$$

No.	$f(x)$	$F(s)$
4	$\Gamma\left(\lambda, ax^2\right) J_\mu(bx)$ $\times J_\nu(bx)$	$\dfrac{a^{-(s+\mu+\nu)/2}(b/2)^{\mu+\nu}}{s+\mu+\nu}\, \Gamma\left[\begin{matrix}\frac{s+2\lambda+\mu+\nu}{2}\\ \mu+1,\ \nu+1\end{matrix}\right]$ $\times {}_4F_4\left(\begin{matrix}\frac{\mu+\nu+1}{2},\ \frac{\mu+\nu+2}{2},\ \frac{s+\mu+\nu}{2},\ \frac{s+2\lambda+\mu+\nu}{2}\\ \mu+1,\ \nu+1,\ \mu+\nu+1,\ \frac{s+\mu+\nu+2}{2};\ -\frac{b^2}{a}\end{matrix}\right)$ $\left[\begin{matrix}\left(\operatorname{Re}a>0;\ -\operatorname{Re}(2\lambda+\mu+\nu),\ -\operatorname{Re}(\mu+\nu)<\operatorname{Re}s\right)\text{ or}\\ \left(\operatorname{Re}a=\operatorname{Im}b=0;\ -\operatorname{Re}(2\lambda+\mu+\nu),\ -\operatorname{Re}(\mu+\nu)<\operatorname{Re}s<5-2\operatorname{Re}\nu\right)\end{matrix}\right]$

3.10.19. $J_\mu(\varphi(x))\, J_\nu(\psi(x))$

1	$J_{\pm\nu}(u_+)\, J_\nu(u_-)$ $u_\pm = b\left(\sqrt{x^2+a^2}\pm a\right)$	$\dfrac{1}{2\sqrt{\pi}}\left(\dfrac{a}{b}\right)^{s/2}\Gamma\left[\begin{matrix}\frac{s+2\nu}{2},\ \frac{1-s}{2}\\ \frac{2-s+2\nu}{2}\end{matrix}\right]$ $\times\left\{\begin{matrix}J_{-s/2}(2ab)\\ \cos(\nu\pi)J_{-s/2}(2ab)-\sin(\nu\pi)Y_{-s/2}(2ab)\end{matrix}\right\}$ $[b,\ \operatorname{Re}a>0;\ -2\operatorname{Re}\nu<\operatorname{Re}s<1]$

3.10.20. $J_\mu(\varphi(x))\, J_\nu(\psi(x))$ **and algebraic functions**

1	$\left(a^2-x^2\right)_+^{\alpha-1}$ $\times J_\nu(bx) J_\mu(bx)$	$\dfrac{1}{2}a^{s+2\alpha+\mu+\nu-2}\left(\dfrac{b}{2}\right)^{\mu+\nu}\Gamma\left[\begin{matrix}\alpha,\ \frac{s+\mu+\nu}{2}\\ \mu+1,\ \nu+1,\ \frac{s+2\alpha+\mu+\nu}{2}\end{matrix}\right]$ $\times {}_3F_4\left(\begin{matrix}\frac{\mu+\nu+1}{2},\ \frac{\mu+\nu+2}{2},\ \frac{s+\mu+\nu}{2};\ -a^2b^2\\ \mu+1,\ \nu+1,\ \mu+\nu+1,\ \frac{s+2\alpha+\mu+\nu}{2}\end{matrix}\right)$ $[a,\ \operatorname{Re}\alpha,\ \operatorname{Re}(s+\mu+\nu)>0]$
2	$\dfrac{1}{(x^2+a^2)^\rho}$ $\times J_\mu(bx) J_\nu(bx)$	$\dfrac{1}{2}\left(\dfrac{b}{2}\right)^{2\rho-s}\Gamma\left[\begin{matrix}1-s+2\rho,\ \frac{s+\mu+\nu-2\rho}{2}\\ \frac{2-s+\mu-\nu+2\rho}{2},\ \frac{2-s+\mu+\nu+2\rho}{2},\ \frac{2-s-\mu+\nu+2\rho}{2}\end{matrix}\right]$ $\times {}_3F_4\left(\begin{matrix}\rho,\ \frac{1-s+2\rho}{2},\ \frac{2-s+2\rho}{2};\ a^2b^2\\ \frac{2-s-\mu-\nu+2\rho}{2},\ \frac{2-s+\mu-\nu+2\rho}{2},\ \frac{2-s+\mu+\nu+2\rho}{2},\ \frac{2-s+\nu-\mu+2\rho}{2}\end{matrix}\right)$ $+\dfrac{a^{s-2\rho}}{2}\left(\dfrac{ab}{2}\right)^{\mu+\nu}\Gamma\left[\begin{matrix}\frac{2\rho-\mu-\nu-s}{2},\ \frac{s+\mu+\nu}{2}\\ \mu+1,\ \nu+1,\ \rho\end{matrix}\right]$ $\times {}_3F_4\left(\begin{matrix}\frac{\mu+\nu+1}{2},\ \frac{\mu+\nu+2}{2},\ \frac{s+\mu+\nu}{2};\ a^2b^2\\ \mu+1,\ \nu+1,\ \mu+\nu+1,\ \frac{s+\mu+\nu-2\rho+2}{2}\end{matrix}\right)$ $[b,\ \operatorname{Re}a,\ \operatorname{Re}(s+\mu+\nu)>0;\ \operatorname{Re}(s-2\rho)<1]$
3	$(a-x)_+^{\alpha-1}$ $\times J_\mu(bx(a-x))$ $\times J_\nu(bx(a-x))$	$a^{s+\alpha+2\mu+2\nu-1}\left(\dfrac{b}{2}\right)^{\mu+\nu}\Gamma\left[\begin{matrix}s+\mu+\nu,\ \alpha+\mu+\nu\\ \mu+1,\ \nu+1,\ s+\alpha+2\mu+2\nu\end{matrix}\right]$ $\times {}_6F_7\left(\begin{matrix}\Delta(2,\mu+\nu+1),\ \Delta(2,s+\mu+\nu),\ \Delta(2,\alpha+\mu+\nu)\\ \mu+1,\ \nu+1,\ \mu+\nu+1,\ \Delta(4,s+\alpha+2\mu+2\nu);\ -\frac{a^4b^2}{16}\end{matrix}\right)$ $[a>0;\ \operatorname{Re}s,\ \operatorname{Re}\alpha>-\operatorname{Re}(\mu+\nu)]$

No.	$f(x)$	$F(s)$
4	$\dfrac{1}{(x+a)^\rho}$ $\times J_\mu\left(\dfrac{bx}{x+a}\right)$ $\times J_\nu\left(\dfrac{bx}{x+a}\right)$	$a^{s-\rho}\left(\dfrac{b}{2}\right)^{\mu+\nu}\dfrac{\mathrm{B}\left(\rho-s,\,s+\mu+\nu\right)}{\Gamma\left(\mu+1\right)\Gamma\left(\nu+1\right)}$ $\times {}_4F_5\left(\begin{matrix}\frac{\mu+\nu+1}{2},\,\frac{\mu+\nu+2}{2},\,\frac{s+\mu+\nu}{2},\,\frac{s+\mu+\nu+1}{2};\,-b^2\\[4pt]\mu+1,\,\nu+1,\,\mu+\nu+1,\,\frac{\mu+\nu+\rho}{2},\,\frac{\mu+\nu+\rho+1}{2}\end{matrix}\right)$ $[\operatorname{Re}\left(\mu+\nu\right)<\operatorname{Re}s<\operatorname{Re}\rho;\,|\arg a|<\pi]$
5	$\dfrac{1}{(x^2+a^2)^\rho}$ $\times J_\mu\left(\dfrac{bx}{x^2+a^2}\right)$ $\times J_\nu\left(\dfrac{bx}{x^2+a^2}\right)$	$\dfrac{a^{s-\mu-\nu-2\rho}b^{\mu+\nu}}{2^{\mu+\nu+1}\Gamma\left(\mu+1\right)\Gamma\left(\nu+1\right)}\,\mathrm{B}\left(\dfrac{s+\mu+\nu}{2},\,\dfrac{-s+\mu+\nu+2\rho}{2}\right)$ $\times {}_4F_5\left(\begin{matrix}\frac{\mu+\nu+1}{2},\,\frac{\mu+\nu+2}{2},\,\frac{s+\mu+\nu}{2},\,\frac{-s+\mu+\nu+2\rho}{2}\\[4pt]\mu+1,\,\nu+1,\,\mu+\nu+1,\,\frac{\mu+\nu+\rho}{2},\,\frac{\mu+\nu+\rho+1}{2};\,-\frac{b^2}{4a^2}\end{matrix}\right)$ $[\operatorname{Re}a>0;\,-\operatorname{Re}\left(\mu+\nu\right)<\operatorname{Re}s<\operatorname{Re}\left(\mu+\nu+2\rho\right)]$

3.10.21. $J_\lambda\left(ax^r\right)J_\mu\left(bx^r\right)J_\nu\left(cx\right)$

No.	$f(x)$	$F(s)$
1	$J_\lambda\left(ax\right)J_\mu\left(ax\right)J_\nu\left(bx\right)$	$\dfrac{2^{s-1}a^{\mu+\lambda}}{b^{s+\mu+\lambda}}\,\Gamma\!\left[\begin{matrix}\frac{s+\lambda+\mu+\nu}{2}\\[4pt]\mu+1,\,\lambda+1,\,\frac{\nu-\mu-\lambda-s+2}{2}\end{matrix}\right]$ $\times {}_4F_3\left(\begin{matrix}\frac{\lambda+\mu+1}{2},\,\frac{\lambda+\mu+2}{2},\,\frac{s+\lambda+\mu-\nu}{2},\,\frac{s+\lambda+\mu+\nu}{2}\\[4pt]\lambda+1,\,\mu+1,\,\lambda+\mu+1;\,\frac{4a^2}{b^2}\end{matrix}\right)$ $[0<2a<b;\,-\operatorname{Re}\left(\lambda+\mu+\nu\right)<\operatorname{Re}s<5/2]$
2	$J_\lambda\left(ax\right)J_\mu\left(ax\right)J_\nu\left(bx\right)$	$\dfrac{2^{s-2}}{\pi ab^{s-1}}\cos\dfrac{(\lambda-\mu)\pi}{2}\,\Gamma\!\left[\begin{matrix}\frac{s+\nu-1}{2}\\[4pt]\frac{3-s+\nu}{2}\end{matrix}\right]$ $\times {}_4F_3\left(\begin{matrix}\frac{1-\lambda-\mu}{2},\,\frac{\lambda-\mu+1}{2},\,\frac{1-\lambda+\mu}{2},\,\frac{\lambda+\mu+1}{2}\\[4pt]\frac{1}{2},\,\frac{3-s-\nu}{2},\,\frac{3-s+\nu}{2};\,\frac{b^2}{4a^2}\end{matrix}\right)$ $+\dfrac{2^{s-1}b^\nu}{a^{s+\nu}}\,\Gamma\!\left[\begin{matrix}\frac{s+\lambda+\mu+\nu}{2},\,1-s-\nu\\[4pt]\nu+1,\,\frac{2-s+\lambda+\mu-\nu}{2},\,\frac{2-s+\lambda-\mu-\nu}{2},\,\frac{2-s+\mu-\lambda-\nu}{2}\end{matrix}\right]$ $\times {}_4F_3\left(\begin{matrix}\frac{s-\lambda-\mu+\nu}{2},\,\frac{s+\lambda-\mu+\nu}{2},\,\frac{s-\lambda+\mu+\nu}{2},\,\frac{s+\lambda+\mu+\nu}{2}\\[4pt]\nu+1,\,\frac{s+\nu}{2},\,\frac{s+\nu+1}{2};\,\frac{b^2}{4a^2}\end{matrix}\right)$ $+\dfrac{2^{s-4}\left(\lambda^2-\mu^2\right)}{\pi a^2 b^{s-2}}\sin\dfrac{(\lambda-\mu)\pi}{2}\,\Gamma\!\left[\begin{matrix}\frac{s+\nu-2}{2}\\[4pt]\frac{4-s+\nu}{2}\end{matrix}\right]$ $\times {}_4F_3\left(\begin{matrix}\frac{2-\lambda-\mu}{2},\,\frac{\lambda-\mu+2}{2},\,\frac{2-\lambda+\mu}{2},\,\frac{\lambda+\mu+2}{2}\\[4pt]\frac{3}{2},\,\frac{4-s-\nu}{2},\,\frac{4-s+\nu}{2};\,\frac{b^2}{4a^2}\end{matrix}\right)$ $[0<b<2a;\,-\operatorname{Re}\left(\lambda+\mu+\nu\right)<\operatorname{Re}s<5/2]$

No.	$f(x)$	$F(s)$
3	$J_\lambda(ax)\, J_\mu(bx)\, J_\nu(cx)$	$\dfrac{2^{s-1}a^\lambda b^\mu}{c^{s+\lambda+\mu}}\,\Gamma\left[\begin{array}{c}\frac{s+\lambda+\mu+\nu}{2}\\ \lambda+1,\ \mu+1,\ \frac{2-s-\lambda-\mu+\nu}{2}\end{array}\right]$

$$\times F_4\left(\frac{s+\lambda+\mu-\nu}{2},\ \frac{s+\lambda+\mu+\nu}{2};\ \lambda+1,\ \mu+1;\ \frac{a^2}{c^2},\ \frac{b^2}{c^2}\right)$$

$$[a,\,b,\ \mathrm{Re}\,(s+\lambda+\mu+\nu)>0;\ c>a+b;\ \mathrm{Re}\,s<5/2]$$

No.	$f(x)$	$F(s)$
4	$J_\lambda\left(\dfrac{a}{x}\right)J_\mu\left(\dfrac{a}{x}\right)$ $\times J_\nu(bx)$	$\dfrac{a^{\lambda+\mu}b^{\lambda+\mu-s}}{2^{2\lambda+2\mu-s+1}}\,\Gamma\left[\begin{array}{c}\frac{s-\lambda-\mu+\nu}{2}\\ \lambda+1,\ \mu+1,\ \frac{2-s+\lambda+\mu+\nu}{2}\end{array}\right]$

$$\times {}_2F_5\left(\begin{array}{c}\frac{\lambda+\mu+1}{2},\ \frac{\lambda+\mu+2}{2};\ \frac{a^2b^2}{4}\\ \lambda+1,\ \mu+1,\ \lambda+\mu+1,\ \frac{2-s+\lambda+\mu-\nu}{2},\ \frac{2-s+\lambda+\mu+\nu}{2}\end{array}\right)$$

$$+\frac{a^{s+\nu}b^\nu}{2^{s+2\nu+1}}\,\Gamma\left[\begin{array}{c}s+\nu+1,\ \frac{\lambda+\mu-\nu-s}{2}\\ \nu+1,\ \frac{s+\lambda+\mu+\nu+2}{2},\ \frac{s-\lambda+\mu+\nu+2}{2},\ \frac{s+\lambda-\mu+\nu+2}{2}\end{array}\right]$$

$$\times {}_2F_5\left(\begin{array}{c}\frac{s+\nu+1}{2},\ \frac{s+\nu+2}{2};\ \frac{a^2b^2}{4}\\ \nu+1,\ \frac{s+\lambda+\mu+\nu+2}{2},\ \frac{s-\lambda+\mu+\nu+2}{2},\ \frac{s-\lambda+\mu+\nu+2}{2},\ \frac{s+\lambda-\mu+\nu+2}{2}\end{array}\right)$$

$$[a,\,b>0;\ -\mathrm{Re}\,\nu-1<\mathrm{Re}\,s<\mathrm{Re}\,(\lambda+\mu)+3/2]$$

No.	$f(x)$	$F(s)$
5	$e^{-ax}\displaystyle\prod_{k=1}^{n}J_{\nu_k}(b_k x)$	$\dfrac{\prod_{k=1}^{n}(b_k/2)^{\nu_k}}{\left(a+i\sum_{k=1}^{n}b_k\right)^{s+\nu}}\,\Gamma\left[\begin{array}{c}s+\nu\\ \nu_1+1,\ \nu_2+1,\dots,\nu_n+1\end{array}\right]$

$$\times F_A^{(n)}\left(s+\nu,\ (\nu_n)+\frac{1}{2};\ 2(\nu_n)+1;\ \frac{2i(b_n)}{a+i\sum_{k=1}^{n}b_k}\right)$$

$$\left[\nu=\sum_{k=1}^{n}\nu_k;\ \mathrm{Re}\,a>\sum_{k=1}^{n}\mathrm{Im}\,b_k;\ \mathrm{Re}\,(s+\nu)>0\right]$$

No.	$f(x)$	$F(s)$
6		$=\dfrac{\prod_{k=1}^{n}(b_k/2)^{\nu_k}}{a^{s+\nu}}\,\Gamma\left[\begin{array}{c}s+\nu\\ \nu_1+1,\ \nu_2+1,\dots,\nu_n+1\end{array}\right]$

$$\times F_C^{(n)}\left(\frac{s+\nu}{2},\ \frac{s+\nu+1}{2};\ (\nu_n)+1;\ -\frac{(b_n^2)}{a^2}\right)$$

$$\left[\nu=\sum_{k=1}^{n}\nu_k;\ \mathrm{Re}\,a,\ \mathrm{Re}\,(s+\nu)>0\right]$$

No.	$f(x)$	$F(s)$
7	$e^{-ax}\displaystyle\prod_{k=1}^{m}\sin(b_k x)$ $\times \displaystyle\prod_{k=1}^{n}\cos(c_k x)$ $\times \displaystyle\prod_{k=1}^{p}J_{\nu_k}(d_k x)$	$\dfrac{\prod_{k=1}^{m}b_k\,\prod_{k=1}^{p}(d_k/2)^{\nu_k}}{a^{s+m+\nu}}\,\Gamma\left[\begin{array}{c}s+m+\nu\\ \nu_1+1,\ \nu_2+1,\dots,\nu_p+1\end{array}\right]$

$$\times F_C^{(m+n+p)}\left(\frac{s+m+\nu}{2},\ \frac{s+m+\nu+1}{2};\ \underbrace{\frac{3}{2},\dots,\frac{3}{2}}_{m},\ \underbrace{\frac{1}{2},\dots,\frac{1}{2}}_{n},\right.$$

$$\left.(\nu_p)+1;\ -\frac{(b_m^2)}{a^2},\ -\frac{(c_n^2)}{a^2},\ -\frac{(d_p^2)}{a^2}\right)$$

$$\left[\nu=\sum_{k=1}^{p}\nu_k;\ \mathrm{Re}\,a,\ \mathrm{Re}\,(s+\nu)>0\right]$$

3.11.　The Bessel Function $Y_\nu(z)$

More formulas can be obtained from the corresponding sections due to the relations

$$Y_{\pm 1/2}(z) = \mp \sqrt{\frac{2}{\pi}} \frac{1}{\sqrt{z}} \begin{Bmatrix} \cos z \\ \sin z \end{Bmatrix}, \quad Y_{\pm 3/2}(z) = \sqrt{\frac{2}{\pi}} \frac{1}{z^{3/2}} \left[\mp z \begin{Bmatrix} \sin z \\ \cos z \end{Bmatrix} - \begin{Bmatrix} \cos z \\ \sin z \end{Bmatrix} \right],$$

$$Y_\nu(z) = \csc(\nu\pi) \left[J_\nu(z) \cos(\nu\pi) - J_{-\nu}(z) \right], \quad [\nu \neq 0, \pm 1, \pm 2, \dots];$$

$$Y_n(z) = \lim_{\nu \to n} Y_\nu(z), \quad [n = 0, \pm 1, \pm 2, \dots];$$

$$Y_\nu(z) = \frac{1}{2i} \left[H_\nu^{(1)}(z) - H_\nu^{(2)}(z) \right],$$

$$Y_\nu(z) = -\frac{2}{\pi} \left\{ i^\nu K_\nu(iz) + \left[\ln(iz) - \ln z \right] J_\nu(z) \right\}, \quad [\nu \neq 0, \pm 1, \pm 2, \dots];$$

$$Y_\nu(z) = \frac{(iz)^{-\nu} z^{-\nu}}{\pi} \left\{ \pi \csc(\nu\pi) \left[\cos(\nu\pi) z^{2\nu} - (iz)^{2\nu} \right] I_\nu(iz) - 2(iz)^{2\nu} K_\nu(iz) \right\},$$

$$[\nu \neq 0, \pm 1, \pm 2, \dots];$$

$$Y_\nu(z) = -\frac{\cos(\nu\pi) \Gamma(-\nu)}{\pi} \left(\frac{z}{2} \right)^\nu {}_0F_1 \left(1+\nu; -\frac{z^2}{4} \right) - \frac{\Gamma(\nu)}{\pi} \left(\frac{2}{z} \right)^\nu {}_0F_1 \left(1-\nu; -\frac{z^2}{4} \right),$$

$$Y_\nu \left(\sqrt{z^2} \right) = G_{13}^{20} \left(\frac{z^2}{4} \middle| \begin{matrix} -(\nu+1)/2 \\ \nu/2, -\nu/2, -(\nu+1)/2 \end{matrix} \right).$$

3.11.1.　$Y_\nu(bx)$ and algebraic functions

No.	$f(x)$	$F(s)$
1	$Y_\nu(ax)$	$-\dfrac{2^{s-1}}{\pi a^s} \cos \dfrac{(s-\nu)\pi}{2} \Gamma\left(\dfrac{s-\nu}{2}\right) \Gamma\left(\dfrac{s+\nu}{2}\right)$ $\qquad\qquad\qquad\qquad [a>0; \, |\mathrm{Re}\,\nu| < \mathrm{Re}\,s < 3/2]$
2	$(a-x)_+^{\alpha-1} Y_\nu(bx)$	$-\dfrac{2^\nu a^{s+\alpha-\nu-1} b^{-\nu}}{\pi} \Gamma(\nu) \, \mathrm{B}(\alpha, s-\nu) \, {}_2F_3 \left(\begin{matrix} \frac{s-\nu}{2}, \frac{s-\nu+1}{2}; -\frac{a^2 b^2}{4} \\ 1-\nu, \frac{s+\alpha-\nu}{2}, \frac{s+\alpha-\nu+1}{2} \end{matrix} \right)$ $-\dfrac{2^{-\nu} a^{s+\alpha+\nu-1} b^\nu}{\pi} \cos(\pi\nu) \Gamma(-\nu) \, \mathrm{B}(\alpha, s+\nu)$ $\times {}_2F_3 \left(\begin{matrix} \frac{s+\nu}{2}, \frac{s+\nu+1}{2}; -\frac{a^2 b^2}{4} \\ 1+\nu, \frac{s+\alpha+\nu}{2}, \frac{s+\alpha+\nu+1}{2} \end{matrix} \right)$ $\qquad\qquad\qquad\qquad [a, \, \mathrm{Re}\,\alpha > 0; \, \mathrm{Re}\,s > |\mathrm{Re}\,\nu|]$
3	$\dfrac{1}{x-a} Y_\nu(bx)$	$\dfrac{(2a)^{s-1}}{\pi} \left[\cos \dfrac{(s-\nu)\pi}{2} \Gamma\left(\dfrac{s-\nu}{2}\right) \Gamma\left(\dfrac{s+\nu}{2}\right) S_{1-s,\nu}(ab) \right.$ $\left. - 2\sin \dfrac{(s-\nu)\pi}{2} \Gamma\left(\dfrac{s-\nu+1}{2}\right) \Gamma\left(\dfrac{s+\nu+1}{2}\right) S_{-s,\nu}(ab) \right]$ $+ \pi a^{s-1} J_\nu(ab) \qquad [a, b > 0; \, |\mathrm{Re}\,\nu| < \mathrm{Re}\,s < 5/2]$

No.	$f(x)$	$F(s)$
4	$\dfrac{1}{(x+a)^\rho} Y_\nu(bx)$	$-\dfrac{a^{s+\nu-\rho}}{\pi}\left(\dfrac{b}{2}\right)^\nu \cos(\nu\pi)\,\Gamma\left[\begin{matrix}-\nu,\,s+\nu,\,-\nu+\rho-s\\\rho\end{matrix}\right]$
		$\times\,{}_2F_3\left(\begin{matrix}\frac{s+\nu}{2},\,\frac{s+\nu+1}{2};\,-\frac{a^2b^2}{4}\\\nu+1,\,\frac{s+\nu-\rho+1}{2},\,\frac{s+\nu-\rho+2}{2}\end{matrix}\right)-\dfrac{a^{s-\nu-\rho}}{\pi}\left(\dfrac{2}{b}\right)^\nu$
		$\times\,\Gamma\left[\begin{matrix}\nu,\,s-\nu,\,\nu+\rho-s\\\rho\end{matrix}\right]{}_2F_3\left(\begin{matrix}\frac{s-\nu}{2},\,\frac{s-\nu+1}{2};\,-\frac{a^2b^2}{4}\\1-\nu,\,\frac{s-\nu-\rho+1}{2},\,\frac{s-\nu-\rho+2}{2}\end{matrix}\right)$
		$-\dfrac{1}{2\pi}\left(\dfrac{b}{2}\right)^{\rho-s}\cos\dfrac{(s-\nu-\rho)\pi}{2}\,\Gamma\left(\dfrac{s+\nu-\rho}{2}\right)$
		$\times\,\Gamma\left(\dfrac{s-\nu-\rho}{2}\right){}_2F_3\left(\begin{matrix}\frac{\rho}{2},\,\frac{\rho+1}{2};\,-\frac{a^2b^2}{4}\\\frac{1}{2},\,\frac{\rho-\nu-s+2}{2},\,\frac{\rho+\nu-s+2}{2}\end{matrix}\right)$
		$-\dfrac{\rho a}{2\pi}\left(\dfrac{b}{2}\right)^{\rho-s+1}\sin\dfrac{(\nu+\rho-s)\pi}{2}\,\Gamma\left(\dfrac{s+\nu-\rho-1}{2}\right)$
		$\times\,\Gamma\left(\dfrac{s-\nu-\rho-1}{2}\right){}_2F_3\left(\begin{matrix}\frac{\rho+1}{2},\,\frac{\rho+2}{2};\,-\frac{a^2b^2}{4}\\\frac{3}{2},\,\frac{\rho-\nu-s+3}{2},\,\frac{\rho+\nu-s+3}{2}\end{matrix}\right)$
		$[b>0;\ |\mathrm{Re}\,\nu|<\mathrm{Re}\,s<\mathrm{Re}\,\rho+3/2;\ |\arg a|<\pi]$
5	$\dfrac{1}{x+a} Y_\nu(bx)$	$-\dfrac{(2a)^{s-1}}{\pi}\left[\cos\dfrac{(s-\nu)\pi}{2}\,\Gamma\left(\dfrac{s+\nu}{2}\right)\Gamma\left(\dfrac{s-\nu}{2}\right)S_{1-s,\nu}(ab)\right.$
		$\left.+2\sin\dfrac{(s-\nu)\pi}{2}\,\Gamma\left(\dfrac{s-\nu+1}{2}\right)\Gamma\left(\dfrac{s+\nu+1}{2}\right)S_{-s,\nu}(ab)\right]$
		$[b>0;\ |\mathrm{Re}\,\nu|<\mathrm{Re}\,s<5/2;\ |\arg a|<\pi]$
6	$(a^2-x^2)_+^{\alpha-1}\,Y_\nu(bx)$	$-\dfrac{2^{\nu-1}a^{s+2\alpha-\nu-2}}{\pi b^\nu}\,\Gamma(\nu)\,\mathrm{B}\left(\alpha,\dfrac{s-\nu}{2}\right){}_1F_2\left(\begin{matrix}\frac{s-\nu}{2};\,-\frac{a^2b^2}{4}\\1-\nu,\,\frac{s+2\alpha-\nu}{2}\end{matrix}\right)$
		$-\dfrac{a^{s+2\alpha+\nu-2}b^\nu}{\pi 2^{\nu+1}}\cos(\pi\nu)\,\Gamma(-\nu)\,\mathrm{B}\left(\alpha,\dfrac{s+\nu}{2}\right)$
		$\times\,{}_1F_2\left(\begin{matrix}\frac{s+\nu}{2};\,-\frac{a^2b^2}{4}\\1+\nu,\,\frac{s+2\alpha+\nu}{2}\end{matrix}\right)\qquad[a,\,\mathrm{Re}\,\alpha>0;\ \mathrm{Re}\,s>|\mathrm{Re}\,\nu|]$
7	$(x^2-a^2)_+^{\alpha-1}\,Y_\nu(bx)$	$\dfrac{2^{s+2\alpha-3}}{\pi b^{s+2\alpha-2}}\cos\dfrac{(s+2\alpha-\nu)\pi}{2}\,\Gamma\left(\dfrac{s+2\alpha-\nu-2}{2}\right)$
		$\times\,\Gamma\left(\dfrac{s+2\alpha+\nu-2}{2}\right){}_1F_2\left(\begin{matrix}1-\alpha;\,-\frac{a^2b^2}{4}\\\frac{4-s-2\alpha-\nu}{2},\,\frac{4-s-2\alpha+\nu}{2}\end{matrix}\right)$
		$-\dfrac{2^{\nu-1}a^{s+2\alpha-\nu-2}}{\pi b^\nu}\Gamma(\nu)\,\mathrm{B}\left(\alpha,\dfrac{-s-2\alpha+\nu+2}{2}\right)$
		$\times\,{}_1F_2\left(\begin{matrix}\frac{s-\nu}{2};\,-\frac{a^2b^2}{4}\\1-\nu,\,\frac{s+2\alpha-\nu}{2}\end{matrix}\right)-\dfrac{2^{-\nu-1}a^{s+2\alpha+\nu-2}b^\nu}{\pi}\cos(\pi\nu)$
		$\times\,\Gamma(-\nu)\,\mathrm{B}\left(\alpha,\dfrac{-s-2\alpha-\nu+2}{2}\right){}_1F_2\left(\begin{matrix}\frac{s+\nu}{2};\,-\frac{a^2b^2}{4}\\1+\nu,\,\frac{s+2\alpha+\nu}{2}\end{matrix}\right)$
		$[a,\,b,\,\mathrm{Re}\,\alpha>0;\ \mathrm{Re}\,(s+2\alpha)<7/2]$

No.	$f(x)$	$F(s)$
8	$\dfrac{1}{(x^2+a^2)^\rho}\,Y_\nu(bx)$	$\dfrac{a^{s+\nu-2\rho}}{2}\left(\dfrac{b}{2}\right)^\nu \cot(\nu\pi)\,\Gamma\!\left[\begin{matrix}\frac{s+\nu}{2},\ \frac{-s-\nu+2\rho}{2}\\ \nu+1,\ \rho\end{matrix}\right]\ {}_1F_2\!\left(\begin{matrix}\frac{s+\nu}{2};\ \frac{a^2b^2}{4}\\ \nu+1,\ \frac{s+\nu-2\rho+2}{2}\end{matrix}\right)$
		$-\dfrac{a^{s-\nu-2\rho}}{2\sin(\nu\pi)}\left(\dfrac{2}{b}\right)^\nu \Gamma\!\left[\begin{matrix}\frac{s-\nu}{2},\ \frac{\nu+2\rho-s}{2}\\ 1-\nu,\ \rho\end{matrix}\right]\ {}_1F_2\!\left(\begin{matrix}\frac{s-\nu}{2};\ \frac{a^2b^2}{4}\\ 1-\nu,\ \frac{s-\nu-2\rho+2}{2}\end{matrix}\right)$
		$-\dfrac{1}{2\pi}\left(\dfrac{b}{2}\right)^{2\rho-s}\cos\dfrac{(\nu+2\rho-s)\pi}{2}\,\Gamma\!\left(\dfrac{s+\nu-2\rho}{2}\right)$
		$\times\,\Gamma\!\left(\dfrac{s-\nu-2\rho}{2}\right)\ {}_1F_2\!\left(\begin{matrix}\rho;\ \frac{a^2b^2}{4}\\ \frac{2-s-\nu+2\rho}{2},\ \frac{2-s+\nu+2\rho}{2}\end{matrix}\right)$
		$[\operatorname{Re}a,\,b>0;\ |\operatorname{Re}\nu|<\operatorname{Re}s<2\operatorname{Re}\rho+3/2]$
9	$\dfrac{1}{x^2+a^2}\,Y_\nu(bx)$	$\dfrac{1}{2\pi}\left(\dfrac{b}{2}\right)^{2-s}\cos\dfrac{(s-\nu)\pi}{2}\,\Gamma\!\left(\dfrac{s-\nu-2}{2}\right)\Gamma\!\left(\dfrac{s+\nu-2}{2}\right)$
		$\times\,{}_1F_2\!\left(\begin{matrix}1;\ \frac{a^2b^2}{4}\\ \frac{4-s-\nu}{2},\ \frac{4-s+\nu}{2}\end{matrix}\right)+\dfrac{\pi a^{s-2}}{2}\csc(\nu\pi)\csc\dfrac{(\nu-s)\pi}{2}$
		$\times\,I_{-\nu}(ab)+\dfrac{\pi a^{s-2}}{2}\cot(\nu\pi)\csc\dfrac{(s+\nu)\pi}{2}\,I_\nu(ab)$
		$[\operatorname{Re}a,\,b>0;\ |\operatorname{Re}\nu|<\operatorname{Re}s<7/2]$
10	$\dfrac{1}{x^2-a^2}\,Y_\nu(bx)$	$\dfrac{1}{2\pi}\left(\dfrac{b}{2}\right)^{2-s}\cos\dfrac{(s-\nu)\pi}{2}\,\Gamma\!\left(\dfrac{s-\nu-2}{2}\right)\Gamma\!\left(\dfrac{s+\nu-2}{2}\right)$
		$\times\,{}_1F_2\!\left(\begin{matrix}1;\ -\frac{a^2b^2}{4}\\ \frac{4-s-\nu}{2},\ \frac{4-s+\nu}{2}\end{matrix}\right)-\dfrac{\pi a^{s-2}}{2}\cot(\nu\pi)\cot\dfrac{(s+\nu)\pi}{2}$
		$\times\,J_\nu(ab)+\dfrac{\pi a^{s-2}}{2}\csc(\nu\pi)\cot\dfrac{(s-\nu)\pi}{2}\,J_{-\nu}(ab)$
		$[a,\,b>0;\ |\operatorname{Re}\nu|<\operatorname{Re}s<7/2]$
11	$\left(\sqrt{x^2+a^2}\pm x\right)^\rho Y_\nu(bx)$	$-\dfrac{2^{s\pm2\rho-1}a^{\rho\mp\rho}}{\pi b^{s\pm\rho}}\cos\dfrac{(\nu\mp\rho-s)\pi}{2}\,\Gamma\!\left(\dfrac{s\pm\rho+\nu}{2}\right)$
		$\times\,\Gamma\!\left(\dfrac{s\pm\rho-\nu}{2}\right)\ {}_2F_3\!\left(\begin{matrix}\mp\frac{\rho}{2},\ \frac{1\mp\rho}{2};\ \frac{a^2b^2}{4}\\ 1\mp\rho,\ \frac{2\mp\rho-\nu-s}{2},\ \frac{2\mp\rho+\nu-s}{2}\end{matrix}\right)$
		$-\dfrac{\rho a^{s+\rho+\nu}b^\nu}{2^{s+2\nu+1}}\cos(\nu\pi)\csc\dfrac{(\mp\rho-\nu-s)\pi}{2}$
		$\times\,\Gamma\!\left[\begin{matrix}-\nu,\ s+\nu\\ \frac{s\mp\rho+\nu+2}{2},\ \frac{s\pm\rho+\nu+2}{2}\end{matrix}\right]\ {}_2F_3\!\left(\begin{matrix}\frac{s+\nu}{2},\ \frac{s+\nu+1}{2};\ \frac{a^2b^2}{4}\\ 1+\nu,\ \frac{s\pm\rho+\nu+2}{2},\ \frac{s\mp\rho+\nu+2}{2}\end{matrix}\right)$
		$-\dfrac{\rho a^{s+\rho-\nu}}{2^{s-2\nu+1}b^\nu}\csc\dfrac{(\nu\mp\rho-s)\pi}{2}\,\Gamma\!\left[\begin{matrix}\nu,\ s-\nu\\ \frac{s\mp\rho-\nu+2}{2},\ \frac{s\pm\rho-\nu+2}{2}\end{matrix}\right]$
		$\times\,{}_2F_3\!\left(\begin{matrix}\frac{s-\nu}{2},\ \frac{s-\nu+1}{2};\ \frac{a^2b^2}{4}\\ 1-\nu,\ \frac{s\pm\rho-\nu+2}{2},\ \frac{s\mp\rho-\nu+2}{2}\end{matrix}\right)$
		$[\operatorname{Re}a,\,b>0;\ |\operatorname{Re}\nu|<\operatorname{Re}s<3/2\mp\operatorname{Re}\rho]$

No.	$f(x)$	$F(s)$
12	$\dfrac{\left(\sqrt{x^2+a^2}\pm x\right)^\rho}{\sqrt{x^2+a^2}}\,Y_\nu(bx)$	$-\dfrac{2^{s\pm2\rho-2}a^{\rho\mp\rho}}{\pi b^{s\pm\rho-1}}\cos\dfrac{(\nu\mp\rho-s+1)\pi}{2}\,\Gamma\left(\dfrac{s\pm\rho+\nu-1}{2}\right)$

$$\times\,\Gamma\left(\dfrac{s\pm\rho-\nu-1}{2}\right){}_2F_3\left({\textstyle\frac{1\mp\rho}{2},\ \frac{2\mp\rho}{2};\ \frac{a^2b^2}{4}\atop 1\mp\rho,\ \frac{3-s\mp\rho-\nu}{2},\ \frac{3-s\mp\rho+\nu}{2}}\right)$$

$$-\dfrac{a^{s+\rho+\nu-1}b^\nu}{2^{s+2\nu}}\cos(\nu\pi)\csc\dfrac{(1\mp\rho-\nu-s)\pi}{2}$$

$$\times\,\Gamma\left[{-\nu,\ s+\nu\atop \frac{s\mp\rho+\nu+1}{2},\ \frac{s\pm\rho+\nu+1}{2}}\right]{}_2F_3\left({\textstyle\frac{s+\nu}{2},\ \frac{s+\nu+1}{2};\ \frac{a^2b^2}{4}\atop 1+\nu,\ \frac{s\pm\rho+\nu+1}{2},\ \frac{s\mp\rho+\nu+1}{2}}\right)$$

$$-\dfrac{a^{s+\rho-\nu-1}}{2^{s-2\nu}b^\nu}\csc\dfrac{(\nu\mp\rho-s+1)\pi}{2}\,\Gamma\left[{\nu,\ s-\nu\atop \frac{s\mp\rho-\nu+1}{2},\ \frac{s\pm\rho-\nu+1}{2}}\right]$$

$$\times\,{}_2F_3\left({\textstyle\frac{s-\nu}{2},\ \frac{s-\nu+1}{2};\ \frac{a^2b^2}{4}\atop 1-\nu,\ \frac{s\pm\rho-\nu+1}{2},\ \frac{s\mp\rho-\nu+1}{2}}\right)$$

$$[\operatorname{Re}a,\,b>0;\ |\operatorname{Re}\nu|<\operatorname{Re}s<5/2\mp\operatorname{Re}\rho]$$

3.11.2. $Y_\nu(\varphi(x))$ **and algebraic functions**

No.	$f(x)$	$F(s)$
1	$\left(x^2+a^2\right)^{\nu/2}$ $\times\,Y_\nu\left(b\sqrt{x^2+a^2}\right)$	$\dfrac{2^{s/2-1}a^{s/2+\nu}}{b^{s/2}}\,\Gamma\left(\dfrac{s}{2}\right)\left[Y_{s/2+\nu}(ab)\cos\dfrac{s\pi}{2}+J_{s/2+\nu}(ab)\sin\dfrac{s\pi}{2}\right]$ $[a,\,b>0;\ 0<\operatorname{Re}s<3/2-\operatorname{Re}\nu]$
2	$\left(x^2+a^2\right)^{-\nu/2}$ $\times\,Y_\nu\left(b\sqrt{x^2+a^2}\right)$	$\dfrac{2^{s/2-1}a^{s/2-\nu}}{b^{s/2}}\,\Gamma\left(\dfrac{s}{2}\right)Y_{\nu-s/2}(ab)$ $[a,\,b>0;\ 0<\operatorname{Re}s<\operatorname{Re}\nu+3/2]$
3	$\left(a^2-x^2\right)_+^{\nu/2}$ $\times\,Y_\nu\left(b\sqrt{a^2-x^2}\right)$	$2^{s/2-1}a^{s/2+\nu}b^{-s/2}\cot(\nu\pi)\,\Gamma\left(\dfrac{s}{2}\right)J_{s/2+\nu}(ab)$ $-\dfrac{2^\nu a^s b^{-\nu}}{s\pi}\,\Gamma(\nu)\,{}_1F_2\left({1;\ -\frac{a^2b^2}{4}\atop 1-\nu,\ \frac{s+2}{2}}\right)$ $[a,\,b,\operatorname{Re}s>0;\ \operatorname{Re}\nu>-1]$
4	$\left(a^2-x^2\right)_+^{-\nu/2}$ $\times\,Y_\nu\left(b\sqrt{a^2-x^2}\right)$	$-2^{s/2-1}a^{s/2-\nu}b^{-s/2}\csc(\nu\pi)\,\Gamma\left(\dfrac{s}{2}\right)J_{s/2-\nu}(ab)$ $-\dfrac{2^{-\nu}a^s b^\nu}{s\pi}\cos(\nu\pi)\,\Gamma(-\nu)\,{}_1F_2\left({1;\ -\frac{a^2b^2}{4}\atop 1+\nu,\ \frac{s+2}{2}}\right)$ $[a,\,b,\ \operatorname{Re}s>0;\ \operatorname{Re}\nu<1]$

No.	$f(x)$	$F(s)$
5	$Y_\nu\left(ax + \dfrac{a}{x}\right)$	$\dfrac{\pi}{2}\left[J_{(\nu-s)/2}(a)\,J_{(\nu+s)/2}(a) - Y_{(\nu-s)/2}(a)\,Y_{(\nu+s)/2}(a)\right]$ $[a > 0;\ |\operatorname{Re} s| < 3/2]$

3.11.3. $Y_\nu(bx)$ and the exponential function

1	$e^{-ax}\,Y_\nu(bx)$	$-\left(\dfrac{b}{2}\right)^\nu \dfrac{\cos(\nu\pi)}{\pi a^{s+\nu}}\,\Gamma(-\nu)\,\Gamma(s+\nu)\;{}_2F_1\!\left(\begin{matrix}\frac{s+\nu}{2},\ \frac{s+\nu+1}{2}\\ 1+\nu;\ -\frac{b^2}{a^2}\end{matrix}\right)$ $-\dfrac{a^{\nu-s}}{\pi}\left(\dfrac{2}{b}\right)^\nu \Gamma(\nu)\,\Gamma(s-\nu)\;{}_2F_1\!\left(\begin{matrix}\frac{s-\nu}{2},\ \frac{s-\nu+1}{2}\\ 1-\nu;\ -\frac{b^2}{a^2}\end{matrix}\right)$ $[\operatorname{Re} a > |\operatorname{Im} b|;\ \operatorname{Re} s > |\operatorname{Re}\nu|]$
2	$e^{\pm iax}\,Y_\nu(ax)$	$-\dfrac{e^{\pm(s+\nu)\pi i/2}}{\pi^{3/2}(2a)^s}\,\Gamma\!\left[s+\nu,\ s-\nu,\ \dfrac{1-2s}{2}\right]$ $\times\left[2\cos(\nu\pi)\cos(s\pi)\mp i\sin\left[(s+\nu)\pi\right]\right]$ $[a > 0;\ |\operatorname{Re}\nu| < \operatorname{Re} s < 1/2]$
3	$e^{-ax^2}\,Y_\nu(bx)$	$-\dfrac{2^{-\nu-1}b^\nu}{\pi a^{(s+\nu)/2}}\cos(\nu\pi)\,\Gamma(-\nu)\,\Gamma\!\left(\dfrac{s+\nu}{2}\right)\,{}_1F_1\!\left(\begin{matrix}\frac{s+\nu}{2};\ -\frac{b^2}{4a}\\ 1+\nu\end{matrix}\right)$ $-\dfrac{2^{\nu-1}b^{-\nu}}{\pi a^{(s-\nu)/2}}\,\Gamma(\nu)\,\Gamma\!\left(\dfrac{s-\nu}{2}\right)\,{}_1F_1\!\left(\begin{matrix}\frac{s-\nu}{2};\ -\frac{b^2}{4a}\\ 1-\nu\end{matrix}\right)$ $[\operatorname{Re} a,\,b > 0;\ \operatorname{Re} s > |\operatorname{Re}\nu|]$

3.11.4. $Y_\nu(bx)$ and trigonometric functions

Notation: $\delta = \left\{\begin{matrix}1\\0\end{matrix}\right\}$.

1	$\left\{\begin{matrix}\sin(ax)\\\cos(ax)\end{matrix}\right\}Y_\nu(ax)$	$\pm\dfrac{2^{1-s}a^{-s}}{\pi^{3/2}}\left\{\begin{matrix}\sin^2\left[(s-\nu)\pi/2\right]\sin\left[(s+\nu)\pi/2\right]\\\cos^2\left[(s-\nu)\pi/2\right]\cos\left[(s+\nu)\pi/2\right]\end{matrix}\right\}$ $\times\,\Gamma\!\left[\dfrac{1-2s}{2},\ s-\nu,\ s+\nu\right]\qquad [a > 0;\ |\operatorname{Re}\nu| - \delta < \operatorname{Re} s < 1/2]$
2	$\left\{\begin{matrix}\sin(ax)\\\cos(ax)\end{matrix}\right\}Y_\nu(bx)$	$\pm\dfrac{2^{s+\delta-1}a^\delta}{\pi b^{s+\delta}}\left\{\begin{matrix}\sin\left[(s-\nu)\pi/2\right]\\\cos\left[(s-\nu)\pi/2\right]\end{matrix}\right\}\Gamma\!\left(\dfrac{s-\nu+\delta}{2}\right)$ $\times\,\Gamma\!\left(\dfrac{s+\nu+\delta}{2}\right)\,{}_2F_1\!\left(\begin{matrix}\frac{s-\nu+\delta}{2},\ \frac{s+\nu+\delta}{2}\\ \frac{2\delta+1}{2};\ \frac{a^2}{b^2}\end{matrix}\right)$ $[0 < a < b;\ |\operatorname{Re}\nu| - \delta < \operatorname{Re} s < 3/2]$

No.	$f(x)$	$F(s)$
3	$\begin{Bmatrix} \sin(ax) \\ \cos(ax) \end{Bmatrix} Y_\nu(bx)$	$-\dfrac{b^\nu \cos(\nu\pi)}{2^{\nu+1} a^{s+\nu}} \begin{Bmatrix} \sec[(s+\nu)\pi/2] \\ \csc[(s+\nu)\pi/2] \end{Bmatrix} \Gamma\begin{bmatrix} -\nu \\ 1-s-\nu \end{bmatrix}$ $\times\,{}_2F_1\left(\begin{matrix} \frac{s+\nu}{2},\ \frac{s+\nu+1}{2} \\ 1+\nu;\ \frac{b^2}{a^2} \end{matrix}\right) - \dfrac{2^{\nu-1} a^{\nu-s}}{b^\nu} \begin{Bmatrix} \sec[(s-\nu)\pi/2] \\ \csc[(s-\nu)\pi/2] \end{Bmatrix}$ $\times\,\Gamma\begin{bmatrix} \nu \\ 1-s+\nu \end{bmatrix} {}_2F_1\left(\begin{matrix} \frac{s-\nu}{2},\ \frac{s-\nu+1}{2} \\ 1-\nu;\ \frac{b^2}{a^2} \end{matrix}\right)$ $[0 < b < a;\ |\mathrm{Re}\,\nu| - \delta < \mathrm{Re}\,s < 3/2]$
4	$\begin{Bmatrix} \sin(ax+b) \\ \cos(ax+b) \end{Bmatrix} Y_\nu(ax)$	$\mp\dfrac{(2a)^{-s}}{\sqrt{\pi}} \begin{Bmatrix} \cos[(s+\nu)\pi/2+b] \\ \sin[(s+\nu)\pi/2+b] \end{Bmatrix} \Gamma\begin{bmatrix} \frac{1-2s}{2},\ s+\nu \\ 1-s+\nu \end{bmatrix}$ $-\dfrac{2^{1-s} a^{-s}}{\pi^{3/2}} \cos(\nu\pi) \begin{Bmatrix} \sin[(\nu-s)\pi/2+b] \\ \cos[(\nu-s)\pi/2+b] \end{Bmatrix}$ $\times\,\Gamma\left(\dfrac{1-2s}{2}\right)\Gamma(s-\nu)\Gamma(s+\nu) \quad [a>0;\ \mathrm{Re}\,\nu < \mathrm{Re}\,s < 1/2]$

3.11.5. $Y_\nu(bx)$ and the logarithmic function

1	$\ln x\, Y_\nu(ax)$	$\dfrac{2^{s-2}}{a^s} \Gamma\left(\dfrac{s+\nu}{2}\right)\Gamma\left(\dfrac{s-\nu}{2}\right) \Bigg\{ \sin\dfrac{(s-\nu)\pi}{2}$ $\qquad -\dfrac{1}{\pi}\cos\dfrac{(s-\nu)\pi}{2}\left[\psi\left(\dfrac{s+\nu}{2}\right) + \psi\left(\dfrac{s-\nu}{2}\right) - 2\ln\dfrac{a}{2}\right]\Bigg\}$ $[a>0;\ |\mathrm{Re}\,\nu| < \mathrm{Re}\,s < 3/2]$

3.11.6. $Y_\nu(bx)$ and $\mathrm{Ei}(ax^r)$

1	$\mathrm{Ei}(-ax)\, Y_\nu(bx)$	$\dfrac{\cos(\nu\pi)\, a^{-s-\nu}\, (b/2)^\nu}{\pi(s+\nu)} \Gamma(-\nu)\,\Gamma(s+\nu)\, {}_3F_2\left(\begin{matrix} \frac{s+\nu}{2},\ \frac{s+\nu}{2},\ \frac{s+\nu+1}{2} \\ \nu+1,\ \frac{s+\nu+2}{2};\ -\frac{b^2}{a^2} \end{matrix}\right)$ $+\dfrac{a^{\nu-s}\, (b/2)^{-\nu}}{\pi(s-\nu)} \Gamma(\nu)\,\Gamma(s-\nu)\, {}_3F_2\left(\begin{matrix} \frac{s-\nu}{2},\ \frac{s-\nu}{2},\ \frac{s-\nu+1}{2} \\ 1-\nu,\ \frac{s-\nu+2}{2};\ -\frac{b^2}{a^2} \end{matrix}\right)$ $[b,\ \mathrm{Re}\,a > 0;\ \mathrm{Re}\,s > |\mathrm{Re}\,\nu|]$
2	$\mathrm{Ei}(-ax^2)\, Y_\nu(bx)$	$\dfrac{2^\nu a^{(\nu-s)/2}}{\pi b^\nu (s-\nu)} \Gamma(\nu)\,\Gamma\left(\dfrac{s-\nu}{2}\right) {}_2F_2\left(\begin{matrix} \frac{s-\nu}{2},\ \frac{s-\nu}{2};\ -\frac{b^2}{4a} \\ 1-\nu,\ \frac{s-\nu+2}{2} \end{matrix}\right)$ $+\dfrac{b^\nu \cos(\nu\pi)}{2^\nu (s+\nu)\pi a^{(s+\nu)/2}} \Gamma(-\nu)\,\Gamma\left(\dfrac{s+\nu}{2}\right) {}_2F_2\left(\begin{matrix} \frac{s+\nu}{2},\ \frac{s+\nu}{2};\ -\frac{b^2}{4a} \\ 1+\nu,\ \frac{s+\nu+2}{2} \end{matrix}\right)$ $[a,\ \mathrm{Re}\,b > 0;\ \mathrm{Re}\,s > |\mathrm{Re}\,\nu|]$

No.	$f(x)$	$F(s)$
3	$e^{\pm ax}\,\mathrm{Ei}\,(\mp ax)\,Y_\nu\,(bx)$	$-\dfrac{2^\nu\Gamma\left(\nu\right)\Gamma\left(s-\nu\right)}{a^{s-\nu}b^\nu}\left\{\begin{matrix}\csc\left[(\nu-s)\,\pi\right]\\\cot\left[(\nu-s)\,\pi\right]\end{matrix}\right\}\,{}_2F_1\left(\begin{matrix}\frac{s-\nu}{2},\ \frac{s-\nu+1}{2}\\1-\nu;\ -\frac{b^2}{a^2}\end{matrix}\right)$

$$+\frac{\cos\left(\nu\pi\right)}{2^\nu a^{s+\nu}b^{-\nu}}\,\Gamma\left(-\nu\right)\Gamma\left(s+\nu\right)$$

$$\times\left\{\begin{matrix}\csc\left[(s+\nu)\,\pi\right]\\\cot\left[(s+\nu)\,\pi\right]\end{matrix}\right\}\,{}_2F_1\left(\begin{matrix}\frac{s+\nu}{2},\ \frac{s+\nu+1}{2}\\1+\nu;\ -\frac{b^2}{a^2}\end{matrix}\right)$$

$$\pm\frac{2^{s-2}}{\pi ab^{s-1}}\sin\frac{(s-\nu)\,\pi}{2}\,\Gamma\left(\frac{s+\nu-1}{2}\right)\Gamma\left(\frac{s-\nu-1}{2}\right)$$

$$\times{}_3F_2\left(\begin{matrix}\frac{1}{2},\ 1,\ 1;\ -\frac{b^2}{a^2}\\\frac{3-s-\nu}{2},\ \frac{3-s+\nu}{2}\end{matrix}\right)+\frac{2^{s-3}}{\pi a^2 b^{s-2}}\cos\frac{(s-\nu)\,\pi}{2}$$

$$\times\Gamma\left(\frac{s+\nu-2}{2}\right)\Gamma\left(\frac{s-\nu-2}{2}\right){}_3F_2\left(\begin{matrix}1,\ 1,\ \frac{3}{2};\ -\frac{b^2}{a^2}\\\frac{4-s-\nu}{2},\ \frac{4-s+\nu}{2}\end{matrix}\right)$$

$$[b,\ \mathrm{Re}\,a>0;\ |\mathrm{Re}\,\nu|<\mathrm{Re}\,s<5/2]$$

3.11.7. $Y_\nu\,(bx)$ **and** $\mathrm{si}\,(ax),\ \mathrm{ci}\,(ax)$

1	$\left\{\begin{matrix}\mathrm{si}\,(ax)\\\mathrm{ci}\,(ax)\end{matrix}\right\}Y_\nu\,(bx)$	$\dfrac{2^\nu a^{\nu-s}}{\pi b^\nu\,(s-\nu)}\,\Gamma\left(\nu\right)\Gamma\left(s-\nu\right)\left\{\begin{matrix}\sin\left[(s-\nu)\,\pi/2\right]\\\cos\left[(s-\nu)\,\pi/2\right]\end{matrix}\right\}$

$$\times{}_3F_2\left(\begin{matrix}\frac{s-\nu}{2},\ \frac{s-\nu}{2},\ \frac{s-\nu+1}{2}\\1-\nu,\ \frac{s-\nu+2}{2};\ \frac{b^2}{a^2}\end{matrix}\right)+\frac{b^\nu\Gamma\left(-\nu\right)\Gamma\left(s+\nu\right)}{2^\nu\pi a^{s+\nu}\,(s+\nu)}$$

$$\times\cos\left(\nu\pi\right)\left\{\begin{matrix}\sin\left[(s+\nu)\,\pi/2\right]\\\cos\left[(s+\nu)\,\pi/2\right]\end{matrix}\right\}{}_3F_2\left(\begin{matrix}\frac{s+\nu}{2},\ \frac{s+\nu}{2},\ \frac{s+\nu+1}{2}\\1+\nu,\ \frac{s+\nu+2}{2};\ \frac{b^2}{a^2}\end{matrix}\right)$$

$$\begin{bmatrix}0<b\leq a;\ |\mathrm{Re}\,\nu|<\mathrm{Re}\,s<5/2\ \text{for}\ b<a;\\|\mathrm{Re}\,\nu|<\mathrm{Re}\,s<3/2\ \text{for}\ b=a\end{bmatrix}$$

3.11.8. $Y_\nu\,(bx)$ **and** $\mathrm{erf}\,(ax),\ \mathrm{erfc}\,(ax),\ \mathrm{erfi}\,(ax)$

1	$\left\{\begin{matrix}\mathrm{erf}\,(ax)\\\mathrm{erfc}\,(ax)\end{matrix}\right\}Y_\nu\,(bx)$	$\mp\dfrac{2^\nu a^{\nu-s}}{\pi^{3/2}b^\nu\,(\nu-s)}\,\Gamma\left(\nu\right)\Gamma\left(\dfrac{s-\nu+1}{2}\right)$

$$\times{}_2F_2\left(\begin{matrix}\frac{s-\nu}{2},\ \frac{s-\nu+1}{2};\ -\frac{b^2}{4a^2}\\1-\nu,\ \frac{s-\nu+2}{2}\end{matrix}\right)\pm\frac{b^\nu\cos\left(\nu\pi\right)}{2^\nu\pi^{3/2}a^{s+\nu}\,(s+\nu)}$$

$$\times\Gamma\left(-\nu\right)\Gamma\left(\frac{s+\nu+1}{2}\right){}_2F_2\left(\begin{matrix}\frac{s+\nu}{2},\ \frac{s+\nu+1}{2};\ -\frac{b^2}{4a^2}\\1+\nu,\ \frac{s+\nu+2}{2}\end{matrix}\right)$$

$$-\frac{1\pm1}{\pi b^s}\,2^{s-2}\cos\frac{(s-\nu)\,\pi}{2}\,\Gamma\left(\frac{s+\nu}{2}\right)\Gamma\left(\frac{s-\nu}{2}\right)$$

$$\begin{bmatrix}b>0;\ \mathrm{Re}\,s>|\mathrm{Re}\,\nu|-(1\pm1)/2;\\|\arg a|<\pi/2;\ \mathrm{Re}\,s<3/2\ \text{for}\ \mathrm{erf}\end{bmatrix}$$

No.	$f(x)$	$F(s)$
2	$\begin{Bmatrix} \mathrm{erf}\,(a\sqrt{x}) \\ \mathrm{erfc}\,(a\sqrt{x}) \end{Bmatrix} Y_\nu(bx)$	$\mp \dfrac{2^{s+1/2}a}{\pi^{3/2}b^{s+1/2}}\, \Gamma\left(\dfrac{2s+2\nu+1}{4}\right)\Gamma\left(\dfrac{2s-2\nu+1}{4}\right)$

$$\times \cos\frac{(2s-2\nu+1)\,\pi}{4}\; {}_3F_2\left(\begin{matrix}\frac{1}{4},\,\frac{2s+2\nu+1}{4},\,\frac{2s-2\nu+1}{4}\\ \frac{1}{2},\,\frac{5}{4};\,-\frac{a^4}{b^2}\end{matrix}\right)$$

$$\mp \frac{2^{s+3/2}a^3}{3\pi^{3/2}b^{s+3/2}}\,\Gamma\left(\frac{2s+2\nu+3}{4}\right)\Gamma\left(\frac{2s-2\nu+3}{4}\right)$$

$$\times \sin\frac{(2s-2\nu+1)\,\pi}{4}\; {}_3F_2\left(\begin{matrix}\frac{3}{4},\,\frac{2s+2\nu+3}{4},\,\frac{2s-2\nu+3}{4}\\ \frac{3}{2},\,\frac{7}{4};\,-\frac{a^4}{b^2}\end{matrix}\right)$$

$$-\frac{1\mp 1}{\pi b^s}\,2^{s-2}\cos\frac{(s-\nu)\,\pi}{2}\,\Gamma\left(\frac{s+\nu}{2}\right)\Gamma\left(\frac{s-\nu}{2}\right)$$

$$\left[\begin{matrix}b>0;\; |\mathrm{Re}\,\nu|<\mathrm{Re}\,s+(1\pm 1)/4;\; |\arg a|<\pi/4;\\ \mathrm{Re}\,s<3/2 \ \text{for}\ \mathrm{erf}\end{matrix}\right]$$

| 3 | $e^{\mp a^2 x^2}\begin{Bmatrix} \mathrm{erfi}\,(ax) \\ \mathrm{erfc}\,(ax) \end{Bmatrix}$ $\times\, Y_\nu(bx)$ | $-\dfrac{b^\nu \cos(\nu\pi)}{2^{\nu+(1\pm 1)/2}a^{s+\nu}}\begin{Bmatrix}\sec[(s+\nu)\,\pi/2]\\ \csc[(s+\nu)\,\pi]\end{Bmatrix}$ |

$$\times \Gamma\begin{bmatrix}-\nu\\ \frac{2-s-\nu}{2}\end{bmatrix}\,{}_1F_1\left(\begin{matrix}\frac{s+\nu}{2};\,\mp\frac{b^2}{4a^2}\\ 1+\nu\end{matrix}\right)$$

$$-\frac{2^{\nu-(1\pm 1)/2}}{a^{s-\nu}b^\nu}\begin{Bmatrix}\sec[(s-\nu)\,\pi/2]\\ \csc[(s-\nu)\,\pi]\end{Bmatrix}$$

$$\times \Gamma\begin{bmatrix}\nu\\ \frac{2-s+\nu}{2}\end{bmatrix}\,{}_1F_1\left(\begin{matrix}\frac{s-\nu}{2};\,\mp\frac{b^2}{4a^2}\\ 1-\nu\end{matrix}\right)-\frac{2^{s-2}b^{1-s}}{\pi^{3/2}a}\,\Gamma\left(\frac{s+\nu-1}{2}\right)$$

$$\times \Gamma\left(\frac{s-\nu-1}{2}\right)\sin\frac{(s-\nu)\,\pi}{2}\;{}_2F_2\left(\begin{matrix}\frac{1}{2},\,1;\,\mp\frac{b^2}{4a^2}\\ \frac{3-s-\nu}{2},\,\frac{3-s+\nu}{2}\end{matrix}\right)$$

$$\left[\begin{matrix}b>0;\; |\mathrm{Re}\,\nu|-(1\pm 1)/2<\mathrm{Re}\,s<5/2;\\ |\arg a|<(2\mp 1)\,\pi/4\end{matrix}\right]$$

3.11.9. $Y_\nu(bx)$ **and** $S(ax),\ C(ax)$

Notation: $\delta=\begin{Bmatrix}1\\ 0\end{Bmatrix}$.

No.	$f(x)$	$F(s)$
1	$\begin{Bmatrix} S(ax) \\ C(ax) \end{Bmatrix} Y_\nu(bx)$	$-\dfrac{2^{s+\delta}a^{1/2+\delta}}{3^\delta\pi^{3/2}b^{s+\delta+1/2}}\cos\dfrac{(2s-2\nu+2\delta+1)\,\pi}{4}$

$$\times \Gamma\left(\frac{2s-2\nu+2\delta+1}{4}\right)\Gamma\left(\frac{2s+2\nu+2\delta+1}{4}\right)$$

$$\times {}_3F_2\left(\begin{matrix}\frac{2\delta+1}{4},\,\frac{2s-2\nu+2\delta+1}{4},\,\frac{2s+2\nu+2\delta+1}{4}\\ \frac{2\delta+5}{4},\,\frac{2\delta+1}{2};\,\frac{a^2}{b^2}\end{matrix}\right)$$

$$[a,\,b>0;\; |\mathrm{Re}\,\nu|-(2\pm 1)/2<\mathrm{Re}\,s<3/2]$$

3.11.10. $Y_\nu(bx)$ **and** $\gamma(\mu, ax)$, $\Gamma(\mu, ax)$

1	$\left\{\begin{matrix}\gamma(\mu, ax)\\ \Gamma(\mu, ax)\end{matrix}\right\} Y_\nu(bx)$	$\mp\dfrac{2^{s+\mu-1}a^\mu}{\mu\pi b^{s+\mu}}\Gamma\left(\dfrac{s+\mu-\nu}{2}\right)\Gamma\left(\dfrac{s+\mu+\nu}{2}\right)$

$$\times\cos\frac{(s+\mu-\nu)\pi}{2}\,_3F_2\left(\begin{matrix}\frac{\mu}{2},\ \frac{s+\mu-\nu}{2},\ \frac{s+\mu+\nu}{2}\\ \frac{1}{2},\ \frac{\mu+2}{2};\ -\frac{a^2}{b^2}\end{matrix}\right)$$

$$\mp\frac{2^{s+\mu}a^{\mu+1}}{(\mu+1)\pi b^{s+\mu+1}}\Gamma\left(\frac{s+\mu-\nu+1}{2}\right)\Gamma\left(\frac{s+\mu+\nu+1}{2}\right)$$

$$\times\sin\frac{(s+\mu-\nu)\pi}{2}\,_3F_2\left(\begin{matrix}\frac{\mu+1}{2},\ \frac{s+\mu+\nu+1}{2},\ \frac{s+\mu-\nu+1}{2}\\ \frac{3}{2},\ \frac{\mu+3}{2};\ -\frac{a^2}{b^2}\end{matrix}\right)$$

$$-\frac{1\mp 1}{\pi b^s}2^{s-1}\cos\frac{(s-\nu)\pi}{2}\Gamma\left[\mu,\ \frac{s-\nu}{2},\ \frac{s+\nu}{2}\right]$$

$$\left[\begin{matrix}b,\ \operatorname{Re}a>0;\ \operatorname{Re}(s+\mu)>|\operatorname{Re}\nu|;\\ \left\{\begin{matrix}\operatorname{Re}\mu>0;\ \operatorname{Re}s<3/2\\ \operatorname{Re}s>|\operatorname{Re}\nu|\end{matrix}\right\}\end{matrix}\right]$$

2	$\left\{\begin{matrix}\gamma(\mu, ax^2)\\ \Gamma(\mu, ax^2)\end{matrix}\right\} Y_\nu(bx)$	$\mp\dfrac{2^\nu a^{(\nu-s)/2}}{\pi b^\nu(\nu-s)}\Gamma(\nu)\Gamma\left(\dfrac{s+2\mu-\nu}{2}\right)$

$$\times\,_2F_2\left(\begin{matrix}\frac{s-\nu}{2},\ \frac{s+2\mu-\nu}{2};\ -\frac{b^2}{4a}\\ 1-\nu,\ \frac{s-\nu+2}{2}\end{matrix}\right)\pm\frac{b^\nu\cos(\nu\pi)}{2^\nu\pi a^{(s+\nu)/2}(s+\nu)}$$

$$\times\Gamma(-\nu)\Gamma\left(\frac{s+2\mu+\nu}{2}\right)\,_2F_2\left(\begin{matrix}\frac{s+\nu}{2},\ \frac{s+2\mu+\nu}{2};\ -\frac{b^2}{4a}\\ 1+\nu,\ \frac{s+\nu+2}{2}\end{matrix}\right)$$

$$-\frac{1\pm 1}{\pi b^s}2^{s-1}\cos\frac{(s-\nu)\pi}{2}\Gamma\left[\mu,\ \frac{s+\nu}{2},\ \frac{s-\nu}{2}\right]$$

$$\left[\begin{matrix}b,\ \operatorname{Re}a>0;\ \operatorname{Re}(s+2\mu)>|\operatorname{Re}\nu|;\\ \left\{\begin{matrix}\operatorname{Re}\mu>0;\ \operatorname{Re}s<3/2\\ \operatorname{Re}s>|\operatorname{Re}\nu|\end{matrix}\right\}\end{matrix}\right]$$

3	$e^{ax^2}\Gamma(\mu, ax^2)\,Y_\nu(bx)$	$-\dfrac{2^{\nu-1}a^{(\nu-s)/2}}{b^\nu}\Gamma\left[\nu,\ \dfrac{s-\nu}{2}\atop 1-\mu\right]\csc\dfrac{(s+2\mu-\nu)\pi}{2}$

$$\times\,_1F_1\left(\begin{matrix}\frac{s-\nu}{2};\ \frac{b^2}{4a}\\ 1-\nu\end{matrix}\right)-\frac{b^\nu}{2^{\nu+1}a^{(s+\nu)/2}}\Gamma\left[-\nu,\ \frac{s+\nu}{2}\atop 1-\mu\right]$$

$$\times\cos(\nu\pi)\csc\frac{(s+2\mu+\nu)\pi}{2}\,_1F_1\left(\begin{matrix}\frac{s+\nu}{2};\ \frac{b^2}{4a}\\ 1+\nu\end{matrix}\right)$$

$$+\frac{2^{s+2\mu-3}a^{\mu-1}}{\pi b^{s+2\mu-2}}\Gamma\left(\frac{s+2\mu+\nu-2}{2}\right)\Gamma\left(\frac{s+2\mu-\nu-2}{2}\right)$$

$$\times\cos\frac{(s-\nu+2\mu)\pi}{2}\,_2F_2\left(\begin{matrix}1,\ 1-\mu;\ \frac{b^2}{4a}\\ \frac{4-s-2\mu+\nu}{2},\ \frac{4-s-2\mu-\nu}{2}\end{matrix}\right)$$

$$\left[\begin{matrix}b>0;\ \operatorname{Re}s>|\operatorname{Re}\nu|;\ |\arg a|<\pi;\\ |\operatorname{Re}\nu|<\operatorname{Re}(s+2\mu)<7/2\end{matrix}\right]$$

3.11.11. $Y_\nu(bx)$ and $D_\mu(ax^r)$

1	$e^{a^2x/4} D_\mu\left(a\sqrt{x}\right) Y_\nu(bx)$	$\dfrac{2^{2s-\mu-7/2}a^{-2s}}{\pi^2\,\Gamma(-\mu)}\,G^{44}_{55}\left(\dfrac{4b^2}{a^4}\,\middle|\,\begin{matrix}-\frac{\nu+1}{2},\ \frac{1-2s}{4},\ \frac{3-2s}{4},\ \frac{1-s}{2},\ \frac{2-s}{2}\\ -\frac{\nu+1}{2},\ -\frac{\nu}{2},\ \frac{\nu}{2},\ -\frac{2s+\mu}{4},\ -\frac{2s+\mu-2}{4}\end{matrix}\right)$

$$[b>0;\ \operatorname{Re}(2s+\mu)<3,\ \operatorname{Re}s>|\operatorname{Re}\nu|;\ |\arg a|<3\pi/4]$$

2	$e^{-a^2x/4} D_\mu\left(a\sqrt{x}\right) Y_\nu(bx)$	$-\dfrac{2^{\mu/2+2\nu-s+1}a^{2\nu-2s}b^{-\nu}}{\sqrt{\pi}}\,\Gamma\!\left[\begin{matrix}\nu,\ 2s-2\nu\\ \frac{2s-\mu-2\nu+1}{2}\end{matrix}\right]$

$$\times\ {}_4F_3\!\left(\begin{matrix}\frac{s-\nu}{2},\ \frac{s-\nu+1}{2},\ \frac{2s-2\nu+1}{4},\ \frac{2s-2\nu+3}{4}\\ 1-\nu,\ \frac{2s-\mu-2\nu+1}{4},\ \frac{2s-\mu-2\nu+3}{4};\ -\frac{4b^2}{a^4}\end{matrix}\right)$$

$$-\dfrac{2^{\mu/2-2\nu-s+1}a^{-2\nu-2s}b^{\nu}}{\sqrt{\pi}}\,\cos(\nu\pi)\,\Gamma\!\left[\begin{matrix}-\nu,\ 2s+2\nu\\ \frac{2s-\mu+2\nu+1}{2}\end{matrix}\right]$$

$$\times\ {}_4F_3\!\left(\begin{matrix}\frac{s+\nu}{2},\ \frac{s+\nu+1}{2},\ \frac{2s+2\nu+1}{4},\ \frac{2s+2\nu+3}{4}\\ \nu+1,\ \frac{2s-\mu+2\nu+1}{4},\ \frac{2s-\mu+2\nu+3}{4};\ -\frac{4b^2}{a^4}\end{matrix}\right)$$

$$[b>0;\ \operatorname{Re}s>|\operatorname{Re}\nu|;\ |\arg a|<\pi/4]$$

3.11.12. $Y_\nu(\varphi(x))$ and $J_\mu(\psi(x))$

1	$\cos(ax)\,J_\nu(ax)$	$\dfrac{2^{s-1}}{a^s}\,\Gamma\!\left[\begin{matrix}\frac{s-\nu}{2},\ \frac{s+\nu}{2}\\ \frac{s\mp2a-\nu}{2},\ \frac{2-s\pm2a+\nu}{2}\end{matrix}\right]$ $[a>0;\ |\operatorname{Re}\nu|<\operatorname{Re}s<3/2]$
	$\pm\sin(ax)\,Y_\nu(ax)$	
2	$\left\{\begin{matrix}\sin(ax+b)\\ \cos(ax+b)\end{matrix}\right\} J_\nu(ax)$	$\pm\dfrac{2^{1-s}a^{-s}}{\pi^{3/2}}\,\cos(\nu\pi)\left\{\begin{matrix}\cos[(\nu-s)\pi/2+b]\\ \sin[(\nu-s)\pi/2+b]\end{matrix}\right\}$
	$\mp\left\{\begin{matrix}\cos(ax+b)\\ \sin(ax+b)\end{matrix}\right\} Y_\nu(ax)$	$\times\,\Gamma\!\left(\dfrac{1-2s}{2}\right)\Gamma(s-\nu)\,\Gamma(s+\nu)$

$$[a>0;\ |\operatorname{Re}\nu|<\operatorname{Re}s<1/2]$$

3	$\left\{\begin{matrix}\sin(ax+b)\\ \cos(ax+b)\end{matrix}\right\} J_\nu(ax)$	$\dfrac{2^{1-s}a^{-s}}{\sqrt{\pi}}\left\{\begin{matrix}\sin[(s+\nu)\pi/2+b]\\ \cos[(s+\nu)\pi/2+b]\end{matrix}\right\}\Gamma\!\left[\begin{matrix}\frac{1-2s}{2},\ s+\nu\\ 1-s+\nu\end{matrix}\right]$
	$\pm\left\{\begin{matrix}\cos(ax+b)\\ \sin(ax+b)\end{matrix}\right\} Y_\nu(ax)$	$\mp\dfrac{2^{1-s}a^{-s}}{\pi^{3/2}}\,\cos(\nu\pi)\left\{\begin{matrix}\cos[(\nu-s)\pi/2+b]\\ \sin[(\nu-s)\pi/2+b]\end{matrix}\right\}$
		$\times\,\Gamma\!\left(\dfrac{1-2s}{2}\right)\Gamma(s-\nu)\,\Gamma(s+\nu)$

$$[a>0;\ |\operatorname{Re}\nu|<\operatorname{Re}s<1/2]$$

4	$J_\nu(ax)\,Y_\nu(ax)$	$-\dfrac{a^{-s}}{2\sqrt{\pi}}\,\Gamma\!\left[\begin{matrix}\frac{s}{2},\ \frac{s+2\nu}{2}\\ \frac{s+1}{2},\ \frac{2-s+2\nu}{2}\end{matrix}\right]$ $[a>0;\ 0,\ -2\operatorname{Re}\nu<\operatorname{Re}s<2]$

No.	$f(x)$	$F(s)$

5 $J_{-\nu}(ax)\, Y_\nu(ax)$

$$-\frac{a^{-s}}{2\pi^{3/2}}\,\cos\frac{(s-2\nu)\pi}{2}\,\Gamma\left[\begin{array}{c}\frac{s}{2},\,\frac{1-s}{2},\,\frac{s-2\nu}{2}\\\frac{2-s-2\nu}{2}\end{array}\right]$$

$$[a>0;\ 0,\ 2\operatorname{Re}\nu<\operatorname{Re}s<1]$$

6 $J_\mu(ax)\, Y_\nu(ax)$

$$-\frac{2^{s-1}}{\pi a^s}\,\cos\frac{(s+\mu-\nu)\pi}{2}\,\Gamma\left[\begin{array}{c}1-s,\,\frac{s+\mu-\nu}{2},\,\frac{s+\mu+\nu}{2}\\\frac{2-s+\mu-\nu}{2},\,\frac{2-s+\mu+\nu}{2}\end{array}\right]$$

$$[a>0;\ |\operatorname{Re}\nu|-\operatorname{Re}\mu<\operatorname{Re}s<1]$$

7 $J_\mu(ax)\, Y_\nu(bx)$

$$-\frac{2^{s-1}a^\mu b^{-s-\mu}}{\pi}\,\cos\frac{(s+\mu-\nu)\pi}{2}\,\Gamma\left[\begin{array}{c}\frac{s+\mu-\nu}{2},\,\frac{s+\mu+\nu}{2}\\\mu+1\end{array}\right]$$

$$\times\ {}_2F_1\left(\begin{array}{c}\frac{s+\mu-\nu}{2},\,\frac{s+\mu+\nu}{2}\\\mu+1;\,\frac{a^2}{b^2}\end{array}\right)\qquad[0<a<b;\ |\operatorname{Re}\nu|-\operatorname{Re}\mu<\operatorname{Re}s<2]$$

8 $J_\nu(ax)\, Y_\nu(bx)$

$$-\frac{2^{s-1}}{\pi}\,(a^2-b^2)^{-s/2}\,\Gamma\left(\frac{s}{2}\right)\Gamma\left(\frac{s+2\nu}{2}\right)$$

$$\times\left[\cos\frac{s\pi}{2}\,P_{-s/2}^{-\nu}\left(\frac{a^2+b^2}{a^2-b^2}\right)\right.$$

$$\left.+\frac{2e^{-i\nu\pi}}{\Gamma\left(\frac{2-s+2\nu}{2}\right)\Gamma\left(\frac{s+2\nu}{2}\right)}\,Q_{-s/2}^{\nu}\left(\frac{a^2+b^2}{a^2-b^2}\right)\right]$$

$$[0<b<a;\ 0,\ -2\operatorname{Re}\nu<\operatorname{Re}s<2]$$

9 $J_\mu(ax)\, Y_\nu(bx)$

$$-\frac{2^{s-1}b^\nu}{\pi a^{s+\nu}}\,\cos(\nu\pi)\,\Gamma\left[\begin{array}{c}-\nu,\,\frac{s+\mu+\nu}{2}\\\frac{2-s+\mu-\nu}{2}\end{array}\right]\ {}_2F_1\left(\begin{array}{c}\frac{s-\mu+\nu}{2},\,\frac{s+\mu+\nu}{2}\\1+\nu;\,\frac{b^2}{a^2}\end{array}\right)$$

$$-\frac{2^{s-1}a^{\nu-s}}{\pi b^\nu}\,\Gamma\left[\begin{array}{c}\nu,\,\frac{s+\mu-\nu}{2}\\\frac{2-s+\mu+\nu}{2}\end{array}\right]\ {}_2F_1\left(\begin{array}{c}\frac{s-\mu-\nu}{2},\,\frac{s+\mu-\nu}{2}\\1-\nu;\,\frac{b^2}{a^2}\end{array}\right)$$

$$[0<b<a;\ |\operatorname{Re}\nu|-\operatorname{Re}\mu<\operatorname{Re}s<2]$$

10 $J_\nu(ax)\, Y_{-\nu}(bx)$

$$-\frac{2^{s-1}}{\pi}\,(b^2-a^2)^{-s/2}\,\cos\frac{(s+2\nu)\pi}{2}$$

$$\times\Gamma\left(\frac{s}{2}\right)\Gamma\left(\frac{s+2\nu}{2}\right)P_{-s/2}^{-\nu}\left(\frac{b^2+a^2}{b^2-a^2}\right)$$

$$[0<a<b;\ 0,\ -2\operatorname{Re}\nu<\operatorname{Re}s<2]$$

11 $J_\nu(ax)\, Y_{-\nu}(bx)$

$$-\frac{2^{s-1}}{\pi}\,(a^2-b^2)^{-s/2}\,\Gamma\left(\frac{s}{2}\right)\Gamma\left(\frac{s+2\nu}{2}\right)$$

$$\times\left[\cos\frac{(s+2\nu)\pi}{2}\,P_{-s/2}^{-\nu}\left(\frac{a^2+b^2}{a^2-b^2}\right)\right.$$

$$\left.+\frac{2e^{-i\nu\pi}\cos(\nu\pi)}{\Gamma\left(\frac{2-s+2\nu}{2}\right)\Gamma\left(\frac{s+2\nu}{2}\right)}\,Q_{-s/2}^{\nu}\left(\frac{a^2+b^2}{a^2-b^2}\right)\right]$$

$$[0<b<a;\ 0,\ -2\operatorname{Re}\nu<\operatorname{Re}s<2]$$

No.	$f(x)$	$F(s)$
12	$J_\mu(ax) Y_\nu(ax)$ $\quad + J_\nu(ax) Y_\mu(ax)$	$-\dfrac{2^{s-1}}{\pi a^s} \Gamma\left[\begin{array}{c} \frac{s+\mu-\nu}{2}, \frac{s-\mu+\nu}{2}, \frac{s+\mu+\nu}{2} \\ s, \frac{2-s+\mu+\nu}{2} \end{array}\right]$ $[a>0;\, -\operatorname{Re}(\mu+\nu),\, |\operatorname{Re}(\mu-\nu)| < \operatorname{Re} s < 2]$
13	$J_\mu(ax) Y_\nu(ax)$ $\quad - J_\nu(ax) Y_\mu(ax)$	$\dfrac{2^{s-1}}{\pi^2 a^s} \sin[(\mu-\nu)\pi]\, \Gamma\left[\begin{array}{c} 1-s, \frac{s-\mu+\nu}{2}, \frac{s+\mu-\nu}{2}, \frac{s+\mu+\nu}{2} \\ \frac{2-s+\mu+\nu}{2} \end{array}\right]$ $[a>0;\, |\operatorname{Re}\nu| - \operatorname{Re}\mu < \operatorname{Re} s < 1]$
14	$J_\nu(ax) Y_{-\nu}(ax)$ $\quad + J_{-\nu}(ax) Y_\nu(ax)$	$-\dfrac{a^{-s}}{\sqrt{\pi}} \Gamma\left[\begin{array}{c} \frac{s-2\nu}{2}, \frac{s+2\nu}{2} \\ \frac{2-s}{2}, \frac{s+1}{2} \end{array}\right] \qquad [a>0;\, 2|\operatorname{Re}\nu| < \operatorname{Re} s < 2]$
15	$J_\nu(ax) Y_{-\nu}(ax)$ $\quad - J_{-\nu}(ax) Y_\nu(ax)$	$\dfrac{a^{-s}}{2\pi^{5/2}} \sin(2\nu\pi)\, \Gamma\left[\dfrac{s}{2}, \dfrac{1-s}{2}, \dfrac{s-2\nu}{2}, \dfrac{s+2\nu}{2}\right]$ $[a>0;\, 2|\operatorname{Re}\nu| < \operatorname{Re} s < 1]$
16	$J_\nu(ax) Y_{-\nu}(bx)$ $\quad + J_{-\nu}(ax) Y_\nu(bx)$	$-\dfrac{2^{s-1}}{a^{s-\nu} b^\nu}\left[\cos(\nu\pi)\csc\dfrac{s\pi}{2} + \csc\dfrac{(s-2\nu)\pi}{2}\right]$ $\times\, \Gamma\left[\begin{array}{c} \nu \\ \frac{2-s}{2}, \frac{2-s+2\nu}{2} \end{array}\right]\, {}_2F_1\left(\begin{array}{c} \frac{s}{2}, \frac{s-2\nu}{2} \\ 1-\nu;\, \frac{b^2}{a^2} \end{array}\right)$ $-\dfrac{2^{s-1}}{a^{s+\nu} b^{-\nu}}\left[\cos(\nu\pi)\csc\dfrac{s\pi}{2} + \csc\dfrac{(s+2\nu)\pi}{2}\right]$ $\times\, \Gamma\left[\begin{array}{c} -\nu \\ \frac{2-s}{2}, \frac{2-s-2\nu}{2} \end{array}\right]\, {}_2F_1\left(\begin{array}{c} \frac{s}{2}, \frac{s+2\nu}{2} \\ 1+\nu;\, \frac{b^2}{a^2} \end{array}\right)$ $[a>b>0;\, 2|\operatorname{Re}\nu| < \operatorname{Re} s < 2]$
17	$J_\nu(u_-) Y_\nu(u_+)$ $u_\pm = b\left(\sqrt{x^2+a^2}\pm a\right)$	$\dfrac{1}{2\sqrt{\pi}}\left(\dfrac{a}{b}\right)^{s/2} \Gamma\left[\begin{array}{c} \frac{s+2\nu}{2}, \frac{1-s}{2} \\ \frac{2-s+2\nu}{2} \end{array}\right] Y_{-s/2}(2ab)$ $[a,b>0;\, -2\operatorname{Re}\nu < \operatorname{Re} s < 1]$
18	$J_\nu(u_-) Y_{-\nu}(u_+)$ $u_\pm = b\left(\sqrt{x^2+a^2}\pm a\right)$	$\dfrac{1}{2\sqrt{\pi}}\left(\dfrac{a}{b}\right)^{s/2} \Gamma\left[\begin{array}{c} \frac{s+2\nu}{2}, \frac{1-s}{2} \\ \frac{2-s+2\nu}{2} \end{array}\right]\left[\sin(\nu\pi) J_{-s/2}(2ab)\right.$ $\left.+ \cos(\nu\pi) Y_{-s/2}(2ab)\right] \qquad [a,b>0;\, -2\operatorname{Re}\nu < \operatorname{Re} s < 1]$
19	$J_\nu(u_-) Y_\nu(u_+)$ $\quad - J_\nu(u_+) Y_\nu(u_-)$ $u_\pm = b\left(\sqrt{x^2+a^2}\pm a\right)$	$\dfrac{\cos(\nu\pi)}{\pi^{3/2}}\left(\dfrac{a}{b}\right)^{s/2} \Gamma\left(\dfrac{1-s}{2}\right)\Gamma\left(\dfrac{s}{2}-\nu\right)\Gamma\left(\dfrac{s}{2}+\nu\right)$ $\times J_{s/2}(2ab) \qquad [a,b>0;\, 2|\operatorname{Re}\nu| < \operatorname{Re} s < 1]$

3.11.13. $Y_\nu(bx)$, $J_\nu(bx)$, and trigonometric functions

Notation: $\delta = \left\{ \begin{matrix} 1 \\ 0 \end{matrix} \right\}$.

1	$\left\{ \begin{matrix} \sin(ax) \\ \cos(ax) \end{matrix} \right\}$ $\times J_\nu(bx) Y_\nu(bx)$	$-\dfrac{a^\delta b^{-s-\delta}}{2\sqrt{\pi}} \Gamma\left[\begin{matrix} \frac{s+\delta}{2}, \frac{s+2\nu+\delta}{2} \\ \frac{s+\delta+1}{2}, \frac{2-s+2\nu-\delta}{2} \end{matrix} \right] {}_3F_2\left(\begin{matrix} \frac{s+\delta}{2}, \frac{s+2\nu+\delta}{2}, \frac{s-2\nu+\delta}{2} \\ \frac{2\delta+1}{2}, \frac{s+\delta+1}{2}; \frac{a^2}{4b^2} \end{matrix} \right)$ $[0 < a < 2b;\ -\delta,\ -2\operatorname{Re}\nu - \delta < \operatorname{Re}s < 2]$
2	$\left\{ \begin{matrix} \sin(ax) \\ \cos(ax) \end{matrix} \right\}$ $\times J_\nu(bx) Y_\nu(bx)$	$-\dfrac{\Gamma(s)}{\nu\pi a^s} \left\{ \begin{matrix} \sin(s\pi/2) \\ \cos(s\pi/2) \end{matrix} \right\} {}_3F_2\left(\begin{matrix} \frac{1}{2}, \frac{s}{2}, \frac{s+1}{2} \\ 1-\nu, 1+\nu; \frac{4b^2}{a^2} \end{matrix} \right)$ $-\dfrac{\cos(\nu\pi)}{\pi a^{s+2\nu}} \left(\dfrac{b}{2} \right)^{2\nu} \left\{ \begin{matrix} \sin[(s+2\nu)\pi/2] \\ \cos[(s+2\nu)\pi/2] \end{matrix} \right\}$ $\times \Gamma\left[\begin{matrix} -\nu, s+2\nu \\ \nu+1 \end{matrix} \right] {}_3F_2\left(\begin{matrix} \frac{2\nu+1}{2}, \frac{s+2\nu}{2}, \frac{s+2\nu+1}{2} \\ \nu+1, 2\nu+1; \frac{4b^2}{a^2} \end{matrix} \right)$ $[0 < 2b < a;\ -\delta,\ -2\operatorname{Re}\nu - \delta < \operatorname{Re}s < 2]$

3.11.14. $Y_\nu(bx)$, $J_\nu(bx)$, and $S(ax)$, $C(ax)$

Notation: $\delta = \left\{ \begin{matrix} 1 \\ 0 \end{matrix} \right\}$.

1	$\left\{ \begin{matrix} S(ax) \\ C(ax) \end{matrix} \right\} J_\nu(bx) Y_\nu(bx)$	$-\dfrac{a^{\delta+1/2} b^{-s-\delta-1/2}}{(2\delta+1)\sqrt{2}\,\pi} \Gamma\left[\begin{matrix} \frac{2s+2\delta+1}{4}, \frac{2s+4\nu+2\delta+1}{4} \\ \frac{2s+2\delta+3}{4}, \frac{3-2s+4\nu-2\delta}{2} \end{matrix} \right]$ $\times {}_4F_3\left(\begin{matrix} \frac{2\delta+1}{4}, \frac{2s+2\delta+1}{4}, \frac{2s-4\nu+2\delta+1}{4}, \frac{2s+4\nu+2\delta+1}{4} \\ \frac{2\delta+1}{2}, \frac{2\delta+5}{4}, \frac{2s+2\delta+3}{4}; \frac{a^2}{4b^2} \end{matrix} \right)$ $[0 < a < 2b;\ -2\nu - \delta - 1/2,\ -\delta - 1/2 < \operatorname{Re}s < 1]$
2	$\left\{ \begin{matrix} S(ax) \\ C(ax) \end{matrix} \right\} J_\nu(bx) Y_\nu(bx)$	$\dfrac{a^{-s-2\nu} b^{2\nu}}{\sqrt{2}\,\pi(s+2\nu)} \left\{ \begin{matrix} \sin[(2s+4\nu+1)\pi/4] \\ \cos[(2s+4\nu+1)\pi/4] \end{matrix} \right\} \Gamma\left[\begin{matrix} -\nu, \frac{2s+4\nu+1}{2} \\ \frac{1-2\nu}{2}, 2\nu+1 \end{matrix} \right]$ $\times {}_4F_3\left(\begin{matrix} \frac{2\nu+1}{2}, \frac{s+2\nu}{2}, \frac{2s+4\nu+1}{4}, \frac{2s+4\nu+3}{4} \\ \nu+1, 2\nu+1, \frac{s+2\nu+2}{2}; \frac{4b^2}{a^2} \end{matrix} \right)$ $+\dfrac{a^{-s}}{\sqrt{2}\,\pi^{3/2}\nu s} \left\{ \begin{matrix} \sin[(2s+1)\pi/4] \\ \cos[(2s+1)\pi/4] \end{matrix} \right\} \Gamma\left(s + \dfrac{1}{2} \right)$ $\times {}_4F_3\left(\begin{matrix} \frac{1}{2}, \frac{s}{2}, \frac{2s+1}{4}, \frac{2s+3}{4} \\ 1-\nu, 1+\nu, \frac{s+2}{2}; \frac{4b^2}{a^2} \end{matrix} \right)$ $-\dfrac{b^{-s}}{4\sqrt{\pi}} \Gamma\left[\begin{matrix} \frac{s}{2}, \frac{s+2\nu}{2} \\ \frac{s+1}{2}, \frac{2-s+2\nu}{2} \end{matrix} \right]$ $[0 < 2b < a;\ -2\nu - \delta - 1/2,\ -\delta - 1/2 < \operatorname{Re}s < 1]$

3.11.15. $Y_\nu(ax)$ **and** $J_\lambda(bx) J_\mu(cx)$

Notation: $\delta = \left\{ \begin{matrix} 1 \\ 0 \end{matrix} \right\}$.

1	$J_\lambda(ax) J_\mu(ax) Y_\nu(bx)$	$-\dfrac{2^{s-1} a^{\lambda+\mu}}{\pi b^{s+\lambda+\mu}} \cos \dfrac{(s+\lambda+\mu-\nu)\pi}{2} \Gamma \left[\begin{matrix} \frac{s+\lambda+\mu+\nu}{2}, \ \frac{s+\lambda+\mu-\nu}{2} \\ \lambda+1, \ \mu+1 \end{matrix} \right]$

$$\times\, {}_4F_3 \left(\begin{matrix} \frac{\lambda+\mu+1}{2}, \ \frac{\lambda+\mu+2}{2}, \ \frac{s+\lambda+\mu+\nu}{2}, \ \frac{s+\lambda+\mu-\nu}{2} \\ \lambda+1, \ \mu+1, \ \lambda+\mu+1; \ \frac{4a^2}{b^2} \end{matrix} \right)$$

$$[0 < 2a < b; \ |\operatorname{Re}\nu| - \operatorname{Re}(\lambda+\mu) < \operatorname{Re}s < 5/2]$$

2	$J_\lambda(ax) J_\mu(bx) Y_\nu(bx)$	$-\dfrac{2^{s-1} a^{\nu-\mu-s}}{\pi b^{\nu-\mu}} \Gamma \left[\begin{matrix} \nu, \ \frac{s+\lambda+\mu-\nu}{2} \\ \mu+1, \ \frac{2-s+\lambda+\nu-\mu}{2} \end{matrix} \right]$

$$\times\, {}_4F_3 \left(\begin{matrix} \frac{\mu-\nu+1}{2}, \ \frac{\mu-\nu+2}{2}, \ \frac{s-\lambda+\mu-\nu}{2}, \ \frac{s+\lambda+\mu-\nu}{2} \\ \mu+1, \ 1-\nu, \ \mu-\nu+1; \ \frac{4b^2}{a^2} \end{matrix} \right)$$

$$-\dfrac{2^{s-1} b^{\mu+\nu}}{\pi a^{s+\mu+\nu}} \cos(\nu\pi)\, \Gamma \left[\begin{matrix} -\nu, \ \frac{s+\lambda+\mu+\nu}{2} \\ \mu+1, \ \frac{2-s+\lambda-\mu-\nu}{2} \end{matrix} \right]$$

$$\times\, {}_4F_3 \left(\begin{matrix} \frac{\mu+\nu+1}{2}, \ \frac{\mu+\nu+2}{2}, \ \frac{s+\mu+\nu-\lambda}{2}, \ \frac{s+\lambda+\mu+\nu}{2} \\ \mu+1, \ \nu+1, \ \mu+\nu+1; \ \frac{4b^2}{a^2} \end{matrix} \right)$$

$$[0 < 2b < a; \ |\operatorname{Re}\nu| - \operatorname{Re}(\lambda+\mu) < \operatorname{Re}s < 5/2]$$

3	$J_\lambda(ax) J_\mu(bx) Y_\nu(bx)$	$\dfrac{2^{s-2}}{\pi a^{s-1} b} \sin \dfrac{(\mu-\nu)\pi}{2} \Gamma \left[\begin{matrix} \frac{s+\lambda-1}{2} \\ \frac{3-s+\lambda}{2} \end{matrix} \right]$

$$\times\, {}_4F_3 \left(\begin{matrix} \frac{\mu+\nu+1}{2}, \ \frac{\mu-\nu+1}{2}, \ \frac{\nu-\mu+1}{2}, \ \frac{1-\mu-\nu}{2} \\ \frac{1}{2}, \ \frac{3-s-\lambda}{2}, \ \frac{3-s+\lambda}{2}; \ \frac{a^2}{4b^2} \end{matrix} \right)$$

$$+ 2^{s-4} \dfrac{\nu^2-\mu^2}{\pi a^{s-2} b^4} \cos \dfrac{(\mu-\nu)\pi}{2} \Gamma \left[\begin{matrix} \frac{s+\lambda-2}{2} \\ \frac{4-s+\lambda}{2} \end{matrix} \right]$$

$$\times\, {}_4F_3 \left(\begin{matrix} \frac{\mu+\nu+2}{2}, \ \frac{\mu-\nu+2}{2}, \ \frac{\nu-\mu+2}{2}, \ \frac{2-\mu-\nu}{2} \\ \frac{3}{2}, \ \frac{4-s-\lambda}{2}, \ \frac{4-s+\lambda}{2}; \ \frac{a^2}{4b^2} \end{matrix} \right)$$

$$- \dfrac{2^{s-1} a^\lambda}{\pi b^{s+\lambda}} \cos \dfrac{(s+\lambda+\mu-\nu)\pi}{2}$$

$$\times \Gamma \left[\begin{matrix} \frac{s+\lambda+\mu+\nu}{2}, \ \frac{s+\lambda+\mu-\nu}{2}, \ 1-s-\lambda \\ \lambda+1, \ \frac{2-s-\lambda+\mu+\nu}{2}, \ \frac{2-s-\lambda+\mu-\nu}{2} \end{matrix} \right]$$

$$\times\, {}_4F_3 \left(\begin{matrix} \frac{s+\lambda+\mu+\nu}{2}, \ \frac{s+\lambda-\mu+\nu}{2}, \ \frac{s+\lambda+\mu-\nu}{2}, \ \frac{s+\lambda-\mu-\nu}{2} \\ \lambda+1, \ \frac{s+\lambda}{2}, \ \frac{s+\lambda+1}{2}; \ \frac{a^2}{4b^2} \end{matrix} \right)$$

$$[0 < a < 2b; \ |\operatorname{Re}\nu| - \operatorname{Re}(\lambda+\mu) < \operatorname{Re}s < 5/2]$$

3.11.16.   Products of $Y_\nu\left(\varphi\left(x\right)\right)$

1	$Y_\nu^2\left(ax\right)$	$\dfrac{a^{-s}}{\sqrt{\pi}}\,\Gamma\left[\begin{array}{c}\frac{s}{2},\ \frac{s-2\nu}{2},\ \frac{s+2\nu}{2}\\ \frac{s+1}{2},\ \frac{s-2\nu+1}{2},\ \frac{1-s+2\nu}{2}\end{array}\right]+\dfrac{a^{-s}}{2\sqrt{\pi}}\,\Gamma\left[\begin{array}{c}\frac{1-s}{2},\ \frac{s+2\nu}{2}\\ \frac{2-s}{2},\ \frac{2-s+2\nu}{2}\end{array}\right]$ $[a>0;\ 2|\operatorname{Re}\nu|<\operatorname{Re}s<1]$
2	$Y_\mu\left(ax\right)Y_\nu\left(bx\right)$	$\dfrac{2^{s-1}a^\mu}{\pi^2 b^{s+\mu}}\,\cos\left(\mu\pi\right)\cos\dfrac{\left(s+\mu-\nu\right)\pi}{2}$ $\times\Gamma\left[-\mu,\ \dfrac{s+\mu-\nu}{2},\ \dfrac{s+\mu+\nu}{2}\right]$ $\times{}_2F_1\left(\begin{array}{c}\frac{s+\mu-\nu}{2},\ \frac{s+\mu+\nu}{2}\\ 1+\mu;\ \frac{a^2}{b^2}\end{array}\right)+\dfrac{2^{s-1}b^{\mu-s}}{\pi^2 a^\mu}\,\cos\dfrac{\left(s-\mu-\nu\right)\pi}{2}$ $\times\Gamma\left[\mu,\ \dfrac{s-\mu-\nu}{2},\ \dfrac{s-\mu+\nu}{2}\right]{}_2F_1\left(\begin{array}{c}\frac{s-\mu-\nu}{2},\ \frac{s-\mu+\nu}{2}\\ 1-\mu;\ \frac{a^2}{b^2}\end{array}\right)$ $[0<a<b;\ |\operatorname{Re}\mu|+|\operatorname{Re}\nu|<\operatorname{Re}s<2]$
3	$J_\nu^2\left(ax\right)-Y_\nu^2\left(ax\right)$	$-\dfrac{a^{-s}}{\sqrt{\pi}}\,\Gamma\left[\begin{array}{c}\frac{s}{2},\ \frac{s-2\nu}{2},\ \frac{s+2\nu}{2}\\ \frac{s+1}{2},\ \frac{s-2\nu+1}{2},\ \frac{1-s+2\nu}{2}\end{array}\right]\qquad[a>0;\ 2|\operatorname{Re}\nu|<\operatorname{Re}s<2]$
4	$J_\nu^2\left(ax\right)+Y_\nu^2\left(ax\right)$	$\dfrac{a^{-s}}{\pi^{5/2}}\,\cos\left(\nu\pi\right)\Gamma\left[\dfrac{s}{2},\ \dfrac{1-s}{2},\ \dfrac{s-2\nu}{2},\ \dfrac{s+2\nu}{2}\right]$ $[a>0;\ 2|\operatorname{Re}\nu|<\operatorname{Re}s<1]$
5	$Y_\nu^2\left(ax\right)\pm Y_{-\nu}^2\left(ax\right)$	$\dfrac{a^{-s}}{\sqrt{\pi}}\left\{\begin{array}{c}\cos\left(\nu\pi\right)\left[\cot\left(s\pi\right)+3\csc\left(s\pi\right)\right]\\ \sin\left(\nu\pi\right)\end{array}\right\}\Gamma\left[\begin{array}{c}\frac{s-2\nu}{2},\ \frac{s+2\nu}{2}\\ \frac{2-s}{2},\ \frac{s+1}{2}\end{array}\right]$ $[a>0;\ 2|\operatorname{Re}\nu|<\operatorname{Re}s<\left(3\mp1\right)/2]$
6	$J_\mu\left(ax\right)J_\nu\left(ax\right)$ $-Y_\mu\left(ax\right)Y_\nu\left(ax\right)$	$-\dfrac{1}{\sqrt{\pi}\,a^s}\,\Gamma\left[\begin{array}{c}\frac{s+\mu+\nu}{2},\ \frac{s+\mu-\nu}{2},\ \frac{s-\mu+\nu}{2},\ \frac{s-\mu-\nu}{2}\\ \frac{s}{2},\ \frac{s+1}{2},\ \frac{s-\mu-\nu+1}{2},\ \frac{1-s+\mu+\nu}{2}\end{array}\right]$ $[a>0;\ \left(|\operatorname{Re}\mu|+|\operatorname{Re}\nu|\right)<\operatorname{Re}s<2]$
7	$J_\mu\left(ax\right)J_\nu\left(ax\right)$ $+Y_\mu\left(ax\right)Y_\nu\left(ax\right)$	$\dfrac{2^{s-1}a^{-s}}{\pi^2}\,\cos\left(\mu\pi\right)\Gamma\left[\begin{array}{c}1-s,\ \frac{s-\mu-\nu}{2},\ \frac{s+\mu-\nu}{2},\ \frac{s+\mu+\nu}{2}\\ \frac{2-s+\mu-\nu}{2}\end{array}\right]$ $+\dfrac{2^{s-1}a^{-s}}{\pi^2}\,\cos\left(\nu\pi\right)\Gamma\left[\begin{array}{c}1-s,\ \frac{s-\mu-\nu}{2},\ \frac{s-\mu+\nu}{2},\ \frac{s+\mu+\nu}{2}\\ \frac{2-s-\mu+\nu}{2}\end{array}\right]$ $[|\operatorname{Re}\left(\mu-\nu\right)|,\ |\operatorname{Re}\left(\mu+\nu\right)|<\operatorname{Re}s<1,\ \mu+\nu\neq0,\pm1,\dots]$

No.	$f(x)$	$F(s)$
8	$J_{-\nu}(ax) J_\nu(ax)$ $+ Y_{-\nu}(ax) Y_\nu(ax)$	$\dfrac{a^{-s}}{\pi^{3/2}} \cos^2(\nu\pi) \sec\dfrac{s\pi}{2} \Gamma\left[\begin{matrix} \frac{s}{2}, \ \frac{s-2\nu}{2}, \ \frac{s+2\nu}{2} \\ \frac{s+1}{2} \end{matrix}\right]$ $[a>0; \ 2|\mathrm{Re}\,\nu| < \mathrm{Re}\,s < 1]$
9	$J_{-\nu}(ax) J_\nu(ax)$ $- Y_{-\nu}(ax) Y_\nu(ax)$	$-\dfrac{a^{-s}}{\pi^{3/2}} \cos\dfrac{s\pi}{2} \Gamma\left[\begin{matrix} \frac{s}{2}, \ \frac{s-2\nu}{2}, \ \frac{s+2\nu}{2} \\ \frac{s+1}{2} \end{matrix}\right]$ $[a>0; \ 2|\mathrm{Re}\,\nu| < \mathrm{Re}\,s < 2]$
10	$Y_\mu(ax) Y_\nu(ax)$ $- Y_{-\mu}(ax) Y_{-\nu}(ax)$	$\dfrac{1}{\pi^2}\left(\dfrac{2}{a}\right)^s \sin\dfrac{s\pi}{2} \sin\dfrac{(\mu+\nu)\pi}{2}$ $\times \Gamma\left[\begin{matrix} \frac{s-\mu-\nu}{2}, \ \frac{s+\mu-\nu}{2}, \ \frac{s-\mu+\nu}{2}, \ \frac{s+\mu+\nu}{2} \\ s \end{matrix}\right]$ $-\dfrac{1}{\pi}\left(\dfrac{2}{a}\right)^s \cos\dfrac{s\pi}{2} \sin\dfrac{(\mu+\nu)\pi}{2} \Gamma\left[\begin{matrix} 1-s, \ \frac{s-\mu-\nu}{2}, \ \frac{s+\mu+\nu}{2} \\ \frac{2-s+\mu-\nu}{2}, \ \frac{2-s-\mu+\nu}{2} \end{matrix}\right]$ $[a>0; \ |\mathrm{Re}\,(\mu-\nu)|, \ |\mathrm{Re}\,(\mu+\nu)| < \mathrm{Re}\,s < 1]$
11	$Y_\mu(ax) Y_\nu(ax)$ $+ Y_{-\mu}(ax) Y_{-\nu}(ax)$	$\dfrac{1}{\pi^2}\left(\dfrac{2}{a}\right)^s \cos\dfrac{s\pi}{2} \cos\dfrac{(\mu+\nu)\pi}{2}$ $\times \Gamma\left[\begin{matrix} \frac{s-\mu-\nu}{2}, \ \frac{s+\mu-\nu}{2}, \ \frac{s-\mu+\nu}{2}, \ \frac{s+\mu+\nu}{2} \\ s \end{matrix}\right]$ $+\dfrac{1}{\pi}\left(\dfrac{2}{a}\right)^s \sin\dfrac{s\pi}{2} \cos\dfrac{(\mu+\nu)\pi}{2} \Gamma\left[\begin{matrix} 1-s, \ \frac{s-\mu-\nu}{2}, \ \frac{s+\mu+\nu}{2} \\ \frac{2-s+\mu-\nu}{2}, \ \frac{2-s-\mu+\nu}{2} \end{matrix}\right]$ $[a>0; \ |\mathrm{Re}\,(\mu-\nu)|, \ |\mathrm{Re}\,(\mu+\nu)| < \mathrm{Re}\,s < 1]$
12	$Y_\nu\left(b\sqrt{x^2+a^2}+ab\right)$ $\times Y_\nu\left(b\sqrt{x^2+a^2}-ab\right)$	$-\dfrac{1}{2\pi^{3/2}}\left(\dfrac{a}{b}\right)^{s/2} \Gamma\left[\begin{matrix} \frac{1-s}{2}, \ \frac{s-2\nu}{2}, \ \frac{s+2\nu}{2} \end{matrix}\right]$ $\times \left[\sin\dfrac{(s-2\nu)\pi}{2} J_{-s/2}(2ab) + 2\cos(\nu\pi) Y_{s/2}(2ab)\right]$ $[b, \ \mathrm{Re}\,a>0; \ 2|\mathrm{Re}\,\nu| < \mathrm{Re}\,s < 1]$
13	$J_\nu(u_+) J_\nu(u_-)$ $+ Y_\nu(u_+) Y_\nu(u_-)$ $u_\pm = b\left(\sqrt{x^2+a^2} \pm a\right)$	$\dfrac{\cos(\nu\pi)}{\pi^{3/2}}\left(\dfrac{a}{b}\right)^{s/2} \Gamma\left[\begin{matrix} \frac{1-s}{2}, \ \frac{s-2\nu}{2}, \ \frac{s+2\nu}{2} \end{matrix}\right]$ $\times \left[\sin\dfrac{s\pi}{2} J_{-s/2}(2ab) - \cos\dfrac{s\pi}{2} Y_{-s/2}(2ab)\right]$ $[a, \ b>0; \ 2|\mathrm{Re}\,\nu| < \mathrm{Re}\,s < 1]$

3.12. The Hankel Functions $H_\nu^{(1)}(z)$ and $H_\nu^{(2)}(z)$

More formulas can be obtained from the corresponding sections due to the relations $(j = 1, 2)$

$$H_{\pm 1/2}^{(j)}(z) = \left((-1)^j i\right)^{(1\pm 1)/2} \sqrt{\frac{2}{\pi}} \frac{1}{\sqrt{z}} e^{-(-1)^j iz},$$

$$H_{n-1/2}^{(j)}(z) = \sqrt{\frac{2}{\pi}} \frac{1}{\sqrt{z}} e^{i(-1)^j(n\pi/2 - z)} \sum_{k=0}^{n-1} (-1)^{kj} \frac{(n+k-1)!}{k!\,(n-k-1)!} (2iz)^{-k},$$

$$H_\nu^{(j)}(z) = J_\nu(z) - (-1)^j i Y_\nu(z).$$

3.12.1. $H_\nu^{(1)}(ax)$, $H_\nu^{(2)}(ax)$

No.	$f(x)$	$F(s)$
1	$H_\nu^{(j)}(ax)$ $j = 1, 2$	$\dfrac{2^{s-1}a^{-s}}{\pi} e^{(-1)^{j+1}(s-\nu-1)\pi i/2} \Gamma\left(\dfrac{s-\nu}{2}\right) \Gamma\left(\dfrac{s+\nu}{2}\right)$ $[a > 0;\ -\operatorname{Re}\nu < \operatorname{Re}(\nu+s) < 3/2]$

3.12.2. $H_\nu^{(1)}(bx)$, $H_\nu^{(2)}(bx)$, and the exponential function

1	$e^{-ax^2} H_\nu^{(1)}(bx)$	$-\dfrac{i2^{\nu-1}a^{(\nu-s)/2}b^{-\nu}}{\pi} \Gamma(\nu)\,\Gamma\left(\dfrac{s-\nu}{2}\right) {}_1F_1\left(\begin{matrix}\frac{s-\nu}{2}\\ 1-\nu;\ -\frac{b^2}{4a}\end{matrix}\right)$ $-\dfrac{ie^{-i\pi\nu}a^{-(s+\nu)/2}b^\nu}{2^{\nu+1}\pi} \Gamma(-\nu)\,\Gamma\left(\dfrac{s+\nu}{2}\right) {}_1F_1\left(\begin{matrix}\frac{s+\nu}{2}\\ \nu+1;\ -\frac{b^2}{4a}\end{matrix}\right)$ $[\operatorname{Re}a > 0;\ \operatorname{Re}s > |\operatorname{Re}\nu|]$
2	$e^{-ax^2} H_\nu^{(2)}(bx)$	$\dfrac{a^{(1-s)/2}}{\pi b} e^{\nu\pi i/2 - b^2/(8a)} \Gamma\left(\dfrac{s-\nu}{2}\right) \Gamma\left(\dfrac{s+\nu}{2}\right)$ $\times W_{(1-s)/2,\,\nu/2}\left(-\dfrac{b^2}{4a}\right) \qquad [\operatorname{Re}a > 0;\ \operatorname{Re}s > |\operatorname{Re}\nu|]$

3.12.3. $H_\nu^{(1)}(ax)$, $H_\nu^{(2)}(ax)$, and trigonometric functions

1	$\left\{\begin{matrix}\sin(ax+b)\\ \cos(ax+b)\end{matrix}\right\}$ $\times H_\nu^{(1)}(ax)$	$\mp \dfrac{i^{(1\pm 1)/2}(2a)^{-s} e^{i(b+(s+\nu)\pi/2)}}{\sqrt{\pi}} \Gamma\left[\begin{matrix}\frac{1}{2}-s,\ s+\nu\\ 1-s+\nu\end{matrix}\right]$ $-\dfrac{i\,2^{1-s}a^{-s}}{\pi^{3/2}} \cos(\nu\pi) \left\{\begin{matrix}\sin[b+(\nu-s)\pi/2]\\ \cos[b+(\nu-s)\pi/2]\end{matrix}\right\}$ $\times \Gamma\left(\dfrac{1}{2}-s\right) \Gamma(s-\nu)\,\Gamma(s+\nu) \qquad [a > 0;\ |\operatorname{Re}\nu| < \operatorname{Re}s < 1/2]$

No.	$f(x)$	$F(s)$
2	$\begin{Bmatrix} \sin(ax+b) \\ \cos(ax+b) \end{Bmatrix}$ $\times H_\nu^{(2)}(ax)$	$\dfrac{i^{(1\pm1)/2}(2a)^{-s}e^{-i(b+(s+\nu)\pi/2)}}{\sqrt{\pi}}\Gamma\begin{bmatrix} \frac{1}{2}-s,\ s+\nu \\ 1-s+\nu \end{bmatrix}$ $+\dfrac{i\,2^{1-s}a^{-s}}{\pi^{3/2}}\cos(\nu\pi)\begin{Bmatrix} \sin[b+(\nu-s)\pi/2] \\ \cos[b+(\nu-s)\pi/2] \end{Bmatrix}$ $\times\Gamma\left(\dfrac{1}{2}-s\right)\Gamma(s-\nu)\Gamma(s+\nu)\quad [a>0;\ |\operatorname{Re}\nu|<\operatorname{Re}s<1/2]$

3.12.4. $\quad H_\nu^{(1)}(bx),\ H_\nu^{(2)}(bx),$ **and** $J_\mu(ax)$

No.	$f(x)$	$F(s)$
1	$J_\mu(ax)H_\nu^{(j)}(bx)$ $j=1,2$	$\dfrac{2^{s-1}a^\mu}{\pi b^{s+\mu}}e^{(-1)^{j+1}(s+\mu-\nu-1)\pi i/2}\Gamma\begin{bmatrix} \frac{s+\mu+\nu}{2},\ \frac{s+\mu-\nu}{2} \\ \mu+1 \end{bmatrix}$ $\times{}_2F_1\left(\begin{matrix} \frac{s+\mu+\nu}{2},\ \frac{s+\mu-\nu}{2} \\ \mu+1;\ \frac{a^2}{b^2} \end{matrix}\right)$ $\begin{bmatrix} |a|<|b|;\ \operatorname{Re}(ib+(-1)^j ia)>0\ \text{for}\ \operatorname{Re}(s+\mu\pm\nu)>0\ \text{and} \\ \operatorname{Re}(ib+(-1)^j ia)=0\ \text{for}\ \operatorname{Re}(s+\mu\pm\nu)>0;\ \operatorname{Re}s<2 \end{bmatrix}$
2	$J_\mu(ax)H_\nu^{(j)}(ax)$ $j=1,2$	$\dfrac{2^{s-1}a^{-s}}{\pi}e^{(-1)^{j+1}(s+\mu-\nu-1)\pi i/2}\Gamma\begin{bmatrix} \frac{s+\mu-\nu}{2},\ \frac{s+\mu+\nu}{2},\ 1-s \\ \frac{\mu-\nu-s+2}{2},\ \frac{\mu+\nu-s+2}{2} \end{bmatrix}$ $[a>0;\ -\operatorname{Re}(\mu\pm\nu)<\operatorname{Re}s<1]$

3.12.5. **Products of** $H_\mu^{(1)}(ax)$ **and** $H_\nu^{(2)}(ax)$

No.	$f(x)$	$F(s)$
1	$H_\mu^{(j)}(ax)H_\nu^{(j)}(ax)$ $j=1,2$	$-\dfrac{2^{s-1}a^{-s}}{\pi^2}e^{(-1)^{j+1}(s-\mu-\nu)\pi i/2}\Gamma\begin{bmatrix} \frac{s-\mu-\nu}{2},\ \frac{s-\mu+\nu}{2},\ \frac{s+\mu-\nu}{2},\ \frac{s+\mu+\nu}{2} \\ s \end{bmatrix}$ $[a>0;\ |\operatorname{Re}\mu|+|\operatorname{Re}\nu|<\operatorname{Re}s<1]$
2	$H_\mu^{(j)}(ax)H_\nu^{(j)}(bx)$ $j=1,2$	$-\dfrac{2^{s-1}b^\nu}{\pi^2 a^{s+\nu}}e^{(-1)^{j+1}(s-\mu-\nu)\pi i/2}\Gamma\begin{bmatrix} \frac{s-\nu-\mu}{2},\ \frac{s-\mu+\nu}{2},\ \frac{s+\mu-\nu}{2},\ \frac{s+\mu+\nu}{2} \\ s \end{bmatrix}$ $\times{}_2F_1\left(\begin{matrix} \frac{s-\mu+\nu}{2},\ \frac{s+\mu+\nu}{2} \\ s;\ \frac{a^2-b^2}{a^2} \end{matrix}\right)\quad [a,b>0;\ |\operatorname{Re}\mu|+|\operatorname{Re}\nu|<\operatorname{Re}s<1]$
3	$H_\nu^{(1)}(ax)H_\nu^{(2)}(ax)$	$\dfrac{a^{-s}}{\pi^{5/2}}\cos(\nu\pi)\Gamma\begin{bmatrix} \frac{s}{2}-\nu,\ \frac{s}{2}+\nu,\ \frac{s}{2},\ \frac{1-s}{2} \end{bmatrix}\quad \begin{bmatrix} a>0; \\ 2|\operatorname{Re}\nu|<\operatorname{Re}s<1 \end{bmatrix}$
4	$H_\mu^{(1)}(ax)H_\nu^{(2)}(ax)$	$\dfrac{2^{s-1}}{\pi a^s}\Gamma\begin{bmatrix} 1-s,\ \frac{s+\mu-\nu}{2},\ \frac{s-\mu+\nu}{2} \\ 1-\frac{s+\mu+\nu}{2},\ 1-\frac{s-\mu-\nu}{2} \end{bmatrix}$ $\times\left[\csc\dfrac{(s-\mu-\nu)\pi}{2}+e^{i\pi(\nu-\mu)}\csc\dfrac{(s+\mu+\nu)\pi}{2}\right]$ $[a>0;\ \max(|\operatorname{Re}(\mu+\nu)|,\ |\operatorname{Re}(\mu-\nu)|)<\operatorname{Re}s<1]$

3.13. The Modified Bessel Function $I_\nu(z)$

More formulas can be obtained from the corresponding sections due to the relations

$$I_{\pm 1/2}(z) = \sqrt{\frac{2}{\pi}} \frac{1}{\sqrt{z}} \left\{ \begin{matrix} \sinh z \\ \cosh z \end{matrix} \right\}, \quad I_{\pm 3/2}(z) = \sqrt{\frac{2}{\pi}} \frac{1}{z^{3/2}} \left[z \left\{ \begin{matrix} \cosh z \\ \sinh z \end{matrix} \right\} - \left\{ \begin{matrix} \sinh z \\ \cosh z \end{matrix} \right\} \right],$$

$$I_{\pm n \pm 1/2}(z) = \frac{1}{\sqrt{2\pi}} \frac{1}{\sqrt{z}} \sum_{k=0}^{n} \frac{(n+k)!}{k!(n-k)!} \frac{(-1)^k e^z \pm (-1)^{n+1} e^{-z}}{(2z)^k}, \quad [n = 0, 1, 2, \ldots];$$

$$I_\nu(z) = i^\nu J_\nu(iz), \quad I_\nu(z) = \frac{(z/2)^\nu}{\Gamma(\nu+1)} \, _0F_1\left(\nu+1; \frac{z^2}{4}\right)$$

$$I_\nu(z) = \frac{z^\nu e^{-z}}{2^\nu \Gamma(\nu+1)} \, _1F_1\left(\nu + \frac{1}{2}; 2\nu+1; 2z\right),$$

$$I_\nu(z) = \pi \left(\frac{z}{2}\right)^\nu G_{13}^{10}\left(\frac{z^2}{4} \,\middle|\, \begin{matrix} 1/2 \\ 0, -\nu, 1/2 \end{matrix}\right),$$

$$I_\nu(z) = z^{\nu/2}(-z)^{-\nu/2} G_{02}^{10}\left(-\frac{z^2}{4} \,\middle|\, \begin{matrix} \cdot \\ \nu/2, -\nu/2 \end{matrix}\right),$$

$$I_\nu(z) = \pi z^\nu (z^2)^{-\nu/2} G_{13}^{10}\left(\frac{z^2}{4} \,\middle|\, \begin{matrix} (\nu+1)/2 \\ \nu/2, -\nu/2, (\nu+1)/2 \end{matrix}\right).$$

3.13.1. $I_\nu(\varphi(x))$ and algebraic functions

No.	$f(x)$	$F(s)$
1	$(a-x)_+^{\alpha-1} I_\nu(bx)$	$\dfrac{a^{s+\alpha+\nu-1}}{\Gamma(\nu+1)} \left(\dfrac{b}{2}\right)^\nu B(\alpha, s+\nu) \, _2F_3\left(\begin{matrix} \frac{s+\nu}{2}, \frac{s+\nu+1}{2}; \frac{a^2b^2}{4} \\ \nu+1, \frac{s+\alpha+\nu}{2}, \frac{s+\alpha+\nu+1}{2} \end{matrix}\right)$ $[a, \operatorname{Re}\alpha, \operatorname{Re}(s+\nu) > 0]$
2	$(a^2-x^2)_+^{\alpha-1} I_\nu(bx)$	$\dfrac{a^{s+2\alpha+\nu-2}b^\nu}{2^{\nu+1}} \Gamma\left[\begin{matrix} \alpha, \frac{s+\nu}{2} \\ \nu+1, \frac{s+2\alpha+\nu}{2} \end{matrix}\right] \, _1F_2\left(\begin{matrix} \frac{s+\nu}{2}; \frac{a^2b^2}{4} \\ \nu+1, \frac{s+2\alpha+\nu}{2} \end{matrix}\right)$ $[a, \operatorname{Re}\alpha, \operatorname{Re}(s+\nu) > 0]$
3	$(a-x)_+^{\alpha-1} I_\nu(b(a-x))$	$\dfrac{a^{s+\alpha+\nu-1}}{\Gamma(\nu+1)} \left(\dfrac{b}{2}\right)^\nu B(\alpha+\nu, s) \, _2F_3\left(\begin{matrix} \frac{\alpha+\nu}{2}, \frac{\alpha+\nu+1}{2}; \frac{a^2b^2}{4} \\ \nu+1, \frac{s+\alpha+\nu}{2}, \frac{s+\alpha+\nu+1}{2} \end{matrix}\right)$ $[a, \operatorname{Re}(\alpha+\nu), \operatorname{Re}s > 0]$
4	$(a-x)_+^{\alpha-1}$ $\times I_\nu(bx(a-x))$	$a^{s+\alpha+2\nu-1} \left(\dfrac{b}{2}\right)^\nu \Gamma\left[\begin{matrix} \alpha+\nu, s+\nu \\ \nu+1, s+\alpha+2\nu \end{matrix}\right]$ $\times \, _4F_5\left(\begin{matrix} \Delta(2, \alpha+\nu), \Delta(2, s+\nu) \\ \nu+1, \Delta(4, s+\alpha+2\nu); \frac{a^4b^2}{64} \end{matrix}\right)$ $[a, \operatorname{Re}(\alpha+\nu), \operatorname{Re}(s+\nu) > 0]$
5	$(a-x)_+^{\nu/2} I_\nu(b\sqrt{a-x})$	$\dfrac{2^s a^{(s+\nu)/2}}{b^s} \Gamma(s) I_{s+\nu}(\sqrt{a}\,b)$ $[a, \operatorname{Re}s > 0; \operatorname{Re}\nu > -1]$

No.	$f(x)$	$F(s)$
6	$(a-x)_+^{\alpha-1} I_\nu\left(b\sqrt{a-x}\right)$	$\dfrac{a^{s+\alpha+\nu/2-1}}{2}\left(\dfrac{b}{2}\right)^\nu \Gamma\left[\begin{matrix}\frac{2\alpha+\nu}{2},\,s\\ \nu+1,\,\frac{2s+2\alpha+\nu}{2}\end{matrix}\right]\,{}_1F_2\left(\begin{matrix}\frac{2\alpha+\nu}{2};\,\frac{ab^2}{4}\\ \nu+1,\,\frac{2s+2\alpha+\nu}{2}\end{matrix}\right)$ $$[a,\ \mathrm{Re}\,(\alpha+\nu/2),\ \mathrm{Re}\,s>0]$$
7	$(a-x)_+^{\nu/2}(bx+1)^\mu$ $\times\, I_\nu\left(c\sqrt{a-x}\right)$	$a^{s+\nu}\left(\dfrac{c}{2}\right)^\nu \Gamma\left[\begin{matrix}s\\ s+\nu+1\end{matrix}\right]\Xi_2\left(-\mu,\,s;\,s+\nu+1;\,-ab,\,\dfrac{ac^2}{4}\right)$ $$[a,\ \mathrm{Re}\,s>0;\ |\arg b|<\pi]$$
8	$(a-x)_+^{\alpha-1}$ $\times\, I_\nu\left(b\sqrt{x(a-x)}\right)$	$a^{s+\alpha+\nu-1}\left(\dfrac{b}{2}\right)^\nu \Gamma\left[\begin{matrix}\frac{2\alpha+\nu}{2},\,\frac{2s+\nu}{2}\\ \nu+1,\,s+\alpha+\nu\end{matrix}\right]$ $\times\,{}_2F_3\left(\begin{matrix}\frac{2\alpha+\nu}{2},\,\frac{2s+\nu}{2};\,\frac{a^2b^2}{16}\\ \nu+1,\,\frac{s+\alpha+\nu}{2},\,\frac{s+\alpha+\nu+1}{2}\end{matrix}\right)$ $$[a,\ \mathrm{Re}\,(\alpha+\nu/2)>0;\ \mathrm{Re}\,(s+\nu/2)>-1]$$
9	$\dfrac{1}{(x+a)^\rho}\,I_\nu\left(\dfrac{b}{x+a}\right)$	$\dfrac{a^{s-\nu-\rho}}{\Gamma(\nu+1)}\left(\dfrac{b}{2}\right)^\nu \mathrm{B}\,(s,\,\nu+\rho-s)\,{}_2F_3\left(\begin{matrix}\frac{\nu+\rho-s}{2},\,\frac{\nu+\rho-s+1}{2}\\ \nu+1,\,\frac{\nu+\rho}{2},\,\frac{\nu+\rho+1}{2};\,\frac{b^2}{4a^2}\end{matrix}\right)$ $$[0<\mathrm{Re}\,s<\mathrm{Re}\,(\nu+\rho);\ |\arg a|<\pi]$$
10	$\dfrac{1}{(x+a)^\rho}\,I_\nu\left(\dfrac{bx}{x+a}\right)$	$a^{s-\rho}\left(\dfrac{b}{2}\right)^\nu \dfrac{\mathrm{B}\,(s+\nu,\,\rho-s)}{\Gamma(\nu+1)}\,{}_2F_3\left(\begin{matrix}\frac{s+\nu}{2},\,\frac{s+\nu+1}{2};\,\frac{b^2}{4}\\ \nu+1,\,\frac{\nu+\rho}{2},\,\frac{\nu+\rho+1}{2}\end{matrix}\right)$ $$[-\mathrm{Re}\,\nu<\mathrm{Re}\,s<\mathrm{Re}\,\rho;\ |\arg a|<\pi]$$
11	$\dfrac{1}{(x^2+a^2)^\rho}$ $\times\, I_\nu\left(\dfrac{bx}{x^2+a^2}\right)$	$\dfrac{2^{-\nu-1}a^{s-\nu-2\rho}b^\nu}{\Gamma(\nu+1)}\,\mathrm{B}\left(\dfrac{s+\nu}{2},\,\dfrac{\nu+2\rho-s}{2}\right)\,{}_2F_3\left(\begin{matrix}\frac{s+\nu}{2},\,\frac{\nu+2\rho-s}{2};\,\frac{b^2}{16a^2}\\ \nu+1,\,\frac{\nu+\rho}{2},\,\frac{\nu+\rho+1}{2}\end{matrix}\right)$ $$[\mathrm{Re}\,a>0;\ -\mathrm{Re}\,\nu<\mathrm{Re}\,s<\mathrm{Re}\,(\nu+2\rho)]$$

3.13.2. $I_\nu(\varphi(x))$ and the exponential function

No.	$f(x)$	$F(s)$
1	$e^{-ax}I_\nu(bx)$	$a^{-s-\nu}\left(\dfrac{b}{2}\right)^\nu \Gamma\left[\begin{matrix}s+\nu\\ \nu+1\end{matrix}\right]\,{}_2F_1\left(\begin{matrix}\frac{s+\nu}{2},\,\frac{s+\nu+1}{2}\\ \nu+1;\,\frac{b^2}{a^2}\end{matrix}\right)$ $$[\mathrm{Re}\,(s+\nu)>0;\ \mathrm{Re}\,a>|\mathrm{Re}\,b|]$$
2	$e^{-ax}I_\nu(ax)$	$\dfrac{(2a)^{-s}}{\sqrt{\pi}}\,\Gamma\left[\begin{matrix}s+\nu,\,\frac{1-2s}{2}\\ 1-s+\nu\end{matrix}\right]$ $[\mathrm{Re}\,a>0;\ -\mathrm{Re}\,\nu<\mathrm{Re}\,s<1/2]$
3	$e^{-ax^2}I_\nu(bx)$	$\dfrac{2^{-\nu-1}b^\nu}{a^{(s+\nu)/2}}\,\Gamma\left[\begin{matrix}\frac{s+\nu}{2}\\ \nu+1\end{matrix}\right]\,{}_1F_1\left(\begin{matrix}\frac{s+\nu}{2};\,\frac{b^2}{4a}\\ \nu+1\end{matrix}\right)$ $[\mathrm{Re}\,a,\ \mathrm{Re}\,(s+\nu)>0]$

No.	$f(x)$	$F(s)$
4	$e^{-ax-b\sqrt{x}}I_\nu(ax)$	$\sqrt{\dfrac{2}{\pi a}}\,b^{1-2s}\,\Gamma(2s-1)\,{}_2F_2\left(\begin{matrix}\frac{1-2\nu}{2},\frac{1+2\nu}{2}\\1-s,\frac{3-2s}{2};\frac{b^2}{8a}\end{matrix}\right)$ $+\dfrac{(2a)^{-s}}{\sqrt{\pi}}\Gamma\left[\begin{matrix}\frac{1-2s}{2},s+\nu\\1-s+\nu\end{matrix}\right]{}_2F_2\left(\begin{matrix}s-\nu,s+\nu\\\frac{1}{2},\frac{2s+1}{2};\frac{b^2}{8a}\end{matrix}\right)$ $-\dfrac{b}{\sqrt{\pi}\,(2a)^{s+1/2}}\Gamma\left[\begin{matrix}-s,\frac{2s+2\nu+1}{2}\\\frac{1-2s+2\nu}{2}\end{matrix}\right]{}_2F_2\left(\begin{matrix}\frac{2s-2\nu+1}{2},\frac{2s+2\nu+1}{2}\\\frac{3}{2},s+1;\frac{b^2}{8a}\end{matrix}\right)$ $[\operatorname{Re}a,\ \operatorname{Re}b,\ \operatorname{Re}(s+\nu)>0]$
5	$(a-x)_+^{\alpha-1}e^{\pm bx}I_\nu(bx)$	$a^{s+\alpha+\nu-1}\left(\dfrac{b}{2}\right)^\nu\Gamma\left[\begin{matrix}\alpha,s+\nu\\\nu+1,s+\alpha+\nu\end{matrix}\right]{}_2F_2\left(\begin{matrix}\frac{2\nu+1}{2},s+\nu;\pm 2ab\\2\nu+1,s+\alpha+\nu\end{matrix}\right)$ $[a,\ \operatorname{Re}\alpha,\ \operatorname{Re}(s+\nu)>0]$
6	$(x-a)_+^{\alpha-1}e^{-bx}I_\nu(bx)$	$\dfrac{(2b)^{1-s-\alpha}}{\sqrt{\pi}}\Gamma\left[\begin{matrix}s+\alpha+\nu-1,\frac{3-2s-2\alpha}{2}\\2-s-\alpha+\nu\end{matrix}\right]$ $\times\,{}_2F_2\left(\begin{matrix}1-\alpha,\frac{3-2s-2\alpha}{2};-2ab\\2-s-\alpha-\nu,2-s-\alpha+\nu\end{matrix}\right)$ $+a^{s+\alpha+\nu-1}\left(\dfrac{b}{2}\right)^\nu\Gamma\left[\begin{matrix}\alpha,1-s-\alpha-\nu\\\nu+1,1-s-\nu\end{matrix}\right]{}_2F_2\left(\begin{matrix}\frac{2\nu+1}{2},s+\nu;-2ab\\2\nu+1,s+\alpha+\nu\end{matrix}\right)$ $[a,\ \operatorname{Re}\alpha,\ \operatorname{Re}b>0;\ \operatorname{Re}(s+\nu)<3/2]$
7	$\dfrac{e^{-bx}}{(x+a)^\rho}I_\nu(bx)$	$\dfrac{(2b)^{\rho-s}}{\sqrt{\pi}}\Gamma\left[\begin{matrix}s+\nu-\rho,\frac{1-2s+2\rho}{2}\\1-s+\nu+\rho\end{matrix}\right]$ $\times\,{}_2F_2\left(\begin{matrix}\rho,\frac{1-2s+2\rho}{2};2ab\\1-s-\nu+\rho,1-s+\nu+\rho\end{matrix}\right)$ $+a^{s+\nu-\rho}\left(\dfrac{b}{2}\right)^\nu\Gamma\left[\begin{matrix}s+\nu,\rho-\nu-s\\\nu+1,\rho\end{matrix}\right]{}_2F_2\left(\begin{matrix}\frac{2\nu+1}{2},s+\nu;2ab\\2\nu+1,s+\nu-\rho+1\end{matrix}\right)$ $[\operatorname{Re}b>0;\ -\operatorname{Re}\nu<\operatorname{Re}s<\operatorname{Re}\rho+1/2;\ |\arg a|<\pi]$
8	$(a-x)_+^\nu e^{bx}$ $\times I_\nu(c(a-x))$	$\dfrac{a^{s+2\nu}(2c)^\nu e^{-ac}}{\sqrt{\pi}}\Gamma\left[\begin{matrix}s,\nu+\frac{1}{2}\\s+2\nu+1\end{matrix}\right]$ $\times\,\Phi_2\left(s,\nu+\dfrac{1}{2};s+2\nu+1;a(b+c),2ac\right)$ $[a,\ \operatorname{Re}s>0;\ \operatorname{Re}\nu>-1/2]$
9	$\dfrac{e^{-bx}}{(x+a)^\nu}I_\nu(bx+ab)$	$\dfrac{a^{(s-1)/2-\nu}}{\sqrt{\pi}\,(2b)^{(s+1)/2}}\Gamma\left[\begin{matrix}s,\frac{1}{2}-s+\nu\\1-s+2\nu\end{matrix}\right]M_{-s/2,\nu-s/2}(2ab)$ $[a,\ \operatorname{Re}b>0;\ 0<\operatorname{Re}s<\operatorname{Re}\nu+1/2]$

No.	$f(x)$	$F(s)$
10	$\dfrac{e^{-bx}}{(x+a)^\rho} I_\nu(bx+ab)$	$a^{s+\nu-\rho}\left(\dfrac{b}{2}\right)^\nu e^{ab}\,\Gamma\!\begin{bmatrix} s,\ \rho-\nu-s \\ \nu+1,\ \rho-\nu \end{bmatrix}{}_2F_2\!\left(\begin{matrix} \frac{2\nu+1}{2},\ \nu-\rho+1;\ -2ab \\ 2\nu+1,\ s+\nu-\rho+1 \end{matrix}\right)$ $+\dfrac{(2b)^{\rho-s}e^{ab}}{\sqrt{\pi}}\,\Gamma\!\begin{bmatrix} s+\nu-\rho,\ \frac12-s+\rho \\ 1-s+\nu+\rho \end{bmatrix}$ $\times{}_2F_2\!\left(\begin{matrix} 1-s,\ \frac12-s+\rho;\ -2ab \\ 1-s-\nu+\rho,\ 1-s+\nu+\rho \end{matrix}\right)$ $[a,\ \operatorname{Re}b>0;\ 0<\operatorname{Re}s<\operatorname{Re}\rho+1/2]$
11	$(a-x)_+^{\alpha-1}\,e^{bx(a-x)}$ $\times I_\nu(bx(a-x))$	$a^{s+\alpha+2\nu-1}\left(\dfrac{b}{2}\right)^\nu\dfrac{\mathrm{B}(\alpha+\nu,\,s+\nu)}{\Gamma(\nu+1)}$ $\times{}_3F_3\!\left(\begin{matrix} \frac{2\nu+1}{2},\ \alpha+\nu,\ s+\nu;\ \frac{a^2b}{2} \\ 2\nu+1,\ \frac{s+\alpha+2\nu}{2},\ \frac{s+\alpha+2\nu+1}{2} \end{matrix}\right)$ $[a,\ \operatorname{Re}(s+\nu)>0;\ \operatorname{Re}(\alpha+\nu)>-1]$
12	$(a-x)_+^{\nu/2}\,e^{bx}$ $\times I_\nu(c\sqrt{a-x})$	$a^{s+\nu}\left(\dfrac{c}{2}\right)^\nu\Gamma\!\begin{bmatrix} s \\ s+\nu+1 \end{bmatrix}\Phi_3\!\left(s;\ s+\nu+1;\ ab,\ \dfrac{ac^2}{4}\right)$ $[a,\ \operatorname{Re}s>0;\ \operatorname{Re}\nu>-1]$
13	$\dfrac{e^{b/(x+a)}}{(x+a)^\rho} I_\nu\!\left(\dfrac{b}{x+a}\right)$	$a^{s-\nu-\rho}\left(\dfrac{b}{2}\right)^\nu\dfrac{\mathrm{B}(s,\,\nu+\rho-s)}{\Gamma(\nu+1)}{}_2F_2\!\left(\begin{matrix} \frac{2\nu+1}{2},\ \nu+\rho-s \\ 2\nu+1,\ \nu+\rho;\ \frac{2b}{a} \end{matrix}\right)$ $[0<\operatorname{Re}s<\operatorname{Re}(\nu+\rho);\ |\arg a|<\pi]$
14	$\dfrac{\theta(x-c)}{\sqrt{x-b}}\,e^{ax/(x-b)}$ $\times I_\nu\!\left(\dfrac{ax}{x-b}\right)$	$\dfrac{a^\nu c^{s-1/2}}{2^{\nu-1}(1-2s)\,\Gamma(\nu+1)}$ $\times\Psi_1\!\left(\dfrac{2\nu+1}{2},\ \dfrac{1-2s}{2};\ \dfrac{3-2s}{2},\ 2\nu+1;\ \dfrac{b}{c},\ 2a\right)$ $[a>0;\ c>b>0]$
15	$(a^2-x^2)_+^{-1}\,e^{-b/(a^2-x^2)}$ $\times I_\nu\!\left(\dfrac{cx}{a^2-x^2}\right)$	$\dfrac{a^{s-1}}{c}\,e^{-b/(2a^2)}\,\Gamma\!\begin{bmatrix} \frac{s+\nu}{2} \\ \nu+1 \end{bmatrix}M_{(1-s)/2,\,\nu/2}\!\left(\dfrac{b-\sqrt{b^2-a^2c^2}}{2a^2}\right)$ $\times W_{(1-s)/2,\,\nu/2}\!\left(\dfrac{b+\sqrt{b^2-a^2c^2}}{2a^2}\right)$ $[b>ac>0;\ a,\ \operatorname{Re}(s+\nu)>0]$
16	$(x^2-a^2)_+^{-1}\,e^{-b/(x^2-a^2)}$ $\times I_\nu\!\left(\dfrac{cx}{x^2-a^2}\right)$	$\dfrac{a^{s-1}}{c}\,e^{b/(2a^2)}\,\Gamma\!\begin{bmatrix} \frac{2-s+\nu}{2} \\ \nu+1 \end{bmatrix}M_{(s-1)/2,\,\nu/2}\!\left(\dfrac{b-\sqrt{b^2-a^2c^2}}{2a^2}\right)$ $\times W_{(s-1)/2,\,\nu/2}\!\left(\dfrac{b+\sqrt{b^2-a^2c^2}}{2a^2}\right)$ $[b>ac>0;\ a>0;\ \operatorname{Re}(s-\nu)<2]$

No.	$f(x)$	$F(s)$
17	$\dfrac{1}{x^2+a^2}\, e^{b/(x^2+a^2)}$ $\times I_\nu\left(\dfrac{cx}{x^2+a^2}\right)$	$\dfrac{a^{s-1}}{c}\, e^{b/(2a^2)}\, \Gamma\left[\begin{array}{c} \frac{s+\nu}{2},\ \frac{2-s+\nu}{2} \\ \nu+1,\ \nu+1 \end{array}\right] M_{(s-1)/2,\,\nu/2}\left(\dfrac{\sqrt{b^2+a^2c^2}+b}{2a^2}\right)$ $\times M_{(1-s)/2,\,\nu/2}\left(\dfrac{\sqrt{b^2+a^2c^2}-b}{2a^2}\right)$ $[b,\ \operatorname{Re}a>0;\ -\operatorname{Re}\nu<\operatorname{Re}s<\operatorname{Re}\nu+2]$

3.13.3. $I_\nu(ax)$ and trigonometric functions

Notation: $\delta = \begin{Bmatrix} 1 \\ 0 \end{Bmatrix}$.

1	$e^{-ax}\begin{Bmatrix} \sin(bx) \\ \cos(bx) \end{Bmatrix} I_\nu(ax)$	$\left(\dfrac{a}{2}\right)^\nu b^{-s-\nu}\, \Gamma\left[\begin{array}{c} s+\nu \\ \nu+1 \end{array}\right] \begin{Bmatrix} \sin\left[(s+\nu)\pi/2\right] \\ \cos\left[(s+\nu)\pi/2\right] \end{Bmatrix}$ $\times {}_4F_3\left(\begin{array}{c} \frac{2\nu+1}{4},\ \frac{2\nu+3}{4},\ \frac{s+\nu}{2},\ \frac{s+\nu+1}{2} \\ \frac{1}{2},\ \frac{2\nu+1}{2},\ \nu+1;\ -\frac{4a^2}{b^2} \end{array}\right)$ $+(-1)^\delta\, \dfrac{a^{\nu+1}b^{-s-\nu-1}}{2^\nu} \begin{Bmatrix} \cos\left[(s+\nu)\pi/2\right] \\ \sin\left[(s+\nu)\pi/2\right] \end{Bmatrix}$ $\times \Gamma\left[\begin{array}{c} s+\nu+1 \\ \nu+1 \end{array}\right] {}_4F_3\left(\begin{array}{c} \frac{2\nu+3}{4},\ \frac{2\nu+5}{4},\ \frac{s+\nu+1}{2},\ \frac{s+\nu+2}{2} \\ \frac{3}{2},\ \nu+1,\ \frac{2\nu+3}{2};\ -\frac{4a^2}{b^2} \end{array}\right)$ $[0<2a<b;\ -\delta-\operatorname{Re}\nu<\operatorname{Re}s<3/2]$
2	$e^{-ax}\begin{Bmatrix} \sin(bx) \\ \cos(bx) \end{Bmatrix} I_\nu(ax)$	$\dfrac{(2a)^{-s-\delta}b^\delta}{\sqrt{\pi}}\, \Gamma\left[\begin{array}{c} s+\nu+\delta,\ \frac{1-2s-2\delta}{2} \\ 1-s+\nu-\delta \end{array}\right]$ $\times {}_4F_3\left(\begin{array}{c} \frac{s-\nu+1}{2},\ \frac{s-\nu+2\delta}{2},\ \frac{s+\nu+1}{2},\ \frac{s+\nu+2\delta}{2} \\ \frac{2\delta+1}{2},\ \frac{2s+3}{4},\ \frac{2s+4\delta+1}{4};\ -\frac{b^2}{4a^2} \end{array}\right) - \dfrac{b^{1/2-s}}{2\sqrt{2\pi a}}\, \cos(s\pi)$ $\times \csc\dfrac{(2s+2\delta-1)\pi}{4}\, \Gamma\left(\dfrac{2s-1}{2}\right) {}_4F_3\left(\begin{array}{c} \frac{1+2\nu}{4},\ \frac{1-2\nu}{4},\ \frac{3+2\nu}{4},\ \frac{3-2\nu}{4} \\ \frac{1}{2},\ \frac{3-2s}{4},\ \frac{5-2s}{4};\ -\frac{b^2}{4a^2} \end{array}\right)$ $-\dfrac{(4\nu^2-1)b^{3/2-s}}{16\sqrt{2\pi}\,a^{3/2}}\, \cos(s\pi)\, \csc\dfrac{(2s+2\delta-3)\pi}{4}$ $\times \Gamma\left(\dfrac{2s-3}{2}\right) {}_4F_3\left(\begin{array}{c} \frac{3+2\nu}{4},\ \frac{3-2\nu}{4},\ \frac{5+2\nu}{4},\ \frac{5-2\nu}{4} \\ \frac{3}{2},\ \frac{5-2s}{4},\ \frac{7-2s}{4};\ -\frac{b^2}{4a^2} \end{array}\right)$ $[0<b<2a;\ -\operatorname{Re}\nu-\delta<\operatorname{Re}s<3/2]$
3	$e^{-ax}\begin{Bmatrix} \sin(b\sqrt{x}) \\ \cos(b\sqrt{x}) \end{Bmatrix}$ $\times I_\nu(ax)$	$\dfrac{(-1)^\delta}{b^{2s-1}}\sqrt{\dfrac{2}{\pi a}}\begin{Bmatrix} \cos(s\pi) \\ \sin(s\pi) \end{Bmatrix} \Gamma(2s-1)\, {}_2F_2\left(\begin{array}{c} \frac{1-2\nu}{2},\ \frac{1+2\nu}{2} \\ \frac{3-2s}{2},\ 1-s;\ -\frac{b^2}{8a} \end{array}\right)$ $+\dfrac{b^\delta}{(2a)^{s+\delta/2}\sqrt{\pi}}\, \Gamma\left[\begin{array}{c} \frac{1-2s-\delta}{2},\ \frac{2s+2\nu+\delta}{2} \\ \frac{2-2s+2\nu+\delta}{2} \end{array}\right] {}_2F_2\left(\begin{array}{c} \frac{2s-2\nu+\delta}{2},\ \frac{2s+2\nu+\delta}{2} \\ \frac{2\delta+1}{2},\ \frac{2s+\delta+1}{2};\ -\frac{b^2}{8a} \end{array}\right)$ $[b,\ \operatorname{Re}a>0;\ -\operatorname{Re}\nu-\delta/2<\operatorname{Re}s<1]$

3.13.4. $I_\nu(ax)$ and the logarithmic function

1	$\theta(a-x)\ln\dfrac{\sqrt{a}+\sqrt{a-x}}{\sqrt{x}}$ $\times I_\nu(bx)$	$\dfrac{\sqrt{\pi}\,a^{s+\nu}}{2(s+\nu)}\left(\dfrac{b}{2}\right)^\nu \Gamma\left[\begin{matrix} s+\nu \\ \nu+1,\ \frac{2s+2\nu+1}{2}\end{matrix}\right]$ $\times {}_3F_4\left(\begin{matrix}\frac{s+\nu}{2},\ \frac{s+\nu}{2},\ \frac{s+\nu+1}{2};\ \frac{a^2b^2}{4} \\ \nu+1,\ \frac{2s+2\nu+1}{4},\ \frac{2s+2\nu+3}{4},\ \frac{s+\nu+2}{2}\end{matrix}\right)$ $[a,\ \mathrm{Re}\,(s+\nu)>0]$
2	$\theta(a-x)\ln\dfrac{a+\sqrt{a^2-x^2}}{x}$ $\times I_\nu(bx)$	$\dfrac{\sqrt{\pi}\,a^{s+\nu}}{2(s+\nu)}\left(\dfrac{b}{2}\right)^\nu \Gamma\left[\begin{matrix}\frac{s+\nu}{2} \\ \nu+1,\ \frac{s+\nu+1}{2}\end{matrix}\right]{}_2F_3\left(\begin{matrix}\frac{s+\nu}{2},\ \frac{s+\nu}{2};\ \frac{a^2b^2}{4} \\ \nu+1,\ \frac{s+\nu+1}{2},\ \frac{s+\nu+2}{2}\end{matrix}\right)$ $[a,\ \mathrm{Re}\,(s+\nu)>0]$
3	$\theta(a-x)\,e^{bx}\ln\dfrac{\sqrt{a}+\sqrt{a-x}}{\sqrt{x}}$ $\times I_\nu(bx)$	$\dfrac{\sqrt{\pi}\,a^{s+\nu}b^\nu}{2^{\nu+1}(s+\nu)} \Gamma\left[\begin{matrix} s+\nu \\ \nu+1,\ \frac{2s+2\nu+1}{2}\end{matrix}\right]$ $\times {}_3F_3\left(\begin{matrix}\frac{2\nu+1}{2},\ s+\nu,\ s+\nu;\ 2ab \\ 2\nu+1,\ \frac{2s+2\nu+1}{2},\ s+\nu+1\end{matrix}\right)$ $[a,\ \mathrm{Re}\,(s+\nu)>0]$

3.13.5. $I_\nu(ax)$ and inverse trigonometric functions

1	$\theta(a-x)\arccos\dfrac{x}{a}\,I_\nu(bx)$	$\dfrac{\sqrt{\pi}\,a^{s+\nu}}{(s+\nu)^2}\left(\dfrac{b}{2}\right)^\nu \Gamma\left[\begin{matrix}\frac{s+\nu+1}{2} \\ \nu+1,\ \frac{s+\nu}{2}\end{matrix}\right]{}_2F_3\left(\begin{matrix}\frac{s+\nu}{2},\ \frac{s+\nu+1}{2};\ \frac{a^2b^2}{4} \\ \nu+1,\ \frac{s+\nu+2}{2},\ \frac{s+\nu+2}{2}\end{matrix}\right)$ $[a,\ \mathrm{Re}\,(s+\nu)>0]$
2	$\theta(a-x)\,e^{bx}\arccos\dfrac{x}{a}\,I_\nu(bx)$	$\dfrac{2^{-\nu}\sqrt{\pi}\,a^{s+\nu+1}b^{\nu+1}}{(s+\nu+1)^2}\Gamma\left[\begin{matrix}\frac{s+\nu+2}{2} \\ \nu+1,\ \frac{s+\nu+1}{2}\end{matrix}\right]$ $\times {}_4F_5\left(\begin{matrix}\frac{2\nu+3}{4},\ \frac{2\nu+5}{4},\ \frac{s+\nu+1}{2},\ \frac{s+\nu+2}{2} \\ \frac{3}{2},\ \nu+1,\ \frac{2\nu+3}{2},\ \frac{s+\nu+3}{2},\ \frac{s+\nu+3}{2};\ a^2b^2\end{matrix}\right)$ $+\dfrac{2^{-\nu}\sqrt{\pi}\,a^{s+\nu}b^\nu}{(s+\nu)^2}\Gamma\left[\begin{matrix}\frac{s+\nu+1}{2} \\ \nu+1,\ \frac{s+\nu}{2}\end{matrix}\right]$ $\times {}_4F_5\left(\begin{matrix}\frac{2\nu+1}{4},\ \frac{2\nu+3}{4},\ \frac{s+\nu}{2},\ \frac{s+\nu+1}{2};\ a^2b^2 \\ \frac{1}{2},\ \frac{2\nu+1}{2},\ \nu+1,\ \frac{s+\nu+2}{2},\ \frac{s+\nu+2}{2}\end{matrix}\right)\quad [a,\ \mathrm{Re}\,(s+\nu)>0]$

3.13.6. $I_\nu(ax)$ and $\mathrm{Ei}\,(bx^r)$

1	$\mathrm{Ei}\,(-ax)\,I_\nu(bx)$	$-\dfrac{b^\nu}{2^\nu a^{s+\nu}(s+\nu)}\Gamma\left[\begin{matrix}s+\nu \\ \nu+1\end{matrix}\right]{}_3F_2\left(\begin{matrix}\frac{s+\nu}{2},\ \frac{s+\nu}{2},\ \frac{s+\nu+1}{2} \\ \nu+1,\ \frac{s+\nu+2}{2};\ \frac{b^2}{a^2}\end{matrix}\right)$ $[\mathrm{Re}\,(a-b),\ \mathrm{Re}\,(s+\nu)>0]$

No.	$f(x)$	$F(s)$
2	$\mathrm{Ei}\left(-ax^2\right) I_\nu(bx)$	$-\dfrac{a^{-(s+\nu)/2}b^\nu}{2^\nu(s+\nu)}\Gamma\begin{bmatrix}\frac{s+\nu}{2}\\ \nu+1\end{bmatrix}\,{}_2F_2\left(\begin{matrix}\frac{s+\nu}{2},\ \frac{s+\nu}{2};\ \frac{b^2}{4a}\\ \nu+1,\ \frac{s+\nu+2}{2}\end{matrix}\right)$
		$[\mathrm{Re}\,a,\ \mathrm{Re}\,(s+\nu)>0]$
3	$e^{-ax}\,\mathrm{Ei}\left(-bx\right) I_\nu(ax)$	$-\dfrac{b^{-s-\nu}}{s+\nu}\left(\dfrac{a}{2}\right)^\nu\Gamma\begin{bmatrix}s+\nu\\ \nu+1\end{bmatrix}\,{}_3F_2\left(\begin{matrix}\frac{2\nu+1}{2},\ s+\nu,\ s+\nu\\ 2\nu+1,\ s+\nu+1;\ -\frac{2a}{b}\end{matrix}\right)$
		$[\mathrm{Re}\,b,\ \mathrm{Re}\,a,\ \mathrm{Re}\,(s+\nu)>0]$
4	$e^{(\pm b-a)x}\,\mathrm{Ei}\left(\mp bx\right) I_\nu(ax)$	$-\dfrac{\pi(a/2)^\nu}{b^{s+\nu}}\left\{\begin{matrix}\csc(s+\nu)\pi\\ \cot(s+\nu)\pi\end{matrix}\right\}\Gamma\begin{bmatrix}s+\nu\\ \nu+1\end{bmatrix}\,{}_2F_1\left(\begin{matrix}\frac{2\nu+1}{2},\ s+\nu\\ 2\nu+1;\ \pm\frac{2a}{b}\end{matrix}\right)$
		$\mp\dfrac{(2a)^{1-s}}{\sqrt{\pi}b}\Gamma\begin{bmatrix}s+\nu-1,\ \frac{3-2s}{2}\\ 2-s+\nu\end{bmatrix}\,{}_3F_2\left(\begin{matrix}1,\ 1,\ \frac{3-2s}{2};\ \pm\frac{2a}{b}\\ 2-s-\nu,\ 2-s+\nu\end{matrix}\right)$
		$[\mathrm{Re}\,a,\ \mathrm{Re}\,b>0;\ -\mathrm{Re}\,\nu<\mathrm{Re}\,s<3/2]$
5	$e^x\,\mathrm{Ei}\left(-2x\right) I_\nu(x)$	$-\dfrac{2^{-s}\sqrt{\pi}}{s+\nu}\sec(\nu\pi)\,\Gamma\begin{bmatrix}s+\nu\\ \frac{1-2\nu}{2},\ 2\nu+1\end{bmatrix}\,{}_3F_2\left(\begin{matrix}\frac{2\nu+1}{2},\ s+\nu,\ s+\nu\\ 2\nu+1,\ s+\nu+1;\ 1\end{matrix}\right)$
		$[-\mathrm{Re}\,\nu<\mathrm{Re}\,s<3/2]$

3.13.7. $I_\nu(ax)$ **and** $\mathrm{si}\,(bx)$, $\mathrm{ci}\,(bx)$

No.	$f(x)$	$F(s)$
1	$e^{-ax}\left\{\begin{matrix}\mathrm{si}\,(bx)\\ \mathrm{ci}\,(bx)\end{matrix}\right\} I_\nu(ax)$	$-\dfrac{b^{-s-\nu}}{s+\nu}\left(\dfrac{a}{2}\right)^\nu\Gamma\begin{bmatrix}s+\nu\\ \nu+1\end{bmatrix}\left\{\begin{matrix}\sin\left[(s+\nu)\pi/2\right]\\ \cos\left[(s+\nu)\pi/2\right]\end{matrix}\right\}$
		$\times\,{}_5F_4\left(\begin{matrix}\frac{2\nu+1}{4},\ \frac{2\nu+3}{4},\ \frac{s+\nu}{2},\ \frac{s+\nu}{2},\ \frac{s+\nu+1}{2}\\ \frac{1}{2},\ \frac{2\nu+1}{2},\ \nu+1,\ \frac{s+\nu+2}{2};\ -\frac{4a^2}{b^2}\end{matrix}\right)$
		$\pm\,\dfrac{a^{\nu+1}b^{-s-\nu-1}}{2^\nu(s+\nu+1)}\Gamma\begin{bmatrix}s+\nu+1\\ \nu+1\end{bmatrix}\left\{\begin{matrix}\cos\left[(s+\nu)\pi/2\right]\\ \sin\left[(s+\nu)\pi/2\right]\end{matrix}\right\}$
		$\times\,{}_5F_4\left(\begin{matrix}\frac{2\nu+3}{4},\ \frac{2\nu+5}{4},\ \frac{s+\nu+1}{2},\ \frac{s+\nu+1}{2},\ \frac{s+\nu+2}{2}\\ \frac{3}{2},\ \nu+1,\ \frac{2\nu+3}{2},\ \frac{s+\nu+3}{2};\ -\frac{4a^2}{b^2}\end{matrix}\right)$
		$[b,\ \mathrm{Re}\,a>0;\ -\mathrm{Re}\,\nu<\mathrm{Re}\,s<5/2]$

3.13.8. $I_\nu(ax)$ **and** $\mathrm{erf}\,(bx^r)$, $\mathrm{erfc}\,(bx^r)$

No.	$f(x)$	$F(s)$
1	$\mathrm{erfc}\,(bx) I_\nu(ax)$	$\dfrac{a^\nu}{2^{s+2\nu}b^{s+\nu}}\Gamma\begin{bmatrix}s+\nu\\ \nu+1,\ \frac{s+\nu+2}{2}\end{bmatrix}\,{}_2F_2\left(\begin{matrix}\frac{s+\nu}{2},\ \frac{s+\nu+1}{2};\ \frac{a^2}{4b^2}\\ \nu+1,\ \frac{s+\nu+2}{2}\end{matrix}\right)$
		$[\mathrm{Re}\,a,\ \mathrm{Re}\,(s+\nu)>0;\ |\arg b|<\pi/4]$

No.	$f(x)$	$F(s)$
2	$\operatorname{erfc}\left(b\sqrt{x}\right) I_\nu(ax)$	$\dfrac{b^{-2(s+\nu)}}{\sqrt{\pi}\,(s+\nu)}\left(\dfrac{a}{2}\right)^\nu \Gamma\left[\begin{array}{c}\frac{2s+2\nu+1}{2}\\ \nu+1\end{array}\right] {}_3F_2\left(\begin{array}{c}\frac{s+\nu}{2},\ \frac{2s+2\nu+1}{4},\ \frac{2s+2\nu+3}{4}\\ \nu+1,\ \frac{s+\nu+2}{2};\ \frac{a^2}{b^4}\end{array}\right)$
		$\left[\operatorname{Re}\left(b^2-a\right),\ \operatorname{Re}\left(s+\nu\right)>0;\ \left|\arg b\right|<\pi/4\right]$

| **3** | $e^{-ax}\left\{\begin{array}{c}\operatorname{erf}(bx)\\ \operatorname{erfc}(bx)\end{array}\right\} I_\nu(ax)$ | $\mp\dfrac{(a/2)^\nu}{\sqrt{\pi}\,b^{s+\nu}(s+\nu)}\Gamma\left[\begin{array}{c}\frac{s+\nu+1}{2}\\ \nu+1\end{array}\right]{}_4F_4\left(\begin{array}{c}\frac{2\nu+1}{4},\ \frac{2\nu+3}{4},\ \frac{s+\nu}{2},\ \frac{s+\nu+1}{2}\\ \frac{1}{2},\ \frac{2\nu+1}{2},\ \nu+1,\ \frac{s+\nu+2}{2};\ \frac{a^2}{b^2}\end{array}\right)$ |

$$\pm\frac{a^{\nu+1}}{2^\nu\sqrt{\pi}\,b^{s+\nu+1}(s+\nu+1)}\Gamma\left[\begin{array}{c}\frac{s+\nu+2}{2}\\ \nu+1\end{array}\right]$$

$$\times {}_4F_4\left(\begin{array}{c}\frac{2\nu+3}{4},\ \frac{2\nu+5}{4},\ \frac{s+\nu+1}{2},\ \frac{s+\nu+2}{2}\\ \frac{3}{2},\ \nu+1,\ \frac{2\nu+3}{2},\ \frac{s+\nu+3}{2};\ \frac{a^2}{b^2}\end{array}\right)+\frac{(1\pm 1)}{2^{s+1}\sqrt{\pi}\,a^s}\Gamma\left[\begin{array}{c}s+\nu,\ \frac{1-2s}{2}\\ 1-s+\nu\end{array}\right]$$

$$\left[\operatorname{Re}a>0;\left\{\begin{array}{c}-\operatorname{Re}\nu-1<\operatorname{Re}s<1/2\\ \operatorname{Re}(s+\nu)>0\end{array}\right\};\left|\arg b\right|<\pi/4\right]$$

| **4** | $e^{-ax}\left\{\begin{array}{c}\operatorname{erf}\left(b\sqrt{x}\right)\\ \operatorname{erfc}\left(b\sqrt{x}\right)\end{array}\right\}$ $\times I_\nu(ax)$ | $\mp\dfrac{a^\nu}{2^\nu(s+\nu)\sqrt{\pi}\,b^{2(s+\nu)}}\Gamma\left[\begin{array}{c}\frac{2s+2\nu+1}{2}\\ \nu+1\end{array}\right]{}_3F_2\left(\begin{array}{c}\frac{2\nu+1}{2},\ \frac{2s+2\nu+1}{2},\ s+\nu\\ 2\nu+1,\ s+\nu+1;\ -\frac{2a}{b^2}\end{array}\right)$ |

$$+\frac{(1\pm 1)}{2^{s+1}\sqrt{\pi}\,a^s}\Gamma\left[\begin{array}{c}s+\nu,\ \frac{1-2s}{2}\\ 1-s+\nu\end{array}\right]$$

$$\left[\operatorname{Re}a>0;\left\{\begin{array}{c}-\operatorname{Re}\nu-1/2<\operatorname{Re}s<1/2\\ \operatorname{Re}(s+\nu)>0\end{array}\right\};\left|\arg b\right|<\pi/4\right]$$

| **5** | $\operatorname{erfc}\left(bx^2\right) J_\nu(ax) I_\nu(ax)$ | $\dfrac{a^{2\nu}}{2^{2\nu}\sqrt{\pi}\,b^{s/2+\nu}(s+2\nu)}\Gamma\left[\begin{array}{c}\frac{s+2\nu+2}{4}\\ \nu+1,\ \nu+1\end{array}\right]$ |

$$\times {}_2F_4\left(\begin{array}{c}\frac{s+2\nu}{4},\ \frac{s+2\nu+2}{4};\ -\frac{a^2}{64b^2}\\ \nu+1,\ \frac{\nu+1}{2},\ \frac{\nu+2}{2},\ \frac{s+2\nu+4}{4}\end{array}\right)\quad\left[\begin{array}{c}\operatorname{Re}(s+2\nu)>0;\\ \left|\arg b\right|<\pi/4\end{array}\right]$$

3.13.9. $I_\nu(ax)$ **and** $S(bx),\ C(bx)$

| **1** | $e^{-ax}\left\{\begin{array}{c}S(bx)\\ C(bx)\end{array}\right\} I_\nu(ax)$ | $-\dfrac{a^\nu b^{-s-\nu}}{2^{\nu+1/2}\sqrt{\pi}\,(s+\nu)}\Gamma\left[\begin{array}{c}\frac{2s+2\nu+1}{2}\\ \nu+1\end{array}\right]\left\{\begin{array}{c}\cos\left[(1-2s-2\nu)\,\pi/4\right]\\ \sin\left[(1-2s-2\nu)\,\pi/4\right]\end{array}\right\}$ |

$$\times {}_5F_4\left(\begin{array}{c}\frac{2\nu+1}{4},\ \frac{2\nu+3}{4},\ \frac{s+\nu}{2},\ \frac{2s+2\nu+1}{4},\ \frac{2s+2\nu+3}{4}\\ \frac{1}{2},\ \nu+1,\ \frac{2\nu+1}{2},\ \frac{s+\nu+2}{2};\ -\frac{4a^2}{b^2}\end{array}\right)$$

$$\pm\frac{a^{\nu+1}b^{-s-\nu-1}}{2^{\nu+1/2}\sqrt{\pi}\,(s+\nu+1)}\Gamma\left[\begin{array}{c}\frac{2s+2\nu+3}{2}\\ \nu+1\end{array}\right]\left\{\begin{array}{c}\sin\left[(1-2s-2\nu)\,\pi/4\right]\\ \cos\left[(1-2s-2\nu)\,\pi/4\right]\end{array}\right\}$$

$$\times {}_5F_4\left(\begin{array}{c}\frac{2\nu+3}{4},\ \frac{2\nu+5}{4},\ \frac{s+\nu+1}{2},\ \frac{2s+2\nu+3}{4},\ \frac{2s+2\nu+5}{4}\\ \frac{3}{2},\ \nu+1,\ \frac{2\nu+3}{2},\ \frac{s+\nu+3}{2};\ -\frac{4a^2}{b^2}\end{array}\right)$$

$$+\frac{(2a)^{-s}}{2\sqrt{\pi}}\Gamma\left[\begin{array}{c}s+\nu,\ \frac{1-2s}{2}\\ 1-s+\nu\end{array}\right]$$

$$\left[b,\ \operatorname{Re}a>0;\ -(2\pm 1)/2-\operatorname{Re}\nu<\operatorname{Re}s<2\right]$$

3.13.10. $I_\nu(ax)$ **and** $\gamma(\mu, bx)$, $\Gamma(\mu, bx^r)$

1	$\Gamma(\mu, bx)\, I_\nu(ax)$	$\dfrac{b^{-s-\nu}}{s+\nu}\left(\dfrac{a}{2}\right)^\nu \Gamma\left[\begin{matrix} s+\mu+\nu \\ \nu+1 \end{matrix}\right] {}_3F_2\left(\begin{matrix} \frac{s+\nu}{2},\ \frac{s+\mu+\nu}{2},\ \frac{s+\mu+\nu+1}{2} \\ \nu+1,\ \frac{s+\nu+2}{2};\ \frac{a^2}{b^2} \end{matrix}\right)$
		$[\operatorname{Re}b > |\operatorname{Re}a|;\ \operatorname{Re}s > -\operatorname{Re}\nu,\ -\operatorname{Re}(\mu+\nu)]$
2	$\Gamma(\mu, bx^2)\, I_\nu(ax)$	$\dfrac{b^{-(s+\nu)/2}}{s+\nu}\left(\dfrac{a}{2}\right)^\nu \Gamma\left[\begin{matrix} \frac{s+2\mu+\nu}{2} \\ \nu+1 \end{matrix}\right] {}_2F_2\left(\begin{matrix} \frac{s+\nu}{2},\ \frac{s+2\mu+\nu}{2};\ \frac{a^2}{4b} \\ \nu+1,\ \frac{s+\nu+2}{2} \end{matrix}\right)$
		$[\operatorname{Re}b,\ \operatorname{Re}(s+\nu),\ \operatorname{Re}(s+2\mu+\nu) > 0]$
3	$e^{-ax}\left\{\begin{matrix} \gamma(\mu, bx) \\ \Gamma(\mu, bx) \end{matrix}\right\} I_\nu(ax)$	$\mp\dfrac{b^{-s-\nu}}{s+\nu}\left(\dfrac{a}{2}\right)^\nu \Gamma\left[\begin{matrix} s+\mu+\nu \\ \nu+1 \end{matrix}\right] {}_3F_2\left(\begin{matrix} \frac{2\nu+1}{2},\ s+\nu,\ s+\mu+\nu \\ 2\nu+1,\ s+\nu+1;\ -\frac{2a}{b} \end{matrix}\right)$
		$+\dfrac{1\pm1}{2^{s+1}\sqrt{\pi}a^s}\Gamma\left[\begin{matrix} \mu,\ s+\nu,\ \frac{1-2s}{2} \\ 1-s+\nu \end{matrix}\right]$
		$\left[\operatorname{Re}a,\ \operatorname{Re}b,\ \operatorname{Re}(s+\mu+\nu) > 0;\ \left\{\begin{matrix} \operatorname{Re}\mu > 0;\ \operatorname{Re}s < 1/2 \\ \operatorname{Re}(s+\nu) > 0 \end{matrix}\right\}\right]$

3.13.11. $I_\nu(ax)$ **and** $D_\mu(bx^r)$

1	$e^{-a^2x^2/4}D_\mu(ax)\,I_\nu(bx)$	$\dfrac{\sqrt{\pi}\,b^\nu}{2^{(s+3\nu-\mu)/2}a^{s+\nu}}\Gamma\left[\begin{matrix} s+\nu \\ \nu+1,\ \frac{s-\mu+\nu+1}{2} \end{matrix}\right] {}_2F_2\left(\begin{matrix} \frac{s+\nu}{2},\ \frac{s+\nu+1}{2};\ \frac{b^2}{2a^2} \\ \nu+1,\ \frac{s-\mu+\nu+1}{2} \end{matrix}\right)$
		$[-\operatorname{Re}\nu < \operatorname{Re}s < 5/2-\operatorname{Re}\mu;\ |\arg a| < \pi/4]$
2	$e^{-a^2x^2/4-bx}D_\mu(ax)$	$\dfrac{\sqrt{\pi}\,b^\nu}{2^{(s+3\nu-\mu)/2}a^{s+\nu}}\Gamma\left[\begin{matrix} s+\nu \\ \nu+1,\ \frac{s-\mu+\nu+1}{2} \end{matrix}\right]$
	$\times I_\nu(bx)$	$\times\,{}_4F_4\left(\begin{matrix} \frac{2\nu+1}{4},\ \frac{2\nu+3}{4},\ \frac{s+\nu}{2},\ \frac{s+\nu+1}{2};\ \frac{2b^2}{a^2} \\ \frac{1}{2},\ \frac{2\nu+1}{2},\ \nu+1,\ \frac{s-\mu+\nu+1}{2} \end{matrix}\right) - \dfrac{\sqrt{\pi}\,b^{\nu+1}}{2^{(s-\mu+3\nu+1)/2}a^{s+\nu+1}}$
		$\times\,\Gamma\left[\begin{matrix} s+\nu+1 \\ \nu+1,\ \frac{s-\mu+\nu+2}{2} \end{matrix}\right] {}_4F_4\left(\begin{matrix} \frac{2\nu+3}{4},\ \frac{2\nu+5}{4},\ \frac{s+\nu+1}{2},\ \frac{s+\nu+2}{2};\ \frac{2b^2}{a^2} \\ \frac{3}{2},\ \nu+1,\ \frac{2\nu+3}{2},\ \frac{s-\mu+\nu+2}{2} \end{matrix}\right)$
		$[\operatorname{Re}b > 0;\ -\operatorname{Re}\nu < \operatorname{Re}s < 5/2-\operatorname{Re}\mu;\ |\arg a| < \pi/4]$
3	$e^{(\pm a^2/4-b)x}D_\mu(a\sqrt{x})$	$\dfrac{2^{-s-2\nu\mp(\mu+1\mp1)/2}b^\nu}{a^{2(s+\nu)}}\Gamma^{\pm1}\left(\dfrac{1\mp1-2\mu\mp4\nu\mp4s}{4}\right)\Gamma\left[\begin{matrix} 2s+2\nu \\ \nu+1 \end{matrix}\right]$
	$\times I_\nu(bx)$	$\times\left\{\begin{matrix} \Gamma^{-1}(-\mu) \\ \sqrt{\pi} \end{matrix}\right\} {}_3F_2\left(\begin{matrix} \frac{2\nu+1}{2},\ s+\nu,\ \frac{2s+2\nu+1}{2} \\ 2\nu+1,\ \frac{4s\pm2\mu+4\nu+3\pm1}{4};\ \pm\frac{4b}{a^2} \end{matrix}\right)$
		$+\dfrac{(1\pm1)a^\mu}{2\sqrt{\pi}\,(2b)^{s+\mu/2}}\Gamma\left[\begin{matrix} \frac{2s+\mu+2\nu}{2},\ \frac{1-2s-\mu}{2} \\ \frac{2-2s-\mu+2\nu}{2} \end{matrix}\right] {}_3F_2\left(\begin{matrix} -\frac{\mu}{2},\ \frac{1-\mu}{2},\ \frac{1-\mu-2s}{2};\ \frac{4b}{a^2} \\ \frac{2-2s-\mu-2\nu}{2},\ \frac{2-2s-\mu+2\nu}{2} \end{matrix}\right)$
		$\left[\operatorname{Re}b > 0;\ |\arg a| < (2\pm1)\pi/4;\ \left\{\begin{matrix} -\operatorname{Re}\nu < \operatorname{Re}s < (1-\operatorname{Re}\mu)/2 \\ \operatorname{Re}(s+\nu) > 0 \end{matrix}\right\}\right]$

No.	$f(x)$	$F(s)$
4	$D_{-\mu-1}(a\sqrt{x})\,D_\mu(a\sqrt{x})$ $\times I_\nu(bx)$	$\dfrac{2^{1/2-2s-3\nu}\pi b^\nu}{a^{2(s+\nu)}}\,\Gamma\left[\begin{array}{c} 2s+2\nu \\ \nu+1,\ \frac{s-\mu+\nu+1}{2},\ \frac{s+\mu+\nu+2}{2} \end{array}\right]$ $\times {}_4F_3\left(\begin{array}{c} \frac{s+\nu}{2},\ \frac{s+\nu+1}{2},\ \frac{2s+2\nu+1}{4},\ \frac{2s+2\nu+3}{4} \\ \nu+1,\ \frac{s-\mu+\nu+1}{2},\ \frac{s+\mu+\nu+2}{2};\ \frac{4b^2}{a^4} \end{array}\right)$ $\left[\operatorname{Re}\left(a^2-2b\right),\ \operatorname{Re}\left(s+\nu\right)>0\right]$

3.13.12. $\quad I_\nu(ax)$ **and** $J_\mu(bx^r),\ Y_\mu(bx^r)$

1	$e^{-ax}J_\mu(bx)\,I_\nu(ax)$	$\dfrac{2^{s-1}a^\nu}{b^{s+\nu}}\,\Gamma\left[\begin{array}{c} \frac{s+\mu+\nu}{2} \\ \nu+1,\ \frac{2-s+\mu-\nu}{2} \end{array}\right]\,{}_4F_3\left(\begin{array}{c} \frac{2\nu+1}{4},\ \frac{2\nu+3}{4},\ \frac{s+\nu-\mu}{2},\ \frac{s+\nu+\mu}{2} \\ \frac{1}{2},\ \frac{2\nu+1}{2},\ \nu+1;\ -\frac{4a^2}{b^2} \end{array}\right)$ $-\dfrac{2^s a^{\nu+1}}{b^{s+\nu+1}}\,\Gamma\left[\begin{array}{c} \frac{s+\mu+\nu+1}{2} \\ \nu+1,\ \frac{1-s+\mu-\nu}{2} \end{array}\right]\,{}_4F_3\left(\begin{array}{c} \frac{2\nu+3}{4},\ \frac{2\nu+5}{4},\ \frac{s-\mu+\nu+1}{2},\ \frac{s+\mu+\nu+1}{2} \\ \frac{3}{2},\ \nu+1,\ \frac{2\nu+3}{2};\ -\frac{4a^2}{b^2} \end{array}\right)$ $[0<2a<b;\ \operatorname{Re}(s+\mu+\nu)>0;\ \operatorname{Re}s<2]$
2	$e^{-ax}J_\mu(bx)\,I_\nu(ax)$	$\dfrac{2^{s-2}b^{1/2-s}}{\sqrt{\pi}\,a}\,\Gamma\left[\begin{array}{c} \frac{2s+2\mu-1}{4} \\ \frac{5-2s+2\mu}{4} \end{array}\right]\,{}_4F_3\left(\begin{array}{c} \frac{1+2\nu}{4},\ \frac{1-2\nu}{4},\ \frac{3+2\nu}{4},\ \frac{3-2\nu}{4} \\ \frac{1}{2},\ \frac{5-2s-2\mu}{4},\ \frac{5-2s+2\mu}{4};\ -\frac{b^2}{4a^2} \end{array}\right)$ $-\dfrac{2^{s-6}b^{3/2-s}}{\sqrt{\pi}\,a^{3/2}}\left(4\nu^2-1\right)\Gamma\left[\begin{array}{c} \frac{2s+2\mu-3}{4} \\ \frac{7-2s+2\mu}{4} \end{array}\right]$ $\times {}_4F_3\left(\begin{array}{c} \frac{3+2\nu}{4},\ \frac{3-2\nu}{4},\ \frac{5+2\nu}{4},\ \frac{5-2\nu}{4} \\ \frac{3}{2},\ \frac{7-2s-2\mu}{4},\ \frac{7-2s+2\mu}{4};\ -\frac{b^2}{4a^2} \end{array}\right)$ $+\dfrac{2^{-s-2\mu}b^\mu}{\sqrt{\pi}\,a^{s+\mu}}\,\Gamma\left[\begin{array}{c} \frac{1-2s-2\mu}{2},\ s+\mu+\nu \\ \mu+1,\ 1-s-\mu+\nu \end{array}\right]$ $\times {}_4F_3\left(\begin{array}{c} \frac{s+\mu-\nu}{2},\ \frac{s+\mu-\nu+1}{2},\ \frac{s+\mu+\nu}{2},\ \frac{s+\mu+\nu+1}{2} \\ \mu+1,\ \frac{2s+2\mu+1}{4},\ \frac{2s+2\mu+3}{4};\ -\frac{b^2}{4a^2} \end{array}\right)$ $[0<b<2a;\ \operatorname{Re}(s+\mu+\nu)>0;\ \operatorname{Re}s<2]$
3	$e^{-ax^2}J_\nu(bx)\,I_\mu(ax^2)$	$\dfrac{2^{s-5/2}b^{1-s}}{\sqrt{\pi}\,a}\,\Gamma\left[\begin{array}{c} \frac{s+\nu-1}{2} \\ \frac{3-s+\nu}{2} \end{array}\right]\,{}_2F_2\left(\begin{array}{c} \frac{1-2\mu}{2},\ \frac{1+2\mu}{2};\ -\frac{b^2}{8a} \\ \frac{3-s-\nu}{2},\ \frac{3-s+\nu}{2} \end{array}\right)$ $+\dfrac{2^{(s+3\nu)/2-1}b^\nu}{\sqrt{\pi}\,a^{(s+\nu)/2}}\,\Gamma\left[\begin{array}{c} \frac{s+2\mu+\nu}{2},\ \frac{1-s-\nu}{2} \\ \nu+1,\ \frac{2-s+2\mu-\nu}{2} \end{array}\right]\,{}_2F_2\left(\begin{array}{c} \frac{s-2\mu+\nu}{2},\ \frac{s+2\mu+\nu}{2} \\ \nu+1,\ \frac{s+\nu+1}{2};\ -\frac{b^2}{8a} \end{array}\right)$ $[b>0;\ -\operatorname{Re}(2\mu+\nu)<\operatorname{Re}s<5/2;\ |\arg a|<\pi/2]$
4	$e^{-ax}J_\mu(b\sqrt{x})\,I_\nu(ax)$	$\dfrac{a^{-s-\mu/2}b^\mu}{2^{s+3\mu/2}\sqrt{\pi}}\,\Gamma\left[\begin{array}{c} \frac{1-2s-\mu}{2},\ \frac{2s+\mu+2\nu}{2} \\ \mu+1,\ \frac{2-2s-\mu+2\nu}{2} \end{array}\right]\,{}_2F_2\left(\begin{array}{c} \frac{2s+\mu-2\nu}{2},\ \frac{2s+\mu+2\nu}{2} \\ \mu+1,\ \frac{2s+\mu+1}{2};\ -\frac{b^2}{8a} \end{array}\right)$ $+\dfrac{2^{2s-3/2}b^{1-2s}}{\sqrt{\pi}\,a}\,\Gamma\left[\begin{array}{c} \frac{2s+\mu-1}{2} \\ \frac{3-2s+\mu}{2} \end{array}\right]\,{}_2F_2\left(\begin{array}{c} \frac{1-2\nu}{2},\ \frac{1+2\nu}{2};\ -\frac{b^2}{8a} \\ \frac{3-2s-\mu}{2},\ \frac{3-2s+\mu}{2} \end{array}\right)$ $[b,\ \operatorname{Re}a,\ \operatorname{Re}(s+\nu+\mu/2)>0;\ \operatorname{Re}s<5/2]$

No.	$f(x)$	$F(s)$
5	$\theta(a-x)\ln\dfrac{\sqrt{a-x}+\sqrt{a}}{\sqrt{x}}$ $\times J_\nu(bx)I_\nu(bx)$	$\dfrac{2^{-2\nu-1}\sqrt{\pi}\,a^{s+2\nu}b^{2\nu}}{s+2\nu}\Gamma\left[\begin{matrix} s+2\nu \\ \nu+1,\ \nu+1,\ \frac{2s+4\nu+1}{2} \end{matrix}\right]$ $\times {}_5F_8\left(\begin{matrix} \frac{s+2\nu}{4},\ \Delta(4,s+2\nu);\ -\frac{a^4b^4}{64} \\ \frac{\nu+1}{2},\ \frac{\nu+2}{2},\ \nu+1,\ \Delta(4,\frac{2s+4\nu+1}{2}),\ \frac{s+2\nu+4}{2} \end{matrix}\right)$ $[a,\ \operatorname{Re}(s+2\nu)>0]$
6	$\theta(a-x)\ln\dfrac{a^2+\sqrt{a^4-x^4}}{x^2}$ $\times J_\nu(bx)I_\nu(bx)$	$\dfrac{a^{s+2\nu}b^{2\nu}}{2^{-s/2+\nu+3}}\Gamma\left[\begin{matrix} \frac{s+2\nu}{4},\ \frac{s+2\nu}{4} \\ \frac{s+2\nu+2}{2},\ \nu+1,\ \nu+1 \end{matrix}\right]$ $\times {}_2F_5\left(\begin{matrix} \frac{s+2\nu}{4},\ \frac{s+2\nu}{4};\ -\frac{a^4b^4}{64} \\ \frac{\nu+1}{2},\ \frac{\nu+2}{2},\ \nu+1,\ \frac{s+2\nu+2}{4},\ \frac{s+2\nu+2}{4} \end{matrix}\right)$ $[a,\ \operatorname{Re}(s+2\nu)>0]$
7	$\theta(a-x)\arccos\dfrac{x}{a}$ $\times J_\nu(bx)I_\nu(bx)$	$\dfrac{2^{-2\nu-1}\sqrt{\pi}\,a^{s+2\nu}b^{2\nu}}{s+2\nu}\Gamma\left[\begin{matrix} \frac{s+2\nu+1}{2} \\ \nu+1,\ \nu+1,\ \frac{s+2\nu+2}{2} \end{matrix}\right]$ $\times {}_3F_6\left(\begin{matrix} \frac{s+2\nu}{4},\ \frac{s+2\nu+1}{4},\ \frac{s+2\nu+3}{4};\ -\frac{a^4b^4}{64} \\ \frac{\nu+1}{2},\ \frac{\nu+2}{2},\ \nu+1,\ \frac{s+2\nu+2}{4},\ \frac{s+2\nu+4}{2},\ \frac{s+2\nu+4}{2} \end{matrix}\right)$ $[a,\ \operatorname{Re}(s+2\nu)>0]$
8	$\Gamma(\mu,ax)J_\nu(bx)I_\nu(bx)$	$\dfrac{a^{-s-2\nu}(b/2)^{2\nu}}{s+2\nu}\Gamma\left[\begin{matrix} s+\mu+2\nu \\ \nu+1,\ \nu+1 \end{matrix}\right]$ $\times {}_5F_4\left(\begin{matrix} \frac{s+2\nu}{4},\ \Delta(4,s+\mu+2\nu);\ -\frac{4b^4}{a^4} \\ \frac{\nu+1}{2},\ \frac{\nu+2}{2},\ \nu+1,\ \frac{s+2\nu+4}{4} \end{matrix}\right)$ $[\operatorname{Re}a>|\operatorname{Im}b|+|\operatorname{Re}b|;\ \operatorname{Re}(s+2\nu)>-\operatorname{Re}\mu,0]$
9	$\operatorname{erfc}(ax)J_\nu(bx)I_\nu(bx)$	$\dfrac{a^{-s-2\nu}b^{2\nu}}{2^{2\nu}\sqrt{\pi}(s+2\nu)}\Gamma\left[\begin{matrix} \frac{s+2\nu+1}{2} \\ \nu+1,\ \nu+1 \end{matrix}\right]{}_3F_3\left(\begin{matrix} \frac{1}{2},\ \frac{s+2\nu}{4},\ \frac{s+2\nu+3}{4} \\ \frac{\nu+1}{2},\ \frac{\nu+2}{2},\ \nu+1;\ -\frac{b^4}{16a^4} \end{matrix}\right)$ $[\operatorname{Re}(s+2\nu)>0;\ |\arg a|<\pi/4]$
10	$e^{-ax}Y_\mu(bx)I_\nu(ax)$	$-\dfrac{2^{s-1}a^\nu}{\pi\,b^{s+\nu}\Gamma(\nu+1)}\cos\dfrac{(s-\mu+\nu)\pi}{2}\Gamma\left(\dfrac{s+\mu+\nu}{2}\right)$ $\times\Gamma\left(\dfrac{s-\mu+\nu}{2}\right){}_4F_3\left(\begin{matrix} \frac{2\nu+1}{4},\ \frac{2\nu+3}{4},\ \frac{s+\mu+\nu}{2},\ \frac{s-\mu+\nu}{2} \\ \frac{1}{2},\ \frac{2\nu+1}{2},\ \nu+1;\ -\frac{4a^2}{b^2} \end{matrix}\right)$ $-\dfrac{2^s a^{\nu+1}}{\pi\,b^{s+\nu+1}}\sin\dfrac{(s-\mu+\nu)\pi}{2}\Gamma\left[\begin{matrix} \frac{s+\mu+\nu+1}{2},\ \frac{s-\mu+\nu+1}{2} \\ \nu+1 \end{matrix}\right]$ $\times {}_4F_3\left(\begin{matrix} \frac{2\nu+3}{4},\ \frac{2\nu+5}{4},\ \frac{s+\mu+\nu+1}{2},\ \frac{s-\mu+\nu+1}{2} \\ \frac{3}{2},\ \nu+1,\ \frac{2\nu+3}{2};\ -\frac{4a^2}{b^2} \end{matrix}\right)$ $[b,\ \operatorname{Re}a>0;\ |\operatorname{Re}\mu|-\operatorname{Re}\nu<\operatorname{Re}s<2]$

3.13.13.   Products of $I_\nu(\varphi(x))$

1	$e^{-ax} I_\mu(bx)\, I_\nu(cx)$	$\dfrac{b^\mu c^\nu}{2^{\mu+\nu} a^{s+\mu+\nu}} \Gamma\left[\begin{array}{c} s+\mu+\nu \\ \mu+1,\, \nu+1 \end{array}\right]$

$$\times F_4\left(\frac{s+\mu+\nu}{2},\ \frac{s+\mu+\nu+1}{2};\ \mu+1,\ \nu+1;\ \frac{b^2}{a^2},\ \frac{c^2}{a^2}\right)$$

$$[\operatorname{Re} a > |\operatorname{Re} b| + |\operatorname{Re} c|;\ \operatorname{Re}(s+\mu+\nu) > 0]$$

2	$e^{-ax} I_\mu(bx)\, I_\nu(bx)$	$a^{-s-\mu-\nu} \left(\dfrac{b}{2}\right)^{\mu+\nu} \Gamma\left[\begin{array}{c} s+\mu+\nu \\ \mu+1,\, \nu+1 \end{array}\right]$

$$\times {}_4F_3\left(\begin{array}{c} \frac{\mu+\nu+1}{2},\ \frac{\mu+\nu+2}{2},\ \frac{s+\mu+\nu}{2},\ \frac{s+\mu+\nu+1}{2} \\ \mu+1,\ \nu+1,\ \mu+\nu+1;\ \frac{4b^2}{a^2} \end{array}\right)$$

$$[\operatorname{Re} a > 2|\operatorname{Re} b|;\ \operatorname{Re}(s+\mu+\nu) > 0]$$

3	$e^{-(a+b)x} I_\mu(ax)\, I_\nu(bx)$	$\dfrac{a^{-s-\nu} b^\nu}{2^{s+2\nu}\sqrt{\pi}} \Gamma\left[\begin{array}{c} \frac{1-2s-2\nu}{2},\ s+\mu+\nu \\ 1-s+\mu-\nu,\ \nu+1 \end{array}\right]$

$$\times {}_3F_2\left(\begin{array}{c} \frac{2\nu+1}{2},\ s-\mu+\nu,\ s+\mu+\nu \\ 2\nu+1,\ \frac{2s+2\nu+1}{2};\ -\frac{b}{a} \end{array}\right) + \frac{b^{1/2-s}}{2^s \pi \sqrt{a}}$$

$$\times \Gamma\left[\begin{array}{c} \frac{2s+2\nu-1}{2},\ 1-s \\ \frac{3-2s+2\nu}{2} \end{array}\right] {}_3F_2\left(\begin{array}{c} \frac{1-2\mu}{2},\ \frac{1+2\mu}{2},\ 1-s \\ \frac{3-2s-2\nu}{2},\ \frac{3-2s+2\nu}{2};\ -\frac{b}{a} \end{array}\right)$$

$$[\operatorname{Re}(a+b) > 0;\ -\operatorname{Re}(\mu+\nu) < \operatorname{Re} s < 1]$$

4	$e^{-ax^2} I_\mu(bx)\, I_\nu(cx)$	$\dfrac{b^\mu c^\nu}{2^{\mu+\nu+1} a^{(s+\mu+\nu)/2}} \Gamma\left[\begin{array}{c} \frac{s+\mu+\nu}{2} \\ \mu+1,\, \nu+1 \end{array}\right]$

$$\times \Psi_2\left(\frac{s+\mu+\nu}{2};\ \mu+1,\ \nu+1;\ \frac{b^2}{4a},\ \frac{c^2}{4a}\right)$$

$$[\operatorname{Re} a,\ \operatorname{Re}(s+\mu+\nu) > 0]$$

5	$e^{-ax^2} I_\mu(bx)\, I_\nu(bx)$	$\dfrac{b^{\mu+\nu}}{2^{\mu+\nu+1} a^{(s+\mu+\nu)/2}} \Gamma\left[\begin{array}{c} \frac{s+\mu+\nu}{2} \\ \mu+1,\, \nu+1 \end{array}\right]$

$$\times {}_3F_3\left(\begin{array}{c} \frac{\mu+\nu+1}{2},\ \frac{\mu+\nu+2}{2},\ \frac{s+\mu+\nu}{2};\ \frac{b^2}{a} \\ \mu+1,\ \nu+1,\ \mu+\nu+1 \end{array}\right)$$

$$[\operatorname{Re} a,\ \operatorname{Re}(s+\mu+\nu) > 0]$$

6	$\theta(a-x)$ $\times \ln\dfrac{\sqrt{a-x}+\sqrt{a}}{\sqrt{x}}$ $\times I_\mu(bx)\, I_\nu(bx)$	$\dfrac{\sqrt{\pi}\, a^{s+\mu+\nu} b^{\mu+\nu}}{2^{\mu+\nu+1}(s+\mu+\nu)} \Gamma\left[\begin{array}{c} s+\mu+\nu \\ \mu+1,\, \nu+1,\, s+\mu+\nu+\frac{1}{2} \end{array}\right]$

$$\times {}_5F_6\left(\begin{array}{c} \frac{\mu+\nu+1}{2},\ \frac{\mu+\nu+2}{2},\ \frac{s+\mu+\nu}{2},\ \frac{s+\mu+\nu}{2},\ \frac{s+\mu+\nu+1}{2};\ a^2 b^2 \\ \mu+1,\ \nu+1,\ \mu+\nu+1,\ \Delta\left(2,\frac{2s+2\mu+2\nu+1}{2}\right),\ \frac{s+\mu+\nu+2}{2} \end{array}\right)$$

$$[a>0;\ \operatorname{Re}(s+\mu+\nu) > 0]$$

No.	$f(x)$	$F(s)$
7	$\theta(a-x)$ $\times \ln \dfrac{\sqrt{a^2-x^2}+a}{x}$ $\times I_\mu(bx)\,I_\nu(bx)$	$\dfrac{\sqrt{\pi}\,a^{s+\mu+\nu}b^{\mu+\nu}}{2^{\mu+\nu+1}(s+\mu+\nu)}\,\Gamma\!\left[\begin{array}{c}\frac{s+\mu+\nu}{2}\\ \mu+1,\ \nu+1,\ \frac{s+\mu+\nu+1}{2}\end{array}\right]$ $\times\,{}_4F_5\!\left(\begin{array}{c}\frac{\mu+\nu+1}{2},\ \frac{\mu+\nu+2}{2},\ \frac{s+\mu+\nu}{2},\ \frac{s+\mu+\nu}{2};\ a^2b^2\\ \mu+1,\ \nu+1,\ \mu+\nu+1,\ \frac{s+\mu+\nu+1}{2},\ \frac{s+\mu+\nu+2}{2}\end{array}\right)$ $[a>0;\ \mathrm{Re}\,(s+(\mu+\nu)/2)>0]$
8	$\theta(a-x)\arccos\dfrac{x}{a}$ $\times I_\mu(bx)\,I_\nu(bx)$	$\dfrac{\sqrt{\pi}\,a^{s+\mu+\nu}b^{\mu+\nu}}{2^{\mu+\nu+1}(s+\mu+\nu)}\,\Gamma\!\left[\begin{array}{c}\frac{s+\mu+\nu+1}{2}\\ \mu+1,\ \nu+1,\ \frac{s+\mu+\nu+2}{2}\end{array}\right]$ $\times\,{}_4F_5\!\left(\begin{array}{c}\frac{\mu+\nu+1}{2},\ \frac{\mu+\nu+2}{2},\ \frac{s+\mu+\nu}{2},\ \frac{s+\mu+\nu+1}{2};\ a^2b^2\\ \mu+1,\ \nu+1,\ \mu+\nu+1,\ \frac{s+\mu+\nu+2}{2},\ \frac{s+\mu+\nu+2}{2}\end{array}\right)$ $[a,\ \mathrm{Re}\,(s+\mu+\nu)>0]$
9	$\mathrm{Ei}\,(-ax)\,I_\mu(bx)\,I_\nu(bx)$	$-\dfrac{a^{-(s+\mu+\nu)}}{s+\mu+\nu}\left(\dfrac{b}{2}\right)^{\mu+\nu}\Gamma\!\left[\begin{array}{c}s+\mu+\nu\\ \mu+1,\ \nu+1\end{array}\right]$ $\times\,{}_5F_4\!\left(\begin{array}{c}\frac{\mu+\nu+1}{2},\ \frac{\mu+\nu+2}{2},\ \frac{s+\mu+\nu}{2},\ \frac{s+\mu+\nu}{2},\ \frac{s+\mu+\nu+1}{2}\\ \mu+1,\ \nu+1,\ \mu+\nu+1,\ \frac{s+\mu+\nu+2}{2};\ \frac{4b^2}{a^2}\end{array}\right)$ $[a>2|\mathrm{Re}\,b|;\ \mathrm{Re}\,(s+\mu+\nu)>0]$
10	$\mathrm{Ei}\,(-ax^2)\,I_\mu(bx)\,I_\nu(bx)$	$-\dfrac{a^{-(s+\mu+\nu)/2}}{s+\mu+\nu}\left(\dfrac{b}{2}\right)^{\mu+\nu}\Gamma\!\left[\begin{array}{c}\frac{s+\mu+\nu}{2}\\ \mu+1,\ \nu+1\end{array}\right]$ $\times\,{}_4F_4\!\left(\begin{array}{c}\frac{\mu+\nu+1}{2},\ \frac{\mu+\nu+2}{2},\ \frac{s+\mu+\nu}{2},\ \frac{s+\mu+\nu}{2};\ \frac{b^2}{a}\\ \mu+1,\ \nu+1,\ \mu+\nu+1,\ \frac{s+\mu+\nu+2}{2}\end{array}\right)$ $[\mathrm{Re}\,a,\ \mathrm{Re}\,(s+\mu+\nu)>0;\ |\arg b|<\pi]$
11	$\mathrm{erfc}\,(ax)\,I_\mu(bx)\,I_\nu(bx)$	$\dfrac{a^{-(s+\mu+\nu)}}{\sqrt{\pi}\,(s+\mu+\nu)}\left(\dfrac{b}{2}\right)^{\mu+\nu}\Gamma\!\left[\begin{array}{c}\frac{s+\mu+\nu+1}{2}\\ \mu+1,\ \nu+1\end{array}\right]$ $\times\,{}_4F_4\!\left(\begin{array}{c}\frac{\mu+\nu+1}{2},\ \frac{\mu+\nu+2}{2},\ \frac{s+\mu+\nu}{2},\ \frac{s+\mu+\nu+1}{2};\ \frac{b^2}{a^2}\\ \mu+1,\ \nu+1,\ \mu+\nu+1,\ \frac{s+\mu+\nu+2}{2}\end{array}\right)$ $[\mathrm{Re}\,(s+\mu+\nu)>0;\ |\arg a|<\pi/4]$
12	$\Gamma(\lambda,\,ax)\,I_\mu(bx)\,I_\nu(bx)$	$\dfrac{a^{-(s+\mu+\nu)}}{s+\mu+\nu}\left(\dfrac{b}{2}\right)^{\mu+\nu}\Gamma\!\left[\begin{array}{c}s+\lambda+\mu+\nu\\ \mu+1,\ \nu+1\end{array}\right]$ $\times\,{}_5F_4\!\left(\begin{array}{c}\frac{\mu+\nu+1}{2},\ \frac{\mu+\nu+2}{2},\ \frac{s+\mu+\nu}{2},\ \frac{s+\lambda+\mu+\nu}{2},\ \frac{s+\lambda+\mu+\nu+1}{2}\\ \mu+1,\ \nu+1,\ \mu+\nu+1,\ \frac{s+\mu+\nu+2}{2};\ \frac{4b^2}{a^2}\end{array}\right)$ $[\mathrm{Re}\,(a-2b)>0;\ \mathrm{Re}\,(s+\mu+\nu)>-\mathrm{Re}\,\lambda,\,0]$
13	$I_\mu(ax)\,I_\nu(ax)$ $-\,I_{-\mu}(ax)\,I_{-\nu}(ax)$	$-\dfrac{\sin(\mu+\nu)\pi}{2\pi^{3/2}a^s}\,\Gamma\!\left[\begin{array}{c}\frac{s+\mu+\nu}{2},\ \frac{s-\mu-\nu}{2},\ \frac{1-s}{2},\ \frac{2-s}{2}\\ \frac{2-s+\mu-\nu}{2},\ \frac{2-s-\mu+\nu}{2}\end{array}\right]$ $[|\mathrm{Re}\,(\mu+\nu)|<\mathrm{Re}\,s<1]$

No.	$f(x)$	$F(s)$
14	$(a-x)_+^{\alpha-1}$ $\times I_\mu(bx(a-x))$ $\times I_\nu(bx(a-x))$	$a^{s+\alpha+2\mu+2\nu-1}\left(\dfrac{b}{2}\right)^{\mu+\nu}\Gamma\left[\begin{matrix}\alpha+\mu+\nu,\,s+\mu+\nu\\\mu+1,\,\nu+1,\,s+\alpha+2\mu+2\nu\end{matrix}\right]$ $\times\,{}_3F_2\left(\begin{matrix}\Delta(2,\mu+\nu+1),\,\Delta(2,\alpha+\mu+\nu),\,\Delta(2,s+\mu+\nu)\\\mu+1,\,\nu+1,\,\mu+\nu+1,\,\Delta(4,s+\alpha+\mu+\nu)\end{matrix};\dfrac{a^4b^2}{64}\right)$ $[a>0;\ \mathrm{Re}\,s,\ \mathrm{Re}\,\alpha>-\mathrm{Re}\,(\mu+\nu)]$
15	$\dfrac{1}{(x+a)^\rho}I_\mu\left(\dfrac{bx}{x+a}\right)$ $\times I_\nu\left(\dfrac{bx}{x+a}\right)$	$a^{s-\rho}\left(\dfrac{b}{2}\right)^{\mu+\nu}\dfrac{\mathrm{B}(\rho-s,s+\mu+\nu)}{\Gamma(\mu+1)\Gamma(\nu+1)}$ $\times\,{}_4F_5\left(\begin{matrix}\frac{\mu+\nu+1}{2},\,\frac{\mu+\nu+2}{2},\,\frac{s+\mu+\nu}{2},\,\frac{s+\mu+\nu+1}{2}\\\mu+1,\,\nu+1,\,\mu+\nu+1,\,\frac{\mu+\nu+\rho}{2},\,\frac{\mu+\nu+\rho+1}{2}\end{matrix};b^2\right)$ $[\mathrm{Re}\,(\mu+\nu)<\mathrm{Re}\,s<\mathrm{Re}\,\rho;\ |\arg a|<\pi]$
16	$\dfrac{1}{(x^2+a^2)^\rho}I_\mu\left(\dfrac{bx}{x^2+a^2}\right)$ $\times I_\nu\left(\dfrac{bx}{x^2+a^2}\right)$	$\dfrac{a^{s-\mu-\nu-2\rho}b^{\mu+\nu}}{2^{\mu+\nu+1}\Gamma(\mu+1)\Gamma(\nu+1)}\mathrm{B}\left(\dfrac{s+\mu+\nu}{2},\dfrac{\mu+\nu+2\rho-s}{2}\right)$ $\times\,{}_4F_5\left(\begin{matrix}\frac{\mu+\nu+1}{2},\,\frac{\mu+\nu+2}{2},\,\frac{s+\mu+\nu}{2},\,\frac{\mu+\nu+2\rho-s}{2}\\\mu+1,\,\nu+1,\,\mu+\nu+1,\,\frac{\mu+\nu+\rho}{2},\,\frac{\mu+\nu+\rho+1}{2}\end{matrix};\dfrac{b^2}{4a^2}\right)$ $[\mathrm{Re}\,a>0;\ -\mathrm{Re}\,(\mu+\nu)<\mathrm{Re}\,s<\mathrm{Re}\,(\mu+\nu+2\rho)]$
17	$e^{-ax}\displaystyle\prod_{k=1}^n I_{\nu_k}(b_k x)$	$\dfrac{\Gamma(s+\nu)}{a^{s+\nu}}\displaystyle\prod_{k=1}^n\dfrac{(b_k/2)^{\nu_k}}{\Gamma(\nu_k+1)}F_C^{(n)}\left(\dfrac{s+\nu}{2},\dfrac{s+\nu+1}{2};(\nu_n)+1;\dfrac{(b_n^2)}{a^2}\right)$ $\left[\nu=\displaystyle\sum_{k=1}^n\nu_k;\ \mathrm{Re}\,a>\displaystyle\sum_{k=1}^n|\mathrm{Re}\,b_k|;\ \mathrm{Re}\,(s+\nu)>0\right]$
18	$e^{-ax}\displaystyle\prod_{k=1}^m\sin(b_k x)$ $\times\displaystyle\prod_{k=1}^n\cos(c_k x)$ $\times\displaystyle\prod_{k=1}^p I_{\nu_k}(d_k x)$	$\dfrac{\prod_{k=1}^m b_k\prod_{k=1}^p(d_k/2)^{\nu_k}}{a^{s+m+\nu}}\Gamma\left[\begin{matrix}s+m+\nu\\\nu_1+1,\,\nu_2+1,\dots,\nu_p+1\end{matrix}\right]$ $\times F_C^{(m+n+p)}\left(\dfrac{s+m+\nu}{2},\dfrac{s+m+\nu+1}{2};\underbrace{\dfrac{3}{2},\dots,\dfrac{3}{2}}_{m},\underbrace{\dfrac{1}{2},\dots,\dfrac{1}{2}}_{n},\right.$ $\left.(\nu_p)+1;-\dfrac{(b_m^2)}{a^2},-\dfrac{(c_n^2)}{a^2},\dfrac{(d_p^2)}{a^2}\right)\quad\left[\nu=\displaystyle\sum_{k=1}^p\nu_k;\right.$ $\left.\mathrm{Re}\,a>\displaystyle\sum_{k=1}^m|\mathrm{Im}\,b_k|+\displaystyle\sum_{k=1}^n|\mathrm{Im}\,c_k|+\displaystyle\sum_{k=1}^p|\mathrm{Re}\,d_k|;\ \mathrm{Re}\,(s+m+\nu)>0\right]$
19	$e^{-ax}\displaystyle\prod_{k=1}^m J_{\mu_k}(b_k x)$ $\times\displaystyle\prod_{k=1}^n I_{\nu_k}(c_k x)$	$\dfrac{\prod_{k=1}^m(b_k/2)^{\mu_k}\prod_{k=1}^n(c_k/2)^{\nu_k}}{a^{s+\mu+\nu}}\Gamma\left[\begin{matrix}s+\mu+\nu\\(\mu_m)+1,\,(\nu_n)+1\end{matrix}\right]$ $\times F_C^{(n+m)}\left(\Delta(2,s+\mu+\nu);(\mu_m)+1,(\nu_n)+1;-\dfrac{(b_m^2)}{a^2},\dfrac{(c_n^2)}{a^2}\right)$ $\left[\mu=\displaystyle\sum_{k=1}^m\mu_k,\ \nu=\displaystyle\sum_{k=1}^n\nu_k;\ \mathrm{Re}\,a>\displaystyle\sum_{k=1}^m|\mathrm{Im}\,b_k|+\displaystyle\sum_{k=1}^n|\mathrm{Re}\,c_k|;\right.$ $\left.\mathrm{Re}\,(s+\mu+\nu)>0\right]$

3.14. The Macdonald Function $K_\nu(z)$

More formulas can be obtained from the corresponding sections due to the relations

$$K_{\pm 1/2}(z) = \sqrt{\frac{2}{\pi}}\,\frac{1}{\sqrt{z}}\,e^{-z}, \quad K_{\pm 3/2}(z) = \sqrt{\frac{2}{\pi}}\,\frac{z+1}{z^{3/2}}\,e^{-z};$$

$$K_{(n+1)/2}(z) = \sqrt{\frac{2}{\pi}}\,\frac{1}{\sqrt{z}}\,e^{-z}\sum_{k=0}^{n}\frac{(n+k)!}{k!\,(n-k)!\,(2z)^k} = n!\sqrt{\frac{2}{\pi}}\,\frac{1}{\sqrt{z}}\,\frac{e^{-z}}{(-2z)^n}\,L_n^{-2n-1}(2z);$$

$$K_\nu(z) = \frac{\pi}{2\sin(\nu\pi)}\left[I_{-\nu}(z) - I_\nu(z)\right], \quad [\nu \neq 0, \pm 1, \pm 2, \ldots];$$

$$K_n(z) = \lim_{\nu \to n} K_\nu(z), \quad [n = 0, \pm 1, \pm 2, \ldots];$$

$$K_\nu(z) = 2^{-\nu-1}z^\nu\,\Gamma(-\nu)\,{}_0F_1\left(1+\nu;\frac{z^2}{4}\right) + 2^{\nu-1}z^{-\nu}\,\Gamma(\nu)\,{}_0F_1\left(1-\nu;\frac{z^2}{4}\right);$$

$$K_\nu(z) = \frac{1}{2}\,G_{02}^{20}\left(\frac{z^2}{4}\,\middle|\,\nu/2,\,-\nu/2\right), \quad \mathrm{Re}\,z > 0; \quad K_\nu(z) = \sqrt{\pi}\,e^z\,G_{12}^{20}\left(2z\,\middle|\,\begin{matrix}1/2\\-\nu,\,\nu\end{matrix}\right).$$

3.14.1. $K_\nu(ax^r)$ and algebraic functions

No.	$f(x)$	$F(s)$
1	$(a-x)_+^{\alpha-1}K_\nu(bx)$	$2^{\nu-1}a^{s+\alpha-\nu-1}b^{-\nu}\,\Gamma(\nu)\,\mathrm{B}(\alpha, s-\nu)\,{}_2F_3\left(\begin{matrix}\frac{s-\nu}{2},\,\frac{s-\nu+1}{2};\,\frac{a^2b^2}{4}\\1-\nu,\,\frac{s+\alpha-\nu}{2},\,\frac{s+\alpha-\nu+1}{2}\end{matrix}\right)$ $+\dfrac{a^{s+\alpha+\nu-1}b^\nu}{2^{\nu+1}}\,\Gamma(-\nu)\,\mathrm{B}(\alpha, s+\nu)\,{}_2F_3\left(\begin{matrix}\frac{s+\nu}{2},\,\frac{s+\nu+1}{2};\,\frac{a^2b^2}{4}\\1+\nu,\,\frac{s+\alpha+\nu}{2},\,\frac{s+\alpha+\nu+1}{2}\end{matrix}\right)$ $[a,\,\mathrm{Re}\,\alpha > 0;\,\mathrm{Re}\,s > |\mathrm{Re}\,\nu|]$
2	$(x-a)_+^{\alpha-1}K_\nu(bx)$	$\dfrac{a^{s+\alpha-\nu-1}}{2^{1-\nu}b^\nu}\,\Gamma(\nu)\,\mathrm{B}(\alpha, 1-s-\alpha+\nu)\,{}_2F_3\left(\begin{matrix}\frac{s-\nu}{2},\,\frac{s-\nu+1}{2};\,\frac{a^2b^2}{4}\\1-\nu,\,\frac{s+\alpha-\nu}{2},\,\frac{s+\alpha-\nu+1}{2}\end{matrix}\right)$ $+\dfrac{a^{s+\alpha+\nu-1}}{2^{\nu+1}b^{-\nu}}\,\Gamma(-\nu)\,\mathrm{B}(\alpha, 1-s-\alpha-\nu)\,{}_2F_3\left(\begin{matrix}\frac{s+\nu}{2},\,\frac{s+\nu+1}{2};\,\frac{a^2b^2}{4}\\1+\nu,\,\frac{s+\alpha+\nu}{2},\,\frac{s+\alpha+\nu+1}{2}\end{matrix}\right)$ $+\dfrac{2^{s+\alpha-3}}{b^{s+\alpha-1}}\,\Gamma\left(\frac{s+\alpha-\nu-1}{2}\right)\Gamma\left(\frac{s+\alpha+\nu-1}{2}\right)$ $\times\,{}_2F_3\left(\begin{matrix}\frac{1-\alpha}{2},\,\frac{2-\alpha}{2};\,\frac{a^2b^2}{4}\\\frac{1}{2},\,\frac{3-s-\alpha-\nu}{2},\,\frac{3-s-\alpha+\nu}{2}\end{matrix}\right)$ $-\dfrac{(\alpha-1)2^{s+\alpha-4}a}{b^{s+\alpha-2}}\,\Gamma\left(\frac{s+\alpha-\nu-2}{2}\right)\Gamma\left(\frac{s+\alpha+\nu-2}{2}\right)$ $\times\,{}_2F_3\left(\begin{matrix}\frac{2-\alpha}{2},\,\frac{3-\alpha}{2};\,\frac{a^2b^2}{4}\\\frac{3}{2},\,\frac{4-s-\alpha-\nu}{2},\,\frac{4-s-\alpha+\nu}{2}\end{matrix}\right)$ $[a,\,\mathrm{Re}\,b,\,\mathrm{Re}\,\alpha > 0]$
3	$K_\nu(ax)$	$\dfrac{2^{s-2}}{a^s}\,\Gamma\left(\frac{s-\nu}{2}\right)\Gamma\left(\frac{s+\nu}{2}\right)$ $\qquad\qquad[\mathrm{Re}\,a > 0;\,\mathrm{Re}\,s > |\mathrm{Re}\,\nu|]$

No.	$f(x)$	$F(s)$
4	$\dfrac{1}{x-a}K_\nu(bx)$	$\dfrac{2^{s-3}}{b^{s-1}}\Gamma\left(\dfrac{s+\nu-1}{2}\right)\Gamma\left(\dfrac{s-\nu-1}{2}\right){}_1F_2\left(\begin{matrix}1;\;\frac{a^2b^2}{4}\\ \frac{3-s-\nu}{2},\;\frac{3-s+\nu}{2}\end{matrix}\right)$

$$+\frac{2^{s-4}a}{b^{s-2}}\Gamma\left(\frac{s+\nu-2}{2}\right)\Gamma\left(\frac{s-\nu-2}{2}\right){}_1F_2\left(\begin{matrix}1;\;\frac{a^2b^2}{4}\\ \frac{4-s-\nu}{2},\;\frac{4-s+\nu}{2}\end{matrix}\right)$$

$$+\frac{\pi^2 a^{s-1}}{2\sin(\nu\pi)}\Big[\cot\left[(s+\nu)\,\pi\right]I_\nu(ab)-\cot\left[(s-\nu)\,\pi\right]I_{-\nu}(ab)\Big]$$

$$[a,\;\operatorname{Re}b>0;\;\operatorname{Re}s>|\operatorname{Re}\nu|]$$

| 5 | $\dfrac{1}{(x+a)^\rho}K_\nu(bx)$ | $\dfrac{2^{s-\rho-2}}{b^{s-\rho}}\Gamma\left(\dfrac{s+\nu-\rho}{2}\right)\Gamma\left(\dfrac{s-\nu-\rho}{2}\right){}_2F_3\left(\begin{matrix}\frac{\rho}{2},\;\frac{\rho+1}{2};\;\frac{a^2b^2}{4}\\ \frac{1}{2},\;\frac{2-s-\nu+\rho}{2},\;\frac{2-s+\nu+\rho}{2}\end{matrix}\right)$ |

$$-\rho a\,\frac{2^{s-\rho-3}}{b^{s-\rho-1}}\Gamma\left(\frac{s+\nu-\rho-1}{2}\right)\Gamma\left(\frac{s-\nu-\rho-1}{2}\right)$$

$$\times{}_2F_3\left(\begin{matrix}\frac{\rho+1}{2},\;\frac{\rho+2}{2};\;\frac{a^2b^2}{4}\\ \frac{3}{2},\;\frac{3-s-\nu+\rho}{2},\;\frac{3-s+\nu+\rho}{2}\end{matrix}\right)+\frac{2^{\nu-1}a^{s-\nu-\rho}}{b^\nu}$$

$$\times\Gamma\left[\begin{matrix}\nu,s-\nu,\nu+\rho-s\\ \rho\end{matrix}\right]{}_2F_3\left(\begin{matrix}\frac{s-\nu}{2},\;\frac{s-\nu+1}{2};\;\frac{a^2b^2}{4}\\ 1-\nu,\;\frac{s-\nu-\rho+1}{2},\;\frac{s-\nu-\rho+2}{2}\end{matrix}\right)$$

$$+\frac{a^{s+\nu-\rho}b^\nu}{2^{\nu+1}}\Gamma\left[\begin{matrix}-\nu,s+\nu,\rho-\nu-s\\ \rho\end{matrix}\right]$$

$$\times{}_2F_3\left(\begin{matrix}\frac{s+\nu}{2},\;\frac{s+\nu+1}{2};\;\frac{a^2b^2}{4}\\ 1+\nu,\;\frac{s+\nu-\rho+1}{2},\;\frac{s+\nu-\rho+2}{2}\end{matrix}\right)$$

$$[\operatorname{Re}b>0;\;\operatorname{Re}s>|\operatorname{Re}\nu|;\;|\arg a|<\pi]$$

| 6 | $\dfrac{1}{x+a}K_\nu(bx)$ | $\dfrac{2^{s-3}}{b^{s-1}}\Gamma\left(\dfrac{s-\nu-1}{2}\right)\Gamma\left(\dfrac{s+\nu-1}{2}\right){}_1F_2\left(\begin{matrix}1;\;\frac{a^2b^2}{4}\\ \frac{3-s-\nu}{2},\;\frac{3-s+\nu}{2}\end{matrix}\right)$ |

$$-\frac{2^{s-4}a}{b^s}\Gamma\left(\frac{s-\nu-2}{2}\right)\Gamma\left(\frac{s+\nu-2}{2}\right){}_1F_2\left(\begin{matrix}1;\;\frac{a^2b^2}{4}\\ \frac{4-s-\nu}{2},\;\frac{4-s+\nu}{2}\end{matrix}\right)$$

$$+\frac{\pi a^{s-1}}{\sin\left[(s-\nu)\,\pi\right]}\left[K_\nu(ab)+\frac{\pi\cos(s\pi)}{\sin\left[(s+\nu)\,\pi\right]}I_\nu(ab)\right]$$

$$[\operatorname{Re}b>0;\;\operatorname{Re}s>|\operatorname{Re}\nu|;\;|\arg a|<\pi]$$

| 7 | $\dfrac{1}{(x^2+a^2)^\rho}K_\nu(bx)$ | $\dfrac{a^{s-2\rho-\nu}b^\nu}{2^{2-\nu}}\Gamma\left[\begin{matrix}\nu,\;\frac{s-\nu}{2},\;\frac{\nu+2\rho-s}{2}\\ \rho\end{matrix}\right]{}_1F_2\left(\begin{matrix}\frac{s-\nu}{2};\;-\frac{a^2b^2}{4}\\ 1-\nu,\;\frac{s-\nu-2\rho+2}{2}\end{matrix}\right)$ |

$$+\frac{a^{s+\nu-2\rho}b^\nu}{2^{\nu+2}}\Gamma\left[\begin{matrix}-\nu,\;\frac{s+\nu}{2},\;\frac{2\rho-\nu-s}{2}\\ \rho\end{matrix}\right]{}_1F_2\left(\begin{matrix}\frac{s+\nu}{2};\;-\frac{a^2b^2}{4}\\ 1+\nu,\;\frac{s+\nu-2\rho+2}{2}\end{matrix}\right)$$

$$+\frac{2^{s-2\rho-2}}{b^{s-2\rho}}\Gamma\left(\frac{s+\nu-2\rho}{2}\right)\Gamma\left(\frac{s-\nu-2\rho}{2}\right)$$

$$\times{}_1F_2\left(\begin{matrix}\rho;\;-\frac{a^2b^2}{4}\\ \frac{2-s-\nu+2\rho}{2},\;\frac{2-s+\nu+2\rho}{2}\end{matrix}\right)\qquad[\operatorname{Re}a,\;\operatorname{Re}b>0;\;\operatorname{Re}s>|\operatorname{Re}\nu|]$$

No.	$f(x)$	$F(s)$
8	$\left(a^2 - x^2\right)_+^{\alpha-1} K_\nu(bx)$	$\dfrac{a^{s+2\alpha-2}}{4}\Gamma(\alpha)\left[\left(\dfrac{ab}{2}\right)^{-\nu}\Gamma\!\left[\begin{matrix}\nu,\ \frac{s-\nu}{2}\\ \frac{s+2\alpha-\nu}{2}\end{matrix}\right]{}_1F_2\!\left(\begin{matrix}\frac{s-\nu}{2};\ \frac{a^2b^2}{4}\\ 1-\nu,\ \frac{s+2\alpha-\nu}{2}\end{matrix}\right)\right.$
		$\left.+\left(\dfrac{ab}{2}\right)^{\nu}\Gamma\!\left[\begin{matrix}-\nu,\ \frac{s+\nu}{2}\\ \frac{s+2\alpha+\nu}{2}\end{matrix}\right]{}_1F_2\!\left(\begin{matrix}\frac{s+\nu}{2};\ \frac{a^2b^2}{4}\\ 1+\nu,\ \frac{s+2\alpha+\nu}{2}\end{matrix}\right)\right]$
		$[a,\ \mathrm{Re}\,b,\ \mathrm{Re}\,\alpha>0;\ \mathrm{Re}\,s>|\mathrm{Re}\,\nu|]$
9	$\left(x^2 - a^2\right)_+^{\alpha-1} K_\nu(bx)$	$\dfrac{2^{\nu-2}a^{s+2\alpha-\nu-2}}{b^\nu}\Gamma(\nu)\,\mathrm{B}\!\left(\alpha,\ \dfrac{2-s-2\alpha+\nu}{2}\right)$
		$\times\,{}_1F_2\!\left(\begin{matrix}\frac{s-\nu}{2};\ \frac{a^2b^2}{4}\\ 1-\nu,\ \frac{s+2\alpha-\nu}{2}\end{matrix}\right)+\dfrac{a^{s+2\alpha+\nu-2}b^\nu}{2^{\nu+2}}\Gamma(-\nu)$
		$\times\,\mathrm{B}\!\left(\alpha,\ \dfrac{2-s-2\alpha-\nu}{2}\right){}_1F_2\!\left(\begin{matrix}\frac{s+\nu}{2};\ \frac{a^2b^2}{4}\\ 1+\nu,\ \frac{s+2\alpha+\nu}{2}\end{matrix}\right)$
		$+\dfrac{2^{s+2\alpha-4}}{b^{s+2\alpha-2}}\Gamma\!\left(\dfrac{s+2\alpha+\nu-2}{2}\right)\Gamma\!\left(\dfrac{s+2\alpha-\nu-2}{2}\right)$
		$\times\,{}_1F_2\!\left(\begin{matrix}1-\alpha;\ \frac{a^2b^2}{4}\\ \frac{4-s-2\alpha-\nu}{2},\ \frac{4-s-2\alpha+\nu}{2}\end{matrix}\right)\qquad [a,\ \mathrm{Re}\,b,\ \mathrm{Re}\,\alpha>0]$
10	$\dfrac{1}{x^2 - a^2}K_\nu(bx)$	$\dfrac{2^{s-4}}{b^{s-2}}\Gamma\!\left(\dfrac{s+\nu-2}{2}\right)\Gamma\!\left(\dfrac{s-\nu-2}{2}\right){}_1F_2\!\left(\begin{matrix}1;\ \frac{a^2b^2}{4}\\ \frac{4-s-\nu}{2},\ \frac{4-s+\nu}{2}\end{matrix}\right)$
		$+\dfrac{\pi^2 a^{s-2}}{4\sin(\nu\pi)}\left[\cot\dfrac{(s+\nu)\pi}{2}I_\nu(ab)-\cot\dfrac{(s-\nu)\pi}{2}I_{-\nu}(ab)\right]$
		$[a,\ \mathrm{Re}\,b>0;\ \mathrm{Re}\,s>|\mathrm{Re}\,\nu|]$
11	$\left(\sqrt{x^2 + a^2}\pm a\right)^{\rho}$ $\times\,K_\nu(bx)$	$\pm\dfrac{2^{s+\rho-3}\rho a}{b^{s+\rho-1}}\Gamma\!\left(\dfrac{s+\rho+\nu-1}{2}\right)\Gamma\!\left(\dfrac{s+\rho-\nu-1}{2}\right)$
		$\times\,{}_2F_3\!\left(\begin{matrix}\frac{1+\rho}{2},\ \frac{1-\rho}{2};\ -\frac{a^2b^2}{4}\\ \frac{3}{2},\ \frac{3-s-\rho-\nu}{2},\ \frac{3-s-\rho+\nu}{2}\end{matrix}\right)+\dfrac{2^{s+\rho-2}}{b^{s+\rho}}\Gamma\!\left(\dfrac{s+\rho+\nu}{2}\right)$
		$\times\,\Gamma\!\left(\dfrac{s+\rho-\nu}{2}\right){}_2F_3\!\left(\begin{matrix}-\frac{\rho}{2},\ \frac{\rho}{2};\ -\frac{a^2b^2}{4}\\ \frac{1}{2},\ \frac{2-s-\rho-\nu}{2},\ \frac{2-s-\rho+\nu}{2}\end{matrix}\right)$
		$\mp\dfrac{2^{s+\rho-2}\rho a^{s+\rho-\nu}}{b^\nu}\Gamma\!\left[\begin{matrix}\nu,\ \frac{s+\rho\mp\rho-\nu}{2},\ -s-\rho+\nu\\ -\frac{s+\rho\pm\rho-\nu-2}{2}\end{matrix}\right]$
		$\times\,{}_2F_3\!\left(\begin{matrix}\frac{s-\nu}{2},\ \frac{s+2\rho-\nu}{2};\ -\frac{a^2b^2}{4}\\ 1-\nu,\ \frac{s+\rho-\nu+1}{2},\ \frac{s+\rho-\nu+2}{2}\end{matrix}\right)$
		$\mp\,2^{s+\rho-2}\rho a^{s+\rho+\nu}b^\nu\,\Gamma\!\left[\begin{matrix}-\nu,\ \frac{s+\nu+\rho\mp\rho}{2},\ -s-\rho-\nu\\ -\frac{s+\rho\pm\rho+\nu-2}{2}\end{matrix}\right]$
		$\times\,{}_2F_3\!\left(\begin{matrix}\frac{s+\nu}{2},\ \frac{s+2\rho+\nu}{2};\ -\frac{a^2b^2}{4}\\ 1+\nu,\ \frac{s+\rho+\nu+1}{2},\ \frac{s+\rho+\nu+2}{2}\end{matrix}\right)$
		$[\mathrm{Re}\,a,\ \mathrm{Re}\,b>0;\ \mathrm{Re}\,(s+\rho\mp\rho)>|\mathrm{Re}\,\nu|]$

No.	$f(x)$	$F(s)$
12	$\dfrac{(\sqrt{x^2+a^2}\pm a)^\rho}{\sqrt{x^2+a^2}}$ $\times K_\nu(bx)$	$\dfrac{2^{s+\rho-3}}{b^{s+\rho-1}}\Gamma\left(\dfrac{s+\rho+\nu-1}{2}\right)\Gamma\left(\dfrac{s+\rho-\nu-1}{2}\right)$ $\times{}_2F_3\left(\begin{matrix}\frac{1+\rho}{2},\frac{1-\rho}{2};-\frac{a^2b^2}{4}\\[2pt]\frac{1}{2},\frac{3-s-\rho-\nu}{2},\frac{3-s-\rho+\nu}{2}\end{matrix}\right)\pm\dfrac{2^{s+\rho-4}\rho a}{b^{s+\rho-2}}\Gamma\left(\dfrac{s+\rho+\nu-2}{2}\right)$ $\times\Gamma\left(\dfrac{s+\rho-\nu-2}{2}\right){}_2F_3\left(\begin{matrix}\frac{2+\rho}{2},\frac{2-\rho}{2};-\frac{a^2b^2}{4}\\[2pt]\frac{3}{2},\frac{4-s-\rho-\nu}{2},\frac{4-s-\rho+\nu}{2}\end{matrix}\right)$ $+\dfrac{2^{s+\rho-2}a^{s+\rho-\nu-1}}{b^\nu}\Gamma\left[\begin{matrix}\nu,\frac{s+\rho\mp\nu}{2},1-s-\rho+\nu\\[2pt]-\frac{s+\rho\pm\rho-\nu-2}{2}\end{matrix}\right]$ $\times{}_2F_3\left(\begin{matrix}\frac{s-\nu}{2},\frac{s+2\rho-\nu}{2};-\frac{a^2b^2}{4}\\[2pt]1-\nu,\frac{s+\rho-\nu}{2},\frac{s+\rho-\nu+1}{2}\end{matrix}\right)$ $+2^{s+\rho-2}a^{s+\rho+\nu-1}b^\nu\Gamma\left[\begin{matrix}-\nu,\frac{s+\rho\mp\nu}{2},1-s-\rho-\nu\\[2pt]-\frac{s+\rho\pm\rho+\nu-2}{2}\end{matrix}\right]$ $\times{}_2F_3\left(\begin{matrix}\frac{s+\nu}{2},\frac{s+2\rho+\nu}{2};-\frac{a^2b^2}{4}\\[2pt]1+\nu,\frac{s+\rho+\nu}{2},\frac{s+\rho+\nu+1}{2}\end{matrix}\right)$ $[\operatorname{Re}a,\ \operatorname{Re}b>0;\ \operatorname{Re}(s+\rho\mp\rho)>|\operatorname{Re}\nu|]$
13	$(\sqrt{x^2+a^2}\pm x)^\rho$ $\times K_\nu(bx)$	$\dfrac{2^{s\pm2\rho-2}a^{\rho\mp\rho}}{b^{s\pm\rho}}\Gamma\left(\dfrac{s\pm\rho+\nu}{2}\right)\Gamma\left(\dfrac{s\pm\rho-\nu}{2}\right)$ $\times{}_2F_3\left(\begin{matrix}\mp\frac{\rho}{2},\frac{1\mp\rho}{2};-\frac{a^2b^2}{4}\\[2pt]1\mp\rho,-\frac{s\pm\rho+\nu-2}{2},-\frac{s\pm\rho-\nu-2}{2}\end{matrix}\right)\mp\dfrac{2^{2\nu-s-2}\rho a^{s+\rho-\nu}}{b^\nu}$ $\times\Gamma\left[\begin{matrix}\nu,s-\nu,\frac{\nu\mp\rho-s}{2}\\[2pt]\frac{s\mp\rho-\nu+2}{2}\end{matrix}\right]{}_2F_3\left(\begin{matrix}\frac{s-\nu}{2},\frac{s-\nu+1}{2};-\frac{a^2b^2}{4}\\[2pt]1-\nu,\frac{s\mp\rho-\nu+2}{2},\frac{s\pm\rho-\nu+2}{2}\end{matrix}\right)$ $\mp\dfrac{\rho a^{s+\rho+\nu}b^\nu}{2^{s+2\nu+2}}\Gamma\left[\begin{matrix}-\nu,s+\nu,-\frac{s\pm\rho+\nu}{2}\\[2pt]\frac{s\mp\rho+\nu+2}{2}\end{matrix}\right]$ $\times{}_2F_3\left(\begin{matrix}\frac{s+\nu}{2},\frac{s+\nu+1}{2};-\frac{a^2b^2}{4}\\[2pt]1+\nu,\frac{s+\nu-\rho+2}{2},\frac{s+\rho+\nu+2}{2}\end{matrix}\right)$ $[\operatorname{Re}a,\ \operatorname{Re}b>0;\ \operatorname{Re}s>|\operatorname{Re}\nu|]$
14	$\dfrac{(\sqrt{x^2+a^2}\pm x)^\rho}{\sqrt{x^2+a^2}}$ $\times K_\nu(bx)$	$\dfrac{2^{s\pm2\rho-3}a^{\rho\mp\rho}}{b^{s\pm\rho-1}}\Gamma\left(\dfrac{s\pm\rho+\nu-1}{2}\right)\Gamma\left(\dfrac{s\pm\rho-\nu-1}{2}\right)$ $\times{}_2F_3\left(\begin{matrix}\frac{2\mp\rho}{2},\frac{1\mp\rho}{2};-\frac{a^2b^2}{4}\\[2pt]1\mp\rho,-\frac{s\pm\rho+\nu-3}{2},-\frac{s-\nu\pm\rho-3}{2}\end{matrix}\right)+\dfrac{a^{s+\rho-\nu-1}b^{-\nu}}{2^{s-2\nu+1}}$ $\times\Gamma\left[\begin{matrix}\nu,\frac{\nu\mp\rho-s+1}{2},s-\nu\\[2pt]\frac{s\mp\rho-\nu+1}{2}\end{matrix}\right]{}_2F_3\left(\begin{matrix}\frac{s-\nu}{2},\frac{s-\nu+1}{2};-\frac{a^2b^2}{4}\\[2pt]1-\nu,\frac{s-\nu\mp\rho+1}{2},\frac{s-\nu\pm\rho+1}{2}\end{matrix}\right)$ $+\dfrac{a^{s+\rho+\nu-1}b^\nu}{2^{s+2\nu+1}}\Gamma\left[\begin{matrix}-\nu,\frac{1-s+\mp\rho-\nu}{2},s+\nu\\[2pt]\frac{s\mp\rho+\nu+1}{2}\end{matrix}\right]$ $\times{}_2F_3\left(\begin{matrix}\frac{s+\nu}{2},\frac{s+\nu+1}{2};-\frac{a^2b^2}{4}\\[2pt]1+\nu,\frac{s-\rho+\nu+1}{2},\frac{s+\rho+\nu+1}{2}\end{matrix}\right)$ $[\operatorname{Re}a,\ \operatorname{Re}b>0;\ \operatorname{Re}s>|\operatorname{Re}\nu|]$

3.14.2. $K_\nu \left(\varphi \left(x \right) \right)$ and algebraic functions

1	$(x-a)_+^{\alpha-1} K_\nu \left(b\sqrt{x-a} \right)$	$\dfrac{2^{\nu-1} a^{s+\alpha-\nu/2-1}}{b^\nu} \Gamma \begin{bmatrix} \nu, \frac{2\alpha-\nu}{2}, \frac{2-2s-2\alpha+\nu}{2} \\ 1-s \end{bmatrix} {}_1F_2 \left(\begin{matrix} \frac{2\alpha-\nu}{2}; -\frac{ab^2}{4} \\ 1-\nu, \frac{2s+2\alpha-\nu}{2} \end{matrix} \right)$

$$+ \frac{a^{s+\alpha+\nu/2-1} b^\nu}{2^{\nu+1}} \Gamma \begin{bmatrix} -\nu, \frac{2\alpha+\nu}{2}, \frac{2-2s-2\alpha-\nu}{2} \\ 1-s \end{bmatrix} {}_1F_2 \left(\begin{matrix} \frac{2\alpha+\nu}{2}; -\frac{ab^2}{4} \\ 1+\nu, \frac{2s+2\alpha+\nu}{2} \end{matrix} \right)$$

$$+ \frac{2^{2s+2\alpha-3}}{b^{2(s+\alpha-1)}} \Gamma \left(s+\alpha+\frac{\nu}{2}-1 \right) \Gamma \left(s+\alpha-\frac{\nu}{2}-1 \right)$$

$$\times {}_1F_2 \left(\begin{matrix} 1-s; -\frac{ab^2}{4} \\ \frac{4-2s-2\alpha-\nu}{2}, \frac{4-2s-2\alpha+\nu}{2} \end{matrix} \right)$$

$$[a, \operatorname{Re} b > 0; \operatorname{Re} \alpha + |\operatorname{Re} \nu| > 0]$$

2	$(x+a)^{\pm\nu/2} K_\nu \left(b\sqrt{x+a} \right)$	$a^{(s\pm\nu)/2} \left(\dfrac{2}{b} \right)^s \Gamma(s) K_{s\pm\nu} \left(\sqrt{a}\,b \right) \qquad [\operatorname{Re} a, \operatorname{Re} b, \operatorname{Re} s > 0]$
3	$(a-x)_+^{-\nu/2} K_\nu \left(b\sqrt{a-x} \right)$	$\dfrac{2^{-\nu-1} a^s b^\nu}{s} \Gamma(-\nu) \, {}_1F_2 \left(\begin{matrix} 1; \frac{ab^2}{4} \\ \nu+1, s+1 \end{matrix} \right)$

$$+ \frac{2^{s-1} \pi a^{(s-\nu)/2}}{b^s} \csc(\nu\pi) \Gamma(s) I_{s-\nu} \left(\sqrt{a}\,b \right)$$

$$[a, \operatorname{Re} b, \operatorname{Re} s, \operatorname{Re}(s-\nu) > 0]$$

4	$(x^2-a^2)_+^{\nu/2}$ $\times K_\nu \left(b\sqrt{x^2-a^2} \right)$	$-\dfrac{2^{\nu-1} a^s b^{-\nu}}{s} \Gamma(\nu) \, {}_1F_2 \left(\begin{matrix} 1; -\frac{a^2 b^2}{4} \\ 1-\nu, \frac{s+2}{2} \end{matrix} \right)$

$$+ \frac{2^{s/2-2} \pi^2 a^{s/2+\nu} b^{-s/2}}{\Gamma\left(\frac{2-s}{2} \right)} \csc \frac{(s+2\nu)\pi}{2}$$

$$\times \left[\csc \frac{s\pi}{2} J_{-s/2-\nu}(ab) + \csc(\nu\pi) J_{s/2+\nu}(ab) \right]$$

$$[a, \operatorname{Re} b > 0; \operatorname{Re} \nu > -1]$$

5	$\theta(1-x) K_\nu \left(ax - \dfrac{a}{x} \right)$	$\dfrac{\pi^2}{4} \csc(\nu\pi) \left[J_{(\nu+s)/2}(a) Y_{(s-\nu)/2}(a) - J_{(s-\nu)/2}(a) Y_{(\nu+s)/2}(a) \right]$

$$[\operatorname{Re} a > 0; |\operatorname{Re} \nu| < 1]$$

6	$\theta(x-1) K_\nu \left(ax - \dfrac{a}{x} \right)$	$\dfrac{\pi^2}{4} \csc(\nu\pi) \left[J_{(\nu-s)/2}(a) Y_{-(s+\nu)/2}(a) \right.$

$$\left. - J_{-(s+\nu)/2}(a) Y_{(\nu-s)/2}(a) \right] \qquad [\operatorname{Re} a > 0; |\operatorname{Re} \nu| < 1]$$

7	$K_0 \left(a \left| x - \dfrac{1}{x} \right| \right)$	$\dfrac{\pi^2}{4} \left[J_{s/2}^2(a) + Y_{s/2}^2(a) \right] \qquad\qquad\qquad\qquad [\operatorname{Re} a > 0]$
8	$K_\nu \left(ax + \dfrac{a}{x} \right)$	$K_{(s+\nu)/2}(a) K_{(\nu-s)/2}(a) \qquad\qquad\qquad\qquad [\operatorname{Re} a > 0]$

No.	$f(x)$	$F(s)$
9	$\left(\dfrac{bx+a}{ax+b}\right)^{\nu/2} K_\nu(\sqrt{u})$ $u = ab\left(x + \dfrac{1}{x}\right) + a^2 + b^2$	$2K_{s+\nu/2}(a)\,K_{s-\nu/2}(b)$ $[a, b > 0]$

3.14.3. $K_\nu(\varphi(x))$ and the exponential function

No.	$f(x)$	$F(s)$
1	$e^{-ax} K_\nu(ax)$	$\dfrac{\sqrt{\pi}}{(2a)^s}\,\Gamma\!\left[\begin{array}{c} s-\nu,\ s+\nu \\ \frac{2s+1}{2} \end{array}\right]$ $[\operatorname{Re}a>0;\ \operatorname{Re}s>|\operatorname{Re}\nu|]$
2	$e^{ax} K_\nu(ax)$	$\dfrac{\cos(\nu\pi)}{\sqrt{\pi}\,(2a)^s}\,\Gamma\!\left[s-\nu,\ s+\nu,\ \dfrac{1-2s}{2}\right]$ $[\operatorname{Re}a>0;\ |\operatorname{Re}\nu|<\operatorname{Re}s<1/2]$
3	$e^{-ax} K_\nu(bx)$	$\dfrac{\sqrt{\pi}\,a^{\nu-s}}{2^s b^\nu}\,\Gamma\!\left[\begin{array}{c} s-\nu,\ s+\nu \\ \frac{2s+1}{2} \end{array}\right]\,{}_2F_1\!\left(\begin{array}{c} \frac{s-\nu}{2},\ \frac{s-\nu+1}{2} \\ \frac{2s+1}{2};\ \frac{a^2-b^2}{a^2} \end{array}\right)$
4		$= \dfrac{e^{-i\pi\nu}\,\Gamma(s-\nu)}{(a^2-b^2)^{s/2}}\,Q_{s-1}^\nu\!\left(\dfrac{a}{\sqrt{a^2-b^2}}\right)$
5		$= \sqrt{\dfrac{\pi}{2b}}\,\dfrac{\Gamma(s-\nu)\,\Gamma(s+\nu)}{(b^2-a^2)^{(2s-1)/4}}\,\mathrm{P}_{\nu-1/2}^{1/2-s}\!\left(\dfrac{a}{b}\right)$ $[\operatorname{Re}(a+b)>0;\ \operatorname{Re}s>|\operatorname{Re}\nu|]$
6	$(a-x)_+^{\alpha-1}\, e^{\pm bx} K_\nu(bx)$	$\dfrac{2^{\nu-1} a^{s+\alpha-\nu-1}}{b^\nu}\,\Gamma\!\left[\begin{array}{c} \alpha,\ \nu,\ s-\nu \\ s+\alpha-\nu \end{array}\right]\,{}_2F_2\!\left(\begin{array}{c} \frac{1-2\nu}{2},\ s-\nu;\ \pm2ab \\ 1-2\nu,\ s+\alpha-\nu \end{array}\right)$ $+\dfrac{a^{s+\alpha+\nu-1}b^\nu}{2^{\nu+1}}\,\Gamma\!\left[\begin{array}{c} \alpha,\ -\nu,\ s+\nu \\ s+\alpha+\nu \end{array}\right]\,{}_2F_2\!\left(\begin{array}{c} \frac{1+2\nu}{2},\ s+\nu;\ \pm2ab \\ 1+2\nu,\ s+\alpha+\nu \end{array}\right)$ $[a,\ \operatorname{Re}\alpha>0;\ \operatorname{Re}s>|\operatorname{Re}\nu|]$
7	$(x-a)_+^{\alpha-1}\, e^{\pm bx} K_\nu(bx)$	$\dfrac{2^{\nu-1} a^{s+\alpha-\nu-1}}{b^\nu}\,\Gamma\!\left[\begin{array}{c} \alpha,\ \nu,\ 1-s-\alpha+\nu \\ 1-s+\nu \end{array}\right]\,{}_2F_2\!\left(\begin{array}{c} \frac{1-2\nu}{2},\ s-\nu;\ \pm2ab \\ 1-2\nu,\ s+\alpha-\nu \end{array}\right)$ $+\dfrac{a^{s+\alpha+\nu-1}b^\nu}{2^{\nu+1}}\,\Gamma\!\left[\begin{array}{c} \alpha,\ -\nu,\ 1-s-\alpha-\nu \\ 1-s-\nu \end{array}\right]\,{}_2F_2\!\left(\begin{array}{c} \frac{1+2\nu}{2},\ s+\nu;\ \pm2ab \\ 1+2\nu,\ s+\alpha+\nu \end{array}\right)$ $\mp\dfrac{\sqrt{\pi}}{(2b)^{s+\alpha-1}}\,[\cos(\nu\pi)\sec(s+\alpha)\pi]^{(1\pm1)/2}$ $\times\,\Gamma\!\left[\begin{array}{c} s+\alpha+\nu-1,\ s+\alpha-\nu-1 \\ \frac{2s+2\alpha-1}{2} \end{array}\right]$ $\times\,{}_2F_2\!\left(\begin{array}{c} 1-\alpha,\ \frac{3-2s-2\alpha}{2};\ \pm2ab \\ 2-s-\alpha-\nu,\ 2-s-\alpha+\nu \end{array}\right)$ $\left[a,\ \operatorname{Re}\alpha>0;\ \left\{\begin{array}{c} \operatorname{Re}b>0;\ \operatorname{Re}(s+\alpha)<3/2 \\ \operatorname{Re}b>0 \end{array}\right\}\right]$

No.	$f(x)$	$F(s)$
8	$\dfrac{e^{\pm bx}}{(x+a)^\rho} K_\nu(bx)$	$\dfrac{\sqrt{\pi}}{(2b)^{s-\rho}} \left[\cos(\nu\pi)\sec(\rho-s)\pi\right]^{(1\pm1)/2} \Gamma\begin{bmatrix} s+\nu-\rho,\, s-\nu-\rho \\ \frac{2s-2\rho+1}{2} \end{bmatrix}$

$$\times\, {}_2F_2\left(\begin{matrix} \rho,\, \frac{1-2s+2\rho}{2};\, \mp 2ab \\ 1-s-\nu+\rho,\, 1-s+\nu+\rho \end{matrix}\right) + \frac{2^{\nu-1}a^{s-\nu-\rho}}{b^\nu}$$

$$\times\, \Gamma\begin{bmatrix} \nu,\, s-\nu,\, \rho+\nu-s \\ \rho \end{bmatrix} {}_2F_2\left(\begin{matrix} \frac{1-2\nu}{2},\, s-\nu;\, \mp 2ab \\ 1-2\nu,\, s-\nu-\rho+1 \end{matrix}\right)$$

$$+\, \frac{a^{s+\nu-\rho}b^\nu}{2^{\nu+1}} \Gamma\begin{bmatrix} -\nu,\, s+\nu,\, \rho-\nu-s \\ \rho \end{bmatrix}$$

$$\times\, {}_2F_2\left(\begin{matrix} \frac{1+2\nu}{2},\, s+\nu;\, \mp 2ab \\ 1+2\nu,\, s+\nu-\rho+1 \end{matrix}\right)$$

$$\left[\operatorname{Re}s > |\operatorname{Re}\nu|;\, \left\{\begin{matrix} \operatorname{Re}b>0;\ \operatorname{Re}(s-\rho)<1/2 \\ \operatorname{Re}b>0 \end{matrix}\right\};\, |\arg a|<\pi\right]$$

No.	$f(x)$	$F(s)$
9	$\dfrac{e^{\pm bx}}{x-a} K_\nu(bx)$	$\mp\dfrac{\sqrt{\pi}\,[\cos(\nu\pi)\sec(s\pi)]^{(1\pm1)/2}}{(2b)^{s-1}} \Gamma\begin{bmatrix} s+\nu-1,\, s-\nu-1 \\ \frac{2s-1}{2} \end{bmatrix}$

$$\times\, {}_2F_2\left(\begin{matrix} 1,\, \frac{3-2s}{2};\, \pm 2ab \\ 2-s-\nu,\, 2-s+\nu \end{matrix}\right)$$

$$-\, \frac{\pi a^{s-\nu-1}}{2^{1-\nu}b^\nu} \Gamma(\nu)\cot[(s-\nu)\pi]\, {}_1F_1\left(\begin{matrix} \frac{1-2\nu}{2};\, \pm 2ab \\ 1-2\nu \end{matrix}\right)$$

$$-\, \frac{\pi a^{s+\nu-1}b^\nu}{2^{\nu+1}} \Gamma(-\nu)\cot[(s+\nu)\pi]\, {}_1F_1\left(\begin{matrix} \frac{2\nu+1}{2};\, \pm 2ab \\ 2\nu+1 \end{matrix}\right)$$

$$\left[\operatorname{Re}s > |\operatorname{Re}\nu|;\, \left\{\begin{matrix} a,\ \operatorname{Re}b>0;\ \operatorname{Re}s<3/2 \\ a,\ \operatorname{Re}b>0 \end{matrix}\right\}\right]$$

No.	$f(x)$	$F(s)$
10	$e^{-ax^2} K_\nu(bx)$	$\dfrac{a^{(1-s)/2}}{2b} e^{b^2/(8a)} \Gamma\left(\dfrac{s-\nu}{2}\right) \Gamma\left(\dfrac{s+\nu}{2}\right) W_{(1-s)/2,\,\nu/2}\left(\dfrac{b^2}{4a}\right)$

$$[\operatorname{Re}a>0;\ \operatorname{Re}s>|\operatorname{Re}\nu|]$$

No.	$f(x)$	$F(s)$
11	$e^{-a\sqrt{x}} K_\nu(bx)$	$\dfrac{2^{s-2}}{b^s} \Gamma\left(\dfrac{s-\nu}{2}\right) \Gamma\left(\dfrac{s+\nu}{2}\right) {}_2F_3\left(\begin{matrix} \frac{s-\nu}{2},\, \frac{s+\nu}{2} \\ \frac{1}{4},\, \frac{1}{2},\, \frac{3}{4};\, \frac{a^4}{64b^2} \end{matrix}\right)$

$$-\, \frac{2^{s-3/2}}{b^{s+1/2}} \Gamma\left(\frac{2s-2\nu+1}{4}\right) \Gamma\left(\frac{2s+2\nu+1}{4}\right)$$

$$\times\, {}_2F_3\left(\begin{matrix} \frac{2s-2\nu+1}{4},\, \frac{2s+2\nu+1}{4} \\ \frac{1}{2},\, \frac{3}{4},\, \frac{5}{4};\, \frac{a^4}{64b^2} \end{matrix}\right) + \frac{2^{s-2}a^2}{b^{s+1}} \Gamma\left(\frac{s-\nu+1}{2}\right)$$

$$\times\, \Gamma\left(\frac{s+\nu+1}{2}\right) {}_2F_3\left(\begin{matrix} \frac{s-\nu+1}{2},\, \frac{s+\nu+1}{2} \\ \frac{3}{4},\, \frac{5}{4},\, \frac{3}{2};\, \frac{a^4}{64b^2} \end{matrix}\right)$$

$$-\, \frac{2^{s-3/2}a^3}{3b^{s+3/2}} \Gamma\left(\frac{2s-2\nu+3}{4}\right) \Gamma\left(\frac{2s+2\nu+3}{4}\right)$$

$$\times\, {}_2F_3\left(\begin{matrix} \frac{2s-2\nu+3}{4},\, \frac{2s+2\nu+3}{4} \\ \frac{5}{4},\, \frac{3}{2},\, \frac{7}{4};\, \frac{a^4}{64b^2} \end{matrix}\right) \qquad [\operatorname{Re}b>0;\ \operatorname{Re}s>|\operatorname{Re}\nu|]$$

No.	$f(x)$	$F(s)$
12	$e^{-a/x}K_\nu(bx)$	$\dfrac{2^{s-2}}{b^s}\Gamma\left(\dfrac{s-\nu}{2}\right)\Gamma\left(\dfrac{s+\nu}{2}\right){}_0F_3\left(\begin{matrix}&\dfrac{a^2b^2}{16}\\ \frac{1}{2},\ \frac{2-s-\nu}{2},\ \frac{2-s+\nu}{2}&\end{matrix}\right)$
		$-\dfrac{2^{s-3}a}{b^{s-1}}\Gamma\left(\dfrac{s-\nu-1}{2}\right)\Gamma\left(\dfrac{s+\nu-1}{2}\right){}_0F_3\left(\begin{matrix}&\dfrac{a^2b^2}{16}\\ \frac{3}{2},\ \frac{3-s-\nu}{2},\ \frac{3-s+\nu}{2}&\end{matrix}\right)$
		$+\dfrac{a^{s+\nu}b^\nu}{2^{\nu+1}}\Gamma(-\nu)\Gamma(-s-\nu){}_0F_3\left(\begin{matrix}&\dfrac{a^2b^2}{16}\\ 1+\nu,\ \frac{s+\nu+1}{2},\ \frac{s+\nu+2}{2}&\end{matrix}\right)$
		$+\dfrac{2^{\nu-1}a^{s-\nu}}{b^\nu}\Gamma(\nu)\Gamma(\nu-s){}_0F_3\left(\begin{matrix}&\dfrac{a^2b^2}{16}\\ 1-\nu,\ \frac{s-\nu+1}{2},\ \frac{s-\nu+2}{2}&\end{matrix}\right)$
		$[\operatorname{Re}a,\ \operatorname{Re}b>0]$
13	$e^{-a/x^2}K_\nu(bx)$	$\dfrac{2^{s-2}}{b^s}\Gamma\left(\dfrac{s-\nu}{2}\right)\Gamma\left(\dfrac{s+\nu}{2}\right){}_0F_2\left(\begin{matrix}&-\dfrac{ab^2}{4}\\ \frac{2-s-\nu}{2},\ \frac{2-s+\nu}{2}&\end{matrix}\right)$
		$+\dfrac{a^{(s+\nu)/2}b^\nu}{2^{\nu+2}}\Gamma(-\nu)\Gamma\left(-\dfrac{s+\nu}{2}\right){}_0F_2\left(\begin{matrix}&-\dfrac{ab^2}{4}\\ 1+\nu,\ \frac{s+\nu+2}{2}&\end{matrix}\right)$
		$+\dfrac{a^{(s-\nu)/2}}{2^{2-\nu}b^\nu}\Gamma(\nu)\Gamma\left(\dfrac{\nu-s}{2}\right){}_0F_2\left(\begin{matrix}&-\dfrac{ab^2}{4}\\ 1-\nu,\ \frac{s-\nu+2}{2}&\end{matrix}\right)$
		$[\operatorname{Re}a,\ \operatorname{Re}b>0]$
14	$e^{\mp bx-a/x}K_\nu(bx)$	$\dfrac{a^{s+\nu}b^\nu}{2^{\nu+1}}\Gamma(-\nu)\Gamma(-\nu-s)\,{}_1F_2\left(\begin{matrix}\frac{1+2\nu}{2};\ \pm 2ab\\ 1+2\nu,\ s+\nu+1\end{matrix}\right)$
		$+\dfrac{a^{s-\nu}b^{-\nu}}{2^{1-\nu}}\Gamma(\nu)\Gamma(\nu-s)\,{}_1F_2\left(\begin{matrix}\frac{1-2\nu}{2};\ \pm 2ab\\ 1-2\nu,\ s-\nu+1\end{matrix}\right)$
		$+\dfrac{\sqrt{\pi}}{(2b)^s}\left(\dfrac{\cos(\nu\pi)}{\cos(s\pi)}\right)^{(1\mp 1)/2}\Gamma\left[\begin{matrix}s-\nu,\ s+\nu\\ \frac{2s+1}{2}\end{matrix}\right]$
		$\times\,{}_1F_2\left(\begin{matrix}\frac{1-2s}{2};\ \pm 2ab\\ 1-s-\nu,\ 1-s+\nu\end{matrix}\right)\qquad[\operatorname{Re}a,\ \operatorname{Re}b>0]$
15	$(a^2-x^2)_+^{-1}$ $\times\exp\left(-b\,\dfrac{a^2+x^2}{a^2-x^2}\right)$ $\times K_\nu\left(\dfrac{cx}{a^2-x^2}\right)$	$\dfrac{a^{s-1}}{2c}\Gamma\left(\dfrac{s-\nu}{2}\right)\Gamma\left(\dfrac{s+\nu}{2}\right)W_{(1-s)/2,\nu/2}\left(\dfrac{2ab+\sqrt{4a^2b^2-c^2}}{2a}\right)$ $\times W_{(1-s)/2,\nu/2}\left(\dfrac{2ab-\sqrt{4a^2b^2-c^2}}{2a}\right)$ $[a,\ b,\ \operatorname{Re}c>0;\ \operatorname{Re}s>|\operatorname{Re}\nu|]$
16	$(x^2-a^2)_+^{-1}$ $\times\exp\left(-b\,\dfrac{a^2+x^2}{a^2-x^2}\right)$ $\times K_\nu\left(\dfrac{cx}{x^2-a^2}\right)$	$\dfrac{a^{s-1}}{2c}\Gamma\left(\dfrac{2-\nu-s}{2}\right)\Gamma\left(\dfrac{2+\nu-s}{2}\right)$ $\times W_{(s-1)/2,\nu/2}\left(\dfrac{2ab+\sqrt{4a^2b^2-c^2}}{2a}\right)$ $\times W_{(s-1)/2,\nu/2}\left(\dfrac{2ab-\sqrt{4a^2b^2-c^2}}{2a}\right)$ $[a,\ b,\ \operatorname{Re}c>0;\ \operatorname{Re}s<|\operatorname{Re}\nu|+2]$

3.14.4. $K_\nu(ax)$ and hyperbolic or trigonometric functions

Notation: $\delta = \left\{ \begin{matrix} 1 \\ 0 \end{matrix} \right\}$.

1	$\left\{ \begin{matrix} \sinh(ax) \\ \sin(ax) \end{matrix} \right\} K_\nu(bx)$	$\dfrac{2^{s-1}a}{b^{s+1}} \Gamma\left(\dfrac{s-\nu+1}{2}\right) \Gamma\left(\dfrac{s+\nu+1}{2}\right) {}_2F_1\left(\begin{matrix} \frac{s-\nu+1}{2}, \frac{s+\nu+1}{2} \\ \frac{3}{2}; \pm\frac{a^2}{b^2} \end{matrix} \right)$
		$[\operatorname{Re} b > |\operatorname{Re} a|;\ \operatorname{Re} s > |\operatorname{Re}\nu| - 1]$
2	$\left\{ \begin{matrix} \cosh(ax) \\ \cos(ax) \end{matrix} \right\} K_\nu(bx)$	$\dfrac{2^{s-2}}{b^{s}} \Gamma\left(\dfrac{s-\nu}{2}\right) \Gamma\left(\dfrac{s+\nu}{2}\right) {}_2F_1\left(\begin{matrix} \frac{s-\nu}{2}, \frac{s+\nu}{2} \\ \frac{1}{2}; \pm\frac{a^2}{b^2} \end{matrix} \right)$
		$[\operatorname{Re} b > |\operatorname{Re} a|;\ \operatorname{Re} s > |\operatorname{Re}\nu|]$
3	$[1 - \cos(ax)] K_\nu(bx)$	$\dfrac{2^{s-1}a^2}{b^{s+2}} \Gamma\left(\dfrac{s-\nu+2}{2}\right) \Gamma\left(\dfrac{s+\nu+2}{2}\right) {}_3F_2\left(\begin{matrix} 1, \frac{s-\nu+2}{2}, \frac{s+\nu+2}{2} \\ \frac{3}{2}, 2; -\frac{a^2}{b^2} \end{matrix} \right)$
		$[\operatorname{Re} b > |\operatorname{Im} a|;\ \operatorname{Re} s > |\operatorname{Re}\nu| - 2]$
4	$\left\{ \begin{matrix} \sinh(ax+b) \\ \cosh(ax+b) \end{matrix} \right\} K_\nu(ax)$	$\dfrac{2^{-s-1}a^{-s}e^b}{\sqrt{\pi}} \cos(\nu\pi) \Gamma\left(\dfrac{1-2s}{2}\right) \Gamma(s-\nu)\Gamma(s+\nu)$
		$\mp 2^{-s-1}\sqrt{\pi}\,a^{-s}e^{-b}\Gamma\left[\begin{matrix} s-\nu, s+\nu \\ \frac{2s+1}{2} \end{matrix} \right]$
		$[\operatorname{Re} a \geq 0;\ |\operatorname{Re}\nu| < \operatorname{Re} s < 1/2]$
5	$\left\{ \begin{matrix} \sin(ax^2) \\ \cos(ax^2) \end{matrix} \right\} K_\nu(bx)$	$\dfrac{2^{-\nu-2}b^\nu}{a^{(s+\nu)/2}} \left\{ \begin{matrix} \sin[(s+\nu)\pi/4] \\ \cos[(s+\nu)\pi/4] \end{matrix} \right\} \Gamma(-\nu)\Gamma\left(\dfrac{s+\nu}{2}\right)$
		$\times {}_2F_3\left(\begin{matrix} \frac{s+\nu}{4}, \frac{s+\nu+2}{4}; -\frac{b^4}{64a^2} \\ \frac{1}{2}, \frac{\nu+1}{2}, \frac{\nu+2}{2} \end{matrix} \right) + \dfrac{2^{\nu-2}b^{-\nu}}{a^{(s-\nu)/2}}$
		$\times \left\{ \begin{matrix} \sin[(s-\nu)\pi/4] \\ \cos[(s-\nu)\pi/4] \end{matrix} \right\} \Gamma(\nu)\Gamma\left(\dfrac{s-\nu}{2}\right)$
		$\times {}_2F_3\left(\begin{matrix} \frac{s-\nu}{4}, \frac{s-\nu+2}{4}; -\frac{b^4}{64a^2} \\ \frac{1}{2}, \frac{1-\nu}{2}, \frac{2-\nu}{2} \end{matrix} \right) \mp \dfrac{2^{-\nu-4}b^{\nu+2}}{a^{(s+\nu+2)/2}}$
		$\times \left\{ \begin{matrix} \cos[(s+\nu)\pi/4] \\ \sin[(s+\nu)\pi/4] \end{matrix} \right\} \Gamma(-\nu-1)\Gamma\left(\dfrac{s+\nu+2}{2}\right)$
		$\times {}_2F_3\left(\begin{matrix} \frac{s+\nu+2}{4}, \frac{s+\nu+4}{4}; -\frac{b^4}{64a^2} \\ \frac{3}{2}, \frac{\nu+2}{2}, \frac{\nu+3}{2} \end{matrix} \right) \mp \dfrac{2^{\nu-4}b^{2-\nu}}{a^{(s-\nu+2)/2}}$
		$\times \left\{ \begin{matrix} \cos[(s-\nu)\pi/4] \\ \sin[(s-\nu)\pi/4] \end{matrix} \right\} \Gamma(\nu-1)\Gamma\left(\dfrac{s-\nu+2}{2}\right)$
		$\times {}_2F_3\left(\begin{matrix} \frac{s-\nu+2}{4}, \frac{s-\nu+4}{4}; -\frac{b^4}{64a^2} \\ \frac{3}{2}, \frac{2-\nu}{2}, \frac{3-\nu}{2} \end{matrix} \right)$
		$[a,\ \operatorname{Re} b > 0;\ \operatorname{Re} s > |\operatorname{Re}\nu| - 1 \mp 1]$

No.	$f(x)$	$F(s)$
6	$\left\{\begin{matrix}\sin(a\sqrt{x})\\\cos(a\sqrt{x})\end{matrix}\right\} K_\nu(bx)$	$\dfrac{2^{s+\delta/2-2}\,a^\delta}{b^{s+\delta/2}}\,\Gamma\left(\dfrac{2s-2\nu+\delta}{4}\right)\Gamma\left(\dfrac{2s+2\nu+\delta}{4}\right)$

$$\times\ {}_2F_3\left(\begin{matrix}\frac{2s-2\nu+\delta}{4},\ \frac{2s+2\nu+\delta}{4}\\\frac{1}{2},\ \frac{3}{4},\ \frac{4\delta+1}{4};\ \frac{a^4}{64b}\end{matrix}\right) - \dfrac{2^{s+\delta/2-2}\,a^{\delta+2}}{3^\delta b^{s+\delta/2+1}}$$

$$\times\ \Gamma\left(\dfrac{2s-2\nu+\delta+2}{2}\right)\Gamma\left(\dfrac{2s+2\nu+\delta+2}{2}\right)$$

$$\times\ {}_2F_3\left(\begin{matrix}\frac{2s-2\nu+\delta+2}{4},\ \frac{2s+2\nu+\delta+2}{4}\\\frac{5}{4},\ \frac{3}{2},\ \frac{4\delta+3}{4};\ \frac{a^4}{64b}\end{matrix}\right)$$

$$[a,\ \mathrm{Re}\,b>0;\ |\mathrm{Re}\,\nu|<\mathrm{Re}\,s+\delta/2]$$

No.	$f(x)$	$F(s)$
7	$\left\{\begin{matrix}\sin(a/x)\\\cos(a/x)\end{matrix}\right\} K_\nu(bx)$	$2^{s-\delta-2}\,a^\delta b^{\delta-s}\,\Gamma\left(\dfrac{s-\nu-\delta}{2}\right)\Gamma\left(\dfrac{s+\nu-\delta}{2}\right)$

$$\times\ {}_0F_3\left(\begin{matrix}-\frac{a^2b^2}{16}\\\frac{2\delta+1}{2},\ \frac{2-s-\nu+\delta}{2},\ \frac{2-s+\nu+\delta}{2}\end{matrix}\right)$$

$$\mp\ \dfrac{a^{s+\nu}\,b^\nu}{2^{\nu+1}}\left\{\begin{matrix}\sin[(s+\nu)\pi/2]\\\cos[(s+\nu)\pi/2]\end{matrix}\right\}$$

$$\times\ \Gamma(-\nu)\,\Gamma(-s-\nu)\,{}_0F_3\left(\begin{matrix}-\frac{a^2b^2}{16}\\1+\nu,\ \frac{s+\nu+1}{2},\ \frac{s+\nu+2}{2}\end{matrix}\right)$$

$$\mp\ \dfrac{2^{\nu-1}\,a^{s-\nu}}{b^\nu}\left\{\begin{matrix}\sin[(s-\nu)\pi/2]\\\cos[(s-\nu)\pi/2]\end{matrix}\right\}$$

$$\times\ \Gamma(\nu)\,\Gamma(-s+\nu)\,{}_0F_3\left(\begin{matrix}-\frac{a^2b^2}{16}\\1-\nu,\ \frac{s-\nu+1}{2},\ \frac{s-\nu+2}{2}\end{matrix}\right)$$

$$[a,\ \mathrm{Re}\,b>0;\ |\mathrm{Re}\,\nu|<\mathrm{Re}\,s+1]$$

No.	$f(x)$	$F(s)$
8	$\left\{\begin{matrix}\sin(ax)\sinh(ax)\\\cos(ax)\cosh(ax)\end{matrix}\right\}$ $\times\ K_\nu(bx)$	$2^{s+2\delta-2}a^{2\delta}b^{-s-2\delta}\,\Gamma\left(\dfrac{s-\nu+2\delta}{2}\right)\Gamma\left(\dfrac{s+\nu+2\delta}{2}\right)$

$$\times\ {}_4F_3\left(\begin{matrix}\frac{s-\nu+2\delta}{4},\ \frac{s-\nu+2\delta+2}{4},\ \frac{s+\nu+2\delta}{4},\ \frac{s+\nu+2\delta+2}{4}\\\frac{2\delta+1}{4},\ \frac{2\delta+3}{4},\ \frac{2\delta+1}{2};\ -\frac{4a^4}{b^4}\end{matrix}\right)$$

$$[\mathrm{Re}\,b>|\mathrm{Re}\,a|+|\mathrm{Im}\,a|;\ \mathrm{Re}\,s>|\mathrm{Re}\,\nu|-2\delta]$$

No.	$f(x)$	$F(s)$
9	$\left\{\begin{matrix}\sin(ax)\cosh(ax)\\\cos(ax)\sinh(ax)\end{matrix}\right\}$ $\times\ K_\nu(bx)$	$\dfrac{2^{s-1}a}{b^{s+1}}\,\Gamma\left(\dfrac{s-\nu+1}{2}\right)\Gamma\left(\dfrac{s+\nu+1}{2}\right)$

$$\times\ {}_4F_3\left(\begin{matrix}\frac{s-\nu+1}{4},\ \frac{s-\nu+3}{4},\ \frac{s+\nu+1}{4},\ \frac{s+\nu+3}{4}\\\frac{1}{2},\ \frac{3}{4},\ \frac{5}{4};\ -\frac{4a^4}{b^4}\end{matrix}\right)$$

$$\pm\ \dfrac{2^{s+1}a^3}{3b^{s+3}}\,\Gamma\left(\dfrac{s-\nu+3}{2}\right)\Gamma\left(\dfrac{s+\nu+3}{2}\right)$$

$$\times\ {}_4F_3\left(\begin{matrix}\frac{s-\nu+3}{4},\ \frac{s-\nu+5}{4},\ \frac{s+\nu+3}{4},\ \frac{s+\nu+5}{4}\\\frac{3}{4},\ \frac{5}{4},\ \frac{7}{2};\ -\frac{4a^4}{b^4}\end{matrix}\right)$$

$$[\mathrm{Re}\,b>|\mathrm{Re}\,a|+|\mathrm{Im}\,a|;\ \mathrm{Re}\,s>|\mathrm{Re}\,\nu|-1]$$

No.	$f(x)$	$F(s)$
10	$e^{-bx}\left\{\begin{matrix}\sin(ax)\\\cos(ax)\end{matrix}\right\}K_\nu(bx)$	$\dfrac{\sqrt{\pi}\,a^\delta}{(2b)^{s+\delta}}\Gamma\left[\begin{matrix}s-\nu+\delta,\,s+\nu+\delta\\\frac{2s+2\delta+1}{2}\end{matrix}\right]$

$$\times\,_4F_3\left(\begin{matrix}\frac{s-\nu+1}{2},\,\frac{s+\nu+1}{2},\,\frac{s-\nu+2\delta}{2},\,\frac{s+\nu+2\delta}{2}\\\frac{2\delta+1}{2},\,\frac{2s+3}{4},\,\frac{2s+4\delta+1}{4};\,-\frac{a^2}{4b^2}\end{matrix}\right)$$

$$[a,\ \mathrm{Re}\,b>0;\ \mathrm{Re}\,s>|\mathrm{Re}\,\nu|-\delta]$$

No.	$f(x)$	$F(s)$
11	$e^{-bx}\left\{\begin{matrix}\sin(a\sqrt{x})\\\cos(a\sqrt{x})\end{matrix}\right\}K_\nu(bx)$	$\dfrac{\sqrt{\pi}\,a^\delta}{(2b)^{s+\delta/2}}\Gamma\left[\begin{matrix}\frac{2s-2\nu+\delta}{2},\,\frac{2s+2\nu+\delta}{2}\\\frac{2s+\delta+1}{2}\end{matrix}\right]\,_2F_2\left(\begin{matrix}\frac{2s-2\nu+\delta}{2},\,\frac{2s+2\nu+\delta}{2}\\\frac{2\delta+1}{2},\,\frac{2s+\delta+1}{2};\,-\frac{a^2}{8b}\end{matrix}\right)$

$$[a,\ \mathrm{Re}\,b>0;\ \mathrm{Re}\,s>|\mathrm{Re}\,\nu|-\delta/2]$$

No.	$f(x)$	$F(s)$
12	$e^{-bx}\left\{\begin{matrix}\sin(ax)\cosh(ax)\\\cos(ax)\sinh(ax)\end{matrix}\right\}$ $\times\,K_\nu(bx)$	$\dfrac{\sqrt{\pi}\,a}{(2b)^{s+1}}\Gamma\left[\begin{matrix}s-\nu+1,\,s+\nu+1\\\frac{2s+3}{2}\end{matrix}\right]$

$$\times\,_8F_7\left(\begin{matrix}\Delta(4,\,s-\nu+1),\,\Delta(4,\,s+\nu+1)\\\frac{1}{2},\,\frac{3}{4},\,\frac{5}{4},\,\Delta\left(4,\,\frac{2s+3}{2}\right);\,-\frac{a^4}{4b^4}\end{matrix}\right)$$

$$\pm\,\frac{\sqrt{\pi}\,a^3}{3\,(2b)^{s+3}}\Gamma\left[\begin{matrix}s-\nu+3,\,s+\nu+3\\\frac{2s+7}{2}\end{matrix}\right]$$

$$\times\,_8F_7\left(\begin{matrix}\Delta(4,\,s-\nu+3),\,\Delta(4,\,s+\nu+3)\\\frac{5}{4},\,\frac{3}{2},\,\frac{7}{4},\,\Delta\left(4,\,\frac{2s+7}{2}\right);\,-\frac{a^4}{4b^4}\end{matrix}\right)$$

$$[\mathrm{Re}\,b>(\mathrm{Re}\,a+\mathrm{Im}\,a)/2;\ \mathrm{Re}\,s>|\mathrm{Re}\,\mu|+|\mathrm{Re}\,\nu|]$$

No.	$f(x)$	$F(s)$
13	$e^{-bx}K_\nu(bx)$ $\times\left\{\begin{matrix}\sin(a\sqrt{x})\sinh(a\sqrt{x})\\\cos(a\sqrt{x})\cosh(a\sqrt{x})\end{matrix}\right\}$	$\dfrac{\sqrt{\pi}\,a^{2\delta}}{(2b)^{s+\delta}}\Gamma\left[\begin{matrix}s-\nu+\delta,\,s+\nu+\delta\\\frac{2s+2\delta+1}{2}\end{matrix}\right]$

$$\times\,_4F_5\left(\begin{matrix}\frac{s-\nu+\delta}{2},\,\frac{s-\nu+\delta+1}{2},\,\frac{s+\nu+\delta}{2},\,\frac{s+\nu+\delta+1}{2};\,-\frac{a^4}{64b^2}\\\frac{2\delta+1}{4},\,\frac{2\delta+3}{4},\,\frac{2\delta+1}{2},\,\frac{2s+2\delta+1}{4},\,\frac{2s+2\delta+3}{4}\end{matrix}\right)$$

$$[\mathrm{Re}\,b>0;\ \mathrm{Re}\,s>|\mathrm{Re}\,\nu|-\delta]$$

No.	$f(x)$	$F(s)$
14	$e^{-bx}K_\nu(bx)$ $\times\left\{\begin{matrix}\sin(a\sqrt{x})\cosh(a\sqrt{x})\\\cos(a\sqrt{x})\sinh(a\sqrt{x})\end{matrix}\right\}$	$\dfrac{\sqrt{\pi}\,a}{(2b)^{s+1/2}}\Gamma\left[\begin{matrix}\frac{2s-2\nu+1}{2},\,\frac{2s+2\nu+1}{2}\\s+1\end{matrix}\right]$

$$\times\,_4F_5\left(\begin{matrix}\frac{2s-2\nu+1}{4},\,\frac{2s-2\nu+3}{4},\,\frac{2s+2\nu+1}{4},\,\frac{2s+2\nu+3}{4}\\\frac{1}{2},\,\frac{3}{4},\,\frac{5}{4},\,\frac{s+1}{2},\,\frac{s+2}{2};\,-\frac{a^4}{64b^2}\end{matrix}\right)$$

$$\pm\,\frac{\sqrt{\pi}\,a^3}{3\,(2b)^{s+3/2}}\Gamma\left[\begin{matrix}\frac{2s-2\nu+3}{2},\,\frac{2s+2\nu+3}{2}\\s+2\end{matrix}\right]$$

$$\times\,_4F_5\left(\begin{matrix}\frac{2s-2\nu+3}{4},\,\frac{2s-2\nu+5}{4},\,\frac{2s+2\nu+3}{2},\,\frac{2s+2\nu+5}{4}\\\frac{5}{4},\,\frac{3}{2},\,\frac{7}{4},\,\frac{s+2}{2},\,\frac{s+3}{2};\,-\frac{a^4}{64b^2}\end{matrix}\right)$$

$$[\mathrm{Re}\,b>0;\ \mathrm{Re}\,s>|\mathrm{Re}\,\nu|-1/2]$$

3.14.5. $K_\nu(ax)$ and the logarithmic function

1	$\ln x \, K_\nu(ax)$	$\dfrac{2^{s-3}}{a^s} \Gamma\left(\dfrac{s-\nu}{2}\right) \Gamma\left(\dfrac{s+\nu}{2}\right) \left[\psi\left(\dfrac{s-\nu}{2}\right) + \psi\left(\dfrac{s+\nu}{2}\right) - 2\ln\dfrac{a}{2}\right]$ $\qquad [\operatorname{Re}a > 0; \ |\operatorname{Re}s| > \operatorname{Re}\nu]$
2	$\ln^n x \, K_\nu(ax)$	$\dfrac{\partial^n}{\partial s^n}\left[\dfrac{2^{s-2}}{a^s} \Gamma\left(\dfrac{s-\nu}{2}\right) \Gamma\left(\dfrac{s+\nu}{2}\right)\right] \qquad [\operatorname{Re}a > 0; \ |\operatorname{Re}s| > \operatorname{Re}\nu]$

3.14.6. $K_\nu(ax)$ and $\operatorname{Ei}(bx^r)$

1	$\operatorname{Ei}(-ax) K_\nu(bx)$	$\dfrac{2^{\nu-1} a^{\nu-s} b^{-\nu}}{\nu - s} \Gamma(\nu)\Gamma(s-\nu) \, {}_3F_2\!\left(\begin{matrix} \frac{s-\nu}{2}, \frac{s-\nu}{2}, \frac{s-\nu+1}{2} \\ 1-\nu, \frac{s-\nu+2}{2}; \frac{b^2}{a^2} \end{matrix}\right)$ $- \dfrac{2^{-\nu-1} a^{-s-\nu} b^\nu}{s+\nu} \Gamma(-\nu)\Gamma(s+\nu) \, {}_3F_2\!\left(\begin{matrix} \frac{s+\nu}{2}, \frac{s+\nu}{2}, \frac{s+\nu+1}{2} \\ 1+\nu, \frac{s+\nu+2}{2}; \frac{b^2}{a^2} \end{matrix}\right)$ $\qquad [\operatorname{Re}a, \ \operatorname{Re}b > 0; \ \operatorname{Re}s > |\operatorname{Re}\nu|]$
2	$\operatorname{Ei}(-ax^2) K_\nu(bx)$	$\dfrac{2^{\nu-1} a^{(\nu-s)/2}}{b^\nu (\nu-s)} \Gamma(\nu)\,\Gamma\left(\dfrac{s-\nu}{2}\right) {}_2F_2\!\left(\begin{matrix} \frac{s-\nu}{2}, \frac{s-\nu}{2}; \frac{b^2}{4a} \\ 1-\nu, \frac{s-\nu+2}{2} \end{matrix}\right)$ $- \dfrac{2^{-\nu-1} b^\nu}{a^{(s+\nu)/2}(s+\nu)} \Gamma(-\nu)\,\Gamma\left(\dfrac{s+\nu}{2}\right) {}_2F_2\!\left(\begin{matrix} \frac{s+\nu}{2}, \frac{s+\nu}{2}; \frac{b^2}{4a} \\ 1+\nu, \frac{s+\nu+2}{2} \end{matrix}\right)$ $\qquad [\operatorname{Re}a, \ \operatorname{Re}b > 0; \ \operatorname{Re}s > |\operatorname{Re}\nu|]$
3	$e^{\pm ax} \operatorname{Ei}(\mp ax) K_\nu(bx)$	$\dfrac{2^{\nu-1}\pi}{a^{s-\nu} b^\nu} \Gamma(\nu)\,\Gamma(s-\nu) \left\{\begin{matrix} \csc[(\nu-s)\pi] \\ \cot[(\nu-s)\pi] \end{matrix}\right\} {}_2F_1\!\left(\begin{matrix} \frac{s-\nu}{2}, \frac{s-\nu+1}{2} \\ 1-\nu; \frac{b^2}{a^2} \end{matrix}\right)$ $- \dfrac{\pi b^\nu}{2^{\nu+1} a^{s+\nu}} \Gamma(-\nu)\,\Gamma(s+\nu) \left\{\begin{matrix} \csc[(s+\nu)\pi] \\ \cot[(s+\nu)\pi] \end{matrix}\right\} {}_2F_1\!\left(\begin{matrix} \frac{s+\nu}{2}, \frac{s+\nu+1}{2} \\ \nu+1; \frac{b^2}{a^2} \end{matrix}\right)$ $\mp \dfrac{2^{s-3}}{a b^{s-1}} \Gamma\left(\dfrac{s-\nu-1}{2}\right)\Gamma\left(\dfrac{s+\nu-1}{2}\right) {}_3F_2\!\left(\begin{matrix} \frac{1}{2}, 1, 1; \frac{b^2}{a^2} \\ \frac{3-s-\nu}{2}, \frac{3-s+\nu}{2} \end{matrix}\right)$ $+ \dfrac{2^{s-4}}{a^2 b^{s-2}} \Gamma\left(\dfrac{s-\nu-2}{2}\right)\Gamma\left(\dfrac{s+\nu-2}{2}\right) {}_3F_2\!\left(\begin{matrix} 1, 1, \frac{3}{2}; \frac{b^2}{a^2} \\ \frac{4-s-\nu}{2}, \frac{4-s+\nu}{2} \end{matrix}\right)$ $\qquad [\operatorname{Re}a, \ \operatorname{Re}b > 0; \ \operatorname{Re}s > |\operatorname{Re}\nu|]$
4	$e^{\pm bx} \operatorname{Ei}(-ax) K_\nu(bx)$	$\dfrac{2^{\nu-1} a^{\nu-s}}{b^\nu (\nu-s)} \Gamma(\nu)\,\Gamma(s-\nu) \, {}_3F_2\!\left(\begin{matrix} \frac{1-2\nu}{2}, s-\nu, s-\nu \\ 1-2\nu, s-\nu+1; \pm\frac{2b}{a} \end{matrix}\right)$ $- \dfrac{2^{-\nu-1} b^\nu}{a^{s+\nu}(s+\nu)} \Gamma(-\nu)\,\Gamma(s+\nu) \, {}_3F_2\!\left(\begin{matrix} \frac{1+2\nu}{2}, s+\nu, s+\nu \\ 1+2\nu, s+\nu+1; \pm\frac{2b}{a} \end{matrix}\right)$ $\qquad [\operatorname{Re}a, \ \operatorname{Re}b > 0; \ \operatorname{Re}s > |\operatorname{Re}\nu|]$

No.	$f(x)$	$F(s)$
5	$e^{(a\mp b)x}\,\mathrm{Ei}\,(-ax)\,K_\nu\,(bx)$	$-\dfrac{2^{\nu-1}\pi}{a^{s-\nu}b^\nu}\,\Gamma\,(\nu)\,\Gamma\,(s-\nu)\,\csc\,[(s-\nu)\,\pi]\; {}_2F_1\left(\begin{matrix}\frac{1-2\nu}{2},\,s-\nu\\1-2\nu;\,\pm\frac{2b}{a}\end{matrix}\right)$
		$-\dfrac{\pi b^\nu}{2^{\nu+1}a^{s+\nu}}\,\Gamma\,(-\nu)\,\Gamma\,(s+\nu)\,\csc\,[(s+\nu)\,\pi]$
		$\times\,{}_2F_1\left(\begin{matrix}\frac{1+2\nu}{2},\,s+\nu\\1+2\nu;\,\pm\frac{2b}{a}\end{matrix}\right)\mp\dfrac{\sqrt{\pi}}{a\,(2b)^{s-1}}\left[\dfrac{\cos\,(\nu\pi)}{\cos\,(s\pi)}\right]^{(1\mp1)/2}$
		$\times\,\Gamma\left[\begin{matrix}s-\nu-1,\,s+\nu-1\\ \frac{2s-1}{2}\end{matrix}\right]\,{}_3F_2\left(\begin{matrix}1,\,1,\,\frac{3-2s}{2};\,\pm\frac{2b}{a}\\2-s-\nu,\,2-s+\nu\end{matrix}\right)$
		$\left[\mathrm{Re}\,a>0;\;\mathrm{Re}\,s>|\mathrm{Re}\,\nu|;\,\left\{\begin{matrix}\mathrm{Re}\,b>0\\ \mathrm{Re}\,s<3/2;\,|\arg b|<\pi\end{matrix}\right\}\right]$
6	$e^{\pm(a+b)x}\,\mathrm{Ei}\,(ax)\,K_\nu\,(bx)$	$-\dfrac{2^{\nu-1}\pi}{a^{s-\nu}b^\nu}\,\Gamma\,(\nu)\,\Gamma\,(s-\nu)\,\cot\,[(s-\nu)\,\pi]\; {}_2F_1\left(\begin{matrix}\frac{1-2\nu}{2},\,s-\nu\\1-2\nu;\,\mp\frac{2b}{a}\end{matrix}\right)$
		$-\dfrac{\pi b^\nu}{2^{\nu+1}a^{s+\nu}}\,\Gamma\,(-\nu)\,\Gamma\,(s+\nu)\,\cot\,[(s+\nu)\,\pi]$
		$\times\,{}_2F_1\left(\begin{matrix}\frac{1+2\nu}{2},\,s+\nu\\1+2\nu;\,\mp\frac{2b}{a}\end{matrix}\right)\pm\dfrac{\sqrt{\pi}}{a\,(2b)^{s-1}}\left[\dfrac{\cos\,(\nu\pi)}{\cos\,(s\pi)}\right]^{(1\mp1)/2}$
		$\times\,\Gamma\left[\begin{matrix}s-\nu-1,\,s+\nu-1\\ \frac{2s-1}{2}\end{matrix}\right]\,{}_3F_2\left(\begin{matrix}1,\,1,\,\frac{3-2s}{2};\,\mp\frac{2b}{a}\\2-s-\nu,\,2-s+\nu\end{matrix}\right)$
		$\left[\mathrm{Re}\,a>0;\;\mathrm{Re}\,s>|\mathrm{Re}\,\nu|;\,\left\{\begin{matrix}\mathrm{Re}\,b>0\\ \mathrm{Re}\,s<3/2;\,|\arg b|<\pi\end{matrix}\right\}\right]$

3.14.7. $K_\nu\,(ax)$ **and** $\mathrm{Si}\,(bx),\,\mathrm{si}\,(bx),\,\mathrm{ci}\,(bx)$

No.	$f(x)$	$F(s)$
1	$\mathrm{Si}\,(ax)\,K_\nu\,(bx)$	$\dfrac{2^{s-1}a}{b^{s+1}}\,\Gamma\left(\dfrac{s-\nu+1}{2}\right)\Gamma\left(\dfrac{s+\nu+1}{2}\right)\,{}_3F_2\left(\begin{matrix}\frac{1}{2},\,\frac{s-\nu+1}{2},\,\frac{s+\nu+1}{2}\\ \frac{3}{2},\,\frac{3}{2};\,-\frac{a^2}{b^2}\end{matrix}\right)$
		$[\mathrm{Re}\,s>|\mathrm{Re}\,\nu|-1;\;\mathrm{Re}\,b>|\mathrm{Im}\,a|]$
2	$\left\{\begin{matrix}\mathrm{si}\,(ax)\\ \mathrm{ci}\,(ax)\end{matrix}\right\}K_\nu\,(bx)$	$-\dfrac{2^{\nu-1}a^{\nu-s}}{b^s\,(s-\nu)}\,\Gamma\,(\nu)\,\Gamma\,(s-\nu)\left\{\begin{matrix}\sin\,[(s-\nu)\,\pi/2]\\ \cos\,[(s-\nu)\,\pi/2]\end{matrix}\right\}$
		$\times\,{}_3F_2\left(\begin{matrix}\frac{s-\nu}{2},\,\frac{s-\nu}{2},\,\frac{s-\nu+1}{2}\\1-\nu,\,\frac{s-\nu+2}{2};\,-\frac{b^2}{a^2}\end{matrix}\right)-\dfrac{2^{-\nu-1}b^\nu}{a^{s+\nu}\,(s+\nu)}$
		$\times\left\{\begin{matrix}\sin\,[(s+\nu)\,\pi/2]\\ \cos\,[(s+\nu)\,\pi/2]\end{matrix}\right\}{}_3F_2\left(\begin{matrix}\frac{s+\nu}{2},\,\frac{s+\nu}{2},\,\frac{s+\nu+1}{2}\\1+\nu,\,\frac{s+\nu+2}{2};\,-\frac{b^2}{a^2}\end{matrix}\right)$
		$[a,\,\mathrm{Re}\,b>0;\;\mathrm{Re}\,s>|\mathrm{Re}\,\nu|]$

No.	$f(x)$	$F(s)$
3	$e^{-bx}\,\mathrm{si}\,(ax)\,K_\nu\,(bx)$	$\dfrac{\sqrt{\pi}\,a}{(2b)^{s+1}}\,\Gamma\!\left[\begin{matrix}s-\nu+1,\,s+\nu+1\\ \frac{2s+3}{2}\end{matrix}\right]$

$$\times\,{}_5F_4\!\left(\begin{matrix}\frac{1}{2},\,\frac{s-\nu+1}{2},\,\frac{s-\nu+2}{2},\,\frac{s+\nu+1}{2},\,\frac{s+\nu+2}{2}\\ \frac{3}{2},\,\frac{3}{2},\,\frac{s+3}{2},\,\frac{s+5}{2};\,-\frac{a^2}{4b^2}\end{matrix}\right)$$

$$-\frac{\pi^{3/2}}{2^{s+1}b^s}\,\Gamma\!\left[\begin{matrix}s-\nu,\,s+\nu\\ \frac{2s+1}{2}\end{matrix}\right]$$

$$[a,\,\mathrm{Re}\,b>0;\,\mathrm{Re}\,s>|\mathrm{Re}\,\nu|]$$

No.	$f(x)$	$F(s)$
4	$e^{-bx}\,\mathrm{ci}\,(ax)\,K_\nu\,(bx)$	$\dfrac{\pi^{3/2}}{2^{s+1}b^s}\,\Gamma\!\left[\begin{matrix}s-\nu,\,s+\nu\\ \frac{2s+1}{2}\end{matrix}\right]\left[\psi\,(s-\nu)+\psi\,(s+\nu)\right.$

$$\left.-\psi\left(s+\frac{1}{2}\right)-\ln\frac{2b}{a}+\mathbf{C}\right]$$

$$-\frac{\sqrt{\pi}\,a^2}{2^{s+4}b^{s+2}}\,\Gamma\!\left[\begin{matrix}s-\nu+2,\,s+\nu+2\\ \frac{2s+5}{2}\end{matrix}\right]$$

$$\times\,{}_6F_5\!\left(\begin{matrix}1,\,1,\,\frac{s-\nu+2}{2},\,\frac{s-\nu+3}{2},\,\frac{s+\nu+2}{2},\,\frac{s+\nu+3}{2}\\ \frac{3}{2},\,2,\,2,\,\frac{2s+5}{4},\,\frac{2s+7}{4};\,-\frac{a^2}{4b^2}\end{matrix}\right)$$

$$[a,\,\mathrm{Re}\,b>0;\,\mathrm{Re}\,s>|\mathrm{Re}\,\nu|]$$

No.	$f(x)$	$F(s)$
5	$e^{bx}\,\mathrm{si}\,(ax)\,K_\nu\,(bx)$	$\dfrac{a\cos(\pi\nu)}{2^{s+1}\sqrt{\pi}\,b^{s+1}}\,\Gamma\!\left[-s-\frac{1}{2},\,s-\nu+1,\,s+\nu+1\right]$

$$\times\,{}_5F_4\!\left(\begin{matrix}\frac{1}{2},\,\frac{s-\nu+1}{2},\,\frac{s-\nu+2}{2},\,\frac{s+\nu+1}{2},\,\frac{s+\nu+2}{2}\\ \frac{3}{2},\,\frac{3}{2},\,\frac{2s+3}{4},\,\frac{2s+5}{4};\,-\frac{a^2}{4b^2}\end{matrix}\right)$$

$$+\frac{\sqrt{2\pi}}{(2s-1)\,a^{s-1/2}\sqrt{b}}\,\cos\frac{(2s+1)\,\pi}{4}\,\Gamma\left(s-\frac{1}{2}\right)$$

$$\times\,{}_5F_4\!\left(\begin{matrix}\frac{1-2s}{4},\,\frac{1-2\nu}{4},\,\frac{3-2\nu}{4},\,\frac{2\nu+1}{4},\,\frac{2\nu+3}{4}\\ \frac{1}{2},\,\frac{3-2s}{4},\,\frac{5-2s}{4},\,\frac{5-2s}{4};\,-\frac{a^2}{4b^2}\end{matrix}\right)$$

$$+\frac{\sqrt{2\pi}\,(4\nu^2-1)}{8\,(2s-3)\,a^{s-3/2}b^{3/2}}\,\sin\frac{(2s+1)\,\pi}{4}\,\Gamma\left(s-\frac{3}{2}\right)$$

$$\times\,{}_5F_4\!\left(\begin{matrix}\frac{3-2s}{4},\,\frac{3-2\nu}{4},\,\frac{5-2\nu}{4},\,\frac{2\nu+3}{4},\,\frac{2\nu+5}{4}\\ \frac{3}{2},\,\frac{5-2s}{4},\,\frac{7-2s}{4},\,\frac{7-2s}{4};\,-\frac{a^2}{4b^2}\end{matrix}\right)$$

$$-\frac{\sqrt{\pi}\cos(\pi\nu)}{2^{s+1}b^s}\,\Gamma\!\left[\frac{1}{2}-s,\,s-\nu,\,s+\nu\right]$$

$$[a,\,\mathrm{Re}\,b>0;\,|\mathrm{Re}\,\nu|<\mathrm{Re}\,s<3/2]$$

No.	$f(x)$	$F(s)$
6	$e^{bx}\,\mathrm{ci}\,(ax)\,K_\nu\,(bx)$	$-\dfrac{a^2\cos(\pi\nu)}{2^{s+4}\sqrt{\pi}\,b^{s+2}}\,\Gamma\!\left[-s-\frac{3}{2},\,s-\nu+2,\,s+\nu+2\right]$

$$\times\,{}_6F_5\!\left(\begin{matrix}1,\,1,\,\frac{s-\nu+2}{2},\,\frac{s-\nu+3}{2},\,\frac{s+\nu+2}{2},\,\frac{s+\nu+3}{2}\\ \frac{3}{2},\,2,\,2,\,\frac{2s+5}{4},\,\frac{2s+7}{4};\,-\frac{a^2}{4b^2}\end{matrix}\right)-$$

No.	$f(x)$	$F(s)$
		$-\dfrac{\sqrt{2\pi}}{(2s-1)a^{s-1/2}\sqrt{b}}\sin\dfrac{(2s+1)\pi}{4}\Gamma\left(s-\dfrac{1}{2}\right)$ $\times {}_5F_4\left(\begin{array}{c}\frac{1-2s}{4},\ \frac{1-2\nu}{4},\ \frac{3-2\nu}{4},\ \frac{2\nu+1}{4},\ \frac{2\nu+3}{4}\\ \frac{1}{2},\ \frac{3-2s}{4},\ \frac{5-2s}{4},\ \frac{5-2s}{4};\ -\frac{a^2}{4b^2}\end{array}\right)$ $+\dfrac{\sqrt{\pi}\,(4\nu^2-1)}{2^{5/2}(2s-3)a^{s-3/2}b^{3/2}}\cos\dfrac{(2s+1)\pi}{4}\Gamma\left(s-\dfrac{3}{2}\right)\times$ $\times {}_5F_4\left(\begin{array}{c}\frac{3-2s}{4},\ \frac{3-2\nu}{4},\ \frac{5-2\nu}{4},\ \frac{2\nu+3}{4},\ \frac{2\nu+5}{4}\\ \frac{3}{2},\ \frac{5-2s}{4},\ \frac{7-2s}{4},\ \frac{7-2s}{4};\ -\frac{a^2}{4b^2}\end{array}\right)$ $+\dfrac{\cos(\pi\nu)}{\sqrt{\pi}\,(2b)^s}\Gamma\left[\dfrac{1}{2}-s,\ s-\nu,\ s+\nu\right]$ $\times\left[\psi(s-\nu)+\psi(s+\nu)-\psi\left(\dfrac{1}{2}-s\right)+\ln\dfrac{a}{2b}+\mathbf{C}\right]$ $[a,\ \operatorname{Re}b>0;\ |\operatorname{Re}\nu|<\operatorname{Re}s<3/2]$

3.14.8. $K_\nu(ax)$ **and** $\operatorname{erf}(bx^r)$, $\operatorname{erfi}(bx^r)$, $\operatorname{erfc}(bx^r)$

No.	$f(x)$	$F(s)$
1	$\left\{\begin{array}{c}\operatorname{erf}(ax)\\ \operatorname{erfc}(ax)\end{array}\right\}K_\nu(bx)$	$\pm\dfrac{2^{\nu-1}a^{\nu-s}}{\sqrt{\pi}\,b^\nu(\nu-s)}\Gamma(\nu)\,\Gamma\left(\dfrac{s-\nu+1}{2}\right)$ $\times {}_2F_2\left(\begin{array}{c}\frac{s-\nu}{2},\ \frac{s-\nu+1}{2};\ \frac{b^2}{4a^2}\\ 1-\nu,\ \frac{s-\nu+2}{2}\end{array}\right)\mp\dfrac{2^{-\nu-1}b^\nu}{\sqrt{\pi}\,a^{s+\nu}(\nu+s)}\Gamma(-\nu)$ $\times\Gamma\left(\dfrac{s+\nu+1}{2}\right){}_2F_2\left(\begin{array}{c}\frac{s+\nu}{2},\ \frac{s+\nu+1}{2};\ \frac{b^2}{4a^2}\\ 1+\nu,\ \frac{s+\nu+2}{2}\end{array}\right)$ $+\dfrac{(1\pm1)2^{s-3}}{b^s}\Gamma\left(\dfrac{s-\nu}{2}\right)\Gamma\left(\dfrac{s+\nu}{2}\right)$ $[\operatorname{Re}b>0;\ \operatorname{Re}s>|\operatorname{Re}\nu|-(1\pm1)/2;\ |\arg a|<\pi/4]$
2	$\left\{\begin{array}{c}\operatorname{erf}(a\sqrt{x})\\ \operatorname{erfc}(a\sqrt{x})\end{array}\right\}K_\nu(bx)$	$\pm\dfrac{2^{s-1/2}a}{\sqrt{\pi}\,b^{s+1/2}}\Gamma\left(\dfrac{2s-2\nu+1}{4}\right)$ $\times\Gamma\left(\dfrac{2s+2\nu+1}{4}\right){}_3F_2\left(\begin{array}{c}\frac{1}{4},\ \frac{2s-2\nu+1}{4},\ \frac{2s+2\nu+1}{4}\\ \frac{1}{2},\ \frac{5}{4};\ \frac{a^4}{b^2}\end{array}\right)$ $\mp\dfrac{2^{s+1/2}a^3}{3\sqrt{\pi}\,b^{s+3/2}}\Gamma\left(\dfrac{2s-2\nu+3}{4}\right)$ $\times\Gamma\left(\dfrac{2s+2\nu+3}{4}\right){}_3F_2\left(\begin{array}{c}\frac{3}{4},\ \frac{2s-2\nu+3}{4},\ \frac{2s+2\nu+3}{4}\\ \frac{3}{2},\ \frac{7}{4};\ \frac{a^4}{b^2}\end{array}\right)$ $+\dfrac{(1\mp1)2^{s-3}}{b^s}\Gamma\left(\dfrac{s-\nu}{2}\right)\Gamma\left(\dfrac{s+\nu}{2}\right)$ $[\operatorname{Re}b>0;\ \operatorname{Re}s>|\operatorname{Re}\nu|-(1\pm1)/4;\ |\arg a|<\pi/4]$

No.	$f(x)$	$F(s)$
3	$e^{\pm bx}\,\mathrm{erf}\,(a\sqrt{x})\,K_\nu(bx)$	$\mp\dfrac{2a}{(2b)^{s+1/2}}\left(\dfrac{\cos(\nu\pi)}{\sin(s\pi)}\right)^{(1\pm1)/2}\Gamma\left[\begin{array}{c}\frac{2s-2\nu+1}{2},\ \frac{2s+2\nu+1}{2}\\ s+1\end{array}\right]$ $\times\ _3F_2\!\left(\begin{array}{c}\frac12,\ \frac{2s-2\nu+1}{2},\ \frac{2s+2\nu+1}{2}\\ \frac32,\ s+1;\ \pm\frac{a^2}{2b}\end{array}\right)$ $+\dfrac{(1\pm1)\,a^{1-2s}\,\Gamma(s)}{\sqrt{2b}\,(1-2s)}\ _3F_2\!\left(\begin{array}{c}\frac{1-2\nu}{2},\ \frac{1+2\nu}{2},\ \frac{1-2s}{2}\\ 1-s,\ \frac{3-2s}{2};\ \frac{a^2}{2b}\end{array}\right)$ $\left[\mathrm{Re}\,b>0;\ |\arg a|<\dfrac{\pi}{4};\ \left\{\begin{array}{c}|\mathrm{Re}\,\nu|-1/2<\mathrm{Re}\,s<1/2\\ |\mathrm{Re}\,\nu|-1/2<\mathrm{Re}\,s\end{array}\right\}\right]$
4	$e^{\pm bx}\,\mathrm{erfc}\,(a\sqrt{x})\,K_\nu(bx)$	$\pm\dfrac{2a}{(2b)^{s+1/2}}\left(\dfrac{\cos(\nu\pi)}{\sin(s\pi)}\right)^{(1\pm1)/2}\Gamma\left[\begin{array}{c}\frac{2s-2\nu+1}{2},\ \frac{2s+2\nu+1}{2}\\ s+1\end{array}\right]$ $\times\ _3F_2\!\left(\begin{array}{c}\frac12,\ \frac{2s-2\nu+1}{2},\ \frac{2s+2\nu+1}{2}\\ \frac32,\ s+1;\ \pm\frac{a^2}{2b}\end{array}\right)$ $-\dfrac{(1\pm1)\,a^{1-2s}\,\Gamma(s)}{\sqrt{2b}\,(1-2s)}\ _3F_2\!\left(\begin{array}{c}\frac{1-2\nu}{2},\ \frac{1+2\nu}{2},\ \frac{1-2s}{2}\\ 1-s,\ \frac{3-2s}{2};\ \frac{a^2}{2b}\end{array}\right)$ $+\dfrac{\sqrt{\pi}}{(2b)^s}\Gamma\left[\begin{array}{c}s-\nu,\ s+\nu\\ \frac{2s+1}{2}\end{array}\right]\left(\dfrac{\cos(\nu\pi)}{\cos(s\pi)}\right)^{(1\pm1)/2}$ $[\mathrm{Re}\,b>0;\ \mathrm{Re}\,s>|\mathrm{Re}\,\nu|;\ |\arg a|<\pi/4]$
5	$e^{a^2x}\,\mathrm{erf}\,(a\sqrt{x})\,K_\nu(bx)$	$\dfrac{2^{s-1/2}ab^{-s-1/2}}{\sqrt{\pi}}\Gamma\left(\dfrac{2s-2\nu+1}{4}\right)\Gamma\left(\dfrac{2s+2\nu+1}{4}\right)$ $\times\ _3F_2\!\left(\begin{array}{c}1,\ \frac{2s-2\nu+1}{4},\ \frac{2s+2\nu+1}{4}\\ \frac34,\ \frac54;\ \frac{a^4}{b^2}\end{array}\right)$ $+\dfrac{2^{s+3/2}a^3b^{-s-3/2}}{3\sqrt{\pi}}\Gamma\left(\dfrac{2s-2\nu+3}{4}\right)$ $\times\ \Gamma\left(\dfrac{2s+2\nu+3}{4}\right)\ _3F_2\!\left(\begin{array}{c}1,\ \frac{2s-2\nu+3}{4},\ \frac{2s+2\nu+3}{4}\\ \frac54,\ \frac74;\ \frac{a^4}{b^2}\end{array}\right)$ $[\mathrm{Re}\,b,\ \mathrm{Re}\,(b-a^2)>0;\ \mathrm{Re}\,s>|\mathrm{Re}\,\nu|-1/2]$
6	$e^{-(a^2+b)x}\,\mathrm{erfi}\,(a\sqrt{x})$ $\times\ K_\nu(bx)$	$\dfrac{a}{2^{s-1/2}b^{s+1/2}}\Gamma\left[\begin{array}{c}\frac{2s-2\nu+1}{2},\ \frac{2s+2\nu+1}{2}\\ s+1\end{array}\right]\ _3F_2\!\left(\begin{array}{c}1,\ \frac{2s-2\nu+1}{2},\ \frac{2s+2\nu+1}{2}\\ \frac32,\ s+1;\ -\frac{a^2}{2b}\end{array}\right)$ $[\mathrm{Re}\,b>0;\ \mathrm{Re}\,s>|\mathrm{Re}\,\nu|-1/2;\ |\arg a|<\pi/4]$
7	$e^{(a^2-b)x}\,\mathrm{erf}\,(a\sqrt{x})$ $\times\ K_\nu(bx)$	$\dfrac{ab^{-s-1/2}}{2^{s-1/2}}\Gamma\left[\begin{array}{c}\frac{2s-2\nu+1}{2},\ \frac{2s+2\nu+1}{2}\\ s+1\end{array}\right]\ _3F_2\!\left(\begin{array}{c}1,\ \frac{2s-2\nu+1}{2},\ \frac{2s+2\nu+1}{2}\\ \frac32,\ s+1;\ \frac{a^2}{2b}\end{array}\right)$ $[\mathrm{Re}\,b>0;\ \mathrm{Re}\,s>|\mathrm{Re}\,\nu|-1/2;\ |\arg a|<3\pi/4]$

No.	$f(x)$	$F(s)$
8	$e^{(a^2-b)x}\operatorname{erfc}(a\sqrt{x})$	$-\dfrac{a}{2^{s-1/2}b^{s+1/2}}\,\Gamma\!\left[\begin{array}{c}\frac{2s-2\nu+1}{2},\,\frac{2s+2\nu+1}{2}\\ s+1\end{array}\right]\,{}_3F_2\!\left(\begin{array}{c}1,\,\frac{2s-2\nu+1}{2},\,\frac{2s+2\nu+1}{2}\\ \frac{3}{2},\,s+1;\,\frac{a^2}{2b}\end{array}\right)$
	$\times K_\nu(bx)$	$+\dfrac{\sqrt{\pi}}{(2b)^s}\,\Gamma\!\left[\begin{array}{c}s-\nu,\,s+\nu\\ \frac{2s+1}{2}\end{array}\right]\,{}_2F_1\!\left(\begin{array}{c}s-\nu,\,s+\nu\\ \frac{2s+1}{2};\,\frac{a^2}{2b}\end{array}\right)$
		$[\operatorname{Re}b>0;\ \operatorname{Re}s>\lvert\operatorname{Re}\nu\rvert;\ \lvert\arg a\rvert<3\pi/4]$
9	$\left\{\begin{array}{c}\operatorname{erfi}(a\sqrt{x})\\ \operatorname{erfc}(a\sqrt{x})\end{array}\right\}$	$\dfrac{(2b)^{1/2-s}}{a}\,\dfrac{\cos(\nu\pi)}{\sin(s\pi)}\,\Gamma\!\left[\begin{array}{c}\frac{2s-2\nu-1}{2},\,\frac{2s+2\nu-1}{2}\\ s\end{array}\right]$
	$\times e^{(\mp a^2+b)x}K_\nu(bx)$	$\times\,{}_3F_2\!\left(\begin{array}{c}\frac{1}{2},\,1,\,1-s;\,\frac{2b}{a^2}\\ \frac{3-2s-2\nu}{2},\,\frac{3-2s+2\nu}{2}\end{array}\right)+\dfrac{\pi b^\nu}{2^{\nu+(1\pm1)/2}a^{2s+2\nu}}$
		$\times\,\Gamma\!\left[\begin{array}{c}-\nu\\ 1-s-\nu\end{array}\right]\left\{\begin{array}{c}\sec[(s+\nu)\pi]\\ \csc[2(s+\nu)\pi]\end{array}\right\}{}_2F_1\!\left(\begin{array}{c}\frac{1+2\nu}{2},\,s+\nu\\ 1+2\nu;\,\frac{2b}{a^2}\end{array}\right)$
		$+\dfrac{2^{\nu-(1\pm1)/2}}{a^{2s-2\nu}b^\nu}\,\Gamma\!\left[\begin{array}{c}\nu\\ 1-s+\nu\end{array}\right]\left\{\begin{array}{c}\sec[(s-\nu)\pi]\\ \csc[2(s-\nu)\pi]\end{array}\right\}{}_2F_1\!\left(\begin{array}{c}\frac{1-2\nu}{2},\,s-\nu\\ 1-2\nu;\,\frac{2b}{a^2}\end{array}\right)$
		$\left[\begin{array}{c}\operatorname{Re}b>0;\ \lvert\operatorname{Re}\nu\rvert-(1\pm1)/4<\operatorname{Re}s<1;\\ \lvert\arg a\rvert<(2\mp1)\pi/4\end{array}\right]$
10	$\operatorname{erf}(a\sqrt{x})\operatorname{erfi}(a\sqrt{x})$	$\dfrac{2^{s+1}a^2 b^{-s-1}}{\pi}\,\Gamma\!\left(\dfrac{s-\nu+1}{2}\right)\Gamma\!\left(\dfrac{s+\nu+1}{2}\right)$
	$\times K_\nu(bx)$	$\times\,{}_4F_3\!\left(\begin{array}{c}\frac{1}{2},\,1,\,\frac{s-\nu+1}{2},\,\frac{s+\nu+1}{2}\\ \frac{3}{4},\,\frac{5}{4},\,\frac{3}{2};\,\frac{a^4}{b^2}\end{array}\right)$
		$[\operatorname{Re}b,\ \operatorname{Re}(b-2a^2)>0;\ \operatorname{Re}s>\lvert\operatorname{Re}\nu\rvert-1]$

3.14.9. $K_\nu(ax)$ and $S(bx)$, $C(bx)$

Notation: $\delta=\left\{\begin{array}{c}1\\ 0\end{array}\right\}$.

	$f(x)$	$F(s)$
1	$\left\{\begin{array}{c}S(ax)\\ C(ax)\end{array}\right\}K_\nu(bx)$	$\dfrac{2^{s+\delta-1}\,a^{\delta+1/2}}{3^\delta\sqrt{\pi}\,b^{s+\delta+1/2}}\,\Gamma\!\left(\dfrac{2s-2\nu+2\delta+1}{4}\right)\Gamma\!\left(\dfrac{2s+2\nu+2\delta+1}{4}\right)$
		$\times\,{}_3F_2\!\left(\begin{array}{c}\frac{2\delta+1}{4},\,\frac{2s-2\nu+2\delta+1}{4},\,\frac{2s+2\nu+2\delta+1}{4}\\ \frac{2\delta+1}{2},\,\frac{2\delta+5}{4};\,-\frac{a^2}{b^2}\end{array}\right)$
		$[a,\ \operatorname{Re}b>0;\ \operatorname{Re}s>\lvert\operatorname{Re}\nu\rvert-(2\pm1)/2]$
2	$e^{-bx}\left\{\begin{array}{c}S(ax)\\ C(ax)\end{array}\right\}K_\nu(bx)$	$\dfrac{\sqrt{2}\,a^{\delta+1/2}}{(2\delta+1)(2b)^{s+\delta+1/2}}\,\Gamma\!\left[\begin{array}{c}\frac{2s-2\nu+2\delta+1}{2},\,\frac{2s+2\nu+2\delta+1}{2}\\ s+\delta+1\end{array}\right]$
		$\times\,{}_5F_4\!\left(\begin{array}{c}\frac{2\delta+1}{4},\,\frac{2s-2\nu+3}{4},\,\frac{2s+2\nu+3}{4},\,\frac{2s-2\nu+4\delta+1}{4},\,\frac{2s+2\nu+4\delta+1}{4}\\ \frac{2\delta+1}{2},\,\frac{2\delta+5}{4},\,\frac{s+2\delta+1}{2},\,\frac{s+2}{2};\,-\frac{a^2}{4b^2}\end{array}\right)$
		$[a,\ \operatorname{Re}b>0;\ \operatorname{Re}s>\lvert\operatorname{Re}\nu\rvert-(2\pm1)/2]$

No.	$f(x)$	$F(s)$
3	$e^{bx}\begin{Bmatrix} S(ax) \\ C(ax) \end{Bmatrix} K_\nu(bx)$	$\pm \dfrac{2^{-s-\delta}\,a^{\delta+1/2}b^{-s-\delta-1/2}}{\pi^\delta\,(2\delta+1)}\,\dfrac{\cos(\nu\pi)}{\sin(s\pi)}\,\Gamma\begin{bmatrix} \frac{2s-2\nu+2\delta+1}{2},\ \frac{2s+2\nu+2\delta+1}{2} \\ s+\delta+1 \end{bmatrix}$

$$\times\,{}_5F_4\left(\begin{matrix} \frac{2\delta+1}{4},\ \frac{2s-2\nu+3}{4},\ \frac{2s+2\nu+3}{4},\ \frac{2s-2\nu+4\delta+1}{4},\ \frac{2s+2\nu+4\delta+1}{4} \\ \frac{2\delta+1}{2},\ \frac{2\delta+5}{4},\ \frac{s+2\delta+1}{2},\ \frac{s+2}{2};\ -\frac{a^2}{4b^2} \end{matrix}\right)$$

$$+\,\frac{a^{1/2-s}}{\sqrt{b}\,(1-2s)}\begin{Bmatrix} \sin(s\pi/2) \\ \cos(s\pi/2) \end{Bmatrix}\Gamma(s)$$

$$\times\,{}_5F_4\left(\begin{matrix} \frac{1-2\nu}{4},\ \frac{3-2\nu}{4},\ \frac{2\nu+1}{4},\ \frac{2\nu+3}{4},\ \frac{1-2s}{4} \\ \frac{1}{2},\ \frac{1-s}{2},\ \frac{2-s}{2},\ \frac{5-2s}{4};\ -\frac{a^2}{4b^2} \end{matrix}\right)$$

$$\pm\,\frac{(4\nu^2-1)\,a^{3/2-s}}{8b^{3/2}\,(2s-3)}\begin{Bmatrix} \cos(s\pi/2) \\ \sin(s\pi/2) \end{Bmatrix}\Gamma(s-1)$$

$$\times\,{}_5F_4\left(\begin{matrix} \frac{3-2\nu}{4},\ \frac{5-2\nu}{4},\ \frac{2\nu+3}{4},\ \frac{2\nu+5}{4},\ \frac{3-2s}{4} \\ \frac{3}{2},\ \frac{2-s}{2},\ \frac{3-s}{2},\ \frac{7-2s}{4};\ -\frac{a^2}{4b^2} \end{matrix}\right)$$

$$[a>0;\ |\mathrm{Re}\,\nu|-(2\pm1)/2 < \mathrm{Re}\,s < 1/2;\ |\arg b| < \pi]$$

3.14.10. $K_\nu(ax)$ and $\Gamma(\mu, bx)$, $\gamma(\mu, bx)$

No.	$f(x)$	$F(s)$
1	$\begin{Bmatrix} \gamma(\mu, ax) \\ \Gamma(\mu, ax) \end{Bmatrix} K_\nu(bx)$	$\pm \dfrac{2^{s+\mu-2}a^\mu}{\mu\,b^{s+\mu}}\,\Gamma\left(\dfrac{s+\mu-\nu}{2}\right)\Gamma\left(\dfrac{s+\mu+\nu}{2}\right)$

$$\times\,{}_3F_2\left(\begin{matrix} \frac{\mu}{2},\ \frac{s+\mu-\nu}{2},\ \frac{s+\mu+\nu}{2} \\ \frac{1}{2},\ \frac{\mu+2}{2};\ \frac{a^2}{b^2} \end{matrix}\right)\mp\frac{2^{s+\mu-1}a^{\mu+1}}{(\mu+1)\,b^{s+\mu+1}}$$

$$\times\,\Gamma\left(\frac{s+\mu-\nu+1}{2}\right)\Gamma\left(\frac{s+\mu+\nu+1}{2}\right)$$

$$\times\,{}_3F_2\left(\begin{matrix} \frac{\mu+1}{2},\ \frac{s+\mu-\nu+1}{2},\ \frac{s+\mu+\nu+1}{2} \\ \frac{3}{2},\ \frac{\mu+3}{2};\ \frac{a^2}{b^2} \end{matrix}\right)+2^{s-3}\frac{1\pm1}{b^s}\,\Gamma\left[\mu,\ \frac{s+\nu}{2},\ \frac{s-\nu}{2}\right]$$

$$\left[\mathrm{Re}\,a,\ \mathrm{Re}\,b>0;\ \mathrm{Re}\,(s+\mu)>|\mathrm{Re}\,\nu|;\ \begin{Bmatrix} \mathrm{Re}\,\mu>0 \\ \mathrm{Re}\,s>|\mathrm{Re}\,\nu| \end{Bmatrix}\right]$$

No.	$f(x)$	$F(s)$
2	$\begin{Bmatrix} \gamma(\mu, ax^2) \\ \Gamma(\mu, ax^2) \end{Bmatrix} K_\nu(bx)$	$\pm \dfrac{2^{\nu-1}a^{(\nu-s)/2}}{(\nu-s)\,b^\nu}\,\Gamma(\nu)\,\Gamma\left(\dfrac{s+2\mu-\nu}{2}\right)$

$$\times\,{}_2F_2\left(\begin{matrix} \frac{s-\nu}{2},\ \frac{s+2\mu-\nu}{2};\ \frac{b^2}{4a} \\ 1-\nu,\ \frac{s-\nu+2}{2} \end{matrix}\right)\mp\frac{2^{-\nu-1}b^\nu}{(\nu+s)\,a^{(s+\nu)/2}}\,\Gamma(-\nu)$$

$$\times\,\Gamma\left(\frac{s+2\mu+\nu}{2}\right){}_2F_2\left(\begin{matrix} \frac{s+\nu}{2},\ \frac{s+2\mu+\nu}{2};\ \frac{b^2}{4a} \\ 1+\nu,\ \frac{s+\nu+2}{2} \end{matrix}\right)$$

$$+2^{s-3}\frac{1\pm1}{b^s}\,\Gamma\left[\mu,\ \frac{s+\nu}{2},\ \frac{s-\nu}{2}\right]$$

$$\left[\mathrm{Re}\,a,\ \mathrm{Re}\,b>0;\ \mathrm{Re}\,(s+2\mu)>|\mathrm{Re}\,\nu|;\ \begin{Bmatrix} \mathrm{Re}\,\mu>0 \\ \mathrm{Re}\,s>|\mathrm{Re}\,\nu| \end{Bmatrix}\right]$$

No.	$f(x)$	$F(s)$
3	$e^{-bx}\left\{\begin{matrix}\gamma(\mu,ax)\\\Gamma(\mu,ax)\end{matrix}\right\}$ $\times K_\nu(bx)$	$\pm\dfrac{\sqrt{\pi}\,a^\mu}{\mu\,(2b)^{s+\mu}}\,\Gamma\left[\begin{matrix}s+\mu-\nu,\,s+\mu+\nu\\\frac{2s+2\mu+1}{2}\end{matrix}\right]$ $\times\,{}_3F_2\left(\begin{matrix}\mu,\,s+\mu-\nu,\,s+\mu+\nu\\\mu+1,\,\frac{2s+2\mu+1}{2};\,-\frac{a}{2b}\end{matrix}\right)$ $+\dfrac{(1\mp1)\sqrt{\pi}}{2^{s+1}b^s}\,\Gamma\left[\begin{matrix}\mu,\,s+\nu,\,s-\nu\\\frac{2s+1}{2}\end{matrix}\right]$ $\left[\operatorname{Re}a,\ \operatorname{Re}b>0;\ \operatorname{Re}(s+\mu)>|\operatorname{Re}\nu|;\ \left\{\begin{matrix}\operatorname{Re}\mu>0\\\operatorname{Re}s>|\operatorname{Re}\nu|\end{matrix}\right\}\right]$
4	$e^{bx}\gamma(\mu,ax)K_\nu(bx)$	$\dfrac{a^\mu\cos(\nu\pi)}{\sqrt{\pi}\,\mu\,(2b)^{s+\mu}}\,\Gamma\left[-\dfrac{2s+2\mu-1}{2},\,s+\mu-\nu,\,s+\mu+\nu\right]$ $\times\,{}_3F_2\left(\begin{matrix}\mu,\,s+\mu-\nu,\,s+\mu+\nu\\\mu+1,\,\frac{2s+2\mu+1}{2};\,\frac{a}{2b}\end{matrix}\right)+\dfrac{a^{1/2-s}}{1-2s}\sqrt{\dfrac{2\pi}{b}}$ $\times\,\Gamma\left(\dfrac{2s+2\mu-1}{2}\right)\,{}_3F_2\left(\begin{matrix}\frac{1+2\nu}{2},\,\frac{1-2\nu}{2},\,\frac{1-2s}{2}\\\frac{3-2s}{2},\,\frac{3-2s-2\mu}{2};\,\frac{a}{2b}\end{matrix}\right)$ $[\operatorname{Re}a,\ \operatorname{Re}b,\ \operatorname{Re}\mu>0;\ \operatorname{Re}(s+\mu)>|\operatorname{Re}\nu|;\ \operatorname{Re}s<1/2]$
5	$e^{bx}\,\Gamma(\mu,ax)K_\nu(bx)$	$\dfrac{2^{\nu-1}a^{\nu-s}}{(s-\nu)\,b^\nu}\,\Gamma(\nu)\,\Gamma(s+\mu-\nu)\,{}_3F_2\left(\begin{matrix}\frac{1-2\nu}{2},\,s-\nu,\,s+\mu-\nu\\1-2\nu,\,s-\nu+1;\,\frac{2b}{a}\end{matrix}\right)$ $+\dfrac{2^{-\nu-1}a^{-\nu-s}}{(s+\nu)\,b^{-\nu}}\,\Gamma(-\nu)\,\Gamma(s+\mu+\nu)$ $\times\,{}_3F_2\left(\begin{matrix}\frac{1+2\nu}{2},\,s+\nu,\,s+\mu+\nu\\1+2\nu,\,s+\nu+1;\,\frac{2b}{a}\end{matrix}\right)$ $[\operatorname{Re}a,\ \operatorname{Re}b>0;\ \operatorname{Re}(s+\mu)>|\operatorname{Re}\nu|,\ \operatorname{Re}s>|\operatorname{Re}\nu|]$
6	$e^{(a\pm b)x}\,\Gamma(\mu,ax)K_\nu(bx)$	$\dfrac{\sqrt{\pi}}{(2b)^s}\,[\cos(\nu\pi)\sec(s\pi)]^{(1\pm1)/2}\,\Gamma\left[\begin{matrix}\mu,\,s-\nu,\,s+\nu\\\frac{2s+1}{2}\end{matrix}\right]$ $\times\,{}_2F_1\left(\begin{matrix}s-\nu,\,s+\nu\\\frac{2s+1}{2};\,\mp\frac{a}{2b}\end{matrix}\right)-\dfrac{\sqrt{\pi}\,a^\mu}{\mu\,(2b)^{s+\mu}}$ $\times\,[\cos(\nu\pi)\sec[(s+\mu)\pi]]^{(1\pm1)/2}\,\Gamma\left[\begin{matrix}s+\mu-\nu,\,s+\mu+\nu\\\frac{2s+2\mu+1}{2}\end{matrix}\right]$ $\times\,{}_3F_2\left(\begin{matrix}1,\,s+\mu-\nu,\,s+\mu+\nu\\\mu+1,\,\frac{2s+2\mu+1}{2};\,\mp\frac{a}{2b}\end{matrix}\right)$ $-\dfrac{(1\pm1)\pi^{3/2}a^{1/2-s}}{2\sqrt{2b}\cos[(s+\mu)\pi]}\,\Gamma\left[\begin{matrix}\frac{2s-1}{2}\\1-\mu\end{matrix}\right]\,{}_2F_1\left(\begin{matrix}\frac{1-2\nu}{2},\,\frac{1+2\nu}{2}\\\frac{3-2s}{2};\,-\frac{a}{2b}\end{matrix}\right)$ $\left[\begin{matrix}\operatorname{Re}a>0;\ \operatorname{Re}s,\ \operatorname{Re}(s+\mu)>|\operatorname{Re}\nu|;\\\left\{\begin{matrix}\operatorname{Re}(s+\mu)<3/2;\ |\arg b|<\pi\\\operatorname{Re}b>0\end{matrix}\right\}\end{matrix}\right]$

No.	$f(x)$	$F(s)$
7	$e^{a/x \pm bx}\Gamma\left(\mu, \dfrac{a}{x}\right)K_\nu(bx)$	$\dfrac{\sqrt{\pi}}{(2b)^s}\left[\cos(\nu\pi)\sec(s\pi)\right]^{(1\pm1)/2}\Gamma\left[\begin{matrix}\mu,\, s-\nu,\, s+\nu\\ \frac{2s+1}{2}\end{matrix}\right]$

$$\times\, _1F_2\left(\begin{matrix}\frac{1-2s}{2};\,\pm2ab\\ 1-s-\nu,\, 1-s+\nu\end{matrix}\right) - \frac{\sqrt{\pi}\,a^\mu}{\mu\,(2b)^{s-\mu}}$$

$$\times\left[\cos(\nu\pi)\sec\left[(s-\mu)\pi\right]\right]^{(1\pm1)/2}\Gamma\left[\begin{matrix}s-\mu-\nu,\, s-\mu+\nu\\ \frac{2s-2\mu+1}{2}\end{matrix}\right]$$

$$\times\, _2F_3\left(\begin{matrix}1,\,\frac{1-2s+2\mu}{2};\,\pm2ab\\ \mu+1,\, 1-s+\mu-\nu,\, 1-s+\mu+\nu\end{matrix}\right)$$

$$+\frac{\pi\,a^{s+\nu}b^\nu}{2^{\nu+1}\sin\left[(\mu-\nu-s)\pi\right]}\Gamma\left[\begin{matrix}-\nu,\,-s-\nu\\ 1-\mu\end{matrix}\right]\, _1F_2\left(\begin{matrix}\frac{1+2\nu}{2};\,\pm2ab\\ 1+2\nu,\, s+\nu+1\end{matrix}\right)$$

$$+\frac{2^{\nu-1}\pi\,a^{s-\nu}b^{-\nu}}{\sin\left[(\mu+\nu-s)\pi\right]}\Gamma\left[\begin{matrix}\nu,\,\nu-s\\ 1-\mu\end{matrix}\right]\, _1F_2\left(\begin{matrix}\frac{1-2\nu}{2};\,\pm2ab\\ 1-2\nu,\, s-\nu+1\end{matrix}\right)$$

$$\left[\begin{matrix}\operatorname{Re}a>0;\ \operatorname{Re}(s-\mu)>|\operatorname{Re}\nu|-1;\\ \left\{\begin{matrix}|\arg b|<\pi;\ \operatorname{Re}s,\ \operatorname{Re}(s-\mu)<1/2\\ \operatorname{Re}b>0\end{matrix}\right\}\end{matrix}\right]$$

3.14.11. $K_\nu(ax)$ and $D_\mu(b\sqrt{x})$

Notation: $\delta = \left\{\begin{matrix}1\\0\end{matrix}\right\}$.

No.	$f(x)$	$F(s)$
1	$e^{(\pm a^2/4-b)x}$ $\times D_\mu(a\sqrt{x})K_\nu(bx)$	$\dfrac{2^{(\mu-2s)/2}\pi}{b^s}\Gamma\left[\begin{matrix}s-\nu,\, s+\nu\\ \frac{1-\mu}{2},\,\frac{2s+1}{2}\end{matrix}\right]\, _3F_2\left(\begin{matrix}\frac{1\mp\mu-\delta}{2},\, s-\nu,\, s+\nu\\ \frac{1}{2},\,\frac{2s+1}{2};\,\pm\frac{a^2}{4b}\end{matrix}\right)$

$$-\frac{2^{(\mu-2s)/2}\pi a}{b^{s+1/2}}\Gamma\left[\begin{matrix}\frac{2s-2\nu+1}{2},\,\frac{2s+2\nu+1}{2}\\ -\frac{\mu}{2},\, s+1\end{matrix}\right]$$

$$\times\, _3F_2\left(\begin{matrix}\frac{2-\delta\mp\mu}{2},\,\frac{2s-2\nu+1}{2},\,\frac{2s+2\nu+1}{2}\\ \frac{3}{2},\, s+1;\,\pm\frac{a^2}{4b}\end{matrix}\right)$$

$$[\operatorname{Re}b>0;\ \operatorname{Re}s>|\operatorname{Re}\nu|;\ |\arg a|<(2\pm1)\pi/4]$$

| 2 | $e^{(-a^2/4+b)x}$ $\times D_\mu(a\sqrt{x})K_\nu(bx)$ | $\dfrac{2^{\mu/2+2\nu-s+1}\pi^{3/2}a^{2\nu-2s}}{2\sin(\nu\pi)b^\nu}\Gamma\left[\begin{matrix}2s-2\nu\\ 1-\nu,\,\frac{2s-\mu-2\nu+1}{2}\end{matrix}\right]$ |

$$\times\, _3F_2\left(\begin{matrix}\frac{1-2\nu}{2},\, s-\nu,\,\frac{2s-2\nu+1}{2}\\ 1-2\nu,\,\frac{2s-\mu-2\nu+1}{2};\,\frac{4b}{a^2}\end{matrix}\right)$$

$$-\frac{2^{\mu/2-2\nu-s+1}\pi^{3/2}a^{-2s-2\nu}}{2\sin(\nu\pi)b^{-\nu}}\Gamma\left[\begin{matrix}2s+2\nu\\ 1+\nu,\,\frac{2s-\mu+2\nu+1}{2}\end{matrix}\right]$$

$$\times\, _3F_2\left(\begin{matrix}\frac{1+2\nu}{2},\, s+\nu,\,\frac{2s+2\nu+1}{2}\\ 1+2\nu,\,\frac{2s-\mu+2\nu+1}{2};\,\frac{4b}{a^2}\end{matrix}\right)$$

$$[\operatorname{Re}b>0;\ \operatorname{Re}s>|\operatorname{Re}\nu|;\ |\arg a|<\pi/4]$$

3.14.12. $K_\nu(\varphi(x))$ **and** $J_\mu(\psi(x))$

Notation: $\delta = \left\{ \begin{matrix} 1 \\ 0 \end{matrix} \right\}$.

---

1 $J_\mu(ax)\,K_\nu(bx)$

$$\frac{2^{s-2}\,a^\mu}{b^{s+\mu}}\,\Gamma\left[\begin{matrix} \frac{s+\mu-\nu}{2},\ \frac{s+\mu+\nu}{2} \\ \mu+1 \end{matrix}\right]\,{}_2F_1\left(\begin{matrix} \frac{s+\mu-\nu}{2},\ \frac{s+\mu+\nu}{2} \\ \mu+1;\ -\frac{a^2}{b^2} \end{matrix}\right)$$

$$[\operatorname{Re} b > |\operatorname{Im} a|;\ \operatorname{Re}(s+\mu) > |\operatorname{Re}\nu|]$$

2 $J_\nu(ax)\,K_\nu(ax)$

$$\frac{2^{s-3}}{a^s}\,\Gamma\left[\begin{matrix} \frac{s}{2},\ \frac{s+2\nu}{4} \\ \frac{4-s+2\nu}{4} \end{matrix}\right] \qquad [\operatorname{Re} s,\ \operatorname{Re}(s+2\nu) > 0;\ |\arg a| < \pi/4]$$

3 $[J_\nu(ax) - J_{-\nu}(ax)]\,K_\nu(ax)$

$$-\frac{2^{3s/2-3}}{\sqrt{\pi}\,a^s}\,\sin\frac{\nu\pi}{2}\,\Gamma\left[\begin{matrix} s,\ \frac{s+2\nu}{4},\ \frac{s-2\nu}{4} \\ \frac{2-s}{4} \end{matrix}\right]$$

$$[\operatorname{Re} s > 2|\operatorname{Re}\nu|;\ |\arg a| < \pi/4]$$

4 $[J_\nu(ax) + J_{-\nu}(ax)]\,K_\nu(ax)$

$$\frac{2^{3s/2-3}}{\sqrt{\pi}\,a^s}\,\cos\frac{\nu\pi}{2}\,\Gamma\left[\begin{matrix} \frac{s+2}{4},\ \frac{s+2\nu}{4},\ \frac{s-2\nu}{4} \\ \frac{4-s}{4} \end{matrix}\right]$$

$$[\operatorname{Re} s > 2|\operatorname{Re}\nu|;\ |\arg a| < \pi/4]$$

5 $J_\mu(ax^2)\,K_\nu(bx)$

$$\frac{2^{(s-\nu)/2-3}b^\nu}{a^{(s+\nu)/2}}\,\Gamma\left[\begin{matrix} -\nu,\ \frac{s+2\mu+\nu}{4} \\ \frac{s+2\mu-\nu+4}{4} \end{matrix}\right]\,{}_2F_3\left(\begin{matrix} \frac{\nu-s-2\mu}{4},\ \frac{\nu+s+2\mu}{4} \\ \frac{1}{2},\ \frac{\nu+1}{2},\ \frac{\nu+2}{2};\ -\frac{b^4}{64a^2} \end{matrix}\right)$$

$$-\frac{2^{(s-\nu)/2-5}\,b^{\nu+2}}{a^{(s+\nu)/2+1}}\,\Gamma\left[\begin{matrix} -\nu-1,\ \frac{s+2\mu+\nu+2}{4} \\ \frac{s+2\mu-\nu+2}{4} \end{matrix}\right]$$

$$\times\,{}_2F_3\left(\begin{matrix} \frac{2-s-2\mu+\nu}{4},\ \frac{s+2\mu+\nu+2}{4} \\ \frac{3}{2},\ \frac{\nu+2}{2},\ \frac{\nu+3}{2};\ -\frac{b^4}{64a^2} \end{matrix}\right)$$

$$+\frac{2^{(s+\nu)/2-3}\,a^{(\nu-s)/2}}{b^\nu}\,\Gamma\left[\begin{matrix} \nu,\ \frac{s+2\mu-\nu}{4} \\ \frac{s+2\mu+\nu+4}{4} \end{matrix}\right]\,{}_2F_3\left(\begin{matrix} \frac{s+2\mu-\nu}{4},\ -\frac{s+2\mu+\nu}{4} \\ \frac{1}{2},\ \frac{1-\nu}{2},\ \frac{2-\nu}{2};\ -\frac{b^4}{64a^2} \end{matrix}\right)$$

$$-\frac{2^{(s+\nu)/2-5}\,a^{(\nu-s)/2-1}}{b^{\nu-2}}\,\Gamma\left[\begin{matrix} \nu+1,\ \frac{s+2\mu-\nu+2}{4} \\ \frac{s+2\mu+\nu+2}{4} \end{matrix}\right]$$

$$\times\,{}_2F_3\left(\begin{matrix} \frac{2-s-2\mu-\nu}{4},\ \frac{s+2\mu-\nu+2}{4} \\ \frac{3}{2},\ \frac{2-\nu}{2},\ \frac{3-\nu}{2};\ -\frac{b^4}{64a^2} \end{matrix}\right)$$

$$[a,\ \operatorname{Re} b > 0;\ \operatorname{Re} s > |\operatorname{Re}(\nu-2\mu)|]$$

6 $J_\mu(a\sqrt{x})\,K_\nu(bx)$

$$\frac{2^{s-\mu/2-2}\,a^\mu}{b^{s+\mu/2}}\,\Gamma\left[\begin{matrix} \frac{2s+\mu-2\nu}{4},\ \frac{2s+\mu+2\nu}{4} \\ \mu+1 \end{matrix}\right]\,{}_2F_3\left(\begin{matrix} \frac{2s+\mu-2\nu}{4},\ \frac{2s+\mu+2\nu}{4} \\ \frac{1}{2},\ \frac{\mu+1}{2},\ \frac{\mu+2}{2};\ \frac{a^4}{64b^2} \end{matrix}\right)$$

$$-\frac{2^{s-\mu/2-3}\,a^{\mu+2}}{b^{s+\mu/2+1}}\,\Gamma\left[\begin{matrix} \frac{2s+\mu-2\nu+2}{4},\ \frac{2s+\mu+2\nu+2}{2} \\ \mu+2 \end{matrix}\right]$$

$$\times\,{}_2F_3\left(\begin{matrix} \frac{2s+\mu-2\nu+2}{4},\ \frac{2s+\mu+2\nu+2}{4} \\ \frac{3}{2},\ \frac{\mu+2}{2},\ \frac{\mu+3}{2};\ \frac{a^4}{64b^2} \end{matrix}\right)$$

$$[a,\ \operatorname{Re} b > 0;\ \operatorname{Re} s > |\operatorname{Re}\nu| - \operatorname{Re}\mu/2]$$

No.	$f(x)$	$F(s)$
7	$J_\mu\left(\dfrac{a}{x}\right) K_\nu(bx)$	

$$\frac{a^{s+\nu}b^\nu}{2^{s+2\nu+2}}\Gamma\left[\begin{matrix}-\nu,\ \frac{\mu-\nu-s}{2}\\ \frac{s+\mu+\nu+2}{2}\end{matrix}\right]{}_0F_3\left(\begin{matrix}&-\frac{a^2b^2}{16}\\ 1+\nu,\ \frac{s-\mu+\nu+2}{2},\ \frac{s+\mu+\nu+2}{2}\end{matrix}\right)$$

$$+\frac{2^{2\nu-s-2}}{a^{\nu-s}b^\nu}\Gamma\left[\begin{matrix}\nu,\ \frac{\mu+\nu-s}{2}\\ \frac{s+\mu-\nu+2}{2}\end{matrix}\right]{}_0F_3\left(\begin{matrix}&-\frac{a^2b^2}{16}\\ 1-\nu,\ \frac{s-\mu-\nu+2}{2},\ \frac{s+\mu-\nu+2}{2}\end{matrix}\right)$$

$$+\frac{2^{s-2\mu-2}a^\mu}{b^{s-\mu}}\Gamma\left[\begin{matrix}\frac{s-\mu+\nu}{2},\ \frac{s-\mu-\nu}{2}\\ \mu+1\end{matrix}\right]$$

$$\times{}_0F_3\left(\begin{matrix}&-\frac{a^2b^2}{16}\\ \mu+1,\ \frac{2-s+\mu-\nu}{2},\ \frac{2-s+\mu+\nu}{2}\end{matrix}\right)$$

$$[a,\ \mathrm{Re}\,b>0;\ \mathrm{Re}\,s>|\mathrm{Re}\,\nu|-3/2]$$

No.	$f(x)$	$F(s)$
8	$\dfrac{1}{(x^4+a^4)^\rho}J_\nu(bx)K_\nu(bx)$	

$$\frac{a^{s-4\rho}}{8\nu}\mathrm{B}\left(\frac{s}{4},\frac{4\rho-s}{4}\right){}_1F_4\left(\begin{matrix}\frac{s}{4};\ \frac{a^4b^4}{64}\\ \frac{1}{2},\ \frac{2-\nu}{2},\ \frac{2+\nu}{2},\ \frac{s-2\rho+2}{2}\end{matrix}\right)$$

$$-\frac{a^{s-4\rho+2}b^2}{16(\nu^2-1)}\mathrm{B}\left(\frac{s+2}{4},\frac{4\rho-s-2}{4}\right)$$

$$\times{}_1F_4\left(\begin{matrix}\frac{s+2}{4};\ \frac{a^4b^4}{64}\\ \frac{3}{2},\ \frac{3-\nu}{2},\ \frac{3+\nu}{2},\ \frac{s-4\rho+6}{4}\end{matrix}\right)$$

$$+\frac{b^{2\nu}a^{s+2\nu-4\rho}}{2^{2\nu+3}}\Gamma\left[\begin{matrix}-\nu,\ \frac{s+2\nu}{4},\ \frac{4\rho-2\nu-s}{4}\\ \nu+1,\ \rho\end{matrix}\right]$$

$$\times{}_1F_4\left(\begin{matrix}\frac{s+2\nu}{4};\ \frac{a^4b^4}{64}\\ \nu+1,\ \frac{\nu+1}{2},\ \frac{\nu+2}{2},\ \frac{2\nu-4\rho+\delta+4}{4}\end{matrix}\right)$$

$$+\frac{2^{s-4\rho-3}}{b^{s-4\rho}}\Gamma\left[\begin{matrix}\frac{s-4\rho}{2},\ \frac{s+2\nu-4\rho}{4}\\ \frac{4-s+2\nu+4\rho}{4}\end{matrix}\right]$$

$$\times{}_1F_4\left(\begin{matrix}\rho;\ \frac{a^4b^4}{64}\\ \frac{2-s+4\rho}{4},\ \frac{4-s+4\rho}{4},\ \frac{4-s+4\rho-2\nu}{4},\ \frac{4-s+4\rho+2\nu}{4}\end{matrix}\right)$$

$$[\mathrm{Re}\,s,\ \mathrm{Re}\,(s-2\nu)>0;\ |\arg a|,\ |\arg b|<\pi/4]$$

No.	$f(x)$	$F(s)$
9	$e^{\pm bx}J_\mu(a\sqrt{x})K_\nu(bx)$	

$$\frac{\sqrt{\pi}\,a^\mu b^{-s-\mu/2}}{2^{s+3\mu/2}}\left[\frac{\cos(\nu\pi)}{\pi}\Gamma\left(\frac{1-2s-\mu}{2}\right)\right]^{(1\pm1)/2}$$

$$\times\Gamma\left[\begin{matrix}\frac{2s+\mu+2\nu}{2},\ \frac{2s+\mu-2\nu}{2}\\ \mu+1,\ \frac{2s+\mu+1}{2}\end{matrix}\right]{}_2F_2\left(\begin{matrix}\frac{2s+\mu+2\nu}{2},\ \frac{2s+\mu-2\nu}{2}\\ \mu+1,\ \frac{2s+\mu+1}{2};\ \pm\frac{a^2}{8b}\end{matrix}\right)$$

$$+2^{2s-5/2}\sqrt{\pi}\,\frac{1\pm1}{a^{2s-1}\sqrt{b}}\Gamma\left[\begin{matrix}\frac{2s+\mu-1}{2}\\ \frac{3-2s+\mu}{2}\end{matrix}\right]$$

$$\times{}_2F_2\left(\begin{matrix}\frac{1-2\nu}{2},\ \frac{1+2\nu}{2}\\ \frac{3-2s-\mu}{2},\ \frac{3-2s+\mu}{2};\ \pm\frac{a^2}{8b}\end{matrix}\right)$$

$$\left[\mathrm{Re}\,(2s+\mu)>2|\mathrm{Re}\,\nu|;\ \left\{\begin{matrix}\mathrm{Re}\,b>0\\ a,\ \mathrm{Re}\,b>0;\ \mathrm{Re}\,s<5/4\end{matrix}\right\}\right]$$

No.	$f(x)$	$F(s)$
10	$\left\{ \begin{array}{c} \sin(ax) \\ \cos(ax) \end{array} \right\} J_\mu(ax) K_\nu(bx)$	$2^{s+\delta-2} a^{\mu+\delta} b^{-s-\mu-\delta} \Gamma\left[\begin{array}{c} \frac{s+\mu-\nu+\delta}{2}, \; \frac{s+\mu+\nu+\delta}{2} \\ \mu+1 \end{array} \right]$ $\times \, {}_4F_3\left(\begin{array}{c} \frac{2\mu+2\delta+1}{4}, \; \frac{2\mu+2\delta+3}{4}, \; \frac{s+\mu-\nu+\delta}{2}, \; \frac{s+\mu+\nu+\delta}{2} \\ \frac{2\delta+1}{2}, \; \frac{2\mu+2\delta+1}{2}, \; \mu+1; \; -\frac{4a^2}{b^2} \end{array} \right)$ $[\operatorname{Re} b > 2|\operatorname{Im} a|; \; \operatorname{Re} s > |\operatorname{Re}\nu| - \operatorname{Re}\mu - \delta]$
11	$\left\{ \begin{array}{c} \sin(ax^2) \\ \cos(ax^2) \end{array} \right\} J_\nu(bx) K_\nu(bx)$	$\frac{a^{-s/2}}{4\nu} \Gamma\left(\frac{s}{2}\right) \left\{ \begin{array}{c} \sin(s\pi/4) \\ \cos(s\pi/4) \end{array} \right\} {}_2F_3\left(\begin{array}{c} \frac{s}{2}, \; \frac{s+2}{4}; \; \frac{b^4}{16a^2} \\ \frac{1}{2}, \; \frac{2-\nu}{2}, \; \frac{2+\nu}{2} \end{array} \right)$ $\mp \frac{a^{-s/2-1}b^2}{8(\nu^2-1)} \Gamma\left(\frac{s+2}{2}\right) \left\{ \begin{array}{c} \cos(s\pi/4) \\ \sin(s\pi/4) \end{array} \right\}$ $\times \, {}_2F_3\left(\begin{array}{c} \frac{s+2}{4}, \; \frac{s+4}{4}; \; \frac{b^4}{16a^2} \\ \frac{3}{2}, \; \frac{3-\nu}{2}, \; \frac{3+\nu}{2} \end{array} \right) + \frac{2^{2\nu-2} b^{2\nu}}{a^{s/2+\nu}} \Gamma\left[\begin{array}{c} -\nu, \; \frac{s+2\nu}{2} \\ \nu+1 \end{array} \right]$ $\times \left\{ \begin{array}{c} \sin[(2\nu+s)\pi/4] \\ \cos[(2\nu+s)\pi/4] \end{array} \right\} {}_2F_3\left(\begin{array}{c} \frac{s+2\nu}{4}, \; \frac{s+2\nu+2}{4}; \; \frac{b^4}{16a^2} \\ \nu+1, \; \frac{\nu+1}{2}, \; \frac{\nu+2}{2} \end{array} \right)$ $[a > 0; \; \operatorname{Re} s, \; \operatorname{Re}(s+2\nu) > -1 \mp 1; \; |\arg b| < \pi/2]$
12	$J_\lambda(ax) J_\mu(bx) K_\nu(cx)$	$\frac{2^{s-2} a^\lambda b^\mu}{c^{s+\lambda+\mu}} \Gamma\left[\begin{array}{c} \frac{s+\lambda+\mu-\nu}{2}, \; \frac{s+\lambda+\mu+\nu}{2} \\ \lambda+1, \; \mu+1 \end{array} \right]$ $\times F_4\left(\frac{s+\lambda+\mu-\nu}{2}, \; \frac{s+\lambda+\mu+\nu}{2}; \right.$ $\left. \lambda+1, \; \mu+1; \; -\frac{a^2}{c^2}, \; -\frac{b^2}{c^2} \right)$ $\left[\begin{array}{c} |c| > |a| + |b|; \; \operatorname{Re} c > |\operatorname{Im} a| + |\operatorname{Im} b|; \\ \operatorname{Re}(s+\lambda+\mu) > |\operatorname{Re}\nu| \end{array} \right]$
13	$J_\lambda(ax) J_\mu(ax) K_\nu(bx)$	$\frac{2^{s-2} a^{\lambda+\mu}}{b^{s+\lambda+\mu}} \Gamma\left[\begin{array}{c} \frac{s+\lambda+\mu+\nu}{2}, \; \frac{s+\lambda+\mu-\nu}{2} \\ \mu+1, \; \lambda+1 \end{array} \right]$ $\times \, {}_4F_3\left(\begin{array}{c} \frac{\lambda+\mu+1}{2}, \; \frac{\lambda+\mu+2}{2}, \; \frac{s+\lambda+\mu+\nu}{2}, \; \frac{s+\lambda+\mu-\nu}{2} \\ \lambda+1, \; \mu+1, \; \lambda+\mu+1; \; -\frac{4a^2}{b^2} \end{array} \right)$ $[|b| > 2|a|; \; \operatorname{Re} c > 2|\operatorname{Im} a|; \; \operatorname{Re}(s+\lambda+\mu) > |\operatorname{Re}\nu|]$
14	$J_\mu(ax^2) J_\nu(bx) K_\nu(bx)$	$\frac{1}{8\nu} \left(\frac{2}{a}\right)^{s/2} \Gamma\left[\begin{array}{c} \frac{2\mu+s}{4} \\ \frac{2\mu-s+4}{4} \end{array} \right] {}_2F_3\left(\begin{array}{c} \frac{s-2\mu}{4}, \; \frac{s+2\mu}{4}; \; \frac{b^4}{16a^2} \\ \frac{1}{2}, \; \frac{2-\nu}{2}, \; \frac{2+\nu}{2} \end{array} \right)$ $- \frac{2^{s/2-3} b^2}{(\nu^2-1) a^{s/2+1}} \Gamma\left[\begin{array}{c} \frac{s+2\mu+2}{4} \\ \frac{2-s+2\mu}{4} \end{array} \right] {}_2F_3\left(\begin{array}{c} \frac{s-2\mu+2}{4}, \; \frac{s+2\mu+2}{4}; \; \frac{b^4}{16a^2} \\ \frac{3}{2}, \; \frac{3-\nu}{2}, \; \frac{3+\nu}{2} \end{array} \right)$ $+ \frac{2^{s/2-\nu-3}}{a^{s/2+\nu} b^{-2\nu}} \Gamma\left[\begin{array}{c} -\nu, \; \frac{s+2\mu+2\nu}{4} \\ \nu+1, \; \frac{4-s+2\mu-2\nu}{4} \end{array} \right] {}_2F_3\left(\begin{array}{c} \frac{s-2\mu+2\nu}{4}, \; \frac{s+2\mu+2\nu}{4} \\ \nu+1, \; \frac{\nu+1}{2}, \; \frac{\nu+2}{2}; \; \frac{b^4}{16a^2} \end{array} \right)$ $[a, \; \operatorname{Re} b > 0; \; \operatorname{Re}(s+2\mu), \; \operatorname{Re}(s+2\mu+2\nu) > 0]$

No.	$f(x)$	$F(s)$
15	$\displaystyle\prod_{j=1}^{n} J_{\mu_j}(a_j x)\, K_\nu(bx)$	$2^{s-2}\, b^{-s-\lambda}\, \Gamma\!\left(\dfrac{s+\lambda-\nu}{2}\right)\Gamma\!\left(\dfrac{s+\lambda+\nu}{2}\right)$

$$\times \prod_{j=1}^{n} \frac{a_j^{\mu_j}}{\Gamma(\mu_j+1)}\, F_C^{(n)}\!\left(\frac{s+\lambda-\nu}{2},\frac{s+\lambda+\nu}{2};\right.$$

$$\left.\mu_1+1,\dots,\mu_n+1;\ -\frac{a_1^2}{b^2},\dots,-\frac{a_n^2}{b^2}\right)$$

$$\left[\lambda=\sum_{j=1}^{n}\mu_j;\ \operatorname{Re} b>\sum_{j=1}^{n}|\operatorname{Im} a_j|;\ \operatorname{Re}(s+\lambda)>|\operatorname{Re}\nu|\right]$$

| 16 | $J_\nu\!\left(b\sqrt{\sqrt{x^2+a^2}-a}\right)$ | $2^{3s/2-1}\left(\dfrac{a}{b^2}\right)^{s/2}\Gamma\!\left[\begin{array}{c}\frac{s+\nu}{2}\\ \frac{2-s+\nu}{2}\end{array}\right]K_s\!\left(\sqrt{2a}\,b\right)$ |
| | $\quad \times\, K_\nu\!\left(b\sqrt{\sqrt{x^2+a^2}+a}\right)$ | $[a,\,b>0;\ \operatorname{Re} s>-\operatorname{Re}\nu]$ |

3.14.13. $\quad K_\nu(\varphi(x))$ and $Y_\nu(\psi(x))$

No.	$f(x)$	$F(s)$
1	$Y_\nu(ax)\,K_\nu(ax)$	$-\dfrac{2^{s-3}}{\pi a^s}\cos\dfrac{(s-2\nu)\pi}{4}\,\Gamma\!\left[\dfrac{s}{2},\dfrac{s-2\nu}{4},\dfrac{s+2\nu}{4}\right]$

$$[\operatorname{Re} s>2|\operatorname{Re}\nu|;\ |\arg a|<\pi/4]$$

| 2 | $Y_\mu(ax)\,K_\nu(bx)$ | $-\dfrac{2^{s-2}b^{\mu-s}}{\pi a^\mu}\,\Gamma\!\left[\mu,\dfrac{s-\mu-\nu}{2},\dfrac{s-\mu+\nu}{2}\right]$ |

$$\times\, {}_2F_1\!\left(\begin{array}{c}\frac{s-\mu-\nu}{2},\frac{s-\mu+\nu}{2}\\ 1-\mu;\ -\frac{a^2}{b^2}\end{array}\right)-\frac{2^{s-2}a^\mu}{\pi b^{s+\mu}}\cos(\mu\pi)$$

$$\times\,\Gamma\!\left[-\mu,\frac{s+\mu-\nu}{2},\frac{s+\mu+\nu}{2}\right]{}_2F_1\!\left(\begin{array}{c}\frac{s+\mu-\nu}{2},\frac{s+\mu+\nu}{2}\\ 1+\mu;\ -\frac{a^2}{b^2}\end{array}\right)$$

$$[\operatorname{Re} b>|\operatorname{Im} a|;\ \operatorname{Re} s>|\operatorname{Re}\mu|+|\operatorname{Re}\nu|]$$

| 3 | $Y_\mu\!\left(\dfrac{a}{x}\right)K_\nu(bx)$ | $-\dfrac{2^{s-2\mu-2}a^\mu}{\pi b^{s-\mu}}\cos(\mu\pi)\,\Gamma\!\left[-\mu,\dfrac{s+\nu-\mu}{2},\dfrac{s-\nu-\mu}{2}\right]$ |

$$\times\, {}_0F_3\!\left(\begin{array}{c}-\frac{a^2b^2}{16}\\ 1+\mu,\frac{2-s+\mu-\nu}{2},\frac{2-s+\mu+\nu}{2}\end{array}\right)$$

$$-\frac{2^{s+2\mu-2}}{\pi a^\mu b^{s+\mu}}\,\Gamma\!\left[\mu,\frac{s+\mu+\nu}{2},\frac{s+\mu-\nu}{2}\right]$$

$$\times\, {}_0F_3\!\left(\begin{array}{c}-\frac{a^2b^2}{16}\\ 1-\mu,\frac{2-s-\mu-\nu}{2},\frac{2-s-\mu+\nu}{2}\end{array}\right)-\frac{a^{s+\nu}b^\nu}{2^{s+2\nu+2}\pi}$$

$$\times\cos\frac{(s+\mu+\nu)\pi}{2}\,\Gamma\!\left[-\nu,\frac{\mu-\nu-s}{2},-\frac{\mu+\nu+s}{2}\right]\times$$

No.	$f(x)$	$F(s)$
		$\times \, _0F_3\left(\begin{array}{c} -\frac{a^2b^2}{16} \\ 1+\nu, \ \frac{s-\mu+\nu+2}{2}, \ \frac{s+\mu+\nu+2}{2} \end{array}\right) - \frac{a^{s-\nu}b^{-\nu}}{2^{s-2\nu+2}\pi}$
		$\times \cos\frac{(s+\mu-\nu)\pi}{2}\,\Gamma\left[\nu, \ \frac{\mu+\nu-s}{2}, \ \frac{\nu-\mu-s}{2}\right]$
		$\times \, _0F_3\left(\begin{array}{c} -\frac{a^2b^2}{16} \\ 1-\nu, \ \frac{s-\mu-\nu+2}{2}, \ \frac{s+\mu-\nu+2}{2} \end{array}\right)$
		$[a, \ \mathrm{Re}\,b > 0; \ \mathrm{Re}\,s > |\mathrm{Re}\,\nu| - 3/2]$
4	$Y_\nu\left(b\sqrt{\sqrt{x^2+a^2}-a}\right)$ $\times K_\nu\left(b\sqrt{\sqrt{x^2+a^2}+a}\right)$	$-2^{3s/2-1}\left(\frac{a}{b^2}\right)^{s/2}\Gamma\left[\begin{array}{c}\frac{s-\nu}{2}, \ \frac{s+\nu}{2}\\ \frac{s-\nu+1}{2}, \ \frac{\nu-s+1}{2}\end{array}\right]K_s\left(\sqrt{2a}\,b\right)$ $[a, b > 0; \ \mathrm{Re}\,s > |\mathrm{Re}\,\nu|]$

3.14.14. $K_\nu(ax)$ **and** $J_\nu(ax)$, $Y_\nu(ax)$

1	$\left[\cos\frac{\nu\pi}{2}J_\nu(ax) - \sin\frac{\nu\pi}{2}Y_\nu(ax)\right]$ $\times K_\nu(ax)$	$\frac{2^{s-3}}{a^s}\Gamma\left[\begin{array}{c}\frac{s}{2}, \ \frac{s-2\nu}{4}, \ \frac{s+2\nu}{4}\\ \frac{s}{4}, \ \frac{4-s}{4}\end{array}\right]$	$[a > 0; \ \mathrm{Re}\,s > 2|\mathrm{Re}\,\nu|]$
2	$\left[\sin\frac{\nu\pi}{2}J_\nu(ax) + \cos\frac{\nu\pi}{2}Y_\nu(ax)\right]$ $\times K_\nu(ax)$	$-\frac{2^{s-3}}{a^s}\Gamma\left[\begin{array}{c}\frac{s}{2}, \ \frac{s-2\nu}{4}, \ \frac{s+2\nu}{4}\\ \frac{2-s}{4}, \ \frac{2+s}{4}\end{array}\right]$	$[a > 0; \ \mathrm{Re}\,s > 2|\mathrm{Re}\,\nu|]$
3	$\frac{2}{\pi}K_0(ax) - Y_0(ax)$	$\frac{2^{2s-2}}{a^s}\Gamma\left[\begin{array}{c}\frac{s}{4}, \ \frac{s}{4}\\ \frac{2-s}{4}, \ \frac{2-s}{4}\end{array}\right]$	$[a > 0; \ 0 < \mathrm{Re}\,s < 3/4]$

3.14.15. $K_\nu(\varphi(x))$ **and** $I_\mu(\psi(x))$

1	$I_\mu(ax)K_\nu(bx)$	$\frac{2^{s-2}a^\mu}{b^{s+\mu}}\Gamma\left[\begin{array}{c}\frac{s+\mu-\nu}{2}, \ \frac{s+\mu+\nu}{2}\\ \mu+1\end{array}\right]\,_2F_1\left(\begin{array}{c}\frac{s+\mu-\nu}{2}, \ \frac{s+\mu+\nu}{2}\\ \mu+1; \frac{a^2}{b^2}\end{array}\right)$ $[\mathrm{Re}\,b > |\mathrm{Re}\,a|; \ \mathrm{Re}\,(s+\mu) > |\mathrm{Re}\,\nu|]$
2	$I_\mu(ax)K_\nu(ax)$	$\frac{2^{s-2}}{a^s}\Gamma\left[\begin{array}{c}\frac{s+\mu-\nu}{2}, \ \frac{s+\mu+\nu}{2}, \ 1-s\\ \frac{2-s+\mu-\nu}{2}, \ \frac{2-s+\mu+\nu}{2}\end{array}\right]$ $[\mathrm{Re}\,a > 0; \ |\mathrm{Re}\,\nu| - \mathrm{Re}\,\mu < \mathrm{Re}\,s < 1]$

No.	$f(x)$	$F(s)$
3	$I_\nu\left(a\sqrt{x}\right)K_\nu\left(bx\right)$	$\dfrac{2^{s-\mu/2-2}\,a^\mu}{b^{s+\mu/2}}\,\Gamma\left[\begin{array}{c}\frac{2s+\mu-2\nu}{4},\ \frac{2s+\mu+2\nu}{4}\\\mu+1\end{array}\right]\,{}_2F_3\left(\begin{array}{c}\frac{2s+\mu-2\nu}{4},\ \frac{2s+\mu+2\nu}{4}\\\frac{1}{2},\ \frac{\mu+1}{2},\ \frac{\mu+2}{2};\ \frac{a^2}{64b^2}\end{array}\right)$
		$+\dfrac{2^{s-\mu/2-3}\,a^{\mu+2}}{b^{s+\mu/2+1}}\,\Gamma\left[\begin{array}{c}\frac{2s+\mu-2\nu+2}{4},\ \frac{2s+\mu+2\nu+2}{4}\\\mu+2\end{array}\right]$
		$\times\,{}_2F_3\left(\begin{array}{c}\frac{2s+\mu-2\nu+2}{4},\ \frac{2s+\mu+2\nu+2}{4}\\\frac{3}{2},\ \frac{\mu+2}{2},\ \frac{\mu+3}{2};\ \frac{a^4}{64b^2}\end{array}\right)$
		$[\operatorname{Re}b>0;\ \operatorname{Re}s>\left\lvert\operatorname{Re}\nu\right\rvert-\operatorname{Re}\mu/2]$
4	$\left[I_\nu\left(ax\right)+I_{-\nu}\left(ax\right)\right]$ $\times K_\nu\left(ax\right)$	$\dfrac{\cos\left(\nu\pi\right)}{2\sqrt{\pi}\,a^s}\,\Gamma\left[\begin{array}{c}\frac{s-2\nu}{2},\ \frac{s+2\nu}{2},\ \frac{1-s}{2}\\\frac{2-s}{2}\end{array}\right]\qquad\left[a>0;\ 2\left\lvert\operatorname{Re}\nu\right\rvert<\operatorname{Re}s<1\right]$
5	$I_\nu\left(b\sqrt{x^2+a^2}-ab\right)$ $\times K_\nu\left(b\sqrt{x^2+a^2}+ab\right)$	$\dfrac{1}{2\sqrt{\pi}}\left(\dfrac{a}{b}\right)^{s/2}\Gamma\left[\begin{array}{c}\frac{s+2\nu}{2},\ \frac{1-s}{2}\\\frac{2-s+2\nu}{2}\end{array}\right]K_{s/2}\left(2ab\right)$
		$[a,\ \operatorname{Re}b>0;\ -2\operatorname{Re}\nu<\operatorname{Re}s<1]$
6	$I_\mu\left(ax\right)K_\nu\left(ax\right)$ $-I_\nu\left(ax\right)K_\mu\left(ax\right)$	$\dfrac{a^{-s}}{2\sqrt{\pi}}\,\sin\dfrac{(\nu-\mu)\pi}{2}\,\Gamma\left[\begin{array}{c}\frac{s+\mu+\nu}{2},\ \frac{s-\mu+\nu}{2},\ \frac{s+\mu-\nu}{2},\ \frac{2-s}{2}\\\frac{s+1}{2},\ \frac{2-s+\mu+\nu}{2}\end{array}\right]$
		$[a>0;\ \operatorname{Re}\left(\nu-\mu\right),\ \left\lvert\operatorname{Re}\mu\right\rvert-\operatorname{Re}\nu<\operatorname{Re}s<1]$
7	$I_\mu\left(ax\right)K_\nu\left(ax\right)$ $+I_\nu\left(ax\right)K_\mu\left(ax\right)$	$\dfrac{a^{-s}}{2\sqrt{\pi}}\,\cos\dfrac{(\mu-\nu)\pi}{2}\,\Gamma\left[\begin{array}{c}\frac{s+\mu+\nu}{2},\ \frac{s-\mu+\nu}{2},\ \frac{s+\mu-\nu}{2},\ \frac{1-s}{2}\\\frac{s}{2},\ \frac{2-s+\mu+\nu}{2}\end{array}\right]$
		$[a>0;\ -\operatorname{Re}\left(\mu-\nu\right),\ \left\lvert\operatorname{Re}\nu\right\rvert-\operatorname{Re}\mu<\operatorname{Re}s<1]$

3.14.16. $K_\nu\left(ax\right)$, $I_\mu\left(\varphi\left(x\right)\right)$, and the exponential function

Notation: $\delta=\left\{\begin{array}{c}1\\0\end{array}\right\}$.

No.	$f(x)$	$F(s)$
1	$e^{\pm ax}I_\mu\left(ax\right)K_\nu\left(bx\right)$	$\dfrac{2^{s-2}a^\mu}{b^{s+\mu}}\,\Gamma\left[\begin{array}{c}\frac{s+\mu-\nu}{2},\ \frac{s+\mu+\nu}{2}\\\mu+1\end{array}\right]\,{}_4F_3\left(\begin{array}{c}\frac{2\mu+1}{4},\ \frac{2\mu+3}{4},\ \frac{s+\mu-\nu}{2},\ \frac{s+\mu+\nu}{2}\\\frac{1}{2},\ \frac{2\mu+1}{2},\ \mu+1;\ \frac{4a^2}{b^2}\end{array}\right)$
		$\pm\dfrac{2^{s-1}a^{\mu+1}}{b^{s+\mu+1}}\,\Gamma\left[\begin{array}{c}\frac{s+\mu-\nu+1}{2},\ \frac{s+\mu+\nu+1}{2}\\\mu+1\end{array}\right]$
		$\times\,{}_4F_3\left(\begin{array}{c}\frac{2\mu+3}{4},\ \frac{2\mu+5}{4},\ \frac{s+\mu-\nu+1}{2},\ \frac{s+\mu+\nu+1}{2}\\\frac{3}{2},\ \mu+1,\ \frac{2\mu+3}{2};\ \frac{4a^2}{b^2}\end{array}\right)$
		$\left[\left\{\begin{array}{c}\operatorname{Re}a,\ \operatorname{Re}b>0\\\operatorname{Re}b>\left\lvert\operatorname{Re}a\right\rvert\end{array}\right\};\ \operatorname{Re}\left(s+\mu\right)>\left\lvert\operatorname{Re}\nu\right\rvert\right]$

No.	$f(x)$	$F(s)$
2	$e^{-ax} I_\mu(bx) K_\nu(bx)$	$\dfrac{b^{\mu+\nu}}{2^{\mu+\nu+1} a^{s+\mu+\nu}} \Gamma \begin{bmatrix} -\nu,\ s+\mu+\nu \\ \mu+1 \end{bmatrix}$ $\times\ _4F_3\left(\begin{matrix} \frac{\mu+\nu+1}{2},\ \frac{\mu+\nu+2}{2},\ \frac{s+\mu+\nu}{2},\ \frac{s+\mu+\nu+1}{2} \\ \mu+1,\ \nu+1,\ \mu+\nu+1;\ \frac{4b^2}{a^2} \end{matrix} \right)$ $+ \dfrac{2^{\nu-\mu-1} b^{\mu-\nu}}{a^{s+\mu-\nu}} \Gamma \begin{bmatrix} \nu,\ s+\mu-\nu \\ \mu+1 \end{bmatrix}$ $\times\ _4F_3\left(\begin{matrix} \frac{\mu-\nu+1}{2},\ \frac{\mu-\nu+2}{2},\ \frac{s+\mu-\nu}{2},\ \frac{s+\mu-\nu+1}{2} \\ \mu+1,\ 1-\nu,\ \mu-\nu+1;\ \frac{4b^2}{a^2} \end{matrix} \right)$ $[\operatorname{Re}a,\ \operatorname{Re}b>0;\ \operatorname{Re}(s+\mu)>|\operatorname{Re}\nu|]$
3	$e^{-ax\pm bx} I_\mu(ax) K_\nu(bx)$	$\dfrac{\sqrt{\pi}\,a^\mu}{2^{s+2\mu}\,b^{s+\mu}} \left(\cos(\nu\pi)\sec\left[(s+\mu)\pi\right]\right)^{(1\pm1)/2}$ $\times\ \Gamma \begin{bmatrix} s+\mu-\nu,\ s+\mu+\nu \\ \mu+1,\ \frac{2s+2\mu+1}{2} \end{bmatrix} {}_3F_2\left(\begin{matrix} \frac{2\mu+1}{2},\ s+\mu-\nu,\ s+\mu+\nu \\ 2\mu+1,\ \frac{2s+2\mu+1}{2};\ \pm\frac{a}{b} \end{matrix} \right)$ $- \dfrac{(1\pm1)\pi}{2^{s+1}a^{s-1/2}\sqrt{b}} \sec\left[(s+\mu)\pi\right] \Gamma \begin{bmatrix} 1-s \\ \frac{3-2s-2\mu}{2},\ \frac{3-2s+2\mu}{2} \end{bmatrix}$ $\times\ _3F_2\left(\begin{matrix} \frac{1-2\nu}{2},\ \frac{1+2\nu}{2},\ 1-s \\ \frac{3-2s-2\mu}{2},\ \frac{3-2s+2\mu}{2};\ \pm\frac{a}{b} \end{matrix} \right)$ $\left[\operatorname{Re}a>0;\ \operatorname{Re}(s+\mu)>|\operatorname{Re}\nu|;\ \left\{ \begin{matrix} \operatorname{Re}s<1;\ |\arg b|<\pi \\ \operatorname{Re}b>0 \end{matrix} \right\}\right]$
4	$e^{-ax^2} I_\mu(bx) K_\nu(bx)$	$\dfrac{a^{-(s+\mu+\nu)/2}\,b^{\mu+\nu}}{2^{\mu+\nu+2}} \Gamma \begin{bmatrix} -\nu,\ \frac{s+\mu+\nu}{2} \\ \mu+1 \end{bmatrix} {}_3F_3\left(\begin{matrix} \frac{\mu+\nu+1}{2},\ \frac{\mu+\nu+2}{2},\ \frac{s+\mu+\nu}{2};\ \frac{b^2}{a} \\ \mu+1,\ \nu+1,\ \mu+\nu+1 \end{matrix} \right)$ $+ \dfrac{2^{\nu-\mu-2}\,b^{\mu-\nu}}{a^{(s+\mu-\nu)/2}} \Gamma \begin{bmatrix} \nu,\ \frac{s+\mu-\nu}{2} \\ \mu+1 \end{bmatrix} {}_3F_3\left(\begin{matrix} \frac{\mu-\nu+1}{2},\ \frac{\mu-\nu+2}{2},\ \frac{s+\mu-\nu}{2};\ \frac{b^2}{a} \\ \mu+1,\ 1-\nu,\ \mu-\nu+1 \end{matrix} \right)$ $[\operatorname{Re}a,\ \operatorname{Re}b>0;\ \operatorname{Re}(s+\mu)>|\operatorname{Re}\nu|]$
5	$e^{-ax^2} I_\mu(ax^2) K_\nu(bx)$	$\dfrac{2^{-(s+3\nu)/2-2}b^\nu}{\sqrt{\pi}\,a^{(s+\nu)/2}} \Gamma \begin{bmatrix} -\nu,\ \frac{1-s-\nu}{2},\ \frac{s+2\mu+\nu}{2} \\ \frac{1-s+2\mu-\nu}{2} \end{bmatrix} {}_2F_2\left(\begin{matrix} \frac{s-2\mu+\nu}{2},\ \frac{s+2\mu+\nu}{2} \\ 1+\nu,\ \frac{s+\nu+1}{2};\ \frac{b^2}{8a} \end{matrix} \right)$ $+ \dfrac{2^{(3\nu-s)/2-2}b^\nu}{\sqrt{\pi}\,a^{(s-\nu)/2}} \Gamma \begin{bmatrix} \nu,\ \frac{1-s+\nu}{2},\ \frac{s+2\mu-\nu}{2} \\ \frac{2-s+2\mu+\nu}{2} \end{bmatrix} {}_2F_2\left(\begin{matrix} \frac{s-2\mu-\nu}{2},\ \frac{s+2\mu-\nu}{2} \\ 1-\nu,\ \frac{s-\nu+1}{2};\ \frac{b^2}{8a} \end{matrix} \right)$ $+ \dfrac{2^{s-7/2}\,b^{1-s}}{\sqrt{\pi a}} \Gamma\left(\frac{s-\nu-1}{2}\right) \Gamma\left(\frac{s+\nu-1}{2}\right)$ $\times\ _2F_2\left(\begin{matrix} \frac{1-2\mu}{2},\ \frac{1+2\mu}{2} \\ \frac{3-s-\nu}{2},\ \frac{3-s+\nu}{2};\ \frac{b^2}{8a} \end{matrix} \right)$ $[\operatorname{Re}a,\ \operatorname{Re}b>0;\ \operatorname{Re}(s+2\mu)>|\operatorname{Re}\nu|]$

No.	$f(x)$	$F(s)$
6	$e^{-ax} I_\mu(b\sqrt{x}) K_\nu(ax)$	$\dfrac{\sqrt{\pi}\,b^\mu}{2^{s+3\mu/2}a^{s+\mu/2}} \Gamma\left[\begin{array}{c} \frac{2s-2\nu+\mu}{2}, \frac{2s+2\nu+\mu}{2} \\ \mu+1,\ \frac{2s+\mu+1}{2} \end{array}\right]\,{}_2F_2\left(\begin{array}{c} \frac{2s-2\nu+\mu}{2},\ \frac{2s+2\nu+\mu}{2} \\ \mu+1,\ \frac{2s+\mu+1}{2};\ \frac{b^2}{8a} \end{array}\right)$ $[\operatorname{Re}a,\ \operatorname{Re}b>0;\ \operatorname{Re}(s+\mu/2)>|\operatorname{Re}\nu|]$
7	$\left.\begin{array}{c} \sinh(ax) \\ \cosh(ax) \end{array}\right\}$ $\times I_\mu(ax) K_\nu(bx)$	$2^{s+\delta-2}a^{\mu+\delta}b^{-s-\mu-\delta}\Gamma\left[\begin{array}{c} \frac{s+\mu-\nu+\delta}{2}, \frac{s+\mu+\nu+\delta}{2} \\ \mu+1 \end{array}\right]$ $\times\,{}_4F_3\left(\begin{array}{c} \frac{2\mu+2\delta+1}{4},\ \frac{2\mu+2\delta+3}{4},\ \frac{s+\mu-\nu+\delta}{2},\ \frac{s+\mu+\nu+\delta}{2} \\ \frac{2\delta+1}{2},\ \frac{2\mu+2\delta+1}{2},\ \mu+1;\ \frac{4a^2}{b^2} \end{array}\right)$ $[\operatorname{Re}b>2|\operatorname{Re}a|;\ \operatorname{Re}s>|\operatorname{Re}\nu|-\operatorname{Re}\mu-\delta]$
8	$\left.\begin{array}{c} \sin(ax) \\ \cos(ax) \end{array}\right\}$ $\times I_\mu(bx) K_\nu(bx)$	$\dfrac{2^{-\mu-\nu-1}b^{\mu+\nu}}{a^{s+\mu+\nu}}\left\{\begin{array}{c} \sin[(s+\mu+\nu)\pi/2] \\ \cos[(s+\mu+\nu)\pi/2] \end{array}\right\}\Gamma\left[\begin{array}{c} -\nu,\ s+\mu+\nu \\ \mu+1 \end{array}\right]$ $\times\,{}_4F_3\left(\begin{array}{c} \frac{\mu+\nu+1}{2},\ \frac{\mu+\nu+2}{2},\ \frac{s+\mu+\nu}{2},\ \frac{s+\mu+\nu+1}{2} \\ \mu+1,\ \nu+1,\ \mu+\nu+1;\ -\frac{4b^2}{a^2} \end{array}\right)$ $+\dfrac{2^{\nu-\mu-1}b^{\mu-\nu}}{a^{s+\mu-\nu}}\left\{\begin{array}{c} \sin[(s+\mu-\nu)\pi/2] \\ \cos[(s+\mu-\nu)\pi/2] \end{array}\right\}\Gamma\left[\begin{array}{c} \nu,\ s+\mu-\nu \\ \mu+1 \end{array}\right]$ $\times\,{}_4F_3\left(\begin{array}{c} \frac{\mu-\nu+1}{2},\ \frac{\mu-\nu+2}{2},\ \frac{s+\mu-\nu}{2},\ \frac{s+\mu-\nu+1}{2} \\ \mu+1,\ 1-\nu,\ \mu-\nu+1;\ -\frac{4b^2}{a^2} \end{array}\right)$ $[a,\ \operatorname{Re}b>0;\ |\operatorname{Re}\nu|-\operatorname{Re}\mu-(1\pm1)/2<\operatorname{Re}s<2]$
9	$I_\lambda(ax) I_\mu(bx) K_\nu(cx)$	$\dfrac{2^{s-1}a^\lambda b^\mu}{c^{s+\lambda+\mu}}\Gamma\left[\begin{array}{c} \frac{s+\lambda+\mu-\nu}{2}, \frac{s+\lambda+\mu+\nu}{2} \\ \lambda+1,\ \mu+1 \end{array}\right]$ $\times F_4\left(\frac{s+\lambda+\mu-\nu}{2},\ \frac{s+\lambda+\mu+\nu}{2};\ \lambda+1,\ \mu+1;\ \frac{a^2}{c^2},\ \frac{b^2}{c^2}\right)$ $\left[\begin{array}{c} |c|>|a|+|b|;\ \operatorname{Re}c>|\operatorname{Re}a|+|\operatorname{Re}b|; \\ \operatorname{Re}(s+\lambda+\mu)>|\operatorname{Re}\nu| \end{array}\right]$
10	$I_\lambda(ax) I_\mu(ax) K_\nu(bx)$	$\dfrac{2^{s-2}a^{\lambda+\mu}}{b^{s+\lambda+\mu}}\Gamma\left[\begin{array}{c} \frac{s+\lambda+\mu-\nu}{2}, \frac{s+\lambda+\mu+\nu}{2} \\ \lambda+1,\ \mu+1 \end{array}\right]$ $\times\,{}_4F_3\left(\begin{array}{c} \frac{\lambda+\mu+1}{2},\ \frac{\lambda+\mu+2}{2},\ \frac{s+\lambda+\mu-\nu}{2},\ \frac{s+\lambda+\mu+\nu}{2} \\ \lambda+1,\ \mu+1,\ \lambda+\mu+1;\ \frac{4a^2}{b^2} \end{array}\right)$ $[\operatorname{Re}b>2|\operatorname{Re}a|;\ \operatorname{Re}(s+\lambda+\mu)>|\operatorname{Re}\nu|]$

3.14.17. $K_\nu\left(ax\right)$ **and** $I_\mu\left(ax\right)$, $J_\lambda\left(bx\right)$

1	$J_\lambda\left(ax\right) I_\mu\left(bx\right) K_\nu\left(bx\right)$	$\dfrac{2^{s-2}\,b^{\mu+\nu}}{a^{s+\mu+\nu}}\,\Gamma\!\left[\begin{array}{c} -\nu,\ \frac{s+\lambda+\mu+\nu}{2} \\ \mu+1,\ \frac{2-s+\lambda-\mu-\nu}{2} \end{array}\right]$ $\times\ {}_4F_3\!\left(\begin{array}{c} \frac{\mu+\nu+1}{2},\ \frac{\mu+\nu+2}{2},\ \frac{s-\lambda+\mu+\nu}{2},\ \frac{s+\lambda+\mu+\nu}{2} \\ \mu+1,\ \nu+1,\ \mu+\nu+1;\ -\frac{4b^2}{a^2} \end{array}\right)$ $+\ \dfrac{2^{s-2}\,b^{\mu-\nu}}{a^{s+\mu-\nu}}\,\Gamma\!\left[\begin{array}{c} \nu,\ \frac{s+\lambda+\mu-\nu}{2} \\ \mu+1,\ \frac{2-s+\lambda-\mu+\nu}{2} \end{array}\right]$ $\times\ {}_4F_3\!\left(\begin{array}{c} \frac{\mu-\nu+1}{2},\ \frac{\mu-\nu+2}{2},\ \frac{s-\lambda+\mu-\nu}{2},\ \frac{s+\lambda+\mu-\nu}{2} \\ \mu+1,\ 1-\nu,\ \mu-\nu+1;\ -\frac{4b^2}{a^2} \end{array}\right)$ $\left[a,\ \operatorname{Re}b>0;\ \left|\operatorname{Re}\nu\right|-\operatorname{Re}\left(\lambda+\mu\right)<\operatorname{Re}s<5/2\right]$
2	$J_\lambda\left(ax\right) I_\mu\left(bx\right) K_\nu\left(cx\right)$	$\dfrac{2^{s-2}\,a^\lambda b^\mu}{c^{s+\lambda+\mu}}\,\Gamma\!\left[\begin{array}{c} \frac{s+\lambda+\mu-\nu}{2},\ \frac{s+\lambda+\mu+\nu}{2} \\ \lambda+1,\ \mu+1 \end{array}\right]$ $\times\ F_4\!\left(\dfrac{s+\lambda+\mu-\nu}{2},\ \dfrac{s+\lambda+\mu+\nu}{2};\right.$ $\left.\lambda+1,\ \mu+1;\ -\dfrac{a^2}{c^2},\ \dfrac{b^2}{c^2}\right)$ $\left[\operatorname{Re}c>\left|\operatorname{Im}a\right|+\left|\operatorname{Re}b\right|;\ \operatorname{Re}\left(s+\lambda+\mu\right)>\left|\operatorname{Re}\nu\right|\right]$

3.14.18.   **Products of** $K_\mu\left(\varphi\left(x\right)\right)$

1	$K_\mu\left(ax\right) K_\nu\left(bx\right)$	$\dfrac{2^{s-3}\,a^{\nu-s}}{b^\nu}\,\Gamma\!\left[\nu,\ \dfrac{s-\mu-\nu}{2},\ \dfrac{s+\mu-\nu}{2}\right]\,{}_2F_1\!\left(\begin{array}{c} \frac{s-\mu-\nu}{2},\ \frac{s+\mu-\nu}{2} \\ 1-\nu;\ \frac{b^2}{a^2} \end{array}\right)$ $+\ \dfrac{2^{s-3}\,a^{-\nu-s}}{b^{-\nu}}\,\Gamma\!\left[-\nu,\ \dfrac{s-\mu+\nu}{2},\ \dfrac{s+\mu+\nu}{2}\right]\,{}_2F_1\!\left(\begin{array}{c} \frac{s-\mu+\nu}{2},\ \frac{s+\mu+\nu}{2} \\ 1+\nu;\ \frac{b^2}{a^2} \end{array}\right)$ $\left[\operatorname{Re}\left(a+b\right)>0;\ \operatorname{Re}s>\left|\operatorname{Re}\mu\right|+\left|\operatorname{Re}\nu\right|\right]$
2	$K_\nu\left(ax\right) K_\nu\left(bx\right)$	$\sqrt{\dfrac{\pi}{ab}}\,\dfrac{2^{s-3}}{\left|a^2-b^2\right|^{(s-1)/2}}\,\Gamma\!\left[\dfrac{s}{2},\ \dfrac{s-2\nu}{2},\ \dfrac{s+2\nu}{2}\right]\,P_{\nu-1/2}^{(1-s)/2}\!\left(\dfrac{a^2+b^2}{2ab}\right)$
3		$=\dfrac{e^{i\nu\pi}2^{s-2}}{\left|a^2-b^2\right|^{s/2}}\,\Gamma\!\left(\dfrac{s}{2}\right)\Gamma\!\left(\dfrac{s+2\nu}{2}\right)Q_{s/2-1}^{-\nu}\!\left(\dfrac{a^2+b^2}{\left|a^2-b^2\right|}\right)$ $\left[\operatorname{Re}\left(a+b\right)>0;\ \operatorname{Re}s>2\left|\operatorname{Re}\nu\right|\right]$
4	$K_\mu\left(ax\right) K_\nu\left(ax\right)$	$\dfrac{2^{s-3}}{a^s\,\Gamma\left(s\right)}\,\Gamma\!\left[\dfrac{s+\mu+\nu}{2},\ \dfrac{s+\mu-\nu}{2},\ \dfrac{s+\nu-\mu}{2},\ \dfrac{s-\mu-\nu}{2}\right]$ $\left[\operatorname{Re}a>0;\ \operatorname{Re}s>\left|\operatorname{Re}\mu\right|+\left|\operatorname{Re}\nu\right|\right]$

No.	$f(x)$	$F(s)$
5	$K_\mu(a\sqrt{x})K_\nu(bx)$	

$$\frac{2^{s-\mu/2-3}a^\mu}{b^{s+\mu/2}}\,\Gamma\left[-\mu,\ \frac{2s+\mu-2\nu}{4},\ \frac{2s+\mu+2\nu}{4}\right]$$

$$\times\,_2F_3\left(\begin{array}{c}\frac{2s+\mu-2\nu}{4},\ \frac{2s+\mu+2\nu}{4}\\[2pt]\frac{1}{2},\ \frac{1+\mu}{2},\ \frac{2+\mu}{2};\ \frac{a^4}{64b^2}\end{array}\right)$$

$$+\,\frac{2^{s+\mu/2-3}a^{-\mu}}{b^{s-\mu/2}}\,\Gamma\left[\mu,\ \frac{2s-\mu-2\nu}{4},\ \frac{2s-\mu+2\nu}{4}\right]$$

$$\times\,_2F_3\left(\begin{array}{c}\frac{2s-\mu-2\nu}{4},\ \frac{2s-\mu+2\nu}{4}\\[2pt]\frac{1}{2},\ \frac{1-\mu}{2},\ \frac{2-\mu}{2};\ \frac{a^4}{64b^2}\end{array}\right)-\frac{2^{s-\mu/2-4}a^{\mu+2}}{b^{s+\mu/2+1}}$$

$$\times\,\Gamma\left[-\mu-1,\ \frac{2s+\mu-2\nu+2}{4},\ \frac{2s+\mu+2\nu+2}{4}\right]$$

$$\times\,_2F_3\left(\begin{array}{c}\frac{2s+\mu-2\nu+2}{4},\ \frac{2s+\mu+2\nu+2}{4}\\[2pt]\frac{3}{2},\ \frac{2+\mu}{2},\ \frac{3+\mu}{2};\ \frac{a^4}{64b^2}\end{array}\right)-\frac{2^{s+\mu/2-4}a^{2-\mu}}{b^{s-\mu/2+1}}$$

$$\times\,\Gamma\left[\mu-1,\ \frac{2s-\mu-2\nu+2}{4},\ \frac{2s-\mu+2\nu+2}{4}\right]$$

$$\times\,_2F_3\left(\begin{array}{c}\frac{2s-\mu-2\nu+2}{4},\ \frac{2s-\mu+2\nu+2}{4}\\[2pt]\frac{3}{2},\ \frac{2-\mu}{2},\ \frac{3-\mu}{2};\ \frac{a^4}{64b^2}\end{array}\right)$$

$$[\operatorname{Re}b>0;\ \operatorname{Re}s>|\operatorname{Re}\mu|/2+|\operatorname{Re}\nu|]$$

No.	$f(x)$	$F(s)$
6	$K_\mu\left(\dfrac{a}{x}\right)K_\nu(bx)$	

$$\frac{2^{s-2\mu-3}a^\mu}{b^{s-\mu}}\,\Gamma\left[-\mu,\ \frac{s-\mu-\nu}{2},\ \frac{s-\mu+\nu}{2}\right]$$

$$\times\,_0F_3\left(\begin{array}{c}\frac{a^2b^2}{16}\\[2pt]1+\mu,\ \frac{2-s+\mu-\nu}{2},\ \frac{2-s+\mu+\nu}{2}\end{array}\right)$$

$$+\,\frac{2^{s+2\mu-3}a^{-\mu}}{b^{s+\mu}}\,\Gamma\left[\mu,\ \frac{s+\mu-\nu}{2},\ \frac{s+\mu+\nu}{2}\right]$$

$$\times\,_0F_3\left(\begin{array}{c}\frac{a^2b^2}{16}\\[2pt]1-\mu,\ \frac{2-s-\mu-\nu}{2},\ \frac{2-s-\mu+\nu}{2}\end{array}\right)$$

$$+\,\frac{a^{s+\nu}b^\nu}{2^{s+2\nu+3}}\,\Gamma\left[-\nu,\ \frac{\mu-\nu-s}{2},\ -\frac{\mu+\nu+s}{2}\right]$$

$$\times\,_0F_3\left(\begin{array}{c}\frac{a^2b^2}{16}\\[2pt]1+\nu,\ \frac{s-\mu+\nu+2}{2},\ \frac{s+\mu+\nu+2}{2}\end{array}\right)+\frac{a^{s-\nu}b^{-\nu}}{2^{s-2\nu+3}}$$

$$\times\,\Gamma\left[\nu,\ \frac{\mu+\nu-s}{2},\ \frac{\nu-\mu-s}{2}\right]\,_0F_3\left(\begin{array}{c}\frac{a^2b^2}{16}\\[2pt]1-\nu,\ \frac{s-\mu-\nu+2}{2},\ \frac{s+\mu-\nu+2}{2}\end{array}\right)$$

$$[\operatorname{Re}a,\ \operatorname{Re}b>0]$$

No.	$f(x)$	$F(s)$
7	$K_\nu\left(b\sqrt{x^2+a^2}-ab\right)$ $\times\,K_\nu\left(b\sqrt{x^2+a^2}+ab\right)$	$\dfrac{\sqrt{\pi}}{2}\left(\dfrac{a}{b}\right)^{s/2}\Gamma\left[\begin{array}{c}\frac{s-2\nu}{2},\ \frac{s+2\nu}{2}\\[2pt]\frac{s+1}{2}\end{array}\right]K_{s/2}(2ab)$ $[\operatorname{Re}a,\ \operatorname{Re}b>0;\ \operatorname{Re}s>2|\operatorname{Re}\nu|]$

3.14.19. Products of $K_\mu(ax^r)$ and the exponential function

1	$e^{(a\pm b)x}K_\mu(ax)K_\nu(bx)$	$\dfrac{\sqrt{\pi}\,a^\mu}{2^{s+2\mu+1}\,b^{s+\mu}}\,\Gamma\!\begin{bmatrix}-\mu,\ s+\mu-\nu,\ s+\mu+\nu\\ \frac{2s+2\mu+1}{2}\end{bmatrix}$

$$\times\left[\cos(\nu\pi)\sec(s+\mu)\,\pi\right]^{(1\pm1)/2}$$

$$\times {}_3F_2\!\left(\begin{matrix}\frac{1+2\mu}{2},\ s+\mu-\nu,\ s+\mu+\nu\\ 2\mu+1,\ \frac{2s+2\mu+1}{2};\ \mp\frac{a}{b}\end{matrix}\right)+\frac{\sqrt{\pi}\,a^{-\mu}}{2^{s-2\mu+1}b^{s-\mu}}$$

$$\times\,\Gamma\!\begin{bmatrix}\mu,\ s-\mu-\nu,\ s-\mu+\nu\\ \frac{2s-2\mu+1}{2}\end{bmatrix}\left[\cos(\nu\pi)\sec(s-\mu)\,\pi\right]^{(1\pm1)/2}$$

$$\times\,{}_3F_2\!\left(\begin{matrix}\frac{1-2\mu}{2},\ s-\nu-\mu,\ s+\nu-\mu\\ 1-2\mu,\ \frac{2s-2\mu+1}{2};\ \mp\frac{a}{b}\end{matrix}\right)$$

$$+\frac{(1\pm1)\cos(\mu\pi)}{2^{s+1}a^{s-1/2}\sqrt{b}}\,\Gamma\!\begin{bmatrix}\frac{2s-2\mu-1}{2},\ \frac{2s+2\mu-1}{2},\ 1-s\end{bmatrix}$$

$$\times\,{}_3F_2\!\left(\begin{matrix}\frac{1+2\nu}{2},\ \frac{1-2\nu}{2},\ 1-s;\ \mp\frac{a}{b}\\ \frac{3-2s-2\mu}{2},\ \frac{3-2s+2\mu}{2}\end{matrix}\right)$$

$$\left[\operatorname{Re}s>|\operatorname{Re}\mu|+|\operatorname{Re}\nu|;\ \left\{\begin{matrix}\operatorname{Re}a,\ \operatorname{Re}b>0;\ \operatorname{Re}s<1\\ \operatorname{Re}b>0\end{matrix}\right\}\right]$$

2	$e^{-(a+b)x}K_\mu(ax)K_\nu(bx)$	$\dfrac{\sqrt{\pi}\,b^\nu}{2^{s+2\nu+1}a^{s+\nu}}\,\Gamma\!\begin{bmatrix}-\nu,\ s+\mu+\nu,\ s-\mu+\nu\\ \frac{2s+2\nu+1}{2}\end{bmatrix}$

$$\times\,{}_3F_2\!\left(\begin{matrix}\frac{1+2\nu}{2},\ s+\mu+\nu,\ s-\mu+\nu\\ 1+2\nu,\ \frac{2s+2\nu+1}{2};\ -\frac{b}{a}\end{matrix}\right)$$

$$+\frac{\sqrt{\pi}\,a^{\nu-s}\,b^{-\nu}}{2^{s-2\nu+1}}\,\Gamma\!\begin{bmatrix}\nu,\ s+\mu-\nu,\ s-\mu-\nu\\ \frac{2s-2\nu+1}{2}\end{bmatrix}$$

$$\times\,{}_3F_2\!\left(\begin{matrix}\frac{1-2\nu}{2},\ s+\mu-\nu,\ s-\mu-\nu\\ 1-2\nu,\ \frac{2s-2\nu+1}{2};\ -\frac{b}{a}\end{matrix}\right)$$

$$[\operatorname{Re}(a+b)>0;\ \operatorname{Re}s>|\operatorname{Re}\mu|+|\operatorname{Re}\nu|]$$

3	$e^{\pm ax^2}K_\mu(ax^2)K_\nu(bx)$	$\dfrac{\sqrt{\pi}\,b^\nu}{2^{(s+3\nu)/2+2}a^{(s+\nu)/2}}\left[\cos(\mu\pi)\sec\dfrac{(s+\nu)\,\pi}{2}\right]^{(1\pm1)/2}$

$$\times\,\Gamma\!\begin{bmatrix}-\nu,\ \frac{s+2\mu+\nu}{2},\ \frac{s-2\mu+\nu}{2}\\ \frac{s+\nu+1}{2}\end{bmatrix}{}_2F_2\!\left(\begin{matrix}\frac{s+2\mu+\nu}{2},\ \frac{s-2\mu+\nu}{2}\\ \nu+1,\ \frac{s+\nu+1}{2};\ \mp\frac{b^2}{8a}\end{matrix}\right)$$

$$+\frac{\sqrt{\pi}\,a^{(\nu-s)/2}b^{-\nu}}{2^{(s-3\nu)/2+2}}\left[\cos(\mu\pi)\sec\frac{(s-\nu)\,\pi}{2}\right]^{(1\pm1)/2}$$

$$\times\,\Gamma\!\begin{bmatrix}\nu,\ \frac{s+2\mu-\nu}{2},\ \frac{s-2\mu-\nu}{2}\\ \frac{s-\nu+1}{2}\end{bmatrix}{}_2F_2\!\left(\begin{matrix}\frac{s+2\mu-\nu}{2},\ \frac{s-2\mu-\nu}{2}\\ 1-\nu,\ \frac{s-\nu+1}{2};\ \mp\frac{b^2}{8a}\end{matrix}\right)+\frac{(1\pm1)}{2^{9/2-s}b^{s-1}}$$

$$\times\,\sqrt{\frac{\pi}{a}}\,\Gamma\!\left(\frac{s-\nu-1}{2}\right)\Gamma\!\left(\frac{s+\nu-1}{2}\right){}_2F_2\!\left(\begin{matrix}\frac{1+2\mu}{2},\ \frac{1-2\mu}{2}\\ \frac{3-s-\nu}{2},\ \frac{3-s+\nu}{2};\ -\frac{b^2}{8a}\end{matrix}\right)$$

$$\left[\operatorname{Re}s>2|\operatorname{Re}\mu|+|\operatorname{Re}\nu|;\ \left\{\begin{matrix}\operatorname{Re}a>0\\ \operatorname{Re}b>0\end{matrix}\right\}\right]$$

No.	$f(x)$	$F(s)$
4	$e^{\pm a/x^2} K_\mu\left(\dfrac{a}{x^2}\right) K_\nu(bx)$	$\dfrac{2^{s-3\mu-3}\,a^\mu}{b^{s-2\mu}}\,\Gamma\left[-\mu,\,\dfrac{s-2\mu+\nu}{2},\,\dfrac{s-2\mu-\nu}{2}\right]$

$$\times\, {}_1F_3\left(\begin{array}{c}\frac{1+2\mu}{2};\,\pm\frac{ab^2}{2}\\[4pt]1+2\mu,\,\frac{1-s+2\mu-\nu}{2},\,\frac{1-s+2\mu+\nu}{2}\end{array}\right)$$

$$+\,\frac{2^{s+3\mu-3}\,a^{-\mu}}{b^{s+2\mu}}\,\Gamma\left[\mu,\,\frac{s+2\mu-\nu}{2},\,\frac{s+2\mu+\nu}{2}\right]$$

$$\times\, {}_1F_3\left(\begin{array}{c}\frac{1-2\mu}{2};\,\pm\frac{ab^2}{2}\\[4pt]1-2\mu,\,\frac{2-s-2\mu-\nu}{2},\,\frac{2-s-2\mu+\nu}{2}\end{array}\right)$$

$$+\,\frac{\sqrt{\pi}\,a^{(s+\nu)/2}b^\nu}{2^{(\nu-s)/2+2}}\,\Gamma\left[-\nu,\,\dfrac{2\mu-\nu-s}{2},\,\dfrac{-2\mu-\nu-s}{2}\atop\dfrac{1-s-\nu}{2}\right]$$

$$\times\left[\cos(\mu\pi)\sec\frac{(s+\nu)\pi}{2}\right]^{(1\pm1)/2}$$

$$\times\, {}_1F_3\left(\begin{array}{c}\frac{s+\nu+1}{2};\,\pm\frac{ab^2}{2}\\[4pt]1+\nu,\,\frac{s-2\mu+\nu+2}{2},\,\frac{s+2\mu+\nu+2}{2}\end{array}\right)$$

$$+\,\frac{2^{(s+\nu)/2-2}\sqrt{\pi}}{a^{(\nu-s)/2}b^\nu}\,\Gamma\left[\nu,\,\dfrac{2\mu+\nu-s}{2},\,\dfrac{-2\mu+\nu-s}{2}\atop\dfrac{1-s+\nu}{2}\right]$$

$$\times\left[\cos(\mu\pi)\sec\frac{(s-\nu)\pi}{2}\right]^{(1\pm1)/2}$$

$$\times\, {}_1F_3\left(\begin{array}{c}\frac{s-\nu+1}{2};\,\pm\frac{ab^2}{2}\\[4pt]1-\nu,\,\frac{s-2\mu-\nu+2}{2},\,\frac{s+2\mu-\nu+2}{2}\end{array}\right)$$

$$\left[\operatorname{Re}b>0;\;\left\{\begin{array}{c}\operatorname{Re}s>|\operatorname{Re}\nu|-1\\\operatorname{Re}a>0\end{array}\right\}\right]$$

3.14.20. Products of $K_\mu(ax^r)$ and trigonometric or hyperbolic functions

Notation: $\delta=\left\{\begin{array}{c}1\\0\end{array}\right\}$.

No.	$f(x)$	$F(s)$
1	$\sin(ax)\,K_\mu(bx)\,K_\nu(bx)$	$\dfrac{2^{s-2}a}{b^{s+1}}\,\Gamma\left[\dfrac{s+\mu+\nu+1}{2},\,\dfrac{s+\mu-\nu+1}{2},\,\dfrac{s-\mu+\nu+1}{2},\,\dfrac{s-\mu-\nu+1}{2}\atop s+1\right]$

$$\times\, {}_4F_3\left(\begin{array}{c}\frac{s+\mu+\nu+1}{2},\,\frac{s+\mu-\nu+1}{2},\,\frac{s-\mu+\nu+1}{2},\,\frac{s-\mu-\nu+1}{2}\\[4pt]\frac{3}{2},\,\frac{s+1}{2},\,\frac{s+2}{2};\,-\frac{a^2}{4b^2}\end{array}\right)$$

$$[2\operatorname{Re}b>|\operatorname{Im}a|;\;\operatorname{Re}s>|\operatorname{Re}\mu|+|\operatorname{Re}\nu|-1]$$

| 2 | $\cos(ax)\,K_\mu(bx)\,K_\nu(bx)$ | $\dfrac{2^{s-3}}{b^s}\,\Gamma\left[\dfrac{s+\mu+\nu}{2},\,\dfrac{s+\mu-\nu}{2},\,\dfrac{s-\mu+\nu}{2},\,\dfrac{s-\mu-\nu}{2}\atop s\right]$ |

$$\times\, {}_4F_3\left(\begin{array}{c}\frac{s+\mu+\nu}{2},\,\frac{s+\mu-\nu}{2},\,\frac{s-\mu+\nu}{2},\,\frac{s-\mu-\nu}{2}\\[4pt]\frac{1}{2},\,\frac{s}{2},\,\frac{s+1}{2};\,-\frac{a^2}{4b^2}\end{array}\right)$$

$$[2\operatorname{Re}b>|\operatorname{Im}a|;\;\operatorname{Re}s>|\operatorname{Re}\mu|+|\operatorname{Re}\nu|]$$

No.	$f(x)$	$F(s)$

3

$\left\{ \begin{array}{l} \sin(ax)\sinh(ax) \\ \cos(ax)\cosh(ax) \end{array} \right\}$

$\times K_\mu(bx)K_\nu(bx)$

$\dfrac{\sqrt{\pi}\,a^{2\delta}}{4b^{s+2\delta}}\,\Gamma\left[\begin{array}{c} \frac{s-\mu-\nu+2\delta}{2},\ \frac{s-\mu+\nu+2\delta}{2},\ \frac{s+\mu-\nu+2\delta}{2},\ \frac{s+\mu+\nu+2\delta}{2} \\ \frac{s+2\delta}{2},\ \frac{s+2\delta+1}{2} \end{array} \right]$

$\times {}_8F_7\left(\begin{array}{c} \Delta\big(2,\frac{s-\mu-\nu+2\delta}{2}\big),\ \Delta\big(2,\frac{s-\mu+\nu+2\delta}{2}\big), \\ \frac{2\delta+1}{4},\ \frac{2\delta+3}{4},\ \frac{2\delta+1}{2}, \\ \Delta\big(2,\frac{s+\mu-\nu+2\delta}{2}\big),\ \Delta\big(2,\frac{s+\mu+\nu+2\delta}{2}\big) \\ \Delta\big(4,s+2\delta\big);\ -\frac{a^4}{4b^4} \end{array} \right)$

$[\operatorname{Re} b > (\operatorname{Re} a + \operatorname{Im} a)/2;\ \operatorname{Re} s > |\operatorname{Re}\mu| + |\operatorname{Re}\nu|]$

4

$\left\{ \begin{array}{l} \sin(ax)\cosh(ax) \\ \cos(ax)\sinh(ax) \end{array} \right\}$

$\times K_\mu(bx)K_\nu(bx)$

$\dfrac{\sqrt{\pi}\,a}{4b^{s+1}}\,\Gamma\left[\begin{array}{c} \frac{s-\mu-\nu+1}{2},\ \frac{s-\mu+\nu+1}{2},\ \frac{s+\mu-\nu+1}{2},\ \frac{s+\mu+\nu+1}{2} \\ \frac{s+1}{2},\ \frac{s+2}{2} \end{array} \right]$

$\times {}_8F_7\left(\begin{array}{c} \Delta\big(2,\frac{s-\mu-\nu+1}{2}\big),\ \Delta\big(2,\frac{s-\mu+\nu+1}{2}\big), \\ \frac{1}{2},\ \frac{3}{4},\ \frac{5}{4}, \\ \Delta\big(2,\frac{s+\mu-\nu+1}{2}\big),\ \Delta\big(2,\frac{s+\mu+\nu+1}{2}\big) \\ \Delta\big(4,s+1\big);\ -\frac{a^4}{4b^4} \end{array} \right)$

$\pm\dfrac{\sqrt{\pi}\,a^3}{12b^{s+3}}\,\Gamma\left[\begin{array}{c} \frac{s-\mu-\nu+3}{2},\ \frac{s-\mu+\nu+3}{2},\ \frac{s+\mu-\nu+3}{2},\ \frac{s+\mu+\nu+3}{2} \\ \frac{s+3}{2},\ \frac{s+4}{2} \end{array} \right]$

$\times {}_8F_7\left(\begin{array}{c} \Delta\big(2,\frac{s-\mu-\nu+3}{2}\big),\ \Delta\big(2,\frac{s-\mu+\nu+3}{2}\big), \\ \frac{5}{4},\ \frac{3}{2},\ \frac{7}{4}, \\ \Delta\big(2,\frac{s+\mu-\nu+3}{2}\big),\ \Delta\big(2,\frac{s+\mu+\nu+3}{2}\big) \\ \Delta\big(4,s+3\big);\ -\frac{a^4}{4b^4} \end{array} \right)$

$[\operatorname{Re} b > (\operatorname{Re} a + \operatorname{Im} a)/2;\ \operatorname{Re} s > |\operatorname{Re}\mu| + |\operatorname{Re}\nu|]$

5

$\left\{ \begin{array}{l} \sin(a\sqrt{x})\sinh(a\sqrt{x}) \\ \cos(a\sqrt{x})\cosh(a\sqrt{x}) \end{array} \right\}$

$\times K_\mu(bx)K_\nu(bx)$

$\dfrac{2^{s+\delta-3}a^{2\delta}}{b^{s+\delta}}\,\Gamma\left[\begin{array}{c} \frac{s-\mu-\nu+\delta}{2},\ \frac{s-\mu+\nu+\delta}{2},\ \frac{s+\mu-\nu+\delta}{2},\ \frac{s+\mu+\nu+\delta}{2} \\ s+\delta \end{array} \right]$

$\times {}_4F_5\left(\begin{array}{c} \frac{s-\mu-\nu+\delta}{2},\ \frac{s-\mu+\nu+\delta}{2},\ \frac{s+\mu-\nu+\delta}{2},\ \frac{s+\mu+\nu+\delta}{2} \\ \frac{2\delta+1}{4},\ \frac{2\delta+3}{4},\ \frac{2\delta+1}{2},\ \frac{s+\delta}{2},\ \frac{s+\delta+1}{2};\ -\frac{a^4}{64b^2} \end{array} \right)$

$[\operatorname{Re} b > 0;\ \operatorname{Re} s > |\operatorname{Re}\mu| + |\operatorname{Re}\nu| - \delta]$

6

$\left\{ \begin{array}{l} \sin(a\sqrt{x})\cosh(a\sqrt{x}) \\ \cos(a\sqrt{x})\sinh(a\sqrt{x}) \end{array} \right\}$

$\times K_\mu(bx)K_\nu(bx)$

$\dfrac{2^{s-5/2}a}{b^{s+1/2}}\,\Gamma\left[\begin{array}{c} \frac{2s-2\mu-2\nu+1}{4},\ \frac{2s-2\mu+2\nu+1}{4},\ \frac{2s+2\mu-2\nu+1}{4},\ \frac{2s+2\mu+2\nu+1}{4} \\ \frac{2s+1}{2} \end{array} \right]$

$\times {}_4F_5\left(\begin{array}{c} \frac{2s-2\mu-2\nu+1}{4},\ \frac{2s-2\mu+2\nu+1}{4},\ \frac{2s+2\mu-2\nu+1}{4},\ \frac{2s+2\mu+2\nu+1}{4} \\ \frac{1}{2},\ \frac{3}{4},\ \frac{5}{4},\ \frac{2s+1}{4},\ \frac{2s+3}{4};\ -\frac{a^4}{64b^2} \end{array} \right)$

$\pm\dfrac{2^{s-3/2}a^3}{3b^{s+3/2}}\,\Gamma\left[\begin{array}{c} \frac{2s-2\mu-2\nu+3}{4},\ \frac{2s-2\mu+2\nu+3}{4},\ \frac{2s+2\mu-2\nu+3}{4},\ \frac{2s+2\mu+2\nu+3}{4} \\ \frac{2s+3}{2} \end{array} \right]$

$\times {}_4F_5\left(\begin{array}{c} \frac{2s-2\mu-2\nu+3}{4},\ \frac{2s-2\mu+2\nu+3}{4},\ \frac{2s+2\mu-2\nu+3}{4},\ \frac{2s+2\mu+2\nu+3}{4} \\ \frac{5}{4},\ \frac{3}{2},\ \frac{7}{4},\ \frac{2s+3}{4},\ \frac{2s+5}{4};\ -\frac{a^4}{64b^2} \end{array} \right)$

$[\operatorname{Re} b > 0;\ \operatorname{Re} s > |\operatorname{Re}\mu| + |\operatorname{Re}\nu| - 1/2]$

3.14.21.   **Products of $K_\nu(ax)$ and $\mathrm{erf}(b\sqrt{x})$, $\mathrm{erfi}(b\sqrt{x})$**

Notation: $\delta = \left\{ \begin{matrix} 1 \\ 0 \end{matrix} \right\}$.

1	$\mathrm{erf}(a\sqrt{x})\,\mathrm{erfi}(a\sqrt{x})$	$\dfrac{2^s a^2 b^{-s-1}}{\pi}\, \Gamma\left[\begin{matrix} \frac{s-\mu-\nu+1}{2},\ \frac{s-\mu+\nu+1}{2},\ \frac{s+\mu-\nu+1}{2},\ \frac{s+\mu+\nu+1}{2} \\ s+1 \end{matrix} \right]$
	$\times\, K_\mu(bx)\,K_\nu(bx)$	$\times\, {}_6F_5\left(\begin{matrix} \frac{1}{2},\ 1,\ \frac{s-\mu-\nu+1}{2},\ \frac{s-\mu+\nu+1}{2},\ \frac{s+\mu-\nu+1}{2},\ \frac{s+\mu+\nu+1}{2} \\ \frac{3}{4},\ \frac{5}{4},\ \frac{3}{2},\ \frac{s+1}{2},\ \frac{s+2}{2};\ \frac{a^4}{4b^2} \end{matrix} \right)$
		$[\mathrm{Re}\,b > 0;\ \mathrm{Re}\,s > (|\mathrm{Re}\,\mu| + |\mathrm{Re}\,\nu|) - 1]$

3.14.22.   **Products of $K_\nu(ax)$ and $S(cx)$, $C(cx)$**

Notation: $\delta = \left\{ \begin{matrix} 1 \\ 0 \end{matrix} \right\}$.

1	$\left\{ \begin{matrix} S(ax) \\ C(ax) \end{matrix} \right\}$	$\dfrac{a^{\delta+1/2} b^{-s-\delta-1/2}}{2\sqrt{2}\,(2\delta+1)}\, \Gamma\left[\begin{matrix} \frac{2s-2\mu-2\nu+2\delta+1}{4},\ \frac{2s-2\mu+2\nu+2\delta+1}{4} \\ \frac{2s+2\delta+1}{4} \end{matrix} \right]$
	$\times\, K_\mu(bx)\,K_\nu(bx)$	$\times\, \Gamma\left[\begin{matrix} \frac{2s+2\mu-2\nu+2\delta+1}{4},\ \frac{2s+2\mu+2\nu+2\delta+1}{4} \\ \frac{2s+2\delta+3}{4} \end{matrix} \right]$
		$\times\, {}_5F_4\left(\begin{matrix} \frac{2\delta+1}{4},\ \frac{2s-2\mu-2\nu+2\delta+1}{4},\ \frac{2s-2\mu+2\nu+2\delta+1}{4}, \\ \frac{2\delta+1}{2},\ \frac{2\delta+5}{4}, \end{matrix} \right.$
		$\left. \begin{matrix} \frac{2s+2\mu-2\nu+2\delta+1}{4},\ \frac{2s+2\mu+2\nu+2\delta+1}{4} \\ \frac{2s+2\delta+1}{4},\ \frac{2s+2\delta+3}{4};\ -\frac{a^2}{4b^2} \end{matrix} \right)$
		$[\mathrm{Re}\,b > |\mathrm{Im}\,a|;\ \mathrm{Re}\,s > |\mathrm{Re}\,\mu| + |\mathrm{Re}\,\nu| - \delta - 1/2]$

3.14.23.   **Products of $K_\nu(ax)$ and $J_\lambda(bx^r)$, $I_\mu(cx^r)$**

1	$J_\lambda(ax)\,K_\mu(bx)\,K_\nu(cx)$	$\dfrac{2^{s-3} a^\lambda}{c^{s+\lambda}\,\Gamma(\lambda+1)} \left\{ \left(\dfrac{b}{c}\right)^\mu \Gamma\left[-\mu,\ \frac{s+\lambda+\mu-\nu}{2},\ \frac{s+\lambda+\mu+\nu}{2} \right] \right.$
		$\times\, F_4\left(\frac{s+\lambda+\mu-\nu}{2},\ \frac{s+\lambda+\mu+\nu}{2};\ \lambda+1,\ \mu+1;\ -\frac{a^2}{c^2};\ \frac{b^2}{c^2} \right)$
		$+\left(\dfrac{b}{c}\right)^{-\mu} \Gamma\left[\mu,\ \frac{s+\lambda-\mu-\nu}{2},\ \frac{s+\lambda-\mu+\nu}{2} \right]$
		$\left. \times\, F_4\left(\frac{s+\lambda-\mu-\nu}{2},\ \frac{s+\lambda-\mu+\nu}{2};\ \lambda+1,\ 1-\mu;\ -\frac{a^2}{c^2},\ \frac{b^2}{c^2} \right) \right\}$
		$[\mathrm{Re}\,(b+c) > |\mathrm{Im}\,a|;\ \mathrm{Re}\,(s+\lambda) > |\mathrm{Re}\,\mu| + |\mathrm{Re}\,\nu|]$

No.	$f(x)$	$F(s)$
2	$\left\{\begin{array}{c} J_\lambda\left(ax\right) \\ I_\lambda\left(ax\right) \end{array}\right\} K_\mu\left(bx\right)$ $\times K_\nu\left(bx\right)$	$\dfrac{2^{s-3}a^\lambda}{b^{s+\lambda}}\,\Gamma\left[\begin{array}{c} \frac{s+\lambda+\mu+\nu}{2},\ \frac{s+\lambda+\mu-\nu}{2},\ \frac{s+\lambda-\mu+\nu}{2},\ \frac{s+\lambda-\mu-\nu}{2} \\ \lambda+1,\ s+\lambda \end{array}\right]$ $\times {}_4F_3\left(\begin{array}{c} \frac{s+\lambda+\mu+\nu}{2},\ \frac{s+\lambda+\mu-\nu}{2},\ \frac{s+\lambda-\mu+\nu}{2},\ \frac{s+\lambda-\mu-\nu}{2} \\ \lambda+1,\ \frac{s+\lambda}{2},\ \frac{s+\lambda+1}{2};\ \mp\frac{a^2}{4b^2} \end{array}\right)$ $\left[2\operatorname{Re}b>\left\{\begin{array}{c}\lvert\operatorname{Im}a\rvert\\\lvert\operatorname{Re}a\rvert\end{array}\right\};\ \operatorname{Re}\left(s+\lambda\right)>\lvert\operatorname{Re}\mu\rvert+\lvert\operatorname{Re}\nu\rvert\right]$
3	$J_\mu\left(a\sqrt{x}\right)K_\mu\left(a\sqrt{x}\right)$ $\times K_\nu\left(bx\right)$	$\dfrac{2^{s-3}}{\mu b^s}\,\Gamma\left(\dfrac{s-\nu}{2}\right)\Gamma\left(\dfrac{s+\nu}{2}\right){}_2F_3\left(\begin{array}{c}\frac{s-\nu}{2},\ \frac{s+\nu}{2};\ -\frac{a^4}{16b^2}\\ \frac12,\ \frac{2-\mu}{2},\ \frac{2+\mu}{2}\end{array}\right)-\dfrac{2^{s-3}a^2}{b^{s+1}\left(\mu^2-1\right)}$ $\times\Gamma\left(\dfrac{s-\nu+1}{2}\right)\Gamma\left(\dfrac{s+\nu+1}{2}\right){}_2F_3\left(\begin{array}{c}\frac{s-\nu+1}{2},\ \frac{s+\nu+1}{2};\ -\frac{a^4}{16b^2}\\ \frac32,\ \frac{3-\mu}{2},\ \frac{3+\mu}{2}\end{array}\right)$ $+\dfrac{2^{s-\mu-3}a^{2\mu}}{b^{s+\mu}}\,\Gamma\left[\begin{array}{c}-\mu,\ \frac{s+\mu-\nu}{2},\ \frac{s+\mu+\nu}{2}\\ \mu+1\end{array}\right]{}_2F_3\left(\begin{array}{c}\frac{s+\mu-\nu}{2},\ \frac{s+\mu+\nu}{2};\ -\frac{a^4}{16b^2}\\ \mu+1,\ \frac{\mu+1}{2},\ \frac{\mu+2}{2}\end{array}\right)$ $\left[a,\ \operatorname{Re}b,\ \operatorname{Re}\left(s+\nu\right),\ \operatorname{Re}\left(s+\mu+\nu\right)>0\right]$
4	$I_\lambda\left(ax\right)K_\mu\left(ax\right)K_\nu\left(bx\right)$	$\dfrac{2^{s-3}a^{\lambda+\mu}}{b^{s+\lambda+\mu}}\,\Gamma\left[\begin{array}{c}-\mu,\ \frac{s+\lambda+\mu+\nu}{2},\ \frac{s+\lambda+\mu-\nu}{2}\\ \lambda+1\end{array}\right]$ $\times {}_4F_3\left(\begin{array}{c}\frac{\lambda+\mu+1}{2},\ \frac{\lambda+\mu+2}{2},\ \frac{s+\lambda+\mu+\nu}{2},\ \frac{s+\lambda+\mu-\nu}{2}\\ \lambda+1,\ \mu+1,\ \lambda+\mu+1;\ \frac{4a^2}{b^2}\end{array}\right)+\dfrac{2^{s-3}a^{\lambda-\mu}}{b^{s+\lambda-\mu}}\,\Gamma\left(\mu\right)$ $\times\Gamma\left[\begin{array}{c}\frac{s+\lambda-\mu+\nu}{2},\ \frac{s+\lambda-\mu-\nu}{2}\\ \lambda+1\end{array}\right]{}_4F_3\left(\begin{array}{c}\frac{\lambda-\mu+1}{2},\ \frac{\lambda-\mu+2}{2},\ \frac{s+\lambda-\mu+\nu}{2},\ \frac{s+\lambda-\mu-\nu}{2}\\ 1-\mu,\ \lambda+1,\ \lambda-\mu+1;\ \frac{4a^2}{b^2}\end{array}\right)$ $\left[\operatorname{Re}a,\ \operatorname{Re}b>0;\ \operatorname{Re}\left(s+\lambda\right)>\lvert\operatorname{Re}\mu\rvert+\lvert\operatorname{Re}\nu\rvert\right]$
5	$K_\lambda\left(ax\right)K_\mu\left(bx\right)K_\nu\left(cx\right)$	$\dfrac{2^{s-4}}{c^s}\left[A\left(\lambda,\ \mu\right)+A\left(\lambda,\ -\mu\right)+A\left(-\lambda,\ \mu\right)+A\left(-\lambda,\ -\mu\right)\right]$ $A\left(\lambda,\ \mu\right)=\left(\dfrac{a}{c}\right)^\lambda\left(\dfrac{b}{c}\right)^\mu\Gamma\left[-\lambda,\ -\mu,\ \dfrac{s+\lambda+\mu-\nu}{2},\ \dfrac{s+\lambda+\mu+\nu}{2}\right]$ $\times F_4\left(\dfrac{s+\lambda+\mu-\nu}{2},\ \dfrac{s+\lambda+\mu+\nu}{2};\ \lambda+1,\ \mu+1;\ \dfrac{a^2}{c^2},\ \dfrac{b^2}{c^2}\right)$ $\left[\operatorname{Re}\left(a+b+c\right)>0;\ \operatorname{Re}s>\lvert\operatorname{Re}\lambda\rvert+\lvert\operatorname{Re}\mu\rvert+\lvert\operatorname{Re}\nu\rvert\right]$
6	$K_\lambda\left(ax\right)K_\mu\left(ax\right)K_\nu\left(bx\right)$	$\dfrac{2^{s-4}b^{-\nu}}{a^{s-\nu}}\,\Gamma\left[\nu,\ \dfrac{s+\lambda+\mu-\nu}{2},\ \dfrac{s-\lambda+\mu-\nu}{2},\ \dfrac{s+\lambda-\mu-\nu}{2},\ \dfrac{s-\lambda-\mu-\nu}{2}\right]$ $\phantom{\dfrac{2^{s-4}b^{-\nu}}{a^{s-\nu}}\,\Gamma[}s-\nu$ $\times {}_4F_3\left(\begin{array}{c}\frac{s+\lambda+\mu-\nu}{2},\ \frac{s-\lambda+\mu-\nu}{2},\ \frac{s+\lambda-\mu-\nu}{2},\ \frac{s-\lambda-\mu-\nu}{2}\\ 1-\nu,\ \frac{s-\nu}{2},\ \frac{s-\nu+1}{2};\ \frac{b^2}{4a^2}\end{array}\right)$ $+\dfrac{2^{s-4}b^\nu}{a^{s+\nu}}\,\Gamma\left[-\nu,\ \dfrac{s+\lambda+\mu+\nu}{2},\ \dfrac{s-\lambda+\mu+\nu}{2},\ \dfrac{s+\lambda-\mu+\nu}{2},\ \dfrac{s-\lambda-\mu+\nu}{2}\right]$ $\phantom{+\dfrac{2^{s-4}b^\nu}{a^{s+\nu}}\,\Gamma[}s+\nu$ $\times {}_4F_3\left(\begin{array}{c}\frac{s+\lambda+\mu+\nu}{2},\ \frac{s-\lambda+\mu+\nu}{2},\ \frac{s+\lambda-\mu+\nu}{2},\ \frac{s-\lambda-\mu+\nu}{2}\\ 1+\nu,\ \frac{s+\nu}{2},\ \frac{s+\nu+1}{2};\ \frac{b^2}{4a^2}\end{array}\right)$ $\left[\operatorname{Re}\left(2a+b\right)>0;\ \operatorname{Re}s>\lvert\operatorname{Re}\lambda\rvert+\lvert\operatorname{Re}\mu\rvert+\lvert\operatorname{Re}\nu\rvert\right]$

3.15.   The Struve Functions $\mathbf{H}_\nu(z)$ and $\mathbf{L}_\nu(z)$

More formulas can be obtained from the corresponding sections due to the relations

$$\mathbf{H}_{\pm 1/2}(z) = \sqrt{\frac{2}{\pi}}\,\frac{1}{\sqrt{z}}\left\{\begin{matrix}1-\cos z\\\sin z\end{matrix}\right\}, \quad \mathbf{L}_{\pm 1/2}(z) = \sqrt{\frac{2}{\pi}}\,\frac{1}{\sqrt{z}}\left\{\begin{matrix}\cosh z-1\\\sinh z\end{matrix}\right\},$$

$$\mathbf{H}_{-n-1/2}(z) = (-1)^n\, J_{n+1/2}(z), \quad \mathbf{L}_{-n-1/2}(z) = I_{n+1/2}(z),$$

$$\left\{\begin{matrix}\mathbf{H}_\nu(z)\\\mathbf{L}_\nu(z)\end{matrix}\right\} = \frac{2^{-\nu}z^{\nu+1}}{\sqrt{\pi}\,\Gamma(\nu+3/2)}\,{}_1F_2\left(1;\frac{3}{2},\nu+\frac{3}{2};\mp\frac{z^2}{4}\right),$$

$$\mathbf{H}_\nu(z) = z^{\nu+1}\left(z^2\right)^{-(\nu+1)/2}G_{13}^{11}\left(\frac{z^2}{4}\,\middle|\,\begin{matrix}(\nu+1)/2\\(\nu+1)/2,\,-\nu/2,\,\nu/2\end{matrix}\right).$$

3.15.1. $\mathbf{H}_\nu(bx)$, $\mathbf{L}_\nu(bx)$, and algebraic functions

No.	$f(x)$	$F(s)$
1	$\mathbf{H}_\nu(ax)$	$\dfrac{2^{s-1}}{a^s}\,\tan\dfrac{(s+\nu)\pi}{2}\,\Gamma\left[\begin{matrix}\frac{s+\nu}{2}\\\frac{2-s+\nu}{2}\end{matrix}\right]$ $$[a>0;\ \mathrm{Re}\,s<3/2;\ |\mathrm{Re}\,(s+\nu)|<1]$$
2	$(a-x)_+^{\alpha-1}\left\{\begin{matrix}\mathbf{H}_\nu(bx)\\\mathbf{L}_\nu(bx)\end{matrix}\right\}$	$\dfrac{a^{s+\alpha+\nu}\,b^{\nu+1}}{2^\nu\sqrt{\pi}\,\Gamma\left(\frac{2\nu+3}{2}\right)}\,B(\alpha,s+\nu+1)\,{}_3F_4\left(\begin{matrix}1,\frac{s+\nu+1}{2},\frac{s+\nu+2}{2};\mp\frac{a^2b^2}{4}\\\frac{3}{2},\frac{2\nu+3}{2},\frac{s+\alpha+\nu+1}{2},\frac{s+\alpha+\nu+2}{2}\end{matrix}\right)$ $$[a,\ \mathrm{Re}\,\alpha>0;\ \mathrm{Re}\,(s+\nu)>-1]$$
3	$(x-a)_+^{\alpha-1}\mathbf{H}_\nu(bx)$	$\dfrac{a^{s+\alpha+\nu}\,b^{\nu+1}}{2^\nu\sqrt{\pi}}\,\Gamma\left[\begin{matrix}\alpha,\,-s-\alpha-\nu\\\frac{2\nu+3}{2},\,-s-\nu\end{matrix}\right]{}_3F_4\left(\begin{matrix}1,\frac{s+\nu+1}{2},\frac{s+\nu+2}{2};-\frac{a^2b^2}{4}\\\frac{3}{2},\frac{2\nu+3}{2},\frac{s+\alpha+\nu+1}{2},\frac{s+\alpha+\nu+2}{2}\end{matrix}\right)$ $+\dfrac{\pi}{2}\left(\dfrac{b}{2}\right)^{1-\alpha-s}\csc\dfrac{(s+\alpha+\nu)\pi}{2}\,\dfrac{1}{\Gamma\left(\frac{3-s-\alpha+\nu}{2}\right)\Gamma\left(\frac{3-s-\alpha-\nu}{2}\right)}$ $\times\,{}_2F_3\left(\begin{matrix}\frac{1-\alpha}{2},\frac{2-\alpha}{2};-\frac{a^2b^2}{4}\\\frac{1}{2},\frac{3-s-\alpha-\nu}{2},\frac{3-s-\alpha+\nu}{2}\end{matrix}\right)$ $-\dfrac{\pi a}{2}\left(\dfrac{b}{2}\right)^{2-\alpha-s}\sec\dfrac{(s+\alpha+\nu)\pi}{2}\,\dfrac{1-\alpha}{\Gamma\left(\frac{4-s-\alpha-\nu}{2}\right)\Gamma\left(\frac{4-s-\alpha+\nu}{2}\right)}$ $\times\,{}_2F_3\left(\begin{matrix}\frac{2-\alpha}{2},\frac{3-\alpha}{2};-\frac{a^2b^2}{4}\\\frac{3}{2},\frac{4-s-\alpha+\nu}{2},\frac{4-s-\alpha-\nu}{2}\end{matrix}\right)$ $$[a,b,\ \mathrm{Re}\,\alpha>0;\ \mathrm{Re}\,(s+\alpha)<5/2,\,2-\mathrm{Re}\,\nu]$$
4	$(a^2-x^2)_+^{\alpha-1}$ $\times\left\{\begin{matrix}\mathbf{H}_\nu(bx)\\\mathbf{L}_\nu(bx)\end{matrix}\right\}$	$\dfrac{a^{s+2\alpha+\nu-1}\,b^{\nu+1}}{2^{\nu+1}\sqrt{\pi}\,\Gamma\left(\frac{2\nu+3}{2}\right)}\,B\left(\alpha,\frac{s+\nu+1}{2}\right){}_2F_3\left(\begin{matrix}1,\frac{s+\nu+1}{2};\mp\frac{a^2b^2}{4}\\\frac{3}{2},\frac{2\nu+3}{2},\frac{s+2\alpha+\nu+1}{2}\end{matrix}\right)$ $$[a,\ \mathrm{Re}\,\alpha>0;\ \mathrm{Re}\,(s+\nu)>-1]$$

No.	$f(x)$	$F(s)$
5	$\left(x^2 - a^2\right)_+^{\alpha-1} \mathbf{H}_\nu(bx)$	$\dfrac{a^{s+2\alpha+\nu-1} b^{\nu+1}}{2^{\nu+1}\sqrt{\pi}\,\Gamma\left(\frac{2\nu+3}{2}\right)} \mathrm{B}\left(\alpha, \dfrac{1-s-2\alpha-\nu}{2}\right) {}_2F_3\left(\begin{array}{c} 1, \frac{s+\nu+1}{2}; -\frac{a^2b^2}{4} \\ \frac{3}{2}, \frac{2\nu+3}{2}, \frac{s+2\alpha+\nu+1}{2} \end{array}\right)$
		$-\dfrac{\pi}{2}\left(\dfrac{b}{2}\right)^{2-2\alpha-s} \dfrac{\sec\frac{(s+2\alpha+\nu)\pi}{2}}{\Gamma\left(\frac{4-s-2\alpha-\nu}{2}\right)\Gamma\left(\frac{4-s-2\alpha+\nu}{2}\right)}$
		$\times {}_1F_2\left(\begin{array}{c} 1-\alpha; -\frac{a^2b^2}{4} \\ \frac{4-s-2\alpha+\nu}{2}, \frac{4-s-2\alpha-\nu}{2} \end{array}\right)$
		$[a,\ \mathrm{Re}\,\alpha > 0;\ \mathrm{Re}\,(s+2\alpha) < 7/2,\ 3 - \mathrm{Re}\,\nu]$
6	$\dfrac{1}{(x+a)^\rho}\mathbf{H}_\nu(bx)$	$\dfrac{a^{s+\nu-\rho+1} b^{\nu+1}}{2^\nu\sqrt{\pi}\,\Gamma\left(\frac{2\nu+3}{2}\right)} \mathrm{B}(s+\nu+1, \rho-\nu-s-1)$
		$\times {}_3F_4\left(\begin{array}{c} 1, \frac{s+\nu+1}{2}, \frac{s+\nu+2}{2}; -\frac{a^2b^2}{4} \\ \frac{3}{2}, \frac{2\nu+3}{2}, \frac{s+\nu-\rho+2}{2}, \frac{s+\nu-\rho+3}{2} \end{array}\right) + \dfrac{\pi}{2}\left(\dfrac{b}{2}\right)^{\rho-s}$
		$\times \dfrac{\sec\frac{(s+\nu-\rho)\pi}{2}}{\Gamma\left(\frac{2-s-\nu+\rho}{2}\right)\Gamma\left(\frac{2-s+\nu+\rho}{2}\right)} {}_2F_3\left(\begin{array}{c} \frac{\rho}{2}, \frac{\rho+1}{2}; -\frac{a^2b^2}{4} \\ \frac{1}{2}, \frac{2-s-\nu+\rho}{2}, \frac{2-s+\nu+\rho}{2} \end{array}\right)$
		$-\dfrac{\pi a}{2}\left(\dfrac{b}{2}\right)^{\rho-s+1} \dfrac{\rho\csc\frac{(s+\nu-\rho)\pi}{2}}{\Gamma\left(\frac{3-s-\nu+\rho}{2}\right)\Gamma\left(\frac{3-s+\nu+\rho}{2}\right)}$
		$\times {}_2F_3\left(\begin{array}{c} \frac{\rho+1}{2}, \frac{\rho+2}{2}; -\frac{a^2b^2}{4} \\ \frac{3}{2}, \frac{3-s-\nu+\rho}{2}, \frac{3-s+\nu+\rho}{2} \end{array}\right)$
		$\left[\begin{array}{c} b > 0;\ \mathrm{Re}\,(s-\rho) < 3/2; \\ -1 < \mathrm{Re}\,(s+\nu) < \mathrm{Re}\,\rho+1;\ |\arg a| < \pi \end{array}\right]$
7	$\dfrac{1}{x-a}\mathbf{H}_\nu(bx)$	$-\pi a^{s-1}\cot\left[(s+\nu)\pi\right]\mathbf{H}_\nu(ab)$
		$+\dfrac{2^{s-2}\pi\csc\frac{(s+\nu)\pi}{2}}{b^{s-1}\Gamma\left(\frac{3-s-\nu}{2}\right)\Gamma\left(\frac{3-s+\nu}{2}\right)} {}_1F_2\left(\begin{array}{c} 1; -\frac{a^2b^2}{4} \\ \frac{3-s-\nu}{2}, \frac{3-s+\nu}{2} \end{array}\right)$
		$-\dfrac{\pi}{2}\left(\dfrac{b}{2}\right)^{2-s} \dfrac{a\sec\frac{(s+\nu)\pi}{2}}{\Gamma\left(\frac{4-s-\nu}{2}\right)\Gamma\left(\frac{4-s+\nu}{2}\right)} {}_1F_2\left(\begin{array}{c} 1; -\frac{a^2b^2}{4} \\ \frac{4-s-\nu}{2}, \frac{4-s+\nu}{2} \end{array}\right)$
		$[a,\ b > 0;\ -1 < \mathrm{Re}\,(s+\nu) < 3;\ \mathrm{Re}\,s < 5/2]$
8	$\dfrac{1}{(x^2+a^2)^\rho}\mathbf{H}_\nu(bx)$	$\dfrac{a^{s+\nu-2\rho+1} b^{\nu+1}}{2^{\nu+1}\sqrt{\pi}\,\Gamma\left(\frac{2\nu+3}{2}\right)} \mathrm{B}\left(\dfrac{s+\nu+1}{2}, \dfrac{2\rho-\nu-s-1}{2}\right)$
		$\times {}_2F_3\left(\begin{array}{c} 1, \frac{s+\nu+1}{2}; \frac{a^2b^2}{4} \\ \frac{3}{2}, \frac{2\nu+3}{2}, \frac{s+\nu-2\rho+3}{2} \end{array}\right) + \dfrac{\pi(b/2)^{2\rho-s}}{2\Gamma\left(\frac{2-s-\nu+2\rho}{2}\right)\Gamma\left(\frac{2-s+\nu+2\rho}{2}\right)}$
		$\times \sec\dfrac{(s+\nu-2\rho)\pi}{2} {}_1F_2\left(\begin{array}{c} \rho; \frac{a^2b^2}{4} \\ \frac{2-s-\nu+2\rho}{2}, \frac{2-s+\nu+2\rho}{2} \end{array}\right)$
		$\left[\begin{array}{c} b,\ \mathrm{Re}\,a > 0;\ \mathrm{Re}\,(s-2\rho) < 3/2; \\ -1 < \mathrm{Re}\,(s+\nu) < 2\,\mathrm{Re}\,\rho+1 \end{array}\right]$

No.	$f(x)$	$F(s)$
9	$\dfrac{1}{x^2-a^2}\,\mathbf{H}_\nu(bx)$	$\dfrac{\pi\,a^{s-2}}{2}\tan\dfrac{(s+\nu)\pi}{2}\,\mathbf{H}_\nu(ab)+2^{s-3}b^{2-s}\tan\dfrac{(s+\nu)\pi}{2}$ $\times\Gamma\!\left[\begin{array}{c}\frac{s+\nu-2}{2}\\ \frac{4-s+\nu}{2}\end{array}\right]\,{}_1F_2\!\left(\begin{array}{c}1;\ -\frac{a^2b^2}{4}\\ \frac{4-s-\nu}{2},\ \frac{4-s+\nu}{2}\end{array}\right)$ $[a,b>0;\ \operatorname{Re}s<7/2;\ -1<\operatorname{Re}(s+\nu)<3]$
10	$(a-x)_+^{\alpha-1}$ $\times\left\{\begin{array}{c}\mathbf{H}_\nu(bx(a-x))\\ \mathbf{L}_\nu(bx(a-x))\end{array}\right\}$	$\dfrac{a^{s+\alpha+2\nu+1}b^{\nu+1}}{2^\nu\sqrt{\pi}}\,\Gamma\!\left[\begin{array}{c}\alpha+\nu+1,\ s+\nu+1\\ \frac{2\nu+3}{2},\ s+\alpha+2\nu+2\end{array}\right]$ $\times\,{}_5F_6\!\left(\begin{array}{c}1,\ \Delta(2,\alpha+\nu+1),\ \Delta(2,s+\nu+1)\\ \frac{3}{2},\ \frac{2\nu+3}{2},\ \Delta(4,s+\alpha+2\nu+2);\ \mp\frac{a^4b^2}{64}\end{array}\right)$ $[a>0;\ \operatorname{Re}(s+\nu),\ \operatorname{Re}(\alpha+\nu)>-1]$
11	$(a-x)_+^{\alpha-1}$ $\times\left\{\begin{array}{c}\mathbf{H}_\nu(b\sqrt{x(a-x)})\\ \mathbf{L}_\nu(b\sqrt{x(a-x)})\end{array}\right\}$	$\dfrac{a^{s+\alpha+\nu}b^{\nu+1}}{2^\nu\sqrt{\pi}}\,\Gamma\!\left[\begin{array}{c}\frac{2\alpha+\nu+1}{2},\ \frac{2s+\nu+1}{2}\\ \frac{2\nu+3}{2},\ s+\alpha+\nu+1\end{array}\right]$ $\times\,{}_3F_4\!\left(\begin{array}{c}1,\ \frac{2\alpha+\nu+1}{2},\ \frac{2s+\nu+1}{2};\ \mp\frac{a^2b^2}{16}\\ \frac{3}{2},\ \frac{2\nu+3}{2},\ \frac{s+\alpha+\nu+1}{2},\ \frac{s+\alpha+\nu+2}{2}\end{array}\right)$ $[a>0;\ \operatorname{Re}s,\ \operatorname{Re}\alpha>-\operatorname{Re}(\nu+1)/2]$
12	$(x^2+a^2)^{-\nu/2}$ $\times\mathbf{H}_\nu(b\sqrt{x^2+a^2})$	$\dfrac{1}{(2a)^\nu}\left(\dfrac{a}{b}\right)^{s/2}\Gamma\!\left(\dfrac{s}{2}\right)\left[\dfrac{1}{\pi}\,\Gamma\!\left[\begin{array}{c}\frac{1-s}{2}\\ \frac{2\nu+1}{2}\end{array}\right]S_{s/2+\nu,\,s/2-\nu}(ab)\right.$ $\left.+2^{\nu-s/2-1}Y_{\nu-s/2}(ab)\right]$ $[a,b>0;\ 0<\operatorname{Re}s<1,\ \operatorname{Re}\nu+3/2]$
13	$(x^2+a^2)^{\nu/2}$ $\times\mathbf{H}_\nu(b\sqrt{x^2+a^2})$	$\dfrac{2^{s/2-1}a^{s/2+\nu}}{b^{s/2}}\,\Gamma\!\left(\dfrac{s}{2}\right)\sec\dfrac{(2\nu+s)\pi}{2}$ $\times\left[\cos(\nu\pi)\,\mathbf{H}_{s/2+\nu}(ab)+\sin(s\pi)\,J_{-s/2-\nu}(ab)\right]$ $[a,b>0;\ 0<\operatorname{Re}s<1-2\operatorname{Re}\nu,\ 3/2-\operatorname{Re}\nu]$
14	$(a^2-x^2)_+^{-\nu/2}$ $\times\mathbf{H}_\nu(b\sqrt{a^2-x^2})$	$\dfrac{a^{s+1}b^{\nu+1}}{2^{\nu+2}}\,\Gamma\!\left[\begin{array}{c}\frac{s}{2}\\ \frac{2\nu+3}{2},\ \frac{s+3}{2}\end{array}\right]\,{}_1F_2\!\left(\begin{array}{c}1;\ -\frac{a^2b^2}{4}\\ \frac{2\nu+3}{2},\ \frac{s+3}{2}\end{array}\right)\qquad[a,b,\ \operatorname{Re}s>0]$
15	$(a^2-x^2)_+^{\nu/2}$ $\times\left\{\begin{array}{c}\mathbf{H}_\nu(b\sqrt{a^2-x^2})\\ \mathbf{L}_\nu(b\sqrt{a^2-x^2})\end{array}\right\}$	$\dfrac{2^{s/2-1}a^{s/2+\nu}}{b^{s/2}}\,\Gamma\!\left(\dfrac{s}{2}\right)\left\{\begin{array}{c}\mathbf{H}_{s/2+\nu}(ab)\\ \mathbf{L}_{s/2+\nu}(ab)\end{array}\right\}$ $[a,b,\ \operatorname{Re}s>0;\ \operatorname{Re}\nu>-3/2]$

No.	$f(x)$	$F(s)$
16	$\dfrac{1}{(x+a)^\rho}$ $\times \left\{ \begin{array}{c} \mathbf{H}_\nu\left(bx/(x+a)\right) \\ \mathbf{L}_\nu\left(bx/(x+a)\right) \end{array} \right\}$	$\dfrac{a^{s-\rho}b^{\nu+1}}{2^\nu\sqrt{\pi}\,\Gamma\left(\frac{2\nu+3}{2}\right)} \mathrm{B}\left(s+\nu+1,\rho-s\right) {}_3F_4\left(\begin{array}{c} 1, \frac{s+\nu+1}{2}, \frac{s+\nu+2}{2}; \mp\frac{b^2}{4} \\ \frac{3}{2}, \frac{2\nu+3}{2}, \frac{\nu+\rho+1}{2}, \frac{\nu+\rho+2}{2} \end{array} \right)$ $[-\operatorname{Re}\nu-1 < \operatorname{Re}s < \operatorname{Re}\rho; \ |\arg a| < \pi]$
17	$\dfrac{1}{(x^2+a^2)^\rho}$ $\times \left\{ \begin{array}{c} \mathbf{H}_\nu\left(bx/(x^2+a^2)\right) \\ \mathbf{L}_\nu\left(bx/(x^2+a^2)\right) \end{array} \right\}$	$\dfrac{a^{s-\nu-2\rho-1}}{\sqrt{\pi}\,\Gamma\left(\frac{2\nu+3}{2}\right)} \left(\dfrac{b}{2}\right)^{\nu+1} \mathrm{B}\left(\dfrac{s+\nu+1}{2}, \dfrac{1-s+\nu+2\rho}{2}\right)$ $\times {}_3F_4\left(\begin{array}{c} 1, \frac{s+\nu+1}{2}, \frac{1-s+\nu+2\rho}{2}; \mp\frac{b^2}{16a^2} \\ \frac{3}{2}, \frac{2\nu+3}{2}, \frac{\nu+\rho+1}{2}, \frac{\nu+\rho+2}{2} \end{array} \right)$ $[\operatorname{Re}a>0; \ -\operatorname{Re}\nu-1 < \operatorname{Re}s < \operatorname{Re}(\nu+2\rho)+1]$

3.15.2. $\mathbf{H}_\nu(bx)$, $\mathbf{L}_\nu(bx)$, and the exponential function

No.	$f(x)$	$F(s)$
1	$e^{-ax}\left\{ \begin{array}{c} \mathbf{H}_\nu(bx) \\ \mathbf{L}_\nu(bx) \end{array} \right\}$	$\dfrac{b^{\nu+1}}{2^\nu\sqrt{\pi}\,a^{s+\nu+1}} \Gamma\left[\begin{array}{c} s+\nu+1 \\ \frac{2\nu+3}{2} \end{array} \right] {}_3F_2\left(\begin{array}{c} 1, \frac{s+\nu+1}{2}, \frac{s+\nu+2}{2} \\ \frac{3}{2}, \frac{2\nu+3}{2}; \mp\frac{b^2}{a^2} \end{array} \right)$ $[b, \ \operatorname{Re}a>0; \ \operatorname{Re}(s+\nu)>-1]$
2	$e^{-ax^2}\left\{ \begin{array}{c} \mathbf{H}_\nu(bx) \\ \mathbf{L}_\nu(bx) \end{array} \right\}$	$\dfrac{(b/2)^{\nu+1}}{\sqrt{\pi}\,a^{(s+\nu+1)/2}} \Gamma\left[\begin{array}{c} \frac{s+\nu+1}{2} \\ \frac{2\nu+3}{2} \end{array} \right] {}_2F_2\left(\begin{array}{c} 1, \frac{s+\nu+1}{2}; \mp\frac{b^2}{4a} \\ \frac{3}{2}, \frac{2\nu+3}{2} \end{array} \right)$ $[\operatorname{Re}a>0; \ \operatorname{Re}(s+\nu)>-1]$
3	$e^{-a/x^2}\,\mathbf{H}_\nu(bx)$	$\dfrac{a^{(s+\nu+1)/2}b^{\nu+1}}{2^{\nu+1}\sqrt{\pi}} \Gamma\left[\begin{array}{c} -\frac{s+\nu+1}{2} \\ \frac{2\nu+3}{2} \end{array} \right] {}_1F_3\left(\begin{array}{c} 1; \frac{ab^2}{4} \\ \frac{3}{2}, \frac{2\nu+3}{2}, \frac{s+\nu+3}{2} \end{array} \right)$ $+\dfrac{2^{s-1}\pi}{b^s\,\Gamma\left(\frac{2-s-\nu}{2}\right)\Gamma\left(\frac{2-s+\nu}{2}\right)} \sec\dfrac{(s+\nu)\pi}{2} {}_0F_2\left(\begin{array}{c} \frac{ab^2}{4} \\ \frac{2-s-\nu}{2}, \frac{2-s+\nu}{2} \end{array} \right)$ $[b, \ \operatorname{Re}a>0; \ \operatorname{Re}s<3/2, 1-\operatorname{Re}\nu]$

3.15.3. $\mathbf{H}_\nu(bx)$, $\mathbf{L}_\nu(bx)$, and trigonometric functions

Notation: $\delta = \left\{ \begin{array}{c} 1 \\ 0 \end{array} \right\}$.

No.	$f(x)$	$F(s)$
1	$\left\{ \begin{array}{c} \sin(ax) \\ \cos(ax) \end{array} \right\} \mathbf{H}_\nu(bx)$	$\pm\dfrac{a^{-s-\nu-1}}{2^\nu\sqrt{\pi}} \Gamma\left[\begin{array}{c} s+\nu+1 \\ \frac{2\nu+3}{2} \end{array} \right] \left\{ \begin{array}{c} \cos\left[(s+\nu)\pi/2\right] \\ \sin\left[(s+\nu)\pi/2\right] \end{array} \right\}$ $\times {}_3F_2\left(\begin{array}{c} \frac{s+\nu+1}{2}, \frac{s+\nu+2}{2}, 1 \\ \frac{3}{2}, \frac{2\nu+3}{2}; \frac{b^2}{a^2} \end{array} \right)$ $[0<b<a; \ \operatorname{Re}s<3/2; \ -\delta-1 < \operatorname{Re}(s+\nu)<2]$

No.	$f(x)$	$F(s)$
2	$\begin{Bmatrix} \sin(ax) \\ \cos(ax) \end{Bmatrix} \mathbf{H}_\nu(bx)$	$\mp \dfrac{(b/2)^{\nu-1}}{\sqrt{\pi}\,a^{s+\nu-1}} \Gamma \begin{bmatrix} s+\nu-1 \\ \frac{2\nu+1}{2} \end{bmatrix} \begin{Bmatrix} \cos\left[(s+\nu)\,\pi/2\right] \\ \sin\left[(s+\nu)\,\pi/2\right] \end{Bmatrix}$ $\times {}_3F_2\left(\begin{matrix} \frac{1}{2},\,1,\,\frac{1-2\nu}{2};\,\frac{a^2}{b^2} \\ \frac{2-s-\nu}{2},\,\frac{3-s-\nu}{2} \end{matrix}\right)$ $+ \dfrac{2^{s+\delta-1}\pi a^\delta \sec\frac{(s+\nu+\delta)\pi}{2}}{b^{s+\delta}\Gamma\left(\frac{2-s-\nu-\delta}{2}\right)\Gamma\left(\frac{2-s+\nu-\delta}{2}\right)} \, {}_2F_1\left(\begin{matrix} \frac{s-\nu+\delta}{2},\,\frac{s+\nu+\delta}{2} \\ \frac{2\delta+1}{2};\,\frac{a^2}{b^2} \end{matrix}\right)$ $[0 < a < b;\ \operatorname{Re} s < 3/2;\ -\delta - 1 < \operatorname{Re}(s+\nu) < 2]$

3.15.4. $\mathbf{H}_\nu(bx)$, $\mathbf{L}_\nu(bx)$, and the logarithmic or inverse trigonometric functions

1	$\theta(a-x)\ln\dfrac{\sqrt{a}+\sqrt{a-x}}{\sqrt{x}}$ $\times \begin{Bmatrix} \mathbf{H}_\nu(bx) \\ \mathbf{L}_\nu(bx) \end{Bmatrix}$	$\dfrac{a^{s+\nu+1}(b/2)^{\nu+1}}{s+\nu+1}\Gamma\begin{bmatrix} s+\nu+1 \\ \frac{2\nu+3}{2},\,\frac{2s+2\nu+3}{2} \end{bmatrix}$ $\times {}_4F_5\left(\begin{matrix} 1,\,\frac{s+\nu+1}{2},\,\frac{s+\nu+1}{2},\,\frac{s+\nu+2}{2};\,\mp\frac{a^2b^2}{4} \\ \frac{3}{2},\,\frac{2\nu+3}{2},\,\frac{2s+2\nu+3}{2},\,\frac{2s+2\nu+5}{2},\,\frac{s+\nu+3}{2} \end{matrix}\right)$ $[a>0;\ \operatorname{Re}(s+\nu) > -1]$
2	$\theta(a-x)\ln\dfrac{a+\sqrt{a^2-x^2}}{x}$ $\times \begin{Bmatrix} \mathbf{H}_\nu(bx) \\ \mathbf{L}_\nu(bx) \end{Bmatrix}$	$\dfrac{a^{s+\nu+1}(b/2)^{\nu+1}}{s+\nu+1}\Gamma\begin{bmatrix} \frac{s+\nu+1}{2} \\ \frac{2\nu+3}{2},\,\frac{s+\nu+2}{2} \end{bmatrix}{}_3F_4\left(\begin{matrix} 1,\,\frac{s+\nu+1}{2},\,\frac{s+\nu+1}{2};\,\mp\frac{a^2b^2}{4} \\ \frac{3}{2},\,\frac{2\nu+3}{2},\,\frac{s+\nu+2}{2},\,\frac{s+\nu+3}{2} \end{matrix}\right)$ $[a>0;\ \operatorname{Re}(s+\nu) > -1]$
3	$\theta(a-x)\arccos\dfrac{x}{a}$ $\times \begin{Bmatrix} \mathbf{H}_\nu(bx) \\ \mathbf{L}_\nu(bx) \end{Bmatrix}$	$\dfrac{a^{s+\nu+1}b^{\nu+1}}{2^\nu(s+\nu+1)^2}\Gamma\begin{bmatrix} \frac{s+\nu+2}{2} \\ \frac{2\nu+3}{2},\,\frac{s+\nu+1}{2} \end{bmatrix}{}_3F_4\left(\begin{matrix} 1,\,\frac{s+\nu+1}{2},\,\frac{s+\nu+2}{2};\,\mp\frac{a^2b^2}{4} \\ \frac{3}{2},\,\frac{2\nu+3}{2},\,\frac{s+\nu+3}{2},\,\frac{s+\nu+2}{2} \end{matrix}\right)$ $[a>0;\ \operatorname{Re}(s+\nu) > -1]$

3.15.5. $\mathbf{H}_\nu(bx)$, $\mathbf{L}_\nu(bx)$, and $\Gamma(\mu, ax)$

1	$\Gamma(\mu, ax)\begin{Bmatrix} \mathbf{H}_\nu(bx) \\ \mathbf{L}_\nu(bx) \end{Bmatrix}$	$\dfrac{2^{-\nu}a^{-s-\nu-1}b^{\nu+1}}{\sqrt{\pi}\,(s+\nu+1)}\Gamma\begin{bmatrix} s+\mu+\nu+1 \\ \frac{2\nu+3}{2} \end{bmatrix}$ $\times {}_4F_3\left(\begin{matrix} 1,\,\frac{s+\nu+1}{2},\,\frac{s+\mu+\nu+1}{2},\,\frac{s+\mu+\nu+2}{2} \\ \frac{3}{2},\,\frac{2\nu+3}{2},\,\frac{s+\nu+3}{2};\,\mp\frac{b^2}{a^2} \end{matrix}\right)$ $\left[\operatorname{Re} a > \begin{Bmatrix} |\operatorname{Im} b| \\ |\operatorname{Re} b| \end{Bmatrix};\ \operatorname{Re}(s+\nu+1) > -\operatorname{Re}\mu,\,0\right]$

3.15.6. $\mathbf{H}_\nu\left(bx\right)$, $\mathbf{L}_\nu\left(bx\right)$, **and** $\mathrm{Ei}\left(-ax^2\right)$, $\mathrm{erfc}\left(ax^r\right)$, $D_\mu\left(ax\right)$

1	$\mathrm{Ei}\left(-ax^2\right)\begin{Bmatrix}\mathbf{H}_\nu\left(bx\right)\\\mathbf{L}_\nu\left(bx\right)\end{Bmatrix}$	$-\dfrac{a^{-(s+\nu+1)/2}b^{\nu+1}}{2^\nu\sqrt{\pi}\left(s+\nu+1\right)}\Gamma\begin{bmatrix}\frac{s+\nu+1}{2}\\\frac{2\nu+3}{2}\end{bmatrix}{}_3F_3\left(\begin{matrix}1,\ \frac{s+\nu+1}{2},\ \frac{s+\nu+1}{2};\ \mp\frac{b^2}{4a}\\\frac{3}{2},\ \frac{2\nu+3}{2},\ \frac{s+\nu+3}{2}\end{matrix}\right)$ $$[\mathrm{Re}\,a>0;\ \mathrm{Re}\,(s+\nu)>-1]$$
2	$\mathrm{erfc}\left(ax\right)\begin{Bmatrix}\mathbf{H}_\nu\left(bx\right)\\\mathbf{L}_\nu\left(bx\right)\end{Bmatrix}$	$\dfrac{a^{-s-\nu-1}b^{\nu+1}}{2^\nu\pi\left(s+\nu+1\right)}\Gamma\begin{bmatrix}\frac{s+\nu+2}{2}\\\frac{2\nu+3}{2}\end{bmatrix}{}_3F_3\left(\begin{matrix}1,\ \frac{s+\nu+1}{2},\ \frac{s+\nu+2}{2}\\\frac{3}{2},\ \frac{2\nu+3}{2},\ \frac{s+\nu+3}{2};\ \mp\frac{b^2}{4a^2}\end{matrix}\right)$ $$[b>0;\ \mathrm{Re}\,(s+\nu)>-1;\ |\arg a|<\pi/4]$$
3	$\mathrm{erfc}\left(a\sqrt{x}\right)\begin{Bmatrix}\mathbf{H}_\nu\left(bx\right)\\\mathbf{L}_\nu\left(bx\right)\end{Bmatrix}$	$\dfrac{a^{-2s-2\nu-2}b^{\nu+1}}{2^\nu\pi\left(s+\nu+1\right)}\Gamma\begin{bmatrix}\frac{2s+2\nu+3}{2}\\\frac{2\nu+3}{2}\end{bmatrix}{}_4F_3\left(\begin{matrix}1,\ \frac{s+\nu+1}{2},\ \frac{2s+2\nu+3}{4},\ \frac{2s+2\nu+5}{4}\\\frac{3}{2},\ \frac{2\nu+3}{2},\ \frac{s+\nu+3}{2};\ \mp\frac{b^2}{a^4}\end{matrix}\right)$ $$\left[\mathrm{Re}\,a^2>\begin{Bmatrix}|\mathrm{Im}\,b|\\|\mathrm{Re}\,b|\end{Bmatrix};\ \mathrm{Re}\,(s+\nu)>-1\right]$$
4	$e^{a^2x^2/4}D_\mu\left(ax\right)$ $\times\begin{Bmatrix}\mathbf{H}_\nu\left(bx\right)\\\mathbf{L}_\nu\left(bx\right)\end{Bmatrix}$	$\dfrac{a^{-s-\nu-1}b^{\nu+1}}{2^{(s+\mu+3\nu+3)/2}\sqrt{\pi}}\Gamma\begin{bmatrix}s+\nu+1,\ -\frac{s+\mu+\nu+1}{2}\\-\mu,\ \frac{2\nu+3}{2}\end{bmatrix}$ $\times\,{}_3F_3\left(\begin{matrix}1,\ \frac{s+\nu+1}{2},\ \frac{s+\nu+2}{2}\\\frac{3}{2},\ \frac{2\nu+3}{2},\ \frac{s+\mu+\nu+3}{2};\ \pm\frac{b^2}{2a^2}\end{matrix}\right)+\dfrac{2^{s+\mu-1}\pi\,a^\mu b^{-s-\mu}}{\Gamma\left(\frac{2-s-\mu-\nu}{2}\right)\Gamma\left(\frac{2-s-\mu+\nu}{2}\right)}$ $\times\sec\dfrac{\left(s+\mu+\nu\right)\pi}{2}\,{}_2F_2\left(\begin{matrix}-\frac{\mu}{2},\ \frac{1-\mu}{2};\ \pm\frac{b^2}{2a^2}\\\frac{2-s-\mu-\nu}{2},\ \frac{2-s-\mu+\nu}{2}\end{matrix}\right)$ $$\left[\begin{matrix}b>0;\ \mathrm{Re}\,(s+\mu)<1-\mathrm{Re}\,\nu;\ \mathrm{Re}\,(s+\mu)<3/2;\\\mathrm{Re}\,(s+\nu)>-1;\ |\arg a|<3\pi/4\end{matrix}\right]$$
5	$e^{-a^2x^2/4}D_\mu\left(ax\right)$ $\times\begin{Bmatrix}\mathbf{H}_\nu\left(bx\right)\\\mathbf{L}_\nu\left(bx\right)\end{Bmatrix}$	$\dfrac{2^{(-s+\mu-3\nu-1)/2}b^{\nu+1}}{a^{s+\nu+1}}\Gamma\begin{bmatrix}s+\nu+1\\\frac{2\nu+3}{2},\ \frac{s-\mu+\nu+2}{2}\end{bmatrix}$ $\times\,{}_3F_3\left(\begin{matrix}1,\ \frac{s+\nu+1}{2},\ \frac{s+\nu+2}{2};\ \mp\frac{b^2}{2a^2}\\\frac{3}{2},\ \frac{2\nu+3}{2},\ \frac{s-\mu+\nu+2}{2}\end{matrix}\right)$ $$[\mathrm{Re}\,(s+\nu)>-1;\ 4|\arg a|,\ |\arg b|<\pi]$$

3.15.7. $\mathbf{H}_\nu\left(bx\right)$ **and** $J_\mu\left(ax\right)$

1	$J_\mu\left(ax\right)\mathbf{H}_\nu\left(bx\right)$	$\dfrac{2^s b^{\nu+1}}{\sqrt{\pi}\,a^{s+\nu+1}}\Gamma\begin{bmatrix}\frac{s+\mu+\nu+1}{2}\\\frac{2\nu+3}{2},\ \frac{1-s+\mu-\nu}{2}\end{bmatrix}{}_3F_2\left(\begin{matrix}1,\ \frac{s-\mu+\nu+1}{2},\ \frac{s+\mu+\nu+1}{2}\\\frac{3}{2},\ \frac{2\nu+3}{2};\ \frac{b^2}{a^2}\end{matrix}\right)$ $$[0<b<a;\ \mathrm{Re}\,s<2;\ -\mathrm{Re}\,\mu-1<\mathrm{Re}\,(s+\nu)\leqslant5/2]$$
2	$J_\mu\left(ax\right)\mathbf{H}_\nu\left(bx\right)$	$\dfrac{2^{s-1}b^{\nu-1}}{\sqrt{\pi}\,a^{s+\nu-1}}\Gamma\begin{bmatrix}\frac{s+\mu+\nu-1}{2}\\\frac{2\nu+1}{2},\ \frac{3-s+\mu-\nu}{2}\end{bmatrix}{}_3F_2\left(\begin{matrix}\frac{1}{2},\ 1,\ \frac{1}{2}-\nu;\ \frac{a^2}{b^2}\\\frac{3-s-\mu-\nu}{2},\ \frac{3-s+\mu-\nu}{2}\end{matrix}\right)$ $+\dfrac{2^{s-1}\pi\,a^\mu}{b^{s+\mu}}\dfrac{\sec\frac{(s+\mu+\nu)\pi}{2}}{\Gamma\left[\mu+1,\ \frac{2-s-\mu-\nu}{2},\ \frac{2-s-\mu+\nu}{2}\right]}{}_2F_1\left(\begin{matrix}\frac{s+\mu-\nu}{2},\ \frac{s+\mu+\nu}{2}\\\mu+1;\ \frac{a^2}{b^2}\end{matrix}\right)$ $$[0<a<b;\ \mathrm{Re}\,s<2;\ -\mathrm{Re}\,\mu-1<\mathrm{Re}\,(s+\nu)<5/2]$$

No.	$f(x)$	$F(s)$
3	$J_\mu\left(\dfrac{a}{x}\right)\mathbf{H}_\nu(bx)$	$\dfrac{2^{s-2\mu-1}\pi a^\mu}{b^{s-\mu}}\dfrac{\sec\frac{(s-\mu+\nu)\pi}{2}}{\Gamma\left[\mu+1,\frac{2-s+\mu-\nu}{2},\frac{2-s+\mu+\nu}{2}\right]}$

$$\times\,{}_0F_3\left(\begin{matrix}\frac{a^2b^2}{16}\\\mu+1,\frac{2-s+\mu-\nu}{2},\frac{2-s+\mu+\nu}{2}\end{matrix}\right)+\frac{a^{s+\nu+1}b^{\nu+1}}{2^{s+2\nu+2}\sqrt\pi}$$

$$\times\,\Gamma\left[\begin{matrix}\frac{-s+\mu-\nu-1}{2}\\\frac{2\nu+3}{2},\frac{s+\mu+\nu+3}{2}\end{matrix}\right]{}_1F_4\left(\begin{matrix}1;\,\frac{a^2b^2}{16}\\\frac{3}{2},\frac{2\nu+3}{2},\frac{s-\mu+\nu+3}{2},\frac{s+\mu+\nu+3}{2}\end{matrix}\right)$$

$$[a,\,b>0;\ \operatorname{Re}(s-\mu)<3/2;\ -5/2<\operatorname{Re}(s+\nu)<\operatorname{Re}\mu+1]$$

3.15.8. $\mathbf{H}(bx)$, $\mathbf{L}_\nu(bx)$, and $K_\mu(ax^r)$

1	$K_\mu(ax)\left\{\begin{matrix}\mathbf{H}_\nu(bx)\\\mathbf{L}_\nu(bx)\end{matrix}\right\}$	$\dfrac{2^{s-1}b^{\nu+1}}{\sqrt\pi\,a^{s+\nu+1}}\Gamma\left[\begin{matrix}\frac{s-\mu+\nu+1}{2},\frac{s+\mu+\nu+1}{2}\\\frac{2\nu+3}{2}\end{matrix}\right]{}_3F_2\left(\begin{matrix}1,\frac{s-\mu+\nu+1}{2},\frac{s+\mu+\nu+1}{2}\\\frac{3}{2},\frac{2\nu+3}{2};\,\mp\frac{b^2}{a^2}\end{matrix}\right)$

$$\left[\operatorname{Re}a>\left\{\begin{matrix}|\operatorname{Im}b|\\|\operatorname{Re}b|\end{matrix}\right\};\ \operatorname{Re}(s\pm\mu+\nu)>-1\right]$$

2	$e^{-ax}K_\mu(ax)\left\{\begin{matrix}\mathbf{H}_\nu(bx)\\\mathbf{L}_\nu(bx)\end{matrix}\right\}$	$\dfrac{b^{\nu+1}}{2^{s+2\nu+1}a^{s+\nu+1}}\Gamma\left[\begin{matrix}s-\mu+\nu+1,s+\mu+\nu+1\\\frac{2\nu+3}{2},\frac{2s+2\nu+3}{2}\end{matrix}\right]$

$$\times\,{}_5F_4\left(\begin{matrix}1,\frac{s-\mu+\nu+1}{2},\frac{s-\mu+\nu+2}{2},\frac{s+\mu+\nu+1}{2},\frac{s+\mu+\nu+2}{2}\\\frac{3}{2},\frac{2\nu+3}{2},\frac{2s+2\nu+3}{4},\frac{2s+2\nu+5}{4};\,\mp\frac{b^2}{4a^2}\end{matrix}\right)$$

$$\left[\left\{\begin{matrix}\operatorname{Re}a>|\operatorname{Im}b|\\\operatorname{Re}a>|\operatorname{Re}b|\end{matrix}\right\};\ \operatorname{Re}(s+\nu)>|\operatorname{Re}\mu|-1\right]$$

3	$e^{\mp ax^2}K_\mu(ax^2)\mathbf{H}_\nu(bx)$	$\pm\dfrac{2^{-(s+3\nu+3)/2}b^{\nu+1}}{a^{(s+\nu+1)/2}}\left[\cos(\mu\pi)\csc\frac{(s+\nu)\pi}{2}\right]^{(1\mp1)/2}$

$$\times\,\Gamma\left[\begin{matrix}\frac{s-2\mu+\nu+1}{2},\frac{s+2\mu+\nu+1}{2}\\\frac{2\nu+3}{2},\frac{s+\nu+2}{2}\end{matrix}\right]{}_3F_3\left(\begin{matrix}1,\frac{s-2\mu+\nu+1}{2},\frac{s+2\mu+\nu+1}{2}\\\frac{3}{2},\frac{2\nu+3}{2},\frac{s+\nu+2}{2};\,\mp\frac{b^2}{8a}\end{matrix}\right)$$

$$+\frac{(1\mp1)\,2^{s-7/2}\pi^{3/2}\csc\frac{(s+\nu)\pi}{2}}{\sqrt{a}\,b^{s-1}\Gamma\left(\frac{3-s-\nu}{2}\right)\Gamma\left(\frac{3-s+\nu}{2}\right)}{}_2F_2\left(\begin{matrix}\frac{1-2\mu}{2},\frac{1+2\mu}{2};\,\frac{b^2}{8a}\\\frac{3-s-\nu}{2},\frac{3-s+\nu}{2}\end{matrix}\right)$$

$$\left[\begin{matrix}\operatorname{Re}(s+\nu)>2|\operatorname{Re}\mu|-1;\ |\arg a|<(2\mp1)\,\pi/2;\\\left\{\begin{matrix}|\arg b|<\pi\\b>0;\ \operatorname{Re}(s+\nu)<2;\ \operatorname{Re}s<5/2\end{matrix}\right\}\end{matrix}\right]$$

4	$e^{-ax^2}K_\mu(ax^2)\mathbf{L}_\nu(bx)$	$\dfrac{2^{-(s+3\nu+3)/2}b^{\nu+1}}{a^{(s+\nu+1)/2}}\Gamma\left[\begin{matrix}\frac{s-2\mu+\nu+1}{2},\frac{s+2\mu+\nu+1}{2}\\\frac{2\nu+3}{2},\frac{s+\nu+2}{2}\end{matrix}\right]$

$$\times\,{}_3F_3\left(\begin{matrix}1,\frac{s-2\mu+\nu+1}{2},\frac{s+2\mu+\nu+1}{2}\\\frac{3}{2},\frac{2\nu+3}{2},\frac{s+\nu+2}{2};\,\frac{b^2}{8a}\end{matrix}\right)$$

$$[\operatorname{Re}a>0;\ \operatorname{Re}(s+\nu)>2|\operatorname{Re}\mu|-1;\ |\arg b|<\pi]$$

No.	$f(x)$	$F(s)$
5	$K_\lambda(ax) K_\mu(ax)$ $\times \left\{ \begin{matrix} \mathbf{H}_\nu(bx) \\ \mathbf{L}_\nu(bx) \end{matrix} \right\}$	$\dfrac{2^{s-2}b^{\nu+1}}{\sqrt{\pi}\,a^{s+\mu+1}}\Gamma\left[\begin{matrix} \frac{s+\lambda+\mu+\nu+1}{2},\ \frac{s+\lambda-\mu+\nu+1}{2},\ \frac{s-\lambda+\mu+\nu+1}{2},\ \frac{s-\lambda-\mu+\nu+1}{2} \\ \frac{2\nu+3}{2},\ s+\nu+1 \end{matrix} \right]$ $\times {}_5F_4\left(\begin{matrix} 1,\ \frac{s+\lambda+\mu+\nu+1}{2},\ \frac{s-\lambda+\mu+\nu+1}{2},\ \frac{s-\lambda-\mu+\nu+1}{2},\ \frac{s+\lambda-\mu+\nu+1}{2} \\ \frac{3}{2},\ \frac{2\nu+3}{2},\ \frac{s+\nu+1}{2},\ \frac{s+\nu+2}{2};\ \mp\frac{b^2}{4a^2} \end{matrix} \right)$ $\left[2\operatorname{Re}a > \left\{ \begin{matrix} |\operatorname{Im}b| \\ |\operatorname{Re}b| \end{matrix} \right\};\ \operatorname{Re}(s+\nu) > |\operatorname{Re}\lambda| + |\operatorname{Re}\mu| - 1 \right]$

3.15.9. $\mathbf{H}_\nu(\varphi(x)) - Y_\nu(\varphi(x)),\ I_{\pm\nu}(\varphi(x)) - \mathbf{L}_\nu(\varphi(x))$

No.	$f(x)$	$F(s)$
1	$\mathbf{H}_\nu(ax) - Y_\nu(ax)$	$\dfrac{2^{s-1}a^{-s}}{\pi}\cos(\nu\pi)\sec\dfrac{(s+\nu)\pi}{2}\Gamma\left(\dfrac{s-\nu}{2}\right)\Gamma\left(\dfrac{s+\nu}{2}\right)$ $[\operatorname{Re}a > 0;\ |\operatorname{Re}\nu| < \operatorname{Re}s < 1 - \operatorname{Re}\nu]$
2	$I_\nu(ax) - \mathbf{L}_\nu(ax)$	$2^{s-1}a^{-s}\sec\dfrac{(s+\nu)\pi}{2}\Gamma\left[\begin{matrix} \frac{s+\nu}{2} \\ \frac{2-s+\nu}{2} \end{matrix} \right]$ $[\operatorname{Re}a > 0;\ -\operatorname{Re}\nu < \operatorname{Re}s < 1 - \operatorname{Re}\nu]$
3	$I_{-\nu}(ax) - \mathbf{L}_\nu(ax)$	$2^{s-1}a^{-s}\cos(\nu\pi)\sec\dfrac{(s+\nu)\pi}{2}\Gamma\left[\begin{matrix} \frac{s-\nu}{2} \\ \frac{2-s-\nu}{2} \end{matrix} \right]$ $[\operatorname{Re}a > 0;\ -\operatorname{Re}\nu < \operatorname{Re}s < 1 + \operatorname{Re}\nu]$
4	$(a^2-x^2)_+^{\alpha-1}$ $\times [I_{\pm\nu}(bx) - \mathbf{L}_\nu(bx)]$	$-\dfrac{a^{s+2\alpha+\nu-1}b^{\nu+1}}{2^{\nu+1}\sqrt{\pi}\,\Gamma\left(\frac{2\nu+3}{2}\right)}\mathrm{B}\left(\alpha,\ \dfrac{s+\nu+1}{2}\right){}_2F_3\left(\begin{matrix} 1,\ \frac{s+\nu+1}{2};\ \frac{a^2b^2}{4} \\ \frac{3}{2},\ \frac{2\nu+3}{2},\ \frac{s+2\alpha+\nu+1}{2} \end{matrix} \right)$ $+\dfrac{a^{s+2\alpha\pm\nu-2}b^{\pm\nu}}{2^{1\pm\nu}\Gamma(1\pm\nu)}\mathrm{B}\left(\alpha,\ \dfrac{s\pm\nu}{2}\right){}_1F_2\left(\begin{matrix} \frac{s\pm\nu}{2};\ \frac{a^2b^2}{4} \\ 1\pm\nu,\ \frac{s+2\alpha\pm\nu}{2} \end{matrix} \right)$ $\left[a,\ \operatorname{Re}\alpha > 0;\ \left\{ \begin{matrix} \operatorname{Re}(s+\nu) > 0 \\ -\operatorname{Re}s - 1 < \operatorname{Re}\nu < \operatorname{Re}s \end{matrix} \right\} \right]$
5	$(x^2-a^2)_+^{\alpha-1}$ $\times [I_{\pm\nu}(bx) - \mathbf{L}_\nu(bx)]$	$-\dfrac{a^{s+2\alpha+\nu-1}}{\sqrt{\pi}\,\Gamma\left(\frac{2\nu+3}{2}\right)}\left(\dfrac{b}{2}\right)^{\nu+1}\mathrm{B}\left(\alpha,\ \dfrac{1-s-2\alpha-\nu}{2}\right)$ $\times {}_2F_3\left(\begin{matrix} 1,\ \frac{s+\nu+1}{2};\ \frac{a^2b^2}{4} \\ \frac{3}{2},\ \frac{2\nu+3}{2},\ \frac{s+2\alpha+\nu+1}{2} \end{matrix} \right) - \dfrac{2^{s+2\alpha-3}}{b^{s+2\alpha-2}}\cos^{(1\mp1)/2}(\nu\pi)$ $\times \sec\dfrac{(s+2\alpha+\nu)\pi}{2}\Gamma\left[\begin{matrix} \frac{s+2\alpha\pm\nu-2}{2} \\ \frac{4-s-2\alpha\pm\nu}{2} \end{matrix} \right]{}_1F_2\left(\begin{matrix} 1-\alpha;\ \frac{a^2b^2}{4} \\ \frac{4-s-2\alpha-\nu}{2},\ \frac{4-s-2\alpha+\nu}{2} \end{matrix} \right)$ $+\dfrac{a^{s+2\alpha\pm\nu-2}b^{\pm\nu}}{2^{1\pm\nu}\Gamma(1\pm\nu)}\mathrm{B}\left(\alpha,\ \dfrac{2-s-2\alpha\mp\nu}{2}\right){}_1F_2\left(\begin{matrix} \frac{s\pm\nu}{2};\ \frac{a^2b^2}{4} \\ 1\pm\nu,\ \frac{s+2\alpha\pm\nu}{2} \end{matrix} \right)$ $[a,\ \operatorname{Re}b,\ \operatorname{Re}\alpha > 0;\ \operatorname{Re}(s+2\alpha+\nu) < 3]$

No.	$f(x)$	$F(s)$
6	$\dfrac{1}{(x^2+a^2)^\rho}$ $\times [I_{\pm\nu}(bx) - \mathbf{L}_\nu(bx)]$	$-\dfrac{a^{s+\nu-2\rho+1}b^{\nu+1}}{2^{\nu+1}\sqrt{\pi}\,\Gamma\left(\frac{2\nu+3}{2}\right)}\,\mathrm{B}\left(\dfrac{s+\nu+1}{2}, \dfrac{2\rho-\nu-s-1}{2}\right)$ $\times\,{}_2F_3\left(\begin{matrix}1,\ \frac{s+\nu+1}{2};\ -\frac{a^2b^2}{4}\\ \frac{3}{2},\ \frac{2\nu+3}{2},\ \frac{s+\nu-2\rho+3}{2}\end{matrix}\right) + \dfrac{2^{s-2\rho-1}}{b^{s-2\rho}}\cos^{(1\mp1)/2}(\nu\pi)$ $\times\sec\dfrac{(s+\nu-2\rho)\pi}{2}\,\Gamma\left[\begin{matrix}\frac{s\pm\nu-2\rho}{2}\\ \frac{\rho\pm\nu-s+2}{2}\end{matrix}\right]\,{}_1F_2\left(\begin{matrix}\rho;\ -\frac{a^2b^2}{4}\\ \frac{2-s-\nu+2\rho}{2},\ \frac{2-s+\nu+2\rho}{2}\end{matrix}\right)$ $+\dfrac{a^{s\pm\nu-2\rho}b^{\pm\nu}}{2^{1\pm\nu}\Gamma(1\pm\nu)}\,\mathrm{B}\left(\dfrac{s\pm\nu}{2}, \dfrac{2\rho-s\mp\nu}{2}\right)\,{}_1F_2\left(\begin{matrix}\frac{s\pm\nu}{2};\ -\frac{a^2b^2}{4}\\ 1\pm\nu,\ \frac{s\pm\nu-2\rho+2}{2}\end{matrix}\right)$ $\left[\begin{matrix}\operatorname{Re}a,\ \operatorname{Re}b>0;\ \operatorname{Re}(s+\nu-2\rho)<1;\\ \left\{\begin{matrix}\operatorname{Re}(s+\nu)>0\\ -1-\operatorname{Re}s<\operatorname{Re}\nu<\operatorname{Re}s\end{matrix}\right\}\end{matrix}\right]$
7	$\dfrac{1}{x^2-a^2}$ $\times [I_{\pm\nu}(bx) - \mathbf{L}_\nu(bx)]$	$-\dfrac{2^{s-3}}{b^{s-2}}\cos^{(1\mp1)/2}(\nu\pi)\sec\dfrac{(s+\nu)\pi}{2}\,\Gamma\left[\begin{matrix}\frac{s\pm\nu-2}{2}\\ \frac{4-s\pm\nu}{2}\end{matrix}\right]\,{}_1F_2\left(\begin{matrix}1;\ \frac{a^2b^2}{4}\\ \frac{4-s-\nu}{2},\ \frac{4-s+\nu}{2}\end{matrix}\right)$ $-\dfrac{\pi a^{s-2}}{2}\left[\tan\dfrac{(s+\nu)\pi}{2}\mathbf{L}_\nu(ab) + \cot\dfrac{(s\pm\nu)\pi}{2}I_{\pm\nu}(ab)\right]$ $\left[a,\ \operatorname{Re}b>0;\ \operatorname{Re}(s+\nu)<3;\ \left\{\begin{matrix}\operatorname{Re}(s+\nu)>0\\ -\operatorname{Re}s-1<\operatorname{Re}\nu<\operatorname{Re}s\end{matrix}\right\}\right]$
8	$e^{-ax}[I_{\pm\nu}(bx) - \mathbf{L}_\nu(bx)]$	$a^{-s\mp\nu}\left(\dfrac{b}{2}\right)^{\pm\nu}\Gamma\left[\begin{matrix}s\pm\nu\\ 1\pm\nu\end{matrix}\right]\,{}_2F_1\left(\begin{matrix}\frac{s\pm\nu}{2},\ \frac{s\pm\nu+1}{2}\\ 1\pm\nu;\ \frac{b^2}{a^2}\end{matrix}\right)$ $-\dfrac{a^{-s-\nu-1}b^{\nu+1}}{2^\nu\sqrt{\pi}}\,\Gamma\left[\begin{matrix}s+\nu+1\\ \frac{2\nu+3}{2}\end{matrix}\right]\,{}_3F_2\left(\begin{matrix}1,\ \frac{s+\nu+1}{2},\ \frac{s+\nu+2}{2}\\ \frac{3}{2},\ \frac{2\nu+3}{2};\ \frac{b^2}{a^2}\end{matrix}\right)$ $\left[\begin{matrix}(\operatorname{Re}a>|\operatorname{Re}b|;\ \operatorname{Re}s>-\operatorname{Re}\nu)\ \text{or}\\ (\operatorname{Re}a=\operatorname{Re}b=0;\ \mp\operatorname{Re}\nu<\operatorname{Re}s<3/2,\ 2-\operatorname{Re}\nu)\end{matrix}\right]$
9	$e^{-ax}[Y_\nu(bx) - \mathbf{H}_\nu(bx)]$	$-\dfrac{a^{-\nu-s+1}(b/2)^{\nu-1}}{\pi^{3/2}}\cos(\nu\pi)\Gamma\left(\dfrac{1-2\nu}{2}\right)$ $\times\,\Gamma(s+\nu-1)\,{}_3F_2\left(\begin{matrix}\frac{1}{2},\ 1,\ \frac{1-2\nu}{2};\ -\frac{a^2}{b^2}\\ \frac{2-s-\nu}{2},\ \frac{3-s-\nu}{2}\end{matrix}\right)$ $-\dfrac{2^s ab^{-s-1}}{\pi}\cos(\nu\pi)\csc\dfrac{(s+\nu)\pi}{2}\,\Gamma\left(\dfrac{s-\nu+1}{2}\right)$ $\times\,\Gamma\left(\dfrac{s+\nu+1}{2}\right)\,{}_2F_1\left(\begin{matrix}\frac{s-\nu+1}{2},\ \frac{s+\nu+1}{2}\\ \frac{3}{2};\ -\frac{a^2}{b^2}\end{matrix}\right) - \dfrac{2^{s-1}b^{-s}}{\pi}\cos(\nu\pi)$ $\times\sec\dfrac{(s+\nu)\pi}{2}\,\Gamma\left(\dfrac{s-\nu}{2}\right)\Gamma\left(\dfrac{s+\nu}{2}\right)\,{}_2F_1\left(\begin{matrix}\frac{s-\nu}{2},\ \frac{s+\nu}{2}\\ \frac{1}{2};\ -\frac{a^2}{b^2}\end{matrix}\right)$ $\left[\begin{matrix}(\operatorname{Re}a>|\operatorname{Im}b|;\ \operatorname{Re}s>|\operatorname{Re}\nu|)\ \text{or}\\ (\operatorname{Re}a=0,\ b>0;\ |\operatorname{Re}\nu|<\operatorname{Re}s<3/2,\ 2-\operatorname{Re}\nu)\end{matrix}\right]$

No.	$f(x)$	$F(s)$
10	$\sin(ax)$ $\times [I_{\pm\nu}(bx) - \mathbf{L}_\nu(bx)]$	$-\dfrac{2^{-\nu}b^{\nu+1}}{\sqrt{\pi}\,a^{s+\nu+1}}\cos\dfrac{(s+\nu)\pi}{2}\Gamma\begin{bmatrix} s+\nu+1 \\ \frac{2\nu+3}{2} \end{bmatrix}{}_3F_2\left(\begin{matrix}1,\ \frac{s+\nu+1}{2},\ \frac{s+\nu+2}{2} \\ \frac{3}{2},\ \frac{2\nu+3}{2};\ -\frac{b^2}{a^2}\end{matrix}\right)$ $+\dfrac{(b/2)^{\pm\nu}}{a^{s\pm\nu}}\sin\dfrac{(s+\nu)\pi}{2}\Gamma\begin{bmatrix} s\pm\nu \\ 1\pm\nu \end{bmatrix}{}_2F_1\left(\begin{matrix}\frac{s\pm\nu}{2},\ \frac{s\pm\nu+1}{2} \\ 1\pm\nu;\ -\frac{b^2}{a^2}\end{matrix}\right)$ $\left[a,\ \mathrm{Re}\,b>0;\ \left\{\begin{matrix} -1<\mathrm{Re}\,(s+\nu)<2 \\ -2<\mathrm{Re}\,(s+\nu)<2,\ 2\,\mathrm{Re}\,s+1\end{matrix}\right\}\right]$
11	$\cos(ax)$ $\times [I_{\pm\nu}(bx) - \mathbf{L}_\nu(bx)]$	$\dfrac{2^{-\nu}b^{\nu+1}}{\sqrt{\pi}\,a^{s+\nu+1}}\sin\dfrac{(s+\nu)\pi}{2}\Gamma\begin{bmatrix} s+\nu+1 \\ \frac{2\nu+3}{2} \end{bmatrix}{}_3F_2\left(\begin{matrix}1,\ \frac{s+\nu+1}{2},\ \frac{s+\nu+2}{2} \\ \frac{3}{2},\ \frac{2\nu+3}{2};\ -\frac{b^2}{a^2}\end{matrix}\right)$ $+\dfrac{(b/2)^{\pm\nu}}{a^{s\pm\nu}}\cos\dfrac{(s+\nu)\pi}{2}\Gamma\begin{bmatrix} s\pm\nu \\ 1\pm\nu \end{bmatrix}{}_2F_1\left(\begin{matrix}\frac{s\pm\nu}{2},\ \frac{s\pm\nu+1}{2} \\ 1\pm\nu;\ -\frac{b^2}{a^2}\end{matrix}\right)$ $\left[a,\ \mathrm{Re}\,b>0;\ \left\{\begin{matrix} 0<\mathrm{Re}\,(s+\nu)<2 \\ -1<\mathrm{Re}\,(s+\nu)<2,\ 2\,\mathrm{Re}\,s\end{matrix}\right\}\right]$
12	$J_\mu(ax)$ $\times [I_{\pm\nu}(bx) - \mathbf{L}_\nu(bx)]$	$-\dfrac{2^s b^{\nu+1}}{\sqrt{\pi}\,a^{s+\nu+1}}\Gamma\begin{bmatrix} \frac{s+\mu+\nu+1}{2} \\ \frac{2\nu+3}{2},\ \frac{1-s+\mu-\nu}{2} \end{bmatrix}{}_3F_2\left(\begin{matrix}1,\ \frac{s-\mu+\nu+1}{2},\ \frac{s+\mu+\nu+1}{2} \\ \frac{3}{2},\ \frac{2\nu+3}{2};\ -\frac{b^2}{a^2}\end{matrix}\right)$ $+\dfrac{2^{s-1}b^{\pm\nu}}{a^{s\pm\nu}}\Gamma\begin{bmatrix} \frac{s+\mu\pm\nu}{2} \\ 1\pm\nu,\ \frac{2-s+\mu\mp\nu}{2} \end{bmatrix}{}_2F_1\left(\begin{matrix}\frac{s-\mu\pm\nu}{2},\ \frac{s+\mu\pm\nu}{2} \\ 1\pm\nu;\ -\frac{b^2}{a^2}\end{matrix}\right)$ $\left[\begin{matrix} a,\ \mathrm{Re}\,b>0;\ \mathrm{Re}\,(s+\nu)<5/2; \\ \left\{\begin{matrix} \mathrm{Re}\,(s+\mu+\nu)>0 \\ -1<\mathrm{Re}\,(s+\mu+\nu)<2\,\mathrm{Re}\,(s+\mu) \end{matrix}\right\}\end{matrix}\right]$
13	$(x^2+a^2)^{\nu/2}$ $\times [\mathbf{H}_\nu(b\sqrt{x^2+a^2})$ $- Y_\nu(b\sqrt{x^2+a^2})]$	$2^{(s-2)/2}a^{s/2+\nu}b^{-s/2}\cos(\nu\pi)\sec\dfrac{(s+2\nu)\pi}{2}\Gamma\left(\dfrac{s}{2}\right)$ $\times [\mathbf{H}_{s/2+\nu}(ab) - Y_{s/2+\nu}(ab)]$ $[a,\,b>0;\ 0<\mathrm{Re}\,s<1-2\,\mathrm{Re}\,\nu]$
14	$(x^2+a^2)^{-\nu/2}$ $\times [\mathbf{H}_\nu(b\sqrt{x^2+a^2})$ $- Y_\nu(b\sqrt{x^2+a^2})]$	$\dfrac{a^{s/2-\nu}}{2^\nu\pi b^{s/2}}\Gamma\begin{bmatrix} \frac{s}{2},\ \frac{1-s}{2} \\ \frac{2\nu+1}{2} \end{bmatrix}S_{s/2+\nu,\,s/2-\nu}(ab)\qquad [a,\,b>0;\ 0<\mathrm{Re}\,s<1]$
15	$(x^2+a^2)^{\nu/2}$ $\times [I_{-\nu}(b\sqrt{x^2+a^2})$ $- \mathbf{L}_\nu(b\sqrt{x^2+a^2})]$	$\dfrac{2^{s/2-1}a^{s/2+\nu}}{b^{s/2}}\cos(\nu\pi)\sec\dfrac{(s+2\nu)\pi}{2}\Gamma\left(\dfrac{s}{2}\right)$ $\times [I_{-s/2-\nu}(ab) - \mathbf{L}_{s/2+\nu}(ab)]$ $[a,\,b,\ \mathrm{Re}\,s>0;\ \mathrm{Re}\,\nu<1/2]$

3.16. The Anger $\mathbf{J}_\nu(z)$ and Weber $\mathbf{E}_\nu(z)$ Functions

More formulas can be obtained from the corresponding sections due to the relations

$$\mathbf{E}_0(z) = -\mathbf{H}_0(z), \quad \mathbf{E}_1(z) = \frac{2}{\pi} - \mathbf{H}_1(z), \quad J_{\pm n}(z) = J_{\pm n}(z),$$

$$\left\{ \begin{matrix} \mathbf{E}_\nu(z) \\ \mathbf{J}_\nu(z) \end{matrix} \right\} = \frac{1}{\nu\pi} \left\{ \begin{matrix} 1 - \cos(\nu\pi) \\ \sin(\nu\pi) \end{matrix} \right\} {}_1F_2\left(1; 1 - \frac{\nu}{2}, 1 + \frac{\nu}{2}; -\frac{z^2}{4}\right)$$

$$\mp \frac{1}{(1 - \nu^2)\pi} \left\{ \begin{matrix} 1 + \cos(\nu\pi) \\ \sin(\nu\pi) \end{matrix} \right\} {}_1F_2\left(1; \frac{3 - \nu}{2}, \frac{3 + \nu}{2}; -\frac{z^2}{4}\right);$$

$$\left\{ \begin{matrix} \mathbf{E}_\nu(z) \\ \mathbf{J}_\nu(z) \end{matrix} \right\} = G_{35}^{22}\left(\frac{z^2}{4} \left| \begin{matrix} 0, 1/2, (3 - 2\nu \pm 1)/4 \\ 0, 1/2, -\nu/2, \nu/2, (3 - 2\nu \pm 1)/4 \end{matrix} \right. \right), \quad [-\pi/2 < \arg z \leq \pi/2].$$

3.16.1. $\mathbf{J}_\nu(\varphi(x))$, $\mathbf{E}_\nu(\varphi(x))$, and algebraic functions

No.	$f(x)$	$F(s)$
1	$\left\{ \begin{matrix} \mathbf{J}_\nu(ax) \\ \mathbf{E}_\nu(ax) \end{matrix} \right\}$	$\dfrac{2^s \pi a^{-s} \csc(s\pi)}{\Gamma\left(\frac{2-s-\nu}{2}\right)\Gamma\left(\frac{2-s+\nu}{2}\right)} \left\{ \begin{matrix} \cos[(\nu - s)\pi/2] \\ \sin[(\nu - s)\pi/2] \end{matrix} \right\} \qquad [a > 0;\ 0 < \mathrm{Re}\,s < 1]$
2	$\mathbf{J}_\nu(ax) \pm \mathbf{J}_{-\nu}(ax)$	$\dfrac{2^s \pi a^{-s}}{\Gamma\left(\frac{2-s-\nu}{2}\right)\Gamma\left(\frac{2-s+\nu}{2}\right)} \left\{ \begin{matrix} \cos(\nu\pi/2)\csc(s\pi/2) \\ \sin(\nu\pi/2)\sec(s\pi/2) \end{matrix} \right\}$ $[a > 0;\ -(1 \mp 1)/2 < \mathrm{Re}\,s < (5 \pm 1)/4]$
3	$(a - x)_+^{\alpha-1} \left\{ \begin{matrix} \mathbf{J}_\nu(bx) \\ \mathbf{E}_\nu(bx) \end{matrix} \right\}$	$\left\{ \begin{matrix} -\sin(\nu\pi) \\ 1 + \cos(\nu\pi) \end{matrix} \right\} \dfrac{a^{s+\alpha}b}{(\nu^2 - 1)\pi} B(s+1, \alpha)$ $\times {}_3F_4\left(\begin{matrix} 1, \frac{s+1}{2}, \frac{s+2}{2}; -\frac{a^2b^2}{4} \\ \frac{3-\nu}{2}, \frac{3+\nu}{2}, \frac{s+\alpha+1}{2}, \frac{s+\alpha+2}{2} \end{matrix} \right)$ $+ \left\{ \begin{matrix} \sin(\nu\pi) \\ 1 + \cos(\nu\pi) \end{matrix} \right\} \dfrac{a^{s+\alpha-1}}{\nu\pi} B(s, \alpha)\, {}_3F_4\left(\begin{matrix} 1, \frac{s}{2}, \frac{s+1}{2}; -\frac{a^2b^2}{4} \\ \frac{2-\nu}{2}, \frac{2+\nu}{2}, \frac{s+\alpha}{2}, \frac{s+\alpha+1}{2} \end{matrix} \right)$ $[a,\ \mathrm{Re}\,\nu,\ \mathrm{Re}\,s > 0]$
4	$(a^2 - x^2)_+^{\alpha-1}$ $\times \left\{ \begin{matrix} \mathbf{J}_\nu(bx) \\ \mathbf{E}_\nu(bx) \end{matrix} \right\}$	$\dfrac{a^{s+2\alpha-2}}{2\nu\pi} B\left(\alpha, \frac{s}{2}\right) \left\{ \begin{matrix} \sin(\nu\pi) \\ 1 - \cos(\nu\pi) \end{matrix} \right\} {}_2F_3\left(\begin{matrix} 1, \frac{s}{2}; -\frac{a^2b^2}{4} \\ \frac{2-\nu}{2}, \frac{2+\nu}{2}, \frac{s+2\alpha}{2} \end{matrix} \right)$ $\pm \dfrac{a^{s+2\alpha-1}b}{2(1 - \nu^2)\pi} B\left(\alpha, \frac{s+1}{2}\right)$ $\times \left\{ \begin{matrix} \sin(\nu\pi) \\ 1 + \cos(\nu\pi) \end{matrix} \right\} {}_2F_3\left(\begin{matrix} 1, \frac{s+1}{2}; -\frac{a^2b^2}{4} \\ \frac{3-\nu}{2}, \frac{3+\nu}{2}, \frac{s+2\alpha+1}{2} \end{matrix} \right)$ $[a,\ \mathrm{Re}\,\nu,\ \mathrm{Re}\,s > 0]$

No.	$f(x)$	$F(s)$

5 $\left(x^2-a^2\right)_+^{\alpha-1}\mathbf{J}_\nu(bx)$

$$\frac{a^{s+2\alpha-2}}{2\nu\pi}\sin(\nu\pi)\,\Gamma\!\left[\begin{matrix}\alpha,\ -\frac{s+2\alpha-2}{2}\\[2pt]\frac{2-s}{2}\end{matrix}\right]{}_2F_3\!\left(\begin{matrix}1,\ \frac{s}{2};\ -\frac{a^2b^2}{4}\\[2pt]\frac{2-\nu}{2},\ \frac{2+\nu}{2},\ \frac{s+2\alpha}{2}\end{matrix}\right)$$

$$+\frac{a^{s+2\alpha-1}b}{2\pi\left(1-\nu^2\right)}\sin(\nu\pi)\,\Gamma\!\left[\begin{matrix}\alpha,\ -\frac{s+2\alpha-1}{2}\\[2pt]\frac{1-s}{2}\end{matrix}\right]{}_2F_3\!\left(\begin{matrix}1,\ \frac{s+1}{2};\ -\frac{a^2b^2}{4}\\[2pt]\frac{3-\nu}{2},\ \frac{3+\nu}{2},\ \frac{s+2\alpha+1}{2}\end{matrix}\right)$$

$$+\frac{2^\nu\pi^{3/2}b^{-s-2\alpha+2}}{\Gamma\!\left(-\frac{s+2\alpha+\nu-4}{2}\right)\Gamma\!\left(\frac{s+2\alpha-\nu-1}{2}\right)\Gamma\left(-s-2\alpha+\nu+3\right)}$$

$$\times\csc\left[(s+2\alpha)\,\pi\right]{}_1F_2\!\left(\begin{matrix}1-\alpha;\ -\frac{a^2b^2}{4}\\[2pt]-\frac{s+2\alpha+\nu-4}{2},\ -\frac{s+2\alpha-\nu-4}{2}\end{matrix}\right)$$

$$[a,\ b,\ \operatorname{Re}\mu>0;\ \operatorname{Re}(s+2\mu)<3]$$

6 $\left(x^2-a^2\right)_+^{\alpha-1}\mathbf{E}_\nu(bx)$

$$\frac{a^{s+2\alpha-2}}{\nu\pi}\sin^2\frac{\nu\pi}{2}\,\Gamma\!\left[\begin{matrix}\alpha,\ -\frac{s+2\alpha-2}{2}\\[2pt]\frac{2-s}{2}\end{matrix}\right]{}_2F_3\!\left(\begin{matrix}1,\ \frac{s}{2};\ -\frac{a^2b^2}{4}\\[2pt]\frac{2-\nu}{2},\ \frac{2+\nu}{2},\ \frac{s+2\alpha}{2}\end{matrix}\right)$$

$$-\frac{a^{s+2\alpha-1}b}{\left(1-\nu^2\right)\pi}\cos^2\frac{\nu\pi}{2}\,\Gamma\!\left[\begin{matrix}\alpha,\ -\frac{s+2\alpha-1}{2}\\[2pt]\frac{1-s}{2}\end{matrix}\right]{}_2F_3\!\left(\begin{matrix}1,\ \frac{s+1}{2};\ -\frac{a^2b^2}{4}\\[2pt]\frac{3-\nu}{2},\ \frac{3+\nu}{2},\ \frac{s+2\alpha+1}{2}\end{matrix}\right)$$

$$+\frac{2^{s+2\alpha-2}\pi b^{-s-2\alpha+2}}{\Gamma\!\left(-\frac{s+2\alpha+\nu-4}{2}\right)\Gamma\!\left(-\frac{s+2\alpha-\nu-4}{2}\right)}\csc\left[(s+2\alpha)\,\pi\right]$$

$$\times\sin\frac{(s+2\alpha-\nu)\,\pi}{2}\,{}_1F_2\!\left(\begin{matrix}1-\alpha;\ -\frac{a^2b^2}{4}\\[2pt]-\frac{s+2\alpha+\nu-4}{2},\ -\frac{s+2\alpha-\nu-4}{2}\end{matrix}\right)$$

$$[a,\ b,\ \operatorname{Re}\mu>0;\ \operatorname{Re}(s+2\mu)<3]$$

7 $\dfrac{1}{\left(x^2+a^2\right)^\rho}\left\{\begin{matrix}\mathbf{J}_\nu(bx)\\ \mathbf{E}_\nu(bx)\end{matrix}\right\}$

$$\frac{a^{s-2\rho}}{2\nu\pi}\,\mathrm{B}\!\left(\frac{s}{2},\frac{2\rho-s}{2}\right)\left\{\begin{matrix}\sin(\nu\pi)\\ 1-\cos(\nu\pi)\end{matrix}\right\}{}_2F_3\!\left(\begin{matrix}1,\ \frac{s}{2};\ \frac{a^2b^2}{4}\\[2pt]\frac{2-\nu}{2},\ \frac{2+\nu}{2},\ \frac{s-2\rho+2}{2}\end{matrix}\right)$$

$$\pm\frac{a^{s-2\rho+1}b}{2\left(1-\nu^2\right)\pi}\,\mathrm{B}\!\left(\frac{s+1}{2},\rho-\frac{s+1}{2}\right)\left\{\begin{matrix}\sin(\nu\pi)\\ 1+\cos(\nu\pi)\end{matrix}\right\}$$

$$\times\,{}_2F_3\!\left(\begin{matrix}1,\ \frac{s+1}{2};\ \frac{a^2b^2}{4}\\[2pt]\frac{3-\nu}{2},\ \frac{3+\nu}{2},\ \frac{s-2\rho+3}{2}\end{matrix}\right)-\left(\frac{b}{2}\right)^{2\rho-s}\frac{\pi\csc\left[(2\rho-s)\,\pi\right]}{\Gamma\!\left(\frac{2-s-\nu+2\rho}{2}\right)\Gamma\!\left(\frac{2-s+\nu+2\rho}{2}\right)}$$

$$\times\left\{\begin{matrix}\cos\left[(\nu-s+2\rho)\,\pi/2\right]\\ \sin\left[(\nu-s+2\rho)\,\pi/2\right]\end{matrix}\right\}{}_1F_2\!\left(\begin{matrix}\rho;\ \frac{a^2b^2}{4}\\[2pt]\frac{2-s-\nu+2\rho}{2},\ \frac{2-s+\nu+2\rho}{2}\end{matrix}\right)$$

$$[b,\ \operatorname{Re}a,\ \operatorname{Re}s>0;\ \operatorname{Re}(s-2\rho)<1]$$

8 $\dfrac{1}{x^2-a^2}\left\{\begin{matrix}\mathbf{J}_\nu(bx)\\ \mathbf{E}_\nu(bx)\end{matrix}\right\}$

$$-\frac{\pi a^{s-2}}{2\nu\pi}\cot\frac{s\pi}{2}\left\{\begin{matrix}\sin(\nu\pi)\\ 1-\cos(\nu\pi)\end{matrix}\right\}{}_1F_2\!\left(\begin{matrix}1;\ -\frac{a^2b^2}{4}\\[2pt]\frac{2-\nu}{2},\ \frac{2+\nu}{2}\end{matrix}\right)$$

$$\pm\frac{\pi a^{s-1}b}{2\left(1-\nu^2\right)\pi}\tan\frac{s\pi}{2}\left\{\begin{matrix}\sin(\nu\pi)\\ 1+\cos(\nu\pi)\end{matrix}\right\}{}_1F_2\!\left(\begin{matrix}1;\ -\frac{a^2b^2}{4}\\[2pt]\frac{3-\nu}{2},\ \frac{3+\nu}{2}\end{matrix}\right)$$

$$-\left(\frac{b}{2}\right)^{2-s}\frac{\pi\csc(s\pi)}{\Gamma\!\left(\frac{4-s-\nu}{2}\right)\Gamma\!\left(\frac{4-s+\nu}{2}\right)}\left\{\begin{matrix}\cos\left[(\nu-s)\,\pi/2\right]\\ \sin\left[(\nu-s)\,\pi/2\right]\end{matrix}\right\}$$

$$\times\,{}_1F_2\!\left(\begin{matrix}1;\ -\frac{a^2b^2}{4}\\[2pt]\frac{4-s-\nu}{2},\ \frac{4-s+\nu}{2}\end{matrix}\right)\qquad[a,\ b>0;\ 0<\operatorname{Re}s<3]$$

No.	$f(x)$	$F(s)$
9	$(x^2+a^2)^{\nu/2}$ $\times\left[\mathbf{J}_\nu\left(b\sqrt{x^2+a^2}\right)\right.$ $\left.-\ \mathbf{J}_{-\nu}\left(b\sqrt{x^2+a^2}\right)\right]$	$\dfrac{2^{s/2}\pi\,a^{s/2+\nu}b^{-s/2}}{\Gamma\left(\frac{2-s}{2}\right)}\sin\dfrac{\nu\pi}{2}\sec\dfrac{(s+\nu)\pi}{2}\,J_{-(s+2\nu)/2}\,(ab)$ $-\dfrac{a^{s+\nu+1}b}{4\pi}\sin(\nu\pi)\,\Gamma\!\left[\begin{matrix}\frac{s}{2},\ -\frac{s+\nu+1}{2}\\ \frac{3-\nu}{2}\end{matrix}\right]{}_1F_2\!\left(\begin{matrix}1;\ -\frac{a^2b^2}{4}\\ \frac{3-\nu}{2},\ \frac{s+\nu+3}{2}\end{matrix}\right)$ $[a,\,b>0;\ 0<\operatorname{Re}s<1-\operatorname{Re}\nu]$
10	$(x^2+a^2)^{\nu/2}$ $\times\left[\mathbf{J}_\nu\left(b\sqrt{x^2+a^2}\right)\right.$ $\left.+\ \mathbf{J}_{-\nu}\left(b\sqrt{x^2+a^2}\right)\right]$	$\dfrac{2^{s/2}\pi\,a^{s/2+\nu}b^{-s/2}}{\Gamma\left(\frac{2-s}{2}\right)}\cos\dfrac{\nu\pi}{2}\csc\dfrac{(s+\nu)\pi}{2}\,J_{-(s+2\nu)/2}\,(ab)$ $-\dfrac{a^{s+\nu}}{2\pi}\sin(\nu\pi)\,\Gamma\!\left[\begin{matrix}\frac{s}{2},\ -\frac{s+\nu}{2}\\ \frac{2-\nu}{2}\end{matrix}\right]{}_1F_2\!\left(\begin{matrix}1;\ -\frac{a^2b^2}{4}\\ \frac{2-\nu}{2},\ \frac{s+\nu+2}{2}\end{matrix}\right)$ $[a,\,b>0;\ 0<\operatorname{Re}s<3/2-\operatorname{Re}\nu]$

3.16.2. $\mathbf{J}_\nu(bx)$, $\mathbf{E}_\nu(bx)$, and the exponential or trigonometric functions

No.	$f(x)$	$F(s)$
1	$e^{-ax}\begin{Bmatrix}\mathbf{J}_\nu(bx)\\ \mathbf{E}_\nu(bx)\end{Bmatrix}$	$\dfrac{1}{\nu\pi a^s}\begin{Bmatrix}\sin(\nu\pi)\\ 1-\cos(\nu\pi)\end{Bmatrix}\Gamma(s)\,{}_3F_2\!\left(\begin{matrix}1,\ \frac{s}{2},\ \frac{s+1}{2};\ -\frac{b^2}{a^2}\\ \frac{2-\nu}{2},\ \frac{2+\nu}{2}\end{matrix}\right)$ $\pm\dfrac{b}{(1-\nu^2)\,\pi a^{s+1}}\begin{Bmatrix}\sin(\nu\pi)\\ 1+\cos(\nu\pi)\end{Bmatrix}\Gamma(s+1)\,{}_3F_2\!\left(\begin{matrix}1,\ \frac{s+1}{2},\ \frac{s+2}{2}\\ \frac{3-\nu}{2},\ \frac{3+\nu}{2};\ -\frac{b^2}{a^2}\end{matrix}\right)$ $[\operatorname{Re}s>0;\ \operatorname{Re}a>|\operatorname{Im}b|]$
2	$e^{-ax^2}\begin{Bmatrix}\mathbf{J}_\nu(bx)\\ \mathbf{E}_\nu(bx)\end{Bmatrix}$	$\dfrac{a^{-s/2}}{2\nu\pi}\begin{Bmatrix}\sin(\nu\pi)\\ 1-\cos(\nu\pi)\end{Bmatrix}\Gamma\!\left(\dfrac{s}{2}\right){}_2F_2\!\left(\begin{matrix}1,\ \frac{s}{2};\ -\frac{b^2}{4a}\\ \frac{2-\nu}{2},\ \frac{2+\nu}{2}\end{matrix}\right)$ $-\dfrac{a^{-(s+1)/2}b}{2(1-\nu^2)\,\pi}\begin{Bmatrix}\sin(\nu\pi)\\ 1+\cos(\nu\pi)\end{Bmatrix}$ $\times\Gamma\!\left(\dfrac{s+1}{2}\right){}_2F_2\!\left(\begin{matrix}1,\ \frac{s+1}{2};\ -\frac{b^2}{4a}\\ \frac{3-\nu}{2},\ \frac{3+\nu}{2}\end{matrix}\right)$ $[b,\ \operatorname{Re}a,\ \operatorname{Re}s>0]$
3	$\sin(ax)\begin{Bmatrix}\mathbf{J}_\nu(bx)\\ \mathbf{E}_\nu(bx)\end{Bmatrix}$	$\dfrac{\Gamma(s)}{\nu\pi a^s}\sin\dfrac{s\pi}{2}\begin{Bmatrix}\sin(\nu\pi)\\ 1-\cos(\nu\pi)\end{Bmatrix}{}_3F_2\!\left(\begin{matrix}1,\ \frac{s}{2},\ \frac{s+1}{2}\\ \frac{2-\nu}{2},\ \frac{2+\nu}{2};\ \frac{b^2}{a^2}\end{matrix}\right)$ $\pm\dfrac{b\,\Gamma(s+1)}{(1-\nu^2)\,\pi a^{s+1}}\cos\dfrac{s\pi}{2}$ $\times\begin{Bmatrix}\sin(\nu\pi)\\ 1+\cos(\nu\pi)\end{Bmatrix}{}_3F_2\!\left(\begin{matrix}1,\ \frac{s+1}{2},\ \frac{s+2}{2}\\ \frac{3-\nu}{2},\ \frac{3+\nu}{2};\ \frac{b^2}{a^2}\end{matrix}\right)$ $\left[\begin{matrix}0<b\le a;\ -1<\operatorname{Re}s<3/2\text{ for }b<a;\\ -1<\operatorname{Re}s<1/2\text{ for }b=a\end{matrix}\right]$

No.	$f(x)$	$F(s)$
4	$\sin(ax)\begin{Bmatrix} \mathbf{J}_\nu(bx) \\ \mathbf{E}_\nu(bx) \end{Bmatrix}$	$\mp\dfrac{\Gamma(s-1)}{\nu\pi a^{s-1}b}\cos\dfrac{s\pi}{2}\begin{Bmatrix} \sin(\nu\pi) \\ 1+\cos(\nu\pi) \end{Bmatrix}{}_3F_2\left(\begin{matrix} 1,\ \frac{1-\nu}{2},\ \frac{1+\nu}{2} \\ \frac{2-s}{2},\ \frac{3-s}{2};\ \frac{a^2}{b^2} \end{matrix}\right)$

$+\dfrac{\nu\,\Gamma(s-2)}{\pi a^{s-2}b^2}\sin\dfrac{s\pi}{2}\begin{Bmatrix} \sin(\nu\pi) \\ 1-\cos(\nu\pi) \end{Bmatrix}{}_3F_2\left(\begin{matrix} 1,\ \frac{2-\nu}{2},\ \frac{2+\nu}{2} \\ \frac{3-s}{2},\ \frac{4-s}{2};\ \frac{a^2}{b^2} \end{matrix}\right)$

$-\pi a\left(\dfrac{2}{b}\right)^{s+1}\dfrac{\csc(s\pi)}{\Gamma\left(\frac{1-s-\nu}{2}\right)\Gamma\left(\frac{1-s+\nu}{2}\right)}\begin{Bmatrix} \cos[(\nu-s-1)\pi/2] \\ \sin[(\nu-s-1)\pi/2] \end{Bmatrix}$

$\times {}_2F_1\left(\begin{matrix} \frac{s-\nu+1}{2},\ \frac{s+\nu+1}{2} \\ \frac{3}{2};\ \frac{a^2}{b^2} \end{matrix}\right)$

$\left[\begin{matrix} 0 < a \le b;\ -1 < \operatorname{Re} s < 3/2 \text{ for } a < b; \\ -1 < \operatorname{Re} s < 1/2 \text{ for } a = b \end{matrix}\right]$

| 5 | $\cos(ax)\begin{Bmatrix} \mathbf{J}_\nu(bx) \\ \mathbf{E}_\nu(bx) \end{Bmatrix}$ | $\dfrac{\Gamma(s)}{\nu\pi\,a^s}\cos\dfrac{s\pi}{2}\begin{Bmatrix} \sin(\nu\pi) \\ 1-\cos(\nu\pi) \end{Bmatrix}{}_3F_2\left(\begin{matrix} 1,\ \frac{s}{2},\ \frac{s+1}{2} \\ \frac{2-\nu}{2},\ \frac{2+\nu}{2};\ \frac{b^2}{a^2} \end{matrix}\right)$ |

$\mp\dfrac{b\,\Gamma(s+1)}{(1-\nu^2)\,\pi\,a^{s+1}}\sin\dfrac{s\pi}{2}\begin{Bmatrix} \sin(\nu\pi) \\ 1+\cos(\nu\pi) \end{Bmatrix}{}_3F_2\left(\begin{matrix} 1,\ \frac{s+1}{2},\ \frac{s+2}{2} \\ \frac{3-\nu}{2},\ \frac{3+\nu}{2};\ \frac{b^2}{a^2} \end{matrix}\right)$

$\left[\begin{matrix} 0 < b \le a;\ 0 < \operatorname{Re} s < 3/2 \text{ for } b < a; \\ 0 < \operatorname{Re} s < 1/2 \text{ for } b = a \end{matrix}\right]$

| 6 | $\cos(ax)\begin{Bmatrix} \mathbf{J}_\nu(bx) \\ \mathbf{E}_\nu(bx) \end{Bmatrix}$ | $\pm\dfrac{a^{1-s}\Gamma(s-1)}{\nu\pi b}\sin\dfrac{s\pi}{2}\begin{Bmatrix} \sin(\nu\pi) \\ 1+\cos(\nu\pi) \end{Bmatrix}{}_3F_2\left(\begin{matrix} 1,\ \frac{1-\nu}{2},\ \frac{1+\nu}{2} \\ \frac{2-s}{2},\ \frac{3-s}{2};\ \frac{a^2}{b^2} \end{matrix}\right)$ |

$+\dfrac{\nu a^{2-s}\Gamma(s-2)}{\pi b^2}\cos\dfrac{s\pi}{2}\begin{Bmatrix} \sin(\nu\pi) \\ 1-\cos(\nu\pi) \end{Bmatrix}$

$\times {}_3F_2\left(\begin{matrix} 1,\ \frac{2+\nu}{2},\ \frac{2-\nu}{2} \\ \frac{3-s}{2},\ \frac{4-s}{2};\ \frac{a^2}{b^2} \end{matrix}\right)+\dfrac{\pi(2/b)^s\csc(s\pi)}{\Gamma\left(\frac{2-s-\nu}{2}\right)\Gamma\left(\frac{2-s+\nu}{2}\right)}$

$\times\begin{Bmatrix} \cos[(\nu-s)\pi/2] \\ \sin[(\nu-s)\pi/2] \end{Bmatrix}{}_2F_1\left(\begin{matrix} \frac{s-\nu}{2},\ \frac{s+\nu}{2} \\ \frac{1}{2};\ \frac{a^2}{b^2} \end{matrix}\right)$

$\left[\begin{matrix} 0 < a \le b;\ 0 < \operatorname{Re} s < 3/2 \text{ for } a < b; \\ 0 < \operatorname{Re} s < 1/2 \text{ for } a = b \end{matrix}\right]$

3.16.3. $\mathbf{J}_\nu(bx)$, $\mathbf{E}_\nu(bx)$, **and** $\operatorname{Ei}\left(-ax^2\right)$ **or** $\operatorname{erfc}(ax)$

| 1 | $\operatorname{Ei}\left(-ax^2\right)\begin{Bmatrix} \mathbf{J}_\nu(bx) \\ \mathbf{E}_\nu(bx) \end{Bmatrix}$ | $\mp\dfrac{a^{-s/2}}{\pi}\left[\dfrac{1}{\nu s}\begin{Bmatrix} \sin(\nu\pi) \\ \cos(\nu\pi)-1 \end{Bmatrix}\Gamma\left(\dfrac{s}{2}\right){}_3F_3\left(\begin{matrix} 1,\ \frac{s}{2},\ \frac{s}{2};\ -\frac{b^2}{4a} \\ \frac{2-\nu}{2},\ \frac{2+\nu}{2},\ \frac{s+2}{2} \end{matrix}\right)\right.$ |

$-\dfrac{a^{-1/2}b}{(\nu^2-1)(s+1)}\begin{Bmatrix} \sin(\nu\pi) \\ \cos(\nu\pi)+1 \end{Bmatrix}$

$\left.\times\,\Gamma\left(\dfrac{s+1}{2}\right){}_3F_3\left(\begin{matrix} 1,\ \frac{s+1}{2},\ \frac{s+1}{2};\ -\frac{b^2}{4a} \\ \frac{3-\nu}{2},\ \frac{3+\nu}{2},\ \frac{s+3}{2} \end{matrix}\right)\right]$

$[a,\ \operatorname{Re} s > 0 \text{ or } (\operatorname{Re} a,\ b > 0;\ |\operatorname{Im} a| \ne 0;\ 0 < \operatorname{Re} s < 1)]$

No.	$f(x)$	$F(s)$
2	$\mathrm{erfc}\,(ax)\begin{Bmatrix}\mathbf{J}_\nu(bx)\\\mathbf{E}_\nu(bx)\end{Bmatrix}$	$\dfrac{a^{-s-1}}{\pi^{3/2}}\left[\dfrac{a}{\nu s}\begin{Bmatrix}\sin(\nu\pi)\\1-\cos(\nu\pi)\end{Bmatrix}\Gamma\left(\dfrac{s+1}{2}\right){}_3F_3\left(\begin{matrix}1,\frac{s}{2},\frac{s+1}{2};\,-\frac{b^2}{4a^2}\\\frac{2-\nu}{2},\frac{2+\nu}{2},\frac{s+2}{2}\end{matrix}\right)\right.$

$$\mp\,\frac{b}{(\nu^2-1)(s+1)}\begin{Bmatrix}\sin(\nu\pi)\\\cos(\nu\pi)+1\end{Bmatrix}$$

$$\times\,\Gamma\left(\frac{s+2}{2}\right){}_3F_3\left(\begin{matrix}1,\frac{s+1}{2},\frac{s+2}{2};\,-\frac{b^2}{4a^2}\\\frac{3-\nu}{2},\frac{3+\nu}{2},\frac{s+3}{2}\end{matrix}\right)\Bigg]$$

$$\left[\begin{matrix}(\mathrm{Re}\,s>0;\,|\arg a|<\pi/4)\text{ or}\\(0<\mathrm{Re}\,s<7/2;\,|\mathrm{Im}\,b|\neq0;\,|\arg a|<\pi/4)\end{matrix}\right]$$

3.16.4. $\mathbf{J}_\nu(bx)$, $\mathbf{E}_\nu(bx)$, and $J_\mu(ax)$

No.	$f(x)$	$F(s)$
1	$J_\mu(ax)\begin{Bmatrix}\mathbf{J}_\nu(bx)\\\mathbf{E}_\nu(bx)\end{Bmatrix}$	$\dfrac{2^{s-1}}{\nu\pi a^s}\begin{Bmatrix}\sin(\nu\pi)\\1-\cos(\nu\pi)\end{Bmatrix}\Gamma\left[\begin{matrix}\frac{s+\mu}{2}\\\frac{2-s+\mu}{2}\end{matrix}\right]{}_3F_2\left(\begin{matrix}1,\frac{s-\mu}{2},\frac{s+\mu}{2}\\\frac{2-\nu}{2},\frac{2+\nu}{2};\,\frac{b^2}{a^2}\end{matrix}\right)$

$$\pm\,\frac{2^s b}{(1-\nu^2)\pi a^{s+1}}\begin{Bmatrix}\sin(\nu\pi)\\1+\cos(\nu\pi)\end{Bmatrix}$$

$$\times\,\Gamma\left[\begin{matrix}\frac{s+\mu+1}{2}\\\frac{1-s+\mu}{2}\end{matrix}\right]{}_3F_2\left(\begin{matrix}1,\frac{s-\mu+1}{2},\frac{s+\mu+1}{2}\\\frac{3-\nu}{2},\frac{3+\nu}{2};\,\frac{b^2}{a^2}\end{matrix}\right)$$

$$\left[\begin{matrix}0<b\leq a;\,-\mathrm{Re}\,\mu<\mathrm{Re}\,s<2\text{ for }b<a;\\-\mathrm{Re}\,\mu<\mathrm{Re}\,s<1\text{ for }b=a\end{matrix}\right]$$

| 2 | $J_\mu(ax)\begin{Bmatrix}\mathbf{J}_\nu(bx)\\\mathbf{E}_\nu(bx)\end{Bmatrix}$ | $\pm\dfrac{1}{2\pi b}\left(\dfrac{a}{2}\right)^{1-s}\begin{Bmatrix}\sin(\nu\pi)\\1+\cos(\nu\pi)\end{Bmatrix}\Gamma\left[\begin{matrix}\frac{s+\mu-1}{2}\\\frac{3-s+\mu}{2}\end{matrix}\right]$ |

$$\times\,{}_3F_2\left(\begin{matrix}1,\frac{1-\nu}{2},\frac{1+\nu}{2}\\\frac{3-s-\mu}{2},\frac{3-s+\mu}{2};\,\frac{a^2}{b^2}\end{matrix}\right)-\frac{\nu a^{2-s}}{2^{3-s}\pi b^2}\begin{Bmatrix}\sin(\nu\pi)\\1-\cos(\nu\pi)\end{Bmatrix}$$

$$\times\,\Gamma\left[\begin{matrix}\frac{s+\mu-2}{2}\\\frac{4-s+\mu}{2}\end{matrix}\right]{}_3F_2\left(\begin{matrix}1,\frac{2-\nu}{2},\frac{2+\nu}{2}\\\frac{4-s-\mu}{2},\frac{4-s+\mu}{2};\,\frac{a^2}{b^2}\end{matrix}\right)$$

$$+\,\frac{2^s\pi a^\mu}{b^{s+\mu}}\frac{\csc\left[(s+\mu)\pi\right]}{\Gamma\left[\mu+1,\frac{2-s-\mu-\nu}{2},\frac{2-s-\mu+\nu}{2}\right]}$$

$$\times\begin{Bmatrix}\cos\left[(\nu-s-\mu)\pi/2\right]\\\sin\left[(\nu-s-\mu)\pi/2\right]\end{Bmatrix}{}_2F_1\left(\begin{matrix}\frac{s+\mu-\nu}{2},\frac{s+\mu+\nu}{2}\\\mu+1;\,\frac{a^2}{b^2}\end{matrix}\right)$$

$$\left[\begin{matrix}0<a\leq b;\,-\mathrm{Re}\,\mu<\mathrm{Re}\,s<2\text{ for }a<b;\\-\mathrm{Re}\,\mu<\mathrm{Re}\,s<1\text{ for }a=b\end{matrix}\right]$$

| 3 | $J_\nu(ax)-\mathbf{J}_\nu(ax)$ | $-\dfrac{2^{s-1}\sin(\nu\pi)}{a^s\sin(s\pi)}\Gamma\left[\begin{matrix}\frac{s+\nu}{2}\\\frac{2-s+\nu}{2}\end{matrix}\right]\qquad[0,\,-\mathrm{Re}\,\nu<\mathrm{Re}\,s<1;\,|\arg a|<\pi]$ |

3.17.   The Kelvin Functions $\mathrm{ber}_\nu(z)$, $\mathrm{bei}_\nu(z)$, and $\mathrm{ker}_\nu(z)$, $\mathrm{kei}_\nu(z)$

More formulas can be obtained from the corresponding sections due to the relations

$$\left\{\begin{matrix} \mathrm{bei}_\nu(z) \\ \mathrm{ber}_\nu(z) \end{matrix}\right\} = \frac{1}{\Gamma(\nu+2)}\left\{\begin{matrix} \cos(3\pi\nu/4) \\ \sin(3\pi\nu/4) \end{matrix}\right\}\left(\frac{z}{2}\right)^{\nu+2}{}_0F_3\left(\frac{3}{2},\frac{\nu+2}{2},\frac{\nu+3}{2};-\frac{z^4}{256}\right)$$

$$+\frac{1}{\Gamma(\nu+1)}\left\{\begin{matrix} \sin(3\pi\nu/4) \\ \cos(3\pi\nu/4) \end{matrix}\right\}\left(\frac{z}{2}\right)^{\nu+2}{}_0F_3\left(\frac{1}{2},\frac{\nu+1}{2},\frac{\nu+2}{2};-\frac{z^4}{256}\right),$$

$$\left\{\begin{matrix} \mathrm{kei}_\nu(z) \\ \mathrm{ker}_\nu(z) \end{matrix}\right\} = -2^{-\nu-3}\left\{\begin{matrix} \cos(\nu\pi/4) \\ \sin(\nu\pi/4) \end{matrix}\right\}\Gamma(-\nu-1)z^{\nu+2}{}_0F_3\left(\frac{3}{2},\frac{\nu+2}{2},\frac{\nu+3}{2};-\frac{z^4}{256}\right)$$

$$\mp 2^{-\nu-1}\left\{\begin{matrix} \sin(\nu\pi/4) \\ \cos(\nu\pi/4) \end{matrix}\right\}\Gamma(-\nu)z^\nu{}_0F_3\left(\frac{1}{2},\frac{\nu+1}{2},\frac{\nu+2}{2};-\frac{z^4}{256}\right)$$

$$-2^{\nu-3}\left\{\begin{matrix} \cos(3\pi\nu/4) \\ \sin(3\pi\nu/4) \end{matrix}\right\}\Gamma(\nu-1)z^{-\nu+2}{}_0F_3\left(\frac{3}{2},\frac{2-\nu}{2},\frac{3-\nu}{2};-\frac{z^4}{256}\right)$$

$$\mp 2^{\nu-1}\left\{\begin{matrix} \sin(3\nu\pi/4) \\ \cos(3\nu\pi/4) \end{matrix}\right\}\Gamma(\nu)z^{-\nu}{}_0F_3\left(\frac{1}{2},\frac{1-\nu}{2},\frac{2-\nu}{2};-\frac{z^4}{256}\right);$$

$$\left\{\begin{matrix} \mathrm{ber}_\nu(z) \\ \mathrm{bei}_\nu(z) \end{matrix}\right\} = \pi G_{15}^{20}\left(\frac{z^4}{256}\left|\begin{matrix} \frac{4\nu+1\pm1}{4} \\ \frac{\nu}{4},\frac{2+\nu}{4},-\frac{\nu}{4},\frac{2-\nu}{4},\frac{4\nu+1\pm1}{4} \end{matrix}\right.\right), \quad [-\pi/4 \le \arg z \le \pi/4];$$

$$\left\{\begin{matrix} \mathrm{ker}_\nu(z) \\ \mathrm{kei}_\nu(z) \end{matrix}\right\} = \pm\frac{1}{4} G_{15}^{40}\left(\frac{z^4}{256}\left|\begin{matrix} \frac{2\nu+1\pm1}{4} \\ -\frac{\nu}{4},\frac{\nu}{4},\frac{2-\nu}{4},\frac{\nu+2}{4},\frac{2\nu+1\pm1}{4} \end{matrix}\right.\right), \quad [-\pi/4 \le \arg z \le \pi/4].$$

3.17.1. $\mathrm{ber}_\nu(bx)$, $\mathrm{bei}_\nu(bx)$, $\mathrm{ker}_\nu(bx)$, $\mathrm{kei}_\nu(bx)$, and algebraic functions

No.	$f(x)$	$F(s)$
1	$(a-x)_+^{\alpha-1}\left\{\begin{matrix} \mathrm{ber}_\nu(bx) \\ \mathrm{bei}_\nu(bx) \end{matrix}\right\}$	$\dfrac{a^{s+\alpha+\nu-1}b^\nu}{2^\nu\Gamma(\nu+1)}\left\{\begin{matrix} \cos(3\pi\nu/4) \\ \sin(3\pi\nu/4) \end{matrix}\right\}\mathrm{B}(\alpha,s+\nu)$
		$\times\,{}_4F_7\left(\begin{matrix} \Delta(4,s+\nu);\ -\frac{a^4b^4}{256} \\ \frac{1}{2},\frac{\nu+1}{2},\frac{\nu+2}{2},\Delta(4,s+\alpha+\nu) \end{matrix}\right)$
		$\mp\dfrac{a^{s+\alpha+\nu+1}b^{\nu+2}}{2^{\nu+2}\Gamma(\nu+2)}\left\{\begin{matrix} \sin(3\pi\nu/4) \\ \cos(3\pi\nu/4) \end{matrix}\right\}\mathrm{B}(\alpha,s+\nu+2)$
		$\times\,{}_4F_7\left(\begin{matrix} \Delta(4,s+\nu+2);\ -\frac{a^4b^4}{256} \\ \frac{3}{2},\frac{\nu+2}{2},\frac{\nu+3}{2},\Delta(4,s+\alpha+\nu+2) \end{matrix}\right)\quad\begin{bmatrix} a,\,\mathrm{Re}\,\alpha>0; \\ \mathrm{Re}\,(s+\nu)>0 \end{bmatrix}$
2	$(a^2-x^2)_+^{\alpha-1}$ $\times\left\{\begin{matrix} \mathrm{ber}_\nu(bx) \\ \mathrm{bei}_\nu(bx) \end{matrix}\right\}$	$\dfrac{a^{s+\nu+2\alpha-2}b^\nu}{2^{\nu+1}\Gamma(\nu+1)}\left\{\begin{matrix} \cos(3\pi\nu/4) \\ \sin(3\pi\nu/4) \end{matrix}\right\}\mathrm{B}\left(\alpha,\frac{s+\nu}{2}\right)$
		$\times\,{}_2F_5\left(\begin{matrix} \Delta\left(2,\frac{s+\nu}{2}\right);\ -\frac{a^4b^4}{256} \\ \frac{1}{2},\Delta(2,\nu+1),\Delta\left(2,\frac{s+2\alpha+\nu}{2}\right) \end{matrix}\right)$
		$\mp\dfrac{a^{s+\nu+2\alpha}b^{\nu+2}}{2^{\nu+3}\Gamma(\nu+2)}\left\{\begin{matrix} \sin(3\pi\nu/4) \\ \cos(3\pi\nu/4) \end{matrix}\right\}\mathrm{B}\left(\alpha,\frac{s+\nu+2}{2}\right)$
		$\times\,{}_2F_5\left(\begin{matrix} \Delta\left(2,\frac{s+\nu+2}{2}\right);\ -\frac{a^4b^4}{256} \\ \frac{3}{2},\Delta(2,\nu+2),\Delta\left(2,\frac{s+2\alpha+\nu+2}{2}\right) \end{matrix}\right)\quad\begin{bmatrix} a,\,\mathrm{Re}\,\alpha>0; \\ \mathrm{Re}\,(s+\nu)>0 \end{bmatrix}$

No.	$f(x)$	$F(s)$
3	$\left\{\begin{matrix} \mathrm{ker}_\nu(ax) \\ \mathrm{kei}_\nu(ax) \end{matrix}\right\}$	$\pm\dfrac{2^{s-2}}{a^s}\left\{\begin{matrix}\cos\left[(s+2\nu)\,\pi/4\right]\\ \sin\left[(s+2\nu)\,\pi/4\right]\end{matrix}\right\}\Gamma\left(\dfrac{s-\nu}{2}\right)\Gamma\left(\dfrac{s+\nu}{2}\right)$ $[\mathrm{Re}\,s > |\mathrm{Re}\,\nu|;\ |\arg a| < \pi/4]$
4	$(a-x)_+^{\alpha-1}\left\{\begin{matrix}\mathrm{ker}_\nu(bx)\\ \mathrm{kei}_\nu(bx)\end{matrix}\right\}$	$-\dfrac{a^{s+\alpha+\nu+1}b^{\nu+2}}{2^{\nu+3}}\left\{\begin{matrix}\sin\left(\pi\nu/4\right)\\ \cos\left(\pi\nu/4\right)\end{matrix}\right\}\Gamma(-\nu-1)\,\mathrm{B}(\alpha,\,s+\nu+2)$ $\times {}_4F_7\left(\begin{matrix}\Delta(4,\,s+\nu+2);\,-\frac{a^4b^4}{256}\\ \frac{3}{2},\,\frac{\nu+2}{2},\,\frac{\nu+3}{2},\,\Delta(4,\,s+\alpha+\nu+2)\end{matrix}\right)$ $\pm\dfrac{a^{s+\alpha+\nu-1}b^{\nu}}{2^{\nu+1}}\left\{\begin{matrix}\cos\left(\pi\nu/4\right)\\ \sin\left(\pi\nu/4\right)\end{matrix}\right\}\Gamma(-\nu)\,\mathrm{B}(\alpha,\,s+\nu)$ $\times {}_4F_7\left(\begin{matrix}\Delta(4,\,s+\nu);\,-\frac{a^4b^4}{256}\\ \frac{1}{2},\,\frac{\nu+1}{2},\,\frac{\nu+2}{2},\,\Delta(4,\,s+\alpha+\nu)\end{matrix}\right)$ $-\dfrac{2^{\nu-3}a^{s+\alpha-\nu+1}}{b^{\nu-2}}\left\{\begin{matrix}\sin\left(3\pi\nu/4\right)\\ \cos\left(3\pi\nu/4\right)\end{matrix}\right\}\Gamma(\nu-1)\,\mathrm{B}(\alpha,\,s-\nu+2)$ $\times {}_4F_7\left(\begin{matrix}\Delta(4,\,s-\nu+2)\,;\,-\frac{a^4b^4}{256}\\ \frac{3}{2},\,\frac{2-\nu}{2},\,\frac{3-\nu}{2},\,\Delta(4,\,s+\alpha-\nu+2)\end{matrix}\right)$ $\pm\dfrac{2^{\nu-1}a^{s+\alpha-\nu-1}}{b^{\nu}}\left\{\begin{matrix}\cos\left(3\pi\nu/4\right)\\ \sin\left(3\pi\nu/4\right)\end{matrix}\right\}\Gamma(\nu)\,\mathrm{B}(\alpha,\,s-\nu)$ $\times {}_4F_7\left(\begin{matrix}\Delta(4,\,s-\nu)\,;\,-\frac{a^4b^4}{256}\\ \frac{1}{2},\,\frac{1-\nu}{2},\,\frac{2-\nu}{2},\,\Delta(4,\,s+\alpha-\nu)\end{matrix}\right)$ $[a,\ \mathrm{Re}\,\alpha > 0;\ \mathrm{Re}\,s > |\mathrm{Re}\,\nu|]$

3.17.2. $\mathrm{ber}_\nu(bx)$, $\mathrm{bei}_\nu(bx)$, $\mathrm{ker}_\nu(bx)$, $\mathrm{kei}_\nu(bx)$, **and the exponential function**

No.	$f(x)$	$F(s)$
1	$e^{-ax}\left\{\begin{matrix}\mathrm{ber}_\nu(bx)\\ \mathrm{bei}_\nu(bx)\end{matrix}\right\}$	$a^{-s-\nu}\left(\dfrac{b}{2}\right)^{\nu}\left\{\begin{matrix}\cos\left(3\nu\pi/4\right)\\ \sin\left(3\nu\pi/4\right)\end{matrix}\right\}\Gamma\left[\begin{matrix}s+\nu\\ \nu+1\end{matrix}\right]{}_4F_3\left(\begin{matrix}\Delta(4,\,s+\nu);\,-\frac{b^4}{a^4}\\ \frac{1}{2},\,\Delta(2,\,\nu+1)\end{matrix}\right)$ $\mp a^{-s-\nu-2}\left(\dfrac{b}{2}\right)^{\nu+2}\left\{\begin{matrix}\sin\left(3\nu\pi/4\right)\\ \cos\left(3\nu\pi/4\right)\end{matrix}\right\}\Gamma\left[\begin{matrix}s+\nu+2\\ \nu+2\end{matrix}\right]$ $\times {}_4F_3\left(\begin{matrix}\Delta(4,\,s+\nu+2);\,-\frac{b^4}{a^4}\\ \frac{3}{2},\,\Delta(2,\,\nu+2)\end{matrix}\right)$ $[\sqrt{2}\,\mathrm{Re}\,a > \mathrm{Re}\,b + |\mathrm{Im}\,b|;\ \mathrm{Re}\,(s+\nu) > 0]$
2	$e^{-ax^2}\left\{\begin{matrix}\mathrm{ber}_\nu(bx)\\ \mathrm{bei}_\nu(bx)\end{matrix}\right\}$	$\dfrac{b^{\nu}}{2^{\nu+1}a^{(s+\nu)/2}}\left\{\begin{matrix}\cos\left(3\nu\pi/4\right)\\ \sin\left(3\nu\pi/4\right)\end{matrix}\right\}\Gamma\left[\begin{matrix}\frac{s+\nu}{2}\\ \nu+1\end{matrix}\right]{}_2F_3\left(\begin{matrix}\Delta(2,\,\frac{s+\nu}{2});\,-\frac{b^4}{64a^2}\\ \frac{1}{2},\,\Delta(2,\,\nu+1)\end{matrix}\right)$ $\mp\dfrac{b^{\nu+2}}{2^{\nu+3}a^{(s+\nu)/2+1}}\left\{\begin{matrix}\sin\left(3\nu\pi/4\right)\\ \cos\left(3\nu\pi/4\right)\end{matrix}\right\}\Gamma\left[\begin{matrix}\frac{s+\nu+2}{2}\\ \nu+2\end{matrix}\right]$ $\times {}_2F_3\left(\begin{matrix}\Delta(2,\,\frac{s+\nu+2}{2});\,-\frac{b^4}{64a^2}\\ \frac{3}{2},\,\Delta(2,\,\nu+2)\end{matrix}\right)\qquad [\mathrm{Re}\,a,\ \mathrm{Re}\,(s+\nu) > 0]$

No.	$f(x)$	$F(s)$

3 $e^{-ax}\left\{\begin{matrix} \ker_\nu(bx) \\ \ker_\nu(bx) \end{matrix}\right\}$

$$\pm \frac{2^{s-2}}{b^s}\left\{\begin{matrix} \cos[(s+2\nu)\pi/4] \\ \sin[(s+2\nu)\pi/4] \end{matrix}\right\} \Gamma\left(\frac{s+\nu}{2}\right)\Gamma\left(\frac{s-\nu}{2}\right)$$

$$\times {}_4F_3\left(\begin{matrix} \Delta\left(2,\frac{s+\nu}{2}\right), \Delta\left(2,\frac{s-\nu}{2}\right) \\ \frac{1}{4}, \frac{1}{2}, \frac{3}{4}; -\frac{a^4}{b^4} \end{matrix}\right)$$

$$\mp \frac{2^{s-1}a}{b^{s+1}}\left\{\begin{matrix} \cos[(s+2\nu+1)\pi/4] \\ \sin[(s+2\nu+1)\pi/4] \end{matrix}\right\} \Gamma\left(\frac{s+\nu+1}{2}\right)$$

$$\times \Gamma\left(\frac{s-\nu+1}{2}\right) {}_4F_3\left(\begin{matrix} \Delta\left(2,\frac{s+\nu+1}{2}\right), \Delta\left(2,\frac{s-\nu+1}{2}\right) \\ \frac{1}{2}, \frac{3}{4}, \frac{5}{4}; -\frac{a^4}{b^4} \end{matrix}\right)$$

$$- \frac{2^{s-1}a^2}{b^{s+2}}\left\{\begin{matrix} \sin[(s+2\nu)\pi/4] \\ \cos[(s+2\nu)\pi/4] \end{matrix}\right\} \Gamma\left(\frac{s+\nu+2}{2}\right)$$

$$\times \Gamma\left(\frac{s-\nu+2}{2}\right) {}_4F_3\left(\begin{matrix} \Delta\left(2,\frac{s+\nu+2}{2}\right), \Delta\left(2,\frac{s-\nu+2}{2}\right) \\ \frac{3}{4}, \frac{5}{4}, \frac{3}{2}; -\frac{a^4}{b^4} \end{matrix}\right)$$

$$+ \frac{2^s a^3}{3b^{s+3}}\left\{\begin{matrix} \sin[(s+2\nu+1)\pi/4] \\ \cos[(s+2\nu+1)\pi/4] \end{matrix}\right\} \Gamma\left(\frac{s+\nu+3}{2}\right)$$

$$\times \Gamma\left(\frac{s-\nu+3}{2}\right) {}_4F_3\left(\begin{matrix} \Delta\left(2,\frac{s+\nu+3}{2}\right), \Delta\left(2,\frac{s-\nu+3}{2}\right) \\ \frac{5}{4}, \frac{3}{2}, \frac{7}{4}; -\frac{a^4}{b^4} \end{matrix}\right)$$

$$\left[\mathrm{Re}\left(\sqrt{2}a+b\right) > |\mathrm{Im}\,b|;\ \mathrm{Re}\,s > |\mathrm{Re}\,\nu|\right]$$

4 $e^{-ax^2}\left\{\begin{matrix} \ker_\nu(bx) \\ \ker_\nu(bx) \end{matrix}\right\}$

$$\pm \frac{2^{\nu-2}}{a^{(s-\nu)/2}b^\nu}\left\{\begin{matrix} \cos(3\pi\nu/4) \\ \sin(3\pi\nu/4) \end{matrix}\right\} \Gamma(\nu)$$

$$\times \Gamma\left(\frac{s-\nu}{2}\right) {}_2F_3\left(\begin{matrix} \frac{s-\nu}{4}, \frac{s-\nu+2}{4} \\ \frac{1}{2}, \frac{1-\nu}{2}, \frac{2-\nu}{2}; -\frac{b^4}{64a^2} \end{matrix}\right)$$

$$- \frac{2^{\nu-4}}{a^{(s-\nu+2)/2}b^{\nu-2}}\left\{\begin{matrix} \sin(3\pi\nu/4) \\ \cos(3\pi\nu/4) \end{matrix}\right\} \Gamma(\nu-1)$$

$$\times \Gamma\left(\frac{s-\nu+2}{2}\right) {}_2F_3\left(\begin{matrix} \frac{s-\nu+2}{4}, \frac{s-\nu+4}{4} \\ \frac{3}{2}, \frac{2-\nu}{2}, \frac{3-\nu}{2}; -\frac{b^4}{64a^2} \end{matrix}\right)$$

$$\pm \frac{2^{-\nu-2}b^\nu}{a^{(s+\nu)/2}}\left\{\begin{matrix} \cos(\pi\nu/4) \\ \sin(\pi\nu/4) \end{matrix}\right\} \Gamma(-\nu)$$

$$\times \Gamma\left(\frac{s+\nu}{2}\right) {}_2F_3\left(\begin{matrix} \frac{s+\nu}{4}, \frac{s+\nu+2}{4} \\ \frac{1}{2}, \frac{\nu+1}{2}, \frac{\nu+2}{2}; -\frac{b^4}{64a^2} \end{matrix}\right)$$

$$- \frac{2^{-\nu-4}b^{\nu+2}}{a^{(s+\nu+2)/2}}\left\{\begin{matrix} \sin(\pi\nu/4) \\ \cos(\pi\nu/4) \end{matrix}\right\} \Gamma(-\nu-1)$$

$$\times \Gamma\left(\frac{s+\nu+2}{2}\right) {}_2F_3\left(\begin{matrix} \frac{s+\nu+2}{4}, \frac{s+\nu+4}{4} \\ \frac{3}{2}, \frac{\nu+2}{2}, \frac{\nu+3}{2}; -\frac{b^4}{64a^2} \end{matrix}\right)$$

$$\left[\mathrm{Re}\,a > 0;\ \mathrm{Re}\,s > |\mathrm{Re}\,\nu|\right]$$

3.17.3. $\mathrm{ker}_\nu (bx)$, $\mathrm{kei}_\nu (bx)$, **and trigonometric functions**

Notation: $\delta = \left\{ \begin{matrix} 1 \\ 0 \end{matrix} \right\}$.

1	$\sin (ax) \left\{ \begin{matrix} \mathrm{ker}_\nu (bx) \\ \mathrm{kei}_\nu (bx) \end{matrix} \right\}$	$U (1)$

$$U (\delta) = \pm \frac{2^{s+\delta-2} a^\delta}{b^{s+\delta}} \left\{ \begin{matrix} \cos[(s + 2\nu + \delta)\, \pi/4] \\ \sin[(s + 2\nu + \delta)\, \pi/4] \end{matrix} \right\} \Gamma \left(\frac{s - \nu + \delta}{2} \right)$$

$$\times \Gamma \left(\frac{s + \nu + \delta}{2} \right) {}_4F_3 \left(\begin{matrix} \Delta \left(2, \frac{s+\nu+\delta}{2}\right),\ \Delta \left(2, \frac{s-\nu+\delta}{2}\right) \\ \frac{1}{2},\ \frac{3}{4},\ \frac{4\delta+1}{4};\ -\frac{a^4}{b^4} \end{matrix} \right)$$

$$+ \frac{2^{s+\delta-1} a^{\delta+2}}{3^\delta b^{s+\delta+2}} \left\{ \begin{matrix} \sin[(s + 2\nu + \delta)\, \pi/4] \\ \cos[(s + 2\nu + \delta)\, \pi/4] \end{matrix} \right\} \Gamma \left(\frac{s - \nu + \delta + 2}{2} \right)$$

$$\times \Gamma \left(\frac{s + \nu + \delta + 2}{2} \right) {}_4F_3 \left(\begin{matrix} \Delta \left(2, \frac{s-\nu+\delta+2}{2}\right),\ \Delta \left(2, \frac{s+\nu+\delta+2}{2}\right) \\ \frac{5}{4},\ \frac{3}{2},\ \frac{4\delta+3}{4};\ -\frac{a^4}{b^4} \end{matrix} \right)$$

$$[a > 0;\ \mathrm{Re}\, s > |\mathrm{Re}\, \nu| - 1;\ |\arg b| < \pi/4]$$

2	$\cos (ax) \left\{ \begin{matrix} \mathrm{ker}_\nu (bx) \\ \mathrm{kei}_\nu (bx) \end{matrix} \right\}$	$U (0)$	$\left[\begin{matrix} a > 0;\ \mathrm{Re}\, s > |\mathrm{Re}\, \nu|; \\ |\arg b| < \pi/4;\ U(\delta) : \text{see } 3.17.3.1 \end{matrix} \right]$

3.17.4. $\mathrm{ber}_\nu (bx)$, $\mathrm{bei}_\nu (bx)$, $\mathrm{ker}_\nu (bx)$, $\mathrm{kei}_\nu (bx)$, **and** $\mathrm{Ei} (-ax^r)$

1	$\mathrm{Ei} (-ax) \left\{ \begin{matrix} \mathrm{ber}_\nu (bx) \\ \mathrm{bei}_\nu (bx) \end{matrix} \right\}$	$-\dfrac{a^{-s-\nu} b^\nu}{2^\nu (s+\nu)} \left\{ \begin{matrix} \cos (3\nu\pi/4) \\ \sin (3\nu\pi/4) \end{matrix} \right\} \Gamma \left[\begin{matrix} s + \nu \\ \nu + 1 \end{matrix} \right]$

$$\times {}_5F_4 \left(\begin{matrix} \frac{s+\nu}{4},\ \Delta (4, s + \nu) \\ \frac{1}{2},\ \Delta (2, \nu + 1),\ \frac{s+\nu+4}{4};\ -\frac{b^4}{a^4} \end{matrix} \right)$$

$$\pm \frac{a^{-s-\nu-2} b^{\nu+2}}{2^{\nu+2} (s+\nu+2)} \left\{ \begin{matrix} \sin (3\nu\pi/4) \\ \cos (3\nu\pi/4) \end{matrix} \right\} \Gamma \left[\begin{matrix} s + \nu + 2 \\ \nu + 2 \end{matrix} \right]$$

$$\times {}_5F_4 \left(\begin{matrix} \frac{s+\nu+2}{4},\ \Delta (4, s + \nu + 2) \\ \frac{3}{2},\ \Delta (2, \nu + 2),\ \frac{s+\nu+6}{4};\ -\frac{b^4}{a^4} \end{matrix} \right)$$

$$[\mathrm{Re}\, (\sqrt{2}\, a - b) > |\mathrm{Im}\, b|;\ \mathrm{Re}\, (s + \nu) > 0]$$

2	$\mathrm{Ei} (-ax^2) \left\{ \begin{matrix} \mathrm{ber}_\nu (bx) \\ \mathrm{bei}_\nu (bx) \end{matrix} \right\}$	$-\dfrac{a^{-(s+\nu)/2} b^\nu}{2^\nu (s+\nu)} \left\{ \begin{matrix} \cos (3\nu\pi/4) \\ \sin (3\nu\pi) \end{matrix} \right\} \Gamma \left[\begin{matrix} \frac{s+\nu}{2} \\ \nu + 1 \end{matrix} \right]$

$$\times {}_3F_4 \left(\begin{matrix} \frac{s+\nu}{4},\ \frac{s+\nu}{4},\ \frac{s+\nu+2}{4};\ -\frac{b^4}{64a^2} \\ \frac{1}{2},\ \Delta (2, \nu + 1),\ \frac{s+\nu+4}{4} \end{matrix} \right)$$

$$\pm \frac{a^{-(s+\nu)/2-1} c^{\nu+2}}{2^{\nu+2} (s+\nu+2)} \left\{ \begin{matrix} \sin (3\nu\pi/4) \\ \cos (3\nu\pi/4) \end{matrix} \right\} \Gamma \left[\begin{matrix} \frac{s+\nu+2}{2} \\ \nu + 2 \end{matrix} \right]$$

$$\times {}_2F_5 \left(\begin{matrix} \frac{s+\nu+2}{4},\ \frac{s+\nu+2}{4},\ \frac{s+\nu+4}{4};\ -\frac{c^4}{64a^2} \\ \frac{3}{2},\ \Delta (2, \nu + 2),\ \frac{s+\nu+6}{4} \end{matrix} \right)$$

$$[\mathrm{Re}\, a,\ \mathrm{Re}\, (s + \nu) > 0]$$

3.17.5. $\mathrm{ber}_\nu\,(bx)$, $\mathrm{bei}_\nu\,(bx)$, $\mathrm{ker}_\nu\,(bx)$, $\mathrm{kei}_\nu\,(bx)$, **and the Bessel functions**

1	$J_\mu\,(ax)\left\{\begin{array}{l}\mathrm{ker}_\nu\,(bx)\\\mathrm{kei}_\nu\,(bx)\end{array}\right\}$	$\pm\dfrac{2^{s-2}a^\mu}{b^{s+\mu}}\left\{\begin{array}{l}\cos[(s+\mu+2\nu)\,\pi/4]\\\sin[(s+\mu+2\nu)\,\pi/4]\end{array}\right\}\Gamma\left[\begin{array}{c}\frac{s+\mu+\nu}{2},\ \frac{s+\mu-\nu}{2}\\\mu+1\end{array}\right]$

$$\times\ {}_4F_3\left(\begin{array}{c}\Delta\left(2,\frac{s+\mu+\nu}{2}\right),\ \Delta\left(2,\frac{s+\mu-\nu}{2}\right)\\\frac{1}{2},\ \Delta\left(2,\mu+1\right);\ -\frac{a^4}{b^4}\end{array}\right)+\frac{2^{s-2}a^{\mu+2}}{b^{s+\mu+2}}$$

$$\times\left\{\begin{array}{l}\sin[(s+\mu+2\nu)\pi/4]\\\cos[(s+\mu+2\nu)\pi/4]\end{array}\right\}\Gamma\left[\begin{array}{c}\frac{s+\mu+\nu+2}{2},\ \frac{s+\mu-\nu+2}{2}\\\mu+2\end{array}\right]$$

$$\times\ {}_4F_3\left(\begin{array}{c}\Delta\left(2,\frac{s+\mu+\nu+2}{2}\right),\ \Delta\left(2,\frac{s+\mu-\nu+2}{2}\right)\\\frac{3}{2},\ \Delta\left(2,\mu+2\right);\ -\frac{a^4}{b^4}\end{array}\right)$$

$$[a>0;\ \mathrm{Re}\,(s+\mu)>|\mathrm{Re}\,\nu|;\ |\arg b|<\pi]$$

2	$K_\mu\,(ax)\left\{\begin{array}{l}\mathrm{ber}_\nu\,(bx)\\\mathrm{bei}_\nu\,(bx)\end{array}\right\}$	$\dfrac{2^{s-2}b^\nu}{a^{s+\nu}}\left\{\begin{array}{l}\cos\,(3\nu\pi/4)\\\sin\,(3\nu\pi/4)\end{array}\right\}\Gamma\left[\begin{array}{c}\frac{s-\mu+\nu}{2},\ \frac{s+\mu+\nu}{2}\\\nu+1\end{array}\right]$

$$\times\ {}_4F_3\left(\begin{array}{c}\Delta\left(2,\frac{s-\mu+\nu}{2}\right),\ \Delta\left(2,\frac{s+\mu+\nu}{2}\right)\\\frac{1}{2},\ \Delta\left(2,\nu+1\right);\ -\frac{b^4}{a^4}\end{array}\right)$$

$$\mp\frac{2^{s-2}b^{\nu+2}}{a^{s+\nu+2}}\left\{\begin{array}{l}\sin\,(3\nu\pi/4)\\\cos\,(3\nu\pi/4)\end{array}\right\}\Gamma\left[\begin{array}{c}\frac{s-\mu+\nu+2}{2},\ \frac{s+\mu+\nu+2}{2}\\\nu+2\end{array}\right]$$

$$\times\ {}_4F_3\left(\begin{array}{c}\Delta\left(2,\frac{s-\mu+\nu+2}{2}\right),\ \Delta\left(2,\frac{s+\mu+\nu+2}{2}\right)\\\frac{3}{2},\ \Delta\left(2,\nu+2\right);\ -\frac{b^4}{a^4}\end{array}\right)$$

$$[\mathrm{Re}\,(\sqrt{2}\,a-b)>|\mathrm{Im}\,b|;\ \mathrm{Re}\,(s+\nu)>|\mathrm{Re}\,\mu|]$$

3	$K_\mu\,(ax^2)\left\{\begin{array}{l}\mathrm{ber}_\nu\,(bx)\\\mathrm{bei}_\nu\,(bx)\end{array}\right\}$	$\dfrac{2^{(s-\nu)/2-3}b^\nu}{a^{(s+\nu)/2}}\left\{\begin{array}{l}\cos\,(3\nu\pi/4)\\\sin\,(3\nu\pi/4)\end{array}\right\}\Gamma\left[\begin{array}{c}\frac{s-2\mu+\nu}{4},\ \frac{s+2\mu+\nu}{4}\\\nu+1\end{array}\right]$

$$\times\ {}_2F_3\left(\begin{array}{c}\frac{s-2\mu+\nu}{4},\ \frac{s+2\mu+\nu}{4};\ -\frac{b^4}{64a^2}\\\frac{1}{2},\ \frac{\nu+1}{2},\ \frac{\nu+2}{2}\end{array}\right)+\frac{2^{(s-\nu)/2-4}b^{\nu+2}}{a^{(s+\nu)/2+1}}$$

$$\times\left\{\begin{array}{l}\sin\,(3\nu\pi/4)\\\cos\,(3\nu\pi/4)\end{array}\right\}\Gamma\left[\begin{array}{c}\frac{s-2\mu+\nu+2}{4},\ \frac{s+2\mu+\nu+2}{4}\\\nu+2\end{array}\right]$$

$$\times\ {}_2F_3\left(\begin{array}{c}\frac{s-2\mu+\nu+2}{4},\ \frac{s+2\mu+\nu+2}{4};\ -\frac{b^4}{64a^2}\\\frac{3}{2},\ \frac{\nu+2}{2},\ \frac{\nu+3}{2}\end{array}\right)\begin{array}{c}\mathrm{Re}\,a>0;\\\mathrm{Re}\,(s+\nu)>2|\mathrm{Re}\,\mu|\end{array}$$

3.17.6. $\varphi\,(x)\,(\mathrm{ber}_\nu^2\,(bx)+\mathrm{bei}_\nu^2\,(bx))$ **and** $\mathrm{ker}_\nu^2\,(bx)+\mathrm{kei}_\nu^2\,(bx)$

1	$e^{-ax}\left[\mathrm{ber}_\nu^2\,(bx)+\mathrm{bei}_\nu^2\,(bx)\right]$	$\dfrac{b^{2\nu}}{2^{2\nu}a^{s+2\nu}}\Gamma\left[\begin{array}{c}s+2\nu\\\nu+1,\ \nu+1\end{array}\right]{}_4F_3\left(\begin{array}{c}\Delta\,(4,\,s+2\nu)\\\Delta\,(2,\,\nu+1),\ \nu+1;\ \frac{4b^4}{a^4}\end{array}\right)$

$$[\mathrm{Re}\,a>\sqrt{2}\,(\mathrm{Re}\,b+|\mathrm{Im}\,b|);\ \mathrm{Re}\,(s+2\nu)>0]$$

2	$e^{-ax^2}\left[\mathrm{ber}_\nu^2\,(bx)+\mathrm{bei}_\nu^2\,(bx)\right]$	$\dfrac{b^{2\nu}}{2^{2\nu+1}a^{s/2+\nu}}\Gamma\left[\begin{array}{c}\frac{s+2\nu}{2}\\\nu+1,\ \nu+1\end{array}\right]{}_2F_3\left(\begin{array}{c}\Delta\left(2,\frac{s+2\nu}{2}\right)\\\Delta\,(2,\,\nu+1),\ \nu+1;\ \frac{b^4}{16a^4}\end{array}\right)$

$$[\mathrm{Re}\,a,\ \mathrm{Re}\,(s+2\nu)>0]$$

No.	$f(x)$	$F(s)$
3	$\theta(a-x)\ln\dfrac{\sqrt{a-x}+\sqrt{a}}{\sqrt{x}}$ $\times\left[\mathrm{ber}_\nu^2(bx)+\mathrm{bei}_\nu^2(bx)\right]$	$\dfrac{2^{-2\nu-1}\sqrt{\pi}\,a^{s+2\nu}b^{2\nu}}{s+2\nu}\Gamma\!\left[\begin{array}{c}s+2\nu\\\nu+1,\ \nu+1,\ \frac{2s+4\nu+1}{2}\end{array}\right]$ $\times\,{}_5F_8\!\left(\begin{array}{c}\frac{s+2\nu}{4},\ \Delta(4,s+2\nu);\ \frac{a^4b^4}{64}\\\frac{\nu+1}{2},\ \frac{\nu+2}{2},\ \nu+1,\ \Delta\left(4,s+2\nu+\frac12\right),\ \frac{s+2\nu+4}{4}\end{array}\right)$ $[a,\ \mathrm{Re}(s+2\nu)>0]$
4	$\theta(a-x)\arccos\dfrac{x}{a}$ $\times\left[\mathrm{ber}_\nu^2(bx)+\mathrm{bei}_\nu^2(bx)\right]$	$\dfrac{2^{-2\nu-1}\sqrt{\pi}\,a^{s+2\nu}b^{2\nu}}{s+2\nu}\Gamma\!\left[\begin{array}{c}\frac{s+2\nu+1}{2}\\\nu+1,\ \nu+1,\ \frac{s+2\nu+2}{2}\end{array}\right]$ $\times\,{}_3F_6\!\left(\begin{array}{c}\frac{s+2\nu}{4},\ \frac{s+2\nu+1}{4},\ \frac{s+2\nu+3}{4};\ \frac{a^4b^4}{64}\\\frac{\nu+1}{2},\ \frac{\nu+2}{2},\ \nu+1,\ \frac{s+2\nu+2}{4},\ \frac{s+2\nu+4}{4},\ \frac{s+2\nu+4}{4}\end{array}\right)$ $[a>0;\ \mathrm{Re}(s+2\nu)>-1]$
5	$\Gamma(\mu,ax)$ $\times\left[\mathrm{ber}_\nu^2(bx)+\mathrm{bei}_\nu^2(bx)\right]$	$\dfrac{a^{-s-2\nu}(b/2)^{2\nu}}{s+2\nu}\Gamma\!\left[\begin{array}{c}s+\mu+2\nu\\\nu+1,\ \nu+1\end{array}\right]$ $\times\,{}_5F_4\!\left(\begin{array}{c}\frac{s+2\nu}{4},\ \Delta(4,s+\mu+2\nu);\ \frac{4b^4}{a^4}\\\frac{\nu+1}{2},\ \frac{\nu+2}{2},\ \nu+1,\ \frac{s+2\nu+4}{4}\end{array}\right)$ $[\mathrm{Re}(a-\sqrt{2}\,b)>0;\ \mathrm{Re}(s+2\nu)>-\mathrm{Re}\,\mu,0]$
6	$\mathrm{erfc}(ax)$ $\times\left[\mathrm{ber}_\nu^2(bx)+\mathrm{bei}_\nu^2(bx)\right]$	$\dfrac{a^{-s-2\nu}b^{2\nu}}{2^{2\nu}\sqrt{\pi}\,(s+2\nu)}\Gamma\!\left[\begin{array}{c}\frac{s+2\nu+1}{2}\\\nu+1,\ \nu+1\end{array}\right]{}_3F_3\!\left(\begin{array}{c}\frac12,\ \frac{s+2\nu}{4},\ \frac{s+2\nu+3}{4}\\\frac{\nu+1}{2},\ \frac{\nu+2}{2},\ \nu+1;\ \frac{b^4}{16a^4}\end{array}\right)$ $[\mathrm{Re}(s+2\nu)>0;\ |\arg a|<\pi/4]$
7	$K_\mu(ax^2)$ $\times\left[\mathrm{ber}_\nu^2(bx)+\mathrm{bei}_\nu^2(bx)\right]$	$\dfrac{2^{s/2-\nu-3}b^{2\nu}}{a^{s/2+\nu}}\Gamma\!\left[\begin{array}{c}\frac{s-2\mu+2\nu}{4},\ \frac{s+2\mu+2\nu}{4}\\\nu+1,\ \nu+1\end{array}\right]$ $\times\,{}_2F_5\!\left(\begin{array}{c}\frac{s-2\mu+2\nu}{4},\ \frac{s+2\mu+2\nu}{4};\ \frac{b^4}{16a^2}\\\frac{\nu+1}{2},\ \frac{\nu+2}{2},\ \nu+1\end{array}\right)$ $[\mathrm{Re}\,a>0;\ \mathrm{Re}(s+2\nu)>2|\mathrm{Re}\,\mu|]$
8	$\mathrm{ker}_\nu^2(ax)+\mathrm{kei}_\nu^2(ax)$	$\dfrac{2^{s-4}}{a^s}\Gamma\!\left[\dfrac{s}{2},\ \dfrac{s-2\nu}{4},\ \dfrac{s+2\nu}{4}\right]\qquad[\mathrm{Re}\,s>2|\mathrm{Re}\,\nu|;\ |\arg a|<\pi/4]$

3.17.7. Products of $\mathrm{ber}_\nu(bx)$, $\mathrm{bei}_\nu(bx)$, $\mathrm{ker}_\nu(bx)$, $\mathrm{kei}_\nu(bx)$

1	$\mathrm{ber}_\nu(ax)\left\{\begin{array}{c}\mathrm{ker}_\nu(ax)\\\mathrm{kei}_\nu(ax)\end{array}\right\}$	$\pm\dfrac{a^{-s}}{8\sqrt{\pi}}\left\{\begin{array}{c}\cos(s\pi/4)\\\sin(s\pi/4)\end{array}\right\}\Gamma\!\left[\begin{array}{c}\frac{s}{2},\ \frac{1-s}{2},\ \frac{s+2\nu}{2}\\\frac{2-s+2\nu}{2}\end{array}\right]$ $\pm\dfrac{2^{s-4}}{a^s}\left\{\begin{array}{c}\cos[(s+6\nu)\pi/4]\\\sin[(s+6\nu)\pi/4]\end{array}\right\}\Gamma\!\left[\begin{array}{c}\frac{s}{2},\ \frac{s+2\nu}{4}\\\frac{4-s+2\nu}{4}\end{array}\right]$ $[a>0;\ 0,-2\,\mathrm{Re}\,\nu<\mathrm{Re}\,s<2]$

No.	$f(x)$	$F(s)$
2	$\mathrm{ber}_{-\nu}(ax)\begin{Bmatrix}\ker_\nu(ax)\\\ker_\nu(ax)\end{Bmatrix}$	$\pm\dfrac{a^{-s}}{8\sqrt{\pi}}\begin{Bmatrix}\cos\left[(s+4\nu)\,\pi/4\right]\\\sin\left[(s+4\nu)\,\pi/4\right]\end{Bmatrix}\Gamma\!\left[\begin{matrix}\frac{s}{2},\ \frac{1-s}{2},\ \frac{s-2\nu}{2}\\\frac{2-s-2\nu}{2}\end{matrix}\right]$ $\pm\dfrac{2^{s-4}}{a^s}\begin{Bmatrix}\cos([(s-2\nu)\,\pi/4]\\\sin[(s-2\nu)\,\pi/4]\end{Bmatrix}\Gamma\!\left[\begin{matrix}\frac{s}{2},\ \frac{s-2\nu}{4}\\\frac{4-s-2\nu}{4}\end{matrix}\right]$ $[a>0;\ 0,\,2\,\mathrm{Re}\,\nu<\mathrm{Re}\,s<1]$
3	$\mathrm{bei}_{\nu}(ax)\begin{Bmatrix}\ker_\nu(ax)\\\ker_\nu(ax)\end{Bmatrix}$	$\dfrac{2^{s-4}}{a^s}\begin{Bmatrix}\sin\left[(s+6\nu)\,\pi/4\right]\\\cos\left[(s+6\nu)\,\pi/4\right]\end{Bmatrix}\Gamma\!\left[\begin{matrix}\frac{s}{2},\ \frac{s+2\nu}{4}\\\frac{4-s+2\nu}{4}\end{matrix}\right]$ $-\dfrac{a^{-s}}{8\sqrt{\pi}}\begin{Bmatrix}\sin\left[s\pi/4\right]\\\cos\left[s\pi/4\right]\end{Bmatrix}\Gamma\!\left[\begin{matrix}\frac{s}{2},\ \frac{1-s}{2},\ \frac{s+2\nu}{4}\\\frac{2-s+2\nu}{2}\end{matrix}\right]$ $[a>0;\ 0,\,-2\,\mathrm{Re}\,\nu<\mathrm{Re}\,s<2]$
4	$\mathrm{bei}_{-\nu}(ax)\begin{Bmatrix}\ker_\nu(ax)\\\ker_\nu(ax)\end{Bmatrix}$	$\dfrac{2^{s-4}}{a^s}\begin{Bmatrix}\sin\left[(s-2\nu)\,\pi/4\right]\\\cos\left[(s-2\nu)\,\pi/4\right]\end{Bmatrix}\Gamma\!\left[\begin{matrix}\frac{s}{2},\ \frac{s-2\nu}{4}\\\frac{4-s-2\nu}{4}\end{matrix}\right]$ $-\dfrac{a^{-s}}{8\sqrt{\pi}}\begin{Bmatrix}\sin\left[(s+4\nu)\,\pi/4\right]\\\cos\left[(s+4\nu)\,\pi/4\right]\end{Bmatrix}\Gamma\!\left[\begin{matrix}\frac{s}{2},\ \frac{1-s}{2},\ \frac{s-2\nu}{2}\\\frac{2-s-2\nu}{2}\end{matrix}\right]$ $[a>0;\ 0,\,2\,\mathrm{Re}\,\nu<\mathrm{Re}\,s<1]$
5	$\begin{Bmatrix}\ker_\nu^2(ax)\\\ker_\nu^2(ax)\end{Bmatrix}$	$\dfrac{2^{s-5}}{a^s}\Gamma\!\left[\dfrac{s}{2},\ \dfrac{s-2\nu}{4},\ \dfrac{s+2\nu}{4}\right]$ $\pm\dfrac{\sqrt{\pi}}{8a^s}\cos\left(\dfrac{s\pi}{4}+\nu\pi\right)\Gamma\!\left[\begin{matrix}\frac{s}{2},\ \frac{s-2\nu}{2},\ \frac{s+2\nu}{2}\\\frac{s+1}{2}\end{matrix}\right]$ $[|\mathrm{Re}\,\nu|<\mathrm{Re}\,s<2;\ |\arg a|\le\pi/4]$
6	$\mathrm{kei}_\nu(ax)\ker_\nu(ax)$	$-\dfrac{\sqrt{\pi}}{8a^s}\sin\dfrac{(s+4\nu)\,\pi}{4}\ \Gamma\!\left[\begin{matrix}\frac{s}{2},\ \frac{s-2\nu}{2},\ \frac{s+2\nu}{2}\\\frac{s+1}{2}\end{matrix}\right]$ $[\mathrm{Re}\,s>2|\mathrm{Re}\,\nu|;\ |\arg a|\le\pi/4]$
7	$\mathrm{kei}_{-\nu}(ax)\begin{Bmatrix}\ker_\nu(ax)\\\ker_\nu(ax)\end{Bmatrix}$	$2^{s-5}a^{-s}\begin{Bmatrix}\sin(\pi\nu)\\\cos(\pi\nu)\end{Bmatrix}\Gamma\!\left[\dfrac{s}{2},\ \dfrac{s-2\nu}{4},\ \dfrac{s+2\nu}{4}\right]$ $-\dfrac{\sqrt{\pi}\,a^{-s}}{8}\begin{Bmatrix}\sin(s\pi/4)\\\cos(s\pi/4)\end{Bmatrix}\Gamma\!\left[\begin{matrix}\frac{s}{2},\ \frac{s-2\nu}{2},\ \frac{s+2\nu}{2}\\\frac{s+1}{2}\end{matrix}\right]$ $[2|\mathrm{Re}\,\nu|<\mathrm{Re}\,s<2;\ |\arg a|\le\pi/4]$
8	$\begin{Bmatrix}\ker_{-\nu}(ax)\ker_\nu(ax)\\\ker_{-\nu}(ax)\ker_\nu(ax)\end{Bmatrix}$	$\dfrac{2^{s-5}}{a^s}\cos(\nu\pi)\,\Gamma\!\left[\dfrac{s}{2},\ \dfrac{s-2\nu}{4},\ \dfrac{s+2\nu}{4}\right]$ $\pm\dfrac{\sqrt{\pi}}{8a^s}\cos\dfrac{s\pi}{4}\ \Gamma\!\left[\begin{matrix}\frac{s}{2},\ \frac{s-2\nu}{2},\ \frac{s+2\nu}{2}\\\frac{s+1}{2}\end{matrix}\right]$ $[2|\mathrm{Re}\,\nu|<\mathrm{Re}\,s<2;\ |\arg a|\le\pi/4]$

3.18. The Airy Functions Ai (z) and Bi (z)

More formulas can be obtained from the corresponding sections due to the relations

$$\text{Ai}(z) = \frac{1}{\pi}\sqrt{\frac{z}{3}}\, K_{1/3}\left(\frac{2}{3} z^{3/2}\right),$$

$$\text{Bi}(z) = \sqrt{\frac{z}{3}}\left[I_{-1/3}\left(\frac{2}{3} z^{3/2}\right) + I_{1/3}\left(\frac{2}{3} z^{3/2}\right)\right],$$

$$\left\{\begin{array}{l}\text{Ai}(z)\\ \text{Bi}(z)\end{array}\right\} = \frac{1}{3^{(5\pm3)/12}\,\Gamma\left(\frac{2}{3}\right)}\, {}_0F_1\left(\frac{2}{3}; \frac{z^3}{9}\right) \mp \frac{z}{3^{(1\pm3)/12}\,\Gamma\left(\frac{1}{3}\right)}\, {}_0F_1\left(\frac{4}{3}; \frac{z^3}{9}\right),$$

$$\left\{\begin{array}{l}\text{Ai}'(z)\\ \text{Bi}'(z)\end{array}\right\} = \frac{z^2}{2\times 3^{(5\pm3)/12}\,\Gamma\left(\frac{2}{3}\right)}\, {}_0F_1\left(\frac{5}{3}; \frac{z^3}{9}\right) \mp \frac{1}{3^{(1\pm3)/12}\,\Gamma\left(\frac{1}{3}\right)}\, {}_0F_1\left(\frac{1}{3}; \frac{z^3}{9}\right);$$

$$\text{Ai}(z) = \frac{1}{2\sqrt[6]{3}\,\pi}\, G_{02}^{20}\left(\frac{z^3}{9}\,\middle|\,\begin{array}{c}\cdot\\ 0,\,1/3\end{array}\right), \quad [-\pi/3 < \arg z \le \pi/3];$$

$$\text{Bi}(z) = \frac{2\pi}{\sqrt[6]{3}}\, G_{24}^{20}\left(\frac{z^3}{9}\,\middle|\,\begin{array}{c}1/6,\,2/3\\ 0,\,1/3,\,1/6,\,2/3\end{array}\right), \quad [-\pi/3 < \arg z \le \pi/3];$$

$$\text{Ai}'(z) = -\frac{\sqrt[6]{3}}{2\pi}\, G_{02}^{20}\left(\frac{z^3}{9}\,\middle|\,\begin{array}{c}\cdot\\ 0,\,2/3\end{array}\right), \quad [-\pi/3 < \arg z \le \pi/3];$$

$$\text{Bi}'(z) = -2\sqrt[6]{3}\,\pi\, G_{24}^{20}\left(\frac{z^3}{9}\,\middle|\,\begin{array}{c}-1/6,\,1/3\\ 0,\,2/3,\,-1/6,\,1/3\end{array}\right), \quad [-\pi/3 < \arg z \le \pi/3].$$

3.18.1. Ai (bx), Ai$'(bx)$, Bi (bx), and algebraic functions

No.	$f(x)$	$F(s)$
1	Ai (ax)	$\dfrac{3^{(4s-7)/6}}{2\pi a^s}\Gamma\left(\dfrac{s}{3}\right)\Gamma\left(\dfrac{s+1}{3}\right)$ $\qquad$ $[\operatorname{Re} s > 0;\ |\arg a| < \pi/3]$
2	$(a-x)_+^{\alpha-1}\left\{\begin{array}{l}\text{Ai}(bx)\\ \text{Bi}(bx)\end{array}\right\}$	$\dfrac{a^{s+\alpha-1}}{3^{(5\pm3)/12}\Gamma(2/3)}\,\text{B}(\alpha,s)\,{}_3F_4\left(\begin{array}{c}\frac{s}{3},\,\frac{s+1}{3},\,\frac{s+2}{3};\,\frac{a^3b^3}{9}\\ \frac{2}{3},\,\frac{s+\alpha}{3},\,\frac{s+\alpha+1}{3},\,\frac{s+\alpha+2}{3}\end{array}\right)$ $\mp\dfrac{a^{s+\alpha}b}{3^{(1\pm3)/12}\Gamma(1/3)}\,\text{B}(\alpha,s+1)\,{}_3F_4\left(\begin{array}{c}\frac{s+1}{3},\,\frac{s+2}{3},\,\frac{s+3}{3};\,\frac{a^3b^3}{9}\\ \frac{4}{3},\,\frac{s+\alpha+1}{3},\,\frac{s+\alpha+2}{3},\,\frac{s+\alpha+3}{3}\end{array}\right)$ $[a,\ \operatorname{Re}\alpha,\ \operatorname{Re} s > 0]$
3	$(a^3-x^3)_+^{\alpha-1}\left\{\begin{array}{l}\text{Ai}(bx)\\ \text{Bi}(bx)\end{array}\right\}$	$\dfrac{a^{s+3\alpha-3}\Gamma(1/3)}{2\cdot3^{(11\pm3)/12}\,\pi}\,\text{B}\left(\alpha,\frac{s}{3}\right)\,{}_1F_2\left(\begin{array}{c}\frac{s}{3};\,\frac{a^3b^3}{9}\\ \frac{2}{3},\,\frac{s+3\alpha}{3}\end{array}\right)$ $\mp\dfrac{a^{s+3\alpha-2}b\,\Gamma(2/3)}{2\cdot3^{(7\pm3)/12}\,\pi}\,\text{B}\left(\alpha,\frac{s+1}{3}\right)\,{}_1F_2\left(\begin{array}{c}\frac{s+1}{3};\,\frac{a^3b^3}{9}\\ \frac{4}{3},\,\frac{s+3\alpha+1}{3}\end{array}\right)$ $[a,\ \operatorname{Re}\alpha,\ \operatorname{Re} s > 0]$

No.	$f(x)$	$F(s)$
4	$\left(x^3 - a^3\right)_+^{\alpha-1} \mathrm{Ai}\,(bx)$	$-\dfrac{a^{s+3\alpha-2}b}{3^{4/3}\Gamma(1/3)}\,\mathrm{B}\left(\alpha,\dfrac{2-s-3\alpha}{3}\right){}_1F_2\left(\begin{matrix}\frac{s+1}{3};\ \frac{a^3b^3}{9}\\ \frac{4}{3},\ \frac{s+3\alpha+1}{3}\end{matrix}\right)$
		$-\dfrac{a^{s+3\alpha-3}}{3^{2/3}\Gamma(-1/3)}\,\mathrm{B}\left(\alpha,\dfrac{3-s-3\alpha}{3}\right){}_1F_2\left(\begin{matrix}\frac{s}{3};\ \frac{a^3b^3}{9}\\ \frac{2}{3},\ \frac{s+3\alpha}{3}\end{matrix}\right)$
		$-\dfrac{3^{2s/3+2\alpha-11/3}}{b^{s+3\alpha-3}}\left\{\sin\dfrac{(2s+6\alpha-1)\pi}{6}\,\Gamma\left[\begin{matrix}\frac{s+3\alpha-2}{3}\\ \frac{6-s-3\alpha}{3}\end{matrix}\right]\right.$
		$\left.+\cos\dfrac{(s+3\alpha)\pi}{3}\,\Gamma\left[\begin{matrix}\frac{s+3\alpha-3}{3}\\ \frac{5-s-3\alpha}{3}\end{matrix}\right]\right\}{}_1F_2\left(\begin{matrix}1-\alpha;\ \frac{a^3b^3}{9}\\ \frac{5-s-3\alpha}{3},\ \frac{6-s-3\alpha}{3}\end{matrix}\right)$
		$[a,\ \mathrm{Re}\,\alpha>0;\ |\arg b|<\pi/3]$
5	$\dfrac{1}{(x^3+a^3)^\rho}\,\mathrm{Ai}\,(bx)$	$-\dfrac{a^{s-3\rho+1}b}{3^{4/3}\,\Gamma(1/3)}\,\mathrm{B}\left(\dfrac{s+1}{3},-\dfrac{s-3\rho+1}{3}\right){}_1F_2\left(\begin{matrix}\frac{s+1}{3};\ -\frac{a^3b^3}{9}\\ \frac{4}{3},\ \frac{s-3\rho+4}{3}\end{matrix}\right)$
		$-\dfrac{a^{s-3\rho}}{3^{2/3}\,\Gamma(-1/3)}\,\mathrm{B}\left(\dfrac{s}{3},-\dfrac{s-3\rho}{3}\right){}_1F_2\left(\begin{matrix}\frac{s}{3};\ -\frac{a^3b^3}{9}\\ \frac{2}{3},\ \frac{s-3\rho+3}{3}\end{matrix}\right)$
		$+\dfrac{3^{2s/3-2\rho-5/3}}{b^{s-3\rho}}\left\{\cos\dfrac{(s-3\rho)\pi}{3}\,\Gamma\left[\begin{matrix}\frac{s-3\rho}{3}\\ -\frac{s-3\rho-2}{3}\end{matrix}\right]\right.$
		$\left.+\sin\dfrac{(2s-6\rho-1)\pi}{6}\,\Gamma\left[\begin{matrix}\frac{s-3\rho+1}{3}\\ -\frac{s-3\rho-3}{3}\end{matrix}\right]\right\}{}_1F_2\left(\begin{matrix}\rho;\ -\frac{a^3b^3}{9}\\ -\frac{s-3\rho-2}{3},\ -\frac{s-3\rho-3}{3}\end{matrix}\right)$
		$[\mathrm{Re}\,s>0;\ |\arg a|<\pi/3]$
6	$\mathrm{Ai}'\,(ax)$	$-\dfrac{3^{(4s-5)/6}}{2\pi}\,a^{-s}\,\Gamma\left(\dfrac{s}{3}\right)\Gamma\left(\dfrac{s+2}{3}\right)$ $\qquad[\mathrm{Re}\,s>0;\ |\arg a|<\pi/3]$

3.18.2. $\mathrm{Ai}\,(bx)$, $\mathrm{Ai}'\,(bx)$, $\mathrm{Bi}\,(bx)$, **and the exponential function**

No.	$f(x)$	$F(s)$
1	$e^{-ax}\,\mathrm{Ai}\,(bx)$	$\dfrac{3^{-(s+1)/3}a b^{-s-2}}{4\Gamma(1-s)}\left[\dfrac{b^2}{3^{1/3}a}\csc\dfrac{s\pi}{3}\csc\dfrac{(s+1)\pi}{3}\right.$
		$\times\Gamma\left(\dfrac{1-s}{3}\right){}_2F_2\left(\begin{matrix}\frac{s}{3},\ \frac{s+1}{3}\\ \frac{1}{3},\ \frac{2}{3};\ -\frac{a^3}{3b^3}\end{matrix}\right)-3^{1/3}b\sec\dfrac{(2s+1)\pi}{6}$
		$\times\csc\dfrac{(s+1)\pi}{3}\,\Gamma\left(\dfrac{3-s}{3}\right){}_2F_2\left(\begin{matrix}\frac{s+1}{3},\ \frac{s+2}{3}\\ \frac{2}{3},\ \frac{4}{3};\ -\frac{a^3}{3b^3}\end{matrix}\right)$
		$\left.+\dfrac{as}{2}\sec\dfrac{(2s+1)\pi}{6}\csc\dfrac{s\pi}{3}\,\Gamma\left(\dfrac{2-s}{3}\right){}_2F_2\left(\begin{matrix}\frac{s+2}{3},\ \frac{s+3}{3}\\ \frac{4}{3},\ \frac{5}{3};\ -\frac{a^3}{3b^3}\end{matrix}\right)\right]$
		$[\mathrm{Re}\,a,\ \mathrm{Re}\,s>0;\ |\arg b|<\pi/3]$

No.	$f(x)$	$F(s)$
2	$e^{-ax^{3/2}}\left\{\begin{array}{c}\mathrm{Ai}\,(bx)\\ \mathrm{Bi}\,(bx)\end{array}\right\}$	$\dfrac{3^{(-11\mp3)/12}}{\pi a^{2s/3}}\,\Gamma\left(\dfrac{1}{3}\right)\Gamma\left(\dfrac{2s}{3}\right){}_2F_1\left(\begin{array}{c}\frac{s}{3},\ \frac{2s+3}{6}\\ \frac{2}{3};\ \frac{4b^3}{9a^2}\end{array}\right)$ $\mp\dfrac{3^{(-7\mp3)/12}b}{\pi a^{2(s+1)/3}}\,\Gamma\left(\dfrac{2}{3}\right)\Gamma\left(\dfrac{2s+2}{3}\right){}_2F_1\left(\begin{array}{c}\frac{s+1}{3},\ \frac{2s+5}{6}\\ \frac{4}{3};\ \frac{4b^3}{9a^2}\end{array}\right)$ $\left[\mathrm{Re}\,s>0;\ \mathrm{Re}\,\left(3a\pm2b^{3/2}\right)>0;\ |\arg b|<\pi/6\right]$
3	$e^{-2/3(ax)^{3/2}}\,\mathrm{Ai}\,(ax)$	$\dfrac{2^{(1-4s)/3}3^{(4s-7)/6}}{\sqrt{\pi}}\,a^{-s}\,\Gamma\left[\begin{array}{c}\frac{2s}{3},\ \frac{2s+2}{3}\\ \frac{4s+5}{6}\end{array}\right]$ $\left[\mathrm{Re}\,s>0;\ |\arg a|<\pi/3\right]$
4	$e^{2/3(ax)^{3/2}}\,\mathrm{Ai}\,(ax)$	$\dfrac{2^{-(4s+2)/3}3^{(4s-7)/6}}{\pi^{3/2}}\,a^{-s}\,\Gamma\left(\dfrac{1-4s}{6}\right)\Gamma\left(\dfrac{2s}{3}\right)\Gamma\left(\dfrac{2s+2}{3}\right)$ $\left[0<\mathrm{Re}\,s<1/4;\ |\arg a|<\pi\right]$
5	$e^{-ax^3}\left\{\begin{array}{c}\mathrm{Ai}\,(bx)\\ \mathrm{Bi}\,(bx)\end{array}\right\}$	$\dfrac{a^{-s/3}}{3^{(17\pm3)/12}}\,\Gamma\left[\begin{array}{c}\frac{s}{3}\\ \frac{2}{3}\end{array}\right]{}_1F_1\left(\begin{array}{c}\frac{s}{3}\\ \frac{2}{3};\ \frac{b^3}{9a}\end{array}\right)\mp\dfrac{a^{-(s+1)/3}b}{3^{(13\pm3)/12}}\,\Gamma\left[\begin{array}{c}\frac{s+1}{3}\\ \frac{1}{3}\end{array}\right]{}_1F_1\left(\begin{array}{c}\frac{s+1}{3}\\ \frac{4}{3};\ \frac{b^3}{9a}\end{array}\right)$ $\left[\mathrm{Re}\,a,\ \mathrm{Re}\,s>0\right]$
6	$e^{-2/3(ax)^{3/2}}\,\mathrm{Ai}'\,(ax)$	$-\dfrac{2^{-(4s+1)/3}3^{(4s-5)/6}}{\sqrt{\pi}}\,a^{-s}\,\Gamma\left[\begin{array}{c}\frac{2s}{3},\ \frac{2s+4}{3}\\ \frac{4s+7}{6}\end{array}\right]$ $\left[\mathrm{Re}\,s>0;\ |\arg a|<\pi/3\right]$

3.18.3.   Ai (bx) **and trigonometric functions**

Notation: $\delta=\left\{\begin{array}{c}1\\ 0\end{array}\right\}$.

| 1 | $\left\{\begin{array}{c}\sin\left(ax^{3/2}\right)\\ \cos\left(ax^{3/2}\right)\end{array}\right\}\mathrm{Ai}\,(bx)$ | $\dfrac{3^{(4s-7)/6+\delta}\,a^\delta}{2\pi\,b^{s+3\delta/2}}\,\Gamma\left(\dfrac{2s+3\delta}{6}\right)\Gamma\left(\dfrac{2s+3\delta+2}{6}\right){}_2F_1\left(\begin{array}{c}\frac{2s+3\delta}{6},\ \frac{2s+3\delta+2}{6}\\ \frac{2\delta+1}{2};\ -\frac{9a^2}{4b^3}\end{array}\right)$ $\left[a>0;\ \mathrm{Re}\,s>-3\delta/2;\ |\arg b|<\pi/6\right]$ |

3.18.4.   Ai (bx), Ai$'$ (bx), Bi (bx), **and special functions**

| 1 | $\mathrm{Ei}\,\left(-ax^3\right)\left\{\begin{array}{c}\mathrm{Ai}\,(bx)\\ \mathrm{Bi}\,(bx)\end{array}\right\}$ | $\pm\dfrac{a^{-(s+1)/3}b}{3^{(25\pm3)/12}}\,\Gamma\left[\begin{array}{c}\frac{s+1}{3},\ \frac{s+1}{3}\\ \frac{4}{3},\ \frac{s+4}{3}\end{array}\right]{}_2F_2\left(\begin{array}{c}\frac{s+1}{3},\ \frac{s+1}{3}\\ \frac{4}{3},\ \frac{s+4}{3};\ \frac{b^3}{9a}\end{array}\right)$ $-\dfrac{a^{-s/3}}{3^{(17\pm3)/12}}\,\Gamma\left[\begin{array}{c}\frac{s}{3},\ \frac{s}{3}\\ \frac{2}{3},\ \frac{s+3}{3}\end{array}\right]{}_2F_2\left(\begin{array}{c}\frac{s}{3},\ \frac{s}{3}\\ \frac{2}{3},\ \frac{s+3}{3};\ \frac{b^3}{9a}\end{array}\right)$ $\left[a,\ \mathrm{Re}\,s>0\right]$ |

No.	$f(x)$	$F(s)$
2	$\operatorname{erfc}\left(ax^{3/2}\right)\left\{\begin{array}{c}\operatorname{Ai}(bx)\\\operatorname{Bi}(bx)\end{array}\right\}$	$\mp\dfrac{a^{-2(s+1)/3}b}{3^{(1\pm3)/12}\sqrt{\pi}\,(s+1)}\Gamma\left[\begin{array}{c}\frac{2s+5}{6}\\\frac{1}{3}\end{array}\right]{}_2F_2\left(\begin{array}{c}\frac{s+1}{3},\ \frac{2s+5}{6}\\\frac{4}{3},\ \frac{s+4}{3};\ \frac{b^3}{9a^2}\end{array}\right)$ $+\dfrac{a^{-2s/3}}{3^{(5\pm3)/12}\sqrt{\pi}\,s}\Gamma\left[\begin{array}{c}\frac{2s+3}{6}\\\frac{2}{3}\end{array}\right]{}_2F_2\left(\begin{array}{c}\frac{s}{3},\ \frac{2s+3}{6}\\\frac{2}{3},\ \frac{s+3}{3};\ \frac{b^3}{9a^2}\end{array}\right)$ $[\operatorname{Re}a,\ \operatorname{Re}s>0]$
3	$\Gamma\left(\nu,ax^3\right)\left\{\begin{array}{c}\operatorname{Ai}(bx)\\\operatorname{Bi}(bx)\end{array}\right\}$	$\mp\dfrac{a^{-(s+1)/3}b}{3^{(1\pm3)/12}(s+1)}\Gamma\left[\begin{array}{c}\frac{s+3\nu+1}{3}\\\frac{1}{3}\end{array}\right]{}_2F_2\left(\begin{array}{c}\frac{s+1}{3},\ \frac{s+3\nu+1}{3}\\\frac{4}{3},\ \frac{s+4}{3};\ \frac{b^3}{9a}\end{array}\right)$ $+\dfrac{a^{-s/3}}{3^{(5\pm3)/12}s}\Gamma\left[\begin{array}{c}\frac{s+3\nu}{3}\\\frac{2}{3}\end{array}\right]{}_2F_2\left(\begin{array}{c}\frac{s}{3},\ \frac{s+3\nu}{3}\\\frac{2}{3},\ \frac{s+3}{3};\ \frac{b^3}{9a}\end{array}\right)$ $[\operatorname{Re}a,\ \operatorname{Re}s,\ \operatorname{Re}(s+3\nu)>0]$
4	$J_\nu\left(ax^{3/2}\right)\operatorname{Ai}(bx)$	$\dfrac{3^{(4s-7)/6+\nu}a^\nu}{2^{\nu+1}\pi b^{s+3\nu/2}}\Gamma\left[\begin{array}{c}\frac{2s+3\nu}{6},\ \frac{2s+3\nu+2}{6}\\\nu+1\end{array}\right]{}_2F_1\left(\begin{array}{c}\frac{2s+3\nu}{6},\ \frac{2s+3\nu+2}{6}\\\nu+1;\ -\frac{9a^2}{4b^3}\end{array}\right)$ $[a,\ \operatorname{Re}(2s+3\nu)>0;\ |\arg b|<\pi/6]$
5	$I_\nu\left(\frac{2}{3}(ax)^{3/2}\right)\operatorname{Ai}(ax)$	$\dfrac{3^{(4s-7)/6}a^{-s}}{2\pi}\Gamma\left[\begin{array}{c}\frac{2-2s}{3},\ \frac{2s+3\nu}{6},\ \frac{2s+3\nu+2}{6}\\\frac{-2s+3\nu+4}{6},\ \frac{-2s+3\nu+6}{6}\end{array}\right]$ $[-3\operatorname{Re}\nu/2<\operatorname{Re}s<1;\ |\arg a|<\pi/3]$
6	$K_\nu\left(\frac{2}{3}(ax)^{3/2}\right)\operatorname{Ai}(ax)$	$\dfrac{3^{(4s-7)/6}a^{-s}}{4\pi}\Gamma\left[\begin{array}{c}\frac{2s-3\nu}{6},\ \frac{2s+3\nu}{6},\ \frac{2s-3\nu+2}{6},\ \frac{2s+3\nu+2}{6}\\\frac{2s+1}{3}\end{array}\right]$ $[\operatorname{Re}s>3|\operatorname{Re}\nu|/2;\ |\arg a|<\pi/3]$
7	$I_\nu\left(\frac{2}{3}(ax)^{3/2}\right)\operatorname{Ai}'(ax)$	$-\dfrac{3^{(4s-5)/6}a^{-s}}{\pi^{3/2}2^{(2s+5)/3}}\Gamma\left[\begin{array}{c}\frac{1-2s}{6},\ \frac{2-s}{3},\ \frac{2s+3\nu}{6},\ \frac{2s+3\nu+4}{6}\\\frac{-2s+3\nu+2}{6},\ \frac{-2s+3\nu+6}{6}\end{array}\right]$ $[-3\operatorname{Re}\nu/2<\operatorname{Re}s<1/2;\ |\arg a|<\pi/3]$
8	$K_\nu\left(\frac{2}{3}(ax)^{3/2}\right)\operatorname{Ai}'(ax)$	$\dfrac{3^{(4s-5)/6}a^{-s}}{4\sin(\nu\pi)}\Gamma\left(\frac{1-2s}{3}\right)\left(\Gamma\left[\begin{array}{c}\frac{2s+3\nu}{6},\ \frac{2s+3\nu+4}{6}\\\frac{-2s+3\nu+2}{6},\ \frac{-2s+3\nu+6}{6}\end{array}\right]\right.$ $\left.-\Gamma\left[\begin{array}{c}\frac{2s-3\nu}{6},\ \frac{2s-3\nu+4}{6}\\-\frac{2s+3\nu-2}{6},\ -\frac{2s+3\nu-6}{6}\end{array}\right]\right)$ $[3|\operatorname{Re}\nu|/2<\operatorname{Re}s<1/2;\ |\arg a|<\pi/3]$

3.18.5.　Products of Airy functions

No.	$f(x)$	$F(s)$
1	$\operatorname{Ai}^2(ax)$	$\dfrac{2^{-2(s+1)/3}3^{-(2s+5)/6}}{\sqrt{\pi}}a^{-s}\Gamma\left[\begin{array}{c}s\\\frac{2s+5}{6}\end{array}\right]$　　$[\operatorname{Re}s>0,\ |\arg a|<\pi/3]$

No.	$f(x)$	$F(s)$
2	Ai (ax) Bi (ax)	$\dfrac{2^{-(2s+5)/3}3^{2(s-2)/3}}{\pi^{3/2}} a^{-s} \Gamma\left[\begin{matrix}\frac{1-2s}{6},\frac{s}{3},\frac{s+2}{3}\\\frac{2-s}{3}\end{matrix}\right]$ $[0 < \operatorname{Re} s < 1/2; \ |\arg a| < \pi/3]$
3	Ai (ax) Bi $(-ax)$	$\dfrac{12^{(s-5)/6}a^{-s}}{\sqrt{\pi}} \Gamma\left[\begin{matrix}\frac{s}{2},\frac{s+1}{6}\\\frac{s+4}{6},\frac{2-s}{6}\end{matrix}\right]$ $[a,\ \operatorname{Re} s > 0]$
4	Ai $\left(ae^{i\pi/6}x\right)$ $\times$ Ai $\left(ae^{-i\pi/6}x\right)$	$\dfrac{2^{(s-8)/3}3^{(s-5)/6}}{\pi^{3/2}a^s} \Gamma\left(\dfrac{s}{2}\right)\Gamma\left(\dfrac{s+1}{6}\right)$ $[a,\ \operatorname{Re} s > 0]$
5	Ai$^2(-ax)$ + Bi$^2(-ax)$	$\dfrac{2^{(1-2s)/3}a^{-s}}{3^{(2s+5)/6}\pi^{3/2}} \Gamma(s)\Gamma\left(\dfrac{1-2s}{6}\right)$ $[a > 0;\ 0 < \operatorname{Re} s < 1/2]$
6	e^{-ax^3} Ai$^2(ax)$	$\dfrac{a^{-s/3}}{2^{2/3}3^{11/6}\sqrt{\pi}} \Gamma\left[\begin{matrix}\frac{s}{3}\\\frac{5}{6}\end{matrix}\right] {}_2F_2\left(\begin{matrix}\frac{1}{6},\frac{s}{3}\\\frac{1}{3},\frac{2}{3};\frac{4a^2}{9}\end{matrix}\right) - \dfrac{a^{(2-s)/3}}{3^{3/2}\pi}\Gamma\left(\dfrac{s+1}{3}\right)$ $\times\ {}_2F_2\left(\begin{matrix}\frac{1}{2},\frac{s+1}{3}\\\frac{2}{3},\frac{4}{3};\frac{4a^2}{9}\end{matrix}\right) + \dfrac{a^{(4-s)/3}}{2^{1/3}3^{7/6}\sqrt{\pi}}\Gamma\left[\begin{matrix}\frac{s+2}{3}\\\frac{1}{6}\end{matrix}\right]{}_2F_2\left(\begin{matrix}\frac{5}{6},\frac{s+2}{3}\\\frac{4}{3},\frac{5}{3};\frac{4a^2}{9}\end{matrix}\right)$ $[a,\ \operatorname{Re} s > 0]$
7	Ai (ax) Ai$'(ax)$	$-\dfrac{12^{-(2s+3)/6}}{\sqrt{\pi}} a^{-s} \Gamma\left[\begin{matrix}s\\\frac{2s+3}{6}\end{matrix}\right]$ $[\operatorname{Re} s > 0;\ |\arg a| < \pi/3]$
8	$\left(\text{Ai}'(ax)\right)^2$	$\dfrac{2^{-(2s+7)/3}3^{(2s-2)/3}}{\pi^{3/2}} a^{-s} \Gamma\left[\begin{matrix}\frac{s}{3},\frac{s+2}{3},\frac{s+4}{3}\\\frac{2s+7}{6}\end{matrix}\right]$ $[\operatorname{Re} s > 0;\ |\arg a| < \pi/3]$
9	Ai$'(ax)$ Bi (ax) + $\dfrac{1}{2\pi}$	$-\dfrac{12^{-(2s+3)/6}}{\pi^{3/2}} a^{-s} \sin\dfrac{s\pi}{3}\Gamma(s)\Gamma\left(\dfrac{3-2s}{6}\right)$ $[-1 < \operatorname{Re} s < 3/2;\ |\arg a| < \pi/3]$
10	Ai (ax) Bi$'(ax)$ − $\dfrac{1}{2\pi}$	$-\dfrac{12^{-(2s+3)/6}}{\pi^{3/2}} a^{-s} \sin\dfrac{s\pi}{3}\Gamma(s)\Gamma\left(\dfrac{3-2s}{6}\right)$ $[-1 < \operatorname{Re} s < 3/2;\ |\arg a| < \pi/3]$
11	$J_\nu\left(ax^{3/2}\right)$ Ai (bx) $\times$ Ai$'(bx)$	$-\dfrac{a^\nu b^{-s-3\nu/2}}{2^{2s/3+2\nu+1}3^{(2s+3\nu+3)/6}\sqrt{\pi}} \Gamma\left[\begin{matrix}\frac{2s+3\nu}{2}\\\nu+1,\frac{2s+3\nu+3}{6}\end{matrix}\right]$ $\times\ {}_3F_2\left(\begin{matrix}\frac{2s+3\nu}{6},\frac{2s+3\nu+2}{6},\frac{2s+3\nu+4}{6}\\\nu+1,\frac{2s+3\nu+3}{6};-\frac{9a^2}{16b^3}\end{matrix}\right)$ $[\operatorname{Re} a,\ \operatorname{Re}(s+3\nu/2) > 0;\ |\arg b| < \pi/3]$

3.19. The Legendre Polynomials $P_n(z)$

More formulas can be obtained from the corresponding sections due to the relations

$$P_\nu(z) = P_\nu^0(z) = \mathrm{P}_\nu^0(z) = C_\nu^{1/2}(z) = P_\nu^{(0,0)}(z) = {}_2F_1\left(-\nu,\, \nu+1;\, 1;\, \frac{1-z}{2}\right).$$

3.19.1. $P_n(\varphi(x))$ and algebraic functions

Notation: $\varepsilon = 0$ or 1.

No.	$f(x)$	$F(s)$
1	$\theta(a-x)\, P_n\left(\dfrac{x}{a}\right)$	$\dfrac{a^s}{2}\,\Gamma\left[\begin{matrix}\frac{s}{2},\ \frac{s+1}{2}\\ \frac{s-n+1}{2},\ \frac{s+n+2}{2}\end{matrix}\right]$ $[a,\ \mathrm{Re}\,s > 0]$
2	$\theta(x-a)\, P_n\left(\dfrac{x}{a}\right)$	$\dfrac{a^s}{2^{s+1}\sqrt{\pi}}\,\Gamma\left[\begin{matrix}-\frac{s+n}{2},\ \frac{1-s+n}{2}\\ 1-s\end{matrix}\right]$ $[a>0;\ \mathrm{Re}\,s < -n]$
3	$(x^2-a^2)_+^{\alpha-1}\, P_n\left(\dfrac{x}{b}\right)$	$\dfrac{2^{n-1}a^{s+2\alpha+n-2}}{n!\,b^n}\left(\dfrac{1}{2}\right)_n\Gamma\left[\begin{matrix}\alpha,\ \frac{2-2\alpha-s-n}{2}\\ \frac{2-n-s}{2}\end{matrix}\right]$ $\times\, {}_3F_2\left(\begin{matrix}-\left[\frac{n}{2}\right],\ \frac{(-1)^n}{2}-\left[\frac{n}{2}\right],\ \frac{2-2\alpha-s-n}{2}\\ \frac{2-n-s}{2},\ \frac{1-2n}{2};\ \frac{b^2}{a^2}\end{matrix}\right)$ $[a>0;\ \mathrm{Re}\,\alpha>0;\ \mathrm{Re}\,(s+2\alpha)<2-n]$
4	$\dfrac{\theta(a-x)}{(b^2\pm x^2)^\rho}\, P_{2n+\varepsilon}\left(\dfrac{x}{a}\right)$	$\dfrac{(-1)^n\left(\frac{1-s+\varepsilon}{2}\right)_n a^s}{2\left(\frac{s+\varepsilon}{2}\right)_{n+1}b^{2\rho}}\,{}_3F_2\left(\begin{matrix}\rho,\ \frac{s}{2},\ \frac{s+1}{2};\ \mp\frac{a^2}{b^2}\\ \frac{s+2n+\varepsilon+2}{2},\ \frac{s-2n-\varepsilon+1}{2}\end{matrix}\right)$ $\left[\mathrm{Re}\,s > -\varepsilon;\ \left\{\begin{matrix}a,\ \mathrm{Re}\,b>0\\ b>a>0\end{matrix}\right\}\right]$
5	$\dfrac{\theta(a-x)}{x^2-b^2}\, P_{2n+\varepsilon}\left(\dfrac{x}{a}\right)$	$\dfrac{(-1)^{n+1}a^s\left(\frac{1-s+\varepsilon}{2}\right)_n}{2b^2\left(\frac{s+\varepsilon}{2}\right)_{n+1}}\,{}_3F_2\left(\begin{matrix}1,\ \frac{s}{2},\ \frac{s+1}{2};\ \frac{a^2}{b^2}\\ \frac{s-2n-\varepsilon+1}{2},\ \frac{s+2n+\varepsilon+2}{2}\end{matrix}\right)$ $[b>a>0;\ \mathrm{Re}\,s > -\varepsilon]$
6	$\dfrac{\theta(a-x)}{x^2-b^2}\, P_{2n+\varepsilon}\left(\dfrac{x}{a}\right)$	$\dfrac{(-1)^{\varepsilon+1}\pi b^{s-2}}{2}\tan^{2\varepsilon-1}\dfrac{s\pi}{2}\,P_{2n+\varepsilon}\left(\dfrac{b}{a}\right)$ $+\dfrac{(-1)^n a^{s-2}\left(\frac{3-s+\varepsilon}{2}\right)_n}{2\left(\frac{s+\varepsilon-2}{2}\right)_{n+1}}\,{}_3F_2\left(\begin{matrix}1,\ \frac{2-2n-s-\varepsilon}{2},\ \frac{2n-s+\varepsilon+3}{2}\\ \frac{3-s}{2},\ \frac{4-s}{2};\ \frac{b^2}{a^2}\end{matrix}\right)$ $[a>b>0;\ \mathrm{Re}\,s > -\varepsilon]$
7	$\dfrac{\theta(x-a)}{(x^2\pm b^2)^\rho}\, P_{2n+\varepsilon}\left(\dfrac{x}{a}\right)$	$\dfrac{(-1)^{n+1}a^{s-2\rho}\left(\frac{2\rho-s+\varepsilon+1}{2}\right)_n}{2\left(\frac{s-2\rho+\varepsilon}{2}\right)_{n+1}}\,{}_3F_2\left(\begin{matrix}\rho,\ \frac{2\rho+2n-s+\varepsilon+1}{2},\ \frac{2\rho-2n-s-\varepsilon}{2}\\ \frac{2\rho-s+1}{2},\ \frac{2\rho-s+2}{2};\ \mp\frac{b^2}{a^2}\end{matrix}\right)$ $\left[\mathrm{Re}\,(s-2\rho)<-2n-\varepsilon;\ \left\{\begin{matrix}a,\ \mathrm{Re}\,b>0\\ a>b>0\end{matrix}\right\}\right]$

No.	$f(x)$	$F(s)$
8	$\dfrac{\theta(x-a)}{x^2-b^2}\, P_{2n+\varepsilon}\left(\dfrac{x}{a}\right)$	$\dfrac{(-1)^n\left(\frac{1-s+\varepsilon}{2}\right)_n a^s}{2b^2\left(\frac{s+\varepsilon}{2}\right)_{n+1}}\, {}_3F_2\left(\begin{matrix}1,\ \frac{s}{2},\ \frac{s+1}{2};\ \frac{a^2}{b^2}\\ \frac{s-2n-\varepsilon+1}{2},\ \frac{s+2n+\varepsilon+2}{2}\end{matrix}\right)$ $+(-1)^{\varepsilon+1}\dfrac{\pi}{2}\,b^{s-2}\tan^{2\varepsilon-1}\dfrac{s\pi}{2}\,P_{2n+\varepsilon}\left(\dfrac{b}{a}\right)$ $[0<a<b;\ \operatorname{Re}s<2-2n-\varepsilon]$
9	$\dfrac{\theta(x-a)}{x^2-b^2}\, P_{2n+\varepsilon}\left(\dfrac{x}{a}\right)$	$(-1)^{n+1}\dfrac{\left(\frac{3-s+\varepsilon}{2}\right)_n a^{s-2}}{2\left(\frac{s-2+\varepsilon}{2}\right)_{n+1}}\, {}_3F_2\left(\begin{matrix}1,\ \frac{2n-s+\varepsilon+3}{2},\ \frac{2-2n-s-\varepsilon}{2}\\ \frac{3-s}{2},\ \frac{4-s}{2};\ \frac{b^2}{a^2}\end{matrix}\right)$ $[0<b<a;\ \operatorname{Re}s<2-2n-\varepsilon]$
10	$\dfrac{1}{(x+a)^\rho}\, P_n\left(\dfrac{2x}{b}+1\right)$	$a^{s-\rho}\,\mathrm{B}(s,\rho-s)\,{}_3F_2\left(\begin{matrix}-n,\ n+1,\ s\\ 1,\ s-\rho+1;\ \frac{a}{b}\end{matrix}\right)$ $[0<\operatorname{Re}s<\operatorname{Re}\rho-n;\ |\arg a|<\pi]$
11	$(x-a)_+^{-1/2}\, P_{2n}\left(i\sqrt{\dfrac{x}{a}-1}\right)$	$\dfrac{(-1)^n a^{s-1/2}}{n!}\,\Gamma\left(\dfrac{2n+1}{2}\right)\Gamma\left[\begin{matrix}1-s+n,\ \frac{1-2s-2n}{2}\\ 1-s,\ 1-s\end{matrix}\right]$ $[a>0;\ \operatorname{Re}s<1/2-n]$
12	$\theta(x-a)$ $\times\left(\dfrac{x-a}{x}\right)^{(n-2[n/2]-1)/2}$ $\times P_n\left(\sqrt{\dfrac{x-a}{x}}\right)$	$\dfrac{(-1)^{[n/2]}a^s}{[n/2]!}\,\Gamma\left[\begin{matrix}-s,\ -s,\ n-\left[\frac{n}{2}\right]+\frac{1}{2}\\ -s-\left[\frac{n}{2}\right],\ -s+n-\left[\frac{n}{2}\right]+\frac{1}{2}\end{matrix}\right]$ $[a>0;\ \operatorname{Re}s<0]$

3.19.2. $P_n(bx)$ and the exponential function

No.	$f(x)$	$F(s)$
1	$\theta(x-a)\,e^{-bx}P_n\left(\dfrac{x}{a}\right)$	$\dfrac{2^n(1/2)_n\,e^{-ab}}{n!\,a^n b^{s+n}}\,\Gamma(s+n)\,{}_2F_2\left(\begin{matrix}-n,\ -n;\ 2ab\\ -2n,\ 1-s-n\end{matrix}\right)$ $[a,\ \operatorname{Re}b,\ \operatorname{Re}s>0]$
2	$\theta(a-x)\,e^{-bx^2}P_n\left(\dfrac{x}{a}\right)$	$\sqrt{\pi}\left(\dfrac{a}{2}\right)^s\Gamma\left[\begin{matrix}s\\ \frac{s-n+1}{2},\ \frac{s+n+2}{2}\end{matrix}\right]{}_2F_2\left(\begin{matrix}\frac{s}{2},\ \frac{s+1}{2};\ -a^2b\\ \frac{s-n+1}{2},\ \frac{s+n+2}{2}\end{matrix}\right)$ $[a>0;\ \operatorname{Re}s>((-1)^n-1)/2]$
3	$\theta(x-a)\,e^{b/x^2}P_n\left(\dfrac{x}{a}\right)$	$\dfrac{2^{-s-1}a^s}{\sqrt{\pi}}\,\Gamma\left[\begin{matrix}-\frac{s+n}{2},\ \frac{1-s+n}{2}\\ 1-s\end{matrix}\right]{}_2F_2\left(\begin{matrix}-\frac{s+n}{2},\ \frac{1-s+n}{2};\ \frac{b}{a^2}\\ \frac{1-s}{2},\ \frac{2-s}{2}\end{matrix}\right)$ $[a>0;\ \operatorname{Re}b>0]$

No.	$f(x)$	$F(s)$
4	$e^{-bx} P_n \left(\dfrac{2x}{a} \pm 1 \right)$	$\dfrac{2^{2n}}{n!\, a^n b^{s+n}} \left(\dfrac{1}{2} \right)_n \Gamma(s+n)\, {}_2F_2 \left(\begin{matrix} -n,\ -n;\ \pm ab \\ -2n,\ 1-s-n \end{matrix} \right)$ $\quad$ [Re b, Re $s > 0$]
5	$e^{-b/x} P_n \left(\dfrac{2x}{a} + 1 \right)$	$b^s\, \Gamma(-s)\, {}_2F_2 \left(\begin{matrix} -n,\ n+1 \\ 1,\ s+1;\ \frac{b}{a} \end{matrix} \right)$ $\qquad$ [Re $b > 0$; Re $s < -n$]
6	$e^{-b\sqrt{x}} P_n \left(\dfrac{2x}{a} \pm 1 \right)$	$\dfrac{2^{2n+1}}{n!\, a^n b^{2s+2n}} \left(\dfrac{1}{2} \right)_n \Gamma(2s+2n)\, {}_2F_3 \left(\begin{matrix} -n,\ -n;\ \mp \frac{ab^2}{4} \\ -2n,\ \frac{1-2s-2n}{2},\ 1-s-n \end{matrix} \right)$ $\quad$ [Re b, Re $s > 0$]

3.19.3. $P_n(ax+b)$ and $\operatorname{Ei}(cx^r)$

Notation: $\varepsilon = 0$ or 1.

1	$\theta(a-x)\operatorname{Ei}\left(-bx^2\right) P_{2n+\varepsilon}\left(\dfrac{x}{a} \right)$	$\dfrac{(-1)^{n+1}\left(\frac{\varepsilon-s-1}{2} \right)_n a^{s+2} b}{2\left(\frac{s+\varepsilon+2}{2} \right)_{n+1}}\, {}_4F_4 \left(\begin{matrix} 1,\ 1,\ \frac{s+2}{2},\ \frac{s+3}{2};\ -a^2 b \\ 2,\ 2,\ \frac{s-2n-\varepsilon+3}{2},\ \frac{s+2n+\varepsilon+4}{2} \end{matrix} \right)$

$$+ \dfrac{(-1)^n\left(\frac{\varepsilon-s+1}{2} \right)_n a^s}{2\left(\frac{s+\varepsilon}{2} \right)_{n+1}}$$

$$\times \left[\mathbf{C} - \sum_{k=0}^{n} \frac{2}{2k+s+\varepsilon} - \sum_{k=0}^{n-1} \frac{2}{2k-s+\varepsilon+1} + \ln\left(a^2 b\right) \right]$$

$$[a > 0;\ \operatorname{Re} s > -\varepsilon;\ |\arg b| < \pi]$$

3.19.4. $P_n(ax+b)$ and $\operatorname{si}(cx^r)$, $\operatorname{ci}(cx^r)$

1	$\left(a^2 - x^2\right)_+^{1/2} \operatorname{si}(bx) P_n\left(\dfrac{x}{a} \right)$	$\sqrt{\pi}\left(\dfrac{a}{2} \right)^{s+1} b\, \Gamma \left[\begin{matrix} s+1 \\ \frac{s-n+2}{2},\ \frac{s+n+3}{2} \end{matrix} \right] {}_3F_4 \left(\begin{matrix} \frac{1}{2},\ \frac{s+1}{2},\ \frac{s+2}{2};\ -\frac{a^2 b^2}{4} \\ \frac{3}{2},\ \frac{3}{2},\ \frac{s-n+2}{2},\ \frac{s+n+3}{2} \end{matrix} \right)$

$$- \dfrac{\pi^{3/2} a^s}{2^{s+1}} \Gamma \left[\begin{matrix} s \\ \frac{s-n+1}{2},\ \frac{s+n+2}{2} \end{matrix} \right]$$

$$[a > 0;\ \operatorname{Re} s > ((-1)^n - 1)/2]$$

2	$\left(a^2 - x^2\right)_+^{1/2} \operatorname{ci}(bx) P_n\left(\dfrac{x}{a} \right)$	$-\dfrac{\sqrt{\pi}\, a^{s+2} b^2}{2^{s+4}} \Gamma \left[\begin{matrix} s+2 \\ \frac{s-n+3}{2},\ \frac{s+n+4}{2} \end{matrix} \right] {}_4F_5 \left(\begin{matrix} 1,\ 1,\ \frac{s+2}{2},\ \frac{s+3}{2};\ -\frac{a^2 b^2}{4} \\ \frac{3}{2},\ 2,\ 2,\ \frac{s-n+3}{2},\ \frac{s+n+4}{2} \end{matrix} \right)$

$$+ \sqrt{\pi}\left(\dfrac{a}{2} \right)^s \Gamma \left[\begin{matrix} s \\ \frac{s-n+1}{2},\ \frac{s+n+2}{2} \end{matrix} \right] \left[\psi(s) \right.$$

$$\left. - \dfrac{1}{2}\psi\left(\dfrac{s-n+1}{2} \right) - \dfrac{1}{2}\psi\left(\dfrac{s+n+2}{2} \right) + \ln\dfrac{ab}{2} + \mathbf{C} \right]$$

$$[a > 0;\ \operatorname{Re} s > ((-1)^n - 1)/2]$$

3.19.5. $P_n(ax+b)$ **and** $\text{erf}(cx^r)$, $\text{erfc}(cx^r)$

1	$\theta(a-x)\,\text{erfc}(bx)\,P_n\left(\dfrac{x}{a}\right)$	$-2^{-s}a^{s+1}b\,\Gamma\left[\begin{array}{c} s+1 \\ \frac{s-n+2}{2},\ \frac{s+n+3}{2}\end{array}\right]\ _3F_3\left(\begin{array}{c}\frac{1}{2},\ \frac{s+1}{2},\ \frac{s+2}{2};\ -a^2b^2 \\ \frac{3}{2},\ \frac{s-n+2}{2},\ \frac{s+n+3}{2}\end{array}\right)$ $+\sqrt{\pi}\left(\dfrac{a}{2}\right)^s\Gamma\left[\begin{array}{c} s \\ \frac{s-n+1}{2},\ \frac{s+n+2}{2}\end{array}\right]$ $[a>0;\ \text{Re}\,s>((-1)^n-1)/2]$

3.19.6.   **Products of** $P_n(ax^r+b)$

Notation: $\varepsilon=0$ or 1.

1	$\theta(a-x)\,P_m\left(\dfrac{x}{a}\right)P_n\left(\dfrac{x}{a}\right)$	$\dfrac{\sqrt{\pi}\,(m+n)!\,a^s}{2^s m!\,n!}\,\Gamma\left[\begin{array}{c} s \\ \frac{s-m-n+1}{2},\ \frac{s+m+n+2}{2}\end{array}\right]$ $\times\ _3F_2\left(\begin{array}{c}-m,\ -n,\ \frac{s-m-n}{2};\ 1 \\ -m-n,\ \frac{s-m-n+1}{2}\end{array}\right)$ $[a>0;\ \text{Re}\,s>2[m/2]+2[n/2]-m-n]$
2	$\theta(x-a)\,P_m\left(\dfrac{2x}{a}-1\right)$ $\times\ P_n\left(\dfrac{2x}{b}\pm1\right)$	$(-1)^{m+1}(\pm1)^n\,a^s\dfrac{(1-s)_m}{(s)_{m+1}}\ _4F_3\left(\begin{array}{c}-n,\ n+1,\ s,\ s;\ \mp\frac{a}{b} \\ 1,\ s-m,\ s+m+1\end{array}\right)$ $[a>0;\ \text{Re}\,s<-m-n]$
3	$\theta(a-x)\,P_n\left(\sqrt{\dfrac{a}{x}}\right)$ $\times\ P_m\left(1-\dfrac{x}{b}\right)$	$a^s\Gamma\left[\begin{array}{c}\frac{2s-n}{2},\ \frac{2s+n+1}{2} \\ \frac{2s+1}{2},\ s+1\end{array}\right]\ _4F_3\left(\begin{array}{c}-m,\ m+1,\ \frac{2s-n}{2},\ \frac{2s+n+1}{2} \\ 1,\ \frac{2s+1}{2},\ s+1;\ \frac{a}{2b}\end{array}\right)$ $[a>0;\ \text{Re}\,s>n/2]$
4	$\theta(a-x)\,(b-x)^m$ $\times\ P_n\left(\sqrt{\dfrac{a}{x}}\right)P_m\left(\dfrac{b+x}{b-x}\right)$	$a^s b^m\Gamma\left[\begin{array}{c}\frac{2s-n}{2},\ \frac{2s+n+1}{2} \\ \frac{2s+1}{2},\ s+1\end{array}\right]\ _4F_3\left(\begin{array}{c}-m,\ -m,\ \frac{2s-n}{2},\ \frac{2s+n+1}{2} \\ 1,\ \frac{2s+1}{2},\ s+1;\ \frac{a}{b}\end{array}\right)$ $[a>0;\ \text{Re}\,s>n/2]$
5	$\theta(a-x)\,P_n\left(\dfrac{a}{x}\right)P_{2m+\varepsilon}(bx)$	$\dfrac{(-1)^m 2^{s+\varepsilon-1}a^{s+\varepsilon}b^\varepsilon}{\sqrt{\pi}\,m!}\left(\dfrac{2\varepsilon+1}{2}\right)_m\Gamma\left[\begin{array}{c}\frac{s-n+\varepsilon}{2},\ \frac{s+n+\varepsilon+1}{2} \\ s+\varepsilon+1\end{array}\right]$ $\times\ _4F_3\left(\begin{array}{c}-m,\ \frac{2m+2\varepsilon+1}{2},\ \frac{s-n+\varepsilon}{2},\ \frac{s+n+\varepsilon+1}{2} \\ \frac{2\varepsilon+1}{2},\ \frac{s+\varepsilon+1}{2},\ \frac{s+\varepsilon+2}{2};\ a^2b^2\end{array}\right)$ $[a>0;\ \text{Re}\,s>n-\varepsilon]$
6	$\theta(a-x)\,P_m\left(1-\dfrac{2}{bx^2}\right)$ $\times\ P_n\left(\dfrac{x}{a}\right)$	$\dfrac{(-1)^m 2^{4m-s}a^{s-2m}b^{-m}}{m!}\Gamma\left[\begin{array}{c}\frac{2m+1}{2},\ s-2m \\ \frac{s-2m-n+1}{2},\ \frac{s-2m+n+2}{2}\end{array}\right]$ $\times\ _4F_3\left(\begin{array}{c}-m,\ -m,\ \frac{s-2m}{2},\ \frac{s-2m+1}{2};\ a^2b \\ -2m,\ \frac{s-2m-n+1}{2},\ \frac{s-2m+n+2}{2}\end{array}\right)\quad[a>0;\ \text{Re}\,s>2m]$

3.20. The Chebyshev Polynomials $T_n(z)$

More formulas can be obtained from the corresponding sections due to the relations

$$T_n(z) = \frac{n}{2} \lim_{\lambda \to 0} \left[\frac{1}{\lambda} C_n^\lambda(z) \right], \quad T_\nu(z) = \frac{\Gamma(\nu+1)}{(1/2)_\nu} P_\nu^{(-1/2,\,-1/2)}(z),$$

$$T_\nu(z) = {}_2F_1\left(-\nu, \nu; \frac{1}{2}; \frac{1-z}{2}\right).$$

3.20.1. $T_n(\varphi(x))$ and algebraic functions

Notation: $\varepsilon = 0$ or 1.

No.	$f(x)$	$F(s)$
1	$(a^2-x^2)_+^{-1/2} T_n\left(\frac{x}{a}\right)$	$\dfrac{\pi a^{s-1}}{2^s} \Gamma\left[{s \atop \frac{s+n+1}{2},\ \frac{s-n+1}{2}} \right]$ $\qquad [a,\ \mathrm{Re}\,s>0]$
2	$\dfrac{(a^2-x^2)_+^{-1/2}}{(b^2\pm x^2)^\rho} T_n\left(\frac{x}{a}\right)$	$\dfrac{\pi a^{s-1}}{2^s b^{2\rho}} \Gamma\left[{s \atop \frac{s-n+1}{2},\ \frac{s+n+1}{2}} \right] {}_3F_2\left({\rho,\ \frac{s}{2},\ \frac{s+1}{2};\ \mp\frac{a^2}{b^2} \atop \frac{s-n+1}{2},\ \frac{s+n+1}{2}}\right)$ $\left[\left\{{\mathrm{Re}\,b>0 \atop b>a}\right\};\ a,\ \mathrm{Re}\,s>0\right]$
3	$(x^2-a^2)_+^{-1/2} T_n\left(\frac{x}{a}\right)$	$\dfrac{a^{s-1}}{2^{s+1}} \Gamma\left[{\frac{1-s+n}{2},\ \frac{1-s-n}{2} \atop 1-s} \right]$ $\qquad [a>0;\ \mathrm{Re}\,s<1-n]$
4	$(a-x)_+^{\alpha-1} T_{2n+\varepsilon}(bx)$	$\dfrac{(-1)^n (n+\varepsilon/2) a^{s+\alpha+\varepsilon-1} (2b)^\varepsilon}{n!} B(\alpha, s+\varepsilon)$ $\times \Gamma(n+\varepsilon)\, {}_4F_3\left({-n,\ n+\varepsilon,\ \frac{s+\varepsilon}{2},\ \frac{s+\varepsilon+1}{2} \atop \frac{2\varepsilon+1}{2},\ \frac{s+\alpha+\varepsilon}{2},\ \frac{s+\alpha+\varepsilon+1}{2};\ a^2b^2}\right)$ $[a,\ \mathrm{Re}\,\alpha>0;\ \mathrm{Re}\,s>-\varepsilon]$
5	$(x-a)_+^{\alpha-1} T_{2n+\varepsilon}(bx)$	$\dfrac{(-1)^n (n+\varepsilon/2) a^{s+\alpha+\varepsilon-1} (2b)^\varepsilon}{n!} B(1-s-\alpha-\varepsilon, \alpha)$ $\times \Gamma(n+\varepsilon)\, {}_4F_3\left({-n,\ n+\varepsilon,\ \frac{s+\varepsilon}{2},\ \frac{s+\varepsilon+1}{2} \atop \frac{2\varepsilon+1}{2},\ \frac{s+\alpha+\varepsilon}{2},\ \frac{s+\alpha+\varepsilon+1}{2};\ a^2b^2}\right)$ $[a>0;\ \mathrm{Re}\,(s+\alpha)<1-2n-\varepsilon]$
6	$(a-x)_+^{-1/2} T_n\left(\frac{2x}{a}-1\right)$	$\sqrt{\pi}\, a^{s-1/2} \Gamma\left[{s,\ s+\frac{1}{2} \atop s-n+\frac{1}{2},\ s+n+\frac{1}{2}} \right]$ $\qquad [a,\ \mathrm{Re}\,s>0]$
7	$(a-x)_+^{\alpha-1} T_n\left(\frac{2x}{a}-1\right)$	$a^{s+\alpha-1} B(\alpha, s)\, {}_3F_2\left({-n,\ n,\ \alpha \atop \frac{1}{2},\ s+\alpha;\ 1}\right)$ $\qquad [a,\ \mathrm{Re}\,\alpha,\ \mathrm{Re}\,s>0]$

No.	$f(x)$	$F(s)$
8	$\dfrac{(a-x)_+^{-1/2}}{(b\pm x)^\rho}\, T_n\left(\dfrac{2x}{a}-1\right)$	$(-1)^n\,\sqrt{\pi}\,a^{s-1/2}b^{-\rho}\left(\dfrac{1-2s}{2}\right)_n\,\Gamma\!\left[\begin{array}{c}s\\ \frac{2s+2n+1}{2}\end{array}\right]$
		$\times\,{}_3F_2\!\left(\begin{array}{c}\rho,\,s,\,\frac{2s+1}{2};\,\mp\frac{a}{b}\\ \frac{2s-2n+1}{2},\,\frac{2s+2n+1}{2}\end{array}\right)\quad\left[\left\{\begin{array}{c}a>0\\ b>a>0\end{array}\right\};\ \mathrm{Re}\,s>0\right]$
9	$(x-a)_+^{-1/2}\,T_n\left(\dfrac{2x}{a}-1\right)$	$\sqrt{\pi}\,a^{s-1/2}\,\Gamma\!\left[\begin{array}{c}\frac{1}{2}-s-n,\,\frac{1}{2}-s+n\\ 1-s,\,\frac{1}{2}-s\end{array}\right]\quad[a>0;\ \mathrm{Re}\,s<1/2-n]$
10	$\dfrac{1}{(x+a)^\rho}\,T_n\left(\dfrac{2x}{a}+1\right)$	$a^{s-\rho}\,\mathrm{B}\left(-s-n+\rho,\,s\right)\,{}_3F_2\!\left(\begin{array}{c}-n,\,\frac{1-2n}{2},\,s\\ \frac{1}{2},\,\rho-n;\,1\end{array}\right)$
		$[0<\mathrm{Re}\,s<\mathrm{Re}\,\rho-n;\ |\arg a|<\pi]$
11	$\dfrac{(x+a)^{-1/2}}{(x+b)^\rho}\,T_n\left(\dfrac{2x}{a}+1\right)$	$\dfrac{(-1)^n\,a^{s-\rho-1/2}}{\sqrt{\pi}}\left(\dfrac{1}{2}-s+\rho\right)_n\,\Gamma\!\left(\dfrac{1-2s-2n+2\rho}{2}\right)$
		$\times\,\Gamma\left(s-\rho\right)\,{}_3F_2\!\left(\begin{array}{c}\rho,\,\frac{1-2s-2n+2\rho}{2},\,\frac{1-2s+2n+2\rho}{2}\\ 1-s+\rho,\,\frac{1-2s+2\rho}{2};\,\frac{b}{a}\end{array}\right)$
		$+\,a^{-1/2}b^{s-\rho}\,\mathrm{B}\left(s,\,\rho-s\right)\,{}_3F_2\!\left(\begin{array}{c}\frac{-2n+1}{2},\,\frac{2n+1}{2},\,s\\ \frac{1}{2},\,s-\rho+1;\,\frac{b}{a}\end{array}\right)$
		$[0<\mathrm{Re}\,s<1/2-n+\mathrm{Re}\,\rho;\ |\arg a|,\,|\arg b|<\pi]$
12	$(a-x)_+^{\alpha-1}\,T_n\left(\dfrac{2x}{b}\pm 1\right)$	$(\pm 1)^n\,a^{s+\alpha-1}\,\mathrm{B}\left(s,\,\alpha\right)\,{}_3F_2\!\left(\begin{array}{c}-n,\,n,\,s\\ \frac{1}{2},\,s+\alpha;\,\mp\frac{a}{b}\end{array}\right)$
		$[a,\ \mathrm{Re}\,\alpha,\ \mathrm{Re}\,s>0]$
13	$\dfrac{(a-x)_+^{\alpha-1}}{\sqrt{b\pm x}}\,T_n\left(\dfrac{2x}{b}\pm 1\right)$	$(\pm 1)^n\,a^{s+\alpha-1}b^{-1/2}\,\mathrm{B}\left(\alpha,\,s\right)\,{}_3F_2\!\left(\begin{array}{c}\frac{-2n+1}{2},\,\frac{2n+1}{2},\,s\\ \frac{1}{2},\,s+\alpha;\,\mp\frac{a}{b}\end{array}\right)$
		$\left[\left\{\begin{array}{c}a>0\\ b>a>0\end{array}\right\};\ \mathrm{Re}\,\alpha,\ \mathrm{Re}\,s>0\right]$
14	$\dfrac{(x+a-b)^{-1/2}}{(x+a+b)^\rho}\,T_n\left(\dfrac{x+a}{b}\right)$	$\dfrac{2^{n-1}\left(\delta_{n,0}+1\right)\left(a+b\right)^{s+n-\rho-1/2}}{b^n}\,\mathrm{B}\left(\dfrac{1-2s-2n+2\rho}{2},\,s\right)$
		$\times\,{}_3F_2\!\left(\begin{array}{c}\frac{1-2n}{2},\,1-n,\,\frac{1-2s-2n+2\rho}{2}\\ \frac{1-2n+2\rho}{2},\,1-2n;\,\frac{2b}{a+b}\end{array}\right)$
		$[a>b>0;\ 0<\mathrm{Re}\,s<1/2-n+\mathrm{Re}\,\rho]$
15	$(a-x)_+^{\alpha-1}\,T_{2n+\varepsilon}\left(b(a-x)\right)$	$\dfrac{(-1)^n\left(n+\varepsilon/2\right)a^{s+\alpha+\varepsilon-1}\left(2b\right)^\varepsilon}{n!}\,\mathrm{B}\left(\alpha+\varepsilon,\,s\right)$
		$\times\,\Gamma\left(n+\varepsilon\right)\,{}_4F_3\!\left(\begin{array}{c}-n,\,n+\varepsilon,\,\frac{\alpha+\varepsilon}{2},\,\frac{\alpha+\varepsilon+1}{2}\\ \frac{2\varepsilon+1}{2},\,\frac{s+\alpha+\varepsilon}{2},\,\frac{s+\alpha+\varepsilon+1}{2};\,a^2b^2\end{array}\right)$
		$[a>0;\ \mathrm{Re}\,\alpha>-\varepsilon;\ \mathrm{Re}\,s>0]$

No.	$f(x)$	$F(s)$
16	$(a-x)_+^{-1/2} T_n\left(\dfrac{x+b}{a+b}\right)$	$n!\sqrt{\pi}\, a^{s-1/2} \Gamma\left[\begin{matrix} s \\ \frac{2s+2n+1}{2}\end{matrix}\right] P_n^{(s-1/2,\,-s-1/2)}\left(\dfrac{b}{a+b}\right)$ $[a,\ \mathrm{Re}\,s > 0]$
17	$(a-x)_+^{\alpha-1} T_n\left(\dfrac{x+b}{a+b}\right)$	$a^{s+\alpha-1}\,\mathrm{B}(s,\alpha)\ {}_3F_2\left(\begin{matrix}-n,\,n,\,\alpha \\ \frac{1}{2},\,s+\alpha;\ \frac{a}{2(a+b)}\end{matrix}\right)$ $[a,\ \mathrm{Re}\,\alpha,\ \mathrm{Re}\,s > 0]$
18	$\left(a^2-x^2\right)_+^{-1/2} T_n\left(\dfrac{a}{x}\right)$	$2^{s-2}a^{s-1}\,\Gamma\left[\begin{matrix}\frac{s-n}{2},\,\frac{s+n}{2} \\ s\end{matrix}\right]$ $[a,\ \mathrm{Re}\,s > 0]$
19	$(a-x)_+^{-1/2} T_n\left(\dfrac{2a}{x}-1\right)$	$\sqrt{\pi}\, a^{s-1/2}\,\Gamma\left[\begin{matrix}s-n,\,s+n \\ s,\,s+\frac{1}{2}\end{matrix}\right]$ $[a>0;\ \mathrm{Re}\,s > n]$
20	$(x-a)_+^{-1/2} T_n\left(\dfrac{2a}{x}-1\right)$	$\sqrt{\pi}\, a^{s-1/2}\,\Gamma\left[\begin{matrix}\frac{1}{2}-s,\,1-s \\ 1-s-n,\,1-s+n\end{matrix}\right]$ $[a>0;\ \mathrm{Re}\,s < 1/2]$
21	$\dfrac{1}{(x+a)^n} T_n\left(\dfrac{x-a}{x+a}\right)$	$\dfrac{(-1)^n 2^{2n-1}a^{s-n}}{(2n-1)!}\,\Gamma\left[\begin{matrix}s,\,n-s,\,n-s+\frac{1}{2} \\ \frac{1}{2}-s\end{matrix}\right]$ $[0 < \mathrm{Re}\,s < n;\ |\arg a| < \pi]$
22	$(a-x)_+^{-1/2}$ $\times\, T_n\left(\dfrac{x^2-8ax+8a^2}{x^2}\right)$	$\sqrt{\pi}a^{s-1/2}\,\Gamma\left[\begin{matrix}s-2n,\,s+2n \\ s,\,s+\frac{1}{2}\end{matrix}\right]$ $[a>0;\ \mathrm{Re}\,s > 2n]$
23	$(x-a)_+^{-1/2}$ $\times\, T_n\left(\dfrac{x^2-8ax+8a^2}{a^2}\right)$	$\sqrt{\pi}a^{s-1/2}\,\Gamma\left[\begin{matrix}\frac{1}{2}-s-2n,\,\frac{1}{2}-s+2n \\ \frac{1}{2}-s,\,1-s\end{matrix}\right]$ $[a>0;\ \mathrm{Re}\,s < 1/2-2n]$
24	$(a-x)_+^{\alpha-1} T_{2n+\varepsilon}\left(bx(a-x)\right)$	$(-1)^n (2n+1)^\varepsilon\, a^{s+\alpha+2\varepsilon-1}b^\varepsilon\,\mathrm{B}(s+\varepsilon,\alpha+\varepsilon)$ $\times\, {}_6F_5\left(\begin{matrix}-n,\,n+\varepsilon,\,\Delta(2,s+\varepsilon),\,\Delta(2,\alpha+\varepsilon) \\ \frac{2\varepsilon+1}{2},\,\Delta(4,s+\alpha+2\varepsilon);\ \frac{a^4b^2}{16}\end{matrix}\right)$ $[a>0;\ \mathrm{Re}\,s,\ \mathrm{Re}\,\alpha > -\varepsilon]$
25	$(a-x)_+^{\alpha-1} T_n\left(\dfrac{b}{x(a-x)}\right)$	$2^{n-1}a^{s+\alpha-2n-1}b^n\,\mathrm{B}(s-n,\alpha-n)$ $\times\, {}_6F_5\left(\begin{matrix}\Delta(2,-n),\,\Delta(2,s-n),\,\Delta(2,\alpha-n) \\ 1-n,\,\Delta(4,s+\alpha-2n);\ \frac{a^4}{16b^2}\end{matrix}\right)$ $[a>0;\ \mathrm{Re}\,s,\ \mathrm{Re}\,\alpha > n]$

No.	$f(x)$	$F(s)$
26	$(a-x)_+^{\alpha-1}$ $\times T_{2n+\varepsilon}\left(b\sqrt{x(a-x)}\right)$	$(-1)^n (2n+1)^\varepsilon a^{s+\alpha+\varepsilon-1} b^\varepsilon \, \mathrm{B}\left(\dfrac{2s+\varepsilon}{2}, \dfrac{2\alpha+\varepsilon}{2}\right)$ $\times {}_4F_3\left(\begin{matrix} -n,\, n+\varepsilon,\, \frac{2s+\varepsilon}{2},\, \frac{2\alpha+\varepsilon}{2} \\ \frac{2\varepsilon+1}{2},\, \frac{s+\alpha+\varepsilon}{2},\, \frac{s+\alpha+\varepsilon+1}{2};\, \frac{a^2b^2}{4} \end{matrix}\right)$ $[a>0;\ \mathrm{Re}\,s,\ \mathrm{Re}\,\alpha > -\varepsilon/2]$
27	$(a-x)_+^{\alpha-1} T_n\left(\dfrac{b}{\sqrt{x(a-x)}}\right)$	$2^{n-1} a^{s-n+\alpha-1} b^n \, \mathrm{B}\left(s-\dfrac{n}{2},\, \alpha-\dfrac{n}{2}\right)$ $\times {}_4F_3\left(\begin{matrix} \frac{1-n}{2},\, -\frac{n}{2},\, s-\frac{n}{2},\, \alpha-\frac{n}{2} \\ 1-n,\, \frac{s-n+\alpha}{2},\, \frac{s-n+\alpha+1}{2};\, \frac{a^2}{4b^2} \end{matrix}\right)$ $[a>0;\ \mathrm{Re}\,s,\ \mathrm{Re}\,\alpha > n/2]$
28	$\theta(a-x) T_{2n+1}\left(\sqrt{1-\dfrac{x}{a}}\right)$	$\dfrac{2n+1}{2}\sqrt{\pi}\, a^s\, \Gamma\left[\begin{matrix} s,\, \frac{1}{2}-s+n \\ s+n+\frac{3}{2},\, \frac{1}{2}-s \end{matrix}\right]$ $\qquad [a,\ \mathrm{Re}\,s>0]$
29	$(a-x)_+^{-1/2} T_{2n}\left(\sqrt{1-\dfrac{x}{a}}\right)$	$\sqrt{\pi}\, a^{s-1/2}\, \Gamma\left[\begin{matrix} s,\, \frac{1}{2}-s+n \\ s+n+\frac{1}{2},\, \frac{1}{2}-s \end{matrix}\right]$ $\qquad [a,\ \mathrm{Re}\,s>0]$
30	$\theta(x-a) T_{2n+1}\left(i\sqrt{\dfrac{x}{a}-1}\right)$	$i\,\dfrac{2n+1}{2}\sqrt{\pi}\, a^s\, \Gamma\left[\begin{matrix} s+\frac{1}{2},\, -\frac{s+2n+1}{2} \\ s-n+\frac{1}{2},\, 1-s \end{matrix}\right]$ $[a>0;\ \mathrm{Re}\,s<-1/2-n]$
31	$(x-a)_+^{-1/2} T_{2n}\left(i\sqrt{\dfrac{x}{a}-1}\right)$	$\sqrt{\pi}\, a^{s-1/2}\, \Gamma\left[\begin{matrix} s+\frac{1}{2},\, \frac{1}{2}-s-n \\ s-n+\frac{1}{2},\, 1-s \end{matrix}\right]$ $[a>0;\ \mathrm{Re}\,s<1/2-n]$
32	$\theta(a-x) T_{2n+1}\left(i\sqrt{\dfrac{a}{x}-1}\right)$	$i\,\dfrac{2n+1}{2}\sqrt{\pi}\, a^s\, \Gamma\left[\begin{matrix} s-n-\frac{1}{2},\, \frac{1}{2}-s \\ s+1,\, \frac{1}{2}-s-n \end{matrix}\right]$ $[a>0;\ \mathrm{Re}\,s>n+1/2]$
33	$(a-x)_+^{-1/2} T_{2n}\left(i\sqrt{\dfrac{a}{x}-1}\right)$	$\sqrt{\pi}\, a^{s-1/2}\, \Gamma\left[\begin{matrix} s-n,\, 1-s \\ s+\frac{1}{2},\, 1-s-n \end{matrix}\right]$ $\qquad [a>0;\ \mathrm{Re}\,s>n]$
34	$(x-a)_+^{-1/2} T_{2n}\left(\sqrt{1-\dfrac{a}{x}}\right)$	$\sqrt{\pi}\, a^{s-1/2}\, \Gamma\left[\begin{matrix} s+n,\, \frac{1}{2}-s \\ s,\, 1-s+n \end{matrix}\right]$ $\qquad [a>0;\ \mathrm{Re}\,s<1/2]$
35	$\dfrac{1}{(x+a)^{n/2}} T_n\left(\sqrt{\dfrac{a}{x+a}}\right)$	$\dfrac{2^{n-1} a^{s-n/2}}{(n-1)!}\, \Gamma\left[\begin{matrix} s,\, \frac{n}{2}-s,\, \frac{n+1}{2}-s \\ \frac{1}{2}-s \end{matrix}\right]$ $[0<\mathrm{Re}\,s<n/2;\ n\geq 1;\ |\arg a|<\pi]$
36	$\dfrac{1}{(x+a)^{n/2}} T_n\left(\sqrt{\dfrac{x}{x+a}}\right)$	$\dfrac{2^{n-1} a^{s-n/2}}{(n-1)!}\, \Gamma\left[\begin{matrix} s,\, s+\frac{1}{2},\, \frac{n}{2}-s \\ s+\frac{1-n}{2} \end{matrix}\right]$ $[a>0;\ 0<\mathrm{Re}\,s<n/2;\ n\geq 1;\ |\arg a|<\pi]$

No.	$f(x)$	$F(s)$
37	$(a-x)_+^{-1/2} \dfrac{(bx+1)^\alpha}{[1-c(a-x)]^{\varepsilon/2}}$ $\times T_{2n+\varepsilon}\left(\sqrt{1+ac-cx}\right)$	$\sqrt{\pi}\, a^{s-1/2}\, \Gamma\!\left[\begin{matrix} s \\ \frac{2s+1}{2} \end{matrix}\right] F_3\!\left(-\alpha,\,-n,\,s,\,n+\varepsilon;\,\dfrac{2s+1}{2};\,-ab,\,-ac\right)$ $[a>0;\ |\arg(1+ab)|<\pi]$
38	$(a-x)_+^{(\varepsilon-1)/2}(b-x)^{n+\varepsilon/2}$ $\times T_{2n+\varepsilon}\left(c\sqrt{\dfrac{a-x}{b-x}}\right)$	$(-1)^n\left(n+\dfrac{1}{2}\right)^\varepsilon \sqrt{\pi}\, a^{s+\varepsilon-1/2} b^n c^\varepsilon\, \Gamma\!\left[\begin{matrix} s \\ \frac{2s+2\varepsilon+1}{2} \end{matrix}\right]$ $\times F_1\!\left(-n,\,s,\,n+\varepsilon;\,\dfrac{2s+2\varepsilon+1}{2};\,\dfrac{a}{b},\,\dfrac{ac^2}{b}\right)$ $[a,\ \mathrm{Re}\,s>0]$

3.20.2. $T_n(bx)$ and the exponential function

No.	$f(x)$	$F(s)$
1	$(a^2-x^2)_+^{-1/2}\, e^{bx}\, T_n\!\left(\dfrac{x}{a}\right)$	$\dfrac{\pi}{2}\left(\dfrac{a}{2}\right)^{s-1}\Gamma\!\left[\begin{matrix} s \\ \frac{s-n+1}{2},\ \frac{s+n+1}{2}\end{matrix}\right]\,{}_2F_3\!\left(\begin{matrix}\frac{s}{2},\ \frac{s+1}{2};\ \frac{a^2b^2}{4}\\ \frac{1}{2},\ \frac{s-n+1}{2},\ \frac{s+n+1}{2}\end{matrix}\right)$ $+\dfrac{\pi}{2}\left(\dfrac{a}{2}\right)^s b\,\Gamma\!\left[\begin{matrix} s+1 \\ \frac{s-n+2}{2},\ \frac{s+n+2}{2}\end{matrix}\right]\,{}_2F_3\!\left(\begin{matrix}\frac{s+1}{2},\ \frac{s+2}{2};\ \frac{a^2b^2}{4}\\ \frac{3}{2},\ \frac{s-n+2}{2},\ \frac{s+n+2}{2}\end{matrix}\right)$ $[a>0;\ \mathrm{Re}\,s>((-1)^n-1)/2]$
2	$(a-x)_+^{-1/2}\, e^{bx}\, T_n\!\left(1-\dfrac{2x}{a}\right)$	$\sqrt{\pi}\, a^{s-1/2}\left(\dfrac{1}{2}-s\right)_n \Gamma\!\left[\begin{matrix} s \\ \frac{2s+2n+1}{2}\end{matrix}\right]\,{}_2F_2\!\left(\begin{matrix} s,\ \frac{2s+1}{2};\ ab\\ \frac{2s-2n+1}{2},\ \frac{2s+2n+1}{2}\end{matrix}\right)$ $[a,\ \mathrm{Re}\,s>0]$
3	$e^{-bx}\, T_n\!\left(\dfrac{2x}{a}\pm1\right)$	$\dfrac{2^{2n-1}(\delta_{n,0}+1)}{a^n b^{s+n}}\,\Gamma(s+n)\,{}_2F_2\!\left(\begin{matrix}-n,\ \frac{1-2n}{2};\ \pm ab\\ 1-2n,\ 1-s-n\end{matrix}\right)$ $[\mathrm{Re}\,b,\ \mathrm{Re}\,s>0]$
4	$\dfrac{e^{-bx}}{\sqrt{x+a}}\, T_n\!\left(\dfrac{2x}{a}+1\right)$	$\dfrac{(-1)^n\, a^{s-1/2}}{\sqrt{\pi}}\left(\dfrac{1-2s}{2}\right)_n \Gamma(s)\,\Gamma\!\left(\dfrac{1-2s-2n}{2}\right)$ $\times\,{}_2F_2\!\left(\begin{matrix} s,\ \frac{2s+1}{2};\ ab\\ \frac{2s-2n+1}{2},\ \frac{2s+2n+1}{2}\end{matrix}\right)$ $+\dfrac{2^{2n-1}(\delta_{n,0}+1)}{a^n b^{s+n-1/2}}\,\Gamma\!\left(\dfrac{2s+2n-1}{2}\right)$ $\times\,{}_2F_2\!\left(\begin{matrix}\frac{1-2n}{2},\ 1-n;\ ab\\ 1-2n,\ \frac{3-2s-2n}{2}\end{matrix}\right)$ $[\mathrm{Re}\,b,\ \mathrm{Re}\,s>0;\ |\arg a|<\pi]$

No.	$f(x)$	$F(s)$
5	$(a-x)_+^{-1/2} e^{-b/x}$ $\times T_n\left(\dfrac{2x}{a}-1\right)$	$(-1)^n \sqrt{\pi}\, a^{s-1/2} \left(\dfrac{1-2s}{2}\right)_n \Gamma\!\left[\begin{matrix} s \\ \frac{2s+2n+1}{2}\end{matrix}\right]$ $\times\, _2F_2\!\left(\begin{matrix} \frac{-2s-2n+1}{2},\ \frac{-2s+2n+1}{2} \\ 1-s,\ \frac{1-2s}{2};\ -\frac{b}{a}\end{matrix}\right)$ $+\,(-1)^n a^{-1/2} b^s\, \Gamma(-s)\, _2F_2\!\left(\begin{matrix}\frac{-2n+1}{2},\ \frac{2n+1}{2} \\ \frac{1}{2},\ s+1;\ -\frac{b}{a}\end{matrix}\right)$ $\qquad\qquad [a,\ \mathrm{Re}\,b>0]$
6	$\dfrac{e^{-b/x}}{\sqrt{x+a}} T_n\left(\dfrac{2x}{a}+1\right)$	$\dfrac{a^{s-1/2}}{\sqrt{\pi}} \left(\dfrac{1-2s}{2}\right)_n \Gamma\!\left(\dfrac{1-2s-2n}{2}\right) \Gamma(s)$ $\times\, _2F_2\!\left(\begin{matrix}\frac{1-2s-2n}{2},\ \frac{1-2s+2n}{2} \\ 1-s,\ \frac{1-2s}{2};\ \frac{b}{a}\end{matrix}\right) + \dfrac{b^s}{\sqrt{a}}\Gamma(-s)\, _2F_2\!\left(\begin{matrix}\frac{-2n+1}{2},\ \frac{2n+1}{2} \\ \frac{1}{2},\ s+1;\ \frac{b}{a}\end{matrix}\right)$ $[\mathrm{Re}\,b>0;\ \mathrm{Re}\,s<1/2-n;\ |\arg a|<\pi]$
7	$(a-x)_+^{-1/2} e^{-b\sqrt{x}}$ $\times T_n\left(1-\dfrac{2x}{a}\right)$	$\sqrt{\pi}\, a^{s-1/2}\left(\dfrac{1}{2}-s\right)_n \Gamma\!\left[\begin{matrix} s \\ \frac{2s+2n+1}{2}\end{matrix}\right]$ $\times\, _2F_3\!\left(\begin{matrix} s,\ \frac{2s+1}{2};\ \frac{ab^2}{4} \\ \frac{1}{2},\ \frac{2s-2n+1}{2},\ \frac{2s+2n+1}{2}\end{matrix}\right) - \sqrt{\pi}\, a^s b\,(-s)_n$ $\times\, \Gamma\!\left[\begin{matrix}\frac{2s+1}{2} \\ s+n+1\end{matrix}\right]\, _2F_3\!\left(\begin{matrix}\frac{2s+1}{2},\ s+1;\ \frac{ab^2}{4} \\ \frac{3}{2},\ s-n+1,\ s+n+1\end{matrix}\right)$ $\qquad\qquad [a,\ \mathrm{Re}\,s>0]$
8	$e^{-b\sqrt{x}} T_n\left(\dfrac{2x}{a}\pm 1\right)$	$\dfrac{2^{2n}(\delta_{n,0}+1)}{a^n b^{2s+2n}} \Gamma(2s+2n)\, _2F_3\!\left(\begin{matrix} -n,\ \frac{1-2n}{2};\ \mp\frac{ab^2}{4} \\ 1-2n,\ \frac{1-2s-2n}{2},\ 1-s-n\end{matrix}\right)$ $[\mathrm{Re}\,b,\ \mathrm{Re}\,s>0]$
9	$\dfrac{e^{-b\sqrt{x}}}{\sqrt{x+a}} T_n\left(\dfrac{2x}{a}+1\right)$	$\dfrac{(-1)^{n+1} a^s b}{\sqrt{\pi}} (-s)_n\, \Gamma(-s-n)\, \Gamma\!\left(\dfrac{2s+1}{2}\right)$ $\times\, _2F_3\!\left(\begin{matrix}\frac{2s+1}{2},\ s+1;\ -\frac{ab^2}{4} \\ \frac{3}{2},\ s-n+1,\ s+n+1\end{matrix}\right)$ $+\dfrac{(-1)^n a^{s-1/2}}{\sqrt{\pi}}\left(\dfrac{1}{2}-s\right)_n \Gamma(s)\,\Gamma\!\left(\dfrac{1-2s-2n}{2}\right)$ $\times\, _2F_3\!\left(\begin{matrix} s,\ \frac{2s+1}{2};\ -\frac{ab^2}{4} \\ \frac{1}{2},\ \frac{2s-2n+1}{2},\ \frac{2s+2n+1}{2}\end{matrix}\right) + \dfrac{2^{2n}(\delta_{n,0}+1)}{a^n b^{2s+2n-1}}$ $\times\, \Gamma(2s+2n-1)\, _2F_3\!\left(\begin{matrix}\frac{1-2n}{2},\ 1-n;\ -\frac{ab^2}{4} \\ 1-2n,\ 1-s-n,\ \frac{3-2s-2n}{2}\end{matrix}\right)$ $[\mathrm{Re}\,b,\ \mathrm{Re}\,s>0;\ |\arg a|<\pi]$

No.	$f(x)$	$F(s)$
10	$(a-x)_+^{-1/2}\, e^{-b/\sqrt{x}}$ $\times T_n\left(\dfrac{2x}{a}-1\right)$	$(-1)^{n+1}\sqrt{\pi}\,a^{s-1}b\,(1-s)_n\,\Gamma\!\begin{bmatrix}\frac{2s-1}{2}\\ s+n\end{bmatrix}$ $\times {}_2F_3\!\left(\begin{matrix}1-s-n,\,1-s+n\\ \frac{3}{2},\,\frac{3-2s}{2},\,1-s;\,\frac{b^2}{4a}\end{matrix}\right)$ $+(-1)^n\sqrt{\pi}\,a^{s-1/2}\left(\dfrac{1-2s}{2}\right)_n\Gamma\!\begin{bmatrix}s\\ \frac{2s+2n+1}{2}\end{bmatrix}$ $\times {}_2F_3\!\left(\begin{matrix}\frac{1-2s-2n}{2},\,\frac{1-2s+2n}{2}\\ \frac{1}{2},\,\frac{1-2s}{2},\,1-s;\,\frac{b^2}{4a}\end{matrix}\right)$ $+2(-1)^n\,a^{-1/2}b^{2s}\Gamma(-2s)\,{}_2F_3\!\left(\begin{matrix}\frac{-2n+1}{2},\,\frac{2n+1}{2}\\ \frac{1}{2},\,\frac{2s+1}{2},\,s+1;\,\frac{b^2}{4a}\end{matrix}\right)$ $[a,\ \mathrm{Re}\,b>0]$
11	$e^{-b/\sqrt{x}}\,T_n\left(\dfrac{2x}{a}\pm 1\right)$	$2(\pm 1)^n\,b^{2s}\,\Gamma(-2s)\,{}_2F_3\!\left(\begin{matrix}-n,\,n;\,\mp\frac{b^2}{4a}\\ \frac{1}{2},\,\frac{2s+1}{2},\,s+1\end{matrix}\right)$ $[\mathrm{Re}\,b>0;\ \mathrm{Re}\,s<-n]$
12	$\dfrac{e^{-b/\sqrt{x}}}{\sqrt{x+a}}\,T_n\left(\dfrac{2x}{a}+1\right)$	$\dfrac{(-1)^n\,a^{s-1/2}}{\sqrt{\pi}}\left(\dfrac{1-2s}{2}\right)_n\Gamma\!\left(\dfrac{1-2s-2n}{2}\right)$ $\times \Gamma(s)\,{}_2F_2\!\left(\begin{matrix}\frac{1-2s-2n}{2},\,\frac{1-2s+2n}{2}\\ \frac{1-2s}{2},\,1-s;\,-\frac{b^2}{4a}\end{matrix}\right)$ $+\dfrac{2b^{2s}}{\sqrt{a}}\,\Gamma(-2s)\,{}_2F_3\!\left(\begin{matrix}\frac{-2n+1}{2},\,\frac{2n+1}{2};\,-\frac{b^2}{4a}\\ \frac{1}{2},\,\frac{2s+1}{2},\,s+1\end{matrix}\right)$ $[\mathrm{Re}\,b>0;\ \mathrm{Re}\,s<1/2-n;\ |\arg a|<\pi]$
13	$\dfrac{e^{-bx}}{(x+a)^n}\,T_n\left(\dfrac{a-x}{a+x}\right)$	$\dfrac{a^{s-n}\left(\frac{1}{2}-s\right)_n}{n!\,\left(\frac{1}{2}\right)_n}\,\Gamma(s)\,\Gamma(n-s)\,{}_2F_2\!\left(\begin{matrix}s,\,\frac{2s+1}{2};\,ab\\ s-n+1,\,\frac{2s-2n+1}{2}\end{matrix}\right)$ $+(-1)^n\,b^{-s+n}\Gamma(s-n)\,{}_2F_2\!\left(\begin{matrix}n+\frac{1}{2},\,n;\,ab\\ \frac{1}{2},\,n-s+1\end{matrix}\right)$ $[\mathrm{Re}\,b,\ \mathrm{Re}\,s>0;\ |\arg a|<\pi]$
14	$(x+a)^n\,e^{-b/x}T_n\left(\dfrac{a-x}{a+x}\right)$	$a^n b^s\,\Gamma(-s)\,{}_2F_2\!\left(\begin{matrix}-n,\,\frac{1-2n}{2}\\ \frac{1}{2},\,s+1;\,\frac{b}{a}\end{matrix}\right)$ $[\mathrm{Re}\,b>0;\ \mathrm{Re}\,s<-n]$
15	$\dfrac{e^{-b/x}}{(x+a)^n}\,T_n\left(\dfrac{a-x}{a+x}\right)$	$\dfrac{n a^{s-n}}{n!}\dfrac{\left(\frac{1-2s}{2}\right)_n}{\left(\frac{1}{2}\right)_n}\,\Gamma(n-s)\,\Gamma(s)\,{}_2F_2\!\left(\begin{matrix}n-s,\,\frac{1-2s+2n}{2}\\ 1-s,\,\frac{1-2s}{2};\,\frac{b}{a}\end{matrix}\right)$ $+a^{-n}b^s\,\Gamma(-s)\,{}_2F_2\!\left(\begin{matrix}n,\,\frac{2n+1}{2}\\ \frac{1}{2},\,s+1;\,\frac{b}{a}\end{matrix}\right)$ $[\mathrm{Re}\,b>0;\ \mathrm{Re}\,s<n;\ |\arg a|<\pi]$

No.	$f(x)$	$F(s)$
16	$(x+a)^n e^{-b\sqrt{x}} T_n\left(\dfrac{a-x}{a+x}\right)$	$2(-1)^n b^{-2s-2n} \Gamma(2s+2n) \, {}_2F_3\left(\begin{matrix} -n, \frac{1-2n}{2}; -\frac{ab^2}{4} \\ \frac{1}{2}, \frac{1-2s-2n}{2}, 1-s-n \end{matrix}\right)$ $[\operatorname{Re}b, \ \operatorname{Re}s > 0]$
17	$\dfrac{e^{-b\sqrt{x}}}{(x+a)^n} T_n\left(\dfrac{a-x}{a+x}\right)$	$-\dfrac{na^{s-n+1/2}b}{n!}\dfrac{(-s)_n}{\left(\frac{1}{2}\right)_n}\Gamma\left(\dfrac{2s+1}{2}\right)\Gamma\left(\dfrac{2n-2s-1}{2}\right)$ $\times {}_2F_3\left(\begin{matrix} \frac{2s+1}{2}, s+1; -\frac{ab^2}{4} \\ \frac{3}{2}, s-n+1, \frac{2s-2n+3}{2} \end{matrix}\right) + \dfrac{na^{s-n}}{n!}\dfrac{\left(\frac{1-2s}{2}\right)_n}{\left(\frac{1}{2}\right)_n}$ $\times \Gamma(n-s)\Gamma(s)\, {}_2F_3\left(\begin{matrix} s, \frac{2s+1}{2}; -\frac{ab^2}{4} \\ \frac{1}{2}, s-n+1, \frac{2s-2n+1}{2} \end{matrix}\right)$ $+\dfrac{2(-1)^n}{b^{2(s-n)}}\Gamma(2s-2n)\, {}_2F_3\left(\begin{matrix} n, \frac{2n+1}{2}; -\frac{ab^2}{4} \\ \frac{1}{2}, \frac{1-2s+2n}{2}, 1-s+n \end{matrix}\right)$ $[\operatorname{Re}b, \ \operatorname{Re}s > 0; \ |\arg a| < \pi]$
18	$(x+a)^n e^{-b/\sqrt{x}} T_n\left(\dfrac{a-x}{a+x}\right)$	$2a^n b^{2s}\Gamma(-2s)\, {}_2F_3\left(\begin{matrix} -n, \frac{-2n+1}{2}; -\frac{b^2}{4a} \\ \frac{1}{2}, \frac{2s+1}{2}, s+1 \end{matrix}\right)$ $[\operatorname{Re}b > 0; \ \operatorname{Re}s < -n]$
19	$\dfrac{e^{-b/\sqrt{x}}}{(x+a)^n} T_n\left(\dfrac{a-x}{a+x}\right)$	$-\dfrac{na^{s-n-1/2}b}{n!}\dfrac{(1-s)_n}{\left(\frac{1}{2}\right)_n}\Gamma\left(\dfrac{1-2s+2n}{2}\right)\Gamma\left(\dfrac{2s-1}{2}\right)$ $\times {}_2F_3\left(\begin{matrix} n-s+1, \frac{1-2s+2n}{2} \\ \frac{3}{2}, \frac{3}{2}-s, 1-s; -\frac{b^2}{4a} \end{matrix}\right) + \dfrac{na^{s-n}}{n!}\dfrac{\left(\frac{1-2s}{2}\right)_n}{\left(\frac{1}{2}\right)_n}$ $\times \Gamma(n-s)\Gamma(s)\, {}_2F_3\left(\begin{matrix} \frac{1-2s+2n}{2}, n-s \\ \frac{1}{2}, 1-s, \frac{1-2s}{2}; -\frac{b^2}{4a} \end{matrix}\right)$ $+2a^{-n}b^{2s}\Gamma(-2s)\, {}_2F_3\left(\begin{matrix} n, \frac{2n+1}{2}; -\frac{b^2}{4a} \\ \frac{1}{2}, \frac{2s+1}{2}, s+1 \end{matrix}\right)$ $[\operatorname{Re}b > 0; \ \operatorname{Re}s < n; \ |\arg a| < \pi]$

3.20.3. $T_n(bx)$ and hyperbolic functions

Notation: $\delta = \left\{\begin{matrix} 1 \\ 0 \end{matrix}\right\}$.

No.	$f(x)$	$F(s)$
1	$(a^2-x^2)_+^{-1/2}\left\{\begin{matrix} \sinh(bx) \\ \cosh(bx) \end{matrix}\right\}$ $\times T_n\left(\dfrac{x}{a}\right)$	$\dfrac{\pi a^{s+\delta-1}b^\delta}{2^{s+\delta}}\Gamma\left[\begin{matrix} s+\delta \\ \frac{s-n+\delta+1}{2}, \frac{s+n+\delta+1}{2} \end{matrix}\right]$ $\times {}_2F_3\left(\begin{matrix} \frac{s+\delta}{2}, \frac{s+\delta+1}{2}; \frac{a^2b^2}{4} \\ \frac{2\delta+1}{2}, \frac{s-n+\delta+1}{2}, \frac{s+n+\delta+1}{2} \end{matrix}\right)$ $[a > 0; \ \operatorname{Re}s > ((-1)^n - 2\delta - 1)/2]$

3.20.4. $T_n\,(ax+b)$ and trigonometric functions

Notation: $\delta = \begin{Bmatrix} 1 \\ 0 \end{Bmatrix}$.

1	$\left(a^2 - x^2\right)_+^{-1/2} \begin{Bmatrix} \sin{(bx)} \\ \cos{(bx)} \end{Bmatrix}$ $\times T_n\left(\dfrac{x}{a}\right)$	$\dfrac{\pi\, a^{s+\delta-1} b^{\delta}}{2^{s+\delta}} \Gamma\left[\begin{matrix} s+\delta \\ \frac{s-n+\delta+1}{2}, \ \frac{s+n+\delta+1}{2} \end{matrix}\right]$ $\times {}_2F_3\left(\begin{matrix} \frac{s+\delta}{2}, \ \frac{s+\delta+1}{2}; \ -\frac{a^2 b^2}{4} \\ \frac{2\delta+1}{2}, \ \frac{s-n+\delta+1}{2}, \ \frac{s+n+\delta+1}{2} \end{matrix}\right)$ $[a > 0; \ \operatorname{Re} s > \left((-1)^n - 2\delta - 1\right)/2]$
2	$\left(a - x\right)_+^{-1/2} \begin{Bmatrix} \sin{(b\sqrt{x})} \\ \cos{(b\sqrt{x})} \end{Bmatrix}$ $\times T_n\left(\dfrac{2x}{a} - 1\right)$	$(-1)^n \sqrt{\pi}\, a^{s+(\delta-1)/2} b^{\delta} \left(\dfrac{1-2s-\delta}{2}\right)_n$ $\times \Gamma\left[\begin{matrix} \frac{2s+\delta}{2} \\ \frac{2s+2n+\delta+1}{2} \end{matrix}\right] {}_2F_3\left(\begin{matrix} \frac{2s+\delta}{2}, \ \frac{2s+\delta+1}{2}; \ -\frac{ab^2}{4} \\ \frac{2\delta+1}{2}, \ \frac{2s-2n+\delta+1}{2}, \ \frac{2s+2n+\delta+1}{2} \end{matrix}\right)$ $[a > 0; \ \operatorname{Re} s > -\delta/2]$

3.20.5. $T_n\,(ax+b)$ and the logarithmic function

Notation: $\varepsilon = 0$ or 1.

1	$\left(a - x\right)_+^{-1/2} \ln\dfrac{x}{a}\, T_n\left(\dfrac{x}{a}\right)$	$\sqrt{\pi}\, a^{s-1/2} \Gamma\left[\begin{matrix} s \\ \frac{2s+1}{2} \end{matrix}\right] \displaystyle\sum_{k=0}^{n} \dfrac{(-n)_k\,(n)_k}{2^k k!\,\left(\frac{2s+1}{2}\right)_k} \left[\psi\,(s) - \psi\left(\dfrac{2s+2k+1}{2}\right)\right]$ $[a > 0; \ \operatorname{Re} s > \left((-1)^n - 1\right)/2]$
2	$\left(a^2 - x^2\right)_+^{-1/2} \ln\left(bx^2 + 1\right)$ $\times T_n\left(\dfrac{x}{a}\right)$	$\dfrac{\pi}{2}\left(\dfrac{a}{2}\right)^{s+1} b\, \Gamma\left[\begin{matrix} s+2 \\ \frac{s-n+3}{2}, \ \frac{s+n+3}{2} \end{matrix}\right] {}_4F_3\left(\begin{matrix} 1, \ 1, \ \frac{s+2}{2}, \ \frac{s+3}{2}; \ -a^2 b \\ 2, \ \frac{s-n+3}{2}, \ \frac{s+n+3}{2} \end{matrix}\right)$ $[a > 0; \ \operatorname{Re} s > \left((-1)^n - 5\right)/2; \ |\arg b| < \pi]$
3	$\left(a^2 - x^2\right)_+^{-1/2} \ln\dfrac{b+x}{b-x}$ $\times T_n\left(\dfrac{x}{a}\right)$	$\pi\left(\dfrac{a}{2}\right)^{s} b^{-1} \Gamma\left[\begin{matrix} s+1 \\ \frac{s-n+2}{2}, \ \frac{s+n+2}{2} \end{matrix}\right] {}_4F_3\left(\begin{matrix} \frac{1}{2}, \ 1, \ \frac{s+1}{2}, \ \frac{s+2}{2}; \ \frac{a^2}{b^2} \\ \frac{3}{2}, \ \frac{s-n+2}{2}, \ \frac{s+n+2}{2} \end{matrix}\right)$ $[a > 0; \ \operatorname{Re} s > \left((-1)^n - 1\right)/2; \ |\arg b| < \pi]$
4	$\left(a^2 - x^2\right)_+^{-1/2}$ $\times \ln\left(\sqrt{b^2 x^2 + 1} + bx\right)$ $\times T_n\left(\dfrac{x}{a}\right)$	$\dfrac{\pi}{2}\left(\dfrac{a}{2}\right)^{s} b\, \Gamma\left[\begin{matrix} s+1 \\ \frac{s-n+2}{2}, \ \frac{s+n+2}{2} \end{matrix}\right] {}_4F_3\left(\begin{matrix} \frac{1}{2}, \ \frac{1}{2}, \ \frac{s+1}{2}, \ \frac{s+2}{2}; \ -a^2 b^2 \\ \frac{3}{2}, \ \frac{s-n+2}{2}, \ \frac{s+n+2}{2} \end{matrix}\right)$ $[a, b > 0; \ \operatorname{Re} s > \left((-1)^n - 3\right)/2]$

No.	$f(x)$	$F(s)$
5	$\dfrac{(a^2-x^2)_+^{-1/2}}{\sqrt{b^2x^2+1}}\,T_n\left(\dfrac{x}{a}\right)$ $\times \ln\left(bx+\sqrt{b^2x^2+1}\right)$	$\dfrac{\pi}{2}\left(\dfrac{a}{2}\right)^s b\,\Gamma\left[\begin{matrix}s+1\\ \frac{s-n+2}{2},\ \frac{s+n+2}{2}\end{matrix}\right]\,{}_4F_3\left(\begin{matrix}1,1,\frac{s+1}{2},\frac{s+2}{2};-a^2b^2\\ \frac{3}{2},\frac{s-n+2}{2},\frac{s+n+2}{2}\end{matrix}\right)$ $[a,b>0;\ \operatorname{Re}s>((-1)^n-3)/2]$
6	$(a^2-x^2)_+^{-1/2}$ $\times \ln^2\left(bx+\sqrt{b^2x^2+1}\right)$ $\times T_n\left(\dfrac{x}{a}\right)$	$\dfrac{\pi}{2}\left(\dfrac{a}{2}\right)^{s+1} b^2\,\Gamma\left[\begin{matrix}s+2\\ \frac{s-n+3}{2},\ \frac{s+n+3}{2}\end{matrix}\right]\,{}_5F_4\left(\begin{matrix}1,1,1,\frac{s+2}{2},\frac{s+3}{2};-a^2b^2\\ \frac{3}{2},2,\frac{s-n+3}{2},\frac{s+n+3}{2}\end{matrix}\right)$ $[a,b>0;\ \operatorname{Re}s>((-1)^n-5)/2]$
7	$\theta(a-x)\ln\dfrac{\sqrt{a}+\sqrt{a-x}}{\sqrt{x}}$ $\times T_{2n+\varepsilon}(bx)$	$\dfrac{(-1)^n\sqrt{\pi}\,(2n+1)^\varepsilon\,a^{s+\varepsilon}b^\varepsilon}{2(s+\varepsilon)}\,\Gamma\left[\begin{matrix}s+\varepsilon\\ \frac{2s+2\varepsilon+1}{2}\end{matrix}\right]$ $\times {}_5F_4\left(\begin{matrix}-n,\,n+\varepsilon,\,\frac{s+\varepsilon}{2},\,\frac{s+\varepsilon}{2},\,\frac{s+\varepsilon+1}{2};\,a^2b^2\\ \frac{2\varepsilon+1}{2},\,\frac{2s+2\varepsilon+1}{4},\,\frac{2s+2\varepsilon+3}{4},\,\frac{s+\varepsilon+2}{2}\end{matrix}\right)$ $[a>0;\ \operatorname{Re}s>-\varepsilon]$
8	$(a-x)_+^{-1/2}\ln\dfrac{x}{a}$ $\times T_n\left(\dfrac{2x}{a}-1\right)$	$(-1)^n\sqrt{\pi}\,a^{s-1/2}\left(\dfrac{1-2s}{2}\right)_n\Gamma\left[\begin{matrix}s\\ \frac{2s+2n+1}{2}\end{matrix}\right]\left[\psi(s)\right.$ $\left.+\psi\left(\dfrac{1-2s}{2}\right)-\psi\left(\dfrac{2s+2n+1}{2}\right)-\psi\left(\dfrac{1-2s+2n}{2}\right)\right]$ $[a,\ \operatorname{Re}s>0]$

3.20.6. $T_n(bx)$ and inverse trigonometric functions

Notation: $\varepsilon=0$ or 1.

1	$(a^2-x^2)_+^{-1/2}$ $\times \arcsin(bx)\,T_n\left(\dfrac{x}{a}\right)$	$\dfrac{\pi}{2}\left(\dfrac{a}{2}\right)^s b\,\Gamma\left[\begin{matrix}s+1\\ \frac{s-n+2}{2},\ \frac{s+n+2}{2}\end{matrix}\right]\,{}_4F_3\left(\begin{matrix}\frac{1}{2},\frac{1}{2},\frac{s+1}{2},\frac{s+2}{2};\,a^2b^2\\ \frac{3}{2},\frac{s-n+2}{2},\frac{s+n+2}{2}\end{matrix}\right)$ $[a>0;\ \operatorname{Re}s>((-1)^n-3)/2]$
2	$\dfrac{(a^2-x^2)_+^{-1/2}}{\sqrt{1-b^2x^2}}$ $\times \arcsin(bx)\,T_n\left(\dfrac{x}{a}\right)$	$\dfrac{\pi}{2}\left(\dfrac{a}{2}\right)^s b\,\Gamma\left[\begin{matrix}s+1\\ \frac{s-n+2}{2},\ \frac{s+n+2}{2}\end{matrix}\right]\,{}_4F_3\left(\begin{matrix}1,1,\frac{s+1}{2},\frac{s+2}{2};\,a^2b^2\\ \frac{3}{2},\frac{s-n+2}{2},\frac{s+n+2}{2}\end{matrix}\right)$ $[a>0;\ \operatorname{Re}s>((-1)^n-3)/2]$
3	$(a^2-x^2)_+^{-1/2}$ $\times \arctan(bx)\,T_n\left(\dfrac{x}{a}\right)$	$\dfrac{\pi}{2}\left(\dfrac{a}{2}\right)^s b\,\Gamma\left[\begin{matrix}s+1\\ \frac{s-n+2}{2},\ \frac{s+n+2}{2}\end{matrix}\right]\,{}_4F_3\left(\begin{matrix}\frac{1}{2},1,\frac{s+1}{2},\frac{s+2}{2};-a^2b^2\\ \frac{3}{2},\frac{s-n+2}{2},\frac{s+n+2}{2}\end{matrix}\right)$ $[a>0;\ \operatorname{Re}s>((-1)^n-3)/2]$

No.	$f(x)$	$F(s)$
4	$\left(a^2 - x^2\right)_+^{-1/2}$	$\dfrac{\pi}{2}\left(\dfrac{a}{2}\right)^{s+1} b^2 \Gamma\left[\begin{matrix} s+2 \\ \frac{s-n+3}{2},\ \frac{s+n+3}{2} \end{matrix}\right] {}_5F_4\left(\begin{matrix} 1,\,1,\,1,\,\frac{s+2}{2},\,\frac{s+3}{2};\ a^2 b^2 \\ \frac{3}{2},\,2,\,\frac{s-n+3}{2},\,\frac{s+n+3}{2} \end{matrix}\right)$
	$\times \arcsin^2(bx)\, T_n\left(\dfrac{x}{a}\right)$	$[a > 0;\ \operatorname{Re} s > ((-1)^n - 5)/2]$
5	$\theta(a - x) \arccos\dfrac{x}{a}$	$\dfrac{(-1)^n \sqrt{\pi}\,(2n+1)^\varepsilon\, a^{s+\varepsilon} b^\varepsilon}{2(s+\varepsilon)} \Gamma\left[\begin{matrix} \frac{s+\varepsilon+1}{2} \\ \frac{s+\varepsilon+2}{2} \end{matrix}\right]$
	$\times T_{2n+\varepsilon}(bx)$	$\times {}_4F_3\left(\begin{matrix} -n,\,n+\varepsilon,\,\frac{s+\varepsilon}{2},\,\frac{s+\varepsilon+1}{2};\ a^2 b^2 \\ \frac{2\varepsilon+1}{2},\,\frac{s+\varepsilon+2}{2},\,\frac{s+\varepsilon+2}{2} \end{matrix}\right) \quad [a > 0;\ \operatorname{Re} s > -\varepsilon]$

3.20.7. $T_n(ax + b)$ **and** $\operatorname{Ei}(cx^r)$

No.	$f(x)$	$F(s)$
1	$\left(a^2 - x^2\right)_+^{-1/2}\operatorname{Ei}(bx)$	$\dfrac{\pi a^s b}{2^{s+1}}\Gamma\left[\begin{matrix} s+1 \\ \frac{s-n+2}{2},\ \frac{s+n+2}{2} \end{matrix}\right] {}_3F_4\left(\begin{matrix} \frac{1}{2},\,\frac{s+1}{2},\,\frac{s+2}{2};\ \frac{a^2 b^2}{4} \\ \frac{3}{2},\,\frac{3}{2},\,\frac{s-n+2}{2},\,\frac{s+n+2}{2} \end{matrix}\right)$
	$\times T_n\left(\dfrac{x}{a}\right)$	$+\dfrac{\pi a^{s+1} b^2}{2^{s+4}}\Gamma\left[\begin{matrix} s+2 \\ \frac{s-n+3}{2},\ \frac{s+n+5}{2} \end{matrix}\right] {}_3F_4\left(\begin{matrix} 1,\,1,\,\frac{s+2}{2},\,\frac{s+3}{2};\ \frac{a^2 b^2}{4} \\ \frac{3}{2},\,2,\,2,\,\frac{s-n+3}{2},\,\frac{s+n+3}{2} \end{matrix}\right)$
		$+\dfrac{\pi a^{s-1}}{2^s}\Gamma\left[\begin{matrix} s \\ \frac{s-n+1}{2},\ \frac{s+n+1}{2} \end{matrix}\right]\left[\ln\dfrac{ab}{2} - \dfrac{1}{2}\psi\left(\dfrac{s+n+1}{2}\right)\right.$
		$\left. -\dfrac{1}{2}\psi\left(\dfrac{s-n+1}{2}\right) + \psi(s) + \mathbf{C}\right]$
		$[a > 0;\ \operatorname{Re} s > ((-1)^n - 1)/2]$
2	$\left(a^2 - x^2\right)_+^{-1/2}\operatorname{Ei}(bx^2)$	$\dfrac{\pi a^{s+1} b}{2^{s+2}}\Gamma\left[\begin{matrix} s+2 \\ \frac{s-n+3}{2},\ \frac{s+n+3}{2} \end{matrix}\right] {}_4F_4\left(\begin{matrix} 1,\,1,\,\frac{s+2}{2},\,\frac{s+3}{2};\ a^2 b \\ 2,\,2,\,\frac{s-n+3}{2},\,\frac{s+n+3}{2} \end{matrix}\right)$
	$\times T_n\left(\dfrac{x}{a}\right)$	$+\dfrac{\pi a^{s-1}}{2^s}\Gamma\left[\begin{matrix} s \\ \frac{s-n+1}{2},\ \frac{s+n+1}{2} \end{matrix}\right]\left[\ln\dfrac{a^2 b}{4} - \psi\left(\dfrac{s+n+1}{2}\right)\right.$
		$\left. -\psi\left(\dfrac{s-n+1}{2}\right) + 2\psi(s) + \mathbf{C}\right]\ [a > 0;\ \operatorname{Re} s > ((-1)^n - 1)/2]$
3	$(a - x)_+^{-1/2}\operatorname{Ei}(-bx)$	$(-1)^{n+1}\sqrt{\pi}\,a^{s+1/2} b\left(\dfrac{-2s-1}{2}\right)_n \Gamma\left[\begin{matrix} s+1 \\ \frac{2s+2n+3}{2} \end{matrix}\right]$
	$\times T_n\left(\dfrac{2x}{a} - 1\right)$	$\times {}_4F_4\left(\begin{matrix} 1,\,1,\,\frac{2s+3}{2},\,s+1;\ -ab \\ 2,\,2,\,\frac{2s-2n+3}{2},\,\frac{2s+2n+3}{2} \end{matrix}\right)$
		$+(-1)^n \sqrt{\pi}\,a^{s-1/2}\left(\dfrac{-2s+1}{2}\right)_n \Gamma\left[\begin{matrix} s \\ \frac{2s+2n+1}{2} \end{matrix}\right]$
		$\times\left[\psi(s) - \psi\left(\dfrac{2s+2n+1}{2}\right) - \sum_{i=0}^{n-1}\dfrac{2}{2i - 2s + 1} + \ln(ab) + \mathbf{C}\right]$
		$[a,\ \operatorname{Re} s > 0]$

3.20.8. $T_n(ax+b)$ **and** $\text{si}(cx^r)$, $\text{ci}(cx^r)$

1	$(a-x)_+^{-1/2}\left\{\begin{matrix}\text{si}(b\sqrt{x})\\ \text{ci}(b\sqrt{x})\end{matrix}\right\}$ $\times T_n\left(\dfrac{2x}{a}-1\right)$	$\dfrac{(-1)^{n+1}2^{\delta-2}\sqrt{\pi}\,a^{s+(\delta+1)/2}b^{\delta+2}}{3^{2\delta}}\left(\dfrac{-2s-\delta-1}{2}\right)_n\Gamma\!\left[\begin{matrix}\frac{2s+\delta+2}{2}\\ \frac{2s+2n+\delta+3}{2}\end{matrix}\right]$ $\times\,{}_4F_5\!\left(\begin{matrix}1,\,\frac{\delta+2}{2},\,\frac{2s+\delta+2}{2},\,\frac{2s+\delta+3}{2};\,-\frac{ab^2}{4}\\ 2,\,\frac{\delta+4}{2},\,\frac{2\delta+3}{2},\,\frac{2s-2n+\delta+3}{2},\,\frac{2s+2n+\delta+3}{2}\end{matrix}\right)$ $+(-1)^n\sqrt{\pi}\,a^{s+(\delta-1)/2}b^\delta\left(\dfrac{-2s-\delta+1}{2}\right)_n\Gamma\!\left[\begin{matrix}\frac{2s+\delta}{2}\\ \frac{2s+2n+\delta+1}{2}\end{matrix}\right]$ $\times\left[\dfrac{1}{2}\psi(s)-\dfrac{1}{2}\psi\left(\dfrac{2s+2n+1}{2}\right)-\sum_{i=0}^{n-1}\dfrac{1}{2i-2s+1}\right.$ $\left.+\dfrac{1}{2}\ln(ab^2)+\mathbf{C}\right]^{1-\delta}-\delta\dfrac{(-1)^n\pi^{3/2}a^{s-1/2}}{2}$ $\times\left(\dfrac{1-2s}{2}\right)_n\Gamma\!\left[\begin{matrix}s\\ \frac{2s+2n+1}{2}\end{matrix}\right]\quad\left[a,\;\text{Re}\,s>0;\,\delta=\left\{\begin{matrix}1\\ 0\end{matrix}\right\}\right]$

3.20.9. $T_n(ax+b)$ **and** $\text{erf}(cx^r)$, $\text{erfc}(cx^r)$

Notation: $\varepsilon=0$ or 1.

1	$(a^2-x^2)_+^{-1/2}$ $\times\,\text{erf}(bx)\,T_n\left(\dfrac{x}{a}\right)$	$\dfrac{\sqrt{\pi}\,a^s b}{2^s}\Gamma\!\left[\begin{matrix}s+1\\ \frac{s-n+2}{2},\,\frac{s+n+2}{2}\end{matrix}\right]{}_3F_3\!\left(\begin{matrix}\frac{1}{2},\,\frac{s+1}{2},\,\frac{s+2}{2};\,-a^2b^2\\ \frac{3}{2},\,\frac{s-n+2}{2},\,\frac{s+n+2}{2}\end{matrix}\right)$ $[a>0;\;\text{Re}\,s>((-1)^n-3)/2]$
2	$(a^2-x^2)_+^{-1/2}e^{b^2x^2}$ $\times\,\text{erf}(bx)\,T_n\left(\dfrac{x}{a}\right)$	$\dfrac{\sqrt{\pi}\,a^s b}{2^s}\Gamma\!\left[\begin{matrix}s+1\\ \frac{s-n+2}{2},\,\frac{s+n+2}{2}\end{matrix}\right]{}_3F_3\!\left(\begin{matrix}1,\,\frac{s+1}{2},\,\frac{s+2}{2};\,a^2b^2\\ \frac{3}{2},\,\frac{s-n+2}{2},\,\frac{s+n+2}{2}\end{matrix}\right)$ $[a>0;\;\text{Re}\,s>((-1)^n-3)/2]$
3	$\text{erfc}(ax)\,T_{2n+\varepsilon}(bx)$	$\dfrac{(-1)^n(2n+1)^\varepsilon b^\varepsilon}{\sqrt{\pi}\,(s+\varepsilon)a^{s+\varepsilon}}\Gamma\!\left(\dfrac{s+\varepsilon+1}{2}\right){}_3F_2\!\left(\begin{matrix}-n,\,n+\varepsilon,\,\frac{s+1}{2},\,\frac{s+2\varepsilon}{2}\\ \frac{2\varepsilon+1}{2},\,\frac{s+\varepsilon+2}{2};\,\frac{b^2}{a^2}\end{matrix}\right)$ $[\text{Re}\,s>-\varepsilon;\;|\arg a|<\pi/4]$
4	$\text{erfc}(bx)\,T_n\left(\dfrac{2x}{a}+1\right)$	$\dfrac{2n^2a^{-1}b^{-s-1}}{\sqrt{\pi}\,(s+1)}\Gamma\!\left(\dfrac{s+2}{2}\right){}_6F_4\!\left(\begin{matrix}\frac{1-n}{2},\,\frac{2-n}{2},\,\frac{n+1}{2},\,\frac{n+2}{2},\,\frac{s+1}{2},\,\frac{s+2}{2}\\ \frac{3}{2},\,\frac{3}{4},\,\frac{5}{4},\,\frac{s+3}{2},\,\frac{1}{a^2b^2}\end{matrix}\right)$ $+\dfrac{b^{-s}}{\sqrt{\pi}\,s}\Gamma\!\left(\dfrac{s+1}{2}\right){}_6F_4\!\left(\begin{matrix}-\frac{n}{2},\,\frac{1-n}{2},\,\frac{n}{2},\,\frac{n+1}{2},\,\frac{s}{2},\,\frac{s+1}{2}\\ \frac{1}{2},\,\frac{1}{4},\,\frac{3}{4},\,\frac{s+2}{2};\,\frac{1}{a^2b^2}\end{matrix}\right)$ $[\text{Re}\,s>0;\;|\arg b|<\pi/4]$
5	$\text{erfc}(b\sqrt{x})\,T_n\left(\dfrac{2x}{a}\pm1\right)$	$\dfrac{\delta_{n,0}+1}{2\sqrt{\pi}\,(s+n)}\left(\dfrac{4}{a}\right)^n b^{-2s-2n}\Gamma\!\left(s+n+\dfrac{1}{2}\right)$ $\times\,{}_3F_3\!\left(\begin{matrix}-n,\,\frac{1}{2}-n,\,-s-n;\,\pm ab^2\\ 1-2n,\,\frac{1}{2}-s-n,\,1-s-n\end{matrix}\right)$ $[\text{Re}\,s>((-1)^n-1)/2;\;|\arg b|<\pi/4]$

No.	$f(x)$	$F(s)$
6	$(a-x)_+^{-1/2}$ $\times \left\{ \begin{matrix} \mathrm{erf}\,(b\sqrt{x}) \\ \mathrm{erfc}\,(b\sqrt{x}) \end{matrix} \right\}$ $\times T_n\left(\dfrac{2x}{a}-1\right)$	$\pm 2\,(-1)^n\,a^s b\,(-s)_n\,\Gamma\!\left[\begin{matrix}\frac{2s+1}{2}\\ s+n+1\end{matrix}\right]\,{}_3F_3\!\left(\begin{matrix}\frac{1}{2},\ \frac{2s+1}{2},\ s+1;\ -ab^2\\ \frac{3}{2},\ s-n+1,\ s+n+1\end{matrix}\right)$ $+\left\{\begin{matrix}0\\1\end{matrix}\right\}(-1)^n\,\sqrt{\pi}\,a^{s-1/2}\left(\dfrac{1}{2}-s\right)_n\Gamma\!\left[\begin{matrix}s\\ s+n+\frac{1}{2}\end{matrix}\right]$ $[a>0;\ \mathrm{Re}\,s>-(1\pm 1)/4]$
7	$(a-x)_+^{-1/2}\,e^{b^2 x}$ $\times \mathrm{erf}\,(b\sqrt{x})$ $\times T_n\left(\dfrac{2x}{a}-1\right)$	$2\,(-1)^n\,a^s b\,(-s)_n\,\Gamma\!\left[\begin{matrix}\frac{2s+1}{2}\\ s+n+1\end{matrix}\right]\,{}_3F_3\!\left(\begin{matrix}1,\ \frac{2s+1}{2},\ s+1;\ ab^2\\ \frac{3}{2},\ s-n+1,\ s+n+1\end{matrix}\right)$ $[a>0;\ \mathrm{Re}\,s>-1/2]$

3.20.10. $T_n\,(bx)$ **and** $\Gamma\,(\nu,\,ax),\ \gamma\,(\nu,\,ax)$

Notation: $\varepsilon = 0$ or 1.

1	$(a^2-x^2)_+^{-1/2}$ $\times \gamma\left(\nu,\,b^2 x^2\right) T_n\left(\dfrac{x}{a}\right)$	$\dfrac{\pi}{2\nu}\left(\dfrac{a}{2}\right)^{s+2\nu-1} b^{2\nu}\,\Gamma\!\left[\begin{matrix}s+2\nu\\ \frac{s-n+2\nu+1}{2},\ \frac{s+n+2\nu+1}{2}\end{matrix}\right]$ $\times\,{}_3F_3\!\left(\begin{matrix}\nu,\ \frac{s+2\nu}{2},\ \frac{s+2\nu+1}{2};\ -a^2 b^2\\ \nu+1,\ \frac{s-n+2\nu+1}{2},\ \frac{s+n+2\nu+1}{2}\end{matrix}\right)$ $[a>0;\ \mathrm{Re}\,(s+2\nu)>((-1)^n-1)/2]$
2	$(a^2-x^2)_+^{-1/2}\,e^{bx}$ $\times \gamma\left(\nu,\,bx\right) T_n\left(\dfrac{x}{a}\right)$	$\dfrac{\pi}{2\nu}\left(\dfrac{a}{2}\right)^{s+\nu-1} b^{\nu}\,\Gamma\!\left[\begin{matrix}s+\nu\\ \frac{s-n+\nu+1}{2},\ \frac{s+n+\nu+1}{2}\end{matrix}\right]$ $\times\,{}_3F_4\!\left(\begin{matrix}1,\ \frac{s+\nu}{2},\ \frac{s+\nu+1}{2};\ \frac{a^2 b^2}{4}\\ \frac{\nu+1}{2},\ \frac{\nu+2}{2},\ \frac{s-n+\nu+1}{2},\ \frac{s+n+\nu+1}{2}\end{matrix}\right)$ $+\dfrac{\pi}{2\nu\,(\nu+1)}\left(\dfrac{a}{2}\right)^{s+\nu} b^{\nu+1}\,\Gamma\!\left[\begin{matrix}s+\nu+1\\ \frac{s-n+\nu+2}{2},\ \frac{s+n+\nu+2}{2}\end{matrix}\right]$ $\times\,{}_3F_4\!\left(\begin{matrix}1,\ \frac{s+\nu+1}{2},\ \frac{s+\nu+2}{2};\ \frac{a^2 b^2}{4}\\ \frac{\nu+2}{2},\ \frac{\nu+3}{2},\ \frac{s-n+\nu+2}{2},\ \frac{s+n+\nu+2}{2}\end{matrix}\right)$ $[a>0;\ \mathrm{Re}\,(s+\nu)>((-1)^n-1)/2]$
3	$(a^2-x^2)_+^{-1/2}\,e^{b^2 x^2}$ $\times \gamma\left(\nu,\,b^2 x^2\right) T_n\left(\dfrac{x}{a}\right)$	$\dfrac{\pi}{2\nu}\left(\dfrac{a}{2}\right)^{s+2\nu-1} b^{2\nu}\,\Gamma\!\left[\begin{matrix}s+2\nu\\ \frac{s-n+2\nu+1}{2},\ \frac{s+n+2\nu+1}{2}\end{matrix}\right]$ $\times\,{}_3F_3\!\left(\begin{matrix}1,\ \frac{s+2\nu}{2},\ \frac{s+2\nu+1}{2};\ a^2 b^2\\ \nu+1,\ \frac{s-n+2\nu+1}{2},\ \frac{s+n+2\nu+1}{2}\end{matrix}\right)$ $[a>0;\ \mathrm{Re}\,(s+2\nu)>((-1)^n-1)/2]$

No.	$f(x)$	$F(s)$
4	$\Gamma(\nu, ax)\, T_{2n+\varepsilon}(bx)$	$\dfrac{(-1)^n (2n+1)^\varepsilon a^{-s-\varepsilon} b^\varepsilon}{s+\varepsilon}\,\Gamma(s+\nu+\varepsilon)$ $\times\, {}_5F_2\left(\begin{matrix} -n,\ n+\varepsilon,\ \frac{s+\varepsilon}{2},\ \frac{s+\nu+\varepsilon}{2},\ \frac{s+\nu+\varepsilon+1}{2} \\ \frac{2\varepsilon+1}{2},\ \frac{s+\varepsilon+2}{2};\ \frac{4b^2}{a^2} \end{matrix}\right)$ $[\operatorname{Re}a>0;\ \operatorname{Re}s,\ \operatorname{Re}(s+\nu)>-\varepsilon]$

3.20.11. $T_n(\varphi(x))$ **and** $J_\nu(cx^r),\ I_\nu(cx)$

Notation: $\varepsilon=0$ or 1.

1	$(a^2-x^2)_+^{-1/2}\left\{\begin{matrix} J_\nu(bx) \\ I_\nu(bx) \end{matrix}\right\}$ $\times\, T_n\left(\dfrac{x}{a}\right)$	$\dfrac{\pi}{2}\left(\dfrac{a}{2}\right)^{s+\nu-1}\left(\dfrac{b}{2}\right)^\nu\Gamma\left[\begin{matrix} s+\nu \\ \nu+1,\ \frac{s-n+\nu+1}{2},\ \frac{s+n+\nu+1}{2} \end{matrix}\right]$ $\times\, {}_2F_3\left(\begin{matrix} \frac{s+\nu}{2},\ \frac{s+\nu+1}{2};\ \frac{a^2b^2}{4} \\ \nu+1,\ \frac{s-n+\nu+1}{2},\ \frac{s+n+\nu+1}{2} \end{matrix}\right)$ $[a>0;\ \operatorname{Re}(s+\nu)>((-1)^n-1)/2]$
2	$(a^2-x^2)_+^{-1/2}\, J_\nu\left(\dfrac{b}{x}\right)$ $\times\, T_{2n+\varepsilon}\left(\dfrac{x}{a}\right)$	$\dfrac{(-1)^n\sqrt{\pi}\,a^{s-\nu-1}b^\nu}{2^{\nu+1}}\left(\dfrac{1-s+\nu+\varepsilon}{2}\right)_n\Gamma\left[\begin{matrix} \frac{s-\nu+\varepsilon}{2} \\ \nu+1,\ \frac{s+2n-\nu+\varepsilon+1}{2} \end{matrix}\right]$ $\times\, {}_2F_3\left(\begin{matrix} \frac{1-s+2n+\nu+\varepsilon}{2},\ \frac{1-s-2n+\nu-\varepsilon}{2} \\ \nu+1,\ \frac{\nu-s+1}{2},\ \frac{\nu-s+2}{2};\ -\frac{b^2}{4a^2} \end{matrix}\right)$ $+\dfrac{(-1)^n(2n+\varepsilon)n^{\varepsilon-1}a^{-\varepsilon-1}b^{s+\varepsilon}}{2^{s+2}}\,\Gamma\left[\begin{matrix} -\frac{s-\nu+\varepsilon}{2} \\ \frac{s+\nu+\varepsilon+2}{2} \end{matrix}\right]$ $\times\, {}_2F_3\left(\begin{matrix} \frac{1-2n}{2},\ \frac{2n+2\varepsilon+1}{2};\ -\frac{b^2}{4a^2} \\ \frac{2\varepsilon+1}{2},\ \frac{s-\nu+\varepsilon+2}{2},\ \frac{s+\nu+\varepsilon+2}{2} \end{matrix}\right)$ $[a,b>0;\ \operatorname{Re}s>-\varepsilon-3/2]$
3	$(a-x)_+^{-1/2}\left\{\begin{matrix} J_\nu(b\sqrt{x}) \\ I_\nu(b\sqrt{x}) \end{matrix}\right\}$ $\times\, T_n\left(\dfrac{2x}{a}-1\right)$	$\dfrac{(-1)^n\sqrt{\pi}\,a^{s+(\nu-1)/2}b^\nu}{2^\nu}\left(\dfrac{-2s-\nu+1}{2}\right)_n$ $\times\,\Gamma\left[\begin{matrix} \frac{2s+\nu}{2} \\ \nu+1,\ \frac{2s+2n+\nu+1}{2} \end{matrix}\right]{}_2F_3\left(\begin{matrix} \frac{2s+\nu}{2},\ \frac{2s+\nu+1}{2};\ \mp\frac{ab^2}{4} \\ \nu+1,\ \frac{2s-2n+\nu+1}{2},\ \frac{2s+2n+\nu+1}{2} \end{matrix}\right)$ $[a>0;\ \operatorname{Re}s>-\operatorname{Re}\nu/2]$
4	$J_\nu(b\sqrt{x})\, T_n\left(\dfrac{2x}{a}\pm 1\right)$	$\dfrac{2^{2s+4n-1}(\delta_{n,0}+1)}{a^n b^{2s+2n}}\,\Gamma\left[\begin{matrix} \frac{2s+2n+\nu}{2} \\ \frac{2-2s-2n+\nu}{2} \end{matrix}\right]$ $\times\, {}_2F_3\left(\begin{matrix} -n,\ \frac{1}{2}-n;\ \pm\frac{ab^2}{4} \\ 1-2n,\ \frac{2-2s-2n-\nu}{2},\ \frac{2-2s-2n+\nu}{2} \end{matrix}\right)$ $[b>0;\ -\operatorname{Re}\nu/2<\operatorname{Re}s<3/4-n]$

No.	$f(x)$	$F(s)$

5 $\dfrac{J_\nu(b\sqrt{x})}{\sqrt{x}+a}\,T_n\!\left(\dfrac{2x}{a}+1\right)$

$$\frac{(-1)^n\,a^{s+(\nu-1)/2}b^\nu}{2^\nu\sqrt{\pi}}\left(\frac{1-2s-\nu}{2}\right)_n\Gamma\!\left[\begin{matrix}\dfrac{2s+\nu}{2},\ \dfrac{-2s-2n-\nu+1}{2}\\[2pt]\nu+1\end{matrix}\right]$$

$$\times\,{}_2F_3\!\left(\begin{matrix}\dfrac{2s+\nu}{2},\ \dfrac{2s+\nu+1}{2};\ \dfrac{ab^2}{4}\\[2pt]\nu+1,\ \dfrac{2s-2n+\nu+1}{2},\ \dfrac{2s+2n+\nu+1}{2}\end{matrix}\right)$$

$$+\frac{(\delta_{n,0}+1)\,2^{2s+4n-2}}{n!\,a^n b^{2s+2n-1}}\,\Gamma\!\left[\begin{matrix}\dfrac{2s+2n+\nu-1}{2}\\[2pt]\dfrac{-2s-2n+\nu+3}{2}\end{matrix}\right]$$

$$\times\,{}_2F_3\!\left(\begin{matrix}\dfrac{-2n+1}{2},\ -n+1;\ \dfrac{ab^2}{4}\\[2pt]-2n+1,\ \dfrac{-2s-2n-\nu+3}{2},\ \dfrac{-2s-2n-\nu+3}{2}\end{matrix}\right)$$

$$[b>0;\ -\operatorname{Re}\nu/2<\operatorname{Re}s<5/4-n;\ |\arg a|<\pi]$$

6 $(a-x)_+^{-1/2}\,J_\nu\!\left(\dfrac{b}{\sqrt{x}}\right)$ $\times T_n\!\left(\dfrac{2x}{a}-1\right)$

$$\frac{(-1)^n\sqrt{\pi}\,a^{s-(\nu+1)/2}b^\nu}{2^\nu}\left(\frac{1-2s+\nu}{2}\right)_n\Gamma\!\left[\begin{matrix}\dfrac{2s-\nu}{2}\\[2pt]\nu+1,\ \dfrac{2s+2n-\nu+1}{2}\end{matrix}\right]$$

$$\times\,{}_2F_3\!\left(\begin{matrix}\dfrac{1-2s-2n+\nu}{2},\ \dfrac{1-2s+2n+\nu}{2};\ -\dfrac{b^2}{4a}\\[2pt]\nu+1,\ \dfrac{1-2s+\nu}{2},\ \dfrac{2-2s+\nu}{2}\end{matrix}\right)$$

$$+\frac{(-1)^n\,a^{-1/2}b^{2s}}{2^{2s}}\,\Gamma\!\left[\begin{matrix}\dfrac{\nu-2s}{2}\\[2pt]\dfrac{2s+\nu+2}{2}\end{matrix}\right]{}_2F_3\!\left(\begin{matrix}\dfrac{-2n+1}{2},\ \dfrac{2n+1}{2};\ -\dfrac{b^2}{4a}\\[2pt]\dfrac12,\ \dfrac{2s-\nu+2}{2},\ \dfrac{2s+\nu+2}{2}\end{matrix}\right)$$

$$[a,b>0;\ \operatorname{Re}s>-3/4]$$

7 $J_\nu\!\left(\dfrac{b}{\sqrt{x}}\right)T_n\!\left(\dfrac{2x}{a}\pm1\right)$

$$(\pm1)^n\left(\frac{b}{2}\right)^{2s}\Gamma\!\left[\begin{matrix}\dfrac{\nu-2s}{2}\\[2pt]\dfrac{2s+\nu+2}{2}\end{matrix}\right]{}_2F_3\!\left(\begin{matrix}-n,\ n;\ \pm\dfrac{b^2}{4a}\\[2pt]\dfrac12,\ \dfrac{2s-\nu+2}{2},\ \dfrac{2s+\nu+2}{2}\end{matrix}\right)$$

$$[b>0;\ -3/4<\operatorname{Re}s<\operatorname{Re}\nu/2-n]$$

8 $\dfrac{1}{\sqrt{x}+a}\,J_\nu\!\left(\dfrac{b}{\sqrt{x}}\right)$ $\times T_n\!\left(\dfrac{2x}{a}+1\right)$

$$\frac{(-1)^n\,a^{s-(\nu+1)/2}b^\nu}{2^\nu\sqrt{\pi}}\left(\frac{1-2s+\nu}{2}\right)_n\Gamma\!\left[\begin{matrix}\dfrac{2s-\nu}{2},\ \dfrac{1-2s-2n+\nu}{2}\\[2pt]\nu+1\end{matrix}\right]$$

$$\times\,{}_2F_3\!\left(\begin{matrix}\dfrac{1-2s-2n+\nu}{2},\ \dfrac{1-2s+2n+\nu}{2}\\[2pt]\nu+1,\ \dfrac{1-2s+\nu}{2},\ \dfrac{2-2s+\nu}{2};\ \dfrac{b^2}{4a}\end{matrix}\right)$$

$$+\frac{a^{-1/2}b^{2s}}{2^{2s}}\,\Gamma\!\left[\begin{matrix}\dfrac{\nu-2s}{2}\\[2pt]\dfrac{2s+\nu+2}{2}\end{matrix}\right]{}_2F_3\!\left(\begin{matrix}\dfrac{-2n+1}{2},\ \dfrac{2n+1}{2};\ \dfrac{b^2}{4a}\\[2pt]\dfrac12,\ \dfrac{2s-\nu+2}{2},\ \dfrac{2s+\nu+2}{2}\end{matrix}\right)$$

$$[b>0;\ -3/4<\operatorname{Re}s<1/2-n+\operatorname{Re}\nu/2;\ |\arg a|<\pi]$$

9 $(a-x)_+^{-1/2}$ $\times\left\{\begin{matrix}J_\mu(b\sqrt{x})\,J_\nu(b\sqrt{x})\\I_\mu(b\sqrt{x})\,I_\nu(b\sqrt{x})\end{matrix}\right\}$ $\times T_n\!\left(1-\dfrac{2x}{a}\right)$

$$\sqrt{\pi}\,a^{s+(\mu+\nu-1)/2}\,(b/2)^{\mu+\nu}\left(\frac{1-2s-\mu-\nu}{2}\right)_n$$

$$\times\,\Gamma\!\left[\begin{matrix}\dfrac{2s+\mu+\nu}{2}\\[2pt]\mu+1,\ \nu+1,\ \dfrac{2s+2n+\mu+\nu+1}{2}\end{matrix}\right]$$

$$\times\,{}_4F_5\!\left(\begin{matrix}\dfrac{\mu+\nu+1}{2},\ \dfrac{\mu+\nu+2}{2},\ \dfrac{2s+\mu+\nu}{2},\ \dfrac{2s+\mu+\nu+1}{2};\ \mp ab^2\\[2pt]\mu+1,\ \nu+1,\ \mu+\nu+1,\ \dfrac{2s-2n+\mu+\nu+1}{2},\ \dfrac{2s+2n+\mu+\nu+1}{2}\end{matrix}\right)$$

$$[a,\ \operatorname{Re}(2s+\mu+\nu)>0]$$

No.	$f(x)$	$F(s)$
10	$(x+a)^n J_\nu(b\sqrt{x})$ $\times T_n\left(\dfrac{a-x}{a+x}\right)$	$(-1)^n \left(\dfrac{2}{b}\right)^{2s+2n} \Gamma\left[\begin{array}{c} \frac{2s+2n+\nu}{2} \\ \frac{2-2s-2n+\nu}{2} \end{array}\right] {}_2F_3\left(\begin{array}{c} -n,\ \frac{1-2n}{2};\ \frac{ab^2}{4} \\ \frac{1}{2},\ \frac{2-2s-2n-\nu}{2},\ \frac{2-2s-2n+\nu}{2} \end{array}\right)$ $[b>0;\ -\operatorname{Re}\nu/2 < \operatorname{Re}s < 3/4-n]$
11	$\dfrac{1}{(x+a)^n} J_\nu(b\sqrt{x})$ $\times T_n\left(\dfrac{a-x}{a+x}\right)$	$\dfrac{na^{s-n+\nu/2}b^\nu}{2^\nu n!} \dfrac{\left(\frac{1-2s-\nu}{2}\right)_n}{\left(\frac{1}{2}\right)_n} \Gamma\left[\begin{array}{c} \frac{2s+\nu}{2},\ \frac{2n-2s-\nu}{2} \\ \nu+1 \end{array}\right]$ $\times {}_2F_3\left(\begin{array}{c} \frac{2s+\nu}{2},\ \frac{2s+\nu+1}{2};\ \frac{ab^2}{4} \\ \nu+1,\ \frac{2s-2n+\nu+1}{2},\ \frac{2s-2n+\nu+2}{2} \end{array}\right) + (-1)^n \left(\dfrac{b}{2}\right)^{2(n-s)}$ $\times \Gamma\left[\begin{array}{c} \frac{2s-2n+\nu}{2} \\ \frac{2-2s+2n+\nu}{2} \end{array}\right] {}_2F_3\left(\begin{array}{c} n,\ \frac{2n+1}{2};\ \frac{ab^2}{4} \\ \frac{1}{2},\ \frac{2-2s+2n-\nu}{2},\ \frac{2-2s+2n+\nu}{2} \end{array}\right)$ $[b>0;\ -\operatorname{Re}\nu/2 < \operatorname{Re}s < n+3/4;\ |\arg a| < \pi]$

3.20.12. $T_n(\varphi(x))$ **and** $K_\nu(cx^r)$

Notation: $\varepsilon = 0$ or 1.

	$f(x)$	$F(s)$
1	$K_\nu(b\sqrt{x}) T_n\left(\dfrac{2x}{a} \pm 1\right)$	$\dfrac{2^{2s+4n-2}(\delta_{n,0}+1)}{a^n b^{2s+2n}} \Gamma\left(s+n-\dfrac{\nu}{2}\right)\Gamma\left(s+n+\dfrac{\nu}{2}\right)$ $\times {}_2F_3\left(\begin{array}{c} -n,\ \frac{1}{2}-n;\ \mp\frac{ab^2}{4} \\ 1-2n,\ \frac{2-2s-2n-\nu}{2},\ \frac{2-2s-2n+\nu}{2} \end{array}\right)$ $[b>0;\ \operatorname{Re}s > |\operatorname{Re}\nu|/2]$
2	$\dfrac{1}{\sqrt{x+a}} K_\nu(b\sqrt{x})$ $\times T_n\left(\dfrac{2x}{a}+1\right)$	$\dfrac{(-1)^n a^{s-(\nu+1)/2}b^{-\nu}}{2^{-\nu+1}\sqrt{\pi}} \left(\dfrac{1-2s+\nu}{2}\right)_n \Gamma\left(\dfrac{1-2n-2s+\nu}{2}\right)$ $\times \Gamma\left(\dfrac{2s-\nu}{2}\right) {}_2F_3\left(\begin{array}{c} \frac{2s-\nu}{2},\ \frac{2s-\nu+1}{2};\ -\frac{ab^2}{4} \\ 1-\nu,\ \frac{s-2n-\nu+1}{2},\ \frac{s+2n-\nu+1}{2} \end{array}\right)$ $+ \dfrac{(-1)^n a^{s+(\nu-1)/2}b^\nu}{2^{\nu+1}\sqrt{\pi}} \left(\dfrac{1-2s-\nu}{2}\right)_n \Gamma\left(\dfrac{1-2s-2n-\nu}{2}\right)$ $\times \Gamma\left(\dfrac{2s+\nu}{2}\right) {}_2F_3\left(\begin{array}{c} \frac{2s+\nu}{2},\ \frac{2s+\nu+1}{2};\ -\frac{ab^2}{4} \\ \nu+1,\ \frac{s-2n+\nu+1}{2},\ \frac{s+2n+\nu+1}{2} \end{array}\right)$ $+ \dfrac{(\delta_{n,0}+1)2^{2s+4n-2}}{a^n b^{2s+2n-1}} \Gamma\left(\dfrac{2s+2n-\nu-1}{2}\right)$ $\times \Gamma\left(\dfrac{2s+2n+\nu-1}{2}\right) {}_2F_3\left(\begin{array}{c} \frac{-2n+1}{2},\ -n+1;\ -\frac{ab^2}{4} \\ -2n+1,\ \frac{3-2s-2n-\nu}{2},\ \frac{3-2s-2n+\nu}{2} \end{array}\right)$ $[\operatorname{Re}b>0;\ \operatorname{Re}s > |\operatorname{Re}\nu|/2;\ |\arg a| < \pi]$

No.	$f(x)$	$F(s)$

3 $K_\nu\left(\dfrac{b}{\sqrt{x}}\right) T_n\left(\dfrac{2x}{a} \pm 1\right)$

$$\frac{(\pm 1)^n}{2}\left(\frac{b}{2}\right)^{2s}\Gamma\left(\frac{\nu-2s}{2}\right)\Gamma\left(\frac{-\nu-2s}{2}\right)$$

$$\times {}_2F_3\left(\begin{matrix}-n,\; n;\; \mp\frac{b^2}{4a}\\[2pt] \frac{1}{2},\; \frac{2s-\nu+2}{2},\; \frac{2s+\nu+2}{2}\end{matrix}\right)$$

$$[\operatorname{Re} b > 0;\; \operatorname{Re} s < -n - |\operatorname{Re}\nu|/2]$$

4 $\dfrac{1}{\sqrt{x+a}}K_\nu\left(\dfrac{b}{\sqrt{x}}\right)$
$\times T_n\left(\dfrac{2x}{a}+1\right)$

$$\frac{b^{2s}}{2^{2s+1}\sqrt{a}}\Gamma\left(-\frac{\nu}{2}-s\right)\Gamma\left(\frac{\nu}{2}-s\right){}_2F_3\left(\begin{matrix}\frac{-2n+1}{2},\; \frac{2n+1}{2};\; -\frac{b^2}{4a}\\[2pt] \frac{1}{2},\; \frac{2s-\nu+2}{2},\; \frac{2s+\nu+2}{2}\end{matrix}\right)$$

$$+\frac{(-1)^n a^{s+(\nu-1)/2}b^{-\nu}}{2^{-\nu+1}\sqrt{\pi}}\left(\frac{1-2s-\nu}{2}\right)_n$$

$$\times \Gamma\left[\nu,\; \frac{2s+\nu}{2},\; \frac{1-2s-2n-\nu}{2}\right]$$

$$\times {}_2F_3\left(\begin{matrix}\frac{1-2s+2n-\nu}{2},\; \frac{1-2s-2n-\nu}{2}\\[2pt] 1-\nu,\; \frac{1-2s-\nu}{2},\; \frac{2-2s-\nu}{2};\; -\frac{b^2}{4a}\end{matrix}\right)$$

$$+\frac{(-1)^n a^{s-(\nu+1)/2}b^{\nu}}{2^{\nu+1}\sqrt{\pi}}\left(\frac{1-2s+\nu}{2}\right)_n$$

$$\times \Gamma\left[-\nu,\; \frac{2s-\nu}{2},\; \frac{1-2s-2n+\nu}{2}\right]$$

$$\times {}_2F_3\left(\begin{matrix}\frac{1-2s+2n+\nu}{2},\; \frac{1-2s-2n+\nu}{2}\\[2pt] \nu+1,\; \frac{1-2s+\nu}{2},\; \frac{2-2s+\nu}{2};\; -\frac{b^2}{4a}\end{matrix}\right)$$

$$[\operatorname{Re} b > 0;\; \operatorname{Re} s < (1-2n-|\operatorname{Re}\nu|)/2;\; |\arg a| < \pi]$$

5 $(x+a)^n K_\nu(b\sqrt{x})$
$\times T_n\left(\dfrac{a-x}{a+x}\right)$

$$(-1)^n 2^{2s+2n-1}b^{-2s-2n}\Gamma\left(s+n-\frac{\nu}{2}\right)\Gamma\left(s+n+\frac{\nu}{2}\right)$$

$$\times {}_2F_3\left(\begin{matrix}-n,\; \frac{1-2n}{2};\; -\frac{ab^2}{4}\\[2pt] \frac{1}{2},\; \frac{2-2s-2n-\nu}{2},\; \frac{2-2s-2n+\nu}{2}\end{matrix}\right)$$

$$[\operatorname{Re} b > 0;\; \operatorname{Re} s > |\operatorname{Re}\nu|/2]$$

3.20.13. $T_n(bx)$ and $H_\nu(ax)$, $L_\nu(ax)$

1 $(a^2-x^2)_+^{-1/2}\left\{\begin{matrix}H_\nu(bx)\\ L_\nu(bx)\end{matrix}\right\}$
$\times T_n\left(\dfrac{x}{a}\right)$

$$\frac{\sqrt{\pi}}{2^{\nu+1}}\left(\frac{a}{2}\right)^{s+\nu}b^{\nu+1}\Gamma\left[\begin{matrix}s+\nu+1\\[2pt] \frac{2\nu+3}{2},\; \frac{s-n+\nu+2}{2},\; \frac{s+n+\nu+2}{2}\end{matrix}\right]$$

$$\times {}_3F_3\left(\begin{matrix}1,\; \frac{s+\nu+1}{2},\; \frac{s+\nu+2}{2}\\[2pt] \frac{3}{2},\; \frac{s+n+\nu+2}{2},\; \frac{3s-3n+7\nu+6}{2};\; \mp\frac{a^2b^2}{4}\end{matrix}\right)$$

$$[a > 0;\; \operatorname{Re}(s+\nu) > ((-1)^n - 3)/2]$$

3.20.14. $T_n(ax+b)$ and $P_m(\varphi(x))$

Notation: $\delta, \varepsilon = 0$ or 1.

1	$\theta(a-x)P_m\left(\dfrac{x}{a}\right)$ $\times T_{2n+\varepsilon}(bx)$	$\dfrac{(-1)^n(2n+\varepsilon)\sqrt{\pi}}{2^{s+1}n!}\cdot a^{s+\varepsilon}b^\varepsilon\,\Gamma\left[\begin{matrix}n+\varepsilon,\ s+\varepsilon\\\frac{s-m+\varepsilon+1}{2},\ \frac{s+m+\varepsilon+2}{2}\end{matrix}\right]$ $\times {}_4F_3\left(\begin{matrix}-n,\ n+\varepsilon,\ \frac{s+\varepsilon}{2},\ \frac{s+\varepsilon+1}{2};\ a^2b^2\\\frac{2\varepsilon+1}{2},\ \frac{s-m+\varepsilon+1}{2},\ \frac{s+m+\varepsilon+2}{2}\end{matrix}\right)$ $[a>0;\ \operatorname{Re}s>((-1)^m+(-1)^\varepsilon)/2-1]$
2	$(x^2-a^2)_+^{-1/2}$ $\times P_{2m+\varepsilon}\left(\dfrac{x}{b}\right)T_{2n+\delta}\left(\dfrac{x}{a}\right)$	$\dfrac{2^{2m+\varepsilon-1}\sqrt{\pi}\,a^{s+2m+\varepsilon-1}}{(2m+\varepsilon)!\,b^{2m+\varepsilon}}\left(\dfrac{1}{2}\right)_{2m+\varepsilon}\left(\dfrac{1-s-2m+\delta-\varepsilon}{2}\right)_n$ $\times\Gamma\left[\begin{matrix}\frac{1-s-2m-2n-\delta-\varepsilon}{2}\\\frac{2-s-2m-\delta-\varepsilon}{2}\end{matrix}\right]$ $\times {}_4F_3\left(\begin{matrix}-m,\ \frac{1-2m-2\varepsilon}{2},\ \frac{1-s-2m-2n-\delta-\varepsilon}{2},\ \frac{1-s-2m+2n+\delta-\varepsilon}{2}\\\frac{1-4m-2\varepsilon}{2},\ \frac{2-s-2m-2\varepsilon}{2},\ \frac{1-s-2m}{2};\ \frac{b^2}{a^2}\end{matrix}\right)$ $[a,b>0;\ \operatorname{Re}s<1-2m-2n-\delta-\varepsilon]$
3	$\theta(x-a)(x^2-b^2)^{-1/2}$ $\times P_{2m+\varepsilon}\left(\dfrac{x}{a}\right)T_{2n+\delta}\left(\dfrac{x}{b}\right)$	$\dfrac{(-1)^{m-1}2^{2n+\delta-2}a^{s+2n+\delta-1}}{b^{2n+\delta}}\dfrac{\left(\frac{2-s-2n-\delta+\varepsilon}{2}\right)_m}{\left(\frac{s+2n+\delta+\varepsilon-1}{2}\right)_{m+1}}$ $\times {}_4F_3\left(\begin{matrix}\frac{1-2n}{2},\ 1-n-\delta,\ \frac{2-s+2m-2n-\delta+\varepsilon}{2},\ \frac{1-s-2m-2n-\delta-\varepsilon}{2}\\1-2n-\delta,\ \frac{2-s-2n}{2},\ \frac{3-s-2n-2\delta}{2};\ \frac{b^2}{a^2}\end{matrix}\right)$ $[a>b>0;\ \operatorname{Re}s<1-2m-2n-\delta-\varepsilon]$
4	$\theta(a-x)P_m\left(\dfrac{2x}{a}-1\right)$ $\times T_n\left(\dfrac{2x}{a}-1\right)$	$\dfrac{(-1)^{m+n}(1-s)_m\,a^s}{(s)_{m+1}}\,{}_4F_3\left(\begin{matrix}-n,\ n,\ s,\ s;\ 1\\\frac{1}{2},\ s-m,\ s+m+1\end{matrix}\right)\quad[a,\ \operatorname{Re}s>0]$
5	$(a-x)_+^{-1/2}P_m\left(1-\dfrac{2x}{a}\right)$ $\times T_n\left(1-\dfrac{2x}{a}\right)$	$\sqrt{\pi}\,a^{s-1/2}\left(\dfrac{1}{2}-s\right)_n\Gamma\left[\begin{matrix}s\\\frac{2s+2n+1}{2}\end{matrix}\right]{}_4F_3\left(\begin{matrix}-m,\ m+1,\ s,\ \frac{2s+1}{2};\ 1\\1,\ \frac{2s-2n+1}{2},\ \frac{2s+2n+1}{2}\end{matrix}\right)$ $[a,\ \operatorname{Re}s>0]$
6	$(a-x)_+^{-1/2}P_m(2bx-1)$ $\times T_n\left(\dfrac{2x}{a}-1\right)$	$(-1)^{m+n}\sqrt{\pi}\,a^{s-1/2}\left(\dfrac{1-2s}{2}\right)_n\Gamma\left[\begin{matrix}s\\\frac{2s+2n+1}{2}\end{matrix}\right]$ $\times {}_4F_3\left(\begin{matrix}-m,\ m+1,\ s,\ \frac{2s+1}{2};\ ab\\1,\ \frac{2s-2n+1}{2},\ \frac{2s+2n+1}{2}\end{matrix}\right)\quad[a,\ \operatorname{Re}s>0]$
7	$\dfrac{\theta(a-x)}{\sqrt{b\pm x}}P_m\left(\dfrac{2x}{a}-1\right)$ $\times T_n\left(\dfrac{2x}{b}\pm 1\right)$	$(-1)^m(\pm1)^n\,a^sb^{-1/2}\dfrac{(1-s)_m}{(s)_{m+1}}\,{}_4F_3\left(\begin{matrix}\frac{-2n+1}{2},\ \frac{2n+1}{2},\ s,\ s;\ \mp\frac{a}{b}\\\frac{1}{2},\ s-m,\ s+m+1\end{matrix}\right)$ $\left[\left\{\begin{matrix}a>0;\ |\arg b|<\pi\\b>a>0\end{matrix}\right\};\ \operatorname{Re}s>0\right]$

No.	$f(x)$	$F(s)$
8	$(a-x)_+^{-1/2} P_{2m+\varepsilon}\left(b\sqrt{x}\right)$ $\times T_n\left(\dfrac{2x}{a}-1\right)$	$\dfrac{(-1)^{m+n}\sqrt{\pi}\,a^{s+(\varepsilon-1)/2}(2b)^{\varepsilon}}{m!}\left(\dfrac{1}{2}\right)_{m+\varepsilon}\left(\dfrac{1-2s-\varepsilon}{2}\right)_n$ $\times\Gamma\left[\begin{array}{c}\frac{2s+\varepsilon}{2}\\\frac{2s+2n+\varepsilon+1}{2}\end{array}\right]{}_4F_3\left(\begin{array}{c}-m,\frac{2m+2\varepsilon+1}{2},\frac{2s+\varepsilon}{2},\frac{2s+\varepsilon+1}{2};ab^2\\\frac{2\varepsilon+1}{2},\frac{2s-2n+\varepsilon+1}{2},\frac{2s+2n+\varepsilon+1}{2}\end{array}\right)$ $[a,\,b>0;\ \mathrm{Re}\,s>-\varepsilon/2]$

3.20.15. Products of $T_n\left(\varphi\left(x\right)\right)$

Notation: $\delta,\,\varepsilon=0$ or 1.

No.	$f(x)$	$F(s)$
1	$(a^2-x^2)_+^{-1/2}$ $\times(b^2-x^2)^{-1/2}$ $\times T_{2m+\varepsilon}\left(\dfrac{x}{b}\right)T_{2n+\delta}\left(\dfrac{x}{a}\right)$	$\dfrac{(-1)^{m+n}\sqrt{\pi}\,(2m+1)^{\varepsilon}}{2}a^{s+\varepsilon-1}b^{-\varepsilon-1}\left(\dfrac{1-s+\delta-\varepsilon}{2}\right)_n$ $\times\Gamma\left[\begin{array}{c}\frac{s+\delta+\varepsilon}{2}\\\frac{s+2n+\delta+\varepsilon+1}{2}\end{array}\right]{}_4F_3\left(\begin{array}{c}\frac{1-2m}{2},\frac{2m+2\varepsilon+1}{2},\frac{s+1}{2},\frac{s+2\varepsilon}{2}\\\frac{2\varepsilon+1}{2},\frac{s-2n-\delta+\varepsilon+1}{2},\frac{s+2n+\delta+\varepsilon+1}{2};\frac{a^2}{b^2}\end{array}\right)$ $[b>a>0;\ \mathrm{Re}\,s>-\delta-\varepsilon]$
2	$(x^2-a^2)_+^{-1/2}$ $\times(x^2-b^2)^{-1/2}$ $\times T_{2m+\varepsilon}\left(\dfrac{x}{b}\right)T_{2n+\delta}\left(\dfrac{x}{a}\right)$	$2^{2m+\varepsilon-2}\sqrt{\pi}\,a^{s+2m+\varepsilon-2}b^{-2m-\varepsilon}\left(\dfrac{2-s-2m+\delta-\varepsilon}{2}\right)_n$ $\times\Gamma\left[\begin{array}{c}\frac{2-s-2m-2n-\delta-\varepsilon}{2}\\\frac{3-s-2m-\delta-\varepsilon}{2}\end{array}\right]$ $\times{}_4F_3\left(\begin{array}{c}\frac{1-2m}{2},1-m-\varepsilon,\frac{2-s-2m+2n+\delta-\varepsilon}{2},\frac{2-s-2m-2n-\delta-\varepsilon}{2}\\\frac{3-s-2m-2\varepsilon}{2},1-2m-\varepsilon,\frac{2-s-2m}{2};\frac{b^2}{a^2}\end{array}\right)$ $[a>b>0;\ \mathrm{Re}\,s<2-2m-2n-\delta-\varepsilon]$
3	$(x^2-a^2)_+^{-1/2}$ $\times(b^2-x^2)_+^{-1/2}$ $\times T_{2m+\varepsilon}\left(\dfrac{x}{b}\right)T_{2n+\delta}\left(\dfrac{x}{a}\right)$	$\dfrac{(-1)^m 2^{\varepsilon-2}(2m+\varepsilon)\sqrt{\pi}}{m!}a^{s+\varepsilon-1}b^{-\varepsilon-1}\left(\dfrac{1-s+\delta-\varepsilon}{2}\right)_n$ $\times\Gamma\left[\begin{array}{c}m+\varepsilon,\frac{1-s-2n-\delta-\varepsilon}{2}\\1-\frac{s+\delta+\varepsilon}{2}\end{array}\right]{}_4F_3\left(\begin{array}{c}\frac{1-2m}{2},\frac{2m+2\varepsilon+1}{2},\frac{s+1}{2},\frac{s+2\varepsilon}{2};\frac{a^2}{b^2}\\\frac{2\varepsilon+1}{2},\frac{s-2n-\delta+\varepsilon+1}{2},\frac{s+2n+\delta+\varepsilon+1}{2}\end{array}\right)$ $+(-1)^m 2^{2n+\delta-2}\sqrt{\pi}\,a^{-2n-\delta}b^{s+2n+\delta-2}$ $\times\left(\dfrac{2-s-2n-\delta+\varepsilon}{2}\right)_m\Gamma\left[\begin{array}{c}\frac{s+2n+\delta+\varepsilon-1}{2}\\\frac{s+2m+2n+\delta+\varepsilon}{2}\end{array}\right]$ $\times{}_4F_3\left(\begin{array}{c}\frac{1-2n}{2},1-n-\delta,\frac{2-s-2m-2n-\delta-\varepsilon}{2},\frac{2-s+2m-2n-\delta+\varepsilon}{2}\\-2n-\delta+1,\frac{-s-2n+2}{2},\frac{-s-2n-2\delta+3}{2};\frac{a^2}{b^2}\end{array}\right)$ $[b>a>0]$

No.	$f(x)$	$F(s)$
4	$(a-x)_+^{-1/2} T_m\left(1-\dfrac{2x}{a}\right)$ $\times T_n\left(1-\dfrac{2x}{a}\right)$	$\sqrt{\pi}\, a^{s-1/2} \Gamma\left[\begin{matrix} s,\, n-s+\frac{1}{2} \\ \frac{1}{2}-s,\, s+n+\frac{1}{2} \end{matrix}\right] {}_4F_3\left(\begin{matrix} -m,\, m,\, s,\, s+\frac{1}{2};\, 1 \\ \frac{1}{2},\, s+n+\frac{1}{2},\, s-n+\frac{1}{2} \end{matrix}\right)$ $[a,\ \mathrm{Re}\, s > 0]$
5	$(a-x)_+^{-1/2}(1-bx)^{-1/2}$ $\times T_n\left(\dfrac{2x}{a}-1\right)$ $\times T_m(2bx-1)$	$(-1)^{m+n}\sqrt{\pi}\, a^{s-1/2}\left(\dfrac{1}{2}-s\right)_n \Gamma\left[\begin{matrix} s \\ s+n+\frac{1}{2} \end{matrix}\right]$ $\times\, {}_4F_3\left(\begin{matrix} -m+\frac{1}{2},\, m+\frac{1}{2},\, s,\, s+\frac{1}{2} \\ \frac{1}{2},\, s-n+\frac{1}{2},\, s+n+\frac{1}{2};\, ab \end{matrix}\right)$ $[a,\ \mathrm{Re}\, s > 0;\ |\arg(1-ab)| < \pi]$
6	$(a-x)_+^{-1/2}(b\pm x)^{-1/2}$ $\times T_m\left(\dfrac{2x}{a}-1\right)$ $\times T_n\left(\dfrac{2x}{b}\pm 1\right)$	$(-1)^m(\pm 1)^n\sqrt{\pi}\, a^{s-1/2} b^{-1/2}\left(\dfrac{1}{2}-s\right)_m$ $\times \Gamma\left[\begin{matrix} s \\ s+m+\frac{1}{2} \end{matrix}\right] {}_4F_3\left(\begin{matrix} -n+\frac{1}{2},\, n+\frac{1}{2},\, s,\, s+\frac{1}{2};\, \mp\frac{a}{b} \\ \frac{1}{2},\, s-m+\frac{1}{2},\, s+m+\frac{1}{2} \end{matrix}\right)$ $\left[\left\{\begin{matrix} a>0;\ |\arg b| < \pi \\ b>a>0 \end{matrix}\right\};\ \mathrm{Re}\, s > 0\right]$
7	$(a-x)_+^{-1/2}(1-b^2x)^{-1/2}$ $\times T_{2m+\varepsilon}(b\sqrt{x})$ $\times T_n\left(\dfrac{2x}{a}-1\right)$	$(-1)^{m+n}(2m+1)^\varepsilon \sqrt{\pi}\, a^{s+(\varepsilon-1)/2} b^\varepsilon$ $\times\left(\dfrac{1-2s-\varepsilon}{2}\right)_n \Gamma\left[\begin{matrix} \frac{2s+\varepsilon}{2} \\ \frac{2s+2n+\varepsilon+1}{2} \end{matrix}\right]$ $\times\, {}_4F_3\left(\begin{matrix} \frac{-2m+1}{2},\, \frac{2m+2\varepsilon+1}{2},\, \frac{2s+\varepsilon}{2},\, \frac{2s+\varepsilon+1}{2} \\ \frac{2\varepsilon+1}{2},\, \frac{2s-2n+\varepsilon+1}{2},\, \frac{2s+2n+\varepsilon+1}{2};\, ab^2 \end{matrix}\right)$ $[a>0;\ \mathrm{Re}\, s > -\varepsilon/2;\ |\arg(1-ab^2)| < \pi]$
8	$(a-x)_+^{-1/2} T_n\left(\sqrt{\dfrac{x}{a}}\right)$ $\times T_m(\sqrt{1-bx})$	$\pi\left(\dfrac{\sqrt{a}}{2}\right)^{2s-1} \Gamma\left[\begin{matrix} 2s \\ \frac{2s-n+1}{2},\, \frac{2s+n+1}{2} \end{matrix}\right] {}_4F_3\left(\begin{matrix} -\frac{m}{2},\, \frac{m}{2},\, s,\, \frac{2s+1}{2} \\ \frac{1}{2},\, \frac{2s-n+1}{2},\, \frac{2s+n+1}{2};\, ab \end{matrix}\right)$ $[a>0;\ \mathrm{Re}\, s > 0]$
9	$(a^2-x^2)_+^{-1/2} T_n\left(\dfrac{a}{x}\right)$ $\times T_{2m+\varepsilon}(bx)$	$(-1)^m(2m+1)^\varepsilon 2^{s+\varepsilon-2} a^{s+\varepsilon-1} b^\varepsilon \Gamma\left[\begin{matrix} \frac{s-n+\varepsilon}{2},\, \frac{s+n+\varepsilon}{2} \\ s+\varepsilon \end{matrix}\right]$ $\times\, {}_4F_3\left(\begin{matrix} -m,\, m+\varepsilon,\, \frac{s-n+\varepsilon}{2},\, \frac{s+n+\varepsilon}{2} \\ \frac{2\varepsilon+1}{2},\, \frac{s+\varepsilon}{2},\, \frac{s+\varepsilon+1}{2};\, a^2b^2 \end{matrix}\right)$ $[a>0;\ \mathrm{Re}\, s > n-\varepsilon/2]$
10	$(a-x)_+^{-1/2} T_n\left(\sqrt{\dfrac{a}{x}}\right)$ $\times T_m(bx+1)$	$(4a)^{s-1/2}\Gamma\left[\begin{matrix} \frac{2s-n}{2},\, \frac{2s+n}{2} \\ 2s \end{matrix}\right] {}_4F_3\left(\begin{matrix} -m,\, m,\, \frac{2s-n}{2},\, \frac{2s+n}{2} \\ \frac{1}{2},\, s,\, \frac{2s+1}{2};\, -\frac{ab}{2} \end{matrix}\right)$ $[a>0;\ \mathrm{Re}\, s > n/2]$

3.21.   The Chebyshev Polynomials $U_n(z)$

More formulas can be obtained from the corresponding sections due to the relations

$$U_\nu(z) = \frac{1}{1-z^2}\left[T_\nu(z) - z\,T_{\nu+1}(z)\right], \quad U_\nu(z) = C_\nu^1(z),$$

$$U_\nu(z) = \frac{\Gamma(\nu+2)}{(3/2)_\nu} P_\nu^{(1/2,\,1/2)}(z), \quad U_\nu(z) = (\nu+1)\,{}_2F_1\left(-\nu,\,\nu+2;\,\frac{3}{2};\,\frac{1-z}{2}\right).$$

3.21.1. $U_n(\varphi(x))$ and algebraic functions

Notation: $\varepsilon = 0$ or 1.

No.	$f(x)$	$F(s)$
1	$(a^2-x^2)_+^{1/2}\,U_n\left(\dfrac{x}{a}\right)$	$\dfrac{n+1}{4}\sqrt{\pi}\,a^{s+1}\,\Gamma\!\left[\begin{matrix}\frac{s}{2},\ \frac{s+1}{2}\\ \frac{s+n+3}{2},\ \frac{s-n+1}{2}\end{matrix}\right]$ $\qquad[a,\ \mathrm{Re}\,s > 0]$
2	$(x^2-a^2)_+^{1/2}\,U_n\left(\dfrac{x}{a}\right)$	$\dfrac{n+1}{4}\sqrt{\pi}\,a^{s+1}\,\Gamma\!\left[\begin{matrix}-\frac{s+n+1}{2},\ \frac{1-s+n}{2}\\ \frac{1-s}{2},\ \frac{2-s}{2}\end{matrix}\right]$ $\quad[a>0;\ \mathrm{Re}\,s < -(n+1)]$
3	$(a-x)_+^{\alpha-1}\,U_n\left(1-\dfrac{2x}{a}\right)$	$(n+1)\,a^{s+\alpha-1}\,\mathrm{B}(s,\alpha)\,{}_3F_2\!\left(\begin{matrix}-n,\,n+2,\,\alpha\\ \frac{3}{2},\,s+\alpha;\,1\end{matrix}\right)$ $[a,\ \mathrm{Re}\,\alpha,\ \mathrm{Re}\,s>0]$
4	$(a-x)_+^{\alpha-1}\,U_n\left(\dfrac{2x}{b}\pm 1\right)$	$(\pm 1)^n\,(n+1)\,a^{s+\alpha-1}\,\mathrm{B}(s,\alpha)\,{}_3F_2\!\left(\begin{matrix}-n,\,n+2,\,s\\ \frac{3}{2},\,s+\alpha;\,\mp\frac{a}{b}\end{matrix}\right)$ $[a,\ \mathrm{Re}\,\alpha,\ \mathrm{Re}\,s>0]$
5	$(x-a)_+^{-1/2}\,U_{2n}\left(i\sqrt{\dfrac{x}{a}-1}\right)$	$\sqrt{\pi}\,a^{s-1/2}\,\Gamma\!\left[\begin{matrix}s-\frac{1}{2},\ \frac{1}{2}-n-s\\ s-n-\frac{1}{2},\ 1-s\end{matrix}\right]$ $\qquad[\mathrm{Re}\,s<1/2-n]$
6	$(a^2-x^2)_+\,U_n\left(\dfrac{x^2+a^2}{2ax}\right)$	$2(n+1)\,a^{s+2}\,\Gamma\!\left[\begin{matrix}s+n+2,\ s-n\\ s+n+3,\ s-n+1\end{matrix}\right]$ $\qquad[a>0;\ \mathrm{Re}\,s>n]$
7	$(x^2-a^2)_+\,U_n\left(\dfrac{x^2+a^2}{2ax}\right)$	$2(n+1)\,a^{s+2}\,\Gamma\!\left[\begin{matrix}n-s,\ -n-s-2\\ n-s+1,\ -n-s-1\end{matrix}\right]$ $\qquad[a>0;\ \mathrm{Re}\,s<-n-2]$
8	$(x-a)_+^{1/2}\,(2x-a)$ $\times U_n\left(\dfrac{8x^2-8ax+a^2}{a^2}\right)$	$\dfrac{n+1}{2}\sqrt{\pi}\,a^{s+3/2}\,\Gamma\!\left[\begin{matrix}2n-s+\frac{5}{2},\ -2n-s-\frac{3}{2}\\ 1-s,\ \frac{3}{2}-s\end{matrix}\right]$ $\qquad[a>0;\ \mathrm{Re}\,s<-2n-3/2]$
9	$(a-x)_+^{1/2}\,(2a-x)$ $\times U_n\left(\dfrac{x^2-8ax+8a^2}{x^2}\right)$	$\dfrac{n+1}{2}\sqrt{\pi}\,a^{s+3/2}\,\Gamma\!\left[\begin{matrix}s+2n+4,\ s-2n\\ s+\frac{5}{2},\ s+3\end{matrix}\right]$ $\qquad[a>0;\ \mathrm{Re}\,s>2n]$

No.	$f(x)$	$F(s)$
10	$\dfrac{x+2a}{(x+a)^{n+2}}$ $\times U_n\left(\dfrac{x^2+2ax+2a^2}{2a(x+a)}\right)$	$\dfrac{a^{s-n-1}}{(2n+1)!}\Gamma\begin{bmatrix}s,\,1-s,\,2n-s+3\\2-s\end{bmatrix}$ $\quad[0<\operatorname{Re}s<1;\,|\arg a|<\pi]$
11	$\dfrac{2x+a}{(x+a)^{n+2}}$ $\times U_n\left(\dfrac{2x^2+2ax+a^2}{2x(x+a)}\right)$	$\dfrac{a^{s-n-1}}{(2n+1)!}\Gamma\begin{bmatrix}s-n,\,s+n+2,\,1-s+n\\s-n+1\end{bmatrix}$ $\quad[n<\operatorname{Re}s<n+1;\,|\arg a|<\pi]$

3.21.2. Products of $U_n(\varphi(x))$

Notation: $\delta,\,\varepsilon=0$ or 1.

No.	$f(x)$	$F(s)$
1	$\left(a^2-x^2\right)_+^{1/2}\sqrt{b^2-x^2}$ $\times U_{2m+\varepsilon}\left(\dfrac{x}{b}\right)U_{2n+\delta}\left(\dfrac{x}{a}\right)$	$(-1)^{m+n}\,2^{\varepsilon-2}\,(m+1)^\varepsilon\,(2n+\delta+1)\sqrt{\pi}\,a^{s+\varepsilon+1}b^{-\varepsilon+1}$ $\times\left(\dfrac{1-s+\delta-\varepsilon}{2}\right)_n\Gamma\begin{bmatrix}\frac{s+\delta+\varepsilon}{2}\\\frac{s+2n+\delta+\varepsilon+3}{2}\end{bmatrix}$ $\times {}_4F_3\left(\begin{matrix}-\frac{2m+1}{2},\,\frac{2m+2\varepsilon+1}{2},\,\frac{s+1}{2},\,\frac{s+2\varepsilon}{2}\\\frac{2\varepsilon+1}{2},\,\frac{s-2n-\delta+\varepsilon+1}{2},\,\frac{s+2n+\delta+\varepsilon+3}{2};\,\frac{a^2}{b^2}\end{matrix}\right)$ $\quad[b>a>0;\,\operatorname{Re}s>-\delta-\varepsilon]$
2	$\left(a^2-x^2\right)_+^{1/2}U_n\left(\dfrac{a}{x}\right)$ $\times U_{2m+\varepsilon}(bx)$	$(-1)^m\,2^{s+2\varepsilon-1}\,(m+1)^\varepsilon\,(n+1)\,a^{s+\varepsilon+1}b^\varepsilon\,\Gamma\begin{bmatrix}\frac{s-n+\varepsilon}{2},\,\frac{s+n+\varepsilon+2}{2}\\s+\varepsilon+2\end{bmatrix}$ $\times {}_4F_3\left(\begin{matrix}-m,\,m+\varepsilon+1,\,\frac{s-n+\varepsilon}{2},\,\frac{s+n+\varepsilon+2}{2}\\\frac{2\varepsilon+1}{2},\,\frac{s+\varepsilon+2}{2},\,\frac{s+\varepsilon+3}{2};\,a^2b^2\end{matrix}\right)$ $\quad[a>0;\,\operatorname{Re}s>n-\varepsilon]$
3	$(a-x)_+^{1/2}U_{2n}\left(\sqrt{\dfrac{x}{a}}\right)$ $\times\left[U_m\left(\sqrt{1-bx}\right)\right]^2$	$(-1)^n\,(m+1)^2\,a^{s+1/2}\,\dfrac{\left(\frac{1-2s}{2}\right)_n}{(1/2)_n}\,\mathrm{B}\left(\dfrac{2n+3}{2},\,s\right)$ $\times {}_5F_4\left(\begin{matrix}1,\,-m,\,m+2,\,\frac{2s+1}{2},\,s;\,ab\\\frac{3}{2},\,2,\,\frac{2s-2n+1}{2},\,\frac{2s+2n+3}{2}\end{matrix}\right)\quad[a,\,\operatorname{Re}s>0]$
4	$(a-x)_+^{\rho}\,P_n^{(\rho,\sigma)}\left(\dfrac{2x}{a}-1\right)$ $\times\left[U_m\left(\sqrt{1-bx}\right)\right]^2$	$\dfrac{(-1)^n\,(m+1)^2\,a^{s+\rho}}{n!}\,(1-s+\sigma)_n\,\mathrm{B}(n+\rho+1,\,s)$ $\times {}_5F_4\left(\begin{matrix}1,\,-m,\,m+2,\,s-\sigma,\,s;\,ab\\\frac{3}{2},\,2,\,s-n-\sigma,\,s+n+\rho+1\end{matrix}\right)$ $\quad[a,\,\operatorname{Re}s>0;\,\operatorname{Re}\rho>-1]$

3.22.   The Hermite Polynomials $H_n(z)$

More formulas can be obtained from the corresponding sections due to the relations

$$H_{2n+\varepsilon}(z) = (-1)^n \, 2^{2n+\varepsilon} n! \, z^\varepsilon L_n^{\varepsilon-1/2}(z^2), \quad \varepsilon = 0 \text{ or } 1;$$

$$H_n(z) = n! \lim_{\lambda \to \infty}\left[\lambda^{-n/2} C_n^\lambda\left(\frac{z}{\sqrt{\lambda}}\right)\right],$$

$$H_{2n+\varepsilon}(z) = (-1)^n \frac{(2n+\varepsilon)!}{n!} (2z)^\varepsilon \,_1F_1\left(-n; \varepsilon+\frac{1}{2}; z^2\right), \quad \varepsilon = 0 \text{ or } 1;$$

$$H_\nu(z) = 2^\nu \sqrt{\pi}\left[\frac{1}{\Gamma\left(\frac{1-\nu}{2}\right)} \,_1F_1\left(-\frac{\nu}{2}; \frac{1}{2}; z^2\right) - \frac{2z}{\Gamma\left(-\frac{\nu}{2}\right)} \,_1F_1\left(\frac{1-\nu}{2}; \frac{3}{2}; z^2\right)\right],$$

$$H_n(z) = 2^n \Psi\left(-\frac{n}{2}, \frac{1}{2}; z^2\right) = 2^n \Psi\left(\frac{1-n}{2}, \frac{3}{2}; z^2\right),$$

$$H_\nu(z) = 2^{\nu/2} e^{z^2/2} D_\nu\left(\sqrt{2}\,z\right), \quad H_n(z) = 2^n e^{z^2} G_{12}^{20}\left(z^2 \,\middle|\, \begin{matrix}(1-n)/2 \\ 0, 1/2\end{matrix}\right).$$

3.22.1. $H_n(bx)$ and algebraic functions

Notation: $\varepsilon = 0$ or 1.

No.	$f(x)$	$F(s)$
1	$(a-x)_+^{\alpha-1} H_{2n+\varepsilon}(bx)$	$\dfrac{(-1)^n (2n+\varepsilon)!}{n!} a^{s+\alpha+\varepsilon-1} (2b)^\varepsilon \, \mathrm{B}(s+\varepsilon, \alpha)$ $\times \,_3F_3\left(\begin{matrix}-n, \frac{s+\varepsilon}{2}, \frac{s+\varepsilon+1}{2}; a^2b^2 \\ \frac{2\varepsilon+1}{2}, \frac{s+\alpha+\varepsilon}{2}, \frac{s+\alpha+\varepsilon+1}{2}\end{matrix}\right)$ $[a, \operatorname{Re}\alpha > 0; \operatorname{Re} s > -\varepsilon]$
2	$(x-a)_+^{\alpha-1} H_{2n+\varepsilon}(bx)$	$\dfrac{(-1)^n (2n+\varepsilon)!}{n!} a^{s+\alpha+\varepsilon-1} (2b)^\varepsilon \, \mathrm{B}(1-s-\alpha-\varepsilon, \alpha)$ $\times \,_3F_3\left(\begin{matrix}-n, \frac{s+\varepsilon}{2}, \frac{s+\varepsilon+1}{2}; a^2b^2 \\ \frac{2\varepsilon+1}{2}, \frac{s+\alpha+\varepsilon}{2}, \frac{s+\alpha+\varepsilon+1}{2}\end{matrix}\right)$ $[a > 0; \operatorname{Re}(s+\alpha) < 1-2n-\varepsilon]$
3	$(a^2-x^2)_+^{\alpha-1} H_{2n+\varepsilon}(bx)$	$(-1)^n \, 2^{2n+\varepsilon-1} a^{s+2\alpha+\varepsilon-2} b^\varepsilon \left(\dfrac{2\varepsilon+1}{2}\right)_n \mathrm{B}\left(\alpha, \dfrac{s+\varepsilon}{2}\right)$ $\times \,_2F_2\left(\begin{matrix}-n, \frac{s+\varepsilon}{2}; a^2b^2 \\ \frac{2\varepsilon+1}{2}, \frac{s+2\alpha+\varepsilon}{2}\end{matrix}\right) \quad [a, \operatorname{Re}\alpha > 0; \operatorname{Re} s > -\varepsilon]$
4	$(x^2-a^2)_+^{\alpha-1} H_{2n+\varepsilon}(bx)$	$(-1)^n \, 2^{2n+\varepsilon-1} a^{s+2\alpha+\varepsilon-2} b^\varepsilon \left(\dfrac{2\varepsilon+1}{2}\right)_n$ $\times \mathrm{B}\left(\alpha, \dfrac{2-2\alpha-s-\varepsilon}{2}\right) \,_2F_2\left(\begin{matrix}-n, \frac{s+\varepsilon}{2}; a^2b^2 \\ \frac{2\varepsilon+1}{2}, \frac{s+2\alpha+\varepsilon}{2}\end{matrix}\right)$ $[a, \operatorname{Re}\alpha > 0; \operatorname{Re}(s+2\alpha) < 2-2n-\varepsilon]$

No.	$f(x)$	$F(s)$
5	$\dfrac{1}{(x^2+a^2)^\rho}\,H_{2n+\varepsilon}(bx)$	$(-1)^n\,2^{2n+\varepsilon-1}a^{s-2\rho+\varepsilon}b^\varepsilon\left(\dfrac{2\varepsilon+1}{2}\right)_n\mathrm{B}\left(\dfrac{s+\varepsilon}{2},\dfrac{2\rho-s-\varepsilon}{2}\right)$ $\times\,{}_2F_2\left(\begin{matrix}-n,\ \frac{s+\varepsilon}{2};\ -a^2b^2\\ \frac{2\varepsilon+1}{2},\ \frac{s-2\rho+\varepsilon+2}{2}\end{matrix}\right)$ $[\mathrm{Re}\,a>0;\ -\varepsilon<\mathrm{Re}\,s<2\,\mathrm{Re}\,\rho-2n-\varepsilon]$
6	$\dfrac{1}{(x+a)^\rho}$ $\times\,H_{2n+\varepsilon}\left(\dfrac{bx}{x+a}\right)$	$(-1)^n\,2^{2n+\varepsilon}\left(\dfrac{2\varepsilon+1}{2}\right)_n a^{s-\rho}b^\varepsilon\,\mathrm{B}(s+\varepsilon,\rho-s)$ $\times\,{}_3F_3\left(\begin{matrix}-n,\ \frac{s+\varepsilon}{2},\ \frac{s+\varepsilon+1}{2}\\ \frac{2\varepsilon+1}{2},\ \frac{\rho+\varepsilon}{2},\ \frac{\rho+\varepsilon+1}{2};\ b^2\end{matrix}\right)$ $[-\varepsilon<\mathrm{Re}\,s<\mathrm{Re}\,\rho;\ |\arg a|<\pi]$
7	$\dfrac{1}{(x^2+a^2)^\rho}$ $\times\,H_{2n+\varepsilon}\left(\dfrac{bx}{x^2+a^2}\right)$	$(-1)^n\,2^{2n+\varepsilon-1}\left(\dfrac{2\varepsilon+1}{2}\right)_n a^{s-2\rho-\varepsilon}b^\varepsilon$ $\times\,\mathrm{B}\left(\dfrac{s+\varepsilon}{2},\dfrac{-s+2\rho+\varepsilon}{2}\right){}_3F_3\left(\begin{matrix}-n,\ \frac{s+\varepsilon}{2},\ \frac{-s+2\rho+\varepsilon}{2}\\ \frac{2\varepsilon+1}{2},\ \frac{\rho+\varepsilon}{2},\ \frac{\rho+\varepsilon+1}{2};\ \frac{b^2}{4a^2}\end{matrix}\right)$ $[\mathrm{Re}\,a>0;\ -\varepsilon<\mathrm{Re}\,s<2\,\mathrm{Re}\,\rho+\varepsilon]$
8	$(a-x)_+^{\alpha-1}$ $\times\,H_{2n+\varepsilon}\left(b\sqrt{x(a-x)}\right)$	$\dfrac{(-1)^n(2n+\varepsilon)!}{n!}\,a^{s+\alpha+\varepsilon-1}(2b)^\varepsilon\,\mathrm{B}\left(\dfrac{2s+\varepsilon}{2},\dfrac{2\alpha+\varepsilon}{2}\right)$ $\times\,{}_3F_3\left(\begin{matrix}-n,\ \frac{2s+\varepsilon}{2},\ \frac{2\alpha+\varepsilon}{2};\ \frac{a^2b^2}{4}\\ \frac{2\varepsilon+1}{2},\ \frac{s+\alpha+\varepsilon}{2},\ \frac{s+\alpha+\varepsilon+1}{2}\end{matrix}\right)$ $[a>0;\ \mathrm{Re}\,s,\ \mathrm{Re}\,\alpha>-\varepsilon/2]$

3.22.2. $H_n(bx)$ and the exponential function

Notation: $\varepsilon=0$ or 1.

No.	$f(x)$	$F(s)$
1	$e^{-ax}H_n(bx)$	$\dfrac{(2b)^n}{a^{s+n}}\,\Gamma(s+n)\,{}_2F_2\left(\begin{matrix}-\frac{n}{2},\ \frac{1-n}{2};\ -\frac{a^2}{4b^2}\\ \frac{1-s-n}{2},\ \frac{2-s-n}{2}\end{matrix}\right)$ $[\mathrm{Re}\,a>0;\ \mathrm{Re}\,s>2\,[n/2]-n]$
2	$e^{-a^2x^2}H_n(ax)$	$\dfrac{2^{n-1}}{a^s}\,\Gamma\left[\begin{matrix}\frac{s}{2},\ \frac{s+1}{2}\\ \frac{s-n+1}{2}\end{matrix}\right]$ $[\mathrm{Re}\,s>0;\ |\arg a|<\pi/4]$
3	$e^{-ax^2}H_n(bx)$	$\dfrac{n!}{2}\,a^{-s/2}\,\Gamma\left(\dfrac{s-n}{2}\right)C_n^{((s-n)/2)}\left(\dfrac{b}{\sqrt{a}}\right)$ $[\mathrm{Re}\,a,\ \mathrm{Re}\,s>0]$
4	$(a-x)_+^{\alpha-1}\,e^{-b^2x^2}$ $\times\,H_{2n+\varepsilon}(bx)$	$(-1)^n\,2^{2n+\varepsilon}a^{s+\alpha+\varepsilon-1}b^\varepsilon\left(\dfrac{2\varepsilon+1}{2}\right)_n\mathrm{B}(\alpha,s+\varepsilon)$ $\times\,{}_3F_3\left(\begin{matrix}\frac{2n+2\varepsilon+1}{2},\ \frac{s+1}{2},\ \frac{s+2\varepsilon}{2};\ -a^2b^2\\ \frac{2\varepsilon+1}{2},\ \frac{s+\alpha+1}{2},\ \frac{s+\alpha+2\varepsilon}{2}\end{matrix}\right)$ $[a,\ \mathrm{Re}\,\alpha>0;\ \mathrm{Re}\,s>-\varepsilon]$

No.	$f(x)$	$F(s)$
5	$(x-a)_+^{\alpha-1}\,e^{-b^2x^2}$ $\times H_{2n+\varepsilon}(bx)$	$(-1)^n\,2^{2n+\varepsilon}a^{s+\alpha+\varepsilon-1}b^\varepsilon\left(\dfrac{2\varepsilon+1}{2}\right)_n B(\alpha,1-s-\alpha-\varepsilon)$ $\times\, {}_3F_3\left(\begin{matrix}\frac{2n+2\varepsilon+1}{2},\,\frac{s+1}{2},\,\frac{s+2\varepsilon}{2};\,-a^2b^2\\[2pt]\frac{2\varepsilon+1}{2},\,\frac{s+\alpha+1}{2},\,\frac{s+\alpha+2\varepsilon}{2}\end{matrix}\right)$ $+(-1)^n\,\dfrac{2^{2n+\varepsilon-1}}{b^{s+\alpha-1}}\left(\dfrac{2-s-\alpha+\varepsilon}{2}\right)_n\Gamma\left(\dfrac{s+\alpha+\varepsilon-1}{2}\right)$ $\times\,{}_3F_3\left(\begin{matrix}\frac{1-\alpha}{2},\,\frac{2-\alpha}{2},\,\frac{2-s+2n-\alpha+\varepsilon}{2}\\[2pt]\frac{1}{2},\,\frac{2-s-\alpha}{2},\,\frac{3-s-\alpha}{2};\,-a^2b^2\end{matrix}\right)$ $+(-1)^n\,(1-\alpha)\,\dfrac{2^{2n+\varepsilon-1}a}{b^{s+\alpha-2}}\left(\dfrac{3-s-\alpha+\varepsilon}{2}\right)_n$ $\times\,\Gamma\left(\dfrac{s+\alpha+\varepsilon-2}{2}\right)\,{}_3F_3\left(\begin{matrix}\frac{2-\alpha}{2},\,\frac{3-\alpha}{2},\,\frac{3-s+2n-\alpha+\varepsilon}{2}\\[2pt]\frac{3}{2},\,\frac{3-s-\alpha}{2},\,\frac{4-s-\alpha}{2};\,-a^2b^2\end{matrix}\right)$ $[a,\ \mathrm{Re}\,\alpha>0;\ |\arg b|<\pi/4]$
6	$(a^2-x^2)_+^{\alpha-1}\,e^{-b^2x^2}$ $\times H_{2n+\varepsilon}(bx)$	$(-1)^n\,2^{2n+\varepsilon-1}a^{s+\varepsilon+2\alpha-1}b^\varepsilon\,B\left(\alpha,\dfrac{s+\varepsilon}{2}\right)\left(\dfrac{2\varepsilon+1}{2}\right)_n$ $\times\,{}_2F_2\left(\begin{matrix}\frac{2n+2\varepsilon+1}{2},\,\frac{s+\varepsilon}{2};\,-a^2b^2\\[2pt]\frac{2\varepsilon+1}{2},\,\frac{s+\varepsilon+2\alpha}{2}\end{matrix}\right)\qquad[a,\ \mathrm{Re}\,\alpha>0;\ \mathrm{Re}\,s>-\varepsilon]$
7	$(x^2-a^2)_+^{\alpha-1}\,e^{-b^2x^2}$ $\times H_{2n+\varepsilon}(bx)$	$(-1)^n\,2^{2n+\varepsilon-1}a^{s+2\alpha+\varepsilon-2}b^\varepsilon\,B\left(\alpha,\dfrac{2-s-2\alpha-\varepsilon}{2}\right)$ $\times\left(\dfrac{2\varepsilon+1}{2}\right)_n\,{}_2F_2\left(\begin{matrix}\frac{2n+2\varepsilon+1}{2},\,\frac{s+\varepsilon}{2}\\[2pt]\frac{2\varepsilon+1}{2},\,\frac{s+2\alpha+\varepsilon}{2};\,-a^2b^2\end{matrix}\right)$ $+(-1)^n\,2^{2n+\varepsilon-1}b^{2-s-2\alpha}\left(\dfrac{3-s-2\alpha+\varepsilon}{2}\right)_n$ $\times\,\Gamma\left(\dfrac{s+2\alpha+\varepsilon-2}{2}\right)\,{}_2F_2\left(\begin{matrix}1-\alpha,\,\frac{3-s+2n-2\alpha+\varepsilon}{2}\\[2pt]\frac{3-s-2\alpha}{2},\,\frac{4-s-2\alpha}{2};\,-a^2b^2\end{matrix}\right)$ $[a,\ \mathrm{Re}\,\alpha>0;\ |\arg b|<\pi/4]$
8	$(a^4-x^4)_+^{\alpha-1}\,e^{-b^2x^2}$ $\times H_{2n+\varepsilon}(bx)$	$(-1)^n\,2^{2n+\varepsilon-2}a^{s+4\alpha+\varepsilon-4}b^\varepsilon\,B\left(\alpha,\dfrac{s+\varepsilon}{4}\right)$ $\times\left(\dfrac{2\varepsilon+1}{2}\right)_n\,{}_3F_4\left(\begin{matrix}\frac{2n+3}{4},\,\frac{2n+4\varepsilon+1}{4},\,\frac{s+\varepsilon}{4};\,\frac{a^4b^4}{4}\\[2pt]\frac{1}{2},\,\frac{3}{4},\,\frac{4\varepsilon+1}{4},\,\frac{s+4\alpha+\varepsilon}{4}\end{matrix}\right)$ $-(-1)^n\,2^{2n+\varepsilon-2}a^{s+4\alpha+\varepsilon-2}b^{\varepsilon+2}\,B\left(\alpha,\dfrac{s+\varepsilon+2}{4}\right)$ $\times\left(\dfrac{2\varepsilon+3}{2}\right)_n\,{}_3F_4\left(\begin{matrix}\frac{2n+5}{4},\,\frac{2n+4\varepsilon+3}{4},\,\frac{s+\varepsilon+2}{4};\,\frac{a^4b^4}{4}\\[2pt]\frac{5}{4},\,\frac{3}{2},\,\frac{4\varepsilon+3}{4},\,\frac{s+4\alpha+\varepsilon+2}{4}\end{matrix}\right)$ $[a,\ \mathrm{Re}\,\alpha>0;\ \mathrm{Re}\,s>-\varepsilon]$

No.	$f(x)$	$F(s)$
9	$\dfrac{e^{-b^2x^2}}{(x+a)^\rho} H_{2n+\varepsilon}(bx)$	$(-1)^n 2^{2n+\varepsilon} a^{s-\rho+\varepsilon} b^\varepsilon \, \mathrm{B}\left(s+\varepsilon,\ \rho-s-\varepsilon\right)$

$$\times \left(\frac{2\varepsilon+1}{2}\right)_n {}_3F_3\left(\begin{matrix} \frac{2n+2\varepsilon+1}{2},\ \frac{s+1}{2},\ \frac{s+2\varepsilon}{2};\ -a^2b^2 \\ \frac{2\varepsilon+1}{2},\ \frac{s-\rho+2}{2},\ \frac{s-\rho+2\varepsilon+1}{2} \end{matrix}\right)$$

$$+ (-1)^n 2^{2n+\varepsilon-1} b^{\rho-s}\left(\frac{1-s+\rho+\varepsilon}{2}\right)_n \Gamma\left(\frac{s-\rho+\varepsilon}{2}\right)$$

$$\times {}_3F_3\left(\begin{matrix} \frac{\rho}{2},\ \frac{\rho+1}{2},\ \frac{1-s+2n+\rho+\varepsilon}{2} \\ \frac{1}{2},\ \frac{1-s+\rho}{2},\ \frac{2-s+\rho}{2};\ -a^2b^2 \end{matrix}\right)$$

$$- (-1)^n 2^{2n+\varepsilon-1} \rho a b^{1-s+\rho}\left(\frac{2-s+\rho+\varepsilon}{2}\right)_n$$

$$\times \Gamma\left(\frac{s-\rho+\varepsilon-1}{2}\right) {}_3F_3\left(\begin{matrix} \frac{\rho+1}{2},\ \frac{\rho+2}{2},\ \frac{2-s+2n+\rho+\varepsilon}{2} \\ \frac{3}{2},\ \frac{2-s+\rho}{2},\ \frac{3-s+\rho}{2};\ -a^2b^2 \end{matrix}\right)$$

$$[\operatorname{Re} s > -\varepsilon;\ |\arg a|,\ 4|\arg b| < \pi]$$

No.	$f(x)$	$F(s)$
10	$\dfrac{e^{-b^2x^2}}{(x^2+a^2)^\rho} H_{2n+\varepsilon}(bx)$	$(-1)^n 2^{2n+\varepsilon-1} a^{s-2\rho+\varepsilon} b^\varepsilon \left(\dfrac{2\varepsilon+1}{2}\right)_n$

$$\times \mathrm{B}\left(\frac{s+\varepsilon}{2},\ \frac{2\rho-s-\varepsilon}{2}\right) {}_2F_2\left(\begin{matrix} \frac{s+\varepsilon}{2},\ \frac{2n+2\varepsilon+1}{2};\ a^2b^2 \\ \frac{2\varepsilon+1}{2},\ \frac{s-2\rho+\varepsilon+2}{2} \end{matrix}\right)$$

$$+ (-1)^n 2^{2n+\varepsilon-1} b^{2\rho-s}\left(\frac{1-s+2\rho+\varepsilon}{2}\right)_n \Gamma\left(\frac{s-2\rho+\varepsilon}{2}\right)$$

$$\times {}_2F_2\left(\begin{matrix} \rho,\ \frac{1-s+2n+2\rho+\varepsilon}{2};\ a^2b^2 \\ \frac{1-s+2\rho}{2},\ \frac{2-s+2\rho}{2} \end{matrix}\right)$$

$$[\operatorname{Re} a > 0;\ \operatorname{Re} s > -\varepsilon;\ |\arg b| < \pi/4]$$

No.	$f(x)$	$F(s)$
11	$\dfrac{e^{-b^2x^2}}{x-a} H_{2n+\varepsilon}(bx)$	$(-1)^{n+1} 2^{2n+\varepsilon} \pi \cot(s\pi)\, a^{s+\varepsilon-1} b^\varepsilon \left(\dfrac{2\varepsilon+1}{2}\right)_n$

$$\times {}_1F_1\left(\begin{matrix} \frac{2n+2\varepsilon+1}{2} \\ \frac{2\varepsilon+1}{2};\ -a^2b^2 \end{matrix}\right) + \frac{(-1)^n 2^{2n+\varepsilon-1}}{b^{s-1}}\left(\frac{2-s+\varepsilon}{2}\right)_n$$

$$\times \Gamma\left(\frac{s+\varepsilon-1}{2}\right) {}_2F_2\left(\begin{matrix} 1,\ \frac{2-s+2n+\varepsilon}{2} \\ \frac{2-s}{2},\ \frac{3-s}{2};\ -a^2b^2 \end{matrix}\right)$$

$$+ \frac{(-1)^n 2^{2n+\varepsilon-1} a}{b^{s-2}}\left(\frac{3-s+\varepsilon}{2}\right)_n \Gamma\left(\frac{s+\varepsilon-2}{2}\right)$$

$$\times {}_2F_2\left(\begin{matrix} 1,\ \frac{3-s+2n+\varepsilon}{2} \\ \frac{3-s}{2},\ \frac{4-s}{2};\ -a^2b^2 \end{matrix}\right)$$

$$[a > 0;\ \operatorname{Re} s > -\varepsilon;\ |\arg b| < \pi/4]$$

No.	$f(x)$	$F(s)$
12	$\dfrac{e^{-b^2x^2}}{x^2-a^2}H_{2n+\varepsilon}(bx)$	$(-1)^{n+1}2^{2n+\varepsilon-1}\pi\cot\dfrac{(s+\varepsilon)\pi}{2}\,a^{s+\varepsilon-2}b^\varepsilon\left(\dfrac{2\varepsilon+1}{2}\right)_n$ $\times\,{}_1F_1\left(\begin{matrix}\frac{2n+2\varepsilon+1}{2}\\\frac{2\varepsilon+1}{2};\ -a^2b^2\end{matrix}\right)+\dfrac{(-1)^n2^{2n+\varepsilon-1}}{b^{s-2}}\left(\dfrac{3-s+\varepsilon}{2}\right)_n$ $\times\,\Gamma\left(\dfrac{s+\varepsilon-2}{2}\right){}_2F_2\left(\begin{matrix}1,\ \frac{3-s+2n+\varepsilon}{2}\\\frac{3-s}{2},\ \frac{4-s}{2};\ -a^2b^2\end{matrix}\right)$ $[a>0;\ \mathrm{Re}\,s>-\varepsilon;\ |\arg b|<\pi/4]$
13	$e^{-a/x}H_{2n+\varepsilon}(bx)$	$(-1)^n2^{2n+\varepsilon}a^{s+\varepsilon}b^\varepsilon\left(\dfrac{2\varepsilon+1}{2}\right)_n\Gamma(-s-\varepsilon)$ $\times\,{}_1F_3\left(\begin{matrix}-n;\ \frac{a^2b^2}{4}\\\frac{2\varepsilon+1}{2},\ \frac{s+\varepsilon+1}{2},\ \frac{s+\varepsilon+2}{2}\end{matrix}\right)$ $[\mathrm{Re}\,a>0;\ \mathrm{Re}\,s<-2n-\varepsilon]$
14	$e^{-a/x^2}H_{2n+\varepsilon}(bx)$	$(-1)^n2^{2n+\varepsilon-1}a^{(s+\varepsilon)/2}b^\varepsilon\left(\dfrac{2\varepsilon+1}{2}\right)_n$ $\times\,\Gamma\left(-\dfrac{s+\varepsilon}{2}\right){}_1F_2\left(\begin{matrix}-n;\ -ab^2\\\frac{2\varepsilon+1}{2},\ \frac{s+\varepsilon+2}{2}\end{matrix}\right)$ $[\mathrm{Re}\,a>0;\ \mathrm{Re}\,s<-2n-\varepsilon]$
15	$e^{-a\sqrt{x}}H_{2n+\varepsilon}(bx)$	$(-1)^n2^{2n+2\varepsilon+1}a^{-2s-2\varepsilon}b^\varepsilon\left(\dfrac{1}{2}\right)_{n+\varepsilon}\Gamma(2s+2\varepsilon)$ $\times\,{}_5F_1\left(\begin{matrix}-n,\ \Delta(4,\ 2s+2\varepsilon)\\\frac{2\varepsilon+1}{2};\ \frac{256b^2}{a^4}\end{matrix}\right)\quad[\mathrm{Re}\,a>0;\ \mathrm{Re}\,s>-\varepsilon]$
16	$e^{-a/\sqrt{x}}H_{2n+\varepsilon}(bx)$	$(-1)^n2^{2n+2\varepsilon+1}a^{2s+2\varepsilon}b^\varepsilon\left(\dfrac{1}{2}\right)_{n+\varepsilon}\Gamma(-2s-2\varepsilon)$ $\times\,{}_1F_5\left(\begin{matrix}-n;\ \frac{a^4b^2}{256}\\\frac{2\varepsilon+1}{2},\ \Delta(4,\ 2s+2\varepsilon)\end{matrix}\right)$ $[\mathrm{Re}\,a>0;\ \mathrm{Re}\,s<-2n-\varepsilon]$
17	$e^{-ax-b^2x^2}H_{2n+\varepsilon}(bx)$	$\dfrac{(-1)^n2^{2n+\varepsilon-1}}{b^s}\left(\dfrac{1-s+\varepsilon}{2}\right)_n\Gamma\left(\dfrac{s+\varepsilon}{2}\right)$ $\times\,{}_2F_2\left(\begin{matrix}\frac{s}{2},\ \frac{s+1}{2};\ \frac{a^2}{4b^2}\\\frac{1}{2},\ \frac{s-2n-\varepsilon+1}{2}\end{matrix}\right)-\dfrac{(-1)^n2^{2n+\varepsilon-1}a}{b^{s+1}}\left(\dfrac{-s+\varepsilon}{2}\right)_n$ $\times\,\Gamma\left(\dfrac{s+\varepsilon+1}{2}\right){}_2F_2\left(\begin{matrix}\frac{s+1}{2},\ \frac{s+2}{2};\ \frac{a^2}{4b^2}\\\frac{3}{2},\ \frac{s-2n-\varepsilon+2}{2}\end{matrix}\right)$ $[\mathrm{Re}\,a>0;\ \mathrm{Re}\,s>-\varepsilon;\ |\arg b|<\pi/4]$

No.	$f(x)$	$F(s)$
18	$e^{-ax^4-b^2x^2} H_{2n+\varepsilon}(bx)$	$(-1)^n \dfrac{2^{2n+\varepsilon-2}b^\varepsilon}{a^{(s+\varepsilon)/4}} \left(\dfrac{2\varepsilon+1}{2}\right)_n \Gamma\left(\dfrac{s+\varepsilon}{4}\right)$

$$\times {}_3F_3\left(\begin{matrix} \frac{2n+2\varepsilon+1}{4}, \frac{2n+2\varepsilon+3}{4}, \frac{s+\varepsilon}{4} \\ \frac{1}{2}, \frac{3}{4}, \frac{4\varepsilon+1}{4}; \frac{b^4}{4a} \end{matrix}\right)$$

$$- (-1)^n \frac{2^{2n+\varepsilon-2}b^{\varepsilon+2}}{a^{(s+\varepsilon+2)/4}} \left(\frac{2\varepsilon+3}{2}\right)_n \Gamma\left(\frac{s+\varepsilon+2}{4}\right)$$

$$\times {}_3F_3\left(\begin{matrix} \frac{2n+2\varepsilon+3}{4}, \frac{2n+2\varepsilon+5}{4}, \frac{s+\varepsilon+2}{4} \\ \frac{5}{4}, \frac{3}{2}, \frac{4\varepsilon+3}{4}; \frac{b^4}{4a} \end{matrix}\right)$$

$$[\operatorname{Re} a > 0;\ \operatorname{Re} s > -\varepsilon;\ |\arg b| < \pi/4]$$

19	$e^{-a/x-b^2x^2} H_{2n+\varepsilon}(bx)$	$(-1)^n 2^{2n+\varepsilon} a^{s+\varepsilon} b^\varepsilon \left(\dfrac{2\varepsilon+1}{2}\right)_n \Gamma(-s-\varepsilon)$

$$\times {}_1F_3\left(\begin{matrix} \frac{2n+2\varepsilon+1}{2}; -\frac{a^2b^2}{4} \\ \frac{2\varepsilon+1}{2}, \frac{s+\varepsilon+1}{2}, \frac{s+\varepsilon+2}{2} \end{matrix}\right) + \frac{(-1)^n 2^{2n+\varepsilon-1}}{b^s}$$

$$\times \left(\frac{1-s+\varepsilon}{2}\right)_n \Gamma\left(\frac{s+\varepsilon}{2}\right) {}_1F_3\left(\begin{matrix} \frac{1-s+2n+\varepsilon}{2}; -\frac{a^2b^2}{4} \\ \frac{1}{2}, \frac{1-s}{2}, \frac{2-s}{2} \end{matrix}\right)$$

$$- \frac{(-1)^n 2^{2n+\varepsilon-1}a}{b^{s-1}} \left(\frac{2-s+\varepsilon}{2}\right)_n$$

$$\times \Gamma\left(\frac{s+\varepsilon-1}{2}\right) {}_1F_3\left(\begin{matrix} \frac{2-s+2n+\varepsilon}{2}; -\frac{a^2b^2}{4} \\ \frac{3}{2}, \frac{2-s}{2}, \frac{3-s}{2} \end{matrix}\right)$$

$$[\operatorname{Re} a > 0;\ |\arg b| < \pi/4]$$

20	$e^{-a/x^2-b^2x^2} H_{2n+\varepsilon}(bx)$	$(-1)^n 2^{2n+\varepsilon-1} a^{(s+\varepsilon)/2} b^\varepsilon \left(\dfrac{2\varepsilon+1}{2}\right)_n \Gamma\left(-\dfrac{s+\varepsilon}{2}\right)$

$$\times {}_1F_2\left(\begin{matrix} \frac{2n+2\varepsilon+1}{2}; ab^2 \\ \frac{2\varepsilon+1}{2}, \frac{s+\varepsilon+2}{2} \end{matrix}\right) + \frac{(-1)^n 2^{2n+\varepsilon-1}}{b^s}$$

$$\times \left(\frac{1-s+\varepsilon}{2}\right)_n \Gamma\left(\frac{s+\varepsilon}{2}\right) {}_1F_2\left(\begin{matrix} \frac{1-s+2n+\varepsilon}{2}; ab^2 \\ \frac{1-s}{2}, \frac{2-s}{2} \end{matrix}\right)$$

$$[\operatorname{Re} a > 0;\ |\arg b| < \pi/4]$$

21	$e^{-a/x^4-b^2x^2} H_{2n+\varepsilon}(bx)$	$(-1)^n 2^{2n+\varepsilon-2} a^{(s+\varepsilon)/4} b^\varepsilon \left(\dfrac{2\varepsilon+1}{2}\right)_n \Gamma\left(-\dfrac{s+\varepsilon}{4}\right)$

$$\times {}_2F_4\left(\begin{matrix} \frac{2n+2\varepsilon+1}{4}, \frac{2n+2\varepsilon+3}{4}; -\frac{ab^4}{4} \\ \frac{1}{2}, \frac{3}{4}, \frac{4\varepsilon+1}{4}, \frac{s+\varepsilon+4}{4} \end{matrix}\right) - (-1)^n 2^{2n+\varepsilon-2} a^{(s+\varepsilon+2)/4} b^{\varepsilon+2}$$

$$\times \left(\frac{2\varepsilon+3}{2}\right)_n \Gamma\left(-\frac{s+\varepsilon+2}{4}\right) {}_2F_4\left(\begin{matrix} \frac{2n+2\varepsilon+3}{4}, \frac{2n+2\varepsilon+5}{4}; -\frac{ab^4}{4} \\ \frac{5}{4}, \frac{3}{2}, \frac{4\varepsilon+3}{4}, \frac{s+\varepsilon+6}{4} \end{matrix}\right)$$

$$+ \frac{(-1)^n 2^{2n+\varepsilon-1}}{b^s} \left(\frac{1-s+\varepsilon}{2}\right)_n \Gamma\left(\frac{s+\varepsilon}{2}\right)$$

$$\times {}_2F_4\left(\begin{matrix} \frac{1-s+2n+\varepsilon}{4}, \frac{3-s+2n+\varepsilon}{4}; -\frac{ab^4}{4} \\ \frac{1-s}{4}, \frac{2-s}{4}, \frac{3-s}{4}, \frac{4-s}{4} \end{matrix}\right) \quad [\operatorname{Re} a > 0;\ |\arg b| < \pi/4]$$

No.	$f(x)$	$F(s)$
22	$(a-x)_+^{(\varepsilon-1)/2}\, e^{bx}$ $\times H_{2n+\varepsilon}\left(c\sqrt{a-x}\right)$	$(-1)^n\, 2^{2n}\,\sqrt{\pi}\, a^{s+\varepsilon-1/2} c^\varepsilon \left(\dfrac{2\varepsilon+1}{2}\right)_n \Gamma\left[\begin{array}{c} s \\ \frac{2s+2\varepsilon+1}{2}\end{array}\right]$ $\times \Phi_2\left(s, -n; \dfrac{2s+2\varepsilon+1}{2}; ab, ac^2\right) \qquad [a,\ \mathrm{Re}\, s > 0]$

3.22.3. $H_n(bx)$ and trigonometric functions

Notation: $\delta = \left\{\begin{array}{c} 1 \\ 0 \end{array}\right\}$, $\varepsilon = 0$ or 1.

1	$e^{-b^2x^2}\left\{\begin{array}{c}\sin(ax)\\\cos(ax)\end{array}\right\}$ $\times H_{2n+\varepsilon}(bx)$	$(-1)^n\dfrac{2^{2n+\varepsilon-1}a^\delta}{b^{s+\delta}}\left(\dfrac{1-s-\delta+\varepsilon}{2}\right)_n \Gamma\left(\dfrac{s+\delta+\varepsilon}{2}\right)$ $\times {}_2F_2\left(\begin{array}{c}\frac{s+1}{2},\ \frac{s+2\delta}{2};\ -\frac{a^2}{4b^2}\\ \frac{2\delta+1}{2},\ \frac{s-2n+\delta-\varepsilon+1}{2}\end{array}\right) \qquad \left[\begin{array}{c}a>0;\ \mathrm{Re}\,s>-\delta-\varepsilon;\\ |\arg b|<\pi/4\end{array}\right]$
2	$e^{-b^2x^2}\left\{\begin{array}{c}\sin(ax^2)\\\cos(ax^2)\end{array}\right\}$ $\times H_{2n+\varepsilon}(bx)$	$(-1)^n\dfrac{2^{2n+\varepsilon-1}a^\delta}{b^{s+2\delta}}\left(\dfrac{1-s-2\delta+\varepsilon}{2}\right)_n \Gamma\left(\dfrac{s+2\delta+\varepsilon}{2}\right)$ $\times {}_4F_3\left(\begin{array}{c}\frac{s+2}{4},\ \frac{s+3}{4},\ \frac{s+4\delta}{4},\ \frac{s+4\delta+1}{4};\ -\frac{a^2}{b^4}\\ \frac{2\delta+1}{2},\ \frac{s-2n-\varepsilon+3}{4},\ \frac{s-2n+4\delta-\varepsilon+1}{4}\end{array}\right)$ $[a>0;\ \mathrm{Re}\,s>-2\delta-\varepsilon;\ |\arg b|<\pi/4]$
3	$e^{-b^2x^2}\left\{\begin{array}{c}\sin(a/x)\\\cos(a/x)\end{array}\right\}$ $\times H_{2n+\varepsilon}(bx)$	$(-1)^n\, 2^{2n+\varepsilon-1}a^\delta b^{\delta-s}\left(\dfrac{1-s+\delta+\varepsilon}{2}\right)_n \Gamma\left(\dfrac{s-\delta+\varepsilon}{2}\right)$ $\times {}_1F_3\left(\begin{array}{c}\frac{1-s+2n+\delta+\varepsilon}{2};\ \frac{a^2b^2}{4}\\ \frac{2\delta+1}{2},\ \frac{2-s+\delta-\varepsilon}{2},\ \frac{1-s+\delta+\varepsilon}{2}\end{array}\right)\mp(-1)^n\, 2^{2n+\varepsilon}a^{s+\varepsilon}b^\varepsilon$ $\times\left(\dfrac{2\varepsilon+1}{2}\right)_n\Gamma(-s-\varepsilon)\left\{\begin{array}{c}\sin[(s+\varepsilon)\pi/2]\\\cos[(s+\varepsilon)\pi/2]\end{array}\right\}$ $\times {}_1F_3\left(\begin{array}{c}\frac{2n+2\varepsilon+1}{2};\ \frac{a^2b^2}{4}\\ \frac{2\varepsilon+1}{2},\ \frac{s+\varepsilon+1}{2},\ \frac{s+\varepsilon+2}{2}\end{array}\right) \qquad \left[\begin{array}{c}a>0;\ \mathrm{Re}\,(s+\varepsilon)>-1;\\ |\arg b|<\pi/4\end{array}\right]$

3.22.4. $H_n(bx)$ and the logarithmic function

Notation: $\varepsilon = 0$ or 1.

1	$\theta(a-x)\ln\dfrac{\sqrt{a}+\sqrt{a-x}}{\sqrt{x}}$ $\times H_{2n+\varepsilon}(bx)$	$(-1)^n\dfrac{2^{\varepsilon-1}(2n+\varepsilon)!\sqrt{\pi}\, a^{s+\varepsilon}b^\varepsilon}{n!\,(s+\varepsilon)}\Gamma\left[\begin{array}{c}s+\varepsilon\\ \frac{2s+2\varepsilon+1}{2}\end{array}\right]$ $\times {}_4F_4\left(\begin{array}{c}-n,\ \frac{s+\varepsilon}{2},\ \frac{s+\varepsilon}{2},\ \frac{s+\varepsilon+1}{2};\ a^2b^2\\ \frac{2\varepsilon+1}{2},\ \frac{2s+2\varepsilon+1}{4},\ \frac{2s+2\varepsilon+3}{4},\ \frac{s+\varepsilon+2}{2}\end{array}\right)$ $[a>0;\ \mathrm{Re}\,s>-\varepsilon]$

No.	$f(x)$	$F(s)$
2	$e^{-b^2x^2}\left\{\begin{array}{l}\ln(x+a)\\ \ln|x-a|\end{array}\right\}$ $\times H_{2n+\varepsilon}(bx)$	$(-1)^n\dfrac{2^{2n+\varepsilon}\pi}{s+\varepsilon}\,a^{s+\varepsilon}b^{\varepsilon}\left(\dfrac{2\varepsilon+1}{2}\right)_n\left\{\begin{array}{l}\csc\left[(s+\varepsilon)\pi\right]\\ \cot\left[(s+\varepsilon)\pi\right]\end{array}\right\}$ $\times\,{}_2F_2\left(\begin{array}{c}\frac{2n+2\varepsilon+1}{2},\,\frac{s+\varepsilon}{2};\,-a^2b^2\\ \frac{2\varepsilon+1}{2},\,\frac{s+\varepsilon+2}{2}\end{array}\right)$ $\pm(-1)^n\dfrac{2^{2n+\varepsilon-1}a}{b^{s-1}}\left(\dfrac{2-s+\varepsilon}{2}\right)_n\Gamma\left(\dfrac{s+\varepsilon-1}{2}\right)$ $\times\,{}_3F_3\left(\begin{array}{c}\frac{1}{2},\,1,\,\frac{2n-s+\varepsilon+2}{2};\,-a^2b^2\\ \frac{3}{2},\,\frac{2-s}{2},\,\frac{3-s}{2}\end{array}\right)$ $-(-1)^n\dfrac{2^{2n+\varepsilon-2}a^2}{b^{s-2}}\left(\dfrac{3-s+\varepsilon}{2}\right)_n\Gamma\left(\dfrac{s+\varepsilon-2}{2}\right)$ $\times\,{}_3F_3\left(\begin{array}{c}1,\,1,\,\frac{2n-s+\varepsilon+3}{2};\,-a^2b^2\\ 2,\,\frac{3-s}{2},\,\frac{4-s}{2}\end{array}\right)+(-1)^n\dfrac{2^{2n+\varepsilon-2}}{b^s}\left(\dfrac{1-s+\varepsilon}{2}\right)_n$ $\times\Gamma\left(\dfrac{s+\varepsilon}{2}\right)\left[\psi\left(\dfrac{s+\varepsilon}{2}\right)-\sum_{k=0}^{n-1}\dfrac{2}{2k-s+\varepsilon+1}-2\ln b\right]$ $[\operatorname{Re}s>-\varepsilon;\ |\arg a|,\,4|\arg b|<\pi]$
3	$e^{-b^2x^2}\left\{\begin{array}{l}\ln(x^2+a^2)\\ \ln|x^2-a^2|\end{array}\right\}$ $\times H_{2n+\varepsilon}(bx)$	$(-1)^n\dfrac{2^{2n+\varepsilon}\pi}{s+\varepsilon}\,a^{s+\varepsilon}b^{\varepsilon}\left(\dfrac{2\varepsilon+1}{2}\right)_n\left\{\begin{array}{l}\csc\left[(s+\varepsilon)\pi/2\right]\\ \cot\left[(s+\varepsilon)\pi/2\right]\end{array}\right\}$ $\times\,{}_2F_2\left(\begin{array}{c}\frac{2n+2\varepsilon+1}{2},\,\frac{s+\varepsilon}{2};\,\pm a^2b^2\\ \frac{2\varepsilon+1}{2},\,\frac{s+\varepsilon+2}{2}\end{array}\right)$ $\pm(-1)^n\dfrac{2^{2n+\varepsilon-1}a^2}{b^{s-2}}\left(\dfrac{3-s+\varepsilon}{2}\right)_n\Gamma\left(\dfrac{s+\varepsilon-2}{2}\right)$ $\times\,{}_3F_3\left(\begin{array}{c}1,\,1,\,\frac{2n-s+\varepsilon+3}{2};\,\pm a^2b^2\\ 2,\,\frac{3-s}{2},\,\frac{4-s}{2}\end{array}\right)$ $+(-1)^n\dfrac{2^{2n+\varepsilon-1}}{b^s}\left(\dfrac{1-s+\varepsilon}{2}\right)_n\Gamma\left(\dfrac{s+\varepsilon}{2}\right)$ $\times\left[\psi\left(\dfrac{s+\varepsilon}{2}\right)-\sum_{k=0}^{n-1}\dfrac{2}{2k-s+\varepsilon+1}-2\ln b\right]$ $[\operatorname{Re}a>0;\ \operatorname{Re}s>-\varepsilon;\ |\arg b|<\pi/4]$

3.22.5. $H_n(bx)$ and inverse trigonometric functions

Notation: $\varepsilon=0$ or 1.

No.	$f(x)$	$F(s)$
1	$\theta(a-x)\arccos\dfrac{x}{a}$ $\times H_{2n+\varepsilon}(bx)$	$\dfrac{(-1)^n2^{\varepsilon-1}(2n+\varepsilon)!\sqrt{\pi}\,a^{s+\varepsilon}b^{\varepsilon}}{n!\,(s+\varepsilon)}\Gamma\left[\begin{array}{c}\frac{s+\varepsilon+1}{2}\\ \frac{s+\varepsilon+2}{2}\end{array}\right]$ $\times\,{}_3F_3\left(\begin{array}{c}-n,\,\frac{s+\varepsilon}{2},\,\frac{s+\varepsilon+1}{2};\,a^2b^2\\ \frac{2\varepsilon+1}{2},\,\frac{s+\varepsilon+2}{2},\,\frac{s+\varepsilon+2}{2}\end{array}\right)$ $[a>0;\ \operatorname{Re}s>-\varepsilon]$

3.22.6. $H_n(bx)$ **and** $\mathrm{Ei}(ax^r)$

Notation: $\varepsilon = 0$ or 1.

1	$e^{-b^2x^2}\,\mathrm{Ei}(-ax)$ $\times\,H_{2n+\varepsilon}(bx)$	$(-1)^{n+1}\dfrac{2^{2n+\varepsilon-1}a}{b^{s+1}}\left(\dfrac{\varepsilon-s}{2}\right)_n \Gamma\left(\dfrac{s+\varepsilon+1}{2}\right)$ $\times\, {}_3F_3\!\left(\begin{matrix}\frac{1}{2},\,\frac{s+1}{2},\,\frac{s+2}{2};\,\frac{a^2}{4b^2}\\ \frac{3}{2},\,\frac{3}{2},\,\frac{s-2n-\varepsilon+2}{2}\end{matrix}\right) + (-1)^n\dfrac{2^{2n+\varepsilon-3}a^2}{b^{s+2}}$ $\times\left(\dfrac{\varepsilon-s-1}{2}\right)_n \Gamma\left(\dfrac{s+\varepsilon+2}{2}\right)$ $\times\,{}_4F_4\!\left(\begin{matrix}1,\,1,\,\frac{s+2}{2},\,\frac{s+3}{2};\,\frac{a^2}{4b^2}\\ 2,\,2,\,\frac{3}{2},\,\frac{s-2n-\varepsilon+3}{2}\end{matrix}\right)$ $+(-1)^n\dfrac{2^{2n+\varepsilon-1}}{b^s}\left(\dfrac{\varepsilon-s+1}{2}\right)_n \Gamma\left(\dfrac{s+\varepsilon}{2}\right)$ $\times\left[\mathbf{C}+\dfrac{1}{2}\psi\left(\dfrac{s+\varepsilon}{2}\right)-\sum_{k=0}^{n-1}\dfrac{1}{2k-s+\varepsilon+1}-\ln\dfrac{b}{a}\right]$ $[\mathrm{Re}\,s>-\varepsilon;\ |\arg a|,\,4|\arg b|<\pi]$
2	$e^{-b^2x^2}\,\mathrm{Ei}(-ax^2)$ $\times\,H_{2n+\varepsilon}(bx)$	$(-1)^{n+1}\dfrac{2^{2n+\varepsilon}b^\varepsilon}{a^{(s+\varepsilon)/2}(s+\varepsilon)}\left(\dfrac{2\varepsilon+1}{2}\right)_n \Gamma\left(\dfrac{s+\varepsilon}{2}\right)$ $\times\,{}_3F_2\!\left(\begin{matrix}\frac{2n+2\varepsilon+1}{2},\,\frac{s+\varepsilon}{2},\,\frac{s+\varepsilon}{2}\\ \frac{2\varepsilon+1}{2},\,\frac{s+\varepsilon+2}{2};\,-\frac{b^2}{a}\end{matrix}\right)$ $[\mathrm{Re}\,(a+b^2)>0;\ \mathrm{Re}\,s>-\varepsilon]$
3	$e^{-(a+b^2)x^2}\,\mathrm{Ei}(ax^2)$ $\times\,H_{2n+\varepsilon}(bx)$	$\dfrac{2^{-s+2n+\varepsilon+2}\pi^{3/2}\csc(s\pi)}{ab^{s-2}\,\Gamma(3-s)\,\Gamma\!\left(\frac{s-2n-\varepsilon-1}{2}\right)}\,{}_3F_2\!\left(\begin{matrix}1,\,1,\,\frac{3-s+2n+\varepsilon}{2}\\ \frac{3-s}{2},\,\frac{4-s}{2};\,-\frac{b^2}{a}\end{matrix}\right)$ $-\dfrac{2^{2n+2\varepsilon-1}\pi^{3/2}b^\varepsilon}{a^{(s+\varepsilon)/2}}\tan^{2\varepsilon-1}\dfrac{s\pi}{2}$ $\times\,\Gamma\!\left[\begin{matrix}\frac{s+\varepsilon}{2}\\ \frac{-2n-2\varepsilon+1}{2}\end{matrix}\right]\,{}_2F_1\!\left(\begin{matrix}\frac{2n+2\varepsilon+1}{2},\,\frac{s+\varepsilon}{2}\\ \frac{2\varepsilon+1}{2};\,-\frac{b^2}{a}\end{matrix}\right)$ $[a>0;\ \mathrm{Re}\,s>-\varepsilon;\ |\arg b|<\pi/4]$
4	$e^{-b^2x^2}\,\mathrm{Ei}(-ax^4)$ $\times\,H_{2n+\varepsilon}(bx)$	$(-1)^{n+1}\dfrac{2^{2n+\varepsilon}b^\varepsilon}{a^{(s+\varepsilon)/4}(s+\varepsilon)}\left(\dfrac{2\varepsilon+1}{2}\right)_n \Gamma\left(\dfrac{s+\varepsilon}{4}\right)$ $\times\,{}_4F_4\!\left(\begin{matrix}\frac{2n+3}{4},\,\frac{2n+4\varepsilon+1}{4},\,\frac{s+\varepsilon}{4},\,\frac{s+\varepsilon}{4}\\ \frac{1}{2},\,\frac{3}{4},\,\frac{4\varepsilon+1}{4},\,\frac{s+\varepsilon+4}{4};\,\frac{b^4}{4a}\end{matrix}\right)$ $+(-1)^n\dfrac{2^{2n+\varepsilon}b^{\varepsilon+2}}{a^{(s+\varepsilon+2)/4}(s+\varepsilon+2)}\left(\dfrac{2\varepsilon+3}{2}\right)_n$ $\times\,\Gamma\left(\dfrac{s+\varepsilon+2}{4}\right)\,{}_4F_4\!\left(\begin{matrix}\frac{2n+5}{4},\,\frac{2n+2\varepsilon+3}{4},\,\frac{s+\varepsilon+2}{4},\,\frac{s+\varepsilon+2}{4}\\ \frac{5}{4},\,\frac{3}{2},\,\frac{4\varepsilon+3}{4},\,\frac{s+\varepsilon+6}{4};\,\frac{b^4}{4a}\end{matrix}\right)$ $[\mathrm{Re}\,a>0;\ \mathrm{Re}\,s>-\varepsilon]$

No.	$f(x)$	$F(s)$
5	$e^{\pm ax^4 - b^2 x^2} \operatorname{Ei}\left(\mp ax^4\right)$ $\times H_{2n+\varepsilon}(bx)$	$\mp \dfrac{2^{2n-s+\varepsilon+4}\sqrt{\pi}}{ab^{s-4}} \Gamma\left[\begin{matrix} s-4 \\ \frac{s-2n-\varepsilon-3}{2}\end{matrix}\right] {}_4F_4\left(\begin{matrix}1,1,\frac{2n-s+\varepsilon+5}{4},\frac{2n-s+\varepsilon+7}{4}\\ \frac{5-s}{4},\frac{6-s}{4},\frac{7-s}{4},\frac{8-s}{4};\mp\frac{b^4}{4a}\end{matrix}\right)$

$$-\frac{2^{2n+\varepsilon-2}\pi^{3/2}}{a^{s/4}}\left\{\begin{matrix}\csc\frac{s\pi}{4}\\ \cot\frac{s\pi}{4}\end{matrix}\right\}\Gamma\left[\begin{matrix}\frac{s}{4}\\ -\frac{2n+\varepsilon-1}{2}\end{matrix}\right]$$

$$\times {}_3F_3\left(\begin{matrix}\frac{2n+\varepsilon+1}{4},\frac{2n+\varepsilon+3}{4},\frac{s}{4}\\ \frac{1}{4},\frac{1}{2},\frac{3}{4};\mp\frac{b^4}{4a}\end{matrix}\right)+\frac{2^{2n+\varepsilon-1}\pi^{3/2}b}{a^{(s+1)/4}}$$

$$\times\left\{\begin{matrix}\csc\frac{(s+1)\pi}{4}\\ \cot\frac{(s+1)\pi}{4}\end{matrix}\right\}\Gamma\left[\begin{matrix}\frac{s+1}{4}\\ -\frac{2n+\varepsilon}{2}\end{matrix}\right]{}_3F_3\left(\begin{matrix}\frac{2n+\varepsilon+2}{4},\frac{2n+\varepsilon+4}{4},\frac{s+1}{4}\\ \frac{1}{2},\frac{3}{4},\frac{5}{4};\mp\frac{b^4}{4a}\end{matrix}\right)$$

$$\mp\frac{2^{2n+\varepsilon-1}\pi^{3/2}b^2}{a^{(s+2)/4}}\left\{\begin{matrix}\sec\frac{s\pi}{4}\\ \tan\frac{s\pi}{4}\end{matrix}\right\}\Gamma\left[\begin{matrix}\frac{s+2}{4}\\ -\frac{2n+\varepsilon+1}{2}\end{matrix}\right]$$

$$\times {}_3F_3\left(\begin{matrix}\frac{2n+\varepsilon+3}{4},\frac{2n+\varepsilon+5}{4},\frac{s+2}{4}\\ \frac{3}{4},\frac{5}{4},\frac{3}{2};\mp\frac{b^4}{4a}\end{matrix}\right)\pm\frac{2^{2n+\varepsilon}\pi^{3/2}b^3}{3a^{(s+3)/4}}$$

$$\times\left\{\begin{matrix}\sec\frac{(s+1)\pi}{4}\\ \tan\frac{(s+1)\pi}{4}\end{matrix}\right\}\Gamma\left[\begin{matrix}\frac{s+3}{4}\\ -\frac{2n+\varepsilon+2}{2}\end{matrix}\right]{}_3F_3\left(\begin{matrix}\frac{2n+\varepsilon+4}{4},\frac{2n+\varepsilon+6}{4},\frac{s+3}{4}\\ \frac{5}{4},\frac{3}{2},\frac{7}{4};\mp\frac{b^4}{4a}\end{matrix}\right)$$

$$\left[\operatorname{Re}s>-\varepsilon;\ |\arg b|<\pi/4;\ \left\{\begin{matrix}|\arg a|<\pi\\ a>0\end{matrix}\right\}\right]$$

3.22.7. $H_n(bx)$ and $\operatorname{si}(ax^r)$, $\operatorname{ci}(ax^r)$

Notation: $\varepsilon = 0$ or 1.

1	$e^{-b^2x^2}\operatorname{si}(ax)H_{2n+\varepsilon}(bx)$	$2^{2n-s+\varepsilon-1}\sqrt{\pi}\,ab^{-s-1}\Gamma\left[\begin{matrix}s+1\\ \frac{s-2n-\varepsilon+2}{2}\end{matrix}\right]$

$$\times {}_3F_3\left(\begin{matrix}\frac{1}{2},\frac{s+1}{2},\frac{s+2}{2};-\frac{a^2}{4b^2}\\ \frac{3}{2},\frac{3}{2},\frac{s-2n-\varepsilon+2}{2}\end{matrix}\right)-\frac{2^{2n-s+\varepsilon-1}\pi^{3/2}}{b^s}\Gamma\left[\begin{matrix}s\\ \frac{s-2n-\varepsilon+1}{2}\end{matrix}\right]$$

$$[a,\operatorname{Re}b>0;\ \operatorname{Re}s>-\varepsilon]$$

2	$e^{-b^2x^2}\operatorname{ci}(ax)H_{2n+\varepsilon}(bx)$	$-2^{2n-s+\varepsilon-4}\sqrt{\pi}\,a^2b^{-s-2}\Gamma\left[\begin{matrix}s+2\\ \frac{s-2n-\varepsilon+3}{2}\end{matrix}\right]$

$$\times {}_4F_4\left(\begin{matrix}1,1,\frac{s+2}{2},\frac{s+3}{2};-\frac{a^2}{4b^2}\\ \frac{3}{2},2,2,\frac{s-2n-\varepsilon+3}{2}\end{matrix}\right)$$

$$+2^{2n-s+\varepsilon}\sqrt{\pi}\,b^{-s}\Gamma\left[\begin{matrix}s\\ \frac{s-2n-\varepsilon+1}{2}\end{matrix}\right]$$

$$\times\left[\psi(s)-\frac{1}{2}\psi\left(\frac{s-2n-\varepsilon+1}{2}\right)+\ln\frac{a}{2b}+\mathbf{C}\right]$$

$$[a,\operatorname{Re}b>0;\ \operatorname{Re}s>-\varepsilon]$$

No.	$f(x)$	$F(s)$
3	$e^{-b^2x^2}\left\{\begin{matrix}\mathrm{si}\left(ax^2\right)\\\mathrm{ci}\left(ax^2\right)\end{matrix}\right\}$ $\times H_{2n+\varepsilon}(bx)$	$\dfrac{(-1)^{n+1}2^{2n+\varepsilon}b^\varepsilon}{a^{(s+\varepsilon)/2}(s+\varepsilon)}\left\{\begin{matrix}\sin\left[(s+\varepsilon)\pi/4\right]\\\cos\left[(s+\varepsilon)\pi/4\right]\end{matrix}\right\}\left(\dfrac{2\varepsilon+1}{2}\right)_n\Gamma\left(\dfrac{s+\varepsilon}{2}\right)$ $\times {}_5F_4\left(\begin{matrix}\frac{2n+3}{4},\ \frac{2n+4\varepsilon+1}{4},\ \frac{s+\varepsilon}{4},\ \frac{s+\varepsilon}{4},\ \frac{s+\varepsilon+2}{4}\\\frac{1}{2},\ \frac{3}{4},\ \frac{4\varepsilon+1}{4},\ \frac{s+\varepsilon+4}{4};\ -\frac{b^4}{a^2}\end{matrix}\right)$ $\pm\dfrac{(-1)^n 2^{s+2n}b^{\varepsilon+2}}{a^{(s+\varepsilon+2)/2}(s+\varepsilon+2)}\left\{\begin{matrix}\cos\left[(s+\varepsilon)\pi/4\right]\\\sin\left[(s+\varepsilon)\pi/4\right]\end{matrix}\right\}$ $\times\left(\dfrac{2\varepsilon+3}{2}\right)_n\Gamma\left(\dfrac{s+\varepsilon+2}{2}\right)$ $\times {}_5F_4\left(\begin{matrix}\frac{2n+5}{4},\ \frac{2n+4\varepsilon+3}{4},\ \frac{s+\varepsilon+2}{4},\ \frac{s+\varepsilon+2}{4},\ \frac{s+\varepsilon+4}{4}\\\frac{5}{4},\ \frac{3}{2},\ \frac{4\varepsilon+3}{4},\ \frac{s+\varepsilon+6}{4};\ -\frac{b^4}{a^2}\end{matrix}\right)$ $[a>0;\ \mathrm{Re}\,s>-\varepsilon;\ \left|\arg b\right|<\pi/4]$

3.22.8. $H_n(bx)$ and $\mathrm{erf}(ax^r)$, $\mathrm{erfc}(ax^r)$

Notation: $\varepsilon=0$ or 1.

No.	$f(x)$	$F(s)$
1	$\mathrm{erfc}(ax)\,H_{2n+\varepsilon}(bx)$	$(-1)^n\dfrac{2^{2n+\varepsilon}a^{-s-\varepsilon}b^\varepsilon}{\sqrt{\pi}\,(s+\varepsilon)}\left(\dfrac{2\varepsilon+1}{2}\right)_n\Gamma\left(\dfrac{s+\varepsilon+1}{2}\right)$ $\times {}_3F_2\left(\begin{matrix}-n,\ \frac{s+\varepsilon}{2},\ \frac{s+\varepsilon+1}{2};\ \frac{b^2}{a^2}\\\frac{2\varepsilon+1}{2},\ \frac{s+\varepsilon+2}{2}\end{matrix}\right)$ $[\mathrm{Re}\,s>-\varepsilon;\ \left|\arg a\right|<\pi/4]$
2	$e^{-b^2x^2}\left\{\begin{matrix}\mathrm{erf}(ax)\\\mathrm{erfc}(ax)\end{matrix}\right\}$ $\times H_{2n}(bx)$	$\mp\dfrac{(-1)^n 2^{2n}}{\sqrt{\pi}\,a^s s}\left(\dfrac{1}{2}\right)_n\Gamma\left(\dfrac{s+1}{2}\right){}_3F_2\left(\begin{matrix}\frac{2n+1}{2},\ \frac{s}{2},\ \frac{s+1}{2}\\\frac{1}{2},\ \frac{s+2}{2};\ -\frac{b^2}{a^2}\end{matrix}\right)$ $+\dfrac{(1\pm1)(-1)^n 2^{2n-2}}{b^s}\left(\dfrac{1-s}{2}\right)_n\Gamma\left(\dfrac{s}{2}\right)$ $[\mathrm{Re}\,s>-(1\pm1)/2;\ \left|\arg a\right|,\ \left|\arg b\right|<\pi/4]$
3	$e^{-b^2x^2}\left\{\begin{matrix}\mathrm{erf}(ax)\\\mathrm{erfc}(ax)\end{matrix}\right\}$ $\times H_{2n+1}(bx)$	$\mp\dfrac{(-1)^n 2^{2n+1}b}{\sqrt{\pi}a^{s+1}(s+1)}\left(\dfrac{3}{2}\right)_n\Gamma\left(\dfrac{s+2}{2}\right)$ $\times {}_3F_2\left(\begin{matrix}\frac{2n+3}{2},\ \frac{s+1}{2},\ \frac{s+2}{2}\\\frac{3}{2},\ \frac{s+3}{2};\ -\frac{b^2}{a^2}\end{matrix}\right)$ $+\dfrac{(1\pm1)(-1)^n 2^{2n-1}}{b^s}\left(\dfrac{2-s}{2}\right)_n\Gamma\left(\dfrac{s+1}{2}\right)$ $[\mathrm{Re}\,s>-1-(1\pm1)/2;\ \left|\arg a\right|,\ \left|\arg b\right|<\pi/4]$

No.	$f(x)$	$F(s)$
4	$e^{-b^2x^2}\left\{\begin{array}{c}\mathrm{erf}\left(ax^2\right)\\ \mathrm{erfc}\left(ax^2\right)\end{array}\right\}$ $\times H_{2n+\varepsilon}(bx)$	$\mp\dfrac{(-1)^n 2^{2n+\varepsilon} b^\varepsilon}{\sqrt{\pi}\,a^{(s+\varepsilon)/2}(s+\varepsilon)}\left(\dfrac{2\varepsilon+1}{2}\right)_n\Gamma\left(\dfrac{s+\varepsilon+2}{4}\right)$ $\times\,{}_4F_4\left(\begin{array}{c}\frac{2n+3}{4},\ \frac{2n+4\varepsilon+1}{4},\ \frac{s+\varepsilon}{4},\ \frac{s+\varepsilon+2}{4}\\ \frac{1}{2},\ \frac{3}{4},\ \frac{4\varepsilon+1}{4},\ \frac{s+\varepsilon+4}{4};\ \frac{b^4}{4a^2}\end{array}\right)$ $\pm\dfrac{(-1)^n 2^{2n+\varepsilon} b^{\varepsilon+2}}{\sqrt{\pi}\,a^{(s+\varepsilon)/2+1}(s+\varepsilon+2)}\left(\dfrac{2\varepsilon+3}{2}\right)_n$ $\times\,\Gamma\left(\dfrac{s+\varepsilon+4}{4}\right){}_4F_4\left(\begin{array}{c}\frac{2n+5}{4},\ \frac{2n+4\varepsilon+3}{4},\ \frac{s+\varepsilon+2}{4},\ \frac{s+\varepsilon+4}{4}\\ \frac{5}{4},\ \frac{3}{2},\ \frac{4\varepsilon+3}{4},\ \frac{s+\varepsilon+6}{4};\ \frac{b^4}{4a^2}\end{array}\right)$ $+\dfrac{(-1)^n(1\pm1)2^{2n+\varepsilon-2}}{b^s}\left(\dfrac{1-s+\varepsilon}{2}\right)_n\Gamma\left(\dfrac{s+\varepsilon}{2}\right)$ $[\mathrm{Re}\,s>-\varepsilon-1\mp1;\ |\arg a|,\ |\arg b|<\pi/4]$
5	$e^{-b^2x^2}\left\{\begin{array}{c}\mathrm{erf}\left(a\sqrt{x}\right)\\ \mathrm{erfc}\left(a\sqrt{x}\right)\end{array}\right\}$ $\times H_n(bx)$	$\pm\dfrac{2^{n-s+1/2}a}{b^{s+1/2}}\Gamma\left[\begin{array}{c}\frac{2s+1}{2}\\ \frac{2s-2n+3}{4}\end{array}\right]{}_3F_3\left(\begin{array}{c}\frac{1}{4},\ \frac{2s+1}{4},\ \frac{2s+3}{4};\ \frac{a^4}{4b^2}\\ \frac{1}{2},\ \frac{5}{4},\ \frac{2s-2n+3}{4}\end{array}\right)$ $\mp\dfrac{2^{n-s-1/2}a^3}{3b^{s+3/2}}\Gamma\left[\begin{array}{c}\frac{2s+3}{2}\\ \frac{2s-2n+5}{4}\end{array}\right]{}_3F_3\left(\begin{array}{c}\frac{3}{4},\ \frac{2s+3}{4},\ \frac{2s+5}{4};\ \frac{a^4}{4b^2}\\ \frac{3}{2},\ \frac{7}{4},\ \frac{2s-2n+5}{4}\end{array}\right)$ $+\dfrac{(1\mp1)2^{n-2}}{b^s}\Gamma\left[\begin{array}{c}\frac{s}{2},\ \frac{s+1}{2}\\ \frac{s-n+1}{2}\end{array}\right]$ $[\mathrm{Re}\,s>\left(-1-(1\pm1)^n\right)/4;\ |\arg a|,\ |\arg b|<\pi/4]$

3.22.9. $H_n(bx)$ **and** $S(ax^r)$, $C(ax^r)$

Notation: $\delta=\left\{\begin{array}{c}1\\0\end{array}\right\}$.

No.	$f(x)$	$F(s)$
1	$e^{-b^2x^2}\left\{\begin{array}{c}S(ax)\\ C(ax)\end{array}\right\}$ $\times H_{2n}(bx)$	$(-1)^n\dfrac{2^{2n-1/2}a^{\delta+1/2}}{3^\delta\sqrt{\pi}\,b^{s+\delta+1/2}}\left(\dfrac{1-2s-2\delta}{4}\right)_n\Gamma\left(\dfrac{2s+2\delta+1}{4}\right)$ $\times\,{}_3F_3\left(\begin{array}{c}\frac{2\delta+1}{4},\ \frac{2s+3}{4},\ \frac{2s+4\delta+1}{4};\ -\frac{a^2}{4b^2}\\ \frac{2\delta+1}{2},\ \frac{2\delta+5}{4},\ \frac{2s-4n+2\delta+3}{4}\end{array}\right)$ $[a>0;\ \mathrm{Re}\,s>-\left(2\pm1\right)/2;\ |\arg b|<\pi/4]$
2	$e^{-b^2x^2}\left\{\begin{array}{c}S(ax)\\ C(ax)\end{array}\right\}$ $\times H_{2n+1}(bx)$	$(-1)^n\dfrac{2^{2n+1/2}a^{\delta+1/2}}{3^\delta\sqrt{\pi}\,b^{s+\delta+1/2}}\left(\dfrac{3-2s-2\delta}{4}\right)_n\Gamma\left(\dfrac{2s+2\delta+3}{4}\right)$ $\times\,{}_3F_3\left(\begin{array}{c}\frac{2\delta+1}{4},\ \frac{2s+3}{4},\ \frac{2s+4\delta+1}{4};\ -\frac{a^2}{4b^2}\\ \frac{2\delta+1}{2},\ \frac{2\delta+5}{4},\ \frac{2s-4n+2\delta+1}{4}\end{array}\right)$ $[a>0;\ \mathrm{Re}\,s>-1-\left(2\pm1\right)/2;\ |\arg b|<\pi/4]$

No.	$f(x)$	$F(s)$
3	$e^{-b^2x^2}\begin{Bmatrix} S\left(ax^2\right) \\ C\left(ax^2\right) \end{Bmatrix}$ $\times H_{2n}(bx)$	$(-1)^n \dfrac{2^{2n-1/2}a^{\delta+1/2}}{3^\delta\sqrt{\pi}\,b^{s+2\delta+1}}\left(-\dfrac{s+2\delta}{2}\right)_n \Gamma\left(\dfrac{s+2\delta+1}{2}\right)$ $\times {}_5F_4\left(\begin{matrix} \frac{2\delta+1}{4},\ \frac{s+3}{4},\ \frac{s+4}{4},\ \frac{s+4\delta+1}{4},\ \frac{s+4\delta+2}{4} \\ \frac{2\delta+1}{2},\ \frac{2\delta+5}{4},\ \frac{s-2n+4}{4},\ \frac{s-2n+4\delta+2}{4};\ -\frac{a^2}{b^4} \end{matrix}\right)$ $[a>0;\ \operatorname{Re}s>-2\mp 1;\ |\arg b|<\pi/4]$
4	$e^{-b^2x^2}\begin{Bmatrix} S\left(ax^2\right) \\ C\left(ax^2\right) \end{Bmatrix}$ $\times H_{2n+1}(bx)$	$(-1)^n \dfrac{2^{2n+1/2}a^{\delta+1/2}}{3^\delta\sqrt{\pi}\,b^{s+2\delta+1}}\left(\dfrac{1-s-2\delta}{2}\right)_n \Gamma\left(\dfrac{s+2\delta+2}{2}\right)$ $\times {}_5F_4\left(\begin{matrix} \frac{2\delta+1}{4},\ \frac{s+3}{4},\ \frac{s+4}{4},\ \frac{s+4\delta+1}{4},\ \frac{s+4\delta+2}{4} \\ \frac{2\delta+1}{2},\ \frac{2\delta+5}{4},\ \frac{s-2n+3}{4},\ \frac{s-2n+4\delta+1}{4};\ -\frac{a^2}{b^4} \end{matrix}\right)$ $[a>0;\ \operatorname{Re}s>-3\mp 1;\ |\arg b|<\pi/4]$

3.22.10. $\quad H_n(bx)$ **and** $\gamma(\nu, ax^r),\ \Gamma(\nu, ax^r)$

Notation: $\varepsilon = 0$ or 1.

1	$\Gamma(\nu,\,ax)\,H_{2n+\varepsilon}(bx)$	$\dfrac{(-1)^n\,2^{2n+2\varepsilon}a^{-s-\varepsilon}b^\varepsilon}{\sqrt{\pi}\,(s+\varepsilon)}\,\Gamma\left(n+\dfrac{2\varepsilon+1}{2}\right)\Gamma(s+\nu+\varepsilon)$ $\times {}_4F_2\left(\begin{matrix} -n,\ \frac{s+\varepsilon}{2},\ \frac{s+\nu+\varepsilon}{2},\ \frac{s+\nu+\varepsilon+1}{2} \\ \frac{2\varepsilon+1}{2},\ \frac{s-\varepsilon+4}{2};\ \frac{4b^2}{a^2} \end{matrix}\right)$ $[\operatorname{Re}a>0;\ \operatorname{Re}(s+\nu)>-\varepsilon]$
2	$e^{-b^2x^2}\begin{Bmatrix} \gamma(\nu,\,ax) \\ \Gamma(\nu,\,ax) \end{Bmatrix}$ $\times H_{2n+\varepsilon}(bx)$	$\pm(-1)^n\dfrac{2^{2n+\varepsilon-1}a^\nu}{\nu\,b^{s+\nu}}\left(\dfrac{1-s-\nu+\varepsilon}{2}\right)_n \Gamma\left(\dfrac{s+\nu+\varepsilon}{2}\right)$ $\times {}_3F_3\left(\begin{matrix} \frac{\nu}{2},\ \frac{s+\nu}{2},\ \frac{s+\nu+1}{2};\ \frac{a^2}{4b^2} \\ \frac{1}{2},\ \frac{\nu+2}{2},\ \frac{s-2n+\nu-\varepsilon+1}{2} \end{matrix}\right)$ $\mp(-1)^n\dfrac{2^{2n+\varepsilon-1}a^{\nu+1}}{(\nu+1)\,b^{s+\nu+1}}\left(\dfrac{-s-\nu+\varepsilon}{2}\right)_n$ $\times \Gamma\left(\dfrac{s+\nu+\varepsilon+1}{2}\right){}_3F_3\left(\begin{matrix} \frac{\nu+1}{2},\ \frac{s+\nu+1}{2},\ \frac{s+\nu+2}{2};\ \frac{a^2}{4b^2} \\ \frac{3}{2},\ \frac{\nu+3}{2},\ \frac{s-2n+\nu-\varepsilon+2}{2} \end{matrix}\right)$ $+(-1)^n\dfrac{(1\mp1)\,2^{2n+\varepsilon-2}}{b^s}\left(\dfrac{1-s+\varepsilon}{2}\right)_n$ $\times \Gamma(\nu)\,\Gamma\left(\dfrac{s+\varepsilon}{2}\right)$ $\left[\operatorname{Re}a>0;\ \operatorname{Re}(s+\nu)>-\varepsilon;\begin{Bmatrix} \operatorname{Re}\nu>0 \\ \operatorname{Re}s>-\varepsilon \end{Bmatrix},\ |\arg b|<\pi/4\right]$

No.	$f(x)$	$F(s)$
3	$e^{-b^2x^2}\begin{Bmatrix}\gamma(\nu,ax^2)\\\Gamma(\nu,ax^2)\end{Bmatrix}$ $\times H_{2n+\varepsilon}(bx)$	$\mp(-1)^n\dfrac{2^{2n+\varepsilon}b^\varepsilon}{(s+\varepsilon)a^{(s+\varepsilon)/2}}\left(\dfrac{2\varepsilon+1}{2}\right)_n$ $\times\Gamma\left(\dfrac{s+2\nu+\varepsilon}{2}\right){}_3F_2\left(\begin{matrix}\frac{2n+2\varepsilon+1}{2},\frac{s+\varepsilon}{2},\frac{s+2\nu+\varepsilon}{2}\\\frac{2\varepsilon+1}{2},\frac{s+\varepsilon+2}{2};-\frac{b^2}{a}\end{matrix}\right)$ $+(-1)^n\dfrac{(1\pm1)2^{2n+\varepsilon-2}}{b^s}\left(\dfrac{1-s+\varepsilon}{2}\right)_n\Gamma(\nu)\,\Gamma\left(\dfrac{s+\varepsilon}{2}\right)$ $\left[\mathrm{Re}\,a>0;\ \mathrm{Re}\,(s+2\nu)>-\varepsilon;\begin{Bmatrix}\mathrm{Re}\,\nu>0\\\mathrm{Re}\,s>-\varepsilon\end{Bmatrix},\ |\arg b|<\pi/4\right]$

3.22.11. $H_n(bx)$ and $J_\nu(ax^r)$, $I_\nu(ax^r)$

Notation: $\varepsilon=0$ or 1.

No.	$f(x)$	$F(s)$
1	$J_\nu(ax)H_n(bx)$	$\dfrac{2^{s+2n-1}b^n}{a^{n+s}}\Gamma\left[\begin{matrix}\frac{s+\nu+n}{2}\\\frac{2-s-n+\nu}{2}\end{matrix}\right]{}_2F_2\left(\begin{matrix}-\frac{n}{2},\frac{1-n}{2};\frac{a^2}{4b^2}\\\frac{2-s-n-\nu}{2},\frac{2-s-n+\nu}{2}\end{matrix}\right)$ $[a>0;\ 2[n/2]-n-\mathrm{Re}\,\nu<\mathrm{Re}\,s<3/2-n]$
2	$J_\nu\left(\dfrac{a}{x}\right)H_{2n+\varepsilon}(bx)$	$\dfrac{(-1)^n a^{s+\varepsilon}b^\varepsilon}{2^{s-2n+1}}\left(\dfrac{2\varepsilon+1}{2}\right)_n\Gamma\left[\begin{matrix}\frac{\nu-s-\varepsilon}{2}\\\frac{s+\nu+\varepsilon+2}{2}\end{matrix}\right]$ $\times{}_1F_3\left(\begin{matrix}-n;-\frac{a^2b^2}{4}\\\frac{2\varepsilon+1}{2},\frac{s+\nu+\varepsilon+2}{2},\frac{s-\nu+\varepsilon+2}{2}\end{matrix}\right)$ $[a>0;\ -\varepsilon-3/2<\mathrm{Re}\,s<\mathrm{Re}\,\nu-2n-\varepsilon]$
3	$e^{-b^2x^2}\begin{Bmatrix}J_\nu(ax)\\I_\nu(ax)\end{Bmatrix}$ $\times H_{2n+\varepsilon}(bx)$	$(-1)^n\dfrac{2^{2n+\varepsilon-\nu-1}a^\nu}{b^{s+\nu}}\left(\dfrac{1-s-\nu+\varepsilon}{2}\right)_n\Gamma\left[\begin{matrix}\frac{s+\varepsilon+\nu}{2}\\\nu+1\end{matrix}\right]$ $\times{}_2F_2\left(\begin{matrix}\frac{s+\nu}{2},\frac{s+\nu+1}{2};\mp\frac{a^2}{4b^2}\\\nu+1,\frac{s-2n+\nu-\varepsilon+1}{2}\end{matrix}\right)$ $[\mathrm{Re}\,(s+\nu)>-\varepsilon;\ |\arg a|,\,4|\arg b|<\pi]$
4	$e^{-b^2x^2}\begin{Bmatrix}J_\nu(ax^2)\\I_\nu(ax^2)\end{Bmatrix}$ $\times H_{2n+\varepsilon}(bx)$	$(-1)^n\dfrac{2^{2n+\varepsilon-\nu-1}a^\nu}{b^{s+2\nu}}\left(\dfrac{1-s-2\nu+\varepsilon}{2}\right)_n\Gamma\left[\begin{matrix}\frac{s+\varepsilon+2\nu}{2}\\\nu+1\end{matrix}\right]$ $\times{}_4F_3\left(\begin{matrix}\frac{s+2\nu}{4},\frac{s+2\nu+1}{4},\frac{s+2\nu+2}{4},\frac{s+2\nu+3}{4}\\\nu+1,\frac{s-2n+2\nu-\varepsilon+1}{4},\frac{s-2n+2\nu-\varepsilon+3}{4};\mp\frac{a^2}{b^4}\end{matrix}\right)$ $\left[\begin{matrix}\mathrm{Re}\,(s+2\nu)>-\varepsilon;\ |\arg b|<\pi/4;\\\begin{Bmatrix}a>0\\\mathrm{Re}\,(b^2-a)>0;\ |\arg a|<\pi\end{Bmatrix}\end{matrix}\right]$

3.22.12. $H_n(bx)$ **and** $Y_\nu(ax^r)$, $K_\nu(ax^r)$

Notation: $\varepsilon = 0$ or 1.

1	$K_\nu(ax) H_n(bx)$	$\dfrac{2^{s+2n-2}b^n}{a^{s+n}} \Gamma\left(\dfrac{s+n-\nu}{2}\right) \Gamma\left(\dfrac{s+n+\nu}{2}\right)$

$$\times\, _2F_2\left(\begin{matrix} -\frac{n}{2}, \frac{1-n}{2}; & -\frac{a^2}{4b^2} \\ \frac{2-s-n-\nu}{2}, & \frac{2-s-n+\nu}{2} \end{matrix}\right)$$

$$[\mathrm{Re}\,a > 0;\ \mathrm{Re}\,s > |\mathrm{Re}\,\nu| + 2\,[n/2] - n]$$

2	$K_\nu\left(\dfrac{a}{x}\right) H_{2n+\varepsilon}(bx)$	$\dfrac{(-1)^n a^{s+\varepsilon}b^\varepsilon}{2^{s-2n+2}} \left(\dfrac{2\varepsilon+1}{2}\right)_n \Gamma\left(\dfrac{\nu-s-\varepsilon}{2}\right) \Gamma\left(-\dfrac{s+\nu+\varepsilon}{2}\right)$

$$\times\, _1F_3\left(\begin{matrix} -n; & \frac{a^2b^2}{4} \\ \frac{2\varepsilon+1}{2}, & \frac{s+\nu+\varepsilon+2}{2}, & \frac{s-\nu+\varepsilon+2}{2} \end{matrix}\right)$$

$$[\mathrm{Re}\,a > 0;\ \mathrm{Re}\,s < -|\mathrm{Re}\,\nu| - 2n - \varepsilon]$$

3	$e^{-b^2x^2}\left\{\begin{matrix} Y_\nu(ax) \\ K_\nu(ax) \end{matrix}\right\}$ $\times\, H_{2n+\varepsilon}(bx)$	$\mp(-1)^n \dfrac{2^{2n+\nu+\varepsilon-2}}{\pi a^\nu b^{s-\nu}} \left(\dfrac{1-s+\nu+\varepsilon}{2}\right)_n \Gamma(\nu)$

$$\times\left\{\begin{matrix} 2 \\ \pi \end{matrix}\right\}\Gamma\left(\dfrac{s-\nu+\varepsilon}{2}\right) \, _2F_2\left(\begin{matrix} \frac{s-\nu}{2}, & \frac{s-\nu+1}{2}; & \mp\frac{a^2}{4b^2} \\ 1-\nu, & \frac{s-2n-\nu-\varepsilon+1}{2} \end{matrix}\right)$$

$$\mp(-1)^n \dfrac{2^{2n-\nu+\varepsilon-2}a^\nu}{\pi b^{s+\nu}} \left(\dfrac{1-s-\nu+\varepsilon}{2}\right)_n \Gamma(-\nu)$$

$$\times\left\{\begin{matrix} 2\cos(\nu\pi) \\ \pi \end{matrix}\right\}\Gamma\left(\dfrac{s+\varepsilon+\nu}{2}\right) \, _2F_2\left(\begin{matrix} \frac{s+\nu}{2}, & \frac{s+\nu+1}{2}; & \mp\frac{a^2}{4b^2} \\ 1+\nu, & \frac{s-2n+\nu-\varepsilon+1}{2} \end{matrix}\right)$$

$$[\mathrm{Re}\,s > |\mathrm{Re}\,\nu| - \varepsilon;\ |\arg a|,\ |\arg b| < \pi/4]$$

4	$e^{-b^2x^2}\left\{\begin{matrix} Y_\nu(ax^2) \\ K_\nu(ax^2) \end{matrix}\right\}$ $\times\, H_{2n+\varepsilon}(bx)$	$\mp \dfrac{(-1)^n 2^{-s+2n+3\nu+\varepsilon-(1\mp1)/2}\pi^{\mp1/2}}{a^\nu b^{s-2\nu}}$

$$\times\left(\dfrac{1-s+2\nu+\varepsilon}{2}\right)_n \Gamma\left[\begin{matrix} \nu, s-2\nu \\ \frac{s-2\nu-\varepsilon+1}{2} \end{matrix}\right]$$

$$\times\, _4F_3\left(\begin{matrix} \frac{s-2\nu}{4}, & \frac{s-2\nu+1}{4}, & \frac{s-2\nu+2}{4}, & \frac{s-2\nu+3}{4}; & \mp\frac{a^2}{b^4} \\ 1-\nu, & \frac{s-2n-2\nu-\varepsilon+1}{4}, & \frac{s-2n-2\nu-\varepsilon+3}{4} \end{matrix}\right)$$

$$\mp \dfrac{(-1)^n 2^{-s+2n-3\nu+\varepsilon-(1\mp1)/2}\pi^{\mp1/2}[\cos(\nu\pi)]^{(1\pm1)/2}}{a^{-\nu}b^{s+2\nu}}$$

$$\times\left(\dfrac{1-s-2\nu+\varepsilon}{2}\right)_n \Gamma\left[\begin{matrix} -\nu, s+2\nu \\ \frac{s+2\nu-\varepsilon+1}{2} \end{matrix}\right]$$

$$\times\, _4F_3\left(\begin{matrix} \frac{s+2\nu}{4}, & \frac{s+2\nu+1}{4}, & \frac{s+2\nu+2}{4}, & \frac{s+2\nu+3}{4}; & \mp\frac{a^2}{b^4} \\ 1+\nu, & \frac{s-2n+2\nu-\varepsilon+1}{4}, & \frac{s-2n+2\nu-\varepsilon+3}{4} \end{matrix}\right)$$

$$\left[\left\{\begin{matrix} \mathrm{Re}\,b^2 > |\mathrm{Im}\,a| \\ \mathrm{Re}\,(a+b^2) > 0 \end{matrix}\right\};\ \mathrm{Re}\,s > 2|\mathrm{Re}\,\nu| - \varepsilon;\ |\arg a|,\ 4|\arg b| < \pi\right]$$

3.22.13. $H_n(bx)$ **and** $P_m(\varphi(x))$

Notation: $\varepsilon = 0$ or 1.

1	$\theta(a-x)P_m\left(\dfrac{x}{a}\right)$ $\times H_{2n+\varepsilon}(bx)$	$(-1)^n\,2^{2n-s+\varepsilon}a^{s+\varepsilon}b^\varepsilon\,\Gamma\left[\begin{array}{c}\frac{2n+2\varepsilon+1}{2},\ s+\varepsilon\\ \frac{s-m+\varepsilon+1}{2},\ \frac{s+m+\varepsilon+2}{2}\end{array}\right]$ $\times\,{}_3F_3\left(\begin{array}{c}-n,\ \frac{s+\varepsilon}{2},\ \frac{s+\varepsilon+1}{2};\ a^2b^2\\ \frac{2\varepsilon+1}{2},\ \frac{s-m+\varepsilon+1}{2},\ \frac{s+m+\varepsilon+2}{2}\end{array}\right)$ $[a>0;\ \operatorname{Re}s>((-1)^m+(-1)^\varepsilon)/2-1]$
2	$\theta(a-x)\,e^{-b^2x^2}$ $\times P_n\left(\dfrac{2x^2}{a^2}-1\right)$ $\times H_{2m+\varepsilon}(bx)$	$(-1)^{m+n}\,2^{2m+\varepsilon-1}\,a^{s+\varepsilon}b^\varepsilon\left(\dfrac{2\varepsilon+1}{2}\right)_m\left(\dfrac{2-s-\varepsilon}{2}\right)_n$ $\times\,\Gamma\left[\begin{array}{c}\frac{s+\varepsilon}{2}\\ \frac{s+2n+\varepsilon+2}{2}\end{array}\right]{}_3F_3\left(\begin{array}{c}\frac{2m+2\varepsilon+1}{2},\ \frac{s+\varepsilon}{2},\ \frac{s+\varepsilon}{2};\ -a^2b^2\\ \frac{2\varepsilon+1}{2},\ \frac{s-2n+\varepsilon}{2},\ \frac{s+2n+\varepsilon+2}{2}\end{array}\right)$ $[a>0;\ \operatorname{Re}s>-\varepsilon]$
3	$\theta(x-a)P_m\left(\dfrac{a}{x}\right)$ $\times H_{2n+\varepsilon}(bx)$	$\dfrac{(-1)^{n+1}}{\sqrt{\pi}}2^{s+2n+2\varepsilon-1}a^{s+\varepsilon}b^\varepsilon\left(\dfrac{2\varepsilon+1}{2}\right)_n$ $\times\,\Gamma\left[\begin{array}{c}\frac{s-m+\varepsilon}{2},\ \frac{s+m+\varepsilon+1}{2}\\ s+\varepsilon+1\end{array}\right]{}_3F_3\left(\begin{array}{c}-n,\ \frac{s-m+\varepsilon}{2},\ \frac{s+m+\varepsilon+1}{2}\\ \frac{2\varepsilon+1}{2},\ \frac{s+\varepsilon+1}{2},\ \frac{s+\varepsilon+2}{2};\ a^2b^2\end{array}\right)$ $[a>0;\ \operatorname{Re}s<(1-(-1)^m)/2-2n-\varepsilon]$

3.22.14. $H_n(bx)$ **and** $T_m(\varphi(x))$, $U_m(\varphi(x))$

Notation: $\varepsilon = 0$ or 1.

1	$(a^2-x^2)_+^{-1/2}e^{-b^2x^2}$ $\times T_n\left(\dfrac{2x^2}{a^2}-1\right)$ $\times H_{2m+\varepsilon}(bx)$	$(-1)^{m+n}\,2^{2m+\varepsilon-1}\sqrt{\pi}\,a^{s+\varepsilon-1}b^\varepsilon\left(\dfrac{2\varepsilon+1}{2}\right)_m\left(\dfrac{1-s-\varepsilon}{2}\right)_n$ $\times\,\Gamma\left[\begin{array}{c}\frac{s+\varepsilon}{2}\\ \frac{s+2n+\varepsilon+1}{2}\end{array}\right]{}_3F_3\left(\begin{array}{c}\frac{2m+2\varepsilon+1}{2},\ \frac{s+\varepsilon}{2},\ \frac{s+\varepsilon+1}{2};\ -a^2b^2\\ \frac{2\varepsilon+1}{2},\ \frac{s-2n+\varepsilon+1}{2},\ \frac{s+2n+\varepsilon+1}{2}\end{array}\right)$ $[a>0;\ \operatorname{Re}s>-\varepsilon]$
2	$(a^2-x^2)_+^{1/2}e^{-b^2x^2}$ $\times U_n\left(\dfrac{2x^2}{a^2}-1\right)$ $\times H_{2m+\varepsilon}(bx)$	$(-1)^{m+n}\,2^{2m+\varepsilon-2}\,(n+1)\sqrt{\pi}\,a^{s+\varepsilon+1}b^\varepsilon\left(\dfrac{2\varepsilon+1}{2}\right)_m$ $\times\left(\dfrac{3-s-\varepsilon}{2}\right)_n\Gamma\left[\begin{array}{c}\frac{s+\varepsilon}{2}\\ \frac{s+2n+\varepsilon+3}{2}\end{array}\right]$ $\times\,{}_3F_3\left(\begin{array}{c}\frac{2m+2\varepsilon+1}{2},\ \frac{s+\varepsilon-1}{2},\ \frac{s+\varepsilon}{2};\ -a^2b^2\\ \frac{2\varepsilon+1}{2},\ \frac{s-2n+\varepsilon-1}{2},\ \frac{s+2n+\varepsilon+3}{2}\end{array}\right)$ $[a>0;\ \operatorname{Re}s>-\varepsilon]$

3.22.15. Products of $H_n(bx)$

Notation: δ, $\varepsilon = 0$ or 1.

1	$e^{-ax^2} H_{2m+\varepsilon}(bx)$	$\dfrac{(-1)^{m+n}(2m+\varepsilon)!(2n+\varepsilon)!(bc)^\varepsilon}{2m!\,n!\,a^{s/2+\varepsilon}} \Gamma\left(\dfrac{s+2\varepsilon}{2}\right)$
	$\times H_{2n+\varepsilon}(cx)$	$\times F_2\left(\dfrac{s+2\varepsilon}{2}, -m, -n; \dfrac{2\varepsilon+1}{2}, \dfrac{2\varepsilon+1}{2}; \dfrac{b^2}{a}, \dfrac{c^2}{a}\right) \left[\begin{array}{l}\operatorname{Re}a>0;\\ \operatorname{Re}s>-2\varepsilon\end{array}\right]$
2	$e^{-a^2x^2} H_m(ax) H_n(ax)$	$\dfrac{\sqrt{\pi}}{2^{s-m-n}a^s} \Gamma\left[\begin{array}{c} s \\ \frac{s-m-n+1}{2}\end{array}\right] {}_2F_1\left(\begin{array}{c}-m,\,-n;\\ \frac{s-m-n+1}{2};\,\frac{1}{2}\end{array}\right)$ $\qquad$ $[\operatorname{Re}a,\ \operatorname{Re}s>0]$
3	$e^{-ax^2} H_{2m+\delta}(bx)$	$\dfrac{2^{2n+2m+\delta+\varepsilon+1}\pi bc}{a^{(s+2)/2}} \Gamma\left[\begin{array}{c}\frac{s+2}{2}\\ -\frac{2m+\delta}{2}, -\frac{2n+\varepsilon}{2}\end{array}\right]$
	$\times H_{2n+\varepsilon}(cx)$	$\times F_2\left(\dfrac{s+2}{2}, -\dfrac{2m+\delta-1}{2}, -\dfrac{2n+\varepsilon-1}{2}; \dfrac{3}{2}, \dfrac{3}{2}; \dfrac{b^2}{a}, \dfrac{c^2}{a}\right)$
		$\qquad -\dfrac{2^{2n+2m+\delta+\varepsilon}\pi b}{a^{(s+1)/2}} \Gamma\left[\begin{array}{c}\frac{s+1}{2}\\ -\frac{2m+\delta}{2}, -\frac{2n+\varepsilon-1}{2}\end{array}\right]$
		$\qquad\times F_2\left(\dfrac{s+1}{2}, -\dfrac{2m+\delta-1}{2}, -\dfrac{2n+\varepsilon}{2}; \dfrac{3}{2}, \dfrac{1}{2}; \dfrac{b^2}{a}, \dfrac{c^2}{a}\right)$
		$\qquad -\dfrac{2^{2n+2m+\delta+\varepsilon}\pi c}{a^{(s+1)/2}} \Gamma\left[\begin{array}{c}\frac{s+1}{2}\\ -\frac{2m+\delta-1}{2}, -\frac{2n+\varepsilon}{2}\end{array}\right]$
		$\qquad\times F_2\left(\dfrac{s+1}{2}, -\dfrac{2m+\delta}{2}, -\dfrac{2n+\varepsilon-1}{2}; \dfrac{1}{2}, \dfrac{3}{2}; \dfrac{b^2}{a}, \dfrac{c^2}{a}\right)$
		$\qquad +\dfrac{2^{2n+2m+\delta+\varepsilon-1}\pi}{a^{s/2}} \Gamma\left[\begin{array}{c}\frac{s}{2}\\ -\frac{2m+\delta-1}{2}, -\frac{2n+\varepsilon-1}{2}\end{array}\right]$
		$\qquad\times F_2\left(\dfrac{s}{2}, -\dfrac{2m+\delta}{2}, -\dfrac{2n+\varepsilon}{2}; \dfrac{1}{2}, \dfrac{1}{2}; \dfrac{b^2}{a}, \dfrac{c^2}{a}\right) \left[\begin{array}{l}\operatorname{Re}a>0;\\ \operatorname{Re}s>-\delta-\varepsilon\end{array}\right]$
4	$e^{-(a^2+b^2)x^2} H_{2m+\varepsilon}(ax)$	$\dfrac{(-1)^{m+n}2^{2m+2n+\delta+\varepsilon-1}b^\delta}{a^{s+\delta}} \left(\dfrac{2\delta+1}{2}\right)_n \left(\dfrac{1-s-\delta+\varepsilon}{2}\right)_m$
	$\times H_{2n+\delta}(bx)$	$\times \Gamma\left(\dfrac{s+\delta+\varepsilon}{2}\right) {}_3F_2\left(\begin{array}{c}\frac{2n+2\delta+1}{2}, \frac{s+\delta}{2}, \frac{s+\delta+1}{2}\\ \frac{2\delta+1}{2}, \frac{s-2m+\delta-\varepsilon+1}{2};\, -\frac{b^2}{a^2}\end{array}\right)$
		$\qquad\qquad\qquad [\operatorname{Re}(a^2+b^2)>0;\ \operatorname{Re}s>-\delta-\varepsilon]$
5	$e^{-a^2x^4-b^2x^2} H_{2m+\varepsilon}(ax^2)$	$\dfrac{(-1)^{m+n}2^{2m+2n+\delta+\varepsilon-2}b^\delta}{a^{(s+\delta)/2}} \left(\dfrac{2\delta+1}{2}\right)_n \left(\dfrac{2-s-\delta+2\varepsilon}{4}\right)_m$
	$\times H_{2n+\delta}(bx)$	$\times \Gamma\left(\dfrac{s+2\varepsilon+\delta}{4}\right) {}_4F_4\left(\begin{array}{c}\frac{2n+3}{4}, \frac{2n+4\delta+1}{4}, \frac{s+\delta}{4}, \frac{s+\delta+2}{4}\\ \frac{1}{2}, \frac{3}{4}, \frac{4\delta+1}{4}, \frac{s-4m+\delta-2\varepsilon+2}{4};\, \frac{b^4}{4b^2}\end{array}\right)$
		$\qquad -\dfrac{(-1)^{m+n}2^{2m+2n+\delta+\varepsilon-2}b^{\delta+2}}{a^{(s+\delta)/2+1}} \left(\dfrac{2\delta+3}{2}\right)_n \left(\dfrac{2\varepsilon-\delta-s}{4}\right)_m$
		$\qquad\times \Gamma\left(\dfrac{s+\delta+2\varepsilon+2}{4}\right) {}_4F_4\left(\begin{array}{c}\frac{2n+5}{2}, \frac{2n+4\delta+3}{4}, \frac{s+\delta+2}{4}, \frac{s+\delta+4}{4}\\ \frac{3}{2}, \frac{5}{4}, \frac{4\delta+3}{4}, \frac{s-4m+\delta-2\varepsilon+4}{4};\, \frac{b^4}{4a^2}\end{array}\right)$
		$\qquad\qquad [\operatorname{Re}s>-\delta-2\varepsilon;\ |\arg a|,\ |\arg b|<\pi/4]$

3.23. The Laguerre Polynomials $L_n^\lambda(z)$

More formulas can be obtained from the corresponding sections due to the relations

$$L_n^{-1/2}(z) = \frac{(-1)^n}{n!\, 2^{2n}} H_{2n}\left(\sqrt{z}\right), \quad L_n^{1/2}(z) = \frac{(-1)^n}{n!\, 2^{2n+1}\sqrt{z}} H_{2n+1}\left(\sqrt{z}\right),$$

$$L_n^\lambda(z) = \lim_{\sigma\to\infty} P_n^{(\lambda,\,\sigma)}\left(1 - \frac{2z}{\sigma}\right),$$

$$L_\nu(z) = {}_1F_1\left(-\nu;\, 1;\, z\right),$$

$$L_\nu^\lambda(z) = \frac{(\lambda+1)_\nu}{\Gamma(\nu+1)}\, {}_1F_1\left(-\nu;\, \lambda+1;\, z\right),$$

$$L_\nu^\lambda(z) = \frac{e^z}{\Gamma(\nu+1)}\, G_{12}^{11}\left(z\, \middle|\, \begin{matrix} -\lambda-\nu \\ 0,\, -\lambda \end{matrix}\right).$$

3.23.1. $L_n^\lambda(bx)$ and algebraic functions

No.	$f(x)$	$F(s)$
1	$(a-x)_+^{\alpha-1}\, L_n^\lambda(bx)$	$\dfrac{(\lambda+1)_n\, a^{s+\alpha-1}}{n!}\, \mathrm{B}(\alpha,\, s)\, {}_2F_2\!\left(\begin{matrix}-n,\, s;\, ab \\ \lambda+1,\, s+\alpha\end{matrix}\right)$ $\quad$ $[a,\ \mathrm{Re}\,\alpha,\ \mathrm{Re}\,s > 0]$
2	$(x-a)_+^{\alpha-1}\, L_n^\lambda(bx)$	$\dfrac{(\lambda+1)_n\, a^{s+\alpha-1}}{n!}\, \mathrm{B}(\alpha,\, 1-s-\alpha)\, {}_2F_2\!\left(\begin{matrix}-n,\, s;\, ab \\ \lambda+1,\, s+\alpha\end{matrix}\right)$ $[a,\ \mathrm{Re}\,\alpha > 0;\ \mathrm{Re}\,(s+\alpha) < 1-n]$
3	$\dfrac{1}{(x+a)^\rho}\, L_n^\lambda(bx)$	$\dfrac{(\lambda+1)_n\, a^{s-\rho}}{n!}\, \mathrm{B}(s,\, \rho-s)\, {}_2F_2\!\left(\begin{matrix}-n,\, s;\, -ab \\ \lambda+1,\, s-\rho+1\end{matrix}\right)$ $[\mathrm{Re}\,s > 0;\ \mathrm{Re}\,(s-\rho) < -n;\ |\arg a| < \pi]$
4	$(a-x)_+^{\alpha-1}$ $\times L_n^\lambda(bx\,(a-x))$	$\dfrac{(\lambda+1)_n\, a^{s+\alpha-1}}{n!}\, \mathrm{B}(s,\, \alpha)\, {}_3F_3\!\left(\begin{matrix}-n,\, s,\, \alpha;\, \frac{a^2 b}{4} \\ \lambda+1,\, \frac{s+\alpha}{2},\, \frac{s+\alpha+1}{2}\end{matrix}\right)$ $[a,\ \mathrm{Re}\,s,\ \mathrm{Re}\,\alpha > 0]$
5	$\dfrac{1}{(x+a)^\rho}\, L_n^\lambda\!\left(\dfrac{b}{x+a}\right)$	$\dfrac{(\lambda+1)_n\, a^{s-\rho}}{n!}\, \mathrm{B}(s,\, \rho-s)\, {}_2F_2\!\left(\begin{matrix}-n,\, \rho-s \\ \lambda+1,\, \rho;\, \frac{b}{a}\end{matrix}\right)$ $[0 < \mathrm{Re}\,s < \mathrm{Re}\,\rho;\ |\arg a| < \pi]$
6	$\dfrac{1}{(x+a)^\rho}\, L_n^\lambda\!\left(\dfrac{b^2 x^2}{(x+a)^2}\right)$	$\dfrac{(\lambda+1)_n\, a^{s-\rho}}{n!}\, \mathrm{B}(s,\, \rho-s)\, {}_3F_3\!\left(\begin{matrix}-n,\, \frac{s}{2},\, \frac{s+1}{2} \\ \lambda+1,\, \frac{\rho}{2},\, \frac{\rho+1}{2};\, b^2\end{matrix}\right)$ $[0 < \mathrm{Re}\,s < \mathrm{Re}\,\rho;\ |\arg a| < \pi]$

No.	$f(x)$	$F(s)$
7	$\dfrac{1}{(x^2+a^2)^\rho}$ $\times L_n^\lambda\left(\dfrac{b^2x^2}{(x^2+a^2)^2}\right)$	$\dfrac{(\lambda+1)_n\,a^{s-2\rho}}{2n!}\,\mathrm{B}\left(\dfrac{s}{2},\rho-\dfrac{s}{2}\right){}_3F_3\!\left(\begin{matrix}-n,\,\frac{s}{2},\,\frac{2\rho-s}{2};\,\frac{b^2}{4a^2}\\[2pt]\lambda+1,\,\frac{\rho}{2},\,\frac{\rho+1}{2}\end{matrix}\right)$ $[\mathrm{Re}\,a>0;\ 0<\mathrm{Re}\,s<2\,\mathrm{Re}\,\rho]$

3.23.2. $L_n^\lambda(bx)$ and the exponential function

No.	$f(x)$	$F(s)$
1	$e^{-ax}L_n^\lambda(bx)$	$\dfrac{\Gamma(s)}{a^s}\,P_n^{(\lambda,\,s-n-\lambda-1)}\left(1-\dfrac{2b}{a}\right)$ $\qquad[\mathrm{Re}\,a,\ \mathrm{Re}\,s>0;\ \mathrm{Re}\,\lambda>-1]$
2	$e^{-ax}L_n^\lambda(ax)$	$\dfrac{(1-s+\lambda)_n}{n!\,a^s}\,\Gamma(s)$ $\qquad\qquad[\mathrm{Re}\,a,\ \mathrm{Re}\,s>0]$
3	$e^{-bx}L_n^\lambda(bx+ab)$	$\dfrac{\Gamma(s)}{b^s}\,L_n^{\lambda-s}(ab)$ $\qquad\qquad[a,\ \mathrm{Re}\,b,\ \mathrm{Re}\,s>0]$
4	$e^{-a/x}L_n^\lambda(bx)$	$\dfrac{(\lambda+1)_n\,a^s}{n!}\,\Gamma(-s)\,{}_1F_2\!\left(\begin{matrix}-n;\,-ab\\\lambda+1,\,s+1\end{matrix}\right)$ $[\mathrm{Re}\,a>0;\ \mathrm{Re}\,s<-n]$
5	$e^{-a/\sqrt{x}}L_n^\lambda(bx)$	$\dfrac{2(\lambda+1)_n\,a^{2s}}{n!}\,\Gamma(-2s)\,{}_1F_3\!\left(\begin{matrix}-n;\,\frac{a^2b}{4}\\\lambda+1,\,\frac{2s+1}{2},\,s+1\end{matrix}\right)$ $[\mathrm{Re}\,a>0;\ \mathrm{Re}\,s<-n]$
6	$e^{-ax^2-bx}L_n^\lambda(bx)$	$\dfrac{(\lambda+1)_n}{2(n!)\,a^{s/2}}\,\Gamma\left(\dfrac{s}{2}\right){}_3F_3\!\left(\begin{matrix}\frac{n+\lambda+1}{2},\,\frac{n+\lambda+2}{2},\,\frac{s}{2}\\\frac{1}{2},\,\frac{\lambda+1}{2},\,\frac{\lambda+2}{2};\,\frac{b^2}{4a}\end{matrix}\right)$ $-\dfrac{(\lambda+2)_n\,b}{2(n!)\,a^{(s+1)/2}}\,\Gamma\left(\dfrac{s+1}{2}\right){}_3F_3\!\left(\begin{matrix}\frac{n+\lambda+2}{2},\,\frac{n+\lambda+3}{2},\,\frac{s+1}{2}\\\frac{3}{2},\,\frac{\lambda+2}{2},\,\frac{\lambda+3}{2};\,\frac{b^2}{4a}\end{matrix}\right)$ $[\mathrm{Re}\,a,\ \mathrm{Re}\,s>0]$
7	$e^{-a\sqrt{x}-bx}L_n^\lambda(bx)$	$\dfrac{(1-s+\lambda)_n}{n!\,b^s}\,\Gamma(s)\,{}_2F_2\!\left(\begin{matrix}s,\,s-\lambda;\,\frac{a^2}{4b}\\\frac{1}{2},\,s-n-\lambda\end{matrix}\right)-\dfrac{a}{n!\,b^{s+1/2}}$ $\times\left(\dfrac{1-2s+2\lambda}{2}\right)_n\Gamma\left(\dfrac{2s+1}{2}\right){}_2F_2\!\left(\begin{matrix}\frac{2s+1}{2},\,\frac{2s-2\lambda+1}{2};\,\frac{a^2}{4b}\\\frac{3}{2},\,\frac{2s-2n-2\lambda+1}{2}\end{matrix}\right)$ $[\mathrm{Re}\,b,\ \mathrm{Re}\,s>0]$
8	$e^{-a/x-bx}L_n^\lambda(bx)$	$\dfrac{(\lambda+1)_n\,a^s}{n!}\,\Gamma(-s)\,{}_1F_2\!\left(\begin{matrix}n+\lambda+1;\,ab\\\lambda+1,\,s+1\end{matrix}\right)$ $+\dfrac{(1-s+\lambda)_n}{n!\,b^s}\,\Gamma(s)\,{}_1F_2\!\left(\begin{matrix}1-s+n+\lambda;\,ab\\1-s,\,1-s+\lambda\end{matrix}\right)$ $[\mathrm{Re}\,a,\ \mathrm{Re}\,b>0]$

No.	$f(x)$	$F(s)$
9	$e^{-a/x^2-bx}L_n^\lambda(bx)$	$\dfrac{(\lambda+1)_n \, a^{s/2}}{2\,(n!)}\,\Gamma\left(-\dfrac{s}{2}\right)\,{}_2F_4\left(\begin{matrix}\frac{n+\lambda+1}{2},\,\frac{n+\lambda+2}{2};\,-\frac{ab^2}{4}\\ \frac{1}{2},\,\frac{\lambda+1}{2},\,\frac{\lambda+2}{2},\,\frac{s+2}{2}\end{matrix}\right)$

$$-\frac{(\lambda+2)_n \, a^{(s+1)/2}b}{2\,(n!)}\,\Gamma\left(-\frac{s+1}{2}\right)$$

$$\times\,{}_2F_4\left(\begin{matrix}\frac{n+\lambda+2}{2},\,\frac{n+\lambda+3}{2};\,-\frac{ab^2}{4}\\ \frac{3}{2},\,\frac{\lambda+2}{2},\,\frac{\lambda+3}{2},\,\frac{s+3}{2}\end{matrix}\right)$$

$$+\frac{(1-s+\lambda)_n \, b^{-s}}{n!}\,\Gamma(s)\,{}_2F_4\left(\begin{matrix}\frac{1-s+n+\lambda}{2},\,\frac{2-s+n+\lambda}{2};\,-\frac{ab^2}{4}\\ \frac{1-s}{2},\,\frac{2-s}{2},\,\frac{1-s+\lambda}{2},\,\frac{2-s+\lambda}{2}\end{matrix}\right)$$

$$[\operatorname{Re}a,\ \operatorname{Re}b>0]$$

No.	$f(x)$	$F(s)$
10	$e^{-a/\sqrt{x}-bx}L_n^\lambda(bx)$	$\dfrac{2\,(\lambda+1)_n \, a^{2s}}{n!}\,\Gamma(-2s)\,{}_1F_3\left(\begin{matrix}n+\lambda+1;\,-\frac{a^2b}{4}\\ \lambda+1,\,\frac{2s+1}{2},\,s+1\end{matrix}\right)$

$$-\frac{(1-s+\lambda)_n}{n!\,b^s}\,\Gamma(s)\,{}_1F_3\left(\begin{matrix}1-s+n+\lambda;\,-\frac{a^2b}{4}\\ \frac{1}{2},\,1-s,\,1-s+\lambda\end{matrix}\right)$$

$$-\frac{a\,\Gamma\left(\frac{2s-1}{2}\right)}{n!\,b^{s-1/2}}\left(\frac{3-2s+2\lambda}{2}\right)_n\,{}_1F_3\left(\begin{matrix}\frac{3-2s+2n+2\lambda}{2};\,-\frac{a^2b}{4}\\ \frac{3}{2},\,\frac{3-2s}{2},\,\frac{3-2s+2\lambda}{2}\end{matrix}\right)$$

$$[\operatorname{Re}a,\ \operatorname{Re}b>0]$$

No.	$f(x)$	$F(s)$
11	$e^{-a\sqrt{x}}L_n^\lambda(bx)$	$\dfrac{(-1)^n\,2b^n}{n!\,a^{2s+2n}}\,\Gamma(2s+2n)\,{}_2F_2\left(\begin{matrix}-n,\,-n-\lambda;\,-\frac{a^2}{4b}\\ \frac{1-2s-2n}{2},\,1-s-n\end{matrix}\right)\quad[\operatorname{Re}a,\ \operatorname{Re}s>0]$
12	$(a-x)_+^{\alpha-1}\,e^{-bx}L_n^\lambda(bx)$	$\dfrac{(\lambda+1)_n \, a^{s+\alpha-1}}{n!}\,\mathrm{B}(\alpha,s)\,{}_2F_2\left(\begin{matrix}n+\lambda+1,\,s;\,-ab\\ \lambda+1,\,s+\alpha\end{matrix}\right)$

$$[a,\ \operatorname{Re}\alpha,\ \operatorname{Re}s>0]$$

No.	$f(x)$	$F(s)$
13	$(x-a)_+^{\alpha-1}\,e^{-bx}L_n^\lambda(bx)$	$\dfrac{(\lambda+1)_n \, a^{s+\alpha-1}}{n!}\,\mathrm{B}(\alpha,1-s-\alpha)\,{}_2F_2\left(\begin{matrix}n+\lambda+1,\,s;\,-ab\\ \lambda+1,\,s+\alpha\end{matrix}\right)$

$$+\frac{b^{1-s-\alpha}}{n!}\,(2-s-\alpha+\lambda)_n\,\Gamma(s+\alpha-1)$$

$$\times\,{}_2F_2\left(\begin{matrix}1-\alpha,\,2-s+n-\alpha+\lambda;\,-ab\\ 2-\alpha-s,\,2-s-\alpha+\lambda\end{matrix}\right)$$

$$[a,\ \operatorname{Re}\alpha,\ \operatorname{Re}b>0]$$

No.	$f(x)$	$F(s)$
14	$(a^2-x^2)_+^{\alpha-1}\,e^{-bx}$	$\dfrac{(\lambda+1)_n \, a^{s+2\alpha-2}}{2(n!)}\,\mathrm{B}\left(\alpha,\dfrac{s}{2}\right)\,{}_3F_4\left(\begin{matrix}\frac{n+\lambda+1}{2},\,\frac{n+\lambda+2}{2},\,\frac{s}{2};\,\frac{a^2b^2}{4}\\ \frac{1}{2},\,\frac{\lambda+1}{2},\,\frac{\lambda+2}{2},\,\frac{s+2\alpha}{2}\end{matrix}\right)$
	$\times\,L_n^\lambda(bx)$	

$$-\frac{(\lambda+2)_n \, a^{s+2\alpha-1}b}{2\,(n!)}\,\mathrm{B}\left(\alpha,\frac{s+1}{2}\right)$$

$$\times\,{}_3F_4\left(\begin{matrix}\frac{n+\lambda+2}{2},\,\frac{n+\lambda+3}{2},\,\frac{s+1}{2};\,\frac{a^2b^2}{4}\\ \frac{3}{2},\,\frac{\lambda+2}{2},\,\frac{\lambda+3}{2},\,\frac{s+2\alpha+1}{2}\end{matrix}\right)\quad[a,\ \operatorname{Re}\alpha,\ \operatorname{Re}s>0]$$

No.	$f(x)$	$F(s)$
15	$\left(x^2 - a^2\right)_+^{\alpha-1} e^{-bx}$ $\times L_n^\lambda(bx)$	$\dfrac{(\lambda+1)_n\, a^{s+2\alpha-2}}{2\,(n!)}\, \mathrm{B}\left(\alpha,\ \dfrac{2-s-2\alpha}{2}\right)\, {}_3F_4\left(\begin{matrix}\frac{n+\lambda+1}{2},\ \frac{n+\lambda+2}{2},\ \frac{s}{2};\ \frac{a^2b^2}{4}\\ \frac{1}{2},\ \frac{\lambda+1}{2},\ \frac{\lambda+2}{2},\ \frac{s+2\alpha}{2}\end{matrix}\right)$ $-\dfrac{(\lambda+2)_n\, a^{s+2\alpha-1}b}{2(n!)}\, \mathrm{B}\left(\alpha,\ \dfrac{1-s-2\alpha}{2}\right)$ $\times\ {}_3F_4\left(\begin{matrix}\frac{n+\lambda+2}{2},\ \frac{n+\lambda+3}{2},\ \frac{s+1}{2};\ \frac{a^2b^2}{4}\\ \frac{3}{2},\ \frac{\lambda+2}{2},\ \frac{\lambda+3}{2},\ \frac{s+2\alpha+1}{2}\end{matrix}\right)$ $+\dfrac{b^{2-2\alpha-s}}{n!}\,(3-s-2\alpha+\lambda)_n\,\Gamma(s+2\alpha-2)$ $\times\ {}_3F_4\left(\begin{matrix}1-\alpha,\ \frac{3-s+n-2\alpha+\lambda}{2},\ \frac{4-s+n-2\alpha+\lambda}{2};\ \frac{a^2b^2}{4}\\ \frac{3-s-2\alpha+\lambda}{2},\ \frac{4-s-2\alpha+\lambda}{2},\ \frac{3-s-2\alpha}{2},\ \frac{4-s-2\alpha}{2}\end{matrix}\right)$ $[a,\ \mathrm{Re}\,\alpha,\ \mathrm{Re}\,b > 0]$
16	$\left(\sqrt{a}-\sqrt{x}\right)_+^{\alpha-1} e^{-bx}$ $\times L_n^\lambda(bx)$	$\dfrac{2\,(\lambda+1)_n\, a^{s+(\alpha-1)/2}}{n!}\, \mathrm{B}\left(\alpha,\ 2s\right)\, {}_3F_3\left(\begin{matrix}n+\lambda+1,\ s,\ \frac{2s+1}{2};\ -ab\\ \lambda+1,\ \frac{2s+\alpha}{2},\ \frac{2s+\alpha+1}{2}\end{matrix}\right)$ $[a,\ \mathrm{Re}\,\alpha,\ \mathrm{Re}\,s > 0]$
17	$\left(\sqrt{x}-\sqrt{a}\right)_+^{\alpha-1} e^{-bx}$ $\times L_n^\lambda(bx)$	$\dfrac{2\,(\lambda+1)_n\, a^{s+(\alpha-1)/2}}{n!}\, \mathrm{B}\left(\alpha,\ 1-2s-\alpha\right)$ $\times\ {}_3F_3\left(\begin{matrix}n+\lambda+1,\ s,\ \frac{2s+1}{2};\ -ab\\ \lambda+1,\ \frac{2s+\alpha}{2},\ \frac{2s+\alpha+1}{2}\end{matrix}\right)$ $+\dfrac{b^{(1-\alpha)/2-s}}{n!}\left(\dfrac{3-2s-\alpha+2\lambda}{2}\right)_n\Gamma\left(\dfrac{2s+\alpha-1}{2}\right)$ $\times\ {}_3F_3\left(\begin{matrix}\frac{1-\alpha}{2},\ \frac{2-\alpha}{2},\ \frac{3-2s+n-\alpha+2\lambda}{2};\ -ab\\ \frac{1}{2},\ \frac{3-2s-\alpha}{2},\ \frac{3-2s-\alpha+2\lambda}{2}\end{matrix}\right)+\dfrac{(1-\alpha)\sqrt{a}}{n!\,b^{s+\alpha/2-1}}$ $\times\left(\dfrac{4-2s-\alpha+2\lambda}{2}\right)_n\Gamma\left(\dfrac{2s+\alpha-2}{2}\right)$ $\times\ {}_3F_3\left(\begin{matrix}\frac{2-\alpha}{2},\ \frac{3-\alpha}{2},\ \frac{4-2s+2n-\alpha+2\lambda}{2};\ -ab\\ \frac{3}{2},\ \frac{4-2s-\alpha}{2},\ \frac{4-2s-\alpha+2\lambda}{2}\end{matrix}\right)$ $[a,\ \mathrm{Re}\,\alpha,\ \mathrm{Re}\,b > 0]$
18	$\dfrac{1}{(x+a)^\rho}\, e^{-bx} L_n^\lambda(bx)$	$\dfrac{(\lambda+1)_n\, a^{s-\rho}}{n!}\, \mathrm{B}\left(s,\ \rho-s\right)\, {}_2F_2\left(\begin{matrix}s,\ n+\lambda+1;\ ab\\ \lambda+1,\ s-\rho+1\end{matrix}\right)$ $+\dfrac{b^{\rho-s}}{n!}\,(1-s+\lambda+\rho)_n\,\Gamma(s-\rho)$ $\times\ {}_2F_2\left(\begin{matrix}\rho,\ 1-s+n+\lambda+\rho;\ ab\\ 1-s+\rho,\ 1-s+\lambda+\rho\end{matrix}\right)$ $[\mathrm{Re}\,b,\ \mathrm{Re}\,s > 0;\ |\arg a| < \pi]$

No.	$f(x)$	$F(s)$
19	$\dfrac{1}{(x^2+a^2)^\rho}\,e^{-bx}L_n^\lambda(bx)$	$\dfrac{(\lambda+1)_n\,a^{s-2\rho}}{2\,(n!)}\,\mathrm{B}\left(\dfrac{s}{2},\dfrac{2\rho-s}{2}\right)\,{}_3F_4\left(\begin{matrix}\frac{n+\lambda+1}{2},\ \frac{n+\lambda+2}{2},\ \frac{s}{2};\ -\frac{a^2b^2}{4}\\[2pt]\frac{1}{2},\ \frac{\lambda+1}{2},\ \frac{\lambda+2}{2},\ \frac{s-2\rho+2}{2}\end{matrix}\right)$

$$-\frac{(\lambda+2)_n\,a^{s-2\rho+1}b}{2\,(n!)}\,\mathrm{B}\left(\frac{s+1}{2},\frac{2\rho-s-1}{2}\right)$$

$$\times\,{}_3F_4\left(\begin{matrix}\frac{n+\lambda+2}{2},\ \frac{n+\lambda+3}{2},\ \frac{s+1}{2};\ -\frac{a^2b^2}{4}\\[2pt]\frac{3}{2},\ \frac{\lambda+2}{2},\ \frac{\lambda+3}{2},\ \frac{s-2\rho+3}{2}\end{matrix}\right)$$

$$+\frac{b^{2\rho-s}}{n!}\,(1-s+\lambda+2\rho)_n\,\Gamma(s-2\rho)$$

$$\times\,{}_3F_4\left(\begin{matrix}\rho,\ \frac{1-s+n+\lambda+2\rho}{2},\ \frac{2-s+n+\lambda+2\rho}{2};\ -\frac{a^2b^2}{4}\\[2pt]\frac{1-s+2\rho}{2},\ \frac{2-s+2\rho}{2},\ \frac{1-s+\lambda+2\rho}{2},\ \frac{2-s+\lambda+2\rho}{2}\end{matrix}\right)$$

$$[\operatorname{Re}a,\ \operatorname{Re}b,\ \operatorname{Re}s>0]$$

| 20 | $\dfrac{1}{(\sqrt{x}+\sqrt{a})^\rho}\,e^{-bx}L_n^\lambda(bx)$ | $\dfrac{2\,(\lambda+1)_n\,a^{s-\rho/2}}{n!}\,\mathrm{B}(2s,\rho-2s)\,{}_3F_3\left(\begin{matrix}n+\lambda+1,\ s,\ \frac{2s+1}{2};\ -ab\\[2pt]\lambda+1,\ \frac{2s-\rho+1}{2},\ \frac{2s-\rho+2}{2}\end{matrix}\right)$ |

$$+\frac{b^{\rho/2-s}}{n!}\left(\frac{2-2s+2\lambda+\rho}{2}\right)_n\,\Gamma\left(\frac{2s-\rho}{2}\right)$$

$$\times\,{}_3F_3\left(\begin{matrix}\frac{\rho}{2},\ \frac{\rho+1}{2},\ \frac{2-2s+2n+2\lambda+\rho}{2};\ -ab\\[2pt]\frac{1}{2},\ \frac{2-2s+\rho}{2},\ \frac{2-2s+2\lambda+\rho}{2}\end{matrix}\right)$$

$$-\frac{\sqrt{a}\,b^{(\rho+1)/2-s}}{n!}\,\rho\left(\frac{3-2s+2\lambda+\rho}{2}\right)_n\,\Gamma\left(\frac{2s-\rho-1}{2}\right)$$

$$\times\,{}_3F_3\left(\begin{matrix}\frac{\rho+1}{2},\ \frac{\rho+2}{2},\ \frac{3-2s+2n+2\lambda+\rho}{2}\\[2pt]\frac{3}{2},\ \frac{3-2s+\rho}{2},\ \frac{3-2s+2\lambda+\rho}{2};\ -ab\end{matrix}\right)$$

$$[\operatorname{Re}b,\ \operatorname{Re}s>0;\ |\arg a|<2\pi]$$

| 21 | $(a-x)_+^\lambda\,e^{bx}$ $\times\,L_n^\lambda(c(a-x))$ | $\dfrac{e^{ab}}{n!}\,a^{s+\lambda}\,\Gamma\left[\begin{matrix}s,\ n+\lambda+1\\ s+\lambda+1\end{matrix}\right]\Phi_2(s,-n;s+\lambda+1;ab,ac)$ $[a,\ \operatorname{Re}\lambda,\ \operatorname{Re}s>0]$ |

3.23.3. $L_n^\lambda(bx)$ and trigonometric functions

Notation: $\delta=\left\{\begin{matrix}1\\0\end{matrix}\right\}$.

| 1 | $e^{-bx}\left\{\begin{matrix}\sin(ax)\\\cos(ax)\end{matrix}\right\}L_n^\lambda(bx)$ | $\dfrac{a^\delta\,(1-s+\lambda-\delta)_n}{n!\,b^{s+\delta}}\,\Gamma(s+\delta)$ |

$$\times\,{}_4F_3\left(\begin{matrix}\frac{s+1}{2},\ \frac{s+2\delta}{2},\ \frac{s-\lambda+1}{2},\ \frac{s-\lambda+2\delta}{2}\\[2pt]\frac{2\delta+1}{2},\ \frac{s-n-\lambda+1}{2},\ \frac{s-n-\lambda+2\delta}{2};\ -\frac{a^2}{b^2}\end{matrix}\right)$$

$$[a,\ \operatorname{Re}b>0;\ \operatorname{Re}s>-\delta]$$

No.	$f(x)$	$F(s)$
2	$e^{-bx}\left\{\begin{matrix}\sin(a\sqrt{x})\\\cos(a\sqrt{x})\end{matrix}\right\}$ $\times L_n^\lambda(bx)$	$\dfrac{a^\delta}{n!\,b^{s+\delta/2}}\left(\dfrac{2-2s+2\lambda-\delta}{2}\right)_n \Gamma\left(\dfrac{2s+\delta}{2}\right)$ $\times {}_2F_2\left(\begin{matrix}\frac{2s+\delta}{2},\ \frac{2s-2\lambda+\delta}{2};\ -\frac{a^2}{4b}\\\frac{2\delta+1}{2},\ \frac{2s-2n-2\lambda+\delta}{2}\end{matrix}\right)$ $[a,\ \operatorname{Re}b>0;\ \operatorname{Re}s>-\delta/2]$
3	$e^{-bx}\left\{\begin{matrix}\sin(a/\sqrt{x})\\\cos(a/\sqrt{x})\end{matrix}\right\}$ $\times L_n^\lambda(bx)$	$\dfrac{a^\delta b^{\delta/2-s}}{n!}\left(\dfrac{2-2s+2\lambda+\delta}{2}\right)_n \Gamma\left(\dfrac{2s-\delta}{2}\right)$ $\times {}_1F_3\left(\begin{matrix}\frac{2-2s+2n+2\lambda+\delta}{2};\ \frac{a^2b}{4}\\\frac{2\delta+1}{2},\ \frac{2-2s+\delta}{2},\ \frac{2-2s+2\lambda+\delta}{2}\end{matrix}\right)$ $\mp \dfrac{2(\lambda+1)_n\,a^{2s}}{n!}\Gamma(-2s)\left\{\begin{matrix}\sin(s\pi)\\\cos(s\pi)\end{matrix}\right\}$ $\times {}_1F_3\left(\begin{matrix}n+\lambda+1;\ \frac{a^2b}{4}\\\lambda+1,\ \frac{2s+1}{2},\ s+1\end{matrix}\right)$ $[a,\ \operatorname{Re}b>0;\ \operatorname{Re}s>-1/2]$

3.23.4. $L_n^\lambda(bx)$ and the logarithmic function

No.	$f(x)$	$F(s)$
1	$e^{-ax}\ln(ax)\,L_n^\lambda(ax)$	$\dfrac{(1-s+\lambda)_n}{n!\,a^s}\Gamma(s)\left[\psi(s)-\sum_{k=1}^{n}\dfrac{1}{k+\lambda-s}\right]$ $[\operatorname{Re}a,\ \operatorname{Re}s>0]$
2	$e^{-ax}\ln^2(ax)\,L_n^\lambda(ax)$	$\dfrac{(1-s+\lambda)_n}{n!\,a^s}\Gamma(s)\left\{\left[\psi(s)-\sum_{k=1}^{n}\dfrac{1}{k+\lambda-s}\right]^2\right.$ $\left.+\psi'(s)-\sum_{k=1}^{n}\dfrac{1}{(k+\lambda-s)^2}\right\}$ $[\operatorname{Re}a,\ \operatorname{Re}s>0]$
3	$e^{-ax}\ln^m(ax)\,L_n^\lambda(ax)$	$\dfrac{a^{-s}}{n!}\dfrac{\partial^m\left[\Gamma(s)(1-s+\lambda)_n\right]}{\partial s^m}$ $[\operatorname{Re}a,\ \operatorname{Re}s>0]$
4	$e^{-bx}\left\{\begin{matrix}\ln(x+a)\\\ln|x-a|\end{matrix}\right\}$ $\times L_n^\lambda(bx)$	$\dfrac{\pi(\lambda+1)_n\,a^s}{n!\,s}\left\{\begin{matrix}\csc(s\pi)\\\cot(s\pi)\end{matrix}\right\}{}_2F_2\left(\begin{matrix}n+\lambda+1,\ s\\\lambda+1,\ s+1;\ \pm ab\end{matrix}\right)$ $\pm\dfrac{ab^{1-s}}{n!}(2-s+\lambda)_n\Gamma(s-1)$ $\times {}_3F_3\left(\begin{matrix}1,\ 1,\ 2-s+n+\lambda\\2,\ 2-s,\ 2-s+\lambda;\ \pm ab\end{matrix}\right)$ $+\dfrac{(1-s+\lambda)_n}{n!\,b^s}\Gamma(s)\left[\psi(s)-\sum_{k=1}^{n}\dfrac{1}{k+\lambda-s}-\ln b\right]$ $\left[\operatorname{Re}b,\ \operatorname{Re}s>0,\ \left\{\begin{matrix}|\arg a|<\pi\\a>0\end{matrix}\right\}\right]$

No.	$f(x)$	$F(s)$
5	$e^{-bx}\left\{\begin{array}{c}\ln\left(x^2+a^2\right)\\\ln\lvert x^2-a^2\rvert\end{array}\right\}$ $\times L_n^\lambda(bx)$	$\dfrac{\pi(\lambda+1)_n\,a^s}{n!\,s}\left\{\begin{array}{c}\csc(s\pi/2)\\\cot(s\pi/2)\end{array}\right\}$ $\times {}_3F_4\left(\begin{array}{c}\frac{n+\lambda+1}{2},\frac{n+\lambda+2}{2},\frac{s}{2};\mp\frac{a^2b^2}{4}\\\frac{1}{2},\frac{\lambda+1}{2},\frac{\lambda+2}{2},\frac{s+2}{2}\end{array}\right)\mp\dfrac{\pi a^{s+1}b(\lambda+2)_n}{n!\,(s+1)}$ $\times\left\{\begin{array}{c}\sec(s\pi/2)\\\tan(s\pi/2)\end{array}\right\}{}_3F_4\left(\begin{array}{c}\frac{n+\lambda+2}{2},\frac{n+\lambda+3}{2},\frac{s+1}{2};\mp\frac{a^2b^2}{4}\\\frac{3}{2},\frac{\lambda+2}{2},\frac{\lambda+3}{2},\frac{s+3}{2}\end{array}\right)$ $\pm\dfrac{a^2b^{2-s}}{n!}\,(3-s+\lambda)_n\,\Gamma(s-2)$ $\times{}_4F_5\left(\begin{array}{c}1,1,\frac{3-s+n+\lambda}{2},\frac{4-s+n+\lambda}{2};\mp\frac{a^2b^2}{4}\\2,\frac{3-s}{2},\frac{4-s}{2},\frac{3-s+\lambda}{2},\frac{4-s+\lambda}{2}\end{array}\right)$ $+\dfrac{2(1-s+\lambda)_n}{n!\,b^s}\,\Gamma(s)\left[\psi(s)-\sum_{k=1}^{n}\dfrac{1}{k+\lambda-s}-\ln b\right]$ $\left[\operatorname{Re}b,\ \operatorname{Re}s>0,\ \left\{\begin{array}{c}\operatorname{Re}a>0\\a>0\end{array}\right\}\right]$
6	$\theta(a-x)\ln\dfrac{\sqrt{a}+\sqrt{a-x}}{\sqrt{x}}$ $\times L_n^\lambda(bx)$	$\dfrac{\sqrt{\pi}\,(\lambda+1)_n\,a^s}{2\,(n!)\,s}\,\Gamma\!\left[\begin{array}{c}s\\s+\frac{1}{2}\end{array}\right]{}_3F_3\left(\begin{array}{c}-n,s,s;\,ab\\\lambda+1,s+\frac{1}{2},s+1\end{array}\right)$ $[a,\ \operatorname{Re}s>0]$

3.23.5. $L_m^\lambda(bx^r)$ and $\operatorname{Ei}(ax^r)$

No.	$f(x)$	$F(s)$
1	$e^{-bx}\operatorname{Ei}(-ax)L_n^\lambda(bx)$	$-\dfrac{(\lambda+1)_n}{n!\,a^s s}\,\Gamma(s)\,{}_3F_2\left(\begin{array}{c}n+\lambda+1,s,s\\\lambda+1,s+1;-\frac{b}{a}\end{array}\right)$ $[\operatorname{Re}a,\ \operatorname{Re}(a+b),\ \operatorname{Re}s>0]$
2	$e^{(\pm a-b)x}\operatorname{Ei}(\mp ax)$ $\times L_n^\lambda(bx)$	$-\dfrac{\pi(\lambda+1)_n}{n!\,a^s}\,\Gamma(s)\left\{\begin{array}{c}\csc(s\pi)\\\cot(s\pi)\end{array}\right\}{}_2F_1\left(\begin{array}{c}n+\lambda+1,s\\\lambda+1;\pm\frac{b}{a}\end{array}\right)$ $\mp\dfrac{b^{1-s}}{n!\,a}\,(2-s+\lambda)_n\,\Gamma(s-1)\,{}_3F_2\left(\begin{array}{c}1,1,2-s+n+\lambda\\2-s,2-s+\lambda;\pm\frac{b}{a}\end{array}\right)$ $\left[\operatorname{Re}b,\ \operatorname{Re}s>0,\ \left\{\begin{array}{c}\lvert\arg a\rvert<\pi\\a>0\end{array}\right\}\right]$
3	$e^{-bx}\operatorname{Ei}(-ax^2)L_n^\lambda(bx)$	$-\dfrac{(\lambda+1)_n}{n!\,a^{s/2}s}\,\Gamma\!\left(\dfrac{s}{2}\right){}_4F_4\left(\begin{array}{c}\frac{n+\lambda+1}{2},\frac{n+\lambda+2}{2},\frac{s}{2},\frac{s}{2}\\\frac{1}{2},\frac{\lambda+1}{2},\frac{\lambda+2}{2},\frac{s+2}{2};\frac{b^2}{4a}\end{array}\right)$ $+\dfrac{(\lambda+2)_n\,b}{n!\,a^{(s+1)/2}(s+1)}\,\Gamma\!\left(\dfrac{s+1}{2}\right){}_4F_4\left(\begin{array}{c}\frac{n+\lambda+2}{2},\frac{n+\lambda+3}{2},\frac{s+1}{2},\frac{s+1}{2}\\\frac{3}{2},\frac{\lambda+2}{2},\frac{\lambda+3}{2},\frac{s+3}{2};\frac{b^2}{4a}\end{array}\right)$ $[\operatorname{Re}a,\ \operatorname{Re}s>0]$

No.	$f(x)$	$F(s)$
4	$e^{\pm ax^2 - bx}\,\mathrm{Ei}\left(\mp ax^2\right)$ $\times L_n^\lambda(bx)$	$-\dfrac{\pi\,(\lambda+1)_n}{2\,(n!)\,a^{s/2}}\,\Gamma\left(\dfrac{s}{2}\right)\left\{\begin{array}{c}\csc\,(s\pi/2)\\ \cot\,(s\pi/2)\end{array}\right\}\,{}_3F_3\!\left(\begin{array}{c}\frac{n+\lambda+1}{2},\ \frac{n+\lambda+2}{2},\ \frac{s}{2}\\ \frac{1}{2},\ \frac{\lambda+1}{2},\ \frac{\lambda+2}{2};\ \mp\frac{b^2}{4a}\end{array}\right)$ $\pm\dfrac{\pi\,(\lambda+2)_n\,b}{2\,(n!)\,a^{(s+1)/2}}\,\Gamma\left(\dfrac{s+1}{2}\right)$ $\times\left\{\begin{array}{c}\sec\,(s\pi/2)\\ \tan\,(s\pi/2)\end{array}\right\}\,{}_3F_3\!\left(\begin{array}{c}\frac{n+\lambda+2}{2},\ \frac{n+\lambda+3}{2},\ \frac{s+1}{2}\\ \frac{3}{2},\ \frac{\lambda+2}{2},\ \frac{\lambda+3}{2};\ \mp\frac{b^2}{4a}\end{array}\right)$ $\mp\dfrac{b^{2-s}}{n!\,a}\,(3-s+\lambda)_n\,\Gamma\,(s-2)$ $\times\,{}_4F_4\!\left(\begin{array}{c}1,\,1,\ \frac{3-s+n+\lambda}{2},\ \frac{4-s+n+\lambda}{2};\ \mp\frac{b^2}{4a}\\ \frac{3-s}{2},\ \frac{4-s}{2},\ \frac{3-s+\lambda}{2},\ \frac{4-s+\lambda}{2}\end{array}\right)$ $\left[\mathrm{Re}\,b,\ \mathrm{Re}\,s>0,\ \left\{\begin{array}{c}\lvert\arg a\rvert<\pi\\ a>0\end{array}\right\}\right]$

3.23.6. $L_n^\lambda(bx)$ **and** $\mathrm{si}\,(ax^r),\ \mathrm{ci}\,(ax^r)$

No.	$f(x)$	$F(s)$
1	$e^{-bx}\left\{\begin{array}{c}\mathrm{si}\,(ax)\\ \mathrm{ci}\,(ax)\end{array}\right\}L_n^\lambda(bx)$	$-\dfrac{(\lambda+1)_n}{n!\,a^s s}\left\{\begin{array}{c}\sin\,(s\pi/2)\\ \cos\,(s\pi/2)\end{array}\right\}\Gamma\,(s)\,{}_5F_4\!\left(\begin{array}{c}\frac{n+\lambda+1}{2},\ \frac{n+\lambda+2}{2},\ \frac{s}{2},\ \frac{s}{2},\ \frac{s+1}{2}\\ \frac{1}{2},\ \frac{\lambda+1}{2},\ \frac{\lambda+2}{2},\ \frac{s+2}{2};\ -\frac{b^2}{a^2}\end{array}\right)$ $\pm\dfrac{(\lambda+2)_n\,b}{n!\,a^{s+1}\,(s+1)}\left\{\begin{array}{c}\cos\,(s\pi/2)\\ \sin\,(s\pi/2)\end{array}\right\}\Gamma\,(s+1)$ $\times\,{}_5F_4\!\left(\begin{array}{c}\frac{n+\lambda+2}{2},\ \frac{n+\lambda+3}{2},\ \frac{s+1}{2},\ \frac{s+1}{2},\ \frac{s+2}{2}\\ \frac{3}{2},\ \frac{\lambda+2}{2},\ \frac{\lambda+3}{2},\ \frac{s+3}{2};\ -\frac{b^2}{a^2}\end{array}\right)$ $[a,\ \mathrm{Re}\,b,\ \mathrm{Re}\,s>0]$
2	$e^{-bx}\,\mathrm{si}\,(a\sqrt{x})\,L_n^\lambda(bx)$	$-\dfrac{ab^{-(2s+1)/2}}{n!}\left(\dfrac{1-2s+2\lambda}{2}\right)_n\Gamma\left(\dfrac{2s+1}{2}\right)$ $\times\,{}_3F_3\!\left(\begin{array}{c}\frac{1}{2},\ \frac{2s+1}{2},\ \frac{2s-2\lambda+1}{2};\ -\frac{a^2}{4b}\\ \frac{3}{2},\ \frac{3}{2},\ \frac{2s-2n-2\lambda+1}{2}\end{array}\right)-\dfrac{\pi\,(1-s+\lambda)_n}{2\,(n!)\,b^s}\,\Gamma\,(s)$ $[a,\ \mathrm{Re}\,b,\ \mathrm{Re}\,s>0]$
3	$e^{-bx}\,\mathrm{ci}\,(a\sqrt{x})\,L_n^\lambda(bx)$	$-\dfrac{a^2 b^{-s-1}}{4(n!)}\,(\lambda-s)_n\,\Gamma\,(s+1)$ $\times\,{}_4F_4\!\left(\begin{array}{c}1,\,1,\,s+1,\,s-\lambda+1;\ -\frac{a^2}{4b}\\ \frac{3}{2},\,2,\,2,\,s-n-\lambda+1\end{array}\right)+\dfrac{b^{-s}}{n!}\,(1-s+\lambda)_n$ $\times\,\Gamma\,(s)\left[\dfrac{1}{2}\,\psi\,(s)-\dfrac{1}{2}\sum_{k=1}^{n}\dfrac{1}{k+\lambda-s}-\ln\dfrac{\sqrt{b}}{a}+\mathbf{C}\right]$ $[a,\ \mathrm{Re}\,b,\ \mathrm{Re}\,s>0]$

3.23.7. $L_n^\lambda(bx)$ **and** $\operatorname{erf}(ax^r)$, $\operatorname{erfc}(ax^r)$

1	$\operatorname{erfc}(a\sqrt{x})\, L_n^\lambda(bx)$	$\dfrac{(\lambda+1)_n}{n!\sqrt{\pi}\,a^{2s}s}\,\Gamma\!\left(\dfrac{2s+1}{2}\right)\,{}_3F_2\!\left(\begin{matrix}-n,\,s,\,\frac{2s+1}{2};\,\frac{b}{a^2}\\ \lambda+1,\,s+1\end{matrix}\right)$

$$[\operatorname{Re} s > 0;\ |\arg a| < \pi/4]$$

2	$e^{-bx}\left\{\begin{matrix}\operatorname{erf}(ax)\\ \operatorname{erfc}(ax)\end{matrix}\right\}L_n^\lambda(bx)$	$\mp\dfrac{(\lambda+1)_n}{n!\sqrt{\pi}\,a^s s}\,\Gamma\!\left(\dfrac{s+1}{2}\right)\,{}_4F_4\!\left(\begin{matrix}\frac{n+\lambda+1}{2},\,\frac{n+\lambda+2}{2},\,\frac{s}{2},\,\frac{s+1}{2};\,\frac{b^2}{4a^2}\\ \frac{1}{2},\,\frac{\lambda+1}{2},\,\frac{\lambda+2}{2},\,\frac{s+2}{2}\end{matrix}\right)$

$$\pm\dfrac{(\lambda+2)_n\,b}{n!\sqrt{\pi}\,a^{s+1}(s+1)}\,\Gamma\!\left(\dfrac{s+2}{2}\right)\,{}_4F_4\!\left(\begin{matrix}\frac{n+\lambda+2}{2},\,\frac{n+\lambda+3}{2},\,\frac{s+1}{2},\,\frac{s+2}{2}\\ \frac{3}{2},\,\frac{\lambda+2}{2},\,\frac{\lambda+3}{2},\,\frac{s+3}{2};\,\frac{b^2}{4a^2}\end{matrix}\right)$$

$$+\dfrac{1\pm1}{2}\dfrac{(1-s+\lambda)_n}{n!\,b^s}\,\Gamma(s)\qquad[\operatorname{Re} a > 0;\ \operatorname{Re} s > -\delta]$$

3	$e^{-bx}\left\{\begin{matrix}\operatorname{erf}(a\sqrt{x})\\ \operatorname{erfc}(a\sqrt{x})\end{matrix}\right\}$ $\times L_n^\lambda(bx)$	$\mp\dfrac{(\lambda+1)_n}{n!\sqrt{\pi}\,a^{2s}s}\,\Gamma\!\left(\dfrac{2s+1}{2}\right)\,{}_3F_2\!\left(\begin{matrix}n+\lambda+1,\,s,\,\frac{2s+1}{2}\\ \lambda+1,\,s+1;\,-\frac{b}{a^2}\end{matrix}\right)$

$$+\dfrac{1\pm1}{2}\dfrac{(1-s+\lambda)_n}{n!\,b^s}\,\Gamma(s)$$

$$[\operatorname{Re} b,\ \operatorname{Re}(a^2+b) > 0;\ \operatorname{Re} s > -(1\pm1)/4]$$

4	$e^{(a^2-b)x}\operatorname{erfc}(a\sqrt{x})$ $\times L_n^\lambda(bx)$	$\dfrac{(\lambda+1)_n\,\Gamma(s)}{n!\,a^{2s}\cos(s\pi)}\,{}_2F_1\!\left(\begin{matrix}n+\lambda+1,\,s\\ \lambda+1;\,\frac{b}{a^2}\end{matrix}\right)+\dfrac{\Gamma(s-1/2)}{n!\sqrt{\pi}\,ab^{s-1/2}}$

$$\times\left(\dfrac{3-2s+2\lambda}{2}\right)_n\,{}_3F_2\!\left(\begin{matrix}\frac{1}{2},\,1,\,\frac{3-2s+2n+2\lambda}{2}\\ \frac{3-2s}{2},\,\frac{3-2s+2\lambda}{2};\,\frac{b}{a^2}\end{matrix}\right)$$

$$[\operatorname{Re} b,\ \operatorname{Re}(b-a^2) > 0;\ \operatorname{Re} s > 0]$$

3.23.8. $L_n^\lambda(bx)$ **and** $S(ax^r)$, $C(ax^r)$

Notation: $\delta = \left\{\begin{matrix}1\\0\end{matrix}\right\}$.

1	$e^{-bx}\left\{\begin{matrix}S(ax)\\ C(ax)\end{matrix}\right\}L_n^\lambda(bx)$	$\dfrac{\sqrt{2}\,a^{\delta+1/2}}{3^\delta n!\sqrt{\pi}\,b^{s+\delta+1/2}}\left(\dfrac{1-2s+2\lambda-2\delta}{2}\right)_n\Gamma\!\left(\dfrac{2s+2\delta+1}{2}\right)$

$$\times\,{}_5F_4\!\left(\begin{matrix}\frac{2\delta+1}{4},\,\frac{2s+3}{4},\,\frac{2s+4\delta+1}{4},\,\frac{2s-2\lambda+3}{4},\,\frac{2s-2\lambda+4\delta+1}{4}\\ \frac{2\delta+1}{2},\,\frac{2\delta+5}{4},\,\frac{2s-2n-2\lambda+3}{4},\,\frac{2s-2n-2\lambda+4\delta+1}{4};\,-\frac{a^2}{b^2}\end{matrix}\right)$$

$$[a,\ \operatorname{Re} b > 0;\ \operatorname{Re} s > -\delta - 1/2]$$

2	$e^{-bx}\left\{\begin{matrix}S(a\sqrt{x})\\ C(a\sqrt{x})\end{matrix}\right\}$ $\times L_n^\lambda(bx)$	$\dfrac{\sqrt{2}\,a^{\delta+1/2}}{3^\delta n!\sqrt{\pi}\,b^{s+(2\delta+1)/4}}\left(\dfrac{3-4s+4\lambda-2\delta}{4}\right)_n\Gamma\!\left(\dfrac{4s+2\delta+1}{4}\right)$

$$\times\,{}_3F_3\!\left(\begin{matrix}\frac{2\delta+1}{4},\,\frac{4s+2\delta+1}{4},\,\frac{4s-4\lambda+2\delta+1}{4};\,-\frac{a^2}{4b}\\ \frac{2\delta+1}{2},\,\frac{2\delta+5}{4},\,\frac{4s-4n-4\lambda+2\delta+1}{4}\end{matrix}\right)$$

$$[a,\ \operatorname{Re} b > 0;\ \operatorname{Re} s > -(2\delta+1)/4]$$

3.23.9. $L_n^\lambda(bx)$ and $\gamma(\nu, ax^r)$, $\Gamma(\nu, ax^r)$

1	$e^{-bx}\begin{Bmatrix}\gamma(\mu, ax)\\[4pt]\Gamma(\mu, ax)\end{Bmatrix}$ $\times L_n^\lambda(bx)$	$\mp\dfrac{(\lambda+1)_n}{n!\,a^s s}\Gamma(s+\mu)\,_3F_2\begin{pmatrix}n+\lambda+1,\,s,\,s+\mu\\\lambda+1,\,s+1;\,-\dfrac{b}{a}\end{pmatrix}$ $+\dfrac{1\pm1}{2}\dfrac{(1-s+\lambda)_n}{n!\,b^s}\Gamma(\mu)\Gamma(s)$ $\left[\operatorname{Re}a,\ \operatorname{Re}b,\ \operatorname{Re}(s+\mu)>0,\ \begin{Bmatrix}\operatorname{Re}\mu>0\\\operatorname{Re}s>0\end{Bmatrix}\right]$
2	$e^{-bx}\begin{Bmatrix}\gamma(\mu, ax^2)\\[4pt]\Gamma(\mu, ax^2)\end{Bmatrix}$ $\times L_n^\lambda(bx)$	$\mp\dfrac{(\lambda+1)_n}{n!\,a^{s/2}s}\Gamma\!\left(\dfrac{s+2\mu}{2}\right)\,_4F_4\begin{pmatrix}\frac{n+\lambda+1}{2},\,\frac{n+\lambda+2}{2},\,\frac{s}{2},\,\frac{s+2\mu}{2}\\\frac{1}{2},\,\frac{\lambda+1}{2},\,\frac{\lambda+2}{2},\,\frac{s+2}{2};\,\frac{b^2}{4a}\end{pmatrix}$ $\pm\dfrac{(\lambda+2)_n\,b}{a^{(s+1)/2}(s+1)}\Gamma\!\left(\dfrac{s+2\mu+1}{2}\right)$ $\times{}_4F_4\begin{pmatrix}\frac{n+\lambda+2}{2},\,\frac{n+\lambda+3}{2},\,\frac{s+1}{2},\,\frac{s+2\mu+1}{2}\\\frac{3}{2},\,\frac{\lambda+2}{2},\,\frac{\lambda+3}{2},\,\frac{s+3}{2};\,\frac{b^2}{4a}\end{pmatrix}$ $+\dfrac{1\pm1}{2}\dfrac{(1-s+\lambda)_n}{n!\,b^s}\Gamma(\mu)\Gamma(s)$ $\left[\operatorname{Re}a,\ \operatorname{Re}(s+2\mu)>0,\ \begin{Bmatrix}\operatorname{Re}\mu>0\\\operatorname{Re}s>0\end{Bmatrix}\right]$
3	$e^{-bx}\begin{Bmatrix}\gamma(\mu, a\sqrt{x})\\[4pt]\Gamma(\mu, a\sqrt{x})\end{Bmatrix}$ $\times L_n^\lambda(bx)$	$\pm\dfrac{a^\mu}{n!\,b^{s+\mu/2}\mu}\left(\dfrac{2-2s+2\lambda-\mu}{2}\right)_n\Gamma\!\left(\dfrac{2s+\mu}{2}\right)$ $\times{}_3F_3\begin{pmatrix}\frac{\mu}{2},\,\frac{2s+\mu}{2},\,\frac{2s-2\lambda+\mu}{2};\,\frac{a^2}{4b}\\\frac{1}{2},\,\frac{\mu+2}{2},\,\frac{2s-2n-2\lambda+\mu}{2}\end{pmatrix}\mp\dfrac{a^{\mu+1}}{n!\,b^{s+(\mu+1)/2}(\mu+1)}$ $\times\Gamma\!\left(\dfrac{2s+\mu+1}{2}\right)\left(\dfrac{1-2s+2\lambda-\mu}{2}\right)_n$ $\times{}_3F_3\begin{pmatrix}\frac{\mu+1}{2},\,\frac{2s+\mu+1}{2},\,\frac{2s-2\lambda+\mu+1}{2};\,\frac{a^2}{4b}\\\frac{3}{2},\,\frac{\mu+3}{2},\,\frac{2s-2n-2\lambda+\mu+1}{2}\end{pmatrix}$ $+\dfrac{1\pm1}{2}\dfrac{(1-s+\lambda)_n}{n!\,b^s}\Gamma(\mu)\Gamma(s)$ $\left[\operatorname{Re}b,\ \operatorname{Re}(2s+\mu)>0,\ \begin{Bmatrix}\operatorname{Re}\mu>0\\\operatorname{Re}s>0\end{Bmatrix}\right]$

3.23.10. $L_n^\lambda(bx)$ and $J_\mu(ax^r)$, $I_\mu(ax^r)$

1	$J_\mu(a\sqrt{x})\,L_n^\lambda(bx)$	$\dfrac{1}{n!}\left(\dfrac{2}{a}\right)^{2s+2n}(-b)^n\,\Gamma\!\left[\dfrac{\frac{2s+\mu+2n}{2}}{\frac{2-2s-2n+\mu}{2}}\right]\,_2F_2\begin{pmatrix}-n,\,-n-\lambda;\,\frac{a^2}{4b}\\\frac{2-2s-2n+\mu}{2},\,\frac{2-2s-2n-\mu}{2}\end{pmatrix}$ $[a>0;\ -\operatorname{Re}\mu<2\operatorname{Re}s<3/2-2n]$

No.	$f(x)$	$F(s)$
2	$J_\mu\left(\dfrac{a}{\sqrt{x}}\right)L_n^\lambda(bx)$	$\dfrac{(\lambda+1)_n}{n!}\left(\dfrac{a}{2}\right)^{2s}\Gamma\left[\begin{matrix}\frac{\mu-2s}{2}\\\frac{2s+\mu+2}{2}\end{matrix}\right]{}_1F_3\left(\begin{matrix}-n;\ -\frac{a^2b}{4}\\\lambda+1,\ \frac{2s+\mu+2}{2},\ \frac{2s-\mu+2}{2}\end{matrix}\right)$ $[a>0;\ -3/2<2\operatorname{Re}s<\operatorname{Re}\mu-2n]$
3	$e^{-bx}\left\{\begin{matrix}J_\mu(ax)\\I_\mu(ax)\end{matrix}\right\}L_n^\lambda(bx)$	$\dfrac{a^\mu(1-s+\lambda-\mu)_n}{2^\mu n!\,b^{s+\mu}}\Gamma\left[\begin{matrix}s+\mu\\\mu+1\end{matrix}\right]$ $\times{}_4F_3\left(\begin{matrix}\frac{s+\mu}{2},\ \frac{s+\mu+1}{2},\ \frac{s-\lambda+\mu}{2},\ \frac{s-\lambda+\mu+1}{2}\\\mu+1,\ \frac{s-n-\lambda+\mu}{2},\ \frac{s-n-\lambda+\mu+1}{2};\ \mp\frac{a^2}{b^2}\end{matrix}\right)$ $\left[\operatorname{Re}b,\ \operatorname{Re}(s+\mu)>0,\ \left\{\begin{matrix}a>0\\\operatorname{Re}(b-a)>0\end{matrix}\right\}\right]$
4	$e^{-bx}\left\{\begin{matrix}J_\mu(a\sqrt{x})\\I_\mu(a\sqrt{x})\end{matrix}\right\}$ $\times L_n^\lambda(bx)$	$\dfrac{a^\mu}{2^\mu n!\,b^{s+\mu/2}}\left(\dfrac{2-2s+2\lambda-\mu}{2}\right)_n\Gamma\left[\begin{matrix}\frac{s+\mu}{2}\\\mu+1\end{matrix}\right]$ $\times{}_2F_2\left(\begin{matrix}\frac{2s+\mu}{2},\ \frac{2s-2\lambda+\mu}{2};\ \mp\frac{a^2}{4b^2}\\\mu+1,\ \frac{2s-2n-2\lambda+\mu}{2}\end{matrix}\right)$ $[\operatorname{Re}b,\ \operatorname{Re}(2s+\mu)>0]$
5	$e^{-bx}J_\mu\left(\dfrac{a}{\sqrt{x}}\right)L_n^\lambda(bx)$	$\dfrac{(\lambda+1)_n}{n!}\left(\dfrac{a}{2}\right)^{2s}\Gamma\left[\begin{matrix}\frac{\mu-2s}{2}\\\frac{2s+\mu+2}{2}\end{matrix}\right]{}_1F_3\left(\begin{matrix}n+\lambda+1;\ \frac{a^2b}{4}\\\lambda+1,\ \frac{2s+\mu+2}{2},\ \frac{2s-\mu+2}{2}\end{matrix}\right)$ $+\dfrac{1}{n!}\left(\dfrac{a}{2}\right)^\mu b^{\mu/2-s}\left(\dfrac{2-2s+2\lambda+\mu}{2}\right)_n\Gamma\left[\begin{matrix}\frac{2s-\mu}{2}\\\mu+1\end{matrix}\right]$ $\times{}_1F_3\left(\begin{matrix}\frac{2-2s+2n+2\lambda+\mu}{2};\ \frac{a^2b}{4}\\\mu+1,\ \frac{2-2s+\mu}{2},\ \frac{2-2s+\mu+2\lambda}{2}\end{matrix}\right)$ $[\operatorname{Re}b>0;\ \operatorname{Re}s>-3/4]$

3.23.11. $L_n^\lambda(bx)$ **and** $Y_\mu(ax^r)$, $K_\mu(ax^r)$

No.	$f(x)$	$F(s)$
1	$K_\mu(a\sqrt{x})L_n^\lambda(bx)$	$\dfrac{2^{2s+2n-1}(-b)^n}{n!\,a^{2s+2n}}\Gamma\left(\dfrac{2s+2n-\mu}{2}\right)\Gamma\left(\dfrac{2s+2n+\mu}{2}\right)$ $\times{}_2F_2\left(\begin{matrix}-n,\ -n-\lambda;\ -\frac{a^2}{4b}\\\frac{2-2s-2n-\mu}{2},\ \frac{2-2s-2n+\mu}{2}\end{matrix}\right)$ $[\operatorname{Re}a>0;\ 2\operatorname{Re}s>|\operatorname{Re}\mu|]$
2	$K_\mu\left(\dfrac{a}{\sqrt{x}}\right)L_n^\lambda(bx)$	$\dfrac{(\lambda+1)_n\,a^{2s}}{2^{2s+1}n!}\Gamma\left(\dfrac{\mu-2s}{2}\right)\Gamma\left(-\dfrac{\mu+2s}{2}\right)$ $\times{}_1F_3\left(\begin{matrix}-n;\ \frac{a^2b}{4}\\\lambda+1,\ \frac{2s+\mu+2}{2},\ \frac{2s-\mu+2}{2}\end{matrix}\right)$ $[\operatorname{Re}a>0;\ 2\operatorname{Re}s+|\operatorname{Re}\mu|<-2n]$

No.	$f(x)$	$F(s)$

3 $e^{-bx}\left\{\begin{array}{c} Y_\mu(ax) \\ K_\mu(ax) \end{array}\right\}L_n^\lambda(bx)$

$$\mp\pi^{(1\mp1)/2}\frac{(\lambda+1)_n\,2^{s-2}}{n!\pi b^s}\Gamma\left(\frac{s+\mu}{2}\right)\Gamma\left(\frac{s-\mu}{2}\right)$$

$$\times\left(2\cos\frac{(s-\mu)\pi}{2}\right)^{(1\pm1)/2}{}_4F_3\left(\begin{array}{c}\frac{n+\lambda+1}{2},\,\frac{n+\lambda+2}{2},\,\frac{s+\mu}{2},\,\frac{s-\mu}{2}\\[4pt]\frac{1}{2},\,\frac{\lambda+1}{2},\,\frac{\lambda+2}{2};\,\mp\frac{b^2}{a^2}\end{array}\right)$$

$$\mp\pi^{(1\mp1)/2}\frac{2^{s-1}b(\lambda+2)_n}{n!\pi a^{s+1}}\Gamma\left(\frac{s+\mu+1}{2}\right)\Gamma\left(\frac{s-\mu+1}{2}\right)$$

$$\times\left(2\sin\frac{(s-\mu)\pi}{2}\right)^{(1\pm1)/2}$$

$$\times{}_4F_3\left(\begin{array}{c}\frac{n+\lambda+2}{2},\,\frac{n+\lambda+3}{2},\,\frac{s-\mu+1}{2},\,\frac{s+\mu+1}{2}\\[4pt]\frac{3}{2},\,\frac{\lambda+2}{2},\,\frac{\lambda+3}{2};\,\mp\frac{b^2}{a^2}\end{array}\right)$$

$$\left[\operatorname{Re}b>0;\ \operatorname{Re}s>|\operatorname{Re}\mu|,\ \left\{\begin{array}{c}a>0\\ \operatorname{Re}(a+b)>0\end{array}\right\}\right]$$

4 $e^{-(a+b)x}K_\mu(ax)L_n^\lambda(bx)$

$$\frac{\sqrt{\pi}\,(\lambda+1)_n}{n!\,(2a)^s}\Gamma\left[\begin{array}{c}s+\mu,\,s-\mu\\ \frac{2s+1}{2}\end{array}\right]{}_3F_2\left(\begin{array}{c}n+\lambda+1,\,s+\mu,\,s-\mu\\ \lambda+1,\,\frac{2s+1}{2};\,-\frac{b}{2a}\end{array}\right)$$

$$[\operatorname{Re}(2a+b)>0;\ \operatorname{Re}s>|\operatorname{Re}\mu|]$$

5 $e^{-bx}\left\{\begin{array}{c} Y_\mu(a\sqrt{x}) \\ K_\mu(a\sqrt{x}) \end{array}\right\}$

$\times L_n^\lambda(bx)$

$$\mp\frac{2^{\mu-(1\mp1)/2}\pi^{(1\mp1)/2}}{n!\pi a^\mu b^{s-\mu/2}}\left(\frac{2-2s+2\lambda+\mu}{2}\right)_n\Gamma(\mu)$$

$$\times\Gamma\left(\frac{2s-\mu}{2}\right){}_2F_2\left(\begin{array}{c}\frac{2s-\mu}{2},\,\frac{2s-2\lambda-\mu}{2};\,\mp\frac{a^2}{4b}\\ 1-\mu,\,\frac{2s-2n-2\lambda-\mu}{2}\end{array}\right)$$

$$\mp\frac{\pi^{(1\mp1)/2}a^\mu}{2^{\mu+1}n!\pi b^{s+\mu/2}}(2\cos\mu\pi)^{(1\pm1)/2}\Gamma(-\mu)\Gamma\left(\frac{2s+\mu}{2}\right)$$

$$\times\left(\frac{2-2s+2\lambda-\mu}{2}\right)_n{}_2F_2\left(\begin{array}{c}\frac{2s+\mu}{2},\,\frac{2s-2\lambda+\mu}{2};\,\mp\frac{a^2}{4b}\\ 1+\mu,\,\frac{2s-2n-2\lambda+\mu}{2}\end{array}\right)$$

$$[\operatorname{Re}b>0;\ 2\operatorname{Re}s>|\operatorname{Re}\mu|;\ |\arg a|<\pi]$$

6 $e^{-bx}K_\mu\left(\dfrac{a}{\sqrt{x}}\right)L_n^\lambda(bx)$

$$\frac{(\lambda+1)_n a^{2s}}{2^{2s+1}n!}\Gamma\left(\frac{\mu-2s}{2}\right)\Gamma\left(\frac{-\mu+2s}{2}\right)$$

$$\times{}_1F_3\left(\begin{array}{c}n+\lambda+1;\,-\frac{a^2b}{4}\\ \lambda+1,\,\frac{2s-\mu+2}{2},\,\frac{2s+\mu+2}{2}\end{array}\right)+\frac{a^\mu}{2^{\mu+1}n!\,b^{s-\mu/2}}$$

$$\times\left(\frac{2-2s+2\lambda+\mu}{2}\right)_n\Gamma(-\mu)\Gamma\left(\frac{2s-\mu}{2}\right)$$

$$\times{}_1F_3\left(\begin{array}{c}\frac{2-2s+n+2\lambda+\mu}{2};\,-\frac{a^2b}{4}\\ \mu+1,\,\frac{2-2s+\mu}{2},\,\frac{2-2s+2\lambda+\mu}{2}\end{array}\right)$$

$$+\frac{2^{\mu-1}}{n!\,a^\mu b^{s+\mu/2}}\left(\frac{2-2s+2\lambda-\mu}{2}\right)_n\Gamma(\mu)\Gamma\left(\frac{2s+\mu}{2}\right)$$

$$\times{}_1F_3\left(\begin{array}{c}\frac{2-2s+n+2\lambda-\mu}{2};\,-\frac{a^2b}{4}\\ 1-\mu,\,\frac{2-2s-\mu}{2},\,\frac{2-2s+2\lambda-\mu}{2}\end{array}\right)\qquad[\operatorname{Re}a,\ \operatorname{Re}b>0]$$

3.23.12. $L_n^\lambda(bx^r)$ **and** $P_n(ax^p + c)$

1	$\theta(a-x)e^{-bx}$ $\times P_n\left(\dfrac{2x}{a} - 1\right) L_m^\lambda(bx)$	$\dfrac{(-1)^n (\lambda+1)_m \, a^s}{m!} \dfrac{(1-s)_n}{(s)_{n+1}} \,_3F_3\left(\begin{matrix} m+\lambda+1,\, s,\, s;\, -ab \\ \lambda+1,\, s-n,\, s+n+1 \end{matrix}\right)$ $[a,\ \mathrm{Re}\, s > 0]$
2	$\theta(x-a) P_m\left(\dfrac{a}{x}\right)$ $\times L_n^\lambda(b^2 x^2)$	$\dfrac{(\lambda+1)_n \, 2^{s-1} a^s}{\pi^{3/2} n!} \sin(s\pi)\, \Gamma(-s)\, \Gamma\left(\dfrac{s-m}{2}\right)$ $\times \Gamma\left(\dfrac{s+m+1}{2}\right) \,_3F_3\left(\begin{matrix} -n,\, \frac{s-m}{2},\, \frac{s+m+1}{2} \\ \lambda+1,\, \frac{s+1}{2},\, \frac{s+2}{2};\, a^2 b^2 \end{matrix}\right)$ $[a > 0;\ \mathrm{Re}\, s < -2n]$

3.23.13. $L_n^\lambda(bx)$ **and** $T_n(ax+c)$, $U_n(ax+c)$

1	$(a-x)_+^{-1/2} e^{-bx}$ $\times T_n\left(\dfrac{2x}{a} - 1\right) L_m^\lambda(bx)$	$\dfrac{(-1)^n \sqrt{\pi}\, a^{s-1/2}}{m!} (\lambda+1)_m \left(\dfrac{1-2s}{2}\right)_n$ $\times \Gamma\left[\begin{matrix} s \\ \frac{2s+2n+1}{2} \end{matrix}\right] \,_3F_3\left(\begin{matrix} m+\lambda+1,\, s,\, \frac{2s+1}{2};\, -ab \\ \lambda+1,\, \frac{2s-2n+1}{2},\, \frac{2s+2n+1}{2} \end{matrix}\right)$ $[a,\ \mathrm{Re}\, s > 0]$
2	$(a-x)_+^{1/2} e^{-bx}$ $\times U_n\left(\dfrac{2x}{a} - 1\right) L_m^\lambda(bx)$	$\dfrac{(-1)^n (n+1) \sqrt{\pi}\, a^{s+1/2}}{2\,(m!)} (\lambda+1)_m \left(\dfrac{3-2s}{2}\right)_n$ $\times \Gamma\left[\begin{matrix} s \\ \frac{2s+2n+3}{2} \end{matrix}\right] \,_3F_3\left(\begin{matrix} m+\lambda+1,\, \frac{2s-1}{2},\, s;\, -ab \\ \lambda+1,\, \frac{2s-2n-1}{2},\, \frac{2s+2n+3}{2} \end{matrix}\right)$ $[a,\ \mathrm{Re}\, s > 0]$

3.23.14. $L_n^\lambda(bx^r)$ **and** $H_n(ax)$

Notation: $\varepsilon = 0$ or 1.

1	$e^{-a^2 x^2 - bx} H_{2m+\varepsilon}(ax)$ $\times L_n^\lambda(bx)$	$\dfrac{(-1)^m 2^{2m+\varepsilon-1} (\lambda+1)_n}{n!\, a^s} \Gamma\left(\dfrac{s+\varepsilon}{2}\right) \left(\dfrac{\varepsilon-s+1}{2}\right)_m$ $\times \,_4F_4\left(\begin{matrix} \frac{n+\lambda+1}{2},\, \frac{n+\lambda+2}{2},\, \frac{s}{2},\, \frac{s+1}{2} \\ \frac{1}{2},\, \frac{\lambda+1}{2},\, \frac{\lambda+2}{2},\, \frac{s-2m-\varepsilon+1}{2};\, \frac{b^2}{4a^2} \end{matrix}\right)$ $- \dfrac{(-1)^m 2^{2m+\varepsilon-1} (\lambda+2)_n\, b}{n!\, a^{s+1}} \Gamma\left(\dfrac{s+\varepsilon+1}{2}\right) \left(\dfrac{\varepsilon-s}{2}\right)_m$ $\times \,_4F_4\left(\begin{matrix} \frac{n+\lambda+2}{2},\, \frac{n+\lambda+3}{2},\, \frac{s+1}{2},\, \frac{s+2}{2} \\ \frac{3}{2},\, \frac{\lambda+2}{2},\, \frac{\lambda+3}{2},\, \frac{s-2m-\varepsilon+2}{2};\, \frac{b^2}{4a^2} \end{matrix}\right)$ $[\mathrm{Re}\, s > -\varepsilon;\ |\arg a| < \pi/4]$

No.	$f(x)$	$F(s)$
2	$e^{-(a^2+b)x^2} H_{2m+\varepsilon}(ax)$ $\times L_n^\lambda(bx^2)$	$\dfrac{(-1)^m 2^{2m+\varepsilon-1}(\lambda+1)_n}{n!\,a^s}\Gamma\left(\dfrac{s+\varepsilon}{2}\right)\left(\dfrac{\varepsilon-s+1}{2}\right)_m$ $\times {}_3F_2\left(\begin{matrix} n+\lambda+1,\ \frac{s}{2},\ \frac{s+1}{2} \\ \lambda+1,\ \frac{s-2m-\varepsilon+1}{2};\ -\frac{b}{a^2} \end{matrix}\right)$ $\left[\operatorname{Re}(a^2+b)>0;\ \operatorname{Re}s>-\varepsilon\right]$

3.23.15. Products of $L_n^\lambda(bx)$

No.	$f(x)$	$F(s)$
1	$e^{-ax} L_m^\lambda(bx) L_n^\lambda(cx)$	$\dfrac{(\lambda+1)_m(\mu+1)_n}{m!\,n!\,a^s} F_2\left(s,\ -m,\ -n;\ \lambda+1,\ \mu+1;\ \dfrac{b}{a},\ \dfrac{c}{a}\right)$ $[\operatorname{Re}a,\ \operatorname{Re}s>0]$
2	$e^{-bx} L_m^\lambda(ax) L_n^\mu(bx)$	$\dfrac{(\lambda+1)_m(1-s+\mu)_n}{m!\,n!\,b^s}\Gamma(s)\,{}_3F_2\left(\begin{matrix} -m,\ s,\ s-\mu;\ \frac{a}{b} \\ \lambda+1,\ s-\mu-n \end{matrix}\right)$ $[\operatorname{Re}b,\ \operatorname{Re}s>0]$
3	$e^{-(a+b)x} L_m^\lambda(ax) L_n^\mu(bx)$	$\dfrac{(\mu+1)_n(1-s+\lambda)_m}{m!\,n!\,a^s}\Gamma(s)\,{}_3F_2\left(\begin{matrix} n+\mu+1,\ s,\ s-\lambda \\ \mu+1,\ s-m-\lambda;\ -\frac{b}{a} \end{matrix}\right)$ $[\operatorname{Re}(a+b),\ \operatorname{Re}s>0]$
4	$e^{-bx} L_m^\lambda(ax^2) L_n^\mu(bx)$	$\dfrac{(\lambda+1)_m(1-s+\mu)_n\,b^{-s}}{m!\,n!}\Gamma(s)$ $\times {}_5F_3\left(\begin{matrix} -m,\ \frac{s}{2},\ \frac{s+1}{2},\ \frac{s-\mu}{2},\ \frac{s-\mu+1}{2} \\ \lambda+1,\ \frac{s-n-\mu}{2},\ \frac{s-n-\mu+1}{2};\ \frac{4a}{b^2} \end{matrix}\right)$ $[\operatorname{Re}b,\ \operatorname{Re}s>0]$
5	$e^{-ax^2-bx} L_m^\lambda(ax^2)$ $\times L_n^\mu(bx)$	$\dfrac{(\mu+1)_n}{2\,(m!)\,n!\,a^{s/2}}\Gamma\left(\dfrac{s}{2}\right)\left(\dfrac{2-s+2\lambda}{2}\right)_m$ $\times {}_4F_4\left(\begin{matrix} \frac{n+\mu+1}{2},\ \frac{n+\mu+2}{2},\ \frac{s}{2},\ \frac{s-2\lambda}{2};\ \frac{b^2}{4a} \\ \frac{1}{2},\ \frac{\mu+1}{2},\ \frac{\mu+2}{2},\ \frac{s-2m-2\lambda}{2} \end{matrix}\right)$ $-\dfrac{(\mu+2)_n\,b}{2\,(m!)\,n!\,a^{(s+1)/2}}\left(\dfrac{1-s+2\lambda}{2}\right)_m\Gamma\left(\dfrac{s+1}{2}\right)$ $\times {}_4F_4\left(\begin{matrix} \frac{n+\mu+2}{2},\ \frac{n+\mu+3}{2},\ \frac{s+1}{2},\ \frac{s-2\lambda+1}{2};\ \frac{b^2}{4a} \\ \frac{3}{2},\ \frac{\mu+2}{2},\ \frac{\mu+3}{2},\ \frac{s-2m-2\lambda+1}{2} \end{matrix}\right)$ $[\operatorname{Re}a,\ \operatorname{Re}s>0]$
6	$e^{-ax}\displaystyle\prod_{k=1}^{n} L_{m_k}^{\lambda_k}(b_k x)$	$a^{-s}\displaystyle\prod_{k=1}^{n}\dfrac{(\lambda_k+1)_{m_k}}{m_k!}\,F_A^{(n)}\left(s,\ (-m_n);\ (\lambda_n)+1;\ \dfrac{(b_n)}{a}\right)$ $[\operatorname{Re}a,\ \operatorname{Re}s>0]$

3.24. The Gegenbauer Polynomials $C_n^\lambda(z)$

More formulas can be obtained from the corresponding sections due to the relations

$$\lim_{\lambda \to 0}\left[\frac{1}{\lambda} C_n^\lambda(z)\right] = \frac{2}{n} T_n(z), \quad C_n^{1/2}(z) = P_n(z) = P_n^{(0,0)}(z),$$

$$C_n^1(z) = U_n(z) = \frac{(n+1)!}{(3/2)_n} P_n^{(1/2,1/2)}(z) = \frac{1}{1-z^2}\left[z T_{n+1}(z) - T_{n+2}(z)\right],$$

$$C_\nu^\lambda(z) = \frac{(2\lambda)_\nu}{(\lambda+1/2)_n} P_\nu^{(\lambda-1/2,\lambda-1/2)}(z),$$

$$C_\nu^\lambda(z) = \frac{\Gamma(2\lambda+\nu)}{\Gamma(2\lambda)\Gamma(\nu+1)} \,_2F_1\left(-\nu, 2\lambda+\nu; \lambda+\frac{1}{2}; \frac{1-z}{2}\right).$$

3.24.1. $C_n^\lambda(\varphi(x))$ and algebraic functions

Notation: $\varepsilon = 0$ or 1.

No.	$f(x)$	$F(s)$
1	$(a-x)_+^{\alpha-1} C_{2n+\varepsilon}^\lambda(bx)$	$\dfrac{(-1)^n a^{s+\alpha+\varepsilon-1}(2b)^\varepsilon}{n!}(\lambda)_{n+\varepsilon} \, \mathrm{B}(\alpha, s+\varepsilon)$ $\times {}_4F_3\left(\begin{array}{c} -n,\, n+\lambda+\varepsilon,\, \frac{s+\varepsilon}{2},\, \frac{s+\varepsilon+1}{2} \\ \frac{2\varepsilon+1}{2},\, \frac{s+\alpha+\varepsilon}{2},\, \frac{s+\alpha+\varepsilon+1}{2};\, a^2b^2 \end{array}\right)$ $[a,\ \mathrm{Re}\,\alpha > 0;\ \mathrm{Re}\,s > -\varepsilon]$
2	$(x-a)_+^{\alpha-1} C_{2n+\varepsilon}^\lambda(bx)$	$\dfrac{(-1)^n a^{s+\alpha+\varepsilon-1}(2b)^\varepsilon}{n!}(\lambda)_{n+\varepsilon} \, \mathrm{B}(1-s-\alpha-\varepsilon, \alpha)$ $\times {}_4F_3\left(\begin{array}{c} -n,\, n+\lambda+\varepsilon,\, \frac{s+\varepsilon}{2},\, \frac{s+\varepsilon+1}{2} \\ \frac{2\varepsilon+1}{2},\, \frac{s+\alpha+\varepsilon}{2},\, \frac{s+\alpha+\varepsilon+1}{2};\, a^2b^2 \end{array}\right)$ $[a > 0;\ \mathrm{Re}\,(s+\alpha) < 1-2n-\varepsilon]$
3	$(a^2-x^2)_+^{\alpha-1} C_{2n+\varepsilon}^\lambda(bx)$	$\dfrac{(-1)^n a^{s+2\alpha+\varepsilon-2} b^\varepsilon}{2^{1-\varepsilon} n!}(\lambda)_{n+\varepsilon} \, \mathrm{B}\left(\alpha, \frac{s+\varepsilon}{2}\right) {}_3F_2\left(\begin{array}{c} -n,\, n+\lambda+\varepsilon,\, \frac{s+\varepsilon}{2} \\ \frac{2\varepsilon+1}{2},\, \frac{s+2\alpha+\varepsilon}{2};\, a^2b^2 \end{array}\right)$ $[a,\ \mathrm{Re}\,\alpha > 0;\ \mathrm{Re}\,s > -\varepsilon]$
4	$(a^2-x^2)_+^{\lambda-1/2} C_n^\lambda\left(\dfrac{x}{a}\right)$	$\dfrac{\pi(2\lambda)_n}{2^{s+2\lambda-1}n!} a^{s+2\lambda-1} \Gamma\left[\begin{array}{c} n+2\lambda,\, s \\ \lambda,\, \frac{s-n+1}{2},\, \frac{s+n+2\lambda+1}{2} \end{array}\right]$ $[a > 0;\ \mathrm{Re}\,\lambda > -1/2;\ \mathrm{Re}\,s > ((-1)^n - 1)/2]$
5	$(x^2-a^2)_+^{\lambda-1/2} C_n^\lambda\left(\dfrac{x}{a}\right)$	$\dfrac{(2\lambda)_n}{2^{s+1}n!\sqrt{\pi}} a^{s+2\lambda-1} \Gamma\left[\begin{array}{c} \frac{2\lambda+1}{2},\, \frac{1-s+n}{2},\, \frac{1-s-n-2\lambda}{2} \\ 1-s \end{array}\right]$ $[a > 0;\ \mathrm{Re}\,\lambda > -1/2;\ \mathrm{Re}\,(s+2\lambda) < 1-n]$

No.	$f(x)$	$F(s)$

6

$$\dfrac{1}{x^2-b^2}\left(a^2-x^2\right)_+^{\lambda-1/2}$$
$$\times\, C_{2n+\varepsilon}^{\lambda}\left(\dfrac{x}{a}\right)$$

$$\dfrac{(-1)^{n+1}\sqrt{\pi}\,(2\lambda)_{2n+\varepsilon}\,a^{s+2\lambda-1}}{2^s\,(2n+\varepsilon)!\,b^2}\left(\dfrac{1-s+\varepsilon}{2}\right)_n$$
$$\times\,\Gamma\left[\begin{array}{c}\frac{2\lambda+1}{2},\,s\\[2pt]\frac{s-\varepsilon+1}{2},\,\frac{s+2n+2\lambda+\varepsilon+1}{2}\end{array}\right]\,{}_3F_2\left(\begin{array}{c}1,\,\frac{s}{2},\,\frac{s+1}{2};\,\frac{a^2}{b^2}\\[2pt]\frac{s-2n-\varepsilon+1}{2},\,\frac{s+2n+2\lambda+\varepsilon+1}{2}\end{array}\right)$$
$$[0<a<b;\ \operatorname{Re}\lambda>-1/2;\ \operatorname{Re}s>-\varepsilon]$$

7

$$\dfrac{1}{x^2-b^2}\left(a^2-x^2\right)_+^{\lambda-1/2}$$
$$\times\, C_{n}^{\lambda}\left(\dfrac{x}{a}\right)$$

$$\dfrac{\sqrt{\pi}\,(2\lambda)_n\,a^{s+2\lambda-3}}{2^{s-2}n!}\,\Gamma\left[\begin{array}{c}\frac{2\lambda+1}{2},\,s-2\\[2pt]\frac{s-n-1}{2},\,\frac{s+n+2\lambda-1}{2}\end{array}\right]$$
$$\times\,{}_3F_2\left(\begin{array}{c}1,\,\frac{3-s+n}{2},\,-\frac{s+n+2\lambda-3}{2}\\[2pt]\frac{3-s}{2},\,\frac{4-s}{2};\,\frac{b^2}{a^2}\end{array}\right)$$
$$+\,\dfrac{2^{n-1}\pi^{3/2}a^{2\lambda-2}b^{s-3}}{(n+1)!}\,\tan\dfrac{s\pi}{2}\,\Gamma\left[\begin{array}{c}\frac{n+2\lambda-1}{2}\\[2pt]\lambda,\,-\frac{n}{2}\end{array}\right]$$
$$\times\left[\left(a^2+2\left(\lambda-2\right)b^2\right){}_2F_1\left(\begin{array}{c}\frac{n+2}{2},\,-\frac{n+2\lambda-2}{2}\\[2pt]\frac{1}{2};\,\frac{b^2}{a^2}\end{array}\right)\right.$$
$$\left.-\left(a^2-b^2\right){}_2F_1\left(\begin{array}{c}\frac{n+2}{2},\,-\frac{n+2\lambda-2}{2}\\[2pt]-\frac{1}{2};\,\frac{b^2}{a^2}\end{array}\right)\right]$$
$$-\,\dfrac{\pi^{3/2}(2\lambda)_n\,a^{2\lambda-1}b^{s-2}}{2\,(n)!}\,\cot\dfrac{s\pi}{2}\,\Gamma\left[\begin{array}{c}\frac{2\lambda+1}{2}\\[2pt]\frac{n+2\lambda+1}{2},\,\frac{1-n}{2}\end{array}\right]$$
$$\times\,{}_2F_1\left(\begin{array}{c}\frac{n+1}{2},\,-\frac{n+2\lambda-1}{2}\\[2pt]\frac{1}{2};\,\frac{b^2}{a^2}\end{array}\right)$$
$$[0<b<a;\ \operatorname{Re}\lambda>-1/2;\ \operatorname{Re}s>\left((-1)^n-1\right)/2]$$

8

$$\dfrac{1}{x^2-b^2}\left(x^2-a^2\right)_+^{\lambda-1/2}$$
$$\times\, C_{2n+\varepsilon}^{\lambda}\left(\dfrac{x}{a}\right)$$

$$-\dfrac{(2\lambda)_{2n+\varepsilon}\,a^{s+2\lambda-1}}{2\,(2n+\varepsilon)!\,b^2}\left(\dfrac{1-s+\varepsilon}{2}\right)_n\,\Gamma\left[\begin{array}{c}\frac{2\lambda+1}{2},\,\frac{1-s-2n-2\lambda-\varepsilon}{2}\\[2pt]\frac{2-s-\varepsilon}{2}\end{array}\right]$$
$$\times\,{}_3F_2\left(\begin{array}{c}1,\,\frac{s}{2},\,\frac{s+1}{2};\,\frac{a^2}{b^2}\\[2pt]\frac{s-2n-\varepsilon+1}{2},\,\frac{s+2n+2\lambda+\varepsilon+1}{2}\end{array}\right)$$
$$+\,\dfrac{2^{2n+\varepsilon-1}\pi^2 b^{s+2n+2\lambda+\varepsilon-3}}{(2n+\varepsilon)!\,a^{2n+\varepsilon}}\,\dfrac{\csc\left[\left(\lambda+\varepsilon\right)\pi\right]}{\Gamma\left(\lambda\right)\Gamma\left(1-2n-\lambda-\varepsilon\right)}$$
$$\times\,\tan\dfrac{(s+2\lambda+\varepsilon)\pi}{2}\,{}_2F_1\left(\begin{array}{c}\frac{1-2n-2\lambda-\varepsilon}{2},\,\frac{2-2n-2\lambda-\varepsilon}{2}\\[2pt]1-2n-\lambda-\varepsilon;\,\frac{a^2}{b^2}\end{array}\right)$$
$$[0<a<b;\ \operatorname{Re}\lambda>-1/2;\ \operatorname{Re}\left(s+2\lambda\right)<3-2n-\varepsilon]$$

9

$$\dfrac{1}{x^2-b^2}\left(x^2-a^2\right)_+^{\lambda-1/2}$$
$$\times\, C_{n}^{\lambda}\left(\dfrac{x}{a}\right)$$

$$\dfrac{(2\lambda)_n\,a^{s+2\lambda-3}}{2^{s-1}\sqrt{\pi}\,n!}\,\Gamma\left[\begin{array}{c}\frac{2\lambda+1}{2},\,\frac{3-s+n}{2},\,\frac{3-s-n-2\lambda}{2}\\[2pt]3-s\end{array}\right]$$
$$\times\,{}_3F_2\left(\begin{array}{c}1,\,\frac{3-s+n}{2},\,\frac{3-s-n-2\lambda}{2}\\[2pt]\frac{3-s}{2},\,\frac{4-s}{2};\,\frac{b^2}{a^2}\end{array}\right)$$
$$[0<b<a;\ \operatorname{Re}\lambda>-1/2;\ \operatorname{Re}\left(s+2\lambda\right)<3-n]$$

No.	$f(x)$	$F(s)$
10	$\left(x^2-a^2\right)_+^{\lambda-1/2}\left(x^2-b^2\right)^{\mu-1}$ $\times C_{2n+\varepsilon}^\lambda\left(\dfrac{x}{a}\right)$	$\dfrac{a^{s+2\mu+2\lambda-3}}{2\,(2n+\varepsilon)!}\,(2\lambda)_{2n+\varepsilon}\left(\dfrac{3-s-2\mu+\varepsilon}{2}\right)_n$ $\times\Gamma\left[\begin{array}{c}\frac{2\lambda+1}{2},\ -\frac{s+2n+2\lambda+2\mu+\varepsilon-3}{2}\\ -\frac{s+2\mu+\varepsilon-4}{2}\end{array}\right]$ $\times{}_3F_2\left(\begin{array}{c}1-\mu,\ -\frac{s-2n+2\mu-\varepsilon-3}{2},\ -\frac{s+2n+2\lambda+2\mu+\varepsilon-3}{2}\\ \frac{3-s-2\mu}{2},\ \frac{4-s-2\mu}{2};\ \frac{b^2}{a^2}\end{array}\right)$ $\left[\begin{array}{c}a>b>0;\ \operatorname{Re}\lambda>-1/2;\\ \operatorname{Re}(s+2\mu+2\lambda)<3-2n-\varepsilon\end{array}\right]$
11	$\left(a^2-x^2\right)_+^{\lambda-1/2}\dfrac{1}{\left(b^2\pm x^2\right)^\rho}$ $\times C_n^\lambda\left(\dfrac{x}{a}\right)$	$\dfrac{\pi}{n!}\left(\dfrac{a}{2}\right)^{s+2\lambda-1}b^{-2\rho}\,\Gamma\left[\begin{array}{c}s,\ n+2\lambda\\ \lambda,\ \frac{s-n+1}{2},\ \frac{s+n+2\lambda+1}{2}\end{array}\right]$ $\times{}_3F_2\left(\begin{array}{c}\rho,\ \frac{s}{2},\ \frac{s+1}{2};\ \mp\frac{a^2}{b^2}\\ \frac{s-n+1}{2},\ \frac{s+n+2\lambda+1}{2}\end{array}\right)$ $\left[\left\{\begin{array}{c}a,\ \operatorname{Re}b>0\\ b>a>0\end{array}\right\};\ \operatorname{Re}\lambda>-\dfrac{1}{2};\ \operatorname{Re}s>\dfrac{(-1)^n-1}{2}\right]$
12	$\left(x^2-a^2\right)_+^{\lambda-1/2}\dfrac{1}{\left(x^2+a^2\right)^\rho}$ $\times C_{2n+\varepsilon}^\lambda\left(\dfrac{x}{a}\right)$	$\dfrac{a^{s+2\lambda-2\rho-1}}{2\,(2n+\varepsilon)!}\,(2\lambda)_{2n+\varepsilon}\left(\dfrac{1-s+2\rho+\varepsilon}{2}\right)_n$ $\times\Gamma\left[\begin{array}{c}\frac{2\lambda+1}{2},\ \frac{1-s-2n-2\lambda+2\rho-\varepsilon}{2}\\ \frac{2-s+2\rho-\varepsilon}{2}\end{array}\right]$ $\times{}_3F_2\left(\begin{array}{c}\rho,\ \frac{1-s+2n+2\rho+\varepsilon}{2},\ \frac{1-s-2n-2\lambda+2\rho-\varepsilon}{2}\\ \frac{1-s+2\rho}{2},\ \frac{2-s+2\rho}{2};\ -\frac{b^2}{a^2}\end{array}\right)$ $\left[\begin{array}{c}a,\ \operatorname{Re}b>0;\ \operatorname{Re}\lambda>-1/2;\\ \operatorname{Re}(s+2\lambda-2\rho)<1-2n-\varepsilon\end{array}\right]$
13	$\left(a^2-x^2\right)_+^{\mu-1}\left(b^2-x^2\right)^{\lambda-1/2}$ $\times C_n^\lambda\left(\dfrac{x}{b}\right)$	$\dfrac{\sqrt{\pi}\,a^{s+2\mu-2}b^{2\lambda-1}}{2\,(n)!}\,(2\lambda)_n\,\Gamma\left[\begin{array}{c}\frac{2\lambda+1}{2},\ \mu,\ \frac{s}{2}\\ -\frac{n-1}{2},\ \frac{n+2\lambda+1}{2},\ \frac{s+2\mu}{2}\end{array}\right]$ $\times{}_3F_2\left(\begin{array}{c}\frac{n+1}{2},\ -\frac{n+2\lambda-1}{2},\ \frac{s}{2}\\ \frac{1}{2},\ \frac{s+2\mu}{2};\ \frac{a^2}{b^2}\end{array}\right)$ $-\dfrac{\sqrt{\pi}\,a^{s+2\mu-1}b^{2\lambda-2}}{n!}\,(2\lambda)_n\,\Gamma\left[\begin{array}{c}\frac{2\lambda+1}{2},\ \mu,\ \frac{s+1}{2}\\ -\frac{n}{2},\ \frac{n+2\lambda}{2},\ \frac{s+2\mu+1}{2}\end{array}\right]$ $\times{}_3F_2\left(\begin{array}{c}\frac{n+2}{2},\ -\frac{n+2\lambda-2}{2},\ \frac{s+1}{2}\\ \frac{3}{2},\ \frac{s+2\mu+1}{2};\ \frac{a^2}{b^2}\end{array}\right)$ $\left[\begin{array}{c}b>a>0;\ \operatorname{Re}\mu>0;\ \operatorname{Re}\lambda>-1/2;\\ \operatorname{Re}s>\left((-1)^n-1\right)/2\end{array}\right]$

No.	$f(x)$	$F(s)$
14	$\left(x^2 - a^2\right)_+^{\mu-1} \left(x^2 - b^2\right)^{\lambda-1/2}$ $\times C_{2n+\varepsilon}^{\lambda}\left(\dfrac{x}{b}\right)$	$\dfrac{2^{2n+\varepsilon-1}\, a^{s+2n+2\lambda+2\mu+\varepsilon-3}}{(2n+\varepsilon)!\, b^{2n+\varepsilon}}\, (\lambda)_{2n+\varepsilon}\, \Gamma\left[\begin{array}{c} \lambda+\varepsilon,\, 1-\lambda-\varepsilon \\ \lambda,\, 1-2n-\lambda-\varepsilon \end{array}\right]$ $\times \mathrm{B}\left(\mu,\, -\dfrac{s+2n+2\lambda+2\mu+\varepsilon-3}{2}\right)$ $\times\, {}_3F_2\left(\begin{array}{c} \frac{1-2n-2\lambda-\varepsilon}{2},\, \frac{2-2n-2\lambda-\varepsilon}{2},\, -\frac{s+2n+2\lambda+2\mu+\varepsilon-3}{2} \\ 1-2n-\lambda-\varepsilon,\, -\frac{s+2n+2\lambda+\varepsilon-3}{2};\, \frac{b^2}{a^2} \end{array}\right)$ $\left[\begin{array}{c} a>b>0;\ \mathrm{Re}\,\mu>0;\ \mathrm{Re}\,\lambda>-1/2 \\ \mathrm{Re}\,(s+2\lambda+2\mu)<3-2n-\varepsilon \end{array}\right]$
15	$(a-x)_+^{\alpha-1}\, C_n^{\lambda}(1-bx)$	$\dfrac{(2\lambda)_n}{n!}\, a^{s+\alpha-1}\, \mathrm{B}(\alpha,\, s)\, {}_3F_2\left(\begin{array}{c} -n,\, n+2\lambda,\, s \\ \frac{2\lambda+1}{2},\, s+\alpha;\, \frac{ab}{2} \end{array}\right)$ $[a,\ \mathrm{Re}\,\alpha,\ \mathrm{Re}\,s>0;\ \mathrm{Re}\,\lambda>-1/2]$
16	$(a-x)_+^{\lambda-1/2}$ $\times C_n^{\lambda}(bx-ab+1)$	$(2\lambda)_n\, a^{s+\lambda-1/2}\, \Gamma\left[\begin{array}{c} \frac{2\lambda+1}{2},\, s \\ \frac{2s+2\lambda+2n+1}{2} \end{array}\right] P_n^{(s+\lambda-1/2,\, \lambda-s-1/2)}(1-ab)$ $[a,\ \mathrm{Re}\,s>0;\ \mathrm{Re}\,\lambda>-1/2]$
17	$(a-x)_+^{\alpha-1}\, C_{2n+\varepsilon}^{\lambda}(b(a-x))$	$\dfrac{(-1)^n\, a^{s+\alpha+\varepsilon-1}\, (2b)^{\varepsilon}}{n!}\, (\lambda)_{n+\varepsilon}\, \mathrm{B}(\alpha+\varepsilon,\, s)$ $\times\, {}_4F_3\left(\begin{array}{c} -n,\, n+\lambda+\varepsilon,\, \frac{\alpha+\varepsilon}{2},\, \frac{\alpha+\varepsilon+1}{2} \\ \frac{2\varepsilon+1}{2},\, \frac{s+\alpha+\varepsilon}{2},\, \frac{s+\alpha+\varepsilon+1}{2};\, a^2b^2 \end{array}\right)$ $[a,\ \mathrm{Re}\,s>0;\ \mathrm{Re}\,\alpha>-\varepsilon]$
18	$(a-x)_+^{\lambda-1/2}\, C_n^{\lambda}\left(\dfrac{x+b}{a+b}\right)$	$a^{s+\lambda-1/2}\, \dfrac{(2\lambda)_n}{\left(\frac{2s+2\lambda+1}{2}\right)_n}\, \mathrm{B}\left(\dfrac{2\lambda+1}{2},\, s\right)$ $\times P_n^{(s+\lambda-1/2,\, -s+\lambda-1/2)}\left(\dfrac{b}{a+b}\right)$ $[a,\ \mathrm{Re}\,s>0;\ \mathrm{Re}\,\lambda>-1/2]$
19	$(a-x)_+^{\alpha-1}\, C_n^{\lambda}\left(\dfrac{x+b}{a+b}\right)$	$\dfrac{a^{s+\alpha-1}}{n!}\, (2\lambda)_n\, \mathrm{B}(s,\, \alpha)\, {}_3F_2\left(\begin{array}{c} -n,\, n+2\lambda,\, \alpha \\ \frac{2\lambda+1}{2},\, s+\alpha;\, \frac{a}{2(a+b)} \end{array}\right)$ $[a,\ \mathrm{Re}\,\alpha,\ \mathrm{Re}\,s>0]$
20	$(a-x)_+^{\lambda-1/2}\, C_n^{\lambda}\left(\dfrac{2x}{a}-1\right)$	$\dfrac{(2\lambda)_n}{n!}\, a^{s+\lambda-1/2}\, \Gamma\left[\begin{array}{c} \frac{2\lambda+1}{2},\, s,\, \frac{2s-2\lambda+1}{2} \\ \frac{2s-2n-2\lambda+1}{2},\, \frac{2s+2n+2\lambda+1}{2} \end{array}\right]$ $[a,\ \mathrm{Re}\,s>0;\ \mathrm{Re}\,\lambda>-1/2]$
21	$(x-a)_+^{\lambda-1/2}\, C_n^{\lambda}\left(\dfrac{2x}{a}-1\right)$	$\dfrac{(2\lambda)_n}{n!}\, a^{s+\lambda-1/2}\, \Gamma\left[\begin{array}{c} \frac{2\lambda+1}{2},\, \frac{1-2s-2n-2\lambda}{2},\, \frac{1-2s+2n+2\lambda}{2} \\ 1-s,\, \frac{1-2s+2\lambda}{2} \end{array}\right]$ $[a>0;\ \mathrm{Re}\,\lambda>-1/2;\ \mathrm{Re}\,s<1/2-n-\mathrm{Re}\,\lambda]$

No.	$f(x)$	$F(s)$
22	$(x+a)^{\lambda-1/2} C_n^\lambda\left(\dfrac{2x}{a}+1\right)$	$\dfrac{(-1)^n (2\lambda)_n}{n!} a^{s+\lambda-1/2} \Gamma\left[\begin{matrix} s, \frac{1-2s+2n+2\lambda}{2}, \frac{1-2s-2n-2\lambda}{2} \\ \frac{1-2\lambda}{2}, \frac{1-2s+2\lambda}{2} \end{matrix}\right]$ $[0<\mathrm{Re}\,s<1/2-\mathrm{Re}\,\lambda-n;\ |\arg a|<\pi]$
23	$\dfrac{1}{(x+a)^\rho} C_n^\lambda\left(\dfrac{2x}{a}+1\right)$	$\dfrac{a^{s-\rho}}{n!}(2\lambda)_n\,\mathrm{B}\,(-s-n+\rho,\,s)\ {}_3F_2\left(\begin{matrix} -n, \frac{1-2n-2\lambda}{2}, s \\ \frac{2\lambda+1}{2}, \rho-n;\, 1 \end{matrix}\right)$ $[0<\mathrm{Re}\,s<\mathrm{Re}\,\rho-n;\ |\arg a|<\pi]$
24	$\dfrac{(a-x)_+^{\lambda-1/2}}{(b\pm x)^\rho} C_n^\lambda\left(\dfrac{2x}{a}-1\right)$	$\dfrac{(-1)^n a^{s+\lambda-1/2}b^{-\rho}}{n!}\dfrac{(2\lambda)_n\left(\frac{-2s+2\lambda+1}{2}\right)_n}{\left(\frac{2s+2\lambda+1}{2}\right)_n}\mathrm{B}\left(\dfrac{2\lambda+1}{2},\,s\right)$ $\times\ {}_3F_2\left(\begin{matrix} \rho,\,s,\,\frac{2s-2\lambda+1}{2};\,\mp\frac{a}{b} \\ \frac{2s-2n-2\lambda+1}{2},\,\frac{2s+2n+2\lambda+1}{2} \end{matrix}\right)$ $\left[\left\{\begin{matrix} a>0 \\ b>a>0 \end{matrix}\right\},\ \mathrm{Re}\,\lambda>-1/2;\ \mathrm{Re}\,s>0\right]$
25	$(a-x)_+^{\alpha-1}(b\pm x)^{\lambda-1/2}$ $\times\ C_n^\lambda\left(\dfrac{2x}{b}\pm 1\right)$	$\dfrac{(\pm 1)^n a^{s+\alpha-1}b^{\lambda-1/2}}{n!}(2\lambda)_n\,\mathrm{B}\,(\alpha,\,s)$ $\times\ {}_3F_2\left(\begin{matrix} \frac{-2n-2\lambda+1}{2}, \frac{2n+2\lambda+1}{2}, s \\ \frac{2\lambda+1}{2}, s+\alpha;\, \mp\frac{a}{b} \end{matrix}\right)\quad [a,\,b,\,\mathrm{Re}\,\alpha,\,\mathrm{Re}\,s>0]$
26	$\dfrac{(x+a)^{\lambda-1/2}}{(x+b)^\rho} C_n^\lambda\left(\dfrac{2x}{a}+1\right)$	$\dfrac{(-1)^n a^{s+\lambda-\rho-1/2}}{n!}(2\lambda)_n\left(\dfrac{1}{2}-s+\lambda+\rho\right)_n$ $\times\ \Gamma\left[\begin{matrix} s-\rho, \frac{1-2s-2n-2\lambda+2\rho}{2} \\ \frac{1-2\lambda}{2} \end{matrix}\right]$ $\times\ {}_3F_2\left(\begin{matrix} \rho, \frac{1-2s-2n-2\lambda+2\rho}{2}, \frac{1-2s+2n+2\lambda+2\rho}{2} \\ 1-s+\rho, \frac{1-2s+2\lambda+2\rho}{2};\, \frac{b}{a} \end{matrix}\right)$ $+\dfrac{a^{\lambda-1/2}b^{s-\rho}}{n!}(2\lambda)_n\,\mathrm{B}\,(s,\,\rho-s)\ {}_3F_2\left(\begin{matrix} \frac{-2n-2\lambda+1}{2}, \frac{2n+2\lambda+1}{2}, s \\ \frac{2\lambda+1}{2}, s-\rho+1;\, \frac{b}{a} \end{matrix}\right)$ $[a>0;\ 0<\mathrm{Re}\,s<1/2-n-\mathrm{Re}\,\lambda+\mathrm{Re}\,\rho;\ |\arg b|<\pi]$
27	$\dfrac{(x+a-b)^{\lambda-1/2}}{(x+a+b)^\rho}$ $\times\ C_n^\lambda\left(\dfrac{x+a}{b}\right)$	$\dfrac{2^n (a+b)^{s+n+\lambda-\rho-1/2}}{n!\,b^n}(\lambda)_n\,\mathrm{B}\left(\dfrac{1-2s-2n-2\lambda+2\rho}{2},\,s\right)$ $\times\ {}_3F_2\left(\begin{matrix} \frac{1-2n-2\lambda}{2}, 1-n-2\lambda, \frac{1-2s-2n-2\lambda+2\rho}{2} \\ \frac{1-2n-2\lambda+2\rho}{2}, 1-2n-2\lambda;\, \frac{2b}{a+b} \end{matrix}\right)$ $[a>b>0;\ 0<\mathrm{Re}\,s<1/2-n-\mathrm{Re}\,\lambda+\mathrm{Re}\,\rho]$
28	$(a^2-x^2)_+^{\lambda-1/2} C_n^\lambda\left(\dfrac{a}{x}\right)$	$\dfrac{2^{s-1}}{n!}a^{s+2\lambda-1}\Gamma\left[\begin{matrix} 2\lambda+n, \frac{s-n}{2}, \frac{s+n+2\lambda}{2} \\ \lambda, s+2\lambda \end{matrix}\right]$ $[a>0;\ \mathrm{Re}\,\lambda>-1/2;\ \mathrm{Re}\,s>n]$

No.	$f(x)$	$F(s)$
29	$\left(x^2 - a^2\right)_+^{\lambda - 1/2} C_n^\lambda\left(\dfrac{a}{x}\right)$	$\dfrac{\sqrt{\pi}\,(2\lambda)_n\,(2a)^{s+2\lambda-1}}{n!}\,\Gamma\!\left[\begin{array}{c} \frac{2\lambda+1}{2},\ 1-s-2\lambda \\ \frac{2-s+n}{2},\ \frac{2-s-n-2\lambda}{2} \end{array}\right]$ $$[a>0;\ \operatorname{Re}\lambda > -1/2;\ \operatorname{Re}(s+2\lambda)<1]$$
30	$(x+a)^{\lambda-1/2}\,C_n^\lambda\left(\dfrac{2a}{x}+1\right)$	$\dfrac{(-1)^n\,(2\lambda)_n}{n!}\,a^{s+\lambda-1/2}\,\Gamma\!\left[\begin{array}{c} s+n+2\lambda,\ s-n,\ \frac{1-2s-2\lambda}{2} \\ \frac{1-2\lambda}{2},\ s+2\lambda \end{array}\right]$ $$[n<\operatorname{Re}s<1/2-\operatorname{Re}\lambda;\ |\arg a|<\pi]$$
31	$(a-x)_+^{\lambda-1/2}\,C_n^\lambda\left(\dfrac{2a}{x}-1\right)$	$\dfrac{(2\lambda)_n}{n!}\,a^{s+\lambda-1/2}\,\Gamma\!\left[\begin{array}{c} \frac{2\lambda+1}{2},\ s-n,\ s+n+2\lambda \\ \frac{2s+2\lambda+1}{2},\ s+2\lambda \end{array}\right]$ $$[a>0;\ \operatorname{Re}\lambda>-1/2;\ \operatorname{Re}s>n]$$
32	$\left(a^2-x^2\right)_+^{2\lambda-1}$ $\times C_n^\lambda\left(\dfrac{a}{2x}+\dfrac{x}{2a}\right)$	$\dfrac{a^{s+4\lambda-2}}{2\,(n!)}\,\Gamma\!\left[\begin{array}{c} n+2\lambda,\ \frac{s-n}{2},\ \frac{s+n+2\lambda}{2} \\ \frac{s-n+2\lambda}{2},\ \frac{s+n+4\lambda}{2} \end{array}\right]$ $$[a>0;\ \operatorname{Re}\lambda>-1/2;\ \operatorname{Re}s>n]$$
33	$(x-a)_+^{\lambda-1/2}\,C_n^\lambda\left(\dfrac{2a}{x}-1\right)$	$\dfrac{(2\lambda)_n}{n!}\,a^{s+\lambda-1/2}\,\Gamma\!\left[\begin{array}{c} \frac{2\lambda+1}{2},\ \frac{1-2s-2\lambda}{2},\ 1-s-2\lambda \\ 1-s+n,\ 1-s-n-2\lambda \end{array}\right]$ $$[a>0;\ \operatorname{Re}\lambda>-1/2;\ \operatorname{Re}s<1/2-\operatorname{Re}\lambda]$$
34	$(x+a)^{-n-2\lambda}\,C_n^\lambda\left(\dfrac{a-x}{a+x}\right)$	$\dfrac{a^{s-n-2\lambda}}{n!\left(\frac{2\lambda+1}{2}\right)_n}\,\Gamma\!\left[\begin{array}{c} s,\ n-s+2\lambda,\ \frac{1-2s+2n+2\lambda}{2} \\ 2\lambda,\ \frac{1-2s+2\lambda}{2} \end{array}\right]$ $$[0<\operatorname{Re}s<n+2\operatorname{Re}\lambda;\ |\arg a|<\pi]$$
35	$(a-x)_+^{-n-2\lambda}\,C_n^\lambda\left(\dfrac{a+x}{a-x}\right)$	$\dfrac{a^{s-n-2\lambda}}{n!\left(\frac{2\lambda+1}{2}\right)_n}\,\Gamma\!\left[\begin{array}{c} 1-2\lambda,\ s,\ \frac{2s-2\lambda+1}{2} \\ s-n-2\lambda+1,\ \frac{2s-2n-2\lambda+1}{2} \end{array}\right]$ $$[a,\ \operatorname{Re}s>0;\ \operatorname{Re}\lambda<1/2-n]$$
36	$(x-a)_+^{-n-2\lambda}\,C_n^\lambda\left(\dfrac{x+a}{x-a}\right)$	$\dfrac{a^{s+n-2\lambda}}{n!\left(\frac{2\lambda+1}{2}\right)_n}\,\Gamma\!\left[\begin{array}{c} 1-2\lambda,\ n-s+2\lambda,\ \frac{1-2s+2n+2\lambda}{2} \\ 1-s,\ \frac{1-2s+2\lambda}{2} \end{array}\right]$ $$[a>0;\ \operatorname{Re}\lambda<1/2-n;\ \operatorname{Re}s<n+2\operatorname{Re}\lambda]$$
37	$(a-x)_+^{\alpha-1}$ $\times C_{2n+\varepsilon}^\lambda\left(bx\,(a-x)\right)$	$\dfrac{(-1)^n\,2^\varepsilon\,(\lambda)_{n+\varepsilon}}{n!}\,a^{s+\alpha+2\varepsilon-1}b^\varepsilon\,\mathrm{B}\,(s+\varepsilon,\ \alpha+\varepsilon)$ $\times\,{}_6F_5\!\left(\begin{array}{c} -n,\ n+\lambda+\varepsilon,\ \Delta\,(2,\ \alpha+\varepsilon),\ \Delta\,(2,\ s+\varepsilon) \\ \frac{2\varepsilon+1}{2},\ \Delta\,(4,\ s+\alpha+2\varepsilon);\ \frac{a^4b^2}{16} \end{array}\right)$ $$[a>0;\ \operatorname{Re}s,\ \operatorname{Re}\alpha>-\varepsilon]$$

No.	$f(x)$	$F(s)$
38	$(a-x)_+^{\alpha-1} C_n^\lambda\left(\dfrac{b}{x(a-x)}\right)$	$\dfrac{(\lambda)_n}{n!}\, a^{s-2n+\alpha-1}(2b)^n \, \mathrm{B}\left(s-n,\,\alpha-n\right)$ $\times {}_6F_5\left(\begin{array}{c}\Delta(2,-n),\,\Delta(2,\alpha-n),\,\Delta(2,s-n)\\ 1-n-\lambda,\,\Delta(4,s-n+\alpha);\,\frac{a^4}{16b^2}\end{array}\right)$ $[a>0;\ \mathrm{Re}\,s,\ \mathrm{Re}\,\alpha>n]$
39	$(a-x)_+^{\alpha-1}$ $\times C_{2n+\varepsilon}^\lambda\big(b\sqrt{x(a-x)}\big)$	$\dfrac{2^\varepsilon(-1)^n(\lambda)_{n+\varepsilon}}{n!}\, a^{s+\alpha+\varepsilon-1}b^\varepsilon \, \mathrm{B}\left(\dfrac{2s+\varepsilon}{2},\,\dfrac{2\alpha+\varepsilon}{2}\right)$ $\times {}_4F_3\left(\begin{array}{c}-n,\,n+\lambda+\varepsilon,\,\frac{2\alpha+\varepsilon}{2},\,\frac{2s+\varepsilon}{2}\\ \frac{2\varepsilon+1}{2},\,\frac{s+\alpha+\varepsilon}{2},\,\frac{s+\alpha+\varepsilon+1}{2};\,\frac{a^2b^2}{4}\end{array}\right)$ $[a>0;\ \mathrm{Re}\,\alpha,\ \mathrm{Re}\,s>-\varepsilon/2]$
40	$(a-x)_+^{\alpha-1} C_n^\lambda\left(\dfrac{b}{\sqrt{x(a-x)}}\right)$	$\dfrac{2^n(\lambda)_n}{n!}\, a^{s-n+\alpha-1}b^n \, \mathrm{B}\left(\dfrac{2s-n}{2},\,\dfrac{2\alpha-n}{2}\right)$ $\times {}_4F_3\left(\begin{array}{c}\frac{1-n}{2},\,-\frac{n}{2},\,s-\frac{n}{2},\,\alpha-\frac{n}{2};\,\frac{a^2}{4b^2}\\ -n-\lambda+1,\,\frac{s-n+\alpha}{2},\,\frac{s-n+\alpha+1}{2}\end{array}\right)$ $[a>0;\ \mathrm{Re}\,\alpha,\ \mathrm{Re}\,s>n/2]$
41	$(a-x)_+^{-1/2} C_{2n}^\lambda\left(\sqrt{1-\dfrac{x}{a}}\right)$	$\dfrac{\sqrt\pi\,(\lambda)_n}{n!}\, a^{s-1/2}\,\Gamma\left[\begin{array}{c}s,\,\frac{1-2s+2n+2\lambda}{2}\\ \frac{2s+2n+1}{2},\,\frac{1-2s+2\lambda}{2}\end{array}\right]$ $[a,\ \mathrm{Re}\,s>0]$
42	$\theta(a-x) C_{2n+1}^\lambda\left(\sqrt{1-\dfrac{x}{a}}\right)$	$\dfrac{\sqrt\pi\,(\lambda)_{n+1}}{n!}\, a^{s}\,\Gamma\left[\begin{array}{c}s,\,\frac{1-2s+2n+2\lambda}{2}\\ \frac{2s+2n+3}{2},\,\frac{1-2s+2\lambda}{2}\end{array}\right]$ $[a,\ \mathrm{Re}\,s>0]$
43	$\theta(x-a) C_{2n+1}^\lambda\left(i\sqrt{\dfrac{x}{a}-1}\right)$	$\dfrac{i\sqrt\pi\,(\lambda)_{n+1}}{n!}\, a^{s}\,\Gamma\left[\begin{array}{c}\frac{2s-2\lambda+1}{2},\,-\frac{2s+2n+1}{2}\\ \frac{2s-2n-2\lambda+1}{2},\,1-s\end{array}\right]$ $[a>0;\ \mathrm{Re}\,s<-n-1/2]$
44	$(x-a)_+^{-1/2} C_{2n}^\lambda\left(\sqrt{1-\dfrac{a}{x}}\right)$	$\dfrac{\sqrt\pi\,(\lambda)_n}{n!}\, a^{s-1/2}\,\Gamma\left[\begin{array}{c}s+n+\lambda,\,\frac{1-2s}{2}\\ s+\lambda,\,1-s+n\end{array}\right]$ $[a>0;\ \mathrm{Re}\,s<1/2]$
45	$\theta(x-a) C_{2n+1}^\lambda\left(\sqrt{1-\dfrac{a}{x}}\right)$	$\dfrac{\sqrt\pi\,(\lambda)_{n+1}}{n!}\, a^{s}\,\Gamma\left[\begin{array}{c}\frac{2s+2\lambda+2n+1}{2},\,-s\\ \frac{2s+2\lambda+1}{2},\,\frac{3-2s+2n}{2}\end{array}\right]$ $[a>0;\ \mathrm{Re}\,s<0]$
46	$(a-x)_+^{-1/2} C_{2n}^\lambda\left(i\sqrt{\dfrac{a}{x}-1}\right)$	$\dfrac{\sqrt\pi\,(\lambda)_n}{n!}\, a^{s-1/2}\,\Gamma\left[\begin{array}{c}s-n,\,1-s-\lambda\\ \frac{2s+1}{2},\,1-s-n-\lambda\end{array}\right]$ $[a>0;\ \mathrm{Re}\,s>n]$
47	$\theta(a-x) C_{2n+1}^\lambda\left(i\sqrt{\dfrac{a}{x}-1}\right)$	$\dfrac{i\sqrt\pi\,(\lambda)_{n+1}}{n!}\, a^{s}\,\Gamma\left[\begin{array}{c}\frac{2s-2n-1}{2},\,\frac{1-2s-2\lambda}{2}\\ s+1,\,\frac{1-2s-2n-2\lambda}{2}\end{array}\right]$ $[a>0;\ \mathrm{Re}\,s>n+1/2]$

No.	$f(x)$	$F(s)$
48	$(a-x)_+^{-n/2-\lambda} C_n^\lambda\left(\sqrt{\dfrac{a}{a-x}}\right)$	$\dfrac{(-2)^n}{n!} a^{s-n/2-\lambda} \Gamma\left[\begin{matrix} 1-\lambda,\ s,\ \frac{2s-2\lambda+1}{2} \\ \frac{2s-n-2\lambda+1}{2},\ \frac{2s-n-2\lambda+2}{2} \end{matrix}\right]$ $[a,\ \operatorname{Re} s > 0;\ \operatorname{Re}\lambda < 1-n]$
49	$(x-a)_+^{-n/2-\lambda} C_n^\lambda\left(\sqrt{\dfrac{x}{x-a}}\right)$	$\dfrac{(-2)^n}{n!} a^{s-n/2-\lambda} \Gamma\left[\begin{matrix} 1-\lambda,\ \frac{n-2s+2\lambda}{2},\ \frac{n-2s+1}{2} \\ \frac{1-2s}{2},\ 1-s \end{matrix}\right]$ $[a > 0;\ \operatorname{Re}\lambda < 1-n;\ \operatorname{Re} s < \operatorname{Re}\lambda + n/2]$
50	$(x+a)^{-n/2-\lambda} C_n^\lambda\left(\sqrt{\dfrac{a}{x+a}}\right)$	$\dfrac{2^n}{n!} a^{s-n/2-\lambda} \Gamma\left[\begin{matrix} s,\ \frac{n-2s+2\lambda}{2},\ \frac{n-2s+2\lambda+1}{2} \\ \lambda,\ \frac{1-2s+2\lambda}{2} \end{matrix}\right]$ $[0 < \operatorname{Re} s < \operatorname{Re}\lambda + n/2;\ |\arg a| < \pi]$
51	$(x+a)^{-n/2-\lambda} C_n^\lambda\left(\sqrt{\dfrac{x}{x+a}}\right)$	$\dfrac{2^n}{n!} a^{s-n/2-\lambda} \Gamma\left[\begin{matrix} s,\ \frac{2s+1}{2},\ \frac{n-2s+2\lambda}{2} \\ \lambda,\ \frac{2s-n+1}{2} \end{matrix}\right]$ $[0 < \operatorname{Re} s < \operatorname{Re}\lambda + n/2;\ |\arg a| < \pi]$
52	$(a-x)_+^{2\lambda-1} C_n^\lambda\left(\dfrac{x+a}{2\sqrt{ax}}\right)$	$\dfrac{a^{s+2\lambda-1}}{n!} \Gamma\left[\begin{matrix} n+2\lambda,\ \frac{2s-n}{2},\ \frac{2s+n+2\lambda}{2} \\ \frac{2s+n+4\lambda}{2},\ \frac{2s-n+2\lambda}{2} \end{matrix}\right]$ $[a,\ \operatorname{Re}\lambda > 0;\ \operatorname{Re} s > n/2]$
53	$(x-a)_+^{2\lambda-1} C_n^\lambda\left(\dfrac{x+a}{2\sqrt{ax}}\right)$	$\dfrac{a^{s+2\lambda-1}}{n!} \Gamma\left[\begin{matrix} n+2\lambda,\ \frac{2-2s-n-4\lambda}{2},\ \frac{2-2s+n-2\lambda}{2} \\ \frac{2-2s+n}{2},\ \frac{2-2s-n-2\lambda}{2} \end{matrix}\right]$ $[a,\ \operatorname{Re}\lambda > 0;\ \operatorname{Re} s < 1 - 2\operatorname{Re}\lambda - n/2]$
54	$(a-x)_+^{-n/2-\lambda}$ $\times\, C_n^\lambda\left(\dfrac{2a-x}{2\sqrt{a(a-x)}}\right)$	$\dfrac{a^{s-n/2-\lambda}}{n!} \Gamma\left[\begin{matrix} 1-\lambda,\ s,\ n-s+2\lambda \\ s-\lambda+1,\ -s+2\lambda \end{matrix}\right]$ $[a,\ \operatorname{Re} s > 0;\ \operatorname{Re}\lambda < 1-n]$
55	$(x-a)_+^{-n/2-\lambda}$ $\times\, C_n^\lambda\left(\dfrac{2x-a}{2\sqrt{x(x-a)}}\right)$	$\dfrac{a^{s-n/2-\lambda}}{n!} \Gamma\left[\begin{matrix} 1-\lambda,\ \frac{2s+n+2\lambda}{2},\ \frac{-2s+n+2\lambda}{2} \\ \frac{2s-n+2\lambda}{2},\ \frac{2-2s+n}{2} \end{matrix}\right]$ $[a > 0;\ \operatorname{Re}\lambda < 1-n;\ \operatorname{Re} s < \operatorname{Re}\lambda + n/2]$
56	$(x+a)^{-n/2-\lambda}$ $\times\, C_n^\lambda\left(\dfrac{x+2a}{2\sqrt{a(x+a)}}\right)$	$\dfrac{a^{s-n/2-\lambda}}{n!} \Gamma\left[\begin{matrix} s,\ \lambda-s,\ -s+n+2\lambda \\ \lambda,\ 2\lambda-s \end{matrix}\right]$ $[0 < \operatorname{Re} s < \operatorname{Re}\lambda;\ |\arg a| < \pi]$

No.	$f(x)$	$F(s)$
57	$(x+a)^{-n/2-\lambda}$ $\times C_n^\lambda\left(\dfrac{2x+a}{2\sqrt{x(x+a)}}\right)$	$\dfrac{a^{s-n/2-\lambda}}{n!}\Gamma\left[\begin{array}{c}\frac{2s+n+2\lambda}{2},\ \frac{2s-n}{2},\ \frac{-2s+n+2\lambda}{2}\\ \lambda,\ \frac{2s-n+2\lambda}{2}\end{array}\right]$ $[n/2 < \operatorname{Re}s < \operatorname{Re}\lambda + n/2;\ |\arg a| < \pi]$
58	$(a-x)_+^{(\varepsilon-1)/2}(b-x)^{n+\varepsilon/2}$ $\times C_{2n+\varepsilon}^\lambda\left(c\sqrt{\dfrac{a-x}{b-x}}\right)$	$\dfrac{(-1)^n\sqrt{\pi}\,(\lambda)_{n+\varepsilon}}{n!}a^{s+\varepsilon-1/2}b^n c^\varepsilon\,\Gamma\left[\begin{array}{c}s\\ \frac{2s+2\varepsilon+1}{2}\end{array}\right]$ $\times F_1\left(-n,s,n+\lambda+\varepsilon;\dfrac{2s+2\varepsilon+1}{2};\dfrac{a}{b},\dfrac{ac^2}{b}\right)$ $[a,\ \operatorname{Re}s > 0]$
59	$(a-x)_+^{\lambda-1/2}\dfrac{(bx+1)^\alpha}{[1-c(a-x)]^{\varepsilon/2}}$ $\times C_{2n+\varepsilon}^\lambda\left(\sqrt{1+ac-cx}\right)$	$\dfrac{(2\lambda)_{2n+\varepsilon}}{(2n+\varepsilon)!}a^{s+\lambda-1/2}\,\mathrm{B}\left(s,\dfrac{2\lambda+1}{2}\right)$ $\times F_3\left(-\alpha,-n,s,n+\lambda+\varepsilon;s+\lambda+\dfrac{1}{2};-ab,-ac\right)$ $[a,\ \operatorname{Re}s > 0]$

3.24.2. $C_n^\lambda(bx)$ **and the exponential function**

Notation: $\varepsilon = 0$ or 1.

1	$e^{-ax}C_{2n+\varepsilon}^\lambda(bx)$	$\dfrac{(-1)^n(\lambda)_{n+\varepsilon}(2b)^\varepsilon}{n!\,a^{s+\varepsilon}}\Gamma(s+\varepsilon)$ $\times\,{}_4F_1\left(\begin{array}{c}-n,n+\lambda+\varepsilon,\frac{s+\varepsilon}{2},\frac{s+\varepsilon+1}{2}\\ \frac{2\varepsilon+1}{2};\frac{4b^2}{a^2}\end{array}\right)$ $[\operatorname{Re}a > 0;\ \operatorname{Re}s > -\varepsilon]$
2	$e^{-ax^2}C_{2n+\varepsilon}^\lambda(bx)$	$\dfrac{(-1)^n 2^{\varepsilon-1}(\lambda)_{n+\varepsilon}b^\varepsilon}{n!\,a^{(s+\varepsilon)/2}}\Gamma\left(\dfrac{s+\varepsilon}{2}\right){}_3F_1\left(\begin{array}{c}-n,\lambda+n+\varepsilon,\frac{s+\varepsilon}{2}\\ \frac{2\varepsilon+1}{2};\frac{b^2}{a}\end{array}\right)$ $[\operatorname{Re}a > 0;\ \operatorname{Re}s > -\varepsilon]$
3	$(a^2-x^2)_+^{\lambda-1/2}e^{bx}C_n^\lambda\left(\dfrac{x}{a}\right)$	$\dfrac{\pi}{n!}\left(\dfrac{a}{2}\right)^{s+2\lambda-1}\Gamma\left[\begin{array}{c}n+2\lambda,\ s\\ \lambda,\ \frac{s-n+1}{2},\ \frac{s+n+2\lambda+1}{2}\end{array}\right]$ $\times\,{}_2F_3\left(\begin{array}{c}\frac{s}{2},\frac{s+1}{2};\frac{a^2b^2}{4}\\ \frac{1}{2},\frac{s-n+1}{2},\frac{s+n+2\lambda+1}{2}\end{array}\right)+\dfrac{\pi}{n!}\left(\dfrac{a}{2}\right)^{s+2\lambda}b$ $\times\Gamma\left[\begin{array}{c}n+2\lambda,\ s+1\\ \lambda,\ \frac{s-n+2}{2},\ \frac{s+n+2\lambda+2}{2}\end{array}\right]{}_2F_3\left(\begin{array}{c}\frac{s+1}{2},\frac{s+2}{2};\frac{a^2b^2}{4}\\ \frac{3}{2},\frac{s-n+2}{2},\frac{s+n+2\lambda+2}{2}\end{array}\right)$ $[a > 0;\ \operatorname{Re}\lambda > -1/2;\ \operatorname{Re}s > ((-1)^n - 1)/2]$

No.	$f(x)$	$F(s)$
4	$\left(a^2 - x^2\right)_+^{\lambda-1/2} e^{bx^2} C_n^\lambda \left(\dfrac{x}{a}\right)$	$\dfrac{\pi}{n!} \left(\dfrac{a}{2}\right)^{s+\lambda-1} \Gamma\left[\begin{array}{c} n+2\lambda,\ s \\ \lambda,\ \frac{s-n+1}{2},\ \frac{s+n+2\lambda+1}{2} \end{array}\right]$ $\times\ {}_2F_2\left(\begin{array}{c} \frac{s}{2},\ \frac{s+1}{2};\ a^2 b \\ \frac{s-n+1}{2},\ \frac{s+n+2\lambda+1}{2} \end{array}\right)$ $[a>0;\ \operatorname{Re}\lambda > -1/2;\ \operatorname{Re} s > ((-1)^n - 1)/2]$
5	$\left(x^2 - a^2\right)_+^{\lambda-1/2} e^{-bx^2}$ $\times\ C_{2n+\varepsilon}^\lambda \left(\dfrac{x}{a}\right)$	$\dfrac{(2\lambda)_{2n+\varepsilon}\, a^{s+2\lambda-1}}{2(2n+\varepsilon)!} \left(\dfrac{1-s+\varepsilon}{2}\right)_n \Gamma\left[\begin{array}{c} \frac{2\lambda+1}{2},\ \frac{1-s-2n-2\lambda-\varepsilon}{2} \\ \frac{2-s-\varepsilon}{2} \end{array}\right]$ $\times\ {}_2F_2\left(\begin{array}{c} \frac{s}{2},\ \frac{s+1}{2};\ -a^2 b \\ \frac{s-2n-\varepsilon+1}{2},\ \frac{s+2n+2\lambda+\varepsilon+1}{2} \end{array}\right)$ $+\ \dfrac{2^{2n+\varepsilon-1}\, (\lambda)_{2n+\varepsilon}\, b^{-s/2-n-\lambda-\varepsilon/2+1/2}}{(2n+\varepsilon)!\, a^{2n+\varepsilon}}$ $\times\ \Gamma\left(\dfrac{s+2n+2\lambda+\varepsilon-1}{2}\right)$ $\times\ {}_2F_2\left(\begin{array}{c} \frac{1-2n-2\lambda}{2},\ 1-n-\lambda-\varepsilon;\ -a^2 b \\ 1-2n-\lambda-\varepsilon,\ \frac{3-s-2n-2\lambda-\varepsilon}{2} \end{array}\right)$ $[a,\ \operatorname{Re} b > 0;\ \operatorname{Re}\lambda > -1/2]$
6	$\left(a^2 - x^2\right)_+^{\lambda-1/2} e^{-b/x^2}$ $\times\ C_{2n+\varepsilon}^\lambda \left(\dfrac{x}{a}\right)$	$\dfrac{(-1)^n (2\lambda)_{2n+\varepsilon}\, a^{s+2\lambda-1}}{2(2n+\varepsilon)!} \left(\dfrac{1-s+\varepsilon}{2}\right)_n \Gamma\left[\begin{array}{c} \frac{2\lambda+1}{2},\ \frac{s+\varepsilon}{2} \\ \frac{s+2n+2\lambda+\varepsilon+1}{2} \end{array}\right]$ $\times\ {}_2F_2\left(\begin{array}{c} \frac{1-s-2n-2\lambda-\varepsilon}{2},\ \frac{1-s+2n+\varepsilon}{2} \\ \frac{1-s}{2},\ \frac{2-s}{2};\ -\frac{b}{a^2} \end{array}\right)$ $+\ \dfrac{(-1)^n 2^{\varepsilon-1} (\lambda)_{n+\varepsilon}}{n!}\, a^{2\lambda-\varepsilon-1} b^{(s+\varepsilon)/2}\, \Gamma\left(-\dfrac{s+\varepsilon}{2}\right)$ $\times\ {}_2F_2\left(\begin{array}{c} \frac{2n+2\varepsilon+1}{2},\ \frac{1-2n-2\lambda}{2} \\ \frac{2\varepsilon+1}{2},\ \frac{s+\varepsilon+2}{2};\ -\frac{b}{a^2} \end{array}\right)$ $[a,\ \operatorname{Re} b > 0;\ \operatorname{Re}\lambda > -1/2]$
7	$\left(x^2 - a^2\right)_+^{\lambda-1/2} e^{-b/x^2}$ $\times\ C_{2n+\varepsilon}^\lambda \left(\dfrac{x}{a}\right)$	$\dfrac{(2\lambda)_{2n+\varepsilon}\, a^{s+2\lambda-1}}{2(2n+\varepsilon)!} \left(\dfrac{1-s+\varepsilon}{2}\right)_n \Gamma\left[\begin{array}{c} \frac{2\lambda+1}{2},\ \frac{1-s-2n-2\lambda-\varepsilon}{2} \\ \frac{2-\varepsilon-s}{2} \end{array}\right]$ $\times\ {}_2F_2\left(\begin{array}{c} \frac{1-s+2n+\varepsilon}{2},\ \frac{1-s-2n-2\lambda-\varepsilon}{2} \\ \frac{1-s}{2},\ \frac{2-s}{2};\ -\frac{b}{a^2} \end{array}\right)$ $[a>0;\ \operatorname{Re}\lambda > -1/2;\ \operatorname{Re}(s+2\lambda) < 1-2n-\varepsilon]$
8	$e^{-bx} C_n^\lambda \left(\dfrac{x}{a} \pm 1\right)$	$\dfrac{2^n}{n!\, a^n b^{s+n}} (\lambda)_n\, \Gamma(s+n)\ {}_2F_2\left(\begin{array}{c} -n,\ \frac{1-2n-2\lambda}{2};\ \pm 2ab \\ 1-2n-2\lambda,\ 1-s-n \end{array}\right)$ $[\operatorname{Re} b,\ \operatorname{Re} s > 0]$

No.	$f(x)$	$F(s)$
9	$(a-x)_+^{\lambda-1/2}\, e^{bx}\, C_n^\lambda\left(1-\dfrac{2x}{a}\right)$	$\dfrac{a^{s+\lambda-1/2}}{n!}\,(2\lambda)_n\left(\dfrac{1}{2}-s+\lambda\right)_n \Gamma\!\left[\begin{array}{c}\frac{2\lambda+1}{2},\ s\\ \frac{2s+2n+2\lambda+1}{2}\end{array}\right]$ $\times\,{}_2F_2\!\left(\begin{array}{c}s,\ \frac{2s-2\lambda+1}{2};\ ab\\ \frac{2s-2n-2\lambda+1}{2},\ \frac{2s+2n+2\lambda+1}{2}\end{array}\right)$ $[a,\ \operatorname{Re}s>0;\ \operatorname{Re}\lambda>-1/2]$
10	$(x+a)^{\lambda-1/2}\, e^{-bx}$ $\times\, C_n^\lambda\left(\dfrac{2x}{a}+1\right)$	$\dfrac{(-1)^n\, a^{s+\lambda-1/2}}{n!}\,(2\lambda)_n\left(\dfrac{1-2s+2\lambda}{2}\right)_n \Gamma\!\left[\begin{array}{c}s,\ \frac{1-2s-2n-2\lambda}{2}\\ \frac{1-2\lambda}{2}\end{array}\right]$ $\times\,{}_2F_2\!\left(\begin{array}{c}s,\ \frac{2s-2\lambda+1}{2};\ ab\\ \frac{2s-2n-2\lambda+1}{2},\ \frac{2s+2n+2\lambda+1}{2}\end{array}\right)$ $+\dfrac{2^{2n}}{n!\,a^n b^{s+n+\lambda-1/2}}\,(\lambda)_n\,\Gamma\!\left(\dfrac{2s+2n+2\lambda-1}{2}\right)$ $\times\,{}_2F_2\!\left(\begin{array}{c}\frac{1-2n-2\lambda}{2},\ 1-n-2\lambda;\ ab\\ 1-2n-2\lambda,\ \frac{3-2s-2n-2\lambda}{2}\end{array}\right)$ $[\operatorname{Re}b,\ \operatorname{Re}s>0;\ |\arg a|<\pi]$
11	$(a-x)_+^{\lambda-1/2}\, e^{-b/x}$ $\times\, C_n^\lambda\left(\dfrac{2x}{a}-1\right)$	$\dfrac{(-1)^n\, a^{s+\lambda-1/2}}{n!}\,(2\lambda)_n\left(\dfrac{1-2s+2\lambda}{2}\right)_n$ $\times\,\Gamma\!\left[\begin{array}{c}\frac{2\lambda+1}{2},\ s\\ \frac{2s+2n+2\lambda+1}{2}\end{array}\right]{}_2F_2\!\left(\begin{array}{c}\frac{1-2s-2n-2\lambda}{2},\ \frac{1-2s+2n+2\lambda}{2}\\ 1-s,\ \frac{1-2s+2\lambda}{2};\ -\frac{b}{a}\end{array}\right)$ $+\dfrac{(-1)^n\, a^{\lambda-1/2}b^s}{n!}\,(2\lambda)_n\,\Gamma\!\left(-s\right)\,{}_2F_2\!\left(\begin{array}{c}\frac{-2n-2\lambda+1}{2},\ \frac{2n+2\lambda+1}{2}\\ \frac{2\lambda+1}{2},\ s+1;\ -\frac{b}{a}\end{array}\right)$ $[a,\ \operatorname{Re}b>0;\ \operatorname{Re}\lambda>-1/2]$
12	$(x+a)^{\lambda-1/2}\, e^{-b/x}$ $\times\, C_n^\lambda\left(\dfrac{2x}{a}+1\right)$	$\dfrac{a^{s+\lambda-1/2}}{n!}\,(2\lambda)_n\left(\dfrac{1-2s+2\lambda}{2}\right)_n \Gamma\!\left[\begin{array}{c}\frac{1-2s-2n-2\lambda}{2},\ s\\ \frac{1-2\lambda}{2}\end{array}\right]$ $\times\,{}_2F_2\!\left(\begin{array}{c}\frac{1-2s-2n-2\lambda}{2},\ \frac{1-2s+2n+2\lambda}{2}\\ 1-s,\ \frac{1-2s+2\lambda}{2};\ \frac{b}{a}\end{array}\right)$ $+\dfrac{a^{\lambda-1/2}b^s}{n!}\,(2\lambda)_n\,\Gamma\!\left(-s\right)\,{}_2F_2\!\left(\begin{array}{c}\frac{-2n-2\lambda+1}{2},\ \frac{2n+2\lambda+1}{2}\\ \frac{2\lambda+1}{2},\ s+1;\ \frac{b}{a}\end{array}\right)$ $[\operatorname{Re}b>0;\ \operatorname{Re}s<1/2-n-\operatorname{Re}\lambda;\ |\arg a|<\pi]$
13	$e^{-b\sqrt{x}}\, C_n^\lambda\left(\dfrac{x}{a}\pm1\right)$	$\dfrac{2^{n+1}}{n!\,a^n b^{2s+2n}}\,(\lambda)_n\,\Gamma\!\left(2s+2n\right)$ $\times\,{}_2F_3\!\left(\begin{array}{c}-n,\ \frac{1-2n-2\lambda}{2};\ \mp\frac{ab^2}{2}\\ 1-2n-2\lambda,\ \frac{1-2s-2n}{2},\ 1-s-n\end{array}\right)$ $[\operatorname{Re}b,\ \operatorname{Re}s>0]$

No.	$f(x)$	$F(s)$

14 $(a-x)_+^{\lambda-1/2}\, e^{-b\sqrt{x}}$

$\times C_n^\lambda\left(1-\dfrac{2x}{a}\right)$

$$\frac{a^{s+\lambda-1/2}}{n!}\,(2\lambda)_n\left(\frac{1}{2}-s+\lambda\right)_n \Gamma\left[\begin{array}{c} \frac{2\lambda+1}{2},\, s \\ \frac{2s+2n+2\lambda+1}{2}\end{array}\right]$$

$$\times\,{}_2F_3\left(\begin{array}{c} s,\,\frac{2s-2\lambda+1}{2};\,\frac{ab^2}{4} \\ \frac{1}{2},\,\frac{2s-2n-2\lambda+1}{2},\,\frac{2s+2n+2\lambda+1}{2}\end{array}\right)$$

$$-\,\frac{a^{s+\lambda}b}{n!}\,(2\lambda)_n\,(\lambda-s)_n\,\Gamma\left[\begin{array}{c}\frac{2\lambda+1}{2},\,\frac{2s+1}{2}\\ s+n+\lambda+1\end{array}\right]$$

$$\times\,{}_2F_3\left(\begin{array}{c}\frac{2s+1}{2},\,s-\lambda+1;\,\frac{ab^2}{4}\\ \frac{3}{2},\,s-n-\lambda+1,\,s+n+\lambda+1\end{array}\right)$$

$$[a,\,\mathrm{Re}\,s>0;\ \mathrm{Re}\,\lambda>-1/2]$$

15 $(x+a)^{\lambda-1/2}\, e^{-b\sqrt{x}}$

$\times C_n^\lambda\left(\dfrac{2x}{a}+1\right)$

$$-\frac{(-1)^n\,a^{s+\lambda}b}{n!}\,(2\lambda)_n\,(\lambda-s)_n\,\Gamma\left[\begin{array}{c}-s-n-\lambda,\,\frac{2s+1}{2}\\ \frac{1-2\lambda}{2}\end{array}\right]$$

$$\times\,{}_2F_3\left(\begin{array}{c}\frac{2s+1}{2},\,s-\lambda+1;\,-\frac{ab^2}{4}\\ \frac{3}{2},\,s-n-\lambda+1,\,s+n+\lambda+1\end{array}\right)$$

$$+\frac{(-1)^n\,a^{s+\lambda-1/2}}{n!}\,(2\lambda)_n\left(\frac{1}{2}-s+\lambda\right)_n\Gamma\left[\begin{array}{c}s,\,\frac{1-2s-2n-2\lambda}{2}\\ \frac{1-2\lambda}{2}\end{array}\right]$$

$$\times\,{}_2F_3\left(\begin{array}{c}s,\,s-\lambda+\frac{1}{2};\,-\frac{ab^2}{4}\\ \frac{1}{2},\,\frac{2s-2n-2\lambda+1}{2},\,\frac{2s+2n+2\lambda+1}{2}\end{array}\right)$$

$$+\frac{2^{2n+1}}{n!\,a^n b^{2s+2n+2\lambda-1}}\,(\lambda)_n\,\Gamma\left(2s+2n+2\lambda-1\right)$$

$$\times\,{}_2F_3\left(\begin{array}{c}\frac{1-2n-2\lambda}{2},\,1-n-2\lambda;\,-\frac{ab^2}{4}\\ 1-2n-2\lambda,\,\frac{3-2s-2n-2\lambda}{2},\,1-s-n-\lambda\end{array}\right)$$

$$[\mathrm{Re}\,b,\,\mathrm{Re}\,s>0;\ |\arg a|<\pi]$$

16 $e^{-b/\sqrt{x}}\, C_n^\lambda\left(\dfrac{x}{a}\pm1\right)$

$$\frac{2\,(\pm1)^n\,b^{2s}}{n!}\,\Gamma(-2s)\,(2\lambda)_n\,{}_2F_3\left(\begin{array}{c}-n,\,n+2\lambda;\,\mp\frac{b^2}{8a}\\ \frac{2\lambda+1}{2},\,\frac{2s+1}{2},\,s+1\end{array}\right)$$

$$[\mathrm{Re}\,b>0;\ \mathrm{Re}\,s<-n]$$

17 $(a-x)_+^{\lambda-1/2}\, e^{-b/\sqrt{x}}$

$\times C_n^\lambda\left(\dfrac{2x}{a}-1\right)$

$$\frac{(-1)^{n+1}\,a^{s+\lambda-1}b}{n!}\,(2\lambda)_n\,(1-s+\lambda)_n\,\Gamma\left[\begin{array}{c}\frac{2\lambda+1}{2},\,\frac{2s-1}{2}\\ s+n+\lambda\end{array}\right]$$

$$\times\,{}_2F_3\left(\begin{array}{c}1-s-n-\lambda,\,1-s+n+\lambda\\ \frac{3}{2},\,\frac{3}{2}-s,\,1-s+\lambda;\,\frac{b^2}{4a}\end{array}\right)$$

$$+\frac{(-1)^n\,a^{s+\lambda-1/2}}{n!}\,(2\lambda)_n\left(\frac{1-2s+2\lambda}{2}\right)_n\Gamma\left[\begin{array}{c}\frac{2\lambda+1}{2},\,s\\ \frac{2s+2n+2\lambda+1}{2}\end{array}\right]$$

$$\times\,{}_2F_3\left(\begin{array}{c}\frac{1-2s-2n-2\lambda}{2},\,\frac{1-2s+2n+2\lambda}{2}\\ \frac{1}{2},\,1-s,\,\frac{1-2s+2\lambda}{2};\,\frac{b^2}{4a}\end{array}\right)+\frac{2\,(-1)^n\,a^{\lambda-1/2}b^{2s}}{n!}$$

$$\times\,(2\lambda)_n\,\Gamma(-2s)\,{}_2F_3\left(\begin{array}{c}\frac{-2n-2\lambda+1}{2},\,\frac{2n+2\lambda+1}{2}\\ \frac{2\lambda+1}{2},\,\frac{2s+1}{2},\,s+1;\,\frac{b^2}{4a}\end{array}\right)$$

$$[a,\,\mathrm{Re}\,b>0;\ \mathrm{Re}\,\lambda>-1/2]$$

No.	$f(x)$	$F(s)$
18	$(x+a)^{\lambda-1/2}\,e^{-b/\sqrt{x}}$ $\times\,C_n^\lambda\left(\dfrac{2x}{a}+1\right)$	$\dfrac{(-1)^n\,a^{s+\lambda-1/2}}{n!}\,(2\lambda)_n\left(\dfrac{1-2s+2\lambda}{2}\right)_n\Gamma\left[\begin{matrix}\frac{1-2s-2n-2\lambda}{2},\,s\\[2pt]\frac{1-2\lambda}{2}\end{matrix}\right]$ $\times\,{}_2F_2\left(\begin{matrix}\frac{1-2s-2n-2\lambda}{2},\,\frac{1-2s+2n+2\lambda}{2}\\[2pt]1-s,\,\frac{1-2s+2\lambda}{2};\,-\frac{b^2}{4a}\end{matrix}\right)$ $+\dfrac{2a^{\lambda-1/2}b^{2s}}{n!}\,(2\lambda)_n\,\Gamma(-2s)\,{}_2F_3\left(\begin{matrix}\frac{-2n-2\lambda+1}{2},\,\frac{2n+2\lambda+1}{2}\\[2pt]\frac{2\lambda+1}{2},\,\frac{2s+1}{2},\,s+1;\,-\frac{b^2}{4a}\end{matrix}\right)$ $[\operatorname{Re}b>0;\ \operatorname{Re}s<1/2-n-\operatorname{Re}\lambda;\ |\arg a|<\pi]$
19	$(x+a)^{-n-2\lambda}\,e^{-bx}$ $\times\,C_n^\lambda\left(\dfrac{a-x}{a+x}\right)$	$\dfrac{a^{s-n-2\lambda}}{n!}\,\dfrac{\left(\frac{1}{2}-s+\lambda\right)_n}{\left(\lambda+\frac{1}{2}\right)_n}\,\Gamma\left[\begin{matrix}s,\,n-s+2\lambda\\[2pt]2\lambda\end{matrix}\right]$ $\times\,{}_2F_2\left(\begin{matrix}s,\,\frac{2s-2\lambda+1}{2};\,ab\\[2pt]s-n-2\lambda+1,\,\frac{2s-2n-2\lambda+1}{2}\end{matrix}\right)$ $+\dfrac{(-1)^n\,b^{-s+n+2\lambda}}{n!}\,(2\lambda)_n\,\Gamma(s-n-2\lambda)$ $\times\,{}_2F_2\left(\begin{matrix}n+\lambda+\frac{1}{2},\,n+2\lambda;\,ab\\[2pt]\lambda+\frac{1}{2},\,1-s+n+2\lambda\end{matrix}\right)\quad[\operatorname{Re}b,\ \operatorname{Re}s>0;\ |\arg a|<\pi]$
20	$(x+a)^n\,e^{-b/x}\,C_n^\lambda\left(\dfrac{a-x}{a+x}\right)$	$\dfrac{a^n b^s}{n!}\,(2\lambda)_n\,\Gamma(-s)\,{}_2F_2\left(\begin{matrix}-n,\,\frac{1-2n-2\lambda}{2}\\[2pt]\frac{2\lambda+1}{2},\,s+1;\,\frac{b}{a}\end{matrix}\right)$ $[\operatorname{Re}b>0;\ \operatorname{Re}s<-n]$
21	$(x+a)^{-n-2\lambda}\,e^{-b/x}$ $\times\,C_n^\lambda\left(\dfrac{a-x}{a+x}\right)$	$\dfrac{a^{s-n-2\lambda}}{n!}\,\dfrac{\left(\frac{1-2s+2\lambda}{2}\right)_n}{\left(\frac{2\lambda+1}{2}\right)_n}\,\Gamma\left[\begin{matrix}n-s+2\lambda,\,s\\[2pt]2\lambda\end{matrix}\right]$ $\times\,{}_2F_2\left(\begin{matrix}\frac{2n-2s+2\lambda+1}{2},\,n-s+2\lambda\\[2pt]1-s,\,\frac{1-2s+2\lambda}{2};\,\frac{b}{a}\end{matrix}\right)$ $+\dfrac{a^{-n-2\lambda}b^s}{n!}\,(2\lambda)_n\,\Gamma(-s)\,{}_2F_2\left(\begin{matrix}\frac{2n+2\lambda+1}{2},\,n+2\lambda\\[2pt]\frac{2\lambda+1}{2},\,s+1;\,\frac{b}{a}\end{matrix}\right)$ $[\operatorname{Re}b>0;\ \operatorname{Re}s<n+2\operatorname{Re}\lambda;\ |\arg a|<\pi]$
22	$(x+a)^n\,e^{-b\sqrt{x}}\,C_n^\lambda\left(\dfrac{a-x}{a+x}\right)$	$\dfrac{2(-1)^n\,b^{-2s-2n}}{n!}\,(2\lambda)_n\,\Gamma(2s+2n)$ $\times\,{}_2F_3\left(\begin{matrix}-n,\,\frac{1-2n-2\lambda}{2};\,-\frac{ab^2}{4}\\[2pt]\frac{2\lambda+1}{2},\,\frac{1-2s-2n}{2},\,1-s-n\end{matrix}\right)$ $[\operatorname{Re}b,\ \operatorname{Re}s>0]$

No.	$f(x)$	$F(s)$
23	$(x+a)^{-n-2\lambda}\, e^{-b\sqrt{x}}$ $\times C_n^\lambda\left(\dfrac{a-x}{a+x}\right)$	$-\dfrac{a^{s-n-2\lambda+1/2}\,b\,(\lambda-s)_n}{n!\,\left(\frac{2\lambda+1}{2}\right)_n}\,\Gamma\left[\begin{matrix}\frac{2s+1}{2},\ \frac{2n-2s+4\lambda-1}{2}\\ 2\lambda\end{matrix}\right]$ $\times\, {}_2F_3\left(\begin{matrix}\frac{2s+1}{2},\ s-\lambda+1;\ -\frac{ab^2}{4}\\ \frac{3}{2},\ s-n-\lambda+1,\ \frac{2s-2n-4\lambda+3}{2}\end{matrix}\right)$ $+\dfrac{a^{s-n-2\lambda}\,\left(\frac{1-2s+2\lambda}{2}\right)_n}{n!\,\left(\frac{2\lambda+1}{2}\right)_n}\,\Gamma\left[\begin{matrix}n-s+2\lambda,\ s\\ 2\lambda\end{matrix}\right]$ $\times\, {}_2F_3\left(\begin{matrix}s,\ \frac{2s-2\lambda+1}{2};\ -\frac{ab^2}{4}\\ \frac{1}{2},\ s-n-2\lambda+1,\ \frac{2s-2n-2\lambda+1}{2}\end{matrix}\right)$ $+\dfrac{2(-1)^n\,b^{2(-s+n+2\lambda)}}{n!}\,(2\lambda)_n\,\Gamma\left(2s-2n-4\lambda\right)$ $\times\, {}_2F_3\left(\begin{matrix}n+2\lambda,\ \frac{2n+2\lambda+1}{2};\ -\frac{ab^2}{4}\\ \frac{2\lambda+1}{2},\ \frac{1-2s+2n+4\lambda}{2},\ 1-s+n+2\lambda\end{matrix}\right)$ $[\operatorname{Re}b,\ \operatorname{Re}s>0;\ |\arg a|<\pi]$
24	$(x+a)^n\, e^{-b/\sqrt{x}}\, C_n^\lambda\left(\dfrac{a-x}{a+x}\right)$	$\dfrac{2a^n b^{2s}}{n!}\,(2\lambda)_n\,\Gamma(-2s)\, {}_2F_3\left(\begin{matrix}-n,\ \frac{1-2n-2\lambda}{2};\ -\frac{b^2}{4a}\\ \frac{2\lambda+1}{2},\ \frac{2s+1}{2},\ s+1\end{matrix}\right)$ $[a,\ \operatorname{Re}b>0;\ \operatorname{Re}s<-n]$
25	$(x+a)^{-n-2\lambda}\, e^{-b/\sqrt{x}}$ $\times C_n^\lambda\left(\dfrac{a-x}{a+x}\right)$	$-\dfrac{a^{s-n-2\lambda-1/2}\,b\,(1-s+\lambda)_n}{n!\,\left(\frac{2\lambda+1}{2}\right)_n}\,\Gamma\left[\begin{matrix}\frac{1-2s+2n+4\lambda}{2},\ \frac{2s-1}{2}\\ 2\lambda\end{matrix}\right]$ $\times\, {}_2F_3\left(\begin{matrix}1-s+n+\lambda,\ \frac{1-2s+2n+4\lambda}{2}\\ \frac{3}{2},\ \frac{3}{2}-s,\ 1-s+\lambda;\ -\frac{b^2}{4a}\end{matrix}\right)+\dfrac{a^{s-n-2\lambda}\,\left(\frac{1-2s+2\lambda}{2}\right)_n}{n!\,\left(\frac{2\lambda+1}{2}\right)_n}$ $\times\,\Gamma\left[\begin{matrix}n-s+2\lambda,\ s\\ 2\lambda\end{matrix}\right]\, {}_2F_3\left(\begin{matrix}\frac{1-2s+2n+2\lambda}{2},\ n-s+2\lambda\\ \frac{1}{2},\ 1-s,\ \frac{1-2s+2\lambda}{2};\ -\frac{b^2}{4a}\end{matrix}\right)$ $+\dfrac{2a^{-n-2\lambda}b^{2s}}{n!}\,(2\lambda)_n\,\Gamma(-2s)\, {}_2F_3\left(\begin{matrix}n+2\lambda,\ \frac{2n+2\lambda+1}{2};\ -\frac{b^2}{4a}\\ \frac{2\lambda+1}{2},\ \frac{2s+1}{2},\ s+1\end{matrix}\right)$ $[a,\ \operatorname{Re}b>0;\ \operatorname{Re}s<n+2\operatorname{Re}\lambda]$

3.24.3. $C_n^\lambda(bx)$ and hyperbolic functions

Notation: $\delta=\begin{Bmatrix}1\\0\end{Bmatrix}$.

	$f(x)$	$F(s)$
1	$(a^2-x^2)_+^{\lambda-1/2}\begin{Bmatrix}\sinh(bx)\\\cosh(bx)\end{Bmatrix}$ $\times C_n^\lambda\left(\dfrac{x}{a}\right)$	$\dfrac{\pi}{n!}\left(\dfrac{a}{2}\right)^{s+2\lambda+\delta-1}\,b^\delta\,\Gamma\left[\begin{matrix}s+\delta,\ n+2\lambda\\ \lambda,\ \frac{s-n+\delta+1}{2},\ \frac{s+n+2\lambda+\delta+1}{2}\end{matrix}\right]$ $\times\, {}_2F_3\left(\begin{matrix}\frac{s+\delta}{2},\ \frac{s+\delta+1}{2};\ \frac{a^2 b^2}{4}\\ \frac{2\delta+1}{2},\ \frac{s-n+\delta+1}{2},\ \frac{s+n+2\lambda+\delta+1}{2}\end{matrix}\right)$ $[a>0;\ \operatorname{Re}\lambda>-1/2;\ \operatorname{Re}s>-\delta]$

3.24.4. $C_n^\lambda(ax+b)$ and trigonometric functions

Notation: $\delta = \left\{\begin{matrix} 1 \\ 0 \end{matrix}\right\}$, $\varepsilon = 0$ or 1.

1	$(a^2 - x^2)_+^{\lambda - 1/2}$ $\times \left\{\begin{matrix} \sin(bx) \\ \cos(bx) \end{matrix}\right\} C_n^\lambda\left(\dfrac{x}{a}\right)$	$\dfrac{\pi}{n!}\left(\dfrac{a}{2}\right)^{s+2\lambda+\delta-1} b^\delta \, \Gamma\left[\begin{matrix} s+\delta,\ n+2\lambda \\ \lambda,\ \frac{s-n+\delta+1}{2},\ \frac{s+n+2\lambda+\delta+1}{2} \end{matrix}\right]$ $\times {}_2F_3\left(\begin{matrix} \frac{s+\delta}{2},\ \frac{s+\delta+1}{2};\ -\frac{a^2 b^2}{4} \\ \frac{2\delta+1}{2},\ \frac{s-n+\delta+1}{2},\ \frac{s+n+2\lambda+\delta+1}{2} \end{matrix}\right)$ $[a > 0;\ \operatorname{Re}\lambda > -1/2;\ \operatorname{Re}s > ((-1)^n - 1)/2 - \delta]$
2	$(x^2 - a^2)_+^{\lambda - 1/2}$ $\times \left\{\begin{matrix} \sin(bx) \\ \cos(bx) \end{matrix}\right\} C_{2n+\varepsilon}^\lambda\left(\dfrac{x}{a}\right)$	$\dfrac{a^{s+2\lambda+\delta-1} b^\delta}{2(2n+\varepsilon)!}\ (2\lambda)_{2n+\varepsilon}\left(\dfrac{1-s-\delta+\varepsilon}{2}\right)_n \Gamma\left[\begin{matrix} \frac{2\lambda+1}{2},\ \frac{1-s-2n-2\lambda-\delta-\varepsilon}{2} \\ \frac{2-s-\delta-\varepsilon}{2} \end{matrix}\right]$ $\times {}_2F_3\left(\begin{matrix} \frac{s+1}{2},\ \frac{s+2\delta}{2};\ -\frac{a^2 b^2}{4} \\ \frac{2\delta+1}{2},\ \frac{s-2n+\delta-\varepsilon+1}{2},\ \frac{s+2n+2\lambda+\delta+\varepsilon+1}{2} \end{matrix}\right)$ $\mp \dfrac{(-1)^n\, 2^{2n+\varepsilon} b^{1-s-2n-2\lambda-\varepsilon}}{(2n+\varepsilon)!\, a^{2n+\varepsilon}}\ (\lambda)_{2n+\varepsilon}$ $\times \Gamma(s+2n+2\lambda+\varepsilon-1)\left\{\begin{matrix} \cos[(s+2\lambda+\varepsilon)\pi/2] \\ \sin[(s+2\lambda+\varepsilon)\pi/2] \end{matrix}\right\}$ $\times {}_2F_3\left(\begin{matrix} \frac{1-2n-2\lambda}{2},\ 1-n-\lambda-\varepsilon;\ -\frac{a^2 b^2}{4} \\ 1-2n-\lambda-\varepsilon,\ \frac{3-s-2n-2\lambda-2\varepsilon}{2},\ \frac{2-s-2n-2\lambda}{2} \end{matrix}\right)$ $[a, b > 0;\ \operatorname{Re}\lambda > -1/2;\ \operatorname{Re}(s+2\lambda) < 2 - \varepsilon - 2n]$
3	$(a-x)_+^{\lambda-1/2}\left\{\begin{matrix} \sin(b\sqrt{x}) \\ \cos(b\sqrt{x}) \end{matrix}\right\}$ $\times C_n^\lambda\left(\dfrac{2x}{a} - 1\right)$	$\dfrac{(-1)^n\, a^{s+\lambda+(\delta-1)/2} b^\delta}{n!}\ (2\lambda)_n\left(\dfrac{1-2s+2\lambda-\delta}{2}\right)_n$ $\times \Gamma\left[\begin{matrix} \frac{2\lambda+1}{2},\ \frac{2s+\delta}{2} \\ \frac{2s+2n+2\lambda+\delta+1}{2} \end{matrix}\right] {}_2F_3\left(\begin{matrix} \frac{2s+\delta}{2},\ \frac{2s-2\lambda+\delta+1}{2};\ -\frac{ab^2}{4} \\ \frac{2\delta+1}{2},\ \frac{2s-2n-2\lambda+\delta+1}{2},\ \frac{2s+2n+2\lambda+\delta+1}{2} \end{matrix}\right)$ $[a > 0;\ \operatorname{Re}\lambda > -1/2;\ \operatorname{Re}s > -\delta/2]$
4	$(x+a)^{\lambda-1/2}$ $\times \left\{\begin{matrix} \sin(b/\sqrt{x}) \\ \cos(b/\sqrt{x}) \end{matrix}\right\}$ $\times C_n^\lambda\left(\dfrac{2x}{a} + 1\right)$	$\dfrac{(-1)^n\, a^{s+\lambda-(\delta+1)/2} b^\delta}{n!}\ (2\lambda)_n\left(\dfrac{1-2s+2\lambda+\delta}{2}\right)_n$ $\times \Gamma\left[\begin{matrix} \frac{2s-\delta}{2},\ \frac{1-2s-2n-2\lambda+\delta}{2} \\ \frac{1-2\lambda}{2} \end{matrix}\right]$ $\times {}_2F_3\left(\begin{matrix} \frac{1-2s-2n-2\lambda+\delta}{2},\ \frac{1-2s+2n+2\lambda+\delta}{2} \\ \frac{2\delta+1}{2},\ \frac{2-2s+\delta}{2},\ \frac{1-2s+2\lambda+\delta}{2};\ \frac{b^2}{4a} \end{matrix}\right)$ $+ \dfrac{2(-1)^\delta\, a^{\lambda-1/2} b^{2s}}{n!}\ (2\lambda)_n\, \Gamma(-2s)\left\{\begin{matrix} \sin(s\pi) \\ \cos(s\pi) \end{matrix}\right\}$ $\times {}_2F_3\left(\begin{matrix} \frac{-2n-2\lambda+1}{2},\ \frac{2n+2\lambda+1}{2} \\ \frac{2\lambda+1}{2},\ \frac{2s+1}{2},\ s+1;\ \frac{b^2}{4a} \end{matrix}\right)$ $[b > 0;\ -1/2 < \operatorname{Re}s < (\delta+1)/2 - n - \operatorname{Re}\lambda;\ |\arg a| < \pi]$

3.24.5. $C_n^\lambda(bx)$ and the logarithmic function

Notation: $\varepsilon = 0$ or 1.

---

1 $(a-x)_+^{\lambda-1/2} \ln \dfrac{x}{a}$

$\times C_n^\lambda \left(\dfrac{2x-a}{a} \right)$

$\dfrac{(-1)^n\, a^{s+\lambda-1/2}}{n!} (2\lambda)_n \left(\dfrac{1-2s+2\lambda}{2} \right)_n \Gamma\left[\begin{matrix} \frac{2\lambda+1}{2},\, s \\ \frac{2s+2n+2\lambda+1}{2} \end{matrix} \right]$

$\times \left[\psi(s) + \psi\left(\dfrac{1-2s+2\lambda}{2} \right) - \psi\left(\dfrac{2s+2n+2\lambda+1}{2} \right) \right.$

$\left. - \psi\left(\dfrac{-2s+2n+2\lambda+1}{2} \right) \right]$

$$[a,\ \operatorname{Re} s > 0;\ \operatorname{Re}\lambda > -1/2]$$

---

2 $(a^2-x^2)_+^{\lambda-1/2}$

$\times \left\{ \begin{matrix} \ln(x^2+b^2) \\ \ln|x^2-b^2| \end{matrix} \right\}$

$\times C_n^\lambda \left(\dfrac{x}{a} \right)$

$\pm \dfrac{\sqrt{\pi}\, a^{s+2\lambda+1}}{2^{s+2} n!\, b^2} (2\lambda)_n \Gamma\left[\begin{matrix} \lambda+\frac{1}{2},\, s+2 \\ \frac{s-n+3}{2},\, \frac{s+n+2\lambda+3}{2} \end{matrix} \right]$

$\times {}_4F_3\left(\begin{matrix} 1,\, 1,\, \frac{s+2}{2},\, \frac{s+3}{2};\, \mp \frac{a^2}{b^2} \\ 2,\, \frac{s-n+3}{2},\, \frac{s+n+2\lambda+3}{2} \end{matrix} \right)$

$+ \dfrac{\sqrt{\pi}\, a^{s+2\lambda-1} \ln b}{2^{s-1} n!} (2\lambda)_n \Gamma\left[\begin{matrix} \lambda+\frac{1}{2},\, s \\ \frac{s-n+1}{2},\, \frac{s+n+2\lambda+1}{2} \end{matrix} \right]$

$$\left[\left\{ \begin{matrix} a,\ \operatorname{Re} b > 0 \\ b > a > 0 \end{matrix} \right\};\ \operatorname{Re}\lambda > -1/2;\ \operatorname{Re} s > ((-1)^n - 1)/2 \right]$$

---

3 $(a^2-x^2)_+^{\lambda-1/2} \ln|x^2-b^2|$

$\times C_n^\lambda \left(\dfrac{x}{a} \right)$

$-\dfrac{\pi\, (a/2)^{s+2\lambda-3}\, b^2}{n!} \Gamma\left[\begin{matrix} s-2,\, n+2\lambda \\ \lambda,\, \frac{s-n-1}{2},\, \frac{s+n+2\lambda-1}{2} \end{matrix} \right]$

$\times {}_4F_3\left(\begin{matrix} 1,\, 1,\, \frac{3-s+n}{2},\, -\frac{s+n+2\lambda-3}{2} \\ 2,\, \frac{3-s}{2},\, \frac{4-s}{2};\, \frac{b^2}{a^2} \end{matrix} \right)$

$+ \dfrac{2^{n+1} \pi^{3/2} a^{2\lambda-2} b^{s+1}}{n!\,(s+1)} \tan\dfrac{s\pi}{2} \Gamma\left[\begin{matrix} \frac{n+2\lambda+1}{2} \\ \lambda,\, -\frac{n}{2} \end{matrix} \right]$

$\times {}_3F_2\left(\begin{matrix} \frac{n+2}{2},\, -\frac{n+2\lambda-2}{2},\, \frac{s+1}{2} \\ \frac{3}{2},\, \frac{s+3}{2};\, \frac{b^2}{a^2} \end{matrix} \right)$

$+ \dfrac{2^n \pi^{3/2} a^{2\lambda-1} b^s}{n!\, s} \cot\dfrac{s\pi}{2} \Gamma\left[\begin{matrix} \frac{n+2\lambda}{2} \\ \lambda,\, -\frac{n-1}{2} \end{matrix} \right]$

$\times {}_3F_2\left(\begin{matrix} \frac{n+1}{2},\, -\frac{n+2\lambda-1}{2},\, \frac{s}{2} \\ \frac{1}{2},\, \frac{s+2}{2};\, \frac{b^2}{a^2} \end{matrix} \right)$

$- \dfrac{\pi\, (a/2)^{s+2\lambda-1}}{n!} \Gamma\left[\begin{matrix} s,\, n+2\lambda \\ \lambda,\, \frac{s-n+1}{2},\, \frac{s+n+2\lambda+1}{2} \end{matrix} \right]$

$\times \left[\psi\left(\dfrac{s+n+2\lambda+1}{2} \right) + \psi\left(\dfrac{s-n+1}{2} \right) - 2\psi(s) + \ln\dfrac{4}{a^2} \right]$

$$[a>0;\ a>b;\ \operatorname{Re}\lambda > -1/2;\ \operatorname{Re} s > ((-1)^n-1)/2]$$

No.	$f(x)$	$F(s)$
4	$(x^2 - a^2)_+^{\lambda-1/2}$ $\times \left\{ \begin{array}{c} \ln(x^2 + b^2) \\ \ln\lvert x^2 - b^2 \rvert \end{array} \right\}$ $\times C_n^\lambda\left(\dfrac{x}{a}\right)$	$\pm \dfrac{\pi^2 (a/2)^{s+2\lambda+1}}{2b^2\, n!} \sec \dfrac{(s-n)\pi}{2} \sec \dfrac{(s+n+2\lambda)\pi}{2}$ $\times \Gamma\left[\begin{array}{c} n+2\lambda \\ \lambda,\, -s-1,\, \frac{s-n+3}{2},\, \frac{s+n+2\lambda+3}{2} \end{array} \right]$ $\times {}_4F_3\left(\begin{array}{c} 1,1,\frac{s+2}{2},\frac{s+3}{2};\mp\frac{a^2}{b^2} \\ 2,\frac{s-n+3}{2},\frac{s+n+2\lambda+3}{2} \end{array} \right) - \dfrac{2^n \pi^2 b^{s+n+2\lambda-1}}{(s+n+2\lambda-1)\,n!\,a^n}$ $\times \dfrac{\csc[(n+\lambda)\pi]}{\Gamma(\lambda)\,\Gamma(1-n-\lambda)} \left\{ \begin{array}{c} \sec[(s+n+2\lambda)\pi/2] \\ \tan[(s+n+2\lambda)\pi/2] \end{array} \right\}$ $\times {}_3F_2\left(\begin{array}{c} \frac{1-n-2\lambda}{2},\frac{2-n-2\lambda}{2},\frac{1-s-n-2\lambda}{2} \\ 1-n-\lambda,\frac{3-s-n-2\lambda}{2};\mp\frac{a^2}{b^2} \end{array} \right)$ $+ \dfrac{(a/2)^{s+2\lambda-1}\ln b}{n!} \Gamma\left[\begin{array}{c} n+2\lambda,\frac{1-s+n}{2},\frac{1-s-n-2\lambda}{2} \\ \lambda,\,1-s \end{array} \right]$ $\left[\left\{ \begin{array}{c} a,\ \mathrm{Re}\,b > 0 \\ b > a > 0 \end{array} \right\};\ \mathrm{Re}\,\lambda > -1/2;\ \mathrm{Re}\,(s+2\lambda) < 1-n \right]$
5	$(x^2 - a^2)_+^{\lambda-1/2}$ $\times \ln\lvert x^2 - b^2 \rvert\, C_n^\lambda\left(\dfrac{x}{a}\right)$	$-\dfrac{(a/2)^{s+2\lambda-3}b^2}{2(n!)} \Gamma\left[\begin{array}{c} n+2\lambda,\frac{3-s+n}{2},\frac{3-s-n-2\lambda}{2} \\ \lambda,\,3-s \end{array} \right]$ $\times {}_4F_3\left(\begin{array}{c} 1,1,\frac{3-s+n}{2},\frac{3-s-n-2\lambda}{2} \\ 2,\frac{3-s}{2},\frac{4-s}{2};\frac{b^2}{a^2} \end{array} \right)$ $-\dfrac{(a/2)^{s+2\lambda-1}}{2(n!)} \Gamma\left[\begin{array}{c} n+2\lambda,\frac{1-s+n}{2},\frac{1-s-n-2\lambda}{2} \\ \lambda,\,1-s \end{array} \right]$ $\times \left[\psi\left(\dfrac{1-s-n-2\lambda}{2}\right) + \psi\left(\dfrac{1-s+n}{2}\right) - 2\psi(1-s) + \ln\dfrac{4b^2}{a^2} \right]$ $-\dfrac{a^{s+2\lambda-1}\ln b}{n!}(2\lambda)_n \Gamma\left[\begin{array}{c} \frac{2\lambda+1}{2},\frac{1-s+n}{2},\frac{1-s-n-2\lambda}{2} \\ \frac{1-s}{2},\frac{2-s}{2} \end{array} \right]$ $[a,b>0;\ \mathrm{Re}\,\lambda > -1/2;\ \mathrm{Re}\,(s+2\lambda) < 1-n]$
6	$(a^2 - x^2)_+^{\lambda-1/2} \ln \dfrac{1+bx}{1-bx}$ $\times C_n^\lambda\left(\dfrac{x}{a}\right)$	$\dfrac{\pi a^{s+2\lambda}b}{2^{s+2\lambda-1}n!} \Gamma\left[\begin{array}{c} n+2\lambda,\,s+1 \\ \lambda,\frac{s-n+2}{2},\frac{s+n+2\lambda+2}{2} \end{array} \right] {}_4F_3\left(\begin{array}{c} \frac{1}{2},1,\frac{s+1}{2},\frac{s+2}{2};a^2b^2 \\ \frac{3}{2},\frac{s-n+2}{2},\frac{s+n+2\lambda+2}{2} \end{array} \right)$ $[a>0;\ \mathrm{Re}\,\lambda > -1/2;\ \mathrm{Re}\,s > -1;\ \lvert\arg(1-a^2b^2)\rvert < \pi]$
7	$(a^2 - x^2)_+^{\lambda-1/2}$ $\times \ln\left(bx + \sqrt{b^2x^2 + 1}\right)$ $\times C_n^\lambda\left(\dfrac{x}{a}\right)$	$\dfrac{\pi}{n!}\left(\dfrac{a}{2}\right)^{s+2\lambda} b\, \Gamma\left[\begin{array}{c} n+2\lambda,\,s+1 \\ \lambda,\frac{s-n+2}{2},\frac{s+n+2\lambda+2}{2} \end{array} \right]$ $\times {}_4F_3\left(\begin{array}{c} \frac{1}{2},\frac{1}{2},\frac{s+1}{2},\frac{s+2}{2};-a^2b^2 \\ \frac{3}{2},\frac{s-n+2}{2},\frac{s+n+2\lambda+2}{2} \end{array} \right)$ $[a>0;\ \mathrm{Re}\,\lambda > -1/2;\ \mathrm{Re}\,s > ((-1)^n - 1)/2;\ \lvert\arg(1+a^2b^2)\rvert < \pi]$

No.	$f(x)$	$F(s)$
8	$\dfrac{\left(a^2-x^2\right)_+^{\lambda-1/2}}{\sqrt{b^2x^2+1}}$ $\times \ln\left(bx+\sqrt{b^2x^2+1}\right)$ $\times C_n^\lambda\left(\dfrac{x}{a}\right)$	$\dfrac{\pi}{n!}\left(\dfrac{a}{2}\right)^{s+2\lambda}b\,\Gamma\left[\begin{matrix}n+2\lambda,\ s+1\\ \lambda,\ \frac{s-n+2}{2},\ \frac{s+n+2\lambda+2}{2}\end{matrix}\right]$ $\times {}_4F_3\left(\begin{matrix}1,\ 1,\ \frac{s+1}{2},\ \frac{s+2}{2};\ -a^2b^2\\ \frac{3}{2},\ \frac{s-n+2}{2},\ \frac{s+n+2\lambda+2}{2}\end{matrix}\right)$ $\left[a>0;\ \operatorname{Re}\lambda>-1/2;\ \operatorname{Re}s>\left((-1)^n-3\right)/2;\ \left|\arg\left(1+a^2b^2\right)\right|<\pi\right]$
9	$\theta\left(a-x\right)\ln\dfrac{\sqrt{a}+\sqrt{a-x}}{\sqrt{x}}$ $\times C_{2n+\varepsilon}^\lambda\left(bx\right)$	$\dfrac{(-1)^n\sqrt{\pi}\,(\lambda)_{n+\varepsilon}}{2^{1-\varepsilon}n!\,(s+\varepsilon)}a^{s+\varepsilon}b^\varepsilon\,\Gamma\left[\begin{matrix}s+\varepsilon\\ \frac{2s+2\varepsilon+1}{2}\end{matrix}\right]$ $\times {}_5F_4\left(\begin{matrix}-n,\ n+\lambda+\varepsilon,\ \frac{s+\varepsilon}{2},\ \frac{s+\varepsilon}{2},\ \frac{s+\varepsilon+1}{2}\\ \frac{2\varepsilon+1}{2},\ \frac{2s+2\varepsilon+1}{4},\ \frac{2s+2\varepsilon+3}{4},\ \frac{s+\varepsilon+2}{2};\ a^2b^2\end{matrix}\right)$ $\left[a>0;\ \operatorname{Re}\lambda>-1/2;\ \operatorname{Re}s>-\varepsilon\right]$
10	$\left(a^2-x^2\right)_+^{\lambda-1/2}$ $\times \ln^2\left(bx+\sqrt{b^2x^2+1}\right)$ $\times C_n^\lambda\left(\dfrac{x}{a}\right)$	$\dfrac{\pi}{n!}\left(\dfrac{a}{2}\right)^{s+2\lambda+1}b^2\,\Gamma\left[\begin{matrix}n+2\lambda,\ s+2\\ \lambda,\ \frac{s-n+3}{2},\ \frac{s+n+2\lambda+3}{2}\end{matrix}\right]$ $\times {}_5F_4\left(\begin{matrix}1,\ 1,\ 1,\ \frac{s+2}{2},\ \frac{s+3}{2};\ -a^2b^2\\ \frac{3}{2},\ 2,\ \frac{s-n+3}{2},\ \frac{s+n+2\lambda+3}{2}\end{matrix}\right)$ $\left[a>0;\ \operatorname{Re}\lambda>-1/2;\ \operatorname{Re}s>\left((-1)^n-5\right)/2;\ \left|\arg\left(1+a^2b^2\right)\right|<\pi\right]$

3.24.6. $C_n^\lambda\left(bx\right)$ and inverse trigonometric functions

Notation: $\varepsilon=0$ or 1.

No.	$f(x)$	$F(s)$
1	$\theta\left(a-x\right)\arccos\dfrac{x}{a}$ $\times C_{2n+\varepsilon}^\lambda\left(bx\right)$	$\dfrac{(-1)^n\sqrt{\pi}\,a^{s+\varepsilon}b^\varepsilon\,(\lambda)_{n+\varepsilon}}{2^{1-\varepsilon}n!\,(s+\varepsilon)}\,\Gamma\left[\begin{matrix}\frac{s+\varepsilon+1}{2}\\ \frac{s+\varepsilon+2}{2}\end{matrix}\right]$ $\times {}_4F_3\left(\begin{matrix}-n,\ n+\lambda+\varepsilon,\ \frac{s+\varepsilon}{2},\ \frac{s+\varepsilon+1}{2}\\ \frac{2\varepsilon+1}{2},\ \frac{s+\varepsilon+2}{2},\ \frac{s+\varepsilon+2}{2};\ a^2b^2\end{matrix}\right)$ $\left[a>0;\ \operatorname{Re}\lambda>-1/2;\ \operatorname{Re}s>-\varepsilon\right]$
2	$\left(a^2-x^2\right)_+^{\lambda-1/2}$ $\times \arcsin\left(bx\right)C_n^\lambda\left(\dfrac{x}{a}\right)$	$\dfrac{\pi}{n!}\left(\dfrac{a}{2}\right)^{s+2\lambda}b\,\Gamma\left[\begin{matrix}n+2\lambda,\ s+1\\ \lambda,\ \frac{s-n+2}{2},\ \frac{s+n+2\lambda+2}{2}\end{matrix}\right]$ $\times {}_4F_3\left(\begin{matrix}\frac{1}{2},\ \frac{1}{2},\ \frac{s+1}{2},\ \frac{s+2}{2};\ a^2b^2\\ \frac{3}{2},\ \frac{s-n+2}{2},\ \frac{s+n+2\lambda+2}{2};\ a^2b^2\end{matrix}\right)$ $\left[a>0;\ \operatorname{Re}\lambda>-1/2;\ \operatorname{Re}s>-1\right]$
3	$\dfrac{\left(a^2-x^2\right)_+^{\lambda-1/2}}{\sqrt{1-b^2x^2}}$ $\times \arcsin\left(bx\right)C_n^\lambda\left(\dfrac{x}{a}\right)$	$\dfrac{\pi}{n!}\left(\dfrac{a}{2}\right)^{s+2\lambda}b\,\Gamma\left[\begin{matrix}n+2\lambda,\ s+1\\ \frac{s-n+2}{2},\ \frac{s+n+2\lambda+2}{2}\end{matrix}\right]{}_4F_3\left(\begin{matrix}1,\ 1,\ \frac{s+1}{2},\ \frac{s+2}{2};\ a^2b^2\\ \frac{3}{2},\ \frac{s-n+2}{2},\ \frac{s+n+2\lambda+2}{2}\end{matrix}\right)$ $\left[a>0;\ \operatorname{Re}\lambda>-1/2;\ \operatorname{Re}s>\left((-1)^n-3\right)/2\right]$

No.	$f(x)$	$F(s)$
4	$\left(a^2 - x^2\right)_+^{\lambda - 1/2}$ $\times \arcsin^2(bx)\, C_n^\lambda\left(\dfrac{x}{a}\right)$	$\dfrac{\pi}{n!}\left(\dfrac{a}{2}\right)^{s+2\lambda+1} b^2\, \Gamma\left[\begin{matrix} n+2\lambda,\ s+2 \\ \lambda,\ \frac{s-n+3}{2},\ \frac{s+n+2\lambda+3}{2}\end{matrix}\right]$ $\times\ {}_5F_4\left(\begin{matrix}1,1,1,\frac{s+2}{2},\frac{s+3}{2};\ a^2b^2 \\ \frac{3}{2},2,\frac{s-n+3}{2},\frac{s+n+2\lambda+3}{2}\end{matrix}\right)$ $[a>0;\ \operatorname{Re}\lambda > -1/2;\ \operatorname{Re} s > ((-1)^n - 5)/2]$
5	$\left(a^2 - x^2\right)_+^{\lambda - 1/2}$ $\times \arctan(bx)\, C_n^\lambda\left(\dfrac{x}{a}\right)$	$\dfrac{\pi}{n!}\left(\dfrac{a}{2}\right)^{s+2\lambda} b\, \Gamma\left[\begin{matrix} n+2\lambda,\ s+1 \\ \lambda,\ \frac{s-n+2}{2},\ \frac{s+n+2\lambda+2}{2}\end{matrix}\right]$ $\times\ {}_4F_3\left(\begin{matrix}\frac{1}{2},1,\frac{s+1}{2},\frac{s+2}{2};\ -a^2b^2 \\ \frac{3}{2},\frac{s-n+2}{2},\frac{s+n+2\lambda+2}{2}\end{matrix}\right)$ $[a>0;\ \operatorname{Re}\lambda > -1/2;\ \operatorname{Re} s > ((-1)^n - 3)/2]$

3.24.7. $C_n^\lambda(ax+b)$ and $\operatorname{Ei}(ax^r)$

Notation: $\varepsilon = 0$ or 1.

No.	$f(x)$	$F(s)$
1	$(a-x)_+^{\lambda - 1/2}\operatorname{Ei}(-bx)$ $\times C_n^\lambda\left(\dfrac{2x}{a}-1\right)$	$\dfrac{(-1)^{n+1} a^{s+\lambda+1/2} b}{n!}\,(2\lambda)_n\left(\dfrac{-2s+2\lambda-1}{2}\right)_n$ $\times \Gamma\left[\begin{matrix}\frac{2\lambda+1}{2},\ s+1 \\ \frac{2s+2n+2\lambda+3}{2}\end{matrix}\right] {}_4F_4\left(\begin{matrix}1,1,\frac{2s-2\lambda+3}{2},s+1;\ -ab \\ 2,2,\frac{2s-2n-2\lambda+3}{2},\frac{2s+2n+2\lambda+3}{2}\end{matrix}\right)$ $+ \dfrac{(-1)^n a^{s+\lambda-1/2}}{n!}\,(2\lambda)_n\left(\dfrac{-2s+2\lambda+1}{2}\right)_n$ $\times \Gamma\left[\begin{matrix}\frac{2\lambda+1}{2},\ s \\ \frac{2s+2n+2\lambda+1}{2}\end{matrix}\right]\left[\psi(s) - \psi\left(\dfrac{2s+2n+2\lambda+1}{2}\right)\right.$ $\left. - \sum_{i=0}^{n-1}\dfrac{2}{2i-2s+2\lambda+1} + \ln(ab) + \mathbf{C}\right]$ $\quad\left[\begin{matrix}a,\ \operatorname{Re} s > 0; \\ \operatorname{Re}\lambda > -1/2\end{matrix}\right]$
2	$\left(a^2 - x^2\right)_+^{\lambda - 1/2}\operatorname{Ei}(bx)$ $\times C_n^\lambda\left(\dfrac{x}{a}\right)$	$\dfrac{\pi}{n!}\left(\dfrac{a}{2}\right)^{s+2\lambda} b\, \Gamma\left[\begin{matrix} n+2\lambda,\ s+1 \\ \lambda,\ \frac{s-n+2}{2},\ \frac{s+n+2\lambda+2}{2}\end{matrix}\right]$ $\times\ {}_3F_4\left(\begin{matrix}\frac{1}{2},\frac{s+1}{2},\frac{s+2}{2};\ \frac{a^2b^2}{4} \\ \frac{3}{2},\frac{3}{2},\frac{s-n+2}{2},\frac{s+n+2\lambda+2}{2}\end{matrix}\right) + \dfrac{\pi a^{s+2\lambda+1}b^2}{2^{s+2\lambda+3}\,n!}$ $\times \Gamma\left[\begin{matrix} n+2\lambda,\ s+2 \\ \lambda,\ \frac{s-n+3}{2},\ \frac{s+n+2\lambda+3}{2}\end{matrix}\right] {}_3F_4\left(\begin{matrix}1,1,\frac{s+2}{2},\frac{s+3}{2};\ \frac{a^2b^2}{4} \\ \frac{3}{2},2,2,\frac{s-n+3}{2},\frac{s+n+2\lambda+3}{2}\end{matrix}\right)$ $+ \dfrac{\pi}{n!}\left(\dfrac{a}{2}\right)^{s+2\lambda-1}\Gamma\left[\begin{matrix} n+2\lambda,\ s \\ \lambda,\ \frac{s-n+1}{2},\ \frac{s+n+2\lambda+1}{2}\end{matrix}\right]\left[\psi(s)\right.$ $\left. - \dfrac{1}{2}\psi\left(\dfrac{s+n+2\lambda+1}{2}\right) - \dfrac{1}{2}\psi\left(\dfrac{s-n+1}{2}\right) + \ln\dfrac{ab}{2} + \mathbf{C}\right]$ $[a>0;\ \operatorname{Re}\lambda > -1/2;\ \operatorname{Re} s > ((-1)^n - 1)/2]$

No.	$f(x)$	$F(s)$
3	$\left(a^2 - x^2\right)_+^{\lambda - 1/2} \operatorname{Ei}\left(bx^2\right)$ $\times C_n^\lambda\left(\dfrac{x}{a}\right)$	$\dfrac{\pi}{n!}\left(\dfrac{a}{2}\right)^{2\lambda+s+1} b\,\Gamma\!\left[\begin{array}{c} n+2\lambda,\ s+2 \\ \lambda,\ \frac{s-n+3}{2},\ \frac{s+n+2\lambda+3}{2}\end{array}\right]$ $\times {}_4F_4\!\left(\begin{array}{c} 1,\,1,\,\frac{s+2}{2},\,\frac{s+3}{2};\ a^2b \\ 2,\,2,\,\frac{s-n+3}{2},\,\frac{s+n+2\lambda+3}{2}\end{array}\right)$ $+\dfrac{\pi}{n!}\left(\dfrac{a}{2}\right)^{2\lambda+s+1}\Gamma\!\left[\begin{array}{c} n+2\lambda,\ s \\ \lambda,\ \frac{s-n+1}{2},\ \frac{s+n+2\lambda+1}{2}\end{array}\right]$ $\times\left[2\psi\left(s\right)-\psi\left(\dfrac{s+n+2\lambda+1}{2}\right)-\psi\left(\dfrac{s-n+1}{2}\right)+\ln\dfrac{a^2b}{4}+\mathbf{C}\right]$ $[a>0;\ \operatorname{Re}\lambda>-1/2;\ \operatorname{Re}s>\left((-1)^n-1\right)/2]$
4	$\left(x^2 - a^2\right)_+^{\lambda - 1/2}$ $\times \operatorname{Ei}\left(-bx^2\right) C_n^\lambda\left(\dfrac{x}{a}\right)$	$-\dfrac{(a/2)^{s+2\lambda+1} b}{2\,(n!)}\Gamma\!\left[\begin{array}{c} n+2\lambda,\ \frac{n-s-1}{2},\ -\frac{s+n+2\lambda+1}{2} \\ \lambda,\ -s-1\end{array}\right]$ $\times {}_4F_4\!\left(\begin{array}{c} 1,\,1,\,\frac{s+2}{2},\,\frac{s+3}{2};\ -a^2b \\ 2,\,2,\,\frac{s-n+3}{2},\,\frac{s+n+2\lambda+3}{2}\end{array}\right)$ $+\dfrac{\pi\,(2/a)^n\,b^{-(s+n+2\lambda-1)/2}}{(s+n+2\lambda-1)\,n!}\sec\dfrac{(s+n+2\lambda)\,\pi}{2}\dfrac{(\lambda)_n}{\Gamma\left(\frac{3-s-n-2\lambda}{2}\right)}$ $\times {}_3F_3\!\left(\begin{array}{c} \frac{1-n-2\lambda}{2},\,\frac{2-n-2\lambda}{2},\,\frac{1-s-n-2\lambda}{2};\ -a^2b \\ 1-n-\lambda,\,\frac{3-s-n-2\lambda}{2},\,\frac{3-s-n-2\lambda}{2}\end{array}\right)$ $+\dfrac{(a/2)^{s+2\lambda-1}}{2\,(n!)}\Gamma\!\left[\begin{array}{c} n+2\lambda,\ \frac{1-s+n}{2},\ \frac{1-s-n-2\lambda}{2} \\ \lambda,\ 1-s\end{array}\right]$ $\times\left[2\psi\left(1-s\right)-\psi\left(\dfrac{1-s-n-2\lambda}{2}\right)\right.$ $\left.-\psi\left(\dfrac{1-s+n}{2}\right)+\ln\dfrac{a^2b}{4}+\mathbf{C}\right]$ $[a,\ \operatorname{Re}b>0;\ \operatorname{Re}\lambda>-1/2]$

3.24.8. $C_n^\lambda\left(ax + b\right)$ **and** $\operatorname{si}\left(ax\right),\ \operatorname{ci}\left(ax\right)$

Notation: $\delta = \left\{\begin{array}{c}1\\0\end{array}\right\},\ \varepsilon = 0$ or 1.

No.	$f(x)$	$F(s)$
1	$\left(a^2 - x^2\right)_+^{\lambda - 1/2}$ $\times \operatorname{si}\left(bx\right) C_n^\lambda\left(\dfrac{x}{a}\right)$	$\dfrac{\sqrt{\pi}\,(2\lambda)_n\,a^{s+2\lambda} b}{2^{s+1} n!}\Gamma\!\left[\begin{array}{c} \frac{2\lambda+1}{2},\ s+1 \\ \frac{s-n+2}{2},\ \frac{s+n+2\lambda+2}{2}\end{array}\right]$ $\times {}_3F_4\!\left(\begin{array}{c} \frac{1}{2},\,\frac{s+1}{2},\,\frac{s+2}{2};\ -\frac{a^2b^2}{4} \\ \frac{3}{2},\,\frac{3}{2},\,\frac{s-n+2}{2},\,\frac{s+n+2\lambda+2}{2}\end{array}\right)$ $-\dfrac{\pi^{3/2}\,(2\lambda)_n\,a^{s+2\lambda-1}}{2^{s+1} n!}\Gamma\!\left[\begin{array}{c} \frac{2\lambda+1}{2},\ s \\ \frac{s-n+1}{2},\ \frac{s+n+2\lambda+1}{2}\end{array}\right]$ $[a>0;\ \operatorname{Re}\lambda>-1/2;\ \operatorname{Re}s>\left((-1)^n-1\right)/2]$

No.	$f(x)$	$F(s)$
2	$\left(a^2 - x^2\right)_+^{\lambda-1/2}$ $\times \operatorname{ci}(bx) \, C_n^\lambda\left(\dfrac{x}{a}\right)$	$\dfrac{\pi}{n!}\left(\dfrac{a}{2}\right)^{s+2\lambda-1} \Gamma\left[\begin{array}{c} n+2\lambda,\ s+2 \\ \lambda,\ \frac{s-n+1}{2},\ \frac{s+n+2\lambda+1}{2} \end{array}\right]$ $\times \left\{ \dfrac{4}{s(s+1)}\left[\ln\dfrac{ab}{2} - \dfrac{1}{2}\psi\left(\dfrac{s+n+2\lambda+1}{2}\right)\right.\right.$ $\left. -\dfrac{1}{2}\psi\left(\dfrac{s-n+1}{2}\right) + \psi(s) + \mathbf{C}\right]$ $\left. -\dfrac{a^2b^2}{(s-n+1)(s+n+2\lambda+3)} \, {}_4F_5\left(\begin{array}{c} 1,1,\frac{s+2}{2},\frac{s+3}{2};-\frac{a^2b^2}{4} \\ \frac{3}{2},2,2,\frac{s-n+3}{2},\frac{s+n+2\lambda+3}{2} \end{array}\right)\right\}$ $[a > 0;\ \operatorname{Re}\lambda > -1/2;\ \operatorname{Re}s > ((-1)^n - 1)/2]$
3	$\left(x^2 - a^2\right)_+^{\lambda-1/2}\operatorname{si}(bx)$ $\times C_n^\lambda\left(\dfrac{x}{a}\right)$	$\dfrac{a^{s+2\lambda}b}{2^{s+2\lambda+1}n!}\Gamma\left[\begin{array}{c} n+2\lambda,\ -\frac{s-n}{2},\ -\frac{s+n+2\lambda}{2} \\ \lambda,\ -s \end{array}\right]$ $\times {}_3F_4\left(\begin{array}{c} \frac{1}{2},\frac{s+1}{2},\frac{s+2}{2};-\frac{a^2b^2}{4} \\ \frac{3}{2},\frac{3}{2},\frac{s-n+2}{2},\frac{s+n+2\lambda+2}{2} \end{array}\right) + \dfrac{2^n(s+n+2\lambda-1)^{-2}}{a^n b^{s+n+2\lambda-1}n!}$ $\times (\lambda)_n \cos\dfrac{(s+n+2\lambda)\pi}{2}\,\Gamma(s+n+2\lambda)$ $\times {}_3F_4\left(\begin{array}{c} \frac{1-n-2\lambda}{2},\frac{2-n-2\lambda}{2},-\frac{s+n+2\lambda-1}{2};-\frac{a^2b^2}{4} \\ 1-n-\lambda,-\frac{s+n+2\lambda-2}{2},-\frac{s+n+2\lambda-3}{2},-\frac{s+n+2\lambda-3}{2} \end{array}\right)$ $-\dfrac{\pi a^{s+2\lambda-1}}{2^{s+2\lambda+1}n!}\Gamma\left[\begin{array}{c} n+2\lambda,\ -\frac{s-n-1}{2},\ -\frac{s+n+2\lambda-1}{2} \\ \lambda,\ 1-s \end{array}\right]$ $[a,b > 0;\ \operatorname{Re}\lambda > -1/2;\ \operatorname{Re}(s+2\lambda) < 1-n]$
4	$\left(x^2 - a^2\right)_+^{\lambda-1/2}\operatorname{ci}(bx)$ $\times C_n^\lambda\left(\dfrac{x}{a}\right)$	$-\dfrac{a^{s+2\lambda+1}b^2}{2^{s+2\lambda+4}n!}\Gamma\left[\begin{array}{c} n+2\lambda,\ -\frac{s-n+1}{2},\ -\frac{s+n+2\lambda+1}{2} \\ \lambda,\ -s-1 \end{array}\right]$ $\times {}_4F_5\left(\begin{array}{c} 1,1,\frac{s+2}{2},\frac{s+3}{2};-\frac{a^2b^2}{4} \\ \frac{3}{2},2,2,\frac{s-n+3}{2},\frac{s+n+2\lambda+3}{2} \end{array}\right) - \dfrac{2^n(s+n+2\lambda-1)^{-2}}{a^n b^{s+n+2\lambda-1}n!}$ $\times (\lambda)_n \sin\dfrac{(s+n+2\lambda)\pi}{2}\,\Gamma(s+n+2\lambda)$ $\times {}_3F_4\left(\begin{array}{c} \frac{1-n-2\lambda}{2},\frac{2-n-2\lambda}{2},\frac{1-s-n-2\lambda}{2};-\frac{a^2b^2}{4} \\ 1-n-\lambda,\frac{2-s-n-2\lambda}{2},\frac{3-s-n-2\lambda}{2},\frac{3-n-s-2\lambda}{2} \end{array}\right)$ $+\dfrac{1}{2(n!)}\left(\dfrac{a}{2}\right)^{s+2\lambda-1}\Gamma\left[\begin{array}{c} n+2\lambda,\ -\frac{s-n-1}{2},\ -\frac{s+n+2\lambda-1}{2} \\ \lambda,\ 1-s \end{array}\right]$ $\times \left[\psi(1-s) - \dfrac{1}{2}\psi\left(\dfrac{1-s-n-2\lambda}{2}\right)\right.$ $\left. -\dfrac{1}{2}\psi\left(\dfrac{1-s+n}{2}\right) + \ln\dfrac{ab}{2} + \mathbf{C}\right]$ $[a,b > 0;\ \operatorname{Re}\lambda > -1/2;\ \operatorname{Re}(s+2\lambda) < 1-n]$

No.	$f(x)$	$F(s)$
5	$(a-x)_+^{\lambda-1/2}$ $\times\begin{Bmatrix}\operatorname{si}(b\sqrt{x})\\\operatorname{ci}(b\sqrt{x})\end{Bmatrix}$ $\times C_n^\lambda\left(\dfrac{2x}{a}-1\right)$	$\dfrac{(-1)^{n+1}2^{\delta-2}a^{s+\lambda+(\delta+1)/2}b^{\delta+2}}{3^{2\delta}n!}(2\lambda)_n$ $\times\left(\dfrac{-2s+2\lambda-\delta-1}{2}\right)_n\Gamma\begin{bmatrix}\frac{2\lambda+1}{2},\ \frac{2s+\delta+2}{2}\\\frac{2s+2n+2\lambda+\delta+3}{2}\end{bmatrix}$ $\times{}_4F_5\left(\begin{matrix}1,\ \frac{\delta+2}{2},\ \frac{2s+\delta+2}{2},\ \frac{2s-2\lambda+\delta+3}{2};\ -\frac{ab^2}{4}\\2,\ \frac{\delta+4}{2},\ \frac{2\delta+3}{2},\ \frac{2s-2n-2\lambda+\delta+3}{2},\ \frac{2s+2n+2\lambda+\delta+3}{2}\end{matrix}\right)$ $+\dfrac{(-1)^n a^{s+\lambda+(\delta-1)/2}b^\delta}{n!}(2\lambda)_n\left(\dfrac{-2s+2\lambda-\delta+1}{2}\right)_n$ $\times\Gamma\begin{bmatrix}\frac{2\lambda+1}{2},\ \frac{2s+\delta}{2}\\\frac{2s+2n+2\lambda+\delta+1}{2}\end{bmatrix}\left[\dfrac{1}{2}\psi(s)-\dfrac{1}{2}\psi\left(\dfrac{2s+2n+2\lambda+1}{2}\right)\right.$ $\left.-\sum_{i=0}^{n-1}\dfrac{1}{2i-2s+2\lambda+1}+\dfrac{1}{2}\ln(ab^2)+\mathbf{C}\right]^{1-\delta}$ $-\delta\dfrac{(-1)^n\pi a^{s+\lambda-1/2}}{2(n!)}(2\lambda)_n\left(\dfrac{1-2s+2\lambda}{2}\right)_n\Gamma\begin{bmatrix}\frac{2\lambda+1}{2},\ s\\\frac{2s+2n+2\lambda+1}{2}\end{bmatrix}$ $[a,\ \operatorname{Re}s>0;\ \operatorname{Re}\lambda>-1/2]$

3.24.9. $C_n^\lambda(ax+b)$ **and** $\operatorname{erf}(ax),\ \operatorname{erfc}(ax)$

Notation: $\delta=\begin{Bmatrix}1\\0\end{Bmatrix},\ \varepsilon=0$ or 1.

No.	$f(x)$	$F(s)$
1	$\operatorname{erfc}(ax)\,C_{2n+\varepsilon}^\lambda(bx)$	$(-1)^n\dfrac{2^\varepsilon(\lambda)_{n+\varepsilon}a^{-s-\varepsilon}b^\varepsilon}{\sqrt{\pi}(s+\varepsilon)n!}\Gamma\left(\dfrac{s+\varepsilon+1}{2}\right)$ $\times{}_4F_2\left(\begin{matrix}-n,\ n+\lambda+\varepsilon,\ \frac{s+1}{2},\ \frac{s+2\varepsilon}{2}\\\frac{2\varepsilon+1}{2},\ \frac{s+\varepsilon+2}{2};\ \frac{b^2}{a^2}\end{matrix}\right)$ $[\operatorname{Re}\lambda>-1/2;\ \operatorname{Re}s>-\varepsilon;\ |\arg a|<\pi/4]$
2	$(a^2-x^2)_+^{\lambda-1/2}\operatorname{erf}(bx)$ $\times C_n^\lambda\left(\dfrac{x}{a}\right)$	$\dfrac{\sqrt{\pi}a^{s+2\lambda}b}{2^{s+2\lambda-1}n!}\Gamma\begin{bmatrix}n+2\lambda,\ s+1\\\lambda,\ \frac{s-n+2}{2},\ \frac{s+n+2\lambda+2}{2}\end{bmatrix}{}_3F_3\left(\begin{matrix}\frac{1}{2},\ \frac{s+1}{2},\ \frac{s+2}{2};\ -a^2b^2\\\frac{3}{2},\ \frac{s-n+2}{2},\ \frac{s+n+2\lambda+2}{2}\end{matrix}\right)$ $[a>0;\ \operatorname{Re}\lambda>-1/2;\operatorname{Re}s>((-1)^n-3)/2]$
3	$(x^2-a^2)_+^{\lambda-1/2}$ $\times\begin{Bmatrix}\operatorname{erf}(bx)\\\operatorname{erfc}(bx)\end{Bmatrix}C_n^\lambda\left(\dfrac{x}{a}\right)$	$\pm\dfrac{(a/2)^{s+2\lambda}b}{\sqrt{\pi}n!}\Gamma\begin{bmatrix}n+2\lambda,\ \frac{n-s}{2},\ -\frac{s+n+2\lambda}{2}\\\lambda,\ -s\end{bmatrix}$ $\times{}_3F_3\left(\begin{matrix}\frac{1}{2},\ \frac{s+1}{2},\ \frac{s+2}{2};\ -a^2b^2\\\frac{3}{2},\ \frac{s-n+2}{2},\ \frac{s+n+2\lambda+2}{2}\end{matrix}\right)\mp\dfrac{a^{-n}b^{-s-n-2\lambda+1}}{2^{s+2\lambda-1}\pi\,n!}(\lambda)_n$ $\times\cos\dfrac{(s+n+2\lambda)\pi}{2}\Gamma\left(\dfrac{1-s-n-2\lambda}{2}\right)\Gamma(s+n+2\lambda-1)\times$

No.	$f(x)$	$F(s)$
		$\times \, {}_3F_3\left(\begin{array}{c} \frac{1-n-2\lambda}{2}, \frac{2-n-2\lambda}{2}, \frac{1-s-n-2\lambda}{2}; -a^2b^2 \\ 1-n-\lambda, \frac{2-s-n-2\lambda}{2}, \frac{3-s-n-2\lambda}{2} \end{array}\right)$
		$+\,(1-\delta)\dfrac{(a/2)^{s+2\lambda-1}}{2\,(n!)}\Gamma\left[\begin{array}{c} n+2\lambda, \frac{1-s+n}{2}, -\frac{s+n+2\lambda-1}{2} \\ \lambda, 1-s \end{array}\right]$
		$[a,\ \mathrm{Re}\,b > 0;\ \mathrm{Re}\,\lambda > -1/2;\ \mathrm{Re}\,(s+2\lambda) < 1-n \text{ for erf}]$
4	$(a^2-x^2)_+^{\lambda-1/2}\,e^{b^2x^2}$ $\times\,\mathrm{erf}\,(bx)\,C_n^\lambda\left(\dfrac{x}{a}\right)$	$\dfrac{\sqrt{\pi}\,a^{s+2\lambda}b}{2^{s+2\lambda-1}n!}\Gamma\left[\begin{array}{c} n+2\lambda, s+1 \\ \lambda, \frac{s-n+2}{2}, \frac{s+n+2\lambda+2}{2} \end{array}\right]\,{}_3F_3\left(\begin{array}{c} 1, \frac{s+1}{2}, \frac{s+2}{2}; a^2b^2 \\ \frac{3}{2}, \frac{s-n+2}{2}, \frac{s+n+2\lambda+2}{2} \end{array}\right)$ $[a > 0;\ \mathrm{Re}\,\lambda > -1/2;\ \mathrm{Re}\,s > ((-1)^n - 3)/2]$
5	$\mathrm{erfc}\,(bx)\,C_n^\lambda\left(\dfrac{x}{a}+1\right)$	$\dfrac{n\,(n+2\lambda)\,a^{-1}b^{-s-1}}{(2\lambda+1)\sqrt{\pi}\,(s+1)\,n!}\,(2\lambda)_n\,\Gamma\left(\dfrac{s+2}{2}\right)$
		$\times\,{}_6F_4\left(\begin{array}{c} \frac{1-n}{2}, \frac{2-n}{2}, \frac{n+2\lambda+1}{2}, \frac{n+2\lambda+2}{2}, \frac{s+1}{2}, \frac{s+2}{2} \\ \frac{3}{2}, \frac{2\lambda+3}{4}, \frac{2\lambda+5}{4}, \frac{s+3}{2}; \frac{1}{4a^2b^2} \end{array}\right)$
		$+\,\dfrac{b^{-s}\,(2\lambda)_n}{\sqrt{\pi}\,s\,n!}\,\Gamma\left(\dfrac{s+1}{2}\right)\,{}_6F_4\left(\begin{array}{c} -\frac{n}{2}, \frac{1-n}{2}, \frac{n+2\lambda}{2}, \frac{n+2\lambda+1}{2}, \frac{s}{2}, \frac{s+1}{2} \\ \frac{1}{2}, \frac{2\lambda+1}{4}, \frac{2\lambda+3}{4}, \frac{s+2}{2}; \frac{1}{4a^2b^2} \end{array}\right)$
		$[\mathrm{Re}\,s > 0;\ |\arg b| < \pi/4]$
6	$\mathrm{erfc}\,(b\sqrt{x})\,C_n^\lambda\left(\dfrac{x}{a}-1\right)$	$\dfrac{(2/a)^n\,b^{-2s-2n}}{\sqrt{\pi}\,(s+n)\,n!}\,(\lambda)_n\,\Gamma\left(s+n+\dfrac{1}{2}\right)$
		$\times\,{}_3F_3\left(\begin{array}{c} -n, \frac{1}{2}-n-\lambda, -s-n; -2ab^2 \\ 1-2n-2\lambda, \frac{1}{2}-s-n, 1-s-n \end{array}\right)$
		$[\mathrm{Re}\,\lambda > -1/2;\ \mathrm{Re}\,s > ((-1)^n-1)/2;\ |\arg b| < \pi/4]$
7	$(a-x)_+^{\lambda-1/2}$ $\times\left\{\begin{array}{c} \mathrm{erf}\,(b\sqrt{x}) \\ \mathrm{erfc}\,(b\sqrt{x}) \end{array}\right\}$ $\times\,C_n^\lambda\left(\dfrac{2x}{a}-1\right)$	$\pm\dfrac{2\,(-1)^n\,a^{s+\lambda}b}{\sqrt{\pi}\,n!}\,(2\lambda)_n\,(\lambda-s)_n\,\Gamma\left[\begin{array}{c} \frac{2\lambda+1}{2}, \frac{2s+1}{2} \\ s+n+\lambda+1 \end{array}\right]$ $\times\,{}_3F_3\left(\begin{array}{c} \frac{1}{2}, \frac{2s+1}{2}, s-\lambda+1; -ab^2 \\ \frac{3}{2}, s-n-\lambda+1, s+n+\lambda+1 \end{array}\right)$ $+\left\{\begin{array}{c} 0 \\ 1 \end{array}\right\}\dfrac{(-1)^n\,a^{s+\lambda-1/2}}{n!}\,(2\lambda)_n\left(\lambda-s+\dfrac{1}{2}\right)_n\,\Gamma\left[\begin{array}{c} \frac{2\lambda+1}{2}, s \\ s+n+\lambda+\frac{1}{2} \end{array}\right]$ $[a > 0;\ \mathrm{Re}\,\lambda > -1/2;\ \mathrm{Re}\,s > -(1\pm1)/4]$
8	$(a-x)_+^{\lambda-1/2}\,e^{b^2x}$ $\times\,\mathrm{erf}\,(b\sqrt{x})\,C_n^\lambda\left(\dfrac{2x}{a}-1\right)$	$\dfrac{2\,(-1)^n\,a^{s+\lambda}b}{\sqrt{\pi}\,n!}\,(2\lambda)_n\,(\lambda-s)_n\,\Gamma\left[\begin{array}{c} \frac{2\lambda+1}{2}, \frac{2s+1}{2} \\ s+n+\lambda+1 \end{array}\right]$ $\times\,{}_3F_3\left(\begin{array}{c} 1, \frac{2s+1}{2}, s-\lambda+1; ab^2 \\ \frac{3}{2}, s-n-\lambda+1, s+n+\lambda+1 \end{array}\right)$ $[a > 0;\ \mathrm{Re}\,\lambda > -1/2;\ \mathrm{Re}\,s > -1/2]$

3.24.10. $C_n^\lambda (bx)$ and $\Gamma (\nu, ax)$, $\gamma (\nu, ax)$

Notation: $\varepsilon = 0$ or 1.

1	$\Gamma (\nu, ax) C_{2n+\varepsilon}^\lambda (bx)$	$\dfrac{(-1)^n (\varepsilon + 1) (\lambda)_{n+\varepsilon}\, a^{-s-\varepsilon} b^\varepsilon}{n! (s+\varepsilon)}\, \Gamma (s + \nu + \varepsilon)$ $\times\, {}_5F_2 \left(\begin{matrix} -n,\, n+\lambda+\varepsilon,\, \frac{s+\varepsilon}{2},\, \frac{s+\nu+\varepsilon}{2},\, \frac{s+\nu+\varepsilon+1}{2} \\ \frac{2\varepsilon+1}{2},\, \frac{s+\varepsilon+2}{2};\, \frac{4b^2}{a^2} \end{matrix} \right)$ $[\operatorname{Re} a > 0;\ \operatorname{Re} s > -\operatorname{Re}\nu - \varepsilon,\, 0]$
2	$\left(a^2 - x^2\right)_+^{\lambda-1/2} e^{bx}$ $\times\, \gamma (\nu, bx) C_n^\lambda \left(\dfrac{x}{a}\right)$	$\dfrac{\pi}{n!\,\nu} \left(\dfrac{a}{2}\right)^{s+2\lambda+\nu-1} b^\nu\, \Gamma \left[\begin{matrix} n+2\lambda,\, s+\nu \\ \lambda,\, \frac{s-n+\nu+1}{2},\, \frac{s+n+2\lambda+\nu+1}{2} \end{matrix} \right]$ $\times\, {}_3F_4 \left(\begin{matrix} 1,\, \frac{s+\nu}{2},\, \frac{s+\nu+1}{2};\, \frac{a^2 b^2}{4} \\ \frac{\nu+1}{2},\, \frac{\nu+2}{2},\, \frac{s-n+\nu+1}{2},\, \frac{s+n+2\lambda+\nu+1}{2} \end{matrix} \right)$ $+\, \dfrac{\pi}{n!\,\nu\,(\nu+1)} \left(\dfrac{a}{2}\right)^{s+2\lambda+\nu} b^{\nu+1}\, \Gamma \left[\begin{matrix} n+2\lambda,\, s+\nu+1 \\ \lambda,\, \frac{s-n+\nu+2}{2},\, \frac{s+n+2\lambda+\nu+2}{2} \end{matrix} \right]$ $\times\, {}_3F_4 \left(\begin{matrix} 1,\, \frac{s+\nu+1}{2},\, \frac{s+\nu+2}{2};\, \frac{a^2 b^2}{4} \\ \frac{\nu+2}{2},\, \frac{\nu+3}{2},\, \frac{s-n+\nu+2}{2},\, \frac{s+n+2\lambda+\nu+2}{2} \end{matrix} \right)$ $[a > 0;\ \operatorname{Re} s > -\operatorname{Re}\nu - \varepsilon]$
3	$\left(a^2 - x^2\right)_+^{\lambda-1/2}$ $\times\, \gamma (\nu, b^2 x^2) C_n^\lambda \left(\dfrac{x}{a}\right)$	$\dfrac{\pi}{n!\,\nu} \left(\dfrac{a}{2}\right)^{s+2\lambda+2\nu-1} b^{2\nu}\, \Gamma \left[\begin{matrix} n+2\lambda,\, s+2\nu \\ \lambda,\, \frac{s-n+2\nu+1}{2},\, \frac{s+n+2\lambda+2\nu+1}{2} \end{matrix} \right]$ $\times\, {}_3F_3 \left(\begin{matrix} \nu,\, \frac{s+2\nu}{2},\, \frac{s+2\nu+1}{2};\, -a^2 b^2 \\ \nu+1,\, \frac{s-n+2\nu+1}{2},\, \frac{s+n+2\lambda+2\nu+1}{2} \end{matrix} \right)$ $[a > 0;\ \operatorname{Re} s > -\operatorname{Re}\nu - \varepsilon]$
4	$\left(a^2 - x^2\right)_+^{\lambda-1/2} e^{b^2 x^2}$ $\times\, \gamma (\nu, b^2 x^2) C_n^\lambda \left(\dfrac{x}{a}\right)$	$\dfrac{\pi}{n!\,\nu} \left(\dfrac{a}{2}\right)^{s+2\lambda+2\nu-1} b^{2\nu}\, \Gamma \left[\begin{matrix} n+2\lambda,\, s+2\nu \\ \lambda,\, \frac{s-n+2\nu+1}{2},\, \frac{s+n+2\lambda+2\nu+1}{2} \end{matrix} \right]$ $\times\, {}_3F_3 \left(\begin{matrix} 1,\, \frac{s+2\nu}{2},\, \frac{s+2\nu+1}{2};\, a^2 b^2 \\ \nu+1,\, \frac{s-n+2\nu+1}{2},\, \frac{s+n+2\lambda+2\nu+1}{2} \end{matrix} \right)$ $[a > 0;\ \operatorname{Re} s > -\operatorname{Re}\nu - \varepsilon]$

3.24.11. $C_n^\lambda (bx)$ and Bessel functions

Notation: $\varepsilon = 0$ or 1.

1	$\left(a^2 - x^2\right)_+^{\lambda-1/2}$ $\times\, \left\{ \begin{matrix} J_\nu (bx) \\ I_\nu (bx) \end{matrix} \right\} C_n^\lambda \left(\dfrac{x}{a}\right)$	$\dfrac{\pi}{n!} \left(\dfrac{a}{2}\right)^{s+2\lambda+\nu-1} \left(\dfrac{b}{2}\right)^\nu \Gamma \left[\begin{matrix} n+2\lambda,\, s+\nu \\ \lambda,\, \nu+1,\, \frac{s-n+\nu+1}{2},\, \frac{s+n+2\lambda+\nu+1}{2} \end{matrix} \right]$ $\times\, {}_2F_3 \left(\begin{matrix} \frac{s+\nu}{2},\, \frac{s+\nu+1}{2};\, \mp \frac{a^2 b^2}{4} \\ \nu+1,\, \frac{s-n+\nu+1}{2},\, \frac{s+n+2\lambda+\nu+1}{2} \end{matrix} \right)$ $[a > 0;\ \operatorname{Re}\lambda > -1/2;\ \operatorname{Re}(s+\nu) > ((-1)^n - 1)/2]$

No.	$f(x)$	$F(s)$
2	$(x^2 - a^2)_+^{\lambda - 1/2} J_\nu(bx)$ $\times C_n^\lambda\left(\dfrac{x}{a}\right)$	$\dfrac{a^{s+2\lambda+\nu-1} b^\nu}{2^{s+2\lambda+2\nu}\, n!} \Gamma\left[\begin{array}{c} n + 2\lambda,\ \frac{1-s+n-\nu}{2},\ \frac{1-s-n-2\lambda-\nu}{2} \\ \lambda,\ \nu+1,\ 1-s-\nu \end{array}\right]$ $\times {}_2F_3\left(\begin{array}{c} \frac{s+\nu}{2},\ \frac{s+\nu+1}{2};\ -\frac{a^2b^2}{4} \\ \nu+1,\ \frac{s-n+\nu+1}{2},\ \frac{s+n+2\lambda+\nu+1}{2} \end{array}\right)$ $+ \dfrac{2^{s+2n+2\lambda-2}}{a^n b^{s+n+2\lambda-1}\, n!}\, (\lambda)_n\, \Gamma\left[\begin{array}{c} \frac{s+n+2\lambda+\nu-1}{2} \\ \frac{3-s-n-2\lambda+\nu}{2} \end{array}\right]$ $\times {}_2F_3\left(\begin{array}{c} \frac{1-n-2\lambda}{2},\ \frac{2-n-2\lambda}{2};\ -\frac{a^2b^2}{4} \\ 1-n-\lambda,\ \frac{3-s-n-2\lambda-\nu}{2},\ \frac{3-s-n-2\lambda+\nu}{2} \end{array}\right)$ $[a,\ b > 0;\ \operatorname{Re}\lambda > -1/2;\ \operatorname{Re}(s+2\lambda) < 3/2 - n]$
3	$(a^2 - x^2)_+^{\lambda - 1/2} J_\nu\left(\dfrac{b}{x}\right)$ $\times C_{2n+\varepsilon}^\lambda\left(\dfrac{x}{a}\right)$	$\dfrac{(-1)^n\, a^{s+2\lambda-\nu-1} b^\nu}{2^{\nu+1}\,(2n+\varepsilon)!}\,(2\lambda)_{2n+\varepsilon}\left(\dfrac{1-s+\nu+\varepsilon}{2}\right)_n$ $\times \Gamma\left[\begin{array}{c} \frac{2\lambda+1}{2},\ \frac{s-\nu+\varepsilon}{2} \\ \nu+1,\ \frac{s+2n+2\lambda-\nu+\varepsilon+1}{2} \end{array}\right] {}_2F_3\left(\begin{array}{c} \frac{1-s+2n+\nu+\varepsilon}{2},\ \frac{1-s-2n-2\lambda+\nu-\varepsilon}{2} \\ \nu+1,\ \frac{1-s+\nu}{2},\ \frac{2-s+\nu}{2};\ -\frac{b^2}{4a^2} \end{array}\right)$ $+ \dfrac{(-1)^n\, a^{2\lambda-\varepsilon-1} b^{s+\varepsilon}}{2^{s+1}\, n!}\,(\lambda)_{n+\varepsilon}\ \Gamma\left[\begin{array}{c} -\frac{s-\nu+\varepsilon}{2} \\ \frac{s+\nu+\varepsilon+2}{2} \end{array}\right]$ $\times {}_2F_3\left(\begin{array}{c} \frac{2n+2\varepsilon+1}{2},\ \frac{1-2\lambda-2n}{2};\ -\frac{b^2}{4a^2} \\ \frac{2\varepsilon+1}{2},\ \frac{s-\nu+\varepsilon+2}{2},\ \frac{s+\nu+\varepsilon+2}{2} \end{array}\right)$ $[a > 0;\ \operatorname{Re}\lambda > -1/2;\ \operatorname{Re} s > -\varepsilon - 3/2]$
4	$(x^2 - a^2)_+^{\lambda - 1/2} J_\nu\left(\dfrac{b}{x}\right)$ $\times C_{2n+\varepsilon}^\lambda\left(\dfrac{x}{a}\right)$	$\dfrac{a^{s+2\lambda-\nu-1} b^\nu}{2^{s+2\lambda}\, n!} \Gamma\left[\begin{array}{c} n+2\lambda,\ \frac{1-s+n+\nu}{2},\ -\frac{s+n+2\lambda-\nu-1}{2} \\ \lambda,\ \nu+1,\ 1-s+\nu \end{array}\right]$ $\times {}_2F_3\left(\begin{array}{c} \frac{1-s+n+\nu}{2},\ -\frac{s+n+2\lambda-\nu-1}{2} \\ \nu+1,\ \frac{1-s+\nu}{2},\ \frac{2-s+\nu}{2};\ -\frac{b^2}{4a^2} \end{array}\right)$ $[a,\ b > 0;\ \operatorname{Re}\lambda > -1/2;\ \operatorname{Re}(s+2\lambda-\nu) < 1 - 2n - \varepsilon]$
5	$J_\nu(b\sqrt{x})\, C_n^\lambda\left(\dfrac{x \pm a}{a}\right)$	$\dfrac{2^{2s+3n}}{a^n b^{2s+2n}\, n!}\,(\lambda)_n\, \Gamma\left[\begin{array}{c} \frac{2s+2n+\nu}{2} \\ \frac{2-2s-2n+\nu}{2} \end{array}\right]$ $\times {}_2F_3\left(\begin{array}{c} -n,\ \frac{1}{2}-n-\lambda;\ \pm\frac{ab^2}{2} \\ 1-2n-2\lambda,\ \frac{2-2s-2n-\nu}{2},\ \frac{2-2s-2n+\nu}{2} \end{array}\right)$ $[b > 0;\ \operatorname{Re}\lambda > -1/2;\ -\operatorname{Re}\nu/2 < \operatorname{Re} s < 3/4 - n]$
6	$K_\nu(b\sqrt{x})\, C_n^\lambda\left(\dfrac{x \pm a}{a}\right)$	$\dfrac{2^{2s+3n-1}}{a^n b^{2s+2n}\, n!}\,(\lambda)_n\, \Gamma\left(s+n-\dfrac{\nu}{2}\right)\Gamma\left(s+n+\dfrac{\nu}{2}\right)$ $\times {}_2F_3\left(\begin{array}{c} -n,\ \frac{1}{2}-n-\lambda;\ \mp\frac{ab^2}{2} \\ 1-2n-2\lambda,\ \frac{2-2s-2n-\nu}{2},\ \frac{2-2s-2n+\nu}{2} \end{array}\right)$ $[b > 0;\ \operatorname{Re} s > |\operatorname{Re}\nu|/2]$

No.	$f(x)$	$F(s)$

7 $J_\nu\left(\dfrac{b}{\sqrt{x}}\right) C_n^\lambda\left(\dfrac{x \pm a}{a}\right)$

$$\frac{(\pm 1)^n}{n!}\left(\frac{b}{2}\right)^{2s}(2\lambda)_n \Gamma\left[\begin{array}{c}\frac{\nu-2s}{2}\\ \frac{2s+\nu+2}{2}\end{array}\right]\, {}_2F_3\left(\begin{array}{c}-n,\ n+2\lambda;\ \pm\frac{b^2}{8a}\\ \frac{2\lambda+1}{2},\ \frac{2s-\nu+2}{2},\ \frac{2s+\nu+2}{2}\end{array}\right)$$

$$[b>0;\ \operatorname{Re}\lambda > -1/2;\ -3/4 < \operatorname{Re}s < \operatorname{Re}\nu/2 - n]$$

8 $K_\nu\left(\dfrac{b}{\sqrt{x}}\right) C_n^\lambda\left(\dfrac{x \pm a}{a}\right)$

$$\frac{(\pm 1)^n}{2(n!)}\left(\frac{b}{2}\right)^{2s}(2\lambda)_n\, \Gamma\left(\frac{\nu-2s}{2}\right)\Gamma\left(\frac{-\nu-2s}{2}\right)$$

$$\times\, {}_2F_3\left(\begin{array}{c}-n,\ n+2\lambda;\ \mp\frac{b^2}{8a}\\ \frac{2\lambda+1}{2},\ \frac{2s-\nu+2}{2},\ \frac{2s+\nu+2}{2}\end{array}\right)$$

$$[\operatorname{Re}b>0;\ \operatorname{Re}s < -n - |\operatorname{Re}\nu|/2]$$

9 $(x+a)^n K_\nu(b\sqrt{x})$

    $\times\, C_n^\lambda\left(\dfrac{a-x}{a+x}\right)$

$$\frac{(-1)^n 2^{2s+2n-1} b^{-2s-2n}}{n!}\,(2\lambda)_n\, \Gamma\left(s+n-\frac{\nu}{2}\right)\Gamma\left(s+n+\frac{\nu}{2}\right)$$

$$\times\, {}_2F_3\left(\begin{array}{c}-n,\ \frac{1-2n-2\lambda}{2};\ -\frac{ab^2}{4}\\ \frac{2\lambda+1}{2},\ \frac{2-2s-2n-\nu}{2},\ \frac{2-2s-2n+\nu}{2}\end{array}\right)$$

$$[\operatorname{Re}b>0;\ \operatorname{Re}s > |\operatorname{Re}\nu|/2]$$

10 $(x+a)^{\lambda-1/2} K_\nu(b\sqrt{x})$

    $\times\, C_n^\lambda\left(\dfrac{2x}{a}+1\right)$

$$\frac{(-1)^n a^{s+\lambda-(\nu+1)/2} b^{-\nu}}{2^{-\nu+1} n!}\,(2\lambda)_n\left(\frac{1-2s+2\lambda+\nu}{2}\right)_n$$

$$\times\, \Gamma\left[\begin{array}{c}\frac{2s-\nu}{2},\ \frac{1-2s-2n-2\lambda+\nu}{2}\\ \frac{1-2\lambda}{2}\end{array}\right]$$

$$\times\, {}_2F_3\left(\begin{array}{c}\frac{2s-\nu}{2},\ \frac{2s-2\lambda-\nu+1}{2};\ -\frac{ab^2}{4}\\ 1-\nu,\ \frac{s-2n-2\lambda-\nu+1}{2},\ \frac{s+2n+2\lambda-\nu+1}{2}\end{array}\right)$$

$$+\ \frac{(-1)^n a^{s+\lambda+(\nu-1)/2} b^\nu}{2^{\nu+1} n!}\,(2\lambda)_n\left(\frac{1-2s+2\lambda-\nu}{2}\right)_n$$

$$\times\, \Gamma\left[\begin{array}{c}\frac{2s+\nu}{2},\ \frac{1-2s-2n-2\lambda-\nu}{2}\\ \frac{1-2\lambda}{2}\end{array}\right]$$

$$\times\, {}_2F_3\left(\begin{array}{c}\frac{2s+\nu}{2},\ \frac{2s-2\lambda+\nu+1}{2};\ -\frac{ab^2}{4}\\ \nu+1,\ \frac{s-2n-2\lambda+\nu+1}{2},\ \frac{s+2n+2\lambda+\nu+1}{2}\end{array}\right)$$

$$+\ \frac{2^{2s+4n+2\lambda-2}}{n!\, a^n b^{2s+2n+2\lambda-1}}\,(\lambda)_n$$

$$\times\, \Gamma\left(\frac{2s+2n+2\lambda-\nu-1}{2}\right)\Gamma\left(\frac{2s+2n+2\lambda+\nu-1}{2}\right)$$

$$\times\, {}_2F_3\left(\begin{array}{c}\frac{-2n-2\lambda+1}{2},\ -n-2\lambda+1;\ -\frac{ab^2}{4}\\ 1-2n-2\lambda,\ \frac{3-2s-2n-2\lambda-\nu}{2},\ \frac{3-2s-2n-2\lambda+\nu}{2}\end{array}\right)$$

$$[\operatorname{Re}b>0;\ \operatorname{Re}s > |\operatorname{Re}\nu|/2;\ |\arg a| < \pi]$$

No.	$f(x)$	$F(s)$
11	$(a-x)_+^{\lambda-1/2} K_\nu\left(b\sqrt{x}\right)$ $\times C_n^\lambda\left(1-\dfrac{2x}{a}\right)$	$\dfrac{a^{s+\lambda-(\nu+1)/2}b^{-\nu}}{2^{-\nu+1}n!}(2\lambda)_n\left(\dfrac{1-2s+2\lambda+\nu}{2}\right)_n$ $\times\Gamma\left[\begin{matrix}\frac{2\lambda+1}{2},\ \nu,\ \frac{2s-\nu}{2}\\ \frac{2s+2n+2\lambda-\nu+1}{2}\end{matrix}\right]{}_2F_3\left(\begin{matrix}\frac{2s-\nu}{2},\ \frac{2s-2\lambda-\nu+1}{2};\ \frac{ab^2}{4}\\ 1-\nu,\ \frac{2s-2n-2\lambda-\nu+1}{2},\ \frac{2s+2n+2\lambda-\nu+1}{2}\end{matrix}\right)$ $+\dfrac{a^{s+\lambda+(\nu-1)/2}b^\nu}{2^{\nu+1}n!}(2\lambda)_n\left(\dfrac{1-2s+2\lambda-\nu}{2}\right)_n$ $\times\Gamma\left[\begin{matrix}\frac{2\lambda+1}{2},\ -\nu,\ \frac{2s+\nu}{2}\\ \frac{2s+2n+2\lambda+\nu+1}{2}\end{matrix}\right]{}_2F_3\left(\begin{matrix}\frac{2s+\nu}{2},\ \frac{2s-2\lambda+\nu+1}{2};\ \frac{ab^2}{4}\\ \nu+1,\ \frac{2s-2n-2\lambda+\nu+1}{2},\ \frac{2s+2n+2\lambda+\nu+1}{2}\end{matrix}\right)$ $[a>0;\ \operatorname{Re}\lambda>-1/2;\ \operatorname{Re}s>|\operatorname{Re}\nu|/2]$
12	$(x+a)^{\lambda-1/2} K_\nu\left(\dfrac{b}{\sqrt{x}}\right)$ $\times C_n^\lambda\left(\dfrac{2x}{a}+1\right)$	$\dfrac{a^{\lambda-1/2}b^{2s}}{2^{2s+1}n!}(2\lambda)_n\,\Gamma\left(-s-\dfrac{\nu}{2}\right)\Gamma\left(-s+\dfrac{\nu}{2}\right)$ $\times{}_2F_3\left(\begin{matrix}\frac{-2n-2\lambda+1}{2},\ \frac{2n+2\lambda+1}{2};\ -\frac{b^2}{4a}\\ \frac{2\lambda+1}{2},\ \frac{2s-\nu+2}{2},\ \frac{2s+\nu+2}{2}\end{matrix}\right)$ $+\dfrac{(-1)^n\,a^{s+\lambda+(\nu-1)/2}b^{-\nu}}{2^{-\nu+1}n!}(2\lambda)_n\left(\dfrac{1-2s+2\lambda-\nu}{2}\right)_n$ $\times\Gamma\left[\begin{matrix}\nu,\ \frac{2s+\nu}{2},\ \frac{1-2s-2n-2\lambda-\nu}{2}\\ \frac{1-2\lambda}{2}\end{matrix}\right]$ $\times{}_2F_3\left(\begin{matrix}\frac{1-2s+2n+2\lambda-\nu}{2},\ \frac{1-2s-2n-2\lambda-\nu}{2}\\ 1-\nu,\ \frac{2-2s-\nu}{2},\ \frac{1-2s+2\lambda-\nu}{2};\ -\frac{b^2}{4a}\end{matrix}\right)$ $+\dfrac{(-1)^n\,a^{s+\lambda-(\nu+1)/2}b^\nu}{2^{\nu+1}n!}(2\lambda)_n\left(\dfrac{1-2s+2\lambda+\nu}{2}\right)_n$ $\times\Gamma\left[\begin{matrix}-\nu,\ \frac{2s-\nu}{2},\ \frac{1-2s-2n-2\lambda+\nu}{2}\\ \frac{1-2\lambda}{2}\end{matrix}\right]$ $\times{}_2F_3\left(\begin{matrix}\frac{1-2s+2n+2\lambda+\nu}{2},\ \frac{1-2s-2n-2\lambda+\nu}{2}\\ \nu+1,\ \frac{2-2s+\nu}{2},\ \frac{1-2s+2\lambda+\nu}{2};\ -\frac{b^2}{4a}\end{matrix}\right)$ $[\operatorname{Re}b>0;\ \operatorname{Re}s<(1-2n-2\operatorname{Re}\lambda-|\operatorname{Re}\nu|)/2;\ |\arg a|<\pi]$
13	$(a-x)_+^{\lambda-1/2}$ $\times\left\{\begin{matrix}J_\nu\left(b\sqrt{x}\right)\\ I_\nu\left(b\sqrt{x}\right)\end{matrix}\right\}$ $\times C_n^\lambda\left(\dfrac{2x}{a}-1\right)$	$\dfrac{(-1)^n\,a^{s+\lambda+(\nu-1)/2}b^\nu}{2^\nu n!}(2\lambda)_n\left(\dfrac{1-2s+2\lambda-\nu}{2}\right)_n$ $\times\Gamma\left[\begin{matrix}\frac{2\lambda+1}{2},\ \frac{2s+\nu}{2}\\ \nu+1,\ \frac{2s+2n+2\lambda+\nu+1}{2}\end{matrix}\right]$ $\times{}_2F_3\left(\begin{matrix}\frac{2s+\nu}{2},\ \frac{2s-2\lambda+\nu+1}{2};\ \mp\frac{ab^2}{4}\\ \nu+1,\ \frac{2s-2n-2\lambda+\nu+1}{2},\ \frac{2s+2n+2\lambda+\nu+1}{2}\end{matrix}\right)$ $[a>0;\ \operatorname{Re}\lambda>-1/2;\ \operatorname{Re}s>-\operatorname{Re}\nu/2]$

No.	$f(x)$	$F(s)$

14 $(x+a)^{\lambda-1/2} J_\nu(b\sqrt{x})$

$\times C_n^\lambda\left(\dfrac{2x}{a}+1\right)$

$$\frac{(-1)^n\,a^{s+\lambda+(\nu-1)/2}b^\nu}{2^\nu n!}\,(2\lambda)_n\left(\frac{1-2s+2\lambda-\nu}{2}\right)_n$$

$$\times\Gamma\left[\begin{array}{c}\frac{2s+\nu}{2},\ \frac{1-2s-2n-2\lambda-\nu}{2}\\[2pt]\frac{1-2\lambda}{2},\ \nu+1\end{array}\right]$$

$$\times\,{}_2F_3\left(\begin{array}{c}\frac{2s+\nu}{2},\ \frac{2s-2\lambda+\nu+1}{2};\ \frac{ab^2}{4}\\[2pt]\nu+1,\ \frac{2s-2n-2\lambda+\nu+1}{2},\ \frac{2s+2n+2\lambda+\nu+1}{2}\end{array}\right)$$

$$+\frac{2^{2s+4n+2\lambda-1}}{n!\,a^n b^{2s+2n+2\lambda-1}}\,(\lambda)_n\,\Gamma\left[\begin{array}{c}\frac{2s+2n+2\lambda+\nu-1}{2}\\[2pt]\frac{3-2s-2n-2\lambda+\nu}{2}\end{array}\right]$$

$$\times\,{}_2F_3\left(\begin{array}{c}\frac{1-2n-2\lambda}{2},\ 1-n-2\lambda;\ \frac{ab^2}{4}\\[2pt]1-2n-2\lambda,\ \frac{3-2s-2n-2\lambda-\nu}{2},\ \frac{3-2s-2n-2\lambda+\nu}{2}\end{array}\right)$$

$$[b>0;\ -\operatorname{Re}\nu/2<\operatorname{Re}s<5/4-n-\operatorname{Re}\lambda;\ |\arg a|<\pi]$$

15 $(a-x)_+^{\lambda-1/2} J_\nu\left(\dfrac{b}{\sqrt{x}}\right)$

$\times C_n^\lambda\left(\dfrac{2x}{a}-1\right)$

$$\frac{(-1)^n\,a^{s+\lambda-(\nu+1)/2}b^\nu}{2^\nu n!}\,(2\lambda)_n\left(\frac{1-2s+2\lambda+\nu}{2}\right)_n$$

$$\times\Gamma\left[\begin{array}{c}\frac{2\lambda+1}{2},\ \frac{2s-\nu}{2}\\[2pt]\nu+1,\ \frac{2s+2n+2\lambda-\nu+1}{2}\end{array}\right]{}_2F_3\left(\begin{array}{c}\frac{1-2s-2n-2\lambda+\nu}{2},\ \frac{1-2s+2n+2\lambda+\nu}{2}\\[2pt]\nu+1,\ \frac{2-2s+\nu}{2},\ \frac{1-2s+2\lambda+\nu}{2};\ -\frac{b^2}{4a}\end{array}\right)$$

$$+\frac{(-1)^n\,a^{\lambda-1/2}b^{2s}}{2^{2s}n!}\,(2\lambda)_n\,\Gamma\left[\begin{array}{c}\frac{\nu-2s}{2}\\[2pt]\frac{2s+\nu+2}{2}\end{array}\right]$$

$$\times\,{}_2F_3\left(\begin{array}{c}\frac{-2n-2\lambda+1}{2},\ \frac{2n+2\lambda+1}{2};\ -\frac{b^2}{4a}\\[2pt]\frac{2\lambda+1}{2},\ \frac{2s-\nu+2}{2},\ \frac{2s+\nu+2}{2}\end{array}\right)$$

$$[a>0;\ \operatorname{Re}\lambda>-1/2;\ \operatorname{Re}s>-3/4]$$

16 $(x+a)^{\lambda-1/2} J_\nu\left(\dfrac{b}{\sqrt{x}}\right)$

$\times C_n^\lambda\left(\dfrac{2x}{a}+1\right)$

$$\frac{(-1)^n\,a^{s+\lambda-(\nu+1)/2}b^\nu}{2^\nu n!}\,(2\lambda)_n\left(\frac{1-2s+2\lambda+\nu}{2}\right)_n$$

$$\times\Gamma\left[\begin{array}{c}\frac{2s-\nu}{2},\ \frac{1-2s-2n-2\lambda+\nu}{2}\\[2pt]\frac{1-2\lambda}{2},\ \nu+1\end{array}\right]$$

$$\times\,{}_2F_3\left(\begin{array}{c}\frac{1-2s-2n-2\lambda+\nu}{2},\ \frac{1-2s+2n+2\lambda+\nu}{2}\\[2pt]\nu+1,\ \frac{2-2s+\nu}{2},\ \frac{1-2s+2\lambda+\nu}{2};\ \frac{b^2}{4a}\end{array}\right)+\frac{a^{\lambda-1/2}b^{2s}}{2^{2s}n!}$$

$$\times(2\lambda)_n\,\Gamma\left[\begin{array}{c}\frac{\nu-2s}{2}\\[2pt]\frac{2s+\nu+2}{2}\end{array}\right]{}_2F_3\left(\begin{array}{c}\frac{-2n-2\lambda+1}{2},\ \frac{2n+2\lambda+1}{2};\ \frac{b^2}{4a}\\[2pt]\frac{2\lambda+1}{2},\ \frac{2s-\nu+2}{2},\ \frac{2s+\nu+2}{2}\end{array}\right)$$

$$[b>0;\ -3/4<\operatorname{Re}s<1/2-n+\operatorname{Re}(\nu/2-\lambda);\ |\arg a|<\pi]$$

17 $(x+a)^n J_\nu(b\sqrt{x})$

$\times C_n^\lambda\left(\dfrac{a-x}{a+x}\right)$

$$\frac{(-1)^n}{n!}\left(\frac{2}{b}\right)^{2s+2n}(2\lambda)_n\,\Gamma\left[\begin{array}{c}\frac{2s+2n+\nu}{2}\\[2pt]\frac{2-2s-2n+\nu}{2}\end{array}\right]$$

$$\times\,{}_2F_3\left(\begin{array}{c}-n,\ \frac{-2n-2\lambda+1}{2};\ \frac{ab^2}{4}\\[2pt]\frac{2\lambda+1}{2},\ \frac{2-2s-2n-\nu}{2},\ \frac{2-2s-2n+\nu}{2}\end{array}\right)$$

$$[b>0;\ -\operatorname{Re}\nu/2<\operatorname{Re}s<3/4-n]$$

No.	$f(x)$	$F(s)$
18	$(x+a)^{-n-2\lambda} J_\nu(b\sqrt{x})$ $\times C_n^\lambda\left(\dfrac{a-x}{a+x}\right)$	$\dfrac{a^{s-n-2\lambda+\nu/2}b^\nu}{2^\nu n!} \dfrac{\left(\frac{1-2s+2\lambda-\nu}{2}\right)_n}{\left(\frac{2\lambda+1}{2}\right)_n} \Gamma\begin{bmatrix} \frac{2s+\nu}{2},\ \frac{2n-2s+4\lambda-\nu}{2} \\ 2\lambda,\ \nu+1 \end{bmatrix}$ $\times {}_2F_3\left(\begin{matrix} \frac{2s-2\lambda+\nu+1}{2},\ \frac{2s+\nu}{2};\ \frac{ab^2}{4} \\ \nu+1,\ \frac{2s-2n-2\lambda+\nu+1}{2},\ \frac{2s-2n-4\lambda+\nu+2}{2} \end{matrix}\right)$ $+\dfrac{(-1)^n}{n!}\left(\dfrac{b}{2}\right)^{2(n-s+2\lambda)}(2\lambda)_n\,\Gamma\begin{bmatrix} \frac{2s-2n-4\lambda+\nu}{2} \\ \frac{2-2s+2n+4\lambda+\nu}{2} \end{bmatrix}$ $\times {}_2F_3\left(\begin{matrix} n+2\lambda,\ \frac{2n+2\lambda+1}{2};\ \frac{ab^2}{4} \\ \frac{2\lambda+1}{2},\ \frac{2-2s+2n+4\lambda-\nu}{2},\ \frac{2-2s+2n+4\lambda+\nu}{2} \end{matrix}\right)$ $[b>0;\ -\operatorname{Re}\nu/2 < \operatorname{Re}s < n+2\operatorname{Re}\lambda+3/4]$
19	$(a-x)_+^{\lambda-1/2}$ $\times \left\{\begin{matrix} J_\mu(b\sqrt{x})\,J_\nu(b\sqrt{x}) \\ I_\mu(b\sqrt{x})\,I_\nu(b\sqrt{x}) \end{matrix}\right\}$ $\times C_n^\lambda\left(1-\dfrac{2x}{a}\right)$	$\dfrac{a^{s+(2\lambda+\mu+\nu-1)/2}(b/2)^{\mu+\nu}}{n!}(2\lambda)_n\left(\dfrac{1-2s+2\lambda-\mu-\nu}{2}\right)_n$ $\times \Gamma\begin{bmatrix} \frac{2\lambda+1}{2},\ \frac{2s+\mu+\nu}{2} \\ \mu+1,\ \nu+1,\ \frac{2s+2n+2\lambda+\mu+\nu+1}{2} \end{bmatrix} {}_4F_5\left(\begin{matrix} \frac{\mu+\nu+1}{2},\ \frac{\mu+\nu+2}{2},\ \frac{2s+\mu+\nu}{2}, \\ \mu+1,\ \nu+1,\ \mu+\nu+1, \end{matrix}\right.$ $\left.\begin{matrix} \frac{2s-2\lambda+\mu+\nu+1}{2};\ \mp ab^2 \\ \frac{2s-2n-2\lambda+\mu+\nu+1}{2},\ \frac{2s+2n+2\lambda+\mu+\nu+1}{2} \end{matrix}\right)$ $[a,\ \operatorname{Re}(2s+\mu+\nu)>0;\ \operatorname{Re}\lambda>-1/2]$

3.24.12. $C_n^\lambda(bx)$ and $\mathbf{H}_\nu(ax)$, $\mathbf{L}_\nu(ax)$

No.	$f(x)$	$F(s)$
1	$(a^2-x^2)_+^{\lambda-1/2}$ $\times \left\{\begin{matrix} \mathbf{H}_\nu(bx) \\ \mathbf{L}_\nu(bx) \end{matrix}\right\} C_n^\lambda\left(\dfrac{x}{a}\right)$	$\dfrac{\sqrt{\pi}}{2^\nu n!}\left(\dfrac{a}{2}\right)^{s+\nu+2\lambda}b^{\nu+1}\Gamma\begin{bmatrix} s+\nu+1,\ n+2\lambda \\ \lambda,\ \frac{2\nu+3}{2},\ \frac{s-n+\nu+2}{2},\ \frac{s+n+\nu+2\lambda+2}{2} \end{bmatrix}$ $\times {}_3F_3\left(\begin{matrix} 1,\ \frac{s+\nu+1}{2},\ \frac{s+\nu+2}{2};\ \mp\frac{a^2b^2}{4} \\ \frac{3}{2},\ \frac{s+n+\nu+2\lambda+2}{2},\ \frac{3s-3n+7\nu+6}{2} \end{matrix}\right)$ $[a>0;\ \operatorname{Re}\lambda>-1/2;\ \operatorname{Re}(s+\nu)>-1]$

3.24.13. $C_n^\lambda(ax+b)$ and $P_m(cx^r+d)$

Notation: $\varepsilon,\ \delta = 0$ or 1.

No.	$f(x)$	$F(s)$
1	$\theta(a-x)P_m\left(\dfrac{x}{a}\right)$ $\times C_{2n+\varepsilon}^\lambda(bx)$	$\dfrac{(-1)^n\sqrt{\pi}}{n!}\left(\dfrac{a}{2}\right)^{s+\varepsilon}(2b)^\varepsilon(\lambda)_{n+\varepsilon}\,\Gamma\begin{bmatrix} s+\varepsilon \\ \frac{s-m+\varepsilon+1}{2},\ \frac{s+m+\varepsilon+2}{2} \end{bmatrix}$ $\times {}_4F_3\left(\begin{matrix} -n,\ n+\lambda+\varepsilon,\ \frac{s+\varepsilon}{2},\ \frac{s+\varepsilon+1}{2};\ a^2b^2 \\ \frac{2\varepsilon+1}{2},\ \frac{s-m+\varepsilon+1}{2},\ \frac{s+m+\varepsilon+2}{2} \end{matrix}\right)$ $[a>0;\ \operatorname{Re}s>((-1)^m-2\varepsilon-1)/2]$

No.	$f(x)$	$F(s)$
2	$(a^2 - x^2)_+^{\lambda-1/2}$ $\times P_{2m+\varepsilon}\left(\dfrac{x}{b}\right) C_{2n+\delta}^\lambda\left(\dfrac{x}{a}\right)$	$\dfrac{(-1)^{m+n} 2^{\varepsilon-1} a^{s+2\lambda+\varepsilon-1}}{m!\,(2n+\delta)!\,b^\varepsilon}\,(2\lambda)_{2n+\delta}\left(\dfrac{1}{2}\right)_{m+\varepsilon}\left(\dfrac{1-s+\delta-\varepsilon}{2}\right)_n$ $\times \Gamma\left[\begin{matrix}\frac{2\lambda+1}{2},\ \frac{s+\delta+\varepsilon}{2} \\ \frac{s+2n+2\lambda+\delta+\varepsilon+1}{2}\end{matrix}\right]{}_4F_3\left(\begin{matrix}-m,\ \frac{2m+2\varepsilon+1}{2},\ \frac{s+1}{2},\ \frac{s+2\varepsilon}{2};\ \frac{a^2}{b^2} \\ \frac{2\varepsilon+1}{2},\ \frac{s-2n-\delta+\varepsilon+1}{2},\ \frac{s+2n+2\lambda+\delta+\varepsilon+1}{2}\end{matrix}\right)$ $[b > a > 0;\ \operatorname{Re}\lambda > -1/2;\ \operatorname{Re} s > -\delta-\varepsilon]$
3	$\theta(a-x)(b^2-x^2)^{\lambda-1/2}$ $\times P_{2m+\varepsilon}\left(\dfrac{x}{a}\right) C_{2n+\delta}^\lambda\left(\dfrac{x}{b}\right)$	$\dfrac{(-1)^{m+n} 2^{\delta-1} a^{s+\delta} b^{2\lambda-\delta-1}}{n!\left(\frac{s+\delta+\varepsilon}{2}\right)_{m+1}}\,(\lambda)_{n+\delta}\left(\dfrac{1-s-\delta+\varepsilon}{2}\right)_m$ $\times {}_4F_3\left(\begin{matrix}\frac{1-2n-2\lambda}{2},\ \frac{2n+2\delta+1}{2},\ \frac{s+1}{2},\ \frac{s+2\delta}{2};\ \frac{a^2}{b^2} \\ \frac{2\delta+1}{2},\ \frac{s-2m+\delta-\varepsilon+1}{2},\ \frac{s+2m+\delta+\varepsilon+2}{2}\end{matrix}\right)$ $[b > a > 0;\ \operatorname{Re}\lambda > -1/2;\ \operatorname{Re} s > -\delta-\varepsilon]$
4	$\theta(x-a)(x^2-b^2)^{\lambda-1/2}$ $\times P_{2m+\varepsilon}\left(\dfrac{x}{a}\right) C_{2n+\delta}^\lambda\left(\dfrac{x}{b}\right)$	$\dfrac{(-1)^{m-1} 2^{2n+\delta-1} a^{s+2n+2\lambda+\delta-1}}{(2n+\delta)!\,b^{2n+\delta}}\,\dfrac{(\lambda)_{2n+\delta}\left(\frac{2-s-2n-2\lambda-\delta+\varepsilon}{2}\right)_m}{\left(\frac{s+2n+2\lambda+\delta+\varepsilon-1}{2}\right)_{m+1}}$ $\times {}_4F_3\left(\begin{matrix}\frac{1-2n-2\lambda}{2},\ 1-n-\lambda-\delta,\ \frac{2-s+2m-2n-2\lambda-\delta+\varepsilon}{2}, \\ 1-2n-\lambda-\delta,\ \frac{2-s-2n-2\lambda}{2},\end{matrix}\right.$ $\left.\begin{matrix}\frac{1-s-2m-2n-2\lambda-\delta-\varepsilon}{2} \\ \frac{3-s-2n-2\lambda-2\delta}{2};\ \frac{b^2}{a^2}\end{matrix}\right)$ $[a > b > 0;\ \operatorname{Re}(s+2\lambda) < 1 - 2m - 2n - \delta - \varepsilon]$
5	$(x^2 - a^2)_+^{\lambda-1/2}$ $\times P_{2m+\varepsilon}\left(\dfrac{x}{b}\right) C_{2n+\delta}^\lambda\left(\dfrac{x}{a}\right)$	$\dfrac{2^{2m+\varepsilon-1} a^{s+2m+2\lambda+\varepsilon-1}}{(2m+\varepsilon)!\,(2n+\delta)!\,b^{2m+\varepsilon}}\,(2\lambda)_{2n+\delta}\left(\dfrac{1}{2}\right)_{2m+\varepsilon}$ $\times\left(\dfrac{1-s-2m+\delta-\varepsilon}{2}\right)_n\Gamma\left[\begin{matrix}\frac{2\lambda+1}{2},\ \frac{1-s-2m-2n-2\lambda-\delta-\varepsilon}{2} \\ \frac{2-s-2m-\delta-\varepsilon}{2}\end{matrix}\right]$ $\times {}_4F_3\left(\begin{matrix}-m,\ \frac{1-2m-2\varepsilon}{2},\ \frac{1-s-2m+2n+\delta-\varepsilon}{2},\ \frac{1-s-2m-2n-2\lambda-\delta-\varepsilon}{2} \\ \frac{1-4m-2\varepsilon}{2},\ \frac{2-s-2m-2\varepsilon}{2},\ \frac{1-s-2m}{2};\ \frac{b^2}{a^2}\end{matrix}\right)$ $\begin{bmatrix} a > b > 0;\ \operatorname{Re}\lambda > -1/2; \\ \operatorname{Re}(s+2\lambda) < 1 - 2m - 2n - \delta - \varepsilon\end{bmatrix}$
6	$\theta(a-x) P_m\left(\dfrac{2x}{a}-1\right)$ $\times C_n^\lambda\left(\dfrac{2x}{a}-1\right)$	$\dfrac{(-1)^{m+n}(2\lambda)_n(1-s)_m\,a^s}{n!\,(s)_{m+1}}\,{}_4F_3\left(\begin{matrix}-n,\ n+2\lambda,\ s,\ s;\ 1 \\ \frac{2\lambda+1}{2},\ s-m,\ s+m+1\end{matrix}\right)$ $[a,\ \operatorname{Re} s > 0]$
7	$(a-x)_+^{\lambda-1/2} P_m\left(1-\dfrac{2x}{a}\right)$ $\times C_n^\lambda\left(1-\dfrac{2x}{a}\right)$	$\dfrac{a^{s+\lambda-1/2}}{n!}\,(2\lambda)_n\left(\dfrac{1-2s+2\lambda}{2}\right)_n\Gamma\left[\begin{matrix}\frac{2\lambda+1}{2},\ s \\ \frac{2s+2n+2\lambda+1}{2}\end{matrix}\right]$ $\times {}_4F_3\left(\begin{matrix}-m,\ m+1,\ \frac{2s-2\lambda+1}{2},\ s;\ 1 \\ 1,\ \frac{2s-2n-2\lambda+1}{2},\ \frac{2s+2n+2\lambda+1}{2}\end{matrix}\right)$ $[a,\ \operatorname{Re} s > 0;\ \operatorname{Re}\lambda > -1/2]$

No.	$f(x)$	$F(s)$
8	$(a-x)_+^{\lambda-1/2} P_m(2bx-1)$ $\times C_n^\lambda\left(\dfrac{2x}{a}-1\right)$	$\dfrac{(-1)^{m+n} a^{s+\lambda-1/2}}{n!}(2\lambda)_n\left(\dfrac{1-2s+2\lambda}{2}\right)_n$ $\times \Gamma\left[\begin{matrix}\frac{2\lambda+1}{2},\,s\\\frac{2s+2n+2\lambda+1}{2}\end{matrix}\right]{}_4F_3\left(\begin{matrix}-m,\,m+1,\,s,\,\frac{2s-2\lambda+1}{2};\,ab\\1,\,\frac{2s-2n-2\lambda+1}{2},\,\frac{2s+2n+2\lambda+1}{2}\end{matrix}\right)$ $[a,\,\operatorname{Re}s>0;\,\operatorname{Re}\lambda>-1/2]$
9	$\theta(a-x)(b\pm x)^{\lambda-1/2}$ $\times P_m\left(\dfrac{2x}{a}-1\right)$ $\times C_n^\lambda\left(\dfrac{2x}{b}\pm 1\right)$	$\dfrac{(-1)^m(\pm 1)^n a^s b^{\lambda-1/2}}{n!}\dfrac{(2\lambda)_n(1-s)_m}{(s)_{m+1}}$ $\times {}_4F_3\left(\begin{matrix}\frac{-2n-2\lambda+1}{2},\,\frac{2n+2\lambda+1}{2},\,s,\,s\\\frac{2\lambda+1}{2},\,s-m,\,s+m+1;\,\mp\frac{a}{b}\end{matrix}\right)$ $[a,\,b,\,\operatorname{Re}s>0]$
10	$(a-x)_+^{\lambda-1/2}P_{2m+\varepsilon}(b\sqrt{x})$ $\times C_n^\lambda\left(\dfrac{2x}{a}-1\right)$	$\dfrac{(-1)^{m+n}a^{s+\lambda+(\varepsilon-1)/2}(2b)^\varepsilon}{m!\,n!}\left(\dfrac{1}{2}\right)_{m+\varepsilon}(2\lambda)_n$ $\times\left(\dfrac{1-2s+2\lambda-\varepsilon}{2}\right)_n\Gamma\left[\begin{matrix}\frac{2\lambda+1}{2},\,\frac{2s+\varepsilon}{2}\\\frac{2s+2n+2\lambda+\varepsilon+1}{2}\end{matrix}\right]$ $\times{}_4F_3\left(\begin{matrix}-m,\,\frac{2m+2\varepsilon+1}{2},\,\frac{2s+\varepsilon}{2},\,\frac{2s-2\lambda+\varepsilon+1}{2};\,ab^2\\\frac{2\varepsilon+1}{2},\,\frac{2s-2n-2\lambda+\varepsilon+1}{2},\,\frac{2s+2n+2\lambda+\varepsilon+1}{2}\end{matrix}\right)$ $[a>0;\,\operatorname{Re}\lambda>-1/2;\,\operatorname{Re}s>-\varepsilon/2]$

3.24.14. $\quad C_n^\lambda(bx)$ **and** $H_m(ax)$

Notation: $\delta,\,\varepsilon=0$ or 1.

No.	$f(x)$	$F(s)$
1	$(a^2-x^2)_+^{\lambda-1/2}$ $\times H_{2m+\varepsilon}(bx)C_n^\lambda\left(\dfrac{x}{a}\right)$	$\dfrac{(-1)^m\pi a^{s+2\lambda+\varepsilon-1}b^\varepsilon}{n!\,2^{s+2\lambda-2m-1}}\left(\dfrac{2\varepsilon+1}{2}\right)_m\Gamma\left[\begin{matrix}s+\varepsilon,\,n+2\lambda\\\lambda,\,\frac{s-n+\varepsilon+1}{2},\,\frac{s+2\lambda+n+\varepsilon+1}{2}\end{matrix}\right]$ $\times{}_3F_3\left(\begin{matrix}-m,\,\frac{s+\varepsilon}{2},\,\frac{s+\varepsilon+1}{2};\,a^2b^2\\\frac{2\varepsilon+1}{2},\,\frac{s-n+\varepsilon+1}{2},\,\frac{s+2\lambda+n+\varepsilon+1}{2}\end{matrix}\right)$ $[a>0;\,\operatorname{Re}\lambda>-1/2;\,\operatorname{Re}s>((-1)^n-2\varepsilon-1)/2]$
2	$(a^2-x^2)_+^{\lambda-1/2}e^{-b^2x^2}$ $\times H_{2m+\varepsilon}(bx)C_n^\lambda\left(\dfrac{x}{a}\right)$	$\dfrac{(-1)^m\pi a^{s+2\lambda+\varepsilon-1}b^\varepsilon}{n!\,2^{s+2\lambda-2m-1}}\left(\dfrac{2\varepsilon+1}{2}\right)_m$ $\times\Gamma\left[\begin{matrix}s+\varepsilon,\,n+2\lambda\\\lambda,\,\frac{s-n+\varepsilon+1}{2},\,\frac{s+2\lambda+n+\varepsilon+1}{2}\end{matrix}\right]$ $\times{}_3F_3\left(\begin{matrix}\frac{2m+2\varepsilon+1}{2},\,\frac{s+\varepsilon}{2},\,\frac{s+\varepsilon+1}{2};\,-a^2b^2\\\frac{2\varepsilon+1}{2},\,\frac{s-n+\varepsilon+1}{2},\,\frac{s+2\lambda+n+\varepsilon+1}{2}\end{matrix}\right)$ $[a>0;\,\operatorname{Re}\lambda>-1/2;\,\operatorname{Re}s>((-1)^n-2\varepsilon-1)/2]$

No.	$f(x)$	$F(s)$
3	$\left(x^2 - a^2\right)_+^{\lambda-1/2} e^{-b^2 x^2}$ $\times H_{2m+\varepsilon}(bx)$ $\times C_{2n+\delta}^\lambda \left(\dfrac{x}{a}\right)$	$(-1)^m \dfrac{2^{2m+2\varepsilon-1} a^{s+2\lambda+\varepsilon-1} b^\varepsilon}{(2n+\delta)!} \left(\dfrac{1}{2}\right)_{m+\varepsilon} (2\lambda)_{2n+\delta}$ $\times \left(\dfrac{1-s+\delta-\varepsilon}{2}\right)_n \Gamma\left[\begin{array}{c}\frac{2\lambda+1}{2},\ \frac{1-s-2n-2\lambda-\delta-\varepsilon}{2} \\ \frac{2-s-\delta-\varepsilon}{2}\end{array}\right]$ $\times {}_3F_3\left(\begin{array}{c}\frac{2\varepsilon+2m+1}{2},\ \frac{s+2\varepsilon}{2},\ \frac{s+1}{2};\ -a^2 b^2 \\ \frac{2\varepsilon+1}{2},\ \frac{s+2n+2\lambda+\delta+\varepsilon+1}{2},\ \frac{s-2n-\delta+\varepsilon+1}{2}\end{array}\right)$ $+ \dfrac{(-1)^m 2^{m+2n+\delta+\varepsilon-1}}{(2n+\delta)!\, a^{2n+\delta} b^{s+2n+2\lambda+\delta-1}} (\lambda)_{2n+\delta}$ $\times \left(\dfrac{2-s-2n-2\lambda-\delta+\varepsilon}{2}\right)_m \Gamma\left(\dfrac{s+2n+2\lambda+\delta+\varepsilon-1}{2}\right)$ $\times {}_3F_3\left(\begin{array}{c}\frac{1-2n-2\lambda}{2},\ 1-n-\lambda-\delta,\ \frac{2-s+2m-2n+\varepsilon-2\lambda-\delta}{2} \\ 1-2n-\lambda-\delta,\ \frac{2-s-2n-2\lambda}{2},\ \frac{3-s-2n-2\lambda-2\delta}{2};\ -a^2 b^2\end{array}\right)$ $[a,\ \operatorname{Re} b > 0;\ \operatorname{Re}\lambda > -1/2]$
4	$(a-x)_+^{\lambda-1/2} e^{-b^2 x}$ $\times H_{2m+\varepsilon}(b\sqrt{x})$ $\times C_n^\lambda \left(\dfrac{2x}{a} - 1\right)$	$\dfrac{(-1)^{m+n} 2^{2m+\varepsilon}}{n!} a^{s+\lambda+(\varepsilon-1)/2} b^\varepsilon \left(\dfrac{2\varepsilon+1}{2}\right)_m (2\lambda)_n$ $\times \left(\dfrac{1-2s+2\lambda-\varepsilon}{2}\right)_n \Gamma\left[\begin{array}{c}\frac{2\lambda+1}{2},\ \frac{2s+\varepsilon}{2} \\ \frac{2s+2n+2\lambda+\varepsilon+1}{2}\end{array}\right]$ $\times {}_3F_3\left(\begin{array}{c}\frac{2m+2\varepsilon+1}{2},\ \frac{2s-2\lambda+\varepsilon+1}{2},\ \frac{2s+\varepsilon}{2};\ -ab^2 \\ \frac{2\varepsilon+1}{2},\ \frac{2s-2n-2\lambda+\varepsilon+1}{2},\ \frac{2s+2n+2\lambda+\varepsilon+1}{2}\end{array}\right)$ $[a > 0;\ \operatorname{Re}\lambda > -1/2;\ \operatorname{Re} s > -\varepsilon/2]$

3.24.15. $C_n^\lambda(bx)$ **and** $L_m^\mu(ax^r)$

Notation: $\delta = \left\{\begin{array}{c}1 \\ 0\end{array}\right\}$, $\varepsilon = 0$ or 1.

No.	$f(x)$	$F(s)$
1	$\left(a^2 - x^2\right)_+^{\lambda-1/2}$ $\times L_m^\mu(bx^2) C_n^\lambda\left(\dfrac{x}{a}\right)$	$\dfrac{\pi(\mu+1)_m}{m!\,n!} \left(\dfrac{a}{2}\right)^{s+2\lambda-1} \Gamma\left[\begin{array}{c}s,\ n+2\lambda \\ \lambda,\ \frac{s-n+1}{2},\ \frac{s+n+2\lambda+1}{2}\end{array}\right]$ $\times {}_3F_3\left(\begin{array}{c}-m,\ \frac{s}{2},\ \frac{s+1}{2};\ a^2 b \\ \mu+1,\ \frac{s-n+1}{2},\ \frac{s+n+2\lambda+1}{2}\end{array}\right)$ $[a > 0;\ \operatorname{Re}\lambda > -1/2;\ \operatorname{Re} s > ((-1)^n - 1)/2]$
2	$\left(a^2 - x^2\right)_+^{\lambda-1/2} e^{-bx^2}$ $\times L_m^\mu(bx^2) C_n^\lambda\left(\dfrac{x}{a}\right)$	$\dfrac{\pi(\mu+1)_m}{m!\,n!} \left(\dfrac{a}{2}\right)^{s+2\lambda-1} \Gamma\left[\begin{array}{c}s,\ n+2\lambda \\ \lambda,\ \frac{s-n+1}{2},\ \frac{s+n+2\lambda+1}{2}\end{array}\right]$ $\times {}_3F_3\left(\begin{array}{c}m+\mu+1,\ \frac{s}{2},\ \frac{s+1}{2};\ -a^2 b \\ \mu+1,\ \frac{s-n+1}{2},\ \frac{s+n+2\lambda+1}{2}\end{array}\right)$ $[a > 0;\ \operatorname{Re}\lambda > -1/2;\ \operatorname{Re} s > ((-1)^n - 1)/2]$

No.	$f(x)$	$F(s)$
3	$\left(x^2 - a^2\right)_+^{\lambda - 1/2} e^{-bx^2}$ $\times L_m^\mu\left(bx^2\right) C_{2n+\varepsilon}^\lambda\left(\dfrac{x}{a}\right)$	$\dfrac{2^{2n+\varepsilon-1} b^{(1-s-\varepsilon)/2 - n - \lambda}}{m!\,(2n+\varepsilon)!\,a^{2n+\varepsilon}}\,(\lambda)_{2n+\varepsilon}$ $\times \left(\dfrac{3-s-2n-2\lambda+2\mu-\varepsilon}{2}\right)_m \Gamma\left(\dfrac{s+2n+2\lambda+\varepsilon-1}{2}\right)$ $\times {}_3F_3\left(\begin{array}{c} \frac{1-2n-2\lambda-\varepsilon}{2},\ \frac{2-2n-2\lambda-\varepsilon}{2}, \\ 1-2n-\lambda-\varepsilon,\ \frac{3-s-2n-2\lambda-\varepsilon}{2}, \\ \frac{3-s+2m-2n-2\lambda+2\mu-\varepsilon}{2} \\ \frac{3-s-2n-2\lambda+2\mu-\varepsilon}{2};\ -a^2b \end{array}\right)$ $+ \dfrac{a^{s+2\lambda-1} (2\lambda)_{2n+\varepsilon}}{2\,(m!)\,(2n+\varepsilon)!}\,(\mu+1)_m \left(\dfrac{1-s+\varepsilon}{2}\right)_n$ $\times \Gamma\left[\begin{array}{c} \frac{2\lambda+1}{2},\ \frac{1-s-2n-2\lambda-\varepsilon}{2} \\ \frac{2-s-\varepsilon}{2} \end{array}\right] {}_3F_3\left(\begin{array}{c} m+\mu+1,\ \frac{s}{2},\ \frac{s+1}{2};\ -a^2b \\ \mu+1,\ \frac{s-2n-\varepsilon+1}{2},\ \frac{s+2n+2\lambda+\varepsilon+1}{2} \end{array}\right)$ $[a,\ \operatorname{Re} b > 0;\ \operatorname{Re}\lambda > -1/2]$
4	$(a-x)_+^{\lambda-1/2} e^{-bx}$ $\times L_m^\mu(bx)\, C_n^\lambda\left(\dfrac{2x}{a} - 1\right)$	$\dfrac{(-1)^n}{m!\,n!}\,a^{s+\lambda-1/2}\,(\mu+1)_m\,(2\lambda)_n \left(\dfrac{1-2s+2\lambda}{2}\right)_n$ $\times \Gamma\left[\begin{array}{c} \frac{2\lambda+1}{2},\ s \\ \frac{2s+2n+2\lambda+1}{2} \end{array}\right] {}_3F_3\left(\begin{array}{c} m+\mu+1,\ \frac{2s-2\lambda+1}{2},\ s;\ -ab \\ \mu+1,\ \frac{2s-2n-2\lambda+1}{2},\ \frac{2s+2n+2\lambda+1}{2} \end{array}\right)$ $[a,\ \operatorname{Re} s > 0;\ \operatorname{Re}\lambda > -1/2]$

3.24.16.   Products of $C_n^\lambda(bx)$

Notation: $\varepsilon,\ \delta = 0$ or 1.

No.	$f(x)$	$F(s)$
1	$\left(a^2 - x^2\right)_+^{\lambda-1/2}$ $\times \left(b^2 - x^2\right)^{\mu-1/2}$ $\times C_{2m+\varepsilon}^\mu\left(\dfrac{x}{b}\right) C_{2n+\delta}^\lambda\left(\dfrac{x}{a}\right)$	$\dfrac{(-1)^{m+n} 2^{\varepsilon-1} (2\lambda)_{2n+\delta} (\mu)_{m+\varepsilon}}{m!\,(2n+\delta)!}\,a^{s+2\lambda+\varepsilon-1} b^{2\mu-\varepsilon-1}$ $\times \left(\dfrac{1-s+\delta-\varepsilon}{2}\right)_n \Gamma\left[\begin{array}{c} \frac{2\lambda+1}{2},\ \frac{s+\delta+\varepsilon}{2} \\ \frac{s+2n+2\lambda+\delta+\varepsilon+1}{2} \end{array}\right]$ $\times {}_4F_3\left(\begin{array}{c} \frac{1-2m-2\mu}{2},\ \frac{2m+2\varepsilon+1}{2},\ \frac{s+1}{2},\ \frac{s+2\varepsilon}{2} \\ \frac{2\varepsilon+1}{2},\ \frac{s-2n-\delta+\varepsilon+1}{2},\ \frac{s+2n+2\lambda+\delta+\varepsilon+1}{2};\ \frac{a^2}{b^2} \end{array}\right)$ $[b > a > 0;\ \operatorname{Re}\lambda > -1/2;\ \operatorname{Re} s > -\delta - \varepsilon]$
2	$\left(x^2 - a^2\right)_+^{\lambda-1/2}$ $\times \left(x^2 - b^2\right)^{\mu-1/2}$ $\times C_{2m+\varepsilon}^\mu\left(\dfrac{x}{b}\right) C_{2n+\delta}^\lambda\left(\dfrac{x}{a}\right)$	$\dfrac{2^{2m+\varepsilon-1} (2\lambda)_{2n+\delta} (\mu)_{2m+\varepsilon}}{(2m+\varepsilon)!\,(2n+\delta)!}\,a^{s+2m+2\lambda+2\mu+\varepsilon-2} b^{-2m-\varepsilon}$ $\times \left(\dfrac{2-s-2m-2\mu+\delta-\varepsilon}{2}\right)_n$ $\times \Gamma\left[\begin{array}{c} \frac{2\lambda+1}{2},\ \frac{2-s-2m-2n-2\lambda-2\mu-\delta-\varepsilon}{2} \\ \frac{3-s-2m-2\mu-\delta-\varepsilon}{2} \end{array}\right] \times$

No.	$f(x)$	$F(s)$
		$\times {}_4F_3\left(\begin{array}{c} \frac{1-2m-2\mu}{2},\, 1-m-\mu-\varepsilon,\, \frac{2-s-2m+2n-2\mu+\delta-\varepsilon}{2}, \\ \frac{3-s-2m-2\mu-2\varepsilon}{2},\, 1-2m-\mu-\varepsilon, \end{array}\right.$
		$\left.\begin{array}{c} \frac{2-s-2m-2n-2\lambda-2\mu-\delta-\varepsilon}{2} \\ \frac{2-s-2m-2\mu}{2};\, \frac{b^2}{a^2} \end{array}\right)$
		$\left[\begin{array}{c} a > b > 0;\ \mathrm{Re}\,\lambda > -1/2; \\ \mathrm{Re}\,(s+2\lambda+2\mu) < 2-2m-2n-\delta-\varepsilon \end{array}\right]$
3	$\left(x^2-a^2\right)_+^{\lambda-1/2}$	$\dfrac{(-1)^m\,2^{\varepsilon-1}a^{s+2\lambda+\varepsilon-1}b^{2\mu-\varepsilon-1}}{m!\,(2n+\delta)!}\,(\mu)_{m+\varepsilon}\,(2\lambda)_{2n+\delta}$
	$\times\left(b^2-x^2\right)_+^{\mu-1/2}$	$\times\left(\dfrac{1-s+\delta-\varepsilon}{2}\right)_n\Gamma\left[\begin{array}{c}\frac{2\lambda+1}{2},\,\frac{1-s-2n-2\lambda-\delta-\varepsilon}{2}\\ 1-\frac{s+\delta+\varepsilon}{2}\end{array}\right]$
	$\times C_{2n+\delta}^{\lambda}\left(\dfrac{x}{a}\right)C_{2m+\varepsilon}^{\mu}\left(\dfrac{x}{b}\right)$	$\times {}_4F_3\left(\begin{array}{c}-m-\mu+\frac{1}{2},\,m+\varepsilon+\frac{1}{2},\,\frac{s+1}{2},\,\frac{s+2\varepsilon}{2}\\ \frac{2\varepsilon+1}{2},\,\frac{s-2n-\delta+\varepsilon+1}{2},\,\frac{s+2n+2\lambda+\delta+\varepsilon+1}{2};\,\frac{a^2}{b^2}\end{array}\right)$
		$+\,\dfrac{(-1)^m\,2^{2n+\delta-1}a^{-2n-\delta}b^{s+2n+2\mu+2\lambda+\delta-2}}{(2m+\varepsilon)!\,(2n+\delta)!}$
		$\times(2\mu)_{2m+\varepsilon}\,(\lambda)_{2n+\delta}\left(\dfrac{2-s-2n-2\lambda-\delta+\varepsilon}{2}\right)_m$
		$\times\Gamma\left[\begin{array}{c}\frac{2\mu+1}{2},\,\frac{s+2n+2\lambda+\delta+\varepsilon-1}{2}\\ \frac{s+2m+2n+2\mu+2\lambda+\delta+\varepsilon}{2}\end{array}\right]$
		$\times {}_4F_3\left(\begin{array}{c}\frac{1-2n-2\lambda}{2},\,1-n-\lambda-\delta,\\ 1-2n-\lambda-\delta,\end{array}\right.$
		$\left.\begin{array}{c}\frac{2-s-2m-2n-2\mu-2\lambda-\delta-\varepsilon}{2},\,\frac{2-s+2m-2n-2\lambda-\delta+\varepsilon}{2}\\ \frac{2-s-2n-2\lambda}{2},\,\frac{3-s-2n-2\lambda-2\delta}{2};\,\frac{a^2}{b^2}\end{array}\right)$
		$[b > a > 0;\ \mathrm{Re}\,\lambda,\,\mathrm{Re}\,\mu > -1/2]$
4	$(a-x)_+^{\lambda-1/2}\,C_m^{\mu}\left(1-\dfrac{2x}{a}\right)$	$\dfrac{a^{s+\lambda-1/2}}{m!\,n!}\,\Gamma\left[\begin{array}{c}\frac{2\lambda+1}{2},\,m+2\mu,\,n+2\lambda,\,s,\,\frac{1-2s+2n+2\lambda}{2}\\ 2\lambda,\,2\mu,\,\frac{1-2s+2\lambda}{2},\,\frac{2s+2n+2\lambda+1}{2}\end{array}\right]$
	$\times C_n^{\lambda}\left(1-\dfrac{2x}{a}\right)$	$\times {}_4F_3\left(\begin{array}{c}-m,\,m+2\mu,\,s,\,\frac{2s-2\lambda+1}{2};\,1\\ \frac{2\mu+1}{2},\,\frac{2s-2n-2\lambda+1}{2},\,\frac{2s+2n+2\lambda+1}{2}\end{array}\right)$
		$[a,\ \mathrm{Re}\,s > 0;\ \mathrm{Re}\,\lambda > -1/2]$
5	$(a-x)_+^{\lambda+\mu-1}\,C_m^{\mu}\left(1-\dfrac{2x}{a}\right)$	$\dfrac{a^{s+\lambda+\mu-1}}{m!\,n!}\,(2\mu)_m\,(2\lambda)_n\left(\dfrac{1-2s+2\lambda}{2}\right)_n$
	$\times C_n^{\lambda}\left(1-\dfrac{2x}{a}\right)$	$\times\Gamma\left[\begin{array}{c}\frac{2\lambda+1}{2},\,s\\ s+n+\lambda+\frac{1}{2}\end{array}\right]$
		$\times {}_4F_3\left(\begin{array}{c}-m-\mu+\frac{1}{2},\,m+\mu+\frac{1}{2},\,s-\lambda+\frac{1}{2},\,s\\ \frac{2\mu+1}{2},\,s-n-\lambda+\frac{1}{2},\,s+n+\lambda+\frac{1}{2};\,1\end{array}\right)$
		$[a,\ \mathrm{Re}\,s > 0;\ \mathrm{Re}\,(\lambda+\mu) > 0]$

No.	$f(x)$	$F(s)$
6	$(a-x)_+^{\lambda-1/2}(1-bx)^{\mu-1/2}$ $\times C_m^\mu(2bx-1)$ $\times C_n^\lambda\left(\frac{2x}{a}-1\right)$	$\dfrac{(-1)^{m+n}\,a^{s+\lambda-1/2}}{m!\,n!}(2\mu)_m(2\lambda)_n$ $\times\left(\dfrac{1-2s+2\lambda}{2}\right)_n\Gamma\left[\begin{array}{c}\frac{2\lambda+1}{2},\,s\\ \frac{2s+2n+2\lambda+1}{2}\end{array}\right]$ $\times\,{}_4F_3\left(\begin{array}{c}\frac{1-2m-2\mu}{2},\,\frac{2m+2\mu+1}{2},\,\frac{2s-2\lambda+1}{2},\,s\\ \frac{2\mu+1}{2},\,\frac{2s-2n-2\lambda+1}{2},\,\frac{2s+2n+2\lambda+1}{2};\,ab\end{array}\right)$ $[a,\ \mathrm{Re}\,s>0;\ \lvert\arg(1-ab)<\pi\rvert]$
7	$(a-x)_+^{\lambda-1/2}(b\pm x)^{\mu-1/2}$ $\times C_m^\lambda\left(\frac{2x}{a}-1\right)$ $\times C_n^\mu\left(\frac{2x}{b}\pm1\right)$	$\dfrac{(-1)^m\,(\pm1)^n}{m!\,n!}\,a^{s+\lambda-1/2}b^{\mu-1/2}(2\lambda)_m(2\mu)_n$ $\times\left(\dfrac{1-2s+2\lambda}{2}\right)_m\Gamma\left[\begin{array}{c}\frac{2\lambda+1}{2},\,s\\ \frac{2s+2m+2\lambda+1}{2}\end{array}\right]$ $\times\,{}_4F_3\left(\begin{array}{c}\frac{1-2n-2\mu}{2},\,\frac{2n+2\mu+1}{2},\,\frac{2s-2\lambda+1}{2},\,s\\ \frac{2\mu+1}{2},\,\frac{2s-2m-2\lambda+1}{2},\,\frac{2s+2m+2\lambda+1}{2};\,\mp\frac{a}{b}\end{array}\right)$ $\left[a,\ \mathrm{Re}\,s>0;\ \left\{\begin{array}{c}\lvert\arg b\rvert<\pi\\ b>a\end{array}\right\}\right]$
8	$(a-x)_+^{\lambda+\mu-1}C_{2m+\varepsilon}^\mu\left(\sqrt{\frac{x}{a}}\right)$ $\times C_n^\lambda\left(\frac{2x}{a}-1\right)$	$\dfrac{(-1)^{m+n}\,2^\varepsilon}{m!\,n!}\,a^{s+\lambda+\mu-1}(\mu)_{m+\varepsilon}(2\lambda)_n$ $\times\left(\dfrac{1-2s+2\lambda-\varepsilon}{2}\right)_n\Gamma\left[\begin{array}{c}\frac{2\lambda+1}{2},\,\frac{2s+\varepsilon}{2}\\ \frac{2s+2n+2\lambda+\varepsilon+1}{2}\end{array}\right]$ $\times\,{}_4F_3\left(\begin{array}{c}\frac{1-2m-2\mu}{2},\,\frac{2m+2\varepsilon+1}{2},\,\frac{2s-2\lambda+\varepsilon+1}{2},\,\frac{2s+\varepsilon}{2}\\ \frac{2\varepsilon+1}{2},\,\frac{2s-2n-2\lambda+\varepsilon+1}{2},\,\frac{2s+2n+2\lambda+\varepsilon+1}{2};\,1\end{array}\right)$ $[a,\ \mathrm{Re}\,(\lambda+\mu)>0;\ \mathrm{Re}\,s>-\varepsilon/2]$
9	$(a-x)_+^{\lambda-1/2}(1-b^2x)^{\mu-1/2}$ $\times C_{2m+\varepsilon}^\mu(b\sqrt{x})$ $\times C_n^\lambda\left(\frac{2x}{a}-1\right)$	$\dfrac{(-1)^{m+n}}{m!\,n!}\,a^{s+\lambda+(\varepsilon-1)/2}(2b)^\varepsilon(\mu)_{m+\varepsilon}(2\lambda)_n$ $\times\left(\dfrac{1-2s+2\lambda-\varepsilon}{2}\right)_n\Gamma\left[\begin{array}{c}\frac{2\lambda+1}{2},\,\frac{2s+\varepsilon}{2}\\ \frac{2s+2n+2\lambda+\varepsilon+1}{2}\end{array}\right]$ $\times\,{}_4F_3\left(\begin{array}{c}\frac{1-2m-2\mu}{2},\,\frac{2m+2\varepsilon+1}{2},\,\frac{2s-2\lambda+\varepsilon+1}{2},\,\frac{2s+\varepsilon}{2}\\ \frac{2\varepsilon+1}{2},\,\frac{2s-2n-2\lambda+\varepsilon+1}{2},\,\frac{2s+2n+2\lambda+\varepsilon+1}{2};\,ab^2\end{array}\right)$ $[a>0;\ \mathrm{Re}\,\lambda>-1/2;\ \mathrm{Re}\,s>-\varepsilon/2;\ \lvert\arg(1-ab^2)<\pi\rvert]$
10	$(a^2-x^2)_+^{\lambda-1/2}C_m^\mu\left(\frac{b}{x}\right)$ $\times C_n^\lambda\left(\frac{x}{a}\right)$	$\dfrac{(-1)^m\,\pi}{m!\,n!}\left(\dfrac{a}{2}\right)^{s-m+2\lambda-1}(2b)^m(1-m-\mu)_m$ $\times\Gamma\left[\begin{array}{c}n+2\lambda,\,s-m\\ \lambda,\,\frac{s-m-n+1}{2},\,\frac{s-m+n+2\lambda+1}{2}\end{array}\right]$ $\times\,{}_4F_3\left(\begin{array}{c}-\frac{m}{2},\,\frac{1-m}{2},\,\frac{s-m}{2},\,\frac{s-m+1}{2};\,\frac{a^2}{b^2}\\ 1-m-\mu,\,\frac{s-m-n+1}{2},\,\frac{s-m+n+2\lambda+1}{2}\end{array}\right)$ $[a>0;\ \mathrm{Re}\,\lambda>-1/2;\ \mathrm{Re}\,s>m]$

3.25. The Jacobi Polynomials $P_n^{(\rho,\sigma)}(z)$

More formulas can be obtained from the corresponding section due to the relations

$$P_n^{(0,0)}(z) = P_n(z), \quad P_n^{(-1/2,-1/2)}(z) = \frac{(1/2)_n}{n!}T_n(z), \quad P_n^{(1/2,1/2)}(z) = \frac{(3/2)_n}{(n+1)!}U_n(z),$$

$$P_n^{(\lambda,\lambda)}(z) = \frac{(\lambda+1)_n}{(2\lambda+1)_n}C_n^{\lambda+1/2}(z),$$

$$P_\nu^{(\rho,\sigma)}(z) = \frac{\Gamma(\rho+\nu+1)}{\Gamma(\rho+1)\Gamma(\nu+1)}\,{}_2F_1\left(-\nu,\,\rho+\sigma+\nu+1;\,\rho+1;\,\frac{1-z}{2}\right).$$

3.25.1. $P_n^{(\rho,\sigma)}(\varphi(x))$ and algebraic functions

No.	$f(x)$	$F(s)$
1	$(2-x)_+^\sigma P_n^{(\rho,\sigma)}(1-x)$	$\dfrac{2^{s+\sigma}}{n!}\Gamma\begin{bmatrix} n+\sigma+1,\,s,\,1-s+n+\rho \\ 1-s+\rho,\,s+n+\sigma+1 \end{bmatrix}$ $\qquad [\operatorname{Re}\sigma>-1;\ \operatorname{Re}s>0]$
2	$(a-x)_+^{\alpha-1} P_n^{(\rho,\sigma)}(1-bx)$	$\dfrac{a^{s+\alpha-1}}{n!}\Gamma\begin{bmatrix} \alpha,\,n+\rho+1,\,s \\ \rho+1,\,s+\alpha \end{bmatrix}\,{}_3F_2\left(\begin{matrix}-n,\,n+\rho+\sigma+1,\,s \\ \rho+1,\,s+\alpha;\,\frac{ab}{2}\end{matrix}\right)$ $\qquad\qquad [a,\ \operatorname{Re}\alpha,\ \operatorname{Re}s>0]$
3	$(a-x)_+^{\alpha-1}(2-bx)^\sigma$ $\times P_n^{(\rho,\sigma)}(1-bx)$	$\dfrac{2^\sigma a^{s+\alpha-1}}{n!}\Gamma\begin{bmatrix} \alpha,\,n+\rho+1,\,s \\ \rho+1,\,s+\alpha \end{bmatrix}\,{}_3F_2\left(\begin{matrix}n+\rho+1,\,-n-\sigma,\,s \\ \rho+1,\,s+\alpha;\,\frac{ab}{2}\end{matrix}\right)$ $\qquad\qquad [a,\ \operatorname{Re}\alpha,\ \operatorname{Re}s>0]$
4	$(a-x)_+^\rho$ $\times P_n^{(\rho,\sigma)}(bx-ab+1)$	$a^{s+\rho}\Gamma\begin{bmatrix} n+\rho+1,\,s \\ s+n+\rho+1 \end{bmatrix}P_n^{(s+\rho,\sigma-s)}(1-ab)$ $\qquad\qquad [a,\ \operatorname{Re}s>0;\ \operatorname{Re}\rho>-1]$
5	$(a-x)_+^\rho(bx+1)^\alpha$ $\times P_n^{(\rho,\sigma)}(1-cx+ac)$	$\dfrac{(\rho+1)_n}{n!}a^{s+\rho}\,\mathrm{B}(s,\rho+1)$ $\times F_3\left(-\alpha,\,-n,\,s,\,n+\rho+\sigma+1;\,s+\rho+1;\,-ab,\,-\dfrac{ac}{2}\right)$ $\qquad [a,\ \operatorname{Re}s>0;\ \operatorname{Re}\rho>-1;\ |\arg(ab+1)|<\pi]$
6	$(a-x)_+^\rho P_n^{(\rho,\sigma)}\left(\dfrac{2x}{a}-1\right)$	$\dfrac{a^{s+\rho}}{n!}\Gamma\begin{bmatrix} s,\,s-\sigma,\,n+\rho+1 \\ s+n+\rho+1,\,s-n-\sigma \end{bmatrix}$ $\qquad [a,\ \operatorname{Re}s>0;\ \operatorname{Re}\rho>-1]$
7	$(a-x)_+^{\alpha-1}$ $\times P_n^{(\rho,\sigma)}\left(\dfrac{2x}{b}\pm1\right)$	$\dfrac{(\pm1)^n a^{s+\alpha-1}}{n!}(\varphi+1)_n\,\mathrm{B}(\alpha,s)\,{}_3F_2\left(\begin{matrix}-n,\,n+\rho+\sigma+1,\,s \\ \varphi+1,\,s+\alpha;\,\mp\frac{a}{b}\end{matrix}\right)$ $\qquad\left[a,\ \operatorname{Re}\alpha,\ \operatorname{Re}s>0;\ \varphi=\left\{\begin{matrix}\rho \\ \sigma\end{matrix}\right\}\right]$

No.	$f(x)$	$F(s)$
8	$(a-x)_+^\sigma$ $\times P_n^{(\rho,\,\sigma)}\left(\dfrac{a-b-2x}{a+b}\right)$	$a^{s+\sigma}\,\mathrm{B}\,(n+\sigma+1,\,s)\,P_n^{(\rho-s,\,s+\sigma)}\left(\dfrac{a-b}{a+b}\right)$ $[a>0;\ \rho>-1;\ \mathrm{Re}\,s>0;\ \mathrm{Re}\,\sigma>-1]$
9	$(x-a)_+^\rho\,P_n^{(\rho,\,\sigma)}\left(\dfrac{2x}{a}-1\right)$	$\dfrac{a^{s+\rho}}{n!}\,\Gamma\left[\begin{matrix}1-s+n+\sigma,\,-s-n-\rho,\,n+\rho+1\\1-s+\sigma,\,1-s\end{matrix}\right]$ $[a>0;\ \mathrm{Re}\,\rho>-1;\ \mathrm{Re}\,s<-\,\mathrm{Re}\,\rho-n]$
10	$(x+a)^\sigma\,P_n^{(\rho,\,\sigma)}\left(\dfrac{2x}{a}+1\right)$	$\dfrac{a^{s+\sigma}}{n!}\,\Gamma\left[\begin{matrix}s,\,1-s+n+\rho,\,-s-n-\sigma\\1-s+\rho,\,-n-\sigma\end{matrix}\right]$ $[0<\mathrm{Re}\,s<-\,\mathrm{Re}\,\sigma-n;\ |\arg a|<\pi]$
11	$\dfrac{(a-x)_+^\rho}{x-b}\,P_n^{(\rho,\,\sigma)}\left(\dfrac{2x}{a}-1\right)$	$\dfrac{(-1)^n\,a^{s+\rho-1}}{n!}\,(2-s+\sigma)_n\,\mathrm{B}\,(n+\rho+1,\,s-1)$ $\times\,{}_3F_2\left(\begin{matrix}1,\,1-s-n-\rho,\,2-s+n+\sigma\\2-s,\,2-s+\sigma;\ \frac{b}{a}\end{matrix}\right)$ $-\,\pi\,(a-b)^\rho\,b^{s-1}\cot(s\pi)\,P_n^{(\rho,\,\sigma)}\left(\dfrac{2b-a}{a}\right)\quad[a>b]$
12		$=\dfrac{(-1)^{n+1}\,a^{s+\rho}}{n!\,b}\,(1-s+\sigma)_n\,\mathrm{B}\,(n+\rho+1,\,s)$ $\times\,{}_3F_2\left(\begin{matrix}1,\,s-\sigma,\,s;\ \frac{a}{b}\\s-n-\sigma,\,s+n+\rho+1\end{matrix}\right)\quad[a<b]$ $[a,\,b,\,\mathrm{Re}\,s>0;\ \mathrm{Re}\,\rho>-1]$
13	$\dfrac{(x+a)^\sigma}{x-b}\,P_n^{(\rho,\,\sigma)}\left(\dfrac{2x}{a}+1\right)$	$\dfrac{a^{s+\sigma-1}}{n!}\,(2-s+\rho)_n\,\mathrm{B}\,(1-s-n-\sigma,\,s-1)$ $\times\,{}_3F_2\left(\begin{matrix}1,\,1-s-n-\sigma,\,2-s+n+\rho\\2-s,\,2-s+\rho;\ -\frac{b}{a}\end{matrix}\right)$ $-\,\pi\,(a+b)^\sigma\,b^{s-1}\cot(s\pi)\,P_n^{(\rho,\,\sigma)}\left(\dfrac{a+2b}{a}\right)$ $[b>0;\ 0<\mathrm{Re}\,s<-\,\mathrm{Re}\,\sigma-n+1;\ |\arg a|<\pi]$
14	$(a-x)_+^{\alpha-1}\left\{\begin{matrix}(x+b)^\sigma\\(b-x)^\rho\end{matrix}\right\}$ $\times P_n^{(\rho,\,\sigma)}\left(\dfrac{2x}{b}\pm1\right)$	$\dfrac{(\pm1)^n\,a^{s+\alpha-1}b^\psi}{n!}\,(\varphi+1)_n\,\mathrm{B}\,(\alpha,\,s)\,{}_3F_2\left(\begin{matrix}-n-\psi,\,n+\varphi+1,\,s\\\varphi+1,\,s+\alpha;\ \mp\frac{a}{b}\end{matrix}\right)$ $\left[\left\{\begin{matrix}a>0;\ |\arg b|<\pi\\b>a>0\end{matrix}\right\};\ \mathrm{Re}\,\alpha,\ \mathrm{Re}\,s>0;\ \varphi=\left\{\begin{matrix}\rho\\\sigma\end{matrix}\right\},\ \psi=\left\{\begin{matrix}\sigma\\\rho\end{matrix}\right\}\right]$

No.	$f(x)$	$F(s)$
15	$(a-x)_+^\rho (b\pm x)^\tau$ $\times P_n^{(\rho,\,\sigma)}\left(\dfrac{2x}{a}-1\right)$	$\dfrac{(-1)^n\,a^{s+\rho}b^\tau}{n!}(1-s+\sigma)_n\,\mathrm{B}\,(n+\rho+1,\,s)$ $\times\,{}_3F_2\left(\begin{matrix}-\tau,\,s-\sigma,\,s;\,\mp\frac{a}{b}\\ s-n-\sigma,\,s+n+\rho+1\end{matrix}\right)$ $\left[\left\{\begin{matrix}a>0;\,|\arg b|<\pi\\ b>a>0\end{matrix}\right\};\ \mathrm{Re}\,\rho>-1;\ \mathrm{Re}\,s>0\right]$
16	$(x+a)^\sigma (x+b)^\tau$ $\times P_n^{(\rho,\,\sigma)}\left(\dfrac{2x}{a}+1\right)$	$\dfrac{a^{s+\sigma+\tau}}{n!}(1-s+\rho-\tau)_n\,\mathrm{B}\,(s+\tau,\,-s-n-\tau-\sigma)$ $\times\,{}_3F_2\left(\begin{matrix}-\tau,\,-s-n-\sigma-\tau,\,1-s+n+\rho-\tau\\ 1-s-\tau,\,1-s+\rho-\tau;\,\frac{b}{a}\end{matrix}\right)$ $+\dfrac{a^\sigma b^{s+\tau}}{n!}(\rho+1)_n\,\mathrm{B}\,(-s-\tau,\,s)$ $\times\,{}_3F_2\left(\begin{matrix}-n-\sigma,\,n+\rho+1,\,s\\ \rho+1,\,s+\tau+1;\,\frac{b}{a}\end{matrix}\right)$ $[a>0;\,0<\mathrm{Re}\,s<-\mathrm{Re}\,(\sigma+\tau)-n;\,|\arg b|<\pi]$
17	$(x+a-b)^\rho (x+a+b)^\tau$ $\times P_n^{(\rho,\,\sigma)}\left(\dfrac{x+a}{b}\right)$	$\dfrac{(a+b)^{s+n+\rho+\tau}}{(2b)^n\,n!}(n+\rho+\sigma+1)_n\,\mathrm{B}\,(-s-n-\rho-\tau,\,s)$ $\times\,{}_3F_2\left(\begin{matrix}-n-\rho-\sigma,\,-n-\rho,\,-s-n-\rho-\tau\\ -n-\rho-\tau,\,-2n-\rho-\sigma;\,\frac{2b}{a+b}\end{matrix}\right)$ $[a>b>0;\,0<\mathrm{Re}\,s<-\mathrm{Re}\,(\tau+\rho)-n]$
18	$(a-x)_+^{\alpha-1}\,P_n^{(\rho,\,\sigma)}\left(\dfrac{x+b}{a+b}\right)$	$\dfrac{a^{s+\alpha-1}}{n!}(\rho+1)_n\,\mathrm{B}\,(\alpha,\,s)\,{}_3F_2\left(\begin{matrix}-n,\,n+\rho+\sigma+1,\,\alpha\\ \rho+1,\,s+\alpha;\,\frac{a}{2(a+b)}\end{matrix}\right)$ $[a,\,\mathrm{Re}\,\alpha,\,\mathrm{Re}\,s>0]$
19	$(a-x)_+^{\alpha-1}(x+a+2b)^\sigma$ $\times P_n^{(\rho,\,\sigma)}\left(\dfrac{x+b}{a+b}\right)$	$\dfrac{2^\sigma\,(a+b)^\sigma\,a^{s+\alpha-1}}{n!}(\rho+1)_n\,\mathrm{B}\,(\alpha,\,s)\,{}_3F_2\left(\begin{matrix}-n-\sigma,\,n+\rho+1,\,\alpha\\ \rho+1,\,s+\alpha;\,\frac{a}{2(a+b)}\end{matrix}\right)$ $[a,\,b,\,\mathrm{Re}\,\alpha,\,\mathrm{Re}\,s>0]$
20	$(a-x)_+^\rho\,P_n^{(\rho,\,\sigma)}\left(\dfrac{2a}{x}-1\right)$	$\dfrac{a^{s+\rho}}{n!}\,\Gamma\left[\begin{matrix}s-n,\,s+\rho+\sigma+n+1,\,n+\rho+1\\ s+\rho+1,\,s+\rho+\sigma+1\end{matrix}\right]$ $[a>0;\,\mathrm{Re}\,\rho>-1;\,\mathrm{Re}\,s>n]$
21	$(x-a)_+^\rho\,P_n^{(\rho,\,\sigma)}\left(\dfrac{2a}{x}-1\right)$	$\dfrac{a^{s+\rho}}{n!}\,\Gamma\left[\begin{matrix}-s-\rho,\,-s-\rho-\sigma,\,n+\rho+1\\ 1-s+n,\,-s-n-\rho-\sigma\end{matrix}\right]$ $[a>0;\,\mathrm{Re}\,s<-\mathrm{Re}\,\rho<1]$

No.	$f(x)$	$F(s)$
22	$(x+a)^\sigma P_n^{(\rho,\sigma)}\left(\dfrac{2a}{x}+1\right)$	$\dfrac{a^{s+\sigma}}{n!}\,\Gamma\left[\begin{array}{c} s-n,\,s+n+\rho+\sigma+1,\,-s-\sigma \\ s+\rho+\sigma+1,\,-n-\sigma \end{array}\right]$
		$[n < \operatorname{Re} s < -\operatorname{Re}\sigma;\ |\arg a| < \pi]$
23	$(a-x)_+^{-(n+\rho+\sigma+1)}$	$\dfrac{a^{s-(n+\rho+\sigma+1)}}{n!}\,\Gamma\left[\begin{array}{c} s,\,1-s+n+\rho,\,-n-\rho-\sigma \\ s-n-\rho-\sigma,\,1-s+\rho \end{array}\right]$
	$\times\,P_n^{(\rho,\sigma)}\left(\dfrac{a+x}{a-x}\right)$	$[a,\ \operatorname{Re} s > 0;\ \operatorname{Re}(\rho+\sigma) < -2n]$
24	$(x-a)_+^{-(n+\rho+\sigma+1)}$	$\dfrac{a^{s-(n+\rho+\sigma+1)}}{n!}\,\Gamma\left[\begin{array}{c} s-\sigma,\,1-s+n+\rho+\sigma,\,-n-\rho-\sigma \\ 1-s,\,s-n-\sigma \end{array}\right]$
	$\times\,P_n^{(\rho,\sigma)}\left(\dfrac{x+a}{x-a}\right)$	$[a > 0;\ \operatorname{Re} s < \operatorname{Re}(\rho+\sigma)+n+1 < 1-n]$
25	$(x+a)^{-(n+\rho+\sigma+1)}$	$\dfrac{a^{s-(n+\rho+\sigma+1)}}{n!}\,\Gamma\left[\begin{array}{c} s,\,1-s+n+\rho,\,1-s+n+\rho+\sigma \\ 1-s+\rho,\,n+\rho+\sigma+1 \end{array}\right]$
	$\times\,P_n^{(\rho,\sigma)}\left(\dfrac{a-x}{a+x}\right)$	$[0 < \operatorname{Re} s < \operatorname{Re}(\rho+\sigma)+n+1;\ |\arg a| < \pi]$
26	$(x+a)^{-(n+\rho+\sigma+1)}$	$a^{s-(n+\rho+\sigma+1)}\,\mathrm{B}\left(1-s+n+\rho+\sigma,\,s\right)P_n^{(\rho-s,\sigma)}\left(\dfrac{b}{a}\right)$
	$\times\,P_n^{(\rho,\sigma)}\left(\dfrac{b-x}{a+x}\right)$	$[0 < \operatorname{Re} s < \operatorname{Re}(\rho+\sigma)+n+1;\ |\arg a| < \pi]$
27	$(a-x)_+^\rho$	$\dfrac{(2b)^{-n}(a+2b)^{s+n+\rho}}{n!}\,(n+\rho+\sigma+1)_n\,\mathrm{B}\left(n+\rho+1,\,s\right)$
	$\times\,P_n^{(\rho,\sigma)}\left(\dfrac{a+b-x}{b}\right)$	$\times\,{}_2F_1\left(\begin{array}{c} -n-\rho-\sigma,\,-s-n-\rho \\ -2n-\rho-\sigma;\ \dfrac{2b}{a+2b} \end{array}\right)$
		$[a,\ \operatorname{Re} s > 0;\ \operatorname{Re}\rho > -1]$

3.25.2. $P_n^{(\rho,\sigma)}(\varphi(x))$ and the exponential function

No.	$f(x)$	$F(s)$
1	$e^{-bx}P_n^{(\rho,\sigma)}\left(\dfrac{2x}{a}\pm1\right)$	$\dfrac{a^{-n}b^{-s-n}}{n!}\,(n+\rho+\sigma+1)_n\,\Gamma(s+n)$
		$\times\,{}_2F_2\left(\begin{array}{c} -n,\,-n-\varphi;\ ab \\ -2n-\rho-\sigma,\,1-s-n \end{array}\right)\quad\left[\operatorname{Re} b,\ \operatorname{Re} s > 0;\ \varphi=\left\{\begin{array}{c}\rho\\\sigma\end{array}\right\}\right]$
2	$(a-x)_+^\sigma\,e^{-bx}$	$\dfrac{a^{s+\sigma}}{n!}\,(1-s+\rho)_n\,\mathrm{B}\left(n+\sigma+1,\,s\right)\,{}_2F_2\left(\begin{array}{c} s-\rho,\,s;\ -ab \\ s-n-\rho,\,s+n+\sigma+1 \end{array}\right)$
	$\times\,P_n^{(\rho,\sigma)}\left(1-\dfrac{2x}{a}\right)$	$[a,\ \operatorname{Re} s > 0;\ \operatorname{Re}\sigma > -1]$

No.	$f(x)$	$F(s)$
3	$(x+a)^\sigma e^{-bx}$ $\times P_n^{(\rho,\sigma)}\left(\dfrac{2x}{a}+1\right)$	$\dfrac{a^{-n}b^{-s-n-\sigma}}{n!}(n+\rho+\sigma+1)_n\,\Gamma(s+n+\sigma)$ $\times {}_2F_2\left({-n-\sigma,\ -n-\rho-\sigma;\ ab \atop -2n-\rho-\sigma,\ 1-s-n-\sigma}\right)$ $+\dfrac{a^{s+\sigma}}{n!}(1-s+\rho)_n\,\mathrm{B}(-s-n-\sigma,\,s)$ $\times {}_2F_2\left({s-\rho,\ s;\ ab \atop s-n-\rho,\ s+n+\sigma+1}\right)$ $[\operatorname{Re}b,\ \operatorname{Re}s>0;\ |\arg a|<\pi]$
4	$e^{-b/x}P_n^{(\rho,\sigma)}\left(\dfrac{2x}{a}\pm 1\right)$	$\dfrac{(\pm 1)^n b^s}{n!}(\varphi+1)_n\,\Gamma(-s)\,{}_2F_2\left({-n,\ n+\rho+\sigma+1 \atop \varphi+1,\ s+1;\ \pm\frac{b}{a}}\right)$ $\left[\operatorname{Re}b>0;\ \operatorname{Re}s<-n;\ \varphi=\left\{{\rho \atop \sigma}\right\}\right]$
5	$(a-x)_+^\rho e^{-b/x}$ $\times P_n^{(\rho,\sigma)}\left(\dfrac{2x}{a}-1\right)$	$\dfrac{(-1)^n a^\rho b^s}{n!}(\sigma+1)_n\,\Gamma(-s)\,{}_2F_2\left({-n-\rho,\ n+\sigma+1 \atop \sigma+1,\ s+1;\ -\frac{b}{a}}\right)$ $+\dfrac{(-1)^n a^{s+\rho}}{n!}(1-s+\sigma)_n\,\mathrm{B}(n+\rho+1,\,s)$ $\times {}_2F_2\left({-s-n-\rho,\ 1-s+n+\sigma \atop 1-s,\ 1-s+\sigma;\ -\frac{b}{a}}\right)$ $[a,\ \operatorname{Re}b>0;\ \operatorname{Re}\rho>-1]$
6	$(x+a)^\sigma e^{-b/x}$ $\times P_n^{(\rho,\sigma)}\left(\dfrac{2x}{a}+1\right)$	$\dfrac{a^{s+\sigma}}{n!}(1-s+\rho)_n\,\mathrm{B}(-s-n-\sigma,\,s)$ $\times {}_2F_2\left({-s-n-\sigma,\ 1-s+n+\rho \atop 1-s,\ 1-s+\rho;\ \frac{b}{a}}\right)$ $+\dfrac{a^\sigma b^s}{n!}(\rho+1)_n\,\Gamma(-s)\,{}_2F_2\left({-n-\sigma,\ n+\rho+1 \atop \rho+1,\ s+1;\ \frac{b}{a}}\right)$ $[\operatorname{Re}b>0;\ \operatorname{Re}(s+\sigma)<-n;\ |\arg a|<\pi]$
7	$e^{-b\sqrt{x}}P_n^{(\rho,\sigma)}\left(\dfrac{2x}{a}\pm 1\right)$	$\dfrac{2a^{-n}b^{-2s-2n}}{n!}(n+\rho+\sigma+1)_n\,\Gamma(2s+2n)$ $\times {}_2F_3\left({-n,\ -n-\varphi;\ \mp\frac{ab^2}{4} \atop -2n-\rho-\sigma,\ 1-s-n,\ \frac{1-2s-2n}{2}}\right)$ $\left[\operatorname{Re}b,\ \operatorname{Re}s>0;\ \varphi=\left\{{\rho \atop \sigma}\right\}\right]$

No.	$f(x)$	$F(s)$
8	$(a-x)_+^\rho\, e^{-b\sqrt{x}}$ $\times P_n^{(\rho,\sigma)}\left(\dfrac{2x}{a}-1\right)$	$\dfrac{(-1)^n a^{s+\rho}}{n!}(1-s+\sigma)_n\,\mathrm{B}\,(n+\rho+1,\,s)$ $\times\, {}_2F_3\left(\begin{matrix} s-\sigma,\,s;\,\frac{ab^2}{4} \\ \frac{1}{2},\,s-n-\sigma,\,s+n+\rho+1 \end{matrix}\right)$ $-\,\dfrac{(-1)^n a^{s+\rho+1/2}b}{n!}\left(\dfrac{1}{2}-s+\sigma\right)_n \mathrm{B}\left(n+\rho+1,\,s+\dfrac{1}{2}\right)$ $\times\, {}_2F_3\left(\begin{matrix} s+\frac{1}{2},\,s-\sigma+\frac{1}{2};\,\frac{ab^2}{4} \\ \frac{3}{2},\,s-n-\sigma+\frac{1}{2},\,s+n+\rho+\frac{3}{2} \end{matrix}\right)$ $[a,\ \mathrm{Re}\,s>0;\ \mathrm{Re}\,\rho>-1]$
9	$(x+a)^\sigma\, e^{-b\sqrt{x}}$ $\times P_n^{(\rho,\sigma)}\left(\dfrac{2x}{a}+1\right)$	$-\dfrac{a^{s+\sigma+1/2}b}{n!}\left(\dfrac{1}{2}-s+\rho\right)_n \mathrm{B}\left(-s-n-\sigma-\dfrac{1}{2},\,s+\dfrac{1}{2}\right)$ $\times\, {}_2F_3\left(\begin{matrix} \frac{2s+1}{2},\,\frac{2s-2\rho+1}{2};\,-\frac{ab^2}{4} \\ \frac{3}{2},\,\frac{2s-2n-2\rho+1}{2},\,\frac{2s+2n+2\sigma+3}{2} \end{matrix}\right)+\dfrac{a^{s+\sigma}}{n!}(1-s+\rho)_n$ $\times\,\mathrm{B}\,(-s-n-\sigma,\,s)\,{}_2F_3\left(\begin{matrix} s-\rho,\,s;\,-\frac{ab^2}{4} \\ \frac{1}{2},\,s-n-\rho,\,s+n+\sigma+1 \end{matrix}\right)$ $+\,\dfrac{2a^{-n}b^{-2s-2n-2\sigma}}{n!}(n+\rho+\sigma+1)_n\,\Gamma\,(2s+2n+2\sigma)$ $\times\, {}_2F_3\left(\begin{matrix} -n-\sigma,\,-n-\rho-\sigma;\,-\frac{ab^2}{4} \\ -2n-\rho-\sigma,\,\frac{1}{2}-s-n-\sigma,\,1-s-n-\sigma \end{matrix}\right)$ $[\mathrm{Re}\,b,\ \mathrm{Re}\,s>0;\ |\arg a|<\pi]$
10	$e^{-b/\sqrt{x}}\,P_n^{(\rho,\sigma)}\left(\dfrac{2x}{a}\pm 1\right)$	$\dfrac{2\,(\pm 1)^n b^{2s}}{n!}(\varphi+1)_n\,\Gamma\,(-2s)\,{}_2F_3\left(\begin{matrix} -n,\,n+\rho+\sigma+1 \\ \varphi+1,\,\frac{2s+1}{2},\,s+1;\,\mp\frac{b^2}{4a} \end{matrix}\right)$ $\left[\mathrm{Re}\,b>0;\ \mathrm{Re}\,s<-n;\ \varphi=\left\{\begin{matrix}\rho\\\sigma\end{matrix}\right\}\right]$
11	$(x+a)^\sigma\, e^{-b/\sqrt{x}}$ $\times P_n^{(\rho,\sigma)}\left(\dfrac{2x}{a}+1\right)$	$\dfrac{a^{s+\sigma}}{n!}(1-s+\rho)_n\,\mathrm{B}\,(-s-n-\sigma,\,s)$ $\times\, {}_2F_3\left(\begin{matrix} -s-n-\sigma,\,1-s+n+\rho \\ \frac{1}{2},\,1-s,\,1-s+\rho;\,-\frac{b^2}{4a} \end{matrix}\right)+\dfrac{2a^\sigma b^{2s}}{n!}(\rho+1)_n$ $\times\,\Gamma\,(-2s)\,{}_2F_3\left(\begin{matrix} -n-\sigma,\,n+\rho+1 \\ \rho+1,\,s+\frac{1}{2},\,s+1;\,-\frac{b^2}{4a} \end{matrix}\right)$ $[\mathrm{Re}\,b>0;\ \mathrm{Re}\,(s+\sigma)<-n;\ |\arg a|<\pi]$
12	$(x+a)^n\, e^{-bx}$ $\times P_n^{(\rho,\sigma)}\left(\dfrac{a-x}{a+x}\right)$	$\dfrac{(-1)^n b^{-s-n}}{n!}(\sigma+1)_n\,\Gamma\,(s+n)\,{}_2F_2\left(\begin{matrix} -n,\,-n-\rho;\,ab \\ \sigma+1,\,1-s-n \end{matrix}\right)$ $[\mathrm{Re}\,b,\ \mathrm{Re}\,s>0]$

No.	$f(x)$	$F(s)$

13 $(x+a)^{-(n+\rho+\sigma+1)}\,e^{-bx}$

$\qquad \times P_n^{(\rho,\sigma)}\left(\dfrac{a-x}{a+x}\right)$

$\dfrac{a^{s-(n+\rho+\sigma+1}}{n!}\,(-s+\rho+1)_n\,\mathrm{B}\,(s,\,-s+n+\rho+\sigma+1)$

$$\times\,{}_2F_2\left(\begin{matrix}s,\,s-\rho;\,ab\\s-n-\rho,\,s-n-\rho-\sigma\end{matrix}\right)$$

$$+\,\frac{(-1)^n\,b^{-s+n+\rho+\sigma+1}}{n!}\,(\sigma+1)_n\,\Gamma\,(s-n-\rho-\sigma-1)$$

$$\times\,{}_2F_2\left(\begin{matrix}n+\sigma+1,\,n+\rho+\sigma+1\\\sigma+1,\,-s+n+\rho+\sigma+2;\,ab\end{matrix}\right)$$

$$[\operatorname{Re}b,\ \operatorname{Re}s>0;\ |\arg a|<\pi]$$

14 $e^{-b/x}\,(x+a)^{-(n+\rho+\sigma+1)}$

$\qquad \times P_n^{(\rho,\sigma)}\left(\dfrac{a-x}{a+x}\right)$

$\dfrac{a^{-(n+\rho+\sigma+1)}b^s}{n!}\,(\rho+1)_n\,\Gamma\,(-s)\,{}_2F_2\left(\begin{matrix}n+\rho+1,\,n+\rho+\sigma+1\\\rho+1,\,s+1;\,\frac{b}{a}\end{matrix}\right)$

$$+\,\frac{a^{s-(n+\rho+\sigma+1)}}{n!}\,(1-s+\rho)_n\,\mathrm{B}\,(1-s+n+\rho+\sigma,\,s)$$

$$\times\,{}_2F_2\left(\begin{matrix}1-s+n+\rho,\,1-s+n+\rho+\sigma\\1-s,\,1-s+\rho;\,\frac{b}{a}\end{matrix}\right)$$

$$[\operatorname{Re}b>0;\ \operatorname{Re}s<\operatorname{Re}(\rho+\sigma)+n+1;\ |\arg a|<\pi]$$

15 $e^{-b/x}\,(x+a)^n$

$\qquad \times P_n^{(\rho,\sigma)}\left(\dfrac{a-x}{a+x}\right)$

$\dfrac{a^n b^s}{n!}\,(\rho+1)_n\,\Gamma\,(-s)\,{}_2F_2\left(\begin{matrix}-n,\,-n-\sigma\\\rho+1,\,s+1;\,\frac{b}{a}\end{matrix}\right)$

$$[\operatorname{Re}b>0;\ \operatorname{Re}s<-n]$$

16 $e^{-b\sqrt{x}}\,(x+a)^n$

$\qquad \times P_n^{(\rho,\sigma)}\left(\dfrac{a-x}{a+x}\right)$

$\dfrac{2\,(-1)^n\,b^{-2s-2n}}{n!}\,(\sigma+1)_n\,\Gamma\,(2s+2n)$

$$\times\,{}_2F_3\left(\begin{matrix}-n,\,-n-\rho;\,-\frac{ab^2}{4}\\\sigma+1,\,1-s-n,\,\frac{1-2s-2n}{2}\end{matrix}\right)\quad[\operatorname{Re}b,\ \operatorname{Re}s>0]$$

17 $e^{-b\sqrt{x}}\,(x+a)^{-(n+\rho+\sigma+1)}$

$\qquad \times P_n^{(\rho,\sigma)}\left(\dfrac{a-x}{a+x}\right)$

$\dfrac{a^{s-(n+\rho+\sigma+1)}}{n!}\,(1-s+\rho)_n\,\mathrm{B}\,(1-s+n+\rho+\sigma,\,s)$

$$\times\,{}_2F_3\left(\begin{matrix}s,\,s-\rho;\,-\frac{ab^2}{4}\\\frac{1}{2},\,s-n-\rho-\sigma,\,s-n-\rho\end{matrix}\right)-\frac{a^{s-(n+\rho+\sigma+1/2)}b}{n!}$$

$$\times\left(\frac{1}{2}-s+\rho\right)_n\,\mathrm{B}\left(s+\frac{1}{2},\,\frac{1}{2}-s+n+\rho+\sigma\right)$$

$$\times\,{}_2F_3\left(\begin{matrix}\frac{2s+1}{2},\,\frac{2s-2\rho+1}{2};\,-\frac{ab^2}{4}\\\frac{3}{2},\,\frac{2s-2n-2\rho+1}{2},\,\frac{2s-2n-2\rho-2\sigma+1}{2}\end{matrix}\right)+\frac{2\,(-1)^n}{n!}$$

$$\times\,b^{2(-s+n+\rho+\sigma+1)}\,(\sigma+1)_n\,\Gamma\,(2s-2n-2\rho-2\sigma-2)$$

$$\times\,{}_2F_3\left(\begin{matrix}n+\sigma+1,\,n+\rho+\sigma+1;\,-\frac{ab^2}{4}\\\sigma+1,\,\frac{3-2s+2n+2\rho+2\sigma}{2},\,2-s+n+\rho+\sigma\end{matrix}\right)$$

$$[\operatorname{Re}b,\ \operatorname{Re}s>0;\ |\arg a|<\pi]$$

No.	$f(x)$	$F(s)$
18	$e^{-b/\sqrt{x}}(x+a)^n$ $\times P_n^{(\rho,\sigma)}\left(\dfrac{a-x}{a+x}\right)$	$\dfrac{2a^n b^{2s}}{n!}(\rho+1)_n\,\Gamma(-2s)\,{}_2F_3\left(\begin{matrix}-n,\,-n-\sigma;\,-\frac{b^2}{4a}\\ \rho+1,\,\frac{2s+1}{2},\,s+1\end{matrix}\right)$ $[\operatorname{Re}b>0;\ \operatorname{Re}s<-n]$
19	$\dfrac{e^{-b/\sqrt{x}}}{(x+a)^{n+\rho+\sigma+1}}$ $\times P_n^{(\rho,\sigma)}\left(\dfrac{a-x}{a+x}\right)$	$\dfrac{2a^{-(n+\rho+\sigma+1)}b^{2s}}{n!}(\rho+1)_n\,\Gamma(-2s)\,{}_2F_3\left(\begin{matrix}n+\rho+1,\,n+\rho+\sigma+1\\ \rho+1,\,s+\frac{1}{2},\,s+1;\,-\frac{b^2}{4a}\end{matrix}\right)$ $+\dfrac{a^{s-(n+\rho+\sigma+1)}}{n!}(1-s+\rho)_n\,\mathrm{B}(1-s+n+\rho+\sigma,s)$ $\times {}_2F_3\left(\begin{matrix}1-s+n+\rho,\,1-s+n+\rho+\sigma\\ \frac{1}{2},\,1-s,\,1-s+\rho;\,-\frac{b^2}{4a}\end{matrix}\right)-\dfrac{a^{s-(n+\rho+\sigma+3/2)}b}{n!}$ $\times\left(\dfrac{3}{2}-s+\rho\right)_n\mathrm{B}\left(\dfrac{3}{2}-s+n+\rho+\sigma,\,s-\dfrac{1}{2}\right)$ $\times {}_2F_3\left(\begin{matrix}\frac{3}{2}-s+n+\rho,\,\frac{3}{2}-s+n+\rho+\sigma\\ \frac{3}{2},\,\frac{3}{2}-s,\,\frac{3}{2}-s+\rho;\,-\frac{b^2}{4a}\end{matrix}\right)$ $[\operatorname{Re}b>0;\ \operatorname{Re}s<\operatorname{Re}(\rho+\sigma)+n+1;\ |\arg a|<\pi]$

3.25.3. $\quad P_n^{(\rho,\sigma)}(\varphi(x))$ and trigonometric functions

Notation: $\delta=\left\{\begin{matrix}1\\0\end{matrix}\right\}$.

1	$(a-x)_+^\rho\left\{\begin{matrix}\sin(b\sqrt{x})\\\cos(b\sqrt{x})\end{matrix}\right\}$ $\times P_n^{(\rho,\sigma)}\left(\dfrac{2x}{a}-1\right)$	$\dfrac{(-1)^n\,a^{s+\rho+\delta/2}b^\delta}{n!}\left(1-s+\sigma-\dfrac{\delta}{2}\right)_n\mathrm{B}\left(n+\rho+1,\,s+\dfrac{\delta}{2}\right)$ $\times {}_2F_3\left(\begin{matrix}s-\sigma+\frac{\delta}{2},\,s+\frac{\delta}{2};\,-\frac{ab^2}{4}\\ \frac{2\delta+1}{2},\,\frac{2s-2n-2\sigma+\delta}{2},\,\frac{2s+2n+2\rho+\delta+2}{2}\end{matrix}\right)$ $[a,\ \operatorname{Re}s>0;\ \operatorname{Re}\rho>-1]$
2	$(x+a)^\sigma\left\{\begin{matrix}\sin(b\sqrt{x})\\\cos(b\sqrt{x})\end{matrix}\right\}$ $\times P_n^{(\rho,\sigma)}\left(\dfrac{2x}{a}+1\right)$	$\dfrac{a^{s+\sigma+\delta/2}b^\delta}{n!}\left(1-s+\rho-\dfrac{\delta}{2}\right)_n\mathrm{B}\left(-s-n-\sigma-\dfrac{\delta}{2},\,s+\dfrac{\delta}{2}\right)$ $\times {}_2F_3\left(\begin{matrix}s-\rho+\frac{\delta}{2},\,s+\frac{\delta}{2};\,\frac{ab^2}{4}\\ \frac{2\delta+1}{2},\,\frac{2s-2n-2\rho+\delta}{2},\,\frac{2s+2n+2\sigma+\delta+2}{2}\end{matrix}\right)$ $+\dfrac{2(-1)^n}{a^n b^{2s+2n+2\sigma}n!}\left\{\begin{matrix}\sin[(s+\sigma)\pi]\\\cos[(s+\sigma)\pi]\end{matrix}\right\}$ $\times(n+\rho+\sigma+1)_n\,\Gamma(2s+2n+2\sigma)$ $\times {}_2F_3\left(\begin{matrix}-n-\sigma,\,-n-\rho-\sigma;\,\frac{ab^2}{4}\\ -2n-\rho-\sigma,\,\frac{1-2s-2n-2\sigma}{2},\,1-s-n-\sigma\end{matrix}\right)$ $[b>0;\ -\delta/2<\operatorname{Re}s<1/2-\operatorname{Re}\sigma-n;\ |\arg a|<\pi]$

No.	$f(x)$	$F(s)$

3 $(x+a)^{\sigma}\left\{\begin{matrix}\sin(b/\sqrt{x})\\\cos(b/\sqrt{x})\end{matrix}\right\}$

$$\times P_n^{(\rho,\sigma)}\left(\frac{2x}{a}+1\right)$$

$$\frac{a^{s+\sigma-\delta/2}b^{\delta}}{n!}\left(1-s+\rho+\frac{\delta}{2}\right)_n \mathrm{B}\left(-s-n-\sigma+\frac{\delta}{2},\,s-\frac{\delta}{2}\right)$$

$$\times {}_2F_3\left(\begin{matrix}1-s+n+\rho+\frac{\delta}{2},\,-s-n-\sigma+\frac{\delta}{2}\\\delta+\frac{1}{2},\,1-s+\frac{\delta}{2},\,1-s+\rho+\frac{\delta}{2};\,\frac{b^2}{4a}\end{matrix}\right)$$

$$\mp\frac{2a^{\sigma}b^{2s}}{n!}(\rho+1)_n\,\Gamma(-2s)\left\{\begin{matrix}\sin(s\pi)\\\cos(s\pi)\end{matrix}\right\}$$

$$\times {}_2F_3\left(\begin{matrix}-n-\sigma,\,n+\rho+1\\\rho+1,\,\frac{2s+1}{2},\,s+1;\,\frac{b^2}{4a}\end{matrix}\right)$$

$$[b>0;\,-1/2<\mathrm{Re}\,s<\delta/2-\mathrm{Re}\,\sigma-n;\,|\arg a|<\pi]$$

4 $(x+a)^{-(n+\rho+\sigma+1)}$

$$\times\left\{\begin{matrix}\sin(b\sqrt{x})\\\cos(b\sqrt{x})\end{matrix}\right\}$$

$$\times P_n^{(\rho,\sigma)}\left(\frac{a-x}{a+x}\right)$$

$$\frac{a^{s-(n+\rho+\sigma-\delta/2+1)}b^{\delta}}{n!}\left(1-s+\rho-\frac{\delta}{2}\right)_n$$

$$\times \mathrm{B}\left(s+\frac{\delta}{2},\,1-s+n+\rho+\sigma-\frac{\delta}{2}\right)$$

$$\times {}_2F_3\left(\begin{matrix}s+\frac{\delta}{2}-\rho,\,s+\frac{\delta}{2};\,\frac{ab^2}{4}\\\frac{2\delta+1}{2},\,\frac{2s-2n-2\rho+\delta}{2},\,\frac{2s-2n-2\rho-2\sigma+\delta}{2}\end{matrix}\right)$$

$$+\frac{2b^{2(-s+n+\rho+\sigma+1)}}{n!}(\sigma+1)_n$$

$$\times\Gamma(2s-2n-2\rho-2\sigma-2)\left\{\begin{matrix}\sin[(\rho-s+\sigma)\pi]\\\cos[(\rho-s+\sigma)\pi]\end{matrix}\right\}$$

$$\times {}_2F_3\left(\begin{matrix}n+\sigma+1,\,n+\rho+\sigma+1;\,\frac{ab^2}{4}\\\sigma+1,\,\frac{3-2s+2n+2\rho+2\sigma}{2},\,2-s+n+\rho+\sigma\end{matrix}\right)$$

$$[b>0;\,-\delta/2<\mathrm{Re}\,s<\mathrm{Re}\,(\rho+\sigma)+n+3/2;\,|\arg a|<\pi]$$

3.25.4. $P_n^{(\rho,\sigma)}(\varphi(x))$ and the logarithmic function

No.	$f(x)$	$F(s)$

1 $(a-x)_+^{\rho}\ln\dfrac{x}{a}$

$$\times P_n^{(\rho,\sigma)}\left(\frac{2x}{a}-1\right)$$

$$\frac{(-1)^n\,a^{s+\rho}}{n!}(1-s+\sigma)_n\,\mathrm{B}(n+\rho+1,\,s)\,[\psi(s)$$

$$+\psi(s-\sigma)-\psi(s+n+\rho+1)-\psi(s-n-\sigma)]$$

$$[a,\,\mathrm{Re}\,s>0;\,\mathrm{Re}\,\rho>-1]$$

3.25.5. $P_n^{(\rho,\sigma)}(\varphi(x))$ **and** $\mathrm{Ei}(bx)$

1	$(a-x)_+^\rho\,\mathrm{Ei}(-bx)$ $\times P_n^{(\rho,\sigma)}\left(\dfrac{2x}{a}-1\right)$	$\dfrac{(-1)^{n+1}a^{s+\rho+1}b}{n!}(\sigma-s)_n\,\mathrm{B}(n+\rho+1,\,s+1)$ $\times\ {}_4F_4\!\left(\begin{matrix}1,\,1,\,s-\sigma+1,\,s+1;\,-ab\\2,\,2,\,s-n-\sigma+1,\,s+n+\rho+2\end{matrix}\right)$ $+\dfrac{(-1)^n a^{s+\rho}}{n!}(\sigma-s+1)_n\,\mathrm{B}(n+\rho+1,\,s)$ $\times\left[\psi(s)-\psi(s+n+\rho+1)-\displaystyle\sum_{j=0}^{n-1}\dfrac{1}{1-s+j+\sigma}+\ln(ab)+\mathbf{C}\right]$ $[a,\ \mathrm{Re}\,s>0;\ \mathrm{Re}\,\rho>-1]$

3.25.6. $P_n^{(\rho,\sigma)}(\varphi(x))$ **and** $\mathrm{si}(b\sqrt{x}),\ \mathrm{ci}(b\sqrt{x})$

Notation: $\delta=\left\{\begin{matrix}1\\0\end{matrix}\right\}$.

1	$(a-x)_+^\rho\left\{\begin{matrix}\mathrm{si}(b\sqrt{x})\\\mathrm{ci}(b\sqrt{x})\end{matrix}\right\}$ $\times P_n^{(\rho,\sigma)}\left(\dfrac{2x}{a}-1\right)$	$\dfrac{(-1)^{n+1}2^{\delta-2}a^{s+\rho+\delta/2+1}b^{\delta+2}}{3^{2\delta}n!}\left(\sigma-s-\dfrac{\delta}{2}\right)_n\mathrm{B}\!\left(n+\rho+1,\,s+\dfrac{\delta}{2}+1\right)$ $\times\ {}_4F_5\!\left(\begin{matrix}1,\,\frac{\delta+2}{2},\,\frac{2s+\delta+2}{2},\,\frac{2s-2\sigma+\delta+2}{2};\,-\frac{ab^2}{4}\\2,\,\frac{\delta+4}{2},\,\frac{2\delta+3}{2},\,\frac{2s-2n-2\sigma+\delta+2}{2},\,\frac{2s+2n+2\rho+\delta+4}{2}\end{matrix}\right)$ $+\dfrac{(-1)^n a^{s+\rho+\delta/2}b^\delta}{n!}\left(1-s+\sigma-\dfrac{\delta}{2}\right)_n\mathrm{B}\!\left(n+\rho+1,\,s+\dfrac{\delta}{2}\right)$ $\times\left[\dfrac{1}{2}\psi(s)-\dfrac{1}{2}\psi(s+n+\rho+1)-\dfrac{1}{2}\displaystyle\sum_{i=0}^{n-1}\dfrac{1}{1-s+i+\sigma}\right.$ $\left.+\dfrac{1}{2}\ln(ab^2)+\mathbf{C}\right]^{1-\delta}$ $-\delta\dfrac{(-1)^n\pi a^{s+\rho}}{2\,(n!)}(1-s+\sigma)_n\,\mathrm{B}(n+\rho+1,\,s)$ $[a,\ \mathrm{Re}\,s>0;\ \mathrm{Re}\,\rho>-1]$

3.25.7. $P_n^{(\rho,\sigma)}(\varphi(x))$ **and** $\mathrm{erf}(bx^r),\ \mathrm{erfc}(bx^r)$

1	$(a-x)_+^\rho\left\{\begin{matrix}\mathrm{erf}(bx)\\\mathrm{erfc}(bx)\end{matrix}\right\}$ $\times P_n^{(\rho,\sigma)}\left(\dfrac{2x}{a}-1\right)$	$\pm\dfrac{2\,(-1)^n a^{s+\rho+1}b}{\sqrt{\pi}\,n!}(\sigma-s)_n\,\mathrm{B}(n+\rho+1,\,s+1)$ $\times\ {}_5F_5\!\left(\begin{matrix}\frac{1}{2},\,\frac{s+1}{2},\,\frac{s+2}{2},\,\frac{s-\sigma+1}{2},\,\frac{s-\sigma+2}{2};\,-a^2b^2\\\frac{3}{2},\,\frac{s-n-\sigma+1}{2},\,\frac{s-n-\sigma+2}{2},\,\frac{s+n+\rho+2}{2},\,\frac{s+n+\rho+3}{2}\end{matrix}\right)$ $+\left\{\begin{matrix}0\\1\end{matrix}\right\}\dfrac{(-1)^n a^{s+\rho}}{n!}(1-s+\sigma)_n\,\mathrm{B}(n+\rho+1,\,s)$ $[a>0;\ \mathrm{Re}\,\rho>-1;\ \mathrm{Re}\,s>-(1\pm1)/2]$

No.	$f(x)$	$F(s)$
2	$\operatorname{erfc}(b\sqrt{x})$ $\times P_n^{(\rho,\sigma)}\left(\dfrac{2x}{a}\pm 1\right)$	$\dfrac{(\pm 1)^n b^{-2s}}{\sqrt{\pi}\,n!\,s}(\varphi+1)_n\,\Gamma\left(\dfrac{2s+1}{2}\right){}_4F_2\left(\begin{array}{c}-n,\,n+\rho+\sigma+1,\,s,\,\frac{2s+1}{2}\\ \varphi+1,\,s+1;\,\mp\frac{1}{ab^2}\end{array}\right)$ $\left[\operatorname{Re}s>0;\;|\arg b|<\pi/4;\;\varphi=\left\{\begin{array}{c}\rho\\ \sigma\end{array}\right\}\right]$
3	$(a-x)_+^\rho\left\{\begin{array}{c}\operatorname{erf}(b\sqrt{x})\\ \operatorname{erfc}(b\sqrt{x})\end{array}\right\}$ $\times P_n^{(\rho,\sigma)}\left(\dfrac{2x}{a}-1\right)$	$\pm\dfrac{2(-1)^n a^{s+\rho+1/2}b}{\sqrt{\pi}\,n!}\left(\dfrac{1}{2}-s+\sigma\right)_n\operatorname{B}\left(n+\rho+1,\dfrac{2s+1}{2}\right)$ $\times {}_3F_3\left(\begin{array}{c}\frac{1}{2},\,\frac{2s+1}{2}\,\frac{2s-2\sigma+1}{2};\,-ab^2\\ \frac{3}{2},\,\frac{2s-2n-2\sigma+1}{2},\,\frac{2s+2n+2\rho+3}{2}\end{array}\right)$ $+\left\{\begin{array}{c}0\\ 1\end{array}\right\}\dfrac{(-1)^n a^{s+\rho}}{n!}(1-s+\sigma)_n\operatorname{B}(n+\rho+1,\,s)$ $[a>0;\;\operatorname{Re}\rho>-1;\;\operatorname{Re}s>-(1\pm 1)/4]$
4	$(a-x)_+^\rho\,e^{b^2 x}\operatorname{erf}(b\sqrt{x})$ $\times P_n^{(\rho,\sigma)}\left(\dfrac{2x}{a}-1\right)$	$\dfrac{2(-1)^n a^{s+\rho+1/2}b}{\sqrt{\pi}\,n!}\left(\dfrac{1}{2}-s+\sigma\right)_n\operatorname{B}\left(n+\rho+1,\,s+\dfrac{1}{2}\right)$ $\times {}_3F_3\left(\begin{array}{c}1,\,s+\frac{1}{2},\,s-\sigma+\frac{1}{2};\,ab^2\\ \frac{3}{2},\,s-n-\sigma+\frac{1}{2},\,s+n+\rho+\frac{3}{2}\end{array}\right)$ $[a>0,\;\operatorname{Re}\rho>-1;\;\operatorname{Re}s>-1/2]$
5	$(a-x)^n\operatorname{erfc}(b\sqrt{x})$ $\times P_n^{(\rho,\sigma)}\left(\dfrac{a+x}{a-x}\right)$	$\dfrac{(\rho+1)_n a^n}{n!\sqrt{\pi}\,b^{2s}s}\Gamma\left(\dfrac{2s+1}{2}\right){}_4F_2\left(\begin{array}{c}-n,\,-n-\sigma,\,s,\,\frac{2s+1}{2}\\ \rho+1,\,s+1;\,\frac{1}{ab^2}\end{array}\right)\quad[\operatorname{Re}s>0]$

3.25.8. $P_n^{(\rho,\sigma)}(\varphi(x))$ **and** $\gamma(\nu,bx)$

1	$(a-x)_+^\rho\,\gamma(\nu,bx)$ $\times P_n^{(\rho,\sigma)}\left(\dfrac{2x}{a}-1\right)$	$\dfrac{(-1)^n a^{s+\nu+\rho}b^\nu}{n!\,\nu}(1-s-\nu+\sigma)_n\Gamma\left[\begin{array}{c}n+\rho+1,\,s+\nu\\ s+n+\nu+\rho+1\end{array}\right]$ $\times {}_3F_3\left(\begin{array}{c}\nu,\,s+\nu,\,s+\nu-\sigma;\,-ab\\ \nu+1,\,s+n+\nu+\rho+1,\,s-n+\nu-\sigma\end{array}\right)$ $[a,\;\operatorname{Re}(s+\nu)>0;\;\operatorname{Re}\rho>-1]$

3.25.9. $P_n^{(\rho,\sigma)}(\varphi(x))$ **and** $I_\nu(bx^r),\,J_\nu(bx^r)$

1	$J_\nu(b\sqrt{x})$ $\times P_n^{(\rho,\sigma)}\left(\dfrac{2x}{a}\pm 1\right)$	$\dfrac{2^{2s+2n}}{n!\,a^n b^{2s+2n}}(n+\rho+\sigma+1)_n\Gamma\left[\begin{array}{c}\frac{2s+2n+\nu}{2}\\ \frac{2-2s-2n+\nu}{2}\end{array}\right]$ $\times {}_2F_3\left(\begin{array}{c}-n,\,-n-\varphi;\,\pm\frac{ab^2}{4}\\ -2n-\rho-\sigma,\,\frac{2-2s-2n-\nu}{2},\,\frac{2-2s-2n+\nu}{2}\end{array}\right)$ $\left[b>0;\;-\operatorname{Re}\nu/2<\operatorname{Re}s<3/4-n;\;\varphi=\left\{\begin{array}{c}\rho\\ \sigma\end{array}\right\}\right]$

No.	$f(x)$	$F(s)$
2	$(a-x)_+^\rho \left\{ \begin{array}{c} J_\nu(b\sqrt{x}) \\ I_\nu(b\sqrt{x}) \end{array} \right\}$ $\times P_n^{(\rho,\sigma)}\left(\dfrac{2x}{a}-1\right)$	$\dfrac{(-1)^n a^{s+\nu/2+\rho}b^\nu}{2^\nu n!\,\Gamma(\nu+1)}\left(1-s+\sigma-\dfrac{\nu}{2}\right)_n \mathrm{B}\left(n+\rho+1,\,s+\dfrac{\nu}{2}\right)$ $\times\,{}_2F_3\left(\begin{array}{c} s+\frac{\nu}{2},\,s+\frac{\nu}{2}-\sigma;\,\mp\frac{ab^2}{4} \\ \nu+1,\,s-n+\frac{\nu}{2}-\sigma,\,s+n+\frac{\nu}{2}+\rho+1 \end{array}\right)$ $[a,\ \mathrm{Re}(2s+\nu)>0;\ \mathrm{Re}\,\rho>-1]$
3	$(x+a)^\sigma J_\nu(b\sqrt{x})$ $\times P_n^{(\rho,\sigma)}\left(\dfrac{2x}{a}+1\right)$	$\dfrac{a^{s+\nu/2+\sigma}b^\nu}{2^\nu n!\,\Gamma(\nu+1)}\left(1-s+\rho-\dfrac{\nu}{2}\right)_n \mathrm{B}\left(-s-n-\sigma-\dfrac{\nu}{2},\,s+\dfrac{\nu}{2}\right)$ $\times\,{}_2F_3\left(\begin{array}{c} s+\frac{\nu}{2},\,s+\frac{\nu}{2}-\rho;\,\frac{ab^2}{4} \\ \nu+1,\,\frac{2s-2n+\nu-2\rho}{2},\,\frac{2s+2n+\nu+2\sigma+2}{2} \end{array}\right)$ $+\dfrac{(2/b)^{2(s+n+\sigma)}}{n!\,a^n}(n+\rho+\sigma+1)_n\,\Gamma\left[\begin{array}{c} \frac{2s+2n+\nu+2\sigma}{2} \\ \frac{2-2s-2n-2\sigma+\nu}{2} \end{array}\right]$ $\times\,{}_2F_3\left(\begin{array}{c} -n-\sigma,\,-n-\rho-\sigma;\,\frac{ab^2}{4} \\ -2n-\rho-\sigma,\,\frac{2-2s-2n-2\sigma-\nu}{2},\,\frac{2-2s-2n-2\sigma+\nu}{2} \end{array}\right)$ $[b>0;\,-\mathrm{Re}\,\nu/2<\mathrm{Re}\,s<3/4-\mathrm{Re}\,\sigma-n;;\,|\arg a|<\pi]$
4	$(a-x)_+^\rho J_\nu\left(\dfrac{b}{\sqrt{x}}\right)$ $\times P_n^{(\rho,\sigma)}\left(\dfrac{2x}{a}-1\right)$	$\dfrac{(-1)^n a^{s+\rho-\nu/2}b^\nu}{2^\nu n!\,\Gamma(\nu+1)}\left(1-s+\dfrac{\nu}{2}+\sigma\right)_n \mathrm{B}\left(n+\rho+1,\,s-\dfrac{\nu}{2}\right)$ $\times\,{}_2F_3\left(\begin{array}{c} -s+n+\frac{\nu}{2}+\sigma+1,\,-s-n+\frac{\nu}{2}-\rho \\ \nu+1,\,-s+\frac{\nu}{2}+1,\,-s+\frac{\nu}{2}+\sigma+1;\,-\frac{b^2}{4a} \end{array}\right)$ $+\dfrac{(-1)^n a^\rho b^{2s}}{2^{2s}n!}(\sigma+1)_n\,\Gamma\left[\begin{array}{c} \frac{\nu}{2}-s \\ s+\frac{\nu}{2}+1 \end{array}\right]$ $\times\,{}_2F_3\left(\begin{array}{c} -n-\rho,\,n+\sigma+1;\,-\frac{b^2}{4a} \\ \sigma+1,\,\frac{2s-\nu+2}{2},\,\frac{2s+\nu+2}{2} \end{array}\right)$ $[a,\,b>0;\ \mathrm{Re}\,\rho>-1;\ \mathrm{Re}\,s>-3/4]$
5	$(x+a)^\sigma J_\nu\left(\dfrac{b}{\sqrt{x}}\right)$ $\times P_n^{(\rho,\sigma)}\left(\dfrac{2x}{a}+1\right)$	$\dfrac{a^{s-\nu/2+\sigma}b^\nu}{2^\nu n!\,\Gamma(\nu+1)}\left(1-s+\dfrac{\nu}{2}+\rho\right)_n \mathrm{B}\left(s-\dfrac{\nu}{2},\,\dfrac{\nu}{2}-s-n-\sigma\right)$ $\times\,{}_2F_3\left(\begin{array}{c} 1-s+n+\frac{\nu}{2}+\rho,\,-s-n+\frac{\nu}{2}-\sigma \\ \nu+1,\,1-s+\frac{\nu}{2},\,1-s+\frac{\nu}{2}+\rho;\,\frac{b^2}{4a} \end{array}\right)$ $+\dfrac{a^\sigma b^{2s}}{2^{2s}n!}(\rho+1)_n\,\Gamma\left[\begin{array}{c} \frac{\nu}{2}-s \\ s+\frac{\nu}{2}+1 \end{array}\right]$ $\times\,{}_2F_3\left(\begin{array}{c} -n-\sigma,\,n+\rho+1 \\ \rho+1,\,\frac{2s-\nu+2}{2},\,\frac{2s+\nu+2}{2};\,\frac{b^2}{4a} \end{array}\right)$ $[b>0;\,-3/4<\mathrm{Re}\,s<\mathrm{Re}(\nu/2-\sigma)-n;\,|\arg a|<\pi]$

No.	$f(x)$	$F(s)$
6	$(a-x)_+^\sigma$ $\times \left\{ \begin{array}{c} J_\mu(b\sqrt{x})\,J_\nu(b\sqrt{x}) \\ I_\mu(b\sqrt{x})\,I_\nu(b\sqrt{x}) \end{array} \right\}$ $\times P_n^{(\rho,\sigma)}\left(1-\dfrac{2x}{a}\right)$	$\dfrac{a^{s+(\mu+\nu)/2+\sigma}b^{\mu+\nu}}{2^{\mu+\nu}n!}\left(1-s+\rho-\dfrac{\mu+\nu}{2}\right)_n$ $\times\Gamma\left[\begin{array}{c} n+\sigma+1,\ \frac{2s+\mu+\nu}{2} \\ \mu+1,\ \nu+1,\ \frac{2s+2n+\mu+\nu+2\sigma+2}{2} \end{array}\right]$ $\times {}_4F_5\left(\begin{array}{c} \frac{\mu+\nu+1}{2},\ \frac{\mu+\nu+2}{2},\ \frac{2s+\mu+\nu-2\rho}{2},\ \frac{2s+\mu+\nu}{2};\ \mp ab^2 \\ \mu+1,\ \nu+1,\ \mu+\nu+1,\ \frac{2s-2n+\mu+\nu-2\rho}{2},\ \frac{2s+2n+\mu+\nu+2\sigma+2}{2} \end{array}\right)$ $[a,\ \mathrm{Re}\,(2s+\mu+\nu)>0;\ \mathrm{Re}\,\sigma>-1]$
7	$(x+a)^n\,J_\nu(b\sqrt{x})$ $\times P_n^{(\rho,\sigma)}\left(\dfrac{a-x}{a+x}\right)$	$\dfrac{(-1)^n}{n!}\left(\dfrac{2}{b}\right)^{2s+2n}(\sigma+1)_n\,\Gamma\left[\begin{array}{c} \frac{2s+2n+\nu}{2} \\ \frac{2-2s-2n+\nu}{2} \end{array}\right]$ $\times {}_2F_3\left(\begin{array}{c} -n,\ -n-\rho;\ \frac{ab^2}{4} \\ \sigma+1,\ \frac{2-2s-2n-\nu}{2},\ \frac{2-2s-2n+\nu}{2} \end{array}\right)$ $[a,\ b>0;\ -\mathrm{Re}\,\nu/2<\mathrm{Re}\,s<3/4-n]$
8	$\dfrac{J_\nu(b\sqrt{x})}{(x+a)^{n+\rho+\sigma+1}}$ $\times P_n^{(\rho,\sigma)}\left(\dfrac{a-x}{a+x}\right)$	$\dfrac{a^{s-(n-\nu/2+\rho+\sigma+1)}(b/2)^\nu}{n!\,\Gamma(\nu+1)}\left(1-s+\rho-\dfrac{\nu}{2}\right)_n$ $\times\mathrm{B}\left(1-s+n-\dfrac{\nu}{2}+\rho+\sigma,\ s+\dfrac{\nu}{2}\right)$ $\times {}_2F_3\left(\begin{array}{c} s+\frac{\nu}{2}-\rho,\ s+\frac{\nu}{2};\ \frac{ab^2}{4} \\ \nu+1,\ \frac{2s-2n+\nu-2\rho}{2},\ \frac{2s-2n+\nu-2\rho-2\sigma}{2} \end{array}\right)$ $+\dfrac{(-1)^n(b/2)^{2(-s+n+\rho+\sigma+1)}}{n!}$ $\times(\sigma+1)_n\,\Gamma\left[\begin{array}{c} \frac{2s-2n+\nu-2\rho-2\sigma-2}{2} \\ \frac{4-2s+2n+\nu+2\rho+2\sigma}{2} \end{array}\right]$ $\times {}_2F_3\left(\begin{array}{c} n+\sigma+1,\ n+\rho+\sigma+1;\ \frac{ab^2}{4} \\ \sigma+1,\ \frac{4-2s+2n-\nu+2\rho+2\sigma}{2},\ \frac{4-2s+2n+\nu+2\rho+2\sigma}{2} \end{array}\right)$ $[b>0;\ -\mathrm{Re}\,\nu/2<\mathrm{Re}\,s<\mathrm{Re}\,(\rho+\sigma)+n+7/4;\ |\arg a|<\pi]$

3.25.10. $P_n^{(\rho,\sigma)}(\varphi(x))$ **and** $K_\nu(bx^r)$

No.	$f(x)$	$F(s)$
1	$K_\nu(b\sqrt{x})$ $\times P_n^{(\rho,\sigma)}\left(\dfrac{2x}{a}\pm 1\right)$	$\dfrac{2^{2s+2n-1}}{n!\,a^n b^{2s+2n}}(n+\rho+\sigma+1)_n\,\Gamma\left(s+n-\dfrac{\nu}{2}\right)\Gamma\left(s+n+\dfrac{\nu}{2}\right)$ $\times {}_2F_3\left(\begin{array}{c} -n,\ -n-\varphi;\ \mp\frac{ab^2}{4} \\ -2n-\rho-\sigma,\ \frac{2-2s-2n-\nu}{2},\ \frac{2-2s-2n+\nu}{2} \end{array}\right)$ $\left[\mathrm{Re}\,b>0;\ \mathrm{Re}\,s>|\mathrm{Re}\,\nu|/2;\ \varphi=\left\{\begin{array}{c}\rho \\ \sigma\end{array}\right\}\right]$

No.	$f(x)$	$F(s)$
2	$K_\nu\left(\dfrac{b}{\sqrt{x}}\right)$ $\times P_n^{(\rho,\sigma)}\left(\dfrac{2x}{a}\pm 1\right)$	$\dfrac{(\pm 1)^n b^{2s}}{2^{2s+1}n!}(\varphi+1)_n \Gamma\left(-s-\dfrac{\nu}{2}\right)\Gamma\left(-s+\dfrac{\nu}{2}\right)$ $\times {}_2F_3\left(\begin{matrix}-n,\,n+\rho+\sigma+1;\,\mp\frac{b^2}{4a}\\\varphi+1,\,s-\frac{\nu}{2}+1,\,s+\frac{\nu}{2}+1\end{matrix}\right)$ $\left[\operatorname{Re}b>0;\ \operatorname{Re}s<-|\operatorname{Re}\nu|/2-n;\ \varphi=\left\{\begin{matrix}\rho\\\sigma\end{matrix}\right\}\right]$
3	$(x+a)^n K_\nu(b\sqrt{x})$ $\times P_n^{(\rho,\sigma)}\left(\dfrac{a-x}{a+x}\right)$	$\dfrac{(-1)^n}{2(n!)}\left(\dfrac{2}{b}\right)^{2s+2n}(\sigma+1)_n \Gamma\left(s+n-\dfrac{\nu}{2}\right)\Gamma\left(s+n+\dfrac{\nu}{2}\right)$ $\times {}_2F_3\left(\begin{matrix}-n,\,-n-\rho;\,-\frac{ab^2}{4}\\\sigma+1,\,\frac{2-2s-2n-\nu}{2},\,\frac{2-2s-2n+\nu}{2}\end{matrix}\right)$ $[\operatorname{Re}b>0;\ \operatorname{Re}s>|\operatorname{Re}\nu|/2]$

3.25.11. $P_n^{(\rho,\sigma)}(\varphi(x))$ **and** $P_m(\psi(x))$

Notation: $\varepsilon=0$ or 1.

No.	$f(x)$	$F(s)$
1	$(a-x)_+^\sigma P_m\left(1-\dfrac{2x}{a}\right)$ $\times P_n^{(\rho,\sigma)}\left(1-\dfrac{2x}{a}\right)$	$\dfrac{a^{s+\sigma}}{n!}(1-s+\rho)_n \operatorname{B}(n+\sigma+1,s)\,{}_4F_3\left(\begin{matrix}-m,\,m+1,\,s-\rho,\,s;\,1\\1,\,s-n-\rho,\,s+n+\sigma+1\end{matrix}\right)$ $[a,\ \operatorname{Re}s>0;\ \operatorname{Re}\sigma>-1]$
2	$(a-x)_+^\rho P_{2m+\varepsilon}(bx)$ $\times P_n^{(\rho,\sigma)}\left(\dfrac{2x}{a}-1\right)$	$(-1)^{m+n}\dfrac{a^{s+\rho+\varepsilon}(2b)^\varepsilon}{m!\,n!}\left(\dfrac{1}{2}\right)_{m+\varepsilon}(1-s+\sigma-\varepsilon)_n \operatorname{B}(n+\rho+1,s+\varepsilon)$ $\times {}_6F_5\left(\begin{matrix}-m,\,m+\varepsilon+\frac{1}{2},\,\Delta(2,s+\varepsilon),\,\Delta(2,s-\sigma+\varepsilon);\,a^2b^2\\\frac{2\varepsilon+1}{2},\,\Delta(2,s+n+\rho+\varepsilon+1),\,\Delta(2,s-n-\sigma+\varepsilon)\end{matrix}\right)$ $[a>0;\ \operatorname{Re}\rho>-1;\ \operatorname{Re}s>-\varepsilon]$
3	$(a-x)_+^\rho P_m(2bx-1)$ $\times P_n^{(\rho,\sigma)}\left(\dfrac{2x}{a}-1\right)$	$\dfrac{(-1)^{m+n}a^{s+\rho}}{n!}(1-s+\sigma)_n \operatorname{B}(n+\rho+1,s)$ $\times {}_4F_3\left(\begin{matrix}-m,\,m+1,\,s-\sigma,\,s;\,ab\\1,\,s-n-\sigma,\,s+n+\rho+1\end{matrix}\right)$ $[a,\ \operatorname{Re}s>0;\ \operatorname{Re}\rho>-1]$
4	$\theta(a-x)\left\{\begin{matrix}(x+b)^\sigma\\(b-x)^\rho\end{matrix}\right\}$ $\times P_m\left(\dfrac{2x}{a}-1\right)$ $\times P_n^{(\rho,\sigma)}\left(\dfrac{2x}{b}\pm 1\right)$	$\dfrac{(-1)^m(\pm 1)^n b^\psi a^s}{n!}(\varphi+1)_n(1-s)_m$ $\times \Gamma\left[\begin{matrix}s\\s+m+1\end{matrix}\right]{}_4F_3\left(\begin{matrix}-n-\psi,\,n+\varphi+1,\,s,\,s;\,\mp\frac{a}{b}\\\varphi+1,\,s-m,\,s+m+1\end{matrix}\right)$ $\left[\left\{\begin{matrix}a>0;\,|\arg b|<\pi\\b>a>0\end{matrix}\right\};\ \operatorname{Re}s>0;\ \varphi=\left\{\begin{matrix}\rho\\\sigma\end{matrix}\right\},\ \psi=\left\{\begin{matrix}\sigma\\\rho\end{matrix}\right\}\right]$

No.	$f(x)$	$F(s)$
5	$(a-x)_+^\rho$ $\times P_{2m+\varepsilon}\left(\sqrt{\dfrac{x}{a}}\right)$ $\times P_n^{(\rho,\sigma)}\left(\dfrac{2x}{a}-1\right)$	$\dfrac{2^\varepsilon(-1)^{m+n}a^{s+\rho}}{m!\,n!}\left(\dfrac{1}{2}\right)_{m+\varepsilon}\left(1-s+\sigma-\dfrac{\varepsilon}{2}\right)_n B\left(n+\rho+1,\,s+\dfrac{\varepsilon}{2}\right)$ $\times {}_4F_3\left(\begin{matrix}-m,\ \frac{2m+2\varepsilon+1}{2},\ \frac{2s-2\sigma+\varepsilon}{2},\ \frac{2s+\varepsilon}{2};\ 1\\ \frac{2\varepsilon+1}{2},\ \frac{2s-2n-2\sigma+\varepsilon}{2},\ \frac{2s+2n+2\rho+\varepsilon+2}{2}\end{matrix}\right)$ $[a>0;\ \operatorname{Re}\rho>-1;\ \operatorname{Re}s>-\varepsilon/2]$
6	$(a-x)_+^\rho\,P_{2m+\varepsilon}(b\sqrt{x})$ $\times P_n^{(\rho,\sigma)}\left(\dfrac{2x}{a}-1\right)$	$\dfrac{(-1)^{m+n}a^{s+\rho+\varepsilon/2}(2b)^\varepsilon}{m!\,n!}\left(\dfrac{1}{2}\right)_{m+\varepsilon}\left(1-s+\sigma-\dfrac{\varepsilon}{2}\right)_n$ $\times B\left(n+\rho+1,\,s+\dfrac{\varepsilon}{2}\right)$ $\times {}_4F_3\left(\begin{matrix}-m,\ \frac{2m+2\varepsilon+1}{2},\ \frac{2s-2\sigma+\varepsilon}{2},\ \frac{2s+\varepsilon}{2};\ ab^2\\ \frac{2\varepsilon+1}{2},\ \frac{2s-2n-2\sigma+\varepsilon}{2},\ \frac{2s+2n+2\rho+\varepsilon+2}{2}\end{matrix}\right)$ $[a>0;\ \operatorname{Re}\rho>-1;\ \operatorname{Re}s>-\varepsilon/2]$

3.25.12. $\;P_n^{(\rho,\sigma)}(\varphi(x))$ **and** $T_m(\psi(x))$

Notation: $\varepsilon=0$ or 1.

1	$(a-x)_+^{\sigma-1/2}$ $\times T_m\left(1-\dfrac{2x}{a}\right)$ $\times P_n^{(\rho,\sigma)}\left(1-\dfrac{2x}{a}\right)$	$\dfrac{a^{s+\sigma-1/2}}{n!}\left(1-s+\rho\right)_n B(n+\sigma+1,\,s)$ $\times {}_4F_3\left(\begin{matrix}-m+\frac{1}{2},\ m+\frac{1}{2},\ s-\rho,\ s\\ \frac{1}{2},\ s-n-\rho,\ s+n+\sigma+1;\ 1\end{matrix}\right)$ $[a,\ \operatorname{Re}s>0;\ \operatorname{Re}\sigma>-1/2]$
2	$(a-x)_+^\rho\,T_{2m+\varepsilon}(bx)$ $\times P_n^{(\rho,\sigma)}\left(\dfrac{2x}{a}-1\right)$	$(-1)^{m+n}\dfrac{(m+\varepsilon/2)\,a^{s+\rho+\varepsilon}(2b)^\varepsilon}{m!\,n!}\left(1-s+\sigma-\varepsilon\right)_n$ $\times\Gamma(m+\varepsilon)\,B(n+\rho+1,\,s+\varepsilon)$ $\times {}_6F_5\left(\begin{matrix}-m,\ m+\varepsilon,\ \Delta(2,s+\varepsilon),\ \Delta(2,s-\sigma+\varepsilon);\ a^2b^2\\ \frac{2\varepsilon+1}{2},\ \Delta(2,s+n+\rho+\varepsilon+1),\ \Delta(2,s-n-\sigma+\varepsilon)\end{matrix}\right)$ $[a>0;\ \operatorname{Re}\rho>-1;\ \operatorname{Re}s>-\varepsilon]$
3	$(a-x)_+^\rho\,(1-bx)^{-1/2}$ $\times T_m^\lambda(2bx-1)$ $\times P_n^{(\rho,\sigma)}\left(\dfrac{2x}{a}-1\right)$	$\dfrac{(-1)^{m+n}a^{s+\rho}}{n!}\left(1-s+\sigma\right)_n B(n+\rho+1,\,s)$ $\times {}_4F_3\left(\begin{matrix}-m+\frac{1}{2},\ m+\frac{1}{2},\ s-\sigma,\ s\\ \frac{1}{2},\ s-n-\sigma,\ s+n+\rho+1;\ ab\end{matrix}\right)$ $[a,\ \operatorname{Re}s>0;\ \operatorname{Re}\rho>-1;\ |\arg(1-ab)|<\pi]$

No.	$f(x)$	$F(s)$
4	$(a-x)_+^{-1/2}\left\{\begin{matrix}(x+b)^\sigma\\(b-x)^\rho\end{matrix}\right\}$ $\times\, T_m\left(\dfrac{2x}{a}-1\right)$ $\times\, P_n^{(\rho,\sigma)}\left(\dfrac{2x}{b}\pm 1\right)$	$\dfrac{(-1)^m\,(\pm 1)^n\,\sqrt{\pi}\,a^{s-1/2}b^\psi}{n!}\,(\varphi+1)_n\left(\dfrac{1}{2}-s\right)_m$ $\times\,\Gamma\left[\begin{matrix}s\\\tfrac{2s+2m+1}{2}\end{matrix}\right]\,{}_4F_3\left(\begin{matrix}-n-\psi,\,n+\varphi+1,\,s,\,\tfrac{2s+1}{2}\\\varphi+1,\,\tfrac{2s-2m+1}{2},\,\tfrac{2s+2m+1}{2};\,\mp\tfrac{a}{b}\end{matrix}\right)$ $\left[\left\{\begin{matrix}a>0;\ |\arg b|<\pi\\b>a>0\end{matrix}\right\};\ \operatorname{Re}s>0;\ \varphi=\left\{\begin{matrix}\rho\\\sigma\end{matrix}\right\},\ \psi=\left\{\begin{matrix}\sigma\\\rho\end{matrix}\right\}\right]$
5	$(a-x)_+^{\rho-1/2}$ $\times\, T_{2m+\varepsilon}\left(\sqrt{\dfrac{x}{a}}\right)$ $\times\, P_n^{(\rho,\sigma)}\left(\dfrac{2x}{a}-1\right)$	$\dfrac{2^\varepsilon\,(-1)^{m+n}\,(2m+\varepsilon)\,a^{s+\rho-1/2}}{m!\,n!}\left(1-s+\sigma-\dfrac{\varepsilon}{2}\right)_n$ $\times\,\Gamma(m+\varepsilon)\,\mathrm{B}\left(n+\rho+1,\,s+\dfrac{\varepsilon}{2}\right)$ $\times\,{}_4F_3\left(\begin{matrix}\tfrac{-2m+1}{2},\,\tfrac{2m+2\varepsilon+1}{2},\,\tfrac{2s-2\sigma+\varepsilon}{2},\,\tfrac{2s+\varepsilon}{2}\\\tfrac{2\varepsilon+1}{2},\,\tfrac{2s-2n-2\sigma+\varepsilon}{2},\,\tfrac{2s+2n+2\rho+\varepsilon+2}{2};\,1\end{matrix}\right)$ $[a>0;\ \operatorname{Re}\rho>-1/2;\ \operatorname{Re}s>-\varepsilon/2]$
6	$(a-x)_+^\rho\,(1-b^2x)^{-1/2}$ $\times\, T_{2m+\varepsilon}\left(b\sqrt{x}\right)$ $\times\, P_n^{(\rho,\sigma)}\left(\dfrac{2x}{a}-1\right)$	$\dfrac{(-1)^{m+n}\,(2m+\varepsilon)\,a^{s+\rho+\varepsilon/2}\,(2b)^\varepsilon}{2\,(m!\,n!)}\left(1-s+\sigma-\dfrac{\varepsilon}{2}\right)_n$ $\times\,\Gamma(m+\varepsilon)\,\mathrm{B}\left(n+\rho+1,\,s+\dfrac{\varepsilon}{2}\right)$ $\times\,{}_4F_3\left(\begin{matrix}\tfrac{-2m+1}{2},\,\tfrac{2m+2\varepsilon+1}{2},\,\tfrac{2s-2\sigma+\varepsilon}{2},\,\tfrac{2s+\varepsilon}{2}\\\tfrac{2\varepsilon+1}{2},\,\tfrac{2s-2n-2\sigma+\varepsilon}{2},\,\tfrac{2s+2n+2\rho+\varepsilon+2}{2};\,ab^2\end{matrix}\right)$ $[a>0;\ \operatorname{Re}\rho>-1;\ \operatorname{Re}s>-\varepsilon/2;;\ |\arg(1-ab^2)|<\pi]$

3.25.13. $P_n^{(\rho,\sigma)}(\varphi(x))$ **and** $U_m(\psi(x))$

Notation: $\varepsilon=0$ or 1.

No.	$f(x)$	$F(s)$
1	$(a-x)_+^{\sigma+1/2}$ $\times\, U_m\left(1-\dfrac{2x}{a}\right)$ $\times\, P_n^{(\rho,\sigma)}\left(1-\dfrac{2x}{a}\right)$	$\dfrac{(m+1)\,a^{s+\sigma+1/2}}{n!}\,(1-s+\rho)_n\,\mathrm{B}(n+\sigma+1,\,s)$ $\times\,{}_4F_3\left(\begin{matrix}-m-\tfrac{1}{2},\,m+\tfrac{3}{2},\,s-\rho,\,s;\,1\\\tfrac{3}{2},\,s-n-\rho,\,s+n+\sigma+1\end{matrix}\right)$ $[a,\,\operatorname{Re}s>0;\ \operatorname{Re}\sigma>-3/2]$
2	$(a-x)_+^\rho\,U_{2m+\varepsilon}(bx)$ $\times\, P_n^{(\rho,\sigma)}\left(\dfrac{2x}{a}-1\right)$	$(-1)^{m+n}\,\dfrac{(m+1)^\varepsilon\,a^{s+\rho+\varepsilon}\,(2b)^\varepsilon}{n!}\,(1-s+\sigma-\varepsilon)_n\,\mathrm{B}(n+\rho+1,\,s+\varepsilon)$ $\times\,{}_6F_5\left(\begin{matrix}-m,\,m+\varepsilon+1,\,\Delta(2,\,s+\varepsilon),\,\Delta(2,\,s-\sigma+\varepsilon);\,a^2b^2\\\tfrac{2\varepsilon+1}{2},\,\Delta(2,\,s+n+\rho+\varepsilon+1),\,\Delta(2,\,s-n-\sigma+\varepsilon)\end{matrix}\right)$ $[a>0;\ \operatorname{Re}\rho>-1;\ \operatorname{Re}s>-\varepsilon]$

No.	$f(x)$	$F(s)$
3	$(a-x)_+^\rho \sqrt{1-bx}$ $\times U_m(2bx-1)$ $\times P_n^{(\rho,\sigma)}\left(\dfrac{2x}{a}-1\right)$	$\dfrac{(-1)^{m+n}(m+1)a^{s+\rho}}{n!}(1-s+\sigma)_n \, \mathrm{B}(n+\rho+1,s)$ $\times {}_4F_3\left(\begin{array}{c} -m-\frac{1}{2},\, m+\frac{3}{2},\, s-\sigma,\, s;\, ab \\ \frac{3}{2},\, s-n-\sigma,\, s+n+\rho+1 \end{array}\right)$ $[a,\ \mathrm{Re}\,s>0;\ \mathrm{Re}\,\rho>-1;\ |\arg(1-ab)|<\pi]$
4	$(a-x)_+^{1/2}\left\{\begin{array}{c}(x+b)^\sigma\\(b-x)^\rho\end{array}\right\}$ $\times U_m\left(\dfrac{2x}{a}-1\right)$ $\times P_n^{(\rho,\sigma)}\left(\dfrac{2x}{b}\pm 1\right)$	$\dfrac{(-1)^m(\pm 1)^n(m+1)\sqrt{\pi}\,a^{s+1/2}b^\psi}{2\,(n!)}(\varphi+1)_n\left(\dfrac{3}{2}-s\right)_m$ $\times \Gamma\left[\begin{array}{c}s\\ \frac{2s+2m+3}{2}\end{array}\right]{}_4F_3\left(\begin{array}{c}-n-\psi,\, n+\varphi+1,\, \frac{2s-1}{2},\, s\\ \varphi+1,\, \frac{2s-2m-1}{2},\, \frac{2s+2m+3}{2};\, \mp\frac{a}{b}\end{array}\right)$ $\left[\left\{\begin{array}{c}a>0;\ |\arg b|<\pi\\ b>a>0\end{array}\right\};\ \mathrm{Re}\,s>0;\ \varphi=\left\{\begin{array}{c}\rho\\\sigma\end{array}\right\},\ \psi=\left\{\begin{array}{c}\sigma\\\rho\end{array}\right\}\right]$
5	$(a-x)_+^{\rho+1/2}$ $\times U_{2m+\varepsilon}\left(\sqrt{\dfrac{x}{a}}\right)$ $\times P_n^{(\rho,\sigma)}\left(\dfrac{2x}{a}-1\right)$	$\dfrac{2^\varepsilon(-1)^{m+n}(m+1)^\varepsilon a^{s+\rho+1/2}}{n!}\left(1-s+\sigma-\dfrac{\varepsilon}{2}\right)_n$ $\times \mathrm{B}\left(n+\rho+1,s+\dfrac{\varepsilon}{2}\right){}_4F_3\left(\begin{array}{c}\frac{-2m-1}{2},\, \frac{2m+2\varepsilon+1}{2},\, \frac{2s-2\sigma+\varepsilon}{2},\, \frac{2s+\varepsilon}{2}\\ \frac{2\varepsilon+1}{2},\, \frac{2s-2n-2\sigma+\varepsilon}{2},\, \frac{2s+2n+2\rho+\varepsilon+2}{2};\, 1\end{array}\right)$ $[a>0;\ \mathrm{Re}\,\rho>-3/2;\ \mathrm{Re}\,s>-\varepsilon/2]$
6	$(a-x)_+^\rho \sqrt{1-b^2x}$ $\times U_{2m+\varepsilon}(b\sqrt{x})$ $\times P_n^{(\rho,\sigma)}\left(\dfrac{2x}{a}-1\right)$	$\dfrac{(-1)^{m+n}(m+1)^\varepsilon a^{s+\rho+\varepsilon/2}(2b)^\varepsilon}{n!}\left(1-s+\sigma-\dfrac{\varepsilon}{2}\right)_n$ $\times \mathrm{B}\left(n+\rho+1,s+\dfrac{\varepsilon}{2}\right)$ $\times {}_4F_3\left(\begin{array}{c}\frac{-2m-1}{2},\, \frac{2m+2\varepsilon+1}{2},\, \frac{2s-2\sigma+\varepsilon}{2},\, \frac{2s+\varepsilon}{2};\, ab^2\\ \frac{2\varepsilon+1}{2},\, \frac{2s-2n-2\sigma+\varepsilon}{2},\, \frac{2s+2n+2\rho+\varepsilon+2}{2}\end{array}\right)$ $[a>0;\ \mathrm{Re}\,\rho>-1;\ \mathrm{Re}\,s>-\varepsilon/2;\ |\arg(1-ab^2)|<\pi]$

3.25.14. $P_n^{(\rho,\sigma)}(\varphi(x))$ **and** $H_m(b\sqrt{x})$

Notation: $\varepsilon=0$ or 1.

	$(a-x)_+^\rho e^{-b^2x}$	$\dfrac{(-1)^{m+n}2^{2m+\varepsilon}a^{s+\rho+\varepsilon/2}b^\varepsilon}{n!}\left(\dfrac{2\varepsilon+1}{2}\right)_m$
1	$\times H_{2m+\varepsilon}(b\sqrt{x})$	$\times\left(1-s+\sigma-\dfrac{\varepsilon}{2}\right)_n \mathrm{B}\left(n+\rho+1,s+\dfrac{\varepsilon}{2}\right)$
	$\times P_n^{(\rho,\sigma)}\left(\dfrac{2x}{a}-1\right)$	$\times {}_3F_3\left(\begin{array}{c}\frac{2m+2\varepsilon+1}{2},\, \frac{2s-2\sigma+\varepsilon}{2},\, \frac{2s+\varepsilon}{2};\, -ab^2\\ \frac{2\varepsilon+1}{2},\, \frac{2s+2n+2\rho+\varepsilon+2}{2},\, \frac{2s-2n-2\sigma+\varepsilon}{2}\end{array}\right)$ $[a>0;\ \mathrm{Re}\,\rho>-1;\ \mathrm{Re}\,s>-\varepsilon/2]$

3.25.15. $\quad P_n^{(\rho,\sigma)}(\varphi(x))$ **and** $L_m^\lambda(bx)$

1	$(a-x)_+^\rho\, e^{-bx} L_m^\lambda(bx)$ $\times P_n^{(\rho,\sigma)}\left(\dfrac{2x}{a}-1\right)$	$\dfrac{(-1)^n\, a^{s+\rho}}{m!\,n!}(\lambda+1)_m(1-s+\sigma)_n\, \mathrm{B}(n+\rho+1,\,s)$ $\times {}_3F_3\!\left(\begin{matrix}m+\lambda+1,\,s-\sigma,\,s;\,-ab\\ \lambda+1,\,s-n-\sigma,\,s+n+\rho+1\end{matrix}\right)$ $[a,\ \mathrm{Re}\,s>0;\ \mathrm{Re}\,\rho>-1]$

3.25.16. $\quad P_n^{(\rho,\sigma)}(\varphi(x))$ **and** $C_m^\lambda(\psi(x))$

Notation: $\varepsilon=0$ or 1.

1	$(a-x)_+^{\lambda+\sigma-1/2}$ $\times C_m^\lambda\left(1-\dfrac{2x}{a}\right)$ $\times P_n^{(\rho,\sigma)}\left(1-\dfrac{2x}{a}\right)$	$\dfrac{a^{s+\lambda+\sigma-1/2}}{m!\,n!}(2\lambda)_m(1-s+\rho)_n\, \mathrm{B}(n+\sigma+1,\,s)$ $\times {}_4F_3\!\left(\begin{matrix}-m-\lambda+\frac12,\,m+\lambda+\frac12,\,s-\rho,\,s\\ \lambda+\frac12,\,s-n-\rho,\,s+n+\sigma+1;\,1\end{matrix}\right)$ $[a,\ \mathrm{Re}\,s>0;\ \mathrm{Re}\,(\lambda+\sigma)>-1/2]$
2	$(a-x)_+^\rho\, C_{2m+\varepsilon}^\lambda(bx)$ $\times P_n^{(\rho,\sigma)}\left(\dfrac{2x}{a}-1\right)$	$(-1)^{m+n}\dfrac{a^{s+\rho+\varepsilon}(2b)^\varepsilon}{m!\,n!}(\lambda)_{m+\varepsilon}$ $\times(1-s+\sigma-\varepsilon)_n\, \mathrm{B}(n+\rho+1,\,s+\varepsilon)$ $\times {}_6F_5\!\left(\begin{matrix}-m,\,m+\lambda+\varepsilon,\,\Delta(2,\,s+\varepsilon),\,\Delta(2,\,s-\sigma+\varepsilon);\,a^2b^2\\ \frac{2\varepsilon+1}{2},\,\Delta(2,\,s+n+\rho+\varepsilon+1),\,\Delta(2,\,s-n-\sigma+\varepsilon)\end{matrix}\right)$ $[a>0;\ \mathrm{Re}\,\rho>-1;\ \mathrm{Re}\,s>-\varepsilon]$
3	$(a-x)_+^\rho\,(1-bx)^{\lambda-1/2}$ $\times C_m^\lambda(2bx-1)$ $\times P_n^{(\rho,\sigma)}\left(\dfrac{2x}{a}-1\right)$	$\dfrac{(-1)^{m+n}\,a^{s+\rho}}{m!\,n!}(2\lambda)_m(1-s+\sigma)_n\, \mathrm{B}(n+\rho+1,\,s)$ $\times {}_4F_3\!\left(\begin{matrix}-m-\lambda+\frac12,\,m+\lambda+\frac12,\,s-\sigma,\,s\\ \lambda+\frac12,\,s-n-\sigma,\,s+n+\rho+1;\,ab\end{matrix}\right)$ $[a,\ \mathrm{Re}\,s>0;\ \mathrm{Re}\,\rho>-1;\ |\arg(1-ab)|<\pi]$
4	$(a-x)_+^{\lambda-1/2}\left\{\begin{matrix}(x+b)^\sigma\\(b-x)^\rho\end{matrix}\right\}$ $\times C_m^\lambda\left(\dfrac{2x}{a}-1\right)$ $\times P_n^{(\rho,\sigma)}\left(\dfrac{2x}{b}\pm1\right)$	$\dfrac{(-1)^m(\pm1)^n\,a^{s+\lambda-1/2}b^\psi}{m!\,n!}(2\lambda)_m(\varphi+1)_n$ $\times\left(\dfrac12-s+\lambda\right)_m\Gamma\!\left[\begin{matrix}\frac{2\lambda+1}{2},\,s\\ \frac{2s+2m+2\lambda+1}{2}\end{matrix}\right]$ $\times {}_4F_3\!\left(\begin{matrix}-n-\psi,\,n+\varphi+1,\,s,\,\frac{2s-2\lambda+1}{2};\,\mp\frac{a}{b}\\ \varphi+1,\,\frac{2s-2m-2\lambda+1}{2},\,\frac{2s+2m+2\lambda+1}{2}\end{matrix}\right)$ $\left[\left\{\begin{matrix}a>0;\ |\arg b|<\pi\\ b>a>0\end{matrix}\right\};\ \mathrm{Re}\,s>0;\ \varphi=\left\{\begin{matrix}\rho\\\sigma\end{matrix}\right\},\,\psi=\left\{\begin{matrix}\sigma\\\rho\end{matrix}\right\}\right]$

No.	$f(x)$	$F(s)$
5	$(a-x)_+^{\lambda+\rho-1/2}$ $\times C_{2m+\varepsilon}^{\lambda}\left(\sqrt{\dfrac{x}{a}}\right)$ $\times P_n^{(\rho,\sigma)}\left(\dfrac{2x}{a}-1\right)$	$\dfrac{2^\varepsilon\,(-1)^{m+n}\,a^{s+\lambda+\rho-1/2}}{m!\,n!}\,(\lambda)_{m+\varepsilon}\left(1-s+\sigma-\dfrac{\varepsilon}{2}\right)_n$ $\times\mathrm{B}\left(n+\rho+1,\,s+\dfrac{\varepsilon}{2}\right)$ $\times\,{}_4F_3\left(\begin{matrix}\frac{-2m-2\lambda+1}{2},\,\frac{2m+2\varepsilon+1}{2},\,\frac{2s+\varepsilon}{2},\,\frac{2s-2\sigma+\varepsilon}{2}\\ \frac{2\varepsilon+1}{2},\,\frac{2s-2n-2\sigma+\varepsilon}{2},\,\frac{2s+2n+2\rho+\varepsilon+2}{2};\,1\end{matrix}\right)$ $[a>0;\ \mathrm{Re}\,(\lambda+\rho)>-1/2;\ \mathrm{Re}\,s>-\varepsilon/2]$
6	$(a-x)_+^{\rho}\left(1-b^2x\right)^{\lambda-1/2}$ $\times C_{2m+\varepsilon}^{\lambda}(b\sqrt{x})$ $\times P_n^{(\rho,\sigma)}\left(\dfrac{2x}{a}-1\right)$	$\dfrac{(-1)^{m+n}\,a^{s+\rho+\varepsilon/2}\,(2b)^\varepsilon}{m!\,n!}\,(\lambda)_{m+\varepsilon}\left(1-s+\sigma-\dfrac{\varepsilon}{2}\right)_n$ $\times\mathrm{B}\left(n+\rho+1,\,s+\dfrac{\varepsilon}{2}\right)$ $\times\,{}_4F_3\left(\begin{matrix}\frac{-2m-2\lambda+1}{2},\,\frac{2m+2\varepsilon+1}{2},\,\frac{2s+\varepsilon}{2},\,\frac{2s-2\sigma+\varepsilon}{2}\\ \frac{2\varepsilon+1}{2},\,\frac{2s-2n-2\sigma+\varepsilon}{2},\,\frac{2s+2n+2\rho+\varepsilon+2}{2};\,ab^2\end{matrix}\right)$ $[a>0;\ \mathrm{Re}\,\rho>-1;\ \mathrm{Re}\,s>-\varepsilon/2;\ |\arg\left(1-ab^2\right)|<\pi]$
7	$(a-x)_+^{\rho}\left[C_m^{\lambda}\left(\sqrt{1-bx}\right)\right]^2$ $\times P_n^{(\rho,\sigma)}\left(\dfrac{2x}{a}-1\right)$	$\dfrac{(-1)^n\,a^{s+\rho}}{(m!)^2\,n!}\,[(2\lambda)_m]^2\,(1-s+\sigma)_n\,\mathrm{B}\,(n+\rho+1,\,s)$ $\times\,{}_5F_4\left(\begin{matrix}-m,\,\lambda,\,m+2\lambda,\,s-\sigma,\,s;\,ab\\ \frac{2\lambda+1}{2},\,2\lambda,\,s-n-\sigma,\,s+n+\rho+1\end{matrix}\right)$ $[a,\ \mathrm{Re}\,s>0;\ \mathrm{Re}\,\rho>-1]$

3.25.17.   Products of $P_n^{(\rho,\sigma)}\,(ax+b)$

No.	$f(x)$	$F(s)$
1	$(a-x)_+^{\nu+\sigma}$ $\times P_m^{(\lambda,\nu)}\left(1-\dfrac{2x}{a}\right)$ $\times P_n^{(\rho,\sigma)}\left(1-\dfrac{2x}{a}\right)$	$\dfrac{a^{s+\nu+\sigma}}{m!\,n!}\,(\lambda+1)_m\,(1-s+\rho)_n\,\mathrm{B}\,(n+\sigma+1,s)$ $\times\,{}_4F_3\left(\begin{matrix}-m-\nu,\,m+\lambda+1,\,s-\rho,\,s\\ \lambda+1,\,s-n-\rho,\,s+n+\sigma+1;\,1\end{matrix}\right)$ $[a,\ \mathrm{Re}\,s>0;\ \mathrm{Re}\,(\sigma+\nu)>-1]$
2	$(a-x)_+^{\lambda+\rho}$ $\times P_m^{(\lambda,\nu)}\left(\dfrac{2x}{a}-1\right)$ $\times P_n^{(\rho,\sigma)}\left(\dfrac{2x}{a}-1\right)$	$\dfrac{(-1)^{m+n}\,a^{s+\lambda+\rho}}{m!\,n!}\,(\nu+1)_m\,(1-s+\sigma)_n\,\mathrm{B}\,(n+\rho+1,s)$ $\times\,{}_4F_3\left(\begin{matrix}-m-\lambda,\,m+\nu+1,\,s-\sigma,\,s\\ \nu+1,\,s-n-\sigma,\,s+n+\rho+1;\,1\end{matrix}\right)$ $[a,\ \mathrm{Re}\,s>0;\ \mathrm{Re}\,(\lambda+\rho)>-1]$

No.	$f(x)$	$F(s)$
3	$(a-x)_+^\rho \, P_m^{(\lambda,\nu)}(bx\pm 1)$ $\times P_n^{(\rho,\sigma)}\left(\dfrac{2x}{a}-1\right)$	$\dfrac{(-1)^n (\pm 1)^m a^{s+\rho}}{m!\,n!} (\varphi+1)_m (1-s+\sigma)_n \, \mathrm{B}(n+\rho+1,s)$ $\times {}_4F_3\left(\begin{matrix} -m,\, m+\lambda+\nu+1,\, s-\sigma,\, s;\, \mp\frac{ab}{2} \\ \varphi+1,\, s-n-\sigma,\, s+n+\rho+1 \end{matrix}\right)$ $\left[a,\ \operatorname{Re}s>0;\ \operatorname{Re}\rho>-1;\ \varphi=\left\{\begin{matrix}\lambda\\\nu\end{matrix}\right\}\right]$
4	$(a-x)_+^\rho (1-bx)^\lambda$ $\times P_m^{(\lambda,\nu)}(2bx-1)$ $\times P_n^{(\rho,\sigma)}\left(\dfrac{2x}{a}-1\right)$	$\dfrac{(-1)^{m+n} a^{s+\rho}}{m!\,n!} (\nu+1)_m (1-s+\sigma)_n \, \mathrm{B}(n+\rho+1,s)$ $\times {}_4F_3\left(\begin{matrix} -m-\lambda,\, m+\nu+1,\, s-\sigma,\, s \\ \nu+1,\, s-n-\sigma,\, s+n+\rho+1;\, ab \end{matrix}\right)$ $[a,\ \operatorname{Re}s>0;\ \operatorname{Re}\rho>-1;\ |\arg(1-ab)|<\pi]$
5	$(a-x)_+^\lambda \left\{\begin{matrix}(x+b)^\sigma\\(b-x)^\rho\end{matrix}\right\}$ $\times P_m^{(\lambda,\nu)}\left(\dfrac{2x}{a}-1\right)$ $\times P_n^{(\rho,\sigma)}\left(\dfrac{2x}{b}\pm 1\right)$	$\dfrac{(-1)^m (\pm 1)^n a^{s+\lambda}b^\psi}{m!\,n!} (1-s+\nu)_m \, \mathrm{B}(m+\lambda+1,s)$ $\times (\varphi+1)_n \, {}_4F_3\left(\begin{matrix} -n-\psi,\, n+\varphi+1,\, s-\nu,\, s;\, \mp\frac{a}{b} \\ \varphi+1,\, s-m-\nu,\, s+m+\lambda+1 \end{matrix}\right)$ $\left[\varphi=\left\{\begin{matrix}\rho\\\sigma\end{matrix}\right\},\ \psi=\left\{\begin{matrix}\sigma\\\rho\end{matrix}\right\};\right.$ $\left.\left\{\begin{matrix}a>0;\ |\arg b|<\pi\\b>a>0\end{matrix}\right\};\ \operatorname{Re}\lambda>-1;\ \operatorname{Re}s>0\right]$
6	$(a-x)_+^\rho \, P_m^{(\lambda,\nu)}\left(1-\dfrac{b}{x}\right)$ $\times P_n^{(\rho,\sigma)}\left(\dfrac{2x}{a}-1\right)$	$\dfrac{(-1)^n a^{s-m+\rho}(b/2)^m}{m!\,n!} (-2m-\lambda-\nu)_m$ $\times (m-s+\sigma+1)_n \Gamma\left[\begin{matrix}n+\rho+1,\,s-m\\s-m+n+\rho+1\end{matrix}\right]$ $\times {}_4F_3\left(\begin{matrix} -m,\, -m-\lambda,\, s-m-\sigma,\, s-m;\, \frac{2a}{b} \\ -2m-\lambda-\nu,\, s-m-n-\sigma,\, s-m+n+\rho+1 \end{matrix}\right)$ $[a>0;\ \operatorname{Re}\rho>-1;\ \operatorname{Re}s>m]$
7	$(a-x)_+^\rho (b-x)^m$ $\times P_m^{(\lambda,\nu)}\left(\dfrac{b+x}{b-x}\right)$ $\times P_n^{(\rho,\sigma)}\left(\dfrac{2x}{a}-1\right)$	$\dfrac{(-1)^n a^{s+\rho}b^m}{m!\,n!} (\lambda+1)_m (1-s+\sigma)_n \Gamma\left[\begin{matrix}n+\rho+1,\,s\\s+n+\rho+1\end{matrix}\right]$ $\times {}_4F_3\left(\begin{matrix} -m,\, -m-\nu,\, s-\sigma,\, s;\, \frac{a}{b} \\ \lambda+1,\, s-n-\sigma,\, s+n+\rho+1 \end{matrix}\right)$ $[a,\ \operatorname{Re}s>0;\ \operatorname{Re}\rho>-1]$

3.26.   The Complete Elliptic Integrals $\mathbf{K}(z)$, $\mathbf{E}(z)$, and $\mathbf{D}(z)$

More formulas can be obtained from the corresponding section due to the relations

$$\mathbf{K}(z) = \frac{\pi}{2}\,{}_2F_1\left(\frac{1}{2}, \frac{1}{2}; 1; z^2\right), \qquad\qquad \mathbf{E}(z) = \frac{\pi}{2}\,{}_2F_1\left(-\frac{1}{2}, \frac{1}{2}; 1; z^2\right),$$

$$\mathbf{D}(z) = \frac{\pi}{4}\,{}_2F_1\left(\frac{1}{2}, \frac{3}{2}; 2; z^2\right), \qquad\qquad \mathbf{K}(z) = \frac{1}{2}\,G_{22}^{12}\left(-z^2 \,\middle|\, \begin{matrix} 1/2,\, 1/2 \\ 0,\, 0 \end{matrix}\right),$$

$$\mathbf{E}(z) = -\frac{1}{4}\,G_{22}^{12}\left(-z^2 \,\middle|\, \begin{matrix} 1/2,\, 3/2 \\ 0,\, 0 \end{matrix}\right), \qquad\qquad \mathbf{D}(z) = \frac{1}{2}\,G_{22}^{12}\left(-z^2 \,\middle|\, \begin{matrix} -1/2,\, 1/2 \\ 0,\, -1 \end{matrix}\right).$$

3.26.1. $\mathbf{K}(\varphi(x))$

No.	$f(x)$	$F(s)$	
1	$\mathbf{K}(iax)$	$\dfrac{a^{-s}}{4}\,\Gamma\!\left[\begin{matrix} \frac{s}{2},\, \frac{1-s}{2},\, \frac{1-s}{2} \\ \frac{2-s}{2} \end{matrix}\right]$	$[\operatorname{Re}a > 0;\ 0 < \operatorname{Re}s < 1/2]$
2	$\mathbf{K}(iax) - \dfrac{\pi}{2}$	$\dfrac{a^{-s}}{4}\,\Gamma\!\left[\begin{matrix} \frac{s}{2},\, \frac{1-s}{2},\, \frac{1-s}{2} \\ \frac{2-s}{2} \end{matrix}\right]$	$[\operatorname{Re}a > 0;\ -1 < \operatorname{Re}s < 0]$
3	$\mathbf{K}(iax)$ $-\dfrac{\pi}{2}\displaystyle\sum_{k=0}^{n}\frac{(1/2)_k^2}{(k!)^2}\left(-a^2x^2\right)^k$	$\dfrac{a^{-s}}{4}\,\Gamma\!\left[\begin{matrix} \frac{s}{2},\, \frac{1-s}{2},\, \frac{1-s}{2} \\ \frac{2-s}{2} \end{matrix}\right]$	$[\operatorname{Re}a > 0;\ -n-1 < \operatorname{Re}s < -n]$
4	$\mathbf{K}\left(\pm i\dfrac{a-x}{2\sqrt{ax}}\right)$	$\dfrac{a^s}{4\pi}\,\Gamma\!\left[\dfrac{2s+1}{4},\, \dfrac{2s+1}{4},\, \dfrac{1-2s}{4},\, \dfrac{1-2s}{4}\right]$	$[-1/2 < \operatorname{Re}s < 1/2;\ |\arg a| < \pi]$
5	$\mathbf{K}\left(\sqrt{\dfrac{a-x}{a}}\right)$	$\dfrac{a^s}{2\pi}\,\Gamma\!\left[s,\, s,\, \dfrac{1-2s}{2},\, \dfrac{1-2s}{2}\right]$	$[0 < \operatorname{Re}s < 1/2]$
6	$\mathbf{K}\left(\sqrt{\dfrac{a+x\operatorname{sgn}(x-a)}{2a}}\right)$	$\dfrac{a^s}{8\pi}\,\Gamma\!\left[\dfrac{s}{2},\, \dfrac{s+1}{2},\, \dfrac{1-2s}{4},\, \dfrac{1-2s}{4}\right]$	$[a > 0;\ 0 < \operatorname{Re}s < 1/2]$
7	$\mathbf{K}\left(\sqrt{\dfrac{\sqrt{a}-\sqrt{x+a}}{2\sqrt{a}}}\right)$	$\dfrac{\pi a^s}{2}\,\Gamma\!\left[\begin{matrix} s,\, \frac{1-4s}{4},\, \frac{1-4s}{4} \\ \frac{1}{4},\, \frac{1}{4},\, 1-s \end{matrix}\right]$	$[0 < \operatorname{Re}s < 1/4;\ |\arg a| < \pi]$

3.26.2. $\mathbf{K}(\varphi(x))$ and algebraic functions

1	$\dfrac{1}{(x+a)^\rho}\,\mathbf{K}\left(\dfrac{b}{x+a}\right)$	$\dfrac{\pi a^{s-\rho}}{2}\,\mathrm{B}(s, \rho-s)\,{}_4F_3\!\left(\begin{matrix} \frac{1}{2},\, \frac{1}{2},\, \frac{\rho-s}{2},\, \frac{\rho-s+1}{2} \\ 1,\, \frac{\rho}{2},\, \frac{\rho+1}{2};\, \frac{b^2}{a^2} \end{matrix}\right)$	
		$[0 < \operatorname{Re}s < \operatorname{Re}\rho;\ |\arg a| < \pi]$	

No.	$f(x)$	$F(s)$
2	$\dfrac{1}{(x+a)^{\rho}}\,\mathbf{K}\!\left(\dfrac{bx}{x+a}\right)$	$\dfrac{\pi a^{s-\rho}}{2}\,\mathrm{B}(s,\rho-s)\;{}_4F_3\!\left(\begin{matrix}\frac{1}{2},\,\frac{1}{2},\,\frac{s}{2},\,\frac{s+1}{2}\\ 1,\,\frac{\rho}{2},\,\frac{\rho+1}{2};\,b^2\end{matrix}\right)$ $[0<\operatorname{Re}s<\operatorname{Re}\rho;\ |\arg a|<\pi]$
3	$\dfrac{1}{x+a}\,\mathbf{K}\!\left(\pm\dfrac{x-a}{x+a}\right)$	$\dfrac{a^{s-1}}{8\pi}\,\Gamma\!\left[\dfrac{s}{2},\dfrac{s}{2},\dfrac{1-s}{2},\dfrac{1-s}{2}\right]$ $[0<\operatorname{Re}s<1;\ |\arg a|<\pi]$
4	$\dfrac{1}{x+a}\,\mathbf{K}\!\left(\dfrac{|x-a|}{x+a}\right)$	$\dfrac{a^{s-1}}{8\pi}\,\Gamma\!\left[\dfrac{s}{2},\dfrac{s}{2},\dfrac{1-s}{2},\dfrac{1-s}{2}\right]$ $[\operatorname{Re}a>0;\ 0<\operatorname{Re}s<1]$
5	$\dfrac{1}{x+a}\,\mathbf{K}\!\left(\pm\dfrac{2\sqrt{ax}}{x+a}\right)$	$\dfrac{\pi a^{s-1}}{4}\,\Gamma\!\left[\dfrac{\frac{s}{2},\,\frac{1-s}{2}}{\frac{s+1}{2},\,\frac{2-s}{2}}\right]\qquad [a>0;\ 0<\operatorname{Re}s<1]$
6	$\dfrac{1}{|x-a|}\,\mathbf{K}\!\left(\pm\dfrac{2i\sqrt{ax}}{x-a}\right)$	$\dfrac{\pi a^{s-1}}{4}\,\Gamma\!\left[\dfrac{\frac{s}{2},\,\frac{1-s}{2}}{\frac{s+1}{2},\,\frac{2-s}{2}}\right]\qquad [a>0;\ 0<\operatorname{Re}s<1]$
7	$\dfrac{1}{(x+a)^{\rho}}\,\mathbf{K}\!\left(\dfrac{b}{\sqrt{x+a}}\right)$	$\dfrac{\pi a^{s-\rho}}{2}\,\mathrm{B}(s,\rho-s)\;{}_3F_2\!\left(\begin{matrix}\frac{1}{2},\,\frac{1}{2},\,\rho-s\\ 1,\,\rho;\,\frac{b^2}{a}\end{matrix}\right)$ $[0<\operatorname{Re}s<\operatorname{Re}\rho;\ |\arg a|<\pi]$
8	$\dfrac{1}{\sqrt{x+a}}\,\mathbf{K}\!\left(\sqrt{\dfrac{a}{x+a}}\right)$	$\dfrac{a^{s-1/2}}{2}\,\Gamma\!\left[\dfrac{s,\,s,\,\frac{1-2s}{2}}{\frac{2s+1}{2}}\right]$ $[0<\operatorname{Re}s<1/2;\ |\arg a|<\pi]$
9	$\dfrac{1}{\sqrt{x+a}}\,\mathbf{K}\!\left(\sqrt{\dfrac{x}{x+a}}\right)$	$\dfrac{a^{s-1/2}}{2}\,\Gamma\!\left[\dfrac{s,\,\frac{1-2s}{2},\,\frac{1-2s}{2}}{1-s}\right]$ $[0<\operatorname{Re}s<1/2;\ |\arg a|<\pi]$
10	$\dfrac{1}{\sqrt{x+a}}\,\mathbf{K}\!\left(\sqrt{\dfrac{\sqrt{a}-\sqrt{x+a}}{2\sqrt{a}}}\right)$	$\dfrac{\pi a^{s-1/2}}{2}\,\Gamma\!\left[\dfrac{s,\,\frac{3-4s}{4},\,\frac{3-4s}{4}}{\frac{3}{4},\,\frac{3}{4},\,1-s}\right]$ $[0<\operatorname{Re}s<3/4;\ |\arg a|<\pi]$
11	$\dfrac{1}{\sqrt{x+a}}\,\mathbf{K}\!\left(\dfrac{|\sqrt{a}-\sqrt{x}|}{\sqrt{2\,(x+a)}}\right)$	$\dfrac{a^{s-1/2}}{8\pi}\,\Gamma\!\left[\dfrac{s}{2},\dfrac{2s+1}{4},\dfrac{1-2s}{4},\dfrac{1-s}{2}\right]$ $[a>0;\ 0<\operatorname{Re}s<1/2]$
12	$\dfrac{1}{\sqrt[4]{x+a}}\,\mathbf{K}\!\left(\dfrac{\sqrt{\sqrt{x+a}-\sqrt{a}}}{\sqrt{2}\,\sqrt[4]{x+a}}\right)$	$2^{2s-1}\sqrt{\pi}\,a^{s-1/4}\,\Gamma\!\left[\dfrac{s,\,\frac{1-4s}{2}}{1-s}\right]$ $[0<\operatorname{Re}s<1/4;\ |\arg a|<\pi]$

No.	$f(x)$	$F(s)$
13	$\dfrac{1}{\sqrt[4]{x+a}}\,\mathbf{K}\left(\dfrac{\sqrt{\sqrt{x+a}-\sqrt{x}}}{\sqrt{2}\,\sqrt[4]{x+a}}\right)$	$2^{-2s-1/2}\sqrt{\pi}\,a^{s-1/4}\,\Gamma\!\left[\begin{matrix}2s,\ \frac{1-4s}{4}\\ \frac{4s+3}{4}\end{matrix}\right]$
		$[0<\operatorname{Re}s<1/4;\ |\arg a|<\pi]$
14	$\dfrac{1}{\sqrt[4]{x+a}}\,\mathbf{K}\left(\pm i\,\dfrac{\sqrt{x+a}-\sqrt{a}}{2\sqrt[4]{a}\,\sqrt[4]{x+a}}\right)$	$\dfrac{a^{s-1/4}}{2}\,\Gamma\!\left[\begin{matrix}s,\ \frac{1-2s}{2},\ \frac{1-2s}{2}\\ 1-s\end{matrix}\right]$
		$[0<\operatorname{Re}s<1/2;\ |\arg a|<\pi]$
15	$\dfrac{1}{\sqrt[4]{x+a}}\,\mathbf{K}\left(\pm i\,\dfrac{\sqrt{x+a}-\sqrt{x}}{2\sqrt[4]{x}\,\sqrt[4]{x+a}}\right)$	$\dfrac{a^{s-1/4}}{2}\,\Gamma\!\left[\begin{matrix}\frac{1-4s}{4},\ \frac{4s+1}{4},\ \frac{4s+1}{4}\\ \frac{4s+3}{4}\end{matrix}\right]$
		$[-1/4<\operatorname{Re}s<1/4;\ |\arg a|<\pi]$
16	$\dfrac{1}{\sqrt{x+a}+\sqrt{a}}\,\mathbf{K}\left(\pm\dfrac{\left(\sqrt{x+a}-\sqrt{a}\right)^2}{x}\right)$	$\dfrac{a^{s-1/2}}{4}\,\Gamma\!\left[\begin{matrix}s,\ \frac{1-2s}{2},\ \frac{1-2s}{2}\\ 1-s\end{matrix}\right]$
		$[0<\operatorname{Re}s<1/2;\ |\arg a|<\pi]$
17	$\dfrac{1}{\sqrt{x+a}\pm\sqrt{a}}\,\mathbf{K}\left(\left\{\begin{matrix}1\\ \pm i\end{matrix}\right\}\dfrac{2\sqrt[4]{a}\,\sqrt[4]{x+a}}{\sqrt{x+a}\pm\sqrt{a}}\right)$	$\dfrac{a^{s-1/2}}{2}\,\Gamma\!\left[\begin{matrix}s,\ s,\ \frac{1-2s}{2}\\ \frac{2s+1}{2}\end{matrix}\right]$
		$[0<\operatorname{Re}s<1/2;\ |\arg a|<\pi]$
18	$\dfrac{1}{\sqrt{x+a}+\sqrt{x}}\,\mathbf{K}\left(\dfrac{\left(\sqrt{x}-\sqrt{x+a}\right)^2}{a}\right)$	$\dfrac{a^{s-1/2}}{4}\,\Gamma\!\left[\begin{matrix}s,\ s,\ \frac{1-2s}{2}\\ \frac{2s+1}{2}\end{matrix}\right]$
		$[0<\operatorname{Re}s<1/2;\ |\arg a|<\pi]$
19	$\dfrac{1}{\sqrt{x+a}\pm\sqrt{x}}\,\mathbf{K}\left(\left\{\begin{matrix}1\\ \pm i\end{matrix}\right\}\dfrac{2\sqrt[4]{x}\,\sqrt[4]{x+a}}{\sqrt{x+a}\pm\sqrt{x}}\right)$	$\dfrac{a^{s-1/2}}{2}\,\Gamma\!\left[\begin{matrix}s,\ \frac{1-2s}{2},\ \frac{1-2s}{2}\\ 1-s\end{matrix}\right]$
		$[0<\operatorname{Re}s<1/2;\ |\arg a|<\pi]$
20	$\dfrac{1}{\sqrt{\sqrt{x+a}+\sqrt{a}}}\,\mathbf{K}\left(\pm i\,\dfrac{\sqrt{x+a}-\sqrt{a}}{\sqrt{x}}\right)$	$2^{2s-3/2}\sqrt{\pi}\,a^{s-1/4}\,\Gamma\!\left[\begin{matrix}s,\ \frac{1-4s}{2}\\ 1-s\end{matrix}\right]$
		$[0<\operatorname{Re}s<1/4;\ |\arg a|<\pi]$
21	$\dfrac{1}{\sqrt{\sqrt{x+a}+\sqrt{a}}}\,\mathbf{K}\left(\sqrt{\dfrac{\sqrt{a}-\sqrt{x+a}}{\sqrt{a}+\sqrt{x+a}}}\right)$	$2^{2s-3/2}\sqrt{\pi}\,a^{s-1/4}\,\Gamma\!\left[\begin{matrix}s,\ \frac{1-4s}{2}\\ 1-s\end{matrix}\right]$
		$[0<\operatorname{Re}s<1/4;\ |\arg a|<\pi]$
22	$\dfrac{1}{\sqrt{\sqrt{x+a}+\sqrt{a}}}\,\mathbf{K}\left(\sqrt{\dfrac{\sqrt{x+a}-\sqrt{a}}{\sqrt{x+a}+\sqrt{a}}}\right)$	$\dfrac{a^{s-1/4}\pi}{2\sqrt{2}}\,\Gamma\!\left[\begin{matrix}s,\ \frac{1-4s}{4},\ \frac{1-4s}{4}\\ \frac{1}{4},\ \frac{1}{4},\ 1-s\end{matrix}\right]$
		$[0<\operatorname{Re}s<1/4;\ |\arg a|<\pi]$

No.	$f(x)$	$F(s)$
23	$\dfrac{1}{\sqrt{\sqrt{x+a}+\sqrt{a}}}$ $\times \mathbf{K}\left(\sqrt{\dfrac{2\sqrt{a}\sqrt{x+a}-x-2a}{x}}\right)$	$2^{2s-3/2}\sqrt{\pi}\,a^{s-1/4}\,\Gamma\left[\begin{matrix} s,\ \frac{1-4s}{2} \\ 1-s \end{matrix}\right]$ $[0<\operatorname{Re}s<1/4;\ |\arg a|<\pi]$
24	$\dfrac{1}{\sqrt{\sqrt{x+a}+\sqrt{a}}}\mathbf{K}\left(\pm\dfrac{\sqrt{x+a}-\sqrt{a}}{\sqrt{x}}\right)$	$\dfrac{a^{s-1/4}\pi}{2\sqrt{2}}\,\Gamma\left[\begin{matrix} s,\ \frac{1-4s}{4},\ \frac{1-4s}{4} \\ \frac{1}{4},\ \frac{1}{4},\ 1-s \end{matrix}\right]$ $[0<\operatorname{Re}s<1/4;\ |\arg a|<\pi]$
25	$\dfrac{1}{\sqrt{\sqrt{x+a}\pm\sqrt{a}}}\mathbf{K}\left(\sqrt{\dfrac{2\sqrt{a}}{\sqrt{a}\pm\sqrt{x+a}}}\right)$	$\dfrac{\pi a^{s-1/4}}{2}\,\Gamma\left[\begin{matrix} s,\ s,\ \frac{1-4s}{4} \\ \frac{1}{4},\ \frac{1}{4},\ \frac{4s+3}{4} \end{matrix}\right]$ $[0<\operatorname{Re}s<1/4;\ |\arg a|<\pi]$
26	$\dfrac{1}{\sqrt{\sqrt{x+a}\pm\sqrt{a}}}$ $\times \mathbf{K}\left(\left\{\begin{matrix}1\\i\end{matrix}\right\}\sqrt{\dfrac{2\sqrt{a}\left(\sqrt{x+a}\mp\sqrt{a}\right)}{x}}\right)$	$\dfrac{\pi a^{s-1/4}}{2}\,\Gamma\left[\begin{matrix} s,\ s,\ \frac{1-4s}{4} \\ \frac{1}{4},\ \frac{1}{4},\ \frac{4s+3}{4} \end{matrix}\right]$ $[0<\operatorname{Re}s<1/4;\ |\arg a|<\pi]$
27	$\dfrac{1}{\sqrt{\sqrt{x+a}+\sqrt{x}}}\mathbf{K}\left(\pm i\dfrac{\sqrt{x}-\sqrt{x+a}}{\sqrt{a}}\right)$	$\dfrac{\sqrt{\pi}\,a^{s-1/4}}{2^{2s+1}}\,\Gamma\left[\begin{matrix} \frac{1-4s}{4},\ 2s \\ \frac{4s+3}{4} \end{matrix}\right]$ $[0<\operatorname{Re}s<1/4;\ |\arg a|<\pi]$
28	$\dfrac{1}{\sqrt{\sqrt{x+a}+\sqrt{x}}}\mathbf{K}\left(\sqrt{\dfrac{\sqrt{x}-\sqrt{x+a}}{\sqrt{x}+\sqrt{x+a}}}\right)$	$\dfrac{\sqrt{\pi}\,a^{s-1/4}}{2^{2s+1}}\,\Gamma\left[\begin{matrix} \frac{1-4s}{4},\ 2s \\ \frac{4s+3}{4} \end{matrix}\right]$ $[0<\operatorname{Re}s<1/4;\ |\arg a|<\pi]$
29	$\dfrac{1}{\sqrt{\sqrt{x+a}+\sqrt{x}}}\mathbf{K}\left(\pm\dfrac{\sqrt{x}-\sqrt{x+a}}{\sqrt{a}}\right)$	$\dfrac{\pi a^{s-1/4}}{2\sqrt{2}}\,\Gamma\left[\begin{matrix} s,\ s,\ \frac{1-4s}{4} \\ \frac{1}{4},\ \frac{1}{4},\ \frac{4s+3}{4} \end{matrix}\right]$ $[0<\operatorname{Re}s<1/4;\ |\arg a|<\pi]$
30	$\dfrac{1}{\sqrt{\sqrt{x+a}+\sqrt{x}}}\mathbf{K}\left(\sqrt{\dfrac{\sqrt{x+a}-\sqrt{x}}{\sqrt{x+a}+\sqrt{x}}}\right)$	$\dfrac{\pi a^{s-1/4}}{2\sqrt{2}}\,\Gamma\left[\begin{matrix} s,\ s,\ \frac{1-4s}{4} \\ \frac{1}{4},\ \frac{1}{4},\ \frac{4s+3}{4} \end{matrix}\right]$ $[0<\operatorname{Re}s<1/4;\ |\arg a|<\pi]$
31	$\dfrac{1}{\sqrt{\sqrt{x+a}\pm\sqrt{x}}}\mathbf{K}\left(\sqrt{\dfrac{2\sqrt{x}}{\sqrt{x}\pm\sqrt{x+a}}}\right)$	$\dfrac{\pi a^{s-1/4}}{2}\,\Gamma\left[\begin{matrix} s,\ \frac{1-4s}{4},\ \frac{1-4s}{4} \\ \frac{1}{4},\ \frac{1}{4},\ 1-s \end{matrix}\right]$ $[0<\operatorname{Re}s<1/4;\ |\arg a|<\pi]$

No.	$f(x)$	$F(s)$
32	$\left(\sqrt{x+a}\pm\sqrt{a}\right)$ $\times \mathbf{K}\left(\pm\left\{\begin{matrix}i\\1\end{matrix}\right\}\dfrac{2\sqrt[4]{a}\sqrt[4]{x+a}}{\sqrt{x+a}\mp\sqrt{a}}\right)$	$\dfrac{a^{s+1/2}}{2}\Gamma\left[\begin{matrix}s+1,\,s+1,\,-\frac{2s+1}{2}\\\frac{2s+3}{2}\end{matrix}\right]$ $[-1<\operatorname{Re}s<-1/2;\,|\arg a|<\pi]$
33	$\left(\sqrt{x+a}-\sqrt{a}\right)\mathbf{K}\left(\pm\dfrac{\left(\sqrt{x+a}-\sqrt{a}\right)^2}{x}\right)$	$\dfrac{a^{s+1/2}}{4}\Gamma\left[\begin{matrix}s+1,\,-\frac{2s+1}{2},\,-\frac{2s+1}{2}\\-s\end{matrix}\right]$ $[-1<\operatorname{Re}s<-1/2;\,|\arg a|<\pi]$
34	$\left(\sqrt{x+a}\pm\sqrt{x}\right)$ $\times \mathbf{K}\left(\pm\left\{\begin{matrix}i\\1\end{matrix}\right\}\dfrac{2\sqrt[4]{x}\sqrt[4]{x+a}}{\sqrt{x+a}\mp\sqrt{x}}\right)$	$\dfrac{a^{s+1/2}}{2}\Gamma\left[\begin{matrix}s,\,\frac{1-2s}{2},\,\frac{1-2s}{2}\\1-s\end{matrix}\right]$ $[0<\operatorname{Re}s<1/2;\,|\arg a|<\pi]$
35	$\left(\sqrt{x+a}-\sqrt{x}\right)\mathbf{K}\left(\pm\dfrac{\left(\sqrt{x}-\sqrt{x+a}\right)^2}{a}\right)$	$\dfrac{a^{s+1/2}}{4}\Gamma\left[\begin{matrix}s,\,s,\,\frac{1-2s}{2}\\\frac{2s+1}{2}\end{matrix}\right]$ $[0<\operatorname{Re}s<1/2;\,|\arg a|<\pi]$
36	$\sqrt{\sqrt{x+a}-\sqrt{a}}\,\mathbf{K}\left(\pm i\dfrac{\sqrt{x+a}-\sqrt{a}}{x}\right)$	$2^{2s-1/2}\sqrt{\pi}\,a^{s+1/4}\Gamma\left[\begin{matrix}\frac{2s+1}{2},\,-\frac{4s+1}{2}\\\frac{1-2s}{2}\end{matrix}\right]$ $[-1/2<\operatorname{Re}s<-1/4;\,|\arg a|<\pi]$
37	$\sqrt{\sqrt{x+a}-\sqrt{a}}\,\mathbf{K}\left(\sqrt{\dfrac{\sqrt{a}-\sqrt{x+a}}{\sqrt{a}+\sqrt{x+a}}}\right)$	$2^{2s-1/2}\sqrt{\pi}\,a^{s+1/4}\Gamma\left[\begin{matrix}\frac{2s+1}{2},\,-\frac{4s+1}{2}\\\frac{1-2s}{2}\end{matrix}\right]$ $[-1/2<\operatorname{Re}s<-1/4;\,|\arg a|<\pi]$
38	$\sqrt{\sqrt{x+a}-\sqrt{a}}\,\mathbf{K}\left(\pm\dfrac{\sqrt{x+a}-\sqrt{a}}{\sqrt{x}}\right)$	$\dfrac{\pi a^{s+1/4}}{2\sqrt{2}}\Gamma\left[\begin{matrix}\frac{2s+1}{2},\,-\frac{4s+1}{2},\,-\frac{4s+1}{2}\\\frac{1}{4},\,\frac{1}{4},\,\frac{1-2s}{2}\end{matrix}\right]$ $[-1/2<\operatorname{Re}s<-1/4;\,|\arg a|<\pi]$
39	$\sqrt{\sqrt{x+a}-\sqrt{a}}\,\mathbf{K}\left(\sqrt{\dfrac{\sqrt{x+a}-\sqrt{a}}{\sqrt{x+a}+\sqrt{a}}}\right)$	$\dfrac{\pi a^{s+1/4}}{2\sqrt{2}}\Gamma\left[\begin{matrix}\frac{2s+1}{2},\,-\frac{4s+1}{2},\,-\frac{4s+1}{2}\\\frac{1}{4},\,\frac{1}{4},\,\frac{1-2s}{2}\end{matrix}\right]$ $[-1/2<\operatorname{Re}s<-1/4;\,|\arg a|<\pi]$
40	$\sqrt{\sqrt{x+a}\pm\sqrt{a}}\,\mathbf{K}\left(\sqrt{\dfrac{2\sqrt{a}}{\sqrt{a}\mp\sqrt{x+a}}}\right)$	$\dfrac{\pi a^{s+1/4}}{2}\Gamma\left[\begin{matrix}\frac{2s+1}{2},\,\frac{2s+1}{2},\,-\frac{4s+1}{2}\\\frac{1}{4},\,\frac{1}{4},\,\frac{4s+5}{4}\end{matrix}\right]$ $[-1/2<\operatorname{Re}s<-1/4;\,|\arg a|<\pi]$
41	$\sqrt{\sqrt{x+a}\pm\sqrt{a}}$ $\times \mathbf{K}\left(\left\{\begin{matrix}i\\1\end{matrix}\right\}\sqrt{\dfrac{2\sqrt{a}\left(\sqrt{x+a}\pm\sqrt{a}\right)}{x}}\right)$	$\dfrac{\pi a^{s+1/4}}{2}\Gamma\left[\begin{matrix}\frac{2s+1}{2},\,\frac{2s+1}{2},\,-\frac{4s+1}{2}\\\frac{1}{4},\,\frac{1}{4},\,\frac{4s+5}{4}\end{matrix}\right]$ $[-1/2<\operatorname{Re}s<-1/4;\,|\arg a|<\pi]$

No.	$f(x)$	$F(s)$
42	$\sqrt{\sqrt{x+a}-\sqrt{x}}\,\mathbf{K}\left(\pm i\dfrac{\sqrt{x}-\sqrt{x+a}}{\sqrt{a}}\right)$	$\dfrac{\sqrt{\pi}\,a^{s+1/4}}{2^{2s+1}}\,\Gamma\!\left[\begin{array}{c}\frac{1-4s}{4},\ 2s\\[2pt]\frac{4s+3}{4}\end{array}\right]$
		$[0<\operatorname{Re}s<1/4;\ |\arg a|<\pi]$
43	$\sqrt{\sqrt{x+a}-\sqrt{x}}\,\mathbf{K}\left(\sqrt{\dfrac{\sqrt{x+a}-\sqrt{x}}{\sqrt{x+a}+\sqrt{x}}}\right)$	$\dfrac{\pi a^{s+1/4}}{2\sqrt{2}}\,\Gamma\!\left[\begin{array}{c}s,\ s,\ \frac{1-4s}{4}\\[2pt]\frac{1}{4},\ \frac{1}{4},\ \frac{4s+3}{4}\end{array}\right]$
		$[0<\operatorname{Re}s<1/4;\ |\arg a|<\pi]$
44	$\sqrt{\sqrt{x+a}\pm\sqrt{x}}\,\mathbf{K}\left(\sqrt{\dfrac{2\sqrt{x}}{\sqrt{x}\mp\sqrt{x+a}}}\right)$	$\dfrac{\pi a^{s+1/4}}{2}\,\Gamma\!\left[\begin{array}{c}s,\ \frac{1-4s}{4},\ \frac{1-4s}{4}\\[2pt]\frac{1}{4},\ \frac{1}{4},\ 1-s\end{array}\right]$
		$[0<\operatorname{Re}s<1/4;\ |\arg a|<\pi]$
45	$\dfrac{\sqrt{\sqrt{x+a}+\sqrt{a}}}{\sqrt{x+a}}\,\mathbf{K}\left(\sqrt{\dfrac{2\sqrt{a}}{\sqrt{a}-\sqrt{x+a}}}\right)$	$\dfrac{\pi a^{s-1/4}}{2}\,\Gamma\!\left[\begin{array}{c}\frac{2s+1}{2},\ \frac{2s+1}{2},\ \frac{1-4s}{4}\\[2pt]\frac{3}{4},\ \frac{3}{4},\ \frac{4s+3}{2}\end{array}\right]$
		$[-1/2<\operatorname{Re}s<1/4;\ |\arg a|<\pi]$
46	$\dfrac{\sqrt{\sqrt{x+a}-\sqrt{a}}}{\sqrt{x+a}}\,\mathbf{K}\left(\sqrt{\dfrac{\sqrt{x+a}-\sqrt{a}}{\sqrt{x+a}+\sqrt{a}}}\right)$	$\dfrac{\pi a^{s-1/4}}{2\sqrt{2}}\,\Gamma\!\left[\begin{array}{c}\frac{2s+1}{2},\ \frac{1-4s}{4},\ \frac{1-4s}{4}\\[2pt]\frac{3}{4},\ \frac{3}{4},\ \frac{1-2s}{2}\end{array}\right]$
		$[-1/2<\operatorname{Re}s<1/4;\ |\arg a|<\pi]$
47	$\dfrac{\sqrt{\sqrt{x+a}-\sqrt{a}}}{\sqrt{x+a}}\,\mathbf{K}\left(\pm\dfrac{\sqrt{x+a}-\sqrt{a}}{\sqrt{x}}\right)$	$\dfrac{\pi a^{s-1/4}}{2\sqrt{2}}\,\Gamma\!\left[\begin{array}{c}\frac{2s+1}{2},\ \frac{1-4s}{4},\ \frac{1-4s}{4}\\[2pt]\frac{3}{4},\ \frac{3}{4},\ \frac{1-2s}{2}\end{array}\right]$
		$[-1/2<\operatorname{Re}s<1/4;\ |\arg a|<\pi]$
48	$\dfrac{\sqrt{\sqrt{x+a}-\sqrt{a}}}{\sqrt{x+a}}\,\mathbf{K}\left(\sqrt{\dfrac{2\sqrt{a}}{\sqrt{x+a}+\sqrt{a}}}\right)$	$\dfrac{\pi a^{s-1/4}}{2}\,\Gamma\!\left[\begin{array}{c}\frac{2s+1}{2},\ \frac{2s+1}{2},\ \frac{1-4s}{4}\\[2pt]\frac{3}{4},\ \frac{3}{4},\ \frac{4s+3}{4}\end{array}\right]$
		$[-1/2<\operatorname{Re}s<1/4;\ |\arg a|<\pi]$
49	$\dfrac{\sqrt{\sqrt{x+a}-\sqrt{x}}}{\sqrt{x+a}}\,\mathbf{K}\left(\sqrt{\dfrac{\sqrt{x+a}-\sqrt{x}}{\sqrt{x+a}+\sqrt{x}}}\right)$	$\dfrac{\pi a^{s-1/4}}{2\sqrt{2}}\,\Gamma\!\left[\begin{array}{c}s,\ s,\ \frac{3-4s}{4}\\[2pt]\frac{3}{4},\ \frac{3}{4},\ \frac{4s+1}{4}\end{array}\right]$
		$[0<\operatorname{Re}s<3/4;\ |\arg a|<\pi]$
50	$\dfrac{\sqrt{\sqrt{x+a}-\sqrt{x}}}{\sqrt{x+a}}\,\mathbf{K}\left(\pm\dfrac{\sqrt{x}-\sqrt{x+a}}{\sqrt{a}}\right)$	$\dfrac{\pi a^{s-1/4}}{2\sqrt{2}}\,\Gamma\!\left[\begin{array}{c}s,\ s,\ \frac{3-4s}{4}\\[2pt]\frac{3}{4},\ \frac{3}{4},\ \frac{4s+1}{4}\end{array}\right]$
		$[0<\operatorname{Re}s<3/4;\ |\arg a|<\pi]$
51	$\dfrac{\sqrt{\sqrt{x+a}\mp\sqrt{x}}}{\sqrt{x+a}}\,\mathbf{K}\left(\sqrt{\dfrac{2\sqrt{x}}{\sqrt{x}\pm\sqrt{x+a}}}\right)$	$\dfrac{\pi a^{s-1/4}}{2}\,\Gamma\!\left[\begin{array}{c}s,\ \frac{3-4s}{4},\ \frac{3-4s}{4}\\[2pt]\frac{3}{4},\ \frac{3}{4},\ 1-s\end{array}\right]$
		$[0<\operatorname{Re}s<3/4;\ |\arg a|<\pi]$

3.26.3. $\theta\left(a-x\right)\mathbf{K}\left(\varphi\left(x\right)\right)$ **and algebraic functions**

1	$(a-x)_+^{\alpha-1}\,\mathbf{K}\,(bx)$	$\dfrac{\pi a^{s+\alpha-1}}{2}\,\mathrm{B}\,(s,\alpha)\,{}_4F_3\!\left(\begin{matrix}\frac{1}{2},\,\frac{1}{2},\,\frac{s}{2},\,\frac{s+1}{2};\,a^2b^2\\[2pt]1,\,\frac{s+\alpha}{2},\,\frac{s+\alpha+1}{2}\end{matrix}\right)$
		$[a,\ \mathrm{Re}\,\alpha,\ \mathrm{Re}\,s>0]$
2	$(a^2-x^2)_+^{\alpha-1}\,\mathbf{K}\,(bx)$	$\dfrac{\pi a^{s+2\alpha-2}}{4}\,\mathrm{B}\left(\frac{s}{2},\alpha\right){}_3F_2\!\left(\begin{matrix}\frac{1}{2},\,\frac{1}{2},\,\frac{s}{2};\,a^2b^2\\[2pt]1,\,\frac{s+2\alpha}{2}\end{matrix}\right)$
		$[a,\ \mathrm{Re}\,\alpha,\ \mathrm{Re}\,s>0]$
3	$(a-x)_+^{\alpha-1}\,\mathbf{K}\,(b\,(a-x))$	$\dfrac{\pi a^{s+\alpha-1}}{2}\,\mathrm{B}\,(s,\alpha)\,{}_4F_3\!\left(\begin{matrix}\frac{1}{2},\,\frac{1}{2},\,\frac{\alpha}{2},\,\frac{\alpha+1}{2};\,a^2b^2\\[2pt]\frac{3}{2},\,\frac{s+\alpha}{2},\,\frac{s+\alpha+1}{2}\end{matrix}\right)$
		$[a,\ \mathrm{Re}\,\alpha,\ \mathrm{Re}\,s>0]$
4	$(a-x)_+^{\alpha-1}\,\mathbf{K}\,(bx\,(a-x))$	$\dfrac{\pi a^{s+\alpha-1}}{2}\,\mathrm{B}\,(s,\alpha)\,{}_6F_5\!\left(\begin{matrix}\frac{1}{2},\,\frac{1}{2},\,\Delta\,(2,\alpha),\,\Delta\,(2,s)\\[2pt]1,\,\Delta\,(4,s+\alpha);\,\frac{a^4b^2}{16}\end{matrix}\right)$
		$[a,\ \mathrm{Re}\,s,\ \mathrm{Re}\,\alpha>0]$
5	$\dfrac{\theta\left(a-x\right)}{x+a}\,\mathbf{K}\left(\pm\dfrac{a-x}{a+x}\right)$	$\dfrac{\pi a^{s-1}}{8}\,\Gamma\!\left[\begin{matrix}\frac{s}{2},\,\frac{s}{2}\\[2pt]\frac{s+1}{2},\,\frac{s+1}{2}\end{matrix}\right]\qquad\qquad [a,\ \mathrm{Re}\,s>0]$
6	$(a-x)_+^{\alpha-1}\,\mathbf{K}\left(b\sqrt{a-x}\right)$	$\dfrac{\pi a^{s+\alpha-1}}{2}\,\mathrm{B}\,(s,\alpha)\,{}_3F_2\!\left(\begin{matrix}\frac{1}{2},\,\frac{1}{2},\,\alpha;\,ab^2\\[2pt]1,\,s+\alpha\end{matrix}\right)$
		$[a,\ \mathrm{Re}\,\alpha,\ \mathrm{Re}\,s>0]$
7	$\dfrac{\theta\left(a-x\right)}{(bx+1)^\rho}\,\mathbf{K}\left(c\sqrt{a-x}\right)$	$\dfrac{\pi a^s}{2s}\,F_3\!\left(\frac{1}{2},\,\rho,\,\frac{1}{2},\,s;\,s+1;\,ac^2,\,-ab\right)$
		$[a,\ \mathrm{Re}\,s>0;\ |\arg\,(1+ab)|<\pi]$
8	$\theta\left(a-x\right)(x-b)_+^{\alpha-1}\,\mathbf{K}\left(c\sqrt{a-x}\right)$	$\dfrac{\pi\,(a-b)^\alpha\,b^{s-1}}{2\alpha}\,F_3\!\left(\frac{1}{2},\,1-s,\,\frac{1}{2},\,\alpha;\,\alpha+1;\right.$
		$\left.c^2\,(a-b),\,\dfrac{b-a}{b}\right)\qquad [a>b>0;\ \mathrm{Re}\,\alpha>0]$
9	$(a-x)_+^{\alpha-1}\,\mathbf{K}\!\left(b\sqrt{x\,(a-x)}\right)$	$\dfrac{\pi a^{s+\alpha-1}}{2}\,\mathrm{B}\,(s,\alpha)\,{}_4F_3\!\left(\begin{matrix}\frac{1}{2},\,\frac{1}{2},\,\alpha,\,s;\,\frac{a^2b^2}{4}\\[2pt]1,\,\frac{s+\alpha}{2},\,\frac{s+\alpha+1}{2}\end{matrix}\right)$
		$[a,\ \mathrm{Re}\,s,\ \mathrm{Re}\,\alpha>0]$
10	$\theta\left(a-x\right)\mathbf{K}\left(\pm i\dfrac{a-x}{2\sqrt{ax}}\right)$	$\dfrac{\pi a^s}{4}\,\Gamma\!\left[\begin{matrix}\frac{2s+1}{4},\,\frac{2s+1}{4}\\[2pt]\frac{2s+3}{4},\,\frac{2s+3}{4}\end{matrix}\right]\qquad [a>0;\ \mathrm{Re}\,s>-1/2]$
11	$\theta\left(a-x\right)\mathbf{K}\left(\sqrt{\dfrac{a-x}{a}}\right)$	$\dfrac{\pi a^s}{2}\,\Gamma\!\left[\begin{matrix}s,\,s\\[2pt]\frac{2s+1}{2},\,\frac{2s+1}{2}\end{matrix}\right]\qquad\qquad [a,\ \mathrm{Re}\,s>0]$

No.	$f(x)$	$F(s)$
12	$\theta(a-x)\,\mathbf{K}\left(\sqrt{\dfrac{a-x}{2a}}\right)$	$\dfrac{\pi^{3/2}a^s}{2^{s+1}}\,\Gamma\!\left[\begin{array}{c} s \\ \frac{2s+3}{4},\ \frac{2s+3}{4}\end{array}\right]$ $[a,\ \mathrm{Re}\,s > 0]$
13	$\dfrac{\theta(a-x)}{(bx+1)^{\rho}}\,\mathbf{K}\left(\sqrt{\dfrac{a-x}{a}}\right)$	$\dfrac{\pi a^s}{2}\,\Gamma\!\left[\begin{array}{c} s,\ s \\ \frac{2s+1}{2},\ \frac{2s+1}{2}\end{array}\right]{}_3F_2\!\left(\begin{array}{c}\rho,\ s,\ s;\ ab \\ \frac{2s+1}{2},\ \frac{2s+1}{2}\end{array}\right)$ $[a,\ \mathrm{Re}\,s>0;\ |\arg(1-ab)| < \pi]$
14	$\theta(a-x)\,\mathbf{K}\left(\sqrt{\dfrac{x-a}{x}}\right)$	$\dfrac{\pi a^s}{2}\,\Gamma\!\left[\begin{array}{c}\frac{2s+1}{2},\ \frac{2s+1}{2} \\ s+1,\ s+1\end{array}\right]$ $[a>0;\ \mathrm{Re}\,s > -1/2]$
15	$\theta(a-x)\,\mathbf{K}\left(\sqrt{\dfrac{x-a}{2x}}\right)$	$2^{s-2}\sqrt{\pi}\,a^s\,\Gamma\!\left[\begin{array}{c}\frac{2s+1}{4},\ \frac{2s+1}{4} \\ s+1\end{array}\right]$ $[a>0;\ \mathrm{Re}\,s > -1/2]$
16	$\dfrac{\theta(a-x)}{\sqrt{x+a}}\,\mathbf{K}\left(\sqrt{\dfrac{a-x}{a+x}}\right)$	$2^{s-3}\sqrt{\pi}\,a^{s-1/2}\,\Gamma\!\left[\begin{array}{c}\frac{s}{2},\ \frac{s}{2} \\ \frac{2s+1}{2}\end{array}\right]$ $[a,\ \mathrm{Re}\,s > 0]$
17	$\dfrac{\theta(a-x)}{\sqrt{x+a}}\,\mathbf{K}\left(\sqrt{\dfrac{x-a}{x+a}}\right)$	$\dfrac{\pi^{3/2}a^{s-1/2}}{2^{s+3/2}}\,\Gamma\!\left[\begin{array}{c} s \\ \frac{2s+3}{4},\ \frac{2s+3}{4}\end{array}\right]$ $[a,\ \mathrm{Re}\,s > 0]$
18	$\dfrac{\theta(a-x)}{\sqrt{b-x}}\,\mathbf{K}\left(c\sqrt{\dfrac{a-x}{b-x}}\right)$	$\dfrac{\pi a^s}{2s\sqrt{b}}\,F_1\!\left(\dfrac{1}{2},\,s,\,\dfrac{1}{2};\,s+1;\,\dfrac{a}{b},\,\dfrac{ac^2}{b}\right)$ $[b>a>0;\ \mathrm{Re}\,s > 0]$
19	$\dfrac{\theta(a-x)}{\sqrt{a}\pm\sqrt{a-x}}\,\mathbf{K}\left(\pm\left\{\begin{array}{c}1\\i\end{array}\right\}\dfrac{2\sqrt[4]{a}\sqrt[4]{a-x}}{\sqrt{a}\pm\sqrt{a-x}}\right)$	$\dfrac{\pi a^{s-1/2}}{2}\,\Gamma\!\left[\begin{array}{c} s,\ s \\ \frac{2s+1}{2},\ \frac{2s+1}{2}\end{array}\right]$ $[a,\ \mathrm{Re}\,s > 0]$
20	$\dfrac{\theta(a-x)}{\sqrt{\sqrt{a}\pm\sqrt{a-x}}}\,\mathbf{K}\left(\sqrt{\dfrac{2\sqrt{a-x}}{\sqrt{a-x}\pm\sqrt{a}}}\right)$	$2^{2s-3/2}\sqrt{\pi}\,a^{s-1/4}\,\Gamma\!\left[\begin{array}{c} s,\ s \\ \frac{4s+1}{2}\end{array}\right]$ $[a,\ \mathrm{Re}\,s > 0]$
21	$\dfrac{\theta(a-x)}{\sqrt{\sqrt{x}\pm\sqrt{x-a}}}\,\mathbf{K}\left(\sqrt{\dfrac{2\sqrt{x-a}}{\sqrt{x-a}\pm\sqrt{x}}}\right)$	$\dfrac{\pi^{3/2}a^{s-1/4}}{2^{2s}}\,\Gamma\!\left[\begin{array}{c} 2s \\ \frac{4s+3}{4},\ \frac{4s+3}{4}\end{array}\right]$ $[a,\ \mathrm{Re}\,s > 0]$
22	$\theta(a-x)\left(\sqrt{a}\pm\sqrt{a-x}\right)$ $\times\,\mathbf{K}\left(\left\{\begin{array}{c} i \\ \pm 1\end{array}\right\}\dfrac{2\sqrt[4]{a}\sqrt[4]{a-x}}{\sqrt{a}\mp\sqrt{a-x}}\right)$	$\dfrac{\pi a^{s+1/2}}{2}\,\Gamma\!\left[\begin{array}{c} s+1,\ s+1 \\ \frac{2s+3}{2},\ \frac{2s+3}{2}\end{array}\right]$ $[a>0;\ \mathrm{Re}\,s > -1]$
23	$\theta(a-x)\,\sqrt{\sqrt{a}\pm\sqrt{a-x}}$ $\times\,\mathbf{K}\left(\sqrt{\dfrac{2\sqrt{a-x}}{\sqrt{a-x}\mp\sqrt{a}}}\right)$	$2^{2s-1/2}\sqrt{\pi}\,a^{s+1/4}\,\Gamma\!\left[\begin{array}{c}\frac{2s+1}{2},\ \frac{2s+1}{2} \\ \frac{4s+3}{2}\end{array}\right]$ $[a>0;\ \mathrm{Re}\,s > -1/2]$

No.	$f(x)$	$F(s)$	
24	$\theta(a-x)\sqrt{\sqrt{x}\pm\sqrt{x-a}}$ $\times \mathbf{K}\left(\sqrt{\dfrac{2\sqrt{x-a}}{\sqrt{x-a}\mp\sqrt{x}}}\right)$	$\dfrac{\pi^{3/2}a^{s+1/4}}{2^{2s}}\,\Gamma\left[\begin{array}{c}2s\\ \frac{4s+3}{4},\ \frac{4s+3}{4}\end{array}\right]$	$[a,\ \mathrm{Re}\,s>0]$

3.26.4. $\theta(x-a)\,\mathbf{K}(\varphi(x))$ and algebraic functions

1	$\dfrac{\theta(x-a)}{x+a}\mathbf{K}\left(\dfrac{x-a}{x+a}\right)$	$\dfrac{\pi a^{s-1}}{8}\,\Gamma\left[\begin{array}{c}\frac{1-s}{2},\ \frac{1-s}{2}\\ \frac{2-s}{2},\ \frac{2-s}{2}\end{array}\right]$	$[a>0;\ \mathrm{Re}\,s<1]$
2	$\theta(x-a)\mathbf{K}\left(\sqrt{\dfrac{a-x}{a}}\right)$	$\dfrac{\pi a^{s}}{2}\,\Gamma\left[\begin{array}{c}\frac{1-2s}{2},\ \frac{1-2s}{2}\\ 1-s,\ 1-s\end{array}\right]$	$[a>0;\ \mathrm{Re}\,s<1/2]$
3	$\theta(x-a)\mathbf{K}\left(\sqrt{\dfrac{a-x}{2a}}\right)$	$\dfrac{\sqrt{\pi}a^{s}}{2^{s+2}}\,\Gamma\left[\begin{array}{c}\frac{1-2s}{4},\ \frac{1-2s}{4}\\ 1-s\end{array}\right]$	$[a>0;\ \mathrm{Re}\,s<1/2]$
4	$\theta(x-a)\mathbf{K}\left(\dfrac{i(x-a)}{2\sqrt{ax}}\right)$	$\dfrac{\pi a^{s}}{4}\,\Gamma\left[\begin{array}{c}\frac{1-2s}{4},\ \frac{1-2s}{4}\\ \frac{3-2s}{4},\ \frac{3-2s}{4}\end{array}\right]$	$[a>0;\ \mathrm{Re}\,s<1/2]$
5	$\theta(x-a)\mathbf{K}\left(\sqrt{\dfrac{x-a}{x}}\right)$	$\dfrac{\pi a^{s}}{2}\,\Gamma\left[\begin{array}{c}-s,\ -s\\ \frac{1-2s}{2},\ \frac{1-2s}{2}\end{array}\right]$	$[a>0;\ \mathrm{Re}\,s<0]$
6	$\theta(x-a)\mathbf{K}\left(\sqrt{\dfrac{x-a}{2x}}\right)$	$\dfrac{2^{s-1}\pi^{3/2}a^{s}}{2}\,\Gamma\left[\begin{array}{c}-s\\ \frac{3-2s}{4},\ \frac{3-2s}{4}\end{array}\right]$	$[a>0;\ \mathrm{Re}\,s<0]$
7	$\dfrac{\theta(x-a)}{\sqrt{x+a}}\mathbf{K}\left(\sqrt{\dfrac{a-x}{a+x}}\right)$	$2^{s-2}\pi^{3/2}a^{s-1/2}\,\Gamma\left[\begin{array}{c}\frac{1-2s}{2}\\ \frac{2-s}{2},\ \frac{2-s}{2}\end{array}\right]$	$[a>0;\ \mathrm{Re}\,s<1/2]$
8	$\dfrac{\theta(x-a)}{\sqrt{x+a}}\mathbf{K}\left(\sqrt{\dfrac{x-a}{x+a}}\right)$	$\dfrac{\sqrt{\pi}\,a^{s-1/2}}{2^{s+5/2}}\,\Gamma\left[\begin{array}{c}\frac{1-2s}{4},\ \frac{1-2s}{4}\\ 1-s\end{array}\right]$	$[a>0;\ \mathrm{Re}\,s<1/2]$
9	$\dfrac{\theta(x-a)}{\sqrt{x}+\sqrt{x-a}}\mathbf{K}\left(\pm\dfrac{2\sqrt[4]{x}\sqrt[4]{x-a}}{\sqrt{x}+\sqrt{x-a}}\right)$	$\dfrac{\pi a^{s-1/2}}{2}\,\Gamma\left[\begin{array}{c}\frac{1-2s}{4},\ \frac{1-2s}{4}\\ 1-s,\ 1-s\end{array}\right]$	$[a>0;\ \mathrm{Re}\,s<1/2]$
10	$\dfrac{\theta(x-a)}{\sqrt{x}-\sqrt{x-a}}\mathbf{K}\left(\pm\dfrac{2i\sqrt[4]{x}\sqrt[4]{x-a}}{\sqrt{x}+\sqrt{x-a}}\right)$	$\dfrac{\pi a^{s-1/2}}{2}\,\Gamma\left[\begin{array}{c}\frac{1-2s}{4},\ \frac{1-2s}{4}\\ 1-s,\ 1-s\end{array}\right]$	$[a>0;\ \mathrm{Re}\,s<1/2]$
11	$\dfrac{\theta(x-a)}{\sqrt{\sqrt{a-x}\pm\sqrt{a}}}\mathbf{K}\left(\sqrt{\dfrac{2\sqrt{a-x}}{\sqrt{a-x}\pm\sqrt{a}}}\right)$	$2^{2s-1/2}\pi^{3/2}a^{s-1/4}\,\Gamma\left[\begin{array}{c}\frac{1-4s}{2}\\ 1-s,\ 1-s\end{array}\right]$ $[a>0;\ \mathrm{Re}\,s<1/4]$	

No.	$f(x)$	$F(s)$
12	$\dfrac{\theta(x-a)}{\sqrt{\sqrt{x}\pm\sqrt{x-a}}}\,\mathbf{K}\left(\sqrt{\dfrac{2\sqrt{x-a}}{\sqrt{x-a}\pm\sqrt{x}}}\right)$	$\dfrac{\sqrt{\pi}\,a^{s-1/4}}{2^{2s+1}}\,\Gamma\left[\begin{matrix}\frac{1-4s}{4},\frac{1-4s}{4}\\1-2s\end{matrix}\right]$ $\quad[a>0;\ \mathrm{Re}\,s<1/4]$
13	$\theta(x-a)\left(\sqrt{x}+\sqrt{x-a}\right)$ $\times\mathbf{K}\left(\dfrac{2i\sqrt[4]{x}\sqrt[4]{x-a}}{\sqrt{x}-\sqrt{x-a}}\right)$	$\dfrac{\pi a^{s+1/2}}{2}\,\Gamma\left[\begin{matrix}\frac{1-2s}{2},\frac{1-2s}{2}\\1-s,\,1-s\end{matrix}\right]$ $\quad[a>0;\ \mathrm{Re}\,s<1/2]$
14	$\theta(x-a)\left(\sqrt{x}-\sqrt{x-a}\right)$ $\times\mathbf{K}\left(\dfrac{2\sqrt[4]{x}\sqrt[4]{x-a}}{\sqrt{x}+\sqrt{x-a}}\right)$	$\dfrac{\pi a^{s+1/2}}{2}\,\Gamma\left[\begin{matrix}\frac{1-2s}{2},\frac{1-2s}{2}\\1-s,\,1-s\end{matrix}\right]$ $\quad[a>0;\ \mathrm{Re}\,s<1/2]$
15	$\theta(x-a)\sqrt{\sqrt{a}\pm\sqrt{a-x}}$ $\times\mathbf{K}\left(\sqrt{\dfrac{2\sqrt{a-x}}{\sqrt{a-x}\mp\sqrt{a}}}\right)$	$\pi^{3/2}2^{2s+1/2}a^{s+1/4}\,\Gamma\left[\begin{matrix}-\frac{4s+1}{2}\\\frac{1-2s}{2},\frac{1-2s}{2}\end{matrix}\right]$ $[a>0;\ \mathrm{Re}\,s<-1/4]$
16	$\theta(x-a)\sqrt{\sqrt{x}\pm\sqrt{x-a}}$ $\times\mathbf{K}\left(\sqrt{\dfrac{2\sqrt{x-a}}{\sqrt{x-a}\mp\sqrt{x}}}\right)$	$\dfrac{\pi a^{s+1/4}}{2}\,\Gamma\left[\begin{matrix}\frac{1-4s}{2},\frac{1-4s}{2}\\\frac{1-2s}{2},\,1-s\end{matrix}\right]$ $\quad[a>0;\ \mathrm{Re}\,s<1/4]$

3.26.5. $\mathbf{E}(\varphi(x))$ and algebraic functions

Notation: $\varepsilon=0$ or 1.

No.	$f(x)$	$F(s)$
1	$\mathbf{E}(iax)-\dfrac{\pi}{2}$	$-\dfrac{a^{-s}}{8}\,\Gamma\left[\begin{matrix}\frac{s}{2},\frac{1-s}{2},-\frac{s+1}{2}\\\frac{2-s}{2}\end{matrix}\right]$ $[\mathrm{Re}\,a>0;\ -2<\mathrm{Re}\,s<1]$
2	$\mathbf{E}(iax)$ $-\dfrac{\pi}{2}\displaystyle\sum_{k=0}^{n}\dfrac{(-1/2)_k\,(1/2)_k}{(k!)^2}\left(-a^2x^2\right)^k$	$\dfrac{a^{-s}}{8}\,\Gamma\left[\begin{matrix}\frac{s}{2},\frac{1-s}{2},-\frac{s+1}{2}\\\frac{2-s}{2}\end{matrix}\right]$ $[\mathrm{Re}\,a>0;\ -2n-2<\mathrm{Re}\,s<-1,-2n]$
3	$\dfrac{1}{x^2+a^2}\,\mathbf{E}\left(\dfrac{ix}{a}\right)$	$\dfrac{a^{s-2}}{2}\,\Gamma\left[\begin{matrix}\frac{s}{2},\frac{1-s}{2},\frac{3-s}{2}\\\frac{2-s}{2}\end{matrix}\right]$ $\quad[a>0;\ 0<\mathrm{Re}\,s<1]$
4	$\dfrac{1}{x^2+a^2}\,\mathbf{E}\left(\dfrac{ia}{x}\right)$	$\dfrac{a^{s-2}}{2}\,\Gamma\left[\begin{matrix}\frac{s+1}{2},\frac{s-1}{2},\frac{2-s}{2}\\\frac{s}{2}\end{matrix}\right]$ $\quad[a>0;\ 1<\mathrm{Re}\,s<2]$

No.	$f(x)$	$F(s)$
5	$\dfrac{1}{\left[(x+a)^2 - b^2\right]^\varepsilon (x+a)^\rho}\, \mathbf{E}\left(\dfrac{b}{x+a}\right)$	$\dfrac{\pi a^{s-\rho-2\varepsilon}}{2}\, \mathrm{B}\left(s,\rho-s+2\varepsilon\right)$ $\times\, {}_4F_3\left(\begin{matrix}\frac{2\varepsilon-1}{2},\ \frac{2\varepsilon+1}{2},\ \frac{\rho-s+2\varepsilon}{2},\ \frac{\rho-s+2\varepsilon+1}{2}\\ 1,\ \frac{\rho+2\varepsilon}{2},\ \frac{\rho+2\varepsilon+1}{2};\ \frac{b^2}{a^2}\end{matrix}\right)$ $[0 < \operatorname{Re} s < \operatorname{Re}\rho + 2\varepsilon;\ |\arg a| < \pi]$
6	$\dfrac{1}{\left[(x+a)^2 - b^2 x^2\right]^\varepsilon (x+a)^\rho}\, \mathbf{E}\left(\dfrac{bx}{x+a}\right)$	$\dfrac{\pi a^{s-\rho-2\varepsilon}}{2}\, \mathrm{B}\left(s,\rho-s+2\varepsilon\right)$ $\times\, {}_4F_3\left(\begin{matrix}\frac{2\varepsilon-1}{2},\ \frac{2\varepsilon+1}{2},\ \frac{s}{2},\ \frac{s+1}{2}\\ 1,\ \frac{\rho+2\varepsilon}{2},\ \frac{\rho+2\varepsilon+1}{2};\ b^2\end{matrix}\right)$ $[0 < \operatorname{Re} s < \operatorname{Re}\rho + 2\varepsilon;\ |\arg a| < \pi]$
7	$\dfrac{1}{(x+a)^\rho}\, \mathbf{E}\left(\dfrac{b}{\sqrt{x+a}}\right)$	$\dfrac{\pi a^{s-\rho}}{2}\, \mathrm{B}\left(s,\rho-s\right)\, {}_3F_2\left(\begin{matrix}-\frac{1}{2},\ \frac{1}{2},\ \rho-s\\ 1,\ \rho;\ \frac{b^2}{a}\end{matrix}\right)$ $[0 < \operatorname{Re} s < \operatorname{Re}\rho;\ |\arg a| < \pi]$
8	$\mathbf{E}\left(\sqrt{\dfrac{a-x}{a}}\right)$	$\dfrac{\pi a^s}{2}\, \Gamma\left[\begin{matrix}s,\ s+1\\ \frac{2s+1}{2},\ \frac{2s+3}{2}\end{matrix}\right]$ $\qquad [a,\ \operatorname{Re} s > 0]$
9	$\dfrac{1}{\sqrt{x+a}}\, \mathbf{E}\left(\sqrt{\dfrac{a}{x+a}}\right)$	$a^{s-1/2}\, \Gamma\left[\begin{matrix}\frac{1-2s}{2},\ s,\ s+1\\ \frac{1+2s}{2}\end{matrix}\right]$ $[0 < \operatorname{Re} s < 1/2;\ |\arg a| < \pi]$
10	$\mathbf{E}\left(\sqrt{\dfrac{x-a}{x}}\right)$	$\dfrac{\pi a^s}{2}\, \Gamma\left[\begin{matrix}\frac{2s-1}{2},\ \frac{2s+1}{2}\\ s,\ s+1\end{matrix}\right]$ $\qquad [a > 0;\ \operatorname{Re} s > 1/2]$
11	$\dfrac{1}{\sqrt{x+a}}\, \mathbf{E}\left(\sqrt{\dfrac{x}{x+a}}\right)$	$a^{s-1/2}\, \Gamma\left[\begin{matrix}\frac{1-2s}{2},\ \frac{3-2s}{2},\ s\\ 1-s\end{matrix}\right]$ $[0 < \operatorname{Re} s < 1/2;\ |\arg a| < \pi]$
12	$\dfrac{\sqrt{\sqrt{x+a} \pm \sqrt{a}}}{\sqrt{x+a}}\, \mathbf{E}\left(\sqrt{\dfrac{2\sqrt{a}}{\sqrt{a} \pm \sqrt{x+a}}}\right)$	$2\pi a^{s-1/4}\, \Gamma\left[\begin{matrix}s,\ s+1,\ \frac{1-4s}{4}\\ \frac{1}{4},\ \frac{1}{4},\ \frac{4s+3}{4}\end{matrix}\right]$ $[0 < \operatorname{Re} s < 1/4;\ |\arg a| < \pi]$
13	$\dfrac{\sqrt{\sqrt{x+a} \pm \sqrt{x}}}{\sqrt{x+a}}\, \mathbf{E}\left(\sqrt{\dfrac{2\sqrt{x}}{\sqrt{x} \pm \sqrt{x+a}}}\right)$	$2\pi a^{s-1/4}\, \Gamma\left[\begin{matrix}s,\ \frac{1-4s}{4},\ \frac{5-4s}{4}\\ \frac{1}{4},\ \frac{1}{4},\ 1-s\end{matrix}\right]$ $[0 < \operatorname{Re} s < 1/4;\ |\arg a| < \pi]$

3.26.6. $\theta(a-x)\,\mathbf{E}(\varphi(x))$ and algebraic functions

Notation: $\varepsilon = 0$ or 1.

1	$\dfrac{(a-x)_+^{\alpha-1}}{(1-b^2x^2)^\varepsilon}\,\mathbf{E}(bx)$	$\dfrac{\pi a^{s+\alpha-1}}{2}\,\mathrm{B}(s,\alpha)\ _4F_3\!\left(\begin{array}{c}\frac{2\varepsilon-1}{2},\ \frac{2\varepsilon+1}{2},\ \frac{s}{2},\ \frac{s+1}{2}\\[2pt]1,\ \frac{s+\alpha}{2},\ \frac{s+\alpha+1}{2};\ a^2b^2\end{array}\right)$ $[a,\ \mathrm{Re}\,\alpha,\ \mathrm{Re}\,s > 0]$
2	$\dfrac{(a^2-x^2)_+^{\alpha-1}}{(1-b^2x^2)^\varepsilon}\,\mathbf{E}(bx)$	$\dfrac{\pi a^{s+2\alpha-2}}{4}\,\mathrm{B}\!\left(\dfrac{s}{2},\alpha\right)\ _3F_2\!\left(\begin{array}{c}\frac{2\varepsilon-1}{2},\ \frac{2\varepsilon+1}{2},\ \frac{s}{2}\\[2pt]1,\ \frac{s+2\alpha}{2};\ a^2b^2\end{array}\right)$ $[a,\ \mathrm{Re}\,\alpha,\ \mathrm{Re}\,s > 0]$
3	$\dfrac{(a-x)_+^{\alpha-1}}{\left[1-b^2(a-x)^2\right]^\varepsilon}\,\mathbf{E}(b(a-x))$	$\dfrac{\pi a^{s+\alpha-1}}{2}\,\mathrm{B}(s,\alpha)\ _4F_3\!\left(\begin{array}{c}\frac{2\varepsilon-1}{2},\ \frac{2\varepsilon+1}{2},\ \frac{\alpha}{2},\ \frac{\alpha+1}{2}\\[2pt]1,\ \frac{s+\alpha}{2},\ \frac{s+\alpha+1}{2};\ a^2b^2\end{array}\right)$ $[a,\ \mathrm{Re}\,\alpha,\ \mathrm{Re}\,s > 0]$
4	$\dfrac{(a-x)_+^{\alpha-1}}{\left[1-b^2x^2(a-x)^2\right]^\varepsilon}\,\mathbf{E}(bx(a-x))$	$\dfrac{\pi a^{s+\alpha-1}}{2}\,\mathrm{B}(s,\alpha)$ $\times\ _6F_5\!\left(\begin{array}{c}\frac{2\varepsilon-1}{2},\ \frac{2\varepsilon+1}{2},\ \Delta(2,\alpha),\ \Delta(2,s)\\[2pt]1,\ \Delta(4,s+\alpha);\ \frac{a^4b^2}{16}\end{array}\right)$ $[a,\ \mathrm{Re}\,s,\ \mathrm{Re}\,\alpha > 0]$
5	$\dfrac{(a-x)_+^{\alpha-1}}{\left[1-b^2(a-x)\right]^\varepsilon}\,\mathbf{E}\!\left(b\sqrt{a-x}\right)$	$\dfrac{\pi a^{s+\alpha-1}}{2}\,\mathrm{B}(s,\alpha)\ _3F_2\!\left(\begin{array}{c}\frac{2\varepsilon-1}{2},\ \frac{2\varepsilon+1}{2},\ \alpha\\[2pt]1,\ s+\alpha;\ ab^2\end{array}\right)$ $[a,\ \mathrm{Re}\,\alpha,\ \mathrm{Re}\,s > 0]$
6	$\dfrac{\theta(a-x)}{\left[1-c^2(a-x)\right]^\varepsilon(bx+1)^\rho}\,\mathbf{E}\!\left(c\sqrt{a-x}\right)$	$\dfrac{\pi a^s}{2s}\,F_3\!\left(\dfrac{2\varepsilon-1}{2},\ \rho,\ \dfrac{2\varepsilon+1}{2},\ s;\ s+1;\ ac^2,\ -ab\right)$ $[a,\ \mathrm{Re}\,s > 0;\ |\arg(1+ab)| < \pi]$
7	$\dfrac{\theta(a-x)(x-b)_+^{\alpha-1}}{\left[1-c^2(a-x)\right]^\varepsilon}\,\mathbf{E}\!\left(c\sqrt{a-x}\right)$	$\dfrac{\pi(a-b)^\alpha b^{s-1}}{2\alpha}\,F_3\!\left(\dfrac{2\varepsilon-1}{2},\ 1-s,\ \dfrac{2\varepsilon+1}{2},\ \alpha;\ \alpha+1;\right.$ $\left. c^2(a-b),\ \dfrac{b-a}{b}\right)$ $[a > b > 0;\ \mathrm{Re}\,\alpha > 0]$
8	$\dfrac{(a-x)_+^{\alpha-1}}{\left[1-b^2x(a-x)\right]^\varepsilon}\,\mathbf{E}\!\left(b\sqrt{x(a-x)}\right)$	$\dfrac{\pi a^{s+\alpha-1}}{2}\,\mathrm{B}(s,\alpha)\ _4F_3\!\left(\begin{array}{c}\frac{2\varepsilon-1}{2},\ \frac{2\varepsilon+1}{2},\ \alpha,\ s\\[2pt]1,\ \frac{s+\alpha}{2},\ \frac{s+\alpha+1}{2};\ \frac{a^2b^2}{4}\end{array}\right)$ $[a,\ \mathrm{Re}\,\alpha,\ \mathrm{Re}\,s > 0]$
9	$\theta(a-x)\,\mathbf{E}\!\left(\sqrt{\dfrac{a-x}{a}}\right)$	$\dfrac{\pi a^s}{2}\,\Gamma\!\left[\begin{array}{c}s,\ s+1\\[2pt]\frac{2s+1}{2},\ \frac{2s+3}{2}\end{array}\right]$ $[a,\ \mathrm{Re}\,s > 0]$

No.	$f(x)$	$F(s)$
10	$\dfrac{\theta(a-x)}{(bx+1)^{\rho}}\,\mathbf{E}\left(\sqrt{\dfrac{a-x}{a}}\right)$	$\dfrac{\pi a^s}{2}\,\Gamma\!\left[\begin{matrix} s,\ s+1 \\ \frac{2s+1}{2},\ \frac{2s+3}{2}\end{matrix}\right]{}_3F_2\!\left(\begin{matrix}\rho,\ s,\ s+1;\ ab \\ \frac{2s+1}{2},\ \frac{2s+3}{2}\end{matrix}\right)$ $[a,\ \operatorname{Re}s>0;\ |\arg(1-ab)|<\pi]$
11	$\theta(a-x)\,\mathbf{E}\left(\sqrt{\dfrac{x-a}{x}}\right)$	$\dfrac{\pi a^s}{2}\,\Gamma\!\left[\begin{matrix}\frac{2s-1}{2},\ \frac{2s+1}{2} \\ s,\ s+1\end{matrix}\right]$ $[a>0;\ \operatorname{Re}s>1/2]$
12	$\dfrac{\theta(a-x)(b-x)^{\varepsilon-1/2}}{\left[c^2(x-a)+b-x\right]^{\varepsilon}}\,\mathbf{E}\left(c\sqrt{\dfrac{a-x}{b-x}}\right)$	$\dfrac{\pi a^s}{2s\sqrt{b}}\,F_1\!\left(\dfrac{1}{2},\ s,\ \dfrac{4\varepsilon-1}{2};\ s+1;\ \dfrac{a}{b},\ \dfrac{ac^2}{b}\right)$ $[b>a>0;\ \operatorname{Re}s>0]$
13	$\dfrac{\theta(a-x)}{\sqrt{a}\pm\sqrt{a-x}}\,\mathbf{E}\left(\pm\begin{Bmatrix}i\\1\end{Bmatrix}\dfrac{2\sqrt[4]{a}\sqrt[4]{a-x}}{\sqrt{a}\mp\sqrt{a-x}}\right)$	$\dfrac{\pi a^{s-1/2}}{2}\,\Gamma\!\left[\begin{matrix}s-1,\ s+1 \\ \frac{2s+1}{2},\ \frac{2s+1}{2}\end{matrix}\right]$ $[a>0;\ \operatorname{Re}s>1]$
14	$\dfrac{\theta(a-x)}{\sqrt{\sqrt{a}\pm\sqrt{a-x}}}\,\mathbf{E}\left(\sqrt{\dfrac{2\sqrt{a-x}}{\sqrt{a-x}\mp\sqrt{a}}}\right)$	$2^{2s-3/2}\sqrt{\pi}\,a^{s-1/4}\,\Gamma\!\left[\begin{matrix}\frac{2s-1}{2},\ \frac{2s+1}{2} \\ \frac{4s+1}{2}\end{matrix}\right]$ $[a>0;\ \operatorname{Re}s>1/2]$
15	$\theta(a-x)\left(\sqrt{a}-\sqrt{a-x}\right)$ $\times\,\mathbf{E}\left(\pm\dfrac{2i\sqrt[4]{a}\sqrt[4]{a-x}}{\sqrt{a}-\sqrt{a-x}}\right)$	$\dfrac{\pi a^{s+1/2}}{2}\,\Gamma\!\left[\begin{matrix}s,\ s+2 \\ \frac{2s+3}{2},\ \frac{2s+3}{2}\end{matrix}\right]$ $[a,\ \operatorname{Re}s>0]$
16	$\theta(a-x)\left(\sqrt{a-x}+\sqrt{a}\right)$ $\times\,\mathbf{E}\left(\pm\dfrac{2\sqrt[4]{a}\sqrt[4]{a-x}}{\sqrt{a}+\sqrt{a-x}}\right)$	$\dfrac{\pi a^{s+1/2}}{2}\,\Gamma\!\left[\begin{matrix}s,\ s+2 \\ \frac{2s+3}{2},\ \frac{2s+3}{2}\end{matrix}\right]$ $[a,\ \operatorname{Re}s>0]$
17	$\theta(a-x)\sqrt{\sqrt{a}\pm\sqrt{a-x}}$ $\times\,\mathbf{E}\left(\sqrt{\dfrac{2\sqrt{a-x}}{\sqrt{a-x}\pm\sqrt{a}}}\right)$	$2^{2s-1/2}\sqrt{\pi}\,a^{s+1/4}\,\Gamma\!\left[\begin{matrix}s,\ s+1 \\ \frac{4s+3}{2}\end{matrix}\right]$ $[a,\ \operatorname{Re}s>0]$
18	$\theta(a-x)\sqrt{\sqrt{x}\pm\sqrt{x-a}}$ $\times\,\mathbf{E}\left(\sqrt{\dfrac{2\sqrt{x-a}}{\sqrt{x-a}\pm\sqrt{x}}}\right)$	$\dfrac{\pi^{3/2}a^{s+1/4}}{2^{2s}}\,\Gamma\!\left[\begin{matrix}2s \\ \frac{4s+1}{2},\ \frac{4s+5}{2}\end{matrix}\right]$ $[a,\ \operatorname{Re}s>0]$

3.26.7. $\theta(x-a)\,\mathbf{E}(\varphi(x))$ and algebraic functions

1	$\dfrac{\theta(x-a)}{\sqrt{x}-\sqrt{x-a}}\,\mathbf{E}\!\left(\dfrac{2\sqrt[4]{x(x-a)}}{\sqrt{x}+\sqrt{x-a}}\right)$	$\dfrac{\pi a^{s-1/2}}{2}\,\Gamma\!\left[\begin{matrix}\frac{3-2s}{2},\ -\frac{2s+1}{2}\\ 1-s,\ 1-s\end{matrix}\right]$ $[a>0;\ \mathrm{Re}\,s<-1/2]$
2	$\dfrac{\theta(x-a)}{\sqrt{x}+\sqrt{x-a}}\,\mathbf{E}\!\left(\pm\dfrac{2i\sqrt[4]{x(x-a)}}{\sqrt{x}-\sqrt{x-a}}\right)$	$\dfrac{\pi a^{s-1/2}}{2}\,\Gamma\!\left[\begin{matrix}\frac{3-2s}{2},\ -\frac{2s+1}{2}\\ 1-s,\ 1-s\end{matrix}\right]$ $[a>0;\ \mathrm{Re}\,s<-1/2]$
3	$\dfrac{\theta(x-a)}{\sqrt{\sqrt{x}\pm\sqrt{x-a}}}\,\mathbf{E}\!\left(\sqrt{\dfrac{2\sqrt{x-a}}{\sqrt{x-a}\mp\sqrt{x}}}\right)$	$2^{-2s-1}\sqrt{\pi}\,a^{s-1/4}\,\Gamma\!\left[\begin{matrix}\frac{3-4s}{4},\ -\frac{4s+1}{4}\\ 1-2s\end{matrix}\right]$ $[a>0;\ \mathrm{Re}\,s<-1/4]$
4	$\theta(x-a)\left(\sqrt{x-a}+\sqrt{x}\right)$ $\times\,\mathbf{E}\!\left(\pm\dfrac{2\sqrt[4]{x}\sqrt[4]{x-a}}{\sqrt{x}+\sqrt{x-a}}\right)$	$\dfrac{\pi a^{s+1/2}}{2}\,\Gamma\!\left[\begin{matrix}\frac{3-2s}{2},\ -\frac{2s+1}{2}\\ 1-s,\ 1-s\end{matrix}\right]$ $[a>0;\ \mathrm{Re}\,s<-1/2]$
5	$\theta(x-a)\left(\sqrt{x}-\sqrt{x-a}\right)$ $\times\,\mathbf{E}\!\left(\pm\dfrac{2i\sqrt[4]{x}\sqrt[4]{x-a}}{\sqrt{x}-\sqrt{x-a}}\right)$	$\dfrac{\pi a^{s+1/2}}{2}\,\Gamma\!\left[\begin{matrix}\frac{3-2s}{2},\ -\frac{2s+1}{2}\\ 1-s,\ 1-s\end{matrix}\right]$ $[a>0;\ \mathrm{Re}\,s<-1/2]$
6	$\theta(x-a)\,\sqrt{\sqrt{a}\pm\sqrt{a-x}}$ $\times\,\mathbf{E}\!\left(\sqrt{\dfrac{2\sqrt{a-x}}{\sqrt{a-x}\pm\sqrt{a}}}\right)$	$2^{2s+1/2}\pi^{3/2}a^{s+1/4}\,\Gamma\!\left[\begin{matrix}-\frac{4s+1}{2}\\ -s,\ 1-s\end{matrix}\right]$ $[a>0;\ \mathrm{Re}\,s<-1/4]$
7	$\theta(x-a)\,\sqrt{\sqrt{x}\pm\sqrt{x-a}}$ $\times\,\mathbf{E}\!\left(\sqrt{\dfrac{2\sqrt{x-a}}{\sqrt{x-a}\pm\sqrt{x}}}\right)$	$2^{-2s-1}\sqrt{\pi}\,a^{s+1/4}\,\Gamma\!\left[\begin{matrix}\frac{3-4s}{4},\ -\frac{4s+1}{4}\\ 1-2s\end{matrix}\right]$ $[a>0;\ \mathrm{Re}\,s<-1/4]$

3.26.8. $\mathbf{K}(\varphi(x))$, $\mathbf{E}(\varphi(x))$, and the exponential function

Notation: $\delta=\left\{\begin{matrix}1\\0\end{matrix}\right\}.$

1	$\theta(a-x)\,e^{bx}\left\{\begin{matrix}\mathbf{K}(\sqrt{1-x/a})\\ \mathbf{E}(\sqrt{1-x/a})\end{matrix}\right\}$	$\dfrac{\pi a^{s}}{2}\,\Gamma\!\left[\begin{matrix}s,\ s-\delta+1\\ \frac{2s+1}{2},\ \frac{2s-2\delta+3}{2}\end{matrix}\right]\,{}_2F_2\!\left(\begin{matrix}s,\ s-\delta+1;\ ab\\ \frac{2s+1}{2},\ \frac{2s-2\delta+3}{2}\end{matrix}\right)$ $[a,\ \mathrm{Re}\,s>0]$

No.	$f(x)$	$F(s)$
2	$\theta(a-x)e^{-b\sqrt{x}}\left\{\begin{matrix}\mathbf{K}(1-x/a)\\\mathbf{E}(1-x/a)\end{matrix}\right\}$	$\dfrac{\pi a^s}{2}\Gamma\left[\begin{matrix}s,\ s-\delta+1\\\frac{2s+1}{2},\ \frac{2s-2\delta+3}{2}\end{matrix}\right]{}_2F_3\left(\begin{matrix}s,\ s-\delta+1;\ \frac{ab^2}{4}\\\frac{1}{2},\ \frac{2s+1}{2},\ \frac{2s-2\delta+3}{2}\end{matrix}\right)$ $-\dfrac{\pi a^{s+1/2}b}{2}\Gamma\left[\begin{matrix}\frac{2s+1}{2},\ \frac{2s-2\delta+3}{2}\\s+1,\ s-\delta+2\end{matrix}\right]$ $\times\ {}_2F_3\left(\begin{matrix}\frac{2s+1}{2},\ \frac{2s-2\delta+3}{2};\ \frac{ab^2}{4}\\\frac{3}{2},\ s+1,\ s-\delta+2\end{matrix}\right)$ $[a,\ \mathrm{Re}\,s>0]$

3.26.9. $\mathbf{K}(\varphi(x))$, $\mathbf{E}(\varphi(x))$, and hyperbolic or trigonometric functions

No.	$f(x)$	$F(s)$
1	$\theta(a-x)\left\{\begin{matrix}\sinh(b\sqrt{x})\\\sin(b\sqrt{x})\end{matrix}\right\}\mathbf{K}\left(\sqrt{1-\frac{x}{a}}\right)$	$\dfrac{\pi a^{s+1/2}b}{2}\Gamma\left[\begin{matrix}\frac{2s+1}{2},\ \frac{2s+1}{2}\\s+1,\ s+1\end{matrix}\right]{}_2F_3\left(\begin{matrix}\frac{2s+1}{2},\ \frac{2s+1}{2};\ \pm\frac{ab^2}{4}\\\frac{3}{2},\ s+1,\ s+1\end{matrix}\right)$ $[a>0;\ \mathrm{Re}\,s>-1/2]$
2	$\theta(a-x)\left\{\begin{matrix}\sinh(b\sqrt{x})\\\sin(b\sqrt{x})\end{matrix}\right\}\mathbf{E}\left(\sqrt{1-\frac{x}{a}}\right)$	$\dfrac{\pi a^{s+1/2}b}{2}\Gamma\left[\begin{matrix}\frac{2s+1}{2},\ \frac{2s+3}{2}\\s+1,\ s+2\end{matrix}\right]{}_2F_3\left(\begin{matrix}\frac{2s+1}{2},\ \frac{2s+3}{2};\ \pm\frac{ab^2}{4}\\\frac{3}{2},\ s+1,\ s+2\end{matrix}\right)$ $[a>0;\ \mathrm{Re}\,s>-1/2]$
3	$\theta(a-x)\left\{\begin{matrix}\cosh(b\sqrt{x})\\\cos(b\sqrt{x})\end{matrix}\right\}\mathbf{K}\left(\sqrt{1-\frac{x}{a}}\right)$	$\dfrac{\pi a^s}{2}\Gamma\left[\begin{matrix}s,\ s\\\frac{2s+1}{2},\ \frac{2s+1}{2}\end{matrix}\right]{}_2F_3\left(\begin{matrix}s,\ s;\ \pm\frac{ab^2}{4}\\\frac{1}{2},\ \frac{2s+1}{2},\ \frac{2s+1}{2}\end{matrix}\right)$ $[a,\ \mathrm{Re}\,s>0]$
4	$\theta(a-x)\left\{\begin{matrix}\cosh(b\sqrt{x})\\\cos(b\sqrt{x})\end{matrix}\right\}\mathbf{E}\left(\sqrt{1-\frac{x}{a}}\right)$	$\dfrac{\pi a^s}{2}\Gamma\left[\begin{matrix}s,\ s+1\\\frac{2s+1}{2},\ \frac{2s+3}{2}\end{matrix}\right]{}_2F_3\left(\begin{matrix}s,\ s+1;\ \pm\frac{ab^2}{4}\\\frac{1}{2},\ \frac{2s+1}{2},\ \frac{2s+3}{2}\end{matrix}\right)$ $[a,\ \mathrm{Re}\,s>0]$

3.26.10. $\mathbf{K}(\varphi(x))$, $\mathbf{E}(\varphi(x))$, and the logarithmic function

Notation: $\delta=\left\{\begin{matrix}1\\0\end{matrix}\right\}$.

No.	$f(x)$	$F(s)$
1	$\theta(1-x)\ln(ax+1)\left\{\begin{matrix}\mathbf{K}(\sqrt{1-x})\\\mathbf{E}(\sqrt{1-x})\end{matrix}\right\}$	$\dfrac{\pi a}{2}\Gamma\left[\begin{matrix}s+1,\ s-\delta+2\\\frac{2s+3}{2},\ \frac{2s-2\delta+5}{2}\end{matrix}\right]{}_4F_3\left(\begin{matrix}1,\ 1,\ s+1,\ s-\delta+2\\2,\ \frac{2s+3}{2},\ \frac{2s-2\delta+5}{2};\ -a\end{matrix}\right)$ $[\mathrm{Re}\,s>-1;\ |\arg(1+a)|<\pi]$
2	$\theta(a-x)\ln(bx^2+1)$ $\times\left\{\begin{matrix}\mathbf{K}(\sqrt{1-x/a})\\\mathbf{E}(\sqrt{1-x/a})\end{matrix}\right\}$	$\dfrac{\pi a^{s+2}b}{2}\Gamma\left[\begin{matrix}s+2,\ s-\delta+3\\\frac{2s+5}{2},\ \frac{2s-2\delta+7}{2}\end{matrix}\right]$ $\times\ {}_6F_5\left(\begin{matrix}1,\ 1,\ \frac{s+2}{2},\ \frac{s+3}{2},\ \frac{s-\delta+3}{2},\ \frac{s-\delta+4}{2};\ -a^2b\\2,\ \frac{2s+5}{4},\ \frac{2s+7}{4},\ \frac{2s-2\delta+7}{4},\ \frac{2s-2\delta+9}{4}\end{matrix}\right)$ $[a>0;\ \mathrm{Re}\,s>-2;\ |\arg(1+a^2b)|<\pi]$

No.	$f(x)$	$F(s)$
3	$\theta(a-x)\ln\dfrac{1+bx}{1-bx}\left\{\begin{array}{l}\mathbf{K}\left(\sqrt{1-x/a}\right)\\ \mathbf{E}\left(\sqrt{1-x/a}\right)\end{array}\right\}$	$\pi a^{s+1}b\,\Gamma\left[\begin{array}{l}s+1,\,s-\delta+2\\ \frac{2s+3}{2},\,\frac{2s-2\delta+5}{2}\end{array}\right]$ $\times\,{}_6F_5\left(\begin{array}{c}\frac{1}{2},1,\frac{s+1}{2},\frac{s+2}{2},\frac{s-\delta+2}{2},\frac{s-\delta+3}{2};a^2b^2\\ \frac{3}{2},\frac{2s+3}{4},\frac{2s+5}{4},\frac{2s-2\delta+5}{4},\frac{2s-2\delta+7}{4}\end{array}\right)$ $\left[a>0;\ \mathrm{Re}\,s>-1;\ \left|\arg\left(1-a^2b^2\right)\right|<\pi\right]$
4	$\theta(a-x)\ln\dfrac{1+b\sqrt{x}}{1-b\sqrt{x}}\left\{\begin{array}{l}\mathbf{K}\left(\sqrt{1-x/a}\right)\\ \mathbf{E}\left(\sqrt{1-x/a}\right)\end{array}\right\}$	$\pi a^{s+1/2}b\,\Gamma\left[\begin{array}{l}\frac{2s+1}{2},\,\frac{2s-2\delta+3}{2}\\ s+1,\,s-\delta+2\end{array}\right]$ $\times\,{}_4F_3\left(\begin{array}{c}\frac{1}{2},1,\frac{2s+1}{2},\frac{2s-2\delta+3}{2}\\ \frac{3}{2},s+1,s-\delta+2;ab^2\end{array}\right)$ $\left[a>0;\ \mathrm{Re}\,s>-1/2;\ \left|\arg\left(1-ab^2\right)\right|<\pi\right]$
5	$\theta(a-x)\ln\left(b\sqrt{x}+\sqrt{1+b^2x}\right)$ $\times\left\{\begin{array}{l}\mathbf{K}\left(\sqrt{1-x/a}\right)\\ \mathbf{E}\left(\sqrt{1-x/a}\right)\end{array}\right\}$	$\dfrac{\pi a^{s+1/2}b}{2}\,\Gamma\left[\begin{array}{l}\frac{2s+1}{2},\,\frac{2s-2\delta+3}{2}\\ s+1,\,s-\delta+2\end{array}\right]$ $\times\,{}_4F_3\left(\begin{array}{c}\frac{1}{2},\frac{1}{2},\frac{2s+1}{2},\frac{2s-2\delta+3}{2}\\ \frac{3}{2},s+1,s-\delta+2;-ab^2\end{array}\right)$ $\left[a>0;\ \mathrm{Re}\,s>-1/2;\ \left|\arg\left(1+ab^2\right)\right|<\pi\right]$
6	$\theta(a-x)\ln\left(bx+\sqrt{b^2x^2+1}\right)$ $\times\left\{\begin{array}{l}\mathbf{K}\left(\sqrt{1-x/a}\right)\\ \mathbf{E}\left(\sqrt{1-x/a}\right)\end{array}\right\}$	$\dfrac{\pi a^{s+1}b}{2}\,\Gamma\left[\begin{array}{l}s+1,\,s-\delta+2\\ \frac{2s+3}{2},\,\frac{2s-2\delta+5}{2}\end{array}\right]$ $\times\,{}_6F_5\left(\begin{array}{c}\frac{1}{2},\frac{1}{2},\frac{s+1}{2},\frac{s+2}{2},\frac{s-\delta+2}{2},\frac{s-\delta+3}{2};-a^2b^2\\ \frac{3}{2},\frac{2s+3}{4},\frac{2s+5}{4},\frac{2s-2\delta+5}{4},\frac{2s-2\delta+7}{4}\end{array}\right)$ $\left[a>0;\ \mathrm{Re}\,s>-1;\ \left|\arg\left(1+a^2b^2\right)\right|<\pi\right]$
7	$\dfrac{\theta(a-x)}{\sqrt{1+b^2x^2}}\ln\left(bx+\sqrt{b^2x^2+1}\right)$ $\times\left\{\begin{array}{l}\mathbf{K}\left(\sqrt{1-x/a}\right)\\ \mathbf{E}\left(\sqrt{1-x/a}\right)\end{array}\right\}$	$\dfrac{\pi a^{s+1}b}{2}\,\Gamma\left[\begin{array}{l}s+1,\,s-\delta+2\\ \frac{2s+3}{2},\,\frac{2s-2\delta+5}{2}\end{array}\right]$ $\times\,{}_6F_5\left(\begin{array}{c}1,1,\frac{s+1}{2},\frac{s+2}{2},\frac{s-\delta+2}{2},\frac{s-\delta+3}{2};-a^2b^2\\ \frac{3}{2},\frac{2s+3}{4},\frac{2s+5}{4},\frac{2s-2\delta+5}{4},\frac{2s-2\delta+7}{4}\end{array}\right)$ $\left[a>0;\ \mathrm{Re}\,s>-1;\ \left|\arg\left(1+a^2b^2\right)\right|<\pi\right]$
8	$\theta(a-x)\ln\dfrac{\sqrt{a-x}+\sqrt{a}}{\sqrt{x}}\left\{\begin{array}{l}\mathbf{K}(bx)\\ \mathbf{E}(bx)\end{array}\right\}$	$\dfrac{\pi^{3/2}a^s}{4s}\,\Gamma\left[\begin{array}{l}s\\ \frac{2s+1}{2}\end{array}\right]{}_5F_4\left(\begin{array}{c}\pm\frac{1}{2},\frac{1}{2},\frac{s}{2},\frac{s}{2},\frac{s+1}{2};a^2b^2\\ 1,\frac{2s+1}{4},\frac{2s+3}{4},\frac{s+2}{2}\end{array}\right)$ $\left[a,\ \mathrm{Re}\,s>0\right]$
9	$\theta(a-x)\ln\dfrac{\sqrt{a^2-x^2}+a}{x}\left\{\begin{array}{l}\mathbf{K}(bx)\\ \mathbf{E}(bx)\end{array}\right\}$	$\dfrac{\pi^{3/2}a^s}{4s}\,\Gamma\left[\begin{array}{l}\frac{s}{2}\\ \frac{s+1}{2}\end{array}\right]{}_4F_3\left(\begin{array}{c}\pm\frac{1}{2},\frac{1}{2},\frac{s}{2},\frac{s}{2}\\ 1,\frac{s+1}{2},\frac{s+2}{2};a^2b^2\end{array}\right)$ $\left[a,\ \mathrm{Re}\,s>0\right]$

No.	$f(x)$	$F(s)$
10	$\theta(a-x)\ln\dfrac{a+\sqrt{a^2-x^2}}{a-\sqrt{a^2-x^2}}\,\mathbf{K}(bx)$	$\dfrac{\pi^{3/2}a^s}{2s}\,\Gamma\left[\begin{matrix}\frac{s}{2}\\\frac{s+1}{2}\end{matrix}\right]\,{}_4F_3\left(\begin{matrix}\frac{1}{2},\,\frac{1}{2},\,\frac{s}{2},\,\frac{s}{2};\,a^2b^2\\1,\,\frac{s+1}{2},\,\frac{s+2}{2}\end{matrix}\right)$ $[a,\ \mathrm{Re}\,s>0]$
11	$\dfrac{\theta(a-x)}{1-b^2x^2}\ln\dfrac{\sqrt{a-x}+\sqrt{a}}{\sqrt{x}}\,\mathbf{E}(bx)$	$\dfrac{\pi^{3/2}a^s}{4s}\,\Gamma\left[\begin{matrix}s\\\frac{2s+1}{2}\end{matrix}\right]\,{}_5F_4\left(\begin{matrix}\frac{1}{2},\,\frac{3}{2},\,\frac{s}{2},\,\frac{s}{2},\,\frac{s+1}{2};\,a^2b^2\\1,\,\frac{2s+1}{4},\,\frac{2s+3}{4},\,\frac{s+2}{2}\end{matrix}\right)$ $[a,\ \mathrm{Re}\,s>0]$
12	$\dfrac{\theta(a-x)}{1-b^2x^2}\ln\dfrac{\sqrt{a^2-x^2}+a}{x}\,\mathbf{E}(bx)$	$\dfrac{\pi^{3/2}a^s}{4s}\,\Gamma\left[\begin{matrix}\frac{s}{2}\\\frac{s+1}{2}\end{matrix}\right]\,{}_4F_3\left(\begin{matrix}\frac{1}{2},\,\frac{3}{2},\,\frac{s}{2},\,\frac{s}{2};\,a^2b^2\\1,\,\frac{s+1}{2},\,\frac{s+2}{2}\end{matrix}\right)$ $[a,\ \mathrm{Re}\,s>0]$
13	$\theta(a-x)\ln^2\left(b\sqrt{x}+\sqrt{b^2x+1}\right)$ $\times\left\{\begin{matrix}\mathbf{K}\left(\sqrt{1-x/a}\right)\\\mathbf{E}\left(\sqrt{1-x/a}\right)\end{matrix}\right\}$	$\dfrac{\pi a^{s+1}b^2}{2}\,\Gamma\left[\begin{matrix}s+1,\,s-\delta+2\\\frac{2s+3}{2},\,\frac{2s-2\delta+5}{2}\end{matrix}\right]$ $\times{}_5F_4\left(\begin{matrix}1,\,1,\,1,\,s+1,\,s-\delta+2\\\frac{3}{2},\,2,\,\frac{2s+3}{2},\,\frac{2s-2\delta+5}{2};\,-a^2b\end{matrix}\right)$ $[a>0;\ \mathrm{Re}\,s>-1]$
14	$\theta(a-x)\ln^2\left(bx+\sqrt{b^2x^2+1}\right)$ $\times\left\{\begin{matrix}\mathbf{K}\left(\sqrt{1-x/a}\right)\\\mathbf{E}\left(\sqrt{1-x/a}\right)\end{matrix}\right\}$	$\dfrac{\pi a^{s+2}b^2}{2}\,\Gamma\left[\begin{matrix}s+2,\,s-\delta+3\\\frac{2s+5}{2},\,\frac{2s-2\delta+7}{2}\end{matrix}\right]$ $\times{}_7F_6\left(\begin{matrix}1,\,1,\,1,\,\frac{s+2}{2},\,\frac{s+3}{2},\,\frac{s-\delta+3}{2},\,\frac{s-\delta+4}{2};\,a^2b^2\\\frac{3}{2},\,2,\,\frac{2s+5}{4},\,\frac{2s+7}{4},\,\frac{2s-2\delta+7}{4},\,\frac{2s-2\delta+9}{4}\end{matrix}\right)$ $[a>0;\ \mathrm{Re}\,s>-2]$

3.26.11. $\mathbf{K}(\varphi(x))$, $\mathbf{E}(\varphi(x))$, and inverse trigonometric functions

Notation: $\delta=\left\{\begin{matrix}1\\0\end{matrix}\right\}$.

No.	$f(x)$	$F(s)$
1	$\theta(a-x)\arccos\dfrac{x}{a}\left\{\begin{matrix}\mathbf{K}(bx)\\\mathbf{E}(bx)\end{matrix}\right\}$	$\dfrac{\pi^{3/2}a^s}{2s^2}\,\Gamma\left[\begin{matrix}\frac{s+1}{2}\\\frac{s}{2}\end{matrix}\right]\,{}_4F_3\left(\begin{matrix}\pm\frac{1}{2},\,\frac{1}{2},\,\frac{s}{2},\,\frac{s+1}{2}\\1,\,\frac{s+2}{2},\,\frac{s+2}{2};\,a^2b^2\end{matrix}\right)$ $[a,\ \mathrm{Re}\,s>0]$
2	$\dfrac{\theta(a-x)}{1-b^2x^2}\arccos\dfrac{x}{a}\,\mathbf{E}(bx)$	$\dfrac{\pi^{3/2}a^s}{2s^2}\,\Gamma\left[\begin{matrix}\frac{s+1}{2}\\\frac{s}{2}\end{matrix}\right]\,{}_4F_3\left(\begin{matrix}\frac{1}{2},\,\frac{3}{2},\,\frac{s}{2},\,\frac{s+1}{2}\\1,\,\frac{s+2}{2},\,\frac{s+2}{2};\,a^2b^2\end{matrix}\right)$ $[a,\ \mathrm{Re}\,s>0]$
3	$\theta(a-x)\arcsin(bx)\left\{\begin{matrix}\mathbf{K}\left(\sqrt{1-x/a}\right)\\\mathbf{E}\left(\sqrt{1-x/a}\right)\end{matrix}\right\}$	$\dfrac{\pi a^{s+1}b}{2}\,\Gamma\left[\begin{matrix}s+1,\,s-\delta+2\\\frac{2s+3}{2},\,\frac{2s-2\delta+5}{2}\end{matrix}\right]$ $\times{}_6F_5\left(\begin{matrix}\frac{1}{2},\,\frac{1}{2},\,\frac{s+1}{2},\,\frac{s+2}{2},\,\frac{s-\delta+2}{2},\,\frac{s-\delta+3}{2};\,a^2b^2\\\frac{3}{2},\,\frac{2s+3}{4},\,\frac{2s+5}{4},\,\frac{2s-2\delta+5}{4},\,\frac{2s-2\delta+7}{4}\end{matrix}\right)$ $[a>0;\ \mathrm{Re}\,s>-1]$

No.	$f(x)$	$F(s)$
4	$\dfrac{\theta(a-x)}{\sqrt{1-b^2x^2}}\arcsin(bx)$ $\times\left\{\begin{array}{l}\mathbf{K}\left(\sqrt{1-x/a}\right)\\\mathbf{E}\left(\sqrt{1-x/a}\right)\end{array}\right\}$	$\dfrac{\pi a^{s+1}b}{2}\Gamma\begin{bmatrix}s+1,\ s-\delta+2\\\frac{2s+3}{2},\ \frac{2s-2\delta+5}{2}\end{bmatrix}$ $\times\,_6F_5\left(\begin{array}{c}1,1,\frac{s+1}{2},\frac{s+2}{2},\frac{s-\delta+2}{2},\frac{s-\delta+3}{2};a^2b^2\\\frac{3}{2},\frac{2s+3}{4},\frac{2s+5}{4},\frac{2s-2\delta+5}{4},\frac{2s-2\delta+7}{4}\end{array}\right)$ $[a>0;\ \mathrm{Re}\,s>-1]$
5	$\theta(a-x)\arcsin(b\sqrt{x})$ $\times\left\{\begin{array}{l}\mathbf{K}\left(\sqrt{1-x/a}\right)\\\mathbf{E}\left(\sqrt{1-x/a}\right)\end{array}\right\}$	$\dfrac{\pi a^{s+1/2}b}{2}\Gamma\begin{bmatrix}\frac{2s+1}{2},\ \frac{2s-2\delta+3}{2}\\s+1,\ s-\delta+2\end{bmatrix}\,_4F_3\left(\begin{array}{c}\frac{1}{2},\frac{1}{2},\frac{2s+1}{2},\frac{2s-2\delta+3}{2}\\\frac{3}{2},s+1,s-\delta+2;ab^2\end{array}\right)$ $[a>0;\ \mathrm{Re}\,s>-1/2]$
6	$\dfrac{\theta(a-x)}{\sqrt{1-b^2x}}\arcsin(b\sqrt{x})$ $\times\left\{\begin{array}{l}\mathbf{K}\left(\sqrt{1-x/a}\right)\\\mathbf{E}\left(\sqrt{1-x/a}\right)\end{array}\right\}$	$\dfrac{\pi a^{s+1/2}b}{2}\Gamma\begin{bmatrix}\frac{2s+1}{2},\ \frac{2s-2\delta+3}{2}\\s+1,\ s-\delta+2\end{bmatrix}\,_4F_3\left(\begin{array}{c}1,1,\frac{2s+1}{2},\frac{2s-2\delta+3}{2}\\\frac{3}{2},s+1,s-\delta+2;ab^2\end{array}\right)$ $\left[a>0;\ \mathrm{Re}\,s>-1/2;\ |\arg(1-ab^2)|<\pi\right]$
7	$\theta(a-x)\arcsin^2(b\sqrt{x})$ $\times\left\{\begin{array}{l}\mathbf{K}\left(\sqrt{1-x/a}\right)\\\mathbf{E}\left(\sqrt{1-x/a}\right)\end{array}\right\}$	$\dfrac{\pi a^{s+1}b^2}{2}\Gamma\begin{bmatrix}s+1,\ s-\delta+2\\\frac{2s+3}{2},\ \frac{2s-2\delta+5}{2}\end{bmatrix}\,_5F_4\left(\begin{array}{c}1,1,1,s+1,s-\delta+2\\\frac{3}{2},2,\frac{2s+3}{2},\frac{2s-2\delta+5}{2};ab^2\end{array}\right)$ $[a>0;\ \mathrm{Re}\,s>-1]$
8	$\theta(a-x)\arcsin^2(bx)$ $\times\left\{\begin{array}{l}\mathbf{K}\left(\sqrt{1-x/a}\right)\\\mathbf{E}\left(\sqrt{1-x/a}\right)\end{array}\right\}$	$\dfrac{\pi a^{s+2}b^2}{2}\Gamma\begin{bmatrix}s+2,\ s-\delta+3\\\frac{2s+5}{2},\ \frac{2s-2\delta+7}{2}\end{bmatrix}$ $\times\,_7F_6\left(\begin{array}{c}1,1,1,\frac{s+2}{2},\frac{s+3}{2},\frac{s-\delta+3}{2},\frac{s-\delta+4}{2};a^2b^2\\\frac{3}{2},2,\frac{2s+5}{4},\frac{2s+7}{4},\frac{2s-2\delta+7}{4},\frac{2s-2\delta+9}{4}\end{array}\right)$ $[a>0;\ \mathrm{Re}\,s>-2]$
9	$\theta(a-x)\arctan(bx)$ $\times\left\{\begin{array}{l}\mathbf{K}\left(\sqrt{1-x/a}\right)\\\mathbf{E}\left(\sqrt{1-x/a}\right)\end{array}\right\}$	$\dfrac{\pi a^{s+1}b}{2}\Gamma\begin{bmatrix}s+1,\ s-\delta+2\\\frac{2s+3}{2},\ \frac{2s-2\delta+5}{2}\end{bmatrix}$ $\times\,_6F_5\left(\begin{array}{c}\frac{1}{2},1,\frac{s+1}{2},\frac{s+2}{2},\frac{s-\delta+2}{2},\frac{s-\delta+3}{2};-a^2b^2\\\frac{3}{2},\frac{2s+3}{4},\frac{2s+5}{4},\frac{2s-2\delta+5}{4},\frac{2s-2\delta+7}{4}\end{array}\right)$ $[a>0;\ \mathrm{Re}\,s>-1]$
10	$\theta(a-x)\arctan(b\sqrt{x})$ $\times\left\{\begin{array}{l}\mathbf{K}\left(\sqrt{1-x/a}\right)\\\mathbf{E}\left(\sqrt{1-x/a}\right)\end{array}\right\}$	$\dfrac{\pi a^{s+1/2}b}{2}\Gamma\begin{bmatrix}\frac{2s+1}{2},\ \frac{2s-2\delta+3}{2}\\s+1,\ s-\delta+2\end{bmatrix}\,_4F_3\left(\begin{array}{c}\frac{1}{2},1,\frac{2s+1}{2},\frac{2s-2\delta+3}{2}\\\frac{3}{2},s+1,s-\delta+2;-ab^2\end{array}\right)$ $[a,\ \mathrm{Re}\,s>0]$

3.26.12. $\mathbf{K}\left(\varphi\left(x\right)\right)$, $\mathbf{E}\left(\varphi\left(x\right)\right)$, and $\mathrm{Li}_2\left(ax\right)$

Notation: $\delta = \left\{\begin{matrix}1\\0\end{matrix}\right\}$.

1	$\theta\left(a-x\right)\mathrm{Li}_2\left(bx\right)$ $\times \left\{\begin{matrix}\mathbf{K}\left(\sqrt{1-x/a}\right)\\\mathbf{E}\left(\sqrt{1-x/a}\right)\end{matrix}\right\}$	$\dfrac{\pi a^{s+1}b}{2}\Gamma\left[\begin{matrix}s+1,\ s-\delta+2\\\frac{2s+3}{2},\ \frac{2s-2\delta+5}{2}\end{matrix}\right]\,_4F_3\left(\begin{matrix}1,\ 1,\ 1,\ s+1,\ s-\delta+2\\2,\ 2,\ \frac{2s+3}{2},\ \frac{2s-2\delta+5}{2};\ ab\end{matrix}\right)$ $\left[a>0,\ \mathrm{Re}\,s>-1;\ \left|\arg\left(1-ab\right)\right|<\pi\right]$

3.26.13. $\mathbf{K}\left(\varphi\left(x\right)\right)$, $\mathbf{E}\left(\varphi\left(x\right)\right)$, and $\mathrm{Si}\left(ax^r\right)$, $\mathrm{shi}\left(ax^r\right)$

1	$\theta\left(a-x\right)\left\{\begin{matrix}\mathrm{shi}\left(bx\right)\\\mathrm{Si}\left(bx\right)\end{matrix}\right\}$ $\times\mathbf{K}\left(\sqrt{1-\dfrac{x}{a}}\right)$	$\dfrac{\pi a^{s+1}b^2}{2}\Gamma\left[\begin{matrix}s+1,\ s+1\\\frac{2s+3}{2},\ \frac{2s+3}{2}\end{matrix}\right]\,_5F_6\left(\begin{matrix}\frac{1}{2},\ \frac{s+1}{2},\ \frac{s+1}{2},\ \frac{s+2}{2},\ \frac{s+2}{2};\ \pm\frac{a^2b^2}{4}\\\frac{3}{2},\ \frac{3}{2},\ \frac{2s+3}{4},\ \frac{2s+3}{4},\ \frac{2s+5}{4},\ \frac{2s+5}{4}\end{matrix}\right)$ $\left[a>0;\ \mathrm{Re}\,s>-1\right]$
2	$\theta\left(a-x\right)\left\{\begin{matrix}\mathrm{shi}\left(bx\right)\\\mathrm{Si}\left(bx\right)\end{matrix}\right\}$ $\times\mathbf{E}\left(\sqrt{1-\dfrac{x}{a}}\right)$	$\dfrac{\pi a^{s+1}b^2}{2}\Gamma\left[\begin{matrix}s+1,\ s+2\\\frac{2s+3}{2},\ \frac{2s+5}{2}\end{matrix}\right]\,_5F_6\left(\begin{matrix}\frac{1}{2},\ \frac{s+1}{2},\ \frac{s+2}{2},\ \frac{s+2}{2},\ \frac{s+3}{2};\ \pm\frac{a^2b^2}{4}\\\frac{3}{2},\ \frac{3}{2},\ \frac{2s+3}{4},\ \frac{2s+5}{4},\ \frac{2s+5}{4},\ \frac{2s+7}{4}\end{matrix}\right)$ $\left[a>0;\ \mathrm{Re}\,s>-1\right]$
3	$\theta\left(a-x\right)\left\{\begin{matrix}\mathrm{shi}\left(b\sqrt{x}\right)\\\mathrm{Si}\left(b\sqrt{x}\right)\end{matrix}\right\}$ $\times\mathbf{K}\left(\sqrt{1-\dfrac{x}{a}}\right)$	$\dfrac{\pi a^{s+1/2}b}{2}\Gamma\left[\begin{matrix}\frac{2s+1}{2},\ \frac{2s+1}{2}\\s+1,\ s+1\end{matrix}\right]\,_3F_4\left(\begin{matrix}\frac{1}{2},\ \frac{2s+1}{2},\ \frac{2s+1}{2};\ \pm\frac{ab^2}{4}\\\frac{3}{2},\ \frac{3}{2},\ s+1,\ s+1\end{matrix}\right)$ $\left[a>0;\ \mathrm{Re}\,s>-1/2\right]$
4	$\theta\left(a-x\right)\left\{\begin{matrix}\mathrm{shi}\left(a\sqrt{x}\right)\\\mathrm{Si}\left(a\sqrt{x}\right)\end{matrix}\right\}$ $\times\mathbf{E}\left(\sqrt{1-\dfrac{x}{a}}\right)$	$\dfrac{\pi a^{s+1/2}b}{2}\Gamma\left[\begin{matrix}\frac{2s+1}{2},\ \frac{2s+3}{2}\\s+1,\ s+2\end{matrix}\right]\,_3F_4\left(\begin{matrix}\frac{1}{2},\ \frac{2s+1}{2},\ \frac{2s+3}{2};\ \pm\frac{ab^2}{4}\\\frac{3}{2},\ \frac{3}{2},\ s+1,\ s+2\end{matrix}\right)$ $\left[a>0;\ \mathrm{Re}\,s>-1/2\right]$

3.26.14. $\mathbf{K}\left(\varphi\left(x\right)\right)$, $\mathbf{E}\left(\varphi\left(x\right)\right)$, and $\mathrm{ci}\left(ax\right)$, $\mathrm{chi}\left(ax\right)$

1	$\theta\left(a-x\right)\left\{\begin{matrix}\mathrm{chi}\left(bx\right)\\\mathrm{ci}\left(bx\right)\end{matrix}\right\}$ $\times\mathbf{K}\left(\sqrt{1-\dfrac{x}{a}}\right)$	$\dfrac{\pi a^s}{2}\Gamma\left[\begin{matrix}s,\ s\\\frac{2s+1}{2},\ \frac{2s+1}{2}\end{matrix}\right]\left[2\psi\left(s\right)-2\psi\left(s+\frac{1}{2}\right)\right.$ $\left.+\ln\left(ab\right)+\mathbf{C}\right]-\dfrac{\pi a^{s+2}b^2}{8}\Gamma\left[\begin{matrix}s+2,\ s+2\\\frac{2s+5}{2},\ \frac{2s+5}{2}\end{matrix}\right]$ $\times\,_6F_7\left(\begin{matrix}1,\ 1,\ \frac{s+2}{2},\ \frac{s+2}{2},\ \frac{s+3}{2},\ \frac{s+3}{2};\ \pm\frac{a^2b^2}{4}\\\frac{3}{2},\ 2,\ 2,\ \frac{2s+5}{4},\ \frac{2s+5}{4},\ \frac{2s+7}{4},\ \frac{2s+7}{4}\end{matrix}\right)$ $\left[a,\ \mathrm{Re}\,s>0\right]$

No.	$f(x)$	$F(s)$
2	$\theta(a-x)\begin{Bmatrix} \operatorname{chi}(bx) \\ \operatorname{ci}(bx) \end{Bmatrix}$ $\times \mathbf{E}\left(\sqrt{1-\dfrac{x}{a}}\right)$	$\dfrac{\pi a^s}{2}\Gamma\left[\begin{matrix} s,\ s+1 \\ \frac{2s+1}{2},\ \frac{2s+3}{2} \end{matrix}\right]\left[2\psi(s)-2\psi\left(s+\dfrac{1}{2}\right)\right.$ $\left.+\dfrac{1}{s(2s+1)}+\ln(ab)+\mathbf{C}\right]-\dfrac{\pi a^{s+2}b^2}{8}\Gamma\left[\begin{matrix} s+2,\ s+3 \\ \frac{2s+5}{2},\ \frac{2s+7}{2} \end{matrix}\right]$ $\times {}_6F_7\left(\begin{matrix} 1,1,\frac{s+2}{2},\frac{s+3}{2},\frac{s+3}{2},\frac{s+4}{2};\ \pm\frac{a^2b^2}{4} \\ \frac{3}{2},2,2,\frac{2s+5}{4},\frac{2s+7}{4},\frac{2s+7}{4},\frac{2s+9}{4} \end{matrix}\right)$ $\qquad$ $[a,\ \operatorname{Re}s>0]$

3.26.15. $\mathbf{K}(\varphi(x))$, $\mathbf{E}(\varphi(x))$, and $\operatorname{erf}(ax^r)$

Notation: $\delta=\begin{Bmatrix} 1 \\ 0 \end{Bmatrix}$.

No.	$f(x)$	$F(s)$
1	$\theta(a-x)\operatorname{erf}(bx)$ $\times\begin{Bmatrix} \mathbf{K}\left(\sqrt{1-x/a}\right) \\ \mathbf{E}\left(\sqrt{1-x/a}\right) \end{Bmatrix}$	$\dfrac{\pi a^{s+1}b}{2}\Gamma\left[\begin{matrix} s+1,\ s-\delta+2 \\ \frac{2s+3}{2},\ \frac{2s-2\delta+5}{2} \end{matrix}\right]$ $\times {}_5F_5\left(\begin{matrix} \frac{1}{2},\frac{s+1}{2},\frac{s+2}{2},\frac{s-\delta+2}{2},\frac{s-\delta+3}{2};\ -a^2b^2 \\ \frac{3}{2},\frac{2s+3}{4},\frac{2s+5}{4},\frac{2s-2\delta+5}{4},\frac{2s-2\delta+7}{4} \end{matrix}\right)$ $[a>0;\ \operatorname{Re}s>-1]$
2	$\theta(a-x)e^{b^2x^2}\operatorname{erf}(bx)$ $\times\begin{Bmatrix} \mathbf{K}\left(\sqrt{1-x/a}\right) \\ \mathbf{E}\left(\sqrt{1-x/a}\right) \end{Bmatrix}$	$\dfrac{\pi a^{s+1}b}{2}\Gamma\left[\begin{matrix} s+1,\ s-\delta+2 \\ \frac{2s+3}{2},\ \frac{2s-2\delta+5}{2} \end{matrix}\right]$ $\times {}_5F_5\left(\begin{matrix} \frac{1}{2},\frac{s+1}{2},\frac{s+2}{2},\frac{s-\delta+2}{2},\frac{s-\delta+3}{2};\ a^2b^2 \\ \frac{3}{2},\frac{2s+3}{4},\frac{2s+5}{4},\frac{2s-2\delta+5}{4},\frac{2s-2\delta+7}{4} \end{matrix}\right)$ $[a>0;\ \operatorname{Re}s>-1]$
3	$\theta(a-x)\operatorname{erf}(b\sqrt{x})$ $\times\begin{Bmatrix} \mathbf{K}\left(\sqrt{1-x/a}\right) \\ \mathbf{E}\left(\sqrt{1-x/a}\right) \end{Bmatrix}$	$\sqrt{\pi}\,a^{s+1/2}b\,\Gamma\left[\begin{matrix} \frac{2s+1}{2},\ \frac{2s-2\delta+3}{2} \\ s+1,\ s-\delta+2 \end{matrix}\right]{}_3F_3\left(\begin{matrix} \frac{1}{2},\frac{2s+1}{2},\frac{2s-2\delta+3}{2};\ -ab^2 \\ \frac{3}{2},s+1,s-\delta+2 \end{matrix}\right)$ $[a>0;\ \operatorname{Re}s>-1/2]$
4	$\theta(a-x)e^{b^2x}\operatorname{erf}(b\sqrt{x})$ $\times\begin{Bmatrix} \mathbf{K}\left(\sqrt{1-x/a}\right) \\ \mathbf{E}\left(\sqrt{1-x/a}\right) \end{Bmatrix}$	$\sqrt{\pi}\,a^{s+1/2}b\,\Gamma\left[\begin{matrix} \frac{2s+1}{2},\ \frac{2s-2\delta+3}{2} \\ s+1,\ s-\delta+2 \end{matrix}\right]{}_3F_3\left(\begin{matrix} 1,\frac{2s+1}{2},\frac{2s-2\delta+3}{2};\ ab^2 \\ \frac{3}{2},s+1,s-\delta+2 \end{matrix}\right)$ $[a>0;\ \operatorname{Re}s>-1/2]$

3.26.16. $\mathbf{K}(\varphi(x))$, $\mathbf{E}(\varphi(x))$, and $S(a\sqrt{x})$, $C(a\sqrt{x})$

Notation: $\delta=\begin{Bmatrix} 1 \\ 0 \end{Bmatrix}$.

No.	$f(x)$	$F(s)$
1	$\theta(a-x)S(b\sqrt{x})$ $\times\begin{Bmatrix} \mathbf{K}\left(\sqrt{1-x/a}\right) \\ \mathbf{E}\left(\sqrt{1-x/a}\right) \end{Bmatrix}$	$\dfrac{a^{s+3/4}}{3}\sqrt{\dfrac{\pi b^3}{2}}\,\Gamma\left[\begin{matrix} \frac{4s+3}{4},\ \frac{4s-4\delta+7}{4} \\ \frac{4s+5}{4},\ \frac{4s-4\delta+9}{4} \end{matrix}\right]{}_3F_4\left(\begin{matrix} \frac{3}{4},\frac{4s+3}{4},\frac{4s-4\delta+7}{4};\ -\frac{ab^2}{4} \\ \frac{3}{2},\frac{7}{4},\frac{4s+5}{4},\frac{4s-4\delta+9}{4} \end{matrix}\right)$ $[a>0;\ \operatorname{Re}s>-3/4]$

No.	$f(x)$	$F(s)$
2	$\theta(a-x)C(b\sqrt{x})$ $\times\left\{\begin{array}{c}\mathbf{K}\left(\sqrt{1-x/a}\right)\\ \mathbf{E}\left(\sqrt{1-x/a}\right)\end{array}\right\}$	$a^{s+1/4}\sqrt{\dfrac{\pi b}{2}}\,\Gamma\left[\begin{array}{cc}\frac{4s+1}{4},&\frac{4s-4\delta+5}{4}\\ \frac{4s+3}{4},&\frac{4s-4\delta+7}{4}\end{array}\right]{}_3F_4\left(\begin{array}{c}\frac{1}{4},\ \frac{4s+1}{4},\ \frac{4s-4\delta+5}{4};\ -\frac{ab^2}{4}\\ \frac{1}{2},\ \frac{5}{4},\ \frac{4s+3}{4},\ \frac{4s-4\delta+7}{4}\end{array}\right)$ $[a>0;\ \mathrm{Re}\,s>-1/4]$

3.26.17. $\mathbf{K}(\varphi(x))$, $\mathbf{E}(\varphi(x))$, and $\gamma(\nu,ax)$

Notation: $\delta=\left\{\begin{array}{c}1\\0\end{array}\right\}$.

1	$\theta(a-x)\gamma(\nu,bx)$ $\times\left\{\begin{array}{c}\mathbf{K}\left(\sqrt{1-x/a}\right)\\ \mathbf{E}\left(\sqrt{1-x/a}\right)\end{array}\right\}$	$\dfrac{\pi a^{s+\nu}b^{\nu}}{2\nu}\,\Gamma\left[\begin{array}{c}s+\nu,\ s+\nu-\delta+1\\ \frac{2s+2\nu+1}{2},\ \frac{2s+2\nu-2\delta+3}{2}\end{array}\right]$ $\times{}_3F_3\left(\begin{array}{c}\nu,\ s+\nu,\ s+\nu-\delta+1;\ -ab\\ \nu+1,\ \frac{2s+2\nu+1}{2},\ \frac{2s+2\nu-2\delta+3}{2}\end{array}\right)\quad[a,\ \mathrm{Re}\,(s+\nu)>0]$
2	$\theta(a-x)e^{bx}\gamma(\nu,bx)$ $\times\left\{\begin{array}{c}\mathbf{K}\left(\sqrt{1-x/a}\right)\\ \mathbf{E}\left(\sqrt{1-x/a}\right)\end{array}\right\}$	$\dfrac{\pi a^{s+\nu}b^{\nu}}{2\nu}\,\Gamma\left[\begin{array}{c}s+\nu,\ s+\nu-\delta+1\\ \frac{2s+2\nu+1}{2},\ \frac{2s+2\nu-2\delta+3}{2}\end{array}\right]$ $\times{}_3F_3\left(\begin{array}{c}1,\ s+\nu,\ s+\nu-\delta+1;\ ab\\ \nu+1,\ \frac{2s+2\nu+1}{2},\ \frac{2s+2\nu-2\delta+3}{2}\end{array}\right)\quad[a,\ \mathrm{Re}\,(s+\nu)>0]$

3.26.18. $\mathbf{K}(\varphi(x))$, $\mathbf{E}(\varphi(x))$, and $J_\nu(bx^r)$, $I_\nu(bx^r)$

Notation: $\delta=\left\{\begin{array}{c}1\\0\end{array}\right\}$.

1	$\theta(a-x)\left\{\begin{array}{c}J_\nu(bx)\\ I_\nu(bx)\end{array}\right\}$ $\times\mathbf{K}\left(\sqrt{1-\dfrac{x}{a}}\right)$	$\dfrac{\pi a^{s+\nu}b^{\nu}}{2^{\nu+1}}\,\Gamma\left[\begin{array}{c}s+\nu,\ s+\nu\\ \nu+1,\ \frac{2s+2\nu+1}{2},\ \frac{2s+2\nu+1}{2}\end{array}\right]$ $\times{}_4F_5\left(\begin{array}{c}\frac{s+\nu}{2},\ \frac{s+\nu}{2},\ \frac{s+\nu+1}{2},\ \frac{s+\nu+1}{2};\ \mp\frac{a^2b^2}{4}\\ \nu+1,\ \frac{2s+2\nu+1}{4},\ \frac{2s+2\nu+1}{4},\ \frac{2s+2\nu+3}{4},\ \frac{2s+2\nu+3}{4}\end{array}\right)$ $[a,\ \mathrm{Re}\,(s+\nu)>0]$
2	$\theta(a-x)\left\{\begin{array}{c}J_\nu(bx)\\ I_\nu(bx)\end{array}\right\}$ $\times\mathbf{E}\left(\sqrt{1-\dfrac{x}{a}}\right)$	$\dfrac{\pi a^{s+\nu}b^{\nu}}{2^{\nu+1}}\,\Gamma\left[\begin{array}{c}s+\nu,\ s+\nu+1\\ \nu+1,\ \frac{2s+2\nu+1}{2},\ \frac{2s+2\nu+3}{2}\end{array}\right]$ $\times{}_4F_5\left(\begin{array}{c}\frac{s+\nu}{2},\ \frac{s+\nu+1}{2},\ \frac{s+\nu+1}{2},\ \frac{s+\nu+3}{2};\ \mp\frac{a^2b^2}{4}\\ \nu+1,\ \frac{2s+2\nu+1}{4},\ \frac{2s+2\nu+3}{4},\ \frac{2s+2\nu+3}{4},\ \frac{2s+2\nu+5}{4}\end{array}\right)$ $[a,\ \mathrm{Re}\,(s+\nu)>0]$
3	$\theta(a-x)\left\{\begin{array}{c}J_\nu(b\sqrt{x})\\ I_\nu(b\sqrt{x})\end{array}\right\}$ $\times\mathbf{K}\left(\sqrt{1-\dfrac{x}{a}}\right)$	$\dfrac{\pi a^{s+\nu/2}b^{\nu}}{2^{\nu+1}}\,\dfrac{\Gamma^2\left(\frac{2s+\nu}{2}\right)}{\Gamma(\nu+1)\Gamma^2\left(\frac{2s+\nu+1}{2}\right)}\,{}_2F_3\left(\begin{array}{c}\frac{2s+\nu}{2},\ \frac{2s+\nu}{2};\ \mp\frac{ab^2}{4}\\ \nu+1,\ \frac{2s+\nu+1}{2},\ \frac{2s+\nu+1}{2}\end{array}\right)$ $[a,\ \mathrm{Re}\,(s+\nu/2)>0]$

No.	$f(x)$	$F(s)$
4	$\theta(a-x)\begin{Bmatrix} J_\nu(b\sqrt{x}) \\ I_\nu(b\sqrt{x}) \end{Bmatrix}$ $\times \mathbf{E}\left(\sqrt{1-\dfrac{x}{a}}\right)$	$\dfrac{\pi a^{s+\nu/2}b^\nu}{2^{\nu+1}}\Gamma\left[\begin{matrix} \frac{2s+\nu}{2},\ \frac{2s+\nu+2}{2} \\ \nu+1,\ \frac{2s+\nu+1}{2},\ \frac{2s+\nu+3}{2} \end{matrix}\right]$ $\times {}_2F_3\left(\begin{matrix} \frac{2s+\nu}{2},\ \frac{2s+\nu+2}{2};\ \mp\frac{ab^2}{4} \\ \nu+1,\ \frac{2s+\nu+1}{2},\ \frac{2s+\nu+3}{2} \end{matrix}\right)$ $[a,\ \mathrm{Re}(s+\nu/2)>0]$
5	$\theta(a-x)\,e^{bx}I_\nu(bx)$ $\times\begin{Bmatrix} \mathbf{K}(\sqrt{1-x/a}) \\ \mathbf{E}(\sqrt{1-x/a}) \end{Bmatrix}$	$\dfrac{\pi a^{s+\nu}b^\nu}{2^{\nu+1}}\Gamma\left[\begin{matrix} s+\nu,\ s+\nu-\delta+1 \\ \nu+1,\ \frac{2s+2\nu+1}{2},\ \frac{2s+2\nu-2\delta+3}{2} \end{matrix}\right]$ $\times {}_3F_3\left(\begin{matrix} \frac{2\nu+1}{2},\ s+\nu,\ s+\nu-\delta+1;\ 2ab \\ 2\nu+1,\ \frac{2s+2\nu+1}{2},\ \frac{2s+2\nu-2\delta+3}{2} \end{matrix}\right)$ $[a,\ \mathrm{Re}(s+\nu)>0]$
6	$\theta(a-x)$ $\times\begin{Bmatrix} J_\mu(b\sqrt{x})\,J_\nu(b\sqrt{x}) \\ I_\mu(b\sqrt{x})\,I_\nu(b\sqrt{x}) \end{Bmatrix}$ $\times \mathbf{K}\left(\sqrt{1-\dfrac{x}{a}}\right)$	$\dfrac{\pi a^{s+(\mu+\nu)/2}b^{\mu+\nu}}{2^{\mu+\nu+1}}\Gamma\left[\begin{matrix} \frac{2s+\mu+\nu}{2},\ \frac{2s+\mu+\nu}{2} \\ \mu+1,\ \nu+1,\ \frac{2s+\mu+\nu+1}{2},\ \frac{2s+\mu+\nu+1}{2} \end{matrix}\right]$ $\times {}_4F_5\left(\begin{matrix} \frac{\mu+\nu+1}{2},\ \frac{\mu+\nu+2}{2},\ \frac{2s+\mu+\nu}{2},\ \frac{2s+\mu+\nu}{2};\ \mp ab^2 \\ \mu+1,\ \nu+1,\ \mu+\nu+1,\ \frac{2s+\mu+\nu+1}{2},\ \frac{2s+\mu+\nu+1}{2} \end{matrix}\right)$ $[a,\ \mathrm{Re}(2s+\mu+\nu)>0]$
7	$\theta(a-x)$ $\times\begin{Bmatrix} J_\mu(b\sqrt{x})\,J_\nu(b\sqrt{x}) \\ I_\mu(b\sqrt{x})\,I_\nu(b\sqrt{x}) \end{Bmatrix}$ $\times \mathbf{E}\left(\sqrt{1-\dfrac{x}{a}}\right)$	$\dfrac{\pi a^{s+(\mu+\nu)/2}b^{\mu+\nu}}{2^{\mu+\nu+1}}\Gamma\left[\begin{matrix} \frac{2s+\mu+\nu}{2},\ \frac{2s+\mu+\nu+2}{2} \\ \mu+1,\ \nu+1,\ \frac{2s+\mu+\nu+1}{2},\ \frac{2s+\mu+\nu+3}{2} \end{matrix}\right]$ $\times {}_4F_5\left(\begin{matrix} \frac{\mu+\nu+1}{2},\ \frac{\mu+\nu+2}{2},\ \frac{2s+\mu+\nu}{2},\ \frac{2s+\mu+\nu+2}{2};\ \mp ab^2 \\ \mu+1,\ \nu+1,\ \mu+\nu+1,\ \frac{2s+\mu+\nu+1}{2},\ \frac{2s+\mu+\nu+3}{2} \end{matrix}\right)$ $[a,\ \mathrm{Re}(2s+\mu+\nu)>0]$

3.26.19. $\mathbf{K}(\varphi(x))$, $\mathbf{E}(\varphi(x))$, **and** $\mathbf{H}_\nu(bx^r)$, $\mathbf{L}_\nu(bx^r)$

1	$\theta(a-x)\begin{Bmatrix} \mathbf{H}_\nu(bx) \\ \mathbf{L}_\nu(bx) \end{Bmatrix}$ $\times \mathbf{K}\left(\sqrt{1-\dfrac{x}{a}}\right)$	$\sqrt{\pi}\,a^{s+\nu+1}\left(\dfrac{b}{2}\right)^{\nu+1}\Gamma\left[\begin{matrix} s+\nu+1,\ s+\nu+1 \\ \frac{2\nu+3}{2},\ \frac{2s+2\nu+3}{2},\ \frac{2s+2\nu+3}{2} \end{matrix}\right]$ $\times {}_4F_5\left(\begin{matrix} 1,\ \frac{s+\nu+1}{2},\ \frac{s+\nu+1}{2},\ \frac{s+\nu+2}{2},\ \frac{s+\nu+2}{2};\ \mp\frac{a^2b^2}{4} \\ \frac{3}{2},\ \frac{2\nu+3}{2},\ \frac{2s+2\nu+3}{4},\ \frac{2s+2\nu+3}{4},\ \frac{2s+2\nu+5}{4},\ \frac{2s+2\nu+5}{4} \end{matrix}\right)$ $[a,\ \mathrm{Re}(s+\nu+1)>0]$
2	$\theta(a-x)\begin{Bmatrix} \mathbf{H}_\nu(bx)) \\ \mathbf{L}_\nu(bx) \end{Bmatrix}$ $\times \mathbf{E}\left(\sqrt{1-\dfrac{x}{a}}\right)$	$\sqrt{\pi}\,a^{s+\nu+1}\left(\dfrac{b}{2}\right)^{\nu+1}\Gamma\left[\begin{matrix} s+\nu+1,\ s+\nu+2 \\ \frac{2\nu+3}{2},\ \frac{2s+2\nu+3}{2},\ \frac{2s+2\nu+5}{2} \end{matrix}\right]$ $\times {}_5F_6\left(\begin{matrix} 1,\ \frac{s+\nu+1}{2},\ \frac{s+\nu+2}{2},\ \frac{s+\nu+2}{2},\ \frac{s+\nu+3}{2};\ \mp\frac{a^2b^2}{4} \\ \frac{3}{2},\ \frac{2\nu+3}{2},\ \frac{2s+2\nu+3}{4},\ \frac{2s+2\nu+5}{4},\ \frac{2s+2\nu+5}{4},\ \frac{2s+2\nu+7}{4} \end{matrix}\right)$ $[a,\ \mathrm{Re}(s+\nu+1)>0]$

No.	$f(x)$	$F(s)$
3	$\theta(a-x)\begin{Bmatrix}\mathbf{H}_\nu(b\sqrt{x})\\\mathbf{L}_\nu(b\sqrt{x})\end{Bmatrix}$ $\times\mathbf{K}\left(\sqrt{1-\dfrac{x}{a}}\right)$	$\sqrt{\pi}\,a^{s+(\nu+1)/2}\left(\dfrac{b}{2}\right)^{\nu+1}\Gamma\left[\begin{array}{c}\frac{2s+\nu+1}{2},\ \frac{2s+\nu+1}{2}\\[4pt]\frac{2\nu+3}{2},\ \frac{2s+\nu+2}{2},\ \frac{2s+\nu+2}{2}\end{array}\right]$ $\times\,_3F_4\left(\begin{array}{c}1,\ \frac{2s+\nu+1}{2},\ \frac{2s+\nu+1}{2};\ \mp\frac{ab^2}{4}\\[4pt]\frac{3}{2},\ \frac{2\nu+3}{2},\ \frac{2s+\nu+2}{2},\ \frac{2s+\nu+2}{2}\end{array}\right)$ $[a>0;\ \mathrm{Re}\,(2s+\nu)>-1]$
4	$\theta(a-x)\begin{Bmatrix}\mathbf{H}_\nu(b\sqrt{x})\\\mathbf{L}_\nu(b\sqrt{x})\end{Bmatrix}$ $\times\mathbf{E}\left(\sqrt{1-\dfrac{x}{a}}\right)$	$\sqrt{\pi}a^{s+(\nu+1)/2}\left(\dfrac{b}{2}\right)^{\nu+1}\Gamma\left[\begin{array}{c}\frac{2s+\nu+1}{2},\ \frac{2s+\nu+3}{2}\\[4pt]\frac{2\nu+3}{2},\ \frac{2s+\nu+2}{2},\ \frac{2s+\nu+4}{2}\end{array}\right]$ $\times\,_3F_4\left(\begin{array}{c}1,\ \frac{2s+\nu+1}{2},\ \frac{2s+\nu+3}{2};\ \mp\frac{ab^2}{4}\\[4pt]\frac{3}{2},\ \frac{2\nu+3}{2},\ \frac{2s+\nu+2}{2},\ \frac{2s+\nu+4}{2}\end{array}\right)$ $[a>0;\ \mathrm{Re}\,(2s+\nu)>-1]$

3.26.20. $\mathbf{K}(bx)$, $\mathbf{E}(bx)$, and $T_n(ax)$

No.	$f(x)$	$F(s)$
1	$(a^2-x^2)_+^{-1/2}\,T_n\left(\dfrac{x}{a}\right)$ $\times\begin{Bmatrix}\mathbf{K}(bx)\\\mathbf{E}(bx)\end{Bmatrix}$	$\dfrac{\pi^2}{4}\left(\dfrac{a}{2}\right)^{s-1}\Gamma\left[\begin{array}{c}s\\\frac{s-n+1}{2},\ \frac{s+n+1}{2}\end{array}\right]\,_4F_3\left(\begin{array}{c}\pm\frac{1}{2},\ \frac{1}{2},\ \frac{s}{2},\ \frac{s+1}{2};\ a^2b^2\\[4pt]1,\ \frac{s-n+1}{2},\ \frac{s+n+1}{2}\end{array}\right)$ $[a>0;\ \mathrm{Re}\,s>((-1)^n-1)/2]$
2	$\dfrac{(a^2-x^2)_+^{-1/2}}{1-b^2x^2}\,T_n\left(\dfrac{x}{a}\right)$ $\times\mathbf{E}(bx)$	$\dfrac{\pi^2}{4}\left(\dfrac{a}{2}\right)^{s-1}\Gamma\left[\begin{array}{c}s\\\frac{s-n+1}{2},\ \frac{s+n+1}{2}\end{array}\right]\,_4F_3\left(\begin{array}{c}\frac{1}{2},\ \frac{3}{2},\ \frac{s}{2},\ \frac{s+1}{2};\ a^2b^2\\[4pt]1,\ \frac{s-n+1}{2},\ \frac{s+n+1}{2}\end{array}\right)$ $[a>0;\ \mathrm{Re}\,s>((-1)^n-1)/2]$

3.26.21. $\mathbf{K}(\varphi(x))$, $\mathbf{E}(\varphi(x))$, and $L_n^\lambda(ax)$, $H_n(ax^r)$

Notation: $\delta=\begin{Bmatrix}1\\0\end{Bmatrix}$.

No.	$f(x)$	$F(s)$
1	$\theta(a-x)\,L_n^\lambda(bx)$ $\times\begin{Bmatrix}\mathbf{K}(\sqrt{1-x/a})\\\mathbf{E}(\sqrt{1-x/a})\end{Bmatrix}$	$\dfrac{\pi(\lambda+1)_n\,a^s}{2(n!)}\Gamma\left[\begin{array}{c}s,\ s-\delta+1\\\frac{2s+1}{2},\ \frac{2s-2\delta+3}{2}\end{array}\right]\,_3F_3\left(\begin{array}{c}-n,\ s,\ s-\delta+1;\ ab\\[4pt]\lambda+1,\ \frac{2s+1}{2},\ \frac{2s-2\delta+3}{2}\end{array}\right)$ $[a,\ \mathrm{Re}\,s>0]$
2	$\theta(a-x)\,H_{2n}(bx)$ $\times\begin{Bmatrix}\mathbf{K}(\sqrt{1-x/a})\\\mathbf{E}(\sqrt{1-x/a})\end{Bmatrix}$	$(-1)^n\dfrac{(2n)!}{n!}\dfrac{\pi a^s}{2}\Gamma\left[\begin{array}{c}s+1,\ s-\delta+1\\\frac{2s+1}{2},\ \frac{2s-2\delta+3}{2}\end{array}\right]$ $\times\,_5F_5\left(\begin{array}{c}-n,\ \frac{s}{2},\ \frac{s+1}{2},\ \frac{s-\delta+1}{2},\ \frac{s-\delta+2}{2};\ -a^2b^2\\[4pt]\frac{1}{2},\ \frac{2s+1}{4},\ \frac{2s+3}{4},\ \frac{2s-2\delta+3}{4},\ \frac{2s-2\delta+5}{4}\end{array}\right)$ $[a,\ \mathrm{Re}\,s>0]$

No.	$f(x)$	$F(s)$
3	$\theta(a-x)\,H_{2n+1}(bx)$ $\times\begin{Bmatrix}\mathbf{K}\left(\sqrt{1-x/a}\right)\\\mathbf{E}\left(\sqrt{1-x/a}\right)\end{Bmatrix}$	$(-1)^n\,\dfrac{(2n+1)!}{n!}\,\pi a^{s+1}b\,\Gamma\begin{bmatrix}s+1,\ s-\delta+2\\\frac{2s+3}{2},\ \frac{2s-2\delta+5}{2}\end{bmatrix}$ $\times {}_5F_5\left(\begin{matrix}-n,\ \frac{s+1}{2},\ \frac{s+2}{2},\ \frac{s-\delta+2}{2},\ \frac{s-\delta+3}{2};\ -a^2b^2\\\frac{3}{2},\ \frac{2s+3}{4},\ \frac{2s+5}{4},\ \frac{2s-2\delta+5}{4},\ \frac{2s-2\delta+7}{4}\end{matrix}\right)$ $[a>0;\ \operatorname{Re}s>-1]$
4	$\theta(a-x)\,H_{2n}(b\sqrt{x})$ $\times\begin{Bmatrix}\mathbf{K}\left(\sqrt{1-x/a}\right)\\\mathbf{E}\left(\sqrt{1-x/a}\right)\end{Bmatrix}$	$(-1)^n\,2^{2n-1}\pi a^s\left(\dfrac{1}{2}\right)_n\Gamma\begin{bmatrix}s,\ s-\delta+1\\\frac{2s+1}{2},\ \frac{2s-2\delta+3}{2}\end{bmatrix}$ $\times {}_3F_3\left(\begin{matrix}-n,\ s,\ s-\delta+1;\ ab^2\\\frac{1}{2},\ \frac{2s+1}{2},\ \frac{2s-2\delta+3}{2}\end{matrix}\right)$ $[a,\ \operatorname{Re}s>0]$
5	$\theta(a-x)\,H_{2n+1}(b\sqrt{x})$ $\times\begin{Bmatrix}\mathbf{K}\left(\sqrt{1-x/a}\right)\\\mathbf{E}\left(\sqrt{1-x/a}\right)\end{Bmatrix}$	$(-4)^n\,\pi a^{s+1/2}b\left(\dfrac{3}{2}\right)_n\Gamma\begin{bmatrix}\frac{2s+1}{2},\ \frac{2s-2\delta+3}{2}\\s+1,\ s-\delta+2\end{bmatrix}$ $\times {}_3F_3\left(\begin{matrix}-n,\ \frac{2s+1}{2},\ \frac{2s-2\delta+3}{2};\ ab^2\\\frac{3}{2},\ s+1,\ s-\delta+2\end{matrix}\right)$ $[a>0;\ \operatorname{Re}s>-1/2]$

3.26.22. $\mathbf{K}(bx)$, $\mathbf{E}(bx)$, and $C_n^\lambda(ax)$

No.	$f(x)$	$F(s)$
1	$(a^2-x^2)_+^{\lambda-1/2}\,C_n^\lambda\left(\dfrac{x}{a}\right)$ $\times\begin{Bmatrix}\mathbf{K}(bx)\\\mathbf{E}(bx)\end{Bmatrix}$	$\dfrac{\pi^2}{2(n!)}\left(\dfrac{a}{2}\right)^{s+2\lambda-1}\Gamma\begin{bmatrix}n+2\lambda,\ s\\\lambda,\ \frac{s-n+1}{2},\ \frac{s+n+2\lambda+1}{2}\end{bmatrix}$ $\times {}_4F_3\left(\begin{matrix}\pm\frac{1}{2},\ \frac{1}{2},\ \frac{s}{2},\ \frac{s+1}{2};\ a^2b^2\\1,\ \frac{s-n+1}{2},\ \frac{s+n+2\lambda+1}{2}\end{matrix}\right)$ $[a>0;\ \operatorname{Re}\lambda>-1/2;\ \operatorname{Re}s>((-1)^n-1)/2]$
2	$\dfrac{(a^2-x^2)_+^{\lambda-1/2}}{1-b^2x^2}\,C_n^\lambda\left(\dfrac{x}{a}\right)$ $\times\mathbf{E}(bx)$	$\dfrac{\pi^2}{2(n!)}\left(\dfrac{a}{2}\right)^{s+2\lambda-1}\Gamma\begin{bmatrix}n+2\lambda,\ s\\\lambda,\ \frac{s-n+1}{2},\ \frac{s+n+2\lambda+1}{2}\end{bmatrix}$ $\times {}_4F_3\left(\begin{matrix}\frac{1}{2},\ \frac{3}{2},\ \frac{s}{2},\ \frac{s+1}{2};\ a^2b^2\\1,\ \frac{s-n+1}{2},\ \frac{s+n+2\lambda+1}{2}\end{matrix}\right)$ $[a>0;\ \operatorname{Re}\lambda>-1/2;\ \operatorname{Re}s>((-1)^n-1)/2]$

3.26.23. $\mathbf{D}(\varphi(x))$ and various functions

No.	$f(x)$	$F(s)$
1	$\theta(a-x)\ln\dfrac{a+\sqrt{a^2-x^2}}{x}$ $\times\mathbf{D}(bx)$	$\dfrac{\pi^{3/2}a^s}{8s}\Gamma\begin{bmatrix}\frac{s}{2}\\\frac{s+1}{2}\end{bmatrix}{}_4F_3\left(\begin{matrix}\frac{1}{2},\ \frac{3}{2},\ \frac{s}{2},\ \frac{s}{2};\ a^2b^2\\2,\ \frac{s+1}{2},\ \frac{s+2}{2}\end{matrix}\right)$ $[a,\ \operatorname{Re}s>0]$
2	$\theta(a-x)\arccos\dfrac{x}{a}\,\mathbf{D}(bx)$	$\dfrac{\pi^{3/2}a^s}{4s^2}\Gamma\begin{bmatrix}\frac{s+1}{2}\\\frac{s}{2}\end{bmatrix}{}_4F_3\left(\begin{matrix}\frac{1}{2},\ \frac{3}{2},\ \frac{s}{2},\ \frac{s+1}{2};\ a^2b^2\\2,\ \frac{s+2}{2},\ \frac{s+2}{2}\end{matrix}\right)$ $[a,\ \operatorname{Re}s>0]$

No.	$f(x)$	$F(s)$
3	$(a-x)_+^{\alpha-1}\,\mathbf{D}\big(b\sqrt{x(a-x)}\big)$	$\dfrac{\pi a^{s+\alpha-1}}{4}\,\mathrm{B}(s,\alpha)\;{}_4F_3\!\left(\begin{matrix}\frac{1}{2},\,\frac{3}{2},\,\alpha,\,s;\,\frac{a^2b^2}{4}\\[2pt]2,\,\frac{s+\alpha}{2},\,\frac{s+\alpha+1}{2}\end{matrix}\right)$ $[a,\ \mathrm{Re}\,s,\ \mathrm{Re}\,\alpha>0]$

3.26.24. Products of $\mathbf{K}(\varphi(x))$

No.	$f(x)$	$F(s)$
1	$\theta(a-x)\,\mathbf{K}(bx)\,\mathbf{K}\!\left(\sqrt{1-\dfrac{x}{a}}\right)$	$\dfrac{\pi^2 a^s}{4}\,\Gamma\!\left[\begin{matrix}s,\,s\\[2pt]\frac{2s+1}{2},\,\frac{2s+1}{2}\end{matrix}\right]\;{}_6F_5\!\left(\begin{matrix}\frac{1}{2},\,\frac{1}{2},\,\frac{s}{2},\,\frac{s}{2},\,\frac{s+1}{2},\,\frac{s+1}{2};\,a^2b^2\\[2pt]1,\,\frac{2s+1}{4},\,\frac{2s+1}{4},\,\frac{2s+3}{4},\,\frac{2s+3}{4}\end{matrix}\right)$ $[a,\ \mathrm{Re}\,s>0]$
2	$\theta(a-x)\,\mathbf{K}(b\sqrt{x})\,\mathbf{K}\!\left(\sqrt{1-\dfrac{x}{a}}\right)$	$\dfrac{\pi^2 a^s}{4}\,\Gamma\!\left[\begin{matrix}s,\,s\\[2pt]\frac{2s+1}{2},\,\frac{2s+1}{2}\end{matrix}\right]\;{}_4F_3\!\left(\begin{matrix}\frac{1}{2},\,\frac{1}{2},\,s,\,s;\,ab^2\\[2pt]1,\,\frac{2s+1}{2},\,\frac{2s+1}{2}\end{matrix}\right)$ $[a,\ \mathrm{Re}\,s>0]$
3	$\dfrac{\theta(a-x)}{\sqrt{1+b^2x}}\,\mathbf{K}\!\left(\dfrac{b\sqrt{x}}{\sqrt{1+b^2x}}\right)$ $\times\mathbf{K}\!\left(\sqrt{1-\dfrac{x}{a}}\right)$	$\dfrac{\pi^2 a^s}{4}\,\Gamma\!\left[\begin{matrix}s,\,s\\[2pt]\frac{2s+1}{2},\,\frac{2s+1}{2}\end{matrix}\right]\;{}_4F_3\!\left(\begin{matrix}\frac{1}{2},\,\frac{1}{2},\,s,\,s;\,-ab^2\\[2pt]1,\,\frac{2s+1}{2},\,\frac{2s+1}{2}\end{matrix}\right)$ $[a,\ \mathrm{Re}\,s>0;\ |\arg(1+ab^2)|<\pi]$
4	$\mathbf{K}^2\!\left(\sqrt{\dfrac{\sqrt{a}-\sqrt{x+a}}{2\sqrt{a}}}\right)$	$\dfrac{\sqrt{\pi}\,a^s}{4}\,\Gamma\!\left[\begin{matrix}s,\,\frac{1-2s}{4},\,\frac{1-2s}{4},\,\frac{1-2s}{4}\\[2pt]1-s,\,1-s\end{matrix}\right]$ $[0<\mathrm{Re}\,s<1/2;\ |\arg a|<\pi]$
5	$\mathbf{K}^2\!\left(\sqrt{\dfrac{\sqrt{x}-\sqrt{x+a}}{2\sqrt{x}}}\right)$	$\dfrac{\sqrt{\pi}\,a^s}{4}\,\Gamma\!\left[\begin{matrix}-s,\,\frac{2s+1}{4},\,\frac{2s+1}{4},\,\frac{2s+1}{4}\\[2pt]s+1,\,s+1\end{matrix}\right]$ $[-1/2<\mathrm{Re}\,s<0;\ |\arg a|<\pi]$
6	$\dfrac{1}{\sqrt{x+a}+\sqrt{x}}\,\mathbf{K}^2\!\left(\pm\dfrac{\sqrt{x+a}-\sqrt{x}}{\sqrt{a}}\right)$	$\dfrac{\sqrt{\pi}\,a^{s-1/2}}{8}\Gamma\!\left[\begin{matrix}s,\,s,\,s,\,\frac{1-2s}{2}\\[2pt]\frac{2s+1}{2},\,\frac{2s+1}{2}\end{matrix}\right]$ $[0<\mathrm{Re}\,s<1/2;\ |\arg a|<\pi]$
7	$\dfrac{1}{\sqrt{x+a}+\sqrt{a}}\,\mathbf{K}^2\!\left(\pm\dfrac{\sqrt{x+a}-\sqrt{a}}{\sqrt{x}}\right)$	$\dfrac{\sqrt{\pi}\,a^{s-1/2}}{8}\Gamma\!\left[\begin{matrix}s,\,\frac{1-2s}{2},\,\frac{1-2s}{2},\,\frac{1-2s}{2}\\[2pt]1-s,\,1-s\end{matrix}\right]$ $[0<\mathrm{Re}\,s<1/2;\ |\arg a|<\pi]$
8	$\mathbf{K}\!\left(i\sqrt{\dfrac{2\sqrt{x}\,(\sqrt{x}-\sqrt{x+a})}{a}}\right)$ $\times\mathbf{K}\!\left(i\sqrt{\dfrac{2\sqrt{x}\,(\sqrt{x}+\sqrt{x+a})}{a}}\right)$	$\dfrac{\sqrt{\pi}\,a^s}{4}\,\Gamma\!\left[\begin{matrix}s,\,\frac{1-2s}{2},\,\frac{1-2s}{2},\,\frac{1-2s}{2}\\[2pt]1-s,\,1-s\end{matrix}\right]$ $[0<\mathrm{Re}\,s<1/2;\ |\arg a|<\pi]$

No.	$f(x)$	$F(s)$
9	$\mathbf{K}\left(i\sqrt{\dfrac{2\sqrt{a}\left(\sqrt{a}-\sqrt{x+a}\right)}{x}}\right)$ $\times \mathbf{K}\left(i\sqrt{\dfrac{2\sqrt{a}\left(\sqrt{a}+\sqrt{x+a}\right)}{x}}\right)$	$\dfrac{\sqrt{\pi}\,a^s}{4}\,\Gamma\left[\begin{matrix}-s,\ \frac{2s+1}{2},\ \frac{2s+1}{2},\ \frac{2s+1}{2}\\ s+1,\ s+1\end{matrix}\right]$ $[-1/2 < \operatorname{Re} s < 0;\ |\arg a| < \pi]$
10	$\mathbf{K}\left(\sqrt{1-\dfrac{\left(\sqrt{x+a}-\sqrt{a}\right)^2}{x}}\right)$ $\times \mathbf{K}\left(\sqrt{1-\dfrac{\left(\sqrt{x+a}+\sqrt{a}\right)^2}{x}}\right)$	$\dfrac{\sqrt{\pi}\,a^s}{4}\,\Gamma\left[\begin{matrix}-s,\ \frac{2s+1}{2},\ \frac{2s+1}{2},\ \frac{2s+1}{2}\\ s+1,\ s+1\end{matrix}\right]$ $[-1/2 < \operatorname{Re} s < 0;\ |\arg a| < \pi]$
11	$\mathbf{K}\left(\sqrt{1-\dfrac{\left(\sqrt{x+a}-\sqrt{x}\right)^2}{a}}\right)$ $\times \mathbf{K}\left(\sqrt{1-\dfrac{\left(\sqrt{x+a}+\sqrt{x}\right)^2}{a}}\right)$	$\dfrac{\sqrt{\pi}\,a^s}{4}\,\Gamma\left[\begin{matrix}s,\ \frac{1-2s}{2},\ \frac{1-2s}{2},\ \frac{1-2s}{2}\\ 1-s,\ 1-s\end{matrix}\right]$ $[0 < \operatorname{Re} s < 1/2;\ |\arg a| < \pi]$

3.26.25. Products of $\mathbf{K}(\varphi(x))$ and $\mathbf{E}(\varphi(x))$

Notation: $\varepsilon = 0$ or 1.

No.	$f(x)$	$F(s)$
1	$\theta(a-x)\,\mathbf{E}\left(\sqrt{1-\dfrac{x}{a}}\right)\mathbf{K}(bx)$	$\dfrac{\pi^2 a^s}{4}\,\Gamma\left[\begin{matrix}s,\ s+1\\ \frac{2s+1}{2},\ \frac{2s+3}{2}\end{matrix}\right]$ $\times\ {}_6F_5\left(\begin{matrix}\frac{1}{2},\ \frac{1}{2},\ \frac{s}{2},\ \frac{s+1}{2},\ \frac{s+1}{2},\ \frac{s+2}{2};\ a^2b^2\\ 1,\ \frac{2s+1}{4},\ \frac{2s+3}{4},\ \frac{2s+3}{4},\ \frac{2s+5}{4}\end{matrix}\right)$ $[a,\ \operatorname{Re} s > 0]$
2	$\theta(a-x)\,\mathbf{E}\left(\sqrt{1-\dfrac{x}{a}}\right)\mathbf{K}(b\sqrt{x})$	$\dfrac{\pi^2 a^s}{4}\,\Gamma\left[\begin{matrix}s,\ s+1\\ \frac{2s+1}{2},\ \frac{2s+3}{2}\end{matrix}\right]\ {}_4F_3\left(\begin{matrix}\frac{1}{2},\ \frac{1}{2},\ s,\ s+1;\ ab^2\\ 1,\ \frac{2s+1}{2},\ \frac{2s+3}{2}\end{matrix}\right)$ $[a,\ \operatorname{Re} s > 0]$
3	$\theta(a-x)\,\mathbf{E}(bx)\,\mathbf{K}\left(\sqrt{1-\dfrac{x}{a}}\right)$	$\dfrac{\pi^2 a^s}{4}\,\Gamma\left[\begin{matrix}s,\ s\\ \frac{2s+1}{2},\ \frac{2s+1}{2}\end{matrix}\right]$ $\times\ {}_6F_5\left(\begin{matrix}-\frac{1}{2},\ \frac{1}{2},\ \frac{s}{2},\ \frac{s}{2},\ \frac{s+1}{2},\ \frac{s+1}{2};\ a^2b^2\\ 1,\ \frac{2s+1}{4},\ \frac{2s+1}{4},\ \frac{2s+3}{4},\ \frac{2s+3}{4}\end{matrix}\right)$ $[a,\ \operatorname{Re} s > 0]$
4	$\dfrac{\theta(a-x)}{(1-b^2x)^\varepsilon}\,\mathbf{E}(b\sqrt{x})\,\mathbf{K}\left(\sqrt{1-\dfrac{x}{a}}\right)$	$\dfrac{\pi^2 a^s}{4}\,\Gamma\left[\begin{matrix}s,\ s\\ \frac{2s+1}{2},\ \frac{2s+1}{2}\end{matrix}\right]\ {}_4F_3\left(\begin{matrix}\frac{2\varepsilon-1}{2},\ \frac{2\varepsilon+1}{2},\ s,\ s;\ ab^2\\ 1,\ \frac{2s+1}{2},\ \frac{2s+1}{2}\end{matrix}\right)$ $[a,\ \operatorname{Re} s > 0]$

No.	$f(x)$	$F(s)$
5	$\theta(a-x)\sqrt{1+b^2x}\,\mathbf{E}\!\left(\dfrac{b\sqrt{x}}{\sqrt{1+b^2x}}\right)$ $\times\mathbf{K}\!\left(\sqrt{1-\dfrac{x}{a}}\right)$	$\dfrac{\pi^2a^s}{4}\,\Gamma\!\left[\begin{matrix}s,\ s\\ \frac{2s+1}{2},\ \frac{2s+1}{2}\end{matrix}\right]{}_4F_3\!\left(\begin{matrix}-\frac12,\ \frac12,\ s,\ s;\ -ab^2\\ 1,\ \frac{2s+1}{2},\ \frac{2s+1}{2}\end{matrix}\right)$ $[a,\ \operatorname{Re}s>0;\ |\arg(1+ab^2)|<\pi]$
6	$\dfrac{\theta(a-x)}{\sqrt{1+b^2x}}\,\mathbf{E}\!\left(\sqrt{1-\dfrac{x}{a}}\right)$ $\times\mathbf{K}\!\left(\dfrac{b\sqrt{x}}{\sqrt{1+b^2x}}\right)$	$\dfrac{\pi^2a^s}{4}\,\Gamma\!\left[\begin{matrix}s,\ s+1\\ \frac{2s+1}{2},\ \frac{2s+3}{2}\end{matrix}\right]{}_4F_3\!\left(\begin{matrix}\frac12,\ \frac12,\ s,\ s+1;\ -ab^2\\ 1,\ \frac{2s+1}{2},\ \frac{2s+3}{2}\end{matrix}\right)$ $[a,\ \operatorname{Re}s>0;\ |\arg(1+ab^2)|<\pi]$

3.26.26.　Products of $\mathbf{E}\left(\varphi(x)\right)$

Notation: $\varepsilon=0$ or 1.

No.	$f(x)$	$F(s)$
1	$\dfrac{\theta(a-x)}{(1-b^2x^2)^\varepsilon}\,\mathbf{E}(bx)\,\mathbf{E}\!\left(\sqrt{1-\dfrac{x}{a}}\right)$	$\dfrac{\pi^2a^s}{4}\,\Gamma\!\left[\begin{matrix}s,\ s+1\\ \frac{2s+1}{2},\ \frac{2s+3}{2}\end{matrix}\right]$ $\times{}_6F_5\!\left(\begin{matrix}\frac{2\varepsilon-1}{2},\ \frac{2\varepsilon+1}{2},\ \frac{s}{2},\ \frac{s+1}{2},\ \frac{s+1}{2},\ \frac{s+2}{2};\ a^2b^2\\ 1,\ \frac{2s+1}{4},\ \frac{2s+3}{4},\ \frac{2s+3}{4},\ \frac{2s+5}{4}\end{matrix}\right)$ $[a,\ \operatorname{Re}s>0]$
2	$\dfrac{\theta(a-x)}{(1-b^2x)^\varepsilon}\,\mathbf{E}(b\sqrt{x})\,\mathbf{E}\!\left(\sqrt{1-\dfrac{x}{a}}\right)$	$\dfrac{\pi^2a^s}{4}\,\Gamma\!\left[\begin{matrix}s,\ s+1\\ \frac{2s+1}{2},\ \frac{2s+3}{2}\end{matrix}\right]{}_4F_3\!\left(\begin{matrix}\frac{2\varepsilon-1}{2},\ \frac{2\varepsilon+1}{2},\ s,\ s+1;\ ab^2\\ 1,\ \frac{2s+1}{2},\ \frac{2s+3}{2}\end{matrix}\right)$ $[a,\ \operatorname{Re}s>0]$
3	$\theta(a-x)\sqrt{1+b^2x}\,\mathbf{E}\!\left(\dfrac{b\sqrt{x}}{\sqrt{1+b^2x}}\right)$ $\times\mathbf{E}\!\left(\sqrt{1-\dfrac{x}{a}}\right)$	$\dfrac{\pi^2a^s}{4}\,\Gamma\!\left[\begin{matrix}s,\ s+1\\ \frac{2s+1}{2},\ \frac{2s+3}{2}\end{matrix}\right]{}_4F_3\!\left(\begin{matrix}-\frac12,\ \frac12,\ s,\ s+1;\ -ab^2\\ 1,\ \frac{2s+1}{2},\ \frac{2s+3}{2}\end{matrix}\right)$ $[a,\ \operatorname{Re}s>0;\ |\arg(1+ab^2)|<\pi]$

3.26.27.　Products containing $\mathbf{D}\left(\varphi(x)\right)$

No.	$f(x)$	$F(s)$
1	$\theta(a-x)\,\mathbf{K}\!\left(\sqrt{1-\dfrac{x}{a}}\right)\mathbf{D}(b\sqrt{x})$	$\dfrac{\pi^2a^s}{8}\,\Gamma\!\left[\begin{matrix}s,\ s\\ \frac{2s+1}{2},\ \frac{2s+1}{2}\end{matrix}\right]{}_4F_3\!\left(\begin{matrix}\frac12,\ \frac32,\ s,\ s;\ ab^2\\ 2,\ \frac{2s+1}{2},\ \frac{2s+1}{2}\end{matrix}\right)$ $[a,\ \operatorname{Re}s>0]$
2	$\theta(a-x)\,\mathbf{E}\!\left(\sqrt{1-\dfrac{x}{a}}\right)\mathbf{D}(b\sqrt{x})$	$\dfrac{\pi^2a^s}{8}\,\Gamma\!\left[\begin{matrix}s,\ s+1\\ \frac{2s+1}{2},\ \frac{2s+3}{2}\end{matrix}\right]{}_4F_3\!\left(\begin{matrix}\frac12,\ \frac32,\ s,\ s+1;\ ab^2\\ 2,\ \frac{2s+1}{2},\ \frac{2s+3}{2}\end{matrix}\right)$ $[a,\ \operatorname{Re}s>0]$

3.27. The Hypergeometric Function $_0F_1(b; z)$

More formulas can be obtained from the corresponding sections due to the relations

$$_0F_1(b; -z) = \Gamma(b) z^{(1-b)/2} J_{b-1}(2\sqrt{z}), \quad _0F_1(b; z) = \Gamma(b) z^{(1-b)/2} I_{b-1}(2\sqrt{z}),$$

$$_0F_1(b; z) = \lim_{a \to \infty} {}_1F_1\left(a; b; \frac{z}{a}\right), \quad _0F_1(b; z) = e^{-2\sqrt{z}} {}_1F_1\left(b - \frac{1}{2}; 2b - 1; 4\sqrt{z}\right),$$

$$_0F_1(b; z) = \Gamma(b) G_{02}^{10}\left(-z \,\middle|\, \begin{matrix} \cdot \\ 0, 1-b \end{matrix}\right).$$

3.27.1. $_0F_1(b; \omega x)$ and the exponential function

No.	$f(x)$	$F(s)$
1	$e^{2\sqrt{\omega x}}\, {}_0F_1(b; \omega x)$	$\dfrac{2^{2b-4s-1}(-\sqrt{\omega})^{-2s}}{\sqrt{\pi}}\, \Gamma\left[\begin{matrix} b, \frac{2b-4s-1}{2}, 2s \\ 2b - 2s - 1 \end{matrix}\right]$ $[\omega < 0;\ 0 < \operatorname{Re} s < (2\operatorname{Re} b - 1)/4]$
2	$e^{-2\sqrt{\omega x}}\, {}_0F_1(b; \omega x)$	$\dfrac{2^{2b-4s-1}\omega^{-s}}{\sqrt{\pi}}\, \Gamma\left[\begin{matrix} b, \frac{2b-4s-1}{2}, 2s \\ 2b - 2s - 1 \end{matrix}\right]$ $[\omega < 0;\ 0 < \operatorname{Re} s < (2\operatorname{Re} b - 1)/4]$

3.27.2. $_0F_1(b; \omega x)$ and trigonometric functions

No.	$f(x)$	$F(s)$
1	$\left\{\begin{matrix} \sin(2\sqrt{\omega x} + \sigma) \\ \cos(2\sqrt{\omega x} + \sigma) \end{matrix}\right\}$ $\times {}_0F_1(b; -\omega x)$	$\dfrac{2^{2b-4s-1}\omega^{-s}}{\sqrt{\pi}}\left\{\begin{matrix} \sin(s\pi + \sigma) \\ \cos(s\pi + \sigma) \end{matrix}\right\} \Gamma\left[\begin{matrix} b, \frac{2b-4s-1}{2}, 2s \\ 2b - 2s - 1 \end{matrix}\right]$ $[\omega > 0;\ 0 < \operatorname{Re} s < (2\operatorname{Re} b - 1)/4]$

3.27.3. $_0F_1(b; \omega x)$ and $\operatorname{sinc}(\sqrt{ax})$

No.	$f(x)$	$F(s)$
1	$\operatorname{sinc}(2\sqrt{\omega x})\, {}_0F_1(b; -\omega x)$	$-\dfrac{2^{2b-4s}\omega^{-s}}{\sqrt{\pi}}\, \cos(s\pi) \Gamma\left[\begin{matrix} b, \frac{1-4s+2b}{2}, 2s - 1 \\ 2b - 2s \end{matrix}\right]$ $[\omega > 0;\ 0 < \operatorname{Re} s < (2\operatorname{Re} b + 1)/4]$

3.27.4. $_0F_1(b; \omega x)$ and the Bessel functions

No.	$f(x)$	$F(s)$
1	$J_\nu(2\sqrt{\omega x})\, {}_0F_1(b; -\omega x)$	$\omega^{-s}\Gamma\left[\begin{matrix} b, b - 2s, \frac{2s+\nu}{2} \\ \frac{\nu - 2s + 2}{2}, \frac{2b - 2s - \nu}{2}, \frac{2b - 2s + \nu}{2} \end{matrix}\right]$ $[\omega > 0;\ -\operatorname{Re}\nu/2 < \operatorname{Re} s < \operatorname{Re} b/2]$

No.	$f(x)$	$F(s)$
2	$J_{-b-n}\left(2\sqrt{\omega x}\right){}_0F_1\left(b;\,-\omega x\right)$ $-\dfrac{(-1)^{[(n+1)/2]}}{2^n\sqrt{\pi}}\,(\omega x)^{-(b+n)/2}$ $\times\,\Gamma\left(b\right)\sum_{k=0}^{[n/2]}\dfrac{\left(\left[\frac{n}{2}\right]-k+1\right)_{n-[n/2]}}{k!}$ $\times\,\Gamma\left[\begin{matrix}k-n+\left[\frac{n}{2}\right]+\frac{1}{2}\\ b+k,\,k-n-b+1\end{matrix}\right](-4\omega x)^k$	$\dfrac{(-1)^{n+1}}{\omega^s}\,\Gamma\left[\begin{matrix}b,\,b-2s,\,\frac{2s-b+n+2}{2}\\ \frac{b+n-2s+2}{2},\,\frac{3b+n-2s}{2},\,\frac{2-b-n-2s}{2}\end{matrix}\right]$ $\left[\omega>0;\;\left(\operatorname{Re}b-n\right)/2-1<\operatorname{Re}s<\operatorname{Re}b/2\right]$
3	$Y_\nu\left(2\sqrt{\omega x}\right){}_0F_1\left(b;\,-\omega x\right)$	$-\dfrac{\omega^{-s}}{\pi}\cos\dfrac{(2s-\nu)\pi}{2}\,\Gamma\left[\begin{matrix}b,\,b-2s,\,\frac{2s-\nu}{2},\,\frac{2s+\nu}{2}\\ \frac{2b-2s-\nu}{2},\,\frac{2b-2s+\nu}{2}\end{matrix}\right]$ $\left[\omega>0;\;\left|\operatorname{Re}\nu\right|/2<\operatorname{Re}s<\operatorname{Re}b/2\right]$
4	$Y_{-b-1}\left(2\sqrt{\omega x}\right){}_0F_1\left(b;\,-\omega x\right)$ $+\dfrac{\cot\left(b\pi\right)}{\Gamma\left(-b\right)}\,(\omega x)^{-(b+1)/2}$	$\dfrac{2^{b-2s}\omega^{-s}}{\pi^{3/2}\left(b-2s+1\right)}\sin\dfrac{(2s+b)\pi}{2}$ $\times\,\Gamma\left[\begin{matrix}b,\,\frac{b-2s}{2},\,\frac{2s-b+3}{2},\,\frac{2s+b+1}{2}\\ \frac{3b-2s+1}{2}\end{matrix}\right]$ $\left[\begin{matrix}\omega>0;\;\left(\operatorname{Re}b-3\right)/2,\,-\left(\operatorname{Re}b+1\right)/2\\ <\operatorname{Re}s<\operatorname{Re}b/2\end{matrix}\right]$
5	$Y_{-b}\left(2\sqrt{\omega x}\right){}_0F_1\left(b;\,-\omega x\right)$ $+\dfrac{\cos\left(b\pi\right)}{2\pi}\,\Gamma\left(b\right)(\omega x)^{-b/2}$	$-\dfrac{2^{b-2s-1}\omega^{-s}}{\pi^{3/2}}\cos\dfrac{(2s+b)\pi}{2}\,\Gamma\left[\begin{matrix}b,\,\frac{b-2s+1}{2},\,\frac{2s-b}{2},\,\frac{2s+b}{2}\\ \frac{3b-2s}{2}\end{matrix}\right]$ $\left[\omega>0;\;\left|\operatorname{Re}b\right|/2<\operatorname{Re}s<\left(\operatorname{Re}b+1\right)/2\right]$
6	$Y_b\left(2\sqrt{\omega x}\right){}_0F_1\left(b;\,-\omega x\right)$ $+\dfrac{\Gamma\left(b\right)}{\pi}\,(\omega x)^{-b/2}$	$-\dfrac{2^{b-2s-1}\omega^{-s}}{\sqrt{\pi}}\,\Gamma\left[\begin{matrix}b,\,\frac{2s-b}{2},\,\frac{2s+b}{2}\\ \frac{3b-2s}{2},\,\frac{2s-b+1}{2}\end{matrix}\right]$ $\left[\begin{matrix}\omega>0;\left(\operatorname{Re}b-2\right)/2,\,-\operatorname{Re}b/2\\ <\operatorname{Re}s<\operatorname{Re}b/2\end{matrix}\right]$
7	$Y_{b+1}\left(2\sqrt{\omega x}\right){}_0F_1\left(b;\,-\omega x\right)$ $+\dfrac{\Gamma\left(b+1\right)}{\pi}\,(\omega x)^{-(b+1)/2}$	$\dfrac{2^{b-2s}\omega^{-s}}{\sqrt{\pi}\left(b-2s+1\right)}\,\Gamma\left[\begin{matrix}b,\,\frac{2s+b+1}{2},\,\frac{2s-b+3}{2}\\ \frac{2s-b+2}{2},\,\frac{3b-2s+1}{2}\end{matrix}\right]$ $\left[\begin{matrix}\omega>0;\;\left(\operatorname{Re}b-3\right)/2,\,-\left(\operatorname{Re}b+1\right)/2\\ <\operatorname{Re}s<\left(\operatorname{Re}b+1\right)/2\end{matrix}\right]$
8	$Y_{\pm b\pm n}\left(2\sqrt{\omega x}\right){}_0F_1\left(b;\,-\omega x\right)$ $+\dfrac{(\mp 1)^n}{2^n\sqrt{\pi}}\,(\omega x)^{-(b+n)/2}\left\{\begin{matrix}\csc\left(b\pi\right)\\ \cot\left(b\pi\right)\end{matrix}\right\}$ $\times\,\Gamma\left(b\right)\sum_{k=0}^{[n/2]}(-1)^{k+[(n+1)/2]}$ $\times\dfrac{\left(\left[\frac{n}{2}\right]-k+1\right)_{n-[n/2]}}{k!}$ $\times\,\Gamma\left[\begin{matrix}k-n+\left[\frac{n}{2}\right]+\frac{1}{2}\\ b+k,\,k-n-b+1\end{matrix}\right](4\omega x)^k$	$(\pm 1)^n\dfrac{\omega^{-s}}{\pi}\cos\dfrac{(2s\mp b+n)\pi}{2}$ $\times\,\Gamma\left[\begin{matrix}b,\,b-2s,\,\frac{2s-b+n+2}{2},\,\frac{2s+b+n}{2}\\ \frac{b+n-2s+2}{2},\,\frac{3b+n-2s}{2}\end{matrix}\right]$ $\left[\begin{matrix}\omega>0;\;\left(\operatorname{Re}b-n\right)/2-1,\,-\left(\operatorname{Re}b+n\right)/2\\ <\operatorname{Re}s<\operatorname{Re}b/2\end{matrix}\right]$

No.	$f(x)$	$F(s)$
9	$\begin{Bmatrix} H_\nu^{(1)}\left(2\sqrt{\omega x}\right) \\ H_\nu^{(2)}\left(2\sqrt{\omega x}\right) \end{Bmatrix} {}_0F_1(b; -\omega x)$	$\dfrac{\omega^{-s}}{\pi}\Gamma\left[\begin{matrix} b,\ b-2s,\ \frac{2s+\nu}{2} \\ \frac{\nu-2s+2}{2},\ \frac{2b-2s-\nu}{2},\ \frac{2b-2s+\nu}{2} \end{matrix}\right]$ $\times \left[\pi \mp i\cos\dfrac{(2s-\nu)\pi}{2}\Gamma\left(s-\dfrac{\nu}{2}\right)\Gamma\left(1-s+\dfrac{\nu}{2}\right)\right]$ $[\omega > 0;\ |\operatorname{Re}\nu|/2 < \operatorname{Re}s < \operatorname{Re}b/2]$
10	$K_{b-1}\left(2\sqrt{\omega x}\right){}_0F_1(b; -\omega x)$	$\dfrac{\omega^{-s}}{4}\Gamma\left[\begin{matrix} b,\ \frac{2s-b+1}{2},\ \frac{2s+b-1}{4} \\ \frac{3b-2s+1}{4} \end{matrix}\right]$ $[\operatorname{Re}s > |1-\operatorname{Re}b|/2]$
11	$K_\nu\left(2\sqrt{\omega x}\right){}_0F_1(b; \omega x)$	$\dfrac{\omega^{-s}}{2}\Gamma\left[\begin{matrix} b,\ b-2s,\ \frac{2s-\nu}{2},\ \frac{2s+\nu}{2} \\ \frac{2b-2s-\nu}{2},\ \frac{2b-2s+\nu}{2} \end{matrix}\right]$ $[|\operatorname{Re}\nu|/2 < \operatorname{Re}s < \operatorname{Re}b/2]$

3.27.5. $\quad {}_0F_1(b; \omega x)$ **and** $\ker_\nu\left(\sqrt{ax}\right)$, $\ker_\nu\left(\sqrt{ax}\right)$

No.	$f(x)$	$F(s)$
1	$\ker_{\pm b\mp 1}\left(2\sqrt{\omega x}\right){}_0F_1(b; i\omega x)$	$\pm\dfrac{i\omega^{-s}}{8}\left(\dfrac{2^{b-2s}}{\sqrt{\pi}}e^{i(\mp b-s)\pi/2}\Gamma\left[\begin{matrix} b,\ \frac{b-2s}{2},\ \frac{2s+b-1}{2},\ \frac{2s-b+1}{2} \\ \frac{3b-2s-1}{2} \end{matrix}\right]\right.$ $\left. - e^{i(\pm b+s)\pi/2}\Gamma\left[\begin{matrix} b,\ \frac{2s+b-1}{4},\ \frac{2s-b+1}{2} \\ \frac{3b-2s+1}{4} \end{matrix}\right]\right)$ $[\omega > 0;\ |\operatorname{Re}b-1|/2 < \operatorname{Re}s < \operatorname{Re}b/2]$
2	$\text{kei}_{\pm b\mp 1}\left(2\sqrt{\omega x}\right){}_0F_1(b; i\omega x)$	$\pm\dfrac{\omega^{-s}}{8}\left(\dfrac{2^{b-2s}}{\sqrt{\pi}}e^{i(\mp b-s)\pi/2}\Gamma\left[\begin{matrix} b,\ \frac{b-2s}{2},\ \frac{2s+b-1}{2},\ \frac{2s-b+1}{2} \\ \frac{3b-2s-1}{2} \end{matrix}\right]\right.$ $\left. + e^{i(\pm b+s)\pi/2}\Gamma\left[\begin{matrix} b,\ \frac{2s+b-1}{4},\ \frac{2s-b+1}{2} \\ \frac{3b-2s+1}{4} \end{matrix}\right]\right)$ $[\omega > 0;\ |\operatorname{Re}b-1|/2 < \operatorname{Re}s < \operatorname{Re}b/2]$

3.27.6. $\quad {}_0F_1(b; \omega x)$ **and** $\text{Ai}\left(\sqrt[3]{ax}\right)$, $\text{Ai}'\left(\sqrt[3]{ax}\right)$

No.	$f(x)$	$F(s)$
1	$\text{Ai}\left(3^{2/3}\sqrt[3]{\omega x}\right){}_0F_1(b; \omega x)$	$\dfrac{3^{-1/6}\omega^{-s}}{2\pi}\Gamma\left[\begin{matrix} b,\ s,\ \frac{3s+1}{3},\ \frac{3b-6s-1}{3} \\ b-s,\ \frac{3b-3s-1}{3} \end{matrix}\right]$ $[0 < \operatorname{Re}s < (3\operatorname{Re}b-1)/6;\ |\arg\omega| < \pi]$
2	$\text{Ai}'\left(3^{2/3}\sqrt[3]{\omega x}\right){}_0F_1(b; \omega x)$	$-\dfrac{3^{1/6}\omega^{-s}}{2\pi}\Gamma\left[\begin{matrix} b,\ s,\ \frac{3s+2}{3},\ \frac{3b-6s-2}{3} \\ b-s,\ \frac{3b-3s-2}{3} \end{matrix}\right]$ $[0 < \operatorname{Re}s < (3\operatorname{Re}b-2)/6;\ |\arg\omega| < \pi]$

3.28. The Kummer Confluent Hypergeometric Function $_1F_1(a; b; z)$

More formulas can be obtained from the corresponding sections due to the relations

$$_1F_1(a; b; z) = \lim_{\lambda \to \infty} {}_2F_1\left(a, \lambda; b; \frac{z}{\lambda}\right), \quad _1F_1(a; b; z) = \frac{\Gamma(b)}{\Gamma(a)} G_{12}^{11}\left(-z \, \middle| \, \begin{matrix} 1-a \\ 0, 1-b \end{matrix}\right).$$

3.28.1. $_1F_1(a; b; \omega x)$ and algebraic functions

No.	$f(x)$	$F(s)$
1	$_1F_1\left(\begin{matrix} a; -\omega x \\ b \end{matrix}\right)$	$\omega^{-s}\,\Gamma\left[\begin{matrix} b, s, a-s \\ a, b-s \end{matrix}\right]$ $\qquad [0 < \mathrm{Re}\,s < \mathrm{Re}\,a; \ \mathrm{Re}\,\omega > 0]$
2	$(\sigma - x)_+^{\alpha-1}\,{}_1F_1\left(\begin{matrix} a; -\omega x \\ b \end{matrix}\right)$	$\sigma^{s+\alpha-1}\,\mathrm{B}(s,\alpha)\,{}_2F_2\left(\begin{matrix} a, s; -\sigma\omega \\ b, s+\alpha \end{matrix}\right)$ $\qquad [\sigma, \ \mathrm{Re}\,\alpha, \ \mathrm{Re}\,s > 0]$
3	$(x - \sigma)_+^{\alpha-1}\,{}_1F_1\left(\begin{matrix} a; -\omega x \\ b \end{matrix}\right)$	$\omega^{1-s-\alpha}\,\Gamma\left[\begin{matrix} b \\ b-s-\alpha+1 \end{matrix}\right]\mathrm{B}(a-s-\alpha+1, s+\alpha-1)$ $\times {}_2F_2\left(\begin{matrix} 1-\alpha, a-s-\alpha+1; -\sigma\omega \\ 1-s-\alpha+2, b-s-\alpha \end{matrix}\right)$ $+ \sigma^{s+\alpha-1}\,\mathrm{B}(1-s-\alpha, \alpha)\,{}_2F_2\left(\begin{matrix} a, s; -\sigma\omega \\ b, s+\alpha \end{matrix}\right)$ $\left[\begin{matrix} \sigma, \ \mathrm{Re}\,\alpha > 0; \ (\mathrm{Re}\,\omega > 0; \ \mathrm{Re}\,(s-a+\alpha) < 1) \ \text{or} \\ (\mathrm{Re}\,\omega = 0; \ \mathrm{Re}\,s < \mathrm{Re}\,(b-a-\alpha)+2) \end{matrix}\right]$
4	$\dfrac{1}{(x+\sigma)^\rho}\,{}_1F_1\left(\begin{matrix} a; -\omega x \\ b \end{matrix}\right)$	$\sigma^{s-\rho}\,\mathrm{B}(s, \rho-s)\,{}_2F_2\left(\begin{matrix} a, s; \sigma\omega \\ b, s-\rho+1 \end{matrix}\right)$ $+ \omega^{\rho-s}\,\mathrm{B}(s-\rho, a-s+\rho)\,\Gamma\left[\begin{matrix} b \\ b-s+\rho \end{matrix}\right]$ $\times {}_2F_2\left(\begin{matrix} \rho, a-s+\rho; \sigma\omega \\ 1-s+\rho, b-s+\rho \end{matrix}\right)$ $\left[\begin{matrix} (\mathrm{Re}\,\omega > 0; \ 0 < \mathrm{Re}\,s < \mathrm{Re}\,(\rho+a)) \ \text{or} \\ (\mathrm{Re}\,\omega = 0; \ 0 < \mathrm{Re}\,s < \mathrm{Re}\,(b-a+\rho)+1); \ |\arg\sigma| < \pi \end{matrix}\right]$
5	$\dfrac{1}{x-\sigma}\,{}_1F_1\left(\begin{matrix} a; -\omega x \\ b \end{matrix}\right)$	$\omega^{1-s}\,\mathrm{B}(a-s+1, s-1)\,\Gamma\left[\begin{matrix} b \\ b-s+1 \end{matrix}\right]$ $\times {}_2F_2\left(\begin{matrix} 1, a-s+1; -\sigma\omega \\ 2-s, b-s+1 \end{matrix}\right)$ $- \pi\sigma^{s-1}\cot(s\pi)\,{}_1F_1\left(\begin{matrix} a; -\sigma\omega \\ b \end{matrix}\right)$ $\left[\begin{matrix} \sigma > 0; \ (\mathrm{Re}\,\omega > 0; \ 0 < \mathrm{Re}\,s < \mathrm{Re}\,a+1) \ \text{or} \\ (\mathrm{Re}\,\omega = 0; \ 0 < \mathrm{Re}\,s < \mathrm{Re}\,(b-a)+2) \end{matrix}\right]$

No.	$f(x)$	$F(s)$
6	$\left(\sqrt{x}+\sqrt{x+\sigma}\right)^{\rho}$ $\times {}_1F_1\left(\begin{matrix} a;\,-\omega x \\ b \end{matrix}\right)$	$\dfrac{2^{\rho}}{\omega^{s+\rho/2}}\,\mathrm{B}\left(\dfrac{2b-2a-2s-\rho}{2},\dfrac{2s+\rho}{2}\right)$ $\times\Gamma\left[\begin{matrix} b \\ \frac{2b-2s-\rho}{2} \end{matrix}\right]{}_3F_3\left(\begin{matrix} -\frac{\rho}{2},\,\frac{1-\rho}{2},\,\frac{2a-2s-\rho}{2};\,\sigma\omega \\ 1-\rho,\,\frac{2-2s-\rho}{2},\,\frac{2b-2s-\rho}{2} \end{matrix}\right)$ $-\dfrac{\sigma^{s+\rho/2}\rho}{2^{2s}}\,\Gamma\left[\begin{matrix} 2s,\,\frac{-2s-\rho}{2} \\ \frac{2s-\rho+2}{2} \end{matrix}\right]{}_3F_3\left(\begin{matrix} a,\,s,\,\frac{2s+1}{2};\,\sigma\omega \\ b,\,\frac{2s-\rho+2}{2},\,\frac{2s+\rho+2}{2} \end{matrix}\right)$ $\left[\begin{matrix}(\operatorname{Re}\omega>0;\,0<\operatorname{Re}s<\operatorname{Re}(a-\rho/2))\text{ or}\\(\operatorname{Re}\omega=0;\,0<\operatorname{Re}s<\operatorname{Re}(b-a-\rho/2)+1);\,|\arg\sigma|<\pi\end{matrix}\right]$
7	$\dfrac{\left(\sqrt{x}+\sqrt{x+\sigma}\right)^{\rho}}{\sqrt{x+\sigma}}$ $\times {}_1F_1\left(\begin{matrix} a;\,-\omega x \\ b \end{matrix}\right)$	$\dfrac{2^{\rho}}{\omega^{s+(\rho-1)/2}}\,\mathrm{B}\left(\dfrac{2a-2s-\rho+1}{2},\dfrac{2s+\rho-1}{2}\right)$ $\times\Gamma\left[\begin{matrix} b \\ \frac{2b-2s-\rho+1}{2} \end{matrix}\right]{}_3F_3\left(\begin{matrix} \frac{1-\rho}{2},\,\frac{2-\rho}{2},\,\frac{2a-2s-\rho+1}{2};\,\sigma\omega \\ 1-\rho,\,\frac{3-2s-\rho}{2},\,\frac{2b-2s-\rho+1}{2} \end{matrix}\right)$ $+\dfrac{\sigma^{s+(\rho-1)/2}}{2^{2s-1}}\,\mathrm{B}\left(2s,\dfrac{1-2s-\rho}{2}\right){}_3F_3\left(\begin{matrix} a,\,s,\,\frac{2s+1}{2};\,\sigma\omega \\ b,\,\frac{2s-\rho+1}{2},\,\frac{2s+\rho+1}{2} \end{matrix}\right)$ $\left[\begin{matrix}(\operatorname{Re}\omega>0;\,0<\operatorname{Re}s<\operatorname{Re}(a+(1-\rho)/2))\text{ or}\\(\operatorname{Re}\omega=0;\,0<\operatorname{Re}s<\operatorname{Re}(b-a+(3-\rho)/2));\,|\arg\sigma|<\pi\end{matrix}\right]$
8	$\theta(x-\sigma)(x-\tau)^{-a}$ $\times {}_1F_1\left(a;b;\dfrac{\omega x}{x-\tau}\right)$	$\dfrac{\sigma^{s-a}}{a-s}\,\Psi_1\left(a,a-s;a-s+1,b;\dfrac{\tau}{\sigma},\omega\right)$ $[\sigma>0;\,|\tau|<\sigma;\,0<\operatorname{Re}s<\operatorname{Re}a]$
9	$(\sigma-x)_+^{b-1}(\tau-x)^{-a}$ $\times {}_1F_1\left(a;b;\dfrac{\omega(\sigma-x)}{\tau-x}\right)$	$\tau^{-a}\sigma^{s+b-1}\mathrm{B}(s,b)\,\Phi_1\left(a,s,s+b,\dfrac{\sigma}{\tau},\dfrac{\sigma\omega}{\tau}\right)$ $[\tau>\sigma>0;\,\operatorname{Re}b,\,\operatorname{Re}s>0]$

3.28.2. $_1F_1(a;b;\omega x)$ and the exponential function

No.	$f(x)$	$F(s)$
1	$e^{-\sigma x}\,{}_1F_1\left(\begin{matrix} a;\,\omega x \\ b \end{matrix}\right)$	$\dfrac{\Gamma(s)}{\sigma^s}\,{}_2F_1\left(\begin{matrix} a,\,s \\ b;\,\frac{\omega}{\sigma} \end{matrix}\right)$ $\left[\begin{matrix}(\operatorname{Re}(\sigma-\omega)>0,\,\operatorname{Re}\sigma>0;\,\operatorname{Re}s>0)\text{ or}\\(\operatorname{Re}(\sigma-\omega)=0,\,\operatorname{Re}\sigma>0;\,0<\operatorname{Re}s<\operatorname{Re}(b-a)+1)\text{ or}\\(\operatorname{Re}(\sigma-\omega)>0,\,\operatorname{Re}\sigma=0;\,0<\operatorname{Re}s<\operatorname{Re}a+1)\text{ or}\\(\operatorname{Re}(\sigma-\omega)=0,\,\operatorname{Re}\sigma=0;\,0<\operatorname{Re}s<\operatorname{Re}a+1,\,\operatorname{Re}(b-a)+1)\end{matrix}\right]$
2	$e^{-\omega x}\,{}_1F_1\left(\begin{matrix} a;\,\omega x \\ b \end{matrix}\right)$	$\omega^{-s}\Gamma\left[\begin{matrix} s,\,b-a-s,\,b \\ b-s,\,b-a \end{matrix}\right]$ $\left[\begin{matrix}(\operatorname{Re}\omega>0;\,0<\operatorname{Re}s<\operatorname{Re}(b-a))\text{ or}\\(\operatorname{Re}\omega=0;\,0<\operatorname{Re}s<\operatorname{Re}a+1,\,\operatorname{Re}(b-a))\end{matrix}\right]$

No.	$f(x)$	$F(s)$
3	$(\sigma - x)_+^{\alpha-1} e^{-\omega x}$ $\times {}_1F_1\left({a;\ \omega x \atop b}\right)$	$\sigma^{s+\alpha-1} \mathrm{B}(s, \alpha)\ {}_2F_2\left({b-a,\ s;\ -\sigma\omega \atop b,\ s+\alpha}\right)$ $\qquad [\sigma,\ \mathrm{Re}\,\alpha,\ \mathrm{Re}\,s > 0]$
4	$(x - \sigma)_+^{\alpha-1} e^{-\omega x}$ $\times {}_1F_1\left({a;\ \omega x \atop b}\right)$	$\omega^{1-s-\alpha} \mathrm{B}(1-a+b-s-\alpha,\ s+\alpha-1)\,\Gamma\left[{b \atop b-s-\alpha+1}\right]$ $\times {}_2F_2\left({1-\alpha,\ 1-a+b-\alpha-s;\ -\sigma\omega \atop 2-s-\alpha,\ b-\alpha-s+1}\right)$ $+\ \sigma^{s+\alpha-1}\mathrm{B}(1-s-\alpha,\ \alpha)\ {}_2F_2\left({b-a,\ s;\ -\sigma\omega \atop b,\ s+\alpha}\right)$ $\left[{\sigma > 0;\ (\mathrm{Re}\,\omega > 0;\ \mathrm{Re}\,s < \mathrm{Re}\,(b-a-\alpha)+1)\ \text{or} \atop (\mathrm{Re}\,\omega = 0;\ \mathrm{Re}\,s < \mathrm{Re}\,(a-\alpha)+2,\ \mathrm{Re}\,(b-a-\alpha)+1)}\right]$
5	$\dfrac{e^{-\omega x}}{(x+\sigma)^\rho}\ {}_1F_1\left({a;\ \omega x \atop b}\right)$	$\sigma^{s-\rho}\mathrm{B}(s,\ \rho-s)\ {}_2F_2\left({b-a,\ s;\ \sigma\omega \atop b,\ s-\rho+1}\right)$ $+\ \omega^{\rho-s}\mathrm{B}(s-\rho,\ b-a+\rho-s)\,\Gamma\left[{b \atop b+\rho-s}\right]$ $\times {}_2F_2\left({\rho,\ b-a+\rho-s;\ \sigma\omega \atop \rho-s+1,\ b+\rho-s}\right)$ $\left[{(\mathrm{Re}\,\omega > 0;\ 0 < \mathrm{Re}\,s < \mathrm{Re}\,(b-a+\rho))\ \text{or} \atop (\mathrm{Re}\,\omega = 0;\ 0 < \mathrm{Re}\,s < \mathrm{Re}\,(b-a+\rho),\ \mathrm{Re}\,(a+\rho)+1);\ |\arg\sigma| < \pi}\right]$
6	$\dfrac{e^{-\omega x}}{x-\sigma}\ {}_1F_1\left({a;\ \omega x \atop b}\right)$	$\omega^{1-s}\mathrm{B}(1-s-a+b,\ s-1)\,\Gamma\left[{b \atop b-s+1}\right]$ $\times {}_2F_2\left({1,\ 1-s-a+b \atop 2-s,\ 1-s+b};\ -\sigma\omega\right) - \pi\sigma^{s-1}\cot(s\pi)\ {}_1F_1\left({b-a \atop b;\ -\sigma\omega}\right)$ $\left[{\sigma > 0;\ (\mathrm{Re}\,\omega > 0;\ 0 < \mathrm{Re}\,s < \mathrm{Re}\,(b-a)+1)\ \text{or} \atop (\mathrm{Re}\,\omega = 0;\ 0 < \mathrm{Re}\,s < \mathrm{Re}\,a+2,\ \mathrm{Re}\,(b-a)+1)}\right]$
7	$e^{-\sigma\sqrt{x}}\ {}_1F_1\left({a;\ -\omega x \atop b}\right)$	$\dfrac{2\sigma^{2(a-s)}}{\omega^a}\,\Gamma\left[{b,\ 2s-2a \atop b-a}\right]\ {}_2F_2\left({a,\ a-b+1;\ \frac{\sigma^2}{4\omega} \atop \frac{2a-2s+1}{2},\ a-s+1}\right)$ $-\ \dfrac{\sigma}{\omega^{s+1/2}}\,\mathrm{B}\left(s+\dfrac{1}{2},\ a-s-\dfrac{1}{2}\right)$ $\times \Gamma\left[{b \atop b-s-\frac{1}{2}}\right]\ {}_2F_2\left({\frac{2s+1}{2},\ \frac{2s-2b+3}{2} \atop \frac{3}{2},\ \frac{2s-2a+3}{2};\ \frac{\sigma^2}{4\omega}}\right)$ $+\ \omega^{-s}\mathrm{B}(s,\ a-s)\,\Gamma\left[{b \atop b-s}\right]\ {}_2F_2\left({s,\ s-b+1;\ \frac{\sigma^2}{4\omega} \atop \frac{1}{2},\ s-a+1}\right)$ $\left[{(\mathrm{Re}\,\omega \geq 0;\ \mathrm{Re}\,\sigma,\ \mathrm{Re}\,s > 0)\ \text{or} \atop (\mathrm{Re}\,\omega = \mathrm{Re}\,\sigma = 0;\ 0 < \mathrm{Re}\,s < \mathrm{Re}\,(b-a)+1/2,\ \mathrm{Re}\,a+1)}\right]$

No.	$f(x)$	$F(s)$
8	$e^{-\sigma\sqrt{x}-\omega x}\,_1F_1\left(\begin{matrix} a;\ \omega x \\ b \end{matrix}\right)$	$\dfrac{2\omega^{a-b}}{\sigma^{2(a-b+s)}}\,\Gamma\left[\begin{matrix} b,\ 2a-2b+2s \\ a \end{matrix}\right]$

$$\times\,_2F_2\left(\begin{matrix} 1-a,\ b-a;\ \frac{\sigma^2}{4\omega} \\ b-a-s+\frac{1}{2},\ b-a-s+1 \end{matrix}\right)$$

$$-\frac{\sigma}{\omega^{s+1/2}}\,\mathrm{B}\left(\frac{2b-2a-2s-1}{2},\ \frac{2s+1}{2}\right)$$

$$\times\,\Gamma\left[\begin{matrix} b \\ \frac{2b-2s-1}{2} \end{matrix}\right]\,_2F_2\left(\begin{matrix} \frac{2s+1}{2},\ \frac{2s-2b+3}{2} \\ \frac{3}{2},\ \frac{2s+2a-2b+3}{2};\ \frac{\sigma^2}{4\omega} \end{matrix}\right)$$

$$+\omega^{-s}\,\mathrm{B}\,(b-a-s,\ s)\,\Gamma\left[\begin{matrix} b \\ b-s \end{matrix}\right]\,_2F_2\left(\begin{matrix} s,\ s-b+1;\ \frac{\sigma^2}{4\omega} \\ \frac{1}{2},\ s+a-b+1 \end{matrix}\right)$$

$$\left[\begin{matrix} (\mathrm{Re}\,\omega\geq 0;\ \mathrm{Re}\,\sigma,\ \mathrm{Re}\,s>0)\ \text{or} \\ (\mathrm{Re}\,\omega=\mathrm{Re}\,\sigma=0,\ 0<\mathrm{Re}\,s<\mathrm{Re}\,a+1/2,\ \mathrm{Re}\,(b-a)+1) \end{matrix}\right]$$

| 9 | $e^{-\sigma/x}\,_1F_1\left(\begin{matrix} a;\ -\omega x \\ b \end{matrix}\right)$ | $\omega^{-s}\,\mathrm{B}\,(a-s,\ s)\,\Gamma\left[\begin{matrix} b \\ b-s \end{matrix}\right]\,_1F_2\left(\begin{matrix} a-s;\ \sigma\omega \\ 1-s,\ b-s \end{matrix}\right)$ |

$$+\sigma^s\Gamma\,(-s)\,_1F_2\left(\begin{matrix} a;\ \sigma\omega \\ b,\ s+1 \end{matrix}\right)$$

$$\left[\begin{matrix} (\mathrm{Re}\,\omega>0,\ \mathrm{Re}\,\sigma>0;\ \mathrm{Re}\,s<\mathrm{Re}\,a)\ \text{or} \\ (\mathrm{Re}\,\omega=0,\ \mathrm{Re}\,\sigma>0;\ \mathrm{Re}\,s<\mathrm{Re}\,a,\ \mathrm{Re}\,(b-a)+1)\ \text{or} \\ (\mathrm{Re}\,\omega>0,\ \mathrm{Re}\,\sigma=0;\ -1<\mathrm{Re}\,s<\mathrm{Re}\,a)\ \text{or} \\ (\mathrm{Re}\,\omega=0,\ \mathrm{Re}\,\sigma=0;\ -1<\mathrm{Re}\,s<\mathrm{Re}\,a,\ \mathrm{Re}\,(b-a)+1) \end{matrix}\right]$$

| 10 | $e^{-\omega x-\sigma/x}\,_1F_1\left(\begin{matrix} a;\ \omega x \\ b \end{matrix}\right)$ | $\omega^{-s}\,\mathrm{B}\,(-a+b-s,\ s)\,\Gamma\left[\begin{matrix} b \\ b-s \end{matrix}\right]\,_1F_2\left(\begin{matrix} b-a-s;\ \sigma\omega \\ 1-s,\ b-s \end{matrix}\right)$ |

$$+\sigma^s\Gamma\,(-s)\,_1F_2\left(\begin{matrix} b-a;\ \sigma\omega \\ b,\ s+1 \end{matrix}\right)$$

$$\left[\begin{matrix} (\mathrm{Re}\,\omega>0,\ \mathrm{Re}\,\sigma>0;\ \mathrm{Re}\,s<\mathrm{Re}\,(b-a))\ \text{or} \\ (\mathrm{Re}\,\omega=0,\ \mathrm{Re}\,\sigma>0;\ \mathrm{Re}\,s<\mathrm{Re}\,a+1,\ \mathrm{Re}\,(b-a))\ \text{or} \\ (\mathrm{Re}\,\omega>0,\ \mathrm{Re}\,\sigma=0;\ -1<\mathrm{Re}\,s<\mathrm{Re}\,(b-a))\ \text{or} \\ (\mathrm{Re}\,\omega=0,\ \mathrm{Re}\,\sigma=0;\ -1<\mathrm{Re}\,s<\mathrm{Re}\,a+1,\ \mathrm{Re}\,(b-a)) \end{matrix}\right]$$

| 11 | $\left(\sqrt{x}+\sqrt{x+\sigma}\right)^\rho e^{-\omega x}$ | $\dfrac{2^\rho}{\omega^{s+\rho/2}}\,\mathrm{B}\left(\frac{2b-2a-2s-\rho}{2},\ \frac{2s+\rho}{2}\right)$ |
| | $\times\,_1F_1\left(\begin{matrix} a;\ \omega x \\ b \end{matrix}\right)$ | $\times\,\Gamma\left[\begin{matrix} b \\ \frac{2b-2s-\rho}{2} \end{matrix}\right]\,_3F_3\left(\begin{matrix} -\frac{\rho}{2},\ \frac{1-\rho}{2},\ \frac{2b-2a-2s-\rho}{2};\ \sigma\omega \\ 1-\rho,\ \frac{2-2s-\rho}{2},\ \frac{2b-2s-\rho}{2} \end{matrix}\right)$ |

$$-\frac{\sigma^{s+\rho/2}\rho}{2^{2s}}\,\Gamma\left[\begin{matrix} 2s,\ \frac{-2s-\rho}{2} \\ \frac{2s-\rho+2}{2} \end{matrix}\right]\,_3F_3\left(\begin{matrix} b-a,\ s,\ \frac{2s+1}{2};\ \sigma\omega \\ b,\ \frac{2s-\rho+2}{2},\ \frac{2s+\rho+2}{2} \end{matrix}\right)$$

$$\left[\begin{matrix} (\mathrm{Re}\,\omega>0;\ 0<\mathrm{Re}\,s<\mathrm{Re}\,(b-a-\rho/2))\ \text{or} \\ (\mathrm{Re}\,\omega=0;\ 0<\mathrm{Re}\,s<\mathrm{Re}\,(a-\rho/2)+1,\ \mathrm{Re}\,(b-a-\rho/2));\ |\arg\sigma|<\pi \end{matrix}\right]$$

No.	$f(x)$	$F(s)$
12	$\dfrac{\left(\sqrt{x}+\sqrt{x+\sigma}\right)^{\rho}}{\sqrt{x+\sigma}}e^{-\omega x}$ $\times {}_1F_1\left(\begin{matrix} a;\,\omega x \\ b \end{matrix}\right)$	$\dfrac{2^{\rho}}{\omega^{s+(\rho-1)/2}}\,\mathrm{B}\left(\dfrac{2b-2a-2s-\rho+1}{2},\,\dfrac{2s+\rho-1}{2}\right)$ $\times\,\Gamma\left[\begin{matrix} b \\ \frac{2b-2s-\rho+1}{2}\end{matrix}\right]\, {}_3F_3\left(\begin{matrix} \frac{1-\rho}{2},\,\frac{2-\rho}{2},\,\frac{2s-2a+2b-\rho+1}{2};\,\sigma\omega \\ 1-\rho,\,\frac{3-2s-\rho}{2},\,\frac{2b-2s-\rho+1}{2}\end{matrix}\right)$ $+\dfrac{\sigma^{s+(\rho-1)/2}}{2^{2s-1}}\,\mathrm{B}\left(2s,\,\dfrac{1-2s-\rho}{2}\right)$ $\times\, {}_3F_3\left(\begin{matrix} b-a,\,s,\,\frac{2s+1}{2};\,\sigma\omega \\ b,\,\frac{2s-\rho+1}{2},\,\frac{2s+\rho+1}{2}\end{matrix}\right)$ $\begin{bmatrix}(\operatorname{Re}\omega>0;\,0<\operatorname{Re}s<\operatorname{Re}(b-a-\rho/2)+1/2)\ \text{or} \\ (\operatorname{Re}\omega=0;\,0<\operatorname{Re}s<\operatorname{Re}(a-\rho/2)+3/2,\,\operatorname{Re}(b-a-\rho/2)+1/2);\,\lvert\arg\sigma\rvert<\pi\end{bmatrix}$
13	$(\sigma-x)_+^{\alpha-1}e^{\tau x}$ $\times {}_1F_1\left(\begin{matrix} a;\,\omega(\sigma-x) \\ b \end{matrix}\right)$	$\sigma^{s+\alpha-1}\,\mathrm{B}(s,\alpha)\,\Phi_2(s,a;\,s+b,\,\sigma\tau,\,\sigma\omega)\qquad[\sigma,\,\operatorname{Re}\alpha,\,\operatorname{Re}s>0]$

3.28.3. ${}_1F_1(a;\,b;\,\omega x)$ and trigonometric functions

1	$\sin(\sigma x)\,{}_1F_1\left(\begin{matrix} a;\,-\omega x \\ b \end{matrix}\right)$	$\sigma^{-s}\sin\dfrac{s\pi}{2}\,\Gamma(s)\,{}_4F_3\left(\begin{matrix} \frac{a}{2},\,\frac{a+1}{2},\,\frac{s}{2},\,\frac{s+1}{2} \\ \frac{1}{2},\,\frac{b}{2},\,\frac{b+1}{2}\end{matrix}\right)$ $-\dfrac{a\sigma^{-s-1}\omega}{b}\cos\dfrac{s\pi}{2}\,\Gamma(s+1)\,{}_4F_3\left(\begin{matrix} \frac{a+1}{2},\,\frac{a+2}{2},\,\frac{s+1}{2},\,\frac{s+2}{2} \\ \frac{3}{2},\,\frac{b+1}{2},\,\frac{b+2}{2};\,-\frac{\omega^2}{\sigma^2}\end{matrix}\right)$ $\begin{bmatrix}\sigma>0;\,(\operatorname{Re}\omega>0;\,-1<\operatorname{Re}s<\operatorname{Re}a+1)\ \text{or} \\ (\operatorname{Re}\omega=0;\,-1<\operatorname{Re}s<\operatorname{Re}a+1,\,\operatorname{Re}(b-a))\end{bmatrix}$
2	$\cos(\sigma x)\,{}_1F_1\left(\begin{matrix} a;\,-\omega x \\ b \end{matrix}\right)$	$\dfrac{as\omega}{b\sigma^{s+1}}\sin\dfrac{s\pi}{2}\,\Gamma(s)\,{}_4F_3\left(\begin{matrix} \frac{a+1}{2},\,\frac{a+2}{2},\,\frac{s+1}{2},\,\frac{s+2}{2} \\ \frac{3}{2},\,\frac{b+1}{2},\,\frac{b+2}{2};\,-\frac{\omega^2}{\sigma^2}\end{matrix}\right)$ $+\sigma^{-s}\cos\dfrac{s\pi}{2}\,\Gamma(s)\,{}_4F_3\left(\begin{matrix} \frac{a}{2},\,\frac{a+1}{2},\,\frac{s}{2},\,\frac{s+1}{2} \\ \frac{1}{2},\,\frac{b}{2},\,\frac{b+1}{2};\,-\frac{\omega^2}{\sigma^2}\end{matrix}\right)$ $\begin{bmatrix}\sigma>0;\,(\operatorname{Re}\omega>0;\,0<\operatorname{Re}s<\operatorname{Re}a+1)\ \text{or} \\ (\operatorname{Re}\omega=0;\,0<\operatorname{Re}s<\operatorname{Re}a+1,\,\operatorname{Re}(b-a))\end{bmatrix}$
3	$\sin(\sigma\sqrt{x})\,{}_1F_1\left(\begin{matrix} a;\,-\omega x \\ b \end{matrix}\right)$	$\dfrac{\sigma}{\omega^{s+1/2}}\,\mathrm{B}\left(\dfrac{2a-2s-1}{2},\,\dfrac{2s+1}{2}\right)\Gamma\left[\begin{matrix} b \\ \frac{2b-2s-1}{2}\end{matrix}\right]$ $\times\, {}_2F_2\left(\begin{matrix} \frac{2s+1}{2},\,\frac{2s-2b+3}{2} \\ \frac{3}{2},\,\frac{2s-2a+3}{2};\,-\frac{\sigma^2}{4\omega}\end{matrix}\right)-\dfrac{2\sigma^{2a-2s}}{\omega^a}\sin[(a-s)\pi]$ $\times\,\Gamma\left[\begin{matrix} b,\,2s-2a \\ b-a\end{matrix}\right]\, {}_2F_2\left(\begin{matrix} a,\,a-b+1;\,-\frac{\sigma^2}{4\omega} \\ \frac{2a-2s+1}{2},\,a-s+1\end{matrix}\right)$ $\begin{bmatrix}\sigma>0;\,(\operatorname{Re}\omega>0;\,-1/2<\operatorname{Re}s<\operatorname{Re}a+1/2)\ \text{or} \\ (\operatorname{Re}\omega=0;\,-1/2<\operatorname{Re}s<\operatorname{Re}a+1/2,\,\operatorname{Re}(b-a)+1)\end{bmatrix}$

No.	$f(x)$	$F(s)$
4	$\cos(\sigma\sqrt{x}) \, _1F_1\left(\begin{matrix} a; -\omega x \\ b \end{matrix}\right)$	$\dfrac{2\sigma^{2a-2s}}{\omega a} \cos[(a-s)\pi]\, \Gamma\left[\begin{matrix} b, \, 2s-2a \\ b-a \end{matrix}\right]$

$$\times \, _2F_2\left(\begin{matrix} a, \, a-b+1; \, -\frac{\sigma^2}{4\omega} \\ \frac{2a-2s+1}{2}, \, a-s+1 \end{matrix}\right)$$

$$+ \omega^{-s}\, \mathrm{B}\,(a-s, s)\, \Gamma\left[\begin{matrix} b \\ b-s \end{matrix}\right] \, _2F_2\left(\begin{matrix} s, \, s-b+1; \, -\frac{\sigma^2}{4\omega} \\ \frac{1}{2}, \, s-a+1 \end{matrix}\right)$$

$$\left[\begin{matrix} \sigma > 0; \; (\mathrm{Re}\,\omega > 0; \; 0 < \mathrm{Re}\,s < \mathrm{Re}\,a + 1/2) \text{ or} \\ (\mathrm{Re}\,\omega = 0; \; 0 < \mathrm{Re}\,s < \mathrm{Re}\,a + 1/2, \; \mathrm{Re}\,(b-a) + 1) \end{matrix}\right]$$

5	$\sin\dfrac{\sigma}{\sqrt{x}} \, _1F_1\left(\begin{matrix} a; -\omega x \\ b \end{matrix}\right)$	$\dfrac{\pi\sigma^{2s}\sec(s\pi)}{\Gamma(2s+1)} \, _1F_3\left(\begin{matrix} a; \, \frac{\sigma^2\omega}{4} \\ b, \, \frac{2s+1}{2}, \, s+1 \end{matrix}\right)$

$$- \dfrac{\pi\sigma\sec(s\pi)}{\omega^{s-1/2}}\, \Gamma\left[\begin{matrix} b, \, \frac{2a-2s+1}{2} \\ a, \, \frac{3}{2}-s, \, b-s+\frac{1}{2} \end{matrix}\right]$$

$$\times \, _1F_3\left(\begin{matrix} \frac{2a-2s+1}{2}; \, \frac{\sigma^2\omega}{4} \\ \frac{3}{2}, \, \frac{3-2s}{2}, \, \frac{2b-2s+1}{2} \end{matrix}\right)$$

$$\left[\begin{matrix} \sigma > 0; \; (\mathrm{Re}\,\omega > 0; \; -1/2 < \mathrm{Re}\,s < \mathrm{Re}\,a + 1/2) \text{ or} \\ (\mathrm{Re}\,\omega = 0; \; -1/2 < \mathrm{Re}\,s < \mathrm{Re}\,a + 1/2, \; \mathrm{Re}\,(b-a) + 3/2) \end{matrix}\right]$$

6	$\cos\dfrac{\sigma}{\sqrt{x}} \, _1F_1\left(\begin{matrix} a; -\omega x \\ b \end{matrix}\right)$	$\dfrac{\pi\csc(s\pi)}{\omega^s}\, \Gamma\left[\begin{matrix} b, \, a-s \\ a, \, 1-s, \, b-s \end{matrix}\right] \, _1F_3\left(\begin{matrix} a-s; \, \frac{\sigma^2\omega}{4} \\ \frac{1}{2}, \, 1-s, \, b-s \end{matrix}\right)$

$$- \dfrac{\pi\sigma^{2s}\csc(s\pi)}{\Gamma(2s+1)} \, _1F_3\left(\begin{matrix} a; \, \frac{\sigma^2\omega}{4} \\ b, \, \frac{2s+1}{2}, \, s+1 \end{matrix}\right)$$

$$\left[\begin{matrix} \sigma > 0; \; (\mathrm{Re}\,\omega > 0; \; -1/2 < \mathrm{Re}\,s < \mathrm{Re}\,a) \text{ or} \\ (\mathrm{Re}\,\omega = 0; \; -1/2 < \mathrm{Re}\,s < \mathrm{Re}\,a, \; \mathrm{Re}\,(b-a) + 1) \end{matrix}\right]$$

7	$e^{-\omega x}\sin(\sigma x) \, _1F_1\left(\begin{matrix} a; \, \omega x \\ b \end{matrix}\right)$	$\sigma^{-s}\sin\dfrac{s\pi}{2}\, \Gamma(s)\, _4F_3\left(\begin{matrix} \frac{b-a}{2}, \, \frac{b-a+1}{2}, \, \frac{s}{2}, \, \frac{s+1}{2} \\ \frac{1}{2}, \, \frac{b}{2}, \, \frac{b+1}{2}; \, -\frac{\omega^2}{\sigma^2} \end{matrix}\right)$

$$- \dfrac{a\sigma^{-s-1}\omega}{b} \cos\dfrac{s\pi}{2}\, \Gamma(s+1)$$

$$\times \, _4F_3\left(\begin{matrix} \frac{b-a+1}{2}, \, \frac{b-a+2}{2}, \, \frac{s+1}{2}, \, \frac{s+2}{2} \\ \frac{3}{2}, \, \frac{b+1}{2}, \, \frac{b+2}{2}; \, -\frac{\omega^2}{\sigma^2} \end{matrix}\right)$$

$$\left[\begin{matrix} \sigma > 0; \; (\mathrm{Re}\,\omega > 0; \; -1 < \mathrm{Re}\,s < \mathrm{Re}\,(b-a) + 1) \text{ or} \\ (\mathrm{Re}\,\omega = 0; \; -1 < \mathrm{Re}\,s < \mathrm{Re}\,a + 1, \; \mathrm{Re}\,(b-a) + 1) \end{matrix}\right]$$

8	$e^{-\omega x}\cos(\sigma x) \, _1F_1\left(\begin{matrix} a; \, \omega x \\ b \end{matrix}\right)$	$\dfrac{(b-a)s\omega}{b\sigma^{s+1}}\sin\dfrac{s\pi}{2}\, \Gamma(s)\, _4F_3\left(\begin{matrix} \frac{b-a+1}{2}, \, \frac{b-a+2}{2}, \, \frac{s+1}{2}, \, \frac{s+2}{2} \\ \frac{3}{2}, \, \frac{b+1}{2}, \, \frac{b+2}{2}; \, -\frac{\omega^2}{\sigma^2} \end{matrix}\right)$

$$+ \sigma^{-s}\cos\dfrac{s\pi}{2}\, \Gamma(s)\, _4F_3\left(\begin{matrix} \frac{b-a}{2}, \, \frac{b-a+1}{2}, \, \frac{s}{2}, \, \frac{s+1}{2} \\ \frac{1}{2}, \, \frac{b}{2}, \, \frac{b+1}{2}; \, -\frac{\omega^2}{\sigma^2} \end{matrix}\right)$$

$$\left[\begin{matrix} \sigma > 0; \; (\mathrm{Re}\,\omega > 0; \; 0 < \mathrm{Re}\,s < \mathrm{Re}\,(b-a) + 1) \text{ or} \\ (\mathrm{Re}\,\omega = 0; \; 0 < \mathrm{Re}\,s < \mathrm{Re}\,a + 1, \; \mathrm{Re}\,(b-a) + 1) \end{matrix}\right]$$

No.	$f(x)$	$F(s)$

9 $e^{-\omega x} \sin\left(\sigma\sqrt{x}\right)$

$\times\, {}_1F_1\left(\begin{matrix} a;\ \omega x \\ b \end{matrix}\right)$

$$\frac{2\omega^{a-b}}{\sigma^{2(s+a-b)}}\,\sin\left[(s+a-b)\,\pi\right]\Gamma\left[\begin{matrix} b,\ 2a-2b+2s \\ a \end{matrix}\right]$$

$$\times\, {}_2F_2\left(\begin{matrix} 1-a,\ b-a;\ -\frac{\sigma^2}{4\omega} \\ \frac{2b-2a-2s+1}{2},\ b-a-s+1 \end{matrix}\right)$$

$$+\frac{\sigma}{\omega^{s+1/2}}\ \mathrm{B}\left(\frac{2b-2a-2s-1}{2},\ \frac{2s+1}{2}\right)\Gamma\left[\begin{matrix} b \\ \frac{2b-2s-1}{2} \end{matrix}\right]$$

$$\times\, {}_2F_2\left(\begin{matrix} \frac{2s+1}{2},\ \frac{2s-2b+3}{2} \\ \frac{3}{2},\ \frac{2a-2b+2s+3}{2};\ -\frac{\sigma^2}{4\omega} \end{matrix}\right)$$

$$\left[\begin{matrix} \sigma>0;\ (\mathrm{Re}\,\omega>0;\ -1/2<\mathrm{Re}\,s<\mathrm{Re}\,(b-a)+1/2)\ \text{or} \\ (\mathrm{Re}\,\omega=0;\ -1/2<\mathrm{Re}\,s<\mathrm{Re}\,a+1,\ \mathrm{Re}\,(b-a)+1/2) \end{matrix}\right]$$

10 $e^{-\omega x}\cos\left(\sigma\sqrt{x}\right)$

$\times\, {}_1F_1\left(\begin{matrix} a;\ \omega x \\ b \end{matrix}\right)$

$$\frac{2\omega^{a-b}}{\sigma^{2(a-b+s)}}\,\cos\left[(s+a-b)\,\pi\right]\Gamma\left[\begin{matrix} b,\ 2s+2a-2b \\ a \end{matrix}\right]$$

$$\times\, {}_2F_2\left(\begin{matrix} 1-a,\ b-a;\ -\frac{\sigma^2}{4\omega} \\ \frac{2b-2a-2s+1}{2},\ b-a-s+1 \end{matrix}\right)$$

$$+\omega^{-s}\ \mathrm{B}\left(b-a-s,\ s\right)\Gamma\left[\begin{matrix} b \\ b-s \end{matrix}\right]\, {}_2F_2\left(\begin{matrix} s,\ s-b+1;\ -\frac{\sigma^2}{4\omega} \\ \frac{1}{2},\ s+a-b+1 \end{matrix}\right)$$

$$\left[\begin{matrix} \sigma>0;\ (\mathrm{Re}\,\omega>0;\ 0<\mathrm{Re}\,s<\mathrm{Re}\,(b-a)+1/2)\ \text{or} \\ (\mathrm{Re}\,\omega=0;\ 0<\mathrm{Re}\,s<\mathrm{Re}\,a+1,\ \mathrm{Re}\,(b-a)+1/2) \end{matrix}\right]$$

11 $e^{-\omega x}\sin\dfrac{\sigma}{\sqrt{x}}\, {}_1F_1\left(\begin{matrix} a;\ \omega x \\ b \end{matrix}\right)$

$$\frac{\pi\sigma^{2s}\sec\left(s\pi\right)}{\Gamma\left(2s+1\right)}\, {}_1F_3\left(\begin{matrix} b-a;\ \frac{\sigma^2\omega}{4} \\ b,\ \frac{2s+1}{2},\ s+1 \end{matrix}\right)$$

$$-\frac{\pi\sigma\sec\left(s\pi\right)}{\omega^{s-1/2}}\Gamma\left[\begin{matrix} b,\ \frac{2b-2a-2s+1}{2} \\ b-a,\ \frac{3-2s}{2},\ \frac{2b-2s+1}{2} \end{matrix}\right]$$

$$\times\, {}_1F_3\left(\begin{matrix} \frac{2b-2a-2s+1}{2};\ \frac{\sigma^2\omega}{4} \\ \frac{3}{2},\ \frac{3-2s}{2},\ \frac{2b-2s+1}{2} \end{matrix}\right)$$

$$\left[\begin{matrix} \sigma>0;\ (\mathrm{Re}\,\omega>0;\ -1/2<\mathrm{Re}\,s<\mathrm{Re}\,(b-a)+1/2)\ \text{or} \\ (\mathrm{Re}\,\omega=0;\ -1/2<\mathrm{Re}\,s<\mathrm{Re}\,a+3/2,\ \mathrm{Re}\,(b-a)+1/2) \end{matrix}\right]$$

12 $e^{-\omega x}\cos\dfrac{\sigma}{\sqrt{x}}\, {}_1F_1\left(\begin{matrix} a;\ \omega x \\ b \end{matrix}\right)$

$$\frac{\pi\csc\left(s\pi\right)}{\omega^s}\Gamma\left[\begin{matrix} b,\ b-a-s \\ b-a,\ 1-s,\ b-s \end{matrix}\right]\, {}_1F_3\left(\begin{matrix} b-a-s;\ \frac{\sigma^2\omega}{4} \\ \frac{1}{2},\ 1-s,\ b-s \end{matrix}\right)$$

$$-\frac{\pi\sigma^{2s}\csc\left(s\pi\right)}{\Gamma\left(2s+1\right)}\, {}_1F_3\left(\begin{matrix} b-a;\ \frac{\sigma^2\omega}{4} \\ b,\ \frac{2s+1}{2},\ s+1 \end{matrix}\right)$$

$$\left[\begin{matrix} \sigma>0;\ (\mathrm{Re}\,\omega>0;\ -1/2<\mathrm{Re}\,s<\mathrm{Re}\,(b-a))\ \text{or} \\ (\mathrm{Re}\,\omega=0;\ -1/2<\mathrm{Re}\,s<\mathrm{Re}\,a+1,\ \mathrm{Re}\,(b-a)) \end{matrix}\right]$$

3.28.4. $_1F_1(a; b; \omega x)$ **and the logarithmic function**

1	$\ln(\sigma x + 1) \, _1F_1\left(\begin{matrix} a; -\omega x \\ b \end{matrix}\right)$	$\dfrac{\omega^{1-s}}{\sigma} \, \mathrm{B}(a-s+1, s-1) \, \Gamma\left[\begin{matrix} b \\ b-s+1 \end{matrix}\right] \, _3F_3\left(\begin{matrix} 1, 1, a-s+1; \frac{\omega}{\sigma} \\ 2, 2-s, b-s+1 \end{matrix}\right)$

$$+\,\omega^{-s}\,\mathrm{B}(s, a-s)\,\Gamma\left[\begin{matrix} b \\ b-s \end{matrix}\right]\left[\ln\sigma - \ln\omega - \psi(a-s)\right.$$

$$\left.+\,\psi(b-s)+\psi(s)\right] + \frac{\pi\csc(s\pi)}{\sigma^s s}\,_2F_2\left(\begin{matrix} a, s; \frac{\omega}{\sigma} \\ b, s+1 \end{matrix}\right)$$

$$\left[\begin{matrix} (\mathrm{Re}\,\omega > 0;\; -1 < \mathrm{Re}\,s < \mathrm{Re}\,a)\text{ or} \\ (\mathrm{Re}\,\omega = 0;\; -1 < \mathrm{Re}\,s < \mathrm{Re}\,a,\; \mathrm{Re}(b-a)+1);\; |\arg\sigma| < \pi \end{matrix}\right]$$

2	$\ln|\sigma x - 1| \, _1F_1\left(\begin{matrix} a; -\omega x \\ b \end{matrix}\right)$	$-\dfrac{\omega^{1-s}}{\sigma}\,\mathrm{B}(a-s+1, s-1)$

$$\times\,\Gamma\left[\begin{matrix} b \\ b-s+1 \end{matrix}\right]\,_3F_3\left(\begin{matrix} 1, 1, a-s+1; -\frac{\omega}{\sigma} \\ 2, 2-s, b-s+1 \end{matrix}\right)$$

$$+\,\omega^{-s}\,\mathrm{B}(s, a-s)\,\Gamma\left[\begin{matrix} b \\ b-s \end{matrix}\right]\left[\ln\sigma - \ln\omega - \psi(a-s)\right.$$

$$\left.+\,\psi(b-s)+\psi(s)\right] + \frac{\pi\sigma^{-s}}{s}\cot(s\pi)\,_2F_2\left(\begin{matrix} a, s; -\frac{\omega}{\sigma} \\ b, s+1 \end{matrix}\right)$$

$$\left[\begin{matrix} \sigma > 0;\; (\mathrm{Re}\,\omega > 0;\; -1 < \mathrm{Re}\,s < \mathrm{Re}\,a)\text{ or} \\ (\mathrm{Re}\,\omega = 0;\; -1 < \mathrm{Re}\,s < \mathrm{Re}\,a,\; \mathrm{Re}(b-a)+1) \end{matrix}\right]$$

3	$e^{-\omega x}\ln(\sigma x + 1)$	$\dfrac{\omega^{1-s}}{\sigma}\,\mathrm{B}(b-a-s+1, s-1)\,\Gamma\left[\begin{matrix} b \\ b-s+1 \end{matrix}\right]$
	$\times\,_1F_1\left(\begin{matrix} a; \omega x \\ b \end{matrix}\right)$	$\times\,_3F_3\left(\begin{matrix} 1, 1, b-a-s+1; \frac{\omega}{\sigma} \\ 2, 2-s, b-s+1 \end{matrix}\right) + \omega^{-s}\,\mathrm{B}(s, b-a-s)$

$$\times\,\Gamma\left[\begin{matrix} b \\ b-s \end{matrix}\right]\left[\ln\sigma - \ln\omega - \psi(b-a-s)\right.$$

$$\left.+\,\psi(b-s)+\psi(s)\right] + \frac{\pi\csc(s\pi)}{\sigma^s s}\,_2F_2\left(\begin{matrix} b-a, s; \frac{\omega}{\sigma} \\ b, s+1 \end{matrix}\right)$$

$$\left[\begin{matrix} (\mathrm{Re}\,\omega > 0;\; -1 < \mathrm{Re}\,s < \mathrm{Re}(b-a)+1)\text{ or} \\ (\mathrm{Re}\,\omega = 0;\; -1 < \mathrm{Re}\,s < \mathrm{Re}\,a+1,\; \mathrm{Re}(b-a)+1);\; |\arg\sigma| < \pi \end{matrix}\right]$$

4	$e^{-\omega x}\ln|\sigma x - 1|$	$-\dfrac{\omega^{1-s}}{\sigma}\,\mathrm{B}(b-a-s+1, s-1)\,\Gamma\left[\begin{matrix} b \\ b-s+1 \end{matrix}\right]$
	$\times\,_1F_1\left(\begin{matrix} a; \omega x \\ b \end{matrix}\right)$	$\times\,_3F_3\left(\begin{matrix} 1, 1, b-a-s+1; -\frac{\omega}{\sigma} \\ 2, 2-s, b-s+1 \end{matrix}\right) + \omega^{-s}\,\mathrm{B}(b-a-s, s)\,\Gamma\left[\begin{matrix} b \\ b-s \end{matrix}\right]$

$$\times\,(\ln\sigma - \ln\omega) - \omega^{-s}\,\mathrm{B}(b-a-s, s)\,\Gamma\left[\begin{matrix} b \\ b-s \end{matrix}\right]\left[\psi(b-a-s)\right.$$

$$\left.-\,\psi(b-s)-\psi(s)\right] + \frac{\pi\sigma^{-s}}{s}\cot(s\pi)\,_2F_2\left(\begin{matrix} b-a, s; -\frac{\omega}{\sigma} \\ b, s+1 \end{matrix}\right)$$

$$\left[\begin{matrix} \sigma > 0;\; (\mathrm{Re}\,\omega > 0;\; -1 < \mathrm{Re}\,s < \mathrm{Re}\,a)\text{ or} \\ (\mathrm{Re}\,\omega = 0;\; -1 < \mathrm{Re}\,s < \mathrm{Re}\,a,\; \mathrm{Re}(b-a)+1) \end{matrix}\right]$$

3.28.5. $_1F_1\left(a;\,b;\,\omega x\right)$ **and** $\mathrm{erf}\left(\sigma\sqrt{x}\right)$, $\mathrm{erfc}\left(\sigma\sqrt{x}\right)$

1	$\mathrm{erf}\left(\sigma\sqrt{x}\right)\,_1F_1\!\left(\begin{matrix}a;\,-\omega x\\b\end{matrix}\right)$	$\omega^{-s}\,\mathrm{B}\left(a-s,\,s\right)\Gamma\!\begin{bmatrix}b\\b-s\end{bmatrix}$

$$-\frac{\sigma^{-2s}}{\sqrt{\pi}s}\,\Gamma\!\left(\frac{2s+1}{2}\right)\,_3F_2\!\left(\begin{matrix}a,\,s,\,\frac{2s+1}{2}\\b,\,s+1;\,-\frac{\omega}{\sigma^2}\end{matrix}\right)$$

$$\left[\begin{matrix}(\mathrm{Re}\,\omega>0;\,-1/2<\mathrm{Re}\,s<\mathrm{Re}\,a)\text{ or}\\(\mathrm{Re}\,\omega=0;\,-1/2<\mathrm{Re}\,s<\mathrm{Re}\,a,\,\mathrm{Re}\,(b-a)+1)\,;\,|\arg\sigma|<\pi/4\end{matrix}\right]$$

2	$\mathrm{erfc}\left(\sigma\sqrt{x}\right)\,_1F_1\!\left(\begin{matrix}a;\,\omega x\\b\end{matrix}\right)$	$\dfrac{\sigma^{-2s}}{\sqrt{\pi}s}\,\Gamma\!\left(\dfrac{2s+1}{2}\right)\,_3F_2\!\left(\begin{matrix}a,\,s,\,\frac{2s+1}{2}\\b,\,s+1;\,\frac{\omega}{\sigma^2}\end{matrix}\right)$

$$\left[\begin{matrix}\left(\mathrm{Re}\left(\sigma^2-\omega\right)>0;\,\mathrm{Re}\,s>0;\,|\arg\sigma|<\pi/4\right)\text{ or}\\\left(\mathrm{Re}\,\omega<0;\,0<\mathrm{Re}\,s<\mathrm{Re}\,a+3/2;\,|\arg\sigma|=\pi/4\right)\text{ or}\\\left(\mathrm{Re}\left(\sigma^2-\omega\right)=0;\,0<\mathrm{Re}\,s<\mathrm{Re}\,(b-a)+3/2;\,|\arg\sigma|<\pi/4\right)\text{ or}\\\left(\mathrm{Re}\left(\sigma^2-\omega\right)=0;\,0<\mathrm{Re}\,s<\mathrm{Re}\,a,\,\mathrm{Re}\,(b-a)+3/2;\,|\arg\sigma|=\pi/4\right)\end{matrix}\right]$$

3	$e^{-\omega x}\,\mathrm{erf}\left(\sigma\sqrt{x}\right)$ $\times\,_1F_1\!\left(\begin{matrix}a;\,\omega x\\b\end{matrix}\right)$	$\omega^{-s}\,\mathrm{B}\left(b-a-s,\,s\right)\Gamma\!\begin{bmatrix}b\\b-s\end{bmatrix}$

$$-\frac{\sigma^{-2s}}{\sqrt{\pi}s}\,\Gamma\!\left(\frac{2s+1}{2}\right)\,_3F_2\!\left(\begin{matrix}b-a,\,s,\,\frac{2s+1}{2}\\b,\,s+1;\,-\frac{\omega}{\sigma^2}\end{matrix}\right)$$

$$\left[\begin{matrix}(\mathrm{Re}\,\omega>0;\,-1/2<\mathrm{Re}\,s<\mathrm{Re}\,(b-a))\text{ or}\\(\mathrm{Re}\,\omega=0;\,-1/2<\mathrm{Re}\,s<\mathrm{Re}\,a+1,\,\mathrm{Re}\,(b-a))\,;\,|\arg\sigma|<\pi/4\end{matrix}\right]$$

4	$e^{-\omega x}\,\mathrm{erfc}\left(\sigma\sqrt{x}\right)$ $\times\,_1F_1\!\left(\begin{matrix}a;\,\omega x\\b\end{matrix}\right)$	$\dfrac{\sigma^{-2s}}{\sqrt{\pi}s}\,\Gamma\!\left(\dfrac{2s+1}{2}\right)\,_3F_2\!\left(\begin{matrix}b-a,\,s,\,\frac{2s+1}{2}\\b,\,s+1;\,\frac{\omega}{\sigma^2}\end{matrix}\right)$

$$\left[\begin{matrix}\left(\mathrm{Re}\left(\sigma^2+\omega\right)>0;\,\mathrm{Re}\,s>0;\,|\arg\sigma|<\pi/4\right)\text{ or}\\\left(\mathrm{Re}\,\omega>0;\,0<\mathrm{Re}\,s<\mathrm{Re}\,(b-a)+3/2;\,|\arg\sigma|=\pi/4\right)\text{ or}\\\left(\mathrm{Re}\left(\sigma^2+\omega\right)=0;\,0<\mathrm{Re}\,s<\mathrm{Re}\,a+3/2;\,|\arg\sigma|<\pi/4\right)\text{ or}\\\left(\mathrm{Re}\left(\sigma^2+\omega\right)=0;\,0<\mathrm{Re}\,s<\mathrm{Re}\,a,\,\mathrm{Re}\,(b-a)+3/2;\,|\arg\sigma|=\pi/4\right)\end{matrix}\right]$$

3.28.6. $_1F_1\left(a;\,b;\,\omega x\right)$ **and the Bessel functions**

1	$J_\nu\left(\sigma x\right)\,_1F_1\!\left(\begin{matrix}a;\,-\omega x\\b\end{matrix}\right)$	$2^{s-1}\omega^{-s}\left(\dfrac{\sigma^2}{\omega^2}\right)^{-s/2}\Gamma\!\begin{bmatrix}\frac{s+\nu}{2}\\\frac{2-s+\nu}{2}\end{bmatrix}\,_4F_3\!\left(\begin{matrix}\frac{a}{2},\,\frac{a+1}{2},\,\frac{s-\nu}{2},\,\frac{s+\nu}{2}\\\frac{1}{2},\,\frac{b}{2},\,\frac{b+1}{2};\,-\frac{\omega^2}{\sigma^2}\end{matrix}\right)$

$$-\frac{2^s a}{b\sigma^2}\,\omega^{2-s}\left(\frac{\sigma^2}{\omega^2}\right)^{(1-s)/2}\Gamma\!\begin{bmatrix}\frac{s+\nu+1}{2}\\\frac{1-s+\nu}{2}\end{bmatrix}$$

$$\times\,_4F_3\!\left(\begin{matrix}\frac{a+1}{2},\,\frac{a+2}{2},\,\frac{s-\nu+1}{2},\,\frac{s+\nu+1}{2}\\\frac{3}{2},\,\frac{b+1}{2},\,\frac{b+2}{2};\,-\frac{\omega^2}{\sigma^2}\end{matrix}\right)$$

$$\left[\begin{matrix}\sigma>0;\,(\mathrm{Re}\,\omega>0;\,-\mathrm{Re}\,\nu<\mathrm{Re}\,s<\mathrm{Re}\,a+3/2)\text{ or}\\(\mathrm{Re}\,\omega=0;\,-\mathrm{Re}\,\nu<\mathrm{Re}\,s<\mathrm{Re}\,a+3/2,\,\mathrm{Re}\,(b-a)+3/2)\end{matrix}\right]$$

No.	$f(x)$	$F(s)$
2	$J_\nu(\sigma\sqrt{x})\,{}_1F_1\left(\begin{matrix}a;\ -\omega x\\ b\end{matrix}\right)$	$\dfrac{2^{2s-2a}}{\sigma^{2s}}\left(\dfrac{\omega}{\sigma^2}\right)^{-a}\Gamma\left[\begin{matrix}b,\ \frac{2s-2a+\nu}{2}\\ b-a,\ \frac{2a-2s+\nu+2}{2}\end{matrix}\right]\,{}_2F_2\left(\begin{matrix}a,\ a-b+1;\ -\frac{\sigma^2}{4\omega}\\ \frac{2a-2s-\nu+2}{2},\ \frac{2a-2s+\nu+2}{2}\end{matrix}\right)$

$$+\frac{\sigma^{-2s}}{2^\nu}\left(\frac{\omega}{\sigma^2}\right)^{-s-\nu/2}B\left(a-s-\frac{\nu}{2},\,s+\frac{\nu}{2}\right)$$

$$\times\,\Gamma\left[\begin{matrix}b\\ \nu+1,\ \frac{2b-2s-\nu}{2}\end{matrix}\right]\,{}_2F_2\left(\begin{matrix}\frac{2s+\nu}{2},\ \frac{2s-2b+\nu+2}{2}\\ \nu+1,\ \frac{2s-2a+\nu+2}{2};\ -\frac{\sigma^2}{4\omega}\end{matrix}\right)$$

$$\left[\begin{matrix}\sigma>0;\ (\operatorname{Re}\omega>0;\ -\operatorname{Re}\nu<\operatorname{Re}s<\operatorname{Re}a+3/4)\ \text{or}\\ (\operatorname{Re}\omega=0;\ -\operatorname{Re}\nu<\operatorname{Re}s<\operatorname{Re}a+3/4,\ \operatorname{Re}(b-a)+5/4)\end{matrix}\right]$$

No.	$f(x)$	$F(s)$
3	$J_\nu\left(\dfrac{\sigma}{\sqrt{x}}\right){}_1F_1\left(\begin{matrix}a;\ -\omega x\\ b\end{matrix}\right)$	$\dfrac{\sigma^{2s}}{2^{2s}}\Gamma\left[\begin{matrix}\frac{\nu-2s}{2}\\ \frac{2s+\nu+2}{2}\end{matrix}\right]\,{}_1F_3\left(\begin{matrix}a;\ \frac{\sigma^2\omega}{4}\\ b,\ \frac{2s-\nu+2}{2},\ \frac{2s+\nu+2}{2}\end{matrix}\right)$

$$+\frac{\omega^{-s}}{2^\nu}\left(\frac{1}{\sigma^2\omega}\right)^{-\nu/2}B\left(\frac{2s-\nu}{2},\,\frac{2a-2s+\nu}{2}\right)$$

$$\times\,\Gamma\left[\begin{matrix}b\\ \nu+1,\ \frac{2b-2s+\nu}{2}\end{matrix}\right]\,{}_1F_3\left(\begin{matrix}\frac{2a-2s+\nu};\ \frac{\sigma^2\omega}{4}\\ \nu+1,\ \frac{\nu-2s+2}{2},\ \frac{2b-2s+\nu}{2}\end{matrix}\right)$$

$$\left[\begin{matrix}\sigma>0;\ (\operatorname{Re}\omega>0;\ 3/4<\operatorname{Re}s<\operatorname{Re}(a+\nu/2)+1/4)\ \text{or}\\ (\operatorname{Re}\omega=0;\ 3/4<\operatorname{Re}s<\operatorname{Re}(a+\nu/2)+1/4,\ \operatorname{Re}(b-a-\nu/2)+5/4)\end{matrix}\right]$$

No.	$f(x)$	$F(s)$
4	$Y_\nu(\sigma x)\,{}_1F_1\left(\begin{matrix}a;\ -\omega x\\ b\end{matrix}\right)$	$-\dfrac{2^s a}{b\pi}\,\omega^{-s}\left(\dfrac{\sigma^2}{\omega^2}\right)^{-(s+1)/2}\sin\dfrac{(s-\nu)\pi}{2}\,\Gamma\left(\dfrac{s-\nu+1}{2}\right)$

$$\times\,\Gamma\left(\frac{s+\nu+1}{2}\right){}_4F_3\left(\begin{matrix}\frac{a+1}{2},\ \frac{a+2}{2},\ \frac{s-\nu+1}{2},\ \frac{s+\nu+1}{2}\\ \frac{3}{2},\ \frac{b+1}{2},\ \frac{b+2}{2};\ -\frac{\omega^2}{\sigma^2}\end{matrix}\right)$$

$$-\frac{2^{s-1}}{\pi}\,\omega^{-s}\left(\frac{\sigma^2}{\omega^2}\right)^{-s/2}\cos\frac{(s-\nu)\pi}{2}\,\Gamma\left(\frac{s-\nu}{2}\right)$$

$$\times\,\Gamma\left(\frac{s+\nu}{2}\right){}_4F_3\left(\begin{matrix}\frac{a}{2},\ \frac{a+1}{2},\ \frac{s-\nu}{2},\ \frac{s+\nu}{2}\\ \frac{1}{2},\ \frac{b}{2},\ \frac{b+1}{2};\ -\frac{\omega^2}{\sigma^2}\end{matrix}\right)$$

$$\left[\begin{matrix}\sigma>0;\ (\operatorname{Re}\omega>0;\ |\operatorname{Re}\nu|<\operatorname{Re}s<\operatorname{Re}a+3/2)\ \text{or}\\ (\operatorname{Re}\omega=0;\ |\operatorname{Re}\nu|<\operatorname{Re}s<\operatorname{Re}a+3/2,\ \operatorname{Re}(b-a)+3/2)\end{matrix}\right]$$

No.	$f(x)$	$F(s)$
5	$Y_\nu(\sigma\sqrt{x})\,{}_1F_1\left(\begin{matrix}a;\ -\omega x\\ b\end{matrix}\right)$	$-\dfrac{2^{2s-2a}}{\pi}\,\sigma^{-2s}\left(\dfrac{\omega}{\sigma^2}\right)^{-a}\cos\dfrac{(2s-2a-\nu)\pi}{2}$

$$\times\,\Gamma\left[\begin{matrix}b,\ \frac{2s-2a-\nu}{2},\ \frac{2s-2a+\nu}{2}\\ b-a\end{matrix}\right]\,{}_2F_2\left(\begin{matrix}a,\ a-b+1;\ -\frac{\sigma^2}{4\omega}\\ \frac{2a-2s-\nu+2}{2},\ \frac{2a-2s+\nu+2}{2}\end{matrix}\right)$$

$$-\frac{\sigma^{-2s}}{2^\nu\pi}\left(\frac{\omega}{\sigma^2}\right)^{-s-\nu/2}\cos(\pi\nu)\,B\left(\frac{2a-2s-\nu}{2},\,\frac{2s+\nu}{2}\right)$$

$$\times\,\Gamma\left[\begin{matrix}b,\ -\nu\\ \frac{2b-2s-\nu}{2}\end{matrix}\right]\,{}_2F_2\left(\begin{matrix}\frac{2s+\nu}{2},\ \frac{2s-2b+\nu+2}{2}\\ \nu+1,\ \frac{2s+2a+\nu+2}{2};\ -\frac{\sigma^2}{4\omega}\end{matrix}\right)$$

$$-\,2^\nu\sigma^{-2s}\left(\frac{\omega}{\sigma^2}\right)^{\nu/2-s}B\left(\frac{2a-2s+\nu}{2},\,\frac{2s-\nu}{2}\right)\times$$

No.	$f(x)$	$F(s)$

| | | $\times \csc(\pi\nu)\,\Gamma\!\left[\begin{matrix} b \\ 1-\nu,\ \frac{2b-2s+\nu}{2} \end{matrix}\right]\ {}_2F_2\!\left(\begin{matrix} \frac{2s-\nu}{2},\ \frac{2s-2b-\nu+2}{2} \\ 1-\nu,\ \frac{2s-2a-\nu+2}{2};\ -\frac{\sigma^2}{4\omega} \end{matrix}\right)$ |
| | | $\left[\begin{matrix} \sigma>0;\ (\operatorname{Re}\omega>0;\ |\operatorname{Re}\nu|<\operatorname{Re}s<\operatorname{Re}a+3/4)\ \text{or} \\ (\operatorname{Re}\omega=0;\ |\operatorname{Re}\nu|<\operatorname{Re}s<\operatorname{Re}a+3/4,\ \operatorname{Re}(b-a)+5/4) \end{matrix}\right]$ |

6	$K_\nu(\sigma x)\,{}_1F_1\!\left(\begin{matrix} a;\ -\omega x \\ b \end{matrix}\right)$	$\dfrac{2^{s-2}}{\omega^s}\left(\dfrac{\sigma^2}{\omega^2}\right)^{-s/2}\Gamma\!\left(\dfrac{s-\nu}{2}\right)\Gamma\!\left(\dfrac{s+\nu}{2}\right)\ {}_4F_3\!\left(\begin{matrix} \frac{a}{2},\ \frac{a+1}{2},\ \frac{s-\nu}{2},\ \frac{s+\nu}{2} \\ \frac{1}{2},\ \frac{b}{2},\ \frac{b+1}{2};\ \frac{\omega^2}{\sigma^2} \end{matrix}\right)$
		$\quad-\dfrac{2^{s-1}a}{b\omega^s}\left(\dfrac{\sigma^2}{\omega^2}\right)^{-(s+1)/2}\Gamma\!\left(\dfrac{s-\nu+1}{2}\right)\Gamma\!\left(\dfrac{s+\nu+1}{2}\right)$
		$\quad\times\ {}_4F_3\!\left(\begin{matrix} \frac{a+1}{2},\ \frac{a+2}{2},\ \frac{s-\nu+1}{2},\ \frac{s+\nu+1}{2} \\ \frac{3}{2},\ \frac{b+1}{2},\ \frac{b+2}{2};\ \frac{\omega^2}{\sigma^2} \end{matrix}\right)$
		$\left[\begin{matrix} (\operatorname{Re}\sigma>0,\ \operatorname{Re}(\sigma+\omega)>0;\ |\operatorname{Re}\nu|<\operatorname{Re}s)\ \text{or} \\ (\operatorname{Re}\sigma=0,\ \operatorname{Re}\omega>0;\ |\operatorname{Re}\nu|<\operatorname{Re}s<\operatorname{Re}a+3/2)\ \text{or} \\ (\operatorname{Re}\sigma=0,\ \operatorname{Re}\omega=0;\ |\operatorname{Re}\nu|<\operatorname{Re}s<\operatorname{Re}a+3/2,\ \operatorname{Re}(b-a)+3/2) \end{matrix}\right]$

7	$K_\nu(\sigma\sqrt{x})\,{}_1F_1\!\left(\begin{matrix} a;\ -\omega x \\ b \end{matrix}\right)$	$2^{2s-2a-1}\sigma^{-2s}\left(\dfrac{\omega}{\sigma^2}\right)^{-a}\Gamma\!\left[\begin{matrix} b,\ \frac{2s-2a-\nu}{2},\ \frac{2s-2a+\nu}{2} \\ b-a \end{matrix}\right]$
		$\quad\times\ {}_2F_2\!\left(\begin{matrix} a,\ a-b+1;\ \frac{\sigma^2}{4\omega} \\ \frac{2a-2s-\nu+2}{2},\ \frac{2a-2s+\nu+2}{2} \end{matrix}\right)$
		$\quad+\dfrac{\sigma^{-2s}}{2^{\nu+1}}\left(\dfrac{\omega}{\sigma^2}\right)^{-s-\nu/2}\mathrm{B}\!\left(\dfrac{2a-2s-\nu}{2},\ \dfrac{2s+\nu}{2}\right)\Gamma\!\left[\begin{matrix} -\nu,\ b \\ \frac{2b-2s-\nu}{2} \end{matrix}\right]$
		$\quad\times\ {}_2F_2\!\left(\begin{matrix} \frac{2s+\nu}{2},\ \frac{2s-2b+\nu+2}{2};\ \frac{\sigma^2}{4\omega} \\ \nu+1,\ \frac{2s-2a+\nu+2}{2} \end{matrix}\right)$
		$\quad+\dfrac{2^{\nu-1}}{\sigma^{2s}}\left(\dfrac{\omega}{\sigma^2}\right)^{\nu/2-s}\mathrm{B}\!\left(\dfrac{2a-2s+\nu}{2},\ \dfrac{2s-\nu}{2}\right)\Gamma\!\left[\begin{matrix} \nu,\ b \\ \frac{2b-2s+\nu}{2} \end{matrix}\right]$
		$\quad\times\ {}_2F_2\!\left(\begin{matrix} \frac{2s-\nu}{2},\ \frac{2s-2b-\nu+2}{2};\ \frac{\sigma^2}{4\omega} \\ 1-\nu,\ \frac{2s-2a-\nu+2}{2} \end{matrix}\right)$
		$\left[\begin{matrix} (\operatorname{Re}\sigma>0,\ \operatorname{Re}\omega\geq0;\ |\operatorname{Re}\nu|<\operatorname{Re}s)\ \text{or} \\ (\operatorname{Re}\sigma=0,\ \operatorname{Re}\omega>0;\ |\operatorname{Re}\nu|<\operatorname{Re}s<\operatorname{Re}a+1/2)\ \text{or} \\ (\operatorname{Re}\sigma=0,\ \operatorname{Re}\omega=0;\ |\operatorname{Re}\nu|<\operatorname{Re}s<\operatorname{Re}a+1/2,\ \operatorname{Re}(b-a)+1) \end{matrix}\right]$

8	$e^{-\omega x}J_\nu(\sigma x)\,{}_1F_1\!\left(\begin{matrix} a;\ \omega x \\ b \end{matrix}\right)$	$\dfrac{2^s(a-b)}{b}\,\omega^{-s}\left(\dfrac{\sigma^2}{\omega^2}\right)^{-(s+1)/2}\Gamma\!\left[\begin{matrix} \frac{s+\nu+1}{2} \\ \frac{1-s+\nu}{2} \end{matrix}\right]$
		$\quad\times\ {}_4F_3\!\left(\begin{matrix} \frac{b-a+1}{2},\ \frac{b-a+2}{2},\ \frac{s-\nu+1}{2},\ \frac{s+\nu+1}{2} \\ \frac{3}{2},\ \frac{b+1}{2},\ \frac{b+2}{2};\ -\frac{\omega^2}{\sigma^2} \end{matrix}\right)$
		$\quad+\dfrac{2^{s-1}}{\omega^s}\left(\dfrac{\sigma^2}{\omega^2}\right)^{-s/2}\Gamma\!\left[\begin{matrix} \frac{s+\nu}{2} \\ \frac{2-s+\nu}{2} \end{matrix}\right]\ {}_4F_3\!\left(\begin{matrix} \frac{b-a}{2},\ \frac{b-a+1}{2},\ \frac{s-\nu}{2},\ \frac{s+\nu}{2} \\ \frac{1}{2},\ \frac{b}{2},\ \frac{b+1}{2};\ -\frac{\omega^2}{\sigma^2} \end{matrix}\right)$
		$\left[\begin{matrix} \sigma>0;\ (\operatorname{Re}\omega>0;\ -\operatorname{Re}\nu<\operatorname{Re}s<\operatorname{Re}(b-a)+3/2)\ \text{or} \\ (\operatorname{Re}\omega=0;\ -\operatorname{Re}\nu<\operatorname{Re}s<\operatorname{Re}a+3/2,\ \operatorname{Re}(b-a)+3/2) \end{matrix}\right]$

No.	$f(x)$	$F(s)$
9	$e^{-\omega x} J_\nu\left(\sigma\sqrt{x}\right)$ $\times {}_1F_1\left(\begin{matrix} a;\ \omega x \\ b \end{matrix}\right)$	$\dfrac{2^{2s+2a-2b}}{\sigma^{2s}}\left(\dfrac{\omega}{\sigma^2}\right)^{a-b}\Gamma\left[\begin{matrix} b,\ \frac{2s+2a-2b+\nu}{2} \\ a,\ \frac{2b-2a-2s+\nu+2}{2} \end{matrix}\right]$ $\times {}_2F_2\left(\begin{matrix} 1-a,\ b-a;\ -\frac{\sigma^2}{4\omega} \\ b-a-s-\frac{\nu}{2}+1,\ b-a-s+\frac{\nu}{2}+1 \end{matrix}\right)$ $+\dfrac{\sigma^{-2s}}{2^\nu}\left(\dfrac{\omega}{\sigma^2}\right)^{-s-\nu/2}\mathrm{B}\left(\dfrac{2b-2a-2s-\nu}{2},\ \dfrac{2s+\nu}{2}\right)$ $\times\Gamma\left[\begin{matrix} b \\ \nu+1,\ b-s-\frac{\nu}{2} \end{matrix}\right]{}_2F_2\left(\begin{matrix} \frac{2s+\nu}{2},\ \frac{2s-2b+\nu+2}{2};\ -\frac{\sigma^2}{4\omega} \\ \nu+1,\ \frac{2s+2a-2b+\nu+2}{2} \end{matrix}\right)$ $\left[\begin{matrix} \sigma>0;\ (\mathrm{Re}\,\omega>0;\ -\mathrm{Re}\,\nu<\mathrm{Re}\,s<\mathrm{Re}\,(b-a)+3/4)\ \text{or} \\ (\mathrm{Re}\,\omega=0;\ -\mathrm{Re}\,\nu<\mathrm{Re}\,s<\mathrm{Re}\,a+5/4,\ \mathrm{Re}\,(b-a)+3/4) \end{matrix}\right]$
10	$e^{-\omega x} J_\nu\left(\dfrac{\sigma}{\sqrt{x}}\right)$ $\times {}_1F_1\left(\begin{matrix} a;\ \omega x \\ b \end{matrix}\right)$	$\dfrac{\sigma^{2s}}{2^{2s}}\Gamma\left[\begin{matrix} \frac{\nu}{2}-s \\ s+\frac{\nu}{2}+1 \end{matrix}\right]{}_1F_3\left(\begin{matrix} b-a;\ \frac{\sigma^2\omega}{4} \\ b,\ s-\frac{\nu}{2}+1,\ s+\frac{\nu}{2}+1 \end{matrix}\right)$ $+\dfrac{\omega^{-s}}{2^\nu}\left(\dfrac{1}{\sigma^2\omega}\right)^{-\nu/2}\mathrm{B}\left(\dfrac{2s-\nu}{2},\ \dfrac{2b-2a-2s+\nu}{2}\right)$ $\times\Gamma\left[\begin{matrix} b \\ \nu+1,\ \frac{2b-2s+\nu}{2} \end{matrix}\right]{}_1F_3\left(\begin{matrix} \frac{2b-2a-2s+\nu}{2};\ \frac{\sigma^2\omega}{4} \\ \nu+1,\ \frac{\nu-2s+2}{2},\ \frac{2b-2s+\nu}{2} \end{matrix}\right)$ $\left[\begin{matrix} \sigma>0;\ (\mathrm{Re}\,\omega>0;\ 3/4<\mathrm{Re}\,s<\mathrm{Re}\,(b-a+\nu/2)+1/4)\ \text{or} \\ (\mathrm{Re}\,\omega=0;\ 3/4<\mathrm{Re}\,s<\mathrm{Re}\,(a-\nu/2)+5/4,\ \mathrm{Re}\,(b-a+\nu/2)+1/4) \end{matrix}\right]$
11	$e^{-\omega x} Y_\nu\left(\sigma x\right) {}_1F_1\left(\begin{matrix} a;\ \omega x \\ b \end{matrix}\right)$	$-\dfrac{2^s(b-a)}{b\pi\omega^s}\left(\dfrac{\sigma^2}{\omega^2}\right)^{-(s+1)/2}\sin\dfrac{(s-\nu)\pi}{2}\Gamma\left(\dfrac{s-\nu+1}{2}\right)$ $\times\Gamma\left(\dfrac{s+\nu+1}{2}\right){}_4F_3\left(\begin{matrix} \frac{b-a+1}{2},\ \frac{b-a+2}{2},\ \frac{s-\nu+1}{2},\ \frac{s+\nu+1}{2} \\ \frac{3}{2},\ \frac{b+1}{2},\ \frac{b+2}{2};\ -\frac{\omega^2}{\sigma^2} \end{matrix}\right)$ $-\dfrac{2^{s-1}}{\pi\omega^s}\left(\dfrac{\sigma^2}{\omega^2}\right)^{-s/2}\cos\dfrac{(s-\nu)\pi}{2}\Gamma\left(\dfrac{s-\nu}{2}\right)$ $\times\Gamma\left(\dfrac{s+\nu}{2}\right){}_4F_3\left(\begin{matrix} \frac{b-a}{2},\ \frac{b-a+1}{2},\ \frac{s-\nu}{2},\ \frac{s+\nu}{2} \\ \frac{1}{2},\ \frac{b+1}{2},\ \frac{b}{2};\ -\frac{\omega^2}{\sigma^2} \end{matrix}\right)$ $\left[\begin{matrix} \sigma>0;\ (\mathrm{Re}\,\omega>0;\ |\mathrm{Re}\,\nu|<\mathrm{Re}\,s<\mathrm{Re}\,(b-a)+3/2)\ \text{or} \\ (\mathrm{Re}\,\omega=0;\ |\mathrm{Re}\,\nu|<\mathrm{Re}\,s<\mathrm{Re}\,a+3/2,\ \mathrm{Re}\,(b-a)+3/2) \end{matrix}\right]$
12	$e^{-\omega x} Y_\nu\left(\sigma\sqrt{x}\right)$ $\times {}_1F_1\left(\begin{matrix} a;\ \omega x \\ b \end{matrix}\right)$	$-\dfrac{2^{2(s+a-b)}}{\pi}\sigma^{-2s}\left(\dfrac{\omega}{\sigma^2}\right)^{a-b}\cos\dfrac{(2s+2a-2b-\nu)\pi}{2}$ $\times\Gamma\left[\begin{matrix} b,\ \frac{2s+2a-2b-\nu}{2},\ \frac{2s+2a-2b+\nu}{2} \\ a \end{matrix}\right]$ $\times {}_2F_2\left(\begin{matrix} 1-a,\ b-a;\ -\frac{\sigma^2}{4\omega} \\ \frac{2b-2a-2s-\nu+2}{2},\ \frac{2b-2a-2s+\nu+2}{2} \end{matrix}\right)$ $-\dfrac{\sigma^{-2s}}{2^\nu\pi}\left(\dfrac{\omega}{\sigma^2}\right)^{-s-\nu/2}\cos(\nu\pi)\,\mathrm{B}\left(\dfrac{2b-2a-2s-\nu}{2},\ \dfrac{2s+\nu}{2}\right)\times$

No.	$f(x)$	$F(s)$

$$\times \Gamma\left[\begin{array}{c} -\nu,\, b \\ \frac{2b-2s-\nu}{2} \end{array}\right] {}_2F_2\left(\begin{array}{c} \frac{2s+\nu}{2},\, \frac{2s-2b+\nu+2}{2};\, -\frac{\sigma^2}{4\omega} \\ \nu+1,\, \frac{2s+2a-2b+\nu+2}{2} \end{array}\right)$$

$$-\frac{2^\nu}{\sigma^{2s}}\left(\frac{\omega}{\sigma^2}\right)^{\nu/2-s}\csc(\nu\pi)\,\mathrm{B}\left(\frac{2s-\nu}{2},\, \frac{2b-2a-2s+\nu}{2}\right)$$

$$\times \Gamma\left[\begin{array}{c} b \\ 1-\nu,\, \frac{2b-2s+\nu}{2} \end{array}\right] {}_2F_2\left(\begin{array}{c} \frac{2s-\nu}{2},\, \frac{2s-2b-\nu+2}{2};\, -\frac{\sigma^2}{4\omega} \\ 1-\nu,\, \frac{2s+2a-2b-\nu+2}{2} \end{array}\right)$$

$$\left[\begin{array}{l} \sigma>0;\ (\mathrm{Re}\,\omega>0;\ |\mathrm{Re}\,\nu|<\mathrm{Re}\,s<\mathrm{Re}\,(b-a)+3/4)\ \text{or} \\ (\mathrm{Re}\,\omega=0;\ |\mathrm{Re}\,\nu|<\mathrm{Re}\,s<\mathrm{Re}\,a+5/4,\ \mathrm{Re}\,(b-a)+3/4) \end{array}\right]$$

13 $\quad e^{-\omega x}K_\nu(\sigma x)\,{}_1F_1\left(\begin{array}{c} a;\,\omega x \\ b \end{array}\right)$
$\qquad \dfrac{2^{s-2}}{\omega^s}\left(\dfrac{\sigma^2}{\omega^2}\right)^{-s/2}\Gamma\left(\dfrac{s-\nu}{2}\right)\Gamma\left(\dfrac{s+\nu}{2}\right)$

$$\times {}_4F_3\left(\begin{array}{c} \frac{b-a}{2},\, \frac{b-a+1}{2},\, \frac{s-\nu}{2},\, \frac{s+\nu}{2} \\ \frac{1}{2},\, \frac{b}{2},\, \frac{b+1}{2};\, \frac{\omega^2}{\sigma^2} \end{array}\right)$$

$$+\frac{2^{s-1}(a-b)}{b\omega^s}\left(\frac{\sigma^2}{\omega^2}\right)^{-(s+1)/2}\Gamma\left(\frac{s-\nu+1}{2}\right)$$

$$\times\Gamma\left(\frac{s+\nu+1}{2}\right){}_4F_3\left(\begin{array}{c} \frac{b-a+1}{2},\, \frac{b-a+2}{2},\, \frac{s-\nu+1}{2},\, \frac{s+\nu+1}{2} \\ \frac{3}{2},\, \frac{b+1}{2},\, \frac{b+2}{2};\, \frac{\omega^2}{\sigma^2} \end{array}\right)$$

$$\left[\begin{array}{l} \left(\mathrm{Re}\,\sigma>0,\ \mathrm{Re}\,(\sigma+\omega)>0;\ |\mathrm{Re}\,\nu|<\mathrm{Re}\,s\right)\ \text{or} \\ \left(\mathrm{Re}\,\sigma=0,\ \mathrm{Re}\,\omega>0;\ |\mathrm{Re}\,\nu|<\mathrm{Re}\,s<\mathrm{Re}\,(b-a)+3/2\right)\ \text{or} \\ \left(\mathrm{Re}\,\sigma=0,\ \mathrm{Re}\,\omega=0;\ |\mathrm{Re}\,\nu|<\mathrm{Re}\,s<\mathrm{Re}\,a+3/2,\ \mathrm{Re}\,(b-a)+3/2\right) \end{array}\right]$$

14 $\quad e^{-\omega x}K_\nu(\sigma\sqrt{x})$
$\qquad 2^{2(s+a-b)-1}\sigma^{-2s}\left(\dfrac{\omega}{\sigma^2}\right)^{a-b}\Gamma\left[\begin{array}{c} b,\, \frac{2s+2a-2b-\nu}{2},\, \frac{2s+2a-2b+\nu}{2} \\ a \end{array}\right]$

$\qquad\qquad \times {}_1F_1\left(\begin{array}{c} a;\,\omega x \\ b \end{array}\right)$
$$\times {}_2F_2\left(\begin{array}{c} 1-a,\, b-a;\, \frac{\sigma^2}{4\omega} \\ \frac{2b-2a-2s-\nu}{2},\, \frac{2b-2a-2s+\nu+2}{2} \end{array}\right)$$

$$+\frac{\sigma^{-2s}}{2^{\nu+1}}\left(\frac{\omega}{\sigma^2}\right)^{-s-\nu/2}\mathrm{B}\left(\frac{2b-2a-2s-\nu}{2},\, \frac{2s+\nu}{2}\right)$$

$$\times\Gamma\left[\begin{array}{c} -\nu,\, b \\ \frac{2b-2s-\nu}{2} \end{array}\right]{}_2F_2\left(\begin{array}{c} \frac{2s+\nu}{2},\, \frac{2s-2b+\nu+2}{2};\, \frac{\sigma^2}{4\omega} \\ \nu+1,\, \frac{2s+2a-2b+\nu+2}{2} \end{array}\right)$$

$$+2^{\nu-1}\sigma^{-2s}\left(\frac{\omega}{\sigma^2}\right)^{\nu/2-s}\mathrm{B}\left(\frac{2s-\nu}{2},\, \frac{2b-2a-2s+\nu}{2}\right)$$

$$\times\Gamma\left[\begin{array}{c} \nu,\, b \\ \frac{2b-2s+\nu}{2} \end{array}\right]{}_2F_2\left(\begin{array}{c} \frac{2s-\nu}{2},\, \frac{2s-2b-\nu+2}{2};\, \frac{\sigma^2}{4\omega} \\ 1-\nu,\, \frac{2s+2a-2b-\nu+2}{2} \end{array}\right)$$

$$\left[\begin{array}{l} \left(\mathrm{Re}\,\sigma>0,\ \mathrm{Re}\,\omega\ge0;\ |\mathrm{Re}\,\nu|<\mathrm{Re}\,s\right)\ \text{or} \\ \left(\mathrm{Re}\,\sigma=0,\ \mathrm{Re}\,\omega>0;\ |\mathrm{Re}\,\nu|<\mathrm{Re}\,s<\mathrm{Re}\,(b-a)+1/2\right)\ \text{or} \\ \left(\mathrm{Re}\,\sigma=0,\ \mathrm{Re}\,\omega=0;\ |\mathrm{Re}\,\nu|<\mathrm{Re}\,s<\mathrm{Re}\,a+1,\ \mathrm{Re}\,(b-a)+1/2\right) \end{array}\right]$$

3.28.7. $_1F_1(a; b; \omega x)$ and the Struve functions

1	$\mathbf{H}_\nu\left(\sigma\sqrt{x}\right) {}_1F_1\left(\begin{matrix} a; \omega x \\ b \end{matrix}\right)$	$\dfrac{2^{2s-2a}\pi}{\omega^s}\left(\dfrac{\sigma^2}{\omega}\right)^{a-s}\Gamma\left[\begin{matrix} b \\ b-a,\ \frac{2a-2s-\nu+2}{2},\ \frac{2a-2s+\nu+2}{2} \end{matrix}\right]$

$$\times\csc\frac{(2s-2a+\nu+1)\pi}{2}\,{}_2F_2\left(\begin{matrix} a,\ a-b+1;\ -\frac{\sigma^2}{4\omega} \\ a-s-\frac{\nu}{2}+1,\ a-s+\frac{\nu}{2}+1 \end{matrix}\right)$$

$$+\frac{\omega^{-s}}{2^\nu\sqrt{\pi}}\left(\frac{\sigma^2}{\omega}\right)^{(\nu+1)/2}\mathrm{B}\left(\frac{2a-2s-\nu-1}{2},\ \frac{2s+\nu+1}{2}\right)$$

$$\times\Gamma\left[\begin{matrix} b \\ \frac{2\nu+3}{2},\ \frac{2b-2s-\nu-1}{2} \end{matrix}\right]\,{}_3F_3\left(\begin{matrix} 1,\ \frac{2s+\nu+1}{2},\ \frac{2s-2b+\nu+3}{2} \\ \frac{3}{2},\ \frac{2\nu+3}{2},\ \frac{2s-2a+\nu+3}{2};\ -\frac{\sigma^2}{4\omega} \end{matrix}\right)$$

$$\left[\begin{matrix} \sigma>0;\ \left(\operatorname{Re}\omega>0;\ -\operatorname{Re}\nu-1<\operatorname{Re}s<\operatorname{Re}a+1/4,\ \operatorname{Re}\left(a-\nu/2\right)+1/2\right)\ \text{or} \\ \left(\operatorname{Re}\omega=0;\ -\operatorname{Re}\nu-1<\operatorname{Re}s<\operatorname{Re}\left(b-a\right)+5/4,\ \operatorname{Re}\left(a-\nu/2\right)+1/2, \\ \operatorname{Re}\left(b-a-\nu/2\right)+3/2\right) \end{matrix}\right]$$

2	$e^{-\omega x}\,\mathbf{H}_\nu\left(\sigma\sqrt{x}\right)$ $\times {}_1F_1\left(\begin{matrix} a; \omega x \\ b \end{matrix}\right)$	$2^{2(s+a-b)}\pi\omega^{-s}\left(\dfrac{\sigma^2}{\omega}\right)^{b-a-s}\csc\dfrac{(2s+2a-b+\nu+1)\pi}{2}$

$$\times\Gamma\left[\begin{matrix} b \\ a,\ \frac{2b-2a-2s-\nu+2}{2},\ \frac{2b-2a-2s+\nu+2}{2} \end{matrix}\right]$$

$$\times{}_2F_2\left(\begin{matrix} 1-a,\ b-a;\ -\frac{\sigma^2}{4\omega} \\ \frac{2b-2a-2s-\nu+2}{2},\ \frac{2b-2a-2s+\nu+2}{2} \end{matrix}\right)$$

$$+\frac{\omega^{-s}}{2^\nu\sqrt{\pi}}\left(\frac{\sigma^2}{\omega}\right)^{(\nu+1)/2}\mathrm{B}\left(\frac{2b-2a-2s-\nu-1}{2},\ \frac{2s+\nu+1}{2}\right)$$

$$\times\Gamma\left[\begin{matrix} b \\ \frac{2\nu+3}{2},\ \frac{2b-2s-\nu-1}{2} \end{matrix}\right]\,{}_3F_3\left(\begin{matrix} 1,\ \frac{2s+\nu+1}{2},\ \frac{2s-2b+\nu+3}{2};\ -\frac{\sigma^2}{4\omega} \\ \frac{3}{2},\ \frac{2\nu+3}{2},\ \frac{2s+2a-2b+\nu+3}{2} \end{matrix}\right)$$

$$\left[\begin{matrix} \sigma>0;\ \left(\operatorname{Re}\omega>0;\ -\operatorname{Re}\nu-1<\operatorname{Re}s<\operatorname{Re}\left(b-a\right)+1/4,\ \operatorname{Re}\left(b-a-\nu/2\right)+1/2\right)\ \text{or} \\ \left(\operatorname{Re}\omega=0;\ -\operatorname{Re}\nu-1<\operatorname{Re}s<\operatorname{Re}a+5/4,\ \operatorname{Re}\left(a-\nu/2\right)+3/2,\ \operatorname{Re}\left(b-a-\nu/2\right)+1/2\right) \end{matrix}\right]$$

3.28.8. $_1F_1(a; b; \omega x)$ and $P_n(\varphi(x))$

1	$\theta(\sigma-x)P_n\left(\dfrac{2x}{\sigma}-1\right)$ $\times {}_1F_1\left(\begin{matrix} a; \omega x \\ b \end{matrix}\right)$	$\dfrac{(-1)^n(1-s)_n\sigma^s}{(s)_{n+1}}\,{}_3F_3\left(\begin{matrix} a,\ s,\ s;\ \sigma\omega \\ b,\ s-n,\ s+n+1 \end{matrix}\right)$ $[\sigma,\ \operatorname{Re}s>0]$

2	$\theta(x-\sigma)P_n\left(\dfrac{2x}{\sigma}-1\right)$ $\times {}_1F_1\left(\begin{matrix} a; -\omega x \\ b \end{matrix}\right)$	$\dfrac{(4/\sigma)^n}{n!}\left(\dfrac{1}{2}\right)_n\omega^{-s-n}\Gamma\left[\begin{matrix} b \\ b-n-s \end{matrix}\right]\mathrm{B}\left(a-n-s,\ s+n\right)$

$$\times{}_3F_3\left(\begin{matrix} -n,\ -n,\ a-n-s;\ -\sigma\omega \\ -2n,\ 1-n-s,\ b-n-s \end{matrix}\right)$$

$$+\frac{(-1)^{n+1}\sigma^s(1-s)_n}{(s)_{n+1}}\,{}_3F_3\left(\begin{matrix} a,\ s,\ s;\ -\sigma\omega \\ b,\ s-n,\ s+n+1 \end{matrix}\right)$$

$$\left[\begin{matrix} \sigma>0;\ \left(\operatorname{Re}\omega>0;\ 0<\operatorname{Re}s<\operatorname{Re}a-n\right)\ \text{or} \\ \left(\operatorname{Re}\omega=0;\ 0<\operatorname{Re}s<\operatorname{Re}a-n,\ \operatorname{Re}\left(b-a\right)-n+1\right) \end{matrix}\right]$$

No.	$f(x)$	$F(s)$
3	$\theta(\sigma - x) P_n\left(\dfrac{2\sigma}{x} - 1\right)$ $\times {}_1F_1\left(\begin{matrix} a;\, \omega x \\ b \end{matrix}\right)$	$(-1)^{n+1} \sigma^s \dfrac{(s+1)_n}{(-s)_{n+1}} \, {}_3F_3\left(\begin{matrix} a,\, s-n,\, s+n+1 \\ b,\, s+1,\, s+1;\, \sigma\omega \end{matrix}\right)$ $[\sigma > 0;\ \operatorname{Re} s > n]$
4	$\theta(\sigma - x) P_n\left(\sqrt{\dfrac{x}{\sigma}}\right)$ $\times {}_1F_1\left(\begin{matrix} a;\, \omega x \\ b \end{matrix}\right)$	$\sigma^s \Gamma\left[\begin{matrix} s,\, \frac{2s+1}{2} \\ \frac{2s-n+1}{2},\, \frac{2s+n+2}{2} \end{matrix}\right] \, {}_3F_3\left(\begin{matrix} a,\, s,\, \frac{2s+1}{2};\, \sigma\omega \\ b,\, \frac{2s-n+1}{2},\, \frac{2s+n+2}{2} \end{matrix}\right)$ $[\sigma > 0;\ \operatorname{Re} s > ((-1)^n - 1)/4]$
5	$\theta(x - \sigma) P_n\left(\sqrt{\dfrac{x}{\sigma}}\right)$ $\times {}_1F_1\left(\begin{matrix} a;\, -\omega x \\ b \end{matrix}\right)$	$\dfrac{2^n \omega^{-s-n/2}}{\sigma^{n/2} n!} \left(\dfrac{1}{2}\right)_n B\left(\dfrac{2a-n-2s}{2},\, \dfrac{2s+n}{2}\right)$ $\times \Gamma\left[\begin{matrix} b \\ \frac{2b-n-2s}{2} \end{matrix}\right] {}_3F_3\left(\begin{matrix} -\frac{n}{2},\, \frac{1-n}{2},\, \frac{2a-n-2s}{2};\, -\sigma\omega \\ \frac{1-2n}{2},\, \frac{2-2s-n}{2},\, \frac{2b-n-2s}{2} \end{matrix}\right)$ $+ \dfrac{(\sigma/4)^s}{\sqrt{\pi}} \Gamma\left[\begin{matrix} \frac{n-2s+1}{2},\, \frac{-2s-n}{2} \\ 1-2s \end{matrix}\right] {}_3F_3\left(\begin{matrix} a,\, s,\, \frac{2s+1}{2};\, -\sigma\omega \\ b,\, \frac{2s-n+1}{2},\, \frac{2s+n+2}{2} \end{matrix}\right)$ $\left[\begin{matrix} \sigma > 0;\ (\operatorname{Re}\omega > 0;\ \operatorname{Re} s < \operatorname{Re} a - n/2)\ \text{or} \\ (\operatorname{Re}\omega = 0;\ \operatorname{Re} s < \operatorname{Re} a - n/2,\ \operatorname{Re}(b-a) - n/2 + 1) \end{matrix}\right]$
6	$\theta(\sigma - x) P_n\left(\sqrt{\dfrac{\sigma}{x}}\right)$ $\times {}_1F_1\left(\begin{matrix} a;\, \omega x \\ b \end{matrix}\right)$	$\dfrac{(4\sigma)^s}{\sqrt{\pi}} \Gamma\left[\begin{matrix} \frac{2s-n}{2},\, \frac{2s+n+1}{2} \\ 2s+1 \end{matrix}\right] {}_3F_3\left(\begin{matrix} a,\, \frac{2s-n}{2},\, \frac{2s+n+1}{2} \\ b,\, \frac{2s+1}{2},\, s+1;\, \sigma\omega \end{matrix}\right)$ $[\sigma > 0;\ \operatorname{Re} s > n/2]$
7	$\theta(x - \sigma) P_n\left(\sqrt{\dfrac{\sigma}{x}}\right)$ $\times {}_1F_1\left(\begin{matrix} a;\, -\omega x \\ b \end{matrix}\right)$	$2^{2s+1} \sqrt{\pi}\, \sigma^s \Gamma\left[\begin{matrix} -2s \\ \frac{2-2s+n}{2},\, \frac{1-2s-n}{2} \end{matrix}\right] {}_3F_3\left(\begin{matrix} a,\, \frac{2s-n}{2},\, \frac{2s+n+1}{2};\, -\sigma\omega \\ b,\, s+\frac{1}{2},\, s+1 \end{matrix}\right)$ $+ \dfrac{(1+(-1)^n)}{2\sqrt{\pi}\,\omega^s} \Gamma\left[\begin{matrix} b,\, \frac{n+1}{2} \\ b-s,\, \frac{n+2}{2} \end{matrix}\right] B(a-s,\, s)$ $\times {}_3F_3\left(\begin{matrix} \frac{n+1}{2},\, -\frac{n}{2},\, a-s;\, -\sigma\omega \\ \frac{1}{2},\, 1-s,\, b-s \end{matrix}\right)$ $+ \dfrac{((-1)^n - 1)\sqrt{\sigma}}{\sqrt{\pi}\,\omega^{s-1/2}} B\left(a-s+\frac{1}{2},\, s-\frac{1}{2}\right)$ $\times \Gamma\left[\begin{matrix} b,\, \frac{n+2}{2} \\ b-s+\frac{1}{2},\, \frac{n+1}{2} \end{matrix}\right] {}_3F_3\left(\begin{matrix} \frac{n+2}{2},\, \frac{1-n}{2},\, a-s+\frac{1}{2};\, -\sigma\omega \\ \frac{3}{2},\, \frac{3}{2}-s,\, b-s+\frac{1}{2} \end{matrix}\right)$ $\left[\begin{matrix} \sigma > 0;\ (\operatorname{Re}\omega > 0;\ \operatorname{Re} s < \operatorname{Re} a + (1-(-1)^n)/4)\ \text{or} \\ (\operatorname{Re}\omega = 0;\ \operatorname{Re} s < \operatorname{Re} a + (1-(-1)^n)/4,\ \operatorname{Re}(b-a) + (5-(-1)^n)/4) \end{matrix}\right]$
8	$\theta(\sigma - x) e^{-\omega x} P_n\left(\dfrac{2x}{\sigma} - 1\right)$ $\times {}_1F_1\left(\begin{matrix} a;\, \omega x \\ b \end{matrix}\right)$	$\dfrac{(-1)^n \sigma^s (1-s)_n}{(s)_{n+1}} \, {}_3F_3\left(\begin{matrix} b-a,\, s,\, s;\, -\sigma\omega \\ b,\, s-n,\, s+n+1 \end{matrix}\right)$ $[\sigma,\ \operatorname{Re} s > 0]$

No.	$f(x)$	$F(s)$
9	$\theta(x-\sigma)e^{-\omega x}P_n\left(\dfrac{2x}{\sigma}-1\right)$ $\times\,_1F_1\left(\begin{matrix}a;\,\omega x\\b\end{matrix}\right)$	$\dfrac{(4/\sigma)^n}{n!}\left(\dfrac{1}{2}\right)_n\omega^{-s-n}\Gamma\left[\begin{matrix}b\\b-s-n\end{matrix}\right]\mathrm{B}\,(b-a-s-n,\,s+n)$ $\times\,_3F_3\left(\begin{matrix}-n,\,-n,\,b-a-n-s;\,-\sigma\omega\\-2n,\,1-s-n,\,b-n-s\end{matrix}\right)$ $+\dfrac{(-1)^{n+1}\sigma^s(1-s)_n}{(s)_{n+1}}\,_3F_3\left(\begin{matrix}b-a,\,s,\,s;\,-\sigma\omega\\b,\,s-n,\,s+n+1\end{matrix}\right)$ $\left[\begin{matrix}\sigma>0;\ (\mathrm{Re}\,\omega>0;\ 0<\mathrm{Re}\,s<\mathrm{Re}\,(b-a)-n)\ \text{or}\\(\mathrm{Re}\,\omega=0;\ 0<\mathrm{Re}\,s<\mathrm{Re}\,a-n+1,\ \mathrm{Re}\,(b-a)-n)\end{matrix}\right]$
10	$\theta(\sigma-x)e^{-\omega x}P_n\left(\dfrac{2\sigma}{x}-1\right)$ $\times\,_1F_1\left(\begin{matrix}a;\,\omega x\\b\end{matrix}\right)$	$(-1)^{n+1}\sigma^s\dfrac{(s+1)_n}{(-s)_{n+1}}\,_3F_3\left(\begin{matrix}b-a,\,s-n,\,s+n+1\\b,\,s+1,\,s+1;\,-\sigma\omega\end{matrix}\right)$ $[\sigma>0;\ \mathrm{Re}\,s>n]$
11	$\theta(\sigma-x)e^{-\omega x}P_n\left(\sqrt{\dfrac{x}{\sigma}}\right)$ $\times\,_1F_1\left(\begin{matrix}a;\,\omega x\\b\end{matrix}\right)$	$\dfrac{\sqrt{\pi}\,\sigma^s}{2^{2s-1}}\Gamma\left[\begin{matrix}2s\\\frac{2s-n+1}{2},\,\frac{2s+n+2}{2}\end{matrix}\right]\,_3F_3\left(\begin{matrix}b-a,\,s,\,\frac{2s+1}{2};\,-\sigma\omega\\b,\,\frac{2s-n+1}{2},\,\frac{2s+n+2}{2}\end{matrix}\right)$ $[\sigma>0;\ \mathrm{Re}\,s>((-1)^n-1)/4]$
12	$\theta(x-\sigma)e^{-\omega x}P_n\left(\sqrt{\dfrac{x}{\sigma}}\right)$ $\times\,_1F_1\left(\begin{matrix}a;\,\omega x\\b\end{matrix}\right)$	$\dfrac{2^n\omega^{-s-n/2}}{n!\,\sigma^{n/2}}\left(\dfrac{1}{2}\right)_n\Gamma\left[\begin{matrix}b\\\frac{2b-n-2s}{2}\end{matrix}\right]\mathrm{B}\left(\dfrac{2b-2a-n-2s}{2},\,\dfrac{2s+n}{2}\right)$ $\times\,_3F_3\left(\begin{matrix}-\frac{n}{2},\,\frac{1-n}{2},\,\frac{2b-2a-n-2s}{2};\,-\sigma\omega\\\frac{1-2n}{2},\,\frac{2-2s-n}{2},\,\frac{2b-n-2s}{2}\end{matrix}\right)+\dfrac{(\sigma/4)^s}{\sqrt{\pi}}$ $\times\,\Gamma\left[\begin{matrix}\frac{1-2s+n}{2},\,\frac{-2s-n}{2}\\1-2s\end{matrix}\right]\,_3F_3\left(\begin{matrix}b-a,\,s,\,\frac{2s+1}{2};\,-\sigma\omega\\b,\,\frac{2s-n+1}{2},\,\frac{2s+n+2}{2}\end{matrix}\right)$ $\left[\begin{matrix}\sigma>0;\ (\mathrm{Re}\,\omega>0;\ \mathrm{Re}\,s<\mathrm{Re}\,(b-a)-n/2)\ \text{or}\\(\mathrm{Re}\,\omega=0;\ \mathrm{Re}\,s<\mathrm{Re}\,a-n/2+1,\ \mathrm{Re}\,(b-a)-n/2)\end{matrix}\right]$
13	$\theta(\sigma-x)e^{-\omega x}P_n\left(\sqrt{\dfrac{\sigma}{x}}\right)$ $\times\,_1F_1\left(\begin{matrix}a;\,\omega x\\b\end{matrix}\right)$	$\dfrac{(4\sigma)^s}{\sqrt{\pi}}\Gamma\left[\begin{matrix}\frac{2s-n}{2},\,\frac{2s+n+1}{2}\\2s+1\end{matrix}\right]\,_3F_3\left(\begin{matrix}b-a,\,\frac{2s-n}{2},\,\frac{2s+n+1}{2}\\b,\,\frac{2s+1}{2},\,s+1;\,-\sigma\omega\end{matrix}\right)$ $[\sigma>0;\ \mathrm{Re}\,s>n/2]$
14	$\theta(x-\sigma)e^{-\omega x}P_n\left(\sqrt{\dfrac{\sigma}{x}}\right)$ $\times\,_1F_1\left(\begin{matrix}a;\,\omega x\\b\end{matrix}\right)$	$2^{2s+1}\sqrt{\pi}\,\sigma^s\Gamma\left[\begin{matrix}-2s\\\frac{2-2s+n}{2},\,\frac{1-2s-n}{2}\end{matrix}\right]\,_3F_3\left(\begin{matrix}b-a,\,\frac{2s-n}{2},\,\frac{2s+n+1}{2}\\b,\,\frac{2s+1}{2},\,s+1;\,-\sigma\omega\end{matrix}\right)$ $+\dfrac{(1+(-1)^n)}{2\sqrt{\pi}\,\omega^s}\Gamma\left[\begin{matrix}b,\,\frac{n+1}{2}\\b-s,\,\frac{n+2}{2}\end{matrix}\right]\,_3F_3\left(\begin{matrix}-\frac{n}{2},\,\frac{n+1}{2},\,b-a-s\\\frac{1}{2},\,1-s,\,b-s;\,-\sigma\omega\end{matrix}\right)$ $\times\,\mathrm{B}\,(b-a-s,\,s)+\dfrac{((-1)^n-1)\sqrt{\sigma}}{\sqrt{\pi}\,\omega^{s-1/2}}\mathrm{B}\left(b-a-s+\dfrac{1}{2},\,s-\dfrac{1}{2}\right)$ $\times\,\Gamma\left[\begin{matrix}b,\,\frac{n+2}{2}\\b-s+\frac{1}{2},\,\frac{n+1}{2}\end{matrix}\right]\,_3F_3\left(\begin{matrix}\frac{1-n}{2},\,\frac{n+2}{2},\,b-a-s+\frac{1}{2}\\\frac{3}{2},\,\frac{3-2s}{2},\,b-s+\frac{1}{2};\,-\sigma\omega\end{matrix}\right)$ $\left[\begin{matrix}\sigma>0;\ (\mathrm{Re}\,\omega>0;\ \mathrm{Re}\,s<\mathrm{Re}\,(b-a)+(1-(-1)^n)/4)\ \text{or}\\(\mathrm{Re}\,\omega=0;\ \mathrm{Re}\,s<\mathrm{Re}\,(b-a)+(1-(-1)^n)/4,\ \mathrm{Re}\,a+(5-(-1)^n)/4)\end{matrix}\right]$

3.28.9. $_1F_1(a; b; \omega x)$ **and** $T_n(\varphi(x))$

1	$(\sigma - x)_+^{-1/2} T_n\left(\dfrac{2x}{\sigma} - 1\right)$ $\times {}_1F_1\left(\begin{matrix} a;\ \omega x \\ b \end{matrix}\right)$	$(-1)^n \sqrt{\pi}\left(\dfrac{1}{2} - s\right)_n \sigma^{s-1/2} \Gamma\left[\begin{matrix} s \\ s + n + \frac{1}{2} \end{matrix}\right]$ $\times {}_3F_3\left(\begin{matrix} a,\ s,\ s + \frac{1}{2};\ \sigma\omega \\ b,\ s - n + \frac{1}{2},\ s + n + \frac{1}{2} \end{matrix}\right)$ $[\sigma,\ \mathrm{Re}\,s > 0]$
2	$(x - \sigma)_+^{-1/2} T_n\left(\dfrac{2x}{\sigma} - 1\right)$ $\times {}_1F_1\left(\begin{matrix} a;\ -\omega x \\ b \end{matrix}\right)$	$\dfrac{1}{2}\left(\dfrac{4}{\sigma}\right)^n \omega^{-s-n+1/2} \Gamma\left[\begin{matrix} b \\ \frac{2b-2n-2s+1}{2} \end{matrix}\right]$ $\times \mathrm{B}\left(\dfrac{2a - 2n - 2s + 1}{2}, \dfrac{2s + 2n - 1}{2}\right)$ $\times {}_3F_3\left(\begin{matrix} 1 - n,\ \frac{1-2n}{2},\ \frac{2a-2n-2s+1}{2};\ -\sigma\omega \\ 1 - 2n,\ \frac{3-2n-2s}{2},\ \frac{2b-2n-2s+1}{2} \end{matrix}\right) + \sqrt{\pi}\,\sigma^{s-1/2}$ $\times \left(\dfrac{1-2s}{2}\right)_n \Gamma\left[\begin{matrix} \frac{1-2n-2s}{2} \\ 1 - s \end{matrix}\right] {}_3F_3\left(\begin{matrix} a,\ s,\ \frac{2s+1}{2};\ -\sigma\omega \\ b,\ \frac{2s-2n+1}{2},\ \frac{2s+2n+1}{2} \end{matrix}\right)$ $\left[\begin{matrix} \sigma > 0;\ (\mathrm{Re}\,\omega > 0;\ \mathrm{Re}\,s < \mathrm{Re}\,a - n + 1/2)\ \text{or} \\ (\mathrm{Re}\,\omega = 0;\ \mathrm{Re}\,s < \mathrm{Re}\,a - n + 1/2,\ \mathrm{Re}\,(b - a) - n + 1/2) \end{matrix}\right]$
3	$(\sigma - x)_+^{-1/2} T_n\left(\dfrac{2\sigma}{x} - 1\right)$ $\times {}_1F_1\left(\begin{matrix} a;\ \omega x \\ b \end{matrix}\right)$	$\sqrt{\pi}\,\sigma^{s-1/2} (s)_n \Gamma\left[\begin{matrix} s - n \\ \frac{2s+1}{2} \end{matrix}\right] {}_3F_3\left(\begin{matrix} a,\ s - n,\ s + n \\ b,\ s,\ \frac{2s+1}{2};\ \sigma\omega \end{matrix}\right)$ $[\sigma > 0;\ \mathrm{Re}\,s > n]$
4	$(\sigma - x)_+^{-1/2} T_n\left(\sqrt{\dfrac{x}{\sigma}}\right)$ $\times {}_1F_1\left(\begin{matrix} a;\ \omega x \\ b \end{matrix}\right)$	$\sqrt{\pi}\,\sigma^{s-1/2} \Gamma\left[\begin{matrix} s,\ \frac{2s+1}{2} \\ \frac{2s-n+1}{2},\ \frac{2s+n+1}{2} \end{matrix}\right] {}_3F_3\left(\begin{matrix} a,\ s,\ \frac{2s+1}{2};\ \sigma\omega \\ b,\ \frac{2s-n+1}{2},\ \frac{2s+n+1}{2} \end{matrix}\right)$ $[\sigma > 0;\ \mathrm{Re}\,s > ((-1)^n - 1)/4]$
5	$(x - \sigma)_+^{-1/2} T_n\left(\sqrt{\dfrac{x}{\sigma}}\right)$ $\times {}_1F_1\left(\begin{matrix} a;\ -\omega x \\ b \end{matrix}\right)$	$\dfrac{2^{n-1}\omega^{-s-n/2+1/2}}{\sigma^{n/2}} \Gamma\left[\begin{matrix} b \\ \frac{2b-n-2s+1}{2} \end{matrix}\right]$ $\times \mathrm{B}\left(\dfrac{2a - n - 2s + 1}{2}, \dfrac{2s + n - 1}{2}\right)$ $\times {}_3F_3\left(\begin{matrix} \frac{1-n}{2},\ \frac{2-n}{2},\ \frac{2a-n-2s+1}{2};\ -\sigma\omega \\ 1 - n,\ \frac{3-2s-n}{2},\ \frac{2b-n-2s+1}{2} \end{matrix}\right)$ $+ \dfrac{1}{2}\left(\dfrac{\sigma}{4}\right)^{s-1/2} \Gamma\left[\begin{matrix} \frac{1-2s+n}{2},\ \frac{1-2s-n}{2} \\ 1 - 2s \end{matrix}\right] {}_3F_3\left(\begin{matrix} a,\ s,\ \frac{2s+1}{2};\ -\sigma\omega \\ b,\ \frac{2s-n+1}{2},\ \frac{2s+n+1}{2} \end{matrix}\right)$ $\left[\begin{matrix} \sigma > 0;\ (\mathrm{Re}\,\omega > 0;\ \mathrm{Re}\,s < \mathrm{Re}\,a - n/2 + 1/2)\ \text{or} \\ (\mathrm{Re}\,\omega = 0;\ \mathrm{Re}\,s < \mathrm{Re}\,a - n/2 + 1/2,\ \mathrm{Re}\,(b - a) - n/2 + 3/2) \end{matrix}\right]$
6	$(\sigma - x)_+^{-1/2} T_n\left(\sqrt{\dfrac{\sigma}{x}}\right)$ $\times {}_1F_1\left(\begin{matrix} a;\ \omega x \\ b \end{matrix}\right)$	$(4\sigma)^{s-1/2} \mathrm{B}\left(\dfrac{2s - n}{2}, \dfrac{2s + n}{2}\right) {}_3F_3\left(\begin{matrix} a,\ \frac{2s-n}{2},\ \frac{2s+n}{2} \\ b,\ s,\ \frac{2s+1}{2};\ \sigma\omega \end{matrix}\right)$ $[\sigma > 0;\ \mathrm{Re}\,s > n/2]$

No.	$f(x)$	$F(s)$
7	$(x - \sigma)_+^{-1/2} T_n\left(\sqrt{\dfrac{\sigma}{x}}\right)$ $\times {}_1F_1\left(\begin{matrix} a; -\omega x \\ b \end{matrix}\right)$	$\dfrac{1 + (-1)^n}{2\,\omega^{s-1/2}} B\left(\dfrac{2a - 2s + 1}{2}, \dfrac{2s - 1}{2}\right)$ $\times \Gamma\left[\begin{matrix} b \\ \frac{2b - 2s + 1}{2} \end{matrix}\right] {}_3F_3\left(\begin{matrix} \frac{1-n}{2}, \frac{1+n}{2}, \frac{2a - 2s + 1}{2} \\ \frac{1}{2}, \frac{3-2s}{2}, \frac{2b - 2s + 1}{2}; -\sigma\omega \end{matrix}\right)$ $+ \dfrac{((-1)^n - 1)\, n\sqrt{\sigma}}{2\,\omega^{s-1}} B(a - s + 1,\, s - 1)$ $\times \Gamma\left[\begin{matrix} b \\ b - s + 1 \end{matrix}\right] {}_3F_3\left(\begin{matrix} \frac{2-n}{2}, \frac{2+n}{2}, a - s + 1 \\ \frac{3}{2}, 2 - s, b - s + 1; -\sigma\omega \end{matrix}\right)$ $+ 2^{2s}\pi\sigma^{s-1/2}\,\Gamma\left[\begin{matrix} 1 - 2s \\ \frac{2-2s-n}{2}, \frac{2-2s+n}{2} \end{matrix}\right] {}_3F_3\left(\begin{matrix} a, \frac{2s-n}{2}, \frac{2s+n}{2} \\ b, s, \frac{2s+1}{2}; -\sigma\omega \end{matrix}\right)$ $\left[\begin{matrix} \sigma > 0;\ (\operatorname{Re}\omega > 0;\ \operatorname{Re} s < \operatorname{Re} a + (3 - (-1)^n)/4)\ \text{or} \\ (\operatorname{Re}\omega = 0;\ \operatorname{Re} s < \operatorname{Re} a + (3 - (-1)^n)/4,\ \operatorname{Re}(b - a) + (7 - (-1)^n)/4) \end{matrix}\right]$
8	$(\sigma - x)_+^{-1/2} e^{-\omega x}$ $\times T_n\left(\dfrac{2x}{\sigma} - 1\right)$ $\times {}_1F_1\left(\begin{matrix} a;\, \omega x \\ b \end{matrix}\right)$	$(-1)^n \sqrt{\pi}\, \sigma^{s-1/2}\left(\dfrac{1}{2} - s\right)_n \Gamma\left[\begin{matrix} s \\ s + n + \frac{1}{2} \end{matrix}\right]$ $\times {}_3F_3\left(\begin{matrix} b - a, s, s + \frac{1}{2}; -\sigma\omega \\ b, s - n + \frac{1}{2}, s + n + \frac{1}{2} \end{matrix}\right)$ $[\sigma,\ \operatorname{Re} s > 0]$
9	$(x - \sigma)_+^{-1/2} e^{-\omega x}$ $\times T_n\left(\dfrac{2x}{\sigma} - 1\right)$ $\times {}_1F_1\left(\begin{matrix} a;\, \omega x \\ b \end{matrix}\right)$	$\dfrac{1}{2}\left(\dfrac{4}{\sigma}\right)^n \omega^{-s-n+1/2}\,\Gamma\left[\begin{matrix} b \\ \frac{2b - 2s - 2n + 1}{2} \end{matrix}\right]$ $\times B\left(\dfrac{2b - 2a - 2s - 2n + 1}{2}, \dfrac{2s + 2n - 1}{2}\right)$ $\times {}_3F_3\left(\begin{matrix} 1 - n, \frac{1-2n}{2}, \frac{2b - 2a - 2s - 2n + 1}{2}; -\sigma\omega \\ 1 - 2n, \frac{3 - 2s - 2n}{2}, \frac{2b - 2s - 2n + 1}{2} \end{matrix}\right)$ $+ \sqrt{\pi}\,\sigma^{s-1/2}\left(\dfrac{1 - 2s}{2}\right)_n \Gamma\left[\begin{matrix} \frac{1-2s-2n}{2} \\ 1 - s \end{matrix}\right]$ $\times {}_3F_3\left(\begin{matrix} b - a, s, \frac{2s+1}{2}; -\sigma\omega \\ b, \frac{2s-2n+1}{2}, \frac{2s+2n+1}{2} \end{matrix}\right)$ $\left[\begin{matrix} \sigma > 0;\ (\operatorname{Re}\omega > 0;\ \operatorname{Re} s < \operatorname{Re}(b - a) - n + 1/2)\ \text{or} \\ (\operatorname{Re}\omega = 0;\ \operatorname{Re} s < \operatorname{Re} a - n + 3/2,\ \operatorname{Re}(b - a) - n + 1/2) \end{matrix}\right]$
10	$(\sigma - x)_+^{-1/2} e^{-\omega x}$ $\times T_n\left(\dfrac{2\sigma}{x} - 1\right)$ $\times {}_1F_1\left(\begin{matrix} a;\, \omega x \\ b \end{matrix}\right)$	$\sqrt{\pi}\,\sigma^{s-1/2}\,(s)_n\,\Gamma\left[\begin{matrix} s - n \\ \frac{2s+1}{2} \end{matrix}\right] {}_3F_3\left(\begin{matrix} b - a, s - n, s + n \\ b, s, \frac{2s+1}{2}; -\sigma\omega \end{matrix}\right)$ $[\sigma > 0;\ \operatorname{Re} s > n]$

No.	$f(x)$	$F(s)$
11	$(\sigma - x)_+^{-1/2} e^{-\omega x}$ $\times T_n\left(\sqrt{\dfrac{x}{\sigma}}\right) {}_1F_1\left(\begin{matrix} a;\ \omega x \\ b \end{matrix}\right)$	$\dfrac{\pi\sigma^{s-1/2}}{2^{2s-1}}\,\Gamma\left[\begin{matrix} 2s \\ \frac{2s-n+1}{2},\ \frac{2s+n+1}{2} \end{matrix}\right] {}_3F_3\left(\begin{matrix} b-a,\ s,\ \frac{2s+1}{2};\ -\sigma\omega \\ b,\ \frac{2s-n+1}{2},\ \frac{2s+n+1}{2} \end{matrix}\right)$ $[\sigma > 0;\ \operatorname{Re}s > ((-1)^n - 1)/4]$
12	$(x - \sigma)_+^{-1/2} e^{-\omega x}$ $\times T_n\left(\sqrt{\dfrac{x}{\sigma}}\right)$ $\times {}_1F_1\left(\begin{matrix} a;\ \omega x \\ b \end{matrix}\right)$	$\dfrac{2^{n-1}\omega^{-s-n/2+1/2}}{\sigma^{n/2}}\,\Gamma\left[\begin{matrix} b \\ \frac{2b-n-2s+1}{2} \end{matrix}\right]$ $\times \mathrm{B}\left(\dfrac{2b-2a-n-2s+1}{2},\ \dfrac{2s+n-1}{2}\right)$ $\times {}_3F_3\left(\begin{matrix} \frac{1-n}{2},\ \frac{2-n}{2},\ \frac{2b-2a-n-2s+1}{2};\ -\sigma\omega \\ 1-n,\ \frac{3-2s-n}{2},\ \frac{2b-n-2s+1}{2} \end{matrix}\right)$ $+\dfrac{1}{2}\left(\dfrac{\sigma}{4}\right)^{s-1/2}\Gamma\left[\begin{matrix} \frac{1-2s+n}{2},\ \frac{1-2s-n}{2} \\ 1-2s \end{matrix}\right] {}_3F_3\left(\begin{matrix} b-a,\ s,\ \frac{2s+1}{2};\ -\sigma\omega \\ b,\ \frac{2s-n+1}{2},\ \frac{2s+n+1}{2} \end{matrix}\right)$ $\left[\begin{matrix} \sigma > 0;\ (\operatorname{Re}\omega > 0;\ \operatorname{Re}s < \operatorname{Re}(b-a) - n/2 + 1/2)\ \text{or} \\ (\operatorname{Re}\omega = 0;\ \operatorname{Re}s < \operatorname{Re}a - n/2 + 3/2,\ \operatorname{Re}(b-a) - n/2 + 1/2) \end{matrix}\right]$
13	$(\sigma - x)_+^{-1/2} e^{-\omega x}$ $\times T_n\left(\sqrt{\dfrac{\sigma}{x}}\right) {}_1F_1\left(\begin{matrix} a;\ \omega x \\ b \end{matrix}\right)$	$(4\sigma)^{s-1/2}\,\mathrm{B}\left(\dfrac{2s-n}{2},\ \dfrac{2s+n}{2}\right) {}_3F_3\left(\begin{matrix} b-a,\ \frac{2s-n}{2},\ \frac{2s+n}{2} \\ b,\ s,\ \frac{2s+1}{2};\ -\sigma\omega \end{matrix}\right)$ $[\sigma > 0;\ \operatorname{Re}s > n/2]$
14	$(x - \sigma)_+^{-1/2} e^{-\omega x}$ $\times T_n\left(\sqrt{\dfrac{\sigma}{x}}\right)$ $\times {}_1F_1\left(\begin{matrix} a;\ -\omega x \\ b \end{matrix}\right)$	$\dfrac{1 + (-1)^n}{2\omega^{s-1/2}}\,\mathrm{B}\left(\dfrac{2b-2a-2s+1}{2},\ \dfrac{2s-1}{2}\right)$ $\times \Gamma\left[\begin{matrix} b \\ \frac{2b-2s+1}{2} \end{matrix}\right] {}_3F_3\left(\begin{matrix} \frac{1-n}{2},\ \frac{1+n}{2},\ \frac{2b-2a-2s+1}{2} \\ \frac{1}{2},\ \frac{3-2s}{2},\ \frac{2b-2s+1}{2};\ -\sigma\omega \end{matrix}\right)$ $+\dfrac{((-1)^n - 1)n\sqrt{\sigma}}{2\omega^{s-1}}\,\mathrm{B}(b-a-s+1,\ s-1)$ $\times \Gamma\left[\begin{matrix} b \\ b-s+1 \end{matrix}\right] {}_3F_3\left(\begin{matrix} \frac{2-n}{2},\ \frac{2+n}{2},\ b-a-s+1 \\ \frac{3}{2},\ 2-s,\ b-s+1;\ -\sigma\omega \end{matrix}\right)$ $+\dfrac{2^{2s}\pi}{\sigma^{1/2-s}}\,\Gamma\left[\begin{matrix} 1-2s \\ \frac{2-2s-n}{2},\ \frac{2-2s+n}{2} \end{matrix}\right] {}_3F_3\left(\begin{matrix} b-a,\ \frac{2s-n}{2},\ \frac{2s+n}{2} \\ b,\ s,\ \frac{2s+1}{2};\ -\sigma\omega \end{matrix}\right)$ $\left[\begin{matrix} \sigma > 0;\ (\operatorname{Re}\omega > 0;\ \operatorname{Re}s < \operatorname{Re}(b-a) + (3 - (-1)^n)/4)\ \text{or} \\ (\operatorname{Re}\omega = 0;\ \operatorname{Re}s < \operatorname{Re}(b-a) + (3-(-1)^n)/4,\ \operatorname{Re}a + (7-(-1)^n)/4) \end{matrix}\right]$

3.28.10. ${}_1F_1(a;\ b;\ \omega x)$ **and** $U_n(\varphi(x))$

1	$(\sigma - x)_+^{1/2}\, U_n\left(\dfrac{2x}{\sigma} - 1\right)$ $\times {}_1F_1\left(\begin{matrix} a;\ \omega x \\ b \end{matrix}\right)$	$\dfrac{(-1)^n(n+1)\sqrt{\pi}\,\sigma^{s+1/2}}{2}\left(\dfrac{3-2s}{2}\right)_n \Gamma\left[\begin{matrix} s \\ \frac{2s+2n+3}{2} \end{matrix}\right]$ $\times {}_3F_3\left(\begin{matrix} a,\ s,\ s-\frac{1}{2};\ \sigma\omega \\ b,\ \frac{2s-2n-1}{2},\ \frac{2s+2n+3}{2} \end{matrix}\right)$ $[\sigma,\ \operatorname{Re}s > 0]$

No.	$f(x)$	$F(s)$
2	$(x-\sigma)_+^{1/2} U_n\left(\dfrac{2x}{\sigma}-1\right)$ $\times {}_1F_1\left(\begin{matrix} a; -\omega x \\ b \end{matrix}\right)$	$\dfrac{(n+1)\sqrt{\pi}\,\sigma^{s+1/2}}{2}\left(\dfrac{3-2s}{2}\right)_n \Gamma\left[\begin{matrix} -\frac{2s+2n+1}{2} \\ 1-s \end{matrix}\right]$ $\times {}_3F_3\left(\begin{matrix} a,\ s-\frac{1}{2},\ s;\ -\sigma\omega \\ b,\ \frac{2s-2n-1}{2},\ \frac{2s+2n+3}{2} \end{matrix}\right)$ $+\dfrac{(4/\sigma)^n}{\omega^{s+n+1/2}}\,B\left(\dfrac{2a-2n-2s-1}{2},\ \dfrac{2s+2n+1}{2}\right)$ $\times \Gamma\left[\begin{matrix} b \\ \frac{2b-2n-2s-1}{2} \end{matrix}\right]$ $\times {}_3F_3\left(\begin{matrix} -n-1,\ -\frac{2n+1}{2},\ \frac{2a-2n-2s-1}{2};\ -\sigma\omega \\ -2n-1,\ \frac{1-2n-2s}{2},\ \frac{2b-2n-2s-1}{2} \end{matrix}\right)$ $\left[\begin{matrix} \sigma>0;\ (\operatorname{Re}\omega>0;\ \operatorname{Re}s<\operatorname{Re}a-n-1/2)\ \text{or} \\ (\operatorname{Re}\omega=0;\ \operatorname{Re}s<\operatorname{Re}a-n-1/2,\ \operatorname{Re}(b-a)-n+1/2) \end{matrix}\right]$
3	$(\sigma-x)_+^{1/2} U_n\left(\dfrac{2\sigma}{x}-1\right)$ $\times {}_1F_1\left(\begin{matrix} a;\ \omega x \\ b \end{matrix}\right)$	$\dfrac{(n+1)\sqrt{\pi}\,\sigma^{s+1/2}}{2}(s+2)_n\,\Gamma\left[\begin{matrix} s-n \\ \frac{2s+3}{2} \end{matrix}\right] {}_3F_3\left(\begin{matrix} a,\ s-n,\ s+n+2 \\ b,\ s+\frac{3}{2},\ s+2;\ \sigma\omega \end{matrix}\right)$ $[\sigma>0;\ \operatorname{Re}s>n]$
4	$(\sigma-x)_+^{1/2} U_n\left(\sqrt{\dfrac{x}{\sigma}}\right)$ $\times {}_1F_1\left(\begin{matrix} a;\ \omega x \\ b \end{matrix}\right)$	$\dfrac{(n+1)\pi\sigma^{s+1/2}}{2^{2s}}\,\Gamma\left[\begin{matrix} 2s \\ \frac{2s-n+1}{2},\ \frac{2s+n+3}{2} \end{matrix}\right] {}_3F_3\left(\begin{matrix} a,\ s,\ \frac{2s+1}{2};\ \sigma\omega \\ b,\ \frac{2s-n+1}{2},\ \frac{2s+n+3}{2} \end{matrix}\right)$ $[\sigma>0;\ \operatorname{Re}s>((-1)^n-1)/4]$
5	$(x-\sigma)_+^{1/2} U_n\left(\sqrt{\dfrac{x}{\sigma}}\right)$ $\times {}_1F_1\left(\begin{matrix} a;\ -\omega x \\ b \end{matrix}\right)$	$\dfrac{2^n\omega^{-s-n/2-1/2}}{\sigma^{n/2}}\,\Gamma\left[\begin{matrix} b \\ \frac{2b-n-2s-1}{2} \end{matrix}\right]$ $\times B\left(\dfrac{2a-n-2s-1}{2},\ \dfrac{2s+n+1}{2}\right)$ $\times {}_3F_3\left(\begin{matrix} -\frac{n}{2},\ -\frac{n+1}{2},\ \frac{2a-n-2s-1}{2};\ -\sigma\omega \\ -n,\ \frac{1-2s-n}{2},\ \frac{2b-n-2s-1}{2} \end{matrix}\right)$ $+(n+1)\left(\dfrac{\sigma}{4}\right)^{s+1/2}\Gamma\left[\begin{matrix} \frac{n-2s+1}{2},\ -\frac{2s+n+1}{2} \\ 1-2s \end{matrix}\right]$ $\times {}_3F_3\left(\begin{matrix} a,\ s,\ \frac{2s+1}{2};\ -\sigma\omega \\ b,\ \frac{2s-n+1}{2},\ \frac{2s+n+3}{2} \end{matrix}\right)$ $\left[\begin{matrix} \sigma>0;\ (\operatorname{Re}\omega>0;\ \operatorname{Re}s<\operatorname{Re}a-n/2-1/2)\ \text{or} \\ (\operatorname{Re}\omega=0;\ \operatorname{Re}s<\operatorname{Re}a-n/2-1/2,\ \operatorname{Re}(b-a)-n/2+1/2) \end{matrix}\right]$
6	$(\sigma-x)_+^{1/2} U_n\left(\sqrt{\dfrac{\sigma}{x}}\right)$ $\times {}_1F_1\left(\begin{matrix} a;\ \omega x \\ b \end{matrix}\right)$	$2^{2s}(n+1)\sigma^{s+1/2}\Gamma\left[\begin{matrix} \frac{2s-n}{2},\ \frac{2s+n+2}{2} \\ 2s+2 \end{matrix}\right]$ $\times {}_3F_3\left(\begin{matrix} a,\ \frac{2s-n}{2},\ \frac{2s+n+2}{2} \\ b,\ s+1,\ \frac{2s+3}{2};\ \sigma\omega \end{matrix}\right)\quad [\sigma>0;\ \operatorname{Re}s>n/2]$

No.	$f(x)$	$F(s)$

7

$$f(x) = (x-\sigma)_+^{1/2}\, U_n\left(\sqrt{\frac{\sigma}{x}}\right) \times {}_1F_1\left(\begin{matrix} a;\; -\omega x \\ b \end{matrix}\right)$$

$$F(s) = (n+1)\,\pi\,(4\sigma)^{s+1/2}\,\Gamma\left[\begin{matrix} -2s-1 \\ \frac{n-2s+2}{2},\; -\frac{2s+n}{2} \end{matrix}\right]$$

$$\times {}_3F_3\left(\begin{matrix} a,\; \frac{2s-n}{2},\; \frac{2s+n+2}{2};\; -\sigma\omega \\ b,\; s+1,\; s+\frac{3}{2} \end{matrix}\right) + \frac{1+(-1)^n}{2\,\omega^{s+1/2}}$$

$$\times \Gamma\left[\begin{matrix} b \\ b-s-\frac{1}{2} \end{matrix}\right] \mathrm{B}\left(a-s-\frac{1}{2},\; s+\frac{1}{2}\right)$$

$$\times {}_3F_3\left(\begin{matrix} -\frac{n+1}{2},\; \frac{n+1}{2},\; \frac{2a-2s-1}{2};\; -\sigma\omega \\ \frac{1}{2},\; \frac{1-2s}{2},\; \frac{2b-2s-1}{2} \end{matrix}\right)$$

$$+ \frac{(n+1)\left((-1)^n-1\right)\sqrt{\sigma}}{2\,\omega^s}\,\Gamma\left[\begin{matrix} b \\ b-s \end{matrix}\right]\mathrm{B}\left(a-s,\; s\right)$$

$$\times {}_3F_3\left(\begin{matrix} -\frac{n}{2},\; \frac{n+2}{2},\; a-s;\; -\sigma\omega \\ \frac{3}{2},\; 1-s,\; b-s \end{matrix}\right)$$

$$\left[\begin{matrix} \sigma > 0;\; (\mathrm{Re}\,\omega > 0;\; \mathrm{Re}\,s < \mathrm{Re}\,a - \left(1+(-1)^n\right)/4)\; \text{or} \\ (\mathrm{Re}\,\omega = 0;\; \mathrm{Re}\,s < \mathrm{Re}\,a - \left(1+(-1)^n\right)/4,\; \mathrm{Re}\,(b-a) + \left(3-(-1)^n\right)/4) \end{matrix}\right]$$

8

$$f(x) = (\sigma-x)_+^{1/2}\, e^{-\omega x} \times U_n\left(\frac{2x}{\sigma}-1\right) \times {}_1F_1\left(\begin{matrix} a;\; \omega x \\ b \end{matrix}\right)$$

$$F(s) = \frac{(-1)^n (n+1)\sqrt{\pi}\,\sigma^{s+1/2}}{2}\left(\frac{3-2s}{2}\right)_n \Gamma\left[\begin{matrix} s \\ \frac{2s+2n+3}{2} \end{matrix}\right]$$

$$\times {}_3F_3\left(\begin{matrix} b-a,\; s,\; s-\frac{1}{2};\; -\sigma\omega \\ b,\; \frac{2s-2n-1}{2},\; \frac{2s+2n+3}{2} \end{matrix}\right)$$

$$[\sigma,\; \mathrm{Re}\,s > 0]$$

9

$$f(x) = (x-\sigma)_+^{1/2}\, e^{-\omega x} \times U_n\left(\frac{2x}{\sigma}-1\right) \times {}_1F_1\left(\begin{matrix} a;\; \omega x \\ b \end{matrix}\right)$$

$$F(s) = \frac{(n+1)\sqrt{\pi}\,\sigma^{s+1/2}}{2}\left(\frac{3-2s}{2}\right)_n$$

$$\times \Gamma\left[\begin{matrix} -\frac{2s+2n+1}{2} \\ 1-s \end{matrix}\right] {}_3F_3\left(\begin{matrix} b-a,\; s-\frac{1}{2},\; s;\; -\sigma\omega \\ b,\; \frac{2s-2n-1}{2},\; \frac{2s+2n+3}{2} \end{matrix}\right)$$

$$+ \frac{(4/\sigma)^n}{\omega^{s+n+1/2}}\,\mathrm{B}\left(\frac{2b-2a-2n-2s-1}{2},\; \frac{2s+2n+1}{2}\right)$$

$$\times \Gamma\left[\begin{matrix} b \\ \frac{2b-2n-2s-1}{2} \end{matrix}\right] {}_3F_3\left(\begin{matrix} -n-1,\; -\frac{2n+1}{2},\; \frac{2b-2a-2n-2s-1}{2};\; -\sigma\omega \\ -2n-1,\; \frac{1-2n-2s}{2},\; \frac{2b-2n-2s-1}{2} \end{matrix}\right)$$

$$\left[\begin{matrix} \sigma > 0;\; (\mathrm{Re}\,\omega > 0;\; \mathrm{Re}\,s < \mathrm{Re}\,(b-a) - n - 1/2)\; \text{or} \\ (\mathrm{Re}\,\omega = 0;\; \mathrm{Re}\,s < \mathrm{Re}\,a - n + 1/2,\; \mathrm{Re}\,(b-a) - n - 1/2) \end{matrix}\right]$$

10

$$f(x) = (\sigma-x)_+^{1/2}\, e^{-\omega x} \times U_n\left(\frac{2\sigma}{x}-1\right) \times {}_1F_1\left(\begin{matrix} a;\; \omega x \\ b \end{matrix}\right)$$

$$F(s) = \frac{(n+1)\sqrt{\pi}\,\sigma^{s+1/2}}{2}\,(s+2)_n\,\Gamma\left[\begin{matrix} s-n \\ \frac{2s+3}{2} \end{matrix}\right]$$

$$\times {}_3F_3\left(\begin{matrix} b-a,\; s-n,\; s+n+2 \\ b,\; \frac{2s+3}{2},\; s+2;\; -\sigma\omega \end{matrix}\right) \qquad [\sigma > 0;\; \mathrm{Re}\,s > n]$$

No.	$f(x)$	$F(s)$
11	$(\sigma - x)_+^{1/2} e^{-\omega x}$ $\times U_n\left(\sqrt{\dfrac{x}{\sigma}}\right)$ $\times {}_1F_1\left(\begin{matrix} a; \omega x \\ b \end{matrix}\right)$	$\dfrac{(n+1)\,\pi\sigma^{s+1/2}}{2^{2s}}\,\Gamma\left[\begin{matrix} 2s \\ \frac{2s-n+1}{2},\ \frac{2s+n+3}{2} \end{matrix}\right]\,{}_3F_3\left(\begin{matrix} b-a,\ s,\ \frac{2s+1}{2};\ -\sigma\omega \\ b,\ \frac{2s-n+1}{2},\ \frac{2s+n+3}{2} \end{matrix}\right)$ $\left[\sigma > 0;\ \operatorname{Re} s > ((-1)^n - 1)/4\right]$
12	$(x - \sigma)_+^{1/2} e^{-\omega x}$ $\times U_n\left(\sqrt{\dfrac{x}{\sigma}}\right)$ $\times {}_1F_1\left(\begin{matrix} a; \omega x \\ b \end{matrix}\right)$	$\dfrac{2^n \omega^{-s-n/2-1/2}}{\sigma^{n/2}}\,\Gamma\left[\begin{matrix} b \\ \frac{2b-n-2s-1}{2} \end{matrix}\right]$ $\times \mathrm{B}\left(\dfrac{2b-2a-n-2s-1}{2},\ \dfrac{2s+n+1}{2}\right)$ $\times {}_3F_3\left(\begin{matrix} -\frac{n}{2},\ -\frac{n+1}{2},\ \frac{2b-2a-n-2s-1}{2};\ -\sigma\omega \\ -n,\ \frac{1-2s-n}{2},\ \frac{2b-n-2s-1}{2} \end{matrix}\right)$ $+ (n+1)\left(\dfrac{\sigma}{4}\right)^{s+1/2}\Gamma\left[\begin{matrix} \frac{n-2s+1}{2},\ -\frac{2s+n+1}{2} \\ 1-2s \end{matrix}\right]$ $\times {}_3F_3\left(\begin{matrix} b-a,\ s,\ \frac{2s+1}{2};\ -\sigma\omega \\ b,\ \frac{2s-n+1}{2},\ \frac{2s+n+3}{2} \end{matrix}\right)$ $\left[\begin{matrix} \sigma > 0;\ (\operatorname{Re}\omega > 0;\ \operatorname{Re} s < \operatorname{Re}(b-a) - n/2 - 1/2)\ \text{or} \\ (\operatorname{Re}\omega = 0;\ \operatorname{Re} s < \operatorname{Re} a - n/2 + 1/2,\ \operatorname{Re}(b-a) - n/2 - 1/2) \end{matrix}\right]$
13	$(\sigma - x)_+^{1/2} e^{-\omega x} U_n\left(\sqrt{\dfrac{\sigma}{x}}\right)$ $\times {}_1F_1\left(\begin{matrix} a; \omega x \\ b \end{matrix}\right)$	$2^{2s}(n+1)\sigma^{s+1/2}\Gamma\left[\begin{matrix} \frac{2s-n}{2},\ \frac{2s+n+2}{2} \\ 2s+2 \end{matrix}\right]$ $\times {}_3F_3\left(\begin{matrix} b-a,\ \frac{2s-n}{2},\ \frac{2s+n+2}{2} \\ b,\ s+1,\ \frac{2s+3}{2};\ -\sigma\omega \end{matrix}\right)\quad [\sigma > 0;\ \operatorname{Re} s > n/2]$
14	$(x - \sigma)_+^{1/2} e^{-\omega x}$ $\times U_n\left(\sqrt{\dfrac{\sigma}{x}}\right)$ $\times {}_1F_1\left(\begin{matrix} a; \omega x \\ b \end{matrix}\right)$	$(n+1)\pi(4\sigma)^{s+1/2}\Gamma\left[\begin{matrix} -2s-1 \\ \frac{n-2s+2}{2},\ \frac{-2s-n}{2} \end{matrix}\right]$ $\times {}_3F_3\left(\begin{matrix} b-a,\ \frac{2s-n}{2},\ \frac{2s+n+2}{2} \\ b,\ s+1,\ s+\frac{3}{2};\ -\sigma\omega \end{matrix}\right) + \dfrac{(1+(-1)^n)}{2\,\omega^{s+1/2}}$ $\times \Gamma\left[\begin{matrix} b \\ b-s-\frac{1}{2} \end{matrix}\right]\mathrm{B}\left(b-a-s-\dfrac{1}{2},\ s+\dfrac{1}{2}\right)$ $\times {}_3F_3\left(\begin{matrix} -\frac{n+1}{2},\ \frac{n+1}{2},\ b-a-s-\frac{1}{2} \\ \frac{1}{2},\ \frac{1-2s}{2},\ b-s-\frac{1}{2};\ -\sigma\omega \end{matrix}\right)$ $+ \dfrac{(n+1)\left((-1)^n - 1\right)\sqrt{\sigma}}{2\,\omega^s}\,\Gamma\left[\begin{matrix} b \\ b-s \end{matrix}\right]\mathrm{B}(b-a-s,\ s)$ $\times {}_3F_3\left(\begin{matrix} -\frac{n}{2},\ \frac{n+2}{2},\ b-a-s \\ \frac{3}{2},\ 1-s,\ b-s;\ -\sigma\omega \end{matrix}\right)$ $\left[\begin{matrix} \sigma > 0;\ (\operatorname{Re}\omega > 0;\ \operatorname{Re} s < \operatorname{Re}(b-a) - (1+(-1)^n)/4)\ \text{or} \\ (\operatorname{Re}\omega = 0;\ \operatorname{Re} s < \operatorname{Re}(b-a) - (1+(-1)^n)/4,\ \operatorname{Re} a + (3-(-1)^n)/4) \end{matrix}\right]$

3.28.11. $_1F_1\left(a;\,b;\,\omega x\right)$ **and** $H_n\left(\sigma\sqrt{x}\right)$

1	$e^{-\sigma^2 x}H_n\left(\sigma\sqrt{x}\right)$ $\times\,_1F_1\begin{pmatrix}a;\,-\omega x\\b\end{pmatrix}$	$\dfrac{2^{n-2s+1}\sqrt{\pi}}{\sigma^{2s}}\,\Gamma\begin{bmatrix}2s\\ \frac{2s-n+1}{2}\end{bmatrix}\,_3F_2\begin{pmatrix}a,\,s,\,\frac{2s+1}{2};\,-\frac{\omega}{\sigma^2}\\b,\,\frac{2s-n+1}{2}\end{pmatrix}$

$$\left[\begin{array}{l}\left(\operatorname{Re}\left(\sigma^2+\omega\right)>0;\ \operatorname{Re}s>[n/2]-n/2;\ |\arg\sigma|<\pi/4\right)\ \text{or}\\ \left(\operatorname{Re}\omega>0;\ [n/2]-n/2<\operatorname{Re}s<\operatorname{Re}a-n/2+1;\ |\arg\sigma|=\pi/4\right)\ \text{or}\\ \left(\operatorname{Re}\omega=0;\ [n/2]-n/2<\operatorname{Re}s<\operatorname{Re}a-n/2+1,\ \operatorname{Re}\left(b-a\right)-n/2+1;\ |\arg\sigma|=\pi/4\right)\end{array}\right]$$

2	$e^{-(\sigma^2+\omega)x}H_n\left(\sigma\sqrt{x}\right)$ $\times\,_1F_1\begin{pmatrix}a;\,\omega x\\b\end{pmatrix}$	$\dfrac{2^{n-2s+1}\sqrt{\pi}}{\sigma^{2s}}\,\Gamma\begin{bmatrix}2s\\ \frac{2s-n+1}{2}\end{bmatrix}\,_3F_2\begin{pmatrix}b-a,\,s,\,\frac{2s+1}{2};\,-\frac{\omega}{\sigma^2}\\b,\,\frac{2s-n+1}{2}\end{pmatrix}$

$$\left[\begin{array}{l}\left(\operatorname{Re}\left(\sigma^2+\omega\right)>0;\ \operatorname{Re}s>[n/2]-n/2;\ |\arg\sigma|<\pi/4\right)\ \text{or}\\ \left(\operatorname{Re}\omega>0;\ [n/2]-n/2<\operatorname{Re}s<\operatorname{Re}\left(b-a\right)-n/2+1;\ |\arg\sigma|=\pi/4\right)\ \text{or}\\ \left(\operatorname{Re}\omega=0;\ [n/2]-n/2<\operatorname{Re}s<\operatorname{Re}a-n/2+1,\ \operatorname{Re}\left(b-a\right)-n/2+1;\ |\arg\sigma|=\pi/4\right)\end{array}\right]$$

3.28.12. $_1F_1\left(a;\,b;\,\omega x\right)$ **and** $L_n^\lambda\left(\sigma x\right)$

1	$e^{-\sigma x}L_n^\lambda\left(\sigma x\right)$ $\times\,_1F_1\begin{pmatrix}a;\,-\omega x\\b\end{pmatrix}$	$\dfrac{\sigma^{a-s}}{n!\,\omega^a}\left(1-s+a+\lambda\right)_n\Gamma\begin{bmatrix}b,\,s-a\\b-a\end{bmatrix}$ $\times\,_3F_2\begin{pmatrix}a,\,a-b+1,\,1-s+a+n+\lambda\\1-s+a,\,1-s+a+\lambda;\,-\frac{\sigma}{\omega}\end{pmatrix}$ $+\dfrac{(\lambda+1)_n}{n!\,\omega^s}\,\mathrm{B}\left(a-s,\,s\right)\Gamma\begin{bmatrix}b\\b-s\end{bmatrix}\,_3F_2\begin{pmatrix}s,\,s-b+1,\,n+\lambda+1\\s+a+1,\,\lambda+1;\,-\frac{\sigma}{\omega}\end{pmatrix}$

$$\left[\begin{array}{l}\left(\operatorname{Re}\sigma,\ \operatorname{Re}\left(\sigma+\omega\right),\ \operatorname{Re}s>0\right)\ \text{or}\\ \left(\operatorname{Re}\sigma=0,\ \operatorname{Re}\omega>0;\ 0<\operatorname{Re}s<\operatorname{Re}a-n+1\right)\ \text{or}\\ \left(\operatorname{Re}\sigma=0,\ \operatorname{Re}\omega=0;\ 0<\operatorname{Re}s<\operatorname{Re}a-n+1,\ \operatorname{Re}\left(b-a\right)-n+1\right)\end{array}\right]$$

2	$e^{-(\sigma+\omega)x}L_n^\lambda\left(\sigma x\right)$ $\times\,_1F_1\begin{pmatrix}a;\,\omega x\\b\end{pmatrix}$	$\dfrac{\sigma^{b-a-s}}{n!\,\omega^{b-a}}\left(1-s+b-a+\lambda\right)_n\Gamma\begin{bmatrix}b,\,s+a-b\\a\end{bmatrix}$ $\times\,_3F_2\begin{pmatrix}1-a,\,b-a,\,1-s+b-a+n+\lambda\\1-s+b-a,\,1-s+b-a+\lambda;\,-\frac{\sigma}{\omega}\end{pmatrix}$ $+\dfrac{(\lambda+1)_n}{n!\,\omega^s}\,\mathrm{B}\left(b-a-s,\,s\right)\Gamma\begin{bmatrix}b\\b-s\end{bmatrix}$ $\times\,_3F_2\begin{pmatrix}n+\lambda+1,\,s,\,s-b+1\\\lambda+1,\,s+a-b+1;\,-\frac{\sigma}{\omega}\end{pmatrix}$

$$\left[\begin{array}{l}\left(\operatorname{Re}\sigma,\ \operatorname{Re}\left(\sigma+\omega\right),\ \operatorname{Re}s>0\right)\ \text{or}\\ \left(\operatorname{Re}\sigma=0,\ \operatorname{Re}\omega>0;\ 0<\operatorname{Re}s<\operatorname{Re}\left(b-a\right)-n+1\right)\ \text{or}\\ \left(\operatorname{Re}\sigma=0,\ \operatorname{Re}\omega=0;\ 0<\operatorname{Re}s<\operatorname{Re}a-n+1,\ \operatorname{Re}\left(b-a\right)-n+1\right)\end{array}\right]$$

3.28.13. $_1F_1(a;b;\omega x)$ **and** $C_n^\lambda(\varphi(x))$

1	$(\sigma-x)_+^{\lambda-1/2} C_n^\lambda\left(\dfrac{2x}{\sigma}-1\right)$	$\dfrac{(-1)^n (2\lambda)_n \left(\frac{1}{2}-s+\lambda\right)_n \sigma^{s+\lambda-1/2}}{n!} \Gamma\left[\begin{array}{c} s,\ \lambda+\frac{1}{2} \\ s+n+\lambda+\frac{1}{2}\end{array}\right]$
	$\times\ _1F_1\left(\begin{array}{c} a;\ \omega x \\ b \end{array}\right)$	$\times\ _3F_3\left(\begin{array}{c} a,\ s,\ s-\lambda+\frac{1}{2};\ \sigma\omega \\ b,\ s-n-\lambda+\frac{1}{2},\ s+n+\lambda+\frac{1}{2}\end{array}\right)$ $\left[\begin{array}{c}\sigma,\ \mathrm{Re}\,s>0; \\ \mathrm{Re}\,\lambda>-1/2\end{array}\right]$
2	$(x-\sigma)_+^{\lambda-1/2} C_n^\lambda\left(\dfrac{2x}{\sigma}-1\right)$	$\dfrac{4^n\omega^{-n-s-\lambda+1/2}}{n!\,\sigma^n}(\lambda)_n\,\Gamma\left[\begin{array}{c} b \\ \frac{2b-2n-2s-2\lambda+1}{2}\end{array}\right]$
	$\times\ _1F_1\left(\begin{array}{c} a;\ -\omega x \\ b \end{array}\right)$	$\times\,\mathrm{B}\left(\dfrac{2a-2n-2s-2\lambda+1}{2},\ \dfrac{2s+2n+2\lambda-1}{2}\right)$
		$\times\ _3F_3\left(\begin{array}{c}1-n-2\lambda,\ \frac{1-2n-2\lambda}{2},\ \frac{2a-2n-2s-2\lambda+1}{2};\ -\sigma\omega \\ 1-2n-2\lambda,\ \frac{3-2n-2s-2\lambda}{2},\ \frac{2b-2n-2s-2\lambda+1}{2}\end{array}\right)$
		$+\ \dfrac{\sqrt{\pi}\,\sigma^{s+\lambda-1/2}}{2^{2\lambda-1}n!}\left(\dfrac{1-2s+2\lambda}{2}\right)_n$
		$\times\,\Gamma\left[\begin{array}{c} n+2\lambda,\ \frac{1-2n-2s-2\lambda}{2} \\ \lambda,\ 1-s\end{array}\right]\ _3F_3\left(\begin{array}{c} a,\ s,\ \frac{2s-2\lambda+1}{2};\ -\sigma\omega \\ b,\ \frac{2s-2n-2\lambda+1}{2},\ \frac{2s+2n+2\lambda+1}{2}\end{array}\right)$
		$\left[\begin{array}{l}\sigma>0;\ \mathrm{Re}\,\lambda>-1/2;\ (\mathrm{Re}\,\omega>0;\ \mathrm{Re}\,s<\mathrm{Re}\,(a-\lambda)-n+1/2)\ \text{or} \\ (\mathrm{Re}\,\omega=0;\ \mathrm{Re}\,s<\mathrm{Re}\,(a-\lambda)-n+1/2,\ \mathrm{Re}\,(b-a-\lambda)-n+1/2)\end{array}\right]$
3	$(\sigma-x)_+^{\lambda-1/2} C_n^\lambda\left(\dfrac{2\sigma}{x}-1\right)$	$\dfrac{2^{1-2\lambda}\sqrt{\pi}\,\sigma^{s+\lambda-1/2}}{n!}(s+2\lambda)_n\,\Gamma\left[\begin{array}{c} n+2\lambda,\ s-n \\ \lambda,\ \frac{2s+2\lambda+1}{2}\end{array}\right]$
	$\times\ _1F_1\left(\begin{array}{c} a;\ \omega x \\ b \end{array}\right)$	$\times\ _3F_3\left(\begin{array}{c} a,\ s-n,\ s+n+2\lambda;\ \sigma\omega \\ b,\ \frac{2s+2\lambda+1}{2},\ s+2\lambda\end{array}\right)$
		$[\sigma>0;\ \mathrm{Re}\,\lambda>-1/2;\ \mathrm{Re}\,s>n]$
4	$(\sigma-x)_+^{\lambda-1/2} C_n^\lambda\left(\sqrt{\dfrac{x}{\sigma}}\right)$	$\dfrac{(2\lambda)_n\,\sigma^{s+\lambda-1/2}}{n!}\Gamma\left[\begin{array}{c} \frac{2\lambda+1}{2},\ s,\ \frac{2s+1}{2} \\ \frac{2s-n+1}{2},\ \frac{2s+2\lambda+n+1}{2}\end{array}\right]$
	$\times\ _1F_1\left(\begin{array}{c} a;\ \omega x \\ b \end{array}\right)$	$\times\ _3F_3\left(\begin{array}{c} a,\ s,\ \frac{2s+1}{2};\ \sigma\omega \\ b,\ \frac{2s-n+1}{2},\ \frac{2s+2\lambda+n+1}{2}\end{array}\right)$
		$[\sigma>0;\ \mathrm{Re}\,\lambda>-1/2;\ \mathrm{Re}\,s>((-1)^n-1)/4]$
5	$(x-\sigma)_+^{\lambda-1/2} C_n^\lambda\left(\sqrt{\dfrac{x}{\sigma}}\right)$	$\dfrac{2^n\omega^{-s-n/2-\lambda+1/2}}{n!\,\sigma^{n/2}}(\lambda)_n\,\Gamma\left[\begin{array}{c} b \\ \frac{2b-n-2s-2\lambda+1}{2}\end{array}\right]$
	$\times\ _1F_1\left(\begin{array}{c} a;\ -\omega x \\ b \end{array}\right)$	$\times\,\mathrm{B}\left(\dfrac{2a-n-2s-2\lambda+1}{2},\ \dfrac{2s+n+2\lambda-1}{2}\right)$
		$\times\ _3F_3\left(\begin{array}{c}\frac{1-n-2\lambda}{2},\ \frac{2-n-2\lambda}{2},\ \frac{2a-n-2s-2\lambda+1}{2};\ -\sigma\omega \\ 1-n-\lambda,\ \frac{3-2s-n-2\lambda}{2},\ \frac{2b-n-2s-2\lambda+1}{2}\end{array}\right)+\dfrac{(\sigma/4)^{s+\lambda-1/2}}{n!}$
		$\times\,\Gamma\left[\begin{array}{c} n+2\lambda,\ \frac{n-2s+1}{2},\ \frac{1-n-2s-2\lambda}{2} \\ \lambda,\ 1-2s\end{array}\right]\ _3F_3\left(\begin{array}{c} a,\ s,\ \frac{2s+1}{2};\ -\sigma\omega \\ b,\ \frac{2s-n+1}{2},\ \frac{2s+n+2\lambda+1}{2}\end{array}\right)$
		$\left[\begin{array}{l}\sigma>0;\ \mathrm{Re}\,\lambda>-1/2;\ (\mathrm{Re}\,\omega>0;\ \mathrm{Re}\,s<\mathrm{Re}\,(a-\lambda)-n/2+1/2)\ \text{or} \\ (\mathrm{Re}\,\omega=0;\ \mathrm{Re}\,s<\mathrm{Re}\,(a-\lambda)-n/2+1/2,\ \mathrm{Re}\,(b-a-\lambda)-n/2+3/2)\end{array}\right]$

No.	$f(x)$	$F(s)$

6

$(\sigma - x)_+^{\lambda - 1/2} C_n^\lambda \left(\sqrt{\dfrac{\sigma}{x}} \right)$

$\times {}_1F_1 \left(\begin{matrix} a; \, \omega x \\ b \end{matrix} \right)$

$\dfrac{2^{2s} \sigma^{s+\lambda-1/2}}{n!} \Gamma \left[\begin{matrix} n+2\lambda, \, \frac{2s-n}{2}, \, \frac{2s+n+2\lambda}{2} \\ \lambda, \, 2s+2\lambda \end{matrix} \right]$

$\times {}_3F_3 \left(\begin{matrix} a, \, \frac{2s-n}{2}, \, \frac{2s+n+2\lambda}{2} \\ b, \, s+\lambda, \, \frac{2s+2\lambda+1}{2}; \, \sigma\omega \end{matrix} \right)$ $\left[\begin{matrix} \sigma > 0, \; \mathrm{Re}\,\lambda > -1/2; \\ \mathrm{Re}\,s > n/2 \end{matrix} \right]$

7

$(x - \sigma)_+^{\lambda - 1/2} C_n^\lambda \left(\sqrt{\dfrac{\sigma}{x}} \right)$

$\times {}_1F_1 \left(\begin{matrix} a; \, -\omega x \\ b \end{matrix} \right)$

$\dfrac{2^{2s+1} \pi \sigma^{s+\lambda-1/2}}{n!} \Gamma \left[\begin{matrix} n+2\lambda, \, 1-2s-2\lambda \\ \lambda, \, \frac{n-2s+2}{2}, \, \frac{2-n-2s-2\lambda}{2} \end{matrix} \right]$

$\times {}_3F_3 \left(\begin{matrix} a, \, \frac{2s-n}{2}, \, \frac{2s+n+2\lambda}{2}; \, -\sigma\omega \\ b, \, s+\lambda, \, s+\lambda+\frac{1}{2} \end{matrix} \right) + \dfrac{(1+(-1)^n)\, 2^{n-1}}{n!\sqrt{\pi}\,\omega^{s+\lambda-1/2}}$

$\times \Gamma \left[\begin{matrix} b, \, \frac{n+1}{2}, \, \frac{n+2\lambda}{2} \\ \lambda, \, b-s-\lambda+\frac{1}{2} \end{matrix} \right] \mathrm{B} \left(a-s-\lambda+\frac{1}{2}, \, s+\lambda-\frac{1}{2} \right)$

$\times {}_3F_3 \left(\begin{matrix} \frac{n+1}{2}, \, \frac{1-n-2\lambda}{2}, \, a-s-\lambda+\frac{1}{2}; \, -\sigma\omega \\ \frac{1}{2}, \, \frac{3}{2}-s-\lambda, \, b-s-\lambda+\frac{1}{2} \end{matrix} \right)$

$+ \dfrac{((-1)^n - 1)\, 2^n \sqrt{\sigma}}{n!\sqrt{\pi}\,\omega^{s+\lambda-1}} \mathrm{B} \left(a-s-\lambda+1, \, s+\lambda-1 \right)$

$\times \Gamma \left[\begin{matrix} b, \, \frac{n+2}{2}, \, \frac{n+2\lambda+1}{2} \\ \lambda, \, b-s-\lambda+1 \end{matrix} \right] {}_3F_3 \left(\begin{matrix} \frac{n+2}{2}, \, \frac{2-n-2\lambda}{2}, \, a-s-\lambda+1; \, -\sigma\omega \\ \frac{3}{2}, \, 2-s-\lambda, \, b-s-\lambda+1 \end{matrix} \right)$

$\left[\begin{matrix} \sigma > 0; \; \mathrm{Re}\,\lambda > -1/2; \; (\mathrm{Re}\,\omega > 0; \; \mathrm{Re}\,s < \mathrm{Re}\,(a-\lambda) + (3-(-1)^n)/4) \; \text{or} \\ (\mathrm{Re}\,\omega = 0; \; \mathrm{Re}\,s < \mathrm{Re}\,(a-\lambda) + (3-(-1)^n)/4, \; \mathrm{Re}\,(b-a-\lambda) + (7-(-1)^n)/4) \end{matrix} \right]$

8

$(\sigma - x)_+^{\lambda - 1/2} e^{-\omega x}$

$\times C_n^\lambda \left(\dfrac{2x}{\sigma} - 1 \right)$

$\times {}_1F_1 \left(\begin{matrix} a; \, \omega x \\ b \end{matrix} \right)$

$\dfrac{(-1)^n \, \sigma^{s+\lambda-1/2} (2\lambda)_n \left(\frac{1}{2} - s + \lambda \right)_n}{n!} \Gamma \left[\begin{matrix} s, \, \lambda + \frac{1}{2} \\ s+n+\lambda+\frac{1}{2} \end{matrix} \right]$

$\times {}_3F_3 \left(\begin{matrix} b-a, \, s, \, s-\lambda+\frac{1}{2}; \, -\sigma\omega \\ b, \, s-n-\lambda+\frac{1}{2}, \, s+n+\lambda+\frac{1}{2} \end{matrix} \right)$

$[\sigma, \; \mathrm{Re}\,s > 0; \; \mathrm{Re}\,\lambda > -1/2]$

9

$(x - \sigma)_+^{\lambda - 1/2} e^{-\omega x}$

$\times C_n^\lambda \left(\dfrac{2x}{\sigma} - 1 \right)$

$\times {}_1F_1 \left(\begin{matrix} a; \, \omega x \\ b \end{matrix} \right)$

$\dfrac{4^n \omega^{-s-n-\lambda+1/2}}{n!\,\sigma^n} (\lambda)_n \Gamma \left[\begin{matrix} b \\ \frac{2b-2n-2s-2\lambda+1}{2} \end{matrix} \right]$

$\times \mathrm{B} \left(\dfrac{2b-2a-2n-2s-2\lambda+1}{2}, \, \dfrac{2s+2n+2\lambda-1}{2} \right)$

$\times {}_3F_3 \left(\begin{matrix} 1-n-2\lambda, \, \frac{1-2n-2\lambda}{2}, \, \frac{2b-2a-2n-2s-2\lambda+1}{2}; \, -\sigma\omega \\ 1-2n-2\lambda, \, \frac{3-2n-2s-2\lambda}{2}, \, \frac{2b-2n-2s-2\lambda+1}{2} \end{matrix} \right)$

$+ \dfrac{\sqrt{\pi}\, \sigma^{s+\lambda-1/2}}{2^{2\lambda-1} n!} \left(\dfrac{1-2s+2\lambda}{2} \right)_n \Gamma \left[\begin{matrix} n+2\lambda, \, \frac{1-2n-2s-2\lambda}{2} \\ \lambda, \, 1-s \end{matrix} \right]$

$\times {}_3F_3 \left(\begin{matrix} b-a, \, s, \, \frac{2s-2\lambda+1}{2}; \, -\sigma\omega \\ b, \, \frac{2s-2n-2\lambda+1}{2}, \, \frac{2s+2n+2\lambda+1}{2} \end{matrix} \right)$

$\left[\begin{matrix} \sigma > 0; \; \mathrm{Re}\,\lambda > -1/2; \; (\mathrm{Re}\,\omega > 0; \; \mathrm{Re}\,s < \mathrm{Re}\,(b-a-\lambda) - n+1/2) \; \text{or} \\ (\mathrm{Re}\,\omega = 0; \; \mathrm{Re}\,s < \mathrm{Re}\,(a-\lambda) - n+3/2, \; \mathrm{Re}\,(b-a-\lambda) - n+1/2) \end{matrix} \right]$

No.	$f(x)$	$F(s)$
10	$(\sigma - x)_+^{\lambda - 1/2} e^{-\omega x}$ $\times C_n^\lambda\left(\dfrac{2\sigma}{x} - 1\right)$ $\times {}_1F_1\left(\begin{array}{c} a;\, \omega x \\ b \end{array}\right)$	$\dfrac{2^{1-2\lambda}\sqrt{\pi}\,\sigma^{s+\lambda-1/2}}{n!}(s+2\lambda)_n\,\Gamma\left[\begin{array}{c} n+2\lambda,\, s-n \\ \lambda,\, \frac{2s+2\lambda+1}{2} \end{array}\right]$ $\times {}_3F_3\left(\begin{array}{c} b-a,\, s-n,\, s+n+2\lambda \\ b,\, \frac{2s+2\lambda+1}{2},\, s+2\lambda;\, -\sigma\omega \end{array}\right)$ $[\sigma > 0;\ \operatorname{Re}\lambda > -1/2;\ \operatorname{Re}s > n]$
11	$(\sigma - x)_+^{\lambda - 1/2} e^{-\omega x}$ $\times C_n^\lambda\left(\sqrt{\dfrac{x}{\sigma}}\right)$ $\times {}_1F_1\left(\begin{array}{c} a;\, \omega x \\ b \end{array}\right)$	$\dfrac{\pi\sigma^{s+\lambda-1/2}}{2^{2s+2\lambda-2}n!}\,\Gamma\left[\begin{array}{c} n+2\lambda,\, 2s \\ \lambda,\, \frac{2s-n+1}{2},\, \frac{2s+n+2\lambda+1}{2} \end{array}\right]$ $\times {}_3F_3\left(\begin{array}{c} b-a,\, s,\, \frac{2s+1}{2};\, -\sigma\omega \\ b,\, \frac{2s-n+1}{2},\, \frac{2s+n+2\lambda+1}{2} \end{array}\right)$ $[\sigma > 0;\ \operatorname{Re}\lambda > -1/2;\ \operatorname{Re}s > ((-1)^n - 1)/4]$
12	$(x - \sigma)_+^{\lambda - 1/2} e^{-\omega x}$ $\times C_n^\lambda\left(\sqrt{\dfrac{x}{\sigma}}\right)$ $\times {}_1F_1\left(\begin{array}{c} a;\, \omega x \\ b \end{array}\right)$	$\dfrac{2^n\omega^{-s-n/2-\lambda+1/2}}{n!\,\sigma^{n/2}}(\lambda)_n\,\Gamma\left[\begin{array}{c} b \\ \frac{2b-n-2s-2\lambda+1}{2} \end{array}\right]$ $\times \mathrm{B}\left(\dfrac{2b-2a-n-2s-2\lambda+1}{2},\, \dfrac{2s+n+2\lambda-1}{2}\right)$ $\times {}_3F_3\left(\begin{array}{c} \frac{1-n-2\lambda}{2},\, \frac{2-n-2\lambda}{2},\, \frac{2b-2a-n-2s-2\lambda+1}{2};\, -\sigma\omega \\ 1-n-\lambda,\, \frac{3-2s-n-2\lambda}{2},\, \frac{2b-n-2s-2\lambda+1}{2} \end{array}\right)$ $+\dfrac{(\sigma/4)^{s+\lambda-1/2}}{n!}\,\Gamma\left[\begin{array}{c} n+2\lambda,\, \frac{n-2s+1}{2},\, \frac{1-n-2s-2\lambda}{2} \\ \lambda,\, 1-2s \end{array}\right]$ $\times {}_3F_3\left(\begin{array}{c} b-a,\, s,\, \frac{2s+1}{2};\, -\sigma\omega \\ b,\, \frac{2s-n+1}{2},\, \frac{2s+n+2\lambda+1}{2} \end{array}\right)$ $\left[\begin{array}{c} \sigma > 0;\ \operatorname{Re}\lambda > -1/2;\ (\operatorname{Re}\omega > 0;\ \operatorname{Re}s < \operatorname{Re}(b-a-\lambda) - n/2 + 1/2)\ \text{or} \\ (\operatorname{Re}\omega = 0;\ \operatorname{Re}s < \operatorname{Re}(a-\lambda) - n/2 + 3/2,\ \operatorname{Re}(b-a-\lambda) - n/2 + 1/2) \end{array}\right]$
13	$(\sigma - x)_+^{\lambda - 1/2} e^{-\omega x}$ $\times C_n^\lambda\left(\sqrt{\dfrac{\sigma}{x}}\right)$ $\times {}_1F_1\left(\begin{array}{c} a;\, \omega x \\ b \end{array}\right)$	$\dfrac{2^{2s}\sigma^{s+\lambda-1/2}}{n!}\,\Gamma\left[\begin{array}{c} n+2\lambda,\, \frac{2s-n}{2},\, \frac{2s+n+2\lambda}{2} \\ \lambda,\, 2s+2\lambda \end{array}\right]$ $\times {}_3F_3\left(\begin{array}{c} b-a,\, \frac{2s-n}{2},\, \frac{2s+n+2\lambda}{2} \\ b,\, s+\lambda,\, \frac{2s+2\lambda+1}{2};\, -\sigma\omega \end{array}\right)$ $[\sigma > 0,\ \operatorname{Re}\lambda > -1/2;\ \operatorname{Re}s > n/2]$
14	$(x - \sigma)_+^{\lambda - 1/2} e^{-\omega x}$ $\times C_n^\lambda\left(\sqrt{\dfrac{\sigma}{x}}\right)$ $\times {}_1F_1\left(\begin{array}{c} a;\, \omega x \\ b \end{array}\right)$	$\dfrac{2^{2s+1}\pi\sigma^{s+\lambda-1/2}}{n!}\,\Gamma\left[\begin{array}{c} 1-2s-2\lambda,\, n+2\lambda \\ \lambda,\, \frac{n-2s+2}{2},\, \frac{2-n-2s-2\lambda}{2} \end{array}\right]$ $\times {}_3F_3\left(\begin{array}{c} b-a,\, \frac{2s-n}{2},\, \frac{2s+n+2\lambda}{2} \\ b,\, s+\lambda,\, s+\lambda+\frac{1}{2};\, -\sigma\omega \end{array}\right)$ $+\dfrac{(1+(-1)^n)\,2^{n-1}}{n!\sqrt{\pi}\,\omega^{s+\lambda-1/2}}\,\Gamma\left[\begin{array}{c} b,\, \frac{n+1}{2},\, \frac{n+2\lambda}{2} \\ \lambda,\, b-s-\lambda+\frac{1}{2} \end{array}\right]\times$

No.	$f(x)$	$F(s)$
		$\times \mathrm{B}\left(b-a-s-\lambda+\dfrac{1}{2},\, s+\lambda-\dfrac{1}{2}\right)$

$$\times {}_3F_3\left(\begin{array}{c} \frac{n+1}{2},\, \frac{1-n-2\lambda}{2},\, b-a-s-\lambda+\frac{1}{2} \\ \frac{1}{2},\, \frac{3}{2}-s-\lambda,\, b-s-\lambda+\frac{1}{2};\, -\sigma\omega \end{array}\right)$$

$$+\frac{((-1)^n-1)\,2^n\sqrt{\sigma}}{n!\sqrt{\pi}\,\omega^{s+\lambda-1}}\,\mathrm{B}\left(b-a-s-\lambda+1,\, s+\lambda-1\right)$$

$$\times\Gamma\left[\begin{array}{c} b,\, \frac{n+2}{2},\, \frac{n+2\lambda+1}{2} \\ \lambda,\, b-s-\lambda+1 \end{array}\right]\, {}_3F_3\left(\begin{array}{c} \frac{n+2}{2},\, \frac{2-n-2\lambda}{2},\, b-a-s-\lambda+1 \\ \frac{3}{2},\, 2-s-\lambda,\, b-s-\lambda+1;\, -\sigma\omega \end{array}\right)$$

$$\left[\begin{array}{l} \sigma>0;\ \mathrm{Re}\,\lambda>-1/2;\ (\mathrm{Re}\,\omega>0;\ \mathrm{Re}\,s<\mathrm{Re}\,(b-a-\lambda)+(3-(-1)^n)/4)\ \text{or} \\ (\mathrm{Re}\,\omega=0;\ \mathrm{Re}\,s<\mathrm{Re}\,(b-a-\lambda)+(3-(-1)^n)/4,\ \mathrm{Re}\,(a-\lambda)+(7-(-1)^n)/4) \end{array}\right]$$

3.28.14. ${}_1F_1(a;\,b;\,\omega x)$ **and** $P_n^{(\rho,\sigma)}(\varphi(x))$

No.	$f(x)$	$F(s)$
1	$(\sigma-x)_+^\mu\, P_n^{(\mu,\nu)}\left(\dfrac{2x}{\sigma}-1\right)$ $\times {}_1F_1\left(\begin{array}{c} a;\,\omega x \\ b \end{array}\right)$	$\dfrac{\sigma^{s+\mu}}{n!}\Gamma\left[\begin{array}{c} n+\mu+1,\, s,\, s-\nu \\ s+n+\mu+1,\, s-n-\nu \end{array}\right]$ $\times {}_3F_3\left(\begin{array}{c} a,\, s,\, s-\nu;\, \sigma\omega \\ b,\, s+n+\mu+1,\, s-n-\nu \end{array}\right)$ $\left[\begin{array}{l}\sigma,\ \mathrm{Re}\,s>0;\\ \mathrm{Re}\,\mu>-1\end{array}\right]$
2	$(x-\sigma)_+^\mu\, P_n^{(\mu,\nu)}\left(\dfrac{2x}{\sigma}-1\right)$ $\times {}_1F_1\left(\begin{array}{c} a;\,-\omega x \\ b \end{array}\right)$	$\dfrac{\omega^{-s-n-\mu}}{n!\,\sigma^n}\,(n+\mu+\nu+1)_n\,\dfrac{\mathrm{B}\,(a-n-s-\mu,\, s+n+\mu)}{\Gamma\,(b-n-s-\mu)}$ $\times\Gamma(b)\,{}_3F_3\left(\begin{array}{c} -n-\mu,\, a-n-s-\mu,\, -n-\mu-\nu;\, -\sigma\omega \\ 1-n-s-\mu,\, b-n-s-\mu,\, -2n-\mu-\nu \end{array}\right)$ $+\dfrac{\sigma^{s+\mu}}{n!}\,(\nu-s+1)_n\,\mathrm{B}\,(-s-n-\mu,\, n+\mu+1)$ $\times {}_3F_3\left(\begin{array}{c} a,\, s,\, s-\nu;\, -\sigma\omega \\ b,\, s+n+\mu+1,\, s-n-\nu \end{array}\right)$ $\left[\begin{array}{l} \sigma>0;\ \mathrm{Re}\,\mu>-1;\ (\mathrm{Re}\,\omega>0;\ \mathrm{Re}\,s<\mathrm{Re}\,(a-\mu)-n)\ \text{or} \\ (\mathrm{Re}\,\omega=0;\ \mathrm{Re}\,s<\mathrm{Re}\,(a-\mu)-n,\ \mathrm{Re}\,(b-a-\mu)-n+1) \end{array}\right]$
3	$(\sigma-x)_+^\mu\, P_n^{(\mu,\nu)}\left(\dfrac{2\sigma}{x}-1\right)$ $\times {}_1F_1\left(\begin{array}{c} a;\,\omega x \\ b \end{array}\right)$	$\dfrac{\sigma^{s+\mu}}{n!}\Gamma\left[\begin{array}{c} n+\mu+1,\, s-n,\, s+n+\mu+\nu+1 \\ s+\mu+1,\, s+\mu+\nu+1 \end{array}\right]$ $\times {}_3F_3\left(\begin{array}{c} a,\, s-n,\, s+n+\mu+\nu+1;\, \sigma\omega \\ b,\, s+\mu+1,\, s+\mu+\nu+1 \end{array}\right)$ $[\sigma>0;\ \mathrm{Re}\,\mu>-1;\ \mathrm{Re}\,s>n]$
4	$(x-\sigma)_+^\mu\, P_n^{(\mu,\nu)}\left(\dfrac{2\sigma}{x}-1\right)$ $\times {}_1F_1\left(\begin{array}{c} a;\,-\omega x \\ b \end{array}\right)$	$\dfrac{(-1)^n\,(\nu+1)_n}{n!\,\omega^{s+\mu}}\,\mathrm{B}\,(a-s-\mu,\, s+\mu)\,\Gamma\left[\begin{array}{c} b \\ b-s-\mu \end{array}\right]$ $\times {}_3F_3\left(\begin{array}{c} -n-\mu,\, n+\nu+1,\, a-s-\mu \\ \nu+1,\, 1-s-\mu,\, b-s-\mu;\, -\sigma\omega \end{array}\right)$ $+\dfrac{(-1)^n\,\sigma^{s+\mu}}{n!}\,(s+\mu+\nu+1)_n\,\Gamma\left[\begin{array}{c} n+\mu+1,\, -s-\mu \\ n-s+1 \end{array}\right]\times$

No.	$f(x)$	$F(s)$

$$\times\,_3F_3\left(\begin{matrix} a,\ s-n,\ s+n+\mu+\nu+1 \\ b,\ s+\mu+1,\ s+\mu+\nu+1;\ -\sigma\omega \end{matrix}\right)$$

$$\left[\begin{matrix} \sigma>0;\ \operatorname{Re}\mu>-1;\ (\operatorname{Re}\omega>0;\ \operatorname{Re}s<\operatorname{Re}(a-\mu))\ \text{or} \\ (\operatorname{Re}\omega=0;\ \operatorname{Re}s<\operatorname{Re}(a-\mu),\ \operatorname{Re}(b-a-\mu)+1) \end{matrix}\right]$$

5 $(\sigma-x)_+^{\mu}\,e^{-\omega x}$

$$\frac{\sigma^{s+\mu}}{n!}\,\Gamma\left[\begin{matrix} n+\mu+1,\ s,\ s-\nu \\ s+n+\mu+1,\ s-n-\nu \end{matrix}\right]$$

$$\times\,P_n^{(\mu,\,\nu)}\left(\frac{2x}{\sigma}-1\right)$$

$$\times\,_3F_3\left(\begin{matrix} b-a,\ s,\ s-\nu;\ -\sigma\omega \\ b,\ s+n+\mu+1,\ s-n-\nu \end{matrix}\right)$$

$$\times\,_1F_1\left(\begin{matrix} a;\ \omega x \\ b \end{matrix}\right)$$

$$[\sigma,\ \operatorname{Re}s>0;\ \operatorname{Re}\mu>-1]$$

6 $(x-\sigma)_+^{\mu}\,e^{-\omega x}$

$$\frac{\omega^{-s-n-\mu}}{n!\,\sigma^n}\,(n+\mu+\nu+1)_n\,\mathrm{B}\,(b-a-n-s-\mu,\ s+n+\mu)$$

$$\times\,P_n^{(\mu,\,\nu)}\left(\frac{2x}{\sigma}-1\right)$$

$$\times\,\Gamma\left[\begin{matrix} b \\ b-n-s-\mu \end{matrix}\right]$$

$$\times\,_1F_1\left(\begin{matrix} a;\ \omega x \\ b \end{matrix}\right)$$

$$\times\,_3F_3\left(\begin{matrix} -n-\mu,\ b-a-n-s-\mu,\ -n-\mu-\nu;\ -\sigma\omega \\ 1-n-s-\mu,\ b-n-s-\mu,\ -2n-\mu-\nu \end{matrix}\right)$$

$$+\,\frac{\sigma^{s+\mu}}{n!}\,(\nu-s+1)_n\,\mathrm{B}\,(-s-n-\mu,\ n+\mu+1)$$

$$\times\,_3F_3\left(\begin{matrix} b-a,\ s,\ s-\nu;\ -\sigma\omega \\ b,\ s+n+\mu+1,\ s-n-\nu \end{matrix}\right)$$

$$\left[\begin{matrix} \sigma>0;\ \operatorname{Re}\mu>-1;\ (\operatorname{Re}\omega>0;\ \operatorname{Re}s<\operatorname{Re}(b-a-\mu)-n)\ \text{or} \\ (\operatorname{Re}\omega=0;\ \operatorname{Re}s<\operatorname{Re}(a-\mu)-n+1,\ \operatorname{Re}(b-a-\mu)-n) \end{matrix}\right]$$

7 $(\sigma-x)_+^{\mu}\,e^{-\omega x}$

$$\frac{\sigma^{s+\mu}}{n!}\,\Gamma\left[\begin{matrix} n+\mu+1,\ s-n,\ s+n+\mu+\nu+1 \\ s+\mu+1,\ s+\mu+\nu+1 \end{matrix}\right]$$

$$\times\,P_n^{(\mu,\,\nu)}\left(\frac{2\sigma}{x}-1\right)$$

$$\times\,_3F_3\left(\begin{matrix} b-a,\ s-n,\ s+n+\mu+\nu+1;\ -\sigma\omega \\ b,\ s+\mu+1,\ s+\mu+\nu+1 \end{matrix}\right)$$

$$\times\,_1F_1\left(\begin{matrix} a;\ \omega x \\ b \end{matrix}\right)$$

$$[\sigma>0;\ \operatorname{Re}\mu>-1;\ \operatorname{Re}s>n]$$

8 $(x-\sigma)_+^{\mu}\,e^{-\omega x}$

$$\frac{(-1)^n\,(\nu+1)_n}{n!\,\omega^{s+\mu}}\,\mathrm{B}\,(b-a-s-\mu,\ s+\mu)\,\Gamma\left[\begin{matrix} b \\ b-s-\mu \end{matrix}\right]$$

$$\times\,P_n^{(\mu,\,\nu)}\left(\frac{2\sigma}{x}-1\right)$$

$$\times\,_3F_3\left(\begin{matrix} -n-\mu,\ b-a-s-\mu,\ n+\nu+1 \\ -s-\mu+1,\ b-s-\mu,\ \nu+1;\ -\sigma\omega \end{matrix}\right)$$

$$\times\,_1F_1\left(\begin{matrix} a;\ \omega x \\ b \end{matrix}\right)$$

$$+\,\frac{(-1)^n\,\sigma^{s+\mu}}{n!}\,(s+\mu+\nu+1)_n\,\Gamma\left[\begin{matrix} n+\mu+1,\ -s-\mu \\ n-s+1 \end{matrix}\right]$$

$$\times\,_3F_3\left(\begin{matrix} b-a,\ s-n,\ s+n+\mu+\nu+1 \\ b,\ s+\mu+1,\ s+\mu+\nu+1;\ -\sigma\omega \end{matrix}\right)$$

$$\left[\begin{matrix} \sigma>0;\ \operatorname{Re}\mu>-1;\ (\operatorname{Re}\omega>0;\ \operatorname{Re}s<\operatorname{Re}(b-a-\mu))\ \text{or} \\ (\operatorname{Re}\omega=0;\ \operatorname{Re}s<\operatorname{Re}(a-\mu)+1,\ \operatorname{Re}(b-a-\mu)) \end{matrix}\right]$$

3.28.15.　Products of $_1F_1\left(a;\, b;\, \omega x^r\right)$

1　$_1F_1\left(\genfrac{}{}{0pt}{}{a;\; -wx}{b}\right) {}_1F_1\left(\genfrac{}{}{0pt}{}{c;\; -\sigma x}{d}\right)$

$\sigma^{a-s}\omega^{-a}\,\Gamma\left[\genfrac{}{}{0pt}{}{b,\, d}{b-a,\, a+d-s}\right] B\left(a-s+c,\, s-a\right)$

$$\times\; {}_3F_2\left(\genfrac{}{}{0pt}{}{a,\, a-b+1,\, a+c-s}{a-s+1,\, a+d-s;\; -\frac{\sigma}{\omega}}\right)$$

$$+\omega^{-s}\,\Gamma\left[\genfrac{}{}{0pt}{}{b}{b-s}\right] B\left(a-s,\, s\right)\, {}_3F_2\left(\genfrac{}{}{0pt}{}{c,\, s,\, s-b+1}{d,\, s-a+1;\; -\frac{\sigma}{\omega}}\right)$$

$$\left[\begin{array}{l}\left(\operatorname{Re}\sigma>0,\ \operatorname{Re}\omega>0;\ 0<\operatorname{Re}s<\operatorname{Re}\left(a+c\right)\right)\ \text{or}\\[2pt]\left(\operatorname{Re}\sigma>0,\ \operatorname{Re}\omega=0;\ 0<\operatorname{Re}s<\operatorname{Re}\left(a+c\right),\ \operatorname{Re}\left(b+c-a\right)+1\right)\ \text{or}\\[2pt]\left(\operatorname{Re}\sigma=0,\ \operatorname{Re}\omega>0;\ 0<\operatorname{Re}s<\operatorname{Re}\left(a+c\right),\ \operatorname{Re}\left(a+d-c\right)+1\right)\ \text{or}\\[2pt]\left(\operatorname{Re}\sigma=0,\ \operatorname{Re}\omega=0;\ 0<\operatorname{Re}s<\operatorname{Re}\left(a+c\right),\ \operatorname{Re}\left(b+c-a\right)+1,\right.\\[2pt]\qquad\qquad\qquad\operatorname{Re}\left(a+d-c\right)+1,\ \operatorname{Re}\left(b+d-a-c\right)+1\left.\right)\end{array}\right]$$

2　$\left(\sigma^2-x^2\right)_{+}^{\alpha-1}\, {}_1F_1\left(\genfrac{}{}{0pt}{}{a;\; -\omega x}{b}\right)$

$\dfrac{\sigma^{s+2\alpha-2}}{2} B\left(\dfrac{s}{2},\, \alpha\right) {}_3F_4\left(\genfrac{}{}{0pt}{}{a,\, b-a,\, \frac{s}{2};\; \frac{\sigma^2\omega^2}{4}}{\frac{b}{2},\, \frac{b+1}{2},\, b,\, \frac{s+2\alpha}{2}}\right)$

$$\times\; {}_1F_1\left(\genfrac{}{}{0pt}{}{a;\, \omega x}{b}\right)$$

$$\left[\sigma,\ \operatorname{Re}\alpha,\ \operatorname{Re}s>0\right]$$

3　$_1F_1\left(\genfrac{}{}{0pt}{}{a;\; -\omega x}{b}\right) {}_1F_1\left(\genfrac{}{}{0pt}{}{c;\; -\frac{\sigma}{x}}{d}\right)$

$\Gamma\left[\genfrac{}{}{0pt}{}{d}{s+d}\right]\sigma^s\, B\left(s+c,\, -s\right)\, {}_2F_3\left(\genfrac{}{}{0pt}{}{a,\, s+c;\; \sigma\omega}{b,\, s+1,\, s+d}\right)$

$$+\Gamma\left[\genfrac{}{}{0pt}{}{b}{b-s}\right]\omega^{-s}\, B\left(a-s,\, s\right)\, {}_2F_3\left(\genfrac{}{}{0pt}{}{c,\, a-s;\; \sigma\omega}{d,\, 1-s,\, b-s}\right)$$

$$\left[\begin{array}{l}\left(\operatorname{Re}\sigma>0,\ \operatorname{Re}\omega>0;\ -\operatorname{Re}a<\operatorname{Re}s<\operatorname{Re}a\right)\ \text{or}\\[2pt]\left(\operatorname{Re}\sigma>0,\ \operatorname{Re}\omega=0;\ -\operatorname{Re}a<\operatorname{Re}s<\operatorname{Re}a,\ \operatorname{Re}\left(b-a\right)+1\right)\ \text{or}\\[2pt]\left(\operatorname{Re}\sigma=0,\ \operatorname{Re}\omega>0;\ -\operatorname{Re}a,\ \operatorname{Re}\left(c-d\right)-1<\operatorname{Re}s<\operatorname{Re}a\right)\ \text{or}\\[2pt]\left(\operatorname{Re}\sigma=0,\ \operatorname{Re}\omega=0;\ -\operatorname{Re}a,\ \operatorname{Re}\left(c-d\right)-1<\operatorname{Re}s<\operatorname{Re}a,\ \operatorname{Re}\left(b-a\right)+1\right)\end{array}\right]$$

4　$e^{-\omega x}\, {}_1F_1\left(\genfrac{}{}{0pt}{}{a;\; -\sigma x}{b}\right)$

$\sigma^{-a}\omega^{a-s}\,\Gamma\left[\genfrac{}{}{0pt}{}{b,\, d}{b-a,\, a+d-s}\right] B\left(s-a,\, a-c+d-s\right)$

$$\times\; {}_1F_1\left(\genfrac{}{}{0pt}{}{c;\, \omega x}{d}\right)$$

$$\times\; {}_3F_2\left(\genfrac{}{}{0pt}{}{a,\, a-b+1,\, a-c+d-s}{a-s+1,\, a+d-s;\; -\frac{\omega}{\sigma}}\right)$$

$$+\sigma^{-s}\,\Gamma\left[\genfrac{}{}{0pt}{}{b}{b-s}\right] B\left(a-s,\, s\right)\, {}_3F_2\left(\genfrac{}{}{0pt}{}{d-c,\, s,\, s-b+1}{d,\, s-a+1;\; -\frac{\omega}{\sigma}}\right)$$

$$\left[\begin{array}{l}\left(\operatorname{Re}\sigma>0,\ \operatorname{Re}\omega>0;\ 0<\operatorname{Re}s<\operatorname{Re}\left(a-c+d\right)\right)\ \text{or}\\[2pt]\left(\operatorname{Re}\sigma>0,\ \operatorname{Re}\omega=0;\ 0<\operatorname{Re}s<\operatorname{Re}\left(a-c+d\right),\ \operatorname{Re}\left(a+c\right)+1\right)\ \text{or}\\[2pt]\left(\operatorname{Re}\sigma=0,\ \operatorname{Re}\omega>0;\ 0<\operatorname{Re}s<\operatorname{Re}\left(a-c+d\right),\ \operatorname{Re}\left(b+d-a-c\right)+1\right)\ \text{or}\\[2pt]\left(\operatorname{Re}\sigma=0,\ \operatorname{Re}\omega=0;\ 0<\operatorname{Re}s<\operatorname{Re}\left(a-c+d\right),\ \operatorname{Re}\left(a+c\right)+1,\right.\\[2pt]\qquad\qquad\qquad\operatorname{Re}\left(b+d-a-c\right)+1,\ \operatorname{Re}\left(b+c-a\right)+1\left.\right)\end{array}\right]$$

No.	$f(x)$	$F(s)$
5	$e^{-(\sigma+\omega)x}\,{}_1F_1\!\left(\begin{matrix}a;\,\sigma x\\b\end{matrix}\right)$ $\times\,{}_1F_1\!\left(\begin{matrix}c;\,\omega x\\d\end{matrix}\right)$	$\sigma^{a-b}\omega^{-a+b-s}\,\Gamma\!\left[\begin{matrix}b,\,d\\a,\,b-a+d-s\end{matrix}\right]$ $\times\,\mathrm{B}\,(b-a-c+d-s,\,a-b+s)$ $\times\,{}_3F_2\!\left(\begin{matrix}1-a,\,b-a,\,b-a-c+d-s\\b-a-s+1,\,b-a+d-s;\,-\frac{\omega}{\sigma}\end{matrix}\right)$ $+\,\sigma^{-s}\,\Gamma\!\left[\begin{matrix}b\\b-s\end{matrix}\right]\mathrm{B}\,(b-a-s,\,s)$ $\times\,{}_3F_2\!\left(\begin{matrix}d-c,\,s,\,s-b+1\\d,\,s+a-b+1;\,-\frac{\omega}{\sigma}\end{matrix}\right)$

$$\left[\begin{matrix}(\operatorname{Re}\sigma>0,\ \operatorname{Re}\omega>0;\ 0<\operatorname{Re}s<\operatorname{Re}(b+d-a-c))\ \text{or}\\(\operatorname{Re}\sigma>0,\ \operatorname{Re}\omega=0;\ 0<\operatorname{Re}s<\operatorname{Re}(b+d-a-c),\ \operatorname{Re}(b+c-a)+1)\ \text{or}\\(\operatorname{Re}\sigma=0,\ \operatorname{Re}\omega>0;\ 0<\operatorname{Re}s<\operatorname{Re}(b+d-a-c),\ \operatorname{Re}(a+d-c)+1)\ \text{or}\\(\operatorname{Re}\sigma=0,\ \operatorname{Re}\omega=0;\ 0<\operatorname{Re}s<\operatorname{Re}(b+d-a-c),\ \operatorname{Re}(b+c-a)+1,\\\operatorname{Re}(a+d-c)+1,\ \operatorname{Re}(a+c)+1)\end{matrix}\right]$$

No.	$f(x)$	$F(s)$
6	$e^{-\sigma/x}\,{}_1F_1\!\left(\begin{matrix}a;\,-wx\\b\end{matrix}\right)$ $\times\,{}_1F_1\!\left(\begin{matrix}c;\,\frac{\sigma}{x}\\d\end{matrix}\right)$	$\sigma^s\,\Gamma\!\left[\begin{matrix}d\\s+d\end{matrix}\right]\mathrm{B}\,(s-c+d,\,-s)\,{}_2F_3\!\left(\begin{matrix}a,\,s-c+d;\,\sigma\omega\\b,\,s+1,\,s+d\end{matrix}\right)$ $+\,\omega^{-s}\,\Gamma\!\left[\begin{matrix}b\\b-s\end{matrix}\right]\mathrm{B}\,(a-s,\,s)\,{}_2F_3\!\left(\begin{matrix}d-c,\,a-s;\,\sigma\omega\\1-s,\,b-s,\,d\end{matrix}\right)$

$$\left[\begin{matrix}(\operatorname{Re}\sigma>0,\ \operatorname{Re}\omega>0;\ \operatorname{Re}(c-d)<\operatorname{Re}s<\operatorname{Re}a)\ \text{or}\\(\operatorname{Re}\sigma>0,\ \operatorname{Re}\omega=0;\ \operatorname{Re}(c-d)<\operatorname{Re}s<\operatorname{Re}a,\ \operatorname{Re}(b-a)+1)\ \text{or}\\(\operatorname{Re}\sigma=0,\ \operatorname{Re}\omega>0;\ \operatorname{Re}(c-d),\ -\operatorname{Re}c-1<\operatorname{Re}s<\operatorname{Re}a)\ \text{or}\\(\operatorname{Re}\sigma=0,\ \operatorname{Re}\omega=0;\ \operatorname{Re}(c-d),\ -\operatorname{Re}c-1<\operatorname{Re}s<\operatorname{Re}a,\ \operatorname{Re}(b-a)+1)\end{matrix}\right]$$

No.	$f(x)$	$F(s)$
7	$e^{-\omega x-\sigma/x}\,{}_1F_1\!\left(\begin{matrix}a;\,wx\\b\end{matrix}\right)$ $\times\,{}_1F_1\!\left(\begin{matrix}c;\,\frac{\sigma}{x}\\d\end{matrix}\right)$	$\sigma^s\,\Gamma\!\left[\begin{matrix}d\\s+d\end{matrix}\right]\mathrm{B}\,(s-c+d,\,-s)\,{}_2F_3\!\left(\begin{matrix}b-a,\,s-c+d\\b,\,s+1,\,s+d;\,\sigma\omega\end{matrix}\right)$ $+\,\omega^{-s}\,\Gamma\!\left[\begin{matrix}b\\b-s\end{matrix}\right]\mathrm{B}\,(b-a-s,\,s)\,{}_2F_3\!\left(\begin{matrix}d-c,\,b-a-s\\1-s,\,b-s,\,d;\,\sigma\omega\end{matrix}\right)$

$$\left[\begin{matrix}(\operatorname{Re}\sigma>0,\ \operatorname{Re}\omega>0;\ \operatorname{Re}(c-d)<\operatorname{Re}s<\operatorname{Re}(b-a))\ \text{or}\\(\operatorname{Re}\sigma>0,\ \operatorname{Re}\omega=0;\ \operatorname{Re}(c-d)<\operatorname{Re}s<\operatorname{Re}a+1,\ \operatorname{Re}(b-a))\ \text{or}\\(\operatorname{Re}\sigma=0,\ \operatorname{Re}\omega>0;\ \operatorname{Re}(c-d),\ -\operatorname{Re}c-1<\operatorname{Re}s<\operatorname{Re}(b-a))\ \text{or}\\(\operatorname{Re}\sigma=0,\ \operatorname{Re}\omega=0;\ \operatorname{Re}(c-d),\ -\operatorname{Re}c-1<\operatorname{Re}s<\operatorname{Re}a+1,\ \operatorname{Re}(b-a))\end{matrix}\right]$$

No.	$f(x)$	$F(s)$
8	$J_\nu(\sigma x)\,{}_1F_1\!\left(\begin{matrix}a;\,-\omega x\\b\end{matrix}\right)$ $\times\,{}_1F_1\!\left(\begin{matrix}a;\,\omega x\\b\end{matrix}\right)$	$\dfrac{2^{s-1}}{\sigma^s}\,\Gamma\!\left[\begin{matrix}\frac{s+\nu}{2}\\\frac{2-s+\nu}{2}\end{matrix}\right]{}_4F_3\!\left(\begin{matrix}a,\,b-a,\,\frac{s-\nu}{2},\,\frac{s+\nu}{2}\\\frac{b}{2},\,\frac{b+1}{2},\,b;\,-\frac{\omega^2}{\sigma^2}\end{matrix}\right)$

$$[\sigma,\,\omega>0;\ -\operatorname{Re}\nu<\operatorname{Re}s<2\operatorname{Re}a+3/2,\ 2\operatorname{Re}(b-a)+3/2,\ \operatorname{Re}b+3/2]$$

3.29.   The Tricomi Confluent Hypergeometric Function $\Psi\left(a;b;z\right)$

In this section, we give some selected simple formulas. Many new transforms can be obtained from Section 3.28 due to the connection formula

$$\Psi\begin{pmatrix}a;z\\b\end{pmatrix}=\frac{\Gamma\left(b-1\right)}{\Gamma\left(a\right)}z^{1-b}\,{}_1F_1\begin{pmatrix}a-b+1\\2-b;z\end{pmatrix}+\frac{\Gamma\left(1-b\right)}{\Gamma\left(a-b+1\right)}\,{}_1F_1\begin{pmatrix}a;z\\b\end{pmatrix}.$$

More formulas can be obtained from the corresponding sections due to the relations

$$\Psi\left(a,b;z\right)=z^{-a}\lim_{c\to\infty}{}_2F_1\left(a,a-b+1;c;1-\frac{c}{z}\right),$$

$$\Psi\left(a,b;z\right)=\frac{1}{\Gamma\left(a\right)\Gamma\left(a-b+1\right)}G_{12}^{21}\left(z\left|\begin{array}{c}1-a\\0,1-b\end{array}\right.\right).$$

3.29.1. $\Psi\left(a;b;\omega x\right)$ and algebraic functions

No.	$f\left(x\right)$	$F\left(s\right)$
1	$\Psi\begin{pmatrix}a;\omega x\\b\end{pmatrix}$	$\omega^{-s}\Gamma\begin{bmatrix}s,\,s-b+1,\,a-s\\a,\,a-b+1\end{bmatrix}$ $\qquad\qquad[0,\ \operatorname{Re}b-1<\operatorname{Re}s<\operatorname{Re}a]$
2	$\left(\sigma-x\right)_+^{\mu-1}\Psi\begin{pmatrix}a;\omega x\\b\end{pmatrix}$	$\dfrac{\sigma^{s-b+\mu}}{\omega^{b-1}}\Gamma\begin{bmatrix}b-1\\a\end{bmatrix}\mathrm{B}\left(\mu,s-b+1\right){}_2F_2\begin{pmatrix}a-b+1,\,s-b+1;\sigma\omega\\2-b,\,s-b+\mu+1\end{pmatrix}$ $+\sigma^{s+\mu-1}\Gamma\begin{bmatrix}1-b\\a-b+1\end{bmatrix}\mathrm{B}\left(\mu,s\right){}_2F_2\begin{pmatrix}a,\,s;\sigma\omega\\b,\,s+\mu\end{pmatrix}$ $\qquad\qquad[\sigma,\ \operatorname{Re}\mu>0;\ \operatorname{Re}s>0,\ \operatorname{Re}b-1]$
3	$\left(x-\sigma\right)_+^{\mu-1}\Psi\begin{pmatrix}a;\omega x\\b\end{pmatrix}$	$\dfrac{\sigma^{s-b+\mu}}{\omega^{b-1}}\Gamma\begin{bmatrix}b-1\\a\end{bmatrix}\mathrm{B}\left(\mu,b-s-\mu\right){}_2F_2\begin{pmatrix}a-b+1,\,s-b+1;\sigma\omega\\2-b,\,s-b+\mu+1\end{pmatrix}$ $+\omega^{1-s-\mu}\Gamma\begin{bmatrix}s+\mu-1\\a\end{bmatrix}\mathrm{B}\left(a-s-\mu+1,\,s-b+\mu\right)$ $\times{}_2F_2\begin{pmatrix}1-\mu,\,a-s-\mu+1;\sigma\omega\\2-s-\mu,\,b-s-\mu+1\end{pmatrix}$ $+\sigma^{s+\mu-1}\Gamma\begin{bmatrix}1-b\\a-b+1\end{bmatrix}\mathrm{B}\left(\mu,1-s-\mu\right){}_2F_2\begin{pmatrix}a,\,s;\sigma\omega\\b,\,s+\mu\end{pmatrix}$ $\qquad\qquad[\sigma,\ \operatorname{Re}\mu>0;\ \operatorname{Re}\left(s-a+\mu\right)<1;\ \left|\arg\omega\right|<\pi]$
4	$\dfrac{1}{x-\sigma}\Psi\begin{pmatrix}a;\omega x\\b\end{pmatrix}$	$\dfrac{\pi\sigma^{s-b}}{\omega^{b-1}}\cot\left[\left(b-s\right)\pi\right]\Gamma\begin{bmatrix}b-1\\a\end{bmatrix}{}_1F_1\begin{pmatrix}a-b+1\\2-b;\sigma\omega\end{pmatrix}$ $+\omega^{1-s}\Gamma\begin{bmatrix}s-b\\a-b+1\end{bmatrix}\mathrm{B}\left(s-1,\,a-s+1\right){}_2F_2\begin{pmatrix}1,\,a-s+1;\sigma\omega\\2-s,\,b-s+1\end{pmatrix}$ $-\pi\sigma^{s-1}\cot\left(s\pi\right)\Gamma\begin{bmatrix}1-b\\a-b+1\end{bmatrix}{}_1F_1\begin{pmatrix}a;\sigma\omega\\b\end{pmatrix}$ $\qquad\qquad[\sigma>0;\ 0,\ \operatorname{Re}b-1<\operatorname{Re}s<\operatorname{Re}a+1]$

No.	$f(x)$	$F(s)$
5	$\dfrac{1}{(x+\sigma)^\rho}\Psi\left(\begin{matrix}a;\,\omega x\\b\end{matrix}\right)$	$\dfrac{\sigma^{s-b-\rho+1}}{\omega^{b-1}}\Gamma\left[\begin{matrix}b-1\\a\end{matrix}\right]B\left(s-b+1,\,b-s+\rho-1\right)$

$$\times\,_2F_2\left(\begin{matrix}a-b+1,\,s-b+1\\2-b,\,s-b-\rho+2;\,-\sigma\omega\end{matrix}\right)+\omega^{\rho-s}\Gamma\left[\begin{matrix}s-b-\rho+1\\a-b+1\end{matrix}\right]$$

$$\times\,B\left(s-\rho,\,a-s+\rho\right)\,_2F_2\left(\begin{matrix}\rho,\,a-s+\rho;\,-\sigma\omega\\\rho-s+1,\,\rho-s+b\end{matrix}\right)$$

$$+\,\sigma^{s-\rho}\Gamma\left[\begin{matrix}1-b\\a-b+1\end{matrix}\right]B\left(s,\,\rho\right)\,_2F_2\left(\begin{matrix}a,\,s;\,-\sigma\omega\\b,\,s-\rho+1\end{matrix}\right)$$

$$[0,\ \operatorname{Re}b-1<\operatorname{Re}s<\operatorname{Re}\left(a+\rho\right);\,|\arg\sigma|,\,|\arg\omega|<\pi]$$

No.	$f(x)$	$F(s)$
6	$\left(\sqrt{x}+\sqrt{x+\sigma}\right)^\nu$	$-\dfrac{\nu\sigma^{s-b+\nu/2+1}}{2^{2s-2b+2}\omega^{b-1}}\Gamma\left[\begin{matrix}b-1,\,2s-2b+2,\,\frac{2b-2s-\nu-2}{2}\\a,\,\frac{2s-2b-\nu+4}{2}\end{matrix}\right]$
	$\times\,\Psi\left(\begin{matrix}a;\,\omega x\\b\end{matrix}\right)$	

$$\times\,_3F_3\left(\begin{matrix}a-b+1,\,s-b+1,\,\frac{2s-2b+3}{2};\,-\sigma\omega\\2-b,\,\frac{2s-2b-\nu+4}{2},\,\frac{2s-2b+\nu+4}{2}\end{matrix}\right)$$

$$+\,\dfrac{2^\nu}{\omega^{s+\nu/2}}B\left(\dfrac{2a-2s-\nu}{2},\,\dfrac{2s+\nu}{2}\right)$$

$$\times\,\Gamma\left[\begin{matrix}\frac{2s-2b+\nu+2}{2}\\a-b+1\end{matrix}\right]\,_3F_3\left(\begin{matrix}-\frac{\nu}{2},\,\frac{1-\nu}{2},\,\frac{2a-2s-\nu}{2};\,-\sigma\omega\\1-\nu,\,\frac{2-2s-\nu}{2},\,\frac{2b-2s-\nu}{2}\end{matrix}\right)$$

$$-\,\dfrac{\nu\sigma^{s+\nu/2}}{2^{2s}}\Gamma\left[\begin{matrix}1-b,\,-\frac{2s+\nu}{2},\,2s\\a-b+1,\,\frac{2s-\nu+2}{2}\end{matrix}\right]\,_3F_3\left(\begin{matrix}a,\,s,\,\frac{2s+1}{2};\,-\sigma\omega\\b,\,\frac{2s-\nu+2}{2},\,\frac{2s+\nu+2}{2}\end{matrix}\right)$$

$$[0,\ \operatorname{Re}b-1<\operatorname{Re}s<\operatorname{Re}\left(a-\nu/2\right);\,|\arg\sigma|,\,|\arg\omega|<\pi]$$

No.	$f(x)$	$F(s)$
7	$\dfrac{\left(\sqrt{x}+\sqrt{x+\sigma}\right)^\nu}{\sqrt{x+\sigma}}$	$\dfrac{\sigma^{s-b+(\nu+1)/2}}{2^{2s-2b+1}\omega^{b-1}}B\left(2s-2b+2,\,\dfrac{2b-2s-\nu-1}{2}\right)$
	$\times\,\Psi\left(\begin{matrix}a;\,\omega x\\b\end{matrix}\right)$	

$$\times\,\Gamma\left[\begin{matrix}b-1\\a\end{matrix}\right]\,_3F_3\left(\begin{matrix}a-b+1,\,s-b+1,\,\frac{2s-2b+3}{2};\,-\sigma\omega\\2-b,\,\frac{2s-2b-\nu+3}{2},\,\frac{2s-2b+\nu+3}{2}\end{matrix}\right)$$

$$+\,\dfrac{2^\nu}{\omega^{s+(\nu-1)/2}}B\left(\dfrac{2a-2s-\nu+1}{2},\,\dfrac{2s+\nu-1}{2}\right)$$

$$\times\,\Gamma\left[\begin{matrix}\frac{2s-2b+\nu+1}{2}\\a-b+1\end{matrix}\right]\,_3F_3\left(\begin{matrix}\frac{1-\nu}{2},\,\frac{2-\nu}{2},\,\frac{2a-2s-\nu+1}{2};\,-\sigma\omega\\1-\nu,\,\frac{3-2s-\nu}{2},\,\frac{2b-2s-\nu+1}{2}\end{matrix}\right)$$

$$+\,\dfrac{\sigma^{s+(\nu-1)/2}}{2^{2s-1}}B\left(2s,\,\dfrac{1-2s-\nu}{2}\right)$$

$$\times\,\Gamma\left[\begin{matrix}1-b\\a-b+1\end{matrix}\right]\,_3F_3\left(\begin{matrix}a,\,s,\,\frac{2s+1}{2};\,-\sigma\omega\\b,\,\frac{2s-\nu+1}{2},\,\frac{2s+\nu+1}{2}\end{matrix}\right)$$

$$[0,\ \operatorname{Re}b-1<\operatorname{Re}s<\operatorname{Re}\left(a-\left(\nu-1\right)/2\right);\,|\arg\sigma|,\,|\arg\omega|<\pi]$$

3.29.2. $\Psi(a; b; \omega x)$ and the exponential function

1	$e^{-\omega x}\Psi\begin{pmatrix} a;\,\omega x \\ b \end{pmatrix}$	$\omega^{-s}\,\Gamma\begin{bmatrix} s,\,s-b+1 \\ s+a-b+1 \end{bmatrix}\begin{bmatrix} (\mathrm{Re}\,\omega>0;\ \mathrm{Re}\,s>0,\ \mathrm{Re}\,b-1)\ \text{or} \\ (\mathrm{Re}\,\omega=0;\ 0,\ \mathrm{Re}\,b-1<\mathrm{Re}\,s<\mathrm{Re}\,a+1) \end{bmatrix}$

$$2\quad e^{-\sigma x}\Psi\begin{pmatrix} a;\,\omega x \\ b \end{pmatrix}$$

$$\omega^{-s}\,\Gamma\begin{bmatrix} s,\,s-b+1 \\ s+a-b+1 \end{bmatrix}\, {}_2F_1\begin{pmatrix} s,\,s-b+1;\,\frac{\omega-\sigma}{\omega} \\ s+a-b+1 \end{pmatrix}$$

$$\begin{bmatrix} (\mathrm{Re}\,\sigma>0;\ \mathrm{Re}\,s>0,\ \mathrm{Re}\,b-1)\ \text{or} \\ (\mathrm{Re}\,\sigma=0;\ 0,\ \mathrm{Re}\,b-1<\mathrm{Re}\,s<\mathrm{Re}\,a+1) \end{bmatrix}$$

$$3\qquad =\frac{\sigma^{b-s-1}}{\omega^{b-1}}\,\Gamma\begin{bmatrix} b-1,\,s-b+1 \\ a \end{bmatrix}\, {}_2F_1\begin{pmatrix} a-b+1,\,s-b+1 \\ 2-b;\,\frac{\omega}{\sigma} \end{pmatrix}$$

$$+\,\sigma^{-s}\,\Gamma\begin{bmatrix} 1-b,\,s \\ a-b+1 \end{bmatrix}\, {}_2F_1\begin{pmatrix} a,\,s \\ b;\,\frac{\omega}{\sigma} \end{pmatrix}$$

$$\begin{bmatrix} (\mathrm{Re}\,\sigma>0;\ \mathrm{Re}\,s>0,\ \mathrm{Re}\,b-1)\ \text{or} \\ (\mathrm{Re}\,\sigma=0;\ 0,\ \mathrm{Re}\,b-1<\mathrm{Re}\,s<\mathrm{Re}\,a+1) \end{bmatrix}$$

$$4\quad e^{-\sigma\sqrt{x}}\Psi\begin{pmatrix} a;\,\omega x \\ b \end{pmatrix}$$

$$\frac{2\sigma^{2a-2s}}{\omega^a}\,\Gamma(2s-2a)\, {}_2F_2\begin{pmatrix} a,\,a-b+1;\,-\frac{\sigma^2}{4\omega} \\ \frac{2a-2s+1}{2},\,a-s+1 \end{pmatrix}$$

$$-\,\frac{\sigma}{\omega^{s+1/2}}\,\mathrm{B}\begin{pmatrix} \frac{2s+1}{2},\,\frac{2a-2s-1}{2} \end{pmatrix}$$

$$\times\,\Gamma\begin{bmatrix} \frac{s-2b+3}{2} \\ a-b+1 \end{bmatrix}\, {}_2F_2\begin{pmatrix} \frac{2s+1}{2},\,\frac{2s-2b+3}{2} \\ \frac{3}{2},\,\frac{2s-2a+3}{2};\,-\frac{\sigma^2}{4\omega} \end{pmatrix}$$

$$+\,\omega^{-s}\,\mathrm{B}(s,\,a-s)\,\Gamma\begin{bmatrix} \frac{s-b+1}{2} \\ a-b+1 \end{bmatrix}\, {}_2F_2\begin{pmatrix} s,\,s-b+1 \\ \frac{1}{2},\,s-a+1;\,-\frac{\sigma^2}{4\omega} \end{pmatrix}$$

$$\begin{bmatrix} (\mathrm{Re}\,\sigma>0;\ \mathrm{Re}\,s>0,\ \mathrm{Re}\,b-1)\ \text{or} \\ (\mathrm{Re}\,\sigma=0;\ 0,\ \mathrm{Re}\,b-1<\mathrm{Re}\,s<\mathrm{Re}\,a+1/2) \end{bmatrix}$$

$$5\quad e^{-\sigma\sqrt{x}-\omega x}\Psi\begin{pmatrix} a;\,\omega x \\ b \end{pmatrix}$$

$$\omega^{-s}\,\Gamma\begin{bmatrix} s,\,s-b+1 \\ s+a-b+1 \end{bmatrix}\, {}_2F_2\begin{pmatrix} s,\,s-b+1;\,\frac{\sigma^2}{4\omega} \\ \frac{1}{2},\,s+a-b+1 \end{pmatrix}$$

$$-\,\frac{\sigma}{\omega^{s+1/2}}\,\Gamma\begin{bmatrix} \frac{2s+1}{2},\,\frac{2s-2b+3}{2} \\ \frac{2s+2a-2b+3}{2} \end{bmatrix}\, {}_2F_2\begin{pmatrix} \frac{2s+1}{2},\,\frac{2s-2b+3}{2};\,\frac{\sigma^2}{4\omega} \\ \frac{3}{2},\,\frac{2s+2a-2b+3}{2} \end{pmatrix}$$

$$\begin{bmatrix} (\mathrm{Re}\,\omega>0;\ \mathrm{Re}\,s>0,\ \mathrm{Re}\,b-1)\ \text{or} \\ (\mathrm{Re}\,\omega=0,\ \mathrm{Re}\,\sigma>0;\ \mathrm{Re}\,s>0,\ \mathrm{Re}\,b-1)\ \text{or} \\ (\mathrm{Re}\,\omega=0,\ \mathrm{Re}\,\sigma=0;\ \mathrm{Re}\,a+1>\mathrm{Re}\,s>0,\ \mathrm{Re}\,b-1) \end{bmatrix}$$

$$6\quad e^{-\sigma/x}\Psi\begin{pmatrix} a;\,\omega x \\ b \end{pmatrix}$$

$$\frac{\sigma^{-b+s+1}}{\omega^{b-1}}\,\Gamma\begin{bmatrix} b-1,\,b-s-1 \\ a \end{bmatrix}\, {}_1F_2\begin{pmatrix} a-b+1;\,-\sigma\omega \\ 2-b,\,s-b+2 \end{pmatrix}$$

$$+\,\omega^{-s}\,\mathrm{B}(s,\,a-s)\,\Gamma\begin{bmatrix} s-b+1 \\ a-b+1 \end{bmatrix}\, {}_1F_2\begin{pmatrix} a-s;\,-\sigma\omega \\ 1-s,\,b-s \end{pmatrix}$$

$$+\,\sigma^s\,\Gamma\begin{bmatrix} 1-b,\,-s \\ a-b+1 \end{bmatrix}\, {}_1F_2\begin{pmatrix} a;\,-\sigma\omega \\ b,\,s+1 \end{pmatrix}$$

$$\begin{bmatrix} (\mathrm{Re}\,\sigma>0;\ \mathrm{Re}\,s<\mathrm{Re}\,a)\ \text{or} \\ (\mathrm{Re}\,\sigma=0;\ -1,\ \mathrm{Re}\,b-2<\mathrm{Re}\,s<\mathrm{Re}\,a) \end{bmatrix}$$

No.	$f\left(x\right)$	$F\left(s\right)$
7	$e^{-\omega x - \sigma/x}\Psi\begin{pmatrix} a;\, \omega x \\ b \end{pmatrix}$	$\dfrac{\sigma^{s-b+1}}{\omega^{b-1}}\,\Gamma\begin{bmatrix} b-1,\, b-s-1 \\ a \end{bmatrix}\,{}_1F_2\begin{pmatrix} 1-a;\, \sigma\omega \\ 2-b,\, s-b+2 \end{pmatrix}$
		$+\,\omega^{-s}\,\Gamma\begin{bmatrix} s,\, s-b+1 \\ s+a-b+1 \end{bmatrix}\,{}_1F_2\begin{pmatrix} s-a+b;\, \sigma\omega \\ 1-s,\, b-s \end{pmatrix}$
		$+\,\sigma^s\,\Gamma\begin{bmatrix} 1-b,\, -s \\ a-b+1 \end{bmatrix}\,{}_1F_2\begin{pmatrix} b-a;\, \sigma\omega \\ b,\, s+1 \end{pmatrix}$
		$\begin{bmatrix} (\operatorname{Re}\sigma,\ \operatorname{Re}\omega > 0)\ \text{or} \\ (\operatorname{Re}\sigma = 0,\ \operatorname{Re}\omega > 0;\, -1,\ \operatorname{Re} b - 2 < \operatorname{Re} s)\ \text{or} \\ (\operatorname{Re}\sigma > 0,\ \operatorname{Re}\omega = 0;\ \operatorname{Re} s < \operatorname{Re} a + 1)\ \text{or} \\ (\operatorname{Re}\sigma = 0,\ \operatorname{Re}\omega = 0;\ -1,\ \operatorname{Re} b - 2 < \operatorname{Re} s < \operatorname{Re} a + 1) \end{bmatrix}$
8	$(\sigma-x)_+^{\mu-1}\,e^{-\omega x}$ $\times\,\Psi\begin{pmatrix} a;\, \omega x \\ b \end{pmatrix}$	$\dfrac{\sigma^{s-b+\mu}}{\omega^{b-1}}\,\Gamma\begin{bmatrix} b-1 \\ a \end{bmatrix}\,\mathrm{B}\left(\mu,\, s-b+1\right)\,{}_2F_2\begin{pmatrix} 1-a,\, s-b+1;\, -\sigma\omega \\ 2-b,\, s-b+\mu+1 \end{pmatrix}$
		$+\,\sigma^{s+\mu-1}\,\Gamma\begin{bmatrix} 1-b \\ a-b+1 \end{bmatrix}\,\mathrm{B}\left(\mu,\, s\right)\,{}_2F_2\begin{pmatrix} b-a,\, s;\, -\sigma\omega \\ b,\, s+\mu \end{pmatrix}$
		$\left[\sigma,\ \operatorname{Re}\mu > 0;\ \operatorname{Re} s > 0,\ \operatorname{Re} b - 1\right]$
9	$(x-\sigma)_+^{\mu-1}\,e^{-\omega x}$ $\times\,\Psi\begin{pmatrix} a;\, \omega x \\ b \end{pmatrix}$	$\dfrac{\sigma^{s-b+\mu}}{\omega^{b-1}}\,\Gamma\begin{bmatrix} b-1 \\ a \end{bmatrix}\,\mathrm{B}\left(\mu,\, b-s-\mu\right)\,{}_2F_2\begin{pmatrix} 1-a,\, s-b+1;\, -\sigma\omega \\ 2-b,\, s-b+\mu+1 \end{pmatrix}$
		$+\,\omega^{-s-\mu+1}\,\Gamma\begin{bmatrix} s+\mu-1,\, s-b+\mu \\ a-b+s+\mu \end{bmatrix}$
		$\times\,{}_2F_2\begin{pmatrix} 1-\mu,\, b-a-s-\mu+1;\, -\sigma\omega \\ 2-s-\mu,\, b-s-\mu+1 \end{pmatrix}$
		$+\,\sigma^{s+\mu-1}\,\Gamma\begin{bmatrix} 1-b \\ a-b+1 \end{bmatrix}\,\mathrm{B}\left(\mu,\, 1-s-\mu\right)\,{}_2F_2\begin{pmatrix} b-a,\, s \\ b,\, s+\mu;\, -\sigma\omega \end{pmatrix}$
		$\begin{bmatrix} \sigma,\ \operatorname{Re}\mu > 0;\ \operatorname{Re}\omega > 0\ \text{or} \\ (\operatorname{Re}\omega = 0;\ \operatorname{Re} s < \operatorname{Re}\left(a-\mu\right) + 2) \end{bmatrix}$
10	$\dfrac{e^{-\omega x}}{(x+\sigma)^\rho}\,\Psi\begin{pmatrix} a;\, \omega x \\ b \end{pmatrix}$	$\dfrac{\sigma^{s-b-\rho+1}}{\omega^{b-1}}\,\Gamma\begin{bmatrix} b-1 \\ a \end{bmatrix}\,\mathrm{B}\left(s-b+1,\, b-s+\rho-1\right)$
		$\times\,{}_2F_2\begin{pmatrix} 1-a,\, s-b+1;\, \sigma\omega \\ 2-b,\, s-b-\rho+2 \end{pmatrix}$
		$+\,\omega^{\rho-s}\,\Gamma\begin{bmatrix} s-\rho,\, s-b-\rho+1 \\ s+a-b-\rho+1 \end{bmatrix}\,{}_2F_2\begin{pmatrix} \rho,\, b-a-s+\rho;\, \sigma\omega \\ \rho-s+1,\, \rho-s+b \end{pmatrix}$
		$+\,\sigma^{s-\rho}\,\Gamma\begin{bmatrix} 1-b \\ a-b+1 \end{bmatrix}\,\mathrm{B}\left(s,\, \rho-s\right)\,{}_2F_2\begin{pmatrix} b-a,\, s;\, \sigma\omega \\ b,\, s-\rho+1 \end{pmatrix}$
		$\begin{bmatrix} (\operatorname{Re}\omega > 0;\ \operatorname{Re} s > 0,\ \operatorname{Re} b - 1)\ \text{or} \\ (\operatorname{Re}\omega = 0;\ 0,\ \operatorname{Re} b - 1 < \operatorname{Re} s < \operatorname{Re}\rho + 1);\ |\arg\sigma| < \pi \end{bmatrix}$

No.	$f(x)$	$F(s)$
11	$\dfrac{e^{-\omega x}}{x - \sigma}\,\Psi\!\begin{pmatrix} a;\ \omega x \\ b \end{pmatrix}$	$\dfrac{\pi\sigma^{s-b}}{\omega^{b-1}}\cot\left[(b-s)\pi\right]\Gamma\!\begin{bmatrix} b-1 \\ a \end{bmatrix} {}_1F_1\!\begin{pmatrix} 1-a;\ -\sigma\omega \\ 2-b \end{pmatrix}$

$$+\,\omega^{1-s}\,\Gamma\!\begin{bmatrix} s-1,\ s-b \\ s+a-b \end{bmatrix} {}_2F_2\!\begin{pmatrix} 1,\ b-a-s+1;\ -\sigma\omega \\ 2-s,\ b-s+1 \end{pmatrix}$$

$$-\,\pi\sigma^{s-1}\cot\left(s\pi\right)\Gamma\!\begin{bmatrix} 1-b \\ a-b+1 \end{bmatrix} {}_1F_1\!\begin{pmatrix} b-a \\ b;\ -\sigma\omega \end{pmatrix}$$

$$\begin{bmatrix} \sigma > 0;\ (\mathrm{Re}\,\omega > 0;\ \mathrm{Re}\,s > 0,\ \mathrm{Re}\,b-1)\ \text{or} \\ (\mathrm{Re}\,\omega = 0;\ 0,\ \mathrm{Re}\,b-1 < \mathrm{Re}\,s < 2) \end{bmatrix}$$

No.	$f(x)$	$F(s)$
12	$\left(\sqrt{x}+\sqrt{\sigma+x}\right)^{\nu}e^{-\omega x}$ $\times \Psi\!\begin{pmatrix} a;\ \omega x \\ b \end{pmatrix}$	$\dfrac{\nu\sigma^{s-b+\nu/2+1}}{2^{2s-2b+2}\omega^{b-1}}\Gamma\!\begin{bmatrix} b-1,\ 2s-2b+2,\ \frac{2b-2s-\nu-2}{2} \\ a,\ \frac{2s-2b-\nu+4}{2} \end{bmatrix}$

$$\times\,{}_3F_3\!\begin{pmatrix} 1-a,\ s-b+1,\ \frac{2s-2b+3}{2};\ \sigma\omega \\ 2-b,\ \frac{2s-2b-\nu+4}{2},\ \frac{2s-2b+\nu+4}{2} \end{pmatrix}$$

$$+\,\dfrac{2^{\nu}}{\omega^{s+\nu/2}}\Gamma\!\begin{bmatrix} s+\frac{\nu}{2},\ -b+s+\frac{\nu}{2}+1 \\ a-b+s+\frac{\nu}{2}+1 \end{bmatrix}$$

$$\times\,{}_3F_3\!\begin{pmatrix} -\frac{\nu}{2},\ \frac{1-\nu}{2},\ \frac{2b-2a-2s-\nu}{2};\ \sigma\omega \\ 1-\nu,\ \frac{2-2s-\nu}{2},\ \frac{2b-2s-\nu}{2} \end{pmatrix}$$

$$-\,\dfrac{\nu\sigma^{s+\nu/2}}{2^{2s}}\Gamma\!\begin{bmatrix} 1-b,\ -\frac{2s+\nu}{2},\ 2s \\ a-b+1,\ \frac{2s-\nu+2}{2} \end{bmatrix} {}_3F_3\!\begin{pmatrix} b-a,\ s,\ \frac{2s+1}{2};\ \sigma\omega \\ b,\ \frac{2s-\nu+2}{2},\ \frac{2s+\nu+2}{2} \end{pmatrix}$$

$$\begin{bmatrix} (\mathrm{Re}\,\omega > 0;\ \mathrm{Re}\,s > 0,\ \mathrm{Re}\,b-1)\ \text{or} \\ (\mathrm{Re}\,\omega = 0;\ 0,\ \mathrm{Re}\,b-1 < \mathrm{Re}\,s < -\mathrm{Re}\,\nu/2+1);\ |\arg\sigma| < \pi \end{bmatrix}$$

No.	$f(x)$	$F(s)$
13	$\dfrac{\left(\sqrt{x}+\sqrt{x+\sigma}\right)^{\nu}}{\sqrt{x+\sigma}}e^{-\omega x}$ $\times \Psi\!\begin{pmatrix} a;\ \omega x \\ b \end{pmatrix}$	$\dfrac{\sigma^{s-b+(\nu+1)/2}}{2^{2s-2b+1}\omega^{b-1}}\,\mathrm{B}\!\left(2s-2b+2,\ \dfrac{2b-2s-\nu-1}{2}\right)$

$$\times\,\Gamma\!\begin{bmatrix} b-1 \\ a \end{bmatrix} {}_3F_3\!\begin{pmatrix} 1-a,\ s-b+1,\ \frac{2s-2b+3}{2};\ \sigma\omega \\ 2-b,\ \frac{2s-2b-\nu+3}{2},\ \frac{2s-2b+\nu+3}{2} \end{pmatrix}$$

$$+\,\dfrac{2^{\nu}}{\omega^{s+(\nu-1)/2}}\Gamma\!\begin{bmatrix} \frac{2s+\nu-1}{2},\ \frac{2s-2b+\nu+1}{2} \\ \frac{2s+2a-2b+\nu+1}{2} \end{bmatrix}$$

$$\times\,{}_3F_3\!\begin{pmatrix} \frac{1-\nu}{2},\ \frac{2-\nu}{2},\ \frac{2b-2a-2s-\nu+1}{2};\ \sigma\omega \\ 1-\nu,\ \frac{3-2s-\nu}{2},\ \frac{2b-2s-\nu+1}{2} \end{pmatrix}$$

$$+\,\dfrac{\sigma^{s+(\nu-1)/2}}{2^{2s-1}}\,\mathrm{B}\!\left(2s,\ \dfrac{1-2s-\nu}{2}\right)$$

$$\times\,\Gamma\!\begin{bmatrix} 1-b \\ a-b+1 \end{bmatrix} {}_3F_3\!\begin{pmatrix} b-a,\ s,\ \frac{2s+1}{2};\ \sigma\omega \\ b,\ \frac{2s-\nu+1}{2},\ \frac{2s+\nu+1}{2} \end{pmatrix}$$

$$\begin{bmatrix} (\mathrm{Re}\,\omega > 0;\ \mathrm{Re}\,s > 0,\ \mathrm{Re}\,b-1)\ \text{or} \\ (\mathrm{Re}\,\omega = 0;\ 0,\ \mathrm{Re}\,b-1 < \mathrm{Re}\,s < -\mathrm{Re}\,\nu/2+3/2);\ |\arg\sigma| < \pi \end{bmatrix}$$

3.29.3. $\Psi(a; b; \omega x)$ and trigonometric functions

1	$\sin(\sigma x)\,\Psi\begin{pmatrix} a;\ \omega x \\ b \end{pmatrix}$	$\dfrac{a\,(a-b+1)\,\pi\sigma^{a-s+1}}{2\omega^{a+1}\Gamma(a-s+2)}\csc\dfrac{(a-s)\,\pi}{2}$

$$\times\,_4F_3\left(\begin{matrix}\Delta(2,\,a+1),\,\Delta(2,\,a-b+2) \\ \tfrac{3}{2},\,\Delta(2,\,a-s+2)\,;\,-\tfrac{\sigma^2}{\omega^2}\end{matrix}\right)+\dfrac{\pi\sigma^{a-s}\omega^{-a}}{2\Gamma(a-s+1)}$$

$$\times\sec\dfrac{(a-s)\,\pi}{2}\,_4F_3\left(\begin{matrix}\Delta(2,\,a),\,\Delta(2,\,a-b+1) \\ \tfrac{1}{2},\,\Delta(2,\,a-s+1)\,;\,-\tfrac{\sigma^2}{\omega^2}\end{matrix}\right)$$

$$+\dfrac{\sigma}{\omega^{s+1}}\,\mathrm{B}(a-s-1,\,s-b+2)\,\Gamma\begin{bmatrix} s+1 \\ a \end{bmatrix}$$

$$\times\,_4F_3\left(\begin{matrix}\Delta(2,\,s+1),\,\Delta(2,\,s-b+2) \\ \tfrac{3}{2},\,\Delta(2,\,s-a+2)\,;\,-\tfrac{\sigma^2}{\omega^2}\end{matrix}\right)$$

$$[\sigma>0;\,-1,\ \mathrm{Re}\,b-2<\mathrm{Re}\,s<\mathrm{Re}\,a+1;\,|\arg\omega|<\pi/2]$$

2	$\cos(\sigma x)\,\Psi\begin{pmatrix} a;\ \omega x \\ b \end{pmatrix}$	$\omega^{-s}\,\mathrm{B}(a-s,\,s)\,\Gamma\begin{bmatrix} s-b+1 \\ a-b+1 \end{bmatrix}\,_4F_3\left(\begin{matrix}\Delta(2,\,s),\,\Delta(2,\,s-b+1) \\ \tfrac{1}{2},\,\Delta(2,\,s+a+2)\,;\,-\tfrac{\sigma^2}{\omega^2}\end{matrix}\right)$

$$+\dfrac{a\,(a-b+1)\,\pi\sigma^{a-s+1}}{2\omega^{a+1}\Gamma(a-s+2)}\sec\dfrac{(a-s)\,\pi}{2}$$

$$\times\,_4F_3\left(\begin{matrix}\Delta(2,\,a+1),\,\Delta(2,\,a-b+2) \\ \tfrac{3}{2},\,\Delta(2,\,a-s+2)\,;\,-\tfrac{\sigma^2}{\omega^2}\end{matrix}\right)-\dfrac{\pi\sigma^{a-s}\omega^{-a}}{2\Gamma(a-s+1)}$$

$$\times\csc\dfrac{(a-s)\,\pi}{2}\,_4F_3\left(\begin{matrix}\Delta(2,\,a),\,\Delta(2,\,a-b+1) \\ \tfrac{1}{2},\,\Delta(2,\,a-s+1)\,;\,-\tfrac{\sigma^2}{\omega^2}\end{matrix}\right)$$

$$[\sigma>0;\,0,\ \mathrm{Re}\,b-1<\mathrm{Re}\,s<\mathrm{Re}\,a+1;\,|\arg\omega|<\pi/2]$$

3	$\sin(\sigma\sqrt{x})\,\Psi\begin{pmatrix} a;\ \omega x \\ b \end{pmatrix}$	$\dfrac{\sqrt{\pi}\,(2/\sigma)^{2(s-a)}}{\omega^a}\Gamma\begin{bmatrix} \tfrac{2s-2a+1}{2} \\ a-s+1 \end{bmatrix}\,_2F_2\left(\begin{matrix} a,\,a-b+1;\,\tfrac{\sigma^2}{4\omega} \\ a-s+\tfrac{1}{2},\,a-s+1 \end{matrix}\right)$

$$+\sigma\omega^{-s-1/2}\,\Gamma\begin{bmatrix} \tfrac{2s+1}{2} \\ a,\,\tfrac{2s-2a+3}{2} \end{bmatrix}\mathrm{B}\left(\dfrac{2a-2s-1}{2},\,\dfrac{2s-2b+3}{2}\right)$$

$$\times\,_2F_2\left(\begin{matrix}\tfrac{2s+1}{2},\,\tfrac{2s-2b+3}{2} \\ \tfrac{3}{2},\,\tfrac{2s-2s+3}{2}\,;\,\tfrac{\sigma^2}{4\omega}\end{matrix}\right)$$

$$[\sigma>0;\,-1/2,\ \mathrm{Re}\,b-3/2<\mathrm{Re}\,s<\mathrm{Re}\,a+1/2]$$

4	$\cos(\sigma\sqrt{x})\,\Psi\begin{pmatrix} a;\ \omega x \\ b \end{pmatrix}$	$\dfrac{\sqrt{\pi}\,(2/\sigma)^{2s-2a}}{\omega^a}\Gamma\begin{bmatrix} s-a \\ \tfrac{2a-2s+1}{2} \end{bmatrix}\,_2F_2\left(\begin{matrix} a,\,a-b+1;\,\tfrac{\sigma^2}{4\omega} \\ \tfrac{2a-2s+1}{2},\,a-s+1 \end{matrix}\right)$

$$+\omega^{-s}\,\mathrm{B}(a-s,\,s)\,\Gamma\begin{bmatrix} s-b+1 \\ a-b+1 \end{bmatrix}\,_2F_2\left(\begin{matrix} s,\,s-b+1;\,\tfrac{\sigma^2}{4\omega} \\ \tfrac{1}{2},\,s-a+1 \end{matrix}\right)$$

$$[\sigma>0;\,0,\ \mathrm{Re}\,b-1<\mathrm{Re}\,s<\mathrm{Re}\,a+1/2]$$

No.	$f(x)$	$F(s)$
5	$e^{-\omega x}\sin(\sigma x)\,\Psi\!\left(\begin{matrix}a;\,\omega x\\b\end{matrix}\right)$	$\dfrac{\sigma}{\omega^{s+1}}\,\Gamma\!\left[\begin{matrix}s+1,\,s-b+2\\a-b+s+2\end{matrix}\right]\,{}_4F_3\!\left(\begin{matrix}\Delta\left(2,\,s+1\right),\,\Delta\left(2,\,s-b+2\right)\\\frac{3}{2},\,\Delta\left(2,\,s+a-b+2\right);\,-\frac{\sigma^2}{\omega^2}\end{matrix}\right)$ $$\left[\begin{matrix}(\operatorname{Re}\omega>|\operatorname{Im}\sigma|;\ \operatorname{Re}s>-1,\ \operatorname{Re}b-2)\ \text{or}\\(\operatorname{Re}^2\omega=\operatorname{Im}^2\sigma;\,-1,\ \operatorname{Re}b-2<\operatorname{Re}s<\operatorname{Re}a+1)\end{matrix}\right]$$
6	$e^{-\omega x}\cos(\sigma x)\,\Psi\!\left(\begin{matrix}a;\,\omega x\\b\end{matrix}\right)$	$\omega^{-s}\,\Gamma\!\left[\begin{matrix}s,\,s-b+1\\a-b+s+1\end{matrix}\right]\,{}_4F_3\!\left(\begin{matrix}\Delta\left(2,\,s\right),\,\Delta\left(2,\,s-b+1\right)\\\frac{1}{2},\,\Delta\left(2,\,s+a-b+1\right);\,-\frac{\sigma^2}{\omega^2}\end{matrix}\right)$ $$\left[\begin{matrix}(\operatorname{Re}\omega>|\operatorname{Im}\sigma|;\ \operatorname{Re}s>0,\ \operatorname{Re}b-1)\ \text{or}\\(\operatorname{Re}^2\omega=\operatorname{Im}^2\sigma;\,0,\ \operatorname{Re}b-1<\operatorname{Re}s<\operatorname{Re}a+1)\end{matrix}\right]$$
7	$e^{-\omega x}\sin(\sigma\sqrt{x})$ $\times\,\Psi\!\left(\begin{matrix}a;\,\omega x\\b\end{matrix}\right)$	$\dfrac{\sigma}{\omega^{s+1/2}}\,\Gamma\!\left[\begin{matrix}\frac{2s+1}{2},\,\frac{2s-2b+3}{2}\\\frac{2s+2a-2b+3}{2}\end{matrix}\right]\,{}_2F_2\!\left(\begin{matrix}\frac{2s+1}{2},\,\frac{2s-2b+3}{2}\\\frac{3}{2},\,\frac{2s+2a-2b+3}{2};\,-\frac{\sigma^2}{4\omega}\end{matrix}\right)$ $$\left[\begin{matrix}(\operatorname{Re}\omega>0;\ \operatorname{Re}s>-1/2,\ \operatorname{Re}b-3/2)\ \text{or}\\(\sigma>0,\ \operatorname{Re}\omega=0;\,-1/2,\ \operatorname{Re}b-3/2<\operatorname{Re}s<\operatorname{Re}a+1/2)\end{matrix}\right]$$
8	$e^{-\omega x}\cos(\sigma\sqrt{x})$ $\times\,\Psi\!\left(\begin{matrix}a;\,\omega x\\b\end{matrix}\right)$	$\omega^{-s}\,\Gamma\!\left[\begin{matrix}s,\,s-b+1\\s+a-b+1\end{matrix}\right]\,{}_2F_2\!\left(\begin{matrix}s,\,s-b+1\\1,\,s+a-b+1;\,-\frac{\sigma^2}{4\omega}\end{matrix}\right)$ $$\left[\begin{matrix}(\operatorname{Re}\omega>0;\ \operatorname{Re}s>0,\ \operatorname{Re}b-1)\ \text{or}\\(\sigma>0,\ \operatorname{Re}\omega=0;\,0,\ \operatorname{Re}b-1<\operatorname{Re}s<\operatorname{Re}a+1/2)\end{matrix}\right]$$

3.29.4. $\Psi(a;\,b;\,\omega x)$ and the logarithmic function

1	$\ln(\sigma x+1)\,\Psi\!\left(\begin{matrix}a;\,\omega x\\b\end{matrix}\right)$	$\dfrac{\pi\sigma^{b-s-1}\omega^{1-b}}{s-b+1}\,\csc\left[(b-s)\pi\right]\,\Gamma\!\left[\begin{matrix}b-1\\a\end{matrix}\right]$

$$\times\,{}_2F_2\!\left(\begin{matrix}a-b+1,\,s-b+1\\2-b,\,s-b+2;\,-\frac{\omega}{\sigma}\end{matrix}\right)+\frac{\omega^{1-s}}{\sigma}\,\mathrm{B}\left(a-s+1,\,s-1\right)$$

$$\times\,\Gamma\!\left[\begin{matrix}s-b\\a-b+1\end{matrix}\right]\,{}_3F_3\!\left(\begin{matrix}1,\,1,\,a-s+1;\,-\frac{\omega}{\sigma}\\2,\,2-s,\,b-s+1\end{matrix}\right)$$

$$+\,\omega^{-s}\,\mathrm{B}\left(a-s,\,s-b+1\right)\Gamma\!\left[\begin{matrix}s\\a\end{matrix}\right]\ln\frac{\sigma}{\omega}$$

$$-\,\omega^{-s}\,\mathrm{B}\left(a-s,\,s\right)\Gamma\!\left[\begin{matrix}s-b+1\\a-b+1\end{matrix}\right]\left[\psi\left(a-s\right)-\psi\left(s-b+1\right)\right.$$

$$\left.-\,\psi\left(s\right)\right]+\frac{\pi\sigma^{-s}}{s}\,\csc\left(s\pi\right)\Gamma\!\left[\begin{matrix}1-b\\a-b+1\end{matrix}\right]\,{}_2F_2\!\left(\begin{matrix}a,\,s;\,-\frac{\omega}{\sigma}\\b,\,s+1\end{matrix}\right)$$

$$\left[\begin{matrix}(\operatorname{Re}\omega>0;\ \operatorname{Re}s>-1,\ \operatorname{Re}b-2)\ \text{or}\\(\operatorname{Re}\omega=0;\,-1,\ \operatorname{Re}b-2<\operatorname{Re}s<\operatorname{Re}a);\,|\arg\sigma|<\pi\end{matrix}\right]$$

No.	$f(x)$	$F(s)$
2	$e^{-\omega x} \ln(\sigma x + 1)$ $\times \Psi\begin{pmatrix} a; \, \omega x \\ b \end{pmatrix}$	$\dfrac{\pi \sigma^{b-s-1} \omega^{1-b}}{s-b+1} \csc\left[(b-s)\pi\right] \Gamma\begin{bmatrix} b-1 \\ a \end{bmatrix} {}_2F_2\begin{pmatrix} 1-a, \, s-b+1 \\ 2-b, \, s-b+2; \, \frac{\omega}{\sigma} \end{pmatrix}$ $- \dfrac{\pi \omega^{1-s}}{\sigma} \csc(s\pi) \Gamma\begin{bmatrix} s-b \\ 2-s, \, a-b+s \end{bmatrix} {}_3F_3\begin{pmatrix} 1,1,1-s-a+b; \, \frac{\omega}{\sigma} \\ 2, 2-s, 1-s+b \end{pmatrix}$ $+ \dfrac{\pi \sigma^{-s}}{s} \csc(s\pi) \Gamma\begin{bmatrix} 1-b \\ a-b+1 \end{bmatrix} {}_2F_2\begin{pmatrix} b-a, \, s; \, \frac{\omega}{\sigma} \\ b, \, s+1 \end{pmatrix}$ $+ \omega^{-s} \Gamma\begin{bmatrix} s, \, s-b+1 \\ s+a-b+1 \end{bmatrix}\left[\psi(s) + \psi(s-b) - \psi(s+a-b) + \ln\dfrac{\sigma}{\omega}\right]$ $\left[\begin{array}{l}(\operatorname{Re}\omega > 0; \ \operatorname{Re}s > -1, \ \operatorname{Re}b-2) \text{ or} \\ (\operatorname{Re}\omega = 0; \ -1, \ \operatorname{Re}b-2 < \operatorname{Re}s < \operatorname{Re}a); \ |\arg\sigma| < \pi\end{array}\right]$

3.29.5. $\Psi(a; b; \omega x)$ **and** $\operatorname{Ei}(\sigma x)$

1	$\operatorname{Ei}(-\sigma x) \Psi\begin{pmatrix} a; \, \omega x \\ b \end{pmatrix}$	$\dfrac{\sigma^{b-s-1}\omega^{1-b}}{b-s-1} \Gamma\begin{bmatrix} b-1, \, s-b+1 \\ a \end{bmatrix} {}_3F_2\begin{pmatrix} a-b+1, \, s-b+1, \, s-b+1 \\ 2-b, \, s-b+2; \, \frac{\omega}{\sigma} \end{pmatrix}$ $- \dfrac{\sigma^{-s}}{s} \Gamma\begin{bmatrix} 1-b, \, s \\ a-b+1 \end{bmatrix} {}_3F_2\begin{pmatrix} a, \, s, \, s \\ b, \, s+1; \, \frac{\omega}{\sigma} \end{pmatrix}$ $\left[\begin{array}{l}(\operatorname{Re}\sigma \geq 0; \ \operatorname{Im}\sigma \neq 0; \ 0, \ \operatorname{Re}b-1 < \operatorname{Re}s < \operatorname{Re}a) \text{ or} \\ (\sigma > 0; \ \operatorname{Re}s > -1, \ \operatorname{Re}b-2)\end{array}\right]$
2	$e^{-\omega x} \operatorname{Ei}(-\sigma x)$ $\times \Psi\begin{pmatrix} a; \, \omega x \\ b \end{pmatrix}$	$\dfrac{\sigma^{b-s-1}\omega^{1-b}}{b-s-1} \Gamma\begin{bmatrix} b-1, \, s-b+1 \\ a \end{bmatrix} {}_3F_2\begin{pmatrix} 1-a, \, s-b+1, \, s-b+1 \\ 2-b, \, s-b+2; \, -\frac{\omega}{\sigma} \end{pmatrix}$ $- \dfrac{\sigma^{-s}}{s} \Gamma\begin{bmatrix} 1-b, \, s \\ a-b+1 \end{bmatrix} {}_3F_2\begin{pmatrix} b-a, \, s, \, s \\ b, \, s+1; \, -\frac{\omega}{\sigma} \end{pmatrix}$ $\left[\begin{array}{l}(\operatorname{Re}\omega, \ \operatorname{Re}(\sigma+\omega) > 0; \ \operatorname{Im}\sigma \neq 0; \ \operatorname{Re}s > 0, \ \operatorname{Re}b-1) \text{ or} \\ (\operatorname{Re}(\sigma+\omega) > 0; \ \operatorname{Im}\sigma = 0; \ \operatorname{Re}s > 0, \ \operatorname{Re}b-1) \text{ or} \\ (\operatorname{Re}\sigma \geq 0; \ \operatorname{Re}\omega = 0; \ \operatorname{Im}\sigma \neq 0; \ 0, \ \operatorname{Re}b-1 < \operatorname{Re}s < \operatorname{Re}a+1) \text{ or} \\ (\sigma > 0; \ \operatorname{Re}\omega = 0; \ \operatorname{Re}s > 0, \ \operatorname{Re}b-1)\end{array}\right]$

3.29.6. $\Psi(a; b; \omega x)$ **and** $\operatorname{erf}(\sigma\sqrt{x})$, $\operatorname{erfc}(\sigma\sqrt{x})$

1	$\operatorname{erf}(\sigma\sqrt{x}) \Psi\begin{pmatrix} a; \, \omega x \\ b \end{pmatrix}$	$\dfrac{\sigma^{2a-2s}\omega^{-a}}{\sqrt{\pi}(a-s)} \Gamma\left(\dfrac{2s-2a+1}{2}\right) {}_3F_2\begin{pmatrix} a, \, a-b+1, \, a-s; \, \frac{\sigma^2}{\omega} \\ \frac{2a-2s+1}{2}, \, a-s+1 \end{pmatrix}$ $+ \dfrac{2\sigma}{\sqrt{\pi}\,\omega^{s+1/2}} \operatorname{B}\left(\dfrac{2a-2s-1}{2}, \, \dfrac{2s-2b+3}{2}\right)$ $\times \Gamma\begin{bmatrix} \frac{2s+1}{2} \\ a \end{bmatrix} {}_3F_2\begin{pmatrix} \frac{1}{2}, \, \frac{2s+1}{2}, \, \frac{2s-2b+3}{2} \\ \frac{3}{2}, \, \frac{2s-2a+3}{2}; \, \frac{\sigma^2}{\omega} \end{pmatrix}$ $[-1/2, \ \operatorname{Re}b-3/2 < \operatorname{Re}s < \operatorname{Re}a; \ |\arg\sigma| < \pi/4]$

No.	$f(x)$	$F(s)$

2 $\quad \mathrm{erfc}\,(\sigma\sqrt{x})\,\Psi\begin{pmatrix} a;\ \omega x \\ b \end{pmatrix}$

$$\frac{\sigma^{2b-2s-2}\omega^{1-b}}{\sqrt{\pi}\,(s-b+1)}\,\Gamma\begin{bmatrix} b-1,\ \frac{2s-2b+3}{2} \\ a \end{bmatrix}$$

$$\times\ {}_3F_2\begin{pmatrix} a-b+1,\ s-b+1,\ \frac{2s-2b+3}{2} \\ 2-b,\ s-b+2;\ \frac{\omega}{\sigma^2} \end{pmatrix}$$

$$+\frac{\sigma^{-2s}}{2^{2s-1}}\,\Gamma\begin{bmatrix} 1-b,\ 2s \\ a-b+1,\ s \end{bmatrix}\,{}_3F_2\begin{pmatrix} a,\ s,\ \frac{2s+1}{2} \\ b,\ s+1;\ \frac{\omega}{\sigma^2} \end{pmatrix}$$

$$\begin{bmatrix} (\mathrm{Re}\,s>0,\ \mathrm{Re}\,b-1;\ |\arg\sigma|<\pi/4)\ \text{or} \\ (0,\ \mathrm{Re}\,b-1<\mathrm{Re}\,s<\mathrm{Re}\,a+3/2;\ |\arg\sigma|=\pi/4) \end{bmatrix}$$

3 $\quad e^{-\omega x}\,\mathrm{erf}\,(\sigma\sqrt{x})$

$\qquad \times\ \Psi\begin{pmatrix} a;\ \omega x \\ b \end{pmatrix}$

$$\frac{2\sigma\omega^{-s-1/2}}{\sqrt{\pi}}\,\Gamma\begin{bmatrix} \frac{2s+1}{2},\ \frac{2s-2b+3}{2} \\ \frac{2s+2a-2b+3}{2} \end{bmatrix}\,{}_3F_2\begin{pmatrix} \frac{1}{2},\ \frac{2s+1}{2},\ \frac{2s-2b+3}{2} \\ \frac{3}{2},\ \frac{2s+2a-2b+3}{2};\ -\frac{\sigma^2}{\omega} \end{pmatrix}$$

$$\begin{bmatrix} (\mathrm{Re}\,(\sigma^2+\omega)>0;\ \mathrm{Re}\,\omega>0;\ \mathrm{Re}\,s>-1/2,\ \mathrm{Re}\,b-3/2)\ \text{or} \\ (\mathrm{Re}\,(\sigma^2+\omega)=0;\ \mathrm{Re}\,\omega>0;\ \mathrm{Re}\,s>-1/2,\ \mathrm{Re}\,b-3/2<\mathrm{Re}\,s<0,\ \mathrm{Re}\,a+3/2)\ \text{or} \\ (\mathrm{Re}\,\omega=0;\ \mathrm{Re}\,s>-1/2,\ \mathrm{Re}\,b-3/2<\mathrm{Re}\,s<0,\ \mathrm{Re}\,a+1;\ |\arg\sigma|\le\pi/4) \end{bmatrix}$$

4 $\quad e^{-\omega x}\,\mathrm{erfc}\,(\sigma\sqrt{x})$

$\qquad \times\ \Psi\begin{pmatrix} a;\ \omega x \\ b \end{pmatrix}$

$$\frac{\sigma^{2b-2s-2}\omega^{1-b}}{\sqrt{\pi}\,(s-b+1)}\,\Gamma\begin{bmatrix} b-1,\ \frac{2s-2b+3}{2} \\ a \end{bmatrix}\,{}_3F_2\begin{pmatrix} 1-a,\ s-b+1,\ \frac{2s-2b+3}{2} \\ 2-b,\ s-b+2;\ -\frac{\omega}{\sigma^2} \end{pmatrix}$$

$$+\frac{\sigma^{-2s}}{\sqrt{\pi}\,s}\,\Gamma\begin{bmatrix} 1-b,\ \frac{2s+1}{2} \\ a-b+1 \end{bmatrix}\,{}_3F_2\begin{pmatrix} b-a,\ s,\ \frac{2s+1}{2} \\ b,\ s+1;\ -\frac{\omega}{\sigma^2} \end{pmatrix}$$

$$\begin{bmatrix} (\mathrm{Re}\,(\sigma^2+\omega)>0;\ \mathrm{Re}\,s>0,\ \mathrm{Re}\,b-1)\ \text{or} \\ (\mathrm{Re}\,(\sigma^2+\omega)=0;\ 0,\ \mathrm{Re}\,b-1<\mathrm{Re}\,s<\mathrm{Re}\,a+3/2) \end{bmatrix}$$

3.29.7. $\quad \Psi\,(a;\,b;\,\omega x)$ and the Bessel functions

1 $\quad J_\nu\,(\sigma x)\,\Psi\begin{pmatrix} a;\ \omega x \\ b \end{pmatrix}$

$$-\frac{2^{s-a-2}a\,(a-b+1)}{\sigma^{s-a-1}\omega^{a+1}}\,\Gamma\begin{bmatrix} \frac{s-a+\nu-1}{2} \\ \frac{a-s+\nu+3}{2} \end{bmatrix}$$

$$\times\ {}_4F_3\begin{pmatrix} \Delta\,(2,\ a+1),\ \Delta\,(2,\ a-b+2) \\ \frac{3}{2},\ \frac{a-s-\nu+3}{2},\ \frac{a-s+\nu+3}{2};\ -\frac{\sigma^2}{\omega^2} \end{pmatrix}$$

$$+\frac{2^{s-a-1}}{\sigma^{s-a}\omega^a}\,\Gamma\begin{bmatrix} \frac{s-a+\nu}{2} \\ \frac{a-s+\nu+2}{2} \end{bmatrix}\,{}_4F_3\begin{pmatrix} \Delta\,(2,\ a),\ \Delta\,(2,\ a-b+1) \\ \frac{1}{2},\ \frac{a-s-\nu+2}{2},\ \frac{a-s+\nu+2}{2};\ -\frac{\sigma^2}{\omega^2} \end{pmatrix}$$

$$+\frac{(\sigma/2)^\nu}{\omega^{s+\nu}}\,\mathrm{B}\,(a-s-\nu,\ s+\nu)\,\Gamma\begin{bmatrix} s-b+\nu+1 \\ \nu+1,\ a-b+1 \end{bmatrix}$$

$$\times\ {}_4F_3\begin{pmatrix} \Delta\,(2,\ s+\nu),\ \Delta\,(2,\ s-b+\nu+1) \\ \nu+1,\ \Delta\,(2,\ s-a+\nu+1);\ -\frac{\sigma^2}{\omega^2} \end{pmatrix}$$

$$\begin{bmatrix} \sigma>0;\ \mathrm{Re}\,(b-\nu)-1,\ -\mathrm{Re}\,\nu<\mathrm{Re}\,s<\mathrm{Re}\,a+3/2; \\ |\arg\omega|<\pi/2 \end{bmatrix}$$

No.	$f(x)$	$F(s)$
2	$J_\nu(\sigma\sqrt{x})\,\Psi\!\begin{pmatrix} a;\,\omega x \\ b \end{pmatrix}$	$\dfrac{(\sigma/2)^{2a-2s}}{\omega^a}\,\Gamma\!\begin{bmatrix} \frac{2s-2a+\nu}{2} \\ \frac{2a-2s+\nu+2}{2} \end{bmatrix}\, {}_2F_2\!\begin{pmatrix} a,\, a-b+1;\, \frac{\sigma^2}{4\omega} \\ \frac{2a-2s-\nu+2}{2},\, \frac{2a-2s+\nu+2}{2} \end{pmatrix}$

$$+ \dfrac{(\sigma/2)^\nu}{\omega^{s+\nu/2}}\, \mathrm{B}\!\left(\dfrac{2a-2s-\nu}{2},\, \dfrac{2s+\nu}{2}\right)$$

$$\times \Gamma\!\begin{bmatrix} \frac{2s-2b+\nu+2}{2} \\ \nu+1,\, a-b+1 \end{bmatrix}\, {}_2F_2\!\begin{pmatrix} \frac{2s+\nu}{2},\, \frac{2s-2b+\nu+2}{2};\, \frac{\sigma^2}{4\omega} \\ \nu+1,\, \frac{2s-2a+\nu+2}{2} \end{pmatrix}$$

$$[\sigma>0;\ \operatorname{Re}(b-\nu/2)-1,\, -\operatorname{Re}\nu/2 < \operatorname{Re}s < \operatorname{Re}a + 3/4]$$

No.	$f(x)$	$F(s)$
3	$e^{-\omega x}J_\nu(\sigma x)\,\Psi\!\begin{pmatrix} a;\,\omega x \\ b \end{pmatrix}$	$\dfrac{(\sigma/2)^\nu}{\omega^{s+\nu}}\,\Gamma\!\begin{bmatrix} s+\nu,\, s-b+\nu+1 \\ \nu+1,\, s+a-b+\nu+1 \end{bmatrix}$

$$\times {}_4F_3\!\begin{pmatrix} \Delta(2,\,s+\nu),\, \Delta(2,\,s-b+\nu+1) \\ \Delta(2,\,s+a-b+\nu+1),\, \nu+1;\, -\frac{\sigma^2}{\omega^2} \end{pmatrix}$$

$$\begin{bmatrix} (\operatorname{Re}\omega > |\operatorname{Im}\sigma|;\ \operatorname{Re}s > \operatorname{Re}(b-\nu)-1,\, -\operatorname{Re}\nu)\ \text{or} \\ (\operatorname{Re}^2\omega = \operatorname{Im}^2\sigma;\ \operatorname{Re}(b-\nu)-1,\, -\operatorname{Re}\nu < \operatorname{Re}s < \operatorname{Re}a+3/2) \end{bmatrix}$$

No.	$f(x)$	$F(s)$
4	$e^{-\omega x}J_\nu(\sigma\sqrt{x})$ $\times \Psi\!\begin{pmatrix} a;\,\omega x \\ b \end{pmatrix}$	$\dfrac{(\sigma/2)^\nu}{\omega^{s+\nu/2}}\,\Gamma\!\begin{bmatrix} \frac{2s+\nu}{2},\, \frac{2s-2b+\nu+2}{2} \\ \nu+1,\, \frac{2s+2a-2b+\nu+1}{2} \end{bmatrix}\, {}_2F_2\!\begin{pmatrix} \frac{2s+\nu}{2},\, \frac{2s-2b+\nu+2}{2};\, \frac{\sigma^2}{4\omega} \\ \nu+1,\, \frac{2s+2a-2b+\nu+2}{2} \end{pmatrix}$

$$\begin{bmatrix} (\operatorname{Re}\omega > 0;\ \operatorname{Re}s > \operatorname{Re}(b-\nu/2)-1,\, -\operatorname{Re}\nu/2)\ \text{or} \\ (\sigma>0;\ \operatorname{Re}\omega = 0;\ \operatorname{Re}(b-\nu/2)-1,\, -\operatorname{Re}\nu/2 < \operatorname{Re}s < \operatorname{Re}a+3/4) \end{bmatrix}$$

No.	$f(x)$	$F(s)$
5	$e^{-\omega x}Y_\nu(\sigma\sqrt{x})$ $\times \Psi\!\begin{pmatrix} a;\,\omega x \\ b \end{pmatrix}$	$\dfrac{(\sigma/2)^\nu}{\pi\omega^{s+\nu/2}}\cos(\pi\nu)\,\Gamma\!\begin{bmatrix} \frac{2s+\nu}{2},\, \frac{2s-2b+\nu+2}{2} \\ -\nu,\, \frac{2s+2a-2b+\nu+2}{2} \end{bmatrix}$

$$\times {}_2F_2\!\begin{pmatrix} \frac{2s+\nu}{2},\, \frac{2s-2b+\nu+2}{2};\, -\frac{\sigma^2}{4\omega} \\ \nu+1,\, \frac{2s+2a-2b+\nu+2}{2} \end{pmatrix} - \dfrac{(2/\sigma)^\nu}{\pi\omega^{s-\nu/2}}$$

$$\times \Gamma\!\begin{bmatrix} \nu,\, \frac{2s-\nu}{2},\, \frac{2s-2b-\nu+2}{2} \\ \frac{2s+2a-2b-\nu+2}{2} \end{bmatrix}\, {}_2F_2\!\begin{pmatrix} \frac{2s-\nu}{2},\, \frac{2s-2b-\nu+2}{2};\, -\frac{\sigma^2}{4\omega} \\ 1-\nu,\, \frac{2s+2a-2b-\nu+2}{2} \end{pmatrix}$$

$$\begin{bmatrix} (\operatorname{Re}\omega > 0;\ \operatorname{Re}s > \operatorname{Re}b - |\operatorname{Re}\nu|/2 - 1,\, -|\operatorname{Re}\nu|/2)\ \text{or} \\ (\sigma>0;\ \operatorname{Re}\omega = 0;\ \operatorname{Re}b - |\operatorname{Re}\nu|/2 - 1,\, -|\operatorname{Re}\nu|/2 < \operatorname{Re}s < \operatorname{Re}a+3/4) \end{bmatrix}$$

No.	$f(x)$	$F(s)$
6	$e^{-\omega x}I_\nu(\sigma x)\,\Psi\!\begin{pmatrix} a;\,\omega x \\ b \end{pmatrix}$	$\dfrac{(\sigma/2)^\nu}{\omega^{s+\nu}}\,\Gamma\!\begin{bmatrix} s+\nu,\, s-b+\nu+1 \\ \nu+1,\, s+a-b+\nu+1 \end{bmatrix}$

$$\times {}_4F_3\!\begin{pmatrix} \Delta(2,\,s+\nu),\, \Delta(2,\,s-b+\nu+1) \\ \nu+1,\, \Delta(2,\,s+a-b+\nu+1);\, \frac{\sigma^2}{\omega^2} \end{pmatrix}$$

$$\begin{bmatrix} (\operatorname{Re}\omega > |\operatorname{Re}\sigma|;\ \operatorname{Re}s > \operatorname{Re}(b-\nu)-1,\, -\operatorname{Re}\nu)\ \text{or} \\ (\operatorname{Re}^2\omega = \operatorname{Re}^2\sigma;\ \operatorname{Re}(b-\nu)-1,\, -\operatorname{Re}\nu < \operatorname{Re}s < \operatorname{Re}a+3/2) \end{bmatrix}$$

No.	$f(x)$	$F(s)$
7	$e^{-\omega x} K_\nu\left(\sigma\sqrt{x}\right)$ $\times \Psi\left(\begin{matrix} a;\ \omega x \\ b \end{matrix}\right)$	$\dfrac{2^{-\nu-1}\sigma^\nu}{\omega^{s+\nu/2}}\Gamma\left[\begin{matrix} -\nu,\ \frac{2s+\nu}{2},\ \frac{2s-2b+\nu+2}{2} \\ \frac{2s+2a-2b+\nu+2}{2} \end{matrix}\right]$ $\times\ {}_2F_2\left(\begin{matrix} \frac{2s+\nu}{2},\ \frac{2s-2b-\nu+2}{2};\ \frac{\sigma^2}{4\omega} \\ \nu+1,\ \frac{2s+2a-2b+\nu+2}{2} \end{matrix}\right) + \dfrac{2^{\nu-1}\sigma^{-\nu}}{\omega^{s-\nu/2}}$ $\times\ \Gamma\left[\begin{matrix} \nu,\ \frac{2s-\nu}{2},\ \frac{2s-2b-\nu+2}{2} \\ \frac{2s+2a-2b-\nu+2}{2} \end{matrix}\right]{}_2F_2\left(\begin{matrix} \frac{2s-\nu}{2},\ \frac{2s-2b-\nu+2}{2};\ \frac{\sigma^2}{4\omega} \\ 1-\nu,\ \frac{2s+2a-2b-\nu+2}{2} \end{matrix}\right)$ $\left[\begin{matrix} (\mathrm{Re}\,\omega>0;\ \mathrm{Re}\,s>\mathrm{Re}\,b-|\mathrm{Re}\,\nu|/2-1,\ -|\mathrm{Re}\,\nu|/2)\ \text{or} \\ (\mathrm{Re}\,\sigma>0;\ \mathrm{Re}\,\omega=0;\ \mathrm{Re}\,s>\mathrm{Re}\,b-|\mathrm{Re}\,\nu|/2-1,\ -|\mathrm{Re}\,\nu|/2)\ \text{or} \\ (\mathrm{Re}\,\sigma=0;\ \mathrm{Re}\,\omega=0;\ \mathrm{Re}\,b-|\mathrm{Re}\,\nu|/2-1,\ -|\mathrm{Re}\,\nu|/2<\mathrm{Re}\,s<\mathrm{Re}\,a+5/4) \end{matrix}\right]$

3.29.8. $\Psi(a;\,b;\,\omega x)$ and $P_n(\varphi(x))$

No.	$f(x)$	$F(s)$
1	$\theta(\sigma-x)P_n\left(\dfrac{2x}{\sigma}-1\right)$ $\times\ \Psi\left(\begin{matrix} a;\ \omega x \\ b \end{matrix}\right)$	$\dfrac{\sigma^{s-b+1}}{\omega^{b-1}}\Gamma\left[\begin{matrix} b-1,\ s-b+1,\ s-b+1 \\ a,\ s-b-n+1,\ s-b+n+2 \end{matrix}\right]$ $\times\ {}_3F_3\left(\begin{matrix} a-b+1,\ s-b+1,\ s-b+1;\ \sigma\omega \\ 2-b,\ s-b-n+1,\ s-b+n+2 \end{matrix}\right)$ $+\sigma^s\,\Gamma\left[\begin{matrix} 1-b,\ s,\ s \\ a-b+1,\ s-n,\ s+n+1 \end{matrix}\right]{}_3F_3\left(\begin{matrix} a,\ s,\ s;\ \sigma\omega \\ b,\ s-n,\ s+n+1 \end{matrix}\right)$ $[\sigma>0;\ \mathrm{Re}\,s>0,\ \mathrm{Re}\,b-1]$
2	$\theta(\sigma-x)P_n\left(\dfrac{2\sigma}{x}-1\right)$ $\times\ \Psi\left(\begin{matrix} a;\ \omega x \\ b \end{matrix}\right)$	$\dfrac{\sigma^{s-b+1}}{\omega^{b-1}}\Gamma\left[\begin{matrix} b-1,\ s-b-n+1,\ s-b+n+2 \\ a,\ s-b+2,\ s-b+2 \end{matrix}\right]$ $\times\ {}_3F_3\left(\begin{matrix} a-b+1,\ s-b-n+1,\ s-b+n+2 \\ 2-b,\ s-b+2,\ s-b+2;\ \sigma\omega \end{matrix}\right)$ $+\sigma^s\,\Gamma\left[\begin{matrix} 1-b,\ s-n,\ s+n+1 \\ a-b+1,\ s+1,\ s+1 \end{matrix}\right]{}_3F_3\left(\begin{matrix} a,\ s-n,\ s+n+1 \\ b,\ s+1,\ s+1;\ \sigma\omega \end{matrix}\right)$ $[\sigma>0;\ \mathrm{Re}\,s>n,\ \mathrm{Re}\,b+n-1]$
3	$\theta(\sigma-x)e^{-\omega x}$ $\times\ P_n\left(\dfrac{2x}{\sigma}-1\right)$ $\times\ \Psi\left(\begin{matrix} a;\ \omega x \\ b \end{matrix}\right)$	$\dfrac{\sigma^{s-b+1}}{\omega^{b-1}}\Gamma\left[\begin{matrix} b-1,\ s-b+1,\ s-b+1 \\ a,\ s-b-n+1,\ s-b+n+2 \end{matrix}\right]$ $\times\ {}_3F_3\left(\begin{matrix} 1-a,\ s-b+1,\ s-b+1;\ -\sigma\omega \\ 2-b,\ s-b-n+1,\ s-b+n+2 \end{matrix}\right)$ $+\sigma^s\,\Gamma\left[\begin{matrix} 1-b,\ s,\ s \\ a-b+1,\ s-n,\ s+n+1 \end{matrix}\right]$ $\times\ {}_3F_3\left(\begin{matrix} b-a,\ s,\ s;\ -\sigma\omega \\ b,\ s-n,\ s+n+1 \end{matrix}\right)$ $[\sigma>0;\ \mathrm{Re}\,s>0,\ \mathrm{Re}\,b-1]$

No.	$f(x)$	$F(s)$
4	$\theta(\sigma - x)\, e^{-\omega x}$ $\times P_n\left(\dfrac{2\sigma}{x} - 1\right)$ $\times \Psi\left(\begin{matrix} a; \omega x \\ b \end{matrix}\right)$	$\dfrac{\sigma^{s-b+1}}{\omega^{b-1}} \Gamma\left[\begin{matrix} b-1,\ s-b-n+1,\ s-b+n+2 \\ a,\ s-b+2,\ s-b+2 \end{matrix}\right]$ $\times {}_3F_3\left(\begin{matrix} 1-a,\ s-b-n+1,\ s-b+n+2 \\ 2-b,\ s-b+2,\ s-b+2;\ -\sigma\omega \end{matrix}\right)$ $+ \sigma^s \Gamma\left[\begin{matrix} 1-b,\ s-n,\ s+n+1 \\ a-b+1,\ s+1,\ s+1 \end{matrix}\right] {}_3F_3\left(\begin{matrix} b-a,\ s-n,\ s+n+1 \\ b,\ s+1,\ s+1;\ -\sigma\omega \end{matrix}\right)$ $[\sigma > 0;\ \operatorname{Re} s > n,\ \operatorname{Re} b + n - 1]$

3.29.9. $\Psi(a;\, b;\, \omega x)$ **and** $T_n(\varphi(x))$

No.	$f(x)$	$F(s)$
1	$(\sigma - x)_+^{-1/2}$ $\times T_n\left(\dfrac{2x}{\sigma} - 1\right)$ $\times \Psi\left(\begin{matrix} a; \omega x \\ b \end{matrix}\right)$	$\dfrac{\sqrt{\pi}\,\sigma^{s-b+1/2}}{\omega^{b-1}} \Gamma\left[\begin{matrix} b-1,\ s-b+1,\ \frac{2s-2b+3}{2} \\ a,\ \frac{2s-2b-2n+3}{2},\ \frac{2s-2b+2n+3}{2} \end{matrix}\right]$ $\times {}_3F_3\left(\begin{matrix} a-b+1,\ s-b+1,\ \frac{2s-2b+3}{2};\ \sigma\omega \\ 2-b,\ \frac{2s-2b-2n+3}{2},\ \frac{2s-2b+2n+3}{2} \end{matrix}\right)$ $+ \sqrt{\pi}\,\sigma^{s-1/2} \Gamma\left[\begin{matrix} 1-b,\ s,\ \frac{2s+1}{2} \\ a-b+1,\ \frac{2s-2n+1}{2},\ \frac{2s+2n+1}{2} \end{matrix}\right]$ $\times {}_3F_3\left(\begin{matrix} a,\ s,\ \frac{2s+1}{2};\ \sigma\omega \\ b,\ \frac{2s-2n+1}{2},\ \frac{2s+2n+1}{2} \end{matrix}\right)\quad [\sigma > 0;\ \operatorname{Re} s > 0,\ \operatorname{Re} b - 1]$
2	$(\sigma - x)_+^{-1/2}$ $\times T_n\left(\dfrac{2\sigma}{x} - 1\right)$ $\times \Psi\left(\begin{matrix} a; \omega x \\ b \end{matrix}\right)$	$\dfrac{\sqrt{\pi}\,\sigma^{s-b+1/2}}{\omega^{b-1}} \Gamma\left[\begin{matrix} b-1,\ s-b-n+1,\ s-b+n+1 \\ a,\ \frac{2s-2b+3}{2},\ s-b+1 \end{matrix}\right]$ $\times {}_3F_3\left(\begin{matrix} a-b+1,\ s-b-n+1,\ s-b+n+1 \\ 2-b,\ \frac{2s-2b+3}{2},\ s-b+1;\ \sigma\omega \end{matrix}\right)$ $+ \sqrt{\pi}\,\sigma^{s-1/2} \Gamma\left[\begin{matrix} 1-b,\ s-n,\ s+n \\ a-b+1,\ \frac{2s+1}{2},\ s \end{matrix}\right] {}_3F_3\left(\begin{matrix} a,\ s-n,\ s+n \\ b,\ \frac{2s+1}{2},\ s;\ \sigma\omega \end{matrix}\right)$ $[\sigma > 0;\ \operatorname{Re} s > n,\ \operatorname{Re} b + n - 1]$
3	$(\sigma - x)_+^{-1/2}\, e^{-\omega x}$ $\times T_n\left(\dfrac{2x}{\sigma} - 1\right)$ $\times \Psi\left(\begin{matrix} a; \omega x \\ b \end{matrix}\right)$	$\dfrac{\sqrt{\pi}\,\sigma^{s-b+1/2}}{\omega^{b-1}} \Gamma\left[\begin{matrix} b-1,\ s-b+1,\ \frac{2s-2b+3}{2} \\ a,\ \frac{2s-2b-2n+3}{2},\ \frac{2s-2b+2n+3}{2} \end{matrix}\right]$ $\times {}_3F_3\left(\begin{matrix} 1-a,\ s-b+1,\ \frac{2s-2b+3}{2};\ -\sigma\omega \\ 2-b,\ \frac{2s-2b-2n+3}{2},\ \frac{2s-2b+2n+3}{2} \end{matrix}\right)$ $+ \sqrt{\pi}\,\sigma^{s-1/2} \Gamma\left[\begin{matrix} 1-b,\ s,\ \frac{2s+1}{2} \\ a-b+1,\ \frac{2s-2n+1}{2},\ \frac{2s+2n+1}{2} \end{matrix}\right]$ $\times {}_3F_3\left(\begin{matrix} b-a,\ s,\ \frac{2s+1}{2};\ -\sigma\omega \\ b,\ \frac{2s-2n+1}{2},\ \frac{2s+2n+1}{2} \end{matrix}\right)$ $[\sigma > 0;\ \operatorname{Re} s > 0,\ \operatorname{Re} b - 1]$

No.	$f(x)$	$F(s)$
4	$(\sigma - x)_+^{-1/2} e^{-\omega x}$ $\times T_n\left(\dfrac{2\sigma}{x} - 1\right)$ $\times \Psi\left(\begin{matrix} a; \omega x \\ b \end{matrix}\right)$	$\dfrac{\sqrt{\pi}\,\sigma^{s-b+1/2}}{\omega^{b-1}} \Gamma\left[\begin{matrix} b-1,\ s-b-n+1,\ s-b+n+1 \\ a,\ \frac{2s-2b+3}{2},\ s-b+1 \end{matrix}\right]$ $\times {}_3F_3\left(\begin{matrix} 1-a,\ s-b-n+1,\ s-b+n+1 \\ 2-b,\ \frac{2s-2b+3}{2},\ s-b+1;\ -\sigma\omega \end{matrix}\right)$ $+\ \sqrt{\pi}\,\sigma^{s-1/2}\Gamma\left[\begin{matrix} 1-b,\ s-n,\ s+n \\ a-b+1,\ \frac{2s+1}{2},\ s \end{matrix}\right] {}_3F_3\left(\begin{matrix} b-a,\ s-n,\ s+n \\ b,\ \frac{2s+1}{2},\ s;\ -\sigma\omega \end{matrix}\right)$ $[\sigma > 0;\ \operatorname{Re} s > n,\ \operatorname{Re} b + n - 1]$

3.29.10. $\Psi(a;\ b;\ \omega x)$ and $U_n(\varphi(x))$

No.	$f(x)$	$F(s)$
1	$(\sigma - x)_+^{1/2}$ $\times U_n\left(\dfrac{2x}{\sigma} - 1\right)$ $\times \Psi\left(\begin{matrix} a; \omega x \\ b \end{matrix}\right)$	$\dfrac{(n+1)\sqrt{\pi}\,\sigma^{s-b+3/2}}{2\,\omega^{b-1}} \Gamma\left[\begin{matrix} b-1,\ s-b+1,\ \frac{2s-2b+1}{2} \\ a,\ \frac{2s-2b-2n+1}{2},\ \frac{2s-2b+2n+5}{2} \end{matrix}\right]$ $\times {}_3F_3\left(\begin{matrix} a-b+1,\ s-b+1,\ \frac{2s-2b+1}{2};\ \sigma\omega \\ 2-b,\ \frac{2s-2b-2n+1}{2},\ \frac{2s-2b+2n+5}{2} \end{matrix}\right)$ $+\ \dfrac{(n+1)\sqrt{\pi}\,\sigma^{s+1/2}}{2} \Gamma\left[\begin{matrix} 1-b,\ s,\ \frac{2s-1}{2} \\ a-b+1,\ \frac{2s-2n-1}{2},\ \frac{2s+2n+3}{2} \end{matrix}\right]$ $\times {}_3F_3\left(\begin{matrix} a,\ s,\ \frac{2s-1}{2};\ \sigma\omega \\ b,\ \frac{2s-2n-1}{2},\ \frac{2s+2n+3}{2} \end{matrix}\right)$ $[\sigma > 0;\ \operatorname{Re} s > 0,\ \operatorname{Re} b - 1]$
2	$(\sigma - x)_+^{1/2}$ $\times U_n\left(\dfrac{2\sigma}{x} - 1\right)$ $\times \Psi\left(\begin{matrix} a; \omega x \\ b \end{matrix}\right)$	$\dfrac{(n+1)\sqrt{\pi}\,\sigma^{s-b+3/2}}{2\,\omega^{b-1}} \Gamma\left[\begin{matrix} b-1 \\ a \end{matrix}\right]\Gamma\left[\begin{matrix} s-b-n+1,\ s-b+n+3 \\ \frac{2s-2b+5}{2},\ s-b+3 \end{matrix}\right]$ $\times {}_3F_3\left(\begin{matrix} a-b+1,\ s-b-n+1,\ s-b+n+3 \\ 2-b,\ \frac{2s-2b+5}{2},\ s-b+3;\ \sigma\omega \end{matrix}\right)$ $+\ \dfrac{(n+1)\sqrt{\pi}\,\sigma^{s+1/2}}{2} \Gamma\left[\begin{matrix} 1-b,\ s-n,\ s+n+2 \\ a-b+1,\ \frac{2s+3}{2},\ s+2 \end{matrix}\right]$ $\times {}_3F_3\left(\begin{matrix} a,\ s-n,\ s+n+2 \\ b,\ \frac{2s+3}{2},\ s+2;\ \sigma\omega \end{matrix}\right)$ $[\sigma > 0;\ \operatorname{Re} s > n,\ \operatorname{Re} b + n - 1]$
3	$(\sigma - x)_+^{1/2} e^{-\omega x}$ $\times U_n\left(\dfrac{2x}{\sigma} - 1\right)$ $\times \Psi\left(\begin{matrix} a; \omega x \\ b \end{matrix}\right)$	$\dfrac{(n+1)\sqrt{\pi}\,\sigma^{s-b+3/2}}{2\,\omega^{b-1}} \Gamma\left[\begin{matrix} b-1,\ s-b+1,\ \frac{2s-2b+1}{2} \\ a,\ \frac{2s-2b-2n+1}{2},\ \frac{2s-2b+2n+5}{2} \end{matrix}\right]$ $\times {}_3F_3\left(\begin{matrix} 1-a,\ s-b+1,\ \frac{2s-2b+1}{2};\ -\sigma\omega \\ 2-b,\ \frac{2s-2b-2n+1}{2},\ \frac{2s-2b+2n+5}{2} \end{matrix}\right)$ $+\ \dfrac{(n+1)\sqrt{\pi}\,\sigma^{s+1/2}}{2} \Gamma\left[\begin{matrix} 1-b,\ s,\ \frac{2s-1}{2} \\ a-b+1,\ \frac{2s-2n-1}{2},\ \frac{2s+2n+3}{2} \end{matrix}\right]$ $\times {}_3F_3\left(\begin{matrix} b-a,\ s,\ \frac{2s-1}{2};\ -\sigma\omega \\ b,\ \frac{2s-2n-1}{2},\ \frac{2s+2n+3}{2} \end{matrix}\right)$ $[\sigma > 0;\ \operatorname{Re} s > 0,\ \operatorname{Re} b - 1]$

No.	$f(x)$	$F(s)$
4	$(\sigma - x)_+^{1/2} e^{-\omega x}$ $\times U_n\left(\dfrac{2\sigma}{x} - 1\right)$ $\times \Psi\left(\begin{matrix} a; \omega x \\ b \end{matrix}\right)$	$\dfrac{(n+1)\sqrt{\pi}\,\sigma^{s-b+3/2}}{2\,\omega^{b-1}} \Gamma\left[\begin{matrix} b-1 \\ a \end{matrix}\right]\Gamma\left[\begin{matrix} s-b-n+1,\ s-b+n+3 \\ \frac{2s-2b+5}{2},\ s-b+3 \end{matrix}\right]$ $\times\ _3F_3\left(\begin{matrix} 1-a,\ s-b-n+1,\ s-b+n+3 \\ 2-b,\ \frac{2s-2b+5}{2},\ s-b+3;\ -\sigma\omega \end{matrix}\right)$ $+\dfrac{(n+1)\sqrt{\pi}\,\sigma^{s+1/2}}{2} \Gamma\left[\begin{matrix} 1-b,\ s-n,\ s+n+2 \\ a-b+1,\ \frac{2s+3}{2},\ s+2 \end{matrix}\right]$ $\times\ _3F_3\left(\begin{matrix} b-a,\ s-n,\ s+n+2 \\ b,\ \frac{2s+3}{2},\ s+2;\ -\sigma\omega \end{matrix}\right)$ $[\sigma > 0;\ \operatorname{Re}s > n,\ \operatorname{Re}b + n - 1]$

3.29.11. $\Psi(a; b; \omega x)$ **and** $H_n(\sigma\sqrt{x})$

No.	$f(x)$	$F(s)$
1	$e^{-\sigma^2 x} H_n(\sigma\sqrt{x})$ $\times \Psi\left(\begin{matrix} a; \omega x \\ b \end{matrix}\right)$	$\dfrac{\sqrt{\pi}\,\omega^{1-b}}{2^{2s-2b-n+1}\sigma^{2s-2b+2}} \Gamma\left[\begin{matrix} b-1,\ 2s-2b+2 \\ a,\ \frac{2s-2b-n+3}{2} \end{matrix}\right]$ $\times\ _3F_2\left(\begin{matrix} a-b+1,\ s-b+1,\ \frac{2s-2b+3}{2} \\ 2-b,\ \frac{2s-2b-n+3}{2};\ \frac{\omega}{\sigma^2} \end{matrix}\right)$ $+\dfrac{\sqrt{\pi}\,\sigma^{-2s}}{2^{2s-n-1}} \Gamma\left[\begin{matrix} 1-b,\ 2s \\ a-b+1,\ \frac{2s-n+1}{2} \end{matrix}\right]\ _3F_2\left(\begin{matrix} a,\ s,\ \frac{2s+1}{2} \\ b,\ \frac{2s-n+1}{2};\ \frac{\omega}{\sigma^2} \end{matrix}\right)$ $\left[\begin{matrix}(\operatorname{Re}\sigma^2 > 0;\ \operatorname{Re}s + (1-(-1)^n)/2 > 0,\ \operatorname{Re}b - 1)\ \text{or} \\ (\operatorname{Re}\sigma^2 = 0;\ 0,\ \operatorname{Re}b - 1 < \operatorname{Re}s - (1-(-1)^n)/2 < \operatorname{Re}a + 1)\end{matrix}\right]$
2	$e^{-(\sigma^2+\omega)x} H_n(\sigma\sqrt{x})$ $\times \Psi\left(\begin{matrix} a; \omega x \\ b \end{matrix}\right)$	$\dfrac{2^n\sqrt{\pi}}{\omega^s} \Gamma\left[\begin{matrix} s,\ s-b+1 \\ \frac{1-n}{2},\ s+a-b+1 \end{matrix}\right]\ _3F_2\left(\begin{matrix} \frac{n+1}{2},\ s,\ s-b+1 \\ \frac{1}{2},\ s+a-b+1;\ -\frac{\sigma^2}{\omega} \end{matrix}\right)$ $-\dfrac{2^{n+1}\sqrt{\pi}\,\sigma}{\omega^{s+1/2}} \Gamma\left[\begin{matrix} \frac{2s+1}{2},\ \frac{2s-2b+3}{2} \\ -\frac{n}{2},\ \frac{2s+2a-2b+3}{2} \end{matrix}\right]\ _3F_2\left(\begin{matrix} \frac{n+2}{2},\ \frac{2s+1}{2},\ \frac{2s-2b+3}{2} \\ \frac{3}{2},\ \frac{2s+2a-2b+3}{2};\ -\frac{\sigma^2}{\omega} \end{matrix}\right)$ $\left[\begin{matrix}(\operatorname{Re}(\sigma^2+\omega) > 0;\ \operatorname{Re}s + (1-(-1)^n)/2 > 0,\ \operatorname{Re}b - 1)\ \text{or} \\ (\operatorname{Re}(\sigma^2+\omega) = 0;\ 0,\ \operatorname{Re}b - 1 < \operatorname{Re}s - (1-(-1)^n)/2 < \operatorname{Re}a + 1)\end{matrix}\right]$

3.29.12. $\Psi(a; b; \omega x)$ **and** $L_n^\lambda(\sigma x)$

No.	$f(x)$	$F(s)$
1	$e^{-\sigma x} L_n^\lambda(\sigma x) \Psi\left(\begin{matrix} a; \omega x \\ b \end{matrix}\right)$	$\dfrac{\omega^{-s}}{n!}\left(\dfrac{\sigma}{\omega}\right)^{a-s} \Gamma\left[\begin{matrix} s-a,\ 1-s+a+n+\lambda \\ 1-s+a+\lambda \end{matrix}\right]$ $\times\ _3F_2\left(\begin{matrix} a,\ a-b+1,\ 1-s+a+n+\lambda \\ a-s+1,\ a-s+\lambda+1;\ \frac{\sigma}{\omega} \end{matrix}\right) + \dfrac{\omega^{-s}}{n!}$ $\times \Gamma\left[\begin{matrix} n+\lambda+1,\ s,\ a-s,\ s-b+1 \\ a,\ a-b+1,\ \lambda+1 \end{matrix}\right]\ _3F_2\left(\begin{matrix} n+\lambda+1,\ s,\ s-b+1 \\ \lambda+1,\ s-a+1;\ \frac{\sigma}{\omega} \end{matrix}\right)$ $\left[\begin{matrix}(\operatorname{Re}\sigma > 0;\ \operatorname{Re}s > 0,\ \operatorname{Re}b - 1)\ \text{or} \\ (\operatorname{Re}\sigma = 0;\ 0,\ \operatorname{Re}b - 1 < \operatorname{Re}s + n < \operatorname{Re}a + 1)\end{matrix}\right]$

No.	$f(x)$	$F(s)$
2	$e^{-(\sigma+\omega)x}L_n^\lambda(\sigma x)$ $\times \Psi\left(\begin{matrix}a;\,\omega x\\b\end{matrix}\right)$	$\dfrac{\omega^{-s}}{n!}\Gamma\left[\begin{matrix}n+\lambda+1,\,s,\,s-b+1\\\lambda+1,\,s+a-b+1\end{matrix}\right]{}_3F_2\left(\begin{matrix}n+\lambda+1,\,s,\,s-b+1\\\lambda+1,\,s+a-b+1;\,-\frac{\sigma}{\omega}\end{matrix}\right)$ $\left[\begin{matrix}(\operatorname{Re}(\sigma+\omega)>0;\ \operatorname{Re}s>0,\ \operatorname{Re}b-1)\text{ or}\\(\operatorname{Re}(\sigma+\omega)=0;\ 0,\ \operatorname{Re}b-1<\operatorname{Re}s+n<\operatorname{Re}a+1)\end{matrix}\right]$

3.29.13. $\Psi(a;\,b;\,\omega x)$ **and** $C_n^\lambda(\varphi(x))$

No.	$f(x)$	$F(s)$
1	$(\sigma-x)_+^{\lambda-1/2}$ $\times C_n^\lambda\left(\dfrac{2x}{\sigma}-1\right)$ $\times \Psi\left(\begin{matrix}a;\,\omega x\\b\end{matrix}\right)$	$\dfrac{\sqrt{\pi}\,\sigma^{s-b+\lambda+1/2}}{2^{2\lambda-1}n!\,\omega^{b-1}}\Gamma\left[\begin{matrix}b-1,\,n+2\lambda,\,s-b+1,\,\frac{2s-2b-2\lambda+3}{2}\\a,\,\lambda,\,\frac{2s-2b-2n-2\lambda+3}{2},\,\frac{2s-2b+2n+2\lambda+3}{2}\end{matrix}\right]$ $\times {}_3F_3\left(\begin{matrix}a-b+1,\,s-b+1,\,\frac{2s-2b-2\lambda+3}{2};\,\sigma\omega\\2-b,\,\frac{2s-2b-2n-2\lambda+3}{2},\,\frac{2s-2b+2n+2\lambda+3}{2}\end{matrix}\right)$ $+\dfrac{\sqrt{\pi}\,\sigma^{s+\lambda-1/2}}{2^{2\lambda-1}n!}\Gamma\left[\begin{matrix}1-b,\,n+2\lambda,\,s,\,\frac{2s-2\lambda+1}{2}\\\lambda,\,a-b+1,\,\frac{2s-2n-2\lambda+1}{2},\,\frac{2s+2n+2\lambda+1}{2}\end{matrix}\right]$ $\times {}_3F_3\left(\begin{matrix}a,\,s,\,\frac{2s-2\lambda+1}{2};\,\sigma\omega\\b,\,\frac{2s-2n-2\lambda+1}{2},\,\frac{2s+2n+2\lambda+1}{2}\end{matrix}\right)$ $[\sigma>0;\ \operatorname{Re}s>0,\ \operatorname{Re}b-1]$
2	$(\sigma-x)_+^{\lambda-1/2}$ $\times C_n^\lambda\left(\dfrac{2\sigma}{x}-1\right)$ $\times \Psi\left(\begin{matrix}a;\,\omega x\\b\end{matrix}\right)$	$\dfrac{\sqrt{\pi}\,\sigma^{s-b+\lambda+1/2}}{2^{2\lambda-1}n!\,\omega^{b-1}}\Gamma\left[\begin{matrix}b-1,\,n+2\lambda\\a,\,\lambda\end{matrix}\right]$ $\times \Gamma\left[\begin{matrix}s-b-n+1,\,s-b+n+2\lambda+1\\\frac{2s-2b+2\lambda+3}{2},\,s-b+2\lambda+1\end{matrix}\right]$ $\times {}_3F_3\left(\begin{matrix}a-b+1,\,s-b-n+1,\,s-b+n+2\lambda+1\\2-b,\,\frac{2s-2b+2\lambda+3}{2},\,s-b+2\lambda+1;\,\sigma\omega\end{matrix}\right)$ $+\dfrac{\sqrt{\pi}\,\sigma^{s+\lambda-1/2}}{2^{2\lambda-1}n!}\Gamma\left[\begin{matrix}1-b,\,n+2\lambda,\,s-n,\,s+n+2\lambda\\\lambda,\,a-b+1,\,\frac{2s+2\lambda+1}{2},\,s+2\lambda\end{matrix}\right]$ $\times {}_3F_3\left(\begin{matrix}a,\,s-n,\,s+n+2\lambda\\b,\,\frac{2s+2\lambda+1}{2},\,s+2\lambda;\,\sigma\omega\end{matrix}\right)$ $[\sigma>0;\ \operatorname{Re}s>n,\ \operatorname{Re}b+n-1]$
3	$(\sigma-x)_+^{\lambda-1/2}\,e^{-\omega x}$ $\times C_n^\lambda\left(\dfrac{2x}{\sigma}-1\right)$ $\times \Psi\left(\begin{matrix}a;\,\omega x\\b\end{matrix}\right)$	$\dfrac{\sqrt{\pi}\,\sigma^{s-b+\lambda+1/2}}{2^{2\lambda-1}n!\,\omega^{b-1}}\Gamma\left[\begin{matrix}b-1,\,n+2\lambda,\,s-b+1,\,\frac{2s-2b-2\lambda+3}{2}\\a,\,\lambda,\,\frac{2s-2b-2n-2\lambda+3}{2},\,\frac{2s-2b+2n+2\lambda+3}{2}\end{matrix}\right]$ $\times {}_3F_3\left(\begin{matrix}1-a,\,s-b+1,\,\frac{2s-2b-2\lambda+3}{2};\,-\sigma\omega\\2-b,\,\frac{2s-2b-2n-2\lambda+3}{2},\,\frac{2s-2b+2n+2\lambda+3}{2}\end{matrix}\right)$ $+\dfrac{\sqrt{\pi}\,\sigma^{s+\lambda-1/2}}{2^{2\lambda-1}n!}\Gamma\left[\begin{matrix}1-b,\,n+2\lambda,\,s,\,\frac{2s-2\lambda+1}{2}\\\lambda,\,a-b+1,\,\frac{2s-2n-2\lambda+1}{2},\,\frac{2s+2n+2\lambda+1}{2}\end{matrix}\right]$ $\times {}_3F_3\left(\begin{matrix}b-a,\,s,\,\frac{2s-2\lambda+1}{2};\,-\sigma\omega\\b,\,\frac{2s-2n-2\lambda+1}{2},\,\frac{2s+2n+2\lambda+1}{2}\end{matrix}\right)$ $[\sigma>0;\ \operatorname{Re}s>0,\ \operatorname{Re}b-1]$

No.	$f(x)$	$F(s)$
4	$(\sigma-x)_+^{\lambda-1/2}\,e^{-\omega x}$ $\times C_n^\lambda\left(\dfrac{2\sigma}{x}-1\right)$ $\times \Psi\left(\begin{matrix}a;\,\omega x\\b\end{matrix}\right)$	$\dfrac{\sqrt\pi\,\sigma^{s-b+\lambda+1/2}}{2^{2\lambda-1}n!\,\omega^{b-1}}\,\Gamma\!\left[\begin{matrix}b-1,\,n+2\lambda\\a,\,\lambda\end{matrix}\right]$ $\times\Gamma\!\left[\begin{matrix}s-b-n+1,\,s-b+n+2\lambda+1\\\frac{2s-2b+2\lambda+3}{2},\,s-b+2\lambda+1\end{matrix}\right]$ $\times {}_3F_3\!\left(\begin{matrix}1-a,\,s-b-n+1,\,s-b+n+2\lambda+1\\2-b,\,\frac{2s-2b+2\lambda+3}{2},\,s-b+2\lambda+1;\,-\sigma\omega\end{matrix}\right)$ $+\dfrac{\sqrt\pi\,\sigma^{s+\lambda-1/2}}{2^{2\lambda-1}n!}\,\Gamma\!\left[\begin{matrix}1-b,\,n+2\lambda,\,s-n,\,s+n+2\lambda\\\lambda,\,a-b+1,\,\frac{2s+2\lambda+1}{2},\,s+2\lambda\end{matrix}\right]$ $\times {}_3F_3\!\left(\begin{matrix}b-a,\,s-n,\,s+n+2\lambda\\b,\,\frac{2s+2\lambda+1}{2},\,s+2\lambda;\,-\sigma\omega\end{matrix}\right)$ $[\sigma>0;\ \mathrm{Re}\,s>n,\ \mathrm{Re}\,b+n-1]$

3.29.14. $\Psi(a;b;\omega x)$ **and** $P_n^{(\mu,\nu)}(\varphi(x))$

1	$(\sigma-x)_+^\mu$ $\times P_n^{(\mu,\nu)}\left(\dfrac{2\sigma}{x}-1\right)$ $\times \Psi\left(\begin{matrix}a;\,\omega x\\b\end{matrix}\right)$	$-\dfrac{\pi\sigma^{s-b+\mu+1}}{n!\,\omega^{b-1}}\,\csc(b\pi)\,\Gamma\!\left[\begin{matrix}n+\mu+1\\a,2-b\end{matrix}\right]$ $\times\Gamma\!\left[\begin{matrix}s-b-n+1,\,s-b+n+\mu+\nu+2\\s-b+\mu+2,\,s-b+\mu+\nu+2\end{matrix}\right]$ $\times {}_3F_3\!\left(\begin{matrix}a-b+1,\,s-b-n+1,\,s-b+n+\mu+\nu+2\\2-b,\,s-b+\mu+2,\,s-b+\mu+\nu+2;\,\sigma\omega\end{matrix}\right)$ $+\dfrac{\pi\sigma^{s+\mu}}{n!}\,\csc[(1-b)\pi]\,\Gamma\!\left[\begin{matrix}n+\mu+1\\b,\,a-b+1\end{matrix}\right]$ $\times\Gamma\!\left[\begin{matrix}s-n,\,s+n+\mu+\nu+1\\s+\mu+1,\,s+\mu+\nu+1\end{matrix}\right]{}_3F_3\!\left(\begin{matrix}a,\,s-n,\,s+n+\mu+\nu+1\\b,\,s+\mu+1,\,s+\mu+\nu+1;\,\sigma\omega\end{matrix}\right)$ $[\sigma>0;\ \mathrm{Re}\,s>n,\ \mathrm{Re}\,b+n-1]$
2	$(\sigma-x)_+^\mu\,e^{-\omega x}$ $\times P_n^{(\mu,\nu)}\left(\dfrac{2\sigma}{x}-1\right)$ $\times \Psi\left(\begin{matrix}a;\,\omega x\\b\end{matrix}\right)$	$\dfrac{\pi\sigma^{s-b+\mu+1}}{n!\,\omega^{b-1}}\,\csc[(b-1)\pi]\,\Gamma\!\left[\begin{matrix}n+\mu+1\\a,2-b\end{matrix}\right]$ $\times\Gamma\!\left[\begin{matrix}s-b-n+1,\,s-b+n+\mu+\nu+2\\s-b+\mu+2,\,s-b+\mu+\nu+2\end{matrix}\right]$ $\times {}_3F_3\!\left(\begin{matrix}1-a,\,s-b-n+1,\,s-b+n+\mu+\nu+2\\2-b,\,s-b+\mu+2,\,s-b+\mu+\nu+2;\,-\sigma\omega\end{matrix}\right)$ $+\dfrac{\pi\sigma^{s+\mu}}{n!}\,\csc(b\pi)\,\Gamma\!\left[\begin{matrix}n+\mu+1,\,s-n,\,s+n+\mu+\nu+1\\b,\,a-b+1,\,s+\mu+1,\,s+\mu+\nu+1\end{matrix}\right]$ $\times {}_3F_3\!\left(\begin{matrix}b-a,\,s-n,\,s+n+\mu+\nu+1\\b,\,s+\mu+1,\,s+\mu+\nu+1;\,-\sigma\omega\end{matrix}\right)$ $[\sigma>0;\ \mathrm{Re}\,s>n,\ \mathrm{Re}\,b+n-1]$

3.29.15. $\Psi\left(a;\,b;\,\omega x\right)$ **and** $\mathbf{K}\left(\varphi\left(x\right)\right),\ \mathbf{E}\left(\varphi\left(x\right)\right)$

Notation: $\delta = \left\{ \begin{matrix} 1 \\ 0 \end{matrix} \right\}.$

1	$\theta\left(\sigma - x\right)$ $\times \left\{ \begin{matrix} \mathbf{K}\left(\sqrt{1 - x/\sigma}\right) \\ \mathbf{E}\left(\sqrt{1 - x/\sigma}\right) \end{matrix} \right\}$ $\times \Psi\left(\begin{matrix} a;\,\omega x \\ b \end{matrix}\right)$	$\dfrac{\pi\sigma^{s-b+1}}{2\omega^{b-1}}\,\Gamma\!\left[\begin{matrix} b-1,\ s-b+1,\ s-b-\delta+2 \\ a,\ \frac{2s-2b+3}{2},\ \frac{2s-2b-2\delta+5}{2} \end{matrix}\right]$ $\times\,{}_3F_3\!\left(\begin{matrix} a-b+1,\ s-b+1,\ s-b-\delta+2 \\ 2-b,\ \frac{2s-2b+3}{2},\ \frac{2s-2b-2\delta+5}{2};\ \sigma\omega \end{matrix}\right)$ $+\dfrac{\pi\sigma^s}{2}\,\Gamma\!\left[\begin{matrix} 1-b,\ s,\ s-\delta+1 \\ a-b+1,\ \frac{2s+1}{2},\ \frac{2s-2\delta+3}{2} \end{matrix}\right]{}_3F_3\!\left(\begin{matrix} a,\ s,\ s-\delta+1;\ \sigma\omega \\ b,\ \frac{2s+1}{2},\ \frac{2s-2\delta+3}{2} \end{matrix}\right)$ $[\sigma > 0;\ \operatorname{Re} s > 0,\ \operatorname{Re} b-1]$
2	$\theta\left(\sigma - x\right)e^{-\omega x}$ $\times \left\{ \begin{matrix} \mathbf{K}\left(\sqrt{1 - x/\sigma}\right) \\ \mathbf{E}\left(\sqrt{1 - x/\sigma}\right) \end{matrix} \right\}$ $\times \Psi\left(\begin{matrix} a;\,\omega x \\ b \end{matrix}\right)$	$\dfrac{\pi\sigma^{s-b+1}}{2\omega^{b-1}}\,\Gamma\!\left[\begin{matrix} b-1,\ s-b+1,\ s-b-\delta+2 \\ a,\ \frac{2s-2b+3}{2},\ \frac{2s-2b-2\delta+5}{2} \end{matrix}\right]$ $\times\,{}_3F_3\!\left(\begin{matrix} 1-a,\ s-b+1,\ s-b-\delta+2 \\ 2-b,\ \frac{2s-2b+3}{2},\ \frac{2s-2b-2\delta+5}{2};\ -\sigma\omega \end{matrix}\right)$ $+\dfrac{\pi\sigma^s}{2}\,\Gamma\!\left[\begin{matrix} 1-b,\ s,\ s-\delta+1 \\ a-b+1,\ \frac{2s+1}{2},\ \frac{2s-2\delta+3}{2} \end{matrix}\right]$ $\times\,{}_3F_3\!\left(\begin{matrix} b-a,\ s,\ s-\delta+1;\ -\sigma\omega \\ b,\ \frac{2s+1}{2},\ \frac{2s-2\delta+3}{2} \end{matrix}\right)$ $[\sigma > 0;\ \operatorname{Re} s > 0,\ \operatorname{Re} b-1]$

3.29.16. $\Psi\left(a;\,b;\,\omega x\right)$ **and** ${}_1F_1\left(a;\,b;\,\sigma x\right)$

1	${}_1F_1\left(\begin{matrix} a;\,-\omega x \\ b \end{matrix}\right)$ $\times \Psi\left(\begin{matrix} a;\,\omega x \\ b \end{matrix}\right)$	$\dfrac{2^{s-b-1}}{\sqrt{\pi}\,\omega^s}\,\Gamma\!\left[\begin{matrix} b,\ \frac{s}{2},\ a-\frac{s}{2},\ \frac{s-b+1}{2},\ \frac{s-b+2}{2} \\ a,\ b-\frac{s}{2},\ \frac{s}{2}+a-b+1 \end{matrix}\right]$ $\left[\begin{matrix} (\operatorname{Re}\omega > 0;\ 0,\ \operatorname{Re} b-1 < \operatorname{Re} s < 2\operatorname{Re} a)\ \text{or} \\ (\operatorname{Re}\omega = 0;\ 0,\ \operatorname{Re} b-1 < \operatorname{Re} s < 2\operatorname{Re} a,\ \operatorname{Re} b+1) \end{matrix}\right]$
2	$e^{-\omega x}\,{}_1F_1\left(\begin{matrix} b-a;\,\omega x \\ b \end{matrix}\right)$ $\times \Psi\left(\begin{matrix} a;\,\omega x \\ b \end{matrix}\right)$	$\dfrac{2^{s-b-1}}{\sqrt{\pi}\,\omega^s}\,\Gamma\!\left[\begin{matrix} b,\ \frac{s}{2},\ a-\frac{s}{2},\ \frac{s-b+1}{2},\ \frac{s-b+2}{2} \\ a,\ b-\frac{s}{2},\ \frac{s}{2}+a-b+1 \end{matrix}\right]$ $\left[\begin{matrix} (\operatorname{Re}\omega > 0;\ 0,\ \operatorname{Re} b-1 < \operatorname{Re} s < 2\operatorname{Re} a)\ \text{or} \\ (\operatorname{Re}\omega = 0;\ 0,\ \operatorname{Re} b-1 < \operatorname{Re} s < 2\operatorname{Re} a,\ \operatorname{Re} b+1) \end{matrix}\right]$

3.29.17. **Products of** $\Psi\left(a;\,b;\,\omega x\right)$

1	$\Psi\left(\begin{matrix} a;\,-\omega x \\ b \end{matrix}\right)\Psi\left(\begin{matrix} a;\,\omega x \\ b \end{matrix}\right)$	$\dfrac{2^{s-b-1}}{\sqrt{\pi}\,(-\omega^2)^{s/2}}\,\Gamma\!\left[\begin{matrix} \frac{2a-s}{2},\ \frac{s}{2},\ \frac{s-b+1}{2},\ \frac{s-b+2}{2},\ \frac{s-2b+2}{2} \\ a,\ a-b+1,\ \frac{s+2a-2b+2}{2} \end{matrix}\right]$ $[\operatorname{Re}\omega > 0;\ 0,\ \operatorname{Re} b-1,\ 2\operatorname{Re} b-2 < \operatorname{Re} s < 2\operatorname{Re} a]$

No.	$f(x)$	$F(s)$

2 $\Psi\left(\begin{matrix} \mu; \sigma x \\ \nu \end{matrix}\right)\Psi\left(\begin{matrix} a; \omega x \\ b \end{matrix}\right)$

$\dfrac{\omega^{1-b}}{\sigma^{s-b+1}}\,\Gamma\left[\begin{matrix} b-1,\, s-b+1,\, b-s+\mu-1,\, s-b-\nu+2 \\ a,\, \mu,\, \mu-\nu+1 \end{matrix}\right]$

$\times\ _3F_2\left(\begin{matrix} a-b+1,\, s-b-\nu+2,\, s-b+1 \\ 2-b,\, s-b-\mu+2;\ -\frac{\omega}{\sigma} \end{matrix}\right)$

$+\dfrac{\omega^{\mu-s}}{\sigma^\mu}\,\Gamma\left[\begin{matrix} a-s+\mu,\, s-\mu,\, s-b-\mu+1 \\ a,\, a-b+1 \end{matrix}\right]$

$\times\ _3F_2\left(\begin{matrix} \mu,\, \mu-\nu+1,\, a-s+\mu \\ 1-s+\mu,\, b-s+\mu;\ -\frac{\omega}{\sigma} \end{matrix}\right)$

$+\sigma^{-s}\,\Gamma\left[\begin{matrix} 1-b,\, \mu-s,\, s,\, s-\nu+1 \\ a-b+1,\, \mu,\, \mu-\nu+1 \end{matrix}\right]\,_3F_2\left(\begin{matrix} a,\, s,\, s-\nu+1 \\ b,\, s-\mu+1;\ -\frac{\omega}{\sigma} \end{matrix}\right)$

$[0,\ \operatorname{Re}\nu-1,\ \operatorname{Re}(b+\nu)-2,\ \operatorname{Re}b-1 < \operatorname{Re}s < \operatorname{Re}(a+\mu)]$

3 $\Psi\left(\begin{matrix} \mu; \frac{\sigma}{x} \\ \nu \end{matrix}\right)\Psi\left(\begin{matrix} a; \omega x \\ b \end{matrix}\right)$

$\dfrac{\sigma^{s-b+1}}{\omega^{b-1}}\,\Gamma\left[\begin{matrix} b-1,\, b-s-1,\, b-s-\nu,\, s-b+\mu+1 \\ a,\, \mu,\, \mu-\nu+1 \end{matrix}\right]$

$\times\ _2F_3\left(\begin{matrix} a-b+1,\, s-b+\mu+1;\ \sigma\omega \\ 2-b,\, s-b+2,\, s-b+\nu+1 \end{matrix}\right)$

$+\dfrac{\sigma^{1-\nu}}{\omega^{s+\nu-1}}\,\Gamma\left[\begin{matrix} \nu-1,\, 1-s+a-\nu,\, s+\nu-1,\, s-b+\nu \\ a,\, \mu,\, a-b+1 \end{matrix}\right]$

$\times\ _2F_3\left(\begin{matrix} \mu-\nu+1,\, 1-s+a-\nu;\ \sigma\omega \\ 2-\nu,\, 2-s-\nu,\, 1-s+b-\nu \end{matrix}\right)$

$+\sigma^s\,\Gamma\left[\begin{matrix} 1-b,\, -s,\, 1-s-\nu,\, s+\mu \\ a-b+1,\, \mu,\, \mu-\nu+1 \end{matrix}\right]\,_2F_3\left(\begin{matrix} a,\, s+\mu;\ \sigma\omega \\ b,\, s+1,\, s+\nu \end{matrix}\right)$

$+\omega^{-s}\,\Gamma\left[\begin{matrix} 1-\nu,\, s,\, a-s,\, s-b+1 \\ a,\, a-b+1,\, \mu-\nu+1 \end{matrix}\right]\,_2F_3\left(\begin{matrix} \mu,\, a-s;\ \sigma\omega \\ \nu,\, 1-s,\, b-s \end{matrix}\right)$

$[-\operatorname{Re}\mu,\ \operatorname{Re}(b-\mu)-1 < \operatorname{Re}s < \operatorname{Re}a,\ \operatorname{Re}(a-\nu)+1]$

4 $e^{-\omega x}\Psi\left(\begin{matrix} \mu; \sigma x \\ \nu \end{matrix}\right)$

$\times\ \Psi\left(\begin{matrix} a; \omega x \\ b \end{matrix}\right)$

$\dfrac{\sigma^{1-\nu}}{\omega^{s-\nu+1}}\,\Gamma\left[\begin{matrix} \nu-1,\, s-\nu+1,\, s-b-\nu+2 \\ \mu,\, s+a-b-\nu+2 \end{matrix}\right]$

$\times\ _3F_2\left(\begin{matrix} \mu-\nu+1,\, s-\nu+1,\, s-b-\nu+2 \\ 2-\nu,\, s+a-b-\nu+2;\ \frac{\sigma}{\omega} \end{matrix}\right)$

$+\omega^{-s}\,\Gamma\left[\begin{matrix} 1-\nu,\, s,\, s-b+1 \\ \mu-\nu+1,\, s+a-b+1 \end{matrix}\right]\,_3F_2\left(\begin{matrix} \mu,\, s,\, s-b+1;\ \frac{\sigma}{\omega} \\ \nu,\, s+a-b+1 \end{matrix}\right)$

$\left[\begin{matrix} (\operatorname{Re}\omega > 0;\ \operatorname{Re}s > 0,\ \operatorname{Re}b-1,\ \operatorname{Re}\nu-1,\ \operatorname{Re}(b+\nu)-2)\ \text{or} \\ (\operatorname{Re}\omega = 0;\ 0,\ \operatorname{Re}b-1,\ \operatorname{Re}\nu-1,\ \operatorname{Re}(b+\nu)-2 < \operatorname{Re}s < \operatorname{Re}(a+\mu)+1) \end{matrix}\right]$

5 $e^{-(\sigma+\omega)x}\Psi\left(\begin{matrix} \mu; \sigma x \\ \nu \end{matrix}\right)$

$\times\ \Psi\left(\begin{matrix} a; \omega x \\ b \end{matrix}\right)$

$\dfrac{\sigma^{1-\nu}}{\omega^{s-\nu+1}}\,\Gamma\left[\begin{matrix} \nu-1,\, s-\nu+1,\, s-b-\nu+2 \\ \mu,\, s+a-b-\nu+2 \end{matrix}\right]$

$\times\ _3F_2\left(\begin{matrix} 1-\mu,\, s-\nu+1,\, s-b-\nu+2 \\ 2-\nu,\, a-b+s-\nu+2;\ -\frac{\sigma}{\omega} \end{matrix}\right)+$

No.	$f(x)$	$F(s)$

$$+\,\omega^{-s}\,\Gamma\left[\begin{matrix}1-\nu,\,s,\,s-b+1\\\mu-\nu+1,\,a-b+s+1\end{matrix}\right]{}_3F_2\left(\begin{matrix}\nu-\mu,\,s,\,s-b+1\\\nu,\,a-b+s+1;\,-\frac{\sigma}{\omega}\end{matrix}\right)$$

$$\left[\begin{matrix}(\operatorname{Re}(\sigma+\omega)>0;\ \operatorname{Re}s>0,\ \operatorname{Re}b-1,\ \operatorname{Re}\nu-1,\ \operatorname{Re}(b+\nu)-2)\ \text{or}\\(\operatorname{Re}(\sigma+\omega)=0;\ 0,\ \operatorname{Re}b-1,\ \operatorname{Re}\nu-1,\ \operatorname{Re}(b+\nu)-2<\operatorname{Re}s<\operatorname{Re}(a+\mu)+1)\end{matrix}\right]$$

6 $e^{-\sigma x}\Psi\!\left(\begin{matrix}\mu;\,\frac{\sigma}{x}\\\nu\end{matrix}\right)\Psi\!\left(\begin{matrix}a;\,\omega x\\b\end{matrix}\right)$

$$\frac{\sigma^{s-b+1}}{\omega^{b-1}}\,\Gamma\left[\begin{matrix}b-1,\,b-s-1,\,b-s-\nu,\,s-b+\mu+1\\a,\,\mu,\,\mu-\nu+1\end{matrix}\right]$$

$$\times\,{}_2F_3\left(\begin{matrix}1-a,\,s-b+\mu+1;\,-\sigma\omega\\2-b,\,s-b+2,\,s-b+\nu+1\end{matrix}\right)$$

$$+\,\frac{\sigma^{1-\nu}}{\omega^{s+\nu-1}}\,\Gamma\left[\begin{matrix}\nu-1,\,s+\nu-1,\,s-b+\nu\\\mu,\,s+a-b+\nu\end{matrix}\right]$$

$$\times\,{}_2F_3\left(\begin{matrix}\mu-\nu+1,\,1-s-a+b-\nu;\,-\sigma\omega\\2-\nu,\,2-s-\nu,\,1-s+b-\nu\end{matrix}\right)$$

$$-\,\sigma^s\,\csc(b\pi)\,\sin[(\mu-\nu)\,\pi]\,\Gamma\left[\begin{matrix}\nu-\mu,\,-s,\,1-s-\nu,\,s+\mu\\b,\,a-b+1,\,\mu\end{matrix}\right]$$

$$\times\,{}_2F_3\left(\begin{matrix}b-a,\,s+\mu;\,-\sigma\omega\\b,\,s+1,\,s+\nu\end{matrix}\right)$$

$$+\,\omega^{-s}\,\Gamma\left[\begin{matrix}1-\nu,\,s,\,s-b+1\\\mu-\nu+1,\,s+a-b+1\end{matrix}\right]{}_2F_3\left(\begin{matrix}\mu,\,b-a-s;\,-\sigma\omega\\\nu,\,1-s,\,b-s\end{matrix}\right)$$

$$\left[\begin{matrix}(\operatorname{Re}\sigma>0;\ -\operatorname{Re}\mu,\ \operatorname{Re}(b-\mu)-1<\operatorname{Re}s)\ \text{or}\\(\operatorname{Re}\sigma=0;\ -\operatorname{Re}\mu,\ \operatorname{Re}(b-\mu)-1<\operatorname{Re}s\\<\operatorname{Re}a+1,\operatorname{Re}(a-\nu)+2)\end{matrix}\right]$$

7 $J_\nu(\sigma x)\,\Psi\!\left(\begin{matrix}a;\,-i\omega x\\b\end{matrix}\right)$

     $\times\,\Psi\!\left(\begin{matrix}a;\,i\omega x\\b\end{matrix}\right)$

$$2^{s-2a-1}\left(\frac{\sigma^2}{\omega^2}\right)^{a-s/2}\left(\omega^2\right)^{-s/2}\,\Gamma\left[\begin{matrix}\frac{s-2a+\nu}{2}\\\frac{2a-s+\nu+2}{2}\end{matrix}\right]$$

$$\times\,{}_4F_3\left(\begin{matrix}a,\,a-b+1,\,\frac{2a-b+1}{2},\,\frac{2a-b+2}{2}\\2a-b+1,\,\frac{2a-s-\nu+2}{2},\,\frac{2a-s+\nu+2}{2};\,\frac{\sigma^2}{\omega^2}\end{matrix}\right)+\frac{2^{-\nu-1}}{(\omega^2)^{s/2}}\left(\frac{\sigma^2}{\omega^2}\right)^{\nu/2}$$

$$\times\,\mathrm{B}\left(\frac{s+\nu}{2},\,\frac{2a-s-\nu}{2}\right)\,\Gamma\left[\begin{matrix}\frac{s-2b+\nu+2}{2},\,s-b+\nu+1\\\nu+1,\,a-b+1,\,\frac{s+2a-2b+\nu+2}{2}\end{matrix}\right]$$

$$\times\,{}_4F_3\left(\begin{matrix}\frac{s+\nu}{2},\,\frac{s-2b+\nu+2}{2},\,\frac{s-b+\nu+1}{2},\,\frac{s-b+\nu+2}{2}\\\nu+1,\,\frac{s-2a+\nu+2}{2},\,\frac{s+2a-2b+\nu+2}{2};\,\frac{\sigma^2}{\omega^2}\end{matrix}\right)$$

$$\left[\begin{matrix}\sigma>0;\ \operatorname{Re}\omega\neq0;\\-\operatorname{Re}\nu,\ \operatorname{Re}(2b-\nu)-2,\ \operatorname{Re}(b-\nu)-1<\operatorname{Re}s<2\operatorname{Re}a+3/2\end{matrix}\right]$$

8 $e^{-\omega x}J_\nu(\sigma x)\,\Psi\!\left(\begin{matrix}a;\,\omega x\\b\end{matrix}\right)$

     $\times\,\Psi\!\left(\begin{matrix}b-a;\,\omega x\\b\end{matrix}\right)$

$$\frac{2^{-\nu-1}\sigma^\nu}{\omega^{s+\nu}}\,\Gamma\left[\begin{matrix}\frac{s+\nu}{2},\,\frac{s-2b+\nu+2}{2},\,s-b+\nu+1\\\nu+1,\,\frac{s-2a+\nu+2}{2},\,\frac{s+2a-2b+\nu+2}{2}\end{matrix}\right]$$

$$\times\,{}_4F_3\left(\begin{matrix}\frac{s+\nu}{2},\,\frac{s+\nu-2b+2}{2},\,\frac{s+\nu-b+1}{2},\,\frac{s+\nu-b+2}{2}\\\nu+1,\,\frac{s+\nu-2a+2}{2},\,\frac{s+\nu+2a-2b+2}{2};\,-\frac{\sigma^2}{\omega^2}\end{matrix}\right)$$

$$\left[\begin{matrix}(\operatorname{Re}\omega>|\operatorname{Im}\sigma|;\ \operatorname{Re}s>-\operatorname{Re}\nu,\ \operatorname{Re}(2b-\nu)-2,\ \operatorname{Re}(b-\nu)-1)\ \text{or}\\(\operatorname{Re}^2\omega=\operatorname{Im}^2\sigma;\ -\operatorname{Re}\nu,\ \operatorname{Re}(2b-\nu)-2,\ \operatorname{Re}(b-\nu)-1<\operatorname{Re}s<\operatorname{Re}b+3/2)\end{matrix}\right]$$

3.30.   The Whittaker Functions $M_{\rho,\sigma}(z)$ and $W_{\rho,\sigma}(z)$

The Whittaker functions $M_{\rho,\sigma}(z)$ and $W_{\rho,\sigma}(z)$ are connected with the Kummer confluent hypergeometric function $_1F_1(a;b;z)$ and the Tricomi confluent hypergeometric function $\Psi(a;b;x)$ by the relations

$$M_{\rho,\sigma}(z) = z^{\sigma+1/2}e^{-z/2}\, _1F_1\left(\sigma-\rho+\frac{1}{2}; 2\sigma+1; z\right),$$

$$M_{\rho,\sigma}(z) = z^{\sigma+1/2}e^{-z/2}\left[z^{-2\sigma}\Gamma\begin{bmatrix}2\sigma\\\frac{1}{2}+\sigma-\rho\end{bmatrix}\,_1F_1\left(\begin{matrix}\frac{1}{2}-\sigma-\rho\\1-2\sigma; z\end{matrix}\right)\right.$$
$$\left.+\Gamma\begin{bmatrix}-2\sigma\\\frac{1}{2}-\sigma-\rho\end{bmatrix}\,_1F_1\left(\begin{matrix}\frac{1}{2}+\sigma-\rho\\1+2\sigma; z\end{matrix}\right)\right],$$

$$W_{\rho,\sigma}(z) = z^{\sigma+1/2}e^{-x/2}\,\Psi\left(\sigma-\rho+\frac{1}{2}; 2\sigma+1; z\right).$$

To evaluate the Mellin transform of functions containing $M_{\rho,\sigma}(z)$ and $W_{\rho,\sigma}(z)$, one can apply the above relations and the formulas of Sections 3.28 and 3.29. We present here only several of such formulas.

3.30.1. $W_{\rho,\sigma}(ax)$

No.	$f(x)$	$F(s)$
1	$W_{-1/2,0}(ax)$	$\dfrac{2^{s-1/2}}{a^s}\Gamma\left(\dfrac{2s+1}{2}\right)\left[\psi\left(\dfrac{2s+3}{4}\right)-\psi\left(\dfrac{2s+1}{4}\right)\right]$ $\left[\begin{matrix}(\operatorname{Re}a>0;\ \operatorname{Re}s>-1/2)\ \text{or}\\(\operatorname{Re}a=0;\ -1/2<\operatorname{Re}s<3/2)\end{matrix}\right]$
2	$W_{0,\sigma}(ax)$	$\dfrac{2^{2s-1}}{\sqrt{\pi}\,a^s}\Gamma\left(\dfrac{2s-2\sigma+1}{4}\right)\Gamma\left(\dfrac{2s+2\sigma+1}{4}\right)$ $\left[\begin{matrix}\sigma\neq0;\ (\operatorname{Re}a>0;\ \operatorname{Re}s>|\operatorname{Re}\sigma|-1/2)\ \text{or}\\(\operatorname{Re}a=0;\ |\operatorname{Re}\sigma|-1/2<\operatorname{Re}s<1)\end{matrix}\right]$
3	$W_{\pm1/2,\sigma}(ax)$	$\dfrac{2^{2s-1}a^{-s}}{\sqrt{\pi}\,\sigma^{(1\mp1)/2}}\left[\Gamma\left(\dfrac{2s-2\sigma+1}{4}\right)\Gamma\left(\dfrac{2s+2\sigma+3}{4}\right)\right.$ $\left.\pm\Gamma\left(\dfrac{2s-2\sigma+3}{4}\right)\Gamma\left(\dfrac{2s+2\sigma+1}{4}\right)\right]$ $\left[\begin{matrix}\sigma\neq0;\ (\operatorname{Re}a>0;\ \operatorname{Re}s>|\operatorname{Re}\sigma|-1/2)\ \text{or}\\(\operatorname{Re}a=0;\ |\operatorname{Re}\sigma|-1/2<\operatorname{Re}s<1/2)\end{matrix}\right]$
4	$W_{\rho,\sigma}(ax)$	$a^{-s}\Gamma\begin{bmatrix}\frac{2s-2\sigma+1}{2},\ \frac{2s+2\sigma+1}{2}\\s-\rho+1\end{bmatrix}\,_2F_1\left(\begin{matrix}\frac{2s-2\sigma+1}{2},\ \frac{2s+2\sigma+1}{2}\\s-\rho+1;\ \frac{1}{2}\end{matrix}\right)$ $\left[\begin{matrix}\sigma\neq0;\ (\operatorname{Re}a>0;\ \operatorname{Re}s>|\operatorname{Re}\sigma|-1/2)\ \text{or}\\(\operatorname{Re}a=0;\ |\operatorname{Re}\sigma|-1/2<\operatorname{Re}s<-\operatorname{Re}\rho+1)\end{matrix}\right]$

3.30.2. $M_{\rho,\sigma}(ax)$, $W_{\rho,\sigma}(bx)$, and the exponential function

1	$e^{-ax} M_{\rho,\sigma}(bx)$	$\dfrac{2^{s+\sigma+1/2}\, b^{\sigma+1/2}}{(2a-b)^{s+\sigma+1/2}} \Gamma\left(\dfrac{2s+2\sigma+1}{2}\right) {}_2F_1\left(\begin{array}{c} \frac{2\rho+2\sigma+1}{2},\ \frac{2s+2\sigma+1}{2} \\ 2\sigma+1;\ \frac{2b}{b-2a} \end{array}\right)$
		$\left[\begin{array}{l}(\operatorname{Re}a > |\operatorname{Re}b|/2;\ \operatorname{Re}s > -\operatorname{Re}\sigma - 1/2)\ \text{or} \\ (\operatorname{Re}a = \operatorname{Re}b/2 > 0;\ -\operatorname{Re}\sigma - 1/2 < \operatorname{Re}s < \operatorname{Re}\rho + 1)\ \text{or} \\ (\operatorname{Re}a = -\operatorname{Re}b/2 > 0;\ -\operatorname{Re}\sigma - 1/2 < \operatorname{Re}s < -\operatorname{Re}\rho + 1)\end{array}\right]$
2	$e^{-ax/2} M_{\rho,\sigma}(ax)$	$a^{-s}\, \Gamma\left[\begin{array}{c} 2\sigma+1,\ \rho - s,\ \frac{2s+2\sigma+1}{2} \\ \frac{2\rho+2\sigma+1}{2},\ \frac{1-2s+2\sigma}{2} \end{array}\right]$
		$\left[\begin{array}{l}(\operatorname{Re}a > 0;\ -\operatorname{Re}\sigma - 1/2 < \operatorname{Re}s < \operatorname{Re}\rho)\ \text{or} \\ (\operatorname{Re}a = 0;\ -\operatorname{Re}\sigma - 1/2 < \operatorname{Re}s < \operatorname{Re}\rho,\ 1 - \operatorname{Re}\rho)\end{array}\right]$
3	$e^{-ax} W_{\rho,\sigma}(bx)$	$b^{-s}\, \Gamma\left[\begin{array}{c} \frac{2s-2\sigma+1}{2},\ \frac{2s+2\sigma+1}{2} \\ s-\rho+1 \end{array}\right] {}_2F_1\left(\begin{array}{c} \frac{2s-2\sigma+1}{2},\ \frac{2s+2\sigma+1}{2} \\ s-\rho+1;\ \frac{b-2a}{2b} \end{array}\right)$
		$\left[\begin{array}{l}\sigma \neq 0;\ (\operatorname{Re}(2a+b) > 0;\ \operatorname{Re}s > |\operatorname{Re}\sigma| - 1/2)\ \text{or} \\ (\operatorname{Re}(2a+b) = 0;\ |\operatorname{Re}\sigma| - 1/2 < \operatorname{Re}s < 1 - \operatorname{Re}\rho)\end{array}\right]$
4	$e^{-ax/2} W_{\rho,\sigma}(ax)$	$a^{-s}\, \Gamma\left[\begin{array}{c} \frac{2s-2\sigma+1}{2},\ \frac{2s+2\sigma+1}{2} \\ s-\rho+1 \end{array}\right]$
		$\left[\begin{array}{l}\sigma \neq 0;\ (\operatorname{Re}a > 0;\ \operatorname{Re}s > |\operatorname{Re}\sigma| - 1/2)\ \text{or} \\ (\operatorname{Re}a = 0;\ |\operatorname{Re}\sigma| - 1/2 < \operatorname{Re}s < 1 - \operatorname{Re}\rho)\end{array}\right]$
5	$e^{ax/2} W_{\rho,\sigma}(ax)$	$a^{-s}\, \Gamma\left[\begin{array}{c} \frac{2s-2\sigma+1}{2},\ \frac{2s+2\sigma+1}{2},\ -s-\rho \\ \frac{1-2\rho-2\sigma}{2},\ \frac{1-2\rho+2\sigma}{2} \end{array}\right]$
		$[|\operatorname{Re}\sigma| - 1/2 < \operatorname{Re}s < -\operatorname{Re}\rho]$
6	$e^{-ax/2} W_{\rho,\sigma}(ax)$	$a^{-s}\, \Gamma\left[\begin{array}{c} \frac{2s-2\sigma+1}{2},\ \frac{2s+2\sigma+1}{2} \\ s-\rho+1 \end{array}\right]$
		$\left[\begin{array}{l}(\operatorname{Re}s > |\operatorname{Re}\sigma| - 1/2;\ |\arg a| < \pi/2)\ \text{or} \\ (|\operatorname{Re}\sigma| - 1/2 < \operatorname{Re}s < 1 - \operatorname{Re}\rho;\ |\arg a| = \pi/2)\end{array}\right]$

3.30.3. $W_{\rho,\sigma}(ax)$ and hyperbolic functions

1	$\left\{\begin{array}{c}\sinh(ax/2) \\ \cosh(ax/2)\end{array}\right\}$	$\dfrac{a^{-s}}{2} \Gamma\left[\begin{array}{c} -s-\rho,\ \frac{2s-2\sigma+1}{2},\ \frac{2s+2\sigma+1}{2} \\ \frac{1-2\rho-2\sigma}{2},\ \frac{1-2\rho+2\sigma}{2} \end{array}\right] \mp \dfrac{a^{-s}}{2} \Gamma\left[\begin{array}{c} \frac{2s-2\sigma+1}{2},\ \frac{2s+2\sigma+1}{2} \\ s-\rho+1 \end{array}\right]$
	$\times W_{\rho,\sigma}(ax)$	$[|\operatorname{Re}\sigma| - 1/2 < \operatorname{Re}s < -\operatorname{Re}\rho;\ |\arg a| \leq \pi/2]$

3.30.4. $W_{\rho,\sigma}(ax)$ and $L_\rho^\sigma(bx)$

1	$e^{ax/2} L_{\rho-\sigma-1/2}^{2\sigma}(-ax)$ $\times W_{\rho,\sigma}(ax)$	$\dfrac{a^{\sigma+1/2}\left(a^2\right)^{-(2s+2\sigma+1)/4}\cos\left[(\rho-\sigma)\pi\right]}{2\pi}$ $\times \Gamma\left[\begin{array}{c} \frac{2\rho+2\sigma+1}{2},\ \frac{2s-2\sigma+1}{2},\ \frac{2s+2\sigma+1}{4},\ \frac{1-2s-4\rho+2\sigma}{4} \\ \frac{3-2s+6\sigma}{4},\ \frac{2s-4\rho-2\sigma+3}{4} \end{array}\right]$ $\left[\begin{array}{c}(|\operatorname{Re}\sigma|-1/2<\operatorname{Re}s<\operatorname{Re}(\sigma-2\rho)+1/2;\ |\arg a|<\pi/2)\ \text{or} \\ (|\operatorname{Re}\sigma|-1/2<\operatorname{Re}s<\operatorname{Re}(\sigma-2\rho)+1/2,\ \operatorname{Re}\sigma+3/2;\ |\arg a|=\pi/2)\end{array}\right]$
2	$e^{-ax/2} L_{-\rho-\sigma-1/2}^{2\sigma}(ax)$ $\times W_{\rho,\sigma}(ax)$	$\dfrac{a^{-s}}{2}\Gamma\left[\begin{array}{c} \frac{2s-2\sigma+1}{2},\ \frac{2s+2\sigma+1}{4},\ \frac{1-2s-4\rho+2\sigma}{4} \\ \frac{1-2\rho-2\sigma}{2},\ \frac{2s-4\rho-2\sigma+3}{4},\ \frac{3-2s+6\sigma}{4} \end{array}\right]$ $\left[\begin{array}{c}(|\operatorname{Re}\sigma|-1/2<\operatorname{Re}s<\operatorname{Re}(\sigma-2\rho)+1/2;\ |\arg a|<\pi/2)\ \text{or} \\ (|\operatorname{Re}\sigma|-1/2<\operatorname{Re}s<\operatorname{Re}(\sigma-2\rho)+1/2,\ \operatorname{Re}\sigma+3/2;\ |\arg a|=\pi/2)\end{array}\right]$

3.30.5. $W_{\rho,\sigma}(ax)$ and $\,_1F_1(b;c;dx)$, $\Psi(b;c;dx)$

1	$e^{\pm ax/2}\,_1F_1\!\left(\begin{array}{c}\frac{1\mp2\rho+2\sigma}{2} \\ 2\sigma+1;\mp ax\end{array}\right)$ $\times W_{\rho,\sigma}(ax)$	$\dfrac{2^{s-\sigma-3/2}a^{-s}}{\sqrt{\pi}}$ $\times \Gamma\left[\begin{array}{c} 2\sigma+1,\ \frac{2s-2\sigma+1}{4},\ \frac{2s-2\sigma+3}{4},\ \frac{2s+2\sigma+1}{4},\ \frac{1-2s-4\rho+2\sigma}{4} \\ \frac{1-2\rho+2\sigma}{2},\ \frac{3-2s+6\sigma}{4},\ \frac{2s-4\rho-2\sigma+3}{4} \end{array}\right]$ $\left[\begin{array}{c}(|\operatorname{Re}\sigma|-1/2<\operatorname{Re}s<1/2-\operatorname{Re}(2\rho-\sigma);\ |\arg a|<\pi/2)\ \text{or} \\ (|\operatorname{Re}\sigma|-1/2<\operatorname{Re}s<1/2-\operatorname{Re}(2\rho-\sigma),\ \operatorname{Re}\sigma+3/2;\ |\arg a|=\pi/2)\end{array}\right]$
2	$e^{ax/2}\Psi\!\left(\begin{array}{c}\frac{1-2\rho\pm2\sigma}{2} \\ 1\pm2\sigma;\,-ax\end{array}\right)$ $\times W_{\rho,\sigma}(ax)$	$\dfrac{\sqrt{a}\,i^{\mp\sigma}2^{s\mp\sigma-3/2}\left(-a^2\right)^{-(2s+1)/4}}{\sqrt{\pi}}$ $\times \Gamma\left[\begin{array}{c} \frac{2s\mp6\sigma+1}{4},\ \frac{2s-2\sigma+1}{4},\ \frac{2s\mp2\sigma+3}{4},\ \frac{2s+2\sigma+1}{4},\ \frac{1-2s-4\rho\pm2\sigma}{4} \\ \frac{1-2\rho-2\sigma}{2},\ \frac{1-2\rho+2\sigma}{2},\ \frac{2s-4\rho\mp2\sigma+3}{4} \end{array}\right]$ $\left[|\operatorname{Re}\sigma|-1/2,\ \pm3\operatorname{Re}\sigma-1/2<\operatorname{Re}s<1/2-\operatorname{Re}(2\rho\mp\sigma)\right]$

3.30.6.   **Products of $M_{\mu,\nu}(ax)$ and $W_{\mu,\nu}(bx)$**

1	$M_{\rho,\sigma}(-ax)\,W_{\rho,\sigma}(ax)$	$\dfrac{(-a)^{\sigma+1/2}}{2\,a^{s+\sigma+1/2}}\Gamma\left[\begin{array}{c} 2\sigma+1,\ -\frac{s+2\rho}{2},\ s+1,\ \frac{s+2\sigma+1}{2} \\ \frac{1-2\rho+2\sigma}{2},\ \frac{1-s+2\sigma}{2},\ \frac{s-2\rho+2}{2} \end{array}\right]$ $\left[\begin{array}{c}(-1,\ 2\operatorname{Re}\sigma-1<\operatorname{Re}s<-2\operatorname{Re}\rho;\ |\arg a|<\pi/2)\ \text{or} \\ (-1,\ 2\operatorname{Re}\sigma-1<\operatorname{Re}s<1,\ -2\operatorname{Re}\rho;\ |\arg a|=\pi/2)\end{array}\right]$

No.	$f(x)$	$F(s)$
2	$M_{\rho,-\sigma}(-ax)W_{\rho,\sigma}(ax)$	$\dfrac{i(-1)^{-\sigma}}{2\,a^s}\,\Gamma\!\left[\begin{matrix}1-2\sigma,\ -\frac{s+2\rho}{2},\ s+1,\ \frac{s-2\sigma+1}{2}\\ \frac{1-2\rho-2\sigma}{2},\ \frac{1-s-2\sigma}{2},\ \frac{s-2\rho+2}{2}\end{matrix}\right]$ $\left[\begin{matrix}(-1,\ 2\operatorname{Re}\sigma-1<\operatorname{Re}s<-2\operatorname{Re}\rho;\ |\arg a|<\pi/2)\ \text{or}\\ (-1,\ 2\operatorname{Re}\sigma-1<\operatorname{Re}s<1,\ -2\operatorname{Re}\rho,\ |\arg a|=\pi/2)\end{matrix}\right]$
3	$M_{-\rho,\sigma}(ax)W_{\rho,\sigma}(ax)$	$\dfrac{a^{-s}}{2}\,\Gamma\!\left[\begin{matrix}2\sigma+1,\ s+1,\ \frac{s+2\sigma+1}{2},\ -\frac{s+2\rho}{2}\\ \frac{2\sigma-2\rho+1}{2},\ \frac{s-2\rho+2}{2},\ \frac{1-s+2\sigma}{2}\end{matrix}\right]$ $\left[\begin{matrix}(\operatorname{Re}a>0;\ -1,\ -2\operatorname{Re}\sigma-1<\operatorname{Re}s<-2\operatorname{Re}\rho)\ \text{or}\\ (\operatorname{Re}a=0;\ -1,\ -2\operatorname{Re}\sigma-1<\operatorname{Re}s<1,\ -2\operatorname{Re}\rho)\end{matrix}\right]$
4	$M_{-\rho,-\sigma}(ax)W_{\rho,\sigma}(ax)$	$\dfrac{a^{-s}}{2}\,\Gamma\!\left[\begin{matrix}1-2\sigma,\ -\frac{s+2\rho}{2},\ s+1,\ \frac{s-2\sigma+1}{2}\\ \frac{1-2\rho-2\sigma}{2},\ \frac{1-s-2\sigma}{2},\ \frac{s-2\rho+2}{2}\end{matrix}\right]$ $\left[\begin{matrix}(-1,\ 2\operatorname{Re}\sigma-1<\operatorname{Re}s<-2\operatorname{Re}\rho;\ |\arg a|<\pi/2)\ \text{or}\\ (-1,\ 2\operatorname{Re}\sigma-1<\operatorname{Re}s<1,\ -2\operatorname{Re}\rho,\ |\arg a|=\pi/2)\end{matrix}\right]$
5	$W_{\rho,\pm\sigma}(-ax)W_{\rho,\pm\sigma}(ax)$	$\dfrac{(-a^2)^{-s/2}}{2}\,\Gamma\!\left[\begin{matrix}-\frac{s+2\rho}{2},\ s+1,\ \frac{s-2\sigma+1}{2},\ \frac{s+2\sigma+1}{2}\\ \frac{1-2\rho-2\sigma}{2},\ \frac{1-2\rho+2\sigma}{2},\ \frac{s-2\rho+2}{2}\end{matrix}\right]$ $[2|\operatorname{Re}\sigma|-1<\operatorname{Re}s<-2\operatorname{Re}\rho]$
6	$W_{\rho,-\sigma}(\mp ax)$ $\times\,W_{\rho,\sigma}(\pm ax)$	$\dfrac{(-a^2)^{-s/2}}{2}\,\Gamma\!\left[\begin{matrix}-\frac{s+2\rho}{2},\ s+1,\ \frac{s-2\sigma+1}{2},\ \frac{s+2\sigma+1}{2}\\ \frac{1-2\rho-2\sigma}{2},\ \frac{1-2\rho+2\sigma}{2},\ \frac{s-2\rho+2}{2}\end{matrix}\right]$ $[2|\operatorname{Re}\sigma|-1<\operatorname{Re}s<-2\operatorname{Re}\rho]$
7	$W_{-\rho,\sigma}(ax)W_{\rho,\sigma}(ax)$	$\dfrac{a^{-s}}{2}\,\Gamma\!\left[\begin{matrix}s+1,\ \frac{s+2\sigma+1}{2},\ \frac{s-2\sigma+1}{2}\\ \frac{s-2\rho+2}{2},\ \frac{s+2\rho+2}{2}\end{matrix}\right]$ $\left[\begin{matrix}(\operatorname{Re}a>0;\ \operatorname{Re}s>-1,\ 2|\operatorname{Re}\sigma|-1)\ \text{or}\\ (\operatorname{Re}a=0;\ 2|\operatorname{Re}\sigma|-1<\operatorname{Re}s<1)\end{matrix}\right]$
8	$M_{\rho,\sigma}(-iax)M_{\rho,\sigma}(iax)$	$\dfrac{a^{-s}}{2}\,\Gamma\!\left[\begin{matrix}2\sigma+1,\ 2\sigma+1,\ \frac{s+2\sigma+1}{2},\ \frac{2\rho-s}{2},\ -\frac{s+2\rho}{2}\\ -s,\ \frac{1-2\rho+2\sigma}{2},\ \frac{1+2\rho+2\sigma}{2},\ \frac{2\sigma-s+1}{2}\end{matrix}\right]$ $[a>0;\ -2\operatorname{Re}\sigma-1<\operatorname{Re}s<1,\ -2|\operatorname{Re}\rho|]$
9	$W_{\rho,\sigma}(-iax)W_{\rho,\sigma}(iax)$	$\dfrac{a^{-s}}{2}\,\Gamma\!\left[\begin{matrix}s+1,\ \frac{s+2\sigma+1}{2},\ \frac{s-2\sigma+1}{2},\ -\frac{s+2\rho}{2}\\ \frac{1-2\rho+2\sigma}{2},\ \frac{1-2\rho-2\sigma}{2},\ \frac{s-2\rho+2}{2}\end{matrix}\right]$ $[2|\operatorname{Re}\sigma|-1<\operatorname{Re}s<-2\operatorname{Re}\rho;\ |\arg a|<\pi]$
10	$W_{\rho,-\sigma}(-iax)W_{\rho,\sigma}(iax)$	$\dfrac{a^{-s}}{2}\,\Gamma\!\left[\begin{matrix}s+1,\ \frac{s+2\sigma+1}{2},\ \frac{s-2\sigma+1}{2},\ -\frac{s+2\rho}{2}\\ \frac{1-2\rho+2\sigma}{2},\ \frac{1-2\rho-2\sigma}{2},\ \frac{s-2\rho+2}{2}\end{matrix}\right]$ $[2|\operatorname{Re}\sigma|-1<\operatorname{Re}s<-2\operatorname{Re}\rho;\ |\arg a|<\pi]$

3.31. The Gauss Hypergeometric Function $_2F_1(a, b; c; z)$

More formulas can be obtained from the corresponding sections due to the relations

$$_2F_1\binom{a,\, b}{c;\, z} = \Gamma\begin{bmatrix} 1-a,\, c \\ c-a \end{bmatrix} P_{-a}^{(c-1,\, a+b-c)}(1-2z),$$

$$_2F_1\binom{a,\, b}{c;\, z} = \Gamma\begin{bmatrix} c \\ a,\, b \end{bmatrix} G_{22}^{12}\left(-z \,\middle|\, \begin{matrix} 1-a,\, 1-b \\ 0,\, 1-c \end{matrix}\right),$$

$$_2F_1\binom{a,\, b}{c;\, z} = \Gamma\begin{bmatrix} c \\ a,\, b,\, c-a,\, c-b \end{bmatrix} G_{22}^{22}\left(1-z \,\middle|\, \begin{matrix} 1-a,\, 1-b \\ 0,\, c-a-b \end{matrix}\right).$$

3.31.1. $_2F_1(a, b; c; \omega x)$ and algebraic functions

No.	$f(x)$	$F(s)$
1	$_2F_1\binom{a,\, b}{c;\, -\omega x}$	$\omega^{-s}\,\Gamma\begin{bmatrix} c \\ a,\, b \end{bmatrix}\Gamma\begin{bmatrix} a-s,\, b-s,\, s \\ c-s \end{bmatrix}$ $[0 < \operatorname{Re}s < \operatorname{Re}a,\, \operatorname{Re}b;\, \lvert\arg\omega\rvert < \pi]$
2	$_2F_1\binom{a,\, b}{c;\, -\omega x} - 1$	$-(-\omega)^{-s}\,\Gamma\begin{bmatrix} c \\ a,\, b \end{bmatrix}\Gamma\begin{bmatrix} -s,\, a-s,\, b-s,\, s+1 \\ 1-s,\, c-s \end{bmatrix}$ $[-1 < \operatorname{Re}s < 0,\, \operatorname{Re}a,\, \operatorname{Re}b;\, \lvert\arg\omega\rvert < \pi]$
3	$_2F_1\binom{a,\, b}{c;\, -\omega x}$ $-\sum_{k=0}^{n}\dfrac{(a)_k\,(b)_k}{k!\,(c)_k}(-\omega x)^k$	$(-1)^{n+1}\,\omega^{-s}\,\Gamma\begin{bmatrix} c \\ a,\, b \end{bmatrix}\Gamma\begin{bmatrix} a-s,\, b-s,\, -n-s,\, s+n+1 \\ 1-s,\, c-s \end{bmatrix}$ $[-n-1 < \operatorname{Re}s < -n,\, \operatorname{Re}a,\, \operatorname{Re}b;\, \lvert\arg\omega\rvert < \pi]$
4	$\dfrac{1}{x-\sigma}\,_2F_1\binom{a,\, b}{c;\, -\omega x}$	$\omega^{1-s}\,\Gamma\begin{bmatrix} c,\, a-s+1,\, b-s+1,\, s-1 \\ a,\, b,\, c-s+1 \end{bmatrix}$ $\times\,_3F_2\binom{1,\, a-s+1,\, b-s+1}{2-s,\, c-s+1;\, -\sigma\omega}$ $-\,\pi\sigma^{s-1}\cot(s\pi)\,_2F_1\binom{a,\, b}{c;\, -\sigma\omega}$ $[\sigma > 0;\, 0 < \operatorname{Re}s < \operatorname{Re}a+1,\, \operatorname{Re}b+1;\, \lvert\arg\omega\rvert < \pi]$
5	$(\sigma-x)_+^{\mu-1}\,_2F_1\binom{a,\, b}{c;\, -\omega x}$	$\sigma^{s+\mu-1}\,\mathrm{B}(\mu,\, s)\,_3F_2\binom{a,\, b,\, s}{c,\, s+\mu;\, -\sigma\omega}$ $[\sigma,\, \operatorname{Re}\mu,\, \operatorname{Re}s > 0;\, \lvert\arg(1+\sigma\omega)\rvert < \pi]$

No.	$f(x)$	$F(s)$
6	$(x-\sigma)_+^{\mu-1}\ {}_2F_1\left(\begin{matrix}a,\,b\\c;\,-\omega x\end{matrix}\right)$	$\sigma^{s+\mu-1}\,\mathrm{B}\left(\mu,\,1-\mu-s\right){}_3F_2\left(\begin{matrix}a,\,b,\,s;\,-\sigma\omega\\c,\,s+\mu\end{matrix}\right)$

$$+\Gamma\left[\begin{matrix}c,\,s+\mu-1,\,a-\mu-s+1,\,b-\mu-s+1\\a,\,b,\,c-\mu-s+1\end{matrix}\right]$$

$$\times\omega^{1-s-\mu}\,{}_3F_2\left(\begin{matrix}1-\mu,\,a-\mu-s+1,\,b-\mu+1\\2-\mu-s,\,c-\mu-s+1;\,-\sigma\omega\end{matrix}\right)$$

$$[\sigma,\ \mathrm{Re}\,\mu>0;\ \mathrm{Re}\,s<\mathrm{Re}\,(a-\mu),\ \mathrm{Re}\,(b-\mu);\ |\arg\omega|<\pi]$$

| 7 | $\dfrac{1}{(x+\sigma)^\rho}\,{}_2F_1\left(\begin{matrix}a,\,b\\c;\,-\omega x\end{matrix}\right)$ | $\sigma^{s-\rho}\,\mathrm{B}\left(s,\,\rho-s\right){}_3F_2\left(\begin{matrix}a,\,b,\,s;\,\sigma\omega\\c,\,s-\rho+1\end{matrix}\right)$ |

$$+\omega^{\rho-s}\,\Gamma\left[\begin{matrix}c,\,s-\rho,\,a+\rho-s,\,b+\rho-s\\a,\,b,\,c+\rho-s\end{matrix}\right]$$

$$\times\,{}_3F_2\left(\begin{matrix}\rho,\,a+\rho-s,\,b+\rho-s\\c+\rho-s,\,\rho-s+1;\,\sigma\omega\end{matrix}\right)$$

$$[0<\mathrm{Re}\,s<\mathrm{Re}\,(a+\rho),\ \mathrm{Re}\,(b+\rho);\ |\arg\sigma|,\ |\arg\omega|<\pi]$$

8	${}_2F_1\left(\begin{matrix}a,\,b\\c;\,-i\omega x\end{matrix}\right)$ $+\ {}_2F_1\left(\begin{matrix}a,\,b\\c;\,i\omega x\end{matrix}\right)$	$2\omega^{-s}\cos\dfrac{s\pi}{2}\,\Gamma\left[\begin{matrix}c\\a,\,b\end{matrix}\right]\Gamma\left[\begin{matrix}a-s,\,b-s,\,s\\c-s\end{matrix}\right]$ $[0<\mathrm{Re}\,s<\mathrm{Re}\,a,\ \mathrm{Re}\,b;\	\arg\omega	<\pi/2]$
9	${}_2F_1\left(\begin{matrix}a,\,b\\c;\,-i\omega x\end{matrix}\right)$ $-\ {}_2F_1\left(\begin{matrix}a,\,b\\c;\,i\omega x\end{matrix}\right)$	$-2i\,\omega^{-s}\sin\dfrac{s\pi}{2}\,\Gamma\left[\begin{matrix}c\\a,\,b\end{matrix}\right]\Gamma\left[\begin{matrix}a-s,\,b-s,\,s\\c-s\end{matrix}\right]$ $[-1<\mathrm{Re}\,s<\mathrm{Re}\,a,\ \mathrm{Re}\,b;\	\arg\omega	<\pi/2]$
10	$(x+\omega)^{-b}$ $\times\,{}_2F_1\left(\begin{matrix}a,\,b;\,-\frac{x}{\omega}\\a+2b+1\end{matrix}\right)$	$b\,(2a+2b-s)\,\omega^{s-b}\,\Gamma\left[\begin{matrix}a+2b+1\\2b+1,\,a+b+1\end{matrix}\right]$ $\times\,\Gamma\left[\begin{matrix}s,\,2b-s,\,a+b-s\\a+2b-s+1\end{matrix}\right]$ $[0<\mathrm{Re}\,s<2\,\mathrm{Re}\,b,\ \mathrm{Re}\,(a+b),\ 2\,\mathrm{Re}\,(a+b)+1;\,	\arg\omega	<\pi]$
11	$(x+\omega)\,{}_2F_1\left(\begin{matrix}a,\,b;\,-\frac{x}{\omega}\\a-b+1\end{matrix}\right)$	$(a-2s-1)\,\omega^{s+1}\,\Gamma\left[\begin{matrix}a-b+1\\a,\,b-1\end{matrix}\right]\Gamma\left[\begin{matrix}a-s-1,\,b-s-1,\,s\\a-b-s+1\end{matrix}\right]$ $[0<\mathrm{Re}\,s<\mathrm{Re}\,a-1,\ \mathrm{Re}\,b-1,\ (\mathrm{Re}\,a+1)/2;\	\arg\omega	<\pi]$
12	$(x+\omega)\,{}_2F_1\left(\begin{matrix}a,\,b;\,-\frac{x}{\omega}\\\frac{2a+b-1}{2}\end{matrix}\right)$	$\dfrac{2a-s-2}{2}\,\omega^{s+1}\,\Gamma\left[\begin{matrix}\frac{2a+b-1}{2}\\a,\,b-1\end{matrix}\right]\Gamma\left[\begin{matrix}a-s-1,\,b-s-1,\,s\\\frac{2a+b-2s-1}{2}\end{matrix}\right]$ $[0<\mathrm{Re}\,s<\mathrm{Re}\,a-1,\ \mathrm{Re}\,b-1;\	\arg\omega	<\pi]$

No.	$f(x)$	$F(s)$
13	$(x+\omega)^{2b}\,{}_2F_1\left(\begin{matrix}a,\,b;\,-\frac{x}{\omega}\\a-b+1\end{matrix}\right)$	$(a-2b-2s)\,\omega^{s+2b}\,\Gamma\left[\begin{matrix}a-b+1\\-b,\,a-2b+1\end{matrix}\right]\Gamma\left[\begin{matrix}s,\,-b-s,\,a-2b-s\\a-b-s+1\end{matrix}\right]$
		$[0<\operatorname{Re}s<-\operatorname{Re}b,\ \operatorname{Re}(a-2b);\ \lvert\arg\omega\rvert<\pi]$
14	$(x+\omega)^{a+b-c}\,{}_2F_1\left(\begin{matrix}a,\,b\\c;\,-\frac{x}{\omega}\end{matrix}\right)$	$\omega^{s+a+b-c}\,\Gamma\left[\begin{matrix}c\\c-a,\,c-b\end{matrix}\right]\Gamma\left[\begin{matrix}c-a-s,\,c-b-s,\,s\\c-s\end{matrix}\right]$
		$[0<\operatorname{Re}s<\operatorname{Re}(c-a),\ \operatorname{Re}(c-b);\ \lvert\arg\omega\rvert<\pi]$
15	$\theta(\omega-x)\,{}_2F_1\left(\begin{matrix}a,\,c+n\\c;\,\frac{x}{\omega}\end{matrix}\right)$	$\dfrac{\omega^s}{(c)_n}\,\Gamma\left[\begin{matrix}1-a,\,s,\,c-s+n\\s-a+1,\,c-s\end{matrix}\right]$ $[\operatorname{Re}a<1-n;\ \omega,\ \operatorname{Re}s>0]$
16	$(\omega-x)_+^{b-c-n}\,{}_2F_1\left(\begin{matrix}-n,\,b\\c;\,\frac{x}{\omega}\end{matrix}\right)$	$\dfrac{\omega^{s+b-c-n}}{(c)_n}\,\Gamma\left[\begin{matrix}b-c+1,\,s,\,c-s+n\\s+b-c+1,\,c-s\end{matrix}\right]$
		$[\omega,\ \operatorname{Re}(b-c-n+1),\ \operatorname{Re}s>0]$
17	$(x-\omega)_+^{b-c-n}\,{}_2F_1\left(\begin{matrix}-n,\,b\\c;\,\frac{x}{\omega}\end{matrix}\right)$	$\dfrac{\omega^{s+b-c-n}}{(c)_n}\,\Gamma\left[\begin{matrix}b-c+1,\,s-c+1,\,c-b-s\\s-c-n+1,\,1-s\end{matrix}\right]$
		$[\omega>0;\ \operatorname{Re}s<\operatorname{Re}(c-b)<1-n]$

3.31.2. ${}_2F_1\left(a,\,b;\,c;\,\dfrac{\omega}{x}\right)$ and algebraic functions

No.	$f(x)$	$F(s)$
1	$(x+\omega)^{a+b-c}\,{}_2F_1\left(\begin{matrix}a,\,b\\c;\,-\frac{\omega}{x}\end{matrix}\right)$	$\omega^{s+a+b-c}\,\Gamma\left[\begin{matrix}c\\c-a,\,c-b\end{matrix}\right]\Gamma\left[\begin{matrix}c-a-b-s,\,s+a,\,s+b\\s+a+b\end{matrix}\right]$
		$[-\operatorname{Re}a,\,-\operatorname{Re}b<\operatorname{Re}s<\operatorname{Re}(c-a-b);\ \lvert\arg\omega\rvert<\pi]$
2	$(x-\omega)^{a+b-c}\,{}_2F_1\left(\begin{matrix}a,\,b\\c;\,\frac{\omega}{x}\end{matrix}\right)$	$e^{i(-a+b+c)\pi}\omega^{s+a+b-c}\,\Gamma\left[\begin{matrix}c\\c-a,\,c-b\end{matrix}\right]$
		$\times\,\Gamma\left[\begin{matrix}c-a-b-s,\,s+a,\,s+b\\s+a+b\end{matrix}\right]$
		$[-\operatorname{Re}a,\,-\operatorname{Re}b<\operatorname{Re}s<\operatorname{Re}(c-a-b);\ 0<\arg\omega\le\pi]$
3	$(x-\omega)^{2b}\,{}_2F_1\left(\begin{matrix}a,\,b;\,\frac{\omega}{x}\\a-b+1\end{matrix}\right)$	$e^{-i(s+2b)\pi}\,(2s+a+2b)\,\omega^{s+2b}\,\Gamma\left[\begin{matrix}a-b+1\\-b,\,a-2b+1\end{matrix}\right]$
		$\times\,\Gamma\left[\begin{matrix}-s-2b,\,s+a,\,s+b\\s+a+b+1\end{matrix}\right]$
		$\left[\begin{matrix}-\operatorname{Re}a,\,-\operatorname{Re}b,\,-\operatorname{Re}(a+2b)/2-1<\operatorname{Re}s<-2\operatorname{Re}b;\\0<\arg\omega\le\pi\end{matrix}\right]$

No.	$f(x)$	$F(s)$
4	$(x-\omega)^{-b}$ $\times {}_2F_1\left(\begin{array}{c}a,\,b;\,\frac{\omega}{x}\\a+2b+1\end{array}\right)$	$\dfrac{e^{-i(s-b)\pi}\omega^{s-b}}{2}\Gamma\left[\begin{array}{c}a+2b+1\\2b,\,a+b+1\end{array}\right]$ $\times\Gamma\left[\begin{array}{c}b-s,\,s+a,\,s+b,\,s+2a+b+1\\s+a+b+1,\,s+2a+b\end{array}\right]$ $[-\operatorname{Re}a,\,-\operatorname{Re}b,\,-\operatorname{Re}(2a+b)-1<\operatorname{Re}s<\operatorname{Re}b;\,0<\arg\omega\le\pi]$
5	$(x+\omega)\,{}_2F_1\left(\begin{array}{c}a,\,b;\,-\frac{\omega}{x}\\\frac{2a+b-1}{2}\end{array}\right)$	$\dfrac{s+2a-1}{2}\,\omega^{s+1}\Gamma\left[\begin{array}{c}\frac{2a+b-1}{2}\\a,\,b-1\end{array}\right]\Gamma\left[\begin{array}{c}-s-1,\,s+a,\,s+b\\\frac{2s+2a+b+1}{2}\end{array}\right]$ $[-\operatorname{Re}a,\,-\operatorname{Re}b<\operatorname{Re}s<-1;\,|\arg\omega|<\pi]$
6	$(x+\omega)\,{}_2F_1\left(\begin{array}{c}a,\,b;\,-\frac{\omega}{x}\\a-b+1\end{array}\right)$	$2\,\omega^{s+1}\Gamma\left[\begin{array}{c}a-b+1\\a,\,b-1\end{array}\right]\Gamma\left[\begin{array}{c}-s-1,\,s+a,\,s+b,\,\frac{2s+a+3}{2}\\\frac{2s+a+1}{2},\,s+a-b+2\end{array}\right]$ $[-\operatorname{Re}a,\,-\operatorname{Re}b<\operatorname{Re}s<-1;\,|\arg\omega|<\pi]$
7	$\theta(x-\omega)\,{}_2F_1\left(\begin{array}{c}a,\,c+n\\c;\,\frac{\omega}{x}\end{array}\right)$	$\dfrac{\omega^s}{(c)_n}\Gamma\left[\begin{array}{c}1-a,\,s+c+n,\,-s\\s+c,\,1-a-s\end{array}\right]\qquad[\omega>0,\,\operatorname{Re}a<1-n;\,\operatorname{Re}s<0]$
8	$(x-\omega)_+^{b-c-n}\,{}_2F_1\left(\begin{array}{c}-n,\,b\\c;\,\frac{\omega}{x}\end{array}\right)$	$\dfrac{\omega^{s+b-c-n}}{(c)_n}\Gamma\left[\begin{array}{c}b-c+1,\,c-b-s+n,\,s+b\\n-s+1,\,s+b-n\end{array}\right]$ $[\omega>0,\,\operatorname{Re}(b-c)>n-1;\,\operatorname{Re}s<\operatorname{Re}(c-b)+n]$

3.31.3. ${}_2F_1\left(a,\,b;\,c;\,\omega x^r\right)$ **and various functions**

No.	$f(x)$	$F(s)$
1	$\theta(1-x)\,{}_2F_1\left(\begin{array}{c}a,\,b\\c;\,x\end{array}\right)$ $+\,\theta(x-1)\,x^{-a}$ $\times\Gamma\left[\begin{array}{c}1-b,\,c\\a-b+1,\,c-a\end{array}\right]$ $\times\,{}_2F_1\left(\begin{array}{c}a,\,a-c+1\\a-b+1;\,\frac{1}{x}\end{array}\right)$	$\Gamma\left[\begin{array}{c}1-b,\,c,\,s,\,a-s\\a,\,s-b+1,\,c-s\end{array}\right]$ $\left[\begin{array}{c}\operatorname{Re}(c-a-b)>-1;\,0<\operatorname{Re}s<\operatorname{Re}a;\\b\ne1,2,\ldots;\,c\ne0,-1,-2,\ldots\end{array}\right]$

3.31.4. ${}_2F_1\left(a,\,b;\,c;\,\dfrac{\omega-x}{\omega}\right)$ **and algebraic functions**

No.	$f(x)$	$F(s)$
1	${}_2F_1\left(\begin{array}{c}a,\,b\\c;\,\frac{\omega-x}{\omega}\end{array}\right)$	$\omega^s\Gamma\left[\begin{array}{c}c,\,a-s,\,b-s,\,s,\,s-a-b+c\\a,\,b,\,c-a,\,c-b\end{array}\right]$ $[0,\,\operatorname{Re}(a+b-c)<\operatorname{Re}s<\operatorname{Re}a,\,\operatorname{Re}b;\,|\arg\omega|<\pi]$

No.	$f(x)$	$F(s)$
2	$(\sigma - x)_+^{\mu-1} \, _2F_1\left(\begin{matrix} a, b \\ c; \frac{\omega-x}{\omega} \end{matrix}\right)$	$\sigma^{s+\mu-1}\Gamma\left[\begin{matrix} c, c-a-b, \mu, s \\ c-a, c-b, s+\mu \end{matrix}\right] \, _3F_2\left(\begin{matrix} a, b, s; \frac{\sigma}{\omega} \\ a+b-c+1, s+\mu \end{matrix}\right)$
		$+ \dfrac{\sigma^{s-a-b+c+\mu-1}}{\omega^{c-a-b}}\Gamma\left[\begin{matrix} c, a+b-c, \mu, s-a-b+c \\ a, b, s-a-b+c+\mu \end{matrix}\right]$
		$\times \, _3F_2\left(\begin{matrix} c-a, c-b, s-a-b+c; \frac{\sigma}{\omega} \\ c-a-b+1, s-a-b+c+\mu \end{matrix}\right)$
		$\left[\sigma, \, \operatorname{Re}\mu > 0; \, \operatorname{Re}s > 0, \, \operatorname{Re}(a+b-c); \, |\arg\omega| < \pi\right]$
3	$(x - \sigma)_+^{\mu-1} \, _2F_1\left(\begin{matrix} a, b \\ c; \frac{\omega-x}{\omega} \end{matrix}\right)$	$\sigma^{s+\mu-a-1}\omega^s\Gamma\left[\begin{matrix} c, b-a, \mu, a-\mu-s+1 \\ b, c-a, a-s+1 \end{matrix}\right]$
		$\times \, _3F_2\left(\begin{matrix} a, c-b, a-\mu-s+1 \\ a-b+1, a-s+1; \frac{\omega}{\sigma} \end{matrix}\right)$
		$+ \sigma^{s+\mu-b-1}\omega^b\Gamma\left[\begin{matrix} a-b, c, \mu, b-\mu-s+1 \\ a, c-b, b-s+1 \end{matrix}\right]$
		$\times \, _3F_2\left(\begin{matrix} b, c-a, b-\mu-s+1 \\ b-a+1, b-s+1; \frac{\omega}{\sigma} \end{matrix}\right)$
		$\left[\begin{matrix}\sigma, \, \operatorname{Re}\mu > 0; \, \operatorname{Re}s < \operatorname{Re}(a-\mu+1), \\ \operatorname{Re}(b-\mu+1); \, |\arg\omega| < \pi\end{matrix}\right]$
4	$\dfrac{1}{x-\sigma} \, _2F_1\left(\begin{matrix} a, b \\ c; \frac{\omega-x}{\omega} \end{matrix}\right)$	$\pi\sigma^{s-a-1}\omega^a\cot\left[(a-s)\pi\right]\Gamma\left[\begin{matrix} b-a, c \\ b, c-a \end{matrix}\right] \, _2F_1\left(\begin{matrix} a, c-b; \frac{\omega}{\sigma} \\ a-b+1 \end{matrix}\right)$
		$+ \pi\sigma^{s-b-1}\omega^b\cot\left[(b-s)\pi\right]\Gamma\left[\begin{matrix} a-b, c \\ a, c-b \end{matrix}\right] \, _2F_1\left(\begin{matrix} b, c-a; \frac{\omega}{\sigma} \\ b-a+1 \end{matrix}\right)$
		$- \dfrac{\omega^s}{\sigma}\Gamma\left[\begin{matrix} c, s, s-a-b+c, a-s, b-s \\ a, b, c-a, c-b \end{matrix}\right]$
		$\times \, _3F_2\left(\begin{matrix} 1, s, s-a-b+c; \frac{\omega}{\sigma} \\ s-a+1, s-b+1 \end{matrix}\right)$
		$\left[\begin{matrix}\sigma > 0; \, 0, \, \operatorname{Re}(a+b-c) < \operatorname{Re}s \\ < \operatorname{Re}a+1, \, \operatorname{Re}b+1; \, |\arg\omega| < \pi\end{matrix}\right]$
5	$\dfrac{1}{(x+\sigma)^\rho} \, _2F_1\left(\begin{matrix} a, b \\ c; \frac{\omega-x}{\omega} \end{matrix}\right)$	$\sigma^{-\rho}\omega^s\Gamma\left[\begin{matrix} c, s, a-s, b-s, s-a-b+c \\ a, b, c-a, c-b \end{matrix}\right]$
		$\times \, _3F_2\left(\begin{matrix} \rho, s, s-a-b+c; -\frac{\omega}{\sigma} \\ s-a+1, s-b+1 \end{matrix}\right) + \sigma^{s-\rho-a}\omega^a\Gamma\left[\begin{matrix} b-a, c \\ b, c-a \end{matrix}\right]$
		$\times\Gamma\left[\begin{matrix} s-a, a+\rho-s \\ \rho \end{matrix}\right] \, _3F_2\left(\begin{matrix} a, c-b, a+\rho-s; -\frac{\omega}{\sigma} \\ a-s+1, a-b+1 \end{matrix}\right) + \sigma^{s-\rho-b}\omega^b$
		$\times\Gamma\left[\begin{matrix} a-b, c, s-b, b-s+\rho \\ a, c-b, \rho \end{matrix}\right] \, _3F_2\left(\begin{matrix} b, c-a, b+\rho-s; -\frac{\omega}{\sigma} \\ b-a+1, b-s+1 \end{matrix}\right)$
		$\left[\begin{matrix}0, \, \operatorname{Re}(a+b-c) < \operatorname{Re}s < \operatorname{Re}(a+\rho), \, \operatorname{Re}(b+\rho); \\ |\arg\sigma|, \, |\arg\omega| < \pi\end{matrix}\right]$

No.	$f(x)$	$F(s)$
6	$(\omega - x)_+^{c-1} \, {}_2F_1\left(\begin{matrix} a,\, b \\ c;\; \frac{\omega-x}{\omega} \end{matrix}\right)$	$\omega^{s+c-1} \Gamma\left[\begin{matrix} c,\, s,\, s-a-b+c \\ s-a+c,\, s-b+c \end{matrix}\right]$ $[\omega,\ \mathrm{Re}\,c > 0;\ \mathrm{Re}\,s > 0,\ \mathrm{Re}\,(a+b-c)]$
7	$(\omega - x)^{c-1} \, {}_2F_1\left(\begin{matrix} a,\, b \\ c;\; \frac{\omega-x}{\omega} \end{matrix}\right)$	$\omega^{s+c-1} \Gamma\left[\begin{matrix} c,\, s,\, s-a-b+c \\ s-a+c,\, s-b+c \end{matrix}\right]$ $- e^{ic\pi}\omega^{s+c-1}\Gamma\left[\begin{matrix} c,\, a-c-s+1,\, b-c-s+1 \\ 1-s,\, a+b-c-s+1 \end{matrix}\right]$ $\left[\begin{matrix}\mathrm{Re}\,c > 0;\, 0,\ \mathrm{Re}\,(a+b-c) < \mathrm{Re}\,s \\ < \mathrm{Re}\,(a-c)+1,\ \mathrm{Re}\,(b-c)+1;\ \mathrm{Im}\,\omega > 0\end{matrix}\right]$
8	$(x - \omega)_+^{c-1} \, {}_2F_1\left(\begin{matrix} a,\, b \\ c;\; \frac{\omega-x}{\omega} \end{matrix}\right)$	$\omega^{s+c-1} \Gamma\left[\begin{matrix} c,\, a-c-s+1,\, b-c-s+1 \\ 1-s,\, a+b-c-s+1 \end{matrix}\right]$ $[\omega,\ \mathrm{Re}\,c > 0;\ \mathrm{Re}\,s < \mathrm{Re}\,(a-c)+1,\ \mathrm{Re}\,(b-c)+1]$
9	$(x - \omega)^{c-1} \, {}_2F_1\left(\begin{matrix} a,\, b \\ c;\; \frac{\omega-x}{\omega} \end{matrix}\right)$	$\omega^{s+c-1} \Gamma\left[\begin{matrix} c,\, a-c-s+1,\, b-c-s+1 \\ 1-s,\, a+b-c-s+1 \end{matrix}\right]$ $- e^{ic\pi}\omega^{s+c-1}\Gamma\left[\begin{matrix} c,\, s-a-b+c,\, s \\ s-a+c,\, s-b+c \end{matrix}\right]$ $\left[\begin{matrix}\omega,\ \mathrm{Re}\,c > 0;\, 0,\ \mathrm{Re}\,(a+b-c) < \mathrm{Re}\,s \\ < \mathrm{Re}\,(a-c)+1,\ \mathrm{Re}\,(b-c)+1\end{matrix}\right]$
10	$(\sigma - x)_+^{\mu-1} (\omega - x)^{c-1}$ $\times\, {}_2F_1\left(\begin{matrix} a,\, b \\ c;\; \frac{\omega-x}{\omega} \end{matrix}\right)$	$\sigma^{s+\mu-1}\omega^{c-1} \Gamma\left[\begin{matrix} c,\, c-a-b,\, \mu,\, s \\ c-a,\, c-b,\, s+\mu \end{matrix}\right]$ $\times\, {}_3F_2\left(\begin{matrix} a-c+1,\, b-c+1,\, s \\ a+b-c+1,\, s+\mu;\; \frac{\sigma}{\omega} \end{matrix}\right)$ $+ \dfrac{\sigma^{s-a-b+c+\mu-1}}{\omega^{1-a-b}} \Gamma\left[\begin{matrix} c,\, a+b-c,\, \mu,\, s-a-b+c \\ a,\, b,\, s+\mu-a-b+c \end{matrix}\right]$ $\times\, {}_3F_2\left(\begin{matrix} 1-a,\, 1-b,\, s-a-b+c;\; \frac{\sigma}{\omega} \\ c-a-b+1,\, s+\mu-a-b+c \end{matrix}\right)$ $[0 < \sigma < \omega;\ \mathrm{Re}\,\mu,\ \mathrm{Re}\,s,\ \mathrm{Re}\,(s-a-b+c) > 0]$
11	$(\sigma - x)^{\mu-1} (\omega - x)_+^{c-1}$ $\times\, {}_2F_1\left(\begin{matrix} a,\, b \\ c;\; \frac{\omega-x}{\omega} \end{matrix}\right)$	$\sigma^{\mu-1}\omega^{c+s-1} \Gamma\left[\begin{matrix} c,\, s,\, s-a-b+c \\ s-a+c,\, s-b+c \end{matrix}\right]$ $\times\, {}_3F_2\left(\begin{matrix} 1-\mu,\, s,\, s-a-b+c \\ s-a+c,\, s-b+c;\; \frac{\omega}{\sigma} \end{matrix}\right)$ $[0 < \omega < \sigma;\ \mathrm{Re}\,c,\ \mathrm{Re}\,s,\ \mathrm{Re}\,(s-a-b+c) > 0]$

No.	$f(x)$	$F(s)$
12	$(x - \sigma)_+^{\mu-1} (\omega - x)_+^{c-1}$	$\sigma^{s+\mu-1}\omega^{c-1} \Gamma \begin{bmatrix} c, c-a-b, \mu, 1-s-\mu \\ c-a, c-b, 1-s \end{bmatrix}$

$$\times {}_2F_1 \begin{pmatrix} a, b \\ c; \frac{\omega-x}{\omega} \end{pmatrix}$$

$$\times {}_3F_2 \begin{pmatrix} a-c+1, b-c+1, s \\ a+b-c+1, s+\mu; \frac{\sigma}{\omega} \end{pmatrix} + \sigma^{s+\mu-a-b+c-1}\omega^{a+b-1}$$

$$\times \Gamma \begin{bmatrix} c, a+b-c, \mu, a+b-c-\mu-s+1 \\ a, b, a+b-c-s+1 \end{bmatrix}$$

$$\times {}_3F_2 \begin{pmatrix} 1-a, 1-b, s-a-b+c; \frac{\sigma}{\omega} \\ c-a-b+1, s+\mu-a-b+c \end{pmatrix}$$

$$+ \omega^{s+\mu+c-2} \Gamma \begin{bmatrix} c, s+\mu-1, s-a-b+c+\mu-1 \\ s+\mu-a+c-1, s+\mu-b+c-1 \end{bmatrix}$$

$$\times {}_3F_2 \begin{pmatrix} 1-\mu, a-c-\mu-s+2, b-c-\mu-s+2 \\ 2-\mu-s, a+b-c-\mu-s+2; \frac{\sigma}{\omega} \end{pmatrix}$$

$$[0 < \sigma < \omega;\ \mathrm{Re}\, c,\ \mathrm{Re}\, \mu > 0]$$

| **13** | $\dfrac{(\omega - x)_+^{c-1}}{(x + \sigma)^\rho} {}_2F_1 \begin{pmatrix} a, b \\ c; \frac{\omega-x}{\omega} \end{pmatrix}$ | $\sigma^{-\rho}\omega^{s+c-1} \Gamma \begin{bmatrix} c, s, s-a-b+c \\ s-a+c, s-b+c \end{bmatrix}$ |

$$\times {}_3F_2 \begin{pmatrix} \rho, s, s-a-b+c \\ s-a+c, s-b+c; -\frac{\omega}{\sigma} \end{pmatrix}$$

$$[\omega,\ \mathrm{Re}\, c,\ \mathrm{Re}\, s,\ \mathrm{Re}\,(s-a-b+c) > 0;\ |\arg \sigma| < \pi]$$

| **14** | $\dfrac{(\omega - x)_+^{c-1}}{x - \sigma} {}_2F_1 \begin{pmatrix} a, b \\ c; \frac{\omega-x}{\omega} \end{pmatrix}$ | $-\pi\sigma^{s-1}\omega^{c-1} \cot(s\pi) \Gamma \begin{bmatrix} c, c-a-b \\ c-a, c-b \end{bmatrix} {}_2F_1 \begin{pmatrix} a-c+1, b-c+1 \\ a+b-c+1; \frac{\sigma}{\omega} \end{pmatrix}$ |

$$+ \pi\sigma^{s-a-b+c-1}\omega^{a+b-1} \cot[(a+b-c-s)\pi]$$

$$\times \Gamma \begin{bmatrix} c, a+b-c \\ a, b \end{bmatrix} {}_2F_1 \begin{pmatrix} 1-a, 1-b \\ c-a-b+1; \frac{\sigma}{\omega} \end{pmatrix}$$

$$+ \omega^{s+c-2} \Gamma \begin{bmatrix} c, s-1, c-a-b+s-1 \\ s-a+c-1, s-b+c-1 \end{bmatrix}$$

$$\times {}_3F_2 \begin{pmatrix} 1, a-c-s+2, b-c-s+2 \\ 2-s, a+b-c-s+2; \frac{\sigma}{\omega} \end{pmatrix}$$

$$[0 < \sigma < \omega;\ \mathrm{Re}\, c,\ \mathrm{Re}\, s,\ \mathrm{Re}\,(s-a-b+c) > 0]$$

| **15** | $\dfrac{(\omega - x)_+^{c-1}}{x - \sigma} {}_2F_1 \begin{pmatrix} a, b \\ c; \frac{\omega-x}{\omega} \end{pmatrix}$ | $-\dfrac{\omega^{s+c-1}}{\sigma} \Gamma \begin{bmatrix} c, s, s-a-b+c \\ s-a+c, s-b+c \end{bmatrix} {}_3F_2 \begin{pmatrix} 1, s, s-a-b+c \\ s-a+c, s-b+c; \frac{\omega}{\sigma} \end{pmatrix}$ |

$$[0 < \omega < \sigma;\ \mathrm{Re}\, c,\ \mathrm{Re}\, s,\ \mathrm{Re}\,(s-a-b+c) > 0]$$

3.31.5. $\quad {}_2F_1\left(a,\,b;\,c;\,\dfrac{\omega}{x+\omega}\right)$ **and algebraic functions**

1	$(x+\omega)^{-a}\,{}_2F_1\!\left(\begin{array}{c}a,\,b\\c;\,\frac{\omega}{x+\omega}\end{array}\right)$	$\omega^{s-a}\,\Gamma\!\left[\begin{array}{c}c,\,s,\,s-a-b+c,\,a-s\\a,\,c-b,\,s-a+c\end{array}\right]$
		$[0,\ \operatorname{Re}(a+b-c)<\operatorname{Re}s<\operatorname{Re}a;\ \lvert\arg\omega\rvert<\pi]$
2	$(x+\omega)^{a}\,{}_2F_1\!\left(\begin{array}{c}a,\,1-a\\c;\,\frac{\omega}{x+\omega}\end{array}\right)$	$2\omega^{s+a}\,\Gamma\!\left[\begin{array}{c}c,\,-s-a,\,s,\,s+c-1,\,\frac{2s+a+c+1}{2}\\-a,\,c-a,\,s+a+c,\,\frac{2s+a+c-1}{2}\end{array}\right]$
		$\left[\begin{array}{c}0,\,1-\operatorname{Re}c,\,-\operatorname{Re}(a+c+1)/2<\operatorname{Re}s<-\operatorname{Re}a;\\ \lvert\arg\omega\rvert<\pi\end{array}\right]$
3	$(x+\omega)^{-2a}$	$\dfrac{\omega^{s-2a}}{2}\,\Gamma\!\left[\begin{array}{c}c,\,2a-s,\,s,\,s-3a+c-1,\,s-4a+2c-1\\2a,\,c-a,\,s-2a+c,\,s-4a+2c-2\end{array}\right]$
	$\times\,{}_2F_1\!\left(\begin{array}{c}a,\,2a+1\\c;\,\frac{\omega}{x+\omega}\end{array}\right)$	$\left[\begin{array}{c}0,\,\operatorname{Re}(4a-2c)+1,\,\operatorname{Re}(3a-c)+1<\operatorname{Re}s<2\operatorname{Re}a;\\ \lvert\arg\omega\rvert<\pi\end{array}\right]$
4	$(x+\omega)^{1-a}$	$2\omega^{s-a+1}\,\Gamma\!\left[\begin{array}{c}\frac{a+b+1}{2},\,a-s-1,\,s,\,\frac{2s-a+3}{2},\,\frac{2s-a-b+1}{2}\\a,\,\frac{a-b-1}{2},\,\frac{2s-a+1}{2},\,\frac{2s-a+b+3}{2}\end{array}\right]$
	$\times\,{}_2F_1\!\left(\begin{array}{c}a,\,b;\,\frac{\omega}{x+\omega}\\\frac{a+b+1}{2}\end{array}\right)$	$\left[\begin{array}{c}0,\,\operatorname{Re}(a-3)/2,\,\operatorname{Re}(a+b-1)/2<\operatorname{Re}s\\ <\operatorname{Re}a-1;\ \lvert\arg\omega\rvert<\pi\end{array}\right]$
5	$(x+\omega)^{1-b}$	$\dfrac{(s+b-1)\,\omega^{s-b+1}}{2}\,\Gamma\!\left[\begin{array}{c}2b-a-1\\b,\,2b-2a-2\end{array}\right]$
	$\times\,{}_2F_1\!\left(\begin{array}{c}a,\,b;\,\frac{\omega}{x+\omega}\\2b-a-1\end{array}\right)$	$\times\,\Gamma\!\left[\begin{array}{c}b-s-1,\,s,\,s-2a+b-1\\s-a+b\end{array}\right]$
		$\left[\begin{array}{c}0,\,-\operatorname{Re}b,\,\operatorname{Re}(2a-b)+1<\operatorname{Re}s<\operatorname{Re}b-1;\\ \lvert\arg\omega\rvert<\pi\end{array}\right]$

3.31.6. $\quad {}_2F_1\left(a,\,b;\,c;\,\dfrac{x-\omega}{x}\right)$ **and algebraic functions**

1	$(\omega-x)_{+}^{c-1}\,{}_2F_1\!\left(\begin{array}{c}a,\,b\\c;\,\frac{x-\omega}{x}\end{array}\right)$	$\omega^{s+c-1}\,\Gamma\!\left[\begin{array}{c}c,\,s+a,\,s+b\\s+c,\,s+a+b\end{array}\right]$
		$[\omega,\ \operatorname{Re}c>0;\ \operatorname{Re}s>-\operatorname{Re}a,\,-\operatorname{Re}b]$
2	$(\omega-x)^{c-1}\,{}_2F_1\!\left(\begin{array}{c}a,\,b\\c;\,\frac{x-\omega}{x}\end{array}\right)$	$\omega^{s+c-1}\,\Gamma\!\left[\begin{array}{c}c,\,s+a,\,s+b\\s+a+b,\,s+c\end{array}\right]$
		$-\,e^{ic\pi}\omega^{s+c-1}\,\Gamma\!\left[\begin{array}{c}c,\,1-a-b-s,\,1-c-s\\1-a-s,\,1-b-s\end{array}\right]$
		$\left[\begin{array}{c}\operatorname{Re}c>0;\,-\operatorname{Re}a,\,-\operatorname{Re}b<\operatorname{Re}s\\ <\operatorname{Re}(1-a-b),\,\operatorname{Re}(1-c);\,0<\arg\omega\le\pi\end{array}\right]$

No.	$f(x)$	$F(s)$
3	$(x-\omega)^{c-1}_+ \; _2F_1\left(\begin{matrix} a,\ b \\ c;\ \frac{x-\omega}{x} \end{matrix}\right)$	$\omega^{s+c-1}\Gamma\left[\begin{matrix} c,\ 1-a-b-s,\ 1-c-s \\ 1-a-s,\ 1-b-s \end{matrix}\right]$ $[\omega,\ \mathrm{Re}\,c>0;\ \mathrm{Re}\,s<1-\mathrm{Re}\,c,\ 1-\mathrm{Re}\,(a+b)]$
4	$(x-\omega)^{c-1} \; _2F_1\left(\begin{matrix} a,\ b \\ c;\ \frac{x-\omega}{x} \end{matrix}\right)$	$\omega^{s+c-1}\Gamma\left[\begin{matrix} c,\ 1-a-b-s,\ 1-c-s \\ 1-a-s,\ 1-b-s \end{matrix}\right]$ $-e^{ic\pi}\omega^{s+c-1}\Gamma\left[\begin{matrix} c,\ s+a,\ s+b \\ s+a+b,\ s+c \end{matrix}\right]$ $\left[\begin{matrix} \mathrm{Re}\,c>0;\ -\mathrm{Re}\,a,\ -\mathrm{Re}\,b<\mathrm{Re}\,s \\ <1-\mathrm{Re}\,c,\ 1-\mathrm{Re}\,(a+b);\ \mathrm{Im}\,\omega<0 \end{matrix}\right]$

3.31.7. $_2F_1\left(a,\ b;\ c;\ \dfrac{x}{x+\omega}\right)$ and algebraic functions

No.	$f(x)$	$F(s)$
1	$(x+\omega)^{-a} \; _2F_1\left(\begin{matrix} a,\ b \\ c;\ \frac{x}{x+\omega} \end{matrix}\right)$	$\omega^{s-a}\Gamma\left[\begin{matrix} c,\ a-s,\ c-b-s,\ s \\ a,\ c-b,\ c-s \end{matrix}\right]$ $[0<\mathrm{Re}\,s<\mathrm{Re}\,a,\ \mathrm{Re}\,(c-b);\ |\arg\omega|<\pi]$
2	$(x+\omega)^{a} \; _2F_1\left(\begin{matrix} a,\ 1-a \\ c;\ \frac{x}{x+\omega} \end{matrix}\right)$	$2\omega^{s+a}\Gamma\left[\begin{matrix} c \\ -a,\ c-a \end{matrix}\right]\Gamma\left[\begin{matrix} \frac{-2s-a+c+1}{2},\ -s-a,\ -s-a+c-1,\ s \\ \frac{-2s-a+c-1}{2},\ c-s \end{matrix}\right]$ $\left[\begin{matrix} 0<\mathrm{Re}\,s<-\mathrm{Re}\,a,\ \mathrm{Re}\,(c-a)-1, \\ \mathrm{Re}\,(c-a+1)/2;\ |\arg\omega|<\pi \end{matrix}\right]$
3	$(x+\omega)^{1-a}$ $\times\; _2F_1\left(\begin{matrix} a,\ b;\ \frac{x}{x+\omega} \\ \frac{a+b+1}{2} \end{matrix}\right)$	$(a-2s-1)\,\omega^{s-a+1}\Gamma\left[\begin{matrix} \frac{a+b+1}{2} \\ a,\ \frac{a-b-1}{2} \end{matrix}\right]\Gamma\left[\begin{matrix} s,\ a-s-1,\ \frac{a-b-2s-1}{2} \\ \frac{a+b-2s+1}{2} \end{matrix}\right]$ $\left[\begin{matrix} 0<\mathrm{Re}\,s<\mathrm{Re}\,a-1,\ \mathrm{Re}\,(a+1)/2, \\ \mathrm{Re}\,(a-b-1)/2;\ |\arg\omega|<\pi \end{matrix}\right]$
4	$(x+\omega)^{1-b}$ $\times\; _2F_1\left(\begin{matrix} a,\ b;\ \frac{x}{x+\omega} \\ 2b-a-1 \end{matrix}\right)$	$\dfrac{(2b-s-2)}{2}\,\omega^{s-b+1}\Gamma\left[\begin{matrix} 2b-a-1 \\ b,\ 2b-2a-2 \end{matrix}\right]$ $\times\Gamma\left[\begin{matrix} s,\ b-s-1,\ 2b-a-s-2 \\ 2b-a-s-1 \end{matrix}\right]$ $[0<\mathrm{Re}\,s<\mathrm{Re}\,b-1,\ 2\,\mathrm{Re}\,(b-a)-2;\ |\arg\omega|<\pi]$
5	$(x+\omega)^{-2a}$ $\times\; _2F_1\left(\begin{matrix} a,\ 2a+1 \\ c;\ \frac{x}{x+\omega} \end{matrix}\right)$	$\dfrac{\omega^{s-2a}}{2}\Gamma\left[\begin{matrix} c \\ 2a,\ c-a \end{matrix}\right]\Gamma\left[\begin{matrix} s,\ 2a-s,\ 2c-2a-s-1,\ c-a-s-1 \\ 2c-2a-s-2,\ c-s \end{matrix}\right]$ $\left[\begin{matrix} 0<\mathrm{Re}\,s<2\,\mathrm{Re}\,a,\ \mathrm{Re}\,(c-a)-1, \\ 2\,\mathrm{Re}\,(c-a)-1;\ |\arg\omega|<\pi \end{matrix}\right]$

3.31.8. $_2F_1\left(a,\,b;\,c;\,\dfrac{4\omega x}{(x+\omega)^2}\right)$ **and algebraic functions**

1	$(x+\omega)^{-2a}$ $\times\,_2F_1\left(\begin{matrix}a,\,b\\2b;\,\frac{4\omega x}{(x+\omega)^2}\end{matrix}\right)$	$\dfrac{\omega^{s-2a}}{2}\,\Gamma\left[\begin{matrix}\frac{2b+1}{2},\,\frac{2b-2a+1}{2}\\a\end{matrix}\right]\Gamma\left[\begin{matrix}\frac{s}{2},\,\frac{2a-s}{2}\\\frac{s-2a+2b+1}{2},\,\frac{2b-s+1}{2}\end{matrix}\right]$ $[\operatorname{Re}\omega>0;\;0<\operatorname{Re}s<2\operatorname{Re}a<2\operatorname{Re}b+1]$
2	$(x+\omega)^{-2a}$ $\times\,_2F_1\left(\begin{matrix}a,\,\frac{2a+1}{2}\\c;\,\frac{4\omega x}{(x+\omega)^2}\end{matrix}\right)$	$\omega^{s-2a}\,\Gamma\left[\begin{matrix}c,\,c-2a\\2a\end{matrix}\right]\Gamma\left[\begin{matrix}s,\,2a-s\\s-2a+c,\,c-s\end{matrix}\right]$ $[\operatorname{Re}\omega>0;\;0<\operatorname{Re}s<2\operatorname{Re}a<\operatorname{Re}c]$
3	$(x+\omega)^{-2a}$ $\times\,_2F_1\left(\begin{matrix}a,\,b\\2b;\,\frac{4\omega x}{(x+\omega)^2}\end{matrix}\right)$	$\dfrac{\omega^{s-2a}}{2}\,\Gamma\left[\begin{matrix}\frac{2b+1}{2},\,\frac{2b-2a+1}{2}\\a\end{matrix}\right]\Gamma\left[\begin{matrix}\frac{s}{2},\,\frac{2a-s}{2}\\\frac{2b-s+1}{2},\,\frac{s-2a+2b+1}{2}\end{matrix}\right]$ $[\omega>0;\;\operatorname{Re}(a-b)<1/2;\;0<\operatorname{Re}s<2\operatorname{Re}a]$
4	$\dfrac{(x+\omega)^{-2b}}{|x-\omega|^{2b-2a}}$ $\times\,_2F_1\left(\begin{matrix}a,\,b\\2b;\,\frac{4\omega x}{(x+\omega)^2}\end{matrix}\right)$	$\dfrac{\omega^{s+2a-4b}}{2}\,\Gamma\left[\begin{matrix}\frac{2b+1}{2},\,\frac{2a-2b+1}{2}\\2b-a\end{matrix}\right]\Gamma\left[\begin{matrix}\frac{s}{2},\,\frac{4b-2a-s}{2}\\\frac{s+2a-2b+1}{2},\,\frac{2b-s+1}{2}\end{matrix}\right]$ $[\omega>0;\;\operatorname{Re}(b-a)<1/2;\;0<\operatorname{Re}s<2\operatorname{Re}(2b-a)]$
5	$\dfrac{(x+\omega)^{-2a}}{|x-\omega|^{2c-4a-1}}$ $\times\,_2F_1\left(\begin{matrix}a,\,\frac{2a+1}{2}\\c;\,\frac{4\omega x}{(x+\omega)^2}\end{matrix}\right)$	$\omega^{s+2a-2c+1}\,\Gamma\left[\begin{matrix}c,\,2a-c+1\\2c-2a-1\end{matrix}\right]\Gamma\left[\begin{matrix}s,\,2c-2a-s-1\\c-s,\,s+2a-c+1\end{matrix}\right]$ $[\omega>0;\;\operatorname{Re}(c-2a)<1;\;0<\operatorname{Re}s<2\operatorname{Re}(c-a)-1]$

3.31.9. $_2F_1\left(a,\,b;\,c;\,-\dfrac{4\omega x}{(x-\omega)^2}\right)$ **and algebraic functions**

1	$|x-\omega|^{-2a}$ $\times\,_2F_1\left(\begin{matrix}a,\,b\\2b;\,-\frac{4\omega x}{(x-\omega)^2}\end{matrix}\right)$	$\dfrac{\omega^{s-2a}}{2}\,\Gamma\left[\begin{matrix}\frac{2b+1}{2},\,\frac{2b-2a+1}{2}\\a\end{matrix}\right]\Gamma\left[\begin{matrix}\frac{s}{2},\,\frac{2a-s}{2}\\\frac{2b-s+1}{2},\,\frac{s-2a+2b+1}{2}\end{matrix}\right]$ $[\omega>0;\;\operatorname{Re}(a-b)<1/2;\;0<\operatorname{Re}s<2\operatorname{Re}a]$
2	$|x-\omega|^{-2a}$ $\times\,_2F_1\left(\begin{matrix}a,\,b;\,-\frac{4\omega x}{(x-\omega)^2}\\a+b+\frac{1}{2}\end{matrix}\right)$	$\omega^{s-2a}\,\Gamma\left[\begin{matrix}\frac{2a+2b+1}{2},\,\frac{2b-2a+1}{2}\\2a\end{matrix}\right]\Gamma\left[\begin{matrix}s,\,2a-s\\\frac{2s-2a+2b+1}{2},\,\frac{2a+2b-2s+1}{2}\end{matrix}\right]$ $[\omega>0;\;0<\operatorname{Re}s<2\operatorname{Re}a<2\operatorname{Re}b+1]$
3	$\dfrac{(x+\omega)^{2a-2b}}{|x-\omega|^{2b}}$ $\times\,_2F_1\left(\begin{matrix}a,\,b\\2b;\,-\frac{4\omega x}{(x-\omega)^2}\end{matrix}\right)$	$\dfrac{\omega^{s+2a-4b}}{2}\,\Gamma\left[\begin{matrix}\frac{2b+1}{2},\,\frac{2a-2b+1}{2}\\2b-a\end{matrix}\right]\Gamma\left[\begin{matrix}\frac{s}{2},\,\frac{4b-2a-s}{2}\\\frac{2b-s+1}{2},\,\frac{s+2a-2b+1}{2}\end{matrix}\right]$ $[\omega>0;\;\operatorname{Re}(b-a)<1/2;\;0<\operatorname{Re}s<2\operatorname{Re}(2b-a)]$

No.	$f(x)$	$F(s)$
4	$\dfrac{x+1}{\|x-1\|^{2a}}$ $\times\, _2F_1\left(\begin{matrix} a,\ b;\ -\frac{4x}{(x-1)^2} \\ \frac{2a+2b-1}{2} \end{matrix}\right)$	$\Gamma\left[\begin{matrix} \frac{2a+2b-1}{2},\ \frac{2b-2a+1}{2},\ s,\ 2a-s-1 \\ 2a-1,\ \frac{2s-2a+2b+1}{2},\ \frac{2a+2b-2s-1}{2} \end{matrix}\right]$ $[\operatorname{Re}(b-a) > -1/2;\ 0 < \operatorname{Re} s < 2\operatorname{Re} a - 1]$

3.31.10. $\quad _2F_1\left(a, b;\ c;\ \dfrac{\alpha_1 x^3 + \beta_1 x^2 + \gamma_1 x + \delta_1}{\alpha_2 x^3 + \beta_2 x^2 + \gamma_2 x + \delta_2}\right)$ **and algebraic functions**

No.	$f(x)$	$F(s)$
1	$(x+\omega)^{-a}$ $\times\, _2F_1\left(\begin{matrix} a,\ \frac{1-6a}{6} \\ \frac{1}{2};\ -\frac{x(8x+9\omega)^2}{27\omega^2(x+\omega)} \end{matrix}\right)$	$\sqrt{\pi}\,\omega^{s-a}\,\Gamma\left[\begin{matrix} s,\ 3a-s,\ \frac{1-3a-3s}{3} \\ 3a,\ \frac{1-3a}{3},\ \frac{1-2s}{2} \end{matrix}\right]$ $[\operatorname{Re}\omega \geq 0;\ 0 < \operatorname{Re} s < 1/3 - \operatorname{Re} a,\ 3\operatorname{Re} a]$
2	$(x+\omega)^{-a}$ $\times\, _2F_1\left(\begin{matrix} a,\ \frac{1-6a}{6} \\ \frac{1}{2};\ -\frac{\omega(9x+8\omega)^2}{27x^2(x+\omega)} \end{matrix}\right)$	$\sqrt{\pi}\,\omega^{s-a}\,\Gamma\left[\begin{matrix} a-s,\ s+2a,\ \frac{3s-6a+1}{3} \\ 3a,\ \frac{1-3a}{3},\ \frac{2s-2a+1}{2} \end{matrix}\right]$ $[\operatorname{Re}\omega \geq 0;\ -2\operatorname{Re} a,\ 2\operatorname{Re} a - 1/3 < \operatorname{Re} s < \operatorname{Re} a]$
3	$(4x+\omega)^{-3a}$ $\times\, _2F_1\left(\begin{matrix} a,\ \frac{3a+1}{3} \\ \frac{12a+5}{6};\ \frac{27\omega^2 x}{(4x+\omega)^3} \end{matrix}\right)$	$\dfrac{\omega^{s-3a}}{2^{6a}}\,\Gamma\left[\begin{matrix} \frac{12a+2}{3} \\ \frac{6a+1}{6},\ 3a \end{matrix}\right]\Gamma\left[\begin{matrix} s,\ 3a-s,\ \frac{6s-12a+1}{6} \\ \frac{3s+3a+2}{3} \end{matrix}\right]$ $[0,\ 2\operatorname{Re} a - 1/6 < \operatorname{Re} s < 3\operatorname{Re} a;\ |\arg\omega| < \pi]$
4	$(x+4\omega)^{-3a}$ $\times\, _2F_1\left(\begin{matrix} a,\ \frac{3a+1}{3} \\ \frac{12a+5}{6};\ \frac{27\omega x^2}{(x+4\omega)^3} \end{matrix}\right)$	$\dfrac{\omega^{s-3a}}{2^{6a}}\,\Gamma\left[\begin{matrix} \frac{12a+2}{3} \\ \frac{6a+1}{6},\ 3a \end{matrix}\right]\Gamma\left[\begin{matrix} s,\ 3a-s,\ \frac{6a-6s+1}{6} \\ \frac{12a-3s+2}{3} \end{matrix}\right]$ $[0 < \operatorname{Re} s < 3\operatorname{Re} a,\ \operatorname{Re} a + 1/6;\ |\arg\omega| < \pi]$
5	$(3x+4\omega)^{-3a}(9x+8\omega)$ $\times\, _2F_1\left(\begin{matrix} a,\ \frac{3a+1}{3} \\ \frac{3}{2};\ \frac{\omega(9x+8\omega)^2}{(3x+4\omega)^3} \end{matrix}\right)$	$\dfrac{3^{2-3a}\sqrt{\pi}\,\omega^{s-3a+1}}{2}\,\Gamma\left[\begin{matrix} 3a-s-1,\ \frac{3s-12a+7}{3},\ s \\ \frac{4-3a}{3},\ 3a-1,\ \frac{2s-6a+5}{2} \end{matrix}\right]$ $[\operatorname{Re} > 0;\ 4\operatorname{Re} a - 7/3 < \operatorname{Re} s < 3\operatorname{Re} a - 1]$
6	$(4x+3\omega)^{-3a}(8x+9\omega)$ $\times\, _2F_1\left(\begin{matrix} a,\ \frac{3a+1}{3} \\ \frac{3}{2};\ \frac{x(8x+9\omega)^2}{(4x+3\omega)^3} \end{matrix}\right)$	$\dfrac{3^{2-3a}\sqrt{\pi}\,\omega^{s-3a+1}}{2}\,\Gamma\left[\begin{matrix} 3a-s-1,\ \frac{4-3a-3s}{3},\ s \\ \frac{4-3a}{3},\ 3a-1,\ \frac{3-2s}{2} \end{matrix}\right]$ $[0 < \operatorname{Re} s < 3\operatorname{Re} a - 1,\ 4/3 - \operatorname{Re} a;\ |\arg\omega| < \pi]$
7	$(3x-\omega)^{-3a}(9x+\omega)$ $\times\, _2F_1\left(\begin{matrix} a,\ \frac{3a+1}{3} \\ \frac{3}{2};\ -\frac{\omega(9x+\omega)^2}{(3x-\omega)^3} \end{matrix}\right)$	$\dfrac{3^{2-3a}\sqrt{\pi}\,\omega^{s-3a+1}}{2}\,\Gamma\left[\begin{matrix} 3a-s-1,\ \frac{6s-12a+7}{6},\ s \\ \frac{6a+1}{6},\ 3a-1,\ \frac{2s-6a+5}{2} \end{matrix}\right]$ $[\operatorname{Re} \geq 0;\ 0,\ 2\operatorname{Re} a - 7/6 < \operatorname{Re} s < 3\operatorname{Re} a - 1]$

No.	$f(x)$	$F(s)$
8	$(3\omega - x)^{-3a}(x + 9\omega)$ $\times\, {}_2F_1\left(\begin{matrix} a,\ \frac{3a+1}{3} \\ \frac{3}{2};\ \frac{x(x+9\omega)^2}{(x-3\omega)^3} \end{matrix}\right)$	$\dfrac{3^{2-3a}\sqrt{\pi}\,\omega^{s-3a+1}}{2}\,\Gamma\left[\begin{matrix} 3a-s-1,\ \frac{6a-6s+1}{6},\ s \\ \frac{6a+1}{6},\ 3a-1,\ \frac{3-2s}{2} \end{matrix}\right]$ $[\operatorname{Re} \geq 0;\ 0,\ \operatorname{Re} a - 1/6 < \operatorname{Re} s < 3\operatorname{Re} a - 1]$

3.31.11. $\ {}_2F_1\left(a,\, b;\, c;\, \dfrac{\omega_1 x + \sigma_1}{\omega_2 x + \sigma_2}\right)$ **and algebraic functions**

No.	$f(x)$	$F(s)$
1	$(\omega - x)_+^{-b}\,{}_2F_1\left(\begin{matrix} -n,\ b \\ c;\ \frac{\omega}{\omega-x} \end{matrix}\right)$	$(-1)^n\dfrac{\omega^{s-b}}{(c)_n}\,\Gamma\left[\begin{matrix} 1-b,\ s,\ b-c-s+1 \\ s-b+1,\ b-c-n-s+1 \end{matrix}\right]$ $[\operatorname{Re} b < 1 - n;\ \omega,\ \operatorname{Re} s > 0]$
2	$(x - \omega)_+^{-b}\,{}_2F_1\left(\begin{matrix} -n,\ b \\ c;\ \frac{\omega}{\omega-x} \end{matrix}\right)$	$\dfrac{\omega^{s-b}}{(c)_n}\,\Gamma\left[\begin{matrix} 1-b,\ b-s,\ s-b+c+n \\ 1-s,\ s-b+c \end{matrix}\right]$ $[\omega > 0;\ \operatorname{Re} s < \operatorname{Re} b < 1 - n]$
3	$(\omega - x)_+^{-b}\,{}_2F_1\left(\begin{matrix} -n,\ b \\ c;\ \frac{x}{x-\omega} \end{matrix}\right)$	$\dfrac{\omega^{s-b}}{(c)_n}\,\Gamma\left[\begin{matrix} 1-b,\ s,\ c-s+n \\ s-b+1,\ c-s \end{matrix}\right]\quad[\operatorname{Re} b < 1 - n;\ \omega,\ \operatorname{Re} s > 0]$
4	$(x - \omega)_+^{-b}\,{}_2F_1\left(\begin{matrix} -n,\ b \\ c;\ \frac{x}{x-\omega} \end{matrix}\right)$	$(-1)^n\dfrac{\omega^{s-b}}{(c)_n}\,\Gamma\left[\begin{matrix} 1-b,\ s-c+1,\ b-s \\ s-c-n+1,\ 1-s \end{matrix}\right]$ $[\omega > 0;\ \operatorname{Re} s < \operatorname{Re} b < 1 - n]$
5	$(\sigma - x)_+^{c-1}(\tau + x)^{\mu}$ $\times\, {}_2F_1\left(\begin{matrix} a,\ b \\ c;\ \omega(\sigma - x) \end{matrix}\right)$	$\sigma^{s+c-1}\tau^{\mu}\,\Gamma\left[\begin{matrix} c,\ s \\ s+c \end{matrix}\right]F_3\left(a,\ -\mu,\ b,\ s;\ s+c;\ \sigma\omega,\ -\dfrac{\sigma}{\tau}\right)$ $[\sigma,\ \operatorname{Re} c,\ \operatorname{Re} s > 0]$
6	$\theta(x - \sigma)(x - \tau)^{-a}$ $\times\, {}_2F_1\left(\begin{matrix} a,\ b \\ c;\ \frac{\omega x}{x-\tau} \end{matrix}\right)$	$\dfrac{\sigma^{s-a}}{a-s}\,F_2\left(a,\ b,\ a-s;\ c,\ a-s+1;\ \omega,\ \dfrac{\tau}{\sigma}\right)$ $[\sigma > 0;\ |\omega| + |\tau/\sigma| < 1;\ \operatorname{Re} s < \operatorname{Re} a]$
7	$(\sigma - x)_+^{c-1}(\tau - x)^{-a}$ $\times\, {}_2F_1\left(\begin{matrix} a,\ b \\ c;\ \frac{\omega(\sigma-x)}{\tau-x} \end{matrix}\right)$	$\sigma^{s+c-1}\tau^{-a}\,\mathrm{B}(s,\ c)\,F_1\left(a,\ b,\ s;\ s+c;\ \dfrac{\sigma}{\tau},\ \dfrac{\sigma\omega}{\tau}\right)$ $[\sigma,\ \tau,\ \operatorname{Re} c,\ \operatorname{Re} s > 0;\ \sigma < \tau;\ |\omega| < \tau]$
8	$(\sigma - x)_+^{c-1}\left(\dfrac{\sigma}{1-\sigma} - x\right)^{-a}$ $\times\, {}_2F_1\left(\begin{matrix} a,\ b \\ c;\ \frac{\omega(\sigma-x)}{(\sigma-1)x+\sigma} \end{matrix}\right)$	$(1-\sigma)^a\,\sigma^{s-a+c-1}\,\mathrm{B}(s,\ c)\,F_1(a;\ s,\ b;\ c+s;\ 1-\sigma,\ \omega)$ $[\sigma,\ \operatorname{Re} c,\ \operatorname{Re} s > 0]$

3.31.12. $\quad _2F_1\left(a, b; c; \dfrac{\sqrt{x} - \sqrt{x+\omega}}{2\sqrt{x}}\right)$ **and algebraic functions**

1	$\left(\sqrt{x+\omega} + \sqrt{x}\right)^{-a}$ $\times\,_2F_1\left(\begin{matrix}a, b\\a+1;\ \frac{\sqrt{x}-\sqrt{x+\omega}}{2\sqrt{x}}\end{matrix}\right)$	$\dfrac{2^{b-1}a\,\omega^{s-a/2}}{\sqrt{\pi}}\,\Gamma\left[\begin{matrix}\frac{-2s+a}{2},\ \frac{2s+a}{2},\ \frac{2s+b}{2},\ \frac{2s+b+1}{2}\\\frac{2s+a+2}{2},\ \frac{2s+a+2b}{2}\end{matrix}\right]$ $\left[\begin{matrix}-\operatorname{Re}a/2,\ -\operatorname{Re}b/2 < \operatorname{Re}s < \operatorname{Re}a/2;\\-\pi < \arg\omega \le \pi\end{matrix}\right]$
2	$\left(\sqrt{x+\omega} - \sqrt{x}\right)^{a}$ $\times\,_2F_1\left(\begin{matrix}a, b\\a+1;\ \frac{\sqrt{x}-\sqrt{x+\omega}}{2\sqrt{x}}\end{matrix}\right)$	$\dfrac{2^{b-1}a\,\omega^{s+a/2}}{\sqrt{\pi}}\,\Gamma\left[\begin{matrix}\frac{-2s+a}{2},\ \frac{2s+a}{2},\ \frac{2s+b}{2},\ \frac{2s+b+1}{2}\\\frac{2s+a+2}{2},\ \frac{2s+a+2b}{2}\end{matrix}\right]$ $\left[\begin{matrix}-\operatorname{Re}a/2,\ -\operatorname{Re}b/2 < \operatorname{Re}s < \operatorname{Re}a/2;\\|\arg\omega| < \pi\end{matrix}\right]$
3	$\left(\sqrt{x+\omega} + \sqrt{x}\right)^{b-2c+2}$ $\times\,_2F_1\left(\begin{matrix}1, b\\c;\ \frac{\sqrt{x}-\sqrt{x+\omega}}{2\sqrt{x}}\end{matrix}\right)$	$\dfrac{(c-1)\,\omega^{s+b/2-c+1}}{\sqrt{\pi}}\,\Gamma\left[\begin{matrix}\frac{-2s-b+2c-2}{2},\ \frac{2s+1}{2},\ s+1,\ \frac{2s+b}{2}\\\frac{2s-b+2c}{2},\ \frac{2s+b+2}{2}\end{matrix}\right]$ $\left[\begin{matrix}-1/2,\ -\operatorname{Re}b/2 < \operatorname{Re}s < \operatorname{Re}(2c-b-2)/2;\\|\arg\omega| < \pi\end{matrix}\right]$
4	$\left(\sqrt{x+\omega} - \sqrt{x}\right)^{2c-b-2}$ $\times\,_2F_1\left(\begin{matrix}1, b\\c;\ \frac{\sqrt{x}-\sqrt{x+\omega}}{2\sqrt{x}}\end{matrix}\right)$	$\dfrac{(c-1)\,\omega^{s-b/2+c-1}}{\sqrt{\pi}}\,\Gamma\left[\begin{matrix}\frac{-2s-b+2c-2}{2},\ \frac{2s+1}{2},\ s+1,\ \frac{2s+b}{2}\\\frac{2s-b+2c}{2},\ \frac{2s+b+2}{2}\end{matrix}\right]$ $\left[\begin{matrix}-1/2,\ -\operatorname{Re}b/2 < \operatorname{Re}s < \operatorname{Re}(2c-b-2)/2;\\-\pi < \arg\omega \le \pi\end{matrix}\right]$

3.31.13. $\quad _2F_1\left(a, b; c; \dfrac{\sqrt{\omega} - \sqrt{x+\omega}}{2\sqrt{\omega}}\right)$ **and algebraic functions**

1	$\left(\sqrt{x+\omega} + \sqrt{\omega}\right)^{-a}$ $\times\,_2F_1\left(\begin{matrix}a, b;\ \frac{\sqrt{\omega}-\sqrt{x+\omega}}{2\sqrt{\omega}}\\a+1\end{matrix}\right)$	$\dfrac{2^{2s-a}a\,\omega^{s-a/2}}{a-s}\,\Gamma\left[\begin{matrix}s, a+b-2s\\a+b-s\end{matrix}\right]$ $[0 < \operatorname{Re}s < \operatorname{Re}a,\ \operatorname{Re}(a+b)/2;\ -\pi < \arg\omega \le \pi]$
2	$\left(\sqrt{x+\omega} + \sqrt{\omega}\right)^{b-2c+2}$ $\times\,_2F_1\left(\begin{matrix}1, b\\c;\ \frac{\sqrt{\omega}-\sqrt{x+\omega}}{2\sqrt{\omega}}\end{matrix}\right)$	$\dfrac{(c-1)\,\omega^{s+b/2-c+1}}{\sqrt{\pi}}\,\Gamma\left[\begin{matrix}c-s-1\\c-s\end{matrix}\right]\Gamma\left[\begin{matrix}\frac{-2s-b+2c-1}{2},\ \frac{-2s-b+2c}{2},\ s\\2c-s-b-1\end{matrix}\right]$ $\left[\begin{matrix}0 < \operatorname{Re}s < \operatorname{Re}c-1,\ \operatorname{Re}(2c-b-1)/2;\\-\pi < \arg\omega \le \pi\end{matrix}\right]$
3	$\left(\sqrt{x+\omega} - \sqrt{\omega}\right)^{2c-b-2}$ $\times\,_2F_1\left(\begin{matrix}1, b\\c;\ \frac{\sqrt{\omega}-\sqrt{x+\omega}}{2\sqrt{\omega}}\end{matrix}\right)$	$\dfrac{(1-c)\,\omega^{s-b/2+c-1}}{\sqrt{\pi}}\,\Gamma\left[\begin{matrix}\frac{-2s+b-2c+3}{2},\ \frac{-2s+b-2c+4}{2}\\1-s\end{matrix}\right]$ $\times\,\Gamma\left[\begin{matrix}b-c-s+1,\ s-b+2c-2\\b-c-s+2\end{matrix}\right]$ $\left[\begin{matrix}\operatorname{Re}(b-2c)+2 < \operatorname{Re}s < \operatorname{Re}(b/2-c)+3/2,\\\operatorname{Re}(b-c)+1;\ -\pi < \arg\omega \le \pi\end{matrix}\right]$

3.31.14. $\;\; {}_2F_1\left(a,\,b;\,c;\,\dfrac{\sqrt{x+\omega}-\sqrt{x}}{\sqrt{x+\omega}+\sqrt{x}}\right)$ and algebraic functions

1	$\left(\sqrt{x+\omega}+\sqrt{x}\right)^{-2a}$ $\times\,{}_2F_1\left(\begin{matrix}a,\,b\\a+1;\,\frac{\sqrt{x+\omega}-\sqrt{x}}{\sqrt{x+\omega}+\sqrt{x}}\end{matrix}\right)$	$\dfrac{a\,\omega^{s-a}}{2^b\sqrt{\pi}}\,\Gamma\left[\begin{matrix}a-s,\,\frac{2s-b+1}{2},\,\frac{2s-b+2}{2},\,s\\s+1,\,s+a-b+1\end{matrix}\right]$ $[0,\;\mathrm{Re}\,(b-1)/2<\mathrm{Re}\,s<\mathrm{Re}\,a;\;-\pi<\arg\omega\le\pi]$
2	$\left(\sqrt{x+\omega}+\sqrt{x}\right)^{1-b-c}$ $\times\,{}_2F_1\left(\begin{matrix}1,\,b\\c;\,\frac{\sqrt{x+\omega}-\sqrt{x}}{\sqrt{x+\omega}+\sqrt{x}}\end{matrix}\right)$	$\dfrac{(c-1)\,\omega^{s+(1-b-c)/2}}{2\sqrt{\pi}}\,\Gamma\left[\begin{matrix}\frac{-2s+b+c-1}{2},\,\frac{2s-b+c-1}{2},\,\frac{2s+1}{2},\,s\\\frac{2s-b+c+1}{2},\,\frac{2s+b+c-1}{2}\end{matrix}\right]$ $\left[\begin{matrix}0,\;\mathrm{Re}\,(b-c+1)/2<\mathrm{Re}\,s\\<\mathrm{Re}\,(b+c-1)/2;\;-\pi<\arg\omega\le\pi\end{matrix}\right]$

3.31.15. $\;\; {}_2F_1\left(a,\,b;\,c;\,\dfrac{\sqrt{\pm x+\omega}-\sqrt{\omega}}{\sqrt{\pm x+\omega}+\sqrt{\omega}}\right)$ and algebraic functions

1	$\left(\sqrt{\omega-x}+\sqrt{\omega}\right)^{-2a}$ $\times\,{}_2F_1\left(\begin{matrix}a,\,b\\a+1;\,\frac{\sqrt{\omega-x}-\sqrt{\omega}}{\sqrt{\omega-x}+\sqrt{\omega}}\end{matrix}\right)$	$\dfrac{2^{2s-2a}a}{a-s}\,\omega^{-a}\left(-\dfrac{1}{\omega}\right)^{-s}\Gamma\left[\begin{matrix}2a-b-2s+1,\,s\\2a-b-s+1\end{matrix}\right]$ $\left[\begin{matrix}0<\mathrm{Re}\,s<\mathrm{Re}\,a,\;\mathrm{Re}\,(2a-b+1)/2;\\-\pi<\arg\omega\le\pi\end{matrix}\right]$
2	$\left(\sqrt{x+\omega}+\sqrt{\omega}\right)^{-2a}$ $\times\,{}_2F_1\left(\begin{matrix}a,\,b\\a+1;\,\frac{\sqrt{x+\omega}-\sqrt{\omega}}{\sqrt{x+\omega}+\sqrt{\omega}}\end{matrix}\right)$	$\dfrac{a\,(4\omega)^{s-a}}{a-s}\,\Gamma\left[\begin{matrix}2a-b-2s+1,\,s\\2a-b-s+1\end{matrix}\right]$ $\left[\begin{matrix}0<\mathrm{Re}\,s<\mathrm{Re}\,a,\;\mathrm{Re}\,(2a-b+1)/2;\\-\pi<\arg\omega\le\pi\end{matrix}\right]$
3	$\left(\sqrt{x+\omega}+\sqrt{\omega}\right)^{1-b-c}$ $\times\,{}_2F_1\left(\begin{matrix}1,\,b\\c;\,\frac{\sqrt{x+\omega}-\sqrt{\omega}}{\sqrt{x+\omega}+\sqrt{\omega}}\end{matrix}\right)$	$\dfrac{(c-1)\,(4\omega)^{s+(1-b-c)/2}}{c-s-1}\,\Gamma\left[\begin{matrix}b+c-2s-1,\,s\\b+c-s-1\end{matrix}\right]$ $\left[\begin{matrix}0<\mathrm{Re}\,s<\mathrm{Re}\,c-1,\;\mathrm{Re}\,(b+c-1)/2;\\-\pi<\arg\omega\le\pi\end{matrix}\right]$

3.31.16. $\;\; {}_2F_1\left(a,\,b;\,c;\,\dfrac{x-2\sqrt{\omega}\sqrt{x+\omega}+2\omega}{x}\right)$ and algebraic functions

1	$\left(\sqrt{x+\omega}-\sqrt{\omega}\right)^{2a}$ $\times\,{}_2F_1\left(\begin{matrix}a,\,b;\,\frac{x-2\sqrt{\omega}\sqrt{x+\omega}+2\omega}{x}\\a+1\end{matrix}\right)$	$\dfrac{a\,\omega^{s+a}}{2^b\sqrt{\pi}}\,\Gamma\left[\begin{matrix}-s-a,\,\frac{1-2s-2a-b}{2},\,\frac{2-2s-2a-b}{2},\,s+2a\\1-a-s,\,1-b-s\end{matrix}\right]$ $\left[\begin{matrix}-2\,\mathrm{Re}\,a<\mathrm{Re}\,s<-\,\mathrm{Re}\,a,\;\mathrm{Re}\,(1-2a-b)/2;\\-\pi<\arg\omega\le\pi\end{matrix}\right]$
2	$\left(\sqrt{x+\omega}-\sqrt{\omega}\right)^{b+c-1}$ $\times\,{}_2F_1\left(\begin{matrix}1,\,b\\c;\,\frac{x-2\sqrt{\omega}\sqrt{x+\omega}+2\omega}{x}\end{matrix}\right)$	$\dfrac{(1-c)\,(4\omega)^{s+(b+c-1)/2}}{s+b}\,\Gamma\left[\begin{matrix}1-b-c-2s,\,s+b+c-1\\-s\end{matrix}\right]$ $\left[\begin{matrix}\mathrm{Re}\,(1-b-c)<\mathrm{Re}\,s<-\,\mathrm{Re}\,b,\;\mathrm{Re}\,(1-b-c)/2;\\-\pi<\arg\omega\le\pi\end{matrix}\right]$

3.31.17. $_2F_1\left(a, b; c; \dfrac{2x - 2\sqrt{x}\sqrt{x+\omega} + \omega}{\omega}\right)$ and algebraic functions

1	$\left(\sqrt{x+\omega} - \sqrt{x}\right)^{2a}$ $\times {}_2F_1\left(\begin{matrix}a, b; \frac{2x-2\sqrt{x}\sqrt{x+\omega}+\omega}{\omega}\\ a+1\end{matrix}\right)$	$\dfrac{a\,\omega^{s+a}}{2^{2s}s}\Gamma\begin{bmatrix}a-s,\ 2s-b+1\\ s+a-b+1\end{bmatrix}$ $[0,\ \mathrm{Re}\,(b-1)/2 < \mathrm{Re}\,s < \mathrm{Re}\,a;\ |\arg\omega| < \pi]$
2	$\left(\sqrt{x+\omega} - \sqrt{x}\right)^{b+c-1}$ $\times {}_2F_1\left(\begin{matrix}1, b\\ c; \frac{2x-2\sqrt{x}\sqrt{x+\omega}+\omega}{\omega}\end{matrix}\right)$	$\dfrac{(c-1)\,\omega^{s+(b+c-1)/2}}{2^{2s-1}(2s-b+c-1)}\Gamma\begin{bmatrix}\frac{-2s+b+c-1}{2},\ 2s\\ \frac{2s+b+c-1}{2}\end{bmatrix}$ $\begin{bmatrix}0,\ \mathrm{Re}\,(b-c+1)/2 < \mathrm{Re}\,s < \mathrm{Re}\,(b+c-1)/2;\\ |\arg\omega| < \pi\end{bmatrix}$

3.31.18. $_2F_1\left(a, b; c; \dfrac{2x - 2\sqrt{x}\sqrt{x+\omega} + \omega}{2\sqrt{x}\left(\sqrt{x} - \sqrt{x+\omega}\right)}\right)$ and algebraic functions

1	$\left(\sqrt{x+\omega} - \sqrt{x}\right)^{a}$ $\times {}_2F_1\left(\begin{matrix}a, b; \frac{2x-2\sqrt{x}\sqrt{x+\omega}+\omega}{2\sqrt{x}(\sqrt{x}-\sqrt{x+\omega})}\\ a+1\end{matrix}\right)$	$\dfrac{2^{b-1}a\,\omega^{s+a/2}}{\sqrt{\pi}}\Gamma\begin{bmatrix}\frac{-2s+a}{2},\ \frac{2s+a}{2},\ \frac{2s+b}{2},\ \frac{2s+b+1}{2}\\ \frac{2s+a+2}{2},\ \frac{2s+a+2b}{2}\end{bmatrix}$ $\begin{bmatrix}-\mathrm{Re}\,a/2,\ -\mathrm{Re}\,b/2 < \mathrm{Re}\,s < \mathrm{Re}\,a/2;\\ |\arg\omega| < \pi\end{bmatrix}$
2	$\left(\sqrt{x+\omega} - \sqrt{x}\right)^{2c-b-2}$ $\times {}_2F_1\left(\begin{matrix}1, b\\ c; \frac{2x-2\sqrt{x}\sqrt{x+\omega}+\omega}{2\sqrt{x}(\sqrt{x}-\sqrt{x+\omega})}\end{matrix}\right)$	$\dfrac{(c-1)\,\omega^{s-b/2+c-1}}{\sqrt{\pi}}\Gamma\begin{bmatrix}\frac{2c-b-2s-2}{2},\ \frac{2s+1}{2},\ s+1,\ \frac{2s+b}{2}\\ \frac{2s+2c-b}{2},\ \frac{2s+b+2}{2}\end{bmatrix}$ $\begin{bmatrix}-1/2,\ -\mathrm{Re}\,b/2 < \mathrm{Re}\,s < \mathrm{Re}\,(c-b/2)-1;\\ -\pi < \arg\omega \le \pi\end{bmatrix}$

3.31.19. $_2F_1\left(a, b; c; \dfrac{x - 2\sqrt{\omega}\sqrt{x+\omega} + 2\omega}{2\sqrt{\omega}\left(\sqrt{\omega} - \sqrt{x+\omega}\right)}\right)$ and algebraic functions

1	$\left(\sqrt{x+\omega} - \sqrt{\omega}\right)^{a}$ $\times {}_2F_1\left(\begin{matrix}a, b; \frac{x-2\sqrt{\omega}\sqrt{x+\omega}+2\omega}{2\sqrt{\omega}(\sqrt{\omega}-\sqrt{x+\omega})}\\ a+1\end{matrix}\right)$	$\dfrac{2^{b-1}a\,\omega^{s+a/2}}{\sqrt{\pi}}\Gamma\begin{bmatrix}-s,\ \frac{b-a-2s}{2},\ \frac{b-a-2s+1}{2},\ s+a\\ 1-s,\ b-s\end{bmatrix}$ $[-\mathrm{Re}\,a < \mathrm{Re}\,s < 0,\ \mathrm{Re}\,(b-a)/2;\ 0 \le \arg\omega \le \pi]$
2	$\left(\sqrt{x+\omega} - \sqrt{\omega}\right)^{2c-b-2}$ $\times {}_2F_1\left(\begin{matrix}1, b; \frac{x-2\sqrt{\omega}\sqrt{x+\omega}+2\omega}{2\sqrt{\omega}(\sqrt{\omega}-\sqrt{x+\omega})}\\ c\end{matrix}\right)$	$\dfrac{(c-1)\,\omega^{s-b/2+c-1}}{\sqrt{\pi}}\Gamma\begin{bmatrix}\frac{b-2c-2s+3}{2},\ \frac{b-2c-2s+4}{2}\\ 1-s\end{bmatrix}$ $\times\,\Gamma\begin{bmatrix}b-c-s+1,\ s-b+2c-2\\ b-c-s+2\end{bmatrix}$ $\begin{bmatrix}\mathrm{Re}\,(b-2c)+2 < \mathrm{Re}\,s < \mathrm{Re}\,(b-c)+1,\\ \mathrm{Re}\,(b-2c+3)/2;\ -\pi < \arg\omega \le \pi\end{bmatrix}$

3.31.20. $_2F_1\left(a, b; c; \dfrac{x - \sqrt{x^2 + \omega^2}}{2x}\right)$ and algebraic functions

1	$\left(\sqrt{x^2 + \omega^2} + x\right)^{-a}$ $\times {}_2F_1\left(\begin{matrix} a,\, b;\ \frac{x-\sqrt{x^2+\omega^2}}{2x} \\ a+1 \end{matrix}\right)$	$\dfrac{2^{b-2a}\omega^{s-a}}{\sqrt{\pi}} \Gamma\left[\begin{matrix} \frac{-s+a}{2},\ \frac{s+a}{2},\ \frac{s+b}{2},\ \frac{s+b+1}{2} \\ \frac{s+a+2}{2},\ \frac{s+a+2b}{2} \end{matrix}\right]$ $[-\operatorname{Re}a,\, -\operatorname{Re}b < \operatorname{Re}s < \operatorname{Re}a;\ -\pi/2 < \arg\omega \le \pi/2]$
2	$\left(\sqrt{x^2 + \omega^2} + x\right)^{b-2c+2}$ $\times {}_2F_1\left(\begin{matrix} 1,\, b;\ \frac{x-\sqrt{x^2+\omega^2}}{2x} \\ c \end{matrix}\right)$	$\dfrac{(c-1)\,\omega^{s+b-2c+2}}{2\sqrt{\pi}} \Gamma\left[\begin{matrix} \frac{2c-b-s-2}{2},\ \frac{s+1}{2},\ \frac{s+2}{2},\ \frac{s+b}{2} \\ \frac{s-b+2c}{2},\ \frac{s+b+2}{2} \end{matrix}\right]$ $\left[\begin{matrix} -1,\, -\operatorname{Re}b < \operatorname{Re}s < \operatorname{Re}(2c-b)-2; \\ -\pi/2 < \arg\omega \le \pi/2 \end{matrix}\right]$

3.31.21. $_2F_1\left(a, b; c; \dfrac{\omega - \sqrt{x^2 + \omega^2}}{2\omega}\right)$ and algebraic functions

1	$\left(\sqrt{x^2 + \omega^2} + \omega\right)^{-a}$ $\times {}_2F_1\left(\begin{matrix} a,\, b;\ \frac{\omega-\sqrt{x^2+\omega^2}}{2\omega} \\ a+1 \end{matrix}\right)$	$\dfrac{2^{b-2a}\omega^{s-a}}{\sqrt{\pi}} \Gamma\left[\begin{matrix} \frac{2a-s}{2},\ \frac{a+b-s}{2},\ \frac{a+b-s+1}{2},\ \frac{s}{2} \\ \frac{2a-s+2}{2},\ \frac{2a+2b-s}{2} \end{matrix}\right]$ $\left[\begin{matrix} 0 < \operatorname{Re}s < 2\operatorname{Re}a,\ \operatorname{Re}(a+b); \\ -\pi/2 < \arg\omega \le \pi/2 \end{matrix}\right]$
2	$\left(\sqrt{x^2 + \omega^2} + \omega\right)^{b-2c+2}$ $\times {}_2F_1\left(\begin{matrix} 1,\, b;\ \frac{\omega-\sqrt{x^2+\omega^2}}{2\omega} \\ c \end{matrix}\right)$	$\dfrac{(c-1)\,\omega^{s+b-2c+2}}{2\sqrt{\pi}} \Gamma\left[\begin{matrix} \frac{2c-s-2}{2},\ \frac{2c-b-s-1}{2},\ \frac{2c-b-s}{2},\ \frac{s}{2} \\ \frac{2c-s}{2},\ \frac{4c-2b-s-2}{2} \end{matrix}\right]$ $\left[\begin{matrix} 0 < \operatorname{Re}s < 2\operatorname{Re}c-2,\ \operatorname{Re}(2c-b)-1; \\ -\pi/2 < \arg\omega \le \pi/2 \end{matrix}\right]$

3.31.22. $_2F_1\left(a, b; c; \dfrac{\sqrt{x^2 + \omega^2} - x}{\sqrt{x^2 + \omega^2} + x}\right)$ and algebraic functions

1	$\left(\sqrt{x^2 + \omega^2} + x\right)^{-2a}$ $\times {}_2F_1\left(\begin{matrix} a,\, b;\ \frac{\sqrt{x^2+\omega^2}-x}{\sqrt{x^2+\omega^2}+x} \\ a+1 \end{matrix}\right)$	$\dfrac{a\,\omega^{s-2a}}{2^{b+1}\sqrt{\pi}} \Gamma\left[\begin{matrix} \frac{2a-s}{2},\ \frac{s-b+1}{2},\ \frac{s-b+2}{2},\ \frac{s}{2} \\ \frac{s+2}{2},\ \frac{s+2a-2b+2}{2} \end{matrix}\right]$ $[0,\ \operatorname{Re}b-1 < \operatorname{Re}s < 2\operatorname{Re}a;\ -\pi/2 < \arg\omega \le \pi/2]$
2	$\left(\sqrt{x^2 + \omega^2} + x\right)^{1-b-c}$ $\times {}_2F_1\left(\begin{matrix} 1,\, b;\ \frac{\sqrt{x^2+\omega^2}-x}{\sqrt{x^2+\omega^2}+x} \\ c \end{matrix}\right)$	$\dfrac{(c-1)\,\omega^{s-b-c+1}}{4\sqrt{\pi}} \Gamma\left[\begin{matrix} \frac{b+c-s-1}{2},\ \frac{s}{2},\ \frac{s+1}{2},\ \frac{s-b+c-1}{2} \\ \frac{s-b+c+1}{2},\ \frac{s+b+c-1}{2} \end{matrix}\right]$ $\left[\begin{matrix} 0,\ \operatorname{Re}(b-c)+1 < \operatorname{Re}s < \operatorname{Re}(b+c)-1; \\ -\pi/2 < \arg\omega \le \pi/2 \end{matrix}\right]$

3.31.23. $_2F_1\left(a, b, c; \dfrac{\sqrt{x^2 + \omega^2} - \omega}{\sqrt{x^2 + \omega^2} + \omega}\right)$ **and algebraic functions**

1	$\left(\sqrt{x^2 + \omega^2} + \omega\right)^{-2a}$ $\times\, _2F_1\left(\begin{matrix} a, b; \frac{\sqrt{x^2+\omega^2}-\omega}{\sqrt{x^2+\omega^2}+\omega} \\ a+1 \end{matrix}\right)$	$\dfrac{a\,\omega^{s-2a}}{2^{b+1}\sqrt{\pi}}\,\Gamma\left[\begin{matrix} \frac{2a-s}{2}, \frac{2a-b-s+1}{2}, \frac{2a-b-s+2}{2}, \frac{s}{2} \\ \frac{2a-s+2}{2}, \frac{4a-2b-s+2}{2} \end{matrix}\right]$ $\left[\begin{matrix} 0 < \operatorname{Re} s < 2\operatorname{Re} a, \ \operatorname{Re}\left(2a-b\right)+1; \\ -\pi/2 < \arg\omega \le \pi/2 \end{matrix}\right]$
2	$\left(\sqrt{x^2 + \omega^2} + \omega\right)^{1-b-c}$ $\times\, _2F_1\left(\begin{matrix} 1, b; \frac{\sqrt{x^2+\omega^2}-\omega}{\sqrt{x^2+\omega^2}+\omega} \\ c \end{matrix}\right)$	$\dfrac{(c-1)\,\omega^{s-b-c+1}}{4\sqrt{\pi}}\,\Gamma\left[\begin{matrix} \frac{b+c-s-1}{2}, \frac{b+c-s}{2}, \frac{2c-s-2}{2}, \frac{s}{2} \\ \frac{2c-s}{2}, \frac{2b+2c-s-2}{2} \end{matrix}\right]$ $\left[\begin{matrix} 0 < \operatorname{Re} s < 2\operatorname{Re} c - 2, \ \operatorname{Re}\left(b+c\right)-1; \\ -\pi/2 < \arg\omega \le \pi/2 \end{matrix}\right]$

3.31.24. $_2F_1\left(a, b; c; \dfrac{x^2 - 2\omega\sqrt{x^2 + \omega^2} + 2\omega^2}{x^2}\right)$ **and algebraic functions**

1	$\left(\sqrt{x^2 + \omega^2} - \omega\right)^{2a}$ $\times\, _2F_1\left(\begin{matrix} a, b; \frac{x^2-2\omega\sqrt{x^2+\omega^2}+2\omega^2}{x^2} \\ a+1 \end{matrix}\right)$	$\dfrac{a\,\omega^{s+2a}}{2^{b+1}\sqrt{\pi}}\,\Gamma\left[\begin{matrix} \frac{1-s-2a-b}{2}, \frac{2-s-2a-b}{2}, \frac{-s-2a}{2}, \frac{s+4a}{2} \\ \frac{2-2a-s}{2}, \frac{2-2b-s}{2} \end{matrix}\right]$ $\left[\begin{matrix} -4\operatorname{Re} a < \operatorname{Re} s < -2\operatorname{Re} a, \ 1 - \operatorname{Re}\left(2a+b\right); \\ \left|\arg\omega\right| < \pi/2 \end{matrix}\right]$
2	$\left(\sqrt{x^2 + \omega^2} - \omega\right)^{b+c-1}$ $\times\, _2F_1\left(\begin{matrix} 1, b; \frac{x^2-2\omega\sqrt{x^2+\omega^2}+2\omega^2}{x^2} \\ c \end{matrix}\right)$	$\dfrac{(c-1)\,\omega^{s+b+c-1}}{4\sqrt{\pi}}\,\Gamma\left[\begin{matrix} \frac{1-b-c-s}{2}, \frac{2-b-c-s}{2}, \frac{-s-2b}{2} \\ \frac{2-2b-s}{2} \end{matrix}\right]$ $\times\,\Gamma\left[\begin{matrix} \frac{s+2b+2c-2}{2} \\ -\frac{s}{2} \end{matrix}\right]$ $\left[\begin{matrix} 2 - 2\operatorname{Re}\left(b+c\right) < \operatorname{Re} s < -2\operatorname{Re} b, \\ 1 - \operatorname{Re}\left(b+c\right); \left|\arg\omega\right| < \pi/2 \end{matrix}\right]$

3.31.25. $_2F_1\left(a, b; c; \dfrac{2x^2 - 2x\sqrt{x^2 + \omega^2} + \omega^2}{\omega^2}\right)$ **and algebraic functions**

1	$\left(\sqrt{x^2 + \omega^2} - x\right)^{2a}$ $\times\, _2F_1\left(\begin{matrix} a, b; \frac{2x^2-2x\sqrt{x^2+\omega^2}+\omega^2}{\omega^2} \\ a+1 \end{matrix}\right)$	$\dfrac{a\,\omega^{s+2a}}{2^{b+1}\sqrt{\pi}}\,\Gamma\left[\begin{matrix} \frac{2a-s}{2}, \frac{s-b+1}{2}, \frac{s-b+2}{2}, \frac{s}{2} \\ \frac{s+2}{2}, \frac{s+2a-2b+2}{2} \end{matrix}\right]$ $[0, \ \operatorname{Re} b - 1 < \operatorname{Re} s < 2\operatorname{Re} a; \left|\arg\omega\right| < \pi/2]$
2	$\left(\sqrt{x^2 + \omega^2} - x\right)^{b+c-1}$ $\times\, _2F_1\left(\begin{matrix} 1, b; \frac{2x^2-2x\sqrt{x^2+\omega^2}+\omega^2}{\omega^2} \\ c \end{matrix}\right)$	$\dfrac{(c-1)\,\omega^{s+b+c-1}}{4\sqrt{\pi}}\,\Gamma\left[\begin{matrix} \frac{b+c-s-1}{2}, \frac{s}{2}, \frac{s+1}{2}, \frac{s-b+c-1}{2} \\ \frac{s-b+c+1}{2}, \frac{s+b+c-1}{2} \end{matrix}\right]$ $\left[\begin{matrix} 0, \ \operatorname{Re}\left(b-c\right)+1 < \operatorname{Re} s < \operatorname{Re}\left(b+c\right)-1; \\ \left|\arg\omega\right| < \pi/2 \end{matrix}\right]$

3.31.26. $_2F_1\left(a, b; c; \dfrac{2x^2 - 2x\sqrt{x^2 + \omega^2} + \omega^2}{2x\left(x - \sqrt{x^2 + \omega^2}\right)}\right)$ **and algebraic functions**

1	$\left(\sqrt{x^2 + \omega^2} - x\right)^a$ $\times {}_2F_1\left(\begin{array}{c} a,\, b;\ \frac{2x^2 - 2x\sqrt{x^2+\omega^2}+\omega^2}{2x\left(x-\sqrt{x^2+\omega^2}\right)} \\ a+1 \end{array}\right)$	$\dfrac{2^{b-2}a\,\omega^{s+a}}{\sqrt{\pi}}\,\Gamma\left[\begin{array}{c} \frac{-s+a}{2},\ \frac{s+a}{2},\ \frac{s+b}{2},\ \frac{s+b+1}{2} \\ \frac{s+a+2}{2},\ \frac{s+a+2b}{2} \end{array}\right]$ $[\operatorname{Re}\omega > 0;\ -\operatorname{Re}a,\ -\operatorname{Re}b < \operatorname{Re}s < \operatorname{Re}a]$	
2	$\left(\sqrt{x^2 + \omega^2} - x\right)^{2c-b-2}$ $\times {}_2F_1\left(\begin{array}{c} 1,\, b;\ \frac{2x^2 - 2x\sqrt{x^2+\omega^2}+\omega^2}{2x\left(x-\sqrt{x^2+\omega^2}\right)} \\ c \end{array}\right)$	$\dfrac{(c-1)\,\omega^{s-b+2c-2}}{2\sqrt{\pi}}\,\Gamma\left[\begin{array}{c} \frac{2c-b-s-2}{2},\ \frac{s+1}{2},\ \frac{s+2}{2},\ \frac{s+b}{2} \\ \frac{s+b+2}{2},\ \frac{s-b+2c}{2} \end{array}\right]$ $\left[\begin{array}{c} -1,\, -\operatorname{Re}b < \operatorname{Re}s < \operatorname{Re}\left(2c-b\right)-2; \\ -\pi/2 < \arg\omega \le \pi/2 \end{array}\right]$	

3.31.27. $_2F_1\left(a, b; c; \dfrac{x^2 - 2\omega\sqrt{x^2 + \omega^2} + 2\omega^2}{2\omega\left(\omega - \sqrt{x^2 + \omega^2}\right)}\right)$ **and algebraic functions**

1	$\left(\sqrt{x^2 + \omega^2} - \omega\right)^a$ $\times {}_2F_1\left(\begin{array}{c} a,\, b;\ \frac{x^2 - 2\omega\sqrt{x^2+\omega^2}+2\omega^2}{2\omega\left(\omega-\sqrt{x^2+\omega^2}\right)} \\ a+1 \end{array}\right)$	$\dfrac{2^{b-2}a\,\omega^{s+a}}{\sqrt{\pi}}\,\Gamma\left[\begin{array}{c} -\frac{s}{2},\ \frac{b-a-s}{2},\ \frac{b-a-s+1}{2},\ \frac{s+2a}{2} \\ \frac{2-s}{2},\ \frac{2b-s}{2} \end{array}\right]$ $\left[\begin{array}{c} -2\operatorname{Re}a < \operatorname{Re}s < 0,\ \operatorname{Re}\left(b-a\right); \\ -\pi/2 < \arg\omega \le \pi/2 \end{array}\right]$	
2	$\left(\sqrt{x^2 + \omega^2} - \omega\right)^{2c-b-2}$ $\times {}_2F_1\left(\begin{array}{c} 1,\, b;\ \frac{x^2 - 2\omega\sqrt{x^2+\omega^2}+2\omega^2}{2\omega\left(\omega-\sqrt{x^2+\omega^2}\right)} \\ c \end{array}\right)$	$\dfrac{(c-1)\,\omega^{s-b+2c-2}}{2\sqrt{\pi}}\,\Gamma\left[\begin{array}{c} \frac{b-2c-s+3}{2},\ \frac{b-2c-s+4}{2} \\ \frac{2-s}{2} \end{array}\right]$ $\times\Gamma\left[\begin{array}{c} \frac{2b-2c-s+2}{2},\ \frac{s-2b+4c-4}{2} \\ \frac{2b-2c-s+4}{2} \end{array}\right]$ $\left[\begin{array}{c} 2\operatorname{Re}\left(b-2c\right)+4 < \operatorname{Re}s < \operatorname{Re}\left(b-2c\right)+3, \\ 2\operatorname{Re}\left(b-c+1\right);\ -\pi/2 < \arg\omega \le \pi/2 \end{array}\right]$	

3.31.28. $_2F_1\left(a, b; c; \varphi\left(x\right)\right)$ **and algebraic functions**

No.	$f\left(x\right)$	$F\left(s\right)$
1	$\dfrac{\left|1 \mp \sqrt{x}\right|^{2a}}{\left|1 - x\right|^{2b}}\,{}_2F_1\left(\begin{array}{c} a,\, b \\ 2b;\ \frac{\pm 4\sqrt{x}}{\left(1 \pm \sqrt{x}\right)^2} \end{array}\right)$	$\Gamma\left[\begin{array}{c} \frac{2b+1}{2},\ \frac{2a-2b+1}{2},\ s,\ 2b-a-s \\ 2b-a,\ \frac{2s+2a-2b+1}{2},\ \frac{2b-2s+1}{2} \end{array}\right]$ $[\operatorname{Re}\left(a-b\right) > -1/2;\ 0 < \operatorname{Re}s < \operatorname{Re}\left(2b-a\right)]$
2	$\left(\sigma - x\right)_{+}^{\mu-1}\,{}_2F_1\left(\begin{array}{c} a,\, b \\ c;\ \omega x\left(\sigma - x\right) \end{array}\right)$	$\sigma^{s+\mu-1}\,\mathrm{B}\left(\mu, s\right)\,{}_4F_3\left(\begin{array}{c} a,\, b,\, \mu,\, s;\ \frac{\sigma^2\omega}{4} \\ c,\ \frac{s+\mu}{2},\ \frac{s+\mu+1}{2} \end{array}\right)$ $[\sigma,\ \operatorname{Re}\mu,\ \operatorname{Re}s > 0]$

3.31.29. $_2F_1(a, b; c; \varphi(x))$ **and the exponential function**

1	$e^{-\sigma x}\,_2F_1\!\left(\begin{matrix}a, b\\c; -\omega x\end{matrix}\right)$	$\omega^{-s}\Gamma\!\left[\begin{matrix}c, s, a-s, b-s\\a, b, c-s\end{matrix}\right]\,_2F_2\!\left(\begin{matrix}s, s-c+1;\ \frac{\sigma}{\omega}\\s-a+1, s-b+1\end{matrix}\right)$

$$+\frac{\sigma^{a-s}}{\omega^a}\Gamma\!\left[\begin{matrix}c, b-a, s-a\\b, c-a\end{matrix}\right]\,_2F_2\!\left(\begin{matrix}a, a-c+1;\ \frac{\sigma}{\omega}\\a-b+1, a-s+1\end{matrix}\right)$$

$$+\frac{\sigma^{b-s}}{\omega^b}\Gamma\!\left[\begin{matrix}c, a-b, s-b\\a, c-b\end{matrix}\right]\,_2F_2\!\left(\begin{matrix}b, b-c+1;\ \frac{\sigma}{\omega}\\b-a+1, b-s+1\end{matrix}\right)$$

$$[\mathrm{Re}\,\sigma,\ \mathrm{Re}\,s > 0;\ |\arg\omega| < \pi]$$

2	$e^{-\sigma x}\,_2F_1\!\left(\begin{matrix}a, b\\c; 1-\omega x\end{matrix}\right)$	$\omega^{-s}\Gamma\!\left[\begin{matrix}c, s, a-s, b-s, s-a-b+c\\a, b, c-a, c-b\end{matrix}\right]\,_2F_2\!\left(\begin{matrix}s, s-a-b+c;\ -\frac{\sigma}{\omega}\\s-a+1, s-b+1\end{matrix}\right)$

$$+\frac{\sigma^{a-s}}{\omega^a}\Gamma\!\left[\begin{matrix}b-a, c, s-a\\b, c-a\end{matrix}\right]\,_2F_2\!\left(\begin{matrix}a, c-b;\ -\frac{\sigma}{\omega}\\a-b+1, a-s+1\end{matrix}\right)$$

$$+\frac{\sigma^{b-s}}{\omega^b}\Gamma\!\left[\begin{matrix}a-b, c, s-b\\a, c-b\end{matrix}\right]\,_2F_2\!\left(\begin{matrix}b, c-a;\ -\frac{\sigma}{\omega}\\b-a+1, b-s+1\end{matrix}\right)$$

$$[\mathrm{Re}\,\sigma,\ \mathrm{Re}\,s,\ \mathrm{Re}\,(s-a-b+c) > 0;\ |\arg\omega| < \pi]$$

3	$(\sigma-x)_+^{c-1}\,e^{\tau x}$ $\times\,_2F_1\!\left(\begin{matrix}a, b\\c; \omega(\sigma-x)\end{matrix}\right)$	$\sigma^{s+c-1}\,\mathrm{B}(s, c)\,\Xi_1(a, s, b; s+c; \sigma\omega, \sigma\tau)$ $\qquad[\sigma,\ \mathrm{Re}\,c,\ \mathrm{Re}\,s > 0]$

4	$e^{-\sigma/x}\,_2F_1\!\left(\begin{matrix}a, b\\c; -\omega x\end{matrix}\right)$	$\omega^{-s}\Gamma\!\left[\begin{matrix}c, s, a-s, b-s\\a, b, c-s\end{matrix}\right]\,_2F_2\!\left(\begin{matrix}a-s, b-s;\ \sigma\omega\\1-s, c-s\end{matrix}\right)$

$$+\sigma^s\,\Gamma(-s)\,_2F_2\!\left(\begin{matrix}a, b;\ \sigma\omega\\c, s+1\end{matrix}\right)$$

$$[\mathrm{Re}\,\sigma > 0;\ \mathrm{Re}\,s < \mathrm{Re}\,a,\ \mathrm{Re}\,b;\ |\arg\omega| < \pi]$$

5	$e^{-\sigma\sqrt{x}}\,_2F_1\!\left(\begin{matrix}a, b\\c; -\omega x\end{matrix}\right)$	$\dfrac{2\sigma^{2a-2s}}{\omega^a}\Gamma\!\left[\begin{matrix}c, b-a, 2s-2a\\b, c-a\end{matrix}\right]\,_2F_3\!\left(\begin{matrix}a, a-c+1;\ -\frac{\sigma^2}{4\omega}\\a-b+1, a-s+1, \frac{2a-2s-1}{2}\end{matrix}\right)$

$$+\frac{2\sigma^{2b-2s}}{\omega^b}\Gamma\!\left[\begin{matrix}c, a-b, 2s-2b\\a, c-b\end{matrix}\right]$$

$$\times\,_2F_3\!\left(\begin{matrix}b, b-c+1;\ -\frac{\sigma^2}{4\omega}\\b-a+1, b-s+1, \frac{2b-2s-1}{2}\end{matrix}\right)$$

$$+\omega^{-s}\Gamma\!\left[\begin{matrix}c, s, a-s, b-s\\a, b, c-s\end{matrix}\right]\,_2F_3\!\left(\begin{matrix}s, s-c+1;\ -\frac{\sigma^2}{4\omega}\\\frac12, s-a+1, s-b+1\end{matrix}\right)$$

$$-\frac{\sigma}{\omega^{s+1/2}}\Gamma\!\left[\begin{matrix}c, \frac{2s+1}{2}, \frac{2a-2s-1}{2}, \frac{2b-2s-1}{2}\\a, b, \frac{2c-2s-1}{2}\end{matrix}\right]\,_2F_3\!\left(\begin{matrix}\frac{2s+1}{2}, \frac{2s-2c+3}{2};\ -\frac{\sigma^2}{4\omega}\\\frac32, \frac{2s-2a+3}{2}, \frac{2s-2b+3}{2}\end{matrix}\right)$$

$$[\mathrm{Re}\,\sigma,\ \mathrm{Re}\,s > 0;\ |\arg\omega| < \pi]$$

No.	$f(x)$	$F(s)$
6	$e^{-\sigma\sqrt{x}}\,{}_2F_1\left(\begin{matrix} a,\,b \\ c;\,1-\omega x \end{matrix}\right)$	$\dfrac{2\sigma^{2a-2s}}{\omega^a}\,\Gamma\left[\begin{matrix} c,\,b-a,\,2s-2a \\ b,\,c-a \end{matrix}\right]\,{}_2F_3\left(\begin{matrix} a,\,c-b;\,\frac{\sigma^2}{4\omega} \\ a-b+1,\,a-s+1,\,\frac{2a-2s+1}{2} \end{matrix}\right)$
		$\qquad+\dfrac{2\sigma^{2b-2s}}{\omega^b}\,\Gamma\left[\begin{matrix} c,\,a-b,\,2s-2b \\ a,\,c-b \end{matrix}\right]$
		$\qquad\times\,{}_2F_3\left(\begin{matrix} b,\,c-a;\,\frac{\sigma^2}{4\omega} \\ b-a+1,\,b-s+1,\,\frac{2b-2s+1}{2} \end{matrix}\right)$
		$\qquad+\omega^{-s}\,\Gamma\left[\begin{matrix} c,\,s,\,a-s,\,b-s,\,s-a-b+c \\ a,\,b,\,c-a,\,c-b \end{matrix}\right]$
		$\qquad\times\,{}_2F_3\left(\begin{matrix} s,\,s-a-b+c;\,\frac{\sigma^2}{4\omega} \\ \frac{1}{2},\,s-a+1,\,s-b+1 \end{matrix}\right)$
		$\qquad-\dfrac{\sigma}{\omega^{s+1/2}}\,\Gamma\left[\begin{matrix} c,\,\frac{2s+1}{2},\,\frac{2a-2s-1}{2},\,\frac{2b-2s-1}{2},\,\frac{2s-2a-2b+2c+1}{2} \\ a,\,b,\,c-a,\,c-b \end{matrix}\right]$
		$\qquad\times\,{}_2F_3\left(\begin{matrix} \frac{2s+1}{2},\,\frac{2s-2a-2b+2c+1}{2};\,\frac{\sigma^2}{4\omega} \\ \frac{3}{2},\,\frac{2s-2a+3}{2},\,\frac{2s-2b+3}{2} \end{matrix}\right)$
		$[\operatorname{Re}\sigma,\ \operatorname{Re}s,\ \operatorname{Re}(s-a-b+c)>0;\ \lvert\arg\omega\rvert<\pi]$
7	$e^{-\sigma/\sqrt{x}}\,{}_2F_1\left(\begin{matrix} a,\,b \\ c;\,-\omega x \end{matrix}\right)$	$\omega^{-s}\,\Gamma\left[\begin{matrix} c,\,s,\,a-s,\,b-s \\ a,\,b,\,c-s \end{matrix}\right]\,{}_2F_3\left(\begin{matrix} a-s,\,b-s;\,-\frac{\sigma^2\omega}{4} \\ \frac{1}{2},\,1-s,\,c-s \end{matrix}\right)$
		$\qquad+\dfrac{\sigma^{2s}}{\sqrt{\pi}\,2^{2s}}\,\Gamma\left(\frac{1}{2}-s\right)\Gamma(-s)\,{}_2F_3\left(\begin{matrix} a,\,b;\,-\frac{\sigma^2\omega}{4} \\ c,\,\frac{2s+1}{2},\,s+1 \end{matrix}\right)$
		$\qquad-\sigma\omega^{1/2-s}\,\Gamma\left[\begin{matrix} c,\,\frac{2s-1}{2},\,\frac{2a-2s+1}{2},\,\frac{2b-2s+1}{2} \\ a,\,b,\,\frac{2c-2s+1}{2} \end{matrix}\right]$
		$\qquad\times\,{}_2F_3\left(\begin{matrix} \frac{2a-2s+1}{2},\,\frac{2b-2s+1}{2};\,-\frac{\sigma^2\omega}{4} \\ \frac{3}{2},\,\frac{3-2s}{2},\,\frac{2c-2s+1}{2} \end{matrix}\right)$
		$[\operatorname{Re}\sigma>0;\ \operatorname{Re}s<\operatorname{Re}a,\ \operatorname{Re}b;\ -\pi<\arg\omega\leq\pi]$
8	$(\omega-x)_+^{c-1}\,e^{-\sigma x}$	$\omega^{s+c-1}\,\Gamma\left[\begin{matrix} c,\,s,\,s-a-b+c \\ s-a+c,\,s-b+c \end{matrix}\right]\,{}_2F_2\left(\begin{matrix} s,\,s-a-b+c;\,-\sigma\omega \\ s-a+c,\,s-b+c \end{matrix}\right)$
	$\times\,{}_2F_1\left(\begin{matrix} a,\,b \\ c;\,\frac{\omega-x}{\omega} \end{matrix}\right)$	$[\omega,\ \operatorname{Re}c,\ \operatorname{Re}s,\ \operatorname{Re}(s-a-b+c)>0]$
9	$(\omega-x)_+^{c-1}\,e^{-\sigma\sqrt{x}}$	$\omega^{s+c-1}\,\Gamma\left[\begin{matrix} c,\,s,\,s-a-b+c \\ s-a+c,\,s-b+c \end{matrix}\right]\,{}_2F_3\left(\begin{matrix} s,\,s-a-b+c;\,\frac{\sigma^2\omega}{4} \\ \frac{1}{2},\,s-a+c,\,s-b+c \end{matrix}\right)$
	$\times\,{}_2F_1\left(\begin{matrix} a,\,b \\ c;\,\frac{\omega-x}{\omega} \end{matrix}\right)$	$\qquad-\sigma\omega^{s+c-1/2}\,\Gamma\left[\begin{matrix} c,\,\frac{2s+1}{2},\,\frac{2s-2a-2b+2c+1}{2} \\ \frac{2s-2a+2c+1}{2},\,\frac{2s-2b+2c+1}{2} \end{matrix}\right]$
		$\qquad\times\,{}_2F_3\left(\begin{matrix} \frac{2s+1}{2},\,\frac{2s-2a-2b+2c+1}{2};\,\frac{\sigma^2\omega}{4} \\ \frac{3}{2},\,\frac{2s-2a+2c+1}{2},\,\frac{2s-2b+2c+1}{2} \end{matrix}\right)$
		$[\omega,\ \operatorname{Re}c,\ \operatorname{Re}s,\ \operatorname{Re}(s-a-b+c)>0]$

No.	$f(x)$	$F(s)$
10	$(x - \omega)_+^{c-1} e^{-\sigma x}$ $\times {}_2F_1\left(\begin{array}{c} a, b \\ c;\ \frac{\omega - x}{\omega} \end{array}\right)$	$\omega^{s+c-1} \Gamma \left[\begin{array}{c} c,\, a - c - s + 1,\, b - c - s + 1 \\ 1 - s,\, a + b - c - s + 1 \end{array}\right]$ $\times {}_2F_2\left(\begin{array}{c} s,\, s - a - b + c;\ -\sigma\omega \\ s - a + c,\, s - b + c \end{array}\right)$ $+ \sigma^{a-c-s+1}\omega^a \Gamma \left[\begin{array}{c} b - a,\, c,\, s - a + c - 1 \\ b,\, c - a \end{array}\right]$ $\times {}_2F_2\left(\begin{array}{c} 1 - b,\, a - c + 1;\ -\sigma\omega \\ a - b + 1,\, a - c - s + 2 \end{array}\right)$ $+ \sigma^{b-c-s+1}\omega^b \Gamma \left[\begin{array}{c} a - b,\, c,\, s - b + c - 1 \\ a,\, c - b \end{array}\right]$ $\times {}_2F_2\left(\begin{array}{c} 1 - a,\, b - c + 1;\ -\sigma\omega \\ b - a + 1,\, b - c - s + 2 \end{array}\right)$ $[\omega,\, \mathrm{Re}\, c,\, \mathrm{Re}\, \sigma > 0]$
11	$(x - \omega)_+^{c-1} e^{-\sigma\sqrt{x}}$ $\times {}_2F_1\left(\begin{array}{c} a, b \\ c;\ \frac{\omega - x}{\omega} \end{array}\right)$	$\omega^{c+s-1} \Gamma \left[\begin{array}{c} c,\, a - c - s + 1,\, b - c - s + 1 \\ 1 - s,\, a + b - c - s + 1 \end{array}\right]$ $\times {}_2F_3\left(\begin{array}{c} s,\, s - a - b + c;\ \frac{\sigma^2\omega}{4} \\ \frac{1}{2},\, s - a + c,\, s - b + c \end{array}\right)$ $+ 2\sigma^{2(a-c-s+1)}\omega^a \Gamma \left[\begin{array}{c} b - a,\, c,\, 2s - 2a + 2c - 2 \\ b,\, c - a \end{array}\right]$ $\times {}_2F_3\left(\begin{array}{c} 1 - b,\, a - c + 1;\ \frac{\sigma^2\omega}{4} \\ a - b + 1,\, \frac{2a - 2c - 2s + 3}{2},\, a - c - s + 2 \end{array}\right)$ $+ 2\sigma^{2(b-c-s+1)}\omega^b \Gamma \left[\begin{array}{c} c,\, a - b,\, 2s - 2b + 2c - 2 \\ a,\, c - b \end{array}\right]$ $\times {}_2F_3\left(\begin{array}{c} 1 - a,\, b - c + 1;\ \frac{\sigma^2\omega}{4} \\ b - a + 1,\, \frac{2b - 2c - 2s + 3}{2},\, \frac{2b - 2c - 2s + 4}{2} \end{array}\right)$ $- \sigma\omega^{c+s-1/2} \Gamma \left[\begin{array}{c} c,\, \frac{2a - 2c - 2s + 1}{2},\, \frac{2b - 2c - 2s + 1}{2} \\ \frac{1-2s}{2},\, \frac{2a + 2b - 2c - 2s + 1}{2} \end{array}\right]$ $\times {}_2F_3\left(\begin{array}{c} \frac{2s+1}{2},\, \frac{2s - 2a - 2b + 2c + 1}{2};\ \frac{\sigma^2\omega}{4} \\ \frac{3}{2},\, \frac{2s - 2a + 2c + 1}{2},\, \frac{2s - 2b + 2c + 1}{2} \end{array}\right)$ $[\omega,\, \mathrm{Re}\, c,\, \mathrm{Re}\, \sigma > 0]$

3.31.30. $_2F_1(a, b; c; \omega x + \sigma)$ and trigonometric functions

Notation: $\delta = \left\{\begin{array}{c} 1 \\ 0 \end{array}\right\}$.

No.	$f(x)$	$F(s)$
1	$\left\{\begin{array}{c} \sin(\sigma\sqrt{x}) \\ \cos(\sigma\sqrt{x}) \end{array}\right\}$ $\times {}_2F_1\left(\begin{array}{c} a, b \\ c;\ -\omega x \end{array}\right)$	$\dfrac{2\sigma^{2a-2s}}{\omega^a} \Gamma \left[\begin{array}{c} b - a,\, c,\, 2s - 2a \\ b,\, c - a \end{array}\right] \left\{\begin{array}{c} \sin[(s - a)\pi] \\ \cos[(s - a)\pi] \end{array}\right\}$ $\times {}_2F_3\left(\begin{array}{c} a,\, a - c + 1;\ \frac{\sigma^2}{4\omega} \\ a - b + 1,\, \frac{2a - 2s + 1}{2},\, a - s + 1 \end{array}\right)$ $+ \dfrac{2\sigma^{2b-2s}}{\omega^b} \Gamma \left[\begin{array}{c} a - b,\, c,\, 2s - 2b \\ a,\, c - b \end{array}\right] \left\{\begin{array}{c} \sin[(s - b)\pi] \\ \cos[(s - b)\pi] \end{array}\right\} \times$

No.	$f(x)$	$F(s)$

$$\times \; _2F_3\left(\begin{matrix} b,\; b-c+1;\; \frac{\sigma^2}{4\omega} \\ b-a+1,\; \frac{2b-2s+1}{2},\; b-s+1 \end{matrix}\right)$$

$$+\frac{\sigma^\delta}{\omega^{s+\delta/2}}\,\Gamma\left[\begin{matrix} c,\; \frac{2s+\delta}{2},\; \frac{2a-2s-\delta}{2},\; \frac{2b-\delta-2s}{2} \\ a,\; b,\; \frac{2c-\delta-2s}{2} \end{matrix}\right]$$

$$\times \; _2F_3\left(\begin{matrix} s+\frac{\delta}{2},\; \frac{2s-2c+\delta+2}{2};\; \frac{\sigma^2}{4\omega} \\ \frac{2\delta+1}{2},\; \frac{2s-2a+\delta+2}{2},\; \frac{2s-2b+\delta+2}{2} \end{matrix}\right)$$

$$[\sigma>0;\; -\delta/2<\operatorname{Re}s<\operatorname{Re}a+1/2,\;\operatorname{Re}b+1/2;\;|\arg\omega|<\pi]$$

2 $\left\{\begin{matrix}\sin\left(\sigma/\sqrt{x}\right)\\\cos\left(\sigma/\sqrt{x}\right)\end{matrix}\right\}$

$$\frac{\sigma^\delta}{\omega^{s-\delta/2}}\,\Gamma\left[\begin{matrix} c,\; \frac{2s-\delta}{2},\; \frac{2a+\delta-2s}{2},\; \frac{2b+\delta-2s}{2} \\ a,\; b,\; \frac{2c+\delta-2s}{2} \end{matrix}\right]$$

$\qquad \times \; _2F_1\left(\begin{matrix}a,\,b\\c;\,-\omega x\end{matrix}\right)$

$$\times \; _2F_3\left(\begin{matrix} \frac{2a+\delta-2s}{2},\; \frac{2b+\delta-2s}{2};\; \frac{\sigma^2\omega}{4} \\ \frac{2\delta+1}{2},\; \frac{2c+\delta-2s}{2},\; \frac{\delta-2s+2}{2} \end{matrix}\right)$$

$$\mp 2\sigma^{2s}\,\Gamma\left(-2s\right)\left\{\begin{matrix}\sin\left(s\pi\right)\\\cos\left(s\pi\right)\end{matrix}\right\}\; _2F_3\left(\begin{matrix} a,\,b;\,\frac{\sigma^2\omega}{4} \\ c,\;\frac{2s+1}{2},\;s+1 \end{matrix}\right)$$

$$[\sigma>0;\; -1/2<\operatorname{Re}s<\operatorname{Re}a+\delta/2,\;\operatorname{Re}b+\delta/2;\;|\arg\omega|<\pi]$$

3 $\left\{\begin{matrix}\sin\left(\sigma\sqrt{x}\right)\\\cos\left(\sigma\sqrt{x}\right)\end{matrix}\right\}$

$$\frac{\sigma^\delta}{\omega^{s+\delta/2}}\,\Gamma\left[\begin{matrix} c,\; \frac{2s-2a-2b+2c+\delta}{2},\; \frac{2s+\delta}{2},\; \frac{2a-2s-\delta}{2},\; \frac{2b-2s-\delta}{2} \\ a,\; b,\; c-a,\; c-b \end{matrix}\right]$$

$\qquad \times \; _2F_1\left(\begin{matrix}a,\,b\\c;\,1-\omega x\end{matrix}\right)$

$$\times \; _2F_3\left(\begin{matrix} \frac{2s+\delta}{2},\; \frac{2s-2a-2b+2c+\delta}{2};\; -\frac{\sigma^2}{4\omega} \\ \frac{2\delta+1}{2},\; \frac{2s+\delta-2a+2}{2},\; \frac{2s+\delta-2b+2}{2} \end{matrix}\right)$$

$$+\frac{2\sigma^{2a-2s}}{\omega^a}\left\{\begin{matrix}\sin\left[(s-a)\pi\right]\\\cos\left[(s-a)\pi\right]\end{matrix}\right\}\Gamma\left[\begin{matrix} b-a,\; c,\; 2s-2a \\ b,\; c-a \end{matrix}\right]$$

$$\times \; _2F_3\left(\begin{matrix} a,\; c-b;\; -\frac{\sigma^2}{4\omega} \\ a-b+1,\; \frac{2a-2s+1}{2},\; a-s+1 \end{matrix}\right)$$

$$+\frac{2\sigma^{2b-2s}}{\omega^b}\left\{\begin{matrix}\sin\left[(s-b)\pi\right]\\\cos\left[(s-b)\pi\right]\end{matrix}\right\}\Gamma\left[\begin{matrix} a-b,\; c,\; 2s-2b \\ a,\; c-b \end{matrix}\right]$$

$$\times \; _2F_3\left(\begin{matrix} b,\; c-a;\; -\frac{\sigma^2}{4\omega} \\ b-a+1,\; \frac{2b-2s+1}{2},\; b-s+1 \end{matrix}\right)$$

$$\left[\begin{matrix}\sigma>0;\;\operatorname{Re}s,\;\operatorname{Re}\left(c-a-b+s\right)>-\delta/2;\\\operatorname{Re}\left(s-a\right),\;\operatorname{Re}\left(s-b\right)<1/2;\;|\arg\omega|<\pi\end{matrix}\right]$$

4 $(\omega-x)_+^{c-1}\left\{\begin{matrix}\sin\left(\sigma\sqrt{x}\right)\\\cos\left(\sigma\sqrt{x}\right)\end{matrix}\right\}$ $\sigma^\delta\omega^{s+c+\delta/2-1}\,\Gamma\left[\begin{matrix} c,\; \frac{2s+\delta}{2},\; \frac{2s-2a-2b+2c+\delta}{2} \\ \frac{2s-2a+2c+\delta}{2},\; \frac{2s-2b+2c+\delta}{2} \end{matrix}\right]$

$\qquad \times \; _2F_1\left(\begin{matrix}a,\,b\\c;\,\frac{\omega-x}{\omega}\end{matrix}\right)$

$$\times \; _2F_3\left(\begin{matrix} \frac{2s+\delta}{2},\; \frac{2s-2a-2b+2c+\delta}{2};\; -\frac{\sigma^2\omega}{4} \\ \frac{2\delta+1}{2},\; \frac{2s-2a+2c+\delta}{2},\; \frac{2s-2b+2c+\delta}{2} \end{matrix}\right)$$

$$[\omega,\;\operatorname{Re}c,\;\operatorname{Re}s>0;\;\operatorname{Re}\left(s-a-b+c\right)>-\delta/2]$$

No.	$f(x)$	$F(s)$
5	$(x-\omega)_+^{c-1} \left\{ \begin{matrix} \sin(\sigma\sqrt{x}) \\ \cos(\sigma\sqrt{x}) \end{matrix} \right\}$ $\times {}_2F_1 \left(\begin{matrix} a, b \\ c; \frac{\omega-x}{\omega} \end{matrix} \right)$	$\sigma^\delta \omega^{c+s+\delta/2-1} \Gamma \left[\begin{matrix} c, \frac{2a-2c-\delta-2s+2}{2}, \frac{2b-2c-\delta-2s+2}{2} \\ \frac{2-\delta-2s}{2}, \frac{2a+2b-2c-\delta-2s+2}{2} \end{matrix} \right]$ $\times {}_2F_3 \left(\begin{matrix} s+\frac{\delta}{2}, c-a-b+s+\frac{\delta}{2}; -\frac{\sigma^2\omega}{4} \\ \frac{2\delta+1}{2}, \frac{2s-2a+2c+\delta}{2}, \frac{2s-2b+2c+\delta}{2} \end{matrix} \right)$ $- 2\sigma^{2(a-c-s+1)}\omega^a \left\{ \begin{matrix} \sin[(s-a+c)\pi] \\ \cos[(s-a+c)\pi] \end{matrix} \right\}$ $\times \Gamma \left[\begin{matrix} b-a, c, 2s-2a+2c-2 \\ b, c-a \end{matrix} \right]$ $\times {}_2F_3 \left(\begin{matrix} 1-b, a-c+1; -\frac{\sigma^2\omega}{4} \\ a-b+1, a-c-s+\frac{3}{2}, a-c-s+2 \end{matrix} \right)$ $- 2\sigma^{2(b-c-s+1)}\omega^b \left\{ \begin{matrix} \sin[(s-b+c)\pi] \\ \cos[(s-b+c)\pi] \end{matrix} \right\}$ $\times \Gamma \left[\begin{matrix} a-b, c, 2s-2b+2c-2 \\ a, c-b \end{matrix} \right]$ $\times {}_2F_3 \left(\begin{matrix} 1-a, b-c+1; -\frac{\sigma^2\omega}{4} \\ b-a+1, b-c-s+\frac{3}{2}, b-c-s+2 \end{matrix} \right)$ $[\sigma, \omega, \operatorname{Re}c > 0; \operatorname{Re}(s-a+c), \operatorname{Re}(s-b+c) < 3/2]$

3.31.31. $_2F_1(a, b; c; \varphi(x))$ and the Bessel functions

No.	$f(x)$	$F(s)$
1	$J_\nu(\sigma\sqrt{x}) \, {}_2F_1 \left(\begin{matrix} a, b \\ c; -\omega x \end{matrix} \right)$	$\frac{(\sigma/2)^\nu}{\omega^{s+\nu/2}} \Gamma \left[\begin{matrix} c, \frac{2s+\nu}{2}, \frac{2a-\nu-2s}{2}, \frac{2b-\nu-2s}{2} \\ a, b, \nu+1, \frac{2c-\nu-2s}{2} \end{matrix} \right]$ $\times {}_2F_3 \left(\begin{matrix} \frac{2s+\nu}{2}, \frac{2s+\nu-2c+2}{2}; \frac{\sigma^2}{4\omega} \\ \nu+1, \frac{2s+\nu-2a+2}{2}, \frac{2s+\nu-2b+2}{2} \end{matrix} \right) + \frac{(\sigma/2)^{2a-2s}}{\omega^a} \Gamma \left[\begin{matrix} c, b-a \\ b, c-a \end{matrix} \right]$ $\times \Gamma \left[\begin{matrix} \frac{2s-2a+\nu}{2} \\ \frac{2-2s+2a+\nu}{2} \end{matrix} \right] {}_2F_3 \left(\begin{matrix} a, a-c+1; \frac{\sigma^2}{4\omega} \\ a-b+1, \frac{2a+\nu-2s+2}{2}, \frac{2a-\nu-2s+2}{2} \end{matrix} \right)$ $+ \frac{(\sigma/2)^{2b-2s}}{\omega^b} \Gamma \left[\begin{matrix} c, a-b, \frac{2s+\nu-2b}{2} \\ a, c-b, \frac{2b+\nu-2s+2}{2} \end{matrix} \right]$ $\times {}_2F_3 \left(\begin{matrix} b, b-c+1; \frac{\sigma^2}{4\omega} \\ b-a+1, \frac{2b-\nu-2s+2}{2}, \frac{2b+\nu-2s+2}{2} \end{matrix} \right)$ $[\sigma, \operatorname{Re}(2s+\nu) > 0; \operatorname{Re}(s-a), \operatorname{Re}(s-b) < 3/4; |\arg\omega| < \pi]$
2	$J_\nu \left(\frac{\sigma}{\sqrt{x}} \right) \, {}_2F_1 \left(\begin{matrix} a, b \\ c; -\omega x \end{matrix} \right)$	$\left(\frac{\sigma}{2} \right)^{2s} \Gamma \left[\begin{matrix} \frac{\nu-2s}{2} \\ \frac{2s+\nu+2}{2} \end{matrix} \right] {}_2F_3 \left(\begin{matrix} a, b; \frac{\sigma^2\omega}{4} \\ c, \frac{2s-\nu+2}{2}, \frac{2s+\nu+2}{2} \end{matrix} \right) + \frac{(\sigma/2)^\nu}{\omega^{s-\nu/2}} \Gamma \left[\begin{matrix} c \\ a, b \end{matrix} \right]$ $\times \Gamma \left[\begin{matrix} \frac{2s-\nu}{2}, \frac{2a-2s+\nu}{2}, \frac{2b-2s+\nu}{2} \\ \nu+1, \frac{2c-2s+\nu}{2} \end{matrix} \right] {}_2F_3 \left(\begin{matrix} \frac{2a+\nu-2s}{2}, \frac{2b+\nu-2s}{2}; \frac{\sigma^2\omega}{4} \\ \nu+1, \frac{\nu-2s+2}{2}, \frac{\nu+2c-2s}{2} \end{matrix} \right)$ $[\sigma > 0; \, -3/4 < \operatorname{Re}s < \operatorname{Re}(a+\nu/2), \operatorname{Re}(b+\nu/2); |\arg\omega| < \pi]$

No.	$f(x)$	$F(s)$
3	$J_\nu(\sigma\sqrt{x})$ $\times {}_2F_1\left({a,\,b \atop c;\,1-\omega x}\right)$	$\dfrac{(\sigma/2)^{2a-2s}}{\omega^a}\,\Gamma\!\left[{b-a,\,c,\,\frac{2s-2a+\nu}{2} \atop b,\,c-a,\,\frac{2-2s+2a+\nu}{2}}\right]$ $\times {}_2F_3\!\left({a,\,c-b;\,-\frac{\sigma^2}{4\omega} \atop a-b+1,\,\frac{2-2s+2a-\nu}{2},\,\frac{2-2s+2a+\nu}{2}}\right) + \dfrac{(\sigma/2)^{2b-2s}}{\omega^b}\,\Gamma\!\left[{a-b,\,c \atop a,\,c-b}\right]$ $\times \Gamma\!\left[{\frac{2s-2b+\nu}{2} \atop \frac{2-2s+2b+\nu}{2}}\right] {}_2F_3\!\left({b,\,c-a;\,-\frac{\sigma^2}{4\omega} \atop 1-a+b,\,\frac{2-2s+2b-\nu}{2},\,\frac{2-2s+2b+\nu}{2}}\right)$ $+ \dfrac{(\sigma/2)^\nu}{\omega^{s+\nu/2}}\,\Gamma\!\left[{c,\,\frac{2s+\nu}{2},\,\frac{2a-2s-\nu}{2},\,\frac{2b-2s-\nu}{2},\,\frac{2s-2a-2b+2c+\nu}{2} \atop a,\,b,\,c-a,\,c-b,\,\nu+1}\right]$ $\times {}_2F_3\!\left({\frac{2s+\nu}{2},\,\frac{2s-2a-2b+2c+\nu}{2};\,-\frac{\sigma^2}{4\omega} \atop \nu+1,\,\frac{2s-2a+\nu+2}{2},\,\frac{2s-2b+\nu+2}{2}}\right)$ $\left[{\sigma,\,\mathrm{Re}\,(s-a-b+c+\nu/2),\,\mathrm{Re}\,(2s+\nu)>0; \atop \mathrm{Re}\,(s-a),\,\mathrm{Re}\,(s-b)<3/4;\,|\arg\omega|<\pi}\right]$
4	$(\omega-x)_+^{c-1}\,J_\nu(\sigma\sqrt{x})$ $\times {}_2F_1\left({a,\,b \atop c;\,\frac{\omega-x}{\omega}}\right)$	$\left(\dfrac{\sigma}{2}\right)^\nu \omega^{s+c+\nu/2-1}\,\Gamma\!\left[{c,\,\frac{2s+\nu}{2},\,\frac{2s+2c-2a-2b+\nu}{2} \atop \nu+1,\,\frac{2s-2a+2c+\nu}{2},\,\frac{2s-2b+2c+\nu}{2}}\right]$ $\times {}_2F_3\!\left({\frac{2s+\nu}{2},\,\frac{2s-2a-2b+2c+\nu}{2};\,-\frac{\sigma^2\omega}{4} \atop \nu+1,\,\frac{2s-2a+2c+\nu}{2},\,\frac{2s-2b+2c+\nu}{2}}\right)$ $[\omega,\,\mathrm{Re}\,c,\,\mathrm{Re}\,(2s+\nu),\,\mathrm{Re}\,(c-a-b+s+\nu/2)>0]$
5	$(x-\omega)_+^{c-1}\,J_\nu(\sigma\sqrt{x})$ $\times {}_2F_1\left({a,\,b \atop c;\,\frac{\omega-x}{\omega}}\right)$	$\left(\dfrac{\sigma}{2}\right)^{2(a-c-s+1)}\omega^a\,\Gamma\!\left[{c,\,b-a,\,\frac{2s-2a+2c+\nu-2}{2} \atop c-a,\,b,\,\frac{2a-2c+\nu-2s+4}{2}}\right]$ $\times {}_2F_3\!\left({1-b,\,a-c+1;\,-\frac{\sigma^2\omega}{4} \atop a-b+1,\,\frac{2a-2c+\nu-2s+4}{2},\,\frac{2a-2c-\nu-2s+4}{2}}\right)$ $+ \left(\dfrac{\sigma}{2}\right)^{2(b-c-s+1)}\omega^b\,\Gamma\!\left[{a-b,\,c,\,\frac{2s-2b+2c+\nu-2}{2} \atop a,\,c-b,\,\frac{2b-2c+\nu-2s+4}{2}}\right]$ $\times {}_2F_3\!\left({1-a,\,b-c+1;\,-\frac{\sigma^2\omega}{4} \atop b-a+1,\,\frac{2b-2c-\nu-2s+4}{2},\,\frac{2b-2c+\nu-2s+4}{2}}\right)$ $+ \left(\dfrac{\sigma}{2}\right)^\nu \omega^{s+c+\nu/2-1}\,\Gamma\!\left[{c,\,\frac{2a-2c-\nu-2s+2}{2},\,\frac{2b-2c-\nu-2s+2}{2} \atop \nu+1,\,\frac{2-\nu-2s}{2},\,\frac{2a+2b-2c-\nu-2s+2}{2}}\right]$ $\times {}_2F_3\!\left({\frac{2s+\nu}{2},\,\frac{2s-2a-2b+2c+\nu}{2};\,-\frac{\sigma^2\omega}{4} \atop \nu+1,\,\frac{2s-2a+2c+\nu}{2},\,\frac{2s-2b+2c+\nu}{2}}\right)$ $[\sigma,\,\omega>0;\,\mathrm{Re}\,(s-a+c),\,\mathrm{Re}\,(s-b+c)<7/4]$
6	$(\omega-x)_+^{c-1}\,I_\nu(\sigma\sqrt{x})$ $\times {}_2F_1\left({a,\,b \atop c;\,\frac{\omega-x}{\omega}}\right)$	$\left(\dfrac{\sigma}{2}\right)^\nu \omega^{s+c+\nu/2-1}\,\Gamma\!\left[{c,\,\frac{2s+\nu}{2},\,\frac{2s-2a-2b+2c+\nu}{2} \atop \nu+1,\,\frac{2s-2a+2c+\nu}{2},\,\frac{2s-2b+2c+\nu}{2}}\right]$ $\times {}_2F_3\!\left({\frac{2s+\nu}{2},\,\frac{2s-2a-2b+2c+\nu}{2};\,\frac{\sigma^2\omega}{4} \atop \nu+1,\,\frac{2s-2a+2c+\nu}{2},\,\frac{2s-2b+2c+\nu}{2}}\right)$ $[\omega,\,\mathrm{Re}\,c,\,\mathrm{Re}\,(2s+\nu),\,\mathrm{Re}\,(s-a-b+c+\nu/2)>0]$

No.	$f(x)$	$F(s)$

7 $K_\nu(\sigma\sqrt{x})$

$\times\, _2F_1\left(\begin{matrix} a,\, b \\ c;\, -\omega x \end{matrix}\right)$

$$\frac{(\sigma/2)^{2a-2s}}{2\omega^a}\,\Gamma\left[\begin{matrix} b-a,\, c,\, \frac{2s-2a+\nu}{2},\, \frac{2s-2a-\nu}{2} \\ b,\, c-a \end{matrix}\right]$$

$$\times\, _2F_3\left(\begin{matrix} a,\, a-c+1;\, -\frac{\sigma^2}{4\omega} \\ a-b+1,\, \frac{2a-2s+\nu+2}{2},\, \frac{2a-2s-\nu+2}{2} \end{matrix}\right)$$

$$+\frac{(\sigma/2)^{2b-2s}}{2\omega^b}\,\Gamma\left[\begin{matrix} a-b,\, c,\, \frac{2s-2b+\nu}{2},\, \frac{2s-2b-\nu}{2} \\ a,\, c-b \end{matrix}\right]$$

$$\times\, _2F_3\left(\begin{matrix} b,\, b-c+1;\, -\frac{\sigma^2}{4\omega} \\ b-a+1,\, \frac{2b-2s+\nu+2}{2},\, \frac{2b-2s-\nu+2}{2} \end{matrix}\right)$$

$$+\frac{(\sigma/2)^\nu}{2\omega^{s+\nu/2}}\,\Gamma\left[\begin{matrix} c,\, -\nu,\, \frac{2s+\nu}{2},\, \frac{2a-2s-\nu}{2},\, \frac{2b-2s-\nu}{2} \\ a,\, b,\, \frac{2c-2s-\nu}{2} \end{matrix}\right]$$

$$\times\, _2F_3\left(\begin{matrix} \frac{2s+\nu}{2},\, \frac{2s-2c+\nu+2}{2};\, -\frac{\sigma^2}{4\omega} \\ \nu+1,\, \frac{2s-2a+\nu+2}{2},\, \frac{2s-2b+\nu+2}{2} \end{matrix}\right)$$

$$+\frac{(2/\sigma)^\nu}{2\omega^{s-\nu/2}}\,\Gamma\left[\begin{matrix} c,\, \nu,\, \frac{2s-\nu}{2},\, \frac{2a-2s+\nu}{2},\, \frac{2b-2s+\nu}{2} \\ a,\, b,\, \frac{2c-2s+\nu}{2} \end{matrix}\right]$$

$$\times\, _2F_3\left(\begin{matrix} \frac{2s-\nu}{2},\, \frac{2s-2c-\nu+2}{2};\, -\frac{\sigma^2}{4\omega} \\ 1-\nu,\, \frac{2s-2a-\nu+2}{2},\, \frac{2s-2b-\nu+2}{2} \end{matrix}\right)$$

$$[\operatorname{Re}\sigma > 0;\ \operatorname{Re} s > |\operatorname{Re}\nu|/2;\ |\arg\omega| < \pi]$$

8 $K_\nu\left(\dfrac{\sigma}{\sqrt{x}}\right)$

$\times\, _2F_1\left(\begin{matrix} a,\, b \\ c;\, -\omega x \end{matrix}\right)$

$$\frac{(\sigma/2)^\nu}{2\omega^{s-\nu/2}}\,\Gamma\left[\begin{matrix} c,\, -\nu,\, \frac{2s-\nu}{2},\, \frac{2a-2s+\nu}{2},\, \frac{2b-2s+\nu}{2} \\ a,\, b,\, \frac{2c-2s+\nu}{2} \end{matrix}\right]$$

$$\times\, _2F_3\left(\begin{matrix} \frac{2a-2s+\nu}{2},\, \frac{2b-2s+\nu}{2};\, -\frac{\sigma^2\omega}{4} \\ 1+\nu,\, \frac{2-2s+\nu}{2},\, \frac{2c-2s+\nu}{2} \end{matrix}\right)$$

$$+\frac{(\sigma/2)^{-\nu}}{2\omega^{s+\nu/2}}\,\Gamma\left[\begin{matrix} c,\, \nu,\, \frac{2s+\nu}{2},\, \frac{2a-2s-\nu}{2},\, \frac{2b-2s-\nu}{2} \\ a,\, b,\, \frac{2c-2s-\nu}{2} \end{matrix}\right]$$

$$\times\, _2F_3\left(\begin{matrix} \frac{2a-2s-\nu}{2},\, \frac{2b-2s-\nu}{2};\, -\frac{\sigma^2\omega}{4} \\ 1-\nu,\, \frac{2-2s-\nu}{2},\, \frac{2c-2s-\nu}{2} \end{matrix}\right) + \frac{(\sigma/2)^{2s}}{2}\,\Gamma\left(\frac{\nu-2s}{2}\right)$$

$$\times\,\Gamma\left(-\frac{2s+\nu}{2}\right)\,_2F_3\left(\begin{matrix} a,\, b;\, -\frac{\sigma^2\omega}{4} \\ c,\, \frac{2s-\nu+2}{2},\, \frac{2s+\nu+2}{2} \end{matrix}\right)$$

$$[\operatorname{Re}\sigma > 0;\ \operatorname{Re} s < \operatorname{Re} a - |\operatorname{Re}\nu|/2,\ \operatorname{Re} b - |\operatorname{Re}\nu|/2;\ |\arg\omega| < \pi]$$

9 $(\omega - x)_+^{c-1}\, K_\nu(\sigma\sqrt{x})$

$\times\, _2F_1\left(\begin{matrix} a,\, b \\ c;\, \frac{\omega-x}{\omega} \end{matrix}\right)$

$$\frac{2^{\nu-1}\omega^{s+c-\nu/2-1}}{\sigma^\nu}\,\Gamma\left[\begin{matrix} c,\, \nu,\, \frac{2s-\nu}{2},\, \frac{2s-2a-2b+2c-\nu}{2} \\ \frac{2s-2a+2c-\nu}{2},\, \frac{2s-2b+2c-\nu}{2} \end{matrix}\right]$$

$$\times\, _2F_3\left(\begin{matrix} \frac{2s-\nu}{2},\, \frac{2s-2a-2b+2c-\nu}{2};\, \frac{\sigma^2\omega}{4} \\ 1-\nu,\, \frac{2s-2a+2c-\nu}{2},\, \frac{2s-2b+2c-\nu}{2} \end{matrix}\right)$$

$$+\frac{\sigma^\nu\omega^{s+c+\nu/2-1}}{2^{\nu+1}}\,\Gamma\left[\begin{matrix} c,\, -\nu,\, \frac{2s+\nu}{2},\, \frac{2s-2a-2b+2c+\nu}{2} \\ \frac{2s-2a+2c+\nu}{2},\, \frac{2s-2b+2c+\nu}{2} \end{matrix}\right]$$

$$\times\, _2F_3\left(\begin{matrix} \frac{2s+\nu}{2},\, \frac{2s-2a-2b+2c+\nu}{2};\, \frac{\sigma^2\omega}{4} \\ 1+\nu,\, \frac{2s-2a+2c+\nu}{2},\, \frac{2s-2b+2c+\nu}{2} \end{matrix}\right)$$

$$[\omega,\ \operatorname{Re} c > 0;\ \operatorname{Re} s,\ \operatorname{Re}(s-a-b+c) > |\operatorname{Re}\nu|/2]$$

3.31.32. $_2F_1^2(a, b; c; \varphi(x))$

1	$_2F_1^2\left(\begin{matrix}a,\ b;\ -\frac{x}{\omega}\\ \frac{2a+2b+1}{2}\end{matrix}\right)$	$\dfrac{2^{2a+2b-1}\omega^s}{\sqrt{\pi}}\,\Gamma\left[\begin{matrix}\frac{2a+2b+1}{2},\ \frac{2a+2b+1}{2}\\ 2a,\ 2b\end{matrix}\right]\Gamma\left[\begin{matrix}s,\ 2a-s,\ 2b-s,\ a+b-s\\ 2a+2b-s,\ \frac{2a+2b-2s+1}{2}\end{matrix}\right]$
		$[0 < \operatorname{Re} s < 2\operatorname{Re}a,\ 2\operatorname{Re}b;\ |\arg\omega| < \pi]$
2	$(x+\omega)\,_2F_1^2\left(\begin{matrix}a,\ b;\ -\frac{x}{\omega}\\ \frac{2a+2b-1}{2}\end{matrix}\right)$	$\dfrac{2^{2a+2b-3}\omega^{s+1}}{\sqrt{\pi}}\,\Gamma\left[\begin{matrix}\frac{2a+2b-1}{2},\ \frac{2a+2b-1}{2}\\ 2a-1,\ 2b-1\end{matrix}\right]$
		$\times\,\Gamma\left[\begin{matrix}s,\ 2a-s-1,\ 2b-s-1,\ a+b-s-1\\ 2a+2b-s-2,\ \frac{2a+2b-2s-1}{2}\end{matrix}\right]$
		$[0 < \operatorname{Re} s < 2\operatorname{Re}a-1,\ 2\operatorname{Re}b-1;\ |\arg\omega| < \pi]$
3	$_2F_1^2\left(\begin{matrix}a,\ b;\ -\frac{\omega}{x}\\ \frac{2a+2b+1}{2}\end{matrix}\right)$	$\dfrac{2^{2a+2b-1}\omega^s}{\sqrt{\pi}}\,\Gamma\left[\begin{matrix}\frac{2a+2b+1}{2},\ \frac{2a+2b+1}{2}\\ 2a,\ 2b\end{matrix}\right]\Gamma\left[\begin{matrix}-s,\ s+2a,\ s+2b,\ s+a+b\\ s+2a+2b,\ \frac{2s+2a+2b+1}{2}\end{matrix}\right]$
		$[-2\operatorname{Re}a,\ -2\operatorname{Re}b < \operatorname{Re} s < 0;\ |\arg\omega| < \pi]$
4	$(x+\omega)\,_2F_1^2\left(\begin{matrix}a,\ b;\ -\frac{\omega}{x}\\ \frac{2a+2b-1}{2}\end{matrix}\right)$	$\dfrac{2^{2a+2b-3}\omega^{s+1}}{\sqrt{\pi}}\,\Gamma\left[\begin{matrix}\frac{2a+2b-1}{2},\ \frac{2a+2b-1}{2}\\ 2a-1,\ 2b-1\end{matrix}\right]$
		$\times\,\Gamma\left[\begin{matrix}-s-1,\ s+2a,\ s+2b,\ s+a+b\\ s+2a+2b-1,\ \frac{2s+2a+2b+1}{2}\end{matrix}\right]$
		$[-2\operatorname{Re}a,\ -2\operatorname{Re}b < \operatorname{Re} s < -1;\ -\pi < \arg\omega \le \pi]$
5	$(x+\omega)^{-2a}$ $\times\,_2F_1^2\left(\begin{matrix}a,\ \frac{2a+1}{2}\\ c;\ \frac{\omega}{x+\omega}\end{matrix}\right)$	$\dfrac{4^{c-1}\omega^{s-2a}}{\sqrt{\pi}}\,\Gamma\left[\begin{matrix}c,\ c\\ 2a,\ 2c-2a-1\end{matrix}\right]$ $\times\,\Gamma\left[\begin{matrix}s,\ 2a-s,\ s-4a+2c-1,\ \frac{2s-4a+2c-1}{2}\\ s-2a+c,\ s-2a+2c-1\end{matrix}\right]$
		$[0,\ \operatorname{Re}(2a-c)+1/2 < \operatorname{Re} s < 2\operatorname{Re}a;\ |\arg\omega| < \pi]$
6	$(x+\omega)^{-2a}$ $\times\,_2F_1^2\left(\begin{matrix}a,\ \frac{2a+1}{2}\\ c;\ \frac{x}{x+\omega}\end{matrix}\right)$	$\dfrac{4^{c-1}\omega^{s-2a}}{\sqrt{\pi}}\,\Gamma\left[\begin{matrix}c,\ c\\ 2a,\ 2c-2a-1\end{matrix}\right]$ $\times\,\Gamma\left[\begin{matrix}s,\ 2a-s,\ \frac{2c-2s-1}{2},\ 2c-2a-s-1\\ c-s,\ 2c-s-1\end{matrix}\right]$
		$[0 < \operatorname{Re} s < 2\operatorname{Re}a,\ 2\operatorname{Re}(c-a)-1;\ |\arg\omega| < \pi]$
7	$_2F_1^2\left(\begin{matrix}a,\ b;\ \frac{\sqrt{\omega}-\sqrt{x+\omega}}{2\sqrt{\omega}}\\ \frac{a+b+1}{2}\end{matrix}\right)$	$\dfrac{2^{a+b-1}\omega^s}{\sqrt{\pi}}\,\Gamma\left[\begin{matrix}\frac{a+b+1}{2},\ \frac{a+b+1}{2}\\ a,\ b\end{matrix}\right]\Gamma\left[\begin{matrix}s,\ a-s,\ b-s,\ \frac{a+b-2s}{2}\\ a+b-s,\ \frac{a+b-2s+1}{2}\end{matrix}\right]$
		$[0 < \operatorname{Re} s < \operatorname{Re}a,\ \operatorname{Re}b;\ |\arg\omega| < \pi]$

No.	$f(x)$	$F(s)$
8	$\left(\sqrt{x+\omega}+\sqrt{\omega}\right)^{2-2c}$ $\times \, _2F_1^2\left(\begin{array}{c} a,\,1-a \\ c;\, \frac{\sqrt{\omega}-\sqrt{x+\omega}}{2\sqrt{\omega}} \end{array}\right)$	$\dfrac{\omega^{s-c+1}}{\sqrt{\pi}}\Gamma\left[\begin{array}{c} c,\,c \\ c-a,\,a+c-1 \end{array}\right]$ $\times \Gamma\left[\begin{array}{c} s,\,c-a-s,\,a+c-s-1,\,\frac{2c-2s-1}{2} \\ c-s,\,2c-s-1 \end{array}\right]$ $[0 < \operatorname{Re}s < \operatorname{Re}(c-a),\,\operatorname{Re}(a+c)-1;\,-\pi < \arg\omega \le \pi]$
9	$\left(\sqrt{x+\omega}-\sqrt{\omega}\right)^{2c-2}$ $\times \, _2F_1^2\left(\begin{array}{c} a,\,1-a \\ c;\, \frac{\sqrt{\omega}-\sqrt{x+\omega}}{2\sqrt{\omega}} \end{array}\right)$	$\dfrac{\omega^{s+c-1}}{\sqrt{\pi}}\Gamma\left[\begin{array}{c} c,\,c \\ c-a,\,a+c-1 \end{array}\right]$ $\times \Gamma\left[\begin{array}{c} \frac{3-2s-2c}{2},\,2-s-a-c,\,1-s+a-c,\,s+2c-2 \\ 1-s,\,2-s-c \end{array}\right]$ $\left[\begin{array}{c} 2-2\operatorname{Re}c < \operatorname{Re}s < 2-\operatorname{Re}(a+c),\,1+\operatorname{Re}(a-c); \\ -\pi < \arg\omega \le \pi \end{array}\right]$
10	$_2F_1^2\left(\begin{array}{c} a,\,b;\, \frac{\sqrt{x}-\sqrt{x+\omega}}{2\sqrt{x}} \\ \frac{a+b+1}{2} \end{array}\right)$	$\dfrac{2^{a+b-1}\omega^{s}}{\sqrt{\pi}}\Gamma\left[\begin{array}{c} \frac{a+b+1}{2},\,\frac{a+b+1}{2} \\ a,\,b \end{array}\right]\Gamma\left[\begin{array}{c} -s,\,s+a,\,s+b,\,\frac{2s+a+b}{2} \\ s+a+b,\,\frac{2s+a+b+1}{2} \end{array}\right]$ $[-\operatorname{Re}a,\,-\operatorname{Re}b < \operatorname{Re}s < 0;\,|\arg\omega| < \pi]$
11	$\left(\sqrt{x+\omega}+\sqrt{x}\right)^{2-2c}$ $\times \, _2F_1^2\left(\begin{array}{c} a,\,1-a \\ c;\, \frac{\sqrt{x}-\sqrt{x+\omega}}{2\sqrt{x}} \end{array}\right)$	$\dfrac{\omega^{s-c+1}}{\sqrt{\pi}}\Gamma\left[\begin{array}{c} c,\,c \\ c-a,\,a+c-1 \end{array}\right]\Gamma\left[\begin{array}{c} s+a,\,s-a+1,\,c-s-1,\,\frac{2s+1}{2} \\ s+1,\,s+c \end{array}\right]$ $[-1/2,\,-\operatorname{Re}a < \operatorname{Re}s < \operatorname{Re}c-1;\,-\pi < \arg\omega \le \pi]$
12	$\left(\sqrt{x+\omega}-\sqrt{x}\right)^{2c-2}$ $\times \, _2F_1^2\left(\begin{array}{c} a,\,1-a \\ c;\, \frac{\sqrt{x}-\sqrt{x+\omega}}{2\sqrt{x}} \end{array}\right)$	$\dfrac{\omega^{s+c-1}}{\sqrt{\pi}}\Gamma\left[\begin{array}{c} c,\,c \\ c-a,\,a+c-1 \end{array}\right]\Gamma\left[\begin{array}{c} s+a,\,s-a+1,\,c-s-1,\,\frac{2s+1}{2} \\ s+1,\,s+c \end{array}\right]$ $\left[\begin{array}{c} -1/2,\,-\operatorname{Re}a,\,\operatorname{Re}a-1 < \operatorname{Re}s < \operatorname{Re}c-1; \\ -\pi < \arg\omega \le \pi \end{array}\right]$
13	$\left(\sqrt{x+\omega}+\sqrt{\omega}\right)^{-2a}$ $\times \, _2F_1^2\left(\begin{array}{c} a,\,b;\, \frac{\sqrt{x+\omega}-\sqrt{\omega}}{\sqrt{x+\omega}+\sqrt{\omega}} \\ a-b+1 \end{array}\right)$	$\dfrac{\omega^{s-a}}{4^{b}\sqrt{\pi}}\Gamma\left[\begin{array}{c} a-b+1,\,a-b+1 \\ a,\,a-2b+1 \end{array}\right]$ $\times \Gamma\left[\begin{array}{c} s,\,a-s,\,a-2b-s+1,\,\frac{2a-2b-2s+1}{2} \\ a-b-s+1,\,2a-2b-s+1 \end{array}\right]$ $[0 < \operatorname{Re}s < \operatorname{Re}a,\,\operatorname{Re}(a-2b)+1;\,|\arg\omega| < \pi]$
14	$\left(\sqrt{x+\omega}-\sqrt{\omega}\right)^{2a}$ $\times \, _2F_1^2\left(\begin{array}{c} a,\,b;\, \frac{\sqrt{x+\omega}-\sqrt{\omega}}{\sqrt{x+\omega}+\sqrt{\omega}} \\ a-b+1 \end{array}\right)$	$\dfrac{\omega^{s+a}}{4^{b}\sqrt{\pi}}\Gamma\left[\begin{array}{c} a-b+1,\,a-b+1 \\ a,\,a-2b+1 \end{array}\right]$ $\times \Gamma\left[\begin{array}{c} -s-a,\,s+2a,\,1-s-a-2b,\,\frac{1-2s-2a-2b}{2} \\ 1-s-2b,\,1-s-a-b \end{array}\right]$ $[-2\operatorname{Re}a < \operatorname{Re}s < -\operatorname{Re}a,\,1-\operatorname{Re}(a+2b);\,|\arg\omega| < \pi]$

No.	$f(x)$	$F(s)$
15	$\left(\sqrt{x+\omega}+\sqrt{x}\right)^{-2a}$ $\times \, _2F_1^2\left(\begin{array}{c}a,\,b;\,\frac{\sqrt{x+\omega}-\sqrt{x}}{\sqrt{x+\omega}+\sqrt{x}}\\ a-b+1\end{array}\right)$	$\dfrac{\omega^{s-a}}{4^b\sqrt{\pi}}\Gamma\left[\begin{array}{c}a-b+1,\,a-b+1\\ a,\,a-2b+1\end{array}\right]\Gamma\left[\begin{array}{c}s,\,a-s,\,s-2b+1,\,\frac{2s-2b+1}{2}\\ s-b+1,\,s+a-2b+1\end{array}\right]$ $[0,\,2\operatorname{Re}b-1<\operatorname{Re}s<\operatorname{Re}a;\,|\arg\omega|<\pi]$
16	$\left(\sqrt{x+\omega}-\sqrt{x}\right)^{2a}$ $\times \, _2F_1^2\left(\begin{array}{c}a,\,b;\,\frac{\sqrt{x+\omega}-\sqrt{x}}{\sqrt{x+\omega}+\sqrt{x}}\\ a-b+1\end{array}\right)$	$\dfrac{\omega^{s+a}}{4^b\sqrt{\pi}}\Gamma\left[\begin{array}{c}a-b+1,\,a-b+1\\ a,\,a-2b+1\end{array}\right]\Gamma\left[\begin{array}{c}s,\,a-s,\,s-2b+1,\,\frac{2s-2b+1}{2}\\ s-b+1,\,s+a-2b+1\end{array}\right]$ $[0,\,2\operatorname{Re}b-1<\operatorname{Re}s<\operatorname{Re}a;\,|\arg\omega|<\pi]$
17	$_2F_1^2\left(\begin{array}{c}a,\,b;\,\frac{x-\sqrt{x^2+\omega^2}}{2x}\\ \frac{a+b+1}{2}\end{array}\right)$	$\dfrac{2^{a+b-2}\omega^s}{\sqrt{\pi}}\Gamma\left[\begin{array}{c}\frac{a+b+1}{2},\,\frac{a+b+1}{2}\\ a,\,b\end{array}\right]\Gamma\left[\begin{array}{c}-\frac{s}{2},\,\frac{s+2a}{2},\,\frac{s+2b}{2},\,\frac{s+a+b}{2}\\ \frac{s+a+b+1}{2},\,\frac{s+2a+2b}{2}\end{array}\right]$ $[-2\operatorname{Re}a,\,-2\operatorname{Re}b<\operatorname{Re}s<0;\,-\pi/2<\arg\omega\le\pi/2]$
18	$\left(\sqrt{x^2+\omega^2}+\omega\right)^{2-2c}$ $\times \, _2F_1^2\left(\begin{array}{c}a,\,1-a\\ c;\,\frac{\omega-\sqrt{x^2+\omega^2}}{2\omega}\end{array}\right)$	$\dfrac{\omega^{s-2c+2}}{2\sqrt{\pi}}\Gamma\left[\begin{array}{c}c,\,c\\ c-a,\,a+c-1\end{array}\right]\Gamma\left[\begin{array}{c}\frac{s}{2},\,\frac{2c-s-1}{2},\,\frac{2c-s-2a}{2},\,\frac{2a+2c-s-2}{2}\\ \frac{2c-s}{2},\,\frac{4c-s-2}{2}\end{array}\right]$ $[0<\operatorname{Re}s<-2\operatorname{Re}(a-c),\,2\operatorname{Re}c-1;\,-\pi/2<\arg\omega\le\pi/2]$
19	$\left(\sqrt{x^2+\omega^2}-\omega\right)^{2c-2}$ $\times \, _2F_1^2\left(\begin{array}{c}a,\,1-a\\ c;\,\frac{\omega-\sqrt{x^2+\omega^2}}{2\omega}\end{array}\right)$	$\dfrac{\omega^{s+2c-2}}{2\sqrt{\pi}}\Gamma\left[\begin{array}{c}c,\,c\\ c-a,\,a+c-1\end{array}\right]$ $\times\Gamma\left[\begin{array}{c}\frac{3-s-2c}{2},\,\frac{4-s-2a-2c}{2},\,\frac{2-s+2a-2c}{2},\,\frac{s+4c-4}{2}\\ \frac{2-s}{2},\,\frac{4-s-2c}{2}\end{array}\right]$ $\left[\begin{array}{c}4-4\operatorname{Re}c<\operatorname{Re}s<2+2\operatorname{Re}(a-c),\,3-2\operatorname{Re}c;\\ -\pi/2<\arg\omega\le\pi/2\end{array}\right]$
20	$\left(\sqrt{x^2+\omega^2}+x\right)^{2-2c}$ $\times \, _2F_1^2\left(\begin{array}{c}a,\,1-a\\ c;\,\frac{x-\sqrt{x^2+\omega^2}}{2x}\end{array}\right)$	$\dfrac{\omega^{s-2c+2}}{\sqrt{\pi}\,s}\Gamma\left[\begin{array}{c}c,\,c\\ c-a,\,a+c-1\end{array}\right]\Gamma\left[\begin{array}{c}\frac{2c-s-2}{2},\,\frac{s+1}{2},\,\frac{s-2a+2}{2},\,\frac{s+2a}{2}\\ \frac{s}{2},\,\frac{s+2c}{2}\end{array}\right]$ $[-1,\,-2\operatorname{Re}a<\operatorname{Re}s<2\operatorname{Re}c-2;\,-\pi/2<\arg\omega\le\pi/2]$
21	$\left(\sqrt{x^2+\omega^2}-x\right)^{2c-2}$ $\times \, _2F_1^2\left(\begin{array}{c}a,\,1-a\\ c;\,\frac{x-\sqrt{x^2+\omega^2}}{2x}\end{array}\right)$	$\dfrac{\omega^{s+2c-2}}{2\sqrt{\pi}}\Gamma\left[\begin{array}{c}c,\,c\\ c-a,\,a+c-1\end{array}\right]\Gamma\left[\begin{array}{c}\frac{2c-s-2}{2},\,\frac{s+1}{2},\,\frac{s-2a+2}{2},\,\frac{s+2a}{2}\\ \frac{s+2}{2},\,\frac{s+2c}{2}\end{array}\right]$ $[-1,\,-2\operatorname{Re}a<\operatorname{Re}s<2\operatorname{Re}c-2;\,-\pi/2<\arg\omega\le\pi/2]$
22	$\left(\sqrt{x^2+\omega^2}+\omega\right)^{-2a}$ $\times \, _2F_1^2\left(\begin{array}{c}a,\,b;\,\frac{\sqrt{x^2+\omega^2}-\omega}{\sqrt{x^2+\omega^2}+\omega}\\ a-b+1\end{array}\right)$	$\dfrac{\omega^{s-2a}}{2^{2b+1}\sqrt{\pi}}\Gamma\left[\begin{array}{c}a-b+1,\,a-b+1\\ a,\,a-2b+1\end{array}\right]$ $\times\Gamma\left[\begin{array}{c}\frac{s}{2},\,\frac{2a-s}{2},\,\frac{1-s+2a-2b}{2},\,\frac{2-s+2a-4b}{2}\\ \frac{2-s+4a-4b}{2},\,\frac{2-s+2a-2b}{2}\end{array}\right]$ $[0<\operatorname{Re}s<2\operatorname{Re}a,\,2\operatorname{Re}(a-b)+1;\,-\pi/2<\arg\omega\le\pi/2]$

No.	$f(x)$	$F(s)$
23	$\left(\sqrt{x^2+\omega^2}-\omega\right)^{2a}$ $\times {}_2F_1^2\left(\begin{matrix}a,\,b;\,\frac{\sqrt{x^2+\omega^2}-\omega}{\sqrt{x^2+\omega^2}+\omega}\\ a-b+1\end{matrix}\right)$	$\dfrac{\omega^{s+2a}}{2^{2b+1}\sqrt{\pi}}\Gamma\left[\begin{matrix}a-b+1,\,a-b+1\\ a,\,a-2b+1\end{matrix}\right]$ $\times\Gamma\left[\begin{matrix}\frac{s+4a}{2},\,\frac{-2a-s}{2},\,\frac{1-s-2a-2b}{2},\,\frac{2-s-2a-4b}{2}\\ \frac{2-s-4b}{2},\,\frac{2-s-2a-2b}{2}\end{matrix}\right]$ $\left[\begin{matrix}-4\,\mathrm{Re}\,a<\mathrm{Re}\,s<-2\,\mathrm{Re}\,a,\,-2\,\mathrm{Re}\,(a+b)+1;\\ |\arg\omega|<\pi/2\end{matrix}\right]$
24	$\left(\sqrt{x^2+\omega^2}+x\right)^{-2a}$ $\times {}_2F_1^2\left(\begin{matrix}a,\,b;\,\frac{\sqrt{x^2+\omega^2}-x}{\sqrt{x^2+\omega^2}+x}\\ a-b+1\end{matrix}\right)$	$\dfrac{\omega^{s-2a}}{2^{2b+1}\sqrt{\pi}}\Gamma\left[\begin{matrix}a-b+1,\,a-b+1\\ a,\,a-2b+1\end{matrix}\right]\Gamma\left[\begin{matrix}\frac{s}{2},\,\frac{2a-s}{2},\,\frac{s-2b+1}{2},\,\frac{s-4b+2}{2}\\ \frac{s-2b+2}{2},\,\frac{s+2a-4b+2}{2}\end{matrix}\right]$ $\left[0,\,2\,\mathrm{Re}\,b-1<\mathrm{Re}\,s<2\,\mathrm{Re}\,a;\,|\arg\omega|<\pi/2\right]$
25	$\left(\sqrt{x^2+\omega^2}-x\right)^{2a}$ $\times {}_2F_1^2\left(\begin{matrix}a,\,b;\,\frac{\sqrt{x^2+\omega^2}-x}{\sqrt{x^2+\omega^2}+x}\\ a-b+1\end{matrix}\right)$	$\dfrac{\omega^{s+2a}}{2^{2b+1}\sqrt{\pi}}\Gamma\left[\begin{matrix}a-b+1,\,a-b+1\\ a,\,a-2b+1\end{matrix}\right]\Gamma\left[\begin{matrix}\frac{s}{2},\,\frac{2a-s}{2},\,\frac{s-2b+1}{2},\,\frac{s-4b+2}{2}\\ \frac{s-2b+2}{2},\,\frac{s+2a-4b+2}{2}\end{matrix}\right]$ $\left[0,\,2\,\mathrm{Re}\,b-1<\mathrm{Re}\,s<2\,\mathrm{Re}\,a;\,|\arg\omega|<\pi/2\right]$

3.31.33. $\quad {}_2F_1\left(a_1, b_1; c_1; -\dfrac{x}{\omega}\right) {}_2F_1\left(a_2, b_2; c_2; -\dfrac{x}{\omega}\right)$ and algebraic functions

No.	$f(x)$	$F(s)$
1	${}_2F_1\left(\begin{matrix}a,\,b;\,-\frac{x}{\omega}\\ \frac{2a+2b-1}{2}\end{matrix}\right)$ $\times {}_2F_1\left(\begin{matrix}a,\,b;\,-\frac{x}{\omega}\\ \frac{2a+2b+1}{2}\end{matrix}\right)$	$\dfrac{2^{2a+2b-2}\omega^s}{\sqrt{\pi}}\Gamma\left[\begin{matrix}\frac{2a+2b-1}{2},\,\frac{2a+2b+1}{2}\\ 2a,\,2b\end{matrix}\right]$ $\times\Gamma\left[\begin{matrix}s,\,2a-s,\,2b-s,\,a+b-s\\ 2a+2b-s-1,\,\frac{2a+2b-2s+1}{2}\end{matrix}\right]$ $\left[0<\mathrm{Re}\,s<2\,\mathrm{Re}\,a,\,2\,\mathrm{Re}\,b;\,|\arg\omega|<\pi\right]$
2	${}_2F_1\left(\begin{matrix}a,\,b;\,-\frac{x}{\omega}\\ \frac{2a+2b+1}{2}\end{matrix}\right)$ $\times {}_2F_1\left(\begin{matrix}a,\,b+1;\,-\frac{x}{\omega}\\ \frac{2a+2b+1}{2}\end{matrix}\right)$	$\dfrac{2^{2a+2b-1}\omega^s}{\sqrt{\pi}}\Gamma\left[\begin{matrix}\frac{2a+2b+1}{2},\,\frac{2a+2b+1}{2}\\ 2a,\,2b+1\end{matrix}\right]$ $\times\Gamma\left[\begin{matrix}s,\,2a-s,\,2b-s+1,\,a+b-s\\ 2a+2b-s,\,\frac{2a+2b-2s+1}{2}\end{matrix}\right]$ $\left[\begin{matrix}0<\mathrm{Re}\,s<2\,\mathrm{Re}\,a,\,2\,\mathrm{Re}\,b+1,\,\mathrm{Re}\,(a+b);\\ |\arg\omega|<\pi\end{matrix}\right]$
3	${}_2F_1\left(\begin{matrix}a,\,b\\ \frac{2a+2b+1}{2};\,-\frac{x}{\omega}\end{matrix}\right)$ $\times {}_2F_1\left(\begin{matrix}a+1,\,b\\ \frac{2a+2b+1}{2};\,-\frac{x}{\omega}\end{matrix}\right)$	$\dfrac{2^{2a+2b-1}\omega^s}{\sqrt{\pi}}\Gamma\left[\begin{matrix}\frac{2a+2b+1}{2},\,\frac{2a+2b+1}{2}\\ 2a+1,\,2b\end{matrix}\right]$ $\times\Gamma\left[\begin{matrix}s,\,2a-s+1,\,2b-s,\,a+b-s\\ 2a+2b-s,\,\frac{2a+2b-2s+1}{2}\end{matrix}\right]$ $\left[\begin{matrix}0<\mathrm{Re}\,s<2\,\mathrm{Re}\,a+1,\,2\,\mathrm{Re}\,b,\,\mathrm{Re}\,(a+b);\\ |\arg\omega|<\pi\end{matrix}\right]$

No.	$f(x)$	$F(s)$
4	${}_2F_1\left(\begin{array}{c} a,\,b;\,-\frac{x}{\omega} \\ \frac{2a+2b+1}{2} \end{array}\right)$ $\times\,{}_2F_1\left(\begin{array}{c} a+1,\,b+1;\,-\frac{x}{\omega} \\ \frac{2a+2b+3}{2} \end{array}\right)$	$\dfrac{2^{2a+2b}\omega^s}{\sqrt{\pi}}\,\Gamma\left[\begin{array}{c} \frac{2a+2b+1}{2},\,\frac{2a+2b+3}{2} \\ 2a+1,\,2b+1 \end{array}\right]$ $\times\,\Gamma\left[\begin{array}{c} s,\,2a-s+1,\,2b-s+1,\,a+b-s+1 \\ 2a+2b-s+1,\,\frac{2a+2b-2s+3}{2} \end{array}\right]$ $[0<\operatorname{Re}s<2\operatorname{Re}a+1,\,2\operatorname{Re}b+1;\,|\arg\omega|<\pi]$
5	${}_2F_1\left(\begin{array}{c} a,\,b \\ \frac{2a+2b+1}{2};\,-\frac{x}{\omega} \end{array}\right)$ $\times\,{}_2F_1\left(\begin{array}{c} \frac{1-2a}{2},\,\frac{1-2b}{2} \\ \frac{3-2a-2b}{2};\,-\frac{x}{\omega} \end{array}\right)$	$\dfrac{(1-2a-2b)\,\omega^s}{2\sqrt{\pi}}\,\dfrac{\cos\left[(a-b)\,\pi\right]}{\cos\left[(a+b)\,\pi\right]}$ $\times\,\Gamma\left[\begin{array}{c} s,\,\frac{1-2s}{2},\,\frac{2a-2b-2s+1}{2},\,\frac{2b-2a-2s+1}{2} \\ \frac{2a+2b-2s+1}{2},\,\frac{3-2a-2b-2s}{2} \end{array}\right]$ $[0<\operatorname{Re}s<1/2-|\operatorname{Re}(a-b)|;\,|\arg\omega|<\pi]$
6	$(x+\omega)\,{}_2F_1\left(\begin{array}{c} \frac{3-2a}{2},\,\frac{3-2b}{2} \\ \frac{5-2a-2b}{2};\,-\frac{x}{\omega} \end{array}\right)$ $\times\,{}_2F_1\left(\begin{array}{c} a,\,b;\,-\frac{x}{\omega} \\ \frac{2a+2b-1}{2} \end{array}\right)$	$\dfrac{(2a+2b-3)\,\omega^{s+1}}{2\sqrt{\pi}}\,\dfrac{\cos\left[(a-b)\,\pi\right]}{\cos\left[(a+b)\,\pi\right]}$ $\times\,\Gamma\left[\begin{array}{c} s,\,\frac{1-2s}{2},\,\frac{2a-2b-2s+1}{2},\,\frac{2b-2a-2s+1}{2} \\ \frac{5-2a-2b-2s}{2},\,\frac{2a+2b-2s-1}{2} \end{array}\right]$ $[0<\operatorname{Re}s<1/2-|\operatorname{Re}(a-b)|;\,|\arg\omega|<\pi]$
7	$\sqrt{x+\omega}\,{}_2F_1\left(\begin{array}{c} a,\,b;\,-\frac{x}{\omega} \\ \frac{2a+2b-1}{2} \end{array}\right)$ $\times\,{}_2F_1\left(\begin{array}{c} \frac{2a-1}{2},\,\frac{2b-1}{2} \\ \frac{2a+2b-1}{2};\,-\frac{x}{\omega} \end{array}\right)$	$\dfrac{2^{2a+2b-3}\omega^{s+1/2}}{\sqrt{\pi}}\,\Gamma\left[\begin{array}{c} \frac{2a+2b-1}{2},\,\frac{2a+2b-1}{2} \\ 2a-1,\,2b-1 \end{array}\right]$ $\times\,\Gamma\left[\begin{array}{c} s,\,2a-s-1,\,2b-s-1,\,a+b-s-1 \\ 2a+2b-s-2,\,\frac{2a+2b-2s-1}{2} \end{array}\right]$ $[0<\operatorname{Re}s<2\operatorname{Re}a-1,\,2\operatorname{Re}b-1;\,|\arg\omega|<\pi]$
8	$\sqrt{x+\omega}\,{}_2F_1\left(\begin{array}{c} a,\,b;\,-\frac{x}{\omega} \\ \frac{2a+2b-1}{2} \end{array}\right)$ $\times\,{}_2F_1\left(\begin{array}{c} \frac{2a-1}{2},\,\frac{2b+1}{2} \\ \frac{2a+2b-1}{2};\,-\frac{x}{\omega} \end{array}\right)$	$\dfrac{2^{2a+2b-3}\omega^{s+1/2}}{\sqrt{\pi}}\,\Gamma\left[\begin{array}{c} \frac{2a+2b-1}{2},\,\frac{2a+2b-1}{2} \\ 2a-1,\,2b \end{array}\right]$ $\times\,\Gamma\left[\begin{array}{c} s,\,2a-s-1,\,2b-s,\,a+b-s-1 \\ 2a+2b-s-2,\,\frac{2a+2b-2s-1}{2} \end{array}\right]$ $\left[\begin{array}{c} 0<\operatorname{Re}s<2\operatorname{Re}a-1,\,2\operatorname{Re}b,\,\operatorname{Re}(a+b)-1; \\ |\arg\omega|<\pi \end{array}\right]$
9	$\sqrt{x+\omega}\,{}_2F_1\left(\begin{array}{c} a,\,b;\,-\frac{x}{\omega} \\ \frac{2a+2b+1}{2} \end{array}\right)$ $\times\,{}_2F_1\left(\begin{array}{c} \frac{2a+1}{2},\,\frac{2b+1}{2} \\ \frac{2a+2b+1}{2};\,-\frac{x}{\omega} \end{array}\right)$	$\dfrac{2^{2a+2b-1}\omega^{s+1/2}}{\sqrt{\pi}}\,\Gamma\left[\begin{array}{c} \frac{2a+2b+1}{2},\,\frac{2a+2b+1}{2} \\ 2a,\,2b \end{array}\right]$ $\times\,\Gamma\left[\begin{array}{c} s,\,2a-s,\,2b-s,\,a+b-s \\ 2a+2b-s,\,\frac{2a+2b-2s+1}{2} \end{array}\right]$ $[0<\operatorname{Re}s<2\operatorname{Re}a,\,2\operatorname{Re}b;\,|\arg\omega|<\pi]$

No.	$f(x)$	$F(s)$
10	$\sqrt{x+\omega}\,_2F_1\left(\begin{array}{c}a,\,b;\,-\frac{x}{\omega}\\ \frac{2a+2b-1}{2}\end{array}\right)$ $\times\,_2F_1\left(\begin{array}{c}1-a,\,1-b\\ \frac{5-2a-2b}{2};\,-\frac{x}{\omega}\end{array}\right)$	$\dfrac{(2a+2b-3)\,\omega^{s+1/2}}{2\sqrt{\pi}}\,\dfrac{\cos\left[(a-b)\,\pi\right]}{\cos\left[(a+b)\,\pi\right]}$ $\times\,\Gamma\left[\begin{array}{c}s,\,\frac{1-2s}{2},\,\frac{2a-2b-2s+1}{2},\,\frac{2b-2a-2s+1}{2}\\ \frac{2a+2b-2s-1}{2},\,\frac{5-2a-2b-2s}{2}\end{array}\right]$ $[0<\operatorname{Re}s<1/2-|\operatorname{Re}(a-b)|;\,|\arg\omega|<\pi]$
11	$\sqrt{x+\omega}\,_2F_1\left(\begin{array}{c}1-a,\,1-b\\ \frac{3-2a-2b}{2};\,-\frac{x}{\omega}\end{array}\right)$ $\times\,_2F_1\left(\begin{array}{c}a,\,b;\,-\frac{x}{\omega}\\ \frac{2a+2b+1}{2}\end{array}\right)$	$\dfrac{(1-2a-2b)\,\omega^{s+1/2}}{2\sqrt{\pi}}\,\dfrac{\cos\left[(a-b)\,\pi\right]}{\cos\left[(a+b)\,\pi\right]}$ $\times\,\Gamma\left[\begin{array}{c}s,\,\frac{1-2s}{2},\,\frac{2a-2b-2s+1}{2},\,\frac{2b-2a-2s+1}{2}\\ \frac{2a+2b-2s+1}{2},\,\frac{3-2a-2b-2s}{2}\end{array}\right]$ $[0<\operatorname{Re}s<1/2-|\operatorname{Re}(a-b)|;\,|\arg\omega|<\pi]$
12	$\dfrac{1}{\sqrt{x+\omega}}\,_2F_1\left(\begin{array}{c}a,\,b;\,-\frac{x}{\omega}\\ \frac{2a+2b+1}{2}\end{array}\right)$ $\times\,_2F_1\left(\begin{array}{c}\frac{2a+1}{2},\,\frac{2b+1}{2}\\ \frac{2a+2b+3}{2};\,-\frac{x}{\omega}\end{array}\right)$	$\dfrac{2^{2a+2b}\omega^{s-1/2}}{\sqrt{\pi}}\,\Gamma\left[\begin{array}{c}\frac{2a+2b+1}{2},\,\frac{2a+2b+3}{2}\\ 2a+1,\,2b+1\end{array}\right]$ $\times\,\Gamma\left[\begin{array}{c}s,\,2a-s+1,\,2b-s+1,\,a+b-s+1\\ 2a+2b-s+1,\,\frac{2a+2b-2s+3}{2}\end{array}\right]$ $[0<\operatorname{Re}s<2\operatorname{Re}a+1,\,2\operatorname{Re}b+1;\,|\arg\omega|<\pi]$
13	$\dfrac{1}{\sqrt{x+\omega}}\,_2F_1\left(\begin{array}{c}a,\,b;\,-\frac{x}{\omega}\\ \frac{2a+2b+1}{2}\end{array}\right)$ $\times\,_2F_1\left(\begin{array}{c}\frac{2a+1}{2},\,\frac{2b-1}{2};\,-\frac{x}{\omega}\\ \frac{2a+2b+1}{2}\end{array}\right)$	$\dfrac{2^{2a+2b-1}\omega^{s-1/2}}{\sqrt{\pi}}\Gamma\left[\begin{array}{c}\frac{2a+2b+1}{2},\,\frac{2a+2b+1}{2}\\ 2a+1,\,2b\end{array}\right]$ $\times\,\Gamma\left[\begin{array}{c}s,\,2a-s+1,\,2b-s,\,a+b-s\\ 2a+2b-s,\,\frac{2a+2b-2s+1}{2}\end{array}\right]$ $\left[\begin{array}{c}0<\operatorname{Re}s<2\operatorname{Re}a+1,\,2\operatorname{Re}b,\,\operatorname{Re}(a+b);\\ |\arg\omega|<\pi\end{array}\right]$
14	$\sqrt{x+\omega}\,_2F_1\left(\begin{array}{c}\frac{2a-1}{2},\,\frac{2b-1}{2}\\ \frac{2a+2b-3}{2};\,-\frac{x}{\omega}\end{array}\right)$ $\times\,_2F_1\left(\begin{array}{c}a,\,b;\,-\frac{x}{\omega}\\ \frac{2a+2b-1}{2}\end{array}\right)$	$\dfrac{2^{2a+2b-4}\omega^{s+1/2}}{\sqrt{\pi}}\,\Gamma\left[\begin{array}{c}\frac{2a+2b-3}{2},\,\frac{2a+2b-1}{2}\\ 2a-1,\,2b-1\end{array}\right]$ $\times\,\Gamma\left[\begin{array}{c}s,\,2a-s-1,\,2b-s-1,\,a+b-s-1\\ \frac{2a+2b-2s-1}{2},\,2a+2b-s-3\end{array}\right]$ $[0<\operatorname{Re}s<2\operatorname{Re}a-1,\,2\operatorname{Re}b-1;\,|\arg\omega|<\pi]$
15	$\sqrt{x+\omega}\,_2F_1\left(\begin{array}{c}a,\,b;\,-\frac{x}{\omega}\\ \frac{2a+2b-1}{2}\end{array}\right)$ $\times\,_2F_1\left(\begin{array}{c}\frac{2a+1}{2},\,\frac{2b+1}{2}\\ \frac{2a+2b+1}{2};\,-\frac{x}{\omega}\end{array}\right)$	$\dfrac{2^{2a+2b-2}\omega^{s+1/2}}{\sqrt{\pi}}\,\Gamma\left[\begin{array}{c}\frac{2a+2b-1}{2},\,\frac{2a+2b+1}{2}\\ 2a,\,2b\end{array}\right]$ $\times\,\Gamma\left[\begin{array}{c}s,\,2a-s,\,2b-s,\,a+b-s\\ \frac{2a+2b-2s+1}{2},\,2a+2b-s-1\end{array}\right]$ $[0<\operatorname{Re}s<2\operatorname{Re}a,\,2\operatorname{Re}b;\,|\arg\omega|<\pi]$

3.31.34. $\quad {}_2F_1\left(\begin{array}{c} a_1, b_1 \\ c_1;\ 1-\omega_1 x \end{array}\right) {}_2F_1\left(\begin{array}{c} a_2, b_2 \\ c_2;\ 1-\omega_2 x \end{array}\right)$ **and algebraic functions**

1	$(\sigma - x)_+^{c-1}\ {}_2F_1\left(\begin{array}{c} a,\ b \\ c;\ \frac{\sigma-x}{\sigma} \end{array}\right)$	$\sigma^{s+c-1}\ \Gamma\left[\begin{array}{c} c,\ c',\ c'-a'-b',\ s,\ s-a-b+c \\ c'-a',\ c'-b',\ s-a+c,\ s-b+c \end{array}\right]$
	$\times\ {}_2F_1\left(\begin{array}{c} a',\ b' \\ c';\ 1-\omega x \end{array}\right)$	$\times\ {}_4F_3\left(\begin{array}{c} a',\ b',\ s,\ s-a-b+c;\ \sigma\omega \\ a'+b'-c'+1,\ s-a+c,\ s-b+c \end{array}\right)$
		$+\ \dfrac{\sigma^{s-a'-b'+c+c'-1}}{\omega^{a'+b'-c'}}\ \Gamma\left[\begin{array}{c} c,\ c',\ a'+b'-c \\ a',\ b',\ s-a-a'-b'+c+c' \end{array}\right]$
		$\times\ \Gamma\left[\begin{array}{c} s-a'-b'+c',\ s-a-a'-b-b'+c+c' \\ s-a'-b-b'+c+c' \end{array}\right]$
		$\times\ {}_4F_3\left(\begin{array}{c} c'-a',\ c'-b',\ s-a'-b'+c', \\ c'-a'-b'+1,\ s-a-a'-b'+c+c', \end{array}\right.$
		$\left.\begin{array}{c} s-a-a'-b-b'+c+c';\ \sigma\omega \\ s-a'-b-b'+c+c' \end{array}\right)$
		$\left[\begin{array}{l} \omega,\ \operatorname{Re}c>0; \\ \operatorname{Re}s>0,\ \operatorname{Re}(a+b-c),\ \operatorname{Re}(a'+b'-c'), \\ \operatorname{Re}(a+a'+b+b'-c-c');\ |\arg(1-\sigma\omega)|<\pi \end{array}\right]$

3.31.35. $\quad {}_2F_1\left(\begin{array}{c} a_1, b_1 \\ c_1;\ \frac{\sqrt{\omega}-\sqrt{x+\omega}}{2\sqrt{\omega}} \end{array}\right) {}_2F_1\left(\begin{array}{c} a_2, b_2 \\ c_2;\ \frac{\sqrt{\omega}-\sqrt{x+\omega}}{2\sqrt{\omega}} \end{array}\right)$ **and algebraic functions**

1	${}_2F_1\left(\begin{array}{c} a,\ b;\ \frac{\sqrt{\omega}-\sqrt{x+\omega}}{2\sqrt{\omega}} \\ a+b-c+1 \end{array}\right)$	$(4\omega)^s\ \Gamma\left[\begin{array}{c} c,\ a+b-c+1 \\ a,\ b \end{array}\right]$
	$\times\ {}_2F_1\left(\begin{array}{c} a,\ b \\ c;\ \frac{\sqrt{\omega}-\sqrt{x+\omega}}{2\sqrt{\omega}} \end{array}\right)$	$\times\ \Gamma\left[\begin{array}{c} s,\ a-s,\ b-s,\ a+b-2s \\ a+b-s,\ c-s,\ a+b-c-s+1 \end{array}\right]$
		$[0<\operatorname{Re}s<\operatorname{Re}a,\ \operatorname{Re}b;\ |\arg\omega|<\pi]$
2	${}_2F_1\left(\begin{array}{c} a,\ 1-a \\ 2-c;\ \frac{\sqrt{\omega}-\sqrt{x+\omega}}{2\sqrt{\omega}} \end{array}\right)$	$\dfrac{(1-c)\,\omega^s}{\sqrt{\pi}}\,\dfrac{\sin(a\pi)}{\sin(c\pi)}\,\Gamma\left[\begin{array}{c} s,\ \frac{1-2s}{2},\ a-s,\ 1-a-s \\ c-s,\ 2-c-s \end{array}\right]$
	$\times\ {}_2F_1\left(\begin{array}{c} a,\ 1-a \\ c;\ \frac{\sqrt{\omega}-\sqrt{x+\omega}}{2\sqrt{\omega}} \end{array}\right)$	$[0<\operatorname{Re}s<\operatorname{Re}a,\ 1-\operatorname{Re}a;\ |\arg\omega|<\pi]$
3	${}_2F_1\left(\begin{array}{c} a,\ \frac{2a+1}{2};\ \frac{\sqrt{\omega}-\sqrt{x+\omega}}{2\sqrt{\omega}} \\ 2a-c+\frac{3}{2} \end{array}\right)$	$2^{8s-4a+1}\sqrt{\pi}\,\omega^s\,\Gamma\left[\begin{array}{c} c \\ 2a \end{array}\right]\Gamma\left[\begin{array}{c} s,\ 4a-4s,\ \frac{4a-2c+3}{2} \\ c-s,\ \frac{4a-2s+1}{2},\ \frac{4a-2c-2s+3}{2} \end{array}\right]$
	$\times\ {}_2F_1\left(\begin{array}{c} a,\ \frac{2a+1}{2} \\ c;\ \frac{\sqrt{\omega}-\sqrt{x+\omega}}{2\sqrt{\omega}} \end{array}\right)$	$[0<\operatorname{Re}s<\operatorname{Re}a;\ |\arg\omega|<\pi]$

No.	$f(x)$	$F(s)$
4	$_2F_1\left(\begin{array}{c}1-a,\ 1-b\\ \frac{3-a-b}{2};\ \frac{\sqrt{\omega}-\sqrt{x+\omega}}{2\sqrt{\omega}}\end{array}\right)$ $\times\ _2F_1\left(\begin{array}{c}a,\ b;\ \frac{\sqrt{\omega}-\sqrt{x+\omega}}{2\sqrt{\omega}}\\ \frac{a+b+1}{2}\end{array}\right)$	$\dfrac{(1-a-b)\,\omega^s}{2\sqrt{\pi}}\dfrac{\cos\left[(a-b)\pi/2\right]}{\cos\left[(a+b)\pi/2\right]}$ $\times\Gamma\left[\begin{array}{c}s,\ \frac{1-2s}{2},\ \frac{a-b-2s+1}{2},\ \frac{b-a-2s+1}{2}\\ \frac{a+b-2s+1}{2},\ \frac{3-a-b-2s}{2}\end{array}\right]$ $[0<\operatorname{Re}s<(1-|\operatorname{Re}(a-b)|)/2;\ |\arg\omega|<\pi]$
5	$\left(\sqrt{\omega}+\sqrt{x+\omega}\right)^{1-c}$ $\times\ _2F_1\left(\begin{array}{c}a,\ b\\ c;\ \frac{\sqrt{\omega}-\sqrt{x+\omega}}{2\sqrt{\omega}}\end{array}\right)$ $\times\ _2F_1\left(\begin{array}{c}a-c+1,\ b-c+1\\ a+b-c+1;\ \frac{\sqrt{\omega}-\sqrt{x+\omega}}{2\sqrt{\omega}}\end{array}\right)$	$(4\omega)^{s+(1-c)/2}\,\Gamma\left[\begin{array}{c}c,\ a+b-c+1\\ a,\ b\end{array}\right]$ $\times\Gamma\left[\begin{array}{c}s,\ a-s,\ b-s,\ a+b-2s\\ a+b-s,\ c-s,\ a+b-c-s+1\end{array}\right]$ $[0<\operatorname{Re}s<\operatorname{Re}a,\ \operatorname{Re}b;\ |\arg\omega|<\pi]$
6	$\left(\sqrt{\omega}+\sqrt{x+\omega}\right)^{a+b-c}$ $\times\ _2F_1\left(\begin{array}{c}a,\ b\\ c;\ \frac{\sqrt{\omega}-\sqrt{x+\omega}}{2\sqrt{\omega}}\end{array}\right)$ $\times\ _2F_1\left(\begin{array}{c}c-a,\ c-b;\ \frac{\sqrt{\omega}-\sqrt{x+\omega}}{2\sqrt{\omega}}\\ c-a-b+1\end{array}\right)$	$(4\omega)^{s+(a+b-c)/2}\,\Gamma\left[\begin{array}{c}c,\ c-a-b+1\\ c-a,\ c-b\end{array}\right]$ $\times\Gamma\left[\begin{array}{c}s,\ c-a-s,\ c-b-s,\ 2c-a-b-2s\\ c-s,\ c-a-b-s+1,\ 2c-a-b-s\end{array}\right]$ $[0<\operatorname{Re}s<\operatorname{Re}(c-a),\ \operatorname{Re}(c-b);\ |\arg\omega|<\pi]$
7	$\left(\sqrt{\omega}+\sqrt{x+\omega}\right)^{a+b-2c+1}$ $\times\ _2F_1\left(\begin{array}{c}a,\ b\\ c;\ \frac{\sqrt{\omega}-\sqrt{x+\omega}}{2\sqrt{\omega}}\end{array}\right)$ $\times\ _2F_1\left(\begin{array}{c}1-a,\ 1-b\\ c-a-b+1;\ \frac{\sqrt{\omega}-\sqrt{x+\omega}}{2\sqrt{\omega}}\end{array}\right)$	$(4\omega)^{s+(a+b-2c+1)/2}\,\Gamma\left[\begin{array}{c}c,\ c-a-b+1\\ c-a,\ c-b\end{array}\right]$ $\times\Gamma\left[\begin{array}{c}s,\ c-a-s,\ c-b-s,\ 2c-a-b-2s\\ c-s,\ c-a-b-s+1,\ 2c-a-b-s\end{array}\right]$ $[0<\operatorname{Re}s<\operatorname{Re}(c-a),\ \operatorname{Re}(c-b);\ |\arg\omega|<\pi]$
8	$\left(\sqrt{\omega}+\sqrt{x+\omega}\right)^{1-c}$ $\times\ _2F_1\left(\begin{array}{c}a,\ 1-a\\ c;\ \frac{\sqrt{\omega}-\sqrt{x+\omega}}{2\sqrt{\omega}}\end{array}\right)$ $\times\ _2F_1\left(\begin{array}{c}a-c+1,\ 2-a-c\\ 2-c;\ \frac{\sqrt{\omega}-\sqrt{x+\omega}}{2\sqrt{\omega}}\end{array}\right)$	$\dfrac{(1-c)\,\omega^{s+(1-c)/2}}{2^{c-1}\sqrt{\pi}}\dfrac{\sin(a\pi)}{\sin(c\pi)}\Gamma\left[\begin{array}{c}s,\ \frac{1-2s}{2},\ a-s,\ 1-a-s\\ c-s,\ 2-c-s\end{array}\right]$ $[0<\operatorname{Re}s<\operatorname{Re}a,\ 1-\operatorname{Re}a;\ |\arg\omega|<\pi]$
9	$\left(\sqrt{\omega}+\sqrt{x+\omega}\right)^{1-c}$ $\times\ _2F_1\left(\begin{array}{c}a,\ \frac{2a+1}{2}\\ c;\ \frac{\sqrt{\omega}-\sqrt{x+\omega}}{2\sqrt{\omega}}\end{array}\right)$ $\times\ _2F_1\left(\begin{array}{c}a-c+1,\ \frac{2a-2c+3}{2}\\ \frac{4a-2c+3}{2};\ \frac{\sqrt{\omega}-\sqrt{x+\omega}}{2\sqrt{\omega}}\end{array}\right)$	$2^{8s-4a-c+2}\omega^{s+(1-c)/2}\,\Gamma\left[\begin{array}{c}c,\ \frac{4a-2c+3}{2}\\ 2a\end{array}\right]$ $\times\Gamma\left[\begin{array}{c}s,\ 4a-4s\\ c-s,\ \frac{4a-2s+1}{2},\ \frac{4a-2c-2s+3}{2}\end{array}\right]$ $[0<\operatorname{Re}s<\operatorname{Re}a;\ |\arg\omega|<\pi]$

No.	$f(x)$	$F(s)$
10	$\left(\sqrt{\omega}+\sqrt{x+\omega}\right)^{2a-2c+3/2}$ $\times {}_2F_1\left(\begin{matrix}\frac{1-2a}{2},\,1-a\\ \frac{2c-4a+1}{2};\ \frac{\sqrt{\omega}-\sqrt{x+\omega}}{2\sqrt{\omega}}\end{matrix}\right)$ $\times {}_2F_1\left(\begin{matrix}a,\,\frac{2a+1}{2}\\ c;\ \frac{\sqrt{\omega}-\sqrt{x+\omega}}{2\sqrt{\omega}}\end{matrix}\right)$	$2^{8s+6a-6c+9/2}\sqrt{\pi}\,\omega^{a-c+s+3/4}\Gamma\left[\begin{matrix}c,\,\frac{2c-4a+1}{2}\\ 2c-2a-1\end{matrix}\right]$ $\times \Gamma\left[\begin{matrix}s,\,4c-4a-4s-2\\ c-s,\,\frac{2c-4a-2s+1}{2},\,\frac{4c-4a-2s-1}{2}\end{matrix}\right]$ $[0<\operatorname{Re}s<\operatorname{Re}(c-a)-1/2;\ |\arg\omega|<\pi]$
11	$\left(\sqrt{\omega}+\sqrt{x+\omega}\right)^{(a+b-1)/2}$ $\times {}_2F_1\left(\begin{matrix}a,\,b;\,\frac{\sqrt{\omega}-\sqrt{x+\omega}}{2\sqrt{\omega}}\\ \frac{a+b+1}{2}\end{matrix}\right)$ $\times {}_2F_1\left(\begin{matrix}\frac{a-b+1}{2},\,\frac{b-a+1}{2}\\ \frac{3-a-b}{2};\,\frac{\sqrt{\omega}-\sqrt{x+\omega}}{2\sqrt{\omega}}\end{matrix}\right)$	$\dfrac{2^{(a+b-3)/2}(1-a-b)\,\omega^{s+(a+b-1)/4}}{\sqrt{\pi}}\cos\dfrac{(a-b)\pi}{2}$ $\times \sec\dfrac{(a+b)\pi}{2}\Gamma\left[\begin{matrix}s,\,\frac{1-2s}{2},\,\frac{a-b-2s+1}{2},\,\frac{b-a-2s+1}{2}\\ \frac{a+b-2s+1}{2},\,\frac{3-a-b-2s}{2}\end{matrix}\right]$ $[0<\operatorname{Re}s<1/2-|\operatorname{Re}(a-b)|;\ |\arg\omega|<\pi]$
12	$\left(\sqrt{\omega}+\sqrt{x+\omega}\right)^{(1-a-b)/2}$ $\times {}_2F_1\left(\begin{matrix}a,\,b;\,\frac{\sqrt{\omega}-\sqrt{x+\omega}}{2\sqrt{\omega}}\\ \frac{a+b+1}{2}\end{matrix}\right)$ $\times {}_2F_1\left(\begin{matrix}\frac{a-b+1}{2},\,\frac{b-a+1}{2}\\ \frac{a+b+1}{2};\,\frac{\sqrt{\omega}-\sqrt{x+\omega}}{2\sqrt{\omega}}\end{matrix}\right)$	$\dfrac{2^{(a+b-1)/2}\omega^{s+(1-a-b)/4}}{\sqrt{\pi}}\Gamma\left[\begin{matrix}\frac{a+b+1}{2},\,\frac{a+b+1}{2}\\ a,\,b\end{matrix}\right]$ $\times \Gamma\left[\begin{matrix}s,\,a-s,\,b-s,\,\frac{a+b-2s}{2}\\ \frac{a+b-2s+1}{2},\,a+b-s\end{matrix}\right]$ $[0<\operatorname{Re}s<\operatorname{Re}a,\,\operatorname{Re}b;\ |\arg\omega|<\pi]$
13	$\left(\sqrt{\omega}+\sqrt{x+\omega}\right)^{a-b}$ $\times {}_2F_1\left(\begin{matrix}a,\,\frac{2a+1}{2}\\ \frac{a+b+1}{2};\,\frac{\sqrt{\omega}-\sqrt{x+\omega}}{2\sqrt{\omega}}\end{matrix}\right)$ $\times {}_2F_1\left(\begin{matrix}b,\,\frac{2b+1}{2};\,\frac{\sqrt{\omega}-\sqrt{x+\omega}}{2\sqrt{\omega}}\\ b-a+1\end{matrix}\right)$	$2^{8s+a-5b+1}\sqrt{\pi}\omega^{s+(a-b)/2}\Gamma\left[\begin{matrix}\frac{2a+2b+1}{2},\,b-a+1\\ 2b\end{matrix}\right]$ $\times \Gamma\left[\begin{matrix}s,\,4b-4s\\ \frac{4b-2s+1}{2},\,\frac{2a+2b-2s+1}{2},\,b-a-s+1\end{matrix}\right]$ $[0<\operatorname{Re}s<\operatorname{Re}b;\ |\arg\omega|<\pi]$
14	$\left(\sqrt{\omega}+\sqrt{x+\omega}\right)^{2a-c+1/2}$ $\times {}_2F_1\left(\begin{matrix}a,\,\frac{2a+1}{2}\\ c;\,\frac{\sqrt{\omega}-\sqrt{x+\omega}}{2\sqrt{\omega}}\end{matrix}\right)$ $\times {}_2F_1\left(\begin{matrix}c-a,\,\frac{2c-2a-1}{2}\\ \frac{2c-4a+1}{2};\,\frac{\sqrt{\omega}-\sqrt{x+\omega}}{2\sqrt{\omega}}\end{matrix}\right)$	$2^{8s+6a-5c+7/2}\sqrt{\pi}\omega^{s+(4a-2c+1)/4}\Gamma\left[\begin{matrix}c,\,\frac{2c-4a+1}{2}\\ 2c-2a-1\end{matrix}\right]$ $\times \Gamma\left[\begin{matrix}s,\,4c-4a-4s-2\\ c-s,\,\frac{2c-4a-2s+1}{2},\,\frac{4c-4a-2s-1}{2}\end{matrix}\right]$ $[0<\operatorname{Re}s<\operatorname{Re}(c-a)-1/2;\ |\arg\omega|<\pi]$
15	$\left(\sqrt{\omega}+\sqrt{x+\omega}\right)^{1-c}$ $\times {}_2F_1\left(\begin{matrix}a,\,a-1\\ c;\,\frac{\sqrt{\omega}-\sqrt{x+\omega}}{2\sqrt{\omega}}\end{matrix}\right)$ $\times {}_2F_1\left(\begin{matrix}c-a,\,a+c-1\\ c;\,\frac{\sqrt{\omega}-\sqrt{x+\omega}}{2\sqrt{\omega}}\end{matrix}\right)$	$\dfrac{2^{c-1}\omega^{s+(1-c)/2}}{\sqrt{\pi}}\Gamma\left[\begin{matrix}c,\,c\\ c-a,\,c-a-1\end{matrix}\right]$ $\times \Gamma\left[\begin{matrix}s,\,c-a-s,\,a+c-s-1,\,\frac{2c-2s-1}{2}\\ c-s,\,2c-s-1\end{matrix}\right]$ $[0<\operatorname{Re}s<\operatorname{Re}(c-a),\,\operatorname{Re}c-1/2;\ |\arg\omega|<\pi]$

3.31.36. $_2F_1\left(\begin{matrix} a_1, b_1 \\ c_1; \frac{\sqrt{x}-\sqrt{x+\omega}}{2\sqrt{x}} \end{matrix}\right) {}_2F_1\left(\begin{matrix} a_2, b_2 \\ c_2; \frac{\sqrt{x}-\sqrt{x+\omega}}{2\sqrt{x}} \end{matrix}\right)$ **and algebraic functions**

1	$_2F_1\left(\begin{matrix} a, b; \frac{\sqrt{x}-\sqrt{x+\omega}}{2\sqrt{x}} \\ a+b-c+1 \end{matrix}\right)$ $\times {}_2F_1\left(\begin{matrix} a, b \\ c; \frac{\sqrt{x}-\sqrt{x+\omega}}{2\sqrt{x}} \end{matrix}\right)$	$\left(\frac{\omega}{4}\right)^s \Gamma\left[\begin{matrix} c, a+b-c+1 \\ a, b \end{matrix}\right]$ $\times \Gamma\left[\begin{matrix} -s, s+a, s+b, 2s+a+b \\ s+a+b, s+c, s+a+b-c+1 \end{matrix}\right]$ $[-\operatorname{Re} a, -\operatorname{Re} b < \operatorname{Re} s < 0; |\arg\omega| < \pi]$
2	$_2F_1\left(\begin{matrix} 1-a, a \\ 2-c; \frac{\sqrt{x}-\sqrt{x+\omega}}{2\sqrt{x}} \end{matrix}\right)$ $\times {}_2F_1\left(\begin{matrix} 1-a, a \\ c; \frac{\sqrt{x}-\sqrt{x+\omega}}{2\sqrt{x}} \end{matrix}\right)$	$\frac{(1-c)\,\omega^s}{\sqrt{\pi}} \frac{\sin(a\pi)}{\sin(c\pi)} \Gamma\left[\begin{matrix} -s, \frac{2s+1}{2}, s+a, s-a+1 \\ s+c, s-c+2 \end{matrix}\right]$ $[\operatorname{Re} a - 1, -\operatorname{Re} a < \operatorname{Re} s < 0; |\arg\omega| < \pi]$
3	$_2F_1\left(\begin{matrix} a, \frac{2a+1}{2}; \frac{\sqrt{x}-\sqrt{x+\omega}}{2\sqrt{x}} \\ \frac{4a-2c+3}{2} \end{matrix}\right)$ $\times {}_2F_1\left(\begin{matrix} a, \frac{2a+1}{2} \\ c; \frac{\sqrt{x}-\sqrt{x+\omega}}{2\sqrt{x}} \end{matrix}\right)$	$\frac{\sqrt{\pi}\,\omega^s}{2^{8s+4a-1}} \Gamma\left[\begin{matrix} c, -s, 4s+4a, \frac{4a-2c+3}{2} \\ 2a, s+c, \frac{2s+4a+1}{2}, \frac{2s+4a-2c+3}{2} \end{matrix}\right]$ $[-\operatorname{Re} a < \operatorname{Re} s < 0; |\arg\omega| < \pi]$
4	$_2F_1\left(\begin{matrix} 1-a, 1-b \\ \frac{3-a-b}{2}; \frac{\sqrt{x}-\sqrt{x+\omega}}{2\sqrt{x}} \end{matrix}\right)$ $\times {}_2F_1\left(\begin{matrix} a, b; \frac{\sqrt{x}-\sqrt{x+\omega}}{2\sqrt{x}} \\ \frac{a+b+1}{2} \end{matrix}\right)$	$\frac{(1-a-b)\,\omega^s}{2\sqrt{\pi}} \frac{\cos[(a-b)\pi/2]}{\cos[(a+b)\pi/2]}$ $\times \Gamma\left[\begin{matrix} -s, \frac{2s+1}{2}, \frac{2s+a-b+1}{2}, \frac{2s-a+b+1}{2} \\ \frac{2s-a-b+3}{2}, \frac{2s+a+b+1}{2} \end{matrix}\right]$ $[(|\operatorname{Re}(a-b)|-1)/2 < \operatorname{Re} s < 0; |\arg\omega| < \pi]$
5	$\left(\sqrt{x}+\sqrt{x+\omega}\right)^{1-c}$ $\times {}_2F_1\left(\begin{matrix} a, b \\ c; \frac{\sqrt{x}-\sqrt{x+\omega}}{2\sqrt{x}} \end{matrix}\right)$ $\times {}_2F_1\left(\begin{matrix} a-c+1, b-c+1 \\ a+b-c+1; \frac{\sqrt{x}-\sqrt{x+\omega}}{2\sqrt{x}} \end{matrix}\right)$	$4^{-s}\omega^{s+(1-c)/2}\Gamma\left[\begin{matrix} c, a+b-c+1 \\ a, b \end{matrix}\right]$ $\times \Gamma\left[\begin{matrix} 2s+a+b-c+1, \frac{c-2s-1}{2} \\ \frac{2s+c+1}{2} \end{matrix}\right]$ $\times \Gamma\left[\begin{matrix} \frac{2s+2a-c+1}{2}, \frac{2s+2b-c+1}{2} \\ \frac{2s+2a+2b-c+1}{2}, \frac{2s+2a+2b-3c+3}{2} \end{matrix}\right]$ $\left[\begin{matrix} \operatorname{Re}(c-2a-1)/2, \operatorname{Re}(c-2b-1)/2 \\ < \operatorname{Re} s < (\operatorname{Re} c - 1)/2; |\arg\omega| < \pi \end{matrix}\right]$
6	$\left(\sqrt{x}+\sqrt{x+\omega}\right)^{a+b-c}$ $\times {}_2F_1\left(\begin{matrix} a, b \\ c; \frac{\sqrt{x}-\sqrt{x+\omega}}{2\sqrt{x}} \end{matrix}\right)$ $\times {}_2F_1\left(\begin{matrix} c-a, c-b; \frac{\sqrt{x}-\sqrt{x+\omega}}{2\sqrt{x}} \\ c-a-b+1 \end{matrix}\right)$	$4^{-s}\omega^{s+(a+b-c)/2}\Gamma\left[\begin{matrix} c, c-a-b+1 \\ c-a, c-b \end{matrix}\right]$ $\times \Gamma\left[\begin{matrix} 2s+c, \frac{2s+a-b+c}{2}, \frac{2s-a+b+c}{2}, \frac{c-a-b-2s}{2} \\ \frac{2s+a+b+c}{2}, \frac{2s-a-b+c+2}{2}, \frac{2s+3c-a-b}{2} \end{matrix}\right]$ $\left[\begin{matrix} \operatorname{Re}(a-b-c)/2, \operatorname{Re}(b-a-c)/2, -\operatorname{Re} c/2 \\ < \operatorname{Re} s < \operatorname{Re}(c-a-b)/2; |\arg\omega| < \pi \end{matrix}\right]$

No.	$f(x)$	$F(s)$
7	$\left(\sqrt{x}+\sqrt{x+\omega}\right)^{a+b-2c+1}$ $\times {}_2F_1\left(\begin{array}{c} a,\,b \\ c;\,\frac{\sqrt{x}-\sqrt{x+\omega}}{2\sqrt{x}} \end{array}\right)$ $\times {}_2F_1\left(\begin{array}{c} 1-a,\,1-b;\,\frac{\sqrt{x}-\sqrt{x+\omega}}{2\sqrt{x}} \\ c-a-b+1 \end{array}\right)$	$\dfrac{\omega^{s+(a+b-2c+1)/2}}{2^{2s}}\Gamma\left[\begin{array}{c} c,\,c-a-b+1 \\ c-a,\,c-b \end{array}\right]$ $\times\Gamma\left[\begin{array}{c} 2s+1,\,\frac{2s+a-b+1}{2},\,\frac{2s-a+b+1}{2},\,\frac{2c-a-b-2s-1}{2} \\ \frac{2s+a+b+1}{2},\,\frac{2s-a-b+3}{2},\,\frac{2s-a-b+2c+1}{2} \end{array}\right]$ $\left[\begin{array}{c} \left(|\operatorname{Re}(a-b)|-1\right)/2<\operatorname{Re}s \\ <\operatorname{Re}(2c-a-b-1)/2;\,|\arg\omega|<\pi \end{array}\right]$
8	$\left(\sqrt{x}+\sqrt{x+\omega}\right)^{1-c}$ $\times {}_2F_1\left(\begin{array}{c} a,\,1-a \\ c;\,\frac{\sqrt{x}-\sqrt{x+\omega}}{2\sqrt{x}} \end{array}\right)$ $\times {}_2F_1\left(\begin{array}{c} a-c+1,\,2-a \\ 2-c;\,\frac{\sqrt{x}-\sqrt{x+\omega}}{2\sqrt{x}} \end{array}\right)$	$\dfrac{(1-c)\,\omega^{s+(1-c)/2}}{2^{c-1}\sqrt{\pi}}\dfrac{\sin(a\pi)}{\sin(c\pi)}$ $\times\Gamma\left[\begin{array}{c} \frac{c-2s-1}{2},\,\frac{2s-c+2}{2},\,\frac{2s+2a-c+1}{2},\,\frac{2s-2a-c+3}{2} \\ \frac{2s+c+1}{2},\,\frac{2s-3c+5}{2} \end{array}\right]$ $\left[\begin{array}{c} \operatorname{Re}(2a+c-3)/2,\,\operatorname{Re}(c-2a-1)/2<\operatorname{Re}s \\ <(\operatorname{Re}c-1)/2;\,|\arg\omega|<\pi \end{array}\right]$
9	$\left(\sqrt{x}+\sqrt{x+\omega}\right)^{1-c}$ $\times {}_2F_1\left(\begin{array}{c} a,\,\frac{2a+1}{2} \\ c;\,\frac{\sqrt{x}-\sqrt{x+\omega}}{2\sqrt{x}} \end{array}\right)$ $\times {}_2F_1\left(\begin{array}{c} a-c+1,\,\frac{2a-2c+3}{2} \\ \frac{4a-2c+3}{2};\,\frac{\sqrt{x}-\sqrt{x+\omega}}{2\sqrt{x}} \end{array}\right)$	$\dfrac{\sqrt{\pi}\,\omega^{s+(1-c)/2}}{2^{8s+4a-3c+2}}\Gamma\left[\begin{array}{c} c,\,\frac{4a-2c+3}{2} \\ 2a \end{array}\right]$ $\times\Gamma\left[\begin{array}{c} \frac{c-2s-1}{2},\,4s+4a-2c+2 \\ \frac{2s+c+1}{2},\,\frac{2s+4a-c+2}{2},\,\frac{2s+4a-3c+4}{2} \end{array}\right]$ $\left[\begin{array}{c} \operatorname{Re}(c-2a-1)/2,\,\operatorname{Re}(2c-4a-3)/4 \\ <\operatorname{Re}s<(\operatorname{Re}c-1)/2;\,|\arg\omega|<\pi \end{array}\right]$
10	$\left(\sqrt{x}+\sqrt{x+\omega}\right)^{2a-2c+3/2}$ $\times {}_2F_1\left(\begin{array}{c} \frac{1-2a}{2},\,1-a \\ \frac{2c-4a+1}{2};\,\frac{\sqrt{x}-\sqrt{x+\omega}}{2\sqrt{x}} \end{array}\right)$ $\times {}_2F_1\left(\begin{array}{c} a,\,\frac{2a+1}{2} \\ c;\,\frac{\sqrt{x}-\sqrt{x+\omega}}{2\sqrt{x}} \end{array}\right)$	$\dfrac{\sqrt{\pi}\,\omega^{s+a-c+3/4}}{2^{8s+2a-2c+3/2}}\Gamma\left[\begin{array}{c} c,\,\frac{2c-4a+1}{2} \\ 2c-2a-1 \end{array}\right]$ $\times\Gamma\left[\begin{array}{c} \frac{4c-4a-4s-3}{4},\,4s+1 \\ \frac{4s-4a+5}{4},\,\frac{4s+4a+3}{4},\,\frac{4s-4a+4c+1}{4} \end{array}\right]$ $\left[-1/4<\operatorname{Re}s<\operatorname{Re}(c-a)-3/4;\,|\arg\omega|<\pi\right]$

3.31.37. ${}_2F_1\left(\begin{array}{c} a_1,\,b_1 \\ c_1;\,-\frac{2\sqrt{x}\left(\sqrt{x}\pm\sqrt{x+\omega}\right)}{\omega} \end{array}\right){}_2F_1\left(\begin{array}{c} a_2,\,b_2 \\ c_2;\,-\frac{2\sqrt{x}\left(\sqrt{x}+\sqrt{x+\omega}\right)}{\omega} \end{array}\right)$ **and algebraic functions**

| 1 | ${}_2F_1\left(\begin{array}{c} a,\,b \\ c;\,-\frac{2\sqrt{x}\left(\sqrt{x}-\sqrt{x+\omega}\right)}{\omega} \end{array}\right)$ $\times {}_2F_1\left(\begin{array}{c} a,\,b \\ c;\,-\frac{2\sqrt{x}\left(\sqrt{x}+\sqrt{x+\omega}\right)}{\omega} \end{array}\right)$ | $\left(\dfrac{\omega}{4}\right)^s\Gamma\left[\begin{array}{c} c,\,c \\ a,\,b,\,c-a,\,c-b \end{array}\right]$ $\times\Gamma\left[\begin{array}{c} s,\,a-s,\,b-s,\,c-a-s,\,c-b-s \\ c-s,\,c-2s \end{array}\right]$ $\left[\begin{array}{c} 0<\operatorname{Re}s<\operatorname{Re}a,\,\operatorname{Re}b,\,\operatorname{Re}(c-a),\,\operatorname{Re}(c-b); \\ |\arg\omega|<\pi \end{array}\right]$ |

No.	$f(x)$	$F(s)$
2	$\left(\dfrac{2\sqrt{x}\left(\sqrt{x}+\sqrt{x+\omega}\right)}{\omega}+1\right)^{a}$	$\left(\dfrac{\omega}{4}\right)^{s}\Gamma\left[\begin{matrix}c,\,c\\ a,\,b,\,c-a,\,c-b\end{matrix}\right]$
	$\times\,_2F_1\left(\begin{matrix}a,\,b\\ c;\,-\frac{2\sqrt{x}\left(\sqrt{x}+\sqrt{x+\omega}\right)}{\omega}\end{matrix}\right)$	$\times\,\Gamma\left[\begin{matrix}s,\,a-s,\,b-s,\,c-a-s,\,c-b-s\\ c-s,\,c-2s\end{matrix}\right]$
	$\times\,_2F_1\left(\begin{matrix}a,\,c-b\\ c;\,-\frac{2\sqrt{x}\left(\sqrt{x}+\sqrt{x+\omega}\right)}{\omega}\end{matrix}\right)$	$\left[\begin{matrix}0<\operatorname{Re}s<\operatorname{Re}a,\;\operatorname{Re}b,\;\operatorname{Re}(c-a),\;\operatorname{Re}(c-b);\\ |\arg\omega|<\pi\end{matrix}\right]$
3	$\left(2x\pm2\sqrt{x}\sqrt{x+\omega}+\omega\right)^{-a-b+c}$	$4^{-s}\omega^{s-a-b+c}\,\Gamma\left[\begin{matrix}c,\,c,\,s,\,a-s,\,b-s\\ a,\,b,\,c-a,\,c-b\end{matrix}\right]$
	$\times\,_2F_1\left(\begin{matrix}a,\,b\\ c;\,\pm\frac{2\sqrt{x}\left(\sqrt{x+\omega}\mp\sqrt{x}\right)}{\omega}\end{matrix}\right)$	$\times\,\Gamma\left[\begin{matrix}c-a-s,\,c-b-s\\ c-s,\,c-2s\end{matrix}\right]\quad\left[\left\{\begin{matrix}|\arg\omega|<\pi\\ \operatorname{Re}\omega\geq0\end{matrix}\right\};\right.$
	$\times\,_2F_1\left(\begin{matrix}c-a,\,c-b\\ c;\,\mp\frac{2\sqrt{x}\left(\sqrt{x+\omega}\pm\sqrt{x}\right)}{\omega}\end{matrix}\right)$	$\left.0<\operatorname{Re}s<\operatorname{Re}a,\;\operatorname{Re}b,\;\operatorname{Re}(c-a),\;\operatorname{Re}(c-b)\right]$

3.31.38. $_2F_1\left(\begin{matrix}a_1,\,b_1\\ c_1;\,\frac{2\sqrt{\omega}\left(\sqrt{x+\omega}-\sqrt{\omega}\right)}{x}\end{matrix}\right)\,_2F_1\left(\begin{matrix}a_2,\,b_2\\ c_2;\,-\frac{2\sqrt{\omega}\left(\sqrt{x+\omega}+\sqrt{\omega}\right)}{x}\end{matrix}\right)$ **and algebraic functions**

No.	$f(x)$	$F(s)$
1	$_2F_1\left(\begin{matrix}a,\,b\\ c;\,\frac{2\sqrt{\omega}\left(\sqrt{x+\omega}-\sqrt{\omega}\right)}{x}\end{matrix}\right)$	$(4\omega)^{s}\,\Gamma\left[\begin{matrix}c,\,c\\ a,\,b,\,c-a,\,c-b\end{matrix}\right]$
	$\times\,_2F_1\left(\begin{matrix}a,\,b\\ c;\,-\frac{2\sqrt{\omega}\left(\sqrt{x+\omega}+\sqrt{\omega}\right)}{x}\end{matrix}\right)$	$\times\,\Gamma\left[\begin{matrix}-s,\,s+a,\,s+b,\,s-a+c,\,s-b+c\\ s+c,\,2s+c\end{matrix}\right]$
		$\left[-\operatorname{Re}a,\,-\operatorname{Re}b,\,\operatorname{Re}(a-c),\,\operatorname{Re}(b-c)<\operatorname{Re}s<0;\,|\arg\omega|<\pi\right]$
2	$\left(\sqrt{\omega}\pm\sqrt{x+\omega}\right)^{2(c-a-b)}$	$(4\omega)^{s-a-b+c}\,\Gamma\left[\begin{matrix}c,\,c,\,a+b-c-s,\,s-a+c\\ a,\,b,\,c-a,\,c-b\end{matrix}\right]$
	$\times\,_2F_1\left(\begin{matrix}a,\,b\\ c;\,\pm\frac{2\sqrt{\omega}\left(\sqrt{x+\omega}\mp\sqrt{\omega}\right)}{x}\end{matrix}\right)$	$\times\,\Gamma\left[\begin{matrix}s-b+c,\,s-a-2b+2c,\,s-2a-b+2c\\ s-a-b+2c,\,2s-2a-2b+3c\end{matrix}\right]$
	$\times\,_2F_1\left(\begin{matrix}c-a,\,c-b\\ c;\,\mp\frac{2\sqrt{\omega}\left(\sqrt{x+\omega}\pm\sqrt{\omega}\right)}{x}\end{matrix}\right)$	$\left[\begin{matrix}\operatorname{Re}(a-c),\,\operatorname{Re}(b-c),\,\operatorname{Re}(2a+b-2c),\\ \operatorname{Re}(a+2b-2c)<\operatorname{Re}s<\operatorname{Re}(a+b-c);\,|\arg\omega|<\pi\end{matrix}\right]$

3.31.39. $_2F_1\left(\begin{matrix}a_1,\,b_1\\ c_1;\,\frac{2\sqrt{\omega}\left(\sqrt{\omega}+\sqrt{\omega-x}\right)}{x}\end{matrix}\right)\,_2F_1\left(\begin{matrix}a_2,\,b_2\\ c_2;\,-\frac{2\sqrt{\omega}\left(\sqrt{\omega}+\sqrt{\omega-x}\right)}{x}\end{matrix}\right)$ **and algebraic functions**

No.	$f(x)$	$F(s)$
1	$\left(x-2\omega-2\sqrt{\omega}\sqrt{\omega-x}\right)^{a}$	$e^{-i(s+a)\pi}(4\omega)^{s+a}\,\Gamma\left[\begin{matrix}c,\,c\\ a,\,b,\,c-a,\,c-b\end{matrix}\right]$
	$\times\,_2F_1\left(\begin{matrix}a,\,b\\ c;\,\frac{2\sqrt{\omega}\left(\sqrt{\omega}+\sqrt{\omega-x}\right)}{x}\end{matrix}\right)$	$\times\,\Gamma\left[\begin{matrix}s+2a,\,-s-a\\ 2s+2a+c\end{matrix}\right]\Gamma\left[\begin{matrix}s+a+b,\,s+c,\,s+a-b+c\\ s+a+c\end{matrix}\right]$
	$\times\,_2F_1\left(\begin{matrix}a,\,c-b\\ c;\,\frac{2\sqrt{\omega}\left(\sqrt{\omega}+\sqrt{\omega-x}\right)}{x}\end{matrix}\right)$	$\left[\begin{matrix}-2\operatorname{Re}a,\,-\operatorname{Re}(a+b),\,-\operatorname{Re}c,\,\operatorname{Re}(b-a-c)\\ <\operatorname{Re}s<-\operatorname{Re}a;\,0<\arg\omega\leq\pi\end{matrix}\right]$

3.32.   The Generalized Hypergeometric Function $_3F_2\left(\begin{matrix} a_1,\ a_2\ ,a_3 \\ b_1,\ b_2;\ z \end{matrix}\right)$

More formulas can be obtained from the corresponding sections due to the relations

$$_3F_2\left(\begin{matrix} a_1,\ a_2,\ a_3 \\ b_1,\ b_2;\ z \end{matrix}\right) = \Gamma\left[\begin{matrix} b_1,\ b_2 \\ a_1,\ a_2,\ a_3 \end{matrix}\right] G^{13}_{33}\left(-z\ \middle|\ \begin{matrix} 1-a_1,\ 1-a_2,\ 1-a_3 \\ 0,\ 1-b_1,\ 1-b_2 \end{matrix}\right).$$

3.32.1. $_3F_2\left(\begin{matrix} a_1,\ a_2,\ a_3 \\ b_1,\ b_2;\ \varphi\left(x\right) \end{matrix}\right)$ and algebraic functions

No.	$f\left(x\right)$	$F\left(s\right)$
1	$(x+\sigma)^{2b+1}\ _3F_2\left(\begin{matrix} a,\ 2a-2,\ b;\ -\frac{x}{\sigma} \\ a-1,\ 2a-b-1 \end{matrix}\right)$	$(2a-2b-2s-3)\,\sigma^{s+2b+1}$ $\times\,\Gamma\left[\begin{matrix} 2a-b-1 \\ -b-1,\ 2a-2b-2 \end{matrix}\right]$ $\times\,\Gamma\left[\begin{matrix} s,\ -b-s-1,\ 2a-2b-s-3 \\ 2a-b-s-1 \end{matrix}\right]$ $\left[\begin{matrix} 0<\operatorname{Re}s<-\operatorname{Re}b-1,\ \operatorname{Re}\left(a-b\right)-1/2, \\ 2\operatorname{Re}\left(a-b\right)-3;\ \left|\arg\sigma\right|<\pi \end{matrix}\right]$
2	$\left(\sqrt{x+\sigma}-\sqrt{x}\right)^a$ $\times\,_3F_2\left(\begin{matrix} a,\ b,\ c;\ \frac{2\sqrt{x}\left(\sqrt{x}-\sqrt{x+\sigma}\right)}{\sigma}+1 \\ a-b+1,\ a-c+1 \end{matrix}\right)$	$\dfrac{\sigma^{s+a/2}}{2^{2s}}\,\Gamma\left[\begin{matrix} a-b+1,\ a-c+1 \\ a,\ a-b-c+1 \end{matrix}\right]$ $\times\,\Gamma\left[\begin{matrix} 2s,\ \frac{a-2s}{2},\ \frac{2s+a-2b-2c+2}{2} \\ \frac{2s+a-2b+2}{2},\ \frac{2s+a-2c+2}{2} \end{matrix}\right]$ $\left[\begin{matrix} 0,\ \operatorname{Re}\left(b-a/2+c\right)-1<\operatorname{Re}s<\operatorname{Re}a/2; \\ \left|\arg\sigma\right|<\pi \end{matrix}\right]$
3	$\left(\sqrt{x^2+\sigma^2}-x\right)^a$ $\times\,_3F_2\left(\begin{matrix} a,\ b,\ c;\ 1-\frac{2x\left(\sqrt{x^2+\sigma^2}-x\right)}{\sigma^2} \\ a-b+1,\ a-c+1 \end{matrix}\right)$	$\dfrac{\sigma^{a+s}}{2^{s+1}}\,\Gamma\left[\begin{matrix} a-b+1,\ a-c+1 \\ a,\ a-b-c+1 \end{matrix}\right]$ $\times\,\Gamma\left[\begin{matrix} s,\ \frac{a-s}{2},\ \frac{s+a-2b-2c+2}{2} \\ \frac{s+a-2b+2}{2},\ \frac{s+a-2c+2}{2} \end{matrix}\right]$ $\left[\begin{matrix} 0,\ \operatorname{Re}\left(-a+2b+2c\right)-2<\operatorname{Re}s<\operatorname{Re}a; \\ \left|\arg\sigma\right|<\pi/2 \end{matrix}\right]$
4	$\left(\sqrt{x+\sigma}-\sqrt{\sigma}\right)^a$ $\times\,_3F_2\left(\begin{matrix} a,\ b,\ c;\ 1-\frac{2\sqrt{\sigma}\left(\sqrt{x+\sigma}-\sqrt{\sigma}\right)}{x} \\ a-b+1,\ a-c+1 \end{matrix}\right)$	$(4\sigma)^{s+a/2}\,\Gamma\left[\begin{matrix} a-b+1,\ a-c+1 \\ a,\ a-b-c+1 \end{matrix}\right]$ $\times\,\Gamma\left[\begin{matrix} s+a,\ -2s-a,\ 1-b-c-s \\ 1-b-s,\ 1-c-s \end{matrix}\right]$ $\left[\begin{matrix} -\operatorname{Re}a<\operatorname{Re}s<-\operatorname{Re}a/2,\ 1-\operatorname{Re}\left(b+c\right); \\ \left|\arg\sigma\right|<\pi \end{matrix}\right]$

3.33.   The Generalized Hypergeometric Functions $_pF_q\left((a_p);\ (b_q);\ z\right)$

More formulas can be obtained from the corresponding section due to the relation

$$_pF_q\left(\begin{matrix} a_1, a_2, \ldots, a_p;\ z \\ b_1, b_2, \ldots, b_q \end{matrix}\right) = \Gamma\left[\begin{matrix} b_1, b_2, \ldots, b_q \\ a_1, a_2, \ldots, a_p \end{matrix}\right] G_{p,\,q+1}^{1,\,p}\left(-z \left|\begin{matrix} 1-a_1, 1-a_2, \ldots, 1-a_p \\ 0,\ 1-b_1, 1-b_2, \ldots, 1-b_q \end{matrix}\right.\right).$$

It is supposed that all hypergeometric functions in formulas exist. If at least one of the upper parameters of a hypergeometric function is a negative integer, then the corresponding function turns into a polynomial, and the conditions can be weakened.

Notation:

$$\chi = \sum_{j=1}^{q} b_j - \sum_{i=1}^{p} a_i + \frac{p-q}{2} + 1.$$

The expression $\operatorname{Re} s < \operatorname{Re}\left(a_k + a\right)$ means that the inequality is valid for all $k = 1, 2, \ldots, p$.

3.33.1. $_pF_q\left((a_p);\ (b_q);\ \varphi\left(x\right)\right)$ and algebraic functions

No.	$f(x)$	$F(s)$
1	$_pF_q\left(\begin{matrix}(a_p);\ -\omega x \\ (b_q)\end{matrix}\right)$	$\omega^{-s}\,\Gamma\left[\begin{matrix}(b_q),\ s,\ (a_p)-s \\ (a_p),\ (b_q)-s\end{matrix}\right]$
		$\left[\begin{matrix}\left[q=p-1;\ \lvert\arg\omega\rvert<\pi;\ 0<\operatorname{Re}s<\operatorname{Re}a_k\right]\ \text{or} \\ \left[q=p;\ (\operatorname{Re}\omega>0;\ 0<\operatorname{Re}s<\operatorname{Re}a_k)\ \text{or}\right. \\ \left.(\operatorname{Re}\omega=0;\ 0<\operatorname{Re}s<\operatorname{Re}a_k,\ 1-\operatorname{Re}\chi)\right]\ \text{or} \\ \left[q=p+1;\ \omega>0;\ 0<\operatorname{Re}s<\operatorname{Re}a_k,\ 1/2-\operatorname{Re}\chi\right]\end{matrix}\right]$
2	$(\sigma-x)_+^{\alpha-1}\,_pF_q\left(\begin{matrix}(a_p);\ -\omega x \\ (b_q)\end{matrix}\right)$	$\sigma^{s+\alpha-1}\,\mathrm{B}\left(s,\alpha\right)\,_{p+1}F_{q+1}\left(\begin{matrix}(a_p),\ s;\ -\sigma\omega \\ (b_q),\ s+\alpha\end{matrix}\right)$
		$\left[\sigma,\ \operatorname{Re}\alpha,\ \operatorname{Re}s>0\right]$
3	$(x-\sigma)_+^{\alpha-1}$ $\times\ _pF_q\left(\begin{matrix}(a_p);\ -\omega x \\ (b_q)\end{matrix}\right)$	$\dfrac{\Gamma\left(s+\alpha-1\right)}{\omega^{s+\alpha-1}}\,\Gamma\left[\begin{matrix}(b_q),\ (a_p)-\alpha-s+1 \\ (a_p),\ (b_q)-\alpha-s+1\end{matrix}\right]$ $\times\ _{p+1}F_{q+1}\left(\begin{matrix}1-\alpha,\ (a_p)-\alpha-s+1;\ -\sigma\omega \\ 2-\alpha-s,\ (b_q)-\alpha-s+1\end{matrix}\right)$ $+\ \sigma^{\alpha+s-1}\,\mathrm{B}\left(\alpha,1-\alpha-s\right)\,_{p+1}F_{q+1}\left(\begin{matrix}(a_p),\ s;\ -\sigma\omega \\ (b_q),\ s+\alpha\end{matrix}\right)$
		$\left[\begin{matrix}\left[q=p-1;\ \sigma,\ \operatorname{Re}\alpha>0;\ \lvert\arg\omega\rvert<\pi;\ \operatorname{Re}s<\operatorname{Re}\left(a_k-\alpha\right)+1\right]\ \text{or} \\ \left[q=p;\ \operatorname{Re}\alpha>0;\ (\sigma,\ \operatorname{Re}\omega>0;\ \operatorname{Re}s<\operatorname{Re}\left(a_k-\alpha\right)+1)\ \text{or}\right. \\ \left.(\sigma>0;\ \operatorname{Re}\omega=0;\ \operatorname{Re}s<\operatorname{Re}\left(a_k-\alpha\right)+1,\ 2-\operatorname{Re}\left(\alpha+\chi\right))\right]\ \text{or} \\ \left[q=p+1;\ \operatorname{Re}\alpha>0;\ \sigma,\ \omega>0;\ \operatorname{Re}s<\operatorname{Re}\left(a_k-\alpha\right)+1,\ 3/2-\operatorname{Re}\left(\alpha+\chi\right)\right]\end{matrix}\right]$

No.	$f(x)$	$F(s)$

4 — $\dfrac{1}{|x-\sigma|^\rho}\,_pF_q\!\left(\begin{matrix}(a_p);\ -\omega x\\(b_q)\end{matrix}\right)$

$\dfrac{\Gamma(s-\rho)}{\omega^{s-\rho}}\,\Gamma\!\left[\begin{matrix}(b_q),\ (a_p)+\rho-s\\(a_p),\ (b_q)+\rho-s\end{matrix}\right]$

$\times\,_{p+1}F_{q+1}\!\left(\begin{matrix}\rho,\ (a_p)+\rho-s;\ -\sigma\omega\\\rho-s+1,\ (b_q)+\rho-s\end{matrix}\right)+\sigma^{s-\rho}\sec\dfrac{\rho\pi}{2}$

$\times\cos\dfrac{(2s-\rho)\pi}{2}\,\mathrm{B}(\rho-s,s)\,_{p+1}F_{q+1}\!\left(\begin{matrix}s,\ (a_p);\ -\sigma\omega\\s-\rho+1,\ (b_q)\end{matrix}\right)$

$$[0<\rho<1]$$

$$\left[\begin{matrix}[q=p-1;\ \sigma>0;\ |\arg\omega|<\pi;\ 0<\mathrm{Re}\,s<\mathrm{Re}\,(a_k+\rho)]\ \text{or}\\ [q=p;\ (\sigma,\ \mathrm{Re}\,\omega>0;\ 0<\mathrm{Re}\,s<\mathrm{Re}\,(a_k+\rho))\ \text{or}\\ (\sigma>0;\ \mathrm{Re}\,\omega=0;\ 0<\mathrm{Re}\,s<\mathrm{Re}\,(a_k+\rho),\ \mathrm{Re}\,(\rho-\chi)+1)]\ \text{or}\\ [q=p+1;\ \sigma,\omega>0;\ 0<\mathrm{Re}\,s<\mathrm{Re}\,(a_k+\rho),\ \mathrm{Re}\,(\rho-\chi)+1/2]\end{matrix}\right]$$

5 — $\dfrac{1}{x-\sigma}\,_pF_q\!\left(\begin{matrix}(a_p);\ -\omega x\\(b_q)\end{matrix}\right)$

$\dfrac{\Gamma(s-1)}{\omega^{s-1}}\,\Gamma\!\left[\begin{matrix}(b_q),\ (a_p)-s+1\\(a_p),\ (b_q)-s+1\end{matrix}\right]$

$\times\,_{p+1}F_{q+1}\!\left(\begin{matrix}1,\ (a_p)-s+1;\ -\sigma\omega\\2-s,\ (b_q)-s+1\end{matrix}\right)$

$-\pi\sigma^{s-1}\cot(s\pi)\,_pF_q\!\left(\begin{matrix}(a_p);\ -\sigma\omega\\(b_q)\end{matrix}\right)$

$$\left[\begin{matrix}[q=p-1;\ \sigma>0;\ |\arg\omega|<\pi;\ 0<\mathrm{Re}\,s<\mathrm{Re}\,a_k+1]\ \text{or}\\ [q=p;\ (\sigma,\ \mathrm{Re}\,\omega>0;\ 0<\mathrm{Re}\,s<\mathrm{Re}\,a_k+1)\ \text{or}\\ (\sigma>0;\ \mathrm{Re}\,\omega=0;\ 0<\mathrm{Re}\,s<\mathrm{Re}\,a_k+1,\ 2-\mathrm{Re}\,\chi)\ \text{or}\\ [q=p+1;\ \sigma,\omega>0;\ 0<\mathrm{Re}\,s<\mathrm{Re}\,a_k+1,\ 3/2-\mathrm{Re}\,\chi]\end{matrix}\right]$$

6 — $\dfrac{1}{(x+\sigma)^\rho}\,_pF_q\!\left(\begin{matrix}(a_p);\ -\omega x\\(b_q)\end{matrix}\right)$

$\sigma^{s-\rho}\,\mathrm{B}(\rho-s,s)\,_{p+1}F_{q+1}\!\left(\begin{matrix}(a_p),\ s;\ \sigma\omega\\(b_q),\ s-\rho+1\end{matrix}\right)$

$+\,\omega^{\rho-s}\,\Gamma\!\left[\begin{matrix}(b_q),\ s-\rho,\ (a_p)+\rho-s\\(a_p),\ (b_q)+\rho-s\end{matrix}\right]$

$\times\,_{p+1}F_{q+1}\!\left(\begin{matrix}\rho,\ (a_p)+\rho-s;\ \sigma\omega\\\rho-s+1,\ (b_q)+\rho-s\end{matrix}\right)$

$$\left[\begin{matrix}[q=p-1;\ |\arg\sigma|,\ |\arg\omega|<\pi;\ 0<\mathrm{Re}\,s<\mathrm{Re}\,(a_k+\rho)]\ \text{or}\\ [q=p;\ (|\arg\sigma|<\pi;\ \mathrm{Re}\,\omega>0;\ 0<\mathrm{Re}\,s<\mathrm{Re}\,(a_k+\rho))\ \text{or}\\ (|\arg\sigma|<\pi;\ \mathrm{Re}\,\omega=0;\ 0<\mathrm{Re}\,s<\mathrm{Re}\,(a_k+\rho),\ \mathrm{Re}\,(\rho-\chi)+1)]\ \text{or}\\ [q=p+1;\ |\arg\sigma|<\pi;\ \omega>0;\ 0<\mathrm{Re}\,s<\mathrm{Re}\,(a_k+\rho),\ \mathrm{Re}\,(\rho-\chi)+1/2]\end{matrix}\right]$$

7 — $(\sigma^2-x^2)_+^{\alpha-1}$

$_pF_q\!\left(\begin{matrix}(a_p);\ -\omega x\\(b_q)\end{matrix}\right)$

$\displaystyle\prod_{i=1}^{p}a_i\prod_{j=1}^{q}b_j^{-1}\,\frac{\sigma^{s+2\alpha-1}\omega}{2}\,\mathrm{B}\!\left(\frac{s+1}{2},\alpha\right)$

$\times\,_{2p+1}F_{2q+2}\!\left(\begin{matrix}\frac{(a_p)+1}{2},\ \frac{(a_p)+2}{2},\ \frac{s+1}{2};\ \frac{\sigma^2\omega^2}{4}\\[2pt]\frac{3}{2},\ \frac{(b_q)+1}{2},\ \frac{(b_q)+2}{2},\ \frac{s+2\alpha+1}{2}\end{matrix}\right)$

$+\dfrac{\sigma^{s+2\alpha-2}}{2}\,\mathrm{B}\!\left(\frac{s}{2},\alpha\right)\,_{2p+1}F_{2q+2}\!\left(\begin{matrix}\frac{(a_p)}{2},\ \frac{(a_p)+1}{2},\ \frac{s}{2};\ \frac{\sigma^2\omega^2}{4}\\[2pt]\frac{1}{2},\ \frac{(b_q)}{2},\ \frac{(b_q)+1}{2},\ \frac{s+2\alpha}{2}\end{matrix}\right)$

$$[\sigma,\ \mathrm{Re}\,\alpha,\ \mathrm{Re}\,s>0]$$

3.33. *The Generalized Hypergeometric Functions* $_pF_q\left((a_p);\,(b_q);\,z\right)$ ⠀⠀⠀⠀⠀⠀⠀⠀⠀⠀⠀ 501

No.	$f(x)$	$F(s)$
8	$\left(x^2 - \sigma^2\right)_+^{\alpha - 1}$ $\times\ {_pF_q}\left(\begin{matrix}(a_p);\ -\omega x\\ (b_q)\end{matrix}\right)$	$\dfrac{\Gamma\left(s + 2\alpha - 2\right)}{\omega^{s + 2\alpha - 2}}\,\Gamma\!\left[\begin{matrix}(b_q),\ (a_p) - 2\alpha - s + 2\\ (a_p),\ (b_q) - 2\alpha - s + 2\end{matrix}\right]$ $\times\ {_{2p+1}F_{2q+2}}\left(\begin{matrix}1 - \alpha,\ \frac{(a_p) - 2\alpha - s + 2}{2},\ \frac{(a_p) - 2\alpha - s + 3}{2};\ \frac{\sigma^2\omega^2}{16}\\ \frac{3 - 2\alpha - s}{2},\ \frac{4 - 2\alpha - s}{2},\ \frac{(b_q) - 2\alpha - s + 2}{2},\ \frac{(b_q) - 2\alpha - s + 3}{2}\end{matrix}\right)$ $-\prod_{i=1}^{p} a_i \prod_{j=1}^{q} b_j^{-1}\,\dfrac{\sigma^{s + 2\alpha - 1}\omega}{2}\,\mathrm{B}\!\left(\alpha,\ \dfrac{1 - 2\alpha - s}{2}\right)$ $\times\ {_{2p+1}F_{2q+2}}\left(\begin{matrix}\frac{(a_p) + 1}{2},\ \frac{(a_p) + 2}{2},\ \frac{s + 1}{2};\ \frac{\sigma^2\omega^2}{16}\\ \frac{3}{2},\ \frac{(b_q) + 1}{2},\ \frac{(b_q) + 2}{2},\ \frac{s + 2\alpha + 1}{2}\end{matrix}\right)$ $+\dfrac{\sigma^{s + 2\alpha - 2}}{2}\,\mathrm{B}\!\left(\alpha,\ \dfrac{2 - 2\alpha - s}{2}\right)$ $\times\ {_{2p+1}F_{2q+2}}\left(\begin{matrix}\frac{(a_p)}{2},\ \frac{(a_p) + 1}{2},\ \frac{s}{2};\ \frac{\sigma^2\omega^2}{16}\\ \frac{1}{2},\ \frac{(b_q)}{2},\ \frac{(b_q) + 1}{2},\ \frac{s + 2\alpha}{2}\end{matrix}\right)$ $\begin{bmatrix}\left[q = p - 1;\ \sigma,\ \mathrm{Re}\,\alpha > 0;\ \lvert\arg\omega\rvert < \pi;\ \mathrm{Re}\,s < \mathrm{Re}\left(a_k - 2\alpha\right) + 2\right]\ \text{or}\\ \left[q = p;\ \mathrm{Re}\,\alpha > 0;\ \left(\sigma,\ \mathrm{Re}\,\omega > 0;\ \mathrm{Re}\,s < \mathrm{Re}\left(a_k - 2\alpha\right) + 2\right)\ \text{or}\right.\\ \left(\sigma > 0;\ \mathrm{Re}\,\omega = 0;\ \mathrm{Re}\,s < \mathrm{Re}\left(a_k - 2\alpha\right) + 2,\ 3 - \mathrm{Re}\left(2\alpha + \chi\right)\right)\right]\ \text{or}\\ \left[q = p + 1;\ \sigma,\ \omega,\ \mathrm{Re}\,\alpha > 0;\ \mathrm{Re}\,s < \mathrm{Re}\left(a_k - 2\alpha\right) + 2,\ 5/2 - \mathrm{Re}\left(2\alpha + \chi\right)\right]\end{bmatrix}$
9	$\dfrac{1}{\lvert x^2 - \sigma^2\rvert^{\rho}}\,{_pF_q}\left(\begin{matrix}(a_p);\ -\omega x\\ (b_q)\end{matrix}\right)$	$\left(\omega^2\right)^{\rho - s/2}\,\Gamma\left(s - 2\rho\right)\,\Gamma\!\left[\begin{matrix}(b_q),\ (a_p) + 2\rho - s\\ (a_p),\ (b_q) + 2\rho - s\end{matrix}\right]$ $\times\ {_{2p+1}F_{2q+2}}\left(\begin{matrix}\rho,\ \frac{(a_p) + 2\rho - s}{2},\ \frac{(a_p) + 2\rho - s + 1}{2};\ \frac{\sigma^2\omega^2}{16}\\ \frac{2\rho - s + 1}{2},\ \frac{2\rho - s + 2}{2},\ \frac{(b_q) + 2\rho - s}{2},\ \frac{(b_q) + 2\rho - s + 1}{2}\end{matrix}\right)$ $+\prod_{i=1}^{p} a_i \prod_{j=1}^{q} b_j^{-1}\,\dfrac{\sigma^{s - 2\rho + 1}\sqrt{\omega^2}}{2}$ $\times\ \sec\dfrac{\rho\pi}{2}\,\sin\dfrac{(s - \rho)\pi}{2}\,\mathrm{B}\!\left(\dfrac{s + 1}{2},\ \dfrac{2\rho - s - 1}{2}\right)$ $\times\ {_{2p+1}F_{2q+2}}\left(\begin{matrix}\frac{s + 1}{2},\ \frac{(a_p) + 1}{2},\ \frac{(a_p) + 2}{2};\ \frac{\sigma^2\omega^2}{16}\\ \frac{3}{2},\ \frac{s - 2\rho + 3}{2},\ \frac{(b_q) + 1}{2},\ \frac{(b_q) + 2}{2}\end{matrix}\right)$ $+\dfrac{\sigma^{s - 2\rho}}{2}\,\sec\dfrac{\rho\pi}{2}\,\cos\dfrac{(s - \rho)\pi}{2}\,\mathrm{B}\!\left(\dfrac{s}{2},\ \dfrac{2\rho - s}{2}\right)$ $\times\ {_{2p+1}F_{2q+2}}\left(\begin{matrix}\frac{s}{2},\ \frac{(a_p)}{2},\ \frac{(a_p) + 1}{2};\ \frac{\sigma^2\omega^2}{16}\\ \frac{1}{2},\ \frac{s - 2\rho + 2}{2},\ \frac{(b_q)}{2},\ \frac{(b_q) + 1}{2}\end{matrix}\right)$ $\hfill\left[0 < \rho < 1/2\right]$ $\begin{bmatrix}\left[q = p - 1;\ \sigma > 0;\ \lvert\arg\omega\rvert < \pi;\ 0 < \mathrm{Re}\,s < \mathrm{Re}\left(a_k + 2\rho\right)\right]\ \text{or}\\ \left[q = p;\ \left(\sigma,\ \mathrm{Re}\,\omega > 0;\ 0 < \mathrm{Re}\,s < \mathrm{Re}\left(a_k + 2\rho\right)\right)\ \text{or}\right.\\ \left(\sigma > 0;\ \mathrm{Re}\,\omega = 0;\ 0 < \mathrm{Re}\,s < \mathrm{Re}\left(a_k + 2\rho\right),\ \mathrm{Re}\left(2\rho - \chi\right) + 1\right)\right]\ \text{or}\\ \left[q = p + 1;\ \sigma,\ \omega > 0;\ 0 < \mathrm{Re}\,s < \mathrm{Re}\left(a_k + 2\rho\right),\ \mathrm{Re}\left(2\rho - \chi\right) + 1/2\right]\end{bmatrix}$

No.	$f(x)$	$F(s)$

10

$f(x)$:
$$\frac{1}{x^2 - \sigma^2}\, {}_pF_q\left(\begin{matrix}(a_p)\,;\ -\omega x\\(b_q)\end{matrix}\right)$$

$F(s)$:
$$\frac{\Gamma(s-2)}{\omega^{s-2}}\,\Gamma\left[\begin{matrix}(b_q),\ (a_p)-s+2\\(a_p),\ (b_q)-s+2\end{matrix}\right]$$

$$\times\ {}_{2p+1}F_{2q+2}\left(\begin{matrix}1,\ \frac{(a_p)-s+2}{2},\ \frac{(a_p)-s+3}{2};\ \frac{\sigma^2\omega^2}{4}\\\frac{3-s}{2},\ \frac{4-s}{2},\ \frac{(b_q)-s+2}{2},\ \frac{(b_q)-s+3}{2}\end{matrix}\right)$$

$$-\prod_{i=1}^{p}a_i\prod_{j=1}^{q}b_j^{-1}\frac{\pi\omega\sigma^{s-1}}{2}\tan\frac{s\pi}{2}$$

$$\times\ {}_{2p}F_{2q+1}\left(\begin{matrix}\frac{(a_p)+1}{2},\ \frac{(a_p)+2}{2};\ \frac{\sigma^2\omega^2}{4}\\\frac{3}{2},\ \frac{(b_q)+1}{2},\ \frac{(b_q)+2}{2}\end{matrix}\right)$$

$$-\frac{\pi\sigma^{s-2}}{2}\cot\frac{s\pi}{2}\ {}_{2p}F_{2q+1}\left(\begin{matrix}\frac{(a_p)}{2},\ \frac{(a_p)+1}{2};\ \frac{\sigma^2\omega^2}{4}\\\frac{1}{2},\ \frac{(b_q)}{2},\ \frac{(b_q)+1}{2}\end{matrix}\right)$$

$$\begin{bmatrix}[q=p-1;\ \sigma>0;\ |\arg\omega|<\pi;\ 0<\operatorname{Re}s<\operatorname{Re}a_k+2]\ \text{or}\\[q=p;\ (\sigma,\ \operatorname{Re}\omega>0;\ 0<\operatorname{Re}s<\operatorname{Re}a_k+2)\ \text{or}\\(\sigma>0;\ \operatorname{Re}\omega=0;\ 0<\operatorname{Re}s<\operatorname{Re}a_k+2,\ 3-\operatorname{Re}\chi)\ \text{or}\\[q=p+1;\ \sigma,\ \omega>0;\ 0<\operatorname{Re}s<\operatorname{Re}a_k+2,\ 5/2-\operatorname{Re}\chi]\end{bmatrix}$$

11

$f(x)$:
$$\frac{1}{(x^2+\sigma^2)^\rho}\, {}_pF_q\left(\begin{matrix}(a_p)\,;\ -\omega x\\(b_q)\end{matrix}\right)$$

$F(s)$:
$$\omega^{2\rho-s}\,\Gamma(s-2\rho)\,\Gamma\left[\begin{matrix}(b_q),\ (a_p)+2\rho-s\\(a_p),\ (b_q)+2\rho-s\end{matrix}\right]$$

$$\times\ {}_{2p+1}F_{2q+2}\left(\begin{matrix}\rho,\ \frac{(a_p)+2\rho-s}{2},\ \frac{(a_p)+2\rho-s+1}{2};\ -\frac{\sigma^2\omega^2}{16}\\\frac{2\rho-s+1}{2},\ \frac{2\rho-s+2}{2},\ \frac{(b_q)+2\rho-s}{2},\ \frac{(b_q)+2\rho-s+1}{2}\end{matrix}\right)$$

$$-\prod_{i=1}^{p}a_i\prod_{j=1}^{q}b_j^{-1}\frac{\sigma^{s-2\rho+1}\omega}{2}\,\mathrm{B}\left(\frac{2\rho-s-1}{2},\ \frac{s+1}{2}\right)$$

$$\times\ {}_{2p+1}F_{2q+2}\left(\begin{matrix}\frac{s+1}{2},\ \frac{(a_p)+1}{2},\ \frac{(a_p)+2}{2};\ -\frac{\sigma^2\omega^2}{16}\\\frac{3}{2},\ \frac{s-2\rho+3}{2},\ \frac{(b_q)+1}{2},\ \frac{(b_q)+2}{2}\end{matrix}\right)$$

$$+\frac{\sigma^{s-2\rho}}{2}\,\mathrm{B}\left(\frac{2\rho-s}{2},\ \frac{s}{2}\right)$$

$$\times\ {}_{2p+1}F_{2q+2}\left(\begin{matrix}\frac{s}{2},\ \frac{(a_p)}{2},\ \frac{(a_p)+1}{2};\ -\frac{\sigma^2\omega^2}{16}\\\frac{1}{2},\ \frac{s-2\rho+2}{2},\ \frac{(b_q)}{2},\ \frac{(b_q)+1}{2}\end{matrix}\right)$$

$$\begin{bmatrix}[q=p-1;\ |\arg\sigma|<\pi/2;\ |\arg\omega|<\pi;\ 0<\operatorname{Re}s<\operatorname{Re}(a_k+2\rho)]\ \text{or}\\[q=p;\ |\arg\sigma|<\pi/2;\ (\operatorname{Re}\omega>0;\ 0<\operatorname{Re}s<\operatorname{Re}(a_k+2\rho))\ \text{or}\\(\operatorname{Re}\omega=0;\ 0<\operatorname{Re}s<\operatorname{Re}(a_k+2\rho),\ \operatorname{Re}(2\rho-\chi)+1)]\ \text{or}\\[q=p+1;\ |\arg\sigma|<\pi/2;\ \omega>0;\ 0<\operatorname{Re}s<\operatorname{Re}(a_k+2\rho),\ \operatorname{Re}(2\rho-\chi)+1/2]\end{bmatrix}$$

12

$f(x)$:
$$(\sigma-x)_+^{\alpha-1}$$
$$\times\ {}_pF_q\left(\begin{matrix}(a_p)\,;\ -\omega x^2\\(b_q)\end{matrix}\right)$$

$F(s)$:
$$\sigma^{s+\alpha-1}\,\mathrm{B}(\alpha,s)\, {}_{p+1}F_{q+1}\left(\begin{matrix}(a_p),\ \frac{s}{2},\ \frac{s+1}{2};\ -\sigma^2\omega\\(b_q),\ \frac{s+\alpha}{2},\ \frac{s+\alpha+1}{2}\end{matrix}\right)$$

$$[\sigma,\ \operatorname{Re}\alpha,\ \operatorname{Re}s>0]$$

No.	$f(x)$	$F(s)$
13	$(x-\sigma)_+^{\alpha-1}$ $\times {}_pF_q\left(\begin{array}{c}(a_p);-\omega x^2\\(b_q)\end{array}\right)$	$\dfrac{(1-\alpha)\sigma}{2\omega^{s+\alpha-2}}\Gamma\left(\dfrac{s+\alpha-2}{2}\right)\Gamma\left[\begin{array}{c}(b_q),\ \frac{2(a_p)-\alpha-s+2}{2}\\(a_p),\ \frac{(b_q)-\alpha-s+2}{2}\end{array}\right]$ $\times {}_{p+1}F_{q+1}\left(\begin{array}{c}\frac{2-\alpha}{2},\ \frac{3-\alpha}{2},\ \frac{2(a_p)-\alpha-s+2}{2};\ -\sigma^2\omega\\\frac{3}{2},\ \frac{4-\alpha-s}{2},\ \frac{2(b_q)-\alpha-s+2}{2}\end{array}\right)$ $+\dfrac{1}{2\omega^{s+\alpha-1}}\Gamma\left(\dfrac{s+\alpha-1}{2}\right)\Gamma\left[\begin{array}{c}(b_q),\ \frac{2(a_p)-\alpha-s+1}{2}\\(a_p),\ \frac{(b_q)-\alpha-s+1}{2}\end{array}\right]$ $\times {}_{p+1}F_{q+1}\left(\begin{array}{c}\frac{1-\alpha}{2},\ \frac{2-\alpha}{2},\ \frac{2(a_p)-\alpha-s+1}{2};\ -\sigma^2\omega\\\frac{1}{2},\ \frac{3-\alpha-s}{2},\ \frac{2(b_q)-\alpha-s+1}{2}\end{array}\right)$ $+\sigma^{s+\alpha-1}\,\mathrm{B}\left(\alpha,1-\alpha-s\right)\,{}_{p+1}F_{q+1}\left(\begin{array}{c}(a_p),\ \frac{s}{2},\ \frac{s+1}{2};\ -\sigma^2\omega\\(b_q),\ \frac{s+\alpha}{2},\ \frac{s+\alpha+1}{2}\end{array}\right)$ $\begin{bmatrix}[q=p-1;\ \sigma,\ \mathrm{Re}\,\alpha>0;\ |\arg\omega|<\pi;\ \mathrm{Re}\,s<\mathrm{Re}\,(2a_k-\alpha)+1]\ \text{or}\\ [q=p;\ \mathrm{Re}\,\alpha>0;\ (\sigma,\ \mathrm{Re}\,\omega>0;\ \mathrm{Re}\,s<\mathrm{Re}\,(2a_k-\alpha)+1)\ \text{or}\\ (\sigma>0;\ \mathrm{Re}\,\omega=0;\ \mathrm{Re}\,s<\mathrm{Re}\,(2a_k-\alpha)+1,\ 3-\mathrm{Re}\,(\alpha+2\chi))]\ \text{or}\\ [q=p+1;\ \sigma,\ \omega,\ \mathrm{Re}\,\alpha>0;\ \mathrm{Re}\,s<\mathrm{Re}\,(2a_k-\alpha)+1,\ 2-\mathrm{Re}\,(\alpha+2\chi)]\end{bmatrix}$
14	$\dfrac{1}{|x-\sigma|^\rho}\,{}_pF_q\left(\begin{array}{c}(a_p);-\omega x^2\\(b_q)\end{array}\right)$	$\dfrac{\rho\sigma\omega^{(\rho-s+1)/2}}{2}\Gamma\left(\dfrac{s-\rho+1}{2}\right)\Gamma\left[\begin{array}{c}(b_q),\ \frac{2(a_p)+\rho-s+1}{2}\\(a_p),\ \frac{2(b_q)+\rho-s+1}{2}\end{array}\right]$ $\times {}_{p+2}F_{q+2}\left(\begin{array}{c}\frac{\rho+1}{2},\ \frac{\rho+2}{2},\ \frac{2(a_p)+\rho-s+1}{2};\ -\sigma^2\omega\\\frac{3}{2},\ \frac{\rho-s+3}{2},\ \frac{2(b_q)+\rho-s+1}{2}\end{array}\right)$ $+\dfrac{\omega^{(\rho-s)/2}}{2}\Gamma\left(\dfrac{s-\rho}{2}\right)\Gamma\left[\begin{array}{c}(b_q),\ \frac{2(a_p)+\rho-s}{2}\\(a_p),\ \frac{2(b_q)+\rho-s}{2}\end{array}\right]$ $\times {}_{p+2}F_{q+2}\left(\begin{array}{c}\frac{\rho}{2},\ \frac{\rho+1}{2},\ \frac{2(a_p)+\rho-s}{2};\ -\sigma^2\omega\\\frac{1}{2},\ \frac{\rho-s+2}{2},\ \frac{2(b_q)+\rho-s}{2}\end{array}\right)$ $+\sigma^{s-\rho}\sec\dfrac{\rho\pi}{2}\cos\dfrac{(2s-\rho)\pi}{2}\,\mathrm{B}\left(s,\rho-s\right)$ $\times {}_{p+2}F_{q+2}\left(\begin{array}{c}(a_p),\ \frac{s}{2},\ \frac{s+1}{2};\ -\sigma^2\omega\\(b_q),\ \frac{s-\rho+1}{2},\ \frac{s-\rho+2}{2}\end{array}\right)$ $[0<\rho<1]$ $\begin{bmatrix}[q=p-1;\ \sigma>0;\ |\arg\omega|<\pi;\ 0<\mathrm{Re}\,s<\mathrm{Re}\,(2a_k+\rho)]\ \text{or}\\ [q=p;\ (\sigma,\ \mathrm{Re}\,\omega>0;\ 0<\mathrm{Re}\,s<\mathrm{Re}\,(2a_k+\rho))\ \text{or}\\ (\sigma>0;\ \mathrm{Re}\,\omega=0;\ 0<\mathrm{Re}\,s<\mathrm{Re}\,(2a_k+\rho),\ \mathrm{Re}\,(\rho-2\chi)+2)]\ \text{or}\\ [q=p+1;\ \sigma,\ \omega>0;\ 0<\mathrm{Re}\,s<\mathrm{Re}\,(2a_k+\rho),\ \mathrm{Re}\,(\rho-2\chi)+1]\end{bmatrix}$
15	$\dfrac{1}{x-\sigma}\,{}_pF_q\left(\begin{array}{c}(a_p);-\omega x^2\\(b_q)\end{array}\right)$	$\dfrac{\sigma}{2\,\omega^{(s-2)/2}}\Gamma\left(\dfrac{s-2}{2}\right)\Gamma\left[\begin{array}{c}(b_q),\ \frac{2(a_p)-s+2}{2}\\(a_p),\ \frac{2(b_q)-s+2}{2}\end{array}\right]$ $\times {}_{p+1}F_{q+1}\left(\begin{array}{c}1,\ \frac{2(a_p)-s+2}{2};\ -\sigma^2\omega\\\frac{4-s}{2},\ \frac{2(b_q)-s+2}{2}\end{array}\right)$ $+\dfrac{1}{2\,\omega^{(s-1)/2}}\Gamma\left(\dfrac{s-1}{2}\right)\Gamma\left[\begin{array}{c}(b_q),\ \frac{2(a_p)-s+1}{2}\\(a_p),\ \frac{2(b_q)-s+1}{2}\end{array}\right]\times$

No.	$f(x)$	$F(s)$
		$\times\,_{p+1}F_{q+1}\left(\begin{matrix}1,\ \frac{2(a_p)-s+1}{2};\ -\sigma^2\omega\\[4pt]\frac{3-s}{2},\ \frac{2(b_q)-s+1}{2}\end{matrix}\right)$
		$-\,\pi\sigma^{s-1}\cot(s\pi)\,_pF_q\left(\begin{matrix}(a_p);\ -\sigma^2\omega\\[4pt](b_q)\end{matrix}\right)$
		$\left[\begin{matrix}[q=p-1;\ \sigma>0;\ |\arg\omega|<\pi;\ 0<\operatorname{Re}s<2\operatorname{Re}a_k+1]\ \text{or}\\ [q=p;\ (\sigma,\ \operatorname{Re}\omega>0;\ 0<\operatorname{Re}s<2\operatorname{Re}a_k+1)\ \text{or}\\ (\sigma>0;\ \operatorname{Re}\omega=0;\ 0<\operatorname{Re}s<2\operatorname{Re}a_k+1,\ 3-2\operatorname{Re}\chi)\ \text{or}\\ [q=p+1;\ \sigma,\ \omega>0;\ 0<\operatorname{Re}s<2\operatorname{Re}a_k+1,\ 2-2\operatorname{Re}\chi]\end{matrix}\right]$
16	$\dfrac{1}{(x+\sigma)^\rho}\,_pF_q\left(\begin{matrix}(a_p);\ -\omega x^2\\[4pt](b_q)\end{matrix}\right)$	$\sigma^{s-\rho}\,\mathrm{B}\,(\rho-s,\,s)\,_{p+2}F_{q+2}\left(\begin{matrix}(a_p),\ \frac{s}{2},\ \frac{s+1}{2};\ -\sigma^2\omega\\[4pt](b_q),\ \frac{s-\rho+1}{2},\ \frac{s-\rho+2}{2}\end{matrix}\right)$
		$+\dfrac{\omega^{(\rho-s)/2}}{2}\,\Gamma\left[\begin{matrix}(b_q),\ \frac{s-\rho}{2},\ \frac{2(a_p)+\rho-s}{2}\\[4pt](a_p),\ \frac{2(b_q)+\rho-s}{2}\end{matrix}\right]$
		$\times\,_{p+2}F_{q+2}\left(\begin{matrix}\frac{\rho}{2},\ \frac{\rho+1}{2},\ \frac{2(a_p)+\rho-s}{2};\ -\sigma^2\omega\\[4pt]\frac{1}{2},\ \frac{\rho-s+2}{2},\ \frac{2(b_q)+\rho-s}{2}\end{matrix}\right)$
		$-\dfrac{\rho\sigma\omega^{(\rho-s+1)/2}}{2}\,\Gamma\left[\begin{matrix}(b_q),\ \frac{s-\rho+1}{2},\ \frac{2(a_p)+\rho-s+1}{2}\\[4pt](a_p),\ \frac{2(b_q)+\rho-s+1}{2}\end{matrix}\right]$
		$\times\,_{p+2}F_{q+2}\left(\begin{matrix}\frac{\rho+1}{2},\ \frac{\rho+2}{2},\ \frac{2(a_p)+\rho-s+1}{2};\ -\sigma^2\omega\\[4pt]\frac{3}{2},\ \frac{\rho-s+3}{2},\ \frac{2(b_q)+\rho-s+1}{2}\end{matrix}\right)$
		$\left[\begin{matrix}[q=p-1;\ |\arg\sigma|,\ |\arg\omega|<\pi;\ 0<\operatorname{Re}s<\operatorname{Re}(2a_k+\rho)]\ \text{or}\\ [q=p;\ (|\arg\sigma|<\pi;\ \operatorname{Re}\omega>0;\ 0<\operatorname{Re}s<\operatorname{Re}(2a_k+\rho))\ \text{or}\\ (|\arg\sigma|<\pi;\ \operatorname{Re}\omega=0;\ 0<\operatorname{Re}s<\operatorname{Re}(2a_k+\rho),\ \operatorname{Re}(\rho-2\chi)+2)]\ \text{or}\\ [q=p+1;\ |\arg\sigma|<\pi;\ \omega>0;\ 0<\operatorname{Re}s<\operatorname{Re}(2a_k+\rho),\ \operatorname{Re}(\rho-2\chi)+1]\end{matrix}\right]$
17	$\dfrac{1}{(x+\sigma)^\rho}\,_pF_q\left(\begin{matrix}(a_p);\ \frac{b}{x+\sigma}\\[4pt](b_q)\end{matrix}\right)$	$\sigma^{s-\rho}\,\mathrm{B}\,(s,\,\rho-s)\,_{p+1}F_{q+1}\left(\begin{matrix}(a_p),\ \rho-s\\[4pt](b_q),\ \rho;\ \frac{b}{\sigma}\end{matrix}\right)$
		$[0<\operatorname{Re}s<\operatorname{Re}\rho;\ |\arg\sigma|<\pi]$
18	$\dfrac{1}{(x+\sigma)^\rho}\,_pF_q\left(\begin{matrix}(a_p);\ \frac{bx}{x+\sigma}\\[4pt](b_q)\end{matrix}\right)$	$\sigma^{s-\rho}\,\mathrm{B}\,(s,\,\rho-s)\,_{p+1}F_{q+1}\left(\begin{matrix}(a_p),\ s\\[4pt](b_q),\ \rho;\ b\end{matrix}\right)$
		$[0<\operatorname{Re}s<\operatorname{Re}\rho;\ |\arg\sigma|<\pi]$
19	$\dfrac{1}{(x+\sigma)^\rho}\,_pF_q\left(\begin{matrix}(a_p);\ \frac{b}{(x+\sigma)^2}\\[4pt](b_q)\end{matrix}\right)$	$\sigma^{s-\rho}\,\mathrm{B}\,(s,\,\rho-s)\,_{p+1}F_{q+1}\left(\begin{matrix}(a_p),\ \frac{\rho-s}{2},\ \frac{\rho-s+1}{2}\\[4pt](b_q),\ \frac{\rho}{2},\ \frac{\rho+1}{2};\ \frac{b}{\sigma^2}\end{matrix}\right)$
		$[0<\operatorname{Re}s<\operatorname{Re}\rho;\ |\arg\sigma|<\pi]$
20	$\dfrac{1}{(x+\sigma)^\rho}\,_pF_q\left(\begin{matrix}(a_p);\ \frac{bx^2}{(x+\sigma)^2}\\[4pt](b_q)\end{matrix}\right)$	$\sigma^{s-\rho}\,\mathrm{B}\,(s,\,\rho-s)\,_{p+2}F_{q+2}\left(\begin{matrix}(a_p),\ \frac{s}{2},\ \frac{s+1}{2}\\[4pt](b_q),\ \frac{\rho}{2},\ \frac{\rho+1}{2};\ b\end{matrix}\right)$
		$[0<\operatorname{Re}s<\operatorname{Re}\rho;\ |\arg\sigma|<\pi]$

3.33.2. $_pF_q\left((a_p)\,;\,(b_q)\,;\,\omega x^r\right)$ **and the exponential function**

Notation:

$$\mu = \sum_{i=1}^{p} a_i - \sum_{j=1}^{q} b_j + \frac{q-p+1}{2}.$$

1	$e^{-\sigma x}\,_pF_q\left(\begin{array}{c}(a_p)\,;\,-\omega x\\(b_q)\end{array}\right)$	$\dfrac{\Gamma(s)}{\sigma^s}\,_{p+1}F_q\left(\begin{array}{c}(a_p),\,s\\(b_q)\,;\,-\frac{\omega}{\sigma}\end{array}\right)$

$$\left[\begin{array}{l}\big[q = p-1;\ |\arg\omega| < \pi;\ (\mathrm{Re}\,\sigma,\ \mathrm{Re}\,s > 0)\ \text{or}\\ \quad (\mathrm{Re}\,\sigma = 0;\ 0 < \mathrm{Re}\,s < \mathrm{Re}\,a_k + 1)\big]\ \text{or}\\ \big[q = p;\ (\mathrm{Re}\,\sigma,\ \mathrm{Re}\,(\sigma+\omega),\ \mathrm{Re}\,s > 0)\ \text{or}\\ \quad (\mathrm{Re}\,\sigma > 0;\ \mathrm{Re}\,(\sigma+\omega) = 0;\ 0 < \mathrm{Re}\,s < 1 - \mathrm{Re}\,\chi)\ \text{or}\\ \quad (\mathrm{Re}\,\sigma = 0;\ \mathrm{Re}\,\omega > 0;\ 0 < \mathrm{Re}\,s < \mathrm{Re}\,a_k + 1)\ \text{or}\\ \quad (\mathrm{Re}\,\sigma = \mathrm{Re}\,\omega = 0;\ 0 < \mathrm{Re}\,s < \mathrm{Re}\,a_k + 1,\ 1 - \mathrm{Re}\,\chi)\big]\ \text{or}\\ \big[q = p+1;\ (\mathrm{Re}\,\sigma,\ \mathrm{Re}\,s > 0;\ |\arg\omega| < \pi)\ \text{or}\\ \quad (\mathrm{Re}\,\sigma = 0;\ \omega > 0;\ 0 < \mathrm{Re}\,s < \mathrm{Re}\,a_k + 1,\ 1 - \mathrm{Re}\,\chi)\big]\ \text{or}\\ \big[q \geq p+2;\ \mathrm{Re}\,\sigma,\ \mathrm{Re}\,s > 0;\ |\arg\omega| < \pi\big]\end{array}\right]$$

2	$e^{-\sigma x^k}\,_pF_q\left(\begin{array}{c}(a_p)\,;\,-\omega x^\ell\\(b_q)\end{array}\right)$	$\dfrac{k^{\mu-1}\ell^{s/k-1/2}\sigma^{-s/k}}{(2\pi)^{[(k-1)(p-q+1)+\ell-1]/2}}\,\Gamma\!\left[\begin{array}{c}(b_q)\\(a_p)\end{array}\right]$

$$\times\, G^{k,\,kp+\ell}_{kp+\ell,\,kq+k}\left(\frac{\ell^\ell\omega^k}{k^{k(q-p+1)}\sigma^\ell}\ \middle|\ \begin{array}{c}\Delta(k,\,1-(a_p)),\,\Delta(\ell,\,s)\\\Delta(k,\,0),\,\Delta(k,\,1-(b_q))\end{array}\right)$$

$$[A = \min_{1\leq i\leq p} a_i]$$

$$\left[\begin{array}{l}\big[q = p-1;\ k > 0;\ |\arg\omega| < \pi;\ (\mathrm{Re}\,\sigma,\ \mathrm{Re}\,s > 0)\ \text{or}\\ \quad (\mathrm{Re}\,\sigma = 0;\ 0 < \mathrm{Re}\,s < k + \ell A)\big]\ \text{or}\\ \big[q = p;\ \big(0 < k < \ell;\ (\mathrm{Re}\,\sigma,\ \mathrm{Re}\,s > 0;\ \mathrm{Re}\,\omega \geq 0)\ \text{or}\\ \quad (\mathrm{Re}\,\sigma = 0;\ \mathrm{Re}\,\omega > 0;\ 0 < \mathrm{Re}\,s < k + \ell A)\ \text{or}\\ \quad (\mathrm{Re}\,\sigma = \mathrm{Re}\,\omega = 0;\ 0 < \mathrm{Re}\,s < k + \ell A,\ \ell - \ell\,\mathrm{Re}\,\chi))\ \text{or}\\ \quad \big(k = \ell;\ (\mathrm{Re}\,\sigma,\ \mathrm{Re}\,(\sigma+\omega),\ \mathrm{Re}\,s > 0)\ \text{or}\\ \quad (\mathrm{Re}\,\sigma = 0;\ \mathrm{Re}\,\omega > 0;\ 0 < \mathrm{Re}\,s < \ell + \ell A)\ \text{or}\\ \quad (\mathrm{Re}\,\sigma > 0;\ \mathrm{Re}\,(\sigma+\omega) = 0;\ 0 < \mathrm{Re}\,s < \ell - \ell\,\mathrm{Re}\,\chi)\ \text{or}\\ \quad (\mathrm{Re}\,\sigma = \mathrm{Re}\,\omega = 0;\ 0 < \mathrm{Re}\,s < \ell + \ell A,\ \ell - \ell\,\mathrm{Re}\,\chi))\ \text{or}\\ \quad \big(k > \ell;\ (\mathrm{Re}\,\sigma,\ \mathrm{Re}\,s > 0;\ |\arg\omega| < \pi)\ \text{or}\\ \quad (\mathrm{Re}\,\sigma = 0;\ \mathrm{Re}\,\omega > 0;\ 0 < \mathrm{Re}\,s < k + \ell A)\ \text{or}\\ \quad (\mathrm{Re}\,\sigma = \mathrm{Re}\,\omega = 0;\ 0 < \mathrm{Re}\,s < k + \ell A,\ k - \ell\,\mathrm{Re}\,\chi))\big]\ \text{or}\\ \big[q = p+1;\ \big(0 < k < \ell/2;\ (\omega,\ \mathrm{Re}\,\sigma,\ \mathrm{Re}\,s > 0)\ \text{or}\\ \quad (\mathrm{Re}\,\sigma = 0;\ \omega > 0;\ 0 < \mathrm{Re}\,s < k + \ell A,\ \ell/2 - \ell\,\mathrm{Re}\,\chi))\ \text{or}\\ \quad \big(k = \ell/2;\ (2|\mathrm{Im}\,\sqrt{\omega}| < \mathrm{Re}\,\sigma;\ \mathrm{Re}\,s > 0)\ \text{or}\\ \quad (\mathrm{Re}\,\sigma = 0;\ \omega > 0;\ 0 < \mathrm{Re}\,s < k + \ell A,\ \ell/2 - \ell\,\mathrm{Re}\,\chi))\ \text{or}\\ \quad \big(k > \ell/2;\ (\mathrm{Re}\,\sigma,\ \mathrm{Re}\,s > 0;\ |\arg\omega| < \pi)\ \text{or}\\ \quad (\mathrm{Re}\,\sigma = 0;\ \omega > 0;\ 0 < \mathrm{Re}\,s < k + \ell A,\ k - \ell\,\mathrm{Re}\,\chi))\big]\ \text{or}\\ \big[q \geq p+2;\ \big(k = \ell/(q-p+1);\ (\mathrm{Re}\,\sigma,\ \mathrm{Re}\,s > 0;\ |\arg\omega| < \pi)\ \text{or}\\ \quad (\mathrm{Re}\,\sigma = 0;\ \mathrm{Re}\,(-\omega)^{k/\ell} > 0;\ 0 < \mathrm{Re}\,s < \ell\,\mathrm{Re}\,a_k + k))\ \text{or}\\ \quad (k > \ell/(q-p+1);\ \mathrm{Re}\,\sigma,\ \mathrm{Re}\,s > 0;\ |\arg\omega| < \pi)\big]\end{array}\right]$$

No.	$f(x)$	$F(s)$
3	$e^{-\sigma x}\,{}_pF_q\!\left(\begin{matrix}(a_p);\ \omega x^\ell\\(b_q)\end{matrix}\right)$	$\dfrac{\Gamma(s)}{\sigma^s}\,{}_{p+\ell}F_q\!\left(\begin{matrix}(a_p),\ \Delta(\ell,s)\\(b_q);\ \left(\frac{\ell}{\sigma}\right)^\ell\omega\end{matrix}\right)$

$$\left[\begin{array}{l} p+\ell \le q+1;\ \operatorname{Re}s>0;\\ p+\ell<q;\ \operatorname{Re}\sigma>0;\\ p+\ell=q+1;\ \operatorname{Re}\left(\sigma+\ell\omega^{1/\ell}e^{2\pi ji/\ell}\right)>0\\ \hspace{4cm}(j=0,1,\dots,\ell-1)\end{array}\right]$$

4	$e^{-\sigma x^2}\,{}_pF_q\!\left(\begin{matrix}(a_p);\ -\omega x\\(b_q)\end{matrix}\right)$	$-\displaystyle\prod_{i=1}^{p}a_i\prod_{j=1}^{q}b_j^{-1}\frac{\omega}{2\,\sigma^{(s+1)/2}}\,\Gamma\!\left(\frac{s+1}{2}\right)$

$$\times\ {}_{2p+1}F_{2q+1}\!\left(\begin{matrix}\frac{(a_p)+1}{2},\ \frac{(a_p)+2}{2},\ \frac{s+1}{2}\\ \frac{3}{2},\ \frac{(b_q)+1}{2},\ \frac{(b_q)+2}{2};\ \frac{\omega^2}{4^{q-p+1}\sigma}\end{matrix}\right)$$

$$+\ \frac{\sigma^{-s/2}}{2}\,\Gamma\!\left(\frac{s}{2}\right)\,{}_{2p+1}F_{2q+1}\!\left(\begin{matrix}\frac{(a_p)}{2},\ \frac{(a_p)+1}{2},\ \frac{s}{2}\\ \frac{1}{2},\ \frac{(b_q)}{2},\ \frac{(b_q)+1}{2};\ \frac{\omega^2}{4^{q-p+1}\sigma}\end{matrix}\right)$$

$$\left[\begin{array}{l} [q=p-1;\ |\arg\omega|<\pi;\ (\operatorname{Re}\sigma,\ \operatorname{Re}s>0)\ \text{or}\\ \quad(\operatorname{Re}\sigma=0;\ 0<\operatorname{Re}s<\operatorname{Re}a_k+2)]\ \text{or}\\ [q=p;\ (\operatorname{Re}\sigma,\ \operatorname{Re}s>0;\ |\arg\omega|<\pi)\ \text{or}\\ \quad(\operatorname{Re}\sigma=0;\ \operatorname{Re}\omega>0;\ 0<\operatorname{Re}s<\operatorname{Re}a_k+2)\ \text{or}\\ \quad(\operatorname{Re}\sigma=\operatorname{Re}\omega=0;\ 0<\operatorname{Re}s<\operatorname{Re}a_k+2,\ 2-\operatorname{Re}\chi)]\ \text{or}\\ [q=p+1;\ (\operatorname{Re}\sigma,\ \operatorname{Re}s>0;\ |\arg\omega|<\pi)\ \text{or}\\ \quad(\operatorname{Re}\sigma=0;\ \omega>0;\ 0<\operatorname{Re}s<\operatorname{Re}a_k+2,\ 2-\operatorname{Re}\chi)]\ \text{or}\\ [q\ge p+2;\ \operatorname{Re}\sigma,\ \operatorname{Re}s>0;\ |\arg\omega|<\pi]\end{array}\right]$$

5	$e^{-\sigma/x}\,{}_pF_q\!\left(\begin{matrix}(a_p);\ -\omega x\\(b_q)\end{matrix}\right)$	$\omega^{-s}\Gamma\!\left[\begin{matrix}(b_q),\ s,\ (a_p)-s\\(a_p),\ (b_q)-s\end{matrix}\right]{}_pF_{q+1}\!\left(\begin{matrix}(a_p)-s;\ \sigma\omega\\(b_q)-s,\ 1-s\end{matrix}\right)$

$$+\ \sigma^s\,\Gamma(-s)\,{}_pF_{q+1}\!\left(\begin{matrix}(a_p);\ \sigma\omega\\(b_q),\ s+1\end{matrix}\right)$$

$$\left[\begin{array}{l} [q=p-1;\ |\arg\omega|<\pi;\ (\operatorname{Re}\sigma>0;\ \operatorname{Re}s<\operatorname{Re}a_k)\ \text{or}\ (\operatorname{Re}\sigma=0;\ \operatorname{Re}s>-1)]\ \text{or}\\ [q=p;\ (\operatorname{Re}\omega>0;\ \operatorname{Re}s<\operatorname{Re}a_k)\ \text{or}\ (\operatorname{Re}\omega=0;\ \operatorname{Re}s<\operatorname{Re}a_k,\ 1-\operatorname{Re}\chi)]\ \text{or}\\ [q=p+1;\ \omega>0;\ \operatorname{Re}s<\operatorname{Re}a_k,\ 1/2-\operatorname{Re}\chi]\end{array}\right]$$

6	$e^{-\sigma/x^2}\,{}_pF_q\!\left(\begin{matrix}(a_p);\ -\omega x\\(b_q)\end{matrix}\right)$	$\omega^{-s}\Gamma\!\left[\begin{matrix}(b_q),\ s,\ (a_p-s)\\(a_p),\ (b_q)-s\end{matrix}\right]{}_{2p}F_{2q+2}\!\left(\begin{matrix}\frac{(a_p)-s}{2},\ \frac{(a_p)-s+1}{2};\ -\frac{\sigma\omega^2}{4^{q-p+1}}\\ \frac{(b_q)-s}{2},\ \frac{(b_q)-s+1}{2},\ \frac{1-s}{2},\ \frac{2-s}{2}\end{matrix}\right)$

$$-\displaystyle\prod_{i=1}^{p}a_i\prod_{j=1}^{q}b_j^{-1}\frac{\omega\sigma^{(s+1)/2}}{2}\,\Gamma\!\left(-\frac{s+1}{2}\right)$$

$$\times\ {}_{2p}F_{2q+2}\!\left(\begin{matrix}\frac{(a_p)+1}{2},\ \frac{(a_p)+2}{2};\ -\frac{\sigma\omega^2}{4^{q-p+1}}\\ \frac{3}{2},\ \frac{(b_q)+1}{2},\ \frac{(b_q)+2}{2},\ \frac{s+3}{2}\end{matrix}\right)$$

$$+\ \frac{\sigma^{s/2}}{2}\,\Gamma\!\left(-\frac{s}{2}\right)\,{}_{2p}F_{2q+2}\!\left(\begin{matrix}\frac{(a_p)}{2},\ \frac{(a_p)+1}{2};\ -\frac{\sigma\omega^2}{4^{q-p+1}}\\ \frac{1}{2},\ \frac{(b_q)}{2},\ \frac{(b_q)+1}{2},\ \frac{s+2}{2}\end{matrix}\right)$$

$$\left[\begin{array}{l} [q=p-1;\ |\arg\omega|<\pi;\ (\operatorname{Re}\sigma>0;\ \operatorname{Re}s<\operatorname{Re}a_k)\ \text{or}\ (\operatorname{Re}\sigma=0;\ -2<\operatorname{Re}s<\operatorname{Re}a_k)]\ \text{or}\\ [q=p;\ (|\arg\omega|<\pi/2;\ \operatorname{Re}s<\operatorname{Re}a_k)\ \text{or}\ (|\arg\omega|=\pi/2;\ \operatorname{Re}s<\operatorname{Re}a_k,\ 1-\operatorname{Re}\chi)]\ \text{or}\\ [q=p+1;\ \omega>0;\ \operatorname{Re}s<\operatorname{Re}a_k,\ 1/2-\operatorname{Re}\chi]\end{array}\right]$$

No.	$f(x)$	$F(s)$
7	$e^{-\sigma\sqrt{x}}\,{}_pF_q\left(\begin{matrix}(a_p);\ -\omega x\\(b_q)\end{matrix}\right)$	$2\left(\sigma^2\right)^{-s}\Gamma\left(2s\right)\,{}_{p+2}F_q\left(\begin{matrix}(a_p),\ s,\ \frac{2s+1}{2}\\(b_q);\ -\frac{4\omega}{\sigma^2}\end{matrix}\right)$

$$\left[\begin{array}{l} \left[q=p-1;\ |\arg\omega|<\pi;\ (\operatorname{Re}\sigma,\ \operatorname{Re}s>0)\ \text{or}\right.\\ \quad\left.(\operatorname{Re}\sigma=0;\ 0<\operatorname{Re}s<\operatorname{Re}a_k+1/2)\right]\ \text{or}\\ \left[q=p;\ (\operatorname{Re}\sigma,\ \operatorname{Re}s>0;\ \operatorname{Re}\omega\geq0)\ \text{or}\right.\\ \quad(\operatorname{Re}\sigma=0,\ \operatorname{Re}\omega>0;\ 0<\operatorname{Re}s<\operatorname{Re}a_k+1/2)\ \text{or}\\ \quad\left.(\operatorname{Re}\sigma=\operatorname{Re}\omega=0;\ 0<\operatorname{Re}s<\operatorname{Re}a_k+1/2,\ 1-\operatorname{Re}\chi)\right]\ \text{or}\\ \left[q=p+1;\ (2|\operatorname{Im}\sqrt{\omega}|<\operatorname{Re}\sigma;\ \operatorname{Re}s>0)\ \text{or}\right.\\ \quad(\operatorname{Re}\sigma=0;\ \omega>0;\ 0<\operatorname{Re}s<\operatorname{Re}a_k+1/2,\ 1/2-\operatorname{Re}\chi)\ \text{or}\\ \quad\left.(\operatorname{Re}\sigma>0;\ 2|\operatorname{Im}\sqrt{\omega}|+\operatorname{Re}\sigma=0;\ 0<\operatorname{Re}s<1/2-\operatorname{Re}\chi)\right]\ \text{or}\\ \left[q\geq p+2;\ \operatorname{Re}\sigma,\ \operatorname{Re}s>0;\ |\arg\omega|<\pi\right] \end{array}\right]$$

No.	$f(x)$	$F(s)$
8	$e^{-\sigma/\sqrt{x}}\,{}_pF_q\left(\begin{matrix}(a_p);\ -\omega x\\(b_q)\end{matrix}\right)$	

$$-\left(\frac{1}{\sigma^2}\right)^{-s}\left(\sigma^2\omega\right)^{(1-2s)/2}\Gamma\left[\begin{matrix}\frac{2s-1}{2},\ (b_q),\ \frac{1-2s+2(a_p)}{2}\\(a_p),\ \frac{1-2s+2(b_q)}{2}\end{matrix}\right]$$

$$\times\ {}_pF_{q+3}\left(\begin{matrix}\frac{1-2s+2(a_p)}{2};\ -\frac{\sigma^2\omega}{4}\\\frac{3}{2},\ \frac{1-2s+2(b_q)}{2},\ \frac{3-2s}{2}\end{matrix}\right)$$

$$+\left(\frac{1}{\sigma^2}\right)^{-s}\left(\sigma^2\omega\right)^{-s}\Gamma\left[\begin{matrix}s,\ (b_q),\ (a_p)-s\\(a_p),\ (b_q)-s\end{matrix}\right]$$

$$\times\ {}_pF_{q+3}\left(\begin{matrix}(a_p)-s;\ -\frac{\sigma^2\omega}{4}\\\frac{1}{2},\ (b_q)-s,\ 1-s\end{matrix}\right)$$

$$+2\left(\frac{1}{\sigma^2}\right)^{-s}\Gamma\left(-2s\right)\,{}_pF_{q+3}\left(\begin{matrix}(a_p);\ -\frac{\sigma^2\omega}{4}\\(b_q),\ \frac{2s+1}{2},\ s+1\end{matrix}\right)$$

$$\left[\begin{array}{l} \left[q=p-1;\ |\arg\omega|<\pi;\ (\operatorname{Re}\sigma>0;\ \operatorname{Re}s<\operatorname{Re}a_k)\ \text{or}\right.\\ \quad\left.(\operatorname{Re}\sigma=0;\ \operatorname{Re}s>-1/2)\right]\ \text{or}\\ \left[q=p;\ (\operatorname{Re}\omega>0;\ \operatorname{Re}s<\operatorname{Re}a_k)\ \text{or}\right.\\ \quad\left.(\operatorname{Re}\omega=0;\ \operatorname{Re}s<\operatorname{Re}a_k,\ 1-\operatorname{Re}\chi)\right]\ \text{or}\\ \left[q=p+1;\ \omega>0;\ \operatorname{Re}s<\operatorname{Re}a_k,\ 1/2-\operatorname{Re}\chi\right] \end{array}\right]$$

3.33.3. $_pF_q\left((a_p);\ (b_q);\ \omega x^r\right)$ and the logarithmic function

No.	$f(x)$	$F(s)$
1	$\theta\left(\sigma-x\right)\ln\dfrac{\sqrt{\sigma}+\sqrt{\sigma-x}}{\sqrt{x}}$ $\times\ {}_pF_q\left(\begin{matrix}(a_p)\\(b_q);\ \omega x\end{matrix}\right)$	$\dfrac{\sqrt{\pi}\,\sigma^s}{2s}\Gamma\left[\begin{matrix}s\\\frac{2s+1}{2}\end{matrix}\right]\,{}_{p+2}F_{q+2}\left(\begin{matrix}(a_p),\ s,\ s;\ \sigma\omega\\(b_q),\ \frac{2s+1}{2},\ s+1\end{matrix}\right)$ $[\sigma,\ \operatorname{Re}s>0;\ |\arg\omega|<\pi]$
2	$\theta\left(\sigma-x\right)\ln\dfrac{\sqrt{\sigma}+\sqrt{\sigma-x}}{\sqrt{x}}$ $\times\ {}_pF_q\left(\begin{matrix}(a_p)\\(b_q);\ \omega x^2\end{matrix}\right)$	$\dfrac{\sqrt{\pi}\,\sigma^s}{2s}\Gamma\left[\begin{matrix}s\\\frac{2s+1}{2}\end{matrix}\right]\,{}_{p+3}F_{q+3}\left(\begin{matrix}(a_p),\ \frac{s}{2},\ \frac{s}{2},\ \frac{s+1}{2};\ \sigma^2\omega\\(b_q),\ \frac{2s+1}{4},\ \frac{2s+3}{4},\ \frac{s+2}{2}\end{matrix}\right)$ $[\sigma,\ \operatorname{Re}s>0;\ |\arg\omega|<\pi]$

3.33.4. $_pF_q\left((a_p)\,;\,(b_q)\,;\,\omega x\right)$ **and inverse trigonometric functions**

1	$\theta\left(\sigma - x\right)\arccos\dfrac{x}{\sigma}$ $\times\ _pF_q\left(\begin{matrix}(a_p)\,;\,\omega x\\(b_q)\end{matrix}\right)$	$\displaystyle\prod_{i=1}^{p}a_i\prod_{j=1}^{q}b_j^{-1}\ \dfrac{\sqrt{\pi}\,\omega\sigma^{s+1}}{2\,(s+1)}\,\Gamma\!\left[\begin{matrix}\frac{s+2}{2}\\\frac{s+3}{2}\end{matrix}\right]$ $\times\ _{2p+2}F_{2q+3}\left(\begin{matrix}\frac{(a_p)+1}{2},\ \frac{(a_p)+2}{2},\ \frac{s+1}{2},\ \frac{s+2}{2}\,;\ \frac{\sigma^2\omega^2}{4^{q-p+1}}\\\frac{3}{2},\ \frac{(b_q)+1}{2},\ \frac{(b_q)+2}{2},\ \frac{s+3}{2},\ \frac{s+3}{2}\end{matrix}\right)$ $+\ \dfrac{\sqrt{\pi}\,\sigma^s}{2s}\,\Gamma\!\left[\begin{matrix}\frac{s+1}{2}\\\frac{s+2}{2}\end{matrix}\right]$ $\times\ _{2p+2}F_{2q+3}\left(\begin{matrix}\frac{(a_p)}{2},\ \frac{(a_p)+1}{2},\ \frac{s}{2},\ \frac{s+1}{2}\,;\ \frac{\sigma^2\omega^2}{4^{q-p+1}}\\\frac{1}{2},\ \frac{(b_q)}{2},\ \frac{(b_q)+1}{2},\ \frac{s+2}{2},\ \frac{s+2}{2}\end{matrix}\right)$ $\left[\sigma,\ \operatorname{Re}s>0;\ |\arg\omega|<\pi\right]$
2	$\theta\left(\sigma - x\right)\arccos\sqrt{\dfrac{x}{\sigma}}$ $\times\ _pF_q\left(\begin{matrix}(a_p)\,;\,\omega x\\(b_q)\end{matrix}\right)$	$\dfrac{\sqrt{\pi}\,\sigma^s}{2s}\,\Gamma\!\left[\begin{matrix}\frac{2s+1}{2}\\s+1\end{matrix}\right]\ _{p+2}F_{q+2}\left(\begin{matrix}(a_p),\ s,\ \frac{2s+1}{2}\,;\ \sigma\omega\\(b_q),\ s+1,\ s+1\end{matrix}\right)$ $\left[\sigma,\ \operatorname{Re}s>0;\ |\arg\omega|<\pi\right]$

3.33.5. $_pF_q\left((a_p)\,;\,(b_q)\,;\,\omega x\right)$ **and** $\operatorname{Ei}\left(\sigma x^r\right)$

1	$\operatorname{Ei}\left(-\sigma x\right)\ _pF_q\left(\begin{matrix}(a_p)\,;\,\omega x\\(b_q)\end{matrix}\right)$	$-\dfrac{\sigma^{-s}}{s}\,\Gamma\left(s\right)\ _{p+2}F_{q+1}\left(\begin{matrix}(a_p),\ s,\ s\\(b_q),\ s+1;\ \frac{\omega}{\sigma}\end{matrix}\right)$ $\left[\begin{matrix}\left[q=p-1;\ \sigma,\ \operatorname{Re}s>0;\ |\arg\omega|<\pi\right]\text{ or}\\\left[q=p;\ (\sigma,\ \sigma+\operatorname{Re}\omega,\ \operatorname{Re}s>0)\text{ or}\right.\\\left.(\sigma>0;\ \sigma+\operatorname{Re}\omega=0;\ 0<\operatorname{Re}s<2-\operatorname{Re}\chi)\right]\text{ or}\\\left[p=0;\ q=1;\ \operatorname{Im}\sigma\neq0,\ \operatorname{Re}\sigma\geq0;\ \omega>0;\right.\\\left.0<\operatorname{Re}s<(2\operatorname{Re}b_1+3)/4\right]\text{ or}\\\left[q\geq p+1;\ \sigma,\ \operatorname{Re}s>0;\ |\arg\omega|<\pi\right]\end{matrix}\right]$
2	$\operatorname{Ei}\left(-\sigma\sqrt{x}\right)\ _pF_q\left(\begin{matrix}(a_p)\,;\,\omega x\\(b_q)\end{matrix}\right)$	$\dfrac{\sigma^{-2s}}{s}\,\Gamma\left(2s\right)\ _{p+3}F_{q+1}\left(\begin{matrix}(a_p),\ s,\ s,\ \frac{2s+1}{2}\\(b_q),\ s+1;\ \frac{4\omega}{\sigma^2}\end{matrix}\right)$ $\left[\begin{matrix}\left[q=p-1;\ \sigma,\ \operatorname{Re}s>0;\ |\arg\omega|<\pi\right]\text{ or}\\\left[q=p;\ (\sigma,\ \operatorname{Re}s>0;\ \operatorname{Re}\omega\geq0)\text{ or}\right.\\\left.(\sigma>0;\ \operatorname{Re}\omega=0;\ 0<\operatorname{Re}s<3/2-\operatorname{Re}\chi)\right]\text{ or}\\\left[p=0;\ q=1;\ \operatorname{Im}\sigma\neq0;\ \omega>0;\right.\\\left.0<\operatorname{Re}s<(2\operatorname{Re}b_1+1)/4\right]\text{ or}\\\left[q=p+1;\ |\operatorname{Im}\sqrt{\omega}|<\sigma;\ \operatorname{Re}s>0\right]\text{ or}\\\left[q\geq p+2;\ \sigma,\ \operatorname{Re}s>0;\ |\arg\omega|<\pi\right]\end{matrix}\right]$

3.33.6. $_pF_q\left((a_p)\,;\,(b_q)\,;\,\omega x\right)$ **and** $\operatorname{erfc}\left(\sigma x^r\right)$

1	$\operatorname{erfc}\left(\sigma x\right)\,_pF_q\!\left(\begin{matrix}(a_p)\,;\,-\omega x\\(b_q)\end{matrix}\right)$	$-\displaystyle\prod_{i=1}^{p}a_i\prod_{j=1}^{q}b_j^{-1}\,\frac{\sigma^{-s-1}\omega}{\sqrt{\pi}\,(s+1)}\,\Gamma\!\left(\frac{s+2}{2}\right)$

$$\times\,_{2p+2}F_{2q+2}\!\left(\begin{matrix}\frac{(a_p)+1}{2},\,\frac{(a_p)+2}{2},\,\frac{s+1}{2},\,\frac{s+2}{2}\,;\,\frac{\omega^2}{4^{q-p+1}\sigma^2}\\[4pt]\frac{3}{2},\,\frac{(b_q)+1}{2},\,\frac{(b_q)+2}{2},\,\frac{s+3}{2}\end{matrix}\right)$$

$$+\,\frac{\sigma^{-s}}{\sqrt{\pi}\,s}\,\Gamma\!\left(\frac{s+1}{2}\right)\,_{2p+2}F_{2q+2}\!\left(\begin{matrix}\frac{(a_p)}{2},\,\frac{(a_p)+1}{2},\,\frac{s}{2},\,\frac{s+1}{2}\,;\,\frac{\omega^2}{4^{q-p+1}\sigma^2}\\[4pt]\frac{1}{2},\,\frac{(b_q)}{2},\,\frac{(b_q)+1}{2},\,\frac{s+2}{2}\end{matrix}\right)$$

$$\begin{bmatrix}[q=p-1;\ (\operatorname{Re}s>0;\ |\arg\sigma|<\pi/4)\ \text{or}\\(0<\operatorname{Re}s<\operatorname{Re}a_k+3;\ |\arg\sigma|=\pi/4)]\ \text{or}\\[q=p;\ (\operatorname{Re}s>0;\ |\arg\sigma|<\pi/4)\ \text{or}\\(\operatorname{Re}\omega>0;\ 0<\operatorname{Re}s<\operatorname{Re}a_k+3;\ |\arg\sigma|=\pi/4)\ \text{or}\\(\operatorname{Re}\omega=0;\ \operatorname{Re}s<3-\operatorname{Re}\chi;\ |\arg\sigma|=\pi/4)]\ \text{or}\\[q=p+1;\ (\operatorname{Re}s>0;\ |\arg\sigma|<\pi/4)\ \text{or}\\(0<\operatorname{Re}s<\operatorname{Re}a_k+3,\,3-\operatorname{Re}\chi;\ |\arg\sigma|=\pi/4)]\ \text{or}\\[q\geq p+2;\ \operatorname{Re}s>0;\ |\arg\sigma|<\pi/4]\end{bmatrix}$$

2	$\operatorname{erfc}\left(\sigma\sqrt{x}\right)\,_pF_q\!\left(\begin{matrix}(a_p)\,;\,-\omega x\\(b_q)\end{matrix}\right)$	$\dfrac{\sigma^{-2s}}{\sqrt{\pi}\,s}\,\Gamma\!\left(\dfrac{2s+1}{2}\right)\,_pF_q\!\left(\begin{matrix}(a_p),\,s,\,\frac{2s+1}{2}\\(b_q),\,s+1\,;\,-\frac{\omega}{\sigma^2}\end{matrix}\right)$

$$\begin{bmatrix}[q=p-1;\ (\operatorname{Re}s>0;\ |\arg\sigma|<\pi/4)\ \text{or}\\(0<\operatorname{Re}s<\operatorname{Re}a_k+3/2;\ |\arg\sigma|=\pi/4)]\ \text{or}\\[q=p;\ (\operatorname{Re}s>0;\ |\arg\sigma|<\pi/4)\ \text{or}\\\left(\operatorname{Re}(\sigma^2+\omega)>0;\ 0<\operatorname{Re}s<\operatorname{Re}a_k+3/2;\ |\arg\sigma|=\pi/4\right)\ \text{or}\\\left(\operatorname{Re}(\sigma^2+\omega)=0;\ \operatorname{Re}s<3/2-\operatorname{Re}\chi;\ |\arg\sigma|=\pi/4\right)]\ \text{or}\\[q=p+1;\ (\operatorname{Re}s>0;\ |\arg\sigma|<\pi/4)\ \text{or}\\(0<\operatorname{Re}s<\operatorname{Re}a_k+3/2,\,3/2-\operatorname{Re}\chi;\ |\arg\sigma|=\pi/4)]\ \text{or}\\[q\geq p+2;\ \operatorname{Re}s>0;\ |\arg\sigma|<\pi/4]\end{bmatrix}$$

3.33.7. $_pF_q\left((a_p)\,;\,(b_q)\,;\,\omega x\right)$ **and** $\Gamma\left(\nu,\,\sigma x^r\right)$

1	$\Gamma\left(\nu,\,\sigma x\right)\,_pF_q\!\left(\begin{matrix}(a_p)\,;\,-\omega x\\(b_q)\end{matrix}\right)$	$\dfrac{\sigma^{-s}}{s}\,\Gamma\left(s+\nu\right)\,_{p+2}F_{q+1}\!\left(\begin{matrix}(a_p),\,s,\,s+\nu\\(b_q),\,s+1\,;\,-\frac{\omega}{\sigma}\end{matrix}\right)$

$$\begin{bmatrix}[q=p-1;\ (\operatorname{Re}\sigma>0;\ \operatorname{Re}s>0,\,-\operatorname{Re}\nu)\ \text{or}\\(\operatorname{Re}\sigma=0;\ 0,\,-\operatorname{Re}\nu<\operatorname{Re}s<2-\operatorname{Re}(\nu-a_k))]\ \text{or}\\[q=p;\ (\operatorname{Re}\sigma>0;\ \operatorname{Re}s>0,\,-\operatorname{Re}\nu)\ \text{or}\\(\operatorname{Re}\sigma=0;\ 0,\,-\operatorname{Re}\nu<\operatorname{Re}s<2-\operatorname{Re}(\nu-a_k))\ \text{or}\\(\operatorname{Re}(\sigma+\omega)>0;\ \operatorname{Re}s>0,\,-\operatorname{Re}\nu)\ \text{or}\\(\operatorname{Re}(\sigma+\omega)=0;\ 0,\,-\operatorname{Re}\nu<\operatorname{Re}s<2-\operatorname{Re}(\nu+\chi))]\ \text{or}\\[q=p+1;\ (\operatorname{Re}\sigma>0;\ \operatorname{Re}s>0,\,-\operatorname{Re}\nu)\ \text{or}\\(\operatorname{Re}\sigma=0;\ 0,\,-\operatorname{Re}\nu<\operatorname{Re}s<2-\operatorname{Re}(\nu+\chi),\,2-\operatorname{Re}(\nu-a_k))]\ \text{or}\\[q\geq p+2;\ \operatorname{Re}\sigma>0;\ \operatorname{Re}s>0,\,-\operatorname{Re}\nu]\end{bmatrix}$$

No.	$f(x)$	$F(s)$
2	$\Gamma\left(\nu,\sigma\sqrt{x}\right)\,{}_pF_q\!\left(\begin{matrix}(a_p);\ -\omega x\\(b_q)\end{matrix}\right)$	$\dfrac{\sigma^{-2s}}{s}\,\Gamma(2s+\nu)\,{}_{p+3}F_{q+1}\!\left(\begin{matrix}(a_p),\,s,\,\frac{2s+\nu}{2},\,\frac{2s+\nu+1}{2}\\(b_q),\,s+1;\ -\frac{4\omega}{\sigma^2}\end{matrix}\right)$

$$\begin{bmatrix}[q=p-1;\ (\operatorname{Re}\sigma>0;\ \operatorname{Re}s>0,\,-\operatorname{Re}\nu/2)\ \text{or}\\(\operatorname{Re}\sigma=0;\ 0,\,-\operatorname{Re}\nu/2<\operatorname{Re}s<1-\operatorname{Re}(\nu/2-a_k))]\ \text{or}\\[q=p;\ (\operatorname{Re}\sigma>0;\ \operatorname{Re}\omega\geq0;\ \operatorname{Re}s>0,\,-\operatorname{Re}\nu/2)\ \text{or}\\(\operatorname{Re}\sigma=0;\ 0,\,-\operatorname{Re}\nu/2<\operatorname{Re}s<1-\operatorname{Re}(\nu/2-a_k))\ \text{or}\\(\operatorname{Re}\omega>0;\ \operatorname{Re}s>0,\,-\operatorname{Re}\nu/2)\ \text{or}\\(\operatorname{Re}\omega=0;\ 0,\,-\operatorname{Re}\nu/2<\operatorname{Re}s<3/2-\operatorname{Re}(\nu/2-\chi))]\ \text{or}\\[q=p+1;\ (\operatorname{Re}\sigma>0;\ \operatorname{Re}s>0,\,-\operatorname{Re}\nu/2)\ \text{or}\\(\operatorname{Re}\sigma=0;\ 0,\,-\operatorname{Re}\nu/2<\operatorname{Re}s<1-\operatorname{Re}(\nu/2+\chi))]\ \text{or}\\[q\geq p+2;\ \operatorname{Re}\sigma>0;\ \operatorname{Re}s>0,\,-\operatorname{Re}\nu/2]\end{bmatrix}$$

3.33.8. ${}_pF_q\left((a_p);\ (b_q);\ \omega x^r\right)$ **and** $J_\nu(\sigma x),\ Y_\nu(\sigma x)$

No.	$f(x)$	$F(s)$
1	$J_\nu(\sigma x)\,{}_pF_q\!\left(\begin{matrix}(a_p);\ -\omega x\\(b_q)\end{matrix}\right)$	$-\prod_{i=1}^{p}a_i\prod_{j=1}^{q}b_j^{-1}\dfrac{2^s}{\omega^s}\left(\dfrac{\omega^2}{\sigma^2}\right)^{(s+1)/2}\Gamma\!\left[\begin{matrix}\frac{s+\nu+1}{2}\\\frac{1-s+\nu}{2}\end{matrix}\right]$

$$\times\,{}_{2p+2}F_{2q+1}\!\left(\begin{matrix}\frac{(a_p)+1}{2},\,\frac{(a_p)+2}{2},\,\frac{s-\nu+1}{2},\,\frac{s+\nu+1}{2}\\\frac{3}{2},\,\frac{(b_q)+1}{2},\,\frac{(b_q)+2}{2};\ -\frac{\omega^2}{4^{q-p}\sigma^2}\end{matrix}\right)$$

$$+\,\dfrac{2^{s-1}}{\omega^s}\left(\dfrac{\omega^2}{\sigma^2}\right)^{s/2}\Gamma\!\left[\begin{matrix}\frac{s+\nu}{2}\\\frac{2-s+\nu}{2}\end{matrix}\right]$$

$$\times\,{}_{2p+2}F_{2q+1}\!\left(\begin{matrix}\frac{(a_p)}{2},\,\frac{(a_p)+1}{2},\,\frac{s-\nu}{2},\,\frac{s+\nu}{2}\\\frac{1}{2},\,\frac{(b_q)}{2},\,\frac{(b_q)+1}{2};\ -\frac{\omega^2}{4^{q-p}\sigma^2}\end{matrix}\right)$$

$$\begin{bmatrix}[q=p-1;\ \sigma>0;\ |\arg\omega|<\pi;\ -\operatorname{Re}\nu<\operatorname{Re}s<\operatorname{Re}a_k+3/2]\ \text{or}\\[q=p;\ (\sigma,\ \operatorname{Re}\omega>0;\ -\operatorname{Re}\nu<\operatorname{Re}s<\operatorname{Re}a_k+3/2)\ \text{or}\\(\sigma,\ \omega>0;\ -\operatorname{Re}\nu<\operatorname{Re}s<\operatorname{Re}a_k+3/2,\,3/2-\operatorname{Re}\chi)]\ \text{or}\\[q=p+1;\ (\sigma,\ \omega>0;\ -\operatorname{Re}\nu<\operatorname{Re}s<\operatorname{Re}a_k+3/2,\,3/2-\operatorname{Re}\chi)]\end{bmatrix}$$

2	$Y_\nu(\sigma x)\,{}_pF_q\!\left(\begin{matrix}(a_p);\ -\omega x\\(b_q)\end{matrix}\right)$	$-\prod_{i=1}^{p}a_i\prod_{j=1}^{q}b_j^{-1}\dfrac{2^s}{\pi\omega^s}\left(\dfrac{\omega^2}{\sigma^2}\right)^{(s+1)/2}\sin\dfrac{(s-\nu)\pi}{2}\,\Gamma\!\left(\dfrac{s-\nu+1}{2}\right)$

$$\times\,\Gamma\!\left(\dfrac{s+\nu+1}{2}\right){}_{2p+2}F_{2q+1}\!\left(\begin{matrix}\frac{(a_p)+1}{2},\,\frac{(a_p)+2}{2},\,\frac{s-\nu+1}{2},\,\frac{s+\nu+1}{2}\\\frac{3}{2},\,\frac{(b_q)+1}{2},\,\frac{(b_q)+2}{2};\ -\frac{\omega^2}{4^{q-p}\sigma^2}\end{matrix}\right)$$

$$-\,\dfrac{2^{s-1}}{\pi\omega^s}\left(\dfrac{\omega^2}{\sigma^2}\right)^{s/2}\cos\dfrac{(s-\nu)\pi}{2}\,\Gamma\!\left(\dfrac{s-\nu}{2}\right)\Gamma\!\left(\dfrac{s+\nu}{2}\right)$$

$$\times\,{}_{2p+2}F_{2q+1}\!\left(\begin{matrix}\frac{(a_p)}{2},\,\frac{(a_p)+1}{2},\,\frac{s-\nu}{2},\,\frac{s+\nu}{2}\\\frac{1}{2},\,\frac{(b_q)}{2},\,\frac{(b_q)+1}{2};\ -\frac{\omega^2}{4^{q-p}\sigma^2}\end{matrix}\right)$$

$$\begin{bmatrix}[q=p-1;\ \sigma>0;\ |\arg\omega|<\pi;\ -|\operatorname{Re}\nu|<\operatorname{Re}s<\operatorname{Re}a_k+3/2]\ \text{or}\\[q=p;\ (\sigma,\ \operatorname{Re}\omega>0;\ -|\operatorname{Re}\nu|<\operatorname{Re}s<\operatorname{Re}a_k+3/2)\ \text{or}\\(\sigma,\ \omega>0;\ -|\operatorname{Re}\nu|<\operatorname{Re}s<\operatorname{Re}a_k+3/2,\,3/2-\operatorname{Re}\chi)]\ \text{or}\\[q=p+1;\ (\sigma,\ \omega>0;\ -|\operatorname{Re}\nu|<\operatorname{Re}s<\operatorname{Re}a_k+3/2,\,3/2-\operatorname{Re}\chi)]\end{bmatrix}$$

3.33.9. $_pF_q\left((a_p);\ (b_q);\ \omega x\right)$ **and** $K_\nu\left(\sigma x^r\right)$

1	$K_\nu\left(\sigma x\right)\ _pF_q\left(\begin{matrix}(a_p);\ -\omega x\\(b_q)\end{matrix}\right)$	$-\dfrac{2^{s-1}\omega}{\sigma^{s+1}}\prod\limits_{i=1}^{p}a_i\prod\limits_{j=1}^{q}b_j^{-1}\Gamma\left(\dfrac{s-\nu+1}{2}\right)\Gamma\left(\dfrac{s+\nu+1}{2}\right)$

$$\times\ _{2p+2}F_{2q+1}\left(\begin{matrix}\frac{(a_p)+1}{2},\ \frac{(a_p)+2}{2},\ \frac{s-\nu+1}{2},\ \frac{s+\nu+1}{2}\\ \frac{3}{2},\ \frac{(b_q)+1}{2},\ \frac{(b_q)+2}{2};\ \frac{\omega^2}{4^{q-p}\sigma^2}\end{matrix}\right)+\frac{2^s}{4\sigma^s}\Gamma\left(\frac{s-\nu}{2}\right)$$

$$\times\Gamma\left(\frac{s+\nu}{2}\right)\ _{2p+2}F_{2q+1}\left(\begin{matrix}\frac{(a_p)}{2},\ \frac{(a_p)+1}{2},\ \frac{s-\nu}{2},\ \frac{s+\nu}{2}\\ \frac{1}{2},\ \frac{(b_q)}{2},\ \frac{(b_q)+1}{2};\ \frac{\omega^2}{4^{q-p}\sigma^2}\end{matrix}\right)$$

$$\begin{bmatrix}\left[q=p-1;\ |\arg\omega|<\pi;\ (\operatorname{Re}\sigma>0;\ \operatorname{Re}s>|\operatorname{Re}\nu|)\ \text{or}\right.\\ (\sigma>0;\ |\operatorname{Re}\nu|<\operatorname{Re}s<\operatorname{Re}a_k+3/2)]\ \text{or}\\ \left[q=p;\ (\operatorname{Re}\sigma,\ \operatorname{Re}(\sigma+\omega)>0;\ \operatorname{Re}s>|\operatorname{Re}\nu|)\ \text{or}\right.\\ (\sigma,\ \operatorname{Re}\omega>0;\ |\operatorname{Re}\nu|<\operatorname{Re}s<\operatorname{Re}a_k+3/2)\ \text{or}\\ (\operatorname{Re}\sigma>0;\ \operatorname{Re}(\sigma+\omega)=0;\ |\operatorname{Re}\nu|<\operatorname{Re}s<3/2-\operatorname{Re}\chi)\ \text{or}\\ (\sigma,\ \omega>0;\ |\operatorname{Re}\nu|<\operatorname{Re}s<3/2+\operatorname{Re}a_k,\ 3/2-\operatorname{Re}\chi)]\ \text{or}\\ \left[q=p+1;\ (\operatorname{Re}\sigma>0;\ \operatorname{Re}s>|\operatorname{Re}\nu|)\ \text{or}\right.\\ (\sigma,\ \omega>0;\ |\operatorname{Re}\nu|<\operatorname{Re}s<3/2+\operatorname{Re}a_k,\ 3/2-\operatorname{Re}\chi)]\ \text{or}\\ \left[q\geq p+2;\ (\operatorname{Re}\sigma>0;\ \operatorname{Re}s>|\operatorname{Re}\nu|)\ \text{or}\right.\\ (\sigma,\ \omega>0;\ |\operatorname{Re}\nu|<\operatorname{Re}s<3/2+\operatorname{Re}a_k)\end{bmatrix}$$

2	$K_\nu\left(\sigma\sqrt{x}\right)\ _pF_q\left(\begin{matrix}(a_p);\ -\omega x\\(b_q)\end{matrix}\right)$	$\dfrac{2^{2s-1}}{\sigma^{2s}}\Gamma\left(\dfrac{2s-\nu}{2}\right)\Gamma\left(\dfrac{2s+\nu}{2}\right)\ _{p+2}F_q\left(\begin{matrix}(a_p),\ \frac{2s-\nu}{2},\ \frac{2s+\nu}{2}\\(b_q);\ -\frac{4\omega}{\sigma^2}\end{matrix}\right)$

$$\begin{bmatrix}\left[q=p-1;\ |\arg\omega|<\pi;\ (\operatorname{Re}\sigma>0;\ \operatorname{Re}s>|\operatorname{Re}\nu|/2)\ \text{or}\right.\\ (\sigma>0;\ |\operatorname{Re}\nu|/2<\operatorname{Re}s<\operatorname{Re}a_k+3/4)]\ \text{or}\\ \left[q=p;\ (\operatorname{Re}\sigma>0;\ \operatorname{Re}\omega\geq0;\ \operatorname{Re}s>|\operatorname{Re}\nu|/2)\ \text{or}\right.\\ (\operatorname{Re}\sigma=0;\ \operatorname{Re}\omega>0;\ |\operatorname{Re}\nu|<\operatorname{Re}s<\operatorname{Re}a_k+3/4)\ \text{or}\\ (\operatorname{Re}\sigma=\operatorname{Re}\omega=0;\ |\operatorname{Re}\nu|/2<\operatorname{Re}s<3/4+\operatorname{Re}a_k,\ 5/4-\operatorname{Re}\chi)]\ \text{or}\\ \left[q=p+1;\ (\operatorname{Re}\sigma>2|\operatorname{Im}\sqrt{\omega}|;\ \operatorname{Re}s>|\operatorname{Re}\nu|/2)\ \text{or}\right.\\ (\sigma,\ \omega>0;\ |\operatorname{Re}\nu|/2<\operatorname{Re}s<3/4+\operatorname{Re}a_k,\ 3/4-\operatorname{Re}\chi)]\ \text{or}\\ \left[q\geq p+2;\ (\operatorname{Re}\sigma>0;\ \operatorname{Re}s>|\operatorname{Re}\nu|/2)\right]\end{bmatrix}$$

3	$e^{-\sigma x}K_\nu\left(\sigma x\right)$ $\times\ _pF_q\left(\begin{matrix}(a_p);\ -\omega x\\(b_q)\end{matrix}\right)$	$\sqrt{\pi}\,(2\sigma)^{-s}\Gamma\left[\begin{matrix}s-\nu,\ s+\nu\\ \frac{2s+1}{2}\end{matrix}\right]\ _{p+2}F_{q+1}\left(\begin{matrix}(a_p),\ s-\nu,\ s+\nu\\(b_q),\ \frac{2s+1}{2};\ -\frac{\omega}{2\sigma}\end{matrix}\right)$

$$\begin{bmatrix}\left[q=p-1;\ |\arg\omega|<\pi;\ (\operatorname{Re}\sigma>0;\ \operatorname{Re}s>|\operatorname{Re}\nu|)\ \text{or}\right.\\ (\sigma>0;\ |\operatorname{Re}\nu|<\operatorname{Re}s<\operatorname{Re}a_k+3/2)]\ \text{or}\\ \left[q=p;\ (\operatorname{Re}\sigma,\ \operatorname{Re}(2\sigma+\omega)>0;\ \operatorname{Re}s>|\operatorname{Re}\nu|)\ \text{or}\right.\\ (\sigma,\ \operatorname{Re}\omega>0;\ |\operatorname{Re}\nu|<\operatorname{Re}s<\operatorname{Re}a_k+3/2)\ \text{or}\\ (\operatorname{Re}\sigma>0;\ \operatorname{Re}(2\sigma+\omega)=0;\ |\operatorname{Re}\nu|<\operatorname{Re}s<3/2-\operatorname{Re}\chi)\ \text{or}\\ (\sigma,\ \omega>0;\ |\operatorname{Re}\nu|<\operatorname{Re}s<3/2+\operatorname{Re}a_k,\ 3/2-\operatorname{Re}\chi)]\ \text{or}\\ \left[q=p+1;\ (\operatorname{Re}\sigma>0;\ \operatorname{Re}s>|\operatorname{Re}\nu|)\ \text{or}\right.\\ (\sigma,\ \omega>0;\ |\operatorname{Re}\nu|<\operatorname{Re}s<3/2+\operatorname{Re}a_k,\ 3/2-\operatorname{Re}\chi)]\ \text{or}\\ \left[q\geq p+2;\ (\operatorname{Re}\sigma>0;\ \operatorname{Re}s>|\operatorname{Re}\nu|)\ \text{or}\right.\\ (\sigma,\ \omega>0;\ |\operatorname{Re}\nu|<\operatorname{Re}s<\operatorname{Re}a_k+3/2)]\end{bmatrix}$$

No.	$f(x)$	$F(s)$

4 $e^{-\sigma\sqrt{x}} K_\nu\left(\sigma\sqrt{x}\right)$

$$\times\ _pF_q\left(\begin{matrix}(a_p)\,;\ -\omega x\\ (b_q)\end{matrix}\right)$$

$$2\sqrt{\pi}\,(2\sigma)^{-2s}\,\Gamma\left[\begin{matrix}2s-\nu,\ 2s+\nu\\ \frac{4s+1}{2}\end{matrix}\right]$$

$$\times\ _{p+4}F_{q+2}\left(\begin{matrix}(a_p),\ \frac{2s-\nu}{2},\ \frac{2s-\nu+1}{2},\ \frac{2s+\nu}{2},\ \frac{2s+\nu+1}{2}\\ (b_q),\ \frac{4s+1}{4},\ \frac{4s+3}{4}\,;\ -\frac{\omega}{\sigma^2}\end{matrix}\right)$$

$$\left[\begin{matrix}\left[q=p-1;\ |\arg\omega|<\pi;\ (\operatorname{Re}\sigma>0;\ \operatorname{Re}s>|\operatorname{Re}\nu|/2)\ \text{or}\right.\\ \left.(\sigma>0;\ |\operatorname{Re}\nu|/2<\operatorname{Re}s<\operatorname{Re}a_k+3/4)\right]\ \text{or}\\ \left[q=p;\ (\operatorname{Re}\sigma>0;\ \operatorname{Re}\omega\geq0;\ \operatorname{Re}s>|\operatorname{Re}\nu|/2)\ \text{or}\right.\\ (\operatorname{Re}\sigma=0;\ \operatorname{Re}\omega>0;\ |\operatorname{Re}\nu|/2<\operatorname{Re}s<\operatorname{Re}a_k+3/4)\ \text{or}\\ \left.(\operatorname{Re}\sigma=\operatorname{Re}\omega=0;\ |\operatorname{Re}\nu|/2<\operatorname{Re}s<3/4+\operatorname{Re}a_k,\ 5/4-\operatorname{Re}\chi)\right]\ \text{or}\\ \left[q=p+1;\ (\operatorname{Re}\sigma>|\operatorname{Im}\sqrt{\omega}|;\ \operatorname{Re}s>|\operatorname{Re}\nu|/2)\ \text{or}\right.\\ \left.(\sigma,\omega>0;\ |\operatorname{Re}\nu|/2<\operatorname{Re}s<3/4+\operatorname{Re}a_k,\ 3/4-\operatorname{Re}\chi)\right.\ \text{or}\\ \left[q\geq p+2;\ (\operatorname{Re}\sigma>0;\ \operatorname{Re}s>|\operatorname{Re}\nu|/2)\right]\end{matrix}\right]$$

5 $K_\mu\left(\sigma x\right) K_\nu\left(\sigma x\right)$

$$\times\ _pF_q\left(\begin{matrix}(a_p)\,;\ -\omega x\\ (b_q)\end{matrix}\right)$$

$$-\prod_{i=1}^{p} a_i \prod_{j=1}^{q} b_j^{-1}\frac{2^{s-2}\omega}{\sigma^{s+1}}$$

$$\times\ \Gamma\left[\begin{matrix}\frac{s-\mu-\nu+1}{2},\ \frac{s-\mu+\nu+1}{2},\ \frac{s+\mu-\nu+1}{2},\ \frac{s+\mu+\nu+1}{2}\\ s+1\end{matrix}\right]$$

$$\times\ _{2p+4}F_{2q+3}\left(\begin{matrix}\frac{(a_p)+1}{2},\ \frac{(a_p)+2}{2},\ \frac{s-\mu-\nu+1}{2},\\ \frac{3}{2},\ \frac{(b_q)+1}{2},\ \frac{(b_q)+2}{2},\end{matrix}\right.$$

$$\left.\begin{matrix}\frac{s-\mu+\nu+1}{2},\ \frac{s+\mu-\nu+1}{2},\ \frac{s+\mu+\nu+1}{2}\\ \frac{s+1}{2},\ \frac{s+2}{2}\,;\ \frac{\omega^2}{4^{q-p+1}\sigma^2}\end{matrix}\right)$$

$$+\ \frac{2^{s-3}}{\sigma^s}\,\Gamma\left[\begin{matrix}\frac{s-\mu-\nu}{2},\ \frac{s-\mu+\nu}{2},\ \frac{s+\mu-\nu}{2},\ \frac{s+\mu+\nu}{2}\\ s\end{matrix}\right]$$

$$\times\ _{2p+4}F_{2q+3}\left(\begin{matrix}\frac{(a_p)}{2},\ \frac{(a_p)+1}{2},\ \frac{s-\mu-\nu}{2},\\ \frac{1}{2},\ \frac{(b_q)}{2},\ \frac{(b_q)+1}{2},\end{matrix}\right.$$

$$\left.\begin{matrix}\frac{s-\mu+\nu}{2},\ \frac{s+\mu-\nu}{2},\ \frac{s+\mu+\nu}{2}\\ \frac{s}{2},\ \frac{s+1}{2}\,;\ \frac{\omega^2}{4^{q-p+1}\sigma^2}\end{matrix}\right)$$

$$\left[\begin{matrix}\left[q=p-1;\ |\arg\omega|<\pi;\ (\operatorname{Re}\sigma>0;\operatorname{Re}s>|\operatorname{Re}\mu|+|\operatorname{Re}\nu|)\ \text{or}\right.\\ \left.(\sigma>0;\ |\operatorname{Re}\mu|+|\operatorname{Re}\nu|<\operatorname{Re}s<\operatorname{Re}a_k+2)\right]\ \text{or}\\ \left[q=p;\ (\operatorname{Re}\sigma,\ \operatorname{Re}(2\sigma+\omega)>0;\ \operatorname{Re}s>|\operatorname{Re}\mu|+|\operatorname{Re}\nu|)\ \text{or}\right.\\ (\operatorname{Re}\sigma=0;\ \operatorname{Re}\omega>0;\ |\operatorname{Re}\mu|+|\operatorname{Re}\nu|<\operatorname{Re}s<\operatorname{Re}a_k+2)\ \text{or}\\ (\operatorname{Re}\sigma>0,\ \operatorname{Re}(2\sigma+\omega)=0;\ |\operatorname{Re}\mu|+|\operatorname{Re}\nu|<\operatorname{Re}s<2-\operatorname{Re}\chi)\ \text{or}\\ \left.(\operatorname{Re}\sigma=\operatorname{Re}\omega=0;\ |\operatorname{Re}\mu|+|\operatorname{Re}\nu|<\operatorname{Re}s<\operatorname{Re}a_k+2,\ 2-\operatorname{Re}\chi)\right]\ \text{or}\\ \left[q=p+1;\ (\operatorname{Re}\sigma>0;\ \operatorname{Re}s>|\operatorname{Re}\mu|+|\operatorname{Re}\nu|)\ \text{or}\right.\\ \left.(\sigma,\ \omega>0;\ |\operatorname{Re}\mu|+|\operatorname{Re}\nu|<\operatorname{Re}s<\operatorname{Re}a_k+2,\ 2-\operatorname{Re}\chi)\right]\ \text{or}\\ \left[q\geq p+2;\ \operatorname{Re}\sigma>0;\ \operatorname{Re}s>|\operatorname{Re}\mu|+|\operatorname{Re}\nu|\right]\end{matrix}\right]$$

No.	$f(x)$	$F(s)$
6	$K_\mu\left(\sigma\sqrt{x}\right)K_\nu\left(\sigma\sqrt{x}\right)$ $\times\,_pF_q\!\left(\begin{matrix}(a_p)\,;\;-\omega x\\(b_q)\end{matrix}\right)$	$\dfrac{2^{2s-2}}{\sigma^{2s}}\,\Gamma\!\left[\begin{matrix}\frac{2s-\mu-\nu}{2},\,\frac{2s-\mu+\nu}{2},\,\frac{2s+\mu-\nu}{2},\,\frac{2s+\mu+\nu}{2}\\ 2s\end{matrix}\right]$ $\times\,_{p+4}F_{q+2}\!\left(\begin{matrix}(a_p),\,\frac{2s-\mu-\nu}{2},\,\frac{2s-\mu+\nu}{2},\,\frac{2s+\mu-\nu}{2},\,\frac{2s+\mu+\nu}{2}\\ (b_q),\,s,\,\frac{2s+1}{2}\,;\;-\frac{\omega}{\sigma^2}\end{matrix}\right)$

$$\left[\begin{aligned}&[q=p-1;\;|\arg\omega|<\pi;\;(\operatorname{Re}\sigma>0;\operatorname{Re}s>(|\operatorname{Re}\mu|+|\operatorname{Re}\nu|)\,/2)\;\text{or}\\&\quad(\sigma>0;\;(|\operatorname{Re}\mu|+|\operatorname{Re}\nu|)\,/2<\operatorname{Re}s<\operatorname{Re}a_k+1)]\;\text{or}\\&[q=p;\;(\operatorname{Re}\sigma>0,\;\operatorname{Re}\omega\ge0;\;\operatorname{Re}s>(|\operatorname{Re}\mu|+|\operatorname{Re}\nu|)\,/2)\;\text{or}\\&\quad(\sigma>0;\;\operatorname{Re}\omega>0;\;(|\operatorname{Re}\mu|+|\operatorname{Re}\nu|)\,/2<\operatorname{Re}s<\operatorname{Re}a_k+1)\;\text{or}\\&\quad(\sigma,\,\omega>0;\;(|\operatorname{Re}\mu|+|\operatorname{Re}\nu|)\,/2<\operatorname{Re}s<\operatorname{Re}a_k+1,\,3/2-\operatorname{Re}\chi)]\;\text{or}\\&[q=p+1;\;(|\operatorname{Im}\sqrt\omega|<\operatorname{Re}\sigma;\;\operatorname{Re}s>(|\operatorname{Re}\mu|+|\operatorname{Re}\nu|)\,/2)\;\text{or}\\&\quad(\sigma,\,\omega>0;\;(|\operatorname{Re}\mu|+|\operatorname{Re}\nu|)\,/2<\operatorname{Re}s<\operatorname{Re}a_k+1,\,1-\operatorname{Re}\chi)]\;\text{or}\\&[q\ge p+2;\;\operatorname{Re}\sigma>0;\;\operatorname{Re}s>(|\operatorname{Re}\mu|+|\operatorname{Re}\nu|)\,/2]\end{aligned}\right]$$

3.33.10. $_pF_q\left((a_p)\,;\;(b_q)\,;\,\omega x\right)$ and $\operatorname{Ai}\left(\sigma x^r\right)$

1	$\operatorname{Ai}(\sigma x)\,_pF_q\!\left(\begin{matrix}(a_p)\,;\;-\omega x\\(b_q)\end{matrix}\right)$	$\dfrac{3^{(4s-7)/6}}{2\pi\sigma^s}\,\Gamma\!\left(\dfrac{s}{3}\right)\Gamma\!\left(\dfrac{s+1}{3}\right)$ $\times\,_{3p+2}F_{3q+2}\!\left(\begin{matrix}\Delta(3,\,(a_p)),\,\frac{s}{3},\,\frac{s+1}{3}\\ \frac13,\,\frac23,\,\Delta(3,\,(b_q))\,;\;-\frac{\omega^3}{3^{3(q-p)+1}\sigma^3}\end{matrix}\right)$ $-\dfrac{3^{(4s-3)/6}\omega}{2\pi\sigma^{s+1}}\dfrac{\prod_{i=1}^p a_i}{\prod_{j=1}^q b_j}\Gamma\!\left(\dfrac{s+1}{3}\right)\Gamma\!\left(\dfrac{s+2}{3}\right)$ $\times\,_{3p+2}F_{3q+2}\!\left(\begin{matrix}\Delta(3,\,(a_p)+1),\,\frac{s+1}{3},\,\frac{s+2}{3}\\ \frac23,\,\frac43,\,\Delta(3,\,(b_q)+1)\,;\;-\frac{\omega^3}{3^{3(q-p)+1}\sigma^3}\end{matrix}\right)$ $+\dfrac{3^{(4s+1)/6}\omega^2}{4\pi\sigma^{s+2}}\dfrac{\prod_{i=1}^p a_i(a_i+1)}{\prod_{j=1}^q b_j(b_j+1)}\Gamma\!\left(\dfrac{s+2}{3}\right)\Gamma\!\left(\dfrac{s+3}{3}\right)$ $\times\,_{3p+2}F_{3q+2}\!\left(\begin{matrix}\Delta(3,\,(a_p)+2),\,\frac{s+2}{3},\,\frac{s+3}{3}\\ \frac43,\,\frac53,\,\Delta(3,\,(b_q)+2)\,;\;-\frac{\omega^3}{3^{3(q-p)+1}\sigma^3}\end{matrix}\right)$

$$\left[\begin{aligned}&[q=p-1;\;|\arg\omega|<\pi;\;(|\arg\sigma|<\pi/3;\;\operatorname{Re}s>0)\;\text{or}\\&\quad(|\arg\sigma|=\pi/3;\;0<\operatorname{Re}s<\operatorname{Re}a_k+7/4)]\\&[q=p;\;(|\arg\sigma|<\pi/3;\;\operatorname{Re}s>0)\;\text{or}\\&\quad(|\arg\sigma|=\pi/3;\;\operatorname{Re}\omega>0;\;0<\operatorname{Re}s<\operatorname{Re}a_k+7/4)\;\text{or}\\&\quad(|\arg\sigma|=\pi/3;\;\operatorname{Re}\omega=0;\;0<\operatorname{Re}s<\operatorname{Re}a_k+7/4,\,7/4-\operatorname{Re}\chi)]\\&[q=p+1;\;(|\arg\sigma|<\pi/3;\;\operatorname{Re}s>0)\;\text{or}\\&\quad(|\arg\sigma|=\pi/3;\;\omega>0;\;0<\operatorname{Re}s<\operatorname{Re}a_k+7/4,\,7/4-\operatorname{Re}\chi)]\\&[q\ge p+2;\;|\arg\sigma|<\pi/3;\;\operatorname{Re}s>0]\end{aligned}\right]$$

No.	$f(x)$	$F(s)$
2	$\mathrm{Ai}^2\left(\sigma\sqrt[3]{x}\right)\,{}_pF_q\left(\begin{matrix}(a_p);\,-\omega x\\(b_q)\end{matrix}\right)$	$\dfrac{2^{-2s-2/3}}{3^{s-1/6}\sqrt{\pi}\,\sigma^{3s}}\,\Gamma\left[\begin{matrix}3s\\\frac{6s+5}{6}\end{matrix}\right]\,{}_{p+3}F_{q+1}\left(\begin{matrix}(a_p),\,\Delta(3,3s)\\(b_q),\,\frac{6s+5}{6};\,-\frac{9\omega}{4\sigma^3}\end{matrix}\right)$

$$\left[\begin{array}{l}
[q=p-1;\ |\arg\omega|<\pi;\ (|\arg\sigma|<\pi/3;\ \mathrm{Re}\,s>0)\ \text{or}\\
\quad(|\arg\sigma|=\pi/3;\ 0<\mathrm{Re}\,s<\mathrm{Re}\,a_k+2/3)]\\
[q=p;\ (|\arg\sigma|<\pi/3;\ \mathrm{Re}\,\omega\ge0;\ \mathrm{Re}\,s>0)\ \text{or}\\
\quad(|\arg\sigma|=\pi/3;\ \mathrm{Re}\,\omega>0;\ 0<\mathrm{Re}\,s<\mathrm{Re}\,a_k+2/3)\ \text{or}\\
\quad(|\arg\sigma|=\pi/3;\ \mathrm{Re}\,\omega=0;\ 0<\mathrm{Re}\,s<\mathrm{Re}\,a_k+2/3,\,7/6-\mathrm{Re}\,\chi)]\\
[q=p+1;\ (|\mathrm{Im}\,\sqrt{\omega}|<2\,\mathrm{Re}\,\sigma^{3/2}/3;\ \mathrm{Re}\,s>0)\ \text{or}\\
\quad(|\arg\sigma|=\pi/3;\ |\mathrm{Im}\,\sqrt{\omega}|<2\,\mathrm{Re}\,\sigma^{3/2}/3;\ 0<\mathrm{Re}\,s<\mathrm{Re}\,a_k+2/3)\ \text{or}\\
\quad(|\arg\sigma|=\pi/3;\ \omega>0;\ 0<\mathrm{Re}\,s<\mathrm{Re}\,a_k+2/3,\,2/3-\mathrm{Re}\,\chi)]\\
[q\ge p+2;\ |\arg\sigma|<\pi/3;\ \mathrm{Re}\,s>0]
\end{array}\right]$$

3.33.11. ${}_pF_q\left((a_p);\,(b_q);\,\omega x^r\right)$ and $P_n\left(\varphi(x)\right)$

Notation: $\varepsilon=0$ or 1.

No.	$f(x)$	$F(s)$
1	$\theta(\sigma-x)\,P_n\left(\dfrac{x}{\sigma}\right)$ $\times\,{}_pF_q\left(\begin{matrix}(a_p);\,\omega x\\(b_q)\end{matrix}\right)$	$\sqrt{\pi}\,\displaystyle\prod_{i=1}^{p}a_i\prod_{j=1}^{q}b_j^{-1}\left(\dfrac{\sigma}{2}\right)^{s+1}\omega\,\Gamma\left[\begin{matrix}s+1\\\frac{s-n+2}{2},\,\frac{s+n+3}{2}\end{matrix}\right]$ $\times\,{}_{2p+2}F_{2q+3}\left(\begin{matrix}\frac{(a_p)+1}{2},\,\frac{(a_p)+2}{2},\,\frac{s+1}{2},\,\frac{s+2}{2};\,\frac{\sigma^2\omega^2}{4^{q-p+1}}\\\frac{3}{2},\,\frac{(b_q)+1}{2},\,\frac{(b_q)+2}{2},\,\frac{s-n+2}{2},\,\frac{s+n+3}{2}\end{matrix}\right)$ $+\sqrt{\pi}\left(\dfrac{\sigma}{2}\right)^{s}\Gamma\left[\begin{matrix}s\\\frac{s-n+1}{2},\,\frac{s+n+2}{2}\end{matrix}\right]$ $\times\,{}_{2p+2}F_{2q+3}\left(\begin{matrix}\frac{(a_p)}{2},\,\frac{(a_p)+1}{2},\,\frac{s}{2},\,\frac{s+1}{2};\,\frac{\sigma^2\omega^2}{4^{q-p+1}}\\\frac{1}{2},\,\frac{(b_q)}{2},\,\frac{(b_q)+1}{2},\,\frac{s-n+1}{2},\,\frac{s+n+2}{2}\end{matrix}\right)$ $[\sigma>0;\ \mathrm{Re}\,s>2\,[n/2]-n]$
2	$\theta(\sigma-x)\,P_n\left(\dfrac{2x}{\sigma}-1\right)$ $\times\,{}_pF_q\left(\begin{matrix}(a_p);\,\omega x\\(b_q)\end{matrix}\right)$	$\sigma^s\,\Gamma\left[\begin{matrix}s,\,s\\s-n,\,s+n+1\end{matrix}\right]\,{}_{p+2}F_{q+2}\left(\begin{matrix}(a_p),\,s,\,s;\,\sigma\omega\\(b_q),\,s-n,\,s+n+1\end{matrix}\right)$ $[\sigma,\ \mathrm{Re}\,s>0]$
3	$\theta(\sigma-x)\,P_n\left(\dfrac{2x}{\sigma}-1\right)$ $\times\,{}_pF_q\left(\begin{matrix}(a_p);\,\omega x^2\\(b_q)\end{matrix}\right)$	$\sigma^s\,\Gamma\left[\begin{matrix}s,\,s\\s-n,\,s+n+1\end{matrix}\right]$ $\times\,{}_{p+4}F_{q+4}\left(\begin{matrix}(a_p),\,\frac{s}{2},\,\frac{s}{2},\,\frac{s+1}{2},\,\frac{s+1}{2};\,\sigma^2\omega\\(b_q),\,\frac{s-n}{2},\,\frac{s-n+1}{2},\,\frac{s+n+1}{2},\,\frac{s+n+2}{2}\end{matrix}\right)$ $[\sigma,\ \mathrm{Re}\,s>0]$

No.	$f(x)$	$F(s)$
4	$\theta(\sigma - x)\, P_n\left(\dfrac{\sigma}{x}\right)$ $\times\ _pF_q\left(\begin{matrix}(a_p);\ \omega x\\ (b_q)\end{matrix}\right)$	$\displaystyle\prod_{i=1}^{p} a_i \prod_{j=1}^{q} b_j^{-1}\,\frac{2^s \sigma^{s+1}\omega}{\sqrt{\pi}}\,\Gamma\left[\begin{matrix}\frac{s-n+1}{2},\ \frac{s+n+2}{2}\\ s+2\end{matrix}\right]$ $\times\ _{2p+2}F_{2q+3}\left(\begin{matrix}\frac{(a_p)+1}{2},\ \frac{(a_p)+2}{2},\ \frac{s-n+1}{2},\ \frac{s+n+2}{2};\ \frac{\sigma^2\omega^2}{4^{q-p+1}}\\ \frac{3}{2},\ \frac{(b_q)+1}{2},\ \frac{(b_q)+2}{2},\ \frac{s+2}{2},\ \frac{s+3}{2}\end{matrix}\right)$ $+\dfrac{2^{s-1}\sigma^s}{\sqrt{\pi}}\,\Gamma\left[\begin{matrix}\frac{s-n}{2},\ \frac{s+n+1}{2}\\ s+1\end{matrix}\right]$ $\times\ _{2p+2}F_{2q+3}\left(\begin{matrix}\frac{(a_p)}{2},\ \frac{(a_p)+1}{2},\ \frac{s-n}{2},\ \frac{s+n+1}{2};\ \frac{\sigma^2\omega^2}{4^{q-p+1}}\\ \frac{1}{2},\ \frac{(b_q)}{2},\ \frac{(b_q)+1}{2},\ \frac{s+1}{2},\ \frac{s+2}{2}\end{matrix}\right)$ $[\sigma > 0;\ \operatorname{Re} s > n]$
5	$\theta(\sigma - x)\, P_n\left(\dfrac{2\sigma}{x} - 1\right)$ $\times\ _pF_q\left(\begin{matrix}(a_p);\ \omega x\\ (b_q)\end{matrix}\right)$	$\sigma^s\,\Gamma\left[\begin{matrix}s-n,\ s+n+1\\ s+1,\ s+1\end{matrix}\right]\ _{p+2}F_{q+2}\left(\begin{matrix}(a_p),\ s-n,\ s+n+1\\ (b_q),\ s+1,\ s+1;\ \sigma\omega\end{matrix}\right)$ $[\sigma > 0;\ \operatorname{Re} s > n]$
6	$\theta(\sigma - x)\, P_n\left(\sqrt{\dfrac{x}{\sigma}}\right)$ $\times\ _pF_q\left(\begin{matrix}(a_p);\ \omega x\\ (b_q)\end{matrix}\right)$	$\dfrac{\sqrt{\pi}\,\sigma^s}{2^{2s-1}}\,\Gamma\left[\begin{matrix}2s\\ \frac{2s-n+1}{2},\ \frac{2s+n+2}{2}\end{matrix}\right]\ _{p+2}F_{q+2}\left(\begin{matrix}(a_p),\ s,\ \frac{2s+1}{2};\ \sigma\omega\\ (b_q),\ \frac{2s-n+1}{2},\ \frac{2s+n+2}{2}\end{matrix}\right)$ $[\sigma > 0;\ \operatorname{Re} s > [n/2] - n/2]$
7	$\theta(\sigma - x)\, P_n\left(2\sqrt{\dfrac{x}{\sigma}} - 1\right)$ $\times\ _pF_q\left(\begin{matrix}(a_p);\ \omega x\\ (b_q)\end{matrix}\right)$	$2\sigma^s\,\Gamma\left[\begin{matrix}2s,\ 2s\\ 2s-n,\ 2s+n+1\end{matrix}\right]$ $\times\ _{p+4}F_{q+4}\left(\begin{matrix}(a_p),\ \Delta(2, 2s),\ \Delta(2, 2s);\ \sigma\omega\\ (b_q),\ \Delta(2, 2s-n),\ \Delta(2, 2s+n+1)\end{matrix}\right)$ $[\sigma > 0;\ \operatorname{Re} s > 0]$
8	$(\sigma - x)_+^{(\varepsilon-1)/2}$ $\times P_{2n+\varepsilon}\left(\sqrt{1 - \dfrac{x}{\sigma}}\right)$ $\times\ _pF_q\left(\begin{matrix}(a_p);\ \omega x\\ (b_q)\end{matrix}\right)$	$\dfrac{(-1)^n\sqrt{\pi}\,\sigma^{s+(\varepsilon-1)/2}}{n!}\left(\dfrac{1}{2}\right)_{n+\varepsilon}\Gamma\left[\begin{matrix}s,\ s\\ s-n,\ \frac{2s+2n+2\varepsilon+1}{2}\end{matrix}\right]$ $\times\ _{p+2}F_{q+2}\left(\begin{matrix}(a_p),\ s,\ s;\ \sigma\omega\\ (b_q),\ s-n,\ \frac{2s+2n+2\varepsilon+1}{2}\end{matrix}\right)$ $[\sigma,\ \operatorname{Re} s > 0]$
9	$\theta(\sigma - x)\, P_n\left(\sqrt{\dfrac{\sigma}{x}}\right)$ $\times\ _pF_q\left(\begin{matrix}(a_p);\ \omega x\\ (b_q)\end{matrix}\right)$	$\dfrac{(4\sigma)^s}{\sqrt{\pi}}\,\Gamma\left[\begin{matrix}\frac{2s-n}{2},\ \frac{s+2n+1}{2}\\ 2s+1\end{matrix}\right]\ _{p+2}F_{q+2}\left(\begin{matrix}(a_p),\ \frac{2s-n}{2},\ \frac{2s+n+1}{2}\\ (b_q),\ \frac{2s+1}{2},\ s+1;\ \sigma\omega\end{matrix}\right)$ $[\sigma > 0;\ \operatorname{Re} s > n/2]$

No.	$f(x)$	$F(s)$
10	$\theta(\sigma - x) P_n\left(2\sqrt{\dfrac{\sigma}{x}} - 1\right)$ $\times {}_pF_q\left(\begin{matrix}(a_p)\,;\,\omega x\\(b_q)\end{matrix}\right)$	$2\,\sigma^s\,\Gamma\begin{bmatrix}2s-n,\,2s+n+1\\2s+1,\,2s+1\end{bmatrix}$ $\times {}_{p+4}F_{q+4}\left(\begin{matrix}(a_p),\,\frac{2s-n}{2},\,\frac{2s-n+1}{2},\,\frac{2s+n+1}{2},\,\frac{2s+n+2}{2}\\(b_q),\,\frac{2s+1}{2},\,\frac{2s+1}{2},\,s+1,\,s+1;\,\sigma\omega\end{matrix}\right)$ $[\sigma > 0;\ \operatorname{Re} s > n/2]$

3.33.12. ${}_pF_q\left((a_p)\,;\,(b_q)\,;\,\omega x^r\right)$ **and** $T_n\left(\varphi(x)\right)$

Notation: $\varepsilon = 0$ or 1.

1	$\left(\sigma^2 - x^2\right)_+^{-1/2} T_n\left(\dfrac{x}{\sigma}\right)$ $\times {}_pF_q\left(\begin{matrix}(a_p)\,;\,\omega x\\(b_q)\end{matrix}\right)$	$\dfrac{\pi}{2}\prod_{i=1}^{p}a_i\prod_{j=1}^{q}b_j^{-1}\left(\dfrac{\sigma}{2}\right)^s\omega\,\Gamma\begin{bmatrix}s+1\\\frac{s-n+2}{2},\,\frac{s+n+2}{2}\end{bmatrix}$ $\times {}_{2p+2}F_{2q+3}\left(\begin{matrix}\frac{(a_p)+1}{2},\,\frac{(a_p)+2}{2},\,\frac{s+1}{2},\,\frac{s+2}{2};\,\frac{\sigma^2\omega^2}{4^{q-p+1}}\\\frac{3}{2},\,\frac{(b_q)+1}{2},\,\frac{(b_q)+2}{2},\,\frac{s-n+2}{2},\,\frac{s+n+2}{2}\end{matrix}\right)$ $+\dfrac{\pi}{2}\left(\dfrac{\sigma}{2}\right)^{s-1}\Gamma\begin{bmatrix}s\\\frac{s-n+1}{2},\,\frac{s+n+1}{2}\end{bmatrix}$ $\times {}_{2p+2}F_{2q+3}\left(\begin{matrix}\frac{(a_p)}{2},\,\frac{(a_p)+1}{2},\,\frac{s}{2},\,\frac{s+1}{2};\,\frac{\sigma^2\omega^2}{4^{q-p+1}}\\\frac{1}{2},\,\frac{(b_q)}{2},\,\frac{(b_q)+1}{2},\,\frac{s-n+1}{2},\,\frac{s+n+1}{2}\end{matrix}\right)$ $[\sigma > 0;\ \operatorname{Re} s > 2\,[n/2] - n]$
2	$\left(\sigma - x\right)_+^{-1/2} T_n\left(\dfrac{2x}{\sigma} - 1\right)$ $\times {}_pF_q\left(\begin{matrix}(a_p)\,;\,\omega x\\(b_q)\end{matrix}\right)$	$\dfrac{\pi\,\sigma^{s-1/2}}{2^{2s-1}}\,\Gamma\begin{bmatrix}2s\\\frac{2s-2n+1}{2},\,\frac{2s+2n+1}{2}\end{bmatrix}$ $\times {}_{p+2}F_{q+2}\left(\begin{matrix}(a_p),\,s,\,\frac{2s+1}{2};\,\sigma\omega\\(b_q),\,\frac{2s-2n+1}{2},\,\frac{2s+2n+1}{2}\end{matrix}\right)$ $[\sigma,\ \operatorname{Re} s > 0]$
3	$\left(\sigma - x\right)_+^{-1/2} T_n\left(\dfrac{2x}{\sigma} - 1\right)$ $\times {}_pF_q\left(\begin{matrix}(a_p)\,;\,\omega x^2\\(b_q)\end{matrix}\right)$	$\dfrac{\pi\sigma^{s-1/2}}{2^{2s-1}}\,\Gamma\begin{bmatrix}2s\\\frac{2s-2n+1}{2},\,\frac{2s+2n+1}{2}\end{bmatrix}$ $\times {}_{p+4}F_{q+4}\left(\begin{matrix}(a_p),\,\Delta(4,2s);\,\sigma^2\omega\\(b_q),\,\Delta\left(2,\frac{2s-2n+1}{2}\right),\,\Delta\left(2,\frac{2s+2n+1}{2}\right)\end{matrix}\right)$ $[\sigma,\ \operatorname{Re} s > 0]$
4	$\left(\sigma - x\right)_+^{-1/2} T_n\left(\dfrac{2\sigma}{x} - 1\right)$ $\times {}_pF_q\left(\begin{matrix}(a_p)\,;\,\omega x\\(b_q)\end{matrix}\right)$	$2^{2s-1}\sigma^{s-1/2}\,\mathrm{B}(s-n,\,s+n)\,{}_{p+2}F_{q+2}\left(\begin{matrix}(a_p),\,s-n,\,s+n\\(b_q),\,\frac{2s+1}{2},\,s;\,\sigma\omega\end{matrix}\right)$ $[\sigma > 0;\ \operatorname{Re} s > n]$

No.	$f(x)$	$F(s)$
5	$(\sigma - x)_+^{-1/2}\, T_n\left(\dfrac{2\sigma}{x} - 1\right)$ $\times\, {}_pF_q\left(\begin{matrix}(a_p);\ \omega x^2\\ (b_q)\end{matrix}\right)$	$2^{2s-1}\,\sigma^{s-1/2}\,\mathrm{B}\,(s-n,\ s+n)$ $\times\, {}_{p+4}F_{q+4}\left(\begin{matrix}(a_p),\ \frac{s-n}{2},\ \frac{s-n+1}{2},\ \frac{s+n}{2},\ \frac{s+n+1}{2}\\ (b_q),\ \frac{2s+1}{4},\ \frac{2s+3}{4},\ \frac{s}{2},\ \frac{s+1}{2};\ \sigma^2\omega\end{matrix}\right)$ $[\sigma > 0;\ \mathrm{Re}\,s > n]$
6	$(\sigma - x)_+^{-1/2}\, T_n\left(\sqrt{\dfrac{x}{\sigma}}\right)$ $\times\, {}_pF_q\left(\begin{matrix}(a_p);\ \omega x\\ (b_q)\end{matrix}\right)$	$\pi\left(\dfrac{\sqrt{\sigma}}{2}\right)^{2s-1}\Gamma\left[\begin{matrix}2s\\ \frac{2s-n+1}{2},\ \frac{2s+n+1}{2}\end{matrix}\right]$ $\times\, {}_{p+2}F_{q+2}\left(\begin{matrix}(a_p),\ s,\ s+\frac{1}{2};\ \sigma\omega\\ (b_q),\ \frac{2s-n+1}{2},\ \frac{2s+n+1}{2}\end{matrix}\right)$ $[\sigma > 0;\ \mathrm{Re}\,s > [n/2] - n/2]$
7	$(\sigma - x)_+^{(\varepsilon - 1)/2}$ $\times\, T_{2n+\varepsilon}\left(\sqrt{1 - \dfrac{x}{\sigma}}\right)$ $\times\, {}_pF_q\left(\begin{matrix}(a_p);\ \omega x\\ (b_q)\end{matrix}\right)$	$\dfrac{(-1)^n\,(2n+1)^\varepsilon\,\pi\,\sigma^{s+(\varepsilon-1)/2}}{2^{2s+\varepsilon-1}}\Gamma\left[\begin{matrix}2s\\ \frac{2s-2n+1}{2},\ \frac{2s+2n+2\varepsilon+1}{2}\end{matrix}\right]$ $\times\, {}_{p+2}F_{q+2}\left(\begin{matrix}(a_p),\ s,\ \frac{2s+1}{2};\ \sigma\omega\\ (b_q),\ \frac{2s-2n+1}{2},\ \frac{2s+2n+2\varepsilon+1}{2}\end{matrix}\right)$ $[\sigma,\ \mathrm{Re}\,s > 0]$

3.33.13. $_pF_q\left((a_p);\ (b_q);\ \omega x^r\right)$ **and** $U_n\left(\varphi(x)\right)$

Notation: $\varepsilon = 0$ or 1.

No.	$f(x)$	$F(s)$
1	$(\sigma^2 - x^2)_+^{1/2}\, U_n\left(\dfrac{x}{\sigma}\right)$ $\times\, {}_pF_q\left(\begin{matrix}(a_p);\ \omega x\\ (b_q)\end{matrix}\right)$	$(n+1)\,\pi\,\displaystyle\prod_{i=1}^{p} a_i \prod_{j=1}^{q} b_j^{-1}\left(\dfrac{\sigma}{2}\right)^{s+2}\omega\,\Gamma\left[\begin{matrix}s+1\\ \frac{s-n+2}{2},\ \frac{s+n+4}{2}\end{matrix}\right]$ $\times\, {}_{2p+2}F_{2q+3}\left(\begin{matrix}\frac{(a_p)+1}{2},\ \frac{(a_p)+2}{2},\ \frac{s+1}{2},\ \frac{s+2}{2},\ \frac{\sigma^2\omega^2}{4^{q-p+1}}\\ \frac{3}{2},\ \frac{(b_q)+1}{2},\ \frac{(b_q)+2}{2},\ \frac{s-n+2}{2},\ \frac{s+n+4}{2}\end{matrix}\right)$ $+\, \pi\,(n+1)\left(\dfrac{\sigma}{2}\right)^{s+1}\Gamma\left[\begin{matrix}s\\ \frac{s-n+1}{2},\ \frac{s+n+3}{2}\end{matrix}\right]$ $\times\, {}_{2p+2}F_{2q+3}\left(\begin{matrix}\frac{(a_p)}{2},\ \frac{(a_p)+1}{2},\ \frac{s}{2},\ \frac{s+1}{2};\ \frac{\sigma^2\omega^2}{4^{q-p+1}}\\ \frac{1}{2},\ \frac{(b_q)}{2},\ \frac{(b_q)+1}{2},\ \frac{s-n+1}{2},\ \frac{s+n+3}{2}\end{matrix}\right)$ $[\sigma > 0;\ \mathrm{Re}\,s > 2\,[n/2] - n]$
2	$(\sigma - x)_+^{1/2}\, U_n\left(\dfrac{2x}{\sigma} - 1\right)$ $\times\, {}_pF_q\left(\begin{matrix}(a_p);\ \omega x\\ (b_q)\end{matrix}\right)$	$\dfrac{(n+1)\,\pi\,\sigma^{s+1/2}}{2^{2s-1}}\Gamma\left[\begin{matrix}2s-1\\ \frac{2s-2n-1}{2},\ \frac{2s+2n+3}{2}\end{matrix}\right]$ $\times\, {}_{p+2}F_{q+2}\left(\begin{matrix}(a_p),\ s,\ \frac{2s-1}{2};\ \sigma\omega\\ (b_q),\ \frac{2s-2n-1}{2},\ \frac{2s+2n+3}{2}\end{matrix}\right)$ $[\sigma,\ \mathrm{Re}\,s > 0]$

No.	$f(x)$	$F(s)$
3	$(\sigma - x)_+^{1/2} U_n \left(\dfrac{2x}{\sigma} - 1 \right)$ $\times {}_pF_q \left(\begin{matrix} (a_p)\,;\, \omega x^2 \\ (b_q) \end{matrix} \right)$	$\dfrac{(n+1)\,\pi\sigma^{s+1/2}}{2^{2s-1}} \Gamma \left[\begin{matrix} 2s-1 \\ \frac{2s-2n-1}{2},\ \frac{2s+2n+3}{2} \end{matrix} \right]$ $\times {}_{p+4}F_{q+4} \left(\begin{matrix} (a_p),\, \Delta(2,s),\, \Delta\left(2, \frac{2s-1}{2}\right);\, \sigma^2\omega \\ (b_q),\, \Delta\left(2, \frac{2s-2n-1}{2}\right),\, \Delta\left(2, \frac{2s+2n+3}{2}\right) \end{matrix} \right)$ $[\sigma,\ \mathrm{Re}\,s > 0]$
4	$(\sigma - x)_+^{1/2} U_n \left(\dfrac{2\sigma}{x} - 1 \right)$ $\times {}_pF_q \left(\begin{matrix} (a_p)\,;\, \omega x \\ (b_q) \end{matrix} \right)$	$2^{2s+1}\,(n+1)\,\sigma^{s+1/2} \Gamma \left[\begin{matrix} s-n,\ s+n+2 \\ 2s+3 \end{matrix} \right]$ $\times {}_{p+2}F_{q+2} \left(\begin{matrix} (a_p),\, s-n,\, s+n+2 \\ (b_q),\, \frac{2s+3}{2},\, s+2;\, \sigma\omega \end{matrix} \right)$ $[\sigma > 0;\ \mathrm{Re}\,s > n]$
5	$(\sigma - x)_+^{1/2}$ $\times U_n \left(\dfrac{2\sigma}{x} - 1 \right)$ $\times {}_pF_q \left(\begin{matrix} (a_p)\,;\, \omega x^2 \\ (b_q) \end{matrix} \right)$	$2^{2s+1}\,(n+1)\,\sigma^{s+1/2} \Gamma \left[\begin{matrix} s-n,\ s+n+2 \\ 2s+3 \end{matrix} \right]$ $\times {}_{p+4}F_{q+4} \left(\begin{matrix} (a_p),\, \frac{s-n}{2},\, \frac{s-n+1}{2},\, \frac{s+n+2}{2},\, \frac{s+n+3}{2} \\ (b_q),\, \frac{2s+3}{4},\, \frac{2s+5}{4},\, \frac{2s+2}{2},\, \frac{2s+3}{2};\, \sigma\omega \end{matrix} \right)$ $[\sigma > 0;\ \mathrm{Re}\,s > n]$
6	$(\sigma - x)_+^{1/2} U_n \left(\sqrt{\dfrac{x}{\sigma}} \right)$ $\times {}_pF_q \left(\begin{matrix} (a_p)\,;\, \omega x \\ (b_q) \end{matrix} \right)$	$\dfrac{(n+1)\,\pi\sigma^{s+1/2}}{2^{2s}} \Gamma \left[\begin{matrix} 2s \\ \frac{2s-n+1}{2},\ \frac{2s+n+3}{2} \end{matrix} \right]$ $\times {}_{p+2}F_{q+2} \left(\begin{matrix} (a_p),\, s,\, \frac{2s+1}{2};\, \sigma\omega \\ (b_q),\, \frac{2s-n+1}{2},\, \frac{2s+n+3}{2} \end{matrix} \right)$ $[\sigma > 0;\ \mathrm{Re}\,s > [n/2] - n/2]$
7	$(\sigma - x)_+^{(\varepsilon-1)/2}$ $\times U_{2n+\varepsilon} \left(\sqrt{1 - \dfrac{x}{\sigma}} \right)$ $\times {}_pF_q \left(\begin{matrix} (a_p)\,;\, \omega x \\ (b_q) \end{matrix} \right)$	$\dfrac{(-1)^n\,(n+1)^\varepsilon\,\pi\sigma^{s+(\varepsilon-1)/2}}{2^{2s-2}} \Gamma \left[\begin{matrix} 2s-1 \\ \frac{2s-2n-1}{2},\ \frac{2s+2n+2\varepsilon+1}{2} \end{matrix} \right]$ $\times {}_{p+2}F_{q+2} \left(\begin{matrix} (a_p),\, s,\, \frac{2s-1}{2};\, \sigma\omega \\ (b_q),\, \frac{2s-2n-1}{2},\, \frac{2s+2n+2\varepsilon+1}{2} \end{matrix} \right)$ $[\sigma,\ \mathrm{Re}\,s > 0]$

3.33.14. ${}_pF_q\left((a_p)\,;\, (b_q)\,;\, \omega x\right)$ **and** $H_n\left(\sigma x^r\right)$

1	$e^{-\sigma^2 x^2} H_n(\sigma x)$ $\times {}_pF_q \left(\begin{matrix} (a_p)\,;\, -\omega x \\ (b_q) \end{matrix} \right)$	$-\prod_{i=1}^{p} a_i \prod_{j=1}^{q} b_j^{-1} \dfrac{2^{n-s-1}\sqrt{\pi}\,\omega}{\sigma^{s+1}} \Gamma \left[\begin{matrix} s+1 \\ \frac{s-n+2}{2} \end{matrix} \right]$ $\times {}_{2p+2}F_{2q+2} \left(\begin{matrix} \frac{(a_p)+1}{2},\, \frac{(a_p)+2}{2},\, \frac{s+1}{2},\, \frac{s+2}{2};\, \frac{\omega^2}{4^{q-p+1}\sigma^2} \\ \frac{3}{2},\, \frac{(b_q)+1}{2},\, \frac{(b_q)+2}{2},\, \frac{s-n+2}{2} \end{matrix} \right)$ $+ \dfrac{\sqrt{\pi}\,2^{n-s}}{\sigma^s} \Gamma \left[\begin{matrix} s \\ \frac{s-n+1}{2} \end{matrix} \right] \times$

No.	$f(x)$	$F(s)$
		$\times\ _{2p+2}F_{2q+2}\left(\begin{array}{c}\frac{(a_p)}{2},\ \frac{(a_p)+1}{2},\ \frac{s}{2},\ \frac{s+1}{2};\ \frac{\omega^2}{4^{q-p+1}\sigma^2}\\ \frac{1}{2},\ \frac{(b_q)}{2},\ \frac{(b_q)+1}{2},\ \frac{s-n+1}{2}\end{array}\right)$

$$\left[\begin{array}{l}
\left[q=p-1;\ |\arg\omega|<\pi;\ \left(\mathrm{Re}\,\sigma^2>0;\ \mathrm{Re}\,s>2\left[n/2\right]-n\right)\ \text{or}\right.\\
\quad\left.\left(\mathrm{Re}\,\sigma^2=0;\ 2\left[n/2\right]-n<\mathrm{Re}\,s<\mathrm{Re}\,a_k-n+2\right)\right]\ \text{or}\\
\left[q=p;\ \left(\mathrm{Re}\,\sigma^2>0;\ |\arg\omega|<\pi;\ \mathrm{Re}\,s>2\left[n/2\right]-n\right)\ \text{or}\right.\\
\quad\left(\mathrm{Re}\,\sigma^2=0;\ \mathrm{Re}\,\omega>0;\ 2\left[n/2\right]-n<\mathrm{Re}\,s<\mathrm{Re}\,a_k-n+2\right)\ \text{or}\\
\quad\left.\left(\mathrm{Re}\,\sigma^2=0;\ \mathrm{Re}\,\omega=0;\ 2\left[n/2\right]-n<\mathrm{Re}\,s<\mathrm{Re}\,a_k-n+2,\,2-n-\mathrm{Re}\,\chi\right)\right]\ \text{or}\\
\left[q=p+1;\ \left(\mathrm{Re}\,\sigma^2>0;\ |\arg\omega|<\pi;\ \mathrm{Re}\,s>2\left[n/2\right]-n\right)\ \text{or}\right.\\
\quad\left.\left(\mathrm{Re}\,\sigma^2=0;\ \omega>0;\ 2\left[n/2\right]-n<\mathrm{Re}\,s<\mathrm{Re}\,a_k-n+2,\,2-n-\mathrm{Re}\,\chi\right)\right]\ \text{or}\\
\left[q\geq p+2;\ \mathrm{Re}\,\sigma^2>0;\ |\arg\omega|<\pi;\ \mathrm{Re}\,s>2\left[n/2\right]-n\right]
\end{array}\right]$$

| 2 | $e^{-\sigma^2 x}H_n\left(\sigma\sqrt{x}\right)$ $\times\ _pF_q\left(\begin{array}{c}(a_p)\,;\ -\omega x\\ (b_q)\end{array}\right)$ | $\dfrac{\sqrt{\pi}\,2^{1-2s+n}}{\sigma^{2s}}\,\Gamma\!\left[\begin{array}{c}2s\\ \frac{2s-n+1}{2}\end{array}\right]\ _{p+2}F_{q+1}\left(\begin{array}{c}(a_p),\ s,\ \frac{2s+1}{2}\\ (b_q),\ \frac{2s-n+1}{2};\ -\frac{\omega}{\sigma^2}\end{array}\right)$ |

$$\left[\begin{array}{l}
\left[q=p-1;\ |\arg\omega|<\pi;\ \left(|\arg\sigma|<\pi/4;\ \mathrm{Re}\,s>[n/2]-n/2\right)\ \text{or}\right.\\
\quad\left.\left(|\arg\sigma|=\pi/4;\ [n/2]-n/2<\mathrm{Re}\,s<\mathrm{Re}\,a_k-n/2+1\right)\right]\ \text{or}\\
\left[q=p;\ \left(|\arg\sigma|<\pi/4;\ \mathrm{Re}\left(\sigma^2+\omega\right)>0;\ \mathrm{Re}\,s>[n/2]-n/2\right)\ \text{or}\right.\\
\quad\left(|\arg\sigma|<\pi/4;\ \mathrm{Re}\left(\sigma^2+\omega\right)=0;\ [n/2]-n/2<\mathrm{Re}\,s<1-n/2-\mathrm{Re}\,\chi\right)\ \text{or}\\
\quad\left(|\arg\sigma|=\pi/4;\ \mathrm{Re}\,\omega>0;\ [n/2]-n/2<\mathrm{Re}\,s<\mathrm{Re}\,a_k-n/2+1\right)\ \text{or}\\
\quad\left.\left(|\arg\sigma|=\pi/4;\ \mathrm{Re}\,\omega=0;\ [n/2]-n/2<\mathrm{Re}\,s<\mathrm{Re}\,a_k-n/2+1,\,1-n/2-\mathrm{Re}\,\chi\right)\right]\ \text{or}\\
\left[q=p+1;\ \left(|\arg\sigma|<\pi/4;\ |\arg\omega|<\pi;\ \mathrm{Re}\,s>[n/2]-n/2\right)\ \text{or}\right.\\
\quad\left.\left(|\arg\sigma|=\pi/4;\ \omega>0;\ [n/2]-n/2<\mathrm{Re}\,s<\mathrm{Re}\,a_k-n/2+1,\,1-n/2-\mathrm{Re}\,\chi\right)\right]\ \text{or}\\
\left[q\geq p+2;\ |\arg\sigma|<\pi/4;\ |\arg\omega|<\pi;\ \mathrm{Re}\,s>[n/2]-n/2\right]
\end{array}\right]$$

3.33.15. $_pF_q\left((a_p)\,;\ (b_q)\,;\ \omega x\right)$ and $L_n^\lambda\left(\sigma x^r\right)$

| 1 | $e^{-\sigma x}L_n^\lambda\left(\sigma x\right)$ $\times\ _pF_q\left(\begin{array}{c}(a_p)\,;\ -\omega x\\ (b_q)\end{array}\right)$ | $\dfrac{\sigma^{-s}}{n!}\left(1-s+\lambda\right)_n\Gamma(s)\ _{p+2}F_{q+1}\left(\begin{array}{c}(a_p),\ s-\lambda,\ s\\ (b_q),\ s-n-\lambda;\ -\frac{\omega}{\sigma}\end{array}\right)$ |

$$\left[\begin{array}{l}
\left[q=p-1;\ |\arg\omega|<\pi;\ \left(\mathrm{Re}\,\sigma,\ \mathrm{Re}\,s>0\right)\ \text{or}\right.\\
\quad\left.\left(\mathrm{Re}\,\sigma=0;\ 0<\mathrm{Re}\,s<\mathrm{Re}\,a_k-n+1\right)\right]\ \text{or}\\
\left[q=p;\ \left(\mathrm{Re}\,\sigma,\ \mathrm{Re}\,s>0;\ \mathrm{Re}\left(\sigma^2+\omega\right)>0\right)\ \text{or}\right.\\
\quad\left(\mathrm{Re}\,\sigma>0;\ \mathrm{Re}\left(\sigma^2+\omega\right)=0;\ 0<\mathrm{Re}\,s<1-n-\mathrm{Re}\,\chi\right)\ \text{or}\\
\quad\left(\mathrm{Re}\,\sigma=0;\ \mathrm{Re}\,\omega>0;\ 0<\mathrm{Re}\,s<\mathrm{Re}\,a_k-n+1\right)\ \text{or}\\
\quad\left.\left(\mathrm{Re}\,\sigma=0;\ \mathrm{Re}\,\omega=0;\ 0<\mathrm{Re}\,s<\mathrm{Re}\,a_k-n+1,\,1-n-\mathrm{Re}\,\chi\right)\right]\ \text{or}\\
\left[q=p+1;\ \left(\mathrm{Re}\,\sigma,\ \mathrm{Re}\,s>0;\ |\arg\omega|<\pi\right)\ \text{or}\right.\\
\quad\left.\left(\mathrm{Re}\,\sigma=0;\ \omega>0;\ 0<\mathrm{Re}\,s<\mathrm{Re}\,a_k-n+1,\,1-n-\mathrm{Re}\,\chi\right)\right]\ \text{or}\\
\left[q\geq p+2;\ \mathrm{Re}\,\sigma,\ \mathrm{Re}\,s>0;\ |\arg\omega|<\pi\right]
\end{array}\right]$$

No.	$f(x)$	$F(s)$
2	$e^{-\sigma\sqrt{x}} L_n^\lambda\left(\sigma\sqrt{x}\right)$ $\times {}_pF_q\left(\begin{matrix}(a_p)\,;\,-\omega x\\(b_q)\end{matrix}\right)$	$\dfrac{2\sigma^{-2s}}{n!}\,(1-2s+\lambda)_n\,\Gamma\,(2s)$ $\times {}_{p+4}F_{q+2}\left(\begin{matrix}(a_p),\,\frac{2s-\lambda}{2},\,\frac{2s-\lambda+1}{2},\,s,\,\frac{2s+1}{2}\\(b_q),\,\frac{2s-n-\lambda}{2},\,\frac{2s-n-\lambda+1}{2};\,-\frac{4\omega}{\sigma^2}\end{matrix}\right)$

$$\left[\begin{matrix}[q=p-1;\ |\arg\omega|<\pi;\ (\mathrm{Re}\,\sigma,\ \mathrm{Re}\,s>0)\ \text{or}\\(\mathrm{Re}\,\sigma=0;\ 0<\mathrm{Re}\,s<\mathrm{Re}\,a_k+(1-n)/2)]\ \text{or}\\{}[q=p;(\mathrm{Re}\,\sigma,\ \mathrm{Re}\,s>0;\ \mathrm{Re}\,\omega\ge0)\ \text{or}\\(\mathrm{Re}\,\sigma=0;\ \mathrm{Re}\,\omega>0;\ 0<\mathrm{Re}\,s<\mathrm{Re}\,a_k+(1-n)/2)\ \text{or}\\(\mathrm{Re}\,\sigma=\mathrm{Re}\,\omega=0;\ 0<\mathrm{Re}\,s<\mathrm{Re}\,a_k+(1-n)/2,\ 1-n/2-\mathrm{Re}\,\chi)]\ \text{or}\\{}[q=p+1;\ (2|\mathrm{Im}\,\sqrt{\omega}|<\mathrm{Re}\,\sigma;\ \mathrm{Re}\,s>0)\ \text{or}\\(\mathrm{Re}\,\sigma>0;\ 2|\mathrm{Im}\,\sqrt{\omega}|+\mathrm{Re}\,\sigma=0;\ 0<\mathrm{Re}\,s<(1-n)/2-\mathrm{Re}\,\chi)\ \text{or}\\(\mathrm{Re}\,\sigma=0;\ \omega>0;\ \mathrm{Re}\,s<\mathrm{Re}\,a_k+(1-n)/2,\ (1-n)/2-\mathrm{Re}\,\chi)]\ \text{or}\\{}[q\ge p+2;\ \mathrm{Re}\,\sigma,\ \mathrm{Re}\,s>0;\ |\arg\omega|<\pi]\end{matrix}\right]$$

3.33.16. ${}_pF_q\left((a_p)\,;\ (b_q)\,;\ \omega x\right)$ **and** $C_n^\lambda\left(\varphi(x)\right)$

Notation: $\varepsilon=0$ or 1.

No.	$f(x)$	$F(s)$
1	$\left(\sigma^2-x^2\right)_+^{\lambda-1/2} C_n^\lambda\left(\dfrac{x}{\sigma}\right)$ $\times {}_pF_q\left(\begin{matrix}(a_p)\,;\,\omega x\\(b_q)\end{matrix}\right)$	$\dfrac{\pi}{n!}\displaystyle\prod_{i=1}^{p}a_i\prod_{j=1}^{q}b_j^{-1}\left(\dfrac{\sigma}{2}\right)^{s+2\lambda}\omega\,\Gamma\left[\begin{matrix}n+2\lambda,\ s+1\\\lambda,\ \frac{s-n+2}{2},\ \frac{s+n+2\lambda+2}{2}\end{matrix}\right]$ $\times {}_{2p+2}F_{2q+3}\left(\begin{matrix}\frac{(a_p)+1}{2},\,\frac{(a_p)+2}{2},\,\frac{s+1}{2},\,\frac{s+2}{2};\,\frac{\sigma^2\omega^2}{4^{q-p+1}}\\\frac{3}{2},\,\frac{(b_q)+1}{2},\,\frac{(b_q)+2}{2},\,\frac{s-n+2}{2},\,\frac{s+n+2\lambda+2}{2}\end{matrix}\right)$ $+\dfrac{\pi}{n!}\left(\dfrac{\sigma}{2}\right)^{s+2\lambda-1}\Gamma\left[\begin{matrix}n+2\lambda,\ s\\\lambda,\ \frac{s-n+1}{2},\ \frac{s+n+2\lambda+1}{2}\end{matrix}\right]$ $\times {}_{2p+2}F_{2q+3}\left(\begin{matrix}\frac{(a_p)}{2},\,\frac{(a_p)+1}{2},\,\frac{s}{2},\,\frac{s+1}{2};\,\frac{\sigma^2\omega^2}{4^{q-p+1}}\\\frac{1}{2},\,\frac{(b_q)}{2},\,\frac{(b_q)+1}{2},\,\frac{s-n+1}{2},\,\frac{s+n+2\lambda+1}{2}\end{matrix}\right)$ $[\sigma>0;\ \mathrm{Re}\,\lambda>-1/2;\ \mathrm{Re}\,s>2\,[n/2]-n]$
2	$(\sigma-x)_+^{\lambda-1/2}$ $\times C_n^\lambda\left(\dfrac{2x}{\sigma}-1\right)$ $\times {}_pF_q\left(\begin{matrix}(a_p)\,;\,\omega x\\(b_q)\end{matrix}\right)$	$\dfrac{\sqrt{\pi}\,\sigma^{s+\lambda-1/2}}{2^{2\lambda-1}n!}\Gamma\left[\begin{matrix}n+2\lambda,\ s,\ \frac{2s-2\lambda+1}{2}\\\lambda,\ \frac{2s-2n-2\lambda+1}{2},\ \frac{2s+2n+2\lambda+1}{2}\end{matrix}\right]$ $\times {}_{p+2}F_{q+2}\left(\begin{matrix}(a_p),\,s,\,\frac{2s-2\lambda+1}{2};\,\sigma\omega\\(b_q),\,\frac{2s-2n-2\lambda+1}{2},\,\frac{2s+2n+2\lambda+1}{2}\end{matrix}\right)$ $[\sigma,\ \mathrm{Re}\,s>0;\ \mathrm{Re}\,\lambda>-1/2]$
3	$(\sigma-x)_+^{\lambda-1/2}$ $\times C_n^\lambda\left(\dfrac{2x}{\sigma}-1\right)$ $\times {}_pF_q\left(\begin{matrix}(a_p)\,;\,\omega x^2\\(b_q)\end{matrix}\right)$	$\dfrac{(-1)^n\sqrt{\pi}\,\sigma^{s+\lambda-1/2}}{2^{2\lambda-1}n!}\Gamma\left[\begin{matrix}n+2\lambda,\ s,\ \frac{1-2s+2n+2\lambda}{2}\\\lambda,\ \frac{1-2s+2\lambda}{2},\ \frac{2s+2n+2\lambda+1}{2}\end{matrix}\right]$ $\times {}_pF_q\left(\begin{matrix}(a_p),\,\Delta(2,s),\,\Delta\left(2,\frac{2s-2\lambda+1}{2}\right);\,\sigma^2\omega\\(b_q),\,\Delta\left(2,\frac{2s-2n-2\lambda+1}{2}\right),\,\Delta\left(2,\frac{2s+2n+2\lambda+1}{2}\right)\end{matrix}\right)$ $[\sigma,\ \mathrm{Re}\,s>0;\ \lambda>-1/2]$

No.	$f(x)$	$F(s)$
4	$(\sigma - x)_+^{\lambda-1/2}$ $\times C_n^\lambda\left(\dfrac{2\sigma}{x} - 1\right)$ $\times {}_pF_q\left(\begin{matrix}(a_p)\,;\,\omega x\\(b_q)\end{matrix}\right)$	$\dfrac{\sqrt{\pi}\,\sigma^{s+\lambda-1/2}}{2^{2\lambda-1}n!}\,\Gamma\left[\begin{matrix}n+2\lambda,\,s-n,\,s+n+2\lambda\\\lambda,\,\frac{2s+2\lambda+1}{2},\,s+2\lambda\end{matrix}\right]$ $\times {}_{p+2}F_{q+2}\left(\begin{matrix}(a_p),\,s-n,\,s+n+2\lambda\\(b_q),\,\frac{2s+2\lambda+1}{2},\,s+2\lambda;\,\sigma\omega\end{matrix}\right)$ $[\sigma > 0;\ \operatorname{Re}\lambda > -1/2;\ \operatorname{Re}s > n]$
5	$(\sigma - x)_+^{\lambda-1/2}$ $\times C_n^\lambda\left(\dfrac{2\sigma}{x} - 1\right)$ $\times {}_pF_q\left(\begin{matrix}(a_p)\,;\,\omega x^2\\(b_q)\end{matrix}\right)$	$\dfrac{\sqrt{\pi}\,\sigma^{s+\lambda-1/2}}{2^{2\lambda-1}n!}\,\Gamma\left[\begin{matrix}n+2\lambda,\,s-n,\,s+n+2\lambda\\\lambda,\,\frac{2s+2\lambda+1}{2},\,s+2\lambda\end{matrix}\right]$ $\times {}_{p+4}F_{q+4}\left(\begin{matrix}(a_p),\,\Delta\left(2,\,s-n\right),\,\Delta\left(2,\,s+n+2\lambda\right)\\(b_q),\,\Delta\left(2,\,\frac{2s+2\lambda+1}{2}\right),\,\Delta\left(2,\,s+2\lambda\right);\,\sigma^2\omega\end{matrix}\right)$ $[\sigma > 0;\ \operatorname{Re}\lambda > -1/2;\ \operatorname{Re}s > n]$
6	$(\sigma - x)^{-n-2\lambda}$ $\times C_n^\lambda\left(\dfrac{\sigma + x}{\sigma - x}\right)$ $\times {}_pF_q\left(\begin{matrix}(a_p)\,;\,\omega x\\(b_q)\end{matrix}\right)$	$\dfrac{\sigma^{s-n-2\lambda}}{n!\left(\frac{2\lambda+1}{2}\right)_n}\,\Gamma\left[\begin{matrix}1-2\lambda,\,s,\,\frac{2s-2\lambda+1}{2}\\\frac{2s-2n-2\lambda+1}{2},\,s-n-2\lambda+1\end{matrix}\right]$ $\times {}_{p+2}F_{q+2}\left(\begin{matrix}(a_p),\,s,\,\frac{2s-2\lambda+1}{2};\,\sigma\omega\\(b_q),\,s-n-2\lambda+1,\,\frac{2s-2n-2\lambda+1}{2}\end{matrix}\right)$ $[\sigma,\ \operatorname{Re}s > 0;\ \operatorname{Re}\lambda < 1/2 - n]$
7	$(\sigma - x)_+^{\lambda-1/2}\,C_n^\lambda\left(\sqrt{\dfrac{x}{\sigma}}\right)$ $\times {}_pF_q\left(\begin{matrix}(a_p)\,;\,\omega x\\(b_q)\end{matrix}\right)$	$\dfrac{2\pi}{n!}\left(\dfrac{\sqrt{\sigma}}{2}\right)^{2s+2\lambda-1}\,\Gamma\left[\begin{matrix}n+2\lambda,\,2s\\\lambda,\,\frac{2s-n+1}{2},\,\frac{2s+n+2\lambda+1}{2}\end{matrix}\right]$ $\times {}_{p+2}F_{q+2}\left(\begin{matrix}(a_p),\,s,\,\frac{2s+1}{2};\,\sigma\omega\\(b_q),\,\frac{2s-n+1}{2},\,\frac{2s+n+2\lambda+1}{2}\end{matrix}\right)$ $[\sigma > 0;\ \operatorname{Re}\lambda > -1/2;\ \operatorname{Re}s > [n/2] - n/2]$
8	$(\sigma - x)_+^{(\varepsilon-1)/2}$ $\times C_{2n+\varepsilon}^\lambda\left(\sqrt{1-\dfrac{x}{\sigma}}\right)$ $\times {}_pF_q\left(\begin{matrix}(a_p)\,;\,\omega x\\(b_q)\end{matrix}\right)$	$\dfrac{(-1)^n\,\sqrt{\pi}\,\sigma^{s+(\varepsilon-1)/2}}{n!}\,(\lambda)_{n+\varepsilon}\,\Gamma\left[\begin{matrix}s,\,\frac{2s-2\lambda+1}{2}\\\frac{2s-2n-2\lambda+1}{2},\,\frac{2s+2n+2\varepsilon+1}{2}\end{matrix}\right]$ $\times {}_{p+2}F_{q+2}\left(\begin{matrix}(a_p),\,s,\,\frac{2s-2\lambda+1}{2};\,\sigma\omega\\(b_q),\,\frac{2s-2n-2\lambda+1}{2},\,\frac{2s+2n+2\varepsilon+1}{2}\end{matrix}\right)$ $[\sigma,\ \operatorname{Re}s > 0]$
9	$(\sigma - x)_+^{-n/2-\lambda}$ $\times C_n^\lambda\left(\sqrt{\dfrac{\sigma}{\sigma - x}}\right)$ $\times {}_pF_q\left(\begin{matrix}(a_p)\,;\,\omega x\\(b_q)\end{matrix}\right)$	$\dfrac{\sigma^{s-n/2-\lambda}}{n!}\,(2\lambda - 2s)_n\,\mathrm{B}\left(1-\lambda,\,s\right)$ $\times {}_{p+2}F_{q+2}\left(\begin{matrix}(a_p),\,s,\,\frac{2s-2\lambda+1}{2};\,\sigma\omega\\(b_q),\,\frac{2s-n-2\lambda+1}{2},\,\frac{2s-n-2\lambda+2}{2}\end{matrix}\right)$ $[\sigma,\ \operatorname{Re}s > 0;\ \operatorname{Re}\lambda < 1 - n]$

3.33.17. $_pF_q\left((a_p)\,;\ (b_q)\,;\ \omega x^r\right)$ **and** $P_n^{(\alpha,\beta)}\left(\varphi\left(x\right)\right)$

1	$(\sigma-x)_+^{\alpha}\,P_n^{(\alpha,\beta)}\left(\dfrac{2x}{\sigma}-1\right)$ $\times\ {}_pF_q\left(\begin{matrix}(a_p)\,;\ \omega x\\(b_q)\end{matrix}\right)$	$\dfrac{(-1)^n\,\sigma^{s+\alpha}}{n!}\,(1-s+\beta)_n\,\mathrm{B}\left(n+\alpha+1,\ s\right)$ $\times\ {}_{p+2}F_{q+2}\left(\begin{matrix}(a_p),\ s,\ s-\beta;\ \sigma\omega\\(b_q),\ s-n-\beta,\ s+n+\alpha+1\end{matrix}\right)$ $[\sigma,\ \operatorname{Re}s>0;\ \operatorname{Re}\alpha>-1]$
2	$(\sigma-x)_+^{\alpha}\,P_n^{(\alpha,\beta)}\left(\dfrac{2x}{\sigma}-1\right)$ $\times\ {}_pF_q\left(\begin{matrix}(a_p)\,;\ \omega x^2\\(b_q)\end{matrix}\right)$	$\dfrac{(-1)^n\,\sigma^{s+\alpha}}{n!}\,(\beta-s+1)_n\,\mathrm{B}\left(n+\alpha+1,\ s\right)$ $\times\ {}_{p+4}F_{q+4}\left(\begin{matrix}(a_p),\ \Delta\left(2,s\right),\ \Delta\left(2,s-\beta\right);\ \sigma^2\omega\\(b_q),\ \Delta\left(2,s-n-\beta\right),\ \Delta\left(2,s+n+\alpha+1\right)\end{matrix}\right)$ $[\sigma,\ \operatorname{Re}s>0;\ \operatorname{Re}\alpha>-1]$
3	$(\sigma-x)_+^{\alpha}\,P_n^{(\alpha,\beta)}\left(\dfrac{2\sigma}{x}-1\right)$ $\times\ {}_pF_q\left(\begin{matrix}(a_p)\,;\ \omega x\\(b_q)\end{matrix}\right)$	$\dfrac{\sigma^{s+\alpha}}{n!}\,(s+\alpha+\beta+1)_n\,\mathrm{B}\left(n+\alpha+1,\ s-n\right)$ $\times\ {}_{p+2}F_{q+2}\left(\begin{matrix}(a_p),\ s-n,\ s+n+\alpha+\beta+1\\(b_q),\ s+\alpha+1,\ s+\alpha+\beta+1;\ \sigma\omega\end{matrix}\right)$ $[\sigma>0;\ \operatorname{Re}\alpha>-1;\ \operatorname{Re}s>n]$
4	$(\sigma-x)_+^{-n-\alpha-\beta-1}$ $\times\ P_n^{(\alpha,\beta)}\left(\dfrac{\sigma+x}{\sigma-x}\right)$ $\times\ {}_pF_q\left(\begin{matrix}(a_p)\,;\ \omega x\\(b_q)\end{matrix}\right)$	$\dfrac{\sigma^{s-n-\alpha-\beta-1}}{n!}\,(1-s+\alpha)_n\,\mathrm{B}\left(-n-\alpha-\beta,\ s\right)$ $\times\ {}_{p+2}F_{q+2}\left(\begin{matrix}(a_p),\ s,\ s-\alpha;\ \sigma\omega\\(b_q),\ s-n-\alpha,\ s-n-\alpha-\beta\end{matrix}\right)$ $[\sigma,\ \operatorname{Re}s>0;\ \operatorname{Re}\left(\alpha+\beta\right)<-n]$

3.33.18. $_pF_q\left((a_p)\,;\ (b_q)\,;\ \omega x^r\right)$ **and** $\mathbf{K}\left(\varphi\left(x\right)\right),\ \mathbf{E}\left(\varphi\left(x\right)\right)$

Notation: $\delta=\left\{\begin{matrix}1\\0\end{matrix}\right\}.$

1	$\theta\left(\sigma-x\right)\left\{\begin{matrix}\mathbf{K}\left(\sqrt{1-x/\sigma}\right)\\\mathbf{E}\left(\sqrt{1-x/\sigma}\right)\end{matrix}\right\}$ $\times\ {}_pF_q\left(\begin{matrix}(a_p)\,;\ \omega x\\(b_q)\end{matrix}\right)$	$\dfrac{\pi\sigma^s}{2}\,\Gamma\left[\begin{matrix}s,\ s-\delta+1\\\frac{2s+1}{2},\ \frac{2s-2\delta+3}{2}\end{matrix}\right]\,{}_{p+2}F_{q+2}\left(\begin{matrix}(a_p),\ s,\ s-\delta+1;\ \sigma\omega\\(b_q),\ \frac{2s+1}{2},\ \frac{2s-2\delta+3}{2}\end{matrix}\right)$ $[\sigma,\ \operatorname{Re}s>0]$
2	$\theta\left(\sigma-x\right)\left\{\begin{matrix}\mathbf{K}\left(\sqrt{1-x/\sigma}\right)\\\mathbf{E}\left(\sqrt{1-x/\sigma}\right)\end{matrix}\right\}$ $\times\ {}_pF_q\left(\begin{matrix}(a_p)\,;\ \omega x^2\\(b_q)\end{matrix}\right)$	$\dfrac{\pi\sigma^s}{2}\,\Gamma\left[\begin{matrix}s,\ s-\delta+1\\\frac{2s+1}{2},\ \frac{2s-2\delta+3}{2}\end{matrix}\right]$ $\times\ {}_{p+4}F_{q+4}\left(\begin{matrix}(a_p),\ \frac{s}{2},\ \frac{s+1}{2},\ \frac{s-\delta+1}{2},\ \frac{s-\delta+2}{2};\ \sigma^2\omega\\(b_q),\ \frac{2s+1}{4},\ \frac{2s+3}{4},\ \frac{2s-2\delta+3}{4},\ \frac{2s-2\delta+5}{4}\end{matrix}\right)$ $[\sigma,\ \operatorname{Re}s>0]$

3.33.19. $_pF_q\left((a_p);\ (b_q);\ \omega x^r\right)$ **and** $P_\nu^\mu\left(\varphi(x)\right),\ \mathrm{P}_\nu^\mu\left(\varphi(x)\right)$

1	$(\sigma^2 - x^2)_+^{-\mu/2}\, P_\nu^\mu\left(\dfrac{x}{\sigma}\right)$ $\times {}_pF_q\left(\begin{matrix}(a_p);\ \omega x\\(b_q)\end{matrix}\right)$	$\sqrt{\pi}\,\omega\left(\dfrac{\sigma}{2}\right)^{s-\mu+1}\displaystyle\prod_{i=1}^p a_i \prod_{j=1}^q b_j^{-1}\,\Gamma\left[\begin{matrix}s+1\\\frac{s-\mu-\nu+2}{2},\ \frac{s-\mu+\nu+3}{2}\end{matrix}\right]$ $\times {}_{2p+2}F_{2q+3}\left(\begin{matrix}\frac{(a_p)+1}{2},\ \frac{(a_p)+2}{2},\ \frac{s+1}{2},\ \frac{s+2}{2};\ \frac{\sigma^2\omega^2}{4^{q-p+1}}\\\frac{3}{2},\ \frac{(b_q)+1}{2},\ \frac{(b_q)+2}{2},\ \frac{s-\mu-\nu+2}{2},\ \frac{s-\mu+\nu+3}{2}\end{matrix}\right)$ $+\sqrt{\pi}\left(\dfrac{\sigma}{2}\right)^{s-\mu}\Gamma\left[\begin{matrix}s\\\frac{s-\mu-\nu+1}{2},\ \frac{s-\mu+\nu+2}{2}\end{matrix}\right]$ $\times {}_{2p+2}F_{2q+3}\left(\begin{matrix}\frac{(a_p)}{2},\ \frac{(a_p)+1}{2},\ \frac{s}{2},\ \frac{s+1}{2};\ \frac{\sigma^2\omega^2}{4^{q-p+1}}\\\frac{1}{2},\ \frac{(b_q)}{2},\ \frac{(b_q)+1}{2},\ \frac{s-\mu-\nu+1}{2},\ \frac{s-\mu+\nu+2}{2}\end{matrix}\right)$ $[\sigma,\ \operatorname{Re}s > 0;\ \operatorname{Re}\mu < 1]$
2	$(\sigma - x)_+^{-\mu/2}\, P_\nu^\mu\left(\dfrac{2x}{\sigma}-1\right)$ $\times {}_pF_q\left(\begin{matrix}(a_p);\ \omega x\\(b_q)\end{matrix}\right)$	$\sigma^{s-\mu/2}\,\Gamma\left[\begin{matrix}\frac{2s-\mu}{2},\ \frac{2s+\mu}{2}\\\frac{2s-\mu-2\nu}{2},\ \frac{2s-\mu+2\nu+2}{2}\end{matrix}\right]$ $\times {}_{p+2}F_{q+2}\left(\begin{matrix}(a_p),\ \frac{2s-\mu}{2},\ \frac{2s+\mu}{2};\ \sigma\omega\\(b_q),\ \frac{2s-\mu-2\nu}{2},\ \frac{2s-\mu+2\nu+2}{2}\end{matrix}\right)$ $[\sigma > 0;\ \operatorname{Re}\mu < 1;\ \operatorname{Re}s > |\operatorname{Re}\mu|/2]$
3	$(\sigma - x)_+^{-\mu/2}\, P_\nu^\mu\left(\sqrt{\dfrac{x}{\sigma}}\right)$ $\times {}_pF_q\left(\begin{matrix}(a_p);\ \omega x\\(b_q)\end{matrix}\right)$	$2^{1-2s+\mu}\sqrt{\pi}\,\sigma^{s-\mu/2}\,\Gamma\left[\begin{matrix}2s\\\frac{2s-\mu-\nu+1}{2},\ \frac{2s-\mu+\nu+2}{2}\end{matrix}\right]$ $\times {}_{p+2}F_{q+2}\left(\begin{matrix}(a_p),\ s,\ \frac{2s+1}{2};\ \sigma\omega\\(b_q),\ \frac{2s-\mu-\nu+1}{2},\ \frac{2s-\mu+\nu+2}{2}\end{matrix}\right)$ $[\sigma,\ \operatorname{Re}s > 0;\ \operatorname{Re}\mu < 1]$
4	$(\sigma - x)_+^{-\mu/2}\, P_\nu^\mu\left(\dfrac{2\sigma}{x}-1\right)$ $\times {}_pF_q\left(\begin{matrix}(a_p);\ \omega x\\(b_q)\end{matrix}\right)$	$\sigma^{s-\mu/2}\,\Gamma\left[\begin{matrix}s-\nu,\ s+\nu+1\\s+1,\ s-\mu+1\end{matrix}\right]$ $\times {}_{p+2}F_{q+2}\left(\begin{matrix}(a_p),\ s-\nu,\ s+\nu+1;\ \sigma\omega\\(b_q),\ s+1,\ s-\mu+1\end{matrix}\right)$ $[\sigma > 0;\ \operatorname{Re}\mu < 1;\ \operatorname{Re}s > \operatorname{Re}\nu,\ -\operatorname{Re}\nu - 1]$
5	$(\sigma^2 - x^2)_+^{-\mu/2}\, P_\nu^\mu\left(\dfrac{\sigma}{x}\right)$ $\times {}_pF_q\left(\begin{matrix}(a_p);\ \omega x\\(b_q)\end{matrix}\right)$	$\dfrac{2^s\omega\sigma^{s-\mu+1}}{\sqrt{\pi}}\displaystyle\prod_{i=1}^p a_i \prod_{j=1}^q b_j^{-1}\,\Gamma\left[\begin{matrix}\frac{s-\nu+1}{2},\ \frac{s+\nu+2}{2}\\s-\mu+2\end{matrix}\right]$ $\times {}_{2p+2}F_{2q+3}\left(\begin{matrix}\frac{(a_p)+1}{2},\ \frac{(a_p)+2}{2},\ \frac{s-\nu+2}{2},\ \frac{s+\nu+3}{2};\ \frac{\sigma^2\omega^2}{4^{q-p+1}}\\\frac{3}{2},\ \frac{(b_q)+1}{2},\ \frac{(b_q)+2}{2},\ \frac{s-\nu+3}{2},\ \frac{s-\mu+4}{2}\end{matrix}\right)$ $+\dfrac{2^{s-1}\sigma^{s-\mu}}{\sqrt{\pi}}\,\Gamma\left[\begin{matrix}\frac{s-\nu}{2},\ \frac{s+\nu+1}{2}\\s-\mu+1\end{matrix}\right]$ $\times {}_{2p+2}F_{2q+3}\left(\begin{matrix}\frac{(a_p)}{2},\ \frac{(a_p)+1}{2},\ \frac{s-\nu}{2},\ \frac{s+\nu+1}{2};\ \frac{\sigma^2\omega^2}{4^{q-p+1}}\\\frac{1}{2},\ \frac{(b_q)}{2},\ \frac{(b_q)+1}{2},\ \frac{s-\mu+1}{2},\ \frac{s-\mu+2}{2}\end{matrix}\right)$ $[\sigma > 0;\ \operatorname{Re}\mu < 1;\ \operatorname{Re}s > \operatorname{Re}\nu,\ -\operatorname{Re}\nu - 1]$

No.	$f(x)$	$F(s)$
6	$(\sigma - x)_+^{-\mu/2} \, P_\nu^\mu \left(\sqrt{\dfrac{\sigma}{x}} \right)$ $\times \, _pF_q \left(\begin{matrix} (a_p)\,;\ \omega x \\ (b_q) \end{matrix} \right)$	$\dfrac{2^{2s}\sigma^{s-\mu/2}}{\sqrt{\pi}} \, \Gamma \left[\begin{matrix} \frac{2s-\nu}{2},\ \frac{2s+\nu+1}{2} \\ 2s - \mu + 1 \end{matrix} \right]$ $\times \, _{p+2}F_{q+2} \left(\begin{matrix} (a_p),\ \frac{2s-\nu}{2},\ \frac{2s+\nu+1}{2}\,;\ \sigma\omega \\ (b_q),\ \frac{2s-\mu+1}{2},\ \frac{2s-\mu+2}{2} \end{matrix} \right)$ $[\sigma > 0;\ \mathrm{Re}\,\mu < 1;\ \mathrm{Re}\,s > \mathrm{Re}\,\nu,\ -\mathrm{Re}\,\nu - 1]$
7	$(\sigma - x)_+^{-\mu/2} \, P_\nu^\mu \left(\dfrac{2x}{\sigma} - 1 \right)$ $\times \, _pF_q \left(\begin{matrix} (a_p)\,;\ \omega x^2 \\ (b_q) \end{matrix} \right)$	$\sigma^{s-\mu/2} \, \Gamma \left[\begin{matrix} \frac{2s-\mu}{2},\ \frac{2s+\mu}{2} \\ \frac{2s-\mu-2\nu}{2},\ \frac{2s-\mu+2\nu+2}{2} \end{matrix} \right]$ $\times \, _{p+4}F_{q+4} \left(\begin{matrix} (a_p),\ \Delta\left(2, \frac{2s-\mu}{2}\right),\ \Delta\left(2, \frac{2s+\mu}{2}\right)\,;\ \sigma^2\omega \\ (b_q),\ \Delta\left(2, \frac{2s-\mu-2\nu}{2}\right),\ \Delta\left(2, \frac{2s-\mu+2\nu+2}{2}\right) \end{matrix} \right)$ $[\sigma > 0;\ \mathrm{Re}\,\mu < 1;\ \mathrm{Re}\,s > |\mathrm{Re}\,\mu|/2]$
8	$(\sigma - x)_+^{-\mu/2} \, P_\nu^\mu \left(\dfrac{2\sigma}{x} - 1 \right)$ $\times \, _pF_q \left(\begin{matrix} (a_p)\,;\ \omega x^2 \\ (b_q) \end{matrix} \right)$	$\sigma^{s-\mu/2} \, \Gamma \left[\begin{matrix} s - \nu,\ s + \nu + 1 \\ s + 1,\ s - \mu + 1 \end{matrix} \right]$ $\times \, _{p+4}F_{q+4} \left(\begin{matrix} (a_p),\ \frac{s-\nu}{2},\ \frac{s-\nu+1}{2},\ \frac{s+\nu+1}{2},\ \frac{s+\nu+2}{2} \\ (b_q),\ \frac{s+1}{2},\ \frac{s+2}{2},\ \frac{s-\mu+1}{2},\ \frac{s-\mu+2}{2}\,;\ \sigma^2\omega \end{matrix} \right)$ $[\sigma > 0;\ \mathrm{Re}\,\mu < 1;\ \mathrm{Re}\,s > \mathrm{Re}\,\nu,\ -\mathrm{Re}\,\nu - 1]$

3.33.20. $_pF_q\left((a_p)\,;\ (b_q)\,;\ \omega x^r\right)$ **and** $Q_\nu^\mu\left(\varphi(x)\right)$

No.	$f(x)$	$F(s)$
1	$(\sigma - x)_+^\nu \, Q_\nu^\mu \left(\dfrac{\sigma + x}{\sigma - x} \right)$ $\times \, _pF_q \left(\begin{matrix} (a_p)\,;\ \omega x \\ (b_q) \end{matrix} \right)$	$\dfrac{e^{i\mu\pi}\sigma^{s+\nu}}{2} \, \Gamma \left[\begin{matrix} \nu + 1,\ \mu + \nu + 1,\ \frac{2s-\mu}{2},\ \frac{2s+\mu}{2} \\ \frac{2s-\mu+2\nu+2}{2},\ \frac{2s+\mu+2\nu+2}{2} \end{matrix} \right]$ $\times \, _{p+2}F_{q+2} \left(\begin{matrix} (a_p),\ \frac{2s-\mu}{2},\ \frac{2s+\mu}{2}\,;\ \sigma\omega \\ (b_q),\ \frac{2s-\mu+2\nu+2}{2},\ \frac{2s+\mu+2\nu+2}{2} \end{matrix} \right)$ $[\sigma > 0;\ \mathrm{Re}\,\nu > -1;\ \mathrm{Re}\,s > |\mathrm{Re}\,\mu|/2]$
2	$(\sigma - x)_+^\nu \, Q_\nu^\mu \left(\dfrac{\sigma + x}{\sigma - x} \right)$ $\times \, _pF_q \left(\begin{matrix} (a_p)\,;\ \omega x^2 \\ (b_q) \end{matrix} \right)$	$\dfrac{e^{i\mu\pi}\sigma^{s+\nu}}{2} \, \Gamma \left[\begin{matrix} \nu + 1,\ \mu + \nu + 1,\ \frac{2s-\mu}{2},\ \frac{2s+\mu}{2} \\ \frac{2s-\mu+2\nu+2}{2},\ \frac{2s+\mu+2\nu+2}{2} \end{matrix} \right]$ $\times \, _{p+4}F_{q+4} \left(\begin{matrix} (a_p),\ \Delta\left(2, \frac{2s-\mu}{2}\right),\ \Delta\left(2, \frac{2s+\mu}{2}\right)\,;\ \sigma^2\omega \\ (b_q),\ \Delta\left(2, \frac{2s-\mu+2\nu+2}{2}\right),\ \Delta\left(2, \frac{2s+\mu+2\nu+2}{2}\right) \end{matrix} \right)$ $[\sigma > 0;\ \mathrm{Re}\,\nu > -1;\ \mathrm{Re}\,s > |\mathrm{Re}\,\mu|/2]$

3.33.21. $_pF_q\left((a_p)\,;\ (b_q)\,;\ \omega x^r\right)$ **and** $\Psi(a, b;\ \sigma x)$

No.	$f(x)$	$F(s)$
1	$e^{-\sigma x} \, \Psi(a, b;\ \sigma x) \times$	$\sigma^{-s} \, \Gamma \left[\begin{matrix} s,\ s - b + 1 \\ s + a - b + 1 \end{matrix} \right] \, _{p+2}F_{q+1} \left(\begin{matrix} (a_p),\ s,\ s - b + 1 \\ (b_q),\ s + a - b + 1\,;\ -\frac{\omega}{\sigma} \end{matrix} \right)$

No.	$f(x)$	$F(s)$
	$\times\, _pF_q\begin{pmatrix}(a_p);\,-\omega x\\(b_q)\end{pmatrix}$	

$$\left[\begin{array}{l}[q=p-1;\,|\arg\sigma|,\,|\arg\omega|<\pi;\,0,\ \mathrm{Re}\,b-1<\mathrm{Re}\,s<\mathrm{Re}\,(a_k+a)]\ \text{or}\\ [q=p;\,|\arg\sigma|<\pi;\,(\mathrm{Re}\,\omega>0;\,0,\ \mathrm{Re}\,b-1<\mathrm{Re}\,s<\mathrm{Re}\,(a_k+a))\ \text{or}\\ \quad(\mathrm{Re}\,\omega=0;\,0,\ \mathrm{Re}\,b-1<\mathrm{Re}\,s<\mathrm{Re}\,(a_k+a),\ \mathrm{Re}\,(a-\chi)+1)\ \text{or}\\ [q=p+1;\,\omega>0;\,0,\ \mathrm{Re}\,b-1<\mathrm{Re}\,s<\mathrm{Re}\,(a_k+a),\ \mathrm{Re}\,(a-\chi)+1/2;\,|\arg\sigma|<\pi].\end{array}\right]$$

No.	$f(x)$	$F(s)$
2	$e^{-\sigma x}\,\Psi(a,b;\sigma x)$	$\sigma^{-s}\,\Gamma\begin{bmatrix}s,\,s-b+1\\s+a-b+1\end{bmatrix}{}_{p+4}F_{q+2}\begin{pmatrix}(a_p),\,\frac{s}{2},\,\frac{s+1}{2},\,\frac{s-b+1}{2},\,\frac{s-b+2}{2}\\(b_q),\,\frac{s+a-b+1}{2},\,\frac{s+a-b+2}{2};\,-\frac{4\omega}{\sigma^2}\end{pmatrix}$
	$\times\, _pF_q\begin{pmatrix}(a_p);\,-\omega x^2\\(b_q)\end{pmatrix}$	

$$\left[\begin{array}{l}[q=p-1;\,|\arg\sigma|,\,|\arg\omega|<\pi;\,0,\ \mathrm{Re}\,b-1<\mathrm{Re}\,s<\mathrm{Re}\,(2a_k+a)]\ \text{or}\\ [q=p;\,|\arg\sigma|<\pi;\,(\mathrm{Re}\,\omega>0;\,0,\ \mathrm{Re}\,b-1<\mathrm{Re}\,s<\mathrm{Re}\,(2a_k+a))\ \text{or}\\ \quad(\mathrm{Re}\,\omega=0;\,0,\ \mathrm{Re}\,b-1<\mathrm{Re}\,s<\mathrm{Re}\,(2a_k+a),\ \mathrm{Re}\,(a-2\chi)+2)\ \text{or}\\ [q=p+1;\,\omega>0;\,0,\ \mathrm{Re}\,b-1<\mathrm{Re}\,s<\mathrm{Re}\,(2a_k+a),\ \mathrm{Re}\,(a-2\chi)+1;\,|\arg\sigma|<\pi].\end{array}\right]$$

3.33.22. $_pF_q\left((a_p);\,(b_q);\,\omega x^r\right)$ **and** $_2F_1\left(a,b;\,\varphi(x)\right)$

No.	$f(x)$	$F(s)$
1	$(\sigma-x)_+^{c-1}\,{}_2F_1\begin{pmatrix}a,\,b\\c;\,1-\frac{x}{\sigma}\end{pmatrix}$	$\sigma^{s+c-1}\,\Gamma\begin{bmatrix}c,\,s,\,s-a-b+c\\s-a+c,\,s-b+c\end{bmatrix}$
	$\times\, _pF_q\begin{pmatrix}(a_p);\,\omega x\\(b_q)\end{pmatrix}$	$\times\, _{p+2}F_{q+2}\begin{pmatrix}(a_p),\,s,\,s-a-b+c;\,\sigma\omega\\(b_q),\,s-a+c,\,s-b+c\end{pmatrix}$
		$[\sigma,\ \mathrm{Re}\,c>0;\ \mathrm{Re}\,s>0,\ \mathrm{Re}\,(a+b-c)]$
2	$(\sigma-x)_+^{c-1}\,{}_2F_1\begin{pmatrix}a,\,b\\c;\,1-\frac{\sigma}{x}\end{pmatrix}$	$\sigma^{s+c-1}\,\Gamma\begin{bmatrix}c,\,s+a,\,s+b\\s+a+b,\,s+c\end{bmatrix}{}_{p+2}F_{q+2}\begin{pmatrix}(a_p),\,s+a,\,s+b;\,\sigma\omega\\(b_q),\,s+a+b,\,s+c\end{pmatrix}$
	$\times\, _pF_q\begin{pmatrix}(a_p);\,\omega x\\(b_q)\end{pmatrix}$	$[\sigma,\ \mathrm{Re}\,c>0;\ \mathrm{Re}\,s>-\mathrm{Re}\,a,\,-\mathrm{Re}\,b]$
3	$(\sigma-x)_+^{c-1}\,{}_2F_1\begin{pmatrix}a,\,b\\c;\,1-\frac{x}{\sigma}\end{pmatrix}$	$\sigma^{s+c-1}\,\Gamma\begin{bmatrix}c,\,s,\,s-a-b+c\\s-a+c,\,s-b+c\end{bmatrix}$
	$\times\, _pF_q\begin{pmatrix}(a_p);\,\omega x^2\\(b_q)\end{pmatrix}$	$\times\, _{p+4}F_{q+4}\begin{pmatrix}(a_p),\,\frac{s}{2},\,\frac{s+1}{2},\,\frac{s-a-b+c}{2},\,\frac{s-a-b+c+1}{2};\,\sigma^2\omega\\(b_q),\,\frac{s-a+c}{2},\,\frac{s-a+c+1}{2},\,\frac{s-b+c}{2},\,\frac{s-b+c+1}{2}\end{pmatrix}$
		$[\sigma,\ \mathrm{Re}\,c>0;\ \mathrm{Re}\,s>0,\ \mathrm{Re}\,(a+b-c)]$
4	$(\sigma-x)_+^{c-1}\,{}_2F_1\begin{pmatrix}a,\,b\\c;\,1-\frac{\sigma}{x}\end{pmatrix}$	$\sigma^{s+c-1}\,\Gamma\begin{bmatrix}c,\,s+a,\,s+b\\s+a+b,\,s+c\end{bmatrix}$
	$\times\, _pF_q\begin{pmatrix}(a_p);\,\omega x^2\\(b_q)\end{pmatrix}$	$\times\, _{p+4}F_{q+4}\begin{pmatrix}(a_p),\,\frac{s+a}{2},\,\frac{s+a+1}{2},\,\frac{s+b}{2},\,\frac{s+b+1}{2};\,\sigma^2\omega\\(b_q),\,\frac{s+a+b}{2},\,\frac{s+a+b+1}{2},\,\frac{s+c}{2},\,\frac{s+c+1}{2}\end{pmatrix}$
		$[\sigma,\ \mathrm{Re}\,c>0;\ \mathrm{Re}\,s>-\mathrm{Re}\,a,\,-\mathrm{Re}\,b]$

3.33.23.   Products of $_pF_q\left((a_p);\ (b_q);\ \omega x^r\right)$

Notation:
$$g = \frac{(1-\ell)(m-n+1)+(1-k)(p-q+1)}{2};$$

$$\mu = \sum_{i=1}^{p} a_i - \sum_{j=1}^{q} b_j + \frac{q-p+1}{2};\quad \rho = \sum_{i=1}^{m} c_i - \sum_{j=1}^{n} d_j + \frac{n-m+1}{2};$$

$$k,\ \ell,\ m,\ n,\ p,\ q = 0,\ 1,\ 2,\ldots;\ k,\ \ell \neq 0;\ m \leq n+1;\ p \leq q+1.$$

1
$$_mF_n\!\left(\begin{matrix}(c_m);\ -\sigma x\\(d_n)\end{matrix}\right)$$
$$\times\, _pF_q\!\left(\begin{matrix}(a_p);\ -\omega x^{\ell/k}\\(b_q)\end{matrix}\right)$$

$$(2\pi)^g\, k^\mu\, \ell^{\rho+s(n-m+1)-1}\, \sigma^{-s}\, \Gamma\!\left[\begin{matrix}(b_q),\ (d_n)\\(a_p),\ (c_m)\end{matrix}\right]$$

$$\times\, G^{k+\ell m,\ kp+\ell}_{kp+\ell n+\ell,\ kq+k+\ell m}\!\left(\frac{k^{k(p-q-1)}\omega^k}{\ell\ell^{(m-n-1)}\sigma^\ell}\,\middle|\,\right.$$

$$\left.\begin{matrix}\Delta(\ell,\,1-s),\,\Delta(k,\,1-(a_p)),\,\Delta(\ell,\,(d_n)-s)\\\Delta(k,\,0),\,\Delta(\ell,\,(c_m)-s),\,\Delta(k,\,1-(b_q))\end{matrix}\right)$$

and one of the following conditions hold

(1) $\left[\begin{matrix}mp \neq 0;\ m = n\ \text{or}\ m = n+1;\ p = q\ \text{or}\ p = q+1;\\|\arg\sigma| < (m-n+1)\pi/2;\ |\arg\omega| < (p-q+1)\pi/2;\ \operatorname{Re}s > 0;\\\operatorname{Re}(s-c_j-a_i\ell/k) < 0\ (j=1,2,\ldots,m;\ i=1,2,\ldots,p)\end{matrix}\right]$

(2) $\left[\begin{matrix}m > 0;\ m = n\ \text{or}\ m = n+1;\ p = q-1\ \text{or}\ p = q;\\|\arg\sigma| < (m-n+1)\pi/2;\ |\arg\omega| = (p-q+1)\pi/2;\ \operatorname{Re}s > 0;\\\operatorname{Re}(s-c_j-a_i\ell/k) < 0\ (j=1,2,\ldots,m;\ i=1,2,\ldots,p)\\(p-q-1)\operatorname{Re}(s-c_j) - \ell\operatorname{Re}\mu/k > -3\ell/2k\ (j=1,2,\ldots,p)\end{matrix}\right]$

(3) $\left[\begin{matrix}m = n-1;\ \text{or}\ m = n;\ p > 0;\ p = q\ \text{or}\ p = q+1;\\|\arg\sigma| = (m-n+1)\pi/2;\ |\arg\omega| < (p-q+1)\pi/2;\ \operatorname{Re}s > 0;\\\operatorname{Re}(s-c_j-a_i\ell/k) < 0\ (j=1,2,\ldots,m;\ i=1,2,\ldots,p)\\(m-n-1)\operatorname{Re}(s-a_i\ell/k) - \operatorname{Re}\rho > -3/2\end{matrix}\right]$

2
$$_mF_n\!\left(\begin{matrix}(c_m);\ -\frac{\sigma}{x}\\(d_n)\end{matrix}\right)$$
$$\times\, _pF_q\!\left(\begin{matrix}(a_p);\ -\omega x^{\ell/k}\\(b_q)\end{matrix}\right)$$

$$(2\pi)^g\, k^\mu\, \ell^{\rho+s+(m-n-1)-1}\, \sigma^s\, \Gamma\!\left[\begin{matrix}(b_q),\ (d_n)\\(a_p),\ (c_m)\end{matrix}\right]$$

$$\times\, G^{k+\ell,\ kp+\ell m}_{kq+\ell m,\ kq+k+\ell n+\ell}\!\left(\frac{k^{k(p-q-1)}\omega^k}{\ell\ell^{(n-m+1)}\sigma^{-\ell}}\,\middle|\,\right.$$

$$\left.\begin{matrix}\Delta(k,\,(a_p)),\,\Delta(\ell,\,1-s-(c_m))\\\Delta(\ell,\,-s),\,\Delta(k,\,0),\,\Delta(k,\,1-(b_q)),\,\Delta(\ell,\,1-s-(d_n))\end{matrix}\right)$$

and one of the following conditions hold

(1) $\left[\begin{matrix}mp \neq 0;\ m = n\ \text{or}\ m = n+1;\ p = q\ \text{or}\ p = q+1;\\|\arg\sigma| < (m-n+1)\pi/2;\ |\arg\omega| < (p-q+1)\pi/2;\\\operatorname{Re}(a+c_j) > 0\ (j=1,\ldots,m);\ \operatorname{Re}(s-a_j\ell/k) < 0\ (j=1,2,\ldots,p)\end{matrix}\right]$

(2) $\left[\begin{matrix}m = n\ \text{or}\ m = n+1;\ p = q-1\ \text{or}\ p = q;\\|\arg\sigma| < (m-n+1)\pi/2;\ |\arg\omega| = (p-q+1)\pi/2;\\\operatorname{Re}(a+c_j) > 0\ (j=1,\ldots,m);\ \operatorname{Re}(s-a_j\ell/k) < 0\ (j=1,2,\ldots,p)\\\operatorname{Re}[(p-q-1)-\mu\ell/k] > -3\ell/(2k)\end{matrix}\right]$

(3) $\left[\begin{matrix}m = n-1\ \text{or}\ m = n;\ p = q\ \text{or}\ p = q+1;\\|\arg\sigma| = (m-n+1)\pi/2;\ |\arg\omega| < (p-q+1)\pi/2;\\\operatorname{Re}(a+c_j) > 0\ (j=1,\ldots,m);\ \operatorname{Re}(s-a_j\ell/k) < 0\ (j=1,2,\ldots,p)\\\operatorname{Re}[(n-m-1)s-\rho] > -3/2\end{matrix}\right]$

3.34. The Appell Functions

3.34.1. The Appell and algebraic functions

1	$(\sigma - x)_+^{c-1}$ $\times F_1\left(a, b, b'; c; w(\sigma - x), z(\sigma - x)\right)$	$\sigma^{s+c-1} \, \mathrm{B}\left(s, c\right) F_1\left(a, b, b'; s+c; \sigma w, \sigma z\right)$ $\left[\sigma, \ \mathrm{Re}\, c, \ \mathrm{Re}\, s > 0\right]$
2	$\dfrac{1}{(x+\sigma)^b} \, F_1\left(a, b, b'; c; \dfrac{w}{x+\sigma}, z\right)$	$\sigma^{s-b} \, \mathrm{B}\left(s, b-s\right) F_1\left(a, b-s, b'; c; \dfrac{w}{\sigma}, z\right)$ $\left[0 < \mathrm{Re}\, s < \mathrm{Re}\, b; \ |\arg \sigma| < \pi\right]$
3	$\dfrac{1}{(x+\sigma)^b} \, F_1\left(a, b, b'; c; \dfrac{wx}{x+\sigma}, z\right)$	$\sigma^{s-b} \, \mathrm{B}\left(s, b-s\right) F_1\left(a, s, b'; c; w, z\right)$ $\left[0 < \mathrm{Re}\, s < \mathrm{Re}\, b; \ |\arg \sigma| < \pi\right]$
4	$\dfrac{1}{(x+\sigma)^a} \, F_1\left(a, b, b'; c; \dfrac{w}{x+\sigma}, \dfrac{z}{x+\sigma}\right)$	$\sigma^{s-a} \, \mathrm{B}\left(s, a-s\right) F_1\left(a-s, b, b'; c; \dfrac{w}{\sigma}, \dfrac{z}{\sigma}\right)$ $\left[0 < \mathrm{Re}\, s < \mathrm{Re}\, a; \ |\arg \sigma| < \pi\right]$
5	$\dfrac{1}{(x+\sigma)^a} \, F_1\left(a, b, b'; c; \dfrac{wx}{x+\sigma}, \dfrac{zx}{x+\sigma}\right)$	$\sigma^{s-a} \, \mathrm{B}\left(s, a-s\right) F_1\left(s, b, b'; c; w, z\right)$ $\left[0 < \mathrm{Re}\, s < \mathrm{Re}\, a; \ |\arg \sigma| < \pi\right]$
6	$(\sigma - x)_+^{c-1}$ $\times F_2\left(a, b, b'; c, c'; w(\sigma - x), z\right)$	$\sigma^{s+c-1} \, \mathrm{B}\left(s, c\right) F_2\left(a, b, b'; s+c, c'; \sigma w, z\right)$ $\left[\sigma, \ \mathrm{Re}\, c, \ \mathrm{Re}\, s > 0\right]$
7	$(x - \sigma)_+^{c-1}$ $\times F_2\left(a, b, b'; c, c'; \dfrac{w(x-\sigma)}{x}, z\right)$	$\sigma^{s+c-1} \, \mathrm{B}\left(c, 1-c-s\right) F_2\left(a, b, b'; 1-s, c'; w, z\right)$ $\left[\sigma, \ \mathrm{Re}\, c > 0; \ \mathrm{Re}\left(s+c\right) < 1\right]$
8	$\dfrac{1}{(x+\sigma)^b} \, F_2\left(a, b, b'; c, c'; \dfrac{w}{x+\sigma}, z\right)$	$\sigma^{s-b} \, \mathrm{B}\left(s, b-s\right) F_2\left(a, s, b'; c, c'; \dfrac{w}{\sigma}, z\right)$ $\left[0 < \mathrm{Re}\, s < \mathrm{Re}\, b; \ |\arg \sigma| < \pi\right]$
9	$\dfrac{1}{(x+\sigma)^b} \, F_2\left(a, b, b'; c, c'; \dfrac{wx}{x+\sigma}, z\right)$	$\sigma^{s-b} \, \mathrm{B}\left(s, b-s\right) F_2\left(a, s, b'; c, c'; w, z\right)$ $\left[0 < \mathrm{Re}\, s < \mathrm{Re}\, b; \ |\arg \sigma| < \pi\right]$
10	$\dfrac{1}{(x+\sigma)^a}$ $\times F_2\left(a, b, b'; c, c'; \dfrac{w}{x+\sigma}, \dfrac{z}{x+\sigma}\right)$	$\sigma^{s-a} \, \mathrm{B}\left(s, a-s\right) F_2\left(a-s, b, b'; c, c'; \dfrac{w}{\sigma}, \dfrac{z}{\sigma}\right)$ $\left[0 < \mathrm{Re}\, s < \mathrm{Re}\, a; \ |\arg \sigma| < \pi\right]$

No.	$f(x)$	$F(s)$
11	$\dfrac{1}{(x+\sigma)^a}$ $\times F_2\left(a,b,b';c,c';\dfrac{wx}{x+\sigma},\dfrac{zx}{x+\sigma}\right)$	$\sigma^{s-a}\,\mathrm{B}\,(s,a-s)\,F_2\,(s,b,b';c,c';w,z)$ $[0<\mathrm{Re}\,s<\mathrm{Re}\,a;\ |\arg\sigma|<\pi]$
12	$(\sigma-x)_+^{c-1}$ $\times F_3\,(a,a',b,b';c;w\,(\sigma-x),z\,(\sigma-x))$	$\sigma^{s+c-1}\,\mathrm{B}\,(s,c)\,F_3\,(a,a',b,b';s+c;\sigma w,\sigma z)$ $[\sigma,\ \mathrm{Re}\,c,\ \mathrm{Re}\,s>0]$
13	$\dfrac{1}{(x+\sigma)^a}\,F_3\left(a,a',b,b';c;\dfrac{w}{x+\sigma},z\right)$	$\sigma^{s-a}\,\mathrm{B}\,(s,a-s)\,F_3\left(a-s,a',b,b';c;\dfrac{w}{\sigma},z\right)$ $[0<\mathrm{Re}\,s<\mathrm{Re}\,a;\ |\arg\sigma|<\pi]$
14	$\dfrac{1}{(x+\sigma)^a}\,F_3\left(a,a',b,b';c;\dfrac{wx}{x+\sigma},z\right)$	$\sigma^{s-a}\,\mathrm{B}\,(s,a-s)\,F_3\,(s,a',b,b';c;w,z)$ $[0<\mathrm{Re}\,s<\mathrm{Re}\,a;\ |\arg\sigma|<\pi]$
15	$(1-x)_+^{c-1}$ $\times F_3\left(a,a',b,b';c;1-x,1-\dfrac{1}{x}\right)$	$\Gamma\,(c)\,\Gamma\begin{bmatrix} s+a',\,s+b',\,s+c-a-b \\ s+a'+b',\,s+c-a,\,s+c-b \end{bmatrix}$ $\begin{bmatrix}\mathrm{Re}\,c>0;\ \mathrm{Re}\,s>-\mathrm{Re}\,a',\ -\mathrm{Re}\,b'; \\ \mathrm{Re}\,(s-a-b+c)>0\end{bmatrix}$
16	$(x-1)_+^{c-1}$ $\times F_3\left(a,a',b,b';c;1-x,1-\dfrac{1}{x}\right)$	$\Gamma\,(c)\,\Gamma\begin{bmatrix} 1-a'-b'-s,\,1+a-c-s \\ 1-a'-s,\,1-b'-s \end{bmatrix}$ $\times\Gamma\begin{bmatrix} 1+b-c-s \\ 1+a+b-c-s \end{bmatrix}$ $\begin{bmatrix}\mathrm{Re}\,c>0;\ \mathrm{Re}\,s<1-\mathrm{Re}\,(a'+b'); \\ \mathrm{Re}\,s<1-\mathrm{Re}\,(a-c),\,1-\mathrm{Re}\,(b-c)\end{bmatrix}$
17	$(\sigma-x)_+^{c-1}\,F_4\,(a,b;c,c';w\,(\sigma-x),z)$	$\sigma^{s+c-1}\,\mathrm{B}\,(s,c)\,F_4\,(a,b;s+c,c';\sigma w,z)$ $[\sigma,\ \mathrm{Re}\,c,\ \mathrm{Re}\,s>0]$
18	$(x-\sigma)_+^{c-1}\,F_4\left(a,b;c,c';\dfrac{w\,(x-\sigma)}{x},z\right)$	$\sigma^{s+c-1}\,\mathrm{B}\,(c,1-c-s)\,F_4\,(a,b;1-s,c';w,z)$ $[\sigma,\ \mathrm{Re}\,c>0;\ \mathrm{Re}\,(s+c)<1]$
19	$\dfrac{1}{(x+\sigma)^a}\,F_4\left(a,b;c,c';\dfrac{w}{x+\sigma},\dfrac{z}{x+\sigma}\right)$	$\sigma^{s-a}\,\mathrm{B}\,(s,a-s)\,F_4\left(a-s,b;c,c';\dfrac{w}{\sigma},\dfrac{z}{\sigma}\right)$ $[0<\mathrm{Re}\,s<\mathrm{Re}\,a;\ |\arg\sigma|<\pi]$
20	$\dfrac{1}{(x+\sigma)^a}\,F_4\left(a,b;c,c';\dfrac{wx}{x+\sigma},\dfrac{zx}{x+\sigma}\right)$	$\sigma^{s-a}\,\mathrm{B}\,(s,a-s)\,F_4\,(s,b;c,c';w,z)$ $[0<\mathrm{Re}\,s<\mathrm{Re}\,a;\ |\arg\sigma|<\pi]$

3.35. The Humbert Functions

3.35.1. The Humbert and algebraic functions

1	$(\sigma - x)_+^{c-1}$ $\times \Phi_1\left(a,\, b;\, c;\, w\left(\sigma - x\right),\, z\left(\sigma - x\right)\right)$	$\sigma^{s+c-1}\, \mathrm{B}\left(s,\, c\right) \Phi_1\left(a,\, b;\, s+c;\, \sigma w,\, \sigma z\right)$ $[\sigma,\, \mathrm{Re}\,c,\, \mathrm{Re}\,s > 0]$
2	$\dfrac{1}{(x+\sigma)^b}\, \Phi_1\left(a,\, b;\, c;\, \dfrac{w}{x+\sigma},\, z\right)$	$\sigma^{s-b}\, \mathrm{B}\left(s,\, b-s\right) \Phi_1\left(a,\, b-s;\, c;\, \dfrac{w}{\sigma},\, z\right)$ $[0 < \mathrm{Re}\,s < \mathrm{Re}\,b;\, \lvert\arg \sigma\rvert < \pi]$
3	$\dfrac{1}{(x+\sigma)^b}\, \Phi_1\left(a,\, b;\, c;\, \dfrac{wx}{x+\sigma},\, z\right)$	$\sigma^{s-b}\, \mathrm{B}\left(s,\, b-s\right) \Phi_1\left(a,\, s;\, c;\, w,\, z\right)$ $[0 < \mathrm{Re}\,s < \mathrm{Re}\,b;\, \lvert\arg \sigma\rvert < \pi]$
4	$\dfrac{1}{(x+\sigma)^a}\, \Phi_1\left(a,\, b,\, c;\, \dfrac{w}{x+\sigma},\, \dfrac{z}{x+\sigma}\right)$	$\sigma^{s-a}\, \mathrm{B}\left(s,\, a-s\right) \Phi_1\left(a-s,\, b;\, c;\, \dfrac{w}{\sigma},\, \dfrac{z}{\sigma}\right)$ $[0 < \mathrm{Re}\,s < \mathrm{Re}\,a;\, \lvert\arg \sigma\rvert < \pi],$
5	$\dfrac{1}{(x+\sigma)^a}\, \Phi_1\left(a,\, b,\, b';\, c;\, \dfrac{wx}{x+\sigma},\, \dfrac{zx}{x+\sigma}\right)$	$\sigma^{s-a}\, \mathrm{B}\left(s,\, a-s\right) \Phi_1\left(a-s,\, b,\, b';\, c;\, w,\, z\right)$ $[0 < \mathrm{Re}\,s < \mathrm{Re}\,a;\, \lvert\arg \sigma\rvert < \pi]$
6	$(\sigma - x)_+^{c-1}$ $\times \Phi_2\left(b,\, b';\, c;\, w\left(\sigma - x\right),\, z\left(\sigma - x\right)\right)$	$\sigma^{s+c-1}\, \mathrm{B}\left(s,\, c\right) \Phi_2\left(b,\, b';\, s+c;\, \sigma w,\, \sigma z\right)$ $[\sigma,\, \mathrm{Re}\,c,\, \mathrm{Re}\,s > 0]$
7	$\dfrac{1}{(x+\sigma)^b}\, \Phi_2\left(b,\, b';\, c;\, \dfrac{w}{x+\sigma},\, z\right)$	$\sigma^{s-b}\, \mathrm{B}\left(s,\, b-s\right) \Phi_2\left(b-s,\, b';\, c;\, \dfrac{w}{\sigma},\, z\right)$ $[0 < \mathrm{Re}\,s < \mathrm{Re}\,b;\, \lvert\arg \sigma\rvert < \pi]$
8	$\dfrac{1}{(x+\sigma)^b}\, \Phi_2\left(b,\, b';\, c;\, \dfrac{wx}{x+\sigma},\, z\right)$	$\sigma^{s-b}\, \mathrm{B}\left(s,\, b-s\right) \Phi_2\left(s,\, b';\, c;\, w,\, z\right)$ $[0 < \mathrm{Re}\,s < \mathrm{Re}\,b;\, \lvert\arg \sigma\rvert < \pi]$
9	$(\sigma - x)_+^{c-1}\, \Phi_3\left(a;\, c;\, w\left(\sigma - x\right),\, z\left(\sigma - x\right)\right)$	$\sigma^{s+c-1}\, \mathrm{B}\left(s,\, c\right) \Phi_3\left(a;\, s+c;\, \sigma w,\, \sigma z\right)$ $[\sigma,\, \mathrm{Re}\,c,\, \mathrm{Re}\,s > 0]$

No.	$f(x)$	$F(s)$
10	$\dfrac{1}{(x+\sigma)^b}\,\Phi_3\!\left(b;\,c;\,\dfrac{w}{x+\sigma},\,z\right)$	$\sigma^{s-b}\,\mathrm{B}\,(s,\,b-s)\,\Phi_3\!\left(b-s;\,c;\,\dfrac{w}{\sigma},\,z\right)$ $[0<\mathrm{Re}\,s<\mathrm{Re}\,b;\;|\arg\sigma|<\pi]$
11	$\dfrac{1}{(x+\sigma)^b}\,\Phi_3\!\left(b;\,c;\,\dfrac{wx}{x+\sigma},\,z\right)$	$\sigma^{s-b}\,\mathrm{B}\,(s,\,b-s)\,\Phi_3\,(s;\,c;\,w,\,z)$ $[0<\mathrm{Re}\,s<\mathrm{Re}\,b;\;|\arg\sigma|<\pi]$
12	$(\sigma-x)_+^{c-1}$ $\times\,\Xi_1\,(a,\,a',\,b;\,c;\,w\,(\sigma-x),\,z\,(\sigma-x))$	$\sigma^{s+c-1}\,\mathrm{B}\,(s,\,c)\,\Xi_1\,(a,\,a',\,b;\,s+c;\,\sigma w,\sigma z)$ $[\sigma,\;\mathrm{Re}\,c,\;\mathrm{Re}\,s>0]$
13	$\dfrac{1}{(x+\sigma)^a}\,\Xi_1\!\left(a,\,a',\,b;\,c;\,\dfrac{w}{x+\sigma},\,z\right)$	$\sigma^{s-a}\,\mathrm{B}\,(s,\,a-s)\,\Xi_1\!\left(a-s,\,a',\,b;\,c;\,\dfrac{w}{\sigma},\,z\right)$ $[0<\mathrm{Re}\,s<\mathrm{Re}\,a;\;|\arg\sigma|<\pi]$
14	$\dfrac{1}{(x+\sigma)^a}\,\Xi_1\!\left(a,\,a',\,b;\,c;\,\dfrac{wx}{x+\sigma},\,z\right)$	$\sigma^{s-a}\,\mathrm{B}\,(s,\,a-s)\,\Xi_1\,(s,\,a',\,b;\,c;\,w,\,z)$ $[0<\mathrm{Re}\,s<\mathrm{Re}\,a;\;|\arg\sigma|<\pi],$
15	$(\sigma-x)_+^{c-1}$ $\times\,\Xi_2\,(a,\,b;\,c;\,w\,(\sigma-x),\,z\,(\sigma-x))$	$\sigma^{s+c-1}\,\mathrm{B}\,(s,\,c)\,\Xi_2\,(a,\,b;\,s+c;\,\sigma w,\,\sigma z)$ $[\sigma,\;\mathrm{Re}\,c,\;\mathrm{Re}\,s>0]$
16	$\dfrac{1}{(x+\sigma)^a}\,\Xi_2\!\left(a,\,b;\,c;\,\dfrac{w}{x+\sigma},\,z\right)$	$\sigma^{s-a}\,\mathrm{B}\,(s,\,a-s)\,\Xi_2\!\left(a-s,\,b;\,c;\,\dfrac{w}{\sigma},\,z\right)$ $[0<\mathrm{Re}\,s<\mathrm{Re}\,a;\;|\arg\sigma|<\pi]$
17	$\dfrac{1}{(x+\sigma)^a}\,\Xi_2\!\left(a,\,b;\,c;\,\dfrac{wx}{x+\sigma},\,z\right)$	$\sigma^{s-a}\,\mathrm{B}\,(s,\,a-s)\,\Xi_2\,(s,\,b;\,c;\,w,\,z)$ $[0<\mathrm{Re}\,s<\mathrm{Re}\,a;\;|\arg\sigma|<\pi]$
18	$(\sigma-x)_+^{c-1}\,\Psi_1\,(a,\,b;\,c,\,c';\,w\,(\sigma-x),\,z)$	$\sigma^{s+c-1}\,\mathrm{B}\,(s,\,c)\,\Psi_1\,(a,\,b;\,s+c,\,c';\,\sigma w,\,z)$ $[\sigma,\;\mathrm{Re}\,c,\;\mathrm{Re}\,s>0]$

No.	$f(x)$	$F(s)$
19	$(x-\sigma)_+^{c-1}\,\Psi_1\!\left(a,\,b;\,c,\,c';\,\dfrac{w\,(x-\sigma)}{x},\,z\right)$	$\sigma^{s+c-1}\,\mathrm{B}\,(c,\,1-c-s)\,\Psi_1\,(a,\,b;\,1-s,\,c';\,w,\,z)$ $[\sigma,\ \mathrm{Re}\,c>0;\ \mathrm{Re}\,(s+c)<1]$
20	$\dfrac{1}{(x+\sigma)^b}\,\Psi_1\!\left(a,\,b;\,c,\,c';\,\dfrac{w}{x+\sigma},\,z\right)$	$\sigma^{s-b}\,\mathrm{B}\,(s,\,b-s)\,\Psi_1\!\left(a,\,s;\,c,\,c';\,\dfrac{w}{\sigma},\,z\right)$ $[0<\mathrm{Re}\,s<\mathrm{Re}\,b;\ |\arg\sigma|<\pi]$
21	$\dfrac{1}{(x+\sigma)^b}\,\Psi_1\!\left(a,\,b;\,c,\,c';\,\dfrac{wx}{x+\sigma},\,z\right)$	$\sigma^{s-b}\,\mathrm{B}\,(s,\,b-s)\,\Psi_1\,(a,\,s;\,c,\,c';\,w,\,z)$ $[0<\mathrm{Re}\,s<\mathrm{Re}\,b;\ |\arg\sigma|<\pi]$
22	$\dfrac{1}{(x+\sigma)^a}\,\Psi_1\!\left(a,\,b;\,c,\,c';\,\dfrac{w}{x+\sigma},\,\dfrac{z}{x+\sigma}\right)$	$\sigma^{s-a}\,\mathrm{B}\,(s,\,a-s)\,\Psi_1\!\left(a-s,\,b;\,c,\,c';\,\dfrac{w}{\sigma},\,\dfrac{z}{\sigma}\right)$ $[0<\mathrm{Re}\,s<\mathrm{Re}\,a;\ |\arg\sigma|<\pi]$
23	$\dfrac{1}{(x+\sigma)^a}\,\Psi_1\!\left(a,\,b;\,c,\,c';\,\dfrac{wx}{x+\sigma},\,\dfrac{zx}{x+\sigma}\right)$	$\sigma^{s-a}\,\mathrm{B}\,(s,\,a-s)\,\Psi_1\,(s,\,b;\,c,\,c';\,w,\,z)$ $[0<\mathrm{Re}\,s<\mathrm{Re}\,a;\ |\arg\sigma|<\pi]$
24	$(\sigma-x)_+^{c-1}\,\Psi_2\,(a;\,c,\,c';\,w\,(\sigma-x),\,z)$	$\sigma^{s+c-1}\,\mathrm{B}\,(s,\,c)\,\Psi_2\,(a;\,s+c,\,c';\,\sigma w,\,z)$ $[\sigma,\ \mathrm{Re}\,c,\ \mathrm{Re}\,s>0]$
25	$(x-\sigma)_+^{c-1}\,\Psi_2\!\left(a;\,c,\,c';\,\dfrac{w\,(x-\sigma)}{x},\,z\right)$	$\sigma^{s+c-1}\,\mathrm{B}\,(c,\,1-c-s)\,\Psi_2\,(a;\,1-s,\,c';\,w,\,z)$ $[\sigma,\ \mathrm{Re}\,c>0;\ \mathrm{Re}\,(s+c)<1]$
26	$\dfrac{1}{(x+\sigma)^a}\,\Psi_2\!\left(a;\,c,\,c';\,\dfrac{w}{x+\sigma},\,\dfrac{z}{x+\sigma}\right)$	$\sigma^{s-a}\,\mathrm{B}\,(s,\,a-s)\,\Psi_2\!\left(a-s;\,c,\,c';\,\dfrac{w}{\sigma},\,\dfrac{z}{\sigma}\right)$ $[0<\mathrm{Re}\,s<\mathrm{Re}\,a;\ |\arg\sigma|<\pi]$
27	$\dfrac{1}{(x+\sigma)^a}\,\Psi_2\!\left(a;\,c,\,c';\,\dfrac{wx}{x+\sigma},\,\dfrac{zx}{x+\sigma}\right)$	$\sigma^{s-a}\,\mathrm{B}\,(s,\,a-s)\,\Psi_2\,(s;\,c,\,c';\,w,\,z)$ $[0<\mathrm{Re}\,s<\mathrm{Re}\,a;\ |\arg\sigma|<\pi]$

3.35.2.   The Humbert and the exponential functions

1	$e^{-px}\Phi_1\left(a,\,b;\,w,\,zx\right)$	$\dfrac{\Gamma\left(s\right)}{p^s}\,F_1\left(a,\,b,\,s;\,c;\,w,\,\dfrac{z}{p}\right)$	$[\operatorname{Re}p>0,\ \operatorname{Re}z;\ \operatorname{Re}s>0]$
2	$e^{-px}\Phi_2\left(b,\,b';\,c;\,wx,\,z\right)$	$\dfrac{\Gamma\left(s\right)}{p^s}\,\Xi_1\left(b,\,b';\,s;\,c;\,\dfrac{w}{p},\,z\right)$	$[\operatorname{Re}p>0,\ \operatorname{Re}w;\ \operatorname{Re}s>0]$
3	$e^{-px}\Phi_2\left(b,\,b';\,c;\,wx,\,zx\right)$	$\dfrac{\Gamma\left(s\right)}{p^s}\,F_1\left(s,\,b,\,b';\,c;\,\dfrac{w}{p},\,\dfrac{z}{p}\right)$	$[\operatorname{Re}p>0,\ \operatorname{Re}z,\ \operatorname{Re}w;\ \operatorname{Re}s>0]$
4	$e^{-px}\Phi_3\left(b;\,c;\,w,\,zx\right)$	$\dfrac{\Gamma\left(s\right)}{p^s}\,\Phi_2\left(b,\,s;\,c;\,w,\,\dfrac{z}{p}\right)$	$[\operatorname{Re}p>0,\ \operatorname{Re}z;\ \operatorname{Re}s>0]$
5	$e^{-px}\Phi_3\left(b;\,c;\,wx,\,z\right)$	$\dfrac{\Gamma\left(s\right)}{p^s}\,\Xi_2\left(s,\,b;\,c;\,\dfrac{w}{p},\,z\right)$	$[\operatorname{Re}p>0,\ \operatorname{Re}w;\ \operatorname{Re}s>0]$
6	$e^{-px}\Phi_3\left(b;\,c;\,wx,\,zx\right)$	$\dfrac{\Gamma\left(s\right)}{p^s}\,\Phi_1\left(s,\,b;\,c;\,\dfrac{w}{p},\,\dfrac{z}{p}\right)$	$[\operatorname{Re}p>0,\ \operatorname{Re}w;\ \operatorname{Re}s>0]$
7	$e^{-p\sqrt{x}}\Phi_3\left(b;\,c;\,w,\,zx\right)$	$\dfrac{2\Gamma\left(2s\right)}{p^{2s}}\,\Xi_1\left(s,\,b,\,\dfrac{2s+1}{2};\,c;\,\dfrac{4z}{p^2},\,w\right)$	
			$[\operatorname{Re}p>2\lvert\operatorname{Re}\left(\sqrt{z}\right)\rvert;\ \operatorname{Re}s>0]$
8	$e^{-px}\Psi_1\left(a,\,b;\,c,\,c';\,w,\,zx\right)$	$\dfrac{\Gamma\left(s\right)}{p^s}\,F_2\left(a,\,b,\,s;\,c,\,c';\,w,\,\dfrac{z}{p}\right)$	$[\operatorname{Re}p>0,\ \operatorname{Re}z;\ \operatorname{Re}s>0]$
9	$e^{-px}\Psi_2\left(a;\,c,\,c';\,wx,\,z\right)$	$\dfrac{\Gamma\left(s\right)}{p^s}\,\Psi_1\left(a,\,s;\,c,\,c';\,\dfrac{w}{p},\,z\right)$	$[\operatorname{Re}p>0,\ \operatorname{Re}w;\ \operatorname{Re}s>0]$
10	$e^{-px}\Psi_2\left(a;\,c,\,c';\,wx,\,zx\right)$	$\dfrac{\Gamma\left(s\right)}{p^s}\,F_4\left(s,\,a;\,c,\,c';\,\dfrac{w}{p},\,\dfrac{z}{p}\right)$	$[\operatorname{Re}p>0,\ \operatorname{Re}w,\ \operatorname{Re}z;\ \operatorname{Re}s>0]$
11	$e^{-px}\Xi_1\left(a,\,a',\,b;\,c;\,w,\,zx\right)$	$\dfrac{\Gamma\left(s\right)}{p^s}\,F_3\left(a,\,a',\,b,\,s;\,c;\,w,\,\dfrac{z}{p}\right)$	$[\operatorname{Re}p>0,\ \operatorname{Re}z;\ \operatorname{Re}s>0]$
12	$e^{-px}\Xi_2\left(a,\,b;\,c;\,w,\,zx\right)$	$\dfrac{\Gamma\left(s\right)}{p^s}\,\Xi_1\left(a,\,s,\,b;\,c;\,w,\,\dfrac{z}{p}\right)$	$[\operatorname{Re}p>0,\ \operatorname{Re}z;\ \operatorname{Re}s>0]$
13	$e^{-p\sqrt{x}}\Xi_2\left(a,\,b;\,c;\,w,\,zx\right)$	$\dfrac{2\Gamma\left(2s\right)}{p^{2s}}\,F_3\left(a,\,s,\,b,\,s+\dfrac{1}{2};\,c;\,w,\,\dfrac{4z}{p^2}\right)$	
			$[\operatorname{Re}p>2\lvert\operatorname{Re}\left(\sqrt{z}\right)\rvert;\ \operatorname{Re}s>0]$

3.36.   The Meijer G-Function

More formulas can be obtained from the corresponding section due to the relations

$$G_{pq}^{mn}\left(z\left|\begin{array}{c}(a_p)\\(b_q)\end{array}\right.\right) = \sum_{k=1}^{m}\Gamma\left[\begin{array}{c}(b_m)'-b_k,\, b_k-(a_n)+1\\a_{n+1}-b_k,\ldots,a_p-b_k,\, b_k-b_{m+1}+1,\ldots,b_k-b_q+1\end{array}\right]$$

$$\times z^{b_k}\,{}_pF_q\left(\begin{array}{c}b_k-(a_p)+1;\ (-1)^{p-m-n}\,z\\b_k-(b_q)'+1\end{array}\right).$$

The notations $(b_m)'-b_k$ and $b_k-(b_q)'+1$ mean
that the term with b_k-b_k is absent.

$$\left[\begin{array}{l}(p<q)\ \text{or}\ (p=q,\, m+n>p)\ \text{or}\\(p=q,\, m+n=p;\, |z|<1);\\b_j-b_k\neq 0,\pm1,\pm2,\ldots;\, j\neq k;\, j,\,k=1,\,2,\ldots,\,m.\end{array}\right]$$

$$G_{pq}^{mn}\left(z\left|\begin{array}{c}(a_p)\\(b_q)\end{array}\right.\right) = \sum_{k=1}^{n}\Gamma\left[\begin{array}{c}a_k-(a_n)',\ (b_m)-a_k+1\\a_k-b_{m+1},\ldots,a_k-b_q,\, a_{n+1}-a_k+1,\ldots,a_p-a_k+1\end{array}\right]$$

$$\times z^{a_k-1}\,{}_pF_q\left(\begin{array}{c}(b_q)-a_k+1;\ \frac{(-1)^{q-m-n}}{z}\\(a_p)'-a_k+1\end{array}\right).$$

The notations $a_k-(a_n)'$ and $(a_p)'-a_k+1$ mean
that the term with a_k-a_k is absent.

$$\left[\begin{array}{l}(p>q)\ \text{or}\ (p=q,\, m+n=p+1;\, z\notin(-1,\,0))\ \text{or}\\(p=q,\, m+n>p+1)\ \text{or}\ (p=q,\, m+n=p;\, |z|>1);\\a_j-a_k\neq 0,\pm1,\pm2,\ldots;\, j\neq k;\, j,\,k=1,\,2,\ldots,\,n.\end{array}\right].$$

Notation:

$$m,\,n,\,p,\,q,\,r,\,t,\,u,\,v=0,\,1,\,2,\ldots;\,\sigma,\,\omega\in\mathbb{C};\,\sigma\neq0;\,\omega\neq0;$$

$$0\leq m\leq q;\,0\leq n\leq p;\,0\leq r\leq v;\,0\leq t\leq u;$$

$$b^*=r+t-\frac{u+v}{2},\quad c^*=m+n-\frac{p+q}{2};$$

$$\mu=\sum_{j=1}^{q}b_j-\sum_{i=1}^{p}a_i+\frac{p-q}{2}+1,\quad \rho=\sum_{h=1}^{v}d_h-\sum_{g=1}^{u}c_g+\frac{u-v}{2}+1;$$

$$k,\,\ell=1,\,2,\ldots;\,\Delta\left(k,a\right)=\frac{a}{k},\,\frac{a+1}{k},\ldots,\frac{a+k-1}{k};$$

$$\Delta\left(k,(a_p)\right)=\Delta\left(k,a_1\right),\,\Delta\left(k,a_2\right),\ldots,\Delta\left(k,a_p\right);$$

$$\varphi=q-p-\frac{\ell}{k}\left(v-u\right);\,\eta=1-s\left(v-u\right)-\mu-\rho.$$

Conditions A:

1° $a_i-b_j\neq 1,2,\ldots$ $(i=1,\ldots,n;\, j=1,\ldots,m)$;

$\quad\ c_g-d_h\neq 1,2,\ldots$ $(g=1,\ldots,t;\, h=1,\ldots,r)$;

2° $\mathrm{Re}\left(s+d_h+\dfrac{\ell}{k}\,b_j\right)>0$ $(j=1,\ldots,m;\, h=1,\ldots,r)$;

3° $\operatorname{Re}\left(s + c_g + \dfrac{\ell}{k} a_i\right) < \dfrac{\ell}{k} + 1 \quad (i = 1, \ldots, n; \ g = 1, \ldots, t)$;

4° $(p - q) \operatorname{Re}(s + c_g - 1) - \dfrac{\ell}{k} \operatorname{Re}\mu > -\dfrac{3\ell}{2k} \quad (g = 1, \ldots, t)$;

5° $(p - q) \operatorname{Re}(s + d_h) - \dfrac{\ell}{k} \operatorname{Re}\mu > -\dfrac{3\ell}{2k} \quad (h = 1, \ldots, r)$;

6° $(u - v) \operatorname{Re}\left(s + \dfrac{\ell}{k} a_i - \dfrac{\ell}{k}\right) - \operatorname{Re}\rho > -\dfrac{3}{2} \quad (i = 1, \ldots, n)$;

7° $(u - v) \operatorname{Re}\left(s + \dfrac{\ell}{k} b_j\right) - \operatorname{Re}\rho > -\dfrac{3}{2} \quad (j = 1, \ldots, m)$;

8° $|\varphi| + 2\operatorname{Re}\left[(q - p)(v - u)s + \dfrac{\ell}{k}(v - u)(\mu - 1) + (q - p)(\rho - 1)\right] > 0$;

9° $|\varphi| - 2\operatorname{Re}\left[(q - p)(v - u)s + \dfrac{\ell}{k}(v - u)(\mu - 1) + (q - p)(\rho - 1)\right] > 0$;

10° $\varphi = 0$; $c^* + r(b^* - 1) \le 0$; $\left|\arg\left(1 - z_0\sigma^{-\ell}\omega^k\right)\right| < \pi$;

$$z_0 = \left(\frac{\ell}{k}\right)^{l(v-u)} \exp\left[-(\ell b^* + kc^*)\pi i\right]$$

and $z_0 = \sigma^\ell \omega^{-k}$ provided that $\operatorname{Re}\left[(v - u)s + \mu + \rho\right] < 1$.

11° One of the following conditions holds:

$\lambda_c > 0$ or $\lambda_c = 0$, $\lambda_r \ne 0$, $\operatorname{Re}\eta > -1$ or $\lambda_c = \lambda_r = 0$, $\operatorname{Re}\eta > 0$.

$$\lambda_c = (q - p)|\omega|^{1/(q-p)}\cos\widetilde{\psi} + (v - u)|\sigma|^{1/(v-u)}\cos\theta,$$

$$\widetilde{\psi} = \frac{1}{q - p}\left[|\arg\omega| + (q - m - n)\pi\right], \quad \theta = \frac{1}{v - u}\left[|\arg\sigma| + (v - r - t)\pi\right];$$

$$\lambda_r = (q - p)|\omega|^{1/(q-p)}\operatorname{sgn}(\arg\omega)\sin\widetilde{\psi}$$

$$+ (v - u)|\sigma|^{1/(v-u)}\operatorname{sgn}(\arg\sigma)\sin\theta \qquad \text{for } \arg\omega\,\arg\sigma \ne 0;$$

$$\lambda_r = \lambda_r^+ \lambda_r^-, \qquad \lambda_r^\pm = \lim_{\arg\sigma\to\pm 0}\lambda_r \qquad \text{for } \arg\sigma = 0 \text{ and } \arg\omega \ne 0;$$

$$\lambda_r = \widetilde{\lambda}_r^+ \widetilde{\lambda}_r^-, \qquad \widetilde{\lambda}_r^\pm = \lim_{\arg\omega\to\pm 0}\lambda_r \qquad \text{for } \arg\sigma \ne 0 \text{ and } \arg\omega = 0;$$

$$\lambda_r = \bar{\lambda}_r^+ \bar{\lambda}_r^-, \qquad \bar{\lambda}_r^\pm = \lim_{\substack{\arg\omega\to 0 \\ \arg\sigma\to\pm 0}}\lambda_r \qquad \text{for } \arg\sigma = \arg\omega = 0.$$

$$G_{pq}^{mn}\left(z \left|\begin{matrix}(a_p) \\ (b_q)\end{matrix}\right.\right) = (2\pi)^{(1-k)c^*} k^\mu\, G_{kp, kq}^{km, kn}\left(\frac{z^k}{k^{k(q-p)}}\left|\begin{matrix}\Delta(k, (a_p)) \\ \Delta(k, (b_q))\end{matrix}\right.\right) \qquad [k = 1, 2, \ldots].$$

3.36.1. $G_{pq}^{mn}\left(\omega x \left| \begin{array}{c} (a_p) \\ (b_q) \end{array}\right.\right)$

No.	$f(x)$	$F(s)$
1	$G_{pq}^{mn}\left(\omega x \left\| \begin{array}{c} (a_p) \\ (b_q) \end{array}\right.\right)$	$\omega^{-s}\,\Gamma\left[\begin{array}{c} 1-(a_n)-s,\ s+(b_m) \\ s+a_{n+1},\ldots,s+a_p,\ 1-b_{m+1}-s,\ldots,1-b_q-s \end{array}\right]$

$$\left[\begin{array}{l} \big[q=p-2;\ c^* \geq 0; \\ \qquad (-1)^{q-m-n}\,\omega < 0;\ -\operatorname{Re}b_k,\ -\operatorname{Re}\chi - 1/2 < \operatorname{Re}s < 1 - \operatorname{Re}a_k\big]\ \text{or} \\ \big[q=p-1;\ c^* \geq 0;\ \big((-1)^{q-m-n}\operatorname{Re}\omega < 0;\ -\operatorname{Re}b_k < \operatorname{Re}s < 1 - \operatorname{Re}a_k\big)\ \text{or} \\ \quad (\operatorname{Re}\omega = 0;\ -\operatorname{Re}b_k,\ -\operatorname{Re}\chi - 1 < \operatorname{Re}s < 1 - \operatorname{Re}a_k)\big]\ \text{or} \\ \big[q=p;\ c^* > 0;\ \big(|\arg\omega| < (2m+2n-p-q)\,\pi/2; \\ \hspace{6cm} -\operatorname{Re}b_k < \operatorname{Re}s < 1 - \operatorname{Re}a_k\big)\ \text{or} \\ \quad \big(\omega > 0;\ c^* = 0;\ \sum_{k=1}^p \operatorname{Re}(a_k - b_k) > 0;\ -\operatorname{Re}b_k < \operatorname{Re}s < 1 - \operatorname{Re}a_k\big)\big]\ \text{or} \\ \big[q=p+1;\ c^* \geq 0;\ \big((-1)^{p-m-n}\operatorname{Re}\omega < 0;\ -\operatorname{Re}b_k < \operatorname{Re}s < 1 - \operatorname{Re}a_k\big)\ \text{or} \\ \quad (\operatorname{Re}\omega = 0;\ -\operatorname{Re}b_k < \operatorname{Re}s < 1 - \operatorname{Re}a_k,\ 1 - \operatorname{Re}\chi)\big]\ \text{or} \\ \big[q=p+2;\ c^* \geq 0;\ (-1)^{p-m-n}\,\omega < 0;\ -\operatorname{Re}b_k < \operatorname{Re}s < 1 - \operatorname{Re}a_k,\ 1/2 - \operatorname{Re}\chi\big] \end{array}\right]$$

No.	$f(x)$	$F(s)$
2	$G_{pq}^{mn}\left(x \left\| \begin{array}{c} (a_p) \\ (b_q) \end{array}\right.\right)$	$\Gamma\left[\begin{array}{c} 1-(a_n)-s,\ s+(b_m) \\ s+a_{n+1},\ldots,s+a_p,\ 1-b_{m+1}-s,\ldots,1-b_q-s \end{array}\right]$

$$\left[\begin{array}{l} -\min_{1 \leq j \leq m}\operatorname{Re}b_j < \operatorname{Re}s < 1 - \max_{1 \leq k \leq n}\operatorname{Re}a_k \\ \hspace{6cm} \text{and either} \\ \big[0 \leq n \leq p;\ 0 \leq m \leq q;\ 2(m+n) > p+q\big]\ \text{or} \\ \big[0 \leq n \leq p \leq q-2\ (\text{or } 0 \leq m \leq q \leq p-2); \\ \quad 2(m+n) = p+q; \\ \qquad (q-p)\operatorname{Re}s < \dfrac{q-p+1}{2} + \operatorname{Re}\Big(\sum_{k=1}^p a_k - \sum_{j=1}^q b_j\Big)\big] \\ \text{or} \\ \big[p=q \geq 1;\ m+n=p;\ \sum_{j=1}^p \operatorname{Re}(a_j - b_j) > 0\big] \end{array}\right]$$

3.36.2. $G_{pq}^{mn}\left(\omega x \left| \begin{array}{c} (a_p) \\ (b_q) \end{array}\right.\right)$ **and algebraic functions**

No.	$f(x)$	$F(s)$
1	$(a-x)_+^{\alpha-1}$ $\times G_{pq}^{mn}\left(\omega x^{\ell/k} \left\| \begin{array}{c} (a_p) \\ (b_q) \end{array}\right.\right)$	$\dfrac{k^\mu\,a^{s+\alpha-1}\Gamma(\alpha)}{\ell^\alpha\,(2\pi)^{c^*(k-1)}}\,G_{kp+\ell,\,kq+\ell}^{km,\,kn+\ell}\left(\dfrac{\omega^k a^\ell}{k^{k(q-p)}}\left\| \begin{array}{c} \Delta(\ell,\,1-s), \\ \Delta(k,\,(b_q)), \end{array}\right.\right.$ $\left.\left.\begin{array}{c} \Delta(k,\,(a_p)) \\ \Delta(\ell,\,1-s-\alpha) \end{array}\right)\right.$

$$\left[\begin{array}{l} \text{see Conditions A with} \\ \sigma = 1/a;\ r = u = v = 1;\ t = d_1 = 0;\ c_1 = \alpha \end{array}\right]$$

No.	$f(x)$	$F(s)$
2	$(x-a)_+^{\alpha-1}$ $\times G_{pq}^{mn}\left(\omega x^{\ell/k}\,\middle|\,\begin{matrix}(a_p)\\(b_q)\end{matrix}\right)$	$\dfrac{k^{\mu}\,\ell^{-\alpha}}{(2\pi)^{c^*(k-1)}\,a^{1-s-\alpha}}\,\Gamma(\alpha)$ $\times G_{kp+\ell,\,kq+\ell}^{km+\ell,\,kn}\left(\dfrac{\omega^k a^\ell}{k^{k(q-p)}}\,\middle|\,\begin{matrix}\Delta(k,(a_p)),\,\Delta(k,1-s)\\\Delta(k,1-s-\alpha),\,\Delta(k,(b_q))\end{matrix}\right)$ $\left[\begin{matrix}\text{see Conditions A with}\\\sigma=1/a;\ r=d_1=0;\ t=u=v=1;\ c_1=\alpha\end{matrix}\right]$
3	$\dfrac{1}{(x+a)^\beta}$ $\times G_{pq}^{mn}\left(\omega x^{\ell/k}\,\middle|\,\begin{matrix}(a_p)\\(b_q)\end{matrix}\right)$	$\dfrac{k^{\mu}\,\ell^{\beta-1}\,a^{s-\beta}}{(2\pi)^{c^*(k-1)+\ell-1}\,\Gamma(\beta)}$ $\times G_{kp+\ell,\,kq+\ell}^{km+\ell,\,kn+\ell}\left(\dfrac{\omega^k a^\ell}{k^{k(q-p)}}\,\middle|\,\begin{matrix}\Delta(\ell,1-s),\,\Delta(k,(a_p))\\\Delta(\ell,\beta-s),\,\Delta(k,(b_q))\end{matrix}\right)$ $\left[\begin{matrix}\text{see Conditions A with}\\\sigma=1/a;\ r=t=u=v=1;\ c_1=1-\beta;\ d_1=0\end{matrix}\right]$
4	$\dfrac{1}{x-a}\,G_{pq}^{mn}\left(\omega x^{\ell/k}\,\middle|\,\begin{matrix}(a_p)\\(b_q)\end{matrix}\right)$	$-\dfrac{\pi\,k^{\mu}\,a^{s-1}}{(2\pi)^{c^*(k-1)}}\,G_{kp+2\ell,\,kq+2\ell}^{km+\ell,\,kn+\ell}\left(\dfrac{\omega^k a^\ell}{k^{k(q-p)}}\,\middle|\,\begin{matrix}\Delta(\ell,1-s),\\\Delta(\ell,1-s),\end{matrix}\right.$ $\left.\begin{matrix}\Delta(k,(a_p)),\,\Delta\!\left(\ell,\frac{1-2s}{2}\right)\\\Delta(k,(b_q)),\,\Delta\!\left(\ell,\frac{1-2s}{2}\right)\end{matrix}\right)$ $\left[\begin{matrix}\text{see Conditions A with}\\\sigma=1/a;\ r=t=1;\ u=v=2;\ c_1=d_1=0;\ c_2=d_2=1/2\end{matrix}\right]$
5	$\dfrac{1}{(x+a)^\beta}$ $\times G_{pq}^{mn}\left(\dfrac{\omega(x+a)^\ell}{x^k}\,\middle|\,\begin{matrix}(a_p)\\(b_q)\end{matrix}\right)$	$\dfrac{\sqrt{2\pi}\,k^{s-1/2}\,\ell^{1/2-\beta}\,a^{s-\beta}}{(\ell-k)^{s-\beta+1/2}}\,G_{p+\ell,\,q+\ell}^{m+\ell,\,n}\left(\dfrac{\omega\ell^\ell}{k^k}\left(\dfrac{a}{\ell-k}\right)^{\ell-k}\,\middle|\,\begin{matrix}(a_p),\\\Delta(k,s),\end{matrix}\right.$ $\left.\begin{matrix}\Delta(\ell,\beta)\\\Delta(\ell-k,\beta-s),\,(b_q)\end{matrix}\right)$ $\left[\begin{matrix}0<k<\ell;\ c^*>0;\ |\arg(\omega a^{\ell-k})|<c^*\pi;\\-k+k\max\limits_{1\le j\le n}\operatorname{Re}a_j<\operatorname{Re}s\\<\operatorname{Re}\beta+(\ell-k)\left[1-\max\limits_{1\le j\le n}\operatorname{Re}a_j\right]\end{matrix}\right]$
6	$\dfrac{1}{(x+a)^\beta}$ $\times G_{pq}^{mn}\left(\dfrac{\omega(x+a)^\ell}{x^k}\,\middle|\,\begin{matrix}(a_p)\\(b_q)\end{matrix}\right)$	$\dfrac{\sqrt{2\pi}\,k^{s-1/2}\,\ell^{1/2-\beta}\,a^{s-\beta}}{(k-\ell)^{1/2+s-\beta}}$ $\times G_{p+k,\,q+k}^{m+k,\,n+k-\ell}\left(\dfrac{\omega\ell^\ell}{k^k}\left(\dfrac{a}{k-\ell}\right)^{\ell-k}\,\middle|\,\right.$ $\left.\begin{matrix}\Delta(\ell-k,s-\beta+1),\,(a_p),\,\Delta(\ell,\beta)\\\Delta(k,s),\,(b_q)\end{matrix}\right)$ $\left[\begin{matrix}0<\ell<k;\ c^*>0;\ |\arg(\omega a^{\ell-k})|<c^*\pi;\\-k+k\max\limits_{1\le j\le n}\operatorname{Re}a_j<\operatorname{Re}s\\<\operatorname{Re}\beta+(k-\ell)\min\limits_{1\le j\le m}\operatorname{Re}b_j\end{matrix}\right]$

No.	$f(x)$	$F(s)$
7	$\dfrac{1}{(x+a)^\beta}$ $\times G_{pq}^{mn}\left(\dfrac{\omega(x+a)^\ell}{x^k}\Bigg\vert \begin{matrix}(a_p)\\(b_q)\end{matrix}\right)$	$\sqrt{2\pi}\,(ka)^{s-\beta}\,\Gamma(\beta-s)\,G_{p+k,\,q+k}^{m+k,\,n}\left(\omega\,\Bigg\vert\begin{matrix}(a_p),\,\Delta(k,\beta)\\ \Delta(k,s),\,(b_q)\end{matrix}\right)$ $\left[\begin{matrix}\ell=k>0;\ c^*>0;\ \vert\arg\omega\vert<c^*\pi;\\ -k+k\max\limits_{1\le j\le n}\operatorname{Re}a_j<\operatorname{Re}s<\operatorname{Re}\beta\end{matrix}\right]$
8	$\dfrac{1}{(x+1)^\beta}$ $\times G_{pq}^{mn}\left(\dfrac{\omega x}{x+1}\Bigg\vert\begin{matrix}(a_p)\\(b_q)\end{matrix}\right)$	$\Gamma(\beta-s)\,G_{p+1,\,q+1}^{m,\,n+1}\left(\omega\,\Bigg\vert\begin{matrix}1-s,\,(a_p),\,\Delta(k,\beta)\\(b_q),\,1-\beta\end{matrix}\right)$ $\left[\begin{matrix}c^*>0;\ \vert\arg\omega\vert<c^*\pi;\\ -\min\limits_{1\le j\le m}\operatorname{Re}b_j<\operatorname{Re}s<\operatorname{Re}\beta\end{matrix}\right]$

3.36.3. $G_{pq}^{mn}\left(\omega x^\sigma\,\Big\vert\begin{matrix}(a_p)\\(b_q)\end{matrix}\right)$ and the exponential function

No.	$f(x)$	$F(s)$
1	$e^{-\sigma x}\,G_{pq}^{mn}\left(\omega x^{\ell/k}\,\Big\vert\begin{matrix}(a_p)\\(b_q)\end{matrix}\right)$	$\dfrac{k^\mu\,\ell^{s-1/2}\,\sigma^{-s}}{(2\pi)^{(\ell-1)/2+(k-1)c^*}}\,G_{kp+\ell,\,kq}^{km,\,kn+\ell}\left(\dfrac{\omega^k\ell^\ell}{\sigma^\ell k^{k(q-p)}}\,\Bigg\vert\begin{matrix}\Delta(\ell,1-s),\\ \Delta(k,(b_q))\end{matrix}\right.$ $\left.\Delta(k,(a_p))\right)$ $\left[\begin{matrix}\text{see Conditions A with}\\ r=v=1;\ t=u=d_1=0\end{matrix}\right]$
2	$e^{-\sigma x}\,G_{pq}^{mn}\left(\omega x\,\Big\vert\begin{matrix}(a_p)\\(b_q)\end{matrix}\right)$	$\sigma^{-s}\,G_{p+1,\,q}^{m,\,n+1}\left(\dfrac{\omega}{\sigma}\,\Bigg\vert\begin{matrix}1-s,\,(a_p)\\(b_q)\end{matrix}\right)$

$$\left[\begin{aligned}
&q=p-2;\ (-1)^{q-m-n}\,\omega<0;\ (\operatorname{Re}\sigma>0;\ -\operatorname{Re}b_k,\,-\operatorname{Re}\chi-1/2<\operatorname{Re}s)\ \text{or}\\
&\quad(\operatorname{Re}\sigma=0;\ -\operatorname{Re}b_k,\,-\operatorname{Re}\chi-1/2<\operatorname{Re}s<2-\operatorname{Re}a_k)]\\
&q=p-1;\ (\operatorname{Re}\sigma>0;\ (-1)^{q-m-n}\,\omega<0;\ -\operatorname{Re}b_k<\operatorname{Re}s)\ \text{or}\\
&\quad(\operatorname{Re}\sigma>0;\ \operatorname{Re}\omega=0;\ -\operatorname{Re}b_k,\,-\operatorname{Re}\chi-1<\operatorname{Re}s)\ \text{or}\\
&\quad(\operatorname{Re}\sigma=0;\ (-1)^{q-m-n}\,\omega<0;\ -\operatorname{Re}b_k<\operatorname{Re}s<2-\operatorname{Re}a_k)\ \text{or}\\
&\quad(\operatorname{Re}\sigma=\operatorname{Re}\omega=0;\ -\operatorname{Re}b_k,\,-\operatorname{Re}\chi-1<\operatorname{Re}s<2-\operatorname{Re}a_k)]\ \text{or}\\
&q=p;\ (\operatorname{Re}\sigma>0;\ \operatorname{Re}s>-\operatorname{Re}b_k)\ \text{or}\\
&\quad(\operatorname{Re}\sigma=0;\ -\operatorname{Re}b_k<\operatorname{Re}s<2-\operatorname{Re}a_k);\\
&\quad((m+n>p;\ \vert\arg\omega\vert<(m+n-p)\pi)\ \text{or}\\
&\quad(m+n=p;\ \omega>0;\ \textstyle\sum_{k=1}^p\operatorname{Re}(a_k-b_k)>0))]\ \text{or}\\
&q=p+1;\ (\operatorname{Re}\sigma,\ \operatorname{Re}(\sigma-(-1)^{p-m-n}\,\omega)>0;\ \operatorname{Re}s>-\operatorname{Re}b_k)\ \text{or}\\
&\quad(\operatorname{Re}\sigma>0;\ \operatorname{Re}(\sigma-(-1)^{p-m-n}\,\omega)=0;\ -\operatorname{Re}b_k<\operatorname{Re}s<1-\operatorname{Re}\chi)\ \text{or}\\
&\quad(\operatorname{Re}\sigma=0;\ (-1)^{p-m-n}\operatorname{Re}\omega<0;\ -\operatorname{Re}b_k<\operatorname{Re}s<2-\operatorname{Re}a_k)\ \text{or}\\
&\quad(\operatorname{Re}\sigma=\operatorname{Re}\omega=0;\ -\operatorname{Re}b_k<\operatorname{Re}s<2-\operatorname{Re}a_k,\,1-\operatorname{Re}\chi)]\ \text{or}\\
&q=p+2;\ (\operatorname{Re}\sigma>0;\ (-1)^{p-m-n}\,\omega<0;\ -\operatorname{Re}b_k<\operatorname{Re}s)\ \text{or}\\
&\quad(\operatorname{Re}\sigma=0;\ \operatorname{Re}s<2-\operatorname{Re}a_k,\,1-\operatorname{Re}\chi)]\ \text{or}\\
&q\ge p+3;\ \operatorname{Re}\sigma>0;\ \operatorname{Re}s>-\operatorname{Re}b_k
\end{aligned}\right]$$

3.36.4. $G_{pq}^{mn}\left(\omega x^{\sigma}\,\middle|\,\begin{matrix}(a_p)\\(b_q)\end{matrix}\right)$ and trigonometric functions

1	$\sin(bx)$ $\times\, G_{pq}^{mn}\left(\omega x^{2\ell/k}\,\middle\|\,\begin{matrix}(a_p)\\(b_q)\end{matrix}\right)$	$\dfrac{k^{\mu}\,(2\ell)^{s-1/2}\,b^{-s}}{2\,(2\pi)^{(k-1)c^*-1/2}}\,G_{kp+2\ell,\,kq}^{km,\,kn+\ell}\left(\dfrac{\omega^k\,(2\ell)^{2\ell}}{b^{2\ell}k^{k(q-p)}}\,\middle\|\,\begin{matrix}\Delta\left(\ell,\,\frac{1-s}{2}\right),\\[4pt]\Delta\left(k,\,(a_p)\right),\,\Delta\left(\ell,\,\frac{2-s}{2}\right)\\[4pt]\Delta\left(k,\,(b_q)\right)\end{matrix}\right)$ $\left[\begin{array}{l}\text{see Conditions A with } s \text{ being}\\ \text{replaced by } s/2 \text{ and with}\\ \sigma=b^2/4;\ r=1;\ t=u=0;\ v=2;\ d_1=1/2;\ d_2=0\end{array}\right]$
2	$\sin(bx)\,G_{pq}^{mn}\left(\omega x^2\,\middle\|\,\begin{matrix}(a_p)\\(b_q)\end{matrix}\right)$	$\dfrac{\sqrt{\pi}}{b}\,G_{p+2,\,q}^{m,\,n+1}\left(\dfrac{4\omega}{b^2}\,\middle\|\,\begin{matrix}0,\,(a_p),\,\frac{1}{2}\\(b_q)\end{matrix}\right)$ $\left[\begin{array}{l}c^*>0;\ b>0;\ \operatorname{Re}b_j>-1\ (j=1,\ldots,m);\\ \operatorname{Re}a_i<1/2\ (i=1,\ldots,n);\ |\arg\omega|<c^*\pi\end{array}\right]$
3	$\cos(bx)$ $\times\, G_{pq}^{mn}\left(\omega x^{2\ell/k}\,\middle\|\,\begin{matrix}(a_p)\\(b_q)\end{matrix}\right)$	$\dfrac{k^{\mu}\,(2\ell)^{s-1/2}\,b^{-s}}{2\,(2\pi)^{c^*(k-1)-1/2}}$ $\times\, G_{kp+2\ell,\,kq}^{km,\,kn+\ell}\left(\dfrac{\omega^k\,(2\ell)^{2\ell}}{b^{2\ell}k^{k(q-p)}}\,\middle\|\,\begin{matrix}\Delta\left(\ell,\,\frac{2-s}{2}\right),\,\Delta\left(k,\,(a_p)\right),\,\Delta\left(\ell,\,\frac{1-s}{2}\right)\\[4pt]\Delta\left(k,\,(b_q)\right)\end{matrix}\right)$ $\left[\begin{array}{l}\text{see Conditions A with } s \text{ being}\\ \text{replaced by } s/2 \text{ and with}\\ \sigma=b^2/4;\ r=1;\ t=u=0;\ v=2;\ d_1=d_2=1/2\end{array}\right]$
4	$\cos(bx)\,G_{pq}^{mn}\left(\omega x^2\,\middle\|\,\begin{matrix}(a_p)\\(b_q)\end{matrix}\right)$	$\dfrac{\sqrt{\pi}}{b}\,G_{p+2,\,q}^{m,\,n+1}\left(\dfrac{4\omega}{b^2}\,\middle\|\,\begin{matrix}\frac{1}{2},\,(a_p),\,0\\(b_q)\end{matrix}\right)$ $\left[\begin{array}{l}c^*;\ b>0;\ \operatorname{Re}b_j>-1/2\ (j=1,\ldots,m);\\ \operatorname{Re}a_i<1/2\ (i=1,\ldots,n);\ |\arg\omega|<c^*\pi\end{array}\right]$

3.36.5. $G_{pq}^{mn}\left(\omega x^{\sigma}\,\middle|\,\begin{matrix}(a_p)\\(b_q)\end{matrix}\right)$ and the Bessel functions

1	$J_{\nu}(bx)$ $\times\, G_{pq}^{mn}\left(\omega x^{2\ell/k}\,\middle\|\,\begin{matrix}(a_p)\\(b_q)\end{matrix}\right)$	$\dfrac{k^{\mu}\,(2\ell)^{s-1}}{(2\pi)^{(k-1)c^*}\,b^s}\,G_{kp+2\ell,\,kq}^{km,\,kn+\ell}\left(\dfrac{\omega^k\,(2\ell)^{2\ell}}{b^{2\ell}k^{k(q-p)}}\,\middle\|\,\begin{matrix}\Delta\left(\ell,\,\frac{2-s-\nu}{2}\right),\\[4pt]\cdot\\[4pt]\Delta\left(k,\,(a_p)\right),\,\Delta\left(\ell,\,\frac{2-s+\nu}{2}\right)\\[4pt]\Delta\left(k,\,(b_q)\right)\end{matrix}\right)$ $\left[\begin{array}{l}\text{see Conditions A with } s \text{ being}\\ \text{replaced by } s/2 \text{ and with}\\ \sigma=b^2/4;\ r=1;\ t=u=0;\ v=2;\ d_1=\nu/4;\ d_2=-\nu/4\end{array}\right]$

No.	$f(x)$	$F(s)$

2 $J_\nu(bx) G_{pq}^{mn}\left(\omega x^2 \left|\begin{matrix}(a_p)\\(b_q)\end{matrix}\right.\right)$

$$\frac{2^{s-1}}{b^s} G_{p+2,\,q}^{m,\,n+1}\left(\frac{4\omega}{b^2}\left|\begin{matrix}\frac{2-s-\nu}{2},\,(a_p),\,\frac{2-s+\nu}{2}\\(b_q)\end{matrix}\right.\right)$$

$$\left[\begin{matrix}c^*>0;\,b>0;\,|\arg\omega|<c^*\pi;\\ \operatorname{Re}(b_j+(s+\nu)/2)>0\ (j=1,\ldots,m),\\ \operatorname{Re}(a_i+s/2)<5/4\ (i=1,\ldots,n)\end{matrix}\right]$$

3 $J_\nu(a\sqrt{x})$

$\times G_{pq}^{mn}\left(\omega x \left|\begin{matrix}(a_p)\\(b_q)\end{matrix}\right.\right)$

$$\left(\frac{2}{a}\right)^{2s} G_{p+2,\,q}^{m,\,n+1}\left(\frac{4\omega}{a^2}\left|\begin{matrix}\frac{2-2s-\nu}{2},\,(a_p),\,\frac{2-2s+\nu}{2}\\(b_q)\end{matrix}\right.\right)$$

$$\left[\begin{matrix}c^*>0;\,a>0;\,|\arg\omega|<c^*\pi;\\ -\operatorname{Re}\nu/2-\min_{1\le j\le m}\operatorname{Re}b_j<\operatorname{Re}s<7/4-\max_{1\le i\le n}\operatorname{Re}a_i\end{matrix}\right]$$

4 $Y_\nu(bx)$

$\times G_{pq}^{mn}\left(\omega x^{2\ell/k} \left|\begin{matrix}(a_p)\\(b_q)\end{matrix}\right.\right)$

$$\frac{k^\mu(2\ell)^{s-1}}{(2\pi)^{(k-1)c^*}\,b^s} G_{kp+3\ell,\,kq+\ell}^{km,\,kn+2\ell}\left(\frac{\omega^k(2\ell)^{2\ell}}{b^{2\ell}k^{k(q-p)}}\left|\begin{matrix}\Delta\left(\ell,\frac{2-s-\nu}{2}\right),\\ \Delta(k,(b_q)),\end{matrix}\right.\right.$$

$$\left.\begin{matrix}\Delta\left(\ell,\frac{2-s+\nu}{2}\right),\,\Delta(k,(a_p)),\,\Delta\left(\ell,\frac{3-s+\nu}{2}\right)\\ \Delta\left(\ell,\frac{3-s+\nu}{2}\right)\end{matrix}\right)$$

$$\left[\begin{matrix}\text{see Conditions A with }s\\ \text{being replaced by }s/2\text{ and with}\\ \sigma=b^2/4;\,r=2;\,t=0;\,u=1;\,v=3;\\ c_1=d_3=(1-\nu)/2;\,d_1=-\nu/2;\,d_2=\nu/2\end{matrix}\right]$$

5 $Y_\nu(a\sqrt{x})$

$\times G_{pq}^{mn}\left(\omega x \left|\begin{matrix}(a_p)\\(b_q)\end{matrix}\right.\right)$

$$\left(\frac{2}{a}\right)^{2s} G_{p+3,\,q+1}^{m,\,n+2}\left(\frac{4\omega}{a^2}\left|\begin{matrix}\frac{2-2s-2\nu}{2},\,\frac{2-2s+2\nu}{2},\,(a_p),\,\frac{3-2s+\nu}{2}\\(b_q),\,\frac{3-2s+\nu}{2}\end{matrix}\right.\right)$$

$$\left[\begin{matrix}c^*>0;\,a>0;\,|\arg\omega|<c^*\pi\\ -\min_{1\le j\le m}\operatorname{Re}b_j-\operatorname{Re}\nu/2<\operatorname{Re}s<7/4-\max_{1\le i\le n}\operatorname{Re}a_i\end{matrix}\right]$$

6 $K_\nu(bx)$

$\times G_{pq}^{mn}\left(\omega x^{2\ell/k} \left|\begin{matrix}(a_p)\\(b_q)\end{matrix}\right.\right)$

$$\frac{\pi k^\mu(2\ell)^{s-1}}{(2\pi)^{(k-1)c^*+\ell}\,b^s} G_{kp+2\ell,\,kq}^{km,\,kn+2\ell}\left(\frac{\omega^k(2\ell)^{2\ell}}{b^{2\ell}k^{k(q-p)}}\left|\begin{matrix}\Delta\left(\ell,\frac{2-s-\nu}{2}\right),\end{matrix}\right.\right.$$

$$\left.\begin{matrix}\Delta\left(\ell,\frac{2-s+\nu}{2}\right),\,\Delta(k,(a_p))\\ \Delta(k,(b_q))\end{matrix}\right)$$

$$\left[\begin{matrix}\text{see Conditions A with }s\\ \text{being replaced by }s/2\text{ and with}\\ \sigma=b^2/4;\,r=v=2;\,t=u=0;\,d_1=-\nu/2;\,d_2=\nu/2\end{matrix}\right]$$

7 $K_\nu(a\sqrt{x})$

$\times G_{pq}^{mn}\left(\omega x \left|\begin{matrix}(a_p)\\(b_q)\end{matrix}\right.\right)$

$$\frac{1}{2}\left(\frac{2}{a}\right)^{2s} G_{pq}^{mn}\left(\frac{4\omega}{a^2}\left|\begin{matrix}\frac{2-2s-\nu}{2},\,\frac{2-2s+\nu}{2},\,(a_p)\\(b_q)\end{matrix}\right.\right)$$

$$\left[\begin{matrix}c^*>0;\,a>0;\,|\arg\omega|<c^*\pi;\\ \operatorname{Re}s>\operatorname{Re}\nu/2-\min_{1\le j\le m}\operatorname{Re}b_j\end{matrix}\right]$$

3.36.6. $G_{pq}^{mn}\left(\omega x^\sigma \left|\begin{matrix}(a_p)\\(b_q)\end{matrix}\right.\right)$ and orthogonal polynomials

1	$\left(a^2 - x^2\right)_+^{\lambda-1/2} C_r^\lambda\left(\dfrac{x}{a}\right)$ $\times G_{pq}^{mn}\left(\omega x^{2\ell/k} \left\|\begin{matrix}(a_p)\\(b_q)\end{matrix}\right.\right)$	$\dfrac{k^\mu\, a^{s+2\lambda-1}}{2\,r!\,(2\pi)^{(k-1)c^*}\,\ell^{\lambda+1/2}}\,(2\lambda)_r\,\Gamma\left(\dfrac{2\lambda+1}{2}\right)$ $\times G_{kp+2\ell,\,kq+2\ell}^{km,\,kn+2\ell}\left(\dfrac{\omega^k k^{k(p-q)}}{\sigma^{2\ell}} \left\|\begin{matrix}\Delta(2\ell,\,1-s),\\ \Delta(k,\,(b_q)),\end{matrix}\right.\right.$ $\left.\begin{matrix}\Delta(k,\,(a_p))\\ \Delta\left(\ell,\,\frac{1-s-r-2\lambda}{2}\right),\,\Delta\left(\ell,\,\frac{1-s+r}{2}\right)\end{matrix}\right)$ $\left[\begin{array}{l}\text{see Conditions A with } s \text{ being}\\ \text{replaced by } s/2 \text{ and with } \sigma = a^{-2};\ t = 0;\\ r = u = v = 2;\ c_1 = (r+2\lambda+1)/2;\ c_2 = (1-r)/2;\\ d_1 = 0;\ d_2 = 1/2;\ r = 0,\,1,\,2,\ldots\end{array}\right]$
2	$(a-x)_+^\alpha P_r^{(\alpha,\beta)}\left(\dfrac{2x}{a} - 1\right)$ $\times G_{pq}^{mn}\left(\omega x^{\ell/k} \left\|\begin{matrix}(a_p)\\(b_q)\end{matrix}\right.\right)$	$\dfrac{k^\mu\, a^{s+\alpha}\,\Gamma(\alpha+r+1)}{(2\pi)^{(k-1)c^*}\,\ell^{\alpha+1}r!}\,G_{kp+2\ell,\,kq+2\ell}^{km,\,kn+2\ell}\left(\dfrac{\omega^k a^\ell}{k^{k(q-p)}} \left\|\begin{matrix}\Delta(\ell,\,1-s),\\ \Delta(k,\,(b_q)),\end{matrix}\right.\right.$ $\left.\begin{matrix}\Delta(\ell,\,1-s+\beta),\,\Delta(k,\,(a_p))\\ \Delta(\ell,\,1-s+r+\beta),\,\Delta(\ell,\,-s-r-\alpha)\end{matrix}\right)$ $\left[\begin{array}{l}\text{see Conditions A with}\\ \sigma = 1/a;\ t = 0;\ r = u = v = 2;\ c_1 = \alpha+r+1;\\ c_2 = -v - r;\ d_1 = 0;\ d_2 = -v;\ r = 0,\,1,\,2,\ldots\end{array}\right]$

3.36.7. $G_{pq}^{mn}\left(\omega x^\sigma \left|\begin{matrix}(a_p)\\(b_q)\end{matrix}\right.\right)$ and the Legendre function

1	$\left(a^2 - x^2\right)_+^{-\lambda/2} P_\nu^\lambda\left(\dfrac{x}{a}\right)$ $\times G_{pq}^{mn}\left(\omega x^{2\ell/k} \left\|\begin{matrix}(a_p)\\(b_q)\end{matrix}\right.\right)$	$\dfrac{k^\mu\,(2\ell)^{\lambda-1}\,a^{s-\lambda}}{(2\pi)^{(k-1)c^*}}\,G_{kp+2\ell,\,kq+2\ell}^{km,\,kn+2\ell}\left(\dfrac{a^{2\ell}\omega^k}{k^{k(q-p)}} \left\|\begin{matrix}\Delta(2\ell,\,1-s),\\ \Delta(k,\,(b_q)),\end{matrix}\right.\right.$ $\left.\begin{matrix}\Delta(k,\,(a_p))\\ \Delta\left(\ell,\,\frac{\lambda-s-\nu}{2}\right),\,\Delta\left(\ell,\,\frac{1-s+\lambda+\nu}{2}\right)\end{matrix}\right)$ $\left[\begin{array}{l}\text{see Conditions A with } s\\ \text{being replaced by } s/2 \text{ and with}\\ \sigma = 1/a^2;\ t = 0;\ r = u = v = 2;\ c_1 = (1-\lambda-\nu)/2;\\ c_2 = (2-\lambda+\nu)/2;\ d_1 = 0;\ d_2 = 1/2\end{array}\right]$
2	$\left(x^2 - a^2\right)_+^{-\lambda/2} P_\nu^\lambda\left(\dfrac{x}{a}\right)$ $\times G_{pq}^{mn}\left(\omega x^{2\ell/k} \left\|\begin{matrix}(a_p)\\(b_q)\end{matrix}\right.\right)$	$\dfrac{k^\mu\,(2\ell)^{\lambda-1}\,a^{s-\lambda}}{(2\pi)^{(k-1)c^*}}\,G_{kp+2\ell,\,kq+2\ell}^{km+2\ell,\,kn}\left(\dfrac{a^{2\ell}\omega^k}{k^{k(q-p)}} \left\|\begin{matrix}\Delta(k,\,(a_p)),\\ \Delta\left(\ell,\,\frac{\lambda-s-\nu}{2}\right),\end{matrix}\right.\right.$ $\left.\begin{matrix}\Delta(2\ell,\,-s)\\ \Delta\left(\ell,\,\frac{1-s+\lambda+\nu}{2}\right),\,\Delta(k,\,(b_q))\end{matrix}\right)$ $\left[\begin{array}{l}\text{see Conditions A with } s\\ \text{being replaced by } s/2 \text{ and with}\\ \sigma = 1/a^2;\ r = 0;\ t = u = v = 2;\ c_1 = (1-\lambda-\nu)/2;\\ c_2 = (2-\lambda+\nu)/2;\ d_1 = 0;\ d_2 = 1/2\end{array}\right]$

3.36.8. $G_{pq}^{mn}\left(\omega x^{\sigma}\,\middle|\,\begin{matrix}(a_p)\\(b_q)\end{matrix}\right)$ **and the Struve function**

1	$\mathbf{H}_{\nu}\left(2\sqrt{x}\right)$	$G_{p+3,\,q+1}^{m+1,\,n+1}\left(\omega\,\middle|\,\begin{matrix}\frac{1-2s-\nu}{2},\,(a_p),\,\frac{2-2s+\nu}{2},\,\frac{2-2s-\nu}{2}\\[4pt]\frac{1-2s-\nu}{2},\,(b_q)\end{matrix}\right)$
	$\times\,G_{pq}^{mn}\left(\omega x\,\middle|\,\begin{matrix}(a_p)\\(b_q)\end{matrix}\right)$	$\left[\begin{matrix}c^* > 0;\ |\arg\omega| < c^*\pi;\\[4pt]\operatorname{Re}s > -\left(1+\operatorname{Re}\nu\right)/2 - \min\limits_{1\le j\le m}\operatorname{Re}b_j;\\[4pt]\operatorname{Re}s < 1 - \max\limits_{1\le i\le n}\operatorname{Re}a_i - \max\left[-3/4,\ \operatorname{Re}\left(\nu-1\right)/2\right]\end{matrix}\right]$

3.36.9. $G_{pq}^{mn}\left(\omega x^{\sigma}\,\middle|\,\begin{matrix}(a_p)\\(b_q)\end{matrix}\right)$ **and the Whittaker functions**

1	$e^{-\sigma x/2}\,W_{\mu,\,\nu}\left(\sigma x\right)$	$\dfrac{k^{\mu}\,\ell^{s+\mu-1/2}\,\sigma^{-s}}{(2\pi)^{(\ell-1)/2+(k-1)c^*}}\,\Gamma\left[\begin{matrix}2\nu+1\\[2pt]\frac{2\mu+2\nu+1}{2}\end{matrix}\right]$
	$\times\,G_{pq}^{mn}\left(\omega x^{\ell/k}\,\middle|\,\begin{matrix}(a_p)\\(b_q)\end{matrix}\right)$	$\times\,G_{kp+2\ell,\,kq+\ell}^{km+\ell,\,kn+\ell}\left(\dfrac{\omega^k\ell^\ell}{\sigma^\ell k^{k(q-p)}}\,\middle|\,\begin{matrix}\Delta\left(\ell,\,\frac{1-2s-2\nu}{2}\right),\\[2pt]\Delta\left(\ell,\,\mu-s\right),\end{matrix}\right.$
		$\left.\begin{matrix}\Delta\left(k,\,(a_p)\right),\,\Delta\left(\ell,\,\frac{1-2s+2\nu}{2}\right)\\[2pt]\Delta\left(k,\,(b_q)\right)\end{matrix}\right)$
		$\left[\begin{matrix}\text{see Conditions A with }v=2;\\[2pt]r=t=u=1;\ c_1=1-\mu;\ d_1=1/2+\nu;\ d_2=1/2-\nu\end{matrix}\right]$
2	$e^{-\sigma x/2}\,W_{\mu,\,\nu}\left(\sigma x\right)$	$\dfrac{k^{\mu}\,\ell^{s+\mu-1/2}\,\sigma^{-s}}{(2\pi)^{(\ell-1)/2+(k-1)c^*}}$
	$\times\,G_{pq}^{mn}\left(\omega x^{\ell/k}\,\middle|\,\begin{matrix}(a_p)\\(b_q)\end{matrix}\right)$	$\times\,G_{kp+2\ell,\,kq+\ell}^{km,\,kn+2\ell}\left(\dfrac{\omega^k\ell^\ell}{\sigma^\ell k^{k(q-p)}}\,\middle|\,\begin{matrix}\Delta\left(\ell,\,\frac{1-2s-2\nu}{2}\right),\\[2pt]\Delta\left(k,\,(b_q)\right),\end{matrix}\right.$
		$\left.\begin{matrix}\Delta\left(\ell,\,\frac{1-2s+2\nu}{2}\right),\,\Delta\left(k,\,(a_p)\right)\\[2pt]\Delta\left(\ell,\,\mu-s\right)\end{matrix}\right)$
		$\left[\begin{matrix}\text{see Conditions A with }t=0;\ r=v=2;\\[2pt]u=1;\ c_1=1-\mu;\ d_1=1/2+\nu;\ d_2=1/2-\nu\end{matrix}\right]$
3	$e^{\sigma x/2}\,W_{\mu,\,\nu}\left(\sigma x\right)$	$(2\pi)^{3(1-\ell)/2+(1-k)c^*}\,\dfrac{k^{\mu}\,\ell^{s-\mu-1/2}\,\sigma^{-s}}{\Gamma\left(\frac{1-2\mu-2\nu}{2}\right)\Gamma\left(\frac{1-2\mu+2\nu}{2}\right)}$
	$\times\,G_{pq}^{mn}\left(\omega x^{\ell/k}\,\middle|\,\begin{matrix}(a_p)\\(b_q)\end{matrix}\right)$	$\times\,G_{kp+2\ell,\,kq+\ell}^{km+\ell,\,kn+2\ell}\left(\dfrac{\omega^k\ell^\ell}{\sigma^\ell k^{k(q-p)}}\,\middle|\,\begin{matrix}\Delta\left(\ell,\,\frac{1-2s-2\nu}{2}\right),\\[2pt]\Delta\left(\ell,\,-s-\mu\right),\end{matrix}\right.$
		$\left.\begin{matrix}\Delta\left(\ell,\,\frac{1-2s+2\nu}{2}\right),\,\Delta\left(k,\,(a_p)\right)\\[2pt]\Delta\left(k,\,(b_q)\right)\end{matrix}\right)$
		$\left[\begin{matrix}\text{see Conditions A with }r=v=2;\\[2pt]t=u=1;\ c_1=\mu+1;\ d_1=1/2+\nu;\ d_2=1/2-\nu\end{matrix}\right]$

3.36.10. $G_{pq}^{mn}\left(\omega x^{\sigma}\ \middle|\ \begin{matrix}(a_p)\\(b_q)\end{matrix}\right)$ and hypergeometric functions

1	$\begin{aligned}&{}_2F_1\left(\begin{matrix}a,\,b\\c;\,1-\sigma x\end{matrix}\right)\\[2mm]&\times\,G_{pq}^{mn}\left(\omega x^{\ell/k}\ \middle|\ \begin{matrix}(a_p)\\(b_q)\end{matrix}\right)\end{aligned}$	$\dfrac{k^{\mu}\,\ell^{c-2}\,\sigma^{-\rho}}{(2\pi)^{2(\ell-1)+(k-1)c^{*}}}\,\Gamma\left[\begin{matrix}c\\a,\,b,\,c-a,\,c-b\end{matrix}\right]$ $$\times\,G_{kp+2\ell,\,kq+2\ell}^{km+2\ell,\,kn+2\ell}\left(\frac{\omega^k\sigma^{-\ell}}{k^{k(q-p)}}\ \middle|\ \begin{matrix}\Delta\left(\ell,\,1-s\right),\\ \Delta\left(\ell,\,a-s\right),\end{matrix}\right.$$ $$\left.\begin{matrix}\Delta\left(\ell,\,1-s+a+b-c\right),\,\Delta\left(k,\,(a_p)\right)\\ \Delta\left(\ell,\,b-s\right),\,\Delta\left(k,\,(b_q)\right)\end{matrix}\right)$$ $$\left[\begin{matrix}\text{see Conditions A with } r=t=u=v=2;\\ c_1=1-a;\,c_2=1-b;\,d_1=0;\,d_2=c-a-b\end{matrix}\right]$$
2	$\begin{aligned}&(d-x)_{+}^{c-1}\,{}_2F_1\left(\begin{matrix}a,\,b\\c;\,\frac{d-x}{d}\end{matrix}\right)\\[2mm]&\times\,G_{pq}^{mn}\left(\omega x^{\ell/k}\ \middle|\ \begin{matrix}(a_p)\\(b_q)\end{matrix}\right)\end{aligned}$	$\dfrac{k^{\mu}\,\ell^{-c}\,\Gamma\left(c\right)}{(2\pi)^{(k-1)c^{*}}\,d^{1-s-c}}\,G_{kp+2\ell,\,kq+2\ell}^{km,\,kn+2\ell}\left(\frac{\omega^k d^{\ell}}{k^{k(q-p)}}\ \middle|\ \begin{matrix}\Delta\left(\ell,\,1-s\right),\\ \Delta\left(k,\,(b_q)\right),\end{matrix}\right.$ $$\left.\begin{matrix}\Delta\left(\ell,\,1-s+a+b-c\right),\,\Delta\left(k,\,(a_p)\right)\\ \Delta\left(\ell,\,1-s+a-c\right),\,\Delta\left(\ell,\,1-s+b-c\right)\end{matrix}\right)$$ $$\left[\begin{matrix}\text{see Conditions A with } \sigma=1/d;\,r=u=v=2;\\ t=0;\,c_1=c-a;\,c_2=c-b;\,d_1=0;\,d_2=c-a-b\end{matrix}\right]$$
3	$\begin{aligned}&(x-d)_{+}^{c-1}\,{}_2F_1\left(\begin{matrix}a,\,b\\c;\,\frac{d-x}{d}\end{matrix}\right)\\[2mm]&\times\,G_{pq}^{mn}\left(\omega x^{\ell/k}\ \middle|\ \begin{matrix}(a_p)\\(b_q)\end{matrix}\right)\end{aligned}$	$\dfrac{k^{\mu}\,\ell^{-c}\,\Gamma\left(c\right)}{(2\pi)^{(k-1)c^{*}}\,d^{1-s-c}}\,G_{kp+2\ell,\,kq+2\ell}^{km+2\ell,\,kn}\left(\frac{\omega^k d^{\ell}}{k^{k(q-p)}}\ \middle|\ \begin{matrix}\Delta\left(k,\,(a_p)\right),\\ \Delta\left(\ell,\,1-s+a-c\right),\end{matrix}\right.$ $$\left.\begin{matrix}\Delta\left(\ell,\,1-s\right),\,\Delta\left(\ell,\,1-s+a+b-c\right)\\ \Delta\left(\ell,\,1-s+b-c\right),\,\Delta\left(k,\,(b_q)\right)\end{matrix}\right)$$ $$\left[\begin{matrix}\text{see Conditions A with } \sigma=1/d;\,r=u=v=2;\\ s=0;\,c_1=c-a;\,c_2=c-b;\,d_1=0;\,d_2=c-a-b\end{matrix}\right]$$
4	$\begin{aligned}&{}_2F_1\left(\begin{matrix}a,\,b\\c;\,-\sigma x\end{matrix}\right)\\[2mm]&\times\,G_{pq}^{mn}\left(\omega x^{\ell/k}\ \middle|\ \begin{matrix}(a_p)\\(b_q)\end{matrix}\right)\end{aligned}$	$\dfrac{k^{\mu}\,\ell^{a+b-c-1}\,\sigma^{-s}}{(2\pi)^{\ell-1+(k-1)c^{*}}}\,\Gamma\left[\begin{matrix}c\\a,\,b\end{matrix}\right]\,G_{kp+2\ell,\,kq+2\ell}^{km+2\ell,\,kn+\ell}\left(\frac{\sigma^{-\ell}\omega^k}{k^{k(q-p)}}\ \middle|\ \begin{matrix}\Delta\left(\ell,\,1-s\right),\\ \Delta\left(\ell,\,a-s\right),\end{matrix}\right.$ $$\left.\begin{matrix}\Delta\left(k,\,(a_p)\right),\,\Delta\left(\ell,\,c-s\right)\\ \Delta\left(\ell,\,b-s\right),\,\Delta\left(k,\,(b_q)\right)\end{matrix}\right)$$ $$\left[\begin{matrix}\text{see Conditions A with } r=1;\,t=u=v=2;\\ c_1=1-a;\,c_2=1-b;\,d_1=0;\,d_2=1-c\end{matrix}\right]$$
5	$\begin{aligned}&{}_rF_t\left(\begin{matrix}(c_r);\,-\sigma x\\(d_t)\end{matrix}\right)\\[2mm]&\times\,G_{pq}^{mn}\left(\omega x^{\ell/k}\ \middle|\ \begin{matrix}(a_p)\\(b_q)\end{matrix}\right)\end{aligned}$	$\dfrac{k^{\mu}\,\ell^{\eta}\,\sigma^{-s}}{(2\pi)^{(1+r-t)(\ell-1)/2+(k-1)c^{*}}}\,\Gamma\left[\begin{matrix}(d_t)\\(c_r)\end{matrix}\right]$ $$\times\,G_{kp+t\ell+\ell,\,kq+r\ell}^{km+r\ell,\,kn+\ell}\left(\frac{\omega^k k^{k(p-q)}}{\sigma^{\ell}\ell^{\ell(r-t-1)}}\ \middle|\ \begin{matrix}\Delta\left(\ell,\,1-s\right),\\ \Delta\left(\ell,\,(c_r)-s\right),\end{matrix}\right.$$ $$\left.\begin{matrix}\Delta\left(k,\,(a_p)\right),\,\Delta\left(\ell,\,(d_t)-s\right)\\ \Delta\left(k,\,(b_q)\right)\end{matrix}\right)$$ $$\left[\begin{matrix}\text{see Conditions A with } t=u=r;\\ r=1;\,,\,v=l+1;\,(c_u)=1-(c_r);\,(d_v)=0,\,1-(d_t)\end{matrix}\right]$$

3.36.11.   Products of two Meijer's G-functions

Notation:

$$\psi = \frac{1}{p-q}\left(\sum_{j=1}^{q} b_j - \sum_{i=1}^{p} a_i + \frac{p-q+1}{2}\right), \quad \chi = \frac{1}{v-u}\left(\sum_{j=1}^{v} d_j - \sum_{i=1}^{u} c_i + \frac{u-v+1}{2}\right).$$

$$\sum_L = \sum_{k=1}^{m} \frac{\prod\limits_{j=1;\,j\neq k}^{m}\Gamma\left(b_j-b_k\right)\prod\limits_{j=1}^{n}\Gamma\left(b_k-a_j+1\right)\prod\limits_{j=1}^{r}\Gamma\left(s+b_k+d_j\right)\prod\limits_{j=1}^{t}\Gamma\left(1-b_k-c_j-s\right)}{\prod\limits_{j=n+1}^{p}\Gamma\left(a_j-b_k\right)\prod\limits_{j=m+1}^{q}\Gamma\left(b_k-b_j+1\right)\prod\limits_{j=t+1}^{u}\Gamma\left(s+b_k+c_j\right)\prod\limits_{j=r+1}^{v}\Gamma\left(1-b_k-d_j-s\right)}$$

$$\times \left(\frac{\omega}{\sigma}\right)^{b_k} {}_{p+v}F_{q+u-1}\left(\begin{matrix} b_k-(a_p)+1,\, s+b_k+(d_v);\ (-1)^{p+v-m-n-r-t}\,\frac{\omega}{\sigma} \\ b_k-(b_q)'+1,\, s+b_k+(c_u) \end{matrix}\right)$$

$$+ \sum_{k=1}^{t} \frac{\prod\limits_{j=1;\,j\neq k}^{t}\Gamma\left(c_k-c_j\right)\prod\limits_{j=1}^{r}\Gamma\left(d_j-c_k+1\right)\prod\limits_{j=1}^{n}\Gamma\left(2-a_j-c_k-s\right)\prod\limits_{j=1}^{m}\Gamma\left(s+b_j+c_k-1\right)}{\prod\limits_{j=r+1}^{v}\Gamma\left(c_k-d_j\right)\prod\limits_{j=t+1}^{u}\Gamma\left(c_j-c_k+1\right)\prod\limits_{j=m+1}^{q}\Gamma\left(2-b_j-c_k-s\right)\prod\limits_{j=n+1}^{p}\Gamma\left(s+a_j+c_k-1\right)}$$

$$\times \left(\frac{\omega}{\sigma}\right)^{1-s-c_k} {}_{p+v}F_{q+u-1}\left(\begin{matrix} (d_v)-c_k+1,\, 2-(a_p)-c_k-s;\ (-1)^{p+v-m-n-r-t}\,\frac{\omega}{\sigma} \\ (c_u)'-c_k+1,\, 2-(b_q)-c_k-s \end{matrix}\right),$$

$$\sum_R = \sum_{k=1}^{n} \frac{\prod\limits_{j=1;\,j\neq k}^{n}\Gamma\left(a_k-a_j\right)\prod\limits_{j=1}^{m}\Gamma\left(b_j-a_k+1\right)\prod\limits_{j=1}^{t}\Gamma\left(2-a_k-c_j-s\right)\prod\limits_{j=1}^{r}\Gamma\left(s+a_k+d_j-1\right)}{\prod\limits_{j=n+1}^{p}\Gamma\left(a_j-a_k+1\right)\prod\limits_{j=m+1}^{q}\Gamma\left(a_k-b_j\right)\prod\limits_{j=r+1}^{v}\Gamma\left(2-a_k-d_j-s\right)\prod\limits_{j=t+1}^{u}\Gamma\left(s+a_k+c_j-1\right)}$$

$$\times \left(\frac{\omega}{\sigma}\right)^{a_k-1} {}_{q+u}F_{p+v-1}\left(\begin{matrix} (b_q)-a_k+1,\, 2-a_k-(c_u)-s;\ (-1)^{q+u-m-n-r-t}\,\frac{\sigma}{\omega} \\ (a_p)'-a_k+1,\, 2-a_k-(d_v)-s \end{matrix}\right)$$

$$+ \sum_{k=1}^{r} \frac{\prod\limits_{j=1;\,j\neq k}^{r}\Gamma\left(d_j-d_k\right)\prod\limits_{j=1}^{t}\Gamma\left(d_k-c_j+1\right)\prod\limits_{j=1}^{m}\Gamma\left(s+b_j+d_k\right)\prod\limits_{j=1}^{n}\Gamma\left(1-a_j-d_k-s\right)}{\prod\limits_{j=r+1}^{v}\Gamma\left(d_k-d_j+1\right)\prod\limits_{j=n+1}^{p}\Gamma\left(s+a_j+d_k\right)\prod\limits_{j=t+1}^{u}\Gamma\left(c_j-d_k\right)\prod\limits_{j=m+1}^{q}\Gamma\left(1-s-b_j-d_k\right)}$$

$$\times \left(\frac{\omega}{\sigma}\right)^{-s-d_k} {}_{q+u}F_{p+v-1}\left(\begin{matrix} s+(b_q)+d_k,\, d_k-(c_u)+1;\ (-1)^{q+u-m-n-r-t}\,\frac{\sigma}{\omega} \\ d_k-(d_v)'+1,\, s+(a_p)+d_k \end{matrix}\right).$$

Conditions B:

B1 $(v \leq u-3)$:

B1.1 $(q = p-1)$

$$\left[\begin{matrix} m=0;\ n\geq q+1;\ 2n-2q+2r+2t-u-v\geq 1; \\ (-1)^{q-n}\operatorname{Re}\omega<0;\ \operatorname{Re}s<2-\operatorname{Re}\left(a_i+c_g\right) \end{matrix}\right]$$

B2 $(v = u - 2):$

B2.1 $(q = p - 2)$

$$\left[\begin{array}{l} m + n \geq q + 1;\ r + t \geq u - 1;\ (-1)^{v-r-t}\,\sigma < 0;\ (-1)^{q-m-n}\,\omega < 0; \\ -\operatorname{Re}(\chi + \psi) - \left(1 - \delta_{0,\,\omega - (-1)^{q-m-n-v+r+t}\sigma}\right)/2,\ -\operatorname{Re}(b_j + \psi) - 1/2, \\ -\operatorname{Re}(\chi + d_h) - 1/2,\ -\operatorname{Re}(b_j + d_h) < \operatorname{Re} s < 2 - \operatorname{Re}(a_i + c_g) \end{array}\right]$$

or

B2.2 $(q = p - 1)$

$$\left[\begin{array}{l} m + n \geq q + 1;\ r + t \geq u - 1;\ (-1)^{v-r-t}\,\sigma < 0; \\ -\operatorname{Re}(b_j + \psi) - 1/2,\ -\operatorname{Re}(b_j + d_h) < \operatorname{Re} s < 2 - \operatorname{Re}(a_i + c_g); \\ (-1)^{q-m-n}\operatorname{Re}\omega < 0\ \text{or}\ (\operatorname{Re}\omega = 0;\ -\operatorname{Re}(\chi + \psi) - 1,\ -\operatorname{Re}(\chi + d_h) - 1 < \operatorname{Re} s) \end{array}\right]$$

or

B2.3 $(q = p)$

$$\left[\begin{array}{l} r + t \geq u - 1;\ (-1)^{v-r-t}\,\sigma < 0; \\ -\operatorname{Re}(b_j + \psi) - 1/2,\ -\operatorname{Re}(b_j + d_h) < \operatorname{Re} s < 2 - \operatorname{Re}(a_i + c_g); \\ (m + n > p;\ |\arg\omega| < (m + n - p)\,\pi)\ \text{or} \\ (m + n = p;\ \omega > 0;\ \sum_{k=1}^{p}\operatorname{Re}(a_k - b_k) > 0) \end{array}\right]$$

or

B2.4 $(q = p + 1)$

$$\left[\begin{array}{l} m + n \geq p + 1;\ r + t \geq u - 1;\ (-1)^{v-r-t}\,\sigma < 0; \\ -\operatorname{Re}(b_j + \psi) - 1/2,\ -\operatorname{Re}(b_j + d_h) < \operatorname{Re} s < 2 - \operatorname{Re}(a_i + c_g); \\ (-1)^{p-m-n}\operatorname{Re}\omega < 0\ \text{or}\ (\operatorname{Re}\omega = 0;\ \operatorname{Re} s < 2 - \operatorname{Re}(c_g + \chi)) \end{array}\right]$$

or

B2.5 $(q = p + 2)$

$$\left[\begin{array}{l} m + n \geq p + 1;\ r + t \geq u - 1; \\ (-1)^{v-r-t}\,\sigma < 0;\ (-1)^{p-m-n}\,\omega < 0; \\ -\operatorname{Re}(b_j + \psi) - 1/2,\ -\operatorname{Re}(b_j + d_h) < \operatorname{Re} s \\ < 2 - \operatorname{Re}(a_i + c_g),\ 3/2 - \operatorname{Re}(c_g + \chi) \end{array}\right]$$

B3 $(v = u - 1):$

B3.1 $(q = p - 2)$

$$\left[\begin{array}{l} m + n \geq q + 1;\ r + t \geq u;\ (-1)^{q-m-n}\,\omega < 0; \\ -\operatorname{Re}(d_h + \chi) - 1/2,\ -\operatorname{Re}(b_j + d_h) < \operatorname{Re} s \\ \qquad\qquad < 2 - \operatorname{Re}(a_i + c_g);\ (-1)^{v-r-t}\operatorname{Re}\sigma < 0\ \text{or} \\ (\operatorname{Re}\sigma = 0;\ -\operatorname{Re}(b_j + \psi) - 1,\ -\operatorname{Re}(\chi + \psi) - 1 < \operatorname{Re} s) \end{array}\right]$$

or

B3.2 $(q = p - 1)$

$$\left[\begin{array}{l} m = 0;\ n \geq q + 1;\ r + t \geq u; \\ (-1)^{q-n}\operatorname{Re}\omega < 0;\ \operatorname{Re} s < 2 - \operatorname{Re}(a_i + c_g); \\ \left(\operatorname{Re}\left((-1)^{q-n}/\omega + (-1)^{v-r-t}/\sigma\right)\right) < 0\ \text{or} \\ \left(\operatorname{Re}\left((-1)^{q-n}\sigma + (-1)^{v-r-t}\omega\right) = 0;\ -\operatorname{Re}(\chi + \psi) - 1 < \operatorname{Re} s\right), \end{array}\right]$$

$$
\begin{bmatrix}
m+n \geq q+1; \; r+t \geq u; \; -\operatorname{Re}(b_j+d_h) < \operatorname{Re}s \\
< 2 - \operatorname{Re}(a_i+c_g); \; \left(\left((-1)^{v-r-t}\operatorname{Re}\sigma<0; \; ((-1)^{q-m-n}\operatorname{Re}\omega<0 \text{ or}\right.\right. \\
(\operatorname{Re}\omega=0; \; -\operatorname{Re}(d_h+\chi)-1<\operatorname{Re}s))) \text{ or} \\
\left(\operatorname{Re}\sigma=0; \; -\operatorname{Re}(b_j+\psi)-1<\operatorname{Re}s;\right. \\
((-1)^{q-m-n}\operatorname{Re}\omega<0 \text{ or} \\
\left(\operatorname{Re}\omega=0; \; -\operatorname{Re}(d_h+\chi)-1, \; -\operatorname{Re}(\chi+\psi)-1<\operatorname{Re}s\right))))
\end{bmatrix}
$$

or

B3.3 $(q=p)$
$$
\begin{bmatrix}
r+t \geq u; \; -\operatorname{Re}(b_j+d_h) < \operatorname{Re}s < 2-\operatorname{Re}(a_i+c_g); \\
(-1)^{v-r-t}\operatorname{Re}\sigma<0 \text{ or } (\operatorname{Re}\sigma=0; \; -\operatorname{Re}(b_j+\psi)-1<\operatorname{Re}s); \\
(m+n>p; \; |\arg\omega|<(m+n-p)\pi) \text{ or} \\
(m+n=p; \; \omega>0; \; \sum_{k=1}^{p}\operatorname{Re}(a_k-b_k)>0)
\end{bmatrix}
$$

or

B3.4 $(q=p+1)$
$$
\begin{bmatrix}
m+n \geq p+1; \; r+t \geq u; \; -\operatorname{Re}(b_j+d_h) < \operatorname{Re}s < 2-\operatorname{Re}(a_i+c_g); \\
((-1)^{v-r-t}\operatorname{Re}\sigma<0 \text{ or } (\operatorname{Re}\sigma=0; \; -\operatorname{Re}(b_j+\psi)-1<\operatorname{Re}s)); \\
(-1)^{p-m-n}\operatorname{Re}\omega<0 \text{ or } (\operatorname{Re}\omega=0; \; \operatorname{Re}s<2-\operatorname{Re}(c_g+\chi))
\end{bmatrix}
$$

or

B3.5 $(q=p+2)$
$$
\begin{bmatrix}
m+n \geq p+1; \; r+t \geq u; \; (-1)^{p-m-n}\omega<0; \\
-\operatorname{Re}(b_j+d_h) < \operatorname{Re}s < 2-\operatorname{Re}(a_i+c_g), \; 3/2-\operatorname{Re}(c_g+\chi); \\
((-1)^{v-r-t}\operatorname{Re}\sigma<0 \text{ or } (\operatorname{Re}\sigma=0; \; -\operatorname{Re}(b_j+\psi)-1<\operatorname{Re}s))
\end{bmatrix}
$$

B4 $(v=u):$

B4.1 $(q=p-2)$
$$
\begin{bmatrix}
m+n \geq q+1; \; (-1)^{q-m-n}\omega<0; \; -\operatorname{Re}(b_j+d_h), \; -\operatorname{Re}(d_h+\chi)-1/2< \\
<\operatorname{Re}s<2-\operatorname{Re}(a_i+c_g); \; ((r+t>v; \; |\arg\sigma|<(r+t-v)\pi) \text{ or} \\
(r+t=v; \; \sigma>0; \; \sum_{j=1}^{u}\operatorname{Re}(c_j-d_j)>0))
\end{bmatrix}
$$

or

B4.2 $(q=p-1)$
$$
\begin{bmatrix}
m+n \geq q+1; \; -\operatorname{Re}(b_j+d_h) < \operatorname{Re}s < 2-\operatorname{Re}(a_i+c_g); \\
((r+t>v; \; |\arg\sigma|<(r+t-v)\pi) \text{ or} \\
(r+t=v; \; \sigma>0; \; \sum_{j=1}^{u}\operatorname{Re}(c_j-d_j)>0)); \\
(-1)^{q-m-n}\operatorname{Re}\omega<0 \text{ or } (\operatorname{Re}\omega=0; \; -\operatorname{Re}(d_h+\chi)-1<\operatorname{Re}s)
\end{bmatrix}
$$

or

B4.3 $(q=p)$
$$
\begin{bmatrix}
r+t>u; \; |\arg\sigma|<(r+t-u)\pi; \; -\operatorname{Re}(b_j+d_h) < \operatorname{Re}s < 2-\operatorname{Re}(a_i+c_g); \\
((m+n>p; \; |\arg\omega|<(m+n-p)\pi) \text{ or} \\
(m+n=p; \; \omega>0; \; \sum_{k=1}^{p}\operatorname{Re}(a_k-b_k)>0)),
\end{bmatrix}
$$

$$\left[\begin{array}{l} r + t = u;\ \sigma > 0;\ -\operatorname{Re}(b_j + d_h) < \operatorname{Re}s < 2 - \operatorname{Re}(a_i + c_g);\\ ((\sum_{j=1}^{u} \operatorname{Re}(c_j - d_j) > 0;\\ ((m + n > p;\ |\arg \omega| < (m + n - p)\pi)\ \text{or}\\ (m + n = p;\ \omega > 0;\ \omega \neq \sigma;\ \sum_{k=1}^{p} \operatorname{Re}(a_k - b_k) > 0)))\ \text{or}\\ (m + n = p;\ \omega = \sigma;\ \sum_{k=1}^{p} \operatorname{Re}(a_k - b_k) + \sum_{j=1}^{u} \operatorname{Re}(c_j - d_j) > 1)) \end{array}\right]$$

or

B4.4 $(q = p + 1)$

$$\left[\begin{array}{l} m + n \geq p + 1;\ -\operatorname{Re}(b_j + d_h) < \operatorname{Re}s < 2 - \operatorname{Re}(a_i + c_g);\\ ((r + t > u;\ |\arg \sigma| < (r + t - u)\pi)\ \text{or}\\ (r + t = u;\ \sigma > 0;\ \sum_{j=1}^{u} \operatorname{Re}(c_j - d_j) > 0));\\ ((-1)^{p-m-n} \operatorname{Re}\omega < 0\ \text{or}\ (\operatorname{Re}\omega = 0;\ \operatorname{Re}s < 2 - \operatorname{Re}(c_g + \chi))) \end{array}\right]$$

or

B4.5 $(q = p + 2)$

$$\left[\begin{array}{l} m + n \geq p + 1;\ (-1)^{p-m-n}\omega < 0;\\ -\operatorname{Re}(b_j + d_h) < \operatorname{Re}s < 2 - \operatorname{Re}(a_i + c_g),\ 3/2 - \operatorname{Re}(c_g + \chi);\\ (r + t > u;\ |\arg \sigma| < (r + t - u)\pi)\ \text{or}\\ (r + t = u;\ \sigma > 0;\ \sum_{j=1}^{u} \operatorname{Re}(c_j - d_j) > 0) \end{array}\right]$$

B5 $(v = u + 1):$

B5.1 $(q = p - 2)$

$$\left[\begin{array}{l} m + n \geq q + 1;\ r + t \geq v;\ (-1)^{q-m-n}\omega < 0;\\ -\operatorname{Re}(b_j + d_h),\ -\operatorname{Re}(d_h + \chi) - 1/2 < \operatorname{Re}s < 2 - \operatorname{Re}(a_i + c_g);\\ (-1)^{u-r-t} \operatorname{Re}\sigma < 0\ \text{or}\ (\operatorname{Re}\sigma = 0;\ \operatorname{Re}s < 2 - \operatorname{Re}(a_i + \psi)) \end{array}\right]$$

or

B5.2 $(q = p - 1)$

$$\left[\begin{array}{l} m + n \geq q + 1;\ r + t \geq v;\ -\operatorname{Re}(b_j + d_h) < \operatorname{Re}s < 2 - \operatorname{Re}(a_i + c_g);\\ (-1)^{u-r-t} \operatorname{Re}\sigma < 0\ \text{or}\ (\operatorname{Re}\sigma = 0;\ \operatorname{Re}s < 2 - \operatorname{Re}(a_i + \psi));\\ (-1)^{q-m-n} \operatorname{Re}\omega < 0\ \text{or}\ (\operatorname{Re}\omega = 0;\ -\operatorname{Re}(d_h + \chi) - 1 < \operatorname{Re}s) \end{array}\right]$$

or

B5.3 $(q = p)$

$$\left[\begin{array}{l} r + t \geq u + 1;\ -\operatorname{Re}(b_j + d_h) < \operatorname{Re}s < 2 - \operatorname{Re}(a_i + c_g);\\ (-1)^{u-r-t} \operatorname{Re}\sigma < 0\ \text{or}\ (\operatorname{Re}\sigma = 0;\ \operatorname{Re}s < 2 - \operatorname{Re}(a_i + \psi));\\ (m + n > p;\ |\arg \omega| < (m + n - p)\pi)\ \text{or}\\ (m + n = p;\ \omega > 0;\ \sum_{k=1}^{p} \operatorname{Re}(a_k - b_k) > 0) \end{array}\right]$$

or

B5.4 $(q = p + 1)$

$$\left[\begin{array}{l} nt = 0;\ v = u + 1;\ m + n \geq p + 1;\ r + t \geq u + 1;\\ (-1)^{p-m} \operatorname{Re}\omega < 0\ \text{for}\ n = 0;\ (-1)^{u-r} \operatorname{Re}\sigma < 0\ \text{for}\ t = 0;\\ -\operatorname{Re}(b_j + d_h) < \operatorname{Re}s;\ (-1)^{u-r-t} \operatorname{Re}\sigma + (-1)^{p-m-n} \operatorname{Re}\omega < 0\ \text{or}\\ ((-1)^{u-r-t} \operatorname{Re}\sigma + (-1)^{p-m-n} \operatorname{Re}\omega = 0;\ \operatorname{Re}s < 1 - \operatorname{Re}(\chi + \psi)) \end{array}\right]$$

$$
\begin{bmatrix}
m + n \geq p + 1;\ r + t \geq u + 1;\ -\operatorname{Re}(b_j + d_h) < \operatorname{Re} s < 2 - \operatorname{Re}(a_i + c_g); \\
\left(\left((-1)^{u-r-t}\operatorname{Re}\sigma < 0;\ \left((-1)^{p-m-n}\operatorname{Re}\omega < 0 \text{ or} \right.\right.\right. \\
\left(\operatorname{Re}\omega = 0;\ \operatorname{Re} s < 2 - \operatorname{Re}(c_g + \chi)\right)\right) \text{ or} \\
\left(\operatorname{Re}\sigma = 0;\ \operatorname{Re} s < 2 - \operatorname{Re}(a_i + \psi);\ \left((-1)^{p-m-n}\operatorname{Re}\omega < 0 \text{ or} \right.\right. \\
\left(\operatorname{Re}\omega = 0;\ \operatorname{Re} s < 1 - \operatorname{Re}(\chi + \psi),\ 2 - \operatorname{Re}(c_g + \chi)\right)\bigg)\bigg)\bigg)
\end{bmatrix}
$$

or

B5.5 $(q = p + 2)$

$$
\begin{bmatrix}
m + n \geq p + 1;\ r + t \geq u + 1;\ (-1)^{p-m-n}\omega < 0; \\
-\operatorname{Re}(b_j + d_h) < \operatorname{Re} s < 2 - \operatorname{Re}(a_i + c_g),\ 3/2 - \operatorname{Re}(c_g + \chi); \\
(-1)^{u-r-t}\operatorname{Re}\sigma < 0 \text{ or } \left(\operatorname{Re}\sigma = 0;\ \operatorname{Re} s < 1 - \operatorname{Re}(\chi + \psi),\ 2 - \operatorname{Re}(a_i + \psi)\right)
\end{bmatrix}
$$

B6 $(v = u + 2):$

B6.1 $(q = p - 2)$

$$
\begin{bmatrix}
m + n \geq q + 1;\ r + t \geq v - 1;\ (-1)^{u-r-t}\sigma < 0;\ (-1)^{q-m-n}\omega < 0; \\
-\operatorname{Re}(b_j + d_h),\ -\operatorname{Re}(d_h + \chi) - 1/2 < \\
< \operatorname{Re} s < 2 - \operatorname{Re}(a_i + c_g),\ 3/2 - \operatorname{Re}(a_i + \psi)
\end{bmatrix}
$$

or

B6.2 $(q = p - 1)$

$$
\begin{bmatrix}
m + n \geq q + 1;\ r + t \geq v - 1;\ (-1)^{u-r-t}\sigma < 0; \\
-\operatorname{Re}(b_j + d_h) < \operatorname{Re} s < 2 - \operatorname{Re}(a_i + c_g),\ 3/2 - \operatorname{Re}(a_i + \psi); \\
(-1)^{q-m-n}\operatorname{Re}\omega < 0 \text{ or } \left(\operatorname{Re}\omega = 0;\ -\operatorname{Re}(d_h + \chi) - 1 < \operatorname{Re} s\right)
\end{bmatrix}
$$

or

B6.3 $(q = p)$

$$
\begin{bmatrix}
r + t \geq u + 1;\ (-1)^{u-r-t}\sigma < 0; \\
-\operatorname{Re}(b_j + d_h) < \operatorname{Re} s < 2 - \operatorname{Re}(a_i + c_g),\ 3/2 - \operatorname{Re}(a_i + \psi); \\
\left((m + n > p;\ |\arg\omega| < (m + n - p)\pi) \text{ or}\right. \\
\left(m + n = p;\ \omega > 0;\ \sum_{k=1}^{p}\operatorname{Re}(a_k - b_k) > 0\right)\bigg)
\end{bmatrix}
$$

or

B6.4 $(q = p + 1)$

$$
\begin{bmatrix}
m + n \geq p + 1;\ r + t \geq u + 1;\ (-1)^{u-r-t}\sigma < 0; \\
-\operatorname{Re}(b_j + d_h) < \operatorname{Re} s < 2 - \operatorname{Re}(a_i + c_g),\ 3/2 - \operatorname{Re}(a_i + \psi); \\
(-1)^{p-m-n}\operatorname{Re}\omega < 0 \text{ or } (\operatorname{Re}\omega = 0;\ \operatorname{Re} s < 2 - \operatorname{Re}(c_g + \chi),\ 1 - \operatorname{Re}(\chi + \psi))
\end{bmatrix}
$$

or

B6.5 $(q = p + 2)$

$$
\begin{bmatrix}
m + n \geq p + 1;\ r + t \geq u + 1; \\
(-1)^{u-r-t}\sigma < 0;\ (-1)^{p-m-n}\omega < 0;\ -\operatorname{Re}(b_j + d_h) < \operatorname{Re} s < 2 - \operatorname{Re}(a_i + c_g), \\
3/2 - \operatorname{Re}(c_g + \chi),\ 3/2 - \operatorname{Re}(a_i + \psi),\ \left(1 - \delta_{0,\,\sigma - (-1)^{-m-n+p+r+t-u}\omega}\right)/2 - \operatorname{Re}(\chi + \psi)
\end{bmatrix}
$$

B7 $(v \geq u + 3):$

B7.1 $(q = p + 1)$

$$
\begin{bmatrix}
n = 0;\ m \geq p + 1;\ 2m - 2p + 2r + 2t - u - v \geq 1;\ (-1)^{p-m}\operatorname{Re}\omega < 0;\ -\operatorname{Re}(b_j + d_h) < \operatorname{Re} s
\end{bmatrix}
$$

No.	$f(x)$	$F(s)$
1	$G_{pq}^{mn}\left(\omega x \left\vert \begin{array}{c}(a_p)\\(b_q)\end{array}\right.\right)$ $\times G_{uv}^{rt}\left(\sigma x \left\vert \begin{array}{c}(c_u)\\(d_v)\end{array}\right.\right)$	$\sigma^{-s} G_{p+v,\,q+u}^{m+t,\,n+r}\left(\dfrac{\omega}{\sigma} \left\vert \begin{array}{c}(a_n),\,1-s-(d_v),\,a_{n+1},\ldots,a_p\\(b_m),\,1-s-(c_u),\,b_{m+1},\ldots,b_q\end{array}\right.\right)$ $\left[\begin{array}{l} 0 \le m \le q;\; 0 \le n \le p;\; 0 \le r \le v;\; 0 \le t \le u;\; 0 \le q-p \le 2;\\ -2 \le v-u;\; \sigma \in \mathbb{C};\; \omega \in \mathbb{C};\; \sigma \ne 0;\; \omega \ne 0;\; a_i - b_j \ne 1,2,\ldots;\\ i = 1,\ldots,n;\; j = 1,\ldots,m;\; c_g - d_h \ne 1,2,\ldots;\\ g = 1,\ldots,t;\; h = 1,\ldots,r;\\ \text{see Conditions B1--B7} \end{array}\right]$
2	$G_{pq}^{mn}\left(\omega x \left\vert \begin{array}{c}(a_p)\\(b_q)\end{array}\right.\right)$ $\times G_{uv}^{rt}\left(\sigma x \left\vert \begin{array}{c}(c_u)\\(d_v)\end{array}\right.\right)$	$\dfrac{\sigma^{-s}}{2\pi i}\displaystyle\int_{\gamma-i\infty}^{\gamma+i\infty}\dfrac{\prod_{j=1}^{m}\Gamma(b_j+\tau)\prod_{g=1}^{t}\Gamma(1-s-c_g+\tau)}{\prod_{k=n+1}^{p}\Gamma(a_k+\tau)\prod_{k=r+1}^{v}\Gamma(1-s-d_k+\tau)}$ $\times\dfrac{\prod_{i=1}^{n}\Gamma(1-a_i-\tau)\prod_{h=1}^{r}\Gamma(s+d_h-\tau)}{\prod_{k=m+1}^{q}\Gamma(1-b_k-\tau)\prod_{k=t+1}^{u}\Gamma(s+c_k-\tau)}\left(\dfrac{\omega}{\sigma}\right)^{-\tau}d\tau$ $\left[\begin{array}{l}-\operatorname{Re}b_k,\;\operatorname{Re}(s+c_k)-1 < \gamma = \operatorname{Re}\tau < 1-\operatorname{Re}a_k,\;\operatorname{Re}(s+d_k);\\ \text{see Conditions B1--B7}\end{array}\right]$
3	$G_{pq}^{mn}\left(\omega x \left\vert \begin{array}{c}(a_p)\\(b_q)\end{array}\right.\right)$ $\times G_{uv}^{rt}\left(\sigma x \left\vert \begin{array}{c}(c_u)\\(d_v)\end{array}\right.\right)$	$\sigma^{-s}\displaystyle\sum_L$ $\left[\begin{array}{l}(q+u > p+v;\; \vert\omega/\sigma\vert < \infty)\text{ or }(q+u = p+v;\; \vert\omega/\sigma\vert < 1);\\ a_i - a_k,\, d_h - d_f,\, s+a_i+d_h \ne 0,\pm1,\pm2,\ldots \text{ for}\\ 1 \le i \le n,\, 1 \le k \le n,\, 1 \le h \le r,\, 1 \le f \le r,\, j \ne k,\, h \ne f;\\ \text{see Conditions B1--B7}\end{array}\right]$
4		$\sigma^{-s}\displaystyle\sum_R$ $\left[\begin{array}{l}(q+u < p+v;\; \vert\omega/\sigma\vert < \infty)\text{ or }(q+u = p+v;\; \vert\omega/\sigma\vert > 1);\\ b_j - b_k,\, c_g - c_f,\, s+b_j+c_g \ne 0,\pm1,\pm2,\ldots \text{ for}\\ 1 \le j \le m,\, 1 \le k \le m,\, 1 \le g \le t,\, 1 \le f \le t,\, j \ne k,\, g \ne f;\\ \text{see Conditions B1--B7}\end{array}\right]$
5		$\sigma^{-s}\displaystyle\sum_L = \sigma^{-s}\displaystyle\sum_R$ $\left[\begin{array}{l}q+u = p+v;\; m+n+r+t-(p+q+u+v)/2 > 0;\\ \text{see Conditions B1--B7}\end{array}\right]$

The following formula is valid if the integers k and ℓ are mutually prime. If this is not the case and M is the greatest common divisor of k and ℓ, one should make the change of variable of integration $x \to x^{1/M}$:

No.	$f(x)$	$F(s)$
6	$G_{pq}^{mn}\left(\omega x^\ell \left\vert \begin{array}{c}(a_p)\\(b_q)\end{array}\right.\right)$ $\times G_{uv}^{rt}\left(\sigma x^k \left\vert \begin{array}{c}(c_u)\\(d_v)\end{array}\right.\right)$	$\dfrac{k^{\mu-1}\ell^{\rho+s(v-u)/k-1}\sigma^{-s/k}}{(2\pi)^R}G_{kp+\ell v,\,kq+\ell u}^{km+\ell t,\,kn+\ell r}\left(\dfrac{k^{k(p-q)}\omega^k}{\ell\ell^{(u-v)}\sigma^\ell}\left\vert \begin{array}{c}\Delta(k,(a_n)),\\ \Delta(k,(b_m)),\end{array}\right.\right.$ $\left.\begin{array}{c}\Delta\left(\ell, 1-(d_v)-\frac{s}{k}\right),\,\Delta(k,(a_{n+1})),\ldots,\Delta(k,(a_p))\\ \Delta\left(\ell, 1-(c_u)-\frac{s}{k}\right),\,\Delta(k,(b_{m+1})),\ldots,\Delta(k,(b_q))\end{array}\right)$

No.	$f(x)$	$F(s)$

$$
\begin{aligned}
&R = (k-1)\,c^* + (\ell-1)\,b^*;\\
&k,\,\ell = 1,\,2,\,...;\; 0 \le m \le q;\; 0 \le n \le p;\; 0 \le r \le v;\\
&0 \le t \le u;\; 0 \le q-p \le 2;\; -2 \le v-u;\; \sigma \ne 0;\; \omega \ne 0;\\
&a_i - b_j \ne 1,\,2,\,\ldots;\; i = 1,\,2,\,...,n;\; j = 1,\,2,\,\ldots,m;\\
&c_g - d_h \ne 1,\,2,\,\ldots;\; g = 1,\,\ldots,t;\; h = 1,\,\ldots,r;\\
&\text{see Conditions B1–B7 with the substitution}\\
&m \to km,\; n \to kn,\; p \to kp,\; q \to kq,\\
&r \to \ell r,\; t \to \ell t,\; u \to \ell u,\; v \to \ell v,\\
&a_p \to \Delta\left(k,\,(a_p)\right),\, b_q \to \Delta\left(k,\,(b_q)\right),\\
&c_u \to \Delta\left(k,\,(c_u)\right),\, d_v \to \Delta\left(k,\,(d_v)\right),\\
&\sigma \to \sigma^\ell \ell^{-\ell(v-u)},\; \omega \to \omega^k k^{-k(q-p)},\; s \to s/(k\ell)
\end{aligned}
$$

7

$$
G_{pq}^{mn}\left(\omega x^{\ell/k}\,\middle|\,\begin{matrix}(a_p)\\(b_q)\end{matrix}\right)
$$

$$
\times\, G_{uv}^{rt}\left(\sigma x\,\middle|\,\begin{matrix}(c_u)\\(d_v)\end{matrix}\right)
$$

$$
\frac{k^{\mu}\,\ell^{\rho+s(v-u)-1}\,\sigma^{-s}}{(2\pi)^{(\ell-1)b^*+(k-1)c^*}}\,G_{kp+\ell v,\,kq+\ell u}^{km+\ell t,\,kn+\ell r}\left(\frac{k^{k(p-q)}\omega^k}{\ell^{\ell(u-v)}\sigma^\ell}\,\middle|\,\begin{matrix}\Delta\left(k,(a_n)\right),\\ \Delta\left(k,(b_m)\right),\end{matrix}\right.
$$

$$
\left.\begin{matrix}\Delta\left(\ell,\,1-(d_v)-s\right),\,\Delta\left(k,\,a_{n+1}\right),\ldots,\Delta\left(k,\,a_p\right)\\ \Delta\left(\ell,\,1-(c_u)-s\right),\,\Delta\left(k,\,b_{m+1}\right),\ldots,\Delta\left(k,\,b_q\right)\end{matrix}\right)
$$

One of the following conditions holds (if $mr=0$ or $nt=0$, the 2° and 3° are omitted, respectively):

1) $mnrt \ne 0$; $b^*,\,c^* > 0$; $|\arg\sigma| < b^*\pi$; $|\arg\omega| < c^*\pi$; 1°–3°;

2) $u = v$; $b^* = 0$; $c^*,\,\sigma > 0$; $|\arg\omega| < c^*\pi$; $|\operatorname{Re}\rho| < 1$; 1°–3°;

3) $p = q$; $b^*,\,\omega > 0$; $c^* = 0$; $|\arg\sigma| < b^*\pi$; $|\operatorname{Re}\mu| < 1$; 1°–3°;

4) $p = q$; $u = v$; $b^* = c^* = 0$; $\sigma,\,\omega > 0$; $\operatorname{Re}\mu,\,\operatorname{Re}\rho < 1$; $\sigma^l \ne \omega^k$; 1°–3°;

5) $p = q$; $u = v$; $b^* = c^* = 0$; $\sigma,\,\omega > 0$; $\operatorname{Re}(\mu+\rho) < 2$; $\sigma^l = \omega^k$; 1°–3°;

6) $p > q$; $r > 0$; $b^* > 0$; $c^* \ge 0$; $|\arg\sigma| < b^*\pi$; $|\arg\omega| = c^*\pi$; 1°–3°; 5°;

7) $p < q$; $t > 0$; $b^* > 0$; $c^* \ge 0$; $|\arg\sigma| < b^*\pi$; $|\arg\omega| = c^*\pi$; 1°–4°;

8) $m > 0$; $u > v$; $b^* \ge 0$; $c^* > 0$; $|\arg\sigma| = b^*\pi$; $|\arg\omega| < c^*\pi$; 1°–3°; 7°;

9) $n > 0$; $u < v$; $b^* \ge 0$; $c^* > 0$; $|\arg\sigma| < b^*\pi$; $|\arg\omega| = c^*\pi$; 1°–3°; 6°;

10) $p > q$; $u = v$; $b^* = 0$; $c^* \ge 0$; $\sigma > 0$; $|\arg\omega| = c^*\pi$; $\operatorname{Re}\rho < 1$; 1°–3°; 5°;

11) $p < q$; $u = v$; $b^* = 0$; $c^* \ge 0$; $\sigma > 0$; $|\arg\omega| = c^*\pi$; $\operatorname{Re}\rho < 1$; 1°–4°;

12) $p = q$; $u > v$; $b^* \ge 0$; $c^* = 0$; $|\arg\sigma| = b^*\pi$; $\omega > 0$; $\operatorname{Re}\mu < 1$; 1°–3°; 7°;

13) $p = q$; $u < v$; $b^* \ge 0$; $c^* = 0$; $|\arg\sigma| = b^*\pi$; $\omega > 0$; $\operatorname{Re}\mu < 1$; 1°–3°; 6°;

14) $p < q$; $u > v$; $b^*,\,c^* \ge 0$; $|\arg\sigma| = b^*\pi$; $|\arg\omega| = c^*\pi$; 1°–4°; 7°;

15) $p > q$; $u < v$; $b^*,\,c^* \ge 0$; $|\arg\sigma| = b^*\pi$; $|\arg\omega| = c^*\pi$; 1°–3°; 5°; 6°;

16) $p > q$; $u > v$; $b^*,\,c^* \ge 0$; $|\arg\sigma| = b^*\pi$; $|\arg\omega| = c^*\pi$; 1°–3°; 5°; 7°; 8°; 10°;

17) $p < q$; $u < v$; $b^*,\,c^* \ge 0$; $|\arg\sigma| = b^*\pi$; $|\arg\omega| = c^*\pi$; 1°–4°; 6°; 9°; 10°;

18) $t = 0$; $r,\,b^*,\,\varphi > 0$; $|\arg\sigma| < b^*\pi$; 1°–2°;

19) $t > 0$; $r = 0$; $b^* > 0$; $\varphi < 0$; $|\arg\sigma| < b^*\pi$; 1°; 3°;

20) $m > 0$; $n = 0$; $c^* > 0$; $\varphi < 0$; $|\arg\omega| < c^*\pi$; 1°–2°;

No.	$f(x)$	$F(s)$

21) $m = 0$; $n > 0$; c^*, $\varphi > 0$; $|\arg \omega| < c^*\pi$; $1°$; $3°$;

22) $rt = 0$; b^*, $c^* > 0$; $|\arg \sigma| < b^*\pi$; $|\arg \omega| < c^*\pi$; $1°$–$3°$;

23) $mn = 0$; b^*, $c^* > 0$; $|\arg \sigma| < b^*\pi$; $|\arg \omega| < c^*\pi$; $1°$–$3°$;

24) $m + n > p$; $t = \varphi = 0$; r, $b^* > 0$; $c^* < 0$; $|\arg \sigma| < b^*\pi$;

$\quad |\arg \omega| < (m + n - p + 1)\pi$; $1°$; $2°$; $10°$; $11°$;

25) $m + n > q$; $r = \varphi = 0$; t, $b^* > 0$; $c^* < 0$; $|\arg \sigma| < b^*\pi$;

$\quad |\arg \omega| < (m + n - q + 1)\pi$; $1°$; $3°$; $10°$; $11°$;

26) $p = q - 1$; $t = \varphi = 0$; $r > 0$; $b^* > 0$; $c^* \geq 0$; $|\arg \sigma| < b^*\pi$;

$\quad c^*\pi < |\arg \omega| < (c^* + 1)\pi$; $1°$; $2°$; $10°$; $11°$;

27) $p = q + 1$; $r = \varphi = 0$; $t > 0$; $b^* > 0$; $c^* \geq 0$; $|\arg \sigma| < b^*\pi$;

$\quad c^*\pi < |\arg \omega| < (c^* + 1)\pi$; $1°$; $3°$; $10°$; $11°$;

28) $p < q - 1$; $t = \varphi = 0$; $r > 0$; $b^* > 0$; $c^* \geq 0$; $|\arg \sigma| < b^*\pi$;

$\quad c^*\pi < |\arg \omega| < (m + n - p + 1)\pi$; $1°$; $2°$; $10°$; $11°$;

29) $p > q - 1$; $r = \varphi = 0$; $t > 0$; $b^* > 0$; $c^* \geq 0$; $|\arg \sigma| < b^*\pi$;

$\quad c^*\pi < |\arg \omega| < (m + n - q + 1)\pi$; $1°$; $3°$; $10°$; $11°$;

30) $n = \varphi = 0$; $r + t > u$; $m > 0$; $b^* < 0$; $c^* > 0$; $|\arg \sigma| < (r + t - u + 1)\pi$;

$\quad |\arg \omega| < c^*\pi$; $1°$; $2°$; $10°$; $11°$;

31) $m = \varphi = 0$; $r + t > v$; $n > 0$; $b^* < 0$; $c^* > 0$; $|\arg \sigma| < (r + t - v + 1)\pi$;

$\quad |\arg \omega| < c^*\pi$; $1°$; $3°$; $10°$; $11°$;

32) $n = \varphi = 0$; $u = v - 1$; $m > 0$; $b^* \geq 0$; $c^* > 0$; $b^*\pi < |\arg \sigma| < (b^* + 1)\pi$;

$\quad |\arg \omega| < c^*\pi$; $1°$; $2°$; $10°$; $11°$;

33) $m = \varphi = 0$; $u = v + 1$; $n > 0$; $b^* \geq 0$; $c^* > 0$; $b^*\pi < |\arg \sigma| < (b^* + 1)\pi$;

$\quad |\arg \omega| < c^*\pi$; $1°$; $3°$; $10°$; $11°$;

34) $n = \varphi = 0$; $u < v - 1$; $m > 0$; $b^* \geq 0$; $c^* > 0$;

$\quad b^*\pi < |\arg \sigma| < (r + t - u + 1)\pi$; $|\arg \omega| < c^*\pi$; $1°$; $2°$; $10°$; $11°$;

35) $m = \varphi = 0$; $u > v + 1$; $n > 0$; $b^* \geq 0$; $c^* > 0$;

$\quad b^*\pi < |\arg \sigma| < (r + t - v + 1)\pi$; $|\arg \omega| < c^*\pi$; $1°$; $3°$; $10°$; $11°$.

$$b^* = r + t - \frac{u + v}{2}, \quad c^* = m + n - \frac{p + q}{2}.$$

| 8 | $G_{uv}^{rt}\left(x + \sigma \left\vert \begin{matrix} (c_u) \\ (d_v) \end{matrix} \right.\right)$ $\times G_{pq}^{mn}\left(\omega x \left\vert \begin{matrix} (a_p) \\ (b_q) \end{matrix} \right.\right)$ | $\displaystyle\sum_{k=0}^{\infty} \frac{(-\sigma)^k}{k!} G_{p+v+1,\, q+u+1}^{m+t,\, n+r+1}\left(\omega \left\vert \begin{matrix} 1-s, \\ (b_m), \end{matrix}\right.\right.$ $\left.\begin{matrix} k - s - (d_v) + 1,\, a_{n+1}, \ldots, a_p \\ k - s - (c_u) + 1,\, k - s + 1,\, b_{m+1}, \ldots, b_q \end{matrix}\right)$ $\left[\begin{matrix} b^*,\, c^* > 0;\ |\arg \sigma| < \pi;\ |\arg \omega| < c^*\pi; \\ -\min_{1 \leq j \leq m} \mathrm{Re}\, b_j < \mathrm{Re}\, s < 2 - \max_{1 \leq i \leq n} \mathrm{Re}\, a_i - \max_{1 \leq k \leq t} \mathrm{Re}\, c_k \end{matrix}\right]$ |

3.37. Various Special Functions

3.37.1. The exponential integral $E_\nu(z)$

More formulas can be obtained from the corresponding sections due to the relations

$$E_\nu(z) = z^{\nu-1}\Gamma(1-\nu, z), \quad E_\nu(z) = z^{\nu-1}\Gamma(1-\nu) - \frac{1}{1-\nu}\,{}_1F_1\left(\begin{matrix}1-\nu\\2-\nu; -z\end{matrix}\right),$$

$$E_\nu(z) = z^{\nu-1}e^{-z}\Psi(\nu, \nu; z), \quad E_\nu(z) = G_{12}^{20}\left(z\,\bigg|\,\begin{matrix}\nu\\\nu-1, 0\end{matrix}\right).$$

No.	$f(x)$	$F(s)$
1	$E_\nu(ax)$	$\dfrac{a^{-s}}{s+\nu-1}\Gamma(s)$ $\quad\left[\begin{matrix}(\operatorname{Re}a > 0;\ \operatorname{Re}s > 1 - \operatorname{Re}\nu, 0)\ \text{or}\\(\operatorname{Re}a = 0;\ 0,\ 1 - \operatorname{Re}\nu < \operatorname{Re}s < 2)\end{matrix}\right]$
2	$E_\nu(ax) - \Gamma(1-\nu)(ax)^{\nu-1}$ $+ \dfrac{1}{1-\nu}$	$\dfrac{a^{-s}}{s+\nu-1}\Gamma(s)$ $\quad[\operatorname{Re}a \geq 0;\ -1 < \operatorname{Re}s < 1 - \operatorname{Re}\nu, 0]$
3	$E_\nu(ax) - \Gamma(1-\nu)(ax)^{\nu-1}$ $+ \sum_{k=0}^{n}\dfrac{(-ax)^k}{k!(k-\nu+1)}$	$\dfrac{a^{-s}}{s+\nu-1}\Gamma(s)$ $\quad[\operatorname{Re}a \geq 0;\ -n-1 < \operatorname{Re}s < -n,\ 1 - \operatorname{Re}\nu]$
4	$e^{ax}E_\nu(ax)$	$\pi a^{-s}\csc(s\pi)\Gamma\left[\begin{matrix}s+\nu-1\\\nu\end{matrix}\right]$ $\quad[0, 1 - \operatorname{Re}\nu < \operatorname{Re}s < 1]$
5	$\Gamma(1-\nu, -ax)E_\nu(ax)$	$\dfrac{\pi}{s+\nu-1}a^{(\nu-s-1)/2}(-a)^{(1-\nu-s)/2}\sec\dfrac{(s-\nu)\pi}{2}\Gamma\left[\begin{matrix}s\\\nu\end{matrix}\right]$ $\quad[|1 - \operatorname{Re}\nu| < \operatorname{Re}s < \operatorname{Re}\nu + 1]$
6	$E_\nu(-ax)E_\nu(ax)$	$\dfrac{\pi}{s+2\nu-2}a^{-s/2}(-a)^{-s/2}\csc\dfrac{s\pi}{2}\Gamma\left[\begin{matrix}s+\nu-1\\\nu\end{matrix}\right]$ $\quad[0, 1 - \operatorname{Re}\nu, 2 - 2\operatorname{Re}\nu < \operatorname{Re}s < 2]$
7	$E_\nu(-i\sqrt{ax})E_\nu(i\sqrt{ax})$	$\dfrac{\pi a^{-s}}{s+\nu-1}\csc(s\pi)\Gamma\left[\begin{matrix}2s+\nu-1\\\nu\end{matrix}\right]$ $\quad[0, 1 - \operatorname{Re}\nu,\ (1 - \operatorname{Re}\nu)/2 < \operatorname{Re}s < 1]$

3.37.2.   The theta functions $\theta_j\,(b,\,ax)$

No.	$f\,(x)$	$F\,(s)$
1	$\theta\,(a-x)\begin{Bmatrix} \theta_1\,(b,\,x/a) \\ \theta_2\,(b,\,x/a) \end{Bmatrix}$	$\dfrac{\pi a^s s^{-1/2}}{\cosh\,(\sqrt{s}\,\pi)}\begin{Bmatrix} \sinh\,(2b\sqrt{s}) \\ \sinh\,[(\pi-2b)\,\sqrt{s}] \end{Bmatrix}$ $[a,\ \operatorname{Re}s>0;\ -(1\pm1)\,\pi\le b\le(3\mp1)\,\pi/4]$
2	$\theta\,(a-x)\begin{Bmatrix} \theta_3\,(b,\,x/a) \\ \theta_4\,(b,\,x/a) \end{Bmatrix}$	$\dfrac{\pi a^s s^{-1/2}}{\sinh\,(\sqrt{s}\,\pi)}\begin{Bmatrix} \cosh\,[(\pi-2b)\,\sqrt{s}] \\ \cosh\,(2b\sqrt{s}) \end{Bmatrix}$ $[a,\ \operatorname{Re}s>0;\ -(1\mp1)\,\pi\le b\le(3\pm1)\,\pi/4]$
3	$\begin{Bmatrix} \theta_1\,(b,\,e^{-x}) \\ \theta_2\,(b,\,e^{-x}) \end{Bmatrix}$	$2^{2s-1}\pi^{2s-1/2}\,\Gamma\left(\dfrac{1-2s}{2}\right)\left[\zeta\left(1-2s,\,\dfrac{(3\pm3)\,\pi+4b}{8\pi}\right)\right.$ $+\,\zeta\left(1-2s,\,\dfrac{(5\mp3)\,\pi-4b}{8\pi}\right)$ $-\,\zeta\left(1-2s,\,\dfrac{(3\mp1)\,\pi+4b}{8\pi}\right)$ $\left.-\,\zeta\left(1-2s,\,\dfrac{(5\pm1)\,\pi-4b}{8\pi}\right)\right]$ $[\operatorname{Re}s>0;\ -(1\pm1)\,\pi/4\le b\le(3\mp1)\,\pi/4]$
4	$\begin{Bmatrix} \theta_3\,(b,\,e^{-x})-1 \\ \theta_4\,(b,\,e^{-x})-1 \end{Bmatrix}$	$\Gamma\,(s)\left[\operatorname{Li}_{2s}\left(\pm e^{-2ib}\right)+\operatorname{Li}_{2s}\left(\pm e^{2ib}\right)\right]$ $[\operatorname{Re}s>1/2;\ -(1\mp1)\,\pi/4\le b\le(3\pm1)\,\pi/4]$
5	$\begin{Bmatrix} \theta_1\,(\pi/2,\,e^{-x}) \\ \theta_2\,(0,\,e^{-x}) \end{Bmatrix}$	$2\Gamma\,(s)\,\zeta\left(2s,\,\dfrac{1}{2}\right)$ $\qquad\qquad\qquad\qquad [\operatorname{Re}s>1/2]$
6	$\begin{Bmatrix} \theta_3\,(0,\,e^{-x})-1 \\ \theta_4\,(\pi/2,\,e^{-x})-1 \end{Bmatrix}$	$2\Gamma\,(s)\,\zeta\,(2s,\,0)$ $\qquad\qquad\qquad\qquad\qquad [\operatorname{Re}s>1/2]$
7	$\begin{Bmatrix} \theta_3\,(\pi/2,\,e^{-x})-1 \\ \theta_4\,(0,\,e^{-x})-1 \end{Bmatrix}$	$2\left(2^{1-2s}-1\right)\Gamma\,(s)\,\zeta\,(2s,\,0)$ $\qquad\qquad [\operatorname{Re}s>1/2]$
8	$-\theta_2\,(0,\,e^{-x})$ $+\,\theta_3\,(0,\,e^{-x})$ $-\,\theta_4\,(0,\,e^{-x})$	$2\left(2^{2s}-1\right)\left(2^{1-2s}-1\right)\Gamma\,(s)\,\zeta\,(2s,\,0)$ $\quad [\operatorname{Re}s>1/2]$

3.37.3. The generalized Fresnel integrals $S(z, \nu)$ and $C(z, \nu)$

More formulas can be obtained from the corresponding sections due to the relations

$$\left\{\begin{matrix} S(z, \nu) \\ C(z, \nu) \end{matrix}\right\} = \left\{\begin{matrix} \sin(\nu\pi/2) \\ \cos(\nu\pi/2) \end{matrix}\right\} \Gamma(\nu) - \frac{z^{\nu+\delta}}{\nu+\delta} \, {}_1F_2\left(\begin{matrix} \frac{\nu+\delta}{2}; -\frac{z^2}{4} \\ \frac{2\delta+1}{2}, \frac{\nu+\delta+2}{2} \end{matrix}\right), \quad \delta = \left\{\begin{matrix} 1 \\ 0 \end{matrix}\right\}.$$

1	$C(ax, \nu)$	$\dfrac{2^{s+\nu-1}\sqrt{\pi}}{s\,a^s} \Gamma\left[\begin{matrix} \frac{s+\nu}{2} \\ \frac{1-s-\nu}{2} \end{matrix}\right]$	$[a > 0;\ 0,\ -\operatorname{Re}\nu < \operatorname{Re}s < 2 - \operatorname{Re}\nu]$
2	$S(ax, \nu)$	$\dfrac{2^{s+\nu-1}\sqrt{\pi}}{s\,a^s} \Gamma\left[\begin{matrix} \frac{s+\nu+1}{2} \\ \frac{2-s-\nu}{2} \end{matrix}\right]$	$[a > 0;\ 0,\ -\operatorname{Re}\nu - 1 < \operatorname{Re}s < 2 - \operatorname{Re}\nu]$

3.37.4. The integral Bessel functions

More formulas can be obtained from the corresponding sections due to the relations

$$Ji_\nu(z) = -\frac{z^\nu}{2^\nu \nu^2 \Gamma(\nu)} \, {}_1F_2\left(\begin{matrix} \frac{\nu}{2}; -\frac{z^2}{4} \\ \frac{\nu+2}{2}, \nu+1 \end{matrix}\right) + \frac{1}{\nu};$$

$$\left\{\begin{matrix} Yi(z) \\ Ki(z) \end{matrix}\right\} = \pm\frac{1}{2\nu}\left\{\begin{matrix} \cot(\nu\pi/2) \\ \pi\csc(\nu\pi/2) \end{matrix}\right\} \pm \frac{\Gamma(-\nu)}{2\nu\pi}\left\{\begin{matrix} \cos\nu\pi \\ \pi \end{matrix}\right\}\left(\frac{z}{2}\right)^\nu {}_1F_2\left(\begin{matrix} \frac{\nu}{2}; \mp\frac{z^2}{4} \\ \frac{\nu+2}{2}, \nu+1 \end{matrix}\right)$$

$$\mp \frac{\Gamma(\nu)}{2\nu\pi}\left\{\begin{matrix} 1 \\ \pi \end{matrix}\right\}\left(\frac{z}{2}\right)^{-\nu} {}_1F_2\left(\begin{matrix} -\frac{\nu}{2}; \mp\frac{z^2}{4} \\ \frac{2-\nu}{2}, 1-\nu \end{matrix}\right), \quad \nu \neq \pm n.$$

1	$Ji_\nu(ax)$	$\dfrac{2^{s-1}}{s\,a^s} \Gamma\left[\begin{matrix} \frac{s+\nu}{2} \\ \frac{2-s+\nu}{2} \end{matrix}\right]$	$[a > 0;\ -\operatorname{Re}\nu,\ 0 < \operatorname{Re}s < 2]$
2	$Ki_\nu(ax)$	$\dfrac{2^{s-2}}{s\,a^s} \Gamma\left(\dfrac{s-\nu}{2}\right) \Gamma\left(\dfrac{s+\nu}{2}\right)$	$[a > 0;\ \operatorname{Re}s > |\operatorname{Re}\nu|]$
3	$Yi_\nu(ax)$	$\dfrac{2^{s-1}}{s\,a^s} \Gamma\left[\begin{matrix} \frac{s-\nu}{2}, \frac{s+\nu}{2} \\ \frac{3-s+\nu}{2}, \frac{s-\nu-1}{2} \end{matrix}\right]$	$[a > 0;\ |\operatorname{Re}\nu| < \operatorname{Re}s < 2]$

3.37.5. The Lommel functions

1	$s_{\mu, \nu}(ax)$	$\dfrac{2^{s+\mu-2}}{a^s} \Gamma\left[\begin{matrix} \frac{\mu-\nu+1}{2}, \frac{\mu+\nu+1}{2}, \frac{-s-\mu+1}{2}, \frac{s+\mu+1}{2} \\ \frac{2-s-\nu}{2}, \frac{2-s+\nu}{2} \end{matrix}\right]$	
		$[a > 0;\ |\operatorname{Re}(s+\mu)| < 1,\ \operatorname{Re}s < 3/2]$	
2	$S_{\mu, \nu}(ax)$	$\dfrac{2^{s+\mu-2}}{a^s} \Gamma\left[\begin{matrix} \frac{s-\nu}{2}, \frac{s+\nu}{2}, \frac{-s-\mu+1}{2}, \frac{s+\mu+1}{2} \\ \frac{1-\mu-\nu}{2}, \frac{1-\mu+\nu}{2} \end{matrix}\right]$	
		$[a > 0;\ |\operatorname{Re}(s+\mu)| < 1,\ \operatorname{Re}s < 3/2]$	

3.37.6. The Owen and $\mathcal{H}$-functions

No.	$f(x)$	$F(s)$
1	$T(ax, b)$	$\dfrac{2^{s/2-2}b}{\pi a^s}\,\Gamma\left(\dfrac{s}{2}\right)\,{}_2F_1\left(\begin{matrix}\frac{1}{2},\ \frac{s+2}{2}\\ \frac{3}{2};\ -b^2\end{matrix}\right)$ $$[\operatorname{Re}a^2,\ \operatorname{Re}\left(a^2+a^2b^2\right)<0;\ \operatorname{Re}s>0]$$
2	$e^{-cx^2}T(ax, b)$	$\dfrac{2^{s/2-2}b}{\pi\left(a^2+2c\right)^{s/2}}\,\Gamma\left(\dfrac{s}{2}\right)F_1\left(\dfrac{1}{2},\,1,\,\dfrac{s}{2};\,\dfrac{3}{2};\,-b^2,\,-\dfrac{a^2b^2}{a^2+2c}\right)$ $$[\operatorname{Re}a^2,\ \operatorname{Re}\left(a^2+a^2b^2\right)<2\operatorname{Re}c;\ \operatorname{Re}s>0]$$
3	$\mathcal{H}_\nu(x, a, b)$	$\dfrac{2^{s/2-3}\left(1-a^2\right)^\nu a^{s+1}}{\pi}\left[\sqrt{\pi}\,\Gamma\begin{bmatrix}\frac{2\nu+1}{2},\ \frac{s}{2}\\ \nu+1\end{bmatrix}{}_2F_1\left(\begin{matrix}\frac{2\nu+1}{2},\ \frac{s+2}{2}\\ \nu+1;\ 1-a^2\end{matrix}\right)\right.$ $$-\frac{2}{\left(2\nu+1\right)\left(1+a^2b^2\right)^{\nu+1/2}}\,\Gamma\left(\frac{s}{2}\right)$$ $$\left.\times F_1\left(\nu+\frac{1}{2};\,\frac{1}{2},\,\frac{s}{2}+1;\,\nu+\frac{3}{2};\,\frac{1}{1+a^2b^2},\,\frac{1-a^2}{1+a^2b^2}\right)\right]$$ $$[0<a\leq1;\ \operatorname{Re}s>0]$$

3.37.7. The Bessel–Maitland and generalized Bessel–Maitland functions

1	$J_\nu^\mu(ax)$	$a^{-s}\,\Gamma\begin{bmatrix}s\\ 1-\mu s+\nu\end{bmatrix}$ $\begin{bmatrix}(a>0,\ \operatorname{Re}\mu<1;\ \operatorname{Re}s>0)\ \text{or}\\ (a>0,\ \mu=1;\ 0<\operatorname{Re}s<(2\operatorname{Re}\nu+3)/4)\end{bmatrix}$
2	$J_{\nu,\lambda}^\mu(ax)$	$\dfrac{2^{s-1}}{a^s}\,\Gamma\begin{bmatrix}-\frac{s+2\lambda+\nu-2}{2},\ \frac{s+2\lambda+\nu}{2}\\ \frac{2-s-\nu}{2},\ \frac{2-\mu s-(2\lambda+\nu)\mu+2\lambda+2\nu}{2}\end{bmatrix}$ $\begin{bmatrix}(a>0,\ \operatorname{Re}\mu<1;\ -\operatorname{Re}(2\lambda+\nu)<\operatorname{Re}s<2-\operatorname{Re}(2\lambda+\nu))\ \text{or}\\ (a>0,\ \mu=1;\ -\operatorname{Re}(2\lambda+\nu)<\operatorname{Re}s<3/2,\ 2-\operatorname{Re}(2\lambda+\nu))\end{bmatrix}$

3.37.8. Other functions

1	$E_\rho(-x;\mu)$	$\Gamma\begin{bmatrix}s,\ 1-s\\ \mu-\frac{s}{\rho}\end{bmatrix}$ $\begin{bmatrix}(\rho>1/2;\ 0<\operatorname{Re}s<1)\ \text{or}\\ (\rho=1/2;\ 0<\operatorname{Re}s<1,\ \operatorname{Re}\mu/2)\end{bmatrix}$
2	$\mu(ae^{-x},1)$	$\dfrac{\pi(1-s)}{\sin(s\pi)}\,\mu(a,1-s)$
3	$\theta(1-x)\,\mu(-\ln x,\lambda)$	$\dfrac{1}{s\ln^{\lambda+1}s}$ $\quad[\operatorname{Re}\lambda>-1;\ \operatorname{Re}s>1]$

No.	$f(x)$	$F(s)$
4	$\mu(z, \lambda, x + \rho)$	$\Gamma(s)\,\mu(z, s + \lambda, \rho)$ $\qquad$ [$\text{Re}\,\lambda,\ \text{Re}\,\rho > -1;\ \text{Re}\,s > 0$]
5	$e^{\rho x}\mu(ae^{-x}, 1, \rho)$	$\Gamma(s)\,\Gamma(2 - s)\,\mu(a, 1 - s, \rho)$
6	$\theta(1 - x)\,\mu(-\ln x, \lambda, \rho)$	$\dfrac{1}{s^{\rho+1}\ln^{\lambda+1} s}$ $\qquad$ [$\text{Re}\,\lambda,\ \text{Re}\,\rho > -1;\ \text{Re}\,s > 1$]
7	$\dfrac{\theta(1 - x)}{\sqrt{-\ln x}}\,\mu\left(a\sqrt{-\ln x}, \lambda, \rho\right)$	$\dfrac{2^{\lambda+1}\sqrt{\pi}}{\sqrt{s}}\,\mu\left(\dfrac{a^2}{4s}, \lambda, \dfrac{\rho}{2}\right)$ $\qquad$ [$a > 0;\ \text{Re}\,\lambda > -1;\ \text{Re}\,\rho > -2$]
8	$\theta(1 - x)\,\mu\left(a\sqrt{-\ln x}, \lambda, \rho\right)$	$\dfrac{2^{\lambda}\sqrt{\pi}\,a}{s^{3/2}}\,\mu\left(\dfrac{a^2}{4s}, \lambda, \dfrac{\rho - 1}{2}\right)$ $\qquad$ [$a > 0;\ \text{Re}\,\lambda,\ \text{Re}\,\rho > -1$]
9	$\theta(a - x)\,\nu\left(\dfrac{x}{a}\right)$	$a^s\displaystyle\int_0^{\infty}\dfrac{dt}{(t + s)\,\Gamma(t + 1)}$ $\qquad$ [$a,\ \text{Re}\,s > 0$]
10	$\nu(e^{-x})$	$\dfrac{\pi}{\sin(s\pi)}\,\mu(1, -s)$ $\qquad$ [$\text{Re}\,s > 0$]
11	$\nu(ae^{-bx})$	$\dfrac{\pi}{b^s\sin(s\pi)}\,\mu(a, -s)$ $\qquad$ [$a,\ \text{Re}\,b > 0;\ 0 < \text{Re}\,s < 1$]
12	$\theta(1 - x)\,\nu(-\ln x)$	$\dfrac{1}{s\ln s}$ $\qquad$ [$\text{Re}\,s > 1$]
13	$\dfrac{\theta(1 - x)\,\nu\left(a\sqrt{-\ln x}\right)}{\sqrt{-\ln x}}$	$\dfrac{2\sqrt{\pi}}{\sqrt{s}}\,\nu\left(\dfrac{a^2}{4s}\right)$ $\qquad$ [$a,\ \text{Re}\,s > 0$]
14	$\nu(a, x + \rho)$	$\Gamma(s)\,\mu(a, s, \rho)$ $\qquad$ [$\text{Re}\,\rho > -1;\ a,\ \text{Re}\,s > 0$]
15	$\theta(1 - x)\,\nu(-\ln x, \rho)$	$\dfrac{1}{s^{\rho+1}\ln s}$ $\qquad$ [$\text{Re}\,\rho > -1;\ \text{Re}\,s > 1$]
16	$\dfrac{\theta(1 - x)\,\nu\left(a\sqrt{-\ln x}, \rho\right)}{\sqrt{-\ln x}}$	$\dfrac{2\sqrt{\pi}}{\sqrt{s}}\,\nu\left(\dfrac{a^2}{4s}, \dfrac{\rho}{2}\right)$ $\qquad$ [$a,\ \text{Re}\,s > 0;\ \text{Re}\,\rho > -2$]
17	$\theta(1 - x)\,\nu\left(a\sqrt{-\ln x}, \rho\right)$	$\dfrac{\sqrt{\pi}\,a}{s^{3/2}}\,\nu\left(\dfrac{a^2}{4s}, \dfrac{\rho - 1}{2}\right)$ $\qquad$ [$a,\ \text{Re}\,s > 0;\ \text{Re}\,\rho > -1$]

Appendix I
Some Properties of the Mellin Transforms

The integral

$$F(s) = \int_0^\infty x^{s-1} f(x)\, dx \qquad\qquad (\text{I.1})$$

is called the Mellin transform of the function $f(x)$.

The notations $\mathfrak{M}[f(x)](s)$ and $\mathfrak{M}[f(x); s]$ are used as well. Here $f(x)$ denotes a function of the real variable x, $0 \le x < \infty$, which is Lebesgue integrable over any interval $(0, A)$, $A > 0$, and $s = \sigma + i\tau$ is a complex number.

The Mellin transform is closely connected with the Fourier and Laplace transforms. The substitution $x = e^{-t}$ transforms (I.1) into the two-sided Laplace transform,

$$F(s) = \int_{-\infty}^\infty e^{-ts} f\left(e^{-t}\right)\, dt.$$

Change of variables $x = e^y$, $f(x) = g(y)$ in (I.1) yields

$$F(s) = \int_{-\infty}^\infty e^{sy} g(y)\, dy = (Fg)(is),$$

where

$$(Fg)(\xi) = \int_{-\infty}^\infty e^{-iy\xi} g(y)\, dy$$

is the Fourier transform of the function $g(y)$. Below, relations are given between the Mellin transform and some other integral transforms [15, 22].

1. **The Fourier cosine transform:**

$$\mathfrak{F}_c[f(t); x] = \sqrt{\frac{2}{\pi}} \int_0^\infty \cos(xt) f(t)\, dt,$$

$$\mathfrak{M}[\mathfrak{F}_c[f(t); s]] = \sqrt{\frac{2}{\pi}} \cos\frac{s\pi}{2} \Gamma(s)\, \mathfrak{M}[f(x); 1-s].$$

2. **The Fourier sine transform:**

$$\mathfrak{F}_s[f(t); x] = \sqrt{\frac{2}{\pi}} \int_0^\infty \sin(xt) f(t)\, dt,$$

$$\mathfrak{M}[\mathfrak{F}_s[f(t); x]; z] = \sqrt{\frac{2}{\pi}} \sin\frac{z\pi}{2} \Gamma(z)\, \mathfrak{M}[f(x); 1-z].$$

3. **The Laplace transform:**

$$\mathcal{L}\left[f\left(t\right);x\right]=\int_{0}^{\infty}e^{-xt}f\left(t\right)\,dt,$$

$$\mathfrak{M}\left[\mathcal{L}\left[f\left(t\right);x\right];s\right]=\Gamma\left(s\right)\mathfrak{M}\left[f\left(x\right);1-s\right].$$

4. **The Hankel transform:**

$$H_{\nu}\left[f\left(t\right);x\right]=\int_{0}^{\infty}\sqrt{xt}\,J_{\nu}\left(xt\right)f\left(t\right)\,dt,$$

$$\mathfrak{M}\left[H_{\nu}\left[f\left(t\right);x\right];s\right]=2^{s-1/2}\Gamma\left[\begin{array}{c}\frac{2s+2\nu+1}{4}\\\frac{3-2s+2\nu}{4}\end{array}\right]\mathfrak{M}\left[f\left(x\right);1-s\right].$$

5. **The Meijer transform:**

$$K_{\nu}\left[f\left(t\right);x\right]=\int_{0}^{\infty}\sqrt{xt}\,K_{\nu}\left(xt\right)f\left(t\right)\,dt,$$

$$\mathfrak{M}\left[K_{\nu}\left[f\left(t\right);x\right];s\right]=2^{s-3/2}\Gamma\left(\frac{2s+2\nu+1}{4}\right)\Gamma\left(\frac{2s-2\nu+1}{4}\right)\mathfrak{M}\left[f\left(x\right);1-s\right].$$

6. **The Y_{ν}–Bessel transform:**

$$Y_{\nu}\left[f\left(t\right);x\right]=\int_{0}^{\infty}\sqrt{xt}\,Y_{\nu}\left(xt\right)f\left(t\right)\,dt,$$

$$\mathfrak{M}\left[Y_{\nu}\left[f\left(t\right);x\right];s\right]=\frac{2^{s-1/2}}{\pi}\sin\frac{\left(2\nu-2s-3\right)\pi}{4}$$
$$\times\Gamma\left(\frac{2s-2\nu+1}{4}\right)\Gamma\left(\frac{2s+2\nu+1}{4}\right)\mathfrak{M}\left[f\left(x\right);1-s\right].$$

7. **The $\mathbf{H}_{\nu}$–Struve transform:**

$$\mathbf{H}_{\nu}\left[f\left(t\right);x\right]=\int_{0}^{\infty}\sqrt{xt}\,\mathbf{H}_{\nu}\left(xt\right)f\left(t\right)\,dt,$$

$$\mathfrak{M}\left[\mathbf{H}_{\nu}\left[f\left(t\right);x\right];s\right]=2^{s-1/2}\tan\frac{\left(2s+2\nu+1\right)\pi}{4}\Gamma\left[\begin{array}{c}\frac{2s+2\nu+1}{2}\\\frac{3-2s+2\nu}{4}\end{array}\right]\mathfrak{M}\left[f\left(x\right);1-s\right].$$

8. **The Hilbert transform:**

$$\mathcal{H}\left[f\left(t\right);x\right]=\int_{0}^{\infty}\frac{f\left(t\right)}{t-x}\,dt,$$

$$\mathfrak{M}\left[\mathcal{H}\left[f\left(t\right);x\right];s\right]=\frac{\Gamma\left(s\right)\Gamma\left(1-s\right)}{\Gamma\left(s+\frac{1}{2}\right)\Gamma\left(\frac{1}{2}-s\right)}\mathfrak{M}\left[f\left(x\right);s\right]=\cos\left(s\pi\right)\mathfrak{M}\left[f\left(x\right);s\right].$$

9. **The generalized Stieltjes transform:**

$$\mathcal{S}_{\nu}\left[f\left(t\right);x\right]=\int_{0}^{\infty}\frac{f\left(t\right)}{\left(x+t\right)^{\nu}}\,dt,$$

$$\mathfrak{M}\left[\mathcal{S}_{\nu}\left[f\left(t\right);x\right];s\right]=\mathrm{B}\left(s,\nu-s\right)\mathfrak{M}\left[f\left(x\right);s-\nu+1\right].$$

10. **The Liouville fractional integrals** [24]:

$$I_{0+}^{\nu} \left[f\left(t\right); x \right] = \frac{1}{\Gamma\left(\nu\right)} \int_0^x \left(x - t\right)^{\nu-1} f\left(t\right) dt,$$

$$\mathfrak{M} \left[I_{0+}^{\nu} \left[f\left(t\right); x \right]; s \right] = \frac{\Gamma\left(1 - s - \nu\right)}{\Gamma\left(1 - s\right)} \mathfrak{M} \left[f\left(x\right); s + \nu \right].$$

$$I_{-}^{\nu} \left[f\left(t\right); x \right] = \frac{1}{\Gamma\left(\nu\right)} \int_x^\infty \left(t - x\right)^{\nu-1} f\left(t\right) dt,$$

$$\mathfrak{M} \left[I_{-}^{\nu} \left[f\left(t\right); x \right]; s \right] = \frac{\Gamma\left(s\right)}{\Gamma\left(s + \nu\right)} \mathfrak{M} \left[f\left(x\right); s + \nu \right].$$

The inverse formula. The Mellin transform can be inverted under some conditions. For example, if $f\left(x\right)$ is analytic on $0 < x < \infty$ and satisfies the asymptotic conditions

$$f\left(x\right) = O\left(x^{-\alpha}\right), \quad x \to 0,$$
$$f\left(x\right) = O\left(x^{-\beta}\right), \quad x \to \infty,$$

where $\alpha < \beta$, then the function $F\left(s\right)$, defined by (I.1), is analytic in the strip $\alpha < \operatorname{Re} s < \beta$, and

$$f\left(x\right) = \frac{1}{2\pi i} \int_{\sigma-i\infty}^{\sigma+i\infty} x^{-s} F\left(s\right) ds = \mathfrak{M}^{-1} \left[F\left(s\right) \right], \quad \alpha < \sigma < \beta. \tag{I.2}$$

The simplest sufficient condition for the validity of the formulae (I.1) and (I.2) is provided by the continuity of $f\left(x\right)$ on $0 < x < \infty$ and the existence of the integral

$$\int_0^\infty x^{\sigma-1} |f\left(x\right)| dx < \infty. \tag{I.3}$$

Let us note two important properties of the Mellin transform [11]:

The convolution formula. If $F\left(s\right)$ and $G\left(s\right)$ are the Mellin transforms of $f\left(x\right)$ and $g\left(x\right)$, then

$$\mathfrak{M} \left[\int_0^\infty f\left(\xi\right) g\left(\frac{x}{\xi}\right) \frac{d\xi}{\xi}; s \right] = F\left(s\right) G\left(s\right). \tag{I.4}$$

The commutation formula. We have

$$\mathfrak{M} \left[x \frac{df\left(x\right)}{dx}; s \right] = -s \, \mathfrak{M} \left[f\left(x\right); s \right] \tag{I.5}$$

provided that $f\left(x\right)$ and $xf'\left(x\right)$ satisfy the condition (I.3), and

$$\lim_{x \to 0} x^s f\left(x\right) = \lim_{x \to \infty} x^s f\left(x\right) = 0.$$

One more important formula: If

$$F\left(s\right) = \int_0^\infty x^{s-1} f\left(x\right) dx, \quad G\left(s\right) = \int_0^\infty x^{s-1} g\left(x\right) dx,$$

and

$$h\left(t\right) = \int_0^\infty f\left(x\right) g\left(xt\right) dx,$$

then

$$\int_0^\infty t^{s-1} h\left(t\right) dt = F\left(1 - s\right) G\left(s\right).$$

In conclusion, we mention one more version of the Mellin transform that is useful in the theory of Dirichlet series [10]. Let

$$\Phi(s) = \sum_{n=1}^{\infty} a_n n^{-s}, \qquad \operatorname{Re} s > \alpha,$$

and

$$\varphi(x) = \sum_{n=1}^{\infty} a_n e^{-nx}, \qquad x > 0.$$

Then we have

$$\Phi(s) = \frac{1}{\Gamma(s)} \int_0^{\infty} x^{s-1} \varphi(x) \, dx \tag{I.6}$$

and

$$\varphi(x) = \frac{1}{2\pi i} \int_{\sigma-i\infty}^{\sigma+i\infty} x^{-s} \Gamma(s) \Phi(s) \, ds, \qquad \sigma > \alpha. \tag{I.7}$$

Putting $\Phi(s) = 1$ in (I.6), we obtain the integral representation of the gamma function:

$$\Gamma(s) = \int_0^{\infty} e^{-x} x^{s-1} \, dx, \quad \operatorname{Re} s > 0.$$

For $\Phi(s) = \zeta(s)$ in (I.6), we get the integral representation of the Riemann zeta function:

$$\zeta(s) = \frac{1}{\Gamma(s)} \int_0^{\infty} \frac{x^{s-1}}{e^x - 1} \, dx, \quad \operatorname{Re} s > 1.$$

Putting $\Phi(s) = 1$ in (I.7), we obtain the integral representation of the exponential function:

$$e^{-x} = \frac{1}{2\pi i} \int_{\sigma-i\infty}^{\sigma+i\infty} x^{-s} \Gamma(s) \, ds, \qquad \sigma > 0, \ |\arg x| < \pi/2.$$

For $\Phi(s) = \Gamma(s)$ in (I.7), we arrive at the integral representation of the Macdonald's function:

$$2K_0(2\sqrt{x}) = \frac{1}{2\pi i} \int_{\sigma-i\infty}^{\sigma+i\infty} x^{-s} \Gamma^2(s) \, ds, \qquad x, \sigma > 0.$$

Evaluation of integrals. We illustrate the Mellin transformation method in evaluation of integrals by some examples.

Example I.1. Let us derive the relation

$$\int_0^{\infty} t^{\alpha-1} e^{-t-t/x} \, dt = \Gamma(\alpha) \left(1 + \frac{1}{x}\right)^{-\alpha}, \tag{I.8}$$

where $\operatorname{Re} \alpha$, $\operatorname{Re}(1 + 1/x) > 0$. The integral has the form of the Mellin convolution of the functions

$$f(t) = t^{\alpha} e^{-t}, \qquad g(t) = e^{-1/t}.$$

Their Mellin transforms are

$$F(s) = \Gamma(s+\alpha), \qquad \operatorname{Re}(s+\alpha) > 0,$$

and

$$G(s) = \Gamma(-s), \qquad \operatorname{Re} s < 0.$$

Denoting the integral by $I(x, \alpha)$ we obtain its Mellin transform in the form

$$\mathfrak{M}[I(x, \alpha); s] = \Gamma(s+\alpha)\Gamma(-s), \qquad -\operatorname{Re}\alpha < \operatorname{Re} s < 0.$$

From the formula 2.1.2.3 we have

$$\mathfrak{M}\left[(1+x)^{-\alpha}; s\right] = \frac{1}{\Gamma(\alpha)} \Gamma(s)\Gamma(\alpha-s), \qquad 0 < \operatorname{Re} s < \operatorname{Re}\alpha,$$

whence, due to the relation 1.1.2.3, we get

$$\mathfrak{M}\left[\left(1+\frac{1}{x}\right)^{-\alpha}; s\right] = \frac{1}{\Gamma(\alpha)} \Gamma(-s)\Gamma(s+\alpha), \qquad -\operatorname{Re}\alpha < \operatorname{Re} s < 0,$$

and, finally,

$$I(x, \alpha) = \Gamma(\alpha)\left(1+\frac{1}{x}\right)^{-\alpha}, \qquad \operatorname{Re}\alpha, \ \operatorname{Re}(1+1/x) > 0.$$

Example I.2. Let us evaluate the integral

$$I(a, b, \alpha, \mu, \nu) = \int_0^\infty t^{\alpha-1} K_\mu(at) I_\nu(bt)\, dt. \qquad (1.9)$$

Making use of the formula $I_\nu(z) = (-i)^\nu J_\nu(iz)$, we transform the function I_ν into J_ν, for which the Mellin transform exists. Then the integral (I.9) takes the form

$$I(a, b, \alpha, \mu, \nu) = (-i)^\nu \int_0^\infty t^{\alpha-1} K_\mu(at) J_\nu(ibt)\, dt.$$

After substitutions

$$b \to -ic, \quad t \to \frac{2\sqrt{\tau}}{c}, \quad c \to \sqrt{x}$$

and

$$f(\eta) = K_\mu\left(\frac{2}{\sqrt{\eta}}\right) \eta^{-\alpha/2}, \qquad g(\tau) = J_\nu\left(2\sqrt{\tau}\right)$$

we obtain a relation of the form (I.4):

$$I(a, b, \alpha, \mu, \nu) = (-i)^\nu 2^{\alpha-1} a^{-\alpha} \mathfrak{M}^{-1}\left[F(s)\, G(s)\right].$$

The images of the corresponding functions can be found by making use of formulae (1.1.5.2), (3.14.1.3), and (3.10.1.2):

$$F(s) = \int_0^\infty t^{s-1} K_\mu\left(\frac{2}{\sqrt{t}}\right) t^{-\alpha/2}\, dt$$

$$= \frac{1}{2}\Gamma\left[\frac{\alpha+\mu}{2} - s, \frac{\alpha-\mu}{2} - s\right], \qquad \operatorname{Re} s < -\frac{|\operatorname{Re}(\alpha\pm\mu)|}{2};$$

$$G(s) = \int_0^\infty t^{s-1} J_\nu\left(2\sqrt{t}\right)\, dt$$

$$= \Gamma\left[\begin{matrix} s + \frac{\nu}{2} \\ 1 - s + \frac{\nu}{2} \end{matrix}\right], \qquad -\frac{\operatorname{Re}\nu}{2} < \operatorname{Re} s < \frac{3}{4}.$$

Multiplying them, we obtain

$$F(s)\, G(s) = \frac{1}{2}\Gamma\left[\begin{matrix} \frac{\alpha+\mu}{2} - s, \frac{\alpha-\mu}{2} - s, s + \frac{\nu}{2} \\ 1 - s + \frac{\nu}{2} \end{matrix}\right].$$

Now, with the aid of formulae 8.4.49.13 from [20], we find $\mathfrak{M}^{-1}[F(s)\, G(s)]$, and thereby the value of the integral (I.9):

$$I(a, b, \alpha, \mu, \nu) = 2^{\alpha-2} a^{-\alpha-\nu} b^\nu \Gamma\left[\frac{\alpha+\mu+\nu}{2}, \frac{\alpha-\mu+\nu}{2}, \nu+1\right]$$

$$\times {}_2F_1\left(\frac{\alpha+\mu+\nu}{2}, \frac{\alpha-\mu+\nu}{2}; \nu+1; \frac{b^2}{a^2}\right),$$

$$\operatorname{Re}(\alpha+\nu\pm\mu), \ \operatorname{Re}(a\pm b) > 0.$$

Example I.3. Consider the integral equation

$$y(x) + \int_0^\infty y(\xi)\, f\left(\frac{x}{\xi}\right)\frac{d\xi}{\xi} = g(x), \tag{I.10}$$

where f and g are known functions. Applying the Mellin transform (I.1) and the relation (I.4), we obtain the equality

$$Y(s) + F(s)Y(s) = G(s),$$

where Y, F, and G are the Mellin transforms of y, f, and g, respectively, and hence

$$Y(s) = \frac{G(s)}{1 + F(s)}.$$

Applying the inversion formula (I.2), we find the required solution

$$y(x) = \mathfrak{M}^{-1}\left[\frac{G(s)}{1 + F(s)}\right].$$

Example I.4. Consider the Laplace equation in polar coordinates [11]

$$\Delta u = \left(\frac{\partial^2}{\partial r^2} + \frac{1}{r}\frac{\partial}{\partial r} + \frac{1}{r^2}\frac{\partial^2}{\partial \varphi^2}\right)u = 0 \tag{I.11}$$

in the sector $0 < \varphi < \varphi_0 < 2\pi$, $0 < r < \infty$ with Dirichlet boundary conditions

$$u(r, \varphi)|_{\varphi=0} = u_0(r), \qquad u(r, \varphi)|_{\varphi=\varphi_0} = u_1(r). \tag{I.12}$$

We suppose that the solution is bounded at infinity and the so-called "Meixner condition on the edge" $\lim_{r\to 0}\sqrt{r}\,\frac{\partial u}{\partial r} = 0$ is satisfied. These conditions guarantee the uniqueness of the solution. Applying the Mellin transform with respect to the variable r, we get

$$U(s, \varphi) = \int_0^\infty r^{s-1} u(r, \varphi)\, dr.$$

The functions $U_0(s)$ and $U_1(s)$ are defined similarly. Now, by taking the commutation relation (I.5) into account, (I.11) and (I.12) are reduced to the ordinary differential equation for $U(s, \varphi)$

$$\left(U''_{\varphi\varphi}(s, \varphi)\right)^2 + U(s, \varphi) = 0 \tag{I.13}$$

with the boundary conditions

$$U(s, 0) = U_0(s), \qquad U(s, \varphi_0) = U_1(s). \tag{I.14}$$

Solving this boundary value problem and applying the inversion formula (I.2), we find the solution $u(r, \varphi)$.

Some other applications can be found, for example, in [2].

Appendix II
Conditions of Convergence

Exploring conditions of convergence of integrals at a point, we often can replace integrands with simpler asymptotic expressions containing only power, exponential, and trigonometric functions and providing the same conditions. For example, instead of behavior of the functions e^{ax-x^2} and $\sin\left(x^2 + 2x + a\right)$, when $x \to \infty$, we can consider behavior of e^{ax} and $\sin x^2$, respectively, and get the same conditions of convergence of the corresponding integral at infinity.

Below, we give some model integrals, their conditions of convergence, and a list of asymptotic analogues of elementary and special functions. Conditions for the majority of other integrals can be obtained by replacing integrands with their asymptotic analogues and comparing them with the formulas 1–9. Note that some integrals can require deeper investigation of asymptotics.

I. Convergence at $x = 0$:

1. $\displaystyle\int_0^1 x^\alpha \, dx$ $\qquad\qquad\qquad$ $[\operatorname{Re}\alpha > -1]$.

2. $\displaystyle\int_0^1 x^\alpha e^{ax^\beta} \, dx$ $\qquad\qquad$ $\begin{bmatrix} (\operatorname{Re}a,\, \beta > 0;\ \operatorname{Re}\alpha > -1)\ \text{or} \\ (\operatorname{Re}a < 0;\ \beta < 0)\ \text{or} \\ (\operatorname{Re}a < 0;\ \beta \geq 0;\ \operatorname{Re}\alpha > -1)\ \text{or} \\ (\operatorname{Re}a = 0;\ \operatorname{Re}\alpha > -1) \end{bmatrix}$.

II. Convergence at $x = \infty$:

3. $\displaystyle\int_1^\infty x^\alpha \, dx$ $\qquad\qquad\qquad$ $[\operatorname{Re}\alpha < -1]$.

4. $\displaystyle\int_1^\infty x^\alpha e^{-ax} \, dx$ $\qquad\qquad$ $\begin{bmatrix} (\operatorname{Re}a > 0)\ \text{or} \\ (\operatorname{Re}a = 0;\ \operatorname{Im}a \neq 0;\ \operatorname{Re}\alpha < 0) \end{bmatrix}$.

5. $\displaystyle\int_1^\infty x^\alpha e^{-ax^\beta} \, dx$ $\qquad\qquad$ $\begin{bmatrix} (\operatorname{Re}a > 0;\ \beta > 0)\ \text{or} \\ (\operatorname{Re}a > 0;\ \beta > 0;\ \operatorname{Re}\alpha < -1)\ \text{or} \\ (\operatorname{Re}a < 0;\ \beta < 0;\ \operatorname{Re}\alpha < -1)\ \text{or} \\ (\operatorname{Re}a = 0;\ \operatorname{Re}\alpha < \beta - 1) \end{bmatrix}$.

6. $\displaystyle\int_1^\infty x^\alpha \left\{ \begin{array}{c} \sin\left(ax\right) \\ \cos\left(ax\right) \end{array} \right\} dx$ $\qquad$ $[\operatorname{Im}a = 0;\ \operatorname{Re}\alpha < 0]$.

7. $\displaystyle\int_1^\infty x^\alpha \left\{ \begin{array}{c} \sin\left(ax^\beta\right) \\ \cos\left(ax^\beta\right) \end{array} \right\} dx$ $[\operatorname{Im} a = 0;\ \beta > 0;\ \operatorname{Re}\alpha < \beta - 1].$

8. $\displaystyle\int_1^\infty x^\alpha e^{ax^\beta} \left\{ \begin{array}{c} \sin\left(bx^\gamma\right) \\ \cos\left(bx^\gamma\right) \end{array} \right\} dx$ $\left[\begin{array}{l} (\operatorname{Re} a > 0;\ \operatorname{Im} b = 0;\ \alpha > 0;\ \beta < 0;\ \operatorname{Re}\alpha < \gamma - 1)\ \text{or} \\ (\operatorname{Re} a < 0;\ \operatorname{Im} b = 0;\ \beta,\ \gamma > 0)\ \text{or} \\ (\operatorname{Re} a = \operatorname{Im} b = 0;\ \alpha,\ \beta > 0;\ \operatorname{Re}\alpha < \beta + 1,\ \gamma + 1) \end{array}\right].$

The Cauchy principal value of the integral

$$\int_a^b f(x)\, dx$$

with a singular point $x = c \in (a, b)$ is defined as

$$\lim_{\varepsilon \to 0} \left(\int_a^{c-\varepsilon} f(x)\, dx + \int_{c+\varepsilon}^b f(x)\, dx \right);$$

for example,

$$\int_a^b \frac{1}{x-c}\, dx = \ln\frac{b-c}{c-a};\quad 0 < a < c < b.$$

III. Convergence at $x = c$ (Cauchy principal value):

9. $\displaystyle\int_a^b \frac{1}{x^r - c^r}\, dx$ $[0 < a < c < b].$

Asymptotic analogues of elementary and special functions

Definition. A set of functions $\left\{f_1(z),\ f_2(z),\dots,f_n(z)\right\}$, such that the integral

$$\int_a^b f(x)\, g(x)\, dx$$

converges or diverges at a point $x = c$ simultaneously with all integrals

$$\int_a^b f_i(x)\, g(x)\, dx,$$

is called asymptotic analogue of the function $f(x)$ at the point $x = c$. Note that asymptotic analogue is not the main term of asymptotics, though in some cases it can coincide with it. We use the notation

$$f(z) \Longrightarrow \left\{f_1(z),\ f_2(z),\dots,f_n(z)\right\}.$$

For $z \to \infty$, the functions $\sin z$ and $\sinh z$ in asymptotic analogues can be replaced with $\cos z$ and $\cosh z$, respectively.

For example, for the error function $\operatorname{erf}(z)$ that has asymptotic behaviour of the form

$$\operatorname{erf}(z) \sim \frac{2z}{\sqrt\pi} - \frac{2z^3}{3\sqrt\pi} + \dots,\qquad\qquad z \to 0,$$

$$\operatorname{erf}(z) \sim 1 + e^{-z^2}\left(-\frac{1}{\sqrt\pi z} + \frac{1}{2\sqrt\pi z^3} + \dots\right),\qquad\qquad z \to \infty,$$

we write

$$\operatorname{erf}(z) \Longrightarrow \left[\begin{array}{ll} z, & z \to 0, \\ \left\{1,\ \dfrac{e^{-z^2}}{z}\right\}, & z \to \infty. \end{array}\right.$$

More examples:

$$\sin(az) \Longrightarrow \left[\begin{array}{ll} z, & z \to 0, \\ \sin(az), & |z| \to \infty; \ \text{Im}(az) = 0, \\ e^{|\text{Im}(az)|}, & |z| \to \infty; \ \text{Im}(az) \neq 0. \end{array} \right.$$

$$J_\nu(az) \Longrightarrow \left[\begin{array}{ll} z^\nu, & z \to 0, \\ \dfrac{\sin(az)}{\sqrt{z}}, & |z| \to \infty; \ \text{Im}(az) = 0, \\ \dfrac{e^{|\text{Im}(az)|}}{\sqrt{z}}, & |z| \to \infty; \ \text{Im}(az) \neq 0. \end{array} \right.$$

Table of asymptotic analogues

$$(a + bz^r)^s \Longrightarrow \left[\begin{array}{ll} 1, & z \to 0; \ r > 0, \\ z^{rs}, & z \to 0; \ r < 0, \\ \left\{ \left[a + \left(\left(-\dfrac{a}{b}\right)^{1/r}\right)^r b\right]^s, \ \left[z - \left(-\dfrac{a}{b}\right)^{1/r}\right]^s \right\}, & z \to \left(-\dfrac{a}{b}\right)^{1/r}, \\ z^{rs}, & |z| \to \infty; \ r > 0, \\ 1, & |z| \to \infty; \ r < 0. \end{array} \right.$$

$$\sqrt{bz^r} \Longrightarrow \left[\begin{array}{ll} z^{r/2}, & z \to 0, \\ z^{r/2}, & |z| \to \infty. \end{array} \right.$$

$$\text{Ai}(z) \Longrightarrow \left[\begin{array}{ll} 1, & z \to 0, \\ \dfrac{e^{-2z^{3/2}/3}}{\sqrt[4]{z}}, & |z| \to \infty; \ -\dfrac{2\pi}{3} < \arg z \leq \dfrac{2\pi}{3}, \\ \left\{ \dfrac{e^{-2z^{3/2}/3}}{\sqrt[4]{z}}, \ \dfrac{e^{2z^{3/2}/3}}{\sqrt[4]{z}} \right\}, & |z| \to \infty; \ \text{otherwise}. \end{array} \right.$$

$$\text{Ai}'(z) \Longrightarrow \left[\begin{array}{ll} 1, & z \to 0, \\ \sqrt[4]{z}\,e^{-2z^{3/2}/3}, & |z| \to \infty; \ -\dfrac{2\pi}{3} < \arg z \leq \dfrac{2\pi}{3}, \\ \left\{ \sqrt[4]{z}\,e^{-2z^{3/2}/3}, \ \sqrt[4]{z}\,e^{2z^{3/2}/3} \right\}, & |z| \to \infty; \ \text{otherwise}. \end{array} \right.$$

$$\arccos z \Longrightarrow \left[\begin{array}{ll} 1, & z \to 0, \\ \sqrt{1-z}, & z \to 1, \\ 1, & z \to -1, \\ \{1, \ \ln z\}, & |z| \to \infty. \end{array} \right.$$

$$\text{arccosh}\, z \Longrightarrow \left[\begin{array}{ll} 1, & z \to 0, \\ \sqrt{z-1}, & z \to 1, \\ 1, & z \to -1, \\ \{1, \ \ln z\}, & |z| \to \infty. \end{array} \right.$$

$$\operatorname{arccot} z \Longrightarrow \begin{bmatrix} 1, & z \to 0, \\ \{1,\ \ln(z-i)\}, & z \to i, \\ \{1,\ \ln(z+i)\}, & z \to -i, \\ \dfrac{1}{z}, & |z| \to \infty. \end{bmatrix}$$

$$\operatorname{arccoth} z \Longrightarrow \begin{bmatrix} 1, & z \to 0, \\ \{1,\ \ln(z-1)\}, & z \to 1, \\ \{1,\ \ln(z+1)\}, & z \to -1, \\ \dfrac{1}{z}, & |z| \to \infty. \end{bmatrix}$$

$$\operatorname{arccsc} z \Longrightarrow \begin{bmatrix} \{1,\ \ln z\}, & z \to 0, \\ 1, & z \to 1, \\ 1, & z \to -1, \\ \dfrac{1}{z}, & |z| \to \infty. \end{bmatrix}$$

$$\operatorname{arccsch} z \Longrightarrow \begin{bmatrix} \{1,\ \ln z\}, & z \to 0, \\ 1, & z \to i, \\ 1, & z \to -i, \\ \dfrac{1}{z}, & |z| \to \infty. \end{bmatrix}$$

$$\operatorname{arcsec} z \Longrightarrow \begin{bmatrix} \{1,\ \ln z\}, & z \to 0, \\ \sqrt{z-1}, & z \to 1, \\ 1, & z \to -1, \\ 1, & |z| \to \infty. \end{bmatrix}$$

$$\operatorname{arcsech} z \Longrightarrow \begin{bmatrix} \{1,\ \ln z\}, & z \to 0, \\ \sqrt{1-z}, & z \to 1, \\ 1, & z \to -1, \\ 1, & |z| \to \infty. \end{bmatrix}$$

$$\operatorname{arcsin} z \Longrightarrow \begin{bmatrix} z, & z \to 0, \\ 1, & z \to 1, \\ 1, & z \to -1, \\ \{1,\ \ln z\}, & |z| \to \infty. \end{bmatrix}$$

$$\mathrm{arcsinh}\,z \Longrightarrow \begin{bmatrix} z, & z \to 0, \\ 1, & z \to i, \\ 1, & z \to -i, \\ \{1,\ \ln z\}, & |z| \to \infty. \end{bmatrix}$$

$$\arctan z \Longrightarrow \begin{bmatrix} z, & z \to 0, \\ \{1,\ \ln(z-i)\}, & z \to i, \\ \{1,\ \ln(z+i)\}, & z \to -i, \\ 1, & |z| \to \infty. \end{bmatrix}$$

$$\mathrm{arctanh}\,z \Longrightarrow \begin{bmatrix} z, & z \to 0, \\ \{1,\ \ln(1-z)\}, & z \to 1, \\ \{1,\ \ln(1+z)\}, & z \to -1, \\ 1, & |z| \to \infty. \end{bmatrix}$$

$$\mathrm{bei}_\nu(z) \Longrightarrow \begin{bmatrix} \{\nu z^\nu,\ z^{\nu+2}\}, & z \to 0, \\ \left\{\dfrac{e^{(-1)^{1/4}z}}{\sqrt{z}},\ \dfrac{e^{(-1)^{3/4}z}}{\sqrt{z}},\ \dfrac{e^{-(-1)^{1/4}z}}{\sqrt{z}},\ \dfrac{e^{-(-1)^{3/4}z}}{\sqrt{z}}\right\}, & |z| \to \infty. \end{bmatrix}$$

$$\mathrm{ber}_\nu(z) \Longrightarrow \begin{bmatrix} z^\nu, & z \to 0, \\ \left\{\dfrac{e^{(-1)^{1/4}z}}{\sqrt{z}},\ \dfrac{e^{(-1)^{3/4}z}}{\sqrt{z}},\ \dfrac{e^{-(-1)^{1/4}z}}{\sqrt{z}},\ \dfrac{e^{-(-1)^{3/4}z}}{\sqrt{z}}\right\}, & |z| \to \infty. \end{bmatrix}$$

$$\mathrm{Bi}(z) \Longrightarrow \begin{bmatrix} 1, & z \to 0, \\ \left\{\dfrac{e^{-2z^{3/2}/3}}{\sqrt[4]{z}},\ \dfrac{e^{2z^{3/2}/3}}{\sqrt[4]{z}}\right\}, & |z| \to \infty. \end{bmatrix}$$

$$\mathrm{Bi}'(z) \Longrightarrow \begin{bmatrix} 1, & z \to 0, \\ \left\{\sqrt[4]{z}\,e^{-2z^{3/2}/3},\ \sqrt[4]{z}\,e^{2z^{3/2}/3}\right\}, & |z| \to \infty. \end{bmatrix}$$

$$C(z) \Longrightarrow \begin{bmatrix} \sqrt{z}, & z \to 0, \\ \left\{1,\ \dfrac{\sin z}{\sqrt{z}}\right\}, & |z| \to \infty. \end{bmatrix}$$

$$C_n^\lambda(z) \Longrightarrow \begin{bmatrix} z^{n-2[n/2]}, & z \to 0, \\ z^n, & |z| \to \infty. \end{bmatrix}$$

$$\mathrm{chi}(z) \Longrightarrow \begin{bmatrix} \{1,\ \ln z\}, & z \to 0, \\ \left\{1,\ \dfrac{\sinh z}{z}\right\}, & |z| \to \infty;\ \arg z = \pi/2, \\ \dfrac{\sinh z}{z}, & |z| \to \infty;\ \arg z \ne \pi/2. \end{bmatrix}$$

$$\operatorname{ci}(z) \Longrightarrow \left[\begin{array}{ll} \{1,\ \ln z\}, & z \to 0, \\[2mm] \left\{1,\ \dfrac{\sin z}{z}\right\}, & z \to -\infty, \\[3mm] \dfrac{\sin z}{z}, & |z| \to \infty;\ \arg z \neq \pi. \end{array} \right.$$

$$\cos z \Longrightarrow \left[\begin{array}{ll} 1, & z \to 0, \\[1mm] \cos z, & z \to \infty;\ \operatorname{Im} z = 0, \\[1mm] e^{|\operatorname{Im} z|}, & |z| \to \infty;\ \operatorname{Im} z \neq 0. \end{array} \right.$$

$$\cosh z \Longrightarrow \left[\begin{array}{ll} 1, & z \to 0, \\[1mm] \cosh z, & z \to \infty;\ \operatorname{Re} z = 0, \\[1mm] e^{|\operatorname{Re} z|}, & |z| \to \infty;\ \operatorname{Re} z \neq 0. \end{array} \right.$$

$$\cot z \Longrightarrow \left[\begin{array}{ll} \dfrac{1}{z}, & z \to 0, \\[3mm] \cot z, & z \to \infty;\ \operatorname{Im} z = 0, \\[2mm] \dfrac{1}{z - n\pi} & z \to n\pi;\ n = 0, \pm 1, \pm 2, \ldots \\[3mm] 1, & |z| \to \infty;\ \operatorname{Im} z \neq 0. \end{array} \right.$$

$$\coth z \Longrightarrow \left[\begin{array}{ll} \dfrac{1}{z}, & z \to 0, \\[3mm] \coth z, & z \to \infty;\ \operatorname{Re} z = 0, \\[2mm] \dfrac{1}{z - n\pi i}, & z \to n\pi i;\ n = 0, \pm 1, \pm 2, \ldots, \\[3mm] 1, & |z| \to \infty;\ \operatorname{Re} z \neq 0. \end{array} \right.$$

$$\csc z \Longrightarrow \left[\begin{array}{ll} \dfrac{1}{z}, & z \to 0, \\[3mm] \dfrac{1}{z - n\pi}, & z \to n\pi;\ n = 0, \pm 1, \pm 2, \ldots, \\[3mm] \csc z, & z \to \infty;\ \operatorname{Im} z = 0, \\[2mm] e^{-|\operatorname{Im} z|}, & |z| \to \infty;\ \operatorname{Im} z \neq 0. \end{array} \right.$$

$$\operatorname{csch} z \Longrightarrow \left[\begin{array}{ll} \dfrac{1}{z}, & z \to 0, \\[3mm] \dfrac{1}{z - n\pi i}, & z \to n\pi i,\ n = 0, \pm 1, \pm 2, \ldots, \\[3mm] \operatorname{csch} z, & z \to \infty;\ \operatorname{Re} z = 0, \\[2mm] e^{-|\operatorname{Re} z|}, & |z| \to \infty;\ \operatorname{Re} z \neq 0. \end{array} \right.$$

$$\mathbf{D}(z) \Longrightarrow \left[\begin{array}{ll} 1, & z \to 0, \\[1mm] \{1,\ \ln(1 - z)\}, & z \to 1, \\[1mm] \{1,\ \ln(1 + z)\}, & z \to -1, \\[1mm] \dfrac{1}{z}, & |z| \to \infty. \end{array} \right.$$

$$D_\nu(z) \implies \begin{bmatrix} 1, & z \to 0, \\ z^\nu e^{-z^2/4}, & |z| \to \infty; \ -\dfrac{\pi}{2} < \arg z \le \dfrac{\pi}{2}, \\ \left\{ z^\nu e^{-z^2/4}, \dfrac{z^{-\nu-2} e^{z^2/4}}{\Gamma(-\nu)} \right\}, & |z| \to \infty\,. \end{bmatrix}$$

$$\mathbf{E}_\nu(z) \implies \begin{bmatrix} 1, & z \to 0, \\ \left\{ \dfrac{1}{z}, \dfrac{\cos z}{\sqrt{z}} \right\}, & |z| \to \infty; \ \mathrm{Im}\, z = 0; \ \nu = \pm\dfrac{1}{2}, \pm\dfrac{3}{2}, \ldots, \\ \left\{ \dfrac{1}{z}, \dfrac{e^{|\mathrm{Im}\, z|}}{\sqrt{z}} \right\} & |z| \to \infty; \ \mathrm{Im}\, z \ne 0; \ \nu \ne \pm\dfrac{1}{2}, \pm\dfrac{3}{2}, \ldots \end{bmatrix}$$

$$\mathbf{E}(z) \implies \begin{bmatrix} 1, & z \to 0, \\ 1, & z \to 1, \\ 1, & z \to -1, \\ z, & |z| \to \infty. \end{bmatrix}$$

$$\mathrm{Ei}(z) \implies \begin{bmatrix} \{1, \ \ln z\}, & z \to 0, \\ \dfrac{e^z}{z}, & |z| \to \infty; \ \mathrm{Im}\, z = 0, \\ \left\{ 1, \dfrac{e^z}{z} \right\}, & |z| \to \infty; \ \mathrm{Im}\, z \ne 0, \ldots \end{bmatrix}$$

$$e^z \implies \begin{bmatrix} 1, & z \to 0, \\ \cos(\mathrm{Im}\, z), & |z| \to \infty; \ \mathrm{Re}\, z = 0, \\ e^z, & |z| \to \infty; \ \mathrm{Re}\, z \ne 0. \end{bmatrix}$$

$$\mathrm{erf}(z) \implies \begin{bmatrix} z, & z \to 0, \\ \left\{ 1, \dfrac{e^{-z^2}}{z} \right\}, & |z| \to \infty. \end{bmatrix}$$

$$\mathrm{erfc}(z) \implies \begin{bmatrix} 1, & z \to 0, \\ \dfrac{e^{-z^2}}{z}, & |z| \to \infty; \ -\dfrac{\pi}{2} < \arg z \le \dfrac{\pi}{2}, \\ \left\{ 1, \dfrac{e^{-z^2}}{z} \right\} & |z| \to \infty; \ \text{otherwise}. \end{bmatrix}$$

$$\mathrm{erfi}(z) \implies \begin{bmatrix} z, & z \to 0, \\ \left\{ 1, \dfrac{e^{z^2}}{z} \right\}, & |z| \to \infty. \end{bmatrix}$$

$${}_0F_1(b; z) \implies \begin{bmatrix} 1, & z \to 0, \\ z^{(1-2b)/4} \cos\left(2\sqrt{-z}\right), & z \to -\infty, \\ z^{(1-2b)/4} e^{2|\mathrm{Im}(\sqrt{-z})|}, & |z| \to \infty; \ \arg z \ne \pi. \end{bmatrix}$$

$$
{}_1F_1\!\left(\begin{array}{c} a;\, z \\ b \end{array}\right) \Longrightarrow
\left[\begin{array}{ll}
1, & z \to 0, \\[2mm]
\{z^{-a},\, z^{a-b}e^{z}\}, & |z| \to \infty.
\end{array}\right.
$$

$$
{}_2F_1\!\left(\begin{array}{c} a,\, b \\ c;\, z \end{array}\right) \Longrightarrow
\left[\begin{array}{ll}
1, & z \to 0, \\[2mm]
\{1,\, (1-z)^{c-a-b}\}, & |z| \to 1;\, c-a-b \neq 0, \\[2mm]
\{1,\, \ln(1-z)\}, & |z| \to 1;\, c-a-b = 0, \\[2mm]
\{z^{-a},\, z^{-b}\}, & |z| \to \infty.
\end{array}\right.
$$

$$
{}_3F_2\!\left(\begin{array}{c} a_1,\, a_2,\, a_3 \\ b_1,\, b_2;\, z \end{array}\right) \Longrightarrow
\left[\begin{array}{ll}
1, & z \to 0, \\[2mm]
\{1,\, (1-z)^{b_1+b_2-a_1-a_2-a_3}\}, & z \to 1;\, b_1+b_2-a_1-a_2-a_3 \neq 0, \\[2mm]
\{1,\, \ln(1-z)\}, & z \to 1;\, b_1+b_2-a_1-a_2-a_3 = 0, \\[2mm]
\{z^{-a_1},\, z^{-a_2},\, z^{-a_3}\}, & |z| \to \infty.
\end{array}\right.
$$

$$
{}_1F_2\!\left(\begin{array}{c} a_1;\, z \\ b_1,\, b_2 \end{array}\right) \Longrightarrow
\left[\begin{array}{ll}
1, & z \to 0, \\[2mm]
\{z^{-a_1},\, z^{(2a_1-2b_1-2b_2+1)/4}\cos\!\left(2\sqrt{-z}\right)\}, & z \to -\infty, \\[2mm]
\{z^{-a_1},\, z^{(2a_1-2b_1-2b_2+1)/4}e^{2|\mathrm{Im}(\sqrt{-z})|}\}, & |z| \to \infty;\, \arg z \neq \pi.
\end{array}\right.
$$

$$
{}_pF_q\!\left(\begin{array}{c} (a_p);\, z \\ (b_q) \end{array}\right) \Longrightarrow
\left[\begin{array}{ll}
1, & z \to 0, \\[3mm]
\{1,\, (1-z)^{\sum_{j=1}^{q} b_j - \sum_{i=1}^{q+1} a_i}\}, & z \to 1;\, p = q+1; \\[2mm]
& \displaystyle\sum_{j=1}^{q} b_j - \sum_{i=1}^{q+1} a_i \neq 0, \\[4mm]
\{1,\, \ln(1-z)\}, & z \to 1;\, p = q+1; \\[2mm]
& \displaystyle\sum_{j=1}^{q} b_j - \sum_{i=1}^{q+1} a_i = 0, \\[4mm]
\{z^{-a_1},\, z^{-a_2},\, \ldots,\, z^{-a_p}\}, & |z| \to \infty;\, p = q+1, \\[2mm]
\{z^{-a_1},\, z^{-a_2},\, \ldots,\, z^{-a_p},\, z^{\chi}e^{z}\}, & |z| \to \infty;\, p = q, \\[2mm]
\{z^{-a_1},\, z^{-a_2},\, \ldots,\, z^{-a_p},\, z^{\chi}\cos\!\left(2\sqrt{-z}\right)\} & |z| \to \infty;\, p = q-1, \\[2mm]
\{z^{-a_1},\, z^{-a_2},\, \ldots,\, z^{-a_p}, & |z| \to \infty;\, p < q-1, \\[2mm]
\quad z^{\chi}\exp\!\left[(q-p+1)z^{1/(q-p+1)}\right]\}, & \\[2mm]
\quad \chi = \dfrac{1}{q-p+1}\!\left(\dfrac{q-p}{2} + \displaystyle\sum_{i=1}^{p} a_i - \sum_{j=1}^{q} b_j\right).
\end{array}\right.
$$

$$G_{p,q}^{m,n}\left(z\left|\begin{matrix}(a_p)\\(b_q)\end{matrix}\right.\right) \Longrightarrow \begin{cases} \left\{z^{b_1},\, z^{b_2},\ldots,z^{b_m}\right\}, & z \to 0;\ p = q, \\[2mm] \left\{z^{b_1},\, z^{b_2},\ldots,z^{b_m},\, z^{\chi}\exp\left[(-1)^{q-m-n}z^{-1}\right]\right\}, & z \to 0;\ p = q+1, \\[2mm] \left\{z^{b_1},\, z^{b_2},\ldots,z^{b_m},\right. & z \to 0;\ p = q+2, \\[1mm] \qquad\qquad \left. z^{\chi}\cos\left(2\sqrt{(-1)^{q-m-n-1}z^{-1}}\right)\right\}, & \\[2mm] \left\{z^{b_1},\, z^{b_2},\ldots,z^{b_m},\right. & \\[1mm] \qquad\qquad \left. z^{\chi}\exp\left[(p-q)\,(-z)^{1/(q-p)}\right]\right\}, & z \to 0;\ p > q+2, \\[2mm] \left\{1,\,\left(1-(-1)^{p-m-n}z\right)^{\sum_{i=1}^{p}(a_i-b_i)-1}\right\}, & z \to (-1)^{m+n-p}; \\[2mm] & p = q; \\[1mm] & \sum\limits_{i=1}^{p}(a_i - b_i) \neq 1, \\[2mm] \left\{1,\,\ln\left(1-(-1)^{p-m-n}z\right)\right\}, & z \to (-1)^{m+n-p}; \\[2mm] & p = q; \\[1mm] & \sum_{i=1}^{p}(a_i - b_i) = 1, \\[2mm] 1, & z \to (-1)^{m+n-p}; \\[2mm] & p \neq q, \\[2mm] \left\{z^{a_1-1},\, z^{a_2-1},\ldots,z^{a_n-1}\right\}, & |z| \to \infty;\ p = q, \\[2mm] \left\{z^{a_1-1},\, z^{a_2-1},\ldots,z^{a_n-1},\right. & |z| \to \infty;\ p = q-1, \\[1mm] \qquad\qquad \left. z^{\chi}\exp\left[(-1)^{p-m-n}z\right]\right\}, & \\[2mm] \left\{z^{a_1-1},\, z^{a_2-1},\ldots,z^{a_n-1},\right. & |z| \to \infty;\ p = q-2, \\[1mm] \qquad\qquad \left. z^{\chi}\cos\left(2\sqrt{(-1)^{p-m-n-1}z}\right)\right\}, & \\[2mm] \left\{z^{a_1-1},\, z^{a_2-1},\ldots,z^{a_n-1},\right. & |z| \to \infty;\ p < q-2, \\[1mm] \qquad\qquad \left. z^{\chi}\exp\left[(q-p)\,(-z)^{1/(q-p)}\right]\right\}, & \\[2mm] \chi = \dfrac{1}{q-p}\left(\dfrac{p-q+1}{2}+\sum\limits_{j=1}^{q}b_j-\sum\limits_{i=1}^{p}a_i\right) & \end{cases}$$

$$\mathbf{H}_\nu(z) \Longrightarrow \begin{cases} z^{\nu+1}, & z \to 0, \\[2mm] \left\{z^{\nu-1},\,\dfrac{\cos z}{\sqrt{z}}\right\}, & |z| \to \infty;\ \operatorname{Im} z = 0, \\[2mm] \left\{z^{\nu-1},\,\dfrac{e^{|\operatorname{Im} z|}}{\sqrt{z}}\right\} & |z| \to \infty;\ \operatorname{Im} z \neq 0. \end{cases}$$

$$H_\nu^{(1)}(z) \Longrightarrow \begin{cases} \left\{z^{\nu},\, z^{-\nu}\right\}, & z \to 0, \\[2mm] \dfrac{\cos z}{\sqrt{z}}, & |z| \to \infty;\ \operatorname{Im} z = 0, \\[2mm] \dfrac{e^{|\operatorname{Im} z|}}{\sqrt{z}}, & |z| \to \infty;\ \operatorname{Im} z \neq 0. \end{cases}$$

$$H_\nu^{(2)}(z) \Longrightarrow \left[\begin{array}{ll} \{z^\nu, z^{-\nu}\}, & z \to 0, \\ \dfrac{\cos z}{\sqrt{z}}, & |z| \to \infty; \ \mathrm{Im}\, z = 0, \\ \dfrac{e^{|\mathrm{Im}\, z|}}{\sqrt{z}} & |z| \to \infty; \ \mathrm{Im}\, z \neq 0. \end{array} \right.$$

$$H_n(z) \Longrightarrow \left[\begin{array}{ll} z^{n-2[n/2]}, & z \to 0, \\ z^n, & |z| \to \infty. \end{array} \right.$$

$$I_\nu(z) \Longrightarrow \left[\begin{array}{ll} z^\nu, & z \to 0, \\ \dfrac{\cosh z}{\sqrt{z}}, & |z| \to \infty; \ \mathrm{Re}\, z = 0, \\ \dfrac{e^{|\mathrm{Re}\, z|}}{\sqrt{z}}, & |z| \to \infty; \ \mathrm{Re}\, z \neq 0. \end{array} \right.$$

$$J_\nu(z) \Longrightarrow \left[\begin{array}{ll} z^\nu, & z \to 0, \\ \dfrac{\cos z}{\sqrt{z}}, & |z| \to \infty; \ \mathrm{Im}\, z = 0, \\ \dfrac{e^{|\mathrm{Im}\, z|}}{\sqrt{z}}, & |z| \to \infty; \ \mathrm{Im}\, z \neq 0. \end{array} \right.$$

$$\mathbf{J}_\nu(z) \Longrightarrow \left[\begin{array}{ll} 1, & z \to 0, \\ \left\{ \dfrac{1}{z}, \dfrac{\cos z}{\sqrt{z}} \right\}, & |z| \to \infty; \ \mathrm{Im}\, z = 0, \\ \left\{ \dfrac{1}{z}, \dfrac{e^{|\mathrm{Im}\, z|}}{\sqrt{z}} \right\}, & |z| \to \infty; \ \mathrm{Im}\, z \neq 0. \end{array} \right.$$

$$\mathbf{K}(z) \Longrightarrow \left[\begin{array}{ll} 1, & z \to 0, \\ \{1, \ln(1-z)\}, & z \to 1, \\ \{1, \ln(1+z)\} & z \to -1, \\ \dfrac{\ln z}{z} & |z| \to \infty. \end{array} \right.$$

$$K_\nu(z) \Longrightarrow \left[\begin{array}{ll} \{z^\nu, z^{-\nu}\}, & z \to 0, \\ \dfrac{e^{-z}}{\sqrt{z}}, & |z| \to \infty. \end{array} \right.$$

$$\mathrm{kei}_\nu(z) \Longrightarrow \left[\begin{array}{ll} \{z^\nu, z^{-\nu}\}, & z \to 0, \\ \left\{ \dfrac{e^{(-1)^{1/4}z}}{\sqrt{z}}, \dfrac{e^{(-1)^{3/4}z}}{\sqrt{z}}, \dfrac{e^{-(-1)^{1/4}z}}{\sqrt{z}}, \dfrac{e^{-(-1)^{3/4}z}}{\sqrt{z}} \right\}, & |z| \to \infty. \end{array} \right.$$

$$\mathrm{ker}_\nu(z) \Longrightarrow \left[\begin{array}{ll} \{z^\nu, z^{-\nu}\}, & z \to 0, \\ \left\{ \dfrac{e^{(-1)^{1/4}z}}{\sqrt{z}}, \dfrac{e^{(-1)^{3/4}z}}{\sqrt{z}}, \dfrac{e^{-(-1)^{1/4}z}}{\sqrt{z}}, \dfrac{e^{-(-1)^{3/4}z}}{\sqrt{z}} \right\}, & |z| \to \infty. \end{array} \right.$$

$$\mathbf{L}_\nu(z) \Longrightarrow \left[\begin{array}{ll} z^{\nu+1}, & z \to 0, \\ \left\{ z^{\nu-1}, \dfrac{\cosh z}{\sqrt{z}} \right\}, & |z| \to \infty; \ \mathrm{Re}\, z = 0, \\ \left\{ z^{\nu-1}, \dfrac{e^{|\mathrm{Re}\, z|}}{\sqrt{z}} \right\}, & |z| \to \infty; \ \mathrm{Re}\, z \neq 0. \end{array} \right.$$

$$L_n^\lambda(z) \Longrightarrow \begin{bmatrix} 1, & z \to 0, \\ z^n, & |z| \to \infty. \end{bmatrix}$$

$$\mathrm{Li}_\nu(z) \Longrightarrow \begin{bmatrix} z, & z \to 0, \\ \left\{1,\ (z-1)^{\nu-1}\right\}, & z \to 1, \\ \{1,\ \ln^\nu z\}, & |z| \to \infty. \end{bmatrix}$$

$$\mathrm{Li}_2(z) \Longrightarrow \begin{bmatrix} z, & z \to 0, \\ 1, & z \to 1, \\ \{1,\ \ln^2 z\}, & |z| \to \infty. \end{bmatrix}$$

$$\ln(1+az^r) \Longrightarrow \begin{bmatrix} z^r, & z \to 0;\ r > 0, \\ \ln z, & z \to 0;\ r < 0, \\ \ln z, & |z| \to \infty;\ r > 0, \\ z^r, & |z| \to \infty;\ r < 0. \end{bmatrix}$$

$$M_{\rho,\sigma}(z) \Longrightarrow \begin{bmatrix} z^{\sigma+1/2}, & z \to 0, \\ \left\{z^\rho e^{-z/2},\ z^{-\rho} e^{z/2}\right\}, & |z| \to \infty. \end{bmatrix}$$

$$P_n(z) \Longrightarrow \begin{bmatrix} z^{n-2[n/2]}, & z \to 0, \\ z^n, & |z| \to \infty. \end{bmatrix}$$

$$P_\nu(z) \Longrightarrow \begin{bmatrix} \left\{\dfrac{1}{\Gamma\left(\frac{1-\nu}{2}\right)\Gamma\left(\frac{2+\nu}{2}\right)},\ \dfrac{z}{\Gamma\left(-\frac{\nu}{2}\right)\Gamma\left(\frac{1+\nu}{2}\right)}\right\}, & z \to 0, \\ 1, & z \to 1, \\ \{1,\ \ln(z+1)\} & z \to -1, \\ \left\{z^\nu,\ \dfrac{z^{-\nu-1}}{\Gamma(-\nu)}\right\}, & |z| \to \infty. \end{bmatrix}$$

$$P_\nu^\mu(z) \Longrightarrow \begin{bmatrix} 1, & z \to 0, \\ (1-z)^{-\mu/2}, & z \to 1, \\ \left\{(z+1)^{\mu/2},\ (z+1)^{-\mu/2}\right\}, & z \to -1, \\ \left\{z^\nu,\ \dfrac{z^{-\nu-1}}{\Gamma(-\nu)}\right\}, & |z| \to \infty. \end{bmatrix}$$

$$\mathrm{P}_\nu^\mu(z) \Longrightarrow \begin{bmatrix} 1, & z \to 0, \\ (z-1)^{-\mu/2}, & z \to 1, \\ \left\{(z+1)^{\mu/2},\ (z+1)^{-\mu/2}\right\}, & z \to -1, \\ \left\{z^\nu,\ \dfrac{z^{-\nu-1}}{\Gamma(-\nu)}\right\}, & |z| \to \infty. \end{bmatrix}$$

$$P_n^{(\rho,\sigma)}(z) \Longrightarrow \begin{bmatrix} 1, & z \to 0, \\ z^n, & |z| \to \infty. \end{bmatrix}$$

$$Q_\nu(z) \Longrightarrow \begin{bmatrix} 1, & z \to 0, \\ \{1, \ln(1-z)\}, & z \to 1, \\ \{1, \ln(z+1)\}, & z \to -1, \\ \{z^\nu, z^{-\nu-1}\}, & |z| \to \infty. \end{bmatrix}$$

$$Q_\nu^\mu(z) \Longrightarrow \begin{bmatrix} 1, & z \to 0, \\ \left\{(1-z)^{\mu/2}, (1-z)^{-\mu/2}\right\}, & z \to 1, \\ \left\{(z+1)^{\mu/2}, (z+1)^{-\mu/2}\right\}, & z \to -1, \\ \{z^\nu, z^{-\nu-1}\}, & |z| \to \infty. \end{bmatrix}$$

$$Q_\nu^\mu(z) \Longrightarrow \begin{bmatrix} 1, & z \to 0, \\ \left\{(z-1)^{\mu/2}, (z-1)^{-\mu/2}\right\}, & z \to 1, \\ \left\{(z+1)^{\mu/2}, (z+1)^{-\mu/2}\right\}, & z \to -1, \\ z^{-\nu-1}, & |z| \to \infty. \end{bmatrix}$$

$$S(z) \Longrightarrow \begin{bmatrix} z^{3/2}, & z \to 0, \\ \left\{1, \dfrac{\cos z}{\sqrt{z}}\right\}, & |z| \to \infty. \end{bmatrix}$$

$$S_{\mu,\nu}(z) \Longrightarrow \begin{bmatrix} z^{\mu+1}, & z \to 0, \\ \dfrac{\cos z}{\sqrt{z}}, & |z| \to \infty;\ \operatorname{Im} z = 0, \\ \dfrac{e^{|\operatorname{Im} z|}}{\sqrt{z}}, & |z| \to \infty;\ \operatorname{Im} z \neq 0. \end{bmatrix}$$

$$s_{\mu,\nu}(z) \Longrightarrow \begin{bmatrix} z^{\mu+1}, & z \to 0, \\ \dfrac{\cos z}{\sqrt{z}}, & |z| \to \infty;\ \operatorname{Im} z = 0, \\ \dfrac{e^{|\operatorname{Im} z|}}{\sqrt{z}}, & |z| \to \infty;\ \operatorname{Im} z \neq 0. \end{bmatrix}$$

$$\sec z \Longrightarrow \begin{bmatrix} 1, & z \to 0, \\ \dfrac{1}{z - \left(n + \frac{1}{2}\right)\pi}, & z \to \left(n + \dfrac{1}{2}\right)\pi;\ n = 0, \pm 1, \pm 2, \ldots, \\ \sec z, & |z| \to \infty;\ \operatorname{Im} z = 0, \\ e^{-|\operatorname{Im} z|}, & |z| \to \infty;\ \operatorname{Im} z \neq 0. \end{bmatrix}$$

$$\operatorname{sech} z \Longrightarrow \begin{bmatrix} 1, & z \to 0, \\ \dfrac{1}{z - \left(n + \frac{1}{2}\right)\pi i}, & z \to \left(n + \dfrac{1}{2}\right)\pi i;\ n = 0, \pm 1, \pm 2, \ldots, \\ \operatorname{sech} z, & |z| \to \infty;\ \operatorname{Im} z = 0, \\ e^{-|\operatorname{Re} z|}, & |z| \to \infty;\ \operatorname{Im} z \neq 0. \end{bmatrix}$$

$$\sin z \Longrightarrow \begin{bmatrix} z, & z \to 0, \\ \sin z, & |z| \to \infty;\ \operatorname{Im} z = 0, \\ e^{|\operatorname{Im} z|}, & |z| \to \infty;\ \operatorname{Im} z \neq 0. \end{bmatrix}$$

$$\sinh z \Longrightarrow \left[\begin{array}{ll} z, & z \to 0, \\ \sinh z, & |z| \to \infty;\ \operatorname{Re} z = 0, \\ e^{|\operatorname{Re} z|}, & |z| \to \infty;\ \operatorname{Re} z \neq 0. \end{array} \right.$$

$$\operatorname{sinc}(z) \Longrightarrow \left[\begin{array}{ll} 1, & z \to 0, \\ \dfrac{\sin z}{z}, & |z| \to \infty;\ \operatorname{Im} z = 0, \\ \dfrac{e^{|\operatorname{Im} z|}}{z}, & |z| \to \infty;\ \operatorname{Im} z \neq 0. \end{array} \right.$$

$$\operatorname{shi}(z) \Longrightarrow \left[\begin{array}{ll} z, & z \to 0, \\ \left\{ 1, \dfrac{\cosh z}{z} \right\}, & |z| \to \infty \end{array} \right.$$

$$\operatorname{Si}(z) \Longrightarrow \left[\begin{array}{ll} z, & z \to 0, \\ \left\{ 1, \dfrac{\cos z}{z} \right\}, & |z| \to \infty \end{array} \right.$$

$$T(z, a) \Longrightarrow \left[\begin{array}{ll} 1, & z \to 0. \end{array} \right.$$

$$T_n(z) \Longrightarrow \left[\begin{array}{ll} z^{n-2[n/2]}, & z \to 0, \\ z^n, & |z| \to \infty. \end{array} \right.$$

$$\tan z \Longrightarrow \left[\begin{array}{ll} z, & z \to 0, \\ \dfrac{1}{z - \left(n + \frac{1}{2}\right)\pi}, & z \to \left(n + \dfrac{1}{2}\right)\pi;\ n = 0, \pm 1, \pm 2, \ldots, \\ \tan z, & |z| \to \infty;\ \operatorname{Im} z = 0, \\ 1, & |z| \to \infty;\ \operatorname{Im} z \neq 0. \end{array} \right.$$

$$\tanh z \Longrightarrow \left[\begin{array}{ll} z, & z \to 0, \\ \dfrac{1}{z - \left(n + \frac{1}{2}\right)\pi i}, & z \to \left(n + \dfrac{1}{2}\right)\pi i;\ n = 0, \pm 1, \pm 2, \ldots, \\ \tanh z, & |z| \to \infty;\ \operatorname{Re} z = 0, \\ 1, & |z| \to \infty;\ \operatorname{Re} z \neq 0. \end{array} \right.$$

$$U_n(z) \Longrightarrow \left[\begin{array}{ll} z^{n-2[n/2]}, & z \to 0, \\ z^n, & |z| \to \infty. \end{array} \right.$$

$$W_{\rho, \sigma}(z) \Longrightarrow \left[\begin{array}{ll} \left\{ z^{\sigma+1/2}, z^{1/2-\sigma} \right\}, & z \to 0, \\ z^\rho e^{-z/2}, & |z| \to \infty. \end{array} \right.$$

$$Y_\nu(z) \Longrightarrow \left[\begin{array}{ll} \left\{ z^\nu, z^{-\nu} \right\}, & z \to 0, \\ \dfrac{\cos z}{\sqrt{z}}, & |z| \to \infty;\ \operatorname{Im} z = 0, \\ \dfrac{e^{|\operatorname{Im} z|}}{\sqrt{z}}, & |z| \to \infty;\ \operatorname{Im} z \neq 0. \end{array} \right.$$

$$\mathrm{B}\,(z,\beta) \Longrightarrow \left[\begin{array}{ll} \dfrac{1}{z}, & z \to 0;\ \beta \neq 0, -1, -2, \ldots, \\[2mm] \dfrac{1}{z-k}, & z \to k;\ k = 0, -1, -2;\ k+\beta \neq 0, -1, -2, \ldots, \\[2mm] z^{-\beta}, & |z| \to \infty. \end{array}\right.$$

$$\Gamma\,(z) \Longrightarrow \left[\begin{array}{ll} \dfrac{1}{z}, & z \to 0, \\[2mm] \dfrac{1}{z-n}, & z \to n;\ n = 0, -1, -2, \ldots, \\[2mm] \dfrac{z^z}{\sqrt{z}\,e^z}, & |z| \to \infty. \end{array}\right.$$

$$\Gamma\,(\nu,z) \Longrightarrow \left[\begin{array}{ll} \{1, z^\nu\}, & z \to 0, \\[1mm] z^{\nu-1}e^{-z}, & |z| \to \infty. \end{array}\right.$$

$$\gamma\,(\nu,z) \Longrightarrow \left[\begin{array}{ll} z^\nu, & z \to 0, \\[1mm] \{1, z^{\nu-1}e^{-z}\}, & |z| \to \infty. \end{array}\right.$$

$$\zeta\,(z) \Longrightarrow \left[\begin{array}{ll} 1, & z \to 0, \\[1mm] \zeta\,(z), & |z| \to \infty. \end{array}\right.$$

$$\zeta\,(z,v) \Longrightarrow \left[\begin{array}{ll} 1, & z \to 0. \end{array}\right.$$

$$\theta_j\,(z,q) \Longrightarrow \left[\begin{array}{ll} z, & z \to 0;\ j = 1, \\[1mm] 1, & z \to 0;\ j = 2, 3, 4. \end{array}\right.$$

$$\Phi\,(z,s,v) \Longrightarrow \left[\begin{array}{ll} 1, & z \to 0, \\[2mm] \left\{\dfrac{1}{z}, z^{-v}\ln^{s-1} z\right\}, & |z| \to \infty;\ \mathrm{Re}\,v,\ \mathrm{Re}\,s > 0. \end{array}\right.$$

$$\Psi\,(a;b;z) \Longrightarrow \left[\begin{array}{ll} \{1, z^{1-b}\}, & z \to 0, \\[1mm] z^{-a}, & |z| \to \infty. \end{array}\right.$$

$$\psi\,(z) \Longrightarrow \left[\begin{array}{ll} \dfrac{1}{z}, & z \to 0, \\[2mm] \dfrac{1}{z+k}, & z \to -k;\ k = 0, 1, 2, \ldots, \\[2mm] \ln z, & |z| \to \infty. \end{array}\right.$$

$$\psi^{(n)}\,(z) \Longrightarrow \left[\begin{array}{ll} z^{-n-1}, & z \to 0, \\[1mm] (z+k)^{-n-1}, & z \to -k;\ k, n = 0, 1, 2, \ldots, \\[1mm] z^{-n}, & |z| \to \infty;\ n \neq 0. \end{array}\right.$$

Bibliography

[1] Bateman H., Erdélyi A., Magnus W., Oberhettinger F., Tricomi F. G. Tables of Integral Transforms, Vols. 1–2. McGraw–Hill, New York, 1954.

[2] Bertrand J., Bertrand P., Ovarlez J. The Transforms and Applications Handbook. Chapman & Hall/CRC, Boca Raton, 2000.

[3] Brychkov Yu. A. Handbook of Special Functions: Derivatives, Integrals, Series and Other Formulas. Chapman & Hall/CRC, Boca Raton, 2008.

[4] Brychkov Yu. A., Glaeske H.-J., Marichev O. I. Factorization of Integral Transforms of Convolution Type. Journal of Soviet Mathematics, 1985, 30:3, 2071–2094.

[5] Brychkov Yu. A., Glaeske H.-J., Prudnikov A. P., Vu Kim Tuan. Multidimensional Integral Transformations. Gordon and Breach, New York–London, 1992.

[6] Brychkov Yu. A., Prudnikov A. P. Integral Transformations of Generalized Functions. Gordon and Breach, New York–London, 1989.

[7] Colombo S. Les Transformations de Mellin et de Hankel. Centre National de la Recherche Scientifique, Paris, 1959.

[8] Colombo S., Lavoine J. Transformation de Laplace et de Mellin. Formulaires. Mode d'Utilisation. Gauthier–Villars, Paris, 1972.

[9] Debnath L., Bhatta D. Integral Transforms and Their Applications. Chapman & Hall/CRC, Boca Raton, 2015.

[10] Ditkin V. A., Prudnikov A. P. Integral Transforms and Operational Calculus. Pergamon Press, New York, 1965.

[11] Fedoryuk M. V. Integral Transforms, Analysis-1, Itogi Nauki i Tekhniki. Ser. Sovrem. Probl. Mat. Fund. Napr., 13, VINITI, Moscow, 1986, 211–253.

[12] Fikioris G. Integral Transforms and Their Applications. Morgan & Claypool, San Rafael, 2007.

[13] Gradshteyn I. S., Ryzhik I. M. Table of Integrals, Series and Products. Academic Press, New York, 2014.

[14] Marichev O. I. Handbook of Integral Transforms of Higher Transcendental Functions: Theory and Algorithmic Tables. Chichester, Ellis Horwood, 1983.

[15] Oberhettinger F. Tables of Mellin Transforms. Springer, Berlin, 1974.

[16] Paris R. B., Kaminski D. Asymptotics and Mellin–Barnes Integrals. Cambridge University Press, Cambridge, 2001.

[17] Poularikas A. D. Transforms and Applications Handbook. Chapman & Hall/CRC, Boca Raton, 2010.

[18] Prudnikov A. P., Brychkov Yu. A., Marichev O. I. Integrals and Series. Vol. 1: Elementary Functions. Gordon and Breach, New York, 1986.

[19] Prudnikov A. P., Brychkov, Yu. A., Marichev O. I. Integrals and Series. Vol. 2: Special Functions. Gordon and Breach, New York, 1986.

[20] Prudnikov A. P., Brychkov Yu. A., Marichev O. I. Integrals and Series. Vol. 3: More Special Functions. Gordon and Breach, New York, 1990.

[21] Prudnikov A. P., Brychkov Yu. A., Marichev O. I. Evaluation of Integrals and Mellin Transform, Journal of Soviet Mathematics, 1991, 54:6, pp.1239–1341.

[22] Prudnikov A. P., Brychkov Yu. A., Marichev O. I. Integrals and Series, Vol. 4: Laplace Transforms. Gordon and Breach, New York, 1992.

[23] Prudnikov A. P., Brychkov Yu. A., Marichev O. I. Integral and Series, Vol. 5: Inverse Laplace Transforms. Gordon and Breach, New York, 1992.

[24] Samko S. G., Kilbas A. A., Marichev O. I. Fractional Integrals and Derivatives. Theory and Applications. Gordon and Breach, New York, 1993.

[25] Sasiela R. J. Electromagnetic Wave Propagation in Turbulence: Evaluation and Application of Mellin Transforms. Springer, Berlin–Heidelsberg, 2012.

[26] Savischenko N. V. Special Integral Functions Used in Wireless Communications Theory. World Scientific, Singapore, 2014.

[27] Sneddon I. N. The Use of Integral Transform. McGraw–Hill, New York, 1972.

[28] Zemanian A. H. Generalized Integral Transformations, Dover Publications, New York, 1987.

Index of Notations for Functions and Constants

$\mathrm{Ai}\,(z) = \dfrac{1}{\pi}\sqrt{\dfrac{z}{3}}\,K_{1/3}\left(\dfrac{2}{3}z^{3/2}\right)$ is the Airy function

$\arccos z$, $\operatorname{arccot} z = \arctan \dfrac{1}{z}$, $\operatorname{arccsc} z = \arcsin \dfrac{1}{z}$, $\operatorname{arcsec} z = \arccos \dfrac{1}{z}$, $\arcsin z$, $\arctan z$
are inverse trigonometric functions

$\operatorname{arccosh} z$, $\operatorname{arcsinh} z$, $\operatorname{arctanh} z$, $\operatorname{arccsch} z = \operatorname{arcsinh} \dfrac{1}{z}$, $\operatorname{arcsech} z = \operatorname{arccosh} \dfrac{1}{z}$, $\operatorname{arccoth} z = \operatorname{arctanh} \dfrac{1}{z}$
are inverse hyperbolic functions

$\arg z$ is the argument of the complex number z, $z = |z|e^{i\,\arg z}$

B_n are the Bernoulli numbers

$B_n\,(z)$ are the Bernoulli polynomials

$\operatorname{bei}_\nu(z)$, $\operatorname{ber}_\nu(z)$ are the Kelvin functions

$\quad \operatorname{ber}_\nu x + i\operatorname{bei}_\nu x = J_\nu\left(e^{3\pi i/4}x\right) = e^{\nu\pi i}J_\nu\left(e^{-\pi i/4}x\right) = e^{\nu\pi i/2}I_\nu\left(e^{\pi i/4}x\right) = e^{3\nu\pi i/2}I_\nu\left(e^{-3\pi i/4}x\right)$

$\mathrm{Bi}\,(z) = \sqrt{\dfrac{z}{3}}\left[I_{-1/3}\left(\dfrac{2}{3}z^{3/2}\right) + I_{1/3}\left(\dfrac{2}{3}z^{3/2}\right)\right]$ is the Airy function

$\mathbf{C} = -\psi\,(1) = 0{,}577\,215\,664\,9\ldots$ is the Euler constant

$C\,(z) = \dfrac{1}{\sqrt{2\pi}}\displaystyle\int_0^z \dfrac{\cos t}{\sqrt{t}}\,dt$ is the Fresnel cosine integral

$C\,(z, \nu) = \displaystyle\int_z^\infty t^{\nu-1}\cos t\,dt \quad [\operatorname{Re}\nu < 1]$ is the generalized Fresnel cosine integral

$C_n^\lambda\,(z) = \dfrac{(2\lambda)_n}{n!}\,{}_2F_1\left(-n, n + 2\lambda; \lambda + \dfrac{1}{2}; \dfrac{1-z}{2}\right)$ are the Gegenbauer polynomials

$\operatorname{chi}\,(z) = \mathbf{C} + \ln z + \displaystyle\int_0^z \dfrac{\cosh t - 1}{t}\,dt$ is the hyperbolic cosine integral

$\operatorname{ci}\,(z) = -\displaystyle\int_z^\infty \dfrac{\cos t}{t}\,dt$ is the cosine integral

$\cos z = \dfrac{e^{iz} + e^{-iz}}{2}$

$\cosh z = \dfrac{e^z + e^{-z}}{2}$

$\coth z = \dfrac{\cosh z}{\sinh z}$

$\cot z = \dfrac{\cos z}{\sin z}$

$\csc z = \dfrac{1}{\sin z}$

$\operatorname{csch} z = \dfrac{1}{\sinh z}$

$$D = \frac{d}{dz}, \ D_a = \frac{d}{da}$$

$$\mathbf{D}(k) = \int_0^{\pi/2} \frac{\sin^2 t \, dt}{\sqrt{1 - k^2 \sin^2 t}} \text{ is the complete elliptic integral}$$

$$D(\varphi, k) = \int_0^\varphi \frac{\sin^2 t \, dt}{\sqrt{1 - k^2 \sin^2 t}} \text{ is the elliptic integral}$$

$$D_\nu(z) = 2^{\nu/2} e^{-z^2/4} \, \Psi\left(-\frac{\nu}{2}, \frac{1}{2}; \frac{z^2}{2}\right) \text{ is the parabolic cylinder function}$$

$$\mathbf{E}(k) = \int_0^{\pi/2} \sqrt{1 - k^2 \sin^2 t} \, dt \text{ is the complete elliptic integral of the second kind}$$

E_n are the Euler numbers

$E_n(z)$ are the Euler polynomials

$$E_\nu(z) = \int_1^\infty \frac{e^{-zt}}{t^\nu} \, dt \quad [\operatorname{Re} z > 0] \text{ is the exponential E-integral}$$

$$\mathbf{E}_\nu(z) = \frac{1}{\pi} \int_0^\pi \sin(\nu t - z \sin t) \, dt \text{ is the Weber function}$$

$$E_\rho(z; \mu) = \sum_{k=0}^\infty \frac{z^k}{\Gamma(\mu + \rho^{-1} k)} \quad [\rho > 0] \text{ is the Mittag–Leffler function}$$

$$\operatorname{Ei}(z) = \int_{-\infty}^z \frac{e^t}{t} \, dt \text{ is the exponential integral}$$

$$\operatorname{erf}(z) = \frac{2}{\sqrt{\pi}} \int_0^z e^{-t^2} \, dt \text{ is the error function}$$

$$\operatorname{erfc}(z) = 1 - \operatorname{erf}(z) = \frac{2}{\sqrt{\pi}} \int_z^\infty e^{-t^2} \, dt \text{ is the complementary error function}$$

$$\operatorname{erfi}(z) = \frac{2}{\sqrt{\pi}} \int_0^z e^{t^2} \, dt \text{ is the error function of imaginary argument}$$

$$_1F_1\left(\begin{matrix} a; z \\ b \end{matrix}\right) \equiv {_1F_1}\left(\begin{matrix} a \\ b; z \end{matrix}\right) \equiv {_1F_1}(a; b; z) = \sum_{k=0}^\infty \frac{(a)_k}{(b)_k} \frac{z^k}{k!}$$

is the Kummer confluent hypergeometric function

$$_2F_1\left(\begin{matrix} a, b; z \\ c \end{matrix}\right) \equiv {_2F_1}\left(\begin{matrix} a, b \\ c; z \end{matrix}\right) \equiv {_2F_1}(a, b; c; z) = \sum_{k=0}^\infty \frac{(a)_k (b)_k}{(c)_k} \frac{z^k}{k!} \qquad [|z| < 1,$$

$$= \frac{\Gamma(c)}{\Gamma(a)\Gamma(c - b)} \int_0^1 t^{b-1} (1 - t)^{c-b-1} (1 - tz)^{-a} \, dt$$

$$[\operatorname{Re} c > \operatorname{Re} b > 0; \ |\arg(1 - z)| < \pi]$$

is the Gauss hypergeometric function

$$_pF_q\left(\begin{matrix} (a_p); z \\ (b_q) \end{matrix}\right) \equiv {_pF_q}\left(\begin{matrix} (a_p) \\ (b_q); z \end{matrix}\right) \equiv {_pF_q}((a_p); (b_q); z)$$

$$\equiv {_pF_q}(a_1, \dots, a_p; b_1, \dots, b_q; z) = \sum_{k=0}^\infty \frac{(a_1)_k (a_2)_k \cdots (a_p)_k}{(b_1)_k (b_2)_k \cdots (b_q)_k} \frac{z^k}{k!}$$

is the generalized hypergeometric function

$F_j^{(n)}(\ldots;\ \ldots;\ z_1,\ldots,z_n)$ $[j=A,B,C,D]$ are the Lauricella functions:

$$F_A^{(n)}(a,\ b_1,\ldots,b_n;\ c_1,\ldots,c_n;\ z_1,\ldots,z_n) =$$

$$= \sum_{k_1,\ldots,k_n=0}^{\infty} \frac{(a)_{k_1+\ldots+k_n}\ (b_1)_{k_1}\cdots(b_n)_{k_n}}{(c_1)_{k_1}\cdots(c_n)_{k_n}}\ \frac{z_1^{k_1}\ldots z_n^{k_n}}{k_1!\ldots k_n!}, \qquad \left[\sum_{j=1}^{n}|z_j|<1\right]$$

$$F_B^{(n)}(a_1,\ldots,a_n,\ b_1,\ldots,b_n;\ c;\ z_1,\ldots,z_n) =$$

$$= \sum_{k_1,\ldots,k_n=0}^{\infty} \frac{(a_1)_{k_1}\cdots(a_n)_{k_n}\ (b_1)_{k_1}\cdots(b_n)_{k_n}}{(c)_{k_1+\ldots+k_n}}\ \frac{z_1^{k_1}\ldots z_n^{k_n}}{k_1!\ldots k_n!}, \qquad [|z_j|<1,\ j=1,2,\ldots,n]$$

$$F_C^{(n)}(a,\ b;\ c_1,\ldots,c_n;\ z_1,\ldots,z_n) = \sum_{k_1,\ldots,k_n=0}^{\infty} \frac{(a)_{k_1+\ldots+k_n}\ (b)_{k_1+\ldots+k_n}}{(c_1)_{k_1}\cdots(c_n)_{k_n}}\ \frac{z_1^{k_1}\ldots z_n^{k_n}}{k_1!\ldots k_n!},$$

$$\left[\sum_{j=1}^{n}\sqrt{|z_j|}<1\right]$$

$$F_D^{(n)}(a,\ b_1,\ldots,b_n;\ c;\ z_1,\ldots,z_n) = \sum_{k_1,\ldots,k_n=0}^{\infty} \frac{(a)_{k_1+\ldots+k_n}\ (b_1)_{k_1}\cdots(b_n)_{k_n}}{(c)_{k_1+\ldots+k_n}}\ \frac{z_1^{k_1}\ldots z_n^{k_n}}{k_1!\ldots k_n!},$$

$$[|z_j|<1,\ j=1,2,\ldots,n]$$

$F_j(\ldots;\ w,z)$ $[j=1,2,3,4]$ are the Appell functions:

$$F_1(a,\ b,\ b';\ c;\ w,\ z) = \sum_{k,\ell=0}^{\infty} \frac{(a)_{k+\ell}\ (b)_k\ (b')_\ell}{(c)_{k+\ell}}\ \frac{w^k z^\ell}{k!\ \ell!} \qquad [|w|,\ |z|<1],$$

$$F_2(a,\ b,\ b';\ c,\ c';\ w,\ z) = \sum_{k,\ell=0}^{\infty} \frac{(a)_{k+\ell}\ (b)_k\ (b')_\ell}{(c)_k\ (c')_\ell}\ \frac{w^k z^\ell}{k!\ \ell!} \qquad [|w|+|z|<1],$$

$$F_3(a,\ a',\ b,\ b';\ c;\ w,\ z) = \sum_{k,\ell=0}^{\infty} \frac{(a)_k\ (a')_\ell\ (b)_k\ (b')_\ell}{(c)_{k+\ell}}\ \frac{w^k z^\ell}{k!\ \ell!} \qquad [|w|,\ |z|<1],$$

$$F_4(a,\ b;\ c,\ c';\ w,\ z) = \sum_{k,\ell=0}^{\infty} \frac{(a)_{k+\ell}\ (b)_{k+\ell}}{(c)_k\ (c')_\ell}\ \frac{w^k z^\ell}{k!\ \ell!} \qquad \left[\sqrt{|w|}+\sqrt{|z|}<1\right]$$

$$\mathbf{G} = \sum_{k=0}^{\infty} \frac{(-1)^k}{(2k+1)^2} = 0,915\,965\,594\,2\ldots \text{ is the Catalan constant}$$

$$G_{pq}^{mn}\left(z\ \middle|\ \begin{matrix}(a_p)\\(b_q)\end{matrix}\right) \equiv G_{pq}^{mn}\left(z\ \middle|\ \begin{matrix}a_1,\ldots,a_p\\b_1,\ldots,b_q\end{matrix}\right)$$

$$= \frac{1}{2\pi i}\int_L \frac{\Gamma(b_1+s)\ldots\Gamma(b_m+s)\,\Gamma(1-a_1-s)\ldots\Gamma(1-a_n-s)}{\Gamma(a_{n+1}+s)\ldots\Gamma(a_p+s)\,\Gamma(1-b_{m+1}-s)\ldots\Gamma(1-b_q-s)}\ z^{-s}\,ds,$$

$$L = L_{\pm\infty},\ L_{i\infty} \text{ is the Meijer } G\text{-function}$$

$$\mathbf{H}_\nu(z) = \frac{2}{\sqrt{\pi}}\left(\frac{z}{2}\right)^{\nu+1}\frac{1}{\Gamma\left(\nu+\frac{3}{2}\right)}\ {}_1F_2\left(\begin{matrix}1;\ -\frac{z^2}{4}\\\frac{3}{2},\ \nu+\frac{3}{2}\end{matrix}\right) \text{ is the Struve function}$$

$H_\nu^{(1)}(z)$, $H_\nu^{(2)}(z)$ are the Hankel functions of the first and second kind (the Bessel functions of the third kind $H_\nu^{(1)}(z) = J_\nu(z)+i\,Y_\nu(z)$, $H_\nu^{(2)}(z) = J_\nu(z)-i\,Y_\nu(z)$)

$H_n\left(z\right) = \left(-1\right)^n e^{z^2} \dfrac{d^n}{dz^n} e^{-z^2}$ are the Hermite polynomials

$\mathcal{H}_\nu\left(z, a, b\right) = \dfrac{\left(1 - a^2\right)^\nu}{2\pi} \displaystyle\int_0^b \dfrac{e^{-z^2\left(t^2+1\right)/\left[2\left(a^2 t^2+1\right)\right]}}{\left(t^2 + 1\right)\left(a^2 t^2 + 1\right)^\nu} \, dt$

$I_\nu\left(z\right) = \dfrac{1}{\Gamma\left(\nu + 1\right)} \left(\dfrac{z}{2}\right)^\nu {}_0F_1\left(\nu + 1; \dfrac{z^2}{4}\right) = e^{-\nu\pi i/2} J_\nu\left(e^{\pi i/2} z\right)$ is the modified Bessel function of the first kind

$J_\nu\left(z\right) = \dfrac{1}{\Gamma\left(\nu + 1\right)} \left(\dfrac{z}{2}\right)^\nu {}_0F_1\left(\nu + 1; -\dfrac{z^2}{4}\right)$ is the Bessel function of the first kind

$\mathbf{J}_\nu\left(z\right) = \dfrac{1}{\pi} \displaystyle\int_0^\pi \cos\left(\nu t - z \sin t\right) \, dt$ is the Anger function

$J_\nu^\mu\left(z\right) = \displaystyle\sum_{k=0}^\infty \dfrac{\left(-z\right)^k}{k!\,\Gamma\left(k\mu + \nu + 1\right)}$ $\left[\mu > -1\right]$ is the Bessel–Maitland function

$J_{\nu,\lambda}^\mu\left(z\right) = \displaystyle\sum_{k=0}^\infty \dfrac{\left(-1\right)^k \left(z/2\right)^{2k+2\lambda+\nu}}{\Gamma\left(k + \lambda + 1\right)\Gamma\left(k\mu + \nu + \lambda + 1\right)}$ $\left[\mu > 0\right]$ is the generalized Bessel–Maitland function

$Ji_\nu\left(z\right) = \displaystyle\int_z^\infty \dfrac{J_\nu\left(t\right)}{t} \, dt$ is the integral Bessel function of the first kind

$\mathbf{K}\left(k\right) = \displaystyle\int_0^{\pi/2} \dfrac{dt}{\sqrt{1 - k^2 \sin^2 t}}$ is the complete elliptic integral of the first kind

$K_\nu\left(z\right) = \dfrac{\pi\left[I_{-\nu}\left(z\right) - I_\nu\left(z\right)\right]}{2 \sin \nu\pi}$ $\left[\nu \neq n\right]$, $K_n\left(z\right) = \displaystyle\lim_{\nu \to n} K_\nu\left(z\right)$ $\left[n = 0, \pm 1, \pm 2, \ldots\right]$

is the Macdonald function (the modified Bessel function of the third kind)

$\mathrm{kei}_\nu\left(z\right)$, $\mathrm{ker}_\nu\left(z\right)$ are the Kelvin functions

$\mathrm{ker}_\nu x + i\,\mathrm{kei}_\nu x = e^{-\nu\pi i/2} K_\nu\left(e^{\pi i/4} x\right) = \dfrac{1}{2}\pi i H_\nu^{(1)}\left(e^{3\pi i/4} x\right) = -\dfrac{1}{2}\pi i e^{-\nu\pi i} H_\nu^{(2)}\left(e^{-\pi i/4} x\right)$

$Ki_\nu\left(z\right) = \displaystyle\int_z^\infty \dfrac{K_\nu\left(t\right)}{t} \, dt$ is the modified integral Bessel function

$\mathbf{L}_\nu\left(z\right) = e^{-\left(\nu+1\right)\pi i/2}\, \mathbf{H}_\nu\left(e^{\pi i/2} z\right)$ is the modified Struve function

$L_n\left(z\right) = L_n^0\left(z\right)$ are the Laguerre polynomials

$L_n^\lambda\left(z\right) = \dfrac{z^{-\lambda} e^z}{n!} \dfrac{d^n}{dz^n} \left(z^{n+\lambda} e^{-z}\right)$ are the generalized Laguerre polynomials

$\mathrm{Li}_\nu\left(z\right) = \displaystyle\sum_{k=1}^\infty \dfrac{z^k}{k^\nu}$ $\hspace{6cm}$ $\left[\left|z\right| < 1\right]$

$\hspace{2.7cm} = \dfrac{z}{\Gamma\left(\nu\right)} \displaystyle\int_0^\infty \dfrac{t^{\nu-1} \, dt}{e^t - z}$ $\hspace{3.5cm}$ $\left[\mathrm{Re}\,\nu > 0;\ \left|\arg\left(1 - z\right)\right| < \pi\right]$

is the polylogarithm of the order ν

$\mathrm{Li}_2\left(z\right)$ is the Euler dilogarithm

$M_{\varkappa,\mu}\left(z\right) = z^{\mu+1/2} e^{-z/2}\, {}_1F_1\left(\begin{matrix} \mu - \varkappa + \frac{1}{2} \\ 2\mu + 1;\, z \end{matrix}\right)$ is the Whittaker confluent hypergeometric function

$P_n(z) = \dfrac{2^{-n}}{n!}\dfrac{d^n}{dz^n}(z^2-1)^n$ are the Legendre polynomials

$$P_\nu(z) \equiv P_\nu^0(z) = {}_2F_1\left(\begin{matrix}-\nu,\,1+\nu\\1;\,\frac{1-z}{2}\end{matrix}\right) \qquad\qquad [|\arg(1+z)|<\pi]$$

is the Legendre function of the first kind

$$P_\nu^\mu(z) = \dfrac{1}{\Gamma(1-\mu)}\left(\dfrac{z+1}{z-1}\right)^{\mu/2}{}_2F_1\left(\begin{matrix}-\nu,\,\nu+1\\1-\mu;\,\frac{1-z}{2}\end{matrix}\right) \qquad [|\arg(z\pm1)|<\pi;\,\mu\neq m;\,m=1,2,\dots]$$

$$P_\nu^m(z) = (z^2-1)^{m/2}\left(\dfrac{d}{dz}\right)^m P_\nu(z) \qquad\qquad [|\arg(z-1)|<\pi;\,m=1,2,\dots]$$

$$\mathrm{P}_\nu^\mu(x) = \dfrac{1}{\Gamma(1-\mu)}\left(\dfrac{1+x}{1-x}\right)^{\mu/2}{}_2F_1\left(\begin{matrix}-\nu,\,\nu+1\\1-\mu;\,\frac{1-x}{2}\end{matrix}\right) \qquad [-1<x<1;\,\mu\neq m;\,m=1,2,\dots]$$

$$\mathrm{P}_\nu^m(x) = (-1)^m(1-x^2)^{m/2}\left(\dfrac{d}{dx}\right)^m P_\nu(x) \qquad\qquad [-1<x<1;\,m=1,2,\dots]$$

is the associated Legendre function of the first kind

$$P_n^{(\rho,\sigma)}(z) = \dfrac{(-1)^n}{2^n n!}(1-z)^{-\rho}(1+z)^{-\sigma}\dfrac{d^n}{dz^n}\left[(1-z)^{\rho+n}(1+z)^{\sigma+n}\right]$$

$$= \dfrac{(\rho+1)_n}{n!}{}_2F_1\left(\begin{matrix}-n,\,\rho+\sigma+n+1\\\rho+1;\,\frac{1-z}{2}\end{matrix}\right) \text{ are the Jacobi polynomials}$$

$Q_\nu(z) \equiv Q_\nu^0(z)$ is the Legendre function of the second kind

$$Q_\nu(z) \equiv Q_\nu^0(z) = \mathrm{Q}_\nu(z) + \dfrac{1}{2}\left[\ln(z-1)-\ln(1-z)\right]P_\nu(z)$$

$$Q_\nu^\mu(z) = \dfrac{e^{i\mu\pi}\sqrt{\pi}}{2^{\nu+1}}\Gamma\left[\begin{matrix}\mu+\nu+1\\\nu+3/2\end{matrix}\right]z^{-\mu-\nu-1}(z^2-1)^{\mu/2}{}_2F_1\left(\begin{matrix}\frac{\mu+\nu+1}{2},\,\frac{\mu+\nu+2}{2}\\\nu+\frac{3}{2};\,\frac{1}{z^2}\end{matrix}\right)$$

$$[|\arg z|,\,|\arg(z\pm1)|<\pi;\,\nu+1/2,\,\mu+\nu\neq-1,-2,-3,\dots]$$

$$Q_{-n-3/2}^\mu(z) = \dfrac{e^{i\mu\pi}\sqrt{\pi}\,\Gamma(\mu+n+3/2)}{2^{n+3/2}(n+1)!}z^{-\mu-n-3/2}(z^2-1)^{\mu/2}{}_2F_1\left(\begin{matrix}\frac{2\mu+2n+3}{4},\,\frac{2\mu+2n+5}{4}\\n+2;\,\frac{1}{z^2}\end{matrix}\right)$$

$$[|\arg z|,\,|\arg(z\pm1)|<\pi;\,\mu+\nu\neq-1,-2,-3,\dots]$$

$$\mathrm{Q}_\nu^\mu(x) = \dfrac{e^{-i\mu\pi}}{2}\left[e^{-\mu\pi/2}Q_\nu^\mu(x+i0)+e^{i\mu\pi/2}Q_\nu^\mu(x-i0)\right]$$

$$= \dfrac{\pi}{2\sin\mu\pi}\left[\mathrm{P}_\nu^\mu(x)\cos\mu\pi-\Gamma\left[\begin{matrix}\nu+\mu+1\\\nu-\mu+1\end{matrix}\right]\mathrm{P}_\nu^{-\mu}(x)\right]$$

$$[-1<x<1;\,\mu\neq\pm m;\,\mu+\nu\neq-1,-2,-3,\dots],$$

$$= (-1)^m(1-x^2)^{m/2}\left(\dfrac{d}{dx}\right)^m \mathrm{Q}_\nu(x) \qquad\qquad [\mu=m;\,\nu\neq-m-1,-m-2,\dots],$$

$$= (-1)^m\Gamma\left[\begin{matrix}\nu-m+1\\\mu+m+1\end{matrix}\right]\mathrm{Q}_\nu^m(x) \qquad\qquad [\mu=-m;\,\nu\neq-m-1,-m-2,\dots]$$

is the associated Legendre function of the second kind

$S(z) = \dfrac{1}{\sqrt{2\pi}}\displaystyle\int_0^z\dfrac{\sin t}{\sqrt{t}}\,dt$ is the Fresnel cosine integral

$S(z,\nu) = \displaystyle\int_z^\infty t^{\nu-1}\sin t\,dt \quad [\mathrm{Re}\,\nu<1]$ is the generalized Fresnel sine integral

$$S_{\mu,\nu}(z) = s_{\mu,\nu}(z) + 2^{\mu-1}\Gamma\begin{bmatrix} \nu, \ (\nu+\mu+1)/2 \\ (\nu-\mu+1)/2 \end{bmatrix}\left(\frac{z}{2}\right)^{-\nu}{}_0F_1\left(1-\nu; \ -\frac{z^2}{4}\right) +$$

$$+ 2^{\mu-1}\Gamma\begin{bmatrix} -\nu, \ (1+\mu-\nu)/2 \\ (1-\mu-\nu)/2 \end{bmatrix}\left(\frac{z}{2}\right)^{\nu}{}_0F_1\left(1+\nu; \ -\frac{z^2}{4}\right) \text{ is the Lommel function}$$

$$s_{\mu,\nu}(z) = \frac{z^{\mu+1}}{(\mu+1)^2 - \nu^2}\,{}_1F_2\left(1; \ \frac{\mu+\nu+3}{2}, \frac{\mu-\nu+3}{2}; \ -\frac{z^2}{4}\right) \text{ is the Lommel function}$$

$$\operatorname{sgn} x = \begin{cases} 1, & x > 0, \\ 0, & x = 0, \\ -1, & x < 0 \end{cases}$$

$$\sec z = \frac{1}{\cos z}$$

$$\operatorname{sech} z = \frac{1}{\cosh z}$$

$$\operatorname{shi}(z) = \int_0^z \frac{\sinh t}{t}\,dt = -i\operatorname{Si}(iz) \text{ is the hyperbolic sine integral}$$

$$\operatorname{Si}(z) = \int_0^z \frac{\sin t}{t}\,dt \text{ is the sine integral}$$

$$\operatorname{si}(z) = \operatorname{Si}(z) - \frac{\pi}{2} = -\int_z^\infty \frac{\sin t}{t}\,dt \text{ is the sine integral}$$

$$\sin z = \frac{e^{iz} - e^{-iz}}{2i},$$

$$\operatorname{sinc} z = \frac{\sin z}{z}$$

$$\sinh z = \frac{e^z - e^{-z}}{2},$$

$$T(z, a) = \frac{1}{2\pi}\int_0^a \frac{e^{-(1+t^2)z^2/2}}{1+t^2}\,dt \quad [|\arg a| < \pi] \text{ is the Owen function}$$

$$T_n(z) = \cos(n\arccos z) = {}_2F_1\left(\begin{matrix} -n, \ n \\ \frac{1}{2}; \ \frac{1-z}{2} \end{matrix}\right) \text{ are the Chebyshev polynomials of the first kind}$$

$$\tanh z = \frac{\sinh z}{\cosh z},$$

$$U_n(z) = \frac{\sin[(n+1)\arccos z]}{\sqrt{1-z^2}} = (n+1)\,{}_2F_1\left(\begin{matrix} -n, \ n+2 \\ \frac{3}{2}; \ \frac{1-z}{2} \end{matrix}\right) \text{ are the Chebyshev polynomials of the second kind}$$

$$W_{\varkappa,\mu}(z) = z^{\mu+1/2}e^{-z/2}\,\Psi\left(\begin{matrix} \mu-\varkappa+\frac{1}{2} \\ 2\mu+1; \ z \end{matrix}\right) \text{ is the Whittaker confluent hypergeometric function}$$

$$Y_\nu(z) = \frac{\cos\nu\pi J_\nu(z) - J_{-\nu}(z)}{\sin\nu\pi} \quad [\nu \neq n], \qquad Y_n(z) = \lim_{\nu \to n} Y_\nu(z) \quad [n = 0, \pm 1, \pm 2, \ldots]$$

is the Neumann function (the Bessel function of the second kind)

$$Yi_\nu(z) = \int_z^\infty \frac{Y_\nu(t)}{t}\,dt \text{ is the integral Bessel function of the second kind}$$

$\mathrm{B}\left(\alpha,\,\beta\right)=\dfrac{\Gamma\left(\alpha\right)\Gamma\left(\beta\right)}{\Gamma\left(\alpha+\beta\right)}$ is the beta function

$\mathrm{B}_{z}\left(\alpha,\,\beta\right)=\displaystyle\int_{0}^{z}t^{\alpha-1}\left(1-t\right)^{\beta-1}\,dt$ [$\operatorname{Re}\alpha>1;\,z<1$] is the incomplete beta function

$\Gamma\left(z\right)=\displaystyle\int_{0}^{\infty}t^{z-1}e^{-t}\,dt$ [$\operatorname{Re}z>0$] is the gamma function

$\Gamma\left(\nu,\,z\right)=\displaystyle\int_{z}^{\infty}t^{\nu-1}e^{-t}\,dt$ is the complementary incomplete gamma function

$\gamma\left(\nu,\,z\right)=\Gamma\left(\nu\right)-\Gamma\left(\nu,z\right)=\displaystyle\int_{0}^{z}t^{\nu-1}e^{-t}\,dt$ [$\operatorname{Re}\nu>0$] is the incomplete gamma function

$\Gamma\left[\begin{matrix}(a_p)\\(b_q)\end{matrix}\right]\equiv\Gamma\left[\begin{matrix}a_1,\dots,a_p\\b_1,\dots,b_q\end{matrix}\right]\equiv\dfrac{\prod\limits_{k=1}^{p}\Gamma\left(a_k\right)}{\prod\limits_{\ell=1}^{q}\Gamma\left(b_\ell\right)}$

$\Gamma\left[(a_p)\right]\equiv\Gamma\left[a_1,\dots,a_p\right]\equiv\prod\limits_{k=1}^{p}\Gamma\left(a_k\right)$

$\Delta\left(k,\,a\right)=\dfrac{a}{k},\dfrac{a+1}{k},\dots,\dfrac{a+k-1}{k}$

$\Delta\left(k,\,(a_p)\right)=\dfrac{(a_p)}{k},\dfrac{(a_p)+1}{k},\dots,\dfrac{(a_p)+k-1}{k}$

$\delta_{m,n}=\begin{cases}0,&m\neq n,\\1,&m=n\end{cases}$ is the Kronecker symbol

$\zeta\left(z\right)=\displaystyle\sum_{k=1}^{\infty}\dfrac{1}{k^z}$ [$\operatorname{Re}z>1$] is the Riemann zeta function

$\zeta\left(z,\,v\right)=\displaystyle\sum_{k=0}^{\infty}\dfrac{1}{(v+k)^z}$ [$\operatorname{Re}z>1;\,v\neq0,-1,-2,\dots$] is the Hurwitz zeta function

$\theta_j\left(z,\,q\right)$ [$j=1,2,3,4$] are the theta functions:

$\theta_1\left(z,\,q\right)=2\displaystyle\sum_{k=0}^{\infty}\left(-1\right)^k q^{(k+1/2)^2}\sin\left(2k+1\right)z,$

$\theta_2\left(z,\,q\right)=2\displaystyle\sum_{k=0}^{\infty}q^{(k+1/2)^2}\cos\left(2k+1\right)z,$

$\theta_3\left(z,\,q\right)=1+2\displaystyle\sum_{k=1}^{\infty}q^{k^2}\cos\left(2kz\right),$

$\theta_4\left(z,\,q\right)=1+2\displaystyle\sum_{k=1}^{\infty}\left(-1\right)^k q^{k^2}\cos\left(2kz\right)$

$\theta\left(x\right)=\begin{cases}1,&x\geq0,\\0,&x<0\end{cases}$ is the Heaviside function

$\lambda\left(z,\,a\right)=\displaystyle\int_{0}^{a}z^{-t}\Gamma\left(t+1\right)\,dt$

$$\mu\left(z,\,\lambda\right) = \int_0^\infty \frac{t^\lambda z^t}{\Gamma\left(\lambda+1\right)\Gamma\left(t+1\right)}\,dt \qquad\qquad [\operatorname{Re}\lambda > -1]$$

$$\mu\left(z,\,\lambda,\,\rho\right) = \int_0^\infty \frac{t^\lambda z^{t+\rho}}{\Gamma\left(\lambda+1\right)\Gamma\left(t+\rho+1\right)}\,dt \qquad\qquad [\operatorname{Re}\lambda > -1]$$

$$\nu\left(z\right) = \int_0^\infty \frac{z^t}{\Gamma\left(t+1\right)}\,dt$$

$$\nu\left(z,\,\rho\right) = \int_0^\infty \frac{z^{t+\rho}}{\Gamma\left(t+\rho+1\right)}\,dt$$

$\Xi_j\left(\ldots;\,w,\,z\right)\,[j=1,2]$ are the Humbert functions:

$$\Xi_1\left(a,\,a',\,b;\,c;\,w,\,z\right) = \sum_{k,\,\ell=0}^\infty \frac{\left(a\right)_k\left(a'\right)_\ell\left(b\right)_k}{\left(c\right)_{k+\ell}}\frac{w^k z^\ell}{k!\,\ell!} \qquad\qquad [|w|<1]$$

$$\Xi_2\left(a,\,b;\,c;\,w,\,z\right) = \sum_{k,\,\ell=0}^\infty \frac{\left(a\right)_k\left(b\right)_k}{\left(c\right)_{k+\ell}}\frac{w^k z^\ell}{k!\,\ell!} \qquad\qquad [|w|<1]$$

$$\Phi\left(z,\,s,\,v\right) = \sum_{k=0}^\infty \frac{z^k}{\left(v+k\right)^s} \qquad\qquad [|z|<1;\,v\neq 0,-1,-2,\ldots]$$

$\Phi_j\left(\ldots;\,w,\,z\right)\,[j=1,2,3]$ are the Humbert functions:

$$\Phi_1\left(a,\,b;\,c;\,w,\,z\right) = \sum_{k,\,\ell=0}^\infty \frac{\left(a\right)_{k+\ell}\left(b\right)_k}{\left(c\right)_{k+\ell}}\frac{w^k z^\ell}{k!\,\ell!} \qquad\qquad [|w|<1]$$

$$\Phi_2\left(b,\,b';\,c;\,w,\,z\right) = \sum_{k,\,\ell=0}^\infty \frac{\left(b\right)_k\left(b'\right)_\ell}{\left(c\right)_{k+\ell}}\frac{w^k z^\ell}{k!\,\ell!}$$

$$\Phi_3\left(b;\,c;\,w,\,z\right) = \sum_{k,\,\ell=0}^\infty \frac{\left(b\right)_k}{\left(c\right)_{k+\ell}}\frac{w^k z^\ell}{k!\,\ell!}$$

$$\Psi\begin{pmatrix} a;\,z \\ b \end{pmatrix} \equiv \Psi\begin{pmatrix} a \\ b;\,z \end{pmatrix} \equiv \Psi\left(a;\,b;\,z\right) = \frac{\Gamma\left(b-1\right)}{\Gamma\left(a\right)}z^{1-b}\,{}_1F_1\begin{pmatrix} 1+a-b \\ 2-b;\,z \end{pmatrix}$$

$$+ \frac{\Gamma\left(1-b\right)}{\Gamma\left(1+a-b\right)}\,{}_1F_1\begin{pmatrix} a;\,z \\ b \end{pmatrix} \qquad\qquad [b\neq 0,\pm1,\pm2,\ldots]$$

$$\Psi\left(a;\,n;\,z\right) = \lim_{b\to n}\Psi\left(a;\,b;\,z\right) \qquad\qquad [n=0,\pm1,\pm2,\ldots]$$

is the Tricomi confluent hypergeometric function

$\Psi_j\left(\ldots;\,w,\,z\right)\,[j=1,2]$ are the Humbert functions:

$$\Psi_1\left(a,\,b;\,c,\,c';\,w,\,z\right) = \sum_{k,\,\ell=0}^\infty \frac{\left(a\right)_{k+\ell}\left(b\right)_k}{\left(c\right)_k\left(c'\right)_\ell}\frac{w^k z^\ell}{k!\,\ell!} \qquad\qquad [|w|<1]$$

$$\Psi_2\left(a;\,c,\,c';\,w,\,z\right) = \sum_{k,\,\ell=0}^\infty \frac{\left(a\right)_{k+\ell}}{\left(c\right)_k\left(c'\right)_\ell}\frac{w^k z^\ell}{k!\,\ell!}$$

$\psi\left(z\right) = \left[\ln\Gamma\left(z\right)\right]' = \dfrac{\Gamma'\left(z\right)}{\Gamma\left(z\right)}$ is the psi function (digamma function)

$\psi^{(n)}\left(z\right) = \dfrac{d^n}{dz^n}\psi\left(z\right)$ is the polygamma function

Index of Notations for Symbols

$(a_p) = a_1, a_2, \ldots, a_p$

$(a_p) + b = a_1 + b, a_2 + b, \ldots, a_p + b$

$(a_p)/b = a_1/b, a_2/b, \ldots, a_p/b$

$(a_p)' - a_j = a_1 - a_j, \ldots, a_{j-1} - a_j, a_{j+1} - a_j, \ldots, a_p - a_j$ $\qquad\qquad [1 \leq j \leq p]$

$(a)_k = a(a+1)\ldots(a+k-1) = \Gamma(a+k)/\Gamma(a)$ $\quad [k = 1, 2, 3, \ldots]$, $(a)_0 = 1$

is the Pochhammer symbol

$$\Delta(k, a) = \frac{a}{k}, \frac{a+1}{k}, \ldots, \frac{a+k-1}{k}$$

$$\Delta(k, (a_p)) = \frac{(a_p)}{k}, \frac{(a_p)+1}{k}, \ldots, \frac{(a_p)+k-1}{k}$$

$n! = 1 \cdot 2 \cdot 3 \ldots (n-1)n = (1)_n, \quad 0! = 1! = (-1)! = 1$

$(2n)!! = 2 \cdot 4 \cdot 6 \ldots (2n-2) 2n = 2^n n!, \quad 0!! = (-1)!! = 1$

$$(2n+1)!! = 1 \cdot 3 \cdot 5 \ldots (2n+1) = \frac{2^{n+1}}{\sqrt{\pi}} \Gamma\left(n + \frac{3}{2}\right) = \left(\frac{3}{2}\right)_n 2^n$$

$$\binom{n}{k} = \frac{n(n-1)\ldots(n-k+1)}{k!} = \frac{n!}{k!(n-k)!} = \frac{(-1)^k (-n)_k}{k!}, \quad \binom{n}{0} = 1$$

$\operatorname{Re} a, \operatorname{Re} b > c$ means $\operatorname{Re} a > c$ and $\operatorname{Re} b > c$

$[x] = n \quad [n \leq x < n+1, n = 0, \pm 1, \pm 2, \ldots]$ is the integer part of x

$$x_+^\lambda = \begin{cases} x^\lambda, & x > 0, \\ 0, & x < 0 \end{cases}$$

$$\prod_{j=1}^{p} (a_p)_k = \prod_{j=1}^{p} (a_j)_k, \quad \prod ((a_p) + b)_k = \prod_{j=1}^{p} (a_j + b)_k$$

$$\prod_{k=m}^{n} a_k = a_m a_{m+1} \ldots a_n \quad [n \geq m],$$
$$\qquad = 1 \qquad\qquad\qquad [n < m]$$

$$\prod_{k=1}^{\infty} a_k(z) = \lim_{n \to \infty} \prod_{k=1}^{n} a_k(z)$$

$$\sum_{k=m}^{n} a_k = a_m + a_{m+1} + \ldots + a_n \quad [n \geq m],$$
$$\qquad = 0 \qquad\qquad\qquad\qquad [n < m]$$

$$\sum_{k=1}^{\infty} a_k(z) = \lim_{n \to \infty} \sum_{k=1}^{n} a_k(z)$$

世界著名数学家迪厄多内(J. Dieudonné,布尔巴基学派重要成员)曾指出:

数学问题的研究逐渐地把我们引向比数和形状更复杂的概念,这种过程发展的结果可能是在理性世界中无法再做解释的解释.这些新概念自然提出了无数问题,为解决这些问题,我们又在充满生气的环境中引入了甚至更抽象的概念,然而这就离数学的本质越来越远,也就使数学家们越来越远离物理学家或工程师们对他们提出的问题.这样有人会说,原则上现代数学就其大部分而言是没有功利目标的,它构成了一种"效用"为零的智力领域.抽象理论有可能在某一天发现其有意外的"应用".尽管如此,从来不是这种无法预知的应用了数学研究,而是那种用数学现象去理解其自身的愿望推动了数学研究.

本书中涉及的梅林(Mellin,1854—1933)是芬兰人,1854 年 6 月 19 日出生,曾在赫尔辛基多科工艺学校任教授,后任校长,1933 年 4 月 5 日逝世.他主要研究解析学、微分方程和积分方程.所谓梅林变换,即函数

$$F(s) = \int_0^\infty f(x) x^{s-1} \mathrm{d}x$$

在数学物理与函数论中被广泛应用.

本书的中文书名或可译为《梅林变换手册》.

本书的作者有三位,分别为:

Yu. A. 布里奇科夫(Yu. A. Brychkov),俄罗斯人,毕业于罗蒙诺索夫莫斯科国立大学. 他是俄罗斯科学院数学研究所的研究生,自 1969 年以来一直在俄罗斯科学院多罗德尼岑计算中心工作. 他已经出版了大约 100 种出版物,包括在 CRC 出版的 2 本著作和 7 本手册.

O. I. 马里切夫(O. I. Marichev),白俄罗斯人,毕业于白俄罗斯国立大学,获得了理学博士学位,在德国耶拿大学获得了数学学位. 1991 年,他开始与斯蒂芬·沃尔夫拉姆(Stephen Wolfram)一起研究数学,发展了积分和数学函数. 他是 10 本书的作者或合著者,并且是著名的沃尔夫拉姆函数网站 http://−functions. wolfram. com/(拥有超过 307 000 个公式)的贡献者之一.

N. V. 萨维申科(N. V. Savischenko),俄罗斯人,毕业于新西伯利亚国立大学,自 1987 年以来一直在军事电信学院工作,发表了近 100 篇文章和 1 本著作.

正如作者在前言中所述:

梅林变换是由芬兰数学家 R. H. 梅林在他的论文《关于柯西定理对伽马和超几何函数理论的根本重要性》(Über die fundamentale Wichtigkeit des Satzes von Cauchy für die Theorien der Gammaund der hypergeometrischen Funktionen)(社会学报,芬兰语,1896,21,1-115)中提出的. 现在,梅林变换被广泛用于各种纯数学与应用数学之中,特别是被应用于微分方程和积分方程、狄利克雷(Dirichlet)级数的理论中. 我们在数学物理学、数论、数学统计学、渐进展开理论,特别是在特殊函数和积分变换的理论中都可以找到梅林变换的广泛应用. 使用梅林变换,许多经典的积分变换可以被表示为正拉普拉斯(Laplace)变换和逆拉普拉斯变换的组合.

本书包含以下形式的正梅林变换的表格

$$F(s) = m[f(x);s] = \int_0^\infty x^{s-1} f(x) \mathrm{d}x, s = \sigma + \mathrm{i}\tau$$

由于大多数积分可以通过特定的参数选择简化为相应的梅林变换的形式,因此这本书也可以被视为定积分和不定积分的手册. 通过改变变量,梅林变换可以转化为傅里叶(Fourier)变换和拉普拉斯变换.

逆梅林变换拥有下面的形式

$$f(x) = m^{-1}[F(s);x] = \frac{1}{2\pi \mathrm{i}} \int_{\sigma-\mathrm{i}\infty}^{\sigma+\mathrm{i}\infty} x^{-s} F(s) \mathrm{d}s, \alpha < \sigma < \beta$$

请见附录 I.

正文用相当详细的内容列表(表 1,表 2)来介绍,读者从中可以轻松地找到所需的公式. 除序号列外,表格分为两列,左边一列展示了函数 $f(x)$,右边一列给出了相应的梅林变换 $F(s)$. 为了简捷起见,我们使用了缩写符号. 例如公式 3. 14. 9. 1(代表了 3. 14. 9 小节的公式 1).

表 1

序号	$f(x)$	$F(s)$
1	$\begin{Bmatrix} S(ax) \\ C(ax) \end{Bmatrix} K_v(bx)$	$\dfrac{2^{s+\delta-1}a^{\delta+1/2}}{3^{\delta}\sqrt{\pi}\,b^{s+\delta+1/2}}\Gamma\left(\dfrac{2s-2v+2\delta+1}{4}\right)\Gamma\left(\dfrac{2s+2v+2\delta+1}{4}\right)\times$ $${}_3F_2\left(\begin{matrix} \dfrac{2\delta+1}{4},\dfrac{2s-2v+2\delta+1}{4},\dfrac{2s+2v+2\delta+1}{4} \\[2mm] \dfrac{2\delta+1}{2},\dfrac{2\delta+5}{4};-\dfrac{a^2}{b^2} \end{matrix}\right)$$ $[\,a,\operatorname{Re}b>0;\operatorname{Re}s>\mid\operatorname{Re}v\mid-(2\pm1)/2\,]$

其中 $\delta=\begin{Bmatrix}1\\0\end{Bmatrix}$，是两个公式的缩写.

表 2

序号	$f(x)$	$F(s)$
1	$S(ax)K_v(bx)$	$\dfrac{2^{s}a^{3/2}}{3\sqrt{\pi}\,b^{s+3/2}}\Gamma\left(\dfrac{2s-2v+3}{2}\right)\Gamma\left(\dfrac{2s+2v+3}{2}\right)\times$ $${}_3F_2\left(\begin{matrix} \dfrac{3}{4},\dfrac{2s-2v+3}{2},\dfrac{2s+2v+3}{2} \\[2mm] \dfrac{3}{2},\dfrac{7}{4};-\dfrac{a^2}{b^2} \end{matrix}\right)$$ $[\,a,\operatorname{Re}b>0;\operatorname{Re}s>\mid\operatorname{Re}v\mid-3/2\,]$
2	$C(ax)K_v(bx)$	$\dfrac{2^{s-1}a^{1/2}}{\sqrt{\pi}\,b^{s+1/2}}\Gamma\left(\dfrac{2s-2v+1}{2}\right)\Gamma\left(\dfrac{2s+2v+1}{2}\right)\times$ $${}_3F_2\left(\begin{matrix} \dfrac{1}{4},\dfrac{2s-2v+1}{2},\dfrac{2s+2v+1}{2} \\[2mm] \dfrac{1}{2},\dfrac{5}{4};-\dfrac{a^2}{b^2} \end{matrix}\right)$$ $[\,a,\operatorname{Re}b>0;\operatorname{Re}s>\mid\operatorname{Re}v\mid-1/2\,]$

表 2 的第 1 行只取大括号中的上符号和上表达式，第 2 行只取大括号中的下符号和下表达式.

公式 $a,b<\operatorname{Re}s<c,d$ 是不等式

$$\max\{a,b\}<\operatorname{Re}s<\min\{c,d\}$$

的一个简写形式. 在所有章节中，除非有其他限制，否则 $k,l,m,n,p,q=0,1,2,\cdots$.

本书在主值的意义上考虑了一些积分.

作者在每节的最前面都给出了对评估梅林变换有帮助的各种函数关系. 更多公式可以参见网址 http://functions.wolfram.com.

在编写本手册时,作者首先参考了 H. 贝特曼(H. Bateman)、A. 艾尔代伊(A. Erdélyi)、W. 马格努斯(W. Magnus)、F. 奥伯海廷格(F. Oberhettinger) 和 F. G. 特里科米(F. G. Tricomi) 的文献[1],Yu. A. 布里奇科夫的文献[3],O. I. 马里内夫的文献[14],I. S. 格拉德施泰因(I. S. Gradshteyn) 和 I. M. 雷日克(I. M. Ryzhik) 的文献[13],V. A. 迪特金(V. A. Ditkin) 和 A. P. 普鲁德尼科夫(A. P. Prudnikov) 的文献[10],F. 奥伯海廷格的文献[15] 以及 A. P. 普鲁德尼科夫、Yu. A. 布里奇科夫和 O. I. 马里切夫的文献[18-23]. 作者自己也得出了相当一部分公式.

附录 Ⅰ 包含了梅林变换的性质及其应用的例子.

附录 Ⅱ 专门讨论积分收敛的条件.

参考文献的出处和注释在书的末尾给出.

本手册适用于研究人员、工程师、研究生、大学生,一般情况下也适用于使用数学方法的任何人.

本书的目录为:

在国内出版的与本书类似的图书中比较有名的一本是王竹溪和郭敦仁两位先生于 1965 年在科学出版社出版的《特殊函数概论》，1979 年再次重印. 令人向往的是当年这本书精装印了 31 260 册，平装印了 34 120 册. 按照今天的标准，这本书妥妥的是畅销书.

可惜出版的黄金岁月已不再，徒留感叹.

近读《苏轼文集编年笺注》，在"记汉讲堂"中有：

汉时讲堂今犹在，画固俨然. 丹青之古，无复前此.

刘培杰

2023 年 12 月 5 日

于哈工大

刘培杰数学工作室
已出版(即将出版)图书目录——原版影印

书　　名	出 版 时 间	定　价	编号
数学物理大百科全书.第1卷(英文)	2016－01	418.00	508
数学物理大百科全书.第2卷(英文)	2016－01	408.00	509
数学物理大百科全书.第3卷(英文)	2016－01	396.00	510
数学物理大百科全书.第4卷(英文)	2016－01	408.00	511
数学物理大百科全书.第5卷(英文)	2016－01	368.00	512
zeta 函数,q-zeta 函数,相伴级数与积分(英文)	2015－08	88.00	513
微分形式:理论与练习(英文)	2015－08	58.00	514
离散与微分包含的逼近和优化(英文)	2015－08	58.00	515
艾伦·图灵:他的工作与影响(英文)	2016－01	98.00	560
测度理论概率导论,第2版(英文)	2016－01	88.00	561
带有潜在故障恢复系统的半马尔柯夫模型控制(英文)	2016－01	98.00	562
数学分析原理(英文)	2016－01	88.00	563
随机偏微分方程的有效动力学(英文)	2016－01	88.00	564
图的谱半径(英文)	2016－01	58.00	565
量子机器学习中数据挖掘的量子计算方法(英文)	2016－01	98.00	566
量子物理的非常规方法(英文)	2016－01	118.00	567
运输过程的统一非局部理论:广义波尔兹曼物理动力学,第2版(英文)	2016－01	198.00	568
量子力学与经典力学之间的联系在原子、分子及电动力学系统建模中的应用(英文)	2016－01	58.00	569
算术域(英文)	2018－01	158.00	821
高等数学竞赛:1962—1991年的米洛克斯·史怀哲竞赛(英文)	2018－01	128.00	822
用数学奥林匹克精神解决数论问题(英文)	2018－01	108.00	823
代数几何(德文)	2018－04	68.00	824
丢番图逼近论(英文)	2018－01	78.00	825
代数几何学基础教程(英文)	2018－01	98.00	826
解析数论入门课程(英文)	2018－01	78.00	827
数论中的丢番图问题(英文)	2018－01	78.00	829
数论(梦幻之旅):第五届中日数论研讨会演讲集(英文)	2018－01	68.00	830
数论新应用(英文)	2018－01	68.00	831
数论(英文)	2018－01	78.00	832

刘培杰数学工作室
已出版(即将出版)图书目录——原版影印

书 名	出版时间	定 价	编号
湍流十讲(英文)	2018—04	108.00	886
无穷维李代数:第3版(英文)	2018—04	98.00	887
等值、不变量和对称性(英文)	2018—04	78.00	888
解析数论(英文)	2018—09	78.00	889
《数学原理》的演化:伯特兰·罗素撰写第二版时的手稿与笔记(英文)	2018—04	108.00	890
哈密尔顿数学论文集(第4卷):几何学、分析学、天文学、概率和有限差分等(英文)	2019—05	108.00	891
偏微分方程全局吸引子的特性(英文)	2018—09	108.00	979
整函数与下调和函数(英文)	2018—09	118.00	980
幂等分析(英文)	2018—09	118.00	981
李群,离散子群与不变量理论(英文)	2018—09	108.00	982
动力系统与统计力学(英文)	2018—09	118.00	983
表示论与动力系统(英文)	2018—09	118.00	984
分析学练习.第1部分(英文)	2021—01	88.00	1247
分析学练习.第2部分,非线性分析(英文)	2021—01	88.00	1248
初级统计学:循序渐进的方法:第10版(英文)	2019—05	68.00	1067
工程师与科学家微分方程用书:第4版(英文)	2019—07	58.00	1068
大学代数与三角学(英文)	2019—06	78.00	1069
培养数学能力的途径(英文)	2019—07	38.00	1070
工程师与科学家统计学:第4版(英文)	2019—06	58.00	1071
贸易与经济中的应用统计学:第6版(英文)	2019—06	58.00	1072
傅立叶级数和边值问题:第8版(英文)	2019—05	48.00	1073
通往天文学的途径:第5版(英文)	2019—05	58.00	1074
拉马努金笔记.第1卷(英文)	2019—06	165.00	1078
拉马努金笔记.第2卷(英文)	2019—06	165.00	1079
拉马努金笔记.第3卷(英文)	2019—06	165.00	1080
拉马努金笔记.第4卷(英文)	2019—06	165.00	1081
拉马努金笔记.第5卷(英文)	2019—06	165.00	1082
拉马努金遗失笔记.第1卷(英文)	2019—06	109.00	1083
拉马努金遗失笔记.第2卷(英文)	2019—06	109.00	1084
拉马努金遗失笔记.第3卷(英文)	2019—06	109.00	1085
拉马努金遗失笔记.第4卷(英文)	2019—06	109.00	1086
数论:1976年纽约洛克菲勒大学数论会议记录(英文)	2020—06	68.00	1145
数论:卡本代尔1979:1979年在南伊利诺伊卡本代尔大学举行的数论会议记录(英文)	2020—06	78.00	1146
数论:诺德韦克豪特1983:1983年在诺德韦克豪特举行的Journees Arithmetiques数论大会会议记录(英文)	2020—06	68.00	1147
数论:1985—1988年在纽约城市大学研究生院和大学中心举办的研讨会(英文)	2020—06	68.00	1148

刘培杰数学工作室
已出版(即将出版)图书目录——原版影印

书　名	出版时间	定　价	编号
数论:1987年在乌尔姆举行的 Journees Arithmetiques 数论大会会议记录(英文)	2020—06	68.00	1149
数论:马德拉斯1987:1987年在马德拉斯安娜大学举行的国际拉马努金百年纪念大会会议记录(英文)	2020—06	68.00	1150
解析数论:1988年在东京举行的日法研讨会会议记录(英文)	2020—06	68.00	1151
解析数论:2002年在意大利切特拉罗举行的 C.I.M.E. 暑期班演讲集(英文)	2020—06	68.00	1152
量子世界中的蝴蝶:最迷人的量子分形故事(英文)	2020—06	118.00	1157
走进量子力学(英文)	2020—06	118.00	1158
计算物理学概论(英文)	2020—06	48.00	1159
物质,空间和时间的理论:量子理论(英文)	2020—10	48.00	1160
物质,空间和时间的理论:经典理论(英文)	2020—10	48.00	1161
量子场理论:解释世界的神秘背景(英文)	2020—07	38.00	1162
计算物理学概论(英文)	2020—06	48.00	1163
行星状星云(英文)	2020—10	38.00	1164
基本宇宙学:从亚里士多德的宇宙到大爆炸(英文)	2020—08	58.00	1165
数学磁流体力学(英文)	2020—07	58.00	1166
计算科学:第1卷,计算的科学(日文)	2020—07	88.00	1167
计算科学:第2卷,计算与宇宙(日文)	2020—07	88.00	1168
计算科学:第3卷,计算与物质(日文)	2020—07	88.00	1169
计算科学:第4卷,计算与生命(日文)	2020—07	88.00	1170
计算科学:第5卷,计算与地球环境(日文)	2020—07	88.00	1171
计算科学:第6卷,计算与社会(日文)	2020—07	88.00	1172
计算科学.别卷,超级计算机(日文)	2020—07	88.00	1173
多复变函数论(日文)	2022—06	78.00	1518
复变函数入门(日文)	2022—06	78.00	1523
代数与数论:综合方法(英文)	2020—10	78.00	1185
复分析:现代函数理论第一课(英文)	2020—07	58.00	1186
斐波那契数列和卡特兰数:导论(英文)	2020—10	68.00	1187
组合推理:计数艺术介绍(英文)	2020—07	88.00	1188
二次互反律的傅里叶分析证明(英文)	2020—07	48.00	1189
旋瓦兹分布的希尔伯特变换与应用(英文)	2020—07	58.00	1190
泛函分析:巴拿赫空间理论入门(英文)	2020—07	48.00	1191
卡塔兰数入门(英文)	2019—05	68.00	1060
测度与积分(英文)	2019—04	68.00	1059
组合学手册.第一卷(英文)	2020—06	128.00	1153
*一代数、局部紧群和巴拿赫 *一代数丛的表示.第一卷,群和代数的基本表示理论(英文)	2020—05	148.00	1154
电磁理论(英文)	2020—08	48.00	1193
连续介质力学中的非线性问题(英文)	2020—09	78.00	1195
多变量数学入门(英文)	2021—05	68.00	1317
偏微分方程入门(英文)	2021—05	88.00	1318
若尔当典范性:理论与实践(英文)	2021—07	68.00	1366
伽罗瓦理论.第4版(英文)	2021—08	88.00	1408
R 统计学概论	2023—03	88.00	1614
基于不确定静态和动态问题解的仿射算术(英文)	2023—03	38.00	1618

刘培杰数学工作室

已出版(即将出版)图书目录——原版影印

书　名	出版时间	定　价	编号
典型群,错排与素数(英文)	2020—11	58.00	1204
李代数的表示:通过 gln 进行介绍(英文)	2020—10	38.00	1205
实分析演讲集(英文)	2020—10	38.00	1206
现代分析及其应用的课程(英文)	2020—10	58.00	1207
运动中的抛射物数学(英文)	2020—10	38.00	1208
2—纽结与它们的群(英文)	2020—10	38.00	1209
概率,策略和选择:博弈与选举中的数学(英文)	2020—11	58.00	1210
分析学引论(英文)	2020—11	58.00	1211
量子群:通往流代数的路径(英文)	2020—11	38.00	1212
集合论入门(英文)	2020—10	48.00	1213
酉反射群(英文)	2020—11	58.00	1214
探索数学:吸引人的证明方式(英文)	2020—11	58.00	1215
微分拓扑短期课程(英文)	2020—10	48.00	1216
抽象凸分析(英文)	2020—11	68.00	1222
费马大定理笔记(英文)	2021—03	48.00	1223
高斯与雅可比和(英文)	2021—03	78.00	1224
π 与算术几何平均:关于解析数论和计算复杂性的研究(英文)	2021—01	58.00	1225
复分析入门(英文)	2021—03	48.00	1226
爱德华·卢卡斯与素性测定(英文)	2021—03	78.00	1227
通往凸分析及其应用的简单路径(英文)	2021—01	68.00	1229
微分几何的各个方面.第一卷(英文)	2021—01	58.00	1230
微分几何的各个方面.第二卷(英文)	2020—12	58.00	1231
微分几何的各个方面.第三卷(英文)	2020—12	58.00	1232
沃克流形几何学(英文)	2020—11	58.00	1233
彷射和韦尔几何应用(英文)	2020—12	58.00	1234
双曲几何学的旋转向量空间方法(英文)	2021—02	58.00	1235
积分:分析学的关键(英文)	2020—12	48.00	1236
为有天分的新生准备的分析学基础教材(英文)	2020—11	48.00	1237
数学不等式.第一卷.对称多项式不等式(英文)	2021—03	108.00	1273
数学不等式.第二卷.对称有理不等式与对称无理不等式(英文)	2021—03	108.00	1274
数学不等式.第三卷.循环不等式与非循环不等式(英文)	2021—03	108.00	1275
数学不等式.第四卷.Jensen 不等式的扩展与加细(英文)	2021—03	108.00	1276
数学不等式.第五卷.创建不等式与解不等式的其他方法(英文)	2021—04	108.00	1277

刘培杰数学工作室

已出版（即将出版）图书目录——原版影印

书　名	出版时间	定　价	编号
冯·诺依曼代数中的谱位移函数:半有限冯·诺依曼代数中的谱位移函数与谱流(英文)	2021—06	98.00	1308
链接结构:关于嵌入完全图的直线中链接单形的组合结构(英文)	2021—05	58.00	1309
代数几何方法.第1卷(英文)	2021—06	68.00	1310
代数几何方法.第2卷(英文)	2021—06	68.00	1311
代数几何方法.第3卷(英文)	2021—06	58.00	1312

书　名	出版时间	定　价	编号
代数、生物信息和机器人技术的算法问题.第四卷,独立恒等式系统(俄文)	2020—08	118.00	1199
代数、生物信息和机器人技术的算法问题.第五卷,相对覆盖性和独立可拆分恒等式系统(俄文)	2020—08	118.00	1200
代数、生物信息和机器人技术的算法问题.第六卷,恒等式和准恒等式的相等 问题、可推导性和可实现性(俄文)	2020—08	128.00	1201
分数阶微积分的应用:非局部动态过程,分数阶导热系数(俄文)	2021—01	68.00	1241
泛函分析问题与练习:第2版(俄文)	2021—01	98.00	1242
集合论、数学逻辑和算法论问题:第5版(俄文)	2021—01	98.00	1243
微分几何和拓扑短期课程(俄文)	2021—01	98.00	1244
素数规律(俄文)	2021—01	88.00	1245
无穷边值问题解的递减:无界域中的拟线性椭圆和抛物方程(俄文)	2021—01	48.00	1246
微分几何讲义(俄文)	2020—12	98.00	1253
二次型和矩阵(俄文)	2021—01	98.00	1255
积分和级数.第2卷,特殊函数(俄文)	2021—01	168.00	1258
积分和级数.第3卷,特殊函数补充:第2版(俄文)	2021—01	178.00	1264
几何图上的微分方程(俄文)	2021—01	138.00	1259
数论教程:第2版(俄文)	2021—01	98.00	1260
非阿基米德分析及其应用(俄文)	2021—03	98.00	1261
古典群和量子群的压缩(俄文)	2021—03	98.00	1263
数学分析习题集.第3卷,多元函数:第3版(俄文)	2021—03	98.00	1266
数学习题:乌拉尔国立大学数学力学系大学生奥林匹克(俄文)	2021—03	98.00	1267
柯西定理和微分方程的特解(俄文)	2021—03	98.00	1268
组合极值问题及其应用:第3版(俄文)	2021—03	98.00	1269
数学词典(俄文)	2021—01	98.00	1271
确定性混沌分析模型(俄文)	2021—06	168.00	1307
精选初等数学习题和定理.立体几何.第3版(俄文)	2021—03	68.00	1316
微分几何习题:第3版(俄文)	2021—05	98.00	1336
精选初等数学习题和定理.平面几何.第4版(俄文)	2021—05	68.00	1335
曲面理论在欧氏空间 E_n 中的直接表示(俄文)	2022—01	68.00	1444
维纳—霍普夫离散算子和托普利兹算子:某些可数赋范空间中的诺特性和可逆性(俄文)	2022—03	108.00	1496
Maple 中的数论:数论中的计算机计算(俄文)	2022—03	88.00	1497
贝尔曼和克努特问题及其概括:加法运算的复杂性(俄文)	2022—03	138.00	1498

刘培杰数学工作室

 已出版(即将出版)图书目录——原版影印

书　　名	出版时间	定　价	编号
复分析:共形映射(俄文)	2022－07	48.00	1542
微积分代数样条和多项式及其在数值方法中的应用(俄文)	2022－08	128.00	1543
蒙特卡罗方法中的随机过程和场模型:算法和应用(俄文)	2022－08	88.00	1544
线性椭圆型方程组:论二阶椭圆型方程的迪利克雷问题(俄文)	2022－08	98.00	1561
动态系统解的增长特性:估值、稳定性、应用(俄文)	2022－08	118.00	1565
群的自由积分解:建立和应用(俄文)	2022－08	78.00	1570
混合方程和偏差自变数方程问题:解的存在和唯一性(俄文)	2023－01	78.00	1582
拟度量空间分析:存在和逼近定理(俄文)	2023－01	108.00	1583
二维和三维流形上函数的拓扑性质:函数的拓扑分类(俄文)	2023－03	68.00	1584
齐次马尔科夫过程建模的矩阵方法:此类方法能够用于不同目上的的复杂系统研究、设计和完善(俄文)	2023－03	68.00	1594
周期函数的近似方法和特性:特殊课程(俄文)	2023－04	158.00	1622
扩散方程解的矩函数:变分法(俄文)	2023－03	58.00	1623
多赋范空间和广义函数:理论及应用(俄文)	2023－03	98.00	1632
分析中的多值映射:部分应用(俄文)	2023－06	98.00	1634
数学物理问题(俄文)	2023－03	78.00	1636
函数的幂级数与三角级数分解(俄文)	2024－01	58.00	1695
星体理论的数学基础:原子三元组(俄文)	2024－01	98.00	1696
素数规律:专著(俄文)	2024－01	118.00	1697
狭义相对论与广义相对论:时空与引力导论(英文)	2021－07	88.00	1319
束流物理学和粒子加速器的实践介绍:第2版(英文)	2021－07	88.00	1320
凝聚态物理中的拓扑和微分几何简介(英文)	2021－05	88.00	1321
混沌映射:动力学、分形学和快速涨落(英文)	2021－05	128.00	1322
广义相对论:黑洞、引力波和宇宙学介绍(英文)	2021－06	68.00	1323
现代分析电磁均质化(英文)	2021－06	68.00	1324
为科学家提供的基本流体动力学(英文)	2021－06	88.00	1325
视觉天文学:理解夜空的指南(英文)	2021－06	68.00	1326
物理学中的计算方法(英文)	2021－06	68.00	1327
单星的结构与演化:导论(英文)	2021－06	108.00	1328
超越居里:1903年至1963年物理界四位女性及其著名发现(英文)	2021－06	68.00	1329
范德瓦尔斯流体热力学的进展(英文)	2021－06	68.00	1330
先进的托卡马克稳定性理论(英文)	2021－06	88.00	1331
经典场论导论:基本相互作用的过程(英文)	2021－07	88.00	1332
光致电离量子动力学方法原理(英文)	2021－07	108.00	1333
经典域论和应力:能量张量(英文)	2021－05	88.00	1334
非线性太赫兹光谱的概念与应用(英文)	2021－06	68.00	1337
电磁学中的无穷空间并矢格林函数(英文)	2021－06	88.00	1338
物理科学基础数学.第1卷,齐次边值问题、傅里叶方法和特殊函数(英文)	2021－07	108.00	1339
离散量子力学(英文)	2021－07	68.00	1340
核磁共振的物理学和数学(英文)	2021－07	108.00	1341
分子水平的静电学(英文)	2021－07	68.00	1342
非线性波:理论、计算机模拟、实验(英文)	2021－06	108.00	1343
石墨烯光学:经典问题的电解解决方案(英文)	2021－06	68.00	1344
超材料多元宇宙(英文)	2021－07	68.00	1345
银河系外的天体物理学(英文)	2021－07	68.00	1346
原子物理学(英文)	2021－07	68.00	1347
将光打结:将拓扑学应用于光学(英文)	2021－07	68.00	1348
电磁学:问题与解法(英文)	2021－07	88.00	1364
海浪的原理:介绍量子力学的技巧与应用(英文)	2021－07	108.00	1365

刘培杰数学工作室
已出版(即将出版)图书目录——原版影印

书　名	出版时间	定　价	编号
多孔介质中的流体:输运与相变(英文)	2021—07	68.00	1372
洛伦兹群的物理学(英文)	2021—08	68.00	1373
物理导论的数学方法和解决方法手册(英文)	2021—08	68.00	1374
非线性波数学物理学入门(英文)	2021—08	88.00	1376
波:基本原理和动力学(英文)	2021—07	68.00	1377
光电子量子计量学.第1卷,基础(英文)	2021—07	88.00	1383
光电子量子计量学.第2卷,应用与进展(英文)	2021—07	68.00	1384
复杂流的格子玻尔兹曼建模的工程应用(英文)	2021—08	68.00	1393
电偶极矩挑战(英文)	2021—08	108.00	1394
电动力学:问题与解法(英文)	2021—09	68.00	1395
自由电子激光的经典理论(英文)	2021—08	68.00	1397
曼哈顿计划——核武器物理学简介(英文)	2021—09	68.00	1401
粒子物理学(英文)	2021—09	68.00	1402
引力场中的量子信息(英文)	2021—09	128.00	1403
器件物理学的基本经典力学(英文)	2021—09	68.00	1404
等离子体物理及其空间应用导论.第1卷,基本原理和初步过程(英文)	2021—09	68.00	1405
磁约束聚变等离子体物理:理想MHD理论(英文)	2023—03	68.00	1613
相对论量子场论.第1卷,典范形式体系(英文)	2023—03	38.00	1615
相对论量子场论.第2卷,路径积分形式(英文)	2023—06	38.00	1616
相对论量子场论.第3卷,量子场论的应用(英文)	2023—06	38.00	1617
涌现的物理学(英文)	2023—05	58.00	1619
量子化旋涡:一本拓扑激发手册(英文)	2023—04	68.00	1620
非线性动力学:实践的介绍性调查(英文)	2023—05	68.00	1621
静电加速器:一个多功能工具(英文)	2023—06	58.00	1625
相对论多体理论与统计力学(英文)	2023—06	58.00	1626
经典力学.第1卷,工具与向量(英文)	2023—04	38.00	1627
经典力学.第2卷,运动学和匀加速运动(英文)	2023—04	58.00	1628
经典力学.第3卷,牛顿定律和匀速圆周运动(英文)	2023—04	58.00	1629
经典力学.第4卷,万有引力定律(英文)	2023—04	38.00	1630
经典力学.第5卷,守恒定律与旋转运动(英文)	2023—04	38.00	1631
对称问题:纳维尔—斯托克斯问题(英文)	2023—04	38.00	1638
摄影的物理和艺术.第1卷,几何与光的本质(英文)	2023—04	78.00	1639
摄影的物理和艺术.第2卷,能量与色彩(英文)	2023—04	78.00	1640
摄影的物理和艺术.第3卷,探测器与数码的意义(英文)	2023—04	78.00	1641
拓扑与超弦理论焦点问题(英文)	2021—07	58.00	1349
应用数学:理论、方法与实践(英文)	2021—07	78.00	1350
非线性特征值问题:牛顿型方法与非线性瑞利函数(英文)	2021—07	58.00	1351
广义膨胀和齐性:利用齐性构造齐次系统的李雅普诺夫函数和控制律(英文)	2021—06	48.00	1352
解析数论焦点问题(英文)	2021—07	58.00	1353
随机微分方程:动态系统方法(英文)	2021—07	58.00	1354
经典力学与微分几何(英文)	2021—07	58.00	1355
负定相交形式流形上的瞬子模空间几何(英文)	2021—07	68.00	1356
广义卡塔兰轨道分析:广义卡塔兰轨道计算数字的方法(英文)	2021—07	48.00	1367
洛伦兹方法的变分:二维与三维洛伦兹方法(英文)	2021—08	38.00	1378
几何、分析和数论精编(英文)	2021—08	68.00	1380
从一个新角度看数论:通过遗传方法引入现实的概念(英文)	2021—07	58.00	1387
动力系统:短期课程(英文)	2021—08	68.00	1382
几何路径:理论与实践(英文)	2021—08	48.00	1385

刘培杰数学工作室
已出版(即将出版)图书目录——原版影印

书 名	出版时间	定 价	编号
论天体力学中某些问题的不可积性(英文)	2021—07	88.00	1396
广义斐波那契数列及其性质(英文)	2021—08	38.00	1386
对称函数和麦克唐纳多项式:余代数结构与 Kawanaka 恒等式(英文)	2021—09	38.00	1400
杰弗里·英格拉姆·泰勒科学论文集:第1卷.固体力学(英文)	2021—05	78.00	1360
杰弗里·英格拉姆·泰勒科学论文集:第2卷.气象学、海洋学和湍流(英文)	2021—05	68.00	1361
杰弗里·英格拉姆·泰勒科学论文集:第3卷.空气动力学以及落弹数和爆炸的力学(英文)	2021—05	68.00	1362
杰弗里·英格拉姆·泰勒科学论文集:第4卷.有关流体力学(英文)	2021—05	58.00	1363
非局域泛函演化方程:积分与分数阶(英文)	2021—08	48.00	1390
理论工作者的高等微分几何:纤维丛、射流流形和拉格朗日理论(英文)	2021—08	68.00	1391
半线性退化椭圆微分方程:局部定理与整体定理(英文)	2021—07	48.00	1392
非交换几何、规范理论和重整化:一般简介与非交换量子场论的重整化(英文)	2021—09	78.00	1406
数论论文集:拉普拉斯变换和带有数论系数的幂级数(俄文)	2021—09	48.00	1407
挠理论专题:相对极大值,单射与扩充模(英文)	2021—09	88.00	1410
强正则图与欧几里得若尔当代数:非通常关系中的启示(英文)	2021—10	48.00	1411
拉格朗日几何和哈密顿几何:力学的应用(英文)	2021—10	48.00	1412
时滞微分方程与差分方程的振动理论:二阶与三阶(英文)	2021—10	98.00	1417
卷积结构与几何函数理论:用以研究特定几何函数理论方向的分数阶微积分算子与卷积结构(英文)	2021—10	48.00	1418
经典数学物理的历史发展(英文)	2021—10	78.00	1419
扩展线性丢番图问题(英文)	2021—10	38.00	1420
一类混沌动力系统的分歧分析与控制:分歧分析与控制(英文)	2021—11	38.00	1421
伽利略空间和伪伽利略空间中一些特殊曲线的几何性质(英文)	2022—01	68.00	1422
一阶偏微分方程:哈密尔顿—雅可比理论(英文)	2021—11	48.00	1424
各向异性黎曼多面体的反问题:分段光滑的各向异性黎曼多面体反边界谱问题:唯一性(英文)	2021—11	38.00	1425
项目反应理论手册.第一卷,模型(英文)	2021—11	138.00	1431
项目反应理论手册.第二卷,统计工具(英文)	2021—11	118.00	1432
项目反应理论手册.第三卷,应用(英文)	2021—11	138.00	1433
二次无理数:经典数论入门(英文)	2022—05	138.00	1434

刘培杰数学工作室
已出版(即将出版)图书目录——原版影印

书　名	出版时间	定　价	编号
数,形与对称性:数论,几何和群论导论(英文)	2022—05	128.00	1435
有限域手册(英文)	2021—11	178.00	1436
计算数论(英文)	2021—11	148.00	1437
拟群与其表示简介(英文)	2021—11	88.00	1438
数论与密码学导论:第二版(英文)	2022—01	148.00	1423
几何分析中的柯西变换与黎兹变换:解析调和容量和李普希兹调和容量、变化和振荡以及一致可求长性(英文)	2021—12	38.00	1465
近似不动点定理及其应用(英文)	2022—05	28.00	1466
局部域的相关内容解析:对局部域的扩展及其伽罗瓦群的研究(英文)	2022—01	38.00	1467
反问题的二进制恢复方法(英文)	2022—03	28.00	1468
对几何函数中某些类的各个方面的研究:复变量理论(英文)	2022—01	38.00	1469
覆盖、对应和非交换几何(英文)	2022—01	28.00	1470
最优控制理论中的随机线性调节器问题:随机最优线性调节器问题(英文)	2022—01	38.00	1473
正交分解法:涡流流体动力学应用的正交分解法(英文)	2022—01	38.00	1475
芬斯勒几何的某些问题(英文)	2022—03	38.00	1476
受限三体问题(英文)	2022—05	38.00	1477
利用马利亚万微积分进行 Greeks 的计算:连续过程、跳跃过程中的马利亚万微积分和金融领域中的 Greeks(英文)	2022—05	48.00	1478
经典分析和泛函分析的应用:分析学的应用(英文)	2022—03	38.00	1479
特殊芬斯勒空间的探究(英文)	2022—03	48.00	1480
某些图形的施泰纳距离的细谷多项式:细谷多项式与图的维纳指数(英文)	2022—05	38.00	1481
图论问题的遗传算法:在新鲜与模糊的环境中(英文)	2022—05	48.00	1482
多项式映射的渐近簇(英文)	2022—05	38.00	1483
一维系统中的混沌:符号动力学,映射序列,一致收敛和沙可夫斯基定理(英文)	2022—05	38.00	1509
多维边界层流动与传热分析:粘性流体流动的数学建模与分析(英文)	2022—05	38.00	1510
演绎理论物理学的原理:一种基于量子力学波函数的逐次置信估计的一般理论的提议(英文)	2022—05	38.00	1511
R^2 和 R^3 中的仿射弹性曲线:概念和方法(英文)	2022—08	38.00	1512
算术数列中除数函数的分布:基本内容、调查、方法、第二矩、新结果(英文)	2022—05	28.00	1513
抛物型狄拉克算子和薛定谔方程:不定常薛定谔方程的抛物型狄拉克算子及其应用(英文)	2022—07	28.00	1514
黎曼-希尔伯特问题与量子场论:可积重正化、戴森-施温格方程(英文)	2022—08	38.00	1515
代数结构和几何结构的形变理论(英文)	2022—08	48.00	1516
概率结构和模糊结构上的不动点:概率结构和直觉模糊度量空间的不动点定理(英文)	2022—08	38.00	1517

刘培杰数学工作室
已出版(即将出版)图书目录——原版影印

书　名	出版时间	定　价	编号
反若尔当对:简单反若尔当对的自同构(英文)	2022—07	28.00	1533
对某些黎曼—芬斯勒空间变换的研究:芬斯勒几何中的某些变换(英文)	2022—07	38.00	1534
内诣零流形映射的尼尔森数的阿诺索夫关系(英文)	2023—01	38.00	1535
与广义积分变换有关的分数次演算:对分数次演算的研究(英文)	2023—01	48.00	1536
强子的芬斯勒几何和吕拉几何(宇宙学方面):强子结构的芬斯勒几何和吕拉几何(拓扑缺陷)(英文)	2022—08	38.00	1537
一种基于混沌的非线性最优化问题:作业调度问题(英文)	2023—03	38.00	1538
广义概率论发展前景:关于趣味数学与置信函数实际应用的一些原创观点(英文)	2023—03	48.00	1539
纽结与物理学:第二版(英文)	2022—09	118.00	1547
正交多项式和q—级数的前沿(英文)	2022—09	98.00	1548
算子理论问题集(英文)	2022—09	108.00	1549
抽象代数:群、环与域的应用导论:第二版(英文)	2023—01	98.00	1550
菲尔兹奖得主演讲集:第三版(英文)	2023—01	138.00	1551
多元实函数教程(英文)	2022—09	118.00	1552
球面空间形式群的几何学:第二版(英文)	2022—09	98.00	1566
对称群的表示论(英文)	2023—01	98.00	1585
纽结理论:第二版(英文)	2023—01	88.00	1586
拟群理论的基础与应用(英文)	2023—01	88.00	1587
组合学:第二版(英文)	2023—01	98.00	1588
加性组合学:研究问题手册(英文)	2023—01	68.00	1589
扭曲、平铺与镶嵌:几何折纸中的数学方法(英文)	2023—01	98.00	1590
离散与计算几何手册:第三版(英文)	2023—01	248.00	1591
离散与组合数学手册:第二版(英文)	2023—01	248.00	1592
分析学教程.第1卷,一元实变量函数的微积分分析学介绍(英文)	2023—01	118.00	1595
分析学教程.第2卷,多元函数的微分和积分,向量微积分(英文)	2023—01	118.00	1596
分析学教程.第3卷,测度与积分理论,复变量的复值函数(英文)	2023—01	118.00	1597
分析学教程.第4卷,傅里叶分析,常微分方程,变分法(英文)	2023—01	118.00	1598

刘培杰数学工作室

已出版（即将出版）图书目录——原版影印

书　名	出版时间	定价	编号
共形映射及其应用手册(英文)	2024—01	158.00	1674
广义三角函数与双曲函数(英文)	2024—01	78.00	1675
振动与波:概论:第二版(英文)	2024—01	88.00	1676
几何约束系统原理手册(英文)	2024—01	120.00	1677
微分方程与包含的拓扑方法(英文)	2024—01	98.00	1678
数学分析中的前沿话题(英文)	2024—01	198.00	1679
流体力学建模:不稳定性与湍流(英文)	2024—03	88.00	1680
动力系统:理论与应用(英文)	2024—03	108.00	1711
空间统计学理论:概述(英文)	2024—03	68.00	1712
梅林变换手册(英文)	2024—03	128.00	1713
非线性系统及其绝妙的数学结构.第1卷(英文)	2024—03	88.00	1714
非线性系统及其绝妙的数学结构.第2卷(英文)	2024—03	108.00	1715
Chip-firing 中的数学(英文)	2024—04	88.00	1716

联系地址:哈尔滨市南岗区复华四道街 10 号　哈尔滨工业大学出版社刘培杰数学工作室
邮　编:150006
联系电话:0451－86281378　　13904613167
E-mail:lpj1378@163.com